JOURNAL

This edition published in 2019 by Arcturus Publishing Limited
26/27 Bickels Yard, 151–153 Bermondsey Street,
London SE1 3HA

AD007510UK

Printed in the UK

MIX
Paper from
responsible sources
FSC® C018072

This book is
from the library of

....

....

....

JOURNAL

JOURNAL

JOURNAL

JOURNAL

JOURNAL

JOURNAL

JOURNAL

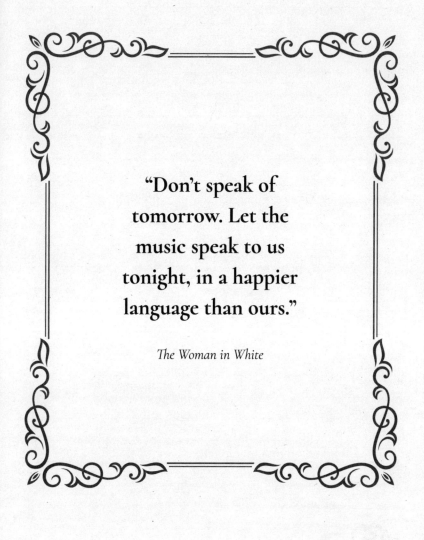

"Don't speak of tomorrow. Let the music speak to us tonight, in a happier language than ours."

The Woman in White

JOURNAL

JOURNAL

JOURNAL

JOURNAL

JOURNAL

JOURNAL

JOURNAL

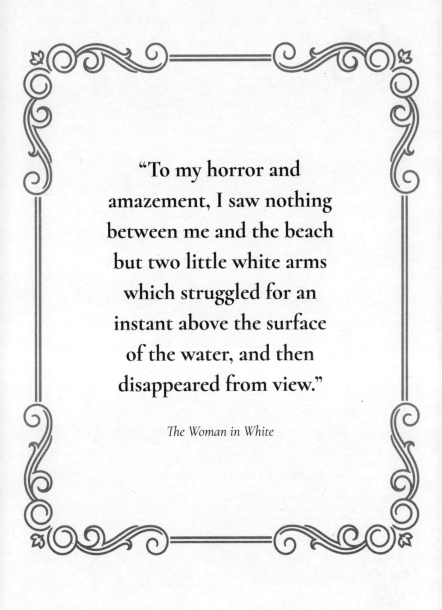

"To my horror and amazement, I saw nothing between me and the beach but two little white arms which struggled for an instant above the surface of the water, and then disappeared from view."

The Woman in White

JOURNAL

JOURNAL

JOURNAL

JOURNAL

JOURNAL

JOURNAL

JOURNAL

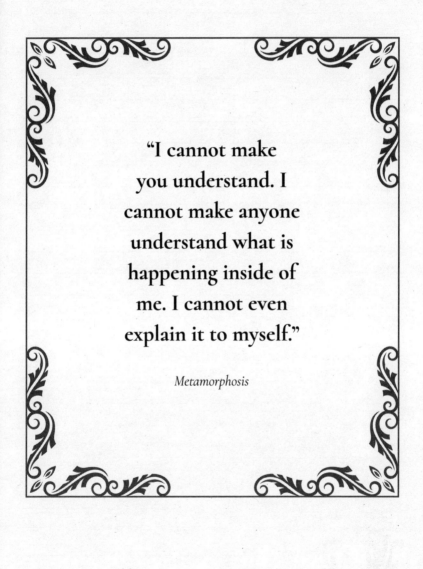

"I cannot make you understand. I cannot make anyone understand what is happening inside of me. I cannot even explain it to myself."

Metamorphosis

JOURNAL

JOURNAL

JOURNAL

JOURNAL

JOURNAL

JOURNAL

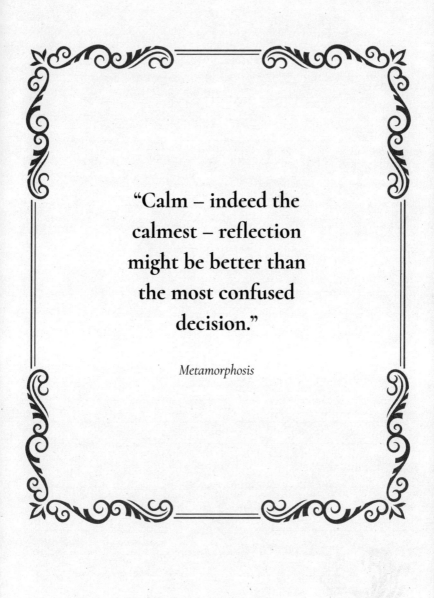

"Calm – indeed the calmest – reflection might be better than the most confused decision."

Metamorphosis

JOURNAL

JOURNAL

JOURNAL

JOURNAL

JOURNAL

JOURNAL

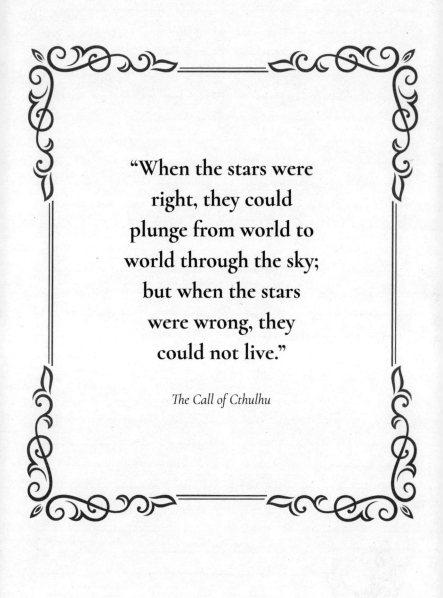

"When the stars were right, they could plunge from world to world through the sky; but when the stars were wrong, they could not live."

The Call of Cthulhu

JOURNAL

JOURNAL

JOURNAL

JOURNAL

JOURNAL

JOURNAL

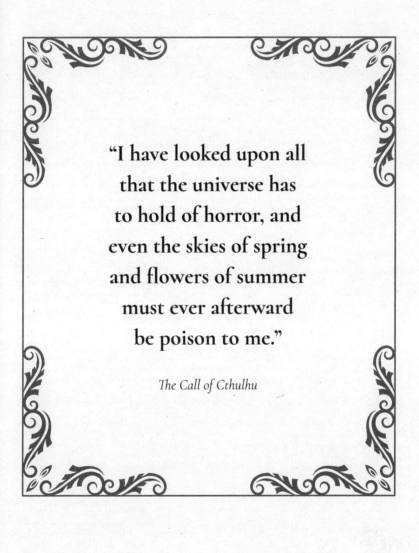

"I have looked upon all
that the universe has
to hold of horror, and
even the skies of spring
and flowers of summer
must ever afterward
be poison to me."

The Call of Cthulhu

JOURNAL

JOURNAL

JOURNAL

JOURNAL

JOURNAL

JOURNAL

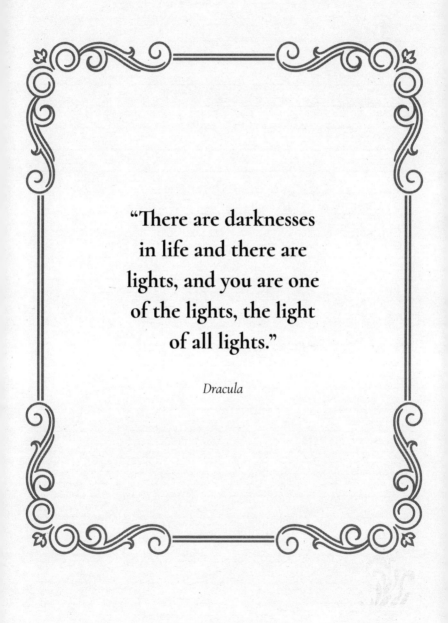

"There are darknesses
in life and there are
lights, and you are one
of the lights, the light
of all lights."

Dracula

JOURNAL

JOURNAL

JOURNAL

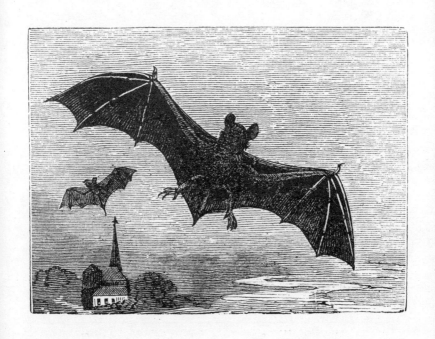

JOURNAL

JOURNAL

JOURNAL

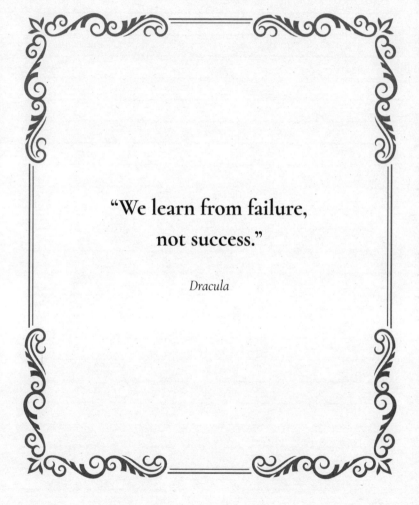

"We learn from failure,
not success."

Dracula

JOURNAL

JOURNAL

JOURNAL

JOURNAL

JOURNAL

JOURNAL

JOURNAL

JOURNAL

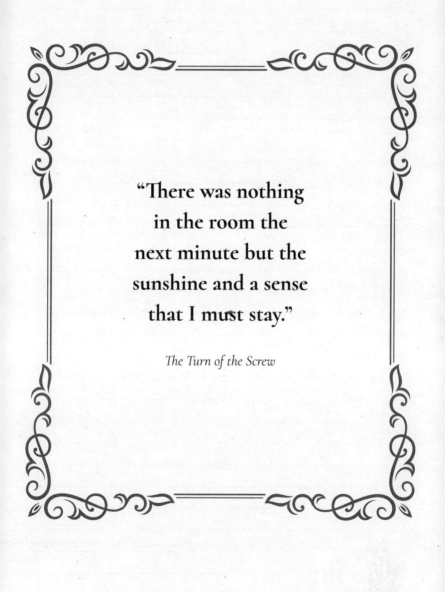

"There was nothing
in the room the
next minute but the
sunshine and a sense
that I must stay."

The Turn of the Screw

JOURNAL

JOURNAL

JOURNAL

JOURNAL

JOURNAL

JOURNAL

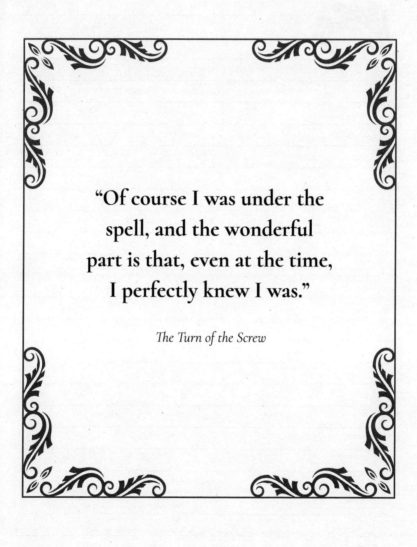

"Of course I was under the
spell, and the wonderful
part is that, even at the time,
I perfectly knew I was."

The Turn of the Screw

JOURNAL

JOURNAL

JOURNAL

JOURNAL

JOURNAL

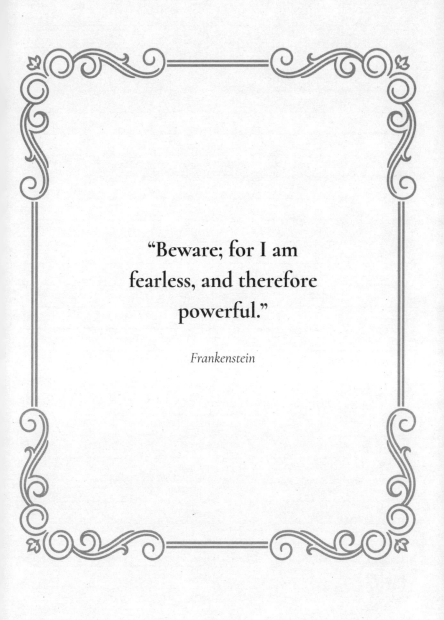

"Beware; for I am
fearless, and therefore
powerful."

Frankenstein

JOURNAL

JOURNAL

JOURNAL

JOURNAL

JOURNAL

JOURNAL

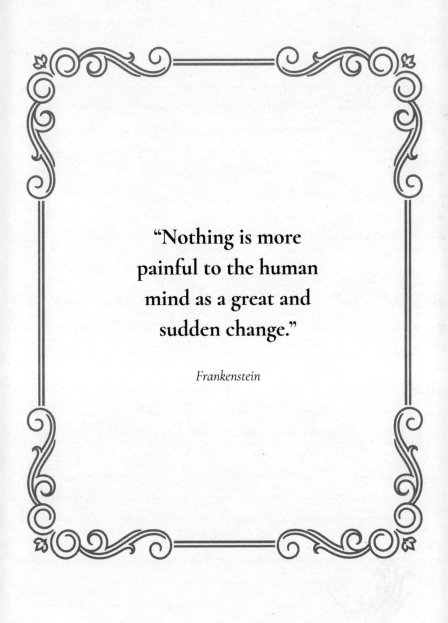

"Nothing is more painful to the human mind as a great and sudden change."

Frankenstein

JOURNAL

JOURNAL

JOURNAL

JOURNAL

JOURNAL

JOURNAL

"It is one thing to
mortify curiosity,
another to conquer it."

*The Strange Case of Dr Jekyll
and Mr Hyde*

JOURNAL

JOURNAL

JOURNAL

JOURNAL

JOURNAL

JOURNAL

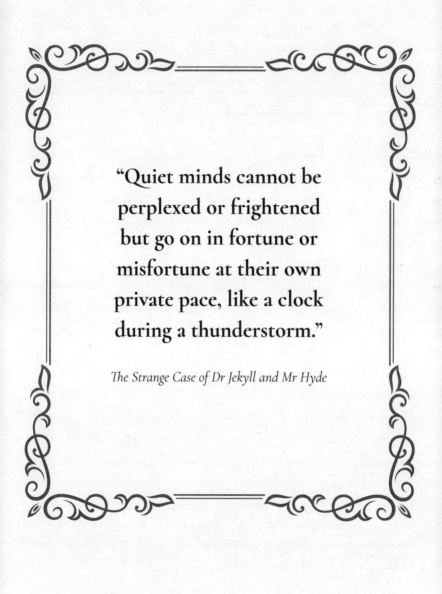

"Quiet minds cannot be perplexed or frightened but go on in fortune or misfortune at their own private pace, like a clock during a thunderstorm."

The Strange Case of Dr Jekyll and Mr Hyde

JOURNAL

JOURNAL

JOURNAL

JOURNAL

JOURNAL

JOURNAL

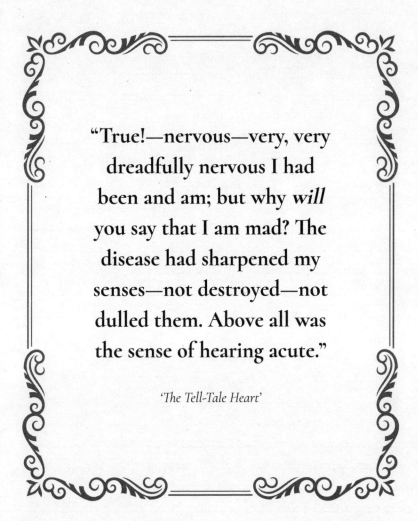

"True!—nervous—very, very dreadfully nervous I had been and am; but why *will* you say that I am mad? The disease had sharpened my senses—not destroyed—not dulled them. Above all was the sense of hearing acute."

'The Tell-Tale Heart'

JOURNAL

JOURNAL

JOURNAL

IN MEMORY OF JEMIMA BROWN

JOURNAL

JOURNAL

JOURNAL

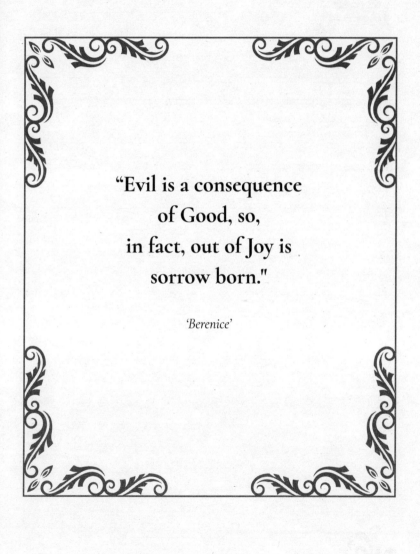

"Evil is a consequence
of Good, so,
in fact, out of Joy is
sorrow born."

'Berenice'

JOURNAL

JOURNAL

JOURNAL

JOURNAL

JOURNAL

JOURNAL

CLASSIC
TALES OF
HORROR

———

CLASSIC
TALES OF
HORROR

EDGAR ALLAN POE

Typesetting by Palimpsest Book Production Limited

Cover design: Peter Ridley
Cover illustration: Peter Gray
Design: Beatriz Custodio

AD005107US

Printed in the UK

Contents

Introduction...7

Metzengerstein..9

The Assignation (The Visionary) 19

Berenice 33

Morella...43

King Pest..49

Shadow: A Parable 63

Ligeia 66

The Fall of the House of Usher....................................84

William Wilson 106

The Man of the Crowd...129

The Oval Portrait...139

The Masque of the Red Death 143

The Pit and the Pendulum 150

The Tell-Tale Heart 167

The Black Cat 173

The Premature Burial...184

The Oblong Box...200

The Imp of the Perverse...213

The Cask of Amontillado...220

Hop-Frog..228

Introduction

Deep into that darkness peering,
Long I stood there, wondering, fearing,
Doubting, dreaming dreams no mortal
Ever dared to dream before.
– Edgar Allan Poe, 1844

To judge by the content of Edgar Allan Poe's infamous obituary, the man was a raving maniac who walked the streets muttering curses, inflamed with envy, ambition, bitter cynicism and arrogance. There was undoubtedly some degree of truth to the accusations, but they very much reflected just one side of an extremely complex man.

An orphan by the age of three, Poe spent his life fascinated by tragedy and death. His talent was celebrated and his works reprinted across the nation, yet he always struggled to keep himself financially afloat. He was, by turns, charming and cynical, gracious and bitterly envious, insightful and arrogant, visionary and dissipated. His foster father, John Allan, provided him with a luxurious childhood, then cut him off completely over university gambling debts. Poe enlisted in the army and rose to the rank of Sergeant Major of Artillery, whilst also publishing two volumes of poetry.

After the army, he spent some time in military college. This coincided with a temporary reconciliation with his foster father, the result of his foster mother Frances' death-bed request. John Allan remarried, and neither college enrolment nor reconciliation survived. In 1831, Poe moved in with his maternal aunt Maria and her daughter, Virginia, whom he married five years later, at the age of 13. Debate still rages as to whether their relationship was spousal or sibling.

After a few happy years, Virginia became ill with tuberculosis. Her health began to decline, throwing Poe into misery. When she died in 1847, at the age of 24, he submerged himself fully into alcohol. He died two and a half years later, aged 40, in 1849.

Gothic fiction was popular when Poe was working, but he was the one who freed it from its constraints. Previous writers of the weird and horrific had largely worked without any clear sense of the psychology of horror. They also laboured under the weight of moral imperative, the acceptance of social values, and it was typical, as a writer, to intrude one's own emotions into the story. Poe cut through to the ideas of the author as an impersonal lens, and of pain and terror as suitable subjects in their own right.

His approach was revolutionary, and his tales of terror delighted as many as they repulsed. They also provided a framework for the modern horror genre to come into being. Without the tales in this volume, we would never have seen Stephen King, H. P. Lovecraft, or Alfred Hitchcock. Poe was equally influential in other fields, though. As well as being a brilliant poet, he invented detective fiction, and laid foundations for modern short stories, literary criticism, adventure stories, and science fiction. He was demon-driven, undoubtedly, but we are far richer for it. If he had been less oversensitive, less bitter, less bereaved – happier – modern literature would be a much poorer thing.

METZENGERSTEIN

"Pestis eram vivus—moriens tua mors ero."
Martin Luther

Horror and fatality have been stalking abroad in all ages. Why then give a date to the story I have to tell? Let it suffice to say, that at the period of which I speak, there existed, in the interior of Hungary, a settled although hidden belief in the doctrines of the Metempsychosis. Of the doctrines themselves—that is, of their falsity, or of their probability—I say nothing. I assert, however, that much of our incredulity (as La Bruyère says of all our unhappiness) *"vient de ne pouvoir être seuls."*

But there were some points in the Hungarian superstition which were fast verging to absurdity. They—the Hungarians—differed very essentially from their Eastern authorities. For example. "The soul," said the former—I give the words of an acute and intelligent Parisian—*"ne demeure qu'une seule fois dans un corps sensible: au reste—un cheval, un chien, un homme même, n'est que la ressemblance peu tangible de ces animaux."*

The families at Berlifitzing and Metzengerstein had been at variance for centuries. Never before were two houses, so illustrious, mutually embittered by hostility so deadly. The origin of this enmity seems to be found in the words of an ancient prophecy—"A lofty name shall have a fearful fall when, as the rider over his horse, the mortality of Metzengerstein shall triumph over the immortality of Berlifitzing."

To be sure, the words themselves had little or no meaning. But more trivial causes have given rise—and that no long while ago—to consequences equally eventful. Besides, the estates, which were contiguous, had long exercised a rival influence in the affairs of a busy government. Moreover, near neighbors are seldom friends; and the inhabitants of the Castle Berlifitzing might look from their lofty buttresses into the very windows of the Palace Metzengerstein. Least of all had the more than feudal magnificence, thus discovered, a tendency to allay the irritable feelings of the less ancient and less wealthy Berlifitzings. What wonder, then, that the words, however silly, of that prediction, should have succeeded in setting and keeping at variance two families already predisposed to quarrel by every instigation of hereditary jealousy? The prophecy seemed to imply— if it implied anything—a final triumph on the part of the already more powerful house; and was of course remembered with the more bitter animosity by the weaker and less influential.

Wilhelm, Count Berlifitzing, although loftily descended, was, at the epoch of this narrative, an infirm and doting old man, remarkable for nothing but an inordinate and inveterate personal antipathy to the family of his rival, and so passionate a love of horses, and of hunting, that neither bodily infirmity, great age, nor mental incapacity, prevented his daily participation in the dangers of the chase.

Frederick, Baron Metzengerstein, was, on the other hand, not yet of age. His father, the Minister G——, died young. His mother, the Lady Mary, followed him quickly. Frederick was, at that time, in his eighteenth year. In a city, eighteen years are no long period; but in a wilderness—in so magnificent a wilderness as that old principality—the pendulum vibrates with a deeper meaning.

From some peculiar circumstances attending the administration of his father, the young Baron, at the decease of the former, entered immediately upon his vast possessions. Such estates were seldom held before by a nobleman of Hungary. His castles were without number. The chief in point of splendor and extent was the "Palace Metzengerstein." The boundary line of his dominions was never clearly defined; but his principal park embraced a circuit of fifty miles.

Upon the succession of a proprietor so young, with a character so well known, to a fortune so unparalleled, little speculation was afloat in regard to his probable course of conduct. And, indeed, for the space of three days the behavior of the heir out-Heroded Herod, and fairly surpassed the expectations of his most enthusiastic admirers. Shameful debaucheries—flagrant treacheries—unheard-of atrocities—gave his trembling vassals quickly to understand that no servile submission on their part—no punctilios of conscience on his own—were thenceforward to prove any security against the remorseless fangs of a petty Caligula. On the night of the fourth day, the stables of the Castle Berlifitzing were discovered to be on fire; and the unanimous opinion of the neighborhood added the crime of the incendiary to the already hideous list of the Baron's misdemeanors and enormities.

But during the tumult occasioned by this occurrence, the young nobleman himself sat apparently buried in meditation, in a vast and desolate upper apartment of the family palace of Metzengerstein. The rich although faded tapestry hangings which swung gloomily upon the walls represented the shadowy and majestic forms of a thousand illustrious ancestors. *Here*, rich-ermined priests and pontifical dignitaries, familiarly seated with the autocrat and the sovereign, put a veto on the wishes of a temporal king, or restrained with the fiat of papal supremacy the rebellious sceptre of the Arch-enemy. *There*, the dark, tall statures of the Princes Metzengerstein—their muscular war-courses plunging over the carcasses of fallen foes—startled the steadiest nerves with their vigorous expression; and *here*, again, the voluptuous and swan-like figures of the dames of days gone by floated away in the mazes of an unreal dance to the strains of imaginary melody.

But as the Baron listened, or affected to listen, to the gradually increasing uproar in the stables of Berlifitzing—or perhaps pondered upon some more novel, some more decided act of audacity—his eyes were turned unwittingly to the figure of an enormous, and unnaturally colored horse, represented in the tapestry as belonging to a Saracen ancestor of the family of his rival. The horse itself, in the foreground of the design, stood motionless and statue-like—while, farther back, its discomfited rider perished by the dagger of a Metzengerstein.

On Frederick's lip arose a fiendish expression, as he became aware of the direction which his glance had, without his consciousness, assumed. Yet he did not remove it. On the contrary, he could by no means account for the overwhelming anxiety which appeared falling like a pall upon his senses. It was with difficulty that he reconciled his dreamy and incoherent feelings with the certainty of being awake. The longer he gazed the more absorbing became the spell—the more impossible did it appear that he could ever withdraw his glance from the fascination of that tapestry. But the tumult without becoming suddenly more violent, with a compulsory exertion he diverted his attention to the glare of ruddy light thrown full by the flaming stables upon the windows of the apartment.

The action, however, was but momentary; his gaze returned mechanically to the wall. To his extreme horror and astonishment, the head of the gigantic steed had, in the meantime, altered its position. The neck of the animal, before arched, as if in compassion, over the prostrate body of its lord, was now extended at full length, in the direction of the Baron. The eyes, before invisible, now wore an energetic and human expression, while they gleamed with a fiery and unusual red; and the distended lips of the apparently enraged horse left in full view his sepulchral and disgusting teeth.

Stupefied with terror, the young nobleman tottered to the door. As he threw it open, a flash of red light, streaming far into the chamber, flung his shadow with a clear outline against the quivering tapestry; and he shuddered to perceive that shadow—as he staggered awhile upon the threshold—assuming the exact position, and precisely filling up the contour, of the relentless and triumphant murderer of the Saracen Berlifitzing.

To lighten the depression of his spirits, the Baron hurried into the open air. At the principal gate of the palace he encountered three equerries. With much difficulty, and at the imminent peril of their lives, they were restraining the convulsive plunges of a gigantic and fiery-colored horse.

"Whose horse? Where did you get him?" demanded the youth, in a querulous and husky tone, as he became instantly aware that the mysterious steed in the tapestried chamber was the very counterpart of the furious animal before his eyes.

"He is your own property, sire," replied one of the equerries, "at least he is claimed by no other owner. We caught him flying, all smoking and foaming with rage, from the burning stables of the Castle Berlifitzing. Supposing him to have belonged to the old Count's stud of foreign horses, we led him back as an estray. But the grooms there disclaim any title to the creature; which is strange, since he bears evident marks of having made a narrow escape from the flames."

"The letters W. V. B. are also branded very distinctly on his forehead," interrupted a second equerry; "I suppose them, of course, to be the initials of William Von Berlifitzing—but all at the castle are positive in denying any knowledge of the horse."

"Extremely singular!" said the young Baron, with a musing air, and apparently unconscious of the meaning of his words. "He is, as you say, a remarkable horse—a prodigious horse! Although, as you very justly observe, of a suspicious and untractable character; let him be mine, however," he added, after a pause, "perhaps a rider like Frederick of Metzengerstein may tame even the devil from the stables of Berlifitzing."

"You are mistaken, my lord; the horse, as I think we mentioned, is *not* from the stables of the Count. If such had been the case, we know our duty better than to bring him into the presence of a noble of your family."

"True!" observed the Baron, dryly; and at that instant a page of the bedchamber came from the palace with a heightened color, and a precipitate step. He whispered into his master's ear an account of the sudden disappearance of a small portion of the tapestry in an apartment which he designated; entering, at the same time, into particulars of a minute and circumstantial character; but from the low tone of voice in which these latter were communicated, nothing escaped to gratify the excited curiosity of the equerries.

The young Frederick, during the conference, seemed agitated by a variety of emotions. He soon, however, recovered his composure, and an expression of determined malignancy settled upon his countenance, as he gave peremptory orders that the apartment in question should be immediately locked up, and the key placed in his own possession.

"Have you heard of the unhappy death of the old hunter Berlifitzing?" said one of his vassals to the Baron, as, after the departure of the page, the huge steed which that nobleman had adopted as his own plunged and curveted, with redoubled fury, down the long avenue which extended from the palace to the stables of Metzengerstein.

"No!" said the Baron, turning abruptly toward the speaker. "Dead, say you?"

"It is indeed true, my lord; and, to the noble of your name, will be, I imagine, no unwelcome intelligence."

A rapid smile shot over the countenance of the listener. "How died he?"

"In his rash exertions to rescue a favorite portion of the hunting stud, he has himself perished miserably in the flames."

"I—n—d—e—e—d!" ejaculated the Baron, as if slowly and deliberately impressed with the truth of some exciting idea.

"Indeed," repeated the vassal.

"Shocking!" said the youth, calmly, and turned quietly into the palace.

From this date a marked alteration took place in the outward of the dissolute young Baron Frederick Von Metzengerstein. Indeed, his behavior disappointed every expectation, and proved little in accordance with the views of many a maneuvering mamma; while his habits and manner still less than formerly offered anything congenial with those of the neighboring aristocracy. He was never to be seen beyond the limits of his own domain, and, in this wide and social world, was utterly companionless—unless, indeed, that unnatural, impetuous, and fiery-colored horse, which he henceforward continually bestrode, had any mysterious right to the title of his friend.

Numerous invitations on the part of the neighborhood for a long time, however, periodically came in. "Will the Baron honor our festivals with his presence?" "Will the Baron join us in a hunting of the boar?"—"Metzengerstein does not hunt;" "Metzengerstein will not attend," were the haughty and laconic answers.

These repeated insults were not to be endured by an imperious nobility. Such invitations became less cordial—less frequent—in time they ceased altogether. The widow of the unfortunate Count Berlifitzing was even heard to express a hope "that the Baron might be at home when he did not wish to be at home, since he disdained the company of his equals; and ride when he did not wish to ride, since he preferred the society of a horse." This, to be sure, was a very silly explosion of hereditary pique; and merely proved how singularly unmeaning our sayings are apt to become, when we desire to be unusually energetic.

The charitable, nevertheless, attributed the alteration in the conduct of the young nobleman to the natural sorrow of a son for the untimely loss of his parents;—forgetting, however, his atrocious and reckless behavior during the short period immediately succeeding that bereavement. Some there were, indeed, who suggested a too haughty idea of self-consequence and dignity. Others again (among whom may be mentioned the family physician) did not hesitate in speaking of morbid melancholy, and hereditary ill-health; while dark hints, of a more equivocal nature, were current among the multitude.

Indeed, the Baron's perverse attachment to his lately acquired charger—an attachment which seemed to attain new strength from every fresh example of the animal's ferocious and demon-like propensities—at length became, in the eyes of all reasonable men, a hideous and unnatural fervor. In the glare of noon—at the dead hour of night—in sickness or in health—in calm or in tempest—the young Metzengerstein seemed riveted to the saddle of that colossal horse, whose intractable audacities so well accorded with his own spirit.

There were circumstances, moreover, which, coupled with late events, gave an unearthly and portentous character to the mania of the rider, and to the capabilities of the steed. The space passed over in a single leap had been accurately measured, and was found to exceed, by an astounding difference, the wildest expectations of the most imaginative. The Baron, besides, had no particular name for the animal, although all the rest in his collection were distinguished by characteristic appellations. His stable, too, was appointed at a distance from the rest; and, with regard to grooming and other necessary offices, none but the owner in person had ventured to officiate, or even to enter the enclosure of that horse's particular stall. It was also to be observed, that although the three grooms, who had caught the steed as he fled from the conflagration at Berlifitzing, had succeeded in arresting his course by means of a chain-bridle and noose—yet not one of the three could with any certainty affirm that he had, during that dangerous struggle, or at any period thereafter, actually placed his hand upon the body of the beast. Instances of peculiar intelligence in the demeanor of a noble and high-spirited horse are not to be supposed capable of exciting unreasonable attention, but there were certain circumstances which intruded themselves perforce upon the most skeptical and phlegmatic; and it is said there were times when the animal caused the gaping crowd who stood around to recoil in horror from the deep and impressive meaning of his terrible stamp—times when the young Metzengerstein turned pale and shrank away from the rapid and searching expression of his human-looking eye.

Among all the retinue of the Baron, however, none were found to doubt the ardor of that extraordinary affection which existed on the part of the young nobleman for the fiery qualities of his horse; at least, none but an insignificant and misshapen little page, whose deformities were in everybody's way, and whose opinions were of the least possible importance. He (if his ideas are worth mentioning at all) had the effrontery to assert that his master never vaulted into the saddle without an unaccountable and almost imperceptible shudder; and that, upon his return from every long-continued and habitual ride, an expression of triumphant malignity distorted every muscle in his countenance.

One tempestuous night, Metzengerstein, awakening from a heavy slumber, descended like a maniac from his chamber, and, mounting in hot haste, bounded away into the mazes of the forest. An occurrence so common attracted no particular attention, but his return was looked for with intense anxiety on the part of his domestics, when, after some hours' absence, the stupendous and magnificent battlements of the Palace Metzengerstein were discovered crackling and rocking to their very foundation, under the influence of a dense and livid mass of ungovernable fire.

As the flames, when first seen, had already made so terrible a progress that all efforts to save any portion of the building were evidently futile, the astonished neighborhood stood idly around in silent if not apathetic wonder. But a new and fearful object soon riveted the attention of the multitude, and proved how much more intense is the excitement wrought in the feelings of a crowd by the contemplation of human agony, than that brought about by the most appalling spectacles of inanimate matter.

Up the long avenue of aged oaks which led from the forest to the main entrance of the Palace Metzengerstein, a steed, bearing an unbonneted and disordered rider, was seen leaping with an impetuosity which outstripped the very Demon of the Tempest.

The career of the horseman was indisputably, on his own part, uncontrollable. The agony of his countenance, the convulsive struggle of his frame, gave evidence of superhuman exertion; but no sound, save a solitary shriek, escaped from his lacerated lips, which were bitten through and through in the intensity of terror. One instant, and the clattering of hoofs resounded sharply and shrilly above the roaring of the flames and the shrieking of the winds—another, and, clearing at a single plunge the gateway and the moat, the steed bounded far up the tottering staircases of the palace, and, with its rider, disappeared amid the whirlwind of chaotic fire.

The fury of the tempest immediately died away, and a dead calm sullenly succeeded. A white flame still enveloped the building like a shroud, and, streaming far away into the quiet atmosphere, shot forth a glare of preternatural light; while a cloud of smoke settled heavily over the battlements in the distinct colossal figure of—a horse.

THE ASSIGNATION (THE VISIONARY)

"Stay for me there! I will not fail
To meet thee in that hollow vale."
"Exequy on the Death of his Wife,"
by Henry King, Bishop of Chichester.

Ill-fated and mysterious man!—Bewildered in the brilliancy of thine own imagination, and fallen in the flames of thine own youth! Again in fancy I behold thee! Once more thy form hath risen before me!—Not—oh not as thou art—in the cold valley and shadow—but as thou *shouldst be*—squandering away a life of magnificent meditation in that city of dim visions, thine own Venice—which is a star-beloved Elysium of the sea, and the wide windows of whose Palladian palaces look down with a deep and bitter meaning upon the secrets of her silent waters. Yes! I repeat it—as thou *shouldst be*. There are surely other worlds than this—other thoughts than the thoughts of the multitude—other speculations than the speculations of the sophist. Who then shall call thy conduct into question? Who blame thee for thy visionary hours, or denounce those occupations as a wasting away of life, which were but the overflowings of thine everlasting energies?

It was at Venice, beneath the covered archway there called the Ponte dei Sospiri, that I met for the third or fourth time the person of whom I speak. It is with a confused recollection that I bring to mind the circumstances of that meeting. Yet I remember—ah! How should I forget?—the deep midnight, the Bridge of Sighs, the beauty of woman, and the Genius of Romance that stalked up and down the narrow canal.

It was a night of unusual gloom. The great clock of the Piazza had sounded the fifth hour of the Italian evening. The square of the Campanile lay silent and deserted, and the lights in the old Ducal Palace were dying fast away. I was returning home from the Piazzetta, by way of the Grand Canal. But as my gondola arrived opposite the mouth of the canal San Marco, a female voice from its recesses broke suddenly upon the night, in one wild, hysterical, and long continued shriek. Startled at the sound, I sprang upon my feet: while the gondolier, letting slip his single oar, lost it in the pitchy darkness beyond a chance of recovery, and we were consequently left to the guidance of the current which here sets from the greater into the smaller channel. Like some huge and sable-feathered condor, we were slowly drifting down towards the Bridge of Sighs, when a thousand flambeaux flashing from the windows, and down the stair-cases of the Ducal Palace, turned all at once that deep gloom into a livid and preternatural day.

A child, slipping from the arms of its own mother, had fallen from an upper window of the lofty structure into the deep and dim canal. The quiet waters had closed placidly over their victim; and, although my own gondola was the only one in sight, many a stout swimmer, already in the stream, was seeking in vain upon the surface the treasure which was to be found—alas!—only within the abyss. Upon the broad black marble flagstones at the entrance of the palace, and a few steps above the water, stood a figure which none who then saw can have ever since forgotten. It was the Marchesa Aphrodite— the adoration of all Venice—the gayest of the gay—the most lovely where all were beautiful—but still the young wife of the old and intriguing Mentoni, and the mother of that fair child, her first and only one, who now, deep beneath the murky water, was thinking in bitterness of heart upon her sweet caresses, and exhausting its little life in struggles to call upon her name.

She stood alone. Her small, bare, and silvery feet gleamed in the black mirror of marble beneath her. Her hair, not as yet more than half loosened for the night from its ballroom array, clustered, amid a shower of diamonds, round and round her classical head, in curls like those of the young hyacinth. A snowy-white and gauze-like drapery seemed to be nearly the sole covering to her delicate form; but the mid-summer and midnight air was hot, sullen, and still, and no motion in the statue-like form itself stirred even the folds of that raiment of very vapor which hung around it as the heavy marble hangs around the Niobe. Yet—strange to say!—her large lustrous eyes were not turned downwards upon that grave wherein her brightest hope lay buried, but riveted in a widely different direction! The prison of the Old Republic is, I think, the stateliest building in all Venice—but how could that lady gaze so fixedly upon it, when beneath her lay stifling her own child? Yon dark, gloomy niche, too, yawns right opposite her chamber window—what, then, *could* there be in its shadows—in its architecture—in its ivy-wreathed and solemn cornices—that the Marchesa di Mentoni had not wondered at a thousand times before? Nonsense!—Who does not remember that, at such a time as this, the eye, like a shattered mirror, multiplies the images of its sorrow, and sees in innumerable far off places, the woe which is close at hand?

Many steps above the Marchesa, and within the arch of the water-gate, stood, in full dress, the Satyr-like figure of Mentoni himself. He was occasionally occupied in thrumming a guitar, and seemed *ennuyé* to the very death, as at intervals he gave directions for the recovery of his child. Stupefied and aghast, I had myself no power to move from the upright position I had assumed upon first hearing the shriek, and must have presented to the eyes of the agitated group a spectral and ominous appearance, as with pale countenance and rigid limbs, I floated down among them in that funereal gondola.

All efforts proved in vain. Many of the most energetic in the search were relaxing their exertions, and yielding to a gloomy sorrow. There seemed but little hope for the child (how much less than for the mother!); but now, from the interior of that dark niche which has been already mentioned as forming a part of the Old Republican prison, and as fronting the lattice of the Marchesa, a figure muffled in a cloak stepped out within reach of the light, and, pausing a moment upon the verge of the giddy descent, plunged headlong into the canal. As, in an instant afterwards, he stood with the still living and breathing child within his grasp, upon the marble flagstones by the side of the Marchesa, his cloak, heavy with the drenching water, became unfastened, and, falling in folds about his feet, discovered to the wonder-stricken spectators the graceful person of a very young man, with the sound of whose name the greater part of Europe was then ringing.

No word spoke the deliverer. But the Marchesa! She will now receive her child—she will press it to her heart—she will cling to its little form, and smother it with her caresses. Alas! *Another's* arms have taken it from the stranger—*another's* arms have taken it away, and borne it afar off, unnoticed, into the palace! And the Marchesa! Her lip—her beautiful lip trembles: tears are gathering in her eyes— those eyes which, like Pliny's acanthus, are "soft and almost liquid." Yes! Tears are gathering in those eyes—and see! The entire woman thrills throughout the soul, and the statue has started into life! The pallor of the marble countenance, the swelling of the marble bosom, the very purity of the marble feet, we behold suddenly flushed over with a tide of ungovernable crimson; and a slight shudder quivers about her delicate frame, as a gentle air at Napoli about the rich silver lilies in the grass.

Why *should* that lady blush! To this demand there is no answer—

except that, having left, in the eager haste and terror of a mother's heart, the privacy of her own boudoir, she has neglected to enthrall her tiny feet in their slippers, and utterly forgotten to throw over her Venetian shoulders that drapery which is their due. What other possible reason could there have been for her so blushing?—For the glance of those wild appealing eyes?—For the unusual tumult of that throbbing bosom?—For the convulsive pressure of that trembling hand?—That hand which fell, as Mentoni turned into the palace, accidentally, upon the hand of the stranger. What reason could there have been for the low—the singularly low tone of those unmeaning words which the lady uttered hurriedly in bidding him adieu? "Thou hast conquered"—she said, or the murmurs of the water deceived me—"thou hast conquered—one hour after sunrise—we shall meet—so let it be!"

* * *

The tumult had subsided, the lights had died away within the palace, and the stranger, whom I now recognized, stood alone upon the flags. He shook with inconceivable agitation, and his eye glanced around in search of a gondola. I could not do less than offer him the service of my own; and he accepted the civility. Having obtained an oar at the water-gate, we proceeded together to his residence, while he rapidly recovered his self-possession, and spoke of our former slight acquaintance in terms of great apparent cordiality.

There are some subjects upon which I take pleasure in being minute. The person of the stranger—let me call him by this title, who to all the world was still a stranger—the person of the stranger is one of these subjects. In height he might have been below rather than above the medium size: although there were moments of intense passion when his frame actually *expanded* and belied the assertion. The light, almost slender symmetry of his figure promised more of that ready activity which he evinced at the Bridge of Sighs, than of that Herculean strength which he has been known to wield without an effort, upon occasions of more dangerous emergency. With the mouth and chin of a deity—singular, wild, full, liquid eyes, whose shadows varied from pure hazel to intense and brilliant jet—and a profusion of curling, black hair, from which a forehead of unusual breadth gleamed forth at intervals all light and ivory—his were features than which I have seen none more classically regular, except, perhaps, the marble ones of the Emperor Commodus. Yet his countenance was, nevertheless, one of those which all men have seen at some period of their lives, and have never afterwards seen again. It had no peculiar—it had no settled predominant expression to be fastened upon the memory; a countenance seen and instantly forgotten—but forgotten with a vague and never-ceasing desire of recalling it to mind. Not that the spirit of each rapid passion failed, at any time, to throw its own distinct image upon the mirror of that face—but that the mirror, mirror-like, retained no vestige of the passion, when the passion had departed.

Upon leaving him on the night of our adventure, he solicited me, in what I thought an urgent manner, to call upon him *very* early the next morning. Shortly after sunrise, I found myself accordingly at his Palazzo, one of those huge structures of gloomy, yet fantastic, pomp, which tower above the waters of the Grand Canal in the vicinity of the Rialto. I was shown up a broad winding staircase of mosaics, into an apartment whose unparalleled splendor burst through the opening door with an actual glare, making me blind and dizzy with luxuriousness.

I knew my acquaintance to be wealthy. Report had spoken of his possessions in terms which I had even ventured to call terms of ridiculous exaggeration. But as I gazed about me, I could not bring myself to believe that the wealth of any subject in Europe could have supplied the princely magnificence which burned and blazed around.

Although, as I say, the sun had arisen, yet the room was still brilliantly lighted up. I judged from this circumstance, as well as from an air of exhaustion in the countenance of my friend, that he had not retired to bed during the whole of the preceding night. In the architecture and embellishments of the chamber, the evident design had been to dazzle and astound. Little attention had been paid to the *decora* of what is technically called *keeping*, or to the proprieties of nationality. The eye wandered from object to object, and rested upon none—neither the *grotesques* of the Greek painters, nor the sculptures of the best Italian days, nor the huge carvings of untutored Egypt. Rich draperies in every part of the room trembled to the vibration of low, melancholy music, whose origin was not to be discovered. The senses were oppressed by mingled and conflicting perfumes, reeking up from strange convolute censers, together with multitudinous flaring and flickering tongues of emerald and violet fire. The rays of the newly risen sun poured in upon the whole, through windows formed each of a single pane of crimson-tinted glass. Glancing to and fro, in a thousand reflections, from curtains which rolled from their cornices like cataracts of molten silver, the beams of natural glory mingled at length fitfully with the artificial light, and lay weltering in subdued masses upon a carpet of rich, liquid-looking cloth of Chili gold.

"Ha! ha! ha!—Ha! ha! ha!"—laughed the proprietor, motioning me to a seat as I entered the room, and throwing himself back at full length upon an ottoman. "I see," said he, perceiving that I could not immediately reconcile myself to the *bienséance* of so singular a welcome—"I see you are astonished at my apartment—at my statues—my pictures—my originality of conception in architecture and upholstery—absolutely drunk—eh?—with my magnificence. But pardon me, my dear sir (here his tone of voice dropped to the very spirit of cordiality), pardon me for my uncharitable laughter. You appeared so *utterly* astonished. Besides, some things are so completely ludicrous that a man *must* laugh or die. To die laughing must be the most glorious of all glorious deaths! Sir Thomas More—a very fine man was Sir Thomas More—Sir Thomas More died laughing, you remember. Also in the *Absurdities* of Ravisius Textor, there is a long list of characters who came to the same magnificent end. Do you know, however," continued he musingly, "that at Sparta (which is now Palæochori), at Sparta, I say, to the west of the citadel, among a chaos of scarcely visible ruins, is a kind of *socle* upon which are still legible the letters ΛΑΣΜ. They are undoubtedly part of ΓΕΛΑΣΜΑ. Now, at Sparta were a thousand temples and shrines to a thousand different divinities. How exceedingly strange that the altar of Laughter should have survived all the others! But in the present instance," he resumed, with a singular alteration of voice and manner, "I have no right to be merry at your expense. You might well have been amazed. Europe cannot produce anything so fine as this, my little regal cabinet. My other apartments are by no means of the same order; mere *ultras* of fashionable insipidity. This is better than fashion—is it not? Yet this has but to be seen to become the rage—that is, with those who could afford it at the cost of their entire patrimony. I have guarded, however, against any such profanation. With one exception you are the only human being besides myself and my valet who has been admitted within the mysteries of these imperial precincts, since they have been bedizzened as you see!"

I bowed in acknowledgment: for the overpowering sense of splendor and perfume, and music, together with the unexpected eccentricity of his address and manner, prevented me from expressing, in words, my appreciation of what I might have construed into a compliment.

"Here," he resumed, arising and leaning on my arm as he sauntered around the apartment, "here are paintings from the Greeks to Cimabue, and from Cimabue to the present hour. Many are chosen, as you see, with little deference to the opinions of Virtû. They are all, however, fitting tapestry for a chamber such as this. Here too, are some *chéfs d'œuvres* of the unknown great—and here unfinished designs by men, celebrated in their day, whose very names the perspicacity of the academies has left to silence and to me. What think you," said he, turning abruptly as he spoke—"what think you of this Madonna della Pietà?"

"It is Guido's own!" I said with all the enthusiasm of my nature, for I had been poring intently over its surpassing loveliness. "It is Guido's own!—How *could* you have obtained it?—She is undoubtedly in painting what the Venus is in sculpture."

"Ha!" said he thoughtfully. "The Venus—the beautiful Venus?—The Venus of the Medici?—She of the diminutive head and the gilded hair? Part of the left arm (here his voice dropped so as to be heard with difficulty) and all the right are restorations, and in the coquetry of that right arm lies, I think, the quintessence of all affectation. Give *me* the Canova! The Apollo, too, is a copy—there can be no doubt of it—blind fool that I am, who cannot behold the boasted inspiration of the Apollo! I cannot help—pity me!—I cannot help preferring the Antinous. Was it not Socrates who said that the statuary found his statue in the block of marble? Then Michæl Angelo was by no means original in his couplet—

Non ha l'ottimo artista alcun concetto
Ch'un marmo solo in sé non circunscriva."

It has been, or should be, remarked that, in the manner of the true gentleman, we are always aware of a difference from the bearing of the vulgar, without being at once precisely able to determine in what such difference consists. Allowing the remark to have applied in its full force to the outward demeanor of my acquaintance, I felt it, on that eventful morning, still more fully applicable to his moral temperament and character. Nor can I better define that peculiarity of spirit which seemed to place him so essentially apart from all other human beings, than by calling it a *habit* of intense and continual thought, pervading even his most trivial actions—intruding upon his moments of dalliance—and interweaving itself with his very flashes of merriment—like adders which writhe from out the eyes of the grinning masks in the cornices around the temples of Persepolis.

I could not help, however, repeatedly observing, through the mingled tone of levity and solemnity with which he rapidly descanted upon matters of little importance, a certain air of trepidation—a degree of nervous *unction* in action and in speech—an unquiet excitability of manner which appeared to me at all times unaccountable, and upon some occasions even filled me with alarm. Frequently, too, pausing in the middle of a sentence whose commencement he had apparently forgotten, he seemed to be listening in the deepest attention, as if either in momentary expectation of a visitor, or to sounds which must have had existence in his imagination alone.

It was during one of these reveries or pauses of apparent abstraction, that, in turning over a page of the poet and scholar Politian's beautiful tragedy *The Orfeo* (the first native Italian tragedy), which lay near me upon an ottoman, I discovered a passage underlined in pencil. It was a passage towards the end of the third act—a passage of the most heart-stirring excitement—a passage which, although tainted with impurity, no man shall read without a thrill of novel emotion—no woman without a sigh. The whole page was blotted with fresh tears, and, upon the opposite interleaf, were the following English lines, written in a hand so very different from the peculiar characters of my acquaintance that I had some difficulty in recognizing it as his own:

> *Thou wast that all to me, love,*
> *For which my soul did pine—*
> *A green isle in the sea, love,*
> *A fountain and a shrine,*

All wreathed with fairy fruits and flowers;
And all the flowers were mine.

Ah, dream too bright to last!
Ah, starry Hope, that didst arise
But to be overcast!
A voice from out the Future cries,
"Onward!"—But o'er the Past
(Dim gulf!) my spirit hovering lies,
Mute—motionless—aghast!

For alas! Alas! With me
The light of life is o'er.
"No more—no more—no more,"
(Such language holds the solemn sea
To the sands upon the shore,)
Shall bloom the thunder-blasted tree,
Or the stricken eagle soar!

Now all my hours are trances;
And all my nightly dreams
Are where the dark eye glances,
And where thy footstep gleams,
In what ethereal dances,
By what Italian streams.

Alas! For that accursed time
They bore thee o'er the billow,
From Love to titled age and crime,
And an unholy pillow!—
From me, and from our misty clime,
Where weeps the silver willow!

That these lines were written in English—a language with which I had not believed their author acquainted—afforded me little matter for surprise. I was too well aware of the extent of his acquirements, and of the singular pleasure he took in concealing them from observation, to be astonished at any similar discovery; but the place of date, I must confess, occasioned me no little amazement. It had been originally written *London*, and afterwards carefully overscored—not, however, so effectually as to conceal the word from a scrutinizing eye. I say this occasioned me no little amazement; for I well remember that, in a former conversation with my friend, I particularly inquired if he had at any time met in London the Marchesa di Mentoni (who for some years previous to her marriage had resided in that city), when his answer, if I mistake not, gave me to understand that he had never visited the metropolis of Great Britain. I might as well here mention that I have more than once heard (without, of course, giving credit to a report involving so many improbabilities), that the person of whom I speak was, not only by birth, but in education, an *Englishman*.

* * *

"There is one painting," said he, without being aware of my notice of the tragedy—"there is still one painting which you have not seen." And throwing aside a drapery, he discovered a full-length portrait of the Marchesa Aphrodite.

Human art could have done no more in the delineation of her superhuman beauty. The same ethereal figure which stood before me the preceding night upon the steps of the Ducal Palace, stood before me once again. But in the expression of the countenance, which was beaming all over with smiles, there still lurked (incomprehensible anomaly!) that fitful stain of melancholy which will ever be found inseparable from the perfection of the beautiful. Her right arm lay folded over her bosom. With her left she pointed downward to a curiously fashioned vase. One small, fairy foot, alone visible, barely touched the earth—and, scarcely discernible in the brilliant atmosphere which seemed to encircle and enshrine her loveliness, floated a pair of the most delicately imagined wings. My glance fell from the painting to the figure of my friend, and the vigorous words of Chapman's *Bussy D'Ambois* quivered instinctively upon my lips:

> "He is up
> There like a Roman statue! He will stand
> 'Till Death hath made him marble!"

"Come!" he said at length, turning towards a table of richly enameled and massive silver, upon which were a few goblets fantastically stained, together with two large Etruscan vases, fashioned in the same extraordinary model as that in the foreground of the portrait, and filled with what I supposed to be Johannisberger. "Come!" he said, abruptly, "let us drink! It is early—but let us drink. It is *indeed* early," he continued, musingly, as a cherub with a heavy golden hammer, made the apartment ring with the first hour after sunrise—"It is *indeed* early, but what matters it? Let us drink! Let us pour out an offering to yon solemn sun which these gaudy lamps and censers are so eager to subdue!" And, having made me pledge him in a bumper, he swallowed in rapid succession several goblets of the wine.

"To dream," he continued, resuming the tone of his desultory conversation, as he held up to the rich light of a censer one of the magnificent vases—"to dream has been the business of my life. I have therefore framed for myself, as you see, a bower of dreams. In the heart of Venice could I have erected a better? You behold around you, it is true, a medley of architectural embellishments. The chastity of Ionia is offended by antediluvian devices, and the sphinxes of

Egypt are outstretched upon carpets of gold. Yet the effect is incongruous to the timid alone. Proprieties of place, and especially of time, are the bugbears which terrify mankind from the contemplation of the magnificent. Once I was myself a decorist; but that sublimation of folly has palled upon my soul. All this is now the fitter for my purpose. Like these arabesque censers, my spirit is writhing in fire, and the delirium of this scene is fashioning me for the wilder visions of that land of real dreams whither I am now rapidly departing." He here paused abruptly, bent his head to his bosom, and seemed to listen to a sound which I could not hear. At length, erecting his frame, he looked upwards and ejaculated the lines of the Bishop of Chichester:—

> "Stay for me there! I will not fail
> To meet thee in that hollow vale."

In the next instant, confessing the power of the wine, he threw himself at full length upon an ottoman.

A quick step was now heard upon the staircase, and a loud knock at the door rapidly succeeded. I was hastening to anticipate a second disturbance, when a page of Mentoni's household burst into the room, and faltered out, in a voice choking with emotion, the incoherent words, "My mistress!—My mistress!—Poisoned!—Poisoned! Oh, beautiful—Oh, beautiful Aphrodite!"

Bewildered, I flew to the ottoman, and endeavored to arouse the sleeper to a sense of the startling intelligence. But his limbs were rigid—his lips were livid—his lately beaming eyes were riveted in *death*. I staggered back towards the table—my hand fell upon a cracked and blackened goblet—and a consciousness of the entire and terrible truth flashed suddenly over my soul.

BERENICE

*"Dicebant mihi sodales si sepulchrum amicae visitarem
curas meas aliquantulum fore levatas."*
Ebn Zaiat

Misery is manifold. The wretchedness of earth is multiform.
Overreaching the wide horizon as the rainbow, its hues are as
various as the hues of that arch—as distinct too, yet as intimately
blended. Overreaching the wide horizon as the rainbow! How is
it that from beauty I have derived a type of unloveliness?—From
the covenant of peace a simile of sorrow? But as, in ethics, evil
is a consequence of good, so, in fact, out of joy is sorrow born.
Either the memory of past bliss is the anguish of today, or the
agonies which *are* have their origin in the ecstasies which *might
have been*.

My baptismal name is Egæus; that of my family I will not
mention. Yet there are no towers in the land more time-honored than
my gloomy, gray, hereditary halls. Our line has been called a race
of visionaries; and in many striking particulars—in the character of
the family mansion—in the frescoes of the chief saloon—in the
tapestries of the dormitories—in the chiseling of some buttresses in
the armory—but more especially in the gallery of antique paintings—
in the fashion of the library chamber—and, lastly, in the very peculiar nature of the library's contents, there is more than sufficient
evidence to warrant the belief.

The recollections of my earliest years are connected with that chamber, and with its volumes—of which latter I will say no more. Here died my mother. Herein was I born. But it is mere idleness to say that I had not lived before—that the soul has no previous existence. You deny it?—Let us not argue the matter. Convinced myself, I seek not to convince. There is, however, a remembrance of aerial forms—of spiritual and meaning eyes—of sounds, musical yet sad—a remembrance which will not be excluded; a memory like a shadow, vague, variable, indefinite, unsteady; and like a shadow, too, in the impossibility of my getting rid of it while the sunlight of my reason shall exist.

In that chamber was I born. Thus awaking from the long night of what seemed, but was not, nonentity, at once into the very regions of fairyland—into a palace of imagination—into the wild dominions of monastic thought and erudition—it is not singular that I gazed around me with a startled and ardent eye—that I loitered away my boyhood in books, and dissipated my youth in reverie; but it *is* singular that as years rolled away, and the noon of manhood found me still in the mansion of my fathers—it *is* wonderful what stagnation there fell upon the springs of my life—wonderful how total an inversion took place in the character of my commonest thought. The realities of the world affected me as visions, and as visions only, while the wild ideas of the land of dreams became, in turn,—not the material of my everyday existence—but in very deed that existence utterly and solely in itself.

Berenice and I were cousins, and we grew up together in my paternal halls. Yet differently we grew—I ill of health, and buried in gloom—she agile, graceful, and overflowing with energy; hers the ramble on the hill-side—mine the studies of the cloister—I living within my own heart, and addicted body and soul to the most intense and painful meditation—she roaming carelessly through life with no thought of the shadows in her path, or the silent flight of the raven-winged hours. Berenice!—I call upon her name—Berenice!—and from the gray ruins of memory a thousand tumultuous recollections are startled at the sound! Ah! Vividly is her image before me now, as in the early days of her light-heartedness and joy! Oh! Gorgeous yet fantastic beauty! Oh! Sylph amid the shrubberies of Arnheim! Oh! Naiad among its fountains!—And then—then all is mystery and terror, and a tale which should not be told. Disease—a fatal disease—fell like the simoom upon her frame, and, even while I gazed upon her, the spirit of change swept over her, pervading her mind, her habits, and her character, and, in a manner the most subtle and terrible, disturbing even the identity of her person! Alas! The destroyer came and went, and the victim—where was she? I knew her not—or knew her no longer as Berenice.

Among the numerous train of maladies superinduced by that fatal and primary one which effected a revolution of so horrible a kind in the moral and physical being of my cousin, may be mentioned as the most distressing and obstinate in its nature, a species of epilepsy not unfrequently terminating in *trance* itself—trance very nearly resembling positive dissolution, and from which her manner of recovery was, in most instances, startlingly abrupt. In the meantime my own disease—for I have been told that I should call it by no other appellation—my own disease, then, grew rapidly upon me, and assumed finally a monomaniac character of a novel and extraordinary form—hourly and momently gaining vigor—and at length obtaining over me the most incomprehensible ascendancy. This monomania, if I must so term it, consisted in a morbid irritability of those properties of the mind in metaphysical science termed the *attentive*. It is more than probable that I am not understood; but I fear, indeed, that it is in no manner possible to convey to the mind of the merely general reader, an adequate idea of that nervous intensity of interest with which, in my case, the powers of meditation (not to speak technically) busied and buried themselves, in the contemplation of even the most ordinary objects of the universe.

To muse for long unwearied hours with my attention riveted to some frivolous device on the margin, or in the typography of a book; to become absorbed for the better part of a summer's day, in a quaint shadow falling aslant upon the tapestry, or upon the door; to lose myself for an entire night in watching the steady flame of a lamp, or the embers of a fire; to dream away whole days over the perfume of a flower; to repeat monotonously some common word, until the sound, by dint of frequent repetition, ceased to convey any idea whatever to the mind; to lose all sense of motion or physical exist-ence, by means of absolute bodily quiescence long and obstinately persevered in—such were a few of the most common and least pernicious vagaries induced by a condition of the mental faculties, not, indeed, altogether unparalleled, but certainly bidding defiance to anything like analysis or explanation.

Yet let me not be misapprehended. The undue, earnest, and morbid attention thus excited by objects in their own nature frivolous, must not be confounded in character with that ruminating propensity common to all mankind, and more especially indulged in by persons of ardent imagination. It was not even, as might be at first supposed, an extreme condition, or exaggeration of such propensity, but primarily and essentially distinct and different. In the one instance, the dreamer, or enthusiast, being interested by an object usually *not* frivolous, imperceptibly loses sight of this object in a wilderness of deductions and suggestions issuing therefrom, until, at the conclusion of a day-dream *often replete with luxury*, he finds the *incitamentum*, or first cause of his musings, entirely vanished and forgotten. In my case, the primary object was *invariably frivolous*, although assuming, through the medium of my distempered vision, a refracted and unreal importance. Few deductions, if any, were made; and those few per-tinaciously returning in upon the original object as a center. The meditations were *never* pleasurable; and, at the termination of the reverie, the first cause, so far from being out of sight, had attained that supernaturally exaggerated interest which was the prevailing feature of the disease. In a word, the powers of mind more particularly exercised were, with me, as I have said before, the *attentive*, and are, with the daydreamer, the *speculative*.

My books, at this epoch, if they did not exactly serve to irritate the disorder, partook, it will be perceived, largely, in their imaginative and inconsequential nature, of the characteristic qualities of the disorder itself. I well remember, among others, the treatise of the noble Italian Caelius Secundus Curio, "*de Amplitudine Beati Regni Dei*"; St Augustine's great work *The City of God*; and Tertullian's "*de Carne Christi*", in which the paradoxical sentence, "*Mortuus est Dei filius; credibile est quia ineptum est: et sepultus resurrexit; certum est quia impossibile est*," occupied my undivided time for many weeks of laborious and fruitless investigation.

Thus it will appear that, shaken from its balance only by trivial things, my reason bore resemblance to that ocean-crag spoken of by Ptolemy Hephestion, which, steadily resisting the attacks of human violence, and the fiercer fury of the waters and the winds, trembled only to the touch of the flower called Asphodel. And although, to a careless thinker, it might appear a matter beyond doubt, that the alteration produced by her unhappy malady, in the *moral* condition of Berenice, would afford me many objects for the exercise of that intense and abnormal meditation whose nature I have been at some trouble in explaining, yet such was not in any degree the case. In the lucid intervals of my infirmity, her calamity, indeed, gave me pain, and, taking deeply to heart that total wreck of her fair and gentle life, I did not fail to ponder frequently and bitterly upon the wonder-working means by which so strange a revolution had been so suddenly brought to pass. But these reflections partook not of the idiosyncrasy of my disease, and were such as would have occurred, under similar circumstances, to the ordinary mass of mankind. True to its own character, my disorder reveled in the less important but

more startling changes wrought in the *physical* frame of Berenice—
in the singular and most appalling distortion of her personal identity.

During the brightest days of her unparalleled beauty, most surely
I had never loved her. In the strange anomaly of my existence, feelings with me had never been of the heart, and my passions always
were of the mind. Through the gray of the early morning—among
the trellised shadows of the forest at noonday—and in the silence
of my library at night, she had flitted by my eyes, and I had seen
her—not as the living and breathing Berenice, but as the Berenice
of a dream—not as a being of the earth, earthy, but as the abstraction
of such a being—not as a thing to admire, but to analyze—not as
an object of love, but as the theme of the most abstruse although
desultory speculation. And *now*—now I shuddered in her presence,
and grew pale at her approach; yet bitterly lamenting her fallen and
desolate condition, I called to mind that she had loved me long, and,
in an evil moment, I spoke to her of marriage.

And at length the period of our nuptials was approaching, when,
upon an afternoon in the winter of the year—one of those unsea-
sonably warm, calm, and misty days which are the nurse of the
beautiful Halcyon—I sat (and sat, as I thought, alone) in the inner
apartment of the library. But uplifting my eyes I saw that Berenice
stood before me.

Was it my own excited imagination—or the misty influence of
the atmosphere—or the uncertain twilight of the chamber—or the
gray draperies which fell around her figure—that caused in it so
vacillating and indistinct an outline? I could not tell. She spoke no
word, and I—not for worlds could I have uttered a syllable. An icy
chill ran through my frame; a sense of insufferable anxiety
oppressed me; a consuming curiosity pervaded my soul; and sinking
back upon the chair, I remained for some time breathless and
motionless, with my eyes riveted upon her person. Alas! Its emaciation was excessive, and not one vestige of the former being lurked

in any single line of the contour. My burning glances at length fell upon the face.

The forehead was high, and very pale, and singularly placid; and the once jetty hair fell partially over it, and overshadowed the hollow temples with innumerable ringlets now of a vivid yellow, and jarring discordantly, in their fantastic character, with the reigning melancholy of the countenance. The eyes were lifeless, and lusterless, and seemingly pupilless, and I shrank involuntarily from their glassy stare to the contemplation of the thin and shrunken lips. They parted; and in a smile of peculiar meaning, *the teeth* of the changed Berenice disclosed themselves slowly to my view. Would to God that I had never beheld them, or that, having done so, I had died!

The shutting of a door disturbed me, and, looking up, I found that my cousin had departed from the chamber. But from the disordered chamber of my brain, had not—alas! —departed, and would not be driven away, the white and ghastly *spectrum* of the teeth. Not a speck on their surface—not a shade on their enamel—not an indenture in their edges—but what that period of her smile had sufficed to brand in upon my memory. I saw them now even more unequivocally than I beheld them then. The teeth!—The teeth!—They were here, and there, and everywhere, and visibly and palpably before me; long, narrow, and excessively white, with the pale lips writhing about them, as in the very moment of their first terrible development. Then came the full fury of my monomania, and I struggled in vain against its strange and irresistible influence. In the multiplied objects of the external world I had no thoughts but for the teeth. For these I longed with a frenzied desire. All other matters and all different interests became absorbed in their single contemplation. They—they alone were present to the mental eye, and they, in their sole individuality, became the essence of my mental life. I held them in every light. I turned them in every attitude. I surveyed their characteristics. I dwelt upon their peculiarities. I pondered upon their conformation. I mused upon the alteration in their nature. I shuddered as I assigned to them in imagination a sensitive and sentient power, and even when unassisted by the lips, a capability of moral expression. Of Mademoiselle Sallé it has been well said, "*Que tous ses pas étaient des sentiments*," and of Berenice I more seriously believed *que toutes ses dents étaient des idées. Des idées!*—Ah, here was the idiotic thought that destroyed me! *Des idées!*—Ah, therefore it was that I coveted them so madly! I felt that their possession could alone ever restore me to peace, in giving me back to reason.

And the evening closed in upon me thus—and then the darkness came, and tarried, and went—and the day again dawned—and the mists of a second night were now gathering around—and still I sat motionless in that solitary room; and still I sat buried in meditation, and still the phantasma of the teeth maintained its terrible ascendancy as, with the most vivid and hideous distinctness, it floated about amid the changing lights and shadows of the chamber. At length there broke in upon my dreams a cry as of horror and dismay; and thereunto, after a pause, succeeded the sound of troubled voices, intermingled with many low moanings of sorrow, or of pain. I arose from my seat and, throwing open one of the doors of the library, saw standing out in the ante-chamber a servant maiden, all in tears, who told me that Berenice was—no more. She had been seized with epilepsy in the early morning, and now, at the closing in of the night, the grave was ready for its tenant, and all the preparations for the burial were completed.

I found myself sitting in the library, and again sitting there alone. It seemed that I had newly awakened from a confused and exciting dream. I knew that it was now midnight, and I was well aware that since the setting of the sun, Berenice had been interred. But of that dreary period which intervened I had no positive—at least no definite

comprehension. Yet its memory was replete with horror—horror more
horrible from being vague, and terror more terrible from ambiguity.
It was a fearful page in the record of my existence, written all over
with dim, and hideous, and unintelligible recollections. I strived to
decipher them, but in vain; while ever and anon, like the spirit of a
departed sound, the shrill and piercing shriek of a female voice
seemed to be ringing in my ears. I had done a deed—what was it?
I asked myself the question aloud, and the whispering echoes of the
chamber answered me, "*What was it?*"

On the table beside me burned a lamp, and near it lay a little
box. It was of no remarkable character, and I had seen it frequently
before, for it was the property of the family physician; but how came
it there, upon my table, and why did I shudder in regarding it? These
things were in no manner to be accounted for, and my eyes at length
dropped to the open pages of a book, and to a sentence underscored
therein. The words were the singular but simple ones of the poet
Ebn Zaiat: "*Dicebant mihi sodales si sepulchrum amicae visitarem
curas meas aliquantulum fore levatas.*" Why then, as I perused them,
did the hairs of my head erect themselves on end, and the blood of
my body become congealed within my veins?

There came a light tap at the library door, and pale as the tenant
of a tomb, a menial entered upon tiptoe. His looks were wild with
terror, and he spoke to me in a voice tremulous, husky, and very
low. What said he?—Some broken sentences I heard. He told me of
a wild cry disturbing the silence of the night—of the gathering
together of the household—of a search in the direction of the sound;
and then his tones grew thrillingly distinct as he whispered me of a
violated grave—of a disfigured body enshrouded, yet still breathing,
still palpitating, *still alive!*

He pointed to my garments: they were muddy and clotted with
gore. I spoke not, and he took me gently by the hand; it was indented
with the impress of human nails. He directed my attention to some

object against the wall. I looked at it for some minutes; it was a spade. With a shriek I bounded to the table, and grasped the box that lay upon it. But I could not force it open; and in my tremor it slipped from my hands, and fell heavily, and burst into pieces; and from it, with a rattling sound, there rolled out some instruments of dental surgery, intermingled with thirty-two small, white and ivory-looking substances that were scattered to and fro about the floor.

MORELLA

"Itself, by itself, solely one everlastingly, and single."
Plato, *Symposium*

With a feeling of deep yet most singular affection I regarded my friend
Morella. Thrown by accident into her society many years ago, my
soul, from our first meeting, burned with fires it had never before
known; but the fires were not of Eros, and bitter and tormenting to
my spirit was the gradual conviction that I could no more define their
unusual meaning, or regulate their vague intensity. Yet we met; and
fate bound us together at the altar; and I never spoke of passion, nor
thought of love. She, however, shunned society, and attaching herself
to me alone, rendered me happy. It is a happiness to wonder; it is a
happiness to dream.

Morella's erudition was profound. As I hope to live, her talents
were of no common order—her powers of mind were gigantic. I felt
this, and in many matters, became her pupil. I soon, however, found
that perhaps on account of her Presburg education, she placed before
me a number of those mystical writings which are usually considered
the mere dross of the early German literature. These, for what reason
I could not imagine, were her favorite and constant study—and that,
in process of time, they became my own should be attributed to the
simple but effectual influence of habit and example.

In all this, if I err not, my reason had little to do. My convictions,
or I forget myself, were in no manner acted upon by the ideal, nor

was any tincture of the mysticism which I read to be discovered, unless I am greatly mistaken, either in my deeds or in my thoughts. Persuaded of this, I abandoned myself implicitly to the guidance of my wife, and entered with an unflinching heart into the intricacies of her studies. And then—then, when poring over forbidden pages, I felt a forbidden spirit enkindling within me—would Morella place her cold hand upon my own, and rake up from the ashes of a dead philosophy some low, singular words, whose strange meaning burned themselves in upon my memory. And then, hour after hour, would I linger by her side, and dwell upon the music of her voice—until, at length, its melody was tainted with terror—and there fell a shadow upon my soul—and I grew pale, and shuddered inwardly at those too unearthly tones. And thus, joy suddenly faded into horror, and the most beautiful became the most hideous, as Hinnon became Ge-Henna.

It is unnecessary to state the exact character of those disquisitions which, growing out of the volumes I have mentioned, formed, for so long a time, almost the sole conversation of Morella and myself. By the learned in what might be termed theological morality they will be readily conceived, and by the unlearned they would, at all events, be little understood. The wild Pantheism of Fichte; the modified of Pythagoreans; and, above all, the doctrines of Identity as urged by Schelling, were generally the points of discussion presenting the most of beauty to the imaginative Morella. That identity which is termed personal, Mr Locke, I think, truly defines to consist in the saneness of a rational being. And since by person we understand an intelligent essence having reason, and since there is a consciousness which always accompanies thinking, it is this which makes us all to be that which we call ourselves—thereby distinguishing us from other beings that think, and giving us our personal identity. But the *principium individuationis*—the notion of identity *which at death is or is not lost for ever*—was to me, at all times, a consideration of intense interest; not more from the perplexing and exciting nature of its consequences than from the marked and agitated manner in which Morella mentioned them.

But, indeed, the time had now arrived when the mystery of my wife's manner oppressed me as a spell. I could no longer bear the touch of her wan fingers, nor the low tone of her musical language, nor the luster of her melancholy eyes. And she knew all this, but did not upbraid; she seemed conscious of my weakness or folly, and, smiling, called it Fate. She seemed, also, conscious of a cause, to me unknown, for the gradual alienation of my regard; but she gave no hint or token of its nature. Yet was she woman, and pined away daily. In time, the crimson spot settled steadily upon the cheek, and the blue veins upon the pale forehead became prominent; and, one instant, my nature melted into pity, but, in the next, I met the glance of her meaning eyes, and then my soul sickened and became giddy with the giddiness of one who gazes downward into some dreary and unfathomable abyss.

Shall I then say that I longed with an earnest and consuming desire for the moment of Morella's decease? I did; but the fragile spirit clung to its tenement of clay for many days—for many weeks and irksome months—until my tortured nerves obtained the mastery over my mind, and I grew furious through delay, and, with the heart of a fiend, cursed the days, and the hours, and the bitter moments, which seemed to lengthen and lengthen as her gentle life declined—like shadows in the dying of the day.

But one autumnal evening, when the winds lay still in heaven, Morella called me to her bedside. There was a dim mist over all the earth, and a warm glow upon the waters, and, amid the rich October leaves of the forest, a rainbow from the firmament had surely fallen.

"It is a day of days," she said as I approached, "a day of all days either to live or die. It is a fair day for the sons of earth and life—ah, more fair for the daughters of heaven and death!"

I kissed her forehead, and she continued: "I am dying, yet shall I live."

"Morella!"

"The days have never been when thou couldst love me—but her whom in life thou didst abhor, in death thou shalt adore."

"Morella!"

"I repeat that I am dying. But within me is a pledge of that affection—ah, how little!—which thou didst feel for me, Morella. And when my spirit departs shall the child live—thy child and mine, Morella's. But thy days shall be days of sorrow—that sorrow which is the most lasting of impressions, as the cypress is the most enduring of trees. For the hours of thy happiness are over; and joy is not gathered twice in a life, as the roses of Pæstum twice in a year. Thou shalt no longer, then, play the Teian with time, but being ignorant of the myrtle and the vine, thou shalt bear about with thee thy shroud on the earth as do the Moslemin at Mecca."

"Morella!" I cried. "Morella! How knowest thou this?"—But she turned away her face upon the pillow, and, a slight tremor coming over her limbs, she thus died, and I heard her voice no more.

Yet, as she had foretold, her child—to which in dying she had given birth, which breathed not until the mother breathed no more— her child, a daughter, lived. And she grew strangely in stature and intellect, and was the perfect resemblance of her who had departed, and I loved her with a love more fervent than I had believed it possible to feel for any denizen of earth.

But, ere long, the heaven of this pure affection became darkened, and gloom, and horror, and grief, swept over it in clouds. I said the child grew strangely in stature and intelligence. Strange, indeed, was her rapid increase in bodily size—but terrible, oh, terrible were the tumultuous thoughts which crowded upon me while watching the development of her mental being! Could it be otherwise, when I daily discovered in the conceptions of the child the adult powers and faculties of the woman?—When the lessons of experience fell from the lips of infancy? And when the wisdom or the passions of maturity I found hourly gleaming from its full and speculative eye? When, I say, all this became evident to my appalled senses—when I could no longer hide it from my soul, nor throw it off from those perceptions which trembled to receive it—is it to be wondered at that suspicions, of a nature fearful and exciting, crept in upon my spirit, or that my thoughts fell back aghast upon the wild tales and thrilling theories of the entombed Morella? I snatched from the scrutiny of the world a being whom destiny compelled me to adore, and in the rigorous seclusion of my home, watched with agonizing anxiety over all which concerned the beloved.

And, as years rolled away, and I gazed, day after day, upon her holy, and mild, and eloquent face, and pored over her maturing form, day after day I discovered new points of resemblance in the child to her mother, the melancholy and the dead. And, hourly, grew darker these shadows of similitude, and more full, and more definite, and more perplexing, and more hideously terrible in their aspect. For that her smile was like her mother's I could bear; but then I shuddered at its too perfect identity—that her eyes were like Morella's I could endure; but then they too often looked down into the depths of my soul with Morella's own intense and bewildering meaning. And in the contour of the high forehead, and in the ringlets of the silken hair, and in the wan fingers which buried themselves therein, and in the sad musical tones of her speech, and above all—oh, above all!—in the phrases and expressions of the dead on the lips of the loved and the living, I found food for consuming thought and horror—for a worm that would not die.

Thus passed away two lustra of her life, and, as yet, my daughter remained nameless upon the earth. "My child" and "my love" were the designations usually prompted by a father's affection, and the rigid seclusion of her days precluded all other intercourse. Morella's name died with her at her death. Of the mother I had never spoken to the daughter—it was impossible to speak. Indeed, during the brief period of her existence, the latter had received no impressions from the outer world, save such as might have been afforded by the narrow limits of her privacy. But at length the ceremony of baptism presented to my mind, in its unnerved and agitated condition, a present deliverance from the terrors of my destiny. And at the baptismal font I hesitated for a name. And many titles of the wise and beautiful, of old and modern times, of my own and foreign lands, came thronging to my lips, with many, many fair titles of the gentle, and the happy, and the good. What prompted me, then, to disturb the memory of the buried dead? What demon urged me to breathe that sound, which, in its very recollection, was wont to make ebb the purple blood in torrents from the temples to the heart? What fiend spoke from the recesses of my soul, when, amid those dim aisles, and in the silence of the night, I whispered within the ears of the holy man the syllables—Morella? What more than fiend convulsed the features of the child, and overspread them with hues of death, as starting at that scarcely audible sound, she turned her glassy eyes from the earth to heaven, and, falling prostrate on the black slabs of our ancestral vault, responded—"I am here!"

Distinct, coldly, calmly distinct, fell those few simple sounds within my ear, and thence like molten lead, rolled hissingly into my brain. Years—years may pass away, but the memory of that epoch—never! Nor was I indeed ignorant of the flowers and the vine—but the hemlock and the cypress overshadowed me night and day. And I kept no reckoning of time or place, and the stars of my fate faded from heaven, and therefore the earth grew dark, and its figures passed by me, like flitting shadows, and among them all I beheld only—Morella. The winds of the firmament breathed but one sound within my ears and the ripples upon the sea murmured evermore—Morella. But she died; and with my own hands I bore her to the tomb; and I laughed with a long and bitter laugh as I found no traces of the first, in the charnel where I laid the second—Morella.

KING PEST

A Tale Containing An Allegory

"The gods do bear and will allow in kings
The things which they abhor in rascal routes."
Buckhurst's *Tragedy of Ferrex and Porrex*

About twelve o'clock, one night in the month of October, and during the chivalrous reign of the third Edward, two seamen belonging to the crew of the *Free and Easy*, a trading schooner plying between Sluys and the Thames, and then at anchor in that river, were much astonished to find themselves seated in the taproom of an alehouse in the parish of St Andrews, London—which alehouse bore for sign the portraiture of a "Jolly Tar."

The room—though ill-contrived, smoke-blackened, low-pitched, and in every other respect agreeing with the general character of such places at the period—was nevertheless, in the opinion of the grotesque groups scattered here and there within it, sufficiently well adapted to its purpose.

Of these groups, our two seamen formed, I think, the most interesting, if not the most conspicuous.

The one who appeared to be the elder, and whom his companion addressed by the characteristic appellation of "Legs," was at the same time much the taller of the two. He might have measured six feet and a half, and a habitual stoop in the shoulders seemed to have been the necessary consequence of an altitude so enormous. Superfluities in height were, however, more than accounted for by deficiencies in other respects. He was exceedingly thin; and might, as his associates asserted, have answered, when drunk, for a pennant at the mast-head, or, when sober, have served for a jib-boom. But these jests, and others of a similar nature, had evidently produced, at no time, any effect upon the cachinnatory muscles of the tar. With high cheek-bones, a large hawk-nose, retreating chin, fallen under-jaw, and huge protruding white eyes, the expression of his countenance, although tinged with a species of dogged indifference to matters and things in general, was not the less utterly solemn and serious beyond all attempts at imitation or description.

The younger seaman was, in all outward appearance, the converse of his companion. His stature could not have exceeded four feet. A pair of stumpy bow legs supported his squat, unwieldy figure, while his unusually short and thick arms, with no ordinary fists at their extremities, swung off dangling from his sides like the fins of a sea-turtle. Small eyes, of no particular color, twinkled far back in his head. His nose remained buried in the mass of flesh which enveloped his round, full, and purple face; and his thick upper-lip rested upon the still thicker one beneath with an air of complacent self-satisfaction, much heightened by the owner's habit of licking them at intervals. He evidently regarded his tall shipmate with a feeling half-wondrous, half-quizzical; and stared up occasionally in his face as the red setting sun stares up at the crags of Ben Nevis.

Various and eventful, however, had been the peregrinations of the worthy couple in and about the different tap-houses of the neighborhood during the earlier hours of the night. Funds, even the most ample, are not always everlasting; and it was with empty pockets our friends had ventured upon the present hostelry.

At the precise period, then, when this history properly commences, Legs, and his fellow, Hugh Tarpaulin, sat, each with both elbows

resting upon the large oaken table in the middle of the floor, and
with a hand upon either cheek. They were eyeing, from behind a
huge flagon of unpaid-for "humming-stuff," the portentous words,
"No Chalk," which to their indignation and astonishment were scored
over the doorway by means of that very mineral whose presence
they purported to deny. Not that the gift of deciphering written
characters—a gift among the commonalty of that day considered
little less cabalistical than the art of inditing—could, in strict justice,
have been laid to the charge of either disciple of the sea; but there
was, to say the truth, a certain twist in the formation of the letters—
an indescribable lee-lurch about the whole—which foreboded, in the
opinion of both seamen, a long run of dirty weather; and determined
them at once, in the allegorical words of Legs himself, to "pump
ship, clew up all sail, and scud before the wind."

Having accordingly disposed of what remained of the ale, and
looped up the points of their short doublets, they finally made a bolt
for the street. Although Tarpaulin rolled twice into the fireplace,
mistaking it for the door, yet their escape was at length happily
effected—and half after twelve o'clock found our heroes ripe for
mischief, and running for life down a dark alley in the direction of
St Andrew's Stair, hotly pursued by the landlady of the "Jolly Tar."

At the epoch of this eventful tale, and periodically, for many
years before and after, all England, but more especially the metropolis, resounded with the fearful cry of "Plague!". The city was in a
great measure depopulated—and in those horrible regions, in the
vicinity of the Thames, where, amid the dark, narrow, and filthy
lanes and alleys, the Demon of Disease was supposed to have had
his nativity, Awe, Terror, and Superstition were alone to be found
stalking abroad.

By authority of the king such districts were placed under ban,
and all persons forbidden, under pain of death, to intrude upon their
dismal solitude. Yet neither the mandate of the monarch, nor the

huge barriers erected at the entrances of the streets, nor the prospect of that loathsome death which, with almost absolute certainty, overwhelmed the wretch whom no peril could deter from the adventure, prevented the unfurnished and untenanted dwellings from being stripped, by the hand of nightly rapine, of every article, such as iron, brass, or leadwork, which could in any manner be turned to a profitable account.

Above all, it was usually found, upon the annual winter opening of the barriers, that locks, bolts, and secret cellars had proved but slender protection to those rich stores of wines and liquors which, in consideration of the risk and trouble of removal, many of the numerous dealers having shops in the neighborhood had consented to trust, during the period of exile, to so insufficient a security.

But there were very few of the terror-stricken people who attributed these doings to the agency of human hands. Pest-spirits, plague-goblins, and fever-demons were the popular imps of mischief; and tales so blood-chilling were hourly told, that the whole mass of forbidden buildings was, at length, enveloped in terror as in a shroud, and the plunderer himself was often scared away by the horrors his own depredations had created; leaving the entire vast circuit of prohibited district to gloom, silence, pestilence, and death.

It was by one of the terrific barriers already mentioned, and which indicated the region beyond to be under the Pest-ban, that, in scrambling down an alley, Legs and the worthy Hugh Tarpaulin found their progress suddenly impeded. To return was out of the question, and no time was to be lost, as their pursuers were close upon their heels. With thoroughbred seamen to clamber up the roughly fashioned plank-work was a trifle; and maddened with the twofold excitement of exercise and liquor, they leaped unhesitatingly down within the enclosure and, holding on their drunken course with shouts and yellings, were soon bewildered in its noisome and intricate recesses.

Had they not, indeed, been intoxicated beyond moral sense, their reeling footsteps must have been palsied by the horrors of their situation. The air was cold and misty. The paving-stones, loosened from their beds, lay in wild disorder amid the tall, rank grass, which sprang up around the feet and ankles. Fallen houses choked up the streets. The most fetid and poisonous smells everywhere prevailed; and by the aid of that ghastly light which, even at midnight, never fails to emanate from a vapory and pestilential atmosphere, might be discerned lying in the bypaths and alleys, or rotting in the window-less habitations, the carcass of many a nocturnal plunderer arrested by the hand of the plague in the very perpetration of his robbery.

But it lay not in the power of images, or sensations, or impediments such as these, to stay the course of men who, naturally brave, and at that time especially, brimful of courage and of "humming-stuff," would have reeled, as straight as their condition might have permitted, undauntedly into the very jaws of Death. Onward—still onward stalked the grim Legs, making the desolate solemnity echo and re-echo with yells like the terrific war-whoop of the Indian; and onward, still onward rolled the dumpy Tarpaulin, hanging on to the doublet of his more active companion, and far surpassing the latter's most strenuous exertions in the way of vocal music, by bull-roarings *in basso*, from the profundity of his stentorian lungs.

They had now evidently reached the stronghold of the pestilence. Their way at every step or plunge grew more noisome and more horrible—the paths more narrow and more intricate. Huge stones and beams falling momently from the decaying roofs above them, gave evidence, by their sullen and heavy descent, of the vast height of the surrounding houses; and while actual exertion became necessary to force a passage through frequent heaps of rubbish, it was by no means seldom that the hand fell upon a skeleton or rested upon a more fleshy corpse.

Suddenly, as the seamen stumbled against the entrance of a tall and ghastly-looking building, a yell more than usually shrill from the throat of the excited Legs was replied to from within, in a rapid succession of wild, laughter-like, and fiendish shrieks. Nothing daunted at sounds which, of such a nature, at such a time, and in such a place, might have curdled the very blood in hearts less irrevocably on fire, the drunken couple rushed headlong against the door, burst it open, and staggered into the midst of things with a volley of curses.

The room within which they found themselves proved to be the shop of an undertaker; but an open trap-door, in the corner of the floor near the entrance, looked down upon a long range of wine-cellars, whose depths the occasional sound of bursting bottles proclaimed to be well stored with their appropriate contents. In the middle of the room stood a table—in the center of which again arose a huge tub of what appeared to be punch. Bottles of various wines and cordials, together with jugs, pitchers, and flagons of every shape and quality, were scattered profusely upon the board. Around it, upon coffin-trestles, was seated a company of six. This company I will endeavor to delineate one by one.

Fronting the entrance, and elevated a little above his companions, sat a personage who appeared to be the president of the table. His stature was gaunt and tall, and Legs was confounded to behold in him a figure more emaciated than himself. His face was as yellow as saffron—but no feature, excepting one alone, was sufficiently marked to merit a particular description. This one consisted in a forehead so unusually and hideously lofty, as to have the appearance of a bonnet or crown of flesh superadded upon the natural head. His mouth was puckered and dimpled into an expression of ghastly affability, and his eyes, as indeed the eyes of all at table, were glazed over with the fumes of intoxication. This gentleman was clothed from head to foot in a richly-embroidered black silk-velvet pall wrapped negligently around his form after the fashion of a Spanish cloak. His head was stuck full of sable hearse-plumes, which he nodded to and fro with a jaunty and knowing air; and, in his right hand, he held a huge human thigh-bone, with which he appeared to have been just knocking down some member of the company for a song.

Opposite him, and with her back to the door, was a lady of no whit the less extraordinary character. Although quite as tall as the person just described, she had no right to complain of his unnatural emaciation. She was evidently in the last stage of a dropsy; and her figure resembled nearly that of the huge puncheon of October beer which stood, with the head driven in, close by her side, in a corner of the chamber. Her face was exceedingly round, red, and full; and the same peculiarity, or rather want of peculiarity, attached itself to her countenance, which I before mentioned in the case of the president—that is to say, only one feature of her face was sufficiently distinguished to need a separate characterization: indeed the acute Tarpaulin immediately observed that the same remark might have applied to each individual person of the party, every one of whom seemed to possess a monopoly of some particular portion of physiognomy. With the lady in question this portion proved to be the mouth. Commencing at the right ear, it swept with a terrific chasm to the left—the short pendants which she wore in either auricle continually bobbing into the aperture. She made, however, every exertion to keep her mouth closed and look dignified, in a dress consisting of a newly starched and ironed shroud coming up close under her chin, with a crumpled ruffle of cambric muslin.

At her right hand sat a diminutive young lady whom she appeared to patronize. This delicate little creature, in the trembling of her wasted fingers, in the livid hue of her lips, and in the slight hectic spot which tinged her otherwise leaden complexion, gave evident indications of a galloping consumption. An air of extreme *haut ton*, however, pervaded her whole appearance; she wore, in a graceful and *dégagé* manner, a large and beautiful winding-sheet of the finest

India lawn; her hair hung in ringlets over her neck; a soft smile played about her mouth; but her nose, extremely long, thin, sinuous, flexible, and pimpled, hung down far below her under-lip, and, in spite of the delicate manner in which she now and then moved it to one side or the other with her tongue, gave to her countenance a somewhat equivocal expression.

Over against her, and upon the left of the dropsical lady, was seated a little puffy, wheezing, and gouty old man, whose cheeks reposed upon the shoulders of their owner, like two huge bladders of Oporto wine. With his arms folded, and with one bandaged leg deposited upon the table, he seemed to think himself entitled to some consideration. He evidently prided himself much upon every inch of his personal appearance, but took more especial delight in calling attention to his gaudy-colored surtout. This, to say the truth, must have cost him no little money, and was made to fit him exceedingly well—being fashioned from one of the curiously embroidered silken covers appertaining to those glorious escutcheons which, in England and elsewhere, are customarily hung up, in some conspicuous place, upon the dwellings of departed aristocracy.

Next to him, and at the right hand of the president, was a gentleman in long white hose and cotton drawers. His frame shook, in a ridiculous manner, with a fit of what Tarpaulin called "the horrors." His jaws, which had been newly shaved, were tightly tied up by a bandage of muslin; and his arms being fastened in a similar way at the wrists, prevented him from helping himself too freely to the liquors upon the table; a precaution rendered necessary, in the opinion of Legs, by the peculiarly sottish and wine-bibbing cast of his visage. A pair of prodigious ears, nevertheless, which it was no doubt found impossible to confine, towered away into the atmosphere of the apartment, and were occasionally pricked up in a spasm at the sound of the drawing of a cork.

Fronting him, sixthly and lastly, was situated a singularly stiff-looking personage, who, being afflicted with paralysis, must, to speak seriously, have felt very ill at ease in his unaccommodating habiliments. He was habited, somewhat uniquely, in a new and handsome mahogany coffin. Its top or headpiece pressed upon the skull of the wearer, and extended over it in the fashion of a hood, giving to the entire face an air of indescribable interest. Arm-holes had been cut in the sides for the sake not more of elegance than of convenience; but the dress, nevertheless, prevented its proprietor from sitting as erect as his associates; and as he lay reclining against his trestle, at an angle of forty-five degrees, a pair of huge goggle eyes rolled up their awful whites toward the ceiling in absolute amazement at their own enormity.

Before each of the party lay a portion of a skull, which was used as a drinking-cup. Overhead was suspended a human skeleton, by means of a rope tied round one of the legs and fastened to a ring in the ceiling. The other limb, confined by no such fetter, stuck off from the body at right angles, causing the whole loose and rattling frame to dangle and twirl about at the caprice of every occasional puff of wind which found its way into the apartment. In the cranium of this hideous thing lay a quantity of ignited charcoal, which threw a fitful but vivid light over the entire scene; while coffins, and other wares appertaining to the shop of an undertaker, were piled high up around the room, and against the windows, preventing any ray from escaping into the street.

At sight of this extraordinary assembly, and of their still more extraordinary paraphernalia, our two seamen did not conduct themselves with that degree of decorum which might have been expected. Legs, leaning against the wall near which he happened to be standing, dropped his lower jaw still lower than usual, and spread open his eyes to their fullest extent; while Hugh Tarpaulin, stooping down so as to bring his nose upon a level with the table, and spreading out a palm upon either knee, burst into a long, loud, and obstreperous roar of very ill-timed and immoderate laughter.

Without, however, taking offence at behavior so excessively rude, the tall president smiled very graciously upon the intruders—nodded to them in a dignified manner with his head of sable plumes—and, arising, took each by an arm, and led him to a seat which some others of the company had placed in the meantime for his accommodation. Legs to all this offered not the slightest resistance, but sat down as he was directed; while the gallant Hugh, removing his coffin-trestle from its station near the head of the table, to the vicinity of the little consumptive lady in the winding-sheet, plumped down by her side in high glee, and pouring out a skull of red wine, quaffed it to their better acquaintance. But at this presumption the stiff gentleman in the coffin seemed exceedingly nettled; and serious consequences might have ensued, had not the president, rapping upon the table with his truncheon, diverted the attention of all present to the following speech:

"It becomes our duty upon the present happy occasion——"

"Avast there!" interrupted Legs, looking very serious. "Avast there a bit, I say, and tell us who the devil ye all are, and what business ye have here, rigged off like the foul fiends, and swilling the snug blue ruin stowed away for the winter by my honest shipmate, Will Wimble, the undertaker!"

At this unpardonable piece of ill-breeding, all the original company half-started to their feet, and uttered the same rapid succession of wild fiendish shrieks which had before caught the attention of the seamen. The president, however, was the first to recover his composure, and at length, turning to Legs with great dignity, recommenced:

"Most willingly will we gratify any reasonable curiosity on the part of guests so illustrious, unbidden though they be. Know then that in these dominions I am monarch, and here rule with undivided empire under the title of 'King Pest the First.'

"This apartment, which you no doubt profanely suppose to be

the shop of Will Wimble the undertaker—a man whom we know not, and whose plebeian appellation has never before this night thwarted our royal ears—this apartment, I say, is the Dais-Chamber of our Palace, devoted to the councils of our kingdom, and to other sacred and lofty purposes.

"The noble lady who sits opposite is Queen Pest, our Serene Consort. The other exalted personages whom you behold are all of our family, and wear the insignia of the blood royal under the respective titles of 'His Grace the Arch Duke Pest-Iferous,'—'His Grace the Duke Pest-Ilential,'—'His Grace the Duke Tem-Pest'—'and Her Serene Highness the Arch Duchess Ana-Pest.'

"As regards," continued he, "your demand of the business upon which we sit here in council, we might be pardoned for replying that it concerns, and concerns alone, our own private and regal interest, and is in no manner important to any other than ourself. But in consideration of those rights to which as guests and strangers you may feel yourselves entitled, we will furthermore explain that we are here this night, prepared, by deep research and accurate investigation, to examine, analyze, and thoroughly determine the indefinable spirit—the incomprehensible qualities and nature—of those inestimable treasures of the palate, the wines, ales and liqueurs of this goodly metropolis: by so doing to advance not more our own designs than the true welfare of that unearthly sovereign whose reign is over us all, whose dominions are unlimited, and whose name is 'Death.'"

"Whose name is Davy Jones!" ejaculated Tarpaulin, helping the lady by his side to a skull of liqueur, and pouring out a second for himself.

"Profane varlet!" said the president, now turning his attention to the worthy Hugh. "Profane and execrable wretch!—We have said, that, in consideration of those rights which, even in thy filthy person, we feel no inclination to violate, we have condescended to make reply to thy rude and unreasonable inquiries. We nevertheless, for your unhallowed intrusion upon our councils, believe it our duty to mulct thee and thy companion in each a gallon of Black Strap—having imbibed which to the prosperity of our kingdom—at a single draught—and upon your bended knees—ye shall be forthwith free either to proceed upon your way, or remain and be admitted to the privileges of our table, according to your respective and individual pleasures."

"It would be a matter of utter impossibility," replied Legs, whom the assumptions and dignity of King Pest the First had evidently inspired with some feelings of respect, and who arose and steadied himself by the table as he spoke—"it would, please your majesty, be a matter of utter impossibility to stow away in my hold even one-fourth part of that same liquor which your majesty has just mentioned. To say nothing of the stuffs placed on board in the forenoon by way of ballast, and not to mention the various ales and liqueurs shipped this evening at various seaports, I have, at present, a full cargo of 'humming-stuff' taken in and duly paid for at the sign of the 'Jolly Tar.' You will, therefore, please your majesty, be so good as to take the will for the deed—for by no manner of means either can I or will I swallow another drop—least of all a drop of that villainous bilge-water that answers to the name of 'Black Strap.'"

"Belay that," interrupted Tarpaulin, astonished not more at the length of his companion's speech than at the nature of his refusal—"Belay that, you lubber!—And I say, Legs, none of your palaver. My hull is still light, although I confess you yourself seem to be a little top-heavy; and as for the matter of your share of the cargo, why rather than raise a squall I would find stowage-room for it myself, but——"

"This proceeding," interposed the president, "is by no means in accordance with the terms of the mulct or sentence, which is in its nature Median, and not to be altered or recalled. The conditions we have imposed must be fulfilled to the letter, and that without a moment's hesitation—in failure of which fulfillment we decree that you do here be tied neck and heels together, and duly drowned as rebels in yon hogshead of October beer!"

"A sentence!—A sentence!—A righteous and just sentence!—A glorious decree!—A most worthy and upright and holy condemnation!" shouted the Pest family altogether. The king elevated his forehead into innumerable wrinkles; the gouty little old man puffed like a pair of bellows; the lady of the winding-sheet waved her nose to and fro; the gentleman in the cotton drawers pricked up his ears; she of the shroud gasped like a dying fish; and he of the coffin looked stiff and rolled up his eyes.

"Ugh! ugh! ugh!" chuckled Tarpaulin, without heeding the general excitement. "Ugh! ugh! ugh!—Ugh! ugh! ugh! ugh!—Ugh ugh ugh!—I was saying," said he—"I was saying when Mr King Pest poked in his marlinspike, that as for the matter of two or three gallons more or less of Black Strap, it was a trifle to a tight sea-boat like myself not overstowed—but when it comes to drinking the health of the Devil (whom God assoilizie) and going down upon my marrowbones to his ill-favored majesty there, whom I know, as well as I know myself to be a sinner, to be nobody in the whole world but Tim Hurlygurly the stage-player!—Why! It's quite another guess sort of a thing, and utterly and altogether past my comprehension."

He was not allowed to finish this speech in tranquility. At the name of Tim Hurlygurly the whole assembly leaped from their seats.

"Treason!" shouted his Majesty King Pest the First.

"Treason!" said the little man with the gout.

"Treason!" screamed the Arch Duchess Ana-Pest.

"Treason!" muttered the gentleman with his jaws tied up.

"Treason!" growled he of the coffin.

"Treason! Treason!" shrieked her majesty of the mouth; and, seizing by the hinder-part of his breeches the unfortunate Tarpaulin, who had just commenced pouring out for himself a skull of liqueur, she lifted him high into the air, and let him fall without ceremony into the huge open puncheon of his beloved ale. Bobbing up and down, for a few seconds, like an apple in a bowl of toddy, he, at length, finally disappeared amid the whirlpool of foam which, in the already effervescent liquor, his struggles easily succeeded in creating.

Not tamely, however, did the tall seaman behold the discomfiture of his companion. Jostling King Pest through the open trap, the valiant Legs slammed the door down upon him with an oath, and strode toward the center of the room. Here tearing down the skeleton which swung over the table, he laid it about him with so much energy and good-will that, as the last glimpses of light died away within the apartment, he succeeded in knocking out the brains of the little gentleman with the gout. Rushing then with all his force against the fatal hogshead full of October ale and Hugh Tarpaulin, he rolled it over and over in an instant. Out poured a deluge of liquor so fierce— so impetuous—so overwhelming—that the room was flooded from wall to wall—the loaded table was over-turned—the trestles were thrown upon their backs—the tub of punch into the fireplace—and the ladies into hysterics. Piles of death furniture floundered about. Jugs, pitchers, and carboys mingled promiscuously in the mêlée, and wicker flagons encountered desperately with bottles of junk. The man with the horrors was drowned upon the spot—the little stiff gentleman floated off in his coffin—and the victorious Legs, seizing by the waist the fat lady in the shroud, rushed out with her into the street, and made a bee-line for the *Free and Easy*, followed under easy sail by the redoubtable Hugh Tarpaulin, who, having sneezed three or four times, panted and puffed after him with the Arch Duchess Ana-Pest.

SHADOW

A Parable

"Yea! Though I walk through the valley of the Shadow"
Psalm of David [XXIII]

Ye who read are still among the living: but I who write shall have long since gone my way into the region of shadows. For indeed strange things shall happen, and secret things be known, and many centuries shall pass away, ere these memorials be seen of men. And, when seen, there will be some to disbelieve, and some to doubt, and yet a few who will find much to ponder upon in the characters here graven with a stylus of iron.

The year had been a year of terror, and of feelings more intense than terror for which there is no name upon the earth. For many prodigies and signs had taken place, and far and wide, over sea and land, the black wings of the Pestilence were spread abroad. To those, nevertheless, cunning in the stars, it was not unknown that the heavens wore an aspect of ill; and to me, the Greek Oinos, among others, it was evident that now had arrived the alternation of that seven hundred and ninety-fourth year when, at the entrance of Aries, the planet Jupiter is conjoined with the red ring of the terrible Saturnus. The peculiar spirit of the skies, if I mistake not greatly, made itself manifest, not only in the physical orb of the earth, but in the souls, imaginations, and meditations of mankind.

Over some flasks of the red Chian wine, within the walls of a
noble hall, in a dim city called Ptolemais, we sat, at night, a company
of seven. And to our chamber there was no entrance save by a lofty
door of brass: and the door was fashioned by the artisan Corinnos,
and, being of rare workmanship, was fastened from within. Black
draperies, likewise, in the gloomy room, shut out from our view the
moon, the lurid stars, and the peopleless streets—but the boding and
the memory of Evil, they would not be so excluded. There were things
around us and about of which I can render no distinct account—things
material and spiritual—heaviness in the atmosphere—a sense of suffocation—anxiety—and, above all, that terrible state of existence which
the nervous experience when the senses are keenly living and awake,
and meanwhile the powers of thought lie dormant. A dead weight
hung upon us. It hung upon our limbs—upon the household furniture—upon the goblets from which we drank; and all things were
depressed, and borne down thereby—all things save only the flames
of the seven iron lamps which illumined our revel. Uprearing themselves in tall slender lines of light, they thus remained burning all
pallid and motionless; and in the mirror which their luster formed
upon the round table of ebony at which we sat, each of us there
assembled beheld the pallor of his own countenance, and the unquiet
glare in the downcast eyes of his companions. Yet we laughed and
were merry in our proper way—which was hysterical; and sang the
songs of Anacreon—which are madness; and drank deeply—although
the purple wine reminded us of blood. For there was yet another tenant
of our chamber in the person of young Zoilus. Dead, and at full length
he lay, enshrouded—the genius and the demon of the scene. Alas! He
bore no portion in our mirth, save that his countenance, distorted with
the plague, and his eyes in which Death had but half extinguished the
fire of the pestilence, seemed to take such interest in our merriment
as the dead may haply take in the merriment of those who are to die.
But although I, Oinos, felt that the eyes of the departed were upon

me, still I forced myself not to perceive the bitterness of their expression, and, gazing down steadily into the depths of the ebony mirror, sang with a loud and sonorous voice the songs of the son of Teios. But gradually my songs they ceased, and their echoes, rolling afar off among the sable draperies of the chamber, became weak, and undistinguishable, and so faded away. And lo! From among those sable draperies where the sounds of the song departed, there came forth a dark and undefined shadow—a shadow such as the moon, when low in heaven, might fashion from the figure of a man: but it was the shadow neither of man nor of God, nor of any familiar thing. And, quivering awhile among the draperies of the room, it at length rested in full view upon the surface of the door of brass. But the shadow was vague, and formless, and indefinite, and was the shadow neither of man nor of God—neither God of Greece, nor God of Chaldæa, nor any Egyptian God. And the shadow rested upon the brazen doorway, and under the arch of the entablature of the door, and moved not, nor spoke any word, but there became stationary and remained. And the door whereupon the shadow rested was, if I remember aright, over against the feet of the young Zoilus enshrouded. But we, the seven there assembled, having seen the shadow as it came out from among the draperies, dared not steadily behold it, but cast down our eyes, and gazed continually into the depths of the mirror of ebony. And at length I, Oinos, speaking some low words, demanded of the shadow its dwelling and its appellation. And the shadow answered, "I am SHADOW, and my dwelling is near to the Catacombs of Ptolemais, and hard by those dim plains of Helusion which border upon the foul Charonian canal." And then did we, the seven, start from our seats in horror, and stand trembling, and shuddering, and aghast: for the tones in the voice of the shadow were not the tones of any one being, but of a multitude of beings, and, varying in their cadences from syllable to syllable, fell duskily upon our ears in the well remembered and familiar accents of many thousand departed friends.

LIGEIA

"And the will therein lieth, which dieth not. Who knoweth
the mysteries of the will, with its vigor? For God is but a
great will pervading all things by nature of its intentness.
Man doth not yield himself to the angels, nor unto death
utterly, save only through the weakness of his feeble will."
                                              Joseph Glanvill

I cannot, for my soul, remember how, when, or even precisely
where, I first became acquainted with the Lady Ligeia. Long years
have since elapsed, and my memory is feeble through much
suffering. Or, perhaps, I cannot now bring these points to mind,
because, in truth, the character of my beloved, her rare learning,
her singular yet placid cast of beauty, and the thrilling and
enthralling eloquence of her low musical language, made their way
into my heart by paces so steadily and stealthily progressive that
they had been unnoticed and unknown. Yet I believe that I met her
first and most frequently in some large, old, decaying city near the
Rhine. Of her family—I have surely heard her speak. That it is of
a remotely ancient date cannot be doubted. Ligeia! Ligeia! Buried
in studies of a nature more than all else adapted to deaden impressions of the outward world, it is by that sweet word alone—by
Ligeia—that I bring before mine eyes in fancy the image of her
who is no more. And now, while I write, a recollection flashes upon
me that I have never known the paternal name of her who was my

friend and my betrothed, and who became the partner of my studies, and finally the wife of my bosom. Was it a playful charge on the part of my Ligeia? Or was it a test of my strength of affection, that I should institute no inquiries upon this point? Or was it rather a caprice of my own—a wildly romantic offering on the shrine of the most passionate devotion? I but distinctly recall the fact itself—what wonder that I have utterly forgotten the circumstances which originated or attended it? And, indeed, if ever that spirit which is entitled *Romance*—if ever she, the wan and the misty-winged *Ashtophet* of idolatrous Egypt, presided, as they tell, over marriages ill-omened, then most surely she presided over mine.

There is one dear topic, however, on which my memory fails me not. It is the *person* of Ligeia. In stature she was tall, somewhat slender, and, in her latter days, even emaciated. I would in vain attempt to portray the majesty, the quiet ease, of her demeanor, or the incomprehensible lightness and elasticity of her footfall. She came and departed as a shadow. I was never made aware of her entrance into my closed study save by the dear music of her low sweet voice, as she placed her marble hand upon my shoulder. In beauty of face no maiden ever equaled her. It was the radiance of an opium-dream—an airy and spirit-lifting vision more wildly divine than the fantasies which hovered about the slumbering souls of the daughters of Delos. Yet her features were not of that regular mould which we have been falsely taught to worship in the classical labors of the heathen. "There is no exquisite beauty," says Bacon, Lord Verulam, speaking truly of all the forms and *genera* of beauty, "without some *strangeness* in the proportion." Yet, although I saw that the features of Ligeia were not of a classic regularity—although I perceived that her loveliness was indeed "exquisite," and felt that there was much of "strangeness" pervading it, yet I have tried in vain to detect the irregularity and to trace home my own perception of "the strange." I examined the contour of the lofty and pale forehead—it was faultless—how cold indeed that word when applied to a majesty so divine!—The skin rivaling the purest ivory, the commanding extent and repose, the gentle prominence of the regions above the temples; and then the raven-black, the glossy, the luxuriant and naturally-curling tresses, setting forth the full force of the Homeric epithet, "hyacinthine"! I looked at the delicate outlines of the nose—and nowhere but in the graceful medallions of the Hebrews had I beheld a similar perfection. There were the same luxurious smoothness of surface, the same scarcely perceptible tendency to the aquiline, the same harmoniously curved nostrils speaking the free spirit. I regarded the sweet mouth. Here was indeed the triumph of all things heavenly—the magnificent turn of the short upper lip—the soft, voluptuous slumber of the under—the dimples which sported, and the color which spoke—the teeth glancing back, with a brilliancy almost startling, every ray of the holy light which fell upon them in her serene and placid, yet most exultingly radiant of all smiles. I scrutinized the formation of the chin—and here, too, I found the gentleness of breadth, the softness and the majesty, the fullness and the spirituality, of the Greek—the contour which the god Apollo revealed but in a dream, to Cleomenes, the son of the Athenian. And then I peered into the large eyes of Ligeia.

For eyes we have no models in the remotely antique. It might have been, too, that in these eyes of my beloved lay the secret to which Lord Verulam alludes. They were, I must believe, far larger than the ordinary eyes of our own race. They were even fuller than the fullest of the gazelle eyes of the tribe of the valley of Nourjahad. Yet it was only at intervals—in moments of intense excitement—that this peculiarity became more than slightly noticeable in Ligeia. And at such moments was her beauty—in my heated fancy thus it appeared perhaps—the beauty of beings either above or apart from the earth—the beauty of the fabulous Houri of the Turk. The hue of the orbs was the most brilliant of black, and, far over them, hung jetty lashes of great length. The brows, slightly irregular in outline, had the same tint. The "strangeness," however, which I found in the eyes, was of a nature distinct from the formation, or the color, or the brilliancy of the features, and must, after all, be referred to the *expression*. Ah, word of no meaning! Behind whose vast latitude of mere sound we entrench our ignorance of so much of the spiritual. The expression of the eyes of Ligeia! How for long hours have I pondered upon it! How have I, through the whole of a midsummer night, struggled to fathom it! What was it—that something more profound than the well of Democritus—which lay far within the pupils of my beloved? What *was* it? I was possessed with a passion to discover. Those eyes! Those large, those shining, those divine orbs! They became to me twin stars of Leda, and I to them devoutest of astrologers.

There is no point, among the many incomprehensible anomalies of the science of mind, more thrillingly exciting than the fact—never, I believe, noticed in the schools—that, in our endeavors to recall to memory something long forgotten, we often find ourselves *upon the very verge* of remembrance, without being able, in the end, to remember. And thus how frequently, in my intense scrutiny of Ligeia's eyes, have I felt approaching the full knowledge of their expression—felt it approaching—yet not quite be mine—and so at length entirely depart! And (strange, oh strangest mystery of all!) I found, in the commonest objects of the universe, a circle of analogies to that expression. I mean to say that, subsequently to the period when Ligeia's beauty passed into my spirit, there dwelling as in a shrine, I derived from many existences in the material world, a sentiment such as I felt always aroused within me by her large and luminous orbs. Yet not the more could I define that sentiment, or analyze, or even steadily view it. I recognized it, let me repeat, sometimes in the survey of a rapidly growing vine—in the contemplation of a moth, a butterfly, a chrysalis, a stream of running water. I have felt it in the ocean; in the falling of a meteor. I have felt it in the glances of unusually aged people. And there are one or two stars in heaven—(one especially, a star of the sixth magnitude, double and changeable, to be found near the large star in Lyra) in a telescopic scrutiny of which I have been made aware of the feeling. I have been filled with it by certain sounds from stringed instruments, and not unfrequently by passages from books. Among innumerable other instances, I well remember something in a volume of Joseph Glanvill, which (perhaps merely from its quaintness—who shall say?) never failed to inspire me with the sentiment: "And the will therein lieth, which dieth not. Who knoweth the mysteries of the will, with its vigor? For God is but a great will pervading all things by nature of its intentness. Man doth not yield him to the angels, nor unto death utterly, save only through the weakness of his feeble will."

Length of years, and subsequent reflection, have enabled me to trace, indeed, some remote connection between this passage in the English moralist and a portion of the character of Ligeia. An intensity in thought, action, or speech, was possibly, in her, a result, or at least an index, of that gigantic volition which, during our long intercourse, failed to give other and more immediate evidence of its existence. Of all the women whom I have ever known, she, the outwardly calm, the ever-placid Ligeia, was the most violently a prey to the tumultuous vultures of stern passion. And of such passion I could form no estimate, save by the miraculous expansion of those eyes which at once so delighted and appalled me—by the almost magical melody, modulation, distinctness, and placidity of her very low voice—and by the fierce energy (rendered doubly effective by contrast with her manner of utterance) of the wild words which she habitually uttered.

I have spoken of the learning of Ligeia: it was immense—such as I have never known in woman. In the classical tongues was she deeply proficient, and as far as my own acquaintance extended in regard to the modern dialects of Europe, I have never known her at fault. Indeed upon any theme of the most admired, because simply the most abstruse of the boasted erudition of the academy, have I *ever* found Ligeia at fault? How singularly—how thrillingly, this one point in the nature of my wife has forced itself, at this late period only, upon my attention! I said her knowledge was such as I have never known in woman—but where breathes the man who has traversed, and successfully, *all* the wide areas of moral, physical, and mathematical science? I saw not then what I now clearly perceive, that the acquisitions of Ligeia were gigantic, were astounding; yet I was sufficiently aware of her infinite supremacy to resign myself, with a childlike confidence, to her guidance through the chaotic world of metaphysical investigation at which I was most busily occupied during the earlier years of our marriage. With how vast a triumph—with how vivid a delight—with how much of all that is ethereal in hope—did I *feel*, as she bent over me in studies but little sought—but less known—that delicious vista by slow degrees expanding before me, down whose long, gorgeous, and all untrodden path, I might at length pass onward to the goal of a wisdom too divinely precious not to be forbidden!

How poignant, then, must have been the grief with which, after some years, I beheld my well-grounded expectations take wings to themselves and fly away! Without Ligeia I was but as a child groping benighted. Her presence, her readings alone, rendered vividly luminous the many mysteries of the transcendentalism in which we were immersed. Wanting the radiant luster of her eyes, letters, lambent and golden, grew duller than Saturnian lead. And now those eyes shone less and less frequently upon the pages over which I pored. Ligeia grew ill. The wild eyes blazed with a too—too glorious effulgence; the pale fingers became of the transparent waxen hue of the grave, and the blue veins upon the lofty forehead swelled and sank impetuously with the tides of the most gentle emotion. I saw that she must die—and I struggled desperately in spirit with the grim Azrael. And the struggles of the passionate wife were, to my astonishment, even more energetic than my own. There had been much in her stern nature to impress me with the belief that, to her, death would have come without its terrors—but not so. Words are impotent to convey any just idea of the fierceness of resistance with which she wrestled with the Shadow. I groaned in anguish at the pitiable spectacle. I would have soothed—I would have reasoned; but, in the intensity of her wild desire for life—for life—*but* for life—solace and reason were alike the uttermost of folly. Yet not until the last instance, amid the most convulsive writhings of her fierce spirit, was shaken the external placidity of her demeanor. Her voice grew more gentle— grew more low—yet I would not wish to dwell upon the wild meaning of the quietly uttered words. My brain reeled as I hearkened entranced, to a melody more than mortal—to assumptions and aspirations which mortality had never before known.

That she loved me I should not have doubted; and I might have been easily aware that, in a bosom such as hers, love would have reigned no ordinary passion. But in death only was I fully impressed with the strength of her affection. For long hours, detaining my hand, would she pour out before me the overflowing of a heart whose more than passionate devotion amounted to idolatry. How had I deserved to be so blessed by such confessions?—How had I deserved to be so cursed with the removal of my beloved in the hour of her making them? But upon this subject I cannot bear to dilate. Let me say only, that in Ligeia's more than womanly abandonment to a love, alas all unmerited, all unworthily bestowed, I at length recognized the principle of her longing with so wildly earnest a desire for the life which was now fleeing so rapidly away. It is this wild longing—it is this eager vehemence of desire for life—*but* for life—that I have no power to portray—no utterance capable of expressing.

At high noon of the night in which she departed, beckoning me, peremptorily, to her side, she bade me repeat certain verses composed by herself not many days before. I obeyed her. They were these:

Lo! 'tis a gala night
    Within the lonesome latter years!
An angel throng, bewinged, bedight
    In veils, and drowned in tears,
Sit in a theatre, to see
    A play of hopes and fears,
While the orchestra breathes fitfully
    The music of the spheres.

Mimes, in the form of God on high,
    Mutter and mumble low,
And hither and thither fly—
    Mere puppets they, who come and go
At bidding of vast formless things
    That shift the scenery to and fro,
Flapping from out their Condor wings
    Invisible Woe!

That motley drama!—Oh, be sure
    It shall not be forgot!
With its Phantom chased forever more,
    By a crowd that seize it not,
Through a circle that ever returneth in
    To the self-same spot,
And much of Madness and more of Sin
    And Horror the soul of the plot.

But see, amid the mimic rout,
    A crawling shape intrude!
A blood-red thing that writhes from out
    The scenic solitude!
It writhes!—It writhes!—With mortal pangs

> The mimes become its food,
> And the seraphs sob at vermin fangs
> In human gore imbued.
>
> Out—out are the lights—out all!
> And over each quivering form,
> The curtain, a funeral pall,
> Comes down with the rush of a storm,
> And the angels, all pallid and wan,
> Uprising, unveiling, affirm
> That the play is the tragedy, "Man,"
> And its hero the Conqueror Worm.

"Oh God!" half shrieked Ligeia, leaping to her feet and extending her arms aloft with a spasmodic movement, as I made an end of these lines—"Oh God! Oh Divine Father!—Shall these things be undeviatingly so?—Shall this Conqueror be not once conquered? Are we not part and parcel in Thee? Who—who knoweth the mysteries of the will with its vigor? Man doth not yield him to the angels, nor unto death utterly, save only through the weakness of his feeble will."

And now, as if exhausted with emotion, she suffered her white arms to fall, and returned solemnly to her bed of death. And as she breathed her last sighs, there came mingled with them a low murmur from her lips. I bent to them my ear and distinguished, again, the concluding words of the passage in Glanvill—"*Man doth not yield himself to the angels, nor unto death utterly, save only through the weakness of his feeble will.*"

She died; and I, crushed into the very dust with sorrow, could no longer endure the lonely desolation of my dwelling in the dim and decaying city by the Rhine. I had no lack of what the world calls wealth. Ligeia had brought me far more, very far more than ordinarily falls to the lot of mortals. After a few months, therefore, of weary and aimless wandering, I purchased, and put in some repair, an abbey, which I shall not name, in one of the wildest and least frequented portions of fair England. The gloomy and dreary grandeur of the building, the almost savage aspect of the domain, the many melancholy and time-honored memories connected with both, had much in unison with the feelings of utter abandonment which had driven me into that remote and unsocial region of the country. Yet although the external abbey, with its verdant decay hanging about it, suffered but little alteration, I gave way, with a childlike perversity, and perchance with a faint hope of alleviating my sorrows, to a display of more than regal magnificence within. For such follies, even in childhood, I had imbibed a taste, and now they came back to me as if in the dotage of grief. Alas, I feel how much even of incipient madness might have been discovered in the gorgeous and fantastic draperies, in the solemn carvings of Egypt, in the wild cornices and furniture, in the Bedlam patterns of the carpets of tufted gold! I had become a bounden slave in the trammels of opium, and my labors and my orders had taken a coloring from my dreams. But these absurdities I must not pause to detail. Let me speak only of that one chamber, ever accursed, whither in a moment of mental alienation, I led from the altar as my bride—as the successor of the unforgotten Ligeia—the fair-haired and blue-eyed Lady Rowena Trevanion, of Tremaine.

There is no individual portion of the architecture and decoration of that bridal chamber which is not now visibly before me. Where were the souls of the haughty family of the bride, when, through thirst of gold, they permitted to pass the threshold of an apartment so bedecked, a maiden and a daughter so beloved? I have said that I minutely remember the details of the chamber—yet I am sadly forgetful on topics of deep moment—and here there was no system, no keeping, in the fantastic display, to take hold upon the memory. The room lay in a high turret of the castellated abbey, was pentagonal

in shape, and of capacious size. Occupying the whole southern face
of the pentagon was the sole window—an immense sheet of unbroken
glass from Venice—a single pane, and tinted of a leaden hue, so that
the rays of either the sun or moon, passing through it, fell with a
ghastly luster on the objects within. Over the upper portion of this
huge window, extended the trelliswork of an aged vine, which
clambered up the massy walls of the turret. The ceiling, of gloomy-
looking oak, was excessively lofty, vaulted, and elaborately fretted
with the wildest and most grotesque specimens of a semi-Gothic,
semi-Druidical device. From out the most central recess of this
melancholy vaulting, depended, by a single chain of gold with long
links, a huge censer of the same metal, Saracenic in pattern, and
with many perforations so contrived that there writhed in and out
of them, as if endued with a serpent vitality, a continual succession
of parti-colored fires.

Some few ottomans and golden candelabra, of Eastern figure,
were in various stations about—and there was the couch, too—the
bridal couch—of an Indian model, and low, and sculptured of solid
ebony, with a pall-like canopy above. In each of the angles of the
chamber stood on end a gigantic sarcophagus of black granite, from
the tombs of the kings over against Luxor, with their aged lids full
of immemorial sculpture. But in the draping of the apartment lay—
alas!—the chief fantasy of all. The lofty walls, gigantic in height—
even unproportionably so—were hung from summit to foot, in vast
folds, with a heavy and massive-looking tapestry—tapestry of a
material which was found alike as a carpet on the floor, as a covering
for the ottomans and the ebony bed, as a canopy for the bed, and as
the gorgeous volutes of the curtains which partially shaded the
window. The material was the richest cloth of gold. It was spotted
all over, at irregular intervals, with arabesque figures, about a foot
in diameter, and wrought upon the cloth in patterns of the most jetty
black. But these figures partook of the true character of the arabesque

only when regarded from a single point of view. By a contrivance now common, and indeed traceable to a very remote period of antiquity, they were made changeable in aspect. To one entering the room, they bore the appearance of simple monstrosities; but upon a farther advance, this appearance gradually departed; and step by step, as the visitor moved his station in the chamber, he saw himself surrounded by an endless succession of the ghastly forms which belong to the superstition of the Norman, or arise in the guilty slumbers of the monk. The phantasmagoric effect was vastly heightened by the artificial introduction of a strong continual current of wind behind the draperies—giving a hideous and uneasy animation to the whole.

In halls such as these—in a bridal chamber such as this—I passed, with the Lady of Tremaine, the unhallowed hours of the first month of our marriage—passed them with but little disquietude. That my wife dreaded the fierce moodiness of my temper—that she shunned me and loved me but little—I could not help perceiving; but it gave me rather pleasure than otherwise. I loathed her with a hatred belonging more to demon than to man. My memory flew back (oh, with what intensity of regret!) to Ligeia, the beloved, the august, the beautiful, the entombed. I reveled in recollections of her purity, of her wisdom, of her lofty, her ethereal nature, of her passionate, her idolatrous love. Now, then, did my spirit fully and freely burn with more than all the fires of her own. In the excitement of my opium dreams (for I was habitually fettered in the shackles of the drug) I would call aloud upon her name, during the silence of the night, or among the sheltered recesses of the glens by day, as if, through the wild eagerness, the solemn passion, the consuming ardor of my longing for the departed, I could restore her to the pathway she had abandoned—ah, *could* it be for ever?—upon the earth.

About the commencement of the second month of the marriage, the Lady Rowena was attacked with sudden illness, from which her recovery was slow. The fever which consumed her rendered her

nights uneasy; and in her perturbed state of half-slumber, she spoke
of sounds, and of motions, in and about the chamber of the turret,
which I concluded had no origin save in the distemper of her fancy,
or perhaps in the phantasmagoric influences of the chamber itself.
She became at length convalescent—finally well. Yet but a brief
period elapsed, ere a second more violent disorder again threw her
upon a bed of suffering; and from this attack her frame, at all times
feeble, never altogether recovered. Her illnesses were, after this
epoch, of alarming character, and of more alarming recurrence,
defying alike the knowledge and the great exertions of her physicians.
With the increase of the chronic disease which had thus, apparently,
taken too sure hold upon her constitution to be eradicated by human
means, I could not fail to observe a similar increase in the nervous
irritation of her temperament, and in her excitability by trivial causes
of fear. She spoke again, and now more frequently and pertinaciously,
of the sounds—of the slight sounds—and of the unusual motions
among the tapestries, to which she had formerly alluded.

One night, near the closing in of September, she pressed this
distressing subject with more than usual emphasis upon my attention.
She had just awakened from an unquiet slumber, and I had been
watching, with feelings half of anxiety, half of vague terror, the
workings of her emaciated countenance. I sat by the side of her
ebony bed, upon one of the ottomans of India. She partly arose, and
spoke, in an earnest low whisper, of sounds which she *then* heard,
but which I could not hear—of motions which she *then* saw, but
which I could not perceive. The wind was rushing hurriedly behind
the tapestries, and I wished to show her (what, let me confess it, I
could not *all* believe) that those almost inarticulate breathings, and
those very gentle variations of the figures upon the wall, were but
the natural effects of that customary rushing of the wind. But a
deadly pallor, overspreading her face, had proved to me that my
exertions to reassure her would be fruitless. She appeared to be

fainting, and no attendants were within call. I remembered where was deposited a decanter of light wine which had been ordered by her physicians, and hastened across the chamber to procure it. But, as I stepped beneath the light of the censer, two circumstances of a startling nature attracted my attention. I had felt that some palpable although invisible object had passed lightly by my person; and I saw that there lay upon the golden carpet, in the very middle of the rich luster thrown from the censer, a shadow—a faint, indefinite shadow of angelic aspect—such as might be fancied for the shadow of a shade. But I was wild with the excitement of an immoderate dose of opium, and heeded these things but little, nor spoke of them to Rowena. Having found the wine, I recrossed the chamber, and poured out a gobletful, which I held to the lips of the fainting lady. She had now partially recovered, however, and took the vessel herself, while I sank upon an ottoman near me, with my eyes fastened upon her person. It was then that I became distinctly aware of a gentle footfall upon the carpet, and near the couch; and in a second thereafter, as Rowena was in the act of raising the wine to her lips, I saw, or may have dreamed that I saw, fall within the goblet, as if from some invisible spring in the atmosphere of the room, three or four large drops of a brilliant and ruby-colored fluid. If this I saw—not so Rowena. She swallowed the wine unhesitatingly, and I forbore to speak to her of a circumstance which must after all, I considered, have been but the suggestion of a vivid imagination rendered morbidly active by the terror of the lady, by the opium, and by the hour.

Yet I cannot conceal it from my own perception that, immediately subsequent to the fall of the ruby-drops, a rapid change for the worse took place in the disorder of my wife; so that, on the third subsequent night, the hands of her menials prepared her for the tomb, and on the fourth, I sat alone, with her shrouded body, in that fantastic chamber which had received her as my bride. Wild visions, opium-engendered, flitted, shadow-like, before me. I gazed with unquiet eye upon the sarcophagi in the angles of the room, upon the varying figures of the drapery, and upon the writhing of the parti-colored fires in the censer overhead. My eyes then fell, as I called to mind the circumstances of a former night, to the spot beneath the glare of the censer where I had seen the faint traces of the shadow. It was there, however, no longer; and breathing with greater freedom, I turned my glances to the pallid and rigid figure upon the bed. Then rushed upon me a thousand memories of Ligeia—and then came back upon my heart, with the turbulent violence of a flood, the whole of that unutterable woe with which I had regarded *her* thus enshrouded. The night waned; and still, with a bosom full of bitter thoughts of the one only and supremely beloved, I remained gazing upon the body of Rowena.

It might have been midnight, or perhaps earlier, or later, for I had taken no note of time, when a sob, low, gentle, but very distinct, startled me from my reverie. I *felt* that it came from the bed of ebony—the bed of death! I listened in an agony of superstitious terror—but there was no repetition of the sound. I strained my vision to detect any motion in the corpse—but there was not the slightest perceptible. Yet I could not have been deceived. I *had* heard the noise, however faint, and my soul was awakened within me. I resolutely and perseveringly kept my attention riveted upon the body. Many minutes elapsed before any circumstances occurred tending to throw light upon the mystery. At length it became evident that a slight, a very feeble, and barely noticeable tinge of color had flushed up within the cheeks, and along the sunken small veins of the eyelids. Through a species of unutterable horror and awe, for which the language of mortality has no sufficiently energetic expression, I felt my heart cease to beat, my limbs grow rigid where I sat. Yet a sense of duty finally operated to restore my self-possession. I could no longer doubt that we had been precipitate in our preparations—that Rowena still lived. It was necessary that some immediate exertion be made; yet the turret was altogether apart from the portion of the abbey tenanted by the servants—there were none within call—I had no means of summoning them to my aid without leaving the room for many minutes—and this I could not venture to do. I therefore struggled alone in my endeavors to call back the spirit still hovering. In a short period it was certain, however, that a relapse had taken place; the color disappeared from both eyelid and cheek, leaving a wanness even more than that of marble; the lips became doubly shriveled and pinched up in the ghastly expression of death; a repulsive clamminess and coldness overspread rapidly the surface of the body; and all the usual rigorous stiffness immediately supervened. I fell back with a shudder upon the couch from which I had been so startlingly aroused, and again gave myself up to passionate waking visions of Ligeia.

An hour thus elapsed when (could it be possible?) I was a second time aware of some vague sound issuing from the region of the bed. I listened—in extremity of horror. The sound came again—it was a sigh. Rushing to the corpse, I saw—distinctly saw—a tremor upon the lips. In a minute afterwards they relaxed, disclosing a bright line of the pearly teeth. Amazement now struggled in my bosom with the profound awe which had hitherto reigned there alone. I felt that my vision grew dim, that my reason wandered; and it was only by a violent effort that I at length succeeded in nerving myself to the task which duty thus once more had pointed out. There was now a partial glow upon the forehead and upon the cheek and throat; a perceptible warmth pervaded the whole frame; there was even a slight pulsation at the heart. The lady *lived*; and with redoubled ardor I betook myself to the task of restoration. I chafed and bathed the temples and the hands, and used every exertion which experience, and no little medical reading, could suggest. But in vain. Suddenly, the color fled, the pulsation ceased, the lips resumed the expression of the dead, and, in an instant afterward, the whole body took upon itself the icy chilliness, the livid hue, the intense rigidity, the sunken outline, and all the loathsome peculiarities of that which has been, for many days, a tenant of the tomb.

And again I sunk into visions of Ligeia—and *again* (what marvel that I shudder while I write?) *again* there reached my ears a low sob from the region of the ebony bed. But why shall I minutely detail the unspeakable horrors of that night? Why shall I pause to relate how, time after time, until near the period of the grey dawn, this hideous drama of revivification was repeated; how each terrific relapse was only into a sterner and apparently more irredeemable death; how each agony wore the aspect of a struggle with some invisible foe; and how each struggle was succeeded by I know not what of wild change in the personal appearance of the corpse? Let me hurry to a conclusion.

The greater part of the fearful night had worn away, and she who had been dead once again stirred—and now more vigorously than hitherto, although arousing from a dissolution more appalling in its utter hopelessness than any. I had long ceased to struggle or to move, and remained sitting rigidly upon the ottoman, a helpless prey to a whirl of violent emotions, of which extreme awe was perhaps the least terrible, the least consuming. The corpse, I repeat, stirred, and now more vigorously than before. The hues of life flushed up with unwonted energy into the countenance—the limbs relaxed—and, save that the eyelids were yet pressed heavily together, and that the bandages and draperies of the grave still imparted their charnel character to the figure, I might have dreamed that Rowena had indeed shaken off, utterly, the fetters of Death. But if this idea was not, even then, altogether adopted, I could at least doubt no longer, when arising from the bed, tottering, with feeble steps, with closed eyes, and with the manner of one bewildered in a dream, the thing that was enshrouded advanced boldly and palpably into the middle of the apartment.

I trembled not—I stirred not—for a crowd of unutterable fancies connected with the air, the stature, the demeanor of the figure, rushing hurriedly through my brain, had paralyzed—had chilled me into stone. I stirred not—but gazed upon the apparition. There was a mad disorder in my thoughts—a tumult unappeasable. Could it, indeed, be the *living* Rowena who confronted me? Could it indeed be Rowena at all—the fair-haired, the blue-eyed Lady Rowena Trevanion of Tremaine? Why, *why* should I doubt it? The bandage lay heavily about the mouth—but then might it not be the mouth of the breathing Lady of Tremaine? And the cheeks—there were the roses as in her noon of life—yes, these might indeed be the fair cheeks of the living Lady of Tremaine. And the chin, with its dimples, as in health, might it not be hers?—But *had she then grown taller since her malady?* What inexpressible madness seized me with that thought? One bound, and I had reached her feet! Shrinking from my touch, she let fall from her head, unloosened, the ghastly cerements which had confined it, and there streamed forth, into the rushing atmosphere of the chamber, huge masses of long and disheveled hair; *it was blacker than the raven wings of the midnight!* And now slowly opened *the* eyes of the figure which stood before me. "Here then, at least," I shrieked aloud, "can I never—can I never be mistaken—these are the full, and the black, and the wild eyes—of my lost love—of the lady—of the Lady Ligeia."

THE FALL OF THE HOUSE OF USHER

"Son cœur est un luth suspendu;
Sitôt qu'on le touche il résonne."
De Béranger

During the whole of a dull, dark, and soundless day in the autumn of the year, when the clouds hung oppressively low in the heavens, I had been passing alone, on horseback, through a singularly dreary tract of country; and at length found myself, as the shades of the evening drew on, within view of the melancholy House of Usher. I know not how it was—but, with the first glimpse of the building, a sense of insufferable gloom pervaded my spirit. I say insufferable; for the feeling was unrelieved by any of that half-pleasurable, because poetic, sentiment, with which the mind usually receives even the sternest natural images of the desolate or terrible. I looked upon the scene before me—upon the mere house, and the simple landscape features of the domain—upon the bleak walls—upon the vacant eye-like windows—upon a few rank sedges—and upon a few white trunks of decayed trees—with an utter depression of soul which I can compare to no earthly sensation more properly than to the after-dream of the reveler upon opium—the bitter lapse into everyday life—the hideous dropping off of the veil. There was an iciness, a sinking, a sickening of the heart—an unredeemed dreariness of thought which no goading of the imagination could torture into aught of the sublime. What was it—I paused to think—what was it that so unnerved me in the contemplation of the House of Usher? It was a mystery all insoluble; nor could I grapple with the shadowy fancies that crowded upon me as I pondered. I was forced to fall back upon the unsatisfactory conclusion, that while, beyond doubt, there *are* combinations of very simple natural objects which have the power of thus affecting us, still the analysis of this power lies among considerations beyond our depth. It was possible, I reflected, that a mere different arrangement of the particulars of the scene, of the details of the picture, would be sufficient to modify, or perhaps to annihilate its capacity for sorrowful impression; and, acting upon this idea, I reined my horse to the precipitous brink of a black and lurid tarn that lay in unruffled luster by the dwelling, and gazed down—but with a shudder even more thrilling than before—upon the remodeled and inverted images of the grey sedge, and the ghastly tree-stems, and the vacant and eye-like windows.

Nevertheless, in this mansion of gloom I now proposed to myself a sojourn of some weeks. Its proprietor, Roderick Usher, had been one of my boon companions in boyhood; but many years had elapsed since our last meeting. A letter, however, had lately reached me in a distant part of the country—a letter from him—which, in its wildly importunate nature, had admitted of no other than a personal reply. The MS gave evidence of nervous agitation. The writer spoke of acute bodily illness—of a mental disorder which oppressed him—and of an earnest desire to see me, as his best, and indeed his only personal friend, with a view of attempting, by the cheerfulness of my society, some alleviation of his malady. It was the manner in which all this, and much more, was said—it was the apparent *heart* that went with his request—which allowed me no room for hesitation; and I accordingly obeyed forthwith what I still considered a very singular summons.

Although, as boys, we had been even intimate associates, yet I really knew little of my friend. His reserve had been always excessive and habitual. I was aware, however, that his very ancient family had been noted, time out of mind, for a peculiar sensibility of temperament, displaying itself, through long ages, in many works of exalted art, and manifested, of late, in repeated deeds of munificent yet unobtrusive charity, as well as in a passionate devotion to the intricacies, perhaps even more than to the orthodox and easily recognizable beauties, of musical science. I had learned, too, the very remarkable fact, that the stem of the Usher race, all time-honored as it was, had put forth, at no period, any enduring branch; in other words, that the entire family lay in the direct line of descent, and had always, with very trifling and very temporary variation, so lain. It was this deficiency, I considered, while running over in thought the perfect keeping of the character of the premises with the accredited character of the people, and while speculating upon the possible influence which the one, in the long lapse of centuries, might have exercised upon the other—it was this deficiency, perhaps, of collateral issue, and the consequent undeviating transmission, from sire to son, of the patrimony with the name, which had, at length, so identified the two as to merge the original title of the estate in the quaint and equivocal appellation of the "House of Usher"—an appellation which seemed to include, in the minds of the peasantry who used it, both the family and the family mansion.

I have said that the sole effect of my somewhat childish experiment—that of looking down within the tarn—had been to deepen the first singular impression. There can be no doubt that the consciousness of the rapid increase of my superstition—for why should I not so term it?—served mainly to accelerate the increase itself. Such, I have long known, is the paradoxical law of all sentiments having terror as a basis. And it might have been for this reason only, that, when I again uplifted my eyes to the house itself, from its image in the pool, there grew in my mind a strange fancy—a fancy so ridiculous, indeed, that I but mention it to show the vivid force of the sensations which oppressed me. I had so worked upon my imagination as really to believe that about the whole mansion and domain there hung an atmosphere peculiar to themselves and their immediate vicinity—an atmosphere which had no affinity with the air of heaven, but which had reeked up from the decayed trees, and the grey wall, and the silent tarn—a pestilent and mystic vapor, dull, sluggish, faintly discernible, and leaden-hued.

Shaking off from my spirit what *must* have been a dream, I scanned more narrowly the real aspect of the building. Its principal feature seemed to be that of an excessive antiquity. The discoloration of ages had been great. Minute fungi overspread the whole exterior, hanging in a fine tangled web-work from the eaves. Yet all this was apart from any extraordinary dilapidation. No portion of the masonry had fallen; and there appeared to be a wild inconsistency between its still perfect adaptation of parts, and the crumbling condition of the individual stones. In this there was much that reminded me of the specious totality of old woodwork which has rotted for long years in some neglected vault, with no disturbance from the breath of the external air. Beyond this indication of extensive decay, however, the fabric gave little token of instability. Perhaps the eye of a scrutinizing observer might have discovered a barely perceptible fissure, which, extending from the roof of the building in front, made its way down the wall in a zigzag direction, until it became lost in the sullen waters of the tarn.

Noticing these things, I rode over a short causeway to the house. A servant in waiting took my horse, and I entered the Gothic archway of the hall. A valet, of stealthy step, thence conducted me, in silence, through many dark and intricate passages in my progress to the studio of his master. Much that I encountered on the way contributed, I know not how, to heighten the vague sentiments of which I have already spoken. While the objects around me—while the carvings of the ceilings, the somber tapestries of the walls, the ebon blackness of the floors, and the phantasmagoric armorial trophies which rattled as I strode, were but matters to which, or to such as which, I had been accustomed from my infancy—while I hesitated not to acknowledge how familiar was all this—I still wondered to find how unfamiliar were the fancies which ordinary images were stirring up. On one of the staircases, I met the physician of the family. His countenance, I thought, wore a mingled expression of low cunning and perplexity. He accosted me with trepidation and passed on. The valet now threw open a door and ushered me into the presence of his master.

The room in which I found myself was very large and lofty. The windows were long, narrow, and pointed, and at so vast a distance from the black oaken floor as to be altogether inaccessible from within. Feeble gleams of encrimsoned light made their way through the trellised panes, and served to render sufficiently distinct the more prominent objects around; the eye, however, struggled in vain to reach the remoter angles of the chamber, or the recesses of the vaulted and fretted ceiling. Dark draperies hung upon the walls. The general furniture was profuse, comfortless, antique, and tattered. Many books and musical instruments lay scattered about, but failed to give any vitality to the scene. I felt that I breathed an atmosphere of sorrow. An air of stern, deep, and irredeemable gloom hung over and pervaded all.

Upon my entrance, Usher arose from a sofa on which he had been lying at full length, and greeted me with a vivacious warmth which had much in it, I at first thought, of an overdone cordiality—of the constrained effort of the *ennuyé* man of the world. A glance, however, at his countenance, convinced me of his perfect sincerity. We sat down; and for some moments, while he spoke not, I gazed upon him with a feeling half of pity, half of awe. Surely, man had never before so terribly altered, in so brief a period, as had Roderick Usher! It was with difficulty that I could bring myself to admit the identity of the wan being before me with the companion of my early boyhood. Yet the character of his face had been at all times remarkable. A cadaverousness of complexion; an eye large, liquid, and luminous beyond comparison; lips somewhat thin and very pallid, but of a surpassingly beautiful curve; a nose of a delicate Hebrew model, but with a breadth of nostril unusual in similar formations; a finely molded chin, speaking, in its want of prominence, of a want of moral energy; hair of a more than web-like softness and tenuity; these features, with an inordinate expansion above the regions of the temple, made up altogether a countenance not easily to be forgotten. And now in the mere exaggeration of the prevailing character of these features, and of the expression they were wont to convey, lay so much of change that I doubted to whom I spoke. The now ghastly pallor of the skin, and the now miraculous luster of the eye, above all things startled and even awed me. The silken hair, too, had been suffered to grow all unheeded, and as, in its wild gossamer texture, it floated rather than fell about the face, I could not, even with effort, connect its arabesque expression with any idea of simple humanity.

In the manner of my friend I was at once struck with an incoherence—an inconsistency; and I soon found this to arise from a series of feeble and futile struggles to overcome an habitual trepidancy—an excessive nervous agitation. For something of this nature I had indeed been prepared, no less by his letter, than by reminiscences of certain boyish traits, and by conclusions deduced from his peculiar physical conformation and temperament. His action was alternately vivacious and sullen. His voice varied rapidly from a tremulous indecision (when the animal spirits seemed utterly in abeyance) to that species of energetic concision—that abrupt, weighty, unhurried, and hollow-sounding enunciation—that leaden, self-balanced and perfectly modulated guttural utterance, which may be observed in the lost drunkard, or the irreclaimable eater of opium, during the periods of his most intense excitement.

It was thus that he spoke of the object of my visit, of his earnest
desire to see me, and of the solace he expected me to afford him.
He entered, at some length, into what he conceived to be the nature
of his malady. It was, he said, a constitutional and a family evil, and
one for which he despaired to find a remedy—a mere nervous affection, he immediately added, which would undoubtedly soon pass off.
It displayed itself in a host of unnatural sensations. Some of these,
as he detailed them, interested and bewildered me; although, perhaps,
the terms, and the general manner of the narration had their weight.
He suffered much from a morbid acuteness of the senses; the most
insipid food was alone endurable; he could wear only garments of
certain texture; the odors of all flowers were oppressive; his eyes
were tortured by even a faint light; and there were but peculiar
sounds, and these from stringed instruments, which did not inspire
him with horror.

To an anomalous species of terror I found him a bounden slave.
"I shall perish," said he, "I *must* perish in this deplorable folly. Thus,
thus, and not otherwise, shall I be lost. I dread the events of the
future, not in themselves, but in their results. I shudder at the thought
of any, even the most trivial, incident, which may operate upon this
intolerable agitation of soul. I have, indeed, no abhorrence of danger,
except in its absolute effect—in terror. In this unnerved—in this
pitiable condition—I feel that the period will sooner or later arrive
when I must abandon life and reason together, in some struggle with
the grim phantasm, Fear."

I learned, moreover, at intervals, and through broken and equivocal hints, another singular feature of his mental condition. He
was enchained by certain superstitious impressions in regard to
the dwelling which he tenanted, and whence, for many years, he
had never ventured forth—in regard to an influence whose
supposititious force was conveyed in terms too shadowy here to
be re-stated—an influence which some peculiarities in the mere

form and substance of his family mansion, had, by dint of long sufferance, he said, obtained over his spirit—an effect which the *physique* of the gray walls and turrets, and of the dim tarn into which they all looked down, had, at length, brought about upon the *morale* of his existence.

He admitted, however, although with hesitation, that much of the peculiar gloom which thus afflicted him could be traced to a more natural and far more palpable origin—to the severe and long-continued illness—indeed to the evidently approaching dissolution—of a tenderly beloved sister—his sole companion for long years—his last and only relative on earth. "Her decease," he said, with a bitterness which I can never forget, "would leave him (him the hopeless and the frail) the last of the ancient race of the Ushers." While he spoke, the Lady Madeline (for so was she called) passed slowly through a remote portion of the apartment, and, without having noticed my presence, disappeared. I regarded her with an utter astonishment not unmingled with dread—and yet I found it impossible to account for such feelings. A sensation of stupor oppressed me, as my eyes followed her retreating steps. When a door, at length, closed upon her, my glance sought instinctively and eagerly the countenance of the brother—but he had buried his face in his hands, and I could only perceive that a far more than ordinary wanness had overspread the emaciated fingers through which trickled many passionate tears.

The disease of the Lady Madeline had long baffled the skill of her physicians. A settled apathy, a gradual wasting away of the person, and frequent although transient affections of a partially cataleptical character, were the unusual diagnosis. Hitherto she had steadily borne up against the pressure of her malady, and had not betaken herself finally to bed; but, on the closing in of the evening of my arrival at the house, she succumbed (as her brother told me at night with inexpressible agitation) to the prostrating power of the destroyer; and I learned that the glimpse I had obtained of her person would thus probably be the last I should obtain—that the lady, at least while living, would be seen by me no more.

For several days ensuing, her name was unmentioned by either Usher or myself: and during this period I was busied in earnest endeavors to alleviate the melancholy of my friend. We painted and read together; or I listened, as if in a dream, to the wild improvisations of his speaking guitar. And thus, as a closer and still closer intimacy admitted me more unreservedly into the recesses of his spirit, the more bitterly did I perceive the futility of all attempt at cheering a mind from which darkness, as if an inherent positive quality, poured forth upon all objects of the moral and physical universe, in one unceasing radiation of gloom.

I shall ever bear about me a memory of the many solemn hours I thus spent alone with the master of the House of Usher. Yet I should fail in any attempt to convey an idea of the exact character of the studies, or of the occupations, in which he involved me, or led me the way. An excited and highly distempered ideality threw a sulfurous luster over all. His long improvised dirges will ring forever in my ears. Among other things, I hold painfully in mind a certain singular perversion and amplification of the wild air of the last waltz of Von Weber. From the paintings over which his elaborate fancy brooded, and which grew, touch by touch, into vagueness at which I shuddered the more thrillingly, because I shuddered knowing not why; from these paintings (vivid as their images now are before me) I would in vain endeavor to educe more than a small portion which should lie within the compass of merely written words. By the utter simplicity, by the nakedness of his designs, he arrested and overawed attention. If ever mortal painted an idea, that mortal was Roderick Usher. For me at least—in the circumstances then surrounding me—there arose out of the pure abstractions which the hypochondriac contrived to throw upon his canvas, an intensity of intolerable awe, no shadow of which felt I ever yet in the contemplation of the certainly glowing yet too concrete reveries of Fuseli.

One of the phantasmagoric conceptions of my friend, partaking not so rigidly of the spirit of abstraction, may be shadowed forth, although feebly, in words. A small picture presented the interior of an immensely long and rectangular vault or tunnel, with low walls, smooth, white, and without interruption or device. Certain accessory points of the design served well to convey the idea that this excavation lay at an exceeding depth below the surface of the earth. No outlet was observed in any portion of its vast extent, and no torch, or other artificial source of light was discernible; yet a flood of intense rays rolled throughout, and bathed the whole in a ghastly and inappropriate splendor.

I have just spoken of that morbid condition of the auditory nerve which rendered all music intolerable to the sufferer, with the exception of certain effects of stringed instruments. It was, perhaps, the narrow limits to which he thus confined himself upon the guitar, which gave birth in great measure, to the fantastic character of his performances. But the fervid *facility* of his *impromptus* could not be so accounted for. They must have been, and were, in the notes, as well as in the words of his wild fantasias (for he not unfrequently accompanied himself with rhymed verbal improvisations), the result of that intense mental collectedness and concentration to which I have previously alluded as observable only in particular moments of the highest artificial excitement. The words of one of these rhapsodies I have easily remembered. I was, perhaps, the more forcibly impressed with it, as he gave it, because, in the under or mystic current of its meaning, I fancied that I perceived, and for the first time, a full consciousness on the part of Usher, of the tottering of his lofty reason upon her throne. The verses, which were entitled "The Haunted Palace," ran very nearly, if not accurately, thus:

I

In the greenest of our valleys,
    By good angels tenanted,
Once a fair and stately palace—
    Radiant palace—reared its head.
In the monarch Thought's dominion—
    It stood there!
Never seraph spread a pinion
    Over fabric half so fair.

II

Banners yellow, glorious, golden,
    On its roof did float and flow;
(This—all this—was in the olden
    Time long ago)
And every gentle air that dallied,
    In that sweet day,
Along the ramparts plumed and pallid,
    A wingèd odor went away.

III

Wanderers in that happy valley
    Through two luminous windows saw
Spirits moving musically
    To a lute's well tunèd law,
Round about a throne, where sitting
    (Porphyrogene!)
In state his glory well befitting,
    The ruler of the realm was seen.

IV

And all with pearl and ruby glowing
    Was the fair palace door,
Through which came flowing, flowing, flowing
    And sparkling evermore,
A troop of echoes whose sweet duty
    Was but to sing,
In voices of surpassing beauty,
    The wit and wisdom of their king.

V

But evil things, in robes of sorrow,
    Assailed the monarch's high estate;
(Ah, let us mourn, for never morrow
    Shall dawn upon him, desolate!)
And, round about his home, the glory
    That blushed and bloomed
Is but a dim-remembered story
    Of the old time entombed.

VI

And travelers now within that valley,
    Through the red-litten windows, see
Vast forms that move fantastically
    To a discordant melody;
While, like a rapid ghastly river,
    Through the pale door,
A hideous throng rush out forever,
    And laugh—but smile no more.

I well remember that suggestions arising from this ballad, led us into a train of thought wherein there became manifest an opinion of Usher's which I mention not so much on account of its novelty (for other men have thought thus), as on account of the pertinacity with which he maintained it. This opinion, in its general form, was that of the sentience of all vegetable things. But, in his disordered fancy, the idea had assumed a more daring character, and trespassed, under certain conditions, upon the kingdom of inorganization. I lack words to express the full extent, or the earnest *abandon* of his persuasion. The belief, however, was connected (as I have previously hinted) with the gray stones of the home of his forefathers. The conditions of the sentience had been here, he imagined, fulfilled in the method of collocation of these stones—in the order of their arrangement, as well as in that of the many *fungi* which overspread them, and of the decayed trees which stood around—above all, in the long undisturbed endurance of this arrangement, and in its reduplication in the still waters of the tarn. Its evidence—the evidence of the sentience—was to be seen, he said (and I here started as he spoke) in the gradual yet certain condensation of an atmosphere of their own about the waters and the walls. The result was discoverable, he added, in that silent, yet importunate and terrible influence which for centuries had molded the destinies of his family, and which made *him* what I now saw him—what he was. Such opinions need no comment, and I will make none.

Our books—the books which, for years, had formed no small portion of the mental existence of the invalid—were, as might be supposed, in strict keeping with this character of phantasm. We pored together over such works as the *Ververt et Chartreuse* of Gresset; the *Belphegor* of Machiavelli; the *Heaven and Hell* of Swedenborg; *The Subterranean Voyage of Nicholas Klimm* by Holberg; *The Chiromancy of Robert Flud* of Jean D'Indaginé, and of De la Chambre; *The Journey into the Blue Distance* of Tieck; and *The City of the Sun* of Campanella. One favorite volume was a small octavo edition of the *Directorium Inquisitorum*, by the Dominican Eymeric de Gironne; and there were passages in Pomponius Mela, about the old African Satyrs and Ægipans, over which Usher would sit dreaming for hours. His chief delight, however, was found in the perusal of an exceedingly rare and curious book in quarto Gothic—the manual of a forgotten church—the *Vigiliae Mortuorum Secundum Chorum Ecclesiae Maguntinae.*

I could not help thinking of the wild ritual of this work, and of its probable influence upon the hypochondriac, when, one evening, having informed me abruptly that the Lady Madeline was no more, he stated his intention of preserving her corpse for a fortnight (previously to its final interment), in one of the numerous vaults within the main walls of the building. The worldly reason, however, assigned for this singular proceeding, was one which I did not feel at liberty to dispute. The brother had been led to his resolution (so he told me) by consideration of the unusual character of the malady of the deceased, of certain obtrusive and eager inquiries on the part of her medical men, and of the remote and exposed situation of the burial ground of the family. I will not deny that when I called to mind the sinister countenance of the person whom I met upon the staircase, on the day of my arrival at the house, I had no desire to oppose what I regarded as at best but a harmless, and by no means an unnatural, precaution.

At the request of Usher, I personally aided him in the arrangements for the temporary entombment. The body having been encoffined, we two alone bore it to its rest. The vault in which we placed it (and which had been so long unopened that our torches, half smothered in its oppressive atmosphere, gave us little opportunity for investigation) was small, damp, and entirely without means of admission for light; lying, at great depth, immediately beneath that portion of the building in which was my own sleeping apartment. It had been used, apparently, in remote feudal times, for the worst purpose of a donjon-keep, and, in later days, as a place of deposit for powder, or some other highly combustible substance, as a portion of its floor, and the whole interior of a long archway through which we reached it, were carefully sheathed with copper. The door, of massive iron, had been, also, similarly protected. Its immense weight caused an unusually sharp grating sound, as it moved upon its hinges.

Having deposited our mournful burden upon trestles within this region of horror, we partially turned aside the yet unscrewed lid of the coffin, and looked upon the face of the tenant. A striking similitude between the brother and sister now first arrested my attention; and Usher, divining, perhaps, my thoughts, murmured out some few words from which I learned that the deceased and himself had been twins, and that sympathies of a scarcely intelligible nature had always existed between them. Our glances, however, rested not long upon the dead—for we could not regard her unawed. The disease which had thus entombed the lady in the maturity of youth, had left, as usual in all maladies of a strictly cataleptical character, the mockery of a faint blush upon the bosom and the face, and that suspiciously lingering smile upon the lip which is so terrible in death. We replaced and screwed down the lid, and, having secured the door of iron, made our way, with toil, into the scarcely less gloomy apartments of the upper portion of the house.

And now, some days of bitter grief having elapsed, an observable change came over the features of the mental disorder of my friend. His ordinary manner had vanished. His ordinary occupations were neglected or forgotten. He roamed from chamber to chamber with hurried, unequal, and objectless step. The pallor of his countenance had assumed, if possible, a more ghastly hue—but the luminousness of his eye had utterly gone out. The once occasional huskiness of his tone was heard no more; and a tremulous quaver, as if of extreme terror, habitually characterized his utterance. There were times, indeed, when I thought his unceasingly agitated mind was laboring with some oppressive secret, to divulge which he struggled for the necessary courage. At times, again, I was obliged to resolve all into the mere inexplicable vagaries of madness, for I beheld him gazing upon vacancy for long hours, in an attitude of the profoundest attention, as if listening to some imaginary sound. It was no wonder that his condition terrified—that it infected me. I felt creeping upon me, by slow yet certain degrees, the wild influences of his own fantastic yet impressive superstitions.

It was, especially, upon retiring to bed late in the night of the seventh or eighth day after the placing of the Lady Madeline within the donjon, that I experienced the full power of such feelings. Sleep came not near my couch—while the hours waned and waned away. I struggled to reason off the nervousness which had dominion over me. I endeavored to believe that much, if not all of what I felt, was due to the bewildering influence of the gloomy furniture of the room—of the dark and tattered draperies, which, tortured into motion by the breath of a rising tempest, swayed fitfully to and fro upon the walls, and rustled uneasily about the decorations of the bed. But my efforts were fruitless. An irrepressible tremor gradually pervaded my frame; and, at length, there sat upon my very heart an incubus of utterly causeless alarm. Shaking this off with a gasp and a struggle, I uplifted myself upon the pillows, and, peering earnestly within the intense darkness of the chamber, harkened—I know not why, except that an instinctive spirit prompted me—to certain low and indefinite sounds which came, through the pauses of the storm, at long intervals, I knew not whence. Overpowered by an intense sentiment of horror, unaccountable yet unendurable, I threw on my clothes with haste (for I felt that I should sleep no more during the night), and endeavored to arouse myself from the pitiable condition into which I had fallen, by pacing rapidly to and fro through the apartment.

I had taken but few turns in this manner, when a light step on an adjoining staircase arrested my attention. I presently recognized it as that of Usher. In an instant afterward he rapped, with a gentle touch, at my door, and entered, bearing a lamp. His countenance was, as usual, cadaverously wan—but, moreover, there was a species of mad hilarity in his eyes—an evident restrained hysteria in his whole demeanor. His air appalled me—but anything was preferable to the solitude which I had so long endured, and I even welcomed his presence as a relief.

"And you have not seen it?" he said abruptly, after having stared about him for some moments in silence. "You have not then seen it?—But, stay! You shall." Thus speaking, and having carefully shaded his lamp, he hurried to one of the casements, and threw it freely open to the storm.

The impetuous fury of the entering gust nearly lifted us from our feet. It was, indeed, a tempestuous yet sternly beautiful night, and one wildly singular in its terror and its beauty. A whirlwind had apparently collected its force in our vicinity; for there were frequent and violent alterations in the direction of the wind; and the exceeding density of the clouds (which hung so low as to press upon the turrets of the house) did not prevent our perceiving the life-like velocity with which they flew careering from all points against each other, without passing away into the distance. I say that even their exceeding density did not prevent our perceiving this—yet we had no glimpse of the moon or stars—nor was there any flashing forth of the lightning. But the under surfaces of the huge masses of agitated vapor, as well as all terrestrial objects immediately around us, were glowing in the unnatural light of a faintly luminous and distinctly visible gaseous exhalation which hung about and enshrouded the mansion.

"You must not—you shall not behold this!" said I, shudderingly, to Usher, as I led him, with a gentle violence, from the window to a seat. "These appearances, which bewilder you, are merely electrical phenomena not uncommon—or it may be that they have their ghastly origin in the rank miasma of the tarn. Let us close this casement;

the air is chilling and dangerous to your frame. Here is one of your favorite romances. I will read, and you shall listen—and so we will pass away this terrible night together."

The antique volume which I had taken up was *The Mad Trist* of Sir Launcelot Canning; but I had called it a favorite of Usher's more in sad jest than in earnest; for, in truth, there is little in its uncouth and unimaginative prolixity which could have had interest for the lofty and spiritual ideality of my friend. It was, however, the only book immediately at hand; and I indulged a vague hope that the excitement which now agitated the hypochondriac, might find relief (for the history of mental disorder is full of similar anomalies) even in the extremeness of the folly which I should read. Could I have judged, indeed, by the wild overstrained air of vivacity with which he harkened, or apparently harkened, to the words of the tale, I might well have congratulated myself upon the success of my design.

I had arrived at that well-known portion of the story where Ethelred, the hero of the Trist, having sought in vain for peaceable admission into the dwelling of the hermit, proceeds to make good an entrance by force. Here, it will be remembered, the words of the narrative run thus:

"And Ethelred, who was by nature of a doughty heart, and who was now mighty withal, on account of the powerfulness of the wine which he had drunken, waited no longer to hold parley with the hermit, who in sooth, was of an obstinate and maliceful turn, but, feeling the rain upon his shoulders, and fearing the rising of the tempest, uplifted his mace outright, and, with blows, made quickly room in the plankings of the door for his gauntleted hand; and now pulling therewith sturdily, he so cracked, and ripped, and tore all asunder, that the noise of the dry and hollow-sounding wood alarmed and reverberated throughout the forest."

At the termination of this sentence I started, and for a moment, paused; for it appeared to me (although I at once concluded that my excited fancy had deceived me)—it appeared to me that, from some very remote portion of the mansion, there came, indistinctly, to my ears, what might have been, in its exact similarity of character, the echo (but a stifled and dull one certainly) of the very cracking and ripping sound which Sir Launcelot had so particularly described. It was, beyond doubt, the coincidence alone which had arrested my attention; for, amid the rattling of the sashes of the casements, and the ordinary commingled noises of the still increasing storm, the sound, in itself, had nothing, surely, which should have interested or disturbed me. I continued the story:

"But the good champion Ethelred, now entering within the door, was sore enraged and amazed to perceive no signal of the maliceful hermit; but, in the stead thereof, a dragon of a scaly and prodigious demeanor, and of a fiery tongue, which sate in guard before a palace of gold, with a floor of silver; and upon the wall there hung a shield of shining brass with this legend enwritten—

> Who entereth herein, a conqueror hath bin;
> Who slayeth the dragon, the shield he shall win;

And Ethelred uplifted his mace, and struck upon the head of the dragon, which fell before him, and gave up his pesty breath, with a shriek so horrid and harsh, and withal so piercing, that Ethelred had fain to close his ears with his hands against the dreadful noise of it, the like whereof was never before heard."

Here again I paused abruptly, and now a feeling of wild amaze-ment—for there could be no doubt whatever that, in this instance, I did actually hear (although from what direction it proceeded I found it impossible to say) a low and apparently distant, but harsh, protracted, and most unusual screaming or grating sound—the exact counterpart of what my fancy had already conjured up for the dragon's unnatural shriek as described by the romancer.

Oppressed, as I certainly was, upon the occurrence of the second and most extraordinary coincidence, by a thousand conflicting sensations, in which wonder and extreme terror were predominant, I still retained sufficient presence of mind to avoid exciting, by any observation, the sensitive nervousness of my companion. I was by no means certain that he had noticed the sounds in question; although, assuredly, a strange alteration had, during the last few minutes, taken place in his demeanor. From a position fronting my own, he had gradually brought round his chair, so as to sit with his face to the door of the chamber; and thus I could but partially perceive his features, although I saw that his lips trembled as if he were murmuring inaudibly. His head had dropped upon his breast—yet I knew that he was not asleep, from the wide and rigid opening of the eye as I caught a glance of it in profile. The motion of his body, too, was at variance with this idea—for he rocked from side to side with a gentle yet constant and uniform sway. Having rapidly taken notice of all this, I resumed the narrative of Sir Launcelot, which thus proceeded:

"And now, the champion, having escaped from the terrible fury of the dragon, bethinking himself of the brazen shield, and of the breaking up of the enchantment which was upon it, removed the carcass from out of the way before him, and approached valorously over the silver pavement of the castle to where the shield was upon the wall; which in sooth tarried not for his full coming, but fell down at his feet upon the silver floor, with a mighty great and terrible ringing sound."

No sooner had these syllables passed my lips, than—as if a shield of brass had indeed, at the moment, fallen heavily upon a floor of

silver—I became aware of a distinct, hollow, metallic, and clan-
gorous, yet apparently muffled reverberation. Completely unnerved,
I leaped to my feet; but the measured rocking movement of Usher
was undisturbed. I rushed to the chair in which he sat. His eyes
were bent fixedly before him, and throughout his whole countenance
there reigned a stony rigidity. But, as I placed my hand upon his
shoulder, there came a strong shudder over his whole person; a
sickly smile quivered about his lips; and I saw that he spoke in a
low, hurried, and gibbering murmur, as if unconscious of my presence. Bending closely over him, I at length drank in the hideous
import of his words.

"Not hear it?—Yes, I hear it, and *have* heard it. Long—long—
long—many minutes, many hours, many days, have I heard it—yet
I dared not—oh, pity me, miserable wretch that I am!—I dared not—I
dared not speak! *We have put her living in the tomb!* Said I not that
my senses were acute? I now tell you that I heard her first feeble
movements in the hollow coffin. I heard them—many, many days
ago—yet I dared not—*I dared not speak!* And now—tonight—
Ethelred—ha! ha!—The breaking of the hermit's door, and the
death-cry of the dragon, and the clangor of the shield!—Say, rather,
the rending of her coffin, and the grating of the iron hinges of her
prison, and her struggles within the coppered archway of the vault!
Oh whither shall I fly? Will she not be here anon? Is she not hurrying
to upbraid me for my haste? Have I not heard her footstep on the
stair? Do I not distinguish that heavy and horrible beating of her
heart? Madman!" —Here he sprang furiously to his feet, and shrieked
out his syllables, as if in the effort he were giving up his soul—
"*Madman! I tell you that she now stands without the door!*"

As if in the superhuman energy of his utterance there had been
found the potency of a spell—the huge antique panels to which the
speaker pointed, threw slowly back, upon the instant, their ponderous
and ebony jaws. It was the work of the rushing gust—but then without

those doors there *did* stand the lofty and enshrouded figure of the Lady Madeline of Usher. There was blood upon her white robes, and the evidence of some bitter struggle upon every portion of her emaciated frame. For a moment she remained trembling and reeling to and fro upon the threshold, then, with a low moaning cry, fell heavily inward upon the person of her brother, and in her violent and now final death-agonies, bore him to the floor a corpse, and a victim to the terrors he had anticipated.

From that chamber, and from that mansion, I fled aghast. The storm was still abroad in all its wrath as I found myself crossing the old causeway. Suddenly there shot along the path a wild light, and I turned to see whence a gleam so unusual could have issued; for the vast house and its shadows were alone behind me. The radiance was that of the full, setting, and blood-red moon which now shone vividly through that once barely discernible fissure of which I have before spoken as extending from the roof of the building, in a zigzag direction, to the base. While I gazed, this fissure rapidly widened— there came a fierce breath of the whirlwind—the entire orb of the satellite burst at once upon my sight—my brain reeled as I saw the mighty walls rushing asunder—there was a long tumultuous shouting sound like the voice of a thousand waters—and the deep and dank tarn at my feet closed sullenly and silently over the fragments of the "House of Usher."

WILLIAM WILSON

"What say of it? What say of conscience grim,
That spectre in my path?"
Chamberlayne's *Pharronida*

Let me call myself, for the present, William Wilson. The fair page now lying before me need not be sullied with my real appellation. This has been already too much an object for the scorn—for the horror—for the detestation of my race. To the uttermost regions of the globe have not the indignant winds bruited its unparalleled infamy? Oh, outcast of all outcasts most abandoned!—To the earth art thou not forever dead? To its honors, to its flowers, to its golden aspirations?—And a cloud, dense, dismal, and limitless, does it not hang eternally between thy hopes and heaven?

I would not, if I could, here or today, embody a record of my later years of unspeakable misery, and unpardonable crime. This epoch—these later years—took unto themselves a sudden elevation in turpitude, whose origin alone it is my present purpose to assign. Men usually grow base by degrees. From me, in an instant, all virtue dropped bodily as a mantle. From comparatively trivial wickedness I passed, with the stride of a giant, into more than the enormities of an Elah-Gabalus. What chance—what one event brought this evil thing to pass, bear with me while I relate. Death approaches; and the shadow which foreruns him has thrown a softening influence over my spirit. I long, in passing through the dim valley, for the sympathy—I had nearly said for the pity—of my fellow men. I would fain have them believe that I have been, in some measure, the slave of circumstances beyond human control. I would wish them to seek out for me, in the details I am about to give, some little oasis of *fatality* amid a wilderness of error. I would have them allow—what they cannot refrain from allowing—that, although temptation may have erewhile existed as great, man was never *thus*, at least, tempted before—certainly, never *thus* fell. And is it therefore that he has never thus suffered? Have I not indeed been living in a dream? And am I not now dying a victim to the horror and the mystery of the wildest of all sublunary visions?

I am the descendant of a race whose imaginative and easily excitable temperament has at all times rendered them remarkable; and, in my earliest infancy, I gave evidence of having fully inherited the family character. As I advanced in years it was more strongly developed; becoming, for many reasons, a cause of serious dis-quietude to my friends, and of positive injury to myself. I grew self-willed, addicted to the wildest caprices, and a prey to the most ungovernable passions. Weak-minded, and beset with constitutional infirmities akin to my own, my parents could do but little to check the evil propensities which distinguished me. Some feeble and ill-directed efforts resulted in complete failure on their part, and, of course, in total triumphs on mine. Thenceforward my voice was a household law; and at an age when few children have abandoned their leading-strings, I was left to the guidance of my own will, and became, in all but name, the master of my own actions.

My earliest recollections of a school-life are connected with a large, rambling, Elizabethan house, in a misty-looking village of England, where were a vast number of gigantic and gnarled trees, and where all the houses were excessively ancient. In truth, it was a dream-like and spirit-soothing place, that venerable old town. At this moment, in fancy, I feel the refreshing chilliness of its deeply shadowed avenues, inhale the fragrance of its thousand shrubberies, and thrill anew with undefinable delight, at the deep hollow note of the church-bell, breaking, each hour, with sullen and sudden roar, upon the stillness of the dusky atmosphere in which the fretted Gothic steeple lay imbedded and asleep.

It gives me, perhaps, as much of pleasure as I can now in any manner experience, to dwell upon minute recollections of the school and its concerns. Steeped in misery as I am—misery, alas, only too real!—I shall be pardoned for seeking relief, however slight and temporary, in the weakness of a few rambling details. These, more-over, utterly trivial, and even ridiculous in themselves, assume, to my fancy, adventitious importance, as connected with a period and a locality when and where I recognize the first ambiguous monitions of the destiny which afterward so fully overshadowed me. Let me then remember.

The house, I have said, was old and irregular. The grounds were extensive, and a high and solid brick wall, topped with a bed of mortar and broken glass, encompassed the whole. This prison-like rampart formed the limit of our domain; beyond it we saw but thrice a week— once every Saturday afternoon, when, attended by two ushers, we were permitted to take brief walks in a body through some of the neighboring fields—and twice during Sunday, when we were paraded in the same formal manner to the morning and evening service in the one church of the village. Of this church the principal of our school was pastor. With how deep a spirit of wonder and perplexity was I wont to regard him from our remote pew in the gallery, as, with step solemn and slow, he ascended the pulpit! This reverend man, with countenance so demurely benign, with robes so glossy and so clerically flowing, with wig so minutely powdered, so rigid and so vast—could this be he who, of late, with sour visage, and in snuffy habiliments, administered, ferule in hand, the Draconian laws of the academy? Oh, gigantic paradox, too utterly monstrous for solution!

At an angle of the ponderous wall frowned a more ponderous gate. It was riveted and studded with iron bolts, and surmounted with jagged iron spikes. What impressions of deep awe did it inspire! It was never opened save for the three periodical egressions and ingressions already mentioned; then, in every creak of its mighty hinges, we found a plenitude of mystery—a world of matter for solemn remark, or for more solemn meditation.

The extensive enclosure was irregular in form, having many capacious recesses. Of these, three or four of the largest constituted the playground. It was level, and covered with fine hard gravel. I well remember it had no trees, nor benches, nor anything similar within it. Of course it was in the rear of the house. In front lay a small parterre, planted with box and other shrubs; but through this sacred division we passed only upon rare occasions indeed—such as a first advent to school or final departure thence, or perhaps, when a parent or friend having called for us, we joyfully took our way home for the Christmas or Midsummer holidays.

But the house!—How quaint an old building was this!—To me how veritably a palace of enchantment! There was really no end to its windings—to its incomprehensible subdivisions. It was difficult, at any given time, to say with certainty upon which of its two stories one happened to be. From each room to every other there were sure to be found three or four steps either in ascent or descent. Then the lateral branches were innumerable—inconceivable—and so returning in upon themselves, that our most exact ideas in regard to the whole mansion were not very far different from those with which we pondered upon infinity. During the five years of my residence here, I was never able to ascertain with precision in what remote locality lay the little sleeping apartment assigned to myself and some eighteen or twenty other scholars.

The school-room was the largest in the house—I could not help thinking, in the world. It was very long, narrow, and dismally low, with pointed Gothic windows and a ceiling of oak. In a remote and terror-inspiring angle was a square enclosure of eight or ten feet, comprising the *sanctum*, "during hours," of our principal, the Reverend Dr. Bransby. It was a solid structure, with massy door, sooner than open which in the absence of the "Dominie," we would all have willingly perished by the *peine forte et dure*. In other angles were two other similar boxes, far less reverenced, indeed, but still greatly matters of awe. One of these was the pulpit of the "classical" usher, one of the "English and mathematical." Interspersed about the room, crossing and recrossing in endless irregularity, were innumerable benches and desks, black, ancient, and time-worn, piled desperately with much-bethumbed books, and so beseamed with initial letters, names at full length, grotesque figures, and other multiplied efforts of the knife, as to have entirely lost what little of original form might have been their portion in days long departed. A huge bucket with water stood at one extremity of the room, and a clock of stupendous dimensions at the other.

Encompassed by the massy walls of this venerable academy, I passed, yet not in tedium or disgust, the years of the third lustrum of my life. The teeming brain of childhood requires no external world of incident to occupy or amuse it; and the apparently dismal monotony of a school was replete with more intense excitement than my riper youth has derived from luxury, or my full manhood from crime. Yet I must believe that my first mental development had in it much of the uncommon—even much of the *outré*. Upon mankind at large the events of very early existence rarely leave in mature age any definite impression. All is gray shadow—a weak and irregular remembrance—an indistinct regathering of feeble pleasures and phantasmagoric pains. With me this is not so. In childhood I must have felt with the energy of a man what I now find stamped upon memory in lines as vivid, as deep, and as durable as the *exergues* of the Carthaginian medals.

Yet in fact—in the fact of the world's view—how little was there to remember! The morning's awakening, the nightly summons to bed; the connings, the recitations; the periodical half-holidays, and perambulations; the playground, with its broils, its pastimes, its intrigues—these, by a mental sorcery long forgotten, were made to involve a wilderness of sensation, a world of rich incident, a university of varied emotion, of excitement the most passionate and spirit-stirring. *"Oh, le bon temps, que ce siècle de fer!"*

In truth, the ardor, the enthusiasm, and the imperiousness of my disposition, soon rendered me a marked character among my schoolmates, and by slow, but natural gradations, gave me an ascendancy over all not greatly older than myself—over all with a single exception. This exception was found in the person of a scholar, who, although no relation bore the same Christian and surname as myself—a circumstance, in fact, little remarkable; for, notwithstanding a noble descent, mine was one of those everyday appellations which seem, by prescriptive right, to have been, time out of mind, the common property of the mob. In this narrative I have therefore designated myself as William Wilson—a fictitious title not very dissimilar to the real. My namesake alone, of those who in school phraseology constituted "our set," presumed to compete with me in the studies of the class—in the sports and broils of the playground—to refuse implicit belief in my assertions, and submission to my will—indeed, to interfere with my arbitrary dictation in any respect whatsoever. If there is on earth a supreme and unqualified despotism, it is the despotism of a master-mind in boyhood over the less energetic spirits of its companions.

Wilson's rebellion was to me a source of the greatest embarrassment—the more so as, in spite of the bravado with which in public I made a point of treating him and his pretensions, I secretly felt that I feared him, and could not help thinking the equality which he maintained so easily with myself, a proof of his true superiority;

since not to be overcome cost me a perpetual struggle. Yet this superiority—even this equality—was in truth acknowledged by no one but myself; our associates, by some unaccountable blindness, seemed not even to suspect it. Indeed, his competition, his resistance, and especially his impertinent and dogged interference with my purposes, were not more pointed than private. He appeared to be destitute alike of the ambition which urged, and of the passionate energy of mind which enabled me to excel. In his rivalry he might have been supposed actuated solely by a whimsical desire to thwart, astonish, or mortify myself; although there were times when I could not help observing, with a feeling made of wonder, abasement, and pique, that he mingled with his injuries, his insults, or his contradictions, a certain most inappropriate, and assuredly most unwelcome *affectionateness* of manner. I could only conceive this singular behavior to arise from a consummate self-conceit assuming the vulgar air of patronage and protection.

Perhaps it was this latter trait in Wilson's conduct, conjoined with our identity of name, and the mere accident of our having entered the school upon the same day, which set afloat the notion that we were brothers, among the senior classes in the academy. These do not usually inquire with much strictness into the affairs of their juniors. I have before said, or should have said, that Wilson was not, in the most remote degree connected with my family. But assuredly if we *had* been brothers we must have been twins; for, after leaving Dr. Bransby's, I casually learned that my namesake was born on the 19th of January 1813—and this is a somewhat remarkable coincidence; for the day is precisely that of my own nativity.

It may seem strange that in spite of the continual anxiety occasioned me by the rivalry of Wilson, and his intolerable spirit of contradiction, I could not bring myself to hate him altogether. We had, to be sure, nearly every day a quarrel in which, yielding me publicly the palm of victory, he, in some manner, contrived to make me feel that it was he who had deserved it; yet a sense of pride on my part, and a veritable dignity on his own, kept us always upon what are called "speaking terms," while there were many points of strong congeniality in our tempers, operating to awake in me a sentiment which our position alone, perhaps, prevented from ripening into friendship. It is difficult, indeed, to define, or even to describe, my real feelings toward him. They formed a motley and heterogeneous admixture—some petulant animosity, which was not yet hatred, some esteem, more respect, much fear, with a world of uneasy curiosity. To the moralist it will be unnecessary to say, in addition, that Wilson and myself were the most inseparable of companions.

It was no doubt the anomalous state of affairs existing between us, which turned all my attacks upon him (and they were many, either open or covert) into the channel of banter or practical joke (giving pain while assuming the aspect of mere fun) rather than into a more serious and determined hostility. But my endeavors on this head were by no means uniformly successful, even when my plans were the most wittily concocted; for my namesake had much about him, in character, of that unassuming and quiet austerity which, while enjoying the poignancy of its own jokes, has no heel of Achilles in itself, and absolutely refuses to be laughed at. I could find, indeed, but one vulnerable point, and that, lying in a personal peculiarity, arising, perhaps, from constitutional disease, would have been spared by any antagonist less at his wit's end than myself—my rival had a weakness in the faucial or gutteral organs, which precluded him from raising his voice at any time *above a very low whisper*. Of this defect I did not fail to take what poor advantage lay in my power.

Wilson's retaliations in kind were many; and there was one form of his practical wit that disturbed me beyond measure. How his sagacity first discovered at all that so petty a thing would vex me, is a question I never could solve; but, having discovered, he habitually practiced the annoyance. I had always felt aversion to my uncourtly patronymic, and its very common, if not plebeian, prænomen. The words were venom in my ears; and when, upon the day of my arrival, a second William Wilson came also to the academy, I felt angry with him for bearing the name, and doubly disgusted with the name because a stranger bore it, who would be the cause of its two-fold repetition, who would be constantly in my presence, and whose concerns, in the ordinary routine of the school business, must inevitably, on account of the detestable coincidence, be often confounded with my own.

The feeling of vexation thus engendered grew stronger with every circumstance tending to show resemblance, moral or physical, between my rival and myself. I had not then discovered the remarkable fact that we were of the same age; but I saw that we were of the same height, and I perceived that we were even singularly alike in general contour of person and outline of feature. I was galled, too, by the rumor touching a relationship, which had grown current in the upper forms. In a word, nothing could more seriously disturb me (although I scrupulously concealed such disturbance), than any allusion to a similarity of mind, person, or condition existing between us. But, in truth, I had no reason to believe that (with the exception of the matter of relationship, and in the case of Wilson himself) this similarity had ever been made a subject of comment, or even observed at all by our schoolfellows. That *he* observed it in all its bearings, and as fixedly as I, was apparent; but that he could discover in such circumstances so fruitful a field of annoyance, can only be attributed, as I said before, to his more than ordinary penetration.

His cue, which was to perfect an imitation of myself, lay both in words and in actions; and most admirably did he play his part. My dress it was an easy matter to copy; my gait and general manner were, without difficulty, appropriated; in spite of his constitutional defect, even my voice did not escape him. My louder tones were, of course, unattempted, but then the key, it was identical; *and his singular whisper, it grew the very echo of my own.*

How greatly this most exquisite portraiture harassed me (for it could not justly be termed a caricature), I will not now venture to describe. I had but one consolation—in the fact that the imitation, apparently, was noticed by myself alone, and that I had to endure only the knowing and strangely sarcastic smiles of my namesake himself. Satisfied with having produced in my bosom the intended effect, he seemed to chuckle in secret over the sting he had inflicted, and was characteristically disregardful of the public applause which the success of his witty endeavors might have so easily elicited. That the school, indeed, did not feel his design, perceive its accomplishment, and participate in his sneer, was, for many anxious months, a riddle I could not resolve. Perhaps the *gradation* of his copy rendered it not so readily perceptible; or, more possibly, I owed my security to the masterly air of the copyist, who, disdaining the letter (which in a painting is all the obtuse can see), gave but the full spirit of his original for my individual contemplation and chagrin.

I have already more than once spoken of the disgusting air of patronage which he assumed toward me, and of his frequent officious interference with my will. This interference often took the ungracious character of advice; advice not openly given, but hinted or insinuated. I received it with a repugnance which gained strength as I grew in years. Yet, at this distant day, let me do him the simple justice to acknowledge that I can recall no occasion when the suggestions of my rival were on the side of those errors or follies so usual to his immature age and seeming inexperience; that his moral sense, at least, if not his general talents and worldly wisdom, was far keener than my own; and that I might, today, have been a better, and thus a happier man, had I less frequently rejected the counsels embodied in those meaning whispers which I then but too cordially hated and too bitterly despised.

As it was, I at length grew restive in the extreme under his distasteful supervision, and daily resented more and more openly what I considered his intolerable arrogance. I have said that, in the first years of our connection as schoolmates, my feelings in regard to him might have been easily ripened into friendship; but, in the latter months of my residence at the academy, although the intrusion of his ordinary manner had, beyond doubt, in some measure, abated, my sentiments, in nearly similar proportion, partook very much of positive hatred. Upon one occasion he saw this, I think, and afterwards avoided, or made a show of avoiding me.

It was about the same period, if I remember aright, that, in an altercation of violence with him, in which he was more than usually thrown off his guard, and spoke and acted with an openness of demeanor rather foreign to his nature, I discovered, or fancied I discovered, in his accent, his air, and general appearance, a something which first startled, and then deeply interested me, by bringing to mind dim visions of my earliest infancy—wild, confused, and thronging memories of a time when memory herself was yet unborn. I cannot better describe the sensation which oppressed me than by saying that I could with difficulty shake off the belief of my having been acquainted with the being who stood before me, at some epoch very long ago—some point of the past even infinitely remote. The delusion, however, faded rapidly as it came; and I mention it at all but to define the day of the last conversation I there held with my singular namesake.

The huge old house, with its countless subdivisions, had several large chambers communicating with each other, where slept the greater number of the students. There were, however (as must necessarily happen in a building so awkwardly planned), many little nooks or recesses, the odds and ends of the structure; and these the economic ingenuity of Dr. Bransby had also fitted up as dormitories; although, being the merest closets, they were capable of accommodating but a single individual. One of these small apartments was occupied by Wilson.

One night, about the close of my fifth year at the school, and immediately after the altercation just mentioned, finding every one wrapped in sleep, I arose from bed, and, lamp in hand, stole through a wilderness of narrow passages from my own bedroom to that of my rival. I had long been plotting one of those ill-natured pieces of practical wit at his expense in which I had hitherto been so uniformly unsuccessful. It was my intention, now, to put my scheme in operation, and I resolved to make him feel the whole extent of the malice with which I was imbued. Having reached his closet, I noiselessly entered, leaving the lamp, with a shade over it, on the outside. I advanced a step, and listened to the sound of his tranquil breathing. Assured of his being asleep, I returned, took the light, and with it again approached the bed. Close curtains were around it, which, in the prosecution of my plan, I slowly and quietly withdrew, when the bright rays fell vividly upon the sleeper, and my eyes, at the same moment, upon his countenance. I looked—and a numbness, an iciness of feeling instantly pervaded my frame. My breast heaved, my knees tottered, my whole spirit became possessed with an objectless yet intolerable horror. Gasping for breath, I lowered the lamp in still nearer proximity to the face. Were these—*these* the lineaments of William Wilson? I saw, indeed, that they were his, but I shook as if with a fit of the ague in fancying they were not. What was there about them to confound me in this manner? I gazed—while my brain reeled with a multitude of incoherent thoughts. Not thus he appeared—assuredly not *thus*—in the vivacity of his waking hours. The same name! The same contour of person! The same day of arrival at the academy! And then his dogged and meaningless imitation of my gait, my voice, my habits, and my manner! Was it, in truth, within the bounds of human possibility, that what I now saw was the result, merely, of the habitual practice of this sarcastic imitation? Awe-stricken, and with a creeping shudder, I extinguished the lamp, passed silently from the chamber, and left, at once, the halls of that old academy, never to enter them again.

After a lapse of some months, spent at home in mere idleness, I found myself a student at Eton. The brief interval had been sufficient to enfeeble my remembrance of the events at Dr. Bransby's, or at least to effect a material change in the nature of the feelings with which I remembered them. The truth—the tragedy—of the drama was no more. I could now find room to doubt the evidence of my senses; and seldom called up the subject at all but with wonder at the extent of human credulity, and a smile at the vivid force of the imagination which I hereditarily possessed. Neither was this species of skepticism likely to be diminished by the character of the life I led at Eton. The vortex of thoughtless folly into which I there so immediately and so recklessly plunged, washed away all but the froth of my past hours, engulfed at once every solid or serious impression, and left to memory only the veriest levities of a former existence.

I do not wish, however, to trace the course of my miserable profligacy here—a profligacy which set at defiance the laws, while it eluded the vigilance of the institution. Three years of folly, passed without profit, had but given me rooted habits of vice, and added, in a somewhat unusual degree, to my bodily stature, when, after a week of soulless dissipation, I invited a small party of the most dissolute students to a secret carousal in my chambers. We met at a late hour of the night; for our debaucheries were to be faithfully protracted until morning. The wine flowed freely, and there were not wanting other and perhaps more dangerous seductions; so that the gray dawn had already faintly appeared in the east, while our delirious extravagance was at its height. Madly flushed with cards and intoxication, I was in the act of insisting upon a toast of more than wonted profanity, when my attention was suddenly diverted by the violent, although partial unclosing of the door of the apartment, and by the eager voice of a servant from without. He said that some person, apparently in great haste, demanded to speak with me in the hall.

Wildly excited with wine, the unexpected interruption rather delighted than surprised me. I staggered forward at once, and a few steps brought me to the vestibule of the building. In this low and small room there hung no lamp; and now no light at all was admitted, save that of the exceedingly feeble dawn which made its way through the semi-circular window. As I put my foot over the threshold, I became aware of the figure of a youth about my own height, and habited in a white kerseymere morning frock, cut in the novel fashion of the one I myself wore at the moment. This the faint light enabled me to perceive; but the features of his face I could not distinguish. Upon my entering he strode hurriedly up to me, and, seizing me by the arm with a gesture of petulant impatience, whispered the words "William Wilson!" in my ear.

I grew perfectly sober in an instant.

There was that in the manner of the stranger, and in the tremulous shake of his uplifted finger, as he held it between my eyes and the light, which filled me with unqualified amazement; but it was not this which had so violently moved me. It was the pregnancy of solemn admonition in the singular, low, hissing utterance; and, above all, it was the character, the tone, *the key*, of those few, simple, and familiar, yet *whispered* syllables, which came with a thousand thronging memories of bygone days, and struck upon my soul with the shock of a galvanic battery. Ere I could recover the use of my senses he was gone.

Although this event failed not of a vivid effect upon my disordered imagination, yet was it evanescent as vivid. For some weeks, indeed, I busied myself in earnest inquiry, or was wrapped in a cloud of morbid speculation. I did not pretend to disguise from my perception the identity of the singular individual who thus perseveringly interfered with my affairs, and harassed me with his insinuated counsel. But who and what was this Wilson?—And whence came he?—And what were his purposes? Upon neither of these points could I be satisfied; merely ascertaining, in regard to him, that a sudden accident in his family had caused his removal from Dr. Bransby's academy on the afternoon of the day in which I myself had eloped. But in a brief period I ceased to think upon the subject; my attention being all absorbed in a contemplated departure for Oxford. Thither I soon went; the uncalculating vanity of my parents furnishing me with an outfit and annual establishment, which would enable me to indulge at will in the luxury already so dear to my heart—to vie in profuseness of expenditure with the haughtiest heirs of the wealthiest earldoms in Great Britain.

Excited by such appliances to vice, my constitutional temperament broke forth with redoubled ardor, and I spurned even the common restraints of decency in the mad infatuation of my revels. But it were absurd to pause in the detail of my extravagance. Let it suffice, that among spendthrifts I out-Heroded Herod, and that, giving name to a multitude of novel follies, I added no brief appendix to the long catalogue of vices then usual in the most dissolute university of Europe.

It could hardly be credited, however, that I had, even here, so utterly fallen from the gentlemanly estate, as to seek acquaintance with the vilest arts of the gambler by profession, and, having become an adept in his despicable science, to practice it habitually as a means of increasing my already enormous income at the expense of the weak-minded among my fellow-collegians. Such, nevertheless, was the fact. And the very enormity of this offence against all manly and honorable sentiment proved, beyond doubt, the main if not the sole reason of the impunity with which it was committed. Who, indeed, among my most abandoned associates, would not rather have disputed the clearest evidence of his senses, than have suspected of such courses, the gay, the frank, the generous William Wilson—the noblest and most liberal commoner at Oxford—him whose follies (said his parasites) were but the follies of youth and unbridled fancy—whose errors but inimitable whim—whose darkest vice but a careless and dashing extravagance?

I had been now two years successfully busied in this way, when there came to the university a young *parvenu* nobleman, Glendinning—rich, said report, as Herodes Atticus—his riches, too, as easily acquired. I soon found him of weak intellect, and, of course, marked him as a fitting subject for my skill. I frequently engaged him in play, and contrived, with the gambler's usual art, to let him win considerable sums, the more effectually to entangle him in my snares. At length, my schemes being ripe, I met him (with the full intention that this meeting should be final and decisive) at the chambers of a fellow-commoner (Mr. Preston), equally intimate with both, but who, to do him justice, entertained not even a remote suspicion of my design. To give to this a better coloring, I had contrived to have assembled a party of some eight or ten, and was solicitously careful that the introduction of cards should appear accidental, and originate in the proposal of my contemplated dupe himself. To be brief upon a vile topic, none of the low finesse was omitted, so customary upon similar occasions that it is a just matter for wonder how any are still found so besotted as to fall its victim.

We had protracted our sitting far into the night, and I had at length effected the maneuver of getting Glendinning as my sole antagonist. The game, too, was my favorite *écarté*. The rest of the company, interested in the extent of our play, had abandoned their own cards, and were standing around us as spectators. The *parvenu*, who had been induced by my artifices in the early part of the evening, to drink deeply, now shuffled, dealt, or played, with a wild nervousness of manner for which his intoxication, I thought, might partially, but could not altogether account. In a very short period he had become

my debtor to a large amount, when, having taken a long draught of
port, he did precisely what I had been coolly anticipating—he
proposed to double our already extravagant stakes. With a well-
feigned show of reluctance, and not until after my repeated refusal
had seduced him into some angry words which gave a color of pique
to my compliance, did I finally comply. The result, of course, did
but prove how entirely the prey was in my toils; in less than an hour
he had quadrupled his debt. For some time his countenance had been
losing the florid tinge lent it by the wine; but now, to my astonishment, I perceived that it had grown to a pallor truly fearful. I say to
my astonishment. Glendinning had been represented to my eager
inquiries as immeasurably wealthy; and the sums which he had as
yet lost, although in themselves vast, could not, I supposed, very
seriously annoy, much less so violently affect him. That he was
overcome by the wine just swallowed, was the idea which most
readily presented itself; and, rather with a view to the preservation
of my own character in the eyes of my associates, than from any
less interested motive, I was about to insist, peremptorily, upon a
discontinuance of the play, when some expressions at my elbow from
among the company, and an ejaculation evincing utter despair on the
part of Glendinning, gave me to understand that I had effected his
total ruin under circumstances which, rendering him an object for
the pity of all, should have protected him from the ill offices even
of a fiend.

What now might have been my conduct it is difficult to say. The
pitiable condition of my dupe had thrown an air of embarrassed
gloom over all; and, for some moments, a profound silence was
maintained, during which I could not help feeling my cheeks tingle
with the many burning glances of scorn or reproach cast upon me
by the less abandoned of the party. I will even own that an intolerable weight of anxiety was for a brief instant lifted from my bosom
by the sudden and extraordinary interruption which ensued. The

wide, heavy folding-doors of the apartment were all at once thrown open, to their full extent, with a vigorous and rushing impetuosity that extinguished, as if by magic, every candle in the room. Their light, in dying, enabled us just to perceive that a stranger had entered, about my own height, and closely muffled in a cloak. The darkness, however, was now total; and we could only *feel* that he was standing in our midst. Before any one of us could recover from the extreme astonishment into which this rudeness had thrown all, we heard the voice of the intruder.

"Gentlemen," he said, in a low, distinct, and never-to-be-forgotten *whisper* which thrilled to the very marrow of my bones, "Gentlemen, I make no apology for this behavior, because in thus behaving, I am but fulfilling a duty. You are, beyond doubt, uninformed of the true character of the person who has tonight won at *écarté* a large sum of money from Lord Glendinning. I will therefore put you upon an expeditious and decisive plan of obtaining this very necessary information. Please to examine, at your leisure, the inner linings of the cuff of his left sleeve, and the several little packages which may be found in the somewhat capacious pockets of his embroidered morning wrapper."

While he spoke, so profound was the stillness that one might have heard a pin drop upon the floor. In ceasing, he departed at once, and as abruptly as he had entered. Can I—shall I describe my sensations? Must I say that I felt all the horrors of the damned? Most assuredly I had little time given for reflection. Many hands roughly seized me upon the spot, and lights were immediately re-procured. A search ensued. In the lining of my sleeve were found all the court cards essential in *écarté*, and, in the pockets of my wrapper, a number of packs, facsimiles of those used at our sittings, with the single exception that mine were of the species called, technically, *arrondées*; the honors being slightly convex at the ends, the lower cards slightly convex at the sides. In this disposition, the dupe who cuts, as customary, at the length of the pack, will, invariably find that he cuts his antagonist an honor; while the gambler, cutting at the breadth, will, as certainly, cut nothing for his victim which may count in the records of the game.

Any burst of indignation upon this discovery would have affected me less than the silent contempt, or the sarcastic composure, with which it was received.

"Mr Wilson," said our host, stooping to remove from beneath his feet an exceedingly luxurious cloak of rare furs, "Mr Wilson, this is your property." (The weather was cold; and, upon quitting my own room, I had thrown a cloak over my dressing wrapper, putting it off upon reaching the scene of play.) "I presume it is supererogatory to seek here" (eyeing the folds of the garment with a bitter smile) "for any further evidence of your skill. Indeed, we have had enough. You will see the necessity, I hope, of quitting Oxford—at all events, of quitting instantly my chambers."

Abased, humbled to the dust as I then was, it is probable that I should have resented this galling language by immediate personal violence, had not my whole attention been at the moment arrested by a fact of the most startling character. The cloak which I had worn was of a rare description of fur; how rare, how extravagantly costly, I shall not venture to say. Its fashion, too, was of my own fantastic invention; for I was fastidious to an absurd degree of coxcombry, in matters of this frivolous nature. When, therefore, Mr Preston reached me that which he had picked up upon the floor, and near the folding-doors of the apartment, it was with an astonishment nearly bordering upon terror, that I perceived my own already hanging on my arm (where I had no doubt unwittingly placed it), and that the one presented me was but its exact counterpart in every, in even the minutest possible particular. The singular being who had so disastrously exposed me, had been muffled, I remembered, in a cloak; and none had been worn at all by any of the members of our party with the exception of myself. Retaining some presence of mind, I took the one offered me by Preston; placed it, unnoticed, over my own; left the apartment with a resolute scowl of defiance; and, next morning ere dawn of day, commenced a hurried journey from Oxford to the Continent, in a perfect agony of horror and of shame.

I fled in vain. My evil destiny pursued me as if in exultation, and proved, indeed, that the exercise of its mysterious dominion had as yet only begun. Scarcely had I set foot in Paris ere I had fresh evidence of the detestable interest taken by this Wilson in my concerns. Years flew, while I experienced no relief. Villain!—At Rome, with how untimely, yet with how spectral an officiousness, stepped he in between me and my ambition! At Vienna, too—at Berlin—and at Moscow! Where, in truth, had I *not* bitter cause to curse him within my heart? From his inscrutable tyranny did I at length flee, panic-stricken, as from a pestilence; and to the very ends of the earth *I fled in vain*.

And again, and again, in secret communion with my own spirit, would I demand the questions "Who is he?—Whence came he?—And what are his objects?" But no answer was there found. And then I scrutinized, with a minute scrutiny, the forms, and the methods, and the leading traits of his impertinent supervision. But even here there was very little upon which to base a conjecture. It was noticeable, indeed, that, in no one of the multiplied instances in which he had of late crossed my path, had he so crossed it except to frustrate those schemes, or to disturb those actions, which, if fully carried out, might have resulted in bitter mischief. Poor justification this, in truth, for an authority so imperiously assumed! Poor indemnity for natural rights of self-agency so pertinaciously, so insultingly denied!

I had also been forced to notice that my tormentor, for a very long period of time (while scrupulously and with miraculous dexterity maintaining his whim of an identity of apparel with myself) had so contrived it, in the execution of his varied interference with my will, that I saw not, at any moment, the features of his face. Be Wilson what he might, *this*, at least, was but the veriest of affectation, or of folly. Could he, for an instant, have supposed that, in my admonisher at Eton—in the destroyer of my honor at Oxford—in him who thwarted my ambition at Rome, my revenge at Paris, my passionate love at Naples, or what he falsely termed my avarice in Egypt—that in this, my arch-enemy and evil genius, I could fail to recognize the William Wilson of my school-boy days—the namesake, the companion, the rival—the hated and dreaded rival at Dr. Bransby's? Impossible!—But let me hasten to the last eventful scene of the drama.

Thus far I had succumbed supinely to this imperious domination. The sentiments of deep awe with which I habitually regarded the elevated character, the majestic wisdom, the apparent omnipresence and omnipotence of Wilson, added to a feeling of even terror, with which certain other traits in his nature and assumptions inspired me, had operated, hitherto, to impress me with an idea of my own utter weakness and helplessness, and to suggest an implicit, although bitterly reluctant submission to his arbitrary will. But, of late days, I had given myself up entirely to wine; and its maddening influence upon my hereditary temper rendered me more and more impatient of control. I began to murmur—to hesitate—to resist. And was it only fancy which induced me to believe that, with the increase of my own firmness, that of my tormentor underwent a proportional diminution? Be this as it may, I now began to feel the inspiration of a burning hope, and at length nurtured in my secret thoughts a stern and desperate resolution that I would submit no longer to be enslaved.

It was at Rome, during the Carnival of 18—, that I attended a masquerade in the palazzo of the Neapolitan Duke Di Broglio. I had indulged more freely than usual in the excesses of the wine-table; and now the suffocating atmosphere of the crowded rooms irritated me beyond endurance. The difficulty, too, of forcing my way through the mazes of the company contributed not a little to the ruffling of my temper; for I was anxiously seeking (let me not say with what unworthy motive) the young, the gay, the beautiful wife of the aged and doting Di Broglio. With a too unscrupulous confidence she had previously communicated to me the secret of the costume in which she would be habited, and now, having caught a glimpse of her person, I was hurrying to make my way into her presence. At this moment I felt a light hand placed upon my shoulder, and that ever-remembered, low, damnable *whisper* within my ear.

In an absolute frenzy of wrath, I turned at once upon him who had thus interrupted me, and seized him violently by the collar. He was attired, as I had expected, in a costume altogether similar to my own: wearing a Spanish cloak of blue velvet, begirt about the waist with a crimson belt sustaining a rapier. A mask of black silk entirely covered his face.

"Scoundrel!" I said, in a voice husky with rage, while every syllable I uttered seemed as new fuel to my fury. "Scoundrel! Impostor! Accursed villain! You shall not—*you shall not* dog me unto death! Follow me, or I stab you where you stand!"—And I broke my way from the ballroom into a small antechamber adjoining—dragging him unresistingly with me as I went.

Upon entering, I thrust him furiously from me. He staggered against the wall, while I closed the door with an oath, and commanded him to draw. He hesitated but for an instant; then, with a slight sigh, drew in silence, and put himself upon his defense.

The contest was brief indeed. I was frantic with every species of wild excitement, and felt within my single arm the energy and power of a multitude. In a few seconds I forced him by sheer strength against the wainscoting, and thus, getting him at mercy, plunged my sword, with brute ferocity, repeatedly through and through his bosom.

At that instant some person tried the latch of the door. I hastened to prevent an intrusion, and then immediately returned to my dying antagonist. But what human language can adequately portray that astonishment, that horror which possessed me at the spectacle then presented to view? The brief moment in which I averted my eyes had been sufficient to produce, apparently, a material change in the arrangements at the upper or farther end of the room. A larger mirror—so at first it seemed to me in my confusion—now stood where none had been perceptible before; and, as I stepped up to it in extremity of terror, mine own image, but with features all pale and dabbled in blood, advanced to meet me with a feeble and tottering gait.

Thus it appeared, I say, but was not. It was my antagonist—it was Wilson, who then stood before me in the agonies of his dissolution. His mask and cloak lay, where he had thrown them, upon the floor. Not a thread in all his raiment—not a line in all the marked and singular lineaments of his face which was not, even in the most absolute identity, *mine own*!

It was Wilson; but he spoke no longer in a whisper, and I could have fancied that I myself was speaking while he said:

"*You have conquered, and I yield. Yet, henceforward art thou also dead—dead to the World, to Heaven, and to hope! In me didst thou exist—and, in my death, see by this image, which is thine own, how utterly thou hast murdered thyself.*"

THE MAN OF THE CROWD

"Ce grand malheur, de ne pouvoir être seul."
La Bruyère

It was well said of a certain German book that *"es lässt sich nicht lesen"*—it does not permit itself to be read. There are some secrets which do not permit themselves to be told. Men die nightly in their beds, wringing the hands of ghostly confessors, and looking them piteously in the eyes—die with despair of heart and convulsion of throat, on account of the hideousness of mysteries which will not suffer themselves to be revealed. Now and then, alas, the conscience of man takes up a burthen so heavy in horror that it can be thrown down only into the grave. And thus the essence of all crime is undivulged.

Not long ago, about the closing in of an evening in autumn, I sat at the large bow window of the D—— Coffee-House in London. For some months I had been ill in health, but was now convalescent, and, with returning strength, found myself in one of those happy moods which are so precisely the converse of *ennui*—moods of the keenest appetency, when the film from the mental vision departs—the αχλυς ος πριν επηεν—and the intellect, electrified, surpasses as greatly its everyday condition, as does the vivid yet candid reason of Leibnitz, the mad and flimsy rhetoric of Gorgias. Merely to breathe was enjoyment; and I derived positive pleasure even from many of the legitimate sources of pain. I felt a calm but inquisitive interest in everything.

With a cigar in my mouth and a newspaper in my lap, I had been amusing myself for the greater part of the afternoon, now in poring over advertisements, now in observing the promiscuous company in the room, and now in peering through the smoky panes into the street.

This latter is one of the principal thoroughfares of the city, and had been very much crowded during the whole day. But, as the darkness came on, the throng momently increased; and, by the time the lamps were well lighted, two dense and continuous tides of population were rushing past the door. At this particular period of the evening I had never before been in a similar situation, and the tumultuous sea of human heads filled me, therefore, with a delicious novelty of emotion. I gave up, at length, all care of things within the hotel, and became absorbed in contemplation of the scene without.

At first my observations took an abstract and generalizing turn. I looked at the passengers in masses, and thought of them in their aggregate relations. Soon, however, I descended to details, and regarded with minute interest the innumerable varieties of figure, dress, air, gait, visage, and expression of countenance.

By far the greater number of those who went by had a satisfied business-like demeanor, and seemed to be thinking only of making their way through the press. Their brows were knit, and their eyes rolled quickly; when pushed against by fellow-wayfarers they evinced no symptom of impatience, but adjusted their clothes and hurried on. Others, still a numerous class, were restless in their movements, had flushed faces, and talked and gesticulated to themselves, as if feeling in solitude on account of the very denseness of the company around. When impeded in their progress, these people suddenly ceased muttering, but redoubled their gesticulations, and waited, with an absent and overdone smile upon the lips, the course of the persons impeding them. If jostled, they bowed profusely to the jostlers, and appeared overwhelmed with confusion. There was nothing very distinctive about these two large classes beyond what I have noted.

Their habiliments belonged to that order which is pointedly termed the decent. They were undoubtedly noblemen, merchants, attorneys, tradesmen, stock-jobbers—the Eupatrids and the commonplaces of society—men of leisure and men actively engaged in affairs of their own—conducting business upon their own responsibility. They did not greatly excite my attention.

The tribe of clerks was an obvious one; and here I discerned two remarkable divisions. There were the junior clerks of flash houses—young gentlemen with tight coats, bright boots, well-oiled hair, and supercilious lips. Setting aside a certain dapperness of carriage, which may be termed *deskism* for want of a better word, the manner of these persons seemed to me an exact facsimile of what had been the perfection of *bon ton* about twelve or eighteen months before. They wore the cast-off graces of the gentry—and this, I believe, involves the best definition of the class.

The division of the upper clerks of staunch firms, or of the "steady old fellows," it was not possible to mistake. These were known by their coats and pantaloons of black or brown, made to sit comfortably, with white cravats and waistcoats, broad solid-looking shoes, and thick hose or gaiters. They had all slightly bald heads, from which the right ears, long used to pen-holding, had an odd habit of standing off on end. I observed that they always removed or settled their hats with both hands, and wore watches, with short gold chains of a substantial and ancient pattern. Theirs was the affectation of respectability—if indeed there be an affectation so honorable.

There were many individuals of dashing appearance, whom I easily understood as belonging to the race of swell pickpockets, with which all great cities are infested. I watched these gentry with much inquisitiveness, and found it difficult to imagine how they should ever be mistaken for gentlemen by gentlemen themselves. Their voluminousness of wristband, with an air of excessive frankness, should betray them at once.

The gamblers, of whom I descried not a few, were still more easily recognizable. They wore every variety of dress, from that of the desperate thimble-rig bully, with velvet waistcoat, fancy neckerchief, gilt chains, and filigreed buttons, to that of the scrupulously inornate clergyman than which nothing could be less liable to suspicion. Still all were distinguished by a certain sodden swarthiness of complexion, a filmy dimness of eye, and pallor and compression of lip. There were two other traits, moreover, by which I could always detect them: a guarded lowness of tone in conversation, and a more than ordinary extension of the thumb in a direction at right angles with the fingers. Very often, in company with these sharpers, I observed an order of men somewhat different in habits, but still birds of a kindred feather. They may be defined as the gentlemen who live by their wits. They seem to prey upon the public in two battalions— that of the dandies and that of the military men. Of the first grade the leading features are long locks and smiles; of the second frogged coats and frowns.

Descending in the scale of what is termed gentility, I found darker and deeper themes for speculation. I saw Jew pedlars, with hawk eyes flashing from countenances whose every other feature wore only an expression of abject humility; sturdy professional street beggars scowling upon mendicants of a better stamp, whom despair alone had driven forth into the night for charity; feeble and ghastly invalids, upon whom death had placed a sure hand, and who sidled and tottered through the mob, looking every one beseechingly in the face, as if in search of some chance consolation, some lost hope; modest young girls returning from long and late labor to a cheerless home, and shrinking more tearfully than indignantly from the glances of ruffians, whose direct contact, even, could not be avoided; women of the town of all kinds and of all ages—the unequivocal beauty in the prime of her womanhood, putting one in mind of the statue in Lucian, with the surface of Parian marble, and the interior filled with filth—the loathsome and utterly lost leper in rags—the wrinkled, bejeweled and paint-begrimed beldame, making a last effort at youth—the mere child of immature form, yet from long association, an adept in the dreadful coquetries of her trade, and burning with a rabid ambition to be ranked the equal of her elders in vice; drunkards innumerable and indescribable—some in shreds and patches, reeling, inarticulate, with bruised visage and lack-luster eyes—some in whole although filthy garments, with a slightly unsteady swagger, thick, sensual lips, and hearty-looking rubicund faces—others clothed in materials which had once been good, and which even now were scrupulously well brushed—men who walked with a more than naturally firm and springy step, but whose countenances were fearfully pale, whose eyes hideously wild and red, and who clutched with quivering fingers, as they strode through the crowd, at every object which came within their reach; beside these, pie-men, porters, coal-heavers, sweeps; organ-grinders, monkey-exhibitors, and ballad-mongers, those who vended with those who sang; ragged artisans and exhausted laborers of every description, and all full of a noisy and inordinate vivacity which jarred discordantly upon the ear, and gave an aching sensation to the eye.

As the night deepened, so deepened to me the interest of the scene; for not only did the general character of the crowd materially alter (its gentler features retiring in the gradual withdrawal of the more orderly portion of the people, and its harsher ones coming out into bolder relief, as the late hour brought forth every species of infamy from its den), but the rays of the gas-lamps, feeble at first in their struggle with the dying day, had now at length gained ascendancy, and threw over everything a fitful and garish luster. All was dark yet splendid—as that ebony to which has been likened the style of Tertullian.

The wild effects of the light enchained me to an examination of individual faces; and although the rapidity with which the world of light flitted before the window, prevented me from casting more than a glance upon each visage, still it seemed that, in my then peculiar mental state, I could frequently read, even in that brief interval of a glance, the history of long years.

With my brow to the glass, I was thus occupied in scrutinizing the mob, when suddenly there came into view a countenance (that of a decrepit old man, some sixty-five or seventy years of age)—a countenance which at once arrested and absorbed my whole attention, on account of the absolute idiosyncrasy of its expression. Anything even remotely resembling that expression I had never seen before. I well remember that my first thought, upon beholding it, was that Retzsch, had he viewed it, would have greatly preferred it to his own pictural incarnations of the fiend. As I endeavored, during the brief minute of my original survey, to form some analysis of the meaning conveyed, there arose confusedly and paradoxically within my mind, the ideas of vast mental power, of caution, of penuriousness, of avarice, of coolness, of malice, of blood-thirstiness, of triumph, of merriment, of excessive terror, of intense—of extreme despair. I felt singularly aroused, startled, fascinated. "How wild a history," I said to myself, "is written within that bosom!" Then came a craving desire to keep the man in view—to know more of him. Hurriedly putting on an overcoat, and seizing my hat and cane, I made my way into the street, and pushed through the crowd in the direction which I had seen him take; for he had already disappeared. With some little difficulty I at length came within sight of him, approached, and followed him closely, yet cautiously, so as not to attract his attention.

I had now a good opportunity of examining his person. He was short in stature, very thin, and apparently very feeble. His clothes, generally, were filthy and ragged; but as he came, now and then, within the strong glare of a lamp, I perceived that his linen, although dirty, was of beautiful texture; and my vision deceived me, or, through a rent in a closely-buttoned and evidently second-handed *roquelaure* which enveloped him, I caught a glimpse both of a diamond and of a dagger. These observations heightened my curiosity, and I resolved to follow the stranger whithersoever he should go.

It was now fully nightfall, and a thick humid fog hung over the city, soon ending in a settled and heavy rain. This change of weather had an odd effect upon the crowd, the whole of which was at once put into new commotion, and overshadowed by a world of umbrellas. The waver, the jostle, and the hum increased in a tenfold degree. For my own part I did not much regard the rain—the lurking of an old fever in my system rendering the moisture somewhat too dangerously pleasant. Tying a handkerchief about my mouth, I kept on. For half an hour the old man held his way with difficulty along the great thoroughfare; and I here walked close at his elbow through fear of losing sight of him. Never once turning his head to look back, he did not observe me. By and by he passed into a cross street, which, although densely filled with people, was not quite so much thronged as the main one he had quitted. Here a change in his demeanor became evident. He walked more slowly and with less object than before—more hesitatingly. He crossed and re-crossed the way repeatedly without apparent aim; and the press was still so thick, that, at every such movement, I was obliged to follow him closely. The street was a narrow and long one, and his course lay within it for nearly an hour, during which the passengers had gradually diminished to about that number which is ordinarily seen at noon in Broadway near the Park— so vast a difference is there between a London populace and that of the most frequented American city. A second turn brought us into a square, brilliantly lighted, and overflowing with life. The old manner of the stranger reappeared. His chin fell upon his breast, while his eyes rolled wildly from under his knit brows, in every direction, upon those who hemmed him in. He urged his way steadily and perseveringly. I was surprised, however, to find, upon his having made the circuit of the square, that he turned and retraced his steps. Still more was I astonished to see him repeat the same walk several times—once nearly detecting me as he came round with a sudden movement.

In this exercise he spent another hour, at the end of which we met with far less interruption from passengers than at first. The rain fell fast; the air grew cool; and the people were retiring to their homes. With a gesture of impatience, the wanderer passed into a by-street comparatively deserted. Down this, some quarter of a mile long, he rushed with an activity I could not have dreamed of seeing in one so aged, and which put me to much trouble in pursuit. A few minutes brought us to a large and busy bazaar, with the localities of which the stranger appeared well acquainted, and where his original demeanor again became apparent, as he forced his way to and fro, without aim, among the host of buyers and sellers.

During the hour and a half, or thereabouts, which we passed in this place, it required much caution on my part to keep him within reach without attracting his observation. Luckily I wore a pair of caoutchouc overshoes, and could move about in perfect silence. At no moment did he see that I watched him. He entered shop after shop, priced nothing, spoke no word, and looked at all objects with a wild and vacant stare. I was now utterly amazed at his behavior, and firmly resolved that we should not part until I had satisfied myself in some measure respecting him.

A loud-toned clock struck eleven, and the company were fast deserting the bazaar. A shopkeeper, in putting up a shutter, jostled the old man, and at the instant I saw a strong shudder come over his frame. He hurried into the street, looked anxiously around him for an instant, and then ran with incredible swiftness through many crooked and people-less lanes, until we emerged once more upon the great thoroughfare whence we had started—the street of the D—— Hotel. It no longer wore, however, the same aspect. It was still brilliant with gas; but the rain fell fiercely, and there were few persons to be seen. The stranger grew pale. He walked moodily some paces up the once populous avenue, then, with a heavy sigh, turned in the direction of the river, and, plunging through a great variety of devious ways, came out, at length, in view of one of the principal theatres. It was about being closed, and the audience were thronging from the doors. I saw the old man gasp as if for breath while he threw himself amid the crowd; but I thought that the intense agony of his countenance had, in some measure, abated. His head again fell upon his breast; he appeared as I had seen him at first. I observed that he now took the course in which had gone the greater number of the audience—but, upon the whole, I was at a loss to comprehend the waywardness of his actions.

As he proceeded, the company grew more scattered, and his old uneasiness and vacillation were resumed. For some time he followed closely a party of some ten or twelve roisterers; but from this number one by one dropped off, until three only remained together, in a narrow and gloomy lane little frequented. The stranger paused, and, for a moment, seemed lost in thought; then, with every mark of agitation, pursued rapidly a route which brought us to the verge of the city, amid regions very different from those we had hitherto traversed. It was the most noisome quarter of London, where everything wore the worst impress of the most deplorable poverty, and of the most desperate crime. By the dim light of an accidental lamp, tall, antique, worm-eaten, wooden tenements were seen tottering to their fall, in directions so many and capricious that scarce the semblance of a passage was discernible between them. The paving stones lay at random, displaced from their beds by the rankly growing grass. Horrible filth festered in the dammed-up gutters. The whole atmosphere teemed with desolation. Yet, as we proceeded, the sounds of human life revived by sure degrees, and at length large bands of the most abandoned of a London populace were seen reeling to and fro. The spirits of the old man again flickered up, as a lamp which is near its death-hour. Once more he strode onward with elastic tread. Suddenly a corner was turned, a blaze of light burst upon our sight, and we stood before one of the huge suburban temples of Intemperance—one of the palaces of the fiend, Gin.

It was now nearly daybreak; but a number of wretched inebriates still pressed in and out of the flaunting entrance. With a half shriek of joy the old man forced a passage within, resumed at once his original bearing, and stalked backward and forward, without apparent object, among the throng. He had not been thus long occupied, however, before a rush to the doors gave token that the host was closing them for the night. It was something even more intense than despair that I then observed upon the countenance of the singular being whom I had watched so pertinaciously. Yet he did not hesitate in his career, but, with a mad energy, retraced his steps at once, to the heart of the mighty London. Long and swiftly he fled, while I followed him in the wildest amazement, resolute not to abandon a scrutiny in which I now felt an interest all-absorbing. The sun arose while we proceeded, and, when we had once again reached that most thronged mart of the populous town, the street of the D—— Hotel, it presented an appearance of human bustle and activity scarcely inferior to what I had seen on the evening before. And here, long, amid the momently increasing confusion, did I persist in my pursuit of the stranger. But, as usual, he walked to and fro, and during the day did not pass from out the turmoil of that street. And, as the shades of the second evening came on, I grew wearied unto death, and, stopping fully in front of the wanderer, gazed at him steadfastly in the face. He noticed me not, but resumed his solemn walk, while I, ceasing to follow, remained absorbed in contemplation. "This old man," I said at length, "is the type and the genius of deep crime. He refuses to be alone. *He is the man of the crowd.* It will be in vain to follow; for I shall learn no more of him, nor of his deeds. The worst heart of the world is a grosser book than the *Hortulus Animae*, and perhaps it is but one of the great mercies of God that *es lässt sich nicht lesen*."

THE OVAL PORTRAIT

The chateau into which my valet had ventured to make forcible
entrance, rather than permit me, in my desperately wounded condition, to pass a night in the open air, was one of those piles of
commingled gloom and grandeur which have so long frowned among
the Apennines, not less in fact than in the fancy of Mrs Radcliffe.
To all appearance it had been temporarily and very lately abandoned.
We established ourselves in one of the smallest and least sumptuously
furnished apartments. It lay in a remote turret of the building. Its
decorations were rich, yet tattered and antique. Its walls were hung
with tapestry and bedecked with manifold and multiform armorial
trophies, together with an unusually great number of very spirited
modern paintings in frames of rich golden arabesque. In these paintings, which depended from the walls not only in their main surfaces,
but in very many nooks which the bizarre architecture of the chateau
rendered necessary—in these paintings my incipient delirium,
perhaps, had caused me to take deep interest; so that I bade Pedro
to close the heavy shutters of the room—since it was already night—
to light the tongues of a tall candelabrum which stood by the head
of my bed—and to throw open far and wide the fringed curtains of
black velvet which enveloped the bed itself. I wished all this done
that I might resign myself, if not to sleep, at least alternately to the

contemplation of these pictures, and the perusal of a small volume which had been found upon the pillow, and which purported to criticize and describe them.

Long—long I read—and devoutly, devotedly I gazed. Rapidly and gloriously the hours flew by, and the deep midnight came. The position of the candelabrum displeased me, and outreaching my hand with difficulty, rather than disturb my slumbering valet, I placed it so as to throw its rays more fully upon the book.

But the action produced an effect altogether unanticipated. The rays of the numerous candles (for there were many) now fell within a niche of the room which had hitherto been thrown into deep shade by one of the bed-posts. I thus saw in vivid light a picture all unnoticed before. It was the portrait of a young girl just ripening into womanhood. I glanced at the painting hurriedly, and then closed my eyes. Why I did this was not at first apparent even to my own perception. But while my lids remained thus shut, I ran over in my mind my reason for so shutting them. It was an impulsive movement to gain time for thought—to make sure that my vision had not deceived me—to calm and subdue my fancy for a more sober and more certain gaze. In a very few moments I again looked fixedly at the painting.

That I now saw aright I could not and would not doubt; for the first flashing of the candles upon that canvas had seemed to dissipate the dreamy stupor which was stealing over my senses, and to startle me at once into waking life.

The portrait, I have already said, was that of a young girl. It was a mere head and shoulders, done in what is technically termed a *vignette* manner; much in the style of the favorite heads of Sully. The arms, the bosom and even the ends of the radiant hair, melted imperceptibly into the vague yet deep shadow which formed the background of the whole. The frame was oval, richly gilded and filigreed in *Moresque*. As a thing of art nothing could be more admirable than the painting itself. But it could have been neither the execution of the work, nor the immortal beauty of the countenance, which had so suddenly and so vehemently moved me. Least of all, could it have been that my fancy, shaken from its half slumber, had mistaken the head for that of a living person. I saw at once that the peculiarities of the design, of the *vignetting*, and of the frame, must have instantly dispelled such idea—must have prevented even its momentary entertainment. Thinking earnestly upon these points, I remained, for an hour perhaps, half sitting, half reclining, with my vision riveted upon the portrait. At length, satisfied with the true secret of its effect, I fell back within the bed. I had found the spell of the picture in an absolute *life-likeliness* of expression, which, at first startling, finally confounded, subdued and appalled me. With deep and reverent awe I replaced the candelabrum in its former position. The cause of my deep agitation being thus shut from view, I sought eagerly the volume which discussed the paintings and their histories. Turning to the number which designated the oval portrait, I there read the vague and quaint words which follow:

"She was a maiden of rarest beauty, and not more lovely than full of glee. And evil was the hour when she saw, and loved, and wedded the painter. He, passionate, studious, austere, and having already a bride in his Art: she a maiden of rarest beauty, and not more lovely than full of glee: all light and smiles, and frolicsome as the young fawn: loving and cherishing all things: hating only the Art which was her rival: dreading only the pallet and brushes and other untoward instruments which deprived her of the countenance of her lover. It was thus a terrible thing for this lady to hear the painter speak of his desire to portray even his young bride. But she was humble and obedient, and sat meekly for many weeks in the dark high turret-chamber where the light dripped upon the pale canvas only from overhead. But he, the painter, took glory in his work, which went on from hour to hour and from day to day. And he was a passionate, and wild and moody man, who became lost in reveries; so that he *would* not see that the light which fell so ghastly in that lone turret withered the health and the spirits of his bride, who pined visibly to all but him. Yet she smiled on and still on, uncomplainingly, because she saw that the painter (who had high renown) took a fervid and burning pleasure in his task, and wrought day and night to depict her who so loved him, yet who grew daily more dispirited and weak. And in sooth some who beheld the portrait spoke of its resemblance in low words, as of a mighty marvel, and a proof not less of the power of the painter than of his deep love for her whom he depicted so surpassingly well.

But at length, as the labor drew nearer to its conclusion, there were admitted none into the turret; for the painter had grown wild with the ardor of his work, and turned his eyes from the canvas rarely, even to regard the countenance of his wife. And he *would* not see that the tints which he spread upon the canvas were drawn from the cheeks of her who sat beside him. And when many weeks had passed, and but little remained to do, save one brush upon the mouth and one tint upon the eye, the spirit of the lady again flickered up as the flame within the socket of the lamp. And then the brush was given, and then the tint was placed; and, for one moment, the painter stood entranced before the work which he had wrought; but in the next, while he yet gazed, he grew tremulous and very pallid, and aghast, and crying with a loud voice "This is indeed *Life* itself!" turned suddenly to regard his beloved: *She was dead*.

THE MASQUE OF THE RED DEATH

The "Red Death" had long devastated the country. No pestilence had ever been so fatal, or so hideous. Blood was its Avatar and its seal—the redness and horror of blood. There were sharp pains, and sudden dizziness, and then profuse bleeding at the pores, with dissolution. The scarlet stains upon the body and especially upon the face of the victim, were the pest ban which shut him out from the aid and from the sympathy of his fellow-men. And the whole seizure, progress, and termination of the disease, were the incidents of half an hour.

But the Prince Prospero was happy and dauntless and sagacious. When his dominions were half-depopulated, he summoned to his presence a thousand hale and light-hearted friends from among the knights and dames of his court, and with these retired to the deep seclusion of one of his castellated abbeys. This was an extensive and magnificent structure, the creation of the prince's own eccentric yet august taste. A strong and lofty wall girdled it in. This wall had gates of iron. The courtiers, having entered, brought furnaces and massy hammers and welded the bolts. They resolved to leave means neither of ingress nor egress to the sudden impulses of despair or of frenzy from within. The abbey was amply provisioned. With such precautions the courtiers might bid defiance to contagion. The external world could take care of itself. In the meantime it was folly to grieve, or to think. The prince had provided all the appliances of pleasure. There were buffoons, there were *improvisatori*, there were ballet-dancers, there were musicians, there was Beauty, there was wine. All these and security were within. Without was the "Red Death."

It was toward the close of the fifth or sixth month of his seclusion, and while the pestilence raged most furiously abroad, that the Prince Prospero entertained his thousand friends at a masked ball of the most unusual magnificence.

It was a voluptuous scene, that masquerade. But first let me tell of the rooms in which it was held. There were seven—an imperial suite. In many palaces, however, such suites form a long and straight vista, while the folding doors slide back nearly to the walls on either hand, so that the view of the whole extent is scarcely impeded. Here the case was very different, as might have been expected from the duke's love of the *bizarre*. The apartments were so irregularly disposed that the vision embraced but little more than one at a time. There was a sharp turn at every twenty or thirty yards, and at each turn a novel effect. To the right and left, in the middle of each wall, a tall and narrow Gothic window looked out upon a closed corridor which pursued the windings of the suite. These windows were of stained glass whose color varied in accordance with the prevailing hue of the decorations of the chamber into which it opened. That at the eastern extremity was hung, for example, in blue—and vividly blue were its windows. The second chamber was purple in its ornaments and tapestries, and here the panes were purple. The third was green throughout, and so were the casements. The fourth was furnished and lighted with orange—the fifth with white—the sixth with violet. The seventh apartment was closely shrouded in black velvet tapestries that hung all over the ceiling and down the walls, falling in heavy folds upon a carpet of the same material and hue. But in this chamber only, the color of the windows failed to correspond with the decorations. The panes here were scarlet—a deep blood color. Now in no one of the seven apartments was there any lamp or candelabrum, amid the profusion of golden ornaments that lay scattered to and fro or depended from the roof. There was no light of any kind emanating from lamp or candle within the suite of chambers. But in the corridors that followed the suite there stood, opposite to each window, a heavy tripod, bearing a brazier of fire that projected its rays through the tinted glass and so glaringly illumined the room. And thus were produced a multitude of gaudy and fantastic appearances. But in the western or black chamber the effect of the firelight that streamed upon the dark hangings through the blood-tinted panes was ghastly in the extreme, and produced so wild a look upon the countenances of those who entered, that there were few of the company bold enough to set foot within its precincts at all.

It was in this apartment, also, that there stood against the western wall a gigantic clock of ebony. Its pendulum swung to and fro with a dull, heavy, monotonous clang; and when the minute-hand made the circuit of the face, and the hour was to be stricken, there came from the brazen lungs of the clock a sound which was clear and loud and deep and exceedingly musical, but of so peculiar a note and emphasis that, at each lapse of an hour, the musicians of the orchestra were constrained to pause, momentarily, in their performance, to harken to the sound; and thus the waltzers perforce ceased their evolutions; and there was a brief disconcert of the whole gay company; and, while the chimes of the clock yet rang, it was observed that the giddiest grew pale, and the more aged and sedate passed their hands over their brows as if in confused reverie or meditation. But when the echoes had fully ceased, a light laughter at once pervaded the assembly; the musicians looked at each other and smiled as if at their own nervousness and folly, and made whispering vows, each to the other, that the next chiming of the clock should produce in them no similar emotion; and then, after the lapse of sixty minutes (which embrace three thousand and six hundred seconds of the Time that flies), there came yet another chiming of the clock, and then were the same disconcert and tremulousness and meditation as before.

But, in spite of these things, it was a gay and magnificent revel. The tastes of the duke were peculiar. He had a fine eye for colors and effects. He disregarded the *decora* of mere fashion. His plans were bold and fiery, and his conceptions glowed with barbaric luster. There are some who would have thought him mad. His followers felt that he was not. It was necessary to hear and see and touch him to be *sure* that he was not.

He had directed, in great part, the movable embellishments of the seven chambers, upon occasion of this great *fête*; and it was his own guiding taste which had given character to the masqueraders. Be sure they were grotesque. There were much glare and glitter and piquancy and phantasm—much of what has been since seen in *Hernani*. There were arabesque figures with unsuited limbs and appointments. There were delirious fancies such as the madman fashions. There were much of the beautiful, much of the wanton, much of the *bizarre*, something of the terrible, and not a little of that which might have excited disgust. To and fro in the seven chambers there stalked, in fact, a multitude of dreams. And these—the dreams—writhed in and about, taking hue from the rooms, and causing the wild music of the orchestra to seem as the echo of their steps. And, anon, there strikes the ebony clock which stands in the hall of the velvet. And then, for a moment, all is still, and all is silent save the voice of the clock. The dreams are stiff-frozen as they stand. But the echoes of the chime die away—they have endured but an instant—and a light, half-subdued laughter floats after them as they depart. And now again the music swells, and the dreams live, and writhe to and fro more merrily than ever, taking hue from the many-tinted windows through which stream the rays from the tripods. But to the chamber which lies most westwardly of the seven there are now none of the maskers who venture; for the night is waning away; and there flows a ruddier light through the blood-colored panes; and the blackness of the sable drapery appalls; and to him whose foot falls upon the sable carpet, there comes from the near clock of ebony a muffled peal more solemnly emphatic than any which reaches *their* ears who indulged in the more remote gaieties of the other apartments.

But these other apartments were densely crowded, and in them beat feverishly the heart of life. And the revel went whirlingly on, until at length there commenced the sounding of midnight upon the clock. And then the music ceased, as I have told; and the evolutions of the waltzers were quieted; and there was an uneasy cessation of all things as before. But now there were twelve strokes to be sounded by the bell of the clock; and thus it happened, perhaps, that more of thought crept, with more of time, into the meditations of the thoughtful among those who revelled. And thus too, it happened, perhaps, that before the last echoes of the last chime had utterly sunk into silence, there were many individuals in the crowd who had found leisure to become aware of the presence of a masked figure which had arrested the attention of no single individual before. And the rumor of this new presence having spread itself whisperingly around, there arose at length from the whole company a buzz, or murmur, expressive of disapprobation and surprise—then finally, of terror, of horror, and of disgust.

In an assembly of phantasms such as I have painted, it may well be supposed that no ordinary appearance could have excited such sensation. In truth the masquerade license of the night was nearly unlimited; but the figure in question had out-Heroded Herod, and gone beyond the bounds of even the prince's indefinite decorum. There are chords in the hearts of the most reckless which cannot be touched without emotion. Even with the utterly lost, to whom life and death are equally jests, there are matters of which no jest can be made. The whole company, indeed, seemed now deeply to feel that in the costume and bearing of the stranger neither wit nor propriety existed. The figure was tall and gaunt, and shrouded from head to foot in the habiliments of the grave. The mask which concealed the visage was made so nearly to resemble the countenance of a stiffened corpse that the closest scrutiny must have had difficulty in detecting the cheat. And yet all this might have been endured, if not approved, by the mad revelers around. But the mummer had gone so far as to assume the type of the Red Death. His vesture was dabbled in *blood*—and his broad brow, with all the features of the face, was be-sprinkled with the scarlet horror.

When the eyes of Prince Prospero fell upon this spectral image (which, with a slow and solemn movement, as if more fully to sustain its role, stalked to and fro among the waltzers) he was seen to be convulsed in the first moment with a strong shudder either of terror or distaste; but, in the next, his brow reddened with rage.

"Who dares?" he demanded hoarsely of the courtiers who stood near him. "Who dares insult us with this blasphemous mockery? Seize him and unmask him—that we may know whom we have to hang, at sunrise, from the battlements!"

It was in the eastern or blue chamber in which stood the Prince Prospero as he uttered these words. They rang throughout the seven rooms loudly and clearly—for the prince was a bold and robust man, and the music had become hushed at the waving of his hand.

It was in the blue room where stood the prince, with a group of pale courtiers by his side. At first, as he spoke, there was a slight rushing movement of this group in the direction of the intruder, who at the moment was also near at hand, and now, with deliberate and stately step, made closer approach to the speaker. But from a certain nameless awe with which the mad assumptions of the mummer had inspired the whole party, there were found none who put forth hand to seize him; so that, unimpeded, he passed within a yard of the prince's person; and, while the vast assembly, as if with one impulse, shrank from the centers of the rooms to the walls, he made his way uninterruptedly, but with the same solemn and measured step which had distinguished him from the first, through the blue chamber to the purple—through the purple to the green—through the green to the orange—through this again to the white—and even thence to the violet, ere a decided movement had been made to arrest him. It was then, however, that the Prince Prospero, maddening with rage and the shame of his own momentary cowardice, rushed hurriedly through the six chambers, while none followed him on account of a deadly terror that had seized upon all. He bore aloft a drawn dagger, and had approached, in rapid impetuosity, to within three or four feet of the retreating figure, when the latter, having attained the extremity of the velvet apartment, turned suddenly and confronted his pursuer. There was a sharp cry—and the dagger dropped gleaming upon the sable carpet, upon which, instantly afterward, fell prostrate in death the Prince Prospero. Then, summoning the wild courage of despair, a throng of the revelers at once threw themselves into the black apartment, and, seizing the mummer, whose tall figure stood erect and motionless within the shadow of the ebony clock, gasped in unutterable horror at finding the grave cerements and corpse-like mask, which they handled with so violent a rudeness, untenanted by any tangible form.

And now was acknowledged the presence of the Red Death. He had come like a thief in the night. And one by one dropped the revelers in the blood-bedewed halls of their revel, and died each in the despairing posture of his fall. And the life of the ebony clock went out with that of the last of the gay. And the flames of the tripods expired. And Darkness and Decay and the Red Death held illimitable dominion over all.

THE PIT AND THE PENDULUM

"Impia tortorum longas hic turba furores
Sanguinis innocui, non satiata, aluit.
Sospite nunc patria, fracto nunc funeris antro,
Mors ubi dira fuit vita salusque patent."
Quatrain composed for the gates of a market to be erected
upon the site of the Jacobin Club House at Paris

I was sick—sick unto death with that long agony; and when they at
length unbound me, and I was permitted to sit, I felt that my senses
were leaving me. The sentence—the dread sentence of death—was
the last of distinct accentuation which reached my ears. After that
the sound of the inquisitorial voices seemed merged in one dreamy
indeterminate hum. It conveyed to my soul the idea of *revolution*—
perhaps from its association in fancy with the burr of a mill-wheel.
This only for a brief period, for presently I heard no more. Yet, for
a while, I saw—but with how terrible an exaggeration! I saw the
lips of the black-robed judges. They appeared to me white—whiter
than the sheet upon which I trace these words—and thin even to
grotesqueness; thin with the intensity of their expression of firmness—of immovable resolution—of stern contempt of human torture.
I saw that the decrees of what to me was Fate were still issuing from
those lips. I saw them writhe with a deadly locution. I saw them
fashion the syllables of my name; and I shuddered because no sound
succeeded. I saw, too, for a few moments of delirious horror, the

soft and nearly imperceptible waving of the sable draperies which enwrapped the walls of the apartment. And then my vision fell upon the seven tall candles upon the table. At first they wore the aspect of charity, and seemed white slender angels who would save me; but then, all at once, there came a most deadly nausea over my spirit, and I felt every fiber in my frame thrill as if I had touched the wire of a galvanic battery, while the angel forms became meaningless specters, with heads of flame, and I saw that from them there would be no help. And then there stole into my fancy, like a rich musical note, the thought of what sweet rest there must be in the grave. The thought came gently and stealthily, and it seemed long before it attained full appreciation; but just as my spirit came at length properly to feel and entertain it, the figures of the judges vanished, as if magically, from before me; the tall candles sank into nothingness; their flames went out utterly; the blackness of darkness supervened; all sensations appeared swallowed up in a mad rushing descent as of the soul into Hades. Then silence and stillness and night were the universe.

I had swooned; but still will not say that all of consciousness was lost. What of it remained I will not attempt to define, or even to describe; yet all was not lost. In the deepest slumber—no! In delirium—no! In a swoon—no! In death—no! even in the grave all *is not* lost. Else there is no immortality for man. Arousing from the most profound of slumbers, we break the gossamer web of *some* dream. Yet in a second afterward (so frail may that web have been), we remember not that we have dreamed. In the return to life from the swoon there are two stages: first, that of the sense of mental or spiritual; secondly, that of the sense of physical, existence. It seems probable that if, upon reaching the second stage, we could recall the impressions of the first, we should find these impressions eloquent in memories of the gulf beyond. And that gulf is—what? How at least shall we distinguish its shadows from those of the tomb? But if the impressions of what I have termed the first stage are not at will recalled, yet, after long interval, do *they* not come unbidden, while we marvel whence they come? He who has never swooned, is not he who finds strange palaces and wildly familiar faces in coals that glow; is not he who beholds floating in mid-air the sad visions that the many may not view; is not he who ponders over the perfume of some novel flower; is not he whose brain grows bewildered with the meaning of some musical cadence which has never before arrested his attention.

Amid frequent and thoughtful endeavors to remember; amid earnest struggles to re-gather some token of the state of seeming nothingness into which my soul had lapsed, there have been moments when I have dreamed of success; there have been brief, very brief periods when I have conjured up remembrances which the lucid reason of a later epoch assures me could have had reference only to that condition of seeming unconsciousness. These shadows of memory tell, indistinctly, of tall figures that lifted and bore me in silence down—down—still down—till a hideous dizziness oppressed me at the mere idea of the interminableness of the descent. They tell also of a vague horror at my heart, on account of that heart's unnatural stillness. Then comes a sense of sudden motionlessness throughout all things; as if those who bore me (a ghastly train!) had outrun, in their descent, the limits of the limitless, and paused from the wearisomeness of their toil. After this I call to mind flatness and dampness; and then all is *madness*—the madness of a memory which busies itself among forbidden things.

Very suddenly there came back to my soul motion and sound— the tumultuous motion of my heart, and, in my ears, the sound of its beating. Then a pause in which all is blank. Then again sound, and motion, and touch—a tingling sensation pervading my frame. Then the mere consciousness of existence, without thought—a condition which lasted long. Then very suddenly, *thought*, and shuddering terror, and earnest endeavor to comprehend my true state. Then a strong desire to lapse into insensibility. Then a rushing revival of soul, and a successful effort to move. And now a full memory of the trial, of the judges, of the sable draperies, of the sentence, of the sickness, of the swoon. Then entire forgetfulness of all that followed; of all that a later day and much earnestness of endeavor have enabled me vaguely to recall.

So far, I had not opened my eyes. I felt that I lay upon my back, unbound. I had reached out my hand, and it fell heavily upon something damp and hard. There I suffered it to remain for many minutes, while I strove to imagine where and *what* I could be. I longed, yet dared not, to employ my vision. I dreaded the first glance at objects around me. It was not that I feared to look upon things horrible, but that I grew aghast lest there should be *nothing* to see. At length, with a wild desperation at heart, I quickly unclosed my eyes. My worst thoughts, then, were confirmed. The blackness of eternal night encompassed me. I struggled for breath. The intensity of the darkness seemed to oppress and stifle me. The atmosphere was intolerably close. I still lay quietly, and made effort to exercise my reason. I brought to mind the inquisitorial proceedings, and attempted from that point to deduce my real condition. The sentence had passed; and it appeared to me that a very long interval of time had since elapsed. Yet not for a moment did I suppose myself actually dead. Such a supposition, notwithstanding what we read in fiction, is altogether inconsistent with real existence—but where and in what state was I? The condemned to death, I knew, perished usually at the autos-da-fé, and one of these had been held on the very night of the day of my trial. Had I been remanded to my dungeon, to await the next sacrifice, which would not take place for many months? This I at once saw could not be. Victims had been in immediate demand. Moreover, my dungeon, as well as all the condemned cells at Toledo, had stone floors, and light was not altogether excluded.

A fearful idea now suddenly drove the blood in torrents upon my heart, and for a brief period I once more relapsed into insensibility. Upon recovering, I at once started to my feet, trembling convulsively in every fiber. I thrust my arms wildly above and around me in all directions. I felt nothing; yet dreaded to move a step, lest I should be impeded by the walls of a *tomb*. Perspiration burst from every pore, and stood in cold big beads upon my forehead. The agony of suspense grew at length intolerable, and I cautiously moved forward, with my arms extended, and my eyes straining from their sockets in the hope of catching some faint ray of light. I proceeded for many paces; but still all was blackness and vacancy. I breathed more freely. It seemed evident that mine was not, at least, the most hideous of fates.

And now, as I still continued to step cautiously onward, there came thronging upon my recollection a thousand vague rumors of the horrors of Toledo. Of the dungeons there had been strange things narrated—fables I had always deemed them—but yet strange, and too ghastly to repeat, save in a whisper. Was I left to perish of starvation in this subterranean world of darkness; or what fate, perhaps even more fearful, awaited me? That the result would be death, and a death of more than customary bitterness, I knew too well the character of my judges to doubt. The mode and the hour were all that occupied or distracted me.

My outstretched hands at length encountered some solid obstruction. It was a wall, seemingly of stone masonry—very smooth, slimy, and cold. I followed it up; stepping with all the careful distrust with which certain antique narratives had inspired me. This process, however, afforded me no means of ascertaining the dimensions of my dungeon, as I might make its circuit and return to the point whence I set out without being aware of the fact, so perfectly uniform seemed the wall. I therefore sought the knife which had been in my pocket when led into the inquisitorial chamber; but it was gone; my clothes had been exchanged for a wrapper of coarse serge. I had thought of forcing the blade in some minute crevice of the masonry, so as to identify my point of departure. The difficulty, nevertheless, was but trivial; although, in the disorder of my fancy, it seemed at first insuperable. I tore a part of the hem from the robe and placed the fragment at full length, and at right angles to the wall. In groping my way around the prison, I could not fail to encounter this rag upon completing the circuit. So, at least, I thought; but I had not counted upon the extent of the dungeon, or upon my own weakness. The ground was moist and slippery. I staggered onward for some time, when I stumbled and fell. My excessive fatigue induced me to remain prostrate; and sleep soon overtook me as I lay.

Upon awaking, and stretching forth an arm, I found beside me a loaf and a pitcher with water. I was too much exhausted to reflect upon this circumstance, but ate and drank with avidity. Shortly afterward, I resumed my tour around the prison, and with much toil, came at last upon the fragment of the serge. Up to the period when I fell, I had counted fifty-two paces, and, upon resuming my walk, I had counted forty-eight more—when I arrived at the rag. There were in all, then, a hundred paces; and, admitting two paces to the yard, I presumed the dungeon to be fifty yards in circuit. I had met, however, with many angles in the wall, and thus I could form no guess at the shape of the vault, for vault I could not help supposing it to be.

I had little object—certainly no hope—in these researches; but a vague curiosity prompted me to continue them. Quitting the wall, I resolved to cross the area of the enclosure. At first, I proceeded with extreme caution, for the floor, although seemingly of solid material, was treacherous with slime. At length, however, I took courage, and did not hesitate to step firmly—endeavoring to cross in as direct a line as possible. I had advanced some ten or twelve paces in this manner, when the remnant of the torn hem of my robe became entangled between my legs. I stepped on it, and fell violently on my face.

In the confusion attending my fall, I did not immediately apprehend a somewhat startling circumstance, which yet, in a few seconds afterward, and while I still lay prostrate, arrested my attention. It was this: my chin rested upon the floor of the prison, but my lips, and the upper portion of my head, although seemingly at a less elevation than the chin, touched nothing. At the same time, my forehead seemed bathed in a clammy vapor, and the peculiar smell of decayed fungus arose to my nostrils. I put forward my arm, and shuddered to find that I had fallen at the very brink of a circular pit, whose extent, of course, I had no means of ascertaining at the moment. Groping about the masonry just below the margin, I succeeded in dislodging a small fragment, and let it fall into the abyss. For many seconds I hearkened to its reverberations as it dashed against the sides of the chasm in its descent; at length, there was a sullen plunge into water, succeeded by loud echoes. At the same moment, there came a sound resembling the quick opening and as rapid closing of a door overhead, while a faint gleam of light flashed suddenly through the gloom, and as suddenly faded away.

I saw clearly the doom which had been prepared for me, and congratulated myself upon the timely accident by which I had escaped. Another step before my fall, and the world had seen me no more. And the death just avoided was of that very character which I had regarded as fabulous and frivolous in the tales respecting the Inquisition. To the victims of its tyranny, there was the choice of death with its direst physical agonies, or death with its most hideous moral horrors. I had been reserved for the latter. By long suffering my nerves had been unstrung, until I trembled at the sound of my own voice, and had become in every respect a fitting subject for the species of torture which awaited me.

Shaking in every limb, I groped my way back to the wall—

resolving there to perish rather than risk the terrors of the wells, of which my imagination now pictured many in various positions about the dungeon. In other conditions of mind, I might have had courage to end my misery at once, by a plunge into one of these abysses; but now I was the veriest of cowards. Neither could I forget what I had read of these pits—that the *sudden* extinction of life formed no part of their most horrible plan.

Agitation of spirit kept me awake for many long hours, but at length I again slumbered. Upon arousing, I found by my side, as before, a loaf and a pitcher of water. A burning thirst consumed me, and I emptied the vessel at a draught. It must have been drugged—for scarcely had I drunk, before I became irresistibly drowsy. A deep sleep fell upon me, a sleep like that of death. How long it lasted, of course I know not; but when, once again, I unclosed my eyes, the objects around me were visible. By a wild, sulfurous luster, the origin of which I could not at first determine, I was enabled to see the extent and aspect of the prison.

In its size I had been greatly mistaken. The whole circuit of its walls did not exceed twenty-five yards. For some minutes this fact occasioned me a world of vain trouble; vain indeed—for what could be of less importance, under the terrible circumstances which environed me, than the mere dimensions of my dungeon? But my soul took a wild interest in trifles, and I busied myself in endeavors to account for the error I had committed in my measurement. The truth at length flashed upon me. In my first attempt at exploration I had counted fifty-two paces, up to the period when I fell: I must then have been within a pace or two of the fragment of serge; in fact, I had nearly performed the circuit of the vault. I then slept—and upon awaking, I must have turned upon my steps—thus supposing the circuit nearly double what it actually was. My confusion of mind prevented me from observing that I began my tour with the wall to the left, and ended with the wall to the right.

I had been deceived, too, in respect to the shape of the enclosure. In feeling my way I had found many angles, and thus deduced an idea of great irregularity; so potent is the effect of total darkness upon one arousing from lethargy or sleep! The angles were simply those of a few slight depressions, or niches at odd intervals. The general shape of the prison was square. What I had taken for masonry seemed now to be iron, or some other metal, in huge plates, whose sutures or joints occasioned the depression. The entire surface of this metallic enclosure was rudely daubed in all the hideous and repulsive devices to which the charnel superstition of the monks has given rise. The figures of fiends in aspects of menace, with skeleton forms, and other more really fearful images, overspread and disfigured the walls. I observed that the outlines of these monstrosities were sufficiently distinct, but that the colors seemed faded and blurred, as if from the effects of a damp atmosphere. I now noticed the floor, too, which was of stone. In the center yawned the circular pit from whose jaws I had escaped; but it was the only one in the dungeon.

All this I saw indistinctly and by much effort—for my personal condition had been greatly changed during slumber. I now lay upon my back, and at full length, on a species of low framework of wood. To this I was securely bound by a long strap resembling a surcingle. It passed in many convolutions about my limbs and body, leaving at liberty only my head, and my left arm to such extent, that I could, by dint of much exertion, supply myself with food from an earthen dish which lay by my side on the floor. I saw, to my horror, that the pitcher had been removed. I say to my horror— for I was consumed with intolerable thirst. This thirst it appeared to be the design of my persecutors to stimulate—for the food in the dish was meat pungently seasoned.

Looking upward, I surveyed the ceiling of my prison. It was some thirty or forty feet overhead, and constructed much as the side walls. In one of its panels a very singular figure riveted my whole attention. It was the painted figure of Time as he is commonly represented, save that, in lieu of a scythe, he held what, at a casual glance, I supposed to be the pictured image of a huge pendulum, such as we see on antique clocks. There was something, however, in the appearance of this machine which caused me to regard it more attentively. While I gazed directly upward at it (for its position was immediately over my own) I fancied that I saw it in motion. In an instant afterward the fancy was confirmed. Its sweep was brief, and of course slow. I watched it for some minutes somewhat in fear, but more in wonder. Wearied at length with observing its dull movement, I turned my eyes upon the other objects in the cell.

A slight noise attracted my notice, and, looking to the floor, I saw several enormous rats traversing it. They had issued from the well which lay just within view to my right. Even then, while I gazed, they came up in troops, hurriedly, with ravenous eyes, allured by the scent of the meat. From this it required much effort and attention to scare them away.

It might have been half an hour, perhaps even an hour (for I could take but imperfect note of time), before I again cast my eyes upward. What I then saw confounded and amazed me. The sweep of the pendulum had increased in extent by nearly a yard. As a natural consequence its velocity was also much greater. But what mainly disturbed me was the idea that it had perceptibly *descended*. I now observed—with what horror it is needless to say—that its nether extremity was formed of a crescent of glittering steel, about a foot in length from horn to horn; the horns upward, and the under edge evidently as keen as that of a razor. Like a razor also, it seemed massive and heavy, tapering from the edge into a solid and broad structure above. It was appended to a weighty rod of brass, and the whole *hissed* as it swung through the air.

I could no longer doubt the doom prepared for me by monkish ingenuity in torture. My cognizance of the pit had become known to the inquisitorial agents—*the pit*, whose horrors had been destined for so bold a recusant as myself—*the pit*, typical of hell and regarded by rumor as the Ultima Thule of all their punishments. The plunge into this pit I had avoided by the merest of accidents, and I knew that surprise, or entrapment into torment, formed an important portion of all the grotesquerie of these dungeon deaths. Having failed to fall, it was no part of the demon plan to hurl me into the abyss; and thus (there being no alternative) a different and milder destruction awaited me. Milder! I half smiled in my agony as I thought of such application of such a term.

What boots it to tell of the long, long hours of horror more than mortal, during which I counted the rushing oscillations of the steel! Inch by inch—line by line—with a descent only appreciable at intervals that seemed ages—down and still down it came! Days passed—it might have been that many days passed—ere it swept so closely over me as to fan me with its acrid breath. The odor of the sharp steel forced itself into my nostrils. I prayed—I wearied heaven with my prayer for its more speedy descent. I grew frantically mad, and struggled to force myself upward against the sweep of the fearful scimitar. And then I fell suddenly calm, and lay smiling at the glittering death, as a child at some rare bauble.

There was another interval of utter insensibility; it was brief; for, upon again lapsing into life, there had been no perceptible descent in the pendulum. But it might have been long—for I knew there were demons who took note of my swoon, and who could have arrested the vibration at pleasure. Upon my recovery, too, I felt very—oh, inexpressibly!—sick and weak, as if through long inanition. Even amid the agonies of that period, the human nature craved food. With painful effort I outstretched my left arm as far as my bonds permitted, and took possession of the small remnant which had been spared me by the rats. As I put a portion of it within my lips, there rushed to my mind a half-formed thought of joy—of hope.

Yet what business had *I* with hope? It was, as I say, a half-formed thought—man has many such, which are never completed. I felt that it was of joy—of hope; but I felt also that it had perished in its formation. In vain I struggled to perfect—to regain it. Long suffering had nearly annihilated all my ordinary powers of mind. I was an imbecile—an idiot.

The vibration of the pendulum was at right angles to my length. I saw that the crescent was designed to cross the region of the heart. It would fray the serge of my robe—it would return and repeat its operations—again—and again. Notwithstanding its terrifically wide sweep (some thirty feet or more), and the hissing vigor of its descent, sufficient to sunder these very walls of iron, still the fraying of my robe would be all that, for several minutes, it would accomplish. And at this thought I paused. I dared not go further than this reflection. I dwelt upon it with a pertinacity of attention—as if, in so dwelling, I could arrest *here* the descent of the steel. I forced myself to ponder upon the sound of the crescent as it should pass across the garment—upon the peculiar thrilling sensation which the friction of cloth produces on the nerves. I pondered over all this frivolity until my teeth were on edge.

Down—steadily down it crept. I took a frenzied pleasure in contrasting its downward with its lateral velocity. To the right—to the left—far and wide—with the shriek of a damned spirit!—to my heart, with the stealthy pace of the tiger! I alternately laughed and howled, as the one or the other idea grew predominant.

Down—certainly, relentlessly down! It vibrated within three inches of my bosom! I struggled violently—furiously—to free my left arm. This was free only from the elbow to the hand. I could reach the latter, from the platter beside me, to my mouth, with great effort, but no farther. Could I have broken the fastenings above the elbow, I would have seized and attempted to arrest the pendulum. I might as well have attempted to arrest an avalanche!

Down—still unceasingly—still inevitably down! I gasped and struggled at each vibration. I shrunk convulsively at its every sweep. My eyes followed its outward or upward whirls with the eagerness of the most unmeaning despair; they closed themselves spasmodically at the descent, although death would have been a relief, oh, how unspeakable! Still I quivered in every nerve to think how slight a sinking of the machinery would precipitate that keen, glistening axe upon my bosom. It was *hope* that prompted the nerve to quiver—the frame to shrink. It was *hope*—the hope that triumphs on the rack—that whispers to the death-condemned even in the dungeons of the Inquisition.

I saw that some ten or twelve vibrations would bring the steel in actual contact with my robe—and with this observation there suddenly came over my spirit all the keen, collected calmness of despair. For the first time during many hours—or perhaps days—I *thought*. It now occurred to me, that the bandage, or surcingle, which enveloped me, was *unique*. I was tied by no separate cord. The first stroke of the razor-like crescent athwart any portion of the band would so detach it that it might be unwound from my person by means of my left hand. But how fearful, in that case, the proximity of the steel! The result of the slightest struggle, how deadly! Was it likely, moreover, that the minions of the torturer had not foreseen and provided for this possibility? Was it probable that the bandage crossed my bosom in the track of the pendulum? Dreading to find my faint and, as it seemed, my last hope frustrated, I so far elevated my head as to obtain a distinct view of my breast. The surcingle enveloped my limbs and body close in all directions—*save in the path of the destroying crescent.*

Scarcely had I dropped my head back into its original position, when there flashed upon my mind what I cannot better describe than as the unformed half of that idea of deliverance to which I have previously alluded, and of which a moiety only floated indeterminately through my brain when I raised food to my burning lips. The whole thought was now present—feeble, scarcely sane, scarcely definite—but still entire. I proceeded at once, with the nervous energy of despair, to attempt its execution.

For many hours the immediate vicinity of the low framework upon which I lay had been literally swarming with rats. They were wild, bold, ravenous—their red eyes glaring upon me as if they waited but for motionlessness on my part to make me their prey. "To what food," I thought, "have they been accustomed in the well?"

They had devoured, in spite of all my efforts to prevent them, all but a small remnant of the contents of the dish. I had fallen into an habitual see-saw or wave of the hand about the platter; and, at length, the unconscious uniformity of the movement deprived it of effect. In their voracity, the vermin frequently fastened their sharp fangs in my fingers. With the particles of the oily and spicy viand which now remained, I thoroughly rubbed the bandage wherever I could reach it; then, raising my hand from the floor, I lay breathlessly still.

At first, the ravenous animals were startled and terrified at the change—at the cessation of movement. They shrank alarmedly back; many sought the well. But this was only for a moment. I had not counted in vain upon their voracity. Observing that I remained without motion, one or two of the boldest leaped upon the framework, and smelt at the surcingle. This seemed the signal for a general rush. Forth from the well they hurried in fresh troops. They clung to the wood—they overran it, and leaped in hundreds upon my person. The measured movement of the pendulum disturbed them not at all. Avoiding its strokes, they busied themselves with the anointed bandage. They pressed—they swarmed upon me in ever accumulating heaps. They writhed upon my throat; their cold lips sought my own; I was half stifled by their thronging pressure; disgust, for which the world has no name, swelled my bosom, and chilled, with a heavy clamminess, my heart. Yet one minute, and I felt that the struggle would be over. Plainly I perceived the loosening of the bandage. I knew that in more than one place it must be already severed. With a more than human resolution I lay *still*.

Nor had I erred in my calculations—nor had I endured in vain. I at length felt that I was *free*. The surcingle hung in ribands from my body. But the stroke of the pendulum already pressed upon my bosom. It had divided the serge of the robe. It had cut through the linen beneath. Twice again it swung, and a sharp sense of pain shot through every nerve. But the moment of escape had arrived. At a wave of my hand my deliverers hurried tumultuously away. With a steady movement—cautious sidelong, shrinking, and slow—I slid from the embrace of the bandage and beyond the reach of the scimitar. For the moment, at least, *I was free*.

Free!—And in the grasp of the Inquisition! I had scarcely stepped from my wooden bed of horror upon the stone floor of the prison, when the motion of the hellish machine ceased, and I beheld it drawn up, by some invisible force, through the ceiling. This was a lesson which I took desperately to heart. My every motion was undoubtedly watched. Free!—I had but escaped death in one form of agony, to be delivered unto worse than death in some other. With that thought I rolled my eyes nervously around on the barriers of iron that hemmed me in. Something unusual—some change, which, at first, I could not appreciate distinctly—it was obvious, had taken place in the apartment. For many minutes of a dreamy and trembling abstraction, I busied myself in vain, unconnected conjecture. During this period, I became aware, for the first time, of the origin of the sulfurous light which illumined the cell. It proceeded from a fissure, about half an inch in width, extending entirely around the prison at the base of the walls, which thus appeared, and were completely separated from the floor. I endeavored, but of course in vain, to look through the aperture.

As I arose from the attempt, the mystery of the alteration in the chamber broke at once upon my understanding. I have observed that, although the outlines of the figures upon the walls were sufficiently distinct, yet the colors seemed blurred and indefinite. These colors had now assumed, and were momentarily assuming a startling and most intense brilliancy, that gave to the spectral and fiendish portraitures an aspect that might have thrilled even firmer nerves than my own. Demon eyes, of a wild and ghastly vivacity, glared upon me in a thousand directions, where none had been visible before, and gleamed with the lurid luster of a fire that I could not force my imagination to regard as unreal.

Unreal!—Even while I breathed there came to my nostrils the breath of the vapor of heated iron! A suffocating odor pervaded the prison! A deeper glow settled each moment in the eyes that glared at my agonies! A richer tint of crimson diffused itself over the pictured horrors of blood. I panted! I gasped for breath! There could be no doubt of the design of my tormentors. Oh, most unrelenting! Oh, most demoniac of men! I shrank from the glowing metal to the center of the cell. Amid the thought of the fiery destruction that impended, the idea of the coolness of the well came over my soul like balm. I rushed to its deadly brink. I threw my straining vision below. The glare from the enkindled roof illumined its inmost recesses. Yet, for a wild moment, did my spirit refuse to comprehend the meaning of what I saw. At length it forced—it wrestled its way into my soul— it burned itself in upon my shuddering reason. Oh, for a voice to speak!—Oh, horror!—Oh, any horror but this! With a shriek, I rushed from the margin, and buried my face in my hands—weeping bitterly.

The heat rapidly increased, and once again I looked up, shuddering as with a fit of the ague. There had been a second change in the cell—and now the change was obviously in the *form*. As before, it was in vain that I at first endeavored to appreciate or understand what was taking place. But not long was I left in doubt. The

Inquisitorial vengeance had been hurried by my twofold escape, and there was to be no more dallying with the King of Terrors. The room had been square. I saw that two of its iron angles were now acute—two, consequently, obtuse. The fearful difference quickly increased with a low rumbling or moaning sound. In an instant the apartment had shifted its form into that of a lozenge. But the alteration stopped not here—I neither hoped nor desired it to stop. I could have clasped the red walls to my bosom as a garment of eternal peace. "Death," I said, "any death but that of the pit!" Fool! Might I not have known that *into the pit* it was the object of the burning iron to urge me? Could I resist its glow? Or if even that, could I withstand its pressure? And now, flatter and flatter grew the lozenge, with a rapidity that left me no time for contemplation. Its center, and of course its greatest width, came just over the yawning gulf. I shrank back—but the closing walls pressed me resistlessly onward. At length for my seared and writhing body there was no longer an inch of foothold on the firm floor of the prison. I struggled no more, but the agony of my soul found vent in one loud, long, and final scream of despair. I felt that I tottered upon the brink—I averted my eyes—

There was a discordant hum of human voices! There was a loud blast as of many trumpets! There was a harsh grating as of a thousand thunders! The fiery walls rushed back! An outstretched arm caught my own as I fell, fainting, into the abyss. It was that of General Lasalle. The French army had entered Toledo. The Inquisition was in the hands of its enemies.

THE TELL-TALE HEART

True!—Nervous—very, very dreadfully nervous I had been and am; but why *will* you say that I am mad? The disease had sharpened my senses—not destroyed—not dulled them. Above all was the sense of hearing acute. I heard all things in the heaven and in the earth. I heard many things in hell. How, then, am I mad? Harken! and observe how healthily—how calmly I can tell you the whole story.

It is impossible to say how first the idea entered my brain; but once conceived, it haunted me day and night. Object there was none. Passion there was none. I loved the old man. He had never wronged me. He had never given me insult. For his gold I had no desire. I think it was his eye! Yes, it was this! He had the eye of a vulture—a pale blue eye, with a film over it. Whenever it fell upon me, my blood ran cold; and so by degrees—very gradually—I made up my mind to take the life of the old man, and thus rid myself of the eye forever.

Now this is the point. You fancy me mad. Madmen know nothing. But you should have seen *me*. You should have seen how wisely I proceeded—with what caution—with what foresight—with what dissimulation I went to work! I was never kinder to the old man than during the whole week before I killed him. And every night, about midnight, I turned the latch of his door and opened it—oh, so gently!

And then, when I had made an opening sufficient for my head, I put in a dark lantern, all closed, closed, so that no light shone out, and then I thrust in my head. Oh, you would have laughed to see how cunningly I thrust it in! I moved it slowly—very, very slowly, so that I might not disturb the old man's sleep. It took me an hour to place my whole head within the opening so far that I could see him as he lay upon his bed. Ha!—Would a madman have been so wise as this? And then, when my head was well in the room, I undid the lantern cautiously—oh, so cautiously— cautiously (for the hinges creaked)—I undid it just so much that a single thin ray fell upon the vulture eye. And this I did for seven long nights—every night just at midnight—but I found the eye always closed; and so it was impossible to do the work; for it was not the old man who vexed me, but his Evil Eye. And every morning, when the day broke, I went boldly into the chamber, and spoke courageously to him, calling him by name in a hearty tone, and inquiring how he had passed the night. So you see he would have been a very profound old man, indeed, to suspect that every night, just at twelve, I looked in upon him while he slept.

Upon the eighth night I was more than usually cautious in opening the door. A watch's minute-hand moves more quickly than did mine. Never before that night, had I *felt* the extent of my own powers—of my sagacity. I could scarcely contain my feelings of triumph. To think that there I was, opening the door, little by little, and he not even to dream of my secret deeds or thoughts. I fairly chuckled at the idea; and perhaps he heard me; for he moved on the bed suddenly, as if startled. Now you may think that I drew back—but no. His room was as black as pitch with the thick darkness (for the shutters were close fastened, through fear of robbers), and so I knew that he could not see the opening of the door, and I kept pushing it on steadily, steadily.

I had my head in, and was about to open the lantern, when my thumb slipped upon the tin fastening, and the old man sprang up in bed, crying out—"Who's there?"

I kept quite still and said nothing. For a whole hour I did not move a muscle, and in the meantime I did not hear him lie down. He was still sitting up in the bed listening—just as I have done, night after night, hearkening to the death watches in the wall.

Presently I heard a slight groan, and I knew it was the groan of mortal terror. It was not a groan of pain or of grief—oh, no!—It was the low stifled sound that arises from the bottom of the soul when overcharged with awe. I knew the sound well. Many a night, just at midnight, when all the world slept, it has welled up from my own bosom, deepening, with its dreadful echo, the terrors that distracted me. I say I knew it well. I knew what the old man felt, and pitied him, although I chuckled at heart. I knew that he had been lying awake ever since the first slight noise, when he had turned in the bed. His fears had been ever since growing upon him. He had been trying to fancy them causeless, but could not. He had been saying to himself—"It is nothing but the wind in the chimney—it is only a mouse crossing the floor," or, "It is merely a cricket which has made a single chirp." Yes, he had been trying to comfort himself with these suppositions: but he had found all in vain. *All in vain*; because Death, in approaching him had stalked with his black shadow before him, and enveloped the victim. And it was the mournful influence of the unperceived shadow that caused him to feel— although he neither saw nor heard—to *feel* the presence of my head within the room.

When I had waited a long time, very patiently, without hearing him lie down, I resolved to open a little—a very, very little crevice in the lantern. So I opened it—you cannot imagine how stealthily, stealthily—until, at length a single dim ray, like the thread of the spider, shot from out the crevice and fell full upon the vulture eye.

It was open—wide, wide open—and I grew furious as I gazed upon it. I saw it with perfect distinctness—all a dull blue, with a hideous veil over it that chilled the very marrow in my bones; but I could see nothing else of the old man's face or person: for I had directed the ray, as if by instinct, precisely upon the damned spot.

And have I not told you that what you mistake for madness is but over-acuteness of the senses?—Now, I say, there came to my ears a low, dull, quick sound, such as a watch makes when enveloped in cotton. I knew *that* sound well, too. It was the beating of the old man's heart. It increased my fury, as the beating of a drum stimulates the soldier into courage.

But even yet I refrained and kept still. I scarcely breathed. I held the lantern motionless. I tried how steadily I could maintain the ray upon the eye. Meantime the hellish tattoo of the heart increased. It grew quicker and quicker, and louder and louder every instant. The old man's terror *must* have been extreme! It grew louder, I say, louder every moment!—Do you mark me well? I have told you that I am nervous: so I am. And now at the dead hour of the night, amid the dreadful silence of that old house, so strange a noise as this excited me to uncontrollable terror. Yet, for some minutes longer I refrained and stood still. But the beating grew louder, louder! I thought the heart must burst. And now a new anxiety seized me—the sound would be heard by a neighbor! The old man's hour had come! With a loud yell, I threw open the lantern and leaped into the room. He shrieked once—once only. In an instant I dragged him to the floor, and pulled the heavy bed over him. I then smiled gaily, to find the deed so far done. But, for many minutes, the heart beat on with a muffled sound. This, however, did not vex me; it would not be heard through the wall. At length it ceased. The old man was dead. I removed the bed and examined the corpse. Yes, he was stone, stone dead. I placed my hand upon the heart and held it there many minutes. There was no pulsation. He was stone dead. His eye would trouble me no more.

If still you think me mad, you will think so no longer when I describe the wise precautions I took for the concealment of the body. The night waned, and I worked hastily, but in silence. First of all I dismembered the corpse. I cut off the head and the arms and the legs.

I then took up three planks from the flooring of the chamber, and deposited all between the scantlings. I then replaced the boards so cleverly, so cunningly, that no human eye—not even *his*—could have detected anything wrong. There was nothing to wash out—no stain of any kind—no blood-spot whatever. I had been too wary for that. A tub had caught all—ha! ha!

When I had made an end of these labors, it was four o'clock—still dark as midnight. As the bell sounded the hour, there came a knocking at the street door. I went down to open it with a light heart, for what had I *now* to fear? There entered three men, who introduced themselves, with perfect suavity, as officers of the police. A shriek had been heard by a neighbor during the night; suspicion of foul play had been aroused; information had been lodged at the police office, and they (the officers) had been deputed to search the premises.

I smiled—for *what* had I to fear? I bade the gentlemen welcome. The shriek, I said, was my own in a dream. The old man, I mentioned, was absent in the country. I took my visitors all over the house. I bade them search—search well. I led them, at length, to his chamber. I showed them his treasures, secure, undisturbed. In the enthusiasm of my confidence, I brought chairs into the room, and desired them *here* to rest from their fatigues, while I myself, in the wild audacity of my perfect triumph, placed my own seat upon the very spot beneath which reposed the corpse of the victim.

The officers were satisfied. My *manner* had convinced them. I was singularly at ease. They sat, and while I answered cheerily, they chatted of familiar things. But, ere long, I felt myself getting pale and wished them gone. My head ached, and I fancied a ringing in my ears: but still they sat and still chatted. The ringing became more distinct; it continued and became more distinct; I talked more freely to get rid of the feeling; but it continued and gained definiteness—until, at length, I found that the noise was *not* within my ears.

No doubt I now grew very pale; but I talked more fluently, and with a heightened voice. Yet the sound increased—and what could I do? It was *a low, dull, quick sound—much such a sound as a watch makes when enveloped in cotton.* I gasped for breath—and yet the officers heard it not. I talked more quickly—more vehemently; but the noise steadily increased. I arose and argued about trifles, in a high key and with violent gesticulations; but the noise steadily increased. Why *would* they not be gone? I paced the floor to and fro with heavy strides, as if excited to fury by the observations of the men—but the noise steadily increased. Oh God! What could I do? I foamed—I raved—I swore! I swung the chair upon which I had been sitting, and grated it upon the boards, but the noise arose over all and continually increased. It grew louder—louder—*louder*! And still the men chatted pleasantly, and smiled. Was it possible they heard not? Almighty God!—No, no! They heard!—They suspected!—They *knew*!—They were making a mockery of my horror!—This I thought, and this I think. But anything was better than this agony! Anything was more tolerable than this derision! I could bear those hypocritical smiles no longer! I felt that I must scream or die! And now—again!—Hark! Louder! Louder! Louder! *Louder*!

"Villains!" I shrieked, "Dissemble no more! I admit the deed!—Tear up the planks! Here, here!—It is the beating of his hideous heart!"

THE BLACK CAT

For the most wild, yet most homely narrative which I am about to pen, I neither expect nor solicit belief. Mad indeed would I be to expect it, in a case where my very senses reject their own evidence. Yet, mad am I not—and very surely do I not dream. But tomorrow I die, and today I would unburden my soul. My immediate purpose is to place before the world plainly, succinctly, and without comment, a series of mere household events. In their consequences these events have terrified—have tortured—have destroyed me. Yet I will not attempt to expound them. To me they have presented little but Horror—to many they will seem less terrible than *baroques*. Hereafter, perhaps, some intellect may be found which will reduce my phantasm to the commonplace—some intellect more calm, more logical, and far less excitable than my own, which will perceive in the circumstances I detail with awe, nothing more than an ordinary succession of very natural causes and effects.

From my infancy I was noted for the docility and humanity of my disposition. My tenderness of heart was even so conspicuous as to make me the jest of my companions. I was especially fond of animals, and was indulged by my parents with a great variety of pets. With these I spent most of my time, and never was so happy as when feeding and caressing them. This peculiarity of character grew with my growth, and, in my manhood, I derived from it one of my principal sources of pleasure. To those who have cherished an affection for a faithful and sagacious dog, I need hardly be at the trouble of explaining the nature or the intensity of the gratification thus derivable. There is something in the unselfish and self-sacrificing love of a brute which goes directly to the heart of him who has had frequent occasion to test the paltry friendship and gossamer fidelity of mere *Man*.

I married early, and was happy to find in my wife a disposition not uncongenial with my own. Observing my partiality for domestic pets, she lost no opportunity of procuring those of the most agreeable kind. We had birds, goldfish, a fine dog, rabbits, a small monkey, and *a cat*.

This latter was a remarkably large and beautiful animal, entirely black, and sagacious to an astonishing degree. In speaking of his intelligence, my wife, who at heart was not a little tinctured with superstition, made frequent allusion to the ancient popular notion which regarded all black cats as witches in disguise. Not that she was ever serious upon this point, and I mention the matter at all for no better reason than that it happens just now to be remembered.

Pluto—this was the cat's name—was my favorite pet and playmate. I alone fed him, and he attended me wherever I went about the house. It was even with difficulty that I could prevent him from following me through the streets.

Our friendship lasted in this manner for several years, during which my general temperament and character—through the instrumentality of the Fiend Intemperance—had (I blush to confess it) experienced a radical alteration for the worse. I grew, day by day, more moody, more irritable, more regardless of the feelings of others. I suffered myself to use intemperate language to my wife. At length, I even offered her personal violence. My pets, of course, were made to feel the change in my disposition. I not only neglected, but ill-used them. For Pluto, however, I still retained sufficient regard to restrain me from maltreating him, as I made no scruple of maltreating the rabbits, the monkey, or even the dog, when by accident, or through affection, they came in my way. But my disease grew upon me—for what disease is like Alcohol?—and at length even Pluto, who was now becoming old, and consequently somewhat peevish—even Pluto began to experience the effects of my ill-temper.

One night, returning home much intoxicated, from one of my haunts about town, I fancied that the cat avoided my presence. I seized him; when, in his fright at my violence, he inflicted a slight wound upon my hand with his teeth. The fury of a demon instantly possessed me. I knew myself no longer. My original soul seemed at once to take its flight from my body, and a more than fiendish malevolence, gin-nurtured, thrilled every fiber of my frame. I took from my waistcoat-pocket a penknife, opened it, grasped the poor beast by the throat, and deliberately cut one of its eyes from the socket! I blush, I burn, I shudder, while I pen the damnable atrocity.

When reason returned with the morning—when I had slept off the fumes of the night's debauch—I experienced a sentiment half of horror, half of remorse, for the crime of which I had been guilty; but it was, at best, a feeble and equivocal feeling, and the soul remained untouched. I again plunged into excess, and soon drowned in wine all memory of the deed.

In the meantime the cat slowly recovered. The socket of the lost eye presented, it is true, a frightful appearance, but he no longer appeared to suffer any pain. He went about the house as usual, but, as might be expected, fled in extreme terror at my approach. I had so much of my old heart left as to be at first grieved by this evident dislike on the part of a creature which had once so loved me. But this feeling soon gave place to irritation. And then came, as if to my final and irrevocable overthrow, the spirit of *Perverseness*. Of this spirit philosophy takes no account. Yet I am not more sure that my soul lives, than I am that perverseness is one of the primitive impulses of the human heart—one of the indivisible primary faculties, or sentiments, which gives direction to the character of Man. Who has not, a hundred times, found himself committing a vile or a silly action for no other reason than because he knows he should *not*? Have we not a perpetual inclination, in the teeth of our best judgment, to violate that which is *Law*, merely because we understand it to be such? This spirit of perverseness, I say, came to my final overthrow. It was this unfathomable longing of the soul *to vex itself*—to offer violence to its own nature—to do wrong for the wrong's sake only— that urged me to continue and finally to consummate the injury I had inflicted upon the unoffending brute. One morning, in cold blood, I slipped a noose about its neck and hung it to the limb of a tree; hung it with the tears streaming from my eyes, and with the bitterest remorse at my heart; hung it *because* I knew that it had loved me, and *because* I felt it had given me no reason of offence; hung it *because* I knew that in so doing I was committing a sin—a deadly sin that would so jeopardize my immortal soul as to place it, if such a thing were possible, even beyond the reach of the infinite mercy of the Most Merciful and Most Terrible God.

On the night of the day on which this cruel deed was done, I was aroused from sleep by the cry of fire. The curtains of my bed were in flames. The whole house was blazing. It was with great difficulty that my wife, a servant, and myself, made our escape from the confla- gration. The destruction was complete. My entire worldly wealth was swallowed up, and I resigned myself thenceforward to despair.

I am above the weakness of seeking to establish a sequence of cause and effect, between the disaster and the atrocity. But I am detailing a chain of facts, and wish not to leave even a possible link imperfect. On the day succeeding the fire, I visited the ruins. The walls, with one exception, had fallen in. This exception was found in a compartment wall, not very thick, which stood about the middle of the house, and against which had rested the head of my bed. The plastering had here, in great measure, resisted the action of the fire, a fact which I attributed to its having been recently spread. About this wall a dense crowd were collected and many persons seemed to be examining a particular portion of it with very minute and eager attention. The words "strange!" "singular!" and other similar expressions excited my curiosity. I approached, and saw, as if graven in *bas-relief* upon the white surface, the figure of a gigantic *cat*. The impression was given with an accuracy truly marvelous. There was a rope about the animal's neck.

When I first beheld this apparition—for I could scarcely regard it as less—my wonder and my terror were extreme. But at length reflection came to my aid. The cat, I remembered, had been hung in a garden adjacent to the house. Upon the alarm of fire, this garden had been immediately filled by the crowd, by some one of whom the animal must have been cut from the tree and thrown, through an open window, into my chamber. This had probably been done with the view of arousing me from sleep. The falling of the other walls had compressed the victim of my cruelty into the substance of the freshly spread plaster; the lime of which, with the flames and the ammonia from the carcass, had then accomplished the portraiture as I saw it.

Although I thus readily accounted to my reason, if not altogether to my conscience, for the startling fact just detailed, it did not the less fail to make a deep impression upon my fancy. For months I could not rid myself of the phantasm of the cat; and during this period there came back into my spirit a half-sentiment that seemed, but was not, remorse. I went so far as to regret the loss of the animal, and to look about me, among the vile haunts which I now habitually frequented, for another pet of the same species, and of somewhat similar appearance, with which to supply its place.

One night as I sat half stupefied in a den of more than infamy, my attention was suddenly drawn to some black object reposing upon the head of one of the immense hogsheads of gin or of rum which constituted the chief furniture of the apartment. I had been looking steadily at the top of this hogshead for some minutes, and what now caused me surprise was the fact that I had not sooner perceived the object thereupon. I approached it, and touched it with my hand. It was a black cat, a very large one, fully as large as Pluto, and closely resembling him in every respect but one. Pluto had not a white hair upon any portion of his body; but this cat had a large, although indefinite, splotch of white, covering nearly the whole region of the breast.

Upon my touching him, he immediately arose, purred loudly, rubbed against my hand, and appeared delighted with my notice. This, then, was the very creature of which I was in search. I at once offered to purchase it of the landlord; but this person made no claim to it—knew nothing of it—had never seen it before.

I continued my caresses; and when I prepared to go home, the animal evinced a disposition to accompany me. I permitted it to do so, occasionally stooping and patting it as I proceeded. When it reached the house it domesticated itself at once, and became immediately a great favorite with my wife.

For my own part, I soon found a dislike to it arising within me. This was just the reverse of what I had anticipated; but—I know not how or why it was—its evident fondness for myself rather disgusted and annoyed. By slow degrees these feelings of disgust and annoyance rose into the bitterness of hatred. I avoided the creature; a certain sense of shame, and the remembrance of my former deed of cruelty, preventing me from physically abusing it. I did not for some weeks strike or otherwise violently ill-use it; but gradually—very gradually—I came to look upon it with unutterable loathing, and to flee silently from its odious presence, as from the breath of a pestilence.

What added, no doubt, to my hatred of the beast, was the discovery, on the morning after I brought it home, that, like Pluto, it also had been deprived of one of its eyes. This circumstance, however, only endeared it to my wife, who, as I have already said, possessed, in a high degree, that humanity of feeling which had once been my distinguishing trait, and the source of many of my simplest and purest pleasures.

With my aversion to this cat, however, its partiality for myself seemed to increase. It followed my footsteps with a pertinacity which it would be difficult to make the reader comprehend. Whenever I sat, it would crouch beneath my chair, or spring upon my knees, covering me with its loathsome caresses. If I arose to walk it would get between my feet, and thus nearly throw me down; or, fastening its long and sharp claws in my dress, clamber in this manner to my breast. At such times, although I longed to destroy it with a blow, I was yet withheld from so doing, partly by a memory of my former crime, but chiefly—let me confess it at once—by absolute *dread* of the beast.

This dread was not exactly a dread of physical evil—and yet I should be at a loss how otherwise to define it. I am almost ashamed to own—yes, even in this felon's cell I am almost ashamed to own—that the terror and horror with which the animal inspired me had been heightened by one of the merest chimeras it would be possible to conceive. My wife had called my attention more than once to the character of the mark of white hair of which I have spoken, and which constituted the sole visible difference between the strange beast and the one I had destroyed. The reader will remember that this mark, although large, had been originally very indefinite; but by slow degrees—degrees nearly imperceptible, and which for a long time my Reason struggled to reject as fanciful—it had at length assumed a rigorous distinctness of outline. It was now the representation of an object that I shudder to name—and for this, above all, I loathed and dreaded and would have rid myself of the monster had I dared—it was now, I say, the image of a hideous—of a ghastly thing—of the *Gallows!*—Oh, mournful and terrible engine of Horror and of Crime—of Agony and of Death!

And now was I indeed wretched beyond the wretchedness of mere Humanity. And *a brute beast*—whose fellow I had contemptuously destroyed—*a brute beast* to work out for *me*—for me, a man fashioned in the image of the High God—so much of insufferable woe! Alas! Neither by day nor by night knew I the blessing of rest any more! During the former the creature left me no moment alone; and, in the latter, I started hourly from dreams of unutterable fear, to find the hot breath of *the thing* upon my face, and its vast weight an incarnate Nightmare that I had no power to shake off—incumbent eternally upon my *heart*!

Beneath the pressure of torments such as these, the feeble remnant of the good within me succumbed. Evil thoughts became my sole intimates—the darkest and most evil of thoughts. The moodiness of my usual temper increased to hatred of all things and of all mankind; while, from the sudden, frequent, and ungovernable outbursts of a fury to which I now blindly abandoned myself, my uncomplaining wife—alas!—was the most usual and the most patient of sufferers.

One day she accompanied me, upon some household errand, into the cellar of the old building which our poverty compelled us to inhabit. The cat followed me down the steep stairs, and, nearly throwing me headlong, exasperated me to madness. Uplifting an axe, and, forgetting in my wrath the childish dread which had hitherto stayed my mind, I aimed a blow at the animal, which of course would have proved instantly fatal had it descended as I wished. But this blow was arrested by the hand of my wife. Goaded, by the interference, into a rage more than demoniacal, I withdrew my arm from her grasp, and buried the axe in her brain. She fell dead upon the spot, without a groan.

This hideous murder accomplished, I set myself forthwith, and with entire deliberation, to the task of concealing the body. I knew that I could not remove it from the house, either by day or by night, without the risk of being observed by the neighbors. Many projects entered my mind. At one period I thought of cutting the corpse into minute fragments and destroying them by fire. At another, I resolved to dig a grave for it in the floor of the cellar. Again, I deliberated about casting it in the well in the yard—about packing it in a box, as if merchandise, with the usual arrangements, and so getting a porter to take it from the house. Finally I hit upon what I considered a far better expedient than either of these. I determined to wall it up in the cellar—as the monks of the Middle Ages are recorded to have walled up their victims.

For a purpose such as this the cellar was well adapted. Its walls were loosely constructed, and had lately been plastered throughout with rough plaster, which the dampness of the atmosphere had prevented from hardening. Moreover, in one of the walls was a projection, caused by a false chimney, or fireplace, that had been filled up, and made to resemble the rest of the cellar. I made no doubt that I could readily displace the bricks at this point, insert the corpse, and wall the whole up as before, so that no eye could detect anything suspicious.

And in this calculation I was not deceived. By means of a crowbar I easily dislodged the bricks; and, having carefully deposited the body against the inner wall, I propped it in that position, while with little trouble I relaid the whole structure as it originally stood. Having procured mortar, sand, and hair, with every possible precaution, I prepared a plaster which could not be distinguished from the old, and with this I very carefully went over the new brickwork. When I had finished, I felt satisfied that all was right. The wall did not present the slightest appearance of having been disturbed. The rubbish on the floor was picked up with the minutest care. I looked around triumphantly, and said to myself, "Here at least, then, my labor has not been in vain."

My next step was to look for the beast which had been the cause of so much wretchedness; for I had at length firmly resolved to put it to death. Had I been able to meet with it, at the moment, there could have been no doubt of its fate, but it appeared that the crafty animal had been alarmed at the violence of my previous anger, and forbore to present itself in my present mood. It is impossible to describe, or to imagine, the deep, the blissful sense of relief which the absence of the detested creature occasioned in my bosom. It did not make its appearance during the night; and thus for one night at least since its introduction into the house, I soundly and tranquilly slept—ay, *slept* even with the burden of murder upon my soul!

The second and third day passed, and still my tormentor came not. Once again I breathed as a free man. The monster, in terror, had fled the premises forever! I should behold it no more! My happiness was supreme! The guilt of my dark deed disturbed me but little. Some few inquiries had been made, but these had been readily answered. Even a search had been instituted; but of course nothing was to be discovered. I looked upon my future felicity as secured.

Upon the fourth day of the assassination, a party of the police came over unexpectedly into the house, and proceeded again to make rigorous investigation of the premises. Secure, however, in the inscrutability of my place of concealment, I felt no embarrassment whatever. The officers bade me accompany them in their search. They left no nook or corner unexplored. At length, for the third or fourth time, they descended into the cellar. I quivered not in a muscle. My heart beat calmly as that of one who slumbers in innocence. I walked the cellar from end to end. I folded my arms upon my bosom, and roamed easily to and fro. The police were thoroughly satisfied, and prepared to depart. The glee of my heart was too strong to be restrained. I burned to say, if but one word, by way of triumph, and to render doubly sure their assurance of my guiltlessness.

"Gentlemen," I said at last, as the party ascended the steps, "I delight to have allayed your suspicions. I wish you all health, and a little more courtesy. By the by, gentlemen, this—this is a very well constructed house." (In the rabid desire to say something easily, I scarcely knew what I uttered at all.) "I may say an *excellently* well constructed house. These walls—are you going, gentlemen?—these walls are solidly put together;" and here, through the mere frenzy of bravado, I rapped heavily, with a cane which I held in my hand, upon that very portion of the brickwork behind which stood the corpse of the wife of my bosom.

But may God shield and deliver me from the fangs of the Arch-Fiend! No sooner had the reverberation of my blows sunk into silence than I was answered by a voice from within the tomb!—By a cry, at first muffled and broken, like the sobbing of a child, and then quickly swelling into one long, loud, and continuous scream, utterly anomalous and inhuman—a howl—a wailing shriek, half of horror and half of triumph, such as might have arisen only out of hell, conjointly from the throats of the damned in their agony and of the demons that exult in the damnation.

Of my own thoughts it is folly to speak. Swooning, I staggered to the opposite wall. For one instant the party upon the stairs remained motionless, through extremity of terror and of awe. In the next, a dozen stout arms were toiling at the wall. It fell bodily. The corpse, already greatly decayed and clotted with gore, stood erect before the eyes of the spectators. Upon its head, with red extended mouth and solitary eye of fire, sat the hideous beast whose craft had seduced me into murder, and whose informing voice had consigned me to the hangman. I had walled the monster up within the tomb!

THE PREMATURE BURIAL

There are certain themes of which the interest is all-absorbing but which are too entirely horrible for the purposes of legitimate fiction. These the mere romanticist must eschew, if he do not wish to offend, or to disgust. They are with propriety handled only when the severity and majesty of truth sanctify and sustain them. We thrill, for example, with the most intense of "pleasurable pain" over the accounts of the Passage of the Beresina, of the Earthquake at Lisbon, of the Plague at London, of the Massacre of St. Bartholomew, or of the stifling of the hundred and twenty-three prisoners in the Black Hole at Calcutta. But, in these accounts, it is the fact—it is the reality—it is the history which excites. As inventions, we should regard them with simple abhorrence.

I have mentioned some few of the more prominent and august calamities on record; but in these it is extent, not less than the character of the calamity, which so vividly impresses the fancy. I need not remind the reader that, from the long and weird catalogue of human miseries, I might have selected many individual instances more replete with essential suffering than any of these vast generalities of disaster. The true wretchedness, indeed—the ultimate woe—is particular, not diffuse. That the ghastly extremes of agony are endured by man the unit, and never by man the mass—for this let us thank a merciful God!

To be buried while alive is, beyond question, the most terrific of these extremes which has ever fallen to the lot of mere mortality. That it has frequently, very frequently, so fallen will scarcely be denied by those who think. The boundaries which divide Life from Death are at best shadowy and vague. Who shall say where the one ends, and where the other begins? We know that there are diseases in which occur total cessations of all the apparent functions of vitality, and yet in which these cessations are merely suspensions, properly so called. They are only temporary pauses in the incomprehensible mechanism. A certain period elapses, and some unseen mysterious principle again sets in motion the magic pinions and the wizard wheels. The silver cord was not forever loosed, nor the golden bowl irreparably broken. But where, meantime, was the soul?

Apart, however, from the inevitable conclusion, *a priori*, that such causes must produce such effects—that the well-known occurrence of such cases of suspended animation must naturally give rise, now and then, to premature interments—apart from this consideration, we have the direct testimony of medical and ordinary experience to prove that a vast number of such interments have actually taken place. I might refer at once, if necessary, to a hundred well-authenticated instances. One of very remarkable character, and of which the circumstances may be fresh in the memory of some of my readers, occurred, not very long ago, in the neighboring city of Baltimore, where it occasioned a painful, intense, and widely extended excitement. The wife of one of the most respectable citizens—a lawyer of eminence and a member of Congress—was seized with a sudden and unaccountable illness, which completely baffled the skill of her physicians. After much suffering she died, or was supposed to die. No one suspected, indeed, or had reason to suspect; that she was not actually dead. She presented all the ordinary appearances of death. The face assumed the usual pinched and sunken outline. The lips were of the usual marble pallor. The eyes were lusterless. There was no warmth.

Pulsation had ceased. For three days the body was preserved unburied, during which it had acquired a stony rigidity. The funeral, in short, was hastened, on account of the rapid advance of what was supposed to be decomposition.

The lady was deposited in her family vault, which, for three subsequent years, was undisturbed. At the expiration of this term it was opened for the reception of a sarcophagus—but alas! How fearful a shock awaited the husband, who, personally, threw open the door! As its portals swung outwardly back, some white-appareled object fell rattling within his arms. It was the skeleton of his wife in her yet unmolded shroud.

A careful investigation rendered it evident that she had revived within two days after her entombment; that her struggles within the coffin had caused it to fall from a ledge, or shelf, to the floor, where it was so broken as to permit her escape. A lamp which had been accidentally left full of oil, within the tomb, was found empty; it might have been exhausted, however, by evaporation. On the uppermost of the steps which led down into the dread chamber was a large fragment of the coffin, with which it seemed that she had endeavored to arrest attention by striking the iron door. While thus occupied, she probably swooned, or possibly died, through sheer terror; and in falling, her shroud became entangled in some iron-work which projected interiorly. Thus she remained, and thus she rotted, erect.

In the year 1810, a case of living inhumation happened in France, attended with circumstances which go far to warrant the assertion that truth is, indeed, stranger than fiction. The heroine of the story was a Mademoiselle Victorine Lafourcade, a young girl of illustrious family, of wealth, and of great personal beauty. Among her numerous suitors was Julien Bossuet, a poor *littérateur*, or jour-nalist, of Paris. His talents and general amiability had recommended him to the notice of the heiress, by whom he seems to have been truly beloved; but her pride of birth decided her, finally, to reject him, and to wed a Monsieur Renelle, a banker and a diplomatist of some eminence. After marriage, however, this gentleman neglected, and, perhaps, even more positively ill-treated her. Having passed with him some wretched years, she died—at least her condition so closely resembled death as to deceive everyone who saw her. She was buried—not in a vault, but in an ordinary grave in the village of her nativity. Filled with despair, and still inflamed by the memory of a profound attachment, the lover journeys from the capital to the remote province in which the village lies, with the romantic purpose of disinterring the corpse, and possessing himself of its luxuriant tresses. He reaches the grave. At midnight he unearths the coffin, opens it, and is in the act of detaching the hair, when he is arrested by the unclosing of the beloved eyes. In fact, the lady had been buried alive. Vitality had not altogether departed, and she was aroused by the caresses of her lover from the lethargy which had been mistaken for death. He bore her frantically to his lodgings in the village. He employed certain powerful restoratives suggested by no little medical learning. In fine, she revived. She recognized her preserver. She remained with him until, by slow degrees, she fully recovered her original health. Her woman's heart was not adamant, and this last lesson of love sufficed to soften it. She bestowed it upon Bossuet. She returned no more to her husband, but, concealing from him her resurrection, fled with her lover to America. Twenty years afterward, the two returned to France, in the persuasion that time had so greatly altered the lady's appearance that her friends would be unable to recognize her. They were mistaken, however; for at the first meeting, Monsieur Renelle did actually recognize and make claim to his wife. This claim she resisted, and a judicial tribunal sustained her in her resistance, deciding that the peculiar circumstances, with the long lapse of years, had extinguished, not only equitably, but legally, the authority of the husband.

The *Chirurgical Journal* of Leipzig, a periodical of high authority and merit, which some American booksellers would do well to translate and republish, records in a late number a very distressing event of the character in question.

An officer of artillery, a man of gigantic stature and of robust health, being thrown from an unmanageable horse, received a very severe contusion upon the head, which rendered him insensible at once; the skull was slightly fractured, but no immediate danger was apprehended. Trepanning was accomplished successfully. He was bled, and many other of the ordinary means of relief were adopted. Gradually, however, he fell into a more and more hopeless state of stupor, and, finally, it was thought that he died.

The weather was warm, and he was buried with indecent haste in one of the public cemeteries. His funeral took place on Thursday. On the Sunday following, the grounds of the cemetery were, as usual, much thronged with visitors, and about noon an intense excitement was created by the declaration of a peasant that, while sitting upon the grave of the officer, he had distinctly felt a commotion of the earth, as if occasioned by some one struggling beneath. At first little attention was paid to the man's asseveration; but his evident terror, and the dogged obstinacy with which he persisted in his story, had at length their natural effects upon the crowd. Spades were hurriedly procured, and the grave, which was shamefully shallow, was in a few minutes so far thrown open that the head of its occupant appeared. He was then seemingly dead; but he sat nearly erect within his coffin, the lid of which, in his furious struggles, he had partially uplifted.

He was forthwith conveyed to the nearest hospital, and there pronounced to be still living, although in an asphytic condition. After some hours he revived, recognized individuals of his acquaintance, and, in broken sentences, spoke of his agonies in the grave.

From what he related, it was clear that he must have been conscious of life for more than an hour, while inhumed, before lapsing into insensibility. The grave was carelessly and loosely filled with an exceedingly porous soil; and thus some air was necessarily admitted. He heard the footsteps of the crowd overhead, and endeavored to make himself heard in turn. It was the tumult within the grounds of the cemetery, he said, which appeared to awaken him from a deep sleep, but no sooner was he awake than he became fully aware of the awful horrors of his position.

This patient, it is recorded, was doing well, and seemed to be in a fair way of ultimate recovery, but fell a victim to the quackeries of medical experiment. The galvanic battery was applied, and he suddenly expired in one of those ecstatic paroxysms which, occasionally, it superinduces.

The mention of the galvanic battery, nevertheless, recalls to my memory a well-known and very extraordinary case in point, where its action proved the means of restoring to animation a young attorney of London, who had been interred for two days. This occurred in 1831, and created, at the time, a very profound sensation wherever it was made the subject of converse.

The patient, Mr Edward Stapleton, had died, apparently, of typhus fever, accompanied with some anomalous symptoms which had excited the curiosity of his medical attendants. Upon his seeming decease, his friends were requested to sanction a post-mortem examination, but declined to permit it. As often happens, when such refusals are made, the practitioners resolve to disinter the body and dissect it at leisure, in private. Arrangements were easily effected with some of the numerous corps of body-snatchers with which London abounds; and, upon the third night after the funeral, the supposed corpse was unearthed from a grave eight feet deep, and deposited in the operating chamber of one of the private hospitals.

An incision of some extent had been actually made in the abdomen, when the fresh and undecayed appearance of the subject suggested an application of the battery. One experiment succeeded another, and the customary effects supervened, with nothing to characterize them in any respect, except, upon one or two occasions, a more than ordinary degree of lifelikeness in the convulsive action.

It grew late. The day was about to dawn; and it was thought expedient, at length, to proceed at once to the dissection. A student, however, was especially desirous of testing a theory of his own, and insisted upon applying the battery to one of the pectoral muscles. A rough gash was made, and a wire hastily brought in contact; when the patient, with a hurried but quite unconvulsive movement, arose from the table, stepped into the middle of the floor, gazed about him uneasily for a few seconds, and then—spoke. What he said was unintelligible; but words were uttered; the syllabification was distinct. Having spoken, he fell heavily to the floor.

For some moments all were paralyzed with awe—but the urgency of the case soon restored them their presence of mind. It was seen that Mr. Stapleton was alive, although in a swoon. Upon exhibition of ether he revived and was rapidly restored to health, and to the society of his friends—from whom, however, all knowledge of his resuscitation was withheld, until a relapse was no longer to be apprehended. Their wonder—their rapturous astonishment—may be conceived.

The most thrilling peculiarity of this incident, nevertheless, is involved in what Mr. S. himself asserts. He declares that at no period was he altogether insensible—that, dully and confusedly, he was aware of everything which happened to him, from the moment in which he was pronounced *dead* by his physicians, to that in which he fell swooning to the floor of the hospital. "I am alive," were the uncomprehended words which, upon recognizing the locality of the dissecting-room, he had endeavored, in his extremity, to utter.

It were an easy matter to multiply such histories as these—but I forbear—for, indeed, we have no need of such to establish the fact that premature interments occur. When we reflect how very rarely, from the nature of the case, we have it in our power to detect them, we must admit that they may *frequently* occur without our cognizance. Scarcely, in truth, is a graveyard ever encroached upon, for any purpose, to any great extent, that skeletons are not found in postures which suggest the most fearful of suspicions.

Fearful indeed the suspicion—but more fearful the doom! It may be asserted, without hesitation, that *no* event is so terribly well adapted to inspire the supremeness of bodily and of mental distress, as is burial before death. The unendurable oppression of the lungs—the stifling fumes of the damp earth—the clinging to the death garments—the rigid embrace of the narrow house—the blackness of the absolute Night—the silence like a sea that overwhelms—the unseen but palpable presence of the Conqueror Worm—these things, with the thoughts of the air and grass above, with memory of dear friends who would fly to save us if but informed of our fate, and with consciousness that of this fate they can *never* be informed—that our hopeless portion is that of the really dead—these considerations, I say, carry into the heart, which still palpitates, a degree of appalling and intolerable horror from which the most daring imagination must recoil. We know of nothing so agonizing upon Earth—we can dream of nothing half so hideous in the realms of the nethermost Hell. And thus all narratives upon this topic have an interest profound; an interest, nevertheless, which, through the sacred awe of the topic itself, very properly and very peculiarly depends upon our conviction of the *truth* of the matter narrated. What I have now to tell is of my own actual knowledge—of my own positive and personal experience.

For several years I had been subject to attacks of the singular disorder which physicians have agreed to term catalepsy, in default of a more definite title. Although both the immediate and the predisposing causes, and even the actual diagnosis of this disease are still mysterious, its obvious and apparent character is sufficiently well understood. Its variations seem to be chiefly of degree. Sometimes the patient lies, for a day only, or even for a shorter period, in a species of exaggerated lethargy. He is senseless and externally motionless; but the pulsation of the heart is still faintly perceptible; some traces of warmth remain; a slight color lingers within the center of the cheek; and, upon application of a mirror to the lips, we can detect a torpid, unequal, and vacillating action of the lungs. Then again the duration of the trance is for weeks—even for months; while the closest scrutiny, and the most rigorous medical tests, fail to establish any material distinction between the state of the sufferer and what we conceive of absolute death. Very usually he is saved from premature interment solely by the knowledge of his friends that he has been previously subject to catalepsy, by the consequent suspicion excited, and, above all, by the non-appearance of decay. The advances of the malady are luckily, gradual. The first manifestations, although marked, are unequivocal. The fits grow successively more and more distinctive, and endure each for a longer term than the preceding. In this lies the principal security from inhumation. The unfortunate whose *first* attack should be of the extreme character which is occasionally seen, would almost inevitably be consigned alive to the tomb.

My own case differed in no important particular from those mentioned in medical books. Sometimes, without any apparent cause, I sank, little by little, into a condition of semi-syncope, or half swoon; and, in this condition, without pain, without ability to stir, or, strictly speaking, to think, but with a dull lethargic consciousness of life and of the presence of those who surrounded my bed, I remained, until the crisis of the disease restored me, suddenly, to perfect sensation. At other times I was quickly and impetuously smitten. I grew sick, and numb, and chilly, and dizzy, and so fell prostrate at once. Then, for weeks, all was void, and black, and silent, and Nothing became the universe. Total annihilation could be no more. From these latter attacks I awoke, however, with a gradation slow in proportion to the suddenness of the seizure. Just as the day dawns to the friendless and houseless beggar who roams the streets throughout the long desolate winter night—just so tardily—just so wearily—just so cheerily came back the light of the Soul to me.

Apart from the tendency to trance, however, my general health appeared to be good; nor could I perceive that it was at all affected by the one prevalent malady—unless, indeed, an idiosyncrasy in my ordinary sleep may be looked upon as superinduced. Upon awakening from slumber, I could never gain, at once, thorough possession of my senses, and always remained, for many minutes, in much bewilderment and perplexity—the mental faculties in general, but the memory in especial, being in a condition of absolute abeyance.

In all that I endured there was no physical suffering, but of moral distress an infinitude. My fancy grew charnel. I talked "of worms, of tombs, of epitaphs." I was lost in reveries of death, and the idea of premature burial held continual possession of my brain. The ghastly Danger to which I was subjected haunted me day and night. In the former, the torture of meditation was excessive; in the latter, supreme. When the grim Darkness overspread the Earth, then, with every horror of thought, I shook—shook as the quivering plumes upon the hearse. When Nature could endure wakefulness no longer, it was with a struggle that I consented to sleep—for I shuddered to reflect that, upon awaking, I might find myself the tenant of a grave. And when, finally, I sank into slumber, it was only to rush at once into a world of phantasms, above which, with vast, sable, overshadowing wings, hovered, predominant, the one sepulchral Idea.

From the innumerable images of gloom which thus oppressed me in dreams, I select for record but a solitary vision. Methought I was immersed in a cataleptic trance of more than usual duration and profundity. Suddenly there came an icy hand upon my forehead, and an impatient, gibbering voice whispered the word "Arise!" within my ear.

I sat erect. The darkness was total. I could not see the figure of him who had aroused me. I could call to mind neither the period at which I had fallen into the trance, nor the locality in which I then lay. While I remained motionless, and busied in endeavors to collect my thoughts, the cold hand grasped me fiercely by the wrist, shaking it petulantly, while the gibbering voice said again:

"Arise! Did I not bid thee arise?"

"And who," I demanded, "art thou?"

"I have no name in the regions which I inhabit," replied the voice, mournfully; "I was mortal, but am fiend. I am merciless, but am pitiful. Thou dost feel that I shudder. My teeth chatter as I speak, yet it is not with the chilliness of the night—of the night without end. But this hideousness is insufferable. How canst *thou* tranquilly sleep? I cannot rest for the cry of these great agonies. These sights are more than I can bear. Get thee up! Come with me into the outer Night, and let me unfold to thee the graves. Is not this a spectacle of woe?—Behold!"

I looked; and the unseen figure, which still grasped me by the wrist, had caused to be thrown open the graves of all mankind; and from each issued the faint phosphoric radiance of decay; so that I could see into the innermost recesses, and there view the shrouded bodies in their sad and solemn slumbers with the worm. But alas! The real sleepers were fewer, by many millions, than those who slumbered not at all; and there was a feeble struggling; and there was a general and sad unrest; and from out the depths of the countless pits there came a melancholy rustling from the garments of the buried. And of those who seemed tranquilly to repose, I saw that a vast number had changed, in a greater or less degree, the rigid and uneasy position in which they had originally been entombed. And the voice again said to me as I gazed:

"Is it not—oh!—is it not a pitiful sight?" But, before I could find words to reply, the figure had ceased to grasp my wrist, the phosphoric lights expired, and the graves were closed with a sudden violence, while from out them arose a tumult of despairing cries, saying again: "Is it not—Oh, God!—is it *not* a very pitiful sight?"

Phantasies such as these, presenting themselves at night, extended their terrific influence far into my waking hours. My nerves became thoroughly unstrung, and I fell a prey to perpetual horror. I hesitated to ride, or to walk, or to indulge in any exercise that would carry me from home. In fact, I no longer dared trust myself out of the immediate presence of those who were aware of my proneness to catalepsy lest, falling into one of my usual fits, I should be buried before my real condition could be ascertained. I doubted the care, the fidelity of my dearest friends. I dreaded that, in some trance of more than customary duration, they might be prevailed upon to regard me as irrecoverable. I even went so far as to fear that, as I occasioned much trouble, they might be glad to consider any very protracted attack as sufficient excuse for getting rid of me altogether. It was in vain they endeavored to reassure me by the most solemn promises. I exacted the most sacred oaths, that under no circumstances they would bury me until decomposition had so materially advanced as to render further preservation impossible. And, even then, my mortal terrors would listen to no reason—would accept no consolation. I entered into a series of elaborate precautions. Among other things, I had the family vault so remodeled as to admit of being readily opened from within. The slightest pressure upon a long lever that extended far into the tomb would cause the iron portals to fly back. There were arrangements also for the free admission of air and light, and convenient receptacles for food and water, within immediate reach of the coffin intended for my reception. This coffin was warmly and softly padded, and was provided with a lid, fashioned upon the principle of the vault door, with the addition of springs so contrived that the feeblest movement of the body would be sufficient to set it at liberty. Besides all this, there was suspended from the roof of the

tomb, a large bell, the rope of which, it was designed, should extend
through a hole in the coffin, and so be fastened to one of the hands
of the corpse. But, alas, what avails the vigilance against the Destiny
of man? Not even these well-contrived securities sufficed to save
from the uttermost agonies of living inhumation a wretch to these
agonies foredoomed!

There arrived an epoch—as often before there had arrived—in
which I found myself emerging from total unconsciousness into the
first feeble and indefinite sense of existence. Slowly—with a tortoise
gradation—approached the faint gray dawn of the psychal day. A
torpid uneasiness. An apathetic endurance of dull pain. No care—no
hope—no effort. Then, after a long interval, a ringing in the ears;
then, after a lapse still longer, a pricking or tingling sensation in the
extremities; then a seemingly eternal period of pleasurable quiescence, during which the awakening feelings are struggling into
thought; then a brief re-sinking into nonentity; then a sudden recovery.
At length the slight quivering of an eyelid, and immediately thereupon, an electric shock of a terror, deadly and indefinite, which sends
the blood in torrents from the temples to the heart. And now the first
positive effort to think. And now the first endeavor to remember.
And now a partial and evanescent success. And now the memory
has so far regained its dominion, that, in some measure, I am cognizant of my state. I feel that I am not awaking from ordinary sleep.
I recollect that I have been subject to catalepsy. And now, at last, as
if by the rush of an ocean, my shuddering spirit is overwhelmed by
the one grim Danger—by the one spectral and ever-prevalent idea.

For some minutes after this fancy possessed me, I remained
without motion. And why? I could not summon courage to move. I
dared not make the effort which was to satisfy me of my fate—and
yet there was something at my heart which whispered me it *was*
sure. Despair—such as no other species of wretchedness ever calls
into being—despair alone urged me, after long irresolution, to uplift

the heavy lids of my eyes. I uplifted them. It was dark—all dark. I knew that the fit was over. I knew that the crisis of my disorder had long passed. I knew that I had now fully recovered the use of my visual faculties—and yet it was dark—all dark—the intense and utter raylessness of the Night that endureth for evermore.

I endeavored to shriek; and my lips and my parched tongue moved convulsively together in the attempt—but no voice issued from the cavernous lungs, which, oppressed as if by the weight of some incumbent mountain, gasped and palpitated, with the heart, at every elaborate and struggling inspiration.

The movement of the jaws, in this effort to cry aloud, showed me that they were bound up, as is usual with the dead. I felt, too, that I lay upon some hard substance; and by something similar my sides were, also, closely compressed. So far, I had not ventured to stir any of my limbs—but now I violently threw up my arms, which had been lying at length, with the wrists crossed. They struck a solid wooden substance, which extended above my person at an elevation of not more than six inches from my face. I could no longer doubt that I reposed within a coffin at last.

And now, amid all my infinite miseries, came sweetly the cherub Hope—for I thought of my precautions. I writhed, and made spasmodic exertions to force open the lid: it would not move. I felt my wrists for the bell-rope: it was not to be found. And now the Comforter fled for ever, and a still sterner Despair reigned triumphant; for I could not help perceiving the absence of the paddings which I had so carefully prepared—and then, too, there came suddenly to my nostrils the strong peculiar odor of moist earth. The conclusion was irresistible. I was *not* within the vault. I had fallen into a trance, while absent from home—while among strangers—when, or how, I could not remember—and it was they who had buried me as a dog—nailed up in some common coffin—and thrust, deep, deep, and for ever, into some ordinary and nameless *grave*.

As this awful conviction forced itself, thus, into the innermost chambers of my soul, I once again struggled to cry aloud. And in this second endeavor I succeeded. A long, wild, and continuous shriek, or yell of agony, resounded through the realms of the subterranean Night.

"Hillo! Hillo, there!" said a gruff voice, in reply.

"What the devil's the matter now?" said a second.

"Get out o' that!" said a third.

"What do you mean by yowling in that ere kind of style, like a catty-mount?" said a fourth; and hereupon I was seized and shaken without ceremony, for several minutes, by a junto of very rough-looking individuals. They did not arouse me from my slumber—for I was wide-awake when I screamed—but they restored me to the full possession of my memory.

This adventure occurred near Richmond, in Virginia. Accompanied by a friend, I had proceeded, upon a gunning expedition, some miles down the banks of the James River. Night approached, and we were overtaken by a storm. The cabin of a small sloop lying at anchor in the stream, and laden with garden mould, afforded us the only available shelter. We made the best of it, and passed the night on board. I slept in one of the only two berths in the vessel—and the berths of a sloop of sixty or seventy tons need scarcely be described. That which I occupied had no bedding of any kind. Its extreme width was eighteen inches. The distance of its bottom from the deck overhead was precisely the same. I found it a matter of exceeding difficulty to squeeze myself in. Nevertheless, I slept soundly; and the whole of my vision— for it was no dream, and no nightmare—arose naturally from the circumstances of my position—from my ordinary bias of thought—and from the difficulty, to which I have alluded, of collecting my senses, and especially of regaining my memory, for a long time after awaking from slumber. The men who shook me were the crew of the sloop, and some laborers engaged to unload it. From the load itself came the earthy smell. The bandage about the jaws was a silk handkerchief in which I had bound up my head, in default of my customary nightcap.

The tortures endured, however, were indubitably quite equal, for the time, to those of actual sepulture. They were fearfully—they were inconceivably hideous; but out of Evil proceeded Good; for their very excess wrought in my spirit an inevitable revulsion. My soul acquired tone—acquired temper. I went abroad. I took vigorous exercise. I breathed the free air of Heaven. I thought upon other subjects than Death. I discarded my medical books. "Buchan" I burned. I read no *Night Thoughts*—no fustian about churchyards—no bugaboo tales—*such as this*. In short I became a new man, and lived a man's life. From that memorable night, I dismissed forever my charnel apprehensions, and with them vanished the cataleptic disorder, of which, perhaps, they had been less the consequence than the cause.

There are moments when, even to the sober eye of Reason, the world of our sad Humanity may assume the semblance of a Hell—but the imagination of man is no Carathis, to explore with impunity its every cavern. Alas! The grim legion of sepulchral terrors cannot be regarded as altogether fanciful—but, like the Demons in whose company Afrasiab made his voyage down the Oxus, they must sleep, or they will devour us—they must be suffered to slumber, or we perish.

THE OBLONG BOX

Some years ago, I engaged passage from Charleston, SC, to the city of New York, in the fine packet-ship *Independence*, Captain Hardy. We were to sail on the fifteenth of the month (June), weather permitting; and, on the fourteenth, I went on board to arrange some matters in my state-room.

I found that we were to have a great many passengers, including a more than usual number of ladies. On the list were several of my acquaintances; and among other names, I was rejoiced to see that of Mr. Cornelius Wyatt, a young artist, for whom I entertained feelings of warm friendship. He had been with me a fellow-student at C—— University, where we were very much together. He had the ordinary temperament of genius, and was a compound of misanthropy, sensibility, and enthusiasm. To these qualities he united the warmest and truest heart which ever beat in a human bosom.

I observed that his name was carded upon *three* state-rooms; and, upon again referring to the list of passengers, I found that he had engaged a passage for himself, wife, and two sisters—his own. The state-rooms were sufficiently roomy, and each had two berths, one above the other. These berths, to be sure, were so exceedingly narrow as to be insufficient for more than one person;

still, I could not comprehend why there were *three* state-rooms for these four persons. I was, just at that epoch, in one of those moody frames of mind which makes a man abnormally inquisitive about trifles: and I confess, with shame, that I busied myself in a variety of ill-bred and preposterous conjectures about this matter of the supernumerary state-room. It was no business of mine, to be sure; but with none the less pertinacity did I occupy myself in attempts to solve the enigma. At last I reached a conclusion which wrought in me great wonder why I had not arrived at it before. "It is a servant, of course," I said; "what a fool I am, not sooner to have thought of so obvious a solution!" And then I again repaired to the list—but here I saw distinctly that *no* servant was to come with the party: although, in fact, it had been the original design to bring one—for the words "and servant" had been first written and then overscored. "Oh, extra baggage, to be sure," I now said to myself—"something he wishes not to be put in the hold—something to be kept under his own eye—ah, I have it—a painting or so—and this is what he has been bargaining about with Nicolino, the Italian Jew." This idea satisfied me, and I dismissed my curiosity for the nonce.

Wyatt's two sisters I knew very well, and most amiable and clever girls they were. His wife he had newly married, and I had never yet seen her. He had often talked about her in my presence, however, and in his usual style of enthusiasm. He described her as of surpassing beauty, wit, and accomplishment. I was, therefore, quite anxious to make her acquaintance.

On the day in which I visited the ship (the fourteenth), Wyatt and party were also to visit it—so the captain informed me—and I waited on board an hour longer than I had designed, in hope of being presented to the bride; but then an apology came. "Mrs. W. was a little indisposed, and would decline coming on board until to-morrow, at the hour of sailing."

The morrow having arrived, I was going from my hotel to the wharf, when Captain Hardy met me and said that, "owing to circumstances" (a stupid but convenient phrase), he rather thought the *Independence* would not sail for a day or two, and that when all was ready, he would send up and let me know. This I thought strange, for there was a stiff southerly breeze; but as "the circumstances" were not forthcoming, although I pumped for them with much perseverance, I had nothing to do but to return home and digest my impatience at leisure.

I did not receive the expected message from the captain for nearly a week. It came at length, however, and I immediately went on board. The ship was crowded with passengers, and everything was in the bustle attendant upon making sail. Wyatt's party arrived about ten minutes after myself. There were the two sisters, the bride, and the artist—the latter in one of his customary fits of moody misanthropy. I was too well used to these, however, to pay them any special attention. He did not even introduce me to his wife—this courtesy devolving, perforce, upon his sister Marian—a very sweet and intelligent girl, who, in a few hurried words, made us acquainted.

Mrs. Wyatt had been closely veiled; and when she raised her veil, in acknowledging my bow, I confess that I was very profoundly astonished. I should have been much more so, however, had not long experience advised me not to trust, with too implicit a reliance, the enthusiastic descriptions of my friend, the artist, when indulging in comments upon the loveliness of woman. When beauty was the theme, I well knew with what facility he soared into the regions of the purely ideal.

The truth is, I could not help regarding Mrs. Wyatt as a decidedly plain-looking woman. If not positively ugly, she was not, I think, very far from it. She was dressed, however, in exquisite taste—and then I had no doubt that she had captivated my friend's heart by the more enduring graces of the intellect and soul. She said very few words, and passed at once into her state-room with Mr. W.

My old inquisitiveness now returned. There was *no* servant—*that* was a settled point. I looked, therefore, for the extra baggage. After some delay, a cart arrived at the wharf, with an oblong pine box, which was everything that seemed to be expected. Immediately upon its arrival we made sail, and in a short time were safely over the bar and standing out to sea.

The box in question was, as I say, oblong. It was about six feet in length by two and a half in breadth; I observed it attentively, and like to be precise. Now this shape was *peculiar*; and no sooner had I seen it than I took credit to myself for the accuracy of my guessing. I had reached the conclusion, it will be remembered, that the extra baggage of my friend, the artist, would prove to be pictures, or at least a picture; for I knew he had been for several weeks in conference with Nicolino— and now here was a box, which, from its shape, could possibly contain nothing in the world but a copy of Leonardo's *Last Supper*; and a copy of this very *Last Supper*, done by Rubini the younger, at Florence, I had known, for some time, to be in the possession of Nicolino. This point, therefore, I considered as sufficiently settled. I chuckled excessively when I thought of my acumen. It was the first time I had ever known Wyatt to keep from me any of his artistical secrets; but here he evidently intended to steal a march upon me, and smuggle a fine picture to New York, under my very nose; expecting me to know nothing of the matter. I resolved to quiz him well, now and hereafter.

One thing, however, annoyed me not a little. The box did *not* go into the extra state-room. It was deposited in Wyatt's own; and there, too, it remained, occupying very nearly the whole of the floor—no doubt to the exceeding discomfort of the artist and his wife;—this the more especially as the tar or paint with which it was lettered in sprawling capitals, emitted a strong, disagreeable, and, to my fancy, a peculiarly disgusting odor. On the lid were painted the words—"*Mrs. Adelaide Curtis, Albany, New York, Charge of Cornelius Wyatt, Esq. This side up. To be handled with care.*"

Now, I was aware that Mrs. Adelaide Curtis, of Albany, was the artist's wife's mother—but then I looked upon the whole address as a mystification, intended especially for myself. I made up my mind, of course, that the box and contents would never get farther north than the studio of my misanthropic friend, in Chambers Street, New York.

For the first three or four days we had fine weather, although the wind was dead ahead; having chopped round to the northward, immediately upon our losing sight of the coast. The passengers were, consequently, in high spirits and disposed to be social. I must except, however, Wyatt, and his sisters, who behaved stiffly, and I could not help thinking, uncourteously to the rest of the party. Wyatt's conduct I did not so much regard. He was gloomy, even beyond his usual habit—in fact he was morose—but in him I was prepared for eccentricity. For the sisters, however, I could make no excuse. They secluded themselves in their state-rooms during the greater part of the passage, and absolutely refused, although I repeatedly urged them, to hold communication with any person on board.

Mrs. Wyatt herself was far more agreeable. That is to say, she was *chatty*; and to be chatty is no slight recommendation at sea. She became *excessively* intimate with most of the ladies; and to my profound astonishment, evinced no equivocal disposition to coquet with the men. She amused us all very much. I say "*amused*"—and scarcely know how to explain myself. The truth is, I soon found that Mrs. W. was far oftener laughed *at* than *with*. The gentlemen said little about her; but the ladies, in a little while, pronounced her "a good-hearted thing, rather indifferent-looking, totally uneducated, and decidedly vulgar." The great wonder was, how Wyatt had been entrapped into such a match. Wealth was the general solution—but this I knew to be no solution at all; for Wyatt had told me that she neither brought him a dollar nor had any expectations from any source whatever. "He had married," he said, "for love, and for love only; and his bride was far more than worthy of his love." When I thought of these expressions, on the part of my friend, I confess that I felt indescribably puzzled. Could it be possible that he was taking leave of his senses? What else could I think? *He*, so refined, so intellectual, so fastidious, with so exquisite a perception of the faulty, and so keen an appreciation of the beautiful! To be sure, the lady seemed especially fond of *him*—particularly so in his absence—when she made herself ridiculous by frequent quotations of what had been said by her "beloved husband, Mr. Wyatt." The word "husband" seemed forever—to use one of her own delicate expressions—forever "on the tip of her tongue." In the meantime, it was observed by all on board, that he avoided *her* in the most pointed manner, and, for the most part, shut himself up alone in his state-room, where, in fact, he might have been said to live altogether, leaving his wife at full liberty to amuse herself as she thought best, in the public society of the main cabin.

My conclusion, from what I saw and heard, was, that the artist, by some unaccountable freak of fate, or perhaps in some fit of enthusiastic and fanciful passion, had been induced to unite himself with a person altogether beneath him, and that the natural result, entire and speedy disgust, had ensued. I pitied him from the bottom of my heart—but could not, for that reason, quite forgive his incommunicativeness in the matter of *The Last Supper*. For this I resolved to have my revenge.

One day he came upon deck, and, taking his arm as had been my wont, I sauntered with him backward and forward. His gloom, however (which I considered quite natural under the circumstances), seemed entirely unabated. He said little, and that moodily, and with evident effort. I ventured a jest or two, and he made a sickening attempt at a smile. Poor fellow!—As I thought of *his wife*, I wondered that he could have heart to put on even the semblance of mirth. At last I ventured a home thrust. I determined to commence a series of covert insinuations, or innuendoes, about the oblong box—just to let him perceive, gradually, that I was *not* altogether the butt, or victim, of his little bit of pleasant mystification. My first observation was by way of opening a masked battery. I said something about the "peculiar shape of *that* box"; and, as I spoke the words, I smiled knowingly, winked, and touched him gently with my forefinger in the ribs.

The manner in which Wyatt received this harmless pleasantry convinced me at once that he was mad. At first he stared at me as if he found it impossible to comprehend the witticism of my remark; but as its point seemed slowly to make its way into his brain, his eyes, in the same proportion, seemed protruding from their sockets. Then he grew very red—then hideously pale—then, as if highly amused with what I had insinuated, he began a loud and boisterous laugh, which, to my astonishment, he kept up, with gradually increasing vigor, for ten minutes or more. In conclusion, he fell flat and heavily upon the deck. When I ran to uplift him, to all appearance he was *dead*.

I called assistance, and, with much difficulty, we brought him to himself. Upon reviving he spoke incoherently for some time. At length we bled him and put him to bed. The next morning he was quite recovered, so far as regarded his mere bodily health. Of his mind I say nothing, of course. I avoided him during the rest of the passage, by advice of the captain, who seemed to coincide with me altogether in my views of his insanity, but cautioned me to say nothing on this head to any person on board.

Several circumstances occurred immediately after this fit of Wyatt's, which contributed to heighten the curiosity with which I was already possessed. Among other things, this: I had been nervous—drank too much strong green tea, and slept ill at night—in fact, for two nights I could not be properly said to sleep at all. Now, my state-room opened into the main cabin, or dining-room, as did those of all the single men on board. Wyatt's three rooms were in the after-cabin, which was separated from the main one by a slight sliding-door, never locked even at night. As we were almost constantly on a wind, and the breeze was not a little stiff, the ship heeled to leeward very considerably; and whenever her starboard side was to leeward, the sliding door between the cabins slid open, and so remained, nobody taking the trouble to get up and shut it. But my berth was in such a position, that when my own state-room door was open, as well as the sliding door in question (and my own door was *always* open on account of the heat), I could see into the after-cabin, quite distinctly, and just at that portion of it, too, where were situated the state-rooms of Mr. Wyatt. Well, during two nights (*not* consecutive) while I lay awake, I clearly saw Mrs. W., about eleven o'clock upon each night, steal cautiously from the state-room of Mr. W., and enter the extra room, where she remained until daybreak, when she was called by her husband and went back. That they were virtually separated was clear. They had separate apartments—no doubt in contemplation of a more permanent divorce; and here, after all, I thought was the mystery of the extra state-room.

There was another circumstance, too, which interested me much. During the two wakeful nights in question, and immediately after the disappearance of Mrs. Wyatt into the extra state-room, I was attracted by certain singular, cautious, subdued noises in that of her husband. After listening to them for some time, with thoughtful attention, I at length succeeded perfectly in translating their import. They were sounds occasioned by the artist in prying open the oblong box, by means of a chisel and mallet—the latter being apparently muffled, or deadened, by some soft woolen or cotton substance in which its head was enveloped.

In this manner I fancied I could distinguish the precise moment when he fairly disengaged the lid—also, that I could determine when he removed it altogether, and when he deposited it upon the lower berth in his room; this latter point I knew, for example, by certain slight taps which the lid made in striking against the wooden edges of the berth, as he endeavored to lay it down *very* gently—there being no room for it on the floor. After this there was a dead stillness, and I heard nothing more, upon either occasion, until nearly daybreak; unless, perhaps, I may mention a low sobbing, or murmuring sound, so very much suppressed as to be nearly inaudible—if, indeed, the whole of this latter noise were not rather produced by my own imagination. I say it seemed to *resemble* sobbing or sighing—but, of course, it could not have been either. I rather think it was a ringing in my own ears. Mr. Wyatt, no doubt according to custom, was merely giving the rein to one of his hobbies—indulging in one of his fits of artistic enthusiasm. He had opened his oblong box in order to feast his eyes on the pictorial treasure within. There was nothing in this, however, to make him sob. I repeat, therefore, that it must have been simply a freak of my own fancy, distempered by good Captain Hardy's green tea. Just before dawn, on each of the two nights of which I speak, I distinctly heard Mr. Wyatt replace the lid upon the oblong box, and force the nails into their old places by means of the muffled mallet. Having done this, he issued from his state-room, fully dressed, and proceeded to call Mrs. W. from hers.

We had been at sea seven days, and were now off Cape Hatteras, when there came a tremendously heavy blow from the south-west. We were, in a measure, prepared for it, however, as the weather had been holding out threats for some time. Everything was made snug, alow and aloft; and as the wind steadily freshened, we lay to, at length, under spanker and foretopsail, both double-reefed.

In this trim we rode safely enough for forty-eight hours—the ship proving herself an excellent sea-boat in many respects, and shipping no water of any consequence. At the end of this period, however, the gale had freshened into a hurricane, and our after-sail split into ribbons, bringing us so much in the trough of the water that we shipped several prodigious seas, one immediately after the other. By this accident we lost three men overboard with the caboose, and nearly the whole of the larboard bulwarks. Scarcely had we recovered our senses, before the foretopsail went into shreds, when we got up a storm stay-sail, and with this did pretty well for some hours, the ship heading the sea much more steadily than before.

The gale still held on, however, and we saw no signs of its abating. The rigging was found to be ill-fitted, and greatly strained; and on the third day of the blow, about five in the afternoon, our mizzen-mast, in a heavy lurch to windward, went by the board. For an hour or more, we tried in vain to get rid of it, on account of the prodigious rolling of the ship; and, before we had succeeded, the carpenter came aft and announced four feet of water in the hold. To add to our dilemma, we found the pumps choked and nearly useless.

All was now confusion and despair—but an effort was made to lighten the ship by throwing overboard as much of her cargo as could be reached and by cutting away the two masts that remained. This we at last accomplished—but we were still unable to do anything at the pumps: and, in the meantime, the leak gained on us very fast.

At sundown, the gale had sensibly diminished in violence, and, as the sea went down with it, we still entertained faint hopes of saving ourselves in the boats. At eight p.m., the clouds broke away to windward, and we had the advantage of a full moon—a piece of good fortune which served wonderfully to cheer our drooping spirits.

After incredible labor we succeeded, at length, in getting the long-boat over the side without material accident, and into this we crowded the whole of the crew and most of the passengers. This party made off immediately, and, after undergoing much suffering, finally arrived, in safety, at Ocracoke Inlet, on the third day after the wreck.

Fourteen passengers, with the captain, remained on board, resolving to trust their fortunes to the jolly-boat at the stern. We lowered it without difficulty, although it was only by a miracle that we prevented it from swamping as it touched the water. It contained, when afloat, the captain and his wife, Mr. Wyatt, and party, a Mexican officer, wife, four children, and myself, with a negro valet.

We had no room, of course, for anything except a few positively necessary instruments, some provisions, and the clothes upon our backs. No one had thought of even attempting to save anything more. What must have been the astonishment of all, then, when, having proceeded a few fathoms from the ship, Mr. Wyatt stood up in the stern-sheets, and coolly demanded of Captain Hardy that the boat should be put back for the purpose of taking in his oblong box!

"Sit down, Mr. Wyatt," replied the captain, somewhat sternly, "you will capsize us if you do not sit quite still. Our gunwale is almost in the water now."

"The box!" vociferated Mr. Wyatt, still standing—"The box, I say! Captain Hardy, you cannot, you will not refuse me. Its weight will be but a trifle—it is nothing—mere nothing. By the mother who bore you—for the love of Heaven—by your hope of salvation, I implore you to put back for the box!"

The captain, for a moment, seemed touched by the earnest appeal of the artist, but he regained his stern composure, and merely said:

"Mr. Wyatt, you are mad. I cannot listen to you. Sit down, I say, or you will swamp the boat. Stay—hold him—seize him!—He is about to spring overboard! There—I knew it—he is over!"

As the captain said this, Mr. Wyatt, in fact, sprang from the boat, and, as we were yet in the lee of the wreck, succeeded, by almost superhuman exertion, in getting hold of a rope which hung from the fore-chains. In another moment he was on board, and rushing frantically down into the cabin.

In the meantime, we had been swept astern of the ship, and being quite out of her lee, were at the mercy of the tremendous sea which was still running. We made a determined effort to put back, but our little boat was like a feather in the breath of the tempest. We saw at a glance that the doom of the unfortunate artist was sealed.

As our distance from the wreck rapidly increased, the madman (for as such only could we regard him) was seen to emerge from the companionway, up which by dint of strength that appeared gigantic, he dragged, bodily, the oblong box. While we gazed in the extremity of astonishment, he passed, rapidly, several turns of a three-inch rope, first around the box, and then around his body. In another instant both body and box were in the sea—disappearing suddenly, at once and forever.

We lingered awhile sadly upon our oars, with our eyes riveted upon the spot. At length we pulled away. The silence remained unbroken for an hour. Finally, I hazarded a remark.

"Did you observe, captain, how suddenly they sank? Was not that an exceedingly singular thing? I confess that I entertained some feeble hope of his final deliverance, when I saw him lash himself to the box, and commit himself to the sea."

"They sank as a matter of course," replied the captain, "and that like a shot. They will soon rise again, however—*but not till the salt melts*."

"The salt!" I ejaculated.

"Hush!" said the captain, pointing to the wife and sisters of deceased. "We must talk of these things at some appropriate time."

We suffered much, and made a narrow escape; but fortune befriended us, as well as our mates in the long-boat. We landed, in fine, more dead than alive, after four days of intense distress, upon the beach opposite Roanoke Island. We remained here a week, were not ill-treated by the wreckers, and at length obtained a passage to New York.

About a month after the loss of the *Independence*, I happened to meet Captain Hardy on Broadway. Our conversation turned, naturally, upon the disaster, and especially upon the sad fate of poor Wyatt. I thus learned the following particulars.

The artist had engaged passage for himself, wife, two sisters, and a servant. His wife was, indeed, as she had been represented, a most lovely, and most accomplished woman. On the morning of the fourteenth of June (the day in which I first visited the ship), the lady suddenly sickened and died. The young husband was frantic with grief—but circumstances imperatively forbade the deferring his voyage to New York. It was necessary to take to her mother the corpse of his adored wife, and, on the other hand, the universal prejudice which would prevent his doing so openly was well known. Nine-tenths of the passengers would have abandoned the ship rather than take passage with a dead body.

In this dilemma, Captain Hardy arranged that the corpse, being first partially embalmed, and packed, with a large quantity of salt, in a box of suitable dimensions, should be conveyed on board as merchandise. Nothing was to be said of the lady's decease; and, as it was well understood that Mr. Wyatt had engaged passage for his wife, it became necessary that some person should personate her during the voyage. This the deceased lady's-maid was easily prevailed on to do. The extra state-room, originally engaged for this girl, during her mistress's life, was now merely retained. In this state-room the pseudo-wife slept, of course, every night. In the daytime she performed, to the best of her ability, the part of her mistress—whose person, it had been carefully ascertained, was unknown to any of the passengers on board.

My own mistake arose, naturally enough, through too careless, too inquisitive, and too impulsive a temperament. But of late, it is a rare thing that I sleep soundly at night. There is a countenance which haunts me, turn as I will. There is an hysterical laugh which will forever ring within my ears.

THE IMP OF THE PERVERSE

In the consideration of the faculties and impulses—of the *prima mobilia* of the human soul, the phrenologists have failed to make room for a propensity which, although obviously existing as a radical, primitive, irreducible sentiment, has been equally overlooked by all the moralists who have preceded them. In the pure arrogance of the reason, we have all overlooked it. We have suffered its existence to escape our senses, solely through want of belief—of faith; whether it be faith in Revelation, or faith in the Kabbala. The idea of it has never occurred to us, simply because of its supererogation. We saw no *need* of the impulse—for the propensity. We could not perceive its necessity. We could not understand, that is to say, we could not have understood, had the notion of this *primum mobile* ever obtruded itself; we could not have understood in what manner it might be made to further the objects of humanity, either temporal or eternal. It cannot be denied that phrenology and, in great measure, all metaphysicianism, have been concocted *a priori*. The intellectual or logical man, rather than the understanding or observant man, set himself to imagine designs—to dictate purposes to God. Having thus fathomed, to his satisfaction, the intentions of Jehovah, out of these intentions he built his innumerable systems of mind. In the matter of phrenology, for example, we first determined, naturally enough, that it was the design of the Deity that man should eat. We then assigned to man an organ of alimentiveness, and this organ is the scourge with which the Deity compels man, will-I nill-I, into eating. Secondly, having settled it to be God's will that man should continue his species, we discovered an organ of amativeness, forthwith. And so with combativeness, with ideality, with causality, with constructiveness—so, in short, with every organ, whether representing a propensity, a moral sentiment, or a faculty of the pure intellect. And in these arrangements of the *principia* of human action, the Spurzheimites, whether right or wrong, in part, or upon the whole, have but followed, in principle, the footsteps of their predecessors; deducing and establishing every thing from the preconceived destiny of man, and upon the ground of the objects of his Creator.

It would have been wiser, it would have been safer to classify (if classify we must) upon the basis of what man usually or occasionally did, and was always occasionally doing, rather than upon the basis of what we took it for granted the Deity intended him to do. If we cannot comprehend God in his visible works, how then in his inconceivable thoughts, that call the works into being? If we cannot understand him in his objective creatures, how then in his substantive moods and phases of creation?

Induction, *a posteriori*, would have brought phrenology to admit, as an innate and primitive principle of human action, a paradoxical something, which we may call *perverseness*, for want of a more characteristic term. In the sense I intend, it is, in fact, a *mobile* without motive, a motive not *motivirt*. Through its promptings we act without comprehensible object; or, if this shall be understood as a contradiction in terms, we may so far modify the proposition as to say, that through its promptings we act, for the reason that we should *not*. In theory, no reason can be more unreasonable; but, in fact, there is none more strong. With certain minds, under certain conditions, it becomes absolutely irresistible. I am not more certain that I breathe, than that the assurance of the wrong or error of any action is often the one unconquerable *force* which impels us, and alone impels us to its prosecution. Nor will this overwhelming tendency to do wrong for the wrong's sake, admit of analysis, or resolution into ulterior elements. It is a radical, a primitive impulse — elementary. It will be said, I am aware, that when we persist in acts because we feel we should *not* persist in them, our conduct is but a modification of that which ordinarily springs from the combativeness of phrenology. But a glance will show the fallacy of this idea. The phrenological *combativeness* has for its essence the necessity of self-defense. It is our safeguard against injury. Its principle regards our well-being; and thus the desire to be well is excited simultaneously with its development. It follows, that the desire to be well must be excited simultaneously with any principle which shall be merely a modification of combativeness, but in the case of that something which I term *perverseness*, the desire to be well is not only not aroused, but a strongly antagonistical sentiment exists.

An appeal to one's own heart is, after all, the best reply to the sophistry just noticed. No one who trustingly consults and thoroughly questions his own soul will be disposed to deny the entire radicalness of the propensity in question. It is not more incomprehensible than distinctive. There lives no man who, at some period, has not been tormented, for example, by an earnest desire to tantalize a listener by circumlocution. The speaker is aware that he displeases; he has every intention to please; he is usually curt, precise, and clear; the most laconic and luminous language is struggling for utterance upon his tongue; it is only with difficulty that he restrains himself from giving it flow; he dreads and deprecates the anger of him whom he addresses; yet, the thought strikes him, that by certain involutions and parentheses, this anger may be engendered. That single thought is enough. The impulse increases to a wish, the wish to a desire, the desire to an uncontrollable longing, and the longing (to the deep

regret and mortification of the speaker, and in defiance of all consequences) is indulged.

We have a task before us which must be speedily performed.
We know that it will be ruinous to make delay. The most important
crisis of our life calls, trumpet-tongued, for immediate energy and
action. We glow, we are consumed with eagerness to commence the
work, with the anticipation of whose glorious result our whole souls
are on fire. It must, it shall be undertaken today, and yet we put it
off until tomorrow, and why? There is no answer, except that we
feel *perverse*, using the word with no comprehension of the principle.
Tomorrow arrives; and with it a more impatient anxiety to do our
duty, but with this very increase of anxiety arrives, also, a nameless,
a positively fearful, because unfathomable craving for delay. This
craving gathers strength as the moments fly. The last hour for action
is at hand. We tremble with the violence of the conflict within us—
of the definite with the indefinite—of the substance with the shadow.
But, if the contest has proceeded thus far, it is the shadow which
prevails—we struggle in vain. The clock strikes, and is the knell of
our welfare. At the same time, it is the chanticleer-note to the ghost
that has so long overawed us. It flies—it disappears—we are free.
The old energy returns. We will labor *now*. Alas, it is *too late!*

We stand upon the brink of a precipice. We peer into the abyss—
we grow sick and dizzy. Our first impulse is to shrink from the
danger. Unaccountably we remain. By slow degrees our sickness and
dizziness, and horror become merged in a cloud of unnamable feeling.
By gradations, still more imperceptible, this cloud assumes shape,
as did the vapor from the bottle out of which arose the genius in the
Arabian Nights. But out of this *our* cloud upon the precipice's edge,
there grows into palpability, a shape, far more terrible than any
genius, or any demon of a tale, and yet it is but a thought, although
a fearful one, and one which chills the very marrow of our bones
with the fierceness of the delight of its horror. It is merely the idea

of what would be our sensations during the sweeping precipitancy of a fall from such a height. And this fall—this rushing annihilation—for the very reason that it involves that one most ghastly and loathsome of all the most ghastly and loathsome images of death and suffering which have ever presented themselves to our imagination—for this very cause do we now the most vividly desire it. And because our reason violently deters us from the brink, *therefore*, do we the most impetuously approach it. There is no passion in nature so demoniacally impatient, as that of him, who shuddering upon the edge of a precipice, thus meditates a plunge. To indulge for a moment in any attempt *at thought*, is to be inevitably lost; for reflection but urges us to forbear, and *therefore* it is, I say, that we *cannot*. If there be no friendly arm to check us, or if we fail in a sudden effort to prostrate ourselves backward from the abyss, we plunge, and are destroyed.

Examine these similar actions as we will, we shall find them resulting solely from the spirit of the *Perverse*. We perpetrate them because we feel that we should *not*. Beyond or behind this, there is no intelligible principle: and we might, indeed, deem this perverseness a direct instigation of the arch-fiend, were it not occasionally known to operate in furtherance of good.

I have said thus much, that in some measure I may answer your question—that I may explain to you why I am here—that I may assign to you something that shall have at least the faint aspect of a cause for my wearing these fetters, and for my tenanting this cell of the condemned. Had I not been thus prolix, you might either have misunderstood me altogether, or, with the rabble, have fancied me mad. As it is, you will easily perceive that I am one of the many uncounted victims of the Imp of the Perverse.

It is impossible that any deed could have been wrought with a more thorough deliberation. For weeks, for months, I pondered upon the means of the murder. I rejected a thousand schemes, because

their accomplishment involved a *chance* of detection. At length, in
reading some French memoirs, I found an account of a nearly fatal
illness that occurred to Madame Pilau, through the agency of a candle
accidentally poisoned. The idea struck my fancy at once. I knew my
victim's habit of reading in bed. I knew, too, that his apartment was
narrow and ill-ventilated. But I need not vex you with impertinent
details. I need not describe the easy artifices by which I substituted,
in his bedroom candle-stand, a wax-light of my own making, for the
one which I there found. The next morning he was discovered dead
in his bed, and the Coroner's verdict was—"Death by the visitation
of God."

Having inherited his estate, all went well with me for years. The
idea of detection never once entered my brain. Of the remains of the
fatal taper, I had myself carefully disposed. I had left no shadow of
a clue by which it would be possible to convict, or even to suspect
me of the crime. It is inconceivable how rich a sentiment of satisfaction arose in my bosom as I reflected upon my absolute security.
For a very long period of time, I was accustomed to revel in this
sentiment. It afforded me more real delight than all the mere worldly
advantages accruing from my sin. But there arrived at length an
epoch, from which the pleasurable feeling grew, by scarcely perceptible gradations, into a haunting and harassing thought. It harassed
because it haunted. I could scarcely get rid of it for an instant. It is
quite a common thing to be thus annoyed with the ringing in our
ears, or rather in our memories, of the burthen of some ordinary
song, or some unimpressive snatches from an opera. Nor will we be
the less tormented if the song in itself be good, or the opera air
meritorious. In this manner, at last, I would perpetually catch myself
pondering upon my security, and repeating, in a low, under-tone, the
phrase, "I am safe."

One day, whilst sauntering along the streets, I arrested myself
in the act of murmuring, half aloud, these customary syllables. In a

fit of petulance, I re-modeled them thus:—"I am safe—I am safe—yes—if I be not fool enough to make open confession!"

No sooner had I spoken these words, than I felt an icy chill creep to my heart. I had had some experience in these fits of perversity (whose nature I have been at some trouble to explain) and I remembered well, that in no instance I had successfully resisted their attacks. And now my own casual self-suggestion, that I might possibly be fool enough to confess the murder of which I had been guilty, confronted me, as if the very ghost of him whom I had murdered—and beckoned me on to death.

At first, I made an effort to shake off this nightmare of the soul. I walked vigorously—faster—still faster—at length I ran. I felt a maddening desire to shriek aloud. Every succeeding wave of thought overwhelmed me with new terror, for, alas! I well, too well understood that, to *think*, in my situation, was to be lost. I still quickened my pace. I bounded like a madman through the crowded thoroughfares. At length, the populace took the alarm, and pursued me. I felt then the consummation of my fate. Could I have torn out my tongue, I would have done it—but a rough voice resounded in my ears—a rougher grasp seized me by the shoulder. I turned—I gasped for breath. For a moment I experienced all the pangs of suffocation; I became blind, and deaf, and giddy; and then some invisible fiend, I thought, struck me with his broad palm upon the back. The long-imprisoned secret burst forth from my soul.

They say that I spoke with a distinct enunciation, but with marked emphasis and passionate hurry, as if in dread of interruption before concluding the brief but pregnant sentences that consigned me to the hangman and to hell.

Having related all that was necessary for the fullest judicial conviction, I fell prostrate in a swoon.

But why shall I say more? Today I wear these chains, and am *here!* Tomorrow I shall be fetterless!—*But where?*

THE CASK OF AMONTILLADO

The thousand injuries of Fortunato I had borne as I best could, but when he ventured upon insult I vowed revenge. You, who so well know the nature of my soul, will not suppose, however, that I gave utterance to a threat. *At length* I would be avenged; this was a point definitely settled—but the very definiteness with which it was resolved precluded the idea of risk. I must not only punish but punish with impunity. A wrong is unredressed when retribution overtakes its redresser. It is equally unredressed when the avenger fails to make himself felt as such to him who has done the wrong.

It must be understood that neither by word nor deed had I given Fortunato cause to doubt my good will. I continued, as was my wont, to smile in his face, and he did not perceive that my smile *now* was at the thought of his immolation.

He had a weak point—this Fortunato—although in other regards he was a man to be respected and even feared. He prided himself on his connoisseurship in wine. Few Italians have the true virtuoso spirit. For the most part their enthusiasm is adopted to suit the time and opportunity, to practice imposture upon the British and Austrian *millionaires*. In painting and gemmary, Fortunato, like his countrymen, was a quack, but in the matter of old wines he was sincere. In this respect I did not differ from him materially; I was skilful in the Italian vintages myself, and bought largely whenever I could.

It was about dusk, one evening during the supreme madness of the carnival season, that I encountered my friend. He accosted me with excessive warmth, for he had been drinking much. The man wore motley. He had on a tight-fitting parti-striped dress, and his head was surmounted by the conical cap and bells. I was so pleased to see him that I thought I should never have done wringing his hand.

I said to him—"My dear Fortunato, you are luckily met. How remarkably well you are looking today. But I have received a pipe of what passes for Amontillado, and I have my doubts."

"How?" said he. "Amontillado? A pipe? Impossible! And in the middle of the carnival!"

"I have my doubts," I replied; "and I was silly enough to pay the full Amontillado price without consulting you in the matter. You were not to be found, and I was fearful of losing a bargain."

"Amontillado!"

"I have my doubts."

"Amontillado!"

"And I must satisfy them."

"Amontillado!"

"As you are engaged, I am on my way to Luchresi. If any one has a critical turn it is he. He will tell me—"

"Luchresi cannot tell Amontillado from Sherry."

"And yet some fools will have it that his taste is a match for your own."

"Come, let us go."

"Whither?"

"To your vaults."

"My friend, no; I will not impose upon your good nature. I perceive you have an engagement. Luchresi—"

"I have no engagement; come."

"My friend, no. It is not the engagement, but the severe cold with which I perceive you are afflicted. The vaults are insufferably damp. They are encrusted with niter."

"Let us go, nevertheless. The cold is merely nothing. Amontillado! You have been imposed upon. And as for Luchresi, he cannot distinguish Sherry from Amontillado."

Thus speaking, Fortunato possessed himself of my arm; and putting on a mask of black silk and drawing a *roquelaure* closely about my person, I suffered him to hurry me to my palazzo.

There were no attendants at home; they had absconded to make merry in honor of the time. I had told them that I should not return until the morning, and had given them explicit orders not to stir from the house. These orders were sufficient, I knew well, to ensure their immediate disappearance, one and all, as soon as my back was turned.

I took from their sconces two flambeaux and, giving one to Fortunato, bowed him through several suites of rooms to the archway that led into the vaults. I passed down a long and winding staircase, requesting him to be cautious as he followed. We came at length to the foot of the descent, and stood together upon the damp ground of the catacombs of the Montresors.

The gait of my friend was unsteady, and the bells upon his cap jingled as he strode.

"The pipe," he said.

"It is farther on," said I; "but observe the white web-work which gleams from these cavern walls."

He turned towards me, and looked into my eyes with two filmy orbs that distilled the rheum of intoxication.

"Niter?" he asked at length.

"Niter," I replied. "How long have you had that cough?"

"Ugh! Ugh! Ugh!—Ugh! Ugh! Ugh!—Ugh! Ugh! Ugh!—Ugh! Ugh! Ugh!—Ugh! Ugh! Ugh!"

My poor friend found it impossible to reply for many minutes.

"It is nothing," he said, at last.

"Come," I said, with decision, "we will go back; your health is precious. You are rich, respected, admired, beloved; you are happy, as once I was. You are a man to be missed. For me it is no matter. We will go back; you will be ill, and I cannot be responsible. Besides, there is Luchresi—"

"Enough," he said; "the cough is a mere nothing; it will not kill me. I shall not die of a cough."

"True—true," I replied; "and, indeed, I had no intention of alarming you unnecessarily—but you should use all proper caution. A draught of this Medoc will defend us from the damps."

Here I knocked off the neck of a bottle which I drew from a long row of its fellows that lay upon the mold.

"Drink," I said, presenting him the wine.

He raised it to his lips with a leer. He paused and nodded to me familiarly, while his bells jingled.

"I drink," he said, "to the buried that repose around us."

"And I to your long life."

He again took my arm, and we proceeded.

"These vaults," he said, "are extensive."

"The Montresors," I replied, "were a great and numerous family."

"I forget your arms."

"A huge human foot *d'or*, in a field azure; the foot crushes a serpent rampant whose fangs are imbedded in the heel."

"And the motto?"

"*Nemo me impune lacessit.*"

"Good!" he said.

The wine sparkled in his eyes and the bells jingled. My own fancy grew warm with the Medoc. We had passed through long walls of piled skeletons, with casks and puncheons intermingling, into the inmost recesses of catacombs. I paused again, and this time I made bold to seize Fortunato by an arm above the elbow.

"The niter!" I said. "See, it increases. It hangs like moss upon the vaults. We are below the river's bed. The drops of moisture trickle among the bones. Come, we will go back ere it is too late. Your cough—"

"It is nothing," he said; "let us go on. But first, another draught of the Medoc."

I broke and reached him a flagon of De Grâve. He emptied it at a breath. His eyes flashed with a fierce light. He laughed and threw the bottle upward with a gesticulation I did not understand.

I looked at him in surprise. He repeated the movement—a grotesque one.

"You do not comprehend?" he said.

"Not I," I replied.

"Then you are not of the brotherhood."

"How?"

"You are not of the masons."

"Yes, yes," I said; "yes, yes."

"You? Impossible! A mason?"

"A mason," I replied.

"A sign," he said, "a sign."

"It is this," I answered, producing a trowel from beneath the folds of my *roquelaure*.

"You jest," he exclaimed, recoiling a few paces. "But let us proceed to the Amontillado."

"Be it so," I said, replacing the tool beneath the cloak and again offering my arm. He leaned upon it heavily. We continued our route in search of the Amontillado. We passed through a range of low arches, descended, passed on, and descending again, arrived at a deep crypt, in which the foulness of the air caused our flambeaux rather to glow than flame.

At the most remote end of the crypt there appeared another less spacious. Its walls had been lined with human remains, piled to the vault overhead, in the fashion of the great catacombs of Paris. Three sides of this interior crypt were still ornamented in this manner. From the fourth side the bones had been thrown down, and lay promiscuously upon the earth, forming at one point a mound of some size. Within the wall thus exposed by the displacing of the bones, we perceived a still interior crypt or recess, in depth about four feet, in width three, in height six or seven. It seemed to have been constructed for no especial use within itself, but formed merely the interval between two of the colossal supports of the roof of the catacombs, and was backed by one of their circumscribing walls of solid granite.

It was in vain that Fortunato, uplifting his dull torch, endeavored to pry into the depth of the recess. Its termination the feeble light did not enable us to see.

"Proceed," I said. "Herein is the Amontillado. As for Luchresi—"

"He is an ignoramus," interrupted my friend, as he stepped unsteadily forward, while I followed immediately at his heels. In an instant he had reached the extremity of the niche, and, finding his progress arrested by the rock, stood stupidly bewildered. A moment more and I had fettered him to the granite. In its surface were two iron staples, distant from each other about two feet, horizontally. From one of these depended a short chain, from the other a padlock. Throwing the links about his waist, it was but the work of a few seconds to secure it. He was too much astounded to resist. Withdrawing the key I stepped back from the recess.

"Pass your hand," I said, "over the wall; you cannot help feeling the niter. Indeed, it is *very* damp. Once more let me *implore* you to return. No? Then I must positively leave you. But I must first render you all the little attentions in my power."

"The Amontillado!" ejaculated my friend, not yet recovered from his astonishment.

"True," I replied; "the Amontillado."

As I said these words I busied myself among the pile of bones of which I have before spoken. Throwing them aside, I soon uncovered a quantity of building stone and mortar. With these materials and with the aid of my trowel, I began vigorously to wall up the entrance of the niche.

I had scarcely laid the first tier of the masonry when I discovered that the intoxication of Fortunato had in a great measure worn off. The earliest indication I had of this was a low moaning cry from the depth of the recess. It was *not* the cry of a drunken man. There was then a long and obstinate silence. I laid the second tier, and the third, and the fourth, and then I heard the furious vibrations of the chain. The noise lasted for several minutes, during which, that I might harken to it with the more satisfaction, I ceased my labors and sat down upon the bones. When at last the clanking subsided, I resumed the trowel, and finished without interruption the fifth, the sixth, and the seventh tier. The wall was now nearly upon a level with my breast. I again paused, and holding the flambeaux over the masonwork, threw a few feeble rays upon the figure within.

A succession of loud and shrill screams, bursting suddenly from the throat of the chained form, seemed to thrust me violently back. For a brief moment I hesitated, I trembled. Unsheathing my rapier, I began to grope with it about the recess; but the thought of an instant reassured me. I placed my hand upon the solid fabric of the catacombs, and felt satisfied. I re-approached the wall; I replied to the yells of him who clamored. I re-echoed, I aided, I surpassed them in volume and in strength. I did this, and the clamorer grew still.

It was now midnight, and my task was drawing to a close. I had completed the eighth, the ninth, and the tenth tier. I had finished a portion of the last and the eleventh; there remained but a single stone to be fitted and plastered in. I struggled with its weight; I placed it partially in its destined position. But now there came from out the niche a low laugh that erected the hairs upon my head. It was succeeded by a sad voice, which I had difficulty in recognizing as that of the noble Fortunato. The voice said—

"Ha! ha! ha!—He! he! he!—A very good joke, indeed—an excellent jest. We shall have many a rich laugh about it at the palazzo—he! he! he!—over our wine—he! he! he!"

"The Amontillado!" I said.

"He! he! he!—He! he! he!—Yes, the Amontillado. But is it not getting late? Will not they be awaiting us at the palazzo, the Lady Fortunato and the rest? Let us be gone."

"Yes," I said, "let us be gone."

"*For the love of God! Montresor!*"

"Yes," I said, "for the love of God!"

But to these words I harkened in vain for a reply. I grew impatient. I called aloud—

"Fortunato!"

No answer. I called again—

"Fortunato!" No answer still. I thrust a torch through the remaining aperture and let it fall within. There came forth in return only a jingling of the bells. My heart grew sick; it was the dampness of the catacombs that made it so. I hastened to make an end of my labor. I forced the last stone into its position; I plastered it up. Against the new masonry I re-erected the old rampart of bones. For the half of a century no mortal has disturbed them. *In pace requiescat!*

HOP-FROG

I never knew any one so keenly alive to a joke as the king was. He seemed to live only for joking. To tell a good story of the joke kind, and to tell it well, was the surest road to his favor. Thus it happened that his seven ministers were all noted for their accomplishments as jokers. They all took after the king, too, in being large, corpulent, oily men, as well as inimitable jokers. Whether people grow fat by joking, or whether there is something in fat itself which predisposes to a joke, I have never been quite able to determine; but certain it is that a lean joker is a *rara avis in terris*.

About the refinements, or, as he called them, the "ghosts" of wit, the king troubled himself very little. He had an especial admiration for *breadth* in a jest, and would often put up with *length*, for the sake of it. Over-niceties wearied him. He would have preferred Rabelais's *Gargantua* to the *Zadig* of Voltaire: and, upon the whole, practical jokes suited his taste far better than verbal ones.

At the date of my narrative, professing jesters had not altogether gone out of fashion at court. Several of the great continental "powers" still retained their "fools," who wore motley, with caps and bells, and who were expected to be always ready with sharp witticisms, at a moment's notice, in consideration of the crumbs that fell from the royal table.

Our king, as a matter of course, retained his "fool." The fact is, he *required* something in the way of folly—if only to counterbalance the heavy wisdom of the seven wise men who were his ministers— not to mention himself.

His fool, or professional jester, was not *only* a fool, however. His value was trebled in the eyes of the king, by the fact of his being also a dwarf and a cripple. Dwarfs were as common at court, in those days, as fools; and many monarchs would have found it difficult to get through their days (days are rather longer at court than elsewhere) without both a jester to laugh *with* and a dwarf to laugh *at*. But, as I have already observed, your jesters, in ninety-nine cases out of a hundred, are fat, round and unwieldy—so that it was no small source of self-gratulation with our king that in Hop-Frog (this was the fool's name) he possessed a triplicate treasure in one person.

I believe the name "Hop-Frog" was *not* that given to the dwarf by his sponsors at baptism, but it was conferred upon him, by general consent of the several ministers, on account of his inability to walk as other men do. In fact, Hop-Frog could only get along by a sort of interjectional gait—something between a leap and a wriggle—a movement that afforded illimitable amusement, and of course conso-lation, to the king, for (notwithstanding the protuberance of his stomach and a constitutional swelling of the head) the king, by his whole court, was accounted a capital figure.

But although Hop-Frog, through the distortion of his legs, could move only with great pain and difficulty along a road or floor, the prodigious muscular power which nature seemed to have bestowed upon his arms, by way of compensation for deficiency in the lower limbs, enabled him to perform many feats of wonderful dexterity, where trees or ropes were in question, or anything else to climb. At such exercises he certainly much more resembled a squirrel, or a small monkey, than a frog.

I am not able to say, with precision, from what country Hop-Frog originally came. It was from some barbarous region, however, that no person ever heard of—a vast distance from the court of our king. Hop-Frog, and a young girl very little less dwarfish than himself (although of exquisite proportions, and a marvelous dancer), had been forcibly carried off from their respective homes in adjoining provinces, and sent as presents to the king, by one of his ever-victorious generals.

Under these circumstances, it is not to be wondered at that a close intimacy arose between the two little captives. Indeed, they soon became sworn friends. Hop-Frog, who, although he made a great deal of sport, was by no means popular, had it not in his power to render Trippetta many services; but she, on account of her grace and exquisite beauty (although a dwarf), was universally admired and petted: so she possessed much influence; and never failed to use it, whenever she could, for the benefit of Hop-Frog.

On some grand state occasion—I forgot what—the king determined to have a masquerade, and whenever a masquerade or anything of that kind, occurred at our court, then the talents both of Hop-Frog and Trippetta were sure to be called in play. Hop-Frog, in especial, was so inventive in the way of getting up pageants, suggesting novel characters, and arranging costume, for masked balls, that nothing could be done, it seems, without his assistance.

The night appointed for the *fête* had arrived. A gorgeous hall had been fitted up, under Trippetta's eye, with every kind of device which could possibly give *éclat* to a masquerade. The whole court was in a fever of expectation. As for costumes and characters, it might well be supposed that everybody had come to a decision on such points. Many had made up their minds (as to what roles they should assume) a week, or even a month, in advance; and, in fact, there was not a particle of indecision anywhere—except in the case of the king and his seven minsters. Why *they* hesitated I never could tell, unless they did it by way of a joke. More probably, they found it difficult, on account of being so fat, to make up their minds. At all events, time flew; and, as a last resource, they sent for Trippetta and Hop-Frog.

When the two little friends obeyed the summons of the king, they found him sitting at his wine with the seven members of his cabinet council; but the monarch appeared to be in a very ill humor. He knew that Hop-Frog was not fond of wine; for it excited the poor cripple almost to madness; and madness is no comfortable feeling. But the king loved his practical jokes, and took pleasure in forcing Hop-Frog to drink and (as the king called it) "to be merry."

"Come here, Hop-Frog," said he, as the jester and his friend entered the room: "swallow this bumper to the health of your absent friends [here Hop-Frog sighed], and then let us have the benefit of your invention. We want characters—*characters*, man—something novel—out of the way. We are wearied with this everlasting sameness. Come, drink! The wine will brighten your wits."

Hop-Frog endeavored, as usual, to get up a jest in reply to these advances from the king; but the effort was too much. It happened to be the poor dwarf's birthday, and the command to drink to his "absent friends" forced the tears to his eyes. Many large, bitter drops fell into the goblet as he took it, humbly, from the hand of the tyrant.

"Ah! Ha! ha! ha!" roared the latter, as the dwarf reluctantly drained the beaker. "See what a glass of good wine can do! Why, your eyes are shining already!"

Poor fellow! His large eyes *gleamed*, rather than shone; for the effect of wine on his excitable brain was not more powerful than instantaneous. He placed the goblet nervously on the table, and looked round upon the company with a half-insane stare. They all seemed highly amused at the success of the king's "*joke*."

"And now to business," said the prime minister, a *very* fat man.

"Yes," said the King; "come, Hop-Frog, lend us your assistance.

Characters, my fine fellow; we stand in need of characters—all of us—ha! ha! ha!" And as this was seriously meant for a joke, his laugh was chorused by the seven.

Hop-Frog also laughed, although feebly and somewhat vacantly.

"Come, come," said the king, impatiently, "have you nothing to suggest?"

"I am endeavoring to think of something *novel*," replied the dwarf, abstractedly, for he was quite bewildered by the wine.

"Endeavoring!" cried the tyrant, fiercely; "what do you mean by *that?* Ah, I perceive. You are sulky, and want more wine. Here, drink this!" And he poured out another goblet full and offered it to the cripple, who merely gazed at it, gasping for breath.

"Drink, I say!" shouted the monster. "Or by the fiends —"

The dwarf hesitated. The king grew purple with rage. The courtiers smirked. Trippetta, pale as a corpse, advanced to the monarch's seat, and, falling on her knees before him, implored him to spare her friend.

The tyrant regarded her, for some moments, in evident wonder at her audacity. He seemed quite at a loss what to do or say—how most becomingly to express his indignation. At last, without uttering a syllable, he pushed her violently from him, and threw the contents of the brimming goblet in her face.

The poor girl got up as best she could, and, not daring even to sigh, resumed her position at the foot of the table.

There was a dead silence for about half a minute, during which the falling of a leaf, or of a feather, might have been heard. It was interrupted by a low, but harsh and protracted *grating* sound which seemed to come at once from every corner of the room.

"What—what—*what* are you making that noise for?" demanded the king, turning furiously to the dwarf.

The latter seemed to have recovered, in great measure, from his intoxication, and looking fixedly but quietly into the tyrant's face, merely ejaculated:

"I—I? How could it have been me?"

"The sound appeared to come from without," observed one of the courtiers. "I fancy it was the parrot at the window, whetting his bill upon his cage-wires."

"True," replied the monarch, as if much relieved by the suggestion. "But, on the honor of a knight, I could have sworn that it was the gritting of this vagabond's teeth."

Hereupon the dwarf laughed (the king was too confirmed a joker to object to any one's laughing), and displayed a set of large, powerful, and very repulsive teeth. Moreover, he avowed his perfect willingness to swallow as much wine as desired. The monarch was pacified; and having drained another bumper with no very perceptible ill effect, Hop-Frog entered at once, and with spirit, into the plans for the masquerade.

"I cannot tell what was the association of idea," observed he, very tranquilly, and as if he had never tasted wine in his life, "but just after your majesty had struck the girl and thrown the wine in her face—*just after* your majesty had done this, and while the parrot was making that odd noise outside the window, there came into my mind a capital diversion—one of my own country frolics—often enacted among us, at our masquerades: but here it will be new altogether. Unfortunately, however, it requires a company of eight persons, and —"

"Here we *are!* " cried the king, laughing at his acute discovery of the coincidence; "Eight to a fraction—I and my seven ministers. Come! What is the diversion?"

"We call it," replied the cripple, "the Eight Chained Orang-utans, and it really is excellent sport if well enacted."

"*We* will enact it," remarked the king, drawing himself up, and lowering his eyelids.

"The beauty of the game," continued Hop-Frog, "lies in the fright it occasions among the women."

"Capital!" roared in chorus the monarch and his ministry.

"*I* will equip you as orang-utans," proceeded the dwarf; "leave all that to me. The resemblance shall be so striking, that the company of masqueraders will take you for real beasts—and of course, they will be as much terrified as astonished."

"Oh, this is exquisite!" exclaimed the king. "Hop-Frog! I will make a man of you."

"The chains are for the purpose of increasing the confusion by their jangling. You are supposed to have escaped, *en masse*, from your keepers. Your majesty cannot conceive the *effect* produced, at a masquerade, by eight chained orang-utans, imagined to be real ones by most of the company; and rushing in with savage cries, among the crowd of delicately and gorgeously habited men and women. The *contrast* is inimitable."

"It *must* be," said the king: and the council arose hurriedly (as it was growing late), to put in execution the scheme of Hop-Frog.

His mode of equipping the party as orang-utans was very simple, but effective enough for his purposes. The animals in question had, at the epoch of my story, very rarely been seen in any part of the civilized world; and as the imitations made by the dwarf were sufficiently beast-like and more than sufficiently hideous, their truthfulness to nature was thus thought to be secured.

The king and his ministers were first encased in tight-fitting stockinet shirts and drawers. They were then saturated with tar. At this stage of the process, some one of the party suggested feathers; but the suggestion was at once overruled by the dwarf, who soon convinced the eight, by ocular demonstration, that the hair of such a brute as the orang-utan was much more efficiently represented by *flax*. A thick coating of the latter was accordingly plastered upon the coating of tar. A long chain was now procured. First, it was passed about the waist of the king, *and tied*; then about another of the party, and also tied; then about all successively, in the same manner. When this chaining arrangement was complete, and the party stood as far apart from each other as possible, they formed a circle; and to make all things appear natural, Hop-Frog passed the residue of the chain, in two diameters, at right angles, across the circle, after the fashion adopted, at the present day, by those who capture chimpanzees, or other large apes, in Borneo.

The grand saloon in which the masquerade was to take place was a circular room, very lofty, and receiving the light of the sun only through a single window at top. At night (the season for which the apartment was especially designed) it was illuminated principally by a large chandelier, depending by a chain from the center of the sky-light, and lowered, or elevated, by means of a counter-balance as usual; but (in order not to look unsightly) this latter passed outside the cupola and over the roof.

The arrangements of the room had been left to Trippetta's super-intendence; but, in some particulars, it seems, she had been guided by the calmer judgment of her friend the dwarf. At his suggestion it was that, on this occasion, the chandelier was removed. Its waxen drippings (which, in weather so warm, it was quite impossible to prevent) would have been seriously detrimental to the rich dresses of the guests, who, on account of the crowded state of the saloon, could not *all* be expected to keep from out its center—that is to say, from under the chandelier. Additional sconces were set in various parts of the hall, out of the way; and a flambeau, emitting sweet odor, was placed in the right hand of each of the Caryatids that stood against the wall—some fifty or sixty altogether.

The eight orang-utans, taking Hop-Frog's advice, waited patiently until midnight (when the room was thoroughly filled with masquer-aders) before making their appearance. No sooner had the clock ceased striking, however, than they rushed, or rather rolled in, all together—for the impediment of their chains caused most of the party to fall, and all to stumble as they entered.

The excitement among the masqueraders was prodigious, and filled the heart of the king with glee. As had been anticipated, there were not a few of the guests who supposed the ferocious-looking creatures to be beasts of *some* kind in reality, if not precisely orangutans. Many of the women swooned with affright; and had not the king taken the precaution to exclude all weapons from the saloon, his party might soon have expiated their frolic in their blood. As it was, a general rush was made for the doors; but the king had ordered them to be locked immediately upon his entrance; and, at the dwarf's suggestion, the keys had been deposited with *him*.

While the tumult was at its height, and each masquerader attentive only to his own safety—(for, in fact, there was much *real* danger from the pressure of the excited crowd)—the chain by which the chandelier ordinarily hung, and which had been drawn up on its removal, might have been seen very gradually to descend, until its hooked extremity came within three feet of the floor.

Soon after this, the king and his seven friends, having reeled about the hall in all directions, found themselves, at length, in its center, and, of course, in immediate contact with the chain. While they were thus situated, the dwarf, who had followed closely at their heels, inciting them to keep up the commotion, took hold of their own chain at the intersection of the two portions which crossed the circle diametrically and at right angles. Here, with the rapidity of thought, he inserted the hook from which the chandelier had been wont to depend; and, in an instant, by some unseen agency, the chandelier-chain was drawn so far upward as to take the hook out of reach, and, as an inevitable consequence, to drag the orang-utans together in close connection, and face to face.

The masqueraders, by this time, had recovered, in some measure, from their alarm; and, beginning to regard the whole matter as a well-contrived pleasantry, set up a loud shout of laughter at the predicament of the apes.

"Leave them to *me!* " now screamed Hop-Frog, his shrill voice making itself easily heard through all the din. "Leave them to *me*. I fancy *I* know them. If I can only get a good look at them, I can soon tell who they are."

Here, scrambling over the heads of the crowd, he managed to get to the wall; when, seizing a flambeau from one of the Caryatids, he returned, as he went, to the center of the room—leaped, with the agility of a monkey, upon the kings head—and thence clambered a few feet up the chain—holding down the torch to examine the group of orang-utans, and still screaming, "*I* shall soon find out who they are!"

And now, while the whole assembly (the apes included) were convulsed with laughter, the jester suddenly uttered a shrill whistle; when the chain flew violently up for about thirty feet—dragging with it the dismayed and struggling orang-utans, and leaving them suspended in mid-air between the sky-light and the floor. Hop-Frog, clinging to the chain as it rose, still maintained his relative position in respect to the eight maskers, and still (as if nothing were the matter) continued to thrust his torch down towards them, as though endeavoring to discover who they were.

So thoroughly astonished was the whole company at this ascent, that a dead silence, of about a minute's duration, ensued. It was broken by just such a low, harsh, *grating* sound, as had before attracted the attention of the king and his councillors, when the former threw the wine in the face of Trippetta. But, on the present occasion, there could be no question as to *whence* the sound issued. It came from the fang-like teeth of the dwarf, who ground them and gnashed them as he foamed at the mouth, and glared, with an expression of maniacal rage, into the upturned countenances of the king and his seven companions.

"Aha!" said at length the infuriated jester. "Aha! I begin to see who these people are, now!" Here, pretending to scrutinize the king more closely, he held the flambeau to the flaxen coat which enveloped him, and which instantly burst into a sheet of vivid flame. In less than half a minute the whole eight orang-utans were blazing fiercely, amid the shrieks of the multitude who gazed at them from below, horror-stricken, and without the power to render them the slightest assistance.

At length the flames, suddenly increasing in virulence, forced the jester to climb higher up the chain, to be out of their reach; and, as he made this movement, the crowd again sank, for a brief instant, into silence. The dwarf seized his opportunity, and once more spoke:

"I now see *distinctly*," he said, "what manner of people these maskers are. They are a great king and his seven privy-councillors—a king who does not scruple to strike a defenseless girl, and his seven councillors who abet him in the outrage. As for myself, I am simply Hop-Frog, the jester—and *this is my last jest*."

Owing to the high combustibility of both the flax and the tar to which it adhered, the dwarf had scarcely made an end of his brief speech before the work of vengeance was complete. The eight corpses swung in their chains, a fetid, blackened, hideous, and indistinguishable mass. The cripple hurled his torch at them, clambered leisurely to the ceiling, and disappeared through the sky-light.

It is supposed that Trippetta, stationed on the roof of the saloon, had been the accomplice of her friend in his fiery revenge, and that, together, they effected their escape to their own country: for neither was seen again.

DRACULA

DRACULA

BRAM STOKER

This edition published in 2019 by Arcturus Publishing Limited
26/27 Bickels Yard, 151–153 Bermondsey Street,
London SE1 3HA

Introduction by Brian Busby
Typesetting by Palimpsest Book Production Limited

Cover design: Peter Ridley
Design: Beatriz Custodio

AD001214UK

Printed in the UK

Introduction

Despite the popular success of more contemporary works like Stephanie Meyer's *Twilight* and *The Vampire Chronicles* by Anne Rice, *Dracula* remains in place as the pre-eminent vampire story. Yet, when first published in 1897, Bram Stoker's tale of the Transylvanian nobleman and his thirst for blood was not a best seller. Indeed, several decades passed before it approached the status it holds today.

Its author was born Abraham Stoker on 8 November 1847 in Dublin, Ireland. Bedridden by an unidentified illness as a child, he regained his strength and represented Trinity College, Dublin in athletic competitions during his studies. Stoker graduated with honours in mathematics, joined the civil service, and served as theatre critic for *The Dublin Evening Mail*. This latter occupation encouraged a friendship with Sir Henry Irving, one of the greatest actors of the day. Stoker soon became Irving's personal assistant and managed London's Lyceum Theatre, which the actor owned. Such was Irving's fame that at the time of Stoker's own death, on 20 April 1912, he was remembered mainly for his connection to the performer.

Stoker's writings reflect a broad range of interests, and include a gathering of fairy tales titled *Under the Sunset* (1881), the political novel *The Snake's Pass* (1890), and *Snowbound* (1908), a collection of short stories set in the theatrical world. It is, however, Stoker's writing within the horror genre that continues to be read today. After *Dracula*, his most popular novel is *The Lair of the White Worm* (1911), a story that includes many of the same supernatural elements found in the earlier work.

CONTENTS

1 Jonathan Harker's Journal.. 11

2 Jonathan Harker's Journal.. 23

3 Jonathan Harker's Journal.. 34

4 Jonathan Harker's Journal.. 46

5 Letter from Miss Mina Murray 58

6 Mina Murray's Journal 67

7 Cutting from 'The Dailygraph', 8 August 78

8 Mina Murray's Journal 90

9 Letter, Mina Harker to Lucy Westenra........................... 103

10 Letter, Dr Seward to Hon. Arthur Holmwood............... 117

11 Lucy Westenra's Diary 130

12 Dr Seward's Diary 141

13 Dr Seward's Diary 157

14 Mina Harker's Journal 171

15 Dr Seward's Diary 185

16 Dr Seward's Diary 197

17 Dr Seward's Diary 207

18 Dr Seward's Diary 219

19 Jonathan Harker's Journal.. 233

20 Jonathan Harker's Journal.. 245

21 Dr Seward's Diary 258

22 Jonathan Harker's Journal.. 271

23 Dr Seward's Diary 282

24 Dr Seward's Phonograph Diary, Spoken By
   Van Helsing 294

25 Dr Seward's Diary 307

26 Dr Seward's Diary 320

27 Mina Harker's Journal 335

How these papers have been placed in sequence will be made clear in the reading of them. All needless matters have been eliminated, so that a history almost at variance with the possibilities of latter-day belief may stand forth as simple fact. There is throughout no statement of past events wherein memory may err, for all the records chosen are exactly contemporary, given from the standpoints and within the range of knowledge of those who made them.

CHAPTER 1

JONATHAN HARKER'S JOURNAL

(Kept in shorthand)

3 May. Bistritz. – Left Munich at 8.35 p.m. on 1st May, arriving at Vienna early next morning; should have arrived at 6.46, but train was an hour late. Buda-Pesth seems a wonderful place, from the glimpse which I got of it from the train and the little I could walk through the streets. I feared to go very far from the station, as we had arrived late and would start as near the correct time as possible. The impression I had was that we were leaving the West and entering the East; the most Western of splendid bridges over the Danube, which is here of noble width and depth, took us among the traditions of Turkish rule.

We left in pretty good time, and came after nightfall to Klausenburgh. Here I stopped for the night at the Hôtel Royale. I had for dinner, or rather supper, a chicken done up some way with red pepper, which was very good but thirsty. (*Mem.*, get recipe for Mina.) I asked the waiter, and he said it was called 'paprika hendl,' and that, as it was a national dish, I should be able to get it anywhere along the Carpathians. I found my smattering of German very useful here; indeed, I don't know how I should be able to get on without it.

Having some time at my disposal when in London, I had visited the British Museum, and made search among the books and maps in the library regarding Transylvania; it had struck me that some foreknowledge of the country could hardly fail to have some importance in dealing with a noble of that country. I find that the district he named is in the extreme east of the country, just on the borders of three states, Transylvania, Moldavia, and Bukovina, in the midst of the Carpathian mountains; one of the wildest and least known portions of Europe. I was not able to light on any map or work giving the exact locality of the Castle Dracula, as there are no maps of this country as yet to compare with our own Ordnance Survey maps; but I found that Bistritz, the post town named by Count Dracula, is a fairly well-known place. I shall enter here some of my notes, as they may refresh my memory when I talk over my travels with Mina.

In the population of Transylvania there are four distinct nationalities: Saxons in the south, and mixed with them the Wallachs, who are the descendants of the Dacians; Magyars in the west, and Szekelys in the east and north. I am going among the latter, who claim to be descended from Attila and the Huns. This may be so, for when the Magyars conquered the country in the eleventh century they found the Huns settled in it. I read that every known superstition in the world is gathered into the horse-shoe of the Carpathians, as if it were the centre of some sort of imaginative whirlpool; if so my stay may be very interesting. (*Mem.*, I must ask the Count all about them.)

I did not sleep well, though my bed was comfortable enough, for I had all sorts of queer dreams. There was a dog howling all night under my window, which may have had something to do with it; or it may have been the paprika, for I had to drink up all the water in my carafe, and was still thirsty. Towards morning I slept and was wakened by the continuous knocking at my door, so I guess I must have been sleeping soundly then. I had for breakfast more paprika, and a sort of porridge of maize flour which they said was 'mamaliga,' and egg-plant stuffed with force-meat, a very excellent dish, which they call 'impletata.' (*Mem.*, get recipe for this also.) I had to hurry breakfast, for the train started a little before eight, or rather it ought to have done so, for after rushing to the station at 7.30 I had to sit in the carriage for more than an hour before we began to move. It seems to me that the further East you go the more unpunctual are the trains. What ought they to be in China?

All day long we seemed to dawdle through a country which was full of beauty of every kind. Sometimes we saw little towns or castles on the top of steep hills such as we see in old missals; sometimes we ran by rivers and streams which seemed from the wide stony margin on each side of them to be subject to great floods. It takes a lot of water, and running strong, to sweep the outside edge of a river clear. At every station there were groups of people, sometimes crowds, and in all sorts of attire. Some of them were just like the peasants at home or those I saw coming through France and Germany, with short jackets and round hats and home-made trousers; but others were very picturesque. The women looked pretty, except when you got near them, but they were very clumsy about the waist. They had all full white sleeves of some kind or other, and most of them had big belts with a lot of strips of something fluttering from them like the dresses in a ballet, but of course petticoats under them. The strangest figures we saw were the Slovaks, who are more barbarian than the rest, with their big cowboy hats, great baggy dirty-white trousers, white linen shirts, and enormous heavy leather belts, nearly a foot wide, all studded over with brass nails. They wore high boots, with their trousers tucked into them, and had long black hair and heavy black moustaches.

They are very picturesque, but do not look prepossessing. On the stage they would be set down at once as some old Oriental band of brigands. They are, however, I am told, very harmless and rather wanting in natural self-assertion.

It was on the dark side of twilight when we got to Bistritz, which is a very interesting old place. Being practically on the frontier – for the Borgo Pass leads from it into Bukovina – it has had a very stormy existence, and it certainly shows marks of it. Fifty years ago a series of great fires took place, which made terrible havoc on five separate occasions. At the very beginning of the seventeenth century it underwent a siege of three weeks and lost 13,000 people, the casualties of war proper being assisted by famine and disease.

Count Dracula had directed me to go to the Golden Krone Hotel, which I found, to my great delight, to be thoroughly old-fashioned, for of course I wanted to see all I could of the ways of the country. I was evidently expected, for when I got near the door I faced a cheery-looking elderly woman in the usual peasant dress – white undergarment with long double apron, front and back, of coloured stuff fitting almost too tight for modesty. When I came close she bowed, and said: 'The Herr Englishman?' 'Yes,' I said, 'Jonathan Harker.' She smiled, and gave some message to an elderly man in white shirt-sleeves, who had followed her to the door. He went, but immediately returned with a letter: –

'My Friend, – Welcome to the Carpathians. I am anxiously expecting you. Sleep well to-night. At three to-morrow the stage-coach will start for Bukovina; a place on it is kept for you. At the Borgo Pass my carriage will await you and will bring you to me. I trust that your journey from London has been a happy one, and that you will enjoy your stay in my beautiful land. – Your friend,
'Dracula.'

4 May. – I found that my landlord had got a letter from the Count, directing him to secure the best place on the coach for me; but on making inquiries as to details he seemed somewhat reticent, and pretended that he could not understand my German. This could not be true, because up to then he had understood it perfectly; at least, he answered my questions exactly as if he did. He and his wife, the old lady who had received me, looked at each other in a frightened sort of way. He mumbled out that the money had been sent in a letter, and that was all he knew. When I asked him if he knew Count Dracula, and could tell me anything of his castle, both he and his wife crossed themselves, and, saying that they knew nothing at all, simply refused to speak further. It was so near the time of starting that I had no time to ask anyone else, for it was all very mysterious and not by any means comforting.

Just before I was leaving, the old lady came up to my room and said in a very hysterical way: –

'Must you go? Oh! young Herr, must you go?' She was in such an excited state that she seemed to have lost her grip of what German she knew, and mixed it all up with some other language which I did not know at all. I was just able to follow her by asking many questions. When I told her that I must go at once, and that I was engaged on important business, she asked again: –

'Do you know what day it is?' I answered that it was the fourth of May. She shook her head as she said again: –

'Oh, yes! I know that, I know that! but do you know what day it is?' On my saying that I did not understand, she went on:

'It is the eve of St George's Day. Do you not know that to-night, when the clock strikes midnight, all the evil things in the world will have full sway? Do you know where you are going, and what you are going to?' She was in such evident distress that I tried to comfort her, but without effect. Finally she went down on her knees and implored me not to go; at least to wait a day or two before starting. It was all very ridiculous, but I did not feel comfortable. However, there was business to be done, and I could allow nothing to interfere with it. I therefore tried to raise her up, and said, as gravely as I could, that I thanked her, but my duty was imperative, and that I must go. She then rose and dried her eyes, and taking a crucifix from her neck offered it to me. I did not know what to do, for, as an English Churchman, I have been taught to regard such things as in some measure idolatrous, and yet it seemed so ungracious to refuse an old lady meaning so well and in such a state of mind. She saw, I suppose, the doubt in my face, for she put the rosary round my neck, and said, 'For your mother's sake,' and went out of the room. I am writing up this part of the diary whilst I am waiting for the coach, which is, of course, late; and the crucifix is still round my neck. Whether it is the old lady's fear, I do not know, but I am not feeling nearly as easy in my mind as usual. If this book should ever reach Mina before I do, let it bring my good-bye. Here comes the coach!

5 May. The Castle. – The grey of the morning has passed, and the sun is high over the distant horizon, which seems jagged, whether with trees or hills I know not, for it is so far off that big things and little are mixed.

I am not sleepy, and, as I am not to be called till I awake, naturally I write till sleep comes. There are many odd things to put down, and, lest who reads them may fancy that I dined too well before I left Bistritz, let me put down my dinner exactly. I dined on what they call 'robber steak' – bits of bacon, onion, and beef, seasoned with red pepper, and strung on sticks and roasted over the fire, in the simple style of the London cat's-meat! The wine was Golden Mediasch, which produces a queer sting on the tongue, which is, however, not disagreeable. I had only a couple of glasses of this, and nothing else.

When I got on the coach the driver had not taken his seat, and I saw him talking with the landlady. They were evidently talking of me, for every now and then they looked at me, and some of the people who were sitting on the bench outside the door – which they call by a name meaning 'word-bearer' – came and listened, and then looked at me, most of them pityingly. I could hear a lot of words often repeated, queer words, for there were many nationalities in the crowd; so I quietly got my polyglot dictionary from my bag and looked them out. I must say they were not cheering to me, for amongst them were 'Ordog' – Satan, 'pokol' – hell, 'stregoica' – witch, 'vrolok' and 'vlkoslak' – both of which mean the same thing, one being Slovak and the other Servian for something that is either were-wolf or vampire. (*Mem.*, I must ask the Count about these superstitions.)

When we started, the crowd round the inn door, which had by this time swelled to a considerable size, all made the sign of the cross and pointed two fingers towards me. With some difficulty I got a fellow-passenger to tell me what they meant; he would not answer at first, but on learning that I was English, he explained that it was a charm or guard against the evil eye. This was not very pleasant for me, just starting for an unknown place to meet an unknown man; but everyone seemed so kind-hearted, and so sorrowful, and so sympathetic that I could not but be touched. I shall never forget the last glimpse which I had of the inn-yard and its crowd of pictur-esque figures, all crossing themselves, as they stood round the wide archway, with its background of rich foliage of oleander and orange trees in green tubs clustered in the centre of the yard. Then our driver, whose wide linen drawers covered the whole front of the box-seat – 'gotza' they call them – cracked his big whip over his four small horses, which ran abreast, and we set off on our journey.

I soon lost sight and recollection of ghostly fears in the beauty of the scene as we drove along, although had I known the language, or rather languages, which my fellow-passengers were speaking, I might not have been able to throw them off so easily. Before us lay a green sloping land full of forests and woods, with here and there steep hills, crowned with clumps of trees or with farmhouses, the blank gable end to the road. There was everywhere a bewildering mass of fruit blossom – apple, plum, pear, cherry; and as we drove by I could see the green grass under the trees spangled with the fallen petals. In and out amongst these green hills of what they call here the 'Mittel Land' ran the road, losing itself as it swept round the grassy curve, or was shut out by the straggling ends of pine woods, which here and there ran down the hillsides like tongues of flame. The road was rugged, but still we seemed to fly over it with a feverish haste. I could not understand then what the haste meant, but the driver was evidently bent on losing no time in reaching Borgo Prund. I was told that this road is in summer-time excellent, but that it had not yet been put in order after the winter snows. In this respect it is different from the general run of roads in the Carpathians, for it is an old tradition that they are not to be kept in too good order. Of old the Hospadars would not repair them, lest the Turk should think that they were preparing to bring in foreign troops, and so hasten the war which was always really at loading point.

Beyond the green swelling hills of the Mittel Land rose mighty slopes of forest up to the lofty steeps of the Carpathians themselves. Right and left of us they towered, with the afternoon sun falling full upon them and bringing out all the glorious colours of this beautiful range, deep blue and purple in the shadows of the peaks, green and brown where grass and rock mingled, and an endless perspective of jagged rock and pointed crags, till these were themselves lost in the distance, where the snowy peaks rose grandly. Here and there seemed mighty rifts in the mountains, through which, as the sun began to sink, we saw now and again the white gleam of falling water. One of my companions touched my arm as we swept round the base of a hill and opened up the lofty, snow-covered peak of a mountain, which seemed, as we wound on our serpentine way, to be right before us: –

'Look! Isten szek!' – 'God's seat!' – and he crossed himself reverently. As we wound on our endless way, and the sun sank lower and lower behind us, the shadows of the evening began to creep round us. This was emphasized by the fact that the snowy mountain-top still held the sunset, and seemed to glow out with a delicate cool pink. Here and there we passed Cszeks and Slovaks, all in picturesque attire, but I noticed that goitre was painfully prevalent. By the roadside were many crosses, and as we swept by, my companions all crossed themselves. Here and there was a peasant man or woman kneeling before a shrine, who did not even turn round as we approached, but seemed in the self-surrender of devotion to have neither eyes nor ears for the outer world. There were many things new to me: for instance, hay-ricks in the trees, and here and there very beautiful masses of weeping birch, their white stems shining like silver through the delicate green of the leaves. Now and again we passed a leiter-waggon – the ordinary peasant's cart, with its long, snake-like vertebrae, calculated to suit the inequalities of the road. On this were sure to be seated quite a group of home-coming peasants, the Cszeks with their white, and the Slovaks with their coloured, sheepskins, the latter carrying lance-fashion their long staves, with axe at end. As the evening fell it began to get very cold, and the growing twilight seemed to merge into one dark mistiness the gloom of the trees, oak, beech, and pine, though in the valleys which ran deep between the spurs of the hills, as we ascended through the Pass, the dark firs stood out here and there against the background of late-lying snow. Sometimes, as the road was cut through the pine woods that seemed in the darkness to be closing down upon us, great masses of greyness, which here and there bestrewed the trees, produced a peculiarly weird and solemn effect, which carried on the thoughts and grim fancies engendered earlier in the evening, when the falling sunset threw into strange relief the ghost-like clouds which amongst the Carpathians seem to wind ceaselessly through the valleys. Sometimes the hills were so steep that, despite our driver's haste, the horses could only go slowly. I wished to get down and walk up them, as we do at home, but the driver would not hear of it. 'No, no,' he said; 'you must not walk here; the dogs are too fierce,' and then he added, with what he evidently meant for grim pleasantry – for he looked round to catch the approving smile of the rest – 'and you may have enough of such matters before you go to sleep.' The only stop he would make was a moment's pause to light his lamps.

When it grew dark there seemed to be some excitement amongst the passengers, and they kept speaking to him, one after the other, as though urging him to further speed. He lashed the horses unmercifully with his long whip, and with wild cries of encouragement urged them on to further exertions. Then through the darkness I could see a sort of patch of grey light ahead of us, as though there were a cleft in the hills. The excitement of the passengers grew greater; the crazy coach rocked on its great leather springs, and swayed like a boat tossed on a stormy sea. I had to hold on. The road grew more level, and we appeared to fly along. Then the mountains seemed to come nearer to us on each side and to frown down upon us; we were entering the Borgo Pass. One by one several of the passengers offered me gifts, which they pressed upon me with an earnestness which would take no denial; these were certainly of an odd and varied kind, but each was given in simple good faith, with a kindly word, and a blessing, and that strange mixture of fear-meaning movements which I had seen outside the hotel at Bistritz – the sign of the cross and the guard against the evil eye. Then, as we flew along, the driver leaned forward, and on each side the passengers, craning over the edge of the coach, peered eagerly into the darkness. It was evident that something very exciting was either happening or expected, but though I asked each passenger, no one would give me the slightest explanation. This state of excitement kept on for some little time; and at last we saw before us the Pass opening out on the eastern side. There were dark, rolling clouds overhead, and in the air the heavy, oppressive sense of thunder. It seemed as though the mountain range had separated two atmospheres, and that now we had got into the thunderous one. I was now myself looking out for the conveyance which was to take me to the Count. Each moment I expected to see the glare of lamps through the blackness; but all was dark. The only light was the flickering rays of our own lamps, in which steam from our hard-driven horses rose in a white cloud. We could now see the sandy road lying white before us, but there was on it no sign of a vehicle. The passengers drew back with a sigh of gladness, which seemed to mock my own disappointment. I was already thinking what I had best do, when the driver, looking at his watch, said to the others something which I could hardly hear, it was spoken so quietly and in so low a tone; I thought it was, 'An hour less than the time.' Then, turning to me, he said in German worse than my own: –

'There is no carriage here. The Herr is not expected, after all. He will now come on to Bukovina, and return to-morrow or the next day; better the next day.' Whilst he was speaking the horses began to neigh and snort and plunge wildly, so that the driver had to hold them up. Then, amongst a chorus of screams from the peasants and a universal crossing of themselves, a calèche, with four horses, drove up behind us, overtook us, and drew up beside the coach. I could see from the flash of our lamps, as the rays fell on them, that the horses were coal-black and splendid animals. They were driven by a tall man, with a long brown beard and a great black hat, which seemed to hide his face from us. I could only see the gleam of a pair of very bright eyes, which seemed red in the lamplight, as he turned to us. He said to the driver: –

'You are early to-night, my friend.' The man stammered in reply: –
'The English Herr was in a hurry,' to which the stranger replied: –

'That is why, I suppose, you wished him to go on to Bukovina. You cannot deceive me, my friend; I know too much, and my horses are swift.' As he spoke he smiled, the lamplight fell on a hard-looking mouth, with very red lips and sharp-looking teeth, as white as ivory. One of my companions whispered to another the line from Burger's 'Lenore': –

'Denn die Todten reiten schnell.' –
('For the dead travel fast.')

The strange driver evidently heard the words, for he looked up with a gleaming smile. The passenger turned his face away, at the same time putting out his two fingers and crossing himself. 'Give me the Herr's luggage,' said the driver; and with exceeding alacrity my bags were handed out and put in the calèche. Then I descended from the side of the coach, as the calèche was close alongside, the driver helping me with a hand which caught my arm in a grip of steel; his strength must have been prodigious. Without a word he shook his reins, the horses turned, and we swept into the darkness of the Pass. As I looked back I saw the steam from the horses of the coach by the light of the lamps, and projected against it the figures of my late companions crossing themselves. Then the driver cracked his whip and called to his horses, and off they swept on their way to Bukovina.

As they sank into the darkness I felt a strange chill, and a lonely feeling came over me; but a cloak was thrown over my shoulders, and a rug across my knees, and the driver said in excellent German: –

'The night is chill, mein Herr, and my master the Count bade me take all care of you. There is a flask of slivovitz [the plum brandy of the country] underneath the seat, if you should require it.' I did not take any, but it was a comfort to know it was there, all the same. I felt a little strange, and not a little frightened. I think had there been any alternative I should have taken it, instead of prosecuting that unknown night journey. The carriage went at a hard pace straight along, then we made a complete turn and went along another straight road. It seemed to me that we were simply going over and over the same ground again; and so I took note of some salient point, and found that this was so. I would have liked to have asked the driver what this all meant, but I really feared to do so, for I thought that, placed as I was, any protest would have had no effect in case there had been an intention to delay. By and by, however, as I was curious to know how time was passing, I struck a match, and by its flame looked at my watch; it was within a few minutes of midnight. This gave me a sort of shock, for I suppose the general superstition about midnight was increased by my recent experiences. I waited with a sick feeling of suspense.

Then a dog began to howl somewhere in a farmhouse far down the road – a long, agonized wailing, as if from fear. The sound was taken up by another dog, and then another and another, till, borne on the wind which now sighed softly through the Pass, a wild howling began, which seemed to come from all over the country, as far as the imagination could grasp it through the gloom of the night. At the first howl the horses began to strain and rear, but the driver spoke to them soothingly, and they quieted down, but shivered and sweated as though after a runaway from sudden fright. Then, far off in the distance, from the mountains on each side of us began a louder and a sharper howling – that of wolves – which affected both the horses and myself in the same way – for I was minded to jump from the calèche and run, whilst they reared again and plunged madly, so that the driver had to use all his great strength to keep them from bolting. In a few minutes, however, my own ears got accustomed to the sound, and the horses so far became quiet that the driver was able to descend and to stand before them. He petted and soothed them, and whispered something in their ears, as I have heard of horse-tamers doing, and with extraordinary effect, for under his caresses they became quite manageable again, though they still trembled. The driver again took his seat, and shaking his reins, started off at a great pace. This time, after going to the far side of the Pass, he suddenly turned down a narrow roadway which ran sharply to the right.

Soon we were hemmed in with trees, which in places arched right over the roadway till we passed as through a tunnel; and again great frowning rocks guarded us boldly on either side. Though we were in shelter, we could hear the rising wind, for it moaned and whistled through the rocks, and the branches of the trees crashed together as we swept along. It grew colder and colder still, and fine, powdery snow began to fall, so that soon we and all around us were covered with a white blanket. The keen wind still carried the howling of the dogs, though this grew fainter as we went on our way. The baying of the wolves sounded nearer and nearer, as though they were closing round on us from every side. I grew dreadfully afraid, and the horses shared my fear; but the driver was not in the least disturbed. He kept turning his head to left and right, but I could not see anything through the darkness.

Suddenly, away on our left, I saw a faint flickering blue flame. The driver saw it at the same moment; he at once checked the horses and, jumping to the ground, disappeared into the darkness. I did not know what to do, the less as the howling of the wolves grew closer; but while I wondered the driver suddenly appeared again, and without a word took his seat, and we resumed our journey. I think I must have fallen asleep and kept dreaming of the incident, for it seemed to be repeated endlessly, and now, looking back, it is like a sort of awful nightmare. Once the flame appeared so near the road that even in the darkness around us I could watch the driver's motions. He went rapidly to where the blue flame rose – it must have been very faint, for it did not seem to illumine the place around it at all – and gathering a few stones, formed them into some device. Once there appeared a strange optical effect: when he stood between me and the flame he did not obstruct it, for I could see its ghostly flicker all the same. This startled me, but as the effect was only momentary, I took it that my eyes deceived me straining through the darkness. Then for a time there were no blue flames, and we sped onwards through the gloom, with the howling of the wolves around us, as though they were following in a moving circle.

At last there came a time when the driver went further afield than he had yet done, and during his absence the horses began to tremble worse than ever and to snort and scream with fright. I could not see any cause for it, for the howling of the wolves had ceased altogether; but just then the moon, sailing through the black clouds, appeared behind the jagged crest of a beetling, pineclad rock, and by its light I saw around us a ring of wolves, with white teeth and lolling red tongues, with long, sinewy limbs and shaggy hair. They were a hundred times more terrible in the grim silence which held them than even when they howled. For myself, I felt a sort of paralysis of fear. It is only when a man feels himself face to face with such horrors that he can understand their true import.

All at once the wolves began to howl as though the moonlight had had some peculiar effect on them. The horses jumped about and reared, and looked helplessly round with eyes that rolled in a way painful to see; but the living ring of terror encompassed them on every side, and they had perforce to remain within it. I called to the coachman to come, for it seemed to me that our only chance was to try to break out through the ring and to aid his approach. I shouted and beat the side of the calèche, hoping by the noise to scare the wolves from that side, so as to give him a chance of reaching the trap. How he came there, I know not, but I heard his voice raised in a tone of imperious command, and looking towards the sound, saw him stand in the roadway. As he swept his long arms, as though brushing aside some impalpable obstacle, the wolves fell back and back further still. Just then a heavy cloud passed across the face of the moon, so that we were again in darkness.

When I could see again the driver was climbing into the calèche, and the wolves had disappeared. This was all so strange and uncanny that a dreadful fear came upon me, and I was afraid to speak or move. The time seemed interminable as we swept on our way, now in almost complete darkness, for the rolling clouds obscured the moon. We kept on ascending, with occasional periods of quick descent, but in the main always ascending. Suddenly I became conscious of the fact that the driver was in the act of pulling up the horses in the courtyard of a vast ruined castle, from whose tall black windows came no ray of light, and whose broken battlements showed a jagged line against the moonlit sky.

CHAPTER 2
JONATHAN HARKER'S JOURNAL
(CONTINUED)

5 May. – I must have been asleep, for certainly if I had been fully awake I must have noticed the approach to such a remarkable place. In the gloom the courtyard looked of considerable size, and as several dark ways led from it under great round arches it perhaps seemed bigger than it really is. I have not yet been able to see it by daylight.

When the calèche stopped the driver jumped down, and held out his hand to assist me to alight. Again I could not but notice his prodigious strength. His hand actually seemed like a steel vice that could have crushed mine if he had chosen. Then he took out my traps, and placed them on the ground beside me as I stood close to a great door, old and studded with large iron nails, and set in a projecting doorway of massive stone. I could see even in the dim light that the stone was massively carved, but that the carving had been much worn by time and weather. As I stood, the driver jumped again into his seat and shook the reins; the horses started forward, and trap and all disappeared down one of the dark openings.

I stood in silence where I was, for I did not know what to do. Of bell or knocker there was no sign; through these frowning walls and dark window openings it was not likely that my voice could penetrate. The time I waited seemed endless, and I felt doubts and fears crowding upon me. What sort of place had I come to, and among what kind of people? What sort of grim adventure was it on which I had embarked? Was this a customary incident in the life of a solicitor's clerk sent out to explain the purchase of a London estate to a foreigner? Solicitor's clerk! Mina would not like that. Solicitor – for just before leaving London I got word that my examination was successful; and I am now a full-blown solicitor! I began to rub my eyes and pinch myself to see if I were awake. It all seemed like a horrible nightmare to me, and I expected that I should suddenly awake, and find myself at home, with the dawn struggling in through the windows, as I had now and again felt in the morning after a day of overwork. But my flesh answered the pinching test, and my eyes were not to be deceived. I was indeed awake and among the Carpathians. All I could do now was to be patient, and to wait the coming of the morning.

Just as I had come to this conclusion I heard a heavy step approaching behind the great door, and saw through the chinks the gleam of a coming light. Then there was the sound of rattling chains and the clanking of massive bolts drawn back. A key was turned with the loud grating noise of long disuse, and the great door swung back.

Within, stood a tall old man, clean-shaven save for a long white moustache, and clad in black from head to foot, without a single speck of colour about him anywhere. He held in his hand an antique silver lamp, in which the flame burned without chimney or globe of any kind, throwing long, quivering shadows as it flickered in the draught of the open door. The old man motioned me in with his right hand with a courtly gesture, saying in excellent English, but with a strange intonation: –

'Welcome to my house! Enter freely and of your own will!' He made no motion of stepping to meet me, but stood like a statue, as though his gesture of welcome had fixed him into stone. The instant, however, that I had stepped over the threshold, he moved impulsively forward, and holding out his hand grasped mine with a strength which made me wince, an effect which was not lessened by the fact that it seemed as cold as ice – more like the hand of a dead than a living man. Again he said: –

'Welcome to my house. Come freely. Go safely. And leave something of the happiness you bring!' The strength of the handshake was so much akin to that which I had noticed in the driver, whose face I had not seen, that for a moment I doubted if it were not the same person to whom I was speaking; so, to make sure, I said interrogatively: –

'Count Dracula?' He bowed in a courtly way as he replied: –

'I am Dracula. And I bid you welcome, Mr Harker, to my house. Come in; the night air is chill, and you must need to eat and rest.' As he was speaking he put the lamp on a bracket on the wall, and stepping out, took my luggage; he had carried it in before I could forestall him. I protested, but he insisted: –

'Nay, sir, you are my guest. It is late, and my people are not available. Let me see to your comfort myself.' He insisted on carrying my traps along the passage, and then up a great winding stair, and along another great passage, on whose stone floor our steps rang heavily. At the end of this he threw open a heavy door, and I rejoiced to see within a well-lit room in which a table was spread for supper, and on whose mighty hearth a great fire of logs flamed and flared.

The Count halted, putting down my bags, closed the door, and crossing the room, opened another door, which led into a small octagonal room lit by a single lamp, and seemingly without a window of any sort. Passing through this, he opened another door, and motioned me to enter. It was a welcome sight; for here was a great bedroom well lighted and warmed with another log fire, which sent a hollow roar up the wide chimney. The Count himself left my luggage inside and withdrew, saying, before he closed the door: –

'You will need, after your journey, to refresh yourself by making your toilet. I trust you will find all you wish. When you are ready come into the other room, where you will find your supper prepared.'

The light and warmth and the Count's courteous welcome seemed to have dissipated all my doubts and fears. Having then reached my normal state, I discovered that I was half-famished with hunger; so making a hasty toilet, I went into the other room.

I found supper already laid out. My host, who stood on one side of the great fireplace, leaning against the stone-work, made a graceful wave of his hand to the table, and said: –

'I pray you, be seated and sup how you please. You will, I trust, excuse me that I do not join you; but I have dined already, and I do not sup.'

I handed to him the sealed letter which Mr Hawkins had entrusted to me. He opened it and read it gravely; then, with a charming smile, he handed it to me to read. One passage of it, at least, gave me a thrill of pleasure: –

'I much regret that an attack of gout, from which malady I am a constant sufferer, forbids absolutely any travelling on my part for some time to come; but I am happy to say I can send a sufficient substitute, one in whom I have every possible confidence. He is a young man, full of energy and talent in his own way, and of a very faithful disposition. He is discreet and silent, and has grown into manhood in my service. He shall be ready to attend on you when you will during his stay, and shall take your instructions in all matters.'

The Count himself came forward and took off the cover of a dish, and I fell to at once on an excellent roast chicken. This, with some cheese and a salad and a bottle of old Tokay, of which I had two glasses, was my supper. During the time I was eating it the Count asked me many questions as to my journey, and I told him by degrees all I had experienced.

By this time I had finished my supper, and by my host's desire had drawn up a chair by the fire and begun to smoke a cigar which he offered me, at the same time excusing himself that he did not smoke. I had now an opportunity of observing him, and found him of a very marked physiognomy.

His face was a strong – a very strong – aquiline, with high bridge of the thin nose and peculiarly arched nostrils; with lofty domed forehead, and hair growing scantily round the temples, but profusely elsewhere. His eyebrows were very massive, almost meeting over the nose, and with bushy hair that seemed to curl in its own profusion. The mouth, so far as I could see it under the heavy moustache, was fixed and rather cruel-looking, with peculiarly sharp white teeth; these protruded over the lips, whose remarkable ruddiness showed astonishing vitality in a man of his years. For the rest, his ears were pale and at the tops extremely pointed; the chin was broad and strong, and the cheeks firm though thin. The general effect was one of extraordinary pallor.

Hitherto I had noticed the backs of his hands as they lay on his knees in the firelight, and they had seemed rather white and fine; but seeing them now close to me, I could not but notice that they were rather coarse – broad, with squat fingers. Strange to say, there were hairs in the centre of the palm. The nails were long and fine, and cut to a sharp point. As the Count leaned over me and his hands touched me, I could not repress a shudder. It may have been that his breath was rank, but a horrible feeling of nausea came over me, which, do what I would, I could not conceal. The Count, evidently noticing it, drew back; and with a grim sort of smile, which showed more than he had yet done his protuberant teeth, sat himself down again on his own side of the fireplace. We were both silent for a while; and as I looked towards the window I saw the first dim streak of the coming dawn. There seemed a strange stillness over everything; but as I listened I heard, as if from down below in the valley, the howling of many wolves. The Count's eyes gleamed, and he said: –

'Listen to them – the children of the night. What music they make!' Seeing, I suppose, some expression in my face strange to him, he added: –

'Ah, sir, you dwellers in the city cannot enter into the feelings of the hunter.' Then he rose and said: –

'But you must be tired. Your bedroom is all ready, and to-morrow you shall sleep as late as you will. I have to be away till the afternoon; so sleep well and dream well!' and, with a courteous bow, he opened for me himself the door to the octagonal room, and I entered my bedroom . . .

I am all in a sea of wonders. I doubt; I fear; I think strange things which I dare not confess to my own soul. God keep me, if only for the sake of those dear to me!

7 May. – It is again early morning, but I have rested and enjoyed the last twenty-four hours. I slept till late in the day, and awoke of my own accord. When I had dressed myself I went into the room where we had supped, and found a cold breakfast laid out, with coffee kept hot by the pot being placed on the hearth. There was a card on the table, on which was written: –

'I have to be absent for a while. Do not wait for me. – D.' So I set to and enjoyed a hearty meal. When I had done, I looked for a bell, so that I might let the servants know I had finished; but I could not find one. There are certainly odd deficiences in the house, considering the extraordinary evidences of wealth which are round me. The table service is of gold, and so beautifully wrought that it must be of immense value. The curtains and upholstery of the chairs and sofas and the hangings of my bed are of the costliest and most beautiful fabrics, and must have been of fabulous value when they were made, for they are centuries old, though in excellent order. I saw something like them in Hampton Court, but there they were worn and frayed and moth-eaten. But still in none of the rooms is there a mirror. There is not even a toilet glass on my table, and I had to get the little shaving-glass from my bag before I could either shave or brush my hair. I have not yet seen a servant anywhere, or heard a sound near the castle except the howling of wolves. When I had finished my meal – I do not know whether to call it breakfast or dinner, for it was between five and six o'clock when I had it – I looked about for something to read, for I did not like to go about the castle until I had asked the Count's permission. There was absolutely nothing in the room, book, newspaper, or even writing materials; so I opened another door in the room and found a sort of library. The door opposite mine I tried, but found it locked.

In the library I found, to my great delight, a vast number of English books, whole shelves full of them, and bound volumes of magazines and newspapers. A table in the centre was littered with English magazines and newspapers, though none of them were of very recent date. The books were of the most varied kind – history, geography, politics, political economy, botany, geology, law – all relating to England and English life and customs and manners. There were even such books of reference as the London Directory, the 'Red' and 'Blue' books, Whitaker's Almanack, the Army and Navy Lists, and – it somehow gladdened my heart to see it – the Law List.

Whilst I was looking at the books, the door opened, and the Count entered. He saluted me in a hearty way, and hoped that I had had a good night's rest. Then he went on: –

'I am glad you found your way in here, for I am sure there is much that will interest you. These friends' – and he laid his hand on some of the books – 'have been good friends to me, and for some years past, ever since I had the idea of going to London, have given me many, many hours of pleasure. Through them I have come to know your great England; and to know her is to love her. I long to go through the crowded streets of your mighty London, to be in the midst of the whirl and rush of humanity, to share its life, its change, its death, and all that makes it what it is. But alas! as yet I only know your tongue through books. To you, my friend, I look that I know it to speak.'

'But, Count,' I said, 'you know and speak English thoroughly!' He bowed gravely.

'I thank you, my friend, for your all too flattering estimate, but yet I fear that I am but a little way on the road I would travel. True, I know the grammar and the words, but yet I know not how to speak them.'

'Indeed,' I said, 'you speak excellently.'

'Not so,' he answered. 'Well I know that, did I move and speak in your London, none there are who would not know me for a stranger. That is not enough for me. Here I am noble; I am *boyar*; the common people know me, and I am master. But a stranger in a strange land, he is no one; men know him not – and to know not is to care not for. I am content if I am like the rest, so that no man stops if he sees me, or pause in his speaking if he hear my words, to say, "Ha, ha! a stranger!" I have been so long master that I would be master still – or at least that none other should be master of me. You come to me not alone as agent of my friend Peter Hawkins, of Exeter, to tell me all about my new estate in London. You shall, I trust, rest here with me a while, so that by our talking I may learn the English intonation; and I would that you tell me when I make error, even of the smallest, in my speaking. I am sorry that I had to be away so long to-day; but you will, I know, forgive one who has so many important affairs in hand.'

Of course I said all I could about being willing, and asked if I might come into that room when I chose. He answered, 'Yes, certainly,' and added: –

'You may go anywhere you wish in the castle, except where the doors are locked, where of course you will not wish to go. There is reason that all things are as they are, and did you see with my eyes and know with my knowledge, you would perhaps better understand.' I said I was sure of this, and then he went on: –

'We are in Transylvania; and Transylvania is not England. Our ways are not your ways, and there shall be to you many strange things. Nay, from what you have told me of your experiences already, you know something of what strange things here may be.'

This led to much conversation. And as it was evident that he wanted to talk, if only for talking's sake, I asked him many questions regarding things that had already happened to me or come within my notice. Sometimes he sheered off the subject, or turned the conversation by pretending not to understand; but generally he answered all I asked most frankly. Then as time went on, and I had got somewhat bolder, I asked him of some of the strange things of the preceding night, as, for instance, why the coachman went to the places where we had seen the blue flames. Was it indeed true that they showed where gold was hidden? He then explained to me that it was commonly believed that on a certain night of the year – last night, in fact, when all evil spirits are supposed to have unchecked sway – a blue flame is seen over any place where treasure has been concealed. 'That treasure has been hidden,' he went on, 'in the region through which you came last night, there can be but little doubt; for it was the ground fought over for centuries by the Wallachian, the Saxon, and the Turk. Why, there is hardly a foot of soil in all this region that has not been enriched by the blood of men, patriots or invaders. In old days there were stirring times, when the Austrian and the Hungarian came up in hordes, and the patriots went out to meet them – men and women, the aged and the children too – and waited their coming on the rocks above the passes, that they might sweep destruction on them with their artificial avalanches. When the invader was triumphant he found but little, for whatever there was had been sheltered in the friendly soil.'

'But how,' said I, 'can it have remained so long undiscovered, when there is a sure index to it if men will but take the trouble to look?' The Count smiled, and as his lips ran back over his gums, the long, sharp, canine teeth showed out strangely; he answered: –

'Because your peasant is at heart a coward and a fool! Those flames only appear on one night. And on that night no man of this land will, if he can help it, stir without his doors. And, dear sir, even if he did he would not know what to do. Why, even the peasant that you tell me of who marked the place of the flame would not know where to look in daylight even for his own work. You would not, I dare be sworn, be able to find these places again?'

'There you are right,' I said. 'I know no more than the dead where even to look for them.' Then we drifted into other matters.

'Come,' he said at last, 'tell me of London and of the house which you have procured for me.' With an apology for my remissness, I went into my own room to get the papers from my bag. Whilst I was placing them in order I heard a rattling of china and silver in the next room, and as I passed through, noticed that the table had been cleared and the lamp lit, for it was by this time deep into the dark. The lamps were also lit in the study or library, and I found the Count lying on the sofa, reading, of all things in the world, an English Bradshaw's Guide. When I came in he cleared the books and papers from the table; and with him I went into plans and deeds and figures of all sorts. He was interested in everything, and asked me a myriad questions about the place and its surroundings. He clearly had studied beforehand all he could get on the subject of the neighbourhood, for he evidently at the end knew very much more than I did. When I remarked this, he answered: –

'Well, but, my friend, is it not needful that I should? When I go there I shall be all alone, and my friend Harker Jonathan – nay, pardon me, I fall into my country's habit of putting your patronymic first – my friend Jonathan Harker will not be by my side to correct and aid me. He will be in Exeter, miles away, probably working at papers of the law with my other friend, Peter Hawkins. So!'

We went thoroughly into the business of the purchase of the estate at Purfleet. When I had told him the facts and got his signature to the necessary papers, and had written a letter with them ready to post to Mr Hawkins, he began to ask me how I had come across so suitable a place. I read to him the notes which I had made at the time, and which I inscribe here: –

'At Purfleet, on a by-road, I came across just such a place as seemed to be required, and where was displayed a dilapidated notice that the place was for sale. It is surrounded by a high wall, of ancient structure, built of heavy stones, and has not been repaired for a large number of years. The closed gates were of heavy old oak and iron, all eaten with rust.

'The estate is called Carfax, no doubt a corruption of the old *Quatre Face*, as the house is four-sided, agreeing with the cardinal points of the compass. It contains in all some twenty acres, quite surrounded by the solid stone wall above mentioned. There are many trees on it, which make it in places gloomy, and there is a deep, dark-looking pond or small lake, evidently fed by some springs, as the water is clear and flows away in a fair-sized stream. The house is very large and of all periods back, I should say, to mediaeval times, for one part is of stone immensely thick, with only a few windows high up and heavily barred with iron. It looks like part of a keep, and is close to an old chapel or church. I could not enter it, as I had not the key of the door leading to it from the house, but I have taken with my Kodak views of it from various points. The house has been added to, but in a very straggling way, and I can only guess at the amount of ground it covers, which must be very great. There are but few houses close at hand, one being a very large house only recently added to and formed into a private lunatic asylum. It is not, however, visible from the grounds.'

When I had finished, he said: –

'I am glad that it is old and big. I myself am of an old family, and to live in a new house would kill me. A house cannot be made habitable in a day; and, after all, how few days go to make up a century. I rejoice also that there is a chapel of old times. We Transylvanian nobles love not to think that our bones may be amongst the common dead. I seek not gaiety nor mirth, not the bright voluptuousness of much sunshine and sparkling waters which please the young and gay. I am no longer young. And my heart, through weary years of mourning over the dead, is not attuned to mirth. Moreover, the walls of my castle are broken; the shadows are many, and the wind breathes cold through the broken battlements and casements. I love the shade and the shadow, and would be alone with my thoughts when I may.'

Somehow his words and his look did not seem to accord, or else it was that his cast of face made his smile look malignant and saturnine.

Presently, with an excuse, he left me, asking me to put all my papers together. He was some little time away, and I began to look at some of the books around me. One was an atlas, which I found opened naturally at England, as if that map had been much used. On looking at it I found in certain places little rings marked, and on examining these I noticed that one was near London on the east side, manifestly where his new estate was situated; the other two were Exeter, and Whitby on the Yorkshire coast.

It was the better part of an hour when the Count returned. 'Aha!' he said, 'still at your books? Good! But you must not work always. Come; I am informed that your supper is ready.' He took my arm, and we went into the next room, where I found an excellent supper ready on the table. The Count again excused himself, as he had dined out on his being away from home. But he sat as on the previous night, and chatted whilst I ate. After supper I smoked, as on the last evening, and the Count stayed with me, chatting and asking questions on every conceivable subject, hour after hour. I felt that it was getting very late indeed, but I did not say anything, for I felt under obligation to meet my host's wishes in every way. I was not sleepy, as the long sleep yesterday had fortified me; but I could not help experiencing that chill which comes over one at the coming of the dawn, which is like, in its way, the turn of the tide. They say that people who are near death die generally at the change to the dawn or at the turn of the tide; anyone who has, when tired, and tied as it were to his post, experienced this change in the atmosphere can well believe it. All at once we heard the crow of a cock coming up with preternatural shrillness through the clear morning air; Count Dracula, jumping to his feet, said: –

'Why, there is the morning again! How remiss I am to let you stay up so long! You must make your conversation regarding my dear new country of England less interesting, so that I may not forget how time flies by us,' and, with a courtly bow, he left me.

I went into my own room and drew the curtains, but there was little to notice; my window opened into the courtyard; all I could see was the warm grey of quickening sky. So I pulled the curtains again, and have written of this day.

8 May. – I began to fear as I wrote in this book that I was getting too diffuse; but now I am glad that I went into detail from the first, for there is something so strange about this place and all in it that I cannot but feel uneasy. I wish I were safe out of it, or that I had never come. It may be that this strange night-existence is telling on me; but would that that were all! If there were anyone to talk to I could bear it, but there is no one. I have only the Count to speak with, and he! – I fear I am myself the only living soul within the place. Let me be prosaic so far as facts can be; it will help me to bear up, and imagination must not run riot with me. If it does I am lost. Let me say at once how I stand – or seem to.

I only slept a few hours when I went to bed, and feeling that I could not sleep any more, got up. I had hung my shaving-glass by the window, and was just beginning to shave. Suddenly I felt a hand on my shoulder, and heard the Count's voice saying to me, 'Good morning.' I started, for it amazed me that I had not seen him, since the reflection of the glass covered the whole room behind me. In starting I had cut myself slightly, but did not notice it at the moment. Having answered the Count's salutation, I turned to the glass again to see how I had been mistaken. This time there could be no error, for the man was close to me, and I could see him over my shoulder. But there was no reflection of him in the mirror! The whole room behind me was displayed; but there was no sign of a man in it, except myself. This was startling, and, coming on the top of so many strange things, was beginning to increase that vague feeling of uneasiness which I always have when the Count is near; but at that instant I saw that the cut had bled a little, and the blood was trickling over my chin. I laid down the razor, turning as I did so half-round to look for some sticking-plaster. When the Count saw my face, his eyes blazed with a sort of demoniac fury, and he suddenly made a grab at my throat. I drew away, and his hand touched the string of beads which held the crucifix. It made an instant change in him, for the fury passed so quickly that I could hardly believe that it was ever there.

'Take care,' he said, 'take care how you cut yourself. It is more dangerous than you think in this country.' Then seizing the shaving-glass, he went on: 'And this is the wretched thing that has done the mischief. It is a foul bauble of man's vanity. Away with it!' and opening the heavy window with one wrench of his terrible hand, he flung out the glass, which was shattered into a thousand pieces on the stones of the courtyard far below. Then he withdrew without a word. It is very annoying, for I do not see how I am to shave, unless in my watch-case or the bottom of the shaving-pot, which is, fortunately, of metal.

When I went into the dining-room, breakfast was prepared; but I could not find the Count anywhere. So I breakfasted alone. It is strange that as yet I have not seen the Count eat or drink. He must be a very peculiar man! After breakfast I did a little exploring in the castle. I went out on the stairs and found a room looking towards the south. The view was magnificent, and from where I stood there was every opportunity of seeing it. The castle is on the very edge of a terrible precipice. A stone falling from the window would fall a thousand feet without touching anything! As far as the eye can reach is a sea of green tree-tops, with occasionally a deep rift where there is a chasm. Here and there are silver threads where the rivers wind in deep gorges through the forests.

But I am not in heart to describe beauty, for when I had seen the view I explored further; doors, doors, doors everywhere, and all locked and bolted. In no place save from the windows in the castle walls is there an available exit.

The castle is a veritable prison, and I am a prisoner!

CHAPTER 3
JONATHAN HARKER'S JOURNAL
(CONTINUED)

When I found that I was a prisoner a sort of wild feeling came over me. I rushed up and down the stairs, trying every door and peering out of every window I could find; but after a little the conviction of my help-lessness overpowered all other things. When I look back after a few hours I think I must have been mad for the time, for I behaved much as a rat does in a trap. When, however, the conviction had come to me that I was helpless I sat down quietly – as quietly as I have ever done anything in my life – and began to think over what was best to be done. I am thinking still, and as yet have come to no definite conclusion. Of one thing only am I certain: that it is no use making my ideas known to the Count. He knows well that I am imprisoned; and as he has done it himself, and has doubtless his own motives for it, he would only deceive me if I trusted him fully with the facts. So far as I can see, my only plan will be to keep my knowledge and my fears to myself, and my eyes open. I am, I know, either being deceived, like a baby, by my own fears, or else I am in desperate straits; and if the latter be so, I need, and shall need, all my brains to get through. I had hardly come to this conclusion when I heard the great door below shut, and knew that the Count had returned. He did not come at once into the library, so I went cautiously to my own room and found him making the bed. This was odd, but only confirmed what I had all along thought – that there were no servants in the house. When later I saw him through the chink of the hinges of the door laying the table in the dining-room, I was assured of it; for if he does himself all these menial offices, surely it is proof that there is no one else to do them. This gave me a fright, for if there is no one else in the castle, it must have been the Count himself who was the driver of the coach that brought me here. This is a terrible thought; for if so, what does it mean that he could control the wolves, as he did, by only holding up his hand in silence? How was it that all the people at Bistritz and on the coach had some terrible fear for me? What meant the giving of the crucifix, of the garlic, of the wild rose, of the mountain ash? Bless that good, good woman who hung the crucifix round my neck! for it is a comfort and a strength to me whenever I touch it. It is odd that a thing which I have been taught to regard with disfavour and as idolatrous should in a time of loneliness and trouble be of help. Is it that there is something in the essence of the thing itself, or that it is a medium, a tangible help, in conveying memories of sympathy and comfort? Some time, if it may be, I must examine this matter and try to make up my mind about it. In the meantime I must find out all I can about Count Dracula, as it may help me to understand. To-night he may talk of himself, if I turn the conversation that way. I must be very careful, however, not to awake his suspicion.

Midnight. – I have had a long talk with the Count. I asked him a few questions on Transylvanian history, and he warmed up to the subject wonderfully. In his speaking of things and people, and especially of battles, he spoke as if he had been present at them all. This he afterwards explained by saying that to a *boyar* the pride of his house and name is his own pride, that their glory is his glory, that their fate is his fate. Whenever he spoke of his house he always said 'we,' and spoke almost in the plural, like a king speaking. I wish I could put down all he said exactly as he said it, for to me it was most fascinating. It seemed to have in it a whole history of the country. He grew excited as he spoke, and walked about the room pulling his great white moustache and grasping anything on which he laid his hands as though he would crush it by main strength. One thing he said which I shall put down as nearly as I can; for it tells in its way the story of his race: –

'We Szekelys have a right to be proud, for in our veins flows the blood of many brave races who fought as the lion fights, for lordship. Here, in the whirlpool of European races, the Ugric tribe bore down from Iceland the fighting spirit which Thor and Wodin gave them, which their Berserkers displayed to such fell intent on the seaboards of Europe, aye, and of Asia and Africa, too, till the peoples thought that the were-wolves themselves had come. Here, too, when they came, they found the Huns, whose warlike fury had swept the earth like a living flame, till the dying peoples held that in their veins ran the blood of those old witches, who, expelled from Scythia, had mated with the devils in the desert. Fools, fools! What devil or what witch was ever so great as Attila, whose blood is in these veins?' He held up his arms. 'Is it a wonder that we were a conquering race; that we were proud; that when the Magyar, the Lombard, the Avar, the Bulgar, or the Turk poured his thousands on our frontiers, we drove them back? Is it strange that when Arpad and his legions swept through the Hungarian fatherland he found us here when he reached the frontier; that the Honfoglalas was completed there? And when the Hungarian flood swept eastward, the Szekelys were claimed as kindred by the victorious Magyars, and to us for centuries was trusted the guarding of the frontier of Turkey-land; aye, and more than that, endless duty of the frontier guard, for, as the Turk says, "water sleeps, and enemy is sleepless." Who more gladly than we throughout the Four Nations received the "bloody sword," or at its warlike call flocked quicker to the standard of the King? When was redeemed that great shame of my nation, the shame of Cassova, when the flags of the Wallach and the Magyar went down beneath the Crescent; who was it but one of my own race who as Voivode crossed the Danube and beat the Turk on his own ground! This was a Dracula indeed. Who was it that his own unworthy brother, when he had fallen, sold his people to the Turk and brought the shame of slavery on them! Was it not this Dracula, indeed, who inspired that other of his race who in a later age again and again brought his forces over the great river into Turkeyland; who, when he was beaten back, came again, and again, and again, though he had to come alone from the bloody field where his troops were being slaughtered, since he knew that he alone could ultimately triumph? They said that he thought only of himself. Bah! what good are peasants without a leader? Where ends the war without a brain and heart to conduct it? Again, when, after the battle of Mohacs, we threw off the Hungarian yoke, we of the Dracula blood were amongst their leaders, for our spirit would not brook that we were not free. Ah, young sir, the Szekelys – and the Dracula as their heart's blood, their brains, and their swords – can boast a record that mushroom growths like the Hapsburgs and the Romanoffs can never reach. The warlike days are over. Blood is too precious a thing in these days of dishonourable peace; and the glories of the great races are as a tale that is told.'

It was by this time close on morning, and we went to bed. (*Mem.*, this diary seems horribly like the beginning of the 'Arabian Nights,' for everything has to break off at cock-crow – or like the ghost of Hamlet's father.)

12 May. – Let me begin with facts – bare, meagre facts, verified by books and figures, and of which there can be no doubt. I must not confuse them with experiences which will have to rest on my own observation or my memory of them. Last evening when the Count came from his room he began by asking me questions on legal matters and on the doing of certain kinds of business. I had spent the day wearily over books, and, simply to keep my mind occupied, went over some of the matters I had been examined in at Lincoln's Inn. There was a certain method in the Count's inquiries, so I shall try to put them down in sequence; the knowledge may somehow or some time be useful to me.

First, he asked if a man in England might have two solicitors, or more. I told him he might have a dozen if he wished, but that it would not be wise to have more than one solicitor engaged in one transaction, as only one could act at a time, and that to change would be certain to militate against his interest. He seemed thoroughly to understand, and went on to ask if there would be any practical difficulty in having one man to attend, say, to banking, and another to look after shipping, in case local help were needed in a place far from the home of the banking solicitor. I asked him to explain more fully, so that I might not by any chance mislead him, so he said: –

'I shall illustrate. Your friend and mine, Mr Peter Hawkins, from under the shadow of your beautiful cathedral at Exeter, which is far from London, buys for me through your good self my place at London. Good! Now here let me say frankly, lest you should think it strange that I have sought the services of one so far off from London instead of someone resident there, that my motive was that no local interest might be served save my wish only; and as one of London resident might, perhaps, have some purpose of himself or friend to serve I went thus afield to seek my agent, whose labours should be only to my interest. Now, suppose I, who have much of affairs, wish to ship goods, say, to Newcastle, or Durham, or Harwich, or Dover, might it not be that it could with more ease be done by consigning to one in these ports?' I answered that certainly it would be most easy, but that we solicitors had a system of agency one for the other, so that local work could be done locally on instruction from any solicitor, so that the client, simply placing himself in the hands of one man, could have his wishes carried out by him without further trouble.

'But,' said he, 'I could be at liberty to direct myself. Is it not so?'

'Of course,' I replied; 'and such is often done by men of business, who do not like the whole of their affairs to be known by any one person.'

'Good!' he said, and then went on to ask about the means of making consignments and the forms to be gone through, and of all sorts of difficulties which might arise, but by forethought could be guarded against. I explained all these things to him to the best of my ability, and he certainly left me under the impression that he would have made a wonderful solicitor, for there was nothing that he did not think of or foresee. For a man who was never in the country, and who did not evidently do much in the way of business, his knowledge and acumen were wonderful. When he had satisfied himself on these points of which he had spoken, and I had verified all as well as I could by the books available, he suddenly stood up and said: –

'Have you written since your first letter to our friend Mr Peter Hawkins, or to any other?' It was with some bitterness in my heart that I answered that I had not, that as yet I had not seen any opportunity of sending letters to anybody.

'Then write now, my young friend,' he said, laying a heavy hand on my shoulder; 'write to our friend and to any other; and say, if it will please you, that you shall stay with me until a month from now.'

'Do you wish me to stay so long?' I asked, for my heart grew cold at the thought.

'I desire it much; nay, I will take no refusal. When your master, employer, what you will, engaged that someone should come on his behalf, it was understood that my needs only were to be consulted. I have not stinted. Is it not so?'

What could I do but bow acceptance? It was Mr Hawkins's interest, not mine, and I had to think of him, not myself; and besides, while Count Dracula was speaking, there was that in his eyes and in his bearing which made me remember that I was a prisoner, and that if I wished it I could have no choice. The Count saw his victory in my bow, and his mastery in the trouble of my face, for he began at once to use them, but in his own smooth, resistless way: –

'I pray you, my good young friend, that you will not discourse of things other than business in your letters. It will doubtless please your friends to know that you are well, and that you look forward to getting home to them. Is it not so?' As he spoke he handed me three sheets of notepaper and three envelopes. They were all of the thinnest foreign post, and looking at them, then at him, and noticing his quiet smile, with the sharp, canine teeth lying over the red under-lip, I understood as well as if he had spoken that I should be careful what I wrote, for he would be able to read it. So I determined to write only formal notes now, but to write fully to Mr Hawkins in secret, and also to Mina, for to her I could write in shorthand, which would puzzle the Count, if he did see it. When I had written my two letters I sat quiet, reading a book whilst the Count wrote several notes, referring as he wrote them to some books on his table. Then he took up my two and placed them with his own, and put by his writing materials, after which, the instant the door had closed behind him, I leaned over and looked at the letters, which were face down on the table. I felt no compunction in doing so, for under the circumstances I felt that I should protect myself in every way I could.

One of the letters was directed to Samuel F. Billington, No. 7, The Crescent, Whitby; another to Herr Leutner, Varna; the third was to Coutts & Co., London, and the fourth to Herren Klopstock & Billreuth, bankers, Buda-Pesth. The second and fourth were unsealed. I was just about to look at them when I saw the door-handle move. I sank back in my seat, having just had time to replace the letters as they had been and to resume my book before the Count, holding still another letter in his hand, entered the room. He took up the letters on the table and stamped them carefully, and then, turning to me, said: –

'I trust you will forgive me, but I have much work to do in private this evening. You will, I hope, find all things as you wish.' At the door he turned, and after a moment's pause said: –

'Let me advise you, my dear young friend – nay, let me warn you with all seriousness, that should you leave these rooms you will not by any chance go to sleep in any other part of the castle. It is old, and has many memories, and there are bad dreams for those who sleep unwisely. Be warned! Should sleep now or ever overcome you, or be like to do, then haste to your own chamber or to these rooms, for your rest will then be safe. But if you be not careful in this respect, then –' He finished his speech in a gruesome way, for he motioned with his hands as if he were washing them. I quite understood; my only doubt was as to whether any dream could be more terrible than the unnatural, horrible net of gloom and mystery which seemed closing round me.

Later. – I endorse the last words written, but this time there is no doubt in question. I shall not fear to sleep in any place where he is not. I have placed the crucifix over the head of my bed – I imagine that my rest is thus freer from dreams; and there it shall remain.

When he left me I went to my room. After a little while, not hearing any sound, I came out and went up the stone stair to where I could look out towards the south. There was some sense of freedom in the vast expanse, inaccessible though it was to me, as compared with the narrow darkness of the courtyard. Looking out on this, I felt that I was indeed in prison, and I seemed to want a breath of fresh air, though it were of the night. I am beginning to feel this nocturnal existence tell on me. It is destroying my nerve. I start at my own shadow, and am full of all sorts of horrible imaginings. God knows that there is ground for any terrible fear in this accursed place! I looked out over the beautiful expanse, bathed in soft yellow moonlight till it was almost as light as day. In the soft light the distant hills became melted, and the shadows in the valleys and gorges of velvety blackness. The mere beauty seemed to cheer me;

there was peace and comfort in every breath I drew. As I leaned from the window my eye was caught by something moving a storey below me, and somewhat to my left, where I imagined, from the lie of the rooms, that the windows of the Count's own room would look out. The window at which I stood was tall and deep, stone-mullioned, and though weather-worn, was still complete; but it was evidently many a day since the case had been there. I drew back behind the stonework, and looked carefully out.

What I saw was the Count's head coming out from the window. I did not see the face, but I knew the man by the neck and the movement of his back and arms. In any case, I could not mistake the hands which I had had so many opportunities of studying. I was at first interested and somewhat amused, for it is wonderful how small a matter will interest and amuse a man when he is a prisoner. But my very feelings changed to repulsion and terror when I saw the whole man slowly emerge from the window and begin to crawl down the castle wall over that dreadful abyss, *face down*, with his cloak spreading out around him like great wings. At first I could not believe my eyes. I thought it was some trick of the moon-light, some weird effect of shadow; but I kept looking, and it could be no delusion. I saw the fingers and toes grasp the corners of the stones, worn clear of the mortar by the stress of years, and by thus using every projection and inequality move downwards with considerable speed, just as a lizard moves along a wall.

What manner of man is this, or what manner of creature is it in the semblance of man? I feel the dread of this horrible place overpowering me; I am in fear – in awful fear – and there is no escape for me; I am encompassed about with terrors that I dare not think of . . .

15 May. – Once more have I seen the Count go out in his lizard fashion. He moved downwards in a sidelong way, some hundred feet down, and a good deal to the left. He vanished into some hole or window. When his head had disappeared I leaned out to try and see more, but without avail – the distance was too great to allow a proper angle of sight. I knew he had left the castle now, and thought to use the opportunity to explore more than I had dared to do as yet. I went back to the room, and taking a lamp, tried all the doors. They were all locked as I had expected, and the locks were comparatively new; but I went down the stone stairs to the hall where I had entered originally. I found I could pull back the bolts easily enough and unhook the great chains; but the door was locked, and the key was gone! That key must be in the Count's room; I must watch should his door be unlocked, so that I may get it and escape. I went on to make a thorough examination of the various stairs and passages, and to try the doors that opened from them. One or two small rooms near the hall were open, but there was nothing to see in them except old furniture, dusty with age and moth-eaten. At last, however, I found one door at the top of a stairway which, though it seemed to be locked, gave a little under pressure. I tried it harder, and found that it was not really locked, but that the resistance came from the fact that the hinges had fallen somewhat, and the heavy door rested on the floor. Here was an opportunity which I might not have again, so I exerted myself, and with many efforts forced it back so that I could enter. I was now in a wing of the castle further to the right than the rooms I knew and a storey lower down. From the windows I could see that the suite of rooms lay along to the south of the castle, the windows of the end room looking out both west and south. On the latter side, as well as to the former, there was a great precipice. The castle was built on the corner of a great rock, so that on three sides it was quite impregnable, and great windows were placed here where sling, or bow, or culverin could not reach, and consequently light and comfort, impossible to a position which had to be guarded, were secured. To the west was a great valley, and then, rising far away, great jagged mountain fastnesses, rising peak on peak, the sheer rock studded with mountain ash and thorn, whose roots clung in cracks and crevices and crannies of the stone. This was evidently the portion of the castle occupied in bygone days, for the furniture had more air of comfort than any I had seen. The windows were curtainless, and the yellow moonlight, flooding in through the diamond panes, enabled one to see even colours, whilst it softened the wealth of dust which lay over all and disguised in some measure the ravages of time and the moth. My lamp seemed to be of little effect in the brilliant moonlight, but I was glad to have it with me, for there was a dread loneliness in the place which chilled my heart and made my nerves tremble. Still, it was better than living alone in the rooms which I had come to hate from the presence of the Count, and after trying a little to school my nerves, I found a soft quietude come over me. Here I am, sitting at a little oak table where in old times possibly some fair lady sat to pen, with much thought and many blushes, her ill-spelt love-letter, and writing in my diary in shorthand all that has happened since I closed it last. It is nineteenth century up-to-date with a vengeance. And yet, unless my senses deceive me, the old centuries had, and have, powers of their own which mere 'modernity' cannot kill.

Later: the morning of 16 May. – God preserve my sanity, for to this I

am reduced. Safety and the assurance of safety are things of the past.
Whilst I live on here there is but one thing to hope for: that I may not go
mad, if, indeed, I be not mad already. If I be sane, then surely it is maddening to think that of all the foul things that lurk in this hateful place
the Count is the least dreadful to me; that to him alone I can look for
safety, even though this be only whilst I can serve his purpose. Great God!
merciful God! Let me be calm, for out of that way lies madness indeed.
I begin to get new lights on certain things which have puzzled me. Up to
now I never quite knew what Shakespeare meant when he made Hamlet
say: –

> 'My tablets! quick, my tablets!
> 'Tis meet that I put it down,' etc.,

for now, feeling as though my own brain were unhinged or as if the shock
had come which must end in its undoing, I turn to my diary for repose.
The habit of entering accurately must help to soothe me.

The Count's mysterious warning frightened me at the time; it frightens
me more now when I think of it, for in future he has a fearful hold upon
me. I shall fear to doubt what he may say!

When I had written in my diary and had fortunately replaced the book
and pen in my pocket, I felt sleepy. The Count's warning came into my
mind, but I took a pleasure in disobeying it. The sense of sleep was upon
me, and with it the obstinacy which sleep brings as outrider. The soft
moonlight soothed, and the wide expanse without gave a sense of freedom
which refreshed me. I determined not to return to-night to the gloom-
haunted rooms, but to sleep here, where of old ladies had sat and sung
and lived sweet lives whilst their gentle breasts were sad for their menfolk
away in the midst of remorseless wars. I drew a great couch out of its
place near the corner, so that, as I lay, I could look at the lovely view to
east and south, and unthinking of and uncaring for the dust, composed
myself for sleep.

I suppose I must have fallen asleep; I hope so, but I fear, for all that
followed was startlingly real – so real that now, sitting here in the broad,
full sunlight of the morning, I cannot in the least believe that it was all
sleep.

I was not alone. The room was the same, unchanged in any way since
I came into it; I could see along the floor, in the brilliant moonlight, my
own footsteps marked where I had disturbed the long accumulation of
dust. In the moonlight opposite me were three young women, ladies by

their dress and manner. I thought at the time that I must be dreaming when I saw them, for, though the moonlight was behind them, they threw no shadow on the floor. They came close to me and looked at me for some time and then whispered together. Two were dark, and had high aquiline noses, like the Count's, and great dark, piercing eyes, that seemed to be almost red when contrasted with the pale yellow moon. The other was fair, as fair as can be, with great, wavy masses of golden hair and eyes like pale sapphires. I seemed somehow to know her face, and to know it in connection with some dreamy fear, but I could not recollect at the moment how or where. All three had brilliant white teeth, that shone like pearls against the ruby of their voluptuous lips. There was something about them that made me uneasy, some longing and at the same time some deadly fear. I felt in my heart a wicked, burning desire that they would kiss me with those red lips. It is not good to note this down, lest some day it should meet Mina's eyes and cause her pain; but it is the truth. They whispered together, and then they all three laughed – such a silvery, musical laugh, but as hard as though the sound never could have come through the softness of human lips. It was like the intolerable, tingling sweetness of water-glasses when played on by a cunning hand. The fair girl shook her head coquettishly, and the other two urged her on. One said: –

'Go on! You are first, and we shall follow; yours is the right to begin.' The other added: –

'He is young and strong; there are kisses for us all.' I lay quiet, looking out under my eyelashes in an agony of delightful anticipation. The fair girl advanced and bent over me till I could feel the movement of her breath upon me. Sweet it was in one sense, honey-sweet, and sent the same tingling through the nerves as her voice, but with a bitter underlying the sweet, a bitter offensiveness, as one smells in blood.

I was afraid to raise my eyelids, but looked out and saw perfectly under the lashes. The fair girl went on her knees and bent over me, fairly gloating. There was a deliberate voluptuousness which was both thrilling and repulsive, and as she arched her neck she actually licked her lips like an animal, till I could see in the moonlight the moisture shining on the scarlet lips and on the red tongue as it lapped the white sharp teeth. Lower and lower went her head as the lips went below the range of my mouth and chin and seemed about to fasten on my throat. Then she paused, and I could hear the churning sound of her tongue as it licked her teeth and lips, and could feel the hot breath on my neck. Then the skin of my throat began to tingle as one's flesh does when the hand that is to tickle it approaches nearer – nearer. I could feel the soft, shivering touch of the lips on the supersensitive skin of my throat, and the hard dents of two sharp teeth, just touching and pausing there. I closed my eyes in a languorous ecstasy and waited – waited with beating heart.

But at that instant another sensation swept through me as quick as lightning. I was conscious of the presence of the Count, and of his being as if lapped in a storm of fury. As my eyes opened involuntarily I saw his strong hand grasp the slender neck of the fair woman and with giant's power draw it back, the blue eyes transformed with fury, the white teeth champing with rage, and the fair cheeks blazing red with passion. But the Count! Never did I imagine such wrath and fury, even in the demons of the pit. His eyes were positively blazing. The red light in them was lurid, as if the flames of hell-fire blazed behind them. His face was deathly pale, and the lines of it were hard like drawn wires; the thick eyebrows that met over the nose now seemed like a heaving bar of white-hot metal. With a fierce sweep of his arm, he hurled the woman from him, and then motioned to the others, as though he were beating them back; it was the same imperious gesture that I had seen used to the wolves. In a voice which, though low and almost a whisper, seemed to cut through the air and then ring round the room, he exclaimed: –

'How dare you touch him, any of you? How dare you cast eyes on him when I had forbidden it? Back, I tell you all! This man belongs to me! Beware how you meddle with him, or you'll have to deal with me.' The fair girl, with a laugh of ribald coquetry, turned to answer him: –

'You yourself never loved; you never love!' On this the other women joined, and such a mirthless, hard, soulless laughter rang through the room that it almost made me faint to hear; it seemed like the pleasure of fiends. Then the Count turned, after looking at my face attentively, and said in a soft whisper: –

'Yes, I too can love; you yourselves can tell it from the past. Is it not so? Well, now I promise you that when I am done with him, you shall kiss him at your will. Now go! go! I must awaken him, for there is work to be done.'

'Are we to have nothing to-night?' said one of them, with a low laugh, as she pointed to the bag which he had thrown upon the floor, and which moved as though there were some living thing within it. For answer he nodded his head. One of the women jumped forward and opened it. If my ears did not deceive me there was a gasp and a low wail, as of a half-smothered child. The women closed round, whilst I was aghast with horror; but as I looked they disappeared, and with them the dreadful bag. There was no door near them, and they could not have passed me without my noticing. They simply seemed to fade into the rays of the moonlight and pass out through the window, for I could see outside the dim, shadowy forms for a moment before they entirely faded away.

Then the horror overcame me, and I sank down unconscious.

CHAPTER 4

JONATHAN HARKER'S JOURNAL

(CONTINUED)

I awoke in my own bed. If it be that I had not dreamt, the Count must have carried me here. I tried to satisfy myself on the subject, but could not arrive at any unquestionable result. To be sure, there were certain small evidences, such as that my clothes were folded and laid by in a manner which was not my habit. My watch was still unwound, and I am rigorously accustomed to wind it the last thing before going to bed, and many such details. But these things are no proof, for they may have been evidences that my mind was not as usual, and, from some cause or another, I had certainly been much upset. I must watch for proof. Of one thing I am glad: if it was the Count that carried me here and undressed me, he must have been hurried in his task, for my pockets are intact. I am sure this diary would have been a mystery to him which he would not have brooked. He would have taken or destroyed it. As I look round this room, although it has been to me so full of fear, it is now a sort of sanctuary, for nothing can be more dreadful than those awful women, who were – who *are* – waiting to suck my blood.

18 May. – I have been down to look at that room again in daylight, for I *must* know the truth. When I got to the doorway at the top of the stairs, I found it closed. It had been so forcibly driven against the jamb that part of the woodwork was splintered. I could see that the bolt of the lock had not been shot, but the door is fastened from the inside. I fear it was no dream, and must act on this surmise.

19 May. – I am surely in the toils. Last night the Count asked me in the suavest tones to write three letters, one saying that my work here was nearly done and that I should start for home within a few days, another that I was starting on the next morning from the time of the letter, and the third that I had left the castle and arrived at Bistritz. I would fain have rebelled, but felt that in the present state of things it would be madness to quarrel openly with the Count whilst I am so absolutely in his power; and to refuse would be to excite his suspicion and to arouse his anger. He knows that I know too much, and that I must not live, lest I be dangerous to him; my only chance is to prolong my opportunities. Something may occur which will give me a chance to escape. I saw in his eyes something of that gathering wrath which was manifest when he hurled that fair woman from him. He explained to me that posts were few and uncertain, and that my writing now would ensure ease of mind to my friends; and he assured me with so much impressiveness that he would countermand the later letters, which would be held over at Bistritz until due time in case chance would admit of my prolonging my stay, that to oppose him would have been to create new suspicion. I therefore pretended to fall in with his views, and asked him what dates I should put on the letters. He calculated a minute, and then said: –

'The first should be June 12, the second June 19, and the third June 29.'

I know now the span of my life. God help me!

28 May. – There is a chance of escape, or at any rate of being able to send word home. A band of Szgany have come to the castle, and are encamped in the courtyard. These Szgany are gipsies; I have notes of them in my book. They are peculiar to this part of the world, though allied to the ordinary gipsies all the world over. There are thousands of them in Hungary and Transylvania who are almost outside all law. They attach themselves as a rule to some great noble or *boyar*, and call themselves by his name. They are fearless and without religion, save superstition, and they talk only their own varieties of the Romany tongue.

I shall write some letters home, and shall try to get them to have them posted. I have already spoken to them through my window to begin an acquaintanceship. They took their hats off and made obeisance and many signs, which, however, I could not understand any more than I could their spoken language . . .

I have written the letters. Mina's is in shorthand, and I simply ask Mr Hawkins to communicate with her. To her I have explained my situation, but without the horrors which I may only surmise. It would shock and frighten her to death were I to expose my heart to her. Should the letters not carry, then the Count shall not yet know my secret or the extent of my knowledge . . .

I have given the letters; I threw them through the bars of my window with a gold piece, and made what signs I could to have them posted. The man who took them pressed them to his heart and bowed, and then put them in his cap. I could do no more. I stole back to the study and began to read. As the Count did not come in, I have written here . . .

The Count has come. He sat down beside me, and said in his smoothest voice as he opened two letters: –

'The Szgany has given me these, of which, though I know not whence they come, I shall, of course, take care. See!' – he must have looked at it – 'one is from you, and to my friend Peter Hawkins; the other' – here he caught sight of the strange symbols as he opened the envelope, and the dark look came into his face, and his eyes blazed wickedly – 'the other is a vile thing, an outrage upon friendship and hospitality! It is not signed. Well! so it cannot matter to us.' And he calmly held letter and envelope in the flame of the lamp till they were consumed. Then he went on: –

'The letter to Hawkins – that I shall, of course, send on, since it is yours. Your letters are sacred to me. Your pardon, my friend, that unknowingly I did break the seal. Will you not cover it again?' He held out the letter to me, and with a courteous bow handed me a clean envelope. I could only redirect it and hand it to him in silence. When he went out of the room I could hear the key turn softly. A minute later I went over and tried it, and the door was locked.

When, an hour or two after, the Count came quietly into the room, his coming wakened me, for I had gone to sleep on the sofa. He was very courteous and very cheery in his manner, and seeing that I had been sleeping, he said:

'So, my friend, you are tired? Get to bed. There is the surest rest. I may not have the pleasure to talk to-night, since there are many labours to me; but you will sleep, I pray.' I passed to my room and went to bed, and, strange to say, slept without dreaming. Despair has its own calms.

31 May. – This morning when I woke I thought I would provide myself with some paper and envelopes from my bag and keep them in my pocket, so that I might write in case I should get an opportunity; but again a surprise, again a shock!

Every scrap of paper was gone, and with it all my notes, my memoranda relating to railways and travel, my letter of credit, in fact, all that might be useful to me were I once outside the castle. I sat and pondered a while, and then some thought occurred to me, and I made search of my portmanteau and in the wardrobe where I had placed my clothes.

The suit in which I had travelled was gone, and also my overcoat and rug; I could find no trace of them anywhere. This looked like some new scheme of villainy . . .

17 June. – This morning, as I was sitting on the edge of my bed cudgelling my brains, I heard without a cracking of whips and pounding and scraping of horses' feet up the rocky path beyond the courtyard. With joy I hurried to the window, and saw drive into the yard two great leiter-waggons, each drawn by eight sturdy horses, and at the head of each pair a Slovak, with his wide hat, great, nail-studded belt, dirty sheepskin, and high boots. They had also their long staves in hand. I ran to the door, intending to descend and try and join them through the main hall, as I thought that way might be opened for them. Again a shock: my door was fastened on the outside.

Then I ran to the window and cried to them. They looked up at me stupidly and pointed, but just then the 'hetman' of the Szgany came out, and seeing them pointing to my window, said something, at which they laughed. Henceforth, no effort of mine, no piteous cry or agonized entreaty, would make them even look at me. They resolutely turned away. The leiter-waggons contained great, square boxes, with handles of thick rope; these were evidently empty by the ease with which the Slovaks handled them, and by their resonance as they were roughly moved. When they were all unloaded and packed in a great heap in one corner of the yard, the Slovaks were given some money by the Szgany, and spitting on it for luck, lazily went each to his horse's head. Shortly afterwards I heard the cracking of their whips die away in the distance.

24 June, before morning. – Last night the Count left me early, and locked himself into his own room. As soon as I dared, I ran up the winding stair, and looked out of the window which opened south. I thought I would watch for the Count, for there is something going on. The Szgany are quartered somewhere in the castle, and are doing work of some kind. I know it, for now and then I hear a far-away, muffled sound as of mattock and spade, and, whatever it is, it must be to the end of some ruthless villainy.

I had been at the window somewhat less than half an hour, when I saw something coming out of the Count's window. I drew back and watched carefully, and saw the whole man emerge. It was a new shock to me to find that he had on the suit of clothes which I had worn whilst travelling here, and slung over his shoulder the terrible bag which I had seen the women take away. There could be no doubt as to his quest, and in my garb, too! This, then, is his new scheme of evil: that he will allow others to see me, as they think, so that he may both leave evidence that I have been seen in the towns or villages posting my own letters, and that any wickedness which he may do shall by the local people be attributed to me.

It makes me rage to think that this can go on, and whilst I am shut up here, a veritable prisoner, but without that protection of the law which is even a criminal's right and consolation.

I thought I would watch for the Count's return, and for a long time sat doggedly at the window. Then I began to notice that there were some quaint little specks floating in the rays of the moonlight. They were like the tiniest grains of dust, and they whirled round and gathered in clusters in a nebulous sort of way. I watched them with a sense of soothing, and a sort of calm stole over me. I leaned back in the embrasure in a more comfortable position, so that I could enjoy more fully the aerial gambolling.

Something made me start up, a low, piteous howling of dogs somewhere far below in the valley, which was hidden from my sight. Louder it seemed to ring in my ears, and the floating motes of dust to take new shapes to the sound as they danced in the moonlight. I felt myself struggling to awake to some call of my instincts; nay, my very soul was struggling, and my half-remembered sensibilities were striving to answer the call. I was becoming hypnotized! Quicker and quicker danced the dust, and the moonbeams seemed to quiver as they went by me into the mass of gloom beyond. More and more they gathered till they seemed to take dim phantom shapes. And then I started, broad awake and in full possession of my senses, and ran screaming from the place. The phantom shapes, which were becoming gradually materialized from the moonbeams, were those of the three ghostly women to whom I was doomed. I fled, and felt somewhat safer in my own room, where there was no moonlight and where the lamp was burning brightly.

When a couple of hours had passed I heard something stirring in the Count's room, something like a sharp wail quickly suppressed; and then there was silence, deep, awful silence, which chilled me. With a beating heart, I tried the door; but I was locked in my prison, and could do nothing. I sat down and simply cried.

As I sat I heard a sound in the courtyard without – the agonized cry of a woman. I rushed to the window, and throwing it up, peered out between the bars. There, indeed, was a woman with dishevelled hair, holding her hands over her heart as one distressed with running. She was leaning against a corner of the gateway. When she saw my face at the window she threw herself forward, and shouted in a voice laden with menace: –

'Monster, give me my child!'

She threw herself on her knees, and raising up her hands, cried the same words in tones which wrung my heart. Then she tore her hair and beat her breast, and abandoned herself to all the violences of extravagant emotion. Finally, she threw herself forward, and, though I could not see her, I could hear the beating of her naked hands against the door.

Somewhere high overhead, probably on the tower, I heard the voice of the Count calling in his harsh, metallic whisper. His call seemed to be answered from far and wide by the howling of wolves. Before many minutes had passed a pack of them poured, like a pent-up dam when liberated, through the wide entrance into the courtyard.

There was no cry from the woman, and the howling of the wolves was but short. Before long they streamed away singly, licking their lips.

I could not pity her, for I knew now what had become of her child, and she was better dead.

What shall I do? What can I do? How can I escape from this dreadful thrall of night and gloom and fear?

25 June, morning. – No man knows till he has suffered from the night how sweet and how dear to his heart and eye the morning can be. When the sun grew so high this morning that it struck the top of the great gateway opposite my window, the high spot which it touched seemed to me as if the dove from the ark had lighted there. My fear fell from me as if it had been a vaporous garment which dissolved in the warmth. I must take action of some sort while the courage of the day is upon me. Last night one of my post-dated letters went to post, the first of that fatal series which is to blot out the very traces of my existence from the earth.

Let me not think of it. Action!

It has always been at night-time that I have been molested or threatened, or in some way in danger or in fear. I have not yet seen the Count in the daylight. Can it be that he sleeps when others wake, that he may be awake whilst they sleep! If I could only get into his room! But there is no possible way. The door is always locked, no way for me.

Yes, there is a way, if one dares to take it. Where his body has gone why may not another body go? I have seen him myself crawl from his window; why should not I imitate him, and go in by his window? The chances are desperate, but my need is more desperate still. I shall risk it. At the worst it can only be death. And a man's death is not a calf's, and the dread Hereafter may still be open to me. God help me in my task! Good-bye, Mina, if I fail; good-bye, my faithful friend and second father; good-bye, all, and last of all Mina!

Same day, later. – I have made the effort, and, God helping me, have come safely back to this room. I must put down every detail in order. I went whilst my courage was fresh straight to the window on the south side, and at once got outside on the narrow ledge of stone which runs round the building on this side. The stones were big and roughly cut, and the mortar had by process of time been washed away between them. I took off my boots, and ventured out on the desperate way. I looked down once, so as to make sure that sudden glimpse of the awful depth would not overcome me, but after that kept my eyes away from it. I knew pretty well the direction and distance of the Count's window, and made for it as well as I could, having regard to the opportunities available. I did not feel dizzy – I suppose I was too excited – and the time seemed ridiculously short till I found myself standing on the window-sill and trying to raise up the sash. I was filled with agitation, however, when I bent down and slid feet foremost in through the window. Then I looked around for the Count, but, with surprise and gladness, made a discovery. The room was empty! It was barely furnished with odd things, which seemed to have never been used; the furniture was something the same style as that in the south rooms, and was covered with dust. I looked for the key, but it was not in the lock, and I could not find it anywhere. The only thing I found was a great heap of gold in one corner – gold of all kinds, Roman, and British, and Austrian, and Hungarian, and Greek and Turkish money, covered with a film of dust, as though it had lain long in the ground. None of it that I noticed was less than three hundred years old. There were also chains and ornaments, some jewelled, but all of them old and stained.

At one corner of the room was a heavy door. I tried it, for, since I could not find the key of the room or the key of the outer door, which was the main object of my search, I must make further examination, or all my efforts would be in vain. It was open, and led through a stone passage to a circular stairway, which went steeply down. I descended, minding carefully where I went, for the stairs were dark, being only lit by loopholes in the heavy masonry. At the bottom there was a dark, tunnel-like passage, through which came a deathly, sickly odour, the odour of old earth newly turned. As I went through the passage the smell grew closer and heavier. At last I pulled open a heavy door which stood ajar, and found myself in an old, ruined chapel, which had evidently been used as a graveyard. The roof was broken, and in two places were steps leading to vaults, but the ground had recently been dug over, and the earth placed in great wooden boxes, manifestly those which had been brought by the Slovaks. There was nobody about, and I made search for any further outlet, but there was none. Then I went over every inch of the ground, so as not to lose a chance. I went down even into the vaults, where the dim light struggled, although to do so was a dread to my very soul. Into two of these I went, but saw nothing except fragments of old coffins and piles of dust; in the third, however, I made a discovery.

There, in one of the great boxes, of which there were fifty in all, on a pile of newly dug earth, lay the Count! He was either dead or asleep, I could not say which – for the eyes were open and stony, but without the glassiness of death – and the cheeks had the warmth of life through all their pallor, and the lips were as red as ever. But there was no sign of movement, no pulse, no breath, no beating of the heart. I bent over him, and tried to find any sign of life, but in vain. He could not have lain there long, for the earthy smell would have passed away in a few hours. By the side of the box was its cover, pierced with holes here and there. I thought he might have the keys on him, but when I went to search I saw the dead eyes, and in them, dead though they were, such a look of hate, though unconscious of me or my presence, that I fled from the place, and leaving the Count's room by the window, crawled again up the castle wall. Regaining my own chamber, I threw myself panting upon the bed and tried to think . . .

29 June. – To-day is the date of my last letter, and the Count has taken steps to prove that it was genuine, for again I saw him leave the castle by the same window, and in my clothes. As he went down the wall, lizard fashion, I wished I had a gun or some lethal weapon, that I might destroy him; but I fear that no weapon wrought alone by man's hand would have any effect on him. I dared not wait to see him return, for I feared to see those weird sisters. I came back to the library, and read there till I fell asleep.

I was awakened by the Count, who looked at me as grimly as a man can look as he said:

'To-morrow, my friend, we must part. You return to your beautiful England, I to some work which may have such an end that we may never meet. Your letter home has been despatched; to-morrow I shall not be here, but all shall be ready for your journey. In the morning come the Szgany, who have some labours of their own here, and also come some Slovaks. When they have gone, my carriage shall come for you, and shall bear you to the Borgo Pass to meet the stagecoach from Bukovina to Bistritz. But I am in hopes that I shall see more of you at Castle Dracula.' I suspected him, and determined to test his sincerity. Sincerity! It seems like a profanation of the word to write it in connection with such a monster, so I asked him point-blank: –

'Why may I not go to-night?'

'Because, dear sir, my coachman and horses are away on a mission.'

'But I would walk with pleasure. I want to get away at once.' He smiled, such a soft, smooth, diabolical smile that I knew there was some trick behind his smoothness. He said: –

'And your baggage?'

'I do not care about it. I can send for it some other time.'

The Count stood up, and said, with a sweet courtesy which made me rub my eyes, it seemed so real: –

'You English have a saying which is close to my heart, for its spirit is that which rules our *boyars:* "Welcome the coming, speed the parting guest." Come with me, my dear young friend. Not an hour shall you wait in my house against your will, though sad am I at your going, and that you so suddenly desire it. Come!' With a stately gravity, he, with the lamp, preceded me down the stairs and along the hall. Suddenly he stopped.

'Hark!'

Close at hand came the howling of many wolves. It was almost as if the sound sprang up at the raising of his hand, just as the music of a great orchestra seems to leap under the baton of the conductor. After a pause of a moment, he proceeded in his stately way, to the door, drew back the ponderous bolts, unhooked the heavy chains, and began to draw it open.

To my intense astonishment I saw that it was unlocked. Suspiciously I looked all round, but could see no key of any kind.

As the door began to open, the howling of the wolves without grew louder and angrier; their red jaws, with champing teeth, and their blunt-clawed feet as they leaped, came in through the opening door. I knew that to struggle at the moment against the Count was useless. With such allies as these at his command, I could do nothing. But still the door continued slowly to open, and only the Count's body stood in the gap. Suddenly it struck me that this might be the moment and the means of my doom; I was to be given to the wolves, and at my own instigation. There was a diabolical wickedness in the idea great enough for the Count, and as a last chance I cried out: –

'Shut the door; I shall wait till morning!' and covered my face with my hands to hide my tears of bitter disappointment. With one sweep of his powerful arm, the Count threw the door shut, and the great bolts clanged and echoed through the hall as they shot back into their places.

In silence we returned to the library, and after a minute or two I went to my own room. The last I saw of Count Dracula was his kissing his hand to me, with a red light of triumph in his eyes, and with a smile that Judas in hell might be proud of.

When I was in my room and about to lie down, I thought I heard a whispering at my door. I went to it softly and listened. Unless my ears deceived me, I heard the voice of the Count: –

'Back, back, to your own place! Your time is not yet come. Wait. Have patience. To-morrow night, to-morrow night, is yours!' There was a low, sweet ripple of laughter, and in a rage I threw open the door, and saw without the three terrible women licking their lips. As I appeared they all joined in a horrible laugh, and ran away.

I came back to my room and threw myself on my knees. Is it then so near the end? To-morrow! to-morrow! Lord, help me, and those to whom I am dear!

30 June, morning. – These may be the last words I ever write in this diary. I slept till just before the dawn, and when I woke threw myself on my knees, for I determined that if Death came he should find me ready.

At last I felt that subtle change in the air and knew that the morning had come. Then came the welcome cock-crow, and I felt that I was safe. With a glad heart, I opened my door and ran down to the hall. I had seen that the door was unlocked and now escape was before me. With hands that trembled with eagerness, I unhooked the chains and drew back the massive bolts.

But the door would not move. Despair seized me. I pulled and pulled at the door, and shook it till, massive as it was, it rattled in its casement. I could see the bolt shot. It had been locked after I left the Count.

Then a wild desire took me to obtain that key at any risk, and I determined then and there to scale the wall again and gain the Count's room. He might kill me, but death now seemed the happier choice of evils. Without a pause I rushed up to the east window and scrambled down the wall, as before, into the Count's room. It was empty, but that was as I expected. I could not see a key anywhere, but the heap of gold remained. I went through the door in the corner and down the winding stair and along the dark passage to the old chapel. I knew now well enough where to find the monster I sought.

The great box was in the same place, close against the wall, but the lid was laid on it, not fastened down, but with the nails ready in their places to be hammered home. I knew I must search the body for the key, so I raised the lid and laid it back against the wall; and then I saw something which filled my very soul with horror. There lay the Count, but looking as if his youth had been half-renewed, for the white hair and moustache were changed to dark iron-grey; the cheeks were fuller, and the white skin seemed ruby-red underneath; the mouth was redder than ever, for on the lips were gouts of fresh blood, which trickled from the corners of the mouth and ran over the chin and neck. Even the deep, burning eyes seemed set amongst swollen flesh, for the lids and pouches underneath were bloated. It seemed as if the whole awful creature were simply gorged with blood; he lay like a filthy leech, exhausted with his repletion. I shuddered as I bent over to touch him, and every sense in me revolted at the contact; but I had to search, or I was lost. The coming night might see my own body a banquet in a similar way to those horrid three. I felt all over the body, but no sign could I find of the key. Then I stopped and looked at the Count. There was a mocking smile on the bloated face which seemed to drive me mad. This was the being I was helping to transfer to London, where, perhaps for centuries to come, he might, amongst its teeming millions, satiate his lust for blood, and create a new and ever widening circle of semi-demons to batten on the helpless. The very thought drove me mad. A terrible desire came upon me to rid the world of such a monster. There was no lethal weapon at hand, but I seized a shovel which the workmen had been using to fill the cases, and lifting it high, struck, with the edge downward, at the hateful face. But as I did so the head turned, and the eyes fell full upon me, with all their blaze of basilisk horror. The sight seemed to paralyse me, and the shovel turned in my hand and glanced from the face, merely making a deep gash above the fore-head. The shovel fell from my hand across the box, and as I pulled it away the flange of the blade caught the edge of the lid, which fell over again, and hid the horrid thing from my sight. The last glimpse I had was of the bloated face, bloodstained and fixed with a grin of malice which would have held its own in the nethermost hell.

I thought and thought what should be my next move, but my brain seemed on fire, and I waited with a despairing feeling growing over me. As I waited I heard in the distance a gipsy song sung by merry voices coming closer, and through their song the rolling of heavy wheels and the cracking of whips; the Szgany and the Slovaks of whom the Count had spoken were coming. With a last look around and at the box which contained the vile body, I ran from the place and gained the Count's room, determined to rush out at the moment the door should be opened. With strained ears I listened, and heard downstairs the grinding of the key in the great lock and the falling back of the heavy door. There must have been some other means of entry, or someone had a key for one of the locked doors. Then there came the sound of many feet tramping and dying away in some passage which sent up a clanging echo. I turned to run down again towards the vault, where I might find the new entrance; but at that moment there seemed to come a violent puff of wind, and the door to the winding stair blew to with a shock that set the dust from the lintels flying. When I ran to push it open, I found that it was hopelessly fast. I was again a prisoner, and the net of doom was closing round me more closely.

As I write there is in the passage below a sound of many tramping feet and the crash of weights being set down heavily, doubtless the boxes, with their freight of earth. There is a sound of hammering; it is the box being nailed down. Now I can hear the heavy feet tramping again along the hall, with many other idle feet coming behind them.

The door is shut, and the chains rattle; there is a grinding of the key in the lock; I can hear the key withdrawn; then another door opens and shuts; I hear the creaking of lock and bolt.

Hark! in the courtyard and down the rocky way the roll of heavy wheels, the crack of whips, and the chorus of the Szgany as they pass into the distance.

I am alone in the castle with those awful women. Faugh! Mina is a woman, and there is naught in common. They are devils of the Pit!

I shall not remain alone with them; I shall try to scale the castle wall farther than I have yet attempted. I shall take some of the gold with me, lest I want it later. I may find a way from this dreadful place.

And then away for home! away to the quickest and nearest train! away from this cursed spot, from this cursed land, where the devil and his children still walk with earthly feet!

At least God's mercy is better than that of these monsters, and the precipice is steep and high. At its foot man may sleep – as a man. Good-bye, all! Mina!

CHAPTER 5

Letter from Miss Mina Murray to Miss Lucy Westenra

'*9 May.*

'My dearest Lucy, –

'Forgive my long delay in writing, but I have been simply overwhelmed with work. The life of an assistant schoolmistress is sometimes trying. I am longing to be with you, and by the sea, where we can talk together freely and build our castles in the air. I have been working very hard lately, because I want to keep up with Jonathan's studies, and I have been practising shorthand very assiduously. When we are married I shall be able to be useful to Jonathan, and if I can stenograph well enough I can take down what he wants to say in this way and write it out for him on the typewriter, at which I am also practising very hard. He and I sometimes write letters in shorthand, and he is keeping a steno-graphic journal of his travels abroad. When I am with you I shall keep a diary in the same way. I don't mean one of those two-pages-to-the-week-with-Sunday-squeezed-in-a-corner diaries, but a sort of journal which I can write in whenever I feel inclined. I do not suppose there will be much of interest to other people; but it is not intended for them. I may show it to Jonathan some day if there is in it anything worth sharing, but it is really an exercise-book. I shall try to do what I see lady journalists do: interviewing and writing descriptions and trying to remember conversations. I am told that, with a little practice, one can remember all that goes on or that one hears said during a day. However, we shall see. I shall tell you all my little plans when we meet. I have just had a few hurried lines from Jonathan from Transylvania. He is well, and will be returning in about a week. I am longing to hear all his news. It must be so nice to see strange countries. I wonder if we – I mean Jonathan and I – shall ever see them together. There is the ten o'clock bell ringing. Good-bye.

'Your loving
'MINA.

'Tell me all the news when you write. You have not told me anything for a long time. I hear rumours, and especially of a tall, handsome, curly-haired man???'

Letter, Lucy Westenra to Mina Murray

'*17 Chatham Street,*
'*Wednesday.*

'My dearest Mina, –

'I must say you tax me *very* unfairly with being a bad correspondent. I wrote to you *twice* since we parted, and your last letter was only your *second*. Besides, I have nothing to tell you. There is really nothing to interest you. Town is very pleasant just now, and we go a good deal to picture-galleries and for walks and rides in the park. As to the tall, curly-haired man, I suppose it was the one who was with me at the last Pop. Someone has evidently been telling tales. That was Mr Holmwood. He often comes to see us, and he and mamma get on very well together; they have so many things to talk about in common. We met some time ago a man that would just *do for you*, if you were not already engaged to Jonathan. He is an excellent *parti*, being handsome, well off, and of good birth. He is a doctor and really clever. Just fancy! He is only nine-and-twenty, and he has an immense lunatic asylum all under his own care. Mr Holmwood introduced him to me, and he called here to see us, and often comes now. I think he is one of the most resolute men I ever saw, and yet the most calm. He seems absolutely imperturbable. I can fancy what a wonderful power he must have over his patients. He has a curious habit of looking one straight in the face, as if trying to read one's thoughts. He tries this on very much with me, but I flatter myself he has got a tough nut to crack. I know that from my glass. Do you ever try to read your own face? *I do*, and I can tell you it is not a bad study, and gives you more trouble than you can well fancy if you have never tried it. He says that I afford him a curious psychological study, and I humbly think I do. I do not, as you know, take sufficient interest in dress to be able to describe the new fashions. Dress is a bore. That is slang again, but never mind; Arthur says that every day. There, it is all out. Mina, we have told all our secrets to each other since we were *children*; we have slept together and eaten together, and laughed and cried together; and now, though I have spoken, I would like to speak more. Oh, Mina, couldn't you guess? I love him. I am blushing as I write, for although I *think* he loves me, he has not told me so in words. But, oh, Mina, I love him; I love him; I love him! There, that does me good. I wish I were with you, dear, sitting by the fire undressing, as we used to sit; and I would try to tell you what I feel. I do not know how I am writing this even to you. I am afraid to stop, or I should tear up the letter, and I don't want to stop, for I *do* so want to tell you all. Let me hear from you *at once*, and tell me all that you think about it. Mina, I must stop. Good-night. Bless me in your prayers; and, Mina, pray for my happiness.

'LUCY.

'P.S. – I need not tell you this is a secret. Good-night again. L.'

Letter, Lucy Westenra to Mina Murray

'*24 May.*

'My dearest Mina, –

'Thanks, and thanks, and thanks again for your sweet letter! It was so nice to be able to tell you and to have your sympathy.

'My dear, it never rains but it pours. How true the old proverbs are. Here am I, who will be twenty in September, and yet I never had a proposal till to-day, not a real proposal, and to-day I have had three. Just fancy! Three proposals in one day! Isn't it awful! I feel sorry, really and truly sorry, for two of the poor fellows. Oh, Mina, I am so happy that I don't know what to do with myself. And three proposals! But, for goodness' sake, don't tell any of the girls, or they would be getting all sorts of extravagant ideas and imagining themselves injured and slighted if in their very first day at home they did not get six at least. Some girls are so vain. You and I, Mina dear, who are engaged and are going to settle down soon soberly into old married women, can despise vanity. Well, I must tell you about the three, but you must keep it a secret, dear, from *everyone*, except, of course, Jonathan. You will tell him, because I would, if I were in your place, certainly tell Arthur. A woman ought to tell her husband everything – don't you think so, dear? – and I must be fair. Men like women, certainly their wives, to be quite as fair as they are; and women, I am afraid, are not always quite as fair as they should be. Well, my dear, number one came just before lunch. I told you of him, Dr John Seward, the lunatic-asylum man, with the strong jaw and the good forehead. He was very cool outwardly, but was nervous all the same. He had evidently been schooling himself as to all sorts of little things, and remembered them; but he almost managed to sit down on his silk hat, which men don't generally do when they are cool, and then when he wanted to appear at ease he kept playing with a lancet in a way that made me nearly scream. He spoke to me, Mina, very straight-forwardly. He told me how dear I was to him, though he had known me so little, and what his life would be with me to help and cheer him. He was going to tell me how unhappy he would be if I did not care for him, but when he saw me cry he said that he was a brute and would not add to my present trouble. Then he broke off and asked if I could love him in time; and when I shook my head his hands trembled, and then with some hesitation he asked me if I cared already for anyone else. He put it very nicely, saying that he did not want to wring my confidence from me, but only to know, because if a woman's heart was free a man might have hope. And then, Mina, I felt it a sort of duty to tell him that there was someone. I only told him that much, and then he stood up, and he looked very strong and very grave as he took both my hands in his and said he hoped I would be happy, and that if I ever wanted a friend I must count him one of my best. Oh, Mina dear, I can't help crying; and you must excuse this letter being all blotted. Being proposed to is all very nice and all that sort of thing, but it isn't at all a happy thing when you have to see a poor fellow, whom you know loves you honestly, going away and looking all broken-hearted, and to know that, no matter what he may say at the moment, you are passing quite out of his life. My dear, I must stop here at present, I feel so miserable, though I am so happy.

'*Evening.*

'Arthur has just gone, and I feel in better spirits than when I left off, so I can go on telling you about the day. Well, my dear, number two came after lunch. He is such a nice fellow, an American from Texas, and he looks so young and so fresh that

it seems almost impossible that he has been to so many places
and has had such adventures. I sympathize with poor Desde-
mona when she had such a dangerous stream poured in her ear,
even by a black man. I suppose that we women are such
cowards that we think a man will save us from fears, and we
marry him. I know now what I would do if I were a man and
wanted to make a girl love me. No, I don't, for there was Mr
Morris telling us his stories, and Arthur never told any, and yet
– My dear, I am somewhat previous. Mr Quincey P. Morris
found me alone. It seems that a man always does find a girl
alone. No, he doesn't, for Arthur tried twice to *make* a chance,
and I helping him all I could; I am not ashamed to say it now. I
must tell you beforehand that Mr Morris doesn't always speak
slang – that is to say, he never does so to strangers or before
them, for he is really well educated and has exquisite manners –
but he found out that it amused me to hear him talk American
slang, and whenever I was present, and there was no one to be
shocked, he said such funny things. I am afraid, my dear, he has
to invent it all, for it fits exactly into whatever else he has to
say. But this is a way slang has. I do not know myself if I shall
ever speak slang; I do not know if Arthur likes it, as I have
never heard him use any as yet. Well, Mr Morris sat down
beside me and looked as happy and jolly as he could, but I
could see all the same that he was very nervous. He took my
hand in his, and said ever so sweetly: –

"'Miss Lucy, I know I ain't good enough to regulate the
fixin's of your little shoes, but I guess if you wait till you find a
man that is you will go join them seven young women with the
lamps when you quit. Won't you just hitch up alongside of me
and let us go down the long road together driving in double
harness?"

'Well, he did look so good-humoured and so jolly that it didn't
seem half so hard to refuse him as it did poor Dr Seward, so I
said, as lightly as I could, that I did not know anything of
hitching, and that I wasn't broken to harness at all yet. Then he
said that he had spoken in a light manner, and he hoped that if he
had made a mistake in doing so on so grave, so momentous, an
occasion for him, I would forgive him. He really did look serious
when he was saying it, and I couldn't help feeling a bit serious,
too. I know, Mina, you will think me a horrid flirt – though I

couldn't help feeling a sort of exultation that he was number two in one day. And then, my dear, before I could say a word he began pouring out a perfect torrent of love-making, laying his very heart and soul at my feet. He looked so earnest over it that I shall never again think that a man must be playful always, and never earnest, because he is merry at times. I suppose he saw something in my face which checked him, for he suddenly stopped, and said with a sort of manly fervour that I could have loved him for if I had been free: –

"'Lucy, you are an honest-hearted girl, I know. I should not be here speaking to you as I am now if I did not believe you clean grit, right through to the very depths of your soul. Tell me, like one good fellow to another, is there anyone else that you care for? And if there is, I'll never trouble you a hair's breadth again, but will be, if you will let me, a very faithful friend."

'My dear Mina, why are men so noble when we women are so little worthy of them? Here was I almost making fun of this great-hearted, true gentleman. I burst into tears – I am afraid, my dear, you will think this is a very sloppy letter in more ways than one – and I really felt very badly. Why can't they let a girl marry three men, or as many as want her, and save all this trouble? But this is heresy, and I must not say it. I am glad to say that, though I was crying, I was able to look into Mr Morris's brave eyes, and I told him out straight: –

"'Yes, there is someone I love, though he has not told me yet that he even loves me." I was right to speak to him so frankly, for quite a light came into his face, and he put out both his hands and took mine – I think I put them into his – and said in a hearty way: –

"'That's my brave girl. It's better worth being late for a chance of winning you than being in time for any other girl in the world. Don't cry, my dear. If it's for me, I'm a hard nut to crack; and I take it standing up. If that other fellow doesn't know his happiness, well, he'd better look for it soon, or he'll have to deal with me. Little girl, your honesty and pluck have made me a friend, and that's rarer than a lover; it's more unselfish anyhow. My dear, I'm going to have a pretty lonely walk between this and Kingdom Come. Won't you give me one kiss? It'll be something to keep off the darkness now and then. You can, you know, if you like, for that other good fellow – he must be a good fellow, my dear, and a fine fellow, or you could not love him – hasn't spoken yet." That quite won me, Mina, for it *was* brave and sweet of him, and noble, too, to a rival – wasn't it? – and he so sad; so I leant over and kissed him. He stood up with my two hands in his, and as he looked down into my face – I am afraid I was blushing very much – he said: –

"'Little girl, I hold your hand, and you've kissed me, and if these things don't make us friends nothing ever will. Thank you for your sweet honesty to me, and good-bye." He wrung my hand, and taking up his hat, went straight out of the room without looking back, without a tear or a quiver or a pause; and I am crying like a baby. Oh, why must a man like that be made unhappy when there are lots of girls about who would worship the very ground he trod on? I know I would if I were free – only I don't want to be free. My dear, this quite upset me, and I feel I cannot write of happiness just at once, after telling you of it; and I don't wish to tell of the number three till it can be all happy. – Ever your loving.

'LUCY.

'P.S. – Oh, about number three – I needn't tell you of number three, need I? Besides, it was all so confused; it seemed only a moment from his coming into the room till both his arms were round me, and he was kissing me. I am very, very happy, and I don't know what I have done to deserve it. I must only try in the future to show that I am not ungrateful for all His goodness to me in sending to me such a lover, such a husband, and such a friend.

'Good-bye.'

DR SEWARD'S DIARY

(Kept in phonograph)

25 May. – Ebb tide in appetite to-day. Cannot eat, cannot rest, so diary instead. Since my rebuff of yesterday I have a sort of empty feeling; nothing in the world seems of sufficient importance to be worth the doing . . . As I knew that the only cure for this sort of thing was work, I went down amongst the patients. I picked out one who has afforded me a study of much interest. He is so quaint in his ideas, and so unlike the normal lunatic, that I have determined to understand him as well as I can. To-day I seemed to get nearer than ever before to the heart of his mystery.

I questioned him more fully than I had ever done, with a view to making myself master of the facts of his hallucination. In my manner of doing it there was, I now see, something of cruelty. I seemed to wish to keep him to the point of his madness – a thing which I avoid with the patients as I would the mouth of hell. (*Mem.*, under what circumstances would I *not* avoid the pit of hell?) *Omnia Romae vernalia sunt*. Hell has its price! *verb. sap.* If there be anything behind this instinct it will be valuable to trace it afterwards *accurately*, so I had better commence to do so, therefore –

R. M. Renfield, aetat. 59 – Sanguine temperament; great physical strength; morbidly excitable; periods of gloom ending in some fixed idea which I cannot make out. I presume that the sanguine temperament itself and the disturbing influence end in a mentally accomplished finish; a possibly dangerous man, probably dangerous if unselfish. In selfish men caution is as secure an armour for their foes as for themselves. What I think of on this point is, when self is the fixed point the centripetal force is balanced with the centrifugal: when duty, a cause, etc., is the fixed point, the latter force is paramount, and only accident or a series of accidents can balance it.

Letter, Quincey P. Morris to Hon. Arthur Holmwood

'*25 May.*

'My dear Art, –

'We've told yarns by the camp-fire in the prairies; and dressed one another's wounds after trying a landing at the Marquesas; and drunk healths on the shore of Titicaca. There are more yarns to be told, and other wounds to be healed, and another health to be drunk. Won't you let this be at my camp-fire to-morrow night? I have no hesitation in asking you, as I know a certain lady is engaged to a certain dinner party, and that you are free. There will only be one other, our old pal at the Korea, Jack Seward. He's coming, too, and we both want to mingle our weeps over the wine-cup, and to drink a health with all our hearts to the happiest man in all the wide world, who has won the noblest heart that God has made and the best worth winning. We promise you a hearty welcome, and a loving greeting, and a health as true as your own right hand. We shall both swear to leave you at home if you drink too deep to a certain pair of eyes. Come!

'Yours, as ever and always,
'QUINCEY P. MORRIS.'

Telegram from Arthur Holmwood to Quincey P. Morris

'*26 May.*

'Count me in every time. I bear messages which will make both your ears tingle.

'ART.'

CHAPTER 6

MINA MURRAY'S JOURNAL

24 July. Whitby. – Lucy met me at the station, looking sweeter and love-
lier than ever, and we drove up to the house at the Crescent, in which they
have rooms. This is a lovely place. The little river, the Esk, runs through
a deep valley, which broadens out as it comes near the harbour. A great
viaduct runs across, with high piers, through which the view seems,
somehow, farther away than it really is. The valley is beautifully green,
and it is so steep that when you are on the high land on either side you
look right across it, unless you are near enough to see down. The houses
of the old town – the side away from us – are all red-roofed, and seem
piled up one over the other anyhow, like the pictures we see of Nurem-
berg. Right over the town is the ruin of Whitby Abbey, which was sacked
by the Danes, and which is the scene of part of 'Marmion,' where the girl
was built up in the wall. It is a most noble ruin, of immense size, and full
of beautiful and romantic bits; there is a legend that a white lady is seen
in one of the windows. Between it and the town there is another church,
the parish one, round which is a big graveyard, all full of tombstones.
This is, to my mind, the nicest spot in Whitby, for it lies right over the
town, and has a full view of the harbour and all up the bay to where the
headland called Kettleness stretches out into the sea. It descends so steeply
over the harbour that part of the bank has fallen away, and some of
the graves have been destroyed. In one place part of the stonework of the
graves stretches out over the sandy pathway far below. There are walks,
with seats beside them, through the churchyard; and people go and sit
there all day long looking at the beautiful view and enjoying the breeze.
I shall come and sit here very often myself and work. Indeed, I am writing
now, with my book on my knee, and listening to the talk of three old men
who are sitting beside me. They seem to do nothing all day but sit up here
and talk.

The harbour lies below me, with, on the far side, one long granite wall
stretching out into the sea, with a curve outwards at the end of it, in the
middle of which is a lighthouse. A heavy sea-wall runs along outside of
it. On the near side, the sea-wall makes an elbow crooked inversely, and
its end too has a lighthouse. Between the two piers there is a narrow
opening into the harbour, which then suddenly widens.

It is nice at high tide; but when the tide is out it shoals away to nothing, and there is merely the stream of the Esk, running between banks of sand, with rocks here and there. Outside the harbour on this side there rises for about half a mile a great reef, the sharp edge of which runs straight out from behind the south lighthouse. At the end of it is a buoy with a bell, which swings in bad weather, and sends in a mournful sound on the wind. They have a legend here that when a ship is lost bells are heard out at sea. I must ask the old man about this; he is coming this way . . .

He is a funny old man. He must be awfully old, for his face is all gnarled and twisted like the bark of a tree. He tells me that he is nearly a hundred, and that he was a sailor in the Greenland fishing fleet when Waterloo was fought. He is, I am afraid, a very sceptical person, for when I asked him about the bells at sea and the White Lady at the abbey he said very brusquely:

'I wouldn't fash masel' about them, miss. Them things be all wore out. Mind, I don't say they never was, but I do say that they wasn't in my time. They be all very well for comers and trippers an' the like, but not for a nice young lady like you. Them feet-folks from York and Leeds that be always eatin' cured herrin's an' drinkin' tea an' lookin' out to buy cheap jet would creed aught. I wonder masel' who'd be bothered tellin' lies to them – even the newspapers, which is full of fool-talk.' I thought he would be a good person to learn interesting things from, so I asked him if he would mind telling me something about whale-fishing in the old days. He was just settling himself to begin when the clock struck six, whereupon he laboured to get up, and said:

'I must gang ageeanwards home now, miss. My grand-daughter doesn't like to be kept waitin' when the tea is ready, for it takes me time to crammle aboon the grees, for there be a many of 'em; an', miss, I lack belly-timber sairly by the clock.'

He hobbled away, and I could see him hurrying, as well as he could, down the steps. The steps are a great feature of the place. They lead from the town up to the church; there are hundreds of them – I do not know how many – and they wind up in a delicate curve; the slope is so gentle that a horse could easily walk up and down them. I think they must orig-inally have had something to do with the Abbey. I shall go home too. Lucy went out visiting with her mother, and as they were only duty calls, I did not go. They will be home by this.

1 August. – I came up here an hour ago with Lucy, and we had a most interesting talk with my old friend and the two others who always come and join him. He is evidently the Sir Oracle of them, and I should think must have been in his time a most dictatorial person. He will not admit anything, and downfaces everybody. If he can't out-argue them he bullies them, and then takes their silence for agreement with his views. Lucy was looking sweetly pretty in her white lawn frock; she has got a beautiful colour since she has been here. I noticed that the old men did not lose any time in coming up and sitting near her when we sat down. She is so sweet with old people; I think they all fell in love with her on the spot. Even my old man succumbed and did not contradict her, but gave me double share instead. I got him on the subject of the legends, and he went off at once into a sort of sermon. I must try to remember it and put it down:

'It be all fool-talk, lock, stock, and barrel; that's what it be, an' nowt else. These bans an' wafts an' boh-ghosts an' bar-guests and bogles an' all anent them is only fit to set bairns an' dizzy women a-belderin'. They be nowt but air-blebs! They, an' all grims an' signs an' warnin's, be all invented by parsons an' illsome beuk-bodies an' railway touters to skeer an' scunner hafflin's, an' to get folks to do somethin' that they don't other incline to. It makes me ireful to think o' them. Why, it's them that, not content with printin' lies on paper an' preachin' them out of pulpits, does want to be cuttin' them on the tombstones. Look here all round you in what airt ye will; all them steans, holdin' up their heads as well as they can out of their pride, is acant – simply tumblin' down with the weight o' the lies wrote on them, "Here lies the body" or "Sacred to the memory" wrote on all of them, an' yet in nigh half of them there bean't no bodies at all; an' the memories of them bean't cared a pinch of snuff about, much less sacred. Lies all of them, nothin' but lies of one kind or another! My gog, but it'll be a quare scowderment at the Day of Judgment when they come tumblin' up here in their death-sarks, all jouped together an' tryin' to drag their tombsteans with them to prove how good they was; some of them trimmlin' and ditherin', with their hands that dozzened an' slippy from lyin' in the sea that they can't even keep ther grup o' them.'

I could see from the old fellow's self-satisfied air and the way in which he looked round for the approval of his cronies that he was 'showing off,' so I put in a word to keep him going:

'Oh, Mr Swales, you can't be serious. Surely these tombstones are not all wrong?'

'Yabblins! There may be a poorish few not wrong, savin' where they make out the people too good; for there be folk that do think a balm-bowl be like the sea, if only it be their own. The whole thing be only lies. Now look you here; you come here a stranger, an' you see this kirk-garth.' I nodded, for I thought it better to assent, though I did not quite understand

his dialect. I knew it had something to do with the church. He went on:
'And you consate that all these steans be aboon folk that be happed here,
snod an' snog?' I assented again. 'Then that be just where the lie comes
in. Why, there be scores of these lay-beds that be toom as old Dun's
baccabox on Friday night.' He nudged one of his companions, and they
all laughed. 'And my gog! how could they be otherwise? Look at that one,
the aftest abaft the bier-bank; read it!' I went over and read:

'Edward Spencelagh, master mariner, murdered by pirates off the coast
of Andres, April, 1854, aet. 30.' When I came back Mr Swales went on:

'Who brought him home, I wonder, to hap him here? Murdered off the
coast of Andres! an' you consated his body lay under! Why, I could name
ye a dozen whose bones lie in the Greenland seas above' – he pointed
northwards – 'or where the currents may have drifted them. There be the
steans around ye. Ye can, with your young eyes, read the small print of
the lies from here. This Braithwaite Lowrey – I knew his father, lost in
the *Lively* off Greeland in '20; or Andrew Woodhouse, drowned in the
same seas in 1777; or John Paxton, drowned off Cape Farewell a year
later; or old John Rawlings, whose grandfather sailed with me, drowned
in the Gulf of Finland in '50. Do ye think that all these men will have to
make a rush to Whitby when the trumpet sounds? I have me antherums
aboot it! I tell ye that when they got here they'd be jommlin' an' jostlin'
one another that way that it 'ud be like a fight up on the ice in the old
days, when we'd be at one another from daylight to dark, an' tryin' to tie
up our cuts by the light of the aurora borealis.' This was evidently local
pleasantry, for the old man cackled over it, and his cronies joined in with
gusto.

'But,' I said, 'surely you are not quite correct, for you start on the
assumption that all the poor people, or their spirits, will have to take their
tombstones with them on the Day of Judgment. Do you think that will be
really necessary?'

'Well, what else be they tombsteans for? Answer me that, miss!'

'To please their relatives, I suppose.'

'To please their relatives, you suppose!' This he said with intense scorn.
'How will it pleasure their relatives to know that lies is wrote over them,
and that everybody in the place knows that they be lies?' He pointed to a
stone at our feet which had been laid down as a slab, on which the seat
was rested, close to the edge of the cliff. 'Read the lines on that thruff-
stean,' he said. The letters were upside down to me from where I sat, but
Lucy was more opposite to them, so she leant over and read:

'"Sacred to the memory of George Canon, who died, in the hope of a glorious resurrection, on July 29, 1873, falling from the rocks at Kettle-ness. This tomb is erected by his sorrowing mother to her dearly beloved son. He was the only son of his mother, and she was a widow." Really, Mr Swales, I don't see anything very funny in that!' She spoke her comment very gravely and somewhat severely.

'Ye don't see aught funny! Ha! ha! But that's because ye don't gawm the sorrowin' mother was a hell-cat that hated him because he was acrewk'd – a regular lamiter he was – an' he hated her so that he committed suicide in order that she mightn't get an insurance she put on his life. He blew nigh the top of his head off with an old musket that they had for scarin' the crows with. 'Twarn't for crows then, for it brought the clegs and the dowps to him. That's the way he fell off the rocks. And, as to hopes of a glorious resurrection, I've often heard him say masel' that he hoped he'd go to hell, for his mother was so pious that she'd be sure to go to heaven, an' he didn't want to addle where she was. Now isn't that stean at any rate' – he hammered it with his stick as he spoke – 'a pack of lies? and won't it make Gabriel keckle when Geordie comes pantin' up the grees with the tombstean balanced on his hump, and asks it to be took as evidence!'

I did not know what to say, but Lucy turned the conversation as she said, rising up:

'Oh, why did you tell us of this? It is my favourite seat, and I cannot leave it; and now I find I must go on sitting over the grave of a suicide.'

'That won't harm ye, my pretty; an' it may make poor Geordie glad-some to have so trim a lass sittin' on his lap. That won't hurt ye. Why, I've sat here off an' on for nigh twenty years past, an' it hasn't done me no harm. Don't ye fash about them as lies under ye, or that doesn' lie there either! It'll be time for ye to be getting scart when ye see the tomb-steans all run away with, and the place as bare as a stubble-field. There's the clock, an' I must gang. My service to ye, ladies!' And off he hobbled.

Lucy and I sat awhile, and it was all so beautiful before us that we took hands as we sat; and she told me all over again about Arthur and their coming marriage. That made me just a little heart-sick, for I haven't heard from Jonathan for a whole month.

The same day. – I came up here alone, for I am very sad. There was no letter for me. I hope there cannot be anything the matter with Jonathan. The clock has just struck nine. I see the lights scattered all over the town, sometimes in rows where the streets are, and sometimes singly; they run right up the Esk and die away in the curve of the valley. To my left the view is cut off by a black line of roof of the old house next the Abbey.

The sheep and lambs are bleating in the fields away behind me, and there is a clatter of a donkey's hoofs up the paved road below. The band on the pier is playing a harsh waltz in good time, and farther along the quay there is a Salvation Army meeting in a back street. Neither of the bands hears the other, but up here I hear and see them both. I wonder where Jonathan is and if he is thinking of me! I wish he were here.

DR SEWARD'S DIARY

5 June. – The case of Renfield grows more interesting the more I get to understand the man. He has certain qualities very largely developed: self-ishness, secrecy, and purpose. I wish I could get at what is the object of the latter. He seems to have some settled scheme of his own, but what it is I do not yet know. His redeeming quality is a love of animals, though, indeed, he has such curious turns in it that I sometimes imagine he is only abnormally cruel. His pets are of odd sorts. Just now his hobby is catching flies. He has at present such a quantity that I have had myself to expostulate. To my astonishment, he did not break out into a fury, as I expected, but took the matter in simple seriousness. He thought for a moment, and then said: 'May I have three days? I shall clear them away.' Of course, I said that would do. I must watch him.

18 June. – He has turned his mind now to spiders, and has got several very big fellows in a box. He keeps feeding them with his flies, and the number of the latter is becoming sensibly diminished, although he has used half his food in attracting more flies from outside to his room.

1 July. – His spiders are now becoming as great a nuisance as his flies, and to-day I told him that he must get rid of them. He looked very sad at this, so I said that he must clear out some of them, at all events. He cheerfully acquiesced in this, and I gave him the same time as before for reduction. He disgusted me much while with him, for when a horrid blow-fly, bloated with some carrion food, buzzed into the room, he caught it, held it exultingly for a few moments between his finger and thumb, and, before I knew what he was going to do, put it in his mouth and ate it. I scolded him for it, but he argued quietly that it was very good and very wholesome; that it was life, strong life, and gave life to him. This gave me an idea, or the rudiment of one. I must watch how he gets rid of his spiders. He has evidently some deep problem in his mind, for he keeps a little note-book in which he is always jotting down something. Whole pages of it are filled with masses of figures, generally single numbers added up in batches, and then the totals added in batches again, as though he were 'focusing' some account, as the auditors put it.

8 July. – There is a method in his madness, and the rudimentary idea in my mind is growing. It will be a whole idea soon, and then, oh, unconscious cerebration! you will have to give the wall to your conscious brother. I kept away from my friend for a few days, so that I might notice if there were any change. Things remain as they were except that he has parted with some of his pets and got a new one. He has managed to get a sparrow, and has already partially tamed it. His means of taming is simple, for already the spiders have diminished. Those that do remain, however, are well fed, for he still brings in the flies by tempting them with his food.

19 July. – We are progressing. My friend has now a whole colony of sparrows, and his flies and spiders are almost obliterated. When I came in he ran to me and said he wanted to ask me a great favour – a very, very great favour; and as he spoke he fawned on me like a dog. I asked him what it was, and he said, with a sort of rapture in his voice and bearing:

'A kitten, a nice little, sleek, playful kitten, that I can play with, and teach, and feed – and feed – and feed!' I was not unprepared for this request, for I had noticed how his pets went on increasing in size and vivacity, but I did not care that his pretty family of tame sparrows should be wiped out in the same manner as the flies and the spiders; so I said I would see about it, and asked him if he would not rather have a cat than a kitten. His eagerness betrayed him as he answered:

'Oh, yes I would like a cat! I only asked for a kitten lest you should refuse me a cat. No one would refuse me a kitten, would they?' I shook my head, and said that at present I feared it would not be possible, but that I would see about it. His face fell, and I could see a warning of danger in it, for there was a sudden fierce, sidelong look which meant killing. The man is an undeveloped homicidal maniac. I shall test him with his present craving and see how it will work out; then I shall know more.

10 p.m. – I have visited him again and found him sitting in a corner brooding. When I came in he threw himself on his knees before me and implored me to let him have a cat; that his salvation depended upon it. I was firm, however, and told him that he could not have it, whereupon he went without a word, and sat down, gnawing his fingers, in the corner where I had found him. I shall see him in the morning early.

20 July. – Visited Renfield very early, before the attendant went his rounds. Found him up and humming a tune. He was spreading out his sugar, which he had saved, in the window, and was manifestly beginning his fly-catching again; and beginning cheerfully and with a good grace. I looked around for his birds, and not seeing them, asked him where they were. He replied, without turning round, that they had all flown away. There were a few feathers about the room and on his pillow a drop of blood. I said nothing, but went and told the keeper to report to me if there were anything odd about him during the day.

11 a.m. – The attendant has just been to me to say that Renfield has been very sick and has disgorged a whole lot of feathers. 'My belief is, doctor,' he said, 'that he has eaten his birds, and that he just took and ate them raw!'

11 p.m. – I gave Renfield a strong opiate to-night, enough to make even him sleep, and took away his pocket-book to look at it. The thought that has been buzzing about my brain lately is complete, and the theory proved. My homicidal maniac is of a peculiar kind. I shall have to invent a new classification for him, and call him a zoophagous (life-eating) maniac; what he desires is to absorb as many lives as he can, and he has laid himself out to achieve it in a cumulative way. He gave many flies to one spider and many spiders to one bird, and then wanted a cat to eat the many birds. What would have been his later steps? It would almost be worth while to complete the experiment. It might be done if there were only a sufficient cause. Men sneered at vivisection, and yet look at its results to-day! Why not advance science in its most difficult and vital aspect – the knowledge of the brain? Had I even the secret of one such mind – did I hold the key to the fancy of even one lunatic – I might advance my own branch of science to a pitch compared with which Burdon-Sanderson's physiology or Ferrier's brain knowledge would be as nothing. If only there were a sufficient cause! I must not think too much of this, or I may be tempted; a good cause might turn the scale with me, for may not I too be of an exceptional brain, congenitally?

How well the man reasoned; lunatics always do within their own scope. I wonder at how many lives he values a man, or if at only one. He has closed the account most accurately, and to-day begun a new record. How many of us begin a new record with each day of our lives?

To me it seems only yesterday that my whole life ended with my new hope, and that truly I began a new record. So it will be until the Great Recorder sums me up and closes my ledger account with a balance to profit or loss. Oh, Lucy, Lucy, I cannot be angry with you, nor can I be angry with my friend whose happiness is yours; but I must only wait on hopeless and work. Work! work!

If I only could have as strong a cause as my poor mad friend there, a good, unselfish cause to make me work, that would be indeed happiness.

MINA MURRAY'S JOURNAL

26 July. – I am anxious, and it soothes me to express myself here; it is like whispering to one's self and listening at the same time. And there is also something about the shorthand symbols that makes it different from writing. I am unhappy about Lucy and about Jonathan. I had not heard from Jonathan for some time, and was very concerned; but yesterday dear Mr Hawkins, who is always so kind, sent me a letter from him. I had written asking him if he had heard, and he said the enclosed had just been received. It is only a line dated from Castle Dracula, and says that he is just starting for home. That is not like Jonathan; I do not understand it, and it makes me uneasy. Then, too, Lucy, although she is so well, has lately taken to her old habit of walking in her sleep. Her mother has spoken to me about it, and we have decided that I am to lock the door of our room every night. Mrs Westenra has got an idea that sleep-walkers always go out on roofs of houses and along the edges of cliffs, and then get suddenly awakened and fall over with a despairing cry that echoes all over the place. Poor dear, she is naturally anxious about Lucy, and she tells me that her husband, Lucy's father, had the same habit; that he would get up in the night and dress himself and go out, if he were not stopped. Lucy is to be married in the autumn, and she is already planning out her dresses and how her house is to be arranged. I sympathize with her, for I do the same, only Jonathan and I will start in life in a very simple way, and shall have to try to make both ends meet. Mr Holmwood – he is the Hon. Arthur Holmwood, only son of Lord Godalming – is coming up here very shortly – as soon as he can leave town, for his father is not very well, and I think dear Lucy is counting the moments till he comes. She wants to take him up to the seat on the churchyard cliff and show him the beauty of Whitby. I daresay it is the waiting which disturbs her; she will be all right when he arrives.

27 July. – No news from Jonathan. I am getting quite uneasy about him, though why I should I do not know; but I *do* wish that he would write, if it were only a single line. Lucy walks more than ever, and each night I am awakened by her moving about the room. Fortunately, the weather is so hot that she cannot get cold; but still the anxiety and the perpetually being wakened is beginning to tell on me, and I am getting nervous and wakeful myself. Thank God, Lucy's health keeps up. Mr Holmwood has been suddenly called to Ring to see his father, who has been taken seriously ill. Lucy frets at the postponement of seeing him, but it does not touch her looks; she is a trifle stouter, and her cheeks are a lovely rose pink. She has lost that anaemic look which she had. I pray it will all last.

3 August. – Another week gone, and no news from Jonathan, not even to Mr Hawkins, from whom I have heard. Oh, I do hope he is not ill. He surely would have written. I look at that last letter of his, but somehow it does not satisfy me. It does not read like him, and yet it is his writing. There is no mistake of that. Lucy has not walked much in her sleep the last week, but there is an odd concentration about her which I do not understand; even in her sleep she seems to be watching me. She tries the door, and finding it locked, goes about the room searching for the key.

6 August. – Another three days, and no news. This suspense is getting dreadful. If I only knew where to write to or where to go to, I should feel easier; but no one has heard a word of Jonathan since that last letter. I must only pray to God for patience. Lucy is more excitable than ever, but is otherwise well. Last night was very threatening, and the fishermen say that we are in for a storm. I must try to watch it and learn the weather signs. To-day is a grey day, and the sun as I write is hidden in thick clouds, high over Kettleness. Everything is grey – except the green grass, which seems like emerald amongst it; grey earthy rock; grey clouds, tinged with the sunburst at the far edge, hang over the grey sea, into which the sand-points stretch like grey fingers. The sea is tumbling in over the shallows and the sandy flats with a roar, muffled in the sea-mists drifting inland. The horizon is lost in a grey mist. All is vastness; the clouds are piled up like giant rocks, and there is a 'brool' over the sea that sounds like some presage of doom. Dark figures are on the beach here and there, sometimes half shrouded in the mist, and seem 'men like trees walking.' The fishing-boats are racing for home, and rise and dip in the ground swell as they sweep into the harbour, bending to the scuppers. Here comes old Mr Swales. He is making straight for me, and I can see, by the way he lifts his hat, that he wants to talk . . .

I have been quite touched by the change in the poor old man. When he sat down beside me, he said in a very gentle way:

'I want to say something to you, miss.' I could see he was not at ease, so I took his poor old wrinkled hand in mine and asked him to speak fully; so he said, leaving his hand in mine: –

'I'm afraid, my deary, that I must have shocked you by all the wicked things I've been sayin' about the dead, and suchlike, for weeks past; but I didn't mean them, and I want ye to remember that when I've gone. We aud folks that be daffled, and with one foot abaft the krok-hooal, don't altogether like to think of it, and we don't want to feel scart of it; an' that's why I've took to makin' light of it, so that I'd cheer up my own heart a bit. But, Lord love ye, miss, I ain't afraid of dyin' not a bit; only I don't want to die if I can help it. My time must be nigh at hand now, for I be aud, and a hundred years is too much for any man to expect; and I'm so nigh it that the Aud Man is already whettin' his scythe. Ye see, I can't get out o' the habit of caffin' about it all at once; the chafts will wag as they be used to. Some day soon the Angel of Death will sound his trumpet for me. But don't ye dooal an' greet, my deary!' – for he saw that I was crying – 'if he should come this very night I'd not refuse to answer his call. For life be, after all, only a waitin' for somethin' else than what we're doin'; and death be all that we can rightly depend on. But I'm content, for it's comin' to me, my deary, and comin' quick. It may be comin' while we be lookin' and wonderin'. Maybe it's in that wind out over the sea that's bringin' with it loss and wreck, and sore distress, and sad hearts. Look! look!' he cried suddenly. 'There's something in that wind and in the hoast beyont that sounds, and looks, and tastes, and smells like death. It's in the air; I feel it comin'. Lord, make me answer cheerful when my call comes!' He held up his arms devoutly, and raised his hat. His mouth moved as though he were praying. After a few minutes' silence, he got up, shook hands with me, and blessed me, and said good-bye, and hobbled off. It all touched me, and upset me very much. I was glad when the coastguard came along, with his spy-glass under his arm. He stopped to talk with me, as he always does, but all the time kept looking at a strange ship.

'I can't make her out,' he said; 'she's a Russian, by the look of her; but she's knocking about in the queerest way. She doesn't know her mind a bit; she seems to see the storm coming, but can't decide whether to run up north in the open, or to put in here. Look there again! She is steered mighty strangely, for she doesn't mind the hand on the wheel; changes about with every puff of wind. We'll hear more of her before this time to-morrow.'

CHAPTER 7

CUTTING FROM 'The Dailygraph', 8 AUGUST

(Pasted in Mina Murray's Journal)

From a Correspondent

Whitby.

One of the greatest and suddenest storms on record has just been experienced here, with results both strange and unique. The weather had been somewhat sultry, but not to any degree uncommon in the month of August. Saturday evening was as fine as was ever known, and the great body of holiday-makers set out yesterday for visits to Mulgrave Woods, Robin Hood's Bay, Rig Mill, Runswick, Staithes, and the various trips in the neighbourhood of Whitby. The steamers *Emma* and *Scarborough* made excursions along the coast, and there was an unusual amount of 'tripping' both to and from Whitby. The day was unusually fine till the afternoon, when some of the gossips who frequent the East Cliff churchyard, and from that commanding eminence watch the wide sweep of sea visible to the north and east, called attention to a sudden show of 'mares'-tails' high in the sky to the north-west. The wind was then blowing from the south-west in the mild degree which in barometrical language is ranked 'No.2: light breeze.' The coastguard on duty at once made report, and one old fisherman, who for more than half a century has kept watch on weather signs from the East Cliff, foretold in an emphatic manner the coming of a sudden storm. The approach of sunset was so very beautiful, so grand in its masses of splendidly coloured clouds, that there was quite an assemblage on the walk along the cliff in the old churchyard to enjoy the beauty. Before the sun dipped below the black mass of Kettleness, standing boldly athwart the western sky, its downward way was marked by myriad clouds of every sunset-colour – flame, purple, pink, green, violet, and all the tints of gold; with here and there masses not large, but of seemingly absolute blackness, in all sorts of shapes, as well outlined as colossal silhouettes. The experience was not lost on the painters, and doubtless some of the sketches of the 'Prelude to the Great Storm' will grace the R.A. and R.I. walls in May next. More than one captain made up his mind then and there that his 'cobble' or his 'mule,' as they term the different classes of boats, would remain in the harbour till the storm had passed. The wind fell away entirely during the evening, and at midnight there was a dead calm, a sultry heat, and that prevailing intensity which, on the approach of thunder, affects persons of a sensitive nature. There were but few lights in sight at sea, for even the coasting steamers, which usually 'hug' the shore so closely, kept well to seaward, and but few fishing-boats were in sight. The only sail noticeable was a foreign schooner with all sails set, which was seemingly going westwards. The foolhardiness or ignorance of her officers was a prolific theme for comment whilst she remained in sight, and efforts were made to signal her to reduce sail in face of her danger. Before the night shut down she was seen with sails idly flapping as she gently rolled on the undulating swell of the sea.

'As idle as a painted ship upon a painted ocean.'

Shortly before ten o'clock the stillness of the air grew quite oppressive, and the silence was so marked that the bleating of a sheep inland or the barking of a dog in the town was distinctly heard, and the band on the pier, with its lively French air, was like a discord in the great harmony of nature's silence. A little after midnight came a strange sound from over the sea, and high overhead the air began to carry a strange, faint hollow booming.

Then without warning the tempest broke. With a rapidity which, at the time, seemed incredible, and even afterwards is impossible to realize, the whole aspect of nature at once became convulsed. The waves rose in growing fury, each over-topping its fellow, till in a very few minutes the lately glassy sea was like a roaring and devouring monster. White-crested waves beat madly on the level sands and rushed up the shelving cliffs; others broke over the piers, and with their spume swept the lanthorns of the lighthouses which rise from the end of either pier of Whitby Harbour. The wind roared like thunder, and blew with such force that it was with difficulty that even strong men kept their feet, or clung with grim clasp to the iron stanchions. It was found necessary to clear the entire piers from the mass of onlookers, or else the fatalities of the night would have been increased many-fold. To add to the difficulties and dangers of the time, masses of sea-fog came drifting inland – white, wet clouds, which swept by in ghostly fashion, so dank and damp and cold that it needed but little effort of imagination to think that the spirits of those lost at sea were touching their living brethren with the clammy hands of death, and many a one shuddered as the wreaths of sea-mist swept by. At times the mist cleared, and the sea for some distance could be seen in the glare of the lightning, which now came thick and fast, followed by such sudden peals of thunder that the whole sky overhead seemed trembling under the shock of the footsteps of the storm. Some of the scenes thus revealed were of immeasurable grandeur and of absorbing interest – the sea, running mountains high, threw skywards with each wave mighty masses of white foam, which the tempest seemed to snatch at and whirl away into space; here and there a fishing-boat, with a rag of sail, running madly for shelter before the blast; now and again the white wings of a storm-tossed sea-bird. On the summit of the East Cliff the new searchlight was ready for experiment, but had not yet been tried. The officers in charge of it got it into working order, and in the pauses of the inrushing mist swept with it the surface of the sea. Once or twice its service was most effective, as when a fishing-boat, with gunwale under water, rushed into the harbour, able, by the guidance of the sheltering light, to avoid the danger of dashing against the piers. As each boat achieved the safety of the port there was a shout of joy from the mass of people on shore, a shout which for a moment seemed to cleave the gale and was then swept away in its rush. Before long the searchlight discovered some distance away a schooner with all sails set, apparently the same vessel which had been noticed earlier in the evening. The wind had by this time backed to the east, and there was a shudder amongst the watchers on the cliff as they realized the terrible danger in which she now was. Between her and the port lay the great flat reef on which so many good ships have from time to time suffered, and, with the wind blowing from its present quarter, it would be quite impossible that she should fetch the entrance of the harbour. It was now nearly the hour of high tide, but the waves were so great that in their troughs the shallows of the shore were almost visible, and the schooner, with all sails set, was rushing with such speed that, in the words of one old salt, 'she must fetch up somewhere, if it was only in hell.' Then came another rush of sea-fog, greater than any hitherto – a mass of dank mist, which seemed to close on all things like a grey pall, and left available to men only the organ of hearing, for the roar of the tempest, and the crash of the thunder, and the booming of the mighty billows came through the damp oblivion even louder than before. The rays of the searchlight were kept fixed on the harbour mouth across the East Pier, where the shock was expected, and men waited breathless. The wind suddenly shifted to the north-east, and the remnant of the sea-fog melted in the blast; and then, *mirabile dictu*, between the piers, leaping from wave to wave as it rushed at headlong speed, swept the strange schooner before the blast, with all sail set, and gained the safety of the harbour. The searchlight followed her, and a shudder ran through all who saw her, for lashed to the helm was a corpse, with drooping head, which swung horribly to and fro at each motion of the ship. No other form could be seen on deck at all. A great awe came on all as they realized that the ship, as if by a miracle, had found the harbour, unsteered save by the hand of a dead man! However, all took place more quickly than it takes to write these words. The schooner paused not, but rushing across the harbour, pitched herself on that accumulation of sand and gravel washed by many tides and many storms into the southeast corner of the pier jutting under the East Cliff, known locally as Tate Hill Pier.

There was of course a considerable concussion as the vessel drove up on the sand-heap. Every spar, rope, and stay was strained, and some of the 'top-hamper' came crashing down. But, strangest of all, the very instant the shore was touched, an immense dog sprang up on deck from below, as if shot up by the concussion, and running forward, jumped from the bow on to the sand. Making straight for the steep cliff, where the churchyard hangs over the laneway to the East Pier so steeply that some of the flat tombstones – 'thruff-steans' or 'through-stones,' as they call them in the Whitby vernacular – actually project over where the sustaining cliff has fallen away, it disappeared in the darkness, which seemed intensified just beyond the focus of the searchlight.

It so happened that there was no one at the moment on Tate Hill Pier, as all those whose houses are in close proximity were either in bed or were out on the heights above. Thus the coastguard on duty on the eastern side of the harbour, who at once ran down to the little pier, was the first to climb on board. The men working the searchlight, after scouring the entrance of the harbour without seeing anything, then turned the light on the derelict and kept it there. The coastguard ran aft, and when he came beside the wheel, bent over to examine it and recoiled at once as though under some sudden emotion. This seemed to pique the general curiosity, and quite a number of people began to run. It is a good way round from the West Cliff by the Drawbridge to Tate Hill Pier, but your correspondent is a fairly good runner, and came well ahead of the crowd. When I arrived, however, I found already assembled on the pier a crowd, whom the coastguard and police refused to allow to come on board. By the courtesy of the chief boatman, I was, as your correspondent, permitted to climb on deck, and was one of a small group who saw that dead seaman whilst actually lashed to the wheel.

It was no wonder that the coastguard was surprised, or even awed, for not often can such a sight have been seen. The man was simply fastened by his hands, tied one over the other, to a spoke of the wheel. Between the inner hand and the wood was a crucifix, the set of beads on which it was fastened being around both wrists and wheel, and all kept fast by the binding cords. The poor fellow may have been seated at one time, but the flapping and buffeting of the sails had worked through the rudder of the wheel and dragged him to and fro, so that the cords with which he was tied had cut the flesh to the bone. Accurate note was made of the state of things, and a doctor – Surgeon J. M. Caffyn, of 33, East Elliot Place – who came immediately after me, declared, after making examination, that the man must have been dead for quite two days. In his pocket was a bottle, carefully corked, empty save for a little roll of paper, which proved to be the addendum to the log. The coastguard said the man must have tied up his own hands, fastening the knots with his teeth. The fact that a coastguard was the first on board may save some complications, later on, in the Admiralty Court; for the coastguards cannot claim the salvage which is the right of the first civilian entering on a derelict. Already, however, the legal tongues are wagging, and one young law student is loudly asserting that the rights of the owner are already completely sacrificed, his property being held in contravention of the statutes of mortmain, since the tiller, as emblemship, if not proof, of delegated possession, is held in a *dead hand*. It is needless to say that the dead steersman has been reverently removed from the place where he held his honourable watch and ward till death – a steadfastness as noble as that of the young Casabianca – and placed in the mortuary to await inquest.

Already the sudden storm is passing, and its fierceness is abating; the crowds are scattering homewards, and the sky is beginning to redden over the Yorkshire wolds. I shall send, in time for your next issue, further details of the derelict ship which found her way so miraculously into harbour in the storm.

Whitby.

9 August. – The sequel to the strange arrival of the derelict in the storm last night is almost more startling than the thing itself. It turns out that the schooner is a Russian from Varna, and is called the *Demeter*. She is almost entirely in ballast of silver sand, with only a small amount of cargo – a number of great wooden boxes filled with mould. This cargo was consigned to a Whitby solicitor, Mr S. F. Billington, of 7, The Crescent, who this morning went aboard and formally took possession of the goods consigned to him. The Russian consul, too, acting for the charter-party, took formal possession of the ship, and paid all harbour dues, etc. Nothing is talked about here to-day except the strange coincidence; the officials of the Board of Trade have been most exacting in seeing that every compliance has been made with existing regulations. As the matter is to be a 'nine days' wonder,' they are evidently determined that there shall be no cause of after complaint. A good deal of interest was abroad concerning the dog which landed when the ship struck, and more than a few of the members of the S.P.C.A., which is very strong in Whitby, have tried to befriend the animal. To the general disappointment, however, it was not to be found; it seems to have disappeared entirely from the town. It may be that it was frightened and made its way on to the moors, where it is still hiding in terror. There are some who look with dread on such a possibility, lest later on it should in itself become a danger, for it is evidently a fierce brute. Early this morning a large dog, a half-bred mastiff, belonging to a coal merchant close to Tate Hill Pier, was found dead in the roadway opposite its master's yard. It had been fighting, and manifestly had had a savage opponent, for its throat was torn away, and its belly was slit open as if with a savage claw.

Later. – By the kindness of the Board of Trade inspector, I have been permitted to look over the log-book of the *Demeter*, which was in order up to within three days, but contained nothing of special interest except as to facts of missing men. The greater interest, however, is with regard to the paper found in the bottle, which was to-day produced at the inquest; and a more strange narrative than the two between them unfold it has not been my lot to come across. As there is no motive for concealment, I am permitted to use them, and accordingly send you a rescript, simply omitting technical details of seamanship and super-cargo. It almost seems as though the captain had been seized with some kind of mania before he had got well into blue water, and that this had developed persistently throughout the voyage. Of course my statement must be taken *cum grano*, since I am writing from the dictation of a clerk of the Russian consul, who kindly translated for me, time being short.

LOG OF THE 'DEMETER'

Varna to Whitby

Written 18 July, things so strange happening, that I shall keep accurate note henceforth till we land.

On 6 July we finished taking in cargo, silver sand and boxes of earth. At noon set sail. East wind, fresh. Crew, five hands . . . two mates, cook, and myself (captain).

On 11 July at dawn entered Bosphorus. Boarded by Turkish Customs officers. Backsheesh. All correct. Under way at 4 p.m.

On 12 July through Dardanelles. More Customs officers and flagboat of guarding squadron. Backsheesh again. Work of officers thorough, but quick. Want us off soon. At dark passed into Archipelago.

On 13 July passed Cape Matapan. Crew dissatisfied about something. Seemed scared, but would not speak out.

On 14 July was somewhat anxious about crew. Men all steady fellows, who sailed with me before. Mate could not make out what was wrong; they only told him there was *something*, and crossed themselves. Mate lost temper with one of them that day and struck him. Expected fierce quarrel, but all was quiet.

On 16 July mate reported in the morning that one of crew, Petrofsky, was missing. Could not account for it. Took lar-board watch eight bells last night; was relieved by Abramoff, but did not go to bunk. Men more downcast than ever. All said they expected something of the kind, but would not say more than that there was *something* aboard. Mate getting very impatient with them; feared some trouble ahead.

On 17 July, yesterday, one of the men, Olgaren, came to my cabin, and in an awestruck way confided to me that he thought there was a strange man aboard the ship. He said that in his watch he had been sheltering behind the deck-house, as there was a rain-storm, when he saw a tall, thin man, who was not like any of the crew, come up the companion way, and go along the deck forward, and disappear. He followed cautiously, but when he got to bows found no one, and the hatchways were all closed. He was in a panic of superstitious fear, and I am afraid the panic may spread. To allay it, I shall to-day search entire ship carefully from stem to stern.

Later in the day I got together the whole crew, and told them, as they evidently thought there was someone in the ship, we should search from stem to stern. First mate angry; said it was folly, and to yield to such foolish ideas would demoralize the men; said he would engage to keep them out of trouble with a handspike. I let him take the helm, while the rest began thorough search, all keeping abreast, with lanterns; we left no corner unsearched. As there were only the big wooden boxes, there were no odd corners where a man could hide. Men much relieved when search over, and went back to work cheerfully. First mate scowled, but said nothing.

22 July. – Rough weather last three days, and all hands busy with sails – no time to be frightened. Men seem to have forgotten their dread. Mate cheerful again, and all on good terms. Praised men for work in bad weather. Passed Gibraltar and out through Straits. All well.

24 July. – There seems some doom over this ship. Already a hand short, and entering on the Bay of Biscay with wild weather ahead, and yet last night another man lost – disappeared. Like the first, he came off his watch and was not seen again. Men all in a panic of fear; sent a round robin, asking to have double watch, as they fear to be alone. Mate violent. Fear there will be some trouble, as either he or the men will do some violence.

28 July. – Four days in hell, knocking about in a sort of maelstrom, and the wind a tempest. No sleep for any one. Men all worn out. Hardly know how to set a watch since no one fit to go on. Second mate volunteered to steer and watch, and let men snatch a few hours' sleep. Wind abating; seas still terrific, but feel them less, as ship is steadier.

29 July. – Another tragedy. Had single watch to-night, as crew too tired to double. When morning watch came on deck could find no one except steersman. Raised outcry, and all came on deck. Thorough search, but no one found. Are now without second mate, and crew in a panic. Mate and I agreed to go armed henceforth and wait for any sign of cause.

30 July. – Last night. Rejoiced we are nearing England. Weather fine, all sails set. Retired worn out; slept soundly; awaked by mate telling me that both men of watch and steersman missing. Only self and mate and two hands left to work ship.

1 August. – Two days of fog, and not a sail sighted. Had hoped when in the English Channel to be able to signal for help or get in somewhere. Not having power to work sails, have to run before wind. Dare not lower, as could not raise them again. We seem to be drifting to some terrible doom. Mate now more demoralized than either of them. His stronger nature seems to have worked inwardly against himself. Men are beyond fear, working stolidly and patiently, with minds made up to worst. They are Russian, he Roumanian.

2 August, midnight. – Woke up from few minutes' sleep by hearing a cry, seemingly outside my port. Could see nothing in fog. Rushed on deck, and ran against mate. Tells me heard cry and ran, but no sign of man on watch. One more gone. Lord, help us! Mate says we must be past Straits of Dover, as in a moment of fog lifting he saw North Foreland just as he heard the man cry out. If so we are now off in the North Sea, and only God can guide us in the fog, which seems to move with us; and God seems to have deserted us.

3 August. – At midnight I went to relieve the man at the wheel, but when I got to it found no one there. The wind was steady, and as we ran before it there was no yawing. I dared not leave it, so shouted for the mate. After a few seconds he rushed up on deck in his flannels. He looked wild-eyed and haggard, and I greatly fear his reason has given way. He came close to me and whispered hoarsely, with his mouth to my ear, as though fearing the very air might hear: 'It is here; I know it, now. On the watch last night I saw It, like a man, tall and thin, and ghastly pale. It was in the bows, and looking out. I crept behind It, and gave It my knife; but the knife went through It, empty as the air.' And as he spoke he took his knife and drove it savagely into space. Then he went on: 'But It is here, and I'll find it. It is in the hold, perhaps, in one of those boxes. I'll unscrew them one by one and see. You work the helm.' And, with a warning look and his finger on his lip, he went below. There was springing up a choppy wind, and I could not leave the helm. I saw him come out on deck again with a tool-chest and a lantern, and go down the forward hatchway. He is mad, stark, raving mad, and it's no use my trying to stop him. He can't hurt those big boxes: they are invoiced as 'clay,' and to pull them about is as harmless a thing as he can do. So here I stay, and mind the helm, and write these notes. I can only trust in God and wait till the fog clears. Then, if I can't steer to any harbour with the wind that is, I shall cut down sails and lie by, and signal for help . . .

It is nearly all over now. Just as I was beginning to hope that the mate would come out calmer – for I heard him knocking away at something in the hold, and work is good for him – there came up the hatchway a sudden, startled scream, which made my blood run cold, and up on the deck he came as if shot from a gun – a raging madman, with his eyes rolling and his face convulsed with fear. 'Save me! save me!' he cried, and then looked round on the blanket of fog. His horror turned to despair, and in a steady voice he said: 'You had better come too, captain, before it is too late. *He* is there. I know the secret now. The sea will save me from Him, and it is all that is left!' Before I could say a word, or move forward to seize him, he sprang on the bulwark and deliberately threw himself into the sea. I suppose I know the secret too, now. It was this madman who had got rid of the men one by one, and now he has followed them himself. God help me! How am I to account for all these horrors when I get to port? *When* I get to port! Will that ever be?

4 August. – Still fog, which the sunrise cannot pierce. I know there is sunrise because I am a sailor, why else I know not. I dared not go below, I dared not leave the helm so here all night I stayed, and in the dimness of the night I saw It – Him! God forgive me, but the mate was right to jump overboard. It is better to die like a man; to die like a sailor in blue water no man can object. But I am captain, and I must not leave my ship. But I shall baffle this fiend or monster, for I shall tie my hands to the wheel when my strength begins to fail, and along with them I shall tie that which He – It! – dare not touch; and then, come good wind or foul, I shall save my soul, and my honour as a captain. I am growing weaker, and the night is coming on. If He can look me in the face again, I may not have time to act . . . If we are wrecked, mayhap this bottle may be found, and those who find it may understand; if not . . . well, then all men shall know that I have been true to my trust. God and the Blessed Virgin and the saints help a poor ignorant soul trying to do his duty . . .

Of course the verdict was an open one. There is no evidence to adduce; and whether or not the man himself committed the murders there is now none to say. The folk hold almost universally here that the captain is simply a hero, and he is to be given a public funeral. Already it is arranged that his body is to be taken with a train of boats up the Esk for a piece and then brought back to Tate Hill Pier and up the Abbey steps; for he is to be buried in the churchyard on the cliff. The owners of more than a hundred boats have already given in their names as wishing to follow him to the grave.

No trace has ever been found of the great dog; at which there is much mourning, for, with public opinion in its present state, he would, I believe, be adopted by the town. To-morrow will see the funeral; and so will end this one more 'mystery of the sea'.

MINA MURRAY'S JOURNAL

8 August. – Lucy was very restless all night, and I, too, could not sleep. The storm was fearful, and as it boomed loudly among the chimney-pots, it made me shudder. When a sharp puff came it seemed to be like a distant gun. Strangely enough, Lucy did not wake; but she got up twice and dressed herself. Fortunately, each time I awoke in time, and managed to undress her without waking her, and got her back to bed. It is a very strange thing, this sleep-walking, for as soon as her will is thwarted in any physical way, her intention, if there be any, disappears, and she yields herself almost exactly to the routine of her life.

Early in the morning we both got up and went down to the harbour to see if anything had happened in the night. There were very few people about, and though the sun was bright, and the air clear and fresh, the big, grim-looking waves, that seemed dark themselves because the foam that topped them was like snow, forced themselves in through the narrow mouth of the harbour – like a bullying man going through a crowd. Somehow I felt glad that Jonathan was not on the sea last night, but on land. But, oh, is he on land or sea? Where is he, and how? I am getting fearfully anxious about him. If I only knew what to do, and could do anything!

10 August. – The funeral of the poor sea-captain to-day was most touching. Every boat in the harbour seemed to be there, and the coffin was carried by captains all the way from Tate Hill Pier up to the church-yard. Lucy came with me, and we went early to our old seat, whilst the cortège of boats went up the river to the Viaduct and came down again. We had a lovely view, and saw the procession nearly all the way. The poor fellow was laid to rest quite near our seat, so that we stood on it when the time came and saw everything. Poor Lucy seemed much upset. She was restless and uneasy all the time, and I cannot but think that her dreaming at night is telling on her. She is quite odd in one thing: she will not admit to me that there is any cause for restlessness; or if there be, she does not understand it herself. There is an additional cause in that poor old Mr Swales was found dead this morning on our seat, his neck being broken. He had evidently, as the doctor said, fallen back in the seat in some sort of fright, for there was a look of fear and horror on his face that the men said made them shudder. Poor dear old man! Perhaps he had seen Death with his dying eyes! Lucy is so sweet and sensitive that she feels influences more acutely than other people do. Just now she was quite upset by a little thing which I did not much heed, though I am myself very fond of animals. One of the men who come up here often to look for the boats was followed by his dog. The dog is always with him. They are both quiet persons, and I never saw the man angry, nor heard the dog bark. During the service the dog would not come to its master, who was on the seat with us, but kept a few yards off, barking and howling. Its master spoke to it gently, and then harshly, and then angrily; but it would neither come nor cease to make a noise. It was in a sort of fury, with its eyes savage, and all its hairs bristling out like a cat's tail when puss is on the war-path. Finally the man, too, got angry, and jumped down and kicked the dog, and then took it by the scruff of the neck and half dragged and half threw it on the tombstone on which the seat is fixed. The moment it touched the stone the poor thing became quiet and fell all into a tremble. It did not try to get away, but crouched down, quivering and cowering, and was in such a pitiable state of terror that I tried, though without effect, to comfort it. Lucy was full of pity, too, but she did not attempt to touch the dog, but looked at it in an agonized sort of way. I greatly fear that she is of too super-sensitive a nature to go through the world without trouble. She will be dreaming of this to-night, I am sure. The whole agglomeration of things – the ship steered into port by a dead man; his attitude, tied to the wheel with a crucifix and beads; the touching funeral; the dog, now furious and now in terror – will all afford ma-terial for her dreams.

I think it will be best for her to go to bed tired out physically, so I shall take her for a long walk by the cliffs to Robin Hood's Bay and back. She ought not to have much inclination for sleep-walking then.

CHAPTER 8
MINA MURRAY'S JOURNAL

Same day, 11 o'clock p.m. – Oh, but I am tired! If it were not that I have made my diary a duty I should not open it to-night. We had a lovely walk. Lucy, after a while, was in gay spirits, owing, I think, to some dear cows who came nosing towards us in a field close to the lighthouse, and frightened the wits out of us. I believe we forgot everything, except, of course, personal fear, and it seemed to wipe the slate clean and give us a fresh start. We had a capital 'severe tea' at Robin Hood's Bay in a sweet little old-fashioned inn, with a bow-window right over the seaweed-covered rocks of the strand. I believe we should have shocked the 'New Woman' with our appetites. Men are more tolerant, bless them! Then we walked home with some, or rather many, stoppages to rest, and with our hearts full of a constant dread of wild bulls. Lucy was really tired, and we intended to creep off to bed as soon as we could. The young curate came in, however, and Mrs Westenra asked him to stay for supper. Lucy and I had both a fight for it with the dusty miller; I know it was a hard fight on my part, and I am quite heroic. I think that some day the bishops must get together and see about breeding up a new class of curates, who don't take supper, no matter how they may be pressed to, and who will know when girls are tired. Lucy is asleep and breathing softly. She has more colour in her cheeks than usual, and looks, oh, so sweet. If Mr Holmwood fell in love with her seeing her only in the drawing-room, I wonder what he would say if he saw her now. Some of the 'New Woman' writers will some day start an idea that men and women should be allowed to see each other asleep before proposing or accepting. But I suppose the New Woman won't condescend in future to accept; she will do the proposing herself. And a nice job she will make of it, too! There's some consolation in that. I am so happy to-night, because dear Lucy seems better. I really believe she has turned the corner, and that we are over her troubles with dreaming. I should be quite happy if I only knew if Jonathan . . . God bless and keep him.

11 August, 3 a.m. – Diary again. No sleep now, so I may as well write. I am too agitated to sleep. We have had such an adventure, such an agonizing experience. I fell asleep as soon as I had closed my diary . . . Suddenly I became broad awake, and sat up, with a horrible sense of fear upon me, and of some feeling of emptiness around me. The room was dark, so I could not see Lucy's bed; I stole across and felt for her. The bed was empty. I lit a match, and found that she was not in the room. The door was shut, but not locked, as I had left it. I feared to wake her mother, who has been more than usually ill lately, so threw on some clothes and got ready to look for her. As I was leaving the room it struck me that the clothes she wore might give me some clue to her dreaming intention. Dressing-gown would mean house; dress, outside. Dressing-gown and dress were both in their places. 'Thank God,' I said to myself, 'she cannot be far, as she is only in her nightdress.' I ran downstairs and looked in the sitting-room. Not there! Then I looked in all the other open rooms of the house, with an ever-growing fear chilling my heart. Finally I came to the hall-door and found it open. It was not wide open, but the catch of the lock had not caught. The people of the house are careful to lock the door every night, so I feared that Lucy must have gone out as she was. There was no time to think of what might happen; a vague, overmastering fear obscured all details. I took a big, heavy shawl and ran out. The clock was striking one as I was in the Crescent, and there was not a soul in sight. I ran along the North Terrace, but could see no sign of the white figure which I expected. At the edge of the West Cliff above the pier I looked across the harbour to the East Cliff, in the hope or fear – I don't know which – of seeing Lucy in our favourite seat. There was a bright full moon, with heavy black, driving clouds, which threw the whole scene into a fleeting diorama of light and shade as they sailed across. For a moment or two I could see nothing, as the shadow of a cloud obscured St Mary's Church and all around it. Then as the cloud passed I could see the ruins of the Abbey coming into view; and as the edge of a narrow band of light as sharp as a sword-cut moved along, the church and the churchyard became gradually visible. Whatever my expectation was, it was not disappointed, for there, on our favourite seat, the silver light of the moon struck a half-reclining figure, snowy white. The coming of the cloud was too quick for me to see much, for shadow shut down on light almost immediately; but it seemed to me as though something dark stood behind the seat where the white figure shone, and bent over it. What it was, whether man or beast, I could not tell; I did not wait to catch another glance, but flew down the steep steps to the pier and along by the fish-market to the bridge, which was the only way to reach the East Cliff. The town seemed as dead, for not a soul did I see; I rejoiced that it was so, for I wanted no witness of poor Lucy's condition. The time and distance seemed endless, and my knees trembled and my breath came laboured as I toiled up the endless steps to the Abbey. I must have gone fast, and yet it seemed to me as if my feet were weighted with lead, and as though every joint in my body were rusty. When I got almost to the top I could see the seat and the white figure, for I was now close enough to distinguish it even through the spells of shadow. There was undoubtedly something, long and black, bending over the half-reclining white figure. I called in fright, 'Lucy! Lucy!' and something raised a head, and from where I was I could see a white face and red, gleaming eyes. Lucy did not answer, and I ran on to the entrance of the churchyard. As I entered, the church was between me and the seat, and for a minute or so I lost sight of her. When I came in view again the cloud had passed, and the moonlight struck so brilliantly that I could see Lucy half-reclining with her head lying over the back of the seat. She was quite alone, and there was not a sign of any living thing about.

When I bent over her I could see that she was still asleep. Her lips were parted, and she was breathing – not softly, as usual with her, but in long, heavy gasps, as though striving to get her lungs full at every breath. As I came close, she put up her hand in her sleep and pulled the collar of her nightdress close round her throat. Whilst she did so there came a little shudder through her, as though she felt the cold. I flung the warm shawl over her, and drew the edges tight round her neck, for I dreaded lest she should get some deadly chill from the night air, unclad as she was. I feared to wake her all at once, so, in order to have my hands free that I might help her, I fastened the shawl at her throat with a big safety-pin; but I must have been clumsy in my anxiety and pinched or pricked her with it, for by-and-by, when her breathing became quieter, she put her hand to her throat again and moaned. When I had her carefully wrapped up I put my shoes on her feet, and then began very gently to wake her. At first she did not respond; but gradually she became more and more uneasy in her sleep, moaning and sighing occasionally. At last, as time was passing fast, and for many other reasons, I wished to get her home at once, I shook her more forcibly, till finally she opened her eyes and awoke. She did not seem surprised to see me, as, of course, she did not realise all at once where she was. Lucy always wakes prettily, and even at such a time, when her body must have been chilled with cold, and her mind somewhat appalled at waking unclad in a churchyard at night, she did not lose her grace. She trembled a little, and clung to me; when I told her to come at once with me home she rose without a word, with the obedience of a child. As we passed along, the gravel hurt my feet, and Lucy noticed me wince. She stopped and wanted to insist upon my taking my shoes; but I would not. However, when we got to the pathway outside the churchyard, where there was a puddle of water remaining from the storm, I daubed my feet with mud, using each foot in turn on the other, so that as we went home no one, in case we should meet anyone, should notice my bare feet.

Fortune favoured us, and we got home without meeting a soul. Once we saw a man, who seemed not quite sober, passing along a street in front of us; but we hid in a door till he had disappeared up an opening such as there are here, steep little closes, or 'wynds,' as they call them in Scotland. My heart beat so loud all the time that sometimes I thought I should faint. I was filled with anxiety about Lucy, not only for her health, lest she should suffer from the exposure, but for her reputation in case the story should get wind. When we got in, and had washed our feet, and had said a prayer of thankfulness together, I tucked her into bed. Before falling asleep she asked – even implored – me not to say a word to any one, even her mother, about her sleep-walking adventure. I hesitated at first to promise; but on thinking of the state of her mother's health, and how the knowledge of such a thing would fret her, and thinking, too, of how such a story might become distorted – nay, infallibly would – in case it should leak out I thought it wiser to do so. I hope I did right. I have locked the door, and the key is tied to my wrist, so perhaps I shall not be again disturbed. Lucy is sleeping soundly; the reflex of the dawn is high and far over the sea . . .

Same day, noon. – All goes well. Lucy slept till I woke her, and seemed not to have even changed her side. The adventure of the night does not seem to have harmed her; on the contrary, it has benefited her, for she looks better this morning than she has done for weeks. I was sorry to notice that my clumsiness with the safety-pin hurt her. Indeed, it might have been serious, for the skin of her throat was pierced. I must have pinched up a piece of loose skin and have transfixed it, for there are two little red points like pin-pricks, and on the band of her nightdress was a drop of blood. When I apologized and was concerned about it, she laughed and petted me, and said she did not even feel it. Fortunately it cannot leave a scar, as it is so tiny.

Same day, night. – We passed a happy day. The air was clear, and the sun bright and there was a cool breeze. We took our lunch to Mulgrave Woods, Mrs Westenra driving by the road and Lucy and I walking by the cliff-path and joining her at the gate. I felt a little sad myself, for I could not but feel how *absolutely* happy it would have been had Jonathan been with me. But there! I must only be patient. In the evening we strolled in the Casino Terrace, and heard some good music by Spohr and Mackenzie, and went to bed early. Lucy seems more restful than she has been for some time, and fell asleep at once. I shall lock the door and secure the key the same as before, though I do not expect any trouble to-night.

12 August. – My expectations were wrong, for twice during the night I was awakened by Lucy trying to get out. She seemed, even in her sleep, to be a little impatient at finding the door shut, and went back to bed under a sort of protest. I woke with the dawn, and heard the birds chirping outside of the window. Lucy woke, too, and, I was glad to see, was even better than on the previous morning. All her old gaiety of manner seemed to have come back, and she came and snuggled in beside me, and told me all about Arthur; I told her how anxious I was about Jonathan, and then she tried to comfort me. Well, she succeeded somewhat, for, though sympathy can't alter facts, it can help to make them more bearable.

13 August. – Another quiet day, and to bed with the key on my wrist as before. Again I woke in the night, and found Lucy sitting up in bed, still asleep, pointing to the window. I got up quietly, and pulling aside the blind, looked out. It was brilliant moonlight, and the soft effect of the light over the sea and sky – merged together in one great, silent mystery – was beautiful beyond words. Between me and the moonlight flitted a great bat, coming and going in great, whirling circles. Once or twice it came quite close, but was, I suppose, frightened at seeing me, and flitted away across the harbour towards the Abbey. When I came back from the window Lucy had lain down again, and was sleeping peacefully. She did not stir again all night.

14 August. – On the East Cliff, reading and writing all day. Lucy seems to have become as much in love with the spot as I am, and it is hard to get her away from it when it is time to come home for lunch or tea or dinner. This afternoon she made a funny remark. We were coming home for dinner, and had come to the top of the steps up from the West Pier and stopped to look at the view, as we generally do. The setting sun, low down in the sky, was just dropping behind Kettleness; the red light was thrown over on the East Cliff and the old Abbey, and seemed to bathe everything in a beautiful rosy glow. We were silent for a while, and suddenly Lucy murmured as if to herself: –

'His red eyes again! They are just the same.' It was such an odd expression, coming *apropos* of nothing, that it quite startled me. I slewed round a little, so as to see Lucy well without seeming to stare at her, and saw that she was in a half-dreamy state, with an odd look on her face that I could not quite make out; so I said nothing, but followed her eyes. She appeared to be looking over at our own seat, whereon was a dark figure seated alone.

I was a little startled myself, for it seemed for an instant as if the stranger had great eyes like burning flames; but a second look dispelled the illusion. The red sunlight was shining on the windows of St Mary's Church behind our seat, and as the sun dipped there was just sufficient change in the refraction and reflection to make it appear as if the light moved. I called Lucy's attention to the peculiar effect, and she became herself with a start, but she looked sad all the same; it may have been that she was thinking of that terrible night up there. We never refer to it; so I said nothing, and we went home to dinner. Lucy had a headache and went early to bed. I saw her asleep, and went out for a little stroll myself; I walked along the cliffs to the westward, and was full of sweet sadness, for I was thinking of Jonathan. When coming home – it was then bright moonlight, so bright that, though the front of our part of the Crescent was in shadow, everything could be well seen – I threw a glance up at our window, and saw Lucy's head leaning out. I thought that perhaps she was looking out for me, so I opened my handkerchief and waved it. She did not notice or make any movement whatever. Just then, the moonlight crept round an angle of the building, and the light fell on the window. There distinctly was Lucy with her head lying up against the side of the windowsill and her eyes shut. She was fast asleep, and by her, seated on the window-sill, was something that looked like a good-sized bird. I was afraid she might get a chill, so I ran upstairs, but as I came into the room she was moving back to her bed, fast asleep, and breathing heavily; she was holding her hand to her throat, as though to protect it from cold. I did not wake her, but tucked her up warmly, I have taken care that the door is locked and the window securely fastened.

She looks so sweet as she sleeps; but she is paler than is her wont, and there is a drawn, haggard look under her eyes which I do not like. I fear she is fretting about something. I wish I could find out what it is.

15 August. – Rose later than usual. Lucy was languid and tired, and slept on after we had been called. We had a happy surprise at breakfast. Arthur's father is better, and wants the marriage to come off soon. Lucy is full of quiet joy, and her mother is glad and sorry at once. Later on in the day she told me the cause. She is grieved to lose Lucy as her very own, but she is rejoiced that she is soon to have someone to protect her. Poor dear, sweet lady! She con-fided to me that she has got her death-warrant. She has not told Lucy, and made me promise secrecy; her doctor told her that within a few months, at most, she must die, for her heart is weakening. At any time, even now, a sudden shock would be almost sure to kill her. Ah, we were wise to keep from her the affair of the dreadful night of Lucy's sleep-walking.

17 August. – No diary for two whole days. I have not had the heart to
write. Some sort of shadowy pall seems to be coming over our happiness.
No news from Jonathan, and Lucy seems to be growing weaker, whilst
her mother's hours are numbering to a close. I do not understand Lucy's
fading away as she is doing. She eats well and sleeps well, and enjoys
the fresh air; but all the time the roses in her cheeks are fading, and she
gets weaker and more languid day by day; at night I hear her gasping as
if for air. I keep the key of our door always fastened to my wrist at night,
but she gets up and walks about the room, and sits at the open window.
Last night I found her leaning out when I woke up, and when I tried to
wake her I could not; she was in a faint. When I managed to restore her
she was as weak as water, and cried silently between long, painful struggles for breath. When I asked her how she came to be at the window she
shook her head and turned away. I trust her feeling ill may not be from
that unlucky prick of the safety-pin. I looked at her throat just now as she
lay asleep, and the tiny wounds seem not to have healed. They are still
open, and, if anything, larger than before, and the edges of them are faintly
white. They are like little white dots with red centres. Unless they heal
within a day or two, I shall insist on the doctor seeing about them.

*Letter, Samuel F. Billington & Son, Solicitors, Whitby, to Messrs.
Carter, Paterson & Co., London*

'17 August.

'Dear Sirs, –

'Herewith please receive invoice of goods sent by Great
Northern Railway. Same are to be delivered at Carfax, near
Purfleet, immediately on receipt at goods station King's Cross.
The house is at present empty, but enclosed please find keys, all
of which are labelled.

'You will please deposit the boxes, fifty in number, which form
the consignment, in the partially ruined building forming part of
the house and marked "A" on rough diagram enclosed. Your agent
will easily recognise the locality, as it is the ancient chapel of the
mansion. The goods leave by the train at 9.30 to-night, and will
be due at King's Cross at 4.30 to-morrow afternoon. As our client
wishes the delivery made as soon as possible, we shall be obliged
by your having teams ready at King's Cross at the time named
and forthwith conveying the goods to destination. In order to
obviate any delays possible through any routine requirements as

to payment in your departments, we enclose cheque herewith for ten pounds (£10), receipt of which please acknowledge. Should the charge be less than this amount, you can return balance; if greater, we shall at once send cheque for difference on hearing from you. You are to leave the keys on coming away in the main hall of the house, where the proprietor may get them on his entering the house by means of his duplicate key.

'Pray do not take us as exceeding the bounds of business courtesy in pressing you in all ways to use the utmost expedition.

        'We are, dear Sirs,

           'Faithfully yours,

           'Samuel F. Billington & Son.'

Letter, Messrs. Carter, Paterson & Co., London, to Messrs.
Billington & Son, Whitby

                                  '21 August.

'Dear Sirs, –

'We beg to acknowledge £10 received and to return cheque £1 17s. 9*d.*, amount of overplus, as shown in receipted account herewith. Goods are delivered in exact accordance with instructions, and keys left in parcel in main hall, as directed.

        'We are, dear Sirs,

           'Yours respectfully,

           '*Pro* Carter, Paterson & Co.'

MINA MURRAY'S JOURNAL

18 August. – I am happy to-day, and write sitting on the seat in the churchyard. Lucy is ever so much better. Last night she slept well all night, and did not disturb me once. The roses seem coming back already to her cheeks, though she is still sadly pale and wan-looking. If she were in any way anaemic I could understand it, but she is not. She is in gay spirits and full of life and cheerfulness. All the morbid reticence seems to have passed from her, and she has just reminded me, as if I needed any reminding, of *that* night, and that it was here, on this very seat, I found her asleep. As she told me she tapped playfully with the heel of her boot on the stone slab and said: –

'My poor little feet didn't make much noise then! I daresay poor old

Mr Swales would have told me that it was because I didn't want to wake up Geordie.' As she was in such a communicative humour, I asked her if she had dreamed at all that night. Before she answered, that sweet, puckered look came into her forehead, which Arthur – I call him Arthur from her habit – says he loves; and, indeed, I don't wonder that he does. Then she went on in a half-dreaming kind of way, as if trying to recall it to herself: –

'I didn't quite dream; but it all seemed to be real. I only wanted to be here in this spot – I don't know why, for I was afraid of something – I don't know what. I remember, though I suppose I was asleep, passing through the streets and over the bridge. A fish leaped as I went by, and I leaned over to look at it, and I heard a lot of dogs howling – the whole town seemed as if it must be full of dogs all howling at once – as I went up the steps. Then I have a vague memory of something long and dark with red eyes, just as we saw in the sunset, and something very sweet and very bitter all around me at once; and then I seemed sinking into deep green water, and there was a singing in my ears, as I have heard there is to drowning men; and then everything seemed passing away from me; my soul seemed to go out from my body and float about the air. I seemed to remember that once the West Lighthouse was right under me, and then there was a sort of agonising feeling, as if I were in an earthquake, and I came back and found you shaking my body. I saw you do it before I felt you.'

Then she began to laugh. It seemed a little uncanny to me, and I listened to her breathlessly. I did not quite like it, and thought it better not to keep her mind on the subject, so we drifted on to other subjects, and Lucy was like her old self again. When we got home the fresh breeze had braced her up, and her pale cheeks were really more rosy. Her mother rejoiced when she saw her, and we all spent a very happy evening together.

19 August. – Joy, joy, joy! although not all joy. At last, news of Jonathan. The dear fellow has been ill, that is why he did not write. I am not afraid to think it or to say it, now that I know. Mr Hawkins sent me on the letter, and wrote himself, oh, so kindly. I am to leave in the morning and to go over to Jonathan, and to help to nurse him if necessary, and to bring him home. Mr Hawkins says it would not be a bad thing if we were to be married out there. I have cried over the good Sister's letter till I can feel it wet against my bosom, where it lies. It is of Jonathan, and must be next to my heart, for he is in my heart. My journey is all mapped out, and my luggage ready. I am only taking one change of dress; Lucy will bring my trunk to London and keep it till I send for it, for it may be that . . . I must write no more; I must keep it to say to Jonathan, my husband. The letter that he has seen and touched must comfort me till we meet.

Letter, Sister Agatha, Hospital of St Joseph and Ste Mary, Buda-Pesth, to Miss Wilhelmina Murray

'*12 August.*

'Dear Madam, –

'I write by desire of Mr Jonathan Harker, who is himself not strong enough to write, though progressing well, thanks to God and St Joseph and Ste Mary. He has been under our care for nearly six weeks, suffering from a violent brain fever. He wishes me to convey his love, and to say that by this post I write for him to Mr Peter Hawkins, Exeter, to say, with his dutiful respects, that he is sorry for his delay, and that all his work is completed. He will require some few weeks' rest in our sanatorium in the hills, but will then return. He wishes me to say that he has not sufficient money with him, and that he would like to pay for his staying here, so that others who need shall not be wanting for help.

'Believe me,

'Yours, with sympathy and all blessings,

'Sister Agatha.

'P.S. – My patient being asleep, I open this to let you know something more. He has told me all about you, and that you are shortly to be his wife. All blessings to you both! He has had some fearful shock – so says our doctor – and in his delirium his ravings have been dreadful; of wolves and poison and blood; of ghosts and demons; and I fear to say of what. Be careful with him always that there may be nothing to excite him of this kind for a long time to come; the traces of such an illness as his do not lightly die away. We should have written long ago, but we knew nothing of his friends, and there was on him nothing that any one could understand. He came in the train from Klausenburg, and the guard was told by the station-master there that he rushed into the station shouting for a ticket for home. Seeing from his violent demeanour that he was English, they gave him a ticket for the farthest station on the way thither that the train reached.

'Be assured that he is well cared for. He has won all hearts by his sweetness and gentleness. He is truly getting on well, and I have no doubt will in a few weeks be all himself. But be careful of him for safety's sake. There are, I pray God and St Joseph and Ste Mary, many, many happy years for you both.'

DR SEWARD'S DIARY

19 August. – Strange and sudden change in Renfield last night. About eight o'clock he began to get excited and to sniff about as a dog does when setting. The attendant was struck by his manner, and knowing my interest in him, encouraged him to talk. He is usually respectful to the attendant, and at times servile; but to-night, the man tells me, he was quite haughty. Would not condescend to talk with him at all. All he would say was: –

'I don't want to talk to you: you don't count now; the Master is at hand.'

The attendant thinks it is some sudden form of religious mania which has seized him. If so, we must look out for squalls, for a strong man with homicidal and religious mania at once might be dangerous. The combination is a dreadful one. At nine o'clock I visited him myself. His attitude to me was the same as that to the attendant; in his sublime self-feeling the difference between myself and attendant seemed to him as nothing. It looks like religious mania, and he will soon think that he himself is God. These infinitesimal distinctions between man and man are too paltry for an omnipotent being. How these madmen give themselves away! The real God taketh heed lest a sparrow fall; but the God created from human vanity sees no difference between an eagle and a sparrow. Oh, if men only knew!

For half an hour or more Renfield kept getting excited in greater and greater degree. I did not pretend to be watching him, but I kept strict observation all the same. All at once that shifty look came into his eyes which we always see when a madman has seized an idea, and with it the shifty movement of the head and back which asylum attendants come to know so well. He became quite quiet, and went and sat on the edge of his bed resignedly, and looked into space with lack-lustre eyes. I thought I would find out if his apathy were real or only assumed, and tried to lead him to talk of his pets, a theme which had never failed to excite his attention. At first he made no reply, but at length said testily: –

'Bother them all! I don't care a pin about them.'

'What?' I said. 'You don't mean to tell me that you don't care about spiders?' (Spiders at present are his hobby, and the note-book is filling up with columns of small figures.) To this he answered enigmatically: –

'The bride-maidens rejoice the eyes that wait the coming of the bride; but when the bride draweth nigh, then the maidens shine not to the eyes that are filled.'

He would not explain himself, but remained obstinately seated on his bed all the time I remained with him.

I am weary to-night and low in spirits. I cannot but think of Lucy, and how different things might have been. If I don't sleep at once, chloral, the modern Morpheus – $C_2HCl_3O.H_2O$! I must be careful not to let it grow into a habit. No, I shall take none to-night! I have thought of Lucy, and I shall not dishonour her by mixing the two. If need be, to-night shall be sleepless . . .

Glad I made the resolution; gladder that I kept to it. I had lain tossing about, and had heard the clock strike only twice, when the night-watchman came to me, sent up from the ward, to say that Renfield had escaped. I threw on my clothes and ran down at once; my patient is too dangerous a person to be roaming about. Those ideas of his might work out dangerously with strangers. The attendant was waiting for me. He said he had seen him not ten minutes before, seemingly asleep in his bed, when he had looked through the observation-trap in the door. His attention was called by the sound of the window being wrenched out. He ran back and saw his feet disappear through the window, and had at once sent up for me. He was only in his night-gear, and cannot be far off. The attendant thought it would be more useful to watch where he should go than to follow him, as he might lose sight of him whilst getting out of the building by the door. He is a bulky man, and couldn't get through the window. I am thin, so, with his aid, I got out, but feet foremost, and, as we were only a few feet above ground, landed unhurt. The attendant told me the patient had gone to the left and had taken a straight line, so I ran as quickly as I could. As I got through the belt of trees I saw a white figure scale the high wall which separates our grounds from those of the deserted house.

I ran back at once, and told the watchman to get three or four men immediately and follow me into the grounds of Carfax, in case our friend might be dangerous. I got a ladder myself, and crossing the wall, dropped down on the other side. I could see Renfield's figure just disappearing behind the angle of the house, so I ran after him. On the far side of the house I found him pressed close against the old iron-bound oak door of the chapel. He was talking, apparently to someone, but I was afraid to go near enough to hear what he was saying, lest I might frighten him, and he should run off. Chasing an errant swarm of bees is nothing to following a naked lunatic when the fit of escaping is upon him! After a few minutes, however, I could see that he did not take note of anything around him, and so ventured to draw nearer to him – the more so as my men had now crossed the wall and were closing him in. I heard him say: –

'I am here to do Your bidding, Master. I am Your slave, and You will reward me, for I shall be faithful. I have worshipped You long and afar off. Now that You are near, I await Your commands, and You will not pass me by, will You, dear Master, in Your distribution of good things?'

He is a selfish old beggar anyhow. He thinks of the loaves and fishes even when he believes he is in a Real Presence. His manias make a startling combination. When we closed in on him he fought like a tiger. He is immensely strong, and he was more like a wild beast than a man. I never saw a lunatic in such a paroxysm of rage before; and I hope I shall not again. It is a mercy that we have found out his strength and his danger in good time. With strength and determination like his, he might have done wild work before he was caged. He is safe now at any rate. Jack Sheppard himself couldn't get free from the strait-waistcoat that keeps him restrained, and he's chained to the wall in the padded room. His cries are at times awful, but the silences that follow are more deadly still, for he means murder in every turn and movement.

Just now he spoke coherent words for the first time: –

'I shall be patient, Master. It is coming – coming – coming!'

So I took the hint, and came too. I was too excited to sleep, but this diary has quieted me, and I feel I shall get some sleep to-night.

CHAPTER 9

Letter, Mina Harker to Lucy Westenra

'BUDA-PESTH, *24 August.*

'My dearest Lucy, –

'I know you will be anxious to hear all that has happened since we parted at the railway station at Whitby. Well, my dear, I got to Hull all right, and caught the boat to Hamburg, and then the train on here. I feel I can hardly recall anything of the journey, except that I knew I was coming to Jonathan, and that, as I should have to do some nursing, I had better get all the sleep I could . . . I found my dear one, oh, so thin and pale and weak-looking. All the resolution has gone out of his dear eyes, and that quiet dignity which I told you was in his face has vanished. He is only a wreck of himself, and he does not remember anything that has happened to him for a long time past. At least, he wants me to believe so, and I shall never ask. He has had some terrible shock, and I fear it might tax his poor brain if he were to try to recall it. Sister Agatha, who is a good creature and a born nurse, tells me that he raved of dreadful things whilst he was off his head. I wanted her to tell me what they were; but she would only cross herself, and say she would never tell; that the ravings of the sick were the secrets of God, and that if a nurse through her vocation should hear them, she should respect her trust. She is a sweet, good soul, and the next day, when she saw I was troubled, she opened up the subject again, and after saying that she could never mention what my poor dear raved about, added: "I can tell you this much, my dear: that it was not about anything which he has done wrong himself; and you, as his wife to be, have no cause to be concerned. He has not forgotten you or what he owes to you. His fear was of great and terrible things, which no mortal can treat of." I believe the dear soul thought I might be jealous lest my poor dear should have fallen in love with any other girl. The idea of *my* being jealous about Jonathan! And yet, my dear, let me whisper, I felt a thrill of joy through me when I *knew* that no other woman was a cause of trouble. I am now sitting by his

bedside, where I can see his face while he sleeps. He is waking!
. . . When he woke he asked me for his coat, as he wanted to
get something from the pocket; I asked Sister Agatha, and she
brought all his things. I saw that amongst them was his note-
book, and was going to ask him to let me look at it – for I
knew then that I might find some clue to his trouble – but I
suppose he must have seen my wish in my eyes, for he sent me
over to the window, saying he wanted to be quite alone for a
moment. Then he called me back, and when I came he had his
hand over the note-book, and he said to me very solemnly: –

"'Wilhelmina" – I knew then that he was in deadly earnest, for
he has never called me by that name since he asked me to marry
him – "you know, dear, my ideas of the trust between husband
and wife: there should be no secret, no concealment. I have had a
great shock, and when I try to think of what it is I feel my head
spin round, and I do not know if it was all real or the dreaming
of a madman. You know I have had brain fever, and that is to be
mad. The secret is here, and I do not want to know it. I want to
take up my life here, with our marriage." For, my dear, we had
decided to be married as soon as the formalities are complete.
"Are you willing, Wilhelmina, to share my ignorance? Here is the
book. Take it and keep it, read it if you will, but never let me
know; unless, indeed, some solemn duty should come upon me to
go back to the bitter hours, asleep or awake, sane or mad,
recorded here." He fell back, exhausted, and I put the book under
his pillow, and kissed him. I have asked Sister Agatha to beg the
Superior to let our wedding be this afternoon, and am waiting her
reply . . .

'She has come and told me that the chaplain of the English
mission church has been sent for. We are to be married in an
hour, or as soon after as Jonathan awakes . . .

'Lucy, the time has come and gone. I feel very solemn, but
very, very happy. Jonathan woke a little after the hour, and all
was ready, and he sat up in bed, propped up with pillows. He
answered his "I will" firmly and strongly. I could hardly speak;
my heart was so full that even these words seemed to choke me.
The dear Sisters were so kind. Please God, I shall never, never
forget them, nor the grave and sweet responsibilities I have taken
upon me. I must tell you of my wedding present. When the chaplain and the Sisters had left me alone with my husband – oh,

Lucy, it is the first time I have written the words "my husband" – left me alone with my husband, I took the book from under his pillow, and wrapped it up in white paper, and tied it with a little bit of pale blue ribbon which was wound round my neck, and sealed it over the knot with sealing-wax, and for my seal I used my wedding ring. Then I kissed it and showed it to my husband, and told him that I would keep it so, and then it would be an outward and visible sign for us all our lives that we trusted each other; that I would never open it unless it were for his own dear sake, or for the sake of some stern duty. Then he took my hand in his, and oh, Lucy, it was the first time he took *his wife's* hand, and said that it was the dearest thing in all the wide world, and that he would go through all the past again to win it, if need be. The poor dear meant to have said a part of the past; but he cannot think of time yet, and I shall not wonder if at first he mixes up not only the month, but the year.

'Well, my dear, what could I say? I could only tell him that I was the happiest woman in all the wide world, and that I had nothing to give him except myself, my life, and my trust, and that with these went my love and duty for all the days of my life. And, my dear, when he kissed me, and drew me to him with his poor weak hands, it was like a very solemn pledge between us . . .

'Lucy dear, do you know why I tell you all this? It is not only because it is all sweet to me, but because you have been, and are, very dear to me. It was my privilege to be your friend and guide when you came from the schoolroom to prepare for the world of life. I want you to see now, and with the eyes of a very happy wife, whither duty has led me; so that in your own married life you too may be all happy as I am. My dear, please Almighty God, your life may be all it promises: a long day of sunshine, with no harsh wind, no forgetting duty, no distrust. I must not wish you no pain, for that can never be; but I do hope you will be *always* as happy as I am *now*. Good-bye, my dear. I shall post this at once, and, perhaps, write you very soon again. I must stop, for Jonathan is waking – I must attend to my husband!

'Your ever-loving
'MINA HARKER.'

Letter, Lucy Westenra to Mina Harker

'Whitby, 30 August.

'My dearest Mina, –

'Oceans of love and millions of kisses, and may you soon be in your own home with your husband. I wish you could be coming home soon enough to stay with us here. This strong air would soon restore Jonathan; it has quite restored me. I have an appetite like a cormorant, am full of life, and sleep well. You will be glad to know that I have quite given up walking in my sleep. I think I have not stirred out of my bed for a week, that is, when I once got into it at night. Arthur says I am getting fat. By the way, I forgot to tell you that Arthur is here. We have such walks and drives, and rides, and rowing, and tennis, and fishing together; and I love him more than ever. He *tells me* that he loves me more, but I doubt that, for at first he told me that he couldn't love me more than he did then. But this is nonsense. There he is, calling to me. So no more just at present from your loving

'LUCY.

'P.S. – Mother sends her love. She seems better, poor dear.
'P.P.S. – We are to be married on 28 September.'

DR SEWARD'S DIARY

20 August. – The case of Renfield grows even more interesting. He has now so far quieted that there are spells of cessation from his passion. For the first week after his attack he was perpetually violent. Then one night, just as the moon rose, he grew quiet, and kept murmuring to himself: 'Now I can wait; now I can wait.' The attendant came to tell me, so I ran down at once to have a look at him. He was still in the strait-waistcoat and in the padded room, but the suffused look had gone from his face, and his eyes had something of their old pleading – I might almost say, 'cringing' – softness. I was satisfied with his present condition, and directed him to be relieved. The attendants hesitated, but finally carried out my wishes without protest. It was a strange thing that the patient had humour enough to see their distrust, for, coming close to me, he said in a whisper, all the while looking furtively at them: –

'They think I could hurt you! Fancy *me* hurting *you*! The fools!'
It was soothing, somehow, to the feelings to find myself dissociated

even in the mind of this poor madman from the others; but all the same I do not follow his thought. Am I to take it that I have anything in common with him, so that we are, as it were, to stand together; or has he to gain from me some good so stupendous that my well-being is needful to him? I must find out later on. To-night he will not speak. Even the offer of a kitten or even a full-grown cat will not tempt him. He will only say: 'I don't take any stock in cats. I have more to think of now, and I can wait; I can wait.'

After a while I left him. The attendant tells me that he was quiet until just before dawn, and then he began to get uneasy, and at length violent, until at last he fell into a paroxysm which exhausted him so that he swooned into a sort of coma.

. . . Three nights has the same thing happened – violent all day, then quiet from moonrise to sunrise. I wish I could get some clue to the cause. It would almost seem as if there was some influence which came and went. Happy thought! We shall to-night play sane wits against mad ones. He escaped before without our help; to-night he shall escape with it. We shall give him a chance, and have the men ready to follow in case they are required . . .

23 August. – 'The unexpected always happens.' How well Disraeli knew life! Our bird when he found the cage open would not fly, so all our subtle arrangements went for naught. At any rate, we have proved one thing: that the spells of quietness last a reasonable time. We shall in future be able to ease his bond for a few hours each day. I have given orders to the night attendant merely to shut him in the padded room, when once he is quiet, until an hour before sunrise. The poor soul's body will enjoy the relief even if his mind cannot appreciate it. Hark! The unexpected again! I am called; the patient has once more escaped.

Later. – Another night adventure. Renfield artfully waited until the attendant was entering the room to inspect. Then he dashed out past him and flew down the passage. I sent word for the attendants to follow. Again we went into the ground of the deserted house, and we found him in the same place, pressed against the old chapel door. When he saw me he became furious, and had not the attendants seized him in time, he would have tried to kill me. As we were holding him a strange thing happened. He suddenly redoubled his efforts, and then as suddenly grew calm. I looked round instinctively, but could see nothing. Then I caught the patient's eye and followed it, but could trace nothing as it looked into the moonlit sky except a big bat, which was flapping its silent and ghostly way to the west. Bats usually wheel and flit about, but this one seemed to go straight on, as if it knew where it was bound for or had some intention of its own. The patient grew calmer every instant, and presently said: –

'You needn't tie me; I shall go quietly!' Without trouble we came back to the house. I feel there is something ominous in his calm, and shall not forget this night . . .

LUCY WESTENRA'S DIARY

Hillingham, 24 August. – I must imitate Mina, and keep writing things down. Then we can have long talks when we do meet. I wonder when it will be. I wish she were with me again, for I feel so unhappy. Last night I seemed to be dreaming again just as I was at Whitby. Perhaps it is the change of air, or getting home again. It is all dark and horrid to me, for I can remember nothing; but I am full of vague fear, and I feel so weak and worn out. When Arthur came to lunch he looked quite grieved when he saw me, and I hadn't the spirit to be cheerful. I wonder if I could sleep in mother's room to-night. I shall make an excuse and try.

25 August. – Another bad night. Mother did not seem to take to my proposal. She seems not too well herself, and doubtless she fears to worry me. I tried to keep awake, and succeeded for a while; but when the clock struck twelve it waked me from a doze, so I must have been falling asleep. There was a sort of scratching or flapping at the window, but I did not mind it, and as I remember no more, I suppose I must then have fallen asleep. More bad dreams. I wish I could remember them. This morning I am horribly weak. My face is ghastly pale, and my throat pains me. It must be something wrong with my lungs, for I don't seem ever to get air enough. I shall try to cheer up when Arthur comes, or else I know he will be miserable to see me so.

Letter, Arthur Holmwood to Dr Seward

'Albemarle Hotel, 31 August.

'My dear Jack, –

'I want you to do me a favour. Lucy is ill; that is, she has no special disease, but she looks awful, and is getting worse every day. I have asked her if there is any cause; I do not dare to ask her mother, for to disturb the poor lady's mind about her daughter in her present state of health would be fatal. Mrs Westenra has confided to me that her doom is spoken – disease of the heart –

though poor Lucy does not know it yet. I am sure that there is something preying on my dear girl's mind. I am almost distracted when I think of her; to look at her gives me a pang. I told her I should ask you to see her, and though she demurred at first – I know why, old fellow – she finally consented. It will be a painful task for you, I know, old friend, but it is for *her* sake, and I must not hesitate to ask, or you to act. You are to come to lunch at Hillingham to-morrow, two o'clock, so as not to arouse any suspicion in Mrs Westenra, and after lunch Lucy will take an opportunity of being alone with you. I shall come in for tea, and we can go away together. I am filled with anxiety, and want to consult with you alone as soon as I can after you have seen her. Do not fail!

'ARTHUR.'

Telegram, Arthur Holmwood to Seward

'*1 September.*
'Am summoned to see my father, who is worse. Am writing. Write me fully by to-night's post to Ring. Wire me if necessary.'

Letter from Dr Seward to Arthur Holmwood

'*2 September.*
'My dear old fellow, –
'With regard to Miss Westenra's health, I hasten to let you know at once that in my opinion there is not any functional disturbance or any malady that I know of. At the same time, I am not by any means satisfied with her appearance; she is woefully different from what she was when I saw her last. Of course you must bear in mind that I did not have full opportunity of examination such as I should wish; our very friendship makes a little difficulty which not even medical science or custom can bridge over. I had better tell you exactly what happened, leaving you to draw, in a measure, your own conclusions. I shall then say what I have done and propose doing.
'I found Miss Westenra in seemingly gay spirits. Her mother was present, and in a few seconds I made up my mind that she was trying all she knew to mislead her mother and prevent her from being anxious. I have no doubt she guesses, if she does not

know, what need of caution there is. We lunched alone, and as we all exerted ourselves to be cheerful, we got, as some kind of reward for our labours, some real cheerfulness amongst us. Then Mrs Westenra went to lie down, and Lucy was left with me. We went into her boudoir, and till we got there her gaiety remained, for the servants were coming and going. As soon as the door was closed, however, the mask fell from her face, and she sank down into a chair with a great sigh, and hid her eyes with her hand. When I saw that her high spirits had failed, I at once took advantage of her reaction to make a diagnosis. She said to me very sweetly: –

"'I cannot tell you how I loathe talking about myself." I reminded her that a doctor's confidence was sacred, but that you were grievously anxious about her. She caught on to my meaning at once, and settled that matter in a word. "Tell Arthur everything you choose. I do not care for myself, but all for him!" So I am quite free.

'I could easily see that she is somewhat bloodless, but I could not see the usual anaemic signs, and by a chance I was actually able to test the quality of her blood, for in opening a window which was stiff a cord gave way, and she cut her hand slightly with broken glass. It was a slight matter in itself, but it gave me an evident chance, and I secured a few drops of the blood and have analysed them. The qualitative analysis gives a quite normal condition, and shows, I should infer, in itself a vigorous state of health. In other physical matters I was quite satisfied that there is no need for anxiety; but as there must be a cause somewhere, I have come to the conclusion that it must be something mental. She complains of difficulty in breathing satisfactorily at times, and of heavy, lethargic sleep, with dreams that frighten her, but regarding which she can remember nothing. She says that as a child she used to walk in her sleep, and that when in Whitby the habit came back, and that once she walked out in the night and went to the East Cliff, where Miss Murray found her: but she assures me that of late the habit has not returned. I am in doubt, and so have done the best thing I know of: I have written to my old friend and master, Professor Van Helsing, of Amsterdam, who knows as much about obscure diseases as anyone in the world. I have asked him to come over, and as you told me that all things were to be at your charge, I have mentioned to him who you are

and your relations to Miss Westenra. This, my dear fellow, is only
in obedience to your wishes, for I am only too proud and happy
to do anything I can for her. Van Helsing would, I know, do
anything for me for a personal reason. So, no matter on what
ground he comes, we must accept his wishes. He is a seemingly
arbitrary man, but this is because he knows what he is talking
about better than anyone else. He is a philosopher and a meta-
physician, and one of the most advanced scientists of his day; and
he has, I believe, an absolutely open mind. This, with an iron
nerve, a temper of the ice brook, an indomitable resolution, self-
command and toleration exalted from virtues to blessings, and the
kindliest and truest heart that beats – these form his equipment
for the noble work that he is doing for mankind – work both in
theory and practice, for his views are as wide as his all-embracing
sympathy. I tell you these facts that you may know why I have
such confidence in him. I have asked him to come at once. I shall
see Miss Westenra to-morrow again. She is to meet me at the
Stores, so that I may not alarm her mother by too early a repetition of my call.

'Yours always
'JOHN SEWARD.'

*Letter, Abraham Van Helsing, M.D., D.Ph.,
D. Litt., etc., etc., to Dr Seward*

'2 *September.*

'My good Friend, –
'When I have received your letter I am already coming to you.
By good fortune I can leave just at once, without wrong to any of
those who have trusted me. Were fortune other, then it were bad
for those who have trusted, for I come to my friend when he call
me to aid those he holds dear. Tell your friend that when that
time you suck from my wound so swiftly the poison of the
gangrene from that knife that our other friend, too nervous, let
slip, you did more for him when he wants my aids and you call
for them than all his great fortune could do. But it is pleasure
added to do for him, your friend; it is to you that I come. Have
then rooms for me at the Great Eastern Hotel, so that I may be
near to hand, and please it so arrange that we may see the young
lady not too late on to-morrow, for it is likely that I may have to

return here that night. But if need be I shall come again in three days, and stay longer if it must. Till then good-bye, my friend John.

'VAN HELSING.'

Letter, Dr Seward to Hon. Arthur Holmwood

'*3 September.*

'My dear Art, –

'Van Helsing has come and gone. He came on with me to Hillingham, and found that, by Lucy's discretion, her mother was lunching out, so that we were alone with her. Van Helsing made a very careful examination of the patient. He is to report to me, and I shall advise you, for of course I was not present all the time. He is, I fear, much concerned, but says he must think. When I told him of our friendship and how you trust to me in the matter, he said: "You must tell him all you think. Tell him what I think, if you can guess it, if you will. Nay, I am not jesting. This is no jest, but life and death, perhaps more." I asked what he meant by that, for he was very serious. This was when we had come back to town, and he was having a cup of tea before starting on his return to Amsterdam. He would not give me any further clue. You must not be angry with him, Art, because his very reticence means that all his brains are working for her good. He will speak plainly enough when the time comes, be sure. So I told him I would simply write an account of our visit, just as if I were doing a descriptive special article for *The Daily Telegraph*. He seemed not to notice, but remarked that the smuts in London were not quite so bad as they used to be when he was a student here. I am to get his report to-morrow if he can possibly make it. In any case I am to have a letter.

'Well, as to the visit. Lucy was more cheerful than on the day I first saw her, and certainly looked better. She had lost something of the ghastly look that so upset you, and her breathing was normal. She was very sweet to the Professor (as she always is), and tried to make him feel at ease; though I could see that the poor girl was making a hard struggle for it. I believe Van Helsing saw it, too, for I saw the quick look under his bushy brows that I knew of old. Then he began to chat of all things except ourselves and diseases, and with such an infinite geniality that I could see

poor Lucy's pretence of animation merge into reality. Then,
without any seeming change, he brought the conversation gently
round to his visit, and suavely said: –

"'My dear young miss, I have the so great pleasure because
you are much beloved. That is much, my dear, even were there
that which I do not see. They told me you were in the spirit,
and that you were of a ghastly pale. To them I say: 'Pouf!'"
And he snapped his fingers at me and went on: "But you and I
shall show them how wrong they are. How can he" – and he
pointed at me with the same look and gesture as that with
which once he pointed me out to his class, on, or rather after, a
particular occasion which he never fails to remind me of –
"know anything of a young ladies? He has his madmans to play
with, and to bring them back to happiness and to those that
love them. It is much to do, and, oh, but there are rewards, in
that we can bestow such happiness. But the young ladies! He
has no wife nor daughter, and the young do not tell themselves
to the young, but to the old, like me, who have known so many
sorrows and the causes of them. So, my dear, we will send him
away to smoke the cigarette in the garden, whiles you and I
have little talk all to ourselves." I took the hint, and strolled
about, and presently the Professor came to the window and
called me in. He looked grave, but said: "I have made careful
examination, but there is no functional cause. With you I agree
that there has been much blood lost; it has been, but is not. But
the conditions of her are in no way anaemic. I have asked her
to send me her maid, that I may asked just one or two questions, that so I may not chance to miss nothing. I know well
what she will say. And yet there is cause; there is always
cause for everything. I must go back home and think. You
must send to me the telegram every day; and if there be cause
I shall come again. The disease – for not to be all well is a
disease – interest me, and the sweet young dear, she interest
me too. She charm me, and for her, if not for you or disease,
I come."

'As I tell you, he would not say a word more, even when we
were alone. And so now, Art, you know all I know. I shall keep
stern watch. I trust your poor father is rallying. It must be a
terrible thing to you, my dear old fellow, to be placed in such a
position between two people who are both so dear to you. I know

your idea of duty to your father, and you are right to stick to it;
but, if need be, I shall send you word to come at once to Lucy;
so do not be over-anxious unless you hear from me.'

4 September. – Zoophagous patient still keeps up our interest in him.
He had only one outburst, and that was yesterday at an unusual time.
Just before the stroke of noon he began to grow restless. The attendant
knew the symptoms, and at once summoned aid. Fortunately the men
came at a run, and were just in time, for at the stroke of noon he became
so violent that it took all their strength to hold him. In about five minutes,
however, he began to get more and more quiet, and finally sank into a
sort of melancholy, in which state he has remained up to now. The attendant tells me that his screams whilst in the paroxysm were really
appalling; I found my hands full when I got in, attending to some of the
other patients who were frightened by him. Indeed, I can quite understand the effect, for the sounds disturbed even me, though I was some
distance away. It is now after the dinner-hour of the asylum, and as yet
my patient sits in a corner brooding, with a dull, sullen, woebegone look
in his face, which seems rather to indicate than to show something
directly. I cannot quite understand it.

Later. – Another change in my patient. At five o'clock I looked in on
him, and found him seemingly as happy and contented as he used to be.
He was catching flies and eating them, and was keeping note of his capture
by making nail-marks on the edge of the door between the ridges of
padding. When he saw me, he came over and apologised for his bad
conduct, and asked me in a very humble, cringing way to be led back to
his own room and to have his note-book again. I thought it well to humour
him; so he is back in his room, with the window open. He has the sugar
of his tea spread out on the windowsill, and is reaping quite a harvest of
flies. He is not now eating them, but putting them in a box, as of old, and
is already examining the corners of his room to find a spider. I tried to
get him to talk about the past few days, for any clue to his thoughts would
be of immense help to me; but he would not rise. For a moment or two
he looked very sad, and said in a sort of far-away voice, as though saying
it rather to himself than to me: –

'All over! all over! He has deserted me. No hope for me now unless I
do it for myself!' Then suddenly turning to me in a resolute way, he said:

'Doctor, won't you be very good to me and let me have a little more sugar? I think it would be good for me.'

'And the flies?' I said.

'Yes! The flies like it, too, and I like the flies; therefore I like it.' And there are people who know so little as to think that madmen do not argue. I procured him a double supply, and left him as happy a man as, I suppose, any in the world. I wish I could fathom his mind.

Midnight. – Another change in him. I had been to see Miss Westenra, whom I found much better, and had just returned, and was standing at our own gate looking at the sunset, when once more I heard him yelling. As his room is on this side of the house, I could hear it better than in the morning. It was a shock to me to turn from the wonderful smoky beauty of a sunset over London, with its lurid lights and inky shadows and all the marvellous tints that come on foul clouds even as on foul water, and to realise all the grim sternness of my own cold stone building, with its wealth of breathing misery, and my own desolate heart to endure it all. I reached him just as the sun was going down, and from his window saw the red disc sink. As it sank he became less and less frenzied; and just as it dipped he slid from the hands that held him, an inert mass, on the floor. It is wonderful, however, what intellectual recuperative power lunatics have, for within a few minutes he stood up quite calmly and looked around him. I signalled to the attendants not to hold him, for I was anxious to see what he would do. He went straight over to the window and brushed out the crumbs of sugar; then he took his fly-box and emptied it outside, and threw away the box; then he shut the window, and crossing over, sat down on his bed. All this surprised me, so I asked him: 'Are you not going to keep flies any more?'

'No,' said he; 'I am sick of all that rubbish!' He certainly is a wonderfully interesting study. I wish I could get some glimpse of his mind or of the cause of his sudden passion. Stop; there may be a clue after all, if we can find why to-day his paroxysms came on at high noon and at sunset. Can it be that there is a malign influence of the sun at periods which affects certain natures – as at times the moon does others? We shall see.

Telegram, Seward, London, to Van Helsing, Amsterdam

'*4 September.* – Patient still better to-day.'

Telegram, Seward, London, to Van Helsing, Amsterdam

'5 *September*. – Patient greatly improved. Good appetite; sleeps naturally; good spirits, colour coming back.'

Telegram, Seward, London, to Van Helsing, Amsterdam

'6 *September*. – Terrible change for the worse. Come at once; do not lose an hour. I hold over telegram to Holmwood till have seen you.'

CHAPTER 10

Letter, Dr Seward to Hon. Arthur Holmwood

'My dear Art, –

'*6 September.*

'My news to-day is not so good. Lucy this morning had gone back a bit. There is, however, one good thing which has arisen from it: Mrs Westenra was naturally anxious concerning Lucy, and has consulted me professionally about her. I took advantage of the opportunity, and told her that my old master, Van Helsing, the great specialist, was coming to stay with me, and that I would put her in his charge conjointly with myself; so now we can come and go without alarming her unduly, for a shock to her would mean sudden death, and this, in Lucy's weak condition, might be disastrous to her. We are hedged in with difficulties, all of us, my poor old fellow; but, please God, we shall come through them all right. If any need I shall write, so that, if you do not hear from me, take it for granted that I am simply waiting for news. In haste.

'Yours ever,
'JOHN SEWARD.'

7 September. – The first thing Van Helsing said to me when we met at Liverpool Street was: –

'Have you said anything to our young friend the lover of her?'

'No,' I said. 'I waited till I had seen you, as I said in my telegram. I wrote him a letter simply telling him that you were coming, as Miss Westenra was not so well, and that I should let him know if need be.'

'Right, my friend,' he said, 'quite right! Better he not know as yet; perhaps he shall never know. I pray so; but if it be needed, then he shall know all. And, my good friend John, let me caution you. You deal with the madmen. All men are mad in some way or the other; and inasmuch as you deal discreetly with your madmen, so deal with God's madmen, too – the rest of the world. You tell not your madmen what you do nor why you do it; you tell them not what you think. So you shall keep knowledge in its place, where it may rest – where it may gather its kind around it and breed. You and I shall keep as yet what we know here, and here.' He touched me on the heart and on the forehead, and then touched him- self the same way. 'I have for myself thoughts at the present. Later I shall unfold to you.'

'Why not now?' I asked. 'It may do some good; we may arrive at some decision.' He stopped and looked at me, and said: –

'My friend John, when the corn is grown, even before it has ripened – while the milk of its mother-earth is in him, and the sunshine has not yet begun to paint him with his gold, the husbandman he pull the ear and rub him between his rough hands, and blow away the green chaff, and say to you: "Look! he's good corn; he will make good crop when the time comes."' I did not see the application, and told him so. For reply he reached over and took my ear in his hand and pulled it playfully, as he used long ago to do at lectures, and said: 'The good husbandman tell you so then because he knows, but not till then. But you do not find the good husbandman dig up his planted corn to see if he grow; that is for the children who play at husbandry, and not for those who take it as of the work of their life. See you now, friend John? I have sown my corn, and Nature has her work to do in making it sprout; if he sprout at all, there's some promise; and I wait till the ear begins to swell.' He broke off, for he evidently saw that I understood. Then he went on, and very gravely: –

'You were always a careful student, and your casebook was ever more full than the rest. You were only student then; now you are master, and I trust that good habit have not fail. Remember, my friend, that knowledge is stronger than memory, and we should not trust the weaker. Even if you have not kept the good practice, let me tell you that this case of our dear miss is one that may be – mind, I say *may be* – of such interest to us and others that all the rest may not make him kick the beam, as your peoples say. Take then good note of it. Nothing is too small. I counsel you, put down in record even your doubts and surmises. Hereafter it may be of interest to you to see how true you guess. We learn from failure, not from success!'

When I described Lucy's symptoms – the same as before, but infin- itely more marked – he looked very grave, but said nothing. He took with him a bag in which were many instruments and drugs, 'the ghastly paraphernalia of our beneficial trade,' as he once called, in one of his lectures, the equipment of a professor of the healing craft. When we were shown in, Mrs Westenra met us. She was alarmed, but not nearly so much as I expected to find her. Nature in one of her beneficent moods has ordained that even death has some antidote to its own terrors. Here, in a case where any shock may prove fatal, matters are so ordered that, from some cause or other, the things not personal – even the terrible change in her daughter to whom she is so attached – do not seem to reach her. It is something like the way Dame Nature gathers round a foreign body an envelope of some insensitive tissue which can protect from evil that which it would otherwise harm by contact. If this be an ordered selfishness, then we should pause before we condemn any one for the vice of egoism, for there may be deeper roots for its causes than we have knowledge of.

I used my knowledge of this phase of spiritual pathology, and laid down a rule that she should not be present with Lucy or think of her illness more than was absolutely required. She assented readily, so readily that I saw again the hand of Nature fighting for life. Van Helsing and I were shown up to Lucy's room. If I was shocked when I saw her yesterday, I was horrified when I saw her to-day. She was ghastly, chalkily pale; the red seemed to have gone even from her lips and gums, and the bones of her face stood out prominently; her breathing was painful to see or hear. Van Helsing's face grew set as marble, and his eyebrows converged till they almost touched over his nose. Lucy lay motionless and did not seem to have strength to speak, so for a while we were all silent. Then Van Helsing beckoned to me, and we went gently out of the room. The instant we had closed the door he stepped quickly along the passage to the next door, which was open. Then he pulled me quickly in with him and closed the door.

'My God!' he said; 'this is dreadful. There is no time to be lost. She will die for sheer want of blood to keep the heart's action as it should be. There must be transfusion of blood at once. Is it you or me?'

'I am younger and stronger, Professor. It must be me.'

'Then get ready at once. I will bring up my bag. I am prepared.'

I went downstairs with him and as we were going there was a knock at the hall-door. When we reached the hall the maid had just opened the door, and Arthur was stepping quickly in. He rushed up to me, saying in an eager whisper: –

'Jack, I was so anxious. I read between the lines of your letter, and have been in an agony. The dad was better, so I ran down here to see for myself. Is not that gentleman Dr Van Helsing? I am so thankful to you, sir, for coming.' When first the Professor's eye had lit upon him he had been angry at any interruption at such a time; but now, as he took in his stalwart proportions and recognised the strong young manhood which seemed to emanate from him, his eyes gleamed. Without a pause he said to him gravely as he held out his hand: –

'Sir, you have come in time. You are the lover of our dear miss. She is bad, very, very bad. Nay, my child, do not go like that.' For he suddenly grew pale and sat down in a chair almost fainting. 'You are to help her. You can do more than any that live, and your courage is your best help.'

'What can I do?' asked Arthur hoarsely. 'Tell me, and I shall do it. My life is hers, and I would give the last drop of blood in my body for her.' The Professor has a strongly humorous side, and I could from old knowledge detect a trace of its origin in his answer: –

'My young sir, I do not ask so much as that – not the last!'

'What shall I do?' There was fire in his eyes, and his open nostrils quivered with intent. Van Helsing slapped him on the shoulder. 'Come!' he said. 'You are a man, and it is a man we want. You are better than me, better than my friend John.' Arthur looked bewildered, and the Professor went on by explaining in a kindly way: –

'Young miss is bad, very bad. She wants blood, and blood she must have or die. My friend John and I have consulted; and we are about to perform what we call transfusion of blood – to transfer from full veins of one to the empty veins which pine for him. John was to give his blood, as he is the more young and strong than me' – here Arthur took my hand and wrung it hard in silence – 'but, now you are here, you are more good than us, old or young, who toil much in the world of thought. Our nerves are not so calm and our blood not so bright than yours!' Arthur turned to him and said: –

'If you only knew how gladly I would die for her you would understand –'

He stopped, with a sort of choke in his voice.

'Good boy!' said Van Helsing. 'In the not-so-far-off you will be happy that you have done all for her you love. Come now and be silent. You shall kiss her once before it is done, but then you must go; and you must leave at my sign. Say no word to Madame; you know how it is with her! There must be no shock; any knowledge of this would be one. Come!'

We all went up to Lucy's room. Arthur by direction remained outside. Lucy turned her head and looked at us, but said nothing. She was not asleep, but she was simply too weak to make the effort. Her eyes spoke to us; that was all. Van Helsing took some things from his bag and laid them on a little table out of sight. Then he mixed a narcotic, and coming over to the bed, said cheerily: –

'Now, little miss, here is your medicine. Drink it off, like a good child.

See, I lift you so that to swallow is easy. Yes.' She had made the effort with success.

It astonished me how long the drug took to act. This, in fact, marked the extent of her weakness. The time seemed endless until sleep began to flicker in her eyelids. At last, however, the narcotic began to manifest its potency; and she fell into a deep sleep. When the Professor was satisfied he called Arthur into the room, and bade him strip off his coat. Then he added: 'You may take that one little kiss whiles I bring over the table. Friend John, help to me!' So neither of us looked whilst he bent over her.

Van Helsing, turning to me, said: –

'He is so young and strong and of blood so pure that we need not defibrinate it.'

Then with swiftness, but with absolute method, Van Helsing performed the operation. As the transfusion went on something like life seemed to come back to poor Lucy's cheeks, and through Arthur's growing pallor the joy of his face seemed absolutely to shine. After a bit I began to grow anxious, for the loss of blood was telling on Arthur, strong man as he was. It gave me an idea of what a terrible strain Lucy's system must have undergone that what weakened Arthur only partially restored her. But the Professor's face was set, and he stood watch in hand and with his eyes fixed now on the patient and now on Arthur. I could hear my own heart beat. Presently he said in a soft voice: 'Do not stir an instant. It is enough. You attend him; I will look to her.' When all was over I could see how much Arthur was weakened. I dressed the wound and took his arm to bring him away, when Van Helsing spoke without turning round – the man seems to have eyes in the back of his head: –

'The brave lover I think deserve another kiss, which he shall have presently.' And as he had now finished his operation, he adjusted the pillow to the patient's head. As he did so the narrow black velvet band which she seemed always to wear round her throat, buckled with an old diamond buckle which her lover had given her, was dragged a little up, and showed a red mark on her throat. Arthur did not notice it, but I could hear the deep biss of indrawn breath which is one of Van Helsing's ways of betraying emotion. He said nothing at the moment, but turned to me, saying: 'Now take down our brave young lover, give him of the port wine, and let him lie down a while. He must then go home and rest, sleep much and eat much, that he may be recruited of what he has so given to his love. He must not stay here. Hold! a moment. I may take it, sir, that you are anxious of results. Then bring it with you that in all ways the operation is successful. You have saved her life this time, and you can go home and rest easy in mind that all that can be is. I shall tell her all when she is well; she shall love you none the less for what you have done. Good-bye.'

When Arthur had gone I went back to the room. Lucy was sleeping gently, but her breathing was stronger; I could see the counterpane move as her breast heaved. By the bedside sat Van Helsing, looking at her intently. The velvet band again covered the red mark. I asked the Professor in a whisper:

'What do you make of that mark on her throat?'

'What do you make of it?'

'I have not seen it yet,' I answered, and then and there proceeded to loose the band. Just over the external jugular vein there were two punctures, not large, but not wholesome-looking. There was no sign of disease, but the edges were white and worn-looking, as if by some trituration. It at once occurred to me that this wound, or whatever it was, might be the means of that manifest loss of blood; but I abandoned the idea as soon as formed, for such a thing could not be. The whole bed would have been drenched to a scarlet with the blood which the girl must have lost to leave such a pallor as she had before the transfusion.

'Well?' said Van Helsing.

'Well,' said I, 'I can make nothing of it.' The Professor stood up. 'I must go back to Amsterdam to-night,' he said. 'There are books and things there which I want. You must remain here all the night, and you must not let your sight pass from her.'

'Shall I have a nurse?' I asked.

'We are the best nurses, you and I. You keep watch all night; see that she is well fed, and that nothing disturbs her. You must not sleep all the night. Later on we can sleep, you and I. I shall be back as soon as possible. And then we may begin.'

'May begin?' I said. 'What on earth do you mean?'

'We shall see!' he answered as he hurried out. He came back a moment later and put his head inside the door, and said, with warning finger held up: –

'Remember, she is your charge. If you leave her, and harm befall, you shall not sleep easy hereafter!'

DR SEWARD'S DIARY (*continued*)

8 September. – I sat up all night with Lucy. The opiate worked itself off towards dusk, and she waked naturally; she looked a different being from what she had been before the operation. Her spirits even were good, and she was full of a happy vivacity, but I could see evidences of the absolute prostration which she had undergone. When I told Mrs Westenra that Dr Van Helsing had directed that I should sit up with her she almost pooh-poohed the idea, pointing out her daughter's renewed strength and excellent spirits. I was firm, however, and made preparations for my long vigil. When her maid had prepared her for the night I came in, having in the meantime had supper, and took a seat by the bedside. She did not in any way make objection, but looked at me gratefully whenever I caught her eye. After a long spell she seemed sinking off to sleep, but with an effort seemed to pull herself together and shook it off. This was repeated several times, with greater effort and with shorter pauses as the time moved on. It was apparent that she did not want to sleep, so I tackled the subject at once: –

'You do not want to go to sleep?'

'No; I am afraid.'

'Afraid to go to sleep! Why so? It is the boon we all crave for.'

'Ah, not if you were like me – if sleep was to you a presage of horror!'

'A presage of horror! What on earth do you mean?'

'I don't know; oh, I don't know. And that is what is so terrible. All this weakness comes to me in sleep; until I dread the very thought.'

'But my dear girl, you may sleep to-night. I am here watching you, and I can promise that nothing will happen.'

'Ah, I can trust you!' I seized the opportunity, and said: 'I promise you that if I see any evidence of bad dreams I will wake you at once.'

'You will? Oh, will you really? How good you are to me! Then I will sleep!' And almost at the word she gave a deep sigh of relief, and sank back, asleep.

All night long I watched by her. She never stirred, but slept on and on in a deep, tranquil, life-giving, health-giving sleep. Her lips were slightly parted, and her breast rose and fell with the regularity of a pendulum. There was a smile on her face, and it was evident that no bad dreams had come to disturb her peace of mind.

In the early morning her maid came, and I left her in her care and took myself back home, for I was anxious about many things. I sent a short wire to Van Helsing and to Arthur, telling them of the excellent result of the operation. My own work, with its manifold arrears, took me all day to clear off; it was dark when I was able to inquire about my zoophagous patient. The report was good: he had been quite quiet for the past day and night. A telegram came from Van Helsing at Amsterdam whilst I was at dinner, suggesting that I should be at Hillingham to-night, as it might be well to be at hand, and stating that he was leaving by the night mail and would join me early in the morning.

9 September. – I was pretty tired and worn-out when I got to Hillingham. For two nights I had hardly had a wink of sleep, and my brain was beginning to feel that numbness which marks cerebral exhaustion. Lucy was up and in cheerful spirits. When she shook hands with me she looked sharply in my face and said: –

'No sitting up to-night for you. You are worn-out. I am quite well again; indeed, I am; and if there is to be any sitting up, it is I who will sit up with you.' I would not argue the point, but went and had my supper. Lucy came with me, and, enlivened by her charming presence, I made an excellent meal, and had a couple of glasses of the more than excellent port. Then Lucy took me upstairs and showed me a room next her own, where a cosy fire was burning. 'Now,' she said, 'you must stay here. I shall leave this door open and my door too. You can lie on the sofa, for I know that nothing would induce any of you doctors to go to bed whilst there is a patient above the horizon. If I want anything I shall call out, and you can come to me at once.' I could not but acquiesce, for I was 'dog-tired,' and could not have sat up had I tried. So, on her renewing her promise to call me if she should want anything, I lay on the sofa, and forgot all about everything.

LUCY WESTENRA'S DIARY

9 September. – I feel so happy to-night. I have been so miserably weak, that to be able to think and move about is like feeling sunshine after a long spell of east wind out of a steel sky. Somehow Arthur feels very, very close to me. I seem to feel his presence warm about me. I suppose it is that sickness and weakness are selfish things and turn our inner eyes and sympathy on ourselves, whilst health and strength give Love rein, and in thought and feeling he can wander where he wills. I know where my thoughts are. If Arthur only knew! My dear, my dear, your ears must tingle as you sleep, as mine do waking. Oh, the blissful rest of last night! How I slept with that dear, good Dr Seward watching me. And to-night I shall not fear to sleep, since he is close at hand and within call. Thank everybody for being so good to me! Thank God! Good-night, Arthur.

DR SEWARD'S DIARY

10 September. – I was conscious of the Professor's hand on my head, and started awake all in a second. That is one of the things that we learn in an asylum, at any rate.

'And how is our patient?'

'Well, when I left her, or rather when she left me,' I answered.

'Come, let us see,' he said. And together we went into the room.

The blind was down, and I went over to raise it gently, whilst Van Helsing stepped, with his soft, catlike tread, over to the bed.

As I raised the blind, and the morning sunlight flooded the room, I heard the Professor's low hiss of inspiration, and knowing its rarity, a deadly fear shot through my heart. As I passed over he moved back, and his exclamation of horror, 'Gott in Himmel!' needed no enforcement from his agonised face. He raised his hand and pointed to the bed, and his iron face was drawn and ashen white. I felt my knees begin to tremble.

There on the bed, seemingly in a swoon, lay poor Lucy, more horribly white and wan-looking than ever. Even the lips were white, and the gums seemed to have shrunken back from the teeth, as we sometimes see in a corpse after a prolonged illness. Van Helsing raised his foot to stamp in anger, but the instinct of his life and all the long years of habit stood to him, and he put it down again softly. 'Quick!' he said. 'Bring the brandy.' I flew to the dining-room, and returned with the decanter. He wetted the poor white lips with it, and together we rubbed palm and wrist and heart. He felt her heart, and after a few moments of agonising suspense said:

'It is not too late. It beats, though but feebly. All our work is undone; we must begin again. There is no young Arthur here now; I have to call on you yourself this time, friend John.' As he spoke, he was dipping into his bag and producing the instruments for transfusion; I had taken off my coat and rolled up my shirt-sleeve. There was no possibility of an opiate just at present, and no need of one; and so, without a moment's delay, we began the operation. After a time – it did not seem a short time either, for the draining away of one's blood, no matter how willingly it be given, is a terrible feeling – Van Helsing held up a warning finger. 'Do not stir,' he said, 'but I fear that with growing strength she may wake; and that would make danger, oh, so much danger. But I shall precaution take. I shall give hypodermic injection of morphia.' He proceeded then, swiftly and deftly, to carry out his intent. The effect on Lucy was not bad, for the faint seemed to merge subtly into the narcotic sleep. It was with a feeling of personal pride that I could see a faint tinge of colour steal back into the pallid cheeks and lips. No man knows till he experiences it, what it is to feel his own life-blood drawn away into the viens of the woman he loves.

The Professor watched me critically. 'That will do,' he said. 'Already?' I remonstrated. 'You took a great deal more from Art.' To which he smiled a sad sort of smile as he replied: –

'He is her lover, her *Wancé*. You have work, much work, to do for her and for others; and the present will suffice.'

When we stopped the operation, he attended to Lucy, whilst I applied digital pressure to my own incision I lay down, whilst I waited his leisure to attend to me, for I felt faint and a little sick. By-and-by he bound up my wound, and sent me downstairs to get a glass of wine for myself. As I was leaving the room, he came after me, and half whispered: –

'Mind, nothing must be said of this. If our young lover should turn up unexpected, as before, no word to him. It would at once frighten him and enjealous him, too. There must be none. So!'

When I came back he looked at me carefully, and then said: –

'You are not much the worse. Go into the room, and lie on your sofa, and rest awhile; then have much breakfast, and come here to me.'

I followed out his orders, for I knew how right and wise they were. I had done my part, and now my next duty was to keep up my strength. I felt very weak, and in the weakness lost something of the amazement at what had occurred. I fell asleep on the sofa, however, wondering over and over again how Lucy had made such a retrograde movement, and how she could have been drained of so much blood with no sign anywhere to show for it. I think I must have continued my wonder in my dreams, for sleeping and waking, my thoughts always came back to the little punctures in her throat and the ragged, exhausted appearance of their edges – tiny though they were.

Lucy slept well into the day; and when she woke she was fairly well and strong, though not nearly so much so as the day before. When Van Helsing had seen her, he went out for a walk, leaving me in charge, with strict injunctions that I was not to leave her for a moment. I could hear his voice in the hall, asking the way to the nearest telegraph office.

Lucy chatted with me freely, and seemed quite unconscious that anything had happened. I tried to keep her amused and interested. When her mother came up to see her, she did not seem to notice any change whatever, but said to me gratefully: –

'We owe you so much, Dr Seward, for all you have done, but you really must now take care not to overwork yourself. You are looking pale yourself. You want a wife to nurse and look after you a bit; that you do!' As she spoke Lucy turned crimson, though it was only momentarily, for her poor wasted veins could not stand for long such an unwonted drain to the head. The reaction came in excessive pallor as she turned imploring eyes on me. I smiled and nodded, and laid my finger on my lips; with a sigh, she sank back amid her pillows.

Van Helsing returned in a couple of hours, and presently said to me: 'Now you go home, and eat much and drink enough. Make yourself strong. I stay here to-night, and I shall sit up with little miss myself. You and I must watch the case, and we must have none other to know. I have grave reasons. No, do not ask them; think what you will. Do not fear to think even the most not-probable. Good-night.'

In the hall two of the maids came to me, and asked if they or either of them might not sit up with Miss Lucy. They implored me to let them; and when I said it was Dr Van Helsing's wish that either he or I should sit up, they asked me quite piteously to intercede with the 'foreign gentleman.' I was much touched by their kindness. Perhaps it is because I am weak at present, and perhaps it was on Lucy's account that their devotion was manifested; for over and over again have I seen similar instances of woman's kindness. I got back here in time for a late dinner; went my rounds – all well; and set this down whilst waiting for sleep. It is coming.

11 September. – This afternoon I went over to Hillingham. Found Van Helsing in excellent spirits, and Lucy much better. Shortly after I had arrived, a big parcel from abroad came for the Professor. He opened it with much impressment – assumed, of course – and showed a great bundle of white flowers.

'These are for you, Miss Lucy,' he said.

'For me? Oh, Dr Van Helsing!'

'Yes, my dear, but not for you to play with. These are medicines.' Here Lucy made a wry face. 'Nay, but they are not to take in a decoction or in nauseous form, so you need not snub that so charming nose,' or I shall point out to my friend Arthur what woes he may have to endure in seeing so much beauty that he so loves so much distort. Aha, my pretty miss, that bring the so nice nose all straight again. This is medicinal, but you do not know how. I put him in your window, I make pretty wreath, and hang him round your neck, so that you sleep well. Oh yes! they, like the lotus flower, make your trouble forgotten. It smell so like the waters of Lethe, and of that fountain of youth that the Conquistadores sought for in the Floridas, and find him all too late.'

Whilst he was speaking, Lucy had been examining the flowers and smelling them. Now she threw them down, saying, with half-laughter and half-disgust: –

'Oh, Professor, I believe you are only putting up a joke on me. Why, these flowers are only common garlic.'

To my surprise. Van Helsing rose up and said with all his sternness, his iron jaw set and his bushy eyebrows meeting: –

'No trifling with me! I never jest! There is grim purpose in all I do; and I warn you that you do not thwart me. Take care, for the sake of others if not for your own.' Then seeing poor Lucy scared, as she might well be, he went on more gently: 'Oh, little miss, my dear, do not fear me. I only do for your good; but there is much virtue to you in those so common flower. See, I place them myself in your room. I make myself the wreath that you are to wear. But hush! no telling to others that make so inquisitive questions. We must obey, and silence is a part of obedience; and obedience is to bring you strong and well into loving arms that wait for you. Now sit still awhile. Come with me, friend John, and you shall help me deck the room with my garlic, which is all the way from Haarlem, where my friend Vanderpool raise herb in his glasshouses all the year. I had to telegraph yesterday, or they would not have been here.'

We went into the room, taking the flowers with us. The Professor's actions were certainly odd, and not to be found in any pharmacopoeia that I ever heard of. First, he fastened up the windows and latched them securely; next, taking a handful of the flowers, he rubbed them all over the sashes, as though to ensure that every whiff of air that might get in would be laden with the garlic smell. Then with the wisp he rubbed all over the jamb of the door, above, below, and at each side, and round the fireplace in the same way. It all seemed grotesque to me, and presently I said: –

'Well, Professor, I know you always have a reason for what you do, but this certainly puzzles me. It is well we have no sceptic here, or he would say that you were working some spell to keep out an evil spirit.'

'Perhaps I am!' he answered quietly as he began to make the wreath which Lucy was to wear round her neck.

We then waited whilst Lucy made her toilet for the night, and when she was in bed he came and himself fixed the wreath of garlic round her neck. The last words he said to her were: –

'Take care you do not disturb it; and even if the room feel close, do not to-night open the window or the door.'

'I promise,' said Lucy, 'and thank you both a thousand times for all your kindness to me! Oh, what have I done to be blessed with such friends?'

As we left the house in my fly, which was waiting, Van Helsing said: –

'To-night I can sleep in peace, and sleep I want – two nights of travel, much reading in the day between, and much anxiety on the day to follow, and a night to sit up, without to wink. To-morrow in the morning early you call for me, and we come together to see our pretty miss, so much more strong for my "spell" which I have work. Ho! ho!'

He seemed so confident that I, remembering my own confidence two nights before and with the baneful result, felt awe and vague terror. It must have been my weakness that made me hesitate to tell it to my friend, but I felt it all the more, like unshed tears.

CHAPTER 11

LUCY WESTENRA'S DIARY

12 September. – How good they all are to me! I quite love that dear Dr Van Helsing. I wonder why he was so anxious about these flowers. He positively frightened me, he was so fierce. And yet he must have been right, for I feel comfort from them already. Somehow, I do not dread being alone to-night, and I can go to sleep without fear. I shall not mind any flapping outside the window. Oh, the terrible struggle that I have had against sleep so often of late; the pain of the sleeplessness, or the pain of the fear of sleep, with such unknown horrors as it has for me! How blessed are some people, whose lives have no fears, no dreads; to whom sleep is a blessing that comes nightly, and brings nothing but sweet dreams. Well, here I am to-night, hoping for sleep, and lying like Ophelia in the play, with 'virgin crants and maiden strewments.' I never liked garlic before, but to-night it is delightful! There is peace in its smell; I feel sleep coming already. Good-night, everybody.

DR SEWARD'S DIARY

13 September. – Called at the Berkeley and found Van Helsing, as usual, up to time. The carriage ordered from the hotel was waiting. The Professor took his bag, which he always brings with him now.

Let all be put down exactly. Van Helsing and I arrived at Hillingham at eight o'clock. It was a lovely morning; the bright sunshine and all the fresh feeling of early autumn seemed like the completion of nature's annual work. The leaves were turning to all kinds of beautiful colours, but had not yet begun to drop from the trees. When we entered we met Mrs Westenra coming out of the morning-room. She is always an early riser. She greeted us warmly and said: –

'You will be glad to know that Lucy is better. The dear child is still asleep. I looked into her room and saw her, but did not go in, lest I should disturb her.' The Professor smiled, and looked quite jubilant. He rubbed his hands together, and said: –

'Aha! I thought I had diagnosed the case. My treatment is working,' to which she answered: –

'You must not take all the credit to yourself, doctor. Lucy's state this morning is due in part to me.'

'How do you mean, ma'am?' asked the Professor.

'Well, I was anxious about the dear child in the night, and went into her room. She was sleeping soundly – so soundly that even my coming did not wake her. But the room was awfully stuffy. There were a lot of those horrible, strong-smelling flowers about everywhere, and she had actually a bunch of them round her neck. I feared that the heavy odour would be too much for the dear child in her weak state, so I took them all away and opened a bit of the window to let in a little fresh air. You will be pleased with her, I am sure.'

She moved off into her boudoir, where she usually breakfasted early. As she had spoken, I watched the Professor's face, and saw it turn ashen grey. He had been able to retain his self-command whilst the poor lady was present, for he knew her state and how mischievous a shock would be; he actually smiled on her as he held open the door for her to pass into her room. But the instant she had disappeared he pulled me, suddenly and forcibly, into the dining-room and closed the door.

Then, for the first time in my life, I saw Van Helsing break down. He raised his hands over his head in a sort of mute despair, and then beat his palms together in a helpless way; finally he sat down on a chair, and putting his hands before his face, began to sob, with loud, dry sobs that seemed to come from the very racking of his heart. Then he raised his arms again, as though appealing to the whole universe. 'God! God! God!' he said. 'What have we done, what has this poor thing done, that we are so sore beset? Is there fate amongst us still, sent down from the pagan world of old, that such things must be, and in such a way? This poor mother, all unknowing, and all for the best as she think, does such thing as lose her daughter body and soul; and we must not tell her, we must not even warn her, or she die, and then both die. Oh, how we are beset! How are all the powers of the devils against us!' Suddenly he jumped to his feet. 'Come,' he said, 'come, we must see and act. Devils or no devils, or all the devils at once, it matters not; we fight him all the same.' He went to the hall-door for his bag; and together we went up to Lucy's room.

Once again I drew up the blind, whilst Van Helsing went towards the bed. This time he did not start as he looked on the poor face with the same awful, waxen pallor as before. He wore a look of stern sadness and infinite pity.

'As I expected,' he murmured, with that hissing inspiration of his which meant so much. Without a word he went and locked the door, and then began to set out on the little table the instruments for yet another operation of transfusion of blood. I had long ago recognised the necessity, and begun to take off my coat, but he stopped me with a warning hand. 'No!' he said. 'To-day you must operate. I shall provide. You are weakened already.' As he spoke he took off his coat and rolled up his shirt-sleeve.

Again the operation; again the narcotic; again some return of colour to the ashy cheeks, and the regular breathing of healthy sleep. This time I watched whilst Van Helsing recruited himself and rested.

Presently he took an opportunity of telling Mrs Westenra that she must not remove anything from Lucy's room without consulting him; that the flowers were of medicinal value, and that the breathing of their odour was a part of the system of cure. Then he took over the care of the case himself, saying that he would watch this night and the next and would send me word when to come.

After another hour Lucy waked from her sleep, fresh and bright, and seemingly not much the worse for her terrible ordeal.

What does it all mean? I am beginning to wonder if my long habit of life amongst the insane is beginning to tell upon my own brain.

LUCY WESTENRA'S DIARY

17 September. – Four days and nights of peace. I am getting so strong again that I hardly know myself. It is as if I had passed through some long nightmare, and had just awakened to see the beautiful sunshine and feel the fresh air of the morning around me. I have a dim half-remembrance of long, anxious times of waiting and fearing; darkness in which there was not even the pain of hope to make present distress more poignant; and then long spells of oblivion, and the rising back to life as a diver coming up through a great press of water. Since, however, Dr Van Helsing has been with me, all this bad dreaming seems to have passed away; the noises that used to frighten me out of my wits – the flapping against the windows, the distant voices which seemed so close to me, the harsh sounds that came from I know not where and commanded me to do I know not what – have all ceased. I go to bed now without any fear of sleep. I do not even try to keep awake. I have grown quite fond of the garlic, and a boxful arrives for me every day from Haarlem. To-night Dr Van Helsing is going away, as he has to be for a day in Amsterdam. But I need not be watched; I am well enough to be left alone. Thank God for mother's sake, and dear Arthur's, and for all our friends who have been so kind! I shall not even feel the change, for last night Dr Van Helsing slept in his chair a lot of the time. I found him asleep twice when I awoke; but I did not fear to go to sleep again, although the boughs or bats or something flapped almost angrily against the window-panes.

'The Pall Mall Gazette', 18 September

THE ESCAPED WOLF

perilous adventure of our interviewer

Interview with the Keeper in the Zoological Gardens

After many inquiries and almost as many refusals, and perpetually using the words *Pall Mall Gazette* as a sort of talisman, I managed to find the keeper of the section of the Zoological Gardens in which the wolf department is included. Thomas Bilder lives in one of the cottages in the enclosure behind the elephant-house, and was just sitting down to his tea when I found him. Thomas and his wife are hospitable folk, elderly, and without children, and if the specimen I enjoyed of their hospitality be of the average kind, their lives must be pretty comfortable.

The keeper would not enter on what he called 'business' until the supper was over, and we were all satisfied. Then when the table was cleared, and he had lit his pipe, he said: –

'Now, sir, you can go on and arsk me what you want. You'll excoose me refoosin' to talk of perfeshunal subjects afore meals. I gives the wolves and the jackals and the hyenas in all our section their tea afore I begins to arsk them questions.'

'How do you mean, ask them questions?' I queried, wishing to get him into a talkative humour.

''Ittin' of them over the 'ead with a pole is one way; scratchin' of their hears is another, when gents as is flush wants a bit of a show-orf to their gals. I don't so much mind the fust – the 'ittin' with a pole afore I chucks in their dinner; but I waits till they've 'ad their sherry and kawffee, so to speak, afore I tries on with the ear-scratchin'. Mind you,' he added philosophically, 'there's a deal of the same nature in us as in them there animiles. Here's you a-comin' and arskin' of me questions about my business, and I that grumpy-like that only for your bloomin' arf-quid I'd 'a' seen you blowed fust 'fore I'd answer. Not even when you arsked me sarcastic-like if I'd like you to arsk the Superintendent if you might arsk me questions. Without offence, did I tell yer to go to 'ell?'

'You did.'

'An' when you said you'd report me for usin' of obscene language, that was 'ittin' me over the 'ead; but the 'arf-quid made that all right. I weren't a-goin' to fight, so I waited for the food, and did with my 'owl as the wolves, and lions, and tigers does. But, Lor' love yer 'art, now that the old 'ooman has stuck a chunk of her tea-cake in me, an' rinsed me out with her bloomin' old teapot, and I've lit up, you may scratch my ears for all you're worth, and won't get even a growl out of me. Drive along with your questions. I know what yer a-comin' at, that 'ere escaped wolf.'

'Exactly. I want you to give me your view of it. Just tell me how it happened; and when I know the facts I'll get you to say what you consider was the cause of it, and how you think the whole affair will end.'

'All right, guv'nor. This 'ere is about the 'ole story. That 'ere wolf what we called Bersicker was one of three grey ones that came from Norway to Jamrach's, which we bought off him four year ago. He was a nice well-behaved wolf, that never gave no trouble to talk of. I'm more surprised at 'im for wantin' to get out nor any other animile in the place. But, there, you can't trust wolves no more nor women.'

'Don't you mind him, sir!' broke in Mrs Tom, with a cheery laugh. ''E's got mindin' the animiles so long that blest if he ain't like a old wolf 'isself! But there ain't no 'arm in 'im.'

'Well, sir, it was about two hours after feedin' yesterday when I first hear any disturbance. I was makin' up a litter in the monkey-house for a young puma which is ill; but when I heard the yelpin' and 'owlin' I kem away straight. There was Bersicker a-tearin' like a mad thing at the bars as if he wanted to get out. There wasn't much people about that day, and close at hand was only one man, a tall, thin chap, with a 'ook nose and a pointed beard, with a few white hairs runnin' through it. He had a 'ard, cold look and red eyes, and I took a sort of mislike to him, for it seemed as if it was 'im as they was hirritated at. He 'ad white kid gloves on 'is 'ands, and he pointed out the animiles to me and says: "Keeper, these wolves seem upset at something."

'"Maybe it's you," says I, for I did not like the airs as he give 'isself. He didn't get angry, as I 'oped he would but he smiled a kind of insolent smile, with a mouth full of white, sharp teeth. "Oh no, they wouldn't like me," 'e says.

'"Ow yes, they would," says I, a-imitatin' of him. "They always likes a bone or two to clean their teeth on about tea-time, which you 'as a bagful."

'Well, it was a odd thing, but when the animiles see us a-talkin' they lay down, and when I went over to Bersicker he let me stroke his ears same as ever. That there man kem over, and blessed but if he didn't put in his hand and stroke the old wolf's ears too!

"'Tyke care,' says I. "Bersicker is quick."

"'Never mind,' he says. "I'm used to 'em!"

"'Are you in the business yourself?' I says, tyking off my 'at, for a man what trades in wolves, anceterer, is a good friend to keepers.

"'No,' says he, "not exactly in the business, but I 'ave made pets of several." And with that he lifts his 'at as perlite as a lord, and walks away. Old Bersicker kep' a-lookin' arter 'im till 'e was out of sight, and then went and lay down in a corner, and wouldn't come hout the 'ole hevening. Well, larst night, so soon as the moon was hup, the wolves here all began a-'owling. There warn't nothing for them to 'owl at. There warn't no one near, except someone that was evidently a-callin' a dog somewheres out back of the gardings in the Park road. Once or twice I went out to see that all was right, and it was, and then the 'owling stopped. Just before twelve o'clock I just took a look round afore turnin' in, an', bust me, but when I kem opposite to old Bersicker's cage I see the rails broken and twisted about and the cage empty. And that's all I know for certing.'

'Did anyone else see anything?'

'One of our gard'ners was a-comin' 'ome about that time from a 'armony, when he sees a big grey dog comin' out through the gardin 'edges. At least, so he says; but I don't give much for it myself, for if he did 'e never said a word about it to his missis when 'e got 'ome, and it was only after the escape of the wolf was made known, and we had been up all night a-huntin' of the Park for Bersicker, that he remembered seein' anything. My own belief was that the 'armony 'ad got into his 'ead.'

'Now, Mr Bilder, can you account in any way for the escape of the wolf?'

'Well, sir,' he said, with a suspicious sort of modesty, 'I think I can; but I don't know as 'ow you'd be satisfied with the theory.'

'Certainly I shall. If a man like you, who knows the animals from experience, can't hazard a good guess at any rate, who is even to try?'

'Well then, sir, I accounts for it this way: it seems to me that 'ere wolf escaped – simply because he wanted to get out.'

From the hearty way that both Thomas and his wife laughed at the joke I could see that it had done service before, and that the whole explanation was simply an elaborate sell. I couldn't cope in badinage with the worthy Thomas, but I thought I knew a surer way to his heart, so I said: –

'Now, Mr Bilder, we'll consider that first half-sovereign worked off, and this brother of his is waiting to be claimed when you've told me what you think will happen.'

'Right y'are, sir,' he said briskly. 'Ye'll excoose me, I know, for a-chaffin' of ye, but the old woman here winked at me, which was as much as telling me to go on.'

'Well, I never!' said the old lady.

'My opinion is this: that 'ere wolf is a-'idin' of, somewheres. The gard'ner wot didn't remember said he was 'a-gallopin' northward faster than a horse could go; but I don't believe him, for, yer see, sir, wolves don't gallop no more than dogs does, they not bein' built that way. Wolves is fine things in a story-book, and I dessay when they gets in packs and does be chivvin' somethin' that's more afeared than they is they can make a devil of a noise and chop it up, whatever it is. But, Lor' bless you, in real life a wolf is only a low creature, not half so clever or bold as a good dog; and not half a quarter so much fight in 'im. This one ain't been used to fightin' or even to providin' for hisself, and more like he's somewhere round the Park a-'idin' an' a-shiverin' of, and, if he thinks at all, wonderin' where he is to get his breakfast from; or maybe he's got down some area and is in a coal-cellar. My eye, won't some cook get a rum start when she sees his green eyes a-shining at her out of the dark! If he can't get food he's bound to look for it, and mayhap he may chance to light on a butcher's shop in time. If he doesn't, and some nursemaid goes a-walkin' orf with a soldier, leavin' of the hinfant in the perambulator – well then I shouldn't be surprised if the census is one babby the less. That's all.'

I was handing him the half-sovereign, when something came bobbing up against the window, and Mr Bilder's face doubled its natural length with surprise.

'God bless me!' he said. 'If there ain't old Bersicker come back by 'isself!'

He went to the door and opened it; a most unnecessary proceeding it seemed to me. I have always thought that a wild animal never looks so well as when some obstacle of pronounced durability is between us; a personal experience has intensified rather than diminished that idea.

After all, however, there is nothing like custom, for neither Bilder nor his wife thought any more of the wolf than I should of a dog. The animal itself was as peaceful and well-behaved as that father of all picture-wolves, Red Riding Hood's quondam friend, whilst seeking her confidence in masquerade.

The whole scene was an unutterable mixture of comedy and pathos. The wicked wolf that for half a day had paralysed London and set all the

children in the town shivering in their shoes, was there in a sort of penitent mood, and was received and petted like a sort of vulpine prodigal
son. Old Bilder examined him all over with most tender solicitude, and
when he had finished with his penitent said: –

'There, I knew the poor old chap would get into some kind of trouble;
didn't I say it all along? Here's his head all cut and full of broken glass.
'E's been a-gettin' over some bloomin' wall or other. It's a shyme that
people are allowed to top their walls with broken bottles. This 'ere's what
comes of it. Come along, Bersicker.'

He took the wolf and locked him up in a cage, with a piece of meat
that satisfied, in quantity at any rate, the elementary conditions of the
fatted calf, and went off to report.

I came off, too, to report the only exclusive information that is given
to-day regarding the strange escapade at the Zoo.

DR SEWARD'S DIARY

17 September. – I was engaged after dinner in my study posting up my
books, which, through press of other work and the many visits to Lucy,
had fallen sadly into arrear. Suddenly the door was burst open, and in
rushed my patient, with his face distorted with passion. I was thunder-
struck, for such a thing as a patient getting of his own accord into the
Superintendent's study is almost unknown. Without an instant's pause he
made straight at me. He had a dinner-knife in his hand, and, as I saw he
was dangerous, I tried to keep the table between us. He was too quick
and too strong for me, however; for before I could get my balance he had
struck at me and cut my left wrist rather severely. Before he could strike
again, however, I got in my right, and he was sprawling on his back on
the floor. My wrist bled freely, and quite a little pool trickled on to the
carpet. I saw that my friend was not intent on further effort, and occupied
myself binding up my wrist, keeping a wary eye on the prostrate figure
all the time. When the attendants rushed in, and we turned our attention
to him, his employment positively sickened me. He was lying on his belly
on the floor licking up, like a dog, the blood which had fallen from my
wounded wrist. He was easily secured, and, to my surprise, went with the
attendants quite placidly, simply repeating over and over again: 'The blood
is the life! the blood is the life!'

I cannot afford to lose blood just at present: I have lost too much of
late for my physical good, and the then prolonged strain of Lucy's illness

and its horrible phases is telling on me. I am over-excited and weary, and I need rest, rest, rest. Happily Van Helsing has not summoned me, so I need not forgo my sleep; to-night I could not well do without it.

Telegram, Van Helsing, Antwerp, to Seward, Carfax
(Sent to Carfax, Sussex, as no county given;
delivered late by twenty-two hours.)

'*17 September.* – Do not fail to be at Hillingham to-night. If not watching all the time, frequently visit and see that flowers are as placed; very important; do not fail. Shall be with you as soon as possible after arrival.'

DR SEWARD'S DIARY

18 September. – Just off for train to London. The arrival of Van Helsing's telegram filled me with dismay. A whole night lost, and I know by bitter experience what may happen in a night. Of course it is possible that all may be well, but what *may* have happened? Surely there is some horrible doom hanging over us that every possible accident should thwart us in all we try to do. I shall take this cylinder with me, and then I can complete my entry on Lucy's phonograph.

MEMORANDUM LEFT BY LUCY WESTENRA

17 September. Night. – I write this and leave it to be seen, so that no one may by any chance get into any trouble through me. This is an exact record of what took place to-night. I feel I am dying of weakness, and have barely strength to write, but it must be done if I die in the doing.

I went to bed as usual, taking care that the flowers were placed as Dr Van Helsing directed, and soon fell asleep.

I was waked by the flapping at the window, which had begun after that sleep-walking on the cliff at Whitby when Mina saved me, and which now I know so well. I was not afraid, but I did wish that Dr Seward was in the next room – as Dr Van Helsing said he would be – so that I might have called him. I tried to go to sleep, but could not. Then there came to me the old fear of sleep, and I determined to keep awake. Perversely sleep would try to come when I did not want it; so, as I feared to be alone, I opened my door and called out: 'Is there anybody there?' There was no answer. I was afraid to wake mother, and so closed my door again. Then outside in the shrubbery I heard a sort of howl like a dog's, but more fierce and deeper. I went to the window and looked out, but could see nothing, except a big bat, which had evidently been buffeting its wings against the window. So I went back to bed again, but determined not to go to sleep. Presently the door opened, and mother looked in; seeing by my moving that I was not asleep, came in, and sat by me. She said to me even more sweetly and softly than her wont: –

'I was uneasy about you, darling, and came in to see that you were all right.'

I feared she might catch cold sitting there, and asked her to come in and sleep with me, so she came into bed, and lay down beside me; she did not take off her dressing-gown, for she said she would only stay awhile and then go back to her own bed. As she lay there in my arms, and I in hers, the flapping and buffeting came to the window again. She was startled and a little frightened, and cried out: 'What is that?' I tried to pacify her, and at last succeeded, and she lay quiet; but I could hear her poor dear heart still beating terribly. After a while there was the low howl again out in the shrubbery, and shortly after there was a crash at the window, and a lot of broken glass was hurled on the floor. The window blind blew back with the wind that rushed in, and in the aperture of the broken panes there was the head of a great gaunt grey wolf. Mother cried out in a fright, and struggled up into a sitting posture, and clutched wildly at anything that would help her. Amongst other things, she clutched the wreath of flowers that Dr Van Helsing insisted on my wearing round my neck, and tore it away from me. For a second or two she sat up, pointing at the wolf, and there was a strange and horrible gurgling in her throat; then she fell over, as if struck with lightning, and her head hit my forehead and made me dizzy for a moment or two. The room and all round seemed to spin round. I kept my eyes fixed on the window, but the wolf drew his head back, and a whole myriad little specks seemed to come blowing in through the broken window, and wheeling and circling round like the pillar of dust that travellers describe when there is a simoom in the desert. I tried to stir, but there was some spell upon me, and dear mother's poor body, which seemed to grow cold already – for her dear heart had ceased to beat – weighed me down; and I remembered no more for a while.

The time did not seem long, but very, very awful, till I recovered consciousness again. Somewhere near, a passing bell was tolling; the dogs all round the neighbourhood were howling; and in our shrubbery, seemingly just outside, a nightingale was singing. I was dazed and stupid with pain and terror and weakness, but the sound of the nightingale seemed like the voice of my dead mother come back to comfort me. The sounds seemed to have awakened the maids, too, for I could hear their bare feet pattering outside my door. I called to them, and they came in, and when they saw what had happened, and what it was that lay over me in the bed, they screamed out. The wind rushed in through the broken window, and the door slammed to. They lifted off the body of my dear mother and laid her, covered up with a sheet, on the bed after I had got up. They were all so frightened and nervous that I directed them to go to the dining-room and have each a glass of wine. The door flew open for an instant and closed again. The maids shrieked, and then went in a body to the dining-room; and I laid what flowers I had on my dear mother's breast. When they were there I remembered what Dr Van Helsing had told me, but I didn't like to remove them, and, besides, I would have some of the servants to sit up with me now. I was surprised that the maids did not come back. I called them, but got no answer, so I went to the dining-room to look for them.

My heart sank when I saw what had happened. They all four lay helpless on the floor, breathing heavily. The decanter of sherry was on the table half full, but there was a queer, acrid smell about. I was suspicious, and examined the decanter. It smelt of laudanum, and looking on the sideboard, I found that the bottle which mother's doctor uses for her – oh! did use – was empty. What am I to do? What am I to do? I am back in the room with mother. I cannot leave her, and I am alone, save for the sleeping servants, whom someone has drugged. Alone with the dead! I dare not go out, for I can hear the low howl of the wolf through the broken window.

The air seems full of specks, floating and circling in the draught from the window, and the lights burn blue and dim. What am I to do? God shield me from harm this night! I shall hide this paper in my breast, where they shall find it when they come to lay me out. My dear mother gone! It is time that I go too. Good-bye, dear Arthur, if I should not survive this night. God keep you, dear, and God help me!

CHAPTER 12

DR SEWARD'S DIARY

18 September. – I drove at once to Hillingham and arrived early. Keeping my cab at the gate, I went up the avenue alone. I knocked gently and rang as quietly as possible, for I feared to disturb Lucy or her mother, and hoped to bring only a servant to the door. After a while, finding no response, I knocked and rang again; still no answer. I cursed the laziness of the servants that they should lie abed at such an hour – for it was now ten o'clock – and so rang and knocked again, but more impatiently, and still without response. Hitherto I had blamed only the servants, but now a terrible fear began to assail me. Was this desolation but another link in the chain of doom which seemed drawing tight around us? Was it indeed a house of death to which I had come too late? I knew that minutes, even seconds of delay might mean hours of danger to Lucy, if she had had again one of those frightful relapses; and I went round the house to try if I could find by chance an entry anywhere.

I could find no means of ingress. Every window and door was fastened and locked, and I returned baffled to the porch. As I did so, I heard the rapid pit-pat of a swiftly driven horse's feet. They stopped at the gate, and a few seconds later I met Van Helsing running up the avenue. When he saw me, he gasped out:

'Then it was you, and just arrived. How is she? Are we too late? Did you not get my telegram?'

I answered as quickly and coherently as I could that I had only got his telegram early in the morning and had not lost a minute in coming here, and that I could not make anyone in the house hear me. He paused and raised his hat as he said solemnly:

'Then I fear we are too late. God's will be done!' With his usual recuperative energy, he went on: 'Come. If there be no way open to get in, we must make one. Time is all in all to us now.'

We went round to the back of the house, where there was a kitchen window. The Professor took a small surgical saw from his case, and handing it to me, pointed to the iron bars which guarded the window. I attacked them at once and had very soon cut through three of them. Then with a long, thin knife we pushed back the fastening of the sashes and opened the window. I helped the Professor in and followed him. There was no one in the kitchen or in the servant's rooms, which were close at hand.

We tried all the rooms as we went along, and in the dining-room, dimly lit by rays of light through the shutters, found four servant-women lying on the floor. There was no need to think them dead, for their stertorous breathing and the acrid smell of laudanum in the room left no doubt as to their condition. Van Helsing and I looked at each other, and as we moved away he said: 'We can attend to them later.' Then we ascended to Lucy's room. For an instant or two we paused at the door to listen, but there was no sound that we could hear. With white faces and trembling hands, we opened the door gently, and entered the room.

How shall I describe what we saw? On the bed lay two women, Lucy and her mother. The latter lay farthest in, and she was covered with a white sheet, the edge of which had been blown back by the draught through the broken window, showing the drawn, white face, with a look of terror fixed upon it. By her side lay Lucy, with face white and still more drawn. The flowers which had been round her neck we found upon her mother's bosom, and her throat was bare, showing the two little wounds which we had noticed before, but looking horribly white and mangled. Without a word the Professor bent over the bed, his head almost touching poor Lucy's breast; then he gave a quick turn of his head, as of one who listens, and leaping to his feet, he cried out to me:

'It is not yet too late! Quick! Quick! Bring the brandy!'

I flew downstairs and returned with it, taking care to smell and taste it, lest it, too, were drugged like the decanter of sherry which I found on the table. The maids were still breathing, but more restlessly, and I fancied that the narcotic was wearing off. I did not stay to make sure, but returned to Van Helsing. He rubbed the brandy, as on another occasion, on her lips and gums and on her wrists and the palms of her hands. He said to me:

'I can do this, all that can be at the present. You go wake those maids. Flick them in the face with a wet towel, and flick them hard. Make them get heat and fire and a warm bath. This poor soul is nearly as cold as that beside her. She will need be heated before we can do anything more.'

I went at once, and found little difficulty in waking three of the women. The fourth was only a young girl, and the drug had evidently affected her more strongly, so I lifted her on the sofa and let her sleep. The others were dazed at first, but as remembrance came back to them they cried and sobbed in a hysterical manner. I was stern with them, however, and would not let them talk. I told them that one life was bad enough to lose, and that if they delayed they would sacrifice Miss Lucy. So, sobbing and crying, they went about their way, half-clad as they were, and prepared fire and water. Fortunately, the kitchen and boiler fires were still alive, and there was no lack of hot water. We got a bath, and carried Lucy out as she was and placed her in it. Whilst we were busy chafing her limbs there was a knock at the hall-door. One of the maids ran off, hurried on some more clothes, and opened it. Then she returned and whispered to us that there was a gentleman who had come with a message from Mr Holmwood. I bade her simply tell him that he must wait, for we could see no one now. She went away with the message, and, engrossed with our work, I clean forgot all about him.

I never saw in all my experience the Professor work in such deadly earnest. I knew – as he knew – that it was a stand-up fight with death, and in a pause told him so. He answered me in a way that I did not understand, but with the sternest look that his face could wear: –

'If that were all, I would stop here where we are now, and let her fade away into peace, for I see no light in life over her horizon.' He went on with his work with, if possible, renewed and more frenzied vigour.

Presently we both began to be conscious that the heat was beginning to be of some effect. Lucy's heart beat a trifle more audibly to the stethoscope, and her lungs had a perceptible movement. Van Helsing's face almost beamed, and as we lifted her from the bath and rolled her in a hot sheet to dry her he said to me: –

'The first gain is ours! Check to the king!'

We took Lucy into another room, which had by now been prepared, and laid her in bed and forced a few drops of brandy down her throat. I noticed that Ven Helsing tied a soft silk handkerchief round her throat. She was still unconscious, and was quite as bad as, if not worse than, we had ever seen her.

Van Helsing called in one of the women, and told her to stay with her and not to take her eyes off her till we returned, and then beckoned me out of the room.

'We must consult as to what is to be done,' he said as we descended the stairs. In the hall he opened the dining-room door, and we passed in, he closing the door carefully behind him. The shutters had been opened, but the blinds were already down, with that obedience to the etiquette of death which the British woman of the lower classes always rigidly observes. The room was, therefore, dimly dark. It was, however, light enough for our purposes. Van Helsing's sternness was somewhat relieved by a look of perplexity. He was evidently torturing his mind about something, so I waited for an instant, and he spoke: –

'What are we to do now? Where are we to turn for help? We must have another transfusion of blood, and that soon, or that poor girl's life won't be worth an hour's purchase. You are exhausted already; I am exhausted too. I fear to trust those women, even if they would have courage to submit. What are we to do for someone who will open his veins for her?'

'What's the matter with me, anyhow?'

The voice came from the sofa across the room, and its tones brought relief and joy to my heart, for they were those of Quincey Morris. Van Helsing started angrily at the first sound, but his face softened and a glad look came into his eyes as I cried out: 'Quincey Morris!' and rushed towards him with outstretched hands.

'What brought you here?' I cried as our hands met.

'I guess Art is the cause.'

He handed me a telegram: –

'Have not heard from Seward for three days, and am terribly anxious. Cannot leave. Father still in same condition. Send me word how Lucy is. Do not delay. – Holmwood.'

'I think I came just in the nick of time. You know you have only to tell me what to do.'

Van Helsing strode forward and took his hand, looking him straight in the eyes as he said: –

'A brave man's blood is the best thing on this earth when a woman is in trouble. You're a man, and no mistake. Well, the devil may work against us for all he's worth, but God sends us men when we want them.'

Once again we went through that ghastly operation. I have not the heart to go through with the details. Lucy had got a terrible shock, and it told on her more than before, for though plenty of blood went into her veins, her body did not respond to the treatment as well as on the other occasions. Her struggle back into life was something frightful to see and hear. However, the action of both heart and lungs improved, and Van Helsing made a subcutaneous injection of morphia, as before, and with good effect. Her faint became a profound slumber. The Professor watched whilst I went downstairs with Quincey Morris, and sent one of the maids to pay off one of the cabmen who were waiting. I left Quincey lying down after having a glass of wine, and told the cook to get ready a good breakfast. Then a thought struck me, and I went back to the room where Lucy now was. When I came softly in, I found Van Helsing with a sheet or two of notepaper in his hand. He had evidently read it, and was thinking it over as he sat with his hand to his brow. There was a look of grim satisfaction in his face, as of one who has had a doubt solved. He handed me the paper, saying only: 'It dropped from Lucy's breast when we carried her to the bath.'

When I had read it, I stood looking at the Professor, and after a pause asked him: 'In God's name, what does it all mean? Was she, or is she, mad: or what sort of horrible danger is it?' I was so bewildered that I did not know what to say more. Van Helsing put out his hand and took the paper, saying: –

'Do not trouble about it now. Forget it for the present. You shall know and understand it all in good time; but it will be later. And now what is it that you came to me to say?' This brought me back to fact, and I was all myself again.

'I came to speak about the certificate of death. If we do not act properly and wisely, there may be an inquest, and that paper would have to be produced. I am in hopes that we need have no inquest, for if we had it would surely kill poor Lucy, if nothing else did. I know, and you know, and the other doctor who attended her knows, that Mrs Westenra had disease of the heart, and we can certify that she died of it. Let us fill up the certificate at once, and I shall take it myself to the registrar and go on to the undertaker.'

'Good, oh my friend John! Well thought of! Truly Miss Lucy, if she be sad in the foes that beset her, is at least happy in the friends that love her. One, two, three, all open their veins for her, besides one old man. Ah yes, I know, friend John; I am not blind! I love you all the more for it! Now go.'

In the hall I met Quincey Morris, with a telegram for Arthur telling him that Mrs Westenra was dead; that Lucy also had been ill, but was now going on better; and that Van Helsing and I were with her. I told him where I was going, and he hurried me out, but as I was going said: –

'When you come back, Jack, may I have two words with you all to ourselves?' I nodded in reply and went out. I found no difficulty about the registration, and arranged with the local undertaker to come up in the evening to measure for the coffin and to make arrangements.

When I got back Quincey was waiting for me. I told him I would see him as soon as I knew about Lucy, and went up to her room. She was still sleeping, and the Professor seemingly had not moved from his seat at her side. From his putting his finger to his lips, I gathered that he expected her to wake before long and was afraid of forestalling nature. So I went down to Quincey and took him into the breakfast-room, where the blinds were not drawn down, and which was a little more cheerful, or rather less cheerless, than the other rooms. When we were alone, he said to me: –

'Jack Seward, I don't want to shove myself in anywhere where I've no right to be; but this is no ordinary case. You know I loved that girl and wanted to marry her; but, although that's all past and gone, I can't help feeling anxious about her all the same. What is it that's wrong with her? The Dutchman – and a fine old fellow he is; I can see that – said, that time you two came into the room, that you must have *another* transfusion of blood, and that both you and he were exhausted. Now I know well that you medical men speak *in camera*, and that a man must not expect to know what they consult about in private. But this is no common matter, and, whatever it is, I have done my part. Is not that so?'

'That's so,' I said, and he went on: –

'I take it that both you and Van Helsing had done already what I did to-day. Is not that so?'

'That's so.'

'And I guess Art was in it too. When I saw him four days ago down at his own place he looked queer. I have not seen anything pulled down so quick since I was on the Pampas and had a mare that I was fond of go to grass all in a night. One of those big bats that they call vampires had got at her in the night, and, what with his gorge and the vein left open, there wasn't enough blood in her to let her stand up, and I had to put a bullet through her as she lay. Jack, if you may tell me without betraying confidence, Arthur was the first; is not that so?' As he spoke the poor fellow looked terribly anxious. He was in a torture of suspense regarding the woman he loved, and his utter ignorance of the terrible mystery which seemed to surround her intensified his pain. His very heart was bleeding, and it took all the manhood of him – and there was a royal lot of it, too – to keep him from breaking down. I paused before answering, for I felt that I must not betray anything which the Professor wished kept secret, but already he knew so much, and guessed so much, that there could be no reason for not answering, so I answered in the same phrase: 'That's so.'

'And how long has this been going on?'

'About ten days.'

'Ten days! Then I guess, Jack Seward, that that poor pretty creature that we all love has had put into her veins within that time the blood of four strong men. Man alive, her whole body wouldn't hold it.' Then, coming close to me, he spoke in a fierce half-whisper: 'What took it out?'

I shook my head. 'That,' I said, 'is the crux. Van Helsing is simply frantic about it, and I am at my wits' end. I can't even hazard a guess. There has been a series of little circumstances which have thrown out all our calculations as to Lucy being properly watched. But these shall not occur again. Here we stay until all be well – or ill.' Quincey held out his hand.

'Count me in,' he said. 'You and the Dutchman will tell me what to do, and I'll do it.'

When she woke late in the afternoon, Lucy's first movement was to feel in her breast, and, to my surprise, produced the paper which Van Helsing had given me to read. The careful Professor had replaced it where it had come from, lest on waking she should be alarmed. Her eye then lit on Van Helsing and on me too, and gladdened. Then she looked round the room, and seeing where she was, shuddered; she gave a loud cry, and put her poor thin hands before her pale face. We both understood what that meant – that she had realized to the full her mother's death; so we tried what we could to comfort her. Doubtless sympathy eased her somewhat, but she was very low in thought and spirit, and wept silently and weakly for a long time. We told her that either or both of us would now remain with her all the time, and that seemed to comfort her. Towards dusk she fell into a doze. Here a very odd thing occurred. Whilst still asleep she took the paper from her breast and tore it in two. Van Helsing stepped over and took the pieces from her. All the same, however, she went on with the action of tearing, as though the material were still in her hands; finally she lifted her hands and opened them as though scattering the fragments. Van Helsing seemed surprised, and his brows gathered as if in thought, but he said nothing.

19 September. – All last night she slept fitfully, being always afraid to sleep, and something weaker when she woke from it. The Professor and I took it in turns to watch, and we never left her for a moment unattended. Quincey Morris said nothing about his intention, but I knew that all night long he patrolled round and round the house.

When the day came, its searching light showed the ravages in poor Lucy's strength. She was hardly able to turn her head, and the little nourishment which she could take seemed to do her no good. At times she slept, and both Van Helsing and I noticed the difference in her, between sleeping and waking. Whilst asleep she looked stronger, although more haggard, and her breathing was softer; her open mouth showed the pale gums drawn back from the teeth, which thus looked positively longer and sharper than usual; when she woke the softness of her eyes evidently changed the expression, for she looked her own self, although a dying one. In the afternoon she asked for Arthur, and we telegraphed for him. Quincey went off to meet him at the station.

When he arrived it was nearly six o'clock, and the sun was setting full and warm, and the red light streamed in through the window and gave more colour to the pale cheeks. When he saw her, Arthur was simply choked with emotion, and none of us could speak. In the hours that had passed, the fits of sleep, or the comatose condition that passed for it, had grown more frequent, so that the pauses when conversation was possible were shortened. Arthur's presence, however, seemed to act as a stimulant; she rallied a little, and spoke to him more brightly than she had done since we arrived. He too pulled himself together, and spoke as cheerily as he could, so that the best was made of everything.

It is now nearly one o'clock, and he and Van Helsing are sitting with her. I am to relieve them in a quarter of an hour, and I am entering this on Lucy's phonograph. Until six o'clock they are to try to rest. I fear that to-morrow will end our watching, for the shock has been too great; the poor child cannot rally. God help us all.

Letter, Mina Harker to Lucy Westenra
(Unopened by her)

                                                    '*17 September.*

'My dearest Lucy, –

'It seems *an age* since I heard from you, or indeed since I wrote. You will pardon me, I know, for all my faults when you have read all my budget of news. Well, I got my husband back all right; when we arrived at Exeter there was a carriage waiting for us, and in it, though he had an attack of gout, Mr Hawkins. He took us to his own house, where there were rooms for us all nice and comfortable, and we dined together. After dinner Mr Hawkins said: –

'"My dears, I want to drink your health and prosperity; and may every blessing attend you both. I know you both from children, and have, with love and pride, seen you grow up. Now I want you to make your home here with me. I have left to me neither chick nor child; all are gone, and in my will I have left you everything." I cried, Lucy dear, as Jonathan and the old man clasped hands. Our evening was a very, very happy one.

'So here we are, installed in this beautiful old house, and from both my bedroom and drawing-room I can see the great elms of the cathedral close, with their great black stems standing out against the old yellow stone of the cathedral; and I can hear the rooks overhead cawing and cawing and chattering and gossiping all day, after the manner of rooks – and humans. I am busy, I need not tell you, arranging things and house-keeping. Jonathan and Mr Hawkins are busy all day; for, now that Jonathan is a partner, Mr Hawkins wants to tell him all about the clients.

'How is your dear mother getting on? I wish I could run up to town for a day or two to see you, dear, but I dare not go yet, with so much on my shoulders; and Jonathan wants looking after still. He is beginning to put some flesh on his bones again, but he was terribly weakened by the long illness; even now he sometimes starts out of his sleep in a sudden way and awakes all trembling until I can coax him back to his usual placidity. However, thank God, these occasions grow less frequent as the days go on, and they will in time pass away altogether, I trust. And now I have told you my news, let me ask yours. When are you to be married, and where, and who is to perform the ceremony, and what are you to wear, and is it to be a public or a private wedding? Tell me all about it, dear; tell me all about everything, for there is nothing which interests you which will not be dear to me. Jonathan asks me to send his "respectful duty," but I do not think that is good enough from the junior partner of the important firm of Hawkins and Harker; and so, as you love me, and he loves me, and I love you with all the moods and tenses of the verb, I send you simply his "love" instead. Good-bye, my dearest Lucy, and all blessings on you.

'Yours,

'MINA HARKER.'

Report from Patrick Hennessey, M.D., M.R.C.S.,
L.K.Q.C.P.I., etc., etc., to John Seward, M.D.

'20 September.

'My dear Sir, –

'In accordance with your wishes, I enclose report of the conditions of everything left in my charge . . . With regard to patient, Renfield, there is more to say. He has had another outbreak which might have had a dreadful ending, but which, as it fortunately happened, was unattended with any unhappy results. This afternoon a carrier's cart with two men made a call at the empty house whose grounds abut on ours – the house to which, you will .

remember, the patient twice ran away. The men stopped at our gate to ask the porter their way, as they were strangers. I was myself looking out of the study window, having a smoke after dinner, and saw one of them come up to the house. As he passed the window of Renfield's room, the patient began to rate him from within, and called him all the foul names he could lay his tongue to. The man, who seemed a decent fellow enough, contented himself by telling him to "shut up for a foul-mouthed beggar," whereon our man accused him of robbing him and wanting to murder him and said that he would hinder him if he were to swing for it. I opened the window and signed to the man not to notice, so he contented himself after looking the place over and making up his mind as to what kind of place he had got to by saying: "Lor' bless yer, sir, I wouldn't mind what was said to me in a bloomin' madhouse. I pity ye and the guv'nor for havin' to live in the house with a wild beast like that." Then he asked the way civilly enough, and I told him where the gate of the empty house was; he went away, followed by threats and curses and revilings from our man. I went down to see if I could make out any cause for his anger, since he is usually such a well-behaved man, and except his violent fits nothing of the kind had ever occurred. I found him, to my astonishment, quite composed and most genial in his manner. I tried to get him to talk of the incident, but he blandly asked me questions as to what I meant, and led me to believe that he was completely oblivious of the affair. It was, I am sorry to say, however, only another instance of his cunning, for within half an hour I heard of him again. This time he had broken out through the window of his room, and was running down the avenue. I called to the attendants to follow me, and ran after him, for I feared he was intent on some mischief. My fear was justified when I saw the same cart which had passed before coming down the road, having on it some great wooden boxes. The men were wiping their foreheads, and were flushed in the face, as if with violent exercise. Before I could get up to him the patient rushed at them, and pulling one of them off the cart, began to knock his head against the ground. If I had not seized him just at the moment I believe he would have killed the man there and then. The other fellow jumped down and struck him over the head with the butt-end of his heavy whip. It was a terrible blow; but he did not seem to mind it, but seized him also, and struggled with the three of us, pulling us to and fro as if we were kittens. You know I am no light weight, and the others were both burly men. At first he was silent in his fighting; but as we began to master him, and the attendants were putting a strait-waistcoat on him, he began to shout: "I'll frustrate them! They shan't rob me! they shan't murder me by inches! I'll fight for my Lord and Master!" and all sorts of similar incoherent ravings. It was with very considerable difficulty that they got him back to the house and put him in the padded room. One of the attendants, Hardy, had a finger broken. However, I set it all right; and he is going on well.

'The two carriers were at first loud in their threats of actions for damages, and promised to rain all the penalties of the law on us. Their threats were, however, mingled with some sort of indirect apology for the defeat of the two of them by a feeble madman. They said that if it had not been for the way their strength had been spent in carrying and raising the heavy boxes to the cart they would have made short work of him. They gave as another reason for their defeat the extraordinary state of drouth to which they had been reduced by the dusty nature of their occupation and the reprehensible distance from the scene of their labours of any place of public entertainment. I quite understood their drift, and after a stiff glass of grog, or rather more of the same, and with each a sovereign in hand, they made light of the attack, and swore that they would encounter a worse madman any day for the pleasure of meeting so "bloomin' good a bloke" as your correspondent. I took their names and addresses, in case they might be needed. They are as follows: – Jack Smollet, of Dudding's Rents, King George's Road, Great Walworth, and Thomas Snelling, Peter Parley's Row, Guide Court, Bethnal Green. They are both in the employment of Harris & Sons, Moving and Shipment Company, Orange Master's Yard, Soho.

'I shall report to you any matter of interest occurring here, and shall wire you at once if there is anything of importance.

'Believe me, dear Sir,
'Yours faithfully,
'PATRICK HENNESSEY.'

Letter, Mina Harker to Lucy Westenra
(Unopened by her)

'*18 September.*

'My dearest Lucy, –

'Such a sad blow has befallen us. Mr Hawkins has died very suddenly. Some may not think it so sad for us, but we had both come to so love him that it really seems as though we had lost a father. I never knew either father or mother, so that the dear old man's death is a real blow to me. Jonathan is greatly distressed. It is not only that he feels sorrow, deep sorrow, for the dear, good man who has befriended him all his life, and now at the end has treated him like his own son and left him a fortune which to people of our modest bringing up is wealth beyond the dream of avarice, but Jonathan feels it on another account. He says the amount of responsibility which it puts upon him makes him nervous. He begins to doubt himself. I try to cheer him up, and *my* belief in *him* helps him to have a belief in himself. But it is here that the grave shock that he experienced tells upon him the most. Oh, it is too hard that a sweet, simple, noble, strong nature such as his – a nature which enabled him, by our dear, good friend's aid, to rise from clerk to master in a few years – should be so injured that the very essence of its strength is gone. Forgive me, dear, if I worry you with my troubles in the midst of your own happiness; but, Lucy dear, I must tell someone, for the strain of keeping up a brave and cheerful appearance to Jonathan tries me, and I have no one here that I can confide in. I dread coming up to London, as we must do the day after to-morrow; for poor Mr Hawkins left in his will that he was to be buried in the grave with his father. As there are no relations at all, Jonathan will have to be chief mourner. I shall try to run over to see you, dearest, if only for a few minutes. Forgive me for troubling you. With all blessings,

'Your loving
'MINA HARKER.'

DR SEWARD'S DIARY

20 September. – Only resolution and habit can let me make an entry to-night. I am too miserable, too low-spirited, too sick of the world and all in it, including life itself, that I would not care if I heard this moment the flapping of the wings of the angel of death. And he has been flapping those wings to some purpose of late – Lucy's mother and Arthur's father, and now . . . Let me get on with my work.

I duly relieved Van Helsing in his watch over Lucy. We wanted Arthur to go to rest also, but he refused at first. It was only when I told him that we should want him to help us during the day, and that we must not all break down for want of rest, lest Lucy should suffer, that he agreed to go. Van Helsing was very kind to him. 'Come, my child,' he said; 'come with me. You are sick and weak, and have had much sorrow and much mental pain, as well as that tax on your strength that we know of. You must not be alone; for to be alone is to be full of fears and alarms. Come to the drawing-room, where there is a big fire, and there are two sofas. You shall lie on one, and I on the other, and our sympathy will be comfort to each other, even though we do not speak, and even if we sleep.' Arthur went off with him, casting back a longing look on Lucy's face, which lay on her pillow, almost whiter than the lawn. She lay quite still, and I looked round the room to see that all was as it should be. I could see that the Professor had carried out in this room, as in the other, his purpose of using the garlic; the whole of the window-sashes reeked with it, and round Lucy's neck, over the silk handkerchief which Van Helsing made her keep on, was a rough chaplet of the same odorous flowers. Lucy was breathing somewhat stertorously, and her face was at its worst, for the open mouth showed the pale gums. Her teeth, in the dim, uncertain light, seemed longer and sharper than they had been in the morning. In particular, by some trick of the light, the canine teeth looked longer and sharper than the rest. I sat down by her, and presently she moved uneasily. At the same moment there came a sort of dull flapping or buffeting at the window. I went over to it softly, and peeped out by the corner of the blind. There was a full moonlight, and I could see that the noise was made by a great bat, which wheeled round – doubtless attracted by the light, although so dim – and every now and again struck the window with its wings. When I came back to my seat I found that Lucy had moved slightly, and had torn away the garlic flowers from her throat. I replaced them as well as I could, and sat watching her.

Presently she woke, and I gave her food, as Van Helsing had prescribed. She took but a little, and that languidly. There did not seem to be with her now the unconscious struggle for life and strength that had hitherto so marked her illness. It struck me as curious that the moment she became conscious she pressed the garlic flowers close to her. It was certainly odd that whenever she got into that lethargic state, with the stertorous breathing, she put the flowers from her; but that when she waked she clutched them close. There was no possibility of making any mistake about this, for in the long hours that followed, she had many spells of sleeping and waking, and repeated both actions many times.

At six o'clock Van Helsing came to relieve me. Arthur had then fallen into a doze, and he mercifully let him sleep on. When he saw Lucy's face I could hear the hissing indraw of his breath, and he said to me in a sharp whisper: 'Draw up the blind; I want light!' Then he bent down, and, with his face almost touching Lucy's, examined her carefully. He removed the flowers and lifted the silk handkerchief from her throat. As he did so he started back, and I could hear his ejaculation, 'Mein Gott!' as it was smothered in his throat. I bent over and looked too, and as I noticed some queer chill came over me.

The wounds on the throat had absolutely disappeared.

For fully five minutes Van Helsing stood looking at her, with his face at its sternest. Then he turned to me and said calmly: –

'She is dying. It will not be long now. It will be much difference, mark me, whether she dies conscious or in her sleep. Wake that poor boy, and let him come and see the last; he trusts us, and we have promised him.'

I went to the dining-room and waked him. He was dazed for a moment, but when he saw the sunlight streaming in through the edges of the shutters he thought he was late, and expressed his fear. I assured him that Lucy was still asleep, but told him as gently as I could that both Van Helsing and I feared that the end was near. He covered his face with his hands, and slid down on his knees by the sofa, where he remained, perhaps a minute, with his head buried, praying, whilst his shoulders shook with grief. I took him by the hand and raised him up. 'Come,' I said, 'my dear old fellow, summon all your fortitude; it will be best and easiest for *her*.'

When we came into Lucy's room I could see that Van Helsing had, with his usual forethought, been putting matters straight and making everything look as pleasing as possible. He had even brushed Lucy's hair, so that it lay on the pillow in its usual shiny ripples. When we came into the room she opened her eyes, and seeing him, whispered softly: –

'Arthur! Oh, my love, I am so glad you have come!' He was stooping to kiss her, when Van Helsing motioned him back. 'No,' he whispered, 'not yet! Hold her hand: it will comfort her more.'

So Arthur took her hand and knelt beside her, and she looked her best, with all the soft lines matching the angelic beauty of her eyes. Then gradually her eyes closed, and she sank to sleep. For a little bit her breast heaved softly, and her breath came and went like a tired child's.

And then insensibly there came the strange change which I had noticed in the night. Her breathing grew stertorous, the mouth opened, and the pale gums, drawn back, made the teeth look longer and sharper than ever. In a sort of sleep-waking, vague, unconscious way she opened her eyes, which were now dull and hard at once, and said in a soft voluptuous voice, such as I had never heard from her lips: –

'Arthur! Oh, my love, I am so glad you have come! Kiss me!' Arthur bent eagerly over to kiss her; but at that instant Van Helsing, who, like me, had been startled by her voice, swooped upon him, and catching him by the neck with both hands, dragged him back with a fury of strength which I never thought he could have possessed, and actually hurled him almost across the room.

'Not for your life!' he said; 'not for your living soul and hers!' And he stood between them like a lion at bay.

Arthur was so taken aback that he did not for a moment know what to do or say; and before any impulse of violence could seize him he realized the place and the occasion, and he stood silent, waiting.

I kept my eyes fixed on Lucy, as did Van Helsing, and we saw a spasm as of rage flit like a shadow over her face; the sharp teeth champed together. Then her eyes closed, and she breathed heavily.

Very shortly after she opened her eyes in all their softness, and putting out her poor pale, thin hand, took Van Helsing's great brown one; drawing it to her, she kissed it. 'My true friend,' she said, in a faint voice, but with untellable pathos, 'my true friend, and his! Oh, guard him, and give him peace!'

'I swear it!' said he solemnly, kneeling beside her and holding up his hand, as one who registers an oath. Then he turned to Arthur, and said to him: 'Come, my child, take her hand in yours, and kiss her on the forehead, and only once.'

Their eyes met instead of their lips; and so they parted.

Lucy's eyes closed; and Van Helsing, who had been watching closely, took Arthur's arm, and drew him away.

And then Lucy's breathing became stertorous again, and all at once it ceased.

'It is all over,' said Van Helsing. 'She is dead!'

I took Arthur by the arm, and led him away to the drawing-room, where he sat down, and covered his face with his hands sobbing in a way that nearly broke me down to see.

I went back to the room, and found Van Helsing looking at poor Lucy, and his face was sterner than ever. Some change had come over her body. Death had given back part of her beauty, for her brow and cheeks had recovered some of their flowing lines; even the lips had lost their deadly pallor. It was as if the blood, no longer needed for the working of the heart, had gone to make the harshness of death as little rude as might be.

> 'We thought her dying whilst she slept
> And sleeping when she died.'

I stood beside Van Helsing, and said: –

'Ah, well, poor girl, there is peace for her at last. It is the end!'

He turned to me, and said with grave solemnity: –

'Not so! alas! not so. It is only the beginning!'

When I asked him what he meant, he only shook his head and answered: –

'We can do nothing as yet. Wait and see.'

CHAPTER 13

DR SEWARD'S DIARY

(CONTINUED)

The funeral was arranged for the next succeeding day, so that Lucy and her mother might be buried together. I attended to all the ghastly formalities, and the urbane undertaker proved that his staff were afflicted – or blessed – with something of his own obsequious suavity. Even the woman who performed the last offices for the dead remarked to me, in a confidential, brother-professional way, when she had come out from the death-chamber: –

'She makes a very beautiful corpse, sir. It's quite a privilege to attend on her. It's not too much to say that she will do credit to our establishment!'

I noticed that Van Helsing never kept far away. This was possible from the disordered state of things in the household. There were no relatives at hand; and as Arthur had to be back the next day to attend at his father's funeral, we were unable to notify anyone who should have been bidden. Under the circumstances, Van Helsing and I took it upon ourselves to examine papers, etc. He insisted upon looking over Lucy's papers himself. I asked him why, for I feared that he, being a foreigner, might not be quite aware of English legal requirements, and so might in ignorance make some unnecessary trouble. He answered me:

'I know; I know. You forget that I am a lawyer as well as a doctor. But this is not altogether for the law. You knew that, when you avoided the coroner. I have more than him to avoid. There may be papers more – such as this.'

As he spoke he took from his pocket-book the memorandum which had been in Lucy's breast, and which she had torn in her sleep.

'When you find anything of the solicitor who is for the late Mrs Westenra, seal all her papers, and write him to-night. For me, I watch here in the room and in Miss Lucy's old room all night, and I myself search for what may be. It is not well that her very thoughts go into the hands of strangers.'

I went on with my part of the work, and in another half-hour had found the name and address of Mrs Westenra's solicitor and had written to him. All the poor lady's papers were in order; explicit directions regarding the place of burial were given. I had hardly sealed the letter, when, to my surprise, Van Helsing walked into the room, saying: –

'Can I help you, friend John? I am free, and if I may, my service is to you.'

'Have you got what you looked for?' I asked, to which he replied: –

'I did not look for any specific thing. I only hoped to find, and find I have, all that there was – only some letters and a few memoranda, and a diary new begun. But I have them here, and we shall for the present say nothing of them. I shall see that poor lad to-morrow evening, and, with his sanction, I shall use some.'

When we had finished the work in hand, he said to me: –

'And now, friend John, I think we may to bed. We want sleep, both you and I, and rest to recuperate. To-morrow we shall have much to do, but for the to-night there is no need of us. Alas!'

Before turning in we went to look at poor Lucy. The undertaker had certainly done his work well, for the room was turned into a small *chapelle ardente*. There was a wilderness of beautiful white flowers, and death was made as little repulsive as might be. The end of the winding-sheet was laid over the face; when the Professor bent over and turned it gently back, we both started at the beauty before us, the tall wax candles showing a sufficient light to note it well. All Lucy's loveliness had come back to her in death, and the hours that had passed, instead of leaving traces of 'decay's effacing fingers,' had but restored the beauty of life, till positively I could not believe my eyes that I was looking at a corpse.

The Professor looked sternly grave. He had not loved her as I had, and there was no need for tears in his eyes. He said to me: 'Remain till I return,' and left the room. He came back with a handful of wild garlic from the box waiting in the hall, but which had not been opened, and placed the flowers amongst the others on and around the bed. Then he took from his neck, inside his collar, a little golden crucifix, and placed it over the mouth. He restored the sheet to its place, and we came away.

I was undressing in my own room, when, with a premonitory tap at the door, he entered, and at once began to speak: –

'To-morrow I want you to bring me, before night, a set of post-mortem knives.'

'Must we make an autopsy?' I asked.

'Yes, and no. I want to operate, but not as you think. Let me tell you now, but not a word to another. I want to cut off her head and take out her heart. Ah! you a surgeon, and so shocked! You, whom I have seen with no tremble of hand or heart, do operations of life and death that make the rest shudder. Oh, but I must not forget, my dear friend John, that you loved her; and I have not forgotten it, for it is I that shall operate, and you must only help. I would like to do it to-night, but for Arthur I must not; he will be free after his father's funeral to-morrow, and he will want to see her – to see it. Then, when she is coffined ready for the next day, you and I shall come when all sleep. We shall unscrew the coffin-lid, and shall do our operation; and then replace all, so that none know, save we alone.'

'But why do it at all? The girl is dead. Why mutilate her poor body without need? And if there is no necessity for a post-mortem and nothing to gain by it – no good to her, to us, to science, to human knowledge – why do it? Without such it is monstrous.'

For answer he put his hand on my shoulder, and said, with infinite tenderness: –

'Friend John, I pity your poor bleeding heart; and I love you the more because it does so bleed. If I could, I would take on myself the burden that you do bear. But there are things that you know not, but that you shall know, and bless me for knowing, though they are not pleasant things. John, my child, you have been my friend now many years, and yet did you ever know me to do any without good cause? I may err – I am but man; but I believe in all I do. Was it not for these causes that you send for me when the great trouble came? Yes! Were you not amazed, nay horrified, when I would not let Arthur kiss his love – though she was dying – and snatched him away by all my strength? Yes! And yet you saw how she thanked me, with her so beautiful dying eyes, her voice, too, so weak, and she kiss my rough old hand and bless me? Yes! and did you not hear me swear promise to her, that so she closed her eyes grateful? Yes!

'Well, I have good reason now for all I want to do. You have for many years trust me; you have believe me weeks past, when there be things so strange that you might have well doubt. Believe me yet a little, friend John. If you trust me not, then I must tell what I think; and that is not perhaps well. And if I work – as work I shall, no matter trust or no trust – without my friend trust in me, I work with heavy heart, and feel, oh! so lonely when I want all help and courage that may be!' He paused a moment, and went on solemnly: 'Friend John, there are strange and terrible days before us. Let us not be two, but one, that so we work to a good end. Will you not have faith in me?'

I took his hand, and promised him. I held my door open as he went away, and watched him go into his room and close the door. As I stood without moving, I saw one of the maids pass silently along the passage –

she had her back towards me, so did not see me – and go into the room
where Lucy lay. The sight touched me. Devotion is so rare, and we are
so grateful to those who show it unasked to those we love. Here was a
poor girl putting aside the terrors which she naturally had of death to go
watch alone by the bier of the mistress whom she loved, so that the poor
clay might not be lonely till laid to eternal rest . . .

I must have slept long and soundly, for it was broad daylight when Van
Helsing waked me by coming into my room. He came over to my bedside
and said: –

'You need not trouble about the knives; we shall not do it.'

'Why not?' I asked. For his solemnity of the night before had greatly
impressed me.

'Because,' he said sternly, 'it is too late – or too early. See!' Here he
held up the little golden crucifix. 'This was stolen in the night.'

'How stolen,' I asked in wonder, 'since you have it now?'

'Because I get it back from the worthless wretch who stole it, from the
woman who robbed the dead and the living. Her punishment will surely
come, but not through me; she knew not altogether what she did, and thus
unknowing, she only stole. Now we must wait.'

He went away on the word, leaving me with a new mystery to think
of, a new puzzle to grapple with.

The forenoon was a dreary time, but at noon the solicitor came: Mr
Marquand, of Wholeman, Sons, Marquand and Lidderdale. He was very
genial and very appreciative of what we had done, and took off our hands
all cares as to details. During lunch he told us that Mrs Westenra had for
some time expected sudden death from her heart, and had put her affairs
in absolute order; he informed us that, with the exception of a certain
entailed property of Lucy's father which now, in default of direct issue,
went back to a distant branch of the family, the whole estate, real and
personal, was left absolutely to Arthur Holmwood. When he had told us
so much he went on: –

'Frankly we did our best to prevent such a testamentary disposition,
and pointed out certain contingencies that might leave her daughter either
penniless or not so free as she should be to act regarding a matrimonial
alliance. Indeed, we pressed the matter so far that we almost came into
collision, for she asked us if we were or were not prepared to carry out
her wishes. Of course, we had then no alternative but to accept. We were
right in principle, and ninety-nine times out of a hundred we should have
proved, by the logic of events, the accuracy of our judgment. Frankly,
however, I must admit that in this case any other form of disposition would

have rendered impossible the carrying out of her wishes. For by her prede-ceasing her daughter the latter would have come into possession of the property, and, even had she only survived her mother by five minutes, her property would, in case there were no will – and a will was a practical impossibility in such a case – have been treated at her decease as under intestacy. In which case, Lord Godalming, though so dear a friend, would have had no claim in the world; and the inheritors, being remote, would not be likely to abandon their just rights for sentimental reasons regarding an entire stranger. I assure you, my dear sirs, I am rejoiced at the result, perfectly rejoiced.'

He was a good fellow, but his rejoicing at the one little part – in which he was officially interested – of so great a tragedy was an object-lesson in the limitations of sympathetic understanding.

He did not remain long, but said he would look in later in the day and see Lord Godalming. His coming, however, had been a certain comfort to us, since it assured us that we should not have to dread hostile criticism as to any of our acts. Arthur was expected at five o'clock, so a little before that time we visited the death-chamber. It was so in very truth, for now both mother and daughter lay in it. The undertaker, true to his craft, had made the best display he could of his goods, and there was a mortuary air about the place that lowered our spirits at once. Van Helsing ordered the former arrangement to be adhered to, explaining that, as Lord Godalming was coming very soon, it would be less harrowing to his feel-ings to see all that was left of his *Wancé* quite alone. The undertaker seemed shocked at his own stupidity, and exerted himself to restore things to the condition in which we left them the night before, so that when Arthur came such shocks to his feelings as we could avoid were saved.

Poor fellow! He looked desperately sad and broken; even his stalwart manhood seemed to have shrunk somewhat under the strain of his much-tried emotions. He had, I knew, been very genuinely and devotedly attached to his father; and to lose him, and at such a time, was a bitter blow to him. With me he was warm as ever, and to Van Helsing he was sweetly courteous; but I could not help seeing that there was some constraint with him. The Professor noticed it, too, and motioned me to bring him upstairs. I did so, and left him at the door of the room, as I felt he would like to be quite alone with her; but he took my arm and led me in, saying huskily: –

'You loved her too, old fellow; she told me all about it, and there was no friend had a closer place in her heart than you. I don't know how to thank you for all you have done for her. I can't think yet . . .'

Here he suddenly broke down, and threw his arms round my shoulders
and laid his head on my breast, crying: –

'Oh, Jack, Jack! What shall I do? The whole of life seems gone from
me all at once, and there is nothing in the wide world for me to live for.'

I comforted him as well as I could. In such cases men do not need
much expression. A grip of the hand, the tightening of an arm over the
shoulder, a sob in unison, are expressions of sympathy dear to a man's
heart. I stood still and silent till his sobs died away, and then I said softly
to him: –

'Come and look at her.'

Together we moved over to the bed, and I lifted the lawn from her face.
God! how beautiful she was. Every hour seemed to be enhancing her loveliness. It frightened and amazed me somewhat; and as for Arthur, he fell
a-trembling, and finally was shaken with doubt as with an ague. At last,
after a long pause, he said to me in a faint whisper: –

'Jack, is she really dead?'

I assured him sadly that it was so, and went on to suggest – for I felt
that such a horrible doubt should not have life for a moment longer than
I could help – that it often happened that after death faces became softened and even resolved into their youthful beauty; that this was especially
so when death had been preceded by any acute or prolonged suffering. It
seemed to quite do away with any doubt, and, after kneeling beside the
couch for a while and looking at her lovingly and long, he turned aside.
I told him that that must be good-bye, as the coffin had to be prepared;
so he went back and took her dead hand in his and kissed it, and bent
over and kissed her forehead. He came away, fondly looking back over
his shoulder at her as he came.

I left him in the drawing-room, and told Van Helsing that he had
said good-bye; so the latter went to the kitchen to tell the undertaker's
men to proceed with the preparations and to screw up the coffin. When
he came out of the room again I told him of Arthur's question, and he
replied: –

'I am not surprised. Just now I doubted for a moment myself!'

We all dined together, and I could see that poor Art was trying to make
the best of things. Van Helsing had been silent all dinner-time, but when
we had lit our cigars he said: –

'Lord –'; but Arthur interrupted him: –

'No, no, not that, for God's sake! not yet at any rate. Forgive me, sir:
I did not mean to speak offensively; it is only because my loss is so recent.'

The Professor answered very sweetly: –

'I only used that name because I was in doubt. I must not call you "Mr," and I have grown to love you – yes, my dear boy, to love you – as Arthur.'

Arthur held out his hand, and took the old man's warmly.

'Call me what you will,' he said. 'I hope I may always have the title of a friend. And let me say that I am at a loss for words to thank you for your goodness to my poor dear.' He paused a moment, and went on: 'I know that she understood your goodness even better than I do; and if I was rude or in any way wanting at that time you acted so – you remember' – the Professor nodded – 'you must forgive me.'

He answered with a grave kindness: –

'I know it was hard for you to quite trust me then, for to trust such violence needs to understand; and I take it that you do not – that you cannot – trust me now, for you do not yet understand. And there may be more times when I shall want you to trust when you cannot – and may not – and must not yet understand. But the time will come when your trust shall be whole and complete in me, and when you shall understand as though the sunlight himself shone through. Then you shall bless me from first to last for your own sake, and for the sake of others, and for her dear sake to whom I swore to protect.'

'And, indeed, indeed, sir,' said Arthur warmly, 'I shall in all ways trust you. I know and believe you have a very noble heart, and you are Jack's friend, and you were hers. You shall do what you like.'

The Professor cleared his throat a couple of times, as though about to speak, and finally said: –

'May I ask you something now?'

'Certainly.'

'You know that Mrs Westenra left you all her property?'

'No, poor dear; I never thought of it.'

'And as it is all yours, you have a right to deal with it as you will. I want you to give me permission to read all Miss Lucy's papers and letters. Believe me, it is no idle curiosity. I have a motive of which, be sure, she would have approved. I have them all here. I took them before we knew that all was yours, so that no strange hand might touch them – no strange eye look through words into her soul. I shall keep them, if I may; even you may not see them yet, but I shall keep them safe. No word shall be lost; and in the good time I shall give them back to you. It's a hard thing I ask, but you will do it, will you not, for Lucy's sake?'

Arthur spoke out heartily, like his old self: –

'Dr Van Helsing, you may do what you will. I feel that in saying this

I am doing what my dear one would have approved. I shall not trouble you with questions till the time comes.'

The old Professor stood up as he said solemnly: –

'And you are right. There will be pain for us all; but it will not be all pain, nor will this pain be the last. We and you too – you most of all, my dear boy – will have to pass through the bitter water before we reach the sweet. But we must be brave of heart and unselfish, and do our duty, and all will be well!'

I slept on a sofa in Arthur's room that night. Van Helsing did not go to bed at all. He went to and fro, as if patrolling the house, and was never out of sight of the room where Lucy lay in her coffin, strewn with the wild garlic flowers, which sent, through the odour of lily and rose, a heavy, overpowering smell into the night.

MINA HARKER'S JOURNAL

22 September. – In the train to Exeter. Jonathan sleeping. It seems only yesterday that the last entry was made, and yet how much between them, in Whitby and all the world before me, Jonathan away and no news of him; and now, married to Jonathan, Jonathan a solicitor, a partner, rich, master of his business, Mr Hawkins dead and buried, and Jonathan with another attack that may harm him. Some day he may ask me about it. Down it all goes. I am rusty in my shorthand – see what unexpected prosperity does for us – so it may be as well to freshen it up again with an exercise anyhow . . .

The service was very simple and very solemn. There were only ourselves and the servants there, one or two old friends of his from Exeter, his London agent, and a gentleman representing Sir John Paxton, the President of the Incorporated Law Society. Jonathan and I stood hand in hand, and we felt that our best and dearest friend was gone from us . . .

We came back to town quietly, taking a 'bus to Hyde Park Corner. Jonathan thought it would interest me to go into the Row for a while, so we sat down; but there were very few people there, and it was sad-looking and desolate to see so many empty chairs. It made us think of the empty chair at home; so we got up and walked down Piccadilly. Jonathan was holding me by the arm, the way he used to in old days before I went to school. I felt it very improper, for you can't go on for some years teaching etiquette and decorum to other girls without the pedantry of it biting into yourself a bit; but it was Jonathan, and he was my husband, and we didn't know anybody who saw us – and we didn't care if they did – so on we walked. I was looking at a very beautiful girl, in a big cart-wheel hat, sitting in a victoria outside Giuliano's, when I felt Jonathan clutch my arm so tight that he hurt me, and he said under his breath: 'My God!' I am always anxious about Jonathan, for I fear that some nervous fit may upset him again; so I turned to him quickly, and asked him what it was that disturbed him.

He was very pale, and his eyes seemed bulging out as, half in terror and half in amazement, he gazed at a tall, thin man, with a beaky nose and black moustache and pointed beard, who was also observing the pretty girl. He was looking at her so hard that he did not see either of us, and so I had a good view of him. His face was not a good face; it was hard, and cruel, and sensual, and his big white teeth, that looked all the whiter because his lips were so red, were pointed like an animal's. Jonathan kept staring at him, till I was afraid he would notice. I feared he might take it ill, he looked so fierce and nasty. I asked Jonathan why he was disturbed, and he answered, evidently thinking that I knew as much about it as he did: 'Do you see who it is?'

'No, dear,' I said; 'I don't know him; who is it?' His answer seemed to shock and thrill me, for it was said as if he did not know that it was to me, Mina, to whom he was speaking: –

'It is the man himself!'

The poor dear was evidently terrified at something – very greatly terrified; I do believe that if he had not had me to lean on and to support him, he would have sunk down. He kept staring; a man came out of the shop with a small parcel, and gave it to the lady, who then drove off. The dark man kept his eyes fixed on her, and when the carriage moved up Piccadilly he followed in the same direction, and hailed a hansom. Jonathan kept looking after him, and said, as if to himself: –

'I believe it is the Count, but he has grown young. My God, if this be so! Oh, my God! my God! If I only knew! if I only knew!' He was distressing himself so much that I feared to keep his mind on the subject by asking him any questions, so I remained silent. I drew him away quietly, and he, holding my arm, came easily. We walked a little further, and then went in and sat for a while in the Green Park. It was a hot day for autumn, and there was a comfortable seat in a shady place. After a few minutes' staring at nothing, Jonathan's eyes closed, and he went quietly into a sleep, with his head on my shoulder. I thought it was the best thing for him, so did not disturb him. In about twenty minutes he woke up, and said to me quite cheerfully: –

'Why, Mina, have I been asleep? Oh, do forgive me for being so rude. Come, and we'll have a cup of tea somewhere.' He had evidently forgotten all about the dark stranger, as in his illness he had forgotten all that this episode had reminded him of. I don't like this lapsing into forgetfulness; it may make or continue some injury to the brain. I must not ask him, for fear I shall do more harm than good; but I must somehow learn the facts of his journey abroad. The time is come, I fear, when I must open that parcel and know what is written. Oh, Jonathan, you will, I know, forgive me if I do wrong but it is for your own dear sake.

Later. – A sad home-coming in every way – the house empty of the dear soul who was so good to us; Jonathan still pale and dizzy under a slight relapse of his malady; and now a telegram from Van Helsing, whoever he may be: –

'You will be grieved to hear that Mrs Westenra died five days ago, and that Lucy died the day before yesterday. They were both buried to-day.'

Oh, what a wealth of sorrow in a few words! Poor Mrs Westenra! poor Lucy! Gone, gone, never to return to us! And poor, poor Arthur, to have lost such sweetness out of his life! God help us all to bear our troubles.

DR SEWARD'S DIARY

22 September. – It is all over. Arthur has gone back to Ring, and has taken Quincey Morris with him. What a fine fellow is Quincey! I believe in my heart of hearts that he suffered as much about Lucy's death as any of us; but he bore himself through it like a moral Viking. If America can go on breeding men like that, she will be a power in the world indeed. Van Helsing is lying down, having a rest preparatory to his journey. He goes over to Amsterdam to-night, but says he returns to-morrow night; that he only wants to make some arrangements which can only be made person-ally. He is to stop with me then, if he can; he says he has work to do in London which may take him some time. Poor old fellow! I fear that the strain of the past week has broken down even his iron strength. All the time of the burial he was, I could see, putting some terrible restraint on himself. When it was all over, we were standing beside Arthur, who, poor fellow, was speaking of his part in the operation where his blood had been transfused to his Lucy's veins; I could see Van Helsing's face grow white and purple by turns. Arthur was saying that he felt since then as if they two had been really married, and that she was his wife in the sight of God. None of us said a word of the other operations, and none of us ever shall. Arthur and Quincey went away together to the station, and Van Helsing and I came on here. The moment we were alone in the carriage he gave way to a regular fit of hysterics. He has denied to me since that it was hysterics, and insisted that it was only his sense of humour asserting itself under very terrible conditions. He laughed till he cried and I had to draw down the blinds lest anyone should see us and misjudge; and then he cried till he laughed again; and laughed and cried together, just as a woman does. I tried to be stern with him, as one is to a woman under the circumstances; but it had no effect. Men and women are so different in manifestations of nervous strength or weakness! Then when his face grew grave and stern again I asked him why his mirth, and why at such a time. His reply was in a way characteristic of him, for it was logical and forceful and mysterious. He said: –

'Ah, you don't comprehend, friend John. Do not think that I am not sad, though I laugh. See, I have cried even when the laugh did choke me. But no more think that I am all sorry when I cry, for the laugh he come just the same. Keep it always with you that laughter who knock at your door and say: "May I come in?" is not the true laughter. No! he is a king, and he come when and how he like. He ask no person; he choose no time of suitability. He say: "I am here." Behold, in example, I grieve my heart out for that so sweet young girl; I give my blood for her, though I am old and worn; I give my time, my skill, my sleep; I let my other sufferers want that she may have all. And yet I can laugh at her very grave – laugh when the clay from the spade of the sexton drop upon her coffin and say: "Thud! thud!" to my heart, till it send back the blood from my cheek. My heart bleed for that poor boy – that dear boy, so of the age of mine own boy had I been so blessed that he live, and with his hair and eyes the same. There, you know now why I love him so. And yet when he say things that touch my husband-heart to the quick, and make my father-heart yearn to him as to no other man – not even to you, friend John, for we are more level in experiences than father and son – yet even at such moment King Laugh he come to me and shout and bellow in my ear: "Here I am! Here I am!" till the blood come dance back and bring some of the sunshine that he carry with him to my cheek. Oh, friend John, it is a strange world, a sad world, a world full of miseries, and woes, and troubles; and yet when King Laugh come he make them all dance to the tune he play. Bleeding hearts, and dry bones of the churchyard, and tears that burn as they fall – all dance together to the music that he make with that smileless mouth of him. And believe me, friend John, that he is good to come, and kind. Ah, we men and women are like ropes drawn tight with strain that pull us different ways. Then tears come; and, like the rain on the ropes, they brace us up, until perhaps the strain become too great, and we break. But King Laugh he come like the sunshine, and he ease off the strain again; and we bear to go on with our labour, what it may be.'

I did not like to wound him by pretending not to see his idea; but, as I did not yet understand the cause of his laughter, I asked him. As he answered me his face grew stern, and he said in quite a different tone: –

'Oh, it was the grim irony of it all – this so lovely lady garlanded with flowers, that looked so fair as life, till one by one we wondered if she were truly dead; she laid in that so fine marble house in that lonely church-yard, where rest so many of her kin, laid there with the mother who loved her, and whom she loved; and that sacred bell going "Toll! toll! toll!" so sad and slow; and those holy men, with the white garments of the angel, pretending to read books, and yet all the time their eyes never on the page; and all us with the bowed head. And all for what? She is dead; so! Is it not?'

'Well, for the life of me, Professor,' I said, 'I can't see anything to laugh at in all that. Why, your explanation makes it a harder puzzle than before. But even if the burial service was comic, what about poor Art and his trouble? Why, his heart was simply breaking.'

'Just so. Said he not that the transfusion of his blood to her veins had made her truly his bride?'

'Yes, and it was a sweet and comforting idea for him.'

'Quite so. But there was a difficulty, friend John. If so that, then what about the others? Ho, ho! Then this so sweet maid is a polyandrist, and me, with my poor wife dead to me, but alive by Church's law, though no wits, all gone – even I, who am faithful husband to this now-no-wife, am bigamist.'

'I don't see where the joke comes in there either!' I said; and I did not feel particularly pleased with him for saying such things. He laid his hand on my arm, and said: –

'Friend John, forgive me if I pain. I showed not my feeling to others when it would wound, but only to you, my old friend, whom I can trust. If you could have looked into my very heart then when I want to laugh; if you could have done so when the laugh arrived; if you could do so now, when King Laugh have pack up his crown and all that is to him – for he go far, far away from me, and for a long, long time – maybe you would perhaps pity me the most of all.'

I was touched by the tenderness of his tone, and asked why.

'Because I know!'

And now we are all scattered; and for many a long day loneliness will sit over our roofs with brooding wings. Lucy lies in the tomb of her kin, a lordly death-house in a lonely churchyard, away from teeming London; where the air is fresh; and the sun rises over Hampstead Hill, and where wild flowers grow of their own accord.

So I can finish this diary; and God only knows if I shall ever begin another. If I do, or if I ever open this again, it will be to deal with different people and different themes; for here at the end, where the romance of my life is told, ere I go back to take up the thread of my life-work, I say sadly and without hope,

'FINIS'

The 'Westminster Gazette', 25 September
A Hampstead Mystery

The neighbourhood of Hampstead is just at present exercised with a series of events which seem to run on lines parallel to those of what was known to the writers of headlines as 'The Kensington Horror,' or 'The Stabbing Woman,' or 'The Woman in Black.' During the past two or three days several cases have occurred of young children straying from home or neglecting to return from their playing on the Heath. In all these cases the children were too young to give any properly intelligible account of themselves, but the consensus of their excuses is that they had been with a 'bloofer lady.' It has always been late in the evening when they have been missed, and on two occasions the children have not been found until early in the following morning. It is generally supposed in the neighbourhood that, as the first child missed gave as his reason for being away that a 'bloofer lady' had asked him to come for a walk, the others had picked up the phrase and used it as occasion served. This is the more natural as the favourite game of the little ones at present is luring each other away by wiles. A correspondent writes us that to see some of the tiny tots pretending to be the 'bloofer lady' is supremely funny. Some of our caricaturists might, he says, take a lesson in the irony of grotesque by comparing the reality and the picture. It is only in accordance with general principles of human nature that the 'bloofer lady' should be the popular rôle at these *al fresco* performances. Our correspondent naïvely says that even Ellen Terry could not be so winningly attractive as some of these grubby-faced little children pretend – and even imagine themselves – to be.

There is, however, possibly a serious side to the question, for some of the children, indeed all who have been missed at night, have been slightly torn or wounded in the throat. The wounds seem such as might be made by a rat or a small dog, and although of not much importance individually, would tend to show that whatever animal inflicts them has a system or method of its own. The police of the division have been instructed to keep a sharp lookout for straying children, especially when very young, in and around Hampstead Heath, and for any stray dog which may be about.

The 'Westminster Gazette', 25 September
Extra Special
THE HAMPSTEAD HORROR
Another Child Injured
The 'Bloofer Lady'

We have just received intelligence that another child, missed last night, was only discovered late in the morning under a furze bush at the Shooter's Hill side of Hampstead Heath, which is, perhaps, less frequented than the other parts. It has the same tiny wound in the throat as has been noticed in other cases. It was terribly weak, and looked quite emaciated. It too, when partially restored, had the common story to tell of being lured away by the 'bloofer lady.'

CHAPTER 14

MINA HARKER'S JOURNAL

23 September. – Jonathan is better after a bad night. I am so glad that he has plenty of work to do, for that keeps his mind off the terrible things; and oh, I am rejoiced that he is not now weighed down with the responsibility of his new position. I knew he would be true to himself, and now how proud I am to see my Jonathan rising to the height of his advancement and keeping pace in all ways with the duties that come upon him. He will be away all day till late, for he said he could not lunch at home. My household work is done, so I shall take his foreign journal, and lock myself up in my room and read it . . .

24 September. – I hadn't the heart to write last night; that terrible record of Jonathan's upset me so. Poor dear! How he must have suffered, whether it be true or only imagination. I wonder if there is any truth in it at all. Did he get his brain fever, and then write all those terrible things; or had he some cause for it all? I suppose I shall never know, for I dare not open the subject to him . . . And yet that man we saw yesterday! He seemed quite certain of him . . . Poor fellow! I suppose it was the funeral upset him and sent his mind back on some train of thought . . . He believes it all himself. I remember how on our wedding-day he said: 'Unless some solemn duty come upon me to go back to the bitter hours, asleep or awake, mad or sane.' There seems to be through it all some thread of continuity . . . That fearful Count was coming to London . . . If it should be, and he came to London, with its teeming millions . . . There may be a solemn duty; and if it come we must not shrink from it . . . I shall be prepared. I shall get my typewriter this very hour and begin transcribing. Then we shall be ready for other eyes if required. And if it be wanted, then, perhaps, if I am ready, poor Jonathan may not be upset, for I can speak for him and never let him be troubled or worried with it all. If ever Jonathan quite gets over the nervousness he may want to tell me of it all, and I can ask him questions and find out things, and see how I may comfort him.

Letter, Van Helsing to Mrs Harker

'*24 September.*
(*Confidence.*)

'Dear Madam,

'I pray you to pardon my writing, in that I am so far friend as that I send to you sad news of Miss Lucy Westenra's death. By the kindness of Lord Godalming, I am empowered to read her letters and papers, for I am deeply concerned about certain matters vitally important. In them I find some letters from you, which show how great friends you were and how you love her. Oh, Madam Mina, by that love, I implore you, help me. It is for others' good that I ask – to redress great wrong, and to lift much and terrible troubles – that may be more great than you can know. May it be that I see you? You can trust me. I am a friend of Dr John Seward and of Lord Godalming (that was Arthur of Miss Lucy). I must keep it private for the present from all. I should come to Exeter to see you at once if you tell me I am privilege to come, and where and when. I implore your pardon, madam. I have read your letters to poor Lucy, and know how good you are and how your husband suffer; so I pray you, if it may be, enlighten him not, lest it may harm. Again your pardon, and forgive me.

'VAN HELSING.'

Telegram, Mrs Harker to Van Helsing

'*25 September.* – Come to-day by quarter-past ten train if you can catch it. Can see you any time you call.

'WILHELMINA HARKER.'

MINA HARKER'S JOURNAL

25 September. – I cannot help feeling terribly excited as the time draws near for the visit of Dr Van Helsing, for somehow I expect it will throw some light upon Jonathan's sad experience; and as he attended poor dear Lucy in her last illness, he can tell me all about her. That is the reason of his coming; it is concerning Lucy and her sleep-walking, and not about

Jonathan. Then I shall never know the real truth now! How silly I am.
That awful journal gets hold of my imagination and tinges everything with
something of its own colour. Of course it is about Lucy. That habit came
back to the poor dear, and that awful night on the cliff must have made
her ill. I had almost forgotten in my own affairs how ill she was afterwards. She must have told him of her sleep-walking adventure on the cliff,
and that I knew all about it; and now he wants me to tell him about it, so
that he may understand. I hope I did right in not saying anything of it to
Mrs Westenra; I should never forgive myself if any act of mine, were it
even a negative one, brought harm on poor dear Lucy. I hope, too, Dr Van
Helsing will not blame me; I have had so much trouble and anxiety of
late that I feel I cannot bear more just at present.

I suppose a cry does us all good at times – clears the air as other rain
does. Perhaps it was reading the journal yesterday that upset me, and then
Jonathan went away this morning to stay away from me a whole day and
night, the first time we have been parted since our marriage. I do hope
the dear fellow will take care of himself, and that nothing will occur to
upset him. It is two o'clock and the doctor will be here soon now. I shall
say nothing of Jonathan's journal unless he asks me. I am so glad I have
typewritten out my own journal, so that, in case he asks about Lucy, I can
hand it to him; it will save much questioning.

Later. – He has come and gone. Oh, what a strange meeting, and how
it all makes my head whirl round! I feel like one in a dream. Can it be
all possible, or even a part of it? If I had not read Jonathan's journal first,
I should never have accepted even a possibility. Poor, poor, dear Jonathan!
How he must have suffered. Please the good God all this may not upset
him again. I shall try to save him from it; but it may be even a consolation and a help to him – terrible though it be and awful in its consequences
– to know for certain that his eyes and ears and brain did not deceive him,
and that it is all true. It may be that it is the doubt which haunts him; that
when the doubt is removed, no matter which – waking or dreaming – may
prove the truth, he will be more satisfied and better able to bear the shock.
Dr Van Helsing must be a good man as well as a clever one if he is Arthur's
friend and Dr Seward's, and if they brought him all the way from Holland
to look after Lucy. I feel from having seen him that he *is* good and kind
and of a noble nature. When he comes to-morrow I shall ask him about
Jonathan; and then, please God, all this sorrow and anxiety may lead to
a good end. I used to think I would like to practise interviewing; Jonathan's
friend on the *Exeter News* told him that memory was everything in such
work – that you must be able to put down exactly almost every word

spoken, even if you had to refine some of it afterwards. Here was a rare interview; I shall try to record it *verbatim*.

It was half-past two o'clock when the knock came. I took my courage *à deux mains* and waited. In a few minutes Mary opened the door, and announced 'Dr Van Helsing.'

I rose and bowed, and he came towards me; a man of medium height, strongly built, with his shoulders set back over a broad, deep chest and a neck well balanced on the trunk as the head is on the neck. The poise of the head strikes one at once as indicative of thought and power; the head is noble, well-sized, broad, and large behind the ears. The face, clean-shaven, shows a hard, square chin, a large, resolute, mobile mouth, a good-sized nose, rather straight, but with quick, sensitive nostrils, that seem to broaden as the big, bushy eyebrows come down and the mouth tightens. The forehead is broad and fine, rising at first almost straight and then sloping back above two bumps or ridges wide apart; such a forehead that the reddish hair cannot possibly tumble over it, but falls naturally back and to the sides. Big, dark blue eyes are set widely apart, and are quick and tender or stern with the man's moods. He said to me: –

'Mrs Harker, is it not?' I bowed assent.

'That was Miss Mina Murray?' Again I assented.

'It is Mina Murray that I came to see, that was friend of that poor dear child Lucy Westenra. Madam Mina, it is on account of the dead I come.'

'Sir,' I said, 'you could have no better claim on me than that you were a friend and helper of Lucy Westenra.' And I held out my hand. He took it and said tenderly: –

'Oh, Madam Mina, I knew that the friend of that poor lily girl must be good, but I had yet to learn –' He finished his speech with a courtly bow. I asked him what it was that he wanted to see me about, so he at once began: –

'I have read your letters to Miss Lucy. Forgive me, but I had to begin to inquire somewhere, and there was none to ask. I know that you were with her at Whitby. She sometimes kept a diary – you need not look surprised, Madam Mina; it was begun after you left, and was made in imitation of you – and in that diary she traces by inference certain things to a sleep-walking in which she puts down that you saved her. In great perplexity then I come to you, and ask you out of your so much kindness to tell me all of it that you remember.'

'I can tell you, I think, Dr Van Helsing, all about it.'

'Ah, then you have a good memory for facts, for details? It is not always so with young ladies.'

'No, doctor, but I wrote it all down at the time. I can show it to you if you like.'

'Oh, Madam Mina, I will be grateful; you will do me much favour.' I could not resist the temptation of mystifying him a bit – I suppose it is some of the taste of the original apple that remains still in our mouths – so I handed him the shorthand diary. He took it with a grateful bow, and said: –

'May I read it?'

'If you wish,' I answered as demurely as I could. He opened it, and for the instant his face fell. Then he stood up and bowed.

'Oh, you so clever woman!' he said. 'I long knew that Mr Jonathan was a man of much thankfulness; but see, his wife have all the good things. And will you not so much honour me and so help me as to read it for me? Alas! I know not the shorthand.' By this time my little joke was over, and I was almost ashamed; so I took the typewritten copy from my work-basket and handed it to him.

'Forgive me,' I said: 'I could not help it; but I had been thinking that it was of dear Lucy that you wished to ask, and so that you might not have to wait – not on my account, but because I know your time must be precious – I have written it out on the typewriter for you.'

He took it, and his eyes glistened. 'You are so good,' he said. 'And may I read it now? I may want to ask you some things when I have read.'

'By all means,' I said, 'read it over whilst I order lunch; and then you can ask me questions whilst we eat.' He bowed and settled himself in a chair with his back to the light, and became absorbed in the papers, whilst I went to see after lunch, chiefly in order that he might not be disturbed. When I came back I found him walking hurriedly up and down the room, his face all ablaze with excitement. He rushed up to me and took me by both hands.

'Oh, Madam Mina,' he said, 'how can I say what I owe to you? This paper is as sunshine. It opens the gate to me. I am daze, I am dazzle, with so much light; and yet clouds roll in behind the light every time. But that you do not, cannot, comprehend. Oh, but I am grateful to you, you so clever woman. Madam' – he said this very solemnly – 'if ever Abraham Van Helsing can do anything for you or yours, I trust you will let me know. It will be pleasure and delight if I may serve you as a friend; as a friend, but all I have ever learned, all I can ever do, shall be for you and those you love. There are darknesses in life, and there are lights; you are one of the lights. You will have happy life and good life, and your husband will be blessed in you.'

'But, doctor, you praise me too much, and – and you do not know me.'

'Not know you – I, who am old, and who have studied all my life men and women; I, who have made my speciality the brain and all that belongs to him and all that follow from him! And I have read your diary that you have so goodly written for me, and which breathes out truth in every line. I, who have read your so sweet letter to poor Lucy of your marriage and your trust, not know you! Oh, Madam Mina, good women tell all their lives, and by day and by hour and by minute, such things that angels can read; and we men who wish to know have in us something of angel's eyes. Your husband is noble nature, and you are noble too, for you trust, and trust cannot be where there is mean nature. And your husband – tell me of him. Is he quite well? Is all that fever gone, and is he strong and hearty?' I saw here an opening to ask him about Jonathan, so I said: –

'He was almost recovered, but he has been greatly upset by Mr Hawkins' death.' He interrupted: –

'Oh yes, I know, I know. I have read your last two letters.' I went on: –

'I suppose this upset him, for when we were in town on Thursday last he had a sort of shock.'

'A shock, and after brain fever so soon! That was not good. What kind of shock was it?'

'He thought he saw someone who recalled something terrible, something which led to his brain fever.' And here the whole thing seemed to overwhelm me in a rush. The pity for Jonathan, the horror which he experienced, the whole fearful mystery of his diary, and the fear that has been brooding over me ever since, all came in a tumult. I suppose I was hysterical, for I threw myself on my knees and held up my hands to him, and implored him to make my husband well again. He took my hands and raised me up, and made me sit on the sofa, and sat by me; he held my hand in his, and said to me with, oh, such infinite sweetness –

'My life is a barren and lonely one, and so full of work that I have not had much time for friendships; but since I have been summoned to here by my friend John Seward I have known so many good people and seen such nobility that I feel more than ever – and it has grown with my advancing years – the loneliness of my life. Believe me, then, that I come here full of respect for you, and you have given me hope – hope, not in what I am seeking of, but that there are good women still left to make life happy – good women, whose lives and whose truths may make good lesson for the children that are to be. I am glad, glad, that I may here be of some use to you; for if your husband suffer, he suffer within the range of my study and experience. I promise you that I will gladly do *all* for him that I can – all to make his life strong and manly, and your life a happy one. Now you must eat. You are over-wrought and perhaps over-anxious. Husband Jonathan would not like to see you so pale; and what he like not where he love, is not to his good. Therefore for his sake you must eat and smile. You have told me all about Lucy, and so now we shall not speak of it, lest it distress. I shall stay in Exeter to-night, for I want to think much over what you have told me, and when I have thought I will ask you questions, if I may. And then, too, you will tell me of husband Jonathan's trouble so far as you can, but not yet. You must eat now; after-wards you shall tell me all.'

After lunch, when we went back to the drawing-room he said to me: –

'And now tell me all about him.' When it came to speaking to this great, learned man, I began to fear that he would think me a weak fool, and Jonathan a madman – that journal is all so strange – and I hesitated to go on. But he was so sweet and kind, and he had promised to help, and I trusted him, so I said: –

'Dr Van Helsing, what I have to tell you is so queer that you must not laugh at me or at my husband. I have been since yesterday in a sort of fever of doubt; you must be kind to me, and not think me foolish that I have even half believed some very strange things.' He reassured me by his manner as well as his words when he said:

'Oh, my dear, if you only knew how strange is the matter regarding which I am here, it is you who would laugh. I have learned not to think little of any one's belief, no matter how strange it be. I have tried to keep an open mind; and it is not the ordinary things of life that could close it, but the strange things, the extraordinary things, the things that make one doubt if they be mad or sane.'

'Thank you, thank you, a thousand times! You have taken a weight off my mind. If you will let me, I shall give you a paper to read. It is long, but I have typewritten it out. It will tell you my trouble and Jonathan's. It is the copy of his journal when abroad, and all that happened. I dare not say anything of it; you will read for yourself and judge. And then when I see you, perhaps, you will be very kind and tell me what you think.'

'I promise,' he said as I gave him the papers; 'I shall in the morning, so soon as I can, come to see you and your husband, if I may.'

'Jonathan will be here at half-past eleven, and you must come to lunch with us and see him then; you could catch the quick 3.34 train, which

will leave you at Paddington before eight.' He was surprised at my knowledge of the trains offhand, but he does not know that I have made up all
the trains to and from Exeter, so that I may help Jonathan in case he is
in a hurry.

So he took the papers with him and went away, and I sit here thinking
– thinking I don't know what.

Letter (by hand), Van Helsing to Mrs Harker

'*25 September, 6 o'clock.*

'Dear Madam Mina,

'I have read your husband's so wonderful diary. You may sleep
without doubt. Strange and terrible as it is, it is *true*! I will pledge
my life on it. It may be worse for others; but for him and you
there is no dread. He is a noble fellow; and let me tell you from
experience of men, that one who would do as he did in going
down that wall and to that room – ay, and going a second time –
is not one to be injured in permanence by a shock. His brain and
his heart are all right; this I swear, before I have even seen him;
so be at rest. I shall have much to ask him of other things. I am
blessed that to-day I come to see you, for I have learn all at once
so much that again I am dazzle – dazzle more than ever, and I
must think.

'Yours the most faithful,
'ABRAHAM VAN HELSING.'

Letter, Mrs Harker to Van Helsing

'*25 September, 6.30 p.m.*

'My dear Dr Van Helsing,

'A thousand thanks for your kind letter, which has taken a
great weight off my mind. And yet, if it be true, what terrible
things there are in the world, and what an awful thing if that man,
that monster, be really in London! I fear to think. I have this
moment, whilst writing, had a wire from Jonathan saying that he
leaves by the 6.25 to-night from Launceston and will be here at
10.18, so that I shall have no fear to-night. Will you therefore,
instead of lunching with us, please come to breakfast, at eight
o'clock, if this be not too early for you? You can get away, if you
are in a hurry, by the 10.30 train, which will bring you to

Paddington by 2.35. Do not answer this, as I shall take it that, if I
do not hear, you will come to breakfast.

> 'Believe me,

>> 'Your faithful and grateful friend,

>>> 'MINA HARKER.'

JONATHAN HARKER'S JOURNAL

26 September. – I thought never to write in this diary again, but the time
has come. When I got home last night Mina had supper ready, and when
we had supped she told me of Van Helsing's visit, and of her having given
him the two diaries copied out, and of how anxious she had been about
me. She showed me in the doctor's letter that all I wrote down was true.
It seems to have made a new man of me. It was the doubt as to the reality
of the whole thing that knocked me over. I felt impotent, and in the dark,
and distrustful. But, now that I *know*, I am not afraid, even of the Count.
He has succeeded after all, then, in his design in getting to London, and
it was he I saw. He has got younger, and how? Van Helsing is the man
to unmask him and hunt him out, if he is anything like what Mina says.
We sat late, and talked it all over. Mina is dressing, and I shall call at the
hotel in a few minutes and bring him over . . .

He was, I think, surprised to see me. When I came into the room where
he was, and introduced myself, he took me by the shoulder and turned
my face round to the light, and said, after a sharp scrutiny: –

'But Madam Mina told me you were ill, that you had had a shock.' It
was so funny to hear my wife called 'Madam Mina' by this kindly, strong-
faced old man. I smiled, and said: –

'I *was* ill, I *have* had a shock: but you have cured me already.'

'And how?'

'By your letter to Mina last night. I was in doubt, and then everything
took a hue of unreality, and I did not know what to trust, even the evidence
of my own senses. Not knowing what to trust, I did not know what to do;
and so had only to keep on working in what had hitherto been the groove
of my life. The groove ceased to avail me, and I mistrusted myself. Doctor,
you don't know what it is to doubt everything, even yourself. No, you
don't; you couldn't with eyebrows like yours.' He seemed pleased, and
laughed as he said: –

'So! You are physiognomist. I learn more here with each hour. I am
with so much pleasure coming to you to breakfast; and, oh, sir, you will

pardon praise from an old man, but you are blessed in your wife.' I would listen to him go on praising Mina for a day, so I simply nodded and stood silent.

'She is one of God's women fashioned by His own hand to show us men and other women that there is a heaven where we can enter, and that its light can be here on earth. So true, so sweet, so noble, so little an egoist – and that, let me tell you, is much in this age, so sceptical and selfish. And you, sir – I have read all the letters to poor Miss Lucy and some of them speak of you, so I know you since some days from the knowing of others; but I have seen your true self since last night. You will give me your hand, will you not? And let us be friends for all our lives.'

We shook hands, and he was so earnest and so kind that it made me quite choky.

'And now,' he said, 'may I ask you for some more help? I have a great task to do, and at the beginning it is to know. You can help me here. Can you tell me what went before your going to Transylvania? Later on I may ask more help and of a different kind; but at first this will do.'

'Look here, sir,' I said, 'does what you have to do concern the Count?'

'It does,' he said solemnly.

'Then I am with you heart and soul. As you go by the 10.30 train, you will not have time to read them; but I shall get the bundle of papers. You can take them with you and read them in the train.'

After breakfast I saw him to the station. When we were parting he said: 'Perhaps you will come to town if I send to you, and take Madam Mina too.'

'We shall both come when you will,' I said.

I had got him the morning papers and the London papers of the previous night, and while we were talking at the carriage window, waiting for the train to start, he was turning them over. His eye suddenly seemed to catch something in one of them, the *Westminster Gazette* – I knew it by the colour – and he grew quite white. He read something intently, groaning to himself: 'Mein Gott! Mein Gott! So soon! so soon!' I do not think he remembered me at the moment. Just then the whistle blew, and the train moved off. This recalled him to himself, and he leaned out of the window and waved his hand, calling out: 'Love to Madam Mina; I shall write so soon as ever I can.'

26 September. – Truly there is no such thing as finality. Not a week since I said 'Finis,' and yet here I am starting fresh again, or rather going on with the same record. Until this afternoon I had no cause to think of what is done. Renfield had become, to all intents, as sane as he ever was. He was already well ahead with his fly business; and he had just started in the spider line also; so he had not been any trouble to me. I had a letter from Arthur, written on Sunday, and from it I gather that he is bearing up wonderfully well. Quincey Morris is with him, and that is much of a help, for he himself is a bubbling well of good spirits. Quincey wrote me a line too, and from him I hear that Arthur is beginning to recover something of his old buoyancy, so as to them all my mind is at rest. As for myself, I was settling down to my work with the enthusiasm which I used to have for it, so that I might fairly have said that the wound which poor Lucy left on me was becoming cicatrized. Everything is, however, now reopened; and what is to be the end God only knows. I have an idea that Van Helsing thinks he knows too, but he will only let out enough at a time to whet curiosity. He went to Exeter yesterday, and stayed there all night. To-day he came back, and almost bounded into the room at about half-past five o'clock, and thrust last night's *Westminster Gazette* into my hand.

'What do you think of that?' he asked as he stood back and folded his arms.

I looked over the paper, for I really did not know what he meant; but he took it from me and pointed out a paragraph about children being decoyed away at Hampstead. It did not convey much to me, until I reached a passage where it described small punctured wounds on their throats. An idea struck me, and I looked up. 'Well?' he said.

'It is like poor Lucy's.'

'And what do you make of it?'

'Simply that there is some cause in common. Whatever it was that injured her has injured them.' I did not quite understand his answer: –

'That is true indirectly, but not directly.'

'How do you mean, Professor?' I asked. I was a little inclined to take his seriousness lightly – for, after all, four days of rest and freedom from burning, harrowing anxiety does help to restore one's spirits – but when I saw his face it sobered me. Never, even in the midst of our despair about poor Lucy, had he looked more stern.

'Tell me!' I said. 'I can hazard no opinion. I do not know what to think, and I have no data on which to found a conjecture.'

'Do you mean to tell me, friend John, that you have no suspicion as to what poor Lucy died of; not after all the hints given, not only by events, but by me?'

'Of nervous prostration following on great loss or waste of blood.'

'And how the blood lost or waste?' I shook my head. He stepped over and sat down beside me, and went on: –

'You are clever man, friend John; you reason well, and your wit is bold; but you are too prejudiced. You do not let your eyes see nor your ears hear, and that which is outside your daily life is not of account to you. Do you not think that there are things which you cannot understand, and yet which are; that some people see things that others cannot? But there are things old and new which must not be contemplate by men's eyes, because they know – or think they know – some things which other men have told them. Ah, it is the fault of our science that it wants to explain all; and if it explain not, then it says there is nothing to explain. But yet we see around us every day the growth of new beliefs, which think themselves new; and which are yet but the old, which pretend to be young – like the fine ladies at the opera. I suppose now you do not believe in corporeal transference. No? Nor in materialization. No? Nor in astral bodies. No? Nor in the reading of thought. No? Nor in hypnotism –'

'Yes,' I said. 'Charcot has proved that pretty well.' He smiled as he went on: 'Then you are satisfied as to it. Yes? And of course then you understand how it act, and can follow the mind of the great Charcot – alas that he is no more! – into the very soul of the patient that he influence. No? Then, friend John, am I to take it that you simply accept fact, and are satisfied to let from premise to conclusion be a blank? No? Then tell me – for I am student of the brain – how you accept the hypnotism and reject the thought-reading. Let me tell you, my friend, that there are things done to-day in electrical science which would have been deemed unholy by the very men who discovered electricity – who would themselves not so long before have been burned as wizards. There are always mysteries in life. Why was it that Methuselah lived nine hundred years, and "Old Parr" one hundred and sixty-nine, and yet that poor Lucy, with four men's blood in her poor veins, could not live even one day! For, had she live one more day, we could have save her. Do you know all the mystery of life and death? Do you know the altogether of comparative anatomy, and can say wherefore the qualities of brutes are in some men, and not in others? Can you tell me why, when other spiders die small and soon, that one great spider lived for centuries in the tower of the old Spanish church and grew and grew, till, on descending, he could drink the oil of all the church lamps? Can you tell me why in the Pampas, ay and elsewhere, there are bats that come at night and open the veins of cattle and horses and suck dry their veins; how in some islands of the Western seas there are bats which hang on the trees all day, that those who have seen describe as like giant nuts or pods, and that when the sailors sleep on the deck, because that it is hot, flit down on them, and then – and then in the morning are found dead men, white as even Miss Lucy was?'

'Good God, Professor!' I said, starting up. 'Do you mean to tell me that Lucy was bitten by such a bat; and that such a thing is here in London in the nineteenth century?' He waved his hand for silence, and went on: –

'Can you tell me why the tortoise lives more long than generations of men; why the elephant goes on and on till he have seen dynasties; and why the parrot never die only of bite of cat or dog or other complaint? Can you tell me why men believe in all ages and places that there are some few who live on always if they be permit; that there are men and women who cannot die? We all know – because science has vouched for the fact – that there have been toads shut up in rocks for thousands of years, shut in one so small hole that only hold him since the youth of the world. Can you tell me how the Indian fakir can make himself to die and have been buried, and his grave sealed and corn sowed on it, and the corn reaped and be cut and sown and reaped and cut again, and then men come and take away the unbroken seal, and that there lie the Indian fakir, not dead, but that rise up and walk amongst them as before?' Here I interrupted him. I was getting bewildered; he so crowded on my mind his list of nature's eccentricities and possible impossibilities that my imagination was getting fired. I had a dim idea that he was teaching me some lesson, as long ago he used to do in his study at Amsterdam; but he used then to tell me the thing, so that I could have the object of thought in mind all the time. But now I was without his help, yet I wanted to follow him, so I said: –

'Professor, let me be your pet student again. Tell me the thesis, so that I may apply your knowledge as you go on. At present I am going in my mind from point to point as a mad man, and not a sane one, follows an idea. I feel like a novice blundering through a bog in a mist, jumping from one tussock to another in the mere blind effort to move on without knowing where I am going.'

'That is good image,' he said. 'Well, I shall tell you. My thesis is this: I want you to believe.'

'To believe what?'

'To believe in things that you cannot. Let me illustrate. I heard once of an American who so defined faith: "that which enables us to believe things which we know to be untrue." For one, I follow that man. He meant that we shall have an open mind, and not let a little bit of truth check the rush of a big truth, like a small rock does a railway truck. We get the small truth first. Good! We keep him, and we value him; but all the same we must not let him think himself all the truth in the universe.'

'Then you want me not to let some previous conviction injure the receptivity of my mind with regard to some strange matter. Do I read your lesson aright?'

'Ah, you are my favourite pupil still. It is worth to teach you. Now that you are willing to understand, you have taken the first step to understand. You think then that those so small holes in the children's throats were made by the same that made the hole in Miss Lucy?'

'I suppose so.' He stood up and said solemnly: –

'Then you are wrong. Oh, would it were so! but alas! no. It is worse, far, far worse.'

'In God's name, Professor Van Helsing, what do you mean?' I cried.

He threw himself with a despairing gesture into a chair, and placed his elbows on the table, covering his face with his hands as he spoke: – 'They were made by Miss Lucy!'

CHAPTER 15

DR SEWARD'S DIARY

(CONTINUED)

For a while sheer anger mastered me; it was as if he had during her life struck Lucy on the face. I smote the table hard and rose up as I said to him: –

'Dr Van Helsing, are you mad?' He raised his head and looked at me, and somehow the tenderness of his face calmed me at once. 'Would I were!' he said. 'Madness were easy to bear compared with truth like this. Oh, my friend, why, think you, did I go so far round; why take so long to tell you so simple a thing? Was it because I hate you and have hated you all my life? Was it because I wished to give you pain? Was it that I wanted, now so late, revenge for that time when you saved my life, and from a fearful death? Ah no!'

'Forgive me,' said I. He went on: –

'My friend, it was because I wished to be gentle in the breaking to you, for I know that you have loved that so sweet lady. But even yet I do not expect you to believe. It is so hard to accept at once any abstract truth, that we may doubt such to be possible when we have always believed the "no" of it; it is more hard still to accept so sad a concrete truth, and of such a one as Miss Lucy. To-night I go to prove it. Dare you come with me?'

This staggered me. A man does not like to prove such a truth; Byron excepted from the category, jealousy.

'And prove the very truth he most abhorred.'

He saw my hesitation, and spoke: –

'The logic is simple, no madman's logic this time, jumping from tussock to tussock in a misty fog. If it be not true, then proof will be relief; at worst it will not harm. If it be true! Ah, there is the dread; yet very dread should help my cause, for in it is some need of belief. Come, I tell you what I propose: first, that we go off now and see that child in the hospital. Dr Vincent of the North Hospital, where the papers say the child is, is friend of mine, and I think of yours since you were in class at Amsterdam. He will let two scientists see his case, if he will not let two friends. We shall tell him nothing, but only that we wish to learn. And then –'

'And then?' He took a key from his pocket and held it up.

'And then we spend the night, you and I, in the churchyard where Lucy lies. This is the key that lock the tomb. I had it from the coffin-man to give to Arthur.' My heart sank within me, for I felt that there was some fearful ordeal before us. I could do nothing, however, so I plucked up what heart I could and said that we had better hasten, as the afternoon was passing . . .

We found the child awake. It had had a sleep and taken some food, and altogether was going on well. Dr Vincent took the bandage from its throat, and showed us the punctures. There was no mistaking the similarity to those which had been on Lucy's throat. They were smaller, and the edges looked fresher; that was all. We asked Vincent to what he attributed them, and he replied that it must have been a bite of some animal, perhaps a rat; but, for his own part, he was inclined to think that it was one of the bats which are so numerous on the northern heights of London. 'Out of so many harmless ones,' he said, 'there may be some wild specimen from the South of a more malignant species. Some sailor may have brought one home, and it managed to escape; or even from the Zoological Gardens a young one may have got loose, or one be bred there from a vampire. These things do occur, you know. Only ten days ago a wolf got out, and was, I believe, traced up in this direction. For a week after, the children were playing nothing but Red Riding Hood on the Heath and in every alley in the place until this "bloofer lady" scare came along, since when it has been quite a gala-time with them. Even this poor little mite, when he woke up to-day, asked the nurse if he might go away. When she asked him why he wanted to go, he said he wanted to play with the "bloofer lady."'

'I hope,' said Van Helsing, 'that when you are sending the child home you will caution its parents to keep strict watch over it. These fancies to stray are most dangerous; and if the child were to remain out another night, it would probably be fatal. But in any case I suppose you will not let it away for some days?'

'Certainly not, not for a week at least; longer if the wound is not healed.'

Our visit to the hospital took more time than we had reckoned on, and the sun had dipped before we came out. When Van Helsing saw how dark it was, he said: –

'There is no hurry. It is more late than I thought. Come, let us seek somewhere that we may eat, and then we shall go on our way.'

We dined at 'Jack Straw's Castle' along with a little crowd of bicyclists and others who were genially noisy. About ten o'clock we started from the inn. It was then very dark, and the scattered lamps made the darkness greater when we were once outside their individual radius. The Professor had evidently noted the road we were to go, for he went on unhesitatingly; but as for me, I was in quite a mix-up as to locality. As we went further, we met fewer and fewer people, till at last we were somewhat surprised when we met even the patrol of horse police going their usual suburban round. At last we reached the wall of the churchyard, which we climbed over. With some little difficulty – for it was very dark, and the whole place seemed so strange to us – we found the Westenra tomb. The Professor took the key, opened the creaky door, and standing back, politely, but quite unconsciously, motioned me to precede him. There was a delicious irony in the offer, in the courtliness of giving preference on such a ghastly occasion. My companion followed me quickly, and cautiously drew the door to, after carefully ascertaining that the lock was a falling, and not a spring one. In the latter case we should have been in a bad plight. Then he fumbled in his bag, and taking out a match-box and a piece of candle, proceeded to make a light. The tomb in the daytime, and when wreathed with fresh flowers, had looked grim and gruesome enough; but now some days afterwards, when the flowers hung lank and dead, their whites turning to rust and their greens to browns; when the spider and the beetle had resumed their accustomed dominance; when time-discoloured stone, and dust-encrusted mortar, and rusty, dank iron, and tarnished brass and clouded silver-plating gave back the feeble glimmer of a candle, the effect was more miserable and sordid than could have been imagined. It conveyed irresistibly the idea that life – animal life – was not the only thing which could pass away.

Van Helsing went about his work systematically. Holding his candle so that he could read the coffin plates, and so holding it that the sperm dropped in white patches which congealed as they touched the metal, he made assurance of Lucy's coffin. Another search in his bag, and he took out a turnscrew.

'What are you going to do?' I asked.

'To open the coffin. You shall yet be convinced.'

Straightway he began taking out the screws, and finally lifted off the lid, showing the casing of lead beneath. The sight was almost too much for me. It seemed to be as much an affront to the dead as it would have been to have stripped off her clothing in her sleep whilst living; I actually took hold of his hand to stop him. He only said: 'You shall see,' and again fumbling in his bag, took out a tiny fret-saw. Striking the turnscrew through the lead with a swift downward stab, which made me wince, he made a small hole, which was, however, big enough to admit the point of the saw. I had expected a rush of gas from the week-old corpse. We doctors, who have had to study our dangers, have to become accustomed to such things, and I drew back towards the door. But the Professor never stopped for a moment; he sawed down a couple of feet along one side of the lead coffin, and then across, and down the other side. Taking the edge of the loose flange, he bent it back towards the foot of the coffin, and holding up the candle into the aperture, motioned to me to look.

I drew near and looked. The coffin was empty.

It was certainly a surprise to me, and gave me a considerable shock, but Van Helsing was unmoved. He was now more sure than ever of his ground, and so emboldened to proceed in his task. 'Are you satisfied now, friend John?' he asked.

I felt all the dogged argumentativeness of my nature awake within me as I answered him: –

'I am satisfied that Lucy's body is not in that coffin; but that only proves one thing.'

'And what is that, friend John?'

'That it is not there.'

'That is good logic,' he said, 'so far as it goes. But how do you – how can you – account for it not being there?'

'Perhaps a body-snatcher,' I suggested. 'Some of the undertaker's people may have stolen it.' I felt that I was speaking folly, and yet it was the only real cause which I could suggest. The Professor sighed. 'Ah well!' he said, 'we must have more proof. Come with me.'

He put on the coffin-lid again, gathered up all his things and placed them in the bag, blew out the light, and placed the candle also in the bag. We opened the door, and went out. Behind us he closed the door and locked it. He handed me the key, saying: 'Will you keep it? You had better be assured.' I laughed – it was not a very cheerful laugh, I am bound to say – as I motioned him to keep it. 'A key is nothing,' I said; 'there may be duplicates; and anyhow it is not difficult to pick a lock of that kind.' He said nothing, but put the key in his pocket. Then he told me to watch at one side of the churchyard whilst he could watch at the other. I took up my place behind a yew-tree, and I saw his dark figure move until the intervening headstones and trees hid it from my sight.

It was a lonely vigil. Just after I had taken my place I heard a distant clock strike twelve, and in time came one and two. I was chilled and unnerved, and angry with the Professor for taking me on such an errand and with myself for coming. I was too cold and too sleepy to be keenly observant, and not sleepy enough to betray my trust; so altogether I had a dreary, miserable time.

Suddenly, as I turned around, I thought I saw something like a white streak, moving between two dark yew-trees at the side of the churchyard farthest from the tomb; at the same time a dark mass moved from the Professor's side of the ground, and hurriedly went towards it. Then I too moved; but I had to go round headstones and railed-off tombs, and I stumbled over graves. The sky was overcast, and somewhere far off an early cock crew. A little way off, beyond the line of scattered juniper-trees, which marked the pathway to the church, a white, dim figure flitted in the direction of the tomb. The tomb itself was hidden by trees, and I could not see where the figure disappeared. I heard the rustle of actual movement where I had first seen the white figure, and coming over, found the Professor holding in his arms a tiny child. When he saw me he held it out to me, and said: –

'Are you satisfied now?'

'No,' I said, in a way that I felt was aggressive.

'Do you not see the child?'

'Yes, it is a child, but who brought it here? And is it wounded?' I asked.

'We shall see,' said the Professor, and with one impulse we took our way out of the churchyard, he carrying the sleeping child.

When we had got some little distance away, we went into a clump of trees, and struck a match, and looked at the child's throat. It was without a scratch or scar of any kind.

'Was I right?' I asked triumphantly.

'We were just in time,' said the Professor thankfully.

We had now to decide what we were to do with the child, and so consulted about it. If we were to take it to a police station we should have to give some account of our movements during the night; at least, we should have had to make some statement as to how we had come to find the child. So finally we decided that we would take it to the Heath, and when we heard a policeman coming, would leave it where he could not fail to find it; we would then seek our way home as quickly as we could. All fell out well. At the edge of Hampstead Heath we heard a policeman's heavy tramp, and laying the child on the pathway, we waited and watched until he saw it as he flashed his lantern to and fro. We heard his exclamation of astonishment, and then we went away silently. By good chance we got a cab near the 'Spaniards,' and drove to town.

I cannot sleep, so I make this entry. But I must try to get a few hours' sleep, as Van Helsing is to call for me at noon. He insists that I shall go with him on another expedition.

27 September. – It was two o'clock before we found a suitable opportunity for our attempt. The funeral held at noon was all completed, and
the last stragglers of the mourners had taken themselves lazily away, when,
looking carefully from behind a clump of alder-trees, we saw the sexton
lock the gate after him. We knew then that we were safe till morning did
we desire it; but the Professor told me that we should not want more than
an hour at most. Again I felt that horrid sense of the reality of things, in
which any effort of imagination seemed out of place; and I realized
distinctly the perils of the law which we were incurring in our unhallowed
work. Besides, I felt it was all so useless. Outrageous as it was to open a
leaden coffin, to see if a woman dead nearly a week were really dead, it
now seemed the height of folly to open the tomb again, when we knew,
from the evidence of our own eyesight, that the coffin was empty. I
shrugged my shoulders, however, and rested silent, for Van Helsing had
a way of going on his own road, no matter who remonstrated. He took
the key, opened the vault, and again courteously motioned me to precede.
The place was not so gruesome as last night, but oh, how unutterably
mean-looking when the sunshine streamed in. Van Helsing walked over
to Lucy's coffin, and I followed. He bent over and again forced back the
leaden flange; and then a shock of surprise and dismay shot through me.

There lay Lucy, seemingly just as we had seen her the night before her
funeral. She was, if possible, more radiantly beautiful than ever; and I
could not believe that she was dead. The lips were red, nay redder than
before; and on the cheeks was a delicate bloom.

'Is this a juggle?' I said to him.

'Are you convinced now?' said the Professor in response, and as he
spoke he put over his hand, and in a way that made me shudder, pulled
back the dead lips and showed the white teeth.

'See,' he went on, 'see, they are even sharper than before. With this
and this' – and he touched one of the canine teeth and that below it – 'the
little children can be bitten. Are you of belief now, friend John?' Once
more, argumentative hostility woke within me. I *could* not accept such an
overwhelming idea as he suggested; so, with an attempt to argue of which
I was even at the moment ashamed, I said: –

'She may have been placed here since last night.'

'Indeed? That is so, and by whom?'

'I do not know. Someone has done it.'

'And yet she has been dead one week. Most peoples in that time would
not look so.' I had no answer for this, so was silent. Van Helsing did not
seem to notice my silence; at any rate, he showed neither chagrin nor

triumph. He was looking intently at the face of the dead woman, raising the eyelids and looking at the eyes, and once more opening the lips and examining the teeth. Then he turned to me and said: –

'Here, there is one thing which is different from all recorded: here is some dual life that is not as the common. She was bitten by the vampire when she was in a trance, sleep-walking – oh, you start; you do not know that, friend John, but you shall know it all later – and in trance could he best come to take more blood. In trance she died, and in trance she is Un-Dead, too. So it is that she differ from all other. Usually when the Un-Dead sleep at home' – as he spoke he made a comprehensive sweep of his arm to designate what to a vampire was 'home' – 'their face show what they are, but this so sweet that-was when she not Un-Dead she go back to the nothings of the common dead. There is no malign there, see, and so it make hard that I must kill her in her sleep.' This turned my blood cold, and it began to dawn upon me that I was accepting Van Helsing's theories; but if she were really dead, what was there of terror in the idea of killing her? He looked up at me, and evidently saw the change in my face, for he said almost joyously: –

'Ah, you believe now?'

I answered: 'Do not press me too hard all at once. I am willing to accept. How will you do this bloody work?'

'I shall cut off her head and fill her mouth with garlic, and I shall drive a stake through her body.' It made me shudder to think of so mutilating the body of the woman whom I had loved. And yet the feeling was not so strong as I had expected. I was, in fact, beginning to shudder at the presence of this being, this Un-Dead, as Van Helsing called it, and to loathe it. It is possible that love is all subjective, or all objective?

I waited a considerable time for Van Helsing to begin, but he stood as if wrapped in thought. Presently he closed the catch of his bag with a snap, and said: –

'I have been thinking, and have made up my mind as to what is best. If I did simply follow my inclining I would do now, at this moment, what is to be done; but there are other things to follow, and things that are thousand times more difficult in that them we do not know. This is simple. She have yet no life taken, though that is of time; and to act now would be to take danger from her for ever. But then we may have to want Arthur, and how shall we tell him of this? If you, who saw the wounds on Lucy's throat, and saw the wounds so similar on the child's at the hospital; if you, who saw the coffin empty last night and full to-day with a woman who have not change only to be more rose and more beautiful in a whole week after she die – if you know of this and know of the white figure last night that brought the child to the churchyard, and yet of your own senses you did not believe, how, then, can I expect Arthur, who know none of those things, to believe? He doubted me when I took him from her kiss when she was dying. I know he has forgiven me because in some mistaken idea I have done things that prevent him say good-bye as he ought; and he may think that in some more mistaken idea this woman was buried alive; and that in most mistake of all we have killed her. He will then argue back that it is we, mistaken ones, that have killed her by our ideas; and so he will be much unhappy always. Yet he never can be sure; and that is the worst of all. And he will sometimes think that she he loved was buried alive, and that will paint his dreams with horrors of what she must have suffered; and, again, he will think that we may be right, and that his so beloved was, after all, an Un-Dead. No! I told him once, and since then I learn much. Now, since I know it is all true, a hundred thousand times more do I know that he must pass through the bitter waters to reach the sweet. He, poor fellow, must have one hour that will make the very face of heaven grow black to him; then we can act for good all round and send him peace. My mind is made up. Let us go. You return home for to-night to your asylum, and see that all be well. As for me, I shall spend the night here in this churchyard in my own way. To-morrow night you will come to me to the Berkeley Hotel at ten of the clock. I shall send for Arthur to come too, and also that so fine young man of America that gave his blood. Later we shall all have work to do. I come with you so far as Piccadilly and there dine, for I must be back here before the sun set.'

So we locked the tomb and came away, and got over the wall of the churchyard, which was not much of a task, and drove back to Piccadilly.

*Note left by Van Helsing in his portmanteau,
Berkeley Hotel, directed to John Seward, M.D.
(Not delivered)*

'27 September.

'Friend John, –

'I write this in case anything should happen. I go alone to watch in that churchyard. It pleases me that the Un-Dead, Miss Lucy, shall not leave to-night, that so on the morrow night she may be more eager. Therefore I shall fix some things she like not – garlic and a crucifix – and so seal up the door of the tomb. She is young as Un-Dead, and will heed. Moreover, these are only to prevent her coming out; they may not prevail on her wanting to get in; for then the Un-Dead is desperate, and must find the line of least resistance, whatsoever it may be. I shall be at hand all the night from sunset till after the sunrise, and if there be aught that may be learned I shall learn it. For Miss Lucy, or from her, I have no fear: but that other to whom is there that she is Un-Dead, he have now the power to seek her tomb and find shelter. He is cunning, as I know from Mr Jonathan and from the way that all along he have fooled us when he played with us for Miss Lucy's life, and we lost; and in many ways the Un-Dead are strong. He have always the strength in his hand of twenty men; even we four who gave our strength to Miss Lucy it also is all to him. Besides, he can summon his wolf and I know not what. So if it be that he come thither on this night he shall find me; but none other shall – until it be too late. But it may be that he will not attempt the place. There is no reason why he should; his hunting ground is more full of game than the churchyard where the Un-Dead woman sleep, and one old man watch.

'Therefore I write this in case . . . Take the papers that are with this, the diaries of Harker and the rest, and read them, and then find this great Un-Dead, and cut off his head and burn his heart or drive a stake through it, so that the world may rest from him.

'If it be so, farewell.

'VAN HELSING.'

DR SEWARD'S DIARY

28 September. – It is wonderful what a good night's sleep will do for one. Yesterday I was almost willing to accept Van Helsing's monstrous ideas; but now they seem to start out lurid before me as outrages on common sense. I have no doubt that he believes it all. I wonder if his mind can have become in any way unhinged. Surely there must be *some* rational explanation of all these mysterious things. Is it possible that the Professor can have done it himself? He is so abnormally clever that if he went off his head he would carry out his intent with regard to some fixed idea in a wonderful way. I am loath to think it, and indeed it would be almost as great a marvel as the other to find that Van Helsing was mad; but anyhow I shall watch him carefully. I may get some light on the mystery.

29 September, morning . . . Last night, at a little before ten o'clock, Arthur and Quincey came into Van Helsing's room; he told us all what he wanted us to do, but especially addressing himself to Arthur, as if all our wills were centred in his. He began by saying that he hoped we would all come with him too, 'for,' he said, 'there is a grave duty to be done there. You were doubtless surprised at my letter?' This query was directly addressed to Lord Godalming.

'I was. It rather upset me for a bit. There has been so much trouble around my house of late that I could do without any more. I have been curious, too, as to what you mean. Quincey and I talked it over; but the more we talked, the more puzzled we got, till now I can say for myself that I'm about up a tree as to any meaning about anything.'

'Me, too,' said Quincey Morris laconically.

'Oh,' said the Professor, 'then you are nearer the beginning, both of you, than friend John here, who has to go a long way back before he can even get so far as to begin.'

It was evident that he recognized my return to my old doubting frame of mind without my saying a word. Then, turning to the other two, he said with intense gravity: –

'I want your permission to do what I think good this night. It is, I know, much to ask; and when you know what it is I propose to do you will know, and only then, how much. Therefore may I ask that you promise me in the dark, so that afterwards, though you may be angry with me for a time – I must not disguise from myself the possibility that such may be – you shall not blame yourselves for anything.'

'That's frank anyhow,' broke in Quincey. 'I'll answer for the Professor. I don't quite see his drift, but I swear he's honest; and that's good enough for me.'

'I thank you, sir,' said Van Helsing proudly. 'I have done myself the honour of counting you one trusting friend, and such endorsement is dear to me.' He held out a hand, which Quincey took.

Then Arthur spoke out: –

'Dr Van Helsing, I don't quite like to buy a "pig in a poke," as they say in Scotland, and if it be anything in which my honour as a gentleman or my faith as a Christian is concerned, I cannot make such a promise. If you can assure me that what you intend does not violate either of these two, then I give my consent at once; though, for the life of me, I cannot understand what you are driving at.'

'I accept your limitation,' said Van Helsing, 'and all I ask of you is that if you feel it necessary to condemn any act of mine, you will first consider it well and be satisfied that it does not violate your reservations.'

'Agreed!' said Arthur; 'that is only fair. And now that the *pourparlers* are over, may I ask what it is we are to do?'

'I want you to come with me, and to come in secret, to the churchyard at Kingstead.'

Arthur's face fell as he said in an amazed sort of way: –

'Where poor Lucy is buried?' The Professor bowed. Arthur went on: 'And when there?'

'To enter the tomb!' Arthur stood up.

'Professor, are you in earnest; or is it some monstrous joke? Pardon me, I see that you are in earnest.' He sat down again, but I could see that he sat firmly and proudly, as one who is on his dignity. There was silence until he asked again: –

'And when in the tomb?'

'To open the coffin.'

'This is too much!' he said, angrily rising again. 'I am willing to be patient in all things that are reasonable; but in this – this desecration of the grave – of one who –' He fairly choked with indignation. The Professor looked pityingly at him.

'If I could spare you one pang, my poor friend,' he said, 'God knows I would. But this night our feet must tread in thorny paths; or later, and for ever, the feet you love must walk in paths of flame!'

Arthur looked up with set, white face and said: –

'Take care, sir, take care!'

'Would it not be well to her what I have to say?' said Van Helsing. 'And then you will at least know the limit of my purpose. Shall I go on?'

'That's fair enough,' broke in Morris.

After a pause Van Helsing went on, evidently with an effort: –

'Miss Lucy is dead; is it not so? Yes! Then there can be no wrong to her. But if she be not dead –'

Arthur jumped to his feet.

'Good God!' he cried. 'What do you mean? Has there been any mistake; has she been buried alive?' He groaned in anguish that not even hope could soften.

'I did not say she was alive, my child; I did not think it. I go no further than to say that she might be Un-Dead.'

'Un-Dead! Not alive! What do you mean? Is this all a nightmare, or what is it?'

'There are mysteries which men can only guess at, which age by age they may solve only in part. Believe me, we are now on the verge of one. But I have not done. May I cut off the head of dead Miss Lucy?'

'Heavens and earth, no!' cried Arthur in a storm of passion. 'Not for the wide world will I consent to any mutilation of her dead body. Dr Van Helsing, you try me too far. What have I done to you that you should torture me so? What did that poor, sweet girl do that you should want to cast such dishonour on her grave? Are you mad that speak such things, or am I mad that listen to them? Don't dare to think more of such a dese-cration; I shall not give my consent to anything you do. I have a duty to do in protecting her grave from outrage; and, by God, I shall do it!'

Van Helsing rose up from where he had all the time been seated, and said, gravely and sternly: –

'My Lord Godalming, I, too, have a duty to do, a duty to others, a duty to you, a duty to the dead; and, by God, I shall do it! All I ask you now is that you come with me, that you look and listen; and if when later I make the same request you do not be more eager for its fulfilment even than I am, then – then I shall do my duty, whatever it may seem to me. And then, to follow of your Lordship's wishes, I shall hold myself at your disposal to render an account to you, when and where you will.' His voice broke a little, and he went on with an accent full of pity: –

'But, I beseech you, do not go forth in anger with me. In a long life of acts which were often not pleasant to do, and which sometimes did wring my heart, I have never had so heavy a task as now. Believe me that if the time comes for you to change your mind towards me, one look from you will wipe away all this so sad hour, for I would do what a man can to save you from sorrow. Just think. For why should I give myself so much of labour and so much of sorrow? I have come here from my own land to do what I can of good; at the first to please my friend John, and then to help a sweet young lady, whom, too, I came to love. For her – I am ashamed to say so much, but I say it in kindness – I gave what you gave: the blood of my veins; I gave it, I, who was not, like you, her lover, but only her physician and her friend. I gave to her my nights and days – before death, after death; and if my death can do her good even now, when she is the dead Un-Dead, she shall have it freely.' He said this with a very grave, sweet pride, and Arthur was much affected by it. He took the old man's hand and said in a broken voice: –

'Oh, it is hard to think of it, and I cannot understand; but at least I will go with you and wait.'

CHAPTER 16

DR SEWARD'S DIARY

(CONTINUED)

It was just a quarter before twelve o'clock when we got into the church-yard over the low wall. The night was dark, with occasional gleams of moonlight between the rents of the heavy clouds that scudded across the sky. We all kept somehow close together, with Van Helsing slightly in front as he led the way. When we had come close to the tomb I looked well at Arthur, for I feared that the proximity to a place laden with so sorrowful a memory would upset him; but he bore himself well. I took it that the very mystery of the proceeding tended in some way to counteract his grief. The Professor unlocked the door, and seeing a natural hesitation amongst us for various reasons, solved the difficulty by entering first himself. The rest of us followed, and he closed the door. He then lit a dark lantern and pointed to the coffin. Arthur stepped forward hesitatingly; Van Helsing said to me: –

'You were with me here yesterday. Was the body of Miss Lucy in that coffin?'

'It was.' The Professor turned to the rest, saying: –

'You hear; and yet there is one who does not believe with me.' He took his screwdriver and again took off the lid of the coffin. Arthur looked on, very pale but silent; when the lid was removed he stepped forward. He evidently did not know that there was a leaden coffin, or, at any rate, had not thought of it. When he saw the rent in the lead, the blood rushed to his face for an instant, but as quickly fell away again, so that he remained of a ghastly whiteness; he was still silent. Van Helsing forced back the leaden flange, and we all looked in and recoiled.

The coffin was empty!

For several minutes no one spoke a word. The silence was broken by Quincey Morris: –

'Professor, I answered for you. Your word is all I want. I wouldn't ask such a thing ordinarily – I wouldn't so dishonour you as to imply a doubt; but this is a mystery that goes beyond any honour or dishonour. Is this your doing?'

'I swear to you by all that I hold sacred that I have not removed nor touched her. What happened was this: Two nights ago my friend

Seward and I came here – with good purpose, believe me. I opened that coffin, which was then sealed up, and we found it, as now, empty. We then waited, and saw something white come through the trees. The next day we came here in daytime, and she lay there. Did she not, friend John?'

'Yes.'

'That night we were just in time. One more so small child was missing, and we find it, thank God, unharmed amongst the graves. Yesterday I came here before sundown, for at sundown the Un-Dead can move. I waited here all the night till the sun rose, but I saw nothing. It was most probable that it was because I had laid over the clamps of those doors garlic, which the Un-Dead cannot bear, and other things which they shun. Last night there was no exodus, so to-night before the sundown I took away my garlic and other things. And so it is we find this coffin empty. But bear with me. So far there is much that is strange. Wait you with me outside, unseen and unheard, and things much stranger are yet to be. So' – here he shut the dark slide of his lantern – 'now to the outside.' He opened the door, and we filed out, he coming last and locking the door behind him.

Oh! but it seemed fresh and pure in the night air after the terror of that vault. How sweet it was to see the clouds race by, and the brief gleams of the moonlight between the scudding clouds crossing and passing – like the gladness and sorrow of a man's life; how sweet it was to breathe the fresh air, that had no taint of death and decay; how humanizing to see the red lighting of the sky beyond the hill, and to hear far away the muffled roar that marks the life of a great city. Each in his own way was solemn and overcome. Arthur was silent, and was, I could see, striving to grasp the purpose and the inner meaning of the mystery. I was myself tolerably patient, and half inclined again to throw aside doubt and to accept Van Helsing's conclusions. Quincey Morris was phlegmatic in the way of a man who accepts all things, and accepts them in the spirit of cool bravery, with hazard of all he has to stake. Not being able to smoke, he cut himself a good-sized plug of tobacco and began to chew. As to Van Helsing, he was employed in a definite way. First he took from his bag a mass of what looked like thin, wafer-like biscuit, which was carefully rolled up in a white napkin; next he took out a double-handful of some whitish stuff, like dough or putty. He crumbled the wafer up fine and worked it into the mass between his hands. This he then took, and rolling it into thin strips, began to lay them into the crevices between the door and its setting in the tomb. I was somewhat puzzled at this, and being close, asked him what it was that he was doing. Arthur and Quincey drew near also, as they too were curious. He answered: –

'I am closing the tomb, so that the Un-Dead may not enter.'

'And is that stuff you have put there going to do it?' asked Quincey. 'Great Scott! Is this a game?'

'It is.'

'What is that which you are using?' This time the question was by Arthur. Van Helsing reverently lifted his hat as he answered: –

'The Host. I brought it from Amsterdam. I have an Indulgence.' It was an answer that appalled the most sceptical of us, and we felt individually that in the presence of such earnest purpose as the Professor's, a purpose which could thus use the to him most sacred of things, it was impossible to distrust. In respectful silence we took the places assigned to us close round the tomb, but hidden from the sight of anyone approaching. I pitied the others, especially Arthur. I had myself been apprenticed by my former visits to this watching horror; and yet I, who had up to an hour ago repudiated the proofs, felt my heart sink within me. Never did tombs look so ghastly white; never did cypress, or yew, or juniper so seem the embodiment of funereal gloom; never did tree or grass wave or rustle so ominously; never did bough creak so mysteriously; and never did the far-away howling of dogs send such a woeful presage through the night.

There was a long spell of silence, a big, aching void, and then from the Professor a keen 'S-s-s-s!' He pointed; and far down the avenue of yews we saw a white figure advance – a dim white figure, which held something dark at its breast. The figure stopped, and at the moment a ray of moonlight fell between the masses of driving clouds and showed in startling prominence a dark-haired woman, dressed in the cerements of the grave. We could not see the face, for it was bent down over what we saw to be a fair-haired child. There was a pause and a sharp little cry, such as a child gives in sleep, or a dog as it lies before the fire and dreams. We were starting forward, but the Professor's warning hand, seen by us as he stood behind a yew-tree, kept us back; and then as we looked the white figure moved forward again. It was now near enough for us to see clearly, and the moonlight still held. My own heart grew cold as ice, and I could hear the gasp of Arthur as we recognized the features of Lucy Westenra. Lucy Westenra, but yet how changed. The sweetness was turned to adamantine, heartless cruelty, and the purity to voluptuous wantonness. Van Helsing stepped out, and, obedient to his gesture, we all advanced too; the four of us ranged in a line before the door of the tomb. Van Helsing raised his lantern and drew the slide; by the concentrated light that fell on Lucy's face we could see that the lips were crimson with fresh blood, and that the stream had trickled over her chin and stained the purity of her lawn death-robe.

We shuddered with horror. I could see by the tremulous light that even Van Helsing's iron nerve had failed. Arthur was next to me, and if I had not seized his arm and held him up, he would have fallen.

When Lucy – I call the thing that was before us Lucy because it bore her shape – saw us she drew back with an angry snarl, such as a cat gives when taken unawares; then her eyes ranged over us. Lucy's eyes in form and colour; but Lucy's eyes unclean and full of hell-fire, instead of the pure, gentle orbs we knew. At that moment the remnant of my love passed into hate and loathing; had she then to be killed, I could have done it with savage delight. As she looked, her eyes blazed with unholy light, and the face became wreathed with a voluptuous smile. Oh, God, how it made me shudder to see it! With a careless motion, she flung to the ground, callous as a devil, the child that up to now she had clutched strenuously to her breast, growling over it as a dog growls over a bone. The child gave a sharp cry, and lay there moaning. There was a cold-bloodedness in the act which wrung a groan from Arthur; when she advanced to him with outstretched arms and a wanton smile, he fell back and hid his face in his hands.

She still advanced, however, and with a languorous, voluptuous grace, said: –

'Come to me, Arthur. Leave these others and come to me. My arms are hungry for you. Come, and we can rest together. Come, my husband, come!'

There was something diabolically sweet in her tones – something of the tingling of glass when struck – which rang through the brains even of us who heard the words addressed to another. As for Arthur, he seemed under a spell; moving his hands from his face, he opened wide his arms. She was leaping for them, when Van Helsing sprang forward and held between them his little golden crucifix. She recoiled from it, and, with a suddenly distorted face, full of rage, dashed past him as if to enter the tomb.

When within a foot or two of the door, however, she stopped as if arrested by some irresistible force. Then she turned, and her face was shown in the clear burst of moonlight and by the lamp, which had now no quiver from Van Helsing's iron nerves. Never did I see such baffled malice on a face; and never, I trust, shall such ever be seen again by mortal eyes. The beautiful colour became livid, the eyes seemed to throw out sparks of hell-fire, the brows were wrinkled as though the folds of the flesh were the coils of Medusa's snakes, and the lovely, blood-stained mouth grew to an open square, as in the passion masks of the Greeks and Japanese. If ever a face meant death – if looks could kill – we saw it at that moment.

And so for full half a minute, which seemed an eternity, she remained between the lifted crucifix and the sacred closing of her means of entry. Van Helsing broke the silence by asking Arthur: –

'Answer me, o my friend! Am I to proceed in my work?'

Arthur threw himself on his knees, and hid his face in his hands, as he answered: –

'Do as you will, friend; do as you will. There can be no horror like this ever any more!' and he groaned in spirit. Quincey and I simultaneously moved towards him, and took his arms. We could hear the click of the closing lantern as Van Helsing held it down; coming close to the tomb, he began to remove from the chinks some of the sacred emblem which he had placed there. We all looked on in horrified amazement as we saw, when he stood back, the woman, with a corporeal body as real at the moment as our own, pass in through the interstice where scarce a knife-blade could have gone. We all felt a glad sense of relief when we saw the Professor calmly restoring the strings of putty to the edges of the door.

When this was done, he lifted the child and said: –

'Come now, my friends; we can do no more till to-morrow. There is a funeral at noon, so here we shall all come before long after that. The friends of the dead will all be gone by two, and when the sexton lock the gate we shall remain. Then there is more to do; but not like this of to-night. As for this little one, he is not much harm, and by to-morrow night he shall be well. We shall leave him where the police will find him, as on the other night; and then to home.' Coming close to Arthur, he said: –

'My friend Arthur, you have had sore trial; but after, when you will look back, you will see how it was necessary. You are now in the bitter waters, my child. By this time to-morrow, you will, please God, have passed them, and have drunk of the sweet waters; so do not mourn over-much. Till then I shall not ask you to forgive me.'

Arthur and Quincey came home with me, and we tried to cheer each other on the way. We had left the child in safety, and were tired; so we all slept with more or less reality of sleep.

29 September, night. – A little before twelve o'clock we three – Arthur, Quincey Morris, and myself – called for the Professor. It was odd to notice that by common consent we had all put on black clothes. Of course, Arthur wore black, for he was in deep mourning, but the rest of us wore it by instinct. We got to the churchyard by half-past one, and strolled about, keeping out of official observation, so that when the gravediggers had completed their task, and the sexton, under the belief that everyone had gone, had locked the gate, we had the place all to ourselves. Van Helsing, instead of his little black bag, had with him a long leather one, something like a cricketing bag; it was manifestly of fair weight.

When we were alone and had heard the last of the footsteps die out up the road, we silently, and as if by ordered intention, followed the Professor to the tomb. He unlocked the door, and we entered, closing it behind us. Then he took from his bag the lantern, which he lit, and also two wax candles, which, when lighted, he stuck, by melting their own ends, on other coffins, so that they might give light sufficient to work by. When he again lifted the lid off Lucy's coffin we all looked – Arthur trembling like an aspen – and saw that the body lay there in all its death-beauty. But there was no love in my own heart, nothing but loathing for the foul Thing which had taken Lucy's shape without her soul. I could see even Arthur's face grow hard as he looked. Presently he said to Van Helsing: –

'Is this really Lucy's body, or only a demon in her shape?'

'It is her body, and yet not it. But wait a while, and you shall see her as she was, and is.'

She seemed like a nightmare of Lucy as she lay there; the pointed teeth, the bloodstained, voluptuous mouth – which it made one shudder to see – the whole carnal and unspiritual appearance, seeming like a devilish mockery of Lucy's sweet purity. Van Helsing, in his methodical manner, began taking the various contents from his bag and placing them ready for use. First he took out a soldering iron and some plumbing solder, and then a small oil-lamp, which gave out, when lit in a corner of the tomb, gas which burned at fierce heat with a blue flame; then his operating knives, which he placed to hand; and last a round wooden stake, some two and a half or three inches thick and about three feet long. One end of it was hardened by charring in the fire, and was sharpened to a fine point. With this stake came a heavy hammer, such as in households is used in the coal-cellar for breaking the lumps. To me, a doctor's preparations for work of any kind are stimulating and bracing, but the effect of these things on both Arthur and Quincey was to cause them a sort of consternation. They both, however, kept their courage, and remained silent and quiet.

When all was ready, Van Helsing said: –

'Before we do anything, let me tell you this; it is out of the lore and experience of the ancients and of all those who have studied the powers of the Un-Dead. When they become such, there comes with the change the curse of immortality; they cannot die, but must go on age after age adding new victims and multiplying the evils of the world; for all that die from the preying of the Un-Dead become themselves Un-Dead, and prey on their kind. And so the circle goes on ever widening, like as the ripples from a stone thrown in the water. Friend Arthur, if you had met that kiss which you know of before poor Lucy die; or again, last night when you open your arms to her, you would in time, when you had died, have become *nosferatu*, as they call it in Eastern Europe, and would all time make more of those Un-Deads that so have filled us with horror. The career of this so unhappy dear lady is but just begun. Those children whose blood she suck are not as yet so much the worse; but if she live on, Un-Dead, more and more they lose their blood, and by her power over them they come to her; and so she draw their blood with that so wicked mouth. But if she die in truth, then all cease; the tiny wounds of the throats disappear, and they go back to their plays unknowing ever of what has been. But of the most blessed of all, when this now Un-Dead be made to rest as true dead, then the soul of the poor lady whom we love shall again be free. Instead of working wickedness by night and growing more debased in the assimilation of it by day, she shall take her place with the other Angels. So that, my friend, it will be a blessed hand for her that shall strike the blow that sets her free. To this I am willing; but is there none amongst us who has a better right? Will it be no joy to think of hereafter in the silence of the night when sleep is not: "It was my hand that sent her to the stars; it was the hand of him that loved her best; the hand that of all she would herself have chosen, had it been to her to choose"? Tell me if there be such a one amongst us.'

We all looked at Arthur. He saw, too, what we all did, the infinite kindness which suggested that his should be the hand which would restore Lucy to us as a holy, and not an unholy, memory; he stepped forward and said bravely, though his hand trembled, and his face was as pale as snow: –

'My true friend, from the bottom of my broken heart I thank you. Tell me what I am to do, and I shall not falter!' Van Helsing laid a hand on his shoulder, and said: –

'Brave lad! A moment's courage, and it is done. This stake must be driven through her. It will be a fearful ordeal – be not deceived in that –

but it will be only a short time, and you will then rejoice more than your pain was great; from this grim tomb you will emerge as though you tread on air. But you must not falter when once you have begun. Only think that we, your true friends, are round you, and that we pray for you all the time.'

'Go on,' said Arthur hoarsely. 'Tell me what I am to do.'

'Take this stake in your left hand, ready to place the point over the heart, and the hammer in your right. Then when we begin our prayer for the dead – I shall read him; I have here the book, and the others shall follow – strike in God's name, that so all may be well with the dead that we love, and that the Un-Dead pass away.'

Arthur took the stake and the hammer, and when once his mind was set on action his hands never trembled nor even quivered. Van Helsing opened his missal and began to read, and Quincey and I followed as well as we could. Arthur placed the point over the heart, and as I looked I could see its dint in the white flesh. Then he struck with all his might.

The Thing in the coffin writhed; and a hideous, blood-curdling screech came from the opened red lips. The body shook and quivered and twisted in wild contortions; the sharp white teeth champed together till the lips were cut and the mouth was smeared with a crimson foam. But Arthur never faltered. He looked like a figure of Thor as his untrembling arm rose and fell, driving deeper and deeper the mercy-bearing stake, whilst the blood from the pierced heart welled and spurted up around it. His face was set, and high duty seemed to shine through it; the sight of it gave us courage, so that our voices seemed to ring through the little vault.

And then the writhing and quivering of the body became less, and the teeth ceased to champ, and the face to quiver. Finally it lay still. The terrible task was over.

The hammer fell from Arthur's hand. He reeled and would have fallen had we not caught him. Great drops of sweat sprang out on his forehead, and his breath came in broken gasps. It had indeed been an awful strain on him; and had he not been forced to his task by more than human considerations he could never have gone through with it. For a few minutes we were so taken up with him that we did not look towards the coffin. When we did, however, a murmur of startled surprise ran from one to the other of us. We gazed so eagerly that Arthur rose, for he had been seated on the ground, and came and looked too; and then a glad, strange light broke over his face and dispelled altogether the gloom of horror that lay upon it.

There in the coffin lay no longer the foul Thing that we had so dreaded and grown to hate that the work of her destruction was yielded as a privilege to the one best entitled to it, but Lucy as we had seen her in her life, with her face of unequalled sweetness and purity. True that there were there, as we had seen them in life, the traces of care and pain and waste; but these were all dear to us, for they marked her truth to what we knew. One and all we felt that the holy calm that lay like sunshine over the wasted face and form was only an earthly token and symbol of the calm that was to reign for ever.

Van Helsing came and laid his hand on Arthur's shoulder, and said to him: –

'And now, Arthur, my friend, dear lad, am I not forgiven?'

The reaction of the terrible strain came as he took the old man's hand in his, and raising it to his lips, pressed it, saying: –

'Forgiven! God bless you that you have given my dear one her soul again, and me peace.' He put his hands on the Professor's shoulder, and laying his head on his breast, cried for a while silently, whilst we stood unmoving. When he raised his head Van Helsing said to him: –

'And now, my child, you may kiss her. Kiss her dead lips if you will, as she would have you to, if for her to choose. For she is not a grinning devil now – not any more a foul Thing for all eternity. No longer she is the devil's Un-Dead. She is God's true dead, whose soul is with Him!'

Arthur bent and kissed her, and then we sent him and Quincey out of the tomb; the Professor and I sawed the top off the stake, leaving the point of it in the body. Then we cut off the head and filled the mouth with garlic. We soldered up the leaden coffin, screwed on the coffin-lid, and gathering up our belongings, came away. When the Professor locked the door he gave the key to Arthur.

Outside the air was sweet, the sun shone, and the birds sang, and it seemed as if all nature were tuned to a different pitch. There was gladness and mirth and peace everywhere, for we were at rest ourselves on one account, and we were glad, though it was with a tempered joy.

Before we moved away Van Helsing said: –

'Now, my friends, one step of our work is done, one the most harrowing to ourselves. But there remains a greater task: to find out the author of all this our sorrow and to stamp him out. I have clues which we can follow; but it is a long task, and a difficult, and there is danger in it, and pain. Shall you not all help me? We have learned to believe, all of us – is it not so? And since so, do we not see our duty? Yes! And do we not promise to go on to the bitter end?'

Each in turn, we took his hand, and the promise was made. Then said the Professor as we moved off: –

'Two nights hence you shall meet with me and dine together at seven of the clock with friend John. I shall entreat two others, two that you know not as yet; and I shall be ready to all our work show and our plans unfold. Friend John, you come with me home, for I have much to consult about, and you can help me. To-night I leave for Amsterdam, but shall return to-morrow night. And then begins our great quest. But first I shall have much to say, so that you may know what is to do and to dread. Then our promise shall be made to each other anew, for there is a terrible task before us, and once our feet are on the ploughshare, we must not draw back.'

CHAPTER 17

DR SEWARD'S DIARY

(CONTINUED)

When we arrived at the Berkeley Hotel, Van Helsing found a telegram waiting for him: –

'Am coming up by train. Jonathan at Whitby. Important news. – Mina Harker.'

The Professor was delighted. 'Ah, that wonderful Madam Mina,' he said, 'pearl among women! She arrive, but I cannot stay. She must go to your house, friend John. You must meet her at the station. Telegraph her *en route*, so that she may be prepared.'

When the wire was despatched he had a cup of tea; over it he told me of a diary kept by Jonathan Harker when abroad, and gave me a type-written copy of it, as also of Mrs Harker's diary at Whitby. 'Take these,' he said, 'and study them well. When I have returned you will be master of all the facts, and we can then better enter on our inquisition. Keep them safe, for there is in them much of treasure. You will need all your faith, even you who have had such an experience as that of to-day. What is here told,' he laid his hand heavily and gravely on the packet of papers as he spoke, 'may be the beginning of the end of you and me and many another, or it may sound the knell of the Un-Dead who walk the earth. Read all, I pray you, with the open mind; and if you can add in any way to the story here told do so, for it is all-important. You have kept diary of all these so strange things; is it not so? Yes! Then we shall go through all these together when that we meet.' He then made ready for his departure, and shortly after drove off to Liverpool Street. I took my way to Paddington, where I arrived about fifteen minutes before the train came in.

The crowd melted away after the bustling fashion common to arrival platforms; and I was beginning to feel uneasy, lest I might miss my guest, when a sweet-faced, dainty-looking girl stepped up to me, and, after a quick glance, said: 'Dr Seward, is it not?'

'And you are Mrs Harker!' I answered at once; whereupon she held out her hand.

'I knew you from the description of poor dear Lucy; but –' She stopped suddenly, and a quick blush overspread her face.

The blush that rose to my own cheeks somehow set us both at ease, for it was a tacit answer to her own. I got her luggage, which included a typewriter, and we took the Underground to Fenchurch Street, after I had sent a wire to my housekeeper to have a sitting-room and bedroom prepared at once for Mrs Harker.

In due time we arrived. She knew, of course, that the place was a lunatic asylum, but I could see that she was unable to repress a slight shudder when we entered.

She told me that, if she might, she would come presently to my study, as she had much to say. So here I am finishing my entry in my phonograph diary whilst I await her. As yet I have not had the chance of looking at the papers which Van Helsing left with me, though they lie open before me. I must get her interested in something, so that I may have an opportunity of reading them. She does not know how precious time is, or what a task we have in hand. I must be careful not to frighten her. Here she is!

MINA HARKER'S JOURNAL

29 September. – After I had tidied myself, I went down to Dr Seward's study. At the door I paused a moment, for I thought I heard him talking with someone. As, however, he had pressed me to be quick, I knocked at the door, and on his calling out, 'Come in,' I entered.

To my intense surprise, there was no one with him. He was quite alone, and on the table opposite him was what I knew at once from the description to be a phonograph. I had never seen one, and was much interested.

'I hope I did not keep you waiting,' I said; 'but I stayed at the door as I heard you talking, and thought there was someone with you.'

'Oh,' he replied, with a smile, 'I was only entering my diary.'

'Your diary?' I asked him in surprise.

'Yes,' he answered. 'I keep it in this.' As he spoke he laid his hand on the phonograph. I felt quite excited over it, and blurted out: –

'Why, this beats even shorthand! May I hear it say something?'

'Certainly,' he replied with alacrity, and stood up to put it in train for speaking. Then he paused, and a troubled look overspread his face.

'The fact is,' he began awkwardly, 'I only keep my diary in it; and as it is entirely – almost entirely – about my cases, it may be awkward – that is, I mean –' He stopped, and I tried to help him out of his embarrassment:

'You helped to attend dear Lucy at the end. Let me hear how she died; for all that I can know of her, I shall be very grateful. She was very, very dear to me.'

To my surprise, he answered, with a horrorstruck look in his face: –
'Tell you of her death? Not for the wide world!'

'Why not?' I asked, for some grave, terrible feeling was coming over
me. Again he paused, and I could see that he was trying to invent an
excuse. At length he stammered out: –

'You see, I do not know how to pick out any particular part of the
diary.' Even while he was speaking an idea dawned upon him, and he said
with unconscious simplicity, in a different voice, and with the naïveté of
a child: 'That's quite true, upon my honour. Honest Indian!' I could not
but smile, at which he grimaced. 'I gave myself away that time!' he said.
'But do you know that, although I have kept the diary for months past, it
never once struck me how I was going to find any particular part of it in
case I wanted to look it up?' By this time my mind was made up that the
diary of a doctor who attended Lucy might have something to add to the
sum of our knowledge of that terrible Being, and I said boldly: –

'Then, Dr Seward, you had better let me copy it out for you on my
typewriter.' He grew to a positively deathly pallor as he said: –

'No! no! no! For all the world, I wouldn't let you know that terrible
story!'

Then it was terrible; my intuition was right! For a moment I thought,
and as my eyes ranged the room, unconsciously looking for something or
some opportunity to aid me, they lit on the great batch of typewriting on
the table. His eyes caught the look in mine, and, without his thinking,
followed their direction. As they saw the parcel he realized my meaning.

'You do not know me,' I said. 'When you have read those papers – my
own diary and my husband's also, which I have typed – you will know
me better. I have not faltered in giving every thought of my own heart in
this cause; but, of course, you do not know me – yet; and I must not
expect you to trust me so far.'

He is certainly a man of noble nature; poor dear Lucy was right about
him. He stood up and opened a large drawer, in which were arranged in
order a number of hollow cylinders of metal covered with dark wax, and
said: –

'You are quite right. I did not trust you because I did not know you.
But I know you now; and let me say that I should have known you long
ago. I know that Lucy told you of me; she told me of you too. May I
make the only atonement in my power? Take the cylinders and hear them
– the first half-dozen of them are personal to me, and they will not horrify
you; then you will know me better. Dinner will by then be ready. In the
meantime I shall read over some of these documents, and shall be better

able to understand certain things.' He carried the phonograph himself up to my sitting-room and adjusted it for me. Now I shall learn something pleasant, I am sure; for it will tell me the other side of a true love episode of which I know one side already . . .

DR SEWARD'S DIARY

29 September. – I was so absorbed in that wonderful diary of Jonathan Harker and that other of his wife that I let the time run on without thinking. Mrs Harker was not down when the maid came to announce dinner, so I said: 'She is possibly tired; let dinner wait an hour'; and I went on with my work. I had just finished Mrs Harker's diary, when she came in. She looked sweetly pretty, but very sad, and her eyes were flushed with crying. This somehow moved me much. Of late I have had cause for tears, God knows! but the relief of them was denied me; and now the sight of those sweet eyes, brightened with recent tears, went straight to my heart. So I said as gently as I could: –

'I greatly fear I have distressed you.'

'Oh no, not distressed me,' she replied, 'but I have been more touched than I can say by your grief. That is a wonderful machine, but it is cruelly true. It told me, in its very tones, the anguish of your heart. It was like a soul crying out to almighty God. No one must hear them spoken ever again! See, I have tried to be useful. I have copied out the words on my typewriter, and none other need now hear your heart beat, as I did.'

'No one need ever know, shall ever know,' I said in a low voice. She laid her hand on mine and said very gravely: –

'Ah, but they must!'

'Must! But why?' I asked.

'Because it is a part of the terrible story, a part of poor dear Lucy's death and all that led to it; because in the struggle which we have before us to rid the earth of this terrible monster we must have all the knowledge and all the help which we can get. I think that the cylinders which you gave me contained more than you intended me to know; but I can see that there are in your record many lights to this dark mystery. You will let me help, will you not? I know all up to a certain point, and I see already, though your diary only took me to 7 September, how poor Lucy was beset, and how her terrible doom was being wrought out. Jonathan and I have been working day and night since Professor Van Helsing saw us. He is gone to Whitby to get more information, and he will be here to-

morrow to help us. We need have no secrets amongst us; working together
and with absolute trust, we can surely be stronger than if some of us were
in the dark.' She looked at me so appealingly, and at the same time manifested such courage and resolution in her bearing, that I gave in at once
to her wishes. 'You shall,' I said, 'do as you like in the matter. God forgive
me if I do wrong! There are terrible things yet to learn of; but if you have
so far travelled on the road to poor Lucy's death, you will not be content,
I know, to remain in the dark. Nay, the end – the very end – may give
you a gleam of peace. Come, there is dinner. We must keep one another
strong for what is before us; we have a cruel and dreadful task. When you
have eaten you shall learn the rest, and I will answer any questions you
ask – if there be anything which you do not understand, though it was
apparent to us who were present.'

MINA HARKER'S JOURNAL

29 September. – After dinner I came with Dr Seward to his study. He
brought back the phonograph from my room, and I took my typewriter.
He placed me in a comfortable chair, and arranged the phonograph so that
I could touch it without getting up, and showed me how to stop it in case
I should want to pause. Then he very thoughtfully took a chair, with his
back to me, so that I might be as free as possible, and began to read. I
put the forked metal to my ears and listened.

When the terrible story of Lucy's death, and – and all that followed,
was done, I lay back in my chair powerless. Fortunately I am not of a
fainting disposition. When Dr Seward saw me he jumped up with a horrified exclamation, and hurriedly taking a case-bottle from a cupboard, gave
me some brandy, which in a few minutes somewhat restored me. My brain
was all in a whirl, and only that there came through all the multitude of
horrors the holy ray of light that my dear, dear Lucy was at last at peace,
I do not think I could have borne it without making a scene. It is all so
wild, and mysterious, and strange, that if I had not known Jonathan's experience in Transylvania I could not have believed. As it was, I didn't know
what to believe, and so got out of my difficulty by attending to something
else. I took the cover off my typewriter, and said to Dr Seward:

'Let me write this all out now. We must be ready for Dr Van Helsing
when he comes. I have sent a telegram to Jonathan to come on here when
he arrives in London from Whitby. In this matter dates are everything, and
I think if we get all our material ready, and have every item put in chrono-

logical order, we shall have done much. You tell me that Lord Godalming
and Mr Morris are coming too. Let us be able to tell them when they
come.' He accordingly set the phonograph at a slow pace, and I began to
typewrite from the beginning of the seventh cylinder. I used manifold, and
so took three copies of the diary, just as I had done with all the rest. It
was late when I got through, but Dr Seward went about his work of going
his round of the patients; when he had finished he came back and sat near
me, reading, so that I did not feel too lonely whilst I worked. How good
and thoughtful he is; the world seems full of good men – even if there
are monsters in it. Before I left him I remembered what Jonathan put in
his diary of the Professor's perturbation at reading something in an evening
paper at the station at Exeter; so, seeing that Dr Seward keeps his newspapers, I borrowed the files of the *Westminster Gazette* and the *Pall Mall
Gazette*, and took them to my room. I remember how much the *Dailygraph* and the *Whitby Gazette*, of which I had made cuttings, helped us
to understand the terrible events at Whitby when Count Dracula landed,
so I shall look through the evening papers since then, and perhaps I shall
get some new light. I am not sleepy, and the work will help to keep me
quiet.

DR SEWARD'S DIARY

30 September. – Mr Harker arrived at nine o'clock. He had got his wife's
wire just before starting. He is uncommonly clever, if one can judge from
his face, and full of energy. If his journal be true – and judging by one's
own wonderful experiences it must be – he is also a man of great nerve.
That going down to the vault a second time was a remarkable piece of
daring. After reading his account of it I was prepared to meet a good specimen of manhood, but hardly the quiet, business-like gentleman who came
here to-day.

Later. – After lunch Harker and his wife went back to their own room,
and as I passed a while ago I heard the click of the typewriter. They are
hard at it. Mrs Harker says that they are knitting together in chronolog-
ical order every scrap of evidence they have. Harker has got the letters
between the consignee of the boxes at Whitby and the carriers in London
who took charge of them. He is now reading his wife's typescript of my
diary. I wonder what they make out of it. Here he is . . .

Strange that it never struck me that the very next house might be the
Count's hiding-place! Goodness knows that we had enough clues from

the conduct of the patient Renfield! The bundle of letters relating to the purchase of the house were with the typescript. Oh, if we had only had them earlier we might have saved poor Lucy! Stop; that way madness lies! Harker has gone back, and is again collating his material. He says that by dinner-time they will be able to show a whole connected narrative. He thinks that in the meantime I should see Renfield, as hitherto he has been a sort of index to the coming and going of the Count. I hardly see this yet, but when I get at the dates I suppose I shall. What a good thing that Mrs Harker put my cylinders into type! We never could have found the dates otherwise . . .

I found Renfield sitting placidly in his room with his hands folded, smiling benignly. At the moment he seemed as sane as anyone I ever saw. I sat down and talked with him on a lot of subjects, all of which he treated naturally. He then, of his own accord, spoke of going home, a subject he has never mentioned to my knowledge during his sojourn here. In fact, he spoke quite confidently of getting his discharge at once. I believe that, had I not had the chat with Harker and read the letters and the dates of his outbursts, I should have been prepared to sign for him after a brief time of observation. As it is, I am darkly suspicious. All those outbreaks were in some way linked with the proximity of the Count. What then does this absolute content mean? Can it be that his instinct is satisfied as to the vampire's ultimate triumph? Stay; he is himself zoophagous, and in his wild ravings outside the chapel door of the deserted house he always spoke of 'master.' This all seems confirmation of our idea. However, after a while I came away; my friend is just a little too sane at present to make it safe to probe him too deep with questions. He might begin to think, and then –! So I came away. I mistrust these quiet moods of his; so I have given the attendant a hint to look closely after him, and to have a strait-waistcoat ready in case of need.

JONATHAN HARKER'S JOURNAL

29 September, in train to London. – When I received Mr Billington's courteous message that he would give me any information in his power, I thought it best to go down to Whitby and make, on the spot, such inquiries as I wanted. It was now my object to trace that horrid cargo of the Count's to its place in London. Later, we may be able to deal with it. Billington junior, a nice lad, met me at the station, and brought me to his father's house, where they had decided that I must stay the night. They are hospitable, with true Yorkshire hospitality: give a guest everything, and leave him free to do as he likes. They all knew that I was busy, and that my stay was short, and Mr Billington had ready in his office all the papers concerning the consignment of boxes. It gave me almost a turn to see again one of the letters which I had seen on the Count's table before I knew of his diabolical plans. Everything had been carefully thought out, and done systematically and with precision. He seemed to have been prepared for every obstacle which might be placed by accident in the way of his intentions being carried out. To use an Americanism, he had 'taken no chances,' and the absolute accuracy with which his instructions were fulfilled was simply the logical result of his care. I saw the invoice, and took note of it: 'Fifty cases of common earth, to be used for experimental purposes.' Also the copy of the letter to Carter Paterson, and their reply; of both of these I got copies. This was all the in-formation Mr Billington could give me, so I went down to the port and saw the coastguards, the Customs officers, and the harbour-master. They had all something to say of the strange entry of the ship, which is already taking its place in local tradition; but no one could add to the simple description: 'Fifty cases of common earth.' I then saw the station-master, who kindly put me in commu-nication with the men who had actually received the boxes. Their tally was exact with the list, and they had nothing to add except that the boxes were 'main and mortal heavy,' and that shifting them was dry work. One of them added that it was hard lines that there wasn't any gentleman 'such-like as yourself, squire,' to show some sort of appreci-ation of their efforts in a liquid form; another put in a rider that the thirst then generated was such that even the time which had elapsed had not completely allayed it. Needless to add, I took care before leaving to lift, for ever and adequately, this source of reproach.

30 September. – The station-master was good enough to give me a line to his old companion the station-master at King's Cross, so that when I arrived there in the morning I was able to ask him about the arrival of the boxes. He, too, put me at once in communication with the proper offi-cials, and I saw that their tally was correct with the original invoice. The opportunities of acquiring an abnormal thirst had been here limited; a noble use of them had, however, been made, and again I was compelled to deal with the result in an *ex post facto* manner.

From thence I went on to Carter Paterson's central office, where I met with the utmost courtesy. They looked up the transaction in their day-book and letter-book, and at once telephoned to their King's Cross office for more details. By good fortune, the men who did the teaming were waiting for work, and the official at once sent them over, sending also by one of them the way-bill and all the papers connected with the delivery of the boxes at Carfax. Here again I found the tally agreeing exactly; the carriers' men were able to supplement the paucity of the written words with a few details. These were, I shortly found, connected almost solely with the dusty nature of the job, and of the consequent thirst engendered in the operators. On my affording an opportunity, through the medium of the currency of the realm, of the allaying at a later period this beneficient evil, one of the men remarked: –

'That 'ere 'ouse, guv'nor, is the rummiest I ever was in. Blyme! but it ain't been touched sence a hundred years. There was dust that thick in the place that you might have slep' on it without 'urtin' of yer bones; an' the place was that neglected that yer might 'ave smelled ole Jerusalem in it. But the ole chapel – that took the cike, that did! Me and my mate, we thort we wouldn't never git out quick enough. Lor', I wouldn't take less nor a quid a moment to stay there arter dark.' Having been in the house, I could well believe him; but if he knew what I know, he would, I think, have raised his terms.

Of one thing I am now satisfied: that *all* the boxes which arrived at Whitby from Varna in the *Demeter* were safely deposited in the old chapel of Carfax. There should be fifty of them there, unless any have since been removed – as from Dr Seward's diary I fear.

I shall try to see the carter who took away the boxes from Carfax when Renfield attacked them. By following up this clue we may learn a good deal.

Later. – Mina and I have worked all day, and we have put all the papers into order.

MINA HARKER'S JOURNAL

30 September. – I am so glad that I hardly know how to contain myself. It is, I suppose, the reaction from the haunting fear which I have had: that this terrible affair and the reopening of his old wound might act detrimentally on Jonathan. I saw him leave for Whitby with as brave a face as I could, but I was sick with apprehension. The effort has, however, done him good. He was never so resolute, never so strong, never so full of volcanic energy, as at present. It is just as that dear, good Professor Van Helsing said: he is true grit, and he improves under strain that would kill a weaker nature. He came back full of life and hope and determination; we have got everything in order for to-night. I feel myself quite wild with excitement. I suppose one ought to pity anything so hunted as is the Count. That is just it: this Thing is not human – not even beast. To read Dr Seward's account of poor Lucy's death, and what followed, is enough to dry up the springs of pity in one's heart.

Later. – Lord Godalming and Mr Morris arrived earlier than we expected. Dr Seward was out on business and had taken Jonathan with him, so I had to see them. It was to me a painful meeting, for it brought back all poor dear Lucy's hopes of only a few months ago. Of course they had heard Lucy speak of me, and it seemed that Dr Van Helsing, too, had been quite 'blowing my trumpet,' as Mr Morris expressed it. Poor fellows, neither of them is aware that I know all about the proposals they made to Lucy. They did not quite know what to say or do, as they were ignorant of the amount of my knowledge; so they had to keep on neutral subjects. However, I thought the matter over, and came to the conclusion that the best thing I could do would be to post them in affairs right up to date. I knew from Dr Seward's diary that they had been at Lucy's death – her real death – and that I need not fear to betray any secret before the time. So I told them, as well as I could, that I had read all the papers and diaries, and that my husband and I, having typewritten them, had just finished putting them in order. I gave them each a copy to read in the library. When Lord Godalming got his and turned it over – it does make a pretty good pile – he said: –

'Did you write all this, Mrs Harker?'

I nodded, and he went on: –

'I don't quite see the drift of it; but you people are all so good and kind, and have been working so earnestly and so energetically, that all I can do is to accept your ideas blindfold and try to help you. I have had one lesson already in accepting facts that should make a man humble to the last hour of his life. Besides, I know you loved my poor Lucy –' Here he turned away and covered his face with his hands. I could hear the tears in his voice. Mr Morris, with instinctive delicacy, just laid a hand for a moment on his shoulder, and then walked quietly out of the room. I suppose there is something in woman's nature that makes a man free to break down before her and express his feelings on the tender or emotional side with-out feeling it derogatory to his manhood; for when Lord Godalming found himself alone with me he sat down on the sofa and gave way utterly and openly. I sat down beside him and took his hand. I hope he didn't think it forward of me, and that if he ever thinks of it afterwards he never will have such a thought. There I wrong him;

I *know* he never will – he is too true a gentleman. I said to him, for I could see that his heart was breaking: –

'I loved dear Lucy, and I know what she was to you, and what you were to her. She and I were like sisters; and now she is gone, will you not let me be like a sister to you in your trouble? I know what sorrows you have had, though I cannot measure the depth of them. If sympathy and pity can help in your affliction, won't you let me be of some little service – for Lucy's sake?'

In an instant the poor dear fellow was overwhelmed with grief. It seemed to me that all that he had of late been suffering in silence found a vent at once. He grew quite hysterical, and raising his open hands, beat his palms together in a perfect agony of grief. He stood up and then sat down again, and the tears rained down his cheeks. I felt an infinite pity for him, and opened my arms unthinkingly. With a sob he laid his head on my shoulder, and cried like a wearied child, whilst he shook with emotion.

We women have something of the mother in us that makes us rise above smaller matters when the mother-spirit is invoked; I felt this big, sorrowing man's head resting on me, as though it were that of the baby that some day may lie on my bosom, and I stroked his hair as though he were my own child. I never thought at the time how strange it all was.

After a little bit his sobs ceased, and he raised himself with an apology, though he made no disguise of his emotion. He told me that for days and nights past – weary days and sleepless nights – he had been unable to speak with anyone, as a man must speak in his time of sorrow. There was no woman whose sympathy could be given to him, or with whom, owing to the terrible circumstances with which his sorrow was surrounded, he could speak freely. 'I know now how I suffered,' he said, as he dried his eyes, 'but I do not know even yet – and none other can ever know – how much your sweet sympathy has been to me to-day. I shall know better in time; and believe me that, though I am not ungrateful now, my gratitude will grow with my understanding. You will let me be like a brother, will you not, for all our lives – for dear Lucy's sake?'

'For dear Lucy's sake,' I said as we clasped hands. 'Ay, and for your own sake,' he added, 'for if a man's esteem and gratitude are ever worth the winning, you have won mine to-day. If ever the future should bring to you a time when you need a man's help, believe me, you will not call in vain. God grant that no such time may ever come to you to break the sunshine of your life; but if it should ever come, promise me that you will let me know.' He was so earnest, and his sorrow was so fresh, that I felt it would comfort him, so I said: –

'I promise.'

As I came along the corridor I saw Mr Morris looking out of a window. He turned as he heard my footsteps. 'How is Art?' he said. Then noticing my red eyes, he went on: 'Ah, I see you have been comforting him. Poor old fellow! he needs it. No one but a woman can help a man when he is in trouble of the heart; and he had no one to comfort him.'

He bore his own trouble so bravely that my heart bled for him. I saw the manuscript in his hand, and I knew that when he read it he would realize how much I knew; so I said to him: –

'I wish I could comfort all who suffer from the heart. Will you let me be your friend, and will you come to me for comfort if you need it? You will know, later on, why I speak.' He saw that I was in earnest, and stooping, took my hand, and raising it to his lips, kissed it. It seemed but poor comfort to so brave and unselfish a soul, and impulsively I bent over and kissed him. The tears rose in his eyes, and there was a momentary choking in his throat; he said quite calmly: –

'Little girl, you will never regret that true-hearted kindness, so long as ever you live!' Then he went into the study to his friend.

'Little girl!' – the very words he had used to Lucy, and oh, but he proved himself a friend!

CHAPTER 18

DR SEWARD'S DIARY

30 September. – I got home at five o'clock, and found that Godalming and Morris had not only arrived, but had already studied the transcript of the various diaries and letters which Harker and his wonderful wife had made and arranged. Harker had not yet returned from his visit to the carriers' men, of whom Dr Hennessey had written to me. Mrs Harker gave us a cup of tea, and I can honestly say that, for the first time since I have lived in it, this old house seemed like *home*. When we had finished, Mrs Harker said: –

'Dr Seward, may I ask a favour? I want to see your patient, Mr Renfield. Do let me see him. What you have said of him in your diary interests me so much!' She looked so appealing and so pretty that I could not refuse her, and there was no possible reason why I should; so I took her with me. When I went into the room, I told the man that a lady would like to see him; to which he simply answered: 'Why?'

'She is going through the house, and wants to see every one in it,' I answered. 'Oh, very well,' he said; 'let her come in, by all means; but just wait a minute till I tidy up the place.' His method of tidying was peculiar: he simply swallowed all the flies and spiders in the boxes before I could stop him. It was quite evident that he feared, or was jealous of, some interference. When he had got through his disgusting task, he said cheerfully: 'Let the lady come in,' and sat down on the edge of his bed with his head down, but with his eyelids raised so that he could see her as she entered. For a moment I thought that he might have some homicidal intent; I remembered how quiet he had been just before he attacked me in my own study, and I took care to stand where I could seize him at once if he attempted to make a spring at her. She came into the room with an easy gracefulness which would at once command the respect of any lunatic – for easiness is one of the qualities mad people most respect. She walked over to him, smiling pleasantly, and held out her hand.

'Good evening, Mr Renfield,' said she. 'You see, I know you, for Dr Seward has told me of you.' He made no immediate reply, but eyed her all over intently with a set frown on his face. This look gave way to one of wonder, which merged in doubt; then, to my intense astonishment, he said: –

'You're not the girl the doctor wanted to marry, are you? You can't be, you know, for she's dead.' Mrs Harker smiled sweetly as she replied: –

'Oh no! I have a husband of my own, to whom I was married before I ever saw Dr Seward, or he me. I am Mrs Harker.'

'Then what are you doing here?'

'My husband and I are staying on a visit with Dr Seward.'

'Then don't stay.'

'But why not?' I thought that this style of conversation might not be pleasant to Mrs Harker, any more than it was to me, so I joined in: –

'How did you know I wanted to marry anyone?' His reply was simply contemptuous, given in a pause in which he turned his eyes from Mrs Harker to me, instantly turning them back again: –

'What an asinine question!'

'I don't see that at all, Mr Renfield,' said Mrs Harker, at once championing me. He replied to her with as much courtesy and respect as he had shown contempt to me: –

'You will, of course, understand, Mrs Harker, that when a man is loved and honoured as our host is, everything regarding him is of interest in our little community. Dr Seward is loved not only by his household and his friends, but even by his patients, who, being some of them hardly in mental equilibrium, are apt to distort causes and effects. Since I myself have been an inmate of a lunatic asylum, I cannot but notice that the sophistic tendencies of some of its inmates lean towards the errors of *non causae* and *ignoratio elenchi*.' I positively opened my eyes at this new development. Here was my own pet lunatic – the most pronounced of his type that I had ever met with – talking elemental philosophy, and with the manner of a polished gentleman. I wonder if it was Mrs Harker's presence which had touched some chord in his memory. If this new phase was spontaneous, or in any way due to her unconscious influence, she must have some rare gift or power.

We continued to talk for some time; and, seeing that he was seemingly quite reasonable, she ventured, looking at me questioningly as she began, to lead him to his favourite topic. I was again astonished, for he addressed himself to the question with the impartiality of the completest sanity; he even took himself as an example when he mentioned certain things.

'Why, I myself am an instance of a man who had a strange belief. Indeed, it was no wonder that my friends were alarmed, and insisted on my being put under control. I used to fancy that life was a positive and perpetual entity, and that by consuming a multitude of live things, no matter how low in the scale of creation, one might indefinitely prolong life. At times I held the belief so strongly that I actually tried to take human life. The doctor here will bear me out that on one occasion I tried to kill him for the purpose of strengthening my vital powers by the assimilation with my own body of his life through the medium of his blood – relying, of course, upon the Scriptural phrase, "For the blood is the life." Though, indeed, the vendor of a certain nostrum has vulgarized the truism to the very point of contempt. Isn't that true, doctor?' I nodded assent, for I was so amazed that I hardly knew what I ought to think or say; it was hard to imagine that I had seen him eat up his spiders and flies not five minutes before. Looking at my watch, I saw that I should go to the station to meet Van Helsing, so I told Mrs Harker that it was time to leave. She came at once, after saying pleasantly to Mr Renfield: 'Good-bye, and I hope I may see you often, under auspices pleasanter to yourself,' to which, to my astonishment, he replied: –

'Good-bye, my dear. I pray God I may never see your sweet face again. May He bless and keep you!'

When I went to the station to meet Van Helsing I left the boys behind me. Poor Art seemed more cheerful than he has been since Lucy first took ill, and Quincey is more like his own bright self than he has been for many a long day.

Van Helsing stepped from the carriage with the eager nimbleness of a boy. He saw me at once, and rushed up to me, saying: –

'Ah, friend John, how goes all? Well? So! I have been busy, for I come here to stay if need be. All affairs are settled with me, and I have much to tell. Madam Mina is with you? Yes. And her so fine husband? And Arthur and my friend Quincey, they are with you, too? Good!'

As I drove to the house I told him of what had passed, and of how my own diary had come to be of some use through Mrs Harker's suggestion; at which the Professor interrupted me: –

'Ah, that wonderful Madam Mina! She has man's brain – a brain that a man should have were he much gifted – and woman's heart. The good God fashioned her for a purpose, believe me, when He made that so good combination. Friend John, up to now fortune has made that woman of help to us; after to-night she must not have to do with this so terrible affair. It is not good that she run a risk so great. We men are determined – nay, are we not pledged? – to destroy this monster; but it is no part for a woman. Even if she be not harmed, her heart may fail her in so much and so many horrors; and hereafter she may suffer – both in waking, from her nerves, and in sleep, from her dreams. And, besides, she is a young woman and not so long married; there may be other things to think of some time, if not now. You tell me she has wrote all, then she must consult with us;

but to-morrow she say good-bye to this work, and we go alone.' I agreed heartily with him, and then I told him what we had found in his absence: that the house which Dracula had bought was the very next one to my own. He was amazed, and a great concern seemed to come on him. 'O that we had known it before!' he said, 'for then we might have reached him in time to save poor Lucy. However, "the milk that is spilt cries not out afterwards," as you say. We shall not think of that, but go on our way to the end.'

Then he fell into a silence that lasted till we entered my own gateway. Before we went to prepare for dinner he said to Mrs Harker: –

'I am told, Madam Mina, by my friend John that you and your husband have put up in exact order all things that have been, up to this moment.'

'Not up to this moment, Professor,' she said impulsively, 'but up to this morning.'

'But why not up to now? We have seen hitherto how good light all the little things have made. We have told our secrets, and yet no one who has told is the worse for it.'

Mrs Harker began to blush, and taking a paper from her pocket, she said: –

'Dr Van Helsing, will you read this, and tell me if it must go in. It is my record of to-day. I too have seen the need of putting down at present everything, however trivial; but there is little in this except what is personal. Must it go in?' The Professor read it over gravely, and handed it back, saying: –

'It need not go in if you do not wish it; but pray that it may. It can but make your husband love you the more, and all us, your friends, more honour you – as well as more esteem and love.' She took it back with another blush and a bright smile.

And so now, up to this very hour, all the records we have are complete and in order. The Professor took away one copy to study after dinner, and before our meeting, which is fixed for nine o'clock. The rest of us have already read everything; so when we meet in the study we shall all be informed as to facts, and can arrange our plan of battle with this terrible and mysterious enemy.

MINA HARKER'S JOURNAL

30 September. – When we met in Dr Seward's study two hours after dinner, which had been at six o'clock, we unconsciously formed a sort of board or committee. Professor Van Helsing took the head of the table, to which

Dr Seward motioned him as he came into the room. He made me sit next to him on his right, and asked me to act as secretary; Jonathan sat next to me. Opposite us were Lord Godalming, Dr Seward, and Mr Morris – Lord Godalming being next the Professor, and Dr Seward in the centre. The Professor said: –

'I may, I suppose, take it that we are all acquainted with the facts that are in these papers.' We all expressed assent, and he went on: –

'Then it were, I think, good that I tell you something of the kind of enemy with which we have to deal. I shall then make known to you something of the history of this man, which has been ascertained for me. So we then can discuss how we shall act, and can take our measure according.

'There are such beings as vampires; some of us have evidence that they exist. Even had we not the proof of our own unhappy experience, the teachings and the records of the past give proof enough for sane peoples. I admit that at the first I was sceptic. Were it not that through long years I have trained myself to keep an open mind, I could not have believed until such time as that fact thunder on my ear: "See! see! I prove; I prove." Alas! Had I known at the first what now I know – nay, had I even guess at him – one so precious life had been spared to many of us who did love her. But that is gone; and we must so work that other poor souls perish not, whilst we can save. The *nosferatu* do not die like the bee when he sting once. He is only stronger; and being stronger, have yet more power to work evil. This vampire which is amongst us is of himself so strong in person as twenty men; he is of cunning more than mortal, for his cunning be the growth of ages; he have still the aids of necromancy, which is, as his etymology imply, the divination by the dead, and all the dead that he can come nigh to are for him at command; he is brute, and more than brute; he is devil in callous, and the heart of him is not; he can, within limitations, appear at will when, and where, and in any of the forms that are to him; he can, within his range, direct the elements: the storm, the fog, the thunder; he can command all the meaner things: the rat, and the owl, and the bat – the moth, and the fox, and the wolf; he can grow and become small; and he can at times vanish and come unknown. How then are we to begin our strife to destroy him? How shall we find his where; and having found it, how can we destroy? My friends, this is much; it is a terrible task that we undertake, and there may be consequence to make the brave shudder. For if we fail in this our fight he must surely win: and then where end we? Life is nothings! I heed him not. But to fail here is not mere life or death. It is that we become as him; that we henceforward become foul things of the night like him – without heart or conscience, preying on the bodies and the souls of those we love best. To us for ever are the gates of heaven shut; for who shall open them to us again? We go on for all time abhorred by all; a blot on the face of God's sunshine; an arrow in the side of Him who died for man. But we are face to face with duty; and in such case must we shrink? For me, I say, no; but then I am old, and life, with his sunshine, his fair places, his song of birds, his music, and his love, lie far behind. You others are young. Some have seen sorrow; but there are fair days yet in store. What say you?'

Whilst he was speaking Jonathan had taken my hand. I feared, oh so much, that the appalling nature of our danger was overcoming him when I saw his hand stretch out; but it was life to me to feel its touch – so strong, so self-reliant, so resolute. A brave man's hand can speak for itself; it does not even need a woman's love to hear its music.

When the Professor had done speaking my husband looked in my eyes, and I in his; there was no need for speaking between us.

'I answer for Mina and myself,' he said.

'Count me in, Professor,' said Mr Quincey Morris, laconically as usual.

'I am with you,' said Lord Godalming, 'for Lucy's sake, if for no other reason.'

Dr Seward simply nodded. The Professor stood up, and, after laying his golden crucifix on the table, held out his hand on either side. I took his right hand, and Lord Godalming his left; Jonathan held my right with his left and stretched across to Mr Morris. So as we all took hands our solemn compact was made. I felt my heart icy cold, but it did not even occur to me to draw back. We resumed our places, and Dr Van Helsing went on with a sort of cheerfulness which showed that the serious work had begun. It was to be taken as gravely, and in as business-like a way, as any other transaction of life: –

'Well, you know what we have to contend against; but we, too, are not without strength. We have on our side power of combination – a power denied to the vampire kind; we have resources of science; we are free to act and think; and the hours of the day and the night are ours equally. In fact, so far as our powers extend, they are unfettered, and we are free to use them. We have self-devotion in a cause, and an end to achieve which is not a selfish one. These things are much.

'Now let us see how far the general powers arrayed against us are restrict, and how the individual cannot. In fine, let us consider the limitations of the vampire in general, and of this one in particular.

'All we have to go upon are traditions and superstitions. These do not at the first appear much, when the matter is one of life and death – nay, of more than either life or death. Yet must we be satisfied; in the first place because we have to be – no other means is at our control – and secondly, because, after all, these things – tradition and superstition – are everything. Does not the belief in vampires rest for others – though not, alas! for us – on them? A year ago which of us would have received such a possibility, in the midst of our scientific, sceptical, matter-of-fact nineteenth century? We even scouted a belief that we saw justified under our very eyes. Take it, then, that the vampire, and the belief in his limitations and his cure, rest for the moment on the same base. For, let me tell you, he is known everywhere that men have been. In old Greece, in old Rome; he flourish in Germany all over, in France, in India, even in the Chersonese; and in China, so far from us in all ways, there even is he, and the peoples fear him at this day. He have follow the wake of the berserker Icelander, the devil-begotten Hun, the Slav, the Saxon, the Magyar. So far, then, we have all we may act upon; and let me tell you that very much of the beliefs are justified by what we have seen in our own so unhappy experience. The vampire live on, and cannot die by mere passing of the time; he can flourish when that he can fatten on the blood of the living. Even more, we have seen amongst us that he can even grow younger; that his vital faculties grow strenuous, and seem as though they refresh themselves when his special pabulum is plenty. But he cannot flourish without this diet; he eat not as others. Even friend Jonathan, who lived with him for weeks, did never see him to eat, never! He throws no shadow; he make in the mirror no reflect, as again Jonathan observe. He has the strength of many in his hand – witness again Jonathan when he shut the door against the wolfs, and when he help him from the diligence too. He can transform himself to wolf, as we gather from the ship arrival in Whitby, when he tear open the dog; he can be as bat, as Madam Mina saw him on the window at Whitby, and as friend John saw him fly from this so near house, and as my friend Quincey saw him at the window of Miss Lucy. He can come in mist which he create – that noble ship's captain proved him of this; but, from what we know, the distance he can make this mist is limited, and it can only be round himself. He come on moonlight rays as elemental dust – as again Jonathan saw those sisters in the castle of Dracula. He become so small – we ourselves saw Miss Lucy, ere she was at peace, slip through a hair-breadth space at the tomb door. He can, when once he find his way, come out from anything or into anything, no matter how close it be bound or even fused up with fire – solder you call it. He can see in the dark – no small power this, in a world which is one half shut from the light. Ah, but hear me through. He can do all these things, yet he is not free. Nay, he is even more prisoner than the slave of the galley, than the madman in his cell. He cannot go where he lists; he who is not of nature has yet to obey some of nature's laws – why we know not. He may not enter anywhere at the first, unless there be someone of the household who bid him to come; though afterwards he can come as he please. His power ceases, as does that of all evil things, at the coming of the day. Only at certain times can he have limited freedom. If he be not at the place whither he is bound, he can only change himself at noon or at exact sunrise or sunset. These things are we told, and in this record of ours we have proof by inference. Thus, whereas he can do as he will within his limit, when he have his earth-home, his coffin-home, his hell-home, the place unhallowed, as we saw when he went to the grave of the suicide at Whitby; still at other time he can only change when the time come. It is said, too, that he can only pass running water at the slack or the flood of the tide. Then there are things which so afflict him that he has no power, as the garlic that we know of, and as for things sacred, as this symbol, my crucifix, that was amongst us even now when we resolve, to them he is nothing, but in their presence he take his place far off and silent with respect. There are others, too, which I shall tell you of, lest in our seeking we may need them. The branch of wild rose on his coffin keep him that he move not from it; a sacred bullet fired into the coffin kill him so that he be true dead; and as for the stake through him, we know already of its peace; or the cut-off head that giveth rest. We have seen it with our eyes.

'Thus when we find the habitation of this man-that-was, we can confine him to his coffin and destroy him, if we obey what we know. But he is clever. I have asked my friend Arminius, of Buda-Pesth University, to make his record; and, from all the means that are, he tell me of what he has been. He must, indeed, have been that Voivode Dracula who won his name against the Turk, over the great river on the very frontier of Turkey-land. If it be so, then was he no common man; for in that time, and for centuries after, he was spoken of as the cleverest and the most cunning, as well as the bravest of the sons of the "land beyond the forest." That mighty brain and that iron resolution went with him to his grave, and are even now arrayed against us. The Draculas were, says Arminius, a great and noble race, though now and again were scions who were held by their coevals to have had dealings with the Evil One. They learned his secrets in the Scholomance, amongst the mountains over Lake Hermanstadt, where the devil claims the tenth scholar as his due. In the records are such words as "stregoica" – witch; "ordog" and "pokol" – Satan and hell; and in one manuscript this very Dracula is spoken of as "wampyr," which we all understand too well.

There have been from the loins of this very one great men and good women, and their graves make sacred the earth where alone this foulness can dwell. For it is not the least of its terrors that this evil thing is rooted deep in all good; in soil barren of holy memories it cannot rest.'

Whilst they were talking Mr Morris was looking steadily at the window, and he now got up quietly, and went out of the room. There was a little pause, and then the Professor went on: –

'And now we must settle what we do. We have here much data, and we must proceed to lay out our campaign. We know from the inquiry of Jonathan that from the castle to Whitby came fifty boxes of earth, all of which were delivered at Carfax; we also know that at least some of these boxes have been removed. It seems to me, that our first step should be to ascertain whether all the rest remain in the house beyond that wall where we look to-day; or whether any more have been removed. If the latter, we must trace –'

Here we were interrupted in a very startling way. Outside the house came the sound of a pistol-shot; the glass of the window was shattered with a bullet, which, ricocheting from the top of the embrasure, struck the far wall of the room. I am afraid I am at heart a coward, for I shrieked out. The men all jumped to their feet; Lord Godalming flew over to the window and threw up the sash. As he did so we heard Mr Morris's voice without: –

'Sorry! I fear I have alarmed you. I shall come in and tell you about it.' A minute later he came in and said: –

'It was an idiotic thing of me to do, and I ask your pardon, Mrs Harker, most sincerely; I fear I must have frightened you terribly. But the fact is that whilst the Professor was talking there came a big bat and sat on the windowsill. I have got such a horror of the damned brutes from recent events that I cannot stand them, and I went out to have a shot, as I have been doing of late of evenings whenever I have seen one. You used to laugh at me for it then, Art.'

'Did you hit it?' asked Dr Van Helsing.

'I don't know; I fancy not, for it flew away into the wood.' Without saying any more he took his seat, and the Professor began to resume his statement: –

'We must trace each of these boxes; and when we are ready, we must either capture or kill this monster in his lair; or we must, so to speak, sterilize the earth, so that no more he can seek safety in it. Thus in the end we may find him in his form of man between the hours of noon and sunset, and so engage with him when he is at his most weak.

'And now for you, Madam Mina, this night is the end until all be well. You are too precious to us to have such risk. When we part to-night, you no more must question. We shall tell you all in good time. We are men, and are able to bear; but you must be our star and our hope, and we shall act all the more free that you are not in the danger, such as we are.'

All the men, even Jonathan, seemed relieved; but it did not seem to me good that they should brave danger and, perhaps, lessen their safety – strength being the best safety – through care of me; but their minds were made up, and, though it was a bitter pill for me to swallow, I could say nothing, save to accept their chivalrous care of me.

Mr Morris resumed the discussion: –

'As there is no time to lose, I vote we have a look at his house right now. Time is everything with him; and swift action on our part may save another victim.'

I own that my heart began to fail me when the time for action came so close, but I did not say anything, for I had a greater fear that if I appeared as a drag or a hindrance to their work, they might even leave me out of their counsels altogether. They have now gone off to Carfax, with means to get into the house.

Manlike, they have told me to go to bed and sleep; as if a woman can sleep when those she loves are in danger! I shall lie down and pretend to sleep, lest Jonathan have added anxiety about me when he returns.

DR SEWARD'S DIARY

1 October, 4 a.m. – Just as we were about to leave the house, an urgent message was brought to me from Renfield to know if I would see him at once, as he had something of the utmost importance to say to me. I told the messenger to say that I would attend to his wishes in the morning; I was busy just at the moment. The attendant added: –

'He seems very importunate, sir. I have never seen him so eager. I don't know but what, if you don't see him soon, he will have one of his violent fits.' I knew the man would not have said this without some cause, so I said: 'All right; I'll go now'; and I asked the others to wait a few minutes for me, as I had to go and see my patient.

'Take me with you, friend John,' said the Professor. 'His case in your diary interested me much, and it had bearing, too, now and again on *our* case. I should much like to see him, and especially when his mind is disturbed.'

'May I come also?' asked Lord Godalming.

'Me too?' said Quincey Morris. I nodded, and we all went down the passage together.

We found him in a state of considerable excitement, but far more rational in his speech and manner than I had ever seen him. There was an unusual understanding of himself, which was unlike anything I had ever met with in a lunatic; and he took it for granted that his reasons would prevail with others entirely sane. We all four went into the room, but none of the others at first said anything. His request was that I would at once release him from the asylum and send him home. This he backed up with arguments regarding his complete recovery, and adduced his own existing sanity. 'I appeal to your friends,' he said; 'they will, perhaps, not mind sitting in judgment on my case. By the way, you have not introduced me.' I was so much astonished, that the oddness of introducing a madman in an asylum did not strike me at the moment; and, besides, there was a certain dignity in the man's manner, so much of the habit of equality, that I at once made the introduction: 'Lord Godalming; Professor Van Helsing; Mr Quincey Morris, of Texas; Mr Renfield.' He shook hands with each of them, saying in turn: –

'Lord Godalming, I had the honour of seconding your father at the Windham; I grieve to know, by your holding the title, that he is no more. He was a man loved and honoured by all who knew him; and in his youth was, I have heard, the inventor of a burnt rum punch, much patronised on Derby night. Mr Morris, you should be proud of your great state. Its reception into the Union was a precedent which may have farreaching effects hereafter, when the Pole and the Tropics may hold allegiance to the Stars and Stripes. The power of Treaty may yet prove a vast engine of enlargement, when the Monroe doctrine takes its true place as a political fable. What shall any man say of his pleasure at meeting Van Helsing? Sir, I make no apology for dropping all forms of conventional prefix. When an individual has revolutionised therapeutics by his discovery of the continuous evolution of brain-matter, conventional forms are unfitting, since they would seem to limit him to one of a class. You gentlemen, who by nationality, by heredity, or by the possession of natural gifts, are fitted to hold your respective places in the moving world, I take to witness that I am as sane as at least the majority of men who are in full possession of their liberties. And I am sure that you, Dr Seward, humanitarian and medico-jurist as well as scientist, will deem it a moral duty to deal with me as one to be considered as under exceptional circumstances.' He made this last appeal with a courtly air of conviction which was not without its own charm.

I think we were all staggered. For my own part, I was under the conviction, despite my knowledge of the man's character and history, that his reason had been restored; and I felt under a strong impulse to tell him that I was satisfied as to his sanity, and would see about the necessary formalities for his release in the morning. I thought it better to wait, however, before making so grave a statement, for of old I knew the sudden changes to which this particular patient was liable. So I contented myself with making a general statement that he appeared to be improving very rapidly; that I would have a longer chat with him in the morning, and would then see what I could do in the direction of meeting his wishes. This did not at all satisfy him, for he said quickly: –

'But I fear, Dr Seward, that you hardly apprehend my wish. I desire to go at once – here – now – this very hour – this very moment, if I may. Time presses, and in our implied agreement with the old scytheman it is of the essence of the contract. I am sure it is only necessary to put before so admirable a practitioner as Dr Seward so simple, yet so momentous a wish, to ensure its fulfilment.' He looked at me keenly, and seeing the negative in my face, turned to the others, and scrutinised them closely. Not meeting any sufficient response, he went on: –

'Is it possible that I have erred in my supposition?'

'You have,' I said frankly, but at the same time, as I felt, brutally. There was a considerable pause, and then he said slowly: –

'Then I suppose I must only shift my ground of request. Let me ask for this concession – boon, privilege, what you will. I am content to implore in such a case, not on personal grounds, but for the sake of others. I am not at liberty to give you the whole of my reasons; but you may, I assure you, take it from me that they are good ones, sound and unselfish, and springing from the highest sense of duty. Could you look, sir, into my heart, you would approve to the full the sentiments which animate me. Nay, more, you would count me amongst the best and truest of your friends.' Again he looked at us all keenly. I had a growing conviction that this sudden change of his entire intellectual method was but yet another form or phase of his madness, and so determined to let him go on a little longer, knowing from experience that he would, like all lunatics, give himself away in the end. Van Helsing was gazing at him with a look of the utmost intensity, his bushy eyebrows almost meeting with the fixed concentration of his look. He said to Renfield in a tone which did not surprise me at the time, but only when I thought of it afterwards – for it was as of one addressing an equal: –

'Can you not tell frankly your real reason for wishing to be free to-night? I will undertake that if you will satisfy even me – a stranger, without prejudice, and with the habit of keeping an open mind – Dr Seward will give you, at his own risk and on his own responsibility, the privilege you seek.' He shook his head sadly, and with a look of poignant regret on his face. The Professor went on: –

'Come, sir, bethink yourself. You claim the privilege of reason in the highest degree, since you seek to impress us with your complete reason-ableness. You do this, whose sanity we have reason to doubt, since you are not yet released from medical treatment for this very defect. If you will not help us in our effort to choose the wisest course, how can we perform the duty which you yourself put upon us? Be wise, and help us; and if we can we shall aid you to achieve your wish.' He still shook his head as he said: –

'Dr Van Helsing, I have nothing to say. Your argument is complete, and if I were free to speak I should not hesitate a moment; but I am not my own master in the matter. I can only ask you to trust me. If I am refused, the responsibility does not rest with me.' I thought it was now time to end the scene, which was becoming too comically grave, so I went towards the door, simply saying: –

'Come, my friends, we have work to do. Good-night.'

As, however, I got near the door, a new change came over the patient. He moved towards me so quickly that for the moment I feared that he was about to make another homicidal attack. My fears, however, were groundless, for he held up his two hands imploringly, and made his peti-tion in a moving manner. As he saw that the very excess of his emotion was militating against him, by restoring us more to our old relations, he became still more demonstrative. I glanced at Van Helsing, and saw my conviction reflected in his eyes; so I became a little more fixed in my manner, if not more stern, and motioned to him that his efforts were unavailing. I had previously seen something of the same constantly growing excitement in him when he had to make some request of which at the time he had thought much, such, for instance, as when he wanted a cat; and I was prepared to see the collapse into the same sullen acquiescence on this occasion. My expectation was not realised, for, when he found that his appeal would not be successful, he got into quite a frantic condition. He threw himself on his knees, and held up his hands, wringing them in plaintive supplication, and poured forth a torrent of entreaty, with the tears rolling down his cheeks and his whole face and form expressive of the deepest emotion: –

'Let me entreat you, Dr Seward, oh, let me implore you, to let me out of this house at once. Send me away how you will and where you will; send keepers with me with whips and chains; let them take me in a strait-waistcoat, manacled and leg-ironed, even to a gaol; but let me go out of this. You don't know what you do by keeping me here. I am speaking from the depths of my heart – of my very soul. You don't know whom you wrong, or how; and I may not tell. Woe is me! I may not tell. By all you hold sacred – by all you hold dear – by your love that is lost – by your hope that lives – for the sake of the Almighty, take me out of this and save my soul from guilt! Can't you hear me, man? Can't you under-stand? Will you never learn? Don't you know that I am sane and earnest now; that I am no lunatic in a mad fit, but a sane man fighting for his soul? Oh, hear me! hear me! Let me go! let me go! let me go!'

I thought that the longer this went on the wilder he would get, and so would bring on a fit; so I took him by the hand and raised him up.

'Come,' I said sternly, 'no more of this; we have had quite enough already. Get to your bed and try to behave more discreetly.'

He suddenly stopped and looked at me intently for several moments. Then without a word he rose, and moving over, sat down on the side of the bed. The collapse had come, as on former occasions, just as I had expected.

When I was leaving the room, last of our party, he said to me in a quiet, well-bred voice: –

'You will, I trust, Dr Seward, do me the justice to bear in mind, later on, that I did what I could to convince you to-night.'

CHAPTER 19

JONATHAN HARKER'S JOURNAL

1 October, 5 a.m. – I went with the party to the search with an easy mind, for I think I never saw Mina so absolutely strong and well. I am so glad that she consented to hold back and let us men do the work. Somehow, it was a dread to me that she was in this fearful business at all; but now that her work is done, and that it is due to her energy and brains and foresight that the whole story is put together in such a way that every point tells, she may well feel that her part is finished, and that she can henceforth leave the rest to us. We were, I think, all a little upset by the scene with Mr Renfield. When we came away from his room we were silent till we got back to the study. Then Mr Morris said to Dr Seward: –

'Say, Jack, if that man wasn't attempting a bluff, he is about the sanest lunatic I ever saw. I'm not sure, but I believe that he had some serious purpose, and if he had, it was pretty rough on him not to get a chance.' Lord Godalming and I were silent, but Dr Van Helsing added: –

'Friend John, you know more of lunatics than I do, and I'm glad of it, for I fear that if it had been to me to decide I would before that last hysterical outburst have given him free. But we live and learn, and in our present task we must take no chance, as my friend Quincey would say. All is best as they are.' Dr Seward seemed to answer them both in a dreamy kind of way: –

'I don't know but that I agree with you. If that man had been an ordinary lunatic I would have taken my chance of trusting him; but he seems so mixed up with the Count in an indexy kind of way that I am afraid of doing anything wrong by helping his fads. I can't forget how he prayed with almost equal fervour for a cat, and then tried to tear my throat out with his teeth. Besides, he called the Count "lord and master," and he may want to get out to help him in some diabolical way. That horrid thing has the wolves and the rats and his own kind to help him, so I suppose he isn't above trying to use a respectable lunatic. He certainly did seem earnest, though. I only hope we have done what is best. These things, in conjunction with the work we have in hand, help to unnerve a man.' The Professor stepped over, and laying a hand on his shoulder, said in his grave, kindly way: –

'Friend John, have no fear. We are trying to do our duty in a very sad and terrible case; we can only do as we deem best. What else have we to hope for, except the pity of the good God?' Lord Godalming had slipped away for a few minutes, but he now returned. He held up a little silver whistle as he remarked: –

'That old place may be full of rats, and if so, I've got an antidote on call.' Having passed the wall, we took our way to the house, taking care to keep in the shadows of the trees on the lawn when the moonlight shone out. When we got to the porch the Professor opened his bag and took out a lot of things, which he laid on the step, sorting them into four little groups, evidently one for each. Then he spoke: –

'My friends, we are going into a terrible danger, and we need arms of many kinds. Our enemy is not merely spiritual. Remember that he has the strength of twenty men, and that, though our necks or our windpipes are of the common kind – and therefore breakable or crushable – his is not amenable to mere strength. A stronger man, or a body of men more strong in all than him, can at certain times hold him; but yet they cannot hurt him as we can be hurt by him. We must, therefore, guard ourselves from his touch. Keep this near your heart' – as he spoke he lifted a little silver crucifix and held it out to me, I being nearest to him – 'put these flowers round your neck' – here he handed to me a wreath of withered garlic blossoms – 'for other enemies more mundane, this revolver and this knife; and for aid in all, these so small electric lamps, which you can fasten to your breast; and for all, and above all at the last, this, which we must not desecrate needless.' This was a portion of sacred wafer, which he put in an envelope and handed to me. Each of the others was similarly equipped. 'Now,' he said, 'friend John, where are the skeleton keys? If so that we can open the door, we need not break house by the window, as before at Miss Lucy's.'

Dr Seward tried one or two skeleton keys, his mechanical dexterity as a surgeon standing him in good stead. Presently he got one to suit; after a little play back and forward the bolt yielded, and, with a rusty clang, shot back. We pressed on the door, the rusty hinges creaked, and it slowly opened. It was startlingly like the image conveyed to me in Dr Seward's diary of the opening of Miss Westenra's tomb; I fancy that the same idea seemed to strike the others, for with one accord they shrank back. The Professor was the first to move forward, and stepped into the open door.

'*In manus tuas, Domine!*' he said, crossing himself as he passed over the threshold. We closed the door behind us, lest when we should have lit our lamps we might possibly attract attention from the road. The

Professor carefully tried the lock, in case we might not be able to open it from within should we be in a hurry to make our exit. Then we all lit our lamps and proceeded on our search.

The light from the tiny lamps fell in all sorts of odd forms, as the rays crossed each other, or the opacity of our bodies threw great shadows. I could not for my life get away from the feeling that there was someone else amongst us. I suppose it was the recollection, so powerfully brought home to me by the grim surroundings, of that terrible experience in Transylvania. I think the feeling was common to us all, for I noticed that the others kept looking over their shoulders at every sound and every new shadow, just as I felt myself doing.

The whole place was thick with dust. The floor was seemingly inches deep, except where there were recent footsteps, in which on holding down my lamp I could see marks of hobnails where the dust was caked. The walls were fluffy and heavy with dust, and in the corners were masses of spiders' webs, whereon the dust had gathered till they looked like old tattered rags as the weight had torn them partly down. On a table in the hall was a great bunch of keys, with a time-yellowed label on each. They had been used several times, for on the table were several similar rents in the blanket of dust, like that exposed when the Professor lifted the keys. He turned to me and said: –

'You know this place, Jonathan. You have copied maps of it, and you know at least more than we do. Which is the way to the chapel?' I had an idea of its direction, though on my former visit I had not been able to get admission to it; so I led the way, and after a few wrong turnings found myself opposite a low, arched oaken door, ribbed with iron bands. 'This is the spot,' said the Professor, as he turned his lamp on a small map of the house, copied from the file of my original correspondence regarding the purchase. With a little trouble we found the key on the bunch and opened the door. We were prepared for some unpleasantness, for as we were opening the door a faint, malodorous air seemed to exhale through the gaps, but none of us ever expected such an odour as we encountered. None of the others had met the Count at all at close quarters, and when I had seen him he was either in the fasting stage of his existence in his rooms or, when he was glutted with fresh blood, in a ruined building open to the air; but here the place was small and close, and the long disuse had made the air stagnant and foul. There was an earthy smell, as of some dry miasma, which came through the fouler air. But as to the odour itself, how shall I describe it? It was not alone that it was composed of all the ills of mortality and with the pungent, acrid smell of blood, but it seemed as though corruption had become itself corrupt. Faugh! it sickens me to think of it. Every breath exhaled by that monster seemed to have clung to the place and intensified its loathsomeness.

Under ordinary circumstances such a stench would have brought our enterprise to an end; but this was no ordinary case, and the high and terrible purpose in which we were involved gave us a strength which rose above merely physical considerations. After the involuntary shrinking consequent on the first nauseous whiff, we one and all set about our work as though that loathsome place were a garden of roses.

We made an accurate examination of the place, the Professor saying as we began: –

'The first thing is to see how many of the boxes are left; we must then examine every hole and corner and cranny, and see if we cannot get some clue as to what has become of the rest.' A glance was sufficient to show how many remained, for the great earth chests were bulky, and there was no mistaking them.

There were only twenty-nine left out of the fifty! Once I got a fright, for, seeing Lord Godalming suddenly turn and look out of the vaulted door into the dark passage beyond, I looked too, and for an instant my heart stood still. Somewhere, looking out from the shadow, I seemed to see the high lights of the Count's evil face, the ridge of the nose, the red eyes, the red lips, the awful pallor. It was only for a moment, for as Lord Godalming said, 'I thought I saw a face, but it was only the shadows,' and resumed his inquiry, I turned my lamp in the direction, and stepped into the passage. There was no sign of anyone; and as there were no corners, no doors, no aperture of any kind, but only the solid walls of the passage, there could be no hiding-place, even for *him*. I took it that fear had helped imagination, and said nothing.

A few minutes later I saw Morris step suddenly back from a corner, which he was examining. We all followed his movements with our eyes, for undoubtedly some nervousness was growing on us, and we saw a whole mass of phosphorescence, which twinkled like stars. We all instinctively drew back. The whole place was becoming alive with rats.

For a moment or two we stood appalled, all save Lord Godalming, who was seemingly prepared for such an emergency. Rushing over to the great iron-bound oaken door, which Dr Seward had described from the outside, and which I had seen myself, he turned the key in the lock, drew the huge bolts, and swung the door open. Then, taking his little silver whistle from his pocket, he blew a low, shrill call. It was answered from behind Dr Seward's house by the yelping of dogs, and after about a minute three terriers came dashing round the corner of the house. Unconsciously we had all moved towards the door, and as we moved I noticed that the dust had been much disturbed: the boxes which had been taken out had been brought this way. But even in the minute that had elapsed the number of the rats had vastly increased. They seemed to swarm over the place all at once, till the lamplight, shining on their moving dark bodies and glittering, baleful eyes, made the place look like a bank of earth set with fireflies. The dogs dashed on, but at the threshold suddenly stopped and snarled, and then, simultaneously lifting their noses, began to howl in most lugubrious fashion. The rats were multiplying in thousands, and moved out.

Lord Godalming lifted one of the dogs, and carrying him in, placed him on the floor. The instant his feet touched the ground he seemed to recover his courage, and rushed at his natural enemies. They fled before him so fast that, before he had shaken the life out of a score, the other dogs, who had by now been lifted in in the same manner, had but small prey ere the whole mass had vanished.

With their going it seemed as if some evil presence had departed, for the dogs frisked about and barked merrily as they made sudden darts at their prostrate foes, and turned them over and over and tossed them in the air with vicious shakes. We all seemed to find our spirits rise. Whether it was the purifying of the deadly atmosphere by the opening of the chapel door, or the relief which we experienced by finding ourselves in the open, I know not; but most certainly the shadow of dread seemed to slip from us like a robe, and the occasion of our coming lost something of its grim significance, though we did not slacken a whit in our resolution. We closed the outer door and barred and locked it, and bringing the dogs with us, began our search of the house. We found nothing throughout except dust in extraordinary proportions, and all untouched save for my own footsteps when I had made my first visit. Never once did the dogs exhibit any symptom of uneasiness, and even when we returned to the chapel they frisked about as though they had been rabbit-hunting in a summer wood.

The morning was quickening in the east when we emerged from the front. Dr Van Helsing had taken the key of the hall-door from the bunch, and locked the door in orthodox fashion, putting the key into his pocket when he had done.

'So far,' he said, 'our night has been eminently successful. No harm has come to us such as I feared might be, and yet we have ascertained how many boxes are missing. More than all do I rejoice that this, our first

– and perhaps our most difficult and dangerous – step has been accomplished without the bringing thereinto our most sweet Madam Mina or troubling her waking or sleeping thoughts with sights and sounds and smells of horror which she might never forget. One lesson, too, we have learned, if it be allowable to argue *a particulari*: that the brute beasts which are to the Count's command are yet themselves not amenable to his spiritual power; for look, these rats that would come to his call, just as from his castle top he summon the wolves to your going and to that poor mother's cry, though they come to him, they run pell-mell from the so little dogs of my friend Arthur. We have other matters before us, other dangers, other fears; and that monster – he has not used his power over the brute world for the only or the last time to-night. So be it that he has gone elsewhere. Good! It has given us opportunity to cry "check" in some way in this chess game, which we play for the stake of human souls. And now let us go home. The dawn is close at hand, and we have reason to be content with our first night's work. It may be ordained that we have many nights and days to follow, if full of peril; but we must go on, and from no danger shall we shrink.'

The house was silent when we got back, save for some poor creature who was screaming away in one of the distant wards, and a low, moaning sound from Renfield's room. The poor wretch was doubtless torturing himself, after the manner of the insane, with needless thoughts of pain.

I came tiptoe into our own room, and found Mina asleep, breathing so softly that I had to put my ear down to hear it. She looks paler than usual. I hope the meeting to-night has not upset her. I am truly thankful that she is to be left out of our future work, and even of our deliberations. It is too great a strain for a woman to bear. I did not think so at first, but I know better now. Therefore I am glad that it is settled. There may be things which would frighten her to hear; and yet to conceal them from her might be worse than to tell her if once she suspected that there was any concealment. Henceforth our work is to be a sealed book to her, till at least such time as we can tell her that all is finished, and the earth free from a monster of the nether world. I daresay it will be difficult to begin to keep silence after such confidence as ours; but I must be resolute, and to-morrow I shall keep dark over to-night's doings, and shall refuse to speak of anything that has happened. I rest on the sofa, so as not to disturb her.

1 October, later. – I suppose it was natural that we should have all overslept ourselves, for the day was a busy one, and the night had no rest at all. Even Mina must have felt its exhaustion, for though I slept till the sun was high, I was awake before her, and had to call two or three times before she awoke. Indeed, she was so sound asleep that for a few seconds she did not recognise me, but looked at me with a sort of blank terror, as one looks who has been waked out of a bad dream. She complained a little of being tired, and I let her rest till later in the day. We now know of twenty-one boxes having been removed, and if it be that several were taken in any of these removals we may be able to trace them all. Such will, of course, immensely simplify our labour, and the sooner the matter is attended to the better. I shall look up Thomas Snelling to-day.

DR SEWARD'S DIARY

1 October. – It was towards noon when I was awakened by the Professor walking into my room. He was more jolly and cheerful than usual, and it is quite evident that last night's work has helped to take some of the brooding weight off his mind. After going over the adventure of the night he suddenly said: –

'Your patient interests me much. May it be that with you I visit him this morning? Or if that you are too occupy, I can go alone if it may be. It is new experience to me to find a lunatic who talk philosophy, and reason so sound.' I had some work to do which pressed, so I told him that if he would go alone I would be glad, as then I should not have to keep him waiting; so I called an attendant and gave him the necessary instructions. Before the Professor left the room I cautioned him against getting any false impression from my patient. 'But,' he answered, 'I want him to talk of himself and of his delusion as to consuming live things. He said to Madam Mina, as I see in your diary of yesterday, that he had once had such a belief. Why do you smile, friend John?'

'Excuse me,' I said, 'but the answer is here.' I laid my hand on the typewritten matter. 'When our sane and learned lunatic made that very statement of how he *used* to consume life, his mouth was actually nauseous with the flies and spiders which he had eaten just before Mrs Harker entered the room.' Van Helsing smiled in turn. 'Good!' he said. 'Your memory is true, friend John. I should have remembered. And yet it is this very obliquity of thought and memory which makes mental disease such a fascinating study. Perhaps I may gain more knowledge out of the folly of this madman than I shall from the teaching of the most wise. Who knows?' I went on with my work, and before long was through that in hand. It seemed that the time had been very short indeed, but there was

Van Helsing back in the study. 'Do I interrupt?' he asked politely as he stood at the door.

'Not at all,' I answered. 'Come in. My work is finished, and I am free. I can go with you now, if you like.'

'It is needless; I have seen him!'

'Well?'

'I fear that he does not appraise me at much. Our interview was short. When I entered the room he was sitting on a stool in the centre, with his elbows on his knees, and his face was the picture of sullen discontent. I spoke to him as cheerfully as I could, and with such a measure of respect as I could assume. He made no reply whatever. "Don't you know me?" I asked. His answer was not reassuring: "I know you well enough; you are the old fool Van Helsing. I wish you would take yourself and your idiotic brain theories somewhere else. Damn all thick-headed Dutchmen!" Not a word more would he say, but sat in his implacable sullenness as indifferent to me as though I had not been in the room at all. Thus departed for this time my chance of much learning from this so clever lunatic; so I shall go, if I may, and cheer myself with a few happy words with that sweet soul Madam Mina. Friend John, it does rejoice me unspeakable that she is no more to be pained, no more to be worried, with our terrible things. Though we shall much miss her help, it is better so.'

'I agree with you with all my heart,' I answered earnestly, for I did not want him to weaken in this matter. 'Mrs Harker is better out of it. Things are quite bad enough for us, all men of the world, and who have been in many tight places in our time; but it is no place for a woman, and if she had remained in touch with the affair, it would in time infallibly have wrecked her.'

So Van Helsing has gone to confer with Mrs Harker and Harker; Quincey and Art are both out following up the clues as to the earth-boxes. I shall finish my round of work, and we shall meet to-night.

MINA HARKER'S JOURNAL

1 October. – It is strange to me to be kept in the dark as I am to-day; after Jonathan's full confidence for so many years, to see him manifestly avoid certain matters, and those the most vital of all. This morning I slept late after the fatigues of yesterday, and though Jonathan was late too, he was the earlier. He spoke to me before he went out, never more sweetly or tenderly, but he never mentioned a word of what had happened in the visit to the Count's house. And yet he must have known how terribly anxious I was. Poor dear fellow! I suppose it must have distressed him even more than it did me. They all agreed that it was best that I should not be drawn further into this awful work, and I acquiesced. But to think that he keeps anything from me! And now I am crying like a silly fool, when I *know* it comes from my husband's great love and from the good, good wishes of those other strong men . . .

That has done me good. Well, some day Jonathan will tell me all; and lest it should ever be that he should think for a moment that I kept anything from him, I still keep my journal as usual. Then if he has doubted of my trust I shall show it to him, with every thought of my heart put down for his dear eyes to read. I feel strangely sad and low-spirited to-day. I suppose it is the reaction from the terrible excitement.

Last night I went to bed when the men had gone, simply because they told me to. I didn't feel sleepy, and I did feel full of devouring anxiety. I kept thinking over everything that has been ever since Jonathan came to see me in London, and it all seems like a horrible tragedy, with fate pressing on relentlessly to some destined end. Everything that one does seems, no matter how right it may be, to bring on the very thing which is most to be deplored. If I hadn't gone to Whitby, perhaps poor dear Lucy would be with us now. She hadn't taken to visiting the churchyard till I came, and if she hadn't come there in the daytime with me she wouldn't have walked there in her sleep; and if she hadn't gone there at night and asleep, that monster couldn't have destroyed her as he did. Oh, why did I ever go to Whitby? There now, crying again! I wonder what has come over me to-day. I must hide it from Jonathan, for if he knew that I had been crying twice in one morning – I, who never cried on my own account, and whom he has never caused to shed a tear – the dear fellow would fret his heart out. I shall put a bold face on, and if I do feel weepy, he shall never see it. I suppose it is one of the lessons that we poor women have to learn . . .

I can't quite remember how I fell asleep last night. I remember hearing the sudden barking of the dogs and a lot of queer sounds, like praying on a very tumultuous scale, from Mr Renfield's room, which is somewhere under this. And then there was silence over everything, silence so profound that it startled me, and I got up and looked out of the window. All was dark and silent, the black shadows thrown by the moonlight seeming full of a silent mystery of their own. Not a thing seemed to be stirring, but all to be grim and fixed as death or fate; so that a thin streak of white mist, that crept with almost imperceptible slowness across the grass towards the

house, seemed to have a sentience and a vitality of its own. I think that
the digression of my thoughts must have done me good, for when I got
back to bed I found a lethargy creeping over me. I lay awhile, but could
not quite sleep, so I got out and looked out of the window again. The mist
was spreading, and was now close up to the house, so that I could see it
lying thick against the wall, as though it were stealing up to the windows.
The poor man was more loud than ever, and though I could not distinguish a word he said, I could in some way recognise in his tones some
passionate entreaty on his part. Then there was the sound of a struggle,
and I knew that the attendants were dealing with him. I was so frightened
that I crept into bed, and pulled the clothes over my head, putting my
fingers in my ears. I was not then a bit sleepy, at least so I thought; but
I must have fallen asleep, for, except dreams, I do not remember anything
until the morning, when Jonathan woke me. I think that it took me an
effort and a little time to realise where I was, and that it was Jonathan
who was bending over me. My dream was very peculiar, and was almost
typical of the way that waking thoughts become merged in, or continued
in, dreams.

I thought that I was asleep, and waiting for Jonathan to come back.
I was very anxious about him, and I was powerless to act; my feet, and
my hands, and my brain were weighted, so that nothing could proceed
at the usual pace. And so I slept uneasily and thought. Then it began to
dawn upon me that the air was heavy, and dank, and cold. I put back
the clothes from my face, and found, to my surprise, that all was dim
around me. The gas-light which I had left lit for Jonathan, but turned
down, came only like a tiny red spark through the fog, which had
evidently grown thicker and poured into the room. Then it occurred to
me that I had shut the window before I had come to bed. I would have
got out to make certain on the point, but some leaden lethargy seemed
to chain my limbs and even my will. I lay still and endured; that was
all. I closed my eyes, but could still see through my eyelids. (It is
wonderful what tricks our dreams play us, and how conveniently we can
imagine.) The mist grew thicker and thicker, and I could see now how
it came in, for I could see it like smoke – or with the white energy of
boiling water – pouring in, not through the window, but through the join-
ings of the door. It got thicker and thicker, till it seemed as if it became
concentrated into a sort of pillar of cloud in the room, through the top
of which I could see the light of the gas shining like a red eye. Things
began to whirl through my brain just as the cloudy column was now
whirling in the room, and through it all came the scriptural words 'a

pillar of cloud by day and of fire by night.' Was it indeed some spiritual guidance that was coming to me in my sleep? But the pillar was composed of both the day and the night-guiding, for the fire was in the red eye, which at the thought got a new fascination for me; till, as I looked, the fire divided, and seemed to shine on me through the fog like two red eyes, such as Lucy told me of in her momentary mental wandering when, on the cliff, the dying sunlight struck the windows of St Mary's Church. Suddenly the horror burst upon me that it was thus that Jonathan had seen those awful women growing into reality through the whirling mist in the moonlight, and in my dream I must have fainted, for all became black darkness. The last conscious effort which imagination made was to show me a livid white face bending over me out of the mist. I must be careful of such dreams, for they would unseat one's reason if there was too much of them. I would get Dr Van Helsing or Dr Seward to prescribe something for me which would make me sleep, only that I fear to alarm them. Such a dream at the present time would become woven into their fears for me. To-night I shall strive hard to sleep naturally. If I do not, I shall to-morrow night get them to give me a dose of chloral; that cannot hurt me for once, and it will give me a good night's sleep. Last night tired me more than if I had not slept at all.

2 October, 10 p.m. – Last night I slept, but did not dream. I must have slept soundly, for I was not waked by Jonathan coming to bed; but the sleep has not refreshed me, for to-day I feel terribly weak and spiritless. I spent all yesterday trying to read, or lying down dozing. In the afternoon Mr Renfield asked if he might see me. Poor man, he was very gentle, and when I came away he kissed my hand and bade God bless me. Some way it affected me much; I am crying when I think of him. This is a new weakness, of which I must be careful. Jonathan would be miserable if he knew I had been crying. He and the others were out until dinner-time, and they all came in tired. I did what I could to brighten them up, and I suppose that the effort did me good, for I forgot how tired I was. After dinner they sent me to bed, and all went off to smoke together, as they said, but I knew that they wanted to tell each other of what had occurred to each during the day; I could see from Jonathan's manner that he had something important to communicate. I was not so sleepy as I should have been; so before they went I asked Dr Seward to give me a little opiate of some kind, as I had not slept well the night before. He very kindly made me up a sleeping draught, which he gave to me, telling me that it would do me no harm, as it was very mild . . . I have taken it, and am waiting for sleep, which still keeps aloof. I hope I have not done wrong, for as sleep begins to flirt with me, a new fear comes: that I may have been foolish in thus depriving myself of the power of waking. I might want it. Here comes sleep. Good-night.

CHAPTER 20

JONATHAN HARKER'S JOURNAL

1 October, evening. – I found Thomas Snelling in his house at Bethnal Green, but unhappily he was not in a condition to remember anything. The very prospect of beer which my expected coming had opened to him had proved too much, and he had begun too early on his expected debauch. I learned, however, from his wife, who seemed a decent, poor soul, that he was only the assistant to Smollet, who of the two mates was the responsible person. So off I drove to Walworth, and found Mr Joseph Smollet at home and in his shirt-sleeves, taking a late tea out of a saucer. He is a decent, intelligent fellow, distinctly a good, reliable type of workman, and with a headpiece of his own. He remembered all about the incident of the boxes, and from a wonderful dog's-eared notebook, which he produced from some mysterious receptacle about the seat of his trousers, and which had hieroglyphical entries in thick, half-obliterated pencil, he gave me the destinations of the boxes. There were, he said, six in the cartload which he took from Carfax and left at 197 Chicksand Street, Mile End New Town, and another six which he deposited at Jamaica Lane, Bermondsey. If then the Count meant to scatter these ghastly refuges of his over London, these places were chosen at the first of delivery, so that later he might distribute more fully. The systematic manner in which this was done made me think that he could not mean to confine himself to two sides of London. He was now fixed on the far east of the northern shore, on the east of the southern shore, and on the south. The north and west were surely never meant to be left out of his diabolical scheme – let alone the City itself and the very heart of fashionable London in the south-west and west. I went back to Smollet and asked him if he could tell us if any other boxes had been taken from Carfax.

He replied: –

'Well, guv'nor, you've treated me wery 'an'some' – I had given him half a sovereign – 'an' I'll tell yer all I know. I heeard a man by the name of Bloxam say four nights ago in the "'Are an' 'Ounds," in Pincher's Alley, as 'ow he an' his mate 'ad 'ad a rare dusty job in a old 'ouse at Purfleet. There ain't a-many such jobs as this 'ere, an' I'm thinkin' that maybe Sam Bloxam could tell ye summut.' I asked if he could tell me where to find him. I told him that if he could get me the address it would be worth another half-sovereign to him. So he gulped down the rest of his tea and stood up, saying that he was going to begin the search then and there. At the door he stopped, and said: –

'Look, 'ere, guv'nor, there ain't no sense in me a-keepin' you 'ere. I may find Sam soon, or I mayn't; but anyhow he ain't like to be in a way to tell ye much to-night. Sam is a rare one when he starts on the booze. If you can give me a envelope with a stamp on it, and put yer address on it, I'll find out where Sam is to be found and post it ye to-night. But ye'd better be up arter 'im soon in the mornin', or maybe ye won't ketch 'im; for Sam gets off main early, never mind the booze the night afore.'

This was all practical, so one of the children went off with a penny to buy an envelope and a sheet of paper, and to keep the change. When she came back I addressed the envelope and stamped it, and when Smollet had again faithfully promised to post the address when found, I took my way to home. We're on the track anyhow. I am tired to-night, and want sleep. Mina is fast alseep, and looks a little too pale; her eyes look as though she had been crying. Poor dear, I've no doubt it frets her to be kept in the dark, and it may make her doubly anxious about me and the others. But it is best as it is. It is better to be disappointed and worried in such a way now than to have her nerve broken. The doctors were quite right to insist on her being kept out of this dreadful business. I must be firm, for on me this particular burden of silence must rest. I shall not ever enter on the subject with her under any circumstances. Indeed, it may not be a hard task after all, she herself has become reticent on the subject, and has not spoken of the Count or his doings ever since we told her of our decision.

2 October, evening. – A long and trying and exciting day. By the first post I got my directed envelope with a dirty scrap of paper enclosed, on which was written with a carpenter's pencil in a sprawling hand: –

'Sam Bloxam, Korkrans, 4 Poters Cort, Bartel Street, Walworth. Arsk for the depite.'

I got the letter in bed, and rose without waking Mina. She looked heavy and sleepy and pale, and far from well. I determined not to wake her, but that, when I should return from this new search, I would arrange for her going back to Exeter. I think she would be happier in our own home, with her daily tasks to interest her, than in being here amongst us and in ignorance. I only saw Dr Seward for a moment, and told him where I was off to, promising to come back and tell the rest so soon as I should have found out anything. I drove to Walworth and found, with some difficulty, Potter's Court. Mr Smollet's spelling misled me, as I asked for Poter's Court instead of Potter's Court. However, when I had found the court I had no difficulty in discovering Corcoran's lodging-house. When I asked the man who came to the door for the 'depite,' he shook his head, and said: 'I dunno 'im. There ain't no such person 'ere; I never 'eard of 'im in all my bloomin' days. Don't believe there ain't nobody of that kind livin' 'ere or anywheres.' I took out Smollet's letter, and as I read it it seemed to me that the lesson of the spelling of the name of the court might guide me. 'What are you?' I asked.

'I'm the depity,' he answered. I saw at once that I was on the right track; phonetic spelling had again misled me. A half-crown tip put the deputy's knowledge at my disposal, and I learned that Mr Bloxam, who had slept off the remains of his beer on the previous night at Corcoran's, had left for his work at Poplar at five o'clock that morning. He could not tell me where the place of work was situated, but he had a vague idea that it was some kind of a 'new-fangled ware'us'; and with this slender clue I had to start for Poplar. It was twelve o'clock before I got any satisfactory hint of such a building, and this I got at a coffee-shop, where some workmen were having their dinner. One of these suggested that there was being erected at Cross Angel Street a new 'cold storage' building; and as this suited the condition of a 'new-fangled ware'us', I at once drove to it. An interview with a surly gatekeeper and a surlier foreman, both of whom were appeased with coin of the realm, put me on the track of Bloxam; he was sent for on my suggesting that I was willing to pay his day's wages to his foreman for the privilege of asking him a few questions on a private matter. He was a smart enough fellow, though rough of speech and bearing. When I had promised to pay for his information and given him an earnest, he told me that he had made two journeys between Carfax and a house in Piccadilly, and had taken from this house to the latter nine great boxes – 'main heavy ones' – with a horse and cart hired by him for this purpose. I asked him if he could tell me the number of the house in Piccadilly, to which he replied: –

'Well, guv'nor, I forgits the number, but it was only a few doors from a big white church or somethink of the kind, not long built. It was a dusty old 'ouse, too, though nothin' to the dustiness of the 'ouse we tooked the bloomin' boxes from.'

'How did you get into the house if they were both empty?'

'There was the old party what engaged me a-waitin' in the 'ouse at Purfleet. He 'elped me to lift the boxes and put them in the dray. Curse me, but he was the strongest chap I ever struck, an' him a old feller, with a white moustache, one that thin you would think he couldn't throw a shadder.'

How this phrase thrilled through me!

'Why, 'e took up 'is end o' the boxes like they was pounds of tea, and me a-puffin' an' a-blowin' afore I could up-end mine anyhow – an' I'm no chicken, neither.'

'How did you get into the house in Piccadilly?' I asked.

'He was there too. He must 'a' started off and got there afore me, for when I rung of the bell he kem an' opened the door 'isself an' 'elped me to carry the boxes into the 'all.'

'The whole nine?' I asked.

'Yus; there was five in the first load an' four in the second. It was main dry work, an' I don't so well remember 'ow I got 'ome.' I interrupted him: –

'Were the boxes left in the hall?'

'Yus; it was a big 'all, an' there was nothin' else in it.' I made one more attempt to further matters: –

'You didn't have any key?'

'Never used no key nor nothink. The old gent, he opened the door 'isself an' shut it again when I druv off. I don't remember the last time – but that was the beer.'

'And you can't remember the number of the house?'

'No, sir. But ye needn't have no difficulty about that. It's a 'igh 'un with a stone front with a bow in it, and 'igh steps up to the door. I know them steps, 'avin' 'ad to carry the boxes up with three loafers what come round to earn a copper. The old gent give them shillin's, an' they seein' they got so much, they wanted more; but 'e took one of them by the shoulder and was like to throw 'im down the steps, till the lot of them went away cussin'.' I thought that with this description I could find the house, so having paid my friend for his information, I started off for Piccadilly. I had gained a new painful experience: the Count could, it was evident, handle the earth-boxes himself. If so, time was precious; for, now he had achieved a certain amount of distribution, he could, by choosing his own time, complete the task unobserved. At Piccadilly Circus I discharged my cab, and walked westward; beyond the Junior Constitutional I came across the house described, and was satisfied that this was the next of the lairs arranged by Dracula. The house looked as though it had been long untenanted. The windows were encrusted with dust, and the shutters were up. All the framework was black with time, and from the iron the paint had mostly scaled away. It was evident that up to lately there had been a large notice-board in front of the balcony; it had, however, been roughly torn away, the uprights which had supported it still remaining.

Behind the rails of the balcony I saw there were some loose boards, whose raw edges looked white. I would have given a good deal to have been able to see the notice-board intact, as it would, perhaps, have given some clue to the ownership of the house. I remembered my experience of the investigation and purchase of Carfax, and I could not but feel that if I could find the former owner there might be some means of gaining access to the house.

There was at present nothing to be learned from the Piccadilly side, and nothing could be done; so I went round to the back to see if anything could be gathered from this quarter. The mews were active, the Piccadilly houses being mostly in occupation. I asked one or two of the grooms and helpers whom I saw around if they could tell me anything about the empty house. One of them said he had heard it had lately been taken, but he couldn't say from whom. He told me, however, that up to very lately there had been a notice-board of 'For sale' up, and that perhaps Mitchell, Sons & Candy, the house agents, could tell me something, as he thought he remembered seeing the name of that firm on the board. I did not wish to seem too eager, or to let my informant know or guess too much, so, thanking him in the usual manner, I strolled away. It was now growing dusk, and the autumn night was closing in, so I did not lose any time. Having learned the address of Mitchell, Sons & Candy from a directory at the Berkeley, I was soon at their office in Sackville Street.

The gentleman who saw me was particularly suave in manner, but uncommunicative in equal proportion. Having once told me that the Piccadilly house – which throughout our interview he called a 'mansion' – was sold, he considered my business as concluded. When I asked who had purchased it, he opened his eyes a thought wider, and paused a few seconds before replying: –

'It is sold, sir.'

'Pardon me,' I said, with equal politeness, 'but I have a special reason for wishing to know who purchased it.'

Again he paused longer, and raised his eyebrows still more. 'It is sold, sir,' was again his laconic reply.

'Surely,' I said, 'you do not mind letting me know so much.'

'But I do mind,' he answered. 'The affairs of their clients are absolutely safe in the hands of Mitchell, Sons & Candy.' This was manifestly a prig of the first water, and there was no use arguing with him. I thought I had best meet him on his own ground, so I said: –

'Your clients, sir, are happy in having so resolute a guardian of their confidence. I am myself a professional man.' Here I handed him my card.

'In this instance I am not prompted by curiosity; I act on the part of Lord Godalming, who wishes to know something of the property which was, he understood, lately for sale.' These words put a different complexion on affairs. He said: –

'I would like to oblige you if I could, Mr Harker, and especially would I like to oblige his lordship. We once carried out a small matter of renting some chambers for him when he was the Honourable Arthur Holmwood. If you will let me have his lordship's address I will consult the House on the subject, and will, in any case, communicate with his lordship by to-night's post. It will be a pleasure if we can so far deviate from our rules as to give the required information to his lordship.'

I wanted to secure a friend, and not to make an enemy, so I thanked him, gave the address at Dr Seward's, and came away. It was now dark, and I was tired and hungry. I got a cup of tea at the Aerated Bread Company and came down to Purfleet by the next train.

I found all the others at home. Mina was looking tired and pale, but she made a gallant effort to be bright and cheerful; it wrung my heart to think that I had had to keep anything from her and so caused her disquietude. Thank God, this will be the last night of her looking on at our conferences, and feeling the sting of our not showing our confidence. It took all my courage to hold to the wise resolution of keeping her out of our grim task. She seems somehow more reconciled; or else the very subject seems to have become repugnant to her, for when any accidental allusion is made she actually shudders. I am glad we made our resolution in time, as with such a feeling as this our growing knowledge would be torture to her.

I could not tell the others of the day's discovery till we were alone; so after dinner – followed by a little music to save appearances even amongst ourselves – I took Mina to her room and left her to go to bed. The dear girl was more affectionate with me than ever, and clung to me as though she would detain me; but there was much to be talked of and I came away. Thank God, the ceasing of telling things has made no difference between us.

When I came down again I found the others all gathered round the fire in the study. In the train I had written my diary so far, and simply read it off to them as the best means of letting them get abreast of my own information; when I had finished Van Helsing said: –

'This has been a great day's work, friend Jonathan. Doubtless we are on the track of the missing boxes. If we find them all in that house, then our work is near the end. But if there be some missing, we must search until we find them. Then shall we make our final *coup*, and hunt the wretch to his real death.' We all sat silent awhile, and all at once Mr Morris spoke: –

'Say! how are we going to get into that house?'

'We got into the other,' answered Lord Godalming quickly.

'But, Art, this is different. We broke house at Carfax, but we had night and a walled park to protect us. It will be a mighty different thing to commit burglary in Piccadilly, either by day or night. I confess I don't see how we are going to get in unless that agency duck can find us a key of some sort; perhaps we shall know when you get his letter in the morning.' Lord Godalming's brows contracted, and he stood up and walked about the room. By-and-by he stopped and said, turning from one to another of us: –

'Quincey's head is level. This burglary business is getting serious; we got off once all right; but we have now a rare job on hand – unless we can find the Count's key basket.'

As nothing could well be done before morning, and as it would be at least advisable to wait till Lord Godalming should hear from Mitchell's, we decided not to take any active step before breakfast time. For a good while we sat and smoked, discussing the matter in its various bearings; I took the opportunity of bringing this diary right up to the moment. I am very sleepy and shall go to bed . . .

Just a line. Mina sleeps soundly and her breathing is regular. Her forehead is puckered up into little wrinkles, as though she thinks even in her sleep. She is still too pale, but does not look so haggard as she did this morning. To-morrow will, I hope, mend all this; she will be herself at home in Exeter. Oh, but I am sleepy!

DR SEWARD'S DIARY

1 October. – I am puzzled afresh about Renfield. His moods change so rapidly that I find it difficult to keep touch with them, and as they always mean something more than his own well-being, they form a more than interesting study. This morning, when I went to see him after his repulse of Van Helsing, his manner was that of a man commanding destiny. He was, in fact, commanding destiny – subjectively. He did not really care for any of the things of mere earth; he was in the clouds and looked down on all the weaknesses and wants of us poor mortals. I thought I would improve the occasion and learn something, so I asked him: –

'What about the flies these times?' He smiled on me in quite a superior sort of way – such a smile as would have become the face of Malvolio – as he answered me: –

'The fly, my dear sir, has one striking feature: its wings are typical of the aerial powers of the psychic faculties. The ancients did well when they typified the soul as a butterfly!'

I thought I would push his analogy to its utmost logically, so I said quickly: –

'Oh, it is a soul you are after now, is it?' His madness foiled his reason, and a puzzled look spread over his face as, shaking his head with a decision which I had but seldom seen in him, he said: –

'Oh no, oh no! I want no souls. Life is all I want.' Here he brightened up: 'I am pretty indifferent about it at present. Life is all right; I have all I want. You must get a new patient, doctor, if you wish to study zoophagy!'

This puzzled me a little, so I drew him on: –

'Then you command life; you are a god, I suppose?' He smiled with an ineffably benign superiority.

'Oh no! Far be it from me to arrogate to myself the attributes of the Deity. I am not even concerned in His especially spiritual doings. If I may state my intellectual position I am, so far as concerns things purely terrestrial, somewhat in the position which Enoch occupied spiritually!' This was a poser to me. I could not at the moment recall Enoch's appositeness; so I had to ask a simple question, though I felt that by doing so I was lowering myself in the eyes of the lunatic: –

'And why Enoch?'

'Because he walked with God.' I could not see the analogy, but did not like to admit it; so I harked back to what he had denied: –

'So you don't care about life and you don't want souls. Why not?' I put my question quickly and somewhat sternly, on purpose to disconcert him. The effort succeeded; for an instant he unconsciously relapsed into his old servile manner, bent low before me, and actually fawned upon me as he replied: –

'I don't want any souls, indeed, indeed! I don't. I couldn't use them if I had them! they would be no manner of use to me. I couldn't eat them or –' He suddenly stopped and the old cunning look spread over his face, like a wind-sweep on the surface of the water. 'And, Doctor, as to life, what is it after all? When you've got all you require, and you know that you will never want, that is all. I have friends – good friends – like you, Doctor Seward,' he said with a leer of inexpressible cunning; 'I know that I shall never lack the means of life!'

I think that through the cloudiness of his insanity he saw some antagonism in me, for he at once fell back on the last refuge of such as he – a dogged silence. After a short time I saw that for the present it was useless to speak to him. He was sulky, and so I came away.

Later in the day he sent for me. Ordinarily I would not have come without special reason, but just at present I am so interested in him that I would gladly make an effort. Besides, I am glad to have anything to help to pass the time. Harker is out, following up clues; and so are Lord Godalming and Quincey. Van Helsing sits in my study poring over the record prepared by the Harkers; he seems to think that by accurate knowledge of all details he will light upon some clue. He does not wish to be disturbed in the work, without cause. I would have taken him with me to see the patient, only I thought that after his last repulse he might not care to go again. There was also another reason: Renfield might not speak so freely before a third person as when he and I were alone.

I found him sitting out in the middle of the floor on his stool, a pose which is generally indicative of some mental energy on his part. When I came in, he said at once, as though the question had been waiting on his lips: –

'What about souls?' It was evident then that my surmise had been correct. Unconscious cerebration was doing its work, even with the lunatic. I determined to have the matter out. 'What about them yourself?' I asked. He did not reply for a moment but looked all round him, and up and down, as though he expected to find some inspiration for an answer.

'I don't want any souls!' he said in a feeble, apologetic way. The matter seemed preying on his mind, and so I determined to use it – to 'be cruel only to be kind.' So I said: –

'You like life, and you want life?'

'Oh yes! but that is all right; you needn't worry about that!'

'But,' I asked, 'how are we to get the life without getting the soul also?' This seemed to puzzle him, so I followed it up: –

'A nice time you'll have some time when you're flying out there, with the souls of thousands of flies and spiders and birds and cats buzzing and twittering and miauing all round you. You've got their lives, you know, and you must put up with their souls!' Something seemed to affect his imagination, for he put his fingers to his ears and shut his eyes, screwing them up tightly just as a small boy does when his face is being soaped. There was something pathetic in it that touched me; it also gave me a lesson, for it seemed that before me was a child – only a child, though the features were worn, and the stubble on the jaws was white. It was evident that he was undergoing some process of mental disturbance, and, knowing how his past moods had interpreted things seemingly foreign to himself, I thought I would enter into his mind as well as I could and go with him. The first step was to restore confidence, so I asked him, speaking pretty loud so that he would hear me through his closed ears: –

'Would you like some sugar to get your flies round again?' He seemed to wake up all at once, and shook his head. With a laugh he replied: –

'Not much! flies are poor things, after all!' After a pause he added, 'But I don't want their souls buzzing round me all the same.'

'Or spiders?' I went on.

'Blow spiders! What's the use of spiders? There isn't anything in them to eat or –' He stopped suddenly, as though reminded of a forbidden topic.

'So, so!' I thought to myself, 'this is the second time he has suddenly stopped at the word "drink", what does it mean?' Renfield seemed himself aware of having made a lapse, for he hurried on, as though to distract my attention from it: –

'I don't take any stock at all in such matters. "Rats and mice and such small deer" as Shakespeare has it; "chicken-feed of the larder" they might be called. I'm past all that sort of nonsense. You might as well ask a man to eat molecules with a pair of chop-sticks, as to try to interest me about the lesser carnivora, when I know of what is before me.'

'I see,' I said. 'You want big things that you can make your teeth meet in? How would you like to breakfast on elephant?'

'What ridiculous nonsense you are talking!' He was getting too wide awake, so I thought I would press him hard. 'I wonder,' I said reflectively, 'what an elephant's soul is like!' The effect I desired was obtained, for he at once fell from his high-horse and became a child again.

'I don't want an elephant's soul, or any soul at all!' he said. For a few moments he sat despondently. Suddenly he jumped to his feet, with his eyes blazing and all the signs of intense cerebral excitement. 'To hell with you and your souls!' he shouted. 'Why do you plague me about souls? Haven't I got enough to worry, and pain, and distract me already, without thinking of souls?' He looked so hostile that I thought he was in for another homicidal fit, so I blew my whistle. The instant, however, that I did so he became calm, and said apologetically: –

'Forgive me, doctor; I forgot myself. You do not need any help. I am so worried in my mind that I am apt to be irritable. If you only knew the problem I have to face, and that I am working out, you would pity, and tolerate, and pardon me. Pray do not put me in a strait-waistcoat. I want to think, and I cannot think freely when my body is confined. I am sure you will understand!' He had evidently self-control; so when the attendants came I told them not to mind, and they withdrew. Renfield watched them go; when the door was closed he said, with considerable dignity and sweetness: –

'Dr Seward, you have been very considerate towards me. Believe me that I am very very grateful to you!' I thought it well to leave him in this mood, and so I came away. There is certainly something to ponder over in this man's state. Several points seem to make what the American interviewer calls 'a story,' if one could only get them in proper order. Here they are: –

Will not mention 'drinking.'

Fears the thought of being burdened with the 'soul' of anything.

Has no dread of wanting 'life' in the future.

Despises the meaner forms of life altogether, though he dreads being haunted by their souls.

Logically all these things point one way! he has assurance of some kind that he will acquire some higher life. He dreads the consequence – the burden of a soul. Then it is a human life he looks to!

And the assurance –?

Merciful God! the Count has been to him, and there is some new scheme of terror afoot!

Later. – I went after my round to Van Helsing and told him my suspicion. He grew very grave; and, after thinking the matter over for a while, asked me to take him to Renfield. I did so. As we came to the door we heard the lunatic within singing gaily, as he used to do in the time which now seems so long ago. When we entered we saw with amazement that he had spread out his sugar as of old; the flies, lethargic with the autumn, were beginning to buzz into the room. We tried to make him talk of the subject of our previous conversation, but he would not attend. He went on with his singing, just as though we had not been present. He had got a scrap of paper and was folding it into a note-book. We had to come away as ignorant as we went in.

His is a curious case indeed; we must watch him to-night.

Letter, Mitchell, Sons & Candy to Lord Godalming

'1 October.

'My Lord, –

'We are at all times only too happy to meet your wishes. We beg, with regard to the desire of your Lordship, expressed by Mr Harker

on your behalf, to supply the following information concerning the
sale and purchase of No. 347 Piccadilly. The original vendors are the
executors of the late Mr Archibald Winter-Suffield. The purchaser is
a foreign nobleman, Count de Ville, who effected the purchase
himself, paying the purchase money in notes "over the counter," if
your Lordship will pardon us using so vulgar an expression. Beyond
this we know nothing whatever of him. – We are, my Lord,

'Your Lordship's humble servants,

'MITCHELL, SONS & CANDY.'

DR SEWARD'S DIARY

2 October. – I placed a man in the corridor last night, and told him to
make an accurate note of any sound he might hear from Renfield's room,
and gave him instructions that if there should be anything strange he was
to call me. After dinner, when we had all gathered round the fire in the
study – Mrs Harker having gone to bed – we discussed the attempts and
discoveries of the day. Harker was the only one who had any result, and
we are in great hopes that his clue may be an important one.

Before going to bed I went round to the patient's room and looked in
through the observation trap. He was sleeping soundly, and his chest rose
and fell with regular respiration.

This morning the man on duty reported to me that a little after midnight
he was restless and kept saying his prayers somewhat loudly. I asked him
if that was all; he replied that it was all he heard. There was something
about his manner so suspicious that I asked point-blank if he had been
asleep. He denied sleep, but admitted to having 'dozed' for a while. It is
too bad that men cannot be trusted unless they are watched.

To-day Harker is out following up his clue, and Art and Quincey are
looking after horses. Godalming thinks that it will be well to have horses
always in readiness, for when we get the information which we seek there
will be no time to lose. We must sterilize all the imported earth between
sunrise and sunset; we shall thus catch the Count at his weakest, and
without a refuge to fly to. Van Helsing is off to the British Museum,
looking up some authorities on ancient medicine. The old physicians took
account of things which their followers do not accept, and the Professor
is searching for witch and demon cures which may be useful later.

I sometimes think we must be all mad and that we shall wake to sanity
in strait-waistcoats.

Later. – We have met again. We seem at last to be on the track, and our work of to-morrow may be the beginning of the end. I wonder if Renfield's quiet has anything to do with this. His moods have so followed the doings of the Count, that the coming destruction of the monster may be carried to him in some subtle way. If we could only get some hint as to what passed in his mind between the time of my argument with him yesterday and his resumption of fly-catching, it might afford us a valuable clue. He is now seemingly quiet for a spell . . . Is he? – that wild yell seemed to come from his room . . .

The attendant came bursting into my room and told me that Renfield had somehow met with some accident. He had heard him yell; and when he went to him found him lying on his face on the floor, all covered with blood. I must go at once . . .

CHAPTER 21

DR SEWARD'S DIARY

3 October. – Let me put down with exactness all that happened, as well as I can remember it, since last I made an entry. Not a detail that I can recall must be forgotten; in all calmness I must proceed.

When I came to Renfield's room I found him lying on the floor on his left side in a glittering pool of blood. When I went to move him, it became at once apparent that he had received some terrible injuries; there seemed none of that unity of purpose between the parts of the body which marks even lethargic sanity. As the face was exposed I could see that it was horribly bruised, as though it had been beaten against the floor – indeed it was from the face wounds that the pool of blood originated. The attendant who was kneeling beside the body said to me as we turned him over: –

'I think, sir, his back is broken. See, both his right arm and leg and the whole side of his face are paralysed.' How such a thing could have happened puzzled the attendant beyond measure. He seemed quite bewildered, and his brows were gathered in as he said: –

'I can't understand the two things. He could mark his face like that by beating his own head on the ground. I saw a young woman do it once at the Eversfield Asylum before anyone could lay hands on her. And I suppose he might have broke his back by falling out of bed, if he got in an awkward kink. But for the life of me I can't imagine how the two things occurred. If his back was broke, he couldn't beat his head; and if his face was like that before the fall out of bed, there would be marks of it.' I said to him: –

'Go to Dr Van Helsing, and ask him to kindly come here at once. I want him without an instant's delay.' The man ran off, and within a very few minutes the Professor, in his dressing-gown and slippers, appeared. When he saw Renfield on the ground, he looked keenly at him a moment and then turned to me. I think he recognised my thought in my eyes, for he said very quietly, manifestly for the ears of the attendant: –

'Ah, a sad accident! He will need very careful watching, and much attention. I shall stay with you myself; but I shall first dress myself. If you will remain I shall in a few minutes join you.'

The patient was now breathing stertorously, and it was easy to see that he had suffered some terrible injury. Van Helsing returned with extraordinary celerity, bearing with him a surgical case He had evidently been thinking and had his mind made up; for, almost before he looked at the patient, he whispered to me: –

'Send the attendant away. We must be alone with him when he becomes conscious, after the operation.' So I said: –

'I think that will do now, Simmons. We have done all that we can at present. You had better go your round, and Dr Van Helsing will operate. Let me know instantly if there be anything unusual anywhere.'

The man withdrew, and we went into a strict examination of the patient. The wounds of the face were superficial; the real injury was a depressed fracture of the skull, extending right up through the motor area. The Professor thought a moment and said: –

'We must reduce the pressure and get back to normal conditions, as far as can be; the rapidity of the suffusion shows the terrible nature of his injury. The whole motor area seems affected. The suffusion of the brain will increase quickly, so we must trephine at once or it may be too late.' As he was speaking there was a soft tapping at the door. I went over and opened it and found in the corridor without, Arthur and Quincey in pyjamas and slippers: the former spoke: –

'I heard your man call up Dr Van Helsing and tell him of an accident. So I woke Quincey, or rather called for him as he was not asleep. Things are moving too quickly and too strangely for sound sleep for any of us these times. I've been thinking that to-morrow night will not see things as they have been. We'll have to look back – and forward a little more than we have done. May we come in?' I nodded, and held the door open till they had entered; then I closed it again. When Quincey saw the attitude and state of the patient, and noted the horrible pool on the floor, he said softly: –

'My God! what has happened to him! Poor, poor devil!' I told him briefly, and added that we expected he would recover consciousness after the operation – for a short time at all events. He went at once and sat down on the edge of the bed, with Godalming beside him; we all watched in patience.

'We shall wait,' said Van Helsing, 'just long enough to fix the best spot for trephining, so that we may most quickly and perfectly remove the blood clot; for it is evident that the haemorrhage is increasing.'

The minutes during which we waited passed with fearful slowness. I had a horrible sinking in my heart, and from Van Helsing's face I gathered that he felt some fear or apprehension as to what was to come. I dreaded the words that Renfield might speak. I was positively afraid to think; but the conviction of what was coming was on me, as I have read of men who have heard the death-watch. The poor man's breathing came in uncertain gasps. Each instant he seemed as though he would open his eyes and speak; but then would follow a prolonged stertorous breath, and he would relapse into a more fixed insensibility. Inured as I was to sick-beds and death, this suspense grew and grew upon me. I could almost hear the beating of my own heart; and the blood surging through my temples sounded like blows from a hammer. The silence finally became agonising. I looked at my companions, one after another, and saw from their flushed faces and damp brows that they were enduring equal torture. There was a nervous suspense over us all, as though overhead some dread bell would peal out powerfully when we should least expect it.

At last there came a time when it was evident that the patient was sinking fast; he might die at any moment. I looked up at the Professor and caught his eyes fixed on mine. His face was sternly set as he spoke: –

'There is no time to lose. His words may be worth many lives; I have been thinking so, as I stood here. It may be there is a soul at stake! We shall operate just above the ear.'

Without another word he made the operation. For a few moments the breathing continued to be stertorous. Then there came a breath so prolonged that it seemed as though it would tear open his chest. Suddenly his eyes opened, and became fixed in a wild, helpless stare. This was continued for a few moments; then it softened into a glad surprise, and from the lips came a sigh of relief. He moved convulsively, and as he did so, said: –

'I'll be quiet, doctor. Tell them to take off the strait-waistcoat. I have had a terrible dream, and it has left me so weak that I cannot move. What's wrong with my face? it feels all swollen, and it smarts dreadfully.' He tried to turn his head; but even with the effort his eyes seemed to grow glassy again, so I gently put it back. Then Van Helsing said in a quiet, grave tone: –

'Tell us your dream, Mr Renfield.' As he heard the voice his face brightened through its mutilation, and he said: –

'That is Dr Van Helsing. How good it is of you to be here. Give me some water, my lips are dry; and I shall try to tell you. I dreamed –' He stopped and seemed fainting. I called quietly to Quincey – 'The brandy – it is in my study – quick!' He flew and returned with a glass, the decanter of brandy and a carafe of water. We moistened the parched lips, and the patient quickly revived. It seemed, however, that his poor injured brain had been working in the interval, for, when he was quite conscious, he looked at me piercingly with an agonised confusion which I shall never forget, and said: –

'I must not deceive myself; it was no dream, but all a grim reality.' Then his eyes roved round the room; as they caught sight of the two figures sitting patiently on the edge of the bed he went on: –

'If I were not sure already, I should know from them.' For an instant his eyes closed – not with pain or sleep but voluntarily, as though he were bringing all his faculties to bear; when he opened them he said, hurriedly, and with more energy than he had yet displayed: –

'Quick, doctor, quick. I am dying! I feel that I have but a few minutes; and then I must go back to death – or worse! Wet my lips with brandy again. I have something that I must say before I die; or before my poor crushed brain dies anyhow. Thank you! It was that night after you left me, when I implored you to let me go away. I couldn't speak then, for I felt my tongue was tied; but I was as sane then, except in that way, as I am now. I was in an agony of despair for a long time after you left me; it seemed hours. Then there came a sudden peace to me. My brain seemed to become cool again, and I realized where I was. I heard the dogs bark behind our house, but not where He was!' As he spoke Van Helsing's eyes never blinked, but his hand came out and met mine and gripped it hard. He did not, however, betray himself; he nodded slightly, and said: 'Go on,' in a low voice. Renfield proceeded: –

'He came up to the window in the mist, as I had seen Him often before; but He was solid then – not a ghost, and His eyes were fierce like a man's when angry. He was laughing with His red mouth; the sharp white teeth glinted in the moonlight when He turned to look back over the belt of trees, to where the dogs were barking. I wouldn't ask Him to come in at first, though I knew He wanted to – just as He had wanted all along. Then He began promising me things – not in words but by doing them.' He was interrupted by a word from the Professor: –

'How?'

'By making them happen; just as He used to send in the flies when the sun was shining. Great big fat ones with steel and sapphire on their wings; and big moths, in the night, with skull and cross-bones on their backs.' Van Helsing nodded to him as he whispered to me unconsciously: –

'The *Acherontia atropos of the Sphinges* – what you call the "Death's-head moth!"' The patient went on without stopping.

'Then he began to whisper: "Rat, rats, rats! Hundreds, thousands, millions of them, and every one a life; and dogs to eat them, and cats too. All lives! all red blood, with years of life in it; and not merely buzzing flies!" I laughed at Him, for I wanted to see what He could do. Then the dogs howled, away beyond the dark trees in His house. He beckoned me to the window. I got up and looked out, and He raised His hands, and seemed to call out without using any words. A dark mass spread over the grass, coming on like the shape of a flame of fire; and then He moved the mist to the right and left, and I could see that there were thousands of rats with their eyes blazing red – like His, only smaller. He held up His hand, and they all stopped; and I thought He seemed to be saying: "All these lives will I give you, ay, and many more and greater, through countless ages, if you will fall down and worship me!" And then a red cloud, like the colour of blood, seemed to close over my eyes; and before I knew what I was doing, I found myself opening the sash and saying to Him: "Come in, Lord and Master!" The rats were all gone, but He slid into the room through the sash, though it was only open an inch wide – just as the Moon herself has often come in through the tiniest crack, and has stood before me in all her size and splendour.'

His voice was weaker, so I moistened his lips with the brandy again, and he continued; but it seemed as though his memory had gone on working in the interval, for his story was further advanced. I was about to call him back to the point, but Van Helsing whispered to me: 'Let him go on. Do not interrupt him; he cannot go back, and maybe could not proceed at all if once he lost the thread of his thought.' He proceeded: –

'All day I waited to hear from Him, but He did not send me anything, not even a blow-fly, and when the moon got up I was pretty angry with Him. When He slid in through the window, though it was shut, and did not even knock, I got mad with Him. He sneered at me, and His white face looked out of the mist with His red eyes gleaming, and He went on as though He owned the whole place, and I was no one. He didn't even smell the same as He went by me. I couldn't hold Him. I thought that, somehow, Mrs Harker had come into the room.'

The two men sitting on the bed stood up and came over, standing behind him so that he could not see them, but where they could hear better. They were both silent, but the Professor started and quivered; his face, however, grew grimmer and sterner still. Renfield went on without noticing: –

'When Mrs Harker came in to see me this afternoon she wasn't the same; it was like tea after the teapot had been watered.' Here we all moved, but no one said a word; he went on: –

'I didn't know that she was here till she spoke; and she didn't look the same. I don't care for the pale people, I like them with lots of blood in them, and hers had all seemed to have run out. I didn't think of it at the time; but when she went away I began to think, and it made me mad to know that He had been taking the life out of her.' I could feel that the rest quivered, as I did; but we remained otherwise still. 'So when He came to-night I was ready for Him. I saw the mist stealing in, and I grabbed it tight. I had heard that madmen have unnatural strength; and as I knew I was a madman – at times anyhow – I resolved to use my power. Ay, and He felt it too, for He had to come out of the mist to struggle with me. I held tight; and I thought I was going to win, for I didn't mean Him to take any more of her life, till I saw His eyes. They burned into me, and my strength became like water. He slipped through it, and when I tried to cling to Him, He raised me up and flung me down. There was a red cloud before me, and a noise like thunder, and the mist seemed to steal away under the door.' His voice was becoming fainter and his breath more stertorous. Van Helsing stood up instinctively.

'We know the worst now,' he said. 'He is here, and we know his purpose. It may not be too late. Let us be armed – the same as we were the other night, but lose no time; there is not an instant to spare.' There was no need to put our fear, nay our conviction, into words – we shared them in common. We all hurried and took from our rooms the same things that we had when we entered the Count's house. The Professor had his ready and as we met in the corridor he pointed to them significantly as he said: –

'They never leave me; and they shall not till this unhappy business is over. Be wise also, my friends. It is no common enemy that we deal with. Alas! alas that that dear Madam Mina should suffer.' He stopped; his voice was breaking, and I do not know if rage or terror predominated in my own heart.

Outside the Harkers' door we paused. Art and Quincey held back, and the latter said: –

'Should we disturb her?'

'We must,' said Van Helsing grimly. 'If the door be locked, I shall break it in.'

'May it not frighten her terribly? It is unusual to break into a lady's room!' Van Helsing said solemnly:

'You are always right; but this is life and death. All chambers are alike to the doctor; and even were they not they are all as one to me to-night. Friend John, when I turn the handle, if the door does not open, do you put your shoulder down and shove; and you too, my friends. Now!'

He turned the handle as he spoke, but the door did not yield. We threw ourselves against it; with a crash it burst open, and we almost fell headlong into the room. The Professor did actually fall, and I saw across him as he gathered himself up from hands and knees. What I saw appalled mc. I felt my hair rise like bristles on the back of my neck, and my heart seemed to stand still.

The moonlight was so bright that through the thick yellow blind the room was light enough to see. On the bed beside the window lay Jonathan Harker, his face flushed, and breathing heavily as though in a stupor. Kneeling on the near edge of the bed facing outwards was the white-clad figure of his wife. By her side stood a tall, thin man, clad in black. His face was turned from us, but the instant we saw it we all recognised the Count – in every way, even to the scar on his forehead. With his left hand he held both Mrs Harker's hands, keeping them away with her arms at full tension; his right hand gripped her by the back of the neck, forcing her face down on his bosom. Her white nightdress was smeared with blood, and a thin stream trickled down the man's bare breast, which was shown by his torn-open dress. The attitude of the two had a terrible resemblance to a child forcing a kitten's nose into a saucer of milk to compel it to drink. As we burst into the room, the Count turned his face, and the hellish look that I had heard described seemed to leap into it. His eyes flamed red with devilish passion; the great nostrils of the white aquiline nose opened wide and quivered at the edges; and the white sharp teeth, behind the full lips of the blood-dripping mouth, champed together like those of a wild beast. With a wrench, which threw his victim back upon the bed as though hurled from a height, he turned and sprang at us. But by this time the Professor had gained his feet, and was holding towards him the envelope which contained the Sacred Wafer. The Count suddenly stopped, just as poor Lucy had done outside the tomb, and cowered back. Further and further back he cowered, as we, lifting our crucifixes, advanced. The moonlight suddenly failed, as a great black cloud sailed across the sky; and when the gaslight sprang up under Quincey's match, we saw nothing but a faint vapour. This, as we looked, trailed under the door, which with the recoil from its bursting open had swung back to its old position. Van Helsing, Art and I moved forward to Mrs Harker, who by this time had drawn her breath and with it had given a scream so wild, so ear-piercing, so despairing that it seems to me now that it will ring in my ears till my dying day. For a few seconds she lay in her helpless attitude and disarray. Her face was ghastly, with a pallor which was accentuated by the blood which smeared her lips and cheeks and chin; from her throat trickled a thin stream of blood. Her eyes were mad with terror. Then she put before her face her poor crushed hands, which bore on their whiteness the red mark of the Count's terrible grip, and from behind them came a low desolate wail which made the terrible scream seem only the quick expression of an endless grief. Van Helsing stepped forward and drew the coverlet gently over her body, whilst Art, after looking at her face for an instant despairingly, ran out of the room. Van Helsing whispered to me: –

'Jonathan is in a stupor such as we know the Vampire can produce. We can do nothing with poor Madam Mina for a few moments till she recovers herself; I must wake him!' He dipped the end of a towel in cold water and with it began to flick him on the face, his wife all the while holding her face between her hands and sobbing in a way that was heart-breaking to hear. I raised the blind, and looked out of the window. There was much moonshine; and as I looked I could see Quincey Morris run across the lawn and hide himself in the shadow of a great yew tree. It puzzled me to think why he was doing this; but at the instant I heard Harker's quick exclamation as he woke to partial consciousness, and turned to the bed. On his face, as there might well be, was a look of wild amazement. He seemed dazed for a few seconds, and then full consciousness seemed to burst upon him all at once, and he started up. His wife was aroused by the quick movement, and turned to him with her arms stretched out, as though to embrace him; instantly, however, she drew them in again, and putting her elbows together, held her hands before her face, and shuddered till the bed beneath her shook.

'In God's name what does this mean?' Harker cried out. 'Dr Seward, Dr Van Helsing, what is it? What has happened? What is wrong? Mina, dear, what is it? What does that blood mean? My God, my God! has it come to this!' and, raising himself to his knees, he beat his hands wildly together. 'Good God help us! help her! oh, help her!' With a quick movement he jumped from bed, and began to pull on his clothes – all the man in him awake at the need for instant exertion. 'What has happened? Tell me all about it!' he cried without pausing. 'Dr Van Helsing, you love Mina, I know. Oh, do something to save her. It cannot have gone too far yet. Guard her while I look for *him*!' His wife, through her terror and horror and distress, saw some sure danger to him; instantly forgetting her own grief, she seized hold of him and cried out: –

'No! no! Jonathan, you must not leave me. I have suffered enough to-night, God knows, without the dread of his harming you. You must stay with me. Stay with these friends who will watch over you!' Her expression became frantic as she spoke; and as he yielded to her, she pulled him down sitting on the bedside, and clung to him fiercely.

Van Helsing and I tried to calm them both. The Professor held up his little golden crucifix, and said with wonderful calmness: –

'Do not fear, my dear. We are here; and whilst this is close to you no foul thing can approach. You are safe for to-night; and we must be calm and take counsel together.' She shuddered and was silent, holding down her head on her husband's breast. When she raised it, his white night-robe was stained with blood where her lips had touched, and where the thin open wound in her neck had sent forth drops. The instant she saw it she drew back, with a low wail, and whispered, amidst choking sobs: –

'Unclean, unclean! I must touch him or kiss him no more. Oh, that it should be that it is I who am now his worst enemy, and whom he may have most cause to fear.' To this he spoke out resolutely: –

'Nonsense, Mina. It is a shame to me to hear such a word. I would not hear it of you; and I shall not hear it from you. May God judge me by my deserts, and punish me with more bitter suffering than even this hour, if by any act or will of mine anything ever come between us!' He put out his arms and folded her to his breast; and for a while she lay there sobbing. He looked at us over her bowed head, with eyes that blinked damply above his quivering nostrils; his mouth was set as steel. After a while her sobs became less frequent and more faint, and then he said to me, speaking with a studied calmness which I felt tried his nervous power to the utmost: –

'And now, Dr Seward, tell me all about it. Too well I know the broad fact; tell me all that has been.' I told him exactly what had happened, and he listened with seeming impassiveness; but his nostrils twitched and his eyes blazed as I told how the ruthless hands of the Count had held his wife in that terrible and horrid position, with her mouth to the open wound in his breast. It interested me, even at that moment, to see that whilst the face of white set passion worked convulsively over the bowed head, the hands tenderly and lovingly stroked the ruffled hair. Just as I had finished Quincey and Godalming knocked at the door. They entered in obedience to our summons. Van Helsing looked at me questioningly. I understood him to mean if we were to take advantage of their coming to divert if possible the thoughts of the unhappy husband and wife from each other and from themselves; so on my nodding acquiescence to him he asked them what they had seen or done. To which Lord Godalming answered: –

'I could not see him anywhere in the passage, or in any of our rooms. I looked in the study, but, though he had been there, he had gone. He had, however –' He stopped suddenly, looking at the poor drooping figure on the bed. Van Helsing said gravely: – 'Go on, friend Arthur. We want no more concealments. Our hope now is in knowing all. Tell freely!' So Art went on: –

'He had been there, and though it could only have been for a few seconds, he made rare hay of the place. All the manuscript had been burned, and the blue flames were flickering amongst the white ashes; the cylinders of your phonograph too were thrown on the fire, and the wax had helped the flames.' Here I interrupted. 'Thank God there is the other copy in the safe!' His face lit for a moment, but fell again as he went on: 'I ran downstairs then, but could see no sign of him. I looked into Renfield's room; but there was no trace there except –!' Again he paused. 'Go on,' said Harker hoarsely; so he bowed his head, and moistening his lips with his tongue, added: 'except that the poor fellow is dead.' Mrs Harker raised her head, looking from one to the other of us as she said solemnly: –

'God's will be done!' I could not but feel that Art was keeping back something; but, as I took it that it was with a purpose, I said nothing. Van Helsing turned to Morris and asked: –

'And you, friend Quincey, have you any to tell?'

'A little,' he answered. 'It may be much eventually, but at present I can't say. I thought it well to know if possible where the Count would go when he left the house. I did not see him; but I saw a bat rise from Renfield's window, and flap westward. I expected to see him in some shape go back to Carfax; but he evidently sought some other lair. He will not be back to-night; for the sky is reddening in the east, and the dawn in close. We must work to-morrow!'

He said the latter words through his shut teeth. For a space of perhaps a couple of minutes there was silence, and I could fancy that I could hear the sound of our hearts beating; then Van Helsing said, placing his hand very tenderly on Mrs Harker's head: –

'And now, Madam Mina – poor, dear, dear Madam Mina – tell us exactly what happened. God knows that I do not want that you be pained; but it is need that we know all. For now more than ever has all work to be done quick and sharp, and in deadly earnest. The day is close to us that must end all, if it may so be; and now is the chance that we may live and learn.'

The poor, dear lady shivered, and I could see the tension of her nerves as she clasped her husband closer to her and bent her head lower and lower still on his breast. Then she raised her head proudly, and held out one hand to Van Helsing, who took it in his, and, after stooping and kissing it reverently, held it fast. The other hand was locked in that of her husband, who held his other arm thrown round her protectingly. After a pause in which she was evidently ordering her thoughts, she began: –

'I took the sleeping draught which you had so kindly given me, but for a long time it did not act. I seemed to become more wakeful, and a myriad horrible fancies began to crowd in upon my mind – all of them connected with death, and vampires; with blood, and pain, and trouble.' Her husband involuntarily groaned as she turned to him and said lovingly: 'Do not fret, dear. You must be brave and strong, and help me through the horrible task. If you only knew what an effort it is to me to tell of this fearful thing at all, you would understand how much I need your help. Well, I saw I must try to help the medicine do its work with my will, if it was to do me any good, so I resolutely set myself to sleep. Sure enough sleep must soon have come to me, for I remembered no more. Jonathan coming in had not waked me, for he lay by my side when next I remember. There was in the room the same thin white mist that I had before noticed. But I forget now if you know of this; you will find it in my diary which I shall show you later. I felt the same vague terror which had come to me before, and the same sense of some presence. I turned to wake Jonathan, but found that he slept so soundly that it seemed as if it was he who had taken the sleeping draught and not I. I tried, but could not wake him. This caused me a great fear, and I looked around terrified. Then indeed my heart sank within me: beside the bed, as if he had stepped out of the mist – or rather as if the mist had turned into his figure, for it had entirely disappeared – stood a tall, thin man, all in black. I knew him at once from the descriptions of the others. The waxen face; the high aquiline nose, on which the light fell in a thin white line; the parted red lips, with the sharp white teeth showing between; and the red eyes that I had seemed to see in the sunset on the windows of St Mary's Church at Whitby. I knew, too, the red scar on his forehead where Jonathan had struck him. For an instant my heart stood still, and I would have screamed out, only that I was paralysed. In the pause he spoke in a sort of keen, cutting whisper, pointing as he spoke to Jonathan: –

"'Silence! If you make a sound I shall take him and dash his brains out before your very eyes." I was appalled and was too bewildered to do or say anything. With a mocking smile, he placed one hand upon my shoulder and, holding me tight, bared my throat with the other, saying as he did so: "First, a little refreshment to reward my exertions. You may as well be quiet; it is not the first time, or the second, that your veins have appeased my thirst!" I was bewildered, and, strangely enough, I did not want to hinder him. I suppose it is a part of the horrible curse that this happens when his touch is on his victim. And oh, my God, my God, pity me! He placed his reeking lips upon my throat!' Her husband groaned again. She clasped his hand harder, and looked at him pityingly, as if he were the injured one, and went on: –

'I felt my strength fading away, and I was in a half-swoon. How long this horrible thing lasted I know not; but it seemed that a long time must have passed before he took his foul, awful sneering mouth away. I saw it drip with the fresh blood!' The remembrance seemed for a while to over-power her, and she drooped and would have sunk down but for her husband's sustaining arm. With a great effort she recovered herself and went on: –

'Then he spoke to me mockingly: "And so you, like the others, would play your brains against mine. You would help these men to hunt me and frustrate me in my designs! You know now, and they know in part already, and will know in full before long, what it is to cross my path. They should have kept their energies for use closer to home. Whilst they played wits against me – against me who commanded nations, and intrigued for them, and fought for them, hundreds of years before they were born – I was countermining them. And you, their best beloved one, are now to me flesh of my flesh; blood of my blood; kin of my kin; my bountiful wine-press for a while; and shall be later on my companion and my helper. You shall be avenged in turn; for not one of them but shall minister to your needs. But as yet you are to be punished for what you have done. You have aided in thwarting me; now you shall come to my call. When my brain says 'Come!' to you, you shall cross land or sea to do my bidding; and to that end this!" With that he pulled open his shirt, and with his long sharp nails opened a vein in his breast. When the blood began to spurt out, he took my hands in one of his, holding them tight, and with the other seized my neck and pressed my mouth to the wound, so that I must either suffocate or swallow some of the – Oh, my God, my God! what have I done? What have I done to deserve such a fate, I who have tried to walk in meekness and righteousness all my days? God pity me! Look down on a poor soul in worse than mortal peril; and in mercy pity those to whom she is dear!' Then she began to rub her lips as though to cleanse them from pollution.

As she was telling her terrible story, the eastern sky began to quicken, and everything became more and more clear. Harker was still and quiet; but over his face, as the awful narrative went on, came a grey look which deepened and deepened in the morning light, till when the first red streak of the coming dawn shot up, the flesh stood darkly out against the whitening hair.

We have arranged that one of us is to stay within call of the unhappy pair till we can meet together and arrange about taking action.

Of this I am sure: the sun rises to-day on no more miserable house in all the great round of its daily course.

CHAPTER 22

JONATHAN HARKER'S JOURNAL

3 October. – As I must do something or go mad, I write this diary. It is now six o'clock, and we are to meet in the study in half an hour and take something to eat; for Dr Van Helsing and Dr Seward are agreed that if we do not eat we cannot work our best. Our best will be, God knows, required to-day. I must keep writing at every chance, for I dare not stop to think. All, big and little, must go down; perhaps at the end the little things may teach us most. The teaching, big or little, could not have landed Mina or me anywhere worse than we are to-day. However, we must trust and hope. Poor Mina told me just now, with the tears running down her dear cheeks, that it is in trouble and trial that our faith is tested – that we must keep on trusting; and that God will aid us up to the end. The end! oh, my God! what end? . . . To work! To work!

When Dr Van Helsing and Dr Seward had come back from seeing poor Renfield, we went gravely into what was to be done. First, Dr Seward told us that when he and Dr Van Helsing had gone down to the room below they had found Renfield lying on the floor, all in a heap. His face was all bruised and crushed in, and the bones of the neck were broken.

Dr Seward asked the attendant who was on duty in the passage if he had heard anything. He said that he had been sitting down – he confessed to half dozing – when he heard loud voices in the room, and then Renfield had called out loudly several times, 'God! God! God!' After that there was a sound of falling, and when he entered the room he found him lying on the floor, face down, just as the doctors had seen him. Van Helsing asked if he had heard 'voices' or 'a voice,' and he said he could not say; that at first it had seemed to him as if there were two, but as there was no one in the room it could have been only one. He could swear to it, if required, that the word 'God' was spoken by the patient. Dr Seward said to us, when we were alone, that he did not wish to go into the matter; the question of an inquest had to be considered, and it would never do to put forward the truth, as no one would believe it. As it was, he thought that on the attendant's evidence he could give a certificate of death by misadventure in falling from bed. In case the coroner should demand it, there would be a formal inquest, necessarily to the same result.

When the question began to be discussed as to what should be our next step, the very first thing we decided was that Mina should be in full confidence; that nothing of any sort – no matter how painful – should be kept from her. She herself agreed as to its wisdom, and it was pitiful to see her so brave and yet so sorrowful, and in such a depth of despair. 'There must be no more concealment,' she said. 'Alas! we have had too much already. And besides there is nothing in all the world that can give me more pain than I have already endured – than I suffer now! Whatever may happen, it must be of new hope or of new courage to me!' Van Helsing was looking at her fixedly as she spoke, and said, suddenly but quietly: –

'But, dear Madam Mina, are you not afraid; not for yourself, but for others from yourself, after what has happened?' Her face grew set in its lines, but her eyes shone with the devotion of a martyr as she answered: –

'Ah no! for my mind is made up!'

'To what?' he asked gently, whilst we were all very still; for each in our own way we had a sort of vague idea of what she meant. Her answer came with direct simplicity, as though she were simply stating a fact: –

'Because if I find in myself – and I shall watch keenly for it – a sign of harm to any that I love, I shall die!'

'You would not kill yourself?' he asked hoarsely.

'I would; if there were no friend who loved me, who would save me such a pain, and so desperate an effort!' She looked at him meaningly as she spoke. He was sitting down; but now he rose and came close to her and put his hand on her head as he said solemnly: –

'My child, there is such a one if it were for your good. For myself I could hold it in my account with God to find such an euthanasia for you, even at this moment, if it were best. Nay, were it safe! But, my child –' for a moment he seemed choked, and a great sob rose in his throat; he gulped it down and went on: –

'There are here some who would stand between you and death. You must not die. You must not die by any hand; but least of all by your own. Until the other, who has fouled your sweet life, is true dead you must not die; for if he is still with the quick Un-dead, your death would make you even as he is. No, you must live! You must struggle and strive to live, though death would seem a boon unspeakable. You must fight Death himself, though he come to you in pain or in joy; by the day, or the night; in safety or in peril! On your living soul I charge you that you do not die – nay, nor think of death – till this great evil be past.' The poor dear grew white as death, and shook and shivered, as I have seen a quicksand shake and shiver at the incoming of the tide. We were all silent; we could do nothing. At length she grew more calm, and turning to him said, sweetly, but oh! so sorrowfully, as she held out her hand: –

'I promise you, my dear friend, that if God will let me live, I shall strive to do so; till, if it may be in His good time, this horror may have passed away from me.' She was so good and brave that we all felt that our hearts were strengthened to work and endure for her, and we began to discuss what we were to do. I told her that she was to have all the papers in the safe, and all the papers or diaries and phonographs we might hereafter use; and was to keep the record as she had done before. She was pleased with the prospect of anything to do – if 'pleased' could be used in connection with so grim an interest.

As usual Van Helsing had thought ahead of everyone else, and was prepared with an exact ordering of our work.

'It is perhaps well,' he said, 'that at our meeting after our visit to Carfax we decided not to do anything with the earth-boxes that lay there. Had we done so, the Count must have guessed our purpose, and would doubtless have taken measures in advance to frustrate such an effort with regard to the others; but now he does not know our intentions. Nay more, in all probability he does not know that such a power exists to us as can sterilize his lairs, so that he cannot use them as of old. We are now so much further advanced in our knowledge as to their disposition, that, when we have examined the house in Piccadilly, we may track the very last of them. To-day, then, is ours; and in it rests our hope. The sun that rose on our sorrow this morning guards us in its course. Until it sets to-night, that monster must retain whatever form he now has. He is confined within the limitations of his earthly envelope. He cannot melt into thin air nor disappear through cracks or chinks or crannies. If he go through a doorway, he must open the door like a mortal. And so we have this day to hunt out all his lairs and sterilise them. So we shall, if we have not yet catch him and destroy him, drive him to bay in some place where the catching and the destroying shall be, in time, sure.' Here I started up, for I could not contain myself at the thought that the minutes and seconds so previously laden with Mina's life and happiness were flying from us, since whilst we talked action was possible. But Van Helsing held up his hand warningly. 'Nay, friend Jonathan,' he said, 'in this, the quickest way home is the longest way, so your proverb say. We shall all act, and act with desperate quick, when the time has come. But think, in all probable the key of the situation is in that house in Piccadilly. The Count may have many houses which he has bought. Of them he will have deeds of purchase, keys and other things. He will have paper that he write on; he will have his book of cheques. There are many belongings that he must have somewhere; why not in this place so central, so quiet, where he come and go by the front or the back at all hour, when in the very vast of the traffic there is none to notice? We shall go there and search that house; and when we learn what it holds, then we do what our friend Arthur call, in his phrases of hunt, "stop the earth," and so we run down our old fox – so? is it not?'

'Then let us come at once,' I cried; 'we are wasting the precious, precious time!' The Professor did not move, but simply said: –

'And how are we to get into that house in Piccadilly?'

'Any way!' I cried. 'We shall break in if need be.'

'And your police; where will they be, and what will they say?'

I was staggered; but I knew that if he wished to delay he had a good reason for it. So I said, as quietly as I could: –

'Don't wait more than need be; you know, I am sure, what torture I am in.'

'Ah, my child, that I do; and indeed there is no wish of me to add to your anguish. But just think, what can we do, until all the world be at movement? Then will come our time. I have thought and thought, and it seems to me that the simplest way is the best of all. Now we wish to get into the house, but we have no key; is it not so?' I nodded.

'Now suppose that you were, in truth, the owner of that house, and could not still get in; and think there was to you no conscience of the housebreaker, what would you do?'

'I should get a respectable locksmith, and set him to work to pick the lock for me.'

'And your police, they would interfere, would they not?'

'Oh, no! not if they knew the man was properly employed.'

'Then,' he looked at me keenly as he spoke, 'all that is in doubt is the conscience of the employer, and the belief of your policemen as to whether or no that employer has a good conscience or a bad one. Your police must indeed be zealous men and clever – oh, so clever! – in reading the heart, that they trouble themselves in such matter. No, no, my friend Jonathan, you go take the lock off a hundred empty houses in this your London, or of any city in the world; and if you do it as such things are rightly done, and at the time such things are rightly done, no one will interfere. I have read of a gentleman who owned a so fine house in your London, and when he went for months of summer to Zwitzerland and lock up his house, some burglar came and broke window at back and got in. Then he went and made open the shutters in front and walk out and in through the door, before the very eyes of the police. Then he have an auction in that house,

and advertise it, and put up big notice; and when the day come he sell
off by a great auctioneer all the goods of that other man who own them.
Then he go to a builder, and he sell him that house, making an agreement
that he pull it down and take all away within a certain time. And your
police and other authority help him all they can. And when that owner
come back from his holiday in Zwitzerland he find only an empty hole
where his house had been. This was all done *en règle*; and in our work
we shall be *en règle* too. We shall not go so early that the policeman who
have then little to think of, shall deem it strange; but we shall go after ten
o'clock when there are many about, and when such things would be done
were we indeed owners of the house.'

I could not but see how right he was, and the terrible despair of Mina's
face became relaxed a thought; there was hope in such good counsel. Van
Helsing went on: –

'When once within that house we may find more clues; at any rate
some of us can remain there whilst the rest find the other places where
there be more earth-boxes – at Bermondsey and Mile End.'

Lord Godalming stood up. 'I can be of some use here,' he said. 'I shall
wire to my people to have horses and carriages where they will be most
convenient.'

'Look here, old fellow,' said Morris, 'it is a capital idea to have all
ready in case we want to go horse-backing; but don't you think that one
of your snappy carriages with its heraldic adornments in a byeway of
Walworth or Mile End would attract too much attention for our purposes?
It seems to me that we ought to take cabs when we go south or east; and
even leave them somewhere near the neighbourhood we are going to.'

'Friend Quincey is right!' said the Professor. 'His head is what you call
in plane with the horizon. It is a difficult thing that we go to do, and we
do not want no peoples to watch us if so it may.'

Mina took a growing interest in everything, and I was rejoiced to see
that the exigency of affairs was helping her to forget for a time the terrible
experience of the night. She was very, very pale – almost ghastly, and so
thin that her lips were drawn away, showing her teeth somewhat prominently. I did not mention this last, lest it should give her needless pain;
but it made my blood run cold in my veins to think of what had occurred
with poor Lucy when the Count had sucked her blood. As yet there was
no sign of the teeth growing sharper; but the time as yet was short, and
there was time for fear.

When we came to the discussion of the sequence of our efforts and of
the disposition of our forces, there were new sources of doubt. It was finally

agreed that before starting for Piccadilly we should destroy the Count's lair close at hand. In case he should find it out too soon, we should thus be still ahead of him in our work of destruction; and his presence in his purely material shape, and at his weakest, might give us some new clue.

As to the disposal of forces, it was suggested by the Professor that, after our visit to Carfax, we should all enter the house in Piccadilly; that the two doctors and I should remain there, whilst Lord Godalming and Quincey found the lairs at Walworth and Mile End and destroyed them. It was possible, if not likely, the Professor urged, that the Count might appear in Piccadilly during the day, and that if so we might be able to cope with him then and there. At any rate we might be able to follow him in force. To this plan I strenuously objected, in so far as my going was concerned, for I said that I intended to stay and protect Mina. I thought that my mind was made up on the subject; but Mina would not listen to my objection. She said that there might be some law matter in which I could be useful; that amongst the Count's papers might be some clue which I could understand out of my experience in Transylvania; and that, as it was, all the strength we could muster was required to cope with the Count's extraordinary power. I had to give in, for Mina's resolution was fixed; she said that it was the last hope for *her* that we should all work together. 'As for me,' she said, 'I have no fear. Things have been as bad as they can be; and whatever may happen must have in it some element of hope or comfort. Go, my husband! God can, if He wishes it, guard me as well alone as with anyone present.' So I started up, crying out: 'Then in God's name let us come at once, for we are losing time. The Count may come to Piccadilly earlier than we think.'

'Not so!' said Van Helsing, holding up his hand.

'But why?' I asked.

'Do you forget,' he said, with actually a smile, 'that last night he banqueted heavily, and will sleep late?'

Did I forget! shall I ever – can I ever! Can any of us ever forget that terrible scene! Mina struggled hard to keep her brave countenance; but the pain overmastered her and she put her hands before her face, and shuddered whilst she moaned. Van Helsing had not intended to recall her frightful experience. He had simply lost sight of her and her part in the affair in his intellectual effort. When it struck him what he had said, he was horrified at his thoughtlessness and tried to comfort her. 'Oh, Madam Mina,' he said, 'dear, dear Madam Mina, alas! that I, of all who so reverence you, should have said anything so forgetful. These stupid old lips of mine and this stupid old head do not deserve so; but you will forget it, will you not?' He bent low beside her as he spoke; she took his hands, and looking at him through her tears, said hoarsely: –

'No, I shall not forget, for it is well that I remember; and with it I have so much in memory of you that is sweet, that I take it all together. Now, you must all be going soon. Breakfast is ready, and we must all eat that we may be strong.'

Breakfast was a strange meal to us all. We tried to be cheerful and encourage each other, and Mina was the brightest and most cheerful of us. When it was over, Van Helsing stood up and said: –

'Now, my dear friends, we go forth to our terrible enterprise. Are we all armed, as we were on that night when first we visited our enemy's lair; armed against ghostly as well as carnal attack?' We all assured him. 'Then it is well. Now, Madam Mina, you are in any case *quite* safe here until the sunset; and before then we shall return – if – We shall return! But before we go let me see you armed against personal attack. I have myself, since you came down, prepared your chamber by the placing of the things of which we know, so that he may not enter. Now let me guard yourself. On your forehead I touch this piece of Sacred Wafer in the name of the Father, the Son, and –'

There was a fearful scream which almost froze our hearts to hear. As he placed the Wafer on Mina's forehead, it had seared it – had burned into the flesh as though it had been a piece of white-hot metal. My poor darling's brain told her the significance of the fact as quickly as her nerves received the pain of it: and the two so overwhelmed her that her over-wrought nature had its voice in that dreadful scream. But the words to her thought came quickly; the echo of the scream had not ceased to ring on the air when there came the reaction, and she sank on her knees on the floor in an agony of abasement. Pulling her beautiful hair over her face, as the leper of old his mantle, she wailed out: –

'Unclean! Unclean! Even the Almighty shuns my polluted flesh! I must bear this mark of shame upon my forehead until the Judgment Day.' They all paused. I had thrown myself beside her in an agony of helpless grief, and putting my arms around held her tight. For a few minutes our sorrowful hearts beat together, whilst the friends around us turned away their eyes that ran tears silently. Then Van Helsing turned and said gravely; so gravely that I could not help feeling that he was in some way inspired and was stating things outside himself: –

'It may be that you may have to bear that mark till God Himself see fit, as He most surely shall, on the Judgment Day to redress all wrongs of the earth and of His children that He has placed thereon. And oh,

Madam Mina, my dear, my dear, may we who love you be there to see, when that red scar, the sign of God's knowledge of what has been, shall pass away and leave your forehead as pure as the heart we know. For so surely as we live, that scar shall pass away when God see right to lift the burden that is hard upon us. Till then we bear our Cross, as His Son did in obedience to His will. It may be that we are chosen instruments of His good pleasure, and that we ascend to His bidding as that other through stripes and shame; through tears and blood; through doubts and fears, and all that makes the difference between God and man.'

There was hope in his words, and comfort; and they made for resignation. Mina and I both felt so, and simultaneously we each took one of the old man's hands and bent over and kissed it. Then without a word we all knelt down together, and, all holding hands, swore to be true to each other. We men pledged ourselves to raise the veil of sorrow from the head of her whom, each in his own way, we loved; and we prayed for help and guidance in the terrible task which lay before us.

It was then time to start. So I said farewell to Mina, a parting which neither of us shall forget to our dying day; and we set out.

To one thing I have made up my mind: if we find out that Mina must be a vampire in the end, then she shall not go into that unknown and terrible land alone. I suppose it is thus that in old times one vampire meant many; just as their hideous bodies could only rest in sacred earth, so the holiest love was the recruiting sergeant for their ghastly ranks.

We entered Carfax without trouble and found all things the same as on the first occasion. It was hard to believe that amongst so prosaic surroundings of neglect and dust and decay there was any ground for such fear as we already knew. Had not our minds been made up, and had there not been terrible memories to spur us on, we could hardly have proceeded with our task. We found no papers, nor any sign of use in the house; and in the old chapel the great boxes looked just as we had seen them last. Dr Van Helsing said to us solemnly as we stood before them: –

'And now, my friends, we have a duty here to do. We must sterilize this earth, so sacred of holy memories, that he has brought from a far distant land for such fell use. He has chosen this earth because it has been holy. Thus we defeat him with his own weapon, for we make it more holy still. It was sanctified to such use of man, now we sanctify it to God.' As he spoke he took from his bag a screw-driver and a wrench, and very soon the top of one of the cases was thrown open. The earth smelled musty and close; but we did not somehow seem to mind, for our attention was concentrated on the Professor. Taking from his box a piece of the Sacred

Wafer he laid it reverently on the earth, and then shutting down the lid began to screw it home, we aiding him as he worked.

One by one we treated in the same way each of the great boxes, and left them as we had found them to all appearance; but in each was a portion of the Host.

When we closed the door behind us, the Professor said solemnly: –

'So much is already done. If it may be that with all the others we can be so successful, then the sunset of this evening may shine on Madam Mina's forehead all white as ivory and with no stain!'

As we passed across the lawn on our way to the station to catch our train we could see the front of the asylum. I looked eagerly, and in the window of my room saw Mina. I waved my hand to her, and nodded to tell that our work there was successfully accomplished. She nodded in reply to show that she understood. The last I saw, she was waving her hand in farewell. It was with a heavy heart that we sought the station and just caught the train, which was steaming in as we reached the platform.

I have written this in the train.

Piccadilly, 12.30 o'clock. – Just before we reached Fenchurch Street Lord Godalming said to me: –

'Quincey and I will find a locksmith. You had better not come with us in case there should be any difficulty; for under the circumstances it wouldn't seem so bad for us to break into an empty house. But you are a solicitor, and the Incorporated Law Society might tell you that you should have known better.' I demurred as to my not sharing any danger even of odium, but he went on: 'Besides, it will attract less attention if there are not too many of us. My title will make it all right with the lock-smith, and with any policeman that may come along. You had better go with Jack and the Professor and stay in the Green Park, somewhere in sight of the house; and when you see the door open and the smith has gone away, do you all come across. We shall be on the look-out for you, and will let you in.'

'The advice is good!' said Van Helsing, so we said no more. Godalming and Morris hurried off in a cab, we following in another. At the corner of Arlington Street our contingent got out and strolled into the Green Park. My heart beat as I saw the house on which so much of our hope was centred, looming up grim and silent in its deserted condition amongst its more lively and spruce-looking neighbours. We sat down on a bench within good view, and began to smoke cigars so as to attract as little attention as possible. The minutes seemed to pass with leaden feet as we waited for the coming of the others.

At length we saw a four-wheeler drive up. Out of it, in leisurely fashion, got Lord Godalming and Morris; and down from the box descended a thick-set working man with his rush-woven basket of tools. Morris paid the cabman, who touched his hat and drove away. Together the two ascended the steps, and Lord Godalming pointed out what he wanted done. The workman took off his coat leisurely and hung it on one of the spikes of the railing, saying something to a policeman who just then sauntered along. The policeman nodded acquiescence, and the man kneeling down placed his bag beside him. After searching through it, he took out a selection of tools which he proceeded to lay beside him in orderly fashion. Then he stood up, looked into the keyhole, blew into it, and turning to his employers, made some remark. Lord Godalming smiled, and the man lifted a good-sized bunch of keys; selecting one of them, he began to probe the lock, as if feeling his way with it. After fumbling about for a bit he tried a second, and then a third. All at once the door opened under a slight push from him, and he and the two others entered the hall. We sat still; my own cigar burnt furiously, but Van Helsing's went cold altogether. We waited patiently as we saw the workman come out and take in his bag. Then he held the door partly open, steadying it with his knees, whilst he fitted a key to the lock. This he finally handed to Lord Godalming, who took out his purse and gave him something. The man touched his hat, took his bag, put on his coat and departed; not a soul took the slightest notice of the whole transaction.

When the man had fairly gone, we three crossed the street and knocked at the door. It was immediately opened by Quincey Morris, beside whom stood Lord Godalming lighting a cigar.

'The place smells so vilely,' said the latter as we came in. It did indeed smell vilely – like the old chapel at Carfax – and with our previous experience it was plain to us that the Count had been using the place pretty freely. We moved to explore the house, all keeping together in case of attack; for we knew we had a strong and wily enemy to deal with, and as yet we did not know whether the Count might not be in the house. In the dining-room, which lay at the back of the hall, we found eight boxes of earth. Eight boxes only out of the nine which we sought! Our work was not over, and would never be until we should have found the missing box. First we opened the shutters of the window which looked out across a narrow stone-flagged yard at the blank face of a stable, pointed to look like the front of a miniature house. There were no windows in it, so we were not afraid of being overlooked. We did not lose any time in examining the chests. With the tools which we had brought with us we opened them, one by one, and treated them as we had treated those others in the chapel. It was evident to us that the Count was not at present in the house, and we proceeded to search for any of his effects.

After a cursory glance at the rest of the rooms from basement to attic, we came to the conclusion that the dining-room contained any effects which might belong to the Count; and so we proceeded to minutely examine them. They lay in a sort of orderly disorder on the great dining-room table. There were title-deeds of the Piccadilly house in a great bundle; deeds of the purchase of the houses at Mile End and Bermondsey; notepaper, envelopes, and pens and ink. All were covered up in thin wrapping paper to keep them from the dust. There were also a clothes brush, a brush and comb, and a jug and basin – the latter containing dirty water which was reddened as if with blood. Last of all was a little heap of keys of all sorts and sizes, probably those belonging to the other houses. When we had examined this last find, Lord Godalming and Quincey Morris, taking accurate notes of the various addresses of the houses in the East and the South, took with them the keys in a great bunch, and set out to destroy the boxes in these places. The rest of us are, with what patience we can, awaiting their return – or the coming of the Count.

CHAPTER 23

DR SEWARD'S DIARY

3 October. – The time seemed terribly long whilst we were waiting for the coming of Godalming and Quincey Morris. The Professor tried to keep our minds active by using them all the time. I could see his beneficent purpose, by the side glances which he threw from time to time at Harker. The poor fellow is overwhelmed in a misery that is appalling to see. Last night he was a frank, happy-looking man, with strong youthful face, full of energy, and with dark brown hair. To-day he is a drawn, haggard old man, whose white hair matches well with the hollow burning eyes and grief-written lines of his face. His energy is still intact; in fact he is like a living flame. This may yet be his salvation, for, if all goes well, it will tide him over the despairing period; he will then, in a kind of way, wake again to the realities of life. Poor fellow, I thought my own trouble was bad enough, but his –! The Professor knows this well enough, and is doing his best to keep his mind active. What he has been saying was, under the circumstances, of absorbing interest. As well as I can remember, here it is: –

'I have studied, over and over again since they came into my hands, all the papers relating to this monster; and the more I have studied, the greater seems the necessity to utterly stamp him out. All through there are signs of his advance; not only of his power, but of his knowledge of it. As I learned from the researches of my friend Arminius of Buda-Pesth, he was in life a most wonderful man. Soldier, statesman, and alchemist – which latter was the highest development of the science-knowledge of his time. He had a mighty brain, a learning beyond compare, and a heart that knew no fear and no remorse. He dared even to attend the Scholomance, and there was no branch of knowledge of his time that he did not essay. Well, in him the brain powers survived the physical death; though it would seem that memory was not all complete. In some faculties of mind he has been, and is, only a child; but he is growing, and some things that were childish at the first are now of man's stature. He is experimenting, and doing it well; and if it had not been that we have crossed his path he would be yet – he may be yet if we fail – the father or furtherer of a new order of beings, whose road must lead through Death, not Life.'

Harker groaned and said: 'And this is all arrayed against my darling! But how is he experimenting? The knowledge may help us to defeat him!'

'He has all along, since his coming, been trying his power, slowly but surely; that big child-brain of his is working. Well for us, it is, as yet, a child-brain; for had he dared, at the first, to attempt certain things he would long ago have been beyond our power. However, he means to succeed, and a man who has centuries before him can afford to wait and to go slow. *Festina lente* may well be his motto.'

'I fail to understand,' said Harker wearily. 'Oh, do be more plain to me! Perhaps grief and trouble are dulling my brain.' The Professor laid his hand tenderly on his shoulder as he spoke: –

'Ah, my child, I will be plain. Do you not see how, of late, this monster has been creeping into knowledge experimentally. How he has been making use of the zoophagous patient to effect his entry into friend John's home; for your Vampire, though in all afterwards he can come when and how he will, must at the first make entry only when asked thereto by an inmate. But these are not his most important experiments. Do we not see how at the first all these so great boxes were moved by others. He knew not then but that must be so. But all the time that so great child-brain of his was growing, and he began to consider whether he might not himself move the box. So he begin to help; and then, when he found that this be all right, he try to move them all alone. And so he progress, and he scatter these graves of him; and none but he know where they are hidden. He may have intend to bury them deep in the ground. So that he only use them in the night, or at such time as he can change his form, they do him equal well; and none may know these are his hiding place! But, my child, do not despair; this knowledge come to him just too late! Already all of his lairs but one be sterilize as for him; and before the sunset this shall be so. Then he have no place where he can move and hide. I delayed this morning that so we might be sure. Is there not more at stake for us than for him? Then why we not be even more careful than him? By my clock it is one hour, and already, if all be well, friend Arthur and Quincey are on their way to us. To-day is our day, and we must go sure, if slow, and lose no chance. See! there are five of us when those absent ones return.'

Whilst he was speaking we were startled by a knock at the hall door, the double postman's knock of the telegraph boy. We all moved out to the hall with one impulse, and Van Helsing, holding up his hand to us to keep silence, stepped to the door and opened it. The boy handed in a despatch. The Professor closed the door again and, after looking at the direction, opened it and read it aloud:

'"Look out for D. He has just now, 12.45, come from Carfax hurriedly and hastened towards the south. He seems to be going the round and may want to see you – MINA."'

There was a pause, broken by Jonathan Harker's voice: –

'Now, God be thanked, we shall soon meet!' Van Helsing turned to him quickly and said: –

'God will act in His own way and time. Do not fear, and do not rejoice as yet; for what we wish for at the moment may be our undoings.'

'I care for nothing now,' he answered hotly, 'except to wipe out this brute from the face of creation. I would sell my soul to do it!'

'Oh, hush, hush, my child!' said Van Helsing, 'God does not purchase souls in this wise; and the Devil, though he may purchase, does not keep faith. But God is merciful and just, and knows your pain and your devotion to that dear Madam Mina. Think you, how her pain would be doubled, did she but hear your wild words. Do not fear any of us; we are all devoted to this cause, and to-day shall see the end. The time is coming for action; to-day this Vampire is limit to the powers of man, and till sunset he may not change. It will take him time to arrive here – see, it is twenty minutes past one – and there are yet some times before he can hither come, be he never so quick. What we must hope for is that my Lord Arthur and Quincey arrive first.'

About half an hour after we had received Mrs Harker's telegram, there came a quiet resolute knock at the hall door. It was just an ordinary knock, such as is given hourly by thousands of gentlemen, but it made the Professor's heart and mine beat loudly. We looked at each other, and together moved out into the hall; we each held ready to use our various armaments – the spiritual in the left hand, the moral in the right. Van Helsing pulled back the latch, and, holding the door half open, stood back, having both hands ready for action. The gladness of our hearts must have shown upon our faces when on the step, close to the door, we saw Lord Godalming and Quincey Morris. They came quickly in and closed the door behind them, the former saying, as they moved along the hall: –

'It is all right. We found both places; six boxes in each, and we destroyed them all!'

'Destroyed?' asked the Professor.

'For him!' We were silent for a minute, and then Quincey said: –

'There's nothing to do but to wait here. If, however, he doesn't turn up by five o'clock, we must start off; for it won't do to leave Mrs Harker alone after sunset.'

'He will be here before long now,' said Van Helsing, who had been consulting his pocket-book. '*Nota bene*, in Madam's telegram he went south from Carfax, that means he went to cross the river, and he could only do so at slack of tide, which should be something before one o'clock.

That he went south has a meaning for us. He is as yet only suspicious; and he went from Carfax first to the place where he would suspect interference least. You must have been at Bermondsey only a short time before him. That he is not here already shows that he went to Mile End next. This took him some time; for he would then have to be carried over the river in some way. Believe me, my friends, we shall not have long to wait now. We should have ready some plan of attack, so that we may throw away no chance. Hush, there is no time now. Have all your arms! Be ready!' He held up a warning hand as he spoke, for we all could hear a key softly inserted in the lock of the hall-door.

I could not but admire, even at such a moment, the way in which a dominant spirit asserted itself. In all our hunting parties and adventures on different parts of the world, Quincey Morris had always been the one to arrange the plan of action, and Arthur and I had been accustomed to obey him implicitly. Now, the old habit seemed to be renewed instinctively. With a swift glance round the room, he at once laid out our plan of attack, and, without speaking a word, with a gesture, placed us each in position. Van Helsing, Harker, and I were just behind the door so that when it was opened the Professor could guard it whilst we two stepped between the incomer and the door. Godalming behind and Quincey in front stood just out of sight ready to move in front of the window. We waited in a suspense that made the seconds pass with nightmare slowness. The slow, careful steps came along the hall; the Count was evidently prepared for some surprise – at least he feared it.

Suddenly with a single bound he leaped into the room, winning a way past us before any of us could raise a hand to stay him. There was something so panther-like in the movement – something so unhuman, that it seemed to sober us all from the shock of his coming. The first to act was Harker, who, with a quick movement, threw himself before the door leading into the room in the front of the house. As the Count saw us, a horrible sort of snarl passed over his face, showing the eye-teeth long and pointed; but the evil smile as quickly passed into a cold stare of lion-like disdain. His expression again changed, as with a single impulse, we all advanced upon him. It was a pity that we had not some better organized plan of attack, for even at the moment I wondered what we were to do. I did not myself know whether our lethal weapons would avail us anything. Harker evidently meant to try the matter, for he had ready his great Kukri knife, and made a fierce and sudden cut at him. The blow was a powerful one; only the diabolical quickness of the Count's leap back saved him. A second less and the trenchant blade had shorn through his heart. As it was, the

point just cut the cloth of his coat, making a wide gap whence a bundle
of bank-notes and a stream of gold fell out. The expression of the Count's
face was so hellish, that for a moment I feared for Harker, though I saw
him throw the terrible knife aloft again for another stroke. Instinctively I
moved forward with a protective impulse, holding the crucifix and wafer
in my hand. I felt a mighty power fly along my arm; and it was without
surprise that I saw the monster cower back before a similar movement
made spontaneously by each one of us. It would be impossible to describe
the expression of hate and baffled malignity – of anger and hellish rage
– which came over the Count's face. His waxen hue became greenish-
yellow by the contrast of his burning eyes, and the red scar on the forehead showed on the pallid skin like a palpitating wound. The next instant,
with a sinuous dive he swept under Harker's arm ere his blow could fall,
and, grasping a handful of the money from the floor, dashed across the
room, and threw himself at the window. Amid the crash and glitter of the
falling glass, he tumbled into the flagged area below. Through the sound
of the shivering glass I could hear the 'ting' of the gold, as some of the
sovereigns fell on the flagging.

We ran over and saw him spring unhurt from the ground. He, rushing
up the steps, crossed the flagged yard, and pushed open the stable door.
There he turned and spoke to us: –

'You think to baffle me, you – with your pale faces all in a row, like
sheep in a butcher's. You shall be sorry yet, each one of you! You think
you have left me without a place to rest; but I have more. My revenge is
just begun! I spread it over centuries, and time is on my side. Your girls
that you all love are mine already; and through them you and others shall
yet be mine – my creatures, to do my bidding and to be my jackals when
I want to feed. Bah!' With a contemptuous sneer, he passed quickly through
the door, and we heard the rusty bolt creak as he fastened it behind him.
A door beyond opened and shut. The first of us to speak was the Professor,
as, realizing the difficulty of following him through the stable, we moved
towards the hall.

'We have learnt something – much! Notwithstanding his brave words,
he fears us; he fear time, he fear want! For if not, why he hurry so? His
very tone betray him, or my ears deceive. Why take that money? You
follow quick. You are hunters of wild beasts, and understand it so. For
me, I make sure that nothing here may be of use to him, if so that he
return.' As he spoke he put the money remaining into his pocket; took the
title-deeds in the bundle as Harker had left them, and swept the remaining
things into the open fireplace, where he set fire to them with a match.

Godalming and Morris had rushed out into the yard, and Harker had lowered himself from the window to follow the Count. He had, however, bolted the stable door; and by the time they had forced it open there was no sign of him. Van Helsing and I tried to make inquiry at the back of the house; but the mews was deserted and no one had seen him depart.

It was now late in the afternoon, and sunset was not far off. We had to recognize that our game was up; with heavy hearts we agreed with the Professor when he said: –

'Let us go back to Madam Mina – poor, poor, dear Madam Mina. All we can do just now is done; and we can there, at least, protect her. But we need not despair. There is but one more earth-box, and we must try to find it; when that is done all may yet be well.' I could see that he spoke as bravely as he could to comfort Harker. The poor fellow was quite broken down; now and again he gave a low groan which he could not suppress – he was thinking of his wife.

With sad hearts we came back to my house, where we found Mrs Harker awaiting us, with an appearance of cheerfulness which did honour to her bravery and unselfishness. When she saw our faces, her own became as pale as death; for a second or two her eyes were closed as if she were in secret prayer; and then she said cheerfully: –

'I can never thank you all enough. Oh, my poor darling!' As she spoke she took her husband's grey head in her hands and kissed it – 'Lay your poor head here and rest it. All will yet be well, dear! God will protect us if He so will it in His good 'ntent.' The poor fellow only groaned. There was no place for words in his sublime misery.

We had a sort of perfunctory supper together, and I think it cheered us all up somewhat. It was, perhaps, the mere animal heat of food to hungry people – for none of us had eaten anything since breakfast – or the sense of companionship may have helped us; but anyhow we were all less miserable, and saw the morrow as not altogether without hope. True to our promise, we told Mrs Harker everything which had passed; and although she grew snowy white at times when danger had seemed to threaten her husband, and red at others when his devotion to her was manifested, she listened bravely and with calmness. When we came to the part where Harker had rushed at the Count so recklessly, she clung to her husband's arm, and held it tight as though her clinging could protect him from any harm that might come. She said nothing, however, till the narration was all done, and matters had been brought right up to the present time. Then without letting go her husband's hand she stood up amongst us and spoke. Oh! that I could give any idea of the scene; of that sweet, sweet, good,

good woman in all the radiant beauty of her youth and animation, with the red scar on her forehead of which she was conscious, and which we saw with grinding of our teeth – remembering whence and how it came; her loving kindness against our grim hate; her tender faith against all our fears and doubting; and we, knowing that, so far as symbols went, she with all her goodness and purity and faith was outcast from God.

'Jonathan,' she said, and the word sounded like music on her lips, it was so full of love and tenderness, 'Jonathan dear, and you all, my true, true friends, I want you to bear something in mind through all this dreadful time. I know that you must fight – that you must destroy even as you destroyed the false Lucy so that the true Lucy might live hereafter; but it is not a work of hate. That poor soul who has wrought all this misery is the saddest case of all. Just think what will be his joy when he too is destroyed in his worser part that his better part may have spiritual immortality. You must be pitiful to him too, though it may not hold your hands from his destruction.'

As she spoke I could see her husband's face darken and draw together, as though the passion in him were shrivelling his being to its core. Instinctively the clasp on his wife's hand grew closer, till his knuckles looked white. She did not flinch from the pain which I knew she must have suffered, but looked at him with eyes that were more appealing than ever. As she stopped speaking he leaped to his feet, almost tearing his hand from hers as he spoke: –

'May God give him into my hand just for long enough to destroy that earthly life of him which we are aiming at. If beyond it I could send his soul for ever and ever to burning hell I would do it!'

'Oh, hush! oh, hush! in the name of the good God. Don't say such things, Jonathan, my husband; or you will crush me with fear and horror. Just think, my dear – I have been thinking all this long, long day of it – that . . . perhaps . . . some day . . . I too may need such pity; and that some other like you – and with equal cause for anger – may deny it to me! Oh, my husband! my husband, indeed I would have spared you such a thought had there been another way; but I pray that God may not have treasured your wild words, except as the heart-broken wail of a very loving and sorely stricken man. O God, let these poor white hairs go in evidence of what he has suffered, who all his life has done no wrong, and on whom so many sorrows have come.'

We men were all in tears now. There was no resisting them, and we wept openly. She wept too, to see that her sweeter counsels had prevailed. Her husband flung himself on his knees beside her, and putting his arms round her, hid his face in the folds of her dress. Van Helsing beckoned to us and we stole out of the room, leaving the two loving hearts alone with God.

Before they retired the Professor fixed up the room against any coming of the Vampire, and assured Mrs Harker that she might rest in peace. She tried to school herself to the belief, and, manifestly for her husband's sake, tried to seem content. It was a brave struggle; and was, I think and believe, not without its reward. Van Helsing had placed at hand a bell which either of them was to sound in case of any emergency. When they had retired, Quincey, Godalming, and I arranged that we should sit up, dividing the night between us, and watch over the safety of the poor stricken lady. The first watch falls to Quincey, so the rest of us will be off to bed as soon as we can. Godalming has already turned in, for his is the second watch. Now that my work is done, I, too, shall go to bed.

JONATHAN HARKER'S JOURNAL

3–4 October close to midnight. – I thought yesterday would never end. There was over me a yearning for sleep in some sort of blind belief that to wake would be to find things changed, and that any change must now be for the better. Before we parted, we discussed what our next step was to be, but we could arrive at no result. All we knew was that one earth-box remained, and that the Count alone knew where it was. If he chooses to lie hidden, he may baffle us for years; and in the meantime! – the thought is too horrible, I dare not think of it even now. This I know: that if ever there was a woman who was all perfection, that one is my poor wronged darling. I love her a thousand times more for her sweet pity of last night, a pity that made my own hate of the monster seem despicable. Surely God will not permit the world to be the poorer by the loss of such a creature. This is hope to me. We are all drifting reefwards now, and faith is our only anchor. Thank God! Mina is sleeping, and sleeping without dreams. I fear what her dreams might be like, with such terrible memories to ground them in. She has not been so calm, within my seeing, since the sunset. Then, for a while, there came over her face a repose which was like spring after the blasts of March. I thought at the time that it was the softness of the red sunset on her face, but somehow now I think it had a deeper meaning. I am not sleepy myself, though I am weary – weary to death. However, I must try to sleep; for there is to-morrow to think of, and there is no rest for me until . . .

Later. – I must have fallen asleep, for I was awakened by Mina, who was sitting up in bed, with a startled look on her face. I could see easily, for we did not leave the room in darkness; she had placed a warning hand over my mouth, and now she whispered in my ear: –

'Hush! there is someone in the corridor!' I got up softly, and crossing the room, gently opened the door.

Just outside, stretched on a mattress, lay Mr Morris, wide awake. He raised a warning hand for silence as he whispered to me: –

'Hush! go back to bed; it is all right. One of us will be here all night. We don't mean to take any chances!'

His look and gesture forbade discussion, so I came back and told Mina. She sighed, and positively a shadow of a smile stole over her poor, pale face as she put her arms round me and said softly: –

'Oh, thank God for good brave men!' With a sigh she sank back again to sleep. I write this as I am not sleepy, though I must try again.

4 October, morning. – Once again during the night I was wakened by Mina. This time we had all had a good sleep, for the grey of the coming dawn was making the windows into sharp oblongs, and the gas flame was like a speck rather than a disc of light. She said to me hurriedly: –

'Go call the Professor. I want to see him at once.'

'Why?' I asked.

'I have an idea. I suppose it must have come in the night, and matured without my knowing it. He must hypnotize me before the dawn, and then I shall be able to speak. Go quick, dearest; the time is getting close.' I went to the door. Dr Seward was resting on the mattress, and, seeing me, he sprang to his feet.

'Is anything wrong?' he asked, in alarm.

'No,' I replied; 'but Mina wants to see Dr Helsing at once.'

'I will go,' he said, and hurried into the Professor's room.

Two or three minutes later Van Helsing was in the room in his dressing-gown, and Mr Morris and Lord Godalming were with Dr Seward at the door asking questions. When the Professor saw Mina a smile – a positive smile – ousted the anxiety of his face; he rubbed his hands as he said: –

'Oh, my dear Madam Mina, this is indeed a change. See! friend Jonathan, we have got our dear Madam Mina, as of old, back to us to-day!' Then turning to her, he said cheerfully: 'And what am I do for you? For at this hour you do not want me for nothings.'

'I want you to hypnotize me!' she said. 'Do it before the dawn, for I feel that then I can speak, and speak freely. Be quick, for the time is short!' Without a word he motioned her to sit up in bed.

Looking fixedly at her, he commenced to make passes in front of her, from over the top of her head downward, with each hand in turn. Mina gazed at him fixedly for a few minutes, during which my own heart beat like a trip hammer, for I felt that some crisis was at hand. Gradually her eyes closed, and she sat stock still; only by the gentle heaving of her bosom could one know that she was alive. The Professor made a few more passes and then stopped, and I could see that his forehead was covered with great beads of perspiration. Mina opened her eyes; but she did not seem the same woman. There was a faraway look in her eyes, and her voice had a sad dreaminess which was new to me. Raising his hand to impose silence, the Professor motioned me to bring the others in. They came on tip-toe, closing the door behind them, and stood at the foot of the bed, looking on. Mina appeared not to see them. The stillness was broken by Van Helsing's voice speaking in a low level tone which would not break the current of her thoughts: –

'Where are you?' The answer came in neutral way: –

'I do not know. Sleep has no place it can call its own.' For several minutes there was silence. Mina sat rigid, and the Professor stood staring at her fixedly; the rest of us hardly dared to breathe. The room was growing lighter; without taking his eyes from Mina's face, Dr Van Helsing motioned me to pull up the blind. I did so, and the day seemed just upon us. A red streak shot up, and a rosy light seemed to diffuse itself through the room. On the instant the Professor spoke again: –

'Where are you now?' The answer came dreamily, but with intention; it was as though she were interpreting something. I have heard her use the same tone when reading her notes.

'I do not know. It is all strange to me!'

'What do you see?'

'I can see nothing; it is all dark.'

'What do you hear?' I could detect the strain in the Professor's patient voice.

'The lapping of water. It is gurgling by, and little waves leap. I can hear them on the outside.'

'Then you are on a ship?' We all looked at each other, trying to glean something each from the other. We were afraid to think. The answer came quick: –

'Oh, yes!'

'What else do you hear?'

'The sound of men stamping overhead as they run about. There is the creaking of a chain, and the loud tinkle as the check of the capstan falls into the ratchet.'

'What are you doing?'

'I am still – oh, so still. It is like death!' The voice faded away into a deep breath as of one sleeping, and the open eyes closed again.

By this time the sun had risen, and we were all in the full light of day. Dr Van Helsing placed his hands on Mina's shoulders, and laid her head down softly on her pillow. She lay like a sleeping child for a few moments, and then, with a long sigh, awoke and stared in wonder to see us all around her. 'Have I been talking in my sleep?' was all she said. She seemed, however, to know the situation without telling; though she was eager to know what she had told. The Professor repeated the conversation, and she said:

'Then there is not a moment to lose: it may not be yet too late!' Mr Morris and Lord Godalming started for the door, but the Professor's calm voice called them back: –

'Stay, my friends. That ship, wherever it was, was weighing anchor whilst she spoke. There are many ships weighing anchor at the moment in your so great Port of London. Which of them is it that you seek? God be thanked that we have once again a clue, though whither it may lead us we know not. We have been blind somewhat; blind after the manner of men, since when we can look back we see what we might have seen looking forward if we had been able to see what we might have seen! Alas! but that sentence is a puddle; is it not? We can know now what was in the Count's mind when he seize that money, though Jonathan's so fierce knife put him in the danger that even he dread. He meant escape. Hear me, ESCAPE! He saw that with but one earth-box left, and a pack of men following like dogs after a fox, this London was no place for him. He have take his last earth-box on board a ship, and he leave the land. He think to escape, but no! we follow him. Tally ho! as friend Arthur would say when he put on his red frock! Our old fox is wily; oh, so wily, and we must follow with wile. I too am wily and I think his mind in a little while. In meantime we may rest and in peace, for there are waters between us which he do not want to pass, and which he could not if he would – unless the ship were to touch the land, and then only at full or slack tide. See, and the sun is just rose, and all day to sunset is to us. Let us take bath, and dress, and have breakfast which we all need, and which we can eat comfortable since he be not in the same land with us.' Mina looked at him appealingly as she asked: –

'But why need we seek him further, when he is gone away from us?' He took her hand and patted it as he replied: –

'Ask me nothing as yet. When we have breakfast, then I answer all questions.' He would say no more, and we separated to dress.

After breakfast Mina repeated her question. He looked at her gravely for a minute and then said sorrowfully: –

'Because, my dear, dear Madam Mina, now more than ever must we find him even if we have to follow him to the jaws of Hell!' She grew paler as she asked faintly: –

'Why?'

'Because,' he answered solemnly, 'he can live for centuries, and you are but mortal woman. Time is now to be dreaded – since once he put that mark upon your throat.'

I was just in time to catch her as she fell forward in a faint.

CHAPTER 24

Dr Seward's Phonograph Diary, Spoken By Van Helsing

This to Jonathan Harker.

You are to stay with your dear Madam Mina. We shall go to make our search – if I can call it so, for it is not search but knowing, and we seek confirmation only. But do you stay and take care of her to-day. This is your best and most holiest office. This day nothing can find him here. Let me tell you that so you will know what we four know already, for I have tell them. He, our enemy, have gone away; he have gone back to his Castle in Transylvania. I know it so well, as if a great hand of fire wrote it on the wall. He have prepared for this in some way, and that last earth-box was ready to ship somewheres. For this he took the money; for this he hurried at the last, lest we catch him before the sun go down. It was his last hope, save that he might hide in the tomb, that he think poor Miss Lucy, being as he thought like him, keep open to him. But there was not of time. When that fail he make straight for his last resource – his last earthwork I might say did I wish *double entente*. He is clever, oh, so clever! he know that his game here was finish; and so he decide he go back home. He find ship going by the route he came, and he go in it. We go off now to find what ship, and whither bound; when we have discovered that, we come back and tell you all. Then we will comfort you and poor dear Madam Mina with new hope. For it will be hope when you think it over: that all is not lost. This very creature that we pursue, he take hundreds of years to get so far as London; and yet in one day, when we know of the disposal of him, we drive him out. He is finite, though he is powerful to do much harm and suffers not as we do. But we are strong, each in our purpose; and we are all more strong together. Take heart afresh, dear husband of Madam Mina. This battle is but begun, and in the end we shall win – so sure as that God sits on high to watch over His children. Therefore be of much comfort till we return.

VAN HELSING

JONATHAN HARKER'S JOURNAL

4 October. – When I read to Mina Van Helsing's message in the phonograph, the poor girl brightened up considerably. Already the certainty that the Count is out of the country has given her comfort; and comfort is strength to her. For my own part, now that this horrible danger is not face to face with us, it seems almost impossible to believe in it. Even my own terrible experiences in Castle Dracula seem like a long-forgotten dream. Here in the crisp autumn air, in the bright sunlight –

Alas! how can I disbelieve! In the midst of my thought my eye fell on the red scar on my poor darling's white forehead. Whilst that lasts, there can be no disbelief. And afterwards the very memory of it will keep faith crystal clear. Mina and I fear to be idle, so we have been over all the diaries again and again. Somehow, although the reality seems greater each time, the pain and the fear seem less. There is something of a guiding purpose manifest throughout, which is comforting. Mina says that perhaps we are the instruments of ultimate good. It may be! I shall try to think as she does. We have never spoken to each other yet of the future. It is better to wait till we see the Professor and the others after their investigations.

The day is running by more quickly than I ever thought a day could run for me again. It is now three o'clock.

MINA HARKER'S JOURNAL

5 October, 5 p.m. – Our meeting for report. Present: Professor Van Helsing, Lord Godalming, Dr Seward, Mr Quincey Morris, Jonathan Harker, Mina Harker.

Dr Van Helsing described what steps were taken during the day to discover on what boat and whither bound Count Dracula made his escape: –

'As I knew that he wanted to get back to Transylvania, I felt sure that he must go by the Danube mouth; or by somewhere in the Black Sea, since by that way he come. It was a dreary blank that was before us. *Omne ignotum pro magnifico*; and so with heavy hearts we start to find what ships leave for the Black Sea last night. He was in sailing ship, since Madam Mina tell of sails being set. These not so important as to go in your list of the shipping in *The Times*, and so we go, by suggestion of my Lord Godalming, to your Lloyd's, where are note of all ships that sail, however so small. There we find that only one Black Sea bound ship go out with the tide. She is the *Czarina Catherine*, and she sail from Doolittle's Wharf for Varna, and thence on to other parts and up the Danube. "So!" said I, "this is the ship whereon is the Count." So off we go to Doolittle's Wharf, and there we find a man in an office of wood so small that the man look bigger than the office. From him we inquire of the goings of the *Czarina Catherine*. He swear much, and he red face and loud of voice, but he good fellow all the same; and when Quincey give him something from his pocket which crackle as he roll it up, and put it in a so small bag which he have hid deep in his clothing, he still better fellow and humble servant to us. He come with us, and ask many men who are rough and hot; these be better fellows too when they have been no more thirsty. They say much of blood and bloom and of others which I comprehend not, though I guess what they mean; but nevertheless they tell us all things which we want to know.

'They make known to us among them how last afternoon at about five o'clock comes a man so hurry. A tall man, thin and pale, with high nose and teeth so white, and eyes that seem to be burning. That he be all in black, except that he have a hat of straw which suit not him or the time. That he scatter his money in making quick inquiry as to what ship sails for the Black Sea and for where. Some took him to the office and then to the ship, where he will not go aboard but halt at shore end of gangplank, and ask that the captain come to him. The captain come, when told that he will be pay well; and though he swear much at the first he agree to term. Then the thin man go and someone tell him where horse and cart can be hired. He go there, and soon he come again, himself driving cart on which is a great box; this he himself lift down, though it take several to put it on truck for the ship. He give much talk to captain as to how and where his box is to be placed; but the captain like it not and swear at him in many tongues, and tell him that if he like he can come and see where it shall be. But he say "no"; that he come not yet, for that he have much to do. Whereupon the captain tell him that he had better be quick – with blood – for that his ship will leave the place – of blood – before the turn of the tide – with blood. Then the thin man smile, and say that of course he must go when he think fit; but he will be surprise if he go quite so soon. The captain swear again, polyglot, and the thin man make him bow, and thank him, and say that he will so far intrude on his kindness as to come aboard before the sailing. Final the captain, more red than ever, and in more tongues, tell him that he doesn't want no Frenchmen – with bloom upon them and also with blood – in his ship – with blood on her also. And so, after asking where there might be close at hand a shop where he might purchase ships forms, he departed.

'No one knew where he went "or bloomin' well cared," as they said, for they had something else to think of – well with blood again; for it soon became apparent to all that the *Czarina Catherine* would not sail as was expected. A thin mist began to creep up from the river, and it grew, and grew; till soon a dense fog. He must have come off by himself, for none notice him. Polyglot – very polyglot – polyglot with bloom and blood; but he could do nothing. The water rose and rose; and he began to fear that he would lose the tide altogether. He was in no friendly mood when, just at full tide, the thin man came up the gangplank again and asked to see where his box had been stowed. Then the captain replied that he wished that he and his box – old and with much bloom and blood – were in hell. But the thin man did not be offend, and went down with the mate and saw where it was place, and came up and stood awhile on deck in fog. He must have come off by himself, for none notice him. Indeed they thought not of him; for soon the fog begin to melt away, and all was clear again. My friends of the thirst and the language that was of bloom and blood laughed, as they told how the captain's swears exceeded even his usual polyglot, and was more than ever full of picturesque, when on questioning other mariners who were in movement up and down the river that hour, he found that few of them had seen any of fog at all, except where it lay round the wharf. However the ship went out on the ebb tide; and was doubtless by morning far down the river mouth. She was by then, when they told us, well out to sea.

'And so, my dear Madam Mina, it is that we have to rest for a time, for our enemy is on the sea, with the fog at his command, on his way to the Danube mouth. To sail a ship takes time, go she never so quick; and when we start we go on land more quick, and we meet him there. Our best hope is to come on him when in the box between sunrise and sunset; for then he can make no struggle, and we may deal with him as we should. There are days for us in which we can make ready our plan. We know all about where he go; for we have seen the owner of the ship, who have shown us invoices and all papers that can be. The box we seek is to be landed in Varna, and to be given to an agent, one Ristics, who will there present his credentials; and so our merchant friend will have done his part. When he ask if there be any wrong, for that so, he can telegraph and have inquiry made at Varna, we say "no"; for what is to be done is not for police or of the customs. It must be done by us alone and in our own way.'

When Dr Van Helsing had done speaking, I asked him if it were certain that the Count had remained on board the ship. He replied: 'We have the best proof of that: your own evidence, when in the hypnotic trance this morning.' I asked him again if it were really necessary that they should pursue the Count, for oh! I dread Jonathan leaving me, and I know that he would surely go if the others went. He answered in growing passion, at first quietly. As he went on, however, he grew more angry and more forceful, till in the end we could not but see wherein was at least some of that personal dominance which made him so long a master amongst men: –

'Yes, it is necessary – necessary – necessary! For your sake in the first, and then for the sake of humanity. This monster has done much harm already, in the narrow scope where he find himself, and in the short time when as yet he was only as a body groping his so small measure in darkness and not knowing. All this have I told these others; you, my dear Madam Mina, will learn it in the phonograph of my friend John, or in that of your husband. I have told them how the measure of leaving his own barren land – barren of people – and coming to a new land where life of man teems till they are like the multitude of standing corn, was the work of centuries. Were another of the Un-Dead, like him, try to do what he has done, perhaps not all the centuries of the world that have been, or that will be, could aid him. With this one, all the forces of nature that are occult and deep and strong must have worked together in some wondrous way. The very place where he have been alive, Un-Dead for all these centuries, is full of strangeness of the geologic and chemical world. There are deep caverns and fissures that reach none know whither. There have been volcanoes, some of whose openings still send out waters of strange properties, and gases that kill or make to vivify. Doubtless, there is something magnetic or electric in some of these combinations of occult forces which work for physical life in strange way; and in himself were from the first some great qualities. In a hard and warlike time he was celebrate that he have more iron nerve, more subtle brain, more braver heart, than any man. In him some vital principle have in strange way found their utmost; and as his body keep strong and grow and thrive, so his brain grow too. All this without that diabolic aid which is surely to him; for it have to yield to the powers that come from, and are, symbolic of good. And now this is what he is to us. He have infect you – oh, forgive me, my dear, that I must say such; but it is for good of you that I speak. He infect you in such wise, that even if he do no more, you have only to live – to live in your own old, sweet way; and so in time, death, which is of man's common lot and with God's sanction, shall make you like to him. This must not be! We have sworn together that it must not. Thus are we ministers of God's own wish: that the world, and men for whom His Son die, will not be given over to monsters, whose very existence would defame

Him. He have allowed us to redeem one soul already, and we go out as the old knights of the Cross to redeem more. Like them we shall travel towards the sunrise; and like them, if we fall, we fall in good cause.' He paused and I said: –

'But will not the Count take his rebuff wisely? Since he has been driven from England, will he not avoid it, as a tiger does the village from which he has been hunted?'

'Aha!' he said, 'your simile of the tiger good, for me, and I shall adopt him. Your man-eater, as they of India call the tiger who has once taste blood of the human, care no more for other prey, but prowl unceasing till he get him. This that we hunt from our village is a tiger, too, a man-eater, and he never cease to prowl. Nay, in himself he is not one to retire and stay afar. In his life, his living life, he go over the Turkey frontier and attack his enemy on his own ground; he be beaten back, but did he stay? No? He come again, and again, and again. Look at his persistence and endurance. With the child-brain that was to him he have long since conceive the idea of coming to a great city. What does he do? He find out the place of all the world most of promise for him. Then he deliberately set himself down to prepare for the task. He find in patience just how is his strength, and what are his powers. He study new tongues. He learn new social life; new environment of old ways, the politic, the law, the finance, the science, the habit of a new land and a new people who have come to be since he was. His glimpse that he have had whet his appetite only and enkeen his desire. Nay, it help him to grow as to his brain; for it all prove to him how right he was at the first in his surmises. He have done this alone; all alone! from a ruin tomb in a forgotten land. What more may he not do when the greater world of thought is open to him? He that can smile at death, as we know him; who can flourish in the midst of diseases that kill off whole peoples. Oh! if such an one was to come from God, and not the Devil, what a force for good might he not be in this old world of ours! But we are pledged to set the world free. Our toil must be in silence, and our efforts all in secret; for this enlightened age, when men believe not even what they see, the doubting of wise men would be his greatest strength. It would be at once his sheath and his armour, and his weapons to destroy us, his enemies, who are willing to peril even our own souls for the safety of one we love – for the good of mankind, and for the honour and glory of God.'

After a general discussion it was determined that for to-night nothing be definitely settled; that we should all sleep on the facts, and try to think out the proper conclusions. To-morrow at breakfast we are to meet again, and, after making our conclusions known to one another, we shall decide on some course of action.

I feel a wonderful peace and rest to-night. It is as if some haunting presence were removed from me. Perhaps . . .

My surmise was not finished, could not be; for I caught sight in the mirror of the red mark upon my forehead; and I knew that I was still unclean.

DR SEWARD'S DIARY

5 October. – We all rose early, and I think that sleep did much for each and all of us. When we met at early breakfast there was more general cheerfulness than any of us had ever expected to experience again.

It is really wonderful how much resilience there is in human nature. Let any obstructing cause, no matter what, be removed in any way – even by death – and we fly back to first principles of hope and enjoyment. More than once, as we sat around the table, my eyes opened in wonder whether the whole of the past days had not been a dream. It was only when I caught sight of the red blotch on Mrs Harker's forehead that I was brought back to reality. Even now, when I am gravely resolving the matter, it is almost impossible to realise that the cause of all our trouble is still existent. Even Mrs Harker seems to lose sight of her trouble for whole spells; it is only now and again, when something recalls it to her mind, that she thinks of her terrible scar. We are to meet here in my study in half an hour and decide on our course of action. I see only one immediate difficulty, I know it by instinct rather than reason: we shall all have to speak frankly; and yet I fear that in some mysterious way poor Mrs Harker's tongue is tied. I *know* that she forms conclusions of her own, and from all that has been I can guess how brilliant and how true they must be; but she will not, or cannot, give them utterance. I have mentioned this to Van Helsing, and he and I are to talk it over when we are alone. I suppose it is some of that horrid poison which has got into her veins beginning to work. The Count had his own purposes when he gave her what Van Helsing called 'the Vampire's baptism of blood.' Well, there may be a poison that distils itself out of good things; in an age when the existence of ptomaines is a mystery we should not wonder at anything! One thing I know: that if my instinct be true regarding poor Mrs Harker's silences, then there is a terrible difficulty – an unknown danger – in the work before us. The same power that compels her silence may compel her speech. I dare not think further; for so I should in my thoughts dishonour a noble woman!

Van Helsing is coming to my study a little before the others. I shall try to open the subject with him.

Later. – When the Professor came in, we talked over the state of things. I could see that he had something on his mind which he wanted to say, but felt some hesitancy about broaching the subject. After beating about the bush a little, he said suddenly: –

'Friend John, there is something that you and I must talk of alone, just at the first at any rate. Later, we may have to take the others into our confidence'; then he stopped, so I waited; he went on: –

'Madam Mina, our poor, dear Madam Mina, is changing.' A cold shiver ran through me to find my worst fears thus endorsed. Van Helsing continued: –

'With the sad experience of Miss Lucy, we must this time be warned before things go too far. Our task is now in reality more difficult than ever, and this new trouble makes every hour of the direst importance. I can see the characteristics of the vampire coming in her face. It is now but very, very slight; but it is to be seen if we have eyes to notice without to pre-judge. Her teeth are some sharper, and at times her eyes are more hard. But these are not all, there is to her the silence now often; as so it was with Miss Lucy. She did not speak, even when she wrote that which she wished to be known later. Now my fear is this. If it be that she can, by our hypnotic trance, tell what the Count see and hear, is it not more true that he who have hypnotize her first, and who have drink of her very blood and make her drink of his, should, if he will, compel her mind to disclose to him that which she know?' I nodded acquiescence; he went on: –

'Then what we must do is to prevent this; we must keep her ignorant of our intent, and so she cannot tell what she know not. This is a painful task! Oh! so painful that it heartbreak me to think of; but it must be. When to-day we meet, I must tell her that for reason which we will not to speak she must not more be of our council, but be simply guarded by us.' He wiped his forehead, which had broken out in profuse perspiration at the thought of the pain which he might have to inflict upon the poor soul already so tortured. I knew that it would be some sort of comfort to him if I told him that I also had come to the same conclusion; for at any rate it would take away the pain of doubt. I told him, and the effect was as I expected.

It is now close to the time of our general gathering. Van Helsing has gone away to prepare for the meeting, and his painful part of it. I really believe his purpose is to be able to pray alone.

Later. – At the very outset of our meeting a great personal relief was experienced by both Van Helsing and myself. Mrs Harker had sent a message by her husband to say that she would not join us at present, as she thought it better that we should be free to discuss our movements without her presence to embarrass us. The Professor and I looked at each other for an instant, and somehow we both seemed relieved. For my own part, I thought that if Mrs Harker realized the danger herself, it was much pain as well as much danger averted. Under the circumstances we agreed, by a questioning look and answer, with finger on lip, to preserve silence of our suspicions, until we should have been able to confer alone again. We went at once into our Plan of Campaign. Van Helsing roughly put the facts before us first: –

'The *Czarina Catherine* left the Thames yesterday morning. It will take her at the quickest speed she has ever made at least three weeks to reach Varna; but we can travel overland to the same place in three days. Now, if we allow for two days less for the ship's voyage, owing to such weather influences as we know that the Count can bring to bear; and if we allow a whole day and night for any delays which may occur to us, then we have a margin of nearly two weeks. Thus, in order to be quite safe, we must leave here on 17th at latest. Then we shall at any rate be in Varna a day before the ship arrives, and able to make such preparations as may be necessary. Of course we shall all go armed – armed against evil things, spiritual as well as physical.' Here Quincey Morris added: –

'I understand that the Count comes from a wolf country, and it may be that he will get there before us. I propose that we add Winchesters to our armament. I have a kind of belief in a Winchester when there is any trouble of that sort around. Do you remember, Art, when we had the pack after us at Tobolsk? What wouldn't we have given then for a repeater apiece!'

'Good!' said Van Helsing. 'Winchesters it shall be. Quincey's head is level at all times, but most so when there is to hunt, though my metaphor be more dishonour to science than wolves be of danger to man. In the meantime we can do nothing here; and as I think that Varna is not familiar to any of us, why not go there more soon? It is as long to wait here as there. To-night and to-morrow we can get ready, and then, if all be well, we four can set out on our journey.'

'We four?' said Harker interrogatively, looking from one to another of us.

'Of course!' answered the Professor quickly. 'You must remain to take care of your so sweet wife!' Harker was silent for a while and then said in a hollow voice: –

'Let us talk of that part of it in the morning. I want to consult with Mina.' I thought that now was the time for Van Helsing to warn him not to disclose our plans to her; but he took no notice. I looked at him significantly and coughed. For answer he put his finger on his lip and turned away.

JONATHAN HARKER'S JOURNAL

5 October, afternoon. – For some time after our meeting this morning I could not think. The new phases of things leave my mind in a state of wonder which allows no room for active thought. Mina's determination not to take any part in the discussion set me thinking; and as I could not argue the matter with her, I could only guess. I am as far as ever from a solution now. The way the others received it, too, puzzled me; the last time we talked of the subject we agreed that there was to be no more concealment of anything amongst us. Mina is sleeping now, calmly and sweetly like a little child. Her lips are curved and her face beams with happiness. Thank God there are such moments still for her.

Later. – How strange it all is! I sat watching Mina's happy sleep, and came as near to being happy myself as I suppose I shall ever be. As the evening drew on, and the earth took its shadows from the sun sinking lower, the silence of the room grew more and more solemn to me. All at once Mina opened her eyes, and looking at me tenderly said: –

'Jonathan, I want you to promise me something on your word of honour. A promise made to me, but made holily in God's hearing, and not to be broken though I should go down on my knees and implore you with bitter tears. Quick, you must make it to me at once.'

'Mina,' I said, 'a promise like that, I cannot make at once. I may have no right to make it.'

'But, dear one,' she said, with such spiritual intensity that her eyes were like pole stars, 'it is I who wish it; and it is not for myself. You can ask Dr Van Helsing if I am not right; if he disagrees you may do as you will. Nay, more, if you all agree, later, you are absolved from the promise.'

'I promise!' I said, and for a moment she looked supremely happy; though to me all happiness for her was denied by the red scar on her forehead. She said: –

'Promise me that you will not tell me anything of the plans formed for the campaign against the Count. Not by word, or inference, or implication; not at any time whilst this remains to me!' and she solemnly pointed to the scar. I saw that she was in earnest, and said solemnly: –

'I promise!' and as I said it I felt that from that instant a door had been shut between us.

Later, midnight. – Mina has been bright and cheerful all the evening. So much so that all the rest seemed to take courage, as if infected somewhat with her gaiety; as a result even I myself felt as if the pall of gloom which weighs us down were somewhat lifted. We all retired early. Mina is now sleeping like a little child; it is a wonderful thing that her faculty of sleep remains to her in the midst of her terrible trouble. Thank God for it, for then at least she can forget her care. Perhaps her example may affect me as her gaiety did to-night. I shall try it. Oh! for a dreamless sleep.

6 October, morning. – Another surprise. Mina woke me early, about the same time as yesterday, and asked me to bring Dr Van Helsing. I thought that it was another occasion for hypnotism, and without question went for the Professor. He had evidently expected some such call, for I found him dressed in his room. His door was ajar, so that he could hear the opening of the door of our room. He came at once; as he passed into the room, he asked Mina if the others might come too.

'No,' she said quite simply, 'it will not be necessary. You can tell them just as well. I must go with you on your journey.'

Dr Van Helsing was as startled as I was. After a moment's pause he asked: –

'But why?'

'You must take me with you. I am safer with you, and you shall be safer too.'

'But why, dear Madam Mina? You know that your safety is our solemnest duty. We go into danger, to which you are, or may be, more liable than any of us from – from circumstances – things that have been.' He paused embarrassed.

As she replied, she raised her finger and pointed to her forehead: –

'I know. That is why I must go. I can tell you now, whilst the sun is coming up; I may not be able again. I know that when the Count wills me I must go. I know that if he tells me to come in secret, I must come by wile; by any device to hood-wink – even Jonathan.' God saw the look that she turned on me as she spoke, and if there be indeed a Recording Angel that look is noted to her everlasting honour. I could only clasp her hand. I could not speak; my emotion was too great for even the relief of tears. She went on: –

'You men are brave and strong. You are strong in your numbers, for you can defy that which would break down the human endurance of one who had to guard alone. Besides, I may be of service, since you can hypnotize me and so learn that which even I myself do not know.' Dr Van Helsing said very gravely: –

'Madam Mina, you are, as always, most wise. You shall with us come; and together we shall do that which we go forth to achieve.' When he had spoken, Mina's long spell of silence made me look at her. She had fallen back on her pillow asleep; she did not even wake when I had pulled up the blind and let in the sunlight which flooded the room. Van Helsing motioned to me to come with him quietly. We went to his room, and within a minute Lord Godalming, Dr Seward, and Mr Morris were with us also. He told them what Mina had said, and went on: –

'In the morning we shall leave for Varna. We have now to deal with a new factor: Madam Mina. Oh, but her soul is true. It is to her an agony to tell us so much as she has done; but it is most right, and we are warned in time. There must be no chance lost, and in Varna we must be ready to act the instant when that ship arrives.'

'What shall we do exactly?' asked Mr Morris laconically. The Professor paused before replying: –

'We shall at the first board that ship; then, when we have identified the box, we shall place a branch of the wild rose on it. This we shall fasten, for when it is there none can emerge; so at least says the superstition. And to superstition must we trust at the first; it was man's faith in the early, and it have its root in faith still. Then, when we get the opportunity that we seek, when none are near to see, we shall open the box, and – and all will be well.'

'I shall not wait for any opportunity,' said Morris. 'When I see the box I shall open it and destroy the monster, though there were a thousand men looking on, and if I am to be wiped out for it the next moment!' I grasped his hand instinctively and found it as firm as a piece of steel. I think he understood my look; I hope he did.

'Good boy,' said Dr Van Helsing. 'Brave boy. Quincey is all man, God bless him for it. My child, believe me, none of us shall lag behind or pause from any fear. I do but say what we may do – what we must do. But, indeed, indeed we cannot say what we shall do. There are so many things which may happen, and their ways and their ends are so various that until the moment we may not say. We shall all be armed, in all ways;

and when the time for the end has come, our effort shall not be lack. Now let us to-day put all our affairs in order. Let all things which touch on others dear to us, and who on us depend, be complete; for none of us can tell what, or when, or how, the end may be. As for me, my own affairs are regulate; and as I have nothing else to do, I shall go make arrangement for the travel. I shall have all tickets and so forth for our journey.'

There was nothing further to be said, and we parted. I shall now settle up all my affairs of earth, and be ready for whatever may come . . .

Later. – It is all done; my will is made, and all complete. Mina if she survive is my sole heir. If it should not be so, then the others who have been so good to us will have remainder.

It is now drawing towards the sunset; Mina's uneasiness calls my attention to it. I am sure that there is something on her mind which the time of exact sunset will reveal. These occasions are becoming harrowing times for us all, for each sunrise and sunset opens up some new danger – some new pain, which, however, may in God's will be means to a good end. I write all these things in the diary since my darling must not hear them now; but if it may be that she can see them again, they shall be ready.

She is calling to me.

CHAPTER 25

DR SEWARD'S DIARY

11 October, evening. – Jonathan Harker has asked me to note this, as he says he is hardly equal to the task, and he wants an exact record kept.

I think that none of us were surprised when we were asked to see Mrs Harker a little before the time of sunset. We have of late come to understand that sunrise and sunset are to her times of peculiar freedom, when her old self can be manifested without any controlling force subduing or restraining her, or inciting her to action. This mood or condition begins some half-hour or more before actual sunrise or sunset, and lasts till either the sun is high, or whilst the clouds are still aglow with the rays streaming above the horizon. At first there is a sort of negative condition, as if some tie were loosened, and then the absolute freedom quickly follows; when, however, the freedom ceases the change-back or relapse comes quickly, preceeded only by a spell of warning silence.

To-night, when we met she was somewhat constrained, and bore all the signs of an internal struggle. I put it down myself to her making a violent effort at the earliest instant she could do so. A very few minutes, however, gave her complete control of herself; then, motioning her husband to sit beside her on the sofa where she was half reclining, she made the rest of us bring chairs up close. Taking her husband's hand in hers she began: –

'We are all here together in freedom, for perhaps the last time! I know, dear; I know that you will always be with me to the end.' This was to her husband, whose hand had, as we could see, tightened upon hers. 'In the morning we go out upon our task, and God alone knows what may be in store for any of us. You are going to be so good to me as to take me with you. I know that all that brave earnest men can do for a poor weak woman, whose soul perhaps is lost – no, no, not yet, but is at any rate at stake – you will do. But you must remember that I am not as you are. There is a poison in my blood, in my soul, which may destroy me; which must destroy me, unless some relief comes to us. Oh, my friends, you know as well as I do, that my soul is at stake; and though I know there is one way out for me, you must not and I must not take it!' She looked appealingly at us all in turn, beginning and ending with her husband.

'What is that way?' asked Van Helsing in a hoarse voice. 'What is that way, which we must not – may not – take?'

'That I may die now, either by my own hand or that of another, before the greater evil is entirely wrought, I know, and you know, that were I once dead you could and would set free my immortal spirit, even as you did my poor Lucy's. Were death, or the fear of death, the only thing that stood in the way, I would not shrink to die here, now, amidst the friends who love me. But death is not all. I cannot believe that to die in such a case, when there is hope before us and a better task to be done, is God's will. Therefore, I on my part give up here the certainty of eternal rest, and go out into the dark where may be the blackest things that the world or the nether world holds!' We were all silent, for we knew instinctively that this was only a prelude. The faces of the others were set, and Harker's grew ashen grey; perhaps he guessed better than any of us what was coming. She continued: –

'This is what I can give into the hotch-pot.' I could not but note the quaint legal phrase which she used in such a place, and with all serious-ness. 'What will each of you give? Your lives, I know,' she went on quickly; 'that is easy for brave men. Your lives are God's and you can give them back to Him; but what will you give me?' She looked again questioningly, but this time avoided her husband's face. Quincey seemed to understand; he nodded, and her face lit up. 'Then I shall tell you plainly what I want, for there must be no doubtful matter in this connection between us now. You must promise me, one and all – even you, my beloved husband – that, should the time come, you will kill me.'

'What is that time?' The voice was Quincey's but it was low and strained.

'When you shall be convinced that I am so changed that it is better that I die that I may live. When I am thus dead in the flesh, then you will, without a moment's delay, drive a stake through me and cut off my head; or do whatever else may be wanting to give me rest!'

Quincey was the first to rise after the pause. He knelt down before her and taking her hand in his said solemnly: –

'I'm only a rough fellow, who hasn't, perhaps, lived as a man should to win such a distinction, but I swear to you by all that I hold sacred and dear that, should the time ever come, I shall not flinch from the duty that you have set us. And I promise you, too, that I shall make all certain, for if I am only doubtful I shall take it that the time has come!'

'My true friend!' was all she could say amid her fast-falling tears, as, bending over, she kissed his hand.

'I swear the same, my dear Madam Mina!' said Van Helsing.

'And I!' said Lord Godalming, each of them in turn kneeling to her to take the oath. I followed, myself. Then her husband turned to her, wan-eyed and with a greenish pallor which subdued the snowy whiteness of his hair, and asked: –

'And must I, too, make such a promise, oh, my wife?'

'You too, my dearest,' she said, with infinite yearning of pity in her voice and eyes. 'You must not shrink. You are nearest and dearest and all the world to me; our souls are knit into one, for all life and all time. Think, dear, that there have been times when brave men have killed their wives and their womenkind, to keep them from falling into the hands of the enemy. Their hands did not falter any the more because those that they loved implored them to slay them. It is men's duty towards those whom they love, in such times of sore trial! And oh, my dear, if it is to be that I must meet death at any hand, let it be at the hand of him that loves me best. Dr Van Helsing, I have not forgotten your mercy in poor Lucy's case to him who loved' – she stopped with a flying blush, and changed her phrase – 'to him who had best right to give her peace. If that time shall come again, I look to you to make it a happy memory of my husband's life that it was his loving hand which set me free from the awful thrall upon me.'

'Again I swear!' came the Professor's resonant voice. Mrs Harker smiled, positively smiled, as with a sigh of relief she leaned back and said: –

'And now one word of warning, a warning which you must never forget: this time, if it ever come, may come quickly and unexpectedly, and in such case you must lose no time in using your opportunity. At such a time I myself might be – nay! if the time ever comes, *shall* be – leagued with your enemy against you.

'One more request'; she became very solemn as she said this, 'it is not vital and necessary like the other, but I want you to do one thing for me, if you will.' We all acquiesced, but no one spoke; there was no need to speak: –

'I want you to read the Burial Service.' She was interrupted by a deep groan from her husband; taking his hand in hers, she held it over her heart, and continued: 'You must read it over me some day. Whatever may be the issue of all this fearful state of things, it will be a sweet thought to all or some of us. You, my dearest, will, I hope, read it, for then it will be in your voice in my memory for ever – come what may!'

'But oh, my dear one,' he pleaded, 'death is afar off from you.'

'Nay,' she said, holding up a warning hand. 'I am deeper in death at this moment than if the weight of an earthly grave lay heavy upon me!'

'Oh, my wife, must I read it?' he said, before he began.

'It would comfort me, my husband!' was all she said; and he began to read when she had got the book ready.

How can I – how could anyone – tell of that strange scene, its solemnity, its gloom, its sadness, its horror; and, withal, its sweetness? Even a sceptic, who can see nothing but a travesty of bitter truth in anything holy or emotional, would have been melted to the heart had he seen that little group of loving and devoted friends kneeling round that stricken and sorrowing lady; or heard the tender passion of her husband's voice, as in tones so broken with emotion that often he had to pause, he read the simple and beautiful service for the Burial of the Dead. 'I – I cannot go on – words – and – v-voice – f-fail m-me!'

She was right in her instinct. Strange as it all was, bizarre as it may hereafter seem even to us who felt its potent influence at the time, it comforted us much; and the silence, which showed Mrs Harker's coming relapse from her freedom of soul, did not seem so full of despair to any of us as we had dreaded.

JONATHAN HARKER'S JOURNAL

15 October. Varna. – We left Charing Cross on the morning of the 12th, got to Paris the same night, and took the places secured for us in the Orient Express. We travelled night and day, arriving here at about five o'clock. Lord Godalming went to the Consulate to see if any telegram had arrived for him, whilst the rest of us came on to this hotel – the Odessus. The journey may have had incidents; I was, however, too eager to get on, to care of them. Until the *Czarina Catherine* comes into port there will be no interest for me in anything in the wide world. Thank God! Mina is well, and looks to be getting stronger; her colour is coming back. She sleeps a great deal; throughout the journey she slept nearly all the time. Before sunrise and sunset, however, she is very wakeful and alert; and it has become a habit for Van Helsing to hypnotize her at such times. At first, some effort was needed, and he had to make many passes; but now, she seems to yield at once, as if by habit, and scarcely any action is needed. He seems to have power at these particular moments to simply will, and her thoughts obey him. He always asks her what she can see and hear. She answers to the first: –

'Nothing; all is dark.' And to the second: –

'I can hear the waves lapping against the ship, and the water rushing by. Canvas and cordage strain and masts and yards creak. The wind is high – I can hear it in the shrouds, and the bow throws back the foam.' It is evident that the *Czarina Catherine* is still at sea, hastening on her way to Varna. Lord Godalming has just returned. He had four telegrams, one each day since we started, and all to the same effect: that the *Czarina Catherine* had not been reported to Lloyd's from anywhere. He had arranged before leaving London that his agent should send him every day a telegram saying if the ship had been reported. He was to have a message even if she were not reported, so that he might be sure that there was a watch being kept at the other end of the wire.

We had dinner and went to bed early. To-morrow we are to see the Vice-Consul, and to arrange, if we can, about getting on board the ship as soon as she arrives. Van Helsing says that our chance will be to get on board between sunrise and sunset. The Count, even if he takes the form of a bat, cannot cross the running water of his own volition, and so cannot leave the ship. As he dare not change to man's form without suspicion – which he evidently wishes to avoid – he must remain in the box. If, then, we can come on board after sunrise, he is at our mercy; for we can open the box and make sure of him, as we did of poor Lucy, before he wakes. What mercy he will get from us will not count for much. We think that we shall not have much trouble with officials or the seamen. Thank God! this is the country where bribery can do anything, and we are well supplied with money. We have only to make sure that the ship cannot come into port between sunset and sunrise without our being warned, and we shall be safe. Judge Moneybag will settle this case, I think!

16 October. – Mina's report still the same: lapping waves and rushing water, darkness and favouring winds. We are evidently in good time, and when we hear of the *Czarina Catherine* we shall be ready. As she must pass the Dardanelles we are sure to have some report.

17 October. – Everything is pretty well fixed now, I think, to welcome the Count on his return from his tour. Godalming told the shippers that he fancied that the box sent aboard might contain something stolen from a friend of his, and got a half consent that he might open it at his own risk. The owner gave him a paper telling the captain to give him every facility in doing whatever he chose on board the ship, and also a similar authorization to his agent at Varna. We have seen the agent, who was much impressed with Godalming's kindly manner to him, and we are all satisfied that whatever he can do to aid our wishes will be done. We have already arranged what to do in case we get the box open. If the Count is there, Van Helsing and Seward will cut off his head at once and drive a stake through his heart. Morris and Godalming and I shall prevent interference, even if we have to use the arms which we shall have ready. The

Professor says that if we can so treat the Count's body, it will soon after fall into dust. In such case there would be no evidence against us, in case any suspicion of murder were aroused. But even if it did not, we should stand or fall by our act, and perhaps some day this very script may be evidence to come between some of us and a rope. For myself, I should take the chance only too thankfully if it were to come. We mean to leave no stone unturned to carry out our intent. We have arranged with certain officials that the instant the *Czarina Catherine* is seen, we are to be informed by a special messenger.

24 October. – A whole week of waiting. Daily telegrams to Godalming, but only the same story: 'Not yet reported.' Mina's hypnotic answer is unvaried: 'Lapping waves, rushing water, and creaking masts.'

Telegram, October 24th.
Rufus Smith, Lloyd's London, to Lord Godalming, care of
H.B.M. Vice-Consul, Varna

'*Czarina Catherine* reported this morning from Dardanelles.'

DR SEWARD'S DIARY

24 October. – How I miss my phonograph! To write diary with a pen is irksome to me; but Van Helsing says I must. We were all wild with excitement to-day when Godalming got his telegram from Lloyd's. I know now what men feel in battle when the call to action is heard. Mrs Harker, alone of our party, did not show any signs of emotion. After all, it is not strange that she did not; for we took special care not to let her know anything about it, and we all tried not to show any excitement when we were in her presence. In old days she would, I am sure, have noticed, no matter how we might have tried to conceal it; but in this way she is greatly changed during the past three weeks. The lethargy grows upon her, and though she seems strong and well, and is getting back some of her colour, Van Helsing and I are not satisfied. We talk of her often; we have not, however, said a word to the others. It would break poor Harker's heart – certainly his nerve – if he knew that we had even a suspicion on the subject. Van Helsing examines, he tells me, her teeth very carefully, whilst she is in the hypnotic condition, for he says that so long as they do not begin to sharpen there is no active danger of a change in her. If this change should come, it would be necessary to take steps! . . . We both know what those steps would have to be, though we do not mention our thoughts to each other. We should neither of us shrink from the task – awful though it be to contemplate. 'Euthanasia' is an excellent and a comforting word! I am grateful to whoever invented it.

It is only about 24 hours' sail from the Dardanelles to here, at the rate the *Czarina Catherine* has come from London. She should therefore arrive some time in the morning; but as she cannot possibly get in before then, we are all about to retire early. We shall get up at one o'clock, so as to be ready.

25 October, noon. – No news yet of the ship's arrival. Mrs Harker's hypnotic report this morning was the same as usual, so it is possible that we may get news at any moment. We men are all in a fever of excitement, except Harker, who is calm; his hands are as cold as ice, and an hour ago I found him whetting the edge of the great Ghoorka knife which he now always carries with him. It will be a bad look-out for the Count if the edge of that 'Kukri' ever touches his throat, driven by that stern, ice-cold hand!

Van Helsing and I were a little alarmed about Mrs Harker to-day. About noon she got into a sort of lethargy which we did not like; although we kept silent to the others, we were neither of us happy about it. She had been restless all the morning, so that we were at first glad to know that she was sleeping. When, however, her husband mentioned casually that she was sleeping so soundly that he could not wake her, we went to her room to see for ourselves. She was breathing naturally and looked so well and peaceful that we agreed that the sleep was better for her than anything else. Poor girl, she has so much to forget that it is no wonder that sleep, if it brings oblivion to her, does her good.

Later. – Our opinion was justified, for when after a refreshing sleep of some hours she woke up, she seemed brighter and better than she has been for days. At sunset she made the usual hypnotic report. Wherever he may be in the Black Sea, the Count is hurrying to his destination. To his doom, I trust!

26 October. – Another day and no tidings of the *Czarina Catherine*. She ought to be here by now. That she is still journeying *somewhere* is apparent, for Mrs Harker's hypnotic report at sunrise was still the same. It is possible that the vessel may be lying by, at times, for fog; some of the steamers which came in last evening reported patches of fog both to north and south of the port. We must continue our watching, as the ship may now be signalled any moment.

27 October, noon. – Most strange; no news yet of the ship we wait for.

Mrs Harker reported last night and this morning as usual: 'Lapping waves and rushing water,' though she added that 'the waves were very faint.' The telegrams from London have been the same: 'No further report.' Van Helsing is terribly anxious, and told me just now that he fears the Count is escaping us. He added significantly: –

'I did not like that lethargy of Madam Mina's. Souls and memories can do strange things during trance.' I was about to ask him more, but Harker just then came in, and he held up a warning hand. We must try to-night, at sunset, to make her speak more fully when in her hypnotic state.

28 October. – Telegram. Rufus Smith, London, to Lord Godalming, care of H.B.M. Vice-Consul, Varna

'*Czarina Catherine* reported entering Galatz at one o'clock to-day.'

DR SEWARD'S DIARY

28 October. – When the telegram came announcing the arrival in Galatz I do not think it was such a shock to any of us as might have been expected. True, we did not know whence, or how, or when, the bolt would come; but I think we all expected that something strange would happen. The delay of arrival at Varna made us individually satisfied that things would not be just as we had expected; we only waited to learn where the change would occur. None the less, however, was it a surprise. I suppose that nature works on such a hopeful basis that we believe against ourselves that things will be as they ought to be, not as we should know that they will be. Transcendentalism is a beacon to the angels, even if it be a will-o'-the-wisp to man. It was an odd experience, and we all took it differently. Van Helsing raised his hands over his head for a moment, as though in remonstrance with the Almighty; but he said not a word, and in a few seconds stood up with his face sternly set. Lord Godalming grew very pale, and sat breathing heavily. I was myself half stunned and looked in wonder at one after another. Quincey Morris tightened his belt with that quick movement which I knew so well; in our old wandering days it meant 'action.' Mrs Harker grew ghastly white, so that the scar on her forehead seemed to burn, but she folded her hands meekly and looked up in prayer. Harker smiled – actually smiled – the dark bitter smile of one who is without hope; but at the same time his action belied his words, for his hands instinctively sought the hilt of the great Kukri knife and rested there.

'When does the next train start for Galatz?' said Van Helsing to us generally.

'At 6.30 to-morrow morning!' We all stared, for the answer came from Mrs Harker.

'How on earth do you know?' said Art.

'You forget – or perhaps you do not know, though Jonathan does and so does Dr Van Helsing – that I am a train fiend. At home in Exeter I always used to make up the time-tables, so as to be helpful to my husband. I found it so useful sometimes, that I always make a study of the time-tables now. I knew that if anything were to take us to Castle Dracula we should go by Galatz, or at any rate through Bucharest, so I learned the times very carefully. Unhappily there are not many to learn, as the only train to-morrow leaves as I say.'

'Wonderful woman!' murmured the Professor.

'Can't we get a special?' asked Lord Godalming.

Van Helsing shook his head: 'I fear not. This land is very different from yours or mine; even if we did have a special, it would probably not arrive as soon as our regular train. Moreover, we have something to prepare. We must think. Now let us organize. You, friend Arthur, go to the train and get the tickets and arrange that all be ready for us to go in the morning. Do you, friend Jonathan, go to the agent of the ship and get from him letters to the agent in Galatz, with authority to make search the ship just as it was here: Quincey Morris, you see the Vice-Consul, and get his aid with his fellow in Galatz and all he can do to make our way smooth, so that no times be lost when over the Danube. John will stay with Madam Mina and me, and we shall consult. For so if time be long you may be delayed; and it will not matter when the sun set, since I am here with Madam to make report.'

'And I,' said Mrs Harker brightly, and more like her old self than she had been for many a long day, 'shall try to be of use in all ways, and shall think and write for you as I used to do. Something is shifting from me in some strange way, and I feel freer than I have been of late!' The three younger men looked happier at the moment as they seemed to realise the significance of her words; but Van Helsing and I, turning to each other, met each a grave and troubled glance. We said nothing at the time, however.

When the three men had gone out to their tasks Van Helsing asked Mrs Harker to look up the copy of the diaries and find him the part of Harker's journal at the castle. She went away to get it; when the door was shut upon her he said to me: –

'We mean the same! speak out!'

'There is some change. It is a hope that makes me sick, for it may deceive us.'

'Quite so. Do you know why I asked her to get the manuscript?'

'No!' said I, 'unless it was to get an opportunity of seeing me alone.'

'You are in part right, friend John, but only in part. I want to tell you something. And oh, my friend, I am taking a great – a terrible – risk; but I believe it is right. In the moment when Madam said those words that arrest both our understanding, an inspiration come to me. In the trance of three days ago the Count sent her his spirit to read her mind; or more like he took her to see him in his earth-box in the ship with water rushing, just as it go free at rise and set of sun. He learn then that we are here; for she have more to tell in her open life with eyes to see and ears to hear than he, shut, as he is, in his coffin-box. Now he make his most effort to escape us. At present he want her not. He is sure with his so great knowledge that she will come at his call; but he cut her off – take her, as he can do, out of his own power, that so she come not to him. Ah! there I have hope that our man-brains, that have been of man so long and that have not lost the grace of God, will come higher than his child-brain that lie in his tomb for centuries, that grow not yet to our stature, and that do only work selfish and therefore small. Here comes Madam Mina; not a word to her of her trance! She know it not; and it would overwhelm her and make despair just when we want all her hope, all her courage; when most we want all her great brain which is trained like man's brain, but is of sweet woman and have a special power which the Count give her, and which he may not take away altogether – though he think not so. Hush! let me speak, and you shall learn. Oh, John, my friend, we are in awful straits. I fear, as I never feared before. We can only trust the good God. Silence! here she comes!'

I thought that the Professor was going to break down and have hysterics, just as he had when Lucy died, but with a great effort he controlled himself and was at perfect nervous poise when Mrs Harker tripped into the room, bright and happy-looking and, in the doing of work, seemingly forgetful of her misery. As she came in, she handed a number of sheets of type-writing to Van Helsing. He looked over them gravely, his face brightening up as he read. Then, holding the pages between his finger and thumb, he said: –

'Friend John, to you with so much of experience already – and you too, dear Madam Mina, that are young – here is a lesson: do not fear ever to think. A half-thought has been buzzing often in my brain, but I fear to let him loose his wings. Here now, with more knowledge, I go back to where that half-thought come from, and I find that he be no half-thought at all; that he be a whole thought, though so young that he is not yet strong to use his little wings. Nay, like the "Ugly Duck" of my friend Hans Andersen, he be no duck-thought at all, but a big swan-thought that sail nobly on big wings, when the time come for him to try them. See I read here what Jonathan have written: –

"'That other of his race who, in a later age, again and again, brought his forces over The Great River into Turkeyland; who, when he was beaten back, came again, and again, and again, though he had to come alone from the bloody field where his troops were being slaughtered, since he knew that he alone could ultimately triumph.'"

'What does this tell us? Not much! no! The Count's child-thought see nothing; therefore he speak so free. Your man-thought see nothing; my man-thought see nothing, till just now. No! But there comes another word from someone who speak without thought because she too know not what it mean – what it *might* mean. Just as there are elements which rest, yet when in nature's course they move on their way and they touch – then pouf! and there comes a flash of light, heaven's wide, that blind and kill and destroy some; but that show up all earth below for leagues and leagues. Is it not so? Well, I shall explain. To begin, have you ever study the philosophy of crime? "Yes" and "No." You, John, yes; for it is a study of insanity. You, no, Madam Mina; for crime touch you not – not but once. Still, your mind works true, and argues not *a particulari ad universale*. There is this peculiarity in criminals. It is so constant, in all countries and at all times, that even police, who know not much from philosophy, come to know it empirically, that *it is*. That is to be empiric. The criminal always work at one crime – that is the true criminal who seems predestinate to crime, and who will of none other. This criminal has not full man-brain. He is clever and cunning and resourceful; but he be not of man-stature as to brain. He be of child-brain in much. Now this criminal of ours is predestinate to crime also; he too have child-brain, and it is of the child to do what he have done. The little bird, the little fish, the little animal learn not by principle, but empirically; and when he learn to do, then there is to him the ground to start from to do more. "*Dos pou sto*," said Archimedes. "Give me a fulcrum, and I shall move the world!" To do once, is the fulcrum whereby child-brain become man-brain; and until he have the purpose to do more, he continue to do the same again every time, just as he have done before! Oh, my dear, I see that your eyes are opened, and that to you the lightning flash show all the leagues,' for Mrs Harker began to clap her hands, and her eyes sparkled. He went on: –

'Now you shall speak. Tell us two dry men of science what you see with those so bright eyes.' He took her hand and held it whilst she spoke. His finger and thumb closed on her pulse, as I thought instinctively and unconsciously, as she spoke: –

'The Count is a criminal and of criminal type. Nordau and Lombroso would so classify him, and *qua* criminal he is of imperfectly formed mind. Thus, in a difficulty he has to seek resource in habit. His past is a clue, and the one page of it that we know – and that from his own lips – tells that once before, when in what Mr Morris would call a "tight place," he went back to his own country from the land he had tried to invade, and thence, without losing purpose, prepared himself for a new effort. He came again, better equipped for his work; and won. So he came to London to invade a new land. He was beaten, and when all hope of success was lost, and his existence in danger, he fled back over the sea to his home; just as formerly he had fled back over the Danube from Turkeyland.'

'Good, good! oh, you so clever lady!' said Van Helsing, enthusiastically, as he stooped and kissed her hand. A moment later he said to me, as calmly as though we had been having a sick-room consultation: –

'Seventy-two only; and in all this excitement, I have hope.' Turning to her again, he said with keen expectation: –

'But go on. Go on! there is more to tell if you will. Be not afraid; John and I know. I do in any case, and shall tell you if you are right. Speak, without fear!'

'I will try to; but you will forgive me if I seem egotistical.'

'Nay! fear not, you must be egotist, for it is of you that we think.'

'Then, as he is criminal he is selfish; and as his intellect is small and his action is based on selfishness, he confines himself to one purpose. That purpose is remorseless. As he fled back over the Danube, leaving his forces to be cut to pieces, so now he is intent on being safe, careless of all. So, his own selfishness frees my soul somewhat of the terrible power which he acquired over me on that dreadful night. I felt it, oh! I felt it. Thank God for His great mercy! My soul is freer than it has been since that awful hour; and all that haunts me is a fear lest in some trance or dream he may have used my knowledge for his ends.' The Professor stood up: –

'He has so used your mind; and by it he has left us here in Varna, whilst the ship that carried him rushed through enveloping fog up to Galatz, where, doubtless, he had made preparation for escaping from us. But his child-mind only saw so far; and it may be that, as ever is in God's Providence, the very thing that the evil doer most reckoned on for his selfish good, turns out to be his chiefest harm. The hunter is taken in his own snare, as the great Psalmist says. For now that he think he is free from every trace of us all, and that he has escaped us with so many hours to him, then his selfish child-brain will whisper him to sleep. He think, too, that as he cut himself off from knowing your mind, there can be no knowledge of him to you; there is where he fail! That terrible baptism of blood which he give you makes you free to go to him in spirit, as you have as yet done in your times of freedom, when the sun rise and set. At such times you go by my volition and not by his; and this power to good of you and others, you have won from your suffering at his hands. This is now all more precious that he know it not, and to guard himself have even cut himself off from his knowledge of our where. We, however, are not all selfish, and we believe that God is with us through all this blackness, and these many dark hours. We shall follow him; and we shall not flinch; even if we peril ourselves that we become like him. Friend John, this has been a great hour; and it have done much to advance us on our way. You must be scribe and write him all down, so that when the others return from their work you can give it to them; then they shall know as we do.'

And so I have written it whilst we wait their return, and Mrs Harker has written with her typewriter all since she brought the MS. to us.

CHAPTER 26

DR SEWARD'S DIARY

29 October. – This is written in the train from Varna to Galatz. Last night we all assembled a little before the time of sunset. Each of us had done his work as well as he could; so far as thought, and endeavour, and opportunity go, we are prepared for the whole of our journey, and for our work when we get to Galatz. When the usual time came round Mrs Harker prepared herself for her hypnotic effort; and after a longer and more strenuous effort on the part of Van Helsing than has been usually necessary, she sank into the trance. Usually she speaks on a hint; but this time the Professor had to ask her questions, and to ask them pretty resolutely, before we could learn anything; at last her answer came: –

'I can see nothing; we are still; there are no waves lapping, but only a steady swirl of water softly running against the hawser. I can hear men's voices calling, near and far, and the roll and creak of oars in the rowlocks. A gun is fired somewhere; the echo of it seems far away. There is tramping of feet overhead, and ropes and chains are dragged along. What is this? There is a gleam of light; I can feel the air blowing upon me.'

Here she stopped. She had risen, as if impulsively, from where she lay on the sofa, and raised both her hands, palms upwards, as if lifting a weight. Van Helsing and I looked at each other with understanding. Quincey raised his eyebrows slightly and looked at her intently, whilst Harker's hand instinctively closed round the hilt of his Kukri. There was a long pause. We all knew that the time when she could speak was passing; but we felt that it was useless to say anything. Suddenly she sat up, and, as she opened her eyes, said sweetly: –

'Would none of you like a cup of tea? You must all be so tired!' We could only make her happy, and so acquiesced. She bustled off to get tea; when she had gone Van Helsing said: –

'You see, my friends. *He* is close to land; he has left his earth-chest. But he has yet to get on shore. In the night he may lie hidden somewhere; but if he be not carried on shore, or if the ship do not touch it, he cannot achieve the land. In such case he can, if it be in the night, change his form and can jump or fly on shore, as he did at Whitby. But if the day come before he get on shore, then, unless he be carried he cannot escape. And if he be carried, then the customs men may discover what the box contains. Thus, in fine, if he escape not on shore to-night, or before dawn, there will be the whole day lost to him. We may then arrive in time: for if he escape not at night we shall come on him in daytime, boxed up and at our mercy; for he dare not be his true self, awake and visible, lest he be discovered.'

There was no more to be said, so we waited in patience until the dawn; at which time we might learn more from Mrs Harker.

Early this morning we listened, with breathless anxiety, for her response in her trance. The hypnotic stage was even longer in coming than before; and when it came the time remaining until full sunrise was so short that we began to despair. Van Helsing seemed to throw his whole soul into the effort; at last, in obedience to his will she made reply: –

'All is dark. I hear lapping water, level with me, and some creaking as of wood on wood.' She paused, and the red sun shot up. We must wait till to-night.

And so it is that we are travelling towards Galatz in an agony of expectation. We are due to arrive between two and three in the morning; but already, at Bucharest, we are three hours late, so we cannot possibly get in till well after sun-up. Thus we shall have two more hypnotic messages from Mrs Harker; either or both may possibly throw more light on what is happening.

Later. – Sunset has come and gone. Fortunately it came at a time when there was no distraction; for had it occurred whilst we were at a station, we might not have secured the necessary calm and isolation. Mrs Harker yielded to the hypnotic influence even less readily than this morning. I am in fear that her power of reading the Count's sensations may die away, just when we want it most. It seems to me that her imagination is beginning to work. Whilst she has been in the trance hitherto she has confined herself to the simplest of facts. If this goes on it may ultimately mislead us. If I thought that the Count's power over her would die away equally with her power of knowledge it would be a happy thought; but I am afraid that it may not be so. When she did speak, her words were enigmatical: –

'Something is going out; I can feel it pass me like a cold wind. I can hear, far off, confused sounds – as of men talking in strange tongues, fierce-falling water, and the howling of wolves.' She stopped, and a shudder ran through her, increasing in intensity for a few seconds, till, at the end, she shook as though in a palsy. She said no more, even in answer to the Professor's imperative questioning. When she woke from the trance, she was cold, and exhausted, and languid; but her mind was all alert. She could not remember anything, but asked what she had said; when she was told, she pondered over it deeply for a long time and in silence.

30 October, 7 a.m. – We are near Galatz now, and I may not have time to write later. Sunrise this morning was anxiously looked for by us all. Knowing of the increasing difficulty of procuring the hypnotic trance, Van Helsing began his passes earlier than usual. They produced no effect, however, until the regular time, when she yielded with a still greater difficulty, only a minute before the sun rose. The Professor lost no time in his questioning; her answer came with equal quickness: –

'All is dark. I hear the water swirling by, level with my ears, and the creaking of wood on wood. Cattle low far off. There is another sound, a queer one like –' She stopped and grew white, and whiter still.

'Go on! Go on! Speak, I command you!' said Van Helsing in an agonized voice. At the same time there was despair in his eyes, for the risen sun was reddening even Mrs Harker's pale face. She opened her eyes, and we all started as she said, sweetly and seemingly with the utmost concern: –

'Oh, Professor, why ask me to do what you know I can't? I don't remember anything.' Then, seeing the look of amazement on our faces, she said, turning from one to the other: –

'What have I said? What have I done? I know nothing, only that I was lying here, half asleep, and I heard you say "Go on! speak, I command you!" It seemed so funny to hear you order me about, as if I were a bad child!'

'Oh, Madam Mina,' he said sadly, 'it is proof, if proof be needed, of how I love and honour you, when a word for your good, spoken more earnest than ever, can seem so strange because it is to order her whom I am proud to obey!'

The whistles are sounding; we are nearing Galatz. We are on fire with anxiety and eagerness.

MINA HARKER'S JOURNAL

30 October. – Mr Morris took me to the hotel where our rooms had been ordered by telegraph, he being the one who could best be spared, since he does not speak any foreign language. The forces were distributed much as they had been at Varna, except that Lord Godalming went to the Vice-Consul, as his rank might serve as an immediate guarantee of some sort to the official, we being in extreme hurry. Jonathan and the two doctors went to the shipping agent to learn particulars of the arrival of the *Czarina Catherine*.

Later. – Lord Godalming has returned. The Consul is away, and the

Vice-Consul sick; so the routine work has been attended to by a clerk. He was very obliging, and offered to do anything in his power.

JONATHAN HARKER'S JOURNAL

30 October. – At nine o'clock Dr Van Helsing, Dr Seward, and I called on Messrs Mackenzie & Steinkoff, the agents of the London firm of Hapgood. They had received a wire from London, in answer to Lord Godalming's telegraphed request, asking them to show us any civility in their power. They were more than kind and courteous, and took us at once on board the *Czarina Catherine*, which lay at anchor out in the river harbour. There we saw the captain, Donelson by name, who told us of his voyage. He said that in all his life he had never had so favourable a run.

'Man!' he said, 'but it made us afeared, for we expeckit that we should have to pay for it wi' some rare piece o' ill luck, so as to keep up the average. It's no cannoy to run frae London to the Black Sea wi' a wind ahint ye, as though the Deil himself were blawin' on yer sail for his ain purpose. An' a' the time we could no' speer a thing. Gin we were night a ship, or a port, or a headland, a fog fell on us and travelled wi' us, till when after it had lifted and we looked out, the deil a thing could we see. We ran by Gibraltar wi'oot bein' able to signal; an' till we came to the Dardanelles and had to wait to get our permit to pass, we never were within hail o' aught. At first I inclined to slack off sail and beat about till the fog was lifted; but whiles, I thocht that if the Deil was minded to get us into the Black Sea quick, he was like to do it whether we would or no. If we had a quick voyage it would be no' to our miscredit wi' the owners, or no hurt to our traffic; an' the Old Mon who had served his ain purpose wad be decently grateful to us for no hinderin' him.' This mixture of simplicity and cunning, of superstition and commercial reasoning, aroused Van Helsing, who said: 'Mine friend, that Devil is more clever than he is thought by some; and he know when he meet his match!' The skipper was not displeased with the compliment, and went on: –

'When we got past the Bosphorus the men began to grumble; some o' them, the Roumanians, came and asked me to heave overboard a big box which had been put on board by a queer-lookin' old man just before we had started frae London. I had seen them speer at the fellow, and put out their two fingers when they saw him, to guard against the evil eye. Man! but the supersteetion of foreigners is pairfectly rideeculous! I sent them aboot their business pretty quick; but as just after a fog closed in on us, I felt a wee bit as they did anent something, though I wouldn't say it was agin the bit box. Well, on we went, and as the fog didn't let up for five days I joost let the wind carry us; for if the Deil wanted to get somewheres – well, he would fetch it up a' reet. An' if he didn't, well, we'd keep a sharp look-out anyhow. Sure enuch, we had a fair way and deep water all the time; and two days ago, when the mornin' sun came through the fog, we found ourselves just in the river opposite Galatz. The Roumanians were wild, and wanted me right or wrong to take out the box and fling it in the river. I had to argy wi' them aboot it wi' a handspike; an' when the last o' them rose off the deck, wi' his head in his hand, I had convinced them that, evil eye or no evil eye, the property and the trust of my owners were better in my hands than in the river Danube. They had, mind ye, taken the box on the deck ready to fling in, and as it was marked Galatz *via* Varna, I thocht I'd let it lie till we discharged in the port an' get rid o't athegither. We didn't do much clearin' that day, an' had to remain the nicht at anchor; but in the mornin', braw an' airly, an hour before sun-up, a man came aboord wi' an order, written to him from England, to receive a box marked for one Count Dracula. Sure enuch the matter was one ready to his hand. He had his papers a' reet, an' glad I was to be rid o' the dam' thing, for I was beginnin' masel' to feel uneasy at it. If the Deil did have any luggage aboord the ship, I'm thinkin' it was nane ither than that same!'

'What was the name of the man who took it?' asked Dr Van Helsing, with restrained eagerness.

'I'll be tellin' ye quick!' he answered, and, stepping down to his cabin, produced a receipt signed 'Immanuel Hildesheim.' Burgen-strasse 16 was the address. We found out that this was all the captain knew; so with thanks we came away.

We found Hildesheim in his office, a Hebrew of rather the Adelphi type, with a nose like a sheep, and a fez. His arguments were pointed with specie – we doing the punctuation – and with a little bargaining he told us what he knew. This turned out to be simple but important. He had received a letter from Mr de Ville of London, telling him to receive, if possible before sunrise so as to avoid customs, a box which would arrive at Galatz in the *Czarina Catherine*. This he was to give in charge to a certain Petrof Skinsky, who dealt with Slovaks who traded down the river to the port. He had been paid for his work by an English bank-note, which had been duly cashed for gold at the Danube International Bank. When Skinsky had come to him, he had taken him to the ship and handed over the box, so as to save porterage. That was all he knew.

We then sought for Skinsky, but were unable to find him. One of his neighbours, who did not seem to bear him any affection, said that he had gone away two days before, no one knew whither. This was corroborated by his landlord, who had received by messenger the key of the house together with the rent due, in English money. This had been between ten and eleven o'clock last night. We were at a standstill again.

Whilst we were talking, one came running and breathlessly gasped out that the body of Skinsky had been found inside the wall of the church-yard of St Peter, and that the throat had been torn open as if by some wild animal. Those we had been speaking with ran off to see the horror, the women crying out, 'This is the work of a Slovak!' We hurried away lest we should have been in some way drawn into the affair, and so detained.

As we came home we could arrive at no definite conclusion. We were all convinced that the box was on its way, by water, to somewhere; but where that might be we would have to discover. With heavy hearts we came home to the hotel to Mina.

When we met together, the first thing was to consult as to taking Mina again into our confidence. Things are getting desperate, and it is at least a chance, though a hazardous one. As a preliminary step, I was released from my promise to her.

MINA HARKER'S JOURNAL

30 October, evening. – They were so tired and worn-out and dispirited that there was nothing to be done till they had some rest; so I asked them all to lie down for half an hour whilst I should enter everything up to the moment. I feel so grateful to the man who invented the 'Traveller's' type-writer, and to Mr Morris for getting this one for me. I should have felt quite astray doing the work if I had to write with a pen . . .

It is all done; poor dear, dear Jonathan, what he must have suffered, what must he be suffering now! He lies on the sofa hardly seeming to breathe, and his whole body appears in collapse. His brows are knit; his face is drawn with pain. Poor fellow, maybe he is thinking, and I can see his face all wrinkled up with the concentration of his thoughts. Oh! if I could only help at all . . . I shall do what I can . . .

I have asked Dr Van Helsing, and he has got me all the papers that I have not yet seen . . . Whilst they are resting, I shall go over all carefully, and perhaps I may arrive at some conclusion. I shall try to follow the Professor's example, and think without prejudice on the facts before me . . .

I do believe that under God's Providence I have made a discovery. I shall get the maps and look over them . . .

I am more than ever sure that I am right. My new conclusion is ready, so I shall get our party together and read it. They can judge it; it is well to be accurate, and every minute is precious.

MINA HARKER'S MEMORANDUM
(Entered in her Journal)

Ground of inquiry. – Count Dracula's problem is to get back to his own place.

(a) He must be *brought back* by someone. This is evident; for, had he power to move himself as he wished, he could go either as man, or wolf, or bat, or in some other way. He evidently fears discovery or interference, in the state of helplessness in which he must be – confined as he is between dawn and sunset in his wooden box.

(b) *How is he to be taken*? – Here a process of exclusion may help us. By road, by rail, by water?

1. *By Road.* – There are endless difficulties, especially in leaving a city.

(a) There are people; and people are curious, and investigate. A hint, a surmise, a doubt as to what might be in the box would destroy him.

(b) There are, or there might be, customs and octroi officers to pass.

(c) His pursuers might follow. This is his greatest fear; and in order to prevent his being betrayed he has repelled, so far as he can, even his victim – me!

2. *By Rail.* – There is no one in charge of the box. It would have to take its chance of being delayed; and delay would be fatal, with enemies on the track. True, he might escape at night; but where would he be if left in a strange place with no refuge that he could fly to? This is not what he intends; and he does not mean to risk it.

3. *By Water.* – Here is the safest way, in one respect, but with most danger in another. On the water he is powerless except at night; even then he can only summon fog and storm and snow and his wolves. But were he wrecked, the living water would engulf him, helpless; and he would indeed be lost. He could have the vessel drive to land; but if it were unfriendly land, wherein he was not free to move, his position would still be desperate.

We know from the record that he was on the water; so what we have to do is to ascertain *what* water.

The first thing is to realize exactly what he has done as yet; we may, then, get a light on what his later task is to be.

Firstly, we must consider what he did in London as part of his general plan of action, when he was pressed for moments and had to arrange as best he could.

Secondly, we must see, as well as we can surmise it from the facts we know of, what he has done here.

As to the first, he evidently intended to arrive at Galatz, and sent invoice to Varna to deceive us lest we should ascertain his means of exit from England; his immediate and sole purpose then was to escape. The proof of this is the letter of instructions sent to Immanuel Hildesheim to clear and take away the box *before sunrise*. There is also the instruction to Petrof Skinsky. This we must only guess at; but there must have been some letter or message, since Skinsky came to Hildesheim.

That, so far, his plans were successful, we know. The *Czarina Catherine* made a phenomenally quick journey – so much so that Captain Donelson's suspicions were aroused; but his superstition united with his canniness played the Count's game for him, and he ran with his favouring wind through fogs and all till he brought up blindfold at Galatz. That the Count's arrangements were well made has been proved. Hildesheim cleared the box, took it off, and gave it to Skinsky. Skinsky took it – and here we lose the trail. We only know that the box is somewhere on the water, moving along. The customs and the octroi, if there be any, have been avoided.

Now we come to what the Count must have done after his arrival – *on land*, at Galatz.

The box was given to Skinsky before sunrise. At sunrise the Count could appear in his own form. Here, we ask why Skinsky was chosen at all to aid in the work? In my husband's diary, Skinsky is mentioned as dealing with the Slovaks who trade down the river to the port; and the man's remark, that the murder was the work of a Slovak, showed the general feeling against his class. The Count wanted isolation.

My surmise is this: that in London the Count decided to get back to his castle by water, as the most safe and secret way. He was brought from the castle by Szgany, and probably they delivered their cargo to Slovaks who took the boxes to Varna, for there they were shipped for London. Thus the Count had knowledge of the persons who could arrange this service. When the box was on land, before sunrise or after sunset, he came out from his box, met Skinsky and instructed him what to do as to arranging the carriage of the box up some river. When this was done, and he knew that all was in train, he blotted out his traces, as he thought, by murdering his agent.

I have examined the map, and find that the river most suitable for the Slovaks to have ascended is either the Pruth or the Sereth. I read in the typescript that in my trance I heard cows low and water swirling level with my ears and the creaking of wood. The Count in his box, then, was on a river in an open boat – propelled probably either by oars or poles, for the banks are near and it is working against stream. There would be no such sound if floating down stream.

Of course it may not be either the Sereth or the Pruth, but we may possibly investigate further. Now of these two, the Pruth is the more easily navigated, but the Sereth is, at Fundu, joined by the Bistritza, which runs up round the Borgo Pass. The loop it makes is manifestly as close to Dracula's Castle as can be got by water.

MINA HARKER'S JOURNAL (*continued*)

When I had done reading, Jonathan took me in his arms and kissed me. The others kept shaking me by both hands, and Dr Van Helsing said: –

'Our dear Madam Mina is once more our teacher. Her eyes have seen where we were blinded. Now we are on the track once again, and this time we may succeed. Our enemy is at his most helpless; and if we can come on him by day, on the water, our task will be over. He has a start, but he is powerless to hasten, as he may not leave his box lest those who carry him may suspect; for them to suspect would be to prompt them to throw him in the stream, where he perish. This he knows, and will not. Now, men, to our Council of War; for, here and now, we must plan what each and all shall do.'

'I shall get a steam launch and follow him,' said Lord Godalming.

'And I, horses to follow on the bank lest by chance he land,' said Mr Morris.

'Good!' said the Professor. 'Both good. But neither must go alone. There must be force to overcome force if need be; the Slovak is strong and rough, and he carries rude arms.' All the men smiled, for amongst them they carried a small arsenal. Said Mr Morris: –

'I have brought some Winchesters; they are pretty handy in a crowd, and there may be wolves. The Count, if you remember, took some other precautions; he made some requisitions on others that Mrs Harker could not quite hear or understand. We must be ready at all points.' Dr Seward said: –

'I think I had better go with Quincey. We have been accustomed to hunt together, and we two, well armed, will be a match for whatever may come along. You must not be alone, Art. It may be necessary to fight the Slovaks, and a chance thrust – for I don't suppose these fellows carry guns – would undo all our plans. There must be no chances, this time; we shall not rest until the Count's head and body have been separated, and we are sure that he cannot reincarnate.' He looked at Jonathan as he spoke, and Jonathan looked at me. I could see that the poor dear was torn about in his mind. Of course he wanted to be with me; but then the boat service would, most likely, be the one which would destroy the . . . the . . . the . . . Vampire. (Why did I hesitate to write the word?) He was silent awhile, and during his silence Dr Van Helsing spoke: –

'Friend Jonathan, this is to you for twice reasons. First, because you are young and brave and can fight, and all energies may be needed at the last; and again that it is your right to destroy him – that – which has wrought such woe to you and yours. Be not afraid for Madam Mina; she will be my care, if I may. I am old. My legs are not so quick to run as once; and I am not used to ride so long or to pursue as need be; or to fight with lethal weapons. But I can be of other service; I can fight in other way. And I can die, if need be, as well as younger men. Now let me say that what I would is this; while you, my Lord Godalming, and friend Jonathan go in your so swift little steamboat up the river, and whilst John and Quincey guard the bank where perchance he might be landed, I will take Madam Mina right into the heart of the enemy's country. Whilst the old fox is tied in his box, floating on the running stream whence he cannot escape to land – where he dares not raise the lid of his coffin-box lest his Slovak carriers should in fear leave him to perish – we shall go in the track where Jonathan went – from Bistritz over the Borgo – and find our way to the Castle of Dracula. Here, Madam Mina's hypnotic power will surely help, and we shall find our way – all dark and unknown otherwise – after the first sunrise when we near that fateful place. There is much to be done, and other places to be made sanctify, so that that nest of vipers be obliterated.' Here Jonathan interrupted him hotly: –

'Do you mean to say, Professor Van Helsing, that you would bring Mina, in her sad case and tainted as she is with that devil's illness, right into the jaws of his death-trap? Not for the world! Not for Heaven or Hell!' He became almost speechless for a minute, and then went on: –

'Do you know what the place is? Have you seen that awful den of hellish infamy – with the very moonlight alive with grisly shapes, and every speck of dust that whirls in the wind a devouring monster in embryo?

Have you felt the Vampire's lips upon your throat?' Here he turned to me, and as his eyes lit on my forehead, he threw up his arms with a cry: 'Oh, my God, what have we done to have this terror upon us!' and he sank down on the sofa in a collapse of misery. The Professor's voice, as he spoke in clear, sweet tones, which seemed to vibrate in the air, calmed us all: –

'Oh, my friend, it is because I would save Madam Mina from that awful place that I would go. God forbid that I should take her into that place! There is work – wild work – to be done there, that her eyes may not see. We men here, all save Jonathan, have seen with our own eyes what is to be done before that place can be purify. Remember that we are in terrible straits. If the Count escape us this time – and he is strong and subtle and cunning – he may choose to sleep him for a century; and then in time our dear one' – he took my hand – 'would come to him to keep him company, and would be as those others that you, Jonathan, saw. You have told us of their gloating lips; you heard their ribald laugh as they clutched the moving bag that the Count threw to them. You shudder; and well may it be. Forgive me that I make you so much pain, but it is necessary. My friend, is it not a dire need for the which I am giving, if need be, my life? If it were that anyone went into that place to stay, it is I who would have to go, to keep them company.'

'Do as you will,' said Jonathan, with a sob that shook him all over; 'we are in the hands of God!'

Later. – Oh, it did me good to see the way that these brave men worked. How can women help loving men when they are so earnest, and so true, and so brave! And, too, it made me think of the wonderful power of money! What can it not do when it is properly applied; and what might it do when basely used! I felt so thankful that Lord Godalming is rich, and that both he and Mr Morris, who also has plenty of money, are willing to spend it so freely. For if they did not, our little expedition could not start, either so promptly or so well equipped, as it will within another hour. It is not three hours since it was arranged what part each of us was to do; now Lord Godalming and Jonathan have a lovely steam launch, with steam up, ready to start at a moment's notice. Dr Seward and Mr Morris have half a dozen beautiful horses, well appointed. We have all the maps and appliances of various kinds that can be had. Professor Van Helsing and I are to leave by the 11.40 train to-night for Veresti, where we are to get a carriage to drive to the Borgo Pass. We are bringing a good deal of ready money, as we are to buy a carriage and horses. We shall drive ourselves, for we have no one whom we can trust in this matter. The Professor knows something of a great many languages, so we shall get on all right. We have all got arms, even for me a large-bore revolver; Jonathan would not be happy unless I was armed like the rest. Alas! I cannot carry one arm that the rest do; the scar on my forehead forbids that. Dear Dr Van Helsing comforts me by telling me that I am fully armed as there may be wolves; the weather is getting colder every hour, and there are snow-flurries which come and go as warnings.

Later. – It took all my courage to say good-bye to my darling. We may never meet again. Courage, Mina! the Professor is looking at you keenly; his look is a warning. There must be no tears now – unless it may be that God will let them fall in gladness.

JONATHAN HARKER'S JOURNAL

October 30, night. – I am writing this in the light from the furnace door of the steam launch; Lord Godalming is firing up. He is an experienced hand at the work, as he has had for years a launch of his own on the Thames, and another on the Norfolk Broads. Regarding our plans, we finally decided that Mina's guess was correct, and that if any waterway was chosen for the Count's escape back to his Castle, the Sereth, and then the Bistritza at its junction, would be the one. We took it that somewhere about the 47th degree, north latitude, would be the place chosen for crossing the country between the river and the Carpathians. We have no fear in running at good speed up the river at night; there is plenty of water, and the banks are wide enough apart to make steaming, even in the dark, easy enough. Lord Godalming tells me to sleep for a while, as it is enough for the present for one to be on watch. But I cannot sleep – how can I with the terrible danger hanging over my darling, and her going out into that awful place? . . . My only comfort is that we are in the hands of God. Only for that faith it would be easier to die than to live, and so be quit of all the trouble. Mr Morris and Dr Seward were off on their long ride before we started; they are to keep up the right bank, far enough off to get on higher lands, where they can see a good stretch of river and avoid the following of its curves. They have, for the first stages, two men to ride and lead their spare horse – four in all, so as not to excite curiosity. When they dismiss the men, which will be shortly, they will themselves look after the horses. It may be necessary for us to join forces; if so they can mount our whole party. One of the saddles has a movable horn, and can be easily adapted for Mina, if required.

It is a wild adventure we are on. Here, as we are rushing along through the darkness, with the cold from the river seeming to rise up and strike us, with all the mysterious voices of the night around us, it all comes home. We seem to be drifting into unknown places and unknown ways; into a whole world of dark and dreadful things. Godalming is shutting the furnace door . . .

31 October. – Still hurrying along. The day has come, and Godalming is sleeping. I am on watch. The morning is bitterly cold; the furnace heat is grateful, though we have heavy fur coats. As yet we have passed only a few open boats, but none of them had on board any box or package of anything like the size of the one we seek. The men were scared every time we turned our electric lamp on them, and fell on their knees and prayed.

1 November, evening. – No news all day; we have found nothing of the kind we seek. We have now passed into the Bistritza; and if we are wrong in our surmise our chance is gone. We have overhauled every boat, big and little. Early this morning, one crew took us for a Government boat, and treated us accordingly. We saw in this a way of smoothing matters, so at Fundu, where the Bistritza runs into the Sereth, we got a Roumanian flag, which we now fly conspicuously. With every boat which we have overhauled since then this trick has succeeded; we have had every deference shown to us, and not once any objection to whatever we chose to ask or do. Some of the Slovaks tell us that a big boat passed them, going at more than usual speed as she had a double crew on board. This was before they came to Fundu, so they could not tell us whether the boat turned into the Bistritza or continued on up the Sereth. At Fundu we could not hear of any such boat, so she must have passed there in the night. I am feeling very sleepy; the cold is perhaps beginning to tell upon me, and nature must have rest some time. Godalming insists that he shall keep the first watch. God bless him for all his goodness to poor dear Mina and me.

2 November, morning. – It is broad daylight. That good fellow would not wake me. He says it would have been a sin to, for I slept so peacefully and was forgetting my trouble. It seems brutally selfish of me to have slept so long, and let him watch all night; but he was quite right. I am a new man this morning; and, as I sit here and watch him sleeping, I can do all that is necessary both as to minding the engine, steering, and keeping watch. I can feel that my strength and energy are coming back to me. I wonder where Mina is now, and Van Helsing. They should have got to Veresti about noon on Wednesday. It would take them some time to get the carriage and horses; so if they had started and travelled hard, they would be about now at the Borgo Pass. God guide and help them! I am afraid to think what may happen. If we could only go faster! but we cannot; the engines are throbbing and doing their utmost. I wonder how Dr Seward and Mr Morris are getting on. There seem to be endless streams running down from the mountains into this river, but as none of them are very large – at present, at all events, though they are terrible doubtless in winter and when the snow melts – the horsemen may not have met much obstruction. I hope that before we get to Strasba we may see them; for if by that time we have not overtaken the Count, it may be necessary to take counsel together on what to do next.

DR SEWARD'S DIARY

2 November. – Three days on the road. No news, and no time to write it if there had been, for every moment is precious. We have had only the rest needful for the horses; but we are both bearing it wonderfully. Those adventurous days of ours are turning up useful. We must push on; we shall never feel happy till we get the launch in sight again.

3 November. – We heard at Fundu that the launch had gone up the Bistritza. I wish it wasn't so cold. There are signs of snow coming; and if it falls heavy it will stop us. In such case we must get a sledge and go on, Russian fashion.

4 November. – To-day we heard of the launch having been detained by an accident when trying to force a way up the rapids. The Slovak boats get up all right, by aid of a rope, and steering with knowledge. Some went up only a few hours before. Godalming is an amateur fitter himself, and evidently it was he who put the launch in trim again. Finally, they got up the rapids all right, with local help, and are off on the chase afresh. I fear that the boat is not any better for the accident; the peasantry tell us that after she got upon the smooth water again, she kept stopping every now and again so long as she was in sight. We must push on harder than ever; our help may be wanted soon.

MINA HARKER'S JOURNAL

31 October. – Arrived at Veresti at noon. The Professor tells me that this morning at dawn he could hardly hypnotize me at all, and that all I could say was, 'Dark and quiet.' He is off now buying a carriage and horses.

He says that he will later on try to buy additional horses, so that we may be able to change them on the way. We have something more than seventy miles before us. The country is lovely, and most interesting; if only we were under different conditions, how delightful it would be to see it all! If Jonathan and I were driving through it alone what a pleasure it would be! To stop and see people, and learn something of their life, and to fill our minds and memories with all the colour and picturesqueness of the whole wild, beautiful country and the quaint people! But, alas! . . .

Later. – Dr Van Helsing has returned. He has got the carriage and horses; we are to have some dinner, and to start in an hour. The landlady is putting us up a huge basket of provision; it seems enough for a company of soldiers. The Professor encourages her, and whispers to me that it may be a week before we can get any good food again. He has been shopping too, and has sent home such a wonderful lot of fur coats and wraps, and all sorts of warm things. There will not be any chance of our being cold.

We shall soon be off. I am afraid to think what may happen to us. We are truly in the hands of God. He alone knows what may be, and I pray Him, with all the strength of my sad and humble soul, that He will watch over my beloved husband; that whatever may happen, Jonathan may know that I loved him and honoured him more than I can say, and that my latest and truest thought will be always for him.

CHAPTER 27

MINA HARKER'S JOURNAL

1 November. – All day long we have travelled, and at a good speed. The horses seem to know that they are being kindly treated, for they go willingly their full stage at best speed. We have now had so many changes and find the same thing so constantly that we are encouraged to think that the journey will be an easy one. Dr Van Helsing is laconic; he tells the farmers that he is hurrying to Bistritz, and pays them well to make the exchange of horses. We get hot soup, or coffee, or tea; and off we go. It is a lovely country; full of beauties of all imaginable kinds, and the people are brave, and strong, and simple, and seem full of nice qualities. They are *very, very* superstitious. In the first house where we stopped, when the woman who served us saw the scar on my forehead, she crossed herself and put out two fingers towards me, to keep off the evil eye. I believe they went to the trouble of putting an extra amount of garlic into our food; and I can't abide garlic. Ever since then I have taken care not to take off my hat or veil, and so have escaped their suspicions. We are travelling fast, and as we have no driver with us to carry tales, we go ahead of scandal; but I daresay that fear of the evil eye will follow hard behind us all the way. The Professor seems tireless; all day he would not take any rest, though he made me sleep for a long spell. At sunset time he hypnotized me, and he says that I answered as usual 'Darkness, lapping water and creaking wood'; so our enemy is still on the river. I am afraid to think of Jonathan, but somehow I have now no fear for him, or for myself. I write this whilst we wait in a farmhouse for the horses to be got ready. Dr Van Helsing is sleeping. Poor dear, he looks very tired and old and grey, but his mouth is set as firmly as a conqueror's; even in his sleep he is instinct with resolution. When we have well started I must make him rest whilst I drive. I shall tell him that we have days before us, and he must not break down when most of all his strength will be needed . . . All is ready; we are off shortly.

2 November, morning. – I was successful, and we took turns driving all night; now the day is on us, bright though cold. There is a strange heaviness in the air – I say heaviness for want of a better word; I mean that it oppresses us both. It is very cold, and only our warm furs keep us comfortable. At dawn Van Helsing hypnotized me; he says I answered 'Darkness, creaking wood and roaring water,' so the river is changing as they ascend. I do hope that my darling will not run any chance of danger – more than need be; but we are in God's hands.

2 November, night. – All day long driving. The country gets wider as we go, and the great spurs of the Carpathians, which at Veresti seemed so far from us and so low on the horizon, now seem to gather round us and tower in front. We both seem in good spirits; I think we make an effort each to cheer the other; in the doing so we cheer ourselves. Dr Van Helsing says that by morning we shall reach the Borgo Pass. The houses are very few here now, and the Professor says that the last horses we got will have to go on with us, as we may not be able to change. He got two in addition to the two we changed, so that now we have a rude four-in-hand. The dear horses are patient and good, and they give us no trouble. We are not worried with other travellers, and so even I can drive. We shall get to the Pass in daylight; we do not want to arrive before. So we take it easy and have each a long rest in turn. Oh, what will to-morrow bring to us? We go to seek the place where my poor darling suffered so much. God grant that we may be guided aright, and that He will deign to watch over my husband and those dear to us both, and who are in such deadly peril. As for me, I am not worthy in His sight. Alas! I am unclean to His eyes, and shall be until He may deign to let me stand forth in His sight as one of those who have not incurred His wrath.

MEMORANDUM BY ABRAHAM VAN HELSING

4 November. – This to my old and true friend John Seward, M.D., of Purfleet, London, in case I may not see him. It may explain. It is morning, and I write by a fire which all the night I have kept alive – Madam Mina aiding me. It is cold, cold; so cold that the grey heavy sky is full of snow, which when it falls will settle for all winter as the ground is hardening to receive it. It seems to have affected Madam Mina; she has been so heavy of head all day that she was not like herself. She sleeps, and sleeps, and sleeps! She, who is usual so alert, have done literally nothing all the day; she even have lost her appetite. She make no entry into her little diary, she who write so faithful at every pause. Something whisper to me that all is not well. However, to-night she is more *vif*. Her long sleep all day have refresh and restore her, for now she is all sweet and bright as ever. At sunset I try to hypnotize her, but alas! with no effect; the power has grown less and less with each day, and to-night it fail me altogether. Well, God's will be done – whatever it may be, and whithersoever it may lead!

Now to the historical, for as Madam Mina write not in her stenography, I must, in my cumbrous old fashion, that so each day of us may not go unrecorded.

We got to the Borgo Pass just after sunrise yesterday morning. When I saw the signs of the dawn I got ready for the hypnotism. We stopped our carriage, and got down so that there might be no disturbance. I made a couch with furs, and Madam Mina, lying down, yield herself as usual, but more slow and more short time than ever, to the hypnotic sleep. As before, came the answer: 'Darkness and the swirling of water.' Then she woke, bright and radiant, and we go on our way and soon reach the Pass. At this time and place she become all on fire with zeal; some new guiding power be in her manifested, for she point to a road and say: –

'This is the way.'

'How know you it?' I ask.

'Of course I know it,' she answer, and with a pause, add: 'Have not my Jonathan travel it and wrote of his travel?'

At first I think somewhat strange, but soon I see that there be only one such by-road. It is used but little, and very different from the coach road from Bukovina to Bistritz, which is more wide and hard, and more of use.

So we came down this road; when we meet other ways – not always were we sure that they were roads at all, for they be neglect and light snow have fallen – the horses know and they only. I give rein to them, and they go on so patient. By-and-by we find all the things which Jonathan have note in that wonderful diary of him. Then we go on for long, long hours and hours. At the first, I tell Madam Mina to sleep; she try, and she succeed. She sleep all the time; till at the last, I feel myself to suspicious grow, and attempt to wake her. But she sleep on, and I may not wake her though I try. I do not wish to try too hard lest I harm her; for I know that she have suffer much, and sleep at times be all-in-all to her. I think I drowse myself, for all of sudden I feel guilt, as though I have done something; I find myself bolt up, with the reins in my hand, and the good horses go along jog, jog, just as ever. I look down and find Madam Mina still sleep. It is now not far off sunset time, and over the snow the light of the sun flow in big yellow flood, so that we throw great long shadow on where the mountain rise so steep. For we are going up, and up; and all is oh! so wild and rocky, as though it were the end of the world.

Then I arouse Madam Mina. This time she wake with not much trouble, and then I try to put her to hypnotic sleep. But she sleep not, being as though I were not. Still I try and try, till all at once I find her and myself in dark; so I look round, and find that the sun have gone down. Madam

Mina laugh, and I turn and look at her. She is now quite awake, and look
so well as I never saw her since that night at Carfax when we first enter
the Count's house. I am amaze, and not at ease then; but she is so bright
and tender and thoughtful for me that I forget all fear. I light a fire, for
we have brought supply of wood with us, and she prepare food while I
undo the horses and set them tethered in shelter, to feed. Then when I
return to the fire she have my supper ready. I go to help her; but she smile,
and tell me that she have eat already – that she was so hungry that she
would not wait. I like it not, and I have grave doubts; but I fear to affright
her, and so I am silent of it. She help me and I eat alone; and then we
wrap in fur and lie beside the fire, and I tell her to sleep while I watch.
But presently I forget all of watching; and when I sudden remember that
I watch, I find her lying quiet, but awake, and looking at me with so bright
eyes. Once, twice more the same occur, and I get much sleep till before
morning. When I wake I try to hypnotize her; but alas! though she shut
her eyes obedient, she may not sleep. The sun rise up, and up, and up;
and then sleep come to her too late, but so heavy that she will not wake.
I have to lift her up and place her sleeping in the carriage when I have
harnessed the horses and made all ready. Madam still sleep, and sleep;
and she look in her sleep more healthy and more redder than before. And
I like it not. And I am afraid, afraid, afraid! – I am afraid of all things –
even to think; but I must go on my way. The stake we play for is life and
death, or more than these, and we must not flinch.

5 November, morning. – Let us be accurate in everything, for though
you and I have seen some strange things together, you may at the first
think that I, Van Helsing, am mad – that the many horrors and the so long
strain on nerves has at the last turn my brain.

All yesterday we travel, ever getting closer to the mountains, and moving
into a more and more wild and desert land. There are great, frowning
precipices and much falling water, and Nature seemed to have held some-
time her carnival. Madam Mina still sleep and sleep; and though I did
have hunger and appeased it, I could not waken her – even for food. I
began to fear that the fatal spell of the place was upon her, tainted as she
is with that Vampire baptism. 'Well,' said I to myself, 'if it be that she
sleep all the day, it shall also be that I do not sleep at night.' As we travel
on the rough road, for a road of an ancient and imperfect kind there was,
I held down my head and slept. Again I waked with a sense of guilt and
of time passed, and found Madam Mina still sleeping, and the sun low
down. But all was indeed changed; the frowning mountains seemed further
away, and we were near the top of a steep-rising hill, on summit of which

was such a castle as Jonathan tell of in his diary. At once I exulted and
feared; for now, for good or ill, the end was near. I woke Madam Mina,
and again tried to to hypnotize her; but alas! unavailing till too late. Then,
ere the great dark came upon us – for even after down-sun the heavens
reflected the gone sun on the snow, and all was for a time in a great
twilight – I took out the horses and fed them in what shelter I could. Then
I make a fire; and near it I make Madam Mina, now wake and more
charming than ever, sit comfortable amid her rugs. I got ready food; but
she would not eat, simply saying that she had not hunger. I did not press
her, knowing her unavailingness. But I myself eat, for I must needs now
be strong for all. Then, with the fear on me of what might be, I drew a
ring, so big for her comfort, round where Madam Mina sat; and over the
ring I passed some of the Wafer, and I broke it fine so that all was well
guarded. She sat still all the time – so still as one dead; and she grew
whiter and ever whiter till the snow was not more pale; and no word she
said. But when I drew near, she clung to me, and I could know that the
poor soul shook her from head to feet with a tremor that was pain to feel.
I said to her presently, when she had grown more quiet: –

'Will you not come over to the fire?' for I wished to make a test of
what she could. She rose obedient, but when she have made a step she
stopped, and stood as one stricken.

'Why not go on?' I asked. She shook her head, and, coming back, sat
down in her place. Then, looking at me with open eyes, as of one waked
from sleep, she said simply: –

'I cannot!' and remained silent. I rejoiced, for I knew that what she
could not, none of those that we dreaded could. Though there might be
danger to her body, yet her soul was safe!

Presently the horses began to scream, and tore at their tethers till I
came to them and quieted them. When they did feel my hands on them,
they whinnied low as in joy, and licked at my hands and were quiet for
a time. Many times through the night did I come to them, till it arrive to
the cold hour when all nature is at lowest; and every time my coming was
with quiet of them. In the cold hour the fire began to die, and I was about
stepping forth to replenish it, for now the snow came in flying sweeps and
with it a chill mist. Even in the dark there was a light of some kind, as
there ever is over snow; and it seemed as though the snow-flurries and
the wreaths of mist took shape as of women with trailing garments. All
was in dead, grim silence, only that the horses whinnied and cowered, as
if in terror of the worst. I began to fear – horrible fears; but then came to
me the sense of safety in that ring wherein I stood. I began, too, to think

that my imaginings were of the night, and the gloom, and the unrest that
I have gone through, and all the terrible anxiety. It was as though my
memories of all Jonathan's horrid experience were befooling me; for the
snowflakes and the mist began to wheel and circle round, till I could get
as though a shadowy glimpse of those women that would have kissed him.
And then the horses cowered lower and lower, and moaned in terror as
men do in pain. Even the madness of fright was not to them, so that they
could break away. I feared for my dear Madam Mina when these weird
figures drew near and circled round. I looked at her, but she sat calm, and
smiled at me; when I would have stepped to the fire to replenish it, she
caught me and held me back, and whispered, like a voice that one hears
in a dream, so low it was: –

'No! no! Do not go without. Here you are safe!' I turned to her, and
looking in her eyes, said: –

'But you? It is for you that I fear!' whereat she laughed – a laugh low
and unreal, and said: –

'Fear for *me*! Why fear for me? None safer in all the world from them
than I am,' and as I wondered at the meaning of her words, a puff of wind
made the flame leap up, and I see the red scar on her forehead. Then,
alas! I knew. Did I not, I would soon have learned, for the wheeling figures
of mist and snow came closer, but keeping ever without the Holy circle.
Then they began to materialize, till – if God have not take away my reason,
for I saw it through my eyes – there were before me in actual flesh the
same three women that Jonathan saw in the room, when they would have
kissed his throat. I knew the swaying round forms, the bright hard eyes,
the white teeth, the ruddy colour, the voluptuous lips. They smiled ever
at poor dear Madam Mina; and as their laugh came through the silence
of the night, they twined their arms and pointed to her, and said in those
so sweet tingling tones that Jonathan said were of the intolerable sweetness of the water-glasses: –

'Come, sister. Come to us. Come! Come!' In fear I turned to my poor
Madam Mina, and my heart with gladness leapt like flame; for oh! the
terror in her sweet eyes, the repulsion, the horror, told a story to my heart
that was all of hope. God be thanked she was not, yet, of them. I seized
some of the firewood which was by me, and holding out some of the
Wafer, advanced on them towards the fire. They drew back before me,
and laughed their low horrid laugh. I fed the fire, and feared them not;
for I knew that we were safe within our protections. They could not
approach me, whilst so armed, nor Madam Mina whilst she remained
within the ring, which she could not leave no more than they could enter.

The horses had ceased to moan, and lay still on the ground; the snow fell on them softly, and they grew whiter. I knew that there was for the poor beasts no more of terror.

And so we remained till the red of the dawn began to fall through the snow-gloom. I was desolate and afraid, and full of woe and terror; but when that beautiful sun began to climb the horizon life was to me again. At the first coming of the dawn the horrid figures melted in the whirling mist and snow; the wreaths of transparent gloom moved away towards the castle, and were lost.

Instinctively, with the dawn coming, I turned to Madam Mina, intending to hypnotize her; but she lay in a deep and sudden sleep, from which I could not wake her. I tried to hypnotize through her sleep, but she made no response, none at all; and the day broke. I fear yet to stir. I have made my fire and have seen the horses; they are all dead. To-day I have much to do here, and I keep waiting till the sun is up high; for there may be places where I must go, where that sunlight, though snow and mist obscure it, will be to me a safety.

I will strengthen me with breakfast, and then I will to my terrible work. Madam Mina still sleeps; and, God be thanked! she is calm in her sleep . . .

JONATHAN HARKER'S JOURNAL

4 November, evening. – The accident to the launch has been a terrible thing for us. Only for it we should have overtaken the boat long ago; and by now my dear Mina would have been free. I fear to think of her, off on the wolds near that horrid place. We have got horses, and we follow on the track. I note this whilst Godalming is getting ready. We have our arms. The Szgany must look out if they mean fight. Oh, if only Morris and Seward were with us! We must only hope! If I write no more, Good-bye, Mina! God bless and keep you.

DR SEWARD'S DIARY

5 November. – With the dawn we saw the body of Szgany before us dashing away from the river with their leiter-waggon. They surrounded it in a cluster, and hurried along as though beset. The snow is falling lightly and there is a strange excitement in the air. It may be our own excited feelings, but the depression is strange. Far off I hear the howling of wolves; the snow brings them down from the mountains, and there are dangers to all of us, and from all sides. The horses are nearly ready, and we are soon off. We ride to death of someone. God alone knows who, or where, or what, or when, or how it may be . . .

DR VAN HELSING'S MEMORANDUM

5 November, afternoon. – I am at least sane. Thank God for that mercy at all events, though the proving it has been dreadful. When I left Madam Mina sleeping within the Holy circle, I took my way to the castle. The blacksmith hammer which I took in the carriage from Veresti was useful; though the doors were all open I broke them off the rusty hinges, lest some ill-intent or ill-chance should close them, so that being entered I might not get out. Jonathan's bitter experience served me here. By memory of his diary I found my way to the old chapel, for I knew that here my work lay. The air was oppressive; it seemed as if there was some sulphurous fume, which at times made me dizzy. Either there was a roaring in my ears or I heard afar off the howl of wolves. Then I bethought me of my dear Madam Mina, and I was in terrible plight. The dilemma had me between his horns. Her, I had not dare to take into this place, but left safe from the Vampire in that Holy circle; and yet even there would be the wolf! I resolve me that my work lay here, and that as to the wolves we must submit, if it were God's will. At any rate it was only death and freedom beyond. So did I choose for her. Had it but been for myself the choice had been easy; the maw of the wolf were better to rest in than the grave of the Vampire! So I make my choice to go on with my work.

I knew that there were at least three graves to find – graves that are inhabit; so I search, and search, and I find one of them. She lay in her Vampire sleep, so full of life and voluptuous beauty that I shudder as though I have come to do murder. Ah, I doubt not that in old time, when such things were, many a man who set forth to do such a task as mine, found at the last his heart fail him, and then his nerve. So he delay, and delay, and delay, till the mere beauty and the fascination of the wanton Un-Dead have hypnotize him; and he remain on, and on, till sunset come, and the Vampire sleep be over. Then the beautiful eyes of the fair woman open and look love, and the voluptuous mouth present to a kiss – and man is weak. And there remain one more victim in the Vampire fold; one more to swell the grim and grisly ranks of the Un-Dead! . . .

There is some fascination, surely, when I am moved by the mere presence of such an one, even lying as she lay in a tomb fretted with age and heavy with the dust of centuries, though there be that horrid odour such as the lairs of the Count have had. Yes, I was moved – I, Van Helsing, with all my purpose and with my motive for hate – I was moved to a yearning for delay which seemed to paralyse my faculties and to clog my very soul. It may have been that the need of natural sleep, and the strange oppression of the air, were beginning to overcome me. Certain it was that I was lapsing into sleep, the open-eyed sleep of one who yields to a sweet fascination, when there came through the snow-stilled air a long, low wail, so full of woe and pity that it woke me like the sound of a clarion. For it was the voice of my dear Madam Mina that I heard.

Then I braced myself again to my horrid task, and found by wrenching away tomb-tops one other of the sisters, the other dark one. I dared not pause to look on her as I had on her sister, lest once more I should begin to be enthral; but I go on searching until, presently, I find in a high great tomb as if made to one much beloved that other fair sister which, like Jonathan, I had seen to gather herself out of the atoms of the mist. She was so fair to look on, so radiantly beautiful, so exquisitely voluptuous, that the very instinct of man in me, which calls some of my sex to love and to protect one of hers, made my head whirl with new emotion. But, God be thanked, that soul-wail of my dear Madam Mina had not died out of my ears; and, before the spell could be wrought further upon me, I had nerved myself to my wild work. By this time I had searched all the tombs in the chapel, so far as I could tell; and as there had been only three of these Un-Dead phantoms around us in the night, I took it that there were no more of active Un-Dead existent. There was one great tomb more lordly than all the rest; huge it was, and nobly proportioned. On it was but one word,

DRACULA

This then was the Un-Dead home of the King-Vampire, to whom so many more were due. Its emptiness spoke eloquent to make certain what I knew. Before I began to restore these women to their dead selves through my awful work, I laid in Dracula's tomb some of the Wafer, and so banished him from it, Undead, for ever.

Then began my terrible task, and I dreaded it. Had it been but one, it had been easy, comparative. But three! To begin twice more after I had been through a deed of horror; for if it was terrible with the sweet Miss

Lucy, what would it not be with these strange ones who had survived through centuries, and who had been strengthened by the passing of the years; who would, if they could, have fought for their foul lives? . . .

Oh, my friend John, but it was butcher work; had I not been nerved by thoughts of other dead, and of the living over whom hung such a pall of fear, I could not have gone on. I tremble and tremble even yet, though till all was over, God be thanked, my nerve did stand. Had I not seen the repose in the first face, and the gladness that stole over it just ere the final dissolution came, as realization that the soul had been won, I could not have gone further with my butchery. I could not have endured the horrid screeching as the stake drove home; the plunging of writhing form, and lips of bloody foam. I should have fled in terror and left my work undone. But it is over! And the poor souls, I can pity them now and weep, as I think of them placid each in her full sleep of death, for a short moment ere fading. For, friend John, hardly had my knife severed the head of each, before the whole body began to melt away and crumble into its native dust, as though the death that should have come centuries agone had at last assert himself and say at once and loud 'I am her!'

Before I left the castle I so fixed its entrances that never more can the Count enter there Un-Dead.

When I stepped into the circle where Madam Mina slept, she woke from her sleep, and seeing me, cried out in pain that I had endured too much.

'Come!' she said, 'come away from this awful place! Let us go to meet my husband, who is, I know, coming towards us.' She was looking thin and pale and weak; but her eyes were pure and glowed with fervour. I was glad to see her paleness and her illness, for my mind was full of the fresh horror of that ruddy Vampire sleep.

And so with trust and hope, and yet full of fear, we go eastward to meet our friends – and *him* – whom Madam Mina tell me that she *know* are coming to meet us.

MINA HARKER'S JOURNAL

6 November. – It was late in the afternoon when the Professor and I took our way towards the east whence I knew Jonathan was coming. We did not go fast, though the way was steeply downhill, for we had to take heavy rugs and wraps with us; we dared not face the possibility of being left without warmth in the cold and the snow. We had to take some of our provisions too, for we were in a perfect desolation, and, so far as we could see through the snowfall, there was not even the sign of a habitation. When we had gone about a mile, I was tired with the heavy walking and sat down to rest. Then we looked back and saw where the clear line of Dracula's castle cut the sky; for we were so deep under the hill whereon it was set that the angle of perspective of the Carpathian mountains was far below it. We saw it in all its grandeur, perched a thousand feet on the summit of a sheer precipice, and with seemingly a great gap between it and the steep of the adjacent mountain on any side. There was something wild and uncanny about the place. We could hear the distant howling of wolves. They were far off, but the sound, even though coming muffled through the deadening snowfall, was full of terror. I knew from the way Dr Van Helsing was searching about that he was trying to seek some strategic point, where we would be less exposed in case of attack. The rough roadway still led downwards; we could trace it through the drifted snow.

In a little while the Professor signalled to me, so I got up and joined him. He had found a wonderful spot, a sort of natural hollow in a rock, with an entrance like a door-way between two boulders. He took me by the hand and drew me in: 'See!' he said, 'here you will be in shelter; and if the wolves do come I can meet them one by one.' He brought in our furs, and made a snug nest for me, and got out some provisions and forced them upon me. But I could not eat; to even try to do so was repulsive to me, and, much as I would have liked to please him, I could not bring myself to the attempt. He looked very sad, but did not reproach me. Taking his field-glasses from the case, he stood on the top of the rock, and began to search the horizon. Suddenly he called out: –

'Look, Madam Mina, look! look!' I sprang up and stood beside him on the rock; he handed me his glasses and pointed. The snow was now falling more heavily, and swirled about fiercely, for a high wind was beginning to blow. However, there were times when there were pauses between the snow-flurries, and I could see a long way round. From the height where we were it was possible to see a great distance; and far off, beyond the white waste of snow, I could see the river lying like a black ribbon in kinks and curls as it wound its way. Straight in front of us and not far off – in fact so near that I wondered we had not noticed before – came a group of mounted men hurrying along. In the midst of them was a cart, a long leiter-waggon, which swept from side to side, like a dog's tail wagging, with each stern inequality of the road. Outlined against the snow as they were, I could see from the men's clothes that they were peasants or gipsies of some kind.

On the cart was a great square chest. My heart leaped as I saw it, for I felt that the end was coming. The evening was now drawing close, and well I knew that at sunset the Thing, which was till then imprisoned there, would take new freedom and could in any of many forms elude all pursuit. In fear I turned to the Professor; to my consternation, however, he was not there. An instant later, I saw him below me. Round the rock he had drawn a circle, such as we had found shelter in last night. When he had completed it he stood beside me again, saying: –

'At least you shall be safe here from *him*!' He took the glasses from me, and at the next lull of the snow swept the whole space below us. 'See,' he said, 'they come quickly; they are flogging the horses, and galloping as hard as they can.' He paused and went on in a hollow voice: –

'They are racing for the sunset. We may be too late. God's will be done!' Down came another blinding rush of driving snow, and the whole landscape was blotted out. It soon passed, however, and once more his glasses were fixed on the plain. Then came a sudden cry: –

'Look! Look! Look! See, two horsemen follow fast, coming up from the south. It must be Quincey and John. Take the glass. Look, before the snow blots it all out!' I took it and looked. The two men might be Dr Seward and Mr Morris. I knew at all events that neither of them was Jonathan. At the same time I *knew* that Jonathan was not far off; looking around I saw on the north side of the coming party two other men, riding at break-neck speed. One of them I knew was Jonathan, and the other I took, of course, to be Lord Godalming. They, too, were pursuing the party with the cart. When I told the Professor he shouted in glee like a schoolboy, and, after looking intently till snowfall made sight impossible, he laid his Winchester rifle ready for use against the boulder at the opening of our shelter. 'They are all converging,' he said. 'When the time comes we shall have the gipsies on all sides.' I got out my revolver ready to hand, for whilst we were speaking the howling of wolves came louder and closer. When the snowstorm abated a moment we looked again. It was strange to see the snow falling in such heavy flakes close to us, and beyond, the sun shining more and more brightly as it sank down towards the far mountain tops. Sweeping the glass all around us I could see here and there dots moving singly and in twos and threes and larger numbers – the wolves were gathering for their prey.

Every instant seemed an age whilst we waited. The wind came now in fierce bursts, and the snow was driven with fury as it swept upon us in circling eddies. At times we could not see an arm's length before us; but at others as the hollow-sounding wind swept by us, it seemed to clear the air-

space around us so that we could see afar off. We had of late been so accustomed to watch for sunrise and sunset, that we knew with fair accuracy
when it would be; and we knew that before long the sun would set.

It was hard to believe that by our watches it was less than an hour that
we waited in that rocky shelter before the various bodies began to converge
close upon us. The wind came now with fiercer and more bitter sweeps,
and more steadily from the north. It seemingly had driven the snow-clouds
from us, for, with only occasional bursts, the snow fell. We could distinguish clearly the individuals of each party, the pursued and the pursuers.
Strangely enough those pursued did not seem to realize, or at least to care,
that they were pursued; they seemed, however, to hasten with redoubled
speed as the sun dropped lower and lower on the mountain tops.

Closer and closer they drew. The Professor and I crouched down behind
our rock, and held our weapons ready; I could see that he was determined
that they should not pass. One and all were quite unaware of our presence.

All at once two voices shouted out to 'Halt!' One was my Jonathan's,
raised in a high key of passion; the other, Mr Morris's strong resolute tone
of quiet command. The gipsies may not have known the language, but
there was no mistaking the tone, in whatever tongue the words were spoken.
Instinctively they reined in, and at the instant Lord Godalming and Jonathan
dashed up at one side and Dr Seward and Mr Morris on the other. The
leader of the gipsies, a splendid-looking fellow, who sat his horse like a
centaur, waved them back, and in a fierce voice gave to his companions
some word to proceed. They lashed the horses, which sprang forward; but
the four men raised their Winchester rifles, and in an unmistakable way
commanded them to stop. At the same moment Dr Van Helsing and I rose
behind the rock and pointed our weapons at them. Seeing that they were
surrounded, the men tightened their reins and drew up. The leader turned
to them and gave a word, at which every man of the gipsy party drew
what weapon he carried, knife or pistol, and held himself in readiness to
attack. Issue was joined in an instant.

The leader, with a quick movement of his rein, threw his horse out in
front, and pointing first to the sun – now close down on the hill-tops –
and then to the castle, said something which I did not understand. For
answer all four men of our party threw themselves from their horses and
dashed towards the cart. I should have felt terrible fear at seeing Jonathan
in such danger, but that the ardour of battle must have been upon me as
well as the rest of them; I felt no fear, but only a wild, surging desire to
do something. Seeing a quick movement of our parties, the leader of the

gipsies gave a command; his men instantly formed round the cart in a sort of undisciplined endeavour, each one shouldering and pushing the other in his eagerness to carry out the order.

In the midst of this I could see that Jonathan on one side of the ring of men, and Quincey on the other, were forcing a way to the cart; it was evident that they were bent on finishing their task before the sun should set. Nothing seemed to stop or even to hinder them. Neither the levelled weapons or the flashing knives of the gipsies in front, or the howling of the wolves behind, appeared to even attract their attention. Jonathan's impetuosity, and the manifest singleness of his purpose, seemed to overawe those in front of him; instinctively they cowered aside and let him pass. In an instant he had jumped upon the cart, and, with a strength which seemed incredible, raised the great box, and flung it over the wheel to the ground. In the mean-time, Mr Morris had had to use force to pass through his side of the ring of Szgany. All the time I had been breathlessly watching Jonathan I had, with the tail of my eye, seen Mr Morris pressing desperately forward, and had seen the knives of the gipsies flash as he won a way through them, and they cut at him. He parried with his great bowie knife, and at first I thought that he too had come through in safety; but as he sprang beside Jonathan, who had by now jumped from the cart, I could see that with his left hand he was clutching at his side, and that the blood was spurting through his fingers. He did not delay notwithstanding this, for as Jonathan, with desperate energy, attacked one end of the chest, attempting to prise off the lid with his great Kukri knife, he attacked the other frantically with his bowie. Under the efforts of both men the lid began to yield; the nails drew with a quick screeching sound, and the top of the box was thrown back.

By this time the gipsies, seeing themselves covered by the Winchesters, and at the mercy of Lord Godalming and Dr Seward, had given in and made no further resistance. The sun was almost down on the mountain tops, and the shadows of the whole group fell long upon the snow. I saw the Count lying within the box upon the earth, some of which the rude falling from the cart had scattered over him. He was deathly pale, just like a waxen image, and the red eyes glared with the horrible vindictive look which I knew too well.

As I looked, the eyes saw the sinking sun, and the look of hate in them turned to triumph.

But, on the instant, came the sweep and flash of Jonathan's great knife. I shrieked as I saw it shear through the throat; whilst at the same moment Mr Morris' bowie knife plunged in the heart.

It was like a miracle; but before our very eyes, and almost in the drawing of a breath, the whole body crumbled into dust and passed from our sight.

I shall be glad as long as I live that even in that moment of final dissolution there was in the face a look of peace, such as I never could have imagined might have rested there.

The Castle of Dracula now stood out against the red sky, and every stone of its broken battlements was articulated against the light of the setting sun.

The gipsies, taking us as in some way the cause of the extraordinary disappearance of the dead man, turned, without a word, and rode away as if for their lives. Those who were unmounted jumped upon the leiter-waggon and shouted to the horsemen not to desert them. The wolves, which had withdrawn to a safe distance, followed in their wake, leaving us alone.

Mr Morris, who had sunk to the ground, leaned on his elbow, holding his hand pressed to his side; the blood still gushed through his fingers. I flew to him, for the Holy circle did not now keep me back; so did the two doctors. Jonathan knelt behind him and the wounded man laid back his head on his shoulder. With a sigh he took, with a feeble effort, my hand in that of his own which was unstained. He must have seen the anguish of my heart in my face, for he smiled at me and said: –

'I am only too happy to have been of any service! Oh, God!' he cried suddenly, struggling up to a sitting posture and pointing to me, 'it was worth this to die! Look! look!'

The sun was now right down upon the mountain top, and the red gleams fell upon my face, so that it was bathed in rosy light. With one impulse the men sank on their knees, and a deep and earnest 'Amen' broke from all as their eyes followed the pointing of his finger as the dying man spoke: –

'Now God be thanked that all has not been in vain! See! the snow is not more stainless than her forehead! The curse has passed away!'

And, to our bitter grief, with a smile and silence, he died, a gallant gentleman.

NOTE

Seven years ago we all went through the flames; and the happiness of some of us since then is, we think, well worth the pain we endured. It is an added joy to Mina and to me that our boy's birthday is the same day as that on which Quincey Morris died. His mother holds, I know, the secret belief that some of our brave friend's spirit has passed into him. His bundle of names links all our little band of men together; but we call him Quincey.

In the summer of this year we made a journey to Transylvania, and went over the old ground which was, and is, to us so full of vivid and terrible memories. It was almost impossible to believe that the things which we had seen with our own eyes and heard with our own ears were living truths. Every trace of all that had been was blotted out. The castle stood as before, reared high above a waste of desolation.

When we got home we got to talking of the old time – which we could all look back on without despair, for Godalming and Seward are both happily married. I took the papers from the safe where they have been ever since our return so long ago. We were struck with the fact that, in all the mass of material of which the record is composed, there is hardly one authentic document! nothing but a mass of type-writing, except the later note-books of Mina and Seward and myself, and Van Helsing's memorandum. We could hardly ask anyone, even did we wish to, to accept these as proofs of so wild a story. Van Helsing summed it all up as he said, with our boy on his knee: –

'We want no proofs; we ask none to believe us! This boy will some day know what a brave and gallant woman his mother is. Already he knows her sweetness and loving care; later on he will understand how some men so loved her, that they did dare much for her sake.'

Jonathan Harker

FRANKENSTEIN

FRANKENSTEIN

MARY SHELLEY

This edition published in 2019 by Arcturus Publishing Limited
26/27 Bickels Yard, 151–153 Bermondsey Street,
London SE1 3HA

Introduction by Brian Busby
Typesetting by Palimpsest Book Production Limited

Cover design: Peter Ridley
Design: Beatriz Custodio

AD001212UK

Printed in the UK

Introduction

Frankenstein; or, The Modern Prometheus was begun in the summer of 1816, in response to a challenge. The poet Lord Byron sought to discover who amongst his friends could write the best horror story. The winner, an 18-year-old who called herself Mary Shelley, reworked the story as a novel, and the results were published anonymously in 1818. It was the author's second book, following a travelogue titled *History of a Six Weeks' Tour* (1817). Shelley wrote seven more novels, six of which were published during her lifetime. Her work is typified by great drama, improbable events and Gothic elements; a reflection, perhaps, of her own life.

Born Mary Wollstonecraft Godwin, in London on 30 August 1797, Shelley's own story is marked by tragedy. Her mother, Mary Wollstonecraft, author of the early feminist classic *A Vindication of the Rights of Women* (1792), died giving birth, leaving Mary in the care of her father, philosopher William Godwin. Raised amongst London's intelligentsia, she was encouraged to write, and forged links to the literary community. In 1814, she met the Romantic poet Percy Bysshe Shelley, with whom she fell in love. Amidst scandal, the couple fled to France, where she became pregnant. Their marriage, late in 1816, occurred weeks after Percy Shelley's wife committed suicide by drowning. In 1822, the poet himself drowned while sailing off the coast of Italy. Mary Shelley devoted much of the remainder of her life to the promotion of his verse and raising their sole surviving child. She died on 1 February 1851.

Volume I

LETTER I

To Mrs Saville, England.

St Petersburgh, Dec. 11th, 17–.

You will rejoice to hear that no disaster has accompanied the commencement of an enterprise which you have regarded with such evil forebodings. I arrived here yesterday; and my first task is to assure my dear sister of my welfare, and increasing confidence in the success of my undertaking.

I am already far north of London; and as I walk in the streets of Petersburgh, I feel a cold northern breeze play upon my cheeks, which braces my nerves, and fills me with delight. Do you understand this feeling? This breeze, which has travelled from the regions towards which I am advancing, gives me a foretaste of those icy climes. Inspirited by this wind of promise, my day dreams become more fervent and vivid. I try in vain to be persuaded that the pole is the seat of frost and desolation; it ever presents itself to my imagination as the region of beauty and delight. There, Margaret, the sun is for ever visible, its broad disk just skirting the horizon, and diffusing a perpetual splendour. There – for with your leave, my sister, I will put some trust in preceding navigators – there snow and frost are banished; and, sailing over a calm sea, we may be wafted to a land surpassing in wonders and in beauty every region hitherto discovered on the habitable globe. Its productions and features may be without example, as the phenomena of the heavenly bodies undoubtedly are in those undiscovered solitudes. What may not be expected in a country of eternal light? I may there discover the wondrous power which attracts the needle; and may regulate a thousand celestial observations, that require only this voyage to render their seeming eccentricities consistent for ever. I shall satiate my ardent curiosity with the sight of a part of the world never before visited, and may tread a land never before imprinted by the foot of man. These are my enticements, and they are sufficient to conquer all fear of danger or death, and to induce me to commence this laborious voyage with the joy a child feels when he embarks in a little boat, with his holiday mates, on an expedition of discovery up his native river. But, supposing all these conjectures to be false, you cannot contest the inestimable benefit which I shall confer on all mankind to the last generation, by discovering a passage near the pole to those countries, to reach which at present so many months are requisite; or by ascertaining the secret of the magnet, which, if at all possible, can only be effected by an undertaking such as mine.

These reflections have dispelled the agitation with which I began my letter, and I feel my heart glow with an enthusiasm which elevates me to heaven; for nothing contributes so much to tranquillise the mind as a steady purpose – a point on which the soul may fix its intellectual eye. This expedition has been the favourite dream of my early years. I have read with ardour the accounts of the various voyages which have been made in the prospect of arriving at the North Pacific Ocean through the seas which surround the pole. You may remember that a history of all the voyages made for purposes of discovery composed the whole of our good uncle Thomas's library. My education was neglected, yet I was passionately fond of reading. These volumes were my study day and night, and my familiarity with them increased that regret which I had felt, as a child, on learning that my father's dying injunction had forbidden my uncle to allow me to embark in a seafaring life.

These visions faded when I perused, for the first time, those poets whose effusions, entranced my soul, and lifted it to heaven. I also became a poet, and for one year lived in a Paradise of my own creation; I imagined that I also might obtain a niche in the temple where the names of Homer and Shakespeare are consecrated. You are well acquainted with my failure, and how heavily I bore the disappointment. But just at that time I inherited the fortune of my cousin, and my thoughts were turned into the channel of their earlier bent.

Six years have passed since I resolved on my present undertaking. I can, even now, remember the hour from which I dedicated myself to this great enterprise. I commenced by inuring my body to hardship. I accompanied the whale-fishers on several expeditions to the North Sea; I voluntarily endured cold, famine, thirst, and want of sleep; I often worked harder than the common sailors during the day, and devoted my nights to the study of mathematics, the theory of medicine, and those branches of physical science from which a naval adventure might derive the greatest practical advantage. Twice I actually hired myself as an under-mate in a Greenland whaler, and acquitted myself to admiration. I must own I felt a little proud, when my captain offered me the second dignity in the vessel and intreated me to remain with the greatest earnestness so valuable did he consider my services.

And now, dear Margaret, do I not deserve to accomplish some great purpose? My life might have been passed in ease and luxury; but I preferred glory to every enticement that wealth placed in my path. Oh, that some encouraging voice would answer in the affirmative! My courage and my resolution is firm; but my hopes fluctuate, and my spirits are often depressed. I am about to proceed on a long and difficult voyage, the emergencies of which will demand all my fortitude: I am required not only to raise the spirits of others, but sometimes to sustain my own, when theirs are failing.

This is the most favourable period for travelling in Russia. They fly quickly over the snow in their sledges; the motion is pleasant, and, in my opinion, far more agreeable than that of an English stage-coach. The cold is not excessive, if you are wrapped in furs – a dress which I have already adopted; for there is a great difference between walking the deck and remaining seated motionless for hours, when no exercise prevents the blood from actually freezing in your veins. I have no ambition to lose my life on the post-road between St Petersburgh and Archangel.

I shall depart for the latter town in a fortnight or three weeks; and my intention is to hire a ship there, which can easily be done by paying the insurance for the owner, and to engage as many sailors as I think necessary among those who are accustomed to the whale-fishing. I do not intend to sail until the month of June; and when shall I return? Ah, dear sister, how can I answer this question? If I succeed, many, many months, perhaps years, will pass before you and I may meet. If I fail, you will see me again soon, or never.

Farewell, my dear, excellent Margaret. Heaven shower down blessings on you, and save me, that I may again and again testify my gratitude for all your love and kindness.

Your affectionate brother,
R. WALTON

LETTER II

To Mrs Saville, England.

Archangel, March 28th, 17–.

How slowly the time passes here, encompassed as I am by frost and snow! yet a second step is taken towards my enterprise. I have hired a vessel, and am occupied in collecting my sailors; those whom I have already engaged, appear to be men on whom I can depend and are certainly possessed of dauntless courage.

But I have one want which I have never yet been able to satisfy; and the absence of the object of which I now feel as a most severe evil. I have no friend, Margaret: when I am glowing with the enthusiasm of success, there will be none to participate my joy; if I am assailed by disappointment, no one will endeavour to sustain me in dejection. I shall commit my thoughts to paper, it is true; but that is a poor medium for the communication of feeling. I desire the company of a man who could sympathise with me; whose eyes would reply to mine. You may deem me romantic, my dear sister, but I bitterly feel the want of a friend. I have no one near me, gentle yet courageous, possessed of a cultivated as well as of a capacious mind, whose tastes are like my own, to approve or amend my plans. How would such a friend repair the faults of your poor brother! I am too ardent in execution, and too impatient of difficulties. But it is a still greater evil to me that I am self-educated: for the first fourteen years of my life I ran wild on a common, and read nothing but our uncle Thomas's books of voyages. At that age I became acquainted with the celebrated poets of our own country; but it was only when it had ceased to be in my power to derive its most important benefits from such a conviction, that I perceived the necessity of becoming acquainted with more languages than that of my native country. Now I am twenty-eight and am in reality more illiterate than many schoolboys of fifteen. It is true that I have thought more, and that my day dreams are more extended and magnificent, but they want (as the painters call it) *keeping*; and I greatly need a friend who would have sense enough not to despise me as romantic, and affection enough for me to endeavour to regulate my mind.

Well, these are useless complaints; I shall certainly find no friend on the wide ocean, nor even here in Archangel, among merchants and seamen. Yet some feelings, unallied to the dross of human nature, beat even in these rugged bosoms. My lieutenant, for instance, is a man of wonderful courage and enterprise; he is madly desirous of glory: or rather, to word my phrase more characteristically, of advancement in his profession. He is an Englishman, and in the midst of national and professional prejudices, unsoftened by cultivation, retains some of the noblest endowments of humanity. I first became acquainted with him on board a whale vessel: finding that he was unemployed in this city, I easily engaged him to assist in my enterprise.

The master is a person of an excellent disposition, and is remarkable in the ship for his gentleness and the mildness of his discipline. This circumstance, added to his well-known integrity and dauntless courage, made me very desirous to engage him. A youth passed in solitude, my best years spent under your gentle and feminine fosterage, has so refined the groundwork of my character that I cannot overcome an intense distaste to the usual brutality exercised on board ship: I have never believed it to be necessary, and when I heard of a mariner equally noted for his kindliness of heart and the respect and obedience paid to him by his crew, I felt myself peculiarly fortunate in being able to secure his services. I heard of him first in rather a romantic manner, from a lady who owes to him the happiness of her life. This, briefly, is his story. Some years ago he loved a young Russian lady of moderate fortune; and having amassed a considerable sum in prize-money, the father of the girl consented to the match. He saw his mistress once before the destined ceremony; but she was bathed in tears, and, throwing herself at his feet, intreated him to spare her, confessing at the time that she loved another, but that he was poor, and that her father would never consent to the union. My generous friend reassured the suppliant, and on being informed of the name of her lover, instantly abandoned his pursuit. He had already bought a farm with his money, on which he had designed to pass the remainder of his life; but he bestowed the whole on his rival, together with the remains of his prize-money to purchase stock, and then himself solicited the young woman's father to consent to her marriage with her lover. But the old man decidedly refused, thinking himself bound in honour to my friend; who, when he found the father inexorable, quitted his country, nor returned until he heard that his former mistress was married according to her inclinations. 'What a noble fellow!' you will exclaim. He is so; but then he is wholly uneducated: he is as silent as a Turk, and a kind of ignorant carelessness attends him, which, while it renders his conduct the more astonishing, detracts from the interest and sympathy which otherwise he would command.

Yet do not suppose, because I complain a little, or because I can conceive a consolation for my toils which I may never know, that I am wavering in my resolutions. Those are as fixed as fate, and my voyage is only now delayed until the weather shall permit my embarkation. The winter has been dreadfully severe, but the spring promises well, and it is considered as a remarkably early season; so that perhaps I may sail sooner than I expected. I shall do nothing rashly: you know me sufficiently to confide in my prudence and considerateness whenever the safety of others is committed to my care.

I cannot describe to you my sensations on the near prospect of my undertaking. It is impossible to communicate to you a conception of the trembling sensation, half pleasurable and half fearful, with which I am preparing to depart. I am going to unexplored regions to 'the land of mist and snow'; but I shall kill no albatross, therefore do not be alarmed for my safety, or if I should come back to you as worn and woeful as the 'Ancient Mariner'. You will smile at my allusion; but I will disclose a secret. I have often attributed my attachment to, my passionate enthusiasm for, the dangerous mysteries of ocean, to that production of the most imaginative of modern poets. There is something at work in my soul, which I do not understand. I am practically industrious – painstaking; a workman to execute with perseverance and labour: – but besides this, there is a love for the marvellous, a belief in the marvellous, intertwined in all my projects, which hurries me out of the common pathways of men, even to the wild sea and unvisited regions I am about to explore.

But to return to dearer considerations. Shall I meet you again, after having traversed immense seas, and returned by the most southern cape of Africa or America? I dare not expect such success, yet I cannot bear to look on the reverse of the picture. Continue for the present to write to me by every opportunity: I may receive your letters on some occasions when I need them most to support my spirits. I love you very tenderly. Remember me with affection, should you never hear from me again.

Your affectionate brother,
ROBERT WALTON.

LETTER III

To Mrs Saville, England.

July 7th, 17–.

MY DEAR SISTER,

I write a few lines in haste to say that I am safe – and well advanced on my voyage. This letter will reach England by a merchantman now on its homeward voyage from Archangel; more fortunate than I, who may not see my native land, perhaps, for many years. I am, however, in good spirits: my men are bold, and apparently firm of purpose, nor do the floating sheets of ice that continually pass us, indicating the dangers of the region towards which we are advancing, appear to dismay them. We have already reached a very high latitude; but it is the height of summer, and although not so warm as in England, the southern gales, which blow us speedily towards those shores which I so ardently desire to attain, breathe a degree of renovating warmth which I had not expected.

No incidents have hitherto befallen us that would make a figure in a letter. One or two stiff gales, and the springing of a leak, are accidents which experienced navigators scarcely remember to record; and I shall be well content if nothing worse happen to us during our voyage.

Adieu, my dear Margaret. Be assured, that for my own sake, as well as yours, I will not rashly encounter danger. I will be cool, persevering and prudent.

But success *shall* crown my endeavours. Wherefore not? Thus far I have gone, tracing a secure way over the pathless seas: the very stars themselves being witnesses and testimonies of my triumph. Why not still proceed over the untamed yet obedient element? What can stop the determined heart and resolved will of man?

My swelling heart involuntarily pours itself out thus. But I must finish. Heaven bless my beloved sister!

R.W.

LETTER IV

To Mrs Saville, England.

August 5th, 17–.

So strange an accident has happened to us that I cannot forbear recording it, although it is very probable that you will see me before these papers can come into your possession.

Last Monday (July 31st) we were nearly surrounded by ice, which closed in the ship on all sides, scarcely leaving her the searoom in which she floated. Our situation was somewhat dangerous, especially as we were compassed round by a very thick fog. We accordingly lay to, hoping that some change would take place in the atmosphere and weather.

About two o'clock the mist cleared away, and we beheld, stretched out in every direction, vast and irregular plains of ice, which seemed to have no end. Some of my comrades groaned, and my own mind began to grow watchful with anxious thoughts, when a strange sight suddenly attracted our attention, and diverted our solicitude from our own situations. We perceived a low carriage, fixed on a sledge and drawn by dogs, pass on towards the north, at the distance of half a mile; a being which had the shape of a man, but apparently of gigantic stature, sat in the sledge, and guided the dogs. We watched the rapid progress of the traveller with our telescopes until he was lost among the distant inequalities of the ice.

This appearance excited our unqualified wonder. We were, as we believed, many hundred miles from any land; but this apparition seemed to denote that it was not, in reality, so distant as we had supposed. Shut in, however, by ice, it was impossible to follow his track, which we had observed with the greatest attention.

About two hours after this occurrence we heard the ground sea; and before night the ice broke, and freed our ship. We, however, lay to until the morning, fearing to encounter in the dark those large loose masses which float about after the breaking up of the ice. I profited of this time to rest for a few hours.

In the morning, however, as soon as it was light, I went upon deck and found all the sailors busy on one side of the vessel, apparently talking to some one in the sea. It was, in fact, a sledge, like that we had seen before, which had drifted towards us in the night on a large fragment of ice. Only one dog remained alive; but there was a human being within it, whom the sailors were persuading to enter the vessel. He was not as the other traveller seemed to be, a savage inhabitant of some undiscovered island, but an European. When I appeared on deck, the master said, 'Here is our captain, and he will not allow you to perish on the open sea.'

On perceiving me, the stranger addressed me in English, although with a foreign accent. 'Before I come on board your vessel,' said he, 'will you have the kindness to inform me whither you are bound?'

You may conceive my astonishment on hearing such a question addressed to me from a man on the brink of destruction and to whom I should have supposed that my vessel would have been a resource which he would not have exchanged for the most precious wealth the earth can afford. I replied, however, that we were on a voyage of discovery towards the northern pole.

Upon hearing this he appeared satisfied, and consented to come on board. Good God! Margaret, if you had seen the man who thus capitulated for his safety, your surprise would have been boundless. His limbs were nearly frozen, and his body dreadfully emaciated by fatigue and suffering. I never saw a man in so wretched a condition. We attempted to carry him into the cabin; but as soon as he had quitted the fresh air, he fainted. We accordingly brought him back to the deck, and restored him to animation by rubbing him with brandy and forcing him to swallow a small quantity. As soon as he showed signs of life, we wrapped him up in blankets and placed him near the chimney of the kitchen stove. By slow degrees he recovered, and ate a little soup which restored him wonderfully.

Two days passed in this manner before he was able to speak; and I often feared that his sufferings had deprived him of understanding. When he had in some measure recovered, I removed him to my own cabin, and attended on him as much as my duty would permit. I never saw a more interesting creature; his eyes have generally an expression of wildness, and even madness, but there are moments when, if any one performs an act of kindness towards him or does him any the most trifling service, his whole countenance is lighted up, as it were, with a beam of benevolence and sweetness that I never saw equalled. But he is generally melancholy and despairing; and sometimes he gnashes his teeth; as if impatient of the weight of woes that oppresses him.

When my guest was a little recovered, I had great trouble to keep off the men, who wished to ask him a thousand questions; but I would not allow him to be tormented by their idle curiosity, in a state of body and mind whose restoration evidently depended upon entire repose. Once, however, the lieutenant asked why he had come so far upon the ice in so strange a vehicle?

His countenance instantly assumed an aspect of the deepest gloom; and he replied, 'To seek one who fled from me.'

'And did the man whom you pursued travel in the same fashion?'

'Yes.'

'Then I fancy we have seen him, for the day before we picked you up, we saw some dogs drawing a sledge, with a man in it, across the ice.'

This aroused the stranger's attention, and he asked a multitude of questions concerning the route which the daemon, as he called him, had pursued. Soon after, when he was alone with me, he said, 'I have, doubtless, excited your curiosity, as well as that of these good people; but you are too considerate to make enquiries.'

'Certainly; it would indeed be very impertinent and inhuman in me to trouble you with any inquisitiveness of mine.'

'And yet you rescued me from a strange and perilous situation: you have benevolently restored me to life.'

Soon after this he enquired if I thought that the breaking up of the ice had destroyed the other sledge? I replied, that I could not answer with any degree of certainty, for the ice had not broken until near midnight, and the traveller might have arrived at a place of safety before that time; but of this I could not judge.

From this time a new spirit of life animated the decaying frame of the stranger. He manifested the greatest eagerness to be upon deck, to watch for the sledge which had before appeared; but I have persuaded him to remain in the cabin, for he is far too weak to sustain the rawness of the atmosphere. I have promised that some one should watch for him and give him instant notice if any new object should appear in sight.

Such is my journal of what relates to this strange occurrence up to the present day. The stranger has gradually improved in health, but is very silent, and appears uneasy when anyone except myself enters the cabin. Yet his manners are so conciliating and gentle, that the sailors are all interested in him, although they have had very little communication with him. For my own part, I begin to love him as a brother; and his constant and deep grief fills me with sympathy and compassion. He must have been a noble creature in his better days, being even now in wreck so attractive and amiable.

I said in one of my letters, my dear Margaret, that I should find no friend on the wide ocean; yet I have found a man who, before his spirit had been broken by misery, I should have been happy to have possessed as the brother of my heart.

I shall continue my journal concerning the stranger at intervals, should I have any fresh incidents to record.

August 13th, 17–.

My affection for my guest increases every day. He excites at once my admiration and my pity to an astonishing degree. How can I see so noble a creature destroyed by misery, without feeling the most poignant grief? He is so gentle, yet so wise; his mind is so cultivated, and when he speaks, although his words are culled with the choicest art, yet they flow with rapidity and unparalleled eloquence.

He is now much recovered from his illness, and is continually on the deck, apparently watching for the sledge that preceded his own. Yet, although unhappy, he is not so utterly occupied by his own misery but that he interests himself deeply in the projects of others. He has frequently conversed with me on mine, which I have communicated to him without disguise. He entered attentively into all my arguments in favour of my eventual success, and into every minute detail of the measures I had taken to secure it. I was easily led by the sympathy which he evinced, to use the language of my heart, to give utterance to the burning ardour of my soul; and to say, with all the fevour that warmed me, how gladly I would sacrifice my fortune, my existence, my every hope, to the furtherance of my enterprise. One man's life or death were but a small price to pay for the acquirement of the knowledge which I sought for the dominion I should acquire and transmit over the elemental foes of our race. As I spoke, a dark gloom spread over my listener's countenance. At first I perceived that he tried to suppress his emotion; he placed his hands before his eyes, and my voice quivered and failed me as I beheld tears trickle fast from between his fingers – a groan burst from his heaving breast. I paused; at length he spoke, in broken accents – 'Unhappy man! Do you share my madness? Have you drunk also of the intoxicating draught? Hear me – let me reveal my tale, and you will dash the cup from your lips!'

Such words, you may imagine, strongly excited my curiosity; but the paroxysm of grief that had seized the stranger overcame his weakened powers, and many hours of repose and tranquil conversation were necessary to restore his composure.

Having conquered the violence of his feelings, he appeared to despise himself for being the slave of passion; and quelling the dark tyranny of despair, he led me again to converse concerning myself personally. He asked me the history of my earlier years. The tale was quickly told: but it awakened various trains of reflection. I spoke of my desire of finding a friend – of my thirst for a more intimate sympathy with a fellow mind than had ever fallen to my lot; and expressed my conviction that a man could boast of little happiness, who did not enjoy this blessing.

'I agree with you,' replied the stranger; 'we are unfashioned creatures, but half made up, if one wiser, better, dearer than ourselves – such a friend ought to be – do not lend his aid to perfectionate our weak and faulty natures. I once had a friend, the most noble of human creatures, and am entitled, therefore, to judge respecting friendship. You have hope, and the world before you, and have no cause for despair. But I – I have lost every thing and cannot begin life anew.'

As he said this his countenance became expressive of a calm, settled grief, that touched me to the heart. But he was silent, and presently retired to his cabin.

Even broken in spirit as he is, no one can feel more deeply than he does the beauties of nature. The starry sky, the sea, and every sight afforded by these wonderful regions, seems still to have the power of elevating his soul from earth. Such a man has a double existence: he may suffer misery and be overwhelmed by disappointments, yet, when he has retired into himself, he will be like a celestial spirit, that has a halo around him, within whose circle no grief or folly ventures.

Will you smile at the enthusiasm I express concerning this divine wanderer? You would not, if you saw him. You have been tutored and refined by books and retirement from the world, and you are therefore somewhat fastidious; but this only renders you the more fit to appreciate the extraordinary merits of this wonderful man. Sometimes I have endeavoured to discover what quality it is which he possesses, that elevates him so immeasurably above any other person I ever knew. I believe it to be an intuitive discernment; a quick but never-failing power of judgment; a penetration into the causes of things, unequalled for clearness and precision; add to this a facility of expression, and a voice whose varied intonations are soul-subduing music.

August 19th, 17–.

Yesterday the stranger said to me, 'You may easily perceive, Captain Walton, that I have suffered great and unparalled misfortunes. I had determined, at one time, that the memory of these evils should die with me, but you have won me to alter my determination. You seek for knowledge and wisdom, as I once did; and I ardently hope that the gratification of your wishes may not be a serpent to sting you, as mine has been. I do not know that the relation of my disasters will be useful to you; yet, when I reflect that you are pursuing the same course, exposing yourself to the same dangers which have rendered me what I am, I imagine that you may deduce an apt moral from my tale; one that may direct you if you succeed in your undertaking, and console you in case of failure. Prepare to hear of occurrences which are usually deemed marvellous. Were we among the tamer scenes of nature, I might fear to encounter your unbelief, perhaps your ridicule; but many things will appear possible in these wild and mysterious regions, which would provoke the laughter of those unacquainted with the ever-varied powers of nature; – nor can I doubt but that my tale conveys in its series internal evidence of the truth of the events of which it is composed.'

You may easily imagine that I was much gratified by the offered communication, yet I could not endure that he should renew his grief by a recital of his misfortunes. I felt the greatest eagerness to hear the promised narrative, partly from curiosity, and partly from a strong desire to ameliorate his fate, if it were in my power. I expressed these feelings in my answer.

'I thank you,' he replied, 'for your sympathy, but it is useless; my fate is nearly fulfilled. I wait but for one event, and then I shall repose in peace. I understand your feeling,' continued he, perceiving that I wished to interrupt him: 'but you are mistaken, my friend, if thus you will allow me to name you; nothing can alter my destiny; listen to my history, and you will perceive how irrevocably it is determined.'

He then told me, that he would commence his narrative the next day, when I should be at leisure. This promise drew from me the warmest thanks. I have resolved every night, when I am not imperatively occupied by my duties, to record, as nearly as possible in his own words, what he has related during the day. If I should be engaged, I will at least make notes. This manuscript will doubtless afford you the greatest pleasure: but to me, who know him and who hear it from his own lips – with what interest and sympathy shall I read it in some future day! Even now, as I commence my task, his full-toned voice swells in my ears; his lustrous eyes dwell on me with all their melancholy sweetness; I see his thin hand raised in animation, while the lineaments of his face are irradiated by the soul within. Strange and harrowing must be his story, frightful the storm which embraced the gallant vessel on its course and wrecked it – thus!

CHAPTER 1

I am by birth a Genevese, and my family is one of the most distinguished of that republic. My ancestors had been for many years counsellors and syndics; and my father had filled several public situations with honour and reputation. He was respected by all who knew him, for his integrity and indefatigable attention to public business. He passed his younger days perpetually occupied by the affairs of his country; a variety of circumstances had prevented his marrying early, nor was it until the decline of life that he became a husband and the father of a family.

As the circumstances of his marriage illustrate his character, I cannot refrain from relating them. One of his most intimate friends was a merchant who, from a flourishing state, fell, through numerous mischances, into poverty. This man, whose name was Beaufort, was of a proud and unbending disposition and could not bear to live in poverty and oblivion in the same country where he had formerly been distinguished for his rank and magnificence. Having paid his debts, therefore, in the most honourable manner, he retreated with his daughter to the town of Lucerne, where he lived unknown and in wretchedness. My father loved Beaufort with the truest friendship, and was deeply grieved by his retreat in these unfortunate circumstances. He bitterly deplored the false pride which led his friend to a conduct so little worthy of the affection that united them. He lost no time in endeavouring to seek him out, with the hope of persuading him to begin the world again through his credit and assistance.

Beaufort had taken effectual measures to conceal himself; and it was ten months before my father discovered his abode. Overjoyed at this discovery, he hastened to the house, which was situated in a mean street near the Reuss. But when he entered, misery and despair alone welcomed him. Beaufort had saved but a very small sum of money from the wreck of his fortunes, but it was sufficient to provide him with sustenance for some months, and in the mean time he hoped to procure some respectable employment in a merchant's house. The interval was, consequently, spent in inaction; his grief only became more deep and rankling, when he had leisure for reflection; and at length it took so fast hold of his mind, that at the end of three months he lay on a bed of sickness, incapable of any exertion.

His daughter attended him with the greatest tenderness; but she saw with despair that their little fund was rapidly decreasing, and that there was no other prospect of support. But Caroline Beaufort possessed a mind of an uncommon mould, and her courage rose to support her in her adversity. She procured plain work; she plaited straw; and by various means contrived to earn a pittance scarcely sufficient to support life.

Several months passed in this manner. Her father grew worse; her time was more entirely occupied in attending him; her means of subsistence decreased; and in the tenth month her father died in her arms, leaving her an orphan and a beggar. This last blow overcame her, and she knelt by Beaufort's coffin, weeping bitterly, when my father entered the chamber. He came like a protecting spirit to the poor girl, who committed herself to his care; and after the interment of his friend he conducted her to Geneva, and placed her under the protection of a relation. Two years after this event Caroline became his wife.

There was a considerable difference between the ages of my parents, but this circumstance seemed to unite them only closer in bonds of devoted affection. There was a sense of justice in my father's upright mind, which rendered it necessary that he should approve highly to love strongly. Perhaps during former years he had suffered from the late-discovered unworthiness of one beloved, and so was disposed to set a greater value on tried worth. There was a show of gratitude and worship in his attachment to my mother, differing wholly from the doating fondness of age, for it was inspired by reverence for her virtues and a desire to be the means of, in some degree, recompensing her for the sorrows she had endured, but which gave inexpressible grace to his behaviour to her. Every thing was made to yield to her wishes and her convenience. He strove to shelter her, as a fair exotic is sheltered by the gardener, from every rougher wind, and to surround her with all that could tend to excite pleasurable emotion in her soft and benevolent mind. Her health, and even the tranquillity of her hitherto constant spirit, had been shaken by what she had gone through. During the two years that had elapsed previous to their marriage my father had gradually relinquished all his public functions; and immediately after their union they sought the pleasant climate of Italy, and the change of scene and interest attendant on a tour through that land of wonders, as a restorative for her weakened frame.

From Italy they visited Germany and France. I, their eldest child, was born at Naples, and as an infant accompanied them in their rambles. I remained for several years their only child. Much as they were attached to each other, they seemed to draw inexhaustible stores of affection from a very mine of love to bestow them upon me. My mother's tender caresses and my father's smile of benevolent pleasure while regarding me, are my first recollections. I was their plaything and their idol, and something better – their child, the innocent and helpless creature bestowed on them by Heaven, whom to bring up to good, and whose future lot it was in their hands to direct to happiness or misery, according as they fulfilled their duties towards me. With this deep consciousness of what they owed towards the being to which they had given life, added to the active spirit of tenderness that animated both, it may be imagined that while during every hour of my infant life I received a lesson of patience, of charity, and of self-control, I was so guided by a silken cord that all seemed but one train of enjoyment to me.

For a long time I was their only care. My mother had much desire to have a daughter, but I continued their single offspring. When I was about five years old, while making an excursion beyond the frontiers of Italy, they passed a week on the shores of the Lake of Como. Their benevolent disposition often made them enter the cottages of the poor. This, to my mother, was more than a duty; it was a necessity, a passion – remembering what she had suffered, and how she had been relieved, – for her to act in her turn the guardian angel to the afflicted. During one of their walks a poor cot in the foldings of a vale attracted their notice as being singularly disconsolate, while the number of half-clothed children gathered about it spoke of penury in its worst shape. One day, when my father had gone by himself to Milan, my mother, accompanied by me, visited this abode. She found a peasant and his wife, hard working, bent down by care and labour, distributing a scanty meal to five hungry babes. Among these there was one which attracted my mother far above all the rest. She appeared of a different stock. The four others were dark-eyed, hardy little vagrants; this child was thin, and very fair. Her hair was the brightest living gold, and despite the poverty of her clothing, seemed to set a crown of distinction on her head. Her brow was clear and ample, her blue eyes cloudless, and her lips and the moulding of her face so expressive of sensibility and sweetness that none could behold her without looking on her as of a distinct species, a being heaven-sent, and bearing a celestial stamp in all her features.

The peasant woman, perceiving that my mother fixed eyes of wonder and admiration on this lovely girl, eagerly communicated her history. She was not her child, but the daughter of a Milanese nobleman. Her mother was a German, and had died on giving her birth. The infant had been placed with these good people to nurse: they were better off then. They had not been long married, and their eldest child was but just born. The father of their charge was one of those Italians nursed in the memory of the antique glory of Italy – one among the *schiavi ognor frementi*, who exerted himself to obtain the liberty of his country. He became the victim of its weakness. Whether he had died, or still lingered in the dungeons of Austria, was not known. His property was confiscated; his child became an orphan and a beggar. She continued with her foster parents, and bloomed in their rude abode, fairer than a garden rose among dark-leaved brambles.

When my father returned from Milan, he found playing with me in the hall of our villa a child fairer than a pictured cherub – a creature who seemed to shed radiance from her looks and whose form and motions were lighter than the chamois of the hills. The apparition was soon explained. With his permission my mother prevailed on her rustic guardians to yield their charge to her. They were fond of the sweet orphan. Her presence had seemed a blessing to them, but it would be unfair to her to keep her in poverty and want, when Providence afforded her such powerful protection. They consulted their village priest, and the result was that Elizabeth Lavenza became the inmate of my parents' house – my more than sister – the beautiful and adored companion of all my occupations and my pleasures.

Everyone loved Elizabeth. The passionate and most reverential attachment with which all regarded her became, while I shared it, my pride and my delight. On the evening previous to her being brought to my home, my mother had said playfully, 'I have a pretty present for my Victor – tomorrow he shall have it.' And when, on the morrow, she presented Elizabeth to me as her promised gift, I, with childish seriousness, interpreted her words literally and looked upon Elizabeth as mine – mine to protect, love, and cherish. All praises bestowed on her I received as made to a possession of my own. We called each other familiarly by the name of cousin. No word, no expression could body forth the kind of relation in which she stood to me – my more than sister, since till death she was to be mine only.

CHAPTER 2

We were brought up together; there was not quite a year difference in our ages. I need not say that we were strangers to any species of disunion or dispute. Harmony was the soul of our companionship, and the diversity and contrast that subsisted in our characters drew us nearer together. Elizabeth was of a calmer and more concentrated disposition; but, with all my ardour, I was capable of a more intense application, and was more deeply smitten with the thirst for knowledge. She busied herself with following the aerial creations of the poets; and in the majestic and wondrous scenes which surrounded our Swiss home – the sublime shapes of the mountains; the changes of the seasons; tempest and calm; the silence of winter, and the life and turbulence of our Alpine summers – she found ample scope for admiration and delight. While my companion contemplated with a serious and satisfied spirit the magnificent appearances of things, I delighted in investigating their causes. The world was to me a secret which I desired to divine. Curiosity, earnest research to learn the hidden laws of nature, gladness akin to rapture, as they were unfolded to me, are among the earliest sensations I can remember.

On the birth of a second son, my junior by seven years, my parents gave up entirely their wandering life, and fixed themselves in their native country. We possessed a house in Geneva, and a *campagne* on Belrive, the eastern shore of the lake, at the distance of rather more than a league from the city. We resided principally in the latter, and the lives of my parents were passed in considerable seclusion. It was my temper to avoid a crowd, and to attach myself fervently to a few. I was indifferent, therefore, to my schoolfellows in general; but I united myself in the bonds of the closest friendship to one among them. Henry Clerval was the son of a merchant of Geneva. He was a boy of singular talent and fancy. He loved enterprise, hardship, and even danger for its own sake. He was deeply read in books of chivalry and romance. He composed heroic songs, and began to write many a tale of enchantment and knightly adventure. He tried to make us act plays and to enter into masquerades, in which the characters were drawn from the heroes of Roncesvalles, of the Round Table of King Arthur, and the chivalrous train who shed their blood to redeem the holy sepulchre from the hands of the infidels.

No human being could have passed a happier childhood than myself.

My parents were possessed by the very spirit of kindness and indulgence. We felt that they were not the tyrants to rule our lot according to their caprice, but the agents and creators of all the many delights which we enjoyed. When I mingled with other families, I distinctly discerned how peculiarly fortunate my lot was, and gratitude assisted the development of filial love.

My temper was sometimes violent, and my passions vehement; but by some law in my temperature they were turned not towards childish pursuits but to an eager desire to learn, and not to learn all things indiscriminately. I confess that neither the structure of languages, nor the code of governments, nor the politics of various states possessed attractions for me. It was the secrets of heaven and earth that I desired to learn; and whether it was the outward substance of things, or the inner spirit of nature and the mysterious soul of man that occupied me, still my enquiries were directed to the metaphysical, or in its highest sense, the physical secrets of the world.

Meanwhile Clerval occupied himself, so to speak, with the moral relations of things. The busy stage of life, the virtues of heroes, and the actions of men were his theme; and his hope and his dream was to become one among those whose names are recorded in story, as the gallant and adventurous benefactors of our species. The saintly soul of Elizabeth shone like a shrine-dedicated lamp in our peaceful home. Her sympathy was ours; her smile, her soft voice, the sweet glance of her celestial eyes, were ever there to bless and animate us. She was the living spirit of love to soften and attract: I might have become sullen in my study, rough through the ardour of my nature, but that she was there to subdue me to a semblance of her own gentleness. And Clerval – could aught ill entrench on the noble spirit of Clerval – yet he might not have been so perfectly humane, so thoughtful in his generosity – so full of kindness and tenderness amidst his passion for adventurous exploit, had she not unfolded to him the real loveliness of beneficence, and made the doing good the end and aim of his soaring ambition.

I feel exquisite pleasure in dwelling on the recollections of childhood, before misfortune had tainted my mind, and changed its bright visions of extensive usefulness into gloomy and narrow reflections upon self. Besides, in drawing the picture of my early days, I also record those events which led, by insensible steps, to my after tale of misery: for when

I would account to myself for the birth of that passion, which afterwards ruled my destiny, I find it arise, like a mountain river, from ignoble and almost forgotten sources; but, swelling as it proceeded, it became the torrent which, in its course, has swept away all my hopes and joys.

Natural philosophy is the genius that has regulated my fate; I desire, therefore, in this narration, to state those facts which led to my predilection for that science. When I was thirteen years of age we all went on a party of pleasure to the baths near Thonon: the inclemency of the weather obliged us to remain a day confined to the inn. In this house I chanced to find a volume of the works of Cornelius Agrippa. I opened it with apathy; the theory which he attempts to demonstrate, and the wonderful facts which he relates soon changed this feeling into enthusiasm. A new light seemed to dawn upon my mind, and, bounding with joy, I communicated my discovery to my father. My father looked carelessly at the titlepage of my book and said, 'Ah! Cornelius Agrippa! My dear Victor, do not waste your time upon this; it is sad trash.'

If, instead of this remark, my father had taken the pains to explain to me that the principles of Agrippa had been entirely exploded, and that a modern system of science had been introduced, which possessed much greater powers than the ancient, because the powers of the latter were chimerical, while those of the former were real and practical; under such circumstances I should certainly have thrown Agrippa aside and have contented my imagination, warmed as it was, by returning with greater ardour to my former studies. It is even possible that the train of my ideas would never have received the fatal impulse that led to my ruin. But the cursory glance my father had taken of my volume by no means assured me that he was acquainted with its contents; and I continued to read with the greatest avidity.

When I returned home my first care was to procure the whole works of this author, and afterwards of Paracelsus and Albertus Magnus. I read and studied the wild fancies of these writers with delight; they appeared to me treasures known to few besides myself. I have described myself as always having been imbued with a fervent longing to penetrate the secrets of nature. In spite of the intense labour and wonderful discoveries of modern philosophers, I always came from my studies discontented and unsatisfied. Sir Isaac Newton is said to have avowed that he felt like a child picking up shells beside the great and unexplored ocean of truth. Those of his successors in each branch of natural philosophy with whom I was acquainted, appeared even to my boy's apprehensions, as tyros engaged in the same pursuit.

The untaught peasant beheld the elements around him, and was acquainted with their practical uses. The most learned philosopher knew little more. He had partially unveiled the face of Nature, but her immortal lineaments were still a wonder and a mystery. He might dissect, anatomise, and give names; but, not to speak of a final cause, causes in their secondary and tertiary grades were utterly unknown to him. I had gazed upon the fortifications and impediments that seemed to keep human beings from entering the citadel of nature, and rashly and ignorantly I had repined.

But here were books, and here were men who had penetrated deeper and knew more. I took their word for all that they averred, and I became their disciple. It may appear strange that such should arise in the eighteenth century; but while I followed the routine of education in the schools of Geneva, I was, to a great degree, self-taught with regard to my favourite studies. My father was not scientific, and I was left to struggle with a child's blindness, added to a student's thirst for knowledge. Under the guidance of my new preceptors, I entered with the greatest diligence into the search of the philosopher's stone and the elixir of life; but the latter soon obtained my undivided attention. Wealth was an inferior object; but what glory would attend the discovery, if I could banish disease from the human frame and render man invulnerable to any but a violent death!

Nor were these my only visions. The raising of ghosts or devils was a promise liberally accorded by my favourite authors, the fulfilment of which I most eagerly sought; and if my incantations were always unsuccessful, I attributed the failure rather to my own inexperience and mistake, than to a want of skill or fidelity in my instructors. And thus for a time I was occupied by exploded systems, mingling, like an unadept, a thousand contradictory theories, and floundering desperately in a very slough of multifarious knowledge, guided by an ardent imagination and childish reasoning, till an accident again changed the current of my ideas.

When I was about fifteen years old we had retired to our house near Belrive, when we witnessed a most violent and terrible thunder-storm.

It advanced from behind the mountains of Jura; and the thunder burst at once with frightful loudness from various quarters of the heavens. I remained, while the storm lasted, watching its progress with curiosity and delight. As I stood at the door, on a sudden I beheld a stream of fire issue from an old and beautiful oak, which stood about twenty yards from our house; and so soon as the dazzling light vanished, the oak had disappeared, and nothing remained but a blasted stump. When we visited it the next morning, we found the tree shattered in a singular manner. It was not splintered by the shock, but entirely reduced to thin ribbons of wood. I never beheld anything so utterly destroyed.

Before this I was not unacquainted with the more obvious laws of electricity. On this occasion a man of great research in natural philosophy was with us, and, excited by this catastrophe, he entered on the explanation of a theory which he had formed on the subject of electricity and galvanism, which was at once new and astonishing to me. All that he said threw greatly into the shade Cornelius Agrippa, Albertus Magnus, and Paracelsus, the lords of my imagination; but by some fatality the overthrow of these men disinclined me to pursue my accustomed studies. It seemed to me as if nothing would or could ever be known. All that had so long engaged my attention suddenly grew despicable. By one of those caprices of the mind, which we are perhaps most subject to in early youth, I at once gave up my former occupations, set down natural history and all its progeny as a deformed and abortive creation, and entertained the greatest disdain for a would-be science which could never even step within the threshold of real knowledge. In this mood of mind I betook myself to the mathematics, and the branches of study appertaining to that science, as being built upon secure foundations, and so worthy of my consideration.

Thus strangely are our souls constructed, and by such slight ligaments are we bound to prosperity or ruin. When I look back, it seems to me as if this almost miraculous change of inclination and will was the immediate suggestion of the guardian angel of my life – the last effort made by the spirit of preservation to avert the storm that was even then hanging in the stars, and ready to envelope me. Her victory was announced by an unusual tranquillity and gladness of soul, which followed the relinquishing of my ancient and latterly tormenting studies. It was thus that I was to be taught to associate evil with their prosecution, happiness with their dis-regard.

It was a strong effort of the spirit of good; but it was ineffectual. Destiny was too potent, and her immutable laws had decreed my utter and terrible destruction.

CHAPTER 3

When I had attained the age of seventeen, my parents resolved, that I should become a student at the university of Ingolstadt. I had hitherto attended the schools of Geneva; but my father thought it necessary, for the completion of my education, that I should be made acquainted with other customs than those of my native country. My departure was therefore fixed at an early date; but, before the day resolved upon could arrive, the first misfortune of my life occurred – an omen, as it were, of my future misery.

Elizabeth had caught the scarlet fever; her illness was severe, and she was in the greatest danger. During her illness, many arguments had been urged to persuade my mother to refrain from attending upon her. She had, at first, yielded to our intreaties, but when she heard that the life of her favourite was menaced, she could no longer control her anxiety. She attended her sickbed; – her watchful attentions triumphed over the malignity of the distemper, – Elizabeth was saved, but the consequences of this imprudence were fatal to her preserver. On the third day my mother sickened; her fever was accompanied by the most alarming symptoms, and the looks of her medical attendants prognosticated the worst event. On her death-bed the fortitude and benignity of this best of women did not desert her. She joined the hands of Elizabeth and myself: – 'My children,' she said, 'my firmest hopes of future happiness were placed on the prospect of your union. This expectation will now be the consolation of your father. Elizabeth, my love, you must supply my place to my younger children. Alas! I regret that I am taken from you; and, happy and beloved as I have been, is it not hard to quit you all? But these are not thoughts befitting me; I will endeavour to resign myself cheerfully to death, and will indulge a hope of meeting you in another world.'

She died calmly; and her countenance expressed affection even in death. I need not describe the feelings of those whose dearest ties are rent by that most irreparable evil; the void that presents itself to the soul; and the despair that is exhibited on the countenance. It is so long before the mind can persuade itself that she, whom we saw every day, and whose very existence appeared a part of our own, can have departed forever – that the brightness of a beloved eye can have been extinguished, and the sound of a voice so familiar and dear to the ear can be hushed, never more to be heard. These are the reflections of the first days; but when the lapse of time proves the reality of the evil, then the actual bitterness of grief commences. Yet from whom has not that rude hand rent away some dear connexion? and why should I describe a sorrow which all have felt, and must feel? The time at length arrives when grief is rather an indulgence than a necessity; and the smile that plays upon the lips, although it may be deemed a sacrilege, is not banished. My mother was dead, but we had still duties which we ought to perform; we must continue our course with the rest, and learn to think ourselves fortunate, whilst one remains whom the spoiler had not seized.

My departure for Ingolstadt, which had been deferred by these events, was now again determined upon. I obtained from my father a respite of some weeks. It appeared to me sacrilege so soon to leave the repose, akin to death, of the house of mourning and to rush into the thick of life. I was new to sorrow, but it did not the less alarm me. I was unwilling to quit the sight of those that remained to me; and above all, I desired to see my sweet Elizabeth in some degree consoled.

She indeed veiled her grief, and strove to act the comforter to us all. She looked steadily on life, and assumed its duties with courage and zeal. She devoted herself to those whom she had been taught to call her uncle and cousins. Never was she so enchanting as at this time, when she recalled the sunshine of her smiles and spent them upon us. She forgot even her own regret in her endeavours to make us forget.

The day of my departure at length arrived. Clerval spent the last evening with us. He had endeavoured to persuade his father to permit him to accompany me and to become my fellow student; but in vain. His father was a narrow-minded trader, and saw idleness and ruin in the aspirations and ambition of his son. Henry deeply felt the misfortune of being debarred from a liberal education. He said little; but when he spoke, I read in his kindling eye and in his animated glance a restrained but firm resolve, not to be chained to the miserable details of commerce.

We sat late. We could not tear ourselves away from each other, nor persuade ourselves to say the word 'Farewell!' It was said; and we retired under the pretence of seeking repose, each fancying that the other was deceived: but when at morning's dawn I descended to the carriage which was to convey me away, they were all there – my father again to bless me, Clerval to press my hand once more, my Elizabeth to renew her intreaties that I would write often, and to bestow the last feminine attentions on her playmate and friend.

I threw myself into the chaise that was to convey me away and indulged in the most melancholy reflections. I, who had ever been surrounded by amiable companions, continually engaged in endeavouring to bestow mutual pleasure, I was now alone. In the university, whither I was going, I must form my own friends and be my own protector. My life had hitherto been remarkably secluded and domestic; and this had given me invincible repugnance to new countenances. I loved my brothers, Elizabeth, and Clerval; these were 'old familiar faces,' but I believed myself totally unfitted for the company of strangers. Such were my reflections as I commenced my journey; but as I proceeded, my spirits and hopes rose. I ardently desired the acquisition of knowledge. I had often, when at home, thought it hard to remain during my youth cooped up in one place, and had longed to enter the world, and take my station among other human beings. Now my desires were complied with, and it would, indeed, have been folly to repent.

I had sufficient leisure for these and many other reflections during my journey to Ingolstadt, which was long and fatiguing. At length the high white steeple of the town met my eyes. I alighted, and was conducted to my solitary apartment, to spend the evening as I pleased.

The next morning I delivered my letters of introduction, and paid a visit to some of the principal professors. Chance – or rather the evil influence, the Angel of Destruction, which asserted omnipotent sway over me from the moment I turned my reluctant steps from my father's door – led me first to M. Krempe, professor of natural philosophy. He was an uncouth man, but deeply imbued in the secrets of his science. He asked me several questions concerning my progress in the different branches of science appertaining to natural philosophy. I replied carelessly; and, partly in contempt, mentioned the names of my alchymists as the principal authors I had studied. The professor stared. 'Have you,' he said, 'really spent your time in studying such nonsense?'

I replied in the affirmative. 'Every minute,' continued M. Krempe with warmth, 'every instant that you have wasted on those books is utterly and entirely lost. You have burdened your memory with exploded

systems and useless names. Good God! In what desert land have you
lived, where no one was kind enough to inform you that these fancies
which you have so greedily imbibed are a thousand years old and as
musty as they are ancient? I little expected, in this enlightened and
scientific age, to find a disciple of Albertus Magnus and Paracelsus.
My dear sir, you must begin your studies entirely anew.'

So saying, he stept aside, and wrote down a list of several books
treating of natural philosophy, which he desired me to procure; and
dismissed me after mentioning that in the beginning of the following
week he intended to commence a course of lectures upon natural
philosophy in its general relations, and that M. Waldman, a fellow-professor, would lecture upon chemistry the alternate days that he omitted.

I returned home, not disappointed, for I have said that I had long
considered those authors useless whom the professor reprobated; but
I returned, not at all the more inclined to recur to these studies in any
shape. M. Krempe was a little squat man, with a gruff voice and a
repulsive countenance; the teacher, therefore, did not prepossess me
in favour of his pursuits. In rather a too philosophical and connected
a strain, perhaps, I have given an account of the conclusions I had
come to concerning them in my early years. As a child, I had not been
content with the results promised by the modern professors of natural
science. With a confusion of ideas only to be accounted for by my
extreme youth, and my want of a guide on such matters, I had retrod
the steps of knowledge along the paths of time, and exchanged the
discoveries of recent enquirers for the dreams of forgotten alchymists.
Besides, I had a contempt for the uses of modern natural philosophy. It
was very different, when the masters of the science sought immortality
and power; such views, although futile, were grand; but now the scene
was changed. The ambition of the enquirer seemed to limit itself to
the annihilation of those visions on which my interest in science was
chiefly founded. I was required to exchange chimeras of boundless
grandeur for realities of little worth.

Such were my reflections during the first two or three days of my residence at Ingolstadt, which were chiefly spent in becoming acquainted
with the localities, and the principal residents in my new abode. But as
the ensuing week commenced, I thought of the information which M.
Krempe had given me concerning the lectures. And although I could

not consent to go and hear that little conceited fellow deliver sentences out of a pulpit, I recollected what he had said of M. Waldman, whom I had never seen, as he had hither to been out of town.

Partly from curiosity, and partly from idleness, I went into the lecturing room, which M. Waldman entered shortly after. This professor was very unlike his colleague. He appeared about fifty years of age, but with an aspect expressive of the greatest benevolence; a few grey hairs covered his temples, but those at the back of his head were nearly black. His person was short, but remarkably erect; and his voice the sweetest I had ever heard. He began his lecture by a recapitulation of the history of chemistry and the various improvements made by different men of learning, pronouncing with fervour the names of the most distinguished discoverers. He then took a cursory view of the present state of the science, and explained many of its elementary terms. After having made a few preparatory experiments, he concluded with a panegyric upon modern chemistry, the terms of which I shall never forget: –

'The ancient teachers of this science,' said he, 'promised impossibil-ities, and performed nothing. The modern masters promise very little; they know that metals cannot be transmuted, and that the elixir of life is a chimera. But these philosophers, whose hands seem only made to dabble in dirt, and their eyes to pore over the microscope or crucible, have indeed performed miracles. They penetrate into the recesses of nature, and show how she works in her hiding-places. They ascend into the heavens: they have discovered how the blood circulates, and the nature of the air we breathe. They have acquired new and almost unlimited powers; they can command the thunders of heaven, mimic the earthquake, and even mock the invisible world with its own shadows.'

Such were the professor's words – rather let me say such the words of the fate – enounced to destroy me. As he went on I felt as if my soul were grappling with a palpable enemy; one by one the various keys were touched which formed the mechanism of my being: chord after chord was sounded, and soon my mind was filled with one thought, one conception, one purpose. So much has been done, exclaimed the soul of Frankenstein, – more, far more, will I achieve: treading in the steps already marked, I will pioneer a new way, explore unknown powers, and unfold to the world the deepest mysteries of creation.

I closed not my eyes that night. My internal being was in a state of insurrection and turmoil; I felt that order would thence arise, but I had no power to produce it. By degrees, after the morning's dawn, sleep came. I awoke, and my yesternight's thoughts were as a dream. There only remained a resolution to return to my ancient studies and to devote myself to a science for which I believed myself to possess a natural talent. On the same day, I paid M. Waldman a visit. His manners in private were even more mild and attractive than in public; for there was a certain dignity in his mien during his lecture, which in his own house was replaced by the greatest affability and kindness. I gave him pretty nearly the same account of my former pursuits as I had given to his fellow-professor. He heard with attention the little narration concerning my studies, and smiled at the names of Cornelius Agrippa and Paracelsus, but without the contempt that M. Krempe had exhibited. He said that 'these were men to whose indefatigable zeal modern philosophers were indebted for most of the foundations of their knowledge. They had left to us, as an easier task to give new names, and arrange in connected classifications the facts which they in a great degree had been the instruments of bringing to light. The labours of men of genius, however erroneously directed, scarcely ever fail in ultimately turning to the solid advantage of mankind.' I listened to his statement, which was delivered without any presumption or affectation; and then added that his lecture had removed any prejudices against modern chemists; I expressed myself in measured terms, with the modesty and deference due from a youth to his instructor, without letting escape (inexperience in life would have made me ashamed) any of the enthusiasm which stimulated my intended labours. I requested his advice concerning the books I ought to procure.

'I am happy,' said M. Waldman, 'to have gained a disciple; and if your application equals your ability, I have no doubt of your success. Chemistry is that branch of natural philosophy in which the greatest improvements have been and may be made: it is on that account that I have made it my peculiar study; but at the same time, I have not neglected the other branches of science. A man would make but a very sorry chemist if he attended to that department of human knowledge alone. If your wish is to become really a man of science, and not merely a petty experimentalist, I should advise you to apply to every branch of natural philosophy, including mathematics.'

He then took me into his laboratory and explained to me the uses of his various machines; instructing me as to what I ought to procure, and promising me the use of his own when I should have advanced far enough in the science not to derange their mechanism. He also gave me the list of books which I had requested; and I took my leave.

Thus ended a day memorable to me: it decided my future destiny.

CHAPTER 4

From this day natural philosophy, and particularly chemistry, in the most comprehensive sense of the term, became nearly my sole occupation. I read with ardour those works, so full of genius and discrimination, which modern enquirers have written on these subjects. I attended the lectures, and cultivated the acquaintance, of the men of science of the university; and I found even in M. Krempe a great deal of sound sense and real information, combined, it is true, with a repulsive physiognomy and manners, but not on that account the less valuable. In M. Waldman I found a true friend. His gentleness was never tinged by dogmatism, and his instructions were given with an air of frankness and good nature, that banished every idea of pedantry. In a thousand ways he smoothed for me the path of knowledge, and made the most abstruse enquiries clear and facile to my apprehension. My application was at first fluctuating and uncertain; it gained strength as I proceeded, and soon became so ardent and eager, that the stars often disappeared in the light of morning whilst I was yet engaged in my laboratory.

As I applied so closely, it may be easily conceived that my progress was rapid. My ardour was indeed the astonishment of the students, and my proficiency that of the masters. Professor Krempe often asked me, with a sly smile, how Cornelius Agrippa went on? whilst M. Waldman expressed the most heartfelt exultation in my progress. Two years passed in this manner, during which I paid no visit to Geneva, but was engaged, heart and soul, in the pursuit of some discoveries which I hoped to make. None but those who have experienced them can conceive of the enticements of science. In other studies you go as far as others have gone before you, and there is nothing more to know; but in a scientific pursuit there is continual food for discovery and wonder. A mind of moderate capacity, which closely pursued one study must infallibly arrive at great proficiency in that study; and I, who continually sought the attainment of one object of pursuit and was solely wrapt up in this, improved so rapidly, that, at the end of two years, I made some discoveries in the improvement of some chemical instruments, which procured me great esteem and admiration at the university. When I had arrived at this point and had become as well acquainted with the theory and practice of natural philosophy as depended on the lessons of any of the professors at Ingolstadt, my residence there being no longer conducive to my improvements, I thought of returning to my friends and my native town, when an incident happened that protracted my stay.

One of the phenomena which had peculiarly attracted my attention was the structure of the human frame, and, indeed, any animal endued with life. Whence, I often asked myself, did the principle of life proceed? It was a bold question, and one which has ever been considered as a mystery; yet with how many things are we upon the brink of becoming acquainted, if cowardice or carelessness did not restrain our enquiries. I revolved these circumstances in my mind, and determined thenceforth to apply myself more particularly to those branches of natural philosophy which relate to physiology. Unless I had been animated by an almost supernatural enthusiasm, my application to this study would have been irksome, and almost intolerable. To examine the causes of life, we must first have recourse to death. I became acquainted with the science of anatomy: but this was not sufficient; I must also observe the natural decay and corruption of the human body. In my education my father had taken the greatest precautions that my mind should be impressed with no supernatural horrors. I do not ever remember to have trembled at a tale of superstition, or to have feared the apparition of a spirit. Darkness had no effect upon my fancy; and a churchyard was to me merely the receptacle of bodies deprived of life, which, from being the seat of beauty and strength, had become food for the worm. Now I was led to examine the cause and progress of this decay, and forced to spend days and nights in vaults and charnel-houses. My attention was fixed upon every object the most insupportable to the delicacy of the human feelings. I saw how the fine form of man was degraded and wasted; I beheld the corruption of death succeed to the blooming cheek of life; I saw how the worm inherited the wonders of the eye and brain. I paused, examining and analysing all the minutiae of causation, as exemplified in the change from life to death, and death to life, until from the midst of this darkness a sudden light broke in upon me – a light so brilliant and wondrous, yet so simple, that while I became dizzy with the immensity of the prospect which it illustrated, I was surprised, that among so many men of genius who had directed their enquiries towards the same science, that I alone should be reserved to discover so astonishing a secret.

Remember, I am not recording the vision of a madman. The sun does not more certainly shine in the heavens, than that which I now affirm is true. Some miracle might have produced it, yet the stages of the discovery were distinct and probable. After days and nights of incredible labour and fatigue, I succeeded in discovering the cause of generation and life; nay, more, I became myself capable of bestowing animation upon lifeless matter.

The astonishment which I had at first experienced on this discovery soon gave place to delight and rapture. After so much time spent in painful labour, to arrive at once at the summit of my desires, was the most gratifying consummation of my toils. But this discovery was so great and overwhelming, that all the steps by which I had been progressively led to it were obliterated, and I beheld only the result. What had been the study and desire of the wisest men since the creation of the world was now within my grasp. Not that, like a magic scene, it all opened upon me at once: the information I had obtained was of a nature rather to direct my endeavours so soon as I should point them towards the object of my search, than to exhibit that object already accomplished. I was like the Arabian who had been buried with the dead and found a passage to life, aided only by one glimmering and seemingly ineffectual light.

I see by your eagerness and the wonder and hope which your eyes express, my friend, that you expect to be informed of the secret with which I am acquainted; that cannot be: listen patiently until the end of my story, and you will easily perceive why I am reserved upon that subject. I will not lead you on, unguarded and ardent as I then was, to your destruction and infallible misery. Learn from me, if not by my precepts, at least by my example, how dangerous is the acquirement of knowledge and how much happier that man is who believes his native town to be the world, than he who aspires to become greater than his nature will allow.

When I found so astonishing a power placed within my hands, I hesitated a long time concerning the manner in which I should employ it. Although I possessed the capacity of bestowing animation, yet to prepare a frame for the reception of it, with all its intricacies of fibres, muscles, and veins, still remained a work of inconceivable difficulty and labour. I doubted at first whether I should attempt the creation of a being like myself, or one of simpler organisation; but my imagination was too much exalted by my first success to permit me to doubt of my ability to give life to an animal as complex and wonderful as man. The materials at present within my command hardly appeared adequate to so arduous an undertaking; but I doubted not that I should ultimately succeed. I prepared myself for a multitude of reverses; my operations might be incessantly baffled, and at last my work be imperfect: yet, when I considered the improvement which every day takes place in science and mechanics, I was encouraged to hope my present attempts would at least lay the foundations of future success. Nor could I consider the magnitude and complexity of my plan as any argument of its impracticability. It was with these feelings that I began the creation of a human being. As the minuteness of the parts formed a great hindrance to my speed, I resolved, contrary to my first intention, to make the being of a gigantic stature; that is to say, about eight feet in height, and proportionally large. After having formed this determination and having spent some months in successfully collecting and arranging my materials, I began.

No one can conceive the variety of feelings which bore me onwards, like a hurricane, in the first enthusiasm of success. Life and death appeared to me ideal bounds, which I should first break through, and pour a torrent of light into our dark world. A new species would bless me as its creator and source; many happy and excellent natures would owe their being to me. No father could claim the gratitude of his child so completely as I should deserve theirs. Pursuing these reflections, I thought, that if I could bestow animation upon lifeless matter, I might in process of time (although I now found it impossible) renew life where death had apparently devoted the body to corruption.

These thoughts supported my spirits, while I pursued my undertaking with unremitting ardour. My cheek had grown pale with study, and my person had become emaciated with confinement. Sometimes, on the very brink of certainty, I failed; yet still I clung to the hope which the next day or the next hour might realise. One secret which I alone possessed was the hope to which I had dedicated myself; and the moon gazed on my midnight labours, while, with unrelaxed and breathless

eagerness, I pursued nature to her hiding-places. Who shall conceive
the horrors of my secret toil as I dabbled among the unhallowed damps
of the grave or tortured the living animal to animate the lifeless clay?
My limbs now tremble, and my eyes swim with the remembrance;
but then a resistless, and almost frantic impulse, urged me forward;
I seemed to have lost all soul or sensation but for this one pursuit. It
was indeed but a passing trance, that only made me feel with renewed
acuteness so soon as, the unnatural stimulus ceasing to operate, I had
returned to my old habits. I collected bones from charnel-houses and
disturbed, with profane fingers, the tremendous secrets of the human
frame. In a solitary chamber, or rather cell, at the top of the house, and
separated from all the other apartments by a gallery and staircase, I kept
my workshop of filthy creation: my eyeballs were starting from their
sockets in attending to the details of my employment. The dissecting
room and the slaughter-house furnished many of my materials; and
often did my human nature turn with loathing from my occupation,
whilst, still urged on by an eagerness which perpetually increased, I
brought my work near to a conclusion.

The summer months passed while I was thus engaged, heart and
soul, in one pursuit. It was a most beautiful season; never did the fields
bestow a more plentiful harvest, or the vines yield a more luxuriant
vintage: but my eyes were insensible to the charms of nature. And the
same feelings which made me neglect the scenes around me caused
me also to forget those friends who were so many miles absent, and
whom I had not seen for so long a time. I knew my silence disquieted
them; and I well remembered the words of my father: 'I know that
while you are pleased with yourself, you will think of us with affection, and we shall hear regularly from you. You must pardon me if I
regard any interruption in your correspondence as a proof that your
other duties are equally neglected.'

I knew well therefore what would be my father's feelings; but I
could not tear my thoughts from my employment, loathsome in itself,
but which had taken an irresistible hold of my imagination. I wished,
as it were, to procrastinate all that related to my feelings of affection
until the great object, which swallowed up every habit of my nature,
should be completed.

I then thought that my father would be unjust if he ascribed my neglect to vice, or faultiness on my part, but I am now convinced that he was justified in conceiving that I should not be altogether free from blame. A human being in perfection ought always to preserve a calm and peaceful mind, and never to allow passion or a transitory desire to disturb his tranquillity. I do not think that the pursuit of knowledge is an exception to this rule. If the study to which you apply yourself has a tendency to weaken your affections, and to destroy your taste for those simple pleasures in which no alloy can possibly mix, then that study is certainly unlawful, that is to say, not befitting the human mind. If this rule were always observed; if no man allowed any pursuit whatsoever to interfere with the tranquillity of his domestic affections, Greece had not been enslaved; Caesar would have spared his country; America would have been discovered more gradually; and the empires of Mexico and Peru had not been destroyed.

But I forget that I am moralising in the most interesting part of my tale, and your looks remind me to proceed.

My father made no reproach in his letters, and only took notice of my silence by enquiring into my occupations more particularly than before. Winter, spring, and summer passed away during my labours; but I did not watch the blossom or the expanding leaves – sights which before always yielded me supreme delight – so deeply was I engrossed in my occupation. The leaves of that year had withered before my work drew to a close; and now every day showed me more plainly how well I had succeeded. But my enthusiasm was checked by my anxiety, and I appeared rather like one doomed by slavery to toil in the mines, or any other unwholesome trade than an artist occupied by his favourite employment. Every night I was oppressed by a slow fever, and I became nervous to a most painful degree; the fall of a leaf startled me, and I shunned my fellow-creatures as if I had been guilty of a crime. Sometimes I grew alarmed at the wreck I perceived that I had become; the energy of my purpose alone sustained me: my labours would soon end, and I believed that exercise and amusement would then drive away incipient disease; and I promised myself both of these when my creation should be complete.

CHAPTER 5

It was on a dreary night of November, that I beheld the accomplishment of my toils. With an anxiety that almost amounted to agony, I collected the instruments of life around me, that I might infuse a spark of being into the lifeless thing that lay at my feet. It was already one in the morning; the rain pattered dismally against the panes, and my candle was nearly burnt out, when, by the glimmer of the half-extinguished light, I saw the dull yellow eye of the creature open; it breathed hard, and a convulsive motion agitated its limbs.

How can I describe my emotions at this catastrophe, or how delineate the wretch whom with such infinite pains and care I had endeavoured to form? His limbs were in proportion, and I had selected his features as beautiful. Beautiful! – Great God! His yellow skin scarcely covered the work of muscles and arteries beneath; his hair was of a lustrous black, and flowing; his teeth of pearly whiteness; but these luxuriances only formed a more horrid contrast with his watery eyes, that seemed almost of the same colour as the dun-white sockets in which they were set, his shrivelled complexion and straight black lips.

The different accidents of life are not so changeable as the feelings of human nature. I had worked hard for nearly two years, for the sole purpose of infusing life into an inanimate body. For this I had deprived myself of rest and health. I had desired it with an ardour that far exceeded moderation; but now that I had finished, the beauty of the dream vanished, and breathless horror and disgust filled my heart. Unable to endure the aspect of the being I had created, I rushed out of the room, and continued a long time traversing my bedchamber, unable to compose my mind to sleep. At length lassitude succeeded to the tumult I had before endured; and I threw myself on the bed in my clothes, endeavouring to seek a few moments of forgetfulness. But it was in vain: I slept, indeed, but I was disturbed by the wildest dreams. I thought I saw Elizabeth, in the bloom of health, walking in the streets of Ingolstadt. Delighted and surprised, I embraced her, but as I imprinted the first kiss on her lips, they became livid with the hue of death; her features appeared to change, and I thought that I held the corpse of my dead mother in my arms; a shroud enveloped her form, and I saw the grave-worms crawling in the folds of flannel. I started from my sleep with horror; a cold dew covered my forehead, my teeth chattered, and every limb became convulsed: when, by the dim and yellow light of the moon, as it forced its way through the window shutters, I beheld the wretch – the miserable monster whom I had created. He held up the curtain of the bed; and his eyes, if eyes they may be called, were fixed on me. His jaws opened, and he muttered some inarticulate sounds, while a grin wrinkled his cheeks. He might have spoken, but I did not hear; one hand was stretched out, seemingly to detain me, but I escaped, and rushed downstairs. I took refuge in the courtyard belonging to the house which I inhabited; where I remained during the rest of the night, walking up and down in the greatest agitation, listening attentively, catching and fearing each sound as if it were to announce the approach of the demoniacal corpse to which I had so miserably given life.

Oh! no mortal could support the horror of that countenance. A mummy again endued with animation could not be so hideous as that wretch. I had gazed on him while unfinished; he was ugly then; but when those muscles and joints were rendered capable of motion, it became a thing such as even Dante could not have conceived.

I passed the night wretchedly. Sometimes my pulse beat so quickly and hardly that I felt the palpitation of every artery; at others, I nearly sank to the ground through languor and extreme weakness. Mingled with this horror, I felt the bitterness of disappointment; dreams that had been my food and pleasant rest for so long a space were now become a hell to me; and the change was so rapid, the overthrow so complete!

Morning, dismal and wet, at length dawned, and discovered to my sleepless and aching eyes the church of Ingolstadt, its white steeple and clock, which indicated the sixth hour. The porter opened the gates of the court, which had that night been my asylum, and I issued into the streets, pacing them with quick steps, as if I sought to avoid the wretch whom I feared every turning of the street would present to my view. I did not dare return to the apartment which I inhabited, but felt impelled to hurry on, although drenched by the rain which poured from a black and comfortless sky.

I continued walking in this manner for some time, endeavouring by bodily exercise to ease the load that weighed upon my mind. I traversed the streets without any clear conception of where I was or what I was doing. My heart palpitated in the sickness of fear, and I hurried on with irregular steps, not daring to look about me:

> Like one, on a lonesome road who,
>   Doth walk in fear and dread,
> And, having once turned round, walks on,
>   And turns no more his head;
> Because he knows a frightful friend
>   Doth close behind him tread.

Continuing thus, I came at length opposite to the inn at which the various diligences and carriages usually stopped. Here I paused, I knew not why; but I remained some minutes with my eyes fixed on a coach that was coming towards me from the other end of the street. As it drew nearer I observed that it was the Swiss diligence: it stopped just where I was standing; and, on the door being opened, I perceived Henry Clerval, who, on seeing me, instantly sprung out. 'My dear Frankenstein,' exclaimed he, 'how glad I am to see you! how fortunate that you should be here at the very moment of my alighting!'

Nothing could equal my delight on seeing Clerval; his presence brought back to my thoughts my father, Elizabeth, and all those scenes of home so dear to my recollection. I grasped his hand, and in a moment forgot my horror and misfortune; I felt suddenly, and for the first time during many months, calm and serene joy. I welcomed my friend, therefore, in the most cordial manner, and we walked towards my college. Clerval continued talking for some time about our mutual friends and his own good fortune in being permitted to come to Ingolstadt. 'You may easily believe,' said he, 'how great was the difficulty to persuade my father that all necessary knowledge was not comprised in the noble art of book-keeping; and, indeed, I believe I left him incredulous to the last, for his constant answer to my unwearied intreaties was the same as that to the Dutch schoolmaster in *The Vicar of Wakefield*: "I have ten thousand florins a year without Greek, I eat heartily without Greek." But his affection for me at length overcame his dislike of learning, and he has permitted me to undertake a voyage of discovery to the land of knowledge.'

'It gives me the greatest delight to see you; but tell me how you left my father, brothers, and Elizabeth.'

'Very well, and very happy, only a little uneasy that they hear from you so seldom. By the by, I mean to lecture you a little upon their account myself – But, my dear Frankenstein,' continued he, stopping short and gazing full in my face, 'I did not before remark how very ill you appear; so thin and pale; and look as if you had been watching for several nights.'

'You have guessed right; I have lately been so deeply engaged in one occupation, that I have not allowed myself sufficient rest, as you see; but I hope, I sincerely hope, that all these employments are now at an end, and that I am at length free.'

I trembled excessively; I could not endure to think of, and far less to allude to, the occurrences of the preceding night. I walked with a quick pace, and we soon arrived at my college. I then reflected, and the thought made me shiver, that the creature whom I had left in my apartment might still be there, alive and walking about. I dreaded to behold this monster; but I feared still more that Henry should see him. Intreating him, therefore, to remain a few minutes at the bottom of the stairs, I darted up towards my own room. My hand was already on the lock of the door before I recollected myself. I then paused; and a cold shivering came over me. I threw the door forcibly open, as children are accustomed to do when they expect a spectre to stand in waiting for them on the other side; but nothing appeared. I stepped fearfully in: the apartment was empty; and my bedroom was also freed from its hideous guest. I could hardly believe that so great a good fortune could have befallen me; but when I became assured that my enemy had indeed fled, I clapped my hands for joy and ran down to Clerval.

We ascended into my room, and the servant presently brought breakfast; but I was unable to contain myself. It was not joy only that possessed me; I felt my flesh tingle with excess of sensitiveness, and my pulse beat rapidly. I was unable to remain for a single instant in the same place; I jumped over the chairs, clapped my hands, and laughed aloud. Clerval at first attributed my unusual spirits to joy on his arrival, but when he observed me more attentively, he saw a wildness in my eyes for which he could not account; and my loud, unrestrained, heartless laughter frightened and astonished him.

'My dear Victor,' cried he, 'what, for God's sake, is the matter? do not laugh in that manner. How ill you are! What is the cause of all this?'

'Do not ask me,' cried I, putting my hands before my eyes, for I thought I saw the dreaded spectre glide into the room; '*he* can tell. – Oh, save me! save me!' I imagined that the monster seized me; I struggled furiously and fell down in a fit.

Poor Clerval! what must have been his feelings? A meeting, which he anticipated with such joy, so strangely turned to bitterness. But I was not the witness of his grief; for I was lifeless, and did not recover my senses for a long, long time.

This was the commencement of a nervous fever, which confined me for several months. During all that time Henry was my only nurse. I afterwards learned that, knowing my father's advanced age, and unfitness for so long a journey, and how wretched my sickness would make Elizabeth, he spared them this grief by concealing the extent of my disorder. He knew that I could not have a more kind and attentive nurse than himself; and, firm in the hope he felt of my recovery, he did not doubt that, instead of doing harm, he performed the kindest action that he could towards them.

But I was in reality very ill; and surely nothing but the unbounded and unremitting attentions of my friend could have restored me to life. The form of the monster on whom I had bestowed existence was forever before my eyes, and I raved incessantly concerning him. Doubtless my words surprised Henry; he at first believed them to be the wanderings of my disturbed imagination; but the pertinacity with which I continually recurred to the same subject, persuaded him that my disorder indeed owed its origin to some uncommon and terrible event.

By very slow degrees, and with frequent relapses that alarmed and grieved my friend, I recovered. I remember the first time I became capable of observing outward objects with any kind of pleasure, I perceived that the fallen leaves had disappeared and that the young buds were shooting forth from the trees that shaded my window. It was a divine spring; and the season contributed greatly to my convalescence. I felt also sentiments of joy and affection revive in my bosom; my gloom disappeared, and in a short time I became as cheerful as before I was attacked by the fatal passion.

'Dearest Clerval,' exclaimed I, 'how kind, how very good you are to me. This whole winter, instead of being spent in study, as you promised yourself, has been consumed in my sick room. How shall I ever repay you? I feel the greatest remorse for the disappointment of which I have been the occasion; but you will forgive me.'

'You will repay me entirely, if you do not discompose yourself, but get well as fast as you can; and since you appear in such good spirits, I may speak to you on one subject, may I not?'

I trembled. One subject! What could it be? Could he allude to an object on whom I dared not even think?

'Compose yourself,' said Clerval, who observed my change of colour, 'I will not mention it if it agitates you; but your father and cousin would be very happy if they received a letter from you in your own handwriting. They hardly know how ill you have been, and are uneasy at your long silence.'

'Is that all, my dear Henry? How could you suppose that my first thought would not fly towards those dear, dear friends whom I love, and who are so deserving of my love?'

'If this is your present temper, my friend, you will perhaps be glad to see a letter that has been lying here some days for you: it is from your cousin, I believe.'

CHAPTER 6

Clerval then put the following letter into my hands. It was from my own Elizabeth: –

MY DEAREST COUSIN,

You have been ill, very ill, and even the constant letters of dear kind Henry are not sufficient to reassure me on your account. You are forbidden to write – to hold a pen; yet one word from you, dear Victor, is necessary to calm our apprehensions. For a long time I have thought that each post would bring this line, and my persuasions have restrained my uncle from undertaking a journey to Ingolstadt. I have prevented his encountering the inconveniences and perhaps dangers of so long a journey, yet how often have I regretted not being able to perform it myself! I figure to myself that the task of attending on your sickbed has devolved on some mercenary old nurse, who could never guess your wishes, nor minister to them with the care and affection of your poor cousin. Yet that is over now: Clerval writes that indeed you are getting better. I eagerly hope that you will confirm this intelligence soon in your own handwriting.

Get well – and return to us. You will find a happy, cheerful home, and friends who love you dearly. Your father's health is vigorous, and he asks but to see you, but to be assured that you are well; and not a care will ever cloud his benevolent countenance. How pleased you would be to remark the improvement of our Ernest! He is now sixteen, and full of activity and spirit. He is desirous to be a true Swiss, and to enter into foreign service, but we cannot part with him, at least until his elder brother return to us. My uncle is not pleased with the idea of a military career in a distant country, but Ernest never had your powers of application. He looks upon study as an odious fetter; his time is spent in the open air, climbing the hills or rowing on the lake. I fear that he will become an idler, unless we yield the point, and permit him to enter on the profession which he has selected.

Little alteration, except the growth of our dear children, has taken place since you left us. The blue lake, and snow-clad mountains – they never change; and I think our placid home and our contented hearts are regulated by the same immutable laws. My trifling occupations take up my time and amuse me, and I am rewarded for any exertions by seeing none but happy, kind faces around me. Since you left us, but one change has taken place in our little household. Do you remember on what occasions Justine Moritz entered our family? Probably you do not; I will relate her history, therefore, in a few words. Madame Moritz, her mother, was a widow with four children, of whom Justine was the third. This girl had always been the favourite of her father; but, through a strange perversity, her mother could not endure her, and after the death of M. Moritz, treated her very ill. My aunt observed this, and when Justine was twelve years of age, prevailed on her mother to allow her to live at our house. The republican institutions of our country have produced simpler and happier manners than those which prevail in the great monarchies that surround it. Hence there is less distinction between the several classes of its inhabitants; and the lower orders, being neither so poor nor so despised, their manners are more refined and moral. A servant in Geneva does not mean the same thing as a servant in France and England. Justine, thus received in our family, learned the duties of a servant; a condition which, in our fortunate country, does not include the idea of ignorance, and a sacrifice of the dignity of a human being.

Justine, you may remember, was a great favourite of yours; and I recollect you once remarked that if you were in an ill humour, one glance from Justine could dissipate it, for the same reason that Ariosto gives concerning the beauty of Angelica – she looked so frank-hearted and happy. My aunt conceived a great attachment for her, by which she was induced to give her an education superior to that which she had at first intended. This benefit was fully repaid; Justine was the most grateful little creature in the world: I do not mean that she made any professions; I never heard one pass her lips, but you could see by her eyes that she almost adored her protectress. Although her disposition was gay, and in many respects inconsiderate, yet she paid the greatest attention to every gesture of my aunt. She thought her the model of all excellence and endeavoured to imitate her phraseology and manners, so that even now she often reminds me of her.

When my dearest aunt died, every one was too much occupied in their own grief to notice poor Justine, who had attended her illness with the most anxious affection. Poor Justine was very ill, but other trials were reserved for her.

One by one, her brothers and sister died; and her mother, with the exception of her neglected daughter, was left childless. The conscience of the woman was troubled; she began to think that the deaths of her favourites were a judgment from heaven to chastise her partiality. She was a Roman catholic; and I believe her confessor confirmed the idea which she had conceived. Accordingly, a few months after your departure for Ingolstadt, Justine was called home by her repentant mother. Poor girl! she wept when she quitted our house; she was much altered since the death of my aunt; grief had given softness and a winning mildness to her manners which had before been remarkable for vivacity. Nor was her residence at her mother's house of a nature to restore her gaiety. The poor woman was very vacillating in her repentance. She sometimes begged Justine to forgive her unkindness but much oftener accused her of having caused the deaths of her brothers and sister. Perpetual fretting at length threw Madame Moritz into a decline, which at first increased her irritability, but she is now at peace forever. She died on the first approach of cold weather, at the beginning of this last winter. Justine has returned to us, and I assure you I love her tenderly. She is very clever and gentle, and extremely pretty; as I mentioned before, her mien and her expressions continually remind me of my dear aunt.

I must say also a few words to you, my dear cousin, of little darling William. I wish you could see him; he is very tall of his age, with sweet laughing blue eyes, dark eyelashes, and curling hair. When he smiles, two little dimples appear on each cheek, which are rosy with health. He has already had one or two little *wives*, but Louisa Biron is his favourite, a pretty little girl of five years of age.

Now, dear Victor, I dare say you wish to be indulged in a little gossip concerning the good people of Geneva. The pretty Miss Mansfield has already received the congratulatory visits on her approaching marriage with a young Englishman, John Melbourne, Esq. Her ugly sister, Manon, married M. Duvillard, the rich banker, last autumn. Your favourite school-fellow, Louis Manoir, has suffered misfortunes since the departure of Clerval from Geneva. But he has already recovered his spirits and is reported to be on the point of marrying a very lively, pretty Frenchwoman, Madame Tavernier. She is a widow, and much older than Manoir; but she is very much admired and a favourite with every body.

I have written myself into better spirits, dear cousin; but my anxiety returns upon me as I conclude. Write, dearest Victor – one line – one word will be a blessing to us. Ten thousand thanks to Henry for his kindness, his affection, and his many letters: we are sincerely grateful. Adieu! my cousin, take care of yourself; and, I intreat you, write!

ELIZABETH LAVENZA
Geneva, March 18th, 17–.

'Dear, dear Elizabeth!' I exclaimed, when I had read her letter, 'I will write instantly, and relieve them from the anxiety they must feel.' I wrote, and this exertion greatly fatigued me; but my convalescence had commenced, and proceeded regularly. In another fortnight I was able to leave my chamber.

One of my first duties on my recovery was to introduce Clerval to the several professors of the university. In doing this, I underwent a kind of rough usage, ill befitting the wounds that my mind had sustained. Ever since the fatal night, the end of my labours, and the beginning of my misfortunes, I had conceived a violent antipathy even to the name of natural philosophy. When I was otherwise quite restored to health, the sight of a chemical instrument would renew all the agony of my nervous symptoms. Henry saw this and had removed all my apparatus from my view. He had also changed my apartment, for he perceived that I had acquired a dislike for the room which had previously been my laboratory. But these cares of Clerval were made of no avail when I visited the professors. M. Waldman inflicted torture when he praised, with kindness and warmth, the astonishing progress I had made in the sciences. He soon perceived that I disliked the subject; but not guessing the real cause, he attributed my feelings to modesty and changed the subject from my improvement to the science itself, with a desire, as I evidently saw, of drawing me out. What could I do? He meant to please, and he tormented me. I felt as if he had placed carefully, one by one, in my view those instruments which were to be afterwards used in putting me to a slow and cruel death. I writhed under his words, yet dared not exhibit the pain I felt. Clerval, whose eyes and feelings were always quick in discerning the sensations of others, declined the subject, alleging, in excuse, his total ignorance; and

the conversation took a more general turn. I thanked my friend from
my heart, but I did not speak. I saw plainly that he was surprised, but
he never attempted to draw my secret from me; and although I loved
him with a mixture of affection and reverence that knew no bounds,
yet I could never persuade myself to confide to him that event which
was so often present to my recollection, but which I feared the detail
to another would only impress more deeply.

M. Krempe was not equally docile; and in my condition at that time,
of almost insupportable sensitiveness, his harsh, blunt encomiums gave
me even more pain than the benevolent approbation of M. Waldman,
'D-n the fellow!' cried he; 'why, M. Clerval, I assure you he has
outstript us all. Ay, stare if you please; but it is nevertheless true. A
youngster who, but a few years ago, believed in Cornelius Agrippa
as firmly as in the Gospel, has now set himself at the head of the
university; and if he is not soon pulled down, we shall all be out of
countenance. – Ay, ay,' continued he, observing my face expressive
of suffering, 'M. Frankenstein is modest, an excellent quality in a
young man. Young men should be diffident of themselves, you know,
M. Clerval: I was myself when young, but that wears out in a very
short time.'

M. Krempe had now commenced a eulogy on himself, which happily
turned the conversation from a subject that was so annoying to me.

Clerval had never sympathised in my tastes for natural science; and
his literary pursuits differed wholly from whose which had occupied
me. He came to the university with the design of making himself
complete master of the Oriental languages, as thus he should open a
field for the plan of life he had marked out for himself. Resolved to
pursue no inglorious career, he turned his eyes towards the East as
affording scope for his spirit of enterprise. The Persian, Arabic, and
Sanscrit languages engaged his attention, and I was easily induced to
enter on the same studies. Idleness had ever been irksome to me, and
now that I wished to fly from reflection and hated my former studies,
I felt great relief in being the fellow pupil with my friend, and found
not only instruction but consolation in the works of the Orientalists.
I did not, like him, attempt a critical knowledge of their dialects, for
I did not contemplate making any other use of them than temporary
amusement. I read merely to understand their meaning, and they well

repaid my labours. Their melancholy is soothing, and their joy elevating, to a degree I never experienced in studying the authors of any other country. When you read their writings, life appears to consist in a warm sun and a garden of roses, in the smiles and frowns of a fair enemy, and the fire that consumes your own heart. How different from the manly and heroical poetry of Greece and Rome!

Summer passed away in these occupations, and my return to Geneva was fixed for the latter end of autumn; but being delayed by several accidents, winter and snow arrived, the roads were deemed impassable, and my journey was retarded until the ensuing spring. I felt this delay very bitterly; for I longed to see my native town and my beloved friends. My return had only been delayed so long from an unwillingness to leave Clerval in a strange place before he had become acquainted with any of its inhabitants. The winter, however, was spent cheerfully, and although the spring was uncommonly late, when it came its beauty compensated for its dilatoriness.

The month of May had already commenced, and I expected the letter daily which was to fix the date of my departure, when Henry proposed a pedestrian tour in the environs of Ingolstadt, that I might bid a personal farewell to the country I had so long inhabited. I acceded with pleasure to this proposition: I was fond of exercise, and Clerval had always been my favourite companion in the rambles of this nature that I had taken among the scenes of my native country.

We passed a fortnight in these perambulations: my health and spirits had long been restored, and they gained additional strength from the salubrious air I breathed, the natural incidents of our progress, and the conversation of my friend. Study had before secluded me from the intercourse of my fellow-creatures, and rendered me unsocial, but Clerval called forth the better feelings of my heart; he again taught me to love the aspect of nature, and the cheerful faces of children. Excellent friend! how sincerely did you love me and endeavour to elevate my mind until it was on a level with your own! A selfish pursuit had cramped and narrowed me, until your gentleness and affection warmed and opened my senses; I became the same happy creature who, a few years ago, loved and beloved by all, had no sorrow or care. When happy, inanimate nature had the power of bestowing on me the most delightful sensations. A serene sky and verdant fields filled me with ecstasy. The present season was indeed divine; the flowers of spring bloomed in the hedges, while those of summer were already in bud. I was undisturbed by thoughts which during the preceding year had pressed upon me, notwithstanding my endeavours to throw them off, with an invincible burden.

Henry rejoiced in my gaiety, and sincerely sympathised in my feelings: he exerted himself to amuse me, while he expressed the sensations that filled his soul. The resources of his mind on this occasion were truly astonishing: his conversation was full of imagination; and very often, in imitation of the Persian and Arabic writers, he invented tales of wonderful fancy and passion. At other times, he repeated my favourite poems, or drew me out into arguments, which he supported with great ingenuity.

We returned to our college on a Sunday afternoon: the peasants were dancing, and everyone we met appeared gay and happy. My own spirits were high, and I bounded along with feelings of unbridled joy and hilarity.

CHAPTER 7

On my return, I found the following letter from my father: –

MY DEAR VICTOR,

You have probably waited impatiently for a letter to fix the date of your return to us; and I was at first tempted to write only a few lines, merely mentioning the day on which I should expect you. But that would be a cruel kindness, and I dare not do it. What would be your surprise, my son, when you expect a happy and glad welcome, to behold, on the contrary, tears and wretchedness? And how, Victor, can I relate our misfortune? Absence cannot have rendered you callous to our joys and griefs; and how shall I inflict pain on my long-absent son? I wish to prepare you for the woeful news, but I know it is impossible; even now your eye skims over the page, to seek the words which are to convey to you the horrible tidings.

William is dead! – that sweet child, whose smiles delighted and warmed my heart, who was so gentle, yet so gay! Victor, he is murdered!

I will not attempt to console you; but will simply relate the circumstances of the transaction.

Last Thursday (May 7th) I, my niece, and your two brothers went to walk in Plainpalais. The evening was warm and serene, and we prolonged our walk farther than usual. It was already dusk before we thought of returning; and then we discovered that William and Ernest, who had gone on before, were not to be found. We accordingly rested on a seat until they should return. Presently Ernest came, and enquired if we had seen his brother: he said that he had been playing with him, that William had run away to hide himself, and that he vainly sought for him, and afterwards waited for him a long time, but he did not return.

This account rather alarmed us, and we continued to search for him until night fell, when Elizabeth conjectured that he might have returned to the house. He was not there. We returned again, with torches, for I could not rest when I thought that my sweet boy had lost himself and was exposed to all the damps and dews of night; Elizabeth also suffered extreme anguish. About five in the morning I discovered my lovely boy, whom the night before I had seen blooming and active in health, stretched on the grass livid and motionless: the print of the murderer's finger was on his neck.

He was conveyed home, and the anguish that was visible in my countenance betrayed the secret to Elizabeth. She was very earnest to see the corpse. At first I attempted to prevent her, but she persisted, and entering the room where it lay, hastily examined the neck of the victim, and clasping her hands, exclaimed, 'Oh, God! I have murdered my darling child!'

She fainted, and was restored with extreme difficulty. When she again lived, it was only to weep and sigh. She told me that that same evening William had teased her to let him wear a very valuable miniature that she possessed of your mother. This picture is gone, and was doubtless the temptation which urged the murderer to the deed. We have no trace of him at present, although our exertions to discover him are unremitted; but they will not restore my beloved William!

Come, dearest Victor; you alone can console Elizabeth. She weeps continually and accuses herself unjustly as the cause of his death; her words pierce my heart. We are all unhappy, but will not that be an additional motive for you, my son, to return and be our comforter? Your dear mother! Alas, Victor! I now say, Thank God she did not live to witness the cruel, miserable death of her youngest darling!

Come, Victor; not brooding thoughts of vengeance against the assassin, but with feelings of peace and gentleness, that will heal, instead of festering, the wounds of our minds. Enter the house of mourning, my friend, but with kindness and affection for those who love you, and not with hatred for your enemies.

Your affectionate and afflicted father,

ALPHONSE FRANKENSTEIN

Geneva, May 12th, 17–.

Clerval, who had watched my countenance as I read this letter, was surprised to observe the despair that succeeded to the joy I at first expressed on receiving news from my friends. I threw the letter on the table, and covered my face with my hands.

'My dear Frankenstein,' exclaimed Henry, when he perceived me weep with bitterness, 'are we always to be unhappy? My dear friend, what has happened?'

I motioned to him to take up the letter, while I walked up and down the room in the extremest agitation. Tears also gushed from the eyes of Clerval, as he read the account of my misfortune.

'I can offer you no consolation, my friend,' said he; 'your disaster is irreparable. What do you intend to do?'

'To go instantly to Geneva: come with me, Henry, to order the horses.'

During our walk Clerval endeavoured to say a few words of consolation; he could only express his heartfelt sympathy. 'Poor William!' said he. 'Dear lovely child, he now sleeps with his angel mother! Who that had seen him bright and joyous in his young beauty, but must weep over his untimely loss! To die so miserably; to feel the murderer's grasp! How much more a murderer, that could destroy such radiant innocence! Poor little fellow! one only consolation have we; his friends mourn and weep, but he is at rest. The pang is over, his sufferings are at an end forever. A sod covers his gentle form, and he knows no pain. He can no longer be a subject for pity; we must reserve that for his miserable survivors.'

Clerval spoke thus as we hurried through the streets; the words impressed themselves on my mind, and I remembered them afterwards in solitude. But now, as soon as the horses arrived, I hurried into a cabriolet and bade farewell to my friend.

My journey was very melancholy. At first I wished to hurry on, for I longed to console and sympathise with my loved and sorrowing friends; but when I drew near my native town, I slackened my progress. I could hardly sustain the multitude of feelings that crowded into my mind. I passed through scenes familiar to my youth, but which I had not seen for nearly six years. How altered every thing might be during that time! One sudden and desolating change had taken place; but a thousand little circumstances might have by degrees worked other alterations, which, although they were done more tranquilly, might not be the less decisive. Fear overcame me; I dared not advance, dreading a thousand nameless evils that made me tremble, although I was unable to define them.

I remained two days at Lausanne, in this painful state of mind. I contemplated the lake: the waters were placid; all around was calm; and the snowy mountains, 'the palaces of nature', were not changed. By degrees the calm and heavenly scene restored me, and I continued my journey towards Geneva.

The road ran by the side of the lake, which became narrower as I approached my native town. I discovered more distinctly the black sides of Jura, and the bright summit of Mont Blanc. I wept like a child. 'Dear mountains! My own beautiful lake! How do you welcome your wanderer? Your summits are clear; the sky and lake are blue and placid. Is this to prognosticate peace, or to mock at my unhappiness?'

I fear, my friend, that I shall render myself tedious by dwelling on these preliminary circumstances; but they were days of comparative happiness, and I think of them with pleasure. My country, my beloved country! who but a native can tell the delight I took in again beholding thy streams, thy mountains, and, more than all, thy lovely lake!

Yet, as I drew nearer home, grief and fear again overcame me. Night also closed around; and when I could hardly see the dark mountains, I felt still more gloomily. The picture appeared a vast and dim scene of evil, and I foresaw obscurely that I was destined to become the most wretched of human beings. Alas! I prophesied truly, and failed only in one single circumstance, that in all the misery I imagined and dreaded, I did not conceive the hundredth part of the anguish I was destined to endure.

It was completely dark when I arrived in the environs of Geneva; the gates of the town were already shut; and I was obliged to pass the night at Secheron, a village at the distance of half a league from the city. The sky was serene; and as I was unable to rest, I resolved to visit the spot where my poor William had been murdered. As I could not pass through the town, I was obliged to cross the lake in a boat to arrive at Plainpalais. During this short voyage I saw the lightnings playing on the summit of Mont Blanc in the most beautiful figures. The storm appeared to approach rapidly; and, on landing, I ascended a low hill, that I might observe its progress. It advanced; the heavens were clouded, and I soon felt the rain coming slowly in large drops, but its violence quickly increased.

I quitted my seat and walked on, although the darkness and storm increased every minute and the thunder burst with a terrific crash over my head. It was echoed from Salêve, the Juras, and the Alps of Savoy; vivid flashes of lightning dazzled my eyes, illuminating the lake, making it appear like a vast sheet of fire; then for an instant every thing seemed of a pitchy darkness, until the eye recovered itself from the preceding flash. The storm, as is often the case in Switzerland, appeared at once in various parts of the heavens. The most violent storm hung exactly north of the town, over that part of the lake which lies between the promontory of Belrive and the village of Copêt. Another storm enlightened Jura with faint flashes; and another darkened and sometimes disclosed the Môle, a peaked mountain to the east of the lake.

While I watched the tempest, so beautiful yet terrific, I wandered on with a hasty step. This noble war in the sky elevated my spirits; I clasped my hands and exclaimed aloud, 'William, dear angel! this is thy funeral, this thy dirge!' As I said these words, I perceived in the gloom a figure which stole from behind a clump of trees near me; I stood fixed, gazing intently: I could not be mistaken. A flash of lightning illuminated the object, and discovered its shape plainly to me; its gigantic stature, and the deformity of its aspect, more hideous than belongs to humanity, instantly informed me that it was the wretch, the filthy daemon to whom I had given life. What did he there? Could he be (I shuddered at the conception) the murderer of my brother? No sooner did that idea cross my imagination, than I became convinced of its truth; my teeth chattered, and I was forced to lean against a tree for support. The figure passed me quickly, and I lost it in the gloom. Nothing in human shape could have destroyed that fair child. *He* was the murderer! I could not doubt it. The mere presence of the idea was an irresistible proof of the fact. I thought of pursuing the devil; but it would have been in vain, for another flash discovered him to me hanging among the rocks of the nearly perpendicular ascent of Mount Salêve, a hill that bound Plainpalais on the south. He soon reached the summit, and disappeared.

I remained motionless. The thunder ceased, but the rain still continued, and the scene was enveloped in an impenetrable darkness. I revolved in my mind the events which I had until now sought to forget: the whole train of my progress towards the creation; the appearance of the work of my own hands alive at my bedside; its departure. Two years had now nearly elapsed since the night on which he first received life; and was this his first crime? Alas! I had turned loose into the world a depraved wretch, whose delight was in carnage and misery; had he not murdered my brother?

No one can conceive the anguish I suffered during the remainder of the night, which I spent, cold and wet, in the open air. But I did not feel the inconvenience of the weather; my imagination was busy in scenes of evil and despair. I considered the being whom I had cast among mankind, and endowed with the will and power to effect purposes of horror, such as the deed which he had now done, nearly in the light of my own vampire, my own spirit let loose from the grave, and forced to destroy all that was dear to me.

Day dawned; and I directed my steps towards the town. The gates were open, and I hastened to my father's house. My first thought was to discover what I knew of the murderer, and cause instant pursuit to be made. But I paused when I reflected on the story that I had to tell. A being whom I myself had formed, and endued with life, had met me at midnight among the precipices of an inaccessible mountain. I remembered also the nervous fever with which I had been seized just at the time that I dated my creation, and which would give an air of delirium to a tale otherwise so utterly improbable. I well knew that if any other had communicated such a relation to me, I should have looked upon it as the ravings of insanity. Besides, the strange nature of the animal would elude all pursuit, even if I were so far credited as to persuade my relatives to commence it. And then of what use would be pursuit? Who could arrest a creature capable of scaling the overhanging sides of Mont Salêve? These reflections determined me, and I resolved to remain silent.

It was about five in the morning when I entered my father's house. I told the servants not to disturb the family, and went into the library to attend their usual hour of rising.

Six years had elapsed, passed as a dream but for one indelible trace, and I stood in the same place where I had last embraced my father before my departure for Ingolstadt. Beloved and venerable parent! He still remained to me. I gazed on the picture of my mother which stood over the mantel-piece. It was an historical subject, painted at my father's desire, and represented Caroline Beaufort in an agony of despair, kneeling by the coffin of her dead father. Her garb was rustic, and her cheek pale; but there was an air of dignity and beauty, that hardly permitted the sentiment of pity. Below this picture was a miniature of William; and my tears flowed when I looked upon it. While I was thus engaged, Ernest entered: he had heard me arrive, and hastened to welcome me. He expressed a sorrowful delight to see me. 'Welcome, my dearest Victor,' said he. 'Ah! I wish you had come three months ago, and then you would have found us all joyous and delighted. You come to us now to share a misery which nothing can alleviate; yet your presence will, I hope, revive our father, who seems sinking under his misfortune; and your persuasions will induce poor Elizabeth to cease her vain and tormenting self-accusations. – Poor William! he was our darling and our pride!'

Tears, unrestrained, fell from my brother's eyes; a sense of mortal agony crept over my frame. Before, I had only imagined the wretchedness of my desolated home; the reality came on me as a new and a not less terrible disaster. I tried to calm Ernest; I enquired more minutely concerning my father, and her I named my cousin.

'She most of all,' said Ernest, 'requires consolation; she accused herself of having caused the death of my brother, and that made her very wretched. But since the murderer has been discovered –'

'The murderer discovered! Good God! how can that be? who could attempt to pursue him? It is impossible; one might as well try to overtake the winds or confine a mountain-stream with a straw. I saw him too; he was free last night!'

'I do not know what you mean,' replied my brother, in accents of wonder, 'but to us the discovery we have made completes our misery. No one would believe it at first; and even now Elizabeth will not be convinced, notwithstanding all the evidence. Indeed, who would credit that Justine Moritz, who was so amiable and fond of all the family, could suddenly become capable of so frightful, so appalling a crime?'

'Justine Moritz! Poor, poor girl, is she the accused? But it is wrongfully; every one knows that; no one believes it, surely, Ernest?'

'No one did at first; but several circumstances came out that have almost forced conviction upon us; and her own behaviour has been so confused as to add to the evidence of facts a weight that, I fear, leaves no hope for doubt. But she will be tried today, and you will then hear all.'

He related that, the morning on which the murder of poor William had been discovered, Justine had been taken ill, and confined to her bed for several days. During this interval one of the servants, happening to examine the apparel she had worn on the night of the murder, had discovered in her pocket the picture of my mother, which had been judged to be the temptation of the murderer. The servant instantly showed it to one of the others, who, without saying a word to any of the family, went to a magistrate; and, upon their deposition, Justine was apprehended. On being charged with the fact, the poor girl confirmed the suspicion in a great measure by her extreme confusion of manner.

This was a strange tale, but it did not shake my faith, and I replied earnestly, 'You are all mistaken; I know the murderer. Justine, poor, good Justine, is innocent.'

At that instant my father entered. I saw unhappiness deeply impressed on his countenance, but he endeavoured to welcome me cheerfully; and after we had exchanged our mournful greeting, would have introduced some other topic than that of our disaster, had not Ernest exclaimed, 'Good God, Papa! Victor says that he knows who was the murderer of poor William.'

'We do also, unfortunately,' replied my father; 'for indeed I had rather have been forever ignorant than have discovered so much depravity and ingratitude in one I valued so highly.'

'My dear father, you are mistaken; Justine is innocent.'

'If she is, God forbid that she should suffer as guilty. She is to be tried today, and I hope, I sincerely hope, that she will be acquitted.'

This speech calmed me. I was firmly convinced in my own mind that Justine, and indeed every human being, was guiltless of this murder. I had no fear, therefore, that any circumstantial evidence could be brought forward strong enough to convict her. My tale was not one to announce publicly; its astounding horror would be looked upon as madness by the vulgar. Did any one indeed exist, except I, the creator, who would believe, unless his senses convinced him, in the existence of the living monument of presumption and rash ignorance which I had let loose upon the world?

We were soon joined by Elizabeth. Time had altered her since I last beheld her; it had endowed her with loveliness surpassing the beauty of her childish years. There was the same candour, the same vivacity, but it was allied to an expression more full of sensibility and intellect. She welcomed me with the greatest affection. 'Your arrival, my dear cousin,' said she, 'fills me with hope. You perhaps will find some means to justify my poor guiltless Justine. Alas! who is safe, if she be convicted of crime? I rely on her innocence as certainly as I do upon my own. Our misfortune is doubly hard to us; we have not only lost that lovely darling boy, but this poor girl, whom I sincerely love, is to be torn away by even a worse fate. If she is condemned, I never shall know joy more. But she will not, I am sure she will not; and then I shall be happy again, even after the sad death of my little William.'

'She is innocent, my Elizabeth,' said I, 'and that shall be proved; fear nothing, but let your spirits be cheered by the assurance of her acquittal.'

'How kind and generous you are! every one else believes in her guilt, and that made me wretched, for I knew that it was impossible: and to see every one else prejudiced in so deadly a manner rendered me hopeless and despairing.' She wept.

'Dearest niece,' said my father, 'dry your tears. If she is, as you believe, innocent, rely on the justice of our laws, and the activity with which I shall prevent the slightest shadow of partiality.'

CHAPTER 8

We passed a few sad hours, until eleven o'clock, when the trial was to commence. My father and the rest of the family being obliged to attend as witnesses, I accompanied them to the court. During the whole of this wretched mockery of justice I suffered living torture. It was to be decided, whether the result of my curiosity and lawless devices would cause the death of my fellow-beings: one a smiling babe full of innocence and joy; the other far more dreadfully murdered, with every aggravation of infamy that could make the murder memorable in horror. Justine also was a girl of merit, and possessed qualities which promised to render her life happy; now all was to be obliterated in an ignominious grave, and I the cause! A thousand times rather would I have confessed myself guilty of the crime ascribed to Justine; but I was absent when it was committed, and such a declaration would have been considered as the ravings of a madman, and would not have exculpated her who suffered through me.

The appearance of Justine was calm. She was dressed in mourning; and her countenance, always engaging, was rendered, by the solemnity of her feelings, exquisitely beautiful. Yet she appeared confident in innocence and did not tremble, although gazed on and execrated by thousands; for all the kindness which her beauty might otherwise have excited was obliterated in the minds of the spectators by the imagination of the enormity she was supposed to have committed. She was tranquil, yet her tranquillity was evidently constrained; and as her confusion had before been adduced as a proof of her guilt, she worked up her mind to an appearance of courage. When she entered the court she threw her eyes round it, and quickly discovered where we were seated. A tear seemed to dim her eye when she saw us; but she quickly recovered herself, and a look of sorrowful affection seemed to attest her utter guiltlessness.

The trial began; and after the advocate against her had stated the charge, several witnesses were called. Several strange facts combined against her, which might have staggered any one who had not such proof of her innocence as I had. She had been out the whole of the night on which the murder had been committed, and towards morning had been perceived by a market-woman not far from the spot where the body of the murdered child had been afterwards found. The woman asked her what she did there; but she looked very strangely, and only returned a confused and unintelligible answer. She returned to the house about eight o'clock; and when one enquired where she had passed the night, she replied that she had been looking for the child and demanded earnestly if any thing had been heard concerning him. When shown the body, she fell into violent hysterics, and kept her bed for several days. The picture was then produced, which the servant had found in her pocket; and when Elizabeth, in a faltering voice, proved that it was the same which, an hour before the child had been missed, she had placed round his neck, a murmur of horror and indignation filled the court.

Justine was called on for her defence. As the trial proceeded, her countenance had altered. Surprise, horror, and misery were strongly expressed. Sometimes she struggled with her tears; but when she was desired to plead, she collected her powers, and spoke in an audible although variable voice.

'God knows,' she said, 'how entirely I am innocent. But I do not pretend that my protestations should acquit me: I rest my innocence on a plain and simple explanation of the facts which have been adduced against me; and I hope the character I have always borne will incline my judges to a favourable interpretation, where any circumstance appears doubtful or suspicious.'

She then related that, by the permission of Elizabeth, she had passed the evening of the night on which the murder had been committed at the house of an aunt at Chêne, a village situated at about a league from Geneva. On her return, at about nine o'clock, she met a man who asked her if she had seen any thing of the child who was lost. She was alarmed by this account, and passed several hours in looking for him, when the gates of Geneva were shut, and she was forced to remain several hours of the night in a barn belonging to a cottage, being unwilling to call up the inhabitants, to whom she was well known. Most of the night she spent here watching; towards morning she believed that she slept for a few minutes; some steps disturbed her, and she awoke. It was dawn, and she quitted her asylum, that she might again endeavour to find my brother. If she had gone near the spot where his body lay, it was without her knowledge. That she had been bewildered when questioned by the market-woman was not surprising, since she had passed a sleepless night and the fate of poor William was yet uncertain. Concerning the picture she could give no account.

'I know,' continued the unhappy victim, 'how heavily and fatally this one circumstance weighs against me, but I have no power of explaining it; and when I have expressed my utter ignorance, I am only left to conjecture concerning the probabilities by which it might have been placed in my pocket. But here also I am checked. I believe that I have no enemy on earth, and none surely would have been so wicked as to destroy me wantonly. Did the murderer place it there? I know of no opportunity afforded him for so doing; or, if I had, why should he have stolen the jewel, to part with it again so soon?

'I commit my cause to the justice of my judges, yet I see no room for hope. I beg permission to have a few witnesses examined concerning my character; and if their testimony shall not overweigh my supposed guilt, I must be condemned, although I would pledge my salvation on my innocence.'

Several witnesses were called who had known her for many years, and they spoke well of her; but fear and hatred of the crime of which they supposed her guilty rendered them timorous, and unwilling to come forward. Elizabeth saw even this last resource, her excellent dispositions and irreproachable conduct, about to fail the accused, when, although violently agitated, she desired permission to address the court.

'I am,' said she, 'the cousin of the unhappy child who was murdered, or rather his sister, for I was educated by and have lived with his parents ever since and even long before, his birth. It may therefore be judged indecent in me to come forward on this occasion; but when I see a fellow creature about to perish through the cowardice of her pretended friends, I wish to be allowed to speak, that I may say what I know of her character. I am well acquainted with the accused. I have lived in the same house with her, at one time for five, and at another for nearly two years. During all that period she appeared to me the most amiable and benevolent of human creatures. She nursed Madame Frankenstein, my aunt, in her last illness, with the greatest affection and care, and afterwards attended her own mother during a tedious illness, in a manner that excited the admiration of all who knew her; after which she again lived in my uncle's house, where she was beloved by all the family. She was warmly attached to the child who is now dead, and acted towards him like a most affectionate mother.

For my own part, I do not hesitate to say that, notwithstanding all the evidence produced against her, I believe and rely on her perfect innocence. She had no temptation for such an action: as to the bauble on which the chief proof rests, if she had earnestly desired it, I should have willingly given it to her; so much do I esteem and value her.'

A murmur of approbation followed Elizabeth's simple and powerful appeal; but it was excited by her generous interference, and not in favour of poor Justine, on whom the public indignation was turned with renewed violence, charging her with the blackest ingratitude. She herself wept as Elizabeth spoke, but she did not answer. My own agitation and anguish was extreme during the whole trial. I believed in her innocence; I knew it. Could the daemon who had (I did not for a minute doubt) murdered my brother also in his hellish sport have betrayed the innocent to death and ignominy? I could not sustain the horror of my situation, and when I perceived that the popular voice and the countenances of the judges had already condemned my unhappy victim, I rushed out of the court in agony. The tortures of the accused did not equal mine; she was sustained by innocence, but the fangs of remorse tore my bosom and would not forego their hold.

I passed a night of unmingled wretchedness. In the morning I went to the court; my lips and throat were parched. I dared not ask the fatal question; but I was known, and the officer guessed the cause of my visit. The ballots had been thrown; they were all black, and Justine was condemned.

I cannot pretend to describe what I then felt. I had before experienced sensations of horror; and I have endeavoured to bestow upon them adequate expressions, but words cannot convey an idea of the heart-sickening despair that I then endured. The person to whom I addressed myself added, that Justine had already confessed her guilt. 'That evidence,' he observed, 'was hardly required in so glaring a case, but I am glad of it; and, indeed, none of our judges like to condemn a criminal upon circumstantial evidence, be it ever so decisive.'

This was strange and unexpected intelligence; what could it mean? Had my eyes deceived me? And was I really as mad as the whole world would believe me to be, if I disclosed the object of my suspicions? I hastened to return home, and Elizabeth eagerly demanded the result.

'My cousin,' replied I, 'it is decided as you may have expected; all judges had rather that ten innocent should suffer than that one guilty should escape. But she has confessed.'

This was a dire blow to poor Elizabeth, who had relied with firmness upon Justine's innocence. 'Alas!' said she. 'How shall I ever again believe in human goodness? Justine, whom I loved and esteemed as my sister, how could she put on those smiles of innocence only to betray? her mild eyes seemed incapable of any severity or guile, and yet she has committed a murder.'

Soon after we heard that the poor victim had expressed a desire to see my cousin. My father wished her not to go, but said that he left it to her own judgment and feelings to decide. 'Yes,' said Elizabeth, 'I will go, although she is guilty; and you, Victor, shall accompany me: I cannot go alone.' The idea of this visit was torture to me, yet I could not refuse.

We entered the gloomy prison chamber and beheld Justine sitting on some straw at the farther end; her hands were manacled, and her head rested on her knees. She rose on seeing us enter; and when we were left alone with her, she threw herself at the feet of Elizabeth, weeping bitterly. My cousin wept also.

'Oh, Justine!' said she. 'Why did you rob me of my last consolation? I relied on your innocence, and although I was then very wretched, I was not so miserable as I am now.'

'And do you also believe that I am so very, very wicked? Do you also join with my enemies to crush me, to condemn me as a murderer?' Her voice was suffocated with sobs.

'Rise, my poor girl,' said Elizabeth; 'why do you kneel, if you are innocent? I am not one of your enemies; I believed you guiltless, notwithstanding every evidence, until I heard that you had yourself declared your guilt. That report, you say, is false; and be assured, dear Justine, that nothing can shake my confidence in you for a moment, but your own confession.'

'I did confess; but I confessed a lie. I confessed, that I might obtain absolution; but now that falsehood lies heavier at my heart than all my other sins. The God of heaven forgive me! Ever since I was condemned, my confessor has besieged me; he threatened and menaced, until I almost began to think that I was the monster that he said I was. He threatened excommunication and hell fire in my last moments if I continued obdurate.

Dear lady, I had none to support me; all looked on me as a wretch doomed to ignominy and perdition. What could I do? In an evil hour I subscribed to a lie; and now only am I truly miserable.'

She paused, weeping, and then continued – 'I thought with horror, my sweet lady, that you should believe your Justine, whom your blessed aunt had so highly honoured and whom you loved, was a creature capable of a crime which none but the devil himself could have perpetrated. Dear William! Dearest blessed child! I soon shall see you again in heaven, where we shall all be happy; and that consoles me, going as I am to suffer ignominy and death.'

'Oh, Justine! Forgive me for having for one moment distrusted you. Why did you confess? But do not mourn, dear girl. Do not fear. I will proclaim, I will prove your innocence. I will melt the stony hearts of your enemies by my tears and prayers. You shall not die! You, my playfellow, my companion, my sister, perish on the scaffold! No! No! I never could survive so horrible a misfortune.'

Justine shook her head mournfully. 'I do not fear to die,' she said; 'that pang is past. God raises my weakness and gives me courage to endure the worst. I leave a sad and bitter world; and if you remember me and think of me as of one unjustly condemned, I am resigned to the fate awaiting me. Learn from me, dear lady, to submit in patience to the will of heaven!'

During this conversation I had retired to the corner of the prison room, where I could conceal the horrid anguish that possessed me. Despair! Who dared talk of that? The poor victim, who on the morrow was to pass the awful boundary between life and death, felt not, as I did, such deep and bitter agony. I gnashed my teeth and ground them together, uttering a groan that came from my inmost soul. Justine started. When she saw who it was, she approached me and said, 'Dear sir, you are very kind to visit me; you, I hope, do not believe that I am guilty?'

I could not answer. 'No, Justine,' said Elizabeth; 'he is more convinced of your innocence than I was; for even when he heard that you had confessed, he did not credit it.'

'I truly thank him. In these last moments I feel the sincerest gratitude towards those who think of me with kindness. How sweet is the affection of others to such a wretch as I am! It removes more than half my misfortune; and I feel as if I could die in peace, now that my innocence is acknowledged by you, dear lady, and your cousin.'

Thus the poor sufferer tried to comfort others and herself. She indeed gained the resignation she desired. But I, the true murderer, felt the never-dying worm alive in my bosom, which allowed of no hope or consolation. Elizabeth also wept and was unhappy; but hers also was the misery of innocence, which, like a cloud that passes over the fair moon, for a while hides but cannot tarnish its brightness. Anguish and despair had penetrated into the core of my heart; I bore a hell within me which nothing could extinguish. We stayed several hours with Justine; and it was with great difficulty that Elizabeth could tear herself away. 'I wish,' cried she, 'that I were to die with you; I cannot live in this world of misery.'

Justine assumed an air of cheerfulness, while she with difficulty repressed her bitter tears. She embraced Elizabeth and said, in a voice of half-suppressed emotion, 'Farewell, sweet lady, dearest Elizabeth, my beloved and only friend; may Heaven, in its bounty, bless and preserve you; may this be the last misfortune that you will ever suffer! Live, and be happy, and make others so.'

And on the morrow Justine died. Elizabeth's heart-rending eloquence failed to move the judges from their settled conviction in the criminality of the saintly sufferer. My passionate and indignant appeals were lost upon them. And when I received their cold answers and heard the harsh, unfeeling reasoning of these men, my purposed avowal died away on my lips. Thus I might proclaim myself a madman, but not revoke the sentence passed upon my wretched victim. She perished on the scaffold as a murderess!

From the tortures of my own heart, I turned to contemplate the deep and voiceless grief of my Elizabeth. This also was my doing! And my father's woe, and the desolation of that late so smiling home – all was the work of my thrice-accursed hands! Ye weep, unhappy ones; but these are not your last tears! Again shall you raise the funeral wail, and the sound of your lamentations shall again and again be heard! Frankenstein, your son, your kinsman, your early, much-loved friend; he who would spend each vital drop of blood for your sakes – who has no thought nor sense of joy, except as it is mirrored also in your dear countenances – who would fill the air with blessings and spend his life in serving you – he bids you weep – to shed countless tears; happy beyond his hopes, if thus inexorable fate be satisfied, and if the destruction pause before the peace of the grave have succeeded to your sad torments!

Thus spoke my prophetic soul, as, torn by remorse, horror, and despair, I beheld those I loved spend vain sorrow upon the graves of William and Justine, the first hapless victims to my unhallowed arts.

END OF VOLUME ONE

Volume II

CHAPTER 1

Nothing is more painful to the human mind than, after the feelings have been worked up by a quick succession of events, the dead calmness of inaction and certainty which follows and deprives the soul both of hope and fear. Justine died; she rested; and I was alive. The blood flowed freely in my veins, but a weight of despair and remorse pressed on my heart, which nothing could remove. Sleep fled from my eyes; I wandered like an evil spirit, for I had committed deeds of mischief beyond description horrible, and more, much more (I persuaded myself) was yet behind. Yet my heart overflowed with kindness, and the love of virtue. I had begun life with benevolent intentions, and thirsted for the moment when I should put them in practice and make myself useful to my fellow beings. Now all was blasted: instead of that serenity of conscience which allowed me to look back upon the past with self-satisfaction, and from thence to gather promise of new hopes, I was seized by remorse and the sense of guilt, which hurried me away to a hell of intense tortures, such as no language can describe.

This state of mind preyed upon my health, which had perhaps never entirely recovered from the first shock it had sustained. I shunned the face of man; all sound of joy or complacency was torture to me; solitude was my only consolation – deep, dark, deathlike solitude.

My father observed with pain the alteration perceptible in my disposition and habits, and endeavoured by arguments, deduced from the feelings of his serene conscience and guiltless life, to inspire me with fortitude, and awaken in me the courage to dispel the dark cloud which brooded over me. 'Do you think, Victor,' said he, 'that I do not suffer also? No one could love a child more than I loved your brother' – tears came into his eyes as he spoke – 'but is it not a duty to the survivors that we should refrain from augmenting their unhappiness by an appearance of immoderate grief? It is also a duty owed to yourself; for excessive sorrow prevents improvement or enjoyment, or even the discharge of daily usefulness, without which no man is fit for society.'

This advice, although good, was totally inapplicable to my case; I should have been the first to hide my grief and console my friends, if remorse had not mingled its bitterness, and terror its alarm, with my other sensations. Now I could only answer my father with a look of despair, and endeavour to hide myself from his view.

About this time we retired to our house at Belrive. This change was particularly agreeable to me. The shutting of the gates regularly at ten o'clock and the impossibility of remaining on the lake after that hour, had rendered our residence within the walls of Geneva very irksome to me. I was now free. Often, after the rest of the family had retired for the night, I took the boat and passed many hours upon the water. Sometimes, with my sails set, I was carried by the wind; and sometimes, after rowing into the middle of the lake, I left the boat to pursue its own course, and gave way to my own miserable reflections. I was often tempted, when all was at peace around me, and I the only unquiet thing that wandered restless in a scene so beautiful and heavenly – if I except some bat, or the frogs, whose harsh and inter-rupted croaking was heard only when I approached the shore – often, I say, I was tempted to plunge into the silent lake, that the waters might close over me and my calamities forever. But I was restrained, when I thought of the heroic and suffering Elizabeth, whom I tenderly loved, and whose existence was bound up in mine. I thought also of my father and surviving brother: should I by my base desertion leave them exposed and unprotected to the malice of the fiend whom I had let loose among them?

At these moments I wept bitterly, and wished that peace would revisit my mind only that I might afford them consolation and happiness. But that could not be. Remorse extinguished every hope. I had been the author of unalterable evils, and I lived in daily fear lest the monster whom I had created should perpetrate some new wickedness. I had an obscure feeling that all was not over, and that he would still commit some signal crime, which by its enormity should almost efface the recollection of the past. There was always scope for fear, so long as anything I loved remained behind. My abhorrence of this fiend cannot be conceived. When I thought of him I gnashed my teeth, my eyes became inflamed, and I ardently wished to extinguish that life which I had so thoughtlessly bestowed. When I reflected on his crimes and malice, my hatred and revenge burst all bounds of moderation. I would have made a pilgrimage to the highest peak of the Andes, could I, when there, have precipitated him to their base. I wished to see him again, that I might wreak the utmost extent of abhorrence on his head, and avenge the deaths of William and Justine.

Our house was the house of mourning. My father's health was deeply shaken by the horror of the recent events. Elizabeth was sad and desponding; she no longer took delight in her ordinary occupations; all pleasure seemed to her sacrilege toward the dead; eternal woe and tears she then thought was the just tribute she should pay to innocence so blasted and destroyed. She was no longer that happy creature who in earlier youth wandered with me on the banks of the lake, and talked with ecstasy of our future prospects. The first of these sorrows which are sent to wean us from the earth, had visited her, and its dimming influence quenched her dearest smiles.

'When I reflect, my dear cousin,' said she, 'on the miserable death of Justine Moritz, I no longer see the world and its works as they before appeared to me. Before, I looked upon the accounts of vice and injustice, that I read in books or heard from others as tales of ancient days or imaginary evils; at least they were remote and more familiar to reason than to the imagination; but now misery has come home, and men appear to me as monsters thirsting for each other's blood. Yet I am certainly unjust. Every body believed that poor girl to be guilty; and if she could have committed the crime for which she suffered, assuredly she would have been the most depraved of human creatures. For the sake of a few jewels, to have murdered the son of her benefactor and friend, a child whom she had nursed from its birth, and appeared to love as if it had been her own! I could not consent to the death of any human being; but certainly I should have thought such a creature unfit to remain in the society of men. But she was innocent. I know, I feel, she was innocent; you are of the same opinion, and that confirms me. Alas! Victor, when falsehood can look so like the truth, who can assure themselves of certain happiness? I feel as if I were walking on the edge of a precipice, towards which thousands are crowding, and endeavouring to plunge me into the abyss. William and Justine were assassinated, and the murderer escapes: he walks about the world free, and perhaps respected. But even if I were condemned to suffer on the scaffold for the same crimes, I would not change places with such a wretch.'

I listened to this discourse with the extremest agony. I, not in deed, but in effect, was the true murderer. Elizabeth read my anguish in my countenance, and kindly taking my hand, said, 'My dearest friend, you must calm yourself. These events have affected me, God knows how deeply; but I am not so wretched as you are. There is an expression of despair, and sometimes of revenge, in your countenance that makes me tremble. Dear Victor, banish these dark passions. Remember the friends around you, who centre all their hopes in you. Have we lost the power of rendering you happy? Ah! while we love – while we are true to each other, here in this land of peace and beauty, your native country, we may reap every tranquil blessing – what can disturb our peace?'

And could not such words from her whom I fondly prized before every other gift of fortune, suffice to chase away the fiend that lurked in my heart? Even as she spoke I drew near to her, as if in terror; lest at that very moment the destroyer had been near to rob me of her.

Thus not the tenderness of friendship, nor the beauty of earth, nor of heaven, could redeem my soul from woe: the very accents of love were ineffectual. I was encompassed by a cloud which no beneficial influence could penetrate. The wounded deer dragging its fainting limbs to some untrodden brake, there to gaze upon the arrow which had pierced it, and to die – was but a type of me.

Sometimes I could cope with the sullen despair that overwhelmed me: but sometimes the whirlwind passions of my soul drove me to seek, by bodily exercise and by change of place, some relief from my intolerable sensations. It was during an access of this kind that I suddenly left my home, and bending my steps towards the near Alpine valleys, sought in the magnificence, the eternity of such scenes, to forget myself and my ephemeral, because human, sorrows. My wanderings were directed towards the valley of Chamounix. I had visited it frequently during my boyhood. Six years had passed since then: *I* was a wreck – but nought had changed in those savage and enduring scenes.

I performed the first part of my journey on horseback. I afterwards hired a mule, as the more sure-footed and least liable to receive injury on these rugged roads. The weather was fine: it was about the middle of the month of August, nearly two months after the death of Justine; that miserable epoch from which I dated all my woe. The weight upon my spirit was sensibly lightened as I plunged yet deeper in the ravine of Arve. The immense mountains and precipices that overhung me on every side – the sound of the river raging among the rocks, and the dashing of the waterfalls around, spoke of a power mighty as Omnipotence – and I ceased to fear, or to bend before any being less almighty than that which had created and ruled the elements, here displayed in their most terrific guise. Still, as I ascended higher, the valley assumed a more magnificent and astonishing character. Ruined castles hanging on the precipices of piny mountains; the impetuous Arve, and cottages every here and there peeping forth from among the trees, formed a scene of singular beauty. But it was augmented and rendered sublime by the mighty Alps, whose white and shining pyramids and domes towered above all, as belonging to another earth, the habitations of another race of beings.

I passed the bridge of Pélissier, where the ravine, which the river forms, opened before me, and I began to ascend the mountain that overhangs it. Soon after I entered the valley of Chamounix. This valley is more wonderful and sublime, but not so beautiful and picturesque, as that of Servox, through which I had just passed. The high and snowy mountains were its immediate boundaries; but I saw no more ruined castles and fertile fields. Immense glaciers approached the road; I heard the rumbling thunder of the falling avalanche and marked the smoke of its passage. Mont Blanc, the supreme and magnificent Mont Blanc, raised itself from the surrounding *aiguilles*, and its tremendous *dôme* overlooked the valley.

A tingling long-lost sense of pleasure often came across me during this journey. Some turn in the road, some new object suddenly perceived and recognised, reminded me of days gone by, and were associated with the light-hearted gaiety of boyhood. The very winds whispered in soothing accents, and maternal nature bade me weep no more. Then again the kindly influence ceased to act – I found myself fettered again to grief and indulging in all the misery of reflection. Then I spurred on my animal, striving so to forget the world, my fears, and more than all, myself – or, in a more desperate fashion, I alighted and threw myself on the grass, weighed down by horror and despair.

At length I arrived at the village of Chamounix. Exhaustion succeeded to the extreme fatigue both of body and of mind which I had endured. For a short space of time I remained at the window, watching the pallid lightnings that played above Mont Blanc, and listening to the rushing of the Arve, which pursued its noisy way beneath. The same lulling sounds acted as a lullaby to my too keen sensations: when I placed my head upon my pillow, sleep crept over me; I felt it as it came and blest the giver of oblivion.

CHAPTER 2

I spent the following day roaming through the valley. I stood beside the sources of the Arveiron, which take their rise in a glacier, that with slow pace is advancing down from the summit of the hills, to barricade the valley. The abrupt sides of vast mountains were before me; the icy wall of the glacier overhung me; a few shattered pines were scattered around; and the solemn silence of this glorious presence-chamber of imperial Nature was broken only by the brawling waves or the fall of some vast fragment, the thunder sound of the avalanche or the cracking, reverberated along the mountains, of the accumulated ice, which, through the silent working of immutable laws, was ever and anon rent and torn, as if it had been but a plaything in their hands. These sublime and magnificent scenes afforded me the greatest consolation that I was capable of receiving. They elevated me from all littleness of feeling; and although they did not remove my grief, they subdued and tranquillised it. In some degree, also, they diverted my mind from the thoughts over which it had brooded for the last month. I retired to rest at night; my slumbers, as it were, waited on and ministered to by the assemblance of grand shapes which I had contemplated during the day. They congregated round me; the unstained snowy mountain-top, the glittering pinnacle, the pine woods, and ragged bare ravine, the eagle, soaring amidst the clouds – they all gathered round me and bade me be at peace.

Where had they fled when the next morning I awoke? All of soul-inspiriting fled with sleep, and dark melancholy clouded every thought. The rain was pouring in torrents, and thick mists hid the summits of the mountains, so that I even saw not the faces of those mighty friends. Still I would penetrate their misty veil and seek them in their cloudy retreats. What were rain and storm to me? My mule was brought to the door, and I resolved to ascend to the summit of Montanvert. I remembered the effect that the view of the tremendous and ever-moving glacier had produced upon my mind when I first saw it. It had then filled me with a sublime ecstasy, that gave wings to the soul, and allowed it to soar from the obscure world to light and joy. The sight of the awful and majestic in nature had indeed always the effect of solemnising my mind and causing me to forget the passing cares of life. I determined to go without a guide, for I was well acquainted with the path, and the presence of another would destroy the solitary grandeur of the scene.

The ascent is precipitous, but the path is cut into continual and short windings, which enable you to surmount the perpendicularity of the mountain. It is a scene terrifically desolate. In a thousand spots the traces of the winter avalanche may be perceived, where trees lie broken and strewed on the ground; some entirely destroyed, others bent, leaning upon the jutting rocks of the mountain or transversely upon other trees. The path, as you ascend higher, is intersected by ravines of snow, down which stones continually roll from above; one of them is particularly dangerous, as the slightest sound, such as even speaking in a loud voice, produces a concussion of air sufficient to draw destruction upon the head of the speaker. The pines are not tall or luxuriant, but they are sombre and add an air of severity to the scene. I looked on the valley beneath; vast mists were rising from the rivers which ran through it and curling in thick wreaths around the opposite mountains, whose summits were hid in the uniform clouds, while rain poured from the dark sky, and added to the melancholy impression I received from the objects around me. Alas! why does man boast of sensibilities superior to those apparent in the brute; it only renders them more necessary beings. If our impulses were confined to hunger, thirst, and desire, we might be nearly free; but now we are moved by every wind that blows and a chance word or scene that that word may convey to us.

> We rest; a dream has power to poison sleep.
>   We rise; one wand'ring thought pollutes the day.
> We feel, conceive, or reason; laugh or weep,
>   Embrace fond woe, or cast our cares away;
> It is the same: for, be it joy or sorrow,
>   The path of its departure still is free.
> Man's yesterday may ne'er be like his morrow;
>   Nought may endure but mutability!

It was nearly noon when I arrived at the top of the ascent. For some time I sat upon the rock that overlooks the sea of ice. A mist covered both that and the surrounding mountains. Presently a breeze dissipated the cloud, and I descended upon the glacier. The surface is very uneven, rising like the waves of a troubled sea, descending low, and interspersed by rifts that sink deep. The field of ice is almost a league in width, but I spent nearly two hours in crossing it. The opposite mountain is a bare perpendicular rock. From the side where I now stood Montanvert was exactly opposite, at the distance of a league; and above it rose Mont Blanc, in awful majesty. I remained in a recess of the rock, gazing on this wonderful and stupendous scene. The sea, or rather the vast river of ice, wound among its dependent mountains, whose aerial summits hung over its recesses. Their icy and glittering peaks shone in the sunlight over the clouds. My heart, which was before sorrowful, now swelled with something like joy; I exclaimed – 'Wandering spirits, if indeed ye wander, and do not rest in your narrow beds, allow me this faint happiness, or take me, as your companion, away from the joys of life.'

As I said this, I suddenly beheld the figure of a man, at some distance, advancing towards me with superhuman speed. He bounded over the crevices in the ice, among which I had walked with caution; his stature, also, as he approached, seemed to exceed that of man. I was troubled: a mist came over my eyes, and I felt a faintness seize me; but I was quickly restored by the cold gale of the mountains. I perceived, as the shape came nearer (sight tremendous and abhorred!) that it was the wretch whom I had created. I trembled with rage and horror, resolving to wait his approach, and then close with him in mortal combat. He approached; his countenance bespoke bitter anguish, combined with disdain and malignity, while its unearthly ugliness rendered it almost too horrible for human eyes. But I scarcely observed this; rage and hatred had at first deprived me of utterance, and I recovered only to overwhelm him with words expressive of furious detestation and contempt.

'Devil,' I exclaimed, 'do you dare approach me? and do not you fear the fierce vengeance of my arm wreaked on your miserable head? Begone, vile insect! or rather, stay, that I may trample you to dust! and, oh! that I could, with the extinction of your miserable existence, restore those victims whom you have so diabolically murdered!'

'I expected this reception,' said the daemon. 'All men hate the wretched; how, then, must I be hated, who am miserable beyond all living things! Yet you, my creator, detest and spurn me, thy creature, to whom thou art bound by ties only dissoluble by the annihilation of one of us. You purpose to kill me. How dare you sport thus with life? Do your duty towards me, and I will do mine towards you and the rest of mankind. If you will comply with my conditions, I will leave them and you at peace; but if you refuse, I will glut the maw of death, until it be satiated with the blood of your remaining friends.'

'Abhorred monster! fiend that thou art! the tortures of hell are too mild a vengeance for thy crimes. Wretched devil! you reproach me with your creation; come on, then, that I may extinguish the spark which I so negligently bestowed.'

My rage was without bounds; I sprang on him, impelled by all the feelings which can arm one being against the existence of another.

He easily eluded me, and said –

'Be calm! I intreat you to hear me, before you give vent to your hatred on my devoted head. Have I not suffered enough, that you seek to increase my misery? Life, although it may only be an accumulation of anguish, is dear to me, and I will defend it. Remember, thou hast made me more powerful than thyself; my height is superior to thine, my joints more supple. But I will not be tempted to set myself in opposition to thee. I am thy creature, and I will be even mild and docile to my natural lord and king, if thou wilt also perform thy part, the which thou owest me. Oh, Frankenstein, be not equitable to every other and trample upon me alone, to whom thy justice, and even thy clemency and affection, is most due. Remember, that I am thy creature; I ought to be thy Adam, but I am rather the fallen angel, whom thou drivest from joy for no misdeed. Everywhere I see bliss, from which I alone am irrevocably excluded. I was benevolent and good; misery made me a fiend. Make me happy, and I shall again be virtuous.'

'Begone! I will not hear you. There can be no community between you and me; we are enemies. Begone, or let us try our strength in a fight in which one must fall.'

'How can I move thee? Will no intreaties cause thee to turn a favourable eye upon thy creature, who implores thy goodness and compassion? Believe me, Frankenstein: I was benevolent; my soul glowed with love and humanity; but am I not alone, miserably alone? You, my creator, abhor me; what hope can I gather from your fellow-creatures, who owe me nothing? they spurn and hate me. The desert mountains and dreary glaciers are my refuge. I have wandered here many days; the caves of ice, which I only do not fear, are a dwelling to me, and the only one which man does not grudge. These bleak skies I hail, for they are kinder to me than your fellow beings. If the multitude of mankind knew of my existence, they would do as you do, and arm themselves for my destruction. Shall I not then hate them who abhor me? I will keep no terms with my enemies. I am miserable, and they shall share my wretchedness. Yet it is in your power to recompense me, and deliver them from an evil which it only remains for you to make so great, that not only you and your family, but thousands of others, shall be swallowed up in the whirlwinds of its rage. Let your compassion be moved, and do not disdain me. Listen to my tale: when you have heard that, abandon or commiserate me, as you shall judge that I deserve. But hear me. The guilty are allowed, by human laws, bloody as they are, to speak in their own defence before they are condemned. Listen to me, Frankenstein. You accuse me of murder, and yet you would, with a satisfied conscience, destroy your own creature. Oh, praise the eternal justice of man! Yet I ask you not to spare me: listen to me; and then, if you can, and if you will, destroy the work of your hands.'

'Why do you call to my remembrance,' I rejoined, 'circumstances, of which I shudder to reflect, that I have been the miserable origin and author? Cursed be the day, abhorred devil, in which you first saw light! Cursed (although I curse myself) be the hands that formed you! You have made me wretched beyond expression. You have left me no power to consider whether I am just to you, or not. Begone! relieve me from the sight of your detested form.'

'Thus I relieve thee, my creator,' he said, and placed his hated hands before my eyes, which I flung from me with violence; 'thus I take from thee a sight which you abhor. Still thou canst listen to me and grant me thy compassion. By the virtues that I once possessed, I demand this from you. Hear my tale; it is long and strange, and the temperature of this place is not fitting to your fine sensations; come to the hut upon the mountain. The sun is yet high in the heavens; before it descends to hide itself beyond yon snowy precipices, and illuminate another world, you will have heard my story and can decide. On you it rests, whether I quit forever the neighbourhood of man and lead a harmless life, or become the scourge of your fellow creatures, and the author of your own speedy ruin.'

As he said this, he led the way across the ice: I followed. My heart was full, and I did not answer him; but as I proceeded, I weighed the various arguments that he had used, and determined at least to listen to his tale. I was partly urged by curiosity, and compassion confirmed my resolution. I had hitherto supposed him to be the murderer of my brother, and I eagerly sought a confirmation or denial of this opinion. For the first time, also, I felt what the duties of a creator towards his creature were, and that I ought to render him happy before I complained of his wickedness. These motives urged me to comply with his demand. We crossed the ice, therefore, and ascended the opposite rock. The air was cold, and the rain again began to descend: we entered the hut, the fiend with an air of exultation, I with a heavy heart and depressed spirits. But I consented to listen, and seating myself by the fire which my odious companion had lighted, he thus began his tale.

CHAPTER 3

'It is with considerable difficulty that I remember the original era of my being: all the events of that period appear confused and indistinct. A strange multiplicity of sensations seized me, and I saw, felt, heard, and smelt at the same time; and it was, indeed, a long time before I learned to distinguish between the operations of my various senses. By degrees, I remember, a stronger light pressed upon my nerves, so that I was obliged to shut my eyes. Darkness then came over me, and troubled me; but hardly had I felt this when, by opening my eyes, as I now suppose, the light poured in upon me again. I walked and, I believe, descended; but I presently found a great alteration in my sensations. Before, dark and opaque bodies had surrounded me, impervious to my touch or sight; but I now found that I could wander on at liberty, with no obstacles which I could not either surmount or avoid. The light became more and more oppressive to me; and the heat wearying me as I walked, I sought a place where I could receive shade. This was the forest near Ingolstadt; and here I lay by the side of a brook resting from my fatigue, until I felt tormented by hunger and thirst. This roused me from my nearly dormant state, and I ate some berries which I found hanging on the trees or lying on the ground. I slaked my thirst at the brook; and then lying down, was overcome by sleep.

'It was dark when I awoke; I felt cold also, and half frightened, as it were, instinctively, finding myself so desolate. Before I had quitted your apartment, on a sensation of cold, I had covered myself with some clothes; but these were insufficient to secure me from the dews of night. I was a poor, helpless, miserable wretch; I knew, and could distinguish, nothing; but feeling pain invade me on all sides, I sat down and wept.

'Soon a gentle light stole over the heavens, and gave me a sensation of pleasure. I started up and beheld a radiant form rise from among the trees. I gazed with a kind of wonder. It moved slowly, but it enlightened my path, and I again went out in search of berries. I was still cold when under one of the trees I found a huge cloak, with which I covered myself, and sat down upon the ground. No distinct ideas occupied my mind; all was confused. I felt light, and hunger, and thirst, and darkness; innumerable sounds rang in my ears, and on all sides various scents saluted me: the only object that I could distinguish was the bright moon, and I fixed my eyes on that with pleasure.

'Several changes of day and night passed, and the orb of night had greatly lessened, when I began to distinguish my sensations from each other. I gradually saw plainly the clear stream that supplied me with drink, and the trees that shaded me with their foliage. I was delighted when I first discovered that a pleasant sound, which often saluted my ears, proceeded from the throats of the little winged animals who had often intercepted the light from my eyes. I began also to observe, with greater accuracy, the forms that surrounded me, and to perceive the boundaries of the radiant roof of light which canopied me. Sometimes I tried to imitate the pleasant songs of the birds, but was unable. Sometimes I wished to express my sensations in my own mode, but the uncouth and inarticulate sounds which broke from me frightened me into silence again.

'The moon had disappeared from the night, and again, with a lessened form, showed itself, while I still remained in the forest. My sensations had by this time become distinct, and my mind received every day additional ideas. My eyes became accustomed to the light and to perceive objects in their right forms; I distinguished the insect from the herb, and by degrees, one herb from another. I found that the sparrow uttered none but harsh notes, whilst those of the blackbird and thrush were sweet and enticing.

'One day, when I was oppressed by cold, I found a fire which had been left by some wandering beggars, and was overcome with delight at the warmth I experienced from it. In my joy I thrust my hand into the live embers, but quickly drew it out again with a cry of pain. How strange, I thought, that the same cause should produce such opposite effects! I examined the materials of the fire, and to my joy found it to be composed of wood. I quickly collected some branches; but they were wet and would not burn. I was pained at this; and sat still watching the operation of the fire. The wet wood which I had placed near the heat dried, and itself became inflamed. I reflected on this; and by touching the various branches, I discovered the cause, and busied myself in collecting a great quantity of wood, that I might dry it and have a plentiful supply of fire. When night came on and brought sleep with it, I was in the greatest fear lest my fire should be extinguished. I covered it carefully with dry wood and leaves, and placed wet branches upon it; and then, spreading my cloak, I lay on the ground, and sunk into sleep.

'It was morning when I awoke, and my first care was to visit the fire. I uncovered it, and a gentle breeze quickly fanned it into a flame. I observed this also and contrived a fan of branches, which roused the embers when they were nearly extinguished. When night came again I found, with pleasure, that the fire gave light as well as heat; and that the discovery of this element was useful to me in my food, for I found some of the offals that the travellers had left had been roasted, and tasted much more savoury than the berries I gathered from the trees. I tried, therefore, to dress my food in the same manner, placing it on the live embers. I found that the berries were spoiled by this operation, and the nuts and roots much improved.

'Food, however, became scarce; and I often spent the whole day searching in vain for a few acorns to assuage the pangs of hunger. When I found this, I resolved to quit the place that I had hitherto inhabited, to seek for one where the few wants I experienced would be more easily satisfied. In this emigration, I exceedingly lamented the loss of the fire which I had obtained through accident, and knew not how to reproduce it. I gave several hours to the serious consideration of this difficulty; but I was obliged to relinquish all attempts to supply it; and, wrapping myself up in my cloak, I struck across the wood towards the setting sun. I passed three days in these rambles, and at length discovered the open country. A great fall of snow had taken place the night before, and the fields were of one uniform white; the appearance was disconsolate, and I found my feet chilled by the cold damp outside that covered the ground.

'It was about seven in the morning, and I longed to obtain food and shelter; at length I perceived a small hut, on a rising ground, which had doubtless been built for the convenience of some shepherd. This was a new sight to me; and I examined the structure; with great curiosity. Finding the door open, I entered. An old man sat in it, near a fire, over which he was preparing his breakfast. He turned on hearing a noise; and perceiving me, shrieked loudly, and quitting the hut, ran across the fields with a speed of which his debilitated form hardly appeared capable. His appearance, different from any I had ever before seen, and his flight, somewhat surprised me. But I was enchanted by the appearance of the hut: here the snow and rain could not penetrate; the ground was dry; and it presented to me then as exquisite and divine a retreat as Pandaemonium appeared to the daemons of hell after their sufferings in the lake of fire. I greedily devoured the remnants of the shepherd's breakfast, which consisted of bread, cheese, milk, and wine; the latter, however, I did not like. Then, overcome by fatigue, I lay down among some straw, and fell asleep.

'It was noon when I awoke; and, allured by the warmth of the sun, which shone brightly on the white ground, I determined to recommence my travels; and, depositing the remains of the peasant's breakfast in a wallet I found, I proceeded across the fields for several hours, until at sunset I arrived at a village. How miraculous did this appear! the huts, the neater cottages, and stately houses engaged my admiration by turns. The vegetables in the gardens, the milk and cheese that I saw placed at the windows of some of the cottages, allured my appetite. One of the best of these I entered; but I had hardly placed my foot within the door before the children shrieked, and one of the women fainted. The whole village was roused; some fled, some attacked me, until, grievously bruised by stones and many other kinds of missile weapons, I escaped to the open country and fearfully took refuge in a low hovel, quite bare, and making a wretched appearance after the palaces I had beheld in the village. This hovel, however, joined a cottage of a neat and pleasant appearance; but, after my late dearly bought experience, I dared not enter it. My place of refuge was constructed of wood, but so low that I could with difficulty sit upright in it. No wood, however, was placed on the earth which formed the floor, but it was dry; and although the wind entered it by innumerable chinks, I found it an agreeable asylum from the snow and rain.

'Here then I retreated, and lay down happy to have found a shelter, however miserable, from the inclemency of the season, and still more from the barbarity of man.

'As soon as morning dawned, I crept from my kennel, that I might view the adjacent cottage and discover if I could remain in the habitation I had found. It was situated against the back of the cottage and surrounded on the sides which were exposed by a pig-sty and a clear pool of water. One part was open, and by that I had crept in; but now I covered every crevice by which I might be perceived with stones and wood, yet in such a manner that I might move them on occasion to pass out: all the light I enjoyed came through the sty, and that was sufficient for me.

'Having thus arranged my dwelling and carpeted it with clean straw, I retired; for I saw the figure of a man at a distance, and I remembered too well my treatment the night before, to trust myself in his power. I had first, however, provided for my sustenance for that day by a loaf of coarse bread, which I purloined, and a cup with which I could drink, more conveniently than from my hand, of the pure water which flowed by my retreat. The floor was a little raised, so that it was kept perfectly dry, and by its vicinity to the chimney of the cottage it was tolerably warm.

'Being thus provided, I resolved to reside in this hovel until something should occur which might alter my determination. It was indeed a paradise compared to the bleak forest, my former residence, the rain-dropping branches, and dank earth. I ate my breakfast with pleasure and was about to remove a plank to procure myself a little water when I heard a step, and looking through a small chink, I beheld a young creature, with a pail on her head, passing before my hovel. The girl was young and of gentle demeanour, unlike what I have since found cottagers and farm-house servants to be. Yet she was meanly dressed, a coarse blue petticoat and a linen jacket being her only grab; her fair hair was plaited, but not adorned: she looked patient, yet sad. I lost sight of her; and in about a quarter of an hour she returned bearing the pail, which was now partly filled with milk. As she walked along, seemingly incommoded by the burden, a young man met her, whose countenance expressed a deeper despondence. Uttering a few sounds with an air of melancholy, he took the pail from her head and bore it to the cottage himself. She followed, and they disappeared. Presently I saw the young man again, with some tools in his hand, cross the field behind the cottage; and the girl was also busied, sometimes in the house and sometimes in the yard.

'On examining my dwelling, I found that one of the windows of the cottage had formerly occupied a part of it, but the panes had been filled up with wood. In one of these was a small and almost imperceptible chink, through which the eye could just penetrate. Through this crevice a small room was visible, whitewashed and clean, but very bare of furni-

ture. In one corner, near a small fire, sat an old man, leaning his head
on his hands in a disconsolate attitude. The young girl was occupied in
arranging the cottage; but presently she took something out of a drawer,
which employed her hands, and she sat down beside the old man, who,
taking up an instrument, began to play, and to produce sounds sweeter
than the voice of the thrush or the nightingale. It was a lovely sight,
even to me, poor wretch! who had never beheld aught beautiful before.
The silver hair and benevolent countenance of the aged cottager won
my reverence, while the gentle manners of the girl enticed my love.
He played a sweet mournful air, which I perceived drew tears from the
eyes of his amiable companion, of which the old man took no notice,
until she sobbed audibly; he then pronounced a few sounds, and the fair
creature, leaving her work, knelt at his feet. He raised her, and smiled
with such kindness and affection that I felt sensations of a peculiar and
overpowering nature: they were a mixture of pain and pleasure, such as
I had never before experienced, either from hunger or cold, warmth or
food; and I withdrew from the window, unable to bear these emotions.

'Soon after this the young man returned, bearing on his shoulders a
load of wood. The girl met him at the door, helped to relieve him of
his burden, and taking some of the fuel into the cottage, placed it on
the fire; then she and the youth went apart into a nook of the cottage,
and he showed her a large loaf and a piece of cheese. She seemed
pleased, and went into the garden for some roots and plants, which
she placed in water, and then upon the fire. She afterwards continued
her work, whilst the young man went into the garden, and appeared
busily employed in digging and pulling up roots. After he had been
employed thus about an hour, the young woman joined him, and they
entered the cottage together.

'The old man had, in the mean time, been pensive; but on the
appearance of his companions he assumed a more cheerful air, and
they sat down to eat. The meal was quickly dispatched. The young
woman was again occupied in arranging the cottage; the old man
walked before the cottage in the sun for a few minutes, leaning on
the arm of the youth. Nothing could exceed in beauty the contrast
between these two excellent creatures. One was old, with silver hairs
and a countenance beaming with benevolence and love: the younger
was slight and graceful in his figure, and his features were moulded

with the finest symmetry; yet his eyes and attitude expressed the utmost sadness and despondency. The old man returned to the cottage; and the youth, with tools different from those he had used in the morning, directed his steps across the fields.

'Night quickly shut in; but to my extreme wonder, I found that the cottagers had a means of prolonging light by the use of tapers, and was delighted to find that the setting of the sun did not put an end to the pleasure I experienced in watching my human neighbours. In the evening, the young girl and her companion were employed in various occupations which I did not understand; and the old man again took up the instrument which produced the divine sounds that had enchanted me in the morning. So soon as he had finished the youth began, not to play, but to utter sounds that were monotonous, and neither resembling the harmony of the old man's instrument nor the songs of the birds: I since found that he read aloud, but at that time I knew nothing of the science of words or letters.

'The family, after having been thus occupied for a short time, extinguished their lights and retired, as I conjectured, to rest.'

CHAPTER 4

'I lay on my straw, but I could not sleep. I thought of the occurrences of the day. What chiefly struck me was the gentle manners of these people; and I longed to join them, but dared not. I remembered too well the treatment I had suffered the night before from the barbarous villagers, and resolved, whatever course of conduct I might hereafter think it right to pursue, that for the present I would remain quietly in my hovel, watching, and endeavouring to discover the motives which influenced their actions.

'The cottagers arose the next morning before the sun. The young woman arranged the cottage and prepared the food; and the youth departed after the first meal.

'This day was passed in the same routine as that which preceded it. The young man was constantly employed out of doors, and the girl in various laborious occupations within. The old man, whom I soon perceived to be blind, employed his leisure hours on his instrument or in contemplation. Nothing could exceed the love and respect which the younger cottagers exhibited towards their venerable companion. They performed towards him every little office of affection and duty with gentleness; and he rewarded them by his benevolent smiles.

'They were not entirely happy. The young man and his companion often went apart, and appeared to weep. I saw no cause for their unhappiness; but I was deeply affected by it. If such lovely creatures were miserable, it was less strange that I, an imperfect and solitary being, should be wretched. Yet why were these gentle beings unhappy? They possessed a delightful house (for such it was in my eyes) and every luxury; they had a fire to warm them when chill, and delicious viands when hungry; they were dressed in excellent clothes; and, still more, they enjoyed one another's company and speech, interchanging each day looks of affection and kindness. What did their tears imply? Did they really express pain? I was at first unable to solve these questions; but perpetual attention and time explained to me many appearances which were at first enigmatic.

'A considerable period elapsed before I discovered one of the causes of the uneasiness of this amiable family: it was poverty, and they suffered that evil in a very distressing degree. Their nourishment consisted entirely of the vegetables of their garden and the milk of one cow, which gave very little during the winter, when its masters could scarcely procure food to support it. They often, I believe, suffered the pangs of hunger very poignantly, especially the two younger cottagers; for several times they placed food before the old man when they reserved none for themselves.

'This trait of kindness moved me sensibly. I had been accustomed, during the night, to steal a part of their store for my own consumption; but when I found that in doing this I inflicted pain on the cottagers, I abstained, and satisfied myself with berries, nuts, and roots, which I gathered from a neighbouring wood.

'I discovered also another means through which I was enabled to assist their labours. I found that the youth spent a great part of each day in collecting wood for the family fire; and, during the night I often took his tools, the use of which I quickly discovered, and brought home firing sufficient for the consumption of several days.

'I remember, the first time that I did this, the young woman, when she opened the door in the morning, appeared greatly astonished on seeing a great pile of wood on the outside. She uttered some words in a loud voice, and the youth joined her, who also expressed surprise. I observed, with pleasure, that he did not go to the forest that day, but spent it in repairing the cottage and cultivating the garden.

'By degrees I made a discovery of still greater moment. I found that these people possessed a method of communicating their experience and feelings to one another by articulate sounds. I perceived that the words they spoke sometimes produced pleasure or pain, smiles or sadness, in the minds and countenances of the hearers. This was indeed a godlike science, and I ardently desired to become acquainted with it. But I was baffled in every attempt I made for this purpose. Their pronunciation was quick; and the words they uttered, not having any apparent connection with visible objects, I was unable to discover any clue by which I could unravel the mystery of their reference. By great application, however, and after having remained during the space of several revolutions of the moon in my hovel, I discovered the names that were given to some of the most familiar objects of discourse; I learned and applied the words, "fire", "milk", "bread", and "wood". I learned also the names of the cottagers themselves. The youth and his companion had each of them several names, but the old man had only one, which was "father". The girl was called "sister", or "Agatha", and the youth "Felix", "brother", or "son". I cannot describe the delight I felt when I learned the ideas appropriated to each of these sounds, and was able to pronounce them. I distinguished several other words without being able as yet to understand or apply them; such as "good", "dearest", "unhappy".

'I spent the winter in this manner. The gentle manners and beauty of the cottagers greatly endeared them to me: when they were unhappy, I felt depressed; when they rejoiced, I sympathised in their joys. I saw few human beings besides them; and if any other happened to enter the cottage, their harsh manners and rude gait only enhanced to me the superior accomplishments of my friends. The old man, I could perceive, often endeavoured to encourage his children, as sometimes I found that he called them, to cast off their melancholy. He would talk in a cheerful accent, with an expression of goodness that bestowed pleasure even upon me. Agatha listened with respect, her eyes sometimes filled with tears, which she endeavoured to wipe away unperceived; but I generally found that her countenance and tone were more cheerful after having listened to the exhortations of her father. It was not thus with Felix. He was always the saddest of the group, and, even to my unpractised senses, he appeared to have suffered more deeply than his friends. But if his countenance was more sorrowful, his voice was more cheerful than that of his sister, especially when he addressed the old man.

'I could mention innumerable instances which, although slight, marked the dispositions of these amiable cottagers. In the midst of poverty and want, Felix carried with pleasure to his sister the first little white flower that peeped out from beneath the snowy ground. Early in the morning, before she had risen, he cleared away the snow that obstructed her path to the milk-house, drew water from the well, and brought the wood from the out-house, where, to his perpetual astonishment, he found his store always replenished by an invisible hand. In the day, I believe, he worked sometimes for a neighbouring farmer, because he often went forth and did not return until dinner, yet brought no wood with him. At other times he worked in the garden; but as there was little to do in the frosty season, he read to the old man and Agatha.

'This reading had puzzled me extremely at first; but, by degrees, I discovered that he uttered many of the same sounds when he read, as when he talked. I conjectured, therefore, that he found on the paper signs for speech which he understood, and I ardently longed to comprehend these also; but how was that possible when I did not even understand the sounds for which they stood as signs? I improved, however, sensibly in this science, but not sufficiently to follow up any kind of conversation, although I applied my whole mind to the endeavour: for I easily perceived that, although I eagerly longed to discover myself to the cottagers, I ought not to make the attempt until I had first become master of their language; which knowledge might enable me to make them overlook the deformity of my figure; for with this also the contrast perpetually presented to my eyes had made me acquainted.

'I had admired the perfect forms of my cottagers – their grace, beauty, and delicate complexions: but how was I terrified, when I viewed myself in a transparent pool! At first I started back, unable to believe that it was indeed I who was reflected in the mirror; and when I became fully convinced that I was in reality the monster that I am, I was filled with the bitterest sensations of despondence and mortification. Alas! I did not yet entirely know the fatal effects of this miserable deformity.

'As the sun became warmer, and the light of day longer, the snow vanished, and I beheld the bare trees and the black earth. From this time Felix was more employed; and the heart-moving indications of impending famine disappeared. Their food, as I afterwards found, was coarse, but it was wholesome; and they procured a sufficiency of it. Several new kinds of plants sprang up in the garden, which they dressed; and these signs of comfort increased daily as the season advanced.

'The old man, leaning on his son, walked each day at noon, when it did not rain, as I found it was called when the heavens poured forth its water. This frequently took place; but a high wind quickly dried the earth, and the season became far more pleasant than it had been.

'My mode of life in my hovel was uniform. During the morning I attended the motions of the cottagers; and when they were dispersed in various occupations, I slept: the remainder of the day was spent in observing my friends. When they had retired to rest, if there was any moon or the night was star-light, I went into the woods and collected my own food and fuel for the cottage. When I returned, as often as it was necessary, I cleared their path from the snow and performed those offices that I had seen done by Felix. I afterwards found that these labours, performed by an invisible hand, greatly astonished them; and once or twice I heard them, on these occasions, utter the words "good spirit", "wonderful"; but I did not then understand the signification of these terms.

'My thoughts now became more active, and I longed to discover the motives and feelings of these lovely creatures; I was inquisitive to know why Felix appeared so miserable and Agatha so sad. I thought (foolish wretch!) that it might be in my power to restore happiness to these deserving people. When I slept or was absent, the forms of the venerable blind father, the gentle Agatha, and the excellent Felix, flitted before me. I looked upon them as superior beings, who would be the arbiters of my future destiny. I formed in my imagination a thousand pictures of presenting myself to them, and their reception of me. I imagined that they would be disgusted, until, by my gentle demeanour and conciliating words, I should first win their favour, and afterwards their love.

'These thoughts exhilarated me and led me to apply with fresh ardour to the acquiring the art of language. My organs were indeed harsh, but supple; and although my voice was very unlike the soft music of their tones, yet I pronounced such words as I understood with tolerable ease. It was as the ass and the lap-dog; yet surely the gentle ass whose intentions were affectionate, although his manners were rude, deserved better treatment than blows and execration.

'The pleasant showers and genial warmth of spring greatly altered the aspect of the earth. Men, who before this change seemed to have been hid in caves, dispersed themselves, and were employed in various arts of cultivation. The birds sang in more cheerful notes, and the leaves began to bud forth on the trees. Happy, happy earth! fit habitation for gods, which, so short a time before, was bleak, damp, and unwholesome. My spirits were elevated by the enchanting appearance of nature; the past was blotted from my memory, the present was tranquil, and the future gilded by bright rays of hope, and anticipations of joy.'

CHAPTER 5

'I now hasten to the more moving part of my story. I shall relate events, that impressed me with feelings which, from what I had been, have made me what I am.

'Spring advanced rapidly; the weather became fine and the skies cloudless. It surprised me, that what before was desert and gloomy should now bloom with the most beautiful flowers and verdure. My senses were gratified and refreshed by a thousand scents of delight, and a thousand sights of beauty.

'It was on one of these days, when my cottagers periodically rested from labour – the old man played on his guitar, and the children listened to him – that I observed the countenance of Felix was melancholy beyond expression; he sighed frequently; and once his father paused in his music, and I conjectured by his manner that he enquired the cause of his son's sorrow. Felix replied in a cheerful accent, and the old man was recommencing his music when some-one tapped at the door.

'It was a lady on horseback, accompanied by a countryman as a guide. The lady was dressed in a dark suit, and covered with a thick black veil. Agatha asked a question, to which the stranger only replied by pronouncing, in a sweet accent, the name of Felix. Her voice was musical but unlike that of either of my friends. On hearing this word, Felix came up hastily to the lady, who, when she saw him, threw up her veil, and I beheld a countenance of angelic beauty and expression. Her hair of a shining raven black, and curiously braided; her eyes were dark, but gentle, although animated; her features of a regular proportion, and her complexion wondrously fair, each cheek tinged with a lovely pink.

'Felix seemed ravished with delight when he saw her, every trait of sorrow vanished from his face, and it instantly expressed a degree of ecstatic joy, of which I could hardly have believed it capable; his eyes sparkled, as his cheek flushed with pleasure; and at that moment I thought him as beautiful as the stranger. She appeared affected by different feelings; wiping a few tears from her lovely eyes, she held out her hand to Felix, who kissed it rapturously and called her, as well as I could distinguish, his sweet Arabian. She did not appear to understand him, but smiled. He assisted her to dismount, and dismissing her guide, conducted her into the cottage. Some conversation took place between him and his father; and the young stranger knelt at the old man's feet and would have kissed his hand, but he raised her, and embraced her affectionately.

'I soon perceived, that although the stranger uttered articulate sounds, and appeared to have a language of her own, she was neither understood by, nor herself understood, the cottagers. They made many signs which I did not comprehend; but I saw that her presence diffused gladness through the cottage, dispelling their sorrow as the sun dissipates the morning mists. Felix seemed peculiarly happy, and with smiles of delight welcomed his Arabian. Agatha, the ever-gentle Agatha, kissed the hands of the lovely stranger; and pointing to her brother, made signs which appeared to me to mean that he had been sorrowful until she came. Some hours passed thus, while they, by their countenances, expressed joy, the cause of which I did not comprehend. Presently I found, by the frequent recurrence of some sound which the stranger repeated after them, that she was endeavouring to learn their language; and the idea instantly occurred to me that I should make use of the same instructions to the same end. The stranger learned about twenty words at the first lesson, most of them, indeed, were those which I had before understood, but I profited by the others.

'As night came on, Agatha and the Arabian retired early. When they separated, Felix kissed the hand of the stranger and said, "Good night, sweet Safie." He sat up much longer, conversing with his father; and by the frequent repetition of her name, I conjectured that their lovely guest was the subject of their conversation. I ardently desired to understand them, and bent every faculty towards that purpose, but found it utterly impossible.

'The next morning Felix went out to his work; and, after the usual occupations of Agatha were finished, the Arabian sat at the feet of the old man, and taking his guitar, played some airs so entrancingly beautiful that they at once drew tears of sorrow and delight from my eyes. She sang, and her voice flowed in a rich cadence, swelling or dying away, like a nightingale of the woods.

'When she had vanished, she gave the guitar to Agatha, who at first declined it. She played a simple air, and her voice accompanied it in sweet accents, but unlike the wondrous strain of the stranger.

The old man appeared enraptured and said some words, which Agatha endeavoured to explain to Safie, and by which he appeared to wish to express that she bestowed on him the greatest delight by her music.

'The days now passed as peaceably as before, with the sole alteration that joy had taken place of sadness in the countenances of my friends. Safie was always gay and happy; she and I improved rapidly in the knowledge of language, so that in two months I began to comprehend most of the words uttered by my protectors.

'In the meanwhile also the black ground was covered with herbage, and the green banks interspersed with innumerable flowers, sweet to the scent and the eyes, stars of pale radiance among the moonlight woods; the sun became warmer, the nights clear and balmy; and my nocturnal rambles were an extreme pleasure to me, although they were considerably shortened by the late setting and early rising of the sun, for I never ventured abroad during daylight, fearful of meeting with the same treatment I had formerly endured in the first village which I entered.

'My days were spent in close attention, that I might more speedily master the language; and I may boast that I improved more rapidly than the Arabian, who understood very little and conversed in broken accents, whilst I comprehended and could imitate almost every word that was spoken.

'While I improved in speech, I also learned the science of letters as it was taught to the stranger; and this opened before me a wide field for wonder and delight.

'The book from which Felix instructed Safie was Volney's *Ruins of Empires*. I should not have understood the purport of this book had not Felix, in reading it, given very minute explanations. He had chosen this work, he said, because the declamatory style was framed in imitation of the eastern authors. Through this work I obtained a cursory knowledge of history and a view of the several empires at present existing in the world; it gave me an insight into the manners, governments, and religions of the different nations of the earth. I heard of the slothful Asiatics; of the stupendous genius and mental activity of the Grecians; of the wars and wonderful virtue of the early Romans – of their subsequent degenerating – of the decline of that mighty empire, of chivalry, Christianity, and kings. I heard of the discovery of the American hemisphere and wept with Safie over the hapless fate of its original inhabitants.

'These wonderful narrations inspired me with strange feelings. Was man, indeed, at once so powerful, so virtuous, and magnificent, yet so vicious and base? He appeared at one time a mere scion of the evil principle, and at another as all that can be conceived as noble and godlike. To be a great and virtuous man appeared the highest honour that can befall a sensitive being; to be base and vicious, as many on record have been, appeared the lowest degradation, a condition more abject than that of the blind mole or harmless worm. For a long time I could not conceive how one man could go forth to murder his fellow, or even why there were laws and governments; but when I heard details of vice and bloodshed, my wonder ceased, and I turned away with disgust and loathing.

'Every conversation of the cottagers now opened new wonders to me. While I listened to the instructions which Felix bestowed upon the Arabian, the strange system of human society was explained to me. I heard of the division of property, of immense wealth and squalid poverty; of rank, descent, and noble blood.

'The words induced me to turn towards myself. I learned that the possessions most esteemed by your fellow creatures were, high and unsullied descent united with riches. A man might be respected with only one of these advantages; but without either he was considered, except in very rare instances, as a vagabond and a slave, doomed to waste his powers for the profits of the chosen few! And what was I? Of my creation and creator I was absolutely ignorant, but I knew that I possessed no money, no friends, no kind of property. I was, besides, endued with a figure hideously deformed and loathsome; I was not even of the same nature as man. I was more agile than they and could subsist upon coarser diet; I bore the extremes of heat and cold with less injury to my frame; my stature far exceeded theirs. When I looked around I saw and heard of none like me. Was I, then, a monster, a blot upon the earth, from which all men fled and whom all men disowned?

'I cannot describe to you the agony that these reflections inflicted upon me: I tried to dispel them, but sorrow only increased with knowledge. Oh, that I had forever remained in my native wood, nor known nor felt beyond the sensations of hunger, thirst and heat!

'Of what a strange nature is knowledge! It clings to the mind, when it has once seized on it, like a lichen on the rock. I wished sometimes to shake off all thought and feeling; but I learned that there was but one means to overcome the sensation of pain, and that was death – a state which I feared yet did not understand. I admired virtue and good feelings and loved the gentle manners and amiable qualities of my cottagers, but I was shut out from intercourse with them, except through means which I obtained by stealth, when I was unseen and unknown, and which rather increased than satisfied the desire I had of becoming one among my fellows. The gentle words of Agatha and the animated smiles of the charming Arabian, were not for me. The mild exhortations of the old man, and the lively conversation of the loved Felix were not for me. Miserable, unhappy wretch!

'Other lessons were impressed upon me even more deeply. I heard of the difference of sexes; and the birth and growth of children; how the father doated on the smiles of the infant, and the lively sallies of the older child; how all the life and cares of the mother were wrapped up in the precious charge; how the mind of youth expanded and gained knowledge; of brother, sister, and all the various relationships which bind one human being to another in mutual bonds.

'But where were my friends and relations? No father had watched my infant days, no mother had blessed me with smiles and caresses; or if they had, all my past life was now a blot, a blind vacancy in which I distinguished nothing. From my earliest remembrance I had been as I then was in height and proportion. I had never yet seen a being resembling me, or who claimed any intercourse with me. What was I? The question again recurred, to be answered only with groans.

'I will soon explain to what these feeling tended; but allow me now to return to the cottagers, whose story excited in me such various feelings of indignation, delight, and wonder, but which all terminated in additional love and reverence for my protectors (for so I loved, in an innocent, half-painful self-deceit, to call them).'

CHAPTER 6

'Some time elapsed before I learned the history of my friends. It was one which could not fail to impress itself deeply on my mind, unfolding as it did a number of circumstances, each interesting and wonderful to one so utterly inexperienced as I was.

'The name of the old man was De Lacey. He was descended from a good family in France, where he had lived for many years in affluence, respected by his superiors and beloved by his equals. His son was bred in the service of his country; and Agatha had ranked with ladies of the highest distinction. A few months before my arrival they had lived in a large and luxurious city called Paris, surrounded by friends and possessed of every enjoyment which virtue, refinement of intellect, or taste, accompanied by a moderate fortune, could afford.

'The father of Safie had been the cause of their ruin. He was a Turkish merchant, and had inhabited Paris for many years, when, for some reason which I could not learn, he became obnoxious to the government. He was seized and cast into prison the very day that Safie arrived from Constantinople to join him. He was tried and condemned to death. The injustice of his sentence was very flagrant; all Paris was indignant; and it was judged that his religion and wealth rather than the crime alleged against him had been the cause of his condemnation.

'Felix had accidentally been present at the trial; his horror and indignation were uncontrollable when he heard the decision of the court. He made, at that moment, a solemn vow to deliver him and then looked around for the means. After many fruitless attempts to gain admittance to the prison, he found a strongly grated window in an unguarded part of the building, which lighted the dungeon of the unfortunate Mahometan; who, loaded with chains, waited in despair the execution of the barbarous sentence. Felix visited the grate at night and made known to the prisoner his intentions in his favour. The Turk, amazed and delighted, endeavoured to kindle the zeal of his deliverer by promises of reward and wealth. Felix rejected his offers with contempt; yet when he saw the lovely Safie, who was allowed to visit her father and who, by her gestures, expressed her lively gratitude, the youth could not help owning to his own mind that the captive possessed a treasure which would fully reward his toil and hazard.

'The Turk quickly perceived the impression that his daughter had made on the heart of Felix and endeavoured to secure him more entirely in his interests by the promise of her hand in marriage, so soon as he should be conveyed to a place of safety. Felix was too delicate to accept his offer; yet he looked forward to the probability of the event as to the consummation of his happiness.

'During the ensuing days, while the preparations were going forward for the escape of the merchant, the zeal of Felix was warmed by several letters that he received from this lovely girl, who found means to express her thoughts in the language of her lover by the aid of an old man, a servant of her father who understood French. She thanked him in the most ardent terms for his intended services towards her parent; and at the same time she gently deplored her own fate.

'I have copies of these letters; for I found means, during my residence in the hovel, to procure the implements of writing; and the letters were often in the hands of Felix or Agatha. Before I depart, I will give them to you, they will prove the truth of my tale; but at present, as the sun is already far declined, I shall only have time to repeat the substance of them to you.

'Safie related that her mother was a Christian Arab, seized and made a slave by the Turks; recommended by her beauty, she had won the heart of the father of Safie, who married her. The young girl spoke in high and enthusiastic terms of her mother, who, born in freedom, spurned the bondage to which she was now reduced. She instructed her daughter in the tenets of her religion and taught her to aspire to higher powers of intellect and an independence of spirit forbidden to the female followers of Mahomet. This lady died; but her lessons were indelibly impressed on the mind of Safie, who sickened at the prospect of again returning to Asia and being immured within the walls of a harem, allowed only to occupy herself with infantile amusements, ill-suited to the temper of her soul, now accustomed to grand ideas and a noble emulation of virtue. The prospect of marrying a Christian and remaining in a country where women were allowed to take a rank in society was enchanting to her.

'The day for the execution of the Turk was fixed; but on the night previous to it he quitted his prison, and before morning was distant many leagues from Paris. Felix had procured passports in the name of his father, sister, and himself. He had previously communicated his plan to the former, who aided the deceit by quitting his house, under the pretence of a journey and concealing himself, with his daughter, in an obscure part of Paris.

'Felix conducted the fugitives through France to Lyons and across Mont Cenis to Leghorn, where the merchant had decided to wait a favourable opportunity of passing into some part of the Turkish dominions.

'Safie resolved to remain with her father until the moment of his departure, before which time the Turk renewed his promise that she should be united to his deliverer; and Felix remained with them in expectation of that event; and in the mean time he enjoyed the society of the Arabian, who exhibited towards him the simplest and tenderest affection. They conversed with one another through the means of an interpreter, and sometimes with the interpretation of looks; and Safie sang to him the divine airs of her native country.

'The Turk allowed this intimacy to take place, and encouraged the hopes of the youthful lovers, while in his heart he had formed far other plans. He loathed the idea that his daughter should be united to a Christian; but he feared the resentment of Felix if he should appear lukewarm; for he knew that he was still in the power of his deliverer if he should choose to betray him to the Italian state which they inhabited. He revolved a thousand plans by which he should be enabled to prolong the deceit until it might be no longer necessary, and secretly to take his daughter with him when he departed. His plans were facilitated by the news which arrived from Paris.

'The government of France were greatly enraged at the escape of their victim and spared no pains to detect and punish his deliverer. The plot of Felix was quickly discovered, and De Lacey and Agatha were thrown into prison. The news reached Felix and roused him from his dream of pleasure. His blind and aged father and his gentle sister lay in a noisome dungeon while he enjoyed the free air and the society of her whom he loved. This idea was torture to him. He quickly arranged with the Turk that if the latter should find a favourable opportunity for escape before Felix could return to Italy, Safie should remain as a boarder at a convent at Leghorn; and then, quitting the lovely Arabian, he hastened to Paris, and delivered himself up to the vengeance of the law, hoping to free De Lacey and Agatha by this proceeding.

'He did not succeed. They remained confined for five months before the trial took place; the result of which deprived them of their fortune and condemned them to a perpetual exile from their native country.

'They found a miserable asylum in the cottage in Germany, where I discovered them. Felix soon learned that the treacherous Turk, for whom he and his family endured such unheard-of oppression, on discovering that his deliverer was thus reduced to poverty and ruin, became a traitor to good feeling and honour and had quitted Italy with his daughter, insultingly sending Felix a pittance of money to aid him, as he said, in some plan of future maintenance.

'Such were the events that preyed on the heart of Felix and rendered him, when I first saw him, the most miserable of his family. He could have endured poverty; and while this distress had been the meed of his virtue, he gloried in it; but the ingratitude of the Turk and the loss of his beloved Safie, were misfortunes more bitter and irreparable. The arrival of the Arabian now infused new life into his soul.

'When the news reached Leghorn that Felix was deprived of his wealth and rank, the merchant commanded his daughter to think no more of her lover, but to prepare to return to her native country. The generous nature of Safie was outraged by this command; she attempted to expostulate with her father, but he left her angrily, reiterating his tyrannical mandate.

'A few days after, the Turk entered his daughter's apartment and told her hastily that he had reason to believe that his residence at Leghorn had been divulged and that he should speedily be delivered up to the French government; he had, consequently, hired a vessel to convey him to Constantinople, for which city he should sail in a few hours. He intended to leave his daughter under the care of a confidential servant, to follow at her leisure with the greater part of his property, which had not yet arrived at Leghorn.

'When alone, Safie resolved in her own mind the plan of conduct that it would become her to pursue in this emergency. A residence in Turkey was abhorrent to her; her religion and her feelings were alike averse to it. By some papers of her father which fell into her hands she heard of the exile of her lover and learnt the name of the spot where he then resided. She hesitated some time, but at length she formed her determination. Taking with her some jewels that belonged to her and a sum of money, she quitted Italy with an attendant, a native of Leghorn, but who understood the common language of Turkey, and departed for Germany.

'She arrived in safety at a town about twenty leagues from the cottage of De Lacey, when her attendant fell dangerously ill. Safie nursed her with the most devoted affection; but the poor girl died, and the Arabian was left alone, unacquainted with the language of the country and utterly ignorant of the customs of the world. She fell, however, into good hands. The Italian had mentioned the name of the spot for which they were bound; and after her death, the woman of the house in which they had lived took care that Safie should arrive in safety at the cottage of her lover.'

CHAPTER 7

'Such was the history of my beloved cottagers. It impressed me deeply. I learned, from the views of social life which it developed, to admire their virtues and to deprecate the vices of mankind.

'As yet I looked upon crime as a distant evil; benevolence and generosity were ever present before me, inciting within me a desire to become an actor in the busy scene where so many admirable qualities were called forth and displayed. But in giving an account of the progress of my intellect, I must not omit a circumstance which occurred in the beginning of the month of August of the same year.

'One night, during my accustomed visit to the neighbouring wood, where I collected my own food and brought home firing for my protectors. I found on the ground a leathern portmanteau, containing several articles of dress and some books. I eagerly seized the prize, and returned with it to my hovel. Fortunately the books were written in the language, the elements of which I had acquired at the cottage; they consisted of *Paradise Lost*, a volume of Plutarch's *Lives*, and the *Sorrows of Werter*. The possession of these treasures gave me extreme delight; I now continually studied and exercised my mind upon these histories, whilst my friends were employed in their ordinary occupations.

'I can hardly describe to you the effect of these books. They produced in me an infinity of new images and feelings, that sometimes raised me to ecstasy, but more frequently sunk me into the lowest dejection. In the *Sorrows of Werter*, besides the interest of its simple and affecting story, so many opinions are canvassed, and so many lights thrown upon what had hitherto been to me obscure subjects, that I found in it a never-ending source of speculation and astonishment. The gentle and domestic manners it described, combined with lofty sentiments and feelings, which had for their object something out of self, accorded well with my experience among my protectors, and with the wants which were forever alive in my own bosom. But I thought Werter himself a more divine being than I had ever beheld or imagined; his character contained no pretension, but it sunk deep. The disquisitions upon death and suicide were calculated to fill me with wonder. I did not pretend to enter into the merits of the case, yet I inclined towards the opinions of the hero, whose extinction I wept, without precisely understanding it.

'As I read, however, I applied much personally to my own feelings and condition. I found myself similar, yet at the same time strangely unlike to the beings concerning whom I read, and to whose conversation I was a listener. I sympathised with and partly understood them, but I was unformed in mind; I was dependent on none, and related to none. "The path of my departure was free," and there was none to lament my annihilation. My person was hideous and my stature gigantic. What did this mean? Who was I? What was I? Whence did I come? What was my destination? These questions continually recurred, but I was unable to solve them.

'The volume of Plutarch's *Lives* which I possessed, contained the histories of the first founders of the ancient republics. This book had a far different effect upon me from the *Sorrows of Werter*. I learned from Werter's imaginations despondency and gloom: but Plutarch taught me high thoughts; he elevated me above the wretched sphere of my own reflections, to admire and love the heroes of past ages. Many things I read surpassed my understanding and experience. I had a very confused knowledge of kingdoms, wide extents of country, mighty rivers, and boundless seas. But I was perfectly unacquainted with towns, and large assemblages of men. The cottage of my protectors had been the only school in which I had studied human nature; but this book developed new and mightier scenes of action. I read of men concerned in public affairs, governing or massacring their species. I felt the greatest ardour for virtue rise within me, and abhorrence for vice, as far as I understood the signification of those terms, relative as they were, as I applied them, to pleasure and pain alone. Induced by these feelings, I was of course led to admire peaceable lawgivers, Numa, Solon, and Lycurgus, in preference to Romulus and Theseus. The patriarchal lives of my protectors caused these impressions to take a firm hold on my mind; perhaps, if my first introduction to humanity had been made by a young soldier, burning for glory and slaughter, I should have been imbued with different sensations.

'But *Paradise Lost* excited different and far deeper emotions. I read it, as I had read the other volumes which had fallen into my hands, as a true history. It moved every feeling of wonder and awe, that the

picture of an omnipotent God warring with his creatures was capable
of exciting. I often referred the several situations, as their similarity
struck me, to my own. Like Adam, I was apparently united by no link
to any other being in existence; but his state was far different from
mine in every other respect. He had come forth from the hands of God
a perfect creature, happy and prosperous, guarded by the especial care
of his Creator; he was allowed to converse with and acquire knowledge from beings of a superior nature: but I was wretched, helpless,
and alone. Many times I considered Satan as the fitter emblem of my
condition; for often, like him, when I viewed the bliss of my protectors,
the bitter gall of envy rose within me.

'Another circumstance strengthened and confirmed these feelings.
Soon after my arrival in the hovel, I discovered some papers in the
pocket of the dress which I had taken from your laboratory. At first I
had neglected them; but now that I was able to decipher the characters
in which they were written, I began to study them with diligence. It
was your journal of the four months that preceded my creation. You
minutely described in these papers every step you took in the progress
of your work; this history was mingled with accounts of domestic
occurrences. You doubtless recollect these papers. Here they are. Every
thing is related in them which bears reference to my accursed origin;
the whole detail of that series of disgusting circumstances which
produced it is set in view; the minutest description of my odious and
loathsome person is given, in language which painted your own horrors
and rendered mine indelible. I sickened as I read. "Hateful day when I
received life!" I exclaimed in agony. "Accursed creator! Why did you
form a monster so hideous that even *you* turned from me in disgust?
God, in pity, made man beautiful and alluring, after his own image;
but my form is a filthy type of yours, more horrid even from the very
resemblance. Satan had his companions, fellow-devils, to admire and
encourage him; but I am solitary and abhorred."

'These were the reflections of my hours of despondency and solitude;
but when I contemplated the virtues of the cottagers, their amiable and
benevolent dispositions, I persuaded myself that when they should
become acquainted with my admiration of their virtues, they would
compassionate me and overlook my personal deformity. Could they
turn from their door one, however monstrous, who solicited their

compassion and friendship? I resolved, at least, not to despair, but in every way to fit myself for an interview with them, which would decide my fate. I postponed this attempt for some months longer; for the importance attached to its success inspired me with a dread lest I should fail. Besides, I found that my understanding improved so much with every day's experience that I was unwilling to commence this undertaking until a few more months should have added to my sagacity.

'Several changes, in the mean time, took place in the cottage. The presence of Safie diffused happiness among its inhabitants; and I also found that a greater degree of plenty reigned there. Felix and Agatha spent more time in amusement and conversation, and were assisted in their labours by servants. They did not appear rich, but they were contented and happy; their feelings were serene and peaceful, while mine became every day more tumultuous. Increase of knowledge only discovered to me more clearly what a wretched outcast I was. I cherished hope, it is true; but it vanished when I beheld my person reflected in water, or my shadow in the moonshine, even as that frail image and that inconstant shade.

'I endeavoured to crush these fears, and to fortify myself for the trial which in a few months I resolved to undergo; and sometimes I allowed my thoughts, unchecked by reason, to ramble in the fields of Paradise, and dared to fancy amiable and lovely creatures sympathising with my feelings and cheering my gloom; their angelic countenances breathed smiles of consolation. But it was all a dream; no Eve soothed my sorrows nor shared my thoughts; I was alone. I remembered Adam's supplication to his Creator. But where was mine? He had abandoned me, and in the bitterness of my heart I cursed him.

'Autumn passed thus. I saw, with surprise and grief, the leaves decay and fall, and nature again assume the barren and bleak appearance it had worn when I first beheld the woods and the lovely moon. Yet I did not heed the bleakness of the weather; I was better fitted by my conformation for the endurance of cold than heat. But my chief delights were the sight of the flowers, the birds, and all the gay apparel of summer; when those deserted me, I turned with more attention towards the cottagers. Their happiness was not decreased by the absence of summer. They loved and sympathised with one another; and their joys, depending on each other, were not interrupted by the casualties that took place around them. The more I saw of them, the greater became my desire to claim their protection and kindness; my heart yearned to be known and loved by these amiable creatures; to see their sweet looks directed towards me with affection was the utmost limit of my ambition. I dared not think that they would turn them from me with disdain and horror. The poor that stopped at their door were never driven away. I asked, it is true, for greater treasures than a little food or rest: I required kindness and sympathy; but I did not believe myself unworthy of it.

'The winter advanced, and an entire revolution of the seasons had taken place since I awoke into life. My attention, at this time, was solely directed towards my plan of introducing myself into the cottage of my protectors. I revolved many projects; but that on which I finally fixed was, to enter the dwelling when the blind old man should be alone. I had sagacity enough to discover, that the unnatural hideousness of my person was the chief object of horror with those who had formerly beheld me. My voice, although harsh, had nothing terrible in it; I thought, therefore, that if in the absence of his children, I could gain the good-will and mediation of the old De Lacey, I might by his means be tolerated by my younger protectors.

'One day, when the sun shone on the red leaves that strewed the ground, and diffused cheerfulness, although it denied warmth, Safie, Agatha, and Felix departed on a long country walk, and the old man, at his own desire, was left alone in the cottage. When his children had departed, he took up his guitar, and played several mournful but sweet airs, more sweet and mournful than I had ever heard him play before. At first his countenance was illuminated with pleasure, but, as he continued, thoughtfulness and sadness succeeded; at length, laying aside the instrument, he sat absorbed in reflection.

'My heart beat quick; this was the hour and moment of trial, which would decide my hopes, or realise my fears. The servants were gone to a neighbouring fair. All was silent in and around the cottage: it was an excellent opportunity; yet, when I proceeded to execute my plan, my limbs failed me, and I sank to the ground. Again I rose; and, exerting all the firmness of which I was master, removed the planks which I had placed before my hovel to conceal my retreat. The fresh air revived me, and, with renewed determination, I approached the door of their cottage.

'I knocked. "Who is there?" said the old man – "Come in."

'I entered; "Pardon this intrusion", said I; "I am a traveller in want of a little rest; you would greatly oblige me if you would allow me to remain a few minutes before the fire."

"'Enter," said De Lacey, "and I will try in what manner I can to relieve your wants; but, unfortunately, my children are from home, and as I am blind, I am afraid I shall find it difficult to procure food for you."

"'Do not trouble yourself, my kind host; I have food; it is warmth and rest only that I need."

'I sat down, and a silence ensued. I knew that every minute was precious to me, yet I remained irresolute in what manner to commence the interview; when the old man addressed me. "By your language, stranger, I suppose you are my countryman; – are you French?"

"'No, but I was educated by a French family, and understand that language only. I am now going to claim the protection of some friends, whom I sincerely love, and of whose favour I have some hopes."

"'Are they Germans?"

"'No, they are French. But let us change the subject. I am an unfortunate and deserted creature; I look around, and I have no relation or friend upon earth. These amiable people to whom I go have never seen me, and know little of me. I am full of fears, for if I fail there, I am an outcast in the world forever."

"'Do not despair. To be friendless is indeed to be unfortunate; but the hearts of men, when unprejudiced by any obvious self-interest, are full of brotherly love and charity. Rely, therefore, on your hopes; and if these friends are good and amiable, do not despair."

"'They are kind – they are the most excellent creatures in the world; but unfortunately, they are prejudiced against me. I have good dispositions; my life has been hitherto harmless and in some degree beneficial; but a fatal prejudice clouds their eyes, and where they ought to see a feeling and kind friend, they behold only a detestable monster."

"'That is indeed unfortunate; but if you are really blameless, cannot you undeceive them?"

"'I am about to undertake that task; and it is on that account that I feel so many overwhelming terrors. I tenderly love these friends; I have, unknown to them, been for many months in the habits of daily kindness towards them; but they believe that I wish to injure them, and it is that prejudice which I wish to overcome."

"'Where do these friends reside?'"

"'Near this spot.'"

'The old man paused and then continued, "If you will unreservedly confide to me the particulars of your tale, I perhaps may be of use in undeceiving them. I am blind and cannot judge of your countenance, but there is something in your words which persuades me that you are sincere. I am poor and an exile, but it will afford me true pleasure to be in any way serviceable to a human creature."

"'Excellent man! I thank you and accept your generous offer. You raise me from the dust by this kindness; and I trust that, by your aid, I shall not be driven from the society and sympathy of your fellow-creatures."

"'Heaven forbid! Even if you were really criminal, for that can only drive you to desperation, and not instigate you to virtue. I also am unfortunate; I and my family have been condemned, although innocent; judge, therefore, if I do not feel for your misfortunes."

"'How can I thank you, my best and only benefactor? From your lips first have I heard the voice of kindness directed towards me; I shall be forever grateful; and your present humanity assures me of success with those friends whom I am on the point of meeting."

"'May I know the names and residence of those friends?'"

'I paused. This, I thought, was the moment of decision, which was to rob me of, or bestow happiness on me forever. I struggled vainly for firmness sufficient to answer him, but the effort destroyed all my remaining strength; I sank on the chair and sobbed aloud. At that moment I heard the steps of my younger protectors. I had not a moment to lose, but, seizing the hand of the old man, I cried, "Now is the time! Save and protect me! You and your family are the friends whom I seek. Do not you desert me in the hour of trial!"

"'Great God!" exclaimed the old man, "who are you?"

'At that instant the cottage door was opened, and Felix, Safie, and Agatha entered. Who can describe their horror and consternation on beholding me? Agatha fainted, and Safie, unable to attend to her friend, rushed out of the cottage. Felix darted forward, and with supernatural force tore me from his father, to whose knees I clung: in a transport of fury, he dashed me to the ground and struck me violently with a stick. I could have torn him limb from limb, as the lion rends the antelope. But my heart sunk within me as with bitter sickness, and I refrained. I saw him on the point of repeating his blow, when, overcome by pain and anguish, I quitted the cottage, and in the general tumult escaped unperceived to my hovel.'

CHAPTER 8

'Cursed, cursed creator! Why did I live? Why, in that instant, did I not extinguish the spark of existence which you had so wantonly bestowed? I know not; despair had not yet taken possession of me; my feelings were those of rage and revenge. I could with pleasure have destroyed the cottage and its inhabitants, and have glutted myself with their shrieks and misery.

'When night came I quitted my retreat and wandered in the wood; and now, no longer restrained by the fear of discovery, I gave vent to my anguish in fearful howlings. I was like a wild beast that had broken the toils, destroying the objects that obstructed me and ranging through the wood with a staglike swiftness. O! what a miserable night I passed! the cold stars shone in mockery, and the bare trees waved their branches above me: now and then the sweet voice of a bird burst forth amidst the universal stillness. All, save I, were at rest or in enjoyment: I, like the archfiend, bore a hell within me, and finding myself unsympathised with, wished to tear up the trees, spread havoc and destruction around me, and then to have sat down and enjoyed the ruin.

'But this was a luxury of sensation that could not endure; I became fatigued with excess of bodily exertion, and sank on the damp grass in the sick impotence of despair. There was none among the myriads of men that existed who would pity or assist me; and should I feel kindness towards my enemies? No: from that moment I declared ever-lasting war against the species, and, more than all, against him who had formed me, and sent me forth to this insupportable misery.

'The sun rose; I heard the voices of men and knew that it was impossible to return to my retreat during that day. Accordingly I hid myself in some thick underwood, determining to devote the ensuing hours to reflection on my situation.

'The pleasant sunshine, and the pure air of day, restored me to some degree of tranquillity; and when I considered what had passed at the cottage, I could not help believing that I had been too hasty in my conclusions. I had certainly acted imprudently. It was apparent that my conversation had interested the father in my behalf, and I was a fool in having exposed my person to the horror of his children. I ought to have familiarised the old De Lacey to me, and by degrees to have discovered myself to the rest of his family, when they should have been prepared for my approach. But I did not believe my errors to be irretrievable, and after much consideration I resolved to return to the cottage, seek the old man, and by my representations win him to my party.

'These thoughts calmed me, and in the afternoon I sank into a profound sleep; but the fever of my blood did not allow me to be visited by peaceful dreams. The horrible scene of the preceding day was forever acting before my eyes; the females were flying, and the enraged Felix tearing me from his father's feet. I awoke exhausted; and finding that it was already night, I crept forth from my hiding-place, and went in search of food.

'When my hunger was appeased, I directed my steps towards the well-known path that conducted to the cottage. All there was at peace. I crept into my hovel, and remained in silent expectation of the accustomed hour when the family arose. That hour passed, the sun mounted high in the heavens, but the cottagers did not appear. I trembled violently, apprehending some dreadful misfortune. The inside of the cottage was dark, and I heard no motion; I cannot describe the agony of this suspense.

'Presently two countrymen passed by; but pausing near the cottage, they entered into conversation, using violent gesticulations; but I did not understand what they said, as they spoke the language of the country, which differed from that of my protectors. Soon after, however, Felix approached with another man; I was surprised, as I knew that he had not quitted the cottage that morning, and waited anxiously to discover, from his discourse, the meaning of these unusual appearances.

'"Do you consider," said his companion to him, "that you will be obliged to pay three months' rent and to lose the produce of your garden? I do not wish to take any unfair advantage, and I beg therefore that you will take some days to consider of your determination."

'"It is utterly useless," replied Felix; "we can never again inhabit your cottage. The life of my father is in the greatest danger, owing to the dreadful circumstance that I have related. My wife and my sister will never recover from their horror. I intreat you not to reason with me any more. Take possession of your tenement, and let me fly from this place."

'Felix trembled violently as he said this. He and his companion entered the cottage, in which they remained for a few minutes, and then departed. I never saw any of the family of De Lacey more.

'I continued for the remainder of the day in my hovel in a state of utter and stupid despair. My protectors had departed, and had broken the only link that held me to the world. For the first time the feelings of revenge and hatred filled my bosom, and I did not strive to control them; but allowing myself to be borne away by the stream, I bent my mind towards injury and death. When I thought of my friends, of the mild voice of De Lacey, the gentle eyes of Agatha, and the exquisite beauty of the Arabian, these thoughts vanished and a gush of tears somewhat soothed me. But again when I reflected that they had spurned and deserted me, anger returned, a rage of anger, and unable to injure anything human, I turned my fury towards inanimate objects. As night advanced I placed a variety of combustibles around the cottage; and, after having destroyed every vestige of cultivation in the garden, I waited with forced impatience until the moon had sunk to commence my operations.

'As the night advanced, a fierce wind arose from the woods, and quickly dispersed the clouds that had loitered in the heavens; the blast tore along like a mighty avalanche and produced a kind of insanity in my spirits, that burst all bounds of reason and reflection. I lighted the dry branch of a tree and danced with fury around the devoted cottage, my eyes still fixed on the western horizon, the edge of which the moon nearly touched. A part of its orb was at length hid, and I waved my brand; it sank, and with a loud scream I fired the straw, and heath, and bushes, which I had collected. The wind fanned the fire, and the cottage was quickly enveloped by the flames, which clung to it and licked it with their forked and destroying tongues.

'As soon as I was convinced that no assistance could save any part of the habitation, I quitted the scene, and sought for refuge in the woods.

'And now, with the world before me, whither should I bend my steps? I resolved to fly far from the scene of my misfortunes; but to me, hated and despised, every country must be equally horrible. At length the thought of you crossed my mind. I learned from your papers that you were my father, my creator; and to whom could I apply with more fitness than to him who had given me life? Among the lessons that Felix had bestowed upon Safie, geography had not been omitted: I had learned from these the relative situations of the different countries of the earth. You had mentioned Geneva as the name of your native town; and towards this place I resolved to proceed.

'But how was I to direct myself? I knew that I must travel in a south-westerly direction to reach my destination; but the sun was my only guide. I did not know the names of the towns that I was to pass through, nor could I ask information from a single human being; but I did not despair. From you only could I hope for succour, although towards you I felt no sentiment but that of hatred. Unfeeling, heartless creator! You had endowed me with perceptions and passions and then cast me abroad an object for the scorn and horror of mankind. But on you only had I any claim for pity and redress, and from you I determined to seek that justice which I vainly attempted to gain from any other being that wore the human form.

'My travels were long, and the sufferings I endured intense. It was late in autumn when I quitted the district where I had so long resided. I travelled only at night, fearful of encountering the visage of a human being. Nature decayed around me, and the sun became heatless; rain and snow poured around me; mighty rivers were frozen; the surface of the earth was hard and chill, and bare, and I found no shelter. Oh, earth! how often did I imprecate curses on the cause of my being! The mildness of my nature had fled, and all within me was turned to gall and bitterness. The nearer I approached to your habitation, the more deeply did I feel the spirit of revenge enkindled in my heart. Snow fell, and the waters were hardened, but I rested not. A few incidents now and then directed me, and I possessed a map of the country; but I often wandered wide from my path. The agony of my feelings allowed me no respite: no incident occurred from which my rage and misery could not extract its food; but a circumstance that happened when I arrived on the confines of Switzerland, when the sun had recovered its warmth and the earth again began to look green, confirmed in an especial manner the bitterness and horror of my feelings.

'I generally rested during the day, and travelled only when I was secured by night from the view of man. One morning, however, finding that my path lay through a deep wood, I ventured to continue my journey after the sun had risen; the day, which was one of the first of spring, cheered even me by the loveliness of its sunshine and the balminess of the air. I felt emotions of gentleness and pleasure, that had long appeared dead, revive within me. Half surprised by the novelty of these sensations, I allowed myself to be borne away by them, and, forgetting my solitude and deformity, dared to be happy. Soft tears again bedewed my cheeks, and I even raised my humid eyes with thankfulness towards the blessed sun, which bestowed such joy upon me.

'I continued to wind among the paths of the wood, until I came to its boundary, which was skirted by a deep and rapid river, into which many of the trees bent their branches, now budding with the fresh spring. Here I paused, not exactly knowing what path to pursue, when I heard the sound of voices, that induced me to conceal myself under the shade of a cypress. I was scarcely hid, when a young girl came running towards the spot where I was concealed, laughing, as if she ran from some one in sport. She continued her course along the precipitous sides of the river, when suddenly her foot slipt, and she fell into the rapid stream. I rushed from my hiding-place, and, with extreme labour from the force of the current, saved her, and dragged her to shore. She was senseless; and I endeavoured, by every means in my power, to restore animation, when I was suddenly interrupted by the approach of a rustic, who was probably the person from whom she had playfully fled. On seeing me, he darted towards me, and tearing the girl from my arms, hastened towards the deeper parts of the wood. I followed speedily, I hardly knew why; but when the man saw me draw near, he aimed a gun, which he carried, at my body, and fired. I sank to the ground, and my injurer, with increased swiftness, escaped into the wood.

'This was then the reward of my benevolence! I had saved a human being from destruction, and as a recompense I now writhed under the miserable pain of a wound which shattered the flesh and bone. The feelings of kindness and gentleness, which I had entertained but a few moments before, gave place to hellish rage and gnashing of teeth. Inflamed by pain, I vowed eternal hatred and vengeance to all mankind. But the agony of my wound overcame me; my pulses paused, and I fainted.

'For some weeks I led a miserable life in the woods, endeavouring to cure the wound which I had received. The ball had entered my shoulder, and I knew not whether it had remained there or passed through; at any rate I had no means of extracting it. My sufferings were augmented also by the oppressive sense of the injustice and ingratitude of their infliction. My daily vows rose for revenge – a deep and deadly revenge, such as would alone compensate for the outrages and anguish I had endured.

'After some weeks my wound healed, and I continued my journey. The labours I endured were no longer to be alleviated by the bright sun or gentle breezes of spring; all joy was but a mockery which insulted my desolate state, and made me feel more painfully that I was not made for the enjoyment of pleasure.

'But my toils now drew near a close, and in two months from this time, I reached the environs of Geneva.

'It was evening when I arrived, and I retired to a hiding-place among the fields that surround it, to meditate in what manner I should apply to you. I was oppressed by fatigue and hunger, and far too unhappy to enjoy the gentle breezes of evening, or the prospect of the sun setting behind the stupendous mountains of Jura.

'At this time a slight sleep relieved me from the pain of reflection, which was disturbed by the approach of a beautiful child, who came running into the recess I had chosen, with all the sportiveness of infancy. Suddenly, as I gazed on him, an idea seized me that this little creature was unprejudiced, and had lived too short a time to have imbibed a horror of deformity. If, therefore, I could seize him and educate him as my companion and friend, I should not be so desolate in this peopled earth.

'Urged by this impulse, I seized on the boy as he passed and drew him towards me. As soon as he beheld my form, he placed his hands before his eyes, and uttered a shrill scream; I drew his hand forcibly from his face and said, "Child, what is the meaning of this? I do not intend to hurt you; listen to me."

'He struggled violently. "Let me go," he cried; "monster! ugly wretch! you wish to eat me and tear me to pieces – You are an ogre – Let me go, or I will tell my papa."

'"Boy, you will never see your father again; you must come with me."

'"Hideous monster! let me go. My papa is a syndic – he is M. Frankenstein – he will punish you. You dare not keep me."

'"Frankenstein! you belong then to my enemy – to him towards whom I have sworn eternal revenge; you shall be my first victim."

'The child still struggled, and loaded me with epithets which carried despair to my heart; I grasped his throat to silence him, and in a moment he lay dead at my feet.

'I gazed on my victim, and my heart swelled with exultation and hellish triumph; clapping my hands, I exclaimed, "I too can create desolation; my enemy is not invulnerable; this death will carry despair to him, and a thousand other miseries shall torment and destroy him."

'As I fixed my eyes on the child, I saw something glittering on his breast. I took it; it was a portrait of a most lovely woman. In spite of my malignity, it softened and attracted me. For a few moments I gazed with delight on her dark eyes, fringed by deep lashes, and her lovely lips; but presently my rage returned: I remembered that I was forever deprived of the delights that such beautiful creatures could bestow; and that she whose resemblance I contemplated would, in regarding me, have changed that air of divine benignity to one expressive of disgust and affright.

'Can you wonder that such thoughts transported me with rage? I only wonder that at that moment, instead of venting my sensations in exclamations and agony, I did not rush among mankind, and perish in the attempt to destroy them.

'While I was overcome by these feelings, I left the spot where I had committed the murder, and seeking a more secluded hiding-place, I entered a barn which had appeared to me to be empty. A woman was sleeping on some straw; she was young: not indeed so beautiful as her whose portrait I held; but of an agreeable aspect and blooming in the loveliness of youth and health. Here, I thought, is one of those whose joy-imparting smiles are bestowed on all but me. And then I bent over her, and whispered, "Awake, fairest, thy lover is near – he who would give his life but to obtain one look of affection from thine eyes: my beloved, awake!"

'The sleeper stirred; a thrill of terror ran through me. Should she indeed awake, and see me, and curse me, and denounce the murderer? Thus would she assuredly act, if her darkened eyes opened, and she beheld me. The thought was madness; it stirred the fiend within me – not I, but she, shall suffer; the murder I have committed because I am forever robbed of all that she could give me, she shall atone. The crime had its source in her: be hers the punishment! Thanks to the lessons of Felix and the sanguinary laws of man, I had learned how to work mischief. I bent over her and placed the portrait securely in one of the folds of her dress. She moved again, and I fled.

'For some days I haunted the spot where these scenes had taken place; sometimes wishing to see you, sometimes resolved to quit the world and its miseries forever. At length I wandered towards these mountains, and have ranged through their immense recesses, consumed by a burning passion which you alone can gratify. We may not part until you have promised to comply with my requisition. I am alone, and miserable; man will not associate with me; but one as deformed and horrible as myself would not deny herself to me. My companion must be of the same species, and have the same defects. This being you must create.'

CHAPTER 9

The being finished speaking, and fixed his looks upon me in the expectation of a reply. But I was bewildered, perplexed, and unable to arrange my ideas sufficiently to understand the full extent of his proposition. He continued.

'You must create a female for me, with whom I can live in the interchange of those sympathies necessary for my being. This you alone can do; and I demand it of you as a right which you must not refuse to concede.'

The latter part of his tale had kindled anew in me the anger that had died away while he narrated his peaceful life among the cottagers, and, as he said this, I could no longer suppress the rage that burned within me.

'I do refuse it,' I replied; 'and no torture shall ever extort a consent from me. You may render me the most miserable of men, but you shall never make me base in my own eyes. Shall I create another like yourself, whose joint wickedness might desolate the world? Begone! I have answered you; you may torture me, but I will never consent.'

'You are in the wrong,' replied the fiend; 'and, instead of threatening, I am content to reason with you. I am malicious because I am miserable. Am I not shunned and hated by all mankind? You, my creator, would tear me to pieces, and triumph; remember that, and tell me why I should pity man more than he pities me? You would not call it murder, if you could precipitate me into one of those ice-rifts, and destroy my frame, the work of your own hands. Shall I respect man when he contemns me? Let him live with me in the interchange of kindness; and, instead of injury I would bestow every benefit upon him with tears of gratitude at his acceptance. But that cannot be; the human senses are insurmountable barriers to our union. Yet mine shall not be the submission of abject slavery. I will revenge my injuries: if I cannot inspire love, I will cause fear, and chiefly towards you my arch-enemy, because my creator, do I swear inextinguishable hatred. Have a care: I will work at your destruction, nor finish until I desolate your heart, so that you shall curse the hour of your birth.'

A fiendish rage animated him as he said this; his face was wrinkled into contortions too horrible for human eyes to behold; but presently he calmed himself and proceeded.

'I intended to reason. This passion is detrimental to me; for you do not reflect that *you* are the cause of its excess. If any being felt emotions of benevolence towards me, I should return them an hundred and an hundredfold; for that one creature's sake I would make peace with the whole kind! But I now indulge in dreams of bliss that cannot be realised. What I ask of you is reasonable and moderate; I demand a creature of another sex, but as hideous as myself; the gratification is small, but it is all that I can receive, and it shall content me. It is true, we shall be monsters, cut off from all the world; but on that account we shall be more attached to one another. Our lives will not be happy, but they will be harmless, and free from the misery I now feel. Oh! my creator, make me happy; let me feel gratitude towards you for one benefit! Let me see that I excite the sympathy of some existing thing; do not deny me my request!'

I was moved. I shuddered when I thought of the possible consequences of my consent, but I felt that there was some justice in his argument. His tale, and the feelings he now expressed, proved him to be a creature of fine sensations; and did I not as his maker, owe him all the portion of happiness that it was in my power to bestow? He saw my change of feeling and continued.

'If you consent, neither you nor any other human being shall ever see us again: I will go to the vast wilds of South America. My food is not that of man; I do not destroy the lamb and the kid to glut my appetite; acorns and berries afford me sufficient nourishment. My companion will be of the same nature as myself, and will be content with the same fare. We shall make our bed of dried leaves; the sun will shine on us as on man, and will ripen our food. The picture I present to you is peaceful and human, and you must feel that you could deny it only in the wantonness of power and cruelty. Pitiless as you have been towards me, I now see compassion in your eyes; let me seize the favourable moment and persuade you to promise what I so ardently desire.'

'You propose,' replied I, 'to fly from the habitations of man, to dwell in those wilds where the beasts of the field will be your only companions. How can you, who long for the love and sympathy of man, persevere in this exile? You will return, and again seek their kindness, and you will meet with their detestation; your evil passions will be renewed, and you will then have a companion to aid you in the task of destruction. This may not be: cease to argue the point, for I cannot consent.'

'How inconstant are your feelings! but a moment ago you were moved by my representations, and why do you again harden yourself to my complaints? I swear to you, by the earth which I inhabit, and by you that made me, that with the companion you bestow I will quit the neighbourhood of man, and dwell, as it may chance, in the most savage of places. My evil passions will have fled, for I shall meet with sympathy! my life will flow quietly away, and in my dying moments I shall not curse my maker.'

His words had a strange effect upon me. I compassionated him and sometimes felt a wish to console him; but when I looked upon him, when I saw the filthy mass that moved and talked, my heart sickened and my feelings were altered to those of horror and hatred. I tried to stifle these sensations; I thought, that as I could not sympathise with him, I had no right to withhold from him the small portion of happiness which was yet in my power to bestow.

'You swear,' I said, 'to be harmless; but have you not already shown a degree of malice that should reasonably make me distrust you? May not even this be a feint that will increase your triumph by affording a wider scope for your revenge?'

'How is this? I must not be trifled with: and I demand an answer. If I have no ties and no affections, hatred and vice must be my portion; the love of another will destroy the cause of my crimes, and I shall become a thing of whose existence every one will be ignorant. My vices are the children of a forced solitude that I abhor; and my virtues will necessarily arise when I live in communion with an equal. I shall feel the affections of a sensitive being, and become linked to the chain of existence and events, from which I am now excluded.'

I paused some time to reflect on all he had related, and the various arguments which he had employed. I thought of the promise of virtues which he had displayed on the opening of his existence, and the subsequent blight of all kindly feeling by the loathing and scorn which his protectors had manifested towards him. His power and threats were not omitted to my calculations: a creature who could exist in the ice-caves of the glaciers, and hide himself from pursuit among the ridges of inaccessible precipices, was a being possessing faculties it would be vain to cope with. After a long pause of reflection, I concluded that the justice due both to him and my fellow creatures demanded of me that I should comply with his request. Turning to him, therefore, I said –

'I consent to your demand, on your solemn oath to quit Europe forever, and every other place in the neighbourhood of man, as soon as I shall deliver into your hands a female who will accompany you in your exile.'

'I swear,' he cried, 'by the sun, and by the blue sky of Heaven, and by the fire of love that burns my heart, that if you grant my prayer, while they exist you shall never behold me again. Depart to your home, and commence your labours: I shall watch their progress with unutterable anxiety; and fear not but that when you are ready I shall appear.'

Saying this, he suddenly quitted me, fearful, perhaps, of any change in my sentiments. I saw him descend the mountain with greater speed than the flight of an eagle, and quickly lost among the undulations of the sea of ice.

His tale had occupied the whole day, and the sun was upon the verge of the horizon when he departed. I knew that I ought to hasten my descent towards the valley, as I should soon be encompassed in darkness; but my heart was heavy, and my steps slow. The labour of winding among the little paths of the mountain and fixing my feet firmly as I advanced, perplexed me, occupied as I was by the emotions which the occurrences of the day had produced. Night was far advanced when I came to the half way resting-place and seated myself beside the fountain. The stars shone at intervals, as the clouds passed from over them; the dark pines rose before me, and every here and there a broken tree lay on the ground: it was a scene of wonderful solemnity and stirred strange thoughts within me. I wept bitterly; and clasping my hands in agony, I exclaimed, 'Oh! stars and clouds and winds, ye are all about to mock me: if ye really pity me, crush sensation and memory; let me become as nought; but if not, depart, depart, and leave me in darkness.'

These were wild and miserable thoughts; but I cannot describe to you how the eternal twinkling of the stars weighed upon me, and how I listened to every blast of wind, as if it were a dull ugly siroc on its way to consume me.

Morning dawned before I arrived at the village of Chamounix; I took no rest, but returned immediately to Geneva. Even in my own heart I could give no expression to my sensations – they weighed on me with a mountain's weight, and their excess destroyed my agony beneath them. Thus I returned home, and entering the house, presented myself to the family. My haggard and wild appearance awoke intense alarm; but I answered no questions, scarcely did I speak. I felt as if I were placed under a ban – as if I had no right to claim their sympathies – as if never more might I enjoy companionship with them. Yet even thus I loved them to adoration; and to save them, I resolved to dedicate myself to my most abhorred task. The prospect of such an occupation made every other circumstance of existence pass before me like a dream, and that thought only had to me the reality of life.

END OF VOLUME TWO

Volume III

CHAPTER 1

Day after day, week after week, passed away on my return to Geneva; and I could not collect the courage to recommence my work. I feared the vengeance of the disappointed fiend, yet I was unable to overcome my repugnance to the task which was enjoined me. I found that I could not compose a female without again devoting several months to profound study and laborious disquisition. I had heard of some discoveries having been made by an English philosopher, the knowledge of which was material to my success, and I sometimes thought of obtaining my father's consent to visit England for this purpose; but I clung to every pretence of delay, and shrank from taking the first step in an undertaking whose immediate necessity began to appear less absolute to me. A change indeed had taken place in me: my health, which had hitherto declined, was now much restored; and my spirits, when unchecked by the memory of my unhappy promise, rose proportionably. My father saw this change with pleasure, and he turned his thoughts towards the best method of eradicating the remains of my melancholy, which every now and then would return by fits, and with a devouring blackness overcast the approaching sunshine. At these moments I took refuge in the most perfect solitude. I passed whole days on the lake alone in a little boat, watching the clouds, and listening to the rippling of the waves, silent and listless. But the fresh air and bright sun seldom failed to restore me to some degree of composure; and, on my return, I met the salutations of my friends with a readier smile and a more cheerful heart.

It was after my return from one of these rambles that my father, calling me aside, thus addressed me –

'I am happy to remark, my dear son, that you have resumed your former pleasures, and seem to be returning to yourself. And yet you are still unhappy, and still avoid our society. For some time I was lost in conjecture as to the cause of this; but yesterday an idea struck me, and if it is well founded, I conjure you to avow it. Reserve on such a point would be not only useless, but draw down treble misery on us all.'

I trembled violently at his exordium, and my father continued –

'I confess, my son, that I have always looked forward to your marriage with our dear Elizabeth as the tie of our domestic comfort, and the stay of my declining years. You were attached to each other from your earliest infancy; you studied together, and appeared, in dispositions and tastes, entirely suited to one another. But so blind is the experience of man, that what I conceived to be the best assistants to my plan may have entirely destroyed it. You, perhaps, regard her as your sister, without any wish that she might become your wife. Nay, you may have met with another whom you may love; and considering yourself as bound in honour to Elizabeth, this struggle may occasion the poignant misery which you appear to feel.'

'My dear father, re-assure yourself. I love my cousin tenderly and sincerely. I never saw any woman who excited, as Elizabeth does, my warmest admiration and affection. My future hopes and prospects are entirely bound up in the expectation of our union.'

'The expression of your sentiments of this subject, my dear Victor, gives me more pleasure than I have for some time experienced. If you feel thus, we shall assuredly be happy, however present events may cast a gloom over us. But it is this gloom which appears to have taken so strong a hold of your mind, that I wish to dissipate. Tell me, therefore, whether you object to an immediate solemnisation of the marriage. We have been unfortunate, and recent events have drawn us from that everyday tranquillity befitting my years and infirmities. You are younger; yet I do not suppose, possessed as you are of a competent fortune, that an early marriage would at all interfere with any future plans of honour and utility that you may have formed. Do not suppose, however, that I wish to dictate happiness to you, or that a delay on your part would cause me any serious uneasiness. Interpret my words with candour and answer me, I conjure you, with confidence and sincerity.'

I listened to my father in silence, and remained for some time incapable of offering any reply. I revolved rapidly in my mind a multitude of thoughts, and endeavoured to arrive at some conclusion. Alas! to me the idea of an immediate union with my Elizabeth was one of horror and dismay. I was bound by a solemn promise, which I had not yet fulfilled, and dared not break; or if I did, what manifold miseries might not impend over me and my devoted family! Could I enter into a festival with this deadly weight yet hanging round my neck, and bowing me to the ground? I must perform my engagement, and let the monster depart with his mate, before I allowed myself to enjoy the delight of a union from which I expected peace.

I remembered also the necessity imposed upon me of either journeying to England, or entering into a long correspondence with those philosophers of that country, whose knowledge and discoveries were of indispensable use to me in my present undertaking. The latter method of obtaining the desired intelligence was dilatory and unsatisfactory: besides, I had an insurmountable aversion to the idea of engaging myself in my loathsome task in my father's house, while in habits of familiar intercourse with those I loved. I knew that a thousand fearful accidents might occur, the slightest of which would disclose a tale to thrill all connected with me with horror. I was aware also that I should often lose all self-command, all capacity of hiding the harrowing sensations that would possess me during the progress of my unearthly occupation. I must absent myself from all I loved while thus employed. Once commenced, it would quickly be achieved, and I might be restored to my family in peace and happiness. My promise fulfilled, the monster would depart forever. Or (so my fond fancy imaged) some accident might meanwhile occur to destroy him, and put an end to my slavery forever.

These feelings dictated my answer to my father. I expressed a wish to visit England; but concealing the true reasons of this request, I clothed my desires under a guise which excited no suspicion, while I urged my desire with an earnestness that easily induced my father to comply. After so long a period of an absorbing melancholy, that resembled madness in its intensity and effects, he was glad to find that I was capable of taking pleasure in the idea of such a journey, and he hoped that change of scene and varied amusement would, before my return, have restored me entirely to myself.

The duration of my absence was left to my own choice; a few months, or at most a year, was the period contemplated. One paternal kind precaution he had taken to ensure my having a companion. Without previously communicating with me, he had, in concert with Elizabeth, arranged that Clerval should join me in Strasburgh. This interfered with the solitude I coveted for the prosecution of my task; yet at the commencement of my journey the presence of my friend could in no way be an impediment, and truly I rejoiced that thus I should be saved many hours of lonely, maddening reflection. Nay, Henry might stand between me and the intrusion of my foe. If I were alone, would he not at times force his abhorred presence on me, to remind me of my task or to contemplate its progress?

To England, therefore, I was bound, and it was understood that my union with Elizabeth should take place immediately on my return. My father's age rendered him extremely averse to delay. For myself, there was one reward I promised myself from my detested toils – one consolation for my unparalleled sufferings; it was the prospect of that day when, enfranchised from my miserable slavery, I might claim Elizabeth, and forget the past in union with her.

I now made arrangements for my journey; but one feeling haunted me, which filled me with fear and agitation. During my absence I should leave my friends unconscious of the existence of their enemy, and unprotected from his attacks, exasperated as he might be by my departure. But he had promised to follow me wherever I might go; and would he not accompany me to England? This imagination was dreadful in itself, but soothing, inasmuch as it supposed the safety of my friends. I was agonised with the idea of the possibility that the reverse of this might happen. But through the whole period during which I was the slave of my creature I allowed myself to be governed by the impulses of the moment; and my present sensations strongly intimated that the fiend would follow me, and exempt my family from the danger of his machinations.

It was in the latter end of August that I again quitted my native country. My journey had been my own suggestion, and Elizabeth, therefore, acquiesced; but she was filled with disquiet at the idea of my suffering, away from her, the inroads of misery and grief. It had been her care which provided me a companion in Clerval – and yet a man is blind to a thousand minute circumstances, which call forth a woman's sedulous attention. She longed to bid me hasten my return – a thousand conflicting emotions rendered her mute, as she bade me a tearful, silent farewell.

I threw myself into the carriage that was to convey me away, hardly knowing whither I was going, and careless of what was passing around. I remembered only, and it was with a bitter anguish that I reflected on it, to order that my chemical instruments should be packed to go with me. Filled with dreary imaginations, I passed through many beautiful and majestic scenes, but my eyes were fixed and unobserving. I could only think of the bourne of my travels, and the work which was to occupy me whilst they endured.

After some days spent in listless indolence, during which I traversed many leagues, I arrived at Strasburgh where I waited two days for Clerval. He came. Alas, how great was the contrast between us! He was alive to every new scene; joyful when he saw the beauties of the setting sun, and more happy when he beheld it rise and recommence a new day. He pointed out to me the shifting colours of the landscape, and the appearances of the sky. 'This is what it is to live,' he cried; 'now I enjoy existence! But you, my dear Frankenstein, wherefore are you desponding and sorrowful?' In truth, I was occupied by gloomy thoughts, and neither saw the descent of the evening star, nor the golden sunrise reflected in the Rhine. – And you, my friend, would be far more amused with the journal of Clerval, who observed the scenery with an eye of feeling and delight, than in listening to my reflections. I, a miserable wretch, haunted by a curse that shut up every avenue to enjoyment.

We had agreed to descend the Rhine in a boat from Strasburgh to Rotterdam, whence we might take shipping for London. During this voyage we passed many willowy islands, and saw several beautiful towns. We stayed a day at Mannheim, and, on the fifth from our departure from Strasburgh, arrived at Mayence. The course of the Rhine below Mayence becomes much more picturesque. The river descends rapidly, and winds between hills, not high, but steep, and of beautiful forms. We saw many ruined castles standing on the edges of precipices, surrounded by black woods, high and inaccessible. This part of the Rhine, indeed, presents a singularly variegated landscape. In one spot you view rugged hills, ruined castles overlooking tremendous precipices, with the dark Rhine rushing beneath; and, on the sudden turn of a promontory, flourishing vineyards with green sloping banks and a meandering river and populous towns occupy the scene.

We travelled at the time of the vintage, and heard the song of the labourers, as we glided down the stream. Even I, depressed in mind, and my spirits continually agitated by gloomy feelings, even I was pleased. I lay at the bottom of the boat, and, as I gazed on the cloud-less blue sky, I seemed to drink in a tranquillity to which I had long been a stranger. And if these were my sensations, who can describe those of Henry? He felt as if he had been transported to Fairy-land and enjoyed a happiness seldom tasted by man. 'I have seen,' he said, 'the most beautiful scenes of my own country; I have visited the lakes of Lucerne and Uri, where the snowy mountains descend almost perpendicularly to the water, casting black and impenetrable shades, which would cause a gloomy and mournful appearance were it not for the most verdant islands that relieve the eye by their gay appearance; I have seen this lake agitated by a tempest, when the wind tore up whirlwinds of water and gave you an idea of what the waterspout must be on the great ocean; and the waves dash with fury the base of the mountain, where the priest and his mistress were overwhelmed by an avalanche and where their dying voices are still said to be heard amid the pauses of the nightly wind; I have seen the mountains of La Valais, and the Pays de Vaud: but this country, Victor, pleases me more than all those wonders. The mountains of Switzerland are more majestic and strange; but there is a charm in the banks of this divine river, that I never before saw equalled. Look at that castle which overhangs yon precipice; and that also on the island, almost concealed amongst the foliage of those lovely trees; and now that group of labourers coming from among their vines; and that village half hid in the recess of the mountain. Oh, surely the spirit that inhabits and guards this place has a soul more in harmony with man than those who pile the glacier, or retire to the inaccessible peaks of the mountains of our own country.'

Clerval! beloved friend! Even now it delights me to record your words, and to dwell on the praise of which you are so eminently deserving. He was a being formed in the 'very poetry of nature'. His wild and enthusiastic imagination was chastened by the sensibility of his heart. His soul overflowed with ardent affections, and his friendship was of that devoted and wondrous nature that the worldly-minded teach us to look for only in the imagination. But even human sympathies were not sufficient to satisfy his eager mind. The scenery of external nature, which others regard only with admiration, he loved with ardour: –

> The sounding cataract
> Haunted him like a passion: the tall rock,
> The mountain, and the deep and gloomy wood,

Their colours and their forms, were then to him
An appetite; a feeling, and a love,
> That had no need of a remoter charm,
> By thought supplied, or any interest
> Unborrow'd from the eye.

And where does he now exist? Is this gentle and lovely being lost forever? Has this mind, so replete with ideas, imaginations fanciful and magnificent, which formed a world, whose existence depended on the life of its creator – has this mind perished? Does it now only exist in my memory? No, it is not thus; your form so divinely wrought, and beaming with beauty, has decayed, but your spirit still visits and consoles your unhappy friend.

Pardon this gush of sorrow; these ineffectual words are but a slight tribute to the unexampled worth of Henry, but they soothe my heart, overflowing with the anguish which his remembrance creates. I will proceed with my tale.

Beyond Cologne we descended to the plains of Holland; and we resolved to post the remainder of our way; for the wind was contrary, and the stream of the river was too gentle to aid us.

Our journey here lost the interest arising from beautiful scenery, but we arrived in a few days at Rotterdam; whence we proceeded by sea to England. It was on a clear morning, in the latter days of September, that I first saw the white cliffs of Britain. The banks of the Thames presented a new scene; they were flat, but fertile, and almost every town was marked by the remembrance of some story. We saw Tilbury Fort, and remembered the Spanish Armada; Gravesend, Woolwich, and Greenwich – places which I had heard of even in my country.

At length we saw the numerous steeples of London, St Paul's towering above all, and the Tower, famed in English history.

CHAPTER 2

London was our present point of rest; we determined to remain several months in this wonderful and celebrated city. Clerval desired the intercourse of the men of genius and talent who flourished at this time; but this was with me a secondary object; I was principally occupied with the means of obtaining the information necessary for the completion of my promise, and quickly availed myself of the letters of introduction that I had brought with me, addressed to the most distinguished natural philosopher.

If this journey had taken place during my days of study and happiness, it would have afforded me inexpressible pleasure. But a blight had come over my existence, and I only visited these people for the sake of the information they might give me on the subject in which my interest was so terribly profound. Company was irksome to me; when alone, I could fill my mind with the sights of heaven and earth; the voice of Henry soothed me, and I could thus cheat myself into a transitory peace. But busy, uninteresting, joyous faces brought back despair to my heart. I saw an insurmountable barrier placed between me and my fellow-men; this barrier was sealed with the blood of William and Justine, and to reflect on the events connected with those names filled my soul with anguish.

But in Clerval I saw the image of my former self; he was inquisitive, and anxious to gain experience and instruction. The difference of manners which he observed was to him an inexhaustible source of instruction and amusement. He was also pursuing an object he had long had in view. His design was to visit India, in the belief that he had in his knowledge of its various languages, and in the views he had taken of its society, the means of materially assisting the progress of European colonisation and trade. In Britain only could he further the execution of his plan. He was forever busy; and the only check to his enjoyments was my sorrowful and dejected mind. I tried to conceal this as much as possible, that I might not debar him from the pleasures natural to one, who was entering on a new scene of life, undisturbed by any care or bitter recollection. I often refused to accompany him, alleging another engagement, that I might remain alone. I now also began to collect the materials necessary for my new creation, and this was to me like the torture of single drops of water continually falling on the head. Every thought that was devoted to it was an extreme anguish, and every word that I spoke in allusion to it caused my lips to quiver, and my heart to palpitate.

After passing some months in London, we received a letter from a person in Scotland, who had formerly been our visitor at Geneva. He mentioned the beauties of his native country, and asked us if those were not sufficient allurements to induce us to prolong our journey as far north as Perth, where he resided. Clerval eagerly desired to accept this invitation; and I, although I abhorred society, wished to view again mountains and streams, and all the wondrous works with which Nature adorns her chosen dwelling-places.

We had arrived in England at the beginning of October, and it was now February. We accordingly determined to commence our journey towards the north at the expiration of another month. In this expedition we did not intend to follow the great road to Edinburgh, but to visit Windsor, Oxford, Matlock, and the Cumberland lakes, resolving to arrive at the completion of this tour about the end of July. I packed up my chemical instruments and the materials I had collected, resolving to finish my labours in some obscure nook in the northern highlands of Scotland.

We quitted London on the 27th of March and remained a few days at Windsor, rambling in its beautiful forest. This was a new scene to us mountaineers; the majestic oaks, the quantity of game, and the herds of stately deer, were all novelties to us.

From thence we proceeded to Oxford. As we entered this city, our minds were filled with the remembrance of the events that had been transacted there more than a century and a half before. It was here that Charles I had collected his forces. This city had remained faithful to him, after the whole nation had forsaken his cause to join the standard of parliament and liberty. The memory of that unfortunate king, and his companions, the amiable Falkland, the insolent Goring, his queen and son, gave a peculiar interest to every part of the city, which they might be supposed to have inhabited. The spirit of elder days found a dwelling here, and we delighted to trace its footsteps. If these feelings had not found an imaginary gratification, the appearance of the city had yet in itself sufficient beauty to obtain our admiration. The colleges are ancient and picturesque; the streets are almost magnificent; and the lovely Isis, which flows beside it through meadows of exquisite verdure, is spread forth into a placid expanse of waters, which reflects its majestic assemblage of towers, and spires, and domes, embosomed among aged trees.

I enjoyed this scene; and yet my enjoyment was embittered both by the memory of the past, and the anticipation of the future. I was formed for peaceful happiness. During my youthful days discontent never visited my mind; and if I was ever overcome by *ennui*, the sight of what is beautiful in nature, or the study of what is excellent and sublime in the productions of man, could always interest my heart, and communicate elasticity to my spirits. But I am a blasted tree; the bolt has entered my soul; and I felt then that I should survive to exhibit what I shall soon cease to be – a miserable spectacle of wrecked humanity, pitiable to others, and intolerable to myself.

We passed a considerable period at Oxford, rambling among its environs, and endeavouring to identify every spot which might relate to the most animating epoch of English history. Our little voyages of discovery were often prolonged by the successive objects that presented themselves. We visited the tomb of the illustrious Hampden, and the field on which that patriot fell. For a moment my soul was elevated from its debasing and miserable fears, to contemplate the divine ideas of liberty and self-sacrifice, of which these sights were the monuments and the remembrancers. For an instant I dared to shake off my chains, and look around me with a free and lofty spirit; but the iron had eaten into my flesh, and I sank again, trembling and hopeless, into my miserable self.

We left Oxford with regret, and proceeded to Matlock, which was our next place of rest. The country in the neighbourhood of this village resembled, to a greater degree, the scenery of Switzerland; but every thing is on a lower scale, and the green hills want the crown of distant white Alps, which always attend on the piny mountains of my native country. We visited the wondrous cave, and the little cabinets of natural history, where the curiosities are disposed in the same manner as in the collections at Servox and Chamounix. The latter name made me tremble when pronounced by Henry; and I hastened to quit Matlock, with which that terrible scene was thus associated.

From Derby, still journeying northwards, we passed two months in

Cumberland and Westmorland. I could now almost fancy myself among the Swiss mountains. The little patches of snow which yet lingered on the northern sides of the mountains, the lakes, and the dashing of the rocky streams, were all familiar and dear sights to me. Here also we made some acquaintances, who almost contrived to cheat me into happiness. The delight of Clerval was proportionably greater than mine; his mind expanded in the company of men of talent, and he found in his own nature greater capacities and resources than he could have imagined himself to have possessed while he associated with his inferiors. 'I could pass my life here,' said he to me; 'and among these mountains I should scarcely regret Switzerland and the Rhine.'

But he found that a traveller's life is one that includes much pain amidst its enjoyments. His feelings are forever on the stretch; and when he begins to sink into repose, he finds himself obliged to quit that on which he rests in pleasure for something new, which again engages his attention, and which also he forsakes for other novelties.

We had scarcely visited various lakes of Cumberland and Westmorland, and conceived an affection for some of the inhabitants, when the period of our appointment with our Scotch friend approached, and we left them to travel on. For my own part I was not sorry. I had now neglected my promise for some time, and I feared the effects of the daemon's disappointment. He might remain in Switzerland, and wreak his vengeance on my relatives. This idea pursued me, and tormented me at every moment from which I might otherwise have snatched repose and peace. I waited for my letters with feverish impatience: if they were delayed, I was miserable, and overcome by a thousand fears; and when they arrived and I saw the superscription of Elizabeth or my father, I hardly dared to read and ascertain my fate. Sometimes I thought that the fiend followed me, and might expedite my remissness by murdering my companion. When these thoughts possessed me, I would not quit Henry for a moment, but followed him as his shadow, to protect him from the fancied rage of his destroyer. I felt as if I had committed some great crime, the consciousness of which haunted me. I was guiltless, but I had indeed drawn down a horrible curse upon my head, as mortal as that of crime.

I visited Edinburgh with languid eyes and mind; and yet that city might have interested the most unfortunate being. Clerval did not like it so

well as Oxford: for the antiquity of the latter city was more pleasing
to him. But the beauty and regularity of the new town of Edinburgh,
its romantic castle and its environs, the most delightful in the world,
Arthur's Seat, St Bernard's Well, and the Pentland Hills, compensated
him for the change, and filled him with cheerfulness and admiration.
But I was impatient to arrive at the termination of my journey.

We left Edinburgh in a week, passing through Coupar, St Andrew's,
and along the banks of the Tay, to Perth, where our friend expected
us. But I was in no mood to laugh and talk with strangers, or enter
into their feelings or plans with the good humour expected from a
guest; and accordingly I told Clerval that I wished to make the tour
of Scotland alone. 'Do you,' said I, 'enjoy yourself, and let this be
our rendezvous. I may be absent a month or two; but do not interfere
with my motions, I intreat you: leave me to peace and solitude for a
short time; and when I return, I hope it will be with a lighter heart,
more congenial to your own temper.'

Henry wished to dissuade me; but seeing me bent on this plan,
ceased to remonstrate. He intreated me to write often. 'I had rather be
with you,' he said, 'in your solitary rambles, than with these Scotch
people, whom I do not know: hasten, then, my dear friend, to return,
that I may again feel myself somewhat at home, which I cannot do
in your absence.'

Having parted from my friend, I determined to visit some remote
spot of Scotland, and finish my work in solitude. I did not doubt but
that the monster followed me, and would discover himself to me when
I should have finished, that he might receive his companion.

With this resolution I traversed the northern highlands, and fixed
on one of the remotest of the Orkneys as the scene of my labours.
It was a place fitted for such a work, being hardly more than a rock,
whose high sides were continually beaten upon by the waves. The soil
was barren, scarcely affording pasture for a few miserable cows, and
oatmeal for its inhabitants, which consisted of five persons, whose gaunt
and scraggy limbs gave tokens of their miserable fare. Vegetables and
bread, when they indulged in such luxuries, and even fresh water, was
to be procured from the mainland, which was about five miles distant.

On the whole island there were but three miserable huts, and one of
these was vacant when I arrived. This I hired. It contained but two rooms,

and these exhibited all the squalidness of the most miserable penury. The thatch had fallen in, the walls were unplastered, and the door was off its hinges. I ordered it to be repaired, bought some furniture, and took possession; an incident which would, doubtless, have occasioned some surprise had not all the senses of the cottagers been benumbed by want and squalid poverty. As it was, I lived ungazed at and unmolested, hardly thanked for the pittance of food and clothes which I gave; so much does suffering blunt even the coarsest sensations of men.

In this retreat I devoted the morning to labour; but in the evening, when the weather permitted, I walked on the stony beach of the sea to listen to the waves as they roared and dashed at my feet. It was a monotonous yet everchanging scene. I thought of Switzerland; it was far different from this desolate and appalling landscape. Its hills are covered with veins, and its cottages are scattered thickly in the plains. Its fair lakes reflect a blue and gentle sky; and, when troubled by the winds, their tumult is but as the play of a lively infant, when compared to the roarings of the giant ocean.

In this manner I distributed my occupations when I first arrived; but as I proceeded in my labour, it became every day more horrible and irksome to me. Sometimes I could not prevail on myself to enter my laboratory for several days; and at other times I toiled day and night in order to complete my work. It was, indeed, a filthy process in which I was engaged. During my first experiment, a kind of enthusiastic frenzy had blinded me to the horror of my employment; my mind was intently fixed on the consummation of my labour, and my eyes shut to the horror of my proceedings. But now I went to it in cold blood, and my heart often sickened at the work of my hands.

Thus situated, employed in the most detestable occupation, immersed in a solitude where nothing could for an instant call my attention from the actual scene in which I was engaged, my spirits became unequal; I grew restless and nervous. Every moment I feared to meet my persecutor. Sometimes I sat with my eyes fixed on the ground, fearing to raise them, lest they should encounter the object which I so much dreaded to behold. I feared to wander from the sight of my fellow-creatures, lest when alone he should come to claim his companion.

In the mean time I worked on, and my labour was already considerably advanced. I looked towards its completion with a tremulous and eager hope, which I dared not trust myself to question, but which was intermixed with obscure forebodings of evil, that made my heart sicken in my bosom.

CHAPTER 3

I sat one evening in my laboratory; the sun had set, and the moon was just rising from the sea; I had not sufficient light for my employment, and I remained idle, in a pause of consideration of whether I should leave my labour for the night, or hasten its conclusion by an unremitting attention to it. As I sat, a train of reflection occurred to me, which led me to consider the effects of what I was now doing. Three years before I was engaged in the same manner, and had created a fiend whose unparalleled barbarity had desolated my heart, and filled it forever with the bitterest remorse. I was now about to form another being, of whose dispositions I was alike ignorant; she might become ten thousand times more malignant than her mate, and delight, for it own sake, in murder and wretchedness. He had sworn to quit the neighbourhood of man, and hide himself in deserts; but she had not; and she, who in all probability was to become a thinking and reasoning animal, might refuse to comply with a compact made before her creation. They might even hate each other; the creature who already lived loathed his own deformity, and might he not conceive a greater abhorrence for it when it came before his eyes in the female form? She also might turn with disgust from him to the superior beauty of man; she might quit him, and he be again alone, exasperated by the fresh provocation of being deserted by one of his own species.

Even if they were to leave Europe, and inhabit the deserts of the new world, yet one of the first results of those sympathies for which the daemon thirsted would be children, and a race of devils would be propagated upon the earth, who might make the very existence of the species of man a condition precarious and full of terror. Had I a right, for my own benefit, to inflict this curse upon everlasting generations? I had before been moved by the sophisms of the being I had created; I had been struck senseless by his fiendish threats: but now, for the first time, the wickedness of my promise burst upon me; I shuddered to think that future ages might curse me as their pest, whose selfishness had not hesitated to buy its own peace at the price, perhaps, of the existence of the whole human race.

I trembled, and my heart failed within me, when, on looking up, I saw, by the light of the moon, the daemon at the casement. A ghastly grin wrinkled his lips as he gazed on me, where I sat fulfilling the task which he had allotted to me. Yes, he had followed me in my travels; he had loitered in forests, hid himself in caves, or taken refuge in wide and desert heaths; and he now came to mark my progress, and claim the fulfilment of my promise.

As I looked on him, his countenance expressed the utmost extent of malice and treachery. I thought with a sensation of madness on my promise of creating another like to him, and trembling with passion, tore to pieces the thing on which I was engaged. The wretch saw me destroy the creature on whose future existence he depended for happiness, and, with a howl of devilish despair and revenge, withdrew.

I left the room, and, locking the door, made a solemn vow in my own heart never to resume my labours; and then, with trembling steps, I sought my own apartment. I was alone; none were near me to dissipate the gloom, and relieve me from the sickening oppression of the most terrible reveries.

Several hours passed, and I remained near my window gazing on the sea; it was almost motionless, for the winds were hushed, and all nature reposed under the eye of the quiet moon. A few fishing vessels alone specked the water, and now and then the gentle breeze wafted the sound of voices as the fishermen called to one another. I felt the silence, although I was hardly conscious of its extreme profundity, until my ear was suddenly arrested by the paddling of oars near the shore, and a person landed close to my house.

In a few minutes after, I heard the creaking of my door, as if some one endeavoured to open it softly. I trembled from head to foot; I felt a presentiment of who it was, and wished to rouse one of the peasants who dwelt in a cottage not far from mine; but I was overcome by the sensation of helplessness, so often felt in frightful dreams, when you in vain endeavour to fly from an impending danger, and was rooted to the spot.

Presently I heard the sound of footsteps along the passage; the door opened, and the wretch whom I dreaded appeared. Shutting the door, he approached me and said in a smothered voice –

'You have destroyed the work which you began; what is it that you intend? Do you dare to break your promise? I have endured toil and misery: I left Switzerland with you; I crept along the shores of the Rhine, among its willow islands, and over the summits of its hills.

I have dwelt many months in the heaths of England, and among the deserts of Scotland. I have endured incalculable fatigue, and cold, and hunger, do you dare destroy my hopes?'

'Begone! I do break my promise; never will I create another like yourself, equal in deformity and wickedness.'

'Slave, I before reasoned with you, but you have proved yourself unworthy of my condescension. Remember that I have power; you believe yourself miserable, but I can make you so wretched that the light of day will be hateful to you. You are my creator, but I am your master – obey!'

'The hour of my irresolution is past, and the period of your power is arrived. Your threats cannot move me to do an act of wickedness; but they confirm me in a determination of not creating you a companion in vice. Shall I, in cool blood, set loose upon the earth a daemon, whose delight is in death and wretchedness? Begone! I am firm, and your words will only exasperate my rage.'

The monster saw my determination in my face, and gnashed his teeth in the impotence of anger. 'Shall each man,' cried he, 'find a wife for his bosom, and each beast have his mate, and I be alone? I had feelings of affection, and they were requited by detestation and scorn. Man! you may hate, but beware! your hours will pass in dread and misery, and soon the bolt will fall which must ravish from you your happiness forever. Are you to be happy, while I grovel in the intensity of my wretchedness? You can blast my other passions, but revenge remains – revenge, henceforth dearer than light or food! I may die, but first you, my tyrant and tormentor, shall curse the sun that gazes on your misery. Beware; for I am fearless, and therefore powerful. I will watch with the wiliness of a snake, that I may sting with its venom. Man, you shall repent of the injuries you inflict.'

'Devil, cease; and do not poison the air with these sounds of malice. I have declared my resolution to you, and I am no coward to bend beneath words. Leave me; I am inexorable.'

'It is well. I go; but remember, I shall be with you on your wedding-night.'

I started forward, and exclaimed, 'Villain! Before you sign my death-warrant, be sure that you are yourself safe.'

I would have seized him; but he eluded me, and quitted the house with precipitation. In a few moments I saw him in his boat, which shot across the waters with an arrowy swiftness, and was soon lost amidst the waves.

All was again silent; but his words rang in my ears. I burned with rage to pursue the murderer of my peace, and precipitate him into the ocean. I walked up and down my room hastily and perturbed, while my imagination conjured up a thousand images to torment and sting me. Why had I not followed him, and closed with him in mortal strife? But I had suffered him to depart, and he had directed his course towards the mainland. I shuddered to think who might be the next victim sacrificed to his insatiate revenge. And then I thought again of his words – '*I will be with you on your wedding-night.*' That then was the period fixed for the fulfilment of my destiny. In that hour I should die, and at once satisfy and extinguish his malice. The prospect did not move me to fear; yet when I thought of my beloved Elizabeth, – of her tears and endless sorrow, when she should find her lover so barbarously snatched from her, – tears, the first I had shed for many months, streamed from my eyes, and I resolved not to fall before my enemy without a bitter struggle.

The night passed away, and the sun rose from the ocean; my feelings became calmer, if it may be called calmness, when the violence of rage sinks into the depths of despair. I left the house, the horrid scene of the last night's contention, and walked on the beach of the sea, which I almost regarded as an insuperable barrier between me and my fellow-creatures; nay, a wish that such should prove the fact stole across me. I desired that I might pass my life on that barren rock, wearily, it is true, but uninterrupted by any sudden shock of misery. If I returned, it was to be sacrificed, or to see those whom I most loved die under the grasp of a daemon whom I had myself created.

I walked about the isle like a restless spectre, separated from all it loved, and miserable in the separation. When it became noon, and the sun rose higher, I lay down on the grass, and was overpowered by a deep sleep. I had been awake the whole of the preceding night, my nerves were agitated, and my eyes inflamed by watching and misery. The sleep into which I now sunk refreshed me; and when I awoke, I again felt as if I belonged to a race of human beings like myself, and I began to reflect upon what had passed with greater composure; yet still the words of the fiend rung in my ears like a death-knell; they appeared like a dream, yet distinct and oppressive as a reality.

The sun had far descended, and I still sat on the shore, satisfying my appetite, which had become ravenous, with an oaten cake, when I saw a fishing-boat land close to me, and one of the men brought me a packet; it contained letters from Geneva, and one from Clerval entreating me to join him. He said that he was wearing away his time fruitlessly where he was; that letters from the friends he had formed in London desired his return to complete the negotiation they had entered into for his Indian enterprise. He could not any longer delay his departure; but as his journey to London might be followed, even sooner than he now conjectured, by his longer voyage, he entreated me to bestow as much of my society on him as I could spare. He besought me, therefore, to leave my solitary isle, and to meet him at Perth, that we might proceed southwards together. This letter in a degree recalled me to life, and I determined to quit my island at the expiration of two days.

Yet, before I departed, there was a task to perform, on which I shuddered to reflect: I must pack up my chemical instruments; and for that purpose I must enter the room which had been the scene of my odious work, and I must handle those utensils, the sight of which was sickening to me. The next morning, at daybreak, I summoned sufficient courage, and unlocked the door of my laboratory. The remains of the half-finished creature, whom I had destroyed, lay scattered on the floor, and I almost felt as if I had mangled the living flesh of a human being. I paused to collect myself, and then entered the chamber. With trembling hand I conveyed the instruments out of the room; but I reflected that I ought not to leave the relics of my work to excite the horror and suspicion of the peasants; and I accordingly put them into a basket, with a great quantity of stones, and, laying them up, determined to throw them into the sea that very night; and in the mean time I sat upon the beach, employed in cleaning and arranging my chemical apparatus.

Nothing could be more complete than the alteration that had taken place in my feelings since the night of the appearance of the daemon. I had before regarded my promise with a gloomy despair, as a thing that, with whatever consequences, must be fulfilled; but I now felt as if a film had been taken from before my eyes, and that I, for the first time, saw clearly. The idea of renewing my labours did not for one instant occur to me; the threat I had heard weighed on my thoughts, but I did not reflect that a voluntary act of mine could avert it. I had resolved in my own mind, that to create another like the fiend I had first made would be an act of the basest and most atrocious self-ishness; and I banished from my mind every thought that could lead to a different conclusion.

Between two and three in the morning the moon rose; and I then, putting my basket aboard a little skiff, sailed out about four miles from the shore. The scene was perfectly solitary: a few boats were returning towards land, but I sailed away from them. I felt as if I was about the commission of a dreadful crime, and avoided with shuddering anxiety any encounter with my fellow-creatures. At one time the moon, which had before been clear, was suddenly overspread by a thick cloud, and I took advantage of the moment of darkness and cast my basket into the sea: I listened to the gurg-ling sound as it sunk, and then sailed away from the spot. The sky became clouded; but the air was pure, although chilled by the north-east breeze that was then rising. But it refreshed me, and filled me with such agreeable sensations, that I resolved to prolong my stay on the water; and, fixing the rudder in a direct position, stretched myself at the bottom of the boat. Clouds hid the moon, every-thing was obscure, and I heard only the sound of the boat, as its keel cut through the waves; the murmur lulled me, and in a short time I slept soundly.

I do not know how long I remained in this situation, but when I awoke I found that the sun had already mounted considerably. The wind was high, and the waves continually threatened the safety of my little skiff. I found that the wind was north-east, and must have driven me far from the coast from which I had embarked. I endeavoured to change my course, but quickly found that if I again made the attempt, the boat would be instantly filled with water.

Thus situated, my only resource was to drive before the wind. I confess that I felt a few sensations of terror. I had no compass with me, and was so slenderly acquainted with the geography of this part of the world, that the sun was of little benefit to me. I might be driven into the wide Atlantic, and feel all the tortures of starvation, or be swallowed up in the immeasurable waters that roared and buffeted around me. I had already been out many hours, and felt the torment of a burning thirst, a prelude to my other sufferings. I looked on the heavens, which were covered by clouds that flew before the wind, only to be replaced by others: I looked upon the sea, it was to be my grave. 'Fiend,' I exclaimed, 'your task is already fulfilled!' I thought of Elizabeth, of my father, and of Clerval; all left behind, on whom the monster might satisfy his sanguinary and merciless passions. This idea plunged me into a reverie, so despairing and frightful, that even now, when the scene is on the point of closing before me forever, I shudder to reflect on it.

Some hours passed thus; but by degrees, as the sun declined towards the horizon, the wind died away into a gentle breeze, and the sea became free from breakers. But these gave place to a heavy swell; I felt sick, and hardly able to hold the rudder, when suddenly I saw a line of high land towards the south.

Almost spent, as I was, by fatigue, and the dreadful suspense I endured for several hours, this sudden certainty of life rushed like a flood of warm joy to my heart, and tears gushed from my eyes.

How mutable are our feelings, and how strange is that clinging love we have of life even in the excess of misery! I constructed another sail with a part of my dress, and eagerly steered my course towards the land. It had a wild and rocky appearance, but, as I approached nearer, I easily perceived the traces of cultivation. I saw vessels near the shore, and found myself suddenly transported back to the neighbourhood of civilised man. I carefully traced the windings of the land, and hailed a steeple which I at length saw issuing from behind a small promontory. As I was in a state of extreme debility, I resolved to sail directly towards the town, as a place where I could most easily procure nourishment. Fortunately I had money with me. As I turned the promontory, I perceived a small neat town and a good harbour, which I entered, my heart bounding with joy at my unexpected escape.

As I was occupied in fixing the boat and arranging the sails, several people crowded towards the spot. They seemed much surprised at my appearance, but instead of offering me any assistance, whispered together with gestures that at any other time might have produced in me a slight sensation of alarm. As it was, I merely remarked that they spoke English; and I therefore addressed them in that language. 'My good friends,' said I, 'will you be so kind as to tell me the name of this town, and inform me where I am?'

'You will know that soon enough,' replied a man with a hoarse voice. 'May be you are come to a place that will not prove much to your taste; but you will not be consulted as to your quarters, I promise you.'

I was exceedingly surprised on receiving so rude an answer from a stranger; and I was also disconcerted on perceiving the frowning and angry countenances of his companions. 'Why do you answer me so roughly?' I replied; 'surely it is not the custom of Englishmen to receive strangers so inhospitably.'

'I do not know,' said the man, 'what the custom of the English may be; but it is the custom of the Irish to hate villains.'

While this strange dialogue continued, I perceived the crowd rapidly increase. Their faces expressed a mixture of curiosity and anger, which annoyed, and in some degree alarmed me. I enquired the way to the inn; but no one replied. I then moved forward, and a murmuring sound arose from the crowd as they followed and surrounded me; when an ill-looking man approaching, tapped me on the shoulder, and said, 'Come, sir, you must follow me to Mr Kirwin's, to give an account of yourself.'

'Who is Mr Kirwin? Why am I to give an account of myself? Is not this a free country?'

'Ay, sir, free enough for honest folks. Mr Kirwin is a magistrate; and you are to give an account of the death of a gentleman who was found murdered here last night.'

This answer startled me; but I presently recovered myself. I was innocent; that could easily be proved: accordingly I followed my conductor in silence and was led to one of the best houses in the town. I was ready to sink from fatigue and hunger; but, being surrounded by a crowd, I thought it politic to rouse all my strength, that no physical debility might be construed into apprehension or conscious guilt. Little did I then expect the calamity that was in a few moments to overwhelm me, and extinguish in horror and despair all fear of ignominy or death.

I must pause here; for it requires all my fortitude to recall the memory of the frightful events which I am about to relate, in proper detail, to my recollection.

CHAPTER 4

I was soon introduced into the presence of the magistrate, an old benevolent man, with calm and mild manners. He looked on me, however, with some degree of severity; and then, turning towards my conductors, he asked who appeared as witnesses on this occasion.

About half a dozen men came forward; and, one being selected by the magistrate, he deposed, that he had been out fishing the night before with his son and brother-in-law, Daniel Nugent, when, about ten o'clock, they observed a strong northerly blast rising, and they accordingly put in for port. It was a very dark night, as the moon had not yet risen; they did not land at the harbour, but, as they had been accustomed, at a creek about two miles below. He walked on first, carrying a part of the fishing tackle, and his companions followed him at some distance. As he was proceeding along the sands, he struck his foot against something, and fell at his length on the ground. His companions came up to assist him; and, by the light of their lantern, they found that he had fallen on the body of a man, who was to all appearance dead. Their first supposition was, that it was the corpse of some person who had been drowned, and was thrown on shore by the waves, but, on examination, they found that the clothes were not wet, and even that the body was not then cold. They instantly carried it to the cottage of an old woman near the spot, and endeavoured, but in vain, to restore it to life. It appeared to be a handsome young man, about five and twenty years of age. He had apparently been strangled; for there was no sign of any violence, except the black mark of fingers on his neck.

The first part of his deposition did not in the least interest me; but when the mark of the fingers was mentioned, I remembered the murder of my brother and felt myself extremely agitated; my limbs trembled, and a mist came over my eyes, which obliged me to lean on a chair for support. The magistrate observed me with a keen eye, and of course drew an unfavourable augury from my manner.

The son confirmed his father's account: but when Daniel Nugent was called, he swore positively that just before the fall of his companion, he saw a boat, with a single man in it, at a short distance from the shore; and, as far as he could judge by the light of a few stars, it was the same boat in which I had just landed.

A woman deposed, that she lived near the beach, and was standing at the door of her cottage, waiting for the return of the fishermen, about an hour before she heard of the discovery of the body, when she saw a boat with only one man in it push off from that part of the shore where the corpse was afterwards found.

Another woman confirmed the account of the fishermen having brought the body into her house; it was not cold. They put it into a bed and rubbed it; and Daniel went to the town for an apothecary, but life was quite gone.

Several other men were examined concerning my landing; and they agreed that, with the strong north wind that had arisen during the night, it was very probable that I had beaten about for many hours, and had been obliged to return nearly to the same spot from which I had departed. Besides, they observed that it appeared that I had brought the body from another place, and it was likely, that as I did not appear to know the shore, I might have put into the harbour ignorant of the distance of the town of *** from the place where I had deposited the corpse.

Mr Kirwin, on hearing this evidence, desired that I should be taken into the room where the body lay for interment, that it might be observed what effect the sight of it would produce upon me. This idea was probably suggested by the extreme agitation I had exhibited when the mode of the murder had been described. I was accordingly conducted, by the magistrate and several other persons, to the inn. I could not help being struck by the strange coincidences that had taken place during this eventful night; but, knowing that I had been conversing with several persons in the island I had inhabited about the time that the body had been found, I was perfectly tranquil as to the consequences of the affair.

I entered the room where the corpse lay, and was led up to the coffin. How can I describe my sensations of beholding it? I feel yet parched with horror, nor can I reflect on that terrible moment without shuddering and agony. The examination, the presence of the magistrate and witnesses, passed like a dream from my memory, when I saw the lifeless form of Henry Clerval stretched before me. I gasped for breath; and throwing myself on the body, I exclaimed, 'Have my murderous machinations deprived you also, my dearest Henry, of life? Two I have already destroyed; other victims await their destiny: but you, Clerval, my friend, my benefactor –'

The human frame could no longer support the agonies that I endured, and I was carried out of the room in strong convulsions.

A fever succeeded to this. I lay for two months on the point of death: my ravings, as I afterwards heard, were frightful; I called myself the murderer of William, of Justine, and of Clerval. Sometimes I intreated my attendants to assist me in the destruction of the fiend by whom I was tormented; and at others, I felt the fingers of the monster already grasping my neck, and screamed aloud with agony and terror. Fortunately, as I spoke my native language, Mr Kirwin alone understood me; but my gestures and bitter cries were sufficient to affright the other witnesses.

Why did I not die? More miserable than man ever was before, why did I not sink into forgetfulness and rest? Death snatches away many blooming children, the only hopes of their doating parents: how many brides and youthful lovers have been one day in the bloom of health and hope, and the next a prey for worms and the decay of the tomb! Of what materials was I made, that I could thus resist so many shocks, which, like the turning of the wheel, continually renewed the torture?

But I was doomed to live; and in two months, found myself as awaking from a dream, in a prison, stretched on a wretched bed, surrounded by gaolers, turnkeys, bolts, and all the miserable apparatus of a dungeon. It was morning, I remember, when I thus awoke to understanding: I had forgotten the particulars of what had happened, and only felt as if some great misfortune had suddenly overwhelmed me; but when I looked around, and saw the barred windows, and the squalidness of the room in which I was, all flashed across my memory, and I groaned bitterly.

This sound disturbed an old woman who was sleeping in a chair beside me. She was a hired nurse, the wife of one of the turnkeys, and her countenance expressed all those bad qualities which often characterise that class. The lines of her face were hard and rude, like that of persons accustomed to see without sympathising in sights of misery. Her tone expressed her entire indifference; she addressed me in English, and the voice struck me as one that I had heard during my sufferings: –

'Are you better now, sir?' said she.

I replied in the same language, with a feeble voice, 'I believe I am; but if it all be true, if indeed I did not dream, I am sorry that I am still alive to feel this misery and horror.'

'For that matter,' replied the old woman, 'if you mean about the gentleman you murdered, I believe that it were better for you if you were dead, for I fancy it will go hard for you! However, that's none of my business; I am sent to nurse you and get you well; I do my duty with a safe conscience; it were well if everybody did the same.'

I turned with loathing from the woman who could utter so unfeeling a speech to a person just saved, on the very edge of death; but I felt languid, and unable to reflect on all that had passed. The whole series of my life appeared to me as a dream; I sometimes doubted if indeed it were all true, for it never presented itself to my mind with the force of reality.

As the images that floated before me became more distinct, I grew feverish; a darkness pressed around me: no one was near me who soothed me with the gentle voice of love; no dear hand supported me. The physician came and prescribed medicines, and the old woman prepared them for me; but utter carelessness was visible in the first, and the expression of brutality was strongly marked in the visage of the second. Who could be interested in the fate of a murderer, but the hangman who would gain his fee?

These were my first reflections; but I soon learned that Mr Kirwin had shown me extreme kindness. He had caused the best room in the prison to be prepared for me (wretched indeed was the best); and it was he who had provided a physician and a nurse. It is true, he seldom came to see me, for although he ardently desired to relieve the sufferings of every human creature, he did not wish to be present at the agonies and miserable ravings of a murderer. He came, therefore, sometimes to see that I was not neglected; but his visits were short, and with long intervals.

One day, while I was gradually recovering, I was seated in a chair, my eyes half open, and my cheeks livid like those in death. I was overcome by gloom and misery, and often reflected I had better seek death than desire to remain in a world which to me was replete with wretchedness. At one time I considered whether I should not declare myself guilty, and suffer the penalty of the law, less innocent than poor Justine had been. Such were my thoughts, when the door of my apartment was opened, and Mr Kirwin entered. His countenance expressed sympathy and compassion; he drew a chair close to mine and addressed me in French –

'I fear that this place is very shocking to you; can I do anything to make you more comfortable?'

'I thank you, but all that you mention is nothing to me: on the whole earth there is no comfort which I am capable of receiving.'

'I know that the sympathy of a stranger can be but of little relief to one borne down as you are by so strange a misfortune. But you will, I hope, soon quit this melancholy abode; for, doubtless, evidence can easily be brought to free you from the criminal charge.'

'That is my least concern: I am, by a course of strange events, become the most miserable of mortals. Persecuted and tortured as I am and have been, can death by any evil to me?'

'Nothing indeed could be more unfortunate and agonising than the strange chances that have lately occurred. You were thrown, by some surprising accident, on this shore, renowned for its hospitality; seized immediately, and charged with murder. The first sight that was presented to your eyes was the body of your friend, murdered in so unaccountable a manner, and placed, as it were, by some fiend across your path.'

As Mr Kirwin said this, notwithstanding the agitation I endured on this retrospect of my sufferings, I also felt considerable surprise at the knowledge he seemed to possess concerning me. I suppose some astonishment was exhibited in my countenance; for Mr Kirwin hastened to say –

'Immediately upon your being taken ill, all the papers that were on your person were brought me, and I examined them that I might discover some trace by which I could send to your relations an account of your misfortune and illness. I found several letters, and, among others, one which I discovered from its commencement to be from your father. I instantly wrote to Geneva: nearly two months have elapsed since the departure of my letter: – But you are ill, even now you tremble: you are unfit for agitation of any kind.'

'This suspense is a thousand times worse than the most horrible event: tell me what new scene of death has been acted, and whose I am now to lament?'

'Your family is perfectly well,' said Mr Kirwin, with gentleness: 'and some one, a friend, is come to visit you.'

I know not by what chain of thought, the idea presented itself, but it instantly darted into my mind that the murderer had come to mock at my misery, and taunt me with the death of Clerval, as a new incitement for me to comply with his hellish desires. I put my hand before my eyes, and cried out in agony –

'Oh! Take him away! I cannot see him; for God's sake, do not let him enter!'

Mr Kirwin regarded me with a troubled countenance. He could not help regarding my exclamation as a presumption of my guilt, and said, in rather a severe tone –

'I should have thought, young man, that the presence of your father would have been welcome instead of inspiring such violent repugnance.'

'My father!' cried I, while every feature and every muscle was relaxed from anguish to pleasure: 'is my father indeed come? How kind, how very kind! But where is he, why does he not hasten to me?'

My change of manner surprised and pleased the magistrate; perhaps he thought that my former exclamation was a momentary return of delirium, and now he instantly resumed his former benevolence. He rose, and quitted the room with my nurse, and in a moment my father entered it.

Nothing, at this moment, could have given me greater pleasure than the arrival of my father. I stretched out my hand to him and cried –

'Are you, then, safe – and Elizabeth – and Ernest?'

My father calmed me with assurances of their welfare, and endeavoured, by dwelling on these subjects so interesting to my heart, to raise my desponding spirits; but he soon felt that a prison cannot be the abode of cheerfulness. 'What a place is this that you inhabit, my son!' said he, looking mournfully at the barred windows, and wretched appearance of the room. 'You travelled to seek happiness, but a fatality seems to pursue you. And poor Clerval –'

The name of my unfortunate and murdered friend was an agitation too great to be endured in my weak state; I shed tears.

'Alas! yes, my father,' replied I; 'some destiny of the most horrible kind hangs over me, and I must live to fulfil it, or surely I should have died on the coffin of Henry.'

We were not allowed to converse for any length of time, for the precarious state of my health rendered every precaution necessary that could ensure tranquillity. Mr Kirwin came in, and insisted that my strength should not be exhausted by too much exertion. But the appearance of my father was to me like that of my good angel, and I gradually recovered my health.

As my sickness quitted me, I was absorbed by a gloomy and black melancholy, that nothing could dissipate. The image of Clerval was forever before me, ghastly and murdered. More than once the agitation into which these reflections threw me made my friends dread a dangerous relapse. Alas! why did they preserve so miserable and detested a life? It was surely that I might fill my destiny, which is now drawing to a close. Soon, oh! very soon, will death extinguish these throbbings, and relieve me from the mighty weight of anguish that bears me to the dust; and, in executing the award of justice, I shall also sink to rest. Then the appearance of death was distant, although the wish was ever present to my thoughts; and I often sat for hours motionless and speechless, wishing for some mighty revolution that might bury me and my destroyer in its ruins.

The season of the assizes approached. I had already been three months in prison; and although I was still weak and in continual danger of a relapse, I was obliged to travel nearly a hundred miles to the county-town, where the court was held. Mr Kirwin charged himself with every care of collecting witnesses, and arranging my defence. I was spared the disgrace of appearing publicly as a criminal, as the case was not brought before the court that decides on life and death. The grand jury rejected the bill, on its being proved that I was on the Orkney Islands at the hour the body of my friend was found; and a fortnight after my removal I was liberated from prison.

My father was enraptured on finding me freed from the vexations of a criminal charge, that I was again allowed to breathe the fresh atmosphere, and permitted to return to my native country. I did not participate in these feelings; for to me the walls of a dungeon or a palace were alike hateful. The cup of life was poisoned for ever; and although the sun shone upon me, as upon the happy and gay of heart, I saw around me nothing but a dense and frightful darkness, penetrated by no light but the glimmer of two eyes that glared upon me. Sometimes they were the expressive eyes of Henry, languishing in death, the dark orbs nearly covered by the lids, and the long black lashes that fringed them; sometimes it was the watery, clouded eyes of the monster, as I first saw them in my chamber at Ingolstadt.

My father tried to awaken in me the feelings of affection. He talked of Geneva, which I should soon visit – of Elizabeth and Ernest; but these words only drew deep groans from me. Sometimes, indeed, I felt a wish for happiness; and thought, with melancholy delight of my beloved cousin; or longed, with a devouring *maladie du pays*, to see once more the blue lake and rapid Rhone, that had been so dear to me in early childhood: but my general state of feeling was a torpor, in which a prison was as welcome a residence as the divinest scene in nature; and these fits were seldom interrupted but by paroxysms of anguish and despair. At these moments I often endeavoured to put an end to the existence I loathed; and it required unceasing attendance and vigilance to restrain me from committing some dreadful act of violence.

Yet one duty remained to me, the recollection of which finally triumphed over my selfish despair. It was necessary that I should return without delay to Geneva, there to watch over the lives of those I so fondly loved; and to lie in wait for the murderer, that if any chance led me to the place of his concealment, or if he dared again to blast me by his presence, I might, with unfailing aim, put an end to the existence of the monstrous Image which I had endued with the mockery of a soul still more monstrous. My father still desired to delay our departure, fearful that I could not sustain the fatigues of a journey: for I was a shattered wreck – the shadow of a human being. My strength was gone. I was a mere skeleton; and fever night and day preyed upon my wasted frame.

Still, as I urged our leaving Ireland with such inquietude and impatience, my father thought it best to yield. We took our passage on board a vessel bound for Havre-de-Grâce, and sailed with a fair wind from the Irish shores. It was midnight. I lay on the deck, looking at the stars, and listening to the dashing of the waves. I hailed the darkness that shut Ireland from my sight; and my pulse beat with a feverish joy when I reflected that I should soon see Geneva. The past appeared to me in the light of a frightful dream; yet the vessel in which I was, the wind that blew me from the detested shore of Ireland, and the sea which surrounded me, told me too forcibly that I was deceived by no vision, and that Clerval, my friend and dearest companion, had fallen a victim to me and the monster of my creation. I repassed, in my memory, my whole life – my quiet happiness while residing with my family in Geneva, the death of my mother, and my departure for Ingolstadt. I remembered, shuddering, the mad enthusiasm that hurried me on to the creation of my hideous enemy, and I called to mind the night in which he first lived. I was unable to pursue the train of thought; a thousand feelings pressed upon me, and I wept bitterly.

Ever since my recovery from the fever, I had been in the custom of taking every night a small quantity of laudanum; for it was by means of this drug only that I was enabled to gain the rest necessary for the preservation of life. Oppressed by the recollection of my various misfortunes, I now swallowed double my usual quantity, and soon slept profoundly. But sleep did not afford me respite from thought and misery; my dreams presented a thousand objects that scared me. Towards morning I was possessed by a kind of nightmare; I felt the fiend's grasp in my neck; and could not free myself from it; groans and cries rang in my ears. My father, who was watching over me, perceiving my restlessness, awoke me; the dashing waves were around: the cloudy sky above; the fiend was not here: a sense of security, a feeling that a truce was established between the present hour and the irresistible, disastrous future, imparted to me a kind of calm forgetfulness, of which the human mind is by its structure peculiarly susceptible.

CHAPTER 5

The voyage came to an end. We landed, and proceeded to Paris. I soon found that I had overtaxed my strength, and that I must repose before I could continue my journey. My father's care and attentions were indefatigable; but he did not know the origin of my sufferings, and sought erroneous methods to remedy the incurable ill. He wished me to seek amusement in society. I abhorred the face of man. Oh, not abhorred! they were my brethren, my fellow beings, and I felt attracted even to the most repulsive among them, as to creatures of an angelic nature and celestial mechanism. But I felt that I had no right to share their intercourse. I had unchained an enemy among them, whose joy it was to shed their blood, and to revel in their groans. How they would, each and all, abhor me, and hunt me from the world, did they know my unhallowed acts and the crimes which had their source in me!

My father yielded at length to my desire to avoid society, and strove by various arguments to banish my despair. Sometimes he thought that I felt deeply the degradation of being obliged to answer a charge of murder, and he endeavoured to prove to me the futility of pride.

'Alas! my father,' said I, 'how little do you know me. Human beings, their feelings and passions, would indeed be degraded if such a wretch as I felt pride. Justine, poor unhappy Justine, was as innocent as I, and she suffered the same charge; she died for it; and I am the cause of this – I murdered her. William, Justine, and Henry – they all died by my hands.'

My father had often, during my imprisonment, heard me make the same assertion; when I thus accused myself, he sometimes seemed to desire an explanation, and at others he appeared to consider it as the offspring of delirium, and that, during my illness, some idea of this kind had presented itself to my imagination, the remembrance of which I preserved in my convalescence. I avoided explanation, and maintained a continual silence concerning the wretch I had created. I had a persuasion that I should be supposed mad; and this in itself would forever have chained my tongue. But, besides, I could not bring myself to disclose a secret which would fill my hearer with consternation, and make fear and unnatural horror the inmates of his breast. I checked, therefore, my impatient thirst for sympathy, and was silent when I would have given the world to have confided that fatal secret. Yet still words like those I have recorded would burst uncontrollably from me. I could offer no explanation of them; but their truth in part relieved the burden of my mysterious woe.

Upon this occasion my father said, with an expression of unbounded wonder, 'My dearest Victor, what infatuation is this? My dear son, I entreat you never to make such an assertion again.'

'I am not mad,' I cried energetically; 'the sun and the heavens, who have viewed my operations, can bear witness of my truth. I am the assassin of those most innocent victims; they died by my machinations. A thousand times would I have shed my own blood, drop by drop, to have saved their lives; but I could not, my father, indeed I could not sacrifice the whole human race.'

The conclusion of this speech convinced my father that my ideas were deranged, and he instantly changed the subject of our conversation, and endeavoured to alter the course of my thoughts. He wished as much as possible to obliterate the memory of the scenes that had taken place in Ireland, and never alluded to them, or suffered me to speak of my misfortunes.

As time passed away I became more calm; misery had her dwelling in my heart, but I no longer talked in the same incoherent manner of my own crimes; sufficient for me was the consciousness of them. By the utmost self-violence I curbed the imperious voice of wretchedness, which sometimes desired to declare itself to the whole world; and my manners were calmer and more composed than they had ever been since my journey to the sea of ice.

A few days before we left Paris on our way to Switzerland, I received the following letter from Elizabeth: –

MY DEAR FRIEND,

It gave me the greatest pleasure to receive a letter from my uncle dated at Paris; you are no longer at a formidable distance, and I may hope to see you in less than a fortnight. My poor cousin, how much you must have suffered! I expect to see you looking even more ill than when you quitted Geneva. This winter has been passed more miserably, tortured as I have been by anxious suspense; yet I hope to see peace in your countenance, and to find that your heart is not totally void of comfort and tranquillity.

Yet I fear that the same feelings now exist that made you so miserable a year ago, even perhaps augmented by time. I would not disturb you at this period, when so many misfortunes weigh upon you; but a conversation that I had with my uncle previous to his departure renders some explanation necessary before we meet.

Explanation! You may possibly say; what can Elizabeth have to explain? If you really say this, my questions are answered, and all my doubts satisfied. But you are distant from me, and it is possible that you may dread, and yet be pleased with this explanation; and, in a probability of this being the case, I dare not any longer postpone writing what, during your absence, I have often wished to express to you, but have never had the courage to begin.

You well know, Victor, that our union had been the favourite plan of your parents ever since our infancy. We were told this when young, and taught to look forward to it as an event that would certainly take place. We were affectionate playfellows during childhood, and, I believe, dear and valued friends to one another as we grew older. But as brother and sister often entertain a lively affection towards each other, without desiring a more intimate union, may not such also be our case? Tell me, dearest Victor, Answer me, I conjure you, by our mutual happiness, with simple truth – Do you not love another?

You have travelled: you have spent several years of your life at Ingolstadt; and I confess to you, my friend, that when I saw you last autumn so unhappy, flying to solitude, from the society of every creature, I could not help supposing that you might regret our connection, and believe yourself bound in honour to fulfil the wishes of your parents, although they opposed themselves to your inclinations. But this is false reasoning. I confess to you, my friend, that I love you, and that in my airy dreams of futurity you have been my constant friend and companion. But it is your happiness I desire as well as my own, when I declare to you that our marriage would render me eternally miserable, unless it were the dictate of your own free choice. Even now I weep to think that, borne down as you are by the cruellest misfortunes, you may stifle, by the word 'honour', all hope of that love and happiness which would alone restore you to yourself. I, who have so disinterested an affection for you, may increase your miseries tenfold by being an obstacle to your wishes. Ah! Victor, be assured that your cousin and playmate has too sincere a love for you not to be made miserable by this supposition. Be happy, my friend; and if you obey me in this one request, remain satisfied that nothing on earth will have the power to interrupt my tranquillity.

Do not let this letter disturb you; do not answer tomorrow, or the next day, or even until you come, if it will give you pain. My uncle will send me news of your health; and if I see but one smile on your lips when we meet, occasioned by this or any other exertion of mine, I shall need no other happiness.

ELIZABETH LAVENZA
Geneva, May 18th, 17–.

This letter revived in my memory what I had before forgotten, the threat of the fiend – *'I will be with you on your wedding-night!'* Such was my sentence, and on that night would the daemon employ every art to destroy me, and tear me from the glimpse of happiness which promised partly to console my sufferings. On that night he had determined to consummate his crimes by my death. Well, be it so; a deadly struggle would then assuredly take place, in which if he were victorious I should be at peace, and his power over me be at an end. If he were vanquished, I should be a free man. Alas! what freedom? Such as the peasant enjoys when his family have been massacred before his eyes, his cottage burnt, his lands laid waste, and he is turned adrift, homeless, penniless, and alone, but free. Such would be my liberty, except that in my Elizabeth I possessed a treasure; alas! balanced by those horrors of remorse and guilt, which would pursue me until death.

Sweet and beloved Elizabeth! I read and re-read her letter, and some softened feelings stole into my heart, and dared to whisper paradisiacal dreams of love and joy; but the apple was already eaten, and the angel's arm bared to drive me from all hope. Yet I would die to make her happy. If the monster executed his threat, death was inevitable; yet, again, I considered whether my marriage would hasten my fate. My destruction might indeed arrive a few months sooner; but if my torturer should suspect that I postponed it, influenced by his menaces, he would surely find other and perhaps more dreadful means of revenge. He had vowed *to be with me on my wedding-night*, yet he did not consider that threat as binding him to peace in the mean time, for as if to show me that he was not yet satiated with blood, he had murdered Clerval immediately after the enunciation of his threats. I resolved, therefore, that if my immediate union with my cousin would conduce either to hers or my father's happiness, my adversary's designs against my life should not retard it a single hour.

In this state of mind I wrote to Elizabeth. My letter was calm and affectionate. 'I fear, my beloved girl,' I said, 'little happiness remains for us on earth; yet all that I may one day enjoy is centred in you. Chase away your idle fears; to you alone do I consecrate my life, and my endeavours for contentment. I have one secret, Elizabeth, a dreadful one; when revealed to you, it will chill your frame with horror, and then, far from being surprised at my misery, you will only wonder that I survive what I have endured. I will confide this tale of misery and terror to you the day after our marriage shall take place, for, my sweet cousin, there must be perfect confidence between us. But until then, I conjure you, do not mention or allude to it. This I most earnestly intreat, and I know you will comply.'

In about a week after the arrival of Elizabeth's letter, we returned to Geneva. The sweet girl welcomed me with warm affection; yet tears were in her eyes; as she beheld my emaciated frame and feverish cheeks. I saw a change in her also. She was thinner, and had lost much of that heavenly vivacity that had before charmed me; but her gentleness, and soft looks of compassion, made her a more fit companion for one blasted and miserable as I was.

The tranquillity which I now enjoyed did not endure. Memory brought madness with it; and when I thought of what had passed, a real insanity possessed me; sometimes I was furious and burnt with rage; sometimes low and despondent. I neither spoke, nor looked at any one, but sat motionless, bewildered by the multitude of miseries that overcame me.

Elizabeth alone had the power to draw me from these fits; her gentle voice would soothe me when transported by passion, and inspire me with human feelings when sunk in torpor. She wept with me, and for me. When reason returned, she would remonstrate, and endeavour to inspire me with resignation. Ah! it is well for the unfortunate to be resigned, but for the guilty there is no peace. The agonies of remorse poison the luxury there is otherwise sometimes found in indulging the excess of grief.

Soon after my arrival, my father spoke of my immediate marriage with Elizabeth. I remained silent.

'Have you, then, some other attachment?'

'None on earth. I love Elizabeth and look forward to our union with delight. Let the day therefore be fixed; and on it I will consecrate myself, in life or death, to the happiness of my cousin.'

'My dear Victor, do not speak thus. Heavy misfortunes have befallen us, but let us only cling closer to what remains, and transfer our love for those whom we have lost to those who yet live. Our circle will be small, but bound close by the ties of affection and mutual misfortune. And when time shall have softened your despair, new and dear objects of care will be born to replace those of whom we have been so cruelly deprived.'

Such were the lessons of my father. But to me the remembrance of the threat returned: nor can you wonder that, omnipotent as the fiend had yet been in his deeds of blood, I should almost regard him as invincible; and that when he had pronounced the words '*I shall be with you on your wedding-night*', I should regard the threatened fate as unavoidable. But death was no evil to me, if the loss of Elizabeth were balanced with it; and I therefore, with a contented and even cheerful countenance, agreed with my father, that if my cousin would consent, the ceremony should take place in ten days, and thus put, as I imagined, the seal to my fate.

Great God! if for one instant I had thought what might be the hellish intention of my fiendish adversary, I would rather have banished myself for ever from my native country, and wandered a friendless outcast over the earth, than have consented to this miserable marriage. But, as if possessed of magic powers, the monster had blinded me to his real intentions; and when I thought that I had prepared only my own death, I hastened that of a far dearer victim.

As the period fixed for our marriage drew nearer, whether from cowardice or a prophetic feeling, I felt my heart sink within me. But I concealed my feelings by an appearance of hilarity, that brought smiles and joy to the countenance of my father, but hardly deceived the ever-watchful and nicer eye of Elizabeth. She looked forward to our union with placid contentment, not unmingled with a little fear, which past misfortunes had impressed, that what now appeared certain and tangible happiness, might soon dissipate into an airy dream, and leave no trace but deep and everlasting regret.

Preparations were made for the event, congratulatory visits were received, and all wore a smiling appearance. I shut up, as well as I could, in my own heart the anxiety that preyed there, and entered with seeming earnestness into the plans of my father, although they might only serve as the decorations of my tragedy. Through my father's exertions, a part of the inheritance of Elizabeth had been restored to her by the Austrian government. A small possession on the shores of Como belonged to her. It was agreed that, immediately after our union, we should proceed to Villa Lavenza, and spend our first days of happiness beside the beautiful lake near which it stood.

In the mean time I took every precaution to defend my person, in case the fiend should openly attack me. I carried pistols and a dagger constantly about me, and was ever on the watch to prevent artifice; and by these means gained a greater degree of tranquillity. Indeed, as the period approached, the threat appeared more as a delusion, not to be regarded as worthy to disturb my peace, while the happiness I hoped for in my marriage wore a greater appearance of certainty, as the day fixed for its solemnisation drew nearer, and I heard it continually spoken of as an occurrence which no accident could possibly prevent.

Elizabeth seemed happy; my tranquil demeanour contributed greatly to calm her mind. But on the day that was to fulfil my wishes and my destiny, she was melancholy, and a presentiment of evil pervaded her; and perhaps also she thought of the dreadful secret which I had promised to reveal to her on the following day. My father was in the mean time overjoyed, and in the bustle of preparation only recognised in the melancholy of his niece the diffidence of a bride.

After the ceremony was performed, a large party assembled at my father's; but it was agreed that Elizabeth and I should commence our journey by water, sleeping that night at Evian, and continuing our voyage on the following day. The day was fair, the wind favourable, all smiled on our nuptial embarkation.

Those were the last moments of my life during which I enjoyed the feeling of happiness. We passed rapidly along: the sun was hot, but we were sheltered from its rays by a kind of canopy, while we enjoyed the beauty of the scene, sometimes on one side of the lake, where we saw Mont Salêve, the pleasant banks of Montalègre, and at a distance, surmounting all, the beautiful Mont Blanc, and the assemblage of snowy mountains that in vain endeavour to emulate her; sometimes coasting the opposite banks, we saw the mighty Jura opposing its dark side to the ambition that would quit its native country, and an almost insurmountable barrier to the invader who should wish to enslave it.

I took the hand of Elizabeth. 'You are sorrowful, my love. Ah! if you knew what I have suffered, and what I may yet endure, you would endeavour to let me taste the quiet and freedom from despair that this one day at least permits me to enjoy.'

'Be happy, my dear Victor,' replied Elizabeth; 'there is, I hope, nothing to distress you; and be assured that if a lively joy is not painted in my face, my heart is contented. Something whispers to me not to depend too much on the prospect that is opened before us, but I will not listen to such a sinister voice. Observe how fast we move along, and how the clouds, which sometimes obscure and sometimes rise above the dome of Mont Blanc, render this scene of beauty still more interesting. Look also at the innumerable fish that are swimming in the clear waters, where we can distinguish every pebble that lies at the bottom. What a divine day! how happy and serene all nature appears!'

Thus Elizabeth endeavoured to divert her thoughts and mine from all reflection upon melancholy subjects. But her temper was fluctuating; joy for a few instants shone in her eyes, but it continually gave place to distraction and reverie.

The sun sank lower in the heavens; we passed the river Drance, and observed its path through the chasms of the higher, and the glens of the lower hills. The Alps here come closer to the lake, and we approached the amphitheatre of mountains which forms its eastern boundary. The spire of Evian shone under the woods that surrounded it, and the range of mountain above mountain by which it was overhung.

The wind, which had hitherto carried us along with amazing rapidity, sunk at sunset to a light breeze; the soft air just ruffled the water, and caused a pleasant motion among the trees as we approached the shore, from which it wafted the most delightful scent of flowers and hay.

The sun sunk beneath the horizon as we landed; and as I touched the shore, I felt those cares and fears revive, which soon were to clasp me, and cling to me forever.

CHAPTER VI

It was eight o'clock when we landed; we walked for a short time on the shore, enjoying the transitory light, and then retired to the inn, and contemplated the lovely scene of waters, woods, and mountains, obscured in darkness, yet still displaying their black outlines.

The wind, which had fallen in the south, now rose with great violence in the west. The moon had reached her summit in the heavens and was beginning to descend; the clouds swept across it swifter than the flight of the vulture and dimmed her rays, while the lake reflected the scene of the busy heavens, rendered still busier by the restless waves that were beginning to rise. Suddenly a heavy storm of rain descended.

I had been calm during the day; but so soon as night obscured the shapes of objects, a thousand fears arose in my mind. I was anxious and watchful, while my right hand grasped a pistol which was hidden in my bosom; every sound terrified me; but I resolved that I would sell my life dearly, and not shrink from the conflict until my own life, or that of my adversary, was extinguished.

Elizabeth observed my agitation for some time in timid and fearful silence, but there was something in my glance which communicated terror to her, and trembling, she asked, 'What is it that agitates you, my dear Victor? What is it you fear?'

'Oh! peace, peace, my love,' replied I; 'this night, and all will be safe: but this night is dreadful, very dreadful.'

I passed an hour in this state of mind, when suddenly, I reflected how fearful the combat which I momentarily expected would be to my wife, and I earnestly intreated her to retire, resolving not to join her until I had obtained some knowledge as to the situation of my enemy.

She left me, and I continued some time walking up and down the passages of the house, and inspecting every corner that might afford a retreat to my adversary. But I discovered no trace of him, and was beginning to conjecture that some fortunate chance had intervened to prevent the execution of his menaces; when suddenly I heard a shrill and dreadful scream. It came from the room into which Elizabeth had retired. As I heard it, the whole truth rushed into my mind, my arms dropped, the motion of every muscle and fibre was suspended; I could feel the blood trickling in my veins, and tingling in the extremities of my limbs. This state lasted but for an instant; the scream was repeated, and I rushed into the room.

Great God! why did I not then expire! Why am I here to relate the destruction of the best hope, and the purest creature of earth? She was there, lifeless and inanimate, thrown across the bed, her head hanging down, and her pale and distorted features half covered by her hair. Every where I turn I see the same figure – her bloodless arms and relaxed form flung by the murderer on its bridal bier. Could I behold this, and live? Alas! life is obstinate, and clings closest where it is most hated. For a moment only did I lose recollection: I fell senseless on the ground.

When I recovered, I found myself surrounded by the people of the inn; their countenances expressed a breathless terror: but the horror of others appeared only as a mockery, a shadow of the feelings that oppressed me. I escaped from them to the room where lay the body of Elizabeth, my love, my wife, so lately living, so dear, so worthy. She had been moved from the posture in which I had first beheld her; and now, as she lay, her head upon her arm, and a handkerchief thrown across her face and neck, I might have supposed her asleep. I rushed towards her, and embraced her with ardour; but the deadly langour and coldness of the limbs told me, that what I now held in my arms had ceased to be the Elizabeth whom I had loved and cherished. The murderous mark of the fiends' grasp was on her neck, and the breath had ceased to issue from her lips.

While I still hung over her in the agony of despair. I happened to look up. The windows of the room had before been darkened, and I felt a kind of panic on seeing the pale yellow light of the moon illuminate the chamber. The shutters had been thrown back; and, with a sensation of horror not to be described, I saw at the open window a figure the most hideous and abhorred. A grin was on the face of the monster; he seemed to jeer, as with his fiendish finger he pointed towards the corpse of my wife. I rushed towards the window, and drawing a pistol from my bosom, fired: but he eluded me, leaped from his station, and, running with the swiftness of lightning, plunged into the lake.

The report of the pistol brought a crowd into the room. I pointed to the spot where he had disappeared, and we followed the track with boats; nets were cast, but in vain. After passing several hours, we returned hopeless, most of my companions believing it to have been a form conjured up by my fancy. After having landed, they proceeded to search the country, parties going in different directions among the woods and vines.

I attempted to accompany them, and proceeded a short distance from the house; but my head whirled round, my steps were like those of a drunken man, I fell at last in a state of utter exhaustion; a film covered my eyes, and my skin was parched with the heat of fever. In this state I was carried back, and placed on a bed, hardly conscious of what had happened; my eyes wandered round the room, as if to seek something that I had lost.

After an interval I arose, and, as if by instinct, crawled into the room where the corpse of my beloved lay. There were women weeping around; – I hung over it, and joined my sad tears to theirs – all this time no distinct idea presented itself to my mind; but my thoughts rambled to various subjects, reflecting confusedly on my misfortunes and their cause. I was bewildered, in a cloud of wonder and horror. The death of William, the execution of Justine, the murder of Clerval, and lastly of my wife; even at that moment I knew not that my only remaining friends were safe from the malignity of the fiend; my father even now might be writhing under his grasp, and Ernest might be dead at his feet. This idea made me shudder, and recalled me to action. I started up, and resolved to return to Geneva with all possible speed.

There were no horses to be procured, and I must return by the lake; but the wind was unfavourable and the rain fell in torrents. However, it was hardly morning, and I might reasonably hope to arrive by night. I hired men to row and took an oar myself; for I had always experienced relief from mental torment in bodily exercise. But the overflowing misery I now felt, and the excess of agitation that I endured, rendered me incapable of any exertion. I threw down the oar; and leaning my head upon my hands, gave way to every gloomy idea that arose. If I looked up, I saw scenes which were familiar to me in my happier time, and which I had contemplated but the day before in the company of her who was now but a shadow and a recollection. Tears streamed from my eyes. The rain had ceased for a moment, and I saw the fish play in the waters as they had done a few hours before; they had then been observed by Elizabeth. Nothing is so painful to the human mind as a great and sudden change. The sun might shine, or the clouds might lower: but nothing could appear to me as it had done the day before. A fiend had snatched from me every hope of future happiness: no creature had ever been so miserable as I was; so frightful an event is single in the history of man.

But why should I dwell upon the incidents that followed this last overwhelming event? Mine has been a tale of horrors; I have reached their *acme*, and what I must now relate can but be tedious to you. Know that, one by one, my friends were snatched away; I was left desolate. My own strength is exhausted; and I must tell, in a few words, what remains of my hideous narration.

I arrived at Geneva. My father and Ernest yet lived; but the former sunk under the tidings that I bore. I see him now, excellent and venerable old man! his eyes wandered in vacancy, for they had lost their charm and their delight – his Elizabeth, his more than daughter, whom he doated on with all that affection which a man feels, who in the decline of life, having few affections, clings more earnestly to those that remain. Cursed, cursed be the fiend that brought misery on his grey hairs, and doomed him to waste in wretchedness! He could not live under the horrors that were accumulated around him; the springs of existence suddenly gave way: he was unable to rise from his bed, and in a few days he died in my arms.

What then became of me? I know not; I lost sensation and chains and darkness were the only objects that pressed upon me. Sometimes, indeed, I dreamt that I wandered in flowery meadows and pleasant vales with the friends of my youth, but I awoke, and found myself in a dungeon. Melancholy followed, but by degrees I gained a clear conception of my miseries and situation, and was then released from my prison. For they had called me mad; and during many months, as I understood, a solitary cell had been my habitation.

Liberty, however, had been an useless gift to me, had I not, as I awakened to reason, at the same time awakened to revenge. As the memory of past misfortunes pressed upon me, I began to reflect on their cause – the monster whom I had created, the miserable daemon whom I had sent abroad into the world for my destruction. I was possessed by a maddening rage when I thought of him, and desired and ardently prayed that I might have him within my grasp to wreak a great and signal revenge on his cursed head.

Nor did my hate long confine itself to useless wishes; I began to reflect on the best means of securing him; and for this purpose, about a month after my release, I repaired to a criminal judge in the town, and told him that I had an accusation to make; that I knew the destroyer of my family; and that I required him to exert his whole authority for the apprehension of the murderer.

The magistrate listened to me with attention and kindness: – 'Be assured sir,' said he, 'no pains or exertions on my part shall be spared to discover the villain.'

'I thank you,' replied I; 'listen, therefore, to the deposition that I have to make. It is indeed a tale so strange, that I should fear you would not credit it were there not something in truth which, however wonderful, forces conviction. The story is too connected to be mistaken for a dream, and I have no motive for falsehood.' My manner, as I thus addressed him, was impressive, but calm; I had formed in my own heart a resolution to pursue my destroyer to death; and this purpose quieted my agony, and for an interval reconciled me to life. I now related my history, briefly, but with firmness and precision, marking the dates with accuracy, and never deviating into invective or exclamation.

The magistrate appeared at first perfectly incredulous, but as I continued he became more attentive and interested; I saw him sometimes shudder with horror; at others a lively surprise, unmingled with disbelief, was painted on his countenance.

When I had concluded my narration I said, 'This is the being whom I accuse, and for whose seizure and punishment I call upon you to exert your whole power. It is your duty as a magistrate, and I believe and hope that your feelings as a man will not revolt from the execution of those functions on this occasion.'

This address caused a considerable change in the physiognomy of my own auditor. He had heard my story with that half kind of belief that is given to a tale of spirits and supernatural events; but when he was called upon to act officially in consequence, the whole tide of his incredulity returned. He, however, answered mildly, 'I would willingly afford you every aid in your pursuit; but the creature of whom you speak appears to have powers which would put all my exertions to defiance. Who can follow an animal which can traverse the sea of ice, and inhabit caves and dens where no man would venture to intrude? Besides, some months have elapsed since the commission of his crimes, and no one can conjecture to what place he has wandered, or what region he may now inhabit.

'I do not doubt that he hovers near the spot which I inhabit; and if he has indeed taken refuge in the Alps, he may be hunted like the chamois, and destroyed as a beast of prey. But I perceive your thoughts: you do not credit my narrative, and do not intend to pursue my enemy with the punishment which is his desert.'

As I spoke, rage sparkled in my eyes; the magistrate was intimidated: – 'You are mistaken,' said he. 'I will exert myself; and if it is in my power to seize the monster, be assured that he shall suffer punishment proportionate to his crimes. But I fear, from what you have yourself described to be his properties, that this will prove impracticable; and thus, while every proper measure is pursued, you should make up your mind to disappointment.'

'That cannot be; but all that I can say will be of little avail. My revenge is of no moment to you; yet, while I allow it to be a vice, I confess that it is the devouring and only passion of my soul. My rage is unspeakable, when I reflect that the murderer, whom I have turned loose upon society, still exists. You refuse my just demand: I have but one resource; and I devote myself, either in my life or death, to his destruction.'

I trembled with excess of agitation as I said this; there was a frenzy in my manner, and something, I doubt not, of that haughty fierceness which the martyrs of old are said to have possessed. But to a Genevan magistrate, whose mind was occupied by far other ideas than those of devotion and heroism, this elevation of mind had much the appearance of madness. He endeavoured to soothe me as a nurse does a child, and reverted to my tale as the effects of delirium.

'Man,' I cried, 'how ignorant art thou in thy pride of wisdom! Cease; you know not what it is you say.'

I broke from the house angry and disturbed, and retired to meditate on some other mode of action.

CHAPTER VII

My present situation was one in which all voluntary thought was swallowed up and lost. I was hurried away by fury; revenge alone endowed me with strength and composure; it moulded my feelings, and allowed me to be calculating and calm, at periods when otherwise delirium or death would have been my portion.

My first resolution was to quit Geneva forever; my country, which, when I was happy and beloved, was dear to me, now, in my adversity, became hateful. I provided myself with a sum of money, together with a few jewels which had belonged to my mother, and departed.

And now my wanderings began, which are to cease but with life. I have traversed a vast portion of the earth, and have endured all the hardships which travellers, in deserts and barbarous countries, are wont to meet. How I have lived I hardly know; many times have I stretched my failing limbs upon the sandy plain, and prayed for death. But revenge kept me alive; I dared not die, and leave my adversary in being.

When I quitted Geneva, my first labour was to gain some clue by which I might trace the steps of my fiendish enemy. But my plan was unsettled; and I wandered many hours round the confines of the town, uncertain what path I should pursue. As night approached, I found myself at the entrance of the cemetery where William, Elizabeth, and my father reposed. I entered it, and approached the tomb which marked their graves. Every thing was silent, except the leaves of the trees, which were gently agitated by the wind; the night was nearly dark; and the scene would have been solemn and affecting even to an uninterested observer. The spirits of the departed seemed to flit around, and to cast a shadow, which was felt but not seen, around the head of the mourner.

The deep grief which this scene had at first excited quickly gave way to rage and despair. They were dead, and I lived; their murderer also lived, and to destroy him I must drag out my weary existence. I knelt on the grass, and kissed the earth, and with quivering lips exclaimed, 'By the sacred earth on which I kneel, by the shades that wander near me, by the deep and eternal grief that I feel, I swear; and by thee, O Night, and the spirits that preside over thee, to pursue the daemon, who caused this misery, until he or I shall perish in mortal conflict. For this purpose I will preserve my life: to execute this dear revenge will I again behold the sun, and tread the green herbage of earth, which otherwise should vanish from my eyes forever. And I call on you, spirits of the dead; and on you, wandering ministers of vengeance, to aid and conduct me in my work. Let the cursed and hellish monster drink deep of agony; let him feel the despair that now torments me.'

I had begun my adjuration with solemnity, and an awe which almost assured me that the shades of my murdered friends heard and approved my devotion; but the furies possessed me as I concluded, and rage choked my utterance.

I was answered through the stillness of night by a loud and fiendish laugh. It rang on my ears long and heavily; the mountains re-echoed it, and I felt as if all hell surrounded me with mockery and laughter. Surely in that moment I should have been possessed by frenzy, and have destroyed my miserable existence, but that my vow was heard, and that I was reserved for vengeance. The laughter died away; when a well-known and abhorred voice, apparently close to my ear, addressed me in an audible whisper, 'I am satisfied: miserable wretch! you have determined to live, and I am satisfied.'

I darted towards the spot from which the sound proceeded; but the devil eluded my grasp. Suddenly the broad disk of the moon arose, and shone full upon his ghastly and distorted shape, as he fled with more than mortal speed.

I pursued him; and for many months this has been my task. Guided by a slight clue, I followed the windings of the Rhône, but vainly. The blue Mediterranean appeared; and; by a strange chance, I saw the fiend enter by night, and hide himself in a vessel bound for the Black Sea. I took my passage in the same ship; but he escaped, I know not how.

Amidst the wilds of Tartary and Russia, although he still evaded me, I have ever followed in his track. Sometimes the peasants, scared by this horrid apparition, informed me of his path; sometimes he himself, who feared that if I lost all trace of him, I should despair and die, left some mark to guide me. The snows descended on my head, and I saw the print of his huge step on the white plain. To you first entering on life, to whom care is new, and agony unknown, how can you understand what I have felt and still feel? Cold, want, and fatigue, were the least pains which I was destined to endure; I was cursed by some devil, and carried about with me my eternal hell; yet still a spirit of good followed and directed my steps and, when I most murmured, would suddenly extricate me from seemingly insurmountable difficulties. Sometimes, when nature, overcome by hunger, sunk under the exhaustion, a repast was prepared for me in the desert, that restored and inspirited me. The fare was, indeed, coarse, such as the peasants of the country ate; but I will not doubt that it was set there by the spirits that I had invoked to aid me. Often, when all was dry, the heavens cloudless, and I was parched by thirst, a slight cloud would bedim the sky, shed the few drops that revived me, and vanish.

I followed, when I could, the courses of the rivers; but the daemon generally avoided these, as it was here that the population of the country chiefly collected. In other places human beings were seldom seen; and I generally subsisted on the wild animals that crossed my path. I had money with me, and gained the friendship of the villagers by distributing it; or I brought with me some food that I had killed, which, after taking a small part, I always presented to those who had provided me with fire and utensils for cooking.

My life, as it passed thus, was indeed hateful to me, and it was during sleep alone that I could taste joy. O blessed sleep! often, when most miserable, I sank to repose, and my dreams lulled me even to rapture. The spirits that guarded me had provided these moments, or rather hours, of happiness that I might retain strength to fulfil my pilgrimage. Deprived of this respite, I should have sunk under my hardships. During the day I was sustained and inspirited by the hope of night: for in sleep I saw my friends, my wife, and my beloved country; again I saw the benevolent countenance of my father, heard the silver tones of my Elizabeth's voice, and beheld Clerval enjoying health and youth. Often, when wearied by a toilsome march, I persuaded myself that I was dreaming until night should come, and that I should then enjoy reality in the arms of my dearest friends. What agonising fondness did I feel for them! how did I cling to their dear forms, as sometimes they haunted even my waking hours, and persuade myself that they still lived! At such moments vengeance, that burned within me, died in my heart, and I pursued my path towards the destruction of the daemon, more as a task enjoined by heaven, as the mechanical impulse of some power of which I was unconscious, than as the ardent desire of my soul.

What his feelings were whom I pursued I cannot know. Sometimes, indeed, he left marks in writing on the barks of the trees, or cut in stone, that guided me, and instigated my fury. 'My reign is not yet over' – these words were legible in one of these inscriptions – 'you live, and my power is complete. Follow me; I seek the everlasting ices of the north, where you will feel the misery of cold and frost, to which I am impassive. You will find near this place, if you follow not too tardily, a dead hare; eat and be refreshed. Come on, my enemy; we have yet to wrestle for our lives, but many hard and miserable hours must you endure until that period shall arrive.'

Scoffing devil! Again do I vow vengeance; again do I devote thee, miserable fiend, to torture and death. Never will I give up my search, until he or I perish; and then with what ecstasy shall I join my Elizabeth and my departed friends, who even now prepare for me the reward of my tedious toil and horrible pilgrimage!

As I still pursued my journey to the northward, the snows thickened, and the cold increased in a degree almost too severe to support. The peasants were shut up in their hovels, and only a few of the most hardy ventured forth to seize the animals whom starvation had forced from their hiding-places to seek for prey. The rivers were covered with ice, and no fish could be procured; and thus I was cut off from my chief article of maintenance.

The triumph of my enemy increased with the difficulty of my labours. One inscription that he left was in these words: – 'Prepare! your toils only begin; wrap yourself in furs, and provide food, for we shall soon enter upon a journey where your sufferings will satisfy my everlasting hatred.'

My courage and perseverance were invigorated by these scoffing words; I resolved not to fail in my purpose; and, calling on Heaven to support me, I continued with unabated fervour to traverse immense deserts, until the ocean appeared at a distance, and formed the utmost boundary of the horizon. Oh! how unlike it was to the blue seasons of the south! Covered with ice, it was only to be distinguished from land by its superior wildness and ruggedness. The Greeks wept for joy when they beheld the Mediterranean from the hills of Asia, and hailed with rapture the boundary of their toils. I did not weep, but I knelt down, and, with a full heart, thanked my guiding spirit for conducting me in safety to the place where I hoped, notwithstanding my adversary's gibe, to meet and grapple with him.

Some weeks before this period I had procured a sledge and dogs, and thus traversed the snows with inconceivable speed. I know not whether the fiend possessed the same advantages; but I found that, as before I had daily lost ground in the pursuit, I now gained on him, so much so that when I first saw the ocean he was but one day's journey in advance, and I hoped to intercept him before he should reach the beach. With new courage, therefore, I pressed on, and in two days arrived at a wretched hamlet on the sea-shore. I enquired of the inhabitants concerning the fiend, and gained accurate information. A gigantic monster, they said, had arrived the night before, armed with a gun and many pistols; putting to flight the inhabitants of a solitary cottage, through fear of his terrific appearance. He had carried off their store of winter food, and, placing it in a sledge, to draw which he had seized on a numerous drove of trained dogs, he had harnessed them, and the same night, to the joy of the horror-struck villagers, had pursued his journey across the sea in a direction that led to no land; and they conjectured that he must speedily be destroyed by the breaking of the ice, or frozen by the eternal frosts.

On hearing this information, I suffered a temporary access of despair. He had escaped me; and I must commence a destructive and almost endless journey across the mountainous ices of the ocean, – amidst cold that few of the inhabitants could long endure and which I, the native of a genial and sunny climate, could not hope to survive. Yet at the idea that the fiend should live and be triumphant, my rage and vengeance returned, and, like a mighty tide, overwhelmed every other feeling. After a slight repose, during which the spirits of the dead hovered round, and instigated me to toil and revenge, I prepared for my journey.

I exchanged my land-sledge for one fashioned for the inequalities of the Frozen Ocean; and purchasing a plentiful stock of provisions, I departed from land.

I cannot guess how many days have passed since then; but I have endured misery, which nothing but the eternal sentiment of a just retribution burning within my heart could have enabled me to support. Immense and rugged mountains of ice often barred up my passage, and I often heard the thunder of the ground sea, which threatened my destruction. But again the frost came, and made the paths of the sea secure.

By the quantity of provision which I had consumed, I should guess that I had passed three weeks in this journey; and the continual protraction of hope, returning back upon the heart, often wrung bitter drops of despondency and grief from my eyes. Despair had indeed almost secured her prey, and I should soon have sunk beneath this misery. Once, after the poor animals that conveyed me had with incredible toil gained the summit of a sloping ice-mountain, and one, sinking under his fatigue, died, I viewed the expanse before me with anguish, when suddenly my eye caught a dark speck upon the dusky plain. I strained my sight to discover what it could be, and uttered a wild cry of ecstasy when I distinguished a sledge, and the distorted proportions of a well-known form within. Oh! with what a burning gush did hope revisit my heart! warm tears filled my eyes, which I hastily wiped away, that they might not intercept the view I had of the daemon; but still my sight was dimmed by the burning drops, until, giving way to the emotions that oppressed me, I wept aloud.

But this was not the time for delay: I disencumbered the dogs of their dead companion, gave them a plentiful portion of food; and, after an hour's rest, which was absolutely necessary, and yet which was bitterly irksome to me, I continued my route. The sledge was still visible; nor did I again lose sight of it, except at the moments when for a short time some ice-rock concealed it with its intervening crags. I indeed perceptibly gained on it; and when, after nearly two days' journey, I beheld my enemy at no more than a mile distant, my heart bounded within me.

But now, when I appeared almost within grasp of my foe, my hopes were suddenly extinguished, and I lost all trace of him more utterly than I had ever done before. A ground sea was heard; the thunder of its progress, as the waters rolled and swelled beneath me, became every moment more ominous and terrific. I pressed on, but in vain. The wind arose; the sea roared; and, as with the mighty shock of an earthquake, it split, and cracked with a tremendous and overwhelming sound. The work was soon finished: in a few minutes a tumultuous sea rolled between me and my enemy, and I was left drifting on a scattered

piece of ice, that was continually lessening, and thus preparing for me a
hideous death. In this manner many appalling hours passed; several of
my dogs died; and I myself was about to sink under the accumulation
of distress when I saw your vessel riding at anchor, and holding forth
to me hopes of succour and life. I had no conception that vessels ever
came so far north, and was astounded at the sight. I quickly destroyed
part of my sledge to construct oars; and by these means was enabled,
with infinite fatigue, to move my ice-raft in the direction of your ship.
I had determined, if you were going southwards, still to trust myself
to the mercy of the seas rather than abandon my purpose. I hoped to
induce you to grant me a boat with which I could pursue my enemy.
But your direction was northward. You took me on board when my
vigour was exhausted, and I should soon have sunk under my multiplied
hardships into a death which I still dread – for my task is unfulfilled.

Oh! when will my guiding spirit, in conducting me to the daemon,
allow me the rest I so much desire; or must I die, and he yet live? If I
do, swear to me, Walton, that he shall not escape; that you will seek him,
and satisfy my vengeance in his death. And do I dare to ask of you to
undertake my pilgrimage, to endure the hardships that I have undergone?
No; I am not so selfish. Yet, when I am dead, if he should appear; if the
ministers of vengeance should conduct him to you, swear that he shall
not live – swear that he shall not triumph over my accumulated woes and
survive to add to the list of his dark crimes. He is eloquent and persuasive;
and once his words had even power over my heart: but trust him not.
His soul is as hellish as his form, full of treachery and fiendlike malice.
Hear him not; call on the manes of William, Justine, Clerval, Elizabeth,
my father, and of the wretched Victor, and thrust your sword into his
heart. I will hover near, and direct the steel aright.

WALTON, *in continuation.*

August 26th, 17–.

You have read this strange and terrific story, Margaret; and do you not
feel your blood congeal with horror, like that which even now curdles
mine? Sometimes, seized with sudden agony, he could not continue
his tale; at others, his voice broken, yet piercing, uttered with difficulty the words so replete with anguish. His fine and lovely eyes were

now lighted up with indignation, now subdued to downcast sorrow, and quenched in infinite wretchedness. Sometimes he commanded his countenance and tones, and related the most horrible incidents with a tranquil voice, suppressing every mark of agitation; then, like a volcano bursting forth, his face would suddenly change to an expression of the wildest rage, as he shrieked out imprecations on his persecutor.

His tale is connected, and told with an appearance of the simplest truth; yet I own to you that the letters of Felix and Safie, which he showed me, and the apparition of the monster seen from our ship, brought to me a greater conviction of the truth of his narrative than his asseverations, however earnest and connected. Such a monster has, then, real existence! I cannot doubt it; yet I am lost in surprise and admiration. Sometimes I endeavoured to gain from Frankenstein the particulars of his creature's formation: but on this point he was impenetrable.

'Are you mad, my friend?' said he; 'or whither does your senseless curiosity lead you? Would you also create for yourself and the world a demoniacal enemy? Peace, peace! learn my miseries, and do not seek to increase your own.'

Frankenstein discovered that I made notes concerning his history: he asked to see them, and then himself corrected and augmented them in many places; but principally in giving the life and spirit to the conversations he held with his enemy. 'Since you have preserved my narration,' said he, 'I would not that a mutilated one should go down to posterity.'

Thus has a week passed away, while I have listened to the strangest tale that ever imagination formed. My thoughts, and every feeling of my soul, have been drunk up by the interest for my guest, which this tale, and his own elevated and gentle manners, have created. I wish to soothe him; yet can I counsel one so infinitely miserable, so destitute of every hope of consolation, to live? Oh, no! the only joy that he can now know will be when he composes his shattered spirit to peace and death. Yet he enjoys one comfort, the offspring of solitude and delirium: he believes, that when in dreams he holds converse with his friends, and derives from that communion consolation for his miseries, or excitements to his vengeance, that they are not the creations of his fancy, but the beings themselves who visit him from the regions of a remote world. This faith gives a solemnity to his reveries that render them to me almost as imposing and interesting as truth.

Our conversations are not always confined to his own history and misfortunes. On every point of general literature he displays unbounded knowledge, and a quick and piercing apprehension. His eloquence is forcible and touching; nor can I hear him, when he relates a pathetic incident, or endeavours to move the passions of pity or love, without tears. What a glorious creature must he have been in the days of his prosperity, when he is thus noble and godlike in ruin! He seems to feel his own worth, and the greatness of his fall.

'When younger,' said he, 'I believed myself destined for some great enterprise. My feelings are profound; but I possessed a coolness of judgment that fitted me for illustrious achievements. This sentiment of the worth of my nature supported me, when others would have been oppressed; for I deemed it criminal to throw away in useless grief those talents that might be useful to my fellow-creatures. When I reflected on the work I had completed, no less a one than the creation of a sensitive and rational animal, I could not rank myself with the herd of common projectors. But this thought, which supported me in the commencement of my career, now serves only to plunge me lower in the dust. All my speculations and hopes are as nothing; and, like the archangel who aspired to omnipotence, I am chained in an eternal hell. My imagination was vivid, yet my powers of analysis and application were intense; by the union of these qualities I conceived the idea, and executed the creation of a man. Even now I cannot recollect, without passion, my reveries while the work was incomplete. I trod heaven in my thoughts, now exulting in my powers, now burning with the idea of their effects. From my infancy I was imbued with high hopes and a lofty ambition; but how am I sunk! Oh! my friend, if you had known me as I once was, you would not recognise me in this state of degradation. Despondency rarely visited my heart; a high destiny seemed to bear me on, until I fell, never, never again to rise.'

Must I then lose this admirable being! I have longed for a friend; I have sought one who would sympathise with and love me. Behold, on these desert seas I have found such a one; but, I fear, I have gained him only to know his value, and lose him. I would reconcile him to life, but he repulses the idea.

'I thank you, Walton,' he said, 'for your kind intentions towards so miserable a wretch; but when you speak of new ties, and fresh affections, think you that any can replace those who are gone? Can any man be to me as Clerval was; or any woman another Elizabeth? Even where the affections are not strongly moved by any superior excellence, the companions of our childhood always possess a certain power over our minds, which hardly any later friend can obtain. They know our infantine dispositions, which, however they may be afterwards modified, are never eradicated; and they can judge of our actions with more certain conclusions as to the integrity of our motives. A sister or a brother can never, unless indeed such symptoms have been shown early, suspect the other of fraud or false dealing, when another friend, however strongly he may be attached, may, in spite of himself, be contemplated with suspicion. But I enjoyed friends, dear not only through habit and association, but from their own merits; and wherever I am, the soothing voice of my Elizabeth, and the conversation of Clerval, will be ever whispered in my ear. They are dead; and but one feeling in such a solitude can persuade me to preserve my life. If I were engaged in any high undertaking or design, fraught with extensive utility to my fellow-creatures, then could I live to fulfil it. But such is not my destiny; I must pursue and destroy the being to whom I gave existence; then my lot on earth will be fulfilled, and I may die.'

September 2nd.

MY BELOVED SISTER,

I write to you, encompassed by peril, and ignorant whether I am ever doomed to see again dear England, and the dearer friends that inhabit it. I am surrounded by mountains of ice, which admit of no escape, and threaten every moment to crush my vessel. The brave fellows, whom I have persuaded to be my companions, look towards me for aid; but I have none to bestow. There is something terribly appalling in our situation, yet my courage and hopes do not desert me. Yet it is terrible to reflect that the lives of all these men are endangered through me. If we are lost, my mad schemes are the cause.

And what, Margaret, will be the state of your mind? You will not hear of my destruction, and you will anxiously await my return. Years will pass, and you will have visitings of despair, and yet be tortured by hope. Oh! my beloved sister, the sickening failing of your heart-felt expectations is, in prospect, more terrible to me than my own death.

But you have a husband, and lovely children; you may be happy: Heaven bless you, and make you so!

My unfortunate guest regards me with the tenderest compassion. He endeavours to fill me with hope; and talks as if life were a possession which he valued. He reminds me how often the same accidents have happened to other navigators, who have attempted this sea, and in spite of myself, he fills me with cheerful auguries. Even the sailors feel the power of his eloquence; when he speaks, they no longer despair; he rouses their energies, and, while they hear his voice, they believe these vast mountains of ice are molehills, which will vanish before the resolutions of man. These feelings are transitory; each day of expectation delayed fills them with fear, and I almost dread a mutiny caused by this despair.

September 5th.

A scene has just passed of such uncommon interest, that although it is highly probable that these papers may never reach you, yet I cannot forbear recording it.

We are still surrounded by mountains of ice, still in imminent danger of being crushed in their conflict. The cold is excessive, and many of my unfortunate comrades have already found a grave amidst this scene of desolation. Frankenstein has daily declined in health: a feverish fire still glimmers in his eyes; but he is exhausted, and when suddenly roused to any exertion, he speedily sinks again into apparent lifelessness.

I mentioned in my last letter the fears I entertained of a mutiny. This morning, as I sat watching the wan countenance of my friend – his eyes half closed, and his limbs hanging listlessly – I was roused by half a dozen of the sailors, who demanded admission into the cabin. They entered, and their leader addressed me. He told me that he and his companions had been chosen by the other sailors to come in deputation to me, to make me a requisition, which, in justice, I could not refuse. We were immured in ice, and should probably never escape; but they feared that if, as was possible, the ice should dissipate and a free passage be opened, I should be rash enough to continue my voyage, and lead them into fresh dangers, after they might happily have surmounted this. They insisted, therefore, that I should engage with a solemn promise, that if the vessel should be freed I would instantly direct my course southwards.

This speech troubled me. I had not despaired; nor had I yet conceived the idea of returning, if set free. Yet could I, in justice, or even in possibility, refuse this demand? I hesitated before I answered; when Frankenstein, who had at first been silent, and, indeed, appeared hardly to have force enough to attend, now roused himself; his eyes sparkled, and his cheeks flushed with momentary vigour. Turning towards the men, he said –

'What do you mean? What do you demand of your captain? Are you then so easily turned from your design? Did you not call this a glorious expedition? And wherefore was it glorious? Not because the way was smooth and placid as a southern sea, but because it was full of dangers and terror; because, at every new incident, your fortitude was to be called forth, and your courage exhibited; because danger and death surrounded it, and these you were to brave and overcome. For this was it a glorious, for this was it an honourable undertaking. You were hereafter to be hailed as the benefactors of your species; your names adored, as belonging to brave men who encountered death for honour, and the benefit of mankind. And now, behold, with the first imagination of danger, or, if you will, the first mighty and terrific trial of your courage, you shrink away, and are content to be handed down as men who had not strength enough to endure cold and peril; and so, poor souls, they were chilly and returned to their warm firesides. Why, that requires not this preparation; ye need not have come thus far, and dragged your captain to the shame of a defeat, merely to prove yourselves cowards. Oh! be men, or be more than men. Be steady to your purposes, and firm as a rock. This ice is not made of such stuff as your hearts may be; it is mutable, and cannot withstand you, if you say that it shall not. Do not return to your families with the stigma of disgrace marked on your brows. Return as heroes who have fought and conquered, and who know not what it is to turn their backs on the foe.'

He spoke this with a voice so modulated to the different feelings expressed in his speech, with an eye so full of lofty design and heroism, that can you wonder that these men were moved? They looked at one another, and were unable to reply. I spoke; I told them to retire, and consider of what had been said: that I would not lead them farther north if they strenuously desired the contrary; but that I hoped that, with reflection, their courage would return.

They retired, and I turned towards my friend, but he was sunk in languor, and almost deprived of life.

How all this will terminate, I know not; but I had rather die than return shamefully – my purpose unfulfilled. Yet I fear such will be my fate; the men, unsupported by ideas of glory and honour, can never willingly continue to endure their present hardships.

September 7th.

The die is cast; I have consented to return, if we are not destroyed. Thus are my hopes blasted by cowardice and indecision: I come back ignorant and disappointed. It requires more philosophy than I possess, to bear this injustice with patience.

September 12th.

It is past; I am returning to England. I have lost my hopes of utility and glory; – I have lost my friend. But I will endeavour to detail these bitter circumstances to you, my dear sister; and, while I am wafted towards England, and towards you, I will not despond.

September 9th, the ice began to move, and roarings like thunder were heard at a distance, as the islands split and cracked in every direction. We were in the most imminent peril; but, as we could only remain passive, my chief attention was occupied by my unfortunate guest, whose illness increased in such a degree that he was entirely confined to his bed. The ice cracked behind us, and was driven with force towards the north; a breeze sprung from the west, and on the 11th the passage towards the south became perfectly free. When the sailors saw this, and that their return to their native country was apparently assured, a shout of tumultuous joy broke from them, loud and long-continued. Frankenstein, who was dozing, awoke and asked the cause of the tumult. 'They shout,' I said, 'because they will soon return to England.'

'Do you then really return?'

'Alas! yes; I cannot withstand their demands. I cannot lead them unwillingly to danger, and I must return.'

'Do so, if you will; but I will not. You may give up your purpose, but mine is assigned to me by Heaven, and I dare not. I am weak; but surely the spirits who assist my vengeance will endow me with sufficient strength.' Saying this, he endeavoured to spring from the bed, but the exertion was too great for him; he fell back and fainted.

It was long before he was restored; and I often thought that life was entirely extinct. At length he opened his eyes; he breathed with difficulty, and was unable to speak. The surgeon gave him a composing draught, and ordered us to leave him undisturbed. In the mean time he told me, that my friend had certainly not many hours to live.

His sentence was pronounced; and I could only grieve, and be patient. I sat by his bed, watching him; his eyes were closed, and I thought he slept; but presently he called to me in a feeble voice, and bidding me come near, said –

'Alas! the strength I relied on is gone; I feel that I shall soon die, and he, my enemy and persecutor, may still be in being. Think not, Walton, that in the last moments of my existence I feel that burning hatred, and ardent desire of revenge, I once expressed; but I feel myself justified in desiring the death of my adversary. During these last days I have been occupied in examining my past conduct; nor do I find it blameable. In a fit of enthusiastic madness I created a rational creature, and was bound towards him, to assure, as far as was in my power, his happiness and well-being. This was my duty; but there was another still paramount to that. My duties towards the beings of my own species had greater claims to my attention, because they included a greater proportion of happiness or misery. Urged by this view, I refused, and I did right in refusing, to create a companion for the first creature. He showed unparalleled malignity and selfishness, in evil; he destroyed my friends; he devoted to destruction beings who possessed exquisite sensations, happiness, and wisdom; nor do I know where this thirst for vengeance may end. Miserable himself, that he may render no other wretched, he ought to die. The task of his destruction was mine, but I have failed. When actuated by selfish and vicious motives, I asked you to undertake my unfinished work; and I renew this request now, when I am only induced by reason and virtue.

'Yet I cannot ask you to renounce your country and friends, to fulfil this task; and now that you are returning to England, you will have little chance of meeting with him. But the consideration of these points, and the well balancing of what you may esteem your duties, I leave to you; my judgment and ideas are already disturbed by the near approach of death. I dare not ask you to do what I think right, for I may still be misled by passion.

'That he should live to be an instrument of mischief disturbs me; in other respects, this hour, when I momentarily expect my release, is the only happy one which I have enjoyed for several years. The forms of the beloved dead flit before me, and I hasten to their arms. Farewell, Walton! Seek happiness in tranquillity, and avoid ambition, even if it be only the apparently innocent one of distinguishing yourself in science and discoveries. Yet why do I say this? I have myself been blasted in these hopes, yet another may succeed.'

His voice became faint as he spoke; and at length, exhausted by his effort, he sunk into silence. About half an hour afterwards he attempted again to speak, but was unable; he pressed my hand feebly, and his eyes closed forever, while the irradiation of a gentle smile passed away from his lips.

Margaret, what comment can I make on the untimely extinction of this glorious spirit? What can I say, that will enable you to understand the depth of my sorrow? All that I should express would be inadequate and feeble. My tears flow; my mind is overshadowed by a cloud of disappointment. But I journey towards England, and I may there find consolation.

I am interrupted. What do these sounds portend? It is midnight; the breeze blows fairly, and the watch on deck scarcely stir. Again there is a sound as of a human voice; but hoarser; it comes from the cabin where the remains of Frankenstein still lie. I must arise, and examine. Good night, my sister.

Great God! what a scene has just taken place! I am yet dizzy with the remembrance of it. I hardly know whether I shall have the power to detail it; yet the tale which I have recorded would be incomplete without this final and wonderful catastrophe.

I entered the cabin where lay the remains of my ill-fated and admirable friend. Over him hung a form which I cannot find words to describe: – gigantic in stature, yet uncouth and distorted in its propor-tions. As he hung over the coffin, his face was concealed by long locks of ragged hair; but one vast hand was extended, in colour and apparent texture like that of a mummy. When he heard the sound of my approach, he ceased to utter exclamations of grief and horror, and sprung towards the window. Never did I behold a vision so horrible as his face, of such loathsome, yet appalling hideousness. I shut my eyes, involuntarily, and endeavoured to recollect what were my duties with regard to this destroyer. I called on him to stay.

He paused, looking on me with wonder; and, again turning towards the lifeless form of his creator, he seemed to forget my presence, and every feature and gesture seemed instigated by the wildest rage of some uncontrollable passion.

'That is also my victim!' he exclaimed: 'in his murder my crimes are consummated; the miserable series of my being is wound to its close! Oh, Frankenstein! generous and self-devoted being! what does it avail that I now ask thee to pardon me? I, who irretrievably destroyed thee by destroying all thou lovedst. Alas! he is cold, he cannot answer me.'

His voice seemed suffocated; and my first impulses, which had suggested to me the duty of obeying the dying request of my friend, in destroying his enemy, were now suspended by a mixture of curiosity and compassion. I approached this tremendous being; I dared not again raise my eyes to his face, there was something so scaring and unearthly in his ugliness. I attempted to speak, but the words died away on my lips. The monster continued to utter wild and incoherent self-reproaches. At length I gathered resolution to address him in a pause of the tempest of his passion: 'Your repentance,' I said, 'is now superfluous. If you had listened to the voice of conscience, and heeded the stings of remorse, before you had urged your diabolical vengeance to this extremity, Frankenstein would yet have lived.'

'And do you dream?' said the daemon; 'do you think that I was then dead to agony and remorse? – He,' he continued, pointing to the corpse, 'he suffered not in the consummation of the deed – oh! not the ten-thousandth portion of the anguish that was mine during the lingering detail of its execution. A frightful selfishness hurried me on, while my heart was poisoned with remorse. Think you that the groans of Clerval were music to my ears? My heart was fashioned to be susceptible of love and sympathy; and when wrenched by misery to vice and hatred, it did not endure the violence of the change, without torture such as you cannot even imagine.

'After the murder of Clerval, I returned to Switzerland, heartbroken and overcome. I pitied Frankenstein; my pity amounted to horror: I abhorred myself. But when I discovered that he, the author at once of my existence and of its unspeakable torments, dared to hope for happiness; that while he accumulated wretchedness and despair upon me, he sought his own enjoyment in feelings and passions from the indulgence of which I was forever barred, then impotent envy and bitter indignation filled me with an insatiable thirst for vengeance. I recollected my threat, and resolved that it should be accomplished. I knew that I was preparing for myself a deadly torture; but I was the slave, not the master, of an impulse, which I detested, yet could not disobey. Yet when she died! – nay, then I was not miserable. I had cast off all feeling, subdued all anguish, to riot in the excess of my despair. Evil thenceforth became my good. Urged thus far, I had no choice but to adapt my nature to an element which I had willingly chosen. The completion of my demoniacal design became an insatiable passion. And now it is ended; there is my last victim!'

I was at first touched by the expressions of his misery; yet, when I called to mind what Frankenstein had said of his powers of eloquence and persuasion, and when I again cast my eyes on the lifeless form of my friend, indignation was rekindled within me. 'Wretch!' I said, 'it is well that you come here to whine over the desolation that you have made. You throw a torch into a pile of buildings; and when they are consumed, you sit among the ruins, and lament the fall. Hypocritical fiend! if he whom you mourn still lived, still would he be the object, again would he become the prey, of your accursed vengeance. It is not pity that you feel; you lament only because the victim of your malignity is withdrawn from your power.'

'Oh, it is not thus – not thus,' interrupted the being; 'yet such must be the impression conveyed to you by what appears to be the purport of my actions. Yet I seek not a fellow-feeling in my misery. No sympathy may I ever find. When I first sought it, it was the love of virtue, the feelings of happiness and affection with which my whole being overflowed, that I wished to be participated. But now, that virtue has become to me a shadow, and that happiness and affection are turned into bitter and loathing despair, in what should I seek for sympathy?

I am content to suffer alone, while my sufferings shall endure; when I die, I am well satisfied that abhorrence and opprobrium should load my memory. Once my fancy was soothed with dreams of virtue, of fame, and of enjoyment. Once I falsely hoped to meet with beings who, pardoning my outward form, would love me for the excellent qualities which I was capable of unfolding. I was nourished with high thoughts of honour and devotion. But now crime has degraded me beneath the meanest animal. No guilt, no mischief, no malignity, no misery, can be found comparable to mine. When I run over the frightful catalogue of my sins, I cannot believe that I am the same creature whose thoughts were once filled with sublime and transcendent visions of the beauty and the majesty of goodness. But it is even so; the fallen angel becomes a malignant devil. Yet even that enemy of God and man had friends and associates in his desolation; I am alone.

'You, who call Frankenstein your friend, seem to have a knowledge of my crimes and his misfortunes. But, in the detail which he gave you of them, he could not sum up the hours and months of misery which I endured, wasting in impotent passions. For while I destroyed his hopes, I did not satisfy my own desires. They were forever ardent and craving; still I desired love and fellowship, and I was still spurned. Was there no injustice in this? Am I to be thought the only criminal, when all human kind sinned against me? Why do you not hate Felix, who drove his friend from the door with contumely? Why do you not execrate the rustic who sought to destroy the saviour of his child? Nay, these are virtuous and immaculate beings! I, the miserable and the abandoned, am an abortion, to be spurned at, and kicked, and trampled on. Even now my blood boils at the recollection of this injustice.

'But it is true that I am a wretch. I have murdered the lovely and the helpless; I have strangled the innocent as they slept, and grasped to death his throat who never injured me or any other living thing. I have devoted my creator, the select specimen of all that is worthy of love and admiration among men, to misery; I have pursued him even to that irremediable ruin. There he lies, white and cold in death. You hate me; but your abhorrence cannot equal that with which I regard myself. I look on the hands which executed the deed; I think on the heart in which the imagination of it was conceived, and long for the moment when these hands will meet my eyes, when that imagination will haunt my thoughts no more.

'Fear not that I shall be the instrument of future mischief. My work is nearly complete. Neither yours nor any man's death is needed to consummate the series of my being, and accomplish that which must be done; but it requires my own. Do not think that I shall be slow to perform this sacrifice. I shall quit your vessel on the ice-raft which brought me thither, and shall seek the most northern extremity of the globe; I shall collect my funeral pile, and consume to ashes this miserable frame, that its remains may afford no light to any curious and unhallowed wretch, who would create such another as I have been. I shall die. I shall no longer feel the agonies which now consume me, or be the prey of feelings unsatisfied, yet unquenched. He is dead who called me into being; and when I shall be no more, the very remembrance of us both will speedily vanish. I shall no longer see the sun or stars, or feel the winds play on my cheeks. Light, feeling, and sense will pass away; and in this condition must I find my happiness. Some years ago, when the images which this world affords first opened upon me, when I felt the cheering warmth of summer and heard the rustling of the leaves and the warbling of the birds, and these were all to me, I should have wept to die; now it is my only consolation. Polluted by crimes, and torn by the bitterest remorse, where can I find rest but in death?

'Farewell! I leave you, and in you the last of human-kind whom these eyes will ever behold. Farewell, Frankenstein! If thou wert yet alive and yet cherished a desire of revenge against me, it would be better satiated in my life than in my destruction. But it was not so; thou didst seek my extinction, that I might not cause greater wretchedness; and if yet, in some mode unknown to me, thou hadst not ceased to think and feel, thou wouldst not desire against me a vengeance greater than that which I feel. Blasted as thou wert, my agony was still superior to thine; for the bitter sting of remorse will not cease to rankle in my wounds until death shall close them for ever.

'But soon,' he cried, with sad and solemn enthusiasm, 'I shall die, and what I now feel be no longer felt. Soon these burning miseries will be extinct. I shall ascend my funeral pile triumphantly, and exult in the agony of the torturing flames. The light of that conflagration will fade away; my ashes will be swept into the sea by the winds. My spirit will sleep in peace; or if it thinks, it will not surely think thus. Farewell.'

He sprung from the cabin window, as he said this, upon the ice-raft which lay close to the vessel. He was soon borne away by the waves, and lost in darkness and distance.

THE END

THE
LOVECRAFT
COMPENDIUM

THE
LOVECRAFT
COMPENDIUM

H. P. LOVECRAFT

This edition published in 2019 by Arcturus Publishing Limited
26/27 Bickels Yard, 151–153 Bermondsey Street,
London SE1 3HA

Typesetting by Palimpsest Book Production Limited

Cover design: Peter Ridley
Design: Beatriz Custodio

AD005110US

Printed in the UK

Contents

Introduction...7

Dagon...9

The Call of Cthulhu 16

The Dunwich Horror...50

The Whisperer in Darkness......................................123

The Haunter of the Dark 177

Introduction

*"The oldest and strongest emotion of mankind is fear, and
the oldest and strongest kind of fear is fear of the unknown."*
– Howard Phillips Lovecraft, 1927.

H. P. Lovecraft has become a worldwide phenomenon. He is vastly important to the fields of weird horror and dark fantasy of course, but his reach has steadily spread to every corner of popular culture. Movies. Books. Games. Toys. Clothes. Foods. Vehicular accessories. Decorations. You name it, it's out there. Cthulhu has become a very unlikely household name. The growth of Lovecraft's influence is not just down to random chance, however.

Born in Providence, Rhode Island in 1890, Lovecraft died at the age of 47, shortly before World War II. Over his lifetime, the balance of global power shifted radically, away from the cosy white male privilege of the Victorian era. Just as geopolitics and women's suffrage were changing global society, science was undermining everything that had been assumed about reality. Passionately curious about both history and cutting-edge science, Lovecraft was particularly aware of the changes around him. It is this sense of alienation that gives his work so much of its power.

Even by the standards of the day, he was a difficult person. Throughout his life, he suffered vivid, horrifying nightmares that became the basis of his stories. He was terrified of the cold, of disease, of decay. In many ways, the fears which drove him are a perfect exaggeration of the concerns of the society he grew up in.

None of this would have made much impact without Lovecraft's literary genius, of course. It's not his writing style that earns him that accolade though, nor his personality. The true strengths of his work lie in the heady blend of dread and wonder invoked in a single moment, in the sense of absolute reality leant to even the most outlandish fictions, in the shift of concerns from the individual to the truly cosmic. It is hard not to shudder when the universe itself feels like a tiny, flickering spark in the hungry darkness.

This collection is a seed. The tales it contains form a perfect introduction to Lovecraft's stories. Let them in, and the Cthulhu Mythos will take root inside you and transform you. A strange and wondrous experience awaits.

DAGON

I am writing this under an appreciable mental strain, since by tonight I shall be no more. Penniless, and at the end of my supply of the drug which alone makes life endurable, I can bear the torture no longer; and shall cast myself from this garret window into the squalid street below. Do not think from my slavery to morphine that I am a weakling or a degenerate. When you have read these hastily scrawled pages you may guess, though never fully realize, why it is that I must have forgetfulness or death.

It was in one of the most open and least frequented parts of the broad Pacific that the packet of which I was supercargo fell a victim to the German sea-raider. The great war was then at its very beginning, and the ocean forces of the Hun had not completely sunk to their later degradation; so that our vessel was made a legitimate prize, whilst we of her crew were treated with all the fairness and consideration due us as naval prisoners. So liberal, indeed, was the discipline of our captors, that five days after we were taken I managed to escape alone in a small boat with water and provisions for a good length of time.

When I finally found myself adrift and free, I had but little idea of my surroundings. Never a competent navigator, I could only guess vaguely by the sun and stars that I was somewhat south of the equator. Of the longitude I knew nothing, and no island or coastline was in sight. The weather kept fair, and for uncounted days I drifted aimlessly beneath the scorching sun; waiting either for some passing ship, or to be cast on the shores of some habitable land. But neither ship nor land appeared, and I began to despair in my solitude upon the heaving vastnesses of unbroken blue.

The change happened whilst I slept. Its details I shall never know; for my slumber, though troubled and dream-infested, was continuous. When at last I awaked, it was to discover myself half sucked into a slimy expanse of hellish black mire which extended about me in monotonous undulations as far as I could see, and in which my boat lay grounded some distance away.

Though one might well imagine that my first sensation would be of wonder at so prodigious and unexpected a transformation of scenery, I was in reality more horrified than astonished; for there was in the air and in the rotting soil a sinister quality which chilled me to the very core. The region was putrid with the carcasses of decaying fish, and of other less describable things which I saw protruding from the nasty mud of the unending plain. Perhaps I should not hope to convey in mere words the unutterable hideousness that can dwell in absolute silence and barren immensity. There was nothing within hearing, and nothing in sight save a vast reach of black slime; yet the very completeness of the stillness and the homogeneity of the landscape oppressed me with a nauseating fear.

The sun was blazing down from a sky which seemed to me almost black in its cloudless cruelty; as though reflecting the inky marsh beneath my feet. As I crawled into the stranded boat I realized that only one theory could explain my position. Through some unprecedented volcanic upheaval, a portion of the ocean floor must have been thrown to the surface, exposing regions which for innumerable millions of years had lain hidden under unfathomable watery depths. So great was the extent of the new land which had risen beneath me, that I could not detect the faintest noise of the surging ocean, strain my ears as I might. Nor were there any sea-fowl to prey upon the dead things.

For several hours I sat thinking or brooding in the boat, which lay upon its side and afforded a slight shade as the sun moved across the heavens. As the day progressed, the ground lost some of its stickiness, and seemed likely to dry sufficiently for traveling purposes in a short time. That night I slept but little, and the next day I made for myself a pack containing food and water, preparatory to an overland journey in search of the vanished sea and possible rescue.

On the third morning I found the soil dry enough to walk upon with ease. The odor of the fish was maddening; but I was too much concerned with graver things to mind so slight an evil, and set out boldly for an unknown goal. All day I forged steadily westward, guided by a far-away hummock which rose higher than any other elevation on the rolling desert. That night I encamped, and on the following day still traveled toward the hummock, though that object seemed scarcely nearer than when I had first espied it. By the fourth evening I attained the base of the mound, which turned out to be much higher than it had appeared from a distance; an intervening valley setting it out in sharper relief from the general surface. Too weary to ascend, I slept in the shadow of the hill.

I know not why my dreams were so wild that night; but ere the waning and fantastically gibbous moon had risen far above the eastern plain, I was awake in a cold perspiration, determined to sleep no more. Such visions as I had experienced were too much for me to endure again. And in the glow of the moon I saw how unwise I had been to travel by day. Without the glare of the parching sun, my journey would have cost me less energy; indeed, I now felt quite able to perform the ascent which had deterred me at sunset. Picking up my pack, I started for the crest of the eminence.

I have said that the unbroken monotony of the rolling plain was a source of vague horror to me; but I think my horror was greater when I gained the summit of the mound and looked down the other side into an immeasurable pit or canyon, whose black recesses the moon had not yet soared high enough to illumine. I felt myself on the edge of the world; peering over the rim into a fathomless chaos of eternal night. Through my terror ran curious reminiscences of *Paradise Lost,* and of Satan's hideous climb through the unfashioned realms of darkness.

As the moon climbed higher in the sky, I began to see that the slopes of the valley were not quite so perpendicular as I had imagined. Ledges and outcroppings of rock afforded fairly easy foot-holds for a descent, whilst after a drop of a few hundred feet, the declivity became very gradual. Urged on by an impulse which I cannot definitely analyze, I scrambled with difficulty down the rocks and stood on the gentler slope beneath, gazing into the Stygian deeps where no light had yet penetrated.

All at once my attention was captured by a vast and singular object on the opposite slope, which rose steeply about an hundred yards ahead of me; an object that gleamed whitely in the newly bestowed rays of the ascending moon. That it was merely a gigantic piece of stone, I soon assured myself; but I was conscious of a distinct impression that its contour and position were not altogether the work of Nature. A closer scrutiny filled me with sensations I cannot express; for despite its enormous magnitude, and its position in an abyss which had yawned at the bottom of the sea since the world was young, I perceived beyond a doubt that the strange object was a well-shaped monolith whose massive bulk had known the workmanship and perhaps the worship of living and thinking creatures.

Dazed and frightened, yet not without a certain thrill of the scientist's or archeologist's delight, I examined my surroundings more closely. The moon, now near the zenith, shone weirdly and vividly above the towering steeps that hemmed in the chasm, and revealed the fact that a far-flung body of water flowed at the bottom, winding out of sight in both directions, and almost lapping my feet as I stood on the slope. Across the chasm, the wavelets washed the base of the Cyclopean monolith; on whose surface I could now trace both inscriptions and crude sculptures. The writing was in a system of hieroglyphics unknown to me, and unlike anything I had ever seen in books; consisting for the most part of conventionalized aquatic symbols such as fishes, eels, octopi, crustaceans, mollusks, whales, and the like. Several characters obviously represented marine things which are unknown to the modern world, but whose decomposing forms I had observed on the ocean-risen plain.

It was the pictorial carving, however, that did most to hold me spellbound. Plainly visible across the intervening water on account of their enormous size, were an array of bas-reliefs whose subjects would have excited the envy of a Doré. I think that these things were supposed to depict men—at least, a certain sort of men; though the creatures were shown disporting like fishes in the waters of some marine grotto, or paying homage at some monolithic shrine which appeared to be under the waves as well. Of their faces and forms I dare not speak in detail; for the mere remembrance makes me grow faint. Grotesque beyond the imagination of a Poe or a Bulwer, they were damnably human in general outline despite webbed hands and feet, shockingly wide and flabby lips, glassy, bulging eyes, and other features less pleasant to recall. Curiously enough, they seemed to have been chiseled badly out of proportion with their scenic background; for one of the creatures was shown in the act of killing a whale represented as but little larger than himself. I remarked, as I say, their grotesqueness and strange size; but in a moment decided that they were merely the imaginary gods of some primitive fishing or seafaring tribe; some tribe whose last descendant had perished eras before the first ancestor of the Piltdown or Neanderthal Man was born. Awestruck at this unexpected glimpse into a past beyond the conception of the most daring anthropologist, I stood musing whilst the moon cast queer reflections on the silent channel before me.

Then suddenly I saw it. With only a slight churning to mark its rise to the surface, the thing slid into view above the dark waters.

Vast, Polyphemus-like, and loathsome, it darted like a stupendous monster of nightmares to the monolith, about which it flung its gigantic scaly arms, the while it bowed its hideous head and gave vent to certain measured sounds. I think I went mad then.

Of my frantic ascent of the slope and cliff, and of my delirious journey back to the stranded boat, I remember little. I believe I sang a great deal, and laughed oddly when I was unable to sing. I have indistinct recollections of a great storm some time after I reached the boat; at any rate, I know that I heard peals of thunder and other tones which Nature utters only in her wildest moods.

When I came out of the shadows I was in a San Francisco hospital; brought thither by the captain of the American ship which had picked up my boat in mid-ocean. In my delirium I had said much, but found that my words had been given scant attention. Of any land upheaval in the Pacific, my rescuers knew nothing; nor did I deem it necessary to insist upon a thing which I knew they could not believe. Once I sought out a celebrated ethnologist, and amused him with peculiar questions regarding the ancient Philistine legend of Dagon, the Fish-God; but soon perceiving that he was hopelessly conventional, I did not press my inquiries.

It is at night, especially when the moon is gibbous and waning, that I see the thing. I tried morphine; but the drug has given only transient surcease, and has drawn me into its clutches as a hopeless slave. So now I am to end it all, having written a full account for the information or the contemptuous amusement of my fellow men. Often I ask myself if it could not all have been a pure phantasm—a mere freak of fever as I lay sun-stricken and raving in the open boat after my escape from the German man-of-war. This I ask myself, but ever does there come before me a hideously vivid vision in reply. I cannot think of the deep sea without shuddering at the nameless things that may at this very moment be crawling and floundering on its slimy bed, worshipping their ancient stone idols and carving their own detestable likenesses on submarine obelisks of water-soaked granite. I dream of a day when they may rise above the billows to drag down in their reeking talons the remnants of puny, war-exhausted mankind— of a day when the land shall sink, and the dark ocean floor shall ascend amidst universal pandemonium.

The end is near. I hear a noise at the door, as of some immense slippery body lumbering against it. It shall not find me. God, *that hand!* The window! The window!

THE CALL OF CTHULHU

(Found Among the Papers of the Late Francis Wayland Thurston, of Boston)

"Of such great powers or beings there may be conceivably a survival . . . a survival of a hugely remote period when . . . consciousness was manifested, perhaps, in shapes and forms long since withdrawn before the tide of advancing humanity . . . forms of which poetry and legend alone have caught a flying memory and called them gods, monsters, mythical beings of all sorts and kinds. . . ."

—Algernon Blackwood

I The Horror in Clay

The most merciful thing in the world, I think, is the inability of the human mind to correlate all its contents. We live on a placid island of ignorance in the midst of black seas of infinity, and it was not meant that we should voyage far. The sciences, each straining in its own direction, have hitherto harmed us little; but some day the piecing together of dissociated knowledge will open up such terrifying vistas of reality, and of our frightful position therein, that we shall either go mad from the revelation or flee from the deadly light into the peace and safety of a new dark age.

Theosophists have guessed at the awesome grandeur of the cosmic cycle wherein our world and human race form transient incidents. They have hinted at strange survivals in terms which would freeze the blood if not masked by a bland optimism. But it is not from them that there came the single glimpse of forbidden eons which chills me when I think of it and maddens me when I dream of it. That glimpse, like all dread glimpses of truth, flashed out from an accidental piecing together of separated things—in this case an old newspaper item and the notes of a dead professor. I hope that no one else will accomplish this piecing out; certainly, if I live, I shall never knowingly supply a link in so hideous a chain. I think that the professor, too, intended to keep silent regarding the part he knew, and that he would have destroyed his notes had not sudden death seized him.

My knowledge of the thing began in the winter of 1926–27 with the death of my great-uncle George Gammell Angell, Professor Emeritus of Semitic Languages in Brown University, Providence, Rhode Island. Professor Angell was widely known as an authority on ancient inscriptions, and had frequently been resorted to by the heads of prominent museums; so that his passing at the age of ninety-two may be recalled by many. Locally, interest was intensified by the obscurity of the cause of death. The professor had been stricken whilst returning from the Newport boat; falling suddenly, as witnesses said, after having been jostled by a nautical-looking negro who had come from one of the queer dark courts on the precipitous hillside which formed a short cut from the waterfront to the deceased's home in Williams Street. Physicians were unable to find any visible disorder, but concluded after perplexed debate that some obscure lesion of the heart, induced by the brisk ascent of so steep a hill by so elderly a man, was responsible for the end. At the time I saw no reason to dissent from this dictum, but latterly I am inclined to wonder—and more than wonder.

As my grand-uncle's heir and executor, for he died a childless widower, I was expected to go over his papers with some thoroughness; and for that purpose moved his entire set of files and boxes to my quarters in Boston. Much of the material which I correlated will be later published by the American Archaeological Society, but there was one box which I found exceedingly puzzling, and which I felt much averse from showing to other eyes. It had been locked, and I did not find the key till it occurred to me to examine the personal ring which the professor carried always in his pocket. Then indeed I succeeded in opening it, but when I did so seemed only to be confronted by a greater and more closely locked barrier. For what could be the meaning of the queer clay bas-relief and the disjointed jottings, ramblings, and cuttings which I found? Had my uncle, in his latter years, become credulous of the most superficial impostures? I resolved to search out the eccentric sculptor responsible for this apparent disturbance of an old man's peace of mind.

The bas-relief was a rough rectangle less than an inch thick and about five by six inches in area; obviously of modern origin. Its designs, however, were far from modern in atmosphere and suggestion; for although the vagaries of cubism and futurism are many and wild, they do not often reproduce that cryptic regularity which lurks in prehistoric writing. And writing of some kind the bulk of these designs seemed certainly to be; though my memory, despite much familiarity with the papers and collections of my uncle, failed in any way to identify this particular species, or even to hint at its remotest affiliations.

Above these apparent hieroglyphics was a figure of evidently pictorial intent, though its impressionistic execution forbade a very clear idea of its nature. It seemed to be a sort of monster, or symbol representing a monster, of a form which only a diseased fancy could conceive. If I say that my somewhat extravagant imagination yielded simultaneous pictures of an octopus, a dragon, and a human caricature, I shall not be unfaithful to the spirit of the thing. A pulpy, tentacled head surmounted a grotesque and scaly body with rudimentary wings; but it was the *general outline* of the whole which made it most shockingly frightful. Behind the figure was a vague suggestion of a Cyclopean architectural background.

The writing accompanying this oddity was, aside from a stack of press cuttings, in Professor Angell's most recent hand; and made no pretence to literary style. What seemed to be the main document was headed "CTHULHU CULT" in characters painstakingly printed to avoid the erroneous reading of a word so unheard-of. The manuscript was divided into two sections, the first of which was headed "1925— Dream and Dream Work of H. A. Wilcox, 7 Thomas St, Providence, RI," and the second, "Narrative of Inspector John R. Legrasse, 121 Bienville St, New Orleans, La, at 1908 A. A. S. Mtg—Notes on Same, & Prof. Webb's Acct." The other manuscript papers were all brief notes, some of them accounts of the queer dreams of different persons, some of them citations from theosophical books and magazines (notably W. Scott-Elliot's *Atlantis and the Lost Lemuria*), and the rest comments on long-surviving secret societies and hidden cults, with references to passages in such mythological and anthropological source-books as Frazer's *Golden Bough* and Miss Murray's *Witch-Cult in Western Europe*. The cuttings largely alluded to *outré* mental illnesses and outbreaks of group folly or mania in the spring of 1925.

The first half of the principal manuscript told a very peculiar tale. It appears that on March 1st, 1925, a thin, dark young man of neurotic and excited aspect had called upon Professor Angell bearing the singular clay bas-relief, which was then exceedingly damp and fresh. His card bore the name of Henry Anthony Wilcox, and my uncle had recognized him as the youngest son of an excellent family slightly known to him, who had latterly been studying sculpture at the Rhode Island School of Design and living alone at the Fleur-de-Lys Building near that institution. Wilcox was a precocious youth of known genius but great eccentricity, and had from childhood excited attention through the strange stories and odd dreams he was in the habit of relating. He called himself "psychically hypersensitive," but the staid folk of the ancient commercial city dismissed him as merely "queer." Never mingling much with his kind, he had dropped gradually from social visibility, and was now known only to a small group of esthetes from other towns. Even the Providence Art Club, anxious to preserve its conservatism, had found him quite hopeless.

On the occasion of the visit, ran the professor's manuscript, the sculptor abruptly asked for the benefit of his host's archeological knowledge in identifying the hieroglyphics on the bas-relief. He spoke in a dreamy, stilted manner which suggested pose and alienated sympathy; and my uncle showed some sharpness in replying, for the conspicuous freshness of the tablet implied kinship with anything but archeology. Young Wilcox's rejoinder, which impressed my uncle enough to make him recall and record it verbatim, was of a fantastically poetic cast which must have typified his whole conversation, and which I have since found highly characteristic of him. He said, "It is new, indeed, for I made it last night in a dream of strange cities; and dreams are older than brooding Tyre, or the contemplative Sphinx, or garden-girdled Babylon."

It was then that he began that rambling tale which suddenly played upon a sleeping memory and won the fevered interest of my uncle. There had been a slight earthquake tremor the night before, the most considerable felt in New England for some years; and Wilcox's imagination had been keenly affected. Upon retiring, he had had an unprecedented dream of great Cyclopean cities of titan blocks and sky-flung monoliths, all dripping with green ooze and sinister with latent horror. Hieroglyphics had covered the walls and pillars, and from some undetermined point below had come a voice that was not a voice; a chaotic sensation which only fancy could transmute into sound, but which he attempted to render by the almost unpronounceable jumble of letters "*Cthulhu fhtagn.*"

This verbal jumble was the key to the recollection which excited and disturbed Professor Angell. He questioned the sculptor with scientific minuteness; and studied with almost frantic intensity the bas-relief on which the youth had found himself working, chilled and clad only in his night-clothes, when waking had stolen bewilderingly over him. My uncle blamed his old age, Wilcox afterward said, for his slowness in recognizing both hieroglyphics and pictorial design.

Many of his questions seemed highly out-of-place to his visitor, especially those which tried to connect the latter with strange cults or societies; and Wilcox could not understand the repeated promises of silence which he was offered in exchange for an admission of membership in some widespread mystical or paganly religious body. When Professor Angell became convinced that the sculptor was indeed ignorant of any cult or system of cryptic lore, he besieged his visitor with demands for future reports of dreams. This bore regular fruit, for after the first interview the manuscript records daily calls of the young man, during which he related startling fragments of nocturnal imagery whose burden was always some terrible Cyclopean vista of dark and dripping stone, with a subterrene voice or intelligence shouting monotonously in enigmatical sense-impacts uninscribable save as gibberish. The two sounds most frequently repeated are those rendered by the letters "*Cthulhu*" and "*R'lyeh.*"

On March 23rd, the manuscript continued, Wilcox failed to appear; and inquiries at his quarters revealed that he had been stricken with an obscure sort of fever and taken to the home of his family in Waterman Street. He had cried out in the night, arousing several other artists in the building, and had manifested since then only alternations of unconsciousness and delirium. My uncle at once telephoned the family, and from that time forward kept close watch of the case; calling often at the Thayer Street office of Dr Tobey, whom he learned to be in charge. The youth's febrile mind, apparently, was dwelling on strange things; and the doctor shuddered now and then as he spoke of them. They included not only a repetition of what he had formerly dreamed, but touched wildly on a gigantic thing "miles high" which walked or lumbered about. He at no time fully described this object, but occasional frantic words, as repeated by Dr Tobey, convinced the professor that it must be identical with the nameless monstrosity he had sought to depict in his dream-sculpture. Reference to this object, the doctor added, was invariably a prelude to the young man's subsidence into lethargy. His temperature, oddly enough, was not greatly above normal; but his whole condition was otherwise such as to suggest true fever rather than mental disorder.

On April 2nd at about 3 p.m. every trace of Wilcox's malady suddenly ceased. He sat upright in bed, astonished to find himself at home and completely ignorant of what had happened in dream or reality since the night of March 22nd. Pronounced well by his physician, he returned to his quarters in three days; but to Professor Angell he was of no further assistance. All traces of strange dreaming had vanished with his recovery, and my uncle kept no record of his night-thoughts after a week of pointless and irrelevant accounts of thoroughly usual visions.

Here the first part of the manuscript ended, but references to certain of the scattered notes gave me much material for thought—so much, in fact, that only the ingrained skepticism then forming my philosophy can account for my continued distrust of the artist. The notes in question were those descriptive of the dreams of various persons covering the same period as that in which young Wilcox had had his strange visitations. My uncle, it seems, had quickly instituted a prodigiously far-flung body of inquiries amongst nearly all the friends whom he could question without impertinence, asking for nightly reports of their dreams, and the dates of any notable visions for some time past. The reception of his request seems to have been varied; but he must, at the very least, have received more responses than any ordinary man could have handled without a secretary. This original correspondence was not preserved, but his notes formed a thorough and really significant digest. Average people in society and business— New England's traditional "salt of the earth"—gave an almost completely negative result, though scattered cases of uneasy but formless nocturnal impressions appear here and there, always between March 23rd and April 2nd—the period of young Wilcox's delirium. Scientific men were little more affected, though four cases of vague description suggest fugitive glimpses of strange landscapes, and in one case there is mentioned a dread of something abnormal.

It was from the artists and poets that the pertinent answers came, and I know that panic would have broken loose had they been able to compare notes. As it was, lacking their original letters, I half suspected the compiler of having asked leading questions, or of having edited the correspondence in corroboration of what he had latently resolved to see. That is why I continued to feel that Wilcox, somehow cognizant of the old data which my uncle had possessed, had been imposing on the veteran scientist. These responses from aesthetes told a disturbing tale. From February 28th to April 2nd a large proportion of them had dreamed very bizarre things, the intensity of the dreams being immeasurably the stronger during the period of the sculptor's delirium. Over a fourth of those who reported anything, reported scenes and half-sounds not unlike those which Wilcox had described; and some of the dreamers confessed acute fear of the gigantic nameless thing visible toward the last. One case, which the note describes with emphasis, was very sad. The subject, a widely known architect with leanings toward theosophy and occultism, went violently insane on the date of young Wilcox's seizure, and expired several months later after incessant screamings to be saved from some escaped denizen of hell. Had my uncle referred to these cases by name instead of merely by number, I should have attempted some corroboration and personal investigation; but as it was, I succeeded in tracing down only a few. All of these, however, bore out the notes in full. I have often wondered if all the objects of the professor's questioning felt as puzzled as did this fraction. It is well that no explanation shall ever reach them.

The press cuttings, as I have intimated, touched on cases of panic, mania, and eccentricity during the given period. Professor Angell must have employed a cutting bureau, for the number of extracts was tremendous and the sources scattered throughout the globe. Here was a nocturnal suicide in London, where a lone sleeper had leaped from a window after a shocking cry. Here likewise a rambling letter to the editor of a paper in South America, where a fanatic deduces a dire future from visions he has seen. A dispatch from California describes a theosophist colony as donning white robes en masse for some "glorious fulfillment" which never arrives, whilst items from India speak guardedly of serious native unrest toward the end of March. Voodoo orgies multiply in Haiti, and African outposts report ominous mutterings. American officers in the Philippines find certain tribes bothersome about this time, and New York policemen are mobbed by hysterical Levantines on the night of March 22nd–23rd. The west of Ireland, too, is full of wild rumor and legendry, and a fantastic painter named Ardois-Bonnot hangs a blasphe-mous "Dream Landscape" in the Paris spring salon of 1926. And so numerous are the recorded troubles in insane asylums, that only a miracle can have stopped the medical fraternity from noting strange parallelisms and drawing mystified conclusions. A weird bunch of cuttings, all told; and I can at this date scarcely envisage the callous rationalism with which I set them aside. But I was then convinced that young Wilcox had known of the older matters mentioned by the professor.

II The Tale of Inspector Legrasse

The older matters which had made the sculptor's dream and bas-relief so significant to my uncle formed the subject of the second half of his long manuscript. Once before, it appears, Professor Angell had seen the hellish outlines of the nameless monstrosity, puzzled over the unknown hieroglyphics, and heard the ominous syllables which can be rendered only as "*Cthulhu*"; and all this in so stirring and horrible a connection that it is small wonder he pursued young Wilcox with queries and demands for data.

The earlier experience had come in 1908, seventeen years before, when the American Archaeological Society held its annual meeting in St Louis. Professor Angell, as befitted one of his authority and attainments, had had a prominent part in all the deliberations; and was one of the first to be approached by the several outsiders who took advantage of the convocation to offer questions for correct answering and problems for expert solution.

The chief of these outsiders, and in a short time the focus of interest for the entire meeting, was a commonplace-looking middle-aged man who had traveled all the way from New Orleans for certain special information unobtainable from any local source. His name was John Raymond Legrasse, and he was by profession an Inspector of Police. With him he bore the subject of his visit, a grotesque, repulsive, and apparently very ancient stone statuette whose origin he was at a loss to determine. It must not be fancied that Inspector Legrasse had the least interest in archeology. On the contrary, his wish for enlightenment was prompted by purely professional considerations. The statuette, idol, fetish, or whatever it was, had been captured some months before in the wooded swamps south of New Orleans during a raid on a supposed voodoo meeting; and so singular and hideous were the rites connected with it, that the police could not but realize that they had stumbled on a dark cult totally unknown to them, and infinitely more diabolic than even the blackest of the African voodoo circles. Of its origin, apart from the erratic and unbelievable tales extorted from the captured members, absolutely nothing was to be discovered; hence the anxiety of the police for any antiquarian lore which might help them to place the frightful symbol, and through it track down the cult to its fountain-head.

Inspector Legrasse was scarcely prepared for the sensation which his offering created. One sight of the thing had been enough to throw the assembled men of science into a state of tense excitement, and they lost no time in crowding around him to gaze at the diminutive figure whose utter strangeness and air of genuinely abysmal antiquity hinted so potently at unopened and archaic vistas. No recognized school of sculpture had animated this terrible object, yet centuries and even thousands of years seemed recorded in its dim and greenish surface of unplaceable stone.

The figure, which was finally passed slowly from man to man for close and careful study, was between seven and eight inches in height, and of exquisitely artistic workmanship. It represented a monster of vaguely anthropoid outline, but with an octopus-like head whose face was a mass of feelers, a scaly, rubbery-looking body, prodigious claws on hind and fore feet, and long, narrow wings behind. This thing, which seemed instinct with a fearsome and unnatural malignancy, was of a somewhat bloated corpulence, and squatted evilly on a rectangular block or pedestal covered with undecipherable characters. The tips of the wings touched the back edge of the block, the seat occupied the center, whilst the long, curved claws of the doubled-up, crouching hind legs gripped the front edge and extended a quarter of the way down toward the bottom of the pedestal. The cephalopod head was bent forward, so that the ends of the facial feelers brushed the backs of huge fore paws which clasped the croucher's elevated knees. The aspect of the whole was abnormally life-like, and the more subtly fearful because its source was so totally unknown. Its vast, awesome, and incalculable age was unmistakable; yet not one link did it show with any known type of art belonging to civilization's youth—or indeed to any other time. Totally separate and apart, its very material was a mystery; for the soapy, greenish-black stone with its golden or irides-cent flecks and striations resembled nothing familiar to geology or mineralogy. The characters along the base were equally baffling; and no member present, despite a representation of half the world's expert learning in this field, could form the least notion of even their remotest linguistic kinship. They, like the subject and material, belonged to something horribly remote and distinct from mankind as we know it; something frightfully suggestive of old and unhallowed cycles of life in which our world and our conceptions have no part.

And yet, as the members severally shook their heads and confessed defeat at the Inspector's problem, there was one man in that gathering who suspected a touch of bizarre familiarity in the monstrous shape and writing, and who presently told with some diffidence of the odd trifle he knew. This person was the late William Channing Webb, Professor of Anthropology in Princeton University, and an explorer of no slight note. Professor Webb had been engaged, forty-eight years before, in a tour of Greenland and Iceland in search of some Runic inscriptions which he failed to unearth; and whilst high up on the West Greenland coast had encountered a singular tribe or cult of degenerate Eskimos whose religion, a curious form of devil-worship, chilled him with its deliberate bloodthirstiness and repulsiveness. It was a faith of which other Eskimos knew little, and which they mentioned only with shudders, saying that it had come down from horribly ancient eons before ever the world was made. Besides nameless rites and human sacrifices there were certain queer hereditary rituals addressed to a supreme elder devil, or *tornasuk;* and of this Professor Webb had taken a careful phonetic copy from an aged *angekok* or wizard-priest, expressing the sounds in Roman letters as best he knew how. But just now of prime significance was the fetish which this cult had cherished, and around which they danced when the aurora leaped high over the ice cliffs. It was, the professor stated, a very crude bas-relief of stone, comprising a hideous picture and some cryptic writing. And so far as he could tell, it was a rough parallel in all essential features of the bestial thing now lying before the meeting.

This data, received with suspense and astonishment by the assembled members, proved doubly exciting to Inspector Legrasse; and he began at once to ply his informant with questions. Having noted and copied an oral ritual among the swamp cult-worshippers his men had arrested, he besought the professor to remember as best he might the syllables taken down amongst the diabolist Eskimos. There then followed an exhaustive comparison of details, and a moment of really awed silence when both detective and scientist agreed on the virtual identity of the phrase common to two hellish rituals so many worlds of distance apart. What, in substance, both the Eskimo wizards and the Louisiana swamp-priests had chanted to their kindred idols was something very like this—the word-divisions being guessed at from traditional breaks in the phrase as chanted aloud:

"Ph'nglui mglw'nafh Cthulhu R'lyeh wgah'nagl fhtagn."

Legrasse had one point in advance of Professor Webb, for several among his mongrel prisoners had repeated to him what older celebrants had told them the words meant. This text, as given, ran something like this:

"In his house at R'lyeh dead Cthulhu waits dreaming."

And now, in response to a general and urgent demand, Inspector Legrasse related as fully as possible his experience with the swamp worshippers; telling a story to which I could see my uncle attached profound significance. It savored of the wildest dreams of myth-maker and theosophist, and disclosed an astonishing degree of cosmic imagination among such half-castes and pariahs as might be least expected to possess it.

On November 1st, 1907, there had come to the New Orleans police a frantic summons from the swamp and lagoon country to the south. The squatters there, mostly primitive but good-natured descendants of Lafitte's men, were in the grip of stark terror from an unknown thing which had stolen upon them in the night. It was voodoo, apparently, but voodoo of a more terrible sort than they had ever known; and some of their women and children had disappeared since the malevolent tom-tom had begun its incessant beating far within the black haunted woods where no dweller ventured. There were insane shouts and harrowing screams, soul-chilling chants and dancing devil-flames; and, the frightened messenger added, the people could stand it no more.

So a body of twenty police, filling two carriages and an automobile, had set out in the late afternoon with the shivering squatter as a guide. At the end of the passable road they alighted, and for miles splashed on in silence through the terrible cypress woods where day never came. Ugly roots and malignant hanging nooses of Spanish moss beset them, and now and then a pile of dank stones or fragment of a rotting wall intensified by its hint of morbid habitation a depression which every malformed tree and every fungous islet combined to create. At length the squatter settlement, a miserable huddle of huts, hove in sight; and hysterical dwellers ran out to cluster around the group of bobbing lanterns. The muffled beat of tom-toms was now faintly audible far, far ahead; and a curdling shriek came at infrequent intervals when the wind shifted. A reddish glare, too, seemed to filter through the pale undergrowth beyond endless avenues of forest night. Reluctant even to be left alone again, each one of the cowed squatters refused point-blank to advance another inch toward the scene of unholy worship, so Inspector Legrasse and his nineteen colleagues plunged on unguided into black arcades of horror that none of them had ever trod before.

The region now entered by the police was one of traditionally evil repute, substantially unknown and untraversed by white men. There were legends of a hidden lake unglimpsed by mortal sight, in which dwelt a huge, formless white polypous thing with luminous eyes; and squatters whispered that bat-winged devils flew up out of caverns in inner earth to worship it at midnight. They said it had been there before D'Iberville, before La Salle, before the Indians, and before even the wholesome beasts and birds of the woods. It was nightmare itself, and to see it was to die. But it made men dream, and so they knew enough to keep away. The present voodoo orgy was, indeed, on the merest fringe of this abhorred area, but that location was bad enough; hence perhaps the very place of the worship had terrified the squatters more than the shocking sounds and incidents.

Only poetry or madness could do justice to the noises heard by Legrasse's men as they ploughed on through the black morass toward the red glare and the muffled tom-toms. There are vocal qualities peculiar to men, and vocal qualities peculiar to beasts; and it is terrible to hear the one when the source should yield the other. Animal fury and orgiastic license here whipped themselves to demoniac heights by howls and squawking ecstasies that tore and reverberated through those nighted woods like pestilential tempests from the gulfs of hell. Now and then the less organized ululation would cease, and from what seemed a well-drilled chorus of hoarse voices would rise in sing-song chant that hideous phrase or ritual:

"Ph'nglui mglw'nafh Cthulhu R'lyeh wgah'nagl fhtagn."

Then the men, having reached a spot where the trees were thinner, came suddenly in sight of the spectacle itself. Four of them reeled, one fainted, and two were shaken into a frantic cry which the mad cacophony of the orgy fortunately deadened. Legrasse dashed swamp water on the face of the fainting man, and all stood trembling and nearly hypnotized with horror.

In a natural glade of the swamp stood a grassy island of perhaps an acre's extent, clear of trees and tolerably dry. On this now leaped and twisted a more indescribable horde of human abnormality than any but a Sime or an Angarola could paint. Void of clothing, this hybrid spawn were braying, bellowing, and writhing about a monstrous ring-shaped bonfire; in the center of which, revealed by occasional rifts in the curtain of flame, stood a great granite monolith some eight feet in height; on top of which, incongruous with its diminutiveness, rested the noxious carven statuette. From a wide circle of ten scaffolds set up at regular intervals with the flame-girt monolith as a center hung, head downward, the oddly marred bodies of the helpless squatters who had disappeared. It was inside this circle that the ring of worshippers jumped and roared, the general direction of the mass motion being from left to right in endless Bacchanal between the ring of bodies and the ring of fire.

It may have been only imagination and it may have been only echoes which induced one of the men, an excitable Spaniard, to fancy he heard antiphonal responses to the ritual from some far and un-illumined spot deeper within the wood of ancient legendry and horror. This man, Joseph D. Galvez, I later met and questioned; and he proved distractingly imaginative. He indeed went so far as to hint of the faint beating of great wings, and of a glimpse of shining eyes and a mountainous white bulk beyond the remotest trees—but I suppose he had been hearing too much native superstition.

Actually, the horrified pause of the men was of comparatively brief duration. Duty came first; and although there must have been nearly a hundred mongrel celebrants in the throng, the police relied on their firearms and plunged determinedly into the nauseous rout. For five minutes the resultant din and chaos were beyond description. Wild blows were struck, shots were fired, and escapes were made; but in the end Legrasse was able to count some forty-seven sullen prisoners, whom he forced to dress in haste and fall into line between two rows of policemen. Five of the worshippers lay dead, and two severely wounded ones were carried away on improvised stretchers by their fellow-prisoners. The image on the monolith, of course, was carefully removed and carried back by Legrasse.

Examined at headquarters after a trip of intense strain and weariness, the prisoners all proved to be men of a very low, mixed-blooded, and mentally aberrant type. Most were seamen, and a sprinkling of negroes and mulattoes, largely West Indians or Brava Portuguese from the Cape Verde Islands, gave a coloring of voodooism to the heterogeneous cult. But before many questions were asked, it became manifest that something far deeper and older than negro fetishism was involved. Degraded and ignorant as they were, the creatures held with surprising consistency to the central idea of their loathsome faith.

They worshipped, so they said, the Great Old Ones who lived ages before there were any men, and who came to the young world out of the sky. Those Old Ones were gone now, inside the earth and under the sea; but their dead bodies had told their secrets in dreams to the first men, who formed a cult which had never died. This was that cult, and the prisoners said it had always existed and always would exist, hidden in distant wastes and dark places all over the world until the time when the great priest Cthulhu, from his dark house in the mighty city of R'lyeh under the waters, should rise and bring the earth again beneath his sway. Some day he would call, when the stars were ready, and the secret cult would always be waiting to liberate him.

Meanwhile no more must be told. There was a secret which even torture could not extract. Mankind was not absolutely alone among the conscious things of earth, for shapes came out of the dark to visit the faithful few. But these were not the Great Old Ones. No man had ever seen the Old Ones. The carven idol was great Cthulhu, but none might say whether or not the others were precisely like him. No one could read the old writing now, but things were told by word of mouth. The chanted ritual was not the secret—that was never spoken aloud, only whispered. The chant meant only this: "In his house at R'lyeh dead Cthulhu waits dreaming."

Only two of the prisoners were found sane enough to be hanged, and the rest were committed to various institutions. All denied a part in the ritual murders, and averred that the killing had been done by Black Winged Ones which had come to them from their immemorial meeting-place in the haunted wood. But of those mysterious allies no coherent account could ever be gained. What the police did extract, came mainly from an immensely aged mestizo named Castro, who claimed to have sailed to strange ports and talked with undying leaders of the cult in the mountains of China.

Old Castro remembered bits of hideous legend that paled the speculations of theosophists and made man and the world seem recent and transient indeed. There had been eons when other Things ruled on the earth, and They had had great cities. Remains of Them, he said the deathless Chinamen had told him, were still to be found as Cyclopean stones on islands in the Pacific. They all died vast epochs of time before men came, but there were arts which could revive Them when the stars had come round again to the right positions in the cycle of eternity. They had, indeed, come themselves from the stars, and brought Their images with Them.

These Great Old Ones, Castro continued, were not composed altogether of flesh and blood. They had shape—for did not this star-fashioned image prove it?—but that shape was not made of matter. When the stars were right, They could plunge from world to world through the sky; but when the stars were wrong, They could not live. But although They no longer lived, They would never really die. They all lay in stone houses in Their great city of R'lyeh, preserved by the spells of mighty Cthulhu for a glorious resurrection when the stars and the earth might once more be ready for Them. But at that time some force from outside must serve to liberate Their bodies. The spells that preserved Them intact likewise prevented Them from making an initial move, and They could only lie awake in the dark and think whilst uncounted millions of years rolled by. They knew all that was occurring in the universe, but Their mode of speech was transmitted thought. Even now They talked in Their tombs. When, after infinities of chaos, the first men came, the Great Old Ones spoke to the sensitive among them by molding their dreams; for only thus could Their language reach the fleshly minds of mammals.

Then, whispered Castro, those first men formed the cult around small idols which the Great Ones showed them; idols brought in dim eras from dark stars. That cult would never die till the stars came right again, and the secret priests would take great Cthulhu from His tomb to revive His subjects and resume His rule of earth. The time would be easy to know, for then mankind would have become as the Great Old Ones; free and wild and beyond good and evil, with laws and morals thrown aside and all men shouting and killing and reveling in joy. Then the liberated Old Ones would teach them new ways to shout and kill and revel and enjoy themselves, and all the earth would flame with a holocaust of ecstasy and freedom. Meanwhile the cult, by appropriate rites, must keep alive the memory of those ancient ways and shadow forth the prophecy of their return.

In the elder time chosen men had talked with the entombed Old Ones in dreams, but then something had happened. The great stone city R'lyeh, with its monoliths and sepulchers, had sunk beneath the waves; and the deep waters, full of the one primal mystery through which not even thought can pass, had cut off the spectral intercourse. But memory never died, and high-priests said that the city would rise again when the stars were right. Then came out of the earth the black spirits of earth, moldy and shadowy, and full of dim rumors picked up in caverns beneath forgotten sea-bottoms. But of them old Castro dared not speak much. He cut himself off hurriedly, and no amount of persuasion or subtlety could elicit more in this direction. The *size* of the Old Ones, too, he curiously declined to mention. Of the cult, he said that he thought the center lay amid the pathless deserts of Arabia, where Irem, the City of Pillars, dreams hidden and untouched. It was not allied to the European witch-cult, and was virtually unknown beyond its members. No book had ever really hinted of it, though the deathless Chinamen said that there were double meanings in the *Necronomicon* of the mad Arab Abdul Alhazred which the initiated might read as they chose, especially the much-discussed couplet:

"That is not dead which can eternal lie,
And with strange eons even death may die."

Legrasse, deeply impressed and not a little bewildered, had inquired in vain concerning the historic affiliations of the cult. Castro, apparently, had told the truth when he said that it was wholly secret. The authorities at Tulane University could shed no light upon either cult or image, and now the detective had come to the highest authorities in the country and met with no more than the Greenland tale of Professor Webb.

The feverish interest aroused at the meeting by Legrasse's tale, corroborated as it was by the statuette, is echoed in the subsequent correspondence of those who attended; although scant mention occurs in the formal publications of the society. Caution is the first care of those accustomed to face occasional charlatanry and imposture. Legrasse for some time lent the image to Professor Webb, but at the latter's death it was returned to him and remains in his possession, where I viewed it not long ago. It is truly a terrible thing, and unmistakably akin to the dream-sculpture of young Wilcox.

That my uncle was excited by the tale of the sculptor I did not wonder, for what thoughts must arise upon hearing, after a knowledge of what Legrasse had learned of the cult, of a sensitive young man who had *dreamed* not only the figure and exact hieroglyphics of the swamp-found image and the Greenland devil tablet, but had come *in his dreams* upon at least three of the precise words of the formula uttered alike by Eskimo diabolists and mongrel Louisianans? Professor Angell's instant start on an investigation of the utmost thoroughness was eminently natural; though privately I suspected young Wilcox of having heard of the cult in some indirect way, and of having invented a series of dreams to heighten and continue the mystery at my uncle's expense. The dream-narratives and cuttings collected by the professor were, of course, strong corroboration; but the rationalism of my mind and the extravagance of the whole subject led me to adopt what I thought the most sensible conclusions. So, after thoroughly studying the manuscript again and correlating the theosophical and anthropological notes with the cult narrative of Legrasse, I made a trip to Providence to see the sculptor and give him the rebuke I thought proper for so boldly imposing upon a learned and aged man.

Wilcox still lived alone in the Fleur-de-Lys Building in Thomas

Street, a hideous Victorian imitation of seventeenth-century Breton architecture which flaunts its stuccoed front amidst the lovely colonial houses on the ancient hill, and under the very shadow of the finest Georgian steeple in America. I found him at work in his rooms, and at once conceded from the specimens scattered about that his genius is indeed profound and authentic. He will, I believe, some time be heard from as one of the great decadents; for he has crystallized in clay and will one day mirror in marble those nightmares and fantasies which Arthur Machen evokes in prose, and Clark Ashton Smith makes visible in verse and in painting.

Dark, frail, and somewhat unkempt in aspect, he turned languidly at my knock and asked me my business without rising. When I told him who I was, he displayed some interest; for my uncle had excited his curiosity in probing his strange dreams, yet had never explained the reason for the study. I did not enlarge his knowledge in this regard, but sought with some subtlety to draw him out. In a short time I became convinced of his absolute sincerity, for hc spoke of the dreams in a manner none could mistake. They and their subconscious residuum had influenced his art profoundly, and he showed me a morbid statue whose contours almost made me shake with the potency of its black suggestion. He could not recall having seen the original of this thing except in his own dream bas-relief, but the outlines had formed themselves insensibly under his hands. It was, no doubt, the giant shape he had raved of in delirium. That he really knew nothing of the hidden cult, save from what my uncle's relentless catechism had let fall, he soon made clear; and again I strove to think of some way in which he could possibly have received the weird impressions.

He talked of his dreams in a strangely poetic fashion; making me see with terrible vividness the damp Cyclopean city of slimy green stone—whose *geometry,* he oddly said, was *all wrong*—and hear with frightened expectancy the ceaseless, half-mental calling from underground: "*Cthulhu fhtagn,*" "*Cthulhu fhtagn.*" These words had formed part of that dread ritual which told of dead Cthulhu's dream-vigil in his stone vault at R'lyeh, and I felt deeply moved despite my rational beliefs. Wilcox, I was sure, had heard of the cult in some casual way, and had soon forgotten it amidst the mass of his equally weird reading and imagining. Later, by virtue of its sheer impressiveness, it had found subconscious expression in dreams, in the bas-relief, and in the terrible statue I now beheld; so that his imposture upon my uncle had been a very innocent one. The youth was of a type, at once slightly affected and slightly ill-mannered, which I could never like; but I was willing enough now to admit both his genius and his honesty. I took leave of him amicably, and wish him all the success his talent promises.

The matter of the cult still remained to fascinate me, and at times I had visions of personal fame from researches into its origin and connections. I visited New Orleans, talked with Legrasse and others of that old-time raiding-party, saw the frightful image, and even questioned such of the mongrel prisoners as still survived. Old Castro, unfortunately, had been dead for some years. What I now heard so graphically at first-hand, though it was really no more than a detailed confirmation of what my uncle had written, excited me afresh; for I felt sure that I was on the track of a very real, very secret, and very ancient religion whose discovery would make me an anthropologist of note. My attitude was still one of absolute materialism, *as I wish it still were*, and I discounted with almost inexplicable perversity the coincidence of the dream notes and odd cuttings collected by Professor Angell.

One thing I began to suspect, and which I now fear I *know*, is that my uncle's death was far from natural. He fell on a narrow hill street leading up from an ancient waterfront swarming with foreign mongrels, after a careless push from a negro sailor. I did not forget the mixed blood and marine pursuits of the cult-members in Louisiana, and would not be surprised to learn of secret methods and poison needles as ruthless and as anciently known as the cryptic rites and beliefs. Legrasse and his men, it is true, have been let alone; but in Norway a certain seaman who saw things is dead. Might not the deeper inquiries of my uncle after encountering the sculptor's data have come to sinister ears? I think Professor Angell died because he knew too much, or because he was likely to learn too much. Whether I shall go as he did remains to be seen, for I have learned much now.

III The Madness from the Sea

If heaven ever wishes to grant me a boon, it will be a total effacing of the results of a mere chance which fixed my eye on a certain stray piece of shelf-paper. It was nothing on which I would naturally have stumbled in the course of my daily round, for it was an old number of an Australian journal, the *Sydney Bulletin* for April 18, 1925. It had escaped even the cutting bureau which had at the time of its issuance been avidly collecting material for my uncle's research.

I had largely given over my inquiries into what Professor Angell called the "Cthulhu Cult," and was visiting a learned friend in Paterson, New Jersey; the curator of a local museum and a mineralogist of note. Examining one day the reserve specimens roughly set on the storage shelves in a rear room of the museum, my eye was caught by an odd picture in one of the old papers spread beneath the stones. It was the *Sydney Bulletin* I have mentioned, for my friend has wide affiliations in all conceivable foreign parts; and the picture was a half-tone cut of a hideous stone image almost identical with that which Legrasse had found in the swamp.

Eagerly clearing the sheet of its precious contents, I scanned the item in detail; and was disappointed to find it of only moderate length. What it suggested, however, was of portentous significance to my flagging quest; and I carefully tore it out for immediate action. It read as follows:

MYSTERY DERELICT FOUND AT SEA

Vigilant Arrives With Helpless Armed New Zealand Yacht in Tow. One Survivor and Dead Man Found Aboard. Tale of Desperate Battle and Deaths at Sea. Rescued Seaman Refuses Particulars of Strange Experience. Odd Idol Found in His Possession. Inquiry to Follow.

The Morrison Co.'s freighter Vigilant, *bound from Valparaiso, arrived this morning at its wharf in Darling Harbour, having in tow the battled and disabled but heavily armed steam yacht* Alert *of Dunedin, NZ, which was sighted April 12th in S. Latitude 34° 21', W. Longitude 152° 17' with one living and one dead man aboard.*

The Vigilant *left Valparaiso March 25th, and on April 2nd was driven considerably south of her course by exceptionally heavy storms and monster waves. On April 12th the derelict was sighted; and though apparently deserted, was found upon boarding to contain one survivor in a half-delirious condition and one man who had evidently been dead for more than a week. The living man was clutching a horrible stone idol of unknown origin, about a foot in height, regarding whose nature authorities at Sydney University, the Royal Society, and the Museum in College Street all profess complete bafflement, and which the survivor says he found in the cabin of the yacht, in a small carved shrine of common pattern.*

This man, after recovering his senses, told an exceedingly strange story of piracy and slaughter. He is Gustaf Johansen, a Norwegian of some intelligence, and had been second mate of the two-masted schooner Emma *of Auckland, which sailed for Callao February 20th with a complement of eleven men. The* Emma, *he says, was delayed and thrown widely south of her course by the great storm of March 1st, and on March*

22nd, in S. Latitude 49° 51', W. Longitude 128° 34', encountered the Alert, *manned by a queer and evil-looking crew of Kanakas and half-castes. Being ordered peremptorily to turn back, Capt. Collins refused; whereupon the strange crew began to fire savagely and without warning upon the schooner with a peculiarly heavy battery of brass cannon forming part of the yacht's equipment. The* Emma's *men showed fight, says the survivor, and though the schooner began to sink from shots beneath the waterline they managed to heave alongside their enemy and board her, grappling with the savage crew on the yacht's deck, and being forced to kill them all, the number being slightly superior, because of their particularly abhorrent and desperate though rather clumsy mode of fighting.*

Three of the Emma's *men, including Capt. Collins and First Mate Green, were killed; and the remaining eight under Second Mate Johansen proceeded to navigate the captured yacht, going ahead in their original direction to see if any reason for their ordering back had existed. The next day, it appears, they raised and landed on a small island, although none is known to exist in that part of the ocean; and six of the men somehow died ashore, though Johansen is queerly reticent about this part of his story, and speaks only of their falling into a rock chasm. Later, it seems, he and one companion boarded the yacht and tried to manage her, but were beaten about by the storm of April 2nd. From that time till his rescue on the 12th the man remembers little, and he does not even recall when William Briden, his companion, died. Briden's death reveals no apparent cause, and was probably due to excitement or exposure. Cable advices from Dunedin report that the* Alert *was well known there as an island trader, and bore an evil reputation along the waterfront. It was owned by a curious group of half-castes whose frequent meetings and night trips to the woods attracted no little curiosity; and it had set sail in great haste just after the storm and earth tremors of March 1st. Our Auckland correspondent gives the* Emma *and her crew an excellent reputation, and Johansen is described as a sober and worthy man. The admiralty will institute an inquiry on the whole matter beginning tomorrow, at which every effort will be made to induce Johansen to speak more freely than he has done hitherto.*

This was all, together with the picture of the hellish image; but what a train of ideas it started in my mind! Here were new treasuries of data on the Cthulhu Cult, and evidence that it had strange interests at sea as well as on land. What motive prompted the hybrid crew to order back the *Emma* as they sailed about with their hideous idol? What was the unknown island on which six of the *Emma*'s crew had died, and about which the mate Johansen was so secretive? What had the vice-admiralty's investigation brought out, and what was known of the noxious cult in Dunedin? And most marvelous of all, what deep and more than natural linkage of dates was this which gave a malign and now undeniable significance to the various turns of events so carefully noted by my uncle?

March 1st—our February 28th according to the International Date Line—the earthquake and storm had come. From Dunedin the *Alert* and her noisome crew had darted eagerly forth as if imperiously summoned, and on the other side of the earth poets and artists had begun to dream of a strange, dank Cyclopean city whilst a young sculptor had molded in his sleep the form of the dreaded Cthulhu. March 23rd the crew of the *Emma* landed on an unknown island and left six men dead; and on that date the dreams of sensitive men assumed a heightened vividness and darkened with dread of a giant monster's malign pursuit, whilst an architect had gone mad and a sculptor had lapsed suddenly into delirium! And what of this storm of April 2nd—the date on which all dreams of the dank city ceased, and Wilcox emerged unharmed from the bondage of strange fever? What of all this—and of those hints of old Castro about the sunken, star-born Old Ones and their coming reign; their faithful cult *and their mastery of dreams?* Was I tottering on the brink of cosmic horrors beyond man's power to bear? If so, they must be horrors of the mind alone, for in some way April 2nd had put a stop to whatever monstrous menace had begun its siege of mankind's soul.

That evening, after a day of hurried cabling and arranging, I bade my host adieu and took a train for San Francisco. In less than a month I was in Dunedin; where, however, I found that little was known of the strange cult-members who had lingered in the old sea-taverns. Waterfront scum was far too common for special mention; though there was vague talk about one inland trip these mongrels had made, during which faint drumming and red flame were noted on the distant hills. In Auckland I learned that Johansen had returned *with yellow hair turned white* after a perfunctory and inconclusive questioning at Sydney, and had thereafter sold his cottage in West Street and sailed with his wife to his old home in Oslo. Of his stirring experience he would tell his friends no more than he had told the admiralty officials, and all they could do was to give me his Oslo address.

After that I went to Sydney and talked profitlessly with seamen and members of the vice-admiralty court. I saw the *Alert*, now sold and in commercial use, at Circular Quay in Sydney Cove, but gained nothing from its non-committal bulk. The crouching image with its cuttlefish head, dragon body, scaly wings, and hieroglyphed pedestal, was preserved in the Museum at Hyde Park; and I studied it long and well, finding it a thing of balefully exquisite workmanship, and with the same utter mystery, terrible antiquity, and unearthly strangeness of material which I had noted in Legrasse's smaller specimen. Geologists, the curator told me, had found it a monstrous puzzle; for they vowed that the world held no rock like it. Then I thought with a shudder of what old Castro had told Legrasse about the primal

Great Ones: "They had come from the stars, and had brought Their images with Them."

Shaken with such a mental revolution as I had never before known, I now resolved to visit Mate Johansen in Oslo. Sailing for London, I re-embarked at once for the Norwegian capital; and one autumn day landed at the trim wharves in the shadow of the Egeberg. Johansen's address, I discovered, lay in the Old Town of King Harold Haardrada, which kept alive the name of Oslo during all the centuries that the greater city masqueraded as "Christiana." I made the brief trip by taxicab, and knocked with palpitant heart at the door of a neat and ancient building with plastered front. A sad-faced woman in black answered my summons, and I was stung with disappointment when she told me in halting English that Gustaf Johansen was no more.

He had not survived his return, said his wife, for the doings at sea in 1925 had broken him. He had told her no more than he had told the public, but had left a long manuscript—of "technical matters" as he said—written in English, evidently in order to safeguard her from the peril of casual perusal. During a walk through a narrow lane near the Gothenburg dock, a bundle of papers falling from an attic window had knocked him down. Two Lascar sailors at once helped him to his feet, but before the ambulance could reach him he was dead. Physicians found no adequate cause for the end, and laid it to heart trouble and a weakened constitution.

I now felt gnawing at my vitals that dark terror which will never leave me till I, too, am at rest; "accidentally" or otherwise. Persuading the widow that my connection with her husband's "technical matters" was sufficient to entitle me to his manuscript, I bore the document away and began to read it on the London boat. It was a simple, rambling thing—a naive sailor's effort at a *post-facto* diary—and strove to recall day by day that last awful voyage. I cannot attempt to transcribe it verbatim in all its cloudiness and redundance, but I will tell its gist enough to show why the sound of the water against the vessel's sides became so unendurable to me that I stopped my ears with cotton.

Johansen, thank God, did not know quite all, even though he saw the city and the Thing, but I shall never sleep calmly again when I think of the horrors that lurk ceaselessly behind life in time and in space, and of those unhallowed blasphemies from elder stars which dream beneath the sea, known and favored by a nightmare cult ready and eager to loose them on the world whenever another earthquake shall heave their monstrous stone city again to the sun and air.

Johansen's voyage had begun just as he told it to the vice-admiralty. The *Emma,* in ballast, had cleared Auckland on February 20th, and had felt the full force of that earthquake-born tempest which must have heaved up from the sea-bottom the horrors that filled men's dreams. Once more under control, the ship was making good progress when held up by the *Alert* on March 22nd, and I could feel the mate's regret as he wrote of her bombardment and sinking. Of the swarthy cult-fiends on the *Alert* he speaks with significant horror. There was some peculiarly abominable quality about them which made their destruction seem almost a duty, and Johansen shows ingenuous wonder at the charge of ruthlessness brought against his party during the proceedings of the court of inquiry. Then, driven ahead by curiosity in their captured yacht under Johansen's command, the men sight a great stone pillar sticking out of the sea, and in S. Latitude 47° 9', W. Longitude 123° 43' come upon a coastline of mingled mud, ooze, and weedy Cyclopean masonry which can be nothing less than the tangible substance of earth's supreme terror—the nightmare corpse-city of R'lyeh, that was built in measureless eons behind history by the vast, loathsome shapes that seeped down from the dark stars. There lay great Cthulhu and his hordes, hidden in green slimy vaults and sending out at last, after cycles incalculable, the thoughts that spread fear to the dreams of the sensitive and called imperiously to the faithful to come on a pilgrimage of liberation and restoration. All this Johansen did not suspect, but God knows he soon saw enough!

I suppose that only a single mountaintop, the hideous monolith-crowned citadel whereon great Cthulhu was buried, actually emerged from the waters. When I think of the *extent* of all that may be brooding down there I almost wish to kill myself forthwith. Johansen and his men were awed by the cosmic majesty of this dripping Babylon of elder demons, and must have guessed without guidance that it was nothing of this or of any sane planet. Awe at the unbelievable size of the greenish stone blocks, at the dizzying height of the great carven monolith, and at the stupefying identity of the colossal statues and bas-reliefs with the queer image found in the shrine on the *Alert,* is poignantly visible in every line of the mate's frightened description.

Without knowing what futurism is like, Johansen achieved something very close to it when he spoke of the city; for instead of describing any definite structure or building, he dwells only on broad impressions of vast angles and stone surfaces—surfaces too great to belong to any thing right or proper for this earth, and impious with horrible images and hieroglyphs. I mention his talk about *angles* because it suggests something Wilcox had told me of his awful dreams. He had said that the *geometry* of the dream-place he saw was abnormal, non-Euclidean, and loathsomely redolent of spheres and dimensions apart from ours. Now an unlettered seaman felt the same thing whilst gazing at the terrible reality.

Johansen and his men landed at a sloping mud-bank on this monstrous Acropolis, and clambered slipperily up over titan oozy blocks which could have been no mortal staircase. The very sun of heaven seemed distorted when viewed through the polarizing miasma welling out from this sea-soaked perversion, and twisted menace and suspense lurked leeringly in those crazily elusive angles of carven rock where a second glance showed concavity after the first showed convexity.

Something very like fright had come over all the explorers before anything more definite than rock and ooze and weed was seen. Each would have fled had he not feared the scorn of the others, and it was only half-heartedly that they searched—vainly, as it proved—for some portable souvenir to bear away.

It was Rodriguez the Portuguese who climbed up the foot of the monolith and shouted of what he had found. The rest followed him, and looked curiously at the immense carved door with the now familiar squid-dragon bas-relief. It was, Johansen said, like a great barn-door; and they all felt that it was a door because of the ornate lintel, threshold, and jambs around it, though they could not decide whether it lay flat like a trap-door or slantwise like an outside cellar-door. As Wilcox would have said, the geometry of the place was all wrong. One could not be sure that the sea and the ground were horizontal, hence the relative position of everything else seemed phantasmally variable.

Briden pushed at the stone in several places without result. Then Donovan felt over it delicately around the edge, pressing each point separately as he went. He climbed interminably along the grotesque stone molding—that is, one would call it climbing if the thing was not after all horizontal—and the men wondered how any door in the universe could be so vast. Then, very softly and slowly, the acre-great panel began to give inward at the top; and they saw that it was balanced. Donovan slid or somehow propelled himself down or along the jamb and rejoined his fellows, and everyone watched the queer recession of the monstrously carven portal. In this fantasy of prismatic distortion it moved anomalously in a diagonal way, so that all the rules of matter and perspective seemed upset.

The aperture was black with a darkness almost material. That tenebrousness was indeed a *positive quality;* for it obscured such parts of the inner walls as ought to have been revealed, and actually burst forth like smoke from its eon-long imprisonment, visibly darkening the sun as it slunk away into the shrunken and gibbous sky on flapping membranous wings. The odor arising from the newly opened depths was intolerable, and at length the quick-eared Hawkins thought he heard a nasty, slopping sound down there. Everyone listened, and everyone was listening still when It lumbered slobberingly into sight and gropingly squeezed Its gelatinous green immensity through the black doorway into the tainted outside air of that poison city of madness.

Poor Johansen's handwriting almost gave out when he wrote of this. Of the six men who never reached the ship, he thinks two perished of pure fright in that accursed instant. The Thing cannot be described— there is no language for such abysms of shrieking and immemorial lunacy, such eldritch contradictions of all matter, force, and cosmic order. A mountain walked or stumbled. God! What wonder that across the earth a great architect went mad, and poor Wilcox raved with fever in that telepathic instant? The Thing of the idols, the green, sticky spawn of the stars, had awaked to claim his own. The stars were right again, and what an age-old cult had failed to do by design, a band of innocent sailors had done by accident. After vigintillions of years great Cthulhu was loose again, and ravening for delight.

Three men were swept up by the flabby claws before anybody turned. God rest them, if there be any rest in the universe. They were Donovan, Guerrera, and Ångstrom. Parker slipped as the other three were plunging frenziedly over endless vistas of green-crusted rock to the boat, and Johansen swears he was swallowed up by an angle of masonry which shouldn't have been there; an angle which was acute, but behaved as if it were obtuse. So only Briden and Johansen reached the boat, and pulled desperately for the *Alert* as the mountainous monstrosity flopped down the slimy stones and hesitated floundering at the edge of the water.

Steam had not been suffered to go down entirely, despite the departure of all hands for the shore; and it was the work of only a few moments of feverish rushing up and down between wheel and engines to get the *Alert* under way. Slowly, amidst the distorted horrors of that indescribable scene, she began to churn the lethal waters;

whilst on the masonry of that charnel shore that was not of earth the titan Thing from the stars slavered and gibbered like Polypheme cursing the fleeing ship of Odysseus. Then, bolder than the storied Cyclops, great Cthulhu slid greasily into the water and began to pursue with vast wave-raising strokes of cosmic potency. Briden looked back and went mad, laughing shrilly as he kept on laughing at intervals till death found him one night in the cabin whilst Johansen was wandering deliriously.

But Johansen had not given out yet. Knowing that the Thing could surely overtake the *Alert* until steam was fully up, he resolved on a desperate chance; and, setting the engine for full speed, ran lightning-like on deck and reversed the wheel. There was a mighty eddying and foaming in the noisome brine, and as the steam mounted higher and higher the brave Norwegian drove his vessel head on against the pursuing jelly which rose above the unclean froth like the stern of a demon galleon. The awful squid-head with writhing feelers came nearly up to the bowsprit of the sturdy yacht, but Johansen drove on relentlessly. There was a bursting as of an exploding bladder, a slushy nastiness as of a cloven sunfish, a stench as of a thousand opened graves, and a sound that the chronicler would not put on paper. For an instant the ship was befouled by an acrid and blinding green cloud, and then there was only a venomous seething astern; where—God in heaven!—the scattered plasticity of that nameless sky-spawn was nebulously *recombining* in its hateful original form, whilst its distance widened every second as the *Alert* gained impetus from its mounting steam.

That was all. After that Johansen only brooded over the idol in the cabin and attended to a few matters of food for himself and the laughing maniac by his side. He did not try to navigate after the first bold flight, for the reaction had taken something out of his soul. Then came the storm of April 2nd, and a gathering of the clouds about his consciousness. There is a sense of spectral whirling through liquid gulfs of infinity, of dizzying rides through reeling universes on a comet's tail, and of hysterical plunges from the pit to the moon and from the moon back again to the pit, all livened by a cachinnating chorus of the distorted, hilarious elder gods and the green, bat-winged mocking imps of Tartarus.

Out of that dream came rescue—the *Vigilant,* the vice-admiralty court, the streets of Dunedin, and the long voyage back home to the old house by the Egeberg. He could not tell—they would think him mad. He would write of what he knew before death came, but his wife must not guess. Death would be a boon if only it could blot out the memories.

That was the document I read, and now I have placed it in the tin box beside the bas-relief and the papers of Professor Angell. With it shall go this record of mine—this test of my own sanity, wherein is pieced together that which I hope may never be pieced together again. I have looked upon all that the universe has to hold of horror, and even the skies of spring and the flowers of summer must ever afterward be poison to me. But I do not think my life will be long. As my uncle went, as poor Johansen went, so I shall go. I know too much, and the cult still lives.

Cthulhu still lives, too, I suppose, again in that chasm of stone which has shielded him since the sun was young. His accursed city is sunken once more, for the *Vigilant* sailed over the spot after the April storm; but his ministers on earth still bellow and prance and slay around idol-capped monoliths in lonely places. He must have been trapped by the sinking whilst within his black abyss, or else the world would by now be screaming with fright and frenzy. Who knows the end? What has risen may sink, and what has sunk may rise. Loathsomeness waits and dreams in the deep, and decay spreads over the tottering cities of men. A time will come—but I must not and cannot think! Let me pray that, if I do not survive this manuscript, my executors may put caution before audacity and see that it meets no other eye.

THE DUNWICH HORROR

"Gorgons, and Hydras, and Chimaeras—dire stories of
Celaeno and the Harpies—may reproduce themselves in
the brain of superstition—*but they were there before.* They
are transcripts, types—the archetypes are in us, and eternal.
How else should the recital of that which we know in a
waking sense to be false come to affect us at all? Is it that
we naturally conceive terror from such objects, considered
in their capacity of being able to inflict upon us bodily
injury? O, least of all! *These terrors are of older standing.*
They date beyond body—or without the body, they would
have been the same . . . . That the kind of fear here treated
is purely spiritual—that it is strong in proportion as it is
objectless on earth, that it predominates in the period of
our sinless infancy—are difficulties the solution of which
might afford some probable insight into our ante-mundane
condition, and a peep at least into the shadowland of pre-
existence."

—Charles Lamb: *Witches and Other Night-Fears*

I

When a traveler in north central Massachusetts takes the wrong fork
at the junction of the Aylesbury pike just beyond Dean's Corners he
comes upon a lonely and curious country. The ground gets higher,
and the brier-bordered stone walls press closer and closer against the
ruts of the dusty, curving road. The trees of the frequent forest belts
seem too large, and the wild weeds, brambles, and grasses attain a
luxuriance not often found in settled regions. At the same time the
planted fields appear singularly few and barren; while the sparsely

scattered houses wear a surprisingly uniform aspect of age, squalor, and dilapidation. Without knowing why, one hesitates to ask directions from the gnarled, solitary figures spied now and then on crumbling doorsteps or on the sloping, rock-strewn meadows. Those figures are so silent and furtive that one feels somehow confronted by forbidden things, with which it would be better to have nothing to do. When a rise in the road brings the mountains in view above the deep woods, the feeling of strange uneasiness is increased. The summits are too rounded and symmetrical to give a sense of comfort and naturalness, and sometimes the sky silhouettes with especial clearness the queer circles of tall stone pillars with which most of them are crowned.

Gorges and ravines of problematical depth intersect the way, and the crude wooden bridges always seem of dubious safety. When the road dips again there are stretches of marshland that one instinctively dislikes, and indeed almost fears at evening when unseen whippoorwills chatter and the fireflies come out in abnormal profusion to dance to the raucous, creepily insistent rhythms of stridently piping bullfrogs. The thin, shining line of the Miskatonic's upper reaches has an oddly serpent-like suggestion as it winds close to the feet of the domed hills among which it rises.

As the hills draw nearer, one heeds their wooded sides more than their stone-crowned tops. Those sides loom up so darkly and precipitously that one wishes they would keep their distance, but there is no road by which to escape them. Across a covered bridge one sees a small village huddled between the stream and the vertical slope of Round Mountain, and wonders at the cluster of rotting gambrel roofs bespeaking an earlier architectural period than that of the neighboring region. It is not reassuring to see, on a closer glance, that most of the houses are deserted and falling to ruin, and that the broken-steepled church now harbors the one slovenly mercantile establishment of the hamlet. One dreads to trust the tenebrous tunnel of the bridge, yet there is no way to avoid it. Once across, it is hard to prevent the impression of a faint, malign odor about the village street, as of the massed mold and decay of centuries. It is always a relief to get clear of the place, and to follow the narrow road around the base of the hills and across the level country beyond till it rejoins the Aylesbury pike. Afterward one sometimes learns that one has been through Dunwich.

Outsiders visit Dunwich as seldom as possible, and since a certain season of horror all the signboards pointing toward it have been taken down. The scenery, judged by any ordinary esthetic canon, is more than commonly beautiful; yet there is no influx of artists or summer tourists. Two centuries ago, when talk of witch-blood, Satan-worship, and strange forest presences was not laughed at, it was the custom to give reasons for avoiding the locality. In our sensible age—since the Dunwich horror of 1928 was hushed up by those who had the town's and the world's welfare at heart—people shun it without knowing exactly why. Perhaps one reason—though it cannot apply to uninformed strangers—is that the natives are now repellently decadent, having gone far along that path of retrogression so common in many New England backwaters. They have come to form a race by themselves, with the well-defined mental and physical stigmata of degeneracy and inbreeding. The average of their intelligence is woefully low, whilst their annals reek of overt viciousness and of half-hidden murders, incests, and deeds of almost unnamable violence and perversity. The old gentry, representing the two or three armigerous families which came from Salem in 1692, have kept somewhat above the general level of decay; though many branches are sunk into the sordid populace so deeply that only their names remain as a key to the origin they disgrace. Some of the Whateleys and Bishops still send their eldest sons to Harvard and Miskatonic, though those sons seldom return to the moldering gambrel roofs under which they and their ancestors were born.

No one, even those who have the facts concerning the recent horror, can say just what is the matter with Dunwich; though old legends speak of unhallowed rites and conclaves of the Indians, amidst which they called forbidden shapes of shadow out of the great rounded hills, and made wild orgiastic prayers that were answered by loud crackings and rumblings from the ground below. In 1747 the Reverend Abijah Hoadley, newly come to the Congregational Church at Dunwich Village, preached a memorable sermon on the close presence of Satan and his imps; in which he said:

It must be allow'd, that these Blasphemies of an infernall Train of Daemons are Matters of too common Knowledge to be deny'd; the cursed Voices of Azazel and Buzrael, of Beelzebub and Belial, being heard now from under Ground by above a Score of credible Witnesses now living. I myself did not more than a Fortnight ago catch a very plain Discourse of evill Powers in the Hill behind my House; wherein there were a Rattling and Rolling, Groaning, Screeching, and Hissing, such as no Things of this Earth cou'd raise up, and which must needs have come from those Caves that only black Magick can discover, and only the Divell unlock.

Mr Hoadley disappeared soon after delivering this sermon; but the text, printed in Springfield, is still extant. Noises in the hills continued to be reported from year to year, and still form a puzzle to geologists and physiographers.

Other traditions tell of foul odors near the hill-crowning circles of stone pillars, and of rushing airy presences to be heard faintly at certain hours from stated points at the bottom of the great ravines; while still others try to explain the Devil's Hop Yard—a bleak, blasted hillside where no tree, shrub, or grass-blade will grow. Then too, the natives are mortally afraid of the numerous whippoorwills which grow vocal on warm nights. It is vowed that the birds are psychopomps lying in wait for the souls of the dying, and that they time their eerie cries in unison with the sufferer's struggling breath. If they can catch the fleeing soul when it leaves the body, they instantly flutter away chittering in demoniac laughter; but if they fail, they subside gradually into a disappointed silence.

These tales, of course, are obsolete and ridiculous; because they come down from very old times. Dunwich is indeed ridiculously old—older by far than any of the communities within thirty miles of it. South of the village one may still spy the cellar walls and chimney of the ancient Bishop house, which was built before 1700; whilst the ruins of the mill at the falls, built in 1806, form the most modern piece of architecture to be seen. Industry did not flourish here, and the nineteenth-century factory movement proved short-lived. Oldest of all are the great rings of rough-hewn stone columns on the hilltops, but these are more generally attributed to the Indians than to the settlers. Deposits of skulls and bones, found within these circles and around the sizeable table-like rock on Sentinel Hill, sustain the popular belief that such spots were once the burial-places of the Pocumtucks; even though many ethnologists, disregarding the absurd improbability of such a theory, persist in believing the remains Caucasian.

II

It was in the township of Dunwich, in a large and partly inhabited farmhouse set against a hillside four miles from the village and a mile and a half from any other dwelling, that Wilbur Whateley was born at 5 a.m. on Sunday, February 2nd, 1913. This date was recalled because it was Candlemas, which people in Dunwich curiously observe under another name; and because the noises in the hills had sounded, and all the dogs of the countryside had barked persistently, throughout the night before. Less worthy of notice was the fact that the mother was one of the decadent Whateleys, a somewhat deformed, unattractive albino woman of thirty-five, living with an aged and half-insane father about whom the most frightful tales of wizardry had been whispered in his youth. Lavinia Whateley had no known husband, but according to the custom of the region made no attempt to disavow the child; concerning the other side of whose ancestry the country folk might—and did—speculate as widely as they chose. On the contrary, she seemed strangely proud of the dark, goatish-looking infant who formed such a contrast to her own sickly and pink-eyed albinism, and was heard to mutter many curious prophecies about its unusual powers and tremendous future.

Lavinia was one who would be apt to mutter such things, for she was a lone creature given to wandering amidst thunderstorms in the hills and trying to read the great odorous books which her father had inherited through two centuries of Whateleys, and which were fast falling to pieces with age and worm-holes. She had never been to school, but was filled with disjointed scraps of ancient lore that Old Whateley had taught her. The remote farmhouse had always been feared because of Old Whateley's reputation for black magic, and the unexplained death by violence of Mrs Whateley when Lavinia was twelve years old had not helped to make the place popular. Isolated among strange influences, Lavinia was fond of wild and grandiose day-dreams and singular occupations; nor was her leisure much taken up by household cares in a home from which all standards of order and cleanliness had long since disappeared.

There was a hideous screaming which echoed above even the hill noises and the dogs' barking on the night Wilbur was born, but no known doctor or midwife presided at his coming. Neighbors knew nothing of him till a week afterward, when Old Whateley drove his sleigh through the snow into Dunwich Village and discoursed incoherently to the group of loungers at Osborn's general store. There seemed to be a change in the old man—an added element of furtiveness in the clouded brain which subtly transformed him from an object to a subject of fear—though he was not one to be perturbed by any common family event. Amidst it all he showed some trace of

the pride later noticed in his daughter, and what he said of the child's
paternity was remembered by many of his hearers years afterward.

"I dun't keer what folks think—ef Lavinny's boy looked like his
pa, he wouldn't look like nothin' ye expeck. Ye needn't think the only
folks is the folks hereabaouts. Lavinny's read some, an' has seed some
things the most o' ye only tell abaout. I calc'late her man is as good
a husban' as ye kin find this side of Aylesbury; an' ef ye knowed as
much abaout the hills as I dew, ye wouldn't ast no better church weddin'
nor her'n. Let me tell ye suthin'—*some day yew folks'll hear a child
o' Lavinny's a-callin' its father's name on the top o' Sentinel Hill!*"

The only persons who saw Wilbur during the first month of his life
were old Zechariah Whateley, of the undecayed Whateleys, and Earl
Sawyer's common-law wife, Mamie Bishop. Mamie's visit was frankly
one of curiosity, and her subsequent tales did justice to her observations; but Zechariah came to lead a pair of Alderney cows which Old
Whateley had bought of his son Curtis. This marked the beginning of
a course of cattle-buying on the part of small Wilbur's family which
ended only in 1928, when the Dunwich horror came and went; yet at
no time did the ramshackle Whateley barn seem overcrowded with
livestock. There came a period when people were curious enough to
steal up and count the herd that grazed precariously on the steep
hillside above the old farmhouse, and they could never find more than
ten or twelve anemic, bloodless-looking specimens. Evidently some
blight or distemper, perhaps sprung from the unwholesome pasturage
or the diseased fungi and timbers of the filthy barn, caused a heavy
mortality amongst the Whateley animals. Odd wounds or sores, having
something of the aspect of incisions, seemed to afflict the visible cattle;
and once or twice during the earlier months certain callers fancied
they could discern similar sores about the throats of the gray, unshaven
old man and his slatternly, crinkly-haired albino daughter.

In the spring after Wilbur's birth Lavinia resumed her customary
rambles in the hills, bearing in her misproportioned arms the swarthy

child. Public interest in the Whateleys subsided after most of the country folk had seen the baby, and no one bothered to comment on the swift development which that newcomer seemed every day to exhibit. Wilbur's growth was indeed phenomenal, for within three months of his birth he had attained a size and muscular power not usually found in infants under a full year of age. His motions and even his vocal sounds showed a restraint and deliberateness highly peculiar in an infant, and no one was really unprepared when, at seven months, he began to walk unassisted, with falterings which another month was sufficient to remove.

It was somewhat after this time—on Hallowe'en—that a great blaze was seen at midnight on the top of Sentinel Hill where the old table-like stone stands amidst its tumulus of ancient bones. Considerable talk was started when Silas Bishop—of the undecayed Bishops— mentioned having seen the boy running sturdily up that hill ahead of his mother about an hour before the blaze was remarked. Silas was rounding up a stray heifer, but he nearly forgot his mission when he fleetingly spied the two figures in the dim light of his lantern. They darted almost noiselessly through the underbrush, and the astonished watcher seemed to think they were entirely unclothed. Afterward he could not be sure about the boy, who may have had some kind of a fringed belt and a pair of dark trunks or trousers on. Wilbur was never subsequently seen alive and conscious without complete and tightly buttoned attire, the disarrangement or threatened disarrangement of which always seemed to fill him with anger and alarm. His contrast with his squalid mother and grandfather in this respect was thought very notable until the horror of 1928 suggested the most valid of reasons.

The next January gossips were mildly interested in the fact that "Lavinny's black brat" had commenced to talk, and at the age of only eleven months. His speech was somewhat remarkable both because of its difference from the ordinary accents of the region, and because it displayed a freedom from infantile lisping of which many children of three or four might well be proud. The boy was not talkative, yet when he spoke he seemed to reflect some elusive element wholly unpossessed by Dunwich and its denizens. The strangeness did not reside in what he said, or even in the simple idioms he used; but seemed vaguely linked with his intonation or with the internal organs that produced the spoken sounds. His facial aspect, too, was remarkable for its maturity; for though he shared his mother's and grandfather's chinlessness, his firm and precociously shaped nose united with the expression of his large, dark, almost Latin eyes to give him an air of quasi-adulthood and well-nigh preternatural intelligence. He was, however, exceedingly ugly despite his appearance of brilliancy; there being something almost goatish or animalistic about his thick lips, large-pored, yellowish skin, coarse crinkly hair, and oddly elongated ears. He was soon disliked even more decidedly than his mother and grandsire, and all conjectures about him were spiced with references to the bygone magic of Old Whateley, and how the hills once shook when he shrieked the dreadful name of *Yog-Sothoth* in the midst of a circle of stones with a great book open in his arms before him. Dogs abhorred the boy, and he was always obliged to take various defensive measures against their barking menace.

III

Meanwhile Old Whateley continued to buy cattle without measurably increasing the size of his herd. He also cut timber and began to repair the unused parts of his house—a spacious, peaked-roofed affair whose rear end was buried entirely in the rocky hillside, and whose three least-ruined ground-floor rooms had always been sufficient for himself and his daughter.

There must have been prodigious reserves of strength in the old man to enable him to accomplish so much hard labor; and though he still babbled dementedly at times, his carpentry seemed to show the effects of sound calculation. It had already begun as soon as Wilbur was born, when one of the many tool-sheds had been put suddenly in order, clapboarded, and fitted with a stout fresh lock. Now, in restoring the abandoned upper story of the house, he was a no less thorough craftsman. His mania showed itself only in his tight boarding-up of all the windows in the reclaimed section—though many declared that it was a crazy thing to bother with the reclamation at all. Less inexplicable was his fitting up of another downstairs room for his new grandson—a room which several callers saw, though no one was ever admitted to the closely boarded upper story. This chamber he lined with tall, firm shelving; along which he began gradually to arrange, in apparently careful order, all the rotting ancient books and parts of books which during his own day had been heaped promiscuously in odd corners of the various rooms.

"I made some use of 'em," he would say as he tried to mend a torn black-letter page with paste prepared on the rusty kitchen stove, "but the boy's fitten to make better use of 'em. He'd orter hev 'em as well sot as he kin, for they're goin' to be all of his larnin'."

When Wilbur was a year and seven months old—in September of 1914—his size and accomplishments were almost alarming. He had grown as large as a child of four, and was a fluent and incredibly intelligent talker. He ran freely about the fields and hills, and accompanied his mother on all her wanderings. At home he would pore diligently over the queer pictures and charts in his grandfather's books, while Old Whateley would instruct and catechize him through long, hushed afternoons. By this time the restoration of the house was finished, and those who watched it wondered why one of the upper windows had been made into a solid plank door. It was a window in the rear of the east gable end, close against the hill; and no one could imagine why a cleated wooden runway was built up to it from the ground. About the period of this work's completion people noticed that the old tool-house, tightly locked and windowlessly clapboarded since Wilbur's birth, had been abandoned again. The door swung listlessly open, and when Earl Sawyer once stepped within after a cattle-selling call on Old Whateley he was quite discomposed by the singular odor he encountered—such a stench, he averred, as he had never before smelt in all his life except near the Indian circles on the hills, and which could not come from anything sane or of this earth. But then, the homes and sheds of Dunwich folk have never been remarkable for olfactory immaculateness.

The following months were void of visible events, save that everyone swore to a slow but steady increase in the mysterious hill noises. On May Eve of 1915 there were tremors which even the Aylesbury people felt, whilst the following Hallowe'en produced an underground rumbling queerly synchronized with bursts of flame— "them witch Whateleys' doin's"—from the summit of Sentinel Hill. Wilbur was growing up uncannily, so that he looked like a boy of ten as he entered his fourth year. He read avidly by himself now; but talked much less than formerly. A settled taciturnity was absorbing him, and for the first time people began to speak specifically of the dawning look of evil in his goatish face. He would sometimes mutter an unfamiliar jargon, and chant in bizarre rhythms which chilled the listener with a sense of unexplainable terror. The aversion displayed toward him by dogs had now become a matter of wide remark, and he was obliged to carry a pistol in order to traverse the countryside in safety. His occasional use of the weapon did not enhance his popularity amongst the owners of canine guardians.

The few callers at the house would often find Lavinia alone on the ground floor, while odd cries and footsteps resounded in the boarded-up second story. She would never tell what her father and the boy were doing up there, though once she turned pale and displayed an abnormal degree of fear when a jocose fish-peddler tried the locked door leading to the stairway. That peddler told the store loungers at

Dunwich Village that he thought he heard a horse stamping on that floor above. The loungers reflected, thinking of the door and runway, and of the cattle that so swiftly disappeared. Then they shuddered as they recalled tales of Old Whateley's youth, and of the strange things that are called out of the earth when a bullock is sacrificed at the proper time to certain heathen gods. It had for some time been noticed that dogs had begun to hate and fear the whole Whateley place as violently as they hated and feared young Wilbur personally.

In 1917 the war came, and Squire Sawyer Whateley, as chairman of the local draft board, had hard work finding a quota of young Dunwich men fit even to be sent to a development camp. The government, alarmed at such signs of wholesale regional decadence, sent several officers and medical experts to investigate; conducting a survey which New England newspaper readers may still recall. It was the publicity attending this investigation which set reporters on the track of the Whateleys, and caused the *Boston Globe* and *Arkham Advertiser* to print flamboyant Sunday stories of young Wilbur's precociousness, Old Whateley's black magic, the shelves of strange books, the sealed second story of the ancient farmhouse, and the weirdness of the whole region and its hill noises. Wilbur was four and a half then, and looked like a lad of fifteen. His lips and cheeks were fuzzy with a coarse dark down, and his voice had begun to break.

Earl Sawyer went out to the Whateley place with both sets of reporters and camera men, and called their attention to the queer stench which now seemed to trickle down from the sealed upper spaces. It was, he said, exactly like a smell he had found in the tool-shed abandoned when the house was finally repaired; and like the faint odors which he sometimes thought he caught near the stone circles on the mountains. Dunwich folk read the stories when they appeared, and grinned over the obvious mistakes. They wondered, too, why the writers made so much of the fact that Old Whateley always paid for his cattle in gold pieces of extremely ancient date.

The Whateleys had received their visitors with ill-concealed distaste, though they did not dare court further publicity by a violent resistance or refusal to talk.

IV

For a decade the annals of the Whateleys sink indistinguishably into the general life of a morbid community used to their queer ways and hardened to their May Eve and All-Hallows orgies. Twice a year they would light fires on the top of Sentinel Hill, at which times the mountain rumblings would recur with greater and greater violence; while at all seasons there were strange and portentous doings at the lonely farmhouse. In the course of time callers professed to hear sounds in the sealed upper story even when all the family were downstairs, and they wondered how swiftly or how lingeringly a cow or bullock was usually sacrificed. There was talk of a complaint to the Society for the Prevention of Cruelty to Animals; but nothing ever came of it, since Dunwich folk are never anxious to call the outside world's attention to themselves.

About 1923, when Wilbur was a boy of ten whose mind, voice, stature, and bearded face gave all the impressions of maturity, a second great siege of carpentry went on at the old house. It was all inside the sealed upper part, and from bits of discarded lumber people concluded that the youth and his grandfather had knocked out all the partitions and even removed the attic floor, leaving only one vast open void between the ground story and the peaked roof. They had torn down the great central chimney, too, and fitted the rusty range with a flimsy outside tin stovepipe.

In the spring after this event Old Whateley noticed the growing number of whippoorwills that would come out of Cold Spring Glen to chirp under his window at night. He seemed to regard the circumstance as one of great significance, and told the loungers at Osborn's that he thought his time had almost come.

"They whistle jest in tune with my breathin' naow," he said, "an' I guess they're gittin' ready to ketch my soul. They know it's a-goin' aout, an' dun't calc'late to miss it. Yew'll know, boys, arter I'm gone, whether they git me er not. Ef they dew, they'll keep up a-singin' an' laffin' till break o' day. Ef they dun't they'll kinder quiet daown like. I expeck them an' the souls they hunts fer hev some pretty tough tussles sometimes."

On Lammas Night, 1924, Dr Houghton of Aylesbury was hastily summoned by Wilbur Whateley, who had lashed his one remaining horse through the darkness and telephoned from Osborn's in the village. He found Old Whateley in a very grave state, with a cardiac action and stertorous breathing that told of an end not far off. The shapeless albino daughter and oddly bearded grandson stood by the bedside, whilst from the vacant abyss overhead there came a disquieting suggestion of rhythmical surging or lapping, as of the waves on some level beach. The doctor, though, was chiefly disturbed by the chattering night birds outside; a seemingly limitless legion of whippoorwills that cried their endless message in repetitions timed diabolically to the wheezing gasps of the dying man. It was uncanny and unnatural—too much, thought Dr. Houghton, like the whole of the region he had entered so reluctantly in response to the urgent call.

Toward one o'clock Old Whateley gained consciousness, and interrupted his wheezing to choke out a few words to his grandson.

"More space, Willy, more space soon. Yew grows—an' *that* grows faster. It'll be ready to sarve ye soon, boy. Open up the gates to Yog-Sothoth with the long chant that ye'll find on page 751 *of the complete edition,* an' *then* put a match to the prison. Fire from airth can't burn it nohaow."

He was obviously quite mad. After a pause, during which the flock of whippoorwills outside adjusted their cries to the altered tempo while some indications of the strange hill noises came from afar off, he added another sentence or two.

"Feed it reg'lar, Willy, an' mind the quantity; but dun't let it grow too fast fer the place, fer ef it busts quarters or gits aout afore ye opens to Yog-Sothoth, it's all over an' no use. Only them from beyont kin make it multiply an' work. . . . Only them, the old uns as wants to come back. . . ."

But speech gave place to gasps again, and Lavinia screamed at the way the whippoorwills followed the change. It was the same for more than an hour, when the final throaty rattle came. Dr Houghton drew shrunken lids over the glazing gray eyes as the tumult of birds faded imperceptibly to silence. Lavinia sobbed, but Wilbur only chuckled whilst the hill noises rumbled faintly.

"They didn't git him," he muttered in his heavy bass voice.

Wilbur was by this time a scholar of really tremendous erudition in his one-sided way, and was quietly known by correspondence to many librarians in distant places where rare and forbidden books of old days are kept. He was more and more hated and dreaded around Dunwich because of certain youthful disappearances which suspicion laid vaguely at his door; but was always able to silence inquiry through fear or through use of that fund of old-time gold which still, as in his grandfather's time, went forth regularly and increasingly for cattle-buying. He was now tremendously mature of aspect, and his height, having reached the normal adult limit, seemed inclined to wax beyond that figure. In 1925, when a scholarly correspondent from Miskatonic University called upon him one day and departed pale and puzzled, he was fully six and three-quarters feet tall.

Through all the years Wilbur had treated his half-deformed albino mother with a growing contempt, finally forbidding her to go to the hills with him on May Eve and Hallowmass; and in 1926 the poor creature complained to Mamie Bishop of being afraid of him.

"They's more abaout him as I knows than I kin tell ye, Mamie," she said, "an' naowadays they's more nor what I know myself. I vaow afur Gawd, I dun't know what he wants nor what he's a-tryin' to dew."

That Hallowe'en the hill noises sounded louder than ever, and fire burned on Sentinel Hill as usual; but people paid more attention to the rhythmical screaming of vast flocks of unnaturally belated whip-poorwills which seemed to be assembled near the unlighted Whateley farmhouse. After midnight their shrill notes burst into a kind of pandemoniac cachinnation which filled all the countryside, and not until dawn did they finally quiet down. Then they vanished, hurrying southward where they were fully a month overdue. What this meant, no one could quite be certain till later. None of the country folk seemed to have died—but poor Lavinia Whateley, the twisted albino, was never seen again.

In the summer of 1927 Wilbur repaired two sheds in the farmyard and began moving his books and effects out to them. Soon afterward Earl Sawyer told the loungers at Osborn's that more carpentry was going on in the Whateley farmhouse. Wilbur was closing all the doors and windows on the ground floor, and seemed to be taking out partitions as he and his grandfather had done upstairs four years before. He was living in one of the sheds, and Sawyer thought he seemed unusually worried and tremulous. People generally suspected him of knowing something about his mother's disappearance, and very few ever approached his neighborhood now. His height had increased to more than seven feet, and showed no signs of ceasing its development.

V

The following winter brought an event no less strange than Wilbur's first trip outside the Dunwich region. Correspondence with the Widener Library at Harvard, the Bibliothèque Nationale in Paris, the British Museum, the University of Buenos Aires, and the Library of Miskatonic University of Arkham had failed to get him the loan of a book he desperately wanted; so at length he set out in person, shabby, dirty, bearded, and uncouth of dialect, to consult the copy at Miskatonic, which was the nearest to him geographically. Almost eight feet tall, and carrying a cheap new valise from Osborn's general store, this dark and goatish gargoyle appeared one day in Arkham in quest of the dreaded volume kept under lock and key at the college library—the hideous *Necronomicon* of the mad Arab Abdul Alhazred in Olaus Wormius's Latin version, as printed in Spain in the seventeenth century. He had never seen a city before, but had no thought save to find his way to the university grounds; where, indeed, he passed heedlessly by the great white-fanged watchdog that barked with unnatural fury and enmity, and tugged frantically at its stout chain.

Wilbur had with him the priceless but imperfect copy of Dr Dee's English version which his grandfather had bequeathed him, and upon receiving access to the Latin copy he at once began to collate the two texts with the aim of discovering a certain passage which would have come on the 751st page of his own defective volume. This much he could not civilly refrain from telling the librarian—the same erudite Henry Armitage (A.M. Miskatonic, Ph. D. Princeton, Litt. D. Johns Hopkins) who had once called at the farm, and who now politely plied him with questions. He was looking, he had to admit, for a kind of formula or incantation containing the frightful name *Yog-Sothoth*, and it puzzled him to find discrepancies, duplications, and ambiguities which made the matter of determination far from easy. As he copied the formula he finally chose, Dr. Armitage looked involuntarily over his shoulder at the open pages; the left-hand one of which, in the Latin version, contained such monstrous threats to the peace and sanity of the world.

*Nor is it to be thought (*ran the text as Armitage mentally translated it*) that man is either the oldest or the last of earth's masters, or that the common bulk of life and substance walks alone. The Old Ones were, the Old Ones are, and the Old Ones shall be. Not in the spaces we know, but* between *them, They walk serene* *and primal, undimensioned and to us unseen.* Yog-Sothoth *knows the gate.* Yog-Sothoth *is the gate.* Yog-Sothoth *is the key and guardian of the gate. Past, present, future, all are one in* Yog-Sothoth. *He knows where the Old Ones broke through of old, and where They shall break through again. He knows where They have trod earth's fields, and where They still tread them, and why no one can behold Them as They tread. By Their smell can men sometimes know Them near, but of Their semblance can no man know,* saving only in the features of those They have begotten on mankind; *and of those are there many sorts, differing in likeness from man's truest eidolon to that shape without sight or substance which is* Them. *They walk unseen and foul in lonely places where the Words have been spoken and the Rites howled through at their Seasons. The wind gibbers with Their voices, and the earth mutters with Their consciousness. They bend the forest and crush the city, yet may not forest or city behold the hand that smites. Kadath in the cold waste hath known Them, and what man knows Kadath? The ice desert of the South and the sunken isles of Ocean hold stones whereon Their seal is engraven, but who hath seen the deep frozen city or the sealed tower long garlanded with seaweed and barnacles? Great Cthulhu is Their cousin, yet can he spy Them only dimly. Iä! Shub-Niggurath! As a foulness shall ye know Them. Their hand is at your throats, yet ye see Them not; and Their habitation is even one with your guarded threshold.* Yog-Sothoth *is the key to the gate, whereby the spheres meet. Man rules now where They ruled once; They shall soon rule where man rules now. After summer is winter, and after winter summer. They wait patient and potent, for here shall They reign again.*

Dr Armitage, associating what he was reading with what he had heard of Dunwich and its brooding presences, and of Wilbur Whateley and his dim, hideous aura that stretched from a dubious birth to a cloud of probable matricide, felt a wave of fright as tangible as a draft of the tomb's cold clamminess. The bent, goatish giant before him seemed like the spawn of another planet or dimension; like something only partly of mankind, and linked to black gulfs of essence and entity that stretch like titan phantasms beyond all spheres of force and matter, space and time. Presently Wilbur raised his head and began speaking in that strange, resonant fashion which hinted at sound-producing organs unlike the run of mankind's.

"Mr Armitage," he said, "I calc'late I've got to take that book home. They's things in it I've got to try under sarten conditions that I can't git here, an' it 'ud be a mortal sin to let a red-tape rule hold me up. Let me take it along, Sir, an' I'll swar they wun't nobody know the difference. I dun't need to tell ye I'll take good keer of it. It wa'n't me that put this Dee copy in the shape it is. . . ."

He stopped as he saw firm denial on the librarian's face, and his own goatish features grew crafty. Armitage, half-ready to tell him he might make a copy of what parts he needed, thought suddenly of the possible consequences and checked himself. There was too much responsibility in giving such a being the key to such blasphemous outer spheres. Whateley saw how things stood, and tried to answer lightly.

"Wal, all right, ef ye feel that way abaout it. Maybe Harvard wun't be so fussy as yew be." And without saying more he rose and strode out of the building, stooping at each doorway.

Armitage heard the savage yelping of the great watchdog, and studied Whateley's gorilla-like lope as he crossed the bit of campus visible from the window. He thought of the wild tales he had heard, and recalled the old Sunday stories in the *Advertiser;* these things, and the lore he had picked up from Dunwich rustics and villagers during his one visit there. Unseen things not of earth—or at least not of tri-dimensional earth—rushed fetid and horrible through New

England's glens, and brooded obscenely on the mountain tops. Of this he had long felt certain. Now he seemed to sense the close presence of some terrible part of the intruding horror, and to glimpse a hellish advance in the black dominion of the ancient and once passive nightmare. He locked away the *Necronomicon* with a shudder of disgust, but the room still reeked with an unholy and unidentifiable stench. "As a foulness shall ye know them," he quoted. Yes—the odor was the same as that which had sickened him at the Whateley farmhouse less than three years before. He thought of Wilbur, goatish and ominous, once again, and laughed mockingly at the village rumors of his parentage.

"Inbreeding?" Armitage muttered half-aloud to himself. "Great God, what simpletons! Show them Arthur Machen's Great God Pan and they'll think it a common Dunwich scandal! But what thing—what cursed shapeless influence on or off this three-dimensioned earth—was Wilbur Whateley's father? Born on Candlemas—nine months after May Eve of 1912, when the talk about the queer earth noises reached clear to Arkham—what walked on the mountains that May-Night? What Roodmas horror fastened itself on the world in half-human flesh and blood?"

During the ensuing weeks Dr Armitage set about to collect all possible data on Wilbur Whateley and the formless presences around Dunwich. He got in communication with Dr Houghton of Aylesbury, who had attended Old Whateley in his last illness, and found much to ponder over in the grandfather's last words as quoted by the physician. A visit to Dunwich Village failed to bring out much that was new; but a close survey of the *Necronomicon,* in those parts which Wilbur had sought so avidly, seemed to supply new and terrible clues to the nature, methods, and desires of the strange evil so vaguely threatening this planet. Talks with several students of archaic lore in Boston, and letters to many others elsewhere, gave him a growing amazement which passed slowly through varied degrees of alarm to a state of really acute spiritual fear. As the summer drew on he felt dimly that something ought to be done about the lurking terrors of the upper Miskatonic valley, and about the monstrous being known to the human world as Wilbur Whateley.

VI

The Dunwich horror itself came between Lammas and the equinox in 1928, and Dr Armitage was among those who witnessed its monstrous prologue. He had heard, meanwhile, of Whateley's grotesque trip to Cambridge, and of his frantic efforts to borrow or copy from the *Necronomicon* at the Widener Library. Those efforts had been in vain, since Armitage had issued warnings of the keenest intensity to all librarians having charge of the dreaded volume. Wilbur had been shockingly nervous at Cambridge; anxious for the book, yet almost equally anxious to get home again, as if he feared the results of being away long.

Early in August the half-expected outcome developed, and in the small hours of the 3rd Dr Armitage was awakened suddenly by the wild, fierce cries of the savage watchdog on the college campus. Deep and terrible, the snarling, half-mad growls and barks continued; always in mounting volume, but with hideously significant pauses. Then there rang out a scream from a wholly different throat—such a scream as roused half the sleepers of Arkham and haunted their dreams ever afterward—such a scream as could come from no being born of earth, or wholly of earth.

Armitage, hastening into some clothing and rushing across the street and lawn to the college buildings, saw that others were ahead of him; and heard the echoes of a burglar-alarm still shrilling from the library. An open window showed black and gaping in the moonlight. What had come had indeed completed its entrance; for the barking and the screaming, now fast fading into a mixed low growling and moaning, proceeded unmistakably from within. Some instinct warned Armitage that what was taking place was not a thing for unfortified eyes to see, so he brushed back the crowd with authority as he unlocked the vestibule door. Among the others he saw Professor Warren Rice and Dr Francis Morgan, men to whom he had told some of his conjectures and misgivings; and these two he motioned to accompany him inside. The inward sounds, except for a watchful, droning whine from the dog, had by this time quite subsided; but Armitage now perceived with a sudden start that a loud chorus of whippoorwills among the shrubbery had commenced a damnably rhythmical piping, as if in unison with the last breaths of a dying man.

The building was full of a frightful stench which Dr Armitage knew too well, and the three men rushed across the hall to the small genealogical reading-room whence the low whining came. For a second nobody dared to turn on the light, then Armitage summoned up his courage and snapped the switch. One of the three—it is not certain which—shrieked aloud at what sprawled before them among disordered tables and overturned chairs. Professor Rice declares that he wholly lost consciousness for an instant, though he did not stumble or fall.

The thing that lay half-bent on its side in a fetid pool of greenish-yellow ichor and tarry stickiness was almost nine feet tall, and the dog had torn off all the clothing and some of the skin. It was not quite dead, but twitched silently and spasmodically while its chest heaved in monstrous unison with the mad piping of the expectant whippoorwills outside. Bits of shoe-leather and fragments of apparel were scattered about the room, and just inside the window an empty canvas sack lay where it had evidently been thrown. Near the central desk a revolver had fallen, a dented but undischarged cartridge later explaining why it had not been fired. The thing itself, however, crowded out all other images at the time. It would be trite and not wholly accurate to say that no human pen could describe it, but one may properly say that it could not be vividly visualized by anyone whose ideas of aspect and contour are too closely bound up with the common life-forms of this planet and of the three known dimensions. It was partly human, beyond a doubt, with very man-like hands and head, and the goatish, chinless face had the stamp of the Whateleys upon it. But the torso and lower parts of the body were teratologically fabulous, so that only generous clothing could ever have enabled it to walk on earth unchallenged or uneradicated.

Above the waist it was semi-anthropomorphic; though its chest, where the dog's rending paws still rested watchfully, had the leathery, reticulated hide of a crocodile or alligator. The back was piebald with yellow and black, and dimly suggested the squamous covering of certain snakes. Below the waist, though, it was the worst; for here all human resemblance left off and sheer phantasy began. The skin was thickly covered with coarse black fur, and from the abdomen a score of long greenish-gray tentacles with red sucking mouths protruded limply. Their arrangement was odd, and seemed to follow the symmetries of some cosmic geometry unknown to earth or the solar system. On each of the hips, deep set in a kind of pinkish, ciliated orbit, was what seemed to be a rudimentary eye; whilst in lieu of a tail there depended a kind of trunk or feeler with purple annular markings, and with many evidences of being an undeveloped mouth or throat. The limbs, save for their black fur, roughly resembled the hind legs of prehistoric earth's giant saurians; and terminated in ridgy-veined pads that were neither hooves nor claws. When the thing breathed, its tail and tentacles rhythmically changed color, as if from some circulatory cause normal to the non-human side of its ancestry. In the tentacles this was observable as a deepening of the greenish tinge, whilst in the tail it was manifest as a yellowish appearance which alternated with a sickly grayish-white in the spaces between the purple rings. Of genuine blood there was none; only the fetid greenish-yellow ichor which trickled along the painted floor beyond the radius of the stickiness, and left a curious discoloration behind it.

As the presence of the three men seemed to rouse the dying thing, it began to mumble without turning or raising its head. Dr Armitage made no written record of its mouthings, but asserts confidently that nothing in English was uttered. At first the syllables defied all correlation with any speech of earth, but toward the last there came some disjointed fragments evidently taken from the *Necronomicon,* that monstrous blasphemy in quest of which the thing had perished. These fragments, as Armitage recalls them, ran something like *"N'gai, n'gha'ghaa, bugg-shoggog, y'hah; Yog-Sothoth, Yog-Sothoth . . . ."* They trailed off into nothingness as the whippoorwills shrieked in rhythmical crescendos of unholy anticipation.

Then came a halt in the gasping, and the dog raised its head in a long, lugubrious howl. A change came over the yellow, goatish face of the prostrate thing, and the great black eyes fell in appallingly. Outside the window the shrilling of the whippoorwills had suddenly ceased, and above the murmurs of the gathering crowd there came the sound of a panic-struck whirring and fluttering. Against the moon vast clouds of feathery watchers rose and raced from sight, frantic at that which they had sought for prey.

All at once the dog started up abruptly, gave a frightened bark, and leaped nervously out of the window by which it had entered. A cry rose from the crowd, and Dr Armitage shouted to the men outside that no one must be admitted till the police or medical examiner came. He was thankful that the windows were just too high to permit of peering in, and drew the dark curtains carefully down over each one. By this time two policemen had arrived; and Dr Morgan, meeting them in the vestibule, was urging them for their own sakes to postpone entrance to the stench-filled reading-room till the examiner came and the prostrate thing could be covered up.

Meanwhile frightful changes were taking place on the floor. One need not describe the kind and rate of shrinkage and disintegration that occurred before the eyes of Dr Armitage and Professor Rice; but it is permissible to say that, aside from the external appearance of face and hands, the really human element in Wilbur Whateley must have been very small. When the medical examiner came, there was only a sticky whitish mass on the painted boards, and the monstrous odor had nearly disappeared. Apparently Whateley had had no skull or bony skeleton; at least, in any true or stable sense. He had taken somewhat after his unknown father.

VII

Yet all this was only the prologue of the actual Dunwich horror. Formalities were gone through by bewildered officials, abnormal details were duly kept from press and public, and men were sent to Dunwich and Aylesbury to look up property and notify any who might be heirs of the late Wilbur Whateley. They found the countryside in great agitation, both because of the growing rumblings beneath the domed hills, and because of the unwonted stench and the surging, lapping sounds which came increasingly from the great empty shell formed by Whateley's boarded-up farmhouse. Earl Sawyer, who tended the horse and cattle during Wilbur's absence, had developed a woefully acute case of nerves. The officials devised excuses not to enter the noisome boarded place; and were glad to confine their survey of the deceased's living quarters, the newly mended sheds, to a single visit. They filed a ponderous report at the court-house in Aylesbury, and litigations concerning heirship are said to be still in progress amongst the innumerable Whateleys, decayed and undecayed, of the upper Miskatonic valley.

An almost interminable manuscript in strange characters, written in a huge ledger and adjudged a sort of diary because of the spacing and the variations in ink and penmanship, presented a baffling puzzle to those who found it on the old bureau which served as its owner's desk. After a week of debate it was sent to Miskatonic University, together with the deceased's collection of strange books, for study and possible translation; but even the best linguists soon saw that it was not likely to be unriddled with ease. No trace of the ancient gold with which Wilbur and Old Whateley always paid their debts has yet been discovered.

It was in the dark of September 9th that the horror broke loose. The hill noises had been very pronounced during the evening, and dogs barked frantically all night. Early risers on the 10th noticed a peculiar stench in the air. About seven o'clock Luther Brown, the hired boy at George Corey's, between Cold Spring Glen and the village, rushed frenziedly back from his morning trip to Ten-Acre Meadow with the cows. He was almost convulsed with fright as he stumbled into the kitchen; and in the yard outside the no less fright-ened herd were pawing and lowing pitifully, having followed the boy back in the panic they shared with him. Between gasps Luther tried to stammer out his tale to Mrs Corey.

"Up thar in the rud beyont the glen, Mis' Corey—they's suthin' ben thar! It smells like thunder, an' all the bushes an' little trees is pushed back from the rud like they'd a haouse ben moved along of it. An' that ain't the wust, nuther. They's *prints* in the rud, Mis' Corey—great raound prints as big as barrel-heads, all sunk daown deep like a elephant had ben along, *only they's a sight more nor four feet could make!* I looked at one or two afore I run, an' I see every one was covered with lines spreadin' aout from one place, like as if big palm-leaf fans—twice or three times as big as any they is—hed of ben paounded daown into the rud. An' the smell was awful, like what it is araound Wizard Whateley's ol' haouse. . . ."

Here he faltered, and seemed to shiver afresh with the fright that had sent him flying home. Mrs Corey, unable to extract more infor-mation, began telephoning the neighbors; thus starting on its rounds the overture of panic that heralded the major terrors. When she got Sally Sawyer, housekeeper at Seth Bishop's, the nearest place to Whateley's, it became her turn to listen instead of transmit; for Sally's boy Chauncey, who slept poorly, had been up on the hill toward Whateley's, and had dashed back in terror after one look at the place, and at the pasturage where Mr Bishop's cows had been left out all night.

"Yes, Mis' Corey," came Sally's tremulous voice over the party wire, "Cha'ncey he just come back a-postin', and couldn't haff talk fer bein' scairt! He says Ol' Whateley's haouse is all blowed up, with the timbers scattered raound like they'd ben dynamite inside; only the bottom floor ain't through, but is all covered with a kind o' tar-like stuff that smells awful an' drips daown offen the aidges onto the graoun' whar the side timbers is blown away. An' they's awful kinder marks in the yard, tew—great raound marks bigger raound than a hogshead, an' all sticky with stuff like is on the blowed-up haouse. Cha'ncey he says they leads off into the medders, whar a great swath wider'n a barn is matted daown, an' all the stun walls tumbled every whichway wherever it goes.

"An' he says, says he, Mis' Corey, as haow he sot to look fer Seth's caows, frighted ez he was; an' faound 'em in the upper pasture nigh the Devil's Hop Yard in an awful shape. Haff on 'em's clean gone, an' nigh haff o' them that's left is sucked most dry o' blood, with sores on 'em like they's ben on Whateley's cattle ever senct Lavinny's black brat was born. Seth he's gone aout naow to look at 'em, though I'll vaow he wun't keer ter git very nigh Wizard Whateley's! Cha'ncey didn't look keerful ter see whar the big matted-daown swath led arter it leff the pasturage, but he says he thinks it p'inted towards the glen rud to the village.

"I tell ye, Mis' Corey, they's suthin' abroad as hadn't orter be abroad, an' I for one think that black Wilbur Whateley, as come to the bad eend he desarved, is at the bottom of the breedin' of it. He wa'n't all human hisself, I allus says to everybody; an' I think he an' Ol' Whateley must a raised suthin' in that there nailed-up haouse as ain't even so human as he was. They's allus ben unseen things araound Dunwich—

livin' things—as ain't human an' ain't good fer human folks.

"The graoun' was a-talkin' lass night, an' towards mornin' Cha'ncey he heerd the whippoorwills so laoud in Col' Spring Glen he couldn't sleep nun. Then he thought he heerd another faint-like saound over towards Wizard Whateley's—a kinder rippin' or tearin' o' wood, like some big box er crate was bein' opened fur off. What with this an' that, he didn't git to sleep at all till sunup, an' no sooner was he up this mornin', but he's got to go over to Whateley's an' see what's the matter. He see enough, I tell ye, Mis' Corey! This dun't mean no good, an' I think as all the men-folks ought to git up a party an' do suthin'. I know suthin' awful's abaout, an' feel my time is nigh, though only Gawd knows jest what it is.

"Did your Luther take accaount o' whar them big tracks led tew? No? Wal, Mis' Corey, ef they was on the glen rud this side o' the glen, an' ain't got to your haouse yet, I calc'late they must go into the glen itself. They would do that. I allus says Col' Spring Glen ain't no healthy nor decent place. The whippoorwills an' fireflies there never did act like they was creaters o' Gawd, an' they's them as says ye kin hear strange things a-rushin' an' a-talkin' in the air daown thar ef ye stand in the right place, atween the rock falls an' Bear's Den."

By that noon fully three-quarters of the men and boys of Dunwich were trooping over the roads and meadows between the new-made Whateley ruins and Cold Spring Glen, examining in horror the vast, monstrous prints, the maimed Bishop cattle, the strange, noisome wreck of the farmhouse, and the bruised, matted vegetation of the fields and roadsides. Whatever had burst loose upon the world had assuredly gone down into the great sinister ravine; for all the trees on the banks were bent and broken, and a great avenue had been gouged in the precipice-hanging underbrush. It was as though a house, launched by an avalanche, had slid down through the tangled growths of the almost vertical slope. From below no sound came, but only a distant, undefinable fetor; and it is not to be wondered at that the men preferred to stay on the edge and argue, rather than descend and beard the unknown Cyclopean horror in its lair. Three dogs that were with the party had barked furiously at first, but seemed cowed and reluctant when near the glen. Someone telephoned the news to the *Aylesbury Transcript;* but the editor, accustomed to wild tales from Dunwich, did no more than concoct a humorous paragraph about it; an item soon afterward reproduced by the Associated Press.

That night everyone went home, and every house and barn was barricaded as stoutly as possible. Needless to say, no cattle were allowed to remain in open pasturage. About two in the morning a frightful stench and the savage barking of the dogs awakened the household at Elmer Frye's, on the eastern edge of Cold Spring Glen, and all agreed that they could hear a sort of muffled swishing or lapping sound from somewhere outside. Mrs Frye proposed telephoning the neighbors, and Elmer was about to agree when the noise of splintering wood burst in upon their deliberations. It came, apparently, from the barn; and was quickly followed by a hideous screaming and stamping amongst the cattle. The dogs slavered and crouched close to the feet of the fear-numbed family. Frye lit a lantern through force of habit, but knew it would be death to go out into that black farmyard. The children and the womenfolk whimpered, kept from screaming by some obscure, vestigial instinct of defense which told them their lives depended on silence. At last the noise of the cattle subsided to a pitiful moaning, and a great snapping, crashing, and crackling ensued. The Fryes, huddled together in the sitting-room, did not dare to move until the last echoes died away far down in Cold Spring Glen. Then, amidst the dismal moans from the stable and the demoniac piping of late whippoorwills in the glen, Selina Frye tottered to the telephone and spread what news she could of the second phase of the horror.

The next day all the countryside was in a panic; and cowed, uncommunicative groups came and went where the fiendish thing had occurred. Two titan swaths of destruction stretched from the glen to the Frye farmyard, monstrous prints covered the bare patches of ground, and one side of the old red barn had completely caved in. Of the cattle, only a quarter could be found and identified. Some of these were in curious fragments, and all that survived had to be shot. Earl Sawyer suggested that help be asked from Aylesbury or Arkham, but others maintained it would be of no use. Old Zebulon Whateley, of a branch that hovered about half way between soundness and decadence, made darkly wild suggestions about rites that ought to be practiced on the hilltops. He came of a line where tradition ran strong, and his memories of chantings in the great stone circles were not altogether connected with Wilbur and his grandfather.

Darkness fell upon a stricken countryside too passive to organize for real defense. In a few cases closely related families would band together and watch in the gloom under one roof; but in general there was only a repetition of the barricading of the night before, and a futile, ineffective gesture of loading muskets and setting pitchforks handily about. Nothing, however, occurred except some hill noises; and when the day came there were many who hoped that the new horror had gone as swiftly as it had come. There were even bold souls who proposed an offensive expedition down in the glen, though they did not venture to set an actual example to the still reluctant majority.

When night came again the barricading was repeated, though there was less huddling together of families. In the morning both the Frye and the Seth Bishop households reported excitement among the dogs and vague sounds and stenches from afar, while early explorers noted with horror a fresh set of the monstrous tracks in the road skirting Sentinel Hill. As before, the sides of the road showed a bruising indicative of the blasphemously stupendous bulk of the horror; whilst the conformation of the tracks seemed to argue a passage in two directions, as if the moving mountain had come from Cold Spring

Glen and returned to it along the same path. At the base of the hill
a thirty-foot swath of crushed shrubbery saplings led steeply upward,
and the seekers gasped when they saw that even the most perpendicular places did not deflect the inexorable trail. Whatever the horror
was, it could scale a sheer stony cliff of almost complete verticality;
and as the investigators climbed around to the hill's summit by safer
routes they saw that the trail ended—or rather, reversed—there.

It was here that the Whateleys used to build their hellish fires and
chant their hellish rituals by the table-like stone on May Eve and
Hallowmass. Now that very stone formed the center of a vast space
thrashed around by the mountainous horror, whilst upon its slightly
concave surface was a thick and fetid deposit of the same tarry stickiness observed on the floor of the ruined Whateley farmhouse when
the horror escaped. Men looked at one another and muttered. Then
they looked down the hill. Apparently the horror had descended by
a route much the same as that of its ascent. To speculate was futile.
Reason, logic, and normal ideas of motivation stood confounded.
Only old Zebulon, who was not with the group, could have done
justice to the situation or suggested a plausible explanation.

Thursday night began much like the others, but it ended less
happily. The whippoorwills in the glen had screamed with such
unusual persistence that many could not sleep, and about 3 a.m. all
the party telephones rang tremulously. Those who took down their
receivers heard a fright-mad voice shriek out, "Help, oh, my
Gawd! . . ." and some thought a crashing sound followed the breaking
off of the exclamation. There was nothing more. No one dared do
anything, and no one knew till morning whence the call came. Then
those who had heard it called everyone on the line, and found that
only the Fryes did not reply. The truth appeared an hour later, when
a hastily assembled group of armed men trudged out to the Frye place
at the head of the glen. It was horrible, yet hardly a surprise. There
were more swaths and monstrous prints, but there was no longer any

house. It had caved in like an eggshell, and amongst the ruins nothing living or dead could be discovered. Only a stench and a tarry stickiness. The Elmer Fryes had been erased from Dunwich.

VIII

In the meantime a quieter yet even more spiritually poignant phase of the horror had been blackly unwinding itself behind the closed door of a shelf-lined room in Arkham. The curious manuscript record or diary of Wilbur Whateley, delivered to Miskatonic University for translation, had caused much worry and bafflement among the experts in languages both ancient and modern; its very alphabet, notwithstanding a general resemblance to the heavily shaded Arabic used in Mesopotamia, being absolutely unknown to any available authority. The final conclusion of the linguists was that the text represented an artificial alphabet, giving the effect of a cipher; though none of the usual methods of cryptographic solution seemed to furnish any clue, even when applied on the basis of every tongue the writer might conceivably have used. The ancient books taken from Whateley's quarters, while absorbingly interesting and in several cases promising to open up new and terrible lines of research among philosophers and men of science, were of no assistance whatever in this matter. One of them, a heavy tome with an iron clasp, was in another unknown alphabet—this one of a very different cast, and resembling Sanskrit more than anything else. The old ledger was at length given wholly into the charge of Dr Armitage, both because of his peculiar interest in the Whateley matter, and because of his wide linguistic learning and skill in the mystical formulae of antiquity and the Middle Ages.

Armitage had an idea that the alphabet might be something esoterically used by certain forbidden cults which have come down from old times, and which have inherited many forms and traditions from the wizards of the Saracenic world. That question, however, he did not deem vital; since it would be unnecessary to know the origin of the symbols if, as he suspected, they were used as a cipher in a modern language. It was his belief that, considering the great amount of text involved, the writer would scarcely have wished the trouble of using another speech than his own, save perhaps in certain special formulae and incantations. Accordingly he attacked the manuscript with the preliminary assumption that the bulk of it was in English.

Dr Armitage knew, from the repeated failures of his colleagues, that the riddle was a deep and complex one; and that no simple mode of solution could merit even a trial. All through late August he fortified himself with the massed lore of cryptography; drawing upon the fullest resources of his own library, and wading night after night amidst the arcana of Trithemius's *Poligraphia,* Giambattista Porta's *De Furtivis Literarum Notis,* De Vigenère's *Traité des Chiffres,* Falconer's *Cryptomenysis Patefacta,* Davys's and Thicknesse's eighteenth-century treatises, and such fairly modern authorities as Blair, von Marten, and Klüber's *Kryptographik.* He interspersed his study of the books with attacks on the manuscript itself, and in time became convinced that he had to deal with one of those subtlest and most ingenious of cryptograms, in which many separate lists of corresponding letters are arranged like the multiplication table, and the message built up with arbitrary key-words known only to the initiated. The older authorities seemed rather more helpful than the newer ones, and Armitage concluded that the code of the manuscript was one of great antiquity, no doubt handed down through a long line of mystical experimenters. Several times he seemed near daylight, only to be set back by some unforeseen obstacle. Then, as September approached, the clouds began to clear. Certain letters, as used in certain parts of the manuscript, emerged definitely and unmistakably; and it became obvious that the text was indeed in English.

On the evening of September 2nd the last major barrier gave way, and Dr Armitage read for the first time a continuous passage of Wilbur Whateley's annals. It was in truth a diary, as all had thought; and it was couched in a style clearly showing the mixed occult erudition and general illiteracy of the strange being who wrote it. Almost the first long passage that Armitage deciphered, an entry dated November 26th, 1916, proved highly startling and disquieting. It was written, he remembered, by a child of three and a half who looked like a lad of twelve or thirteen.

Today learned the Aklo for the Sabaoth (it ran), which did not like, it being answerable from the hill and not from the air. That upstairs more ahead of me than I had thought it would be, and is not like to have much earth brain. Shot Elam Hutchins's collie Jack when he went to bite me, and Elam says he would kill me if he dast. I guess he won't. Grandfather kept me saying the Dho formula last night, and I think I saw the inner city at the 2 magnetic poles. I shall go to those poles when the earth is cleared off, if I can't break through with the Dho-Hna formula when I commit it. They from the air told me at Sabbat that it will be years before I can clear off the earth, and I guess grandfather will be dead then, so I shall have to learn all the angles of the planes and all the formulas between the Yr and the Nhhngr. They from outside will help, but they cannot take body without human blood. That upstairs looks it will have the right cast. I can see it a little when I make the Voorish sign or blow the powder of Ibn Ghazi at it, and it is near like them at May Eve on the Hill. The other face may wear off some. I wonder how I shall look when the earth is cleared and there are no earth beings on it. He that came with the Aklo Sabaoth said I may be transfigured, there being much of outside to work on.

Morning found Dr Armitage in a cold sweat of terror and a frenzy of wakeful concentration. He had not left the manuscript all night, but sat at his table under the electric light turning page after page with shaking hands as fast as he could decipher the cryptic text. He had nervously telephoned his wife he would not be home, and when she brought him a breakfast from the house he could scarcely dispose of a mouthful. All that day he read on, now and then halted maddeningly as a reapplication of the complex key became necessary. Lunch and dinner were brought him, but he ate only the smallest fraction of either. Toward the middle of the next night he drowsed off in his chair, but soon woke out of a tangle of nightmares almost as hideous as the truths and menaces to man's existence that he had uncovered.

On the morning of September 4th Professor Rice and Dr Morgan insisted on seeing him for a while, and departed trembling and ashen-gray. That evening he went to bed, but slept only fitfully. Wednesday—the next day—he was back at the manuscript, and began to take copious notes both from the current sections and from those he had already deciphered. In the small hours of that night he slept a little in an easy-chair in his office, but was at the manuscript again before dawn. Some time before noon his physician, Dr Hartwell, called to see him and insisted that he cease work. He refused; intimating that it was of the most vital importance for him to complete the reading of the diary, and promising an explanation in due course of time.

That evening, just as twilight fell, he finished his terrible perusal and sank back exhausted. His wife, bringing his dinner, found him in a half-comatose state; but he was conscious enough to warn her off with a sharp cry when he saw her eyes wander toward the notes he had taken. Weakly rising, he gathered up the scribbled papers and sealed them all in a great envelope, which he immediately placed in his inside coat pocket. He had sufficient strength to get home, but was so clearly in need of medical aid that Dr Hartwell was summoned at once. As the doctor put him to bed he could only mutter over and over again, *"But what, in God's name, can we do?"*

Dr Armitage slept, but was partly delirious the next day. He made no explanations to Hartwell, but in his calmer moments spoke of the imperative need of a long conference with Rice and Morgan. His wilder wanderings were very startling indeed, including frantic appeals that something in a boarded-up farmhouse be destroyed, and fantastic references to some plan for the extirpation of the entire human race and all animal and vegetable life from the earth by some terrible elder race of beings from another dimension. He would shout that the world was in danger, since the Elder Things wished to strip it and drag it away from the solar system and cosmos of matter into some other plane or phase of entity from which it had once fallen, vigintillions of eons ago. At other times he would call for the dreaded *Necronomicon* and the *Daemonolatreia* of Remigius, in which he seemed hopeful of finding some formula to check the peril he conjured up.

"Stop them, stop them!" he would shout. "Those Whateleys meant to let them in, and the worst of all is left! Tell Rice and Morgan we must do something—it's a blind business, but I know how to make the powder . . . . It hasn't been fed since the second of August, when Wilbur came here to his death, and at that rate . . . ."

But Armitage had a sound physique despite his seventy-three years, and slept off his disorder that night without developing any real fever. He woke late Friday, clear of head, though sober with a gnawing fear and tremendous sense of responsibility. Saturday afternoon he felt able to go over to the library and summon Rice and Morgan for a conference, and the rest of that day and evening the three men tortured their brains in the wildest speculation and the most desperate debate. Strange and terrible books were drawn voluminously from the stack shelves and from secure places of storage; and diagrams and formulae were copied with feverish haste and in bewildering abundance. Of skepticism there was none. All three had seen the body of Wilbur Whateley as it lay on the floor in a room of that very building, and after that not one of them could feel even slightly inclined to treat the diary as a madman's raving.

Opinions were divided as to notifying the Massachusetts State Police, and the negative finally won. There were things involved which simply could not be believed by those who had not seen a sample, as indeed was made clear during certain subsequent investigations. Late at night the conference disbanded without having developed a definite plan, but all day Sunday Armitage was busy comparing formulae and mixing chemicals obtained from the college laboratory. The more he reflected on the hellish diary, the more he was inclined to doubt the efficacy of any material agent in stamping out the entity which Wilbur Whateley had left behind him—the earth-threatening entity which, unknown to him, was to burst forth in a few hours and become the memorable Dunwich horror.

Monday was a repetition of Sunday with Dr Armitage, for the task in hand required an infinity of research and experiment. Further consultations of the monstrous diary brought about various changes of plan, and he knew that even in the end a large amount of uncertainty must remain. By Tuesday he had a definite line of action mapped out, and believed he would try a trip to Dunwich within a week. Then, on Wednesday, the great shock came. Tucked obscurely away in a corner of the *Arkham Advertiser* was a facetious little item from the Associated Press, telling what a record-breaking monster the bootleg whiskey of Dunwich had raised up. Armitage, half stunned, could only telephone for Rice and Morgan. Far into the night they discussed, and the next day was a whirlwind of preparation on the part of them all. Armitage knew he would be meddling with terrible powers, yet saw that there was no other way to annul the deeper and more malign meddling which others had done before him.

IX

Friday morning Armitage, Rice, and Morgan set out by motor for Dunwich, arriving at the village about one in the afternoon. The day was pleasant, but even in the brightest sunlight a kind of quiet dread and portent seemed to hover about the strangely domed hills and the deep, shadowy ravines of the stricken region. Now and then on some mountain-top a gaunt circle of stones could be glimpsed against the sky. From the air of hushed fright at Osborn's store they knew something hideous had happened, and soon learned of the annihilation of the Elmer Frye house and family. Throughout that afternoon they rode around Dunwich; questioning the natives concerning all that had occurred, and seeing for themselves with rising pangs of horror the drear Frye ruins with their lingering traces of the tarry stickiness, the blasphemous tracks in the Frye yard, the wounded Seth Bishop cattle, and the enormous swaths of disturbed vegetation in various places. The trail up and down Sentinel Hill seemed to Armitage of almost cataclysmic significance, and he looked long at the sinister altar-like stone on the summit.

At length the visitors, apprised of a party of State Police which had come from Aylesbury that morning in response to the first telephone reports of the Frye tragedy, decided to seek out the officers and compare notes as far as practicable. This, however, they found more easily planned than performed; since no sign of the party could be found in any direction. There had been five of them in a car, but now the car stood empty near the ruins in the Frye yard. The natives, all of whom had talked with the policemen, seemed at first as perplexed as Armitage and his companions. Then old Sam Hutchins thought of something and turned pale, nudging Fred Farr and pointing to the dank, deep hollow that yawned close by.

"Gawd," he gasped, "I told 'em not ter go daown into the glen, an' I never thought nobody'd dew it with them tracks an' that smell an' the whippoorwills a-screechin' daown thar in the dark o' noonday. . . ."

A cold shudder ran through natives and visitors alike, and every ear seemed strained in a kind of instinctive, unconscious listening. Armitage, now that he had actually come upon the horror and its monstrous work, trembled with the responsibility he felt to be his. Night would soon fall, and it was then that the mountainous blasphemy lumbered upon its eldritch course. *Negotium perambulans in tenebris* . . . . The old librarian rehearsed the formulae he had memorized, and clutched the paper containing the alternative one he had not memorized. He saw that his electric flashlight was in working order. Rice, beside him, took from a valise a metal sprayer of the sort used in combating insects; whilst Morgan uncased the big-game rifle on which he relied despite his colleague's warnings that no material weapon would be of help.

Armitage, having read the hideous diary, knew painfully well what kind of a manifestation to expect; but he did not add to the fright of the Dunwich people by giving any hints or clues. He hoped that it might be conquered without any revelation to the world of the monstrous thing it had escaped. As the shadows gathered, the natives commenced to disperse homeward, anxious to bar themselves indoors despite the present evidence that all human locks and bolts were useless before a force that could bend trees and crush houses when it chose. They shook their heads at the visitors' plan to stand guard at the Frye ruins near the glen; and as they left, had little expectancy of ever seeing the watchers again.

There were rumblings under the hills that night, and the whippoorwills piped threateningly. Once in a while a wind, sweeping up out of Cold Spring Glen, would bring a touch of ineffable fetor to the heavy night air; such a fetor as all three of the watchers had smelled once before, when they stood above a dying thing that had passed for fifteen years and a half as a human being. But the looked-for terror did not appear. Whatever was down there in the glen was biding its time, and Armitage told his colleagues it would be suicidal to try to attack it in the dark.

Morning came wanly, and the night-sounds ceased. It was a gray, bleak day, with now and then a drizzle of rain; and heavier and heavier clouds seemed to be piling themselves up beyond the hills to the northwest. The men from Arkham were undecided what to do. Seeking shelter from the increasing rainfall beneath one of the few undestroyed Frye outbuildings, they debated the wisdom of waiting, or of taking the aggressive and going down into the glen in quest of their name-less, monstrous quarry. The downpour waxed in heaviness, and distant peals of thunder sounded from far horizons. Sheet lightning shim-mered, and then a forky bolt flashed near at hand, as if descending into the accursed glen itself. The sky grew very dark, and the watchers hoped that the storm would prove a short, sharp one followed by clear weather.

It was still gruesomely dark when, not much over an hour later, a confused babel of voices sounded down the road. Another moment brought to view a frightened group of more than a dozen men, running, shouting, and even whimpering hysterically. Someone in the lead began sobbing out words, and the Arkham men started violently when those words developed a coherent form.

"Oh, my Gawd, my Gawd," the voice choked out. "It's a-goin' agin, *an' this time by day!* It's aout—it's aout an' a-movin' this very minute, an' only the Lord knows when it'll be on us all!"

The speaker panted into silence, but another took up his message.

"Nigh on a haour ago Zeb Whateley here heerd the 'phone a-ringin', an' it was Mis' Corey, George's wife, that lives daown by the junction. She says the hired boy Luther was aout drivin' in the caows from the storm arter the big bolt, when he see all the trees a-bendin' at the maouth o' the glen—opposite side ter this—an' smelt the same awful smell like he smelt when he faound the big tracks las' Monday mornin'. An' she says he says they was a swishin', lappin' saound, more nor what the bendin' trees an' bushes could make, an' all on a suddent the trees along the rud begun ter git pushed one side, an' they was a awful stompin' an' splashin' in the mud. But mind ye, Luther he didn't see nothin' at all, only just the bendin' trees an' underbrush.

"Then fur ahead where Bishop's Brook goes under the rud he heerd a awful creakin' an' strainin' on the bridge, an' says he could tell the saound o' wood a-startin' to crack an' split. An' all the whiles he never see a thing, only them trees an' bushes a-bendin'. An' when the swishin' saound got very fur off—on the rud towards Wizard Whateley's an' Sentinel Hill—Luther he had the guts ter step up whar he'd heerd it furst an' look at the graound. It was all mud an' water, an' the sky was dark, an' the rain was wipin' aout all tracks abaout as fast as could be; but beginnin' at the glen maouth, whar the trees had moved, they was still some o' them awful prints big as bar'ls like he seen Monday."

At this point the first excited speaker interrupted.

"But *that* ain't the trouble naow—that was only the start. Zeb here was callin' folks up an' everybody was a-listenin' in when a call from Seth Bishop's cut in. His haousekeeper Sally was carryin' on fit ter kill—she'd jest seed the trees a-bendin' beside the rud, an' says they was a kind o' mushy saound, like a elephant puffin' an' treadin', a-headin' fer the haouse. Then she up an' spoke suddent of a fearful smell, an' says her boy Cha'ncey was a-screamin' as haow it was jest like what he smelt up to the Whateley rewins Monday mornin'. An' the dogs was all barkin' an' whinin' awful.

"An' then she let aout a turrible yell, an' says the shed daown the rud had jest caved in like the storm hed blowed it over, only the wind wa'n't strong enough to dew that. Everybody was a-listenin', an' we could hear lots o' folks on the wire a-gaspin'. All to onct Sally she yelled agin, an' says the front yard picket fence hed just crumbled up, though they wa'n't no sign o' what done it. Then everybody on the line could hear Cha'ncey an' ol' Seth Bishop a-yellin' tew, an' Sally was shriekin' aout that suthin' heavy hed struck the haouse—not lightnin' nor nothin', but suthin' heavy agin the front, that kep' a-launchin' itself agin an' agin, though ye couldn't see nothin' aout the front winders. An' then . . . an' then . . ."

Lines of fright deepened on every face; and Armitage, shaken as he was, had barely poise enough to prompt the speaker.

"An' then . . . Sally she yelled aout, 'O help, the haouse is a-cavin' in' . . . an' on the wire we could hear a turrible crashin', an' a hull flock o' screamin' . . . jest like when Elmer Frye's place was took, only wuss. . . ."

The man paused, and another of the crowd spoke.

"That's all—not a saound nor squeak over the 'phone arter that. Jest still-like. We that heerd it got aout Fords an' wagons an' raounded up as many able-bodied menfolks as we could git, at Corey's place, an' come up here ter see what yew thought best ter dew. Not but what I think it's the Lord's jedgment fer our iniquities, that no mortal kin ever set aside."

Armitage saw that the time for positive action had come, and spoke decisively to the faltering group of frightened rustics.

"We must follow it, boys." He made his voice as reassuring as possible. "I believe there's a chance of putting it out of business. You men know that those Whateleys were wizards—well, this thing is a thing of wizardry, and must be put down by the same means. I've seen Wilbur Whateley's diary and read some of the strange old books he used to read; and I think I know the right kind of spell to recite to make the thing fade away. Of course, one can't be sure, but we can always take a chance. It's invisible—I knew it would be—but there's a powder in this long-distance sprayer that might make it show up for a second. Later on we'll try it. It's a frightful thing to have alive, but it isn't as bad as what Wilbur would have let in if he'd lived longer. You'll never know what the world has escaped. Now we've only this one thing to fight, and it can't multiply. It can, though, do a lot of harm; so we mustn't hesitate to rid the community of it.

"We must follow it—and the way to begin is to go to the place that has just been wrecked. Let somebody lead the way—I don't know your roads very well, but I've an idea there might be a shorter cut across lots. How about it?"

The men shuffled about a moment, and then Earl Sawyer spoke softly, pointing with a grimy finger through the steadily lessening rain.

"I guess ye kin git to Seth Bishop's quickest by cuttin' acrost the lower medder here, wadin' the brook at the low place, an' climbin' through Carrier's mowin' and the timber-lot beyont. That comes aout on the upper rud mighty nigh Seth's—a leetle t'other side."

Armitage, with Rice and Morgan, started to walk in the direction indicated; and most of the natives followed slowly. The sky was growing lighter, and there were signs that the storm had worn itself away. When Armitage inadvertently took a wrong direction, Joe Osborn warned him and walked ahead to show the right one. Courage and confidence were mounting; though the twilight of the almost perpendicular wooded hill which lay toward the end of their short cut, and among whose fantastic ancient trees they had to scramble as if up a ladder, put these qualities to a severe test.

At length they emerged on a muddy road to find the sun coming out. They were a little beyond the Seth Bishop place, but bent trees and hideously unmistakable tracks showed what had passed by. Only a few moments were consumed in surveying the ruins just around the bend. It was the Frye incident all over again, and nothing dead or living was found in either of the collapsed shells which had been the Bishop house and barn. No one cared to remain there amidst the stench and tarry stickiness, but all turned instinctively to the line of horrible prints leading on toward the wrecked Whateley farmhouse and the altar-crowned slopes of Sentinel Hill.

As the men passed the site of Wilbur Whateley's abode they shuddered visibly, and seemed again to mix hesitancy with their zeal. It was no joke tracking down something as big as a house that one could not see, but that had all the vicious malevolence of a demon. Opposite the base of Sentinel Hill the tracks left the road, and there was a fresh bending and matting visible along the broad swath marking the monster's former route to and from the summit.

Armitage produced a pocket telescope of considerable power and scanned the steep green side of the hill. Then he handed the instrument to Morgan, whose sight was keener. After a moment of gazing Morgan cried out sharply, passing the glass to Earl Sawyer and indicating a certain spot on the slope with his finger. Sawyer, as clumsy as most non-users of optical devices are, fumbled a while; but eventually focused the lenses with Armitage's aid. When he did so his cry was less restrained than Morgan's had been.

"Gawd almighty, the grass an' bushes is a-movin'! It's a-goin' up—slow-like—creepin' up ter the top this minute, heaven only knows what fur!"

Then the germ of panic seemed to spread among the seekers. It was one thing to chase the nameless entity, but quite another to find it. Spells might be all right—but suppose they weren't? Voices began questioning Armitage about what he knew of the thing, and no reply seemed quite to satisfy. Everyone seemed to feel himself in close proximity to phases of Nature and of being utterly forbidden, and wholly outside the sane experience of mankind.

X

In the end the three men from Arkham—old, white-bearded Dr Armitage, stocky, iron-gray Professor Rice, and lean, youngish Dr Morgan—ascended the mountain alone. After much patient instruction regarding its focusing and use, they left the telescope with the frightened group that remained in the road; and as they climbed they were watched closely by those among whom the glass was passed around. It was hard going, and Armitage had to be helped more than once. High above the toiling group the great swath trembled as its hellish maker re-passed with snail-like deliberateness. Then it was obvious that the pursuers were gaining.

Curtis Whateley—of the undecayed branch—was holding the telescope when the Arkham party detoured radically from the swath. He told the crowd that the men were evidently trying to get to a sub-ordinate peak which overlooked the swath at a point considerably ahead of where the shrubbery was now bending. This, indeed, proved to be true; and the party were seen to gain the minor elevation only a short time after the invisible blasphemy had passed it.

Then Wesley Corey, who had taken the glass, cried out that Armitage was adjusting the sprayer which Rice held, and that something must be about to happen. The crowd stirred uneasily, recalling that this sprayer was expected to give the unseen horror a moment of visibility. Two or three men shut their eyes, but Curtis Whateley snatched back the telescope and strained his vision to the utmost. He saw that Rice, from the party's point of vantage above and behind the entity, had an excellent chance of spreading the potent powder with marvelous effect.

Those without the telescope saw only an instant's flash of gray cloud—a cloud about the size of a moderately large building—near the top of the mountain. Curtis, who had held the instrument, dropped it with a piercing shriek into the ankle-deep mud of the road. He reeled, and would have crumpled to the ground had not two or three others seized and steadied him. All he could do was moan half-inaudibly.

"Oh, oh, great Gawd . . . *that* . . . *that* . . ."

There was a pandemonium of questioning, and only Henry Wheeler thought to rescue the fallen telescope and wipe it clean of mud. Curtis was past all coherence, and even isolated replies were almost too much for him.

"Bigger'n a barn . . . all made o' squirmin' ropes . . . hull thing sort o' shaped like a hen's egg bigger'n anything, with dozens o' legs like hogsheads that haff shut up when they step . . . nothin' solid abaout it—all like jelly, an' made o' sep'rit wrigglin' ropes pushed clost together . . . great bulgin' eyes all over it . . . ten or twenty maouths or trunks a-stickin' aout all along the sides, big as stovepipes, an' all a-tossin' an' openin' an' shuttin' . . . all gray, with kinder blue or purple rings . . . *an' Gawd in heaven—that haff face on top!* . . ."

This final memory, whatever it was, proved too much for poor Curtis; and he collapsed completely before he could say more. Fred Farr and Will Hutchins carried him to the roadside and laid him on the damp grass. Henry Wheeler, trembling, turned the rescued telescope on the mountain to see what he might. Through the lenses were discernible three tiny figures, apparently running toward the summit as fast as the steep incline allowed. Only these—nothing more. Then everyone noticed a strangely unseasonable noise in the deep valley behind, and even in the underbrush of Sentinel Hill itself. It was the piping of unnumbered whippoorwills, and in their shrill chorus there seemed to lurk a note of tense and evil expectancy.

Earl Sawyer now took the telescope and reported the three figures as standing on the topmost ridge, virtually level with the altar-stone but at a considerable distance from it. One figure, he said, seemed to be raising its hands above its head at rhythmic intervals; and as Sawyer mentioned the circumstance the crowd seemed to hear a faint, half-musical sound from the distance, as if a loud chant were accompanying the gestures. The weird silhouette on that remote peak must have been a spectacle of infinite grotesqueness and impressiveness, but no observer was in a mood for esthetic appreciation. "I guess he's sayin' the spell," whispered Wheeler as he snatched back the telescope. The whippoorwills were piping wildly, and in a singularly curious irregular rhythm quite unlike that of the visible ritual.

Suddenly the sunshine seemed to lessen without the intervention of any discernible cloud. It was a very peculiar phenomenon, and was plainly marked by all. A rumbling sound seemed brewing beneath the hills, mixed strangely with a concordant rumbling which clearly came from the sky. Lightning flashed aloft, and the wondering crowd looked in vain for the portents of storm. The chanting of the men from Arkham now became unmistakable, and Wheeler saw through the glass that they were all raising their arms in the rhythmic incantation. From some farmhouse far away came the frantic barking of dogs.

The change in the quality of the daylight increased, and the crowd gazed about the horizon in wonder. A purplish darkness, born of nothing more than a spectral deepening of the sky's blue, pressed down upon the rumbling hills. Then the lightning flashed again, somewhat brighter than before, and the crowd fancied that it had showed a certain mistiness around the altar-stone on the distant height. No one, however, had been using the telescope at that instant. The whippoorwills continued their irregular pulsation, and the men of Dunwich braced themselves tensely against some imponderable menace with which the atmosphere seemed surcharged.

Without warning came those deep, cracked, raucous vocal sounds which will never leave the memory of the stricken group who heard them. Not from any human throat were they born, for the organs of man can yield no such acoustic perversions. Rather would one have said they came from the pit itself, had not their source been so unmistakably the altar-stone on the peak. It is almost erroneous to call them *sounds* at all, since so much of their ghastly, infra-bass timbre spoke to dim seats of consciousness and terror far subtler than the ear; yet one must do so, since their form was indisputably though vaguely that of half-articulate *words*. They were loud—loud as the rumblings and the thunder above which they echoed—yet did they come from no visible being. And because imagination might suggest a conjectural source in the world of non-visible beings, the huddled crowd at the mountain's base huddled still closer, and winced as if in expectation of a blow.

"*Ygnaiih . . . ygnaiih . . . thflthkh'ngha . . . Yog-Sothoth . . .*" rang the hideous croaking out of space. "*Y'bthnk . . . h'ehye—n'grkdl'lh. . . .*"

The speaking impulse seemed to falter here, as if some frightful psychic struggle were going on. Henry Wheeler strained his eye at the telescope, but saw only the three grotesquely silhouetted human figures on the peak, all moving their arms furiously in strange gestures as their incantation drew near its culmination. From what black wells of Acherontic fear or feeling, from what unplumbed gulfs of extra-cosmic consciousness or obscure, long-latent heredity, were those half-articulate thunder-croakings drawn? Presently they began to gather renewed force and coherence as they grew in stark, utter, ultimate frenzy.

"*Eh-ya-ya-ya-yahaah—e'yayayayaaaa . . . ngh'aaaaa . . . ngh'aaaa* . . . h'yuh . . . h'yuh . . . HELP! HELP! . . . *ff—ff— ff*—FATHER! FATHER! YOG-SOTHOTH! . . ."

But that was all. The pallid group in the road, still reeling at the *indisputably English* syllables that had poured thickly and thunder-ously down from the frantic vacancy beside that shocking altar-stone, were never to hear such syllables again. Instead, they jumped violently at the terrific report which seemed to rend the hills; the deafening, cataclysmic peal whose source, be it inner earth or sky, no hearer was ever able to place. A single lightning-bolt shot from the purple zenith to the altar-stone, and a great tidal wave of viewless force and indescribable stench swept down from the hill to all the countryside. Trees, grass, and underbrush were whipped into a fury; and the frightened crowd at the mountain's base, weakened by the lethal fetor that seemed about to asphyxiate them, were almost hurled off their feet. Dogs howled from the distance, green grass and foliage wilted to a curious, sickly yellow-gray, and over field and forest were scattered the bodies of dead whippoorwills.

The stench left quickly, but the vegetation never came right again. To this day there is something queer and unholy about the growths on and around that fearsome hill. Curtis Whateley was only just regaining consciousness when the Arkham men came slowly down the mountain in the beams of a sunlight once more brilliant and untainted. They were grave and quiet, and seemed shaken by memories and reflections even more terrible than those which had reduced the group of natives to a state of cowed quivering. In reply to a jumble of questions they only shook their heads and reaffirmed one vital fact.

"The thing has gone forever," Armitage said. "It has been split up into what it was originally made of, and can never exist again. It was an impossibility in a normal world. Only the least fraction was really matter in any sense we know. It was like its father—and most of it has gone back to him in some vague realm or dimension outside our material universe; some vague abyss out of which only the most accursed rites of human blasphemy could ever have called him for a moment on the hills."

There was a brief silence, and in that pause the scattered senses of poor Curtis Whateley began to knit back into a sort of continuity; so that he put his hands to his head with a moan. Memory seemed to pick itself up where it had left off, and the horror of the sight that had prostrated him burst in upon him again.

"*Oh, oh, my Gawd, that haff face—that haff face on top of it . . . that face with the red eyes an' crinkly albino hair, an' no chin, like the Whateleys . . . It was a octopus, centipede, spider kind o' thing, but they was a haff-shaped man's face on top of it, an' it looked like Wizard Whateley's, only it was yards an' yards acrost . . . .*"

He paused exhausted, as the whole group of natives stared in a bewilderment not quite crystallized into fresh terror. Only old Zebulon Whateley, who wanderingly remembered ancient things but who had been silent heretofore, spoke aloud.

"Fifteen year' gone," he rambled, "I heerd Ol' Whateley say as haow some day we'd hear a child o' Lavinny's a-callin' its father's name on the top o' Sentinel Hill. . . ."

But Joe Osborn interrupted him to question the Arkham men anew.

"*What was it anyhaow*, an' haowever did young Wizard Whateley call it aout o' the air it come from?"

Armitage chose his words very carefully.

"It was—well, it was mostly a kind of force that doesn't belong in our part of space; a kind of force that acts and grows and shapes itself by other laws than those of our sort of Nature. We have no business calling in such things from outside, and only very wicked people and very wicked cults ever try to. There was some of it in Wilbur Whateley himself—enough to make a devil and a precocious monster of him, and to make his passing out a pretty terrible sight. I'm going to burn his accursed diary, and if you men are wise you'll dynamite that altar-stone up there, and pull down all the rings of standing stones on the other hills. Things like that brought down the beings those Whateleys were so fond of—the beings they were going to let in tangibly to wipe out the human race and drag the earth off to some nameless place for some nameless purpose.

"But as to this thing we've just sent back—the Whateleys raised it for a terrible part in the doings that were to come. It grew fast and big from the same reason that Wilbur grew fast and big—but it beat him because it had a greater share of the *outsideness* in it. You needn't ask how Wilbur called it out of the air. He didn't call it out. *It was his twin brother, but it looked more like the father than he did.*"

THE WHISPERER IN DARKNESS

I

Bear in mind closely that I did not see any actual visual horror at the end. To say that a mental shock was the cause of what I inferred—that last straw which sent me racing out of the lonely Akeley farmhouse and through the wild domed hills of Vermont in a commandeered motor at night—is to ignore the plainest facts of my final experience. Notwithstanding the deep extent to which I shared the information and speculations of Henry Akeley, the things I saw and heard, and the admitted vividness of the impression produced on me by these things, I cannot prove even now whether I was right or wrong in my hideous inference. For after all, Akeley's disappearance establishes nothing. People found nothing amiss in his house despite the bullet-marks on the outside and inside. It was just as though he had walked out casually for a ramble in the hills and failed to return. There was not even a sign that a guest had been there, or that those horrible cylinders and machines had been stored in the study. That he had mortally feared the crowded green hills and endless trickle of brooks among which he had been born and reared, means nothing at all, either; for thousands are subject to just such morbid fears. Eccentricity, moreover, could easily account for his strange acts and apprehensions toward the last.

The whole matter began, so far as I am concerned, with the historic and unprecedented Vermont floods of November 3rd, 1927. I was then, as now, an instructor of literature at Miskatonic University in Arkham, Massachusetts, and an enthusiastic amateur student of New

England folklore. Shortly after the flood, amidst the varied reports of hardship, suffering, and organized relief which filled the press, there appeared certain odd stories of things found floating in some of the swollen rivers; so that many of my friends embarked on curious discussions and appealed to me to shed what light I could on the subject. I felt flattered at having my folklore study taken so seriously, and did what I could to belittle the wild, vague tales which seemed so clearly an outgrowth of old rustic superstitions. It amused me to find several persons of education who insisted that some stratum of obscure, distorted fact might underlie the rumors.

The tales thus brought to my notice came mostly through newspaper cuttings; though one yarn had an oral source and was repeated to a friend of mine in a letter from his mother in Hardwick, Vermont. The type of thing described was essentially the same in all cases, though there seemed to be three separate instances involved—one connected with the Winooski River near Montpelier, another attached to the West River in Windham County beyond Newfane, and a third centering in the Passumpsic in Caledonia County above Lyndonville. Of course many of the stray items mentioned other instances, but on analysis they all seemed to boil down to these three. In each case country folk reported seeing one or more very bizarre and disturbing objects in the surging waters that poured down from the unfrequented hills, and there was a widespread tendency to connect these sights with a primitive, half-forgotten cycle of whispered legend which old people resurrected for the occasion.

What people thought they saw were organic shapes not quite like any they had ever seen before. Naturally, there were many human bodies washed along by the streams in that tragic period; but those who described these strange shapes felt quite sure that they were not human, despite some superficial resemblances in size and general outline. Nor, said the witnesses, could they have been any kind of animal known to Vermont. They were pinkish things about five feet long; with crustaceous bodies bearing vast pairs of dorsal fins or membranous wings and several sets of articulated limbs, and with a sort of convoluted ellipsoid, covered with multitudes of very short antennae, where a head would ordinarily be. It was really remarkable how closely the reports from different sources tended to coincide; though the wonder was lessened by the fact that the old legends, shared at one time throughout the hill country, furnished a morbidly vivid picture which might well have colored the imaginations of all the witnesses concerned. It was my conclusion that such witnesses— in every case naive and simple backwoods folk—had glimpsed the battered and bloated bodies of human beings or farm animals in the whirling currents; and had allowed the half-remembered folklore to invest these pitiful objects with fantastic attributes.

The ancient folklore, while cloudy, evasive, and largely forgotten by the present generation, was of a highly singular character, and obviously reflected the influence of still earlier Indian tales. I knew it well, though I had never been in Vermont, through the exceedingly rare monograph of Eli Davenport, which embraces material orally obtained prior to 1839 among the oldest people of the state. This material, moreover, closely coincided with tales which I had personally heard from elderly rustics in the mountains of New Hampshire. Briefly summarized, it hinted at a hidden race of monstrous beings which lurked somewhere among the remoter hills—in the deep woods of the highest peaks, and the dark valleys where streams trickle from unknown sources. These beings were seldom glimpsed, but evidences of their presence were reported by those who had ventured farther than usual up the slopes of certain mountains or into certain deep, steep-sided gorges that even the wolves shunned.

There were queer footprints or claw-prints in the mud of brook-margins and barren patches, and curious circles of stones, with the grass around them worn away, which did not seem to have been placed or entirely shaped by Nature. There were, too, certain caves of problematical depth in the sides of the hills; with mouths closed by boulders in a manner scarcely accidental, and with more than an average quota of the queer prints leading both toward and away from them—if indeed the direction of these prints could be justly estimated. And worst of all, there were the things which adventurous people had seen very rarely in the twilight of the remotest valleys and the dense perpendicular woods above the limits of normal hill-climbing.

It would have been less uncomfortable if the stray accounts of these things had not agreed so well. As it was, nearly all the rumors had several points in common; averring that the creatures were a sort of huge, light-red crab with many pairs of legs and with two great bat-like wings in the middle of the back. They sometimes walked on all their legs, and sometimes on the hindmost pair only, using the others to convey large objects of indeterminate nature. On one occasion they were spied in considerable numbers, a detachment of them wading along a shallow woodland watercourse three abreast in evidently disciplined formation. Once a specimen was seen flying—launching itself from the top of a bald, lonely hill at night and vanishing in the sky after its great flapping wings had been silhouetted an instant against the full moon.

These things seemed content, on the whole, to let mankind alone; though they were at times held responsible for the disappearance of venturesome individuals—especially persons who built houses too close to certain valleys or too high up on certain mountains. Many localities came to be known as inadvisable to settle in, the feeling persisting long after the cause was forgotten. People would look up at some of the neighboring mountain-precipices with a shudder, even when not recalling how many settlers had been lost, and how many farmhouses burnt to ashes, on the lower slopes of those grim, green sentinels.

But while according to the earliest legends the creatures would appear to have harmed only those trespassing on their privacy; there were later accounts of their curiosity respecting men, and of their attempts to establish secret outposts in the human world. There were tales of the queer claw-prints seen around farmhouse windows in the morning, and of occasional disappearances in regions outside the obviously haunted areas. Tales, besides, of buzzing voices in imitation of human speech which made surprising offers to lone travelers on roads and cart-paths in the deep woods, and of children frightened out of their wits by things seen or heard where the primal forest pressed close upon their dooryards. In the final layer of legends—the layer just preceding the decline of superstition and the abandonment of close contact with the dreaded places—there are shocked references to hermits and remote farmers who at some period of life appeared to have undergone a repellent mental change, and who were shunned and whispered about as mortals who had sold themselves to the strange beings. In one of the northeastern counties it seemed to be a fashion about 1800 to accuse eccentric and unpopular recluses of being allies or representatives of the abhorred things.

As to what the things were—explanations naturally varied. The common name applied to them was "those ones," or "the old ones," though other terms had a local and transient use. Perhaps the bulk of the Puritan settlers set them down bluntly as familiars of the devil, and made them a basis of awed theological speculation. Those with Celtic legendry in their heritage—mainly the Scotch-Irish element of New Hampshire, and their kindred who had settled in Vermont on Governor Wentworth's colonial grants—linked them vaguely with the malign fairies and "little people" of the bogs and raths, and protected themselves with scraps of incantation handed down through many generations. But the Indians had the most fantastic theories of all. While different tribal legends differed, there was a marked consensus of belief in certain vital particulars; it being unanimously agreed that the creatures were not native to this earth.

The Pennacook myths, which were the most consistent and picturesque, taught that the Winged Ones came from the Great Bear in the sky, and had mines in our earthly hills whence they took a kind of stone they could not get on any other world. They did not live here, said the myths, but merely maintained outposts and flew back with vast cargos of stone to their own stars in the north. They harmed only those earth-people who got too near them or spied upon them. Animals shunned them through instinctive hatred, not because of being hunted. They could not eat the things and animals of earth, but brought their own food from the stars. It was bad to get near them, and sometimes young hunters who went into their hills never came back. It was not good, either, to listen to what they whispered at night in the forest with voices like a bee's that tried to be like the voices of men. They knew the speech of all kinds of men—Pennacooks, Hurons, men of the Five Nations—but did not seem to have or need any speech of their own. They talked with their heads, which changed color in different ways to mean different things.

All the legendry, of course, white and Indian alike, died down during the nineteenth century, except for occasional atavistical flare-ups. The ways of the Vermonters became settled; and once their habitual paths and dwellings were established according to a certain fixed plan, they remembered less and less what fears and avoidances had determined that plan, and even that there had been any fears or avoidances. Most people simply knew that certain hilly regions were considered as highly unhealthy, unprofitable, and generally unlucky to live in, and that the farther one kept from them the better off one usually was. In time the ruts of custom and economic interest became so deeply cut in approved places that there was no longer any reason for going outside them, and the haunted hills were left deserted by accident rather than by design. Save during infrequent local scares, only wonder-loving grandmothers and retrospective nonagenarians ever whispered of beings dwelling in those hills; and even such whisperers admitted that there was not much to fear from those things now that they were used to the presence of houses and settlements, and now that human beings let their chosen territory severely alone.

All this I had known from my reading, and from certain folk tales picked up in New Hampshire; hence when the flood-time rumors began to appear, I could easily guess what imaginative background had evolved them. I took great pains to explain this to my friends, and was correspondingly amused when several contentious souls continued to insist on a possible element of truth in the reports. Such persons tried to point out that the early legends had a significant persistence and uniformity, and that the virtually unexplored nature of the Vermont hills made it unwise to be dogmatic about what might or might not dwell among them; nor could they be silenced by my assurance that all the myths were of a well-known pattern common to most of mankind and determined by early phases of imaginative experience which always produced the same type of delusion.

It was of no use to demonstrate to such opponents that the Vermont myths differed but little in essence from those universal legends of natural personification which filled the ancient world with fauns and dryads and satyrs, suggested the *kallikantzaroi* of modern Greece, and gave to wild Wales and Ireland their dark hints of strange, small, and terrible hidden races of troglodytes and burrowers. No use, either, to point out the even more startlingly similar belief of the Nepalese hill tribes in the dreaded *Mi-Go* or "Abominable Snow-Men" who lurk hideously amidst the ice and rock pinnacles of the Himalayan summits. When I brought up this evidence, my opponents turned it against me by claiming that it must imply some actual historicity for the ancient tales; that it must argue the real existence of some queer elder earth-race, driven to hiding after the advent and dominance of mankind, which might very conceivably have survived in reduced numbers to relatively recent times—or even to the present.

The more I laughed at such theories, the more these stubborn friends asseverated them; adding that even without the heritage of legend the recent reports were too clear, consistent, detailed, and sanely prosaic in manner of telling, to be completely ignored. Two or three fanatical extremists went so far as to hint at possible meanings in the ancient Indian tales which gave the hidden beings a non-terrestrial origin; citing the extravagant books of Charles Fort with their claims that voyagers from other worlds and outer space have often visited earth. Most of my foes, however, were merely romanticists who insisted on trying to transfer to real life the fantastic lore of lurking "little people" made popular by the magnificent horror-fiction of Arthur Machen.

II

As was only natural under the circumstances, this piquant debating finally got into print in the form of letters to the *Arkham Advertiser*; some of which were copied in the press of those Vermont regions whence the flood-stories came. The *Rutland Herald* gave half a page of extracts from the letters on both sides, while the *Brattleboro Reformer* reprinted one of my long historical and mythological summaries in full, with some accompanying comments in "The Pendrifter's" thoughtful column which supported and applauded my skeptical conclusions. By the spring of 1928 I was almost a well-known figure in Vermont, notwithstanding the fact that I had never set foot in the state. Then came the challenging letters from Henry Akeley which impressed me so profoundly, and which took me for the first and last time to that fascinating realm of crowded green precipices and muttering forest streams.

Most of what I now know of Henry Wentworth Akeley was gathered by correspondence with his neighbors, and with his only son in California, after my experience in his lonely farmhouse. He was, I discovered, the last representative on his home soil of a long, locally distinguished line of jurists, administrators, and gentlemen-agriculturists. In him, however, the family mentally had veered away from practical affairs to pure scholarship; so that he had been a notable student of mathematics, astronomy, biology, anthropology, and folklore at the University of Vermont. I had never previously heard of him, and he did not give many autobiographical details in his communications; but from the first I saw he was a man of character, education, and intelligence, albeit a recluse with very little worldly sophistication.

Despite the incredible nature of what he claimed, I could not help at once taking Akeley more seriously than I had taken any of the other challengers of my views. For one thing, he was really close to the actual phenomena—visible and tangible—that he speculated so grotesquely about; and for another thing, he was amazingly willing to leave his conclusions in a tentative state like a true man of science. He had no personal preferences to advance, and was always guided by what he took to be solid evidence. Of course I began by considering him mistaken, but gave him credit for being intelligently mistaken; and at no time did I emulate some of his friends in attributing his ideas, and his fear of the lonely green hills, to insanity. I could see that there was a great deal to the man, and knew that what he reported must surely come from strange circumstances deserving investigation, however little it might have to do with the fantastic causes he assigned. Later on I received from him certain material proofs which placed the matter on a somewhat different and bewilderingly bizarre basis.

I cannot do better than transcribe in full, so far as is possible, the long letter in which Akeley introduced himself, and which formed such an important landmark in my own intellectual history. It is no longer in my possession, but my memory holds almost every word of its portentous message; and again I affirm my confidence in the sanity of the man who wrote it. Here is the text—a text which reached me in the cramped, archaic-looking scrawl of one who had obviously not mingled much with the world during his sedate, scholarly life.

R.F.D. #2, Townshend, Windham Co., Vermont
May 5th, 1928

Albert N. Wilmarth, Esq.,
118 Saltonstall St,
Arkham, Mass,

My dear Sir:—
I have read with great interest the Brattleboro Reformer*'s reprint*
(Apr. 23, '28) of your letter on the recent stories of strange
bodies seen floating in our flooded streams last fall, and on the
curious folklore they so well agree with. It is easy to see why
an outlander would take the position you take, and even why
"Pendrifter" agrees with you. That is the attitude generally
taken by educated persons both in and out of Vermont, and was
my own attitude as a young man (I am now 57) before my
studies, both general and in Davenport's book, led me to do
some exploring in parts of the hills hereabouts not usually
visited.

I was directed toward such studies by the queer old tales I
used to hear from elderly farmers of the more ignorant sort,
but now I wish I had let the whole matter alone. I might say,
with all proper modesty, that the subject of anthropology and
folklore is by no means strange to me. I took a good deal of it
at college, and am familiar with most of the standard authori-
ties such as Tylor, Lubbock, Frazer, Quatrefages, Murray,
Osborn, Keith, Boule, G. Elliot Smith, and so on. It is no news
to me that tales of hidden races are as old as all mankind. I
have seen the reprints of letters from you, and those arguing
with you, in the Rutland Herald, *and guess I know about where*
your controversy stands at the present time.

What I desire to say now is, that I am afraid your adversaries are nearer right than yourself, even though all reason seems to be on your side. They are nearer right than they realize themselves— for of course they go only by theory, and cannot know what I know. If I knew as little of the matter as they, I would not feel justified in believing as they do. I would be wholly on your side.

You can see that I am having a hard time getting to the point, probably because I really dread getting to the point; but the upshot of the matter is that I have certain evidence that monstrous things do indeed live in the woods on the high hills which nobody visits. *I have not seen any of the things floating in the rivers, as reported,* but I have seen things like them *under circumstances I dread to repeat. I have seen footprints, and of late have seen them nearer my own home (I live in the old Akeley place south of Townshend Village, on the side of Dark Mountain) than I dare tell you now. And I have overheard voices in the woods at certain points that I will not even begin to describe on paper.*

At one place I heard them so much that I took a phonograph there—with a dictaphone attachment and wax blank—and I shall try to arrange to have you hear the record I got. I have run it on the machine for some of the old people up here, and one of the voices had nearly scared them paralyzed by reason of its likeness to a certain voice (that buzzing voice in the woods which Davenport mentions) that their grandmothers have told about and mimicked for them. I know what most people think of a man who tells about "hearing voices"—but before you draw conclusions just listen to this record and ask some of the older backwoods people what they think of it. If you can account for it normally, very well; but there must be something behind it. Ex nihilo nihil fit, *you know.*

Now my object in writing you is not to start an argument, but to give you information which I think a man of your tastes will find deeply interesting. This is private. Publicly I am on your side, *for certain things show me that it does not do for people to know too much about these matters. My own studies are now wholly private, and I would not think of saying anything to attract people's attention and cause them to visit the places I have explored. It is true—terribly true—that there are* non-human creatures watching us all the time*; with spies among us gathering information. It is from a wretched man who, if he was sane (as I think he was), was one of those spies, that I got a large part of my clues to the matter. He later killed himself, but I have reason to think there are others now.*

The things come from another planet, being able to live in interstellar space and fly through it *on clumsy, powerful wings which have a way of resisting the ether but which are too poor at steering to be of much use in helping them about on earth. I will tell you about this later if you do not dismiss me at once as a madman. They come here to get metals from mines that go deep under the hills,* and I think I know where they come from. *They will not hurt us if we let them alone, but no one can say what will happen if we get too curious about them. Of course a good army of men could wipe out their mining colony. That is what they are afraid of. But if that happened, more would come from* outside—*any number of them. They could easily conquer the earth, but have not tried so far because they have not needed to. They would rather leave things as they are to save bother.*

I think they mean to get rid of me because of what I have discovered. There is a great black stone with unknown hiero-glyphics half worn away which I found in the woods on Round Hill, east of here; and after I took it home everything became different. If they think I suspect too much they will either kill me or take me off the earth to where they come from. *They like to take away men of learning once in a while, to keep informed on the state of things in the human world.*

This leads me to my secondary purpose in addressing you—namely, to urge you to hush up the present debate rather than give it more publicity. People must be kept away from these hills, *and in order to effect this, their curiosity ought not to be aroused any further. Heaven knows there is peril enough anyway, with promoters and real estate men flooding Vermont with herds of summer people to overrun the wild places and cover the hills with cheap bungalows.*

I shall welcome further communication with you, and shall try to send you that phonograph record and black stone (which is so worn that photographs don't show much) by express if you are willing. I say "try" because I think those creatures have a way of tampering with things around here. There is a sullen, furtive fellow named Brown, on a farm near the village, who I think is their spy. Little by little they are trying to cut me off from our world because I know too much about their world.

They have the most amazing way of finding out what I do. You may not even get this letter. I think I shall have to leave this part of the country and go to live with my son in San Diego, Cal., if things get any worse, but it is not easy to give up the place you were born in, and where your family has lived for six generations. Also, I would hardly dare sell this house to anybody now that the creatures *have taken notice of it. They seem to be trying to get the black stone back and destroy the phonograph record, but I shall not let them if I can help it. My great police dogs always hold them back, for there are very few here as yet, and they are clumsy in getting about. As I have said, their wings are not much use for short flights on earth. I am on the very brink of deciphering that stone—in a very terrible way—and with your knowledge of folklore you may be able to supply missing links enough to help me. I suppose you know all about the fearful myths antedating the coming of man to the earth—the Yog-Sothoth and Cthulhu cycles—which are hinted at in the* Necronomicon. *I had access to a copy of that once, and hear that you have one in your college library under lock and key.*

To conclude, Mr Wilmarth, I think that with our respective studies we can be very useful to each other. I don't wish to put you in any peril, and suppose I ought to warn you that possession of the stone and the record won't be very safe; but I think you will find any risks worth running for the sake of knowledge. I will drive down to Newfane or Brattleboro to send whatever you authorize me to send, for the express offices there are more to be trusted. I might say that I live quite alone now, since I can't keep hired help any more. They won't stay because of the things that try to get near the house at night, and that keep the dogs barking continually. I am glad I didn't get as deep as this into the business while my wife was alive, for it would have driven her mad.

Hoping that I am not bothering you unduly, and that you will decide to get in touch with me rather than throw this letter into the waste basket as a madman's raving, I am

Yrs. very truly,
HENRY W. AKELEY

P.S. I am making some extra prints of certain photographs taken by me, which I think will help to prove a number of the points I have touched on. The old people think they are monstrously true. I shall send you these very soon if you are interested. H.W.A.

It would be difficult to describe my sentiments upon reading this strange document for the first time. By all ordinary rules, I ought to have laughed more loudly at these extravagances than at the far milder theories which had previously moved me to mirth; yet something in the tone of the letter made me take it with paradoxical seriousness. Not that I believed for a moment in the hidden race from the stars which my correspondent spoke of; but that, after some grave preliminary doubts, I grew to feel oddly sure of his sanity and sincerity, and of his confrontation by some genuine though singular and abnormal phenomenon which he could not explain except in this imaginative way. It could not be as he thought it, I reflected, yet on the other hand it could not be otherwise than worthy of investigation. The man seemed unduly excited and alarmed about something, but it was hard to think that all cause was lacking. He was so specific and logical in certain ways—and after all, his yarn did fit in so perplexingly well with some of the old myths—even the wildest Indian legends.

That he had really overheard disturbing voices in the hills, and had really found the black stone he spoke about, was wholly possible despite the crazy inferences he had made—inferences probably suggested by the man who had claimed to be a spy of the outer beings and had later killed himself. It was easy to deduce that this man must have been wholly insane, but that he probably had a streak of perverse outward logic which made the naive Akeley—already prepared for such things by his folklore studies—believe his tale. As for the latest developments—it appeared from his inability to keep hired help that Akeley's humbler rustic neighbors were as convinced as he that his house was besieged by uncanny things at night. The dogs really barked, too.

And then the matter of that phonograph record, which I could not but believe he had obtained in the way he said. It must mean something; whether animal noises deceptively like human speech, or the speech of some hidden, night-haunting human being decayed to a state not much above that of lower animals. From this my thoughts went back to the black hieroglyphed stone, and to speculations upon what it might mean. Then, too, what of the photographs which Akeley said he was about to send, and which the old people had found so convincingly terrible?

As I re-read the cramped handwriting I felt as never before that my credulous opponents might have more on their side than I had conceded. After all, there might be some queer and perhaps hereditarily misshapen outcasts in those shunned hills, even though no such race of star-born monsters as folklore claimed. And if there were, then the presence of strange bodies in the flooded streams would not be wholly beyond belief. Was it too presumptuous to suppose that both the old legends and the recent reports had this much of reality behind them? But even as I harbored these doubts I felt ashamed that so fantastic a piece of bizarrerie as Henry Akeley's wild letter had brought them up.

In the end I answered Akeley's letter, adopting a tone of friendly interest and soliciting further particulars. His reply came almost by return mail; and contained, true to promise, a number of kodak views of scenes and objects illustrating what he had to tell. Glancing at these pictures as I took them from the envelope, I felt a curious sense of fright and nearness to forbidden things; for in spite of the vagueness of most of them, they had a damnably suggestive power which was intensified by the fact of their being genuine photographs—actual optical links with what they portrayed, and the product of an impersonal transmitting process without prejudice, fallibility, or mendacity.

The more I looked at them, the more I saw that my serious estimate of Akeley and his story had not been unjustified. Certainly, these pictures carried conclusive evidence of something in the Vermont hills which was at least vastly outside the radius of our common knowledge and belief. The worst thing of all was the footprint—a view taken where the sun shone on a mud patch somewhere in a deserted upland. This was no cheaply counterfeited thing, I could see at a glance; for the sharply defined pebbles and grass-blades in the field of vision gave a clear index of scale and left no possibility of a tricky double exposure. I have called the thing a "footprint", but "claw-print" would be a better term. Even now I can scarcely describe it save to say that it was hideously crab-like, and that there seemed to be some ambiguity about its direction. It was not a very deep or fresh print, but seemed to be about the size of an average man's foot. From a central pad, pairs of saw-toothed nippers projected in opposite directions—quite baffling as to function, if indeed the whole object were exclusively an organ of locomotion.

Another photograph—evidently a time-exposure taken in deep shadow—was of the mouth of a woodland cave, with a boulder of rounded regularity choking the aperture. On the bare ground in front of it one could just discern a dense network of curious tracks, and when I studied the picture with a magnifier I felt uneasily sure that the tracks were like the one in the other view. A third picture showed a druid-like circle of standing stones on the summit of a wild hill. Around the cryptic circle the grass was very much beaten down and worn away, though I could not detect any footprints even with the glass. The extreme remoteness of the place was apparent from the veritable sea of tenantless mountains which formed the background and stretched away toward a misty horizon.

But if the most disturbing of all the views was that of the footprint, the most curiously suggestive was that of the great black stone found in the Round Hill woods. Akeley had photographed it on what was evidently his study table, for I could see rows of books and a bust of Milton in the background. The thing, as nearly as one might guess, had faced the camera vertically with a somewhat irregularly curved surface of one by two feet; but to say anything definite about that surface, or about the general shape of the whole mass, almost defies the power of language. What outlandish geometrical principles had guided its cutting—for artificially cut it surely was—I could not even begin to guess; and never before had I seen anything which struck me as so strangely and unmistakably alien to this world. Of the hieroglyphics on the surface I could discern very few, but one or two that I did see gave me rather a shock. Of course they might be fraudulent, for others besides myself had read the monstrous and abhorred *Necronomicon* of the mad Arab Abdul Alhazred; but it nevertheless made me shiver to recognize certain ideographs which study had taught me to link with the most blood-curdling and blasphemous whispers of things that had had a kind of mad half-existence before the earth and the other inner worlds of the solar system were made.

Of the five remaining pictures, three were of swamp and hill scenes which seemed to bear traces of hidden and unwholesome tenancy. Another was of a queer mark in the ground very near Akeley's house, which he said he had photographed the morning after a night on which the dogs had barked more violently than usual. It was very blurred, and one could really draw no certain conclusions from it; but it did seem fiendishly like that other mark or claw-print photographed on the deserted upland. The final picture was of the Akeley place itself; a trim white house of two stories and attic, about a century and a quarter old, and with a well-kept lawn and stone-bordered path leading up to a tastefully carved Georgian doorway. There were several huge police dogs on the lawn, squatting near a pleasant-faced man with a close-cropped gray beard whom I took to be Akeley himself—his own photographer, one might infer from the tube-connected bulb in his right hand.

From the pictures I turned to the bulky, closely written letter itself; and for the next three hours was immersed in a gulf of unutterable horror. Where Akeley had given only outlines before, he now entered into minute details; presenting long transcripts of words overheard in the woods at night, long accounts of monstrous pinkish forms spied in thickets at twilight on the hills, and a terrible cosmic narrative derived from the application of profound and varied scholarship to the endless bygone discourses of the mad self-styled spy who had killed himself. I found myself faced by names and terms that I had heard elsewhere in the most hideous of connections—Yuggoth, Great Cthulhu, Tsathoggua, Yog-Sothoth, R'lyeh, Nyarlathotep, Azathoth, Hastur, Yian, Leng, the Lake of Hali, Bethmoora, the Yellow Sign, L'mur-Kathulos, Bran, and the Magnum Innominandum—and was drawn back through nameless eons and inconceivable dimensions to worlds of elder, outer entity at which the crazed author of the *Necronomicon* had only guessed in the vaguest way. I was told of the pits of primal life, and of the streams that had trickled down therefrom; and finally, of the tiny rivulet from one of those streams which had become entangled with the destinies of our own earth.

My brain whirled; and where before I had attempted to explain things away, I now began to believe in the most abnormal and incredible wonders. The array of vital evidence was damnably vast and overwhelming; and the cool, scientific attitude of Akeley—an attitude removed as far as imaginable from the demented, the fanatical, the hysterical, or even the extravagantly speculative—had a tremendous effect on my thought and judgment. By the time I laid the frightful letter aside I could understand the fears he had come to entertain, and was ready to do anything in my power to keep people away from those wild, haunted hills. Even now, when time has dulled the impression and made me half question my own experience and horrible doubts, there are things in that letter of Akeley's which I would not quote, or even form into words on paper. I am almost glad that the letter and record and photographs are gone now—and I wish, for reasons I shall soon make clear, that the new planet beyond Neptune had not been discovered.

With the reading of that letter my public debating about the Vermont horror permanently ended. Arguments from opponents remained unanswered or put off with promises, and eventually the controversy petered out into oblivion. During late May and June I was in constant correspondence with Akeley; though once in a while a letter would be lost, so that we would have to retrace our ground and perform considerable laborious copying. What we were trying to do, as a whole, was to compare notes in matters of obscure mythological scholarship and arrive at a clearer correlation of the Vermont horrors with the general body of primitive world legend.

For one thing, we virtually decided that these morbidities and the hellish Himalayan *Mi-Go* were one and the same order of incarnated nightmare. There were also absorbing zoological conjectures, which I would have referred to Professor Dexter in my own college but for Akeley's imperative command to tell no one of the matter before us. If I seem to disobey that command now, it is only because I think that at this stage a warning about those farther Vermont hills—and about those Himalayan peaks which bold explorers are more and more determined to ascend—is more conducive to public safety than silence would be. One specific thing we were leading up to was a deciphering of the hieroglyphics on that infamous black stone—a deciphering which might well place us in possession of secrets deeper and more dizzying than any formerly known to man.

III

Toward the end of June the phonograph record came—shipped from Brattleboro, since Akeley was unwilling to trust conditions on the branch line north of there. He had begun to feel an increased sense of espionage, aggravated by the loss of some of our letters; and said much about the insidious deeds of certain men whom he considered tools and agents of the hidden beings. Most of all he suspected the surly farmer Walter Brown, who lived alone on a run-down hillside place near the deep woods, and who was often seen loafing around corners in Brattleboro, Bellows Falls, Newfane, and South Londonderry in the most inexplicable and seemingly unmotivated way. Brown's voice, he felt convinced, was one of those he had overheard on a certain occasion in a very terrible conversation; and he had once found a footprint or claw-print near Brown's house which might possess the most ominous significance. It had been curiously near some of Brown's own footprints—footprints that faced toward it.

So the record was shipped from Brattleboro, whither Akeley drove in his Ford car along the lonely Vermont back roads. He confessed in an accompanying note that he was beginning to be afraid of those roads, and that he would not even go into Townshend for supplies now except in broad daylight. It did not pay, he repeated again and again, to know too much unless one were very remote from those silent and problematical hills. He would be going to California pretty soon to live with his son, though it was hard to leave a place where all one's memories and ancestral feelings centered.

Before trying the record on the commercial machine which I borrowed from the college administration building I carefully went over all the explanatory matter in Akeley's various letters. This record, he had said, was obtained about 1 a.m. on May 1st, 1915, near the closed mouth of a cave where the wooded west slope of Dark Mountain rises out of Lee's Swamp. The place had always been unusually plagued with strange voices, this being the reason he had brought the phonograph, dictaphone, and blank in expectation of results. Former experience had told him that May Eve—the hideous Sabbat-night of underground European legend—would probably be more fruitful than any other date, and he was not disappointed. It was noteworthy, though, that he never again heard voices at that particular spot.

Unlike most of the overheard forest voices, the substance of the record was quasi-ritualistic, and included one palpably human voice which Akeley had never been able to place. It was not Brown's, but seemed to be that of a man of greater cultivation. The second voice, however, was the real crux of the thing—for this was the accursed *buzzing* which had no likeness to humanity despite the human words which it uttered in good English grammar and a scholarly accent.

The recording phonograph and dictaphone had not worked uniformly well, and had of course been at a great disadvantage because of the remote and muffled nature of the overheard ritual; so that the actual speech secured was very fragmentary. Akeley had given me a transcript of what he believed the spoken words to be, and I glanced through this again as I prepared the machine for action. The text was darkly mysterious rather than openly horrible, though a knowledge of its origin and manner of gathering gave it all the associative horror which any words could well possess. I will present it here in full as I remember it—and I am fairly confident that I know it correctly by heart, not only from reading the transcript, but from playing the record itself over and over again. It is not a thing which one might readily forget!

(INDISTINGUISHABLE SOUNDS)

(A CULTIVATED MALE HUMAN VOICE)

. . is the Lord of the Woods, even to . . . and the gifts of the men of Leng . . . so from the wells of night to the gulfs of space, and from the gulfs of space to the wells of night, ever the praises of Great Cthulhu, of Tsathoggua, and of Him Who is not to be Named. Ever Their praises, and abundance to the Black Goat of the Woods. Iä! Shub-Niggurath! The Goat with a Thousand Young!

(A BUZZING IMITATION OF HUMAN SPEECH)

Iä! Shub-Niggurath! The Black Goat of the Woods with a Thousand Young!

(HUMAN VOICE)

And it has come to pass that the Lord of the Woods, being . . . seven and nine, down the onyx steps . . . (tri)butes to Him in the Gulf, Azathoth, He of Whom Thou hast taught us marv(els) . . . on the wings of night out beyond space, out beyond th . . . to That whereof Yuggoth is the youngest child, rolling alone in black ether at the rim. . . .

(BUZZING VOICE)

. . go out among men and find the ways thereof, that He in the Gulf may know. To Nyarlathotep, Mighty Messenger, must all things be told. And He shall put on the semblance of men, the waxen mask and the robe that hides, and come down from the world of Seven Suns to mock. . . .

(HUMAN VOICE)

. . . (Nyarl)athotep, Great Messenger, bringer of strange joy to Yuggoth through the void, Father of the Million Favored Ones, Stalker among. . . .

(SPEECH CUT OFF BY END OF RECORD)

Such were the words for which I was to listen when I started the phonograph. It was with a trace of genuine dread and reluctance that I pressed the lever and heard the preliminary scratching of the sapphire point, and I was glad that the first faint, fragmentary words were in a human voice—a mellow, educated voice which seemed vaguely Bostonian in accent, and which was certainly not that of any native of the Vermont hills. As I listened to the tantalizingly feeble rendering, I seemed to find the speech identical with Akeley's carefully prepared transcript. On it chanted, in that mellow Bostonian voice, ". . . Iä! Shub-Niggurath! The Goat with a Thousand Young! . . ."

And then I heard *the other voice.* To this hour I shudder retrospectively when I think of how it struck me, prepared though I was by Akeley's accounts. Those to whom I have since described the record profess to find nothing but cheap imposture or madness in it; but *could they have heard the accursed thing itself,* or read the bulk of Akeley's correspondence (especially that terrible and encyclopedic second letter), I know they would think differently. It is, after all, a tremendous pity that I did not disobey Akeley and play the record for others—a tremendous pity, too, that all of his letters were lost. To me, with my first-hand impression of the actual sounds, and with my knowledge of the background and surrounding circumstances, the voice was a monstrous thing. It swiftly followed the human voice in ritualistic response, but in my imagination it was a morbid echo winging its way across unimaginable abysses from unimaginable outer hells. It is more than two years now since I last ran off that blasphemous waxen cylinder; but at this moment, and at all other moments, I can still hear that feeble, fiendish buzzing as it reached me for the first time.

Iä! Shub-Niggurath! The Black Goat of the Woods with a Thousand Young!

But though that voice is always in my ears, I have not even yet been able to analyze it well enough for a graphic description. It was like the drone of some loathsome, gigantic insect ponderously shaped into the articulate speech of an alien species, and I am perfectly certain that the organs producing it can have no resemblance to the vocal organs of man, or indeed to those of any of the mammalia. There were singularities in timbre, range, and overtones which placed this phenomenon wholly outside the sphere of humanity and earth-life. Its sudden advent that first time almost stunned me, and I heard the rest of the record through in a sort of abstracted daze. When the longer passage of buzzing came, there was a sharp intensification of that feeling of blasphemous infinity which had struck me during the shorter and earlier passage. At last the record ended abruptly, during an unusually clear speech of the human and Bostonian voice; but I sat stupidly staring long after the machine had automatically stopped.

I hardly need say that I gave that shocking record many another playing, and that I made exhaustive attempts at analysis and comment in comparing notes with Akeley. It would be both useless and disturbing to repeat here all that we concluded; but I may hint that we agreed in believing we had secured a clue to the source of some of the most repulsive primordial customs in the cryptic elder religions of mankind. It seemed plain to us, also, that there were ancient and elaborate alliances between the hidden outer creatures and certain members of the human race. How extensive these alliances were, and how their state today might compare with their state in earlier ages, we had no means of guessing; yet at best there was room for a limit-less amount of horrified speculation. There seemed to be an awful, immemorial linkage in several definite stages betwixt man and name-less infinity. The blasphemies which appeared on earth, it was hinted, came from the dark planet Yuggoth, at the rim of the solar system; but this was itself merely the populous outpost of a frightful interstellar race whose ultimate source must lie far outside even the Einsteinian space-time continuum or greatest known cosmos.

Meanwhile we continued to discuss the black stone and the best way of getting it to Arkham—Akeley deeming it inadvisable to have me visit him at the scene of his nightmare studies. For some reason or other, Akeley was afraid to trust the thing to any ordinary or expected transportation route. His final idea was to take it across county to Bellows Falls and ship it on the Boston and Maine system through Keene and Winchendon and Fitchburg, even though this would necessitate his driving along somewhat lonelier and more forest-traversing hill roads than the main highway to Brattleboro. He said he had noticed a man around the express office at Brattleboro when he had sent the phonograph record, whose actions and expression had been far from reassuring. This man had seemed too anxious to talk with the clerks, and had taken the train on which the record was shipped. Akeley confessed that he had not felt strictly at ease about that record until he heard from me of its safe receipt.

About this time—the second week in July—another letter of mine went astray, as I learned through an anxious communication from Akeley. After that he told me to address him no more at Townshend, but to send all mail in care of the General Delivery at Brattleboro; whither he would make frequent trips either in his car or on the motor-coach line which had lately replaced passenger service on the lagging branch railway. I could see that he was getting more and more anxious, for he went into much detail about the increased barking of the dogs on moonless nights, and about the fresh claw-prints he sometimes found in the road and in the mud at the back of his farmyard when morning came. Once he told about a veritable army of prints drawn up in a line facing an equally thick and resolute line of dog-tracks, and sent a loathsomely disturbing kodak picture to prove it. That was after a night on which the dogs had outdone themselves in barking and howling.

On the morning of Wednesday, July 18th, I received a telegram from Bellows Falls, in which Akeley said he was expressing the black stone over the B. & M. on Train No. 5508, leaving Bellows Falls at 12:15 p.m., standard time, and due at the North Station in Boston at 4:12 p.m. It ought, I calculated, to get up to Arkham at least by the next noon; and accordingly I stayed in all Thursday morning to receive it. But noon came and went without its advent, and when I telephoned down to the express office I was informed that no shipment for me had arrived. My next act, performed amidst a growing alarm, was to give a long-distance call to the express agent at the Boston North Station; and I was scarcely surprised to learn that my consignment had not appeared. Train No. 5508 had pulled in only 35 minutes late on the day before, but had contained no box addressed to me. The agent promised, however, to institute a searching inquiry; and I ended the day by sending Akeley a night-letter outlining the situation.

With commendable promptness a report came from the Boston office on the following afternoon, the agent telephoning as soon as he learned the facts. It seemed that the railway express clerk on No. 5508 had been able to recall an incident which might have much bearing on my loss—an argument with a very curious-voiced man, lean, sandy, and rustic-looking, when the train was waiting at Keene, N.H., shortly after one o'clock standard time.

The man, he said, was greatly excited about a heavy box which he claimed to expect, but which was neither on the train nor entered on the company's books. He had given the name of Stanley Adams, and had had such a queerly thick droning voice, that it made the clerk abnormally dizzy and sleepy to listen to him. The clerk could not remember quite how the conversation had ended, but recalled starting into a fuller awakeness when the train began to move. The Boston agent added that this clerk was a young man of wholly unquestioned veracity and reliability, of known antecedents and long with the company.

That evening I went to Boston to interview the clerk in person, having obtained his name and address from the office. He was a frank, prepossessing fellow, but I saw that he could add nothing to his original account. Oddly, he was scarcely sure that he could even recognize the strange inquirer again. Realizing that he had no more to tell, I returned to Arkham and sat up till morning writing letters to Akeley, to the express company, and to the police department and station agent in Keene. I felt that the strange-voiced man who had so queerly affected the clerk must have a pivotal place in the ominous business, and hoped that Keene station employees and telegraph-office records might tell something about him and about how he happened to make his inquiry when and where he did.

I must admit, however, that all my investigations came to nothing. The queer-voiced man had indeed been noticed around the Keene station in the early afternoon of July 18th, and one lounger seemed to couple him vaguely with a heavy box; but he was altogether unknown, and had not been seen before or since. He had not visited the telegraph office or received any message so far as could be learned, nor had any message which might justly be considered a notice of the black stone's presence on No. 5508 come through the office for anyone. Naturally Akeley joined with me in conducting these inquiries, and even made a personal trip to Keene to question the people around the station; but his attitude toward the matter was more fatalistic than mine. He seemed to find the loss of the box a portentous and menacing fulfillment of inevitable tendencies, and had no real hope at all of its recovery. He spoke of the undoubted telepathic and hypnotic powers of the hill creatures and their agents, and in one letter hinted that he did not believe the stone was on this earth any longer. For my part, I was duly enraged, for I had felt there was at least a chance of learning profound and astonishing things from the old, blurred hiero-glyphs. The matter would have rankled bitterly in my mind had not Akeley's immediate subsequent letters brought up a new phase of the whole horrible hill problem which at once seized all my attention.

IV

The unknown things, Akeley wrote in a script grown pitifully trem-ulous, had begun to close in on him with a wholly new degree of determination. The nocturnal barking of the dogs whenever the moon was dim or absent was hideous now, and there had been attempts to molest him on the lonely roads he had to traverse by day. On the second of August, while bound for the village in his car, he had found a tree-trunk laid in his path at a point where the highway ran through a deep patch of woods; while the savage barking of the two great dogs he had with him told all too well of the things which must have been lurking near. What would have happened had the dogs not been there, he did not dare guess—but he never went out now without at least two of his faithful and powerful pack. Other road experiences had occurred on August 5th and 6th; a shot grazing his car on one occasion, and the barking of the dogs telling of unholy woodland presences on the other.

On August 15th I received a frantic letter which disturbed me greatly, and which made me wish Akeley could put aside his lonely reticence and call in the aid of the law. There had been frightful happenings on the night of the 12th–13th, bullets flying outside the farmhouse, and three of the twelve great dogs being found shot dead in the morning. There were myriads of claw-prints in the road, with the human prints of Walter Brown among them. Akeley had started to telephone to Brattleboro for more dogs, but the wire had gone dead before he had a chance to say much. Later he went to Brattleboro in his car, and learned there that linemen had found the main telephone cable neatly cut at a point where it ran through the deserted hills north of Newfane. But he was about to start home with four fine new dogs, and several cases of ammunition for his big-game repeating rifle. The letter was written at the post office in Brattleboro, and came through to me without delay.

My attitude toward the matter was by this time quickly slipping from a scientific to an alarmedly personal one. I was afraid for Akeley in his remote, lonely farmhouse, and half afraid for myself because of my now definite connection with the strange hill problem. The thing was *reaching out* so. Would it suck me in and engulf me? In replying to his letter I urged him to seek help, and hinted that I might take action myself if he did not. I spoke of visiting Vermont in person in spite of his wishes, and of helping him explain the situation to the proper authorities. In return, however, I received only a telegram from Bellows Falls which read thus:

APPRECIATE YOUR POSITION BUT CAN DO NOTHING. TAKE NO ACTION YOURSELF FOR IT COULD ONLY HARM BOTH. WAIT FOR EXPLANATION.

HENRY AKELY

But the affair was steadily deepening. Upon my replying to the telegram I received a shaky note from Akeley with the astonishing news that he had not only never sent the wire, but had not received the letter from me to which it was an obvious reply. Hasty inquiries by him at Bellows Falls had brought out that the message was deposited by a strange sandy-haired man with a curiously thick, droning voice, though more than this he could not learn. The clerk showed him the original text as scrawled in pencil by the sender, but the handwriting was wholly unfamiliar. It was noticeable that the signature was misspelled—A-K-E-L-Y, without the second "E." Certain conjectures were inevitable, but amidst the obvious crisis he did not stop to elaborate upon them.

He spoke of the death of more dogs and the purchase of still others, and of the exchange of gunfire which had become a settled feature each moonless night. Brown's prints, and the prints of at least one or two more shod human figures, were now found regularly among the claw-prints in the road, and at the back of the farmyard. It was, Akeley admitted, a pretty bad business; and before long he would probably have to go to live with his California son whether or not he could sell the old place. But it was not easy to leave the only spot one could really think of as home. He must try to hang on a little longer; perhaps he could scare off the intruders—especially if he openly gave up all further attempts to penetrate their secrets.

Writing Akeley at once, I renewed my offers of aid, and spoke

again of visiting him and helping him convince the authorities of his
dire peril. In his reply he seemed less set against that plan than his
past attitude would have led one to predict, but said he would like
to hold off a little while longer—long enough to get his things in
order and reconcile himself to the idea of leaving an almost morbidly
cherished birthplace. People looked askance at his studies and speculations, and it would be better to get quietly off without setting the
countryside in a turmoil and creating widespread doubts of his own
sanity. He had had enough, he admitted, but he wanted to make a
dignified exit if he could.

This letter reached me on the 28th of August, and I prepared and
mailed as encouraging a reply as I could. Apparently the encouragement had effect, for Akeley had fewer terrors to report when he
acknowledged my note. He was not very optimistic, though, and
expressed the belief that it was only the full moon season which was
holding the creatures off. He hoped there would not be many densely
cloudy nights, and talked vaguely of boarding in Brattleboro when
the moon waned. Again I wrote him encouragingly, but on September
5th there came a fresh communication which had obviously crossed
my letter in the mails; and to this I could not give any such hopeful
response. In view of its importance I believe I had better give it in
full—as best I can do from memory of the shaky script. It ran substantially as follows:

Monday

Dear Wilmarth—
A rather discouraging P.S. to my last. Last night was thickly
cloudy—though no rain—and not a bit of moonlight got through.
Things were pretty bad, and I think the end is getting near, in
spite of all we have hoped. After midnight something landed on
the roof of the house, and the dogs all rushed up to see what
it was. I could hear them snapping and tearing around, and

then one managed to get on the roof by jumping from the low ell. There was a terrible fight up there, and I heard a frightful buzzing which I'll never forget. And then there was a shocking smell. About the same time bullets came through the window and nearly grazed me. I think the main line of the hill creatures had got close to the house when the dogs divided because of the roof business. What was up there I don't know yet, but I'm afraid the creatures are learning to steer better with their space wings. I put out the light and used the windows for loopholes, and raked all around the house with rifle fire aimed just high enough not to hit the dogs. That seemed to end the business, but in the morning I found great pools of blood in the yard, beside pools of a green sticky stuff that had the worst odor I have ever smelled. I climbed up on the roof and found more of the sticky stuff there. Five of the dogs were killed—I'm afraid I hit one by aiming too low, for he was shot in the back. Now I am setting the panes the shots broke, and am going to Brattleboro for more dogs. I guess the men at the kennels think I am crazy. Will drop another note later. Suppose I'll be ready for moving in a week or two, though it nearly kills me to think of it.

Hastily—
AKELEY

But this was not the only letter from Akeley to cross mine. On the next morning—September 6th—still another came; this time a frantic scrawl which utterly unnerved me and put me at a loss what to say or do next. Again I cannot do better than quote the text as faithfully as memory will let me.

Tuesday
Clouds didn't break, so no moon again—and going into the wane anyhow. I'd have the house wired for electricity and put

*in a searchlight if I didn't know they'd cut the cables as fast
as they could be mended.*

*I think I am going crazy. It may be that all I have ever written
you is a dream or madness. It was bad enough before, but this
time it is too much.* They talked to me last night—*talked in that
cursed buzzing voice and told me things* that I dare not repeat to
you. *I heard them plainly over the barking of the dogs, and once
when they were drowned out* a human voice helped them. *Keep
out of this, Wilmarth—it is worse than either you or I ever
suspected.* They don't mean to let me get to California now—they
want to take me off alive, or what theoretically and mentally
amounts to alive—*not only to Yuggoth, but beyond that—away
outside the galaxy* and possibly beyond the last curved rim of
space. *I told them I wouldn't go where they wish,* or in the terrible
way they propose to take me, *but I'm afraid it will be no use.
My place is so far out that they may come by day as well as by
night before long. Six more dogs killed, and I felt presences all
along the wooded parts of the road when I drove to Brattleboro
today.*

*It was a mistake for me to try to send you that phonograph
record and black stone. Better smash the record before it's too
late. Will drop you another line tomorrow if I'm still here. Wish
I could arrange to get my books and things to Brattleboro and
board there. I would run off without anything if I could, but
something inside my mind holds me back. I can slip out to
Brattleboro, where I ought to be safe, but I feel just as much a
prisoner there as at the house. And I seem to know that I couldn't
get much farther even if I dropped everything and tried. It is
horrible—don't get mixed up in this.*

                                                    Yrs—AKELEY

I did not sleep at all the night after receiving this terrible thing, and was utterly baffled as to Akeley's remaining degree of sanity. The substance of the note was wholly insane, yet the manner of expression—in view of all that had gone before—had a grimly potent quality of convincingness. I made no attempt to answer it, thinking it better to wait until Akeley might have time to reply to my latest communication. Such a reply indeed came on the following day, though the fresh material in it quite overshadowed any of the points brought up by the letter it nominally answered. Here is what I recall of the text, scrawled and blotted as it was in the course of a plainly frantic and hurried composition.

Wednesday

W—

Yr letter came, but it's no use to discuss anything any more. I am fully resigned. Wonder that I have even enough will power left to fight them off. Can't escape even if I were willing to give up everything and run. They'll get me.

Had a letter from them yesterday—R.F.D. man brought it while I was at Brattleboro. Typed and postmarked Bellows Falls. Tells what they want to do with me—I can't repeat it. Look out for yourself, too! Smash that record. Cloudy nights keep up, and moon waning all the time. Wish I dared to get help—it might brace up my will power—but everyone who would dare to come at all would call me crazy unless there happened to be some proof. Couldn't ask people to come for no reason at all—am all out of touch with everybody and have been for years.

*But I haven't told you the worst, Wilmarth. Brace up to read this, for it will give you a shock. I am telling the truth, though. It is this—*I have seen and touched one of the things, or part of one of the things. *God, man, but it's awful! It was dead, of course. One of the dogs had it, and I found it near the kennel this morning. I tried to save it in the woodshed to convince* *people of the whole thing, but it all evaporated in a few hours. Nothing left. You know, all those things in the rivers were seen only on the first morning after the flood. And here's the worst. I tried to photograph it for you, but when I developed the film* there wasn't anything visible except the woodshed. *What can the thing have been made of? I saw it and felt it, and they all leave footprints. It was surely made of matter—but what kind of matter? The shape can't be described. It was a great crab with a lot of pyramided fleshy rings or knots of thick, ropy stuff covered with feelers where a man's head would be. That green sticky stuff is its blood or juice. And there are more of them due on earth any minute.*

Walter Brown is missing—hasn't been seen loafing around any of his usual corners in the villages hereabouts. I must have got him with one of my shots, though the creatures always seem to try to take their dead and wounded away.

Got into town this afternoon without any trouble, but am afraid they're beginning to hold off because they're sure of me. Am writing this in Brattleboro P.O. This may be goodbye—if it is, write my son George Goodenough Akeley, 176 Pleasant St, San Diego, Cal., but don't come up here. *Write the boy if you don't hear from me in a week, and watch the papers for news.*

I'm going to play my last two cards now—if I have the will power left. First to try poison gas on the things (I've got the right chemicals and have fixed up masks for myself and the dogs) and then if that doesn't work, tell the sheriff. They can lock me in a madhouse if they want to—it'll be better than what the other creatures *would do. Perhaps I can get them to pay attention to the prints around the house—they are faint, but I can find them every morning. Suppose, though, police would say I faked them somehow; for they all think I'm a queer character.*

Must try to have a state policeman spend a night here and

see for himself—though it would be just like the creatures to learn about it and hold off that night. They cut my wires whenever I try to telephone in the night—the linemen think it is very queer, and may testify for me if they don't go and imagine I cut them myself. I haven't tried to keep them repaired for over a week now.

I could get some of the ignorant people to testify for me about the reality of the horrors, but everybody laughs at what they say, and anyway, they have shunned my place for so long that they don't know any of the new events. You couldn't get one of those run-down farmers to come within a mile of my house for love or money. The mail-carrier hears what they say and jokes me about it—God! If I only dared tell him how real it is! I think I'll try to get him to notice the prints, but he comes in the afternoon and they're usually about gone by that time. If I kept one by setting a box or pan over it, he'd think surely it was a fake or joke.

Wish I hadn't gotten to be such a hermit, so folks don't drop around as they used to. I've never dared show the black stone or the kodak pictures, or play that record, to anybody but the ignorant people. The others would say I faked the whole business and do nothing but laugh. But I may yet try showing the pictures. They give those claw-prints clearly, even if the things that made them can't be photographed. What a shame nobody else saw that thing this morning before it went to nothing!

But I don't know as I care. After what I've been through, a madhouse is as good a place as any. The doctors can help me make up my mind to get away from this house, and that is all that will save me.

Write my son George if you don't hear soon. Goodbye, smash that record, and don't mix up in this.

Yrs—AKELEY

The letter frankly plunged me into the blackest of terror. I did not know what to say in answer, but scratched off some incoherent words of advice and encouragement and sent them by registered mail. I recall urging Akeley to move to Brattleboro at once, and place himself under the protection of the authorities; adding that I would come to that town with the phonograph record and help convince the courts of his sanity. It was time, too, I think I wrote, to alarm the people generally against this thing in their midst. It will be observed that at this moment of stress my own belief in all Akeley had told and claimed was virtually complete, though I did think his failure to get a picture of the dead monster was due not to any freak of Nature but to some excited slip of his own.

V

Then, apparently crossing my incoherent note and reaching me Saturday afternoon, September 8th, came that curiously different and calming letter neatly typed on a new machine; that strange letter of reassurance and invitation which must have marked so prodigious a transition in the whole nightmare drama of the lonely hills. Again I will quote from memory—seeking for special reasons to preserve as much of the flavor of the style as I can. It was postmarked Bellows Falls, and the signature as well as the body of the letter was typed—as is frequent with beginners in typing. The text, though, was marvelously accurate for a tyro's work; and I concluded that Akeley must have used a machine at some previous period—perhaps in college. To say that the letter relieved me would be only fair, yet beneath my relief lay a substratum of uneasiness. If Akeley had been sane in his terror, was he now sane in his deliverance? And the sort of "improved rapport" mentioned . . . what was it? The entire thing implied such a diametrical reversal of Akeley's previous attitude! But here is the substance of the text, carefully transcribed from a memory in which I take some pride.

Townshend, Vermont,
Thursday, Sept. 6th, 1928.

My dear Wilmarth:—
It gives me great pleasure to be able to set you at rest regarding all the silly things I've been writing you. I say "silly," although by that I mean my frightened attitude rather than my descriptions of certain phenomena. Those phenomena are real and important enough; my mistake had been in establishing an anomalous attitude toward them.

I think I mentioned that my strange visitors were beginning to communicate with me, and to attempt such communication. Last night this exchange of speech became actual. In response to certain signals I admitted to the house a messenger from those outside—a fellow-human, let me hasten to say. He told me much that neither you nor I had even begun to guess, and showed clearly how totally we had misjudged and misinterpreted the purpose of the Outer Ones in maintaining their secret colony on this planet.

It seems that the evil legends about what they have offered to men, and what they wish in connection with the earth, are wholly the result of an ignorant misconception of allegorical speech—speech, of course, molded by cultural backgrounds and thought-habits vastly different from anything we dream of. My own conjectures, I freely own, shot as widely past the mark as any of the guesses of illiterate farmers and savage Indians. What I had thought morbid and shameful and ignominious is in reality awesome and mind-expanding and even glorious—*my previous estimate being merely a phase of man's eternal tendency to hate and fear and shrink from the* utterly different.

Now I regret the harm I have inflicted upon these alien and incredible beings in the course of our nightly skirmishes. If only

I had consented to talk peacefully and reasonably with them in the first place! But they bear me no grudge, their emotions being organized very differently from ours. It is their misfortune to have had as their human agents in Vermont some very inferior specimens—the late Walter Brown, for example. He prejudiced me vastly against them. Actually, they have never knowingly harmed men, but have often been cruelly wronged and spied upon by our species. There is a whole secret cult of evil men (a man of your mystical erudition will understand me when I link them with Hastur and the Yellow Sign) devoted to the purpose of tracking them down and injuring them on behalf of monstrous powers from other dimensions. It is against these aggressors—not against normal humanity—that the drastic precautions of the Outer Ones are directed. Incidentally, I learned that many of our lost letters were stolen not by the Outer Ones but by the emissaries of this malign cult.

All that the Outer Ones wish of man is peace and non-molestation and an increasing intellectual rapport. This latter is absolutely necessary now that our inventions and devices are expanding our knowledge and motions, and making it more and more impossible for the Outer Ones' necessary outposts to exist secretly *on this planet. The alien beings desire to know mankind more fully, and to have a few of mankind's philosophic and scientific leaders know more about them. With such an exchange of knowledge all perils will pass, and a satisfactory* modus vivendi *be established. The very idea of any attempt to enslave or* degrade *mankind is ridiculous.*

As a beginning of this improved rapport, the Outer Ones have naturally chosen me—whose knowledge of them is already so considerable—as their primary interpreter on earth. Much was told me last night—facts of the most stupendous and vista-opening nature—and more will be subsequently communicated to me both orally and in writing. I shall not be called upon to make any trip outside just yet, though I shall probably wish to do so later on—employing special means and transcending everything which we have hitherto been accustomed to regard as human experience. My house will be besieged no longer. Everything has reverted to normal, and the dogs will have no further occupation. In place of terror I have been given a rich boon of knowledge and intellectual adventure which few other mortals have ever shared.

The Outer Beings are perhaps the most marvelous organic things in or beyond all space and time—members of a cosmoswide race of which all other life-forms are merely degenerate variants. They are more vegetable than animal, if these terms can be applied to the sort of matter composing them, and have a somewhat fungoid structure; though the presence of a chlorophylllike substance and a very singular nutritive system differentiate them altogether from true cormophytic fungi. Indeed, the type is composed of a form of matter totally alien to our part of space—with electrons having a wholly different vibration-rate. That is why the beings cannot be photographed on the ordinary camera films and plates of our known universe, even though our eyes can see them. With proper knowledge, however, any good chemist could make a photographic emulsion which would record their images.

The genus is unique in its ability to traverse the heatless and airless interstellar void in full corporeal form, and some of its variants cannot do this without mechanical aid or curious surgical transpositions. Only a few species have the etherresisting wings characteristic of the Vermont variety. Those inhabiting certain remote peaks in the Old World were brought in other ways. Their external resemblance to animal life, and to the sort of structure we understand as material, is a matter of parallel evolution rather than of close kinship. Their

brain-capacity exceeds that of any other surviving life-form,
although the winged types of our hill country are by no means
the most highly developed. Telepathy is their usual means of
discourse, though they have rudimentary vocal organs which,
after a slight operation (for surgery is an incredibly expert and
everyday thing among them), can roughly duplicate the speech
of such types of organism as still use speech.

Their main immediate *abode is a still undiscovered and almost*
lightless planet at the very edge of our solar system—beyond
Neptune, and the ninth in distance from the sun. It is, as we have
inferred, the object mystically hinted at as "Yuggoth" in certain
ancient and forbidden writings; and it will soon be the scene of
a strange focusing of thought upon our world in an effort to
facilitate mental rapport. I would not be surprised if astronomers
became sufficiently sensitive to these thought-currents to discover
Yuggoth when the Outer Ones wish them to do so. But Yuggoth,
of course, is only the stepping-stone. The main body of the
beings inhabits strangely organized abysses wholly beyond the
utmost reach of any human imagination. The space-time globule
which we recognize as the totality of all cosmic entity is only
an atom in the genuine infinity which is theirs. And as much
of this infinity as any human brain can hold is eventually to be
opened up to me, as it has been to not more than fifty other
men since the human race has existed.

You will probably call this raving at first, Wilmarth, but in time
you will appreciate the titanic opportunity I have stumbled upon.
I want you to share as much of it as is possible, and to that end
must tell you thousands of things that won't go on paper. In the
past I have warned you not to come to see me. Now that all is
safe, I take pleasure in rescinding that warning and inviting you.

Can't you make a trip up here before your college term
opens? It would be marvelously delightful if you could. Bring

along the phonograph record and all my letters to you as consultative data—we shall need them in piecing together the whole tremendous story. You might bring the kodak prints, too, since I seem to have mislaid the negatives and my own prints in all this recent excitement. But what a wealth of facts I have to add to all this groping and tentative material—and what a stupendous device I have to supplement my additions!

Don't hesitate—I am free from espionage now, and you will not meet anything unnatural or disturbing. Just come along and let my car meet you at the Brattleboro station—prepare to stay as long as you can, and expect many an evening of discussion of things beyond all human conjecture. Don't tell anyone about it, of course—for this matter must not get to the promiscuous public.

The train service to Brattleboro is not bad—you can get a timetable in Boston. Take the B. & M. to Greenfield, and then change for the brief remainder of the way. I suggest your taking the convenient 4:10 p.m.—standard—from Boston. This gets into Greenfield at 7:35, and at 9:19 a train leaves there which reaches Brattleboro at 10:01. That is weekdays. Let me know the date and I'll have my car on hand at the station.

Pardon this typed letter, but my handwriting has grown shaky of late, as you know, and I don't feel equal to long stretches of script. I got this new Corona in Brattleboro yesterday—it seems to work very well.

Awaiting word, and hoping to see you shortly with the phonograph record and all my letters—and the kodak prints.

I am
Yours in anticipation,
HENRY W. AKELEY

To Albert N. Wilmarth, Esq.,
Miskatonic University, Arkham, Mass

The complexity of my emotions upon reading, re-reading, and pondering over this strange and unlooked-for letter is past adequate description. I have said that I was at once relieved and made uneasy, but this expresses only crudely the overtones of diverse and largely subconscious feelings which comprised both the relief and the uneasiness. To begin with, the thing was so antipodally at variance with the whole chain of horrors preceding it—the change of mood from stark terror to cool complacency and even exultation was so unheralded, lightning-like, and complete! I could scarcely believe that a single day could so alter the psychological perspective of one who had written that final frenzied bulletin of Wednesday, no matter what relieving disclosures that day might have brought. At certain moments a sense of conflicting unrealities made me wonder whether this whole distantly reported drama of fantastic forces were not a kind of half-illusory dream created largely within my own mind. Then I thought of the phonograph record and gave way to still greater bewilderment.

The letter seemed so unlike anything which could have been expected! As I analyzed my impression, I saw that it consisted of two distinct phases. First, granting that Akeley had been sane before and was still sane, the indicated change in the situation itself was so swift and unthinkable. And secondly, the change in Akeley's own manner, attitude, and language was so vastly beyond the normal or the predictable. The man's whole personality seemed to have undergone an insidious mutation—a mutation so deep that one could scarcely reconcile his two aspects with the supposition that both represented equal sanity. Word-choice, spelling—all were subtly different. And with my academic sensitiveness to prose style, I could trace profound divergences in his commonest reactions and rhythm-responses. Certainly, the emotional cataclysm or revelation which could produce so radical an overturn must be an extreme one indeed! Yet in another way the letter seemed quite characteristic of Akeley. The same old passion for infinity—the same old scholarly inquisitiveness. I could not a moment—or more than a moment—credit the idea of spuriousness or malign substitution. Did not the invitation—the willingness to have me test the truth of the letter in person—prove its genuineness?

I did not retire Saturday night, but sat up thinking of the shadows and marvels behind the letter I had received. My mind, aching from the quick succession of monstrous conceptions it had been forced to confront during the last four months, worked upon this startling new material in a cycle of doubt and acceptance which repeated most of the steps experienced in facing the earlier wonders; till long before dawn a burning interest and curiosity had begun to replace the original storm of perplexity and uneasiness. Mad or sane, metamorphosed or merely relieved, the chances were that Akeley had actually encountered some stupendous change of perspective in his hazardous research; some change at once diminishing his danger—real or fancied—and opening dizzy new vistas of cosmic and superhuman knowledge. My own zeal for the unknown flared up to meet his, and I felt myself touched by the contagion of the morbid barrier-breaking. To shake off the maddening and wearying limitations of time and space and natural law—to be linked with the vast *outside*—to come close to the nighted and abysmal secrets of the infinite and the ultimate—surely such a thing was worth the risk of one's life, soul, and sanity! And Akeley had said there was no longer any peril—he had invited me to visit him instead of warning me away as before. I tingled at the thought of what he might now have to tell me—there was an almost paralyzing fascination in the thought of sitting in that lonely and lately beleaguered farmhouse with a man who had talked with actual emissaries from outer space; sitting there with the terrible record and the pile of letters in which Akeley had summarized his earlier conclusions.

So late Sunday morning I telegraphed Akeley that I would meet him in Brattleboro on the following Wednesday—September 12th—

if that date were convenient for him. In only one respect did I depart
from his suggestions, and that concerned the choice of a train. Frankly,
I did not feel like arriving in that haunted Vermont region late at
night; so instead of accepting the train he chose I telephoned the
station and devised another arrangement. By rising early and taking
the 8:07 a.m. (standard) into Boston, I could catch the 9:25 for
Greenfield; arriving there at 12:22 noon. This connected exactly with
a train reaching Brattleboro at 1:08 p.m.—a much more comfortable
hour than 10:01 for meeting Akeley and riding with him into the
close-packed, secret-guarding hills.

I mentioned this choice in my telegram, and was glad to learn in
the reply which came toward evening that it had met with my prospective host's endorsement. His wire ran thus:

ARRANGEMENT SATISFACTORY. WILL MEET 1:08
TRAIN WEDNESDAY. DON'T FORGET RECORD AND
LETTERS AND PRINTS. KEEP DESTINATION QUIET.
EXPECT GREAT REVELATIONS.

                                                        AKELEY

Receipt of this message in direct response to one sent to Akeley—
and necessarily delivered to his house from the Townshend station
either by official messenger or by a restored telephone service—
removed any lingering subconscious doubts I may have had about the
authorship of the perplexing letter. My relief was marked—indeed, it
was greater than I could account for at that time; since all such doubts
had been rather deeply buried. But I slept soundly and long that night,
and was eagerly busy with preparations during the ensuing two days.

VI

On Wednesday I started as agreed, taking with me a valise full of
simple necessities and scientific data, including the hideous phono-

graph record, the kodak prints, and the entire file of Akeley's correspondence. As requested, I had told no one where I was going; for I could see that the matter demanded utmost privacy, even allowing for its most favorable turns. The thought of actual mental contact with alien, outside entities was stupefying enough to my trained and somewhat prepared mind; and this being so, what might one think of its effect on the vast masses of uninformed laymen? I do not know whether dread or adventurous expectancy was uppermost in me as I changed trains in Boston and began the long westward run out of familiar regions into those I knew less thoroughly. Waltham—Concord—Ayer—Fitchburg—Gardner—Athol—

My train reached Greenfield seven minutes late, but the northbound connecting express had been held. Transferring in haste, I felt a curious breathlessness as the cars rumbled on through the early afternoon sunlight into territories I had always read of but had never before visited. I knew I was entering an altogether older-fashioned and more primitive New England than the mechanized, urbanized coastal and southern areas where all my life had been spent; an unspoiled, ancestral New England without the foreigners and factory-smoke, billboards and concrete roads, of the sections which modernity has touched. There would be odd survivals of that continuous native life whose deep roots make it the one authentic outgrowth of the landscape—the continuous native life which keeps alive strange ancient memories, and fertilizes the soil for shadowy, marvelous, and seldom-mentioned beliefs.

Now and then I saw the blue Connecticut River gleaming in the sun, and after leaving Northfield we crossed it. Ahead loomed green and cryptical hills, and when the conductor came around I learned that I was at last in Vermont. He told me to set my watch back an hour, since the northern hill country will have no dealings with new-fangled daylight time schemes. As I did so it seemed to me that I was likewise turning the calendar back a century.

The train kept close to the river, and across in New Hampshire I could see the approaching slope of steep Wantastiquet, about which singular old legends cluster. Then streets appeared on my left, and a green island showed in the stream on my right. People rose and filed to the door, and I followed them. The car stopped, and I alighted beneath the long train-shed of the Brattleboro station.

Looking over the line of waiting motors I hesitated a moment to see which one might turn out to be the Akeley Ford, but my identity was divined before I could take the initiative. And yet it was clearly not Akeley himself who advanced to meet me with an outstretched hand and a mellowly phrased query as to whether I was indeed Mr Albert N. Wilmarth of Arkham. This man bore no resemblance to the bearded, grizzled Akeley of the snapshot; but was a younger and more urban person, fashionably dressed, and wearing only a small, dark mustache. His cultivated voice held an odd and almost disturbing hint of vague familiarity, though I could not definitely place it in my memory.

As I surveyed him I heard him explaining that he was a friend of my prospective host's who had come down from Townshend in his stead. Akeley, he declared, had suffered a sudden attack of some asthmatic trouble, and did not feel equal to making a trip in the outdoor air. It was not serious, however, and there was to be no change in plans regarding my visit. I could not make out just how much this Mr Noyes—as he announced himself—knew of Akeley's researches and discoveries, though it seemed to me that his casual manner stamped him as a comparative outsider. Remembering what a hermit Akeley had been, I was a trifle surprised at the ready avail-ability of such a friend; but did not let my puzzlement deter me from entering the motor to which he gestured me. It was not the small ancient car I had expected from Akeley's descriptions, but a large and immaculate specimen of recent pattern—apparently Noyes's own, and bearing Massachusetts license plates with the amusing "sacred codfish" device of that year. My guide, I concluded, must be a summer transient in the Townshend region.

Noyes climbed into the car beside me and started it at once. I was glad that he did not overflow with conversation, for some peculiar atmospheric tensity made me feel disinclined to talk. The town seemed very attractive in the afternoon sunlight as we swept up an incline and turned to the right into the main street. It drowsed like the older New England cities which one remembers from boyhood, and something in the collocation of roofs and steeples and chimneys and brick walls formed contours touching deep viol-strings of ancestral emotion. I could tell that I was at the gateway of a region half-bewitched through the piling-up of unbroken time-accumulations; a region where old, strange things have had a chance to grow and linger because they have never been stirred up.

As we passed out of Brattleboro my sense of constraint and foreboding increased, for a vague quality in the hill-crowded countryside with its towering, threatening, close-pressing green and granite slopes hinted at obscure secrets and immemorial survivals which might or might not be hostile to mankind. For a time our course followed a broad, shallow river which flowed down from unknown hills in the north, and I shivered when my companion told me it was the West River. It was in this stream, I recalled from newspaper items, that one of the morbid crab-like beings had been seen floating after the floods.

Gradually the country around us grew wilder and more deserted. Archaic covered bridges lingered fearsomely out of the past in pockets of the hills, and the half-abandoned railway track paralleling the river seemed to exhale a nebulously visible air of desolation. There were awesome sweeps of vivid valley where great cliffs rose, New England's virgin granite showing gray and austere through the verdure that scaled the crests. There were gorges where untamed streams leaped, bearing down toward the river the unimagined secrets of a thousand pathless peaks. Branching away now and then were narrow, half-concealed roads that bored their way through solid, luxuriant masses of forest among whose primal trees whole armies of elemental spirits might well lurk. As I saw these I thought of how Akeley had been molested by unseen agencies on his drives along this very route, and did not wonder that such things could be.

The quaint, sightly village of Newfane, reached in less than an hour, was our last link with that world which man can definitely call his own by virtue of conquest and complete occupancy. After that we cast off all allegiance to immediate, tangible, and time-touched things, and entered a fantastic world of hushed unreality in which the narrow, ribbon-like road rose and fell and curved with an almost sentient and purposeful caprice amidst the tenantless green peaks and half-deserted valleys. Except for the sound of the motor, and the faint stir of the few lonely farms we passed at infrequent intervals, the only thing that reached my ears was the gurgling, insidious trickle of strange waters from numberless hidden fountains in the shadowy woods.

The nearness and intimacy of the dwarfed, domed hills now became veritably breath-taking. Their steepness and abruptness were even greater than I had imagined from hearsay, and suggested nothing in common with the prosaic objective world we know. The dense, un-visited woods on those inaccessible slopes seemed to harbor alien and incredible things, and I felt that the very outline of the hills themselves held some strange and eon-forgotten meaning, as if they were vast hieroglyphs left by a rumored titan race whose glories live only in rare, deep dreams. All the legends of the past, and all the stupefying imputations of Henry Akeley's letters and exhibits, welled up in my memory to heighten the atmosphere of tension and growing menace. The purpose of my visit, and the frightful abnormalities it postulated, struck me all at once with a chill sensation that nearly overbalanced my ardor for strange delvings.

My guide must have noticed my disturbed attitude; for as the road grew wilder and more irregular, and our motion slower and more jolting, his occasional pleasant comments expanded into a steadier flow of discourse. He spoke of the beauty and weirdness of the country, and revealed some acquaintance with the folklore studies of my prospective host. From his polite questions it was obvious that he knew I had come for a scientific purpose, and that I was bringing data of some importance; but he gave no sign of appreciating the depth and awfulness of the knowledge which Akeley had finally reached.

His manner was so cheerful, normal, and urbane that his remarks ought to have calmed and reassured me; but oddly enough, I felt only the more disturbed as we bumped and veered onward into the unknown wilderness of hills and woods. At times it seemed as if he were pumping me to see what I knew of the monstrous secrets of the place, and with every fresh utterance that vague, teasing, baffling *familiarity* in his voice increased. It was not an ordinary or healthy familiarity despite the thoroughly wholesome and cultivated nature of the voice. I somehow linked it with forgotten nightmares, and felt that I might go mad if I recognized it. If any good excuse had existed, I think I would have turned back from my visit. As it was, I could not well do so—and it occurred to me that a cool, scientific conversation with Akeley himself after my arrival would help greatly to pull me together.

Besides, there was a strangely calming element of cosmic beauty in the hypnotic landscape through which we climbed and plunged fantastically. Time had lost itself in the labyrinths behind, and around us stretched only the flowering waves of faery and the recaptured loveliness of vanished centuries—the hoary groves, the untainted pastures edged with gay autumnal blossoms, and at vast intervals the small brown farmsteads nestling amidst huge trees beneath vertical precipices of fragrant brier and meadow-grass. Even the sunlight assumed a supernal glamour, as if some special atmosphere or exhalation mantled the whole region. I had seen nothing like it before save in the magic vistas that sometimes form the backgrounds of Italian primitives. Sodoma and Leonardo conceived such expanses, but only in the distance, and through the vaultings of Renaissance arcades. We were now burrowing bodily through the midst of the picture, and I seemed to find in its necromancy a thing I had innately known or inherited, and for which I had always been vainly searching.

Suddenly, after rounding an obtuse angle at the top of a sharp ascent, the car came to a standstill. On my left, across a well-kept lawn which stretched to the road and flaunted a border of whitewashed stones, rose a white, two-and-a-half-story house of unusual size and elegance for the region, with a congeries of contiguous or arcade-linked barns, sheds, and windmill behind and to the right. I recognized it at once from the snapshot I had received, and was not surprised to see the name of Henry Akeley on the galvanized-iron mailbox near the road. For some distance back of the house a level stretch of marshy and sparsely wooded land extended, beyond which soared a steep, thickly forested hillside ending in a jagged leafy crest. This latter, I knew, was the summit of Dark Mountain, half way up which we must have climbed already.

Alighting from the car and taking my valise, Noyes asked me to wait while he went in and notified Akeley of my advent. He himself, he added, had important business elsewhere, and could not stop for more than a moment. As he briskly walked up the path to the house I climbed out of the car myself, wishing to stretch my legs a little before settling down to a sedentary conversation. My feeling of nervousness and tension had risen to a maximum again now that I was on the actual scene of the morbid beleaguering described so hauntingly in Akeley's letters, and I honestly dreaded the coming discussions which were to link me with such alien and forbidden worlds.

Close contact with the utterly bizarre is often more terrifying than inspiring, and it did not cheer me to think that this very bit of dusty road was the place where those monstrous tracks and that fetid green ichor had been found after moonless nights of fear and death. Idly I noticed that none of Akeley's dogs seemed to be about. Had he sold them all as soon as the Outer Ones made peace with him? Try as I might, I could not have the same confidence in the depth and sincerity of that peace which appeared in Akeley's final and queerly different letter. After all, he was a man of much simplicity and with little worldly experience. Was there not, perhaps, some deep and sinister undercurrent beneath the surface of the new alliance?

Led by my thoughts, my eyes turned downward to the powdery road surface which had held such hideous testimonies. The last few days had been dry, and tracks of all sorts cluttered the rutted, irregular highway despite the unfrequented nature of the district. With a vague curiosity I began to trace the outline of some of the heterogeneous impressions, trying meanwhile to curb the flights of macabre fancy which the place and its memories suggested. There was something menacing and uncomfortable in the funereal stillness, in the muffled, subtle trickle of distant brooks, and in the crowding green peaks and black-wooded precipices that choked the narrow horizon.

And then an image shot into my consciousness which made those vague menaces and flights of fancy seem mild and insignificant indeed. I have said that I was scanning the miscellaneous prints in the road with a kind of idle curiosity—but all at once that curiosity was shockingly snuffed out by a sudden and paralyzing gust of active terror. For though the dust tracks were in general confused and over-lapping, and unlikely to arrest any casual gaze, my restless vision had caught certain details near the spot where the path to the house joined the highway; and had recognized beyond doubt or hope the frightful significance of those details. It was not for nothing, alas, that I had pored for hours over the kodak views of the Outer Ones' claw-prints which Akeley had sent. Too well did I know the marks of those loathsome nippers, and that hint of ambiguous direction which stamped the horrors as no creatures of this planet. No chance had been left me for merciful mistake. Here, indeed, in objective form before my own eyes, and surely made not many hours ago, were at least three marks which stood out blasphemously among the surprising plethora of blurred footprints leading to and from the Akeley farmhouse. *They were the hellish tracks of the living fungi from Yuggoth.*

I pulled myself together in time to stifle a scream. After all, what more was there than I might have expected, assuming that I had really believed Akeley's letters? He had spoken of making peace with the things. Why, then, was it strange that some of them had visited his house? But the terror was stronger than the reassurance. Could any man be expected to look unmoved for the first time upon the claw-marks of animate beings from outer depths of space? Just then I saw Noyes emerge from the door and approach with a brisk step. I must, I reflected, keep command of myself, for the chances were this genial friend knew nothing of Akeley's profoundest and most stupendous probings into the forbidden.

Akeley, Noyes hastened to inform me, was glad and ready to see me; although his sudden attack of asthma would prevent him from being a very competent host for a day or two. These spells hit him hard when they came, and were always accompanied by a debilitating fever and general weakness. He never was good for much while they lasted—had to talk in a whisper, and was very clumsy and feeble in getting about. His feet and ankles swelled, too, so that he had to bandage them like a gouty old beef-eater. Today he was in rather bad shape, so that I would have to attend very largely to my own needs; but he was none the less eager for conversation. I would find him in the study at the left of the front hall—the room where the blinds were shut. He had to keep the sunlight out when he was ill, for his eyes were very sensitive.

As Noyes bade me adieu and rode off northward in his car I began to walk slowly toward the house. The door had been left ajar for me; but before approaching and entering I cast a searching glance around the whole place, trying to decide what had struck me as so intangibly queer about it. The barns and sheds looked trimly prosaic enough, and I noticed Akeley's battered Ford in its capacious, unguarded shelter. Then the secret of the queerness reached me. It was the total silence. Ordinarily a farm is at least moderately murmurous from its various kinds of livestock, but here all signs of life were missing. What of the hens and the hogs? The cows, of which Akeley had said he possessed several, might conceivably be out to pasture, and the dogs might possibly have been sold; but the absence of any trace of cackling or grunting was truly singular.

I did not pause long on the path, but resolutely entered the open house door and closed it behind me. It had cost me a distinct psychological effort to do so, and now that I was shut inside I had a momentary longing for precipitate retreat. Not that the place was in the least sinister in visual suggestion; on the contrary, I thought the graceful late-colonial hallway very tasteful and wholesome, and admired the evident breeding of the man who had furnished it. What made me wish to flee was something very attenuated and indefinable. Perhaps it was a certain odd odor which I thought I noticed—though I well knew how common musty odors are in even the best of ancient farmhouses.

VII

Refusing to let these cloudy qualms overmaster me, I recalled Noyes's instructions and pushed open the six-paneled, brass-latched white door on my left. The room beyond was darkened, as I had known before; and as I entered it I noticed that the queer odor was stronger there. There likewise appeared to be some faint, half-imaginary rhythm or vibration in the air. For a moment the closed blinds allowed me to see very little, but then a kind of apologetic hacking or whispering sound drew my attention to a great easy-chair in the farther, darker corner of the room. Within its shadowy depths I saw the white blur of a man's face and hands; and in a moment I had crossed to greet the figure who had tried to speak. Dim though the light was, I perceived that this was indeed my host. I had studied the kodak picture repeatedly, and there could be no mistake about this firm, weather-beaten face with the cropped, grizzled beard.

But as I looked again my recognition was mixed with sadness and anxiety; for certainly, this face was that of a very sick man. I felt that there must be something more than asthma behind that strained, rigid, immobile expression and unwinking glassy stare; and realized how terribly the strain of his frightful experiences must have told on him. Was it not enough to break any human being—even a younger man than this intrepid delver into the forbidden? The strange and sudden relief, I feared, had come too late to save him from something like a general breakdown. There was a touch of the pitiful in the limp, lifeless way his lean hands rested in his lap. He had on a loose dressing-gown, and was swathed around the head and high around the neck with a vivid yellow scarf or hood.

And then I saw that he was trying to talk in the same hacking whisper with which he had greeted me. It was a hard whisper to catch at first, since the gray mustache concealed all movements of the lips, and something in its timbre disturbed me greatly; but by concentrating my attention I could soon make out its purport surprisingly well. The accent was by no means a rustic one, and the language was even more polished than correspondence had led me to expect.

"Mr Wilmarth, I presume? You must pardon my not rising. I am quite ill, as Mr Noyes must have told you; but I could not resist having you come just the same. You know what I wrote in my last letter—there is so much to tell you tomorrow when I shall feel better. I can't say how glad I am to see you in person after all our many letters. You have the file with you, of course? And the kodak prints and record? Noyes put your valise in the hall—I suppose you saw it. For tonight I fear you'll have to wait on yourself to a great extent. Your room is upstairs—the one over this—and you'll see the bathroom door open at the head of the staircase. There's a meal spread for you in the dining-room—right through this door at your right—which you can take whenever you feel like it. I'll be a better host tomorrow—but just now weakness leaves me helpless.

"Make yourself at home—you might take out the letters and pictures and record and put them on the table here before you go upstairs with your bag. It is here that we shall discuss them—you can see my phonograph on that corner stand.

"No, thanks—there's nothing you can do for me. I know these spells of old. Just come back for a little quiet visiting before night, and then go to bed when you please. I'll rest right here—perhaps sleep here all night as I often do. In the morning I'll be far better able to go into the things we must go into. You realize, of course, the utterly stupendous nature of the matter before us. To us, as to only a few men on this earth, there will be opened up gulfs of time and space and knowledge beyond anything within the conception of human science and philosophy.

"Do you know that Einstein is wrong, and that certain objects and forces *can* move with a velocity greater than that of light? With proper aid I expect to go backward and forward in time, and actually *see* and *feel* the earth of remote past and future epochs. You can't imagine the degree to which those beings have carried science. There is nothing they can't do with the mind and body of living organisms. I expect to visit other planets, and even other stars and galaxies. The first trip will be to Yuggoth, the nearest world fully peopled by the beings. It is a strange dark orb at the very rim of our solar system—unknown to earthly astronomers as yet. But I must have written you about this. At the proper time, you know, the beings there will direct thought-currents toward us and cause it to be discovered—or perhaps let one of their human allies give the scientists a hint.

"There are mighty cities on Yuggoth—great tiers of terraced towers built of black stone like the specimen I tried to send you. That came from Yuggoth. The sun shines there no brighter than a star, but the beings need no light. They have other, subtler senses, and put no windows in their great houses and temples. Light even hurts and hampers and confuses them, for it does not exist at all in the black cosmos outside time and space where they came from originally. To visit Yuggoth would drive any weak man mad—yet I am going there. The black rivers of pitch that flow under those mysterious Cyclopean bridges—things built by some elder race extinct and forgotten before the things came to Yuggoth from the ultimate voids—ought to be enough to make any man a Dante or Poe if he can keep sane long enough to tell what he has seen.

"But remember—that dark world of fungoid gardens and window-less cities isn't really terrible. It is only to us that it would seem so. Probably this world seemed just as terrible to the beings when they first explored it in the primal age. You know they were here long before the fabulous epoch of Cthulhu was over, and remember all about sunken R'lyeh when it was above the waters. They've been inside the earth, too—there are openings which human beings know nothing of—some of them in these very Vermont hills—and great worlds of unknown life down there; blue-litten K'n-yan, red-litten Yoth, and black, lightless N'kai. It's from N'kai that frightful Tsathoggua came—you know, the amorphous, toad-like god-creature mentioned in the Pnakotic Manuscripts and the *Necronomicon* and the Commoriom myth-cycle preserved by the Atlantean high-priest Klarkash-Ton.

"But we will talk of all this later on. It must be four or five o'clock by this time. Better bring the stuff from your bag, take a bite, and then come back for a comfortable chat."

Very slowly I turned and began to obey my host; fetching my valise, extracting and depositing the desired articles, and finally ascending to the room designated as mine. With the memory of that roadside claw-print fresh in my mind, Akeley's whispered paragraphs had affected me queerly; and the hints of familiarity with this unknown world of fungous life—forbidden Yuggoth—made my flesh creep more than I cared to own. I was tremendously sorry about Akeley's illness, but had to confess that his hoarse whisper had a hateful as well as pitiful quality. If only he wouldn't *gloat* so about Yuggoth and its black secrets!

My room proved a very pleasant and well-furnished one, devoid alike of the musty odor and disturbing sense of vibration; and after leaving my valise there I descended again to greet Akeley and take the lunch he had set out for me. The dining-room was just beyond the study, and I saw that a kitchen ell extended still farther in the same direction. On the dining-table an ample array of sandwiches, cake, and cheese awaited me, and a Thermos-bottle beside a cup and saucer testified that hot coffee had not been forgotten. After a well-relished meal I poured myself a liberal cup of coffee, but found that the culinary standard had suffered a lapse in this one detail. My first spoonful revealed a faintly unpleasant acrid taste, so that I did not take more. Throughout the lunch I thought of Akeley sitting silently in the great chair in the darkened next room. Once I went in to beg him to share the repast, but he whispered that he could eat nothing as yet. Later on, just before he slept, he would take some malted milk—all he ought to have that day.

After lunch I insisted on clearing the dishes away and washing them in the kitchen sink—incidentally emptying the coffee which I had not been able to appreciate. Then returning to the darkened study I drew up a chair near my host's corner and prepared for such conversation as he might feel inclined to conduct. The letters, pictures, and record were still on the large center-table, but for the nonce we did not have to draw upon them. Before long I forgot even the bizarre odor and curious suggestions of vibration.

I have said that there were things in some of Akeley's letters—especially the second and most voluminous one—which I would not dare to quote or even form into words on paper. This hesitancy applies with still greater force to the things I heard whispered that evening in the darkened room among the lonely haunted hills. Of the extent of the cosmic horrors unfolded by that raucous voice I cannot even hint. He had known hideous things before, but what he had learned since making his pact with the Outside Things was almost too much for sanity to bear. Even now I absolutely refuse to believe what he implied about the constitution of ultimate infinity, the juxtaposition of dimensions, and the frightful position of our known cosmos of space and time in the unending chain of linked cosmos-atoms which makes up the immediate super-cosmos of curves, angles, and material and semi-material electronic organization.

Never was a sane man more dangerously close to the arcana of basic entity—never was an organic brain nearer to utter annihilation in the chaos that transcends form and force and symmetry. I learned whence Cthulhu *first* came, and why half the great temporary stars of history had flared forth. I guessed—from hints which made even my informant pause timidly—the secret behind the Magellanic Clouds and globular nebulae, and the black truth veiled by the immemorial allegory of Tao. The nature of the Doels was plainly revealed, and I was told the essence (though not the source) of the Hounds of Tindalos. The legend of Yig, Father of Serpents, remained figurative no longer, and I started with loathing when told of the monstrous nuclear chaos beyond angled space which the *Necronomicon* had mercifully cloaked under the name of Azathoth. It was shocking to have the foulest nightmares of secret myth cleared up in concrete terms whose stark, morbid hatefulness exceeded the boldest hints of ancient and medieval mystics. Ineluctably I was led to believe that the first whisperers of these accursed tales must have had discourse with Akeley's Outer Ones, and perhaps have visited outer cosmic realms as Akeley now proposed visiting them.

I was told of the Black Stone and what it implied, and was glad that it had not reached me. My guesses about those hieroglyphics had been all too correct! And yet Akeley now seemed reconciled to the whole fiendish system he had stumbled upon; reconciled and eager to probe farther into the monstrous abyss. I wondered what beings he had talked with since his last letter to me, and whether many of them had been as human as that first emissary he had mentioned. The tension in my head grew insufferable, and I built up all sorts of wild theories about the queer, persistent odor and those insidious hints of vibration in the darkened room.

Night was falling now, and as I recalled what Akeley had written me about those earlier nights I shuddered to think there would be no moon. Nor did I like the way the farmhouse nestled in the lee of that colossal forested slope leading up to Dark Mountain's unvisited crest. With Akeley's permission I lighted a small oil lamp, turned it low, and set it on a distant bookcase beside the ghostly bust of Milton; but afterward I was sorry I had done so, for it made my host's strained, immobile face and listless hands look damnably abnormal and corpse-like. He seemed half-incapable of motion, though I saw him nod stiffly once in a while.

After what he had told, I could scarcely imagine what profounder secrets he was saving for the morrow; but at last it developed that his trip to Yuggoth and beyond—*and my own possible participation in it*—was to be the next day's topic. He must have been amused by the start of horror I gave at hearing a cosmic voyage on my part proposed, for his head wobbled violently when I showed my fear. Subsequently he spoke very gently of how human beings might accomplish—and several times had accomplished—the seemingly impossible flight across the interstellar void. It seemed *that complete human bodies did not indeed make the trip*, but that the prodigious surgical, biological, chemical, and mechanical skill of the Outer Ones had found a way to convey human brains without their concomitant physical structure.

There was a harmless way to extract a brain, and a way to keep the organic residue alive during its absence. The bare, compact cerebral matter was then immersed in an occasionally replenished fluid within an ether-tight cylinder of a metal mined in Yuggoth, certain electrodes reaching through and connecting at will with elaborate instruments capable of duplicating the three vital faculties of sight, hearing, and speech. For the winged fungus-beings to carry the brain-cylinders intact through space was an easy matter. Then, on every planet covered by their civilization, they would find plenty of adjustable faculty-instruments capable of being connected with the encased brains; so that after a little fitting these traveling intelligences could be given a full sensory and articulate life—albeit a bodiless and mechanical one—at each stage of their journeying through and beyond the space-time continuum. It was as simple as carrying a phonograph record about and playing it wherever a phonograph of the corresponding make exists. Of its success there could be no question. Akeley was not afraid. Had it not been brilliantly accomplished again and again?

For the first time one of the inert, wasted hands raised itself and pointed to a high shelf on the farther side of the room. There, in a neat row, stood more than a dozen cylinders of a metal I had never seen before—cylinders about a foot high and somewhat less in diameter, with three curious sockets set in an isosceles triangle over the front convex surface of each. One of them was linked at two of the sockets to a pair of singular-looking machines that stood in the background. Of their purport I did not need to be told, and I shivered as with ague. Then I saw the hand point to a much nearer corner where some intricate instruments with attached cords and plugs, several of them much like the two devices on the shelf behind the cylinders, were huddled together.

"There are four kinds of instruments here, Wilmarth," whispered the voice. "Four kinds—three faculties each—makes twelve pieces in all. You see there are four different sorts of beings presented in those cylinders up there. Three humans, six fungoid beings who can't navigate space corporeally, two beings from Neptune (God! if you could see the body this type has on its own planet!), and the rest entities from the central caverns of an especially interesting dark star beyond the galaxy. In the principal outpost inside Round Hill you'll now and then find more cylinders and machines—cylinders of extra-cosmic brains with different senses from any we know—allies and explorers from the uttermost Outside—and special machines for giving them impressions and expression in the several ways suited at once to them and to the comprehensions of different types of listeners. Round Hill, like most of the beings' main outposts all through the various universes, is a very cosmopolitan place! Of course, only the more common types have been lent to me for experiment.

"Here—take the three machines I point to and set them on the table. That tall one with the two glass lenses in front—then the box with the vacuum tubes and sounding-board—and now the one with the metal disc on top. Now for the cylinder with the label 'B-67' pasted on it. Just stand in that Windsor chair to reach the shelf. Heavy? Never mind! Be sure of the number—B-67. Don't bother that fresh, shiny cylinder joined to the two testing instruments—the one with my name on it. Set B-67 on the table near where you've put the machines—and see that the dial switch on all three machines is jammed over to the extreme left.

"Now connect the cord of the lens machine with the upper socket on the cylinder—there! Join the tube machine to the lower left-hand socket, and the disc apparatus to the outer socket. Now move all the dial switches on the machines over to the extreme right—first the lens one, then the disc one, and then the tube one. That's right. I might as well tell you that this is a human being—just like any of us. I'll give you a taste of some of the others tomorrow."

To this day I do not know why I obeyed those whispers so slavishly, or whether I thought Akeley was mad or sane. After what had gone before, I ought to have been prepared for anything; but this mechanical mummery seemed so like the typical vagaries of crazed inventors and scientists that it struck a chord of doubt which even the preceding discourse had not excited. What the whisperer implied was beyond all human belief—yet were not the other things still farther beyond, and less preposterous only because of their remoteness from tangible concrete proof?

As my mind reeled amidst this chaos, I became conscious of a mixed grating and whirring from all three machines lately linked to the cylinder—a grating and whirring which soon subsided into a virtual noiselessness. What was about to happen? Was I to hear a voice? And if so, what proof would I have that it was not some cleverly concocted radio device talked into by a concealed but closely watching speaker? Even now I am unwilling to swear just what I heard, or just what phenomenon really took place before me. But something certainly seemed to take place.

To be brief and plain, the machine with the tubes and sound-box began to speak, and with a point and intelligence which left no doubt that the speaker was actually present and observing us. The voice was loud, metallic, lifeless, and plainly mechanical in every detail of its production. It was incapable of inflection or expressiveness, but scraped and rattled on with a deadly precision and deliberation.

"Mr Wilmarth," it said, "I hope I do not startle you. I am a human being like yourself, though my body is now resting safely under proper vitalizing treatment inside Round Hill, about a mile and a half east of here. I myself am here with you—my brain is in that cylinder and I see, hear, and speak through these electronic vibrators. In a week I am going across the void as I have been many times before, and I expect to have the pleasure of Mr Akeley's company. I wish I might have yours as well; for I know you by sight and reputation, and have kept close track of your correspondence with our friend. I am, of course, one of the men who have become allied with the outside beings visiting our planet. I met them first in the Himalayas, and have helped them in various ways. In return they have given me experiences such as few men have ever had.

"Do you realize what it means when I say I have been on thirty-seven different celestial bodies—planets, dark stars, and less definable objects—including eight outside our galaxy and two outside the curved cosmos of space and time? All this has not harmed me in the least. My brain has been removed from my body by fissions so adroit that it would be crude to call the operation surgery. The visiting beings have methods which make these extractions easy and almost normal—and one's body never ages when the brain is out of it. The brain, I may add, is virtually immortal with its mechanical faculties and a limited nourishment supplied by occasional changes of the preserving fluid.

"Altogether, I hope most heartily that you will decide to come with Mr Akeley and me. The visitors are eager to know men of knowledge like yourself, and to show them the great abysses that most of us have had to dream about in fanciful ignorance. It may seem strange at first to meet them, but I know you will be above minding that. I think Mr Noyes will go along, too—the man who doubtless brought you up here in his car. He has been one of us for years—I suppose you recognized his voice as one of those on the record Mr Akeley sent you."

At my violent start the speaker paused a moment before concluding. "So, Mr Wilmarth, I will leave the matter to you; merely adding that a man with your love of strangeness and folklore ought never to miss such a chance as this. There is nothing to fear. All transitions are

painless, and there is much to enjoy in a wholly mechanized state of
sensation. When the electrodes are disconnected, one merely drops
off into a sleep of especially vivid and fantastic dreams.

"And now, if you don't mind, we might adjourn our session till
tomorrow. Good night—just turn all the switches back to the left;
never mind the exact order, though you might let the lens machine
be last. Good night, Mr Akeley—treat our guest well! Ready now
with those switches?"

That was all. I obeyed mechanically and shut off all three switches,
though dazed with doubt of everything that had occurred. My head
was still reeling as I heard Akeley's whispering voice telling me that
I might leave all the apparatus on the table just as it was. He did not
essay any comment on what had happened, and indeed no comment
could have conveyed much to my burdened faculties. I heard him
telling me I could take the lamp to use in my room, and deduced
that he wished to rest alone in the dark. It was surely time he rested,
for his discourse of the afternoon and evening had been such as to
exhaust even a vigorous man. Still dazed, I bade my host good night
and went upstairs with the lamp, although I had an excellent pocket
flashlight with me.

I was glad to be out of that downstairs study with the queer odor
and vague suggestions of vibration, yet could not of course escape a
hideous sense of dread and peril and cosmic abnormality as I thought
of the place I was in and the forces I was meeting. The wild, lonely
region, the black, mysteriously forested slope towering so close behind
the house, the footprints in the road, the sick, motionless whisperer
in the dark, the hellish cylinders and machines, and above all the
invitations to strange surgery and stranger voyagings—these things,
all so new and in such sudden succession, rushed in on me with a
cumulative force which sapped my will and almost undermined my
physical strength.

To discover that my guide Noyes was the human celebrant in that monstrous bygone Sabbat-ritual on the phonograph record was a particular shock, though I had previously sensed a dim, repellent familiarity in his voice. Another special shock came from my own attitude toward my host whenever I paused to analyze it; for much as I had instinctively liked Akeley as revealed in his correspondence, I now found that he filled me with a distinct repulsion. His illness ought to have excited my pity; but instead, it gave me a kind of shudder. He was so rigid and inert and corpse-like—and that incessant whispering was so hateful and unhuman!

It occurred to me that this whispering was different from anything else of the kind I had ever heard; that, despite the curious motion-lessness of the speaker's mustache-screened lips, it had a latent strength and carrying-power remarkable for the wheezings of an asthmatic. I had been able to understand the speaker when wholly across the room, and once or twice it had seemed to me that the faint but penetrant sounds represented not so much weakness as deliberate repression—for what reason I could not guess. From the first I had felt a disturbing quality in their timbre. Now, when I tried to weigh the matter, I thought I could trace this impression to a kind of sub-conscious familiarity like that which had made Noyes's voice so hazily ominous. But when or where I had encountered the thing it hinted at, was more than I could tell.

One thing was certain—I would not spend another night here. My scientific zeal had vanished amidst fear and loathing, and I felt nothing now but a wish to escape from this net of morbidity and unnatural revelation. I knew enough now. It must indeed be true that cosmic linkages do exist—but such things are surely not meant for normal human beings to meddle with.

Blasphemous influences seemed to surround me and press chok-ingly upon my senses. Sleep, I decided, would be out of the question; so I merely extinguished the lamp and threw myself on the bed fully dressed. No doubt it was absurd, but I kept ready for some unknown emergency; gripping in my right hand the revolver I had brought along, and holding the pocket flashlight in my left. Not a sound came from below, and I could imagine how my host was sitting there with cadaverous stiffness in the dark.

Somewhere I heard a clock ticking, and was vaguely grateful for the normality of the sound. It reminded me, though, of another thing about the region which disturbed me—the total absence of animal life. There were certainly no farm beasts about, and now I realized that even the accustomed night-noises of wild living things were absent. Except for the sinister trickle of distant unseen waters, that stillness was anomalous—interplanetary—and I wondered what star-spawned, intangible blight could be hanging over the region. I recalled from old legends that dogs and other beasts had always hated the Outer Ones, and thought of what those tracks in the road might mean.

VIII

Do not ask me how long my unexpected lapse into slumber lasted, or how much of what ensued was sheer dream. If I tell you that I awaked at a certain time, and heard and saw certain things, you will merely answer that I did not wake then; and that everything was a dream until the moment when I rushed out of the house, stumbled to the shed where I had seen the old Ford, and seized that ancient vehicle for a mad, aimless race over the haunted hills which at last landed me—after hours of jolting and winding through forest-threatened labyrinths—in a village which turned out to be Townshend.

You will also, of course, discount everything else in my report; and declare that all the pictures, record-sounds, cylinder-and-machine sounds, and kindred evidences were bits of pure deception practiced on me by the missing Henry Akeley. You will even hint that he conspired with other eccentrics to carry out a silly and elaborate hoax—that he had the express shipment removed at Keene, and that he had Noyes make that terrifying wax record. It is odd, though, that

Noyes has not even yet been identified; that he was unknown at any of the villages near Akeley's place, though he must have been frequently in the region. I wish I had stopped to memorize the license-number of his car—or perhaps it is better after all that I did not. For I, despite all you can say, and despite all I sometimes try to say to myself, know that loathsome outside influences must be lurking there in the half-unknown hills—and that those influences have spies and emissaries in the world of men. To keep as far as possible from such influences and such emissaries is all that I ask of life in future.

When my frantic story sent a sheriff's posse out to the farmhouse, Akeley was gone without leaving a trace. His loose dressing-gown, yellow scarf, and foot-bandages lay on the study floor near his corner easy-chair, and it could not be decided whether any of his other apparel had vanished with him. The dogs and livestock were indeed missing, and there were some curious bullet-holes both on the house's exterior and on some of the walls within; but beyond this nothing unusual could be detected. No cylinders or machines, none of the evidences I had brought in my valise, no queer odor or vibration-sense, no footprints in the road, and none of the problematical things I glimpsed at the very last.

I stayed a week in Brattleboro after my escape, making inquiries among people of every kind who had known Akeley; and the results convince me that the matter is no figment of dream or delusion. Akeley's queer purchases of dogs and ammunition and chemicals, and the cutting of his telephone wires, are matters of record; while all who knew him—including his son in California—concede that his occasional remarks on strange studies had a certain consistency. Solid citizens believe he was mad, and unhesitatingly pronounce all reported evidences mere hoaxes devised with insane cunning and perhaps abetted by eccentric associates; but the lowlier country folk sustain his statements in every detail. He had showed some of these rustics his photographs and black stone, and had played the hideous record for them; and they all said the footprints and buzzing voice were like those described in ancestral legends.

They said, too, that suspicious sights and sounds had been noticed increasingly around Akeley's house after he found the black stone, and that the place was now avoided by everybody except the mail man and other casual, tough-minded people. Dark Mountain and Round Hill were both notoriously haunted spots, and I could find no one who had ever closely explored either. Occasional disappearances of natives throughout the district's history were well attested, and these now included the semi-vagabond Walter Brown, whom Akeley's letters had mentioned. I even came upon one farmer who thought he had personally glimpsed one of the queer bodies at flood-time in the swollen West River, but his tale was too confused to be really valuable.

When I left Brattleboro I resolved never to go back to Vermont, and I feel quite certain I shall keep my resolution. Those wild hills are surely the outpost of a frightful cosmic race—as I doubt all the less since reading that a new ninth planet has been glimpsed beyond Neptune, just as those influences had said it would be glimpsed. Astronomers, with a hideous appropriateness they little suspect, have named this thing "Pluto." I feel, beyond question, that it is nothing less than nighted Yuggoth—and I shiver when I try to figure out the real reason *why* its monstrous denizens wish it to be known in this way at this especial time. I vainly try to assure myself that these demoniac creatures are not gradually leading up to some new policy hurtful to the earth and its normal inhabitants.

But I have still to tell of the ending of that terrible night in the farmhouse. As I have said, I did finally drop into a troubled doze; a doze filled with bits of dream which involved monstrous landscape-glimpses. Just what awaked me I cannot yet say, but that I did indeed awake at this given point I feel very certain. My first confused impression was of stealthily creaking floor-boards in the hall outside my door, and of a clumsy, muffled fumbling at the latch. This, however, ceased almost at once; so that my really clear impressions began with the voices heard from the study below. There seemed to be several speakers, and I judged that they were controversially engaged.

By the time I had listened a few seconds I was broad awake, for the nature of the voices was such as to make all thought of sleep ridiculous. The tones were curiously varied, and no one who had listened to that accursed phonograph record could harbor any doubts about the nature of at least two of them. Hideous though the idea was, I knew that I was under the same roof with nameless things from abysmal space; for those two voices were unmistakably the blasphemous buzzings which the Outside Beings used in their communication with men. The two were individually different—different in pitch, accent, and tempo—but they were both of the same damnable general kind.

A third voice was indubitably that of a mechanical utterance-machine connected with one of the detached brains in the cylinders. There was as little doubt about that as about the buzzings; for the loud, metallic, lifeless voice of the previous evening, with its inflectionless, expressionless scraping and rattling, and its impersonal precision and deliberation, had been utterly unforgettable. For a time I did not pause to question whether the intelligence behind the scraping was the identical one which had formerly talked to me; but shortly afterward I reflected that *any* brain would emit vocal sounds of the same quality if linked to the same mechanical speech-producer; the only possible differences being in language, rhythm, speed, and pronunciation. To complete the eldritch colloquy there were two actually human voices—one the crude speech of an unknown and evidently rustic man, and the other the suave Bostonian tones of my erstwhile guide Noyes.

As I tried to catch the words which the stoutly fashioned floor so bafflingly intercepted, I was also conscious of a great deal of stirring and scratching and shuffling in the room below; so that I could not escape the impression that it was full of living beings—many more than the few whose speech I could single out. The exact nature of this stirring is extremely hard to describe, for very few good bases of comparison exist. Objects seemed now and then to move across the room like conscious entities; the sound of their footfalls having something about it like a loose, hard-surfaced clattering—as of the contact of ill-coordinated surfaces of horn or hard rubber. It was, to use a more concrete but less accurate comparison, as if people with loose, splintery wooden shoes were shambling and rattling about on the polished board floor. On the nature and appearance of those responsible for the sounds, I did not care to speculate.

Before long I saw that it would be impossible to distinguish any connected discourse. Isolated words—including the names of Akeley and myself—now and then floated up, especially when uttered by the mechanical speech-producer; but their true significance was lost for want of continuous context. Today I refuse to form any definite deductions from them, and even their frightful effect on me was one of *suggestion* rather than of *revelation*. A terrible and abnormal conclave, I felt certain, was assembled below me; but for what shocking deliberations I could not tell. It was curious how this unquestioned sense of the malign and the blasphemous pervaded me despite Akeley's assurances of the Outsiders' friendliness.

With patient listening I began to distinguish clearly between voices, even though I could not grasp much of what any of the voices said. I seemed to catch certain typical emotions behind some of the speakers. One of the buzzing voices, for example, held an unmistakable note of authority; whilst the mechanical voice, notwithstanding its artificial loudness and regularity, seemed to be in a position of subordination and pleading. Noyes's tones exuded a kind of conciliatory atmosphere. The others I could make no attempt to interpret. I did not hear the familiar whisper of Akeley, but well knew that such a sound could never penetrate the solid flooring of my room.

I will try to set down some of the few disjointed words and other sounds I caught, labeling the speakers of the words as best I know how. It was from the speech-machine that I first picked up a few recognizable phrases.

(THE SPEECH-MACHINE)

". . . brought it on myself . . . sent back the letters and the record . . . end on it . . . taken in . . . seeing and hearing . . . damn you . . . impersonal force, after all . . . fresh, shiny cylinder . . . great God. . . ."

(FIRST BUZZING VOICE)

". . . time we stopped . . . small and human . . . Akeley . . . brain . . . saying . . ."

(SECOND BUZZING VOICE)

". . . Nyarlathotep . . . Wilmarth . . . records and letters . . . cheap imposture. . . ."

(NOYES)

". . . (an unpronounceable word or name, possibly N'gah-Kthun*) . . . harmless . . . peace . . . couple of weeks . . . theatrical . . . told you that before. . . ."*

(FIRST BUZZING VOICE)

". . . no reason . . . original plan . . . effects . . . Noyes can watch . . . Round Hill . . . fresh cylinder . . . Noyes's car. . . ."

(NOYES)

". . . well . . . all yours . . . down here . . . rest . . . place. . . ."

(SEVERAL VOICES AT ONCE IN INDISTINGUISHABLE SPEECH)

(MANY FOOTSTEPS, INCLUDING THE PECULIAR LOOSE STIRRING OR CLATTERING)

(A CURIOUS SORT OF FLAPPING SOUND)

(THE SOUND OF AN AUTOMOBILE STARTING AND RECEDING)

(SILENCE)

That is the substance of what my ears brought me as I lay rigid upon that strange upstairs bed in the haunted farmhouse among the demoniac hills—lay there fully dressed, with a revolver clenched in my right hand and a pocket flashlight gripped in my left. I became, as I have said, broad awake; but a kind of obscure paralysis nevertheless kept me inert till long after the last echoes of the sounds had died away. I heard the wooden, deliberate ticking of the ancient Connecticut clock somewhere far below, and at last made out the irregular snoring of a sleeper. Akeley must have dozed off after the strange session, and I could well believe that he needed to do so.

Just what to think or what to do was more than I could decide. After all, what *had* I heard beyond things which previous information might have led me to expect? Had I not known that the nameless Outsiders were now freely admitted to the farmhouse? No doubt Akeley had been surprised by an unexpected visit from them. Yet something in that fragmentary discourse had chilled me immeasurably, raised the most grotesque and horrible doubts, and made me wish fervently that I might wake up and prove everything a dream. I think my subconscious mind must have caught something which my consciousness has not yet recognized. But what of Akeley? Was he not my friend, and would he not have protested if any harm were meant me? The peaceful snoring below seemed to cast ridicule on all my suddenly intensified fears.

Was it possible that Akeley had been imposed upon and used as a lure to draw me into the hills with the letters and pictures and phonograph record? Did those beings mean to engulf us both in a common destruction because we had come to know too much? Again I thought of the abruptness and unnaturalness of that change in the situation which must have occurred between Akeley's penultimate and final letters. Something, my instinct told me, was terribly wrong. All was not as it seemed. That acrid coffee which I refused—had there not been an attempt by some hidden, unknown entity to drug it? I must talk to Akeley at once, and restore his sense of proportion. They had hypnotized him with their promises of cosmic revelations, but now he must listen to reason. We must get out of this before it would be too late. If he lacked the will power to make the break for liberty, I would supply it. Or if I could not persuade him to go, I could at least go myself. Surely he would let me take his Ford and leave it in a garage at Brattleboro. I had noticed it in the shed—the door being left unlocked and open now that peril was deemed past—and I believed there was a good chance of its being ready for instant use. That momentary dislike of Akeley which I had felt during and after the evening's conversation was all gone now. He was in a position much like my own, and we must stick together. Knowing his indisposed condition, I hated to wake him at this juncture, but I knew that I must. I could not stay in this place till morning as matters stood.

At last I felt able to act, and stretched myself vigorously to regain command of my muscles. Arising with a caution more impulsive than deliberate, I found and donned my hat, took my valise, and started downstairs with the flashlight's aid. In my nervousness I kept the revolver clutched in my right hand, being able to take care of both valise and flashlight with my left. Why I exerted these precautions I do not really know, since I was even then on my way to awaken the only other occupant of the house.

As I half tiptoed down the creaking stairs to the lower hall I could hear the sleeper more plainly, and noticed that he must be in the room on my left—the living-room I had not entered. On my right was the gaping blackness of the study in which I had heard the voices. Pushing open the unlatched door of the living-room I traced a path with the flashlight toward the source of the snoring, and finally turned the beams on the sleeper's face. But in the next second I hastily turned them away and commenced a cat-like retreat to the hall, my caution this time springing from reason as well as from instinct. For the sleeper on the couch was not Akeley at all, but my quondam guide Noyes.

Just what the real situation was, I could not guess; but common sense told me that the safest thing was to find out as much as possible before arousing anybody. Regaining the hall, I silently closed and latched the living-room door after me; thereby lessening the chances of awaking Noyes. I now cautiously entered the dark study, where I expected to find Akeley, whether asleep or awake, in the great corner chair which was evidently his favorite resting-place. As I advanced, the beams of my flashlight caught the great center-table, revealing one of the hellish cylinders with sight and hearing machines attached, and with a speech-machine standing close by, ready to be connected at any moment. This, I reflected, must be the encased brain I had heard talking during the frightful conference; and for a second I had a perverse impulse to attach the speech-machine and see what it would say.

It must, I thought, be conscious of my presence even now; since the sight and hearing attachments could not fail to disclose the rays of my flashlight and the faint creaking of the floor beneath my feet. But in the end I did not dare meddle with the thing. I idly saw that it was the fresh, shiny cylinder with Akeley's name on it, which I had noticed on the shelf earlier in the evening and which my host had told me not to bother. Looking back at that moment, I can only regret my timidity and wish that I had boldly caused the apparatus to speak. God knows what mysteries and horrible doubts and questions of identity it might have cleared up! But then, it may be merciful that I let it alone.

From the table I turned my flashlight to the corner where I thought Akeley was, but found to my perplexity that the great easy-chair was empty of any human occupant asleep or awake. From the seat to the floor there trailed voluminously the familiar old dressing-gown, and near it on the floor lay the yellow scarf and the huge foot-bandages I had thought so odd. As I hesitated, striving to conjecture where Akeley might be, and why he had so suddenly discarded his necessary sick-room garments, I observed that the queer odor and sense of vibration were no longer in the room. What had been their cause? Curiously it occurred to me that I had noticed them only in Akeley's vicinity. They had been strongest where he sat, and wholly absent except in the room with him or just outside the doors of that room. I paused, letting the flashlight wander about the dark study and racking my brain for explanations of the turn affairs had taken.

Would to heaven I had quietly left the place before allowing that light to rest again on the vacant chair. As it turned out, I did not leave quietly; but with a muffled shriek which must have disturbed, though it did not quite awake, the sleeping sentinel across the hall. That shriek, and Noyes's still-unbroken snore, are the last sounds I ever heard in that morbidity-choked farmhouse beneath the black-wooded crest of a haunted mountain—that focus of trans-cosmic horror amidst the lonely green hills and curse-muttering brooks of a spectral rustic land.

It is a wonder that I did not drop flashlight, valise, and revolver in my wild scramble, but somehow I failed to lose any of these. I actually managed to get out of that room and that house without making any further noise, to drag myself and my belongings safely into the old Ford in the shed, and to set that archaic vehicle in motion toward some unknown point of safety in the black, moonless night. The ride that followed was a piece of delirium out of Poe or Rimbaud or the drawings of Doré, but finally I reached Townshend. That is all. If my sanity is still unshaken, I am lucky. Sometimes I fear what the years will bring, especially since that new planet Pluto has been so curiously discovered.

As I have implied, I let my flashlight return to the vacant easy-chair after its circuit of the room; then noticing for the first time the presence of certain objects in the seat, made inconspicuous by the adjacent loose folds of the empty dressing-gown. These are the objects, three in number, which the investigators did not find when they came later on. As I said at the outset, there was nothing of actual visual horror about them. The trouble was in what they led one to infer. Even now I have my moments of half-doubt—moments in which I half-accept the skepticism of those who attribute my whole experience to dream and nerves and delusion.

The three things were damnably clever constructions of their kind, and were furnished with ingenious metallic clamps to attach them to organic developments of which I dare not form any conjecture. I hope—devoutly hope—that they were the waxen products of a master artist, despite what my inmost fears tell me. Great God! That whisperer in darkness with its morbid odor and vibrations! Sorcerer, emissary, changeling, outsider . . . that hideous repressed buzzing . . . and all the time in that fresh, shiny cylinder on the shelf . . . poor devil . . . "prodigious surgical, biological, chemical, and mechanical skill. . . ."

For the things in the chair, perfect to the last, subtle detail of microscopic resemblance—or identity—were the face and hands of Henry Wentworth Akeley.

THE HAUNTER OF THE DARK

(Dedicated to Robert Bloch)

I have seen the dark universe yawning
Where the black planets roll without aim—
Where they roll in their horror unheeded,
Without knowledge or luster or name.

—Nemesis

Cautious investigators will hesitate to challenge the common belief that Robert Blake was killed by lightning, or by some profound nervous shock derived from an electrical discharge. It is true that the window he faced was unbroken, but Nature has shown herself capable of many freakish performances. The expression on his face may easily have arisen from some obscure muscular source unrelated to anything he saw, while the entries in his diary are clearly the result of a fantastic imagination aroused by certain local superstitions and by certain old matters he had uncovered. As for the anomalous conditions at the deserted church on Federal Hill—the shrewd analyst is not slow in attributing them to some charlatanry, conscious or unconscious, with at least some of which Blake was secretly connected.

For after all, the victim was a writer and painter wholly devoted to the field of myth, dream, terror, and superstition, and avid in his quest for scenes and effects of a bizarre, spectral sort. His earlier stay in the city—a visit to a strange old man as deeply given to occult and forbidden lore as he—had ended amidst death and flame, and it must have been some morbid instinct which drew him back from his home in Milwaukee. He may have known of the old stories despite his statements to the contrary in the diary, and his death may have nipped in the bud some stupendous hoax destined to have a literary reflection.

Among those, however, who have examined and correlated all this evidence, there remain several who cling to less rational and common-place theories. They are inclined to take much of Blake's diary at its face value, and point significantly to certain facts such as the undoubted genuineness of the old church record, the verified existence of the disliked and unorthodox Starry Wisdom sect prior to 1877, the recorded disappearance of an inquisitive reporter named Edwin M. Lillibridge in 1893, and—above all—the look of monstrous, trans-figuring fear on the face of the young writer when he died. It was one of these believers who, moved to fanatical extremes, threw into the bay the curiously angled stone and its strangely adorned metal box found in the old church steeple—the black windowless steeple, and not the tower where Blake's diary said those things originally were. Though widely censured both officially and unofficially, this man—a reputable physician with a taste for odd folklore—averred that he had rid the earth of something too dangerous to rest upon it.

Between these two schools of opinion the reader must judge for himself. The papers have given the tangible details from a skeptical angle, leaving for others the drawing of the picture as Robert Blake saw it—or thought he saw it—or pretended to see it. Now, studying the diary closely, dispassionately, and at leisure, let us summarize the dark chain of events from the expressed point of view of their chief actor.

Young Blake returned to Providence in the winter of 1934–5, taking the upper floor of a venerable dwelling in a grassy court off College Street—on the crest of the great eastward hill near the Brown University campus and behind the marble John Hay Library. It was a cozy and fascinating place, in a little garden oasis of village-like antiquity where huge, friendly cats sunned themselves atop a conven-ient shed. The square Georgian house had a monitor roof, classic doorway with fan carving, small-paned windows, and all the other earmarks of early nineteenth-century workmanship. Inside were six-paneled doors, wide floor-boards, a curving colonial staircase, white Adam-period mantels, and a rear set of rooms three steps below the general level.

Blake's study, a large southwest chamber, overlooked the front garden on one side, while its west windows—before one of which he had his desk—faced off from the brow of the hill and commanded a splendid view of the lower town's outspread roofs and of the mystical sunsets that flamed behind them. On the far horizon were the open countryside's purple slopes. Against these, some two miles away, rose the spectral hump of Federal Hill, bristling with huddled roofs and steeples whose remote outlines wavered mysteriously, taking fantastic forms as the smoke of the city swirled up and enmeshed them. Blake had a curious sense that he was looking upon some unknown, ethereal world which might or might not vanish in dream if ever he tried to seek it out and enter it in person.

Having sent home for most of his books, Blake bought some antique furniture suitable to his quarters and settled down to write and paint—living alone, and attending to the simple housework himself. His studio was in a north attic room, where the panes of the monitor roof furnished admirable lighting. During that first winter he produced five of his best-known short stories—"The Burrower Beneath," "The Stairs in the Crypt," "Shaggai," "In the Vale of Pnath," and "The Feaster from the Stars"—and painted seven canvases; studies of nameless, unhuman monsters, and profoundly alien, non-terrestrial landscapes.

At sunset he would often sit at his desk and gaze dreamily off at the outspread west—the dark towers of Memorial Hall just below, the Georgian court-house belfry, the lofty pinnacles of the downtown section, and that shimmering, spire-crowned mound in the distance whose unknown streets and labyrinthine gables so potently provoked his fancy. From his few local acquaintances he learned that the far-off slope was a vast Italian quarter, though most of the houses were remnants of older Yankee and Irish days. Now and then he would train his field-glasses on that spectral, unreachable world beyond the curling smoke; picking out individual roofs and chimneys and steeples, and speculating upon the bizarre and curious mysteries they might house. Even with optical aid Federal Hill seemed somehow alien, half fabulous, and linked to the unreal, intangible marvels of Blake's own tales and pictures. The feeling would persist long after the hill had faded into the violet, lamp-starred twilight, and the court-house floodlights and the red Industrial Trust beacon had blazed up to make the night grotesque.

Of all the distant objects on Federal Hill, a certain huge, dark church most fascinated Blake. It stood out with especial distinctness at certain hours of the day, and at sunset the great tower and tapering steeple loomed blackly against the flaming sky. It seemed to rest on especially high ground; for the grimy facade, and the obliquely seen north side with sloping roof and the tops of great pointed windows, rose boldly above the tangle of surrounding ridgepoles and chimney-pots. Peculiarly grim and austere, it appeared to be built of stone, stained and weathered with the smoke and storms of a century and more. The style, so far as the glass could show, was that earliest experimental form of Gothic revival which preceded the stately Upjohn period and held over some of the outlines and proportions of the Georgian age. Perhaps it was reared around 1810 or 1815.

As months passed, Blake watched the far-off, forbidding structure with an oddly mounting interest. Since the vast windows were never lighted, he knew that it must be vacant. The longer he watched, the more his imagination worked, till at length he began to fancy curious things. He believed that a vague, singular aura of desolation hovered over the place, so that even the pigeons and swallows shunned its smoky eaves. Around other towers and belfries his glass would reveal great flocks of birds, but here they never rested. At least, that is what he thought and set down in his diary. He pointed the place out to several friends, but none of them had even been on Federal Hill or possessed the faintest notion of what the church was or had been.

In the spring a deep restlessness gripped Blake. He had begun his long-planned novel—based on a supposed survival of the witch-cult in Maine—but was strangely unable to make progress with it. More and more he would sit at his westward window and gaze at the distant hill and the black, frowning steeple shunned by the birds. When the delicate leaves came out on the garden boughs the world was filled with a new beauty, but Blake's restlessness was merely increased. It was then that he first thought of crossing the city and climbing bodily up that fabulous slope into the smoke-wreathed world of dream.

Late in April, just before the eon-shadowed Walpurgis time, Blake made his first trip into the unknown. Plodding through the endless downtown streets and the bleak, decayed squares beyond, he came finally upon the ascending avenue of century-worn steps, sagging Doric porches, and blear-paned cupolas which he felt must lead up to the long-known, unreachable world beyond the mists. There were dingy blue-and-white street signs which meant nothing to him, and presently he noted the strange, dark faces of the drifting crowds, and the foreign signs over curious shops in brown, decade-weathered buildings. Nowhere could he find any of the objects he had seen from afar; so that once more he half fancied that the Federal Hill of that distant view was a dream-world never to be trod by living human feet.

Now and then a battered church facade or crumbling spire came in sight, but never the blackened pile that he sought. When he asked a shopkeeper about a great stone church the man smiled and shook his head, though he spoke English freely. As Blake climbed higher, the region seemed stranger and stranger, with bewildering mazes of brooding brown alleys leading eternally off to the south. He crossed two or three broad avenues, and once thought he glimpsed a familiar tower. Again he asked a merchant about the massive church of stone, and this time he could have sworn that the plea of ignorance was feigned. The dark man's face had a look of fear which he tried to hide, and Blake saw him make a curious sign with his right hand.

Then suddenly a black spire stood out against the cloudy sky on his left, above the tiers of brown roofs lining the tangled southerly alleys. Blake knew at once what it was, and plunged toward it through the squalid, unpaved lanes that climbed from the avenue. Twice he lost his way, but he somehow dared not ask any of the patriarchs or housewives who sat on their doorsteps, or any of the children who shouted and played in the mud of the shadowy lanes.

At last he saw the tower plain against the southwest, and a huge stone bulk rose darkly at the end of an alley. Presently he stood in a windswept open square, quaintly cobblestoned, with a high bank wall on the farther side. This was the end of his quest; for upon the wide, iron-railed, weed-grown plateau which the wall supported—a separate, lesser world raised fully six feet above the surrounding streets—there stood a grim, titan bulk whose identity, despite Blake's new perspective, was beyond dispute.

The vacant church was in a state of great decrepitude. Some of the high stone buttresses had fallen, and several delicate finials lay half lost among the brown, neglected weeds and grasses. The sooty Gothic windows were largely unbroken, though many of the stone mullions were missing. Blake wondered how the obscurely painted panes could have survived so well, in view of the known habits of small boys the world over. The massive doors were intact and tightly closed. Around the top of the bank wall, fully enclosing the grounds, was a rusty iron fence whose gate—at the head of a flight of steps from the square—was visibly padlocked. The path from the gate to the building was completely overgrown. Desolation and decay hung like a pall above the place, and in the birdless eaves and black, ivyless walls Blake felt a touch of the dimly sinister beyond his power to define.

There were very few people in the square, but Blake saw a policeman at the northerly end and approached him with questions about the church. He was a great wholesome Irishman, and it seemed odd that he would do little more than make the sign of the cross and mutter that people never spoke of that building. When Blake pressed him he said very hurriedly that the Italian priests warned everybody against it, vowing that a monstrous evil had once dwelt there and left its mark. He himself had heard dark whispers of it from his father, who recalled certain sounds and rumors from his boyhood.

There had been a bad sect there in the old days—an outlaw sect that called up awful things from some unknown gulf of night. It had taken a good priest to exorcise what had come, though there did be those who said that merely the light could do it. If Father O'Malley were alive there would be many the thing he could tell. But now there was nothing to do but let it alone. It hurt nobody now, and those that owned it were dead or far away. They had run away like rats after the threatening talk in '77, when people began to mind the way folks vanished now and then in the neighborhood. Some day the city would step in and take the property for lack of heirs, but little good would come of anybody's touching it. Better it be left alone for the years to topple, lest things be stirred that ought to rest forever in their black abyss.

After the policeman had gone Blake stood staring at the sullen steepled pile. It excited him to find that the structure seemed as sinister to others as to him, and he wondered what grain of truth might lie behind the old tales the bluecoat had repeated. Probably they were mere legends evoked by the evil look of the place, but even so, they were like a strange coming to life of one of his own stories.

The afternoon sun came out from behind dispersing clouds, but seemed unable to light up the stained, sooty walls of the old temple

that towered on its high plateau. It was odd that the green of spring
had not touched the brown, withered growths in the raised, iron-fenced
yard. Blake found himself edging nearer the raised area and examining
the bank wall and rusted fence for possible avenues of ingress. There
was a terrible lure about the blackened fane which was not to be
resisted. The fence had no opening near the steps, but around on the
north side were some missing bars. He could go up the steps and
walk around on the narrow coping outside the fence till he came to
the gap. If the people feared the place so wildly, he would encounter
no interference.

He was on the embankment and almost inside the fence before
anyone noticed him. Then, looking down, he saw the few people in
the square edging away and making the same sign with their right
hands that the shopkeeper in the avenue had made. Several windows
were slammed down, and a fat woman darted into the street and
pulled some small children inside a rickety, unpainted house. The
gap in the fence was very easy to pass through, and before long Blake
found himself wading amidst the rotting, tangled growths of the
deserted yard. Here and there the worn stump of a headstone told
him that there had once been burials in this field; but that, he saw,
must have been very long ago. The sheer bulk of the church was
oppressive now that he was close to it, but he conquered his mood
and approached to try the three great doors in the facade. All were
securely locked, so he began a circuit of the Cyclopean building in
quest of some minor and more penetrable opening. Even then he
could not be sure that he wished to enter that haunt of desertion and
shadow, yet the pull of its strangeness dragged him on automatically.

A yawning and unprotected cellar window in the rear furnished
the needed aperture. Peering in, Blake saw a subterrene gulf of
cobwebs and dust faintly litten by the western sun's filtered rays.
Debris, old barrels, and ruined boxes and furniture of numerous sorts
met his eye, though over everything lay a shroud of dust which

softened all sharp outlines. The rusted remains of a hot-air furnace showed that the building had been used and kept in shape as late as mid-Victorian times.

Acting almost without conscious initiative, Blake crawled through the window and let himself down to the dust-carpeted and debris-strewn concrete floor. The vaulted cellar was a vast one, without partitions; and in a corner far to the right, amid dense shadows, he saw a black archway evidently leading upstairs. He felt a peculiar sense of oppression at being actually within the great spectral building, but kept it in check as he cautiously scouted about—finding a still-intact barrel amid the dust, and rolling it over to the open window to provide for his exit. Then, bracing himself, he crossed the wide, cobweb-festooned space toward the arch. Half choked with the omnipresent dust, and covered with ghostly gossamer fibers, he reached and began to climb the worn stone steps which rose into the darkness. He had no light, but groped carefully with his hands. After a sharp turn he felt a closed door ahead, and a little fumbling revealed its ancient latch. It opened inward, and beyond it he saw a dimly illumined corridor lined with worm-eaten paneling.

Once on the ground floor, Blake began exploring in a rapid fashion. All the inner doors were unlocked, so that he freely passed from room to room. The colossal nave was an almost eldritch place with its drifts and mountains of dust over box pews, altar, hourglass pulpit, and sounding-board, and its titanic ropes of cobweb stretching among the pointed arches of the gallery and entwining the clustered Gothic columns. Over all this hushed desolation played a hideous leaden light as the declining afternoon sun sent its rays through the strange, half-blackened panes of the great apsidal windows.

The paintings on those windows were so obscured by soot that Blake could scarcely decipher what they had represented, but from the little he could make out he did not like them. The designs were largely conventional, and his knowledge of obscure symbolism told him much concerning some of the ancient patterns. The few saints depicted bore expressions distinctly open to criticism, while one of the windows seemed to show merely a dark space with spirals of curious luminosity scattered about in it. Turning away from the windows, Blake noticed that the cobwebbed cross above the altar was not of the ordinary kind, but resembled the primordial *ankh* or *crux ansata* of shadowy Egypt.

In a rear vestry room beside the apse Blake found a rotting desk and ceiling-high shelves of mildewed, disintegrating books. Here for the first time he received a positive shock of objective horror, for the titles of those books told him much. They were the black, forbidden things which most sane people have never even heard of, or have heard of only in furtive, timorous whispers; the banned and dreaded repositories of equivocal secrets and immemorial formulae which have trickled down the stream of time from the days of man's youth, and the dim, fabulous days before man was. He had himself read many of them—a Latin version of the abhorred *Necronomicon*, the sinister *Liber Ivonis*, the infamous *Cultes des Goules* of Comte d'Erlette, the *Unaussprechlichen Kulten* of von Junzt, and old Ludvig Prinn's hellish *De Vermis Mysteriis*. But there were others he had known merely by reputation or not at all—the Pnakotic Manuscripts, the *Book of Dzyan*, and a crumbling volume in wholly unidentifiable characters yet with certain symbols and diagrams shudderingly recognizable to the occult student. Clearly, the lingering local rumors had not lied. This place had once been the seat of an evil older than mankind and wider than the known universe.

In the ruined desk was a small leather-bound record-book filled with entries in some odd cryptographic medium. The manuscript writing consisted of the common traditional symbols used today in astronomy and anciently in alchemy, astrology, and other dubious arts—the devices of the sun, moon, planets, aspects, and zodiacal signs—here massed in solid pages of text, with divisions and paragraphings suggesting that each symbol answered to some alphabetical letter.

In the hope of later solving the cryptogram, Blake bore off this volume in his coat pocket. Many of the great tomes on the shelves fascinated him unutterably, and he felt tempted to borrow them at some later time. He wondered how they could have remained undisturbed so long. Was he the first to conquer the clutching, pervasive fear which had for nearly sixty years protected this deserted place from visitors?

Having now thoroughly explored the ground floor, Blake plowed again through the dust of the spectral nave to the front vestibule, where he had seen a door and staircase presumably leading up to the blackened tower and steeple—objects so long familiar to him at a distance. The ascent was a choking experience, for dust lay thick, while the spiders had done their worst in this constricted place. The staircase was a spiral with high, narrow wooden treads, and now and then Blake passed a clouded window looking dizzily out over the city. Though he had seen no ropes below, he expected to find a bell or peal of bells in the tower whose narrow, louver-boarded lancet windows his field-glass had studied so often. Here he was doomed to disappointment; for when he attained the top of the stairs he found the tower chamber vacant of chimes, and clearly devoted to vastly different purposes.

The room, about fifteen feet square, was faintly lighted by four lancet windows, one on each side, which were glazed within their screening of decayed louver-boards. These had been further fitted with tight, opaque screens, but the latter were now largely rotted away. In the center of the dust-laden floor rose a curiously angled stone pillar some four feet in height and two in average diameter, covered on each side with bizarre, crudely incised, and wholly unrecognizable hieroglyphs. On this pillar rested a metal box of peculiarly asymmetrical form; its hinged lid thrown back, and its interior holding what looked beneath the decade-deep dust to be an egg-shaped or irregularly spherical object some four inches through. Around the pillar in a rough circle were seven high-backed Gothic chairs still largely intact, while behind them, ranging along the dark-paneled walls, were seven colossal images of crumbling, black-painted plaster, resembling more than anything else the cryptic carven megaliths of mysterious Easter Island. In one corner of the cobwebbed chamber a ladder was built into the wall, leading up to the closed trapdoor of the windowless steeple above.

As Blake grew accustomed to the feeble light he noticed odd bas-reliefs on the strange open box of yellowish metal. Approaching, he tried to clear the dust away with his hands and handkerchief, and saw that the figurings were of a monstrous and utterly alien kind; depicting entities which, though seemingly alive, resembled no known life-form ever evolved on this planet. The four-inch seeming sphere turned out to be a nearly black, red-striated polyhedron with many irregular flat surfaces; either a very remarkable crystal of some sort, or an artificial object of carved and highly polished mineral matter. It did not touch the bottom of the box, but was held suspended by means of a metal band around its center, with seven queerly designed supports extending horizontally to angles of the box's inner wall near the top. This stone, once exposed, exerted upon Blake an almost alarming fascination. He could scarcely tear his eyes from it, and as he looked at its glistening surfaces he almost fancied it was transparent, with half-formed worlds of wonder within. Into his mind floated pictures of alien orbs with great stone towers, and other orbs with titan mountains and no mark of life, and still remoter spaces where only a stirring in vague blacknesses told of the presence of consciousness and will.

When he did look away, it was to notice a somewhat singular mound of dust in the far corner near the ladder to the steeple. Just why it took his attention he could not tell, but something in its contours carried a message to his unconscious mind. Plowing toward it, and brushing aside the hanging cobwebs as he went, he began to discern something grim about it. Hand and handkerchief soon revealed the truth, and Blake gasped with a baffling mixture of emotions. It was a human skeleton, and it must have been there for a very long time. The clothing was in shreds, but some buttons and fragments of cloth bespoke a man's gray suit. There were other bits of evidence—shoes, metal clasps, huge buttons for round cuffs, a stickpin of bygone pattern, a reporter's badge with the name of the old *Providence Telegram,* and a crumbling leather pocketbook. Blake examined the latter with care, finding within it several bills of antiquated issue, a celluloid advertising calendar for 1893, some cards with the name "Edwin M. Lillibridge," and a paper covered with penciled memoranda.

This paper held much of a puzzling nature, and Blake read it carefully at the dim westward window. Its disjointed text included such phrases as the following:

Prof. Enoch Bowen home from Egypt May 1844—buys old Free-Will Church in July—his archeological work & studies in occult well known.

Dr Drowne of 4th Baptist warns against Starry Wisdom in sermon Dec. 29th, 1844.

Congregation 97 by end of '45.

1846—3 disappearances—first mention of Shining Trapezohedron.

7 disappearances 1848—stories of blood sacrifice begin.

Investigation 1853 comes to nothing—stories of sounds.

Fr O'Malley tells of devil-worship with box found in great Egyptian ruins—says they call up something that can't exist in light. Flees a little light, and banished by strong light. Then has to be summoned again. Probably got this from deathbed confession of Francis X. Feeney, who had joined Starry Wisdom in '49. These people say the Shining Trapezohedron shows them heaven & other worlds, & that the Haunter of the Dark tells them secrets in some way.

Story of Orrin B. Eddy 1857. They call it up by gazing at the crystal, & have a secret language of their own.

200 or more in cong. 1863, exclusive of men at front.

Irish boys mob church in 1869 after Patrick Regan's disappearance.

Veiled article in J. March 14th, '72, but people don't talk about it.

6 disappearances 1876—secret committee calls on Mayor Doyle.

Action promised Feb. 1877—church closes in April.

Gang—Federal Hill Boys—threaten Dr —— and vestrymen in May.

181 persons leave city before end of '77—mention no names.

Ghost stories begin around 1880—try to ascertain truth of report that no human being has entered church since 1877.

Ask Lanigan for photograph of place taken 1851. . . .

Restoring the paper to the pocketbook and placing the latter in his coat, Blake turned to look down at the skeleton in the dust. The implications of the notes were clear, and there could be no doubt but that this man had come to the deserted edifice forty-two years before in quest of a newspaper sensation which no one else had been bold enough to attempt. Perhaps no one else had known of his plan—who could tell? But he had never returned to his paper. Had some bravely suppressed fear risen to overcome him and bring on sudden heart-failure? Blake stooped over the gleaming bones and noted their peculiar state. Some of them were badly scattered, and a few seemed oddly *dissolved* at the ends. Others were strangely yellowed, with vague suggestions of charring. This charring extended to some of the fragments of clothing. The skull was in a very peculiar state—stained yellow, and with a charred aperture in the top as if some powerful acid had eaten through the solid bone. What had happened to the skeleton during its four decades of silent entombment here Blake could not imagine.

Before he realized it, he was looking at the stone again, and letting its curious influence call up a nebulous pageantry in his mind. He saw processions of robed, hooded figures whose outlines were not human, and looked on endless leagues of desert lined with carved, sky-reaching monoliths. He saw towers and walls in nighted depths under the sea, and vortices of space where wisps of black mist floated before thin shimmerings of cold purple haze. And beyond all else he glimpsed an infinite gulf of darkness, where solid and semi-solid forms were known only by their windy stirrings, and cloudy patterns of force seemed to superimpose order on chaos and hold forth a key to all the paradoxes and arcana of the worlds we know.

Then all at once the spell was broken by an access of gnawing, indeterminate panic fear. Blake choked and turned away from the stone, conscious of some formless alien presence close to him and watching him with horrible intentness. He felt entangled with something—something which was not in the stone, but which had looked through it at him—something which would ceaselessly follow him with a cognition that was not physical sight. Plainly, the place was getting on his nerves—as well it might in view of his gruesome find. The light was waning, too, and since he had no illuminant with him he knew he would have to be leaving soon.

It was then, in the gathering twilight, that he thought he saw a faint trace of luminosity in the crazily angled stone. He had tried to look away from it, but some obscure compulsion drew his eyes back. Was there a subtle phosphorescence of radioactivity about the thing? What was it that the dead man's notes had said concerning a *Shining Trapezohedron?* What, anyway, was this abandoned lair of cosmic evil? What had been done here, and what might still be lurking in the bird-shunned shadows? It seemed now as if an elusive touch of fetor had arisen somewhere close by, though its source was not apparent. Blake seized the cover of the long-open box and snapped it down. It moved easily on its alien hinges, and closed completely over the unmistakably glowing stone.

At the sharp click of that closing a soft stirring sound seemed to come from the steeple's eternal blackness overhead, beyond the trap-door. Rats, without question—the only living things to reveal their presence in this accursed pile since he had entered it. And yet that stirring in the steeple frightened him horribly, so that he plunged almost wildly down the spiral stairs, across the ghoulish nave, into the vaulted basement, out amidst the gathering dusk of the deserted square, and down through the teeming, fear-haunted alleys and avenues of Federal Hill toward the sane central streets and the home-like brick sidewalks of the college district.

During the days which followed, Blake told no one of his expedition. Instead, he read much in certain books, examined long years of newspaper files downtown, and worked feverishly at the cryptogram in that leather volume from the cobwebbed vestry room. The cipher, he soon saw, was no simple one; and after a long period of endeavor he felt sure that its language could not be English, Latin, Greek, French, Spanish, Italian, or German. Evidently he would have to draw upon the deepest wells of his strange erudition.

Every evening the old impulse to gaze westward returned, and he saw the black steeple as of yore amongst the bristling roofs of a distant and half-fabulous world. But now it held a fresh note of terror for him. He knew the heritage of evil lore it masked, and with the knowledge his vision ran riot in queer new ways. The birds of spring were returning, and as he watched their sunset flights he fancied they avoided the gaunt, lone spire as never before. When a flock of them approached it, he thought, they would wheel and scatter in panic confusion—and he could guess at the wild twitterings which failed to reach him across the intervening miles.

It was in June that Blake's diary told of his victory over the cryptogram. The text was, he found, in the dark Aklo language used by certain cults of evil antiquity, and known to him in a halting way through previous researches. The diary is strangely reticent about what Blake deciphered, but he was patently awed and disconcerted by his results. There are references to a Haunter of the Dark awaked by gazing into the Shining Trapezohedron, and insane conjectures about the black gulfs of chaos from which it was called. The being is spoken of as holding all knowledge, and demanding monstrous sacrifices. Some of Blake's entries show fear lest the thing, which he seemed to regard as summoned, stalk abroad; though he adds that the streetlights form a bulwark which cannot be crossed.

Of the Shining Trapezohedron he speaks often, calling it a window on all time and space, and tracing its history from the days it was fashioned on dark Yuggoth, before ever the Old Ones brought it to earth. It was treasured and placed in its curious box by the crinoid things of Antarctica, salvaged from their ruins by the serpent-men of Valusia, and peered at eons later in Lemuria by the first human beings.

It crossed strange lands and stranger seas, and sank with Atlantis before a Minoan fisher meshed it in his net and sold it to swarthy merchants from nighted Khem. The Pharaoh Nephren-Ka built around it a temple with a windowless crypt, and did that which caused his name to be stricken from all monuments and records. Then it slept in the ruins of that evil fane which the priests and the new Pharaoh destroyed, till the delver's spade once more brought it forth to curse mankind.

Early in July the newspapers oddly supplement Blake's entries, though in so brief and casual a way that only the diary has called general attention to their contribution. It appears that a new fear had been growing on Federal Hill since a stranger had entered the dreaded church. The Italians whispered of unaccustomed stirrings and bumpings and scrapings in the dark windowless steeple, and called on their priests to banish an entity which haunted their dreams. Something, they said, was constantly watching at a door to see if it were dark enough to venture forth. Press items mentioned the long-standing local superstitions, but failed to shed much light on the earlier background of the horror. It was obvious that the young reporters of today are no antiquarians. In writing of these things in his diary, Blake expresses a curious kind of remorse, and talks of the duty of burying the Shining Trapezohedron and of banishing what he had evoked by letting daylight into the hideous jutting spire. At the same time, however, he displays the dangerous extent of his fascination, and admits a morbid longing—pervading even his dreams—to visit the accursed tower and gaze again into the cosmic secrets of the glowing stone.

Then something in the *Journal* on the morning of July 17 threw the diarist into a veritable fever of horror. It was only a variant of the other half-humorous items about the Federal Hill restlessness, but to Blake it was somehow very terrible indeed. In the night a thunderstorm had put the city's lighting system out of commission for a full hour, and in that black interval the Italians had nearly gone mad with fright. Those living near the dreaded church had sworn that the thing in the steeple had taken advantage of the street-lamps' absence and gone down into the body of the church, flopping and bumping around in a viscous, altogether dreadful way. Toward the last it had bumped up to the tower, where there were sounds of the shattering of glass. It could go wherever the darkness reached, but light would always send it fleeing.

When the current blazed on again there had been a shocking commotion in the tower, for even the feeble light trickling through the grime-blackened, louver-boarded windows was too much for the thing. It had bumped and slithered up into its tenebrous steeple just in time—for a long dose of light would have sent it back into the abyss whence the crazy stranger had called it. During the dark hour praying crowds had clustered round the church in the rain with lighted candles and lamps somehow shielded with folded paper and umbrellas—a guard of light to save the city from the nightmare that stalks in darkness. Once, those nearest the church declared, the outer door had rattled hideously.

But even this was not the worst. That evening in the *Bulletin* Blake read of what the reporters had found. Aroused at last to the whimsical news value of the scare, a pair of them had defied the frantic crowds of Italians and crawled into the church through the cellar window after trying the doors in vain. They found the dust of the vestibule and of the spectral nave plowed up in a singular way, with bits of rotted cushions and satin pew-linings scattered curiously around. There was a bad odor everywhere, and here and there were bits of yellow stain and patches of what looked like charring. Opening the door to the tower, and pausing a moment at the suspicion of a scraping sound above, they found the narrow spiral stairs wiped roughly clean.

In the tower itself a similarly half-swept condition existed. They spoke of the heptagonal stone pillar, the overturned Gothic chairs, and the bizarre plaster images; though strangely enough the metal box and the old mutilated skeleton were not mentioned. What disturbed Blake the most—except for the hints of stains and charring and bad odors—was the final detail that explained the crashing glass. Every one of the tower's lancet windows was broken, and two of them had been darkened in a crude and hurried way by the stuffing of satin pew-linings and cushion-horsehair into the spaces between the slanting exterior louver-boards. More satin fragments and bunches of horsehair lay scattered around the newly swept floor, as if someone had been interrupted in the act of restoring the tower to the absolute blackness of its tightly curtained days.

Yellowish stains and charred patches were found on the ladder to the windowless spire, but when a reporter climbed up, opened the horizontally sliding trap-door, and shot a feeble flashlight beam into the black and strangely fetid space, he saw nothing but darkness, and a heterogeneous litter of shapeless fragments near the aperture. The verdict, of course, was charlatanry. Somebody had played a joke on the superstitious hill-dwellers, or else some fanatic had striven to bolster up their fears for their own supposed good. Or perhaps some of the younger and more sophisticated dwellers had staged an elaborate hoax on the outside world. There was an amusing aftermath when the police sent an officer to verify the reports. Three men in succession found ways of evading the assignment, and the fourth went very reluctantly and returned very soon without adding to the account given by the reporters.

From this point onward Blake's diary shows a mounting tide of insidious horror and nervous apprehension. He upbraids himself for not doing something, and speculates wildly on the consequences of another electrical breakdown. It has been verified that on three occasions—during thunderstorms—he telephoned the electric light company in a frantic vein and asked that desperate precautions against a lapse of power be taken. Now and then his entries show concern over the failure of the reporters to find the metal box and stone, and the strangely marred old skeleton, when they explored the shadowy tower room. He assumed that these things had been removed—whither, and by whom or what, he could only guess. But his worst fears concerned himself, and the kind of unholy rapport he felt to exist between his mind and that lurking horror in the distant steeple—that monstrous thing of night which his rashness had called out of the ultimate black spaces. He seemed to feel a constant tugging at his will, and callers of that period remember how he would sit abstractedly at his desk and stare out of the west window at that far-off, spire-bristling mound beyond the swirling smoke of the city. His entries dwell monotonously on certain terrible dreams, and of a strengthening of the unholy rapport in his sleep. There is mention of a night when he awaked to find himself fully dressed, outdoors, and headed automatically down College Hill toward the west. Again and again he dwells on the fact that the thing in the steeple knows where to find him.

The week following July 30th is recalled as the time of Blake's partial breakdown. He did not dress, and ordered all his food by telephone. Visitors remarked the cords he kept near his bed, and he said that sleep-walking had forced him to bind his ankles every night with knots which would probably hold or else waken him with the labor of untying.

In his diary he told of the hideous experience which had brought the collapse. After retiring on the night of the 30th he had suddenly found himself groping about in an almost black space. All he could see were short, faint, horizontal streaks of bluish light, but he could smell an overpowering fetor and hear a curious jumble of soft, furtive sounds above him. Whenever he moved he stumbled over something, and at each noise there would come a sort of answering sound from above—a vague stirring, mixed with the cautious sliding of wood on wood.

Once his groping hands encountered a pillar of stone with a vacant top, whilst later he found himself clutching the rungs of a ladder built into the wall, and fumbling his uncertain way upward toward some region of intenser stench where a hot, searing blast beat down against him. Before his eyes a kaleidoscopic range of phantasmal images played, all of them dissolving at intervals into the picture of a vast, unplumbed abyss of night wherein whirled suns and worlds of an even profounder blackness. He thought of the ancient legends of Ultimate Chaos, at whose center sprawls the blind idiot god Azathoth, Lord of All Things, encircled by his flopping horde of mindless and amorphous dancers, and lulled by the thin monotonous piping of a demoniac flute held in nameless paws.

Then a sharp report from the outer world broke through his stupor and roused him to the unutterable horror of his position. What it was, he never knew—perhaps it was some belated peal from the fireworks heard all summer on Federal Hill as the dwellers hail their various patron saints, or the saints of their native villages in Italy. In any event he shrieked aloud, dropped frantically from the ladder, and stumbled blindly across the obstructed floor of the almost lightless chamber that encompassed him.

He knew instantly where he was, and plunged recklessly down the narrow spiral staircase, tripping and bruising himself at every turn. There was a nightmare flight through a vast cobwebbed nave whose ghostly arches reached up to realms of leering shadow, a sightless scramble through a littered basement, a climb to regions of air and streetlights outside, and a mad racing down a spectral hill of gibbering gables, across a grim, silent city of tall black towers, and up the steep eastward precipice to his own ancient door.

On regaining consciousness in the morning he found himself lying on his study floor fully dressed. Dirt and cobwebs covered him, and every inch of his body seemed sore and bruised. When he faced the mirror he saw that his hair was badly scorched, while a trace of strange, evil odor seemed to cling to his upper outer clothing. It was then that his nerves broke down. Thereafter, lounging exhaustedly about in a dressing-gown, he did little but stare from his west window, shiver at the threat of thunder, and make wild entries in his diary.

The great storm broke just before midnight on August 8th. Lightning struck repeatedly in all parts of the city, and two remarkable fireballs were reported. The rain was torrential, while a constant fusillade of thunder brought sleeplessness to thousands. Blake was utterly frantic in his fear for the lighting system, and tried to telephone the company around 1 a.m., though by that time service had been temporarily cut off in the interest of safety. He recorded everything in his diary—the large, nervous, and often undecipherable hieroglyphs telling their own story of growing frenzy and despair, and of entries scrawled blindly in the dark.

He had to keep the house dark in order to see out of the window, and it appears that most of his time was spent at his desk, peering anxiously through the rain across the glistening miles of downtown roofs at the constellation of distant lights marking Federal Hill. Now and then he would fumblingly make an entry in his diary, so that detached phrases such as "The lights must not go"; "It knows where I am"; "I must destroy it"; and "It is calling to me, but perhaps it means no injury this time"; are found scattered down two of the pages.

Then the lights went out all over the city. It happened at 2:12 a.m. according to power-house records, but Blake's diary gives no indication of the time. The entry is merely, "Lights out—God help me." On Federal Hill there were watchers as anxious as he, and rain-soaked knots of men paraded the square and alleys around the evil church with umbrella-shaded candles, electric flashlights, oil lanterns, crucifixes, and obscure charms of the many sorts common to southern Italy. They blessed each flash of lightning, and made cryptical signs of fear with their right hands when a turn in the storm caused the flashes to lessen and finally to cease altogether. A rising wind blew out most of the candles, so that the scene grew threateningly dark. Someone roused Father Merluzzo of Spirito Santo Church, and he hastened to the dismal square to pronounce whatever helpful syllables he could. Of the restless and curious sounds in the blackened tower, there could be no doubt whatever.

For what happened at 2:35 a.m. we have the testimony of the priest, a young, intelligent, and well-educated person; of Patrolman William J. Monahan of the Central Station, an officer of the highest reliability who had paused at that part of his beat to inspect the crowd; and of most of the seventy-eight men who had gathered around the church's high bank wall—especially those in the square where the eastward façade was visible. Of course there was nothing which can be proved as being outside the order of Nature. The possible causes of such an event are many. No one can speak with certainty of the obscure chemical processes arising in a vast, ancient, ill-aired, and long-deserted building of heterogeneous contents. Mephitic vapors— spontaneous combustion—pressure of gases born of long decay—any one of numberless phenomena might be responsible. And then, of course, the factor of conscious charlatanry can by no means be excluded. The thing was really quite simple in itself, and covered less than three minutes of actual time. Father Merluzzo, always a precise man, looked at his watch repeatedly.

It started with a definite swelling of the dull fumbling sounds inside the black tower. There had for some time been a vague exhalation of strange, evil odors from the church, and this had now become emphatic and offensive. Then at last there was a sound of splintering wood, and a large, heavy object crashed down in the yard beneath the frowning easterly facade. The tower was invisible now that the candles would not burn, but as the object neared the ground the people knew that it was the smoke-grimed louver-boarding of that tower's east window.

Immediately afterward an utterly unbearable fetor welled forth from the unseen heights, choking and sickening the trembling watchers, and almost prostrating those in the square. At the same time the air trembled with a vibration as of flapping wings, and a sudden east-blowing wind more violent than any previous blast snatched off the hats and wrenched the dripping umbrellas of the crowd. Nothing definite could be seen in the candleless night, though some upward-looking spectators thought they glimpsed a great spreading blur of denser blackness against the inky sky—something like a formless cloud of smoke that shot with meteor-like speed toward the east.

That was all. The watchers were half numbed with fright, awe, and discomfort, and scarcely knew what to do, or whether to do anything at all. Not knowing what had happened, they did not relax their vigil; and a moment later they sent up a prayer as a sharp flash of belated lightning, followed by an earsplitting crash of sound, rent the flooded heavens. Half an hour later the rain stopped, and in fifteen minutes more the streetlights sprang on again, sending the weary, bedraggled watchers relievedly back to their homes.

The next day's papers gave these matters minor mention in connection with the general storm reports. It seems that the great lightning flash and deafening explosion which followed the Federal Hill occurrence were even more tremendous farther east, where a burst of the singular fetor was likewise noticed. The phenomenon was most marked over College Hill, where the crash awaked all the sleeping inhabitants and led to a bewildered round of speculations. Of those who were already awake only a few saw the anomalous blaze of light near the top of the hill, or noticed the inexplicable upward rush of air which almost stripped the leaves from the trees and blasted the plants in the gardens. It was agreed that the lone, sudden lightning-bolt must have struck somewhere in this neighborhood, though no trace of its striking could afterward be found. A youth in the Tau Omega fraternity house thought he saw a grotesque and hideous mass of smoke in the air just as the preliminary flash burst, but his observation has not been verified. All of the few observers, however, agree as to the violent gust from the west and the flood of intolerable stench which preceded the belated stroke; whilst evidence concerning the momentary burned odor after the stroke is equally general.

These points were discussed very carefully because of their probable connection with the death of Robert Blake. Students in the Psi Delta house, whose upper rear windows looked into Blake's study, noticed the blurred white face at the westward window on the morning of the 9th, and wondered what was wrong with the expression. When they saw the same face in the same position that evening, they felt worried, and watched for the lights to come up in his apartment. Later they rang the bell of the darkened flat, and finally had a policeman force the door.

The rigid body sat bolt upright at the desk by the window, and when the intruders saw the glassy, bulging eyes, and the marks of stark, convulsive fright on the twisted features, they turned away in sickened dismay. Shortly afterward the coroner's physician made an examination, and despite the unbroken window reported electrical shock, or nervous tension induced by electrical discharge, as the cause of death. The hideous expression he ignored altogether, deeming it a not improbable result of the profound shock as experienced by a person of such abnormal imagination and unbalanced emotions. He deduced these latter qualities from the books, paintings, and manuscripts found in the apartment, and from the blindly scrawled entries in the diary on the desk. Blake had prolonged his frenzied jottings to the last, and the broken-pointed pencil was found clutched in his spasmodically contracted right hand.

The entries after the failure of the lights were highly disjointed, and legible only in part. From them certain investigators have drawn conclusions differing greatly from the materialistic official verdict, but such speculations have little chance for belief among the conservative. The case of these imaginative theorists has not been helped by the action of superstitious Dr Dexter, who threw the curious box and angled stone—an object certainly self-luminous as seen in the black windowless steeple where it was found—into the deepest channel of Narragansett Bay. Excessive imagination and neurotic unbalance on Blake's part, aggravated by knowledge of the evil bygone cult whose startling traces he had uncovered, form the dominant interpretation given those final frenzied jottings. These are the entries—or all that can be made of them:

Lights still out—must be five minutes now. Everything depends on lightning. Yaddith grant it will keep up!. . . Some influence seems beating through it. . . Rain and thunder and wind deafen. . . The thing is taking hold of my mind. . .

Trouble with memory. I see things I never knew before. Other worlds and other galaxies. . . Dark. . . The lightning seems dark and the darkness seems light. . .

It cannot be the real hill and church that I see in the pitch-darkness. Must be retinal impression left by flashes. Heaven grant the Italians are out with their candles if the lightning stops!

What am I afraid of? Is it not an avatar of Nyarlathotep, who in antique and shadowy Khem even took the form of man? I remember Yuggoth, and more distant Shaggai, and the ultimate void of the black planets. . .

The long, winging flight through the void. . . cannot cross the universe of light. . . re-created by the thoughts caught in the Shining Trapezohedron. . . send it through the horrible abysses of radiance. . .

My name is Blake—Robert Harrison Blake of 620 East Knapp Street, Milwaukee, Wisconsin. . . I am on this planet. . .

Azathoth have mercy!—The lightning no longer flashes—horrible—I can see everything with a monstrous sense that is not sight—light is dark and dark is light. . . those people on the hill. . . guard. . . candles and charms. . . their priests. . .

Sense of distance gone—far is near and near is far. No light— no glass—see that steeple—that tower—window—can hear—Roderick Usher—am mad or going mad—the thing is stirring and fumbling in the tower—I am it and it is I—I want to get out. . . must get out and unify the forces. . . It knows where I am. . .

I am Robert Blake, but I see the tower in the dark. There is a monstrous odor. . . senses transfigured. . . boarding at that tower window cracking and giving way. . . Iä. . . ngai. . . ygg. . .

I see it—coming here—hell-wind—titan blur—black wings— Yog-Sothoth save me—the three-lobed burning eye. . .

DR JEKYLL AND
MR HYDE
AND OTHER STRANGE TALES

DR JEKYLL AND MR HYDE

AND OTHER STRANGE TALES

ROBERT LOUIS STEVENSON

This edition published in 2019 by Arcturus Publishing Limited
26/27 Bickels Yard, 151–153 Bermondsey Street,
London SE1 3HA

Introduction by Brian Busby
Typesetting by Palimpsest Book Production Limited

Cover design: Peter Ridley
Cover illustration: Peter Gray
Design: Beatriz Custodio

AD001213UK

Printed in the UK

Contents

INTRODUCTION 7

THE STRANGE CASE OF DR JEKYLL AND MR HYDE

Story of the Door.. 11

Search for Mr Hyde 17

Dr Jekyll was quite at ease.................................... 24

The Carew Murder Case....................................... 26

Incident of the Letter.. 30

Remarkable Incident of Dr Lanyon 34

Incident at the Window 38

The Last Night.. 40

Dr Lanyon's Narrative... 51

Henry Jekyll's Full Statement of the Case......... 58

THE BODY SNATCHER 73

THE BOTTLE IMP 93

MARKHEIM 123

WEIR OF HERMISTON.. 141

Introduction

Robert Louis Balfour Stevenson was born on 13 November 1850 at
Edinburgh, Scotland. In childhood, he began a lifelong battle with
tuberculosis. Despite poor health, he attended Edinburgh University,
where he studied engineering and law. In 1875, Stevenson was called
to the bar, but then followed a career in letters. His earliest writing
consisted of short stories, essays and travelogues; this last area being
related to the constant search for a climate that would suit his rather
fragile condition. Stevenson's first popular success came with his
debut novel, *Treasure Island* (1883), a tale of pirates and lost treasure.
Amongst his other better-known works are the poetry collection *A
Child's Garden of Verses* (1885) and the adventure novels *Kidnapped*
(1886) and *The Master of Ballantrae* (1889).

Stevenson's novella, *The Strange Case of Dr Jekyll and Mr Hyde*
(1886), with its exploration of split personality, is considered to be
amongst his darkest writing. Its stature as one of the great classics
in literature tends to overshadow much of his other writing in the
horror and supernatural genres, including *The Body Snatcher* (1884),
Markheim (1885) and *The Bottle Imp* (1891), presented in this volume.

Stevenson was a mere 44 years old when he died, on 3 December
1894, yet he left a large body of work, including nine novels, four
short story collections, four books of poetry, and numerous volumes
of non-fiction. At the time of his death, the author was writing two
novels, one of which was *Weir of Hermiston*. The work was published
in its incomplete form two years later.

THE STRANGE CASE OF
DR JEKYLL AND MR HYDE

STORY OF THE DOOR

Mr Utterson the lawyer was a man of a rugged countenance, that was never lighted by a smile; cold, scanty and embarrassed in discourse; backward in sentiment; lean, long, dusty, dreary and yet somehow lovable. At friendly meetings, and when the wine was to his taste, something eminently human beaconed from his eye; something indeed which never found its way into his talk, but which spoke not only in these silent symbols of the after-dinner face, but more often and loudly in the acts of his life. He was austere with himself; drank gin when he was alone, to mortify a taste for vintages; and though he enjoyed the theatre, had not crossed the doors of one for twenty years. But he had an approved tolerance for others; sometimes wondering, almost with envy, at the high pressure of spirits involved in their misdeeds; and in any extremity inclined to help rather than to reprove. 'I incline to Cain's heresy,' he used to say quaintly: 'I let my brother go to the devil in his own way.' In this character, it was frequently his fortune to be the last reputable acquaintance and the last good influence in the lives of down-going men. And to such as these, so long as they came about his chambers, he never marked a shade of change in his demeanour.

No doubt the feat was easy to Mr Utterson; for he was undemonstrative at the best, and even his friendships seemed to be founded in a similar catholicity of good-nature. It is the mark of a modest man to accept his friendly circle ready-made from the hands of opportunity; and that was the lawyer's way. His friends were those of his own blood or those whom he had known the longest; his affections, like ivy, were the growth of time, they implied no aptness in the object. Hence, no doubt, the bond that united him to Mr Richard Enfield, his distant kinsman, the well-known man about town. It was a nut to crack for many, what these two could see in each other or what subject they could find in common. It was reported by those who encountered them in their Sunday walks, that they said nothing, looked singularly dull, and would hail with obvious relief the appearance of a friend. For all that, the two men put the greatest store by these excursions, counted them the chief jewel of each week, and not only set aside occasions of pleasure, but even resisted the calls of business, that they might enjoy them uninterrupted.

It chanced on one of these rambles that their way led them down a bystreet in a busy quarter of London. The street was small and what is called quiet, but it drove a thriving trade on the weekdays. The inhabitants were all doing well, it seemed, and all emulously hoping to do better still, and laying out the surplus of their gains in coquetry; so that the shop fronts stood along that thoroughfare with an air of invitation, like rows of smiling saleswomen. Even on Sunday, when it veiled its more florid charms and lay comparatively empty of passage, the street shone out in contrast to its dingy neighbourhood, like a fire in a forest; and with its freshly painted shutters, well-polished brasses, and general cleanliness and gaiety of note, instantly caught and pleased the eye of the passenger.

Two doors from one corner, on the left hand going east, the line was broken by the entry of a court; and just at that point, a certain sinister block of building thrust forward its gable on the street. It was two storeys high; showed no window, nothing but a door on the lower storey and a blind forehead of discoloured wall on the upper; and bore in every feature, the marks of prolonged and sordid negligence. The door which was equipped with neither bell nor knocker, was blistered and distained. Tramps slouched into the recess and struck matches on the panels; children kept shop upon the steps; the schoolboy had tried his knife on the mouldings; and for close on a generation, no one had appeared to drive away these random visitors or to repair their ravages.

Mr Enfield and the lawyer were on the other side of the bystreet; but when they came abreast of the entry, the former lifted up his cane and pointed.

'Did you ever remark that door?' he asked; and when his companion had replied in the affirmative, 'it is connected in my mind,' added he, 'with a very odd story.'

'Indeed?' said Mr Utterson, with a slight change of voice, 'and what was that?'

'Well, it was this way,' returned Mr Enfield: 'I was coming home from some place at the end of the world, about three o'clock of a black winter morning, and my way lay through a part of town where there was literally nothing to be seen but lamps. Street after street, and all the folks asleep – street after street, all lighted up as if for a procession and all as empty as a church – till at last I got into that state of mind when a man listens and listens and begins to long for the sight of a policeman. All at once, I saw two figures: one a little man who was stumping along eastward at a good walk, and the other a girl of maybe eight or ten who was running as hard as she was able down a cross street. Well, sir, the two ran into one another naturally enough at the corner; and then came the horrible part of the thing; for the man trampled calmly over the child's body and left her screaming on the ground. It sounds nothing to hear, but it was hellish to see. It wasn't like a man; it was like some damned Juggernaut. I gave a view halloa, took to my heels, collared my gentleman, and brought him back to where there was already quite a group about the screaming child. He was perfectly cool and made no resistance, but gave me one look, so ugly that it brought out the sweat on me like running. The people who had turned out were the girl's own family; and pretty soon, the doctor, for whom she had been sent, put in his appearance. Well, the child was not much the worse, more frightened, according to the Sawbones; and there you might have supposed would be an end to it. But there was one curious circumstance. I had taken a loathing to my gentleman at first sight. So had the child's family, which was only natural. But the doctor's case was what struck me. He was the usual cut and dry apothecary, of no particular age and colour, with a strong Edinburgh accent, and about as emotional as a bagpipe. Well, sir, he was like the rest of us; every time he looked at my prisoner, I saw that Sawbones turn sick and white with the desire to kill him. I knew what was in his mind, just as he knew what was in mine; and killing being out of the question, we did the next best. We told the man we could and would make such a scandal out of this, as should make his name stink from one end of London to the other. If he had any friends or any credit, we undertook that he should lose them. And all the time, as we were pitching it in red hot, we were keeping the women off him as best we could, for they were as wild as harpies. I never saw a circle of such hateful faces; and there was the man in the middle, with a kind of black, sneering coolness – frightened too, I could see that – but carrying it off, sir, really like Satan. "If you choose to make capital out of this accident," said he, "I am naturally helpless. No gentleman but wishes to avoid a scene," says he. "Name your figure." Well, we screwed him up to a hundred pounds for the child's family; he would have clearly liked to stick out; but there was something about the lot of us that meant mischief, and at last he struck. The next thing was to get the money; and where do you think he carried us but to that place with the door? – whipped out a key, went in, and presently came back with the matter of ten pounds in gold and a cheque for the balance on Coutts's, drawn payable to bearer and signed with a name that I can't mention, though it's one of the points of my story, but it was a name at least very well known and often printed. The figure was stiff; but the signature was good for more than that, if it was only genuine. I took the liberty of pointing out to my gentleman that the whole business looked apocryphal, and that a man does not, in real life, walk into a cellar door at four in the morning and come out of it with another man's cheque for close upon a hundred pounds. But he was quite easy and sneering. "Set your mind at rest," says he, "I will stay with you till the banks open and cash the cheque myself." So we all set off, the doctor, and the child's father, and our friend and myself, and passed the rest of the night in my chambers; the next day, when we had breakfasted, went in a body to the bank. I gave in the cheque myself, and said I had every reason to believe it was a forgery. Not a bit of it. The cheque was genuine.'

'Tut-tut,' said Mr Utterson.

'I see you feel as I do,' said Mr Enfield. 'Yes, it's a bad story. For my man was a fellow that nobody could have to do with, a really damnable man; and the person that drew the cheque is the very pink of the proprieties, celebrated too, and (what makes it worse) one of your fellows who do what they call good. Blackmail, I suppose; an honest man paying through the nose for some of the capers of his youth. Blackmail House is what I call that place with the door, in consequence. Though even that, you know, is far from explaining all,' he added, and with the words fell into a vein of musing.

From this he was recalled by Mr Utterson asking rather suddenly: 'And you don't know if the drawer of the cheque lives there?'

'A likely place isn't it?' returned Mr Enfield. 'But I happen to have noticed his address; he lives in some square or other.'

'And you never asked about – the place with the door?' said Mr Utterson.

'No, sir: I had a delicacy,' was the reply. 'I feel very strongly about putting questions; it partakes too much of the style of the day of judgment. You start a question, and it's like starting a stone. You sit quietly on the top of a hill; and away the stones goes, starting others; and presently some bland old bird (the last you would have thought of) is knocked on the head in his own back garden and the family have to change their name. No, sir, I make it a rule of mine: the more it looks like Queer Street, the less I ask.'

'A very good rule, too,' said the lawyer.

'But I have studied the place for myself,' continued Mr Enfield. 'It seems scarcely a house. There is no other door, and nobody goes in or out of that one but, once in a great while, the gentleman of my adventure. There are three windows looking on the court on the first floor; none below; the windows are always shut but they're clean. And then there is a chimney which is generally smoking; so somebody must live there. And yet it's not so sure; for the buildings are so packed together about that court, that it's hard to say where one ends and another begins.'

The pair walked on again for a while in silence; and then 'Enfield,' said Mr Utterson, 'that's a good rule of yours.'

'Yes, I think it is,' returned Enfield.

'And for all that,' continued the lawyer, 'there's one point I want to ask: I want to ask the name of that man who walked over the child.'

'Well,' said Mr Enfield, 'I can't see what harm it would do. It was a man of the name of Hyde.'

'Hm,' said Mr Utterson. 'What sort of a man is he to see?'

'He is not easy to describe. There is something wrong with his appearance; something displeasing, something downright detestable. I never saw a man I so disliked, and yet I scarce know why. He must be deformed somewhere; he gives a strong feeling of deformity, although I couldn't specify the point. He's an extraordinary-looking man, and yet I really can name nothing out of the way. No, sir; I can make no hand of it; I can't describe him. And it's not want of memory; for I declare I can see him this moment.'

Mr Utterson again walked some way in silence and obviously under a weight of consideration. 'You are sure he used a key?' he inquired at last.

'My dear sir . . .' began Enfield, surprised out of himself.

'Yes, I know,' said Utterson; 'I know it must seem strange. The fact is, if I do not ask you the name of the other party, it is because I know it already. You see, Richard, your tale has gone home. If you have been inexact in my point, you had better correct it.'

'I think you might have warned me,' returned the other with a touch of sullenness. 'But I have been pedantically exact, as you call it. The fellow had a key; and what's more, he has it still. I saw him use it, not a week ago.'

Mr Utterson sighed deeply but said never a word; and the young man presently resumed. 'Here is another lesson to say nothing,' said he. 'I am ashamed of my long tongue. Let us make a bargain never to refer to this again.'

'With all my heart,' said the lawyer. 'I shake hands on that, Richard.'

SEARCH FOR MR HYDE

That evening, Mr Utterson came home to his bachelor house in sombre spirits and sat down to dinner without relish. It was his custom of a Sunday, when this meal was over, to sit close by the fire, a volume of some dry divinity on his reading desk, until the clock of the neighbouring church rang out the hour of twelve, when he would go soberly and gratefully to bed. On this night, however, as soon as the cloth was taken away, he took up a candle and went into his business room. There he opened his safe, took from the most private part of it a document endorsed on the envelope as Dr Jekyll's Will, and sat down with a clouded brow to study its contents. The will was holograph, for Mr Utterson, though he took charge of it now that it was made, had refused to lend the least assistance in the making of it; it provided not only that, in case of the decease of Henry Jekyll, MD, DCL, LLD, FRS, &c., all his possessions were to pass into the hands of his 'friend and benefactor Edward Hyde', but that in case of Dr Jekyll's 'disappearance or unexplained absence for any period exceeding three calendar months', the said Edward Hyde should step into the said Henry Jekyll's shoes without further delay and free from any burden or obligation, beyond the payment of a few small sums to the members of the doctor's household. This document had long been the lawyer's eyesore. It offended him both as a lawyer and as a lover of the sane and customary sides of life, to whom the fanciful was the immodest. And hitherto it was his ignorance of Mr Hyde that had swelled his indignation; now, by a sudden turn, it was his know-ledge. It was already bad enough when the name was but a name of which he could learn no more. It was worse when it began to be clothed upon with detestable attributes; and out of the shifting, insubstantial mists that had so long baffled his eye, there leaped up the sudden, definite presentment of a fiend.

'I thought it was madness,' he said, as he replaced the obnoxious paper in the safe, 'and now I begin to fear it is disgrace.'

With that he blew out his candle, put on a great coat and set forth in the direction of Cavendish Square, that citadel of medicine, where his friend, the great Dr Lanyon, had his house and received his crowding patients. 'If anyone knows, it will be Lanyon,' he had thought.

The solemn butler knew and welcomed him; he was subjected to no stage of delay, but ushered direct from the door to the dining room where Dr Lanyon sat alone over his wine. This was a hearty, healthy, dapper, red-faced gentleman, with a shock of hair prematurely white, and a boisterous and decided manner. At sight of Mr Utterson, he sprang up from his chair and welcomed him with both hands. The geniality, as was the way of the man, was somewhat theatrical to the eye; but it reposed on genuine feeling. For these two were old friends, old mates both at school and college, both thorough respecters of themselves and of each other, and, what does not always follow, men who thoroughly enjoyed each other's company.

After a little rambling talk, the lawyer led up to the subject which so disagreeably preoccupied his mind.

'I suppose, Lanyon,' said he, 'you and I must be the two oldest friends that Henry Jekyll has?'

'I wish the friends were younger,' chuckled Dr Lanyon. 'But I suppose we are. And what of that? I see little of him now.'

'Indeed?' said Utterson. 'I thought you had a bond of common interest.'

'We had,' was the reply. 'But it is more than ten years since Henry Jekyll became too fanciful for me. He began to go wrong, wrong in mind; and though of course I continue to take an interest in him for old sake's sake as they say, I see and I have seen devilish little of the man. Such unscientific balderdash,' added the doctor, flushing suddenly purple, 'would have estranged Damon and Pythias.'

This little spirt of temper was somewhat of a relief to Mr Utterson. 'They have only differed on some point of science,' he thought; and being a man of no scientific passions (except in the matter of conveyancing) he even added: 'It is nothing worse than that!' He gave his friend a few seconds to recover his composure, and then approached the question he had come to put. 'Did you ever come across a protégé of his – one Hyde?' he asked.

'Hyde?' repeated Lanyon. 'No. Never heard of him. Since my time.'

That was the amount of information that the lawyer carried back with him to the great, dark bed on which he tossed to and fro, until the small hours of the morning began to grow large. It was a night of little ease to his toiling mind, toiling in mere darkness and besieged by questions.

Six o'clock struck on the bells of the church that was so conveniently near to Mr Utterson's dwelling, and still he was digging at the problem. Hitherto it had touched him on the intellectual side alone; but now his imagin-ation also was engaged or rather enslaved; and as he lay and tossed in the gross darkness of the night and the curtained room, Mr Enfield's tale went by before his mind in a scroll of lighted pictures. He would be aware of the great field of lamps of a nocturnal city; then of the figure of a man walking swiftly; then of a child running from the doctor's; and then these met, and that human Juggernaut trod the child down and passed on regardless of her screams. Or else he would see a room in a rich house, where his friend lay asleep, dreaming and smiling at his dreams; and then the door of that room would be opened, the curtains of the bed plucked apart, the sleeper recalled, and lo! there would stand by his side a figure to whom power was given, and even at that dead hour, he must rise and do its bidding. The figure in these two phases haunted the lawyer all night; and if at any time he dozed over, it was but to see it glide more stealthily through sleeping houses, or move the more swiftly and still the more swiftly, even to dizziness, through wider labyrinths of lamplighted city, and at every street corner crush a child and leave her screaming. And still the figure had no face by which he might know it; even in his dreams, it had no face, or one that baffled him and melted before his eyes; and thus it was that there sprang up and grew apace in the lawyer's mind a singularly strong, almost an inordinate, curiosity to behold the features of the real Mr Hyde. If he could but once set eyes on him, he thought the mystery would lighten and perhaps roll altogether away, as was the habit of mysterious things when well examined. He might see a reason for his friend's strange preference or bondage (call it which you please) and even for the startling clauses of the will. And at least it would be a face worth seeing: the face of a man who was without bowels of mercy: a face which had but to show itself to raise up, in the mind of the unimpressionable Enfield, a spirit of enduring hatred.

From that time forward, Mr Utterson began to haunt the door in the bystreet of shops. In the morning before office hours, at noon when business was plenty and time scarce, at night under the face of the fogged city moon, by all lights and at all hours of solitude or concourse, the lawyer was to be found on his chosen post.

'If he be Mr Hyde,' he had thought, 'I shall be Mr Seek.'

And at last his patience was rewarded. It was a fine dry night; frost in the air; the streets as clean as a ballroom floor; the lamps, unshaken by any wind, drawing a regular pattern of light and shadow. By ten o'clock, when the shops were closed, the bystreet was very solitary and, in spite of the low growl of London from all round, very silent. Small sounds carried far; domestic sounds out of the houses were clearly audible on either side of the roadway; and the rumour of the approach of any passenger preceded him by a long time. Mr Utterson had been some minutes at his post, when he was aware of an odd, light footstep drawing near. In the course of his nightly patrols, he had long grown accustomed to the quaint effect with which the footfalls of a single person, while he is still a great way off, suddenly spring out distinct from the vast hum and clatter of the city. Yet his attention had never before been so sharply and decisively arrested; and it was with a strong, superstitious prevision of success that he withdrew into the entry of the court.

The steps drew swiftly nearer, and swelled out suddenly louder as they turned the end of the street. The lawyer, looking forth from the entry, could soon see what manner of man he had to deal with. He was small and very plainly dressed, and the look of him, even at that distance, went somehow strongly against the watcher's inclination. But he made straight for the door, crossing the roadway to save time; and as he came, he drew a key from his pocket like one approaching home.

Mr Utterson stepped out and touched him on the shoulder as he passed. 'Mr Hyde, I think?'

Mr Hyde shrank back with a hissing intake of the breath. But his fear was only momentary; and though he did not look the lawyer in the face, he answered coolly enough: 'That is my name. What do you want?'

'I see you are going in,' returned the lawyer. 'I am an old friend of Dr Jekyll's – Mr Utterson of Gaunt Street – you must have heard my name; and meeting you so conveniently, I thought you might admit me.'

'You will not find Dr Jekyll; he is from home,' replied Mr Hyde, blowing in the key. And then suddenly, but still without looking up, 'How did you know me?' he asked.

'On your side,' said Mr Utterson, 'will you do me a favour?'

'With pleasure,' replied the other. 'What shall it be?'

'Will you let me see your face?' asked the lawyer.

Mr Hyde appeared to hesitate, and then, as if upon some sudden reflection, fronted about with an air of defiance; and the pair stared at each other pretty fixedly for a few seconds. 'Now I shall know you again,' said Mr Utterson. 'It may be useful.'

'Yes,' returned Mr Hyde, 'it is as well we have met; and *à propos*, you should have my address.' And he gave a number of a street in Soho.

'Good God!' thought Mr Utterson, 'can he too have been thinking of the will?' But he kept his feelings to himself and only grunted in acknowledgement of the address.

'And now,' said the other, 'how did you know me?'

'By description,' was the reply.

'Whose description?'

'We have common friends,' said Mr Utterson.

'Common friends?' echoed Mr Hyde, a little hoarsely. 'Who are they?'

'Jekyll, for instance,' said the lawyer.

'He never told you,' cried Mr Hyde, with a flush of anger. 'I did not think you would have lied.'

'Come,' said Mr Utterson, 'that is not fitting language.'

The other snarled aloud into a savage laugh; and the next moment, with extraordinary quickness, he had unlocked the door and disappeared into the house.

The lawyer stood awhile when Mr Hyde had left him, the picture of disquietude. Then he began slowly to mount the street, pausing every step or two and putting his hand to his brow like a man in mental perplexity. The problem he was thus debating as he walked, was one of a class that is rarely solved. Mr Hyde was pale and dwarfish, he gave an impression of deformity without any nameable malformation, he had a displeasing smile, he had borne himself to the lawyer with a sort of murderous mixture of timidity and boldness, and he spoke with a husky, whispering and somewhat broken voice; all these were points against him, but not all of these together could explain the hitherto unknown disgust, loathing and fear with which Mr Utterson regarded him. 'There must be something else,' said the perplexed gentleman. 'There *is* something more, if I could find a name for it. God bless me, the man seems hardly human! Something troglodytic, shall we say? or can it be the old story of Dr Fell? or is it the mere radiance of a foul soul that thus transpires through, and transfigures, its clay continent? The last, I think; for O my poor old Harry Jekyll, if ever I read Satan's signature upon a face, it is on that of your new friend.'

Round the corner from the bystreet, there was a square of ancient, handsome houses, now for the most part decayed from their high estate and let in flats and chambers to all sorts and conditions of men: map-engravers, architects, shady lawyers and the agents of obscure enterprises. One house, however, second from the corner, was still occupied entire; and at the door of this, which wore a great air of wealth and comfort, though it was now plunged in darkness except for the fan-light, Mr Utterson stopped and knocked. A well-dressed, elderly servant opened the door.

'Is Dr Jekyll at home, Poole?' asked the lawyer.

'I will see, Mr Utterson,' said Poole, admitting the visitor, as he spoke, into a large, low-roofed, comfortable hall, paved with flags, warmed (after the fashion of a country house) by a bright, open fire, and furnished with costly cabinets of oak. 'Will you wait here by the fire, sir? or shall I give you a light in the dining room?'

'Here, thank you,' said the lawyer, and he drew near and leaned on the tall fender. This hall, in which he was now left alone, was a pet fancy of his friend the doctor's; and Utterson himself was wont to speak of it as the pleasantest room in London. But tonight there was a shudder in his blood; the face of Hyde sat heavy on his memory; he felt (what was rare with him) a nausea and distaste of life; and in the gloom of his spirits, he seemed to read a menace in the flickering of the firelight on the polished cabinets and the uneasy starting of the shadow on the roof. He was ashamed of his relief, when Poole presently returned to announce that Dr Jekyll was gone out.

'I saw Mr Hyde go in by the old dissecting room door, Poole,' he said. 'Is that right, when Dr Jekyll is from home?'

'Quite right, Mr Utterson, sir,' replied the servant. 'Mr Hyde has a key.'

'Your master seems to repose a great deal of trust in that young man, Poole,' resumed the other musingly.

'Yes, sir, he do indeed,' said Poole. 'We have all orders to obey him.'

'I do not think I ever met Mr Hyde?' asked Utterson.

'O, dear no, sir. He never *dines* here,' replied the butler. 'Indeed we see very little of him on this side of the house; he mostly comes and goes by the laboratory.'

'Well, good night, Poole.'

'Good night, Mr Utterson.'

And the lawyer set out homeward with a very heavy heart. 'Poor Harry Jekyll,' he thought, 'my mind misgives me he is in deep waters! He was wild when he was young; a long while ago to be sure; but in the law of God, there is no statute of limitations. Ay, it must be that; the ghost of some old sin, the cancer of some concealed disgrace: punishment coming, *pede claudo*, years after memory has forgotten and self-love condoned the fault.' And the lawyer, scared by the thought, brooded awhile on his own past, groping in all the corners of memory, lest by chance some Jack-in-the-Box of an old iniquity should leap to light there. His past was fairly blameless; few men could read the rolls of their life with less apprehension; yet he was humbled to the dust by the many ill things he had done, and raised up again into a sober and fearful gratitude by the many that he had come so near to doing, yet avoided. And then by a return on his former subject, he conceived a spark of hope. 'This Master Hyde, if he were studied,' thought he, 'must have secrets of his own: black secrets, by the look of him; secrets compared to which poor Jekyll's worst would be like sunshine. Things cannot continue as they are. It turns me cold to think of this creature stealing like a thief to Harry's bedside; poor Harry, what a wakening! And the danger of it; for if this Hyde suspects the existence of the will, he may grow impatient to inherit. Ay, I must put my shoulder to the wheel – if Jekyll will but let me,' he added, 'if Jekyll will only let me.' For once more he saw before his mind's eye, as clear as a transparency, the strange clauses of the will.

DR JEKYLL WAS QUITE AT EASE

A fortnight later, by excellent good fortune, the doctor gave one of his pleasant dinners to some five or six old cronies, all intelligent, reputable men and all judges of good wine; and Mr Utterson so contrived that he remained behind after the others had departed. This was no new arrangement, but a thing that had befallen many scores of times. Where Utterson was liked, he was liked well. Hosts loved to detail the dry lawyer, when the light-hearted and the loose-tongued had already their foot on the threshold; they liked to sit awhile in his unobtrusive company, practising for solitude, sobering their minds in the man's rich silence after the expense and strain of gaiety. To this rule, Dr Jekyll was no exception; and as he now sat on the opposite side of the fire – a large, well-made, smooth-faced man of fifty, with something of a slyish cast perhaps, but every mark of capacity and kindness – you could see by his looks that he cherished for Mr Utterson a sincere and warm affection.

'I have been wanting to speak to you, Jekyll,' began the latter. 'You know that will of yours?'

A close observer might have gathered that the topic was distasteful; but the doctor carried it off gaily. 'My poor Utterson,' said he, 'you are unfortunate in such a client. I never saw a man so distressed as you were by my will; unless it were that hide-bound pedant, Lanyon, at what he called my scientific heresies. O, I know he's a good fellow – you needn't frown – an excellent fellow, and I always mean to see more of him; but a hide-bound pedant for all that; an ignorant blatant pedant. I was never more disappointed in any man than Lanyon.'

'You know I never approved of it,' pursued Utterson, ruthlessly disregarding the fresh topic.

'My will? Yes, certainly, I know that,' said the doctor, a trifle sharply. 'You have told me so.'

'Well, I tell you so again,' continued the lawyer. 'I have been learning something of young Hyde.'

The large handsome face of Dr Jekyll grew pale to the very lips, and there came a blackness about his eyes. 'I do not care to hear more,' said he. 'This is a matter I thought we had agreed to drop.'

'What I heard was abominable,' said Utterson.

'It can make no change. You do not understand my position,' returned the doctor, with a certain incoherency of manner. 'I am painfully situated, Utterson; my position is a very strange – a very strange one. It is one of those affairs that cannot be mended by talking.'

'Jekyll,' said Utterson, 'you know me: I am a man to be trusted. Make a clean breast of this in confidence; and I make no doubt I can get you out of it.'

'My good Utterson,' said the doctor, 'this is very good of you, this is downright good of you, and I cannot find words to thank you in. I believe you fully; I would trust you before any man alive, ay, before myself, if I could make the choice; but indeed it isn't what you fancy; it is not so bad as that; and just to put your good heart at rest, I will tell you one thing: the moment I choose, I can be rid of Mr Hyde. I give you my hand upon that; and I thank you again and again; and I will just add one little word, Utterson, that I'm sure you'll take in good part: this is a private matter, and I beg of you to let it sleep.'

Utterson reflected a little looking in the fire.

'I have no doubt you are perfectly right,' he said at last, getting to his feet.

'Well, but since we have touched upon this business, and for the last time I hope,' continued the doctor, 'there is one point I should like you to understand. I have really a very great interest in poor Hyde. I know you have seen him; he told me so; and I fear he was rude. But I do sincerely take a great, a very great interest in that young man; and if I am taken away, Utterson, I wish you to promise me that you will bear with him and get his rights for him. I think you would, if you knew all; and it would be a weight off my mind if you would promise.'

'I can't pretend that I shall ever like him,' said the lawyer.

'I don't ask that,' pleaded Jekyll, laying his hand upon the other's arm; 'I only ask for justice; I only ask you to help him for my sake, when I am no longer here.'

Utterson heaved an irrepressible sigh. 'Well,' said he. 'I promise.'

THE CAREW MURDER CASE

Nearly a year later, in the month of October 18—, London was startled by a crime of singular ferocity and rendered all the more notable by the high position of the victim. The details were few and startling. A maidservant living alone in a house not far from the river, had gone upstairs to bed about eleven. Although a fog rolled over the city in the small hours, the early part of the night was cloudless, and the lane, which the maid's window overlooked, was brilliantly lit by the full moon. It seems she was romantically given for she sat down upon her box, which stood immediately under the window, and fell into a dream of musing. Never (she used to say, with streaming tears, when she narrated that experience) never had she felt more at peace with all men or thought more kindly of the world. And as she so sat she became aware of an aged and beautiful gentleman with white hair, drawing near along the lane; and advancing to meet him, another and very small gentleman, to whom at first she paid less attention. When they had come within speech (which was just under the maid's eyes) the older man bowed and accosted the other with a very pretty manner of politeness. It did not seem as if the subject of his address were of great importance; indeed, from his pointing, it sometimes appeared as if he were only inquiring his way; but the moon shone on his face as he spoke, and the girl was pleased to watch it, it seemed to breathe such an innocent and old-world kindness of disposition, yet with something high too, as of a well-founded self-content. Presently her eye wandered to the other, and she was surprised to recognize in him a certain Mr Hyde, who had once visited her master and for whom she had conceived a dislike. He had in his hand a heavy cane, with which he was trifling; but he answered never a word, and seemed to listen with an ill-contained impatience. And then all of a sudden he broke out in a great flame of anger, stamping with his foot, brandishing the cane, and carrying on (as the maid described it) like a madman. The old gentleman took a step back, with the air of one very much surprised and a trifle hurt; and at that Mr Hyde broke out of all bounds and clubbed him to the earth. And next moment, with ape-like fury, he was trampling his victim under foot, and hailing down a storm of blows, under which the bones were audibly shattered and the body jumped upon the roadway. At the horror of these sights and sounds, the maid fainted.

It was two o'clock when she came to herself and called for the police. The murderer was gone long ago; but there lay his victim in the middle of the lane, incredibly mangled. The stick with which the deed had been done, although it was of some rare and very tough and heavy wood, had broken in the middle under the stress of this insensate cruelty; and one splintered half had rolled in the neighbouring gutter – the other, without doubt, had been carried away by the murderer. A purse and a gold watch were found upon the victim; but no cards or papers, except a sealed and stamped envelope, which he had been probably carrying to the post, and which bore the name and address of Mr Utterson.

This was brought to the lawyer the next morning, before he was out of bed; and he had no sooner seen it, and been told the circumstances, than he shot out a solemn lip. 'I shall say nothing till I have seen the body,' said he; 'this may be very serious. Have the kindness to wait while I dress.' And with the same grave countenance he hurried through his breakfast and drove to the police station, whither the body had been carried. As soon as he came into the cell, he nodded.

'Yes,' said he, 'I recognize him. I am sorry to say that this is Sir Danvers Carew.'

'Good God, sir,' exclaimed the officer, 'is it possible?' And the next moment his eye lighted up with professional ambition. 'This will make a deal of noise,' he said. 'And perhaps you can help us to the man.' And he briefly narrated what the maid had seen, and showed the broken stick.

Mr Utterson had already quailed at the name of Hyde; but when the stick was laid before him, he could doubt no longer: broken and battered as it was, he recognized it for one that he had himself presented many years before to Henry Jekyll.

'Is this Mr Hyde a person of small stature?' he inquired.

'Particularly small and particularly wicked-looking, is what the maid calls him,' said the officer.

Mr Utterson reflected; and then, raising his head, 'If you will come with me in my cab,' he said, 'I think I can take you to his house.'

It was by this time about nine in the morning, and the first fog of the season. A great chocolate-coloured pall lowered over heaven, but the wind was continually charging and routing these embattled vapours; so that as the cab crawled from street to street, Mr Utterson beheld a marvellous number of degrees and hues of twilight; for here it would be dark like the back-end of evening; and there would be a glow of a rich, lurid brown, like the light of some strange conflagration; and here, for a moment, the fog would be quite broken up, and a haggard shaft of daylight would glance in between the swirling wreaths. The dismal quarter of Soho seen under these changing glimpses, with its muddy ways, and slatternly passengers, and its lamps, which had never been extinguished or had been kindled afresh to combat this mournful reinvasion of darkness, seemed, in the lawyer's eyes, like a district of some city in a nightmare. The thoughts of his mind, besides, were of the gloomiest dye; and when he glanced at the companion of his drive, he was conscious of some touch of that terror of the law and the law's officers, which may at times assail the most honest.

As the cab drew up before the address indicated, the fog lifted a little and showed him a dingy street, a gin palace, a low French eating house, a shop for the retail of penny numbers and twopenny salads, many ragged children huddled in the doorways, and many women of many different nationalities passing out, key in hand, to have a morning glass; and the next moment the fog settled down again upon that part, as brown as umber, and cut him off from his blackguardly surroundings. This was the home of Henry Jekyll's favourite; of a man who was heir to a quarter of a million sterling.

An ivory-faced and silvery-haired old woman opened the door. She had an evil face, smoothed by hypocrisy; but her manners were excellent. Yes, she said, this was Mr Hyde's, but he was not at home; he had been in that night very late, but had gone away again in less than an hour; there was nothing strange in that; his habits were very irregular, and he was often absent; for instance, it was nearly two months since she had seen him till yesterday.

'Very well then, we wish to see his rooms,' said the lawyer; and when the woman began to declare it was impossible, 'I had better tell you who this person is,' he added. 'This is Inspector Newcomen of Scotland Yard.'

A flash of odious joy appeared upon the woman's face. 'Ah!' said she, 'he is in trouble! What has he done?'

Mr Utterson and the inspector exchanged glances. 'He don't seem a very popular character,' observed the latter. 'And now, my good woman, just let me and this gentleman have a look about us.'

In the whole extent of the house, which but for the old woman remained otherwise empty, Mr Hyde had only used a couple of rooms; but these were furnished with luxury and good taste. A closet was filled with wine; the plate was of silver, the napery elegant; a good picture hung upon the walls, a gift (as Utterson supposed) from Henry Jekyll, who was much of a connoisseur; and the carpets were of many plies and agreeable in colour. At this moment, however, the rooms bore every mark of having been recently and hurriedly ransacked; clothes lay about the floor, with their pockets inside out; lockfast drawers stood open; and on the hearth there lay a pile of grey ashes, as though many papers had been burned. From these embers the inspector disinterred the butt end of a green cheque book, which had resisted the action of the fire; the other half of the stick was found behind the door; and as this clinched his suspicions, the officer declared himself delighted. A visit to the bank, where several thousand pounds were found to be lying to the murderer's credit, completed his gratification.

'You may depend upon it, sir,' he told Mr Utterson: 'I have him in my hand. He must have lost his head, or he would never have left the stick or, above all, burned the cheque book. Why, money's life to the man. We have nothing to do but wait for him at the bank, and get out the handbills.'

This last, however, was not so easy of accomplishment; for Mr Hyde had numbered few familiars – even the master of the servantmaid had only seen him twice; his family could nowhere be traced; he had never been photographed; and the few who could describe him differed widely, as common observers will. Only on one point, were they agreed; and that was the haunting sense of unexpressed deformity with which the fugitive impressed his beholders.

INCIDENT OF THE LETTER

It was late in the afternoon, when Mr Utterson found his way to Dr Jekyll's door, where he was at once admitted by Poole, and carried down by the kitchen offices and across a yard which had once been a garden, to the building which was indifferently known as the laboratory or the dissecting rooms. The doctor had bought the house from the heirs of a celebrated surgeon; and his own tastes being rather chemical than anatomical, had changed the destination of the block at the bottom of the garden. It was the first time that the lawyer had been received in that part of his friend's quarters; and he eyed the dingy windowless structure with curiosity, and gazed round with a distasteful sense of strangeness as he crossed the theatre, once crowded with eager students and now lying gaunt and silent, the tables laden with chemical apparatus, the floor strewn with crates and littered with packing straw, and the light falling dimly through the foggy cupola. At the further end, a flight of stairs mounted to a door covered with red baize; and through this, Mr Utterson was at last received into the doctor's cabinet. It was a large room, fitted round with glass presses, furnished, among other things, with a cheval-glass and a business table, and looking out upon the court by three dusty windows barred with iron. The fire burned in the grate; a lamp was set lighted on the chimney shelf, for even in the houses the fog began to lie thickly; and there, close up to the warmth, sat Dr Jekyll, looking deadly sick. He did not rise to meet his visitor, but held out a cold hand and bade him welcome in a changed voice.

'And now,' said Mr Utterson, as soon as Poole had left them, 'you have heard the news?'

The doctor shuddered. 'They were crying it in the square,' he said. 'I heard them in my dining room.'

'One word,' said the lawyer. 'Carew was my client, but so are you, and I want to know what I am doing. You have not been mad enough to hide this fellow?'

'Utterson, I swear to God,' cried the doctor, 'I swear to God I will never set eyes on him again. I bind my honour to you that I am done with him in this world. It is all at an end. And indeed he does not want my help; you do not know him as I do; he is safe, he is quite safe; mark my words, he will never more be heard of.'

The lawyer listened gloomily; he did not like his friend's feverish manner. 'You seem pretty sure of him,' said he; 'and for your sake, I hope you may be right. If it came to a trial, your name might appear.'

'I am quite sure of him,' replied Jekyll; 'I have grounds for certainty that I cannot share with anyone. But there is one thing on which you may advise me. I have – I have received a letter; and I am at a loss whether I should show it to the police. I should like to leave it in your hands, Utterson; you would judge wisely I am sure; I have so great a trust in you.'

'You fear, I suppose, that it might lead to his detection?' asked the lawyer.

'No,' said the other. 'I cannot say that I care what becomes of Hyde; I am quite done with him. I was thinking of my own character, which this hateful business has rather exposed.'

Utterson ruminated awhile; he was surprised at his friend's selfishness, and yet relieved by it. 'Well,' said he, at last, 'let me see the letter.'

The letter was written in an odd, upright hand and signed 'Edward Hyde': and it signified, briefly enough, that the writer's benefactor, Dr Jekyll, whom he had long so unworthily repaid for a thousand generosities, need labour under no alarm for his safety as he had means of escape on which he placed a sure dependence. The lawyer liked this letter well enough; it put a better colour on the intimacy than he had looked for; and he blamed himself for some of his past suspicions.

'Have you the envelope?' he asked.

'I burned it,' replied Jekyll, 'before I thought what I was about. But it bore no postmark. The note was handed in.'

'Shall I keep this and sleep upon it?' asked Utterson.

'I wish you to judge for me entirely,' was the reply. 'I have lost confidence in myself.'

'Well, I shall consider,' returned the lawyer. 'And now one word more: it was Hyde who dictated the terms in your will about that disappearance?'

The doctor seemed seized with a qualm of faintness; he shut his mouth tight and nodded.

'I knew it,' said Utterson. 'He meant to murder you. You have had a fine escape.'

'I have had what is far more to the purpose,' returned the doctor solemnly: 'I have had a lesson – O God, Utterson, what a lesson I have had!' And he covered his face for a moment with his hands.

On his way out, the lawyer stopped and had a word or two with Poole. 'By the by,' said he, 'there was a letter handed in today: what was the messenger like?' But Poole was positive nothing had come except by post; 'and only circulars by that,' he added.

This news sent off the visitor with his fears renewed. Plainly the letter had come by the laboratory door; possibly, indeed, it had been written in the cabinet; and if that were so, it must be differently judged, and handled with the more caution. The newsboys, as he went, were crying themselves hoarse along the footways: 'Special edition. Shocking murder of an MP.' That was the funeral oration of one friend and client; and he could not help a certain apprehension lest the good name of another should be sucked down in the eddy of the scandal. It was, at least, a ticklish decision that he had to make; and self-reliant as he was by habit, he began to cherish a longing for advice. It was not to be had directly; but perhaps, he thought, it might be fished for.

Presently after, he sat on one side of his own hearth, with Mr Guest, his head clerk, upon the other, and midway between, at a nicely calculated distance from the fire, a bottle of a particular old wine that had long dwelt unsunned in the foundations of his house. The fog still slept on the wing above the drowned city, where the lamps glimmered like carbuncles; and through the muffle and smother of these fallen clouds, the procession of the town's life was still rolling in through the great arteries with a sound as of a mighty wind. But the room was gay with firelight. In the bottle the acids were long ago resolved; the imperial dye had softened with time, as the colour grows richer in stained windows; and the glow of hot autumn afternoons on hillside vineyards, was ready to be set free and to disperse the fogs of London. Insensibly the lawyer melted. There was no man from whom he kept fewer secrets than Mr Guest; and he was not always sure that he kept as many as he meant. Guest had often been on business to the doctor's; he knew Poole; he could scarce have failed to hear of Mr Hyde's familiarity about the house; he might draw conclusions: was it not as well, then, that he should see a letter which put that mystery to rights? and above all since Guest, being a great student and critic of handwriting, would consider the step natural and obliging? The clerk, besides, was a man of counsel; he would scarce read so strange a document without dropping a remark; and by that remark Mr Utterson might shape his future course.

'This is a sad business about Sir Danvers,' he said.

'Yes, sir, indeed. It has elicited a great deal of public feeling,' returned Guest. 'The man, of course, was mad.'

'I should like to hear your views on that,' replied Utterson. 'I have a document here in his handwriting; it is between ourselves, for I scarce knew what to do about it; it is an ugly business at the best. But there it is; quite in your way: a murderer's autograph.'

Guest's eyes brightened, and he sat down at once and studied it with passion. 'No, sir,' he said; 'not mad; but it is an odd hand.'

'And by all accounts a very odd writer,' added the lawyer.

Just then the servant entered with a note.

'Is that from Doctor Jekyll, sir?' inquired the clerk. 'I thought I knew the writing. Anything private, Mr Utterson?'

'Only an invitation to dinner. Why? do you want to see it?'

'One moment. I thank you, sir;' and the clerk laid the two sheets of paper alongside and sedulously compared their contents. 'Thank you, sir,' he said at last, returning both; 'it's a very interesting autograph.'

There was a pause, during which Mr Utterson struggled with himself. 'Why did you compare them, Guest?' he inquired suddenly.

'Well, sir,' returned the clerk, 'there's a rather singular resemblance; the two hands are in many points identical: only differently sloped.'

'Rather quaint,' said Utterson.

'It is, as you say, rather quaint,' returned Guest.

'I wouldn't speak of this note, you know,' said the master.

'No, sir,' said the clerk. 'I understand.'

But no sooner was Mr Utterson alone that night, than he locked the note into his safe where it reposed from that time forward. 'What!' he thought. 'Henry Jekyll forge for a murderer!' And his blood ran cold in his veins.

REMARKABLE INCIDENT OF DOCTOR LANYON

Time ran on; thousands of pounds were offered in reward, for the death of Sir Danvers was resented as a public injury; but Mr Hyde had disappeared out of the ken of the police as though he had never existed. Much of his past was unearthed, indeed, and all disreputable: tales came out of the man's cruelty, at once so callous and violent, of his vile life, of his strange associates, of the hatred that seemed to have surrounded his career; but of his present whereabouts, not a whisper. From the time he had left the house in Soho on the morning of the murder, he was simply blotted out; and gradually, as time drew on, Mr Utterson began to recover from the hotness of his alarm, and to grow more at quiet with himself. The death of Sir Danvers was, to his way of thinking, more than paid for by the disappearance of Mr Hyde. Now that that evil influence had been withdrawn, a new life began for Dr Jekyll. He came out of his seclusion, renewed relations with his friends, became once more their familiar guest and entertainer; and whilst he had always been known for charities, he was now no less distinguished for religion. He was busy, he was much in the open air, he did good; his face seemed to open and brighten, as if with an inward consciousness of service; and for more than two months, the doctor was at peace.

On the 8th of January Utterson had dined at the doctor's with a small party; Lanyon had been there; and the face of the host had looked from one to the other as in the old days when the trio were inseparable friends. On the 12th, and again on the 14th, the door was shut against the lawyer. 'The doctor was confined to the house,' Poole said, 'and saw no one.' On the 15th, he tried again, and was again refused; and having now been used for the last two months to see his friend almost daily, he found this return of solitude to weigh upon his spirits. The fifth night, he had in Guest to dine with him; and the sixth he betook himself to Doctor Lanyon's.

There at least he was not denied admittance; but when he came in, he was shocked at the change which had taken place in the doctor's appearance. He had his death-warrant written legibly upon his face. The rosy man had grown pale; his flesh had fallen away; he was visibly balder and older; and yet it was not so much these tokens of a swift physical decay that arrested the lawyer's notice, as a look in the eye and quality of manner that seemed to testify to some deep-seated terror of the mind. It was unlikely that the doctor should fear death; and yet that was what Utterson was tempted to suspect. 'Yes,' he thought; 'he is a doctor, he must know his own state and that his days are counted; and the knowledge is more than he can bear.' And yet when Utterson remarked on his ill-looks, it was with an air of great firmness that Lanyon declared himself a doomed man.

'I have had a shock,' he said, 'and I shall never recover. It is a question of weeks. Well, life has been pleasant; I liked it; yes, sir, I used to like it. I sometimes think if we knew all, we should be more glad to get away.'

'Jekyll is ill, too,' observed Utterson. 'Have you seen him?'

But Lanyon's face changed, and he held up a trembling hand. 'I wish to see or hear no more of Doctor Jekyll,' he said in a loud, unsteady voice. 'I am quite done with that person; and I beg that you will spare me any allusion to one whom I regard as dead.'

'Tut-tut,' said Mr Utterson; and then after a considerable pause, 'Can't I do anything?' he inquired. 'We are three very old friends, Lanyon; we shall not live to make others.'

'Nothing can be done,' returned Lanyon; 'ask himself.'

'He will not see me,' said the lawyer.

'I am not surprised at that,' was the reply. 'Some day, Utterson, after I am dead, you may perhaps come to learn the right and wrong of this. I cannot tell you. And in the meantime, if you can sit and talk with me of other things, for God's sake, stay and do so; but if you cannot keep clear of this accursed topic, then, in God's name, go, for I cannot bear it.'

As soon as he got home, Utterson sat down and wrote to Jekyll, complaining of his exclusion from the house, and asking the cause of this unhappy break with Lanyon; and the next day brought him a long answer, often very pathetically worded, and sometimes darkly mysterious in drift. The quarrel with Lanyon was incurable. 'I do not blame our old friend,' Jekyll wrote, 'but I share his view that we must never meet. I mean from henceforth to lead a life of extreme seclusion; you must not be surprised, nor must you doubt my friendship, if my door is often shut even to you. You must suffer me to go my own dark way. I have brought on myself a punishment and a danger that I cannot name. If I am the chief of sinners, I am the chief of sufferers also. I could not think that this earth contained a place for sufferings and terrors so unmanning; and you can do but one thing, Utterson, to lighten this destiny, and that is to respect my silence.' Utterson was amazed; the dark influence of Hyde had been withdrawn, the doctor had returned to his old tasks and amities; a week ago, the prospect had smiled with every promise of a cheerful and an honoured age; and now in a moment, friendship, and peace of mind and the whole tenor of his life were wrecked. So great and unprepared a change pointed to madness; but in view of Lanyon's manner and words, there must lie for it some deeper ground.

A week afterwards Dr Lanyon took to his bed, and in something less than a fortnight he was dead. The night after the funeral, at which he had been sadly affected, Utterson locked the door of his business room, and sitting there by the light of a melancholy candle, drew out and set before him an envelope addressed by the hand and sealed with the seal of his dear friend. 'Private: for the hands of J. G. Utterson alone and in case of his predecease *to be destroyed unread*', so it was emphatically superscribed; and the lawyer dreaded to behold the contents. 'I have buried one friend today,' he thought: 'what if this should cost me another?' And then he condemned the fear as a disloyalty, and broke the seal. Within there was another enclosure, likewise sealed, and marked upon the cover as 'Not to be opened till the death or disappearance of Dr Henry Jekyll.' Utterson could not trust his eyes. Yes, it was disappearance; here again, as in the mad will which he had long ago restored to its author, here again were the idea of a disappearance and the name of Henry Jekyll bracketed. But in the will, that idea had sprung from the sinister suggestion of the man Hyde; it was set there with a purpose all too plain and horrible. Written by the hand of Lanyon, what should it mean? A great curiosity came on the trustee, to disregard the prohibition and dive at once to the bottom of these mysteries; but professional honour and faith to his dead friend were stringent obligations; and the packet slept in the inmost corner of his private safe.

It is one thing to mortify curiosity, another to conquer it; and it may be doubted if, from that day forth, Utterson desired the society of his surviving friend with the same eagerness. He thought of him kindly; but his thoughts were disquieted and fearful. He went to call indeed; but he was perhaps relieved to be denied admittance; perhaps, in his heart, he preferred to speak with Poole upon the doorstep and surrounded by the air and sounds of the open city, rather than to be admitted into that house of voluntary bondage, and to sit and speak with its inscrutable recluse. Poole had, indeed, no very pleasant news to communicate. The doctor, it appeared, now more than ever confined himself to the cabinet over the laboratory, where he would sometimes even sleep; he was out of spirits, he had grown very silent, he did not read; it seemed as if he had something on his mind. Utterson became so used to the unvarying character of these reports, that he fell off little by little in the frequency of his visits.

INCIDENT AT THE WINDOW

It chanced on Sunday, when Mr Utterson was on his usual walk with Mr Enfield, that their way lay once again through the bystreet; and that when they came in front of the door, both stopped to gaze on it.

'Well,' said Enfield, 'that story's at an end at least. We shall never see more of Mr Hyde.'

'I hope not,' said Utterson. 'Did I ever tell you that I once saw him, and shared your feeling of repulsion?'

'It was impossible to do the one without the other,' returned Enfield. 'And by the way what an ass you must have thought me, not to know that this was a back way to Dr Jekyll's! It was partly your own fault that I found it out, even when I did.'

'So you found it out, did you?' said Utterson. 'But if that be so, we may step into the court and take a look at the windows. To tell you the truth, I am uneasy about poor Jekyll; and even outside, I feel as if the presence of a friend might do him good.'

The court was very cool and a little damp, and full of premature twilight, although the sky, high up overhead, was still bright with sunset. The middle one of the three windows was half way open; and sitting close beside it, taking the air with an infinite sadness of mien, like some disconsolate prisoner, Utterson saw Dr Jekyll.

'What! Jekyll!' he cried. 'I trust you are better.'

'I am very low, Utterson,' replied the doctor drearily, 'very low. It will not last long, thank God.'

'You stay too much indoors,' said the lawyer. 'You should be out, whipping up the circulation like Mr Enfield and me. (This is my cousin – Mr Enfield – Dr Jekyll.) Come now; get your hat and take a quick turn with us.'

'You are very good,' sighed the other. 'I should like to very much; but no, no, no, it is quite impossible; I dare not. But indeed, Utterson, I am very glad to see you; this is really a great pleasure; I would ask you and Mr Enfield up, but the place is really not fit.'

'Why then,' said the lawyer, good-naturedly, 'the best thing we can do is to stay down here and speak with you from where we are.'

'That is just what I was about to venture to propose,' returned the doctor with a smile. But the words were hardly uttered, before the smile was struck out of his face and succeeded by an expression of such abject terror and despair, as froze the very blood of the two gentlemen below. They saw it but for a glimpse, for the window was instantly thrust down; but that glimpse had been sufficient, and they turned and left the court without a word. In silence, too, they traversed the bystreet; and it was not until they had come into a neighbouring thoroughfare, where even upon a Sunday there were still some stirrings of life, that Mr Utterson at last turned and looked at his companion. They were both pale; and there was an answering horror in their eyes.

'God forgive us, God forgive us,' said Mr Utterson.

But Mr Enfield only nodded his head very seriously, and walked on once more in silence.

THE LAST NIGHT

Mr Utterson was sitting by his fireside one evening after dinner, when he was surprised to receive a visit from Poole.

'Bless me, Poole, what brings you here?' he cried; and then taking a second look at him, 'What ails you?' he added, 'is the doctor ill?'

'Mr Utterson,' said the man, 'there is something wrong.'

'Take a seat, and here is a glass of wine for you,' said the lawyer. 'Now, take your time, and tell me plainly what you want.'

'You know the doctor's ways, sir,' replied Poole, 'and how he shuts himself up. Well, he's shut up again in the cabinet; and I don't like it, sir – I wish I may die if I like it. Mr Utterson, sir, I'm afraid.'

'Now, my good man,' said the lawyer, 'be explicit. What are you afraid of?'

'I've been afraid for about a week,' returned Poole, doggedly disregarding the question, 'and I can bear it no more.'

The man's appearance amply bore out his words; his manner was altered for the worse; and except for the moment when he had first announced his terror, he had not once looked the lawyer in the face. Even now, he sat with the glass of wine untasted on his knee, and his eyes directed to a corner of the floor. 'I can bear it no more,' he repeated.

'Come,' said the lawyer, 'I see you have some good reason, Poole; I see there is something seriously amiss. Try to tell me what it is.'

'I think there's been foul play,' said Poole, hoarsely.

'Foul play!' cried the lawyer, a good deal frightened and rather inclined to be irritated in consequence. 'What foul play? What does the man mean?'

'I daren't say, sir,' was the answer; 'but will you come along with me and see for yourself?'

Mr Utterson's only answer was to rise and get his hat and great coat; but he observed with wonder the greatness of the relief that appeared upon the butler's face, and perhaps with no less, that the wine was still untasted when he set it down to follow.

It was a wild, cold, seasonable night of March, with a pale moon, lying on her back as though the wind had tilted her, and a flying wrack of the most diaphanous and lawny texture. The wind made talking difficult, and flecked the blood into the face. It seemed to have swept the streets unusually bare of passengers, besides; for Mr Utterson thought he had never seen that part of London so deserted. He could have wished it otherwise; never in his life had he been conscious of so sharp a wish to see and touch his fellow-creatures; for struggle as he might, there was borne in upon his mind a crushing anticipation of calamity. The square, when they got there, was all full of wind and dust, and the thin trees in the garden were lashing themselves along the railing. Poole, who had kept all the way a pace or two ahead, now pulled up in the middle of the pavement, and in spite of the biting weather, took off his hat and mopped his brow with a red pocket-handkerchief. But for all the hurry of his coming, these were not the dews of exertion that he wiped away, but the moisture of some strangling anguish; for his face was white and his voice, when he spoke, harsh and broken.

'Well, sir,' he said, 'here we are, and God grant there be nothing wrong.'

'Amen, Poole,' said the lawyer.

Thereupon the servant knocked in a very guarded manner; the door was opened on the chain; and a voice asked from within, 'Is that you, Poole?'

'It's all right,' said Poole. 'Open the door.'

The hall, when they entered it, was brightly lighted up; the fire was built high; and about the hearth the whole of the servants, men and women, stood huddled together like a flock of sheep. At the sight of Mr Utterson, the housemaid broke into hysterical whimpering; and the cook, crying out 'Bless God! it's Mr Utterson,' ran forward as if to take him in her arms.

'What, what? Are you all here?' said the lawyer peevishly. 'Very irregular, very unseemly; your master would be far from pleased.'

'They're all afraid,' said Poole.

Blank silence followed, no one protesting; only the maid lifted up her voice and now wept loudly.

'Hold your tongue!' Poole said to her, with a ferocity of accent that testified to his own jangled nerves; and indeed, when the girl had so suddenly raised the note of her lamentation, they had all started and turned towards the inner door with faces of dreadful expectation. 'And now,' continued the butler, addressing the knife-boy, 'reach me a candle, and we'll get this through hands at once.' And then he begged Mr Utterson to follow him, and led the way to the back garden.

'Now, sir,' said he, 'you come as gently as you can. I want you to hear, and I don't want you to be heard. And see here, sir, if by any chance he was to ask you in, don't go.'

Mr Utterson's nerves, at this unlooked-for termination, gave a jerk that nearly threw him from his balance; but he re-collected his courage and followed the butler into the laboratory building and through the surgical theatre, with its lumber of crates and bottles, to the foot of the stair. Here Poole motioned him to stand on one side and listen; while he himself, setting down the candle and making a great and obvious call on his resolution, mounted the steps and knocked with a somewhat uncertain hand on the red baize of the cabinet door.

'Mr Utterson, sir, asking to see you,' he called; and even as he did so, once more violently signed to the lawyer to give ear.

A voice answered from within: 'Tell him I cannot see anyone,' it said complainingly.

'Thank you, sir,' said Poole, with a note of something like triumph in his voice; and taking up his candle, he led Mr Utterson back across the yard and into the great kitchen, where the fire was out and the beetles were leaping on the floor.

'Sir,' he said, looking Mr Utterson in the eyes, 'was that my master's voice?'

'It seems much changed,' replied the lawyer, very pale, but giving look for look.

'Changed? Well, yes, I think so,' said the butler. 'Have I been twenty years in this man's house, to be deceived about his voice? No, sir; master's made away with – he was made away with, eight days ago, when we heard him cry out upon the name of God; and *who's* in there instead of him, and *why* it stays there, is a thing that cries to Heaven, Mr Utterson!'

'This is a very strange tale, Poole; this is rather a wild tale, my man,' said Mr Utterson, biting his finger. 'Suppose it were as you suppose, supposing Dr Jekyll to have been – well, murdered, what could induce the murderer to stay? That won't hold water; it doesn't commend itself to reason.'

'Well, Mr Utterson, you are a hard man to satisfy, but I'll do it yet,' said Poole. 'All this last week (you must know) him, or it, or whatever it is that lives in that cabinet, has been crying night and day for some sort of medicine and cannot get it to his mind. It was sometimes his way – the master's, that is – to write his orders on a sheet of paper and throw it on the stair. We've had nothing else this week back; nothing but papers, and a closed door, and the very meals left there to be smuggled in when nobody was looking. Well, sir, every day, ay, and twice and thrice in the same day, there have been orders and complaints, and I have been sent flying to all the wholesale chemists in town. Every time I brought the stuff back, there would be another paper telling me to return it, because it was not pure, and another order to a different firm. This drug is wanted bitter bad, sir, whatever for.'

'Have you any of these papers?' asked Mr Utterson.

Poole felt in his pocket and handed out a crumpled note, which the lawyer, bending nearer to the candle, carefully examined. Its contents ran thus: 'Dr Jekyll presents his compliments to Messrs Maw. He assures them that their last sample is impure and quite useless for his present purpose. In the year 18 –, Dr J. purchased a somewhat large quantity from Messrs M. He now begs them to search with the most sedulous care, and should any of the same quality be left, to forward it to him at once. Expense is no consideration. The importance of this to Dr J. can hardly be exaggerated.' So far the letter had run composedly enough, but here with a sudden splutter of the pen, the writer's emotion had broken loose. 'For God's sake,' he had added, 'find me some of the old.'

'This is a strange note,' said Mr Utterson; and then sharply, 'How do you come to have it open?'

'The man at Maw's was main angry, sir, and he threw it back to me like so much dirt,' returned Poole.

'This is unquestionably the doctor's hand, do you know?' resumed the lawyer.

'I thought it looked like it,' said the servant rather sulkily; and then, with another voice, 'But what matters hand of write,' he said. 'I've seen him!'

'Seen him?' repeated Mr Utterson. 'Well?'

'That's it!' said Poole. 'It was this way. I came suddenly into the theatre from the garden. It seems he had slipped out to look for this drug or whatever it is; for the cabinet door was open, and there he was at the far end of the room digging among the crates. He looked up when

I came in, gave a kind of cry, and whipped upstairs into the cabinet. It was but for one minute that I saw him, but the hair stood upon my head like quills. Sir, if that was my master, why had he a mask upon his face? If it was my master, why did he cry out like a rat, and run from me? I have served him long enough. And then . . .' the man paused and passed his hand over his face.

'These are all very strange circumstances,' said Mr Utterson, 'but I think I begin to see daylight. Your master, Poole, is plainly seized with one of those maladies that both torture and deform the sufferer; hence, for aught I know, the alteration of his voice; hence the mask and his avoidance of his friends; hence his eagerness to find this drug, by means of which the poor soul retains some hope of ultimate recovery – God grant that he be not deceived! There is my explanation; it is sad enough, Poole, ay, and appalling to consider; but it is plain and natural, hangs well together and delivers us from all exorbitant alarms.'

'Sir,' said the butler, turning to a sort of mottled pallor, 'that thing was not my master, and there's the truth. My master' – here he looked round him and began to whisper – 'is a tall fine build of a man, and this was more of a dwarf.' Utterson attempted to protest. 'O, sir,' cried Poole, 'do you think I do not know my master after twenty years? do you think I do not know where his head comes to in the cabinet door, where I saw him every morning of my life? No, sir, that thing in the mask was never Doctor Jekyll – God knows what it was, but it was never Doctor Jekyll; and it is the belief of my heart that there was murder done.'

'Poole,' replied the lawyer, 'if you say that, it will become my duty to make certain. Much as I desire to spare your master's feelings, much as I am puzzled by this note which seems to prove him to be still alive, I shall consider it my duty to break in that door.'

'Ah, Mr Utterson, that's talking!' cried the butler.

'And now comes the second question,' resumed Utterson: 'Who is going to do it?'

'Why, you and me, sir,' was the undaunted reply.

'That is very well said,' returned the lawyer; 'and whatever comes of it, I shall make it my business to see you are no loser.'

'There is an axe in the theatre,' continued Poole; 'and you might take the kitchen poker for yourself.'

The lawyer took that rude but weighty instrument into his hand, and balanced it. 'Do you know, Poole,' he said, looking up, 'that you and I are about to place ourselves in a position of some peril?'

'You may say so, sir, indeed,' returned the butler.

'It is well, then, that we should be frank,' said the other. 'We both think more than we have said; let us make a clean breast. This masked figure that you saw, did you recognize it?'

'Well, sir, it went so quick, and the creature was so doubled up, that I could hardly swear to that,' was the answer. 'But if you mean, was it Mr Hyde? – why, yes, I think it was! You see, it was much of the same bigness; and it had the same quick light way with it; and then who else could have got in by the laboratory door? You have not forgot, sir, that at the time of the murder he had still the key with him? But that's not all. I don't know, Mr Utterson, if ever you met this Mr Hyde?'

'Yes,' said the lawyer, 'I once spoke with him.'

'Then you must know as well as the rest of us that there was something queer about that gentleman – something that gave a man a turn – I don't know rightly how to say it, sir, beyond this: that you felt it in your marrow – kind of cold and thin.'

'I own I felt something of what you describe,' said Mr Utterson.

'Quite so, sir,' returned Poole. 'Well, when that masked thing like a monkey jumped from among the chemicals and whipped into the cabinet, it went down my spine like ice. 'O, I know it's not evidence, Mr Utterson; I'm book-learned enough for that; but a man has his feelings, and I give you my bible-word it was Mr Hyde!'

'Ay, ay,' said the lawyer. 'My fears incline to the same point. Evil, I fear, founded – evil was sure to come – of that connection. Ay, truly, I believe you; I believe poor Harry is killed; and I believe his murderer (for what purpose, God alone can tell) is still lurking in his victim's room. Well, let our name be vengeance. Call Bradshaw.'

The footman came at the summons, very white and nervous.

'Pull yourself together, Bradshaw,' said the lawyer. 'This suspense, I know, is telling upon all of you; but it is now our intention to make an end of it. Poole, here, and I are going to force our way into the cabinet. If all is well, my shoulders are broad enough to bear the blame. Meanwhile, lest anything should really be amiss, or any malefactor seek to escape by the back, you and the boy must go round the corner with a pair of good sticks, and take your post at the laboratory door. We give you ten minutes, to get to your stations.'

As Bradshaw left, the lawyer looked at his watch. 'And now, Poole, let us get to ours,' he said; and taking the poker under his arm, he led the way into the yard. The scud had banked over the moon, and it was now quite dark. The wind, which only broke in puffs and draughts into that deep well of building, tossed the light of the candle to and fro about their steps, until they came into the shelter of the theatre, where they sat down silently to wait. London hummed solemnly all around; but nearer at hand, the stillness was only broken by the sound of a footfall moving to and fro along the cabinet floor.

'So it will walk all day, sir,' whispered Poole; 'ay, and the better part of the night. Only when a new sample comes from the chemist, there's a bit of a break. Ah, it's an ill-conscience that's such an enemy to rest! Ah, sir, there's blood foully shed in every step of it! But hark again, a little closer – put your heart in your ears, Mr Utterson, and tell me, is that the doctor's foot?'

The steps fell lightly and oddly, with a certain swing, for all they went so slowly; it was different indeed from the heavy creaking tread of Henry Jekyll. Utterson sighed. 'Is there never anything else?' he asked.

Poole nodded. 'Once,' he said. 'Once I heard it weeping!'

'Weeping? how that?' said the lawyer, conscious of a sudden chill of horror.

'Weeping like a woman or a lost soul,' said the butler. 'I came away with that upon my heart, that I could have wept too.'

But now the ten minutes drew to an end. Poole disinterred the axe from under a stack of packing straw; the candle was set upon the nearest table to light them to the attack; and they drew near with bated breath to where that patient foot was still going up and down, up and down, in the quiet of the night.

'Jekyll,' cried Utterson, with a loud voice, 'I demand to see you.' He paused a moment, but there came no reply. 'I give you fair warning, our suspicions are aroused, and I must and shall see you,' he resumed; 'if not by fair means, then by foul – if not of your consent, then by brute force!'

'Utterson,' said the voice, 'for God's sake, have mercy!'

'Ah, that's not Jekyll's voice – it's Hyde's!' cried Utterson. 'Down with the door, Poole.'

Poole swung the axe over his shoulder; the blow shook the building, and the red baize door leaped against the lock and hinges. A dismal screech, as of mere animal terror, rang from the cabinet. Up went the axe again, and again the panels crashed and the flame bounded; four times the blow fell; but the wood was tough and the fittings were of excellent workmanship; and it was not until the fifth, that the lock burst in sunder and the wreck of the door fell inwards on the carpet.

The besiegers, appalled by their own riot and the stillness that had succeeded, stood back a little and peered in. There lay the cabinet before their eyes in the quiet lamplight, a good fire glowing and chattering on the hearth, the kettle singing its thin strain, a drawer or two open, papers neatly set forth on the business table, and nearer the fire, the things laid out for tea: the quietest room, you would have said, and, but for the glazed presses full of chemicals, the most commonplace that night in London.

Right in the midst there lay the body of a man sorely contorted and still twitching. They drew near on tiptoe, turned it on its back and beheld the face of Edward Hyde. He was dressed in clothes far too large for him, clothes of the doctor's bigness; the cords of his face still moved with a semblance of life, but life was quite gone; and by the crushed phial in the hand and the strong smell of kernels that hung upon the air, Utterson knew that he was looking on the body of a self-destroyer.

'We have come too late,' he said sternly, 'whether to save or punish. Hyde is gone to his account; and it only remains for us to find the body of your master.'

The far greater proportion of the building was occupied by the theatre, which filled almost the whole ground storey and was lighted from above, and by the cabinet, which formed an upper storey at one end and looked upon the court. A corridor joined the theatre to the door on the bystreet; and with this, the cabinet communicated separately by a second flight of stairs. There were besides a few dark closets and a spacious cellar. All these they now thoroughly examined. Each closet needed but a glance, for all were empty and all, by the dust that fell from their doors, had stood long unopened. The cellar, indeed, was filled with crazy lumber, mostly dating from the times of the surgeon who was Jekyll's predecessor; but even as they opened the door, they were advertised of the uselessness of further search, by the fall of a perfect mat of cobweb which had for years sealed up the entrance. Nowhere was there any trace of Henry Jekyll, dead or alive.

Poole stamped on the flags of the corridor. 'He must be buried here,' he said, hearkening to the sound.

'Or he may have fled,' said Utterson, and he turned to examine the door in the bystreet. It was locked; and lying near by on the flags, they found the key, already stained with rust.

'This does not look like use,' observed the lawyer.

'Use!' echoed Poole. 'Do you not see, sir, it is broken? much as if a man had stamped on it.'

'Ay,' continued Utterson, 'and the fractures, too, are rusty.' The two men looked at each other with a scare. 'This is beyond me, Poole,' said the lawyer. 'Let us go back to the cabinet.'

They mounted the stair in silence, and still with an occasional awestruck glance at the dead body, proceeded more thoroughly to examine the contents of the cabinet. At one table, there were traces of chemical work, various measured heaps of some white salt being laid on glass saucers, as though for an experiment in which the unhappy man had been prevented.

'That is the same drug that I was always bringing him,' said Poole; and even as he spoke, the kettle with a startling noise boiled over.

This brought them to the fireside, where the easy chair was drawn cosily up, and the tea things stood ready to the sitter's elbow, the very sugar in the cup. There were several books on a shelf; one lay beside the tea things open, and Utterson was amazed to find it a copy of a pious work, for which Jekyll had several times expressed a great esteem, annotated, in his own hand, with startling blasphemies.

Next, in the course of their review of the chamber, the searchers came to the cheval glass, into whose depths they looked with an involuntary horror. But it was so turned as to show them nothing but the rosy glow playing on the roof, the fire sparkling in a hundred repetitions along the glazed front of the presses, and their own pale and fearful countenances stooping to look in.

'This glass have seen some strange things, sir,' whispered Poole.

'And surely none stranger than itself,' echoed the lawyer in the same tones. 'For what did Jekyll' – he caught himself up at the word with a start, and then conquering the weakness: 'what could Jekyll want with it?' he said.

'You may say that!' said Poole.

Next they turned to the business table. On the desk among the neat array of papers, a large envelope was uppermost, and bore, in the doctor's hand, the name of Mr Utterson. The lawyer unsealed it, and several enclosures fell to the floor. The first was a will, drawn in the same eccentric terms as the one which he had returned six months before, to serve as a testament in case of death and as a deed of gift in case of disappearance; but in place of the name of Edward Hyde, the lawyer, with indescribable amazement, read the name of Gabriel John Utterson. He looked at Poole, and then back at the paper, and last of all at the dead malefactor stretched upon the carpet.

'My head goes round,' he said. 'He has been all these days in possession; he had no cause to like me; he must have raged to see himself displaced; and he has not destroyed this document.'

He caught up the next paper; it was a brief note in the doctor's hand and dated at the top. 'O Poole!' the lawyer cried, 'he was alive and here this day. He cannot have been disposed of in so short a space, he must be still alive, he must have fled! And then, why fled? and how? and in that case, can we venture to declare this suicide? O, we must be careful. I foresee that we may yet involve your master in some dire catastrophe.'

'Why don't you read it, sir?' asked Poole.

'Because I fear,' replied the lawyer solemnly. 'God grant I have no cause for it!' And with that he brought the paper to his eyes and read as follows.

> *'My dear Utterson, – When this shall fall into your*
> *hands, I shall have disappeared, under what circumstances*
> *I have not the penetration to foresee, but my instinct and all*
> *the circumstances of my nameless situation tell me that the*
> *end is sure and must be early. Go then, and first read the*
> *narrative which Lanyon warned me he was to place in your*
> *hands; and if you care to hear more, turn to the confession*
> *of*
>
> *'Your unworthy and unhappy friend,*
>
> **'HENRY JEKYLL'**

'There was a third enclosure?' asked Utterson.

'Here, sir,' said Poole, and gave into his hands a considerable packet sealed in several places.

The lawyer put it in his pocket. 'I would say nothing of this paper. If your master has fled or is dead, we may at least save his credit. It is now ten; I must go home and read these documents in quiet; but I shall be back before midnight, when we shall send for the police.'

They went out, locking the door of the theatre behind them; and Utterson, once more leaving the servants gathered about the fire in the hall, trudged back to his office to read the two narratives in which this mystery was now to be explained.

DOCTOR LANYON'S NARRATIVE

On the ninth of January, now four days ago, I received by the evening delivery a registered envelope, addressed in the hand of my colleague and old school-companion, Henry Jekyll. I was a good deal surprised by this; for we were by no means in the habit of correspondence; I had seen the man, dined with him, indeed, the night before; and I could imagine nothing in our intercourse that should justify the formality of registration. The contents increased my wonder; for this is how the letter ran:

'*10th December,* 18—

'*Dear Lanyon, – You are one of my oldest friends; and although we may have differed at times on scientific questions, I cannot remember, at least on my side, any break in our affection. There was never a day when, if you had said to me, "Jekyll, my life, my honour, my reason, depend upon you," I would not have sacrificed my fortune or my left hand to help you. Lanyon, my life, my honour, my reason, are all at your mercy; if you fail me tonight, I am lost. You might suppose, after this preface, that I am going to ask you for something dishonourable to grant. Judge for yourself.*

'*I want you to postpone all other engagements for tonight – ay, even if you were summoned to the bedside of an emperor; to take a cab, unless your carriage should be actually at the door; and with this letter in your hand for consultation, to drive straight to my house. Poole, my butler, has his orders; you will find him waiting your arrival with a locksmith. The door of my cabinet is then to be forced; and you are to go in alone; to open the glazed press (letter E) on the left hand, breaking the lock if it be shut; and to draw out,* with all its contents as they stand, *the fourth drawer from the top or (which is the same thing) the third from the bottom. In my extreme distress of mind, I have a morbid fear of misdirecting you; but even if I am in error, you may know the right drawer by its contents: some powders, a phial and a paper book. This drawer I beg of you to carry back with you to Cavendish Square exactly as it stands.*

'That is the first part of the service: now for the second. You should be back, if you set out at once on the receipt of this, long before midnight; but I will leave you that amount of margin, not only in the fear of one of those obstacles that can neither be prevented nor foreseen, but because an hour when your servants are in bed is to be preferred for what will then remain to do. At midnight, then, I have to ask you to be alone in your consulting room, to admit with your own hand into the house a man who will present himself in my name, and to place in his hands the drawer that you will have brought with you from my cabinet. Then you will have played your part and earned my gratitude completely. Five minutes, afterwards, if you insist upon an explanation, you will have understood that these arrangements are of capital importance; and that by the neglect of one of them, fantastic as they must appear, you might have charged your conscience with my death or the shipwreck of my reason.

'Confident as I am that you will not trifle with this appeal, my heart sinks and my hand trembles at the bare thought of such a possibility. Think of me at this hour, in a strange place, labouring under a blackness of distress that no fancy can exaggerate, and yet well aware that, if you will but punctually serve me, my troubles will roll away like a story that is told. Serve me, my dear Lanyon, and save

'Your friend,
'H.J.

'PS I had already sealed this up when a fresh terror struck upon my soul. It is possible that the post office may fail me, and this letter not come into your hands until tomorrow morning. In that case, dear Lanyon, do my errand when it shall be most convenient for you in the course of the day; and once more expect my messenger at midnight. It may then already be too late; and if that night passes without event, you will know that you have seen the last of Henry Jekyll.'

Upon the reading of this letter, I made sure my colleague was insane; but till that was proved beyond the possibility of doubt, I felt bound to do as he requested. The less I understood of this farrago, the less I was in a position to judge of its importance; and an appeal so worded could not be set aside without a grave responsibility. I rose accordingly from table, got into a hansom, and drove straight to Jekyll's house. The butler was awaiting my arrival; he had received by the same post as mine a registered letter of instruction, and had sent at once for a locksmith and a carpenter. The tradesmen came while we were yet speaking; and we moved in a body to old Dr Denman's surgical theatre from which (as you are doubtless aware) Jekyll's private cabinet is most conveniently entered. The door was very strong, the lock excellent; the carpenter avowed he would have great trouble and have to do much damage, if force were to be used; and the locksmith was near despair. But this last was a handy fellow, and after two hours' work, the door stood open. The press marked E was unlocked; and I took out the drawer, had it filled up with straw and tied in a sheet, and returned with it to Cavendish Square.

Here I proceeded to examine its contents. The powders were neatly enough made up, but not with the nicety of the dispensing chemist; so that it was plain they were of Jekyll's private manufacture; and when I opened one of the wrappers, I found what seemed to me a simple, crystalline salt of a white colour. The phial, to which I next turned my attention, might have been about half-full of a blood-red liquor, which was highly pungent to the sense of smell and seemed to me to contain phosphorus and some volatile ether. At the other ingredients, I could make no guess. The book was an ordinary version book and contained little but a series of dates. These covered a period of many years, but I observed that the entries ceased nearly a year ago and quite abruptly. Here and there a brief remark was appended to a date, usually no more than a single word: 'double' occurring perhaps six times in a total of several hundred entries; and once very early in the list and followed by several marks of exclamation, 'total failure!!!' All this, though it whetted my curiosity, told me little that was definite. Here were a phial of some tincture, a paper of some salt, and the record of a series of experiments that had led (like too many of Jekyll's investigations) to no end of practical usefulness. How could the presence of these articles in my house affect either the honour, the sanity, or the life of my flighty colleague? If his messenger could go to one place, why could he not go to another? And even granting some impediment, why was this gentleman to be received by me in secret? The more I reflected, the more convinced I grew that I was dealing with a case of cerebral disease; and though I dismissed my servants to bed, I loaded an old revolver that I might be found in some posture of self-defence.

Twelve o'clock had scarce rung out over London, ere the knocker sounded very gently on the door. I went myself at the summons, and found a small man crouching against the pillars of the portico.

'Are you come from Dr Jekyll?' I asked.

He told me 'yes' by a constrained gesture; and when I had bidden him enter, he did not obey me without a searching backward glance into the darkness of the square. There was a policeman not far off, advancing with his bull's eye open; and at the sight, I thought my visitor started and made greater haste.

These particulars struck me, I confess, disagreeably; and as I followed him into the bright light of the consulting room, I kept my hand ready on my weapon. Here, at last, I had a chance of clearly seeing him. I had never set eyes on him before, so much was certain. He was small, as I have said; I was struck besides with the shocking expression of his face, with his remarkable combination of great muscular activity and great apparent debility of constitution, and – last but not least – with the odd, subjective disturbance caused by his neighbourhood. This bore some resemblance to incipient rigor, and was accompanied by a marked sinking of the pulse. At the time, I set it down to some idiosyncratic, personal distaste, and merely wondered at the acuteness of the symptoms; but I have since had reason to believe the cause to lie much deeper in the nature of man, and to turn on some nobler hinge than the principle of hatred.

This person (who had thus, from the first moment of his entrance, struck in me what I can only describe as a disgustful curiosity) was dressed in a fashion that would have made an ordinary person laughable: his clothes, that is to say, although they were of rich and sober fabric, were enormously too large for him in every measurement – the trousers hanging on his legs and rolled up to keep them from the ground, the waist of the coat below his haunches, and the collar sprawling wide upon his shoulders. Strange to relate, this ludicrous accoutrement was far from moving me to laughter. Rather, as there was something abnormal and misbegotten in the very essence of the creature that now faced me – something seizing, surprising and revolting – this fresh disparity seemed but to fit in with and to reinforce it; so that to my interest in the man's nature and character, there was added a curiosity as to his origin, his life, his fortune and status in the world.

These observations, though they have taken so great a space to be set down in, were yet the work of a few seconds. My visitor was, indeed, on fire with sombre excitement.

'Have you got it?' he cried. 'Have you got it?' And so lively was his impatience that he even laid his hand upon my arm and sought to shake me.

I put him back, conscious at his touch of a certain icy pang along my blood. 'Come, sir,' said I. 'You forget that I have not yet the pleasure of your acquaintance. Be seated, if you please.' And I showed him an example, and sat down myself in my customary seat and with as fair an imitation of my ordinary manner to a patient, as the lateness of the house, the nature of my preoccupations, and the horror I had of my visitor, would suffer me to muster.

'I beg your pardon, Dr Lanyon,' he replied civilly enough. 'What you say is very well founded; and my impatience has shown its heels to my politeness. I come here at the instance of your colleague, Dr Henry Jekyll, on a piece of business of some moment; and I understood . . .' he paused and put his hand to his throat, and I could see, in spite of his collected manner, that he was wrestling against the approaches of the hysteria – 'I understood, a drawer . . .'

But here I took pity on my visitor's suspense, and some perhaps on my own growing curiosity.

'There it is, sir,' said I, pointing to the drawer, where it lay on the floor behind a table and still covered with the sheet.

He sprang to it, and then paused, and laid his hand upon his heart; I could hear his teeth grate with the convulsive action of his jaws; and his face was so ghastly to see that I grew alarmed both for his life and reason.

'Compose yourself,' said I.

He turned a dreadful smile to me, and as if with the decision of despair, plucked away the sheet. At sight of the contents, he uttered one loud sob of such immense relief that I sat petrified. And the next moment, in a voice that was already fairly well under control, 'Have you a graduated glass?' he asked.

I rose from my place with something of an effort and gave him what he asked.

He thanked me with a smiling nod, measured out a few minims of the red tincture and added one of the powders. The mixture, which was at first of a reddish hue, began, in proportion as the crystals melted, to brighten in colour, to effervesce audibly, and to throw off small fumes of vapour. Suddenly and at the same moment, the ebullition ceased and the compound changed to a dark purple, which faded again more slowly to a watery green. My visitor, who had watched these metamorphoses with a keen eye, smiled, set down the glass upon the table, and then turned and looked upon me with an air of scrutiny.

'And now,' said he, 'to settle what remains. Will you be wise? will you be guided? will you suffer me to take this glass in my hand and to go forth from your house without further parley? or has the greed of curiosity too much command of you? Think before you answer, for it shall be done as you decide. As you decide, you shall be left as you were before, and neither richer nor wiser, unless the sense of service rendered to a man in mortal distress may be counted as a kind of riches of the soul. Or, if you shall so prefer to choose, a new province of knowledge and new avenues to fame and power shall be laid open to you, here, in this room, upon the instant; and your sight shall be blasted by a prodigy to stagger the unbelief of Satan.'

'Sir,' said I, affecting a coolness that I was far from truly possessing, 'you speak engimas, and you will perhaps not wonder that I hear you with no very strong impression of belief. But I have gone too far in the way of inexplicable services to pause before I see the end.'

'It is well,' replied my visitor. 'Lanyon, you remember your vows: what follows is under the seal of our profession. And now, you who have so long been bound to the most narrow and material views, you who have denied the virtue of transcendental medicine, you who have derided your superiors – behold!'

He put the glass to his lips and drank at one gulp. A cry followed; he reeled, staggered, clutched at the table and held on, staring with injected eyes, gasping with open mouth; and as I looked there came, I thought, a change – he seemed to swell – his face became suddenly black and the features seemed to melt and alter – and the next moment, I had sprung to my feet and leaped back against the wall, my arm raised to shield me from that prodigy, my mind submerged in terror.

'O God!' I screamed, and 'O God!' again and again; for there before my eyes – pale and shaken, and half fainting, and groping before him with his hands, like a man restored from death – there stood Henry Jekyll!

What he told me in the next hour, I cannot bring my mind to set on paper. I saw what I saw, I heard what I heard, and my soul sickened at it; and yet now when that sight has faded from my eyes, I ask myself if I believe it, and I cannot answer. My life is shaken to its roots; sleep has left me; the deadliest terror sits by me at all hours of the day and night; I feel that my days are numbered, and that I must die; and yet I shall die incredulous. As for the moral turpitude that man unveiled to me, even with tears of penitence, I cannot, even in memory, dwell on it without a start of horror. I will say but one thing, Utterson, and that (if you can bring your mind to credit it) will be more than enough. The creature who crept into my house that night was, on Jekyll's own confession, known by the name of Hyde and hunted for in every corner of the land as the murderer of Carew.

Hastie Lanyon.

HENRY JEKYLL'S FULL STATEMENT OF THE CASE

I was born in the year 18— to a large fortune, endowed besides with excellent parts, inclined by nature to industry, fond of the respect of the wise and good among my fellow-men, and thus, as might have been supposed, with every guarantee of an honourable and distinguished future. And indeed the worst of my faults was a certain impatient gaiety of disposition, such as has made the happiness of many, but such as I found it hard to reconcile with my imperious desire to carry my head high, and wear a more than commonly grave countenance before the public. Hence it came about that I concealed my pleasures; and that when I reached years of reflection, and began to look round me and take stock of my progress and position in the world, I stood already committed to a profound duplicity of life. Many a man would have even blazoned such irregularities as I was guilty of; but from the high views that I had set before me, I regarded and hid them with an almost morbid sense of shame. It was thus rather the exacting nature of my aspirations than any particular degradation in my faults, that made me what I was and, with even a deeper trench than in the majority of men, severed in me those provinces of good and ill which divide and compound man's dual nature. In this case, I was driven to reflect deeply and inveterately on that hard law of life, which lies at the root of religion and is one of the most plentiful springs of distress. Though so profound a double-dealer, I was in no sense a hypocrite; both sides of me were in dead earnest; I was no more myself when I laid aside restraint and plunged in shame, than when I laboured, in the eye of day, at the furtherance of knowledge or the relief of sorrow and suffering. And it chanced that the direction of my scientific studies, which led wholly towards the mystic and the transcendental, reacted and shed a strong light on this consciousness of the perennial war among my members. With every day, and from both sides of my intelligence, the moral and the intellectual, I thus drew steadily nearer to that truth, by whose partial discovery I have been doomed to such a dreadful shipwreck: that man is not truly one, but truly two. I say two, because the state of my own knowledge does not pass beyond that point. Others will follow, others will outstrip me on the same lines;

and I hazard the guess that man will be ultimately known for a mere polity of multifarious, incongruous and independent denizens. I for my part, from the nature of my life, advanced infallibly in one direction and in one direction only. It was on the moral side, and in my own person, that I learned to recognize the thorough and primitive duality of man; I saw that, of the two natures that contended in the field of my consciousness, even if I could rightly be said to be either, it was only because I was radically both; and from an early date, even before the course of my scientific discoveries had begun to suggest the most naked possibility of such a miracle, I had learned to dwell with pleasure, as a beloved daydream, on the thought of the separation of these elements. If each, I told myself, could but be housed in separate identities, life would be relieved of all that was unbearable; the unjust might go his way, delivered from the aspirations and remorse of his more upright twin; and the just could walk steadfastly and securely on his upward path, doing the good things in which he found his pleasure, and no longer exposed to disgrace and penitence by the hands of this extraneous evil. It was the curse of mankind that these incongruous faggots were thus bound together – that in the agonized womb of consciousness, these polar twins should be continuously struggling. How, then, were they dissociated?

I was so far in my reflections when, as I have said, a side light began to shine upon the subject from the la-boratory table. I began to perceive more deeply than it has ever yet been stated, the trembling immateriality, the mist-like transience, of this seemingly so solid body in which we walk attired. Certain agents I found to have the power to shake and to pluck back that fleshly vestment, even as a wind might toss the curtains of a pavilion. For two good reasons, I will not enter deeply into this scientific branch of my confession. First, because I have been made to learn that the doom and burden of our life is bound forever on man's shoulders, and when the attempt is made to cast it off, it but returns upon us with more unfamiliar and more awful pressure. Second, because as my narrative will make alas! too evident, my discoveries were incomplete. Enough, then, that I not only recognized my natural body for the mere aura and effulgence of certain of the powers that made up my spirit, but managed to compound a drug by which these powers should be dethroned from their supremacy, and a second form and countenance substituted, none the less natural to me because they were the expression, and bore the stamp, of lower elements in my soul.

I hesitated long before I put this theory to the test of practice. I knew well that I risked death; for any drug that so potently controlled and shook the very fortress of identity, might by the least scruple of an overdose or at the least inopportunity in the moment of exhibition, utterly blot out that immaterial tabernacle which I looked to it to change. But the temptation of a discovery so singular and profound, at last overcame the suggestions of alarm. I had long since prepared my tincture; I purchased at once, from a firm of wholesale chemists, a large quantity of a particular salt which I knew, from my experiments, to be the last ingredient required; and late one accursed night, I compounded the elements, watched them boil and smoke together in the glass, and when the ebullition had subsided, with a strong glow of courage, drank off the potion.

The most racking pangs succeeded: a grinding in the bones, deadly nausea, and a horror of the spirit that cannot be exceeded at the hour of birth or death. Then these agonies began swiftly to subside, and I came to myself as if out of a great sickness. There was something strange in my sensations, something indescribably new and, from its very novelty, incredibly sweet. I felt younger, lighter, happier in body; within I was conscious of a heady recklessness, a current of disordered sensual images running like a mill race in my fancy, a solution of the bonds of obligation, an unknown but not an innocent freedom of the soul. I knew myself, at the first breath of this new life, to be more wicked, tenfold more wicked, sold a slave to my original evil; and the thought, in that moment, braced and delighted me like wine. I stretched out my hands, exulting in the freshness of these sensations; and in the act, I was suddenly aware that I had lost in stature.

There was no mirror, at that date, in my room; that which stands beside me as I write, was brought there later on and for the very purpose of these transformations. The night, however, was far gone into the morning – the morning, black as it was, was nearly ripe for the conception of the day – the inmates of my house were locked in the most rigorous hours of slumber; and I determined, flushed as I was with hope and triumph, to venture in my new shape as far as to my bedroom. I crossed the yard, wherein the constellations looked down upon me,

I could have thought, with wonder, the first creature of that sort that their unsleeping vigilance had yet disclosed to them; I stole through the corridors, a stranger in my own house; and coming to my room, I saw for the first time the appearance of Edward Hyde.

I must here speak by theory alone, saying not that which I know, but that which I suppose to be most probable. The evil side of my nature, to which I had now transferred the stamping efficacy, was less robust and less developed than the good which I had just deposed. Again, in the course of my life, which had been, after all, nine tenths a life of effort, virtue and control, it had been much less exercised and much less exhausted. And hence, as I think, it came about that Edward Hyde was so much smaller, slighter and younger than Henry Jekyll. Even as good shone upon the countenance of the one, evil was written broadly and plainly on the face of the other. Evil besides (which I must still believe to be the lethal side of man) had left on that body an imprint of deformity and decay. And yet when I looked upon that ugly idol in the glass, I was conscious of no repugnance, rather of a leap of welcome. This, too, was myself. It seemed natural and human. In my eyes it bore a livelier image of the spirit, it seemed more express and single, than the imperfect and divided countenance, I had been hitherto accustomed to call mine. And in so far I was doubtless right. I have observed that when I wore the semblance of Edward Hyde, none could come near to me at first without a visible misgiving of the flesh. This, as I take it, was because all human beings, as we meet them, are commingled out of good and evil: and Edward Hyde, alone in the ranks of mankind, was pure evil.

I lingered but a moment at the mirror: the second and conclusive experiment had yet to be attempted; it yet remained to be seen if I had lost my identity beyond redemption and must flee before daylight from a house that was no longer mine; and hurrying back to my cabinet, I once more prepared and drank the cup, once more suffered the pangs of dissolution, and came to myself once more with the character, the stature and the face of Henry Jekyll.

That night I had come to the fatal cross roads. Had I approached my discovery in a more noble spirit, had I risked the experiment while under the empire of generous or pious aspirations, all must have been otherwise, and from these agonies of death and birth, I had come forth an angel instead of a fiend. The drug had no discriminating action; it was neither diabolical nor divine; it but shook the doors of the prisonhouse of my disposition; and like the captives of Philippi, that which stood within ran forth. At that time my virtue slumbered; my evil, kept awake by ambition, was alert and swift to seize the occasion; and the thing that was projected was Edward Hyde. Hence, although I had now two characters as well as two appearances, one was wholly evil, and the other was still the old Henry Jekyll, that incongruous compound of whose reformation and improvement I had already learned to despair. The movement was thus wholly toward the worse.

Even at that time, I had not yet conquered my aversion to the dryness of a life of study. I would still be merrily disposed at times; and as my pleasures were (to say the least) undignified, and I was not only well known and highly considered, but growing towards the elderly man, this incoherency of my life was daily growing more unwelcome. It was on this side that my new power tempted me until I fell in slavery. I had but to drink the cup, to doff at once the body of the noted professor, and to assume, like a thick cloak, that of Edward Hyde. I smiled at the notion; it seemed to me at the time to be humorous; and I made my preparations with the most studious care. I took and furnished that house in Soho, to which Hyde was tracked by the police; and engaged as housekeeper a creature whom I well knew to be silent and unscrupulous. On the other side, I announced to my servants that a Mr Hyde (whom I described) was to have full liberty and power about my house in the square; and to parry mishaps, I even called and made myself a familiar object, in my second character. I next drew up that will to which you so much objected; so that if anything befell me in the person of Doctor Jekyll, I could enter on that of Edward Hyde without pecuniary loss. And thus fortified, as I supposed, on every side, I began to profit by the strange immunities of my position.

Men have before hired bravos to transact their crimes, while their own person and reputation sat under shelter. I was the first that ever did so for his pleasures. I was the first that could thus plod in the public eye with a load of genial respectability, and in a moment, like a schoolboy, strip off these lendings and spring headlong into the sea of liberty. But for me, in my impenetrable mantle, the safety was complete. Think of it – I did not even exist! Let me but escape into my laboratory door, give me but a second or two to mix and swallow the draught that I had always standing ready; and whatever he had done, Edward Hyde would pass away like the stain of breath upon a mirror; and there in his stead, quietly at home, trimming the midnight lamp in his study, a man who could afford to laugh at suspicion, would be Henry Jekyll.

The pleasures which I made haste to seek in my disguise were, as I have said, undignified; I would scarce use a harder term. But in the hands of Edward Hyde, they soon began to turn towards the monstrous. When I would come back from these excursions, I was often plunged into a kind of wonder at my vicarious depravity. This familiar that I called out of my own soul, and sent forth alone to do his good pleasure, was a being inherently malign and villainous; his every act and thought centred on self; drinking pleasure with bestial avidity from any degree of torture to another; relentless like a man of stone. Henry Jekyll stood at times aghast before the acts of Edward Hyde; but the situation was apart from ordinary laws, and insidiously relaxed the grasp of conscience. It was Hyde, after all, and Hyde alone, that was guilty. Jekyll was no worse; he woke again to his good qualities seemingly unimpaired; he would even make haste, where it was possible, to undo the evil done by Hyde. And thus his conscience slumbered.

Into the details of the infamy at which I thus connived (for even now I can scarce grant that I committed it) I have no design of entering; I mean but to point out the warnings and the successive steps with which my chastisement approached. I met with one accident which, as it brought on no consequence, I shall no more than mention. An act of cruelty to a child aroused against me the anger of a passer by, whom I recognized the other day in the person of your kinsman; the doctor and the child's family joined him; there were moments when I feared for my life; and at last, in order to pacify their too just resentment, Edward Hyde had to bring them to the door, and pay them in a cheque drawn in the name, of Henry Jekyll. But this danger was easily eliminated from the future, by opening an account at another bank in the name of Edward Hyde himself; and when, by sloping my own hand backward, I had supplied my double with a signature, I thought I sat beyond the reach of fate.

Some two months before the murder of Sir Danvers, I had been out for one of my adventures, had returned at a late hour, and woke the next day in bed with somewhat odd sensations. It was in vain I looked about me; in vain I saw the decent furniture and tall proportions of my room in the square; in vain that I recognized the pattern of the bed curtains and the design of the mahogany frame; something still kept insisting that I was not where I was, that I had not wakened where I seemed to be, but in the little room in Soho where I was accustomed to sleep in the body of Edward Hyde. I smiled to myself, and, in my psychological way, began lazily to inquire into the elements of this illusion, occasionally, even as I did so, dropping back into a comfortable morning doze. I was still so engaged when, in one of my more wakeful moments, my eye fell upon my hand. Now the hand of Henry Jekyll (as you have often remarked) was professional in shape and size: it was large, firm, white and comely. But the hand which I now saw, clearly enough, in the yellow light of a mid-London morning, lying half shut on the bed clothes, was lean, corded, knuckly, of a dusky pallor and thickly shaded with a smart growth of hair. It was the hand of Edward Hyde.

I must have stared upon it for near half a minute, sunk as I was in the mere stupidity of wonder, before terror woke up in my breast as sudden and startling as the crash of cymbals; and bounding from my bed, I rushed to the mirror. At the sight that met my eyes, my blood was changed into something exquisitely thin and icy. Yes, I had gone to bed Henry Jekyll, I had awakened Edward Hyde. How was this to be explained? I asked myself; and then, with another bound of terror – how was it to be remedied? It was well on in the morning; the servants were up; all my drugs were in the cabinet – a long journey, down two pairs of stairs, through the back passage, across the open court and through the anatomical theatre, from where I was then standing horror-struck. It might indeed be possible to cover my face; but of what use was that, when I was unable to conceal the alteration in my stature? And then with an overpowering sweetness of relief, it came back upon my mind that the servants were already used to the coming and going of my second self. I had soon dressed, as well as I was able, in clothes of my own size: had soon passed through the house, where Bradshaw stared and drew back at seeing Mr Hyde at such an hour and in such a strange array; and ten minutes later, Dr Jekyll had returned to his own shape and was sitting down, with a darkened brow, to make a feint of breakfasting.

Small indeed was my appetite. This inexplicable incident, this reversal of my previous experience, seemed, like the Babylonian finger on the wall, to be spelling out the letters of my judgment; and I began to reflect more seriously than ever before on the issues and possibilities of my double existence. That part of me which I had the power of projecting, had lately been much exercised and nourished; it had seemed to me of late as though the body of Edward Hyde had grown in stature, as though (when I wore that form) I were conscious of a more generous tide of blood; and I began to spy a danger that, if this were much prolonged, the balance of my nature might be permanently overthrown, the power of voluntary change be forfeited, and the character of Edward Hyde become irrevocably mine. The power of the drug had not been always equally displayed. Once, very early in my career, it had totally failed me; since then I had been obliged on more than one occasion to double, and once, with infinite risk of death, to treble the amount; and these rare uncertainties had cast hitherto the sole shadow on my contentment. Now, however, and in the light of that morning's accident, I was led to remark that whereas, in the beginning, the difficulty had been to throw off the body of Jekyll, it had of late, gradually but decidedly transferred itself to the other side. All things therefore seemed to point to this: that I was slowly losing hold of my original and better self, and becoming slowly incorporated with my second and worse.

Between these two, I now felt I had to choose. My two natures had memory in common, but all other faculties were most unequally shared between them. Jekyll (who was composite) now with the most sensitive apprehensions, now with a greedy gusto, projected and shared in the pleasures and adventures of Hyde; but Hyde was indifferent to Jekyll, or but remembered him as the mountain bandit remembers the cavern in which he conceals himself from pursuit. Jekyll had more than a father's interest; Hyde had more than a son's indifference. To cast in my lot with Jekyll, was to die to those appetites which I had long secretly indulged and had of late begun to pamper. To cast it in with Hyde, was to die to a thousand interests and aspirations, and to become, at a blow and forever, despised and friendless. The bargain might appear unequal; but there was still another consideration in the scales; for while Jekyll would suffer smartingly in the fires of abstinence, Hyde would be not even conscious of all that he had lost. Strange as my circumstances were, the terms of this debate are as old and commonplace as man; much the same induce-ments and alarms cast the die for any tempted and trembling sinner; and it fell out with me, as it falls with so vast a majority of my fellows, that I chose the better part and was found wanting in the strength to keep to it.

Yes, I preferred the elderly and discontented doctor, surrounded by friends and cherishing honest hopes; and bade a resolute farewell to the liberty, the comparative youth, the light step, leaping pulses and secret pleasures, that I had enjoyed in the disguise of Hyde. I made this choice perhaps with some unconscious reservation, for I neither gave up the house in Soho, nor destroyed the clothes of Edward Hyde, which still lay ready in my cabinet. For two months, however, I was true to my determination; for two months, I led a life of such severity as I had never before attained to, and enjoyed the compensations of an approving conscience. But time began at last to obliterate the freshness of my alarm; the praises of conscience began to grow into a thing of course; I began to be tortured with throes and longings, as of Hyde struggling after freedom; and at last, in an hour of moral weakness, I once again compounded and swallowed the transforming draught.

I do not suppose that, when a drunkard reasons with himself upon his vice, he is once out of five hundred times affected by the dangers that he runs through his brutish, physical insensibility; neither had I, long as I had considered my position, made enough allowance for the complete moral insensibility and insensate readiness to evil, which were the leading characters of Edward Hyde. Yet it was by these that I was punished. My devil had been long caged, he came out roaring. I was conscious, even when I took the draught, of a more unbridled, a more furious propensity to ill. It must have been this, I suppose, that stirred in my soul that tempest of impatience with which I listened to the civil-ities of my unhappy victim; I declare at least, before God, no man morally sane could have been guilty of that crime upon so pitiful a provocation; and that I struck in no more reasonable spirit than that in which a sick child may break a plaything. But I had voluntarily stripped myself of all those balancing instincts, by which even the worst of us continues to walk with some degree of steadiness among temptations; and in my case, to be tempted, however slightly, was to fall.

Instantly the spirit of hell awoke in me and raged. With a transport of glee, I mauled the unresisting body, tasting delight from every blow; and it was not till weariness had begun to succeed, that I was suddenly, in the top fit of my delirium, struck through the heart by a cold thrill of terror. A mist dispersed; I saw my life to be forfeit; and fled from the scene of these excesses, at once glorying and trembling, my lust of evil gratified and stimulated, my love of life screwed to the topmost peg. I ran to the house in Soho, and (to make assurance doubly sure) destroyed my papers; thence I set out through the lamplit strees, in the same divided ecstasy of mind, gloating on my crime, light-headedly devising others in the future, and yet still hastening and still hearkening in my wake for the steps of the avenger. Hyde had a song upon his lips as he compounded the draught, and as he drank it, pledged the dead man. The pangs of transformation had not done tearing him, before Henry Jekyll, with streaming tears of gratitude and remorse, had fallen upon his knees and lifted his clasped hands to God. The veil of self-indulgence was rent from head to foot, I saw my life as a whole: I followed it up from the days of childhood, when I had walked with my father's hand, and through the self-denying toils of my professional life, to arrive again and again, with the same sense of unreality, at the damned horrors of the evening. I could have screamed aloud; I sought with tears and prayers to smother down the crowd of hideous images and sounds with which my memory swarmed against me; and still, between the petitions, the ugly face of my iniquity stared into my soul. As the acuteness of this remorse began to die away, it was succeeded by a sense of joy. The problem of my conduct was solved. Hyde was thenceforth impossible; whether I would or not, I was now confined to the better part of my existence; and O, how I rejoiced to think it! with what willing humility, I embraced anew the restrictions of natural life! with what sincere renunciation, I locked the door by which I had so often gone and come, and ground the key under my heel!

The next day, came the news that the murder had been overlooked, that the guilt of Hyde was patent to the world, and that the victim was a man high in public estimation. It was not only a crime, it had been a tragic folly. I think I was glad to know it; I think I was glad to have my better impulses thus buttressed and guarded by the terrors of the scaffold. Jekyll was now my city of refuge; let but Hyde peep out an instant, and the hands of all men would be raised to take and slay him.

I resolved in my future conduct to redeem the past; and I can say with honesty that my resolve was fruitful of some good. You know yourself how earnestly in the last months of last year, I laboured to relieve suffering; you know that much was done for others, and that the days passed quietly, almost happily for myself. Nor can I truly say that I wearied of this beneficent and innocent life; I think instead that I daily enjoyed it more completely; but I was still cursed with my duality of purpose; and as the first edge of my penitence wore off, the lower side of me, so long indulged, so recently chained down, began to growl for licence. Not that I dreamed of resuscitating Hyde; the bare idea of that would startle me to frenzy: no, it was in my own person, that I was once more tempted to trifle with my conscience; and it was as an ordinary secret sinner, that I at last fell before the assaults of temptation.

There comes an end to all things; the most capacious measure is filled at last; and this brief condescension to my evil finally destroyed the balance of my soul. And yet I was not alarmed; the fall seemed natural, like a return to the old days before I had made my discovery. It was a fine, clear, January day, wet under foot where the frost had melted, but cloudless overhead; and the Regent's Park was full of winter chirruppings and sweet with Spring odours. I sat in the sun on a bench; the animal within me licking the chops of memory; the spiritual side a little drowsed, promising subsequent penitence, but not yet moved to begin. After all, I reflected I was like my neighbours; and then I smiled, comparing myself with other men, comparing my active goodwill with the lazy cruelty of their neglect. And at the very moment of that vainglorious thought, a qualm came over me, a horrid nausea and the most deadly shuddering. These passed away, and left me faint; and then as in its turn the faintness subsided, I began to be aware of a change in the temper of my thoughts, a greater boldness, a contempt of danger, a solution of the bonds of obligation. I looked down; my clothes hung formlessly on my shrunken limbs; the hand that lay on my knee was corded and hairy. I was once more Edward Hyde. A moment before I had been safe of all men's respect, wealthy, beloved – the cloth laying for me in the dining room at home; and now I was the common quarry of mankind, hunted, houseless, a known murderer, thrall to the gallows.

My reason wavered, but it did not fail me utterly. I have more than once observed that, in my second character, my faculties seemed sharpened to a point and my spirits more tensely elastic; thus it came about that, where Jekyll perhaps might have succumbed, Hyde rose to the importance of the moment. My drugs were in one of the presses of my cabinet; how was I to reach them? That was the problem that (crushing my temples in my hands) I set myself to solve. The laboratory door I had closed. If I sought to enter by the house, my own servants would consign me to the gallows. I saw I must employ another hand, and thought of Lanyon. How was he to be reached? how persuaded? Supposing that I escaped capture in the streets, how was I to make my way into his presence? and how should I, an unknown and displeasing visitor, prevail on the famous physician to rifle the study of his colleague, Dr Jekyll? Then I remembered that of my original character, one part remained to me: I could write my own hand; and once I had conceived that kindling spark, the way that I must follow became lighted up from end to end.

Thereupon, I arranged my clothes as best I could, and summoning a passing hansom, drove to an hotel in Portland Street, the name of which I chanced to remember. At my appearance (which was indeed comical enough, however tragic a fate these garments covered) the driver could not conceal his mirth. I gnashed my teeth upon him with a gust of devilish fury; and the smile withered from his face – happily for him – yet more happily for myself, for in another instant I had certainly dragged him from his perch. At the inn, as I entered, I looked about me with so black a countenance as made the attendants tremble; not a look did they exchange in my presence; but obsequiously took my orders, led me to a private room, and brought me wherewithal to write. Hyde in danger of his life was a creature new to me: shaken with inordinate anger, strung to the pitch of murder, lusting to inflict pain. Yet the creature was astute; mastered his fury with a great effort of the will; composed his two important letters, one to Lanyon and one to Poole; and that he might receive actual evidence of their being posted, sent them out with directions that they should be registered.

Thenceforward, he sat all day over the fire in the private room, gnawing his nails; there he dined, sitting alone with his fears, the waiter visibly quailing before his eye; and thence, when the night was fully come, he set forth in the corner of a closed cab, and was driven to and fro about the streets of the city. He, I say – I cannot say, I. That child of Hell had nothing human; nothing lived in him but fear and hatred. And when at last, thinking the driver had begun to grow suspicious, he discharged the cab and ventured on foot, attired in his misfitting clothes, an object marked out for observation, into the midst of the nocturnal passengers, these two base passions raged within him like a tempest. He walked fast, hunted by his fears, chattering to himself, skulking through the less frequented thoroughfares, counting the minutes that still divided him from midnight. Once a woman spoke to him, offering, I think, a box of lights. He smote her in the face, and she fled.

When I came to myself at Lanyon's, the horror of my old friend perhaps affected me somewhat: I do not know; it was at least but a drop in the sea to the abhorrence with which I looked back upon these hours. A change had come over me. It was no longer the fear of the gallows, it was the horror of being Hyde that racked me. I received Lanyon's condemnation partly in a dream; it was partly in a dream that I came home to my own house and got into bed. I slept after the prostration of the day, with a stringent and profound slumber which not even the night-mares that wrung me could avail to break. I awoke in the morning shaken, weakened, but refreshed. I still hated and feared the thought of the brute that slept within me, and I had not of course forgotten the appalling dangers of the day before; but I was once more at home, in my own house and close to my drugs; and gratitude for my escape shone so strong in my soul that it almost rivalled the brightness of hope.

I was stepping leisurely across the court after breakfast, drinking the chill of the air with pleasure, when I was seized again with those indescribable sensations that heralded the change; and I had but the time to gain the shelter of my cabinet, before I was once again raging and freezing with the passions of Hyde. It took on this occasion a double dose to recall me to myself; and alas, six hours after, as I sat looking sadly in the fire, the pangs returned, and the drug had to be readminis-tered. In short, from that day forth it seemed only by a great effort as of gymnastics, and only under the immediate stimulation of the drug, that I was able to wear the countenance of Jekyll. At all hours of the day and night, I would be taken with the premonitory shudder; above all, if I slept, or even dozed for a moment in my chair, it was always as Hyde that I awakened. Under the strain of this continually impending doom and by the sleeplessness to which I now condemned myself, ay, even beyond what I had thought possible to man, I became, in my own person, a creature eaten up and emptied by fever, languidly weak both in body and mind, and solely occupied by one thought: the horror of my other self. But when I slept, or when the virtue of the medicine wore off, I would leap almost without transition (for the pangs of transformation grew daily less marked) into the possession of a fancy brimming with images of terror, a soul boiling with causeless hatreds, and a body that seemed not strong enough to contain the raging energies of life. The powers of Hyde seemed to have grown with the sickliness of Jekyll. And certainly the hate that now divided them was equal on each side. With Jekyll, it was a thing of vital instinct. He had now seen the full deformity of that creature that shared with him some of the phenomena of consciousness, and was co-heir with him to death: and beyond these links of community, which in themselves made the most poignant part of his distress, he thought of Hyde, for all his energy of life, as of something not only hellish but inorganic. This was the shocking thing; that the slime of the pit seemed to utter cries and voices; that the amorphous dust gesticulated and sinned; that what was dead, and had no shape, would usurp the offices of life. And this again, that that insurgent horror was knit to him closer than a wife, closer than an eye; lay caged in his flesh, where he heard it mutter and felt it struggle to be born; and at every hour of weakness, and in the confidence of slumber, prevailed against him, and deposed him out of life. The hatred of Hyde for Jekyll, was of a different order. His terror of the gallows drove him continually to commit temporary suicide, and return to his subordinate station of a part instead of a person; but he loathed the necessity, he loathed the despondency into which Jekyll was now fallen, and he resented the dislike with which he was himself regarded. Hence the ape-like tricks that he would play me, scrawling in my own hand blasphemies on the pages of my books, burning the letters and destroying the portrait of my father; and indeed, had it not been for his fear of death, he would long ago have ruined himself in order to involve me in the ruin. But his love of life is wonderful; I go further: I, who sicken and freeze at the mere thought of him, when I recall the abjection and passion of this attachment, and when I know how he fears my power to cut him off by suicide, I find it in my heart to pity him.

It is useless, and the time awfully fails me, to prolong this description; no one has ever suffered such torments, let that suffice; and yet even to these, habit brought – no, not alleviation – but a certain callousness of soul, a certain acquiescence of despair; and my punishment might have gone on for years, but for the last calamity which has now fallen, and which has finally severed me from my own face and nature. My provision of the salt, which had never been renewed since the date of the first experiment, began to run low. I sent out for a fresh supply, and mixed the draught; the ebullition followed, and the first change of colour, not the second; I drank it and it was without efficiency. You will learn from Poole how I have had London ransacked; it was in vain; and I am now persuaded that my first supply was impure, and that it was that unknown impurity which lent efficacy to the draught.

About a week has passed, and I am now finishing this statement under the influence of the last of the old powders. This, then, is the last time, short of a miracle, that Henry Jekyll can think his own thoughts or see his own face (now how sadly altered!) in the glass. Nor must I delay too long to bring my writing to an end; for if my narrative has hitherto escaped destruction, it has been by a combination of great prudence and great good luck. Should the throes of change take me in the act of writing it, Hyde will tear it in pieces; but if some time shall have elapsed after I have laid it by, his wonderful selfishness and circumscription to the moment will probably save it once again from the action of his ape-like spite. And indeed the doom that is closing on us both, has already changed and crushed him. Half an hour from now, when I shall again and forever reindue that hated personality, I know how I shall sit shuddering and weeping in my chair, or continue, with the most strained and fearstruck ecstasy of listening, to pace up and down this room (my last earthly refuge) and give ear to every sound of menace. Will Hyde die upon the scaffold? or will he find the courage to release himself at the last moment? God knows; I am careless; this is my true hour of death, and what is to follow concerns another than myself. Here then, as I lay down the pen and proceed to seal up my confession, I bring the life of that unhappy Henry Jekyll to an end.

THE BODY SNATCHER

Every night in the year, four of us sat in the small parlour of the *George* at Debenham – the undertaker, and the landlord, and Fettes, and myself. Sometimes there would be more; but blow high, blow low, come rain or snow or frost, we four would be each planted in his own particular armchair. Fettes was an old drunken Scotsman, a man of education obviously, and a man of some property, since he lived in idleness. He had come to Debenham years ago, while still young, and by a mere continuance of living had grown to be an adopted townsman. His blue camlet cloak was a local antiquity, like the church-spire. His place in the parlour at the *George*, his absence from church, his old, crapulous, disreputable vices, were all things of course in Debenham. He had some vague Radical opinions and some fleeting infidelities, which he would now and again set forth and emphasize with tottering slaps upon the table. He drank rum – five glasses regularly every evening; and for the greater portion of his nightly visit to the *George* sat, with his glass in his right hand, in a state of melancholy alcoholic saturation. We called him the Doctor, for he was supposed to have some special knowledge of medicine, and had been known upon a pinch, to set a fracture or reduce a dislocation; but, beyond these slight particulars, we had no knowledge of his character and antecedents.

One dark winter night – it had struck nine some time before the landlord joined us – there was a sick man in the *George*, a great neighbouring proprietor suddenly struck down with apoplexy on his way to Parliament; and the great man's still greater London doctor had been telegraphed to his bedside. It was the first time that such a thing had happened in Debenham, for the railway was but newly open, and we were all proportionately moved by the occurrence.

'He's come,' said the landlord, after he had filled and lighted his pipe.

'He?' said I. 'Who? – not the doctor?'

'Himself,' replied our host.

'What is his name?'

'Dr Macfarlane,' said the landlord.

Fettes was far through his third tumbler, stupidly fuddled, now nodding over, now staring mazily around him; but at the last word he seemed to awaken, and repeated the name 'Macfarlane' twice, quietly enough the first time, but with sudden emotion at the second.

'Yes,' said the landlord, 'that's his name, Doctor Wolfe Macfarlane.'

Fettes became instantly sober: his eyes awoke, his voice became clear, loud, and steady, his language forcible and earnest. We were all startled by the transformation, as if a man had risen from the dead.

'I beg your pardon,' he said, 'I am afraid I have not been paying much attention to your talk. Who is this Wolfe Macfarlane?' And then, when he had heard the landlord out, 'It cannot be, it cannot be,' he added; 'and yet I would like well to see him face to face.'

'Do you know him, Doctor?' asked the undertaker, with a gasp.

'God forbid!' was the reply. 'And yet the name is a strange one; it were too much to fancy two. Tell me, landlord, is he old?'

'Well,' said the host, 'he's not a young man, to be sure, and his hair is white; but he looks younger than you.'

'He is older, though; years older. But,' with a slap upon the table, 'it's the rum you see in my face – rum and sin. This man, perhaps, may have an easy conscience and a good digestion. Conscience! Hear me speak. You would think I was some good, old, decent Christian, would you not? But no, not I; I never canted. Voltaire might have canted if he'd stood in my shoes; but the brains' – with a rattling fillip on his bald head – 'the brains were clear and active, and I saw and made no deductions.'

'If you know this doctor,' I ventured to remark, after a somewhat awful pause, 'I should gather that you do not share the landlord's good opinion.'

Fettes paid no regard to me.

'Yes,' he said, with sudden decision, 'I must see him face to face.'

There was another pause, and then a door was closed rather sharply on the first floor, and a step was heard upon the stair.

'That's the doctor,' cried the landlord. 'Look sharp, and you can catch him.'

It was but two steps from the small parlour to the door of the old *George* inn; the wide oak staircase landed almost in the street; there was room for a Turkey rug and nothing more between the threshold and the last round of the descent; but this little space was every evening brilliantly lit up, not only by the light upon the stair and the great signal-lamp below the sign, but by the warm radiance of the bar-room window. The *George* thus brightly advertised itself to passers-by in the cold street.

Fettes walked steadily to the spot, and we, who were hanging behind, beheld the two men meet, as one of them had phrased it, face to face. Dr Macfarlane was alert and vigorous. His white hair set off his pale and placid, although energetic, countenance. He was richly dressed in the finest of broadcloth and the whitest of linen, with a great gold watchchain, and studs and spectacles of the same precious material. He wore a broad-folded tie, white and speckled with lilac, and he carried on his arm a comfortable driving-coat of fur. There was no doubt but he became his years, breathing as he did, of wealth and consideration; and it was a surprising contrast to see our parlour sot – bald, dirty, pimpled, and robed in his old camlet cloak – confront him at the bottom of the stairs.

'Macfarlane!' he said somewhat loudly, more like a herald than a friend.

The great doctor pulled up short on the fourth step, as though the familiarity of the address surprised and somewhat shocked his dignity.

'Toddy Macfarlane!' repeated Fettes.

The London man almost staggered. He stared for the swiftest of seconds at the man before him, glanced behind him with a sort of scare, and then in a startled whisper, 'Fettes!' he said, 'you!'

'Ay,' said the other, 'me! Did you think I was dead too? We are not so easy shut of our acquaintance.'

'Hush, hush!' exclaimed the doctor; 'hush, hush! this meeting is so unexpected – I can see you are unmanned. I hardly knew you, I confess, at first; but I am overjoyed – overjoyed to have this opportunity. For the present it must be how-d'ye-do and goodbye in one, for my fly is waiting, and I must not fail the train; but you shall – let me see – yes – you shall give me your address, and you can count on early news of me. We must do something for you, Fettes. I fear you are out at elbows; but we must see to that for auld lang syne, as once we sang at suppers.'

'Money!' cried Fettes; 'money from you! The money that I had from you is lying where I cast it in the rain.'

Dr Macfarlane had talked himself into some measure of superiority and confidence, but the uncommon energy of this refusal cast him back into his first confusion.

A horrible, ugly look came and went across his almost venerable countenance. 'My dear fellow,' he said, 'be it as you please; my last thought is to offend you. I would intrude on none. I will leave you my address, however – '

'I do not wish it – I do not wish to know the roof that shelters you,' interrupted the other. 'I heard your name; I feared it might be you; I wished to know if, after all, there were a God; I know now that there is none. Begone!'

He still stood in the middle of the rug, between the stair and the doorway; and the great London physician, in order to escape, would be forced to step to one side. It was plain that he hesitated before the thought of this humiliation. White as he was, there was a dangerous glitter in his spectacles; but while he still paused uncertain, he became aware that the driver of his fly was peering in from the street at this unusual scene and caught a glimpse at the same time of our little body from the parlour, huddled by the corner of the bar. The presence of so many witnesses decided him at once to flee. He crouched together, brushing on the wainscot, and made a dart like a serpent, striking for the door. But his tribulation was not yet entirely at an end, for even as he was passing Fettes clutched him by the arm and these words came in a whisper, and yet painfully distinct, 'Have you seen it again?'

The great rich London doctor cried out aloud with a sharp, throttling cry; he dashed his questioner across the open space, and, with his hands over his head, fled out of the door like a detected thief. Before it had occurred to one of us to make a movement, the fly was already rattling toward the station. The scene was over like a dream, but the dream had left proofs and traces of its passage. Next day the servant found the fine gold spectacles broken on the threshold, and that very night we were all standing breathless by the bar-room window, and Fettes at our side, sober, pale, and resolute in look.

'God protect us, Mr Fettes!' said the landlord, coming first into possession of his customary senses. 'What in the universe is all this? These are strange things you have been saying.'

Fettes turned toward us; he looked us each in succession in the face. 'See if you can hold your tongues,' said he. 'That man Macfarlane is not safe to cross; those that have done so already have repented it too late.'

And then, without so much as finishing his third glass, far less waiting for the other two, he bade us goodbye and went forth, under the lamp of the hotel, into the black night.

We three turned to our places in the parlour, with the big red fire and four clear candles; and as we recapitulated what had passed the first chill of our surprise soon changed into a glow of curiosity. We sat late; it was the latest session I have known in the old *George*. Each man, before we parted, had his theory that he was bound to prove; and none of us had any nearer business in this world than to track out the past of our condemned companion, and surprise the secret that he shared with the great London doctor. It is no great boast, but I believe I was a better hand at worming out a story than either of my fellows at the *George*; and perhaps there is now no other man alive who could narrate to you the following foul and unnatural events.

In his young days Fettes studied medicine in the schools of Edinburgh. He had talent of a kind, the talent that picks up swiftly what it hears and readily retails it for its own. He worked little at home; but he was civil, attentive, and intelligent in the presence of his masters. They soon picked him out as a lad who listened closely and remembered well; nay, strange as it seemed to me when I first heard it, he was in those days well favoured, and pleased by his exterior. There was, at that period, a certain extramural teacher of anatomy, whom I shall here designate by the letter K. His name was subsequently too well known. The man who bore it skulked through the streets of Edinburgh in disguise, while the mob that applauded at the execution of Burke called loudly for the blood of his employer. But Mr K– was then at the top of his vogue; he enjoyed a popularity due partly to his own talent and address, partly to the incapacity of his rival, the university professor. The students, at least, swore by his name, and Fettes believed himself, and was believed by others, to have laid the foundations of success when he had acquired the favour of this meteorically famous man. Mr K– was a *bon vivant* as well as an accomplished teacher; he liked a sly allusion no less than a careful preparation. In both capacities Fettes enjoyed and deserved his notice, and by the second year of his attendance he held the half-regular position of second demonstrator or sub-assistant in his class.

In this capacity, the charge of the theatre and lecture-room devolved in particular upon his shoulder. He had to answer for the cleanliness of the premises and the conduct of the other students, and it was a part of his duty to supply, receive, and divide the various subjects. It was with a view to this last – at that time very delicate – affair that he was lodged by

Mr K– in the same wynd, and at last in the same building, with the dissecting-rooms. Here, after a night of turbulent pleasures, his hand still tottering, his sight still misty and confused, he would be called out of bed in the black hours before the winter dawn by the unclean and desperate interlopers who supplied the table. He would open the door to these men, since infamous throughout the land. He would help them with their tragic burthen, pay them their sordid price, and remain alone, when they were gone, with the unfriendly relics of humanity. From such a scene he would return to snatch another hour or two of slumber, to repair the abuses of the night, and refresh himself for the labours of the day.

Few lads could have been more insensible to the impressions of a life thus passed among the ensigns of mortality. His mind was closed against all general considerations. He was incapable of interest in the fate and fortunes of another, the slave of his own desires and low ambitions. Cold, light, and selfish in the last resort, he had that modicum of prudence, miscalled morality, which keeps a man from inconvenient drunkenness or punishable theft. He coveted, besides, a measure of consideration from his masters and his fellow-pupils, and he had no desire to fail conspicuously in the external parts of life. Thus he made it his pleasure to gain some distinction in his studies, and day after day rendered unimpeachable eye-service to his employer, Mr K– . For his day of work he indemnified himself by nights of roaring, blackguardly enjoyment; and when that balance had been struck, the organ that he called his conscience declared itself content.

The supply of subjects was a continual trouble to him as well as to his master. In that large and busy class, the raw material of the anatomists kept perpetually running out; and the business thus rendered necessary was not only unpleasant in itself, but threatened dangerous consequences to all who were concerned. It was the policy of Mr K– to ask no questions in his dealings with the trade. 'They bring the boy, and we pay the price,' he used to say, dwelling on the alliteration – *quid pro quo*. And, again, and somewhat profanely, 'Ask no questions,' he would tell his assistants, 'for conscience' sake.' There was no understanding that the subjects were provided by the crime of murder. Had that idea been broached to him in words, he would have recoiled in horror; but the lightness of his speech upon so grave a matter was, in itself, an offence against good manners, and a temptation to the men with whom he dealt. Fettes, for instance, had often remarked to himself upon the singular freshness of the bodies. He had been struck again and again by the hang-dog, abominable looks of the ruffians who came to him before the dawn; and, putting things together clearly in his private thoughts, he perhaps attributed a meaning too immoral and too categorical to the unguarded counsels of his master. He understood his duty, in short, to have three branches: to take what was brought, to pay the price, and to avert the eye from any evidence of crime.

One November morning this policy of silence was put sharply to the test. He had been awake all night with a racking toothache – pacing his room like a caged beast or throwing himself in fury on his bed – and had fallen at last into that profound, uneasy slumber that so often follows on a night of pain, when he was awakened by the third or fourth angry repetition of the concerted signal. There was a thin, bright moonshine: it was bitter cold, windy, and frosty; the town had not yet awakened, but an indefinable stir already preluded the noise and business of the day. The ghouls had come later than usual, and they seemed more than usually eager to be gone. Fettes, sick with sleep, lighted them upstairs. He heard their grumbling Irish voices through a dream; and as they stripped the sack from their sad merchandise he leaned dozing, with his shoulder propped against the wall; he had to shake himself to find the men their money. As he did so his eyes lighted on the dead face. He started; he took two steps nearer, with the candle raised.

'God Almighty!' he cried. 'That is Jane Galbraith!'

The men answered nothing, but they shuffled nearer the door.

'I know her, I tell you,' he continued. 'She was alive and hearty yesterday. It's impossible she can be dead; it's impossible you should have got this body fairly.'

'Sure, sir, you're mistaken entirely,' said one of the men.

But the other looked Fettes darkly in the eyes, and demanded the money on the spot.

It was impossible to misconceive the threat or to exaggerate the danger. The lad's heart failed him. He stammered some excuses, counted out the sum, and saw his hateful visitors depart. No sooner were they gone than he hastened to confirm his doubts. By a dozen unquestionable marks he identified the girl he had jested with the day before. He saw, with horror, marks upon her body that might well betoken violence. A panic seized him, and he took refuge in his room. There he reflected at length over the discovery that he had made; considered soberly the bearing of Mr K–'s instructions and the danger to himself of interference in so serious a business, and at last, in sore perplexity, determined to wait for the advice of his immediate superior, the class assistant.

This was a young doctor, Wolfe Macfarlane, a high favourite among all the reckless students, clever, dissipated, and unscrupulous to the last degree. He had travelled and studied abroad. His manners were agreeable and a little forward. He was an authority on the stage, skilful on the ice or the links with skate or golf-club; he dressed with nice audacity, and, to put the finishing touch upon his glory, he kept a gig and a strong trotting-horse. With Fettes he was on terms of intimacy; indeed their relative positions called for some community of life; and when subjects were scarce the pair would drive far into the country in Macfarlane's gig, visit and desecrate some lonely graveyard, and return before dawn with their booty to the door of the dissecting-room.

On that particular morning Macfarlane arrived somewhat earlier than his wont. Fettes heard him, and met him on the stairs, told him his story, and showed him the cause of his alarm. Macfarlane examined the marks on her body.

'Yea', he said with a nod, 'it looks fishy.'

'Well, what should I do?' asked Fettes.

'Do?' repeated the other. 'Do you want to do anything? Least said soonest mended, I should say.'

'Someone else might recognize her,' objected Fettes. 'She was as well known as the Castle Rock.'

'We'll hope not,' said Macfarlane, 'and if anybody does – well, you didn't, don't you see, and there's an end. The fact is, this has been going on too long. Stir up the mud, and you'll get K– into the most unholy trouble; you'll be in a shocking box yourself. So will I, if you come to that. I should like to know how any one of us would look, or what the devil we should have to say for ourselves, in any Christian witness-box. For me, you know there's one thing certain – that, practically speaking, all our subjects have been murdered.'

'Macfarlane!' cried Fettes.

'Come now!' sneered the other. 'As if you hadn't suspected it yourself!'

'Suspecting is one thing –'

'And proof another. Yes, I know; and I'm as sorry as you are this should have come here,' tapping the body with his cane. 'The next best thing for me is not to recognize it; and,' he added coolly, 'I don't. You may, if you please. I don't dictate, but I think a man of the world would do as I do; and I may add, I fancy that is what K– would look for at our hands. The question is, Why did he choose us two for his assistants? And I answer, because he didn't want old wives.'

This was the tone of all others to affect the mind of a lad like Fettes. He agreed to imitate Macfarlane. The body of the unfortunate girl was duly dissected, and no one remarked or appeared to recognize her.

One afternoon, when his day's work was over, Fettes dropped into a popular tavern and found Macfarlane sitting with a stranger. This was a small man, very pale and dark, with coal-black eyes. The cut of his features gave a promise of intellect and refinement which was but feebly realized in his manners, for he proved, upon a nearer acquaintance, coarse, vulgar, and stupid. He exercised, however, a very remarkable control over Macfarlane; issued orders like the Great Bashaw; became inflamed at the least discussion or delay, and commented rudely on the servility with which he was obeyed. This most offensive person took a fancy to Fettes on the spot, plied him with drinks, and honoured him with unusual confidences on his past career. If a tenth part of what he confessed were true, he was a very loathsome rogue; and the lad's vanity was tickled by the attention of so experienced a man.

'I'm a pretty bad fellow myself,' the stranger remarked, 'but Macfarlane is the boy – Toddy Macfarlane I call him. Toddy, order your friend another glass.' Or it might be, 'Toddy, you jump up and shut the door.' 'Toddy hates me,' he said again. 'Oh, yes, Toddy, you do!'

'Don't you call me that confounded name,' growled Macfarlane.

'Hear him! Did you ever see the lads play knife? He would like to do that all over my body,' remarked the stranger.

'We medicals have a better way than that,' said Fettes. 'When we dislike a dead friend of ours, we dissect him.'

Macfarlane looked up sharply, as though this jest was scarcely to his mind.

The afternoon passed. Gray, for that was the stranger's name, invited Fettes to join them at dinner, ordered a feast so sumptuous that the tavern was thrown in commotion, and when all was done commanded Macfarlane to settle the bill. It was late before they separated; the man

Gray was incapably drunk. Macfarlane, sobered by his fury, chewed the cud of the money he had been forced to squander and the slights he had been obliged to swallow. Fettes, with various liquors singing in his head, returned home with devious footsteps and a mind entirely in abeyance. Next day Macfarlane was absent from the class, and Fettes smiled to himself as he imagined him still squiring the intolerable Gray from tavern to tavern. As soon as the hour of liberty had struck he posted from place to place in quest of his last night's companions. He could find them, however, nowhere; so returned early to his rooms, went early to bed, and slept the sleep of the just.

At four in the morning he was awakened by the well-known signal. Descending to the door, he was filled with astonishment to find Macfarlane with his gig, and in the gig one of those long and ghastly packages with which he was so well acquainted.

'What?' he cried. 'Have you been out alone? How did you manage?'

But Macfarlane silenced him roughly, bidding him turn to business. When they had got the body upstairs and laid it on the table, Macfarlane made at first as if he were going away. Then he paused and seemed to hesitate; and then, 'You had better look at the face,' said he, in tones of some constraint. 'You had better,' he repeated, as Fettes only stared at him in wonder.

'But where, and how, and when did you come by it?' cried the other.

'Look at the face,' was the only answer.

Fettes was staggered, strange doubts assailed him. He looked from the young doctor to the body, and then back again. At last, with a start, he did as he was bidden. He had almost expected the sight that met his eyes, and yet the shock was cruel. To see, fixed in the rigidity of death and naked on that coarse layer of sack-cloth, the man whom he had left well-clad and full of meat and sin upon the threshold of a tavern, awoke, even in the thoughtless Fettes, some of the terrors of the conscience. It was a *cras tibi* which re-echoed in his soul – that two whom he had known should have come to lie upon these icy tables. Yet these were only secondary thoughts. His first concern regarded Wolfe. Unprepared for a challenge so momentous, he knew not how to look his comrade in the face. He durst not meet his eye, and he had neither words nor voice at his command.

It was Macfarlane himself who made the first advance. He came up quietly behind and laid his hand gently but firmly on the other's shoulder.

'Richardson,' said he, 'may have the head.'

Now Richardson was a student who had long been anxious for that portion of the human subject to dissect. There was no answer, and the murderer resumed: 'Talking of business, you must pay me; your accounts, you see, must tally.'

Fettes found a voice, the ghost of his own: 'Pay you!' he cried, 'Pay you for that?'

'Why, yes, of course you must. By all means and on every possible account, you must,' returned the other. 'I dare not give it for nothing, you dare not take it for nothing; it would compromise us both. This is another case like Jane Galbraith's. The more things are wrong the more we must act as if all were right. Where does old K– keep his money?'

'There,' answered Fettes hoarsely, pointing to a cupboard in the corner.

'Give me the key, then,' said the other, calmly, holding out his hand.

There was an instant's hesitation, and the die was cast. Macfarlane could not suppress a nervous twitch, the infinitesimal mark of an immense relief, as he felt the key between his fingers. He opened the cupboard, brought out pen and ink and a paper-book that stood in one compartment, and separated from the funds in a drawer a sum suitable to the occasion.

'Now, look here,' he said, 'there is the payment made – first proof of your good faith: first step to your security. You have now to clinch it by a second. Enter the payment in your book, and then you for your part may defy the devil.'

The next few seconds were for Fettes an agony of thought; but in balancing his terrors it was the most immediate that triumphed. Any future difficulty seemed almost welcome if he could avoid a present quarrel with Macfarlane. He set down the candle which he had been carrying all the time, and with a steady hand entered the date, the nature, and the amount of the transaction.

'And now,' said Macfarlane, 'it's only fair that you should pocket the lucre. I've had my share already. By-the-by, when a man of the world falls into a bit of luck, has a few shillings extra in his pocket – I'm ashamed to speak of it, but there's a rule of conduct in the case. No treating, no purchase of expensive class-books, no squaring of old debts; borrow, don't lend.'

'Macfarlane,' began Fettes, still somewhat hoarsely, 'I have put my neck in a halter to oblige you.'

'To oblige me?' cried Wolfe. 'Oh, come! You did, as near as I can see the matter, what you downright had to do in self-defence. Suppose I got into trouble, where would you be? This second little matter flows clearly from the first. Mr Gray is the continuation of Miss Galbraith. You can't begin and then stop. If you begin, you must keep on beginning; that's the truth. No rest for the wicked.'

A horrible sense of blackness and the treachery of fate seized hold upon the soul of the unhappy student.

'My God!' he cried, 'but what have I done? and when did I begin? To be made a class assistant – in the name of reason, where's the harm in that? Service wanted the position; Service might have got it. Would *he* have been where *I* am now?'

'My dear fellow,' said Macfarlane, 'what a boy you are! What harm *has* come to you? What harm *can* come to you if you hold your tongue? Why, man, do you know what this life is? There are two squads of us – the lions and the lambs. If you're a lamb, you'll come to lie upon these tables like Gray or Jane Galbraith; if you're a lion, you'll live and drive a horse like me, like K– , like all the world with any wit or courage. You're staggered at the first. But look at K– ! My dear fellow, you're clever, you have pluck. I like you, and K– likes you. You were born to lead the hunt; and I tell you, on my honour and my experience of life, three days from now you'll laugh at all these scarecrows like a high-school boy at a farce.'

And with that Macfarlane took his departure and drove off up the wynd in his gig to get under cover before daylight. Fettes was thus left alone with his regrets. He saw the miserable peril in which he stood involved. He saw, with inexpressible dismay, that there was no limit to his weakness, and that, from concession to concession, he had fallen from the arbiter of Macfarlane's destiny to his paid and helpless accomplice. He would have given the world to have been a little braver at the time, but it did not occur to him that he might still be brave. The secret of Jane Galbraith and the cursed entry in the day-book closed his mouth.

Hours passed; the class began to arrive; the members of the unhappy Gray were dealt out to one and to another, and received without remark.

Richardson was made happy with the head; and before the hour of freedom rang Fettes trembled with exultation to perceive how far they had already gone toward safety.

For two days he continued to watch, with increasing joy, the dreadful process of disguise.

On the third day Macfarlane made his appearance. He had been ill, he said; but he made up for lost time by the energy with which he directed the students. To Richardson in particular he extended the most valuable assistance and advice, and that student, encouraged by the praise of the demonstrator, burned high with ambitious hopes, and saw the medal already in his grasp.

Before the week was out Macfarlane's prophecy had been fulfilled. Fettes had outlived his terrors and had forgotten his baseness. He began to plume himself upon his courage, and had so arranged the story in his mind that he could look back on these events with an unhealthy pride. Of his accomplice he saw but little. They met, of course, in the business of the class; they received their orders together from Mr K– . At times they had a word or two in private, and Macfarlane was from first to last particularly kind and jovial. But it was plain that he avoided any reference to their common secret; and even when Fettes whispered to him that he had cast in his lot with the lions and forsworn the lambs, he only signed to him smilingly to hold his peace.

At length an occasion arose which threw the pair once more into a closer union. Mr K– was again short of subjects; pupils were eager, and it was a part of this teacher's pretensions to be always well supplied. At the same time there came the news of a burial in the rustic graveyard of Glencorse. Time has little changed the place in question. It stood then, as now, upon a crossroad, out of call of human habitations, and buried fathom deep in the foliage of six cedar trees. The cries of the sheep upon the neighbouring hills, the streamlets upon either hand, one loudly singing among pebbles, the other dripping furtively from pond to pond, the stir of the wind in mountainous old flowering chestnuts, and once in seven days the voice of the bell and the old tunes of the preceptor, were the only sounds that disturbed the silence around the rural church. The Resurrection Man – to use a by-name of the period – was not to be deterred by any of the sanctities of customary piety. It was part of his trade to despise and desecrate the scrolls and trumpets of old tombs, the paths worn by the feet of worshippers and mourners, and the offerings and the inscriptions of bereaved affection. To rustic neighbourhoods, where love is more than commonly tenacious, and where some bonds of blood or fellowship unite the entire society of a parish, the body-snatcher, far from being repelled by natural respect, was attracted by the ease and safety of the task. To bodies that had been laid in earth, in joyful expectation of a far different awakening, there came that hasty, lamp-lit, terror-haunted resurrection of the spade and mattock. The coffin was forced, the cerements torn, and the melancholy relics, clad in sackcloth, after being rattled for hours on moonless by-ways, were at length exposed to uttermost indignities before a class of gaping boys.

Somewhat as two vultures may swoop upon a dying lamb, Fettes and Macfarlane were to be let loose upon a grave in that green and quiet resting-place. The wife of a farmer, a woman who had lived for sixty years, and been known for nothing but good butter and a godly conversation, was to be rooted from her grave at midnight and carried, dead and naked, to that far-away city that she had always honoured with her Sunday best; the place beside her family was to be empty till the crack of doom; her innocent and almost venerable members to be exposed to that last curiosity of the anatomist.

Late one afternoon the pair set forth, well wrapped in cloaks and furnished with a formidable bottle. It rained without remission – a cold, dense, lashing rain. Now and again there blew a puff of wind, but these sheets of falling water kept it down. Bottle and all, it was a sad and silent drive as far as Penicuik, where they were to spend the evening. They stopped once, to hide their implements in a thick bush not far from the churchyard, and once again at the Fisher's Tryst, to have a toast before the kitchen fire and vary their nips of whisky with a glass of ale. When they reached their journey's end the gig was housed, the horse was fed and comforted, and the two young doctors in a private room sat down to the best dinner and the best wine the house afforded. The lights, the fire, the beating rain upon the window, the cold, incongruous work that lay before them, added zest to their enjoyment of the meal. With every glass their cordiality increased. Soon Macfarlane handed a little pile of gold to his companion.

'A compliment,' he said. 'Between friends these little d–d accommodations ought to fly like pipe-lights.'

Fettes pocketed the money, and applauded the sentiment to the echo.

'You are a philosopher,' he cried. 'I was an ass till I knew you. You and K– between you, by the Lord Harry! but you'll make a man of me.'

'Of course we shall,' applauded Macfarlane. 'A man? I tell you, it required a man to back me up the other morning. There are some big, brawling, forty-year-old cowards who would have turned sick at the look of the d–d thing; but not you – you kept your head. I watched you.'

'Well, and why not?' Fettes thus vaunted himself. 'It was no affair of mine. There was nothing to gain on the one side but disturbance, and on the other I could count on your gratitude, don't you see?' And he slapped his pocket till the gold pieces rang.

Macfarlane somehow felt a certain touch of alarm at these unpleasant words. He may have regretted that he had taught his young companion so successfully, but he had no time to interfere, for the other noisily continued in this boastful strain:

'The great thing is not to be afraid. Now, between you and me, I don't want to hang – that's practical; but for all cant, Macfarlane, I was born with a contempt. Hell, God, Devil, right, wrong, sin, crime, and all the old gallery of curiosities – they may frighten boys, but men of the world, like you and me, despise them. Here's to the memory of Gray!'

It was by this time growing somewhat late. The gig, according to order, was brought round to the door with both lamps brightly shining, and the young men had to pay their bill and take the road. They announced that they were bound for Peebles, and drove in that direction till they were clear of the last house of the town; then, extinguishing the lamps, returned upon their course, and followed a by-road toward Glencorse. There was no sound but that of their own passage, and the incessant, strident pouring of the rain. It was pitch dark; here and there a white gate or a white stone in the wall guided them for a short space across the night; but for the most part it was at a foot pace, and almost groping, that they picked their way through that resonant blackness to their solemn and isolated destination. In the sunken woods that traverse the neighbourhood of the burying-ground the last glimmer failed them, and it became necessary to kindle a match and reillumine one of the lanterns of the gig. Thus, under the dripping trees, and environed by huge and moving shadows, they reached the scene of their unhallowed labours.

They were both experienced in such affairs, and powerful with the spade; and they had scarce been twenty minutes at their task before they were rewarded by a dull rattle on the coffin lid. At the same moment Macfarlane, having hurt his hand upon a stone, flung it carelessly above his head. The grave, in which they now stood almost to the shoulders, was close to the edge of the plateau of the graveyard; and the gig lamp had been propped, the better to illuminate their labours, against a tree, and on the immediate verge of the steep bank descending to the stream. Chance had taken a sure aim with the stone. Then came a clang of broken glass; night fell upon them; sounds alternately dull and ringing announced the bounding of the lantern down the bank, and its occasional collision with the trees. A stone or two, which it had dislodged in its descent, rattled behind it into the profundities of the glen; and then silence, like night, resumed its sway; and they might bend their hearing to its utmost pitch, but naught was to be heard except the rain, now marching to the wind, now steadily falling over miles of open country.

They were so nearly at an end of their abhorred task that they judged it wisest to complete it in the dark. The coffin was exhumed and broken open; the body inserted in the dripping sack and carried between them to the gig; one mounted to keep it in its place, and the other, taking the horse by the mouth, groped along by wall and bush until they reached the wider road by the Fisher's Tryst. Here was a faint, diffused radiancy, which they hailed like daylight; by that they pushed the horse to a good pace and began to rattle along merrily in the direction of the town.

They had both been wetted to the skin during their operations, and now, as the gig jumped among the deep ruts, the thing that stood propped between them fell now upon one and now upon the other. At every repetition of the horrid contact each instinctively repelled it with greater haste; and the process, natural although it was, began to tell upon the nerves of the companions. Macfarlane made some ill-favoured jest about the farmer's wife, but it came hollowly from his lips, and was allowed to drop in silence. Still their unnatural burthen bumped from side to side; and now the head would be laid, as if in confidence, upon their shoulders, and now the drenching sackcloth would flap icily about their faces. A creeping chill began to possess the soul of Fettes. He peered at the bundle, and it seemed somehow larger than at first. All over the countryside, and from every degree of distance, the farm dogs accompanied their passage with tragic ululations; and it grew and grew upon his mind that some unnatural miracle had been accomplished that some nameless change had befallen the dead body, and that it was in fear of their unholy burden that the dogs were howling.

'For God's sake,' said he, making a great effort to arrive at speech, 'for God's sake, let's have a light!'

Seemingly Macfarlane was affected in the same direction, for though he made no reply, he stopped the horse, passed the reins to his companion, got down, and proceeded to kindle the remaining lamp. They had by that time got no further than the cross-road down to Auchendinny. The rain still poured as though the deluge were returning, and it was no easy matter to make a light in such a world of wet and darkness. When at last the flickering blue flame had been transferred to the wick and began to expand and clarify, and shed a wide circle of misty brightness round the gig, it became possible for the two young men to see each other and the thing they had along with them. The rain had moulded the rough sacking to the outlines of the body underneath; the head was distinct from the trunk, the shoulders plainly modelled; something at once spectral and human riveted their eyes upon the ghastly comrade of their drive.

For some time Macfarlane stood motionless, holding up the lamp. A nameless dread was swathed, like a wet sheet, about the body, and tightened the white skin upon the face of Fettes; a fear that was meaning-less, a horror of what could not be, kept mounting to his brain. Another beat of the watch, and he had spoken. But his comrade forestalled him.

'That is not a woman,' said Macfarlane, in a hushed voice.

'It was a woman when we put her in,' whispered Fettes.

'Hold that lamp,' said the other. 'I must see her face.'

And as Fettes took the lamp his companion untied the fastenings of the sack and drew down the cover from the head. The light fell very clear upon the dark, well-moulded features and smooth-shaven cheeks of a too familiar countenance, often beheld in dreams of both of these young men. A wild yell rang up into the night; each leaped from his own side into the roadway; the lamp fell, broke, and was extinguished; and the horse, terrified by this unusual commotion, bounded and went off toward Edinburgh at a gallop, bearing along with it, sole occupant of the gig, the body of the dead and long-dissected Gray.

THE BOTTLE IMP

There was a man of the island of Hawaii, whom I shall call Keawe; for the truth is, he still lives, and his name must be kept secret; but the place of his birth was not far from Honaunau, where the bones of Keawe the Great lie hidden in a cave. The man was poor, brave, and active; he could read and write like a schoolmaster; he was a first-rate mariner besides, sailed for some time in the island steamers, and steered a whaleboat on the Kamakua coast. At length it came in Keawe's mind to have a sight of the great world and foreign cities, and he shipped on a vessel bound to San Francisco.

This is a fine town, with a fine harbour, and rich people unaccountable; and, in particular there is one hill which is covered with palaces. Upon this hill Keawe was one day taking a walk, with his pocket full of money, viewing the great houses upon either hand with pleasure. 'What fine houses there are!' he was thinking, 'and how happy must these people be who dwell in them, and take no care for the morrow!' The thought was in his mind when he came abreast of a house that was smaller than some others, but all finished and beautiful like a toy; the steps of that house shone like silver, and the borders of the garden bloomed like garlands, and the windows were bright like diamonds; and Keawe stopped and wondered at the excellence of all he saw. So stopping, he was aware of a man that looked forth upon him through a window, so clear that Keawe could see him as you see a fish in a pool upon the reef. The man was elderly, with a bald head and a black beard; and his face was heavy with sorrow, and he bitterly sighed. And the truth of it is, that as Keawe looked in upon the man, and the man looked out upon Keawe, each envied the other.

All of a sudden the man smiled and nodded, and beckoned Keawe to enter, and met him at the door of the house.

'This is a fine house of mine,' said the man, and bitterly sighed. 'Would you not care to view the chambers?'

So he led Keawe all over it, from the cellar to the roof, and there was nothing there that was not perfect of its kind, and Keawe was astonished.

'Truly,' said Keawe, 'this is a beautiful house; if I lived in the like of it, I should be laughing all day long. How comes it, then, that you should be sighing?'

'There is no reason,' said the man, 'why you should not have a house in all points similar to this, and finer, if you wish. You have some money, I suppose?'

'I have fifty dollars,' said Keawe; 'but a house like this will cost more than fifty dollars.'

The man made a computation. 'I am sorry you have no more,' said he, 'for it may raise you trouble in the future; but it shall be yours at fifty dollars.'

'The house?' asked Keawe.

'No, not the house,' replied the man; 'but the bottle. For I must tell you, although I appear to you so rich and fortunate, all my fortune, and this house itself and its garden, came out of a bottle not much bigger than a pint. This is it.'

And he opened a lockfast place, and took out a round-bellied bottle with a long neck; the glass of it was white like milk, with changing rainbow colours in the grain. Withinsides something obscurely moved, like a shadow and a fire.

'This is the bottle,' said the man; and, when Keawe laughed, 'You do not believe me?' he added. 'Try, then, for yourself. See if you can break it.'

So Keawe took the bottle up and dashed it on the floor till he was weary; but it jumped on the floor like a child's ball, and was not injured.

'This is a strange thing,' said Keawe. 'For by the touch of it, as well as by the look, the bottle should be of glass.'

'Of glass it is,' replied the man, sighing more heavily than ever; 'but the glass of it was tempered in the flames of hell. An imp lives in it, and that is the shadow we behold there moving; or, so I suppose. If any man buy this bottle the imp is at his command; all that he desires – love, fame, money, houses like this house, ay, or a city like this city – all are his at the word uttered. Napoleon had this bottle, and by it he grew to be the king of the world; but he sold it at the last and fell. Captain Cook had this bottle, and by it he found his way to so many islands; but he too sold it, and was slain upon Hawaii. For, once it is sold, the power goes and the protection; and unless a man remain content with what he has, ill will befall him.'

'And yet you talk of selling it yourself?' Keawe said.

'I have all I wish, and I am growing elderly,' replied the man. 'There is one thing the imp cannot do – he cannot prolong life; and it would not be fair to conceal from you there is a drawback to the bottle; for if a man dies before he sells it, he must burn in hell for ever.'

'To be sure, this is a drawback and no mistake,' cried Keawe. 'I would not meddle with the thing. I can do without the house, thank God; but there is one thing I could not be doing with one particle, and that is to be damned.'

'Dear me, you must not run away with things,' returned the man. 'All you have to do is to use the power of the imp in moderation, and then sell it to someone else, as I do to you, and finish your life in comfort.'

'Well, I observe two things,' said Keawe. 'All the time you keep sighing like a maid in love – that is one; and for the other, you sell this bottle very cheap.'

'I have told you already why I sigh,' said the man. 'It is because I fear my health is breaking up; and, as you said yourself, to die and go to the devil is a pity for anyone. As for why I sell so cheap, I must explain to you there is a peculiarity about the bottle. Long ago, when the devil brought it first upon the earth, it was extremely expensive, and was sold first of all to Prester John for many millions of dollars; but it cannot be sold at all, unless sold at a loss. If you sell it for as much as you paid for it, back it comes to you again like a homing pigeon. It follows that the price has kept falling in these centuries, and the bottle is now remarkably cheap. I bought it myself from one of my great neighbours on this hill, and the price I paid was only ninety dollars. I could sell for as high as eighty-nine dollars and ninety-nine cents, but not a penny dearer, or back the thing must come to me. Now, about this there are two bothers. First, when you offer a bottle so singular for eighty-odd dollars, people suppose you to be jesting. And second – but there is no hurry about that – and I need not go into it. Only remember it must be coined money that you sell it for.'

'How am I to know that this is all true?' asked Keawe.

'Some of it you can try at once,' replied the man. 'Give me your fifty dollars, take the bottle, and wish your fifty dollars back into your pocket. If that does not happen, I pledge you my honour I will cry off the bargain and restore your money.'

'You are not deceiving me?' said Keawe.

The man bound himself with a great oath.

'Well, I will risk that much,' said Keawe, 'for that can do no harm,' and he paid over his money to the man, and the man handed him the bottle.

'Imp of the bottle,' said Keawe, 'I want my fifty dollars back,' And sure enough, he had scarce said the word before his pocket was as heavy as ever.

'To be sure this is a wonderful bottle,' said Keawe.

'And now good-morning to you, my fine fellow, and the devil go with you for me,' said the man.

'Hold on,' said Keawe, 'I don't want any more of this fun. Here, take your bottle back.'

'You have bought it for less than I paid for it,' replied the man, rubbing his hands. 'It is yours now; and, for my part, I am only concerned to see the back of you.' And with that he rang for his Chinese servant, and had Keawe shown out of the house.

Now, when Keawe was in the street, with the bottle under his arm, he began to think. 'If all is true about this bottle, I may have made a losing bargain,' thinks he. 'But perhaps the man was only fooling me.' The first thing he did was to count his money; the sum was exact – forty-nine dollars American money, and one Chilli piece. 'That looks like the truth,' said Keawe. 'Now I will try another part.'

The streets in that part of the city were as clean as a ship's decks, and though it was noon, there were no passengers. Keawe set the bottle in the gutter and walked away. Twice he looked back, and there was the milky, round-bellied bottle where he had left it. A third time he looked back and turned a corner; but he had scarce done so, when something knocked upon his elbow, and behold! it was the long neck sticking up; and as for the round belly, it was jammed into the pocket of his pilot-coat.

'And that looks like the truth,' said Keawe.

The next thing he did was to buy a corkscrew in a shop, and go apart in a secret place in the fields. And there he tried to draw the cork, but as often as he put the screw in, out it came again, and the cork was as whole as ever.

'This is some new sort of cork,' said Keawe, and all at once he began to shake and sweat, for he was afraid of that bottle.

On his way back to the port-side he saw a shop where a man sold shells and clubs from the wild islands, old heathen deities, old coined money, pictures from China and Japan, and all manner of things that sailors bring in their sea-chest. And here he had an idea. So he went in and offered the bottle for a hundred dollars. The man of the shop laughed at him at first, and offered him five; but, indeed, it was a curious bottle, such glass was never blown in any human glass-works, so prettily the colours shone under the milky way, and so strangely the shadow hovered in the midst; so, after he had disputed a while after the manner of his kind, the shopman gave Keawe sixty silver dollars for the thing and set it on a shelf in the midst of his window.

'Now,' said Keawe, 'I have sold that for sixty which I bought for fifty – or, to say truth, a little less, because one of my dollars was from Chilli. Now I shall know the truth upon another point.'

So he went back on board his ship, and when he opened his chest, there was the bottle, which had come more quickly than himself. Now Keawe had a mate on board whose name was Lopaka.

'What ails you,' said Lopaka, 'that you stare in your chest?'

They were alone in the ship's forecastle, and Keawe bound him to secrecy, and told all.

'This is a very strange affair,' said Lopaka; 'and I fear you will be in trouble about this bottle. But there is one point very clear – that you are sure of the trouble, and you had better have the profit in the bargain. Make up your mind what you want with it; give the order, and it is done as you desire, I will buy the bottle myself; for I have an idea of my own to get a schooner, and go trading through the islands.'

'That is not my idea,' said Keawe; 'but to have a beautiful house and garden on the Kona Coast, where I was born, the sun shining in at the door, flowers in the garden, glass in the windows, pictures on all the walls, and toys and fine carpets on the tables, for all the world like the house I was in this day – only a storey higher, and with balconies all about like the King's palace; and to live there without care and make merry with my friends and relatives.'

'Well,' said Lopaka, 'let us carry it back with us to Hawaii; and if it comes true as you suppose, I will buy the bottle, as I said, and ask a schooner.'

Upon that they were agreed, and it was not long before the ship returned to Honolulu, carrying Keawe and Lopaka, and the bottle. They were scarce come ashore when they met a friend upon the beach, who began at once to condole with Keawe.

'I do not know what I am to be condoled about,' said Keawe.

'Is it possible you have not heard,' said the friend, 'your uncle – that good old man – is dead, and your cousin – that beautiful boy – was drowned at sea?'

Keawe was filled with sorrow, and, beginning to weep and to lament, he forgot about the bottle. But Lopaka was thinking to himself, and presently, when Keawe's grief was a little abated, 'I have been thinking,' said Lopaka, 'had not your uncle lands in Hawaii, in the district of Kaü?'

'No,' said Keawe, 'not in Kaü: they are on the mountain side – a little be-south Kookena.'

'These lands will now be yours?' asked Lopaka.

'And so they will,' says Keawe, and began again to lament for his relatives.

'No,' said Lopaka, 'do not lament at present. I have a thought in my mind. How if this should be the doing of the bottle? For here is the place ready for your house.'

'If this be so,' cried Keawe, 'it is a very ill way to serve me by killing my relatives. But it may be, indeed; for it was in just such a station that I saw the house with my mind's eye.'

'The house, however, is not yet built,' said Lopaka.

'No, nor like to be!' said Keawe; 'for though my uncle has some coffee and ava and bananas, it will not be more than will keep me in comfort; and the rest of the land is the black lava.'

'Let us go to the lawyer,' said Lopaka; 'I have still this idea in my mind.'

Now, when they came to the lawyer's it appeared Keawe's uncle had grown monstrous rich in the last days, and there was a fund of money.

'And here is the money for the house!' cried Lopaka.

'If you are thinking of a new house,' said the lawyer, 'here is the card of a new architect of whom they tell me great things.'

'Better and better!' cried Lopaka. 'Here is all made plain for us. Let us continue to obey orders.'

So they went to the architect, and he had drawings of houses on his table.

'You want something out of the way,' said the architect. 'How do you like this?' and he handed a drawing to Keawe.

Now, when Keawe set eyes on the drawing, he cried out aloud, for it was the picture of his thought exactly drawn.

'I am in for this house,' thought he. 'Little as I like the way it comes to me, I am in for it now, and I may as well take the good along with the evil.'

So he told the architect all that he wished, and how he would have that house furnished, and about the pictures on the wall and the knick-knacks on the tables; and he asked the man plainly for how much he would undertake the whole affair.

The architect put many questions, and took his pen and made a computation; and when he had done he named the very sum that Keawe had inherited.

Lopaka and Keawe looked at one another and nodded.

'It is quite clear,' thought Keawe, 'that I am to have this house, whether or no. It comes from the devil, and I fear I will get little good by that; and of one thing I am sure, I will make no more wishes as long as I have this bottle. But with the house I am saddled, and I may as well take the good along with the evil.'

So he made his terms with the architect, and they signed a paper; and Keawe and Lopaka took ship again and sailed to Australia; for it was concluded between them they should not interfere at all, but leave the architect and the bottle imp to build and to adorn the house at their own pleasure.

The voyage was a good voyage, only all the time Keawe was holding in his breath, for he had sworn he would utter no more wishes, and take no more favours, from the devil. The time was up when they got back. The architect told them that the house was ready, and Keawe and Lopaka took a passage in the Hall, and went down Kona way to view the house, and see if all had been done fitly according to the thought that was in Keawe's mind.

Now, the house stood on the mountain side, visible to ships. Above, the forest ran up into the clouds of rain; below, the black lava fell in cliffs, where the kings of old lay buried. A garden bloomed about the house with every hue of flowers; and there was an orchard of papaya on the one hand and an orchard of bread-fruit on the other, and right in front, towards the sea, a ship's mast had been rigged up and bore a flag. As for the house, it was three stories high, with great chambers and broad balconies on each. The windows were of glass, so excellent that it was as clear as water and as bright as day. All manner of furniture adorned the chambers. Pictures hung upon the wall in golden frames – pictures of ships, and men fighting, and of the most beautiful women, and of singular places; nowhere in the world are there pictures of so bright a colour as those Keawe found hanging in his house. As for the knick-knacks, they were extraordinarily fine: chiming clocks and musical boxes, little men with nodding heads, books filled with pictures, weapons of price from all quarters of the world, and the most elegant puzzles to entertain the leisure of a solitary man. And as no one would care to live in such chambers, only to walk through and view them, the balconies were made so broad that a whole town might have lived upon them in delight, and Keawe knew not which to prefer, whether the back porch, where you got the land breeze and looked upon the orchards and the flowers, or the front balcony, where you could drink the wind of the sea, and look down the steep wall of the mountain and see the Hall going by once a week or so between Hookena and the hills of Pele, or the schooners plying up the coast for wood and ava and bananas.

When they had viewed all, Keawe and Lopaka sat on the porch.

'Well,' asked Lopaka, 'is it all as you designed?'

'Words cannot utter it,' said Keawe. 'It is better than I dreamed, and I am sick with satisfaction.'

'There is but one thing to consider,' said Lopaka, 'all this may be quite natural, and the bottle imp have nothing whatever to say to it. If I were to buy the bottle, and got no schooner after all, I should have put my hand in the fire for nothing. I gave you my word, I know; but yet I think you would not grudge me one more proof.'

'I have sworn I would take no more favours,' said Keawe. 'I have gone already deep enough.'

'This is no favour I am thinking of,' replied Lopaka. 'It is only to see the imp himself. There is nothing to be gained by that, and so nothing to be ashamed of, and yet, if I once saw him, I should be sure of the whole matter. So indulge me so far, and let me see the imp; and, after that, here is the money in my hand, and I will buy it.'

'There is only one thing I am afraid of,' said Keawe. 'The imp may be very ugly to view, and if you once set eyes upon him you might be very undesirous of the bottle.'

'I am a man of my word,' said Lopaka. 'And here is the money betwixt us.'

'Very well,' replied Keawe, 'I have a curiosity myself. So come, let us have one look at you, Mr. Imp.'

Now as soon as that was said, the imp looked out of the bottle, and in again, swift as a lizard; and there sat Keawe and Lopaka turned to stone. The night had quite come, before either of them found a thought to say or voice to say it with; and then Lopaka pushed the money over and took the bottle.

'I am a man of my word,' said he, 'and had need to be so, or I would not touch this bottle with my foot. Well, I shall get my schooner and a dollar or two for my pocket; and then I will be rid of this devil as fast as I can. For, to tell you the plain truth, the look of him has cast me down.'

'Lopaka,' said Keawe, 'do not think you any worse of me than you can help; I know it is night, and the roads bad, and the pass by the tombs an ill place to go by so late, but I declare since I have seen that little face, I cannot eat or sleep or pray till it is gone from me. I will give you a lantern, and a basket to put the bottle in, and any picture or fine thing in all my house that takes your fancy; and be gone at once, and go sleep at Hookena with Nahinu.'

'Keawe,' said Lopaka, 'many a man would take this ill; above all, when I am doing you a turn so friendly, as to keep my word and buy the bottle; and for that matter, the night and the dark, and the way of the tombs, must be all tenfold more dangerous to a man with such a sin upon his conscience and such a bottle under his arm. But for my part, I am so extremely terrified myself, I have not the heart to blame you. Here I go, then; and I pray God you may be happy in your house, and I fortunate with my schooner, and both get to heaven in the end in spite of the devil and his bottle.'

So Lopaka went down the mountain; and Keawe stood in his front balcony, and listened to the clink of the horses' shoes, and watched the lantern go shining down the path, and along the cliff of caves where the old dead are buried; and all the time he trembled and clasped his hands, and prayed for his friend, and gave glory to God that he himself was escaped out of that trouble.

But the next day came very brightly, and that new house of his was so delightful to behold that he forgot his terrors. One day followed another, and Keawe dwelt there in perpetual joy. He had his place on the back porch; it was there that he ate and lived, and read the stories in the Honolulu newspapers; but when any one came by they would go in and view the chambers and the pictures. And the fame of the house went far and wide; it was called Ka-Hale Nui – the Great House – in all Kona; and sometimes the Bright House, for Keawe kept a Chinaman, who was all day dusting and furbishing; and the glass, and the gilt, and the fine stuffs, and the pictures, shone as bright as the morning. As for Keawe himself, he could not walk in the chambers without singing, his heart was so enlarged; and when ships sailed by upon the sea, he would fly his colours on the mast.

So time went by, until one day Keawe went upon a visit as far as Kailua to certain of his friends. There he was well feasted; and left as soon as he could the next morning, and rode hard, for he was impatient to behold his beautiful house; and, besides, the night then coming on was the night in which the dead of old days go abroad in the sides of Kona; and having already meddled with the devil, he was the more chary of meeting with the dead. A little beyond Honaunau, looking far ahead, he was aware of a woman bathing in the edges of the sea; and she seemed a well-grown girl, and he thought no more of it. Then he saw her white shift flutter as she put it on, and then her red holoku; and by the time he came abreast of her she was done with her toilet, and had come up from the sea, and stood by the track-side in her red holoku, and she was all freshened with the bath, and her eyes shone and were kind. Now Keawe no sooner beheld her than he drew rein.

'I thought I knew every one in this country,' said he. 'How comes it that I do not know you?'

'I am Kokua, daughter of Kiano,' said the girl, 'and I have just returned from Oahu. Who are you?'

'I will tell you who I am in a little,' said Keawe, dismounting from his horse, 'but not now. For I have a thought in my mind, and if you knew who I was, you might have heard of me, and would not give me a true answer. But tell me, first of all, one thing: are you married?'

At this Kokua laughed out loud. 'It is you who ask questions,' she said. 'Are you married yourself?'

'Indeed, Kokua, I am not,' replied Keawe, 'and never thought to be until this hour. But here is the plain truth. I have met you here at the roadside, and I saw your eyes, which are like stars, and my heart went to you as swift as a bird. And so now, if you want none of me, say so, and I will go on to my own place; but if you think me no worse than any other young man, say so, too, and I will turn aside to your father's for the night, and to-morrow I will talk with the good man.'

Kokua said never a word, but she looked at the sea and laughed.

'Kokua,' said Keawe, 'if you say nothing, I will take that for the good answer; so let us be stepping to your father's door.'

She went on ahead of him, still without speech; only sometimes she glanced back and glanced away again, and she kept the strings of her hat in her mouth.

Now, when they had come to the door, Kiano came out on his veranda, and cried out and welcomed Keawe by name. At that the girl looked over, for the fame of the great house had come to her ears; and, to be sure, it was a great temptation. All that evening they were merry together; and the girl was as bold as brass under the eyes of her parents, and made a mark for Keawe, for she had a quick wit. The next day he had a word with Kiano, and found the girl alone.

'Kokua,' said he, 'you made a mark of me all the evening; and it is still time to bid me go. I would not tell you who I was, because I have so fine a house, and I feared you would think too much of that house and too little of the man that loves you. Now you know all, and if you wish to have seen the last of me, say so at once.'

'No,' said Kokua, but this time she did not laugh, nor did Keawe ask for more.

This was the wooing of Keawe; things had gone quickly, but so an arrow goes, and the ball of a rifle swifter still, and yet both may strike the target. Things had gone fast, but they had gone far also, and the thought of Keawe rang in the maiden's head; she heard his voice in the breach of the surf upon the lava, and for this young man that she had seen but twice she would have left father and mother and her native islands. As for Keawe himself, his horse flew up the path of the mountain under the cliff of tombs, and the sound of the hoofs, and the sound of Keawe singing to himself for pleasure, echoed in the caverns of the dead. He came to the Bright House, and still he was singing. He sat and ate in the broad balcony, and the Chinaman wondered at his master, to hear how he sang between mouthfuls. The sun went down into the sea, and the night came; and Keawe walked the balconies by lamplight, high in the mountains, and the voice of his singing startled men on ships.

'Here am I now upon my high place,' he said to himself. 'Life may be no better; this is the mountain top; and all shelves about me towards the worse. For the first time I will light up the chambers, and bathe in my fine bath with the hot water and the cold, and sleep above in the bed of my bridal chamber.'

So the Chinaman had word, and he must rise from sleep and light the furnaces; and as he walked below, beside the boilers, he heard his master singing and rejoicing above him in the lighted chambers. When the water began to be hot the Chinaman cried to his master: and Keawe went into the bathroom; and the Chinaman heard him sing as he filled the marble basin; and heard him sing, and the singing broken, as he undressed; until of a sudden, the song ceased. The Chinaman listened, and listened; he called up the house to Keawe to ask if all were well, and Keawe answered him 'Yes,' and bade him go to bed; but there was no more singing in the Bright House; and all night long the Chinaman heard his master's feet go round and round the balconies without repose.

Now, the truth of it was this: as Keawe undressed for his bath, he spied upon his flesh a patch like a patch of lichen on a rock, and it was then that he stopped singing. For he knew the likeness of that patch, and knew that he was fallen in the Chinese Evil.

Now, it is a sad thing for any man to fall into this sickness. And it would be a sad thing for anyone to leave a house so beautiful and so commodious, and depart from all his friends to the north coast of Molokai, between the mighty cliff and the sea-breakers. But what was that to Keawe, he who had met his love but yesterday and won her but that morning, and now saw all his hopes break, in a moment, like a piece of glass?

A while he sat upon the edge of the bath, then sprang, with a cry, and ran outside; and to and fro, to and fro, along the balcony, like one despairing.

'Very willingly could I leave Hawaii, the home of my fathers,' Keawe was thinking. 'Very lightly could I leave my house, the high-placed, the many-windowed, here upon the mountains. Very bravely could I go to

Molokai, to Kalaupapa by the cliffs, to live with the smitten and to sleep there, far from my fathers. But what wrong have I done, what sin lies upon my soul, that I should have encountered Kokua coming cool from the seawater in the evening? Kokua, the soul ensnarer! Kokua, the light of my life! Her may I never wed, her may I look upon no longer, her may I no more handle with my loving hand; and it is for this, it is for you, O Kokua! that I pour out my lamentations!'

Now you are to observe what sort of a man Keawe was, for he might have dwelt there in the Bright House for years, and no one been the wiser for his sickness; but he reckoned nothing of that, if he must lose Kokua. And again he might have wed Kokua even as he was; and so many would have done, because they have the souls of pigs; but Keawe loved the maid manfully, and he would do her no hurt and bring her in no danger.

A little beyond the midst of the night, there came in his mind the recollection of that bottle. He went round to the back porch, and called to memory the day when the devil had looked forth; and at the thought ice ran in his veins.

'A dreadful thing is in the bottle,' thought Keawe, 'and dreadful is the imp, and it is a dreadful thing to risk the flames of hell. But what other hope have I to cure my sickness or to wed Kokua? What!' he thought, 'would I beard the devil once, only to get me a house, and not face him again to win Kokua?'

Thereupon he called to mind it was the next day the Hall went by on her return to Honolulu. 'There must I go first,' he thought, 'and see Lopaka. For the best hope that I have now is to find that same bottle I was so pleased to be rid of.'

Never a wink could he sleep; the food stuck in his throat; but he sent a letter to Kiano, and about the time when the steamer would be coming, rode down beside the cliff of the tombs. It rained; his horse went heavily; he looked up at the black mouths of the caves, and he envied the dead that slept there and were done with trouble; and called to mind how he had galloped by the day before, and was astonished. So he came down to Hookena, and there was all the country gathered for the steamer as usual. In the shed before the shore they sat and jested and passed the news; but there was no matter of speech in Keawe's bosom, and he sat in their midst and looked without on the rain falling on the houses, and the surf beating among the rocks, and the sighs arose in his throat.

'Keawe of the Bright House is out of spirits,' said one to another. Indeed, and so he was, and little wonder.

Then the Hall came, and the whale-boat carried him on board. The after-part of the ship was full of Haoles – who had been to visit the volcano, as their custom is; and the midst was crowded with Kanakas, and the forepart with wild bulls from Kilo and horses from Kaü; but Keawe sat apart from all in his sorrow, and watched for the house of Kiano. There it sat low upon the shore in the black rocks, and shaded by the cocoa-palms, and there by the door was a red holoku, no greater than a fly, and going to and fro with a fly's busyness. 'Ah, queen of my heart,' he cried, 'I'll venture my dear soul to win you!'

Soon after, darkness fell and the cabins were lit up, and the Haoles sat and played at the cards and drank whisky as their custom is; but Keawe walked the deck all night; and all the next day, as they steamed under the lee of Maui or of Molokai, he was still pacing to and fro like a wild animal in a menagerie.

Towards evening they passed Diamond Head, and came to the pier of Honolulu. Keawe stepped out among the crowd and began to ask for Lopaka. It seemed he had become the owner of a schooner – none better in the islands – and was gone upon an adventure as far as Pola-Pola or Kahiki; so there was no help to be looked for from Lopaka. Keawe called to mind a friend of his, a lawyer in the town (I must not tell his name), and inquired of him. They said he was grown suddenly rich, and had a fine new house upon Waikiki shore; and this put a thought in Keawe's head, and he called a hack and drove to the lawyer's house.

The house was all brand new, and the trees in the garden no greater than walking-sticks, and the lawyer, when he came, had the air of a man well pleased.

'What can I do to serve you?' said the lawyer.

'You are a friend of Lopaka's,' replied Keawe, 'and Lopaka purchased from me a certain piece of goods that I thought you might enable me to trace.'

The lawyer's face became very dark. 'I do not profess to misunderstand you, Mr. Keawe,' said he, 'though this is an ugly business to be stirring in. You may be sure I know nothing, but yet I have a guess, and if you would apply in a certain quarter I think you might have news.'

And he named the name of a man, which, again, I had better not repeat. So it was for days, and Keawe went from one to another, finding everywhere in great contentment, although, to be sure, when he hinted at his business their faces would cloud over.

'No doubt I am upon the track,' thought Keawe. 'These new clothes and carriages are all the gifts of the little imp, and these glad faces are the faces of men who have taken their profit and got rid of the accursed thing in safety. When I see pale cheeks and hear sighing, I shall know that I am near the bottle.'

So it befell at last he was recommended to a Haole in Beritania Street. When he came to the door, about the hour of the evening meal, there were the usual marks of the new house, and the young garden, and the electric light shining in the windows; but when the owner came, a shock of hope and fear ran through Keawe; for here was a young man, white as a corpse, and black about the eyes, the hair shedding from his head, and such a look in countenance as a man may have when he is waiting for the gallows.

'Here it is, to be sure,' thought Keawe, and so with this man he noways veiled his errand. 'I am come to buy the bottle,' said he.

At the word, the young Haole of Beritania Street reeled against the wall.

'The bottle!' he gasped. 'To buy the bottle!' Then he seemed to choke, and seizing Keawe by the arm, carried him into a room and poured out wine into two glasses.

'Here is my respects,' said Keawe, who had been much about with Haoles in his time. 'Yes,' he added, 'I am come to buy the bottle. What is the price by now?'

At that word the young man let his glass slip through his fingers, and looked at Keawe like a ghost.

'The price,' says he; 'the price! You do not know the price?'

'It is for that I am asking you,' returned Keawe. 'But why are you so much concerned? Is there anything wrong about the price?'

'It has dropped a great deal in value since your time, Mr. Keawe,' said the young man, stammering.

'Well, well, I shall have the less to pay for it,' said Keawe. 'How much did it cost you?'

The young man was as white as a sheet.

'Two cents,' said he.

'What!' cried Keawe, 'two cents? Why, then, you can only sell it for one. And he who buys it – ' The words died upon Keawe's tongue; he who bought it could never sell it again, the bottle and the bottle imp must abide with him until he died, and when he died must carry him to the red end of hell.

The young man of Beritania Street fell upon his knees. 'For God's sake, buy it!' he cried. 'You can have all my fortune in the bargain. I was mad when I bought it at that price. I had embezzled money at my store; I was lost else; I must have gone to jail.'

'Poor creature,' said Keawe, 'you would risk your soul upon so desperate an adventure, and to avoid the proper punishment of your own disgrace; and you think I could hesitate with love in front of me. Give me the bottle, and the change which I make sure you have all ready. Here is a five-cent piece.'

It was as Keawe supposed; the young man had the change ready in a drawer; the bottle changed hands, and Keawe's fingers were no sooner clasped upon the stalk than he had breathed his wish to be a clean man. And sure enough, when he got home to his room, and stripped himself before a glass, his flesh was whole like an infant's. And here was the strange thing: he had no sooner seen this miracle than his mind was changed within him, and he cared naught for the Chinese Evil, and little enough for Kokua; and had but the one thought, that here he was bound to the bottle imp for time and eternity, and had no better hope but to be a cinder for ever in the flames of hell. Away ahead of him he saw them blaze with his mind's eye, and his soul shrank, and darkness fell upon the light.

When Keawe came to himself a little, he was aware it was the night when the band played at the hotel. Thither he went, because he feared to be alone; and there, among the happy faces, walked to and fro, and heard the tunes go up and down, and saw Berger beat the measure, and all the while he heard the flames crackle and saw the red fire burning in the bottomless pit. Of a sudden the band played Hiki-ao-ao; that was the song that he had sung with Kokua, and at the strain courage returned to him.

'It is done now,' he thought, 'and once more let me take the good along with the evil.'

So it befell that he returned to Hawaii by the first steamer, and as soon as it could be managed he was wedded to Kokua, and carried her up the mountain side to the Bright House.

Now it was so with these two, that when they were together Keawe's heart was stilled; but as soon as he was alone he fell into a brooding horror, and heard the flames crackle, and saw the red fire burn in the bottomless pit. The girl, indeed, had come to him wholly; her heart leaped in her side at the sight of him, her hand clung to his; and she was so fashioned, from the hair upon her head to the nails upon her toes, that none could see her without joy. She was pleasant in her nature. She had the good word always. Full of song she was, and went to and fro in the Bright House, the brightest thing in its three stories, carolling like the birds. And Keawe beheld and heard her with delight, and then must shrink upon one side, and weep and groan to think upon the price that he had paid for her; and then he must dry his eyes, and wash his face, and go and sit with her on the broad balconies, joining in her songs, and, with a sick spirit, answering her smiles.

There came a day when her feet began to be heavy and her songs more rare; and now it was not Keawe only that would weep apart, but each would sunder from the other and sit in opposite balconies with the whole width of the Bright House betwixt. Keawe was so sunk in his despair, he scarce observed the change, and was only glad he had more hours to sit alone and brood upon his destiny, and was not so frequently condemned to pull a smiling face on a sick heart. But one day, coming softly through the house, he heard the sound of childish sobbing, and there was Kokua rolling her face upon the balcony floor, and weeping like the lost.

'You so well to weep in this house, Kokua,' he said. 'And yet I would give the head of my body that you (at least) might have been happy.'

'Happy!' she cried, 'Keawe, when you lived alone in your Bright House you were the word of the island for a happy man; laughter and song were in your mouth, and your face was as bright as the sunrise. Then you wedded poor Kokua; and the good God knows what is amiss in her – but from that day you have not smiled. Oh!' she cried, 'what ails me? I thought I was pretty, and I knew I loved him. What ails me, that I throw this cloud upon my husband?'

'Poor Kokua,' said Keawe. He sat down by her side, and sought to take her hand; but that she plucked away. 'Poor Kokua,' he said again. 'My poor child – my pretty. And I had thought all this while to spare you!

Well, you shall know all. Then, at least, you will pity poor Keawe; then you will understand how much he loved you in the past – that he dared hell for your possession – and how much he loves you still (the poor condemned one), that he can yet call up a smile when he beholds you.'

With that he told her all, even from the beginning.

'You have done this for me?' she cried, 'Ah, well, then what do I care!' and she clasped and wept upon him.

'Ah, child!' said Keawe, 'and yet, when I consider of the fire of hell, I care a good deal!'

'Never tell me,' she said, 'no man can be lost because he loved Kokua, and no other fault. I tell you, Keawe, I shall save you with these hands, or perish in your company. What! you loved me and gave your soul, and you think I will not die to save you in return?'

'Ah, my dear, you might die a hundred times: and what difference would that make?' he cried, 'except to leave me lonely till the time comes for my damnation?'

'You know nothing,' said she. 'I was educated in a school in Honolulu; I am no common girl. And I tell you I shall save my lover. What is this you say about a cent? But all the world is not American. In England they have a piece they call a farthing, which is about half a cent. Ah! sorrow!' she cried, 'that makes it scarcely better, for the buyer must be lost, and we shall find none so brave as my Keawe! But, then, there is France; they have a small coin there which they call a centime, and these go five to the cent, or thereabout. We could not do better. Come, Keawe, let us go to the French islands; let us go to Tahiti as fast as ships can bear us. There we have four centimes, three centimes, two centimes, one centime; for possible sales to come and go on; and two of us to push the bargain. Come, my Keawe! kiss me, and banish care. Kokua will defend you.'

'Gift of God!' he cried. 'I cannot think that God will punish me for desiring aught so good. Be it as you will then, take me where you please: I put my life and my salvation in your hands.'

Early the next day Kokua went about her preparations. She took Keawe's chest that he went with sailoring; and first she put the bottle in a corner, and then packed it with the richest of their clothes and the bravest of the knick-knacks in the house. 'For,' she said, 'we must seem to be rich folks, or who would believe in the bottle?' All the time of her preparation she was as gay as a bird; only when she looked upon Keawe the tears would spring in her eye, and she must run and kiss him. As for Keawe, a weight was off his soul; now that he had his secret shared, and some hope in front of him, he seemed like a new man, his feet went lightly on the earth, and his breath was good to him again. Yet was terror still at his elbow; and ever and again, as the wind blows out a taper, hope died in him, and he saw the flames toss and the red fire burn in hell.

It was given out in the country they were gone pleasuring in the States, which was thought a strange thing, and yet not so strange as the truth, if any could have guessed it. So they went to Honolulu in the Hall, and thence in the Umatilla to San Francisco with a crowd of Haoles, and at San Francisco took their passage by the mail brigantine, the Tropic Bird, for Papeet, the chief place of the French in the south islands. Thither they came, after a pleasant voyage, on a fair day of the Trade Wind, and saw the reef with the surf breaking and Motuiti with its palms, and the schooner riding withinside and the white houses of the town low down along the shore among green trees, and overhead the mountains and the clouds of Tahiti, the wise island.

It was judged the most wise to hire a house, which they did accordingly, opposite the British Consul's, to make a great parade of money, and themselves conspicuous with carriages and horses. This it was very easy to do, so long as they had the bottle in their possession; for Kokua was more bold than Keawe, and, whenever she had a mind, called on the imp for twenty or a hundred dollars. At this rate they soon grew to be remarked in the town; and the strangers from Hawaii, their riding and their driving, the fine holokus, and the rich lace of Kokua, became the matter of much talk.

They got on well after the first with the Tahiti language, which is indeed like to the Hawaiian, with a change of certain letters; and as soon as they had any freedom of speech, began to push the bottle. You are to consider it was not an easy subject to introduce; it was not easy to persuade people you are in earnest, when you offer to sell them for four centimes the spring of health and riches inexhaustible. It was necessary besides to explain the dangers of the bottle; and either people disbelieved the whole thing and laughed, or they thought the more of the darker part, became overcast with gravity, and drew away from Keawe and Kokua, as from persons who had dealings with the devil. So far from gaining ground, these two began to find they were avoided in the town; the children ran away from them screaming, a thing intolerable to Kokua; Catholics crossed themselves as they went by; and all persons began with one accord to disengage themselves from their advances.

Depression fell upon their spirits. They would sit at night in their new house, after a day's weariness, and not exchange one word, or the silence would be broken by Kokua bursting suddenly into sobs. Sometimes they would pray together; sometimes they would have the bottle out upon the floor, and sit all evening watching how the shadow hovered in the midst. At such times they would be afraid to go to rest. It was long ere slumber came to them, and, if either dozed off, it would be to wake and find the other silently weeping in the dark, or, perhaps, to wake alone, the other having fled from the house and the neighbourhood of that bottle, to pace under the bananas in the little garden, or to wander on the beach by moonlight.

One night it was so when Kokua awoke. Keawe was gone. She felt in the bed and his place was cold. Then fear fell upon her, and she sat up in bed. A little moonshine filtered through the shutters. The room was bright, and she could spy the bottle on the floor. Outside it blew high, the great trees of the avenue cried aloud, and the fallen leaves rattled in the veranda. In the midst of this Kokua was aware of another sound; whether beast or of a man she could scarce tell, but it was as sad as death, and cut her to the soul. Softly she arose, set the door ajar, and looked forth into the moonlit yard. There, under the bananas, lay Keawe, his mouth in the dust, and as he lay he moaned.

It was Kokua's first thought to run forward and console him; her second potently witheld her. Keawe had borne himself before his wife like a brave man; it became her little in the hour of weakness to intrude upon his shame. With the thought she drew back into the house.

'Heaven,' she thought, 'how careless have I been – how weak! It is he, not I, that stands in this eternal peril; it was he, not I, that took the curse upon his soul. It is for my sake, and for the love of a creature of so little worth and such poor help, that he now beholds so close to him the flames of hell – ay, and smells the smoke of it, lying there in the wind and moonlight. Am I so dull of spirit that never till now I have surmised my duty, or have I seen it before and turned aside? But now, at least, I take up my soul in both the hands of my affection; now I say farewell to the white steps of heaven and the waiting faces of my friends. A love for a love, and let mine be equalled with Keawe's! A soul for a soul, and be it mine to perish!'

She was a deft woman with her hands, and was soon apparelled. She took in her hands the charge – the precious centimes they kept ever at their side; for this coin is little used, and they had made provision at a government office. When she was forth in the avenue clouds came on the wind, and the moon was blackened. The town slept, and she knew not whither to turn till she heard one coughing in the shadow of the trees.

'Old man,' said Kokua, 'what do you here abroad in the cold night?'

The old man could not express himself for coughing, but she made out that he was old and poor, and a stranger in the island.

'Will you do me a service?' said Kokua. 'As one stranger to another, and as an old man to a young woman, will you help a daughter of Hawaii?'

'Ah,' said the old man. 'So you are the witch from the Eight Islands, and even my old soul you seek to entangle. But I have heard of you, and defy your wickedness.'

'Sit down here,' said Kokua, 'and let me tell you a tale.' And she told him the story of Keawe from the beginning to the end.

'And now,' said she, 'I am his wife, whom he bought with his soul's welfare. And what should I do? If I went to him myself and offered to buy it, he will refuse. But if you go, he will sell it eagerly; I will await you here; you will buy it for four centimes, and I will buy it again for three. And the Lord strengthen a poor girl!'

'If you meant falsely,' said the old man, 'I think God would strike you dead.'

'He would!' cried Kokua. 'Be sure He would. I could not be so treacherous; God would not suffer it.'

'Give me the four centimes and await me here,' said the old man.

Now, when Kokua stood alone in the street, her spirit died. The wind roared in the trees, and it seemed to her the rushing of the flames of hell; the shadows towered in the light of the street lamp, and they seemed to her the snatching hands of evil ones. If she had had the strength, she must have run away, and if she had had the breath, she must have screamed aloud; but, in truth, she could do neither, and stood and trembled in the avenue, like an affrighted child.

Then she saw the old man returning, and he had the bottle in his hand.

'I have done your bidding,' said he. 'I left your husband weeping like a child; to-night he will sleep easy.' And he held the bottle forth.

'Before you give it to me,' Kokua panted, 'take the good with the evil – ask to be delivered from your cough.'

'I am an old man,' replied the other, 'and too near the gate of the grave to take a favour from the devil. But what is this? Why do you not take the bottle? Do you hesitate?'

'Not hesitate!' cried Kokua. 'I am only weak. Give me a moment. It is my hand resists, my flesh shrinks back from the accursed thing. One moment only!'

The old man looked at Kokua kindly. 'Poor child!' said he, 'you fear: your soul misgives you. Well, let me keep it. I am old, and can never more be happy in this world, and as for the next – '

'Give it to me!' gasped Kokua. 'There is your money. Do you think I am so base as that? Give me the bottle.'

'God bless you, child,' said the old man.

Kokua concealed the bottle under her holoku, said farewell to the old man, and walked off along the avenue, she cared not whither. For all roads were now the same to her, and led equally to hell. Sometimes she walked, and sometimes ran; sometimes she screamed out loud in the night, and sometimes lay by the wayside in the dust and wept. All that she had heard of hell came back to her; she saw the flames blaze, and she smelled the smoke, and her flesh withered on the coals.

Near day she came to her mind again, and returned to the house. It was even as the old man said – Keawe slumbered like a child. Kokua stood and gazed upon his face.

'Now, my husband, said she, 'it is your turn to sleep. When you wake it will be your turn to sing and laugh. But for poor Kokua, alas! that meant no evil – for poor Kokua no more sleep, no more singing, no more delight, whether in earth or heaven.'

With that she lay down in the bed by his side, and her misery was so extreme that she fell in a deep slumber instantly.

Late in the morning her husband woke her and gave her the good news. It seemed he was silly with delight, for he paid no heed to her distress, ill though she dissembled it. The words stuck in her mouth, it mattered not; Keawe did the speaking. She ate not a bite, but who was to observe it? For Keawe cleared the dish. Kokua saw and heard him, like some strange thing in a dream; there were times when she forgot or doubted, and put her hands to her brow; to know herself doomed and hear her husband babble seemed so monstrous.

All the while Keawe was eating and talking, and planning the time of their return, and thanking her for saving him and fondling her, and calling her the true helper after all. He laughed at the old man that was fool enough to buy that bottle.

'A worthy man he seemed,' Keawe said. 'But no one can judge by appearances. For why did the old reprobate require the bottle?'

'My husband,' said Kokua humbly, 'his purpose may have been good.'

Keawe laughed like an angry man.

'Fiddle-de-dee!' cried Keawe. 'An old rogue, I tell you; and an old ass to boot. For the bottle was hard enough to sell at four centimes; and at three it will be quite impossible. The margin is not broad enough, the thing begins to smell of scorching – brrr!' said he, and shuddered. 'It is true I bought it myself at a cent, when I knew not there were smaller coins. I was a fool for my pains; there will never be found another, and whoever has that bottle now will carry it to the pit.'

'O my husband!' said Kokua. 'Is it not a terrible thing to save oneself by the eternal ruin of another? It seems to me I could not laugh. I would be humbled. I would be filled with melancholy. I would pray for the poor holder.'

Then Keawe, because he felt the truth of what she said, grew the more angry. 'Heighty-teighty!' cried he. 'You may be filled with melancholy if you please. It is not the mind of a good wife. If you thought at all of me, you would sit shamed.'

Thereupon he went out, and Kokua was alone.

What chance had she to sell that bottle at two centimes? None, she perceived. And if she had any, here was her husband hurrying her away to a country where there was nothing lower than a cent. And here – on the morrow of her sacrifice – was her husband leaving her and blaming her.

She would not even try to profit by what time she had, but sat in the house, and now had the bottle out and viewed it with unutterable fear, and now, with loathing, hid it out of sight.

By-and-by Keawe came back, and would have her take a drive.

'My husband, I am ill,' she said. 'I am out of heart. Excuse me, I can take no pleasure.'

Then was Keawe more wroth than ever. With her, because he thought she was brooding over the case of the old man; and with himself, because he thought she was right and was ashamed to be so happy.

'This is your truth,' cried he, 'and this your affection! Your husband is just saved from eternal ruin, which he encountered for the love of you – and you can take no pleasure! Kokua, you have a disloyal heart.'

He went forth again furious, and wandered in the town all day. He met friends, and drank with them; they hired a carriage and drove into the country, and there drank again. All the time Keawe was ill at ease, because he was taking this pastime while his wife was sad, and because he knew in his heart that she was more right than he; and the knowledge made him drink the deeper.

Now there was an old brutal Haole drinking with him, one that had been a boatswain of a whaler – a runaway, a digger of gold mines, a convict in prisons. He had a low mind and a foul mouth; he loved to drink and to see others drunken; and he pressed the glass upon Keawe. Soon there was no more money in the company.

'Here, you!' says the boatswain, 'you are rich, you have been always saying. You have a bottle of some foolishness.'

'Yes,' says Keawe, 'I am rich; I will go back and get some money from my wife, who keeps it.'

'That's a bad idea, mate,' said the boatswain. 'Never you trust a petticoat with dollars. They're all as false as water; you keep an eye on her.'

Now this word struck in Keawe's mind; for he was muddled with what he had been drinking.

'I should not wonder but she was false, indeed,' thought he. 'Why else should she be so cast down at my release? But I will show her I am not the man to be fooled. I will catch her in the act.'

Accordingly, when they were back in town, Keawe bade the boatswain wait for him at the corner by the old calaboose, and went forward up the avenue alone to the door of his house. The night had come again; there was a light within, but never a sound; and Keawe crept about the corner, opened the back door softly, and looked in.

There was Kokua on the floor, the lamp at her side; before her was a milk-white bottle, with a round belly and a long neck; and as she viewed it, Kokua wrung her hands.

A long time Keawe stood and looked in the doorway. At first he was struck stupid; and then fear fell upon him that the bargain had been made amiss, and the bottle had come back to him as it came at San Francisco; and at that his knees were loosened, and the fumes of the wine departed from his head like mists off a river in the morning. And then he had another thought; and it was a strange one, that made his cheeks to burn.

'I must make sure of this,' he thought.

So he closed the door, and went softly round the corner again, and then came noisily in, as though he were but now returned. And, lo! by the time he opened the front door no bottle was to be seen; and Kokua sat in a chair and started up like one awakened out of sleep.

'I have been drinking all day and making merry,' said Keawe. 'I have been with good companions, and now I only came back for money, and return to drink and carouse with them again.'

Both his face and voice were as stern as his judgement, but Kokua was too troubled to observe.

'You do well to use your own, my husband,' said she, and her words trembled.

'Oh, I do well in all things,' said Keawe, and he went straight to the chest and took out money. But he looked besides in the corner where they kept the bottle, and there was no bottle there.

At that the chest heaved upon the floor like a sea-billow, and the house spun about him like a wreath of smoke, for he saw she was lost now, and there was no escape. 'It is what I feared,' he thought. 'It is she who had bought it.'

And then he came to himself a little and rose up; but the sweat streamed on his face as thick as the rain and as cold as the well-water.

'Kokua,' said he, 'I said to you to-day what ill became me. Now I return to the house with my jolly companions,' and at that he laughed a little quietly. 'I will take more pleasure in the cup if you forgive me.'

She clasped his knees in a moment, she kissed his knees with flowing tears.

'Oh,' she cried, 'I ask but a kind word!'

'Let us never one think hardly of the other,' said Keawe, and was gone out of the house.

Now, the money that Keawe had taken was only some of that store of centime pieces they had laid in at their arrival. It was very sure he had no mind to be drinking. His wife had given her soul for him, now he must give his for hers; no other thought was in the world with him.

At the corner, by the old calaboose, there was the boatswain waiting.

'My wife has the bottle,' said Keawe, 'and, unless you help me to recover it, there can be no more money and no more liquor tonight.'

'You do not mean to say you are serious about that bottle?' cried the boatswain.

'There is the lamp,' said Keawe. 'Do I look as if I was jesting?'

'That is so,' said the boatswain. 'You look as serious as a ghost.'

'Well, then,' said Keawe, 'here are two centimes; you just go to my wife in the house, and offer her these for the bottle, which (if I am not much mistaken) she will give you instantly. Bring it to me here, and I will buy it back from you for one; for that is the law with this bottle, that it still must be sold for a less sum. But whatever you do, never breathe a word to her that you have come from me.'

'Mate, I wonder are you making a fool of me?' asked the boatswain.

'It will do no harm if I am,' returned Keawe.

'That is so, mate,' said the boatswain.

'And if you doubt me,' added Keawe, 'you can try. As soon as you are clear of the house, wish to have your pocket full of money, or a bottle of the best rum, or what you please, and you will see the virtue of the thing.'

'Very well, Keawe,' said the boatswain. 'I will try; but if you are having your fun out of me, I will take my fun out of you with a belaying-pin.'

So the whaler-man went off up the avenue; and Keawe stood and waited. It was near the same spot where Kokua had waited the night before; but Keawe was more resolved, and never faltered in his purpose; only his soul was bitter with despair.

It seemed a long time he had to wait before he heard a voice singing in the darkness of the avenue. He knew the voice to be the boatswain's; but it was strange how drunken it appeared upon a sudden.

Next the man himself came stumbling into the light of the lamp. He had the devil's bottle buttoned in his coat; another bottle was in his hand; and even as he came in view he raised it to his mouth and drank.

'You have it,' said Keawe. 'I see that.'

'Hands off!' cried out the boatswain, jumping back. 'Take a step near me, and I'll smash your mouth. You thought you could make a catspaw of me, did you?'

'What do you mean?' cried Keawe.

'Mean?' cried the boatswain. 'This is a pretty good bottle, this is; that's what I mean. How I got it for two centimes I can't make out; but I am sure you shan't have it for one.'

'You mean you won't sell?' gasped Keawe.

'No, sir,' cried the boatswain. 'But I'll give you a drink of the rum, if you like.'

'I tell you,' said Keawe, 'the man who has that bottle goes to hell.'

'I reckon I'm going anyway,' returned the sailor; 'and this bottle's the best thing to go with I've struck yet. No, sir!' he cried again, 'this is my bottle now, and you can go and fish for another.'

'Can this be true?' Keawe cried. 'For your own sake, I beseech you, sell it me!'

'I don't value any of your talk,' replied the boatswain. 'You thought I was a flat, now you see I'm not; and there's an end. If you won't have a swallow of the rum, I'll have one myself. Here's your health, and goodnight to you!'

So off he went down the avenue towards town, and there goes the bottle out of the story.

But Keawe ran to Kokua light as the wind; and great was their joy that night; and great, since then, has been the peace of all their days in the Bright House.

MARKHEIM

'Yes,' said the dealer, 'our windfalls are of various kinds. Some customers are ignorant, and then I touch a dividend on my superior knowledge. Some are dishonest,' and here he held up the candle, so that the light fell strongly on his visitor, 'and in that case,' he continued, 'I profit by my virtue.'

Markheim had but just entered from the daylight streets, and his eyes had not yet grown familiar with the mingled shine and darkness in the shop. At these pointed words, and before the near presence of the flame, he blinked painfully and looked aside.

The dealer chuckled. 'You come to me on Christmas Day,' he resumed, 'when you know that I am alone in my house, put up my shutters, and make a point of refusing business. Well, you will have to pay for that; you will have to pay for my loss of time, when I should be balancing my books; you will have to pay, besides, for a kind of manner that I remark in you to-day very strongly. I am the essence of discretion, and ask no awkward questions; but when a customer cannot look me in the eye, he has to pay for it.' The dealer once more chuckled; and then, changing to his usual business voice, though still with a note of irony, 'You can give, as usual, a clear account of how you came into the possession of the object?' he continued. 'Still your uncle's cabinet? A remarkable collector, sir!'

And the little pale, round-shouldered dealer stood almost on tip-toe, looking over the top of his gold spectacles, and nodding his head with every mark of disbelief. Markheim returned his gaze with one of infinite pity, and a touch of horror.

'This time,' said he, 'you are in error. I have not come to sell, but to buy. I have no curios to dispose of; my uncle's cabinet is bare to the wainscot; even were it still intact, I have done well on the Stock Exchange, and should more likely add to it than otherwise, and my errand to-day is simplicity itself. I seek a Christmas present for a lady,' he continued, waxing more fluent as he struck into the speech he had prepared; 'and certainly I owe you every excuse for thus disturbing you upon so small a matter. But the thing was neglected yesterday; I must produce my little compliment at dinner; and, as you very well know, a rich marriage is not a thing to be neglected.'

There followed a pause, during which the dealer seemed to weigh this statement incredulously. The ticking of many clocks among the curious lumber of the shop, and the faint rushing of the cabs in a near thoroughfare, filled up the interval of silence.

'Well, sir,' said the dealer, 'be it so. You are an old customer after all; and if, as you say, you have the chance of a good marriage, far be it from me to be an obstacle. Here is a nice thing for a lady now,' he went on, 'this hand glass – fifteenth century, warranted; comes from a good collection, too; but I reserve the name, in the interests of my customer, who was just like yourself, my dear sir, the nephew and sole heir of a remarkable collector.'

The dealer, while he thus ran on in his dry and biting voice, had stooped to take the object from its place; and, as he had done so, a shock had passed through Markheim, a start both of hand and foot, a sudden leap of many tumultuous passions to the face. It passed as swiftly as it came, and left no trace beyond a certain trembling of the hand that now received the glass.

'A glass,' he said hoarsely, and then paused, and repeated it more clearly. 'A glass? For Christmas? Surely not?'

'And why not?' cried the dealer. 'Why not a glass?'

Markheim was looking upon him with an indefinable expression. 'You ask me why not?' he said. 'Why, look here – look in it – look at yourself! Do you like to see it? No! nor I – nor any man.'

The little man had jumped back when Markheim had so suddenly confronted him with the mirror; but now, perceiving there was nothing worse on hand, he chuckled. 'Your future lady, sir, must be pretty hard favoured,' said he.

'I ask you,' said Markheim, 'for a Christmas present, and you give me this – this damned reminder of years, and sins and follies – this hand-conscience! Did you mean it? Had you a thought in your mind? Tell me. It will be better for you if you do. Come, tell me about yourself. I hazard a guess now, that you are in secret a very charitable man?'

The dealer looked closely at his companion. It was very odd, Markheim did not appear to be laughing; there was something in his face like an eager sparkle of hope, but nothing of mirth.

'What are you driving at?' the dealer asked.

'Not charitable?' returned the other, gloomily. 'Not charitable; not pious; not scrupulous; unloving, unbeloved; a hand to get money, a safe to keep it. Is that all? Dear God, man, is that all?'

'I will tell you what it is,' began the dealer, with some sharpness, and then broke off again into a chuckle. 'But I see this is a love match of yours, and you have been drinking the lady's health.'

'Ah!' cried Markheim, with a strange curiosity. 'Ah, have you been in love? Tell me about that.'

'I,' cried the dealer. 'I in love! I never had the time, nor have I the time to-day for all this nonsense. Will you take the glass?'

'Where is the hurry?' returned Markheim. 'It is very pleasant to stand here talking; and life is so short and insecure that I would not hurry away from any pleasure – no, not even from so mild a one as this. We should rather cling, cling to what little we can get, like a man at a cliff's edge. Every second is a cliff, if you think upon it – a cliff a mile high – high enough, if we fall, to dash us out of every feature of humanity. Hence it is best to talk pleasantly. Let us talk of each other: why should we wear this mask? Let us be confidential. Who knows, we might become friends?'

'I have just one word to say to you,' said the dealer. 'Either make your purchase, or walk out of my shop!'

'True, true,' said Markheim. 'Enough fooling. To business. Show me something else.'

The dealer stooped once more, this time to replace the glass upon the shelf, his thin blond hair falling over his eyes as he did so. Markheim moved a little nearer, with one hand in the pocket of his greatcoat; he drew himself up and filled his lungs; at the same time many different emotions were depicted together on his face – terror, horror, and resolve, fascination and a physical repulsion; and through a haggard lift of his upper lip, his teeth looked out.

'This, perhaps, may suit,' observed the dealer: and then, as he began to re-arise, Markheim bounded from behind upon his victim. The long, skewerlike dagger flashed and fell. The dealer struggled like a hen, striking his temple on the shelf, and then tumbled on the floor in a heap.

Time had some score of small voices in that shop, some stately and slow as was becoming to their great age; others garrulous and hurried. All these told out the seconds in an intricate chorus of tickings. Then the passage of a lad's feet, heavily running on the pavement, broke in upon these smaller voices and startled Markheim into the consciousness of his surroundings. He looked about him awfully. The candle stood on the counter, its flame solemnly wagging in a draught; and by that inconsiderable movement, the whole room was filled with noiseless bustle and kept heaving like a sea: the tall shadows nodding, the gross blots of darkness swelling and dwindling as with respiration, the faces of the portraits and the china gods changing and wavering like images in water. The inner door stood ajar, and peered into that leaguer of shadows with a long slit of daylight like a pointing finger.

From these fear-stricken rovings Markheim's eyes returned to the body of his victim, where it lay both humped and sprawling, incredibly small and strangely meaner than in life. In these poor, miserly clothes, in that ungainly attitude, the dealer lay like so much sawdust. Markheim had feared to see it, and lo! it was nothing. And yet, as he gazed, this bundle of old clothes and pool of blood began to find eloquent voices. There it must lie; there was none to work the cunning hinges or direct the miracle of locomotion – there it must lie till it was found. Found! ay, and then? Then would this dead flesh lift up a cry that would ring over England, and fill the world with the echoes of pursuit. Ay, dead or not, this was still the enemy. 'Time was that when the brains were out,' he thought; and the first word struck into his mind. Time, now that the deed was accomplished – time, which had closed for the victim, had become instant and momentous for the slayer.

The thought was yet in his mind, when, first one and then another, with every variety of pace and voice – one deep as the bell from a cathedral turret, another ringing on its treble notes the prelude of a waltz – the clocks began to strike the hour of three in the afternoon.

The sudden outbreak of so many tongues in that dumb chamber staggered him. He began to bestir himself, going to and fro with the candle, beleaguered by moving shadows, and startled to the soul by chance reflections. In many rich mirrors, some of home design, some from Venice or Amsterdam, he saw his face repeated and repeated, as it were an army of spies; his own eyes met and detected him; and the sound of his own steps, lightly as they fell, vexed the surrounding quiet. And still, as he continued to fill his pockets, his mind accused him with a sickening iteration, of the thousand faults of his design. He should have chosen a more quiet hour; he should have prepared an alibi; he should not have used a knife; he should have been more cautious, and only bound and gagged the dealer, and not killed him; he should have been more bold, and killed the servant also; he should have done all things otherwise: poignant regrets, weary, incessant toiling of the mind to change what was unchangeable, to plan what was now useless, to be the architect of the irrevocable past. Meanwhile, and behind all this activity, brute terrors, like the scurrying of rats in a deserted attic, filled the more remote chambers of his brain with riot; the hand of the constable would fall heavy on his shoulder, and his nerves would jerk like a hooked fish; or he beheld, in galloping defile, the dock, the prison, the gallows, and the black coffin.

Terror of the people in the street sat down before his mind like a besieging army. It was impossible, he thought, but that some rumour of the struggle must have reached their ears and set on edge their curiosity; and now, in all the neighbouring houses, he divined them sitting motionless and with uplifted ear – solitary people, condemned to spend Christmas dwelling alone on memories of the past, and now startingly recalled from that tender exercise; happy family parties, struck into silence round the table, the mother still with raised finger: every degree and age and humour, but all, by their own hearths, prying and hearkening and weaving the rope that was to hang him. Sometimes it seemed to him he could not move too softly; the clink of the tall Bohemian goblets rang out loudly like a bell; and alarmed by the bigness of the ticking, he was tempted to stop the clocks. And then, again, with a swift transition of his terrors, the very silence of the place appeared a source of peril, and a thing to strike and freeze the passer-by; and he would step more boldly, and bustle aloud among the contents of the shop and imitate, with elaborate bravado, the movements of a busy man at ease in his own house.

But he was now so pulled about by different alarms that, while one portion of his mind was still alert and cunning, another trembled on the brink of lunacy. One hallucination in particular took a strong hold on his credulity. The neighbour hearkening with white face beside his window, the passer-by arrested by a horrible surmise on the pavement – these could at worst suspect, they could not know; through the brick walls and shuttered windows only sounds could penetrate. But here, within the house, was he alone? He knew he was; he had watched the servant set forth sweet-hearting, in her poor best, 'out for the day' written in every ribbon and smile. Yes, he was alone, of course; and yet, in the bulk of empty house above him, he could surely hear a stir of delicate footing – he was surely conscious, inexplicably conscious of some presence. Ay, surely; to every room and corner of the house his imagination followed it; and now it was a faceless thing, and yet had eyes to see with; and again it was a shadow of himself; and yet again behold the image of the dead dealer, re-inspired with cunning and hatred.

At times, with a strong effort, he would glance at the open door which still seemed to repel his eyes. The house was tall, the skylight small and dirty, the day blind with fog; and the light that filtered down to the ground story was exceedingly faint, and showed dimly on the threshold of the shop. And yet, in that strip of doubtful brightness, did there not hang wavering a shadow?

Suddenly, from the street outside, a very jovial gentleman began to beat with a staff on the shop-door, accompanying his blows with shouts and railleries in which the dealer was continually called upon by name. Markheim, smitten into ice, glanced at the dead man. But no! he lay quite still; he was fled away far beyond earshot of these blows and shoutings; he was sunk beneath seas of silence; and his name, which would once have caught his notice above the howling of a storm, had become an empty sound. And presently the jovial gentleman desisted from his knocking, and departed.

Here was a broad hint to hurry what remained to be done, to get forth from this accusing neighbourhood, to plunge into a bath of London multitudes, and to reach, on the other side of day, that haven of safety and apparent innocence – his bed. One visitor had come: at any moment another might follow and be more obstinate. To have done the deed, and yet not to reap the profit, would be too abhorrent a failure. The money, that was now Markheim's concern; and as a means to that, the keys.

He glanced over his shoulder at the open door, where the shadow was still lingering and shivering; and with no conscious repugnance of the mind, yet with a tremor of the belly, he drew near the body of his victim. The human character had quite departed. Like a suit half-stuffed with bran, the limbs lay scattered, the trunk doubled, on the floor; and yet the thing repelled him. Although so dingy and inconsiderable to the eye, he feared it might have more significance to the touch. He took the body by the shoulders, and turned it on its back. It was strangely light and supple, and the limbs, as if they had been broken, fell into the oddest postures. The face was robbed of all expression; but it was as pale as wax, and shockingly smeared with blood about one temple. That was, for Markheim, the one displeasing circumstance. It carried him back, upon the instant, to a certain fair-day in a fishers' village: a gray day, a piping wind, a crowd upon the street, the blare of brasses, the booming of drums, the nasal voice of a ballad singer; and a boy going to and fro, buried over head in the crowd and divided between interest and fear, until, coming out upon the chief place of concourse, he beheld a booth and a great screen with pictures, dismally designed, garishly coloured: Brownrigg with her apprentice; the Mannings with their murdered guest; Weare in the death-grip of Thurtell; and a score besides of famous crimes. The thing was as clear as an illusion; he was once again that little boy; he was looking once again, and with the same sense of physical revolt, at these vile pictures; he was still stunned by the thumping of the drums. A bar of that day's music returned upon his memory; and at that, for the first time, a qualm came over him, a breath of nausea, a sudden weakness of the joints, which he must instantly resist and conquer.

He judged it more prudent to confront than to flee from these considerations; looking the more hardily in the dead face, bending his mind to realise the nature and greatness of his crime. So little a while ago that face had moved with every change of sentiment, that pale mouth had spoken, that body had been all on fire with governable energies; and now, and by his act, that piece of life had been arrested, as the horologist, with interjected finger, arrests the beating of the clock. So he reasoned in vain; he could rise to no more remorseful consciousness; the same heart which had shuddered before the painted effigies of crime, looked on its reality unmoved. At best, he felt a gleam of pity for one who had been endowed in vain with all those faculties that can make the world a garden of enchantment, one who had never lived and who was now dead. But of penitence, no, not a tremor.

With that, shaking himself clear of these considerations, he found the keys and advanced towards the open door of the shop. Outside, it had begun to rain smartly; and the sound of the shower upon the roof had banished silence. Like some dripping cavern, the chambers of the house were haunted by an incessant echoing, which filled the ear and mingled with the ticking of the clocks. And, as Markheim approached the door, he seemed to hear, in answer to his own cautious tread, the steps of another foot withdrawing up the stair. The shadow still palpitated loosely on the threshold. He threw a ton's weight of resolve upon his muscles, and drew back the door.

The faint, foggy daylight glimmered dimly on the bare floor and stairs; on the bright suit of armour posted, halbert in hand, upon the landing; and on the dark wood-carvings, and framed pictures that hung against the yellow panels of the wainscot. So loud was the beating of the rain through all the house that, in Markheim's ears, it began to be distinguished into many different sounds. Footsteps and sighs, the tread of regiments marching in the distance, the chink of money in the counting, and the creaking of doors held stealthily ajar, appeared to mingle with the patter of the drops upon the cupola and the gushing of the water in the pipes. The sense that he was not alone grew upon him to the verge of madness. On every side he was haunted and begirt by presences. He heard them moving in the upper chambers; from the shop, he heard the dead man getting to his legs; and as he began with a great effort to mount the stairs, feet fled quietly before him and followed stealthily behind. If he were but deaf, he thought, how tranquilly he would possess his soul! And then again, and hearkening with ever fresh attention, he blessed himself for that unresting sense which held the outposts and stood a trusty sentinel upon his life. His head turned continually on his neck; his eyes, which seemed starting from their orbits, scouted on every side, and on every side were half-rewarded as with the tail of something nameless vanishing. The four-and-twenty steps to the first floor were four-and-twenty agonies.

On that first storey, the doors stood ajar, three of them like three ambushes, shaking his nerves like the throats of cannon. He could never again, he felt, be sufficiently immured and fortified from men's observing eyes, he longed to be home, girt in by walls, buried among bedclothes, and invisible to all but God. And at that thought he wondered a little, recollecting tales of other murderers and the fear they were said to entertain of heavenly avengers. It was not so, at least, with him. He feared the laws of nature, lest, in their callous and immutable procedure, they should preserve some damning evidence of his crime. He feared tenfold more, with a slavish, superstitious terror, some scission in the continuity of man's experience, some wilful illegality of nature. He played a game of skill, depending on the rules, calculating consequence from cause; and what if nature, as the defeated tyrant overthrew the chess-board, should break the mould of their succession? The like had befallen Napoleon (so writers said) when the winter changed the time of its appearance. The like might befall Markheim: the solid walls might become transparent and reveal his doings like those of bees in a glass hive; the stout planks might yield under his foot like quicksands and detain him in their clutch; ay, and there were soberer accidents that might destroy him: if, for instance, the house should fall and imprison him beside the body of his victim; or the house next door should fly on fire, and the firemen invade him from all sides. These things he feared; and, in a sense, these things might be called the hands of God reached forth against sin. But about God himself he was at ease; his act was doubt-less exceptional, but so were his excuses, which God knew; it was there, and not among men, that he felt sure of justice.

When he had got safe into the drawing-room and shut the door behind him, he was aware of a respite from alarms. The room was quite dismantled, uncarpeted besides, and strewn with packing-cases and incongruous furniture; several great pier-glasses, in which he beheld himself at various angles, like an actor on a stage; many pictures, framed and unframed, standing, with their faces to the wall; a fine Sheraton sideboard, a cabinet of marquetry, and a great old bed, with tapestry hangings. The windows opened to the floor; but by great good fortune the lower part of the shutters had been closed, and this concealed him from the neighbours. Here, then, Markheim drew in a packing case before the cabinet, and began to search among the keys. It was a long business, for there were many, and it was irksome, besides; for, after all, there might be nothing in the cabinet, and time was on the wing. But the closeness of the occupation sobered him. With the tail of his eye he saw the door – even glanced at it from time to time directly, like a besieged commander pleased to verify the good estate of his defences. But in truth he was at peace. The rain falling in the street sounded natural and pleasant. Presently, on the other side, the notes of a piano were wakened to the music of a hymn, and the voices of many children took up the air and words. How stately, how comfortable was the melody! How fresh the youthful voices! Markheim gave ear to it smilingly, as he sorted out the keys; and his mind was thronged with answerable ideas and images; church-going children and the pealing of the high organ; children afield, bathers by the brookside, ramblers on the brambly common, kite-flyers in the windy and cloud-navigated sky; and then, at another cadence of the hymn, back again to church, and the somnolence of summer Sundays, and the high genteel voice of the parson (which he smiled a little to recall), and the painted Jacobean tombs, and the dim lettering of the Ten Commandments in the chancel.

And as he sat thus, at once busy and absent, he was startled to his feet. A flash of ice, a flash of fire, a bursting gush of blood, went over him, and then he stood transfixed and thrilling. A step mounted the stair slowly and steadily, and presently a hand was laid upon the knob, and the lock clicked, and the door opened.

Fear held Markheim in a vice. What to expect he knew not, whether the dead man walking, or the official ministers of human justice, or some chance witness blindly stumbling in to consign him to the gallows. But when a face was thrust into the aperture, glanced round the room, looked at him, nodded and smiled as if in friendly recognition, and then withdrew again, and the door closed behind it, his fear broke loose from his control in a hoarse cry. At the sound of this the visitant returned.

'Did you call me?' he asked pleasantly, and with that he entered the room and closed the door behind him.

Markheim stood and gazed at him with all his eyes. Perhaps there was a film upon his sight, but the outlines of the newcomer seemed to change and waver like those of the idols in the wavering candlelight of the shop; and at times he thought he knew him; and at times he thought he bore a likeness to himself; and always, like a lump of living terror, there lay in his bosom the conviction that this thing was not of the earth and not of God.

And yet the creature had a strange air of the commonplace, as he stood looking on Markheim with a smile; and when he added: 'You are looking for the money, I believe?' it was in the tones of everyday politeness.

Markheim made no answer.

'I should warn you,' resumed the other, 'that the maid has left her sweetheart earlier than usual and will soon be here. If Mr. Markheim be found in this house, I need not describe to him the consequences.'

'You know me?' cried the murderer.

The visitor smiled. 'You have long been a favourite of mine,' he said; 'and I have long observed and often sought to help you.'

'What are you?' cried Markheim: 'the Devil?'

'What I may be,' returned the other, 'cannot affect the service I propose to render you.'

'It can,' cried Markheim; 'it does! Be helped by you? No, never; not by you! You do not know me yet; thank God, you do not know me!'

'I know you,' replied the visitant, with a sort of kind severity or rather firmness. 'I know you to the soul.'

'Know me!' cried Markheim. 'Who can do so? My life is but a travesty and slander on myself. I have lived to belie my nature. All men do; all men are better than this disguise that grows about and stifles them. You see each dragged away by life, like one whom bravos have seized and muffled in a cloak. If they had their own control – if you could see their faces, they would be altogether different, they would shine out for heroes and saints! I am worse than most; myself is more overlaid; my excuse is known to me and God. But, had I the time, I could disclose myself.'

'To me?' inquired the visitant.

'To you before all,' returned the murderer. 'I supposed you were intelligent. I thought – since you exist – you would prove a reader of the heart. And yet you would propose to judge me by my acts! Think of it; my acts! I was born and I have lived in a land of giants; giants have dragged me by the wrists since I was born out of my mother – the giants of circumstance. And you would judge me by my acts! But can you not look within? Can you not understand that evil is hateful to me? Can you not see within me the clear writing of conscience, never blurred by any wilful sophistry, although too often disregarded? Can you not read me for a thing that surely must be common as humanity – the unwilling sinner?'

'All this is very feelingly expressed,' was the reply, 'but it regards me not. These points of consistency are beyond my province, and I care not in the least by what compulsion you may have been dragged away, so as you are but carried in the right direction. But time flies; the servant delays, looking in the faces of the crowd and at the pictures on the hoardings, but still she keeps moving nearer; and remember, it is as if the gallows itself was striding towards you through the Christmas streets! Shall I help you; I, who know all? Shall I tell you where to find the money?'

'For what price?' asked Markheim.

'I offer you the service for a Christmas gift,' returned the other.

Markheim could not refrain from smiling with a kind of bitter triumph. 'No,' said he, 'I will take nothing at your hands; if I were dying of thirst, and it was your hand that put the pitcher to my lips, I should find the courage to refuse. It may be credulous, but I will do nothing to commit myself to evil.'

'I have no objection to a death-bed repentance,' observed the visitant.

'Because you disbelieve their efficacy!' Markheim cried.

'I do not say so,' returned the other; 'but I look on these things from a different side, and when the life is done my interest falls. The man has lived to serve me, to spread black looks under colour of religion, or to sow tares in the wheat-field, as you do, in a course of weak compliance with desire. Now that he draws so near to his deliverance, he can add but one act of service – to repent, to die smiling, and thus to build up in confidence and hope the more timorous of my surviving followers. I am not so hard a master. Try me. Accept my help. Please yourself in life as you have done hitherto; please yourself more amply, spread your elbows at the board; and when the night begins to fall and the curtains to be drawn, I tell you, for your greater comfort, that you will find it even easy to compound your quarrel with your conscience, and to make a truckling peace with God. I came but now from such a deathbed, and the room was full of sincere mourners, listening to the man's last words: and when I looked into that face, which had been set as a flint against mercy, I found it smiling with hope.'

'And do you, then, suppose me such a creature?' asked Markheim. 'Do you think I have no more generous aspirations than to sin, and sin, and sin, and, at the last, sneak into heaven? My heart rises at the thought. Is this, then, your experience of mankind? or is it because you find me with red hands that you presume such baseness? and is this crime of murder indeed so impious as to dry up the very springs of good?'

'Murder is to me no special category,' replied the other. 'All sins are murder, even as all life is war. I behold your race, like starving mariners on a raft, plucking crusts out of the hands of famine and feeding on each other's lives. I follow sins beyond the moment of their acting; I find in all that the last consequence is death; and to my eyes, the pretty maid who thwarts her mother with such taking graces on a question of a ball, drips no less visibly with human gore than such a murderer as yourself. Do I say that I follow sins? I follow virtues also; they differ not by the thickness of a nail, they are both scythes for the reaping angel of Death. Evil, for which I live, consists not in action but in character. The bad man is dear to me; not the bad act, whose fruits, if we could follow them far enough down the hurtling cataract of the ages, might yet be found more blessed than those of the rarest virtues. And it is not because you have killed a dealer, but because you are Markheim, that I offer to forward your escape.'

'I will lay my heart open to you,' answered Markheim. 'This crime on which you find me is my last. On my way to it I have learned many lessons; itself is a lesson, a momentous lesson. Hitherto I have been driven with revolt to what I would not; I was a bond-slave to poverty, driven and scourged. There are robust virtues that can stand in these temptations; mine was not so: I had a thirst of pleasure. But today, and out of this deed, I pluck both warning and riches – both the power and a fresh resolve to be myself. I become in all things a free actor in the world; I begin to see myself all changed, these hands the agents of good, this heart at peace. Something comes over me out of the past; something of what I have dreamed on Sabbath evenings to the sound of the church organ, of what I forecast when I shed tears over noble books, or talked, an innocent child, with my mother. There lies my life; I have wandered a few years, but now I see once more my city of destination.'

'You are to use this money on the Stock Exchange, I think?' remarked the visitor; 'and there, if I mistake not, you have already lost some thousands?'

'Ah,' said Markheim, 'but this time I have a sure thing.'

'This time, again, you will lose,' replied the visitor quietly.

'Ah, but I keep back the half!' cried Markheim.

'That also you will lose,' said the other.

The sweat started upon Markheim's brow. 'Well, then, what matter?' he exclaimed. 'Say it be lost, say I am plunged again in poverty, shall one part of me, and that the worse, continue until the end to override the better? Evil and good run strong in me, haling me both ways. I do not love the one thing, I love all. I can conceive great deeds, renunciations, martyrdoms; and though I be fallen to such a crime as murder, pity is no stranger to my thoughts. I pity the poor; who knows their trials better than myself? I pity and help them; I prize love, I love honest laughter; there is no good thing nor true thing on earth but I love it from my heart. And are my vices only to direct my life, and my virtues to lie without effect, like some passive lumber of the mind? Not so; good, also, is a spring of acts.'

But the visitant raised his finger. 'For six-and-thirty years that you have been in this world,' said be, 'through many changes of fortune and varieties of humour, I have watched you steadily fall. Fifteen years ago you would have started at a theft. Three years back you would have blenched at the name of murder. Is there any crime, is there any cruelty or meanness, from which you still recoil? – five years from now I shall detect you in the fact! Downward, downward, lies your way; nor can anything but death avail to stop you.'

'It is true,' Markheim said huskily, 'I have in some degree complied with evil. But it is so with all: the very saints, in the mere exercise of living, grow less dainty, and take on the tone of their surroundings.'

'I will propound to you one simple question,' said the other; 'and as you answer, I shall read to you your moral horoscope. You have grown in many things more lax; possibly you do right to be so; and at any account, it is the same with all men. But granting that, are you in any one particular, however trifling, more difficult to please with your own conduct, or do you go in all things with a looser rein?'

'In any one?' repeated Markheim, with an anguish of consideration. 'No,' he added, with despair, 'in none! I have gone down in all.'

'Then,' said the visitor, 'content yourself with what you are, for you will never change; and the words of your part on this stage are irrevocably written down.'

Markheim stood for a long while silent, and indeed it was the visitor who first broke the silence. 'That being so,' he said, 'shall I show you the money?'

'And grace?' cried Markheim.

'Have you not tried it?' returned the other. 'Two or three years ago, did I not see you on the platform of revival meetings, and was not your voice the loudest in the hymn?'

'It is true,' said Markheim; 'and I see clearly what remains for me by way of duty. I thank you for these lessons from my soul; my eyes are opened, and I behold myself at last for what I am.'

At this moment, the sharp note of the door-bell rang through the house; and the visitant, as though this were some concerted signal for which he had been waiting, changed at once in his demeanour.

'The maid!' he cried. 'She has returned, as I forewarned you, and there is now before you one more difficult passage. Her master, you must say, is ill; you must let her in, with an assured but rather serious countenance – no smiles, no overacting, and I promise you success! Once the girl within, and the door closed, the same dexterity that has already rid you of the dealer will relieve you of this last danger in your path. Thenceforward you have the whole evening – the whole night, if needful – to ransack the treasures of the house and to make good your safety. This is help that comes to you with the mask of danger. Up!' he cried; 'up, friend; your life hangs trembling in the scales: up, and act!'

Markheim steadily regarded his counsellor. 'If I be condemned to evil acts,' he said, 'there is still one door of freedom open – I can cease from action. If my life be an ill thing, I can lay it down. Though I be, as you say truly, at the beck of every small temptation, I can yet, by one decisive gesture, place myself beyond the reach of all. My love of good is damned to barrenness; it may, and let it be! But I have still my hatred of evil; and from that, to your galling disappointment, you shall see that I can draw both energy and courage.'

The features of the visitor began to undergo a wonderful and lovely change: they brightened and softened with a tender triumph, and, even as they brightened, faded and dislimned. But Markheim did not pause to watch or understand the transformation. He opened the door and went downstairs very slowly, thinking to himself. His past went soberly before him; he beheld it as it was, ugly and strenuous like a dream, random as chancemedley – a scene of defeat. Life, as he thus reviewed it, tempted him no longer; but on the further side he perceived a quiet haven for his bark. He paused in the passage, and looked into the shop, where the candle still burned by the dead body. It was strangely silent. Thoughts of the dealer swarmed into his mind as he stood gazing. And then the bell once more broke out into impatient clamour.

He confronted the maid upon the threshold with something like a smile.

'You had better go for the police,' said he: 'I have killed your master.'

WEIR OF HERMISTON

INTRODUCTORY

In the wild end of a moorland parish, far out of the sight of any house, there stands a cairn among the heather, and a little by east of it, in the going down of the brae-side, a monument with some verses half defaced. It was here that Claverhouse shot with his own hand the Praying Weaver of Balweary, and the chisel of Old Mortality has clinked on that lonely gravestone. Public and domestic history have thus marked with a bloody finger this hollow among the hills; and since the Cameronian gave his life there, two hundred years ago, in a glorious folly, and without comprehension or regret, the silence of the moss has been broken once again by the report of firearms and the cry of the dying.

The Deil's Hags was the old name. But the place is now called Francie's Cairn. For a while it was told that Francie walked. Aggie Hogg met him in the gloaming by the cairnside, and he spoke to her, with chattering teeth, so that his words were lost. He pursued Rob Todd (if any one could have believed Robbie) for the space of half a mile with pitiful entreaties. But the age is one of incredulity; these superstitious decorations speedily fell off; and the facts of the story itself, like the bones of a giant buried there and half dug up, survived, naked and imperfect, in the memory of the scattered neighbours. To this day, of winter nights, when the sleet is on the window and the cattle are quiet in the byre, there will be told again, amid the silence of the young and the additions and corrections of the old, the tale of the Justice-Clerk and of his son, young Hermiston, that vanished from men's knowledge; of the two Kirsties and the Four Black Brothers of the Cauldstaneslap; and of Frank Innes, 'the young fool advocate,' that came into these moorland parts to find his destiny.

I

The Lord Justice-Clerk was a stranger in that part of the country; but his lady wife was known there from a child, as her race had been before her. The old 'riding Rutherfords of Hermiston,' of whom she was the last descendant, had been famous men of yore, ill neighbours, ill subjects, and ill husbands to their wives though not their properties. Tales of them were rife for twenty miles about; and their name was even printed in the page of our Scots histories, not always to their credit. One bit the dust at Flodden; one was hanged at his peel door by James the Fifth; another fell dead in a carouse with Tom Dalyell; while a fourth (and that was Jean's own father) died presiding at a Hell-Fire Club, of which he was the founder. There were many heads shaken in Crossmichael at that judgment; the more so as the man had a villainous reputation among high and low, and both with the godly and the worldly. At that very hour of his demise, he had ten going pleas before the Session, eight of them oppressive. And the same doom extended even to his agents; his grieve, that had been his right hand in many a left-hand business, being cast from his horse one night and drowned in a peat-hag on the Kye-skairs; and his very doer (although lawyers have long spoons) surviving him not long, and dying on a sudden in a bloody flux.

In all these generations, while a male Rutherford was in the saddle with his lads, or brawling in a change-house, there would be always a white-faced wife immured at home in the old peel or the later mansion-house. It seemed this succession of martyrs bided long, but took their vengeance in the end, and that was in the person of the last descendant, Jean. She bore the name of the Rutherfords, but she was the daughter of their trembling wives. At the first she was not wholly without charm. Neighbours recalled in her, as a child, a strain of elfin wilfulness, gentle little mutinies, sad little gaieties, even a morning gleam of beauty that was not to be fulfilled. She withered in the growing, and (whether it was the sins of her sires or the sorrows of her mothers) came to her maturity depressed, and, as it were, defaced; no blood of life in her, no grasp or gaiety; pious, anxious, tender, tearful, and incompetent.

It was a wonder to many that she had married – seeming so wholly of the stuff that makes old maids. But chance cast her in the path of

Adam Weir, then the new Lord-Advocate, a recognised, risen man, the conqueror of many obstacles, and thus late in the day beginning to think upon a wife. He was one who looked rather to obedience than beauty, yet it would seem he was struck with her at the first look. 'Wha's she?' he said, turning to his host; and, when he had been told, 'Ay,' says he, 'she looks menseful. She minds me –'; and then, after a pause (which some have been daring enough to set down to sentimental recollections), 'Is she releegious?' he asked, and was shortly after, at his own request, presented. The acquaintance, which it seems profane to call a courtship, was pursued with Mr Weir's accustomed industry, and was long a legend, or rather a source of legends, in the Parliament House. He was described coming, rosy with much port, into the drawing-room, walking direct up to the lady, and assailing her with pleasantries, to which the embarrassed fair one responded, in what seemed a kind of agony, 'Eh, Mr Weir!' or 'O, Mr Weir!' or 'Keep me, Mr Weir!' On the very eve of their engagement, it was related that one had drawn near to the tender couple, and had overheard the lady cry out, with the tones of one who talked for the sake of talking, 'Keep me, Mr Weir, and what became of him?' and the profound accents of the suitor reply, 'Haangit, mem, haangit.' The motives upon either side were much debated. Mr Weir must have supposed his bride to be somehow suitable; perhaps he belonged to that class of men who think a weak head the ornament of women – an opinion invariably punished in this life. Her descent and her estate were beyond question. Her wayfaring ancestors and her litigious father had done well by Jean. There was ready money and there were broad acres, ready to fall wholly to the husband, to lend dignity to his descendants, and to himself a title, when he should be called upon the Bench. On the side of Jean, there was perhaps some fascination of curiosity as to this unknown male animal that approached her with the roughness of a ploughman and the *aplomb* of an advocate. Being so trenchantly opposed to all she knew, loved, or understood, he may well have seemed to her the extreme, if scarcely the ideal, of his sex. And besides, he was an ill man to refuse. A little over forty at the period of his marriage, he looked already older, and to the force of manhood added the senatorial dignity of years; it was, perhaps, with an unreverend awe, but he was awful. The Bench, the Bar, and the most experienced and reluctant witness, bowed to his authority – and why not Jeannie Rutherford?

The heresy about foolish women is always punished, I have said, and Lord Hermiston began to pay the penalty at once. His house in George Square was wretchedly ill-guided; nothing answerable to the expense of maintenance but the cellar, which was his own private care. When things went wrong at dinner, as they continually did, my lord would look up the table at his wife: 'I think these broth would be better to sweem in than to sup.' Or else to the butler: 'Here, M'Killop, awa' wi' this Raadical gigot – tak' it to the French, man, and bring me some puddocks! It seems rather a sore kind of a business that I should be all day in Court haanging Raadicals, and get nawthing to my denner.' Of course this was but a manner of speaking, and he had never hanged a man for being a Radical in his life; the law, of which he was the faithful minister, directing otherwise. And of course these growls were in the nature of pleasantry, but it was of a recondite sort; and uttered as they were in his resounding voice, and commented on by that expression which they called in the Parliament House 'Hermiston's hanging face' – they struck mere dismay into the wife. She sat before him speechless and fluttering; at each dish, as at a fresh ordeal, her eye hovered toward my lord's countenance and fell again; if he but ate in silence, unspeakable relief was her portion; if there were complaint, the world was darkened. She would seek out the cook, who was always her *sister in the Lord*. 'O, my dear, this is the most dreidful thing that my lord can never be contented in his own house!' she would begin; and weep and pray with the cook; and then the cook would pray with Mrs Weir; and the next day's meal would never be a penny the better – and the next cook (when she came) would be worse, if anything, but just as pious. It was often wondered that Lord Hermiston bore it as he did; indeed, he was a stoical old voluptuary, contented with sound wine and plenty of it. But there were moments when he overflowed. Perhaps half a dozen times in the history of his married life – 'Here! tak' it awa', and bring me a piece bread and kebbuck!' he had exclaimed, with an appalling explosion of his voice and rare gestures. None thought to dispute or to make excuses; the service was arrested; Mrs Weir sat at the head of the table whimpering without disguise; and his lordship opposite munched his bread and cheese in ostentatious disregard. Once only, Mrs Weir had ventured to appeal. He was passing her chair on his way into the study.

'O, Edom!' she wailed, in a voice tragic with tears, and reaching out to him both hands, in one of which she held a sopping pocket-handkerchief.

He paused and looked upon her with a face of wrath, into which there stole, as he looked, a twinkle of humour.

'Noansense!' he said. 'You and your noansense! What do I want with a Christian faim'ly? I want Christian broth! Get me a lass that can plain-boil a potato, if she was a whüre off the streets.' And with these words, which echoed in her tender ears like blasphemy, he had passed on to his study and shut the door behind him.

Such was the housewifery in George Square. It was better at Hermiston, where Kirstie Elliott, the sister of a neighbouring bonnet-laird, and an eighteenth cousin of the lady's, bore the charge of all, and kept a trim house and a good country table. Kirstie was a woman in a thousand, clean, capable, notable; once a moorland Helen, and still comely as a blood horse and healthy as the hill wind. High in flesh and voice and colour, she ran the house with her whole intemperate soul, in a bustle, not without buffets. Scarce more pious than decency in those days required, she was the cause of many an anxious thought and many a tearful prayer to Mrs Weir. Housekeeper and mistress renewed the parts of Martha and Mary; and though with a pricking conscience, Mary reposed on Martha's strength as on a rock. Even Lord Hermiston held Kirstie in a particular regard. There were few with whom he unbent so gladly, few whom he favoured with so many pleasantries. 'Kirstie and me maun have our joke,' he would declare in high good-humour, as he buttered Kirstie's scones, and she waited at table. A man who had no need either of love or of popularity, a keen reader of men and of events, there was perhaps only one truth for which he was quite unprepared: he would have been quite unprepared to learn that Kirstie hated him. He thought maid and master were well matched; hard, handy, healthy, broad Scots folk, without a hair of nonsense to the pair of them. And the fact was that she made a goddess and an only child of the effete and tearful lady; and even as she waited at table her hands would sometimes itch for my lord's ears.

Thus, at least, when the family were at Hermiston, not only my lord, but Mrs Weir too, enjoyed a holiday. Free from the dreadful looking-for of the miscarried dinner, she would mind her seam, read her piety books, and take her walk (which was my lord's orders), sometimes by herself, sometimes with Archie, the only child of that scarce natural union. The child was her next bond to life. Her frosted sentiment bloomed again, she breathed deep of life, she let loose her heart, in that society. The miracle of her motherhood was ever new to her. The sight of the little man at her skirt intoxicated her with the sense of power, and froze her with the consciousness of her responsibility. She looked forward, and, seeing him in fancy grow up and play his diverse part on the world's theatre, caught in her breath and lifted up her courage with a lively effort. It was only with the child that she forgot herself and was at moments natural; yet it was only with the child that she had conceived and managed to pursue a scheme of conduct. Archie was to be a great man and a good; a minister if possible, a saint for certain. She tried to engage his mind upon her favourite books, Rutherford's *Letters*, Scougal's *Grace Abounding*, and the like. It was a common practice of hers (and strange to remember now) that she would carry the child to the Deil's Hags, sit with him on the Praying Weaver's stone, and talk of the Covenanters till their tears ran down. Her view of history was wholly artless, a design in snow and ink; upon the one side, tender innocents with psalms upon their lips; upon the other, the persecutors, booted, bloody-minded, flushed with wine: a suffering Christ, a raging Beelzebub. *Persecutor* was a word that knocked upon the woman's heart; it was her highest thought of wickedness, and the mark of it was on her house. Her great-great-grand-father had drawn the sword against the Lord's anointed on the field of Rullion Green, and breathed his last (tradition said) in the arms of the detestable Dalyell. Nor could she blind herself to this, that had they lived in those old days, Hermiston himself would have been numbered along-side of Bloody MacKenzie and the politic Lauderdale and Rothes, in the band of God's immediate enemies. The sense of this moved her to the more fervour; she had a voice for that name of *persecutor* that thrilled in the child's marrow; and when one day the mob hooted and hissed them all in my lord's travelling carriage, and cried, 'Down with the persecutor! down with Hanging Hermiston!' and mamma covered her eyes and wept, and papa let down the glass and looked out upon the rabble with his droll formidable face, bitter and smiling, as they said he sometimes looked when he gave sentence, Archie was for the moment too much amazed to be alarmed, but he had scarce got his mother by herself before his shrill voice was raised demanding an explanation: why had they called papa a persecutor?

'Keep me, my precious!' she exclaimed. 'Keep me, my dear! this is poleetical. Ye must never ask me anything poleetical, Erchie. Your father is a great man, my dear, and it's no for me or you to be judging him. It would be telling us all, if we behaved ourselves in our several stations the way your faither does in his high office; and let me hear no more of any such disrespectful and undutiful questions! No that you meant to be undutiful, my lamb; your mother kens that – she kens it well, dearie!' And so slid off to safer topics, and left on the mind of the child an obscure but ineradicable sense of something wrong.

Mrs Weir's philosophy of life was summed in one expression – tenderness. In her view of the universe, which was all lighted up with a glow out of the doors of hell, good people must walk there in a kind of ecstasy of tenderness. The beasts and plants had no souls; they were here but for a day, and let their day pass gently! And as for the immortal men, on what black, downward path were many of them wending, and to what a horror of an immortality! 'Are not two sparrows,' 'Whosoever shall smite thee,' 'God sendeth His rain,' 'Judge not, that ye be not judged' – these texts made her body of divinity; she put them on in the morning with her clothes and lay down to sleep with them at night; they haunted her like a favourite air, they clung about her like a favourite perfume. Their minister was a marrowy expounder of the law, and my lord sat under him with relish; but Mrs Weir respected him from far off; heard him (like the cannon of a beleaguered city) usefully booming outside on the dogmatic ramparts; and meanwhile, within and out of shot, dwelt in her private garden which she watered with grateful tears. It seems strange to say of this colourless and ineffectual woman, but she was a true enthusiast, and might have made the sunshine and the glory of a cloister. Perhaps none but Archie knew she could be eloquent; perhaps none but he had seen her – her colour raised, her hands clasped or quivering – glow with gentle ardour. There is a corner of the policy of Hermiston, where you come suddenly in view of the summit of Black Fell, sometimes like the mere grass top of a hill, sometimes (and this is her own expression) like a precious jewel in the heavens. On such days, upon the sudden view of it, her hand would tighten on the child's fingers, her voice rise like a song. '*I to the hills!*' she would repeat. 'And O, Erchie, are nae these like the hills of Naphtali?' and her tears would flow.

Upon an impressionable child the effect of this continual and pretty accompaniment to life was deep. The woman's quietism and piety passed on to his different nature undiminished; but whereas in her it was a native sentiment, in him it was only an implanted dogma. Nature and the child's pugnacity at times revolted. A cad from the Potterrow once struck him in the mouth; he struck back, the pair fought it out in the back stable lane towards the Meadows, and Archie returned with a considerable decline in the number of his front teeth, and unregenerately boasting of the losses of the foe. It was a sore day for Mrs Weir; she wept and prayed over the infant backslider until my lord was due from Court, and she must resume that air of tremulous composure with which she always greeted him. The judge was that day in an observant mood, and remarked upon the absent teeth.

'I am afraid Erchie will have been fechting with some of they blagyard lads,' said Mrs Weir.

My lord's voice rang out as it did seldom in the privacy of his own house. 'I'll have nonn of that, sir!' he cried. 'Do you have me? – nonn of that! No son of mine shall be speldering in the glaur with any dirty raibble.'

The anxious mother was grateful for so much support; she had even feared the contrary. And that night when she put the child to bed – 'Now, my dear, ye see!' she said, 'I told you what your faither would think of it, if he heard ye had fallen into this dreidful sin; and let you and me pray to God that ye may be keepit from the like temptation or stren'thened to resist it!'

The womanly falsity of this was thrown away. Ice and iron cannot be welded; and the points of view of the Justice-Clerk and Mrs. Weir were not less unassimilable. The character and position of his father had long been a stumbling-block to Archie, and with every year of his age the difficulty grew more instant. The man was mostly silent; when he spoke at all, it was to speak of the things of the world, always in a worldly spirit, often in language that the child had been schooled to think coarse, and sometimes with words that he knew to be sins in themselves. Tenderness was the first duty, and my lord was invariably harsh. God was love; the name of the lord (to all who knew him) was fear. In the world, as schematised for Archie by his mother, the place was marked for such a creature. There were some whom it was good to pity and well (though very likely useless) to pray for; they were named reprobates, goats, God's enemies, brands for the burning; and Archie tallied every mark of identification, and drew the inevitable private inference that the Lord Justice-Clerk was the chief of sinners.

The mother's honesty was scarce complete. There was one influence she feared for the child and still secretly combated; that was my lord's; and half-unconsciously, half in a wilful blindness, she continued to undermine her husband with his son. As long as Archie remained silent, she did so ruthlessly, with a single eye to heaven and the child's salvation; but the day came when Archie spoke. It was 1801, and Archie was seven, and beyond his years for curiosity and logic, when he brought the case up openly. If judging were sinful and forbidden, how came papa to be a judge? to have that sin for a trade? to bear the name of it for a distinction?

'I can't see it,' said the little Rabbi, and wagged his head.

Mrs Weir abounded in commonplace replies.

'No, I cannae see it,' reiterated Archie. 'And I'll tell you what, mamma, I don't think you and me's justifeed in staying with him.'

The woman awoke to remorse; she saw herself disloyal to her man, her sovereign and bread-winner, in whom (with what she had of worldliness) she took a certain subdued pride. She expatiated in reply on my lord's honour and greatness; his useful services in this world of sorrow and wrong, and the place in which he stood, far above where babes and innocents could hope to see or criticise. But she had builded too well – Archie had his answers pat: Were not babes and innocents the type of the kingdom of heaven? Were not honour and greatness the badges of the world? And at any rate, how about the mob that had once seethed about the carriage?

'It's all very fine,' he concluded, 'but in my opinion papa has no right to be it. And it seems that's not the worst yet of it. It seems he's called "The Hanging Judge" – it seems he's crooool. I'll tell you what it is, mamma, there's a tex' borne in upon me: It were better for that man if a milestone were bound upon his back and him flung into the deepestmost pairts of the sea.'

'O, my lamb, ye must never say the like of that!' she cried. 'Ye're to honour faither and mother, dear, that your days may be long in the land. It's Atheists that cry out against him – French Atheists, Erchie! Ye would

never surely even yourself down to be saying the same thing as French
Atheists? It would break my heart to think that of you. And O, Erchie,
here are'na *you* setting up to *judge?* And have ye no forgot God's plain
command – the First with Promise, dear? Mind you upon the beam and
the mote!'

Having thus carried the war into the enemy's camp, the terrified
lady breathed again. And no doubt it is easy thus to circumvent a child
with catchwords, but it may be questioned how far it is effectual. An
instinct in his breast detects the quibble, and a voice condemns it. He
will instantly submit, privately hold the same opinion. For even in this
simple and antique relation of the mother and the child, hypocrisies
are multiplied.

When the Court rose that year and the family returned to Hermiston,
it was a common remark in all the country that the lady was sore failed.
She seemed to loose and seize again her touch with life, now sitting
inert in a sort of durable bewilderment, anon waking to feverish and
weak activity. She dawdled about the lasses at their work, looking stupidly
on; she fell to rummaging in old cabinets and presses, and desisted when
half through; she would begin remarks with an air of animation and
drop them without a struggle. Her common appearance was of one
who has forgotten something and is trying to remember; and when she
overhauled, one after another, the worthless and touching mementoes of
her youth, she might have been seeking the clue to that lost thought.
During this period, she gave many gifts to the neighbours and house lasses,
giving them with a manner of regret that embarrassed the recipients.

The last night of all she was busy on some female work, and toiled
upon it with so manifest and painful a devotion that my lord (who was
not often curious) inquired as to its nature.

She blushed to the eyes. 'O, Edom, it's for you!' she said. 'It's slippers.
I – I hae never made ye any.'

'Ye daft auld wife!' returned his lordship. 'A bonny figure I would
be, palmering about in bauchles!'

The next day, at the hour of her walk, Kirstie interfered. Kirstie took
this decay of her mistress very hard; bore her a grudge, quarrelled with
and railed upon her, the anxiety of a genuine love wearing the disguise
of temper. This day of all days she insisted disrespectfully, with rustic
fury, that Mrs Weir should stay at home. But, 'No, no,' she said, 'it's

my lord's orders,' and set forth as usual. Archie was visible in the acre bog, engaged upon some childish enterprise, the instrument of which was mire; and she stood and looked at him a while like one about to call; then thought otherwise, sighed, and shook her head, and proceeded on her rounds alone. The house lasses were at the burnside washing, and saw her pass with her loose, weary, dowdy gait.

'She's a terrible feckless wife, the mistress!' said the one.

'Tut,' said the other, 'the wumman's seeck.'

'Weel; I canna see nae differ in her,' returned the first. 'A füshionless quean, a feckless carline.'

The poor creature thus discussed rambled a while in the grounds without a purpose. Tides in her mind ebbed and flowed, and carried her to and fro like seaweed. She tried a path, paused, returned, and tried another; questing, forgetting her quest; the spirit of choice extinct in her bosom, or devoid of sequency. On a sudden, it appeared as though she had remembered, or had formed a resolution, wheeled about, returned with hurried steps, and appeared in the dining-room, where Kirstie was at the cleaning, like one charged with an important errand.

'Kirstie!' she began, and paused; and then with conviction, 'Mr Weir isna speeritually minded, but he has been a good man to me.'

It was perhaps the first time since her husband's elevation that she had forgotten the handle to his name, of which the tender, inconsistent woman was not a little proud. And when Kirstie looked up at the speaker's face, she was aware of a change.

'Godsake, what's the maitter wi' ye, mem?' cried the housekeeper, starting from the rug.

'I do not ken,' answered her mistress, shaking her head. 'But he is not speeritually minded, my dear.'

'Here, sit down with ye! Godsake, what ails the wife?' cried Kirstie, and helped and forced her into my lord's own chair by the cheek of the hearth.

'Keep me, what's this?' she gasped. 'Kirstie, what's this? I'm frich'ened.'

They were her last words.

It was the lowering nightfall when my lord returned. He had the sunset in his back, all clouds and glory; and before him, by the wayside, spied Kirstie Elliott waiting. She was dissolved in tears, and addressed him in the high, false note of barbarous mourning, such as still lingers modified among Scots heather.

'The Lord peety ye, Hermiston! the Lord prepare ye!' she keened out. 'Weary upon me, that I should have to tell it!'

He reined in his horse and looked upon her with the hanging face.

'Has the French landit?' cried he.

'Man, man,' she said, 'is that a' ye can think of? The Lord prepare ye: the Lord comfort and support ye!'

'Is onybody deid?' said his lordship. 'It's no Erchie?'

'Bethankit, no!' exclaimed the woman, startled into a more natural tone. 'Na, na, it's no sae bad as that. It's the mistress, my lord; she just fair flittit before my e'en. She just gi'ed a sab and was by wi' it. Eh, my bonny Miss Jeannie, that I mind sae weel!' And forth again upon that pouring tide of lamentation in which women of her class excel and over-abound.

Lord Hermiston sat in the saddle beholding her. Then he seemed to recover command upon himself.

'Well, it's something of the suddenest,' said he. 'But she was a dwaibly body from the first.'

And he rode home at a precipitate amble with Kirstie at his horse's heels.

Dressed as she was for her last walk, they had laid the dead lady on her bed. She was never interesting in life; in death she was not impressive; and as her husband stood before her, with his hands crossed behind his powerful back, that which he looked upon was the very image of the insignificant.

'Her and me were never cut out for one another,' he remarked at last. 'It was a daft-like marriage.' And then, with a most unusual gentleness of tone, 'Puir bitch,' said he, 'puir bitch!' Then suddenly: 'Where's Erchie?'

Kirstie had decoyed him to her room and given him 'a jeely-piece.'

'Ye have some kind of gumption, too,' observed the judge, and considered his housekeeper grimly. 'When all's said,' he added, 'I micht have done waur – I micht have been marriet upon a skirling Jezebel like you!'

'There's naebody thinking of you, Hermiston!' cried the offended woman. 'We think of her that's out of her sorrows. And could *she* have done waur? Tell me that, Hermiston – tell me that before her clay-cauld corp!'

'Weel, there's some of them gey an' ill to please,' observed his lordship.

II

My Lord Justice-Clerk was known to many; the man Adam Weir perhaps to none. He had nothing to explain or to conceal; he sufficed wholly and silently to himself; and that part of our nature which goes out (too often with false coin) to acquire glory or love, seemed in him to be omitted. He did not try to be loved, he did not care to be; it is probable the very thought of it was a stranger to his mind. He was an admired lawyer, a highly unpopular judge; and he looked down upon those who were his inferiors in either distinction, who were lawyers of less grasp or judges not so much detested. In all the rest of his days and doings, not one trace of vanity appeared; and he went on through life with a mechanical movement, as of the unconscious, that was almost august.

He saw little of his son. In the childish maladies with which the boy was troubled, he would make daily inquiries and daily pay him a visit, entering the sick-room with a facetious and appalling countenance, letting off a few perfunctory jests, and going again swiftly, to the patient's relief. Once, a court holiday falling opportunely, my lord had his carriage, and drove the child himself to Hermiston, the customary place of convalescence. It is conceivable he had been more than usually anxious, for that journey always remained in Archie's memory as a thing apart, his father having related to him from beginning to end, and with much detail, three authentic murder cases. Archie went the usual round of other Edinburgh boys, the high school and the college; and Hermiston looked on, or rather looked away, with scarce an affectation of interest in his progress. Daily, indeed, upon a signal after dinner, he was brought in, given nuts and a glass of port, regarded sardonically, sarcastically questioned. 'Well, sir, and what have you donn with your book today?' my lord might begin, and set him posers in law Latin. To a child just stumbling into Corderius, Papinian and Paul proved quite invincible. But papa had memory of no other. He was not harsh to the little scholar, having a vast fund of patience learned upon the bench, and was at no pains whether to conceal or to express his disappointment. 'Well, ye have a long jaunt before ye yet!' he might observe, yawning, and fall back on his own thoughts (as like as not) until the time came for separation, and my lord would take the decanter and the glass, and be off to the back chamber looking on the Meadows, where he toiled on his cases till the hours were small. There was no 'fuller man' on the bench; his memory was marvellous, though wholly legal; if he had to 'advise' extempore, none did it better; yet there was none who more earnestly prepared. As he thus watched in the night, or sat at table and forgot the presence of his son, no doubt but he tasted deeply of recondite pleasures. To be wholly devoted to some intellectual exercise is to have succeeded in life; and perhaps only in law and the higher mathematics may this devotion be maintained, suffice to itself without reaction, and find continual rewards without excitement. This atmosphere of his father's sterling industry was the best of Archie's education. Assuredly it did not attract him; assuredly it rather rebutted and depressed. Yet it was still present, unobserved like the ticking of a clock, an arid ideal, a tasteless stimulant in the boy's life.

But Hermiston was not all of one piece. He was, besides, a mighty toper; he could sit at wine until the day dawned, and pass directly from the table to the bench with a steady hand and a clear head. Beyond the third bottle, he showed the plebeian in a larger print; the low, gross accent, the low, foul mirth, grew broader and commoner; he became less formidable, and infinitely more disgusting. Now, the boy had inherited from Jean Rutherford a shivering delicacy, unequally mated with potential violence. In the playing-fields, and amongst his own companions, he repaid a coarse expression with a blow; at his father's table (when the time came for him to join these revels) he turned pale and sickened in silence. Of all the guests whom he there encountered, he had toleration for only one: David Keith Carnegie, Lord Glenalmond. Lord Glenalmond was tall and emaciated, with long features and long delicate hands. He was often compared with the statue of Forbes of Culloden in the Parliament House; and his blue eye, at more than sixty, preserved some of the fire of youth. His exquisite disparity with any of his fellow-guests, his appearance as of an artist and an aristocrat stranded in rude company, riveted the boy's attention; and as curiosity and interest are the things in the world that are the most immediately and certainly rewarded, Lord Glenalmond was attracted by the boy.

'And so this is your son, Hermiston?' he asked, laying his hand on Archie's shoulder. 'He's getting a big lad.'

'Hout!' said the gracious father, 'just his mother over again – daurna say boo to a goose!'

But the stranger retained the boy, talked to him, drew him out, found in him a taste for letters, and a fine, ardent, modest, youthful soul; and encouraged him to be a visitor on Sunday evenings in his bare, cold, lonely dining-room, where he sat and read in the isolation of a bachelor grown old in refinement. The beautiful gentleness and grace of the old judge, and the delicacy of his person, thoughts, and language, spoke to Archie's heart in its own tongue. He conceived the ambition to be such another; and, when the day came for him to choose a profession, it was in emulation of Lord Glenalmond, not of Lord Hermiston, that he chose the Bar. Hermiston looked on at this friendship with some secret pride, but openly with the intolerance of scorn. He scarce lost an opportunity to put them down with a rough jape; and, to say truth, it was not difficult, for they were neither of them quick. He had a word of contempt for the whole crowd of poets, painters, fiddlers, and their admirers, the bastard race of amateurs, which was continually on his lips. 'Signor Feedle-eerie!' he would say. 'O, for Goad's sake, no more of the Signor!'

'You and my father are great friends, are you not?' asked Archie once.

'There is no man that I more respect, Archie,' replied Lord Glenalmond. 'He is two things of price. He is a great lawyer, and he is upright as the day.'

'You and he are so different,' said the boy, his eyes dwelling on those of his old friend, like a lover's on his mistress's.

'Indeed so,' replied the judge; 'very different. And so I fear are you and he. Yet I would like it very ill if my young friend were to misjudge his father. He has all the Roman virtues: Cato and Brutus were such; I think a son's heart might well be proud of such an ancestry of one.'

'And I would sooner he were a plaided herd,' cried Archie, with sudden bitterness.

'And that is neither very wise, nor I believe entirely true,' returned Glenalmond. 'Before you are done you will find some of these expressions rise on you like a remorse. They are merely literary and decorative; they

do not aptly express your thought, nor is your thought clearly apprehended, and no doubt your father (if he were here) would say, "Signor
Feedle-eerie!"'

With the infinitely delicate sense of youth, Archie avoided the subject
from that hour. It was perhaps a pity. Had he but talked – talked freely
– let himself gush out in words (the way youth loves to do and should),
there might have been no tale to write upon the Weirs of Hermiston.
But the shadow of a threat of ridicule sufficed; in the slight tartness of
these words he read a prohibition; and it is likely that Glenalmond meant
it so.

Besides the veteran, the boy was without confidant or friend. Serious
and eager, he came through school and college, and moved among a
crowd of the indifferent, in the seclusion of his shyness. He grew up
handsome, with an open, speaking countenance, with graceful, youthful
ways; he was clever, he took prizes, he shone in the Speculative Society.
It should seem he must become the centre of a crowd of friends; but
something that was in part the delicacy of his mother, in part the austerity
of his father, held him aloof from all. It is a fact, and a strange one, that
among his contemporaries Hermiston's son was thought to be a chip of
the old block. 'You're a friend of Archie Weir's?' said one to Frank
Innes; and Innes replied, with his usual flippancy and more than his
usual insight: 'I know Weir, but I never met Archie.' No one had met
Archie, a malady most incident to only sons. He flew his private signal,
and none heeded it; it seemed he was abroad in a world from which the
very hope of intimacy was banished; and he looked round about him on
the concourse of his fellow-students, and forward to the trivial days and
acquaintances that were to come, without hope or interest.

As time went on, the tough and rough old sinner felt himself drawn
to the son of his loins and sole continuator of his new family, with soft-
nesses of sentiment that he could hardly credit and was wholly impotent
to express. With a face, voice, and manner trained through forty years
to terrify and repel, Rhadamanthus may be great, but he will scarce be
engaging. It is a fact that he tried to propitiate Archie, but a fact that
cannot be too lightly taken; the attempt was so unconspicuously made,
the failure so stoically supported. Sympathy is not due to these stead-
fast iron natures. If he failed to gain his son's friendship, or even his
son's toleration, on he went up the great, bare staircase of his duty,

uncheered and undepressed. There might have been more pleasure in his relations with Archie, so much he may have recognised at moments; but pleasure was a by-product of the singular chemistry of life, which only fools expected.

An idea of Archie's attitude, since we are all grown up and have forgotten the days of our youth, it is more difficult to convey. He made no attempt whatsoever to understand the man with whom he dined and breakfasted. Parsimony of pain, glut of pleasure, these are the two alternating ends of youth; and Archie was of the parsimonious. The wind blew cold out of a certain quarter – he turned his back upon it; stayed as little as was possible in his father's presence; and when there, averted his eyes as much as was decent from his father's face. The lamp shone for many hundred days upon these two at table – my lord, ruddy, gloomy, and unreverent; Archie with a potential brightness that was always dimmed and veiled in that society; and there were not, perhaps, in Christendom two men more radically strangers. The father, with a grand simplicity, either spoke of what interested himself, or maintained an unaffected silence. The son turned in his head for some topic that should be quite safe, that would spare him fresh evidences either of my lord's inherent grossness or of the innocence of his inhumanity; treading gingerly the ways of intercourse, like a lady gathering up her skirts in a by-path. If he made a mistake, and my lord began to abound in matter of offence, Archie drew himself up, his brow grew dark, his share of the talk expired; but my lord would faithfully and cheerfully continue to pour out the worst of himself before his silent and offended son.

'Well, it's a poor hert that never rejoices!' he would say, at the conclusion of such a nightmare interview. 'But I must get to my plew-stilts.' And he would seclude himself as usual in his back room, and Archie go forth into the night and the city quivering with animosity and scorn.

III

It chanced in the year 1813 that Archie strayed one day into the Justiciary Court. The macer made room for the son of the presiding judge. In the dock, the centre of men's eyes, there stood a whey-coloured, misbegotten caitiff, Duncan Jopp, on trial for his life. His story, as it was

raked out before him in that public scene, was one of disgrace and vice
and cowardice, the very nakedness of crime; and the creature heard and
it seemed at times as though he understood – as if at times he forgot
the horror of the place he stood in, and remembered the shame of what
had brought him there. He kept his head bowed and his hands clutched
upon the rail; his hair dropped in his eyes and at times he flung it back;
and now he glanced about the audience in a sudden fellness of terror,
and now looked in the face of his judge and gulped. There was pinned
about his throat a piece of dingy flannel; and this it was perhaps that
turned the scale in Archie's mind between disgust and pity. The creature
stood in a vanishing point; yet a little while, and he was still a man, and
had eyes and apprehension; yet a little longer, and with a last sordid
piece of pageantry, he would cease to be. And here, in the meantime,
with a trait of human nature that caught at the beholder's breath, he was
tending a sore throat.

Over against him, my Lord Hermiston occupied the bench in the red
robes of criminal jurisdiction, his face framed in the white wig. Honest
all through, he did not affect the virtue of impartiality; this was no case
for refinement; there was a man to be hanged, he would have said, and
he was hanging him. Nor was it possible to see his lordship, and acquit
him of gusto in the task. It was plain he gloried in the exercise of his
trained faculties, in the clear sight which pierced at once into the joint
of fact, in the rude, unvarnished gibes with which he demolished every
figment of defence. He took his ease and jested, unbending in that solemn
place with some of the freedom of the tavern; and the rag of man with
the flannel round his neck was hunted gallowsward with jeers.

Duncan had a mistress, scarce less forlorn and greatly older than
himself, who came up, whimpering and curtseying, to add the weight
of her betrayal. My lord gave her the oath in his most roaring voice,
and added an intolerant warning.

'Mind what ye say now, Janet,' said he. 'I have an e'e upon ye, I'm
ill to jest with.'

Presently, after she was tremblingly embarked on her story, 'And what
made ye do this, ye auld runt?' the Court interposed. 'Do ye mean to
tell me ye was the panel's mistress?'

'If you please, ma loard,' whined the female.

'Godsake! ye made a bonny couple,' observed his lordship; and there was something so formidable and ferocious in his scorn that not even the galleries thought to laugh.

The summing up contained some jewels.

'These two peetiable creatures seem to have made up thegither, it's not for us to explain why.' – 'The panel, who (whatever else he may be) appears to be equally ill set-out in mind and boady.' – 'Neither the panel nor yet the old wife appears to have had so much common sense as even to tell a lie when it was necessary.' And in the course of sentencing, my lord had this *obiter dictum*: 'I have been the means, under God, of haanging a great number, but never just such a disjaskit rascal as yourself.' The words were strong in themselves; the light and heat and detonation of their delivery, and the savage pleasure of the speaker in his task, made them tingle in the ears.

When all was over, Archie came forth again into a changed world. Had there been the least redeeming greatness in the crime, any obscurity, any dubiety, perhaps he might have understood. But the culprit stood, with his sore throat, in the sweat of his mortal agony, without defence or excuse: a thing to cover up with blushes: a being so much sunk beneath the zones of sympathy that pity might seem harmless. And the judge had pursued him with a monstrous, relishing gaiety, horrible to be conceived, a trait for nightmares. It is one thing to spear a tiger, another to crush a toad; there are æsthetics even of the slaughter-house; and the loathsomeness of Duncan Jopp enveloped and infected the image of his judge.

Archie passed by his friends in the High Street with incoherent words and gestures. He saw Holyrood in a dream, remembrance of its romance awoke in him and faded; he had a vision of the old radiant stories, of Queen Mary and Prince Charlie, of the hooded stag, of the splendour and crime, the velvet and bright iron of the past; and dismissed them with a cry of pain. He lay and moaned in the Hunter's Bog, and the heavens were dark above him and the grass of the field an offence. 'This is my father,' he said. 'I draw my life from him; the flesh upon my bones is his, the bread I am fed with is the wages of these horrors.' He recalled his mother, and ground his forehead in the earth. He thought of flight, and where was he to flee to? of other lives, but was there any life worth living in this den of savage and jeering animals?

The interval before the execution was like a violent dream. He met his father; he would not look at him, he could not speak to him. It seemed there was no living creature but must have been swift to recognise that imminent animosity; but the hide of the Justice-Clerk remained impenetrable. Had my lord been talkative, the truce could never have subsisted; but he was by fortune in one of his humours of sour silence; and under the very guns of his broadside, Archie nursed the enthusiasm of rebellion. It seemed to him, from the top of his nineteen years' experience, as if he were marked at birth to be the perpetrator of some signal action, to set back fallen Mercy, to overthrow the usurping devil that sat, horned and hoofed, on her throne. Seductive Jacobin figments, which he had often refuted at the Speculative, swam up in his mind and startled him as with voices: and he seemed to himself to walk accompanied by an almost tangible presence of new beliefs and duties.

On the named morning he was at the place of execution. He saw the fleering rabble, the flinching wretch produced. He looked on for a while at a certain parody of devotion, which seemed to strip the wretch of his last claim to manhood. Then followed the brutal instant of extinction, and the paltry dangling of the remains like a broken jumping-jack. He had been prepared for something terrible, not for this tragic meanness. He stood a moment silent, and then – 'I denounce this God-defying murder,' he shouted; and his father, if he must have disclaimed the sentiment, might have owned the stentorian voice with which it was uttered.

Frank Innes dragged him from the spot. The two handsome lads followed the same course of study and recreation, and felt a certain mutual attraction, founded mainly on good looks. It had never gone deep; Frank was by nature a thin, jeering creature, not truly susceptible whether of feeling or inspiring friendship; and the relation between the pair was altogether on the outside, a thing of common knowledge and the pleasantries that spring from a common acquaintance. The more credit to Frank that he was appalled by Archie's outburst, and at least conceived the design of keeping him in sight, and, if possible, in hand, for the day. But Archie, who had just defied – was it God or Satan? – would not listen to the word of a college companion.

'I will not go with you,' he said. 'I do not desire your company, sir; I would be alone.'

'Here, Weir, man, don't be absurd,' said Innes, keeping a tight hold upon his sleeve. 'I will not let you go until I know what you mean to do with yourself; it's no use brandishing that staff.' For indeed at that moment Archie had made a sudden – perhaps a warlike – movement. 'This has been the most insane affair; you know it has. You know very well that I'm playing the good Samaritan. All I wish is to keep you quiet.'

'If quietness is what you wish, Mr Innes,' said Archie, 'and you will promise to leave me entirely to myself, I will tell you so much, that I am going to walk in the country and admire the beauties of nature.'

'Honour bright?' asked Frank.

'I am not in the habit of lying, Mr Innes,' retorted Archie. 'I have the honour of wishing you good-day.'

'You won't forget the Spec.?' asked Innes.

'The Spec.?' said Archie. 'O no, I won't forget the Spec.'

And the one young man carried his tortured spirit forth of the city and all the day long, by one road and another, in an endless pilgrimage of misery; while the other hastened smilingly to spread the news of Weir's access of insanity, and to drum up for that night a full attendance at the Speculative, where further eccentric developments might certainly be looked for. I doubt if Innes had the least belief in his prediction; I think it flowed rather from a wish to make the story as good and the scandal as great as possible; not from any ill-will to Archie – from the mere pleasure of beholding interested faces. But for all that his words were prophetic. Archie did not forget the Spec.; he put in an appearance there at the due time, and, before the evening was over, had dealt a memorable shock to his companions. It chanced he was the president of the night. He sat in the same room where the Society still meets – only the portraits were not there: the men who afterwards sat for them were then but beginning their career. The same lustre of many tapers shed its light over the meeting; the same chair, perhaps, supported him that so many of us have sat in since. At times he seemed to forget the business of the evening, but even in these periods he sat with a great air of energy and determination. At times he meddled bitterly, and launched with defiance those fines which are the precious and rarely used artillery of the president. He little thought, as he did so, how he resembled his father, but his friends remarked upon it, chuckling. So far, in his high place above his fellow-students, he seemed set beyond the possibility of any scandal; but his mind was made up – he was determined to fulfil the sphere of his offence. He signed to Innes (whom he had just fined, and who just impeached his ruling) to succeed him in the chair, stepped down from the platform, and took his place by the chimney-piece, the shine of many wax tapers from above illuminating his pale face, the glow of the great red fire relieving from behind his slim figure. He had to propose, as an amendment to the next subject in the case-book, 'Whether capital punishment be consistent with God's will or man's policy?'

A breath of embarrassment, of something like alarm, passed round the room, so daring did these words appear upon the lips of Hermiston's only son. But the amendment was not seconded; the previous question was promptly moved and unanimously voted, and the momentary scandal smuggled by. Innes triumphed in the fulfilment of his prophecy. He and Archie were now become the heroes of the night; but whereas everyone crowded about Innes, when the meeting broke up, but one of all his companions came to speak to Archie.

'Weir, man! That was an extraordinary raid of yours!' observed this courageous member, taking him confidentially by the arm as they went out.

'I don't think it a raid,' said Archie grimly. 'More like a war. I saw that poor brute hanged this morning, and my gorge rises at it yet.'

'Hut-tut,' returned his companion, and, dropping his arm like something hot, he sought the less tense society of others.

Archie found himself alone. The last of the faithful – or was it only the boldest of the curious? – had fled. He watched the black huddle of his fellow-students draw off down and up the street, in whispering or boisterous gangs. And the isolation of the moment weighed upon him like an omen and an emblem of his destiny in life. Bred up in unbroken fear himself, among trembling servants, and in a house which (at the least ruffle in the master's voice) shuddered into silence, he saw himself on the brink of the red valley of war, and measured the danger and length of it with awe. He made a détour in the glimmer and shadow of the streets, came into the back stable lane, and watched for a long while the light burn steady in the Judge's room. The longer he gazed upon that illuminated window-blind, the more blank became the picture of the man who sat behind it, endlessly turning over sheets of process, pausing to sip a glass of port, or rising and passing heavily about his book-lined walls to verify some reference. He could not combine the brutal judge and the industrious, dispassionate student; the connecting link escaped him; from such a dual nature, it was impossible he should predict behaviour; and he asked himself if he had done well to plunge into a business of which the end could not be foreseen? and presently after, with a sickening decline of confidence, if he had done loyally to strike his father? For he had struck him – defied him twice over and before a cloud of witnesses – struck him a public buffet before crowds. Who had called him to judge his father in these precarious and high questions? The office was usurped. It might have become a stranger; in a son – there was no blinking it – in a son, it was disloyal. And now, between these two natures so antipathetic, so hateful to each other, there was depending an unpardonable affront: and the providence of God alone might foresee the manner in which it would be resented by Lord Hermiston.

These misgivings tortured him all night and arose with him in the winter's morning; they followed him from class to class, they made him shrinkingly sensitive to every shade of manner in his companions, they sounded in his ears through the current voice of the professor; and he brought them home with him at night unabated and indeed increased. The cause of this increase lay in a chance encounter with the celebrated Dr Gregory. Archie stood looking vaguely in the lighted window of a bookshop, trying to nerve himself for the approaching ordeal. My lord and he had met and parted in the morning as they had now done for long, with scarcely the ordinary civilities of life; and it was plain to the son that nothing had yet reached the father's ears. Indeed, when he recalled the awful countenance of my lord, a timid hope sprang up in him that perhaps there would be found no one bold enough to carry tales. If this were so, he asked himself, would he begin again? and he found no answer. It was at this moment that a hand was laid upon his arm, and a voice said in his ear, 'My dear Mr Archie, you had better come and see me.'

He started, turned round, and found himself face to face with Dr Gregory. 'And why should I come to see you?' he asked, with the defiance of the miserable.

'Because you are looking exceedingly ill,' said the doctor, 'and you very evidently want looking after, my young friend. Good folk are scarce, you know; and it is not everyone that would be quite so much missed as yourself. It is not everyone that Hermiston would miss.'

And with a nod and a smile, the doctor passed on.

A moment after, Archie was in pursuit, and had in turn, but more roughly, seized him by the arm.

'What do you mean? what did you mean by saying that? What makes you think that Hermis – my father would have missed me?'

The doctor turned about and looked him all over with a clinical eye. A far more stupid man than Dr Gregory might have guessed the truth; but ninety-nine out of a hundred, even if they had been equally inclined to kindness, would have blundered by some touch of charitable exaggeration. The doctor was better inspired. He knew the father well; in that white face of intelligence and suffering, he divined something of the son; and he told, without apology or adornment, the plain truth.

'When you had the measles, Mr Archibald, you had them gey and ill; and I thought you were going to slip between my fingers.' he said. 'Well, your father was anxious. How did I know it? says you. Simply because I am a trained observer. The sign that I saw him make, ten thousand would have missed; and perhaps – *perhaps*, I say, because he's a hard man to judge of – but perhaps he never made another. A strange thing to consider! It was this. One day I came to him: 'Hermiston,' said I, 'there's a change.' He never said a word, just glowered at me (if ye'll pardon the phrase) like a wild beast. 'A change for the better,' said I. And I distinctly heard him take his breath.'

The doctor left no opportunity for anti-climax; nodding his cocked hat (a piece of antiquity to which he clung) and repeating 'Distinctly' with raised eyebrows, he took his departure, and left Archie speechless in the street.

The anecdote might be called infinitely little, and yet its meaning for Archie was immense. 'I did not know the old man had so much blood in him.' He had never dreamed this sire of his, this aboriginal antique, this adamantine Adam, had even so much of a heart as to be moved in the least degree for another – and that other himself, who had insulted him! With the generosity of youth, Archie was instantly under arms upon the other side: had instantly created a new image of Lord Hermiston, that of a man who was all iron without and all sensibility within. The mind of the vile jester, the tongue that had pursued Duncan Jopp with unmanly insults, the unbeloved countenance that he had known and feared for so long, were all forgotten; and he hastened home, impatient to confess his misdeeds, impatient to throw himself on the mercy of this imaginary character.

He was not to be long without a rude awakening. It was in the gloaming when he drew near the doorstep of the lighted house, and was aware of the figure of his father approaching from the opposite side. Little daylight lingered; but on the door being opened, the strong yellow shine of the lamp gushed out upon the landing and shone full on Archie, as he stood, in the old-fashioned observance of respect, to yield precedence. The Judge came without haste, stepping stately and firm; his chin raised, his face (as he entered the lamplight) strongly illumined, his mouth set hard. There was never a wink of change in his expression; without looking to the right or left, he mounted the stair, passed close to Archie, and entered the house. Instinctively, the boy, upon his first coming, had made a movement to meet him; instinctively he recoiled against the railing, as the old man swept by him in a pomp of indignation. Words were needless; he knew all – perhaps more than all – and the hour of judgment was at hand.

It is possible that, in this sudden revulsion of hope, and before these symptoms of impending danger, Archie might have fled. But not even that was left to him. My lord, after hanging up his cloak and hat, turned round in the lighted entry, and made him an imperative and silent gesture with his thumb, and with the strange instinct of obedience, Archie followed him into the house.

All dinner-time there reigned over the Judge's table a palpable silence, and as soon as the solids were despatched he rose to his feet.

'M'Killup, tak' the wine into my room,' said he; and then to his son: 'Archie, you and me has to have a talk.'

It was at this sickening moment that Archie's courage, for the first and last time, entirely deserted him. 'I have an appointment,' said he.

'It'll have to be broken, then,' said Hermiston, and led the way into his study.

The lamp was shaded, the fire trimmed to a nicety, the table covered deep with orderly documents, the backs of law books made a frame upon all sides that was only broken by the window and the doors.

For a moment Hermiston warmed his hands at the fire, presenting his back to Archie; then suddenly disclosed on him the terrors of the Hanging Face.

'What's this I hear of ye?' he asked.

There was no answer possible to Archie.

'I'll have to tell ye, then,' pursued Hermiston. 'It seems ye've been skirling against the father that begot ye, and one of his Maijesty's Judges in this land; and that in the public street, and while an order of the Court was being executit. Forbye which, it would appear that ye've been airing your opeenions in a Coallege Debatin' Society'; he paused a moment: and then, with extraordinary bitterness, added: 'Ye damned eediot.'

'I had meant to tell you,' stammered Archie. 'I see you are well informed.'

'Muckle obleeged to ye,' said his lordship, and took his usual seat. 'And so you disapprove of Caapital Punishment?' he added.

'I am sorry, sir, I do,' said Archie.

'I am sorry, too,' said his lordship. 'And now, if you please, we shall approach this business with a little more parteecularity. I hear that at the hanging of Duncan Jopp – and man! ye had a fine client there – in the middle of all the riff-raff of the ceety, ye thought fit to cry out, "This is a damned murder, and my gorge rises at the man that haangit him."'

'No, sir, these were not my words,' cried Archie.

'What were yer words, then?' asked the Judge.

'I believe I said, "I denounce it as a murder!"' said the son.

'I beg your pardon – a God-defying murder. I have no wish to conceal the truth,' he added, and looked his father for a moment in the face.

'God, it would only need that of it next!' cried Hermiston. 'There was nothing about your gorge rising, then?'

'That was afterwards, my lord, as I was leaving the Speculative. I said I had been to see the miserable creature hanged, and my gorge rose at it.'

'Did ye, though?' said Hermiston. 'And I suppose ye knew who haangit him?'

'I was present at the trial, I ought to tell you that, I ought to explain. I ask your pardon beforehand for any expression that may seem undutiful. The position in which I stand is wretched,' said the unhappy hero, now fairly face to face with the business he had chosen. 'I have been reading some of your cases. I was present while Jopp was tried. It was a hideous business. Father, it was a hideous thing! Grant he was vile, why should you hunt him with a vileness equal to his own? It was done with glee

– that is the word – you did it with glee; and I looked on, God help me! with horror.'

'You're a young gentleman that doesna approve of Caapital Punishment,' said Hermiston. 'Weel, I'm an auld man that does. I was glad to get Jopp haangit, and what for would I pretend I wasna? You're all for honesty, it seems; you couldn't even steik your mouth on the public street. What for should I steik mines upon the bench, the King's officer, bearing the sword, a dreid to evildoers, as I was from the beginning, and as I will be to the end! Mair than enough of it! Heedious! I never gave twa thoughts to heediousness, I have no call to be bonny. I'm a man that gets through with my day's business, and let that suffice.'

The ring of sarcasm had died out of his voice as he went on; the plain words became invested with some of the dignity of the Justice-seat.

'It would be telling you if you could say as much,' the speaker resumed. 'But ye cannot. Ye've been reading some of my cases, ye say. But it was not for the law in them, it was to spy out your faither's nakedness, a fine employment in a son. You're splairging; you're running at lairge in life like a wild nowt. It's impossible you should think any longer of coming to the Bar. You're not fit for it; no splairger is. And another thing: son of mines or no son of mines, you have flung fylement in public on one of the Senators of the Coallege of Justice, and I would make it my business to see that ye were never admitted there yourself. There is a kind of a decency to be observit. Then comes the next of it – what am I to do with ye next? Ye'll have to find some kind of a trade, for I'll never support ye in idleset. What do ye fancy ye'll be fit for? The pulpit? Na, they could never get diveenity into that bloackhead. Him that the law of man whammles is no likely to do muckle better by the law of God. What would ye make of hell? Wouldna your gorge rise at that? Na, there's no room for splairgers under the fower quarters of John Calvin. What else is there? Speak up. Have ye got nothing of your own?'

'Father, let me go to the Peninsula,' said Archie. 'That's all I'm fit for – to fight.'

'All? quo' he!' returned the Judge. 'And it would be enough too, if I thought it. But I'll never trust ye so near the French, you that's so Frenchi-feed.'

'You do me injustice there, sir,' said Archie. 'I am loyal; I will not boast; but any interest I may have ever felt in the French –'

'Have ye been so loyal to me?' interrupted his father.

There came no reply.

'I think not,' continued Hermiston. 'And I would send no man to be a servant to the King, God bless him! that has proved such a shauchling son to his own faither. You can splairge here on Edinburgh street, and where's the hairm? It doesna play buff on me! And if there were twenty thousand eediots like yourself, sorrow a Duncan Jopp would hang the fewer. But there's no splairging possible in a camp; and if ye were to go to it, you would find out for yourself whether Lord Well'n'ton approves of caapital punishment or not. You a sodger!' he cried, with a sudden burst of scorn. 'Ye auld wife thesodgers would bray at ye like cuddies!'

As at the drawing of a curtain, Archie was aware of some illogicality in his position, and stood abashed. He had a strong impression, besides, of the essential valour of the old gentleman before him, how conveyed it would be hard to say.

'Well, have ye no other proposeetion?' said my lord again.

'You have taken this so calmly, sir that I cannot but stand ashamed,' began Archie.

'I'm nearer voamiting, though, than you would fancy,' said my lord.

The blood rose to Archie's brow.

'I beg your pardon, I should have said that you had accepted my affront . . . I admit it was an affront; I did not think to apologise, but I do, I ask your pardon; it will not be so again, I pass you my word of honour . . . I should have said that I admired your magnanimity with – this – offender,' Archie concluded with a gulp.

'I have no other son, ye see,' said Hermiston. 'A bonny one I have gotten! But I must just do the best I can wi' him, and what am I to do? If ye had been younger, I would have wheepit ye for this rideeculous exhibeetion. The way it is, I have just to grin and bear. But one thing is to be clearly understood. As a faither, I must grin and bear it; but if I had been the Lord Advocate instead of the Lord Justice-Clerk, son or no son, Mr Erchibald Weir would have been in a jyle the night.'

Archie was now dominated. Lord Hermiston was coarse and cruel; and yet the son was aware of a bloomless nobility, an ungracious abnegation of the man's self in the man's office. At every word, this sense of the greatness of Lord Hermiston's spirit struck more home; and along with it that of his own impotence, who had struck – and perhaps basely struck – at his own father, and not reached so far as to have even nettled him.

'I place myself in your hands without reserve,' he said.

'That's the first sensible word I've had of ye the night,' said Hermiston. 'I can tell ye, that would have been the end of it, the one way or the other; but it's better ye should come there yourself, than what I would have had to hirstle ye. Weel, by my way of it – and my way is the best – there's just the one thing it's possible that ye might be with decency, and that's a laird. Ye'll be out of hairm's way at the least of it. If ye have to rowt, ye can rowt amang the kye; and the maist feck of the caapital punishment ye're like to come across'll be guddling trouts. Now, I'm for no idle lairdies; every man has to work, if it's only at peddling ballants; to work, or to be wheeped, or to be haangit. If I set ye down at Hermiston I'll have to see you work that place the way it has never been workit yet; ye must ken about the sheep like a herd; ye must be my grieve there, and I'll see that I gain by ye. Is that understood?'

'I will do my best,' said Archie.

'Well, then, I'll send Kirstie word the morn, and ye can go yourself the day after,' said Hermiston. 'And just try to be less of an eediot!' he concluded with a freezing smile, and turned immediately to the papers on his desk.

IV

Late the same night, after a disordered walk, Archie was admitted into Lord Glenalmond's dining-room, where he sat with a book upon his knee, beside three frugal coals of fire. In his robes upon the bench, Glenalmond had a certain air of burliness: plucked of these, it was a maypole of a man that rose unsteadily from his chair to give his visitor welcome. Archie had suffered much in the last days, he had suffered again that evening; his face was white and drawn, his eyes wild and dark. But Lord Glenalmond greeted him without the least mark of surprise or curiosity.

'Come in, come in,' said he. 'Come in and take a seat. Carstairs' (to his servant), 'make up the fire, and then you can bring a bit of supper,' and again to Archie, with a very trivial accent: 'I was half expecting you,' he added.

'No supper,' said Archie. 'It is impossible that I should eat.'

'Not impossible,' said the tall old man, laying his hand upon his shoulder, 'and, if you will believe me, necessary.'

'You know what brings me?' said Archie, as soon as the servant had left the room.

'I have a guess, I have a guess,' replied Glenalmond. 'We will talk of it presently – when Carstairs has come and gone, and you have had a piece of my good Cheddar cheese and a pull at the porter tankard: not before.'

'It is impossible I should eat,' repeated Archie.

'Tut, tut!' said Lord Glenalmond. 'You have eaten nothing today, and I venture to add, nothing yesterday. There is no case that may not be made worse; this may be a very disagreeable business, but if you were to fall sick and die, it would be still more so, and for all concerned – for all concerned.'

'I see you must know all,' said Archie. 'Where did you hear it?'

'In the mart of scandal, in the Parliament House,' said Glenalmond. 'It runs riot below among the bar and the public, but it sifts up to us upon the bench, and rumour has some of her voices even in the divisions.'

Carstairs returned at this moment, and rapidly laid out a little supper; during which Lord Glenalmond spoke at large and a little vaguely on indifferent subjects, so that it might be rather said of him that he made a cheerful noise, than that he contributed to human conversation; and Archie sat upon the other side, not heeding him, brooding over his wrongs and errors.

But so soon as the servant was gone, he broke forth again at once. 'Who told my father? Who dared to tell him? Could it have been you?'

'No, it was not me,' said the Judge; 'although – to be quite frank with you, and after I had seen and warned you – it might have been me. I believe it was Glenkindie.'

'That shrimp!' cried Archie.

'As you say, that shrimp,' returned my lord; 'although really it is scarce a fitting mode of expression for one of the senators of the College of Justice. We were hearing the parties in a long, crucial case before the fifteen; Creech was moving at some length for an infeftment; when I saw Glenkindie lean forward to Hermiston with his hand over his mouth and make him a secret communication. No one could have guessed its nature from your father: from Glenkindie, yes, his malice sparked out of him a little grossly. But your father, no. A man of granite. The next moment he pounced upon Creech. "Mr Creech," says he, "I'll take a look of that sasine," and for thirty minutes after,' said Glenalmond, with a smile, 'Messrs. Creech and Co. were fighting a pretty uphill battle, which resulted, I need hardly add, in their total rout. The case was dismissed. No, I doubt if ever I heard Hermiston better inspired. He was literally rejoicing *in apicibus juris*.'

Archie was able to endure no longer. He thrust his plate away and interrupted the deliberate and insignificant stream of talk. 'Here,' he said, 'I have made a fool of myself, if I have not made something worse. Do you judge between us – judge between a father and a son. I can speak to you; it is not like ... I will tell you what I feel and what I mean to do; and you shall be the judge,' he repeated.

'I decline jurisdiction,' said Glenalmond, with extreme seriousness. 'But, my dear boy, if it will do you any good to talk, and if it will interest you at all to hear what I may choose to say when I have heard you, I am quite at your command. Let an old man say it, for once, and not need to blush: I love you like a son.'

There came a sudden sharp sound in Archie's throat. 'Ay,' he cried, 'and there it is! Love! Like a son! And how do you think I love my father?'

'Quietly, quietly,' says my lord.

'I will be very quiet,' replied Archie. 'And I will be baldly frank. I do not love my father; I wonder sometimes if I do not hate him. There's my shame; perhaps my sin; at least, and in the sight of God, not my fault. How was I to love him? He has never spoken to me, never smiled upon me; I do not think he ever touched me. You know the way he talks? You do not talk so, yet you can sit and hear him without shuddering, and I cannot. My soul is sick when he begins with it; I could smite him in the mouth. And all that's nothing. I was at the trial of this Jopp. You were not there, but you must have heard him often; the man's notorious for it, for being – look at my position! he's my father and this is how I have to speak of him – notorious for being a brute and cruel and a coward. Lord Glenalmond, I give you my word, when I came out of that Court, I longed to die – the shame of it was beyond my strength: but I – I –' he rose from his seat and began to pace the room in a disorder. 'Well, who am I? A boy, who have never been tried, have never done anything except this twopenny impotent folly with my father. But I tell you, my lord, and I know myself, I am at least that kind of a man – or that kind of a boy, if you prefer it – that I could die in torments rather than that anyone should suffer as that scoundrel suffered. Well, and what have I done? I see it now. I have made a fool of myself, as I said in the beginning; and I have gone back, and asked my father's pardon, and placed myself wholly in his hands – and he has sent me to Hermiston,' with a wretched smile, 'for life, I suppose – and what can I say? he strikes me as having done quite right, and let me off better than I had deserved.'

'My poor, dear boy!' observed Glenalmond. 'My poor dear and, if you will allow me to say so, very foolish boy! You are only discovering where you are; to one of your temperament, or of mine, a painful discovery. The world was not made for us; it was made for ten hundred millions of men, all different from each other and from us; there's no royal road there, we just have to sclamber and tumble. Don't think that I am at all disposed to be surprised; don't suppose that I ever think of blaming you; indeed I rather admire! But there fall to be offered one or two observations on the case which occur to me and which (if you will listen to them dispassionately) may be the means of inducing you to view the matter more calmly. First of all, I cannot acquit you of a good deal of what is called intolerance. You seem to have been very much offended because your father talks a little sculduddery after dinner, which it is perfectly licit for him to do, and which (although I am not very fond of it myself) appears to be entirely an affair of taste. Your father, I scarcely like to remind you, since it is so trite a commonplace, is older than yourself. At least, he is *major* and *sui juris*, and may please himself in the matter of his conversation. And, do you know, I wonder if he might not have as good an answer against you and me? We say we sometimes find him *coarse*, but I suspect he might retort that he finds us always dull. Perhaps a relevant exception.'

He beamed on Archie, but no smile could be elicited.

'And now,' proceeded the Judge, 'for "Archibald on Capital Punishment." This is a very plausible academic opinion; of course I do not and I cannot hold it; but that's not to say that many able and excellent persons have not done so in the past. Possibly, in the past also, I may have a little dipped myself in the same heresy. My third client, or possibly my fourth, was the means of a return in my opinions. I never saw the man I more believed in; I would have put my hand in the fire, I would have gone to the cross for him; and when it came to trial he was gradually pictured before me, by undeniable probation, in the light of so gross, so cold-blooded, and so black-hearted a villain, that I had a mind to have cast my brief upon the table. I was then boiling against the man with even a more tropical temperature than I had been boiling for him. But I said to myself: 'No, you have taken up his case; and because you have changed your mind it must not be suffered to let drop. All that rich tide of eloquence that you prepared last night with so much enthusiasm is out of place, and yet you must not desert him, you must say something.' So I said something, and I got him off. It made my reputation. But an experience of that kind is formative. A man must not bring his passions to the bar – or to the bench,' he added.

The story had slightly rekindled Archie's interest. 'I could never deny,' he began – 'I mean I can conceive that some men would be better dead. But who are we to know all the springs of God's unfortunate creatures? Who are we to trust ourselves where it seems that God Himself must think twice before He treads, and to do it with delight? Yes, with delight. *Tigris ut aspera.*'

'Perhaps not a pleasant spectacle,' said Glenalmond. 'And yet, do you know, I think somehow a great one.'

'I've had a long talk with him tonight,' said Archie.

'I was supposing so,' said Glenalmond.

'And he struck me – I cannot deny that he struck me as something very big,' pursued the son. 'Yes, he is big. He never spoke about himself; only about me. I suppose I admired him. The dreadful part –'

'Suppose we did not talk about that,' interrupted Glenalmond. 'You know it very well, it cannot in any way help that you should brood upon it, and I sometimes wonder whether you and I – who are a pair of sentimentalists – are quite good judges of plain men.'

'How do you mean?' asked Archie.

'*Fair* judges, I mean,' replied Glenalmond. 'Can we be just to them?

Do we not ask too much? There was a word of yours just now that impressed me a little when you asked me who we were to know all the springs of God's unfortunate creatures. You applied that, as I understood, to capital cases only. But does it – I ask myself – does it not apply all through? Is it any less difficult to judge of a good man or of a half-good man, than of the worst criminal at the bar? And may not each have relevant excuses?'

'Ah, but we do not talk of punishing the good,' cried Archie.

'No, we do not talk of it,' said Glenalmond. 'But I think we do it. Your father, for instance.'

'You think I have punished him?' cried Archie. Lord Glenalmond bowed his head.

'I think I have,' said Archie. 'And the worst is, I think he feels it! How much, who can tell, with such a being? But I think he does.'

'And I am sure of it,' said Glenalmond.

'Has he spoken to you, then?' cried Archie.

'O no,' replied the judge.

'I tell you honestly,' said Archie, 'I want to make it up to him. I will go, I have already pledged myself to go to Hermiston. That was to him. And now I pledge myself to you, in the sight of God, that I will close my mouth on capital punishment and all other subjects where our views may clash, for – how long shall I say? when shall I have sense enough? – ten years. Is that well?'

'It is well,' said my lord.

'As far as it goes,' said Archie. 'It is enough as regards myself, it is to lay down enough of my conceit. But as regards him, whom I have publicly insulted? What am I to do to him? How do you pay attentions to a – an Alp like that?'

'Only in one way,' replied Glenalmond. 'Only by obedience, punctual, prompt, and scrupulous.'

'And I promise that he shall have it,' answered Archie. 'I offer you my hand in pledge of it.'

'And I take your hand as a solemnity,' replied the judge. 'God bless you, my dear, and enable you to keep your promise. God guide you in the true way, and spare your days, and preserve to you your honest heart.' At that, he kissed the young man upon the forehead in a gracious, distant, antiquated way; and instantly launched, with a marked change of voice, into another subject. 'And now, let us replenish the tankard; and I believe if you will try my Cheddar again, you would find you had a better appetite. The Court has spoken and the case is dismissed.'

'No, there is one thing I must say,' cried Archie. 'I must say it in justice to himself. I know – I believe faithfully, slavishly, after our talk – he will never ask me anything unjust. I am proud to feel it, that we have that much in common, I am proud to say it to you.'

The Judge, with shining eyes, raised his tankard. 'And I think perhaps that we might permit ourselves a toast,' said he. 'I should like to propose the health of a man very different from me and very much my superior – a man from whom I have often differed, who has often (in the trivial expression) rubbed me the wrong way, but whom I have never ceased to respect and, I may add, to be not a little afraid of. Shall I give you his name?'

'The Lord Justice-Clerk, Lord Hermiston,' said Archie, almost with gaiety; and the pair drank the toast deeply.

It was not precisely easy to re-establish, after these emotional passages, the natural flow of conversation. But the Judge eked out what was wanting with kind looks, produced his snuff-box (which was very rarely seen) to fill in a pause, and at last, despairing of any further social success, was upon the point of getting down a book to read a favourite passage, when there came a rather startling summons at the front door, and Carstairs ushered in my Lord Glenkindie, hot from a midnight supper. I am not aware that Glenkindie was ever a beautiful object, being short, and gross-bodied, and with an expression of sensuality comparable to a bear's. At that moment, coming in hissing from many potations, with a flushed countenance and blurred eyes, he was strikingly contrasted with the tall, pale, kingly figure of Glenalmond. A rush of confused thought came over Archie – of shame that this was one of his father's elect friends; of pride, that at the least of it Hermiston could carry his liquor; and last of all, of rage, that he should have here under his eyes the man that had betrayed him. And then that too passed away; and he sat quiet, biding his opportunity.

The tipsy senator plunged at once into an explanation with Glenalmond. There was a point reserved yesterday, he had been able to make neither head nor tail of it, and seeing lights in the house, he had just dropped in for a glass of porter – and at this point he became aware of the third person. Archie saw the cod's mouth and the blunt lips of Glenkindie gape at him for a moment, and the recognition twinkle in his eyes.

'Who's this?' said he. 'What? is this possibly you, Don Quickshot? And how are ye? And how's your father? And what's all this we hear of you? It seems you're a most extraordinary leveller, by all tales. No king, no parliaments, and your gorge rises at the macers, worthy men! Hoot, toot! Dear, dear me! Your father's son too! Most rideeculous!'

Archie was on his feet, flushing a little at the reappearance of his unhappy figure of speech, but perfectly self-possessed. 'My lord – and you, Lord Glenalmond, my dear friend,' he began, 'this is a happy chance for me, that I can make my confession and offer my apologies to two of you at once.'

'Ah, but I don't know about that. Confession? It'll be judeecial, my young friend,' cried the jocular Glenkindie. 'And I'm afraid to listen to ye. Think if ye were to make me a coanvert!'

'If you would allow me, my lord,' returned Archie, 'what I have to say is very serious to me; and be pleased to be humorous after I am gone!'

'Remember, I'll hear nothing against the macers!' put in the incorrigible Glenkindie.

But Archie continued as though he had not spoken. 'I have played, both yesterday and today, a part for which I can only offer the excuse of youth. I was so unwise as to go to an execution; it seems I made a scene at the gallows; not content with which, I spoke the same night in a college society against capital punishment. This is the extent of what I have done, and in case you hear more alleged against me, I protest my innocence. I have expressed my regret already to my father, who is so good as to pass my conduct over – in a degree, and upon the condition that I am to leave my law studies . . .'

V

The road to Hermiston runs for a great part of the way up the valley of a stream, a favourite with anglers and with midges, full of falls and pools, and shaded by willows and natural woods of birch. Here and there, but at great distances, a byway branches off, and a gaunt farmhouse may be described above in a fold of the hill; but the more part of the time, the road would be quite empty of passage and the hills of habitation. Hermiston parish is one of the least populous in Scotland; and, by the time you came that length, you would scarce be surprised at the inimitable smallness of the kirk, a dwarfish, ancient place seated for fifty, and standing in a green by the burn-side among two-score gravestones. The manse close by, although no more than a cottage, is surrounded by the brightness of a flower-garden and the straw roofs of bees; and the whole colony, kirk and manse, garden and graveyard, finds harbourage in a grove of rowans, and is all the year round in a great silence broken only by the drone of the bees, the tinkle of the burn, and the bell on Sundays. A mile beyond the kirk the road leaves the valley by a precipitous ascent, and brings you a little after to the place of Hermiston, where it comes to an end in the back-yard before the coach-house. All beyond and about is the great field of the hills; the plover, the curlew, and the lark cry there; the wind blows as it blows in a ship's rigging, hard and cold and pure; and the hill-tops huddle one behind another like a herd of cattle into the sunset.

The house was sixty years old, unsightly, comfortable; a farmyard and a kitchen-garden on the left, with a fruit wall where little hard green pears came to their maturity about the end of October.

The policy (as who should say the park) was of some extent, but very ill reclaimed; heather and moorfowl had crossed the boundary wall and spread and roosted within; and it would have tasked a landscape gardener to say where policy ended and unpolicied nature began. My lord had been led by the influence of Mr Sheriff Scott into a considerable design of planting; many acres were accordingly set out with fir, and the little feathery besoms gave a false scale and lent a strange air of a toy-shop to the moors. A great, rooty sweetness of bogs was in the air, and at all seasons an infinite melancholy piping of hill birds. Standing so high and with so little shelter, it was a cold, exposed house, splashed by showers, drenched by continuous rains that made the gutters to spout, beaten upon and buffeted by all the winds of heaven; and the prospect would be often black with tempest, and often white with the snows of winter. But the house was wind and weather proof, the hearths were kept bright, and the rooms pleasant with live fires of peat; and Archie might sit of an evening and hear the squalls bugle on the moorland, and watch the fire prosper in the earthy fuel, and the smoke winding up the chimney, and drink deep of the pleasures of shelter.

Solitary as the place was, Archie did not want neighbours. Every night, if he chose, he might go down to the manse and share a 'brewst' of toddy with the minister – a hare-brained ancient gentleman, long and light and still active, though his knees were loosened with age, and his voice broke continually in childish trebles – and his lady wife, a heavy, comely dame, without a word to say for herself beyond good-even and good-day. Harum-scarum, clodpole young lairds of the neighbourhood paid him the compliment of a visit. Young Hay of Romanes rode down to call, on his crop-eared pony; young Pringle of Drumanno came up on his bony grey. Hay remained on the hospitable field, and must be carried to bed; Pringle got somehow to his saddle about 3 a.m., and (as Archie stood with the lamp on the upper doorstep) lurched, uttered a senseless view-holloa, and vanished out of the small circle of illumination like a wraith. Yet a minute or two longer the clatter of his breakneck flight was audible, then it was cut off by the intervening steepness of the hill; and again, a great while after, the renewed beating of phantom horse-hoofs, far in the valley of the Hermiston, showed that the horse at least, if not his rider, was still on the homeward way.

There was a Tuesday club at the 'Cross-keys' in Crossmichael, where the young bloods of the countryside congregated and drank deep on a percentage of the expense, so that he was left gainer who should have drunk the most. Archie had no great mind to this diversion, but he took it like a duty laid upon him, went with a decent regularity, did his manfullest with the liquor, held up his head in the local jests, and got home again and was able to put up his horse, to the admiration of Kirstie and the lass that helped her. He dined at Driffel, supped at Windielaws. He went to the new year's ball at Huntsfield and was made welcome, and thereafter rode to hounds with my Lord Muirfell, upon whose name, as that of a legitimate Lord of Parliament, in a work so full of Lords of Session, my pen should pause reverently. Yet the same fate attended him here as in Edinburgh. The habit of solitude tends to perpetuate itself, and an austerity of which he was quite unconscious, and a pride which seemed arrogance, and perhaps was chiefly shyness, discouraged and offended his new companions. Hay did not return more than twice, Pringle never at all, and there came a time when Archie even desisted from the Tuesday Club, and became in all things – what he had had the name of almost from the first – the Recluse of Hermiston. High-nosed Miss Pringle of Drumanno and high-stepping Miss Marshall of the Mains were understood to have had a difference of opinion about him the day after the ball – he was none the wiser, he could not suppose himself to be remarked by these entrancing ladies. At the ball itself my Lord Muirfell's daughter, the Lady Flora, spoke to him twice, and the second time with a touch of appeal, so that her colour rose and her voice trembled a little in his ear, like a passing grace in music. He stepped back with a heart on fire, coldly and not ungracefully excused himself, and a little after watched her dancing with young Drumanno of the empty laugh, and was harrowed at the sight, and raged to himself that this was a world in which it was given to Drumanno to please, and to himself only to stand aside and envy. He seemed excluded, as of right, from the favour of such society – seemed to extinguish mirth wherever he came, and was quick to feel the wound, and desist, and retire into solitude. If he had but understood the figure he presented and the impression he made on these bright eyes and tender hearts; if he had but guessed that the Recluse of Hermiston, young, graceful, well spoken, but always cold, stirred the maidens of the county with the charm of Byronism when Byronism was new, it may be questioned whether his destiny might not even yet have been modified. It may be questioned, and I think it should be doubted. It was in his horoscope to be parsimonious of pain to himself, or of the chance of pain, even to the avoidance of any opportunity of pleasure; to have a Roman sense of duty, an instinctive aristocracy of manners and taste; to be the son of Adam Weir and Jean Rutherford.

Kirstie was now over fifty, and might have sat to a sculptor. Long of limb, and still light of foot, deep-breasted, robust-loined, her golden hair not yet mingled with any trace of silver, the years had but caressed and embellished her. By the lines of a rich and vigorous maternity, she seemed destined to be the bride of heroes and the mother of their children; and behold, by the iniquity of fate, she had passed through her youth alone, and drew near to the confines of age, a childless woman. The tender ambitions that she had received at birth had been, by time and disappointment, diverted into a certain barren zeal of industry and fury of interference. She carried her thwarted ardours into housework, she washed floors with her empty heart. If she could not win the love of one with love, she must dominate all by her temper. Hasty, wordy, and wrathful, she had a drawn quarrel with most of her neighbours, and with the others not much more than armed neutrality. The grieve's wife had been 'sneisty'; the sister of the gardener who kept house for him had shown herself 'upsitten'; and she wrote to Lord Hermiston about once a year demanding the discharge of the offenders, and justifying the demand by much wealth of detail. For it must not be supposed that the quarrel rested with the wife and did not take in the husband also – or with the gardener's sister, and did not speedily include the gardener himself. As the upshot of all this petty quarrelling and intemperate speech, she was practically excluded (like a lightkeeper on his tower) from the comforts of human association; except with her own indoor drudge, who, being but a lassie and entirely at her mercy, must submit to the shifty weather of 'the mistress's' moods without complaint, and be willing to take buffets or caresses according to the temper of the hour. To Kirstie, thus situate and in the Indian summer of her heart, which was slow to submit to age, the gods sent this equivocal good thing of Archie's presence. She had known him in the cradle and paddled him when he misbehaved; and yet, as she had not so much as set eyes on him since he was eleven and had his last serious illness, the tall, slender, refined, and rather melancholy young gentleman of twenty came upon her with the shock of a new acquaintance. He was 'Young Hermiston,' 'the laird himsel'': he had an air of distinctive superiority, a cold straight glance of his black eyes, that abashed the woman's tantrums in the beginning, and therefore the possibility of any quarrel was excluded. He was new, and therefore immediately aroused her curiosity; he was reticent, and kept it awake. And lastly he was dark and she fair, and he was male and she female, the everlasting fountains of interest.

Her feeling partook of the loyalty of a clanswoman, the hero-worship of a maiden aunt, and the idolatry due to a god. No matter what he had asked of her, ridiculous or tragic, she would have done it and joyed to do it. Her passion, for it was nothing less, entirely filled her. It was a rich physical pleasure to make his bed or light his lamp for him when he was absent, to pull off his wet boots or wait on him at dinner when he returned. A young man who should have so doted on the idea, moral and physical, of any woman, might be properly described as being in love, head and heels, and would have behaved himself accordingly. But Kirstie – though her heart leaped at his coming footsteps – though, when he patted her shoulder, her face brightened for the day – had not a hope or thought beyond the present moment and its perpetuation to the end of time. Till the end of time she would have had nothing altered, but still continue delightedly to serve her idol, and be repaid (say twice in the month) with a clap on the shoulder.

I have said her heart leaped – it is the accepted phrase. But rather, when she was alone in any chamber of the house, and heard his foot passing on the corridors, something in her bosom rose slowly until her breath was suspended, and as slowly fell again with a deep sigh, when the steps had passed and she was disappointed of her eyes' desire. This perpetual hunger and thirst of his presence kept her all day on the alert. When he went forth at morning, she would stand and follow him with admiring looks. As it grew late and drew to the time of his return, she would steal forth to a corner of the policy wall and be seen standing there sometimes by the hour together, gazing with shaded eyes, waiting the exquisite and barren pleasure of his view a mile off on the mountains. When at night she had trimmed and gathered the fire, turned down his bed, and laid out his nightgear – when there was no more to be done for the king's pleasure, but to remember him fervently in her usually very tepid prayers, and go to bed brooding upon his perfections, his future career, and what she should give him the next day for dinner – there still remained before her one more opportunity; she was still to take in the tray and say good-night. Sometimes Archie would glance up from his book with a preoccupied nod and a perfunctory salution which was in truth a dismissal; sometimes – and by degrees more often – the volume would be laid aside, he would meet her coming with a look of relief; and the conversation would be engaged, last out the supper, and be prolonged till the small hours by the waning fire. It was no wonder that Archie was fond of company after his solitary days; and Kirstie, upon her side, exerted all the arts of her vigorous nature to ensnare his attention. She would keep back some piece of news during dinner to be fired off with the entrance of the supper tray, and form as it were the *lever de rideau* of the evening's entertainment. Once he had heard her tongue wag, she made sure of the result. From one subject to another she moved by insidious transitions, fearing the least silence, fearing almost to give him time for an answer lest it should slip into a hint of separation. Like so many people of her class, she was a brave narrator; her place was on the hearthrug and she made it a rostrum, mimeing her stories as she told them, fitting them with vital detail, spinning them out with endless 'quo' he's' and, 'quo' she's,' her voice sinking into a whisper over the supernatural or the horrific; until she would suddenly spring up in affected surprise, and pointing to the clock, 'Mercy, Mr Archie!' she would say, 'whatten a time o' night is this of it! God forgive me for a daft wife!' So it befell, by good management, that she was not only the first to begin these nocturnal conversations, but invariably the first to break them off; so she managed to retire and not to be dismissed.

Such an unequal intimacy has never been uncommon in Scotland, where the clan spirit survives; where the servant tends to spend her life in the same service, a helpmeet at first, then a tyrant, and at last a pensioner; where, besides, she is not necessarily destitute of the pride of birth, but is, perhaps, like Kirstie, a connection of her master's, and at least knows the legend of her own family, and may count kinship with some illustrious dead. For that is the mark of the Scot of all classes: that he stands in an attitude towards the past unthinkable to Englishmen, and remembers and cherishes the memory of his forebears, good or bad; and there burns alive in him a sense of identity with the dead even to the twentieth generation. No more characteristic instance could be found than in the family of Kirstie Elliott. They were all, and Kirstie the first of all, ready and eager to pour forth the particulars of their genealogy, embellished with every detail that memory had handed down or fancy fabricated; and, behold! from every ramification of that tree there dangled a halter. The Elliotts themselves have had a chequered history; but these Elliotts deduced, besides, from three of the most unfortunate of the border clans – the Nicksons, the Ellwalds, and the Crozers. One ancestor after another might be seen appearing a moment out of the rain and the hill mist upon his furtive business, speeding home, perhaps, with a paltry booty of lame horses and lean kine, or squealing and dealing death in some moorland feud of the ferrets and the wild cats. One after another closed his obscure adventures in mid-air, triced up to the arm of the royal gibbet or the Baron's dule-tree. For the rusty blunderbuss of Scots criminal justice, which usually hurt nobody but jurymen, became a weapon of

precision for the Nicksons, the Ellwalds, and the Crozers. The exhilaration of their exploits seemed to haunt the memories of their descendants
alone, and the shame to be forgotten. Pride glowed in their bosoms to
publish their relationship to 'Andrew Ellwald of the Laverockstanes,
called "Unchancy Dand," who was justifeed wi' seeven mair of the same
name at Jeddart in the days of King James the Sax.' In all this tissue of
crime and misfortune, the Elliotts of Cauldstaneslap had one boast which
must appear legitimate: the males were gallows-birds, born outlaws,
petty thieves, and deadly brawlers; but, according to the same tradition,
the females were all chaste and faithful. The power of ancestry on the
character is not limited to the inheritance of cells. If I buy ancestory by
the gross from the benevolence of Lyon King of Arms, my grandson (if
he is Scottish) will feel a quickening emulation of their deeds. The men
of the Elliotts were proud, lawless, violent as of right, cherishing and
prolonging a tradition. In like manner with the women. And the woman,
essentially passionate and reckless, who crouched on the rug, in the shine
of the peat fire, telling these tales, had cherished through life a wild
integrity of virtue.

Her father Gilbert had been deeply pious, a savage disciplinarian in
the antique style, and withal a notorious smuggler. 'I mind when I was
a bairn getting mony a skelp and being shoo'd to bed like pou'try,' she
would say. 'That would be when the lads and their bit kegs were on the
road. We've had the riffraff of two-three counties in our kitchen, mony's
the time, betwix' the twelve and the three; and their lanterns would be
standing in the forecourt, ay, a score o' them at once. But there was nae
ungodly talk permitted at Cauldstaneslap. My faither was a consistent
man in walk and conversation; just let slip an aith, and there was the
door to ye! He had that zeal for the Lord, it was a fair wonder to hear
him pray, but the family has aye had a gift that way.' This father was
twice married, once to a dark woman of the old Ellwald stock, by whom
he had Gilbert, presently of Cauldstaneslap; and, secondly, to the mother
of Kirstie. 'He was an auld man when he married her, a fell auld man
wi' a muckle voice – you could hear him rowting from the top o' the
Kye-skairs,' she said; 'but for her, it appears she was a perfit wonder. It
was gentle blood she had, Mr Archie, for it was your ain. The countryside gaed gyte about her and her gowden hair. Mines is no to be mentioned
wi' it, and there's few weemen has mair hair than what I have, or yet a

bonnier colour. Often would I tell my dear Miss Jeannie – that was your mother, dear, she was cruel ta'en up about her hair, it was unco' tender, ye see – "Houts, Miss Jeannie," I would say, "just fling your washes and your French dentifrishes in the back o' the fire, for that's the place for them; and awa' down to a burnside, and wash yersel' in cauld hill water, and dry your bonny hair in the caller wind o' the muirs, the way that my mother aye washed hers, and that I have aye made it a practice to have wishen mines – just you do what I tell ye, my dear, and ye'll give me news of it! Ye'll have hair, and routh of hair, a pigtail as thick's my arm," I said, "and the bonniest colour like the clear gowden guineas, so as the lads in kirk'll no can keep their eyes off it!" Weel, it lasted out her time, puir thing! I cuttit a lock of it upon her corp that was lying there sae cauld. I'll show it ye some of thir days if ye're good. But, as I was sayin', my mither –'

On the death of the father there remained golden-haired Kirstie, who took service with her distant kinsfolk, the Rutherfords, and black-a-vised Gilbert, twenty years older, who farmed the Cauldstaneslap, married, and begot four sons between 1773 and 1784, and a daughter, like a post-script, in '97, the year of Camperdown and Cape St Vincent. It seemed it was a tradition in the family to wind up with a belated girl. In 1804, at the age of sixty, Gilbert met an end that might be called heroic. He was due home from market any time from eight at night till five in the morning, and in any condition from the quarrelsome to the speechless, for he maintained to that age the goodly customs of the Scots farmer. It was known on this occasion that he had a good bit of money to bring home; the word had gone round loosely. The laird had shown his guineas, and if anybody had but noticed it, there was an ill-looking, vagabond crew, the scum of Edinburgh, that drew out of the market long ere it was dusk and took the hill-road by Hermiston, where it was not to be believed that they had lawful business. One of the countryside, one Dickieson, they took with them to be their guide, and dear he paid for it! Of a sudden in the ford of the Broken Dykes, this vermin clan fell on the laird, six to one, and him three parts asleep, having drunk hard. But it is ill to catch an Elliott. For a while, in the night and the black water that was deep as to his saddle-girths, he wrought with his staff like a smith at his smithy, and great was the sound of oaths and blows. With that the ambuscade was burst, and he rode for home with a pistol-ball in him, three knife wounds, the loss of his front teeth, a broken rib and bridle, and a dying horse. That was a race with death that the laird rode! In the mirk night, with his broken bridle and his head swimming, he dug his spurs to the rowels in the horse's side, and the horse, that was even worse off than himself, the poor creature! screamed out loud like a person as he went, so that the hills echoed with it, and the folks at Cauldstaneslap got to their feet about the table and looked at each other with white faces. The horse fell dead at the yard gate, the laird won the length of the house and fell there on the threshold. To the son that raised him he gave the bag of money. 'Hae,' said he. All the way up the thieves had seemed to him to be at his heels, but now the hallucination left him – he saw them again in the place of the ambuscade – and the thirst of vengeance seized on his dying mind. Raising himself and pointing with an imperious finger into the black night from which he had come, he uttered the single command, 'Brocken Dykes,' and fainted. He had never been loved, but he had been feared in honour. At that sight, at that word, gasped out at them from a toothless and bleeding mouth, the old Elliott spirit awoke with a shout in the four sons. 'Wanting the hat,' continues my author, Kirstie, whom I but haltingly follow, for she told this tale like one inspired, 'wanting guns, for there wasna twa grains o' pouder in the house, wi' nae mair weepons than their sticks into their hands, the fower o' them took the road. Only Hob, and that was the eldest, hunkered at the doorsill where the blood had rin, fyled his hand wi' it, and haddit it up to Heeven in the way o' the auld Border aith. "Hell shall have her ain this nicht!" he raired, and rode forth upon that earrand.' It was three miles to Broken Dykes, downhill, and a sore road. Kirstie has seen men from Edinburgh dismounting there in plain day to lead their horses. But the four brothers rode it as if Auld Hornie were behind and Heaven in front. Come to the ford, and there was Dickieson. By all tales, he was not dead, but breathed and reared upon his elbow, and cried out to them for help. It was at a graceless face that he asked mercy. As soon as Hob saw, by the glint of the lantern, the eyes shining and the whiteness of the teeth in the man's face, 'Damn you!' says he; 'ye hae your teeth, hae ye?' and rode his horse to and fro upon that human remnant. Beyond that, Dandie must dismount with the lantern to be their guide; he was the youngest son, scarce twenty at the time. 'A' nicht long they gaed in the wet heath and jennipers, and whaur they gaed they neither knew nor cared, but just followed the bluid-stains and the foot-prints o' their faither's murderers. And a' nicht Dandie had his nose to the grund like a tyke, and the ithers followed and spak' naething, neither black nor white. There was nae noise to be heard, but just the sough of the swalled burns, and Hob, the dour yin, risping his teeth as he gaed.' With the first glint of the morning they saw they were on the drove road, and at that the four stopped and had a dram to their breakfasts, for they knew that Dand must have guided them right, and the rogues could be but little ahead, hot foot for Edinburgh by the way of the Pentland Hills. By eight o'clock they had word of them – a shepherd had seen four men 'uncoly mishandled' go by in the last hour. 'That's yin a piece,' says Clem, and swung his cudgel. 'Five o' them!' says Hob. 'God's death, but the faither was a man! And him drunk!' And then there befell them what my author termed 'a sair misbegowk,' for they were overtaken by a posse of mounted neighbours come to aid in the pursuit. Four sour faces looked on the reinforcement. 'The Deil's broughten you!' said Clem, and they rode thenceforward in the rear of the party with hanging heads. Before ten they had found and secured the rogues, and by three of the afternoon, as they rode up the Vennel with their prisoners, they were aware of a concourse of people bearing in their midst something that dripped. 'For the boady of the saxt,' pursued Kirstie, 'wi' his head smashed like a hazelnit, had been a' that nicht in the chairge o' Hermiston Water, and it dunting it on the stanes, and grunding it on the shallows, and flinging the deid thing heels-ower-hurdie at the Fa's o' Spango; and in the first o' the day, Tweed had got a hold o' him and carried him off like a wind, for it was uncoly swalled, and raced wi' him, bobbing under brae-sides, and was long playing with the creature in the drumlie lynns under the castle, and at the hinder end of all cuist him up on the starling of Crossmichael brig. Sae there they were a'thegither at last (for Dickieson had been brought in on a cart long syne), and folk could see what mainner o' man my brither had been that had held his head again sax and saved the siller, and him drunk!' Thus died of honourable injuries and in the savour of fame Gilbert Elliott of the Cauldstaneslap; but his sons had scarce less glory out of the business. Their savage haste, the skill with which Dand had found and followed the trail, the barbarity to the wounded Dickieson (which was like an open secret in the county), and the doom which it was currently supposed they had intended for the others, struck and stirred popular imagination. Some century earlier the last of the minstrels might have fashioned the last of the ballads out of that Homeric fight and chase; but the spirit was dead, or had been reincarnated already in Mr Sheriff Scott, and the degenerate moorsmen must be content to tell the tale in prose, and to make of the 'Four Black Brothers' a unit after the fashion of the 'Twelve Apostles' or the 'Three Musketeers.'

Robert, Gilbert, Clement, and Andrew – in the proper Border diminutives, Hob, Gib, Clem, and Dand Elliott – these ballad heroes, had much in common; in particular, their high sense of the family and the family honour; but they went diverse ways, and prospered and failed in different businesses. According to Kirstie, 'they had a' bees in their bonnets but Hob.' Hob the laird was, indeed, essentially a decent man. An elder of the Kirk, nobody had heard an oath upon his lips, save perhaps thrice or so at the sheep-washing, since the chase of his father's murderers. The figure he had shown on that eventful night disappeared as if swallowed by a trap. He who had ecstatically dipped his hand in the red blood, he who had ridden down Dickieson, became, from that moment on, a stiff and rather graceless model of the rustic proprieties; cannily profiting by the high war prices, and yearly stowing away a little nest-egg in the bank against calamity; approved of and sometimes consulted by the greater lairds for the massive and placid sense of what he said, when he could be induced to say anything; and particularly valued by the minister, Mr Torrance, as a right-hand man in the parish, and a model to parents. The transfiguration had been for the moment only; some Barbarossa, some old Adam of our ancestors, sleeps in all of us till the fit circumstance shall call it into action; and, for as sober as he now seemed, Hob had given once for all the measure of the devil that haunted him. He was married, and, by reason of the effulgence of that legendary night, was adored by his wife. He had a mob of little lusty, barefoot children who marched in a caravan the long miles to school, the stages of whose pilgrimage were marked by acts of spoliation and mischief, and who were qualified in the countryside as 'fair pests.' But in the house, if 'faither was in,' they were quiet as mice. In short, Hob moved through life in a great peace – the reward of anyone who shall have killed his man, with any formidable and figurative circumstance, in the midst of a country gagged and swaddled with civilisation.

It was a current remark that the Elliotts were 'guid and bad, like sanguishes'; and certainly there was a curious distinction, the men of business coming alternately with the dreamers. The second brother, Gib, was a weaver by trade, had gone out early into the world to Edinburgh, and come home again with his wings singed. There was an exaltation in his nature which had led him to embrace with enthusiasm the principles of the French Revolution, and had ended by bringing him under the hawse of my Lord Hermiston in that furious onslought of his upon the Liberals, which sent Muir and Palmer into exile and dashed the party into chaff. It was whispered that my lord, in his great scorn for the movement, and prevailed upon a little by a sense of neighbourliness, had given Gib a hint. Meeting him one day in the Potterrow, my lord had stopped in front of him: 'Gib, ye eediot,' he had said, 'what's this I hear of you? Poalitics, poalitics, poalitics, weaver's poalitics, is the way of it, I hear. If ye arena a'thegither dozened with eediocy, ye'll gang your ways back to Cauldstaneslap, and ca' your loom, and ca' your loom, man!' And Gilbert had taken him at the word and returned, with an expedition almost to be called flight, to the house of his father. The clearest of his inheritance was that family gift of prayer of which Kirstie had boasted; and the baffled politician now turned his attention to religious matters – or, as others said, to heresy and schism. Every Sunday morning he was in Crossmichael, where he had gathered together, one by one, a sect of about a dozen persons, who called themselves 'God's Remnant of the True Faithful,' or, for short, 'God's Remnant.' To the profane, they were known as 'Gib's Deils.' Bailie Sweedie, a noted humorist in the town, vowed that the proceedings always opened to the tune of 'The Deil Fly Away with the Exciseman,' and that the sacrament was dispensed in the form of hot whisky-toddy; both wicked hits at the evangelist, who had been suspected of smuggling in his youth, and had been overtaken (as the phrase went) on the streets of Crossmichael one Fair day. It was known that every Sunday they prayed for a blessing on the arms of Bonaparte. For this 'God's Remnant,' as they were 'skailing' from the cottage that did duty for a temple, had been repeatedly stoned by the bairns, and Gib himself hooted by a squadron of Border volunteers in which his own brother, Dand, rode in a uniform and with a drawn sword. The 'Remnant' were believed, besides, to be 'antinomian in principle,' which might otherwise have been a serious charge, but the way public opinion then blew it was quite swallowed up and forgotten in the scandal about Bonaparte. For the rest, Gilbert had set up his loom in an outhouse at Cauldstaneslap, where he laboured assiduously six days of the week. His brothers, appalled by his political opinions, and willing to avoid dissension in the household, spoke but little to him; he less to them, remaining absorbed in the study of the Bible and almost constant prayer. The gaunt weaver was dry-nurse at Cauldstaneslap, and the bairns loved him dearly. Except when he was carrying an infant in his arms, he was rarely seen to smile – as, indeed, there were few smilers in that family. When his sister-in-law rallied him, and proposed that he should get a wife and bairns of his own, since he was so fond of them, 'I have no clearness of mind upon that point,' he would reply. If nobody called him in to dinner, he stayed out. Mrs Hob, a hard, unsympathetic woman, once tried the experiment. He went without food all day, but at dusk, as the light began to fail him, he came into the house of his own accord, looking puzzled. 'I've had a great gale of prayer upon my speerit,' said he. 'I canna mind sae muckle's what I had for denner.' The creed of God's Remnant was justified in the life of its founder. 'And yet I dinna ken,' said Kirstie. 'He's maybe no more stockfish than his neeghbours! He rode wi' the rest o' them, and had a good stamach to the work, by a' that I hear! God's Remnant! The deil's clavers! There wasna muckle Christianity in the way Hob guided Johnny Dickieson, at the least of it; but Guid kens! Is he a Christian even? He might be a Mahommedan or a Deevil or a Fireworshipper, for what I ken.'

The third brother had his name on a door-plate, no less, in the city of Glasgow, 'Mr Clement Elliott,' as long as your arm. In his case, that spirit of innovation which had shown itself timidly in the case of Hob by the admission of new manures, and which had run to waste with Gilbert in subversive politics and heretical religions, bore useful fruit in many ingenious mechanical improvements. In boyhood, from his addiction to strange devices of sticks and string, he had been counted the most eccentric of the family. But that was all by now; and he was a partner of his firm, and looked to die a bailie. He too had married, and was rearing a plentiful family in the smoke and din of Glasgow; he was wealthy, and could have bought out his brother, the cocklaird, six times over, it was whispered; and when he slipped away to Cauldstaneslap for a well-earned holiday, which he did as often as he was able, he astonished the neighbours with his broadcloth, his beaver hat, and the ample piles of his neckcloth. Though an eminently solid man at bottom, after the pattern of Hob, he had contracted a certain Glasgow briskness and *aplomb* which set him off. All the other Elliotts were as lean as a rake, but Clement was laying on fat, and he panted sorely when he must get into his boots. Dand said, chuckling: 'Ay, Clem has the elements of a corporation.' 'A provost and corporation,' returned Clem. And his readiness was much admired.

The fourth brother, Dand, was a shepherd to his trade, and by starts, when he could bring his mind to it, excelled in the business. Nobody could train a dog like Dandie; nobody, through the peril of great storms in the winter time, could do more gallantly. But if his dexterity were exquisite, his diligence was but fitful; and he served his brother for bed and board, and a trifle of pocket-money when he asked for it. He loved money well enough, knew very well how to spend it, and could make a shrewd bargain when he liked. But he preferred a vague knowledge that he was well to windward to any counted coins in the pocket; he felt himself richer so. Hob would expostulate: 'I'm an amature herd.' Dand would reply, 'I'll keep your sheep to you when I'm so minded, but I'll keep my liberty too. Thir's no man can coandescend on what I'm worth.' Clem would expound to him the miraculous results of compound interest, and recommend investments. 'Ay, man?' Dand would say; 'and do you think if I took Hob's siller, that I wouldna drink it or wear it on the lassies? And, anyway, my kingdom is no of this world. Either I'm a poet or else I'm nothing.' Clem would remind him of old age. 'I'll die young, like Robbie Burns,' he would say stoutly. No question but he had a certain accomplishment in minor verse. His 'Hermiston Burn,' with its pretty refrain –

> 'I love to gang thinking whaur ye gang linking,
> Hermiston burn, in the howe;'

his 'Auld, auld Elliotts, clay-cauld Elliotts, dour, bauld Elliotts of auld,' and his really fascinating piece about the Praying Weaver's Stone, had gained him in the neighbourhood the reputation, still possible in Scotland, of a local bard; and, though not printed himself, he was recognised by others who were and who had become famous. Walter Scott owed to Dandie the text of the 'Raid of Wearie' in the *Minstrelsy*; and made him welcome at his house, and appreciated his talents, such as they were, with all his usual generosity. The Ettrick Shepherd was his sworn crony; they would meet, drink to excess, roar out their lyrics in each other's faces, and quarrel and make it up again till bedtime. And besides these recognitions, almost to be called official, Dandie was made welcome for the sake of his gift through the farmhouses of several contiguous dales, and was thus exposed to manifold temptations which he rather sought than fled. He had figured on the stool of repentance, for once fulfilling to the letter the tradition of his hero and model. His humorous verses to Mr. Torrance on that occasion – 'Kenspeckle here my lane I stand' – unfortunately too indelicate for further citation, ran through the country like a fiery cross; they were recited, quoted, paraphrased, and laughed over as far away as Dumfries on the one hand and Dunbar on the other.

These four brothers were united by a close bond, the bond of that mutual admiration – or rather mutual hero-worship – which is so strong among the members of secluded families who have much ability and little culture. Even the extremes admired each other. Hob, who had as much poetry as the tongs, professed to find pleasure in Dand's verses; Clem, who had no more religion than Claverhouse, nourished a heart-felt, at least an open-mouthed, admiration of Gib's prayers; and Dandie followed with relish the rise of Clem's fortunes. Indulgence followed hard on the heels of admiration. The laird, Clem, and Dand, who were Tories and patriots of the hottest quality, excused to themselves, with a certain bashfulness, the radical and revolutionary heresies of Gib. By another division of the family, the laird, Clem, and Gib, who were men exactly virtuous, swallowed the dose of Dand's irregularities as a kind of clog or drawback in the mysterious providence of God affixed to bards, and distinctly probative of poetical genius. To appreciate the simplicity of their mutual admiration it was necessary to hear Clem, arrived upon one of his visits, and dealing in a spirit of continuous irony with the affairs and personalities of that great city of Glasgow where he lived and transacted business. The various personages, ministers of the church, municipal officers, mercantile big-wigs, whom he had occasion to introduce, were all alike denigrated, all served but as reflectors to cast back a flattering sidelight on the house of Cauldstaneslap. The Provost, for whom Clem by exception entertained a measure of respect, he would liken to Hob. 'He minds me o' the laird there,' he would say. 'He has some of Hob's grand, whunstane sense, and the same way with him of steiking his mouth when he's no very pleased.' And Hob, all unconscious, would draw down his upper lip and produce, as if for comparison, the formidable grimace referred to. The unsatisfactory incumbent of St Enoch's Kirk was thus briefly dismissed: 'If he had but twa fingers o' Gib's, he would waken them up.' And Gib, honest man! would look down and secretly smile. Clem was a spy whom they had sent out into the world of men. He had come back with the good news that there was nobody to compare with the Four Black Brothers, no position that they would not adorn, no official that it would not be well they should replace, no interest of mankind, secular or spiritual, which would not immediately bloom under their supervision. The excuse of their folly is in two words: scarce the breadth of a hair divided them from the peasantry. The measure of their sense is this: that these symposia of rustic vanity were kept entirely within the family, like some secret ancestral practice. To the world their serious faces were never deformed by the suspicion of any simper of self-contentment. Yet it was known. 'They hae a guid pride o' themsel's!' was the word in the countryside.

Lastly, in a Border story, there should be added their 'two-names.' Hob was The Laird. 'Roy ne puis, prince ne daigne'; he the laird of Cauldstaneslap – say fifty acres – *ipsissimus*. Clement was Mr Elliott, as upon his door-plate, the earlier Dafty having been discarded as no longer applicable, and indeed only a reminder of misjudgment and the imbecility of the public; and the youngest, in honour of his perpetual wanderings, was known by the sobriquet of Randy Dand.

It will be understood that not all this information was communicated by the aunt, who had too much of the family failing herself to appreciate it thoroughly in others. But as time went on, Archie began to observe an omission in the family chronicle.

'Is there not a girl too?' he asked.

'Ay: Kirstie. She was named for me, or my grandmother at least – it's the same thing,' returned the aunt, and went on again about Dand, whom she secretly preferred by reason of his gallantries.

'But what is your niece like?' said Archie at the next opportunity.

'Her? As black's your hat! But I dinna suppose she would maybe be what you would ca' *ill-looked* a'thegither. Na, she's a kind of a handsome jaud – a kind o' gipsy,' said the aunt, who had two sets of scales for men and women – or perhaps it would be more fair to say that she had three, and the third and the most loaded was for girls.

'How comes it that I never see her in church?' said Archie.

''Deed, and I believe she's in Glesgie with Clem and his wife. A heap good she's like to get of it! I dinna say for menfolk, but where weemenfolk are born, there let them bide. Glory to God, I was never far'er from here than Crossmichael.'

In the meanwhile it began to strike Archie as strange, that while she thus sang the praises of her kinsfolk, and manifestly relished their virtues and (I may say) their vices like a thing creditable to herself, there should appear not the least sign of cordiality between the house of Hermiston and that of Cauldstaneslap. Going to church of a Sunday, as the lady housekeeper stepped with her skirts kilted, three tucks of her white petticoat showing below, and her best India shawl upon her back (if the day were fine) in a pattern of radiant dyes, she would sometimes overtake her relatives preceding her more leisurely in the same direction. Gib of course was absent: by skreigh of day he had been gone to Crossmichael and his fellow-heretics; but the rest of the family would be seen marching in open order: Hob and Dand, stiff-necked, straight-backed six-footers, with severe dark faces, and their plaids about their shoulders; the convoy of children scattering (in a state of high polish) on the wayside, and every now and again collected by the shrill summons of the mother; and the mother herself, by a suggestive circumstance which might have afforded matter of thought to a more experienced observer than Archie, wrapped in a shawl nearly identical with Kirstie's, but a thought more gaudy and conspicuously newer. At the sight, Kirstie grew more tall – Kirstie showed her classical profile, nose in air and nostril spread, the pure blood came in her cheek evenly in a delicate living pink.

'A braw day to ye, Mistress Elliott,' said she, and hostility and gentility were nicely mingled in her tones. 'A fine day, mem,' the laird's wife would reply with a miraculous curtsey, spreading the while her plumage – setting off, in other words, and with arts unknown to the mere man, the pattern of her India shawl. Behind her, the whole Cauldstaneslap contingent marched in closer order, and with an indescribable air of being in the presence of the foe; and while Dandie saluted his aunt with a certain familiarity as of one who was well in court, Hob marched on in awful immobility. There appeared upon the face of the attitude in the

family the consequences of some dreadful feud. Presumably the two
women had been principals in the original encounter, and the laird had
probably been drawn into the quarrel by the ears, too late to be included
in the present skin-deep reconciliation.

'Kirstie,' said Archie one day, 'what is this you have against your
family?'

'I dinna complean,' said Kirstie, with a flush. 'I say naething.'

'I see you do not – not even good-day to your own nephew,' said he.

'I hae naething to be ashamed of,' said she. 'I can say the Lord's
prayer with a good grace. If Hob was ill, or in preeson or poverty, I
would see to him blithely. But for curtchying and complimenting and
colloguing, thank ye kindly!'

Archie had a bit of a smile: he leaned back in his chair. 'I think you
and Mrs Robert are not very good friends,' says he slyly, 'when you
have your India shawls on?'

She looked upon him in silence, with a sparkling eye but an indeci-
pherable expression; and that was all that Archie was ever destined to
learn of the battle of the India shawls.

'Do none of them ever come here to see you?' he inquired.

'Mr Archie,' said she, 'I hope that I ken my place better. It would be
a queer thing, I think, if I was to clamjamfry up your faither's house –
that I should say it! – wi' a dirty, black-a-vised clan, no ane o' them it
was worth while to mar soap upon but just mysel'! Na, they're all
damnifeed wi' the black Ellwalds. I have nae patience wi' black folk.'
Then, with a sudden consciousness of the case of Archie, 'No that it
maitters for men sae muckle,' she made haste to add, 'but there's naebody
can deny that it's unwomanly. Long hair is the ornament o' woman
onyway; we've good warrandise for that – it's in the Bible – and wha
can doubt that the Apostle had some gowden-haired lassie in his mind
– Apostle and all, for what was he but just a man like yersel'?'

VI

Archie was sedulous at church. Sunday after Sunday he sat down and
stood up with that small company, heard the voice of Mr Torrance leaping
like an ill-played clarionet from key to key, and had an opportunity to

study his moth-eaten gown and the black thread mittens that he joined together in prayer, and lifted up with a reverent solemnity in the act of benediction. Hermiston pew was a little square box, dwarfish in proportion with the kirk itself, and enclosing a table not much bigger than a footstool. There sat Archie, an apparent prince, the only undeniable gentleman and the only great heritor in the parish, taking his ease in the only pew, for no other in the kirk had doors. Thence he might command an undisturbed view of that congregation of solid plaided men, strapping wives and daughters, oppressed children, and uneasy sheep-dogs. It was strange how Archie missed the look of race; except the dogs, with their refined foxy faces and inimitably curling tails, there was no one present with the least claim to gentility. The Cauldstaneslap party was scarcely an exception; Dandie perhaps, as he amused himself making verses through the interminable burden of the service, stood out a little by the glow in his eye and a certain superior animation of face and alertness of body; but even Dandie slouched like a rustic. The rest of the congregation, like so many sheep, oppressed him with a sense of hobnailed routine, day following day – of physical labour in the open air, oatmeal porridge, peas bannock, the somnolent fireside in the evening, and the night-long nasal slumbers in a box-bed. Yet he knew many of them to be shrewd and humorous, men of character, notable women, making a bustle in the world and radiating an influence from their low-browed doors. He knew besides they were like other men; below the crust of custom, rapture found a way; he had heard them beat the timbrel before Bacchus – had heard them shout and carouse over their whisky-toddy; and not the most Dutch-bottomed and severe faces among them all, not even the solemn elders themselves, but were capable of singular gambols at the voice of love. Men drawing near to an end of life's adventurous journey – maids thrilling with fear and curiosity on the threshold of entrance – women who had borne and perhaps buried children, who could remember the clinging of the small dead hands and the patter of the little feet now silent – he marvelled that among all those faces there should be no face of expectation, none that was mobile, none into which the rhythm and poetry of life had entered. 'O for a live face,' he thought; and at times he had a memory of Lady Flora; and at times he would study the living gallery before him with despair, and would see himself go on to waste his days in that joyless pastoral place, and death come to him, and his grave be dug under the rowans, and the Spirit of the Earth laugh out in a thunder-peal at the huge fiasco.

On this particular Sunday, there was no doubt but that the spring had come at last. It was warm, with a latent shiver in the air that made the warmth only the more welcome. The shallows of the stream glittered and tinkled among bunches of primrose. Vagrant scents of the earth arrested Archie by the way with moments of ethereal intoxication. The grey Quakerish dale was still only awakened in places and patches from the sobriety of its winter colouring; and he wondered at its beauty; an essential beauty of the old earth it seemed to him, not resident in particulars but breathing to him from the whole. He surprised himself by a sudden impulse to write poetry – he did so sometimes, loose, galloping octosyllabics in the vein of Scott – and when he had taken his place on a boulder, near some fairy falls and shaded by a whip of a tree that was already radiant with new leaves, it still more surprised him that he should have nothing to write. His heart perhaps beat in time to some vast indwelling rhythm of the universe. By the time he came to a corner of the valley and could see the kirk, he had so lingered by the way that the first psalm was finishing. The nasal psalmody, full of turns and trills and graceless graces, seemed the essential voice of the kirk itself upraised in thanksgiving. 'Everything's alive,' he said; and again cries it aloud, 'thank God, everything's alive!' He lingered yet a while in the kirk-yard. A tuft of primroses was blooming hard by the leg of an old black table tombstone, and he stopped to contemplate the random apologue. They stood forth on the cold earth with a trenchancy of contrast; and he was struck with a sense of incompleteness in the day, the season, and the beauty that surrounded him – the chill there was in the warmth, the gross black clods about the opening primroses, the damp earthy smell that was everywhere intermingled with the scents. The voice of the aged Torrance within rose in an ecstasy. And he wondered if Torrance also felt in his old bones the joyous influence of the spring morning; Torrance, or the shadow of what once was Torrance, that must come so soon to lie outside here in the sun and rain with all his rheumatisms, while a new minister stood in his room and thundered from his own familiar pulpit? The pity of it, and something of the chill of the grave, shook him for a moment as he made haste to enter.

He went up the aisle reverently, and took his place in the pew with lowered eyes, for he feared he had already offended the kind old gentleman in the pulpit, and was sedulous to offend no further. He could not follow the prayer, not even the heads of it. Brightnesses of azure, clouds of fragrance, a tinkle of falling water and singing birds, rose like exhalations from some deeper, aboriginal memory, that was not his, but belonged to the flesh on his bones. His body remembered; and it seemed to him that his body was in no way gross, but ethereal and perishable like a strain of music; and he felt for it an exquisite tenderness as for a child, an innocent, full of beautiful instincts and destined to an early death. And he felt for old Torrance – of the many supplications, of the few days – a pity that was near to tears. The prayer ended. Right over him was a tablet in the wall, the only ornament in the roughly masoned chapel – for it was no more; the tablet commemorated, I was about to say the virtues, but rather the existence of a former Rutherford of Hermiston; and Archie, under that trophy of his long descent and local greatness, leaned back in the pew and contemplated vacancy with the shadow of a smile between playful and sad, that became him strangely. Dandie's sister, sitting by the side of Clem in her new Glasgow finery, chose that moment to observe the young laird. Aware of the stir of his entrance, the little formalist had kept her eyes fastened and her face prettily composed during the prayer. It was not hypocrisy, there was no one further from a hypocrite. The girl had been taught to behave: to look up, to look down, to look unconscious, to look seriously impressed in church, and in every conjuncture to look her best. That was the game of female life, and she played it frankly. Archie was the one person in church who was of interest, who was somebody new, reputed eccentric, known to be young, and a laird, and still unseen by Christina. Small wonder that, as she stood there in her attitude of pretty decency, her mind should run upon him! If he spared a glance in her direction, he should know she was a well-behaved young lady who had been to Glasgow. In reason he must admire her clothes, and it was possible that he should think her pretty. At that her heart beat the least thing in the world; and she proceeded, by way of a corrective, to call up and dismiss a series of fancied pictures of the young man who should now, by rights, be looking at her. She settled on the plainest of them – a pink short young man with a dish face and no figure, at whose admiration she could afford to smile; but for all that, the consciousness of his gaze (which was really fixed on Torrance and his mittens) kept her in something of a flutter till the word Amen. Even then, she was far too well-bred to gratify her curiosity with any impatience. She resumed her seat languidly – this was a Glasgow touch – she composed her dress, rearranged her nosegay of primroses, looked first in front, then behind upon the other side, and at last allowed her eyes to move, without hurry, in the direction of the Hermiston pew. For a moment, they were riveted. Next she had plucked her gaze home again like a tame bird who should have meditated flight. Possibilities crowded on her; she hung over the future and grew dizzy; the image of this young man, slim, graceful, dark, with the inscrutable half-smile, attracted and repelled her like a chasm. 'I wonder, will I have met my fate?' she thought, and her heart swelled.

Torrance was got some way into his first exposition, positing a deep layer of texts as he went along, laying the foundations of his discourse, which was to deal with a nice point in divinity, before Archie suffered his eyes to wander. They fell first of all on Clem, looking insupportably prosperous, and patronising Torrance with the favour of a modified attention, as of one who was used to better things in Glasgow. Though he had never before set eyes on him, Archie had no difficulty in identifying him, and no hesitation in pronouncing him vulgar, the worst of the family. Clem was leaning lazily forward when Archie first saw him. Presently he leaned nonchalantly back; and that deadly instrument, the maiden, was suddenly unmasked in profile. Though not quite in the front of the fashion (had anybody cared!), certain artful Glasgow mantua-makers, and her own inherent taste, had arrayed her to great advantage. Her accoutrement was, indeed, a cause of heart-burning, and almost of scandal, in that infinitesimal kirk company. Mrs Hob had said her say at Cauldstaneslap. 'Daft-like!' she had pronounced it. 'A jaiket that'll no meet! Whaur's the sense of a jaiket that'll no button upon you, if it should come to be weet? What do ye ca' thir things? Demmy brokens, d'ye say? They'll be brokens wi' a vengeance or ye can win back! Weel, I have naething to do wi' it – it's no good taste.' Clem, whose purse had thus metamorphosed his sister, and who was not insensible to the advertisement, had come to the rescue with a 'Hoot, woman! What do you ken of good taste that has never been to the ceety?' And Hob, looking on the girl with pleased smiles, as she timidly displayed her finery in the midst of the dark kitchen, had thus ended the dispute: 'The cutty looks weel,' he had said, 'and it's no very like rain. Wear them the day, hizzie; but it's no a thing to make a practice o'.' In the breasts of her rivals, coming to the kirk very conscious of white under-linen, and their faces splendid with much soap, the sight of the toilet had raised a storm of varying emotion, from the mere unenvious admiration that was expressed in a long-drawn 'Eh!' to the angrier feeling that found vent in an emphatic 'Set her up!' Her frock was of straw-coloured jaconet muslin, cut low at the bosom and short at the ankle, so as to display her *demi-broquins* of Regency violet, crossing with many straps upon a yellow cobweb stocking. According to the pretty fashion in which our grandmothers did not hesitate to appear, and our great-aunts went forth armed for the pursuit and capture of our great-uncles, the dress was drawn up so as to mould the contour of both breasts, and in the nook between, a cairngorm brooch maintained it. Here, too, surely in a very enviable position, trembled the nosegay of primroses. She wore on her shoulders – or rather on her back and not her shoulders, which it scarcely passed – a French coat of sarsenet, tied in front with Margate braces, and of the same colour with her violet shoes. About her face clustered a disorder of dark ringlets, a little garland of yellow French roses surmounted her brow, and the whole was crowned by a village hat of chipped straw. Amongst all the rosy and all the weathered faces that surrounded her in church, she glowed like an open flower – girl and raiment, and the cairngorm that caught the daylight and returned it in a fiery flash, and the threads of bronze and gold that played in her hair.

Archie was attracted by the bright thing like a child. He looked at her again and yet again, and their looks crossed. The lip was lifted from her little teeth. He saw the red blood work vividly under her tawny skin. Her eye, which was great as a stag's, struck and held his gaze. He knew who she must be – Kirstie, she of the harsh diminutive, his housekeeper's niece, the sister of the rustic prophet, Gib – and he found in her the answer to his wishes.

Christina felt the shock of their encountering glances, and seemed to rise, clothed in smiles, into a region of the vague and bright. But the gratification was not more exquisite than it was brief. She looked away abruptly, and immediately began to blame herself for that abruptness. She knew what she should have done, too late – turned slowly with her nose in the air. And meantime his look was not removed, but continued to play upon her like a battery of cannon constantly aimed, and now seemed to isolate her alone with him, and now seemed to uplift her, as on a pillory, before the congregation. For Archie continued to drink her in with his eyes, even as a wayfarer comes to a well-head on a mountain, and stoops his face, and drinks with thirst unassuageable. In the cleft of her little breasts the fiery eye of the topaz and the pale florets of primrose fascinated him. He saw the breasts heave, and the flowers shake with the heaving, and marvelled what should so much discompose the girl. And Christina was conscious of his gaze – saw it, perhaps, with the dainty plaything of an ear that peeped among her ringlets; she was conscious of changing colour, conscious of her unsteady breath. Like a creature tracked, run down, surrounded, she sought in a dozen ways to give herself a countenance. She used her handkerchief – it was a really fine one – then she desisted in a panic: 'He would only think I was too warm.' She took to reading in the metrical psalms, and then remembered it was sermon-time. Last she put a 'sugar-bool' in her mouth, and the next moment repented of the step. It was such a homely-like thing! Mr Archie would never be eating sweeties in kirk; and, with a palpable effort, she swallowed it whole, and her colour flamed legh. At this signal of distress Archie awoke to a sense of his ill-behaviour. What had he been doing? He had been exquisitely rude in church to the niece of his housekeeper; he had stared like a lackey and a libertine at a beautiful and modest girl. It was possible, it was even likely, he would be presented to her after service in the kirk-yard, and then how was he to look? And there was no excuse. He had marked the tokens of her shame, of her increasing indignation, and he was such a fool that he had not understood them. Shame bowed him down, and he looked resolutely at Mr Torrance; who little supposed, good, worthy man, as he continued to expound justification by faith, what was his true business: to play the part of derivative to a pair of children at the old game of falling in love.

Christina was greatly relieved at first. It seemed to her that she was clothed again. She looked back on what had passed. All would have been right if she had not blushed, a silly fool! There was nothing to blush at, if she *had* taken a sugar-bool. Mrs MacTaggart, the elder's wife in St Enoch's, took them often. And if he had looked at her, what was more natural than that a young gentleman should look at the best-dressed girl in church? And at the same time, she knew far otherwise, she knew there was nothing casual or ordinary in the look, and valued herself on its memory like a decoration. Well, it was a blessing he had found something else to look at! And presently she began to have other thoughts. It was necessary, she fancied, that she should put herself right by a repetition of the incident, better managed. If the wish was father to the thought, she did not know or she would not recognise it. It was simply as a manœuvre of propriety, as something called for to lessen the significance of what had gone before, that she should a second time meet his eyes, and this time without blushing. And at the memory of the blush, she blushed again, and became one general blush burning from head to foot. Was ever anything so indelicate, so forward, done by a girl before? And here she was, making an exhibition of herself before the congregation about nothing! She stole a glance upon her neighbours, and behold! they were steadily indifferent, and Clem had gone to sleep. And still the one idea was becoming more and more potent with her, that in common prudence she must look again before the service ended. Something of the same sort was going forward in the mind of Archie, as he struggled with the load of penitence. So it chanced that, in the flutter of the moment when the last psalm was given out, and Torrance was reading the verse, and the leaves of every psalm-book in church were rustling under busy fingers, two stealthy glances were sent out like antennæ among the pews and on the indifferent and absorbed occupants, and drew timidly nearer to the straight line between Archie and Christina. They met, they lingered together for the least fraction of time, and that was enough. A charge as of electricity passed through Christina, and behold! the leaf of her psalm-book was torn across.

Archie was outside by the gate of the graveyard, conversing with Hob and the minister and shaking hands all round with the scattering congregation, when Clem and Christina were brought up to be presented. The laird took off his hat and bowed to her with grace and respect. Christina made her Glasgow curtsey to the laird and went on again up the road for Hermiston and Cauldstaneslap, walking fast, breathing hurriedly with a heightened colour, and in this strange frame of mind, that when she was alone she seemed in high happiness, and when anyone addressed her she resented it like a contradiction. A part of the way she had the company of some neighbour girls and a loutish young man; never had they seemed so insipid, never had she made herself so disagreeable. But these struck aside to their various destinations or were out-walked and left behind; and when she had driven off with sharp words the proffered convoy of some of her nephews and nieces, she was free to go on alone up Hermiston brae, walking on air, dwelling intoxicated among clouds of happiness. Near to the summit she heard steps behind her, a man's steps, light and very rapid. She knew the foot at once and walked the faster. 'If it's me he's wanting, he can run for it,' she thought, smiling.

Archie overtook her like a man whose mind was made up.

'Miss Kirstie,' he began.

'Miss Christina, if you please, Mr Weir,' she interrupted. 'I canna bear the contraction.'

'You forget it has a friendly sound for me. Your aunt is an old friend of mine, and a very good one. I hope we shall see much of you at Hermiston?'

'My aunt and my sister-in-law doesna agree very well. Not that I have much ado with it. But still when I'm stopping in the house, if I was to be visiting my aunt, it would not look considerate-like.'

'I am sorry,' said Archie.

'I thank you kindly, Mr Weir,' she said. 'I whiles think myself it's a great peety.'

'Ah, I am sure your voice would always be for peace!' he cried.

'I wouldna be too sure of that,' she said. 'I have my days like other folk, I suppose.'

'Do you know, in our old kirk, among our good old grey dames, you made an effect like sunshine.'

'Ah, but that would be my Glasgow clothes!'

'I did not think I was so much under the influence of pretty frocks.'

She smiled with a half look at him. 'There's more than you!' she said. 'But you see I'm only Cinderella. I'll have to put all these things by in my trunk; next Sunday I'll be as grey as the rest. They're Glasgow clothes, you see, and it would never do to make a practice of it. It would seem terrible conspicuous.'

By that they were come to the place where their ways severed. The old grey moors were all about them; in the midst a few sheep wandered; and they could see on the one hand the straggling caravan scaling the braes in front of them for Cauldstaneslap, and on the other, the contingent from Hermiston bending off and beginning to disappear by detachments into the policy gate. It was in these circumstances that they turned to say farewell, and deliberately exchanged a glance as they shook hands. All passed as it should, genteelly; and in Christina's mind, as she mounted the first steep ascent for Cauldstaneslap, a gratifying sense of triumph prevailed over the recollection of minor lapses and mistakes. She had kilted her gown, as she did usually at that rugged pass; but when she spied Archie still standing and gazing after her, the skirts came down again as if by enchantment. Here was a piece of nicety for that upland parish, where the matrons marched with their coats kilted in the rain, and the lasses walked barefoot to kirk through the dust of summer, and went bravely down by the burnside, and sat on stones to make a public toilet before entering! It was perhaps an air wafted from Glasgow; or perhaps it marked a stage of that dizziness of gratified vanity, in which the instinctive act passed unperceived. He was looking after! She unloaded her bosom of a prodigious sigh that was all pleasure, and betook herself to run. When she had overtaken the stragglers of her family, she caught up the niece whom she had so recently repulsed, and kissed and slapped her, and drove her away again, and ran after her with pretty cries and laughter. Perhaps she thought the laird might still be looking! But it chanced the little scene came under the view of eyes less favourable; for she overtook Mrs Hob marching with Clem and Dand.

'You're shürely fey, lass!' quoth Dandie.

'Think shame to yersel', miss!' said the strident Mrs Hob. 'Is this the gait to guide yersel' on the way hame frae kirk? You're shürely no sponsible the day! And anyway I would mind my guid claes.'

'Hoot!' said Christina, and went on before them head in the air, treading the rough track with the tread of a wild doe.

She was in love with herself, her destiny, the air of the hills, the benediction of the sun. All the way home, she continued under the intoxication of these skyscraping spirits. At table she could talk freely of young Hermiston; gave her opinion of him offhand and with a loud voice, that he was a handsome young gentleman, real well mannered and sensible-like, but it was a pity he looked doleful. Only – the moment after – a memory of his eyes in church embarrassed her. But for this inconsiderable check, all through meal-time she had a good appetite, and she kept them laughing at table, until Gib (who had returned before them from Crossmichael and his separative worship) reproved the whole of them for their levity.

Singing 'in to herself' as she went, her mind still in the turmoil of a glad confusion, she rose and tripped upstairs to a little loft, lighted by four panes in the gable, where she slept with one of her nieces. The niece, who followed her, presuming on 'Auntie's' high spirits, was flounced out of the apartment with small ceremony, and retired, smarting and half tearful, to bury her woes in the byre among the hay. Still humming, Christina divested herself of her finery, and put her treasures one by one in her great green trunk. The last of these was the psalm-book; it was a fine piece, the gift of Mistress Clem, in distinct old-faced type, on paper that had begun to grow foxy in the warehouse – not by service – and she was used to wrap it in a handkerchief every Sunday after its period of service was over, and bury it end-wise at the head of her trunk. As she now took it in hand the book fell open where the leaf was torn, and she stood and gazed upon that evidence of her bygone discomposure. There returned again the vision of the two brown eyes staring at her, intent and bright, out of that dark corner of the kirk. The whole appearance and attitude, the smile, the suggested gesture of young Hermiston came before her in a flash at the sight of the torn page. 'I was surely fey!' she said, echoing the words of Dandie, and at the suggested doom her high spirits deserted her. She flung herself prone upon the bed, and lay there, holding the psalm-book in her hands for hours, for the more part in a mere stupor of unconsenting pleasure and unreasoning fear. The fear was superstitious; there came up again and again in her memory Dandie's ill-omened words, and a hundred grisly and black tales out of the immediate neighbourhood read her a commentary on their force. The pleasure was never realised. You might say the joints of her body thought and remembered, and were gladdened, but her essential self, in the immediate theatre of consciousness, talked feverishly of something else, like a nervous person at a fire. The image that she most complacently dwelt on was that of Miss Christina in her character of the Fair Lass of Cauldstaneslap, carrying all before her in the straw-coloured frock, the violet mantle, and the yellow cobweb stockings. Archie's image, on the other hand, when it presented itself was never welcomed – far less welcomed with any ardour, and it was exposed at times to merciless criticism. In the long vague dialogue she held in her mind, often with imaginary, often with unrealised interlocutors, Archie, if he were referred to at all, came in for savage handling. He was described as 'looking like a stork,' 'staring like a caulf,' 'a face like a ghaist's.' 'Do you call that manners?' she said; or 'I soon put him in his place.' '"*Miss Christina, if you please, Mr Weir!*" says I, and just flyped up my skirt tails.' With gabble like this she would entertain herself long whiles together, and then her eye would perhaps fall on the torn leaf, and the eyes of Archie would appear again from the darkness of the wall, and the voluble words deserted her, and she would lie still and stupid, and think upon nothing with devotion, and be sometimes raised by a quiet sigh. Had a doctor of medicine come into that loft, he would have diagnosed a healthy, well-developed, eminently vivacious lass lying on her face in a fit of the sulks; not one who had just contracted, or was just contracting, a mortal sickness of the mind which should yet carry her towards death and despair. Had it been a doctor of psychology, he might have been pardoned for divining in the girl a passion of childish vanity, self-love *in excelsis*, and no more. It is to be understood that I have been painting chaos and describing the inarticulate. Every lineament that appears is too precise, almost every word used too strong. Take a finger-post in the mountains on a day of rolling mists; I have but copied the names that appear upon the pointers, the names of definite and famous cities far distant, and now perhaps basking in sunshine; but Christina remained all these hours, as it were, at the foot of the post itself, not moving, and enveloped in mutable and blinding wreaths of haze.

The day was growing late and the sunbeams long and level, when she sat suddenly up, and wrapped in its handkerchief and put by that psalm-book which had already played a part so decisive in the first chapter of her love-story. In the absence of the mesmerist's eye, we are told nowadays that the head of a bright nail may fill his place, if it be steadfastly regarded. So that torn page had riveted her attention on what might else have been but little, and perhaps soon forgotten; while the ominous words of Dandie – heard, not heeded, and still remembered – had lent to her thoughts, or rather to her mood, a cast of solemnity, and that idea of Fate – a pagan Fate, uncontrolled by any Christian deity, obscure, lawless, and august – moving indissuadably in the affairs of Christian men. Thus even that phenomenon of love at first sight, which is so rare and seems so simple and violent, like a disruption of life's tissue, may be decomposed into a sequence of accidents happily concurring.

She put on a grey frock and a pink kerchief, looked at herself a moment with approval in the small square of glass that served her for a toilet mirror, and went softly downstairs through the sleeping house that resounded with the sound of afternoon snoring. Just outside the door, Dandie was sitting with a book in his hand, not reading, only honouring the Sabbath by a sacred vacancy of mind. She came near him and stood still.

'I'm for off up the muirs, Dandie,' she said.

There was something unusually soft in her tones that made him look up. She was pale, her eyes dark and bright; no trace remained of the levity of the morning.

'Ay, lass? Ye'll have yer ups and downs like me, I'm thinkin',' he observed.

'What for do ye say that?' she asked.

'O, for naething,' says Dand. 'Only I think ye're mair like me than the lave of them. Ye've mair of the poetic temper, tho' Guid kens little enough of the poetic taalent. It's an ill gift at the best. Look at yoursel'. At denner you were all sunshine and flowers and laughter, and now you're like the star of evening on a lake.'

She drank in this hackneyed compliment like wine, and it glowed in her veins.

'But I'm saying, Dand' – she came nearer him – 'I'm for the muirs. I must have a braith of air. If Clem was to be speiring for me, try and quaiet him, will ye no?'

'What way?' said Dandie. 'I ken but the ae way, and that's leein'. I'll say ye had a sair heid, if ye like.'

'But I havena,' she objected.

'I daursay no,' he returned. 'I said I would say ye had; and if ye like to nay-say me when ye come back, it'll no mateerially maitter, for my chara'ter's clean gane a'ready past reca'.'

'O, Dand, are ye a leear?' she asked, lingering.

'Folks say sae,' replied the bard.

'Wha says sae?' she pursued.

'Them that should ken the best,' he responded. 'The lassies, for ane.'

'But, Dand, you would never lee to me?' she asked.

'I'll leave that for your pairt of it, ye girzie,' said he. 'Ye'll lee to me fast eneuch, when ye hae gotten a jo. I'm tellin' ye and it's true; when you have a jo, Miss Kirstie, it'll be for guid and ill. I ken: I was made that way mysel', but the deil was in my luck! Here, gang awa wi' ye to your muirs, and let me be; I'm in an hour of inspiraution, ye upsetting tawpie!'

But she clung to her brother's neighbourhood, she knew not why.

'Will ye no gie's a kiss, Dand?' she said. 'I aye likit ye fine.'

He kissed her and considered her a moment; he found something strange in her. But he was a libertine through and through, nourished equal contempt and suspicion of all womankind, and paid his way among them habitually with idle compliments.

'Gae wa' wi' ye!' said he. 'Ye're a dentie baby, and be content wi' that!'

That was Dandie's way; a kiss and a comfit to Jenny – a bawbee and my blessing to Jill – and goodnight to the whole clan of ye, my dears! When anything approached the serious, it became a matter for men, he both thought and said. Women, when they did not absorb, were only children to be shoo'd away. Merely in his character of connoisseur, however, Dandie glanced carelessly after his sister as she crossed the meadow. 'The brat's no that bad!' he thought with surprise, for though he had just been paying her compliments, he had not really looked at her. 'Hey! what's yon?' For the grey dress was cut with short sleeves and skirts, and displayed her trim strong legs clad in pink stockings of the same shade as the kerchief she wore round her shoulders, and that shimmered as she went. This was not her way in undress; he knew her ways and the ways of the whole sex in the countryside, no one better; when they did not go barefoot, they wore stout 'rig and furrow' woollen hose of an invisible blue mostly, when they were not black outright; and Dandie, at sight of this daintiness, put two and two together. It was a silk handkerchief, then they would be silken hose; they matched – then the whole outfit was a present of Clem's, a costly present, and not something to be worn through bog and briar, or on a late afternoon of Sunday. He whistled. 'My denty May, either your heid's fair turned, or there's some ongoings!' he observed, and dismissed the subject.

She went slowly at first, but ever straighter and faster for the Cauldstaneslap, a pass among the hills to which the farm owed its name. The Slap opened like a doorway between two rounded hillocks; and through this ran the short cut to Hermiston. Immediately on the other side it went down through the Deil's Hags, a considerable marshy hollow of the hilltops, full of springs, and crouching junipers, and pools where the black peat-water slumbered. There was no view from here. A man might have sat upon the Praying Weaver's stone a half-century, and seen none but the Cauldstaneslap children twice in the twenty-four hours on their way to the school and back again, an occasional shepherd, the irruption of a clan of sheep, or the birds who haunted about the springs, drinking and shrilly piping. So, when she had once passed the Slap, Kirstie was received into seclusion. She looked back a last time at the farm. It still lay deserted except for the figure of Dandie, who was now seen to be scribbling in his lap, the hour of expected inspiration having come to him at last. Thence she passed rapidly through the morass, and came to the farther end of it, where a sluggish burn discharges, and the path for Hermiston accompanies it on the beginning of its downward path. From this corner a wide view was opened to her of the whole stretch of braes upon the other side, still sallow and in places rusty with the winter, with the path marked boldly, here and there by the burnside a tuft of birches, and – two miles off as the crow flies – from its enclosures and young plantations, the windows of Hermiston glittering in the western sun.

Here she sat down and waited, and looked for a long time at these far-away bright panes of glass. It amused her to have so extended a view, she thought. It amused her to see the house of Hermiston – to see 'folk'; and there was an indistinguishable human unit, perhaps the gardener, visibly sauntering on the gravel paths.

By the time the sun was down and all the easterly braes lay plunged in clear shadow, she was aware of another figure coming up the path at a most unequal rate of approach, now half-running, now pausing and seeming to hesitate. She watched him at first with a total suspension of thought. She held her thought as a person holds his breathing. Then she consented to recognise him. 'He'll no be coming here, he canna be; it's no possible.' And there began to grow upon her a subdued choking suspense. He *was* coming; his hesitations had quite ceased, his step grew firm and swift; no doubt remained; and the question loomed up before her instant: what was she to do? It was all very well to say that her brother was a laird himself: it was all very well to speak of casual inter-marriages and to count cousinship, like Auntie Kirstie. The difference in their social station was trenchant; propriety, prudence, all that she had ever learned, all that she knew, bade her flee. But on the other hand the cup of life now offered to her was too enchanting. For one moment, she saw the question clearly, and definitely made her choice. She stood up and showed herself an instant in the gap relieved upon the skyline; and the next, fled trembling and sat down glowing with excitement on the Weaver's stone. She shut her eyes, seeking, praying for composure. Her hand shook in her lap, and her mind was full of incongruous and futile speeches. What was there to make a work about? She could take care of herself, she supposed! There was no harm in seeing the laird. It was the best thing that could happen. She would mark a proper distance to him once and for all. Gradually the wheels of her nature ceased to go round so madly, and she sat in passive expectation, a quiet, solitary figure in the midst of the grey moss. I have said she was no hypocrite, but here I am at fault. She never admitted to herself that she had come up the hill to look for Archie. And perhaps after all she did not know, perhaps came as a stone falls. For the steps of love in the young, and especially in girls, are instinctive and unconscious.

In the meantime Archie was drawing rapidly near, and he at least was consciously seeking her neighbourhood. The afternoon had turned to ashes in his mouth; the memory of the girl had kept him from reading and drawn him as with cords; and at last, as the cool of the evening began to come on, he had taken his hat and set forth, with a smothered ejaculation, by the moor path to Cauldstaneslap. He had no hope to find her; he took the offchance without expectation of result and to relieve his uneasiness. The greater was his surprise, as he surmounted the slope and came into the hollow of the Deil's Hags, to see there, like an answer to his wishes, the little womanly figure in the grey dress and the pink kerchief sitting little, and low, and lost, and acutely solitary, in these desolate surroundings and on the weather-beaten stone of the dead weaver. Those things that still smacked of winter were all rusty about her, and those things that already relished of the spring had put forth the tender and lively colours of the season. Even in the unchanging face of the death-stone, changes were to be remarked; and in the channeled lettering, the moss began to renew itself in jewels of green. By an afterthought that was a stroke of art, she had turned up over her head the back of the kerchief; so that it now framed becomingly her vivacious and yet pensive face. Her feet were gathered under her on the one side, and she leaned on her bare arm, which showed out strong and round, tapered to a slim wrist, and shimmered in the fading light.

Young Hermiston was struck with a certain chill. He was reminded that he now dealt in serious matters of life and death. This was a grown woman he was approaching, endowed with her mysterious potencies and attractions, the treasury of the continued race, and he was neither better nor worse than the average of his sex and age. He had a certain delicacy which had preserved him hitherto unspotted, and which (had either of them guessed it) made him a more dangerous companion when his heart should be really stirred. His throat was dry as he came near; but the appealing sweetness of her smile stood between them like a guardian angel.

For she turned to him and smiled, though without rising. There was a shade in this cavalier greeting that neither of them perceived; neither he, who simply thought it gracious and charming as herself; nor yet she, who did not observe (quick as she was) the difference between rising to meet the laird, and remaining seated to receive the expected admirer.

'Are ye stepping west, Hermiston?' said she, giving him his territorial name after the fashion of the countryside.

'I was,' said he, a little hoarsely, 'but I think I will be about the end of my stroll now. Are you like me, Miss Christina? The house would not hold me. I came here seeking air.'

He took his seat at the other end of the tombstone and studied her, wondering what was she. There was infinite import in the question alike for her and him.

'Ay,' she said. 'I couldna bear the roof either. It's a habit of mine to come up here about the gloaming when it's quaiet and caller.'

'It was a habit of my mother's also,' he said gravely. The recollection half startled him as he expressed it. He looked around. 'I have scarce been here since. It's peaceful,' he said, with a long breath.

'It's no like Glasgow,' she replied. 'A weary place, yon Glasgow! But what a day have I had for my hame-coming, and what a bonny evening!'

'Indeed, it was a wonderful day,' said Archie. 'I think I will remember it years and years until I come to die. On days like this – I do not know if you feel as I do – but everything appears so brief, and fragile, and exquisite, that I am afraid to touch life. We are here for so short a time; and all the old people before us – Rutherfords of Hermiston, Elliotts of the Cauldstaneslap – that were here but a while since riding about and keeping up a great noise in this quiet corner – making love too, and marrying – why, where are they now? It's deadly commonplace, but, after all, the commonplaces are the great poetic truths.'

He was sounding her, semi-consciously, to see if she could understand him; to learn if she were only an animal the colour of flowers, or had a soul in her to keep her sweet. She, on her part, her means well in hand, watched, womanlike, for any opportunity to shine, to abound in his humour, whatever that might be. The dramatic artist, that lies dormant or only half awake in most human beings, had in her sprung to his feet in a divine fury, and chance had served her well. She looked upon him with a subdued twilight look that became the hour of the day and the train of thought; earnestness shone through her like stars in the purple west; and from the great but controlled upheaval of her whole nature there passed into her voice, and rang in her lightest words, a thrill of emotion.

'Have you mind of Dand's song?' she answered. 'I think he'll have been trying to say what you have been thinking.'

'No, I never heard it,' he said. 'Repeat it to me, can you?'

'It's nothing wanting the tune,' said Kirstie.

'Then sing it me,' said he.

'On the Lord's Day? That would never do, Mr. Weir!'

'I am afraid I am not so strict a keeper of the Sabbath, and there is no one in this place to hear us, unless the poor old ancient under the stone.'

'No that I'm thinking that really,' she said. 'By my way of thinking, it's just as serious as a psalm. Will I sooth it to ye, then?'

'If you please,' said he, and, drawing near to her on the tombstone, prepared to listen.

She sat up as if to sing. 'I'll only can sooth it to ye,' she explained. 'I wouldna like to sing out loud on the Sabbath. I think the birds would carry news of it to Gilbert,' and she smiled. 'It's about the Elliotts,' she continued, 'and I think there's few bonnier bits in the book-poets, though Dand has never got printed yet.'

And she began, in the low, clear tones of her half voice, now sinking almost to a whisper, now rising to a particular note which was her best, and which Archie learned to wait for with growing emotion: –

'O they rade in the rain, in the days that are gane,
In the rain and the wind and the lave,
They shoutit in the ha' and they routit on the hill,
But they're a' quaitit noo in the grave.
Auld, auld Elliotts, clay-cauld Elliotts, dour, bauld Elliotts of
    auld!'

All the time she sang she looked steadfastly before her, her knees straight, her hands upon her knee, her head cast back and up. The expression was admirable throughout, for had she not learned it from the lips and under the criticism of the author? When it was done, she turned upon Archie a face softly bright, and eyes gently suffused and shining in the twilight, and his heart rose and went out to her with boundless pity and sympathy. His question was answered. She was a human being tuned to a sense of the tragedy of life; there were pathos and music and a great heart in the girl.

He arose instinctively, she also; for she saw she had gained a point, and scored the impression deeper, and she had wit enough left to flee upon a victory. They were but commonplaces that remained to be exchanged, but the low, moved voices in which they passed made them sacred in the memory. In the falling greyness of the evening he watched her figure winding through the morass, saw it turn a last time and wave a hand, and then pass through the Slap; and it seemed to him as if something went along with her out of the deepest of his heart. And something surely had come, and come to dwell there. He had retained from childhood a picture, now half obliterated by the passage of time and the multitude of fresh impressions, of his mother telling him, with the fluttered earnestness of her voice, and often with dropping tears, the tale of the 'Praying Weaver,' on the very scene of his brief tragedy and long repose. And now there was a companion piece; and he beheld, and he should behold for ever, Christina perched on the same tomb, in the grey colours of the evening, gracious, dainty, perfect as a flower, and she also singing –

'Of old, unhappy far off things,
And battles long ago,'

of their common ancestors now dead, of their rude wars composed, their weapons buried with them, and of these strange changelings, their descendants, who lingered a little in their places, and would soon be gone also, and perhaps sung of by others at the gloaming hour. By one of the unconscious arts of tenderness the two women were enshrined together in his memory. Tears, in that hour of sensibility, came into his eyes indifferently at the thought of either; and the girl, from being something merely bright and shapely, was caught up into the zone of things serious as life and death and his dead mother. So that in all ways and on either side, Fate played his game artfully with this poor pair of children. The generations were prepared, the pangs were made ready, before the curtain rose on the dark drama.

In the same moment of time that she disappeared from Archie, there opened before Kirstie's eyes the cup-like hollow in which the farm lay. She saw, some five hundred feet below her, the house making itself bright with candles, and this was a broad hint to her to hurry. For they were only kindled on a Sabbath night with a view to that family worship which rounded in the incomparable tedium of the day and brought on the relaxation of supper. Already she knew that Robert must be within-sides at the head of the table, 'waling the portions'; for it was Robert in his quality of family priest and judge, not the gifted Gilbert, who officiated. She made good time accordingly down the steep ascent, and came up to the door panting as the three younger brothers, all roused at last from slumber, stood together in the cool and the dark of the evening with a fry of nephews and nieces about them, chatting and awaiting the expected signal. She stood back; she had no mind to direct attention to her late arrival or to her labouring breath.

'Kirstie, ye have shaved it this time, my lass?' said Clem. 'Whaur were ye?'

'O, just taking a dander by myself',' said Kirstie.

And the talk continued on the subject of the American War, without further reference to the truant who stood by them in the covert of the dusk, thrilling with happiness and the sense of guilt.

The signal was given, and the brothers began to go in one after another, amid the jostle and throng of Hob's children.

Only Dandie, waiting till the last, caught Kirstie by the arm. 'When did ye begin to dander in pink hosen, Mistress Elliott?' he whispered slyly.

She looked down; she was one blush. 'I maun have forgotten to change them,' said she; and went into prayers in her turn with a troubled mind, between anxiety as to whether Dand should have observed her yellow stockings at church, and should thus detect her in a palpable falsehood, and shame that she had already made good his prophecy. She remembered the words of it, how it was to be when she had gotten a jo, and that that would be for good and evil. 'Will I have gotten my jo now?' she thought with a secret rapture.

And all through prayers, where it was her principal business to conceal the pink stockings from the eyes of the indifferent Mrs. Hob – and all through supper, as she made a feint of eating and sat at the table radiant and constrained – and again when she had left them and come into her chamber, and was alone with her sleeping niece, and could at last lay aside the armour of society – the same words sounded within her, the same profound note of happiness, of a world all changed and renewed, of a day that had been passed in Paradise, and of a night that was to be heaven opened. All night she seemed to be conveyed smoothly upon a shallow stream of sleep and waking, and through the bowers of Beulah; all night she cherished to her heart that exquisite hope; and if, towards morning, she forgot it a while in a more profound unconsciousness, it was to catch again the rainbow thought with her first moment of awaking.

VII

Two days later a gig from Crossmichael deposited Frank Innes at the doors of Hermiston. Once in a way, during the past winter, Archie, in some acute phase of boredom, had written him a letter. It had contained something in the nature of an invitation or a reference to an invitation – precisely what, neither of them now remembered. When Innes had received it, there had been nothing further from his mind than to bury himself in the moors with Archie; but not even the most acute political heads are guided through the steps of life with unerring directness. That would require a gift of prophecy which has been denied to man. For instance, who could have imagined that, not a month after he had received the letter, and turned it into mockery, and put off answering it, and in the end lost it, misfortunes of a gloomy cast should begin to thicken over Frank's career? His case may be briefly stated. His father, a small Morayshire laird with a large family, became recalcitrant and cut off the supplies; he had fitted himself out with the beginnings of quite a good law library, which, upon some sudden losses on the turf, he had been obliged to sell before they were paid for; and his bookseller, hearing some rumour of the event, took out a warrant for his arrest. Innes had early word of it, and was able to take precautions. In this immediate welter of his affairs, with an unpleasant charge hanging over him, he had judged it the part of prudence to be off instantly, had written a fervid letter to his father at Inverauld, and put himself in the coach for Crossmichael. Any port in a storm! He was manfully turning his back on the Parliament House and its gay babble, on porter and oysters, the race-course and the ring; and manfully prepared, until these clouds should have blown by, to share a living grave with Archie Weir at Hermiston.

To do him justice, he was no less surprised to be going than Archie was to see him come; and he carried off his wonder with an infinitely better grace.

'Well, here I am!' said he, as he alighted. 'Pylades has come to Orestes at last. By the way, did you get my answer? No? How very provoking! Well, here I am to answer for myself, and that's better still.'

'I am very glad to see you, of course,' said Archie. 'I make you heartily welcome, of course. But you surely have not come to stay, with the Courts still sitting; is that not most unwise?'

'Damn the Courts!' says Frank. 'What are the Courts to friendship and a little fishing?'

And so it was agreed that he was to stay, with no term to the visit but the term which he had privily set to it himself – the day, namely, when his father should have come down with the dust, and he should be able to pacify the bookseller. On such vague conditions there began for these two young men (who were not even friends) a life of great familiarity and, as the days drew on, less and less intimacy. They were together at mealtimes, together o' nights when the hour had come for whisky-toddy; but it might have been noticed (had there been anyone to pay heed) that they were rarely so much together by day. Archie had Hermiston to attend to, multifarious activities in the hills, in which he did not require, and had even refused, Frank's escort. He would be off sometimes in the morning and leave only a note on the breakfast table to announce the fact; and sometimes, with no notice at all, he would not return for dinner until the hour was long past. Innes groaned under these desertions; it required all his philosophy to sit down to a solitary breakfast with composure, and all his unaffected good nature to be able to greet Archie with friendliness on the more rare occasions when he came home late for dinner.

'I wonder what on earth he finds to do, Mrs Elliott?' said he one morning, after he had just read the hasty billet and sat down to table.

'I suppose it will be business, sir,' replied the housekeeper drily, measuring his distance off to him by an indicated curtsey.

'But I can't imagine what business!' he reiterated.

'I suppose it will be *his* business,' retorted the austere Kirstie.

He turned to her with that happy brightness that made the charm of his disposition, and broke into a peal of healthy and natural laughter.

'Well played, Mrs Elliott!' he cried; and the housekeeper's face relaxed into the shadow of an iron smile. 'Well played indeed!' said he. 'But you must not be making a stranger of me like that. Why, Archie and I were at the High School together, and we've been to college together, and we were going to the Bar together, when – you know! Dear, dear me! what a pity that was! A life spoiled, a fine young fellow as good as buried here in the wilderness with rustics; and all for what? A frolic, silly, if you like, but no more. God, how good your scones are, Mrs Elliott!'

'They're no mines, it was the lassie made them,' said Kirstie; 'and, saving your presence, there's little sense in taking the Lord's name in vain about idle vivers that you fill your kyte wi'.'

'I daresay you're perfectly right, ma'am,' quoth the imperturbable Frank. 'But as I was saying, this is a pitiable business, this about poor Archie; and you and I might do worse than put our heads together, like a couple of sensible people, and bring it to an end. Let me tell you, ma'am, that Archie is really quite a promising young man, and in my opinion he would do well at the Bar. As for his father, no one can deny his ability, and I don't fancy anyone would care to deny that he has the deil's own temper –'

'If you'll excuse me, Mr Innes, I think the lass is crying on me,' said Kirstie, and flounced from the room.

'The damned, cross-grained old broomstick!' ejaculated Innes.

In the meantime, Kirstie had escaped into the kitchen, and before her vassal gave vent to her feelings.

'Here, ettercap! Ye'll have to wait on yon Innes! I canna haud myself in. "Puir Erchie!" I'd "puir Erchie" him, if I had my way! And Hermiston with the deil's ain temper! God, let him take Hermiston's scones out of his mouth first. There's no a hair on ayther o' the Weirs that hasna mair spunk and dirdum to it than what he has in his hale dwaibly body! Settin' up his snash to me! Let him gang to the black toon where he's mebbe wantit – birling in a curricle – wi' pimatum on his heid – making a mess o' himsel' wi' nesty hizzies – a fair disgrace!' It was impossible to hear without admiration Kirstie's graduated disgust, as she brought forth, one after another, these somewhat baseless charges. Then she remembered her immediate purpose, and turned again on her fascinated auditor. 'Do ye no hear me, tawpie? Do ye no hear what I'm tellin' ye? Will I have to shoo ye in to him? If I come to attend to ye, mistress!' And the maid fled the kitchen, which had become practically dangerous, to attend on Innes' wants in the front parlour.

Tantaene irae? Has the reader perceived the reason? Since Frank's coming there were no more hours of gossip over the supper tray! All his blandishments were in vain; he had started handicapped on the race for Mrs Elliott's favour.

But it was a strange thing how misfortune dogged him in his efforts to be genial. I must guard the reader against accepting Kirstie's epithets as evidence; she was more concerned for their vigour than for their accuracy. Dwaibly, for instance; nothing could be more calumnious. Frank was the very picture of good looks, good humour, and manly youth. He had bright eyes with a sparkle and a dance to them, curly hair, a charming smile, brilliant teeth, an admirable carriage of the head, the look of a gentleman, the address of one accustomed to please at first sight and to improve the impression. And with all these advantages, he failed with everyone about Hermiston; with the silent shepherd, with the obsequious grieve, with the groom who was also the ploughman, with the gardener and the gardener's sister – a pious, downhearted woman with a shawl over her ears – he failed equally and flatly. They did not like him, and they showed it. The little maid, indeed, was an exception; she admired him devoutly, probably dreamed of him in her private hours; but she was accustomed to play the part of silent auditor to Kirstie's tirades and silent recipient of Kirstie's buffets, and she had learned not only to be a very capable girl of her years, but a very secret and prudent one besides. Frank was thus conscious that he had one ally and sympathiser in the midst of that general union of disfavour that surrounded, watched, and waited on him in the house of Hermiston; but he had little comfort or society from that alliance, and the demure little maid (twelve on her last birthday) preserved her own counsel, and tripped on his service, brisk, dumbly responsive, but inexorably unconversational. For the others, they were beyond hope and beyond endurance. Never had a young Apollo been cast among such rustic barbarians. But perhaps the cause of his ill-success lay in one trait which was habitual and unconscious with him, yet diagnostic of the man. It was his practice to approach any one person at the expense of someone else. He offered you an alliance against the someone else; he flattered you by slighting him; you were drawn into a small intrigue against him before you knew how. Wonderful are the virtues of this process generally; but Frank's mistake was in the choice of the some-one else. He was not politic in that; he listened to the voice of irritation. Archie had offended him at first by what he had felt to be rather a dry reception, had offended him since by his frequent absences. He was besides the one figure continually present in Frank's eye; and it was to his immediate dependants that Frank could offer the snare of his sympathy. Now the truth is that the Weirs, father and son, were surrounded by a posse of strenuous loyalists. Of my lord they were vastly proud. It was a distinction in itself to be one of the vassals of the 'Hanging Judge,' and his gross, formidable joviality was far from unpopular in the neighbour-hood of his home. For Archie they had, one and all, a sensitive affection and respect which recoiled from a word of belittlement.

Nor was Frank more successful when he went farther afield. To the Four Black Brothers, for instance, he was antipathetic in the highest degree. Hob thought him too light, Gib too profane. Clem, who saw him but for a day or two before he went to Glasgow, wanted to know what the fule's business was, and whether he meant to stay here all session time! 'Yon's a drone,' he pronounced. As for Dand, it will be enough to describe their first meeting, when Frank had been whipping a river and the rustic celebrity chanced to come along the path.

'I'm told you're quite a poet,' Frank had said.

'What tell't ye that, mannie?' had been the unconciliating answer.

'O, everybody!' says Frank.

'God! Here's fame!' said the sardonic poet, and he had passed on his way.

Come to think of it, we have here perhaps a truer explanation of Frank's failures. Had he met Mr Sheriff Scott he could have turned a neater compliment, because Mr Scott would have been a friend worth making. Dand, on the other hand, he did not value sixpence, and he showed it even while he tried to flatter. Condescension is an excellent thing, but it is strange how one-sided the pleasure of it is! He who goes fishing among the Scots peasantry with condescension for a bait will have an empty basket by evening.

In proof of this theory Frank made a great success of it at the Crossmichael Club, to which Archie took him immediately on his arrival; his own last appearance on that scene of gaiety. Frank was made welcome there at once, continued to go regularly, and had attended a meeting (as the members ever after loved to tell) on the evening before his death. Young Hay and young Pringle appeared again. There was another supper at Windielaws, another dinner at Driffel; and it resulted in Frank being taken to the bosom of the county people as unreservedly as he had been repudiated by the country folk. He occupied Hermiston after the manner of an invader in a conquered capital. He was perpetually issuing from it, as from a base, to toddy parties, fishing parties, and dinner parties, to which Archie was not invited, or to which Archie would not go. It was now that the name of The Recluse became general for the young man. Some say that Innes invented it; Innes, at least, spread it abroad.

'How's all with your Recluse today?' people would ask.

'O, reclusing away!' Innes would declare, with his bright air of saying something witty; and immediately interrupt the general laughter which he had provoked much more by his air than his words, 'Mind you, it's all very well laughing, but I'm not very well pleased. Poor Archie is a good fellow, an excellent fellow, a fellow I always liked. I think it small of him to take his little disgrace so hard and shut himself up. "Grant that it is a ridiculous story, painfully ridiculous," I keep telling him. "Be a man! Live it down, man!" But not he. Of course, it's just solitude, and shame, and all that. But I confess I'm beginning to fear the result. It would be all the pities in the world if a really promising fellow like Weir was to end ill. I'm seriously tempted to write to Lord Hermiston, and put it plainly to him.'

'I would if I were you,' some of his auditors would say, shaking the head, sitting bewildered and confused at this new view of the matter, so deftly indicated by a single word. 'A capital idea!' they would add, and wonder at the *aplomb* and position of this young man, who talked as a matter of course of writing to Hermiston and correcting him upon his private affairs.

And Frank would proceed, sweetly confidential: 'I'll give you an idea, now. He's actually sore about the way that I'm received and he's left out in the county – actually jealous and sore. I've rallied him and I've reasoned with him, told him that everyone was most kindly inclined towards him, told him even that *I* was received merely because I was his guest. But it's no use. He will neither accept the invitations he gets, nor stop brooding about the ones where he's left out. What I'm afraid of is that the wound's ulcerating. He had always one of those dark, secret, angry natures – a little underhand and plenty of bile – you know the sort. He must have inherited it from the Weirs, whom I suspect to have been a worthy family of weavers somewhere; what's the cant phrase? sedentary occupation. It's precisely the kind of character to go wrong in a false position like what his father's made for him, or he's making for himself, whichever you like to call it. And for my part, I think it a disgrace,' Frank would say generously.

Presently the sorrow and anxiety of this disinterested friend took shape. He began in private, in conversations of two, to talk vaguely of bad habits and low habits. 'I must say I'm afraid he's going wrong altogether,' he would say. 'I'll tell you plainly, and between ourselves, I scarcely like to stay there any longer; only, man, I'm positively afraid to leave him alone. You'll see, I shall be blamed for it later on. I'm staying at a great sacrifice. I'm hindering my chances at the Bar, and I can't blind my eyes to it. And what I'm afraid of is that I'm going to get kicked for it all round before all's done. You see, nobody believes in friendship nowadays.'

'Well, Innes,' his interlocutor would reply, 'it's very good of you, I must say that. If there's any blame going, you'll always be sure of *my* good word, for one thing.'

'Well,' Frank would continue, 'candidly, I don't say it's pleasant. He has a very rough way with him; his father's son, you know. I don't say he's rude – of course, I couldn't be expected to stand that – but he steers very near the wind. No, it's not pleasant; but I tell ye, man, in conscience I don't think it would be fair to leave him. Mind you, I don't say there's anything actually wrong. What I say is that I don't like the looks of it, man!' and he would press the arm of his momentary confidant.

In the early stages I am persuaded there was no malice. He talked but for the pleasure of airing himself. He was essentially glib, as becomes the young advocate, and essentially careless of the truth, which is the mark of the young ass; and so he talked at random. There was no particular bias, but that one which is indigenous and universal, to flatter himself and to please and interest the present friend. And by thus milling air out of his mouth, he had presently built up a presentation of Archie which was known and talked of in all corners of the county. Wherever there was a residential house and a walled garden, wherever there was a dwarfish castle and a park, wherever a quadruple cottage by the ruins of a peel-tower showed an old family going down, and wherever a handsome villa with a carriage approach and a shrubbery marked the coming up of a new one – probably on the wheels of machinery – Archie began to be regarded in the light of a dark, perhaps a vicious mystery, and the future developments of his career to be looked for with uneasiness and confidential whispering. He had done something disgraceful, my dear. What, was not precisely known, and that good kind young man, Mr Innes, did his best to make light of it. But there it was. And Mr Innes was very anxious about him now; he was really uneasy, my dear; he was positively wrecking his own prospects because he dared not leave him alone. How wholly we all lie at the mercy of a single prater, not needfully with any malign purpose! And if a man but talks of himself in the right spirit, refers to his virtuous actions by the way, and never applies to them the name of virtue, how easily his evidence is accepted in the court of public opinion!

All this while, however, there was a more poisonous ferment at work between the two lads, which came late indeed to the surface, but had modified and magnified their dissensions from the first. To an idle, shallow, easy-going customer like Frank, the smell of a mystery was attractive. It gave his mind something to play with, like a new toy to a child; and it took him on the weak side, for like many young men coming to the Bar, and before they had been tried and found wanting, he flattered himself he was a fellow of unusual quickness and penetration. They knew nothing of Sherlock Holmes in those days, but there was a good deal said of Talleyrand. And if you could have caught Frank off his guard, he would have confessed with a smirk that, if he resembled anyone, it was the Marquis de Talleyrand-Périgord. It was on the occasion of Archie's first absence that this interest took root. It was vastly deepened when Kirstie resented his curiosity at breakfast, and that same afternoon there occurred another scene which clinched the business. He was fishing Swingleburn, Archie accompanying him, when the latter looked at his watch.

'Well, good-bye,' said he. 'I have something to do. See you at dinner.'

'Don't be in such a hurry,' cries Frank. 'Hold on till I get my rod up. I'll go with you; I'm sick of flogging this ditch.'

And he began to reel up his line.

Archie stood speechless. He took a long while to recover his wits under this direct attack; but by the time he was ready with his answer, and the angle was almost packed up, he had become completely Weir, and the hanging face gloomed on his young shoulders. He spoke with a laboured composure, a laboured kindness even; but a child could see that his mind was made up.

'I beg your pardon, Innes; I don't want to be disagreeable, but let us understand one another from the beginning. When I want your company, I'll let you know.'

'O!' cries Frank, 'you don't want my company, don't you?'

'Apparently not just now,' replied Archie. 'I even indicated to you when I did, if you'll remember – and that was at dinner. If we two fellows are to live together pleasantly – and I see no reason why we should not – it can only be by respecting each other's privacy. If we begin intruding –'

'O, come! I'll take this at no man's hands. Is this the way you treat a guest and an old friend?' cried Innes.

'Just go home and think over what I said by yourself,' continued Archie, 'whether it's reasonable, or whether it's really offensive or not;

and let's meet at dinner as though nothing had happened, I'll put it this way, if you like – that I know my own character, that I'm looking forward (with great pleasure, I assure you) to a long visit from you, and that I'm taking precautions at the first. I see the thing that we – that I, if you like – might fall out upon, and I step in and *obsto principiis*. I wager you five pounds you'll end by seeing that I mean friendliness, and I assure you, Francie, I do,' he added, relenting.

Bursting with anger, but incapable of speech, Innes shouldered his rod, made a gesture of farewell, and strode off down the burn-side. Archie watched him go without moving. He was sorry, but quite unashamed. He hated to be inhospitable, but in one thing he was his father's son. He had a strong sense that his house was his own and no man else's; and to lie at a guest's mercy was what he refused. He hated to seem harsh. But that was Frank's lookout. If Frank had been commonly discreet, he would have been decently courteous. And there was another consideration. The secret he was protecting was not his own merely; it was hers: it belonged to that inexpressible she who was fast taking possession of his soul, and whom he would soon have defended at the cost of burning cities. By the time he had watched Frank as far as the Swingleburn-foot, appearing and disappearing in the tarnished heather, still stalking at a fierce gait but already dwindled in the distance into less than the smallness of Lilliput, he could afford to smile at the occurrence. Either Frank would go, and that would be a relief – or he would continue to stay, and his host must continue to endure him. And Archie was now free – by devious paths, behind hillocks and in the hollow of burns – to make for the trysting-place where Kirstie, cried about by the curlew and the plover, waited and burned for his coming by the Covenanter's stone.

Innes went off downhill in a passion of resentment, easy to be under-stood, but which yielded progressively to the needs of his situation. He cursed Archie for a cold-hearted, unfriendly, rude, rude dog; and himself still more passionately for a fool in having come to Hermiston when he might have sought refuge in almost any other house in Scotland. But the step once taken, was practically irretrievable. He had no more ready money to go anywhere else; he would have to borrow from Archie the next club-night; and ill as he thought of his host's manners, he was sure of his practical generosity. Frank's resemblance to Talleyrand strikes me as imaginary; but at least not Talleyrand himself could have more obediently taken his lesson from the facts. He met Archie at dinner without resentment, almost with cordiality. You must take your friends as you find them, he would have said. Archie couldn't help being his father's son, or his grandfather's, the hypothetical weaver's, grandson. The son of a hunks, he was still a hunks at heart, incapable of true generosity and consideration; but he had other qualities with which Frank could divert himself in the meanwhile, and to enjoy which it was necessary that Frank should keep his temper.

So excellently was it controlled that he awoke next morning with his head full of a different, though a cognate subject. What was Archie's little game? Why did he shun Frank's company? What was he keeping secret? Was he keeping tryst with somebody, and was it a woman? It would be a good joke and a fair revenge to discover. To that task he set himself with a great deal of patience, which might have surprised his friends, for he had been always credited not with patience so much as brilliancy; and little by little, from one point to another, he at last succeeded in piecing out the situation. First he remarked that, although Archie set out in all the directions of the compass, he always came home again from some point between the south and west. From the study of a map, and in consideration of the great expanse of untenanted moorland running in that direction towards the sources of the Clyde, he laid his finger on Cauldstaneslap and two other neighbouring farms, Kingsmuirs and Polintarf. But it was difficult to advance farther. With his rod for a pretext, he vainly visited each of them in turn; nothing was to be seen suspicious about this trinity of moorland settlements. He would have tried to follow Archie, had it been the least possible, but the nature of the land precluded the idea. He did the next best, ensconced himself in a quiet corner, and pursued his movements with a telescope. It was equally in vain, and he soon wearied of his futile vigilance, left the telescope at home, and had almost given the matter up in despair, when, on the twenty-seventh day of his visit, he was suddenly confronted with the person whom he sought. The first Sunday Kirstie had managed to stay away from kirk on some pretext of indisposition, which was more truly modesty; the pleasure of beholding Archie seeming too sacred, too vivid for that public place. On the two following, Frank had himself been absent on some of his excursions among the neighbouring families. It was not until the fourth, accordingly, that Frank had occasion to set eyes on the enchantress. With the first look, all hesitation was over. She came with the Cauldstaneslap party; then she lived at Cauldstaneslap. Here was Archie's secret, here was the woman, and more than that – though I have need here of every manageable attenuation of language – with the first look, he had already entered himself as rival. It was a good deal in pique, it was a little in revenge, it was much in genuine admiration: the devil may decide the proportions! I cannot, and it is very likely that Frank could not.

'Mighty attractive milkmaid,' he observed, on the way home.

'Who?' said Archie.

'O, the girl you're looking at – aren't you? Forward there on the road. She came attended by the rustic bard; presumably, therefore, belongs to his exalted family. The single objection! for the four black brothers are awkward customers. If anything were to go wrong, Gib would gibber, and Clem would prove inclement; and Dand fly in danders, and Hob blow up in gobbets. It would be a Helliott of a business!'

'Very humorous, I am sure,' said Archie.

'Well, I am trying to be so,' said Frank. 'It's none too easy in this place, and with your solemn society, my dear fellow. But confess that the milkmaid has found favour in your eyes, or resign all claim to be a man of taste.'

'It is no matter,' returned Archie.

But the other continued to look at him, steadily and quizzically, and his colour slowly rose and deepened under the glance, until not impudence itself could have denied that he was blushing. And at this Archie lost some of his control. He changed his stick from one hand to the other, and – 'O, for God's sake, don't be an ass!' he cried.

'Ass? That's the retort delicate without doubt,' says Frank, 'Beware of the homespun brothers, dear. If they come into the dance, you'll see who's an ass. Think now, if they only applied (say) a quarter as much talent as I have applied to the question of what Mr Archie does with his evening hours, and why he is so unaffectedly nasty when the subject's touched on –'

'You are touching on it now,' interrupted Archie with a wince.

'Thank you. That was all I wanted, an articulate confession,' said Frank.

'I beg to remind you –' began Archie.

But he was interrupted in turn. 'My dear fellow, don't. It's quite need-less. The subject's dead and buried.'

And Frank began to talk hastily on other matters, an art in which he was an adept, for it was his gift to be fluent on anything or nothing. But although Archie had the grace or the timidity to suffer him to rattle on, he was by no means done with the subject. When he came home to dinner, he was greeted with a sly demand, how things were looking 'Cauldstaneslap ways.' Frank took his first glass of port out after dinner to the toast of Kirstie, and later in the evening he returned to the charge again.

'I say, Weir, you'll excuse me for returning again to this affair. I've been thinking it over, and I wish to beg you very seriously to be more careful. It's not a safe business. Not safe, my boy,' said he.

'What?' said Archie.

'Well, it's your own fault if I must put a name on the thing; but really, as a friend, I cannot stand by and see you rushing head down into these dangers. My dear boy,' said he, holding up a warning cigar, 'consider! What is to be the end of it?'

'The end of what?' – Archie, helpless with irritation, persisted in this dangerous and ungracious guard.

'Well, the end of the milkmaid; or, to speak more by the card, the end of Miss Christina Elliott of the Cauldstaneslap.'

'I assure you,' Archie broke out, 'this is all a figment of your imagin-ation. There is nothing to be said against that young lady; you have no right to introduce her name into the conversation.'

'I'll make a note of it,' said Frank. 'She shall henceforth be nameless, nameless, nameless, Grigalach! I make a note besides of your valuable testimony to her character. I only want to look at this thing as a man of the world. Admitted she's an angel – but, my good fellow, is she a lady?'

This was torture to Archie. 'I beg your pardon,' he said, struggling to be composed, 'but because you have wormed yourself into my confidence –'

'O, come!' cried Frank. 'Your confidence? It was rosy but uncon-senting. Your confidence, indeed? Now, look! This is what I must say, Weir, for it concerns your safety and good character, and therefore my honour as your friend. You say I wormed myself into your confidence. Wormed is good. But what have I done? I have put two and two together, just as the parish will be doing tomorrow, and the whole of Tweeddale in two weeks, and the black brothers – well, I won't put a date on that; it will be a dark and stormy morning! Your secret, in other words, is poor Poll's. And I want to ask of you as a friend whether you like the prospect? There are two horns to your dilemma, and I must say for myself I should look mighty ruefully on either. Do you see yourself explaining to the four Black Brothers? or do you see yourself presenting the milkmaid to papa as the future lady of Hermiston? Do you? I tell you plainly, I don't!'

Archie rose. 'I will hear no more of this,' he said, in a trembling voice.

But Frank again held up his cigar. 'Tell me one thing first. Tell me if this is not a friend's part that I am playing?'

'I believe you think it so,' replied Archie. 'I can go as far as that. I can do so much justice to your motives. But I will hear no more of it. I am going to bed.'

'That's right, Weir,' said Frank heartily. 'Go to bed and think over it; and I say, man, don't forget your prayers! I don't often do the moral – don't go in for that sort of thing – but when I do there's one thing sure, that I mean it.'

So Archie marched off to bed, and Frank sat alone by the table for another hour or so, smiling to himself richly. There was nothing vindictive in his nature; but, if revenge came in his way, it might as well be good, and the thought of Archie's pillow reflections that night was indescribably sweet to him. He felt a pleasant sense of power. He looked down on Archie as on a very little boy whose strings he pulled – as on a horse whom he had backed and bridled by sheer power of intelligence, and whom he might ride to glory or the grave at pleasure. Which was it to be? He lingered long, relishing the details of schemes that he was too idle to pursue. Poor cork upon a torrent, he tasted that night the sweets of omnipotence, and brooded like a deity over the strands of that intrigue which was to shatter him before the summer waned.

VIII

Kirstie had many causes of distress. More and more as we grow old – and yet more and more as we grow old and are women, frozen by the fear of age – we come to rely on the voice as the single outlet of the soul. Only thus, in the curtailment of our means, can we relieve the straitened cry of the passion within us; only thus, in the bitter and sensitive shyness of advancing years, can we maintain relations with those vivacious figures of the young that still show before us and tend daily to become no more than the moving wallpaper of life. Talk is the last link, the last relation. But with the end of the conversation, when the voice stops and the bright face of the listener is turned away, solitude falls again on the bruised heart. Kirstie had lost her 'cannie hour at e'en'; she could no more wander with Archie, a ghost if you will, but a happy ghost, in fields Elysian. And to her it was as if the whole world had fallen silent; to him, but an unremarkable change of amusements. And she raged to know it. The effervescency of her passionate and irritable nature rose within her at times to bursting point.

This is the price paid by age for unseasonable ardours of feeling. It must have been so for Kirstie at any time when the occasion chanced; but it so fell out that she was deprived of this delight in the hour when she had most need of it, when she had most to say, most to ask, and when she trembled to recognise her sovereignty not merely in abeyance but annulled. For, with the clairvoyance of a genuine love, she had pierced the mystery that had so long embarrassed Frank. She was conscious, even before it was carried out, even on that Sunday night when it began, of an invasion of her rights; and a voice told her the invader's name. Since then, by arts, by accident, by small things observed, and by the general drift of Archie's humour, she had passed beyond all possibility of doubt. With a sense of justice that Lord Hermiston might have envied, she had that day in church considered and admitted the attractions of the younger Kirstie; and with the profound humanity and sentimentality of her nature, she had recognised the coming of fate. Not thus would she have chosen. She had seen, in imagination, Archie wedded to some tall, powerful, and rosy heroine of the golden locks, made in her own image, for whom she would have strewed the bride-bed with delight; and now she could have wept to see the ambition falsified. But the gods had pronounced, and her doom was otherwise.

She lay tossing in bed that night, besieged with feverish thoughts. There were dangerous matters pending, a battle was toward, over the fate of which she hung in jealousy, sympathy, fear, and alternate loyalty and disloyalty to either side. Now she was reincarnated in her niece, and now in Archie. Now she saw, through the girl's eyes, the youth on his knees to her, heard his persuasive instances with a deadly weakness, and received his overmastering caresses. Anon, with a revulsion, her temper raged to see such utmost favours of fortune and love squandered on a brat of a girl, one of her own house, using her own name – a deadly ingredient – and that 'didna ken her ain mind an' was as black's your hat.' Now she trembled lest her deity should plead in vain, loving the idea of success for him like a triumph of nature; anon, with returning loyalty to her own family and sex, she trembled for Kirstie and the credit of the Elliotts. And again she had a vision of herself, the day over for her old-world tales and local gossip, bidding farewell to her last link with life and brightness and love; and behind and beyond, she saw but the blank butt-end where she must crawl to die. Had she then come to the lees? she, so great, so beautiful, with a heart as fresh as a girl's and strong as womanhood? It could not be, and yet it was so; and for a moment her bed was horrible to her as the sides of the grave. And she looked forward over a waste of hours, and saw herself go on to rage, and tremble, and be softened, and rage again, until the day came and the labours of the day must be renewed.

Suddenly she heard feet on the stairs – his feet, and soon after the sound of a window-sash flung open. She sat up with her heart beating. He had gone to his room alone, and he had not gone to bed. She might again have one of her night cracks; and at the entrancing prospect, a change came over her mind; with the approach of this hope of pleasure, all the baser metal became immediately obliterated from her thoughts. She rose, all woman, and all the best of woman, tender, pitiful, hating the wrong, loyal to her own sex – and all the weakest of that dear miscellany, nourishing, cherishing next her soft heart, voicelessly flattering, hopes that she would have died sooner than have acknowledged. She tore off her nightcap, and her hair fell about her shoulders in profusion. Undying coquetry awoke. By the faint light of her nocturnal rush, she stood before the looking-glass, carried her shapely arms above her head, and gathered up the treasures of her tresses. She was never backward to admire herself; that kind of modesty was a stranger to her nature; and she paused, struck with a pleased wonder at the sight. 'Ye daft auld wife!' she said, answering a thought that was not; and she blushed with the innocent conscious-ness of a child. Hastily she did up the massive and shining coils, hastily donned a wrapper, and with the rushlight in her hand, stole into the hall. Below stairs she heard the clock ticking the deliberate seconds, and Frank jingling with the decanters in the dining-room. Aversion rose in her, bitter and momentary. 'Nesty, tippling puggy!' she thought; and the next moment she had knocked guardedly at Archie's door and was bidden enter.

Archie had been looking out into the ancient blackness, pierced here and there with a rayless star; taking the sweet air of the moors and the night into his bosom deeply; seeking, perhaps finding, peace after the manner of the unhappy. He turned round as she came in, and showed her a pale face against the window-frame.

'Is that you, Kirstie?' he asked. 'Come in!'

'It's unco late, my dear,' said Kirstie, affecting unwillingness.

'No, no,' he answered, 'not at all. Come in, if you want a crack. I am not sleepy, God knows!'

She advanced, took a chair by the toilet table and the candle, and set the rushlight at her foot. Something – it might be in the comparative disorder of her dress, it might be the emotion that now welled in her bosom – had touched her with a wand of transformation, and she seemed young with the youth of goddesses.

'Mr Erchie,' she began, 'what's this that's come to ye?'

'I am not aware of anything that has come,' said Archie, and blushed and repented bitterly that he had let her in.

'O, my dear, that'll no dae!' said Kirstie. 'It's ill to blend the eyes of love. O, Mr Erchie, tak a thocht ere it's ower late. Ye shouldna be impatient o' the braws o' life, they'll a' come in their saison, like the sun and the rain. Ye're young yet; ye've mony cantie years afore ye. See and dinna wreck yersel' at the outset like sae mony ithers; Hae patience – they telled me aye that was the owercome o' life – hae patience, there's a braw day coming yet. Gude kens it never came to me; and here I am, wi' nayther man nor bairn to ca' my ain, wearying a' folks wi' my ill tongue, and you just the first, Mr Erchie!'

'I have a difficulty in knowing what you mean,' said Archie.

'Weel, and I'll tell ye,' she said. 'It's just this, that I'm feared. I'm feared for ye, my dear. Remember, your faither is a hard man, reaping where he hasna sowed and gaithering where he hasna strawed. It's easy speakin', but mind! Ye'll have to look in the gurly face o'm, where it's ill to look, and vain to look for mercy. Ye mind me o' a bonny ship pitten oot into the black and gowsty seas – ye're a' safe still, sittin' quait and crackini' w' Kirstie in your lown chalmer; but whaur will ye be the morn, and in whatten horror o' the fearsome tempest, cryin' on the hills to cover ye?'

'Why, Kirstie, you're very enigmatical tonight – and very eloquent,' Archie put in.

'And, my dear Mr Erchie,' she continued; with a change of voice, 'ye mauna think that I canna sympathise wi' ye. Ye mauna think that I havena been young mysel'. Lang syne, when I was a bit lassie, no twenty yet –' She paused and sighed. 'Clean and caller, wi' a fit like the hinney bee,' she continued. 'I was aye big and buirdly, ye maun understand; a bonny figure o' a woman, though I say it that suldna – built to rear bairns – braw bairns they suld hae been, and grand I would hae likit it! But I was young, dear, wi' the bonny glint o' youth in my e'en, and little I dreamed I'd ever be tellin' ye this, an auld, lanely, rudas wife! Weel, Mr Erchie, there was a lad cam' courtin' me, as was but naetural. Mony had come before, and I would nane o' them. But this yin had a tongue to wile the birds frae the lift and the bees frae the foxglove bells. Deary me, but it's lang syne! Folk have dee'd sinsyne and been buried, and are forgotten, and bairns been born and got merrit and got bairns o' their ain. Sinsyne woods have been plantit, and have grawn up and are bonny trees, and the joes sit in their shadow, and sinsyne auld estates have changed hands, and there have been wars and rumours of wars on the face of the earth. And here I'm still – like an auld droopit craw – lookin' on and craikin'! But, Mr Erchie, do ye no think that I have mind o' it a' still? I was dwalling then in my faither's house; and it's a curious thing that we were whiles trysted in the Deil's Hags. And do ye no think that I have mind of the bonny simmer days, the lang miles o' the bluid-red heather, the cryin' o' the whaups, and the lad and the lassie that was trysted? Do ye no think that I mind how the hilly sweetness ran about my hairt? Ay, Mr Erchie, I ken the way o' it – fine do I ken the way – how the grace o' God takes them, like Paul of Tarsus, when they think it least, and drives the pair o' them into a land which is like a dream, and the world and the folks in't are nae mair than clouds to the puir lassie, and heeven nae mair than windle-straes, if she can but pleesure him! Until Tam dee'd – that was my story,' she broke off to say, 'he dee'd, and I wasna at the buryin'. But while he was here, I could take care o' mysel'. And can yon puir lassie?'

Kirstie, her eyes shining with unshed tears, stretched out her hand towards him appealingly; the bright and the dull gold of her hair flashed and smouldered in the coils behind her comely head, like the rays of an eternal youth; the pure colour had risen in her face; and Archie was abashed alike by her beauty and her story. He came towards her slowly from the window, took up her hand in his and kissed it.

'Kirstie,' he said hoarsely, 'you have misjudged me sorely. I have always thought of her, I wouldna harm her for the universe, my woman!'

'Eh, lad, and that's easy sayin',' cried Kirstie, 'but it's nane sae easy doin'! Man, do ye no comprehend that it's God's wull we should be blendit and glamoured, and have nae command over our ain members at a time like that? My brain,' she cried, still holding his hand, 'think o' the puir lass! have pity upon her, Erchie! and O, be wise for twa! Think o' the risk she rins! I have seen ye, and what's to prevent ithers! I saw ye once in the Hags, in my ain howl, and I was wae to see ye there – in pairt for the omen, for I think there's a weird on the place – and in pairt for pure nakit envy and bitterness o' hairt. It's strange ye should forgather there tae! God! but yon puir, thrawn, auld Covenanter's seen a heap o' human nature since he lookit his last on the musket barrels, if he never saw nane afore,' she added, with a kind of wonder in her eyes.

'I swear by my honour I have done her no wrong,' said Archie. 'I swear by my honour and the redemption of my soul that there shall none be done her. I have heard of this before. I have been foolish, Kirstie, not unkind, and, above all, not base.'

'There's my bairn!' said Kirstie, rising. 'I'll can trust ye noo, I'll can gang to my bed wi' an easy hairt.' And then she saw in a flash how barren had been her triumph. Archie had promised to spare the girl, and he would keep it; but who had promised to spare Archie? What was to be the end of it? Over a maze of difficulties she glanced, and saw, at the end of every passage, the flinty countenance of Hermiston. And a kind of horror fell upon her at what she had done. She wore a tragic mask. 'Erchie, the Lord peety you, dear, and peety me! I have buildit on this foundation' – laying her hand heavily on his shoulder – 'and buildit hie, and put my hairt in the buildin' of it. If the hale hypothec were to fa', I think, laddie, I would dee! Excuse a daft wife that loves ye, and that kenned your mither. And for His name's sake keep yersel' frae inordinate desires; haud your heart in baith your hands, carry it canny and laigh; dinna send it up like a bairn's kite into the collie-shangie o' the wunds! Mind, Maister Erchie dear, that this life's a' disappointment, and a mouthfu' o' mools is the appointed end.'

'Ay, but Kirstie, my woman, you're asking me ower much at last,' said Archie, profoundly moved, and lapsing into the broad Scots. 'Ye're asking what nae man can grant ye, what only the Lord of Heaven can grant ye if He see fit. Ay! And can even He! I can promise ye what I shall do, and you can depend on that. But how I shall feel – my woman, that is long past thinking of!'

They were both standing by now opposite each other. The face of Archie wore the wretched semblance of a smile; hers was convulsed for a moment.

'Promise me ae thing,' she cried in a sharp voice. 'Promise me ye'll never do naething without telling me.'

'No, Kirstie, I canna promise ye that,' he replied. 'I have promised enough, God kens!'

'May the blessing of God lift and rest upon ye, dear!' she said.

'God bless ye, my old friend,' said he.

IX

It was late in the afternoon when Archie drew near by the hill path to the Praying Weaver's stone. The Hags were in shadow. But still, through the gate of the Slap, the sun shot a last arrow, which sped far and straight across the surface of the moss, here and there touching and shining on a tussock, and lighted at length on the gravestone and the small figure awaiting him there. The emptiness and solitude of the great moors seemed to be concentrated there, and Kirstie pointed out by that figure of sunshine for the only inhabitant. His first sight of her was thus excruciatingly sad, like a glimpse of a world from which all light, comfort, and society were on the point of vanishing. And the next moment, when she had turned her face to him and the quick smile had enlightened it, the whole face of nature smiled upon him in her smile of welcome. Archie's slow pace was quickened; his legs hasted to her though his heart was hanging back.

The girl, upon her side, drew herself together slowly and stood up, expectant; she was all languor, her face was gone white; her arms ached for him, her soul was on tiptoes. But he deceived her, pausing a few steps away, not less white than herself, and holding up his hand with a gesture of denial.

'No, Christina, not today,' he said. 'Today I have to talk to you seriously. Sit ye down, please, there where you were. Please!' he repeated.

The revulsion of feeling in Christina's heart was violent. To have longed and waited these weary hours for him, rehearsing her endearments – to have seen him at last come – to have been ready there, breathless, wholly passive, his to do what he would with – and suddenly to have found herself confronted with a grey-faced, harsh schoolmaster – it was too rude a shock. She could have wept, but pride withheld her. She sat down on the stone, from which she had arisen, part with the instinct of obedience, part as though she had been thrust there. What was this? Why was she rejected? Had she ceased to please? She stood here offering her wares, and he would none of them! And yet they were all his! His to take and keep, not his to refuse though! In her quick petulant nature, a moment ago on fire with hope, thwarted love and wounded vanity wrought. The schoolmaster that there is in all men, to the despair of all girls and most women, was now completely in possession of Archie. He had passed a night of sermons, a day of reflection; he had come wound up to do his duty; and the set mouth, which in him only betrayed the effort of his will, to her seemed the expression of an averted heart. It was the same with his constrained voice and embarrassed utterance; and if so – if it was all over – the pang of the thought took away from her the power of thinking.

He stood before her some way off. 'Kirstie, there's been too much of this. We've seen too much of each other.' She looked up quickly and her eyes contracted. 'There's no good ever comes of these secret meetings. They're not frank, not honest truly, and I ought to have seen it. People have begun to talk; and it's not right of me. Do you see?'

'I see somebody will have been talking to ye,' she said sullenly.

'They have, more than one of them,' replied Archie.

'And whae were they?' she cried. 'And what kind o' love do ye ca' that, that's ready to gang round like a whirligig at folk talking? Do ye think they havena talked to me?'

'Have they indeed?' said Archie, with a quick breath. 'That is what I feared. Who were they? Who has dared –?'

Archie was on the point of losing his temper.

As a matter of fact, not anyone had talked to Christina on the matter; and she strenuously repeated her own first question in a panic of self-defence.

'Ah, well! what does it matter?' he said. 'They were good folk that wished well to us, and the great affair is that there are people talking. My dear girl, we have to be wise. We must not wreck our lives at the outset. They may be long and happy yet, and we must see to it, Kirstie, like God's rational creatures and not like fool children. There is one thing we must see to before all. You're worth waiting for, Kirstie! worth waiting for a generation; it would be enough reward.' – And here he remembered the schoolmaster again, and very unwisely took to following wisdom. 'The first thing that we must see to, is that there shall be no scandal about for my father's sake. That would ruin all; do ye no see that?'

Kirstie was a little pleased, there had been some show of warmth of sentiment in what Archie had said last. But the dull irritation still persisted in her bosom; with the aboriginal instinct, having suffered herself, she wished to make Archie suffer.

And besides, there had come out the word she had always feared to hear from his lips, the name of his father. It is not to be supposed that, during so many days with a love avowed between them, some reference had not been made to their conjoint future. It had in fact been often touched upon, and from the first had been the sore point. Kirstie had wilfully closed the eye of thought; she would not argue even with herself; gallant, desperate little heart, she had accepted the command of that supreme attraction like the call of fate and marched blindfold on her doom. But Archie, with his masculine sense of responsibility, must reason; he must dwell on some future good, when the present good was all in all to Kirstie; he must talk – and talk lamely, as necessity drove him – of what was to be. Again and again he had touched on marriage; again and again been driven back into indistinctness by a memory of Lord Hermiston. And Kirstie had been swift to understand and quick to choke down and smother the understanding; swift to leap up in flame at a mention of that hope, which spoke volumes to her vanity and her love, that she might one day be Mrs Weir of Hermiston; swift also, to recognise in his stumbling or throttled utterance the death-knell of these expectations, and constant, poor girl! in her large-minded madness, to go on and to reck nothing of the future. But these unfinished references, these blinks in which his heart spoke, and his memory and reason rose up to silence it before the words were well uttered, gave her unqualifiable agony. She was raised up and dashed down again bleeding. The recurrence of the subject forced her, for however short a time, to open her eyes on what she did not wish to see; and it had invariably ended in another disappointment. So now again, at the mere wind of its coming, at the mere mention of his father's name – who might seem indeed to have accompanied them in their whole moorland courtship, an awful figure in a wig with an ironical and bitter smile, present to guilty consciousness – she fled from it head down.

'Ye havena told me yet,' she said, 'who was it spoke?'

'Your aunt for one,' said Archie.

'Auntie Kirstie?' she cried. 'And what do I care for my Auntie Kirstie?'

'She cares a great deal for her niece,' replied Archie, in kind reproof.

'Troth, and it's the first I've heard of it,' retorted the girl.

'The question here is not who it is, but what they say, what they have noticed,' pursued the lucid schoolmaster. 'That is what we have to think of in self-defence.'

'Auntie Kirstie, indeed! A bitter, thrawn auld maid that's fomented trouble in the country before I was born, and will be doing it still, I daur say, when I'm deid! It's in her nature; it's as natural for her as it's for a sheep to eat.'

'Pardon me, Kirstie, she was not the only one,' interposed Archie. 'I had two warnings, two sermons, last night, both most kind and considerate. Had you been there, I promise you you would have grat, my dear! And they opened my eyes. I saw we were going a wrong way.'

'Who was the other one?' Kirstie demanded.

By this time Archie was in the condition of a hunted beast. He had come, braced and resolute; he was to trace out a line of conduct for the pair of them in a few cold, convincing sentences; he had now been there some time, and he was still staggering round the outworks and undergoing what he felt to be a savage cross-examination.

'Mr Frank!' she cried. 'What nex', I would like to ken?'

'He spoke most kindly and truly.'

'What like did he say?'

'I am not going to tell you; you have nothing to do with that,' cried Archie, startled to find he had admitted so much.

'O, I have naething to do with it!' she repeated, springing to her feet. 'A'body at Hermiston's free to pass their opinions upon me, but I have naething to do wi' it! Was this at prayers like? Did ye ca' the grieve into the consultation? Little wonder if a'body's talking, when ye make a'body yer confidants! But as you say, Mr Weir – most kindly, most consider-ately, most truly, I'm sure – I have naething to do with it. And I think I'll better be going. I'll be wishing you good evening, Mr Weir.' And she made him a stately curtsey, shaking as she did so from head to foot, with the barren ecstasy of temper.

Poor Archie stood dumbfounded. She had moved some steps away from him before he recovered the gift of articulate speech.

'Kirstie!' he cried. 'O, Kirstie woman!'

There was in his voice a ring of appeal, a clang of mere astonishment that showed the schoolmaster was vanquished.

She turned round on him. 'What do ye Kirstie me for?' she retorted. 'What have ye to do wi' me! Gang to your ain freends and deave them!'

He could only repeat the appealing 'Kirstie!'

'Kirstie, indeed!' cried the girl, her eyes blazing in her white face. 'My name is Miss Christina Elliott, I would have ye to ken, and I daur ye to ca' me out of it. If I canna get love, I'll have respect, Mr Weir. I'm come of decent people, and I'll have respect. What have I done that ye should lightly me? What have I done? What have I done? O, what have I done?' and her voice rose upon the third repetition. 'I thocht – I thocht – I thocht I was sae happy!' and the first sob broke from her like the paroxysm of some mortal sickness.

Archie ran to her. He took the poor child in his arms, and she nestled to his breast as to a mother's, and clasped him in hands that were strong like vices. He felt her whole body shaken by the throes of distress, and had pity upon her beyond speech. Pity, and at the same time a bewil-dered fear of this explosive engine in his arms, whose works he did not understand, and yet had been tampering with. There arose from before him the curtains of boyhood, and he saw for the first time the ambiguous face of woman as she is. In vain he looked back over the interview; he saw not where he had offended. It seemed unprovoked, a wilful convulsion of brute nature . . .

THE
TURN OF THE
SCREW

THE TURN OF THE SCREW

HENRY JAMES

This edition published in 2019 by Arcturus Publishing Limited
26/27 Bickels Yard, 151–153 Bermondsey Street,
London SE1 3HA

Cover design: Peter Ridley
Cover illustration: Peter Gray
Design: Beatriz Custodio

AD005703UK

Printed in the UK

Contents

Introduction 7
Prologue 9
I 18
II 23
III 28
IV 34
V 40
VI 45
VII 53
VIII 58
IX 64
X 70
XI 75
XII 80
XIII 84
XIV 90
XV 95
XVI 99
XVII 103
XVIII 108
XIX 112
XX 117
XXI 122
XXII 129
XXIII 134
XXIV 139

Introduction

The Turn of the Screw was described by Oscar Wilde as 'a most wonderful, lurid poisonous little tale', and was inspired by the Archbishop of Canterbury.

On a winter's day in 1895, the leader of the Church of England told Henry James a ghost story involving children. We know this because James made notes in his diary.

The novella that subsequently evolved was a deliberate attempt to make money – and reach an audience that James knew would not engage in his other work. Henry James (1843–1916) was both writer and critic, interested in perception and consciousness and keen to experiment with narrative style. He had his admirers, but admiration pays no bills.

Hence *The Turn of the Screw*, a work he intended as a 'potboiler'. The novella was first serialised in *Collier's Weekly* in 1898 – and this blend of horror, gothic and ghost story has been attracting and repelling readers ever since. It even frightened the author himself. After correcting the proofs of his story, he was 'afraid to go upstairs to bed'.

What makes the story so unnerving is that it is difficult to be certain what is happening. Is the young governess slowly losing her mind? Are the ghosts real? Or – and perhaps this is the most frightening possibility – it's not a case of *either/or*; it's a case of *and*.

The ambiguity may be deliberate. The introduction is unusual, the ending seems incomplete, and questions are left unanswered.

An unnamed narrator introduces a man named Douglas, who in turn announces that he has an interesting manuscript. This was written some 20 years previously and given to him by a woman he will not admit he loved. Before setting pen to paper, she has not told her story to anyone else. Why is she telling it to him now?

What she wrote takes up most of the novella, and when her manuscript is complete, so too is the story. We do not return to Douglas or the unnamed narrator – and readers are left to try to make their own sense of what they have been told.

Perhaps this explains the many creative responses that have followed. It influenced the structure of Joseph Conrad's *Heart of Darkness*; it inspired an opera by Benjamin Britten; numerous films have been made, notably *The Innocents*, described by critic Pauline Kael as 'the best ghost movie I've seen'; and the story has been reworked by authors ranging from A. N. Wilson to Sarah Waters and Rumer Goden to Joyce Carol Oates.

The Turn of the Screw

The story had held us, round the fire, sufficiently breathless, but except the obvious remark that it was gruesome, as, on Christmas Eve in an old house, a strange tale should essentially be, I remember no comment uttered till somebody happened to say that it was the only case he had met in which such a visitation had fallen on a child. The case, I may mention, was that of an apparition in just such an old house as had gathered us for the occasion – an appearance, of a dreadful kind, to a little boy sleeping in the room with his mother and waking her up in the terror of it; waking her not to dissipate his dread and soothe him to sleep again, but to encounter also, herself, before she had succeeded in doing so, the same sight that had shaken him. It was this observation that drew from Douglas – not immediately, but later in the evening – a reply that had the interesting consequence to which I call attention. Someone else told a story not particularly effective, which I saw he was not following. This I took for a sign that he had himself something to produce and that we should only have to wait. We waited in fact till two nights later; but that same evening, before we scattered, he brought out what was in his mind.

"I quite agree – in regard to Griffin's ghost, or whatever it was – that its appearing first to the little boy, at so tender an age, adds a particular touch. But it's not the first occurrence of its charming kind that I know to have involved a child. If the child gives the effect another turn of the screw, what do you say to *two* children – ?"

"We say, of course," somebody exclaimed, "that they give two turns! Also that we want to hear about them."

I can see Douglas there before the fire, to which he had got up to present his back, looking down at his interlocutor with his hands in his pockets. "Nobody but me, till now, has ever heard. It's quite too horrible." This, naturally, was declared by several voices to give the thing the utmost price, and our friend, with quiet art, prepared his triumph by turning his eyes over the rest of us and going on: "It's beyond everything. Nothing at all that I know touches it."

"For sheer terror?" I remember asking.

He seemed to say it was not so simple as that; to be really at a loss how to qualify it. He passed his hand over his eyes, made a little wincing grimace. "For dreadful – dreadfulness!"

"Oh, how delicious!" cried one of the women.

He took no notice of her; he looked at me, but as if, instead of me, he saw what he spoke of. "For general uncanny ugliness and horror and pain."

"Well then," I said, "just sit right down and begin."

He turned round to the fire, gave a kick to a log, watched it an instant. Then as he faced us again: "I can't begin. I shall have to send to town." There was a unanimous groan at this, and much reproach; after which, in his preoccupied way, he explained. "The story's written. It's in a locked drawer – it has not been out for years. I could write to my man and enclose the key; he could send down the packet as he finds it." It was to me in particular that he appeared to propound this – appeared almost to appeal for aid not to hesitate. He had broken a thickness of ice, the formation of many a winter; had had his reasons for a long silence. The others resented postponement, but it was just his scruples that charmed me. I adjured him to write by the first post and to agree with us for an early hearing; then I asked him if the experience in question had been his own. To this his answer was prompt. "Oh, thank God, no!"

"And is the record yours? You took the thing down?"

"Nothing but the impression. I took that *here*," – he tapped his heart. "I've never lost it."

"Then your manuscript – ?"

"Is in old, faded ink, and in the most beautiful hand." He hung fire again. "A woman's. She has been dead these twenty years. She sent me the pages in question before she died." They were all listening now, and of course there was somebody to be arch, or at any rate to draw the inference. But if he put the inference by without a smile it was also without irritation. "She was a most charming person, but she was ten years older than I. She was my sister's governess," he quietly said. "She was the most agreeable woman I've ever known in her position; she would have been worthy of any whatever. It was long ago, and this episode was long before. I was at Trinity, and I found her at home on my coming down the second summer. I was much there that year – it was a beautiful one; and we had, in her off-hours, some strolls and talks in the garden – talks in which she struck me as awfully clever and nice. Oh yes; don't grin: I liked her extremely and am glad to this day to think she liked me, too. If she hadn't she wouldn't have told me. She had never told anyone. It wasn't simply that she said so, but that I knew she hadn't. I was sure; I could see. You'll easily judge why when you hear."

"Because the thing had been such a scare?"

He continued to fix me. "You'll easily judge," he repeated: "*You* will."

I fixed him, too. "I see. She was in love."

He laughed for the first time. "You *are* acute. Yes, she was in love. That is, she *had* been. That came out – she couldn't tell her story without its coming out. I saw it, and she saw I saw it; but neither of us spoke of it. I remember the time and

11

the place – the corner of the lawn, the shade of the great beeches and the long, hot summer afternoon. It wasn't a scene for a shudder; but oh!" He quitted the fire and dropped back into his chair.

"You'll receive the packet Thursday morning?" I enquired.

"Probably not till the second post."

"Well then; after dinner?"

"You'll all meet me here?" He looked us round again. "Isn't anybody going?" It was almost the tone of hope.

"Everybody will stay!"

"*I* will" – and "*I* will!" cried the ladies whose departure had been fixed. Mrs Griffin, however, expressed the need for a little more light. "Who was it she was in love with?"

"The story will tell," I took upon myself to reply.

"Oh, I can't wait for the story!"

"The story *won't* tell," said Douglas; "not in any literal, vulgar way."

"More's the pity, then. That's the only way I ever understand."

"Won't *you* tell, Douglas?" somebody else enquired.

He sprang to his feet again. "Yes – tomorrow. Now I must go to bed. Good night." And quickly catching up a candlestick, he left us slightly bewildered. From our end of the great brown hall we heard his step on the stair; whereupon Mrs Griffin spoke. "Well, if I don't know who she was in love with, I know who *he* was."

"She was ten years older," said her husband.

"*Raison de plus* – at that age! But it's rather nice, his long reticence."

"Forty years!" Griffin put in.

"With this outbreak at last."

"The outbreak," I returned, "will make a tremendous occasion of Thursday night;" and everyone so agreed with me that, in the light of it, we lost all attention for everything else. The last story, however incomplete and like the mere opening of a serial, had been told; we handshook and "candlestuck", as somebody said, and went to bed.

I knew the next day that a letter containing the key had, by the first post, gone off to his London apartments; but in spite of – or perhaps just on account of – the eventual diffusion of this knowledge we quite let him alone till after dinner, till such an hour of the evening, in fact, as might best accord with the kind of emotion on which our hopes were fixed. Then he became as communicative as we could desire and indeed gave us his best reason for being so. We had it from him again before the fire in the hall, as we had had our mild wonders of the previous night. It appeared that the narrative he had promised to read us really required for a proper intelligence a few words of prologue. Let me say here distinctly, to have done with it, that this narrative, from an exact transcript of my own made much later, is what I shall presently give. Poor Douglas, before his death – when it was in sight – committed to me the manuscript that reached him on the third of these days and that, on the same spot, with immense effect, he began to read to our hushed little circle on the night of the fourth. The departing ladies who had said they would stay didn't, of course, thank heaven, stay: they departed, in consequence of arrangements made, in a rage of curiosity, as they professed, produced by the touches with which he had already worked us up. But that only made his little final auditory more compact and select, kept it, round the hearth, subject to a common thrill.

The first of these touches conveyed that the written statement took up the tale at a point after it had, in a manner, begun. The fact to be in possession of was therefore that his old friend, the youngest of several daughters of a poor country parson, had, at the age of twenty, on taking service for the first time in the schoolroom, come up to London, in trepidation, to answer in person an advertisement that had already placed her in brief correspondence with the advertiser. This person proved, on her presenting herself, for judgement, at a house in Harley Street, that impressed her as vast and imposing – this prospective patron proved a gentleman, a bachelor in the prime of life, such a figure as had never risen, save in a dream or an old novel, before a fluttered, anxious girl out of a Hampshire vicarage. One could easily fix his type; it never, happily, dies out. He was handsome and bold and pleasant, offhand and gay and kind. He struck her, inevitably, as gallant and splendid, but what took her most of all and gave her the courage she afterward showed was that he put the whole thing to her as a kind of favour, an obligation he should gratefully incur. She conceived him as rich, but as fearfully extravagant – saw him all in a glow of high fashion, of good looks, of expensive habits, of charming ways with women. He had for his own town residence a big house filled with the spoils of travel and the trophies of the chase; but it was to his country home, an old family place in Essex, that he wished her immediately to proceed.

He had been left, by the death of his parents in India, guardian to a small nephew and a small niece, children of a younger, military brother, whom he had lost two years before. These children were, by the strangest of chances for a man in his position – a lone man without the right sort of experience or a grain of patience – very heavy on his hands. It had all been a great worry and, on his own part doubtless, a series of blunders, but he immensely pitied the poor chicks and had done all he could; had in particular sent them down to his other house, the proper place for them being of course the country, and kept them there, from the first, with the best people he could find to look after them, parting even with his own servants to wait on them and going down himself, whenever he might, to see how they were doing. The awkward thing was that they had practically no other relations and that his own affairs took up all his time. He had put them in possession of Bly, which was healthy and secure, and had placed at the head of their little establishment – but below stairs only – an excellent woman, Mrs Grose, whom he was sure his visitor would like and who had formerly been maid to his mother. She was now housekeeper and was also acting for the time as superintendent to the little girl, of whom, without children of her own, she was, by good luck, extremely fond. There were plenty of people to help, but of course the young lady who should go down as governess would be in supreme authority. She would also have, in holidays, to look after the small boy, who had been for a term at school – young as he was to be sent, but what else could be done? – and who, as the holidays were about to begin, would be back from one day to the other. There had been for the two children at first a young lady whom they had had the misfortune to lose. She had done for them quite beautifully – she was a most respectable person – till her death, the great awkwardness of which had, precisely, left no alternative but the school for little Miles. Mrs Grose, since then, in the way of manners and things, had done as she could for Flora; and there were, further, a cook, a housemaid, a dairywoman, an old pony, an old groom and an old gardener, all likewise thoroughly respectable.

So far had Douglas presented his picture when someone put a question. "And what did the former governess die of? – Of so much respectability?"

Our friend's answer was prompt. "That will come out. I don't anticipate."

"Pardon me – I thought that was just what you *are* doing."

"In her successor's place," I suggested, "I should have wished to learn if the office brought with it – "

"Necessary danger to life?" Douglas completed my thought. "She did wish to learn, and she did learn. You shall hear tomorrow what she learned. Meanwhile, of course, the prospect struck her as slightly grim. She was young, untried, nervous: it was a vision of serious duties and little company, of really great loneliness. She hesitated – took a couple of days to consult and consider. But the salary offered much exceeded her modest measure, and on a second interview she faced the music, she engaged." And Douglas, with this, made a pause that, for the benefit of the company, moved me to throw in –

"The moral of which was of course the seduction exercised by the splendid young man. She succumbed to it."

He got up and, as he had done the night before, went to the fire, gave a stir to a log with his foot, then stood a moment with his back to us. "She saw him only twice."

"Yes, but that's just the beauty of her passion."

A little to my surprise, on this, Douglas turned round to me. "It *was* the beauty of it. There were others," he went on, "who hadn't succumbed. He told her frankly all his difficulty – that for several applicants the conditions had been prohibitive. They were, somehow, simply afraid. It sounded dull – it sounded strange; and all the more so because of his main condition."

"Which was – ?"

"That she should never trouble him – but never, never: neither appeal nor complain nor write about anything; only meet all questions herself, receive all moneys from his solicitor, take the whole thing over and let him alone. She promised to do this, and she mentioned to me that when, for a moment, disburdened, delighted, he held her hand, thanking her for the sacrifice, she already felt rewarded."

"But was that all her reward?" one of the ladies asked.

"She never saw him again."

"Oh!" said the lady; which, as our friend immediately left us again, was the only other word of importance contributed to the subject till, the next night, by the corner of the hearth, in the best chair, he opened the faded red cover of a thin old-fashioned gilt-edged album. The whole thing took indeed more nights than one, but on the first occasion the same lady put another question. "What is your title?"

"I haven't one."

"Oh, *I* have!" I said. But Douglas, without heeding me, had begun to read with a fine clearness that was like a rendering to the ear of the beauty of his author's hand.

I

I remember the whole beginning as a succession of flights and drops, a little seesaw of the right throbs and the wrong. After rising, in town, to meet his appeal, I had at all events a couple of very bad days – found myself doubtful again, felt indeed sure I had made a mistake. In this state of mind I spent the long hours of bumping, swinging coach that carried me to the stopping place at which I was to be met by a vehicle from the house. This convenience, I was told, had been ordered, and I found, toward the close of the June afternoon, a commodious fly in waiting for me. Driving at that hour, on a lovely day, through a country to which the summer sweetness seemed to offer me a friendly welcome, my fortitude mounted afresh and, as we turned into the avenue, encountered a reprieve that was probably but a proof of the point to which it had sunk. I suppose I had expected, or had dreaded, something so melancholy that what greeted me was a good surprise. I remember as a most pleasant impression the broad, clear front, its open windows and fresh curtains and the pair of maids looking out; I remember the lawn and the bright flowers and the crunch of my wheels on the gravel and the clustered treetops over which the rooks circled and cawed in the golden sky. The scene had a greatness that made it a different affair from my own scant home, and there immediately appeared at the door, with a little girl in her hand, a civil person who dropped me as decent a curtsey as if I had been the mistress or a distinguished visitor. I had received in Harley Street a narrower notion of the place, and that, as I recalled it, made me think the proprietor still more of a gentleman, suggested that what I was to enjoy might be something beyond his promise.

I had no drop again till the next day, for I was carried triumphantly through the following hours by my introduction to the younger of my pupils. The little girl who accompanied Mrs Grose appeared to me on the spot a creature so charming as to make it a great fortune to have to do with her. She was the most beautiful child I had ever seen, and I afterwards wondered that my employer had not told me more of her. I slept little that night – I was too much excited; and this astonished me, too, I recollect, remained with me, adding to my sense of the liberality with which I was treated. The large, impressive room, one of the best in the house, the great state bed, as I almost felt it, the full, figured draperies, the long glasses in which, for the first time, I could see myself from head to foot, all struck me – like the extraordinary charm of my small charge – as so many things thrown in. It was thrown in as well, from the first moment, that I should get on with Mrs Grose in a relation over which, on my way, in the coach, I fear I had rather brooded. The only thing indeed that in this early outlook might have made me shrink again was the clear circumstance of her being so glad to see me. I perceived within half an hour that she was so glad – stout, simple, plain, clean, wholesome woman – as to be positively on her guard against showing it too much. I wondered even then a little why she should wish not to show it, and that, with reflection, with suspicion, might of course have made me uneasy.

But it was a comfort that there could be no uneasiness in a connection with anything so beatific as the radiant image of my little girl, the vision of whose angelic beauty had probably more than anything else to do with the restlessness that, before morning, made me several times rise and wander about my room to take in the whole picture and prospect; to watch, from my open window, the faint summer dawn, to look at such portions of the rest of the house as I could catch, and to listen, while, in the fading dusk, the first birds began to twitter, for the possible recurrence of a sound or two, less natural and not without, but within, that I had fancied I heard. There had been a moment when I believed I recognised, faint and far, the cry of a child; there had been another when I found myself just consciously starting as at the passage, before my door, of a light footstep. But these fancies were not marked enough not to be thrown off, and it is only in the light, or the gloom, I should rather say, of other and subsequent matters that they now come back to me. To watch, teach, "form" little Flora would too evidently be the making of a happy and useful life. It had been agreed between us downstairs that after this first occasion I should have her as a matter of course at night, her small white bed being already arranged, to that end, in my room. What I had undertaken was the whole care of her, and she had remained, just this last time, with Mrs Grose only as an effect of our consideration for my inevitable strangeness and her natural timidity. In spite of this timidity – which the child herself, in the oddest way in the world, had been perfectly frank and brave about, allowing it, without a sign of uncomfortable consciousness, with the deep, sweet serenity indeed of one of Raphael's holy infants, to be discussed, to be imputed to her and to determine us – I feel quite sure she would presently like me. It was part of what I already liked Mrs Grose herself for, the pleasure I could see her feel in my admiration and wonder as I sat at supper with four tall candles and with my pupil, in a high chair and a bib, brightly facing me, between them, over bread and milk. There were naturally things that in Flora's presence could pass between us only as prodigious and gratified looks, obscure and roundabout allusions.

"And the little boy – does he look like her? Is he too so very remarkable?"

One wouldn't flatter a child. "Oh, miss, *most* remarkable. If you think well of this one!" – and she stood there with a plate in her hand, beaming at our companion, who looked from one of us to the other with placid heavenly eyes that contained nothing to check us.

"Yes; if I do – ?"

"You *will* be carried away by the little gentleman!"

"Well, that, I think, is what I came for – to be carried away. I'm afraid, however," I remember feeling the impulse to add, "I'm rather easily carried away. I was carried away in London!"

I can still see Mrs Grose's broad face as she took this in. "In Harley Street?"

"In Harley Street."

"Well, miss, you're not the first – and you won't be the last."

"Oh, I've no pretension," I could laugh, "to being the only one. My other pupil, at any rate, as I understand, comes back tomorrow?"

"Not tomorrow – Friday, miss. He arrives, as you did, by the coach, under care of the guard, and is to be met by the same carriage."

I forthwith expressed that the proper as well as the pleasant and friendly thing would be therefore that on the arrival of the public conveyance I should be in waiting for him with his little sister; an idea in which Mrs Grose concurred so heartily that I somehow took her manner as a kind of comforting pledge – never falsified, thank heaven! – that we should on every question be quite at one. Oh, she was glad I was there!

What I felt the next day was, I suppose, nothing that could be fairly called a reaction from the cheer of my arrival; it was probably at the most only a slight oppression produced by a fuller measure of the scale, as I walked round them, gazed up at them, took them in, of my new circumstances. They had, as it were, an extent and mass for which I had not been prepared and in the presence of which I found myself, freshly, a little scared as well as a little proud. Lessons, in this agitation, certainly suffered some delay; I reflected that my first duty was, by the gentlest arts I could contrive, to win the child into the sense of knowing me. I spent the day with her out of doors; I arranged with her, to her great satisfaction, that it should be she, she only, who might show me the place. She showed it step by step and room by room and secret by secret, with droll, delightful, childish talk about it and with the result, in half an hour, of our becoming immense friends. Young as she was, I was struck, throughout our little tour, with her confidence and courage, with the way, in empty chambers and dull corridors, on crooked staircases that made me pause and even on the summit of an old machicolated square tower that made me dizzy, her morning music, her disposition to tell me so many more things than she asked, rang out and led me on. I have not seen Bly since the day I left it, and I daresay that to my older and more informed eyes it would now appear sufficiently contracted. But as my little conductress, with her hair of gold and her frock of blue, danced before me round corners and pattered down passages, I had the view of a castle of romance inhabited by a rosy sprite, such a place as would somehow, for diversion of the young idea, take all colour out of storybooks and fairytales. Wasn't it just a storybook over which I had fallen adoze and adream? No; it was a big, ugly, antique, but convenient house, embodying a few features of a building still older, half-replaced and half-utilised, in which I had the fancy of our being almost as lost as a handful of passengers in a great drifting ship. Well, I was, strangely, at the helm!

II

This came home to me when, two days later, I drove over with Flora to meet, as Mrs Grose said, the little gentleman; and all the more for an incident that, presenting itself the second evening, had deeply disconcerted me. The first day had been, on the whole, as I have expressed, reassuring; but I was to see it wind up in keen apprehension. The postbag, that evening – it came late – contained a letter for me, which, however, in the hand of my employer, I found to be composed but of a few words enclosing another, addressed to himself, with a seal still unbroken. "This, I recognise, is from the headmaster, and the headmaster's an awful bore. Read him, please; deal with him; but mind you don't report. Not a word. I'm off!" I broke the seal with a great effort – so great a one that I was a long time coming to it; took the unopened missive at last up to my room and only attacked it just before going to bed. I had better have let it wait till morning, for it gave me a second sleepless night. With no counsel to take, the next day, I was full of distress; and it finally got so the better of me that I determined to open myself at least to Mrs Grose.

"What does it mean? The child's dismissed his school."

She gave me a look that I remarked at the moment; then, visibly, with a quick blankness, seemed to try to take it back. "But aren't they all – ?"

"Sent home – yes. But only for the holidays. Miles may never go back at all."

Consciously, under my attention, she reddened. "They won't take him?"

"They absolutely decline."

23

At this she raised her eyes, which she had turned from me; I saw them fill with good tears. "What has he done?"

I hesitated; then I judged best simply to hand her my letter – which, however, had the effect of making her, without taking it, simply put her hands behind her. She shook her head sadly. "Such things are not for me, miss."

My counsellor couldn't read! I winced at my mistake, which I attenuated as I could, and opened my letter again to repeat it to her; then, faltering in the act and folding it up once more, I put it back in my pocket. "Is he really *bad*?"

The tears were still in her eyes. "Do the gentlemen say so?"

"They go into no particulars. They simply express their regret that it should be impossible to keep him. That can have only one meaning." Mrs Grose listened with dumb emotion; she forbore to ask me what this meaning might be; so that, presently, to put the thing with some coherence and with the mere aid of her presence to my own mind, I went on: "That he's an injury to the others."

At this, with one of the quick turns of simple folk, she suddenly flamed up. "Master Miles! *Him* an injury?"

There was such a flood of good faith in it that, though I had not yet seen the child, my very fears made me jump to the absurdity of the idea. I found myself, to meet my friend the better, offering it, on the spot, sarcastically. "To his poor little innocent mates!"

"It's too dreadful," cried Mrs Grose, "to say such cruel things! Why, he's scarce ten years old."

"Yes, yes; it would be incredible."

She was evidently grateful for such a profession. "See him, miss, first. *Then* believe it!" I felt forthwith a new impatience to see him; it was the beginning of a curiosity that, for all the next hours, was to deepen almost to pain. Mrs Grose was aware, I could judge, of what she had produced in me, and she followed it up with assurance. "You might as well believe it of the little lady. Bless her," she added the next moment – "*Look* at her!"

I turned and saw that Flora, whom, ten minutes before, I had established in the schoolroom with a sheet of white paper, a pencil and a copy of nice "round O's," now presented herself to view at the open door. She expressed in her little way an extraordinary detachment from disagreeable duties, looking to me, however, with a great childish light that seemed to offer it as a mere result of the affection she had conceived for my person, which had rendered necessary that she should follow me. I needed nothing more than this to feel the full force of Mrs Grose's comparison, and, catching my pupil in my arms, covered her with kisses in which there was a sob of atonement.

Nonetheless, the rest of the day I watched for further occasion to approach my colleague, especially as, toward evening, I began to fancy she rather sought to avoid me. I overtook her, I remember, on the staircase; we went down together, and at the bottom I detained her, holding her there with a hand on her arm. "I take what you said to me at noon as a declaration that *you've* never known him to be bad."

She threw back her head; she had clearly, by this time, and very honestly, adopted an attitude. "Oh, never known him – I don't pretend *that*!"

I was upset again. "Then you *have* known him – ?"

"Yes indeed, miss, thank God!"

On reflection I accepted this. "You mean that a boy who never is – ?"

"Is no boy for *me*!"

I held her tighter. "You like them with the spirit to be naughty?" Then, keeping pace with her answer, "So do I!" I eagerly brought out. "But not to the degree to contaminate – "

"To contaminate?" – my big word left her at a loss. I explained it. "To corrupt."

She stared, taking my meaning in; but it produced in her an odd laugh. "Are you afraid he'll corrupt *you*?" She put the question with such a fine bold humour that, with a laugh, a little silly doubtless, to match her own, I gave way for the time to the apprehension of ridicule.

But the next day, as the hour for my drive approached, I cropped up in another place. "What was the lady who was here before?"

"The last governess? She was also young and pretty – almost as young and almost as pretty, miss, even as you."

"Ah, then, I hope her youth and her beauty helped her!" I recollect throwing off. "He seems to like us young and pretty!"

"Oh, he *did*," Mrs Grose assented: "it was the way he liked everyone!" She had no sooner spoken indeed than she caught herself up. "I mean that's *his* way – the master's."

I was struck. "But of whom did you speak first?"

She looked blank, but she coloured. "Why, of *him*."

"Of the master?"

"Of who else?"

There was so obviously no one else that the next moment I had lost my impression of her having accidentally said more than she meant; and I merely asked what I wanted to know. "Did *she* see anything in the boy – ?"

"That wasn't right? She never told me."

I had a scruple, but I overcame it. "Was she careful – particular?"

Mrs Grose appeared to try to be conscientious. "About some things – yes."

"But not about all?"

Again she considered. "Well, miss – she's gone. I won't tell tales."

"I quite understand your feeling," I hastened to reply; but I thought it, after an instant, not opposed to this concession to pursue: "Did she die here?"

"No – she went off."

I don't know what there was in this brevity of Mrs Grose's that struck me as ambiguous. "Went off to die?" Mrs Grose looked straight out of the window, but I felt that, hypothetically, I had a right to know what young persons engaged for Bly were expected to do. "She was taken ill, you mean, and went home?"

"She was not taken ill, so far as appeared, in this house. She left it, at the end of the year, to go home, as she said, for a short holiday, to which the time she had put in had certainly given her a right. We had then a young woman – a nursemaid who had stayed on and who was a good girl and clever; and *she* took the children altogether for the interval. But our young lady never came back, and at the very moment I was expecting her I heard from the master that she was dead."

I turned this over. "But of what?"

"He never told me! But please, miss," said Mrs Grose, "I must get to my work."

III

Her thus turning her back on me was fortunately not, for my just preoccupations, a snub that could check the growth of our mutual esteem. We met, after I had brought home little Miles, more intimately than ever on the ground of my stupefaction, my general emotion: so monstrous was I then ready to pronounce it that such a child as had now been revealed to me should be under an interdict. I was a little late on the scene, and I felt, as he stood wistfully looking out for me before the door of the inn at which the coach had put him down, that I had seen him, on the instant, without and within, in the great glow of freshness, the same positive fragrance of purity, in which I had, from the first moment, seen his little sister. He was incredibly beautiful, and Mrs Grose had put her finger on it: everything but a sort of passion of tenderness for him was swept away by his presence. What I then and there took him to my heart for was something divine that I have never found to the same degree in any child – his indescribable little air of knowing nothing in the world but love. It would have been impossible to carry a bad name with a greater sweetness of innocence, and by the time I had got back to Bly with him I remained merely bewildered – so far, that is, as I was not outraged – by the sense of the horrible letter locked up in my room, in a drawer. As soon as I could compass a private word with Mrs Grose I declared to her that it was grotesque.

She promptly understood me. "You mean the cruel charge – ?"

"It doesn't live an instant. My dear woman, *look* at him!"

She smiled at my pretension to have discovered his charm. "I assure you, miss, I do nothing else! What will you say, then?" she immediately added.

"In answer to the letter?" I had made up my mind. "Nothing."

"And to his uncle?"

I was incisive. "Nothing."

"And to the boy himself?"

I was wonderful. "Nothing."

She gave with her apron a great wipe to her mouth. "Then I'll stand by you. We'll see it out."

"We'll see it out!" I ardently echoed, giving her my hand to make it a vow.

She held me there a moment, then whisked up her apron again with her detached hand. "Would you mind, miss, if I used the freedom – "

"To kiss me? No!" I took the good creature in my arms and, after we had embraced like sisters, felt still more fortified and indignant.

This, at all events, was for the time: a time so full that, as I recall the way it went, it reminds me of all the art I now need to make it a little distinct. What I look back at with amazement is the situation I accepted. I had undertaken, with my companion, to see it out, and I was under a charm, apparently, that could smooth away the extent and the far and difficult connections of such an effort. I was lifted aloft on a great wave of infatuation and pity. I found it simple, in my ignorance, my confusion, and perhaps my conceit, to assume that I could deal with a boy whose education for the world was all on the point of beginning. I am unable even to remember at this day what proposal I framed for the end of his holidays and the resumption of his studies. Lessons with me, indeed, that charming summer, we all had a theory that he was to have; but I now feel that, for weeks, the lessons must have been rather my own. I learned something – at first, certainly – that had not been one of the teachings of my small, smothered life; learned to be amused, and even amusing, and not to think for the morrow. It was the first time, in a manner, that I had known space and air and freedom, all the music of summer and all the mystery of nature. And then there was consideration – and consideration was sweet. Oh, it was a trap – not designed, but deep – to my imagination, to my delicacy, perhaps to my vanity; to whatever, in me, was most excitable. The best way to picture it all is to say that I was off my guard. They gave me so little trouble – they were of a gentleness so extraordinary. I used to speculate – but even this with a dim disconnectedness – as to how the rough future (for all futures are rough!) would handle them and might bruise them. They had the bloom of health and happiness; and yet, as if I had been in charge of a pair of little grandees, of princes of the blood, for whom everything, to be right, would have to be enclosed and protected, the only form that, in my fancy, the afteryears could take for them was that of a romantic, a really royal extension of the garden and the park. It may be, of course, above all, that what suddenly broke into this gives the previous time a charm of stillness – that hush in which something gathers or crouches. The change was actually like the spring of a beast.

In the first weeks the days were long; they often, at their finest, gave me what I used to call my own hour, the hour when, for my pupils, teatime and bedtime having come and gone, I had, before my final retirement, a small interval alone. Much as I liked my companions, this hour was the thing in the day I liked most; and I liked it best of all when, as the light faded – or rather, I should say, the day lingered and the last calls of the last birds sounded, in a flushed sky, from the old trees – I could take a turn into the grounds and enjoy, almost with a sense of property that amused and flattered me, the beauty and dignity of the place. It was a pleasure at these moments to feel myself tranquil and justified; doubtless, perhaps, also to reflect that by my discretion, my quiet good sense and general high propriety, I was giving pleasure – if he ever thought of it! – to the person to whose pressure I had responded. What I was doing was what he had earnestly hoped and directly asked of me, and that I *could*, after all, do it proved even a greater joy than I had expected. I daresay I fancied myself, in short, a remarkable young woman and took comfort in the faith that this would more publicly appear. Well, I needed to be remarkable to offer a front to the remarkable things that presently gave their first sign.

It was plump, one afternoon, in the middle of my very hour: the children were tucked away, and I had come out for my stroll. One of the thoughts that, as I don't in the least shrink now from noting, used to be with me in these wanderings was that it would be as charming as a charming story suddenly to meet someone. Someone would appear there at the turn of a path and would stand before me and smile and approve. I didn't ask more than that – I only asked that he should *know*; and the only way to be sure he knew would be to see it, and the kind light of it, in his handsome face. That was exactly present to me – by which I mean the face was – when, on the first of these occasions, at the end of a long June day, I stopped short on emerging from one of the plantations and coming into view of the house. What arrested me on the spot – and with a shock much greater than any vision had allowed for – was the sense that my imagination had, in a flash, turned real. He did stand there! But high up, beyond the lawn and at the very top of the tower to which, on that first morning, little Flora had conducted me. This tower was one of a pair – square, incongruous, crenellated structures – that were distinguished, for some reason, though I could see little difference, as the new and the old. They flanked opposite ends of the house and were probably architectural absurdities, redeemed in a measure indeed by not being wholly disengaged nor of a height too pretentious, dating, in their gingerbread antiquity, from a romantic revival that was already a respectable past. I admired them, had fancies about them, for we could all profit in a degree, especially when they loomed through the dusk, by the grandeur of their actual battlements; yet it was not at such an elevation that the figure I had so often invoked seemed most in place.

It produced in me, this figure, in the clear twilight, I remember, two distinct gasps of emotion, which were, sharply, the shock of my first and that of my second surprise. My second was a violent perception of the mistake of my first: the man who met my eyes was not the person I had precipitately supposed. There came to me thus a bewilderment of vision of which, after these years, there is no living view that I can hope to give. An unknown man in a lonely place is a permitted object of fear to a young woman privately bred; and the figure that faced me was – a few more seconds assured me – as little anyone else I knew as it was the image that had been in my mind. I had not seen it in Harley Street – I had not seen it anywhere. The place, moreover, in the strangest way in the world, had, on the instant, and by the very fact of its appearance, become a solitude. To me at least, making my statement here with a deliberation with which I have never made it, the whole feeling of the moment returns. It was as if, while I took in – what I did take in – all the rest of the scene had been stricken with death. I can hear again, as I write, the intense hush in which the sounds of evening dropped. The rooks stopped cawing in the golden sky, and the friendly hour lost, for the minute, all its voice. But there was no other change in nature, unless indeed it were a change that I saw with a stranger sharpness. The gold was still in the sky, the clearness in the air, and the man who looked at me over the battlements was as definite as a picture in a frame. That's how I thought, with extraordinary quickness, of each person that he might have been and that he was not. We were confronted across our distance quite long enough for me to ask myself with intensity who then he was and to feel, as an effect of my inability to say, a wonder that in a few instants more became intense.

The great question, or one of these, is, afterwards, I know, with regard to certain matters, the question of how long they have lasted. Well, this matter of mine, think what you will of it, lasted while I caught at a dozen possibilities, none of which made a difference for the better, that I could see, in there having been in the house – and for how long, above all? – a person of whom I was in ignorance. It lasted while I just bridled a little with the sense that my office demanded that there should be no such ignorance and no such person. It lasted while this visitant, at all events – and there was a touch of the strange freedom, as I remember, in the sign of familiarity of his wearing no hat – seemed to fix me, from his position, with just the question, just the scrutiny through the fading light, that his own presence provoked. We were too far apart to call to each other, but there was a moment at which, at shorter range, some challenge between us, breaking the hush, would have been the right result of our straight mutual stare. He was in one of the angles, the one away from the house, very erect, as it struck me, and with both hands on the ledge. So I saw him as I see the letters I form on this page; then, exactly, after a minute, as if to add to the spectacle, he slowly changed his place – passed, looking at me hard all the while, to the opposite corner of the platform. Yes, I had the sharpest sense that during this transit he never took his eyes from me, and I can see at this moment the way his hand, as he went, passed from one of the crenellations to the next. He stopped at the other corner, but less long, and even as he turned away still markedly fixed me. He turned away; that was all I knew.

IV

It was not that I didn't wait, on this occasion, for more, for I was rooted as deeply as I was shaken. Was there a "secret" at Bly – a mystery of Udolpho or an insane, an unmentionable relative kept in unsuspected confinement? I can't say how long I turned it over, or how long, in a confusion of curiosity and dread, I remained where I had had my collision; I only recall that when I re-entered the house darkness had quite closed in. Agitation, in the interval, certainly had held me and driven me, for I must, in circling about the place, have walked three miles; but I was to be, later on, so much more overwhelmed that this mere dawn of alarm was a comparatively human chill. The most singular part of it, in fact – singular as the rest had been – was the part I became, in the hall, aware of in meeting Mrs Grose. This picture comes back to me in the general train – the impression, as I received it on my return, of the wide white panelled space, bright in the lamplight and with its portraits and red carpet, and of the good surprised look of my friend, which immediately told me she had missed me. It came to me straightway, under her contact, that, with plain heartiness, mere relieved anxiety at my appearance, she knew nothing whatever that could bear upon the incident I had there ready for her. I had not suspected in advance that her comfortable face would pull me up, and I somehow measured the importance of what I had seen by my thus finding myself hesitate to mention it. Scarce anything in the whole history seems to me so odd as this fact that my real beginning of fear was one, as I may say, with the instinct of sparing my companion. On the spot, accordingly, in the pleasant hall and with her eyes on me, I, for a reason that I couldn't then have phrased, achieved an inward resolution – offered a vague pretext for my lateness and, with the plea of the beauty of the night and of the heavy dew and wet feet, went as soon as possible to my room.

Here it was another affair; here, for many days after, it was a queer affair enough. There were hours, from day to day – or at least there were moments, snatched even from clear duties – when I had to shut myself up to think. It was not so much yet that I was more nervous than I could bear to be as that I was remarkably afraid of becoming so; for the truth I had now to turn over was, simply and clearly, the truth that I could arrive at no account whatever of the visitor with whom I had been so inexplicably and yet, as it seemed to me, so intimately concerned. It took little time to see that I could sound without forms of enquiry and without exciting remark any domestic complications. The shock I had suffered must have sharpened all my senses; I felt sure, at the end of three days and as the result of mere closer attention, that I had not been practised upon by the servants nor made the object of any "game". Of whatever it was that I knew, nothing was known around me. There was but one sane inference: someone had taken a liberty rather gross. That was what, repeatedly, I dipped into my room and locked the door to say to myself. We had been, collectively, subject to an intrusion; some unscrupulous traveller, curious in old houses, had made his way in unobserved, enjoyed the prospect from the best point of view, and then stolen out as he came. If he had given me such a bold hard stare, that was but a part of his indiscretion. The good thing, after all, was that we should surely see no more of him.

This was not so good a thing, I admit, as not to leave me to judge that what, essentially, made nothing else much signify was simply my charming work. My charming work was just my life with Miles and Flora, and through nothing could I so like it as through feeling that I could throw myself into it in trouble. The attraction of my small charges was a constant joy, leading me to wonder afresh at the vanity of my original fears, the distaste I had begun by entertaining for the probable grey prose of my office. There was to be no grey prose, it appeared, and no long grind; so how could work not be charming that presented itself as daily beauty? It was all the romance of the nursery and the poetry of the schoolroom. I don't mean by this, of course, that we studied only fiction and verse; I mean I can express no otherwise the sort of interest my companions inspired. How can I describe that except by saying that instead of growing used to them – and it's a marvel for a governess: I call the sisterhood to witness! – I made constant fresh discoveries. There was one direction, assuredly, in which these discoveries stopped: deep obscurity continued to cover the region of the boy's conduct at school. It had been promptly given me, I have noted, to face that mystery without a pang. Perhaps even it would be nearer the truth to say that – without a word – he himself had cleared it up. He had made the whole charge absurd. My conclusion bloomed there with the real rose flush of his innocence: he was only too fine and fair for the little horrid, unclean school world, and he had paid a price for it. I reflected acutely that the sense of such differences, such superiorities of quality, always, on the part of the majority – which could include even stupid, sordid headmasters – turn infallibly to the vindictive.

Both the children had a gentleness (it was their only fault, and it never made Miles a muff) that kept them – how shall I express it? – almost impersonal and certainly quite unpunishable. They were like the cherubs of the anecdote, who had – morally, at any rate – nothing to whack! I remember feeling with Miles in especial as if he had had, as it were, no history. We expect of a small child a scant one, but there was in this beautiful little boy something extraordinarily sensitive, yet extraordinarily happy, that, more than in any creature of his age I have seen, struck me as beginning anew each day. He had never for a second suffered. I took this as a direct disproof of his having really been chastised. If he had been wicked he would have "caught" it, and I should have caught it by the rebound – I should have found the trace. I found nothing at all, and he was therefore an angel. He never spoke of his school, never mentioned a comrade or a master; and I, for my part, was quite too much disgusted to allude to them. Of course I was under the spell, and the wonderful part is that, even at the time, I perfectly knew I was. But I gave myself up to it; it was an antidote to any pain, and I had more pains than one. I was in receipt in these days of disturbing letters from home, where things were not going well. But with my children, what things in the world mattered? That was the question I used to put to my scrappy retirements. I was dazzled by their loveliness.

There was a Sunday – to get on – when it rained with such force and for so many hours that there could be no procession to church; in consequence of which, as the day declined, I had arranged with Mrs Grose that, should the evening show improvement, we would attend together the late service. The rain happily stopped, and I prepared for our walk, which, through the park and by the good road to the village, would be a matter of twenty minutes. Coming downstairs to meet my colleague in the hall, I remembered a pair of gloves that had required three stitches and that had received them – with a publicity perhaps not edifying – while I sat with the children at their tea, served on Sundays, by exception, in that cold, clean temple of mahogany and brass, the "grown-up" dining room. The gloves had been dropped there, and I turned in to recover them. The day was grey enough, but the afternoon light still lingered, and it enabled me, on crossing the threshold, not only to recognise, on a chair near the wide window, then closed, the articles I wanted, but to become aware of a person on the other side of the window and looking straight in. One step into the room had sufficed; my vision was instantaneous; it was all there. The person looking straight in was the person who had already appeared to me. He appeared thus again with I won't say greater distinctness, for that was impossible, but with a nearness that represented a forward stride in our intercourse and made me, as I met him, catch my breath and turn cold. He was the same – he was the same, and seen, this time, as he had been seen before, from the waist up, the window, though the dining room was on the ground floor, not going down to the terrace on which he stood. His face was close to the glass, yet the effect of this better view was, strangely, only to show me how intense the former had been. He remained but a few seconds – long enough to convince me he also saw and recognised; but it was as if I had been looking at him for years and had known him always. Something, however, happened this time that had not happened before; his stare into my face, through the glass and across the room, was as deep and hard as then, but it quitted me for a moment during which I could still watch it, see it fix successively several other things. On the spot there came to me the added shock of a certitude that it was not for me he had come there. He had come for someone else.

The flash of this knowledge – for it was knowledge in the midst of dread – produced in me the most extraordinary effect, started as I stood there, a sudden vibration of duty and courage. I say courage because I was beyond all doubt already far gone. I bounded straight out of the door again, reached that of the house, got, in an instant, upon the drive, and, passing along the terrace as fast as I could rush, turned a corner and came full in sight. But it was in sight of nothing now – my visitor had vanished. I stopped, I almost dropped, with the real relief of this; but I took in the whole scene – I gave him time to reappear. I call it time, but how long was it? I can't speak to the purpose today of the duration of these things. That kind of measure must have left me: they couldn't have lasted as they actually appeared to me to last. The terrace and the whole place, the lawn and the garden beyond it, all I could see of the park, were empty with a great emptiness. There were shrubberies and big trees, but I remember the clear assurance I felt that none of them concealed him. He was there or was not there: not there if I didn't see him. I got hold of this; then, instinctively, instead of returning as I had come, went to the window. It was confusedly present to me that I ought to place myself where he had stood. I did so; I applied my face to the pane and looked, as he had looked, into the room. As if, at this moment, to show me exactly what his range had been, Mrs Grose, as I had done for himself just before, came in from the hall. With this I had the full image of a repetition of what had already occurred. She saw me as I had seen my own visitant; she pulled up short as I had done; I gave her something of the shock that I had received. She turned white, and this made me ask myself if I had blanched as much. She stared, in short, and retreated on just *my* lines, and I knew she had then passed out and come round to me and that I should presently meet her. I remained where I was, and while I waited I thought of more things than one. But there's only one I take space to mention. I wondered why *she* should be scared.

V

Oh, she let me know as soon as, round the corner of the house, she loomed again into view. "What in the name of goodness is the matter – ?" She was now flushed and out of breath.

I said nothing till she came quite near. "With me?" I must have made a wonderful face. "Do I show it?"

"You're as white as a sheet. You look awful."

I considered; I could meet on this, without scruple, any innocence. My need to respect the bloom of Mrs Grose's had dropped, without a rustle, from my shoulders, and if I wavered for the instant it was not with what I kept back. I put out my hand to her and she took it; I held her hard a little, liking to feel her close to me. There was a kind of support in the shy heave of her surprise. "You came for me for church, of course, but I can't go."

"Has anything happened?"

"Yes. You must know now. Did I look very queer?"

"Through this window? Dreadful!"

"Well," I said, "I've been frightened." Mrs Grose's eyes expressed plainly that *she* had no wish to be, yet also that she knew too well her place not to be ready to share with me any marked inconvenience. Oh, it was quite settled that she *must* share! "Just what you saw from the dining room a minute ago was the effect of that. What *I* saw – just before – was much worse."

Her hand tightened. "What was it?"

"An extraordinary man. Looking in."

"What extraordinary man?"

"I haven't the least idea."

Mrs Grose gazed round us in vain. "Then where is he gone?"

"I know still less."

"Have you seen him before?"

"Yes – once. On the old tower."

She could only look at me harder. "Do you mean he's a stranger?"

"Oh, very much!"

"Yet you didn't tell me?"

"No – for reasons. But now that you've guessed – "

Mrs Grose's round eyes encountered this charge. "Ah, I haven't guessed!" she said very simply. "How can I if *you* don't imagine?"

"I don't in the very least."

"You've seen him nowhere but on the tower?"

"And on this spot just now."

Mrs Grose looked round again. "What was he doing on the tower?"

"Only standing there and looking down at me."

She thought a minute. "Was he a gentleman?"

I found I had no need to think. "No." She gazed in deeper wonder. "No."

"Then nobody about the place? Nobody from the village?"

"Nobody – nobody. I didn't tell you, but I made sure."

She breathed a vague relief: this was, oddly, so much to the good. It only went indeed a little way. "But if he isn't a gentleman – "

"What *is* he? He's a horror."

"A horror?"

"He's – God help me if I know *what* he is!"

Mrs Grose looked round once more; she fixed her eyes on the duskier distance, then, pulling herself together, turned to me with abrupt inconsequence. "It's time we should be at church."

"Oh, I'm not fit for church!"

"Won't it do you good?"

"It won't do *them* – !" I nodded at the house.

"The children?"

"I can't leave them now."

"You're afraid – ?"

I spoke boldly. "I'm afraid of *him*."

Mrs Grose's large face showed me, at this, for the first time, the faraway faint glimmer of a consciousness more acute: I somehow made out in it the delayed dawn of an idea I myself had not given her and that was as yet quite obscure to me. It comes back to me that I thought instantly of this as something I could get from her; and I felt it to be connected with the desire she presently showed to know more. "When was it – on the tower?"

"About the middle of the month. At this same hour."

"Almost at dark," said Mrs Grose.

"Oh, no, not nearly. I saw him as I see you."

"Then how did he get in?"

"And how did he get out?" I laughed. "I had no opportunity to ask him! This evening, you see," I pursued, "he has not been able to get in."

"He only peeps?"

"I hope it will be confined to that!" She had now let go my hand; she turned away a little. I waited an instant; then I brought out: "Go to church. Goodbye. I must watch."

Slowly she faced me again. "Do you fear for them?"

We met in another long look. "Don't *you*?" Instead of answering she came nearer to the window and, for a minute, applied her face to the glass. "You see how he could see," I meanwhile went on.

She didn't move. "How long was he here?"

"Till I came out. I came to meet him."

Mrs Grose at last turned round, and there was still more in her face. "*I* couldn't have come out."

"Neither could I!" I laughed again. "But I did come. I have my duty."

"So have I mine," she replied; after which she added: "What is he like?"

"I've been dying to tell you. But he's like nobody."

"Nobody?" she echoed.

"He has no hat." Then seeing in her face that she already, in this, with a deeper dismay, found a touch of picture, I quickly added stroke to stroke. "He has red hair, very red, close-curling, and a pale face, long in shape, with straight, good features and little, rather queer whiskers that are as red as his hair. His eyebrows are, somehow, darker; they look particularly arched and as if they might move a good deal. His eyes are sharp, strange – awfully; but I only know clearly that they're rather small and very fixed. His mouth's wide, and his lips are thin, and except for his little whiskers he's quite clean-shaven. He gives me a sort of sense of looking like an actor."

"An actor!" It was impossible to resemble one less, at least, than Mrs Grose at that moment.

"I've never seen one, but so I suppose them. He's tall, active, erect," I continued, "but never – no, never! – a gentleman."

My companion's face had blanched as I went on; her round eyes started and her mild mouth gaped. "A gentleman?" she gasped, confounded, stupefied: "A gentleman *he*?"

"You know him then?"

She visibly tried to hold herself. "But he *is* handsome?"

I saw the way to help her. "Remarkably!"

"And dressed – ?"

"In somebody's clothes. They're smart, but they're not his own."

She broke into a breathless affirmative groan: "They're the master's!"

I caught it up. "You *do* know him?"

She faltered but a second. "Quint!" she cried.

"Quint?"

"Peter Quint – his own man, his valet, when he was here!"

"When the master was?"

Gaping still, but meeting me, she pieced it all together. "He never wore his hat, but he did wear – well, there were waistcoats missed. They were both here – last year. Then the master went, and Quint was alone."

I followed, but halting a little. "Alone?"

"Alone with *us*." Then, as from a deeper depth, "In charge," she added.

"And what became of him?"

She hung fire so long that I was still more mystified. "He went, too," she brought out at last.

"Went where?"

Her expression, at this, became extraordinary. "God knows where! He died."

"Died?" I almost shrieked.

She seemed fairly to square herself, plant herself more firmly to utter the wonder of it. "Yes. Mr Quint is dead."

VI

It took of course more than that particular passage to place us together in presence of what we had now to live with as we could – my dreadful liability to impressions of the order so vividly exemplified, and my companion's knowledge, henceforth – a knowledge half consternation and half compassion – of that liability. There had been, this evening, after the revelation left me, for an hour, so prostrate – there had been, for either of us, no attendance on any service but a little service of tears and vows, of prayers and promises, a climax to the series of mutual challenges and pledges that had straightway ensued on our retreating together to the schoolroom and shutting ourselves up there to have everything out. The result of our having everything out was simply to reduce our situation to the last rigour of its elements. She herself had seen nothing, not the shadow of a shadow, and nobody in the house but the governess was in the governess's plight; yet she accepted without directly impugning my sanity the truth as I gave it to her, and ended by showing me, on this ground, an awestricken tenderness, an expression of the sense of my more than questionable privilege, of which the very breath has remained with me as that of the sweetest of human charities.

What was settled between us, accordingly, that night, was that we thought we might bear things together; and I was not even sure that, in spite of her exemption, it was she who had the best of the burden. I knew at this hour, I think, as well as I knew later, what I was capable of meeting to shelter my pupils; but it took me some time to be wholly sure of what my honest ally was prepared for to keep terms with so compromising a contract. I was queer company enough – quite as queer as the company I received; but as I trace over what we went through I see how much common ground we must have found in the one idea that, by good fortune, *could* steady us. It was the idea, the second movement, that led me straight out, as I may say, of the inner chamber of my dread. I could take the air in the court, at least, and there Mrs Grose could join me. Perfectly can I recall now the particular way strength came to me before we separated for the night. We had gone over and over every feature of what I had seen.

"He was looking for someone else, you say – someone who was not you?"

"He was looking for little Miles." A portentous clearness now possessed me. "*That's* whom he was looking for."

"But how do you know?"

"I know, I know, I know!" My exaltation grew. "And *you* know, my dear!"

She didn't deny this, but I required, I felt, not even so much telling as that. She resumed in a moment, at any rate: "What if *he* should see him?"

"Little Miles? That's what he wants!"

She looked immensely scared again. "The child?"

"Heaven forbid! The man. He wants to appear to *them*." That he might was an awful conception, and yet, somehow, I could keep it at bay; which, moreover, as we lingered there, was what I succeeded in practically proving. I had an absolute certainty that I should see again what I had already seen, but something within me said that by offering myself bravely as the sole subject of such experience, by accepting, by inviting, by surmounting it all, I should serve as an expiatory victim and guard the tranquillity of my companions. The children, in especial, I should thus fence about and absolutely save. I recall one of the last things I said that night to Mrs Grose.

"It does strike me that my pupils have never mentioned – "

She looked at me hard as I musingly pulled up. "His having been here and the time they were with him?"

"The time they were with him, and his name, his presence, his history, in any way."

"Oh, the little lady doesn't remember. She never heard or knew."

"The circumstances of his death?" I thought with some intensity. "Perhaps not. But Miles would remember – Miles would know."

"Ah, don't try him!" broke from Mrs Grose.

I returned her the look she had given me. "Don't be afraid." I continued to think. "It *is* rather odd."

"That he has never spoken of him?"

"Never by the least allusion. And you tell me they were 'great friends'?"

"Oh, it wasn't *him*!" Mrs Grose with emphasis declared. "It was Quint's own fancy. To play with him, I mean – to spoil him." She paused a moment; then she added: "Quint was much too free."

This gave me, straight from my vision of his face – *such* a face! – a sudden sickness of disgust. "Too free with *my* boy?"

"Too free with everyone!"

I forbore, for the moment, to analyse this description further than by the reflection that a part of it applied to several of the members of the household, of the half-dozen maids and men who were still of our small colony. But there was everything, for our apprehension, in the lucky fact that no discomfortable legend, no perturbation of scullions, had ever, within anyone's memory attached to the kind old place. It had neither bad name nor ill fame, and Mrs Grose, most apparently, only desired to cling to me and to quake in silence. I even put her, the very last thing of all, to the test. It was when, at midnight, she had her hand on the schoolroom door to take leave. "I *have* it from you then – for it's of great importance – that he was definitely and admittedly bad?"

"Oh, not admittedly. *I* knew it – but the master didn't."

"And you never told him?"

"Well, he didn't like tale-bearing – he hated complaints. He was terribly short with anything of that kind, and if people were all right to *him* – "

"He wouldn't be bothered with more?" This squared well enough with my impressions of him: he was not a trouble-loving gentleman, nor so very particular perhaps about some of the company *he* himself kept. All the same, I pressed my interlocutress. "I promise you *I* would have told!"

She felt my discrimination. "I daresay I was wrong. But, really, I was afraid."

"Afraid of what?"

"Of things that man could do. Quint was so clever – he was so deep."

I took this in still more than, probably, I showed. "You weren't afraid of anything else? Not of his effect – ?"

"His effect?" she repeated with a face of anguish and waiting while I faltered.

"On innocent little precious lives. They were in your charge."

"No, they were not in mine!" she roundly and distressfully returned. "The master believed in him and placed him here because he was supposed not to be well and the country air so good for him. So he had everything to say. Yes" – she let me have it – "even about *them.*"

"Them – that creature?" I had to smother a kind of howl. "And you could bear it?"

"No. I couldn't – and I can't now!" And the poor woman burst into tears.

A rigid control, from the next day, was, as I have said, to

follow them; yet how often and how passionately, for a week, we came back together to the subject! Much as we had discussed it that Sunday night, I was, in the immediate later hours in especial – for it may be imagined whether I slept – still haunted with the shadow of something she had not told me. I myself had kept back nothing, but there was a word Mrs Grose had kept back. I was sure, moreover, by morning, that this was not from a failure of frankness, but because on every side there were fears. It seems to me indeed, in retrospect, that by the time the morrow's sun was high I had restlessly read into the fact before us almost all the meaning they were to receive from subsequent and more cruel occurrences. What they gave me above all was just the sinister figure of the living man – the dead one would keep awhile! – and of the months he had continuously passed at Bly, which, added up, made a formidable stretch. The limit of this evil time had arrived only when, on the dawn of a winter's morning, Peter Quint was found, by a labourer going to early work, stone dead on the road from the village: a catastrophe explained – superficially at least – by a visible wound to his head; such a wound as might have been produced – and as, on the final evidence, *had* been – by a fatal slip, in the dark and after leaving the public house, on the steepish icy slope, a wrong path altogether, at the bottom of which he lay. The icy slope, the turn mistaken at night and in liquor, accounted for much – practically, in the end and after the inquest and boundless chatter, for everything; but there had been matters in his life – strange passages and perils, secret disorders, vices more than suspected – that would have accounted for a good deal more.

I scarce know how to put my story into words that shall be a credible picture of my state of mind; but I was in these days literally able to find a joy in the extraordinary flight of heroism the occasion demanded of me. I now saw that I had been asked for a service admirable and difficult; and there would be a great-ness in letting it be seen – oh, in the right quarter! – that I could succeed where many another girl might have failed. It was an immense help to me – I confess I rather applaud myself as I look back! – that I saw my service so strongly and so simply. I was there to protect and defend the little creatures in the world the most bereaved and the most lovable, the appeal of whose helplessness had suddenly become only too explicit, a deep, constant ache of one's own committed heart. We were cut off, really, together; we were united in our danger. They had nothing but me, and I – well, I had *them*. It was in short a magnificent chance. This chance presented itself to me in an image richly material. I was a screen – I was to stand before them. The more I saw, the less they would. I began to watch them in a stifled suspense, a disguised excitement that might well, had it continued too long, have turned to something like madness. What saved me, as I now see, was that it turned to something else altogether. It didn't last as suspense – it was superseded by horrible proofs. Proofs, I say, yes – from the moment I really took hold.

This moment dated from an afternoon hour that I happened to spend in the grounds with the younger of my pupils alone. We had left Miles indoors, on the red cushion of a deep window seat; he had wished to finish a book, and I had been glad to encourage a purpose so laudable in a young man whose only defect was an occasional excess of the restless. His sister, on the contrary, had been alert to come out, and I strolled with her half an hour, seeking the shade, for the sun was still high and the day exceptionally warm. I was aware afresh, with her, as we went, of how, like her brother, she contrived – it was the charming thing in both children – to let me alone without appearing to drop me and to accompany me without appearing to surround. They were never importunate and yet never listless. My attention to them all really went to seeing them amuse themselves immensely without me: this was a spectacle they seemed actively to prepare and that engaged me as an active admirer. I walked in a world of their invention – they had no occasion whatever to draw upon mine; so that my time was taken only with being, for them, some remarkable person or thing that the game of the moment required and that was merely, thanks to my superior, my exalted stamp, a happy and highly distinguished sinecure. I forget what I was on the present occasion; I only remember that I was something very important and very quiet and that Flora was playing very hard. We were on the edge of the lake, and, as we had lately begun geography, the lake was the Sea of Azof.

Suddenly, in these circumstances, I became aware that, on the other side of the Sea of Azof, we had an interested spectator. The way this knowledge gathered in me was the strangest thing in the world – the strangest, that is, except the very much stranger in which it quickly merged itself. I had sat down with a piece of work – for I was something or other that could sit – on the old stone bench which overlooked the pond; and in this position I began to take in with certitude, and yet without direct vision, the presence, at a distance, of a third person. The old trees, the thick shrubbery, made a great and pleasant shade, but it was all suffused with the brightness of the hot, still hour. There was no ambiguity in anything; none whatever, at least, in the conviction I from one moment to another found myself forming as to what I should see straight before me and across the lake as a consequence of raising my eyes. They were attached at this juncture to the stitching in which I was engaged, and I can feel once more the spasm of my effort not to move them till I should so have steadied myself as to be able to make up my mind what to do. There was an alien object in view – a figure whose right of presence I instantly, passionately questioned. I recollect counting over perfectly the possibilities, reminding myself that nothing was more natural, for instance, then the appearance of one of the men about the place, or even of a messenger, a postman, or a tradesman's boy, from the village. That reminder had as little effect on my practical certitude as I was conscious – still even without looking – of its having upon the character and attitude of our visitor. Nothing was more natural than that these things should be the other things that they absolutely were not.

Of the positive identity of the apparition I would assure myself as soon as the small clock of my courage should have ticked out the right second; meanwhile, with an effort that was already sharp enough, I transferred my eyes straight to little Flora, who, at the moment, was about ten yards away. My heart had stood still for an instant with the wonder and terror of the question whether she too would see; and I held my breath while I waited for what a cry from her, what some sudden innocent sign either of interest or of alarm, would tell me. I waited, but nothing came; then, in the first place – and there is something more dire in this, I feel, than in anything I have to relate – I was determined by a sense that, within a minute, all sounds from her had previously dropped; and, in the second, by the circumstance that, also within the minute, she had, in her play, turned her back to the water. This was her attitude when I at last looked at her – looked with the confirmed conviction that we were still, together, under direct personal notice. She had picked up a small flat piece of wood, which happened to have in it a little hole that had evidently suggested to her the idea of sticking in another fragment that might figure as a mast and make the thing a boat. This second morsel, as I watched her, she was very markedly and intently attempting to tighten in its place. My apprehension of what she was doing sustained me so that after some seconds I felt I was ready for more. Then I again shifted my eyes – I faced what I had to face.

VII

I got hold of Mrs Grose as soon after this as I could; and I can give no intelligible account of how I fought out the interval. Yet I still hear myself cry as I fairly threw myself into her arms: "They *know* – it's too monstrous: they know, they know!"

"And what on earth – ?" I felt her incredulity as she held me.

"Why, all that *we* know – and heaven knows what else besides!" Then, as she released me, I made it out to her, made it out perhaps only now with full coherency even to myself. "Two hours ago, in the garden," – I could scarce articulate – "Flora *saw*!"

Mrs Grose took it as she might have taken a blow in the stomach. "She has told you?" she panted.

"Not a word – that's the horror. She kept it to herself! The child of eight, *that* child!" Unutterable still, for me, was the stupefaction of it.

Mrs Grose, of course, could only gape the wider. "Then how do you know?"

"I was there – I saw with my eyes: saw that she was perfectly aware."

"Do you mean aware of *him*?"

"No – of *her*." I was conscious as I spoke that I looked prodigious things, for I got the slow reflection of them in my companion's face. "Another person – this time; but a figure of quite as unmistakeable horror and evil: a woman in black, pale and dreadful – with such an air also, and such a face! – on the other side of the lake. I was there with the child – quiet for the hour; and in the midst of it she came."

"Came how – from where?"

"From where they come from! She just appeared and stood there – but not so near."

"And without coming nearer?"

"Oh, for the effect and the feeling, she might have been as close as you!"

My friend, with an odd impulse, fell back a step. "Was she someone you've never seen?"

"Yes. But someone the child has. Someone *you* have." Then, to show how I had thought it all out: "My predecessor – the one who died."

"Miss Jessel?"

"Miss Jessel. You don't believe me?" I pressed.

She turned right and left in her distress. "How can you be sure?"

This drew from me, in the state of my nerves, a flash of impatience. "Then ask Flora – *she's* sure!" But I had no sooner spoken than I caught myself up. "No, for God's sake, *don't*! She'll say she isn't – she'll lie!"

Mrs Grose was not too bewildered instinctively to protest. "Ah, how *can* you?"

"Because I'm clear. Flora doesn't want me to know."

"It's only then to spare you."

"No, no – there are depths, depths! The more I go over it, the more I see in it, and the more I see in it, the more I fear. I don't know what I *don't* see – what I *don't* fear!"

Mrs Grose tried to keep up with me. "You mean you're afraid of seeing her again?"

"Oh, no; that's nothing – now!" Then I explained. "It's of *not* seeing her."

But my companion only looked wan. "I don't understand you."

"Why, it's that the child may keep it up – and that the child assuredly *will* – without my knowing it."

At the image of this possibility Mrs Grose for a moment collapsed, yet presently to pull herself together again, as if from the positive force of the sense of what, should we yield an inch, there would really be to give way to. "Dear, dear – we must keep our heads! And after all, if she doesn't mind it – !" She even tried a grim joke. "Perhaps she likes it!"

"Likes *such* things – a scrap of an infant!"

"Isn't it just a proof of her blessed innocence?" my friend bravely enquired.

She brought me, for the instant, almost round. "Oh, we must clutch at *that* – we must cling to it! If it isn't a proof of what you say, it's a proof of – God knows what! For the woman's a horror of horrors."

Mrs Grose, at this, fixed her eyes a minute on the ground; then at last raising them, "Tell me how you know," she said.

"Then you admit it's what she was?" I cried.

"Tell me how you know," my friend simply repeated.

"Know? By seeing her! By the way she looked."

"At you, do you mean – so wickedly?"

"Dear me, no – I could have borne that. She gave me never a glance. She only fixed the child."

Mrs Grose tried to see it. "Fixed her?"

"Ah, with such awful eyes!"

She stared at mine as if they might really have resembled them. "Do you mean of dislike?"

"God help us, no. Of something much worse."

"Worse than dislike?" This left her indeed at a loss.

"With a determination – indescribable. With a kind of fury of intention."

I made her turn pale. "Intention?"

"To get hold of her." Mrs Grose – her eyes just lingering on mine – gave a shudder and walked to the window; and while she stood there looking out I completed my statement. "*That's* what Flora knows."

After a little she turned round. "The person was in black, you say?"

"In mourning – rather poor, almost shabby. But – yes – with extraordinary beauty." I now recognised to what I had at last, stroke by stroke, brought the victim of my confidence, for she quite visibly weighed this. "Oh, handsome – very, very," I insisted. "Wonderfully handsome. But infamous."

She slowly came back to me. "Miss Jessel – *was* infamous." She once more took my hand in both her own, holding it as tight as if to fortify me against the increase of alarm I might draw from this disclosure. "They were both infamous," she finally said.

So, for a little, we faced it once more together; and I found absolutely a degree of help in seeing it now so straight. "I appreciate," I said, "the great decency of your not having hitherto spoken; but the time has certainly come to give me the whole thing." She appeared to assent to this, but still only in silence; seeing which I went on: "I must have it now. Of what did she die? Come, there was something between them."

"There was everything."

"In spite of the difference – ?"

"Oh, of their rank, their condition" – she brought it woefully out. "*She* was a lady."

I turned it over; I again saw. "Yes – she was a lady."

"And he so dreadfully below," said Mrs Grose.

I felt that I doubtless needn't press too hard, in such company, on the place of a servant in the scale; but there was nothing to prevent an acceptance of my companion's own measure of my predecessor's abasement. There was a way to deal with that, and I dealt; the more readily for my full vision – on the evidence

– of our employer's late clever, good-looking "own" man; impudent, assured, spoiled, depraved. "The fellow was a hound."

Mrs Grose considered as if it were perhaps a little a case for a sense of shades. "I've never seen one like him. He did what he wished."

"With *her*?"

"With them all."

It was as if now in my friend's own eyes Miss Jessel had again appeared. I seemed at any rate, for an instant, to see their evocation of her as distinctly as I had seen her by the pond; and I brought out with decision: "It must have been also what *she* wished!"

Mrs Grose's face signified that it had been indeed, but she said at the same time: "Poor woman – she paid for it!"

"Then you do know what she died of?" I asked.

"No – I know nothing. I wanted not to know; I was glad enough I didn't; and I thanked heaven she was well out of this!"

"Yet you had, then, your idea – "

"Of her real reason for leaving? Oh, yes – as to that. She couldn't have stayed. Fancy it here – for a governess! And afterward I imagined – and I still imagine. And what I imagine is dreadful."

"Not so dreadful as what *I* do," I replied; on which I must have shown her – as I was indeed but too conscious – a front of miserable defeat. It brought out again all her compassion for me, and at the renewed touch of her kindness my power to resist broke down. I burst, as I had, the other time, made her burst, into tears; she took me to her motherly breast, and my lamentation overflowed. "I don't do it!" I sobbed in despair; "I don't save or shield them! It's far worse than I dreamed – they're lost!"

VIII

What I had said to Mrs Grose was true enough: there were in the matter I had put before her depths and possibilities that I lacked resolution to sound; so that when we met once more in the wonder of it we were of a common mind about the duty of resistance to extravagant fancies. We were to keep our heads if we should keep nothing else – difficult indeed as that might be in the face of what, in our prodigious experience, was least to be questioned. Late that night, while the house slept, we had another talk in my room, when she went all the way with me as to its being beyond doubt that I had seen exactly what I had seen. To hold her perfectly in the pinch of that, I found I had only to ask her how, if I had "made it up", I came to be able to give, of each of the persons appearing to me, a picture disclosing, to the last detail, their special marks – a portrait on the exhibition of which she had instantly recognised and named them. She wished of course – small blame to her! – to sink the whole subject; and I was quick to assure her that my own interest in it had now violently taken the form of a search for the way to escape from it. I encountered her on the ground of a probability that with recurrence – for recurrence we took for granted – I should get used to my danger, distinctly professing that my personal exposure had suddenly become the least of my discomforts. It was my new suspicion that was intolerable; and yet even to this complication the later hours of the day had brought a little ease.

On leaving her, after my first outbreak, I had of course returned to my pupils, associating the right remedy for my dismay with that sense of their charm which I had already found to be a thing

I could positively cultivate and which had never failed me yet. I had simply, in other words, plunged afresh into Flora's special society and there become aware – it was almost a luxury! – that she could put her little conscious hand straight upon the spot that ached. She had looked at me in sweet speculation and then had accused me to my face of having "cried". I had supposed I had brushed away the ugly signs: but I could literally – for the time, at all events – rejoice, under this fathomless charity, that they had not entirely disappeared. To gaze into the depths of blue of the child's eyes and pronounce their loveliness a trick of premature cunning was to be guilty of a cynicism in preference to which I naturally preferred to abjure my judgement and, so far as might be, my agitation. I couldn't abjure for merely wanting to, but I could repeat to Mrs Grose – as I did there, over and over, in the small hours – that with their voices in the air, their pressure on one's heart, and their fragrant faces against one's cheek, everything fell to the ground but their incapacity and their beauty. It was a pity that, somehow, to settle this once for all, I had equally to re-enumerate the signs of subtlety that, in the afternoon, by the lake had made a miracle of my show of self-possession. It was a pity to be obliged to reinvestigate the certitude of the moment itself and repeat how it had come to me as a revelation that the inconceivable communion I then surprised was a matter, for either party, of habit. It was a pity that I should have had to quaver out again the reasons for my not having, in my delusion, so much as questioned that the little girl saw our visitant even as I actually saw Mrs Grose herself, and that she wanted, by just so much as she did thus see, to make me suppose she didn't, and at the same time, without showing anything, arrive at a guess as to whether I myself did! It was a pity that I needed once more to describe the portentous little activity by which she sought to divert my attention – the perceptible increase of movement, the greater intensity of play, the singing, the gabbling of nonsense, and the invitation to romp.

Yet if I had not indulged, to prove there was nothing in it, in this review, I should have missed the two or three dim elements of comfort that still remained to me. I should not for instance have been able to asseverate to my friend that I was certain – which was so much to the good – that *I* at least had not betrayed myself. I should not have been prompted, by stress of need, by desperation of mind – I scarce know what to call it – to invoke such further aid to intelligence as might spring from pushing my colleague fairly to the wall. She had told me, bit by bit, under pressure, a great deal; but a small shifty spot on the wrong side of it all still sometimes brushed my brow like the wing of a bat; and I remember how on this occasion – for the sleeping house and the concentration alike of our danger and our watch seemed to help – I felt the importance of giving the last jerk to the curtain. "I don't believe anything so horrible," I recollect saying. "No, let us put it definitely, my dear, that I don't. But if I did, you know, there's a thing I should require now, just without sparing you the least bit more – oh, not a scrap, come! – to get out of you. What was it you had in mind when, in our distress, before Miles came back, over the letter from his school, you said, under my insistence, that you didn't pretend for him that he had not literally *ever* been 'bad'? He has *not* literally 'ever', in these weeks that I myself have lived with him and so closely watched him; he has been an imperturbable little prodigy of delightful, loveable goodness. Therefore you might perfectly have made the claim for him if you had not, as it happened, seen an exception to take. What was your exception, and to what passage in your personal observation of him did you refer?"

It was a dreadfully austere enquiry, but levity was not our note, and, at any rate, before the grey dawn admonished us to separate

I had got my answer. What my friend had had in mind proved to be immensely to the purpose. It was neither more nor less than the circumstance that for a period of several months Quint and the boy had been perpetually together. It was in fact the very appropriate truth that she had ventured to criticise the propriety, to hint at the incongruity, of so close an alliance, and even to go so far on the subject as a frank overture to Miss Jessel. Miss Jessel had, with a most strange manner, requested her to mind her business, and the good woman had, on this, directly approached little Miles. What she had said to him, since I pressed, was that *she* liked to see young gentlemen not forget their station.

I pressed again, of course, at this. "You reminded him that Quint was only a base menial?"

"As you might say! And it was his answer, for one thing, that was bad."

"And for another thing?" I waited. "He repeated your words to Quint?"

"No, not that. It's just what he *wouldn't*!" she could still impress upon me. "I was sure, at any rate," she added, "that he didn't. But he denied certain occasions."

"What occasions?"

"When they had been about together quite as if Quint were his tutor – and a very grand one – and Miss Jessel only for the little lady. When he had gone off with the fellow, I mean, and spent hours with him."

"He then prevaricated about it – he said he hadn't?" Her assent was clear enough to cause me to add in a moment: "I see. He lied."

"Oh!" Mrs Grose mumbled. This was a suggestion that it didn't matter; which indeed she backed up by a further remark. "You see, after all, Miss Jessel didn't mind. She didn't forbid him."

I considered. "Did he put that to you as a justification?"

At this she dropped again. "No, he never spoke of it."

"Never mentioned her in connection with Quint?"

She saw, visibly flushing, where I was coming out. "Well, he didn't show anything. He denied," she repeated; "he denied."

Lord, how I pressed her now! "So that you could see he knew what was between the two wretches?"

"I don't know – I don't know!" the poor woman groaned.

"You do know, you dear thing," I replied; "only you haven't my dreadful boldness of mind, and you keep back, out of timidity and modesty and delicacy, even the impression that, in the past, when you had, without my aid, to flounder about in silence, most of all made you miserable. But I shall get it out of you yet! There was something in the boy that suggested to you," I continued, "that he covered and concealed their relation."

"Oh, he couldn't prevent – "

"Your learning the truth? I daresay! But, heavens," I fell, with vehemence, athinking, "what it shows that they must, to that extent, have succeeded in making of him!"

"Ah, nothing that's not nice *now*!" Mrs Grose lugubriously pleaded.

"I don't wonder you looked queer," I persisted, "when I mentioned to you the letter from his school!"

"I doubt if I looked as queer as you!" she retorted with homely force. "And if he was so bad then as that comes to, how is he such an angel now?"

"Yes, indeed – and if he was a fiend at school! How, how, how? Well," I said in my torment, "you must put it to me again, but I shall not be able to tell you for some days. Only, put it to me again!" I cried in a way that made my friend stare. "There are directions in which I must not for the present let myself go." Meanwhile I returned to her first example – the one to which she had just previously referred – of the boy's happy capacity for an occasional slip. "If Quint – on your remonstrance at the time you speak of – was a base menial, one of the things Miles said to you, I find myself guessing, was that you were another." Again her admission was so adequate that I continued: "And you forgave him that?"

"Wouldn't *you*?"

"Oh, yes!" And we exchanged there, in the stillness, a sound of the oddest amusement. Then I went on: "At all events, while he was with the man – "

"Miss Flora was with the woman. It suited them all!"

It suited me, too, I felt, only too well; by which I mean that it suited exactly the particularly deadly view I was in the very act of forbidding myself to entertain. But I so far succeeded in checking the expression of this view that I will throw, just here, no further light on it than may be offered by the mention of my final observation to Mrs Grose. "His having lied and been impudent are, I confess, less engaging specimens than I had hoped to have from you of the outbreak in him of the little natural man. Still," I mused, "they must do, for they make me feel more than ever that I must watch."

It made me blush, the next minute, to see in my friend's face how much more unreservedly she had forgiven him than her anecdote struck me as presenting to my own tenderness an occasion for doing. This came out when, at the schoolroom door, she quitted me. "Surely you don't accuse *him* – "

"Of carrying on an intercourse that he conceals from me? Ah, remember that, until further evidence, I now accuse nobody." Then, before shutting her out to go, by another passage, to her own place, "I must just wait," I wound up.

IX

I waited and waited, and the days, as they elapsed, took something from my consternation. A very few of them, in fact, passing in constant sight of my pupils, without a fresh incident, sufficed to give to grievous fancies and even to odious memories a kind of brush of the sponge. I have spoken of the surrender to their extraordinary childish grace as a thing I could actively cultivate, and it may be imagined if I neglected now to address myself to this source for whatever balm it would yield. Stranger than I can express, certainly, was the effort to struggle against my new lights; it would doubtless have been, however, a greater tension still had it not been so frequently successful. I used to wonder how my little charges could help guessing that I thought strange things about them; and the circumstances that these things only made them more interesting was not by itself a direct aid to keeping them in the dark. I trembled lest they should see that they *were* so immensely more interesting. Putting things at the worst, at all events, as in meditation I so often did, any clouding of their innocence could only be – blameless and foredoomed as they were – a reason the more for taking risks. There were moments when, by an irresistible impulse, I found myself catching them up and pressing them to my heart. As soon as I had done so I used to say to myself: "What will they think of that? Doesn't it betray too much?" It would have been easy to get into a sad, wild tangle about how much I might betray; but the real account, I feel, of the hours of peace that I could still enjoy was that the immediate charm of my companions was a beguilement still effective even under the shadow of the possibility that it was studied. For if it occurred to me that I might occasionally excite suspicion by the little outbreaks of my sharper passion for them, so too I remember wondering if I mightn't see a queerness in the traceable increase of their own demonstrations.

They were at this period extravagantly and preternaturally fond of me; which, after all, I could reflect, was no more than a graceful response in children perpetually bowed over and hugged. The homage of which they were so lavish succeeded, in truth, for my nerves, quite as well as if I never appeared to myself, as I may say, literally to catch them at a purpose in it. They had never, I think, wanted to do so many things for their poor protectress; I mean – though they got their lessons better and better, which was naturally what would please her most – in the way of diverting, entertaining, surprising her; reading her passages, telling her stories, acting her charades, pouncing out at her, in disguises, as animals and historical characters, and above all astonishing her by the "pieces" they had secretly got by heart and could interminably recite. I should never get to the bottom – were I to let myself go even now – of the prodigious private commentary, all under still more private correction, with which, in these days, I overscored their full hours. They had shown me from the first a facility for everything, a general faculty which, taking a fresh start, achieved remarkable flights. They got their little tasks as if they loved them, and indulged, from the mere exuberance of the gift, in the most unimposed little miracles of memory. They not only popped out at me as tigers and as Romans, but as Shakespeareans, astronomers and navigators. This was so singularly the case that it had presumably much to do with the fact as to which, at the present day, I am at a loss for a different explanation: I allude to my unnatural composure on the subject of another school for Miles. What I remember is that I was content not, for the time, to open the question, and that contentment must have sprung from the sense of his perpetually striking show of cleverness. He was too clever for a bad governess, for a parson's daughter, to spoil; and the strangest if not the brightest thread in the pensive embroidery I just spoke of was the impression I might have got, if I had dared to work it out, that he was under some influence operating in his small intellectual life as a tremendous incitement.

If it was easy to reflect, however, that such a boy could postpone school, it was at least as marked that for such a boy to have been "kicked out" by a schoolmaster was a mystification without end. Let me add that in their company now – and I was careful almost never to be out of it – I could follow no scent very far. We lived in a cloud of music and love and success and private theatricals. The musical sense in each of the children was of the quickest, but the elder in especial had a marvellous knack of catching and repeating. The schoolroom piano broke into all gruesome fancies; and when that failed there were confabulations in corners, with a sequel of one of them going out in the highest spirits in order to "come in" as something new. I had had brothers myself, and it was no revelation to me that little girls could be slavish idolaters of little boys. What surpassed everything was that there was a little boy in the world who could have for the inferior age, sex and intelligence so fine a consideration. They were extraordinarily at one, and to say that they never either quarrelled or complained is to make the note of praise coarse for their quality of sweetness. Sometimes, indeed, when I dropped into coarseness, I perhaps came across traces of little understandings between them by which one of them should keep me occupied while the other slipped away. There is a naive side, I suppose, in all diplomacy; but if my pupils practised upon me, it was surely with the minimum of grossness. It was all in the other quarter that, after a lull, the grossness broke out.

I find that I really hang back; but I must take my plunge. In going on with the record of what was hideous at Bly, I not only challenge the most liberal faith – for which I little care; but – and this is another matter – I renew what I myself suffered, I again push my way through it to the end. There came suddenly an hour after which, as I look back, the affair seems to me to have been all pure suffering; but I have at least reached the heart of it, and the straightest road out is doubtless to advance. One evening – with nothing to lead up or to prepare it – I felt the cold touch of the impression that had breathed on me the night of my arrival and which, much lighter then, as I have mentioned, I should probably have made little of in memory had my subsequent sojourn been less agitated. I had not gone to bed; I sat reading by a couple of candles. There was a roomful of old books at Bly – last-century fiction, some of it, which, to the extent of a distinctly deprecated renown, but never to so much as that of a stray specimen, had reached the sequestered home and appealed to the unavowed curiosity of my youth. I remember that the book I had in my hand was Fielding's *Amelia*; also that I was wholly awake. I recall further both a general conviction that it was horribly late and a particular objection to looking at my watch. I figure, finally, that the white curtain draping, in the fashion of those days, the head of Flora's little bed, shrouded, as I had assured myself long before, the perfection of childish rest. I recollect in short that, though I was deeply interested in my author, I found myself, at the turn of a page and with his spell all scattered, looking straight up from him and hard at the door of my room. There was a moment during which I listened, reminded of the faint sense I had had, the first night, of there being something undefinably astir in the house, and noted the soft breath of the open casement just move the half-drawn blind. Then, with all the marks of a deliberation that must have seemed magnificent had there been anyone to admire it, I laid down my book, rose to my feet, and, taking a candle, went straight out of the room and, from the passage, on which my light made little impression, noiselessly closed and locked the door.

I can say now neither what determined nor what guided me, but I went straight along the lobby, holding my candle high, till I came within sight of the tall window that presided over the great turn of the staircase. At this point I precipitately found myself aware of three things. They were practically simultaneous, yet they had flashes of succession. My candle, under a bold flourish, went out, and I perceived, by the uncovered window, that the yielding dusk of earliest morning rendered it unnecessary. Without it, the next instant, I saw that there was someone on the stair. I speak of sequences, but I required no lapse of seconds to stiffen myself for a third encounter with Quint. The apparition had reached the landing halfway up and was therefore on the spot nearest the window, where at sight of me, it stopped short and fixed me exactly as it had fixed me from the tower and from the garden. He knew me as well as I knew him; and so, in the cold, faint twilight, with a glimmer in the high glass and another on the polish of the oak stair below, we faced each other in our common intensity. He was absolutely, on this occasion, a living, detestable, dangerous presence. But that was not the wonder of wonders; I reserve this distinction for quite another circumstance: the circumstance that dread had unmistakeably quitted me and that there was nothing in me there that didn't meet and measure him.

I had plenty of anguish after that extraordinary moment, but I had, thank God, no terror. And he knew I had not – I found myself at the end of an instant magnificently aware of this. I felt, in a fierce rigour of confidence, that if I stood my ground a minute I should cease – for the time, at least – to have him to reckon with; and during the minute, accordingly, the thing

was as human and hideous as a real interview: hideous just
because it *was* human, as human as to have met alone, in the
small hours, in a sleeping house, some enemy, some adventurer,
some criminal. It was the dead silence of our long gaze at such
close quarters that gave the whole horror, huge as it was, its
only note of the unnatural. If I had met a murderer in such a
place and at such an hour, we still at least would have spoken.
Something would have passed, in life, between us; if nothing
had passed, one of us would have moved. The moment was so
prolonged that it would have taken but little more to make me
doubt if even *I* were in life. I can't express what followed it
save by saying that the silence itself – which was indeed in a
manner an attestation of my strength – became the element into
which I saw the figure disappear; in which I definitely saw it
turn as I might have seen the low wretch to which it had once
belonged turn on receipt of an order, and pass, with my eyes
on the villainous back that no hunch could have more disfigured,
straight down the staircase and into the darkness in which the
next bend was lost.

X

I remained awhile at the top of the stair, but with the effect
presently of understanding that when my visitor had gone, he
had gone; then I returned to my room. The foremost thing I saw
there by the light of the candle I had left burning was that Flora's
little bed was empty; and on this I caught my breath with all the
terror that, five minutes before, I had been able to resist. I dashed
at the place in which I had left her lying and over which (for
the small silk counterpane and the sheets were disarranged) the
white curtains had been deceivingly pulled forward; then my
step, to my unutterable relief, produced an answering sound: I
perceived an agitation of the window blind, and the child, ducking
down, emerged rosily from the other side of it. She stood there
in so much of her candour and so little of her nightgown, with
her pink bare feet and the golden glow of her curls. She looked
intensely grave, and I had never had such a sense of losing an
advantage acquired (the thrill of which had just been so prodigious) as on my consciousness that she addressed me with a
reproach. "You naughty: where *have* you been?" – instead of
challenging her own irregularity I found myself arraigned and
explaining. She herself explained, for that matter, with the love-
liest, eagerest simplicity. She had known suddenly, as she lay
there, that I was out of the room, and had jumped up to see what
had become of me. I had dropped, with the joy of her reappearance, back into my chair – feeling then, and then only, a little
faint; and she had pattered straight over to me, thrown herself
upon my knee, given herself to be held with the flame of the
candle full in the wonderful little face that was still flushed with
sleep. I remember closing my eyes an instant, yieldingly,

consciously, as before the excess of something beautiful that shone out of the blue of her own. "You were looking for me out of the window?" I said. "You thought I might be walking in the grounds?"

"Well, you know, I thought someone was," – she never blanched as she smiled out that at me.

Oh, how I looked at her now! "And did you see anyone?"

"Ah, *no*!" she returned, almost with the full privilege of childish inconsequence, resentfully, though with a long sweetness in her little drawl of the negative.

At that moment, in the state of my nerves, I absolutely believed she lied; and if I once more closed my eyes it was before the dazzle of the three or four possible ways in which I might take this up. One of these, for a moment, tempted me with such singular intensity that, to withstand it, I must have gripped my little girl with a spasm that, wonderfully, she submitted to without a cry or a sign of fright. Why not break out at her on the spot and have it all over – give it to her straight in her lovely little lighted face? "You see, you see, you *know* that you do and that you already quite suspect I believe it; therefore, why not frankly confess it to me, so that we may at least live with it together and learn perhaps, in the strangeness of our fate, where we are and what it means?" This solicitation dropped, alas, as it came: if I could immediately have succumbed to it I might have spared myself – well, you'll see what. Instead of succumbing I sprang again to my feet, looked at her bed, and took a helpless middle way. "Why did you pull the curtain over the place to make me think you were still there?"

Flora luminously considered; after which, with her little divine smile: "Because I don't like to frighten you!"

"But if I had, by your idea, gone out – ?"

She absolutely declined to be puzzled; she turned her eyes to the flame of the candle as if the question were as irrelevant, or at any rate as impersonal, as Mrs Marcet or nine-times-nine. "Oh, but you know," she quite adequately answered, "that you might come back, you dear, and that you *have*!" And after a little, when she had got into bed, I had, for a long time, by almost sitting on her to hold her hand, to prove that I recognised the pertinence of my return.

You may imagine the general complexion, from that moment, of my nights. I repeatedly sat up till I didn't know when; I selected moments when my roommate unmistakeably slept, and, stealing out, took noiseless turns in the passage and even pushed as far as to where I had last met Quint. But I never met him there again; and I may as well say at once that I on no other occasion saw him in the house. I just missed, on the staircase, on the other hand, a different adventure. Looking down it from the top I once recognised the presence of a woman seated on one of the lower steps with her back presented to me, her body half-bowed and her head, in an attitude of woe, in her hands. I had been there but an instant, however, when she vanished without looking round at me. I knew, nonetheless, exactly what dreadful face she had to show; and I wondered whether, if instead of being above I had been below, I should have had, for going up, the same nerve I had lately shown Quint. Well, there continued to be plenty of chance for nerve. On the eleventh night after my latest encounter with that gentleman – they were all numbered now – I had an alarm that perilously skirted it and that indeed, from the particular quality of its unexpectedness, proved quite my sharpest shock. It was precisely the first night during this series that, weary with watching, I had felt that I might again without laxity lay myself down at my old hour. I slept immediately and, as I afterwards knew, till about one o'clock; but when I woke it was to sit straight up, as completely roused as if a hand had shook me. I had left a light burning, but it was now out, and I felt an instant certainty that Flora had extinguished it. This brought me to my feet and straight, in the darkness, to her bed, which I found she had left. A glance at the window enlightened me further, and the striking of a match completed the picture.

The child had again got up – this time blowing out the taper, and had again, for some purpose of observation or response, squeezed in behind the blind and was peering out into the night. That she now saw – as she had not, I had satisfied myself, the previous time – was proved to me by the fact that she was disturbed neither by my re-illumination nor by the haste I made to get into slippers and into a wrap. Hidden, protected, absorbed, she evidently rested on the sill – the casement opened forward – and gave herself up. There was a great still moon to help her, and this fact had counted in my quick decision. She was face to face with the apparition we had met at the lake, and could now communicate with it as she had not then been able to do. What I, on my side, had to care for was, without disturbing her, to reach, from the corridor, some other window in the same quarter. I got to the door without her hearing me; I got out of it, closed it, and listened, from the other side, for some sound from her. While I stood in the passage I had my eyes on her brother's door, which was but ten steps off and which, indescribably, produced in me a renewal of the strange impulse that I lately spoke of as my temptation. What if I should go straight in and march to *his* window? What if, by risking to his boyish bewilderment a revelation of my motive, I should throw across the rest of the mystery the long halter of my boldness?

This thought held me sufficiently to make me cross to his threshold and pause again. I preternaturally listened; I figured to myself what might portentously be; I wondered if his bed were also empty and he too were secretly at watch. It was a deep, soundless minute, at the end of which my impulse failed. He was quiet; he might be innocent; the risk was hideous; I turned away. There was a figure in the grounds – a figure prowling for a sight, the visitor with whom Flora was engaged; but it was not the visitor most concerned with my boy. I hesitated afresh, but on other grounds and only for a few seconds; then I had made my choice. There were empty rooms at Bly, and it was only a question of choosing the right one. The right one suddenly presented itself to me as the lower one – though high above the gardens – in the solid corner of the house that I have spoken of as the old tower. This was a large, square chamber, arranged with some state as a bedroom, the extravagant size of which made it so inconvenient that it had not for years, though kept by Mrs Grose in exemplary order, been occupied. I had often admired it and I knew my way about in it; I had only, after just faltering at the first chill gloom of its disuse, to pass across it and unbolt as quietly as I could one of the shutters. Achieving this transit, I uncovered the glass without a sound and, applying my face to the pane, was able, the darkness without being much less than within, to see that I commanded the right direction. Then I saw something more. The moon made the night extraordinarily pene-trable and showed me on the lawn a person, diminished by distance, who stood there motionless and as if fascinated, looking up to where I had appeared – looking, that is, not so much straight at me as at something that was apparently above me. There was clearly another person above me – there was a person on the tower; but the presence on the lawn was not in the least what I had conceived and had confidently hurried to meet. The presence on the lawn – I felt sick as I made it out – was poor little Miles himself.

XI

It was not till late next day that I spoke to Mrs Grose; the rigour with which I kept my pupils in sight making it often difficult to meet her privately, and the more as we each felt the importance of not provoking – on the part of the servants quite as much as on that of the children – any suspicion of a secret flurry or that of a discussion of mysteries. I drew a great security in this particular from her mere smooth aspect. There was nothing in her fresh face to pass on to others my horrible confidences. She believed me, I was sure, absolutely: if she hadn't I don't know what would have become of me, for I couldn't have borne the business alone. But she was a magnificent monument to the blessing of a want of imagination, and if she could see in our little charges nothing but their beauty and amiability, their happiness and cleverness, she had no direct communication with the sources of my trouble. If they had been at all visibly blighted or battered, she would doubtless have grown, on tracing it back, haggard enough to match them; as matters stood, however, I could feel her, when she surveyed them, with her large white arms folded and the habit of serenity in all her look, thank the Lord's mercy that if they were ruined the pieces would still serve. Flights of fancy gave place, in her mind, to a steady fireside glow, and I had already begun to perceive how, with the development of the conviction that – as time went on without a public accident – our young things could, after all, look out for themselves, she addressed her greatest solicitude to the sad case presented by their instructress. That, for myself, was a sound simplification: I could engage that, to the world, my face should tell no tales, but it would have been, in the conditions, an immense added strain to find myself anxious about hers.

At the hour I now speak of she had joined me, under pressure, on the terrace, where, with the lapse of the season, the afternoon sun was now agreeable; and we sat there together while, before us, at a distance, but within call if we wished, the children strolled to and fro in one of their most manageable moods. They moved slowly, in unison, below us, over the lawn, the boy, as they went, reading aloud from a storybook and passing his arm round his sister to keep her quite in touch. Mrs Grose watched them with positive placidity; then I caught the suppressed intellectual creak with which she conscientiously turned to take from me a view of the back of the tapestry. I had made her a receptacle of lurid things, but there was an odd recognition of my superiority – my accomplishments and my function – in her patience under my pain. She offered her mind to my disclosures as, had I wished to mix a witch's broth and proposed it with assurance, she would have held out a large clean saucepan. This had become thoroughly her attitude by the time that, in my recital of the events of the night, I reached the point of what Miles had said to me when, after seeing him, at such a monstrous hour, almost on the very spot where he happened now to be, I had gone down to bring him in; choosing then, at the window, with a concentrated need of not alarming the house, rather that method than a signal more resonant. I had left her meanwhile in little doubt of my small hope of representing with success even to her actual sympathy my sense of the real splendour of the little inspiration with which, after I had got him into the house, the boy met my final articulate challenge. As soon as I appeared in the moonlight on the terrace, he had come to me as straight as possible; on which I had taken his hand without a word and led him, through the dark spaces, up the staircase where Quint had so hungrily hovered for him, along the lobby where I had listened and trembled, and so to his forsaken room.

Not a sound, on the way, had passed between us, and I had wondered – oh, *how* I had wondered! – if he were groping about in his little mind for something plausible and not too grotesque. It would tax his invention, certainly, and I felt, this time, over his real embarrassment, a curious thrill of triumph. It was a sharp trap for the inscrutable! He couldn't play any longer at innocence; so how the deuce would he get out of it? There beat in me indeed, with the passionate throb of this question an equal dumb appeal as to how the deuce *I* should. I was confronted at last, as never yet, with all the risk attached even now to sounding my own horrid note. I remember in fact that as we pushed into his little chamber, where the bed had not been slept in at all and the window, uncovered to the moonlight, made the place so clear that there was no need of striking a match – I remember how I suddenly dropped, sank upon the edge of the bed from the force of the idea that he must know how he really, as they say, "had" me. He could do what he liked, with all his cleverness to help him, so long as I should continue to defer to the old tradition of the criminality of those caretakers of the young who minister to superstitions and fears. He "had" me indeed, and in a cleft stick; for who would ever absolve me, who would consent that I should go unhung, if, by the faintest tremor of an overture, I were the first to introduce into our perfect intercourse an element so dire? No, no: it was useless to attempt to convey to Mrs Grose, just as it is scarcely less so to attempt to suggest here, how, in our short, stiff brush in the dark, he fairly shook me with admiration. I was of course thoroughly kind and merciful; never, never yet had I placed on his little shoulders hands of such tenderness as those with which, while I rested against the bed, I held him there well under fire. I had no alternative but, in form at least, to put it to him.

"You must tell me now – and all the truth. What did you go out for? What were you doing there?"

I can still see his wonderful smile, the whites of his beautiful eyes, and the uncovering of his little teeth shine to me in the dusk. "If I tell you why, will you understand?" My heart, at this, leaped into my mouth. *Would* he tell me why? I found no sound on my lips to press it, and I was aware of replying only with a vague, repeated, grimacing nod. He was gentleness itself, and while I wagged my head at him he stood there more than ever a little fairy prince. It was his brightness indeed that gave me a respite. Would it be so great if he were really going to tell me? "Well," he said at last, "just exactly in order that you should do this."

"Do what?"

"Think me – for a change – *bad*!" I shall never forget the sweetness and gaiety with which he brought out the word, nor how, on top of it, he bent forward and kissed me. It was practically the end of everything. I met his kiss and I had to make, while I folded him for a minute in my arms, the most stupendous effort not to cry. He had given exactly the account of himself that permitted least of my going behind it, and it was only with the effect of confirming my acceptance of it that, as I presently glanced about the room, I could say –

"Then you didn't undress at all?"

He fairly glittered in the gloom. "Not at all. I sat up and read."

"And when did you go down?"

"At midnight. When I'm bad I *am* bad!"

"I see, I see – it's charming. But how could you be sure I would know it?"

"Oh, I arranged that with Flora." His answers rang out with a readiness! "She was to get up and look out."

"Which is what she did do." It was I who fell into the trap!

"So she disturbed you, and, to see what she was looking at, you also looked – you saw."

"While you," I concurred, "caught your death in the night air!"

He literally bloomed so from this exploit that he could afford radiantly to assent. "How otherwise should I have been bad enough?" he asked. Then, after another embrace, the incident and our interview closed on my recognition of all the reserves of goodness that, for his joke, he had been able to draw upon.

XII

The particular impression I had received proved in the morning light, I repeat, not quite successfully presentable to Mrs Grose, though I reinforced it with the mention of still another remark that he had made before we separated. "It all lies in half a dozen words," I said to her, "words that really settle the matter. 'Think, you know, what I *might* do!' He threw that off to show me how good he is. He knows down to the ground what he 'might' do. That's what he gave them a taste of at school."

"Lord, you do change!" cried my friend.

"I don't change – I simply make it out. The four, depend upon it, perpetually meet. If on either of these last nights you had been with either child, you would clearly have understood. The more I've watched and waited the more I've felt that if there were nothing else to make it sure it would be made so by the systematic silence of each. *Never*, by a slip of the tongue, have they so much as alluded to either of their old friends, any more than Miles has alluded to his expulsion. Oh, yes, we may sit here and look at them, and they may show off to us there to their fill; but even while they pretend to be lost in their fairytale they're steeped in their vision of the dead restored. He's not reading to her," I declared; "they're talking of *them* – they're talking horrors! I go on, I know, as if I were crazy; and it's a wonder I'm not. What I've seen would have made *you* so; but it has only made me more lucid, made me get hold of still other things."

My lucidity must have seemed awful, but the charming creatures who were victims of it, passing and repassing in their interlocked sweetness, gave my colleague something to hold on by; and I felt how tight she held as, without stirring in the breath of my passion, she covered them still with her eyes. "Of what other things have you got hold?"

"Why, of the very things that have delighted, fascinated, and yet, at bottom, as I now so strangely see, mystified and troubled me. Their more than earthly beauty, their absolutely unnatural goodness. It's a game," I went on; "it's a policy and a fraud!"

"On the part of little darlings – ?"

"As yet mere lovely babies? Yes, mad as that seems!" The very act of bringing it out really helped me to trace it – follow it all up and piece it all together. "They haven't been good – they've only been absent. It has been easy to live with them, because they're simply leading a life of their own. They're not mine – they're not ours. They're his and they're hers!"

"Quint's and that woman's?"

"Quint's and that woman's. They want to get to them."

Oh, how, at this, poor Mrs Grose appeared to study them! "But for what?"

"For the love of all the evil that, in those dreadful days, the pair put into them. And to ply them with that evil still, to keep up the work of demons, is what brings the others back."

"Laws!" said my friend under her breath. The exclamation was homely, but it revealed a real acceptance of my further proof of what, in the bad time – for there had been a worse even than this! – must have occurred. There could have been no such justification for me as the plain assent of her experience to whatever depth of depravity I found credible in our brace of scoundrels. It was in obvious submission of memory that she brought out after a moment: "They *were* rascals! But what can they now do?" she pursued.

"Do?" I echoed so loud that Miles and Flora, as they passed at their distance, paused an instant in their walk and looked at us. "Don't they do enough?" I demanded in a lower tone, while the children, having smiled and nodded and kissed hands to us, resumed their exhibition. We were held by it a minute; then I answered: "They can destroy them!" At this my companion did turn, but the appeal she launched was a silent one, the effect of which was to make me more explicit. "They don't know, as yet, quite how – but they're trying hard. They're seen only across, as it were, and beyond – in strange places and on high places, the top of towers, the roof of houses, the outside of windows, the further edge of pools; but there's a deep design, on either side, to shorten the distance and overcome the obstacle; and the success of the tempters is only a question of time. They've only to keep to their suggestions of danger."

"For the children to come?"

"And perish in the attempt!" Mrs Grose slowly got up, and I scrupulously added: "Unless, of course, we can prevent!"

Standing there before me while I kept my seat, she visibly turned things over. "Their uncle must do the preventing. He must take them away."

"And who's to make him?"

She had been scanning the distance, but she now dropped on me a foolish face. "You, miss."

"By writing to him that his house is poisoned and his little nephew and niece mad?"

"But if they *are*, miss?"

"And if I am myself, you mean? That's charming news to be sent him by a governess whose prime undertaking was to give him no worry."

Mrs Grose considered, following the children again. "Yes, he do hate worry. That was the great reason – "

"Why those fiends took him in so long? No doubt, though his indifference must have been awful. As I'm not a fiend, at any rate, I shouldn't take him in."

My companion, after an instant and for all answer, sat down again and grasped my arm. "Make him at any rate come to you."

I stared. "To *me*?" I had a sudden fear of what she might do. "'Him'?"

"He ought to *be* here – he ought to help."

I quickly rose, and I think I must have shown her a queerer face than ever yet. "You see me asking him for a visit?" No, with her eyes on my face she evidently couldn't. Instead of it even – as a woman reads another – she could see what I myself saw: his derision, his amusement, his contempt for the breakdown of my resignation at being left alone and for the fine machinery I had set in motion to attract his attention to my slighted charms. She didn't know – no one knew – how proud I had been to serve him and to stick to our terms; yet she nonetheless took the measure, I think, of the warning I now gave her. "If you should so lose your head as to appeal to him for me – "

She was really frightened. "Yes, miss?"

"I would leave, on the spot, both him and you."

XIII

It was all very well to join them, but speaking to them proved quite as much as ever an effort beyond my strength – offered, in close quarters, difficulties as insurmountable as before. This situation continued a month, and with new aggravations and particular notes, the note above all, sharper and sharper, of the small ironic consciousness on the part of my pupils. It was not, I am as sure today as I was sure then, my mere infernal imagination: it was absolutely traceable that they were aware of my predicament and that this strange relation made, in a manner, for a long time, the air in which we moved. I don't mean that they had their tongues in their cheeks or did anything vulgar, for that was not one of their dangers: I do mean, on the other hand, that the element of the unnamed and untouched became, between us, greater than any other, and that so much avoidance could not have been so successfully effected without a great deal of tacit arrangement. It was as if, at moments, we were perpetually coming into sight of subjects before which we must stop short, turning suddenly out of alleys that we perceived to be blind, closing with a little bang that made us look at each other – for, like all bangs, it was something louder than we had intended – the doors we had indiscreetly opened. All roads lead to Rome, and there were times when it might have struck us that almost every branch of study or subject of conversation skirted forbidden ground. Forbidden ground was the question of the return of the dead in general and of whatever, in especial, might survive, in memory, of the friends little children had lost. There were days when I could have sworn that one of them had, with a small invisible nudge, said to the other: "She thinks she'll do it this time – but she *won't*!" To "do it" would have been to indulge for instance – and for once in a way – in some direct reference to the lady who had prepared them for my discipline. They had a delightful endless appetite for passages in my own history, to which I had again and again treated them; they were in possession of everything that had ever happened to me, had had, with every circumstance the story of my smallest adventures and of those of my brothers and sisters and of the cat and the dog at home, as well as many particulars of the eccentric nature of my father, of the furniture and arrangement of our house, and of the conversation of the old women of our village. There were things enough, taking one with another, to chatter about, if one went very fast and knew by instinct when to go round. They pulled with an art of their own the strings of my invention and my memory; and nothing else perhaps, when I thought of such occasions afterwards, gave me so the suspicion of being watched from under cover. It was in any case over *my* life, *my* past, and *my* friends alone that we could take anything like our ease – a state of affairs that led them sometimes without the least pertinence to break out into sociable reminders. I was invited – with no visible connection – to repeat afresh Goody Gosling's celebrated *mot* or to confirm the details already supplied as to the cleverness of the vicarage pony.

It was partly at such junctures as these and partly at quite different ones that, with the turn my matters had now taken, my predicament, as I have called it, grew most sensible. The fact that the days passed for me without another encounter ought, it would have appeared, to have done something toward soothing my nerves. Since the light brush, that second night on the upper landing, of the presence of a woman at the foot of the stair, I had seen nothing, whether in or out of the house, that one had better not have seen. There was many a corner round which I expected to come upon Quint, and many a situation that, in a merely sinister way, would have favoured the appearance of Miss Jessel. The summer had turned, the summer had gone; the autumn had dropped upon Bly and had blown out half our lights. The place, with its grey sky and withered garlands, its bared spaces and scattered dead leaves, was like a theater after the performance – all strewn with crumpled playbills. There were exactly states of the air, conditions of sound and of stillness, unspeakable impressions of the *kind* of ministering moment, that brought back to me, long enough to catch it, the feeling of the medium in which, that June evening out of doors, I had had my first sight of Quint, and in which, too, at those other instants, I had, after seeing him through the window, looked for him in vain in the circle of shrubbery. I recognised the signs, the portents – I recognised the moment, the spot. But they remained unaccompanied and empty, and I continued unmolested; if unmolested one could call a young woman whose sensibility had, in the most extraordinary fashion, not declined but deepened. I had said in my talk with Mrs Grose on that horrid scene of Flora's by the lake – and had perplexed her by so saying – that it would from that moment distress me much more to lose my power than to keep it. I had then expressed what was vividly in my mind: the truth that, whether the children really saw or not – since, that is, it was not yet definitely proved – I greatly preferred, as a safeguard, the fullness of my own exposure. I was ready to know the very worst that was to be known. What I had then had an ugly glimpse of was that my eyes might be sealed just while theirs were most opened. Well, my eyes *were* sealed, it appeared, at present – a consummation for which it seemed blasphemous not to thank God. There was, alas, a difficulty about that: I would have thanked him with all my soul had I not had in a proportionate measure this conviction of the secret of my pupils.

How can I retrace today the strange steps of my obsession? There were times of our being together when I would have been ready to swear that, literally, in my presence, but with my direct sense of it closed, they had visitors who were known and were welcome. Then it was that, had I not been deterred by the very chance that such an injury might prove greater than the injury to be averted, my exultation would have broken out. "They're here, they're here, you little wretches," I would have cried, "and you can't deny it now!" The little wretches denied it with all the added volume of their sociability and their tenderness, in just the crystal depths of which – like the flash of a fish in a stream – the mockery of their advantage peeped up. The shock, in truth, had sunk into me still deeper than I knew on the night when, looking out to see either Quint or Miss Jessel under the stars, I had beheld the boy over whose rest I watched and who had immediately brought in with him – had straightway, there, turned it on me – the lovely upward look with which, from the battlements above me, the hideous apparition of Quint had played. If it was a question of a scare, my discovery on this occasion had scared me more than any other, and it was in the condition of nerves produced by it that I made my actual inductions. They harassed me so that sometimes, at odd moments, I shut myself up audibly to rehearse – it was at once a fantastic relief and a renewed despair – the manner in which I might come to the point. I approached it from one side and the other while, in my room, I flung myself about, but I always broke down in the monstrous utterance of names. As they died away on my lips, I said to myself that I should indeed help them to represent something infamous, if, by pronouncing them, I should violate as rare a little case of instinctive delicacy as any schoolroom, probably, had ever known. When I said to myself: "*They* have the manners to be silent, and you, trusted as you are, the baseness to speak!"

I felt myself crimson and I covered my face with my hands. After these secret scenes I chattered more than ever, going on volubly enough till one of our prodigious, palpable hushes occurred – I can call them nothing else – the strange, dizzy lift or swim (I try for terms!) into a stillness, a pause of all life, that had nothing to do with the more or less noise that at the moment we might be engaged in making and that I could hear through any deepened exhilaration or quickened recitation or louder strum of the piano. Then it was that the others, the outsiders, were there. Though they were not angels, they "passed", as the French say, causing me, while they stayed, to tremble with the fear of their addressing to their younger victims some yet more infernal message or more vivid image than they had thought good enough for myself.

What it was most impossible to get rid of was the cruel idea that, whatever I had seen, Miles and Flora saw *more* – things terrible and unguessable and that sprang from dreadful passages of intercourse in the past. Such things naturally left on the surface, for the time, a chill which we vociferously denied that we felt; and we had, all three, with repetition, got into such splendid training that we went, each time, almost automatically, to mark the close of the incident, through the very same movements. It was striking of the children, at all events, to kiss me inveterately with a kind of wild irrelevance and never to fail – one or the other – of the precious question that had helped us through many a peril. "When do you think he *will* come? Don't you think we *ought* to write?" – there was nothing like that enquiry, we found by experience, for carrying off an awkwardness. "He" of course was their uncle in Harley Street; and we lived in much profusion of theory that he might at any moment arrive to mingle in our circle. It was impossible to have given less encouragement than he had done to such a doctrine, but if we had not had the doctrine to fall back upon we should have deprived each other of some of our finest exhibitions. He never wrote to them – that may have been selfish, but it was a part of the flattery of his trust of me; for the way in which a man pays his highest tribute to a woman is apt to be but by the more festal celebration of one of the sacred laws of his comfort; and I held that I carried out the spirit of the pledge given not to appeal to him when I let my charges understand that their own letters were but charming literary exercises. They were too beautiful to be posted; I kept them myself; I have them all to this hour. This was a rule indeed which only added to the satiric effect of my being plied with the supposition that he might at any moment be among us. It was exactly as if my charges knew how almost more awkward than anything else that might be for me. There appears to me, moreover, as I look back, no note in all this more extraordinary than the mere fact that, in spite of my tension and of their triumph, I never lost patience with them. Adorable they must in truth have been, I now reflect, that I didn't in these days hate them! Would exasperation, however, if relief had longer been postponed, finally have betrayed me? It little matters, for relief arrived. I call it relief, though it was only the relief that a snap brings to a strain or the burst of a thunderstorm to a day of suffocation. It was at least change, and it came with a rush.

XIV

Walking to church a certain Sunday morning, I had little Miles at my side and his sister, in advance of us and at Mrs Grose's, well in sight. It was a crisp, clear day, the first of its order for some time; the night had brought a touch of frost, and the autumn air, bright and sharp, made the church bells almost gay. It was an odd accident of thought that I should have happened at such a moment to be particularly and very gratefully struck with the obedience of my little charges. Why did they never resent my inexorable, my perpetual society? Something or other had brought nearer home to me that I had all but pinned the boy to my shawl and that, in the way our companions were marshalled before me, I might have appeared to provide against some danger of rebellion. I was like a gaoler with an eye to possible surprises and escapes. But all this belonged – I mean their magnificent little surrender – just to the special array of the facts that were most abysmal. Turned out for Sunday by his uncle's tailor, who had had a free hand and a notion of pretty waistcoats and of his grand little air, Miles's whole title to independence, the rights of his sex and situation, were so stamped upon him that if he had suddenly struck for freedom I should have had nothing to say. I was by the strangest of chances wondering how I should meet him when the revolution unmistakeably occurred. I call it a revolution because I now see how, with the word he spoke, the curtain rose on the last act of my dreadful drama, and the catastrophe was precipitated. "Look here, my dear, you know," he charmingly said, "when in the world, please, am I going back to school?"

Transcribed here the speech sounds harmless enough, particularly as uttered in the sweet, high, casual pipe with which, at all interlocutors, but above all at his eternal governess, he threw off intonations as if he were tossing roses. There was something in them that always made one "catch", and I caught, at any rate, now so effectually that I stopped as short as if one of the trees of the park had fallen across the road. There was something new, on the spot, between us, and he was perfectly aware that I recognised it, though, to enable me to do so, he had no need to look a whit less candid and charming than usual. I could feel in him how he already, from my at first finding nothing to reply, perceived the advantage he had gained. I was so slow to find anything that he had plenty of time, after a minute, to continue with his suggestive but inconclusive smile: "You know, my dear, that for a fellow to be with a lady *always* – !" His "my dear" was constantly on his lips for me, and nothing could have expressed more the exact shade of the sentiment with which I desired to inspire my pupils than its fond familiarity. It was so respectfully easy.

But, oh, how I felt that at present I must pick my own phrases! I remember that, to gain time, I tried to laugh, and I seemed to see in the beautiful face with which he watched me how ugly and queer I looked. "And always with the same lady?" I returned.

He neither blanched nor winked. The whole thing was virtually out between us. "Ah, of course, she's a jolly, 'perfect' lady; but, after all, I'm a fellow, don't you see? that's – well, getting on."

I lingered there with him an instant ever so kindly. "Yes, you're getting on." Oh, but I felt helpless!

I have kept to this day the heartbreaking little idea of how he seemed to know that and to play with it. "And you can't say I've not been awfully good, can you?"

I laid my hand on his shoulder, for, though I felt how much

better it would have been to walk on, I was not yet quite able. "No, I can't say that, Miles."

"Except just that one night, you know – !"

"That one night?" I couldn't look as straight as he.

"Why, when I went down – went out of the house."

"Oh, yes. But I forget what you did it for."

"You forget?" – he spoke with the sweet extravagance of childish reproach. "Why, it was to show you I could!"

"Oh, yes, you could."

"And I can again."

I felt that I might, perhaps, after all, succeed in keeping my wits about me. "Certainly. But you won't."

"No, not *that* again. It was nothing."

"It was nothing," I said. "But we must go on."

He resumed our walk with me, passing his hand into my arm. "Then when *am* I going back?"

I wore, in turning it over, my most responsible air. "Were you very happy at school?"

He just considered. "Oh, I'm happy enough anywhere!"

"Well, then," I quavered, "if you're just as happy here – !"

"Ah, but that isn't everything! Of course *you* know a lot – "

"But you hint that you know almost as much?" I risked as he paused.

"Not half I want to!" Miles honestly professed. "But it isn't so much that."

"What is it, then?"

"Well – I want to see more life."

"I see; I see." We had arrived within sight of the church and of various persons, including several of the household of Bly, on their way to it and clustered about the door to see us go in. I quickened our step; I wanted to get there before the question between us opened up much further; I reflected hungrily that, for more than an hour, he would have to be silent; and I thought with envy of the comparative dusk of the pew and of the almost spiritual help of the hassock on which I might bend my knees. I seemed literally to be running a race with some confusion to which he was about to reduce me, but I felt that he had got in first when, before we had even entered the churchyard, he threw out –

"I want my own sort!"

It literally made me bound forward. "There are not many of your own sort, Miles!" I laughed. "Unless perhaps dear little Flora!"

"You really compare me to a baby girl?"

This found me singularly weak. "Don't you, then, *love* our sweet Flora?"

"If I didn't – and you, too; if I didn't – !" he repeated as if retreating for a jump, yet leaving his thought so unfinished that, after we had come into the gate, another stop, which he imposed on me by the pressure of his arm, had become inevitable. Mrs Grose and Flora had passed into the church, the other worshippers had followed, and we were, for the minute, alone among the old, thick graves. We had paused, on the path from the gate, by a low, oblong, tablelike tomb.

"Yes, if you didn't – ?"

He looked, while I waited, at the graves. "Well, you know what!" But he didn't move, and he presently produced something that made me drop straight down on the stone slab, as if suddenly to rest. "Does my uncle think what *you* think?"

I markedly rested. "How do you know what I think?"

"Ah, well, of course I don't; for it strikes me you never tell me. But I mean does *he* know?"

"Know what, Miles?"

"Why, the way I'm going on."

I perceived quickly enough that I could make, to this enquiry, no answer that would not involve something of a sacrifice of my employer. Yet it appeared to me that we were all, at Bly, sufficiently sacrificed to make that venial. "I don't think your uncle much cares."

Miles, on this, stood looking at me. "Then don't you think he can be made to?"

"In what way?"

"Why, by his coming down."

"But who'll get him to come down?"

"*I* will!" the boy said with extraordinary brightness and emphasis. He gave me another look charged with that expression and then marched off alone into church.

XV

The business was practically settled from the moment I never followed him. It was a pitiful surrender to agitation, but my being aware of this had somehow no power to restore me. I only sat there on my tomb and read into what my little friend had said to me the fullness of its meaning; by the time I had grasped the whole of which I had also embraced, for absence, the pretext that I was ashamed to offer my pupils and the rest of the congregation such an example of delay. What I said to myself above all was that Miles had got something out of me and that the proof of it, for him, would be just this awkward collapse. He had got out of me that there was something I was much afraid of and that he should probably be able to make use of my fear to gain, for his own purpose, more freedom. My fear was of having to deal with the intolerable question of the grounds of his dismissal from school, for that was really but the question of the horrors gathered behind. That his uncle should arrive to treat with me of these things was a solution that, strictly speaking, I ought now to have desired to bring on; but I could so little face the ugliness and the pain of it that I simply procrastinated and lived from hand to mouth. The boy, to my deep discomposure, was immensely in the right, was in a position to say to me: "Either you clear up with my guardian the mystery of this interruption of my studies, or you cease to expect me to lead with you a life that's so unnatural for a boy." What was so unnatural for the particular boy I was concerned with was this sudden revelation of a consciousness and a plan.

That was what really overcame me, what prevented my going in. I walked round the church, hesitating, hovering; I reflected that I had already, with him, hurt myself beyond repair. Therefore I could patch up nothing, and it was too extreme an effort to squeeze beside him into the pew: he would be so much more sure than ever to pass his arm into mine and make me sit there for an hour in close, silent contact with his commentary on our talk. For the first minute since his arrival I wanted to get away from him. As I paused beneath the high east window and listened to the sounds of worship, I was taken with an impulse that might master me, I felt, completely should I give it the least encouragement. I might easily put an end to my predicament by getting away altogether. Here was my chance; there was no one to stop me; I could give the whole thing up – turn my back and retreat. It was only a question of hurrying again, for a few preparations, to the house which the attendance at church of so many of the servants would practically have left unoccupied. No one, in short, could blame me if I should just drive desperately off. What was it to get away if I got away only till dinner? That would be in a couple of hours, at the end of which – I had the acute prevision – my little pupils would play at innocent wonder about my non-appearance in their train.

"What *did* you do, you naughty, bad thing? Why in the world, to worry us so – and take our thoughts off, too, don't you know? – did you desert us at the very door?" I couldn't meet such questions nor, as they asked them, their false little lovely eyes; yet it was all so exactly what I should have to meet that, as the prospect grew sharp to me, I at last let myself go.

I got, so far as the immediate moment was concerned, away; I came straight out of the churchyard and, thinking hard, retraced my steps through the park. It seemed to me that by the time I reached the house I had made up my mind I would fly. The Sunday stillness both of the approaches and of the interior, in which I met no one, fairly excited me with a sense of opportunity.

Were I to get off quickly, this way, I should get off without a scene, without a word. My quickness would have to be remarkable, however, and the question of a conveyance was the great one to settle. Tormented, in the hall, with difficulties and obstacles, I remember sinking down at the foot of the staircase – suddenly collapsing there on the lowest step and then, with a revulsion, recalling that it was exactly where more than a month before, in the darkness of night and just so bowed with evil things, I had seen the spectre of the most horrible of women. At this I was able to straighten myself; I went the rest of the way up; I made, in my bewilderment, for the schoolroom, where there were objects belonging to me that I should have to take. But I opened the door to find again, in a flash, my eyes unsealed. In the presence of what I saw I reeled straight back upon my resistance.

Seated at my own table in clear noonday light I saw a person whom, without my previous experience, I should have taken at the first blush for some housemaid who might have stayed at home to look after the place and who, availing herself of rare relief from observation and of the schoolroom table and my pens, ink and paper, had applied herself to the considerable effort of a letter to her sweetheart. There was an effort in the way that, while her arms rested on the table, her hands with evident weariness supported her head; but at the moment I took this in I had already become aware that, in spite of my entrance, her attitude strangely persisted. Then it was – with the very act of its announcing itself – that her identity flared up in a change of posture. She rose, not as if she had heard me, but with an indescribable grand melancholy of indifference and detachment, and, within a dozen feet of me, stood there as my vile prede-cessor. Dishonoured and tragic, she was all before me; but even as I fixed and, for memory, secured it, the awful image passed away. Dark as midnight in her black dress, her haggard beauty and her unutterable woe, she had looked at me long enough to appear to say that her right to sit at my table was as good as mine to sit at hers. While these instants lasted, indeed, I had the extraordinary chill of feeling that it was I who was the intruder. It was as a wild protest against it that, actually addressing her – "You terrible, miserable woman!" – I heard myself break into a sound that, by the open door, rang through the long passage and the empty house. She looked at me as if she heard me, but I had recovered myself and cleared the air. There was nothing in the room the next minute but the sunshine and a sense that I must stay.

XVI

I had so perfectly expected that the return of my pupils would be marked by a demonstration that I was freshly upset at having to take into account that they were dumb about my absence. Instead of gaily denouncing and caressing me, they made no allusion to my having failed them, and I was left, for the time, on perceiving that she too said nothing, to study Mrs Grose's odd face. I did this to such purpose that I made sure they had in some way bribed her to silence; a silence that, however, I would engage to break down on the first private opportunity. This opportunity came before tea: I secured five minutes with her in the housekeeper's room, where, in the twilight, amid a smell of lately baked bread, but with the place all swept and garnished, I found her sitting in pained placidity before the fire. So I see her still, so I see her best: facing the flame from her straight chair in the dusky, shining room, a large clean image of the "put away" – of drawers closed and locked and rest without a remedy.

"Oh, yes, they asked me to say nothing; and to please them – so long as they were there – of course I promised. But what had happened to you?"

"I only went with you for the walk," I said. "I had then to come back to meet a friend."

She showed her surprise. "A friend – *you*?"

"Oh, yes, I have a couple!" I laughed. "But did the children give you a reason?"

"For not alluding to your leaving us? Yes; they said you would like it better. *Do* you like it better?"

My face had made her rueful. "No, I like it worse!" But after an instant I added: "Did they say why I should like it better?"

"No; Master Miles only said, 'We must do nothing but what she likes!'"

"I wish indeed he would. And what did Flora say?"

"Miss Flora was too sweet. She said, 'Oh, of course, of course!' – and I said the same."

I thought a moment. "You were too sweet, too – I can hear you all. But nonetheless, between Miles and me, it's now all out."

"All out?" My companion stared. "But what, miss?"

"Everything. It doesn't matter. I've made up my mind. I came home, my dear," I went on, "for a talk with Miss Jessel."

I had by this time formed the habit of having Mrs Grose literally well in hand in advance of my sounding that note; so that even now, as she bravely blinked under the signal of my word, I could keep her comparatively firm. "A talk! Do you mean she spoke?"

"It came to that. I found her, on my return, in the schoolroom."

"And what did she say?" I can hear the good woman still, and the candour of her stupefaction.

"That she suffers the torments – !"

It was this, of a truth, that made her, as she filled out my picture, gape. "Do you mean," she faltered, " – of the lost?"

"Of the lost. Of the damned. And that's why, to share them – " I faltered myself with the horror of it.

But my companion, with less imagination, kept me up. "To share them – ?"

"She wants Flora." Mrs Grose might, as I gave it to her, fairly have fallen away from me had I not been prepared. I still held her there, to show I was. "As I've told you, however, it doesn't matter."

"Because you've made up your mind? But to what?"

"To everything."

"And what do you call 'everything'?"

"Why, sending for their uncle."

"Oh, miss, in pity do," my friend broke out.

"Ah, but I will, I *will*! I see it's the only way. What's 'out', as I told you, with Miles is that if he thinks I'm afraid to – and has ideas of what he gains by that – he shall see he's mistaken. Yes, yes; his uncle shall have it here from me on the spot (and before the boy himself, if necessary) that if I'm to be reproached with having done nothing again about more school – "

"Yes, miss – " my companion pressed me.

"Well, there's that awful reason."

There were now clearly so many of these for my poor colleague that she was excusable for being vague. "But – a – which?"

"Why, the letter from his old place."

"You'll show it to the master?"

"I ought to have done so on the instant."

"Oh, no!" said Mrs Grose with decision.

"I'll put it before him," I went on inexorably, "that I can't undertake to work the question on behalf of a child who has been expelled – "

"For we've never in the least known what!" Mrs Grose declared.

"For wickedness. For what else – when he's so clever and beautiful and perfect? Is he stupid? Is he untidy? Is he infirm? Is he ill-natured? He's exquisite – so it can be only *that*; and that would open up the whole thing. After all," I said, "it's their uncle's fault. If he left here such people – !"

"He didn't really in the least know them. The fault's mine." She had turned quite pale.

"Well, you shan't suffer," I answered.

"The children shan't!" she emphatically returned.

I was silent awhile; we looked at each other. "Then what am I to tell him?"

"You needn't tell him anything. *I'll* tell him."

I measured this. "Do you mean you'll write – ?" Remembering she couldn't, I caught myself up. "How do you communicate?"

"I tell the bailiff. *He* writes."

"And should you like him to write our story?"

My question had a sarcastic force that I had not fully intended, and it made her, after a moment, inconsequently break down. The tears were again in her eyes. "Ah, miss, *you* write!"

"Well – tonight," I at last answered; and on this we separated.

XVII

I went so far, in the evening, as to make a beginning. The weather had changed back, a great wind was abroad, and beneath the lamp, in my room, with Flora at peace beside me, I sat for a long time before a blank sheet of paper and listened to the lash of the rain and the batter of the gusts. Finally I went out, taking a candle; I crossed the passage and listened a minute at Miles's door. What, under my endless obsession, I had been impelled to listen for was some betrayal of his not being at rest, and I presently caught one, but not in the form I had expected. His voice tinkled out. "I say, you there – come in." It was a gaiety in the gloom!

I went in with my light and found him, in bed, very wide awake, but very much at his ease. "Well, what are *you* up to?" he asked with a grace of sociability in which it occurred to me that Mrs Grose, had she been present, might have looked in vain for proof that anything was "out".

I stood over him with my candle. "How did you know I was there?"

"Why, of course I heard you. Did you fancy you made no noise? You're like a troop of cavalry!" he beautifully laughed.

"Then you weren't asleep?"

"Not much! I lie awake and think."

I had put my candle, designedly, a short way off, and then, as he held out his friendly old hand to me, had sat down on the edge of his bed. "What is it," I asked, "that you think of?"

"What in the world, my dear, but *you*?"

"Ah, the pride I take in your appreciation doesn't insist on that! I had so far rather you slept."

"Well, I think also, you know, of this queer business of ours."

I marked the coolness of his firm little hand. "Of what queer business, Miles?"

"Why, the way you bring me up. And all the rest!"

I fairly held my breath a minute, and even from my glimmering taper there was light enough to show how he smiled up at me from his pillow. "What do you mean by all the rest?"

"Oh, you know, you know!"

I could say nothing for a minute, though I felt, as I held his hand and our eyes continued to meet, that my silence had all the air of admitting his charge and that nothing in the whole world of reality was perhaps at that moment so fabulous as our actual relation. "Certainly you shall go back to school," I said, "if it be that that troubles you. But not to the old place – we must find another, a better. How could I know it did trouble you, this question, when you never told me so, never spoke of it at all?" His clear, listening face, framed in its smooth whiteness, made him for the minute as appealing as some wistful patient in a children's hospital; and I would have given, as the resemblance came to me, all I possessed on earth really to be the nurse or the sister of charity who might have helped to cure him. Well, even as it was, I perhaps might help! "Do you know you've never said a word to me about your school – I mean the old one; never mentioned it in any way?"

He seemed to wonder; he smiled with the same loveliness. But he clearly gained time; he waited, he called for guidance. "Haven't I?" It wasn't for *me* to help him – it was for the thing I had met!

Something in his tone and the expression of his face, as I got this from him, set my heart aching with such a pang as it had never yet known; so unutterably touching was it to see his little brain puzzled and his little resources taxed to play, under the spell laid on him, a part of innocence and consistency. "No, never – from the hour you came back. You've never mentioned to me one of your masters, one of your comrades, nor the least little thing that ever happened to you at school. Never, little Miles – no, never – have you given me an inkling of anything that *may* have happened there. Therefore you can fancy how much I'm in the dark. Until you came out, that way, this morning, you had, since the first hour I saw you, scarce even made a reference to anything in your previous life. You seemed so perfectly to accept the present." It was extraordinary how my absolute conviction of his secret precocity (or whatever I might call the poison of an influence that I dared but half to phrase) made him, in spite of the faint breath of his inward trouble, appear as accessible as an older person – imposed him almost as an intellectual equal. "I thought you wanted to go on as you are."

It struck me that at this he just faintly coloured. He gave, at any rate, like a convalescent slightly fatigued, a languid shake of his head. "I don't – I don't. I want to get away."

"You're tired of Bly?"

"Oh, no, I like Bly."

"Well, then – ?"

"Oh, *you* know what a boy wants!"

I felt that I didn't know so well as Miles, and I took temporary refuge. "You want to go to your uncle?"

Again, at this, with his sweet ironic face, he made a movement on the pillow. "Ah, you can't get off with that!"

I was silent a little, and it was I, now, I think, who changed colour. "My dear, I don't want to get off!"

"You can't, even if you do. You can't, you can't!" – he lay beautifully staring. "My uncle must come down, and you must completely settle things."

"If we do," I returned with some spirit, "you may be sure it will be to take you quite away."

"Well, don't you understand that that's exactly what I'm working for? You'll have to *tell* him – about the way you've let it all drop: you'll have to tell him a tremendous lot!"

The exultation with which he uttered this helped me somehow, for the instant, to meet him rather more. "And how much will *you*, Miles, have to tell him? There are things he'll ask you!"

He turned it over. "Very likely. But what things?"

"The things you've never told me. To make up his mind what to do with you. He can't send you back – "

"Oh, I don't want to go back!" he broke in. "I want a new field."

He said it with admirable serenity, with positive unimpeachable gaiety; and doubtless it was that very note that most evoked for me the poignancy, the unnatural childish tragedy, of his probable reappearance at the end of three months with all this bravado and still more dishonour. It overwhelmed me now that I should never be able to bear that, and it made me let myself go. I threw myself upon him and in the tenderness of my pity I embraced him. "Dear little Miles, dear little Miles – !"

My face was close to his, and he let me kiss him, simply taking it with indulgent good humour. "Well, old lady?"

"Is there nothing – nothing at all that you want to tell me?"

He turned off a little, facing round toward the wall and holding up his hand to look at as one had seen sick children look. "I've told you – I told you this morning."

Oh, I was sorry for him! "That you just want me not to worry you?"

He looked round at me now, as if in recognition of my understanding him; then ever so gently, "To let me alone," he replied.

There was even a singular little dignity in it, something that made me release him, yet, when I had slowly risen, linger beside him. God knows I never wished to harass him, but I felt that merely, at this, to turn my back on him was to abandon or, to put it more truly, to lose him. "I've just begun a letter to your uncle," I said.

"Well, then, finish it!"

I waited a minute. "What happened before?"

He gazed up at me again. "Before what?"

"Before you came back. And before you went away."

For some time he was silent, but he continued to meet my eyes. "What happened?"

It made me, the sound of the words, in which it seemed to me that I caught for the very first time a small faint quaver of consenting consciousness – it made me drop on my knees beside the bed and seize once more the chance of possessing him. "Dear little Miles, dear little Miles, if you *knew* how I want to help you! It's only that, it's nothing but that, and I'd rather die than give you a pain or do you a wrong – I'd rather die than hurt a hair of you. Dear little Miles" – oh, I brought it out now even if I *should* go too far – "I just want you to help me to save you!" But I knew in a moment after this that I had gone too far. The answer to my appeal was instantaneous, but it came in the form of an extraordinary blast and chill, a gust of frozen air and a shake of the room as great as if, in the wild wind, the casement had crashed in. The boy gave a loud, high shriek, which, lost in the rest of the shock of sound, might have seemed, indistinctly, though I was so close to him, a note either of jubilation or of terror. I jumped to my feet again and was conscious of darkness. So for a moment we remained, while I stared about me and saw that the drawn curtains were unstirred and the window tight. "Why, the candle's out!" I then cried.

"It was I who blew it, dear!" said Miles.

XVIII

The next day, after lessons, Mrs Grose found a moment to say to me quietly: "Have you written, miss?"

"Yes – I've written." But I didn't add – for the hour – that my letter, sealed and directed, was still in my pocket. There would be time enough to send it before the messenger should go to the village. Meanwhile there had been, on the part of my pupils, no more brilliant, more exemplary morning. It was exactly as if they had both had at heart to gloss over any recent little friction. They performed the dizziest feats of arithmetic, soaring quite out of *my* feeble range, and perpetrated, in higher spirits than ever, geographical and historical jokes. It was conspicuous of course in Miles in particular that he appeared to wish to show how easily he could let me down. This child, to my memory, really lives in a setting of beauty and misery that no words can translate; there was a distinction all his own in every impulse he revealed; never was a small natural creature, to the uninitiated eye all frankness and freedom, a more ingenious, a more extraordinary little gentleman. I had perpetually to guard against the wonder of contemplation into which my initiated view betrayed me; to check the irrelevant gaze and discouraged sigh in which I constantly both attacked and renounced the enigma of what such a little gentleman could have done that deserved a penalty. Say that, by the dark prodigy I knew, the imagination of all evil *had* been opened up to him: all the justice within me ached for the proof that it could ever have flowered into an act.

He had never, at any rate, been such a little gentleman as when, after our early dinner on this dreadful day, he came round to me and asked if I shouldn't like him, for half an hour, to play to me. David playing to Saul could never have shown a finer sense of the occasion. It was literally a charming exhibition of tact, of magnanimity, and quite tantamount to his saying outright: "The true knights we love to read about never push an advantage too far. I know what you mean now: you mean that – to be let alone yourself and not followed up – you'll cease to worry and spy upon me, won't keep me so close to you, will let me go and come. Well, I 'come', you see – but I don't go! There'll be plenty of time for that. I do really delight in your society, and I only want to show you that I contended for a principle." It may be imagined whether I resisted this appeal or failed to accompany him again, hand in hand, to the schoolroom. He sat down at the old piano and played as he had never played; and if there are those who think he had better have been kicking a football I can only say that I wholly agree with them. For at the end of a time that under his influence I had quite ceased to measure, I started up with a strange sense of having literally slept at my post. It was after luncheon, and by the schoolroom fire, and yet I hadn't really, in the least, slept: I had only done something much worse – I had forgotten. Where, all this time, was Flora? When I put the question to Miles, he played on a minute before answering and then could only say: "Why, my dear, how do *I* know?" – breaking moreover into a happy laugh which, immediately after, as if it were a vocal accompaniment, he prolonged into incoherent, extravagant song.

I went straight to my room, but his sister was not there; then, before going downstairs, I looked into several others. As she was nowhere about she would surely be with Mrs Grose, whom, in the comfort of that theory, I accordingly proceeded in quest of. I found her where I had found her the evening before, but she met my quick challenge with blank, scared ignorance. She had only supposed that, after the repast, I had carried off both the children; as to which she was quite in her right, for it was the very first time I had allowed the little girl out of my sight without some special provision. Of course now indeed she might be with the maids, so that the immediate thing was to look for her without an air of alarm. This we promptly arranged between us; but when, ten minutes later and in pursuance of our arrangement, we met in the hall, it was only to report on either side that after guarded enquiries we had altogether failed to trace her. For a minute there, apart from observation, we exchanged mute alarms, and I could feel with what high interest my friend returned me all those I had from the first given her.

"She'll be above," she presently said – "in one of the rooms you haven't searched."

"No; she's at a distance." I had made up my mind. "She has gone out."

Mrs Grose stared. "Without a hat?"

I naturally also looked volumes. "Isn't that woman always without one?"

"She's with *her*?"

"She's with *her*!" I declared. "We must find them."

My hand was on my friend's arm, but she failed for the moment, confronted with such an account of the matter, to respond to my pressure. She communed, on the contrary, on the spot, with her uneasiness. "And where's Master Miles?"

"Oh, *he's* with Quint. They're in the schoolroom."

"Lord, miss!" My view, I was myself aware – and therefore I suppose my tone – had never yet reached so calm an assurance.

"The trick's played," I went on; "they've successfully worked their plan. He found the most divine little way to keep me quiet while she went off."

"'Divine'?" Mrs Grose bewilderedly echoed.

"Infernal, then!" I almost cheerfully rejoined. "He has provided for himself as well. But come!"

She had helplessly gloomed at the upper regions. "You leave him – ?"

"So long with Quint? Yes – I don't mind that now."

She always ended, at these moments, by getting possession of my hand, and in this manner she could at present still stay me. But after gasping an instant at my sudden resignation, "Because of your letter?" she eagerly brought out.

I quickly, by way of answer, felt for my letter, drew it forth, held it up, and then, freeing myself, went and laid it on the great hall table. "Luke will take it," I said as I came back. I reached the house door and opened it; I was already on the steps.

My companion still demurred: the storm of the night and the early morning had dropped, but the afternoon was damp and grey. I came down to the drive while she stood in the doorway. "You go with nothing on?"

"What do I care when the child has nothing? I can't wait to dress," I cried, "and if you must do so, I leave you. Try meanwhile, yourself, upstairs."

"With *them*?" Oh, on this, the poor woman promptly joined me!

XIX

We went straight to the lake, as it was called at Bly, and I daresay rightly called, though I reflect that it may in fact have been a sheet of water less remarkable than it appeared to my untravelled eyes. My acquaintance with sheets of water was small, and the pool of Bly, at all events on the few occasions of my consenting, under the protection of my pupils, to affront its surface in the old flat-bottomed boat moored there for our use, had impressed me both with its extent and its agitation. The usual place of embarkation was half a mile from the house, but I had an intimate conviction that, wherever Flora might be, she was not near home. She had not given me the slip for any small adventure, and, since the day of the very great one that I had shared with her by the pond, I had been aware, in our walks, of the quarter to which she most inclined. This was why I had now given to Mrs Grose's steps so marked a direction – a direction that made her, when she perceived it, oppose a resistance that showed me she was freshly mystified. "You're going to the water, Miss? – you think she's *in* – ?"

"She may be, though the depth is, I believe, nowhere very great. But what I judge most likely is that she's on the spot from which, the other day, we saw together what I told you."

"When she pretended not to see – ?"

"With that astounding self-possession? I've always been sure she wanted to go back alone. And now her brother has managed it for her."

Mrs Grose still stood where she had stopped. "You suppose they really *talk* of them?"

"I could meet this with a confidence! They say things that, if we heard them, would simply appal us."

"And if she *is* there – "

"Yes?"

"Then Miss Jessel is?"

"Beyond a doubt. You shall see."

"Oh, thank you!" my friend cried, planted so firm that, taking it in, I went straight on without her. By the time I reached the pool, however, she was close behind me, and I knew that, whatever, to her apprehension, might befall me, the exposure of my society struck her as her least danger. She exhaled a moan of relief as we at last came in sight of the greater part of the water without a sight of the child. There was no trace of Flora on that nearer side of the bank where my observation of her had been most startling, and none on the opposite edge, where, save for a margin of some twenty yards, a thick copse came down to the water. The pond, oblong in shape, had a width so scant compared to its length that, with its ends out of view, it might have been taken for a scant river. We looked at the empty expanse, and then I felt the suggestion of my friend's eyes. I knew what she meant and I replied with a negative headshake.

"No, no; wait! She has taken the boat."

My companion stared at the vacant mooring place and then again across the lake. "Then where is it?"

"Our not seeing it is the strongest of proofs. She has used it to go over, and then has managed to hide it."

"All alone – that child?"

"She's not alone, and at such times she's not a child: she's an old, old woman." I scanned all the visible shore while Mrs Grose took again, into the queer element I offered her, one of her plunges of submission; then I pointed out that the boat might perfectly be in a small refuge formed by one of the recesses of the pool, an indentation masked, for the hither side, by a projection of the bank and by a clump of trees growing close to the water.

"But if the boat's there, where on earth's *she*?" my colleague anxiously asked.

"That's exactly what we must learn." And I started to walk further.

"By going all the way round?"

"Certainly, far as it is. It will take us but ten minutes, but it's far enough to have made the child prefer not to walk. She went straight over."

"Laws!" cried my friend again; the chain of my logic was ever too much for her. It dragged her at my heels even now, and when we had got halfway round – a devious, tiresome process, on ground much broken and by a path choked with overgrowth – I paused to give her breath. I sustained her with a grateful arm, assuring her that she might hugely help me; and this started us afresh, so that in the course of but few minutes more we reached a point from which we found the boat to be where I had supposed it. It had been intentionally left as much as possible out of sight and was tied to one of the stakes of a fence that came, just there, down to the brink and that had been an assistance to disembarking. I recognised, as I looked at the pair of short, thick oars, quite safely drawn up, the prodigious character of the feat for a little girl; but I had lived, by this time, too long among wonders and had panted to too many livelier measures. There was a gate in the fence, through which we passed, and that brought us, after a trifling interval, more into the open. Then, "There she is!" we both exclaimed at once.

Flora, a short way off, stood before us on the grass and smiled as if her performance was now complete. The next thing she did, however, was to stoop straight down and pluck – quite as if it were all she was there for – a big, ugly spray of withered fern. I instantly became sure she had just come out of the copse. She waited for us, not herself taking a step, and I was conscious of the rare solemnity with which we presently approached her. She smiled and smiled, and we met; but it was all done in a silence by this time flagrantly ominous. Mrs Grose was the first to break the spell: she threw herself on her knees and, drawing the child to her breast, clasped in a long embrace the little tender, yielding body. While this dumb convulsion lasted I could only watch it – which I did the more intently when I saw Flora's face peep at me over our companion's shoulder. It was serious now – the flicker had left it; but it strengthened the pang with which I at that moment envied Mrs Grose the simplicity of *her* relation. Still, all this while, nothing more passed between us save that Flora had let her foolish fern again drop to the ground. What she and I had virtually said to each other was that pretexts were useless now. When Mrs Grose finally got up she kept the child's hand, so that the two were still before me; and the singular reticence of our communion was even more marked in the frank look she launched me. "I'll be hanged," it said, "if *I'll* speak!"

It was Flora who, gazing all over me in candid wonder, was the first. She was struck with our bareheaded aspect. "Why, where are your things?"

"Where yours are, my dear!" I promptly returned.

She had already got back her gaiety, and appeared to take this as an answer quite sufficient. "And where's Miles?" she went on.

There was something in the small valour of it that quite finished me: these three words from her were, in a flash like the glitter of a drawn blade, the jostle of the cup that my hand, for weeks and weeks, had held high and full to the brim that now, even before speaking, I felt overflow in a deluge. "I'll tell you if you'll tell *me* – " I heard myself say, then heard the tremor in which it broke.

"Well, what?"

Mrs Grose's suspense blazed at me, but it was too late now, and I brought the thing out handsomely. "Where, my pet, is Miss Jessel?"

XX

Just as in the churchyard with Miles, the whole thing was upon us. Much as I had made of the fact that this name had never once, between us, been sounded, the quick, smitten glare with which the child's face now received it fairly likened my breach of the silence to the smash of a pane of glass. It added to the interposing cry, as if to stay the blow, that Mrs Grose, at the same instant, uttered over my violence – the shriek of a creature scared, or rather wounded, which, in turn, within a few seconds, was completed by a gasp of my own. I seized my colleague's arm. "She's there, she's there!"

Miss Jessel stood before us on the opposite bank exactly as she had stood the other time, and I remember, strangely, as the first feeling now produced in me, my thrill of joy at having brought on a proof. She was there, and I was justified; she was there, and I was neither cruel nor mad. She was there for poor scared Mrs Grose, but she was there most for Flora; and no moment of my monstrous time was perhaps so extraordinary as that in which I consciously threw out to her – with the sense that, pale and ravenous demon as she was, she would catch and understand it – an inarticulate message of gratitude. She rose erect on the spot my friend and I had lately quitted, and there was not, in all the long reach of her desire, an inch of her evil that fell short. This first vividness of vision and emotion were things of a few seconds, during which Mrs Grose's dazed blink across to where I pointed struck me as a sovereign sign that she too at last saw, just as it carried my own eyes precipitately to the child. The revelation then of the manner in which Flora was affected startled me, in truth, far more than it would have done to find her also merely agitated, for direct dismay was of course not what I had expected. Prepared and on her guard as our pursuit had actually made her, she would repress every betrayal; and I was therefore shaken, on the spot, by my first glimpse of the particular one for which I had not allowed. To see her, without a convulsion of her small pink face, not even feign to glance in the direction of the prodigy I announced, but only, instead of that, turn at *me* an expression of hard, still gravity, an expression absolutely new and unprecedented and that appeared to read and accuse and judge me – this was a stroke that somehow converted the little girl herself into the very presence that could make me quail. I quailed even though my certitude that she thoroughly saw was never greater than at that instant, and in the immediate need to defend myself I called it passionately to witness. "She's there, you little unhappy thing – there, there, *there*, and you see her as well as you see me!" I had said shortly before to Mrs Grose that she was not at these times a child, but an old, old woman, and that description of her could not have been more strikingly confirmed than in the way in which, for all answer to this, she simply showed me, without a concession, an admission, of her eyes, a countenance of deeper and deeper, of indeed suddenly quite fixed, reprobation. I was by this time – if I can put the whole thing at all together – more appalled at what I may properly call her manner than at anything else, though it was simultaneously with this that I became aware of having Mrs Grose also, and very formidably, to reckon with. My elder companion, the next moment, at any rate, blotted out everything but her own flushed face and her loud, shocked protest, a burst of high disapproval. "What a dreadful turn, to be sure, miss! Where on earth do you see anything?"

I could only grasp her more quickly yet, for even while she spoke the hideous plain presence stood undimmed and undaunted. It had already lasted a minute, and it lasted while I continued, seizing my colleague, quite thrusting her at it and presenting her to it, to insist with my pointing hand. "You don't see her exactly as *we* see? – You mean to say you don't now – *now*? She's as big as a blazing fire! Only look, dearest woman, *look* – !" She looked, even as I did, and gave me, with her deep groan of negation, repulsion, compassion – the mixture with her pity of her relief at her exemption – a sense, touching to me even then, that she would have backed me up if she could. I might well have needed that, for with this hard blow of the proof that her eyes were hopelessly sealed I felt my own situation horribly crumble, I felt – I saw – my livid predecessor press, from her position, on my defeat, and I was conscious, more than all, of what I should have from this instant to deal with in the astounding little attitude of Flora. Into this attitude Mrs Grose immediately and violently entered, breaking, even while there pierced through my sense of ruin a prodigious private triumph, into breathless reassurance.

"She isn't there, little lady, and nobody's there – and you never see nothing, my sweet! How can poor Miss Jessel – when poor Miss Jessel's dead and buried? *We* know, don't we, love?" – and she appealed, blundering in, to the child. "It's all a mere mistake and a worry and a joke – and we'll go home as fast as we can!"

Our companion, on this, had responded with a strange, quick primness of propriety, and they were again, with Mrs Grose on her feet, united, as it were, in pained opposition to me. Flora continued to fix me with her small mask of reprobation, and even at that minute I prayed God to forgive me for seeming to see that, as she stood there holding tight to our friend's dress, her incomparable childish beauty had suddenly failed, had quite vanished. I've said it already – she was literally, she was hideously, hard; she had turned common and almost ugly. "I don't know what you mean. I see nobody. I see nothing. I never *have*. I think you're cruel. I don't like you!" Then, after this deliverance, which might have been that of a vulgarly pert little girl in the street, she hugged Mrs Grose more closely and buried in her skirts the dreadful little face. In this position she produced an almost furious wail. "Take me away, take me away – oh, take me away from *her*!"

"From *me*?" I panted.

"From you – from you!" she cried.

Even Mrs Grose looked across at me dismayed, while I had nothing to do but communicate again with the figure that, on the opposite bank, without a movement, as rigidly still as if catching, beyond the interval, our voices, was as vividly there for my disaster as it was not there for my service. The wretched child had spoken exactly as if she had got from some outside source each of her stabbing little words, and I could therefore, in the full despair of all I had to accept, but sadly shake my head at her. "If I had ever doubted, all my doubt would at present have gone. I've been living with the miserable truth, and now it has only too much closed round me. Of course I've lost you: I've interfered, and you've seen – under *her* dictation" – with which I faced, over the pool again, our infernal witness – "the easy and perfect way to meet it. I've done my best, but I've lost you. Goodbye." For Mrs Grose I had an imperative, an almost frantic "Go, go!" before which, in infinite distress, but mutely possessed of the little girl and clearly convinced, in spite of her blindness, that something awful had occurred and some collapse engulfed us, she retreated, by the way we had come, as fast as she could move.

Of what first happened when I was left alone I had no subsequent memory. I only knew that at the end of, I suppose, a quarter of an hour, an odorous dampness and roughness, chilling and piercing my trouble, had made me understand that I must have thrown myself, on my face, on the ground and given way to a wildness of grief. I must have lain there long and cried and sobbed, for when I raised my head the day was almost done. I got up and looked a moment, through the twilight, at the grey pool and its blank, haunted edge, and then I took, back to the house, my dreary and difficult course. When I reached the gate in the fence the boat, to my surprise, was gone, so that I had a fresh reflection to make on Flora's extraordinary command of the situation. She passed that night, by the most tacit, and I should add, were not the word so grotesque a false note, the happiest of arrangements, with Mrs Grose. I saw neither of them on my return, but, on the other hand, as by an ambiguous compensation, I saw a great deal of Miles. I saw – I can use no other phrase – so much of him that it was as if it were more than it had ever been. No evening I had passed at Bly had the portentous quality of this one; in spite of which – and in spite also of the deeper depths of consternation that had opened beneath my feet – there was literally, in the ebbing actual, an extraordinarily sweet sadness. On reaching the house I had never so much as looked for the boy; I had simply gone straight to my room to change what I was wearing and to take in, at a glance, much material testimony to Flora's rupture. Her little belongings had all been removed. When later, by the schoolroom fire, I was served with tea by the usual maid, I indulged, on the article of my other pupil, in no enquiry whatever. He had his freedom now – he might have it to the end! Well, he did have it; and it consisted – in part at least – of his coming in at about eight o'clock and sitting down with me in silence. On the removal of the tea things I had blown out the candles and drawn my chair closer: I was conscious of a mortal coldness and felt as if I should never again be warm. So, when he appeared, I was sitting in the glow with my thoughts. He paused a moment by the door as if to look at me; then – as if to share them – came to the other side of the hearth and sank into a chair. We sat there in absolute stillness; yet he wanted, I felt, to be with me.

XXI

Before a new day, in my room, had fully broken, my eyes opened to Mrs Grose, who had come to my bedside with worse news. Flora was so markedly feverish that an illness was perhaps at hand; she had passed a night of extreme unrest, a night agitated above all by fears that had for their subject not in the least her former, but wholly her present, governess. It was not against the possible re-entrance of Miss Jessel on the scene that she protested – it was conspicuously and passionately against mine. I was promptly on my feet of course, and with an immense deal to ask; the more that my friend had discernibly now girded her loins to meet me once more. This I felt as soon as I had put to her the question of her sense of the child's sincerity as against my own. "She persists in denying to you that she saw, or has ever seen, anything?"

My visitor's trouble, truly, was great. "Ah, miss, it isn't a matter on which I can push her! Yet it isn't either, I must say, as if I much needed to. It has made her, every inch of her, quite old."

"Oh, I see her perfectly from here. She resents, for all the world like some high little personage, the imputation on her truthfulness and, as it were, her respectability. 'Miss Jessel indeed – *she*!' Ah, she's 'respectable', the chit! The impression she gave me there yesterday was, I assure you, the very strangest of all; it was quite beyond any of the others. I *did* put my foot in it! She'll never speak to me again."

Hideous and obscure as it all was, it held Mrs Grose briefly silent; then she granted my point with a frankness which, I made sure, had more behind it. "I think indeed, miss, she never will. She do have a grand manner about it!"

"And that manner" – I summed it up – "is practically what's the matter with her now!"

Oh, that manner, I could see in my visitor's face, and not a little else besides! "She asks me every three minutes if I think you're coming in."

"I see – I see." I, too, on my side, had so much more than worked it out. "Has she said to you since yesterday – except to repudiate her familiarity with anything so dreadful – a single other word about Miss Jessel?"

"Not one, miss. And of course you know," my friend added, "I took it from her, by the lake, that, just then and there at least, there *was* nobody."

"Rather! And, naturally, you take it from her still."

"I don't contradict her. What else can I do?"

"Nothing in the world! You've the cleverest little person to deal with. They've made them – their two friends, I mean – still cleverer even than nature did; for it was wondrous material to play on! Flora has now her grievance, and she'll work it to the end."

"Yes, miss; but to *what* end?"

"Why, that of dealing with me to her uncle. She'll make me out to him the lowest creature – !"

I winced at the fair show of the scene in Mrs Grose's face; she looked for a minute as if she sharply saw them together. "And him who thinks so well of you!"

"He has an odd way – it comes over me now – " I laughed, "of proving it! But that doesn't matter. What Flora wants, of course, is to get rid of me."

My companion bravely concurred. "Never again to so much as look at you."

"So that what you've come to me now for," I asked, "is to speed me on my way?" Before she had time to reply, however,

I had her in check. "I've a better idea – the result of my reflections. My going *would* seem the right thing, and on Sunday I was terribly near it. Yet that won't do. It's *you* who must go. You must take Flora."

My visitor, at this, did speculate. "But where in the world – ?"

"Away from here. Away from *them*. Away, even most of all, now, from me. Straight to her uncle."

"Only to tell on you – ?"

"No, not 'only'! To leave me, in addition, with my remedy."

She was still vague. "And what *is* your remedy?"

"Your loyalty, to begin with. And then Miles's."

She looked at me hard. "Do you think he – ?"

"Won't, if he has the chance, turn on me? Yes, I venture still to think it. At all events, I want to try. Get off with his sister as soon as possible and leave me with him alone." I was amazed, myself, at the spirit I had still in reserve, and therefore perhaps a trifle the more disconcerted at the way in which, in spite of this fine example of it, she hesitated. "There's one thing, of course," I went on: "they mustn't, before she goes, see each other for three seconds." Then it came over me that, in spite of Flora's presumable sequestration from the instant of her return from the pool, it might already be too late. "Do you mean," I anxiously asked, "that they *have* met?"

At this she quite flushed. "Ah, miss, I'm not such a fool as that! If I've been obliged to leave her three or four times, it has been each time with one of the maids, and at present, though she's alone, she's locked in safe. And yet – and yet!" There were too many things.

"And yet what?"

"Well, are you so sure of the little gentleman?"

"I'm not sure of anything but *you*. But I have, since last evening, a new hope. I think he wants to give me an opening. I do believe that – poor little exquisite wretch! – he wants to speak. Last evening, in the firelight and the silence, he sat with me for two hours as if it were just coming."

Mrs Grose looked hard, through the window, at the grey, gathering day. "And did it come?"

"No, though I waited and waited, I confess it didn't, and it was without a breach of the silence or so much as a faint allusion to his sister's condition and absence that we at last kissed for good night. All the same," I continued, "I can't, if her uncle sees her, consent to his seeing her brother without my having given the boy – and most of all because things have got so bad – a little more time."

My friend appeared on this ground more reluctant than I could quite understand. "What do you mean by more time?"

"Well, a day or two – really to bring it out. He'll then be on *my* side – of which you see the importance. If nothing comes, I shall only fail, and you will, at the worst, have helped me by doing, on your arrival in town, whatever you may have found possible." So I put it before her, but she continued for a little so inscrutably embarrassed that I came again to her aid. "Unless, indeed," I wound up, "you really want *not* to go."

I could see it, in her face, at last clear itself; she put out her hand to me as a pledge. "I'll go – I'll go. I'll go this morning."

I wanted to be very just. "If you *should* wish still to wait, I would engage she shouldn't see me."

"No, no: it's the place itself. She must leave it." She held me a moment with heavy eyes, then brought out the rest. "Your idea's the right one. I myself, miss – "

"Well?"

"I can't stay."

The look she gave me with it made me jump at possibilities. "You mean that, since yesterday, you *have* seen – ?"

She shook her head with dignity. "I've *heard* – !"

"Heard?"

"From that child – horrors! There!" she sighed with tragic relief. "On my honour, miss, she says things – !" But at this evocation she broke down; she dropped, with a sudden sob, upon my sofa and, as I had seen her do before, gave way to all the grief of it.

It was quite in another manner that I, for my part, let myself go. "Oh, thank God!"

She sprang up again at this, drying her eyes with a groan. "'Thank God'?"

"It so justifies me!"

"It does that, miss!"

I couldn't have desired more emphasis, but I just hesitated. "She's so horrible?"

I saw my colleague scarce knew how to put it. "Really shocking."

"And about me?"

"About you, miss – since you must have it. It's beyond everything, for a young lady; and I can't think wherever she must have picked up – "

"The appalling language she applied to me? I can, then!" I broke in with a laugh that was doubtless significant enough.

It only, in truth, left my friend still more grave. "Well, perhaps I ought to also – since I've heard some of it before! Yet I can't bear it," the poor woman went on while, with the same movement, she glanced, on my dressing table, at the face of my watch. "But I must go back."

I kept her, however. "Ah, if you can't bear it – !"

"How can I stop with her, you mean? Why, just *for* that: to get her away. Far from this," she pursued, "far from *them* – "

"She may be different? She may be free?" I seized her almost with joy. "Then, in spite of yesterday, you *believe* – "

"In such doings?" Her simple description of them required, in the light of her expression, to be carried no further, and she gave me the whole thing as she had never done. "I believe."

Yes, it was a joy, and we were still shoulder to shoulder: if I might continue sure of that I should care but little what else happened. My support in the presence of disaster would be the same as it had been in my early need of confidence, and if my friend would answer for my honesty, I would answer for all the rest. On the point of taking leave of her, nonetheless, I was to some extent embarrassed. "There's one thing, of course – it occurs to me – to remember. My letter, giving the alarm, will have reached town before you."

I now perceived still more how she had been beating about the bush and how weary at last it had made her. "Your letter won't have got there. Your letter never went."

"What then became of it?"

"Goodness knows! Master Miles – "

"Do you mean *he* took it?" I gasped.

She hung fire, but she overcame her reluctance. "I mean that I saw yesterday, when I came back with Miss Flora, that it wasn't where you had put it. Later in the evening I had the chance to question Luke, and he declared that he had neither noticed nor touched it." We could only exchange, on this, one of our deeper mutual soundings, and it was Mrs Grose who first brought up the plumb with an almost elated "You see!"

"Yes, I see that if Miles took it instead he probably will have read it and destroyed it."

"And don't you see anything else?"

I faced her a moment with a sad smile. "It strikes me that by this time your eyes are open even wider than mine."

They proved to be so indeed, but she could still blush, almost, to show it. "I make out now what he must have done at school."

And she gave, in her simple sharpness, an almost droll disillu-
sioned nod. "He stole!"

I turned it over – I tried to be more judicial. "Well – perhaps."

She looked as if she found me unexpectedly calm. "He stole
letters!"

She couldn't know my reasons for a calmness after all pretty
shallow; so I showed them off as I might. "I hope then it was
to more purpose than in this case! The note, at any rate, that I
put on the table yesterday," I pursued, "will have given him so
scant an advantage – for it contained only the bare demand for
an interview – that he is already much ashamed of having gone
so far for so little, and that what he had on his mind last evening
was precisely the need of confession." I seemed to myself, for
the instant, to have mastered it, to see it all. "Leave us, leave
us" – I was already, at the door, hurrying her off. "I'll get it out
of him. He'll meet me – he'll confess. If he confesses, he's saved.
And if he's saved – "

"Then *you* are?" The dear woman kissed me on this, and I
took her farewell. "I'll save you without him!" she cried as
she went.

XXII

Yet it was when she had got off – and I missed her on the spot – that the great pinch really came. If I had counted on what it would give me to find myself alone with Miles, I speedily perceived, at least, that it would give me a measure. No hour of my stay in fact was so assailed with apprehensions as that of my coming down to learn that the carriage containing Mrs Grose and my younger pupil had already rolled out of the gates. Now I *was*, I said to myself, face to face with the elements, and for much of the rest of the day, while I fought my weakness, I could consider that I had been supremely rash. It was a tighter place still than I had yet turned round in; all the more that, for the first time, I could see in the aspect of others a confused reflection of the crisis. What had happened naturally caused them all to stare; there was too little of the explained, throw out whatever we might, in the suddenness of my colleague's act. The maids and the men looked blank; the effect of which on my nerves was an aggravation until I saw the necessity of making it a positive aid. It was precisely, in short, by just clutching the helm that I avoided total wreck; and I dare say that, to bear up at all, I became, that morning, very grand and very dry. I welcomed the consciousness that I was charged with much to do, and I caused it to be known as well that, left thus to myself, I was quite remarkably firm. I wandered with that manner, for the next hour or two, all over the place and looked, I have no doubt, as if I were ready for any onset. So, for the benefit of whom it might concern, I paraded with a sick heart.

The person it appeared least to concern proved to be, till dinner, little Miles himself. My perambulations had given me, meanwhile, no glimpse of him, but they had tended to make more public the change taking place in our relation as a consequence of his having at the piano, the day before, kept me, in Flora's interest, so beguiled and befooled. The stamp of publicity had of course been fully given by her confinement and departure, and the change itself was now ushered in by our non-observance of the regular custom of the schoolroom. He had already disappeared when, on my way down, I pushed open his door, and I learned below that he had breakfasted – in the presence of a couple of the maids – with Mrs Grose and his sister. He had then gone out, as he said, for a stroll; than which nothing, I reflected, could better have expressed his frank view of the abrupt transformation of my office. What he would not permit this office to consist of was yet to be settled: there was a queer relief, at all events – I mean for myself in especial – in the renouncement of one pretension. If so much had sprung to the surface, I scarce put it too strongly in saying that what had perhaps sprung highest was the absurdity of our prolonging the fiction that I had anything more to teach him. It sufficiently stuck out that, by tacit little tricks in which even more than myself he carried out the care for my dignity, I had had to appeal to him to let me off straining to meet him on the ground of his true capacity. He had at any rate his freedom now; I was never to touch it again; as I had amply shown, moreover, when, on his joining me in the school-room the previous night, I had uttered, on the subject of the interval just concluded, neither challenge nor hint. I had too much, from this moment, my other ideas. Yet when he at last arrived, the difficulty of applying them, the accumulations of my problem, were brought straight home to me by the beautiful little presence on which what had occurred had as yet, for the eye, dropped neither stain nor shadow.

To mark, for the house, the high state I cultivated I decreed that my meals with the boy should be served, as we called it, downstairs; so that I had been awaiting him in the ponderous pomp of the room outside of the window of which I had had from Mrs Grose, that first scared Sunday, my flash of something it would scarce have done to call light. Here at present I felt afresh – for I had felt it again and again – how my equilibrium depended on the success of my rigid will, the will to shut my eyes as tight as possible to the truth that what I had to deal with was, revoltingly, against nature. I could only get on at all by taking "nature" into my confidence and my account, by treating my monstrous ordeal as a push in a direction unusual, of course, and unpleasant, but demanding, after all, for a fair front, only another turn of the screw of ordinary human virtue. No attempt, nonetheless, could well require more tact than just this attempt to supply, one's self, *all* the nature. How could I put even a little of that article into a suppression of reference to what had occurred? How, on the other hand, could I make reference without a new plunge into the hideous obscure? Well, a sort of answer, after a time, had come to me, and it was so far confirmed as that I was met, incontestably, by the quickened vision of what was rare in my little companion. It was indeed as if he had found even now – as he had so often found at lessons – still some other delicate way to ease me off. Wasn't there light in the fact which, as we shared our solitude, broke out with a specious glitter it had never yet quite worn? – the fact that (opportunity aiding, precious opportunity which had now come) it would be preposterous, with a child so endowed, to forego the help one might wrest from absolute intelligence? What had his intelligence been given him for but to save him? Mightn't one, to reach his mind, risk the stretch of an angular arm over his character? It was as if, when we were face to face in the dining room, he had literally shown me the way. The roast mutton was on the table, and I had dispensed with attendance. Miles, before he sat down, stood a moment with his hands in his pockets and looked at the joint, on which he seemed on the point of passing some humorous judgement. But what he presently produced was: "I say, my dear, is she really very awfully ill?"

"Little Flora? Not so bad but that she'll presently be better. London will set her up. Bly had ceased to agree with her. Come here and take your mutton."

He alertly obeyed me, carried the plate carefully to his seat, and, when he was established, went on. "Did Bly disagree with her so terribly suddenly?"

"Not so suddenly as you might think. One had seen it coming on."

"Then why didn't you get her off before?"

"Before what?"

"Before she became too ill to travel."

I found myself prompt. "She's *not* too ill to travel: she only might have become so if she had stayed. This was just the moment to seize. The journey will dissipate the influence" – oh, I was grand! – "and carry it off."

"I see, I see," – Miles, for that matter, was grand, too. He settled to his repast with the charming little "table manner" that, from the day of his arrival, had relieved me of all grossness of admonition. Whatever he had been driven from school for, it was not for ugly feeding. He was irreproachable, as always, today; but he was unmistakeably more conscious. He was discernibly trying to take for granted more things than he found, without assistance, quite easy; and he dropped into peaceful silence while he felt his situation. Our meal was of the briefest – mine a vain pretence, and I had the things immediately removed. While this was done Miles stood again with his hands in his little pockets and his back to me – stood and looked out of the wide window through which, that other day, I had seen what pulled me up. We continued silent while the maid was with us – as silent, it whimsically occurred to me, as some young couple who, on their wedding journey, at the inn, feel shy in the presence of the waiter. He turned round only when the waiter had left us. "Well – so we're alone!"

XXIII

"Oh, more or less." I fancy my smile was pale. "Not absolutely. We shouldn't like that!" I went on.

"No – I suppose we shouldn't. Of course we have the others."

"We have the others – we have indeed the others," I concurred.

"Yet even though we have them," he returned, still with his hands in his pockets and planted there in front of me, "they don't much count, do they?"

I made the best of it, but I felt wan. "It depends on what you call 'much'!"

"Yes," – with all accommodation – "everything depends!" On this, however, he faced to the window again and presently reached it with his vague, restless, cogitating step. He remained there awhile, with his forehead against the glass, in contemplation of the stupid shrubs I knew and the dull things of November. I had always my hypocrisy of "work", behind which, now, I gained the sofa. Steadying myself with it there as I had repeatedly done at those moments of torment that I have described as the moments of my knowing the children to be given to something from which I was barred, I sufficiently obeyed my habit of being prepared for the worst. But an extraordinary impression dropped on me as I extracted a meaning from the boy's embarrassed back – none other than the impression that I was not barred now. This inference grew in a few minutes to sharp intensity and seemed bound up with the direct perception that it was positively *he* who was. The frames and squares of the great window were a kind of image, for him, of a kind of failure. I felt that I saw him, at any rate, shut in or shut out. He was admirable, but not comfortable: I took it in with a throb of hope. Wasn't he looking, through the haunted pane, for something he couldn't see? – and wasn't it the first time in the whole business that he had known such a lapse? The first, the very first: I found it a splendid portent. It made him anxious, though he watched himself; he had been anxious all day and, even while in his usual sweet little manner he sat at table, had needed all his small strange genius to give it a gloss. When he at last turned round to meet me, it was almost as if this genius had succumbed. "Well, I think I'm glad Bly agrees with *me*!"

"You would certainly seem to have seen, these twenty-four hours, a good deal more of it than for some time before. I hope", I went on bravely, "that you've been enjoying yourself."

"Oh, yes, I've been ever so far; all round about – miles and miles away. I've never been so free."

He had really a manner of his own, and I could only try to keep up with him. "Well, do you like it?"

He stood there smiling; then at last he put into two words – "Do *you*?" – more discrimination than I had ever heard two words contain. Before I had time to deal with that, however, he continued as if with the sense that this was an impertinence to be softened. "Nothing could be more charming than the way you take it, for of course if we're alone together now it's you that are alone most. But I hope," he threw in, "you don't particularly mind!"

"Having to do with you?" I asked. "My dear child, how can I help minding? Though I've renounced all claim to your company – you're so beyond me – I at least greatly enjoy it. What else should I stay on for?"

He looked at me more directly, and the expression of his face, graver now, struck me as the most beautiful I had ever found in it. "You stay on just for *that*?"

"Certainly. I stay on as your friend and from the tremendous interest I take in you till something can be done for you that may be more worth your while. That needn't surprise you." My voice trembled so that I felt it impossible to suppress the shake. "Don't you remember how I told you, when I came and sat on your bed the night of the storm, that there was nothing in the world I wouldn't do for you?"

"Yes, yes!" He, on his side, more and more visibly nervous, had a tone to master; but he was so much more successful than I that, laughing out through his gravity, he could pretend we were pleasantly jesting. "Only that, I think, was to get me to do something for *you*!"

"It was partly to get you to do something," I conceded. "But, you know, you didn't do it."

"Oh, yes," he said with the brightest superficial eagerness, "you wanted me to tell you something."

"That's it. Out, straight out. What you have on your mind, you know."

"Ah, then, is *that* what you've stayed over for?"

He spoke with a gaiety through which I could still catch the finest little quiver of resentful passion; but I can't begin to express the effect upon me of an implication of surrender even so faint. It was as if what I had yearned for had come at last only to astonish me. "Well, yes – I may as well make a clean breast of it, it was precisely for that."

He waited so long that I supposed it for the purpose of repudiating the assumption on which my action had been founded; but what he finally said was: "Do you mean now – here?"

"There couldn't be a better place or time." He looked round him uneasily, and I had the rare – oh, the queer! – impression of the very first symptom I had seen in him of the approach of immediate fear. It was as if he were suddenly afraid of me – which struck me indeed as perhaps the best thing to make him. Yet in the very pang of the effort I felt it vain to try sternness, and I heard myself the next instant so gentle as to be almost grotesque. "You want so to go out again?"

"Awfully!" He smiled at me heroically, and the touching little bravery of it was enhanced by his actually flushing with pain. He had picked up his hat, which he had brought in, and stood twirling it in a way that gave me, even as I was just nearly reaching port, a perverse horror of what I was doing. To do it in *any* way was an act of violence, for what did it consist of but the obtrusion of the idea of grossness and guilt on a small helpless creature who had been for me a revelation of the possibilities of beautiful intercourse? Wasn't it base to create for a being so exquisite a mere alien awkwardness? I suppose I now read into our situation a clearness it couldn't have had at the time, for I seem to see our poor eyes already lighted with some spark of a prevision of the anguish that was to come. So we circled about, with terrors and scruples, like fighters not daring to close. But it was for each other we feared! That kept us a little longer suspended and unbruised. "I'll tell you everything," Miles said – "I mean I'll tell you anything you like. You'll stay on with me, and we shall both be all right, and I *will* tell you – I *will*. But not now."

"Why not now?"

My insistence turned him from me and kept him once more at his window in a silence during which, between us, you might have heard a pin drop. Then he was before me again with the air of a person for whom, outside, someone who had frankly to be reckoned with was waiting. "I have to see Luke."

I had not yet reduced him to quite so vulgar a lie, and I felt proportionately ashamed. But, horrible as it was, his lies made up my truth. I achieved thoughtfully a few loops of my knitting. "Well, then, go to Luke, and I'll wait for what you promise. Only, in return for that, satisfy, before you leave me, one very much smaller request."

He looked as if he felt he had succeeded enough to be able still a little to bargain. "Very much smaller – ?"

"Yes, a mere fraction of the whole. Tell me," – oh, my work preoccupied me, and I was offhand! – "if, yesterday afternoon, from the table in the hall, you took, you know, my letter."

XXIV

My sense of how he received this suffered for a minute from something that I can describe only as a fierce split of my attention – a stroke that at first, as I sprang straight up, reduced me to the mere blind movement of getting hold of him, drawing him close and, while I just fell for support against the nearest piece of furniture, instinctively keeping him with his back to the window. The appearance was full upon us that I had already had to deal with here: Peter Quint had come into view like a sentinel before a prison. The next thing I saw was that, from outside, he had reached the window, and then I knew that, close to the glass and glaring in through it, he offered once more to the room his white face of damnation. It represents but grossly what took place within me at the sight to say that on the second my decision was made; yet I believe that no woman so overwhelmed ever in so short a time recovered her grasp of the *act*. It came to me in the very horror of the immediate presence that the act would be, seeing and facing what I saw and faced, to keep the boy himself unaware. The inspiration – I can call it by no other name – was that I felt how voluntarily, how transcendently, I *might*. It was like fighting with a demon for a human soul, and when I had fairly so appraised it I saw how the human soul – held out, in the tremor of my hands, at arm's length – had a perfect dew of sweat on a lovely childish forehead. The face that was close to mine was as white as the face against the glass, and out of it presently came a sound, not low nor weak, but as if from much further away, that I drank like a waft of fragrance.

"Yes – I took it."

At this, with a moan of joy, I enfolded, I drew him close; and while I held him to my breast, where I could feel in the sudden fever of his little body the tremendous pulse of his little heart, I kept my eyes on the thing at the window and saw it move and shift its posture. I have likened it to a sentinel, but its slow wheel, for a moment, was rather the prowl of a baffled beast. My present quickened courage, however, was such that, not too much to let it through, I had to shade, as it were, my flame. Meanwhile the glare of the face was again at the window, the scoundrel fixed as if to watch and wait. It was the very confidence that I might now defy him, as well as the positive certitude, by this time, of the child's unconsciousness, that made me go on. "What did you take it for?"

"To see what you said about me."

"You opened the letter?"

"I opened it."

My eyes were now, as I held him off a little again, on Miles's own face, in which the collapse of mockery showed me how complete was the ravage of uneasiness. What was prodigious was that at last, by my success, his sense was sealed and his communication stopped: he knew that he was in presence, but knew not of what, and knew still less that I also was and that I did know. And what did this strain of trouble matter when my eyes went back to the window only to see that the air was clear again and – by my personal triumph – the influence quenched? There was nothing there. I felt that the cause was mine and that I should surely get *all*. "And you found nothing!" – I let my elation out.

He gave the most mournful, thoughtful little headshake. "Nothing."

"Nothing, nothing!" I almost shouted in my joy.

"Nothing, nothing," he sadly repeated.

I kissed his forehead; it was drenched. "So what have you done with it?"

"I've burned it."

"Burned it?" It was now or never. "Is that what you did at school?"

Oh, what this brought up! "At school?"

"Did you take letters? – Or other things?"

"Other things?" He appeared now to be thinking of something far off and that reached him only through the pressure of his anxiety. Yet it did reach him. "Did I *steal*?"

I felt myself redden to the roots of my hair as well as wonder if it were more strange to put to a gentleman such a question or to see him take it with allowances that gave the very distance of his fall in the world. "Was it for that you mightn't go back?"

The only thing he felt was rather a dreary little surprise. "Did you know I mightn't go back?"

"I know everything."

He gave me at this the longest and strangest look. "Everything?"

"Everything. Therefore *did* you – ?" But I couldn't say it again.

Miles could, very simply. "No. I didn't steal."

My face must have shown him I believed him utterly; yet my hands – but it was for pure tenderness – shook him as if to ask him why, if it was all for nothing, he had condemned me to months of torment. "What then did you do?"

He looked in vague pain all round the top of the room and drew his breath, two or three times over, as if with difficulty. He might have been standing at the bottom of the sea and raising his eyes to some faint green twilight. "Well – I said things."

"Only that?"

"They thought it was enough!"

"To turn you out for?"

Never, truly, had a person "turned out" shown so little to explain it as this little person! He appeared to weigh my question,

141

but in a manner quite detached and almost helpless. "Well, I suppose I oughtn't."

"But to whom did you say them?"

He evidently tried to remember, but it dropped – he had lost it. "I don't know!"

He almost smiled at me in the desolation of his surrender, which was indeed practically, by this time, so complete that I ought to have left it there. But I was infatuated – I was blind with victory, though even then the very effect that was to have brought him so much nearer was already that of added separation. "Was it to everyone?" I asked.

"No; it was only to – " But he gave a sick little headshake. "I don't remember their names."

"Were they then so many?"

"No – only a few. Those I liked."

Those he liked? I seemed to float not into clearness, but into a darker obscure, and within a minute there had come to me out of my very pity the appalling alarm of his being perhaps innocent. It was for the instant confounding and bottomless, for if he *were* innocent, what then on earth was *I*? Paralysed, while it lasted, by the mere brush of the question, I let him go a little, so that, with a deep-drawn sigh, he turned away from me again; which, as he faced toward the clear window, I suffered, feeling that I had nothing now there to keep him from. "And did they repeat what you said?" I went on after a moment.

He was soon at some distance from me, still breathing hard and again with the air, though now without anger for it, of being confined against his will. Once more, as he had done before, he looked up at the dim day as if, of what had hitherto sustained him, nothing was left but an unspeakable anxiety. "Oh, yes," he nevertheless replied – "they must have repeated them. To those *they* liked," he added.

There was, somehow, less of it than I had expected; but I turned it over. "And these things came round – ?"

"To the masters? Oh, yes!" he answered very simply. "But I didn't know they'd tell."

"The masters? They didn't – they've never told. That's why I ask you."

He turned to me again his little beautiful fevered face. "Yes, it was too bad."

"Too bad?"

"What I suppose I sometimes said. To write home."

I can't name the exquisite pathos of the contradiction given to such a speech by such a speaker; I only know that the next instant I heard myself throw off with homely force: "Stuff and nonsense!" But the next after that I must have sounded stern enough. "What *were* these things?"

My sternness was all for his judge, his executioner; yet it made him avert himself again, and that movement made *me*, with a single bound and an irrepressible cry, spring straight upon him. For there again, against the glass, as if to blight his confession and stay his answer, was the hideous author of our woe – the white face of damnation. I felt a sick swim at the drop of my victory and all the return of my battle, so that the wildness of my veritable leap only served as a great betrayal. I saw him, from the midst of my act, meet it with a divination, and on the perception that even now he only guessed, and that the window was still to his own eyes free, I let the impulse flame up to convert the climax of his dismay into the very proof of his liberation. "No more, no more, no more!" I shrieked, as I tried to press him against me, to my visitant.

"Is she *here*?" Miles panted as he caught with his sealed eyes the direction of my words. Then as his strange "she" staggered me and, with a gasp, I echoed it, "Miss Jessel, Miss Jessel!" he with a sudden fury gave me back.

I seized, stupefied, his supposition – some sequel to what we had done to Flora, but this made me only want to show him that it was better still than that. "It's not Miss Jessel! But it's at the window – straight before us. It's *there* – the coward horror, there for the last time!"

At this, after a second in which his head made the movement of a baffled dog's on a scent and then gave a frantic little shake for air and light, he was at me in a white rage, bewildered, glaring vainly over the place and missing wholly, though it now, to my sense, filled the room like the taste of poison, the wide, over-whelming presence. "It's *he*?"

I was so determined to have all my proof that I flashed into ice to challenge him. "Whom do you mean by 'he'?"

"Peter Quint – you devil!" His face gave again, round the room, its convulsed supplication. "*Where*?"

They are in my ears still his supreme surrender of the name and his tribute to my devotion. "What does he matter now, my own? – What will he *ever* matter? *I* have you," I launched at the beast, "but he has lost you forever!" Then, for the demonstration of my work, "There, *there*!" I said to Miles.

But he had already jerked straight round, stared, glared again, and seen but the quiet day. With the stroke of the loss I was so proud of he uttered the cry of a creature hurled over an abyss, and the grasp with which I recovered him might have been that of catching him in his fall. I caught him, yes, I held him – it may be imagined with what a passion; but at the end of a minute I began to feel what it truly was that I held. We were alone with the quiet day, and his little heart, dispossessed, had stopped.

THE
WOMAN
IN WHITE

THE
WOMAN
IN WHITE

WILKIE COLLINS

This edition published in 2019 by Arcturus Publishing Limited
26/27 Bickels Yard, 151–153 Bermondsey Street,
London SE1 3HA

Cover design: Peter Ridley
Cover illustration: Peter Gray
Design: Catherine Wood

AD001853UK

Printed in the UK

Contents

Introduction 7

Preface to the 1860 Edition 9

Preface to the 1861 Edition 11

The First Epoch

The Story Begun By Walter Hartright 13

The Story Continued By Vincent Gilmore 109

The Story Continued By Marian Halcombe 137

The Second Epoch

The Story Continued By Marian Halcombe 164

The Story Continued By Frederick Fairlie, Esq. 279

The Story Continued By Eliza Michelson 294

The Story Continued In Several Narratives 328

I.   *The Narrative Of Hester Pinhorn* 328

II. *The Narrative Of The Doctor* 332

III. *The Narrative Of Jane Gould* 332

IV. *The Narrative Of The Tombstone* 333

V.   *The Narrative Of Walter Hartright* 333

The Third Epoch

The Story Continued By Walter Hartright 338

The Story Continued By Mrs Catherick 432

The Story Continued By Walter Hartright 442

The Story Continued By Isidor Ottavio Baldassare Fosco 489

The Story Concluded By Walter Hartright 501

Introduction

William Wilkie Collins was born in London on 8 January 1824, the son of William Collins, a celebrated artist and Royal Academician. For two years in his early teens, Wilkie lived in France and Italy with his parents and always that claimed it had been more valuable to him than any schooling. He was short in stature with a disproportionately large head and inevitably drew the attention of school bullies. It was to appease one in particular that he first became a storyteller.

Collins left school at seventeen and was clerk to a tea merchant for five dreary years before studying law at Lincoln's Inn. He never practised, though several lawyers feature in his works and his introduction to *The Woman in White* states: 'the story here presented will be told by more than one pen, as the story of an offence against the laws is told in Court by more than one witness'.

Instead, Collins turned to journalism and became a contributor to Charles Dickens's *Household Words*, joining the staff in 1856 and collaborating with Dickens on the Christmas numbers. The two men were firm friends until Dickens's death in 1870.

The Woman in White was first serialized from November 1859 to August 1860, in Dickens's newest journal, *All Year Round*. Collins had an instant and overwhelming success on his hands. The 'Woman in White' brand was used to sell everything from bonnets and perfumes to sheet music. The tale is based on a French case of abduction and wrongful imprisonment, woven in with the theme of false identity, which was a favourite of the author. The original model for the character was a widow called Caroline Graves with whom Collins lived for many years, although the couple were never married.

Wilkie Collins died on 23 September 1889.

PREFACE TO THE 1860 EDITION

An experiment is attempted in this novel, which has not (so far as I know) been hitherto tried in fiction. The story of the book is told throughout by the characters of the book. They are all placed in different positions along the chain of events; and they all take the chain up in turn, and carry it on to the end.

If the execution of this idea had led to nothing more than the attainment of mere novelty of form, I should not have claimed a moment's attention for it in this place. But the substance of the book, as well as the form, has profited by it. It has forced me to keep the story constantly moving forward; and it has afforded my characters a new opportunity of expressing themselves, through the medium of the written contributions which they are supposed to make to the progress of the narrative.

In writing these prefatory lines, I cannot prevail on myself to pass over in silence the warm welcome which my story has met with, in its periodical form, among English and American readers. In the first place, that welcome has, I hope, justified me for having accepted the serious literary responsibility of appearing in the columns of *All the Year Round*, immediately after Mr Charles Dickens had occupied them with the most perfect work of constructive art that has ever proceeded from his pen. In the second place, by frankly acknowledging the recognition that I have obtained thus far, I provide for myself an opportunity of thanking many correspondents (to whom I am personally unknown) for the hearty encouragement I received from them while my work was in progress. Now, while the visionary men and women, among whom I have been living so long, are all leaving me, I remember very gratefully that 'Marian' and 'Laura' made such warm friends in many quarters, that I was peremptorily cautioned at a serious crisis in the story, to be careful how I treated them – that Mr Fairlie found sympathetic fellow-sufferers, who remonstrated with me for not making Christian allowance for the state of his nerves – that Sir Percival's 'secret' became sufficiently exasperating, in course of time, to be made the subject of bets (all of which I hereby declare to be 'off') – and that Count Fosco suggested metaphysical considerations to the learned in such matters (which I don't quite understand to this day), besides provoking numerous inquiries as to the living model, from which he had been really taken. I can only answer these last by confessing that many models, some living and some dead, have 'sat' for him; and by hinting that the Count would not have been as true to nature as I have tried to make him, if the range of my search for materials had not extended, in his case as well as in others, beyond the narrow human limit which is represented by one man.

Before I conclude, I am desirous of addressing one or two questions, of the most harmless and innocent kind, to the Critics.

In the event of this book being reviewed, I venture to ask whether it is possible to praise the writer, or to blame him, without opening the proceedings by telling his story at second-hand? As that story is written by me – with the inevitable suppressions which the periodical system of publication forces on the novelist – the telling it fills more than a thousand closely printed pages. No small portion of this space is occupied by hundreds of little 'connecting links', of trifling value in themselves, but of the utmost importance in maintaining the smoothness, the reality, and the probability of the entire narrative. If the critic tells the story *with* these, can he do it in his allotted page, or column, as the case may be? If he tells it *without* these, is he doing a fellow-labourer in another form of Art, the justice which writers owe to one another? And lastly, if he tells it at all, in any way whatever, is he doing a service to the reader, by destroying, beforehand, two main elements of the attraction of all stories – the interest of curiosity, and the excitement of surprise?

Harley Street, London
August 3, 1860

PREFACE TO THE 1861 EDITION

The Woman in White has been received with such marked favour by a very large circle of readers, that this volume scarcely stands in need of any prefatory introduction on my part. All that it is necessary for me to say on the subject of the present edition – the first issued in a portable and popular form – may be summed up in few words.

I have endeavoured, by careful correction and revision, to make my story as worthy as I could of a continuance of the public approval. Certain technical errors which had escaped me while I was writing the book are here rectified. None of these little blemishes in the slightest degree interfered with the interest of the narrative – but it was as well to remove them at the first opportunity, out of respect to my readers; and in this edition, accordingly, they exist no more.

Some doubt having been expressed, in certain captious quarters, about the correct presentation of the legal 'points' incidental to the story, I may be permitted to mention that I spared no pains – in this instance, as in all others – to preserve myself from unintentionally misleading my readers. A solicitor of great experience in his profession most kindly and carefully guided my steps, whenever the course of the narrative led me into the labyrinth of the Law. Every doubtful question was submitted to this gentleman, before I ventured on putting pen to paper; and all the proofsheets which referred to legal matters were corrected by his hand before the story was published. I can add, on high judicial authority, that these precautions were not taken in vain. The 'law' in this book has been discussed, since its publication, by more than one competent tribunal, and has been decided to be sound.

One word more, before I conclude, in acknowledgement of the heavy debt of gratitude which I owe to the reading public.

It is no affectation on my part to say that the success of this book has been especially welcome to me, because it implied the recognition of a literary principle which has guided me since I first addressed my readers in the character of a novelist.

I have always held the old-fashioned opinion that the primary object of a work of fiction should be to tell a story; and I have never believed that the novelist who properly performed this first condition of his art, was in danger, on that account, of neglecting the delineation of character – for this plain reason, that the effect produced by any narrative of events is essentially dependent, not on the events themselves, but on the human interest which is directly connected with them. It may be possible, in novel-writing, to present characters successfully without telling a story; but it is not possible to tell a story successfully without presenting characters: their existence, as recognisable realities, being the sole condition on which the story can be effectively told. The only narrative which can hope to lay a strong hold on the attention of readers, is a narrative which interests them about men and women – for the perfectly obvious reason that they are men and women themselves.

The reception accorded to *The Woman in White* has practically confirmed these opinions, and has satisfied me that I may trust to them in the future. Here is a novel which has met with a very kind reception, because it is a story; and here is a story, the interest of which – as I know by the testimony, voluntarily addressed to me, of the readers themselves – is never disconnected from the interest of character. 'Laura', 'Miss Halcombe' and 'Anne Catherick'; 'Count Fosco', 'Mr Fairlie' and 'Walter Hartright'; have made friends for me wherever they have made themselves known. I hope the time is not far distant when I may meet those friends again, and when I may try, through the medium of new characters, to awaken their interest in another story.

Harley Street, London
February, 1861

THE FIRST EPOCH

THE STORY BEGUN BY WALTER HARTRIGHT
(of Clement's Inn, Teacher of Drawing)

This is the story of what a Woman's patience can endure, and what a Man's resolution can achieve.

If the machinery of the Law could be depended on to fathom every case of suspicion, and to conduct every process of inquiry, with moderate assistance only from the lubricating influences of oil of gold, the events which fill these pages might have claimed their share of the public attention in a Court of Justice.

But the Law is still, in certain inevitable cases, the pre-engaged servant of the long purse; and the story is left to be told, for the first time, in this place. As the Judge might once have heard it, so the Reader shall hear it now. No circumstance of importance, from the beginning to the end of the disclosure, shall be related on hearsay evidence. When the writer of these introductory lines (Walter Hartright by name) happens to be more closely connected than others with the incidents to be recorded, he will be the narrator. When not, he will retire from the position of narrator; and his task will be continued, from the point at which he has left it off, by other persons who can speak to the circumstances under notice from their own knowledge, just as clearly and positively as he has spoken before them.

Thus, the story here presented will be told by more than one pen, as the story of an offence against the laws is told in Court by more than one witness – with the same object, in both cases, to present the truth always in its most direct and most intelligible aspect; and to trace the course of one complete series of events, by making the persons who have been most closely connected with them, at each successive stage, relate their own experience, word for word.

Let Walter Hartright, teacher of drawing, aged twenty-eight years, be heard first.

II

It was the last day of July. The long hot summer was drawing to a close; and we, the weary pilgrims of the London pavement, were beginning to think of the cloud-shadows on the corn-fields, and the autumn breezes on the sea-shore.

For my own poor part, the fading summer left me out of health, out of spirits, and, if the truth must be told, out of money as well. During the past year I had not managed my professional resources as carefully as usual; and my extravagance now limited me to the prospect of spending the autumn economically between my mother's cottage at Hampstead and my own chambers in town.

The evening, I remember, was still and cloudy; the London air was at its heaviest; the distant hum of the street-traffic was at its faintest; the small pulse of the life within me, and the great heart of the city around me, seemed to be sinking in unison, languidly and more languidly, with the sinking sun. I roused myself from the book which I was dreaming over rather than reading, and left my chambers to meet the cool night air in the suburbs. It was one of the two evenings in every week which I was accustomed to spend with my mother and my sister. So I turned my steps northward in the direction of Hampstead.

Events which I have yet to relate make it necessary to mention in this place that my father had been dead some years at the period of which I am now writing; and that my sister Sarah and I were the sole survivors of a family of five children. My father was a drawing-master before me. His exertions had made him highly successful in his profession; and his affectionate anxiety to provide for the future of those who were dependent on his labours had impelled him, from the time of his marriage, to devote to the insuring of his life a much larger portion of his income than most men consider it necessary to set aside for that purpose. Thanks to his admirable prudence and self-denial my mother and sister were left, after his death, as independent of the world as they had been during his lifetime. I succeeded to his connection, and had every reason to feel grateful for the prospect that awaited me at my starting in life.

The quiet twilight was still trembling on the topmost ridges of the heath; and the view of London below me had sunk into a black gulf in the shadow of the cloudy night, when I stood before the gate of my mother's cottage. I had hardly rung the bell before the house door was opened violently; my worthy Italian friend, Professor Pesca, appeared in the servant's place; and darted out joyously to receive me, with a shrill foreign parody on an English cheer.

On his own account, and, I must be allowed to add, on mine also, the Professor merits the honour of a formal introduction. Accident has made him the starting-point of the strange family story which it is the purpose of these pages to unfold.

I had first become acquainted with my Italian friend by meeting him at certain great houses where he taught his own language and I taught drawing.

All I then knew of the history of his life was, that he had once held a situation in the University of Padua; that he had left Italy for political reasons (the nature of which he uniformly declined to mention to any one); and that he had been for many years respectably established in London as a teacher of languages.

Without being actually a dwarf – for he was perfectly well proportioned from head to foot – Pesca was, I think, the smallest human being I ever saw out of a show-room. Remarkable anywhere, by his personal appearance, he was still further distinguished among the rank and file of mankind by the harmless eccentricity of his character. The ruling idea of his life appeared to be, that he was bound to show his gratitude to the country which had afforded him an asylum and a means of subsistence by doing his utmost to turn himself into an Englishman. Not content with paying the nation in general the compliment of invariably carrying an umbrella, and invariably wearing gaiters and a white hat, the Professor further aspired to become an Englishman in his habits and amusements, as well as in his personal appearance. Finding us distinguished, as a nation, by our love of athletic exercises, the little man, in the innocence of his heart, devoted himself impromptu to all our English sports and pastimes whenever he had the opportunity of joining them; firmly persuaded that he could adopt our national amusements of the field by an effort of will precisely as he had adopted our national gaiters and our national white hat.

I had seen him risk his limbs blindly at a fox-hunt and in a cricket-field; and soon afterwards I saw him risk his life, just as blindly, in the sea at Brighton.

We had met there accidentally, and were bathing together. If we had been engaged in any exercise peculiar to my own nation I should, of course, have looked after Pesca carefully; but as foreigners are generally quite as well able to take care of themselves in the water as Englishmen, it never occurred to me that the art of swimming might merely add one more to the list of manly exercises which the Professor believed that he could learn impromptu. Soon after we had both struck out from shore, I stopped, finding my friend did not gain on me, and turned round to look for him. To my horror and amazement, I saw nothing between me and the beach but two little white arms which struggled for an instant above the surface of the water, and then disappeared from view. When I dived for him, the poor little man was lying quietly coiled up at the bottom, in a hollow of shingle, looking by many degrees smaller than I had ever seen him look before. During the few minutes that elapsed while I was taking him in, the air revived him, and he ascended the steps of the machine with my assistance. With the partial recovery of his animation came the return of his wonderful delusion on the subject of swimming. As soon as his chattering teeth would let him speak, he smiled vacantly, and said he thought it must have been the Cramp.

When he had thoroughly recovered himself, and had joined me on the beach, his warm Southern nature broke through all artificial English restraints in a moment. He overwhelmed me with the wildest expressions of affection – exclaimed passionately, in his exaggerated Italian way, that he would hold his life henceforth at my disposal – and declared that he should never be happy again until he had found an opportunity of proving his gratitude by rendering me some service which I might remember, on my side, to the end of my days.

I did my best to stop the torrent of his tears and protestations by persisting in treating the whole adventure as a good subject for a joke; and succeeded at last, as I imagined, in lessening Pesca's overwhelming sense of obligation to me. Little did I think then – little did I think afterwards when our pleasant holiday had drawn to an end – that the opportunity of serving me for which my grateful companion so ardently longed was soon to come; that he was eagerly to seize it on the instant; and that by so doing he was to turn the whole current of my existence into a new channel, and to alter me to myself almost past recognition.

Yet so it was. If I had not dived for Professor Pesca when he lay under water on his shingle bed, I should in all human probability never have been connected with the story which these pages will relate – I should never, perhaps, have heard even the name of the woman who has lived in all my thoughts, who has possessed herself of all my energies, who has become the one guiding influence that now directs the purpose of my life.

III

Pesca's face and manner, on the evening when we confronted each other at my mother's gate, were more than sufficient to inform me that something extraordinary had happened. It was quite useless, however, to ask him for an immediate explanation. I could only conjecture, while he was dragging me in by both hands, that (knowing my habits) he had come to the cottage to make sure of meeting me that night, and that he had some news to tell of an unusually agreeable kind.

We both bounced into the parlour in a highly abrupt and undignified manner. My mother sat by the open window laughing and fanning herself. Pesca was one of her especial favourites and his wildest eccentricities were always pardonable in her eyes. Poor dear soul! from the first moment when she found out that the little Professor was deeply and gratefully attached to her son, she opened her heart to him unreservedly, and took all his puzzling foreign peculiarities for granted, without so much as attempting to understand any one of them.

My sister Sarah, with all the advantages of youth, was, strangely enough, less pliable. She did full justice to Pesca's excellent qualities of heart; but she could not accept him implicitly, as my mother accepted him, for my sake. Her insular notions of propriety rose in perpetual revolt against Pesca's constitutional contempt for appearances; and she was always more or less undisguisedly astonished at her mother's familiarity with the eccentric little foreigner. I have observed, not only in my sister's case, but in the instances of others, that we of the young generation are nothing like so hearty and so impulsive as some of our elders. I constantly see old people flushed and excited by the prospect of some anticipated pleasure which altogether fails to ruffle the tranquillity of their serene grandchildren. Are we, I wonder, quite such genuine boys and girls now as our seniors were in their time? Has the great advance in education taken rather too long a stride; and are we in these modern days, just the least trifle in the world too well brought up?

Without attempting to answer those questions decisively, I may at least record that I never saw my mother and my sister together in Pesca's society, without finding my mother much the younger woman of the two. On this occasion, for example, while the old lady was laughing heartily over the boyish manner in which we tumbled into the parlour, Sarah was perturbedly picking up the broken pieces of a teacup, which the Professor had knocked off the table in his precipitate advance to meet me at the door.

'I don't know what would have happened, Walter,' said my mother, 'if you had delayed much longer. Pesca has been half mad with impatience, and I have been half mad with curiosity. The Professor has brought some wonderful news with him, in which he says you are concerned; and he has cruelly refused to give us the smallest hint of it till his friend Walter appeared.'

'Very provoking: it spoils the Set,' murmured Sarah to herself, mournfully absorbed over the ruins of the broken cup.

While these words were being spoken, Pesca, happily and fussily unconscious of the irreparable wrong which the crockery had suffered at his hands, was dragging a large arm-chair to the opposite end of the room, so as to command us all three, in the character of a public speaker addressing an audience. Having turned the chair with its back towards us, he jumped into it on his knees, and excitedly addressed his small congregation of three from an impromptu pulpit.

'Now, my good dears,' began Pesca (who always said 'good dears' when he meant 'worthy friends'), 'listen to me. The time has come – I recite my good news – I speak at last.'

'Hear, hear!' said my mother, humouring the joke.

'The next thing he will break, mamma,' whispered Sarah, 'will be the back of the best armchair.'

'I go back into my life, and I address myself to the noblest of created beings,' continued Pesca, vehemently apostrophising my unworthy self over the top rail of the chair. 'Who found me dead at the bottom of the sea (through Cramp); and who pulled me up to the top; and what did I say when I got into my own life and my own clothes again?'

'Much more than was at all necessary,' I answered as doggedly as possible; for the least encouragement in connection with this subject invariably let loose the Professor's emotions in a flood of tears.

'I said,' persisted Pesca, 'that my life belonged to my dear friend, Walter, for the rest of my days – and so it does. I said that I should never be happy again till I had found the opportunity of doing a good Something for Walter – and I have never been contented with myself till this most blessed day. Now,' cried the enthusiastic little man at the top of his voice, 'the overflowing happiness bursts out of me at every pore of my skin, like a perspiration; for on my faith, and soul, and honour, the something is done at last, and the only word to say now is – Right-all-right!'

It may be necessary to explain here that Pesca prided himself on being a perfect Englishman in his language, as well as in his dress, manners, and amusements. Having picked up a few of our most familiar colloquial expressions, he scattered them about over his conversation whenever they happened to occur to him, turning them, in his high relish for their sound and his general ignorance of their sense, into compound words and repetitions of his own, and always running them into each other, as if they consisted of one long syllable.

'Among the fine London Houses where I teach the language of my native country,' said the Professor, rushing into his long-deferred explanation without another word of preface, 'there is one, mighty fine, in the big place called Portland. You all know where that is? Yes, yes – course-of-course. The fine house, my good dears, has got inside it a fine family. A Mamma, fair and fat; three young Misses, fair and fat; two young Misters, fair and fat; and a Papa, the fairest and the fattest of all, who is a mighty merchant, up to his eyes in gold – a fine man once, but seeing that he has got a naked head and two chins, fine no longer at the present time. Now mind! I teach the sublime Dante to the young Misses, and ah! – my-soul-bless-my-soul! – it is not in human language to say how the sublime Dante puzzles the pretty heads of all three! No matter – all in good time – and the more lessons the better for me. Now mind! Imagine to yourselves that I am teaching the young Misses today, as usual. We are all four of us down together in the Hell of Dante. At the Seventh Circle – but no matter for that: all the Circles are alike to the three young Misses, fair and fat, – at the Seventh Circle, nevertheless, my pupils are sticking fast; and I, to set them going again, recite, explain, and blow myself up red-hot with useless enthusiasm, when – a creak of boots in the passage outside, and in comes the golden Papa, the mighty merchant with the naked head and the two chins. – Ha! my good dears, I am closer than you think for to the business, now. Have you been patient so far? or have you said to yourselves, "Deuce-what-the-deuce! Pesca is long-winded tonight?"'

We declared that we were deeply interested. The Professor went on:

'In his hand, the golden Papa has a letter; and after he has made his excuse for disturbing us in our Infernal Region with the common mortal Business of the house, he addresses himself to the three young Misses, and begins, as you English begin everything in this blessed world that you have to say, with a great O. "O, my dears," says the mighty merchant, "I have got here a letter from my friend, Mr—" (the name has slipped out of my mind; but no matter; we shall come back to that; yes, yes – right-all-right). So the Papa says, "I have got a letter from my friend, the Mister; and he wants a recommend from me, of a drawing-master, to go down to his house in the country." My-soul-bless-my-soul! when I heard the golden Papa say those words, if I had been big enough to reach up to him, I should have put my arms round his neck, and pressed him to my bosom in a long and grateful hug! As it was, I only bounced upon my chair. My seat was on thorns, and my soul was on fire to speak but I held my tongue, and let Papa go on. "Perhaps you know," says this good man of money, twiddling his friend's letter this way and that, in his golden fingers and thumbs, "perhaps you know, my dears, of a drawing-master that I can recommend?" The three young Misses all look at each other, and then say (with the indispensable great O to begin) "O, dear no, Papa! But here is Mr Pesca – " At the mention of myself I can hold no longer – the thought of you, my good dears, mounts like blood to my head – I start from my seat, as if a spike had grown up from the ground through the bottom of my chair – I address myself to the mighty merchant, and I say (English phrase) "Dear sir, I have the man! The first and foremost drawing-master of the world! Recommend him by the post tonight, and send him off, bag and baggage (English phrase again – ha!), send him off, bag and baggage, by the train tomorrow!" "Stop, stop," says Papa; "is he a foreigner, or an Englishman?" "English to the bone of his back," I answer. "Respectable?" says Papa. "Sir," I say (for this last question of his outrages me, and I have

done being familiar with him) – "Sir! the immortal fire of genius burns in
this Englishman's bosom, and, what is more, his father had it before him!"
"Never mind," says the golden barbarian of a Papa, "never mind about his
genius, Mr Pesca. We don't want genius in this country, unless it is accompanied by respectability – and then we are very glad to have it, very glad
indeed. Can your friend produce testimonials – letters that speak to his
character?" I wave my hand negligently. "Letters?" I say. "Ha! my-soul-
bless-my-soul! I should think so, indeed! Volumes of letters and portfolios
of testimonials, if you like!" "One or two will do," says this man of phlegm
and money. "Let him send them to me, with his name and address.
And – stop, stop, Mr Pesca – before you go to your friend, you had better
take a note." "Bank-note!" I say, indignantly. "No bank-note, if you please,
till my brave Englishman has earned it first." "Bank-note!" says Papa, in
a great surprise, "who talked of bank-note? I mean a note of the terms – a
memorandum of what he is expected to do. Go on with your lesson, Mr
Pesca, and I will give you the necessary extract from my friend's letter."
Down sits the man of merchandise and money to his pen, ink, and paper;
and down I go once again into the Hell of Dante, with my three young
Misses after me. In ten minutes' time the note is written, and the boots of
Papa are creaking themselves away in the passage outside. From that
moment, on my faith, and soul, and honour, I know nothing more! The
glorious thought that I have caught my opportunity at last, and that my
grateful service for my dearest friend in the world is as good as done
already, flies up into my head and makes me drunk. How I pull my young
Misses and myself out of our Infernal Region again, how my other business
is done afterwards, how my little bit of dinner slides itself down my throat,
I know no more than a man in the moon. Enough for me, that here I
am, with the mighty merchant's note in my hand, as large as life, as hot
as fire, and as happy as a king! Ha! ha! ha! right-right-right-all-right!'
Here the Professor waved the memorandum of terms over his head, and
ended his long and voluble narrative with his shrill Italian parody on an
English cheer.

My mother rose the moment he had done, with flushed cheeks and brightened eyes. She caught the little man warmly by both hands. 'My dear, good
Pesca,' she said, 'I never doubted your true affection for Walter – but I am
more than ever persuaded of it now!'

'I am sure we are very much obliged to Professor Pesca, for Walter's
sake,' added Sarah. She half rose, while she spoke, as if to approach the
arm-chair, in her turn; but, observing that Pesca was rapturously kissing my
mother's hands, looked serious, and resumed her seat. 'If the familiar little
man treats my mother in that way, how will he treat *me*?' Faces sometimes

tell truth; and that was unquestionably the thought in Sarah's mind, as she sat down again.

Although I myself was gratefully sensible of the kindness of Pesca's motives, my spirits were hardly so much elevated as they ought to have been by the prospect of future employment now placed before me. When the Professor had quite done with my mother's hand, and when I had warmly thanked him for his interference on my behalf, I asked to be allowed to look at the note of terms which his respectable patron had drawn up for my inspection.

Pesca handed me the paper, with a triumphant flourish of the hand.

'Read!' said the little man majestically. 'I promise you my friend, the writing of the golden Papa speaks with a tongue of trumpets for itself.'

The note of terms was plain, straightforward, and comprehensive, at any rate. It informed me,

First, That Frederick Fairlie, Esquire, of Limmeridge House, Cumberland, wanted to engage the services of a thoroughly competent drawing-master, for a period of four months certain.

Secondly, That the duties which the master was expected to perform would be of a twofold kind. He was to superintend the instruction of two young ladies in the art of painting in water-colours; and he was to devote his leisure time, afterwards, to the business of repairing and mounting a valuable collection of drawings, which had been suffered to fall into a condition of total neglect.

Thirdly, That the terms offered to the person who should undertake and properly perform these duties were four guineas a week; that he was to reside at Limmeridge House; and that he was to be treated there on the footing of a gentleman.

Fourthly, and lastly, That no person need think of applying for this situation unless he could furnish the most unexceptionable references to character and abilities. The references were to be sent to Mr Fairlie's friend in London, who was empowered to conclude all necessary arrangements. These instructions were followed by the name and address of Pesca's employer in Portland Place – and there the note, or memorandum, ended.

The prospect which this offer of an engagement held out was certainly an attractive one. The employment was likely to be both easy and agreeable; it was proposed to me at the autumn time of the year when I was least occupied; and the terms, judging by my personal experience in my profession, were surprisingly liberal. I knew this; I knew that I ought to consider myself very fortunate if I succeeded in securing the offered employment – and yet, no sooner had I read the memorandum than I felt an inexplicable unwillingness within me to stir in the matter. I had never in the whole of my previous experience found my duty and my inclination so painfully and so unaccountably at variance as I found them now.

'Oh, Walter, your father never had such a chance as this!' said my mother, when she had read the note of terms and had handed it back to me.

'Such distinguished people to know,' remarked Sarah, straightening herself in the chair; 'and on such gratifying terms of equality too!'

'Yes, yes; the terms, in every sense, are tempting enough,' I replied impatiently. 'But before I send in my testimonials, I should like a little time to consider—'

'Consider!' exclaimed my mother. 'Why, Walter, what is the matter with you?'

'Consider!' echoed my sister. 'What a very extraordinary thing to say, under the circumstances!'

'Consider!' chimed in the Professor. 'What is there to consider about? Answer me this! Have you not been complaining of your health, and have you not been longing for what you call a smack of the country breeze? Well! there in your hand is the paper that offers you perpetual choking mouthfuls of country breeze for four months' time. Is it not so? Ha! Again – you want money. Well! Is four golden guineas a week nothing? My-soul-bless-my-soul! only give it to *me* – and my boots shall creak like the golden Papa's, with a sense of the overpowering richness of the man who walks in them! Four guineas a week, and, more than that, the charming society of two young misses! and, more than that, your bed, your breakfast, your dinner, your gorging English teas and lunches and drinks of foaming beer, all for nothing – why, Walter, my dear good friend – deuce-what-the-deuce! – for the first time in my life I have not eyes enough in my head to look, and wonder at you!'

Neither my mother's evident astonishment at my behaviour, nor Pesca's fervid enumeration of the advantages offered to me by the new employment, had any effect in shaking my unreasonable disinclination to go to Limmeridge House. After starting all the petty objections that I could think of to going to Cumberland, and after hearing them answered, one after another, to my own complete discomfiture, I tried to set up a last obstacle by asking what was to become of my pupils in London while I was teaching Mr Fairlie's young ladies to sketch from nature. The obvious answer to this was, that the greater part of them would be away on their autumn travels, and that the few who remained at home might be confided to the care of one of my brother drawing-masters, whose pupils I had once taken off his hands under similar circumstances. My sister reminded me that this gentleman had expressly placed his services at my disposal, during the present season, in case I wished to leave town; my mother seriously appealed to me not to let an idle caprice stand in the way of my own interests and my own health;

and Pesca piteously entreated that I would not wound him to the heart by rejecting the first grateful offer of service that he had been able to make to the friend who had saved his life.

The evident sincerity and affection which inspired these remonstrances would have influenced any man with an atom of good feeling in his composition. Though I could not conquer my own unaccountable perversity, I had at least virtue enough to be heartily ashamed of it, and to end the discussion pleasantly by giving way, and promising to do all that was wanted of me.

The rest of the evening passed merrily enough in humorous anticipations of my coming life with the two young ladies in Cumberland. Pesca, inspired by our national grog, which appeared to get into his head, in the most marvellous manner, five minutes after it had gone down his throat, asserted his claims to be considered a complete Englishman by making a series of speeches in rapid succession, proposing my mother's health, my sister's health, my health, and the healths, in mass, of Mr Fairlie and the two young Misses, pathetically returning thanks himself, immediately afterwards, for the whole party. 'A secret, Walter,' said my little friend confidentially, as we walked home together. 'I am flushed by the recollection of my own eloquence. My soul bursts itself with ambition. One of these days I go into your noble Parliament. It is the dream of my whole life to be Honourable Pesca, M.P.!'

The next morning I sent my testimonials to the Professor's employer in Portland Place. Three days passed, and I concluded, with secret satisfaction, that my papers had not been found sufficiently explicit. On the fourth day, however, an answer came. It announced that Mr Fairlie accepted my services, and requested me to start for Cumberland immediately. All the necessary instructions for my journey were carefully and clearly added in a postscript.

I made my arrangements, unwillingly enough, for leaving London early the next day. Towards evening Pesca looked in, on his way to a dinner-party, to bid me good-bye.

'I shall dry my tears in your absence,' said the Professor gaily, 'with this glorious thought. It is my auspicious hand that has given the first push to your fortune in the world. Go, my friend! When your sun shines in Cumberland (English proverb), in the name of heaven make your hay. Marry one of the two young Misses; become Honourable Hartright, M.P.; and when you are on the top of the ladder remember that Pesca, at the bottom, has done it all!'

I tried to laugh with my little friend over his parting jest, but my spirits were not to be commanded. Something jarred in me almost painfully while he was speaking his light farewell words.

When I was left alone again nothing remained to be done but to walk to the Hampstead cottage and bid my mother and Sarah good-bye.

IV

The heat had been painfully oppressive all day, and it was now a close and sultry night.

My mother and sister had spoken so many last words, and had begged me to wait another five minutes so many times, that it was nearly midnight when the servant locked the garden-gate behind me. I walked forward a few paces on the shortest way back to London, then stopped and hesitated.

The moon was full and broad in the dark blue starless sky, and the broken ground of the heath looked wild enough in the mysterious light to be hundreds of miles away from the great city that lay beneath it. The idea of descending any sooner than I could help into the heat and gloom of London repelled me. The prospect of going to bed in my airless chambers, and the prospect of gradual suffocation, seemed, in my present restless frame of mind and body, to be one and the same thing. I determined to stroll home in the purer air by the most roundabout way I could take; to follow the white winding paths across the lonely heath; and to approach London through its most open suburb by striking into the Finchley Road, and so getting back, in the cool of the new morning, by the western side of the Regent's Park.

I wound my way down slowly over the heath, enjoying the divine still-ness of the scene, and admiring the soft alternations of light and shade as they followed each other over the broken ground on every side of me. So long as I was proceeding through this first and prettiest part of my night walk my mind remained passively open to the impressions produced by the view; and I thought but little on any subject – indeed, so far as my own sensations were concerned, I can hardly say that I thought at all.

But when I had left the heath and had turned into the by-road, where there was less to see, the ideas naturally engendered by the approaching change in my habits and occupations gradually drew more and more of my attention exclusively to themselves. By the time I had arrived at the end of the road I had become completely absorbed in my own fanciful visions of Limmeridge House, of Mr Fairlie, and of the two ladies whose practice in the art of water-colour painting I was so soon to superintend.

I had now arrived at that particular point of my walk where four roads met – the road to Hampstead, along which I had returned, the road to Finchley, the road to West End, and the road back to London. I had mechanically turned in this latter direction, and was strolling along the lonely high-road – idly wondering, I remember, what the Cumberland young ladies would look like – when, in one moment, every drop of blood in my body was brought to a stop by the touch of a hand laid lightly and suddenly on my shoulder from behind me.

I turned on the instant, with my fingers tightening round the handle of my stick.

There, in the middle of the broad bright high-road – there, as if it had that moment sprung out of the earth or dropped from the heaven – stood the figure of a solitary Woman, dressed from head to foot in white garments, her face bent in grave inquiry on mine, her hand pointing to the dark cloud over London, as I faced her.

I was far too seriously startled by the suddenness with which this extraordinary apparition stood before me, in the dead of night and in that lonely place, to ask what she wanted. The strange woman spoke first.

'Is that the road to London?' she said.

I looked attentively at her, as she put that singular question to me. It was then nearly one o'clock. All I could discern distinctly by the moonlight was a colourless, youthful face, meagre and sharp to look at about the cheeks and chin; large, grave, wistfully attentive eyes; nervous, uncertain lips; and light hair of a pale, brownish-yellow hue. There was nothing wild, nothing immodest in her manner: it was quiet and self-controlled, a little melancholy and a little touched by suspicion; not exactly the manner of a lady, and, at the same time, not the manner of a woman in the humblest rank of life. The voice, little as I had yet heard of it, had something curiously still and mechanical in its tones, and the utterance was remarkably rapid. She held a small bag in her hand: and her dress – bonnet, shawl, and gown all of white – was, so far as I could guess, certainly not composed of very delicate or very expensive materials. Her figure was slight, and rather above the average height – her gait and actions free from the slightest approach to extravagance. This was all that I could observe of her in the dim light and under the perplexingly strange circumstances of our meeting. What sort of a woman she was, and how she came to be out alone in the high-road, an hour after midnight, I altogether failed to guess. The one thing of which I felt certain was, that the grossest of mankind could not have misconstrued her motive in speaking, even at that suspiciously late hour and in that suspiciously lonely place.

'Did you hear me?' she said, still quietly and rapidly, and without the least fretfulness or impatience. 'I asked if that was the way to London.'

'Yes,' I replied, 'that is the way: it leads to St. John's Wood and the Regent's Park. You must excuse my not answering you before. I was rather startled by your sudden appearance in the road; and I am, even now, quite unable to account for it.'

'You don't suspect me of doing anything wrong, do you? I have done nothing wrong. I have met with an accident – I am very unfortunate in being here alone so late. Why do you suspect me of doing wrong?'

She spoke with unnecessary earnestness and agitation, and shrank back from me several paces. I did my best to reassure her.

'Pray don't suppose that I have any idea of suspecting you,' I said, 'or any other wish than to be of assistance to you, if I can. I only wondered at your appearance in the road, because it seemed to me to be empty the instant before I saw you.'

She turned, and pointed back to a place at the junction of the road to London and the road to Hampstead, where there was a gap in the hedge.

'I heard you coming,' she said, 'and hid there to see what sort of man you were, before I risked speaking. I doubted and feared about it till you passed; and then I was obliged to steal after you, and touch you.'

Steal after me and touch me? Why not call to me? Strange, to say the least of it.

'May I trust you?' she asked. 'You don't think the worse of me because I have met with an accident?' She stopped in confusion; shifted her bag from one hand to the other; and sighed bitterly.

The loneliness and helplessness of the woman touched me. The natural impulse to assist her and to spare her got the better of the judgment, the caution, the worldly tact, which an older, wiser, and colder man might have summoned to help him in this strange emergency.

'You may trust me for any harmless purpose,' I said. 'If it troubles you to explain your strange situation to me, don't think of returning to the subject again. I have no right to ask you for any explanations. Tell me how I can help you; and if I can, I will.'

'You are very kind, and I am very, very thankful to have met you.' The first touch of womanly tenderness that I had heard from her trembled in her voice as she said the words; but no tears glistened in those large, wistfully attentive eyes of hers, which were still fixed on me. 'I have only been in London once before,' she went on, more and more rapidly, 'and I know nothing about that side of it, yonder. Can I get a fly, or a carriage of any kind? Is it too late? I don't know. If you could show me where to get a fly – and if you will only promise not to interfere with me, and to let me leave you, when and how I please – I have a friend in London who will be glad to receive me – I want nothing else – will you promise?'

She looked anxiously up and down the road; shifted her bag again from one hand to the other; repeated the words, 'Will you promise?' and looked hard in my face, with a pleading fear and confusion that it troubled me to see.

What could I do? Here was a stranger utterly and helplessly at my mercy – and that stranger a forlorn woman. No house was near; no one was passing whom I could consult; and no earthly right existed on my part to give me a power of control over her, even if I had known how to exercise it. I trace these lines, self-distrustfully, with the shadows of after-events darkening the very paper I write on; and still I say, what could I do?

What I did do, was to try and gain time by questioning her.

'Are you sure that your friend in London will receive you at such a late hour as this?' I said.

'Quite sure. Only say you will let me leave you when and how I please – only say you won't interfere with me. Will you promise?'

As she repeated the words for the third time, she came close to me and laid her hand, with a sudden gentle stealthiness, on my bosom – a thin hand; a cold hand (when I removed it with mine) even on that sultry night. Remember that I was young; remember that the hand which touched me was a woman's.

'Will you promise?'

'Yes.'

One word! The little familiar word that is on everybody's lips, every hour in the day. Oh me! and I tremble, now, when I write it.

We set our faces towards London, and walked on together in the first still hour of the new day – I, and this woman, whose name, whose character, whose story, whose objects in life, whose very presence by my side, at that moment, were fathomless mysteries to me. It was like a dream. Was I Walter Hartright? Was this the well-known, uneventful road, where holiday people strolled on Sundays? Had I really left, little more than an hour since, the quiet, decent, conventionally domestic atmosphere of my mother's cottage? I was too bewildered – too conscious also of a vague sense of something like self-reproach – to speak to my strange companion for some minutes. It was her voice again that first broke the silence between us.

'I want to ask you something,' she said suddenly. 'Do you know many people in London?'

'Yes, a great many.'

'Many men of rank and title?' There was an unmistakable tone of suspicion in the strange question. I hesitated about answering it.

'Some,' I said, after a moment's silence.

'Many' – she came to a full stop, and looked me searchingly in the face— 'many men of the rank of Baronet?'

Too much astonished to reply, I questioned her in my turn.

'Why do you ask?'

'Because I hope, for my own sake, there is one Baronet that you don't know.'

'Will you tell me his name?'

'I can't – I daren't – I forget myself when I mention it.' She spoke loudly and almost fiercely, raised her clenched hand in the air, and shook it passionately; then, on a sudden, controlled herself again, and added, in tones lowered to a whisper 'Tell me which of them *you* know.'

I could hardly refuse to humour her in such a trifle, and I mentioned three names. Two, the names of fathers of families whose daughters I taught; one, the name of a bachelor who had once taken me a cruise in his yacht, to make sketches for him.

'Ah! you *don't* know him,' she said, with a sigh of relief. 'Are you a man of rank and title yourself?'

'Far from it. I am only a drawing-master.'

As the reply passed my lips – a little bitterly, perhaps – she took my arm with the abruptness which characterised all her actions.

'Not a man of rank and title,' she repeated to herself. 'Thank God! I may trust *him*.'

I had hitherto contrived to master my curiosity out of consideration for my companion; but it got the better of me now.

'I am afraid you have serious reason to complain of some man of rank and title?' I said. 'I am afraid the baronet, whose name you are unwilling to mention to me, has done you some grievous wrong? Is he the cause of your being out here at this strange time of night?'

'Don't ask me: don't make me talk of it,' she answered. 'I'm not fit now. I have been cruelly used and cruelly wronged. You will be kinder than ever, if you will walk on fast, and not speak to me. I sadly want to quiet myself, if I can.'

We moved forward again at a quick pace; and for half an hour, at least, not a word passed on either side. From time to time, being forbidden to make any more inquiries, I stole a look at her face. It was always the same; the lips close shut, the brow frowning, the eyes looking straight forward, eagerly and yet absently. We had reached the first houses, and were close on the new Wesleyan college, before her set features relaxed and she spoke once more.

'Do you live in London?' she said.

'Yes.' As I answered, it struck me that she might have formed some intention of appealing to me for assistance or advice, and that I ought to spare her a possible disappointment by warning her of my approaching absence from home. So I added, 'But tomorrow I shall be away from London for some time. I am going into the country.'

'Where?' she asked. 'North or south?'

'North – to Cumberland.'

'Cumberland!' she repeated the word tenderly. 'Ah! I wish I was going there too. I was once happy in Cumberland.'

I tried again to lift the veil that hung between this woman and me.

'Perhaps you were born,' I said, 'in the beautiful Lake country.'

'No,' she answered. 'I was born in Hampshire; but I once went to school for a little while in Cumberland. Lakes? I don't remember any lakes. It's Limmeridge village, and Limmeridge House, I should like to see again.'

It was my turn now to stop suddenly. In the excited state of my curiosity, at that moment, the chance reference to Mr Fairlie's place of residence, on the lips of my strange companion, staggered me with astonishment.

'Did you hear anybody calling after us?' she asked, looking up and down the road affrightedly, the instant I stopped.

'No, no. I was only struck by the name of Limmeridge House. I heard it mentioned by some Cumberland people a few days since.'

'Ah! not *my* people. Mrs Fairlie is dead; and her husband is dead; and their little girl may be married and gone away by this time. I can't say who lives at Limmeridge now. If any more are left there of that name, I only know I love them for Mrs Fairlie's sake.'

She seemed about to say more; but while she was speaking, we came within view of the turnpike, at the top of the Avenue Road. Her hand tightened round my arm, and she looked anxiously at the gate before us.

'Is the turnpike man looking out?' she asked.

He was not looking out; no one else was near the place when we passed through the gate. The sight of the gas-lamps and houses seemed to agitate her, and to make her impatient.

'This is London,' she said. 'Do you see any carriage I can get? I am tired and frightened. I want to shut myself in and be driven away.'

I explained to her that we must walk a little further to get to a cab-stand, unless we were fortunate enough to meet with an empty vehicle; and then tried to resume the subject of Cumberland. It was useless. That idea of shutting herself in, and being driven away, had now got full possession of her mind. She could think and talk of nothing else.

We had hardly proceeded a third of the way down the Avenue Road when I saw a cab draw up at a house a few doors below us, on the opposite side of the way. A gentleman got out and let himself in at the garden door. I hailed the cab, as the driver mounted the box again. When we crossed the road, my companion's impatience increased to such an extent that she almost forced me to run.

'It's so late,' she said. 'I am only in a hurry because it's so late.'

'I can't take you, sir, if you're not going towards Tottenham Court Road,' said the driver civilly, when I opened the cab door. 'My horse is dead beat, and I can't get him no further than the stable.'

'Yes, yes. That will do for me. I'm going that way – I'm going that way.' She spoke with breathless eagerness, and pressed by me into the cab.

I had assured myself that the man was sober as well as civil before I let her enter the vehicle. And now, when she was seated inside, I entreated her to let me see her set down safely at her destination.

'No, no, no,' she said vehemently. 'I'm quite safe, and quite happy now. If you are a gentleman, remember your promise. Let him drive on till I stop him. Thank you – oh! thank you, thank you!'

My hand was on the cab door. She caught it in hers, kissed it, and pushed it away. The cab drove off at the same moment – I started into the road, with some vague idea of stopping it again, I hardly knew why – hesitated from dread of frightening and distressing her – called, at last, but not loudly enough to attract the driver's attention. The sound of the wheels grew fainter in the distance – the cab melted into the black shadows on the road – the woman in white was gone.

Ten minutes or more had passed. I was still on the same side of the way; now mechanically walking forward a few paces; now stopping again absently. At one moment I found myself doubting the reality of my own adventure; at another I was perplexed and distressed by an uneasy sense of having done wrong, which yet left me confusedly ignorant of how I could have done right. I hardly knew where I was going, or what I meant to do next; I was conscious of nothing but the confusion of my own thoughts, when I was abruptly recalled to myself – awakened, I might almost say – by the sound of rapidly approaching wheels close behind me.

I was on the dark side of the road, in the thick shadow of some garden trees, when I stopped to look round. On the opposite and lighter side of the way, a short distance below me, a policeman was strolling along in the direction of the Regent's Park.

The carriage passed me – an open chaise driven by two men.

'Stop!' cried one. 'There's a policeman. Let's ask him.'

The horse was instantly pulled up, a few yards beyond the dark place where I stood.

'Policeman!' cried the first speaker. 'Have you seen a woman pass this way?'

'What sort of woman, sir?'

'A woman in a lavender-coloured gown—'

'No, no,' interposed the second man. 'The clothes we gave her were found on her bed. She must have gone away in the clothes she wore when she came to us. In white, policeman. A woman in white.'

'I haven't seen her, sir.'

'If you or any of your men meet with the woman, stop her, and send her in careful keeping to that address. I'll pay all expenses, and a fair reward into the bargain.'

The policeman looked at the card that was handed down to him.

'Why are we to stop her, sir? What has she done?'

'Done! She has escaped from my Asylum. Don't forget; a woman in white. Drive on.'

V

'She has escaped from my Asylum!'

I cannot say with truth that the terrible inference which those words suggested flashed upon me like a new revelation. Some of the strange questions put to me by the woman in white, after my ill-considered promise to leave her free to act as she pleased, had suggested the conclusion either that she was naturally flighty and unsettled, or that some recent shock of terror had disturbed the balance of her faculties. But the idea of absolute insanity which we all associate with the very name of an Asylum, had, I can honestly declare, never occurred to me, in connection with her. I had seen nothing, in her language or her actions, to justify it at the time; and even with the new light thrown on her by the words which the stranger had addressed to the policeman, I could see nothing to justify it now.

What had I done? Assisted the victim of the most horrible of all false imprisonments to escape; or cast loose on the wide world of London an unfortunate creature, whose actions it was my duty, and every man's duty, mercifully to control? I turned sick at heart when the question occurred to me, and when I felt self-reproachfully that it was asked too late.

In the disturbed state of my mind, it was useless to think of going to bed, when I at last got back to my chambers in Clement's Inn. Before many hours elapsed it would be necessary to start on my journey to Cumberland. I sat down and tried, first to sketch, then to read – but the woman in white got between me and my pencil, between me and my book. Had the forlorn creature come to any harm? That was my first thought, though I shrank selfishly from confronting it. Other thoughts followed, on which it was less harrowing to dwell. Where had she stopped the cab? What had become of her now? Had she been traced and captured by the men in the chaise? Or was she still capable of controlling her own actions; and were we two following our widely parted roads towards one point in the mysterious future, at which we were to meet once more?

It was a relief when the hour came to lock my door, to bid farewell to London pursuits, London pupils, and London friends, and to be in movement again towards new interests and a new life. Even the bustle and confusion at the railway terminus, so wearisome and bewildering at other times, roused me and did me good.

My travelling instructions directed me to go to Carlisle, and then to diverge by a branch railway which ran in the direction of the coast. As a misfortune to begin with, our engine broke down between Lancaster and Carlisle. The delay occasioned by this accident caused me to be too late for the branch train, by which I was to have gone on immediately. I had to wait some hours; and when a later train finally deposited me at the nearest station to Limmeridge House, it was past ten, and the night was so dark that I could hardly see my way to the pony-chaise which Mr Fairlie had ordered to be in waiting for me.

The driver was evidently discomposed by the lateness of my arrival. He was in that state of highly respectful sulkiness which is peculiar to English servants. We drove away slowly through the darkness in perfect silence. The roads were bad, and the dense obscurity of the night increased the difficulty of getting over the ground quickly. It was, by my watch, nearly an hour and a half from the time of our leaving the station before I heard the sound of the sea in the distance, and the crunch of our wheels on a smooth gravel drive. We had passed one gate before entering the drive, and we passed another before we drew up at the house. I was received by a solemn man-servant out of livery, was informed that the family had retired for the night, and was then led into a large and lofty room where my supper was awaiting me, in a forlorn manner, at one extremity of a lonesome mahogany wilderness of dining-table.

I was too tired and out of spirits to eat or drink much, especially with the solemn servant waiting on me as elaborately as if a small dinner party had arrived at the house instead of a solitary man. In a quarter of an hour I was ready to be taken up to my bedchamber. The solemn servant conducted me into a prettily furnished room – said, 'Breakfast at nine o'clock, sir' – looked all round him to see that everything was in its proper place, and noiselessly withdrew.

'What shall I see in my dreams tonight?' I thought to myself, as I put out the candle; 'the woman in white? or the unknown inhabitants of this Cumberland mansion?' It was a strange sensation to be sleeping in the house, like a friend of the family, and yet not to know one of the inmates, even by sight!

VI

When I rose the next morning and drew up my blind, the sea opened before me joyously under the broad August sunlight, and the distant coast of Scotland fringed the horizon with its lines of melting blue.

The view was such a surprise, and such a change to me, after my weary London experience of brick and mortar landscape, that I seemed to burst into a new life and a new set of thoughts the moment I looked at it. A confused sensation of having suddenly lost my familiarity with the past, without acquiring any additional clearness of idea in reference to the present or the future, took possession of my mind. Circumstances that were but a few days old faded back in my memory, as if they had happened months and months since. Pesca's quaint announcement of the means by which he had procured me my present employment; the farewell evening I had passed with my mother and sister; even my mysterious adventure on the way home from Hampstead – had all become like events which might have occurred at some former epoch of my existence. Although the woman in white was still in my mind, the image of her seemed to have grown dull and faint already.

A little before nine o'clock, I descended to the ground-floor of the house. The solemn man-servant of the night before met me wandering among the passages, and compassionately showed me the way to the breakfast-room.

My first glance round me, as the man opened the door, disclosed a well-furnished breakfast-table, standing in the middle of a long room, with many windows in it. I looked from the table to the window farthest from me, and saw a lady standing at it, with her back turned towards me. The instant my eyes rested on her, I was struck by the rare beauty of her form, and by the unaffected grace of her attitude. Her figure was tall, yet not too tall; comely and well-developed, yet not fat; her head set on her shoulders with an easy, pliant firmness; her waist, perfection in the eyes of a man, for it occupied its natural place, it filled out its natural circle, it was visibly and delightfully undeformed by stays. She had not heard my entrance into the room; and I allowed myself the luxury of admiring her for a few moments, before I moved one of the chairs near me, as the least embarrassing means of attracting her attention. She turned towards me immediately. The easy elegance of every movement of her limbs and body as soon as she began to advance from the far end of the room, set me in a flutter of expectation to see her face clearly. She left the window – and I said to myself, The

lady is dark. She moved forward a few steps – and I said to myself, The
lady is young. She approached nearer – and I said to myself (with a sense
of surprise which words fail me to express), The lady is ugly!

Never was the old conventional maxim, that Nature cannot err, more flatly
contradicted – never was the fair promise of a lovely figure more strangely
and startlingly belied by the face and head that crowned it. The lady's
complexion was almost swarthy, and the dark down on her upper lip was
almost a moustache. She had a large, firm, masculine mouth and jaw; prominent, piercing, resolute brown eyes; and thick, coal-black hair, growing
unusually low down on her forehead. Her expression – bright, frank, and
intelligent – appeared, while she was silent, to be altogether wanting in those
feminine attractions of gentleness and pliability, without which the beauty
of the handsomest woman alive is beauty incomplete. To see such a face as
this set on shoulders that a sculptor would have longed to model – to be
charmed by the modest graces of action through which the symmetrical limbs
betrayed their beauty when they moved, and then to be almost repelled by
the masculine form and masculine look of the features in which the perfectly
shaped figure ended – was to feel a sensation oddly akin to the helpless
discomfort familiar to us all in sleep, when we recognise yet cannot reconcile
the anomalies and contradictions of a dream.

'Mr Hartright?' said the lady interrogatively, her dark face lighting up
with a smile, and softening and growing womanly the moment she began
to speak. 'We resigned all hope of you last night, and went to bed as
usual. Accept my apologies for our apparent want of attention; and allow
me to introduce myself as one of your pupils. Shall we shake hands? I
suppose we must come to it sooner or later – and why not sooner?'

These odd words of welcome were spoken in a clear, ringing, pleasant
voice. The offered hand – rather large, but beautifully formed – was given
to me with the easy, unaffected self-reliance of a highly-bred woman. We
sat down together at the breakfast-table in as cordial and customary a manner
as if we had known each other for years, and had met at Limmeridge House
to talk over old times by previous appointment.

'I hope you come here good-humouredly determined to make the best of
your position,' continued the lady. 'You will have to begin this morning by
putting up with no other company at breakfast than mine. My sister is in her
own room, nursing that essentially feminine malady, a slight headache; and
her old governess, Mrs Vesey, is charitably attending on her with restorative
tea. My uncle, Mr Fairlie, never joins us at any of our meals: he is an invalid,
and keeps bachelor state in his own apartments. There is nobody else in the
house but me. Two young ladies have been staying here, but they went away
yesterday, in despair; and no wonder. All through their visit (in consequence

of Mr Fairlie's invalid condition) we produced no such convenience in the house as a flirtable, danceable, small-talkable creature of the male sex; and the consequence was, we did nothing but quarrel, especially at dinner-time. How can you expect four women to dine together alone every day, and not quarrel? We are such fools, we can't entertain each other at table. You see I don't think much of my own sex, Mr Hartright – which will you have, tea or coffee? – no woman does think much of her own sex, although few of them confess it as freely as I do. Dear me, you look puzzled. Why? Are you wondering what you will have for breakfast? or are you surprised at my careless way of talking? In the first case, I advise you, as a friend, to have nothing to do with that cold ham at your elbow, and to wait till the omelette comes in. In the second case, I will give you some tea to compose your spirits, and do all a woman can (which is very little, by-the-bye) to hold my tongue.'

She handed me my cup of tea, laughing gaily. Her light flow of talk, and her lively familiarity of manner with a total stranger, were accompanied by an unaffected naturalness and an easy inborn confidence in herself and her position, which would have secured her the respect of the most audacious man breathing. While it was impossible to be formal and reserved in her company, it was more than impossible to take the faintest vestige of a liberty with her, even in thought. I felt this instinctively, even while I caught the infection of her own bright gaiety of spirits – even while I did my best to answer her in her own frank, lively way.

'Yes, yes,' she said, when I had suggested the only explanation I could offer, to account for my perplexed looks, 'I understand. You are such a perfect stranger in the house, that you are puzzled by my familiar references to the worthy inhabitants. Natural enough: I ought to have thought of it before. At any rate, I can set it right now. Suppose I begin with myself, so as to get done with that part of the subject as soon as possible? My name is Marian Halcombe; and I am as inaccurate as women usually are, in calling Mr Fairlie my uncle, and Miss Fairlie my sister. My mother was twice married: the first time to Mr Halcombe, my father; the second time to Mr Fairlie, my half-sister's father. Except that we are both orphans, we are in every respect as unlike each other as possible. My father was a poor man, and Miss Fairlie's father was a rich man. I have got nothing, and she has a fortune. I am dark and ugly, and she is fair and pretty. Everybody thinks me crabbed and odd (with perfect justice); and everybody thinks her sweet-tempered and charming (with more justice still). In short, she is an angel; and I am – Try some of that marmalade, Mr Hartright, and finish the sentence, in the name of female propriety, for yourself. What am I to tell you about Mr Fairlie? Upon my honour, I hardly know. He is sure to send for you after breakfast, and you can study him for yourself. In the meantime, I may inform you, first, that he is the late Mr Fairlie's younger brother; secondly, that he is a single man; and thirdly, that he is Miss Fairlie's guardian. I won't live without her, and she can't live without me; and that is how I come to be at Limmeridge House. My sister and I are honestly fond of each other; which, you will say, is perfectly unaccountable, under the circumstances, and I quite agree with you – but so it is. You must please both of us, Mr Hartright, or please neither of us: and, what is still more trying, you will be thrown entirely upon our society. Mrs Vesey is an excellent person, who possesses all the cardinal virtues, and counts for nothing; and Mr Fairlie is too great an invalid to be a companion for anybody. I don't know what is the matter with him, and the doctors don't know what is the matter with him, and he doesn't know himself what is the matter with him. We all say it's on the nerves, and we none of us know what we mean when we say it. However, I advise you to humour his little peculiarities, when you see him today. Admire his collection of coins, prints, and water-colour drawings, and you will win his heart. Upon my word, if you can be contented with a quiet country life, I don't see why you should not get on very well here. From breakfast to lunch, Mr Fairlie's drawings will occupy you. After lunch, Miss Fairlie and I shoulder our sketch-books, and go out to misrepresent Nature, under your directions. Drawing is *her* favourite whim, mind, not mine. Women can't draw – their minds are too flighty, and their eyes are too inattentive. No matter – my sister likes it; so I waste paint and spoil paper, for her sake, as composedly as any woman in England. As for the evenings, I think we can help you through them. Miss Fairlie plays delightfully. For my own poor part, I don't know one note of music from the other; but I can match you at chess, backgammon, écarté, and (with the inevitable female drawbacks) even at billiards as well. What do you think of the programme? Can you reconcile yourself to our quiet, regular life? or do you mean to be restless, and secretly thirst for change and adventure, in the humdrum atmosphere of Limmeridge House?'

She had run on thus far, in her gracefully bantering way, with no other interruptions on my part than the unimportant replies which politeness required of me. The turn of the expression, however, in her last question, or rather the one chance word, 'adventure,' lightly as it fell from her lips, recalled my thoughts to my meeting with the woman in white, and urged me to discover the connection which the stranger's own reference to Mrs Fairlie informed me must once have existed between the nameless fugitive from the Asylum, and the former mistress of Limmeridge House.

'Even if I were the most restless of mankind,' I said, 'I should be in no danger of thirsting after adventures for some time to come. The very night before I arrived at this house, I met with an adventure; and the wonder and excitement of it, I can assure you, Miss Halcombe, will last me for the whole term of my stay in Cumberland, if not for a much longer period.'

'You don't say so, Mr Hartright! May I hear it?'

'You have a claim to hear it. The chief person in the adventure was a total stranger to me, and may perhaps be a total stranger to you; but she certainly mentioned the name of the late Mrs Fairlie in terms of the sincerest gratitude and regard.'

'Mentioned my mother's name! You interest me indescribably. Pray go on.'

I at once related the circumstances under which I had met the woman in white, exactly as they had occurred; and I repeated what she had said to me about Mrs Fairlie and Limmeridge House, word for word.

Miss Halcombe's bright resolute eyes looked eagerly into mine, from the beginning of the narrative to the end. Her face expressed vivid interest and astonishment, but nothing more. She was evidently as far from knowing of any clue to the mystery as I was myself.

'Are you quite sure of those words referring to my mother?' she asked.

'Quite sure,' I replied. 'Whoever she may be, the woman was once at school in the village of Limmeridge, was treated with especial kindness by Mrs Fairlie, and, in grateful remembrance of that kindness, feels an affectionate interest in all surviving members of the family. She knew that Mrs Fairlie and her husband were both dead; and she spoke of Miss Fairlie as if they had known each other when they were children.'

'You said, I think, that she denied belonging to this place?'

'Yes, she told me she came from Hampshire.'

'And you entirely failed to find out her name?'

'Entirely.'

'Very strange. I think you were quite justified, Mr Hartright, in giving the poor creature her liberty, for she seems to have done nothing in your presence to show herself unfit to enjoy it. But I wish you had been a little more resolute about finding out her name. We must really clear up this mystery, in some way. You had better not speak of it yet to Mr Fairlie, or to my sister. They are both of them, I am certain, quite as ignorant of who the woman is, and of what her past history in connection with us can be, as I am myself. But they are also, in widely different ways, rather nervous and sensitive; and you would only fidget one and alarm the other to no purpose. As for myself, I am all aflame with curiosity, and I devote my whole energies to the business of discovery from this moment. When my mother came here, after her second marriage, she certainly established the village school just as it exists at the present time. But the old teachers are all dead, or gone elsewhere; and no enlightenment is to be hoped for from that quarter. The only other alternative I can think of—'

At this point we were interrupted by the entrance of the servant, with a message from Mr Fairlie, intimating that he would be glad to see me, as soon as I had done breakfast.

'Wait in the hall,' said Miss Halcombe, answering the servant for me, in her quick, ready way. 'Mr Hartright will come out directly. I was about to say,' she went on, addressing me again, 'that my sister and I have a large collection of my mother's letters, addressed to my father and to hers. In the absence of any other means of getting information, I will pass the morning in looking over my mother's correspondence with Mr Fairlie. He was fond of London, and was constantly away from his country home; and she was accustomed, at such times, to write and report to him how things went on at Limmeridge. Her letters are full of references to the school in which she took so strong an interest; and I think it more than likely that I may have discovered something when we meet again. The luncheon hour is two, Mr Hartright. I shall have the pleasure of introducing you to my sister by that time, and we will occupy the afternoon in driving round the neighbourhood and showing you all our pet points of view. Till two o'clock, then, farewell.'

She nodded to me with the lively grace, the delightful refinement of familiarity, which characterised all that she did and all that she said; and disappeared by a door at the lower end of the room. As soon as she had left me, I turned my steps towards the hall, and followed the servant, on my way, for the first time, to the presence of Mr Fairlie.

VII

My conductor led me upstairs into a passage which took us back to the bedchamber in which I had slept during the past night; and opening the door next to it, begged me to look in.

'I have my master's orders to show you your own sitting-room, sir,' said the man, 'and to inquire if you approve of the situation and the light.'

I must have been hard to please, indeed, if I had not approved of the room, and of everything about it. The bow-window looked out on the same lovely view which I had admired, in the morning, from my bedroom. The furniture was the perfection of luxury and beauty; the table in the centre was bright with gaily bound books, elegant conveniences for writing, and beautiful flowers; the second table, near the window, was covered with all the necessary materials for mounting water-colour drawings, and had a little easel attached to it, which I could expand or fold up at will; the walls were hung with gaily tinted chintz; and the floor was spread with Indian matting in maize-colour and red. It was the prettiest and most luxurious little sitting-room I had ever seen; and I admired it with the warmest enthusiasm.

The solemn servant was far too highly trained to betray the slightest satisfaction. He bowed with icy deference when my terms of eulogy were all exhausted, and silently opened the door for me to go out into the passage again.

We turned a corner, and entered a long second passage, ascended a short flight of stairs at the end, crossed a small circular upper hall, and stopped in front of a door covered with dark baize. The servant opened this door, and led me on a few yards to a second; opened that also, and disclosed two curtains of pale sea-green silk hanging before us; raised one of them noise-lessly; softly uttered the words, 'Mr Hartright,' and left me.

I found myself in a large, lofty room, with a magnificent carved ceiling, and with a carpet over the floor, so thick and soft that it felt like piles of velvet under my feet. One side of the room was occupied by a long book-case of some rare inlaid wood that was quite new to me. It was not more than six feet high, and the top was adorned with statuettes in marble, ranged at regular distances one from the other. On the opposite side stood two antique cabinets; and between them, and above them, hung a picture of the Virgin and Child, protected by glass, and bearing Raphael's name on the gilt tablet at the bottom of the frame. On my right hand and on my left, as I stood inside the door, were chiffoniers and little stands in buhl and marquetterie, loaded with figures in Dresden china, with rare vases, ivory ornaments, and toys and curiosities that sparkled at all points with gold, silver, and precious stones. At the lower end of the room, opposite to me, the windows were concealed and the sunlight was tempered by large blinds of the same pale sea-green colour as the curtains over the door. The light thus produced was deliciously soft, mysterious, and subdued; it fell equally upon all the objects in the room; it helped to intensify the deep silence, and the air of profound seclusion that possessed the place; and it surrounded, with an appropriate halo of repose, the solitary figure of the master of the house, leaning back, listlessly composed, in a large easy-chair, with a reading-easel fastened on one of its arms, and a little table on the other.

If a man's personal appearance, when he is out of his dressing-room, and when he has passed forty, can be accepted as a safe guide to his time of life – which is more than doubtful – Mr Fairlie's age, when I saw him, might have been reasonably computed at over fifty and under sixty years. His beardless face was thin, worn, and transparently pale, but not wrinkled; his nose was high and hooked; his eyes were of a dim greyish blue, large, prominent, and rather red round the rims of the eyelids; his hair was scanty, soft to look at, and of that light sandy colour which is the last to disclose its own changes towards grey. He was dressed in a dark frock-coat, of some substance much thinner than cloth, and in waistcoat and trousers of spotless white. His feet were effeminately small, and were clad in buff-coloured silk stockings, and little womanish bronze-leather slippers. Two rings adorned his white delicate hands, the value of which even my inexperienced observation detected to be all but priceless. Upon the whole, he had a frail, languidly-fretful, over-refined look – something singularly and unpleasantly delicate in its association with a man, and, at the same time, something which could by no possibility have looked natural and appropriate if it had been transferred to the personal appearance of a woman. My morning's experience of Miss Halcombe had predisposed me to be pleased with everybody in the house; but my sympathies shut themselves up resolutely at the first sight of Mr Fairlie.

On approaching nearer to him, I discovered that he was not so entirely without occupation as I had at first supposed. Placed amid the other rare and beautiful objects on a large round table near him, was a dwarf cabinet in ebony and silver, containing coins of all shapes and sizes, set out in little drawers lined with dark purple velvet. One of these drawers lay on the small table attached to his chair; and near it were some tiny jeweller's brushes, a wash-leather 'stump', and a little bottle of liquid, all waiting to be used in various ways for the removal of any accidental impurities which might be discovered on the coins. His frail white fingers were listlessly toying with something which looked, to my uninstructed eyes, like a dirty pewter medal with ragged edges, when I advanced within a respectful distance of his chair, and stopped to make my bow.

'So glad to possess you at Limmeridge, Mr Hartright,' he said in a querulous, croaking voice, which combined, in anything but an agreeable manner, a discordantly high tone with a drowsily languid utterance. 'Pray sit down. And don't trouble yourself to move the chair, please. In the wretched state of my nerves, movement of any kind is exquisitely painful to me. Have you seen your studio? Will it do?'

'I have just come from seeing the room, Mr Fairlie; and I assure you—'

He stopped me in the middle of the sentence, by closing his eyes, and holding up one of his white hands imploringly. I paused in astonishment; and the croaking voice honoured me with this explanation –

'Pray excuse me. But *could* you contrive to speak in a lower key? In the wretched state of my nerves, loud sound of any kind is indescribable torture to me. You will pardon an invalid? I only say to you what the lamentable state of my health obliges me to say to everybody. Yes. And you really like the room?'

'I could wish for nothing prettier and nothing more comfortable,' I answered, dropping my voice, and beginning to discover already that Mr

Fairlie's selfish affectation and Mr Fairlie's wretched nerves meant one and the same thing.

'So glad. You will find your position here, Mr Hartright, properly recognised. There is none of the horrid English barbarity of feeling about the social position of an artist in this house. So much of my early life has been passed abroad, that I have quite cast my insular skin in that respect. I wish I could say the same of the gentry – detestable word, but I suppose I must use it – of the gentry in the neighbourhood. They are sad Goths in Art, Mr Hartright. People, I do assure you, who would have opened their eyes in astonishment, if they had seen Charles the Fifth pick up Titian's brush for him. Do you mind putting this tray of coins back in the cabinet, and giving me the next one to it? In the wretched state of my nerves, exertion of any kind is unspeakably disagreeable to me. Yes. Thank you.'

As a practical commentary on the liberal social theory which he had just favoured me by illustrating, Mr Fairlie's cool request rather amused me. I put back one drawer and gave him the other, with all possible politeness. He began trifling with the new set of coins and the little brushes immediately; languidly looking at them and admiring them all the time he was speaking to me.

'A thousand thanks and a thousand excuses. Do you like coins? Yes. So glad we have another taste in common besides our taste for Art. Now, about the pecuniary arrangements between us – do tell me – are they satisfactory?'

'Most satisfactory, Mr Fairlie.'

'So glad. And – what next? Ah! I remember. Yes. In reference to the consideration which you are good enough to accept for giving me the benefit of your accomplishments in art, my steward will wait on you at the end of the first week, to ascertain your wishes. And – what next? Curious, is it not? I had a great deal more to say: and I appear to have quite forgotten it. Do you mind touching the bell? In that corner. Yes. Thank you.'

I rang; and a new servant noiselessly made his appearance – a foreigner, with a set smile and perfectly brushed hair – a valet every inch of him.

'Louis,' said Mr Fairlie, dreamily dusting the tips of his fingers with one of the tiny brushes for the coins, 'I made some entries in my tablettes this morning. Find my tablettes. A thousand pardons, Mr Hartright, I'm afraid I bore you.'

As he wearily closed his eyes again, before I could answer, and as he did most assuredly bore me, I sat silent, and looked up at the Madonna and Child by Raphael. In the meantime, the valet left the room, and returned shortly with a little ivory book. Mr Fairlie, after first relieving himself by a gentle sigh, let the book drop open with one hand, and held up the tiny brush with the other, as a sign to the servant to wait for further orders.

'Yes. Just so!' said Mr Fairlie, consulting the tablettes. 'Louis, take down that portfolio.' He pointed, as he spoke, to several portfolios placed near the window, on mahogany stands. 'No. Not the one with the green back – that contains my Rembrandt etchings, Mr Hartright. Do you like etchings? Yes? So glad we have another taste in common. The portfolio with the red back, Louis. Don't drop it! You have no idea of the tortures I should suffer, Mr Hartright, if Louis dropped that portfolio. Is it safe on the chair? Do *you* think it safe, Mr Hartright? Yes? So glad. Will you oblige me by looking at the drawings, if you really think they are quite safe. Louis, go away. What an ass you are. Don't you see me holding the tablettes? Do you suppose I want to hold them? Then why not relieve me of the tablettes without being told? A thousand pardons, Mr Hartright; servants are such asses, are they not? Do tell me – what do you think of the drawings? They have come from a sale in a shocking state – I thought they smelt of horrid dealers' and brokers' fingers when I looked at them last. *Can* you undertake them?'

Although my nerves were not delicate enough to detect the odour of plebeian fingers which had offended Mr Fairlie's nostrils, my taste was sufficiently educated to enable me to appreciate the value of the drawings, while I turned them over. They were, for the most part, really fine specimens of English water-colour art; and they had deserved much better treatment at the hands of their former possessor than they appeared to have received.

'The drawings,' I answered, 'require careful straining and mounting; and, in my opinion, they are well worth—'

'I beg your pardon,' interposed Mr Fairlie. 'Do you mind my closing my eyes while you speak? Even this light is too much for them. Yes?'

'I was about to say that the drawings are well worth all the time and trouble—'

Mr Fairlie suddenly opened his eyes again, and rolled them with an expression of helpless alarm in the direction of the window.

'I entreat you to excuse me, Mr Hartright,' he said in a feeble flutter. 'But surely I hear some horrid children in the garden – my private garden – below?'

'I can't say, Mr Fairlie. I heard nothing myself.'

'Oblige me – you have been so very good in humouring my poor nerves – oblige me by lifting up a corner of the blind. Don't let the sun in on me, Mr Hartright! Have you got the blind up? Yes? Then will you be so very kind as to look into the garden and make quite sure?'

I complied with this new request. The garden was carefully walled in, all round. Not a human creature, large or small, appeared in any part of the sacred seclusion. I reported that gratifying fact to Mr Fairlie.

'A thousand thanks. My fancy, I suppose. There are no children, thank

Heaven, in the house; but the servants (persons born without nerves) will encourage the children from the village. Such brats – oh, dear me, such brats! Shall I confess it, Mr Hartright? – I sadly want a reform in the construction of children. Nature's only idea seems to be to make them machines for the production of incessant noise. Surely our delightful Raffaello's conception is infinitely preferable?'

He pointed to the picture of the Madonna, the upper part of which represented the conventional cherubs of Italian Art, celestially provided with sitting accommodation for their chins, on balloons of buff-coloured cloud.

'Quite a model family!' said Mr Fairlie, leering at the cherubs. 'Such nice round faces, and such nice soft wings, and – nothing else. No dirty little legs to run about on, and no noisy little lungs to scream with. How immeasurably superior to the existing construction! I will close my eyes again, if you will allow me. And you really can manage the drawings? So glad. Is there anything else to settle? if there is, I think I have forgotten it. Shall we ring for Louis again?'

Being, by this time, quite as anxious, on my side, as Mr Fairlie evidently was on his, to bring the interview to a speedy conclusion, I thought I would try to render the summoning of the servant unnecessary, by offering the requisite suggestion on my own responsibility.

'The only point, Mr Fairlie, that remains to be discussed,' I said, 'refers, I think, to the instruction in sketching which I am engaged to communicate to the two young ladies.'

'Ah! just so,' said Mr Fairlie. 'I wish I felt strong enough to go into that part of the arrangement – but I don't. The ladies who profit by your kind services, Mr Hartright, must settle, and decide, and so on, for themselves. My niece is fond of your charming art. She knows just enough about it to be conscious of her own sad defects. Please take pains with her. Yes. Is there anything else? No. We quite understand each other – don't we? I have no right to detain you any longer from your delightful pursuit – have I? So pleasant to have settled everything – such a sensible relief to have done business. Do you mind ringing for Louis to carry the portfolio to your own room?'

'I will carry it there myself, Mr Fairlie, if you will allow me.'

'Will you really? Are you strong enough? How nice to be so strong! Are you sure you won't drop it? So glad to possess you at Limmeridge, Mr Hartright. I am such a sufferer that I hardly dare hope to enjoy much of your society. Would you mind taking great pains not to let the doors bang, and not to drop the portfolio? Thank you. Gently with the curtains, please – the slightest noise from them goes through me like a knife. Yes. *Good* morning!'

When the sea-green curtains were closed, and when the two baize doors were shut behind me, I stopped for a moment in the little circular hall beyond, and drew a long, luxurious breath of relief. It was like coming to the surface of the water after deep diving, to find myself once more on the outside of Mr Fairlie's room.

As soon as I was comfortably established for the morning in my pretty little studio, the first resolution at which I arrived was to turn my steps no more in the direction of the apartments occupied by the master of the house, except in the very improbable event of his honouring me with a special invitation to pay him another visit. Having settled this satisfactory plan of future conduct in reference to Mr Fairlie, I soon recovered the serenity of temper of which my employer's haughty familiarity and impudent politeness had, for the moment, deprived me. The remaining hours of the morning passed away pleasantly enough, in looking over the drawings, arranging them in sets, trimming their ragged edges, and accomplishing the other necessary preparations in anticipation of the business of mounting them. I ought, perhaps, to have made more progress than this; but, as the luncheon-time drew near, I grew restless and unsettled, and felt unable to fix my attention on work, even though that work was only of the humble manual kind.

At two o'clock I descended again to the breakfast-room, a little anxiously. Expectations of some interest were connected with my approaching reappearance in that part of the house. My introduction to Miss Fairlie was now close at hand; and, if Miss Halcombe's search through her mother's letters had produced the result which she anticipated, the time had come for clearing up the mystery of the woman in white.

VIII

When I entered the room, I found Miss Halcombe and an elderly lady seated at the luncheon-table.

The elderly lady, when I was presented to her, proved to be Miss Fairlie's former governess, Mrs Vesey, who had been briefly described to me by my lively companion at the breakfast-table, as possessed of 'all the cardinal virtues, and counting for nothing.' I can do little more than offer my humble testimony to the truthfulness of Miss Halcombe's sketch of the old lady's character. Mrs Vesey looked the personification of human composure and female amiability. A calm enjoyment of a calm existence beamed in drowsy smiles on her plump, placid face. Some of us rush through life, and some of us saunter through life. Mrs Vesey *sat* through life. Sat in the house, early and late; sat in the garden; sat in unexpected window-seats in passages; sat (on a camp-stool) when her friends tried to take her out walking; sat before she looked at anything, before she talked of anything, before she answered

Yes, or No, to the commonest question – always with the same serene smile
on her lips, the same vacantly-attentive turn of the head, the same snugly-
comfortable position of her hands and arms, under every possible change of
domestic circumstances. A mild, a compliant, an unutterably tranquil and
harmless old lady, who never by any chance suggested the idea that she had
been actually alive since the hour of her birth. Nature has so much to do in
this world, and is engaged in generating such a vast variety of co-existent
productions, that she must surely be now and then too flurried and confused
to distinguish between the different processes that she is carrying on at the
same time. Starting from this point of view, it will always remain my private
persuasion that Nature was absorbed in making cabbages when Mrs Vesey
was born, and that the good lady suffered the consequences of a vegetable
preoccupation in the mind of the Mother of us all.

'Now, Mrs Vesey,' said Miss Halcombe, looking brighter, sharper, and
readier than ever, by contrast with the undemonstrative old lady at her side,
'what will you have? A cutlet?'

Mrs Vesey crossed her dimpled hands on the edge of the table, smiled
placidly, and said, 'Yes, dear.'

'What is that opposite Mr Hartright? Boiled chicken, is it not? I thought
you liked boiled chicken better than cutlet, Mrs Vesey?'

Mrs Vesey took her dimpled hands off the edge of the table and crossed
them on her lap instead; nodded contemplatively at the boiled chicken, and
said, 'Yes, dear.'

'Well, but which will you have, today? Shall Mr Hartright give you some
chicken? or shall I give you some cutlet?'

Mrs Vesey put one of her dimpled hands back again on the edge of the
table; hesitated drowsily, and said, 'Which you please, dear.'

'Mercy on me! it's a question for your taste, my good lady, not for mine.
Suppose you have a little of both? and suppose you begin with the chicken,
because Mr Hartright looks devoured by anxiety to carve for you.'

Mrs Vesey put the other dimpled hand back on the edge of the table;
brightened dimly one moment; went out again the next; bowed obediently,
and said, 'If you please, sir.'

Surely a mild, a compliant, an unutterably tranquil and harmless old lady!
But enough, perhaps, for the present, of Mrs Vesey.

All this time, there were no signs of Miss Fairlie. We finished our luncheon;
and still she never appeared. Miss Halcombe, whose quick eye nothing
escaped, noticed the looks that I cast, from time to time, in the direction of
the door.

'I understand you, Mr Hartright,' she said; 'you are wondering what has become of your other pupil. She has been downstairs, and has got over her headache; but has not sufficiently recovered her appetite to join us at lunch. If you will put yourself under my charge, I think I can undertake to find her somewhere in the garden.'

She took up a parasol lying on a chair near her, and led the way out, by a long window at the bottom of the room, which opened on to the lawn. It is almost unnecessary to say that we left Mrs Vesey still seated at the table, with her dimpled hands still crossed on the edge of it; apparently settled in that position for the rest of the afternoon.

As we crossed the lawn, Miss Halcombe looked at me significantly, and shook her head.

'That mysterious adventure of yours,' she said, 'still remains involved in its own appropriate midnight darkness. I have been all the morning looking over my mother's letters, and I have made no discoveries yet. However, don't despair, Mr Hartright. This is a matter of curiosity; and you have got a woman for your ally. Under such conditions success is certain, sooner or later. The letters are not exhausted. I have three packets still left, and you may confidently rely on my spending the whole evening over them.'

Here, then, was one of my anticipations of the morning still unfulfilled. I began to wonder, next, whether my introduction to Miss Fairlie would disappoint the expectations that I had been forming of her since breakfast-time.

'And how did you get on with Mr Fairlie?' inquired Miss Halcombe, as we left the lawn and turned into a shrubbery. 'Was he particularly nervous this morning? Never mind considering about your answer, Mr Hartright. The mere fact of your being obliged to consider is enough for me. I see in your face that he *was* particularly nervous; and, as I am amiably unwilling to throw you into the same condition, I ask no more.'

We turned off into a winding path while she was speaking, and approached a pretty summer-house, built of wood, in the form of a miniature Swiss chalet. The one room of the summer-house, as we ascended the steps of the door, was occupied by a young lady. She was standing near a rustic table, looking out at the inland view of moor and hill presented by a gap in the trees, and absently turning over the leaves of a little sketch-book that lay at her side. This was Miss Fairlie.

How can I describe her? How can I separate her from my own sensations, and from all that has happened in the later time? How can I see her again as she looked when my eyes first rested on her – as she should look, now, to the eyes that are about to see her in these pages?

The water-colour drawing that I made of Laura Fairlie, at an after period, in the place and attitude in which I first saw her, lies on my desk while I write. I look at it, and there dawns upon me brightly, from the dark greenish-brown background of the summer-house, a light, youthful figure, clothed in a simple muslin dress, the pattern of it formed by broad alternate stripes of delicate blue and white. A scarf of the same material sits crisply and closely round her shoulders, and a little straw hat of the natural colour, plainly and sparingly trimmed with ribbon to match the gown, covers her head, and throws its soft pearly shadow over the upper part of her face. Her hair is of so faint and pale a brown – not flaxen, and yet almost as light; not golden, and yet almost as glossy – that it nearly melts, here and there, into the shadow of the hat. It is plainly parted and drawn back over her ears, and the line of it ripples naturally as it crosses her forehead. The eyebrows are rather darker than the hair; and the eyes are of that soft, limpid, turquoise blue, so often sung by the poets, so seldom seen in real life. Lovely eyes in colour, lovely eyes in form – large and tender and quietly thoughtful – but beautiful above all things in the clear truthfulness of look that dwells in their inmost depths, and shines through all their changes of expression with the light of a purer and a better world. The charm – most gently and yet most distinctly expressed – which they shed over the whole face, so covers and transforms its little natural human blemishes elsewhere, that it is difficult to estimate the relative merits and defects of the other features. It is hard to see that the lower part of the face is too delicately refined away towards the chin to be in full and fair proportion with the upper part; that the nose, in escaping the aquiline bend (always hard and cruel in a woman, no matter how abstractedly perfect it may be), has erred a little in the other extreme, and has missed the ideal straightness of line; and that the sweet, sensitive lips are subject to a slight nervous contraction, when she smiles, which draws them upward a little at one corner, towards the cheek. It might be possible to note these blemishes in another woman's face but it is not easy to dwell on them in hers, so subtly are they connected with all that is individual and characteristic in her expression, and so closely does the expression depend for its full play and life, in every other feature, on the moving impulse of the eyes.

Does my poor portrait of her, my fond, patient labour of long and happy days, show me these things? Ah, how few of them are in the dim mechanical drawing, and how many in the mind with which I regard it! A fair, delicate girl, in a pretty light dress, trifling with the leaves of a sketch-book, while she looks up from it with truthful, innocent blue eyes – that is all the drawing can say; all, perhaps, that even the deeper reach of thought and pen can say in their language, either. The woman who first gives life, light, and form to our shadowy conceptions of beauty, fills a void in our spiritual nature that has remained unknown to us till she appeared. Sympathies that lie too deep for words, too deep almost for thoughts, are touched, at such times, by other charms than those which the senses feel and which the resources of expression can realise. The mystery which underlies the beauty of women is never raised above the reach of all expression until it has claimed kindred with the deeper mystery in our own souls. Then, and then only, has it passed beyond the narrow region on which light falls, in this world, from the pencil and the pen.

Think of her as you thought of the first woman who quickened the pulses within you that the rest of her sex had no art to stir. Let the kind, candid blue eyes meet yours, as they met mine, with the one matchless look which we both remember so well. Let her voice speak the music that you once loved best, attuned as sweetly to your ear as to mine. Let her footstep, as she comes and goes, in these pages, be like that other footstep to whose airy fall your own heart once beat time. Take her as the visionary nursling of your own fancy; and she will grow upon you, all the more clearly, as the living woman who dwells in mine.

Among the sensations that crowded on me, when my eyes first looked upon her – familiar sensations which we all know, which spring to life in most of our hearts, die again in so many, and renew their bright existence in so few – there was one that troubled and perplexed me: one that seemed strangely inconsistent and unaccountably out of place in Miss Fairlie's presence.

Mingling with the vivid impression produced by the charm of her fair face and head, her sweet expression, and her winning simplicity of manner, was another impression, which, in a shadowy way, suggested to me the idea of something wanting. At one time it seemed like something wanting in her: at another, like something wanting in myself, which hindered me from understanding her as I ought. The impression was always strongest in the most contradictory manner, when she looked at me; or, in other words, when I was most conscious of the harmony and charm of her face, and yet, at the same time, most troubled by the sense of an incompleteness which it was impossible to discover. Something wanting, something wanting – and where it was, and what it was, I could not say.

The effect of this curious caprice of fancy (as I thought it then) was not of a nature to set me at my ease, during a first interview with Miss Fairlie. The few kind words of welcome which she spoke found me hardly self-possessed enough to thank her in the customary phrases of reply. Observing my hesitation, and no doubt attributing it, naturally enough, to some momentary shyness on my part, Miss Halcombe took the business of talking, as easily and readily as usual, into her own hands.

'Look there, Mr Hartright,' she said, pointing to the sketch-book on the table, and to the little delicate wandering hand that was still trifling with it.

'Surely you will acknowledge that your model pupil is found at last? The moment she hears that you are in the house, she seizes her inestimable sketch-book, looks universal Nature straight in the face, and longs to begin!'

Miss Fairlie laughed with a ready good-humour, which broke out as brightly as if it had been part of the sunshine above us, over her lovely face.

'I must not take credit to myself where no credit is due,' she said, her clear, truthful blue eyes looking alternately at Miss Halcombe and at me. 'Fond as I am of drawing, I am so conscious of my own ignorance that I am more afraid than anxious to begin. Now I know you are here, Mr Hartright, I find myself looking over my sketches, as I used to look over my lessons when I was a little girl, and when I was sadly afraid that I should turn out not fit to be heard.'

She made the confession very prettily and simply, and, with quaint, childish earnestness, drew the sketch-book away close to her own side of the table. Miss Halcombe cut the knot of the little embarrassment forthwith, in her resolute, downright way.

'Good, bad, or indifferent,' she said, 'the pupil's sketches must pass through the fiery ordeal of the master's judgment – and there's an end of it. Suppose we take them with us in the carriage, Laura, and let Mr Hartright see them, for the first time, under circumstances of perpetual jolting and interruption? If we can only confuse him all through the drive, between Nature as it is, when he looks up at the view, and Nature as it is not when he looks down again at our sketch-books, we shall drive him into the last desperate refuge of paying us compliments, and shall slip through his professional fingers with our pet feathers of vanity all unruffled.'

'I hope Mr Hartright will pay *me* no compliments,' said Miss Fairlie, as we all left the summer-house.

'May I venture to inquire why you express that hope?' I asked.

'Because I shall believe all that you say to me,' she answered simply.

In those few words she unconsciously gave me the key to her whole character: to that generous trust in others which, in her nature, grew innocently out of the sense of her own truth. I only knew it intuitively then. I know it by experience now.

We merely waited to rouse good Mrs Vesey from the place which she still occupied at the deserted luncheon-table, before we entered the open carriage for our promised drive. The old lady and Miss Halcombe occupied the back seat, and Miss Fairlie and I sat together in front, with the sketch-book open between us, fairly exhibited at last to my professional eyes. All serious criticism on the drawings, even if I had been disposed to volunteer it, was rendered impossible by Miss Halcombe's lively resolution to see nothing but the ridiculous side of the Fine Arts, as practised by herself, her sister, and ladies in general. I can remember the conversation that passed far more easily than the sketches that I mechanically looked over. That part of the talk, especially, in which Miss Fairlie took any share, is still as vividly impressed on my memory as if I had heard it only a few hours ago.

Yes! let me acknowledge that on this first day I let the charm of her presence lure me from the recollection of myself and my position. The most trifling of the questions that she put to me, on the subject of using her pencil and mixing her colours; the slightest alterations of expression in the lovely eyes that looked into mine with such an earnest desire to learn all that I could teach, and to discover all that I could show, attracted more of my attention than the finest view we passed through, or the grandest changes of light and shade, as they flowed into each other over the waving moorland and the level beach. At any time, and under any circumstances of human interest, is it not strange to see how little real hold the objects of the natural world amid which we live can gain on our hearts and minds? We go to Nature for comfort in trouble, and sympathy in joy, only in books. Admiration of those beauties of the inanimate world, which modern poetry so largely and so eloquently describes, is not, even in the best of us, one of the original instincts of our nature. As children, we none of us possess it. No uninstructed man or woman possesses it. Those whose lives are most exclusively passed amid the ever-changing wonders of sea and land are also those who are most universally insensible to every aspect of Nature not directly associated with the human interest of their calling. Our capacity of appreciating the beauties of the earth we live on is, in truth, one of the civilised accomplishments which we all learn as an Art; and, more, that very capacity is rarely practised by any of us except when our minds are most indolent and most unoccupied. How much share have the attractions of Nature ever had in the pleasurable or painful interests and emotions of ourselves or our friends? What space do they ever occupy in the thousand little narratives of personal experience which pass every day by word of mouth from one of us to the other? All that our minds can compass, all that our hearts can learn, can be accomplished with equal certainty, equal profit, and equal satisfaction to ourselves, in the poorest as in the richest prospect that the face of the earth can show. There is surely a reason for this want of inborn sympathy between the creature and the creation around it, a reason which may perhaps be found in the widely differing destinies of man and his earthly sphere. The grandest mountain prospect that the eye can range over is appointed to annihilation. The smallest human interest that the pure heart can feel is appointed to immortality.

We had been out nearly three hours, when the carriage again passed through the gates of Limmeridge House.

On our way back I had let the ladies settle for themselves the first point of view which they were to sketch, under my instructions, on the afternoon of the next day. When they withdrew to dress for dinner, and when I was alone again in my little sitting-room, my spirits seemed to leave me on a sudden. I felt ill at ease and dissatisfied with myself, I hardly knew why. Perhaps I was now conscious for the first time of having enjoyed our drive too much in the character of a guest, and too little in the character of a drawing-master. Perhaps that strange sense of something wanting, either in Miss Fairlie or in myself, which had perplexed me when I was first introduced to her, haunted me still. Anyhow, it was a relief to my spirits when the dinner-hour called me out of my solitude, and took me back to the society of the ladies of the house.

I was struck, on entering the drawing-room, by the curious contrast, rather in material than in colour, of the dresses which they now wore. While Mrs Vesey and Miss Halcombe were richly clad (each in the manner most becoming to her age), the first in silver-grey, and the second in that delicate primrose-yellow colour which matches so well with a dark complexion and black hair, Miss Fairlie was unpretendingly and almost poorly dressed in plain white muslin. It was spotlessly pure: it was beautifully put on; but still it was the sort of dress which the wife or daughter of a poor man might have worn, and it made her, so far as externals went, look less affluent in circumstances than her own governess. At a later period, when I learnt to know more of Miss Fairlie's character, I discovered that this curious contrast, on the wrong side, was due to her natural delicacy of feeling and natural intensity of aversion to the slightest personal display of her own wealth. Neither Mrs Vesey nor Miss Halcombe could ever induce her to let the advantage in dress desert the two ladies who were poor, to lean to the side of the one lady who was rich.

When the dinner was over we returned together to the drawing-room. Although Mr Fairlie (emulating the magnificent condescension of the monarch who had picked up Titian's brush for him) had instructed his butler to consult my wishes in relation to the wine that I might prefer after dinner, I was resolute enough to resist the temptation of sitting in solitary grandeur among bottles of my own choosing, and sensible enough to ask the ladies' permission to leave the table with them habitually, on the civilised foreign plan, during the period of my residence at Limmeridge House.

The drawing-room, to which we had now withdrawn for the rest of the evening, was on the ground-floor, and was of the same shape and size as the breakfast-room. Large glass doors at the lower end opened on to a terrace, beautifully ornamented along its whole length with a profusion of flowers. The soft, hazy twilight was just shading leaf and blossom alike into harmony with its own sober hues as we entered the room, and the sweet evening scent of the flowers met us with its fragrant welcome through the open glass doors. Good Mrs Vesey (always the first of the party to sit down) took possession of an arm-chair in a corner, and dozed off comfortably to sleep. At my request Miss Fairlie placed herself at the piano. As I followed her to a seat near the instrument, I saw Miss Halcombe retire into a recess of one of the side windows, to proceed with the search through her mother's letters by the last quiet rays of the evening light.

How vividly that peaceful home-picture of the drawing-room comes back to me while I write! From the place where I sat I could see Miss Halcombe's graceful figure, half of it in soft light, half in mysterious shadow, bending intently over the letters in her lap; while, nearer to me, the fair profile of the player at the piano was just delicately defined against the faintly deepening background of the inner wall of the room. Outside, on the terrace, the clustering flowers and long grasses and creepers waved so gently in the light evening air, that the sound of their rustling never reached us. The sky was without a cloud, and the dawning mystery of moonlight began to tremble already in the region of the eastern heaven. The sense of peace and seclusion soothed all thought and feeling into a rapt, unearthly repose; and the balmy quiet, that deepened ever with the deepening light, seemed to hover over us with a gentler influence still, when there stole upon it from the piano the heavenly tenderness of the music of Mozart. It was an evening of sights and sounds never to forget.

We all sat silent in the places we had chosen – Mrs Vesey still sleeping, Miss Fairlie still playing, Miss Halcombe still reading – till the light failed us. By this time the moon had stolen round to the terrace, and soft, mysterious rays of light were slanting already across the lower end of the room. The change from the twilight obscurity was so beautiful that we banished the lamps, by common consent, when the servant brought them in, and kept the large room unlighted, except by the glimmer of the two candles at the piano.

For half an hour more the music still went on. After that the beauty of the moonlight view on the terrace tempted Miss Fairlie out to look at it, and I followed her. When the candles at the piano had been lighted Miss Halcombe had changed her place, so as to continue her examination of the letters by their assistance. We left her, on a low chair, at one side of the instrument, so absorbed over her reading that she did not seem to notice when we moved.

We had been out on the terrace together, just in front of the glass doors, hardly so long as five minutes, I should think; and Miss Fairlie was, by my advice, just tying her white handkerchief over her head as a precaution against the night air – when I heard Miss Halcombe's voice – low, eager, and altered from its natural lively tone – pronounce my name.

'Mr Hartright,' she said, 'will you come here for a minute? I want to speak to you.'

I entered the room again immediately. The piano stood about half-way down along the inner wall. On the side of the instrument farthest from the terrace Miss Halcombe was sitting with the letters scattered on her lap, and with one in her hand selected from them, and held close to the candle. On the side nearest to the terrace there stood a low ottoman, on which I took my place. In this position I was not far from the glass doors, and I could see Miss Fairlie plainly, as she passed and repassed the opening on to the terrace, walking slowly from end to end of it in the full radiance of the moon.

'I want you to listen while I read the concluding passages in this letter,' said Miss Halcombe. 'Tell me if you think they throw any light upon your strange adventure on the road to London. The letter is addressed by my mother to her second husband, Mr Fairlie, and the date refers to a period of between eleven and twelve years since. At that time Mr and Mrs Fairlie, and my half-sister Laura, had been living for years in this house; and I was away from them completing my education at a school in Paris.'

She looked and spoke earnestly, and, as I thought, a little uneasily as well. At the moment when she raised the letter to the candle before beginning to read it, Miss Fairlie passed us on the terrace, looked in for a moment, and seeing that we were engaged, slowly walked on.

Miss Halcombe began to read as follows: –

'You will be tired, my dear Philip, of hearing perpetually about my schools and my scholars. Lay the blame, pray, on the dull uniformity of life at Limmeridge, and not on me. Besides, this time I have something really interesting to tell you about a new scholar.

'You know old Mrs Kempe at the village shop. Well, after years of ailing, the doctor has at last given her up, and she is dying slowly day by day. Her only living relation, a sister, arrived last week to take care of her. This sister comes all the way from Hampshire – her name is Mrs Catherick. Four days ago Mrs Catherick came here to see me, and brought her only child with her, a sweet little girl about a year older than our darling Laura—'

As the last sentence fell from the reader's lips, Miss Fairlie passed us on the terrace once more. She was softly singing to herself one of the melodies which she had been playing earlier in the evening. Miss Halcombe waited till she had passed out of sight again, and then went on with the letter –

'Mrs Catherick is a decent, well-behaved, respectable woman; middle-aged, and with the remains of having been moderately, only moderately, nice-looking. There is something in her manner and in her appearance, however, which I can't make out. She is reserved about herself to the point of downright secrecy, and there is a look in her face – I can't describe it – which suggests to me that she has something on her mind. She is altogether what you would call a walking mystery. Her errand at Limmeridge House, however, was simple enough. When she left Hampshire to nurse her sister, Mrs Kempe, through her last illness, she had been obliged to bring her daughter with her, through having no one at home to take care of the little girl. Mrs Kempe may die in a week's time, or may linger on for months; and Mrs Catherick's object was to ask me to let her daughter, Anne, have the benefit of attending my school, subject to the condition of her being removed from it to go home again with her mother, after Mrs Kempe's death. I consented at once, and when Laura and I went out for our walk, we took the little girl (who is just eleven years old) to the school that very day.'

Once more Miss Fairlie's figure, bright and soft in its snowy muslin dress – her face prettily framed by the white folds of the handkerchief which she had tied under her chin – passed by us in the moonlight. Once more Miss Halcombe waited till she was out of sight, and then went on –

'I have taken a violent fancy, Philip, to my new scholar, for a reason which I mean to keep till the last for the sake of surprising you. Her mother having told me as little about the child as she told me of herself, I was left to discover (which I did on the first day when we tried her at lessons) that the poor little thing's intellect is not developed as it ought to be at her age. Seeing this I had her up to the house the next day, and privately arranged with the doctor to come and watch her and question her, and tell me what he thought. His opinion is that she will grow out of it. But he says her careful bringing-up at school is a matter of great importance just now, because her unusual slowness in acquiring ideas implies an unusual tenacity in keeping them, when they are once received into her mind. Now, my love, you must not imagine, in your off-hand way, that I have been attaching myself to an idiot. This poor little Anne Catherick is a sweet, affectionate, grateful girl, and says the quaintest, prettiest things (as you shall judge by an instance), in the most oddly sudden, surprised, half-frightened way. Although she is dressed very neatly, her clothes show a sad want of taste in colour and pattern. So I arranged, yesterday, that some of our darling Laura's old white frocks and white hats should be altered for Anne Catherick, explaining to her that little girls of her complexion looked neater and better all in white than in anything else. She hesitated and seemed puzzled for a minute, then flushed up, and appeared to understand. Her little hand clasped mine suddenly. She kissed it, Philip, and said (oh, so earnestly!), "I will always wear white as long as I live. It will help me to remember you, ma'am, and to think that I am pleasing you still, when I go away and see you no more." This is only one specimen of the quaint things she says so prettily. Poor little soul! She shall have a stock of white frocks, made with good deep tucks, to let out for her as she grows—'

Miss Halcombe paused, and looked at me across the piano.

'Did the forlorn woman whom you met in the high-road seem young?' she asked. 'Young enough to be two- or three-and-twenty?'

'Yes, Miss Halcombe, as young as that.'

'And she was strangely dressed, from head to foot, all in white?'

'All in white.'

While the answer was passing my lips Miss Fairlie glided into view on the terrace for the third time. Instead of proceeding on her walk, she stopped, with her back turned towards us, and, leaning on the balustrade of the terrace, looked down into the garden beyond. My eyes fixed upon the white gleam of her muslin gown and head-dress in the moonlight, and a sensation, for which I can find no name – a sensation that quickened my pulse, and raised a fluttering at my heart – began to steal over me.

'All in white?' Miss Halcombe repeated. 'The most important sentences in the letter, Mr Hartright, are those at the end, which I will read to you immediately. But I can't help dwelling a little upon the coincidence of the white costume of the woman you met, and the white frocks which produced that strange answer from my mother's little scholar. The doctor may have been wrong when he discovered the child's defects of intellect, and predicted that she would "grow out of them." She may never have grown out of them, and the old grateful fancy about dressing in white, which was a serious feeling to the girl, may be a serious feeling to the woman still.'

I said a few words in answer – I hardly know what. All my attention was concentrated on the white gleam of Miss Fairlie's muslin dress.

'Listen to the last sentences of the letter,' said Miss Halcombe. 'I think they will surprise you.'

As she raised the letter to the light of the candle, Miss Fairlie turned from the balustrade, looked doubtfully up and down the terrace, advanced a step towards the glass doors, and then stopped, facing us.

Meanwhile Miss Halcombe read me the last sentences to which she had referred –

> 'And now, my love, seeing that I am at the end of my paper, now for the real reason, the surprising reason, for my fondness for little Anne Catherick. My dear Philip, although she is not half so pretty, she is, nevertheless, by one of those extraordinary caprices of accidental resemblance which one sometimes sees, the living likeness, in her hair, her complexion, the colour of her eyes, and the shape of her face—'

I started up from the ottoman before Miss Halcombe could pronounce the next words. A thrill of the same feeling which ran through me when the touch was laid upon my shoulder on the lonely high-road chilled me again.

There stood Miss Fairlie, a white figure, alone in the moonlight; in her attitude, in the turn of her head, in her complexion, in the shape of her face, the living image, at that distance and under those circumstances, of the woman in white! The doubt which had troubled my mind for hours and hours past flashed into conviction in an instant. That 'something wanting' was my own recognition of the ominous likeness between the fugitive from the asylum and my pupil at Limmeridge House.

'You see it!' said Miss Halcombe. She dropped the useless letter, and her eyes flashed as they met mine. 'You see it now, as my mother saw it eleven years since!'

'I see it – more unwillingly than I can say. To associate that forlorn, friendless, lost woman, even by an accidental likeness only, with Miss Fairlie, seems like casting a shadow on the future of the bright creature who stands looking at us now. Let me lose the impression again as soon as possible. Call her in, out of the dreary moonlight – pray call her in!'

'Mr Hartright, you surprise me. Whatever women may be, I thought that men, in the nineteenth century, were above superstition.'

'Pray call her in!'

'Hush, hush! She is coming of her own accord. Say nothing in her presence. Let this discovery of the likeness be kept a secret between you and me. Come in, Laura, come in, and wake Mrs Vesey with the piano. Mr Hartright is petitioning for some more music, and he wants it, this time, of the lightest and liveliest kind.'

IX

So ended my eventful first day at Limmeridge House.

Miss Halcombe and I kept our secret. After the discovery of the likeness no fresh light seemed destined to break over the mystery of the woman in white. At the first safe opportunity Miss Halcombe cautiously led her half-sister to speak of their mother, of old times, and of Anne Catherick. Miss Fairlie's recollections of the little scholar at Limmeridge were, however, only of the most vague and general kind. She remembered the likeness between herself and her mother's favourite pupil, as something which had been supposed to exist in past times; but she did not refer to the gift of the white dresses, or to the singular form of words in which the child had artlessly expressed her gratitude for them. She remembered that Anne had remained at Limmeridge for a few months only, and had then left it to go back to her home in Hampshire; but she could not say whether the mother and daughter had ever returned, or had ever been heard of afterwards. No further search, on Miss Halcombe's part, through the few letters of Mrs Fairlie's writing which she had left unread, assisted in clearing up the uncertainties still left to perplex us. We had identified the unhappy woman whom I had met in the night-time with Anne Catherick – we had made some advance, at least, towards connecting the probably defective condition of the poor creature's intellect with the peculiarity of her being dressed all in white, and with the continuance, in her maturer years, of her childish gratitude towards Mrs Fairlie – and there, so far as we knew at that time, our discoveries had ended.

The days passed on, the weeks passed on, and the track of the golden autumn wound its bright way visibly through the green summer of the trees. Peaceful, fast-flowing, happy time! my story glides by you now as swiftly as you once glided by me. Of all the treasures of enjoyment that you poured so freely into my heart, how much is left me that has purpose and value enough to be written on this page? Nothing but the saddest of all confessions that a man can make – the confession of his own folly.

The secret which that confession discloses should be told with little effort, for it has indirectly escaped me already. The poor weak words, which have failed to describe Miss Fairlie, have succeeded in betraying the sensations she awakened in me. It is so with us all. Our words are giants when they do us an injury, and dwarfs when they do us a service.

I loved her.

Ah! how well I know all the sadness and all the mockery that is contained in those three words. I can sigh over my mournful confession with the tenderest woman who reads it and pities me. I can laugh at it as bitterly as the hardest man who tosses it from him in contempt. I loved her! Feel for me, or despise me, I confess it with the same immovable resolution to own the truth.

Was there no excuse for me? There was some excuse to be found, surely, in the conditions under which my term of hired service was passed at Limmeridge House.

My morning hours succeeded each other calmly in the quiet and seclusion of my own room. I had just work enough to do, in mounting my employer's drawings, to keep my hands and eyes pleasurably employed, while my mind was left free to enjoy the dangerous luxury of its own unbridled thoughts. A perilous solitude, for it lasted long enough to enervate, not long enough to fortify me. A perilous solitude, for it was followed by afternoons and evenings spent, day after day and week after week alone in the society of two women, one of whom possessed all the accomplishments of grace, wit, and high-breeding, the other all the charms of beauty, gentleness, and simple truth, that can purify and subdue the heart of man. Not a day passed, in that dangerous intimacy of teacher and pupil, in which my hand was not close to Miss Fairlie's; my cheek, as we bent together over her sketch-book, almost touching hers. The more attentively she watched every movement of my brush, the more closely I was breathing the perfume of her hair, and the warm fragrance of her breath. It was part of my service to live in the very light of her eyes – at one time to be bending over her, so close to her bosom as to tremble at the thought of touching it; at another, to feel her bending over me, bending so close to see what I was about, that her voice sank low when she spoke to me, and her ribbons brushed my cheek in the wind before she could draw them back.

The evenings which followed the sketching excursions of the afternoon varied, rather than checked, these innocent, these inevitable familiarities. My natural fondness for the music which she played with such tender feeling, such delicate womanly taste, and her natural enjoyment of giving me back, by the practice of her art, the pleasure which I had offered to her by the practice of mine, only wove another tie which drew us closer and closer to one another. The accidents of conversation; the simple habits which regulated even such a little thing as the position of our places at table; the play of Miss Halcombe's ever-ready raillery, always directed against my anxiety as teacher, while it sparkled over her enthusiasm as pupil; the harmless expression of poor Mrs Vesey's drowsy approval, which connected Miss Fairlie and me as two model young people who never disturbed her – every one of these trifles, and many more, combined to fold us together in the same domestic atmosphere, and to lead us both insensibly to the same hopeless end.

I should have remembered my position, and have put myself secretly on my guard. I did so, but not till it was too late. All the discretion, all the experience, which had availed me with other women, and secured me against other temptations, failed me with her. It had been my profession, for years past, to be in this close contact with young girls of all ages, and of all orders of beauty. I had accepted the position as part of my calling in life; I had trained myself to leave all the sympathies natural to my age in my employer's outer hall, as coolly as I left my umbrella there before I went upstairs. I had long since learnt to understand, composedly and as a matter of course, that my situation in life was considered a guarantee against any of my female pupils feeling more than the most ordinary interest in me, and that I was admitted among beautiful and captivating women much as a harmless domestic animal is admitted among them. This guardian experience I had gained early; this guardian experience had sternly and strictly guided me straight along my own poor narrow path, without once letting me stray aside, to the right hand or to the left. And now I and my trusty talisman were parted for the first time. Yes, my hardly-earned self-control was as completely lost to me as if I had never possessed it; lost to me, as it is lost every day to other men, in other critical situations, where women are concerned. I know, now, that I should have questioned myself from the first. I should have asked why any room in the house was better than home to me when she entered it, and barren as a desert when she went out again – why I always noticed and remembered the little changes in her dress that I had noticed and remembered in no other woman's before – why I saw her, heard her, and touched her (when we shook hands at night and morning) as I had never seen, heard, and touched any other woman in my life? I should have looked into my own heart, and found this new growth springing up there, and plucked it out while it was young. Why was this easiest, simplest work of self-culture always too much for me? The explanation has been written already in the three words that were many enough, and plain enough, for my confession. I loved her.

The days passed, the weeks passed; it was approaching the third month of my stay in Cumberland. The delicious monotony of life in our calm seclusion flowed on with me, like a smooth stream with a swimmer who glides down the current. All memory of the past, all thought of the future, all sense of the falseness and hopelessness of my own position, lay hushed within me into deceitful rest. Lulled by the Siren-song that my own heart sung to me, with eyes shut to all sight, and ears closed to all sound of danger, I drifted nearer and nearer to the fatal rocks. The warning that aroused me at last, and startled me into sudden, self-accusing consciousness of my own weakness, was the plainest, the truest, the kindest of all warnings, for it came silently from *her*.

We had parted one night as usual. No word had fallen from my lips, at that time or at any time before it, that could betray me, or startle her into sudden knowledge of the truth. But when we met again in the morning, a change had come over her – a change that told me all.

I shrank then – I shrink still – from invading the innermost sanctuary of her heart, and laying it open to others, as I have laid open my own. Let it be enough to say that the time when she first surprised my secret was, I firmly believe, the time when she first surprised her own, and the time, also, when she changed towards me in the interval of one night. Her nature, too truthful to deceive others, was too noble to deceive itself. When the doubt that I had hushed asleep first laid its weary weight on her heart, the true face owned all, and said, in its own frank, simple language – I am sorry for him; I am sorry for myself.

It said this, and more, which I could not then interpret. I understood but too well the change in her manner, to greater kindness and quicker readiness in interpreting all my wishes, before others – to constraint and sadness, and nervous anxiety to absorb herself in the first occupation she could seize on, whenever we happened to be left together alone. I understood why the sweet sensitive lips smiled so rarely and so restrainedly now, and why the clear blue eyes looked at me, sometimes with the pity of an angel, sometimes with the innocent perplexity of a child. But the change meant more than this. There was a coldness in her hand, there was an unnatural immobility in her face, there was in all her movements the mute expression of constant fear and clinging self-reproach. The sensations that I could trace to herself and to me, the unacknowledged sensations that we were feeling in common, were not these. There were certain elements of the change in her that were still secretly drawing us together, and others that were, as secretly, beginning to drive us apart.

In my doubt and perplexity, in my vague suspicion of something hidden which I was left to find by my own unaided efforts, I examined Miss Halcombe's looks and manner for enlightenment. Living in such intimacy as ours, no serious alteration could take place in any one of us which did not sympathetically affect the others. The change in Miss Fairlie was reflected in her half-sister. Although not a word escaped Miss Halcombe which hinted at an altered state of feeling towards myself, her penetrating eyes had contracted a new habit of always watching me. Sometimes the look was like suppressed anger, sometimes like suppressed dread, sometimes like neither – like nothing, in short, which I could understand. A week elapsed, leaving us all three still in this position of secret constraint towards one another. My situation, aggravated by the sense of my own miserable weakness and forget-fulness of myself, now too late awakened in me, was becoming intolerable. I felt that I must cast off the oppression under which I was living, at once and for ever – yet how to act for the best, or what to say first, was more than I could tell.

From this position of helplessness and humiliation I was rescued by Miss Halcombe. Her lips told me the bitter, the necessary, the unexpected truth;

her hearty kindness sustained me under the shock of hearing it; her sense
and courage turned to its right use an event which threatened the worst that
could happen, to me and to others, in Limmeridge House.

X

It was on a Thursday in the week, and nearly at the end of the third month
of my sojourn in Cumberland.

In the morning, when I went down into the breakfast-room at the usual
hour, Miss Halcombe, for the first time since I had known her, was absent
from her customary place at the table.

Miss Fairlie was out on the lawn. She bowed to me, but did not come in.
Not a word had dropped from my lips, or from hers, that could unsettle
either of us – and yet the same unacknowledged sense of embarrassment
made us shrink alike from meeting one another alone. She waited on the
lawn, and I waited in the breakfast-room, till Mrs Vesey or Miss Halcombe
came in. How quickly I should have joined her: how readily we should have
shaken hands, and glided into our customary talk, only a fortnight ago.

In a few minutes Miss Halcombe entered. She had a preoccupied look,
and she made her apologies for being late rather absently.

'I have been detained,' she said, 'by a consultation with Mr Fairlie on a
domestic matter which he wished to speak to me about.'

Miss Fairlie came in from the garden, and the usual morning greeting
passed between us. Her hand struck colder to mine than ever. She did not
look at me, and she was very pale. Even Mrs Vesey noticed it when she
entered the room a moment after.

'I suppose it is the change in the wind,' said the old lady. 'The winter is
coming – ah, my love, the winter is coming soon!'

In her heart and in mine it had come already!

Our morning meal – once so full of pleasant good-humoured discussion
of the plans for the day – was short and silent. Miss Fairlie seemed to feel
the oppression of the long pauses in the conversation, and looked appealingly
to her sister to fill them up. Miss Halcombe, after once or twice hesitating
and checking herself, in a most uncharacteristic manner, spoke at last.

'I have seen your uncle this morning, Laura,' she said. 'He thinks the
purple room is the one that ought to be got ready, and he confirms what I
told you. Monday is the day – not Tuesday.'

While these words were being spoken Miss Fairlie looked down at the
table beneath her. Her fingers moved nervously among the crumbs that were
scattered on the cloth. The paleness on her cheeks spread to her lips, and
the lips themselves trembled visibly. I was not the only person present who

noticed this. Miss Halcombe saw it, too, and at once set us the example of rising from table.

Mrs Vesey and Miss Fairlie left the room together. The kind sorrowful blue eyes looked at me, for a moment, with the prescient sadness of a coming and a long farewell. I felt the answering pang in my own heart – the pang that told me I must lose her soon, and love her the more unchangeably for the loss.

I turned towards the garden when the door had closed on her. Miss Halcombe was standing with her hat in her hand, and her shawl over her arm, by the large window that led out to the lawn, and was looking at me attentively.

'Have you any leisure time to spare,' she asked, 'before you begin to work in your own room?'

'Certainly, Miss Halcombe. I have always time at your service.'

'I want to say a word to you in private, Mr Hartright. Get your hat and come out into the garden. We are not likely to be disturbed there at this hour in the morning.'

As we stepped out on to the lawn, one of the under-gardeners – a mere lad – passed us on his way to the house, with a letter in his hand. Miss Halcombe stopped him.

'Is that letter for me?' she asked.

'Nay, miss; it's just said to be for Miss Fairlie,' answered the lad, holding out the letter as he spoke.

Miss Halcombe took it from him and looked at the address.

'A strange handwriting,' she said to herself. 'Who can Laura's corres-pondent be? Where did you get this?' she continued, addressing the gardener.

'Well, miss,' said the lad, 'I just got it from a woman.'

'What woman?'

'A woman well stricken in age.'

'Oh, an old woman. Any one you knew?'

'I canna' tak' it on mysel' to say that she was other than a stranger to me.'

'Which way did she go?'

'That gate,' said the under-gardener, turning with great deliberation towards the south, and embracing the whole of that part of England with one compre-hensive sweep of his arm.

'Curious,' said Miss Halcombe; 'I suppose it must be a begging-letter. There,' she added, handing the letter back to the lad, 'take it to the house, and give it to one of the servants. And now, Mr Hartright, if you have no objection, let us walk this way.'

She led me across the lawn, along the same path by which I had followed her on the day after my arrival at Limmeridge. At the little summer-house, in which Laura Fairlie and I had first seen each other, she stopped, and broke the silence which she had steadily maintained while we were walking together.

'What I have to say to you I can say here.'

With those words she entered the summer-house, took one of the chairs at the little round table inside, and signed to me to take the other. I suspected what was coming when she spoke to me in the breakfast-room; I felt certain of it now.

'Mr Hartright,' she said, 'I am going to begin by making a frank avowal to you. I am going to say – without phrase-making, which I detest, or paying compliments, which I heartily despise – that I have come, in the course of your residence with us, to feel a strong friendly regard for you. I was predisposed in your favour when you first told me of your conduct towards that unhappy woman whom you met under such remarkable circumstances. Your management of the affair might not have been prudent, but it showed the self-control, the delicacy, and the compassion of a man who was naturally a gentleman. It made me expect good things from you, and you have not disappointed my expectations.'

She paused – but held up her hand at the same time, as a sign that she awaited no answer from me before she proceeded. When I entered the summer-house, no thought was in me of the woman in white. But now, Miss Halcombe's own words had put the memory of my adventure back in my mind. It remained there throughout the interview – remained, and not without a result.

'As your friend,' she proceeded, 'I am going to tell you, at once, in my own plain, blunt, downright language, that I have discovered your secret – without help or hint, mind, from any one else. Mr Hartright, you have thoughtlessly allowed yourself to form an attachment – a serious and devoted attachment I am afraid – to my sister Laura. I don't put you to the pain of confessing it in so many words, because I see and know that you are too honest to deny it. I don't even blame you – I pity you for opening your heart to a hopeless affection. You have not attempted to take any underhand advantage – you have not spoken to my sister in secret. You are guilty of weakness and want of attention to your own best interests, but of nothing worse. If you had acted, in any single respect, less delicately and less modestly, I should have told you to leave the house without an instant's notice, or an instant's consultation of anybody. As it is, I blame the misfortune of your years and your position – I don't blame *you*. Shake hands – I have given you pain; I am going to give you more, but there is no help for it – shake hands with your friend, Marian Halcombe, first.'

The sudden kindness – the warm, high-minded, fearless sympathy which met me on such mercifully equal terms, which appealed with such delicate and generous abruptness straight to my heart, my honour, and my courage, overcame me in an instant. I tried to look at her when she took my hand, but my eyes were dim. I tried to thank her, but my voice failed me.

'Listen to me,' she said, considerately avoiding all notice of my loss of self-control. 'Listen to me, and let us get it over at once. It is a real true relief to me that I am not obliged, in what I have now to say, to enter into the question – the hard and cruel question as I think it – of social inequalities. Circumstances which will try you to the quick, spare me the ungracious necessity of paining a man who has lived in friendly intimacy under the same roof with myself by any humiliating reference to matters of rank and station. You must leave Limmeridge House, Mr Hartright, before more harm is done. It is my duty to say that to you; and it would be equally my duty to say it, under precisely the same serious necessity, if you were the representative of the oldest and wealthiest family in England. You must leave us, not because you are a teacher of drawing—'

She waited a moment, turned her face full on me, and reaching across the table, laid her hand firmly on my arm.

'Not because you are a teacher of drawing,' she repeated, 'but because Laura Fairlie is engaged to be married.'

The last word went like a bullet to my heart. My arm lost all sensation of the hand that grasped it. I never moved and never spoke. The sharp autumn breeze that scattered the dead leaves at our feet came as cold to me, on a sudden, as if my own mad hopes were dead leaves too, whirled away by the wind like the rest. Hopes! Betrothed, or not betrothed, she was equally far from *me*. Would other men have remembered that in my place? Not if they had loved her as I did.

The pang passed, and nothing but the dull numbing pain of it remained. I felt Miss Halcombe's hand again, tightening its hold on my arm – I raised my head and looked at her. Her large black eyes were rooted on me, watching the white change on my face, which I felt, and which she saw.

'Crush it!' she said. 'Here, where you first saw her, crush it! Don't shrink under it like a woman. Tear it out; trample it under foot like a man!'

The suppressed vehemence with which she spoke, the strength which her will – concentrated in the look she fixed on me, and in the hold on my arm that she had not yet relinquished – communicated to mine, steadied me. We both waited for a minute in silence. At the end of that time I had justified her generous faith in my manhood – I had, outwardly at least, recovered my self-control.

'Are you yourself again?'

'Enough myself, Miss Halcombe, to ask your pardon and hers. Enough myself to be guided by your advice, and to prove my gratitude in that way, if I can prove it in no other.'

'You have proved it already,' she answered, 'by those words. Mr Hartright, concealment is at an end between us. I cannot affect to hide from you what my sister has unconsciously shown to me. You must leave us for her sake, as well as for your own. Your presence here, your necessary intimacy with us, harmless as it has been, God knows, in all other respects, has unsteadied her and made her wretched. I, who love her better than my own life – I, who have learnt to believe in that pure, noble, innocent nature as I believe in my religion – know but too well the secret misery of self-reproach that she has been suffering since the first shadow of a feeling disloyal to her marriage engagement entered her heart in spite of her. I don't say – it would be useless to attempt to say it after what has happened – that her engagement has ever had a strong hold on her affections. It is an engagement of honour, not of love; her father sanctioned it on his deathbed, two years since; she herself neither welcomed it nor shrank from it – she was content to make it. Till you came here she was in the position of hundreds of other women, who marry men without being greatly attracted to them or greatly repelled by them, and who learn to love them (when they don't learn to hate!) after marriage, instead of before. I hope more earnestly than words can say – and you should have the self-sacrificing courage to hope too – that the new thoughts and feelings which have disturbed the old calmness and the old content have not taken root too deeply to be ever removed. Your absence (if I had less belief in your honour, and your courage, and your sense, I should not trust to them as I am trusting now) your absence will help my efforts, and time will help us all three. It is something to know that my first confidence in you was not all misplaced. It is something to know that you will not be less honest, less manly, less considerate towards the pupil whose relation to yourself you have had the misfortune to forget, than towards the stranger and the outcast whose appeal to you was not made in vain.'

Again the chance reference to the woman in white! Was there no possibility of speaking of Miss Fairlie and of me without raising the memory of Anne Catherick, and setting her between us like a fatality that it was hopeless to avoid?

'Tell me what apology I can make to Mr Fairlie for breaking my engagement,' I said. 'Tell me when to go after that apology is accepted. I promise implicit obedience to you and to your advice.'

'Time is every way of importance,' she answered. 'You heard me refer this morning to Monday next, and to the necessity of setting the purple room in order. The visitor whom we expect on Monday—'

I could not wait for her to be more explicit. Knowing what I knew now, the memory of Miss Fairlie's look and manner at the breakfast-table told me that the expected visitor at Limmeridge House was her future husband. I tried to force it back; but something rose within me at that moment stronger than my own will, and I interrupted Miss Halcombe.

'Let me go today,' I said bitterly. 'The sooner the better.'

'No, not today,' she replied. 'The only reason you can assign to Mr Fairlie for your departure, before the end of your engagement, must be that an unforeseen necessity compels you to ask his permission to return at once to London. You must wait till tomorrow to tell him that, at the time when the post comes in, because he will then understand the sudden change in your plans, by associating it with the arrival of a letter from London. It is miserable and sickening to descend to deceit, even of the most harmless kind – but I know Mr Fairlie, and if you once excite his suspicions that you are trifling with him, he will refuse to release you. Speak to him on Friday morning: occupy yourself afterwards (for the sake of your own interests with your employer) in leaving your unfinished work in as little confusion as possible, and quit this place on Saturday. It will be time enough then, Mr Hartright, for you, and for all of us.'

Before I could assure her that she might depend on my acting in the strictest accordance with her wishes, we were both startled by advancing footsteps in the shrubbery. Some one was coming from the house to seek for us! I felt the blood rush into my cheeks and then leave them again. Could the third person who was fast approaching us, at such a time and under such circumstances, be Miss Fairlie?

It was a relief – so sadly, so hopelessly was my position towards her changed already – it was absolutely a relief to me, when the person who had disturbed us appeared at the entrance of the summer-house, and proved to be only Miss Fairlie's maid.

'Could I speak to you for a moment, miss?' said the girl, in rather a flurried, unsettled manner.

Miss Halcombe descended the steps into the shrubbery, and walked aside a few paces with the maid.

Left by myself, my mind reverted, with a sense of forlorn wretchedness which it is not in any words that I can find to describe, to my approaching return to the solitude and the despair of my lonely London home. Thoughts of my kind old mother, and of my sister, who had rejoiced with her so innocently over my prospects in Cumberland – thoughts whose long banishment from my heart it was now my shame and my reproach to realise for the first time – came back to me with the loving mournfulness of old, neglected friends. My mother and my sister, what would they feel when I returned to them from my broken engagement, with the confession of my miserable secret – they who had parted from me so hopefully on that last happy night in the Hampstead cottage!

Anne Catherick again! Even the memory of the farewell evening with my mother and my sister could not return to me now unconnected with that other memory of the moonlight walk back to London. What did it mean? Were that woman and I to meet once more? It was possible, at the least. Did she know that I lived in London? Yes; I had told her so, either before or after that strange question of hers, when she had asked me so distrustfully if I knew many men of the rank of Baronet. Either before or after – my mind was not calm enough, then, to remember which.

A few minutes elapsed before Miss Halcombe dismissed the maid and came back to me. She, too, looked flurried and unsettled now.

'We have arranged all that is necessary, Mr Hartright,' she said. 'We have understood each other, as friends should, and we may go back at once to the house. To tell you the truth, I am uneasy about Laura. She has sent to say she wants to see me directly, and the maid reports that her mistress is apparently very much agitated by a letter that she has received this morning – the same letter, no doubt, which I sent on to the house before we came here.'

We retraced our steps together hastily along the shrubbery path. Although Miss Halcombe had ended all that she thought it necessary to say on her side, I had not ended all that I wanted to say on mine. From the moment when I had discovered that the expected visitor at Limmeridge was Miss Fairlie's future husband, I had felt a bitter curiosity, a burning envious eagerness, to know who he was. It was possible that a future opportunity of putting the question might not easily offer, so I risked asking it on our way back to the house.

'Now that you are kind enough to tell me we have understood each other, Miss Halcombe,' I said, 'now that you are sure of my gratitude for your forbearance and my obedience to your wishes, may I venture to ask who'—(I hesitated – I had forced myself to think of him, but it was harder still to speak of him, as her promised husband)—'who the gentleman engaged to Miss Fairlie is?'

Her mind was evidently occupied with the message she had received from her sister. She answered in a hasty, absent way –

'A gentleman of large property in Hampshire.'

Hampshire! Anne Catherick's native place. Again, and yet again, the woman in white. There *was* a fatality in it.

'And his name?' I said, as quietly and indifferently as I could.

'Sir Percival Glyde.'

Sir – Sir Percival! Anne Catherick's question – that suspicious question

about the men of the rank of Baronet whom I might happen to know – had
hardly been dismissed from my mind by Miss Halcombe's return to me in
the summer-house, before it was recalled again by her own answer. I stopped
suddenly, and looked at her.

'Sir Percival Glyde,' she repeated, imagining that I had not heard her
former reply.

'Knight, or Baronet?' I asked, with an agitation that I could hide no longer.

She paused for a moment, and then answered, rather coldly –

'Baronet, of course.'

XI

Not a word more was said, on either side, as we walked back to the house.
Miss Halcombe hastened immediately to her sister's room, and I withdrew
to my studio to set in order all of Mr Fairlie's drawings that I had not yet
mounted and restored before I resigned them to the care of other hands.
Thoughts that I had hitherto restrained, thoughts that made my position harder
than ever to endure, crowded on me now that I was alone.

She was engaged to be married, and her future husband was Sir Percival
Glyde. A man of the rank of Baronet, and the owner of property in Hampshire.

There were hundreds of baronets in England, and dozens of landowners
in Hampshire. Judging by the ordinary rules of evidence, I had not the shadow
of a reason, thus far, for connecting Sir Percival Glyde with the suspicious
words of inquiry that had been spoken to me by the woman in white. And
yet, I did connect him with them. Was it because he had now become associated in my mind with Miss Fairlie, Miss Fairlie being, in her turn, associated
with Anne Catherick, since the night when I had discovered the ominous
likeness between them? Had the events of the morning so unnerved me
already that I was at the mercy of any delusion which common chances and
common coincidences might suggest to my imagination? Impossible to say.
I could only feel that what had passed between Miss Halcombe and myself,
on our way from the summer-house, had affected me very strangely. The
foreboding of some undiscoverable danger lying hid from us all in the darkness of the future was strong on me. The doubt whether I was not linked
already to a chain of events which even my approaching departure from
Cumberland would be powerless to snap asunder – the doubt whether we
any of us saw the end as the end would really be – gathered more and more
darkly over my mind. Poignant as it was, the sense of suffering caused by
the miserable end of my brief, presumptuous love seemed to be blunted and
deadened by the still stronger sense of something obscurely impending,
something invisibly threatening, that Time was holding over our heads.

I had been engaged with the drawings little more than half an hour, when there was a knock at the door. It opened, on my answering; and, to my surprise, Miss Halcombe entered the room.

Her manner was angry and agitated. She caught up a chair for herself before I could give her one, and sat down in it, close at my side.

'Mr Hartright,' she said, 'I had hoped that all painful subjects of conversation were exhausted between us, for today at least. But it is not to be so. There is some underhand villainy at work to frighten my sister about her approaching marriage. You saw me send the gardener on to the house, with a letter addressed, in a strange handwriting, to Miss Fairlie?'

'Certainly.'

'The letter is an anonymous letter – a vile attempt to injure Sir Percival Glyde in my sister's estimation. It has so agitated and alarmed her that I have had the greatest possible difficulty in composing her spirits sufficiently to allow me to leave her room and come here. I know this is a family matter on which I ought not to consult you, and in which you can feel no concern or interest—'

'I beg your pardon, Miss Halcombe. I feel the strongest possible concern and interest in anything that affects Miss Fairlie's happiness or yours.'

'I am glad to hear you say so. You are the only person in the house, or out of it, who can advise me. Mr Fairlie, in his state of health and with his horror of difficulties and mysteries of all kinds, is not to be thought of. The clergyman is a good, weak man, who knows nothing out of the routine of his duties; and our neighbours are just the sort of comfortable, jog-trot acquaintances whom one cannot disturb in times of trouble and danger. What I want to know is this: ought I at once to take such steps as I can to discover the writer of the letter? or ought I to wait, and apply to Mr Fairlie's legal adviser tomorrow? It is a question – perhaps a very important one – of gaining or losing a day. Tell me what you think, Mr Hartright. If necessity had not already obliged me to take you into my confidence under very delicate circumstances, even my helpless situation would, perhaps, be no excuse for me. But as things are I cannot surely be wrong, after all that has passed between us, in forgetting that you are a friend of only three months' standing.'

She gave me the letter. It began abruptly, without any preliminary form of address, as follows –

Do you believe in dreams? I hope, for your own sake, that you do. See what Scripture says about dreams and their fulfilment (Genesis xl. 8, xli. 25; Daniel iv. 18–25), and take the warning I send you before it is too late.

    Last night I dreamed about you, Miss Fairlie. I dreamed that I was

standing inside the communion rails of a church – I on one side of
the altar-table, and the clergyman, with his surplice and his prayer-
book, on the other.

After a time there walked towards us, down the aisle of the church,
a man and a woman, coming to be married. You were the woman. You
looked so pretty and innocent in your beautiful white silk dress, and
your long white lace veil, that my heart felt for you, and the tears
came into my eyes.

They were tears of pity, young lady, that heaven blesses; and instead
of falling from my eyes like the everyday tears that we all of us shed,
they turned into two rays of light which slanted nearer and nearer to
the man standing at the altar with you, till they touched his breast.
The two rays sprang in arches like two rainbows between me and him.
I looked along them, and I saw down into his inmost heart.

The outside of the man you were marrying was fair enough to see.
He was neither tall nor short – he was a little below the middle size.
A light, active, high-spirited man – about five-and-forty years old, to
look at. He had a pale face, and was bald over the forehead, but had
dark hair on the rest of his head. His beard was shaven on his chin,
but was let to grow, of a fine rich brown, on his cheeks and his upper
lip. His eyes were brown too, and very bright; his nose straight and
handsome, and delicate enough to have done for a woman's. His hands
the same. He was troubled from time to time with a dry hacking cough,
and when he put up his white right hand to his mouth, he showed the
red scar of an old wound across the back of it. Have I dreamt of the
right man? You know best, Miss Fairlie, and you can say if I was
deceived or not. Read next, what I saw beneath the outside – I entreat
you, read, and profit.

I looked along the two rays of light, and I saw down into his inmost
heart. It was black as night, and on it were written, in the red flaming
letters which are the handwriting of the fallen angel, 'Without pity and
without remorse. He has strewn with misery the paths of others, and
he will live to strew with misery the path of this woman by his side.'
I read that, and then the rays of light shifted and pointed over his
shoulder; and there, behind him, stood a fiend laughing. And the rays
of light shifted once more, and pointed over your shoulder; and there
behind you, stood an angel weeping. And the rays of light shifted for
the third time, and pointed straight between you and that man. They
widened and widened, thrusting you both asunder, one from the other.
And the clergyman looked for the marriage-service in vain: it was gone
out of the book, and he shut up the leaves, and put it from him in

despair. And I woke with my eyes full of tears and my heart beating – for I believe in dreams.

Believe too, Miss Fairlie – I beg of you, for your own sake, believe as I do. Joseph and Daniel, and others in Scripture, believed in dreams. Inquire into the past life of that man with the scar on his hand, before you say the words that make you his miserable wife. I don't give you this warning on my account, but on yours. I have an interest in your well-being that will live as long as I draw breath. Your mother's daughter has a tender place in my heart – for your mother was my first, my best, my only friend.

There the extraordinary letter ended, without signature of any sort.

The handwriting afforded no prospect of a clue. It was traced on ruled lines, in the cramped, conventional, copy-book character technically termed 'small hand.' It was feeble and faint, and defaced by blots, but had otherwise nothing to distinguish it.

'That is not an illiterate letter,' said Miss Halcombe, 'and at the same time, it is surely too incoherent to be the letter of an educated person in the higher ranks of life. The reference to the bridal dress and veil, and other little expressions, seem to point to it as the production of some woman. What do you think, Mr Hartright?'

'I think so too. It seems to me to be not only the letter of a woman, but of a woman whose mind must be—'

'Deranged?' suggested Miss Halcombe. 'It struck me in that light too.'

I did not answer. While I was speaking, my eyes rested on the last sentence of the letter: 'Your mother's daughter has a tender place in my heart – for your mother was my first, my best, my only friend.' Those words and the doubt which had just escaped me as to the sanity of the writer of the letter, acting together on my mind, suggested an idea, which I was literally afraid to express openly, or even to encourage secretly. I began to doubt whether my own faculties were not in danger of losing their balance. It seemed almost like a monomania to be tracing back everything strange that happened, everything unexpected that was said, always to the same hidden source and the same sinister influence. I resolved, this time, in defence of my own courage and my own sense, to come to no decision that plain fact did not warrant, and to turn my back resolutely on everything that tempted me in the shape of surmise.

'If we have any chance of tracing the person who has written this,' I said, returning the letter to Miss Halcombe, 'there can be no harm in seizing our opportunity the moment it offers. I think we ought to speak to the gardener again about the elderly woman who gave him the letter, and then to continue our inquiries in the village. But first let me ask a question. You mentioned just now the alternative of consulting Mr Fairlie's legal adviser tomorrow. Is there no possibility of communicating with him earlier? Why not today?'

'I can only explain,' replied Miss Halcombe, 'by entering into certain particulars, connected with my sister's marriage-engagement, which I did not think it necessary or desirable to mention to you this morning. One of Sir Percival Glyde's objects in coming here on Monday, is to fix the period of his marriage, which has hitherto been left quite unsettled. He is anxious that the event should take place before the end of the year.'

'Does Miss Fairlie know of that wish?' I asked eagerly.

'She has no suspicion of it, and after what has happened, I shall not take the responsibility upon myself of enlightening her. Sir Percival has only mentioned his views to Mr Fairlie, who has told me himself that he is ready and anxious, as Laura's guardian, to forward them. He has written to London, to the family solicitor, Mr Gilmore. Mr Gilmore happens to be away in Glasgow on business, and he has replied by proposing to stop at Limmeridge House on his way back to town. He will arrive tomorrow, and will stay with us a few days, so as to allow Sir Percival time to plead his own cause. If he succeeds, Mr Gilmore will then return to London, taking with him his instructions for my sister's marriage-settlement. You understand now, Mr Hartright, why I speak of waiting to take legal advice until tomorrow? Mr Gilmore is the old and tried friend of two generations of Fairlies, and we can trust him, as we could trust no one else.'

The marriage-settlement! The mere hearing of those two words stung me with a jealous despair that was poison to my higher and better instincts. I began to think – it is hard to confess this, but I must suppress nothing from beginning to end of the terrible story that I now stand committed to reveal – I began to think, with a hateful eagerness of hope, of the vague charges against Sir Percival Glyde which the anonymous letter contained. What if those wild accusations rested on a foundation of truth? What if their truth could be proved before the fatal words of consent were spoken, and the marriage-settlement was drawn? I have tried to think since, that the feeling which then animated me began and ended in pure devotion to Miss Fairlie's interests, but I have never succeeded in deceiving myself into believing it, and I must not now attempt to deceive others. The feeling began and ended in reckless, vindictive, hopeless hatred of the man who was to marry her.

'If we are to find out anything,' I said, speaking under the new influence which was now directing me, 'we had better not let another minute slip by us unemployed. I can only suggest, once more, the propriety of questioning the gardener a second time, and of inquiring in the village immediately afterwards.'

'I think I may be of help to you in both cases,' said Miss Halcombe, rising. 'Let us go, Mr Hartright, at once, and do the best we can together.'

I had the door in my hand to open it for her – but I stopped, on a sudden, to ask an important question before we set forth.

'One of the paragraphs of the anonymous letter,' I said, 'contains some sentences of minute personal description. Sir Percival Glyde's name is not mentioned, I know – but does that description at all resemble him?'

'Accurately – even in stating his age to be forty-five—'

Forty-five; and she was not yet twenty-one! Men of his age married wives of her age every day – and experience had shown those marriages to be often the happiest ones. I knew that – and yet even the mention of his age, when I contrasted it with hers, added to my blind hatred and distrust of him.

'Accurately,' Miss Halcombe continued, 'even to the scar on his right hand, which is the scar of a wound that he received years since when he was travelling in Italy. There can be no doubt that every peculiarity of his personal appearance is thoroughly well known to the writer of the letter.'

'Even a cough that he is troubled with is mentioned, if I remember right?'

'Yes, and mentioned correctly. He treats it lightly himself, though it sometimes makes his friends anxious about him.'

'I suppose no whispers have ever been heard against his character?'

'Mr Hartright! I hope you are not unjust enough to let that infamous letter influence you?'

I felt the blood rush into my cheeks, for I knew that it *had* influenced me.

'I hope not,' I answered confusedly. 'Perhaps I had no right to ask the question.'

'I am not sorry you asked it,' she said, 'for it enables me to do justice to Sir Percival's reputation. Not a whisper, Mr Hartright, has ever reached me, or my family, against him. He has fought successfully two contested elections, and has come out of the ordeal unscathed. A man who can do that, in England, is a man whose character is established.'

I opened the door for her in silence, and followed her out. She had not convinced me. If the recording angel had come down from heaven to confirm her, and had opened his book to my mortal eyes, the recording angel would not have convinced me.

We found the gardener at work as usual. No amount of questioning could extract a single answer of any importance from the lad's impenetrable stupidity. The woman who had given him the letter was an elderly woman;

she had not spoken a word to him, and she had gone away towards the south in a great hurry. That was all the gardener could tell us.

The village lay southward of the house. So to the village we went next.

XII

Our inquiries at Limmeridge were patiently pursued in all directions, and among all sorts and conditions of people. But nothing came of them. Three of the villagers did certainly assure us that they had seen the woman, but as they were quite unable to describe her, and quite incapable of agreeing about the exact direction in which she was proceeding when they last saw her, these three bright exceptions to the general rule of total ignorance afforded no more real assistance to us than the mass of their unhelpful and unobservant neighbours.

The course of our useless investigations brought us, in time, to the end of the village at which the schools established by Mrs Fairlie were situated. As we passed the side of the building appropriated to the use of the boys, I suggested the propriety of making a last inquiry of the schoolmaster, whom we might presume to be, in virtue of his office, the most intelligent man in the place.

'I am afraid the schoolmaster must have been occupied with his scholars,' said Miss Halcombe, 'just at the time when the woman passed through the village and returned again. However, we can but try.'

We entered the playground enclosure, and walked by the schoolroom window to get round to the door, which was situated at the back of the building. I stopped for a moment at the window and looked in.

The schoolmaster was sitting at his high desk, with his back to me, apparently haranguing the pupils, who were all gathered together in front of him, with one exception. The one exception was a sturdy white-headed boy, standing apart from all the rest on a stool in a corner – a forlorn little Crusoe, isolated in his own desert island of solitary penal disgrace.

The door, when we got round to it, was ajar, and the school-master's voice reached us plainly, as we both stopped for a minute under the porch.

'Now, boys,' said the voice, 'mind what I tell you. If I hear another word spoken about ghosts in this school, it will be the worse for all of you. There are no such things as ghosts, and therefore any boy who believes in ghosts believes in what can't possibly be; and a boy who belongs to Limmeridge School, and believes in what can't possibly be, sets up his back against reason and discipline, and must be punished accordingly. You all see Jacob Postlethwaite standing up on the stool there in disgrace. He has been punished, not because he said he saw a ghost last night, but because he is too impudent and too obstinate to listen to reason, and because he persists in saying he saw the ghost after I have told him that no such thing can possibly be. If nothing else will do, I mean to cane the ghost out of Jacob Postlethwaite, and if the thing spreads among any of the rest of you, I mean to go a step farther, and cane the ghost out of the whole school.'

'We seem to have chosen an awkward moment for our visit,' said Miss Halcombe, pushing open the door at the end of the schoolmaster's address, and leading the way in.

Our appearance produced a strong sensation among the boys. They appeared to think that we had arrived for the express purpose of seeing Jacob Postlethwaite caned.

'Go home all of you to dinner,' said the schoolmaster, 'except Jacob. Jacob must stop where he is; and the ghost may bring him his dinner, if the ghost pleases.'

Jacob's fortitude deserted him at the double disappearance of his schoolfellows and his prospect of dinner. He took his hands out of his pockets, looked hard at his knuckles, raised them with great deliberation to his eyes, and when they got there, ground them round and round slowly, accompanying the action by short spasms of sniffing, which followed each other at regular intervals – the nasal minute guns of juvenile distress.

'We came here to ask you a question, Mr Dempster,' said Miss Halcombe, addressing the schoolmaster; 'and we little expected to find you occupied in exorcising a ghost. What does it all mean? What has really happened?'

'That wicked boy has been frightening the whole school, Miss Halcombe, by declaring that he saw a ghost yesterday evening,' answered the master; 'and he still persists in his absurd story, in spite of all that I can say to him.'

'Most extraordinary,' said Miss Halcombe. 'I should not have thought it possible that any of the boys had imagination enough to see a ghost. This is a new accession indeed to the hard labour of forming the youthful mind at Limmeridge, and I heartily wish you well through it, Mr Dempster. In the meantime, let me explain why you see me here, and what it is I want.'

She then put the same question to the schoolmaster which we had asked already of almost every one else in the village. It was met by the same discouraging answer. Mr Dempster had not set eyes on the stranger of whom we were in search.

'We may as well return to the house, Mr Hartright,' said Miss Halcombe; 'the information we want is evidently not to be found.'

She had bowed to Mr Dempster, and was about to leave the schoolroom, when the forlorn position of Jacob Postlethwaite, piteously sniffing on the stool of penitence, attracted her attention as she passed him, and made her stop good-humouredly to speak a word to the little prisoner before she opened the door.

'You foolish boy,' she said, 'why don't you beg Mr Dempster's pardon, and hold your tongue about the ghost?'

'Eh! – but I saw t' ghaist,' persisted Jacob Postlethwaite, with a stare of terror and a burst of tears.

'Stuff and nonsense! You saw nothing of the kind. Ghost indeed! What ghost—'

'I beg your pardon, Miss Halcombe,' interposed the schoolmaster a little uneasily—'but I think you had better not question the boy. The obstinate folly of his story is beyond all belief; and you might lead him into ignorantly—'

'Ignorantly what?' inquired Miss Halcombe sharply.

'Ignorantly shocking your feelings,' said Mr Dempster, looking very much discomposed.

'Upon my word, Mr Dempster, you pay my feelings a great compliment in thinking them weak enough to be shocked by such an urchin as that!' She turned with an air of satirical defiance to little Jacob, and began to question him directly. 'Come!' she said, 'I mean to know all about this. You naughty boy, when did you see the ghost?'

'Yestere'en, at the gloaming,' replied Jacob.

'Oh! you saw it yesterday evening, in the twilight? And what was it like?'

'Arl in white – as a ghaist should be,' answered the ghost-seer, with a confidence beyond his years.

'And where was it?'

'Away yander, in t' kirkyard – where a ghaist ought to be.'

'As a "ghaist" should be – where a "ghaist" ought to be – why, you little fool, you talk as if the manners and customs of ghosts had been familiar to you from your infancy! You have got your story at your fingers' ends, at any rate. I suppose I shall hear next that you can actually tell me whose ghost it was?'

'Eh! but I just can,' replied Jacob, nodding his head with an air of gloomy triumph.

Mr Dempster had already tried several times to speak while Miss Halcombe was examining his pupil, and he now interposed resolutely enough to make himself heard.

'Excuse me, Miss Halcombe,' he said, 'if I venture to say that you are only encouraging the boy by asking him these questions.'

'I will merely ask one more, Mr Dempster, and then I shall be quite satisfied. Well,' she continued, turning to the boy, 'and whose ghost was it?'

'T' ghaist of Mistress Fairlie,' answered Jacob in a whisper.

The effect which this extraordinary reply produced on Miss Halcombe fully justified the anxiety which the schoolmaster had shown to prevent her from hearing it. Her face crimsoned with indignation – she turned upon little Jacob with an angry suddenness which terrified him into a fresh burst of tears – opened her lips to speak to him – then controlled herself, and addressed the master instead of the boy.

'It is useless,' she said, 'to hold such a child as that responsible for what he says. I have little doubt that the idea has been put into his head by others. If there are people in this village, Mr Dempster, who have forgotten the respect and gratitude due from every soul in it to my mother's memory, I will find them out, and if I have any influence with Mr Fairlie, they shall suffer for it.'

'I hope – indeed, I am sure, Miss Halcombe – that you are mistaken,' said the schoolmaster. 'The matter begins and ends with the boy's own perversity and folly. He saw, or thought he saw, a woman in white, yesterday evening, as he was passing the churchyard; and the figure, real or fancied, was standing by the marble cross, which he and every one else in Limmeridge knows to be the monument over Mrs Fairlie's grave. These two circumstances are surely sufficient to have suggested to the boy himself the answer which has so naturally shocked you?'

Although Miss Halcombe did not seem to be convinced, she evidently felt that the schoolmaster's statement of the case was too sensible to be openly combated. She merely replied by thanking him for his attention, and by promising to see him again when her doubts were satisfied. This said, she bowed, and led the way out of the schoolroom.

Throughout the whole of this strange scene I had stood apart, listening attentively, and drawing my own conclusions. As soon as we were alone again, Miss Halcombe asked me if I had formed any opinion on what I had heard.

'A very strong opinion,' I answered; 'the boy's story, as I believe, has a foundation in fact. I confess I am anxious to see the monument over Mrs Fairlie's grave, and to examine the ground about it.'

'You shall see the grave.'

She paused after making that reply, and reflected a little as we walked on. 'What has happened in the schoolroom,' she resumed, 'has so completely distracted my attention from the subject of the letter, that I feel a little bewildered when I try to return to it. Must we give up all idea of making any further inquiries, and wait to place the thing in Mr Gilmore's hands tomorrow?'

'By no means, Miss Halcombe. What has happened in the schoolroom encourages me to persevere in the investigation.'

'Why does it encourage you?'

'Because it strengthens a suspicion I felt when you gave me the letter to read.'

'I suppose you had your reasons, Mr Hartright, for concealing that suspicion from me till this moment?'

'I was afraid to encourage it in myself. I thought it was utterly preposterous – I distrusted it as the result of some perversity in my own imagination. But I can do so no longer. Not only the boy's own answers to your questions, but even a chance expression that dropped from the schoolmaster's lips in explaining his story, have forced the idea back into my mind. Events may yet prove that idea to be a delusion, Miss Halcombe; but the belief is strong in me, at this moment, that the fancied ghost in the churchyard, and the writer of the anonymous letter, are one and the same person.'

She stopped, turned pale, and looked me eagerly in the face.

'What person?'

'The schoolmaster unconsciously told you. When he spoke of the figure that the boy saw in the churchyard he called it "a woman in white." '

'Not Anne Catherick?'

'Yes, Anne Catherick.'

She put her hand through my arm and leaned on it heavily.

'I don't know why,' she said in low tones, 'but there is something in this suspicion of yours that seems to startle and unnerve me. I feel—' She stopped, and tried to laugh it off. 'Mr Hartright,' she went on, 'I will show you the grave, and then go back at once to the house. I had better not leave Laura too long alone. I had better go back and sit with her.'

We were close to the churchyard when she spoke. The church, a dreary building of grey stone, was situated in a little valley, so as to be sheltered from the bleak winds blowing over the moorland all round it. The burial-ground advanced, from the side of the church, a little way up the slope of the hill. It was surrounded by a rough, low stone wall, and was bare and open to the sky, except at one extremity, where a brook trickled down the stony hill-side, and a clump of dwarf trees threw their narrow shadows over the short, meagre grass. Just beyond the brook and the trees, and not far from one of the three stone stiles which afforded entrance, at various points, to the churchyard, rose the white marble cross that distinguished Mrs Fairlie's grave from the humbler monuments scattered about it.

'I need go no farther with you,' said Miss Halcombe, pointing to the grave. 'You will let me know if you find anything to confirm the idea you have just mentioned to me. Let us meet again at the house.'

She left me. I descended at once to the churchyard, and crossed the stile which led directly to Mrs Fairlie's grave.

The grass about it was too short, and the ground too hard, to show any marks of footsteps. Disappointed thus far, I next looked attentively at the cross, and at the square block of marble below it, on which the inscription was cut.

The natural whiteness of the cross was a little clouded, here and there, by weather stains, and rather more than one half of the square block beneath it, on the side which bore the inscription, was in the same condition. The other half, however, attracted my attention at once by its singular freedom from stain or impurity of any kind. I looked closer, and saw that it had been cleaned – recently cleaned, in a downward direction from top to bottom. The boundary line between the part that had been cleaned and the part that had not was traceable wherever the inscription left a blank space of marble – sharply traceable as a line that had been produced by artificial means. Who had begun the cleansing of the marble, and who had left it unfinished?

I looked about me, wondering how the question was to be solved. No sign of a habitation could be discerned from the point at which I was standing – the burial-ground was left in the lonely possession of the dead. I returned to the church, and walked round it till I came to the back of the building; then crossed the boundary wall beyond, by another of the stone stiles, and found myself at the head of a path leading down into a deserted stone quarry. Against one side of the quarry a little two-room cottage was built, and just outside the door an old woman was engaged in washing.

I walked up to her, and entered into conversation about the church and burial-ground. She was ready enough to talk, and almost the first words she said informed me that her husband filled the two offices of clerk and sexton. I said a few words next in praise of Mrs Fairlie's monument. The old woman shook her head, and told me I had not seen it at its best. It was her husband's business to look after it, but he had been so ailing and weak for months and months past, that he had hardly been able to crawl into church on Sundays to do his duty, and the monument had been neglected in consequence. He was getting a little better now, and in a week or ten days' time he hoped to be strong enough to set to work and clean it.

This information – extracted from a long rambling answer in the broadest Cumberland dialect – told me all that I most wanted to know. I gave the poor woman a trifle, and returned at once to Limmeridge House.

The partial cleansing of the monument had evidently been accomplished by a strange hand. Connecting what I had discovered, thus far, with what I had suspected after hearing the story of the ghost seen at twilight, I wanted nothing more to confirm my resolution to watch Mrs Fairlie's grave, in secret, that evening, returning to it at sunset, and waiting within sight of it till the night fell. The work of cleansing the monument had been left unfinished, and the person by whom it had been begun might return to complete it.

On getting back to the house I informed Miss Halcombe of what I intended to do. She looked surprised and uneasy while I was explaining my purpose, but she made no positive objection to the execution of it. She only said, 'I hope it may end well.'

Just as she was leaving me again, I stopped her to inquire, as calmly as I could, after Miss Fairlie's health. She was in better spirits, and Miss Halcombe hoped she might be induced to take a little walking exercise while the afternoon sun lasted.

I returned to my own room to resume setting the drawings in order. It was necessary to do this, and doubly necessary to keep my mind employed on anything that would help to distract my attention from myself, and from the hopeless future that lay before me. From time to time I paused in my work to look out of window and watch the sky as the sun sank nearer and nearer to the horizon. On one of those occasions I saw a figure on the broad gravel walk under my window. It was Miss Fairlie.

I had not seen her since the morning, and I had hardly spoken to her then. Another day at Limmeridge was all that remained to me, and after that day my eyes might never look on her again. This thought was enough to hold me at the window. I had sufficient consideration for her to arrange the blind so that she might not see me if she looked up, but I had no strength to resist the temptation of letting my eyes, at least, follow her as far as they could on her walk.

She was dressed in a brown cloak, with a plain black silk gown under it. On her head was the same simple straw hat which she had worn on the morning when we first met. A veil was attached to it now which hid her face from me. By her side trotted a little Italian greyhound, the pet companion of all her walks, smartly dressed in a scarlet cloth wrapper, to keep the sharp air from his delicate skin. She did not seem to notice the dog. She walked straight forward, with her head drooping a little, and her arms folded in her cloak. The dead leaves, which had whirled in the wind before me when I had heard of her marriage engagement in the morning, whirled in the wind before her, and rose and fell and scattered themselves at her feet as she walked on in the pale waning sunlight. The dog shivered and trembled, and pressed against her dress impatiently for notice and encouragement. But she never heeded him. She walked on, farther and farther away from me, with the dead leaves whirling about her on the path – walked on, till my aching eyes could see her no more, and I was left alone again with my own heavy heart.

In another hour's time I had done my work, and the sunset was at hand. I got my hat and coat in the hall, and slipped out of the house without meeting any one.

The clouds were wild in the western heaven, and the wind blew chill from the sea. Far as the shore was, the sound of the surf swept over the intervening moorland, and beat drearily in my ears when I entered the churchyard. Not a living creature was in sight. The place looked lonelier than ever as I chose my position, and waited and watched, with my eyes on the white cross that rose over Mrs Fairlie's grave.

XIII

The exposed situation of the churchyard had obliged me to be cautious in choosing the position that I was to occupy.

The main entrance to the church was on the side next to the burial-ground, and the door was screened by a porch walled in on either side. After some little hesitation, caused by natural reluctance to conceal myself, indispensable as that concealment was to the object in view, I had resolved on entering the porch. A loophole window was pierced in each of its side walls. Through one of these windows I could see Mrs Fairlie's grave. The other looked towards the stone quarry in which the sexton's cottage was built. Before me, fronting the porch entrance, was a patch of bare burial-ground, a line of low stone wall, and a strip of lonely brown hill, with the sunset clouds sailing heavily over it before the strong, steady wind. No living creature was visible or audible – no bird flew by me, no dog barked from the sexton's cottage. The pauses in the dull beating of the surf were filled up by the dreary rustling of the dwarf trees near the grave, and the cold faint bubble of the brook over its stony bed. A dreary scene and a dreary hour. My spirits sank fast as I counted out the minutes of the evening in my hiding-place under the church porch.

It was not twilight yet – the light of the setting sun still lingered in the heavens, and little more than the first half-hour of my solitary watch had elapsed – when I heard footsteps and a voice. The footsteps were approaching from the other side of the church, and the voice was a woman's.

'Don't you fret, my dear, about the letter,' said the voice. 'I gave it to the lad quite safe, and the lad he took it from me without a word. He went his way and I went mine, and not a living soul followed me afterwards – that I'll warrant.'

These words strung up my attention to a pitch of expectation that was almost painful. There was a pause of silence, but the footsteps still advanced. In another moment two persons, both women, passed within my range of view from the porch window. They were walking straight towards the grave; and therefore they had their backs turned towards me.

One of the women was dressed in a bonnet and shawl. The other wore a long travelling-cloak of a dark-blue colour, with the hood drawn over her head. A few inches of her gown were visible below the cloak. My heart beat fast as I noted the colour – it was white.

After advancing about half-way between the church and the grave they stopped, and the woman in the cloak turned her head towards her companion. But her side face, which a bonnet might now have allowed me to see, was hidden by the heavy, projecting edge of the hood.

'Mind you keep that comfortable warm cloak on,' said the same voice which I had already heard – the voice of the woman in the shawl. 'Mrs Todd is right about your looking too particular, yesterday, all in white. I'll walk about a little while you're here, churchyards being not at all in my way, whatever they may be in yours. Finish what you want to do before I come back, and let us be sure and get home again before night.'

With those words she turned about, and retracing her steps, advanced with her face towards me. It was the face of an elderly woman, brown, rugged, and healthy, with nothing dishonest or suspicious in the look of it. Close to the church she stopped to pull her shawl closer round her.

'Queer,' she said to herself, 'always queer, with her whims and her ways, ever since I can remember her. Harmless, though – as harmless, poor soul, as a little child.'

She sighed – looked about the burial-ground nervously – shook her head, as if the dreary prospect by no means pleased her, and disappeared round the corner of the church.

I doubted for a moment whether I ought to follow and speak to her or not. My intense anxiety to find myself face to face with her companion helped me to decide in the negative. I could ensure seeing the woman in the shawl by waiting near the churchyard until she came back – although it seemed more than doubtful whether she could give me the information of which I was in search. The person who had delivered the letter was of little consequence. The person who had written it was the one centre of interest, and the one source of information, and that person I now felt convinced was before me in the churchyard.

While these ideas were passing through my mind I saw the woman in the cloak approach close to the grave, and stand looking at it for a little while. She then glanced all round her, and taking a white linen cloth or handkerchief from under her cloak, turned aside towards the brook. The little stream ran into the churchyard under a tiny archway in the bottom of the wall, and ran out again, after a winding course of a few dozen yards, under a similar opening. She dipped the cloth in the water, and returned to the grave. I saw her kiss the white cross, then kneel down before the inscription, and apply her wet cloth to the cleansing of it.

After considering how I could show myself with the least possible chance of frightening her, I resolved to cross the wall before me, to skirt round it outside, and to enter the churchyard again by the stile near the grave, in order that she might see me as I approached. She was so absorbed over her employment that she did not hear me coming until I had stepped over the stile. Then she looked up, started to her feet with a faint cry, and stood facing me in speechless and motionless terror.

'Don't be frightened,' I said. 'Surely you remember me?'

I stopped while I spoke – then advanced a few steps gently – then stopped again – and so approached by little and little till I was close to her. If there had been any doubt still left in my mind, it must have been now set at rest. There, speaking affrightedly for itself – there was the same face confronting me over Mrs Fairlie's grave which had first looked into mine on the high-road by night.

'You remember me?' I said. 'We met very late, and I helped you to find the way to London. Surely you have not forgotten that?'

Her features relaxed, and she drew a heavy breath of relief. I saw the new life of recognition stirring slowly under the death-like stillness which fear had set on her face.

'Don't attempt to speak to me just yet,' I went on. 'Take time to recover yourself – take time to feel quite certain that I am a friend.'

'You are very kind to me,' she murmured. 'As kind now as you were then.'

She stopped, and I kept silence on my side. I was not granting time for composure to her only, I was gaining time also for myself. Under the wan wild evening light, that woman and I were met together again, a grave between us, the dead about us, the lonesome hills closing us round on every side. The time, the place, the circumstances under which we now stood face to face in the evening stillness of that dreary valley – the lifelong interests which might hang suspended on the next chance words that passed between us – the sense that, for aught I knew to the contrary, the whole future of Laura Fairlie's life might be determined, for good or for evil, by my winning or losing the confidence of the forlorn creature who stood trembling by her mother's grave – all threatened to shake the steadiness and the self-control on which every inch of the progress I might yet make now depended. I tried hard, as I felt this, to possess myself of all my resources; I did my utmost to turn the few moments for reflection to the best account.

'Are you calmer now?' I said, as soon as I thought it time to speak again. 'Can you talk to me without feeling frightened, and without forgetting that I am a friend?'

'How did you come here?' she asked, without noticing what I had just said to her.

'Don't you remember my telling you, when we last met, that I was going to Cumberland? I have been in Cumberland ever since – I have been staying all the time at Limmeridge House.'

'At Limmeridge House!' Her pale face brightened as she repeated the words, her wandering eyes fixed on me with a sudden interest. 'Ah, how happy you must have been!' she said, looking at me eagerly, without a shadow of its former distrust left in her expression.

I took advantage of her newly-aroused confidence in me to observe her face, with an attention and a curiosity which I had hitherto restrained myself from showing, for caution's sake. I looked at her, with my mind full of that other lovely face which had so ominously recalled her to my memory on the terrace by moonlight. I had seen Anne Catherick's likeness in Miss Fairlie. I now saw Miss Fairlie's likeness in Anne Catherick – saw it all the more clearly because the points of dissimilarity between the two were presented to me as well as the points of resemblance. In the general outline of the countenance and general proportion of the features – in the colour of the hair and in the little nervous uncertainty about the lips – in the height and size of the figure, and the carriage of the head and body, the likeness appeared even more startling than I had ever felt it to be yet. But there the resemblance ended, and the dissimilarity, in details, began. The delicate beauty of Miss Fairlie's complexion, the transparent clearness of her eyes, the smooth purity of her skin, the tender bloom of colour on her lips, were all missing from the worn weary face that was now turned towards mine. Although I hated myself even for thinking such a thing, still, while I looked at the woman before me, the idea would force itself into my mind that one sad change, in the future, was all that was wanting to make the likeness complete, which I now saw to be so imperfect in detail. If ever sorrow and suffering set their profaning marks on the youth and beauty of Miss Fairlie's face, then, and then only, Anne Catherick and she would be the twin-sisters of chance resemblance, the living reflections of one another.

I shuddered at the thought. There was something horrible in the blind unreasoning distrust of the future which the mere passage of it through my mind seemed to imply. It was a welcome interruption to be roused by feeling Anne Catherick's hand laid on my shoulder. The touch was as stealthy and as sudden as that other touch which had petrified me from head to foot on the night when we first met.

'You are looking at me, and you are thinking of something,' she said, with her strange breathless rapidity of utterance. 'What is it?'

'Nothing extraordinary,' I answered. 'I was only wondering how you came here.'

'I came with a friend who is very good to me. I have only been here two days.'

'And you found your way to this place yesterday?'

'How do you know that?'

'I only guessed it.'

She turned from me, and knelt down before the inscription once more.

'Where should I go if not here?' she said. 'The friend who was better than a mother to me is the only friend I have to visit at Limmeridge. Oh, it makes my heart ache to see a stain on her tomb! It ought to be kept white as snow, for her sake. I was tempted to begin cleaning it yesterday, and I can't help coming back to go on with it today. Is there anything wrong in that? I hope not. Surely nothing can be wrong that I do for Mrs Fairlie's sake?'

The old grateful sense of her benefactress's kindness was evidently the ruling idea still in the poor creature's mind – the narrow mind which had but too plainly opened to no other lasting impression since that first impression of her younger and happier days. I saw that my best chance of winning her confidence lay in encouraging her to proceed with the artless employment which she had come into the burial-ground to pursue. She resumed it at once, on my telling her she might do so, touching the hard marble as tenderly as if it had been a sentient thing, and whispering the words of the inscription to herself, over and over again, as if the lost days of her girlhood had returned and she was patiently learning her lesson once more at Mrs Fairlie's knees.

'Should you wonder very much,' I said, preparing the way as cautiously as I could for the questions that were to come, 'if I owned that it is a satisfaction to me, as well as a surprise, to see you here? I felt very uneasy about you after you left me in the cab.'

She looked up quickly and suspiciously.

'Uneasy,' she repeated. 'Why?'

'A strange thing happened after we parted that night. Two men overtook me in a chaise. They did not see where I was standing, but they stopped near me, and spoke to a policeman on the other side of the way.'

She instantly suspended her employment. The hand holding the damp cloth with which she had been cleaning the inscription dropped to her side. The other hand grasped the marble cross at the head of the grave. Her face turned towards me slowly, with the blank look of terror set rigidly on it once more. I went on at all hazards – it was too late now to draw back.

'The two men spoke to the policeman,' I said, 'and asked him if he had seen you. He had not seen you; and then one of the men spoke again, and said you had escaped from his Asylum.'

She sprang to her feet as if my last words had set the pursuers on her track.

'Stop! and hear the end,' I cried. 'Stop! and you shall know how I befriended you. A word from me would have told the men which way you had gone – and I never spoke that word. I helped your escape – I made it safe and certain. Think, try to think. Try to understand what I tell you.'

My manner seemed to influence her more than my words. She made an effort to grasp the new idea. Her hands shifted the damp cloth hesitatingly from one to the other, exactly as they had shifted the little travelling-bag on the night when I first saw her. Slowly the purpose of my words seemed to force its way through the confusion and agitation of her mind. Slowly her features relaxed, and her eyes looked at me with their expression gaining in curiosity what it was fast losing in fear.

'*You* don't think I ought to be back in the Asylum, do you?' she said.

'Certainly not. I am glad you escaped from it – I am glad I helped you.'

'Yes, yes, you did help me indeed; you helped me at the hard part,' she went on a little vacantly. 'It was easy to escape, or I should not have got away. They never suspected me as they suspected the others. I was so quiet, and so obedient, and so easily frightened. The finding London was the hard part, and there you helped me. Did I thank you at the time? I thank you now very kindly.'

'Was the Asylum far from where you met me? Come! show that you believe me to be your friend, and tell me where it was.'

She mentioned the place – a private Asylum, as its situation informed me; a private Asylum not very far from the spot where I had seen her – and then, with evident suspicion of the use to which I might put her answer, anxiously repeated her former inquiry, '*You* don't think I ought to be taken back, do you?'

'Once again, I am glad you escaped – I am glad you prospered well after you left me,' I answered. 'You said you had a friend in London to go to. Did you find the friend?'

'Yes. It was very late, but there was a girl up at needle-work in the house, and she helped me to rouse Mrs Clements. Mrs Clements is my friend. A good, kind woman, but not like Mrs Fairlie. Ah no, nobody is like Mrs Fairlie!'

'Is Mrs Clements an old friend of yours? Have you known her a long time?'

'Yes, she was a neighbour of ours once, at home, in Hampshire, and liked me, and took care of me when I was a little girl. Years ago, when she went away from us, she wrote down in my Prayer-book for me where she was going to live in London, and she said, "If you are ever in trouble, Anne, come to me. I have no husband alive to say me nay, and no children to look after, and I will take care of you." Kind words, were they not? I suppose I remember them because they were kind. It's little enough I remember besides – little enough, little enough!'

'Had you no father or mother to take care of you?'

'Father? – I never saw him – I never heard mother speak of him. Father? Ah, dear! he is dead, I suppose.'

'And your mother?'

'I don't get on well with her. We are a trouble and a fear to each other.'

A trouble and a fear to each other! At those words the suspicion crossed my mind, for the first time, that her mother might be the person who had placed her under restraint.

'Don't ask me about mother,' she went on. 'I'd rather talk of Mrs Clements. Mrs Clements is like you, she doesn't think that I ought to be back in the Asylum, and she is as glad as you are that I escaped from it. She cried over my misfortune, and said it must be kept secret from everybody.'

Her 'misfortune.' In what sense was she using that word? In a sense which might explain her motive in writing the anonymous letter? In a sense which might show it to be the too common and too customary motive that has led many a woman to interpose anonymous hindrances to the marriage of the man who has ruined her? I resolved to attempt the clearing up of this doubt before more words passed between us on either side.

'What misfortune?' I asked.

'The misfortune of my being shut up,' she answered, with every appearance of feeling surprised at my question. 'What other misfortune could there be?'

I determined to persist, as delicately and forbearingly as possible. It was of very great importance that I should be absolutely sure of every step in the investigation which I now gained in advance.

'There is another misfortune,' I said, 'to which a woman may be liable, and by which she may suffer lifelong sorrow and shame.'

'What is it?' she asked eagerly.

'The misfortune of believing too innocently in her own virtue, and in the faith and honour of the man she loves,' I answered.

She looked up at me with the artless bewilderment of a child. Not the slightest confusion or change of colour – not the faintest trace of any secret consciousness of shame struggling to the surface appeared in her face – that face which betrayed every other emotion with such transparent clearness. No words that ever were spoken could have assured me, as her look and manner now assured me, that the motive which I had assigned for her writing the letter and sending it to Miss Fairlie was plainly and distinctly the wrong one. That doubt, at any rate, was now set at rest; but the very removal of it opened a new prospect of uncertainty. The letter, as I knew from positive testimony, pointed at Sir Percival Glyde, though it did not name him. She must have had some strong motive, originating in some deep sense of injury, for secretly denouncing him to Miss Fairlie in such terms as she had employed, and that motive was unquestionably not to be traced to the loss of her innocence and her character. Whatever wrong he might have inflicted on her was not of that nature. Of what nature could it be?

'I don't understand you,' she said, after evidently trying hard, and trying in vain, to discover the meaning of the words I had last said to her.

'Never mind,' I answered. 'Let us go on with what we were talking about. Tell me how long you stayed with Mrs Clements in London, and how you came here.'

'How long?' she repeated. 'I stayed with Mrs Clements till we both came to this place, two days ago.'

'You are living in the village, then?' I said. 'It is strange I should not have heard of you, though you have only been here two days.'

'No, no, not in the village. Three miles away at a farm. Do you know the farm? They call it Todd's Corner.'

I remembered the place perfectly – we had often passed by it in our drives. It was one of the oldest farms in the neighbourhood, situated in a solitary, sheltered spot, inland at the junction of two hills.

'They are relations of Mrs Clements at Todd's Corner,' she went on, 'and they had often asked her to go and see them. She said she would go, and take me with her, for the quiet and the fresh air. It was very kind, was it not? I would have gone anywhere to be quiet, and safe, and out of the way. But when I heard that Todd's Corner was near Limmeridge – oh! I was so happy I would have walked all the way barefoot to get there, and see the schools and the village and Limmeridge House again. They are very good people at Todd's Corner. I hope I shall stay there a long time. There is only one thing I don't like about them, and don't like about Mrs Clements—'

'What is it?'

'They will tease me about dressing all in white – they say it looks so particular. How do they know? Mrs Fairlie knew best. Mrs Fairlie would never have made me wear this ugly blue cloak! Ah! she was fond of white in her lifetime, and here is white stone about her grave – and I am making it whiter for her sake. She often wore white herself, and she always dressed her little daughter in white. Is Miss Fairlie well and happy? Does she wear white now, as she used when she was a girl?'

Her voice sank when she put the questions about Miss Fairlie, and she turned her head farther and farther away from me. I thought I detected, in the alteration of her manner, an uneasy consciousness of the risk she had run in sending the anonymous letter, and I instantly determined so to frame my answer as to surprise her into owning it.

'Miss Fairlie was not very well or very happy this morning,' I said.

She murmured a few words, but they were spoken so confusedly, and in such a low tone, that I could not even guess at what they meant.

'Did you ask me why Miss Fairlie was neither well nor happy this morning?' I continued.

'No,' she said quickly and eagerly—'oh no, I never asked that.'

'I will tell you without your asking,' I went on. 'Miss Fairlie has received your letter.'

She had been down on her knees for some little time past, carefully removing the last weather-stains left about the inscription while we were speaking together. The first sentence of the words I had just addressed to her made her pause in her occupation, and turn slowly without rising from her knees, so as to face me. The second sentence literally petrified her. The cloth she had been holding dropped from her hands – her lips fell apart – all the little colour that there was naturally in her face left it in an instant.

'How do you know?' she said faintly. 'Who showed it to you?' The blood rushed back into her face – rushed overwhelmingly, as the sense rushed upon her mind that her own words had betrayed her. She struck her hands together in despair. 'I never wrote it,' she gasped affrightedly; 'I know nothing about it!'

'Yes,' I said, 'you wrote it, and you know about it. It was wrong to send such a letter, it was wrong to frighten Miss Fairlie. If you had anything to say that it was right and necessary for her to hear, you should have gone yourself to Limmeridge House – you should have spoken to the young lady with your own lips.'

She crouched down over the flat stone of the grave, till her face was hidden on it, and made no reply.

'Miss Fairlie will be as good and kind to you as her mother was, if you mean well,' I went on. 'Miss Fairlie will keep your secret, and not let you come to any harm. Will you see her tomorrow at the farm? Will you meet her in the garden at Limmeridge House?'

'Oh, if I could die, and be hidden and at rest with *you*!' Her lips murmured the words close on the grave-stone, murmured them in tones of passionate endearment, to the dead remains beneath. 'You know how I love your child, for your sake! Oh, Mrs Fairlie! Mrs Fairlie! tell me how to save her. Be my darling and my mother once more, and tell me what to do for the best.'

I heard her lips kissing the stone – I saw her hands beating on it passionately. The sound and the sight deeply affected me. I stooped down, and took the poor helpless hands tenderly in mine, and tried to soothe her.

It was useless. She snatched her hands from me, and never moved her face from the stone. Seeing the urgent necessity of quieting her at any hazard and by any means, I appealed to the only anxiety that she appeared to feel, in connection with me and with my opinion of her – the anxiety to convince me of her fitness to be mistress of her own actions.

'Come, come,' I said gently. 'Try to compose yourself, or you will make me alter my opinion of you. Don't let me think that the person who put you in the Asylum might have had some excuse—'

The next words died away on my lips. The instant I risked that chance reference to the person who had put her in the Asylum she sprang up on her knees. A most extraordinary and startling change passed over her. Her face, at all ordinary times so touching to look at, in its nervous sensitiveness, weakness, and uncertainty, became suddenly darkened by an expression of maniacally intense hatred and fear, which communicated a wild, unnatural force to every feature. Her eyes dilated in the dim evening light, like the eyes of a wild animal. She caught up the cloth that had fallen at her side, as if it had been a living creature that she could kill, and crushed it in both her hands with such convulsive strength, that the few drops of moisture left in it trickled down on the stone beneath her.

'Talk of something else,' she said, whispering through her teeth. 'I shall lose myself if you talk of that.'

Every vestige of the gentler thoughts which had filled her mind hardly a minute since seemed to be swept from it now. It was evident that the impression left by Mrs Fairlie's kindness was not, as I had supposed, the only strong impression on her memory. With the grateful remembrance of her school-days at Limmeridge, there existed the vindictive remembrance of the wrong inflicted on her by her confinement in the Asylum. Who had done that wrong? Could it really be her mother?

It was hard to give up pursuing the inquiry to that final point, but I forced myself to abandon all idea of continuing it. Seeing her as I saw her now, it would have been cruel to think of anything but the necessity and the humanity of restoring her composure.

'I will talk of nothing to distress you,' I said soothingly.

'You want something,' she answered sharply and suspiciously. 'Don't look at me like that. Speak to me – tell me what you want.'

'I only want you to quiet yourself, and when you are calmer, to think over what I have said.'

'Said?' She paused – twisted the cloth in her hands, backwards and forwards, and whispered to herself, 'What is it he said?' She turned again towards me, and shook her head impatiently. 'Why don't you help me?' she asked, with angry suddenness.

'Yes, yes,' I said, 'I will help you, and you will soon remember. I ask you to see Miss Fairlie tomorrow and to tell her the truth about the letter.'

'Ah! Miss Fairlie – Fairlie – Fairlie—'

The mere utterance of the loved familiar name seemed to quiet her. Her face softened and grew like itself again.

'You need have no fear of Miss Fairlie,' I continued, 'and no fear of getting into trouble through the letter. She knows so much about it already, that you will have no difficulty in telling her all. There can be little necessity for concealment where there is hardly anything left to conceal. You mention no names in the letter; but Miss Fairlie knows that the person you write of is Sir Percival Glyde—'

The instant I pronounced that name she started to her feet, and a scream burst from her that rang through the churchyard, and made my heart leap in me with the terror of it. The dark deformity of the expression which had just left her face lowered on it once more, with doubled and trebled intensity. The shriek at the name, the reiterated look of hatred and fear that instantly followed, told all. Not even a last doubt now remained. Her mother was guiltless of imprisoning her in the Asylum. A man had shut her up – and that man was Sir Percival Glyde.

The scream had reached other ears than mine. On one side I heard the door of the sexton's cottage open; on the other I heard the voice of her companion, the woman in the shawl, the woman whom she had spoken of as Mrs Clements.

'I'm coming! I'm coming!' cried the voice from behind the clump of dwarf trees.

In a moment more Mrs Clements hurried into view.

'Who are you?' she cried, facing me resolutely as she set her foot on the stile. 'How dare you frighten a poor helpless woman like that?'

She was at Anne Catherick's side, and had put one arm around her, before I could answer. 'What is it, my dear?' she said. 'What has he done to you?'

'Nothing,' the poor creature answered. 'Nothing. I'm only frightened.'

Mrs Clements turned on me with a fearless indignation, for which I respected her.

'I should be heartily ashamed of myself if I deserved that angry look,' I said. 'But I do not deserve it. I have unfortunately startled her without intending it. This is not the first time she has seen me. Ask her yourself, and she will tell you that I am incapable of willingly harming her or any woman.'

I spoke distinctly, so that Anne Catherick might hear and understand me, and I saw that the words and their meaning had reached her.

'Yes, yes,' she said—'he was good to me once – he helped me—' She whispered the rest into her friend's ear.

'Strange, indeed!' said Mrs Clements, with a look of perplexity. 'It makes all the difference, though. I'm sorry I spoke so rough to you, sir; but you must own that appearances looked suspicious to a stranger. It's more my fault than yours, for humouring her whims, and letting her be alone in such a place as this. Come, my dear – come home now.'

I thought the good woman looked a little uneasy at the prospect of the walk back, and I offered to go with them until they were both within sight of home. Mrs Clements thanked me civilly, and declined. She said they were sure to meet some of the farm-labourers as soon as they got to the moor.

'Try to forgive me,' I said, when Anne Catherick took her friend's arm to go away. Innocent as I had been of any intention to terrify and agitate her, my heart smote me as I looked at the poor, pale, frightened face.

'I will try,' she answered. 'But you know too much – I'm afraid you'll always frighten me now.'

Mrs Clements glanced at me, and shook her head pityingly.

'Good-night, sir,' she said. 'You couldn't help it, I know; but I wish it was me you had frightened, and not her.'

They moved away a few steps. I thought they had left me, but Anne suddenly stopped, and separated herself from her friend.

'Wait a little,' she said. 'I must say good-bye.'

She returned to the grave, rested both hands tenderly on the marble cross, and kissed it.

'I'm better now,' she sighed, looking up at me quietly. 'I forgive you.'

She joined her companion again, and they left the burial-ground. I saw them stop near the church and speak to the sexton's wife, who had come from the cottage, and had waited, watching us from a distance. Then they went on again up the path that led to the moor. I looked after Anne Catherick as she disappeared, till all trace of her had faded in the twilight – looked as anxiously and sorrowfully as if that was the last I was to see in this weary world of the woman in white.

XIV

Half an hour later I was back at the house, and was informing Miss Halcombe of all that had happened.

She listened to me from beginning to end with a steady, silent attention, which, in a woman of her temperament and disposition, was the strongest proof that could be offered of the serious manner in which my narrative affected her.

'My mind misgives me,' was all she said when I had done. 'My mind misgives me sadly about the future.'

'The future may depend,' I suggested, 'on the use we make of the present. It is not improbable that Anne Catherick may speak more readily and unreservedly to a woman than she has spoken to me. If Miss Fairlie—'

'Not to be thought of for a moment,' interposed Miss Halcombe, in her most decided manner.

'Let me suggest, then,' I continued, 'that you should see Anne Catherick yourself, and do all you can to win her confidence. For my own part, I shrink from the idea of alarming the poor creature a second time, as I have most unhappily alarmed her already. Do you see any objection to accompanying me to the farmhouse tomorrow?'

'None whatever. I will go anywhere and do anything to serve Laura's interests. What did you say the place was called?'

'You must know it well. It is called Todd's Corner.'

'Certainly. Todd's Corner is one of Mr Fairlie's farms. Our dairymaid here is the farmer's second daughter. She goes backwards and forwards constantly between this house and her father's farm, and she may have heard or seen something which it may be useful to us to know. Shall I ascertain, at once, if the girl is downstairs?'

She rang the bell, and sent the servant with his message. He returned, and announced that the dairymaid was then at the farm. She had not been there for the last three days, and the housekeeper had given her leave to go home for an hour or two that evening.

'I can speak to her tomorrow,' said Miss Halcombe, when the servant had left the room again. 'In the meantime, let me thoroughly understand the object to be gained by my interview with Anne Catherick. Is there no doubt in your mind that the person who confined her in the Asylum was Sir Percival Glyde?'

'There is not the shadow of a doubt. The only mystery that remains is the mystery of his *motive*. Looking to the great difference between his station in life and hers, which seems to preclude all idea of the most distant relationship between them, it is of the last importance – even assuming that she really required to be placed under restraint – to know why *he* should have been the person to assume the serious responsibility of shutting her up—'

'In a private Asylum, I think you said?'

'Yes, in a private Asylum, where a sum of money, which no poor person could afford to give, must have been paid for her maintenance as a patient.'

'I see where the doubt lies, Mr Hartright, and I promise you that it shall be set at rest, whether Anne Catherick assists us tomorrow or not. Sir Percival Glyde shall not be long in this house without satisfying Mr Gilmore, and satisfying me. My sister's future is my dearest care in life, and I have influence enough over her to give me some power, where her marriage is concerned, in the disposal of it.'

We parted for the night.

*   *   *

After breakfast the next morning, an obstacle, which the events of the evening before had put out of my memory, interposed to prevent our proceeding immediately to the farm. This was my last day at Limmeridge House, and it was necessary, as soon as the post came in, to follow Miss Halcombe's advice, and to ask Mr Fairlie's permission to shorten my engagement by a month, in consideration of an unforeseen necessity for my return to London.

Fortunately for the probability of this excuse, so far as appearances were concerned, the post brought me two letters from London friends that morning. I took them away at once to my own room, and sent the servant with a message to Mr Fairlie, requesting to know when I could see him on a matter of business.

I awaited the man's return, free from the slightest feeling of anxiety about the manner in which his master might receive my application. With Mr Fairlie's leave or without it, I must go. The consciousness of having now taken the first step on the dreary journey which was henceforth to separate my life from Miss Fairlie's seemed to have blunted my sensibility to every consideration connected with myself. I had done with my poor man's touchy pride – I had done with all my little artist vanities. No insolence of Mr Fairlie's, if he chose to be insolent, could wound me now.

The servant returned with a message for which I was not unprepared. Mr Fairlie regretted that the state of his health, on that particular morning, was such as to preclude all hope of his having the pleasure of receiving me. He begged, therefore, that I would accept his apologies, and kindly communicate what I had to say in the form of a letter. Similar messages to this had reached me, at various intervals, during my three months' residence in the house. Throughout the whole of that period Mr Fairlie had been rejoiced to 'possess' me, but had never been well enough to see me for a second time. The servant took every fresh batch of drawings that I mounted and restored back to his master with my 'respects,' and returned empty-handed with Mr Fairlie's 'kind compliments,' 'best thanks,' and 'sincere regrets' that the state of his health still obliged him to remain a solitary prisoner in his own room. A more satisfactory arrangement to both sides could not possibly have been adopted. It would be hard to say which of us, under the circumstances, felt the most grateful sense of obligation to Mr Fairlie's accommodating nerves.

I sat down at once to write the letter, expressing myself in it as civilly, as clearly, and as briefly as possible. Mr Fairlie did not hurry his reply. Nearly an hour elapsed before the answer was placed in my hands. It was written with beautiful regularity and neatness of character, in violet-coloured ink, on note-paper as smooth as ivory and almost as thick as cardboard, and it addressed me in these terms –

Mr Fairlie's compliments to Mr Hartright. Mr Fairlie is more surprised and disappointed than he can say (in the present state of his health) by Mr Hartright's application. Mr Fairlie is not a man of business, but he has consulted his steward, who is, and that person confirms Mr Fairlie's opinion that Mr Hartright's request to be allowed to break his engagement cannot be justified by any necessity whatever, excepting perhaps a case of life and death. If the highly-appreciative feeling towards Art and its professors, which it is the consolation and happiness of Mr Fairlie's suffering existence to cultivate, could be easily shaken, Mr Hartright's present proceeding would have shaken it. It has not done so – except in the instance of Mr Hartright himself.

Having stated his opinion – so far, that is to say, as acute nervous suffering will allow him to state anything – Mr Fairlie has nothing to add but the expression of his decision, in reference to the highly irregular application that has been made to him. Perfect repose of body and mind being to the last degree important in his case, Mr Fairlie will not suffer Mr Hartright to disturb that repose by remaining in the house under circumstances of an essentially irritating nature to both sides. Accordingly, Mr Fairlie waives his right of refusal, purely with a view to the preservation of his own tranquillity – and informs Mr Hartright that he may go.

I folded the letter up, and put it away with my other papers. The time had been when I should have resented it as an insult – I accepted it now as a written release from my engagement. It was off my mind, it was almost out of my memory, when I went downstairs to the breakfast-room, and informed Miss Halcombe that I was ready to walk with her to the farm.

'Has Mr Fairlie given you a satisfactory answer?' she asked as we left the house.

'He has allowed me to go, Miss Halcombe.'

She looked up at me quickly, and then, for the first time since I had known her, took my arm of her own accord. No words could have expressed so delicately that she understood how the permission to leave my employment had been granted, and that she gave me her sympathy, not as my superior, but as my friend. I had not felt the man's insolent letter, but I felt deeply the woman's atoning kindness.

On our way to the farm we arranged that Miss Halcombe was to enter the house alone, and that I was to wait outside, within call. We adopted this mode of proceeding from an apprehension that my presence, after what had happened in the churchyard the evening before, might have the effect of renewing Anne Catherick's nervous dread, and of rendering her additionally distrustful of the advances of a lady who was a stranger to her. Miss Halcombe left me, with the intention of speaking, in the first instance, to the farmer's wife (of whose friendly readiness to help her in any way she was well assured), while I waited for her in the near neighbourhood of the house.

I had fully expected to be left alone for some time. To my surprise, however, little more than five minutes had elapsed before Miss Halcombe returned.

'Does Anne Catherick refuse to see you?' I asked in astonishment.

'Anne Catherick is gone,' replied Miss Halcombe.

'Gone?'

'Gone with Mrs Clements. They both left the farm at eight o'clock this morning.'

I could say nothing – I could only feel that our last chance of discovery had gone with them.

'All that Mrs Todd knows about her guests, I know,' Miss Halcombe went on, 'and it leaves me, as it leaves her, in the dark. They both came back safe last night, after they left you, and they passed the first part of the evening with Mr Todd's family as usual. Just before supper-time, however, Anne Catherick startled them all by being suddenly seized with faintness. She had had a similar attack, of a less alarming kind, on the day she arrived at the farm; and Mrs Todd had connected it, on that occasion, with something she was reading at the time in our local newspaper, which lay on the farm table, and which she had taken up only a minute or two before.'

'Does Mrs Todd know what particular passage in the newspaper affected her in that way?' I inquired.

'No,' replied Miss Halcombe. 'She had looked it over, and had seen nothing in it to agitate any one. I asked leave, however, to look it over in my turn, and at the very first page I opened I found that the editor had enriched his small stock of news by drawing upon our family affairs, and had published my sister's marriage engagement, among his other announcements, copied from the London papers, of Marriages in High Life. I concluded at once that this was the paragraph which had so strangely affected Anne Catherick, and I thought I saw in it, also, the origin of the letter which she sent to our house the next day.'

'There can be no doubt in either case. But what did you hear about her second attack of faintness yesterday evening?'

'Nothing. The cause of it is a complete mystery. There was no stranger in the room. The only visitor was our dairymaid, who, as I told you, is one of Mr Todd's daughters, and the only conversation was the usual gossip about local affairs. They heard her cry out, and saw her turn deadly pale, without the slightest apparent reason. Mrs Todd and Mrs Clements took her upstairs, and Mrs Clements remained with her. They were heard talking together until long after the usual bedtime, and early this morning Mrs Clements took Mrs Todd aside, and amazed her beyond all power of expression by saying that they must go. The only explanation Mrs Todd could extract from her guest was, that something had happened, which was not the fault of any one at the farmhouse, but which was serious enough to make Anne Catherick resolve to leave Limmeridge immediately. It was quite useless to press Mrs Clements to be more explicit. She only shook her head, and said that, for Anne's sake, she must beg and pray that no one would question her. All she could repeat, with every appearance of being seriously agitated herself, was that Anne must go, that she must go with her, and that the destination to which they might both betake themselves must be kept a secret from everybody. I spare you the recital of Mrs Todd's hospitable remonstrances and refusals. It ended in her driving them both to the nearest station, more than three hours since. She tried hard on the way to get them to speak more plainly, but without success; and she set them down outside the station-door, so hurt and offended by the unceremonious abruptness of their departure and their unfriendly reluctance to place the least confidence in her, that she drove away in anger, without so much as stopping to bid them good-bye. That is exactly what has taken place. Search your own memory, Mr Hartright, and tell me if anything happened in the burial-ground yesterday evening which can at all account for the extraordinary departure of those two women this morning.'

'I should like to account first, Miss Halcombe, for the sudden change in Anne Catherick which alarmed them at the farmhouse, hours after she and I had parted, and when time enough had elapsed to quiet any violent agitation that I might have been unfortunate enough to cause. Did you inquire particularly about the gossip which was going on in the room when she turned faint?'

'Yes. But Mrs Todd's household affairs seem to have divided her attention that evening with the talk in the farmhouse parlour. She could only tell me that it was "just the news," – meaning, I suppose, that they all talked as usual about each other.'

'The dairymaid's memory may be better than her mother's,' I said. 'It may be as well for you to speak to the girl, Miss Halcombe, as soon as we get back.'

My suggestion was acted on the moment we returned to the house. Miss Halcombe led me round to the servants' offices, and we found the girl in the dairy, with her sleeves tucked up to her shoulders, cleaning a large milk-pan and singing blithely over her work.

'I have brought this gentleman to see your dairy, Hannah,' said Miss Halcombe. 'It is one of the sights of the house, and it always does you credit.'

The girl blushed and curtseyed, and said shyly that she hoped she always did her best to keep things neat and clean.

'We have just come from your father's,' Miss Halcombe continued. 'You were there yesterday evening, I hear, and you found visitors at the house?'

'Yes, miss.'

'One of them was taken faint and ill, I am told. I suppose nothing was said or done to frighten her? You were not talking of anything very terrible, were you?'

'Oh no, miss!' said the girl, laughing. 'We were only talking of the news.'

'Your sisters told you the news at Todd's Corner, I suppose?'

'Yes, miss.'

'And you told them the news at Limmeridge House?'

'Yes, miss. And I'm quite sure nothing was said to frighten the poor thing, for I was talking when she was taken ill. It gave me quite a turn, miss, to see it, never having been taken faint myself.'

Before any more questions could be put to her, she was called away to receive a basket of eggs at the dairy door. As she left us I whispered to Miss Halcombe –

'Ask her if she happened to mention, last night, that visitors were expected at Limmeridge House.'

Miss Halcombe showed me, by a look, that she understood, and put the question as soon as the dairymaid returned to us.

'Oh yes, miss, I mentioned that,' said the girl simply. 'The company coming, and the accident to the brindled cow, was all the news I had to take to the farm.'

'Did you mention names? Did you tell them that Sir Percival Glyde was expected on Monday?'

'Yes, miss – I told them Sir Percival Glyde was coming. I hope there was no harm in it – I hope I didn't do wrong.'

'Oh no, no harm. Come, Mr Hartright, Hannah will begin to think us in the way, if we interrupt her any longer over her work.'

We stopped and looked at one another the moment we were alone again.

'Is there any doubt in your mind, now, Miss Halcombe?'

'Sir Percival Glyde shall remove that doubt, Mr Hartright – or Laura Fairlie shall never be his wife.'

XV

As we walked round to the front of the house a fly from the railway approached us along the drive. Miss Halcombe waited on the door-steps until the fly drew up, and then advanced to shake hands with an old gentleman, who got out briskly the moment the steps were let down. Mr Gilmore had arrived.

I looked at him, when we were introduced to each other, with an interest and a curiosity which I could hardly conceal. This old man was to remain at Limmeridge House after I had left it, he was to hear Sir Percival Glyde's explanation, and was to give Miss Halcombe the assistance of his experience in forming her judgment; he was to wait until the question of the marriage was set at rest; and his hand, if that question were decided in the affirmative, was to draw the settlement which bound Miss Fairlie irrevocably to her engagement. Even then, when I knew nothing by comparison with what I know now, I looked at the family lawyer with an interest which I had never felt before in the presence of any man breathing who was a total stranger to me.

In external appearance Mr Gilmore was the exact opposite of the conventional idea of an old lawyer. His complexion was florid – his white hair was worn rather long and kept carefully brushed – his black coat, waistcoat, and trousers fitted him with perfect neatness – his white cravat was carefully tied, and his lavender-coloured kid gloves might have adorned the hands of a fashionable clergyman, without fear and without reproach. His manners were pleasantly marked by the formal grace and refinement of the old school of politeness, quickened by the invigorating sharpness and readiness of a man whose business in life obliges him always to keep his faculties in good working order. A sanguine constitution and fair prospects to begin with – a long subsequent career of creditable and comfortable prosperity – a cheerful, diligent, widely-respected old age – such were the general impressions I derived from my introduction to Mr Gilmore, and it is but fair to him to add, that the knowledge I gained by later and better experience only tended to confirm them.

I left the old gentleman and Miss Halcombe to enter the house together, and to talk of family matters undisturbed by the restraint of a stranger's presence. They crossed the hall on their way to the drawing-room, and I descended the steps again to wander about the garden alone.

My hours were numbered at Limmeridge House – my departure the next morning was irrevocably settled – my share in the investigation which the anonymous letter had rendered necessary was at an end. No harm could be done to any one but myself if I let my heart loose again, for the little time that was left me, from the cold cruelty of restraint which necessity had forced me to inflict upon it, and took my farewell of the scenes which were associated with the brief dream-time of my happiness and my love.

I turned instinctively to the walk beneath my study-window, where I had seen her the evening before with her little dog, and followed the path which her dear feet had trodden so often, till I came to the wicket gate that led into her rose garden. The winter bareness spread drearily over it now. The flowers that she had taught me to distinguish by their names, the flowers that I had taught her to paint from, were gone, and the tiny white paths that led between the beds were damp and green already. I went on to the avenue of trees, where we had breathed together the warm fragrance of August evenings, where we had admired together the myriad combinations of shade and sunlight that dappled the ground at our feet. The leaves fell about me from the groaning branches, and the earthy decay in the atmosphere chilled me to the bones. A little farther on, and I was out of the grounds, and following the lane that wound gently upward to the nearest hills. The old felled tree by the wayside, on which we had sat to rest, was sodden with rain, and the tuft of ferns and grasses which I had drawn for her, nestling under the rough stone wall in front of us, had turned to a pool of water, stagnating round an island of draggled weeds. I gained the summit of the hill, and looked at the view which we had so often admired in the happier time. It was cold and barren – it was no longer the view that I remembered. The sunshine of her presence was far from me – the charm of her voice no longer murmured in my ear. She had talked to me, on the spot from which I now looked down, of her father, who was her last surviving parent – had told me how fond of each other they had been, and how sadly she missed him still when she entered certain rooms in the house, and when she took up forgotten occupations and amusements with which he had been associated. Was the view that I had seen, while listening to those words, the view that I saw now, standing on the hill-top by myself? I turned and left it – I wound my way back again, over the moor, and round the sandhills, down to the beach. There was the white rage of the surf, and the multitudinous glory of the leaping waves – but where was the place on which she had once drawn idle figures with her parasol in the sand – the place where we had sat together, while she talked to me about myself and my home, while she asked me a woman's minutely observant questions about my mother and my sister, and innocently wondered whether I should ever leave my lonely chambers and have a wife and a house of my own? Wind and wave had long since smoothed out the trace of her which she had left in those marks on the sand, I looked over the wide monotony of the sea-side prospect, and the place in which we two had idled away the sunny hours was as lost to me as if I had never known it, as strange to me as if I stood already on a foreign shore.

The empty silence of the beach struck cold to my heart. I returned to the house and the garden, where traces were left to speak of her at every turn.

On the west terrace walk I met Mr Gilmore. He was evidently in search of me, for he quickened his pace when we caught sight of each other. The state of my spirits little fitted me for the society of a stranger; but the meeting was inevitable, and I resigned myself to make the best of it.

'You are the very person I wanted to see,' said the old gentleman. 'I had two words to say to you, my dear sir; and if you have no objection I will avail myself of the present opportunity. To put it plainly, Miss Halcombe and I have been talking over family affairs – affairs which are the cause of my being here – and in the course of our conversation she was naturally led to tell me of this unpleasant matter connected with the anonymous letter, and of the share which you have most creditably and properly taken in the proceedings so far. That share, I quite understand, gives you an interest which you might not otherwise have felt, in knowing that the future management of the investigation which you have begun will be placed in safe hands. My dear sir, make yourself quite easy on that point – it will be placed in *my* hands.'

'You are, in every way, Mr Gilmore, much fitter to advise and to act in the matter than I am. Is it an indiscretion on my part to ask if you have decided yet on a course of proceeding?'

'So far as it is possible to decide, Mr Hartright, I have decided. I mean to send a copy of the letter, accompanied by a statement of the circumstances, to Sir Percival Glyde's solicitor in London, with whom I have some acquaintance. The letter itself I shall keep here to show to Sir Percival as soon as he arrives. The tracing of the two women I have already provided for, by sending one of Mr Fairlie's servants – a confidential person – to the station to make inquiries. The man has his money and his directions, and he will follow the women in the event of his finding any clue. This is all that can be done until Sir Percival comes on Monday. I have no doubt myself that every explanation which can be expected from a gentleman and a man of honour, he will readily give. Sir Percival stands very high, sir – an eminent position, a reputation above suspicion – I feel quite easy about results – quite easy, I am rejoiced to assure you. Things of this sort happen constantly in my experience. Anonymous letters – unfortunate woman – sad state of society. I don't deny that there are peculiar complications in this case; but the case itself is, most unhappily, common – common.'

'I am afraid, Mr Gilmore, I have the misfortune to differ from you in the view I take of the case.'

'Just so, my dear sir – just so. I am an old man, and I take the practical view. You are a young man, and you take the romantic view. Let us not dispute about our views. I live professionally in an atmosphere of disputation, Mr Hartright, and I am only too glad to escape from it, as I am escaping here. We will wait for events – yes, yes, yes – we will wait for events. Charming place this. Good shooting? Probably not, none of Mr Fairlie's land is preserved, I think. Charming place, though, and delightful people. You draw and paint, I hear, Mr Hartright? Enviable accomplishment. What style?'

We dropped into general conversation, or rather, Mr Gilmore talked and I listened. My attention was far from him, and from the topics on which he discoursed so fluently. The solitary walk of the last two hours had wrought its effect on me – it had set the idea in my mind of hastening my departure from Limmeridge House. Why should I prolong the hard trial of saying farewell by one unnecessary minute? What further service was required of me by any one? There was no useful purpose to be served by my stay in Cumberland – there was no restriction of time in the permission to leave which my employer had granted to me. Why not end it there and then?

I determined to end it. There were some hours of daylight still left – there was no reason why my journey back to London should not begin on that afternoon. I made the first civil excuse that occurred to me for leaving Mr Gilmore, and returned at once to the house.

On my way up to my own room I met Miss Halcombe on the stairs. She saw, by the hurry of my movements and the change in my manner, that I had some new purpose in view, and asked what had happened.

I told her the reasons which induced me to think of hastening my departure, exactly as I have told them here.

'No, no,' she said, earnestly and kindly, 'leave us like a friend – break bread with us once more. Stay here and dine, stay here and help us to spend our last evening with you as happily, as like our first evenings, as we can. It is my invitation – Mrs Vesey's invitation—' she hesitated a little, and then added, 'Laura's invitation as well.'

I promised to remain. God knows I had no wish to leave even the shadow of a sorrowful impression with any one of them.

My own room was the best place for me till the dinner bell rang. I waited there till it was time to go downstairs.

I had not spoken to Miss Fairlie – I had not even seen her – all that day. The first meeting with her, when I entered the drawing-room, was a hard trial to her self-control and to mine. She, too, had done her best to make our last evening renew the golden bygone time – the time that could never come again. She had put on the dress which I used to admire more than any other that she possessed – a dark blue silk, trimmed quaintly and prettily with old-fashioned lace; she came forward to meet me with her former readiness – she gave me her hand with the frank, innocent good-will of happier days. The cold fingers that trembled round mine – the pale cheeks with a bright red spot burning in the midst of them – the faint smile that struggled to live on her lips and died away from them while I looked at it, told me at what sacrifice of herself her outward composure was maintained. My heart could take her no closer to me, or I should have loved her then as I had never loved her yet.

Mr Gilmore was a great assistance to us. He was in high good-humour, and he led the conversation with unflagging spirit. Miss Halcombe seconded him resolutely, and I did all I could to follow her example. The kind blue eyes, whose slightest changes of expression I had learnt to interpret so well, looked at me appealingly when we first sat down to table. Help my sister – the sweet anxious face seemed to say – help my sister, and you will help me.

We got through the dinner, to all outward appearance at least, happily enough. When the ladies had risen from table, and Mr Gilmore and I were left alone in the dining-room, a new interest presented itself to occupy our attention, and to give me an opportunity of quieting myself by a few minutes of needful and welcome silence. The servant who had been despatched to trace Anne Catherick and Mrs Clements returned with his report, and was shown into the dining-room immediately.

'Well,' said Mr Gilmore, 'what have you found out?'

'I have found out, sir,' answered the man, 'that both the women took tickets at our station here for Carlisle.'

'You went to Carlisle, of course, when you heard that?'

'I did, sir, but I am sorry to say I could find no further trace of them.'

'You inquired at the railway?'

'Yes, sir.'

'And at the different inns?'

'Yes, sir.'

'And you left the statement I wrote for you at the police station?'

'I did, sir.'

'Well, my friend, you have done all you could, and I have done all I could, and there the matter must rest till further notice. We have played our trump cards, Mr Hartright,' continued the old gentleman when the servant had withdrawn. 'For the present, at least, the women have outmanoeuvred us, and our only resource now is to wait till Sir Percival Glyde comes here on Monday next. Won't you fill your glass again? Good bottle of port, that – sound, substantial, old wine. I have got better in my own cellar, though.'

We returned to the drawing-room – the room in which the happiest evenings of my life had been passed – the room which, after this last night, I was never to see again. Its aspect was altered since the days had shortened and the weather had grown cold. The glass doors on the terrace side were closed, and hidden by thick curtains. Instead of the soft twilight obscurity, in which we used to sit, the bright radiant glow of lamplight now dazzled my eyes. All was changed – indoors and out all was changed.

Miss Halcombe and Mr Gilmore sat down together at the card-table – Mrs Vesey took her customary chair. There was no restraint on the disposal of *their* evening, and I felt the restraint on the disposal of mine all the more painfully from observing it. I saw Miss Fairlie lingering near the music-stand. The time had been when I might have joined her there. I waited irresolutely – I knew neither where to go nor what to do next. She cast one quick glance at me, took a piece of music suddenly from the stand, and came towards me of her own accord.

'Shall I play some of those little melodies of Mozart's which you used to like so much?' she asked, opening the music nervously, and looking down at it while she spoke.

Before I could thank her she hastened to the piano. The chair near it, which I had always been accustomed to occupy, stood empty. She struck a few chords – then glanced round at me – then looked back again at her music.

'Won't you take your old place?' she said, speaking very abruptly and in very low tones.

'I may take it on the last night,' I answered.

She did not reply – she kept her attention riveted on the music – music which she knew by memory, which she had played over and over again, in former times, without the book. I only knew that she had heard me, I only knew that she was aware of my being close to her, by seeing the red spot on the cheek that was nearest to me fade out, and the face grow pale all over.

'I am very sorry you are going,' she said, her voice almost sinking to a whisper, her eyes looking more and more intently at the music, her fingers flying over the keys of the piano with a strange feverish energy which I had never noticed in her before.

'I shall remember those kind words, Miss Fairlie, long after tomorrow has come and gone.'

The paleness grew whiter on her face, and she turned it farther away from me.

'Don't speak of tomorrow,' she said. 'Let the music speak to us of tonight, in a happier language than ours.'

Her lips trembled – a faint sigh fluttered from them, which she tried vainly to suppress. Her fingers wavered on the piano – she struck a false note, confused herself in trying to set it right, and dropped her hands angrily on her lap. Miss Halcombe and Mr Gilmore looked up in astonishment from the card-table at which they were playing. Even Mrs Vesey, dozing in her chair, woke at the sudden cessation of the music, and inquired what had happened.

'You play at whist, Mr Hartright?' asked Miss Halcombe, with her eyes directed significantly at the place I occupied.

I knew what she meant – I knew she was right, and I rose at once to go to the card-table. As I left the piano Miss Fairlie turned a page of the music, and touched the keys again with a surer hand.

'I *will* play it,' she said, striking the notes almost passionately. 'I *will* play it on the last night.'

'Come, Mrs Vesey,' said Miss Halcombe, 'Mr Gilmore and I are tired of écarté – come and be Mr Hartright's partner at whist.'

The old lawyer smiled satirically. His had been the winning hand, and he had just turned up a king. He evidently attributed Miss Halcombe's abrupt change in the card-table arrangements to a lady's inability to play the losing game.

The rest of the evening passed without a word or a look from her. She kept her place at the piano, and I kept mine at the card-table. She played unintermittingly – played as if the music was her only refuge from herself. Sometimes her fingers touched the notes with a lingering fondness – a soft, plaintive, dying tenderness, unutterably beautiful and mournful to hear; sometimes they faltered and failed her, or hurried over the instrument mechanically, as if their task was a burden to them. But still, change and waver as they might in the expression they imparted to the music, their resolution to play never faltered. She only rose from the piano when we all rose to say Good-night.

Mrs Vesey was the nearest to the door, and the first to shake hands with me.

'I shall not see you again, Mr Hartright,' said the old lady. 'I am truly sorry you are going away. You have been very kind and attentive, and an old woman like me feels kindness and attention. I wish you happy, sir – I wish you a kind good-bye.'

Mr Gilmore came next.

'I hope we shall have a future opportunity of bettering our acquaintance, Mr Hartright. You quite understand about that little matter of business being safe in my hands? Yes, yes, of course. Bless me, how cold it is! Don't let me keep you at the door. Bon voyage, my dear sir – bon voyage, as the French say.'

Miss Halcombe followed.

'Half-past seven tomorrow morning,' she said – then added in a whisper, 'I have heard and seen more than you think. Your conduct tonight has made me your friend for life.'

Miss Fairlie came last. I could not trust myself to look at her when I took her hand, and when I thought of the next morning.

'My departure must be a very early one,' I said. 'I shall be gone, Miss Fairlie, before you—'

'No, no,' she interposed hastily, 'not before I am out of my room. I shall be down to breakfast with Marian. I am not so ungrateful, not so forgetful of the past three months—'

Her voice failed her, her hand closed gently round mine – then dropped it suddenly. Before I could say 'Good-night' she was gone.

The end comes fast to meet me – comes inevitably, as the light of the last morning came at Limmeridge House.

It was barely half-past seven when I went downstairs, but I found them both at the breakfast-table waiting for me. In the chill air, in the dim light, in the gloomy morning silence of the house, we three sat down together, and tried to eat, tried to talk. The struggle to preserve appearances was hopeless and useless, and I rose to end it.

As I held out my hand, as Miss Halcombe, who was nearest to me, took it, Miss Fairlie turned away suddenly and hurried from the room.

'Better so,' said Miss Halcombe, when the door had closed—'better so, for you and for her.'

I waited a moment before I could speak – it was hard to lose her, without a parting word or a parting look. I controlled myself – I tried to take leave of Miss Halcombe in fitting terms; but all the farewell words I would fain have spoken dwindled to one sentence.

'Have I deserved that you should write to me?' was all I could say.

'You have nobly deserved everything that I can do for you, as long as we both live. Whatever the end is you shall know it.'

'And if I can ever be of help again, at any future time, long after the memory of my presumption and my folly is forgotten . . .'

I could add no more. My voice faltered, my eyes moistened in spite of me.

She caught me by both hands – she pressed them with the strong, steady grasp of a man – her dark eyes glittered – her brown complexion flushed deep – the force and energy of her face glowed and grew beautiful with the pure inner light of her generosity and her pity.

'I will trust you – if ever the time comes I will trust you as my friend and *her* friend, as my brother and *her* brother.' She stopped, drew me nearer to her – the fearless, noble creature – touched my forehead, sister-like, with her lips, and called me by my Christian name. 'God bless you, Walter!' she said. 'Wait here alone and compose yourself – I had better not stay for both our sakes – I had better see you go from the balcony upstairs.'

She left the room. I turned away towards the window, where nothing faced me but the lonely autumn landscape – I turned away to master myself, before I too left the room in my turn, and left it for ever.

A minute passed – it could hardly have been more – when I heard the door open again softly, and the rustling of a woman's dress on the carpet moved towards me. My heart beat violently as I turned round. Miss Fairlie was approaching me from the farther end of the room.

She stopped and hesitated when our eyes met, and when she saw that we were alone. Then, with that courage which women lose so often in the small emergency, and so seldom in the great, she came on nearer to me, strangely pale and strangely quiet, drawing one hand after her along the table by which she walked, and holding something at her side in the other, which was hidden by the folds of her dress.

'I only went into the drawing-room,' she said, 'to look for this. It may remind you of your visit here, and of the friends you leave behind you. You told me I had improved very much when I did it, and I thought you might like—'

She turned her head away, and offered me a little sketch, drawn throughout by her own pencil, of the summer-house in which we had first met. The paper trembled in her hand as she held it out to me – trembled in mine as I took it from her.

I was afraid to say what I felt – I only answered, 'It shall never leave me – all my life long it shall be the treasure that I prize most. I am very grateful for it – very grateful to you, for not letting me go away without bidding you good-bye.'

'Oh!' she said innocently, 'how could I let you go, after we have passed so many happy days together!'

'Those days may never return, Miss Fairlie – my way of life and yours are very far apart. But if a time should come, when the devotion of my whole heart and soul and strength will give you a moment's happiness, or spare you a moment's sorrow, will you try to remember the poor drawing-master who has taught you? Miss Halcombe has promised to trust me – will you promise too?'

The farewell sadness in the kind blue eyes shone dimly through her gathering tears.

'I promise it,' she said in broken tones. 'Oh, don't look at me like that! I promise it with all my heart.'

I ventured a little nearer to her, and held out my hand.

'You have many friends who love you, Miss Fairlie. Your happy future is the dear object of many hopes. May I say, at parting, that it is the dear object of *my* hopes too?'

The tears flowed fast down her cheeks. She rested one trembling hand on the table to steady herself while she gave me the other. I took it in mine – I held it fast. My head drooped over it, my tears fell on it, my lips pressed it – not in love; oh, not in love, at that last moment, but in the agony and the self-abandonment of despair.

'For God's sake, leave me!' she said faintly.

The confession of her heart's secret burst from her in those pleading words. I had no right to hear them, no right to answer them – they were the words that banished me, in the name of her sacred weakness, from the room. It was all over. I dropped her hand, I said no more. The blinding tears shut her out from my eyes, and I dashed them away to look at her for the last time. One look as she sank into a chair, as her arms fell on the table, as her fair head dropped on them wearily. One farewell look, and the door had closed upon her – the great gulf of separation had opened between us – the image of Laura Fairlie was a memory of the past already.

The End of Hartright's Narrative

THE STORY CONTINUED BY VINCENT GILMORE
(of Chancery Lane, Solicitor)

I

I write these lines at the request of my friend, Mr Walter Hartright. They are intended to convey a description of certain events which seriously affected Miss Fairlie's interests, and which took place after the period of Mr Hartright's departure from Limmeridge House.

There is no need for me to say whether my own opinion does or does not sanction the disclosure of the remarkable family story, of which my narrative forms an important component part. Mr Hartright has taken that responsibility on himself, and circumstances yet to be related will show that he has amply earned the right to do so, if he chooses to exercise it. The plan he has adopted for presenting the story to others, in the most truthful and most vivid manner, requires that it should be told, at each successive stage in the march of events, by the persons who were directly concerned in those events at the time of their occurrence. My appearance here, as narrator, is the necessary consequence of this arrangement. I was present during the sojourn of Sir Percival Glyde in Cumberland, and was personally concerned in one important result of his short residence under Mr Fairlie's roof. It is my duty, therefore, to add these new links to the chain of events, and to take up the chain itself at the point where, for the present only, Mr Hartright has dropped it.

I arrived at Limmeridge House on Friday the second of November.

My object was to remain at Mr Fairlie's until the arrival of Sir Percival Glyde. If that event led to the appointment of any given day for Sir Percival's union with Miss Fairlie, I was to take the necessary instructions back with me to London, and to occupy myself in drawing the lady's marriage-settlement.

On the Friday I was not favoured by Mr Fairlie with an interview. He had been, or had fancied himself to be, an invalid for years past, and he was not well enough to receive me. Miss Halcombe was the first member of the family whom I saw. She met me at the house door, and introduced me to Mr Hartright, who had been staying at Limmeridge for some time past.

I did not see Miss Fairlie until later in the day, at dinner-time. She was not looking well, and I was sorry to observe it. She is a sweet lovable girl, as amiable and attentive to every one about her as her excellent mother used to be – though, personally speaking, she takes after her father. Mrs Fairlie had dark eyes and hair, and her elder daughter, Miss Halcombe, strongly reminds me of her. Miss Fairlie played to us in the evening – not so well as usual, I thought. We had a rubber at whist, a mere profanation, so far as play was concerned, of that noble game. I had been favourably impressed by Mr Hartright on our first introduction to one another, but I soon discovered that he was not free from the social failings incidental to his age. There are three things that none of the young men of the present generation can do. They can't sit over their wine, they can't play at whist, and they can't pay a lady a compliment. Mr Hartright was no exception to the general rule. Otherwise, even in those early days and on that short acquaintance, he struck me as being a modest and gentlemanlike young man.

So the Friday passed. I say nothing about the more serious matters which engaged my attention on that day – the anonymous letter to Miss Fairlie, the measures I thought it right to adopt when the matter was mentioned to me, and the conviction I entertained that every possible explanation of the circumstances would be readily afforded by Sir Percival Glyde, having all been fully noticed, as I understand, in the narrative which precedes this.

On the Saturday Mr Hartright had left before I got down to breakfast. Miss Fairlie kept her room all day, and Miss Halcombe appeared to me to be out of spirits. The house was not what it used to be in the time of Mr and Mrs Philip Fairlie. I took a walk by myself in the forenoon, and looked about at some of the places which I first saw when I was staying at Limmeridge to transact family business, more than thirty years since. They were not what they used to be either.

At two o'clock Mr Fairlie sent to say he was well enough to see me. *He* had not altered, at any rate, since I first knew him. His talk was to the same purpose as usual – all about himself and his ailments, his wonderful coins, and his matchless Rembrandt etchings. The moment I tried to speak of the business that had brought me to his house, he shut his eyes and said I 'upset' him. I persisted in upsetting him by returning again and again to the subject. All I could ascertain was that he looked on his niece's marriage as a settled thing, that her father had sanctioned it, that he sanctioned it himself, that it was a desirable marriage, and that he should be personally rejoiced when the worry of it was over. As to the settlements, if I would consult his niece, and afterwards dive as deeply as I pleased into my own knowledge of the family affairs, and get everything ready, and limit his share in the business, as guardian, to saying Yes, at the right moment – why, of course he would meet my views, and everybody else's views, with infinite pleasure. In the meantime, there I saw him, a helpless sufferer, confined to his room. Did I think he looked as if he wanted teasing? No. Then why tease him?

I might, perhaps, have been a little astonished at this extraordinary absence of all self-assertion on Mr Fairlie's part, in the character of guardian, if my knowledge of the family affairs had not been sufficient to remind me that he was a single man, and that he had nothing more than a life-interest in the Limmeridge property. As matters stood, therefore, I was neither surprised nor disappointed at the result of the interview. Mr Fairlie had simply justified my expectations – and there was an end of it.

Sunday was a dull day, out of doors and in. A letter arrived for me from Sir Percival Glyde's solicitor, acknowledging the receipt of my copy of the anonymous letter and my accompanying statement of the case. Miss Fairlie joined us in the afternoon, looking pale and depressed, and altogether unlike herself. I had some talk with her, and ventured on a delicate allusion to Sir Percival. She listened and said nothing. All other subjects she pursued willingly, but this subject she allowed to drop. I began to doubt whether she might not be repenting of her engagement – just as young ladies often do, when repentance comes too late.

On Monday Sir Percival Glyde arrived.

I found him to be a most prepossessing man, so far as manners and appearance were concerned. He looked rather older than I had expected, his head being bald over the forehead, and his face somewhat marked and worn, but his movements were as active and his spirits as high as a young man's. His meeting with Miss Halcombe was delightfully hearty and unaffected, and his reception of me, upon my being presented to him, was so easy and pleasant that we got on together like old friends. Miss Fairlie was not with us when he arrived, but she entered the room about ten minutes afterwards. Sir Percival rose and paid his compliments with perfect grace. His evident concern on seeing the change for the worse in the young lady's looks was expressed with a mixture of tenderness and respect, with an unassuming delicacy of tone, voice, and manner, which did equal credit to his good breeding and his good sense. I was rather surprised, under these circumstances, to see that Miss Fairlie continued to be constrained and uneasy in his presence, and that she took the first opportunity of leaving the room again. Sir Percival neither noticed the restraint in her reception of him, nor her sudden withdrawal from our society. He had not obtruded his attentions on her while she was present, and he did not embarrass Miss Halcombe by any allusion to her departure when she was gone. His tact and taste were never at fault on this or on any other occasion while I was in his company at Limmeridge House.

As soon as Miss Fairlie had left the room he spared us all embarrassment on the subject of the anonymous letter, by adverting to it of his own accord. He had stopped in London on his way from Hampshire, had seen his solicitor, had read the documents forwarded by me, and had travelled on to Cumberland, anxious to satisfy our minds by the speediest and the fullest explanation that words could convey. On hearing him express himself to this effect, I offered him the original letter, which I had kept for his inspection. He thanked me, and declined to look at it, saying that he had seen the copy, and that he was quite willing to leave the original in our hands.

The statement itself, on which he immediately entered, was as simple and satisfactory as I had all along anticipated it would be.

Mrs Catherick, he informed us, had in past years laid him under some obligations for faithful services rendered to his family connections and to himself. She had been doubly unfortunate in being married to a husband who had deserted her, and in having an only child whose mental faculties had been in a disturbed condition from a very early age. Although her marriage had removed her to a part of Hampshire far distant from the neighbourhood in which Sir Percival's property was situated, he had taken care not to lose sight of her – his friendly feeling towards the poor woman, in consideration of her past services, having been greatly strengthened by his admiration of the patience and courage with which she supported her calamities. In course of time the symptoms of mental affliction in her unhappy daughter increased to such a serious extent, as to make it a matter of necessity to place her under proper medical care. Mrs Catherick herself recognised this necessity, but she also felt the prejudice common to persons occupying her respectable station, against allowing her child to be admitted, as a pauper, into a public Asylum. Sir Percival had respected this prejudice, as he respected honest independence of feeling in any rank of life, and had resolved to mark his grateful sense of Mrs Catherick's early attachment to the interests of himself and his family, by defraying the expense of her daughter's maintenance in a trustworthy private Asylum. To her mother's regret, and to his own regret, the unfortunate creature had discovered the share which circumstances had induced him to take in placing her under restraint, and had conceived the most intense hatred and distrust of him in consequence. To that hatred and distrust – which had expressed itself in various ways in the Asylum – the anonymous letter, written after her escape, was plainly attributable. If Miss Halcombe's or Mr Gilmore's recollection of the document did not confirm that view, or if they wished for any additional particulars about the Asylum (the address of which he mentioned, as well as the names and addresses of the two doctors on whose certificates the patient was admitted), he was ready to answer any question and to clear up any uncertainty. He had done his duty to the unhappy young woman, by instructing his solicitor to spare no expense in tracing her, and in restoring her once more to medical care, and he was now only anxious to do his duty towards Miss Fairlie and towards her family, in the same plain, straightforward way.

I was the first to speak in answer to this appeal. My own course was plain to me. It is the great beauty of the Law that it can dispute any human statement, made under any circumstances, and reduced to any form. If I had felt professionally called upon to set up a case against Sir Percival Glyde, on the strength of his own explanation, I could have done so beyond all doubt. But my duty did not lie in this direction – my function was of the purely judicial kind. I was to weigh the explanation we had just heard, to allow all due force to the high reputation of the gentleman who offered it, and to decide honestly whether the probabilities, on Sir Percival's own showing, were plainly with him, or plainly against him. My own conviction was that they were plainly with him, and I accordingly declared that his explanation was, to my mind, unquestionably a satisfactory one.

Miss Halcombe, after looking at me very earnestly, said a few words, on her side, to the same effect – with a certain hesitation of manner, however, which the circumstances did not seem to me to warrant. I am unable to say, positively, whether Sir Percival noticed this or not. My opinion is that he did, seeing that he pointedly resumed the subject, although he might now, with all propriety, have allowed it to drop.

'If my plain statement of facts had only been addressed to Mr Gilmore,' he said, 'I should consider any further reference to this unhappy matter as unnecessary. I may fairly expect Mr Gilmore, as a gentleman, to believe me on my word, and when he has done me that justice, all discussion of the subject between us has come to an end. But my position with a lady is not the same. I owe to her – what I would concede to no man alive – a *proof* of the truth of my assertion. You cannot ask for that proof, Miss Halcombe, and it is therefore my duty to you, and still more to Miss Fairlie, to offer it. May I beg that you will write at once to the mother of this unfortunate woman – to Mrs Catherick – to ask for her testimony in support of the explanation which I have just offered to you.'

I saw Miss Halcombe change colour, and look a little uneasy. Sir Percival's suggestion, politely as it was expressed, appeared to her, as it appeared to me, to point very delicately at the hesitation which her manner had betrayed a moment or two since. 'I hope, Sir Percival, you don't do me the injustice to suppose that I distrust you,' she said quickly.

'Certainly not, Miss Halcombe. I make my proposal purely as an act of attention to you. Will you excuse my obstinacy if I still venture to press it?'

He walked to the writing-table as he spoke, drew a chair to it, and opened the paper case.

'Let me beg you to write the note,' he said, 'as a favour to me. It need not occupy you more than a few minutes. You have only to ask Mrs

Catherick two questions. First, if her daughter was placed in the Asylum with her knowledge and approval. Secondly, if the share I took in the matter was such as to merit the expression of her gratitude towards myself? Mr Gilmore's mind is at ease on this unpleasant subject, and your mind is at ease – pray set my mind at ease also by writing the note.'

'You oblige me to grant your request, Sir Percival, when I would much rather refuse it.'

With those words Miss Halcombe rose from her place and went to the writing-table. Sir Percival thanked her, handed her a pen, and then walked away towards the fireplace. Miss Fairlie's little Italian greyhound was lying on the rug. He held out his hand, and called to the dog good-humouredly.

'Come, Nina,' he said, 'we remember each other, don't we?'

The little beast, cowardly and cross-grained, as pet-dogs usually are, looked up at him sharply, shrank away from his outstretched hand, whined, shivered, and hid itself under a sofa. It was scarcely possible that he could have been put out by such a trifle as a dog's reception of him, but I observed, nevertheless, that he walked away towards the window very suddenly. Perhaps his temper is irritable at times. If so, I can sympathise with him. My temper is irritable at times too.

Miss Halcombe was not long in writing the note. When it was done she rose from the writing-table, and handed the open sheet of paper to Sir Percival. He bowed, took it from her, folded it up immediately without looking at the contents, sealed it, wrote the address, and handed it back to her in silence. I never saw anything more gracefully and more becomingly done in my life.

'You insist on my posting this letter, Sir Percival?' said Miss Halcombe.

'I beg you will post it,' he answered. 'And now that it is written and sealed up, allow me to ask one or two last questions about the unhappy woman to whom it refers. I have read the communication which Mr Gilmore kindly addressed to my solicitor, describing the circumstances under which the writer of the anonymous letter was identified. But there are certain points to which that statement does not refer. Did Anne Catherick see Miss Fairlie?'

'Certainly not,' replied Miss Halcombe.

'Did she see you?'

'No.'

'She saw nobody from the house then, except a certain Mr Hartright, who accidentally met with her in the churchyard here?'

'Nobody else.'

'Mr Hartright was employed at Limmeridge as a drawing-master, I believe? Is he a member of one of the Water-Colour Societies?'

'I believe he is,' answered Miss Halcombe.

He paused for a moment, as if he was thinking over the last answer, and then added –

'Did you find out where Anne Catherick was living, when she was in this neighbourhood?'

'Yes. At a farm on the moor, called Todd's Corner.'

'It is a duty we all owe to the poor creature herself to trace her,' continued Sir Percival. 'She may have said something at Todd's Corner which may help us to find her. I will go there and make inquiries on the chance. In the meantime, as I cannot prevail on myself to discuss this painful subject with Miss Fairlie, may I beg, Miss Halcombe, that you will kindly undertake to give her the necessary explanation, deferring it of course until you have received the reply to that note.'

Miss Halcombe promised to comply with his request. He thanked her, nodded pleasantly, and left us, to go and establish himself in his own room. As he opened the door the cross-grained greyhound poked out her sharp muzzle from under the sofa, and barked and snapped at him.

'A good morning's work, Miss Halcombe,' I said, as soon as we were alone. 'Here is an anxious day well ended already.'

'Yes,' she answered; 'no doubt. I am very glad your mind is satisfied.'

'My mind! Surely, with that note in your hand, your mind is at ease too?'

'Oh yes – how can it be otherwise? I know the thing could not be,' she went on, speaking more to herself than to me; 'but I almost wish Walter Hartright had stayed here long enough to be present at the explanation, and to hear the proposal to me to write this note.'

I was a little surprised – perhaps a little piqued also – by these last words.

'Events, it is true, connected Mr Hartright very remarkably with the affair of the letter,' I said; 'and I readily admit that he conducted himself, all things considered, with great delicacy and discretion. But I am quite at a loss to understand what useful influence his presence could have exercised in relation to the effect of Sir Percival's statement on your mind or mine.'

'It was only a fancy,' she said absently. 'There is no need to discuss it, Mr Gilmore. Your experience ought to be, and is, the best guide I can desire.'

I did not altogether like her thrusting the whole responsibility, in this marked manner, on my shoulders. If Mr Fairlie had done it, I should not have been surprised. But resolute, clear-minded Miss Halcombe was the very last person in the world whom I should have expected to find shrinking from the expression of an opinion of her own.

'If any doubts still trouble you,' I said, 'why not mention them to me at once? Tell me plainly, have you any reason to distrust Sir Percival Glyde?'

'None whatever.'

'Do you see anything improbable, or contradictory, in his explanation?'

'How can I say I do, after the proof he has offered me of the truth of it? Can there be better testimony in his favour, Mr Gilmore, than the testimony of the woman's mother?'

'None better. If the answer to your note of inquiry proves to be satisfactory, I for one cannot see what more any friend of Sir Percival's can possibly expect from him.'

'Then we will post the note,' she said, rising to leave the room, 'and dismiss all further reference to the subject until the answer arrives. Don't attach any weight to my hesitation. I can give no better reason for it than that I have been over-anxious about Laura lately – and anxiety, Mr Gilmore, unsettles the strongest of us.'

She left me abruptly, her naturally firm voice faltering as she spoke those last words. A sensitive, vehement, passionate nature – a woman of ten thousand in these trivial, superficial times. I had known her from her earliest years – I had seen her tested, as she grew up, in more than one trying family crisis, and my long experience made me attach an importance to her hesitation under the circumstances here detailed, which I should certainly not have felt in the case of another woman. I could see no cause for any uneasiness or any doubt, but she had made me a little uneasy, and a little doubtful, nevertheless. In my youth, I should have chafed and fretted under the irritation of my own unreasonable state of mind. In my age, I knew better, and went out philosophically to walk it off.

II

We all met again at dinner-time.

Sir Percival was in such boisterous high spirits that I hardly recognised him as the same man whose quiet tact, refinement, and good sense had impressed me so strongly at the interview of the morning. The only trace of his former self that I could detect reappeared, every now and then, in his manner towards Miss Fairlie. A look or a word from her suspended his loudest laugh, checked his gayest flow of talk, and rendered him all attention to her, and to no one else at table, in an instant. Although he never openly tried to draw her into the conversation, he never lost the slightest chance she gave him of letting her drift into it by accident, and of saying the words to her, under those favourable circumstances, which a man with less tact and delicacy would have pointedly addressed to her the moment they occurred to him. Rather to my surprise, Miss Fairlie appeared to be sensible of his attentions without being moved by them. She was a little confused from time to time when he looked at her, or spoke to her; but she never warmed towards him. Rank, fortune, good breeding, good looks, the respect of a gentleman, and the devotion of a lover were all humbly placed at her feet, and, so far as appearances went, were all offered in vain.

On the next day, the Tuesday, Sir Percival went in the morning (taking one of the servants with him as a guide) to Todd's Corner. His inquiries, as I afterwards heard, led to no results. On his return he had an interview with Mr Fairlie, and in the afternoon he and Miss Halcombe rode out together. Nothing else happened worthy of record. The evening passed as usual. There was no change in Sir Percival, and no change in Miss Fairlie.

The Wednesday's post brought with it an event – the reply from Mrs Catherick. I took a copy of the document, which I have preserved, and which I may as well present in this place. It ran as follows –

MADAM, – I beg to acknowledge the receipt of your letter, inquiring whether my daughter, Anne, was placed under medical superintendence with my knowledge and approval, and whether the share taken in the matter by Sir Percival Glyde was such as to merit the expression of my gratitude towards that gentleman. Be pleased to accept my answer in the affirmative to both those questions, and believe me to remain, your obedient servant,

JANE ANNE CATHERICK.

Short, sharp, and to the point; in form rather a business-like letter for a woman to write – in substance as plain a confirmation as could be desired of Sir Percival Glyde's statement. This was my opinion, and with certain minor reservations, Miss Halcombe's opinion also. Sir Percival, when the letter was shown to him, did not appear to be struck by the sharp, short tone of it. He told us that Mrs Catherick was a woman of few words, a clear-headed, straightforward, unimaginative person, who wrote briefly and plainly, just as she spoke.

The next duty to be accomplished, now that the answer had been received, was to acquaint Miss Fairlie with Sir Percival's explanation. Miss Halcombe had undertaken to do this, and had left the room to go to her sister, when she suddenly returned again, and sat down by the easy-chair in which I was reading the newspaper. Sir Percival had gone out a minute before to look at the stables, and no one was in the room but ourselves.

'I suppose we have really and truly done all we can?' she said, turning and twisting Mrs Catherick's letter in her hand.

'If we are friends of Sir Percival's, who know him and trust him, we have done all, and more than all, that is necessary,' I answered, a little annoyed by this return of her hesitation. 'But if we are enemies who suspect him—'

'That alternative is not even to be thought of,' she interposed. 'We are

Sir Percival's friends, and if generosity and forbearance can add to our regard for him, we ought to be Sir Percival's admirers as well. You know that he saw Mr Fairlie yesterday, and that he afterwards went out with me.'

'Yes. I saw you riding away together.'

'We began the ride by talking about Anne Catherick, and about the singular manner in which Mr Hartright met with her. But we soon dropped that subject, and Sir Percival spoke next, in the most unselfish terms, of his engagement with Laura. He said he had observed that she was out of spirits, and he was willing, if not informed to the contrary, to attribute to that cause the alteration in her manner towards him during his present visit. If, however, there was any more serious reason for the change, he would entreat that no constraint might be placed on her inclinations either by Mr Fairlie or by me. All he asked, in that case, was that she would recall to mind, for the last time, what the circumstances were under which the engagement between them was made, and what his conduct had been from the beginning of the courtship to the present time. If, after due reflection on those two subjects, she seriously desired that he should withdraw his pretensions to the honour of becoming her husband – and if she would tell him so plainly with her own lips – he would sacrifice himself by leaving her perfectly free to withdraw from the engagement.'

'No man could say more than that, Miss Halcombe. As to my experience, few men in his situation would have said as much.'

She paused after I had spoken those words, and looked at me with a singular expression of perplexity and distress.

'I accuse nobody, and I suspect nothing,' she broke out abruptly. 'But I cannot and will not accept the responsibility of persuading Laura to this marriage.'

'That is exactly the course which Sir Percival Glyde has himself requested you to take,' I replied in astonishment. 'He has begged you not to force her inclinations.'

'And he indirectly obliges me to force them, if I give her his message.'

'How can that possibly be?'

'Consult your own knowledge of Laura, Mr Gilmore. If I tell her to reflect on the circumstances of her engagement, I at once appeal to two of the strongest feelings in her nature – to her love for her father's memory, and to her strict regard for truth. You know that she never broke a promise in her life – you know that she entered on this engagement at the beginning of her father's fatal illness, and that he spoke hopefully and happily of her marriage to Sir Percival Glyde on his deathbed.'

I own that I was a little shocked at this view of the case.

'Surely,' I said, 'you don't mean to infer that when Sir Percival spoke to you yesterday he speculated on such a result as you have just mentioned?'

Her frank, fearless face answered for her before she spoke.

'Do you think I would remain an instant in the company of any man whom I suspected of such baseness as that?' she asked angrily.

I liked to feel her hearty indignation flash out on me in that way. We see so much malice and so little indignation in my profession.

'In that case,' I said, 'excuse me if I tell you, in our legal phrase, that you are travelling out of the record. Whatever the consequences may be, Sir Percival has a right to expect that your sister should carefully consider her engagement from every reasonable point of view before she claims her release from it. If that unlucky letter has prejudiced her against him, go at once, and tell her that he has cleared himself in your eyes and in mine. What objection can she urge against him after that? What excuse can she possibly have for changing her mind about a man whom she had virtually accepted for her husband more than two years ago?'

'In the eyes of law and reason, Mr Gilmore, no excuse, I daresay. If she still hesitates, and if I still hesitate, you must attribute our strange conduct, if you like, to caprice in both cases, and we must bear the imputation as well as we can.'

With those words she suddenly rose and left me. When a sensible woman has a serious question put to her, and evades it by a flippant answer, it is a sure sign, in ninety-nine cases out of a hundred, that she has something to conceal. I returned to the perusal of the newspaper, strongly suspecting that Miss Halcombe and Miss Fairlie had a secret between them which they were keeping from Sir Percival, and keeping from me. I thought this hard on both of us, especially on Sir Percival.

My doubts – or to speak more correctly, my convictions – were confirmed by Miss Halcombe's language and manner when I saw her again later in the day. She was suspiciously brief and reserved in telling me the result of her interview with her sister. Miss Fairlie, it appeared, had listened quietly while the affair of the letter was placed before her in the right point of view, but when Miss Halcombe next proceeded to say that the object of Sir Percival's visit at Limmeridge was to prevail on her to let a day be fixed for the marriage she checked all further reference to the subject by begging for time. If Sir Percival would consent to spare her for the present, she would undertake to give him his final answer before the end of the year. She pleaded for this delay with such anxiety and agitation, that Miss Halcombe had promised to use her influence, if necessary, to obtain it, and there, at Miss Fairlie's earnest entreaty, all further discussion of the marriage question had ended.

The purely temporary arrangement thus proposed might have been convenient enough to the young lady, but it proved somewhat embarrassing to the writer of these lines. That morning's post had brought a letter from my partner, which obliged me to return to town the next day by the afternoon train. It was extremely probable that I should find no second opportunity of presenting myself at Limmeridge House during the remainder of the year. In that case, supposing Miss Fairlie ultimately decided on holding to her engagement, my necessary personal communication with her, before I drew her settlement, would become something like a downright impossibility, and we should be obliged to commit to writing questions which ought always to be discussed on both sides by word of mouth. I said nothing about this difficulty until Sir Percival had been consulted on the subject of the desired delay. He was too gallant a gentleman not to grant the request immediately. When Miss Halcombe informed me of this I told her that I must absolutely speak to her sister before I left Limmeridge, and it was, therefore, arranged that I should see Miss Fairlie in her own sitting-room the next morning. She did not come down to dinner, or join us in the evening. Indisposition was the excuse, and I thought Sir Percival looked, as well he might, a little annoyed when he heard of it.

The next morning, as soon as breakfast was over, I went up to Miss Fairlie's sitting-room. The poor girl looked so pale and sad, and came forward to welcome me so readily and prettily, that the resolution to lecture her on her caprice and indecision, which I had been forming all the way upstairs, failed me on the spot. I led her back to the chair from which she had risen, and placed myself opposite to her. Her cross-grained pet greyhound was in the room, and I fully expected a barking and snapping reception. Strange to say, the whimsical little brute falsified my expectations by jumping into my lap and poking its sharp muzzle familiarly into my hand the moment I sat down.

'You used often to sit on my knee when you were a child, my dear,' I said, 'and now your little dog seems determined to succeed you in the vacant throne. Is that pretty drawing your doing?'

I pointed to a little album which lay on the table by her side and which she had evidently been looking over when I came in. The page that lay open had a small water-colour landscape very neatly mounted on it. This was the drawing which had suggested my question – an idle question enough – but how could I begin to talk of business to her the moment I opened my lips?

'No,' she said, looking away from the drawing rather confusedly, 'it is not my doing.'

Her fingers had a restless habit, which I remembered in her as a child, of always playing with the first thing that came to hand whenever any one was talking to her. On this occasion they wandered to the album, and toyed absently about the margin of the little water-colour drawing. The expression of melancholy deepened on her face. She did not look at the drawing, or look at me. Her eyes moved uneasily from object to object in the room, betraying plainly that she suspected what my purpose was in coming to speak to her. Seeing that, I thought it best to get to the purpose with as little delay as possible.

'One of the errands, my dear, which brings me here is to bid you good-bye,' I began. 'I must get back to London today: and, before I leave, I want to have a word with you on the subject of your own affairs.'

'I am very sorry you are going, Mr Gilmore,' she said, looking at me kindly. 'It is like the happy old times to have you here.'

'I hope I may be able to come back and recall those pleasant memories once more,' I continued; 'but as there is some uncertainty about the future, I must take my opportunity when I can get it, and speak to you now. I am your old lawyer and your old friend, and I may remind you, I am sure, without offence, of the possibility of your marrying Sir Percival Glyde.'

She took her hand off the little album as suddenly as if it had turned hot and burnt her. Her fingers twined together nervously in her lap, her eyes looked down again at the floor, and an expression of constraint settled on her face which looked almost like an expression of pain.

'Is it absolutely necessary to speak of my marriage engagement?' she asked in low tones.

'It is necessary to refer to it,' I answered, 'but not to dwell on it. Let us merely say that you may marry, or that you may not marry. In the first case, I must be prepared, beforehand, to draw your settlement, and I ought not to do that without, as a matter of politeness, first consulting you. This may be my only chance of hearing what your wishes are. Let us, therefore, suppose the case of your marrying, and let me inform you, in as few words as possible, what your position is now, and what you may make it, if you please, in the future.'

I explained to her the object of a marriage-settlement, and then told her exactly what her prospects were – in the first place, on her coming of age, and in the second place, on the decease of her uncle – marking the distinction between the property in which she had a life-interest only, and the property which was left at her own control. She listened attentively, with the constrained expression still on her face, and her hands still nervously clasped together in her lap.

'And now,' I said in conclusion, 'tell me if you can think of any condition which, in the case we have supposed, you would wish me to make for you – subject, of course, to your guardian's approval, as you are not yet of age.'

She moved uneasily in her chair, then looked in my face on a sudden very earnestly.

'If it does happen,' she began faintly, 'if I am—'

'If you are married,' I added, helping her out.

'Don't let him part me from Marian,' she cried, with a sudden outbreak of energy. 'Oh, Mr Gilmore, pray make it law that Marian is to live with me!'

Under other circumstances I might, perhaps, have been amused at this essentially feminine interpretation of my question, and of the long explanation which had preceded it. But her looks and tones, when she spoke, were of a kind to make me more than serious – they distressed me. Her words, few as they were, betrayed a desperate clinging to the past which boded ill for the future.

'Your having Marian Halcombe to live with you can easily be settled by private arrangement,' I said. 'You hardly understood my question, I think. It referred to your own property – to the disposal of your money. Supposing you were to make a will when you come of age, who would you like the money to go to?'

'Marian has been mother and sister both to me,' said the good, affectionate girl, her pretty blue eyes glistening while she spoke. 'May I leave it to Marian, Mr Gilmore?'

'Certainly, my love,' I answered. 'But remember what a large sum it is. Would you like it all to go to Miss Halcombe?'

She hesitated; her colour came and went, and her hand stole back again to the little album.

'Not all of it,' she said. 'There is some one else besides Marian—'

She stopped; her colour heightened, and the fingers of the hand that rested upon the album beat gently on the margin of the drawing, as if her memory had set them going mechanically with the remembrance of a favourite tune.

'You mean some other member of the family besides Miss Halcombe?' I suggested, seeing her at a loss to proceed.

The heightening colour spread to her forehead and her neck, and the nervous fingers suddenly clasped themselves fast round the edge of the book.

'There is some one else,' she said, not noticing my last words, though she had evidently heard them; 'there is some one else who might like a little keepsake if – if I might leave it. There would be no harm if I should die first—'

She paused again. The colour that had spread over her cheeks suddenly, as suddenly left them. The hand on the album resigned its hold, trembled a little, and moved the book away from her. She looked at me for an instant – then turned her head aside in the chair. Her handkerchief fell to the floor as she changed her position, and she hurriedly hid her face from me in her hands.

Sad! To remember her, as I did, the liveliest, happiest child that ever laughed the day through, and to see her now, in the flower of her age and her beauty, so broken and so brought down as this!

In the distress that she caused me I forgot the years that had passed, and the change they had made in our position towards one another. I moved my chair close to her, and picked up her handkerchief from the carpet, and drew her hands from her face gently. 'Don't cry, my love,' I said, and dried the tears that were gathering in her eyes with my own hand, as if she had been the little Laura Fairlie of ten long years ago.

It was the best way I could have taken to compose her. She laid her head on my shoulder, and smiled faintly through her tears.

'I am very sorry for forgetting myself,' she said artlessly. 'I have not been well – I have felt sadly weak and nervous lately, and I often cry without reason when I am alone. I am better now – I can answer you as I ought, Mr Gilmore, I can indeed.'

'No, no, my dear,' I replied, 'we will consider the subject as done with for the present. You have said enough to sanction my taking the best possible care of your interests, and we can settle details at another opportunity. Let us have done with business now, and talk of something else.'

I led her at once into speaking on other topics. In ten minutes' time she was in better spirits, and I rose to take my leave.

'Come here again,' she said earnestly. 'I will try to be worthier of your kind feeling for me and for my interests if you will only come again.'

Still clinging to the past – that past which I represented to her, in my way, as Miss Halcombe did in hers! It troubled me sorely to see her looking back, at the beginning of her career, just as I look back at the end of mine.

'If I do come again, I hope I shall find you better,' I said; 'better and happier. God bless you, my dear!'

She only answered by putting up her cheek to me to be kissed. Even lawyers have hearts, and mine ached a little as I took leave of her.

The whole interview between us had hardly lasted more than half an hour – she had not breathed a word, in my presence, to explain the mystery of her evident distress and dismay at the prospect of her marriage, and yet she had contrived to win me over to her side of the question, I neither knew how nor why. I had entered the room, feeling that Sir Percival Glyde had fair reason to complain of the manner in which she was treating him. I left it, secretly hoping that matters might end in her taking him at his word and claiming her release. A man of my age and experience ought to have known better than to vacillate in this unreasonable manner. I can make no excuse for myself; I can only tell the truth, and say – so it was.

The hour for my departure was now drawing near. I sent to Mr Fairlie to say that I would wait on him to take leave if he liked, but that he must excuse my being rather in a hurry. He sent a message back, written in pencil on a slip of paper: 'Kind love and best wishes, dear Gilmore. Hurry of any kind is inexpressibly injurious to me. Pray take care of yourself. Good-bye.'

Just before I left I saw Miss Halcombe for a moment alone.

'Have you said all you wanted to Laura?' she asked.

'Yes,' I replied. 'She is very weak and nervous – I am glad she has you to take care of her.'

Miss Halcombe's sharp eyes studied my face attentively.

'You are altering your opinion about Laura,' she said. 'You are readier to make allowances for her than you were yesterday.'

No sensible man ever engages, unprepared, in a fencing match of words with a woman. I only answered –

'Let me know what happens. I will do nothing till I hear from you.'

She still looked hard in my face. 'I wish it was all over, and well over, Mr Gilmore – and so do you.' With those words she left me.

Sir Percival most politely insisted on seeing me to the carriage door.

'If you are ever in my neighbourhood,' he said, 'pray don't forget that I am sincerely anxious to improve our acquaintance. The tried and trusted old friend of this family will be always a welcome visitor in any house of mine.'

A really irresistible man – courteous, considerate, delightfully free from pride – a gentleman, every inch of him. As I drove away to the station I felt as if I could cheerfully do anything to promote the interests of Sir Percival Glyde – anything in the world, except drawing the marriage settlement of his wife.

III

A week passed, after my return to London, without the receipt of any communication from Miss Halcombe.

On the eighth day a letter in her handwriting was placed among the other letters on my table.

It announced that Sir Percival Glyde had been definitely accepted, and that the marriage was to take place, as he had originally desired, before the end of the year. In all probability the ceremony would be performed during the last fortnight in December. Miss Fairlie's twenty-first birthday was late in March. She would, therefore, by this arrangement, become Sir Percival's wife about three months before she was of age.

I ought not to have been surprised, I ought not to have been sorry, but I was surprised and sorry, nevertheless. Some little disappointment, caused by the unsatisfactory shortness of Miss Halcombe's letter, mingled itself with these feelings, and contributed its share towards upsetting my serenity for the day. In six lines my correspondent announced the proposed marriage – in three more, she told me that Sir Percival had left Cumberland to return to his house in Hampshire, and in two concluding sentences she informed me, first, that Laura was sadly in want of change and cheerful society; secondly, that she had resolved to try the effect of some such change forthwith, by taking her sister away with her on a visit to certain old friends in Yorkshire. There the letter ended, without a word to explain what the circumstances were which had decided Miss Fairlie to accept Sir Percival Glyde in one short week from the time when I had last seen her.

At a later period the cause of this sudden determination was fully explained to me. It is not my business to relate it imperfectly, on hearsay evidence. The circumstances came within the personal experience of Miss Halcombe, and when her narrative succeeds mine, she will describe them in every particular exactly as they happened. In the meantime, the plain duty for me to perform – before I, in my turn, lay down my pen and withdraw from the story – is to relate the one remaining event connected with Miss Fairlie's proposed marriage in which I was concerned, namely, the drawing of the settlement.

It is impossible to refer intelligibly to this document without first entering into certain particulars in relation to the bride's pecuniary affairs. I will try to make my explanation briefly and plainly, and to keep it free from professional obscurities and technicalities. The matter is of the utmost importance. I warn all readers of these lines that Miss Fairlie's inheritance is a very serious part of Miss Fairlie's story, and that Mr Gilmore's experience, in this particular, must be their experience also, if they wish to understand the narratives which are yet to come.

Miss Fairlie's expectations, then, were of a twofold kind, comprising her possible inheritance of real property, or land, when her uncle died, and her absolute inheritance of personal property, or money, when she came of age.

Let us take the land first.

In the time of Miss Fairlie's paternal grandfather (whom we will call Mr Fairlie, the elder) the entailed succession to the Limmeridge estate stood thus –

Mr Fairlie, the elder, died and left three sons, Philip, Frederick, and Arthur. As eldest son, Philip succeeded to the estate. If he died without leaving a son, the property went to the second brother, Frederick; and if Frederick died also without leaving a son, the property went to the third brother, Arthur.

As events turned out, Mr Philip Fairlie died leaving an only daughter, the Laura of this story, and the estate, in consequence, went, in course of law, to the second brother, Frederick, a single man. The third brother, Arthur, had died many years before the decease of Philip, leaving a son and a daughter. The son, at the age of eighteen, was drowned at Oxford. His death left Laura, the daughter of Mr Philip Fairlie, presumptive heiress to the estate, with every chance of succeeding to it, in the ordinary course of nature, on her uncle Frederick's death, if the said Frederick died without leaving male issue.

Except in the event, then, of Mr Frederick Fairlie's marrying and leaving an heir (the two very last things in the world that he was likely to do), his niece, Laura, would have the property on his death, possessing, it must be remembered, nothing more than a life-interest in it. If she died single, or died childless, the estate would revert to her cousin, Magdalen, the daughter of Mr Arthur Fairlie. If she married, with a proper settlement – or, in other words, with the settlement I meant to make for her – the income from the estate (a good three thousand a year) would, during her lifetime, be at her own disposal. If she died before her husband, he would naturally expect to be left in the enjoyment of the income, for *his* lifetime. If she had a son, that son would be the heir, to the exclusion of her cousin Magdalen. Thus, Sir Percival's prospects in marrying Miss Fairlie (so far as his wife's expectations from real property were concerned) promised him these two advantages, on Mr Frederick Fairlie's death: First, the use of three thousand a year (by his wife's permission, while she lived, and in his own right, on her death, if he survived her); and, secondly, the inheritance of Limmeridge for his son, if he had one.

So much for the landed property, and for the disposal of the income from it, on the occasion of Miss Fairlie's marriage. Thus far, no difficulty or difference of opinion on the lady's settlement was at all likely to arise between Sir Percival's lawyer and myself.

The personal estate, or, in other words, the money to which Miss Fairlie would become entitled on reaching the age of twenty-one years, is the next point to consider.

This part of her inheritance was, in itself, a comfortable little fortune. It was derived under her father's will, and it amounted to the sum of twenty thousand pounds. Besides this, she had a life-interest in ten thousand pounds more, which latter amount was to go, on her decease, to her aunt Eleanor, her father's only sister. It will greatly assist in setting the family affairs before the reader in the clearest possible light, if I stop here for a moment, to explain why the aunt had been kept waiting for her legacy until the death of the niece.

Mr Philip Fairlie had lived on excellent terms with his sister Eleanor, as long as she remained a single woman. But when her marriage took place, somewhat late in life, and when that marriage united her to an Italian gentleman named Fosco, or, rather, to an Italian nobleman – seeing that he rejoiced in the title of Count – Mr Fairlie disapproved of her conduct so strongly that he ceased to hold any communication with her, and even went the length of striking her name out of his will. The other members of the family all thought this serious manifestation of resentment at his sister's marriage more or less unreasonable. Count Fosco, though not a rich man, was not a penniless adventurer either. He had a small but sufficient income of his own. He had lived many years in England, and he held an excellent position in society. These recommendations, however, availed nothing with Mr Fairlie. In many of his opinions he was an Englishman of the old school, and he hated a foreigner simply and solely because he was a foreigner. The utmost that he could be prevailed on to do, in after years – mainly at Miss Fairlie's intercession – was to restore his sister's name to its former place in his will, but to keep her waiting for her legacy by giving the income of the money to his daughter for life, and the money itself, if her aunt died before her, to her cousin Magdalen. Considering the relative ages of the two ladies, the aunt's chance, in the ordinary course of nature, of receiving the ten thousand pounds, was thus rendered doubtful in the extreme; and Madame Fosco resented her brother's treatment of her as unjustly as usual in such cases, by refusing to see her niece, and declining to believe that Miss Fairlie's intercession had ever been exerted to restore her name to Mr Fairlie's will.

Such was the history of the ten thousand pounds. Here again no difficulty could arise with Sir Percival's legal adviser. The income would be at the wife's disposal, and the principal would go to her aunt or her cousin on her death.

All preliminary explanations being now cleared out of the way, I come at last to the real knot of the case – to the twenty thousand pounds.

This sum was absolutely Miss Fairlie's own on her completing her twenty-first year, and the whole future disposition of it depended, in the first instance, on the conditions I could obtain for her in her marriage-settlement. The other clauses contained in that document were of a formal kind, and need not be recited here. But the clause relating to the money is too important to be passed over. A few lines will be sufficient to give the necessary abstract of it.

My stipulation in regard to the twenty thousand pounds was simply this: The whole amount was to be settled so as to give the income to the lady for her life – afterwards to Sir Percival for his life – and the principal to the children of the marriage. In default of issue, the principal was to be disposed of as the lady might by her will direct, for which purpose I reserved to her the right of making a will. The effect of these conditions may be thus summed up. If Lady Glyde died without leaving children, her half-sister

Miss Halcombe, and any other relatives or friends whom she might be anxious to benefit, would, on her husband's death, divide among them such shares of her money as she desired them to have. If, on the other hand, she died leaving children, then their interest, naturally and necessarily, superseded all other interests whatsoever. This was the clause – and no one who reads it can fail, I think, to agree with me that it meted out equal justice to all parties.

We shall see how my proposals were met on the husband's side.

At the time when Miss Halcombe's letter reached me I was even more busily occupied than usual. But I contrived to make leisure for the settlement. I had drawn it, and had sent it for approval to Sir Percival's solicitor, in less than a week from the time when Miss Halcombe had informed me of the proposed marriage.

After a lapse of two days the document was returned to me, with notes and remarks of the baronet's lawyer. His objections, in general, proved to be of the most trifling and technical kind, until he came to the clause relating to the twenty thousand pounds. Against this there were double lines drawn in red ink, and the following note was appended to them –

'Not admissible. The *principal* to go to Sir Percival Glyde, in the event of his surviving Lady Glyde, and there being no issue.'

That is to say, not one farthing of the twenty thousand pounds was to go to Miss Halcombe, or to any other relative or friend of Lady Glyde's. The whole sum, if she left no children, was to slip into the pockets of her husband.

The answer I wrote to this audacious proposal was as short and sharp as I could make it. 'My dear sir. Miss Fairlie's settlement. I maintain the clause to which you object, exactly as it stands. Yours truly.' The rejoinder came back in a quarter of an hour. 'My dear sir. Miss Fairlie's settlement. I maintain the red ink to which you object, exactly as it stands. Yours truly.' In the detestable slang of the day, we were now both 'at a deadlock,' and nothing was left for it but to refer to our clients on either side.

As matters stood, my client – Miss Fairlie not having yet completed her twenty-first year – Mr Frederick Fairlie, was her guardian. I wrote by that day's post, and put the case before him exactly as it stood, not only urging every argument I could think of to induce him to maintain the clause as I had drawn it, but stating to him plainly the mercenary motive which was at the bottom of the opposition to my settlement of the twenty thousand pounds. The knowledge of Sir Percival's affairs which I had necessarily gained when the provisions of the deed on *his* side were submitted in due course to my examination, had but too plainly informed me that the debts on his estate were enormous, and that his income, though nominally a large one, was virtually, for a man in his position, next to nothing. The want of ready money was the practical necessity of Sir Percival's existence, and his lawyer's note on the clause in the settlement was nothing but the frankly selfish expression of it.

Mr Fairlie's answer reached me by return of post, and proved to be wandering and irrelevant in the extreme. Turned into plain English, it practically expressed itself to this effect: 'Would dear Gilmore be so very obliging as not to worry his friend and client about such a trifle as a remote contingency? Was it likely that a young woman of twenty-one would die before a man of forty-five, and die without children? On the other hand, in such a miserable world as this, was it possible to over-estimate the value of peace and quietness? If those two heavenly blessings were offered in exchange for such an earthly trifle as a remote chance of twenty thousand pounds, was it not a fair bargain? Surely, yes. Then why not make it?'

I threw the letter away in disgust. Just as it had fluttered to the ground, there was a knock at my door, and Sir Percival's solicitor, Mr Merriman, was shown in. There are many varieties of sharp practitioners in this world, but I think the hardest of all to deal with are the men who overreach you under the disguise of inveterate good-humour. A fat, well fed, smiling, friendly man of business is of all parties to a bargain the most hopeless to deal with. Mr Merriman was one of this class.

'And how is good Mr Gilmore?' he began, all in a glow with the warmth of his own amiability. 'Glad to see you, sir, in such excellent health. I was passing your door, and I thought I would look in in case you might have something to say to me. Do – now pray do let us settle this little difference of ours by word of mouth, if we can! Have you heard from your client yet?'

'Yes. Have you heard from yours?'

'My dear, good sir! I wish I had heard from him to any purpose – I wish, with all my heart, the responsibility was off my shoulders; but he is obstinate – or let me rather say, resolute – and he won't take it off. "Merriman, I leave details to you. Do what you think right for my interests, and consider me as having personally withdrawn from the business until it is all over." Those were Sir Percival's words a fortnight ago, and all I can get him to do now is to repeat them. I am not a hard man, Mr Gilmore, as you know. Personally and privately, I do assure you, I should like to sponge out that note of mine at this very moment. But if Sir Percival won't go into the matter, if Sir Percival will blindly leave all his interests in my sole care, what course can I possibly take except the course of asserting them? My hands are bound – don't you see, my dear sir? – my hands are bound.'

'You maintain your note on the clause, then, to the letter?' I said.

'Yes – deuce take it! I have no other alternative.' He walked to the fireplace and warmed himself, humming the fag end of a tune in a rich convivial bass voice. 'What does your side say?' he went on; 'now pray tell me – what does your side say?'

I was ashamed to tell him. I attempted to gain time – nay, I did worse. My legal instincts got the better of me, and I even tried to bargain.

'Twenty thousand pounds is rather a large sum to be given up by the lady's friends at two days' notice,' I said.

'Very true,' replied Mr Merriman, looking down thoughtfully at his boots. 'Properly put, sir – most properly put!'

'A compromise, recognising the interests of the lady's family as well as the interests of the husband, might not perhaps have frightened my client quite so much,' I went on. 'Come, come! this contingency resolves itself into a matter of bargaining after all. What is the least you will take?'

'The least we will take,' said Mr Merriman, 'is nineteen-thousand-nine-hundred-and-ninety-nine-pounds-nineteen-shillings-and-elevenpence-three-farthings. Ha! ha! ha! Excuse me, Mr Gilmore. I must have my little joke.'

'Little enough,' I remarked. 'The joke is just worth the odd farthing it was made for.'

Mr Merriman was delighted. He laughed over my retort till the room rang again. I was not half so good-humoured on my side; I came back to business, and closed the interview.

'This is Friday,' I said. 'Give us till Tuesday next for our final answer.'

'By all means,' replied Mr Merriman. 'Longer, my dear sir, if you like.' He took up his hat to go, and then addressed me again. 'By the way,' he said, 'your clients in Cumberland have not heard anything more of the woman who wrote the anonymous letter, have they?'

'Nothing more,' I answered. 'Have you found no trace of her?'

'Not yet,' said my legal friend. 'But we don't despair. Sir Percival has his suspicions that Somebody is keeping her in hiding, and we are having that Somebody watched.'

'You mean the old woman who was with her in Cumberland,' I said.

'Quite another party, sir,' answered Mr Merriman. 'We don't happen to have laid hands on the old woman yet. Our Somebody is a man. We have got him close under our eye here in London, and we strongly suspect he had something to do with helping her in the first instance to escape from the Asylum. Sir Percival wanted to question him at once, but I said, "No. Questioning him will only put him on his guard – watch him, and wait." We shall see what happens. A dangerous woman to be at large, Mr Gilmore; nobody knows what she may do next. I wish you good-morning, sir. On Tuesday next I shall hope for the pleasure of hearing from you.' He smiled amiably and went out.

My mind had been rather absent during the latter part of the conversation with my legal friend. I was so anxious about the matter of the settlement that I had little attention to give to any other subject, and the moment I was left alone again I began to think over what my next proceeding ought to be.

In the case of any other client I should have acted on my instructions, however personally distasteful to me, and have given up the point about the twenty thousand pounds on the spot. But I could not act with this business-like indifference towards Miss Fairlie. I had an honest feeling of affection and admiration for her – I remembered gratefully that her father had been the kindest patron and friend to me that ever man had – I had felt towards her while I was drawing the settlement as I might have felt, if I had not been an old bachelor, towards a daughter of my own, and I was determined to spare no personal sacrifice in her service and where her interests were concerned. Writing a second time to Mr Fairlie was not to be thought of – it would only be giving him a second opportunity of slipping through my fingers. Seeing him and personally remonstrating with him might possibly be of more use. The next day was Saturday. I determined to take a return ticket and jolt my old bones down to Cumberland, on the chance of persuading him to adopt the just, the independent, and the honourable course. It was a poor chance enough, no doubt, but when I had tried it my conscience would be at ease. I should then have done all that a man in my position could do to serve the interests of my old friend's only child.

The weather on Saturday was beautiful, a west wind and a bright sun. Having felt latterly a return of that fulness and oppression of the head, against which my doctor warned me so seriously more than two years since, I resolved to take the opportunity of getting a little extra exercise by sending my bag on before me and walking to the terminus in Euston Square. As I came out into Holborn a gentleman walking by rapidly stopped and spoke to me. It was Mr Walter Hartright.

If he had not been the first to greet me I should certainly have passed him. He was so changed that I hardly knew him again. His face looked pale and haggard – his manner was hurried and uncertain – and his dress, which I remembered as neat and gentlemanlike when I saw him at Limmeridge, was so slovenly now that I should really have been ashamed of the appearance of it on one of my own clerks.

'Have you been long back from Cumberland?' he asked. 'I heard from Miss Halcombe lately. I am aware that Sir Percival Glyde's explanation has been considered satisfactory. Will the marriage take place soon? Do you happen to know, Mr Gilmore?'

He spoke so fast, and crowded his questions together so strangely and confusedly, that I could hardly follow him. However accidentally intimate he might have been with the family at Limmeridge, I could not see that he had any right to expect information on their private affairs, and I determined to drop him, as easily as might be, on the subject of Miss Fairlie's marriage.

'Time will show, Mr Hartright,' I said—'time will show. I dare say if we look out for the marriage in the papers we shall not be far wrong. Excuse my noticing it, but I am sorry to see you not looking so well as you were when we last met.'

A momentary nervous contraction quivered about his lips and eyes, and made me half reproach myself for having answered him in such a significantly guarded manner.

'I had no right to ask about her marriage,' he said bitterly. 'I must wait to see it in the newspapers like other people. Yes,' – he went on before I could make any apologies – 'I have not been well lately. I am going to another country to try a change of scene and occupation. Miss Halcombe has kindly assisted me with her influence, and my testimonials have been found satisfactory. It is a long distance off, but I don't care where I go, what the climate is, or how long I am away.' He looked about him while he said this at the throng of strangers passing us by on either side, in a strange, suspicious manner, as if he thought that some of them might be watching us.

'I wish you well through it, and safe back again,' I said, and then added, so as not to keep him altogether at arm's length on the subject of the Fairlies, 'I am going down to Limmeridge today on business. Miss Halcombe and Miss Fairlie are away just now on a visit to some friends in Yorkshire.'

His eyes brightened, and he seemed about to say something in answer, but the same momentary nervous spasm crossed his face again. He took my hand, pressed it hard, and disappeared among the crowd without saying another word. Though he was little more than a stranger to me, I waited for a moment, looking after him almost with a feeling of regret. I had gained in my profession sufficient experience of young men to know what the outward signs and tokens were of their beginning to go wrong, and when I resumed my walk to the railway I am sorry to say I felt more than doubtful about Mr Hartright's future.

IV

Leaving by an early train, I got to Limmeridge in time for dinner. The house was oppressively empty and dull. I had expected that good Mrs Vesey would have been company for me in the absence of the young ladies, but she was confined to her room by a cold. The servants were so surprised at seeing me that they hurried and bustled absurdly, and made all sorts of annoying mistakes. Even the butler, who was old enough to have known better, brought me a bottle of port that was chilled. The reports of Mr Fairlie's health were just as usual, and when I sent up a message to announce my arrival, I was told that he would be delighted to see me the next morning but that the sudden news of my appearance had prostrated him with palpitations for the rest of the evening. The wind howled dismally all night, and strange cracking and groaning noises sounded here, there, and everywhere in the empty house. I slept as wretchedly as possible, and got up in a mighty bad humour to breakfast by myself the next morning.

At ten o'clock I was conducted to Mr Fairlie's apartments. He was in his usual room, his usual chair, and his usual aggravating state of mind and body. When I went in, his valet was standing before him, holding up for inspection a heavy volume of etchings, as long and as broad as my office writing-desk. The miserable foreigner grinned in the most abject manner, and looked ready to drop with fatigue, while his master composedly turned over the etchings, and brought their hidden beauties to light with the help of a magnifying glass.

'You very best of good old friends,' said Mr Fairlie, leaning back lazily before he could look at me, 'are you *quite* well? How nice of you to come here and see me in my solitude. Dear Gilmore!'

I had expected that the valet would be dismissed when I appeared, but nothing of the sort happened. There he stood, in front of his master's chair, trembling under the weight of the etchings, and there Mr Fairlie sat, serenely twirling the magnifying glass between his white fingers and thumbs.

'I have come to speak to you on a very important matter,' I said, 'and you will therefore excuse me, if I suggest that we had better be alone.'

The unfortunate valet looked at me gratefully. Mr Fairlie faintly repeated my last three words, 'better be alone,' with every appearance of the utmost possible astonishment.

I was in no humour for trifling, and I resolved to make him understand what I meant.

'Oblige me by giving that man permission to withdraw,' I said, pointing to the valet.

Mr Fairlie arched his eyebrows and pursed up his lips in sarcastic surprise.

'Man?' he repeated. 'You provoking old Gilmore, what can you possibly mean by calling him a man? He's nothing of the sort. He might have been a man half an hour ago, before I wanted my etchings, and he may be a man half an hour hence, when I don't want them any longer. At present he is simply a portfolio stand. Why object, Gilmore, to a portfolio stand?'

'I *do* object. For the third time, Mr Fairlie, I beg that we may be alone.'

My tone and manner left him no alternative but to comply with my request. He looked at the servant, and pointed peevishly to a chair at his side.

'Put down the etchings and go away,' he said. 'Don't upset me by losing my place. Have you, or have you not, lost my place? Are you sure you have not? And have you put my hand-bell quite within my reach? Yes? Then why the devil don't you go?'

The valet went out. Mr Fairlie twisted himself round in his chair, polished the magnifying glass with his delicate cambric handkerchief, and indulged himself with a sidelong inspection of the open volume of etchings. It was not easy to keep my temper under these circumstances, but I did keep it.

'I have come here at great personal inconvenience,' I said, 'to serve the interests of your niece and your family, and I think I have established some slight claim to be favoured with your attention in return.'

'Don't bully me!' exclaimed Mr Fairlie, falling back helplessly in the chair, and closing his eyes. 'Please don't bully me. I'm not strong enough.'

I was determined not to let him provoke me, for Laura Fairlie's sake.

'My object,' I went on, 'is to entreat you to reconsider your letter, and not to force me to abandon the just rights of your niece, and of all who belong to her. Let me state the case to you once more, and for the last time.'

Mr Fairlie shook his head and sighed piteously.

'This is heartless of you, Gilmore – very heartless,' he said. 'Never mind, go on.'

I put all the points to him carefully – I set the matter before him in every conceivable light. He lay back in the chair the whole time I was speaking with his eyes closed. When I had done he opened them indolently, took his silver smelling-bottle from the table, and sniffed at it with an air of gentle relish.

'Good Gilmore!' he said between the sniffs, 'how very nice this is of you! How you reconcile one to human nature!'

'Give me a plain answer to a plain question, Mr Fairlie. I tell you again, Sir Percival Glyde has no shadow of a claim to expect more than the income of the money. The money itself if your niece has no children, ought to be under her control, and to return to her family. If you stand firm, Sir Percival must give way – he must give way, I tell you, or he exposes himself to the base imputation of marrying Miss Fairlie entirely from mercenary motives.'

Mr Fairlie shook the silver smelling-bottle at me playfully.

'You dear old Gilmore, how you do hate rank and family, don't you? How you detest Glyde because he happens to be a baronet. What a Radical you are – oh, dear me, what a Radical you are!'

A Radical!!! I could put up with a good deal of provocation, but, after holding the soundest Conservative principles all my life, I could *not* put up with being called a Radical. My blood boiled at it – I started out of my chair – I was speechless with Indignation.

'Don't shake the room!' cried Mr Fairlie—'for Heaven's sake don't shake the room! Worthiest of all possible Gilmores, I meant no offence. My own views are so extremely liberal that I think I am a Radical myself. Yes. We are a pair of Radicals. Please don't be angry. I can't quarrel – I haven't stamina enough. Shall we drop the subject? Yes. Come and look at these sweet etchings. Do let me teach you to understand the heavenly pearliness of these lines. Do now, there's a good Gilmore!'

While he was maundering on in this way I was, fortunately for my own self-respect, returning to my senses. When I spoke again I was composed enough to treat his impertinence with the silent contempt that it deserved.

'You are entirely wrong, sir,' I said, 'in supposing that I speak from any prejudice against Sir Percival Glyde. I may regret that he has so unreservedly resigned himself in this matter to his lawyer's direction as to make any appeal to himself impossible, but I am not prejudiced against him. What I have said would equally apply to any other man in his situation, high or low. The principle I maintain is a recognised principle. If you were to apply at the nearest town here, to the first respectable solicitor you could find, he would tell you as a stranger what I tell you as a friend. He would inform you that it is against all rule to abandon the lady's money entirely to the man she marries. He would decline, on grounds of common legal caution, to give the husband, under any circumstances whatever, an interest of twenty thousand pounds in his wife's death.'

'Would he really, Gilmore?' said Mr Fairlie. 'If he said anything half so horrid, I do assure you I should tinkle my bell for Louis, and have him sent out of the house immediately.'

'You shall not irritate me, Mr Fairlie – for your niece's sake and for her father's sake, you shall not irritate me. You shall take the whole responsibility of this discreditable settlement on your own shoulders before I leave the room.'

'Don't! – now please don't!' said Mr Fairlie. 'Think how precious your time is, Gilmore, and don't throw it away. I would dispute with you if I could, but I can't – I haven't stamina enough. You want to upset me, to upset yourself, to upset Glyde, and to upset Laura; and – oh, dear me! – all for the sake of the very last thing in the world that is likely to happen. No, dear friend, in the interests of peace and quietness, positively No!'

'I am to understand, then, that you hold by the determination expressed in your letter?'

'Yes, please. So glad we understand each other at last. Sit down again – do!'

I walked at once to the door, and Mr Fairlie resignedly 'tinkled' his hand-bell. Before I left the room I turned round and addressed him for the last time.

'Whatever happens in the future, sir,' I said, 'remember that my plain duty of warning you has been performed. As the faithful friend and servant of your family, I tell you, at parting, that no daughter of mine should be married to any man alive under such a settlement as you are forcing me to make for Miss Fairlie.'

The door opened behind me, and the valet stood waiting on the threshold.

'Louis,' said Mr Fairlie, 'show Mr Gilmore out, and then come back and hold up my etchings for me again. Make them give you a good lunch downstairs. Do, Gilmore, make my idle beasts of servants give you a good lunch!'

I was too much disgusted to reply – I turned on my heel, and left him in silence. There was an up train at two o'clock in the afternoon, and by that train I returned to London.

On the Tuesday I sent in the altered settlement, which practically disinherited the very persons whom Miss Fairlie's own lips had informed me she was most anxious to benefit. I had no choice. Another lawyer would have drawn up the deed if I had refused to undertake it.

My task is done. My personal share in the events of the family story extends no farther than the point which I have just reached. Other pens than mine will describe the strange circumstances which are now shortly to follow. Seriously and sorrowfully I close this brief record. Seriously and sorrowfully I repeat here the parting words that I spoke at Limmeridge House: – No daughter of mine should have been married to any man alive under such a settlement as I was compelled to make for Laura Fairlie.

The End of Mr Gilmore's Narrative

THE STORY CONTINUED BY
MARIAN HALCOMBE
(in Extracts from her Diary)

...* This morning Mr Gilmore left us.

His interview with Laura had evidently grieved and surprised him more than he liked to confess. I felt afraid, from his look and manner when we parted, that she might have inadvertently betrayed to him the real secret of her depression and my anxiety. This doubt grew on me so, after he had gone, that I declined riding out with Sir Percival, and went up to Laura's room instead.

I have been sadly distrustful of myself, in this difficult and lamentable matter, ever since I found out my own ignorance of the strength of Laura's unhappy attachment. I ought to have known that the delicacy and forbearance and sense of honour which drew me to poor Hartright, and made me so sincerely admire and respect him, were just the qualities to appeal most irresistibly to Laura's natural sensitiveness and natural generosity of nature. And yet, until she opened her heart to me of her own accord, I had no suspicion that this new feeling had taken root so deeply. I once thought time and care might remove it. I now fear that it will remain with her and alter her for life. The discovery that I have committed such an error in judgment as this makes me hesitate about everything else. I hesitate about Sir Percival, in the face of the plainest proofs. I hesitate even in speaking to Laura. On this very morning I doubted, with my hand on the door, whether I should ask her the questions I had come to put, or not.

When I went into her room I found her walking up and down in great impatience. She looked flushed and excited, and she came forward at once, and spoke to me before I could open my lips.

'I wanted you,' she said. 'Come and sit down on the sofa with me. Marian! I can bear this no longer – I must and will end it.'

There was too much colour in her cheeks, too much energy in her manner, too much firmness in her voice. The little book of Hartright's drawings – the fatal book that she will dream over whenever she is alone – was in one of her hands. I began by gently and firmly taking it from her, and putting it out of sight on a side-table.

---

* The passages omitted, here and elsewhere, in Miss Halcombe's Diary are only those which bear no reference to Miss Fairlie or to any of the persons with whom she is associated in these pages.

'Tell me quietly, my darling, what you wish to do,' I said. 'Has Mr Gilmore been advising you?'

She shook her head. 'No, not in what I am thinking of now. He was very kind and good to me, Marian, and I am ashamed to say I distressed him by crying. I am miserably helpless – I can't control myself. For my own sake, and for all our sakes, I must have courage enough to end it.'

'Do you mean courage enough to claim your release?' I asked.

'No,' she said simply. 'Courage, dear, to tell the truth.'

She put her arms round my neck, and rested her head quietly on my bosom. On the opposite wall hung the miniature portrait of her father. I bent over her, and saw that she was looking at it while her head lay on my breast.

'I can never claim my release from my engagement,' she went on. 'Whatever way it ends it must end wretchedly for me. All I can do, Marian, is not to add the remembrance that I have broken my promise and forgotten my father's dying words, to make that wretchedness worse.'

'What is it you propose, then?' I asked.

'To tell Sir Percival Glyde the truth with my own lips,' she answered, 'and to let him release me, if he will, not because I ask him, but because he knows all.'

'What do you mean, Laura, by "all"? Sir Percival will know enough (he has told me so himself) if he knows that the engagement is opposed to your own wishes.'

'Can I tell him that, when the engagement was made for me by my father, with my own consent? I should have kept my promise, not happily, I am afraid, but still contentedly—' she stopped, turned her face to me, and laid her cheek close against mine—'I should have kept my engagement, Marian, if another love had not grown up in my heart, which was not there when I first promised to be Sir Percival's wife.'

'Laura! you will never lower yourself by making a confession to him?'

'I shall lower myself, indeed, if I gain my release by hiding from him what he has a right to know.'

'He has not the shadow of a right to know it!'

'Wrong, Marian, wrong! I ought to deceive no one – least of all the man to whom my father gave me, and to whom I gave myself.' She put her lips to mine, and kissed me. 'My own love,' she said softly, 'you are so much too fond of me, and so much too proud of me, that you forget, in my case, what you would remember in your own. Better that Sir Percival should doubt my motives, and misjudge my conduct if he will, than that I should be first false to him in thought, and then mean enough to serve my own interests by hiding the falsehood.'

I held her away from me in astonishment. For the first time in our lives we had changed places – the resolution was all on her side, the hesitation all on mine. I looked into the pale, quiet, resigned young face – I saw the pure, innocent heart, in the loving eyes that looked back at me – and the poor worldly cautions and objections that rose to my lips dwindled and died away in their own emptiness. I hung my head in silence. In her place the despicably small pride which makes so many women deceitful would have been my pride, and would have made me deceitful too.

'Don't be angry with me, Marian,' she said, mistaking my silence.

I only answered by drawing her close to me again. I was afraid of crying if I spoke. My tears do not flow so easily as they ought – they come almost like men's tears, with sobs that seem to tear me in pieces, and that frighten every one about me.

'I have thought of this, love, for many days,' she went on, twining and twisting my hair with that childish restlessness in her fingers, which poor Mrs Vesey still tries so patiently and so vainly to cure her of—'I have thought of it very seriously, and I can be sure of my courage when my own conscience tells me I am right. Let me speak to him tomorrow – in your presence, Marian. I will say nothing that is wrong, nothing that you or I need be ashamed of – but, oh, it will ease my heart so to end this miserable conceal-ment! Only let me know and feel that I have no deception to answer for on my side, and then, when he has heard what I have to say, let him act towards me as he will.'

She sighed, and put her head back in its old position on my bosom. Sad misgivings about what the end would be weighed upon my mind, but still distrusting myself, I told her that I would do as she wished. She thanked me, and we passed gradually into talking of other things.

At dinner she joined us again, and was more easy and more herself with Sir Percival than I have seen her yet. In the evening she went to the piano, choosing new music of the dexterous, tuneless, florid kind. The lovely old melodies of Mozart, which poor Hartright was so fond of, she has never played since he left. The book is no longer in the music-stand. She took the volume away herself, so that nobody might find it out and ask her to play from it.

I had no opportunity of discovering whether her purpose of the morning had changed or not, until she wished Sir Percival good-night – and then her own words informed me that it was unaltered. She said, very quietly, that she wished to speak to him after breakfast, and that he would find her in her sitting-room with me. He changed colour at those words, and I felt his hand trembling a little when it came to my turn to take it. The event of the next morning would decide his future life, and he evidently knew it.

I went in, as usual, through the door between our two bedrooms, to bid Laura good-night before she went to sleep. In stooping over her to kiss her I saw the little book of Hartright's drawings half hidden under her pillow, just in the place where she used to hide her favourite toys when she was a child. I could not find it in my heart to say anything, but I pointed to the book and shook my head. She reached both hands up to my cheeks, and drew my face down to hers till our lips met.

'Leave it there tonight,' she whispered; 'tomorrow may be cruel, and may make me say good-bye to it for ever.'

9TH – The first event of the morning was not of a kind to raise my spirits – a letter arrived for me from poor Walter Hartright. It is the answer to mine describing the manner in which Sir Percival cleared himself of the suspicions raised by Anne Catherick's letter. He writes shortly and bitterly about Sir Percival's explanations, only saying that he has no right to offer an opinion on the conduct of those who are above him. This is sad, but his occasional references to himself grieve me still more. He says that the effort to return to his old habits and pursuits grows harder instead of easier to him every day and he implores me, if I have any interest, to exert it to get him employment that will necessitate his absence from England, and take him among new scenes and new people. I have been made all the readier to comply with this request by a passage at the end of his letter, which has almost alarmed me.

After mentioning that he has neither seen nor heard anything of Anne Catherick, he suddenly breaks off, and hints in the most abrupt, mysterious manner, that he has been perpetually watched and followed by strange men ever since he returned to London. He acknowledges that he cannot prove this extraordinary suspicion by fixing on any particular persons, but he declares that the suspicion itself is present to him night and day. This has frightened me, because it looks as if his one fixed idea about Laura was becoming too much for his mind. I will write immediately to some of my mother's influential old friends in London, and press his claims on their notice. Change of scene and change of occupation may really be the salvation of him at this crisis in his life.

Greatly to my relief, Sir Percival sent an apology for not joining us at breakfast. He had taken an early cup of coffee in his own room, and he was still engaged there in writing letters. At eleven o'clock, if that hour was convenient, he would do himself the honour of waiting on Miss Fairlie and Miss Halcombe.

My eyes were on Laura's face while the message was being delivered. I had found her unaccountably quiet and composed on going into her room in the morning, and so she remained all through breakfast. Even when we were sitting together on the sofa in her room, waiting for Sir Percival, she still preserved her self-control.

'Don't be afraid of me, Marian,' was all she said; 'I may forget myself with an old friend like Mr Gilmore, or with a dear sister like you, but I will not forget myself with Sir Percival Glyde.'

I looked at her, and listened to her in silent surprise. Through all the years of our close intimacy this passive force in her character had been hidden from me – hidden even from herself, till love found it, and suffering called it forth.

As the clock on the mantelpiece struck eleven Sir Percival knocked at the door and came in. There was suppressed anxiety and agitation in every line of his face. The dry, sharp cough, which teases him at most times, seemed to be troubling him more incessantly than ever. He sat down opposite to us at the table, and Laura remained by me. I looked attentively at them both, and he was the palest of the two.

He said a few unimportant words, with a visible effort to preserve his customary ease of manner. But his voice was not to be steadied, and the restless uneasiness in his eyes was not to be concealed. He must have felt this himself, for he stopped in the middle of a sentence, and gave up even the attempt to hide his embarrassment any longer.

There was just one moment of dead silence before Laura addressed him.

'I wish to speak to you, Sir Percival,' she said, 'on a subject that is very important to us both. My sister is here, because her presence helps me and gives me confidence. She has not suggested one word of what I am going to say – I speak from my own thoughts, not from hers. I am sure you will be kind enough to understand that before I go any farther?'

Sir Percival bowed. She had proceeded thus far, with perfect outward tranquillity and perfect propriety of manner. She looked at him, and he looked at her. They seemed, at the outset, at least, resolved to understand one another plainly.

'I have heard from Marian,' she went on, 'that I have only to claim my release from our engagement to obtain that release from you. It was forbearing and generous on your part, Sir Percival, to send me such a message. It is only doing you justice to say that I am grateful for the offer, and I hope and believe that it is only doing myself justice to tell you that I decline to accept it.'

His attentive face relaxed a little. But I saw one of his feet, softly, quietly, incessantly beating on the carpet under the table, and I felt that he was secretly as anxious as ever.

'I have not forgotten,' she said, 'that you asked my father's permission before you honoured me with a proposal of marriage. Perhaps you have not forgotten either what I said when I consented to our engagement? I ventured to tell you that my father's influence and advice had mainly decided me to give you my promise. I was guided by my father, because I had always found him the truest of all advisers, the best and fondest of all protectors and friends. I have lost him now – I have only his memory to love, but my faith in that dear dead friend has never been shaken. I believe at this moment, as truly as I ever believed, that he knew what was best, and that his hopes and wishes ought to be my hopes and wishes too.'

Her voice trembled for the first time. Her restless fingers stole their way into my lap, and held fast by one of my hands. There was another moment of silence, and then Sir Percival spoke.

'May I ask,' he said, 'if I have ever proved myself unworthy of the trust which it has been hitherto my greatest honour and greatest happiness to possess?'

'I have found nothing in your conduct to blame,' she answered. 'You have always treated me with the same delicacy and the same forbearance. You have deserved my trust, and, what is of far more importance in my estimation, you have deserved my father's trust, out of which mine grew. You have given me no excuse, even if I had wanted to find one, for asking to be released from my pledge. What I have said so far has been spoken with the wish to acknowledge my whole obligation to you. My regard for that obligation, my regard for my father's memory, and my regard for my own promise, all forbid me to set the example, on my side, of withdrawing from our present position. The breaking of our engagement must be entirely your wish and your act, Sir Percival – not mine.'

The uneasy beating of his foot suddenly stopped, and he leaned forward eagerly across the table.

'My act?' he said. 'What reason can there be on my side for withdrawing?'

I heard her breath quickening – I felt her hand growing cold. In spite of what she had said to me when we were alone, I began to be afraid of her. I was wrong.

'A reason that it is very hard to tell you,' she answered. 'There is a change in me, Sir Percival – a change which is serious enough to justify you, to yourself and to me, in breaking off our engagement.'

His face turned so pale again that even his lips lost their colour. He raised the arm which lay on the table, turned a little away in his chair, and supported his head on his hand, so that his profile only was presented to us.

'What change?' he asked. The tone in which he put the question jarred on me – there was something painfully suppressed in it.

She sighed heavily, and leaned towards me a little, so as to rest her shoulder against mine. I felt her trembling, and tried to spare her by speaking myself. She stopped me by a warning pressure of her hand, and then addressed Sir Percival once more, but this time without looking at him.

'I have heard,' she said, 'and I believe it, that the fondest and truest of all affections is the affection which a woman ought to bear to her husband. When our engagement began that affection was mine to give, if I could, and yours to win, if you could. Will you pardon me, and spare me, Sir Percival, if I acknowledge that it is not so any longer?'

A few tears gathered in her eyes, and dropped over her cheeks slowly as she paused and waited for his answer. He did not utter a word. At the beginning of her reply he had moved the hand on which his head rested, so that it hid his face. I saw nothing but the upper part of his figure at the table. Not a muscle of him moved. The fingers of the hand which supported his head were dented deep in his hair. They might have expressed hidden anger or hidden grief – it was hard to say which – there was no significant trembling in them. There was nothing, absolutely nothing, to tell the secret of his thoughts at that moment – the moment which was the crisis of his life and the crisis of hers.

I was determined to make him declare himself, for Laura's sake.

'Sir Percival!' I interposed sharply, 'have you nothing to say when my sister has said so much? More, in my opinion,' I added, my unlucky temper getting the better of me, 'than any man alive, in your position, has a right to hear from her.'

That last rash sentence opened a way for him by which to escape me if he chose, and he instantly took advantage of it.

'Pardon me, Miss Halcombe,' he said, still keeping his hand over his face, 'pardon me if I remind you that I have claimed no such right.'

The few plain words which would have brought him back to the point from which he had wandered were just on my lips, when Laura checked me by speaking again.

'I hope I have not made my painful acknowledgment in vain,' she continued. 'I hope it has secured me your entire confidence in what I have still to say?'

'Pray be assured of it.' He made that brief reply warmly, dropping his hand on the table while he spoke, and turning towards us again. Whatever outward change had passed over him was gone now. His face was eager and expectant – it expressed nothing but the most intense anxiety to hear her next words.

'I wish you to understand that I have not spoken from any selfish motive,' she said. 'If you leave me, Sir Percival, after what you have just heard, you do not leave me to marry another man, you only allow me to remain a single woman for the rest of my life. My fault towards you has begun and ended in my own thoughts. It can never go any farther. No word has passed—' She hesitated, in doubt about the expression she should use next, hesitated in a momentary confusion which it was very sad and very painful to see. 'No word has passed,' she patiently and resolutely resumed, 'between myself and the person to whom I am now referring for the first and last time in your presence of my feelings towards him, or of his feelings towards me – no word ever can pass – neither he nor I are likely, in this world, to meet again. I earnestly beg you to spare me from saying any more, and to believe me, on my word, in what I have just told you. It is the truth, Sir Percival, the truth which I think my promised husband has a claim to hear, at any sacrifice of my own feelings. I trust to his generosity to pardon me, and to his honour to keep my secret.'

'Both those trusts are sacred to me,' he said, 'and both shall be sacredly kept.' After answering in those terms he paused, and looked at her as if he was waiting to hear more.

'I have said all I wish to say,' she added quietly—'I have said more than enough to justify you in withdrawing from your engagement.'

'You have said more than enough,' he answered, 'to make it the dearest object of my life to *keep* the engagement.' With those words he rose from his chair, and advanced a few steps towards the place where she was sitting.

She started violently, and a faint cry of surprise escaped her. Every word she had spoken had innocently betrayed her purity and truth to a man who thoroughly understood the priceless value of a pure and true woman. Her own noble conduct had been the hidden enemy, throughout, of all the hopes she had trusted to it. I had dreaded this from the first. I would have prevented it, if she had allowed me the smallest chance of doing so. I even waited and watched now, when the harm was done, for a word from Sir Percival that would give me the opportunity of putting him in the wrong.

'You have left it to *me*, Miss Fairlie, to resign you,' he continued. 'I am not heartless enough to resign a woman who has just shown herself to be the noblest of her sex.'

He spoke with such warmth and feeling, with such passionate enthusiasm, and yet with such perfect delicacy, that she raised her head, flushed up a little, and looked at him with sudden animation and spirit.

'No!' she said firmly. 'The most wretched of her sex, if she must give herself in marriage when she cannot give her love.'

'May she not give it in the future,' he asked, 'if the one object of her husband's life is to deserve it?'

'Never!' she answered. 'If you still persist in maintaining our engagement,

I may be your true and faithful wife, Sir Percival – your loving wife, if I know my own heart, never!'

She looked so irresistibly beautiful as she said those brave words that no man alive could have steeled his heart against her. I tried hard to feel that Sir Percival was to blame, and to say so, but my womanhood would pity him, in spite of myself.

'I gratefully accept your faith and truth,' he said. 'The least that *you* can offer is more to me than the utmost that I could hope for from any other woman in the world.'

Her left hand still held mine, but her right hand hung listlessly at her side. He raised it gently to his lips – touched it with them, rather than kissed it – bowed to me – and then, with perfect delicacy and discretion, silently quitted the room.

She neither moved nor said a word when he was gone – she sat by me, cold and still, with her eyes fixed on the ground. I saw it was hopeless and useless to speak, and I only put my arm round her, and held her to me in silence. We remained together so for what seemed a long and weary time – so long and so weary, that I grew uneasy and spoke to her softly, in the hope of producing a change.

The sound of my voice seemed to startle her into consciousness. She suddenly drew herself away from me and rose to her feet.

'I must submit, Marian, as well as I can,' she said. 'My new life has its hard duties, and one of them begins today.'

As she spoke she went to a side-table near the window, on which her sketching materials were placed, gathered them together carefully, and put them in a drawer of her cabinet. She locked the drawer and brought the key to me.

'I must part from everything that reminds me of him,' she said. 'Keep the key wherever you please – I shall never want it again.'

Before I could say a word she had turned away to her book-case, and had taken from it the album that contained Walter Hartright's drawings. She hesitated for a moment, holding the little volume fondly in her hands – then lifted it to her lips and kissed it.

'Oh, Laura! Laura!' I said, not angrily, not reprovingly – with nothing but sorrow in my voice, and nothing but sorrow in my heart.

'It is the last time, Marian,' she pleaded. 'I am bidding it good-bye for ever.'

She laid the book on the table and drew out the comb that fastened her hair. It fell, in its matchless beauty, over her back and shoulders, and dropped round her, far below her waist. She separated one long, thin lock from the rest, cut it off, and pinned it carefully, in the form of a circle, on the first blank page of the album. The moment it was fastened she closed the volume hurriedly, and placed it in my hands.

'You write to him and he writes to you,' she said. 'While I am alive, if he asks after me always tell him I am well, and never say I am unhappy. Don't distress him, Marian, for my sake, don't distress him. If I die first, promise you will give him this little book of his drawings, with my hair in it. There can be no harm, when I am gone, in telling him that I put it there with my own hands. And say – oh, Marian, say for me, then, what I can never say for myself – say I loved him!'

She flung her arms round my neck, and whispered the last words in my ear with a passionate delight in uttering them which it almost broke my heart to hear. All the long restraint she had imposed on herself gave way in that first last outburst of tenderness. She broke from me with hysterical vehemence, and threw herself on the sofa in a paroxysm of sobs and tears that shook her from head to foot.

I tried vainly to soothe her and reason with her – she was past being soothed, and past being reasoned with. It was the sad, sudden end for us two of this memorable day. When the fit had worn itself out she was too exhausted to speak. She slumbered towards the afternoon, and I put away the book of drawings so that she might not see it when she woke. My face was calm, whatever my heart might be, when she opened her eyes again and looked at me. We said no more to each other about the distressing interview of the morning. Sir Percival's name was not mentioned. Walter Hartright was not alluded to again by either of us for the remainder of the day.

10TH. – Finding that she was composed and like herself this morning, I returned to the painful subject of yesterday, for the sole purpose of imploring her to let me speak to Sir Percival and Mr Fairlie, more plainly and strongly than she could speak to either of them herself, about this lamentable marriage. She interposed, gently but firmly, in the middle of my remonstrances.

'I left yesterday to decide,' she said; 'and yesterday *has* decided. It is too late to go back.'

Sir Percival spoke to me this afternoon about what had passed in Laura's room. He assured me that the unparalleled trust she had placed in him had awakened such an answering conviction of her innocence and integrity in his mind, that he was guiltless of having felt even a moment's unworthy jealousy, either at the time when he was in her presence, or afterwards when he had withdrawn from it. Deeply as he lamented the unfortunate attachment which had hindered the progress he might otherwise have made in her esteem and regard, he firmly believed that it had remained unacknowledged in the past, and that it would remain, under all changes of circumstance which it was possible to contemplate, unacknowledged in the future. This was his absolute conviction; and the strongest proof he could give of it was the assurance, which he now offered, that he felt no curiosity to know whether the attachment was of recent date or not, or who had been the object of it. His implicit confidence in Miss Fairlie made him satisfied with what she had thought fit to say to him, and he was honestly innocent of the slightest feeling of anxiety to hear more.

He waited after saying those words and looked at me. I was so conscious of my unreasonable prejudice against him – so conscious of an unworthy suspicion that he might be speculating on my impulsively answering the very questions which he had just described himself as resolved not to ask – that I evaded all reference to this part of the subject with something like a feeling of confusion on my own part. At the same time I was resolved not to lose even the smallest opportunity of trying to plead Laura's cause, and I told him boldly that I regretted his generosity had not carried him one step farther, and induced him to withdraw from the engagement altogether.

Here, again, he disarmed me by not attempting to defend himself. He would merely beg me to remember the difference there was between his allowing Miss Fairlie to give him up, which was a matter of submission only, and his forcing himself to give up Miss Fairlie, which was, in other words, asking him to be the suicide of his own hopes. Her conduct of the day before had so strengthened the unchangeable love and admiration of two long years, that all active contention against those feelings, on his part, was henceforth entirely out of his power. I must think him weak, selfish, unfeeling towards the very woman whom he idolised, and he must bow to my opinion as resignedly as he could – only putting it to me, at the same time, whether her future as a single woman, pining under an unhappily placed attachment which she could never acknowledge, could be said to promise her a much brighter prospect than her future as the wife of a man who worshipped the very ground she walked on? In the last case there was hope from time, however slight it might be – in the first case, on her own showing, there was no hope at all.

I answered him – more because my tongue is a woman's, and must answer, than because I had anything convincing to say. It was only too plain that the course Laura had adopted the day before had offered him the advantage if he chose to take it – and that he *had* chosen to take it. I felt this at the time, and I feel it just as strongly now, while I write these lines, in my own room. The one hope left is that his motives really spring, as he says they do, from the irresistible strength of his attachment to Laura.

Before I close my diary for tonight I must record that I wrote today, in poor Hartright's interest, to two of my mother's old friends in London – both men of influence and position. If they can do anything for him, I am quite sure they will. Except Laura, I never was more anxious about any one than I am now about Walter. All that has happened since he left us has only increased my strong regard and sympathy for him. I hope I am doing right in trying to help him to employment abroad – I hope, most earnestly and anxiously, that it will end well.

11TH – Sir Percival had an interview with Mr Fairlie, and I was sent for to join them.

I found Mr Fairlie greatly relieved at the prospect of the 'family worry' (as he was pleased to describe his niece's marriage) being settled at last. So far, I did not feel called on to say anything to him about my own opinion, but when he proceeded, in his most aggravatingly languid manner, to suggest that the time for the marriage had better be settled next, in accordance with Sir Percival's wishes, I enjoyed the satisfaction of assailing Mr Fairlie's nerves with as strong a protest against hurrying Laura's decision as I could put into words. Sir Percival immediately assured me that he felt the force of my objection, and begged me to believe that the proposal had not been made in consequence of any interference on his part. Mr Fairlie leaned back in his chair, closed his eyes, said we both of us did honour to human nature, and then repeated his suggestion as coolly as if neither Sir Percival nor I had said a word in opposition to it. It ended in my flatly declining to mention the subject to Laura, unless she first approached it of her own accord. I left the room at once after making that declaration. Sir Percival looked seriously embarrassed and distressed, Mr Fairlie stretched out his lazy legs on his velvet footstool, and said, 'Dear Marian! how I envy you your robust nervous system! Don't bang the door!'

On going to Laura's room I found that she had asked for me, and that Mrs Vesey had informed her that I was with Mr Fairlie. She inquired at once what I had been wanted for, and I told her all that had passed, without attempting to conceal the vexation and annoyance that I really felt. Her answer surprised and distressed me inexpressibly – it was the very last reply that I should have expected her to make.

'My uncle is right,' she said. 'I have caused trouble and anxiety enough to you, and to all about me. Let me cause no more, Marian – let Sir Percival decide.'

I remonstrated warmly, but nothing that I could say moved her.

'I am held to my engagement,' she replied; 'I have broken with my old life. The evil day will not come the less surely because I put it off. No,

Marian! once again my uncle is right. I have caused trouble enough and anxiety enough, and I will cause no more.'

She used to be pliability itself, but she was now inflexibly passive in her resignation – I might almost say in her despair. Dearly as I love her, I should have been less pained if she had been violently agitated – it was so shockingly unlike her natural character to see her as cold and insensible as I saw her now.

12TH – Sir Percival put some questions to me at breakfast about Laura, which left me no choice but to tell him what she had said.

While we were talking she herself came down and joined us. She was just as unnaturally composed in Sir Percival's presence as she had been in mine. When breakfast was over he had an opportunity of saying a few words to her privately, in a recess of one of the windows. They were not more than two or three minutes together, and on their separating she left the room with Mrs Vesey, while Sir Percival came to me. He said he had entreated her to favour him by maintaining her privilege of fixing the time for the marriage at her own will and pleasure. In reply she had merely expressed her acknowledgments, and had desired him to mention what his wishes were to Miss Halcombe.

I have no patience to write more. In this instance, as in every other, Sir Percival has carried his point with the utmost possible credit to himself, in spite of everything that I can say or do. His wishes are now, what they were, of course, when he first came here; and Laura having resigned herself to the one inevitable sacrifice of the marriage, remains as coldly hopeless and enduring as ever. In parting with the little occupations and relics that reminded her of Hartright, she seems to have parted with all her tenderness and all her impressibility. It is only three o'clock in the afternoon while I write these lines, and Sir Percival has left us already, in the happy hurry of a bridegroom, to prepare for the bride's reception at his house in Hampshire. Unless some extraordinary event happens to prevent it they will be married exactly at the time when he wished to be married – before the end of the year. My very fingers burn as I write it!

13TH – A sleepless night, through uneasiness about Laura. Towards the morning I came to a resolution to try what change of scene would do to rouse her. She cannot surely remain in her present torpor of insensibility, if I take her away from Limmeridge and surround her with the pleasant faces of old friends? After some consideration I decided on writing to the Arnolds, in Yorkshire. They are simple, kind-hearted, hospitable people, and she has known them from her childhood. When I had put the letter in the post-bag

I told her what I had done. It would have been a relief to me if she had shown the spirit to resist and object. But no – she only said, 'I will go anywhere with you, Marian. I dare say you are right – I dare say the change will do me good.'

14TH – I wrote to Mr Gilmore, informing him that there was really a prospect of this miserable marriage taking place, and also mentioning my idea of trying what change of scene would do for Laura. I had no heart to go into particulars. Time enough for them when we get nearer to the end of the year.

15TH – Three letters for me. The first, from the Arnolds, full of delight at the prospect of seeing Laura and me. The second, from one of the gentlemen to whom I wrote on Walter Hartright's behalf, informing me that he has been fortunate enough to find an opportunity of complying with my request. The third, from Walter himself, thanking me, poor fellow, in the warmest terms, for giving him an opportunity of leaving his home, his country, and his friends. A private expedition to make excavations among the ruined cities of Central America is, it seems, about to sail from Liverpool. The draughtsman who had been already appointed to accompany it has lost heart, and withdrawn at the eleventh hour, and Walter is to fill his place. He is to be engaged for six months certain, from the time of the landing in Honduras, and for a year afterwards, if the excavations are successful, and if the funds hold out. His letter ends with a promise to write me a farewell line when they are all on board ship, and when the pilot leaves them. I can only hope and pray earnestly that he and I are both acting in this matter for the best. It seems such a serious step for him to take, that the mere contemplation of it startles me. And yet, in his unhappy position, how can I expect him or wish him to remain at home?

16TH – The carriage is at the door. Laura and I set out on our visit to the Arnolds today.

POLESDEAN LODGE, YORKSHIRE

23RD – A week in these new scenes and among these kind-hearted people has done her some good, though not so much as I had hoped. I have resolved to prolong our stay for another week at least. It is useless to go back to Limmeridge till there is an absolute necessity for our return.

24TH – Sad news by this morning's post. The expedition to Central America sailed on the twenty-first. We have parted with a true man – we have lost a faithful friend. Water Hartright has left England.

25TH – Sad news yesterday – ominous news today. Sir Percival Glyde has written to Mr Fairlie, and Mr Fairlie has written to Laura and me, to recall us to Limmeridge immediately.

What can this mean? Has the day for the marriage been fixed in our absence?

II

LIMMERIDGE HOUSE

NOVEMBER 27TH – My forebodings are realised. The marriage is fixed for the twenty-second of December.

The day after we left for Polesdean Lodge Sir Percival wrote, it seems, to Mr Fairlie, to say that the necessary repairs and alterations in his house in Hampshire would occupy a much longer time in completion than he had originally anticipated. The proper estimates were to be submitted to him as soon as possible, and it would greatly facilitate his entering into definite arrangements with the workpeople, if he could be informed of the exact period at which the wedding ceremony might be expected to take place. He could then make all his calculations in reference to time, besides writing the necessary apologies to friends who had been engaged to visit him that winter, and who could not, of course, be received when the house was in the hands of the workmen.

To this letter Mr Fairlie had replied by requesting Sir Percival himself to suggest a day for the marriage, subject to Miss Fairlie's approval, which her guardian willingly undertook to do his best to obtain. Sir Percival wrote back by the next post, and proposed (in accordance with his own views and wishes from the first?) the latter part of December – perhaps the twenty-second, or twenty-fourth, or any other day that the lady and her guardian might prefer. The lady not being at hand to speak for herself, her guardian had decided, in her absence, on the earliest day mentioned – the twenty-second of December, and had written to recall us to Limmeridge in consequence.

After explaining these particulars to me at a private interview yesterday, Mr Fairlie suggested, in his most amiable manner, that I should open the necessary negotiations today. Feeling that resistance was useless, unless I could first obtain Laura's authority to make it, I consented to speak to her, but declared, at the same time, that I would on no consideration undertake to gain her consent to Sir Percival's wishes. Mr Fairlie complimented me on my 'excellent conscience,' much as he would have complimented me, if he had been out walking, on my 'excellent constitution,' and seemed perfectly satisfied, so far, with having simply shifted one more family responsibility from his own shoulders to mine.

This morning I spoke to Laura as I had promised. The composure – I may almost say, the insensibility – which she has so strangely and so resolutely maintained ever since Sir Percival left us, was not proof against the shock of the news I had to tell her. She turned pale and trembled violently.

'Not so soon!' she pleaded. 'Oh, Marian, not so soon!'

The slightest hint she could give was enough for me. I rose to leave the room, and fight her battle for her at once with Mr Fairlie.

Just as my hand was on the door, she caught fast hold of my dress and stopped me.

'Let me go!' I said. 'My tongue burns to tell your uncle that he and Sir Percival are not to have it all their own way.'

She sighed bitterly, and still held my dress.

'No!' she said faintly. 'Too late, Marian, too late!'

'Not a minute too late,' I retorted. 'The question of time is *our* question – and trust me, Laura, to take a woman's full advantage of it.'

I unclasped her hand from my gown while I spoke; but she slipped both her arms round my waist at the same moment, and held me more effectually than ever.

'It will only involve us in more trouble and more confusion,' she said. 'It will set you and my uncle at variance, and bring Sir Percival here again with fresh causes of complaint—'

'So much the better!' I cried out passionately. 'Who cares for his causes of complaint? Are you to break your heart to set his mind at ease? No man under heaven deserves these sacrifices from us women. Men! They are the enemies of our innocence and our peace – they drag us away from our parents' love and our sisters' friendship – they take us body and soul to themselves, and fasten our helpless lives to theirs as they chain up a dog to his kennel. And what does the best of them give us in return? Let me go, Laura – I'm mad when I think of it!'

The tears – miserable, weak, women's tears of vexation and rage – started to my eyes. She smiled sadly, and put her handkerchief over my face to hide for me the betrayal of my own weakness – the weakness of all others which she knew that I most despised.

'Oh, Marian!' she said. 'You crying! Think what you would say to me, if the places were changed, and if those tears were mine. All your love and courage and devotion will not alter what must happen, sooner or later. Let my uncle have his way. Let us have no more troubles and heart-burnings that any sacrifice of mine can prevent. Say you will live with me, Marian, when I am married – and say no more.'

But I did say more. I forced back the contemptible tears that were no relief to *me*, and that only distressed *her*, and reasoned and pleaded as

calmly as I could. It was of no avail. She made me twice repeat the promise
to live with her when she was married, and then suddenly asked a question
which turned my sorrow and my sympathy for her into a new direction.

'While we were at Polesdean,' she said, 'you had a letter, Marian—'

Her altered tone – the abrupt manner in which she looked away from me
and hid her face on my shoulder – the hesitation which silenced her before
she had completed her question, all told me, but too plainly, to whom the
half-expressed inquiry pointed.

'I thought, Laura, that you and I were never to refer to him again,'
I said gently.

'You had a letter from him?' she persisted.

'Yes,' I replied, 'if you must know it.'

'Do you mean to write to him again?'

I hesitated. I had been afraid to tell her of his absence from England, or
of the manner in which my exertions to serve his new hopes and projects
had connected me with his departure. What answer could I make? He was
gone where no letters could reach him for months, perhaps for years, to
come.

'Suppose I do mean to write to him again,' I said at last. 'What then,
Laura?'

Her cheek grew burning hot against my neck, and her arms trembled and
tightened round me.

'Don't tell him about *the twenty-second*,' she whispered. 'Promise,
Marian – pray promise you will not even mention my name to him when
you write next.'

I gave the promise. No words can say how sorrowfully I gave it. She
instantly took her arm from my waist, walked away to the window, and stood
looking out with her back to me. After a moment she spoke once more, but
without turning round, without allowing me to catch the smallest glimpse of
her face.

'Are you going to my uncle's room?' she asked. 'Will you say that I
consent to whatever arrangement he may think best? Never mind leaving
me, Marian. I shall be better alone for a little while.'

I went out. If, as soon as I got into the passage, I could have transported
Mr Fairlie and Sir Percival Glyde to the uttermost ends of the earth by
lifting one of my fingers, that finger would have been raised without an
instant's hesitation. For once my unhappy temper now stood my friend. I
should have broken down altogether and burst into a violent fit of crying,
if my tears had not been all burnt up in the heat of my anger. As it was,
I dashed into Mr Fairlie's room – called to him as harshly as possible,
'Laura consents to the twenty-second' – and dashed out again without

waiting for a word of answer. I banged the door after me, and I hope I shattered Mr Fairlie's nervous system for the rest of the day.

28TH – This morning I read poor Hartright's farewell letter over again, a doubt having crossed my mind since yesterday, whether I am acting wisely in concealing the fact of his departure from Laura.

On reflection, I still think I am right. The allusions in his letter to the preparations made for the expedition to Central America, all show that the leaders of it know it to be dangerous. If the discovery of this makes me uneasy, what would it make *her*? It is bad enough to feel that his departure has deprived us of the friend of all others to whose devotion we could trust in the hour of need, if ever that hour comes and finds us helpless; but it is far worse to know that he has gone from us to face the perils of a bad climate, a wild country, and a disturbed population. Surely it would be a cruel candour to tell Laura this, without a pressing and a positive necessity for it?

I almost doubt whether I ought not to go a step farther, and burn the letter at once, for fear of its one day falling into wrong hands. It not only refers to Laura in terms which ought to remain a secret for ever between the writer and me, but it reiterates his suspicion – so obstinate, so unaccountable, and so alarming – that he has been secretly watched since he left Limmeridge. He declares that he saw the faces of the two strange men who followed him about the streets of London, watching him among the crowd which gathered at Liverpool to see the expedition embark, and he positively asserts that he heard the name of Anne Catherick pronounced behind him as he got into the boat. His own words are, 'These events have a meaning, these events must lead to a result. The mystery of Anne Catherick is *not* cleared up yet. She may never cross my path again, but if ever she crosses yours, make better use of the opportunity, Miss Halcombe, than I made of it. I speak on strong conviction – I entreat you to remember what I say.' These are his own expressions. There is no danger of my forgetting them – my memory is only too ready to dwell on any words of Hartright's that refer to Anne Catherick. But there is danger in my keeping the letter. The merest accident might place it at the mercy of strangers. I may fall ill – I may die. Better to burn it at once, and have one anxiety the less.

It is burnt. The ashes of his farewell letter – the last he may ever write to me – lie in a few black fragments on the hearth. Is this the sad end to all that sad story? Oh, not the end – surely, surely not the end already!

29TH – The preparations for the marriage have begun. The dressmaker has come to receive her orders. Laura is perfectly impassive, perfectly careless about the question of all others in which a woman's personal interests are most closely bound up. She has left it all to the dressmaker and to me. If poor Hartright had been the baronet, and the husband of her father's choice, how differently she would have behaved! How anxious and capricious she would have been, and what a hard task the best of dressmakers would have found it to please her!

30TH – We hear every day from Sir Percival. The last news is that the alterations in his house will occupy from four to six months before they can be properly completed. If painters, paperhangers, and upholsterers could make happiness as well as splendour, I should be interested about their proceedings in Laura's future home. As it is, the only part of Sir Percival's last letter which does not leave me as it found me, perfectly indifferent to all his plans and projects, is the part which refers to the wedding tour. He proposes, as Laura is delicate, and as the winter threatens to be unusually severe, to take her to Rome, and to remain in Italy until the early part of next summer. If this plan should not be approved, he is equally ready, although he has no establishment of his own in town, to spend the season in London, in the most suitable furnished house that can be obtained for the purpose.

Putting myself and my own feelings entirely out of the question (which it is my duty to do, and which I have done), I, for one, have no doubt of the propriety of adopting the first of these proposals. In either case a separation between Laura and me is inevitable. It will be a longer separation, in the event of their going abroad, than it would be in the event of their remaining in London – but we must set against this disadvantage the benefit to Laura, on the other side, of passing the winter in a mild climate, and more than that, the immense assistance in raising her spirits, and reconciling her to her new exist-ence, which the mere wonder and excitement of travelling for the first time in her life in the most interesting country in the world, must surely afford. She is not of a disposition to find resources in the conventional gaieties and excite-ments of London. They would only make the first oppression of this lamentable marriage fall the heavier on her. I dread the beginning of her new life more than words can tell, but I see some hope for her if she travels – none if she remains at home.

It is strange to look back at this latest entry in my journal, and to find that I am writing of the marriage and the parting with Laura, as people write of a settled thing. It seems so cold and so unfeeling to be looking at the future already in this cruelly composed way. But what other way is possible, now that the time is drawing so near? Before another month is over our heads she will be *his* Laura instead of mine! *his* Laura! I am as little able to realise the idea which those two words convey – my mind feels almost as dulled and stunned by it – as if writing of her marriage were like writing of her death.

DECEMBER 1ST – A sad, sad day – a day that I have no heart to describe at any length. After weakly putting it off last night, I was obliged to speak to her this morning of Sir Percival's proposal about the wedding tour.

In the full conviction that I should be with her wherever she went, the poor child – for a child she is still in many things – was almost happy at the prospect of seeing the wonders of Florence and Rome and Naples. It nearly broke my heart to dispel her delusion, and to bring her face to face with the hard truth. I was obliged to tell her that no man tolerates a rival – not even a woman rival – in his wife's affections, when he first marries, whatever he may do afterwards. I was obliged to warn her that my chance of living with her permanently under her own roof, depended entirely on my not arousing Sir Percival's jealousy and distrust by standing between them at the beginning of their marriage, in the position of the chosen depositary of his wife's closest secrets. Drop by drop I poured the profaning bitterness of this world's wisdom into that pure heart and that innocent mind, while every higher and better feeling within me recoiled from my miserable task. It is over now. She has learnt her hard, her inevitable lesson. The simple illusions of her girlhood are gone, and my hand has stripped them off. Better mine than his – that is all my consolation – better mine than his.

So the first proposal is the proposal accepted. They are to go to Italy, and I am to arrange, with Sir Percival's permission, for meeting them and staying with them when they return to England. In other words, I am to ask a personal favour, for the first time in my life, and to ask it of the man of all others to whom I least desire to owe a serious obligation of any kind. Well! I think I could do even more than that, for Laura's sake.

2ND – On looking back, I find myself always referring to Sir Percival in disparaging terms. In the turn affairs have now taken, I must and will root out my prejudice against him. I cannot think how it first got into my mind. It certainly never existed in former times.

Is it Laura's reluctance to become his wife that has set me against him? Have Hartright's perfectly intelligible prejudices infected me without my suspecting their influence? Does that letter of Anne Catherick's still leave a lurking distrust in my mind, in spite of Sir Percival's explanation, and of the proof in my possession of the truth of it? I cannot account for the state of my own feelings; the one thing I am certain of is, that it is my duty – doubly my duty now – not to wrong Sir Percival by unjustly distrusting him. If it has got to be a habit with me always to write of him in the same unfavourable manner, I must and will break myself of this unworthy tendency, even though the effort should force me to close the pages of my journal till the marriage is over! I am seriously dissatisfied with myself – I will write no more today.

DECEMBER 16TH – A whole fortnight has passed, and I have not once opened these pages. I have been long enough away from my journal to come back to it with a healthier and better mind, I hope, so far as Sir Percival is concerned.

There is not much to record of the past two weeks. The dresses are almost all finished, and the new travelling trunks have been sent here from London. Poor dear Laura hardly leaves me for a moment all day, and last night, when neither of us could sleep, she came and crept into my bed to talk to me there. 'I shall lose you so soon, Marian,' she said; 'I must make the most of you while I can.'

They are to be married at Limmeridge Church, and thank Heaven, not one of the neighbours is to be invited to the ceremony. The only visitor will be our old friend, Mr Arnold, who is to come from Polesdean to give Laura away, her uncle being far too delicate to trust himself outside the door in such inclement weather as we now have. If I were not determined, from this day forth, to see nothing but the bright side of our prospects, the melancholy absence of any male relative of Laura's, at the most important moment of her life, would make me very gloomy and very distrustful of the future. But I have done with gloom and distrust – that is to say, I have done with writing about either the one or the other in this journal.

Sir Percival is to arrive tomorrow. He offered, in case we wished to treat him on terms of rigid etiquette, to write and ask our clergyman to grant him the hospitality of the rectory, during the short period of his sojourn at Limmeridge, before the marriage. Under the circumstances, neither Mr Fairlie nor I thought it at all necessary for us to trouble ourselves about attending to trifling forms and ceremonies. In our wild moorland country, and in this great lonely house, we may well claim to be beyond the reach of the trivial conventionalities which hamper people in other places. I wrote to Sir Percival to thank him for his polite offer, and to beg that he would occupy his old rooms, just as usual, at Limmeridge House.

17TH – He arrived today, looking, as I thought, a little worn and anxious, but still talking and laughing like a man in the best possible spirits. He brought with him some really beautiful presents in jewellery, which Laura received with her best grace, and, outwardly at least, with perfect self-possession. The only sign I can detect of the struggle it must cost her to

preserve appearances at this trying time, expresses itself in a sudden unwillingness, on her part, ever to be left alone. Instead of retreating to her own
room, as usual, she seems to dread going there. When I went upstairs today,
after lunch, to put on my bonnet for a walk, she volunteered to join me, and
again, before dinner, she threw the door open between our two rooms, so
that we might talk to each other while we were dressing. 'Keep me always
doing something,' she said; 'keep me always in company with somebody.
Don't let me think – that is all I ask now, Marian – don't let me think.'

This sad change in her only increases her attractions for Sir Percival. He
interprets it, I can see, to his own advantage. There is a feverish flush in her
cheeks, a feverish brightness in her eyes, which he welcomes as the return of
her beauty and the recovery of her spirits. She talked today at dinner with a
gaiety and carelessness so false, so shockingly out of her character, that I
secretly longed to silence her and take her away. Sir Percival's delight and
surprise appeared to be beyond all expression. The anxiety which I had noticed
on his face when he arrived totally disappeared from it, and he looked, even
to my eyes, a good ten years younger than he really is.

There can be no doubt – though some strange perversity prevents me
from seeing it myself – there can be no doubt that Laura's future husband
is a very handsome man. Regular features form a personal advantage to begin
with – and he has them. Bright brown eyes, either in man or woman, are a
great attraction – and he has them. Even baldness, when it is only baldness
over the forehead (as in his case), is rather becoming than not in a man, for
it heightens the head and adds to the intelligence of the face. Grace and ease
of movement, untiring animation of manner, ready, pliant, conversational
powers – all these are unquestionable merits, and all these he certainly
possesses. Surely Mr Gilmore, ignorant as he is of Laura's secret, was not
to blame for feeling surprised that she should repent of her marriage engagement? Any one else in his place would have shared our good old friend's
opinion. If I were asked, at this moment, to say plainly what defects I have
discovered in Sir Percival, I could only point out two. One, his incessant
restlessness and excitability – which may be caused, naturally enough, by
unusual energy of character. The other, his short, sharp, ill-tempered manner
of speaking to the servants – which may be only a bad habit after all. No,
I cannot dispute it, and I will not dispute it – Sir Percival is a very handsome
and a very agreeable man. There! I have written it down at last, and I am
glad it's over.

18TH – Feeling weary and depressed this morning, I left Laura with Mrs
Vesey, and went out alone for one of my brisk midday walks, which I have
discontinued too much of late. I took the dry airy road over the moor that

leads to Todd's Corner. After having been out half an hour, I was excessively surprised to see Sir Percival approaching me from the direction of the farm. He was walking rapidly, swinging his stick, his head erect as usual, and his shooting jacket flying open in the wind. When we met he did not wait for me to ask any questions – he told me at once that he had been to the farm to inquire if Mr or Mrs Todd had received any tidings, since his last visit to Limmeridge, of Anne Catherick.

'You found, of course, that they had heard nothing?' I said.

'Nothing whatever,' he replied. 'I begin to be seriously afraid that we have lost her. Do you happen to know,' he continued, looking me in the face very attentively 'if the artist – Mr Hartright – is in a position to give us any further information?'

'He has neither heard of her, nor seen her, since he left Cumberland,' I answered.

'Very sad,' said Sir Percival, speaking like a man who was disappointed, and yet, oddly enough, looking at the same time like a man who was relieved. 'It is impossible to say what misfortunes may not have happened to the miserable creature. I am inexpressibly annoyed at the failure of all my efforts to restore her to the care and protection which she so urgently needs.'

This time he really looked annoyed. I said a few sympathising words, and we then talked of other subjects on our way back to the house. Surely my chance meeting with him on the moor has disclosed another favourable trait in his character? Surely it was singularly considerate and unselfish of him to think of Anne Catherick on the eve of his marriage, and to go all the way to Todd's Corner to make inquiries about her, when he might have passed the time so much more agreeably in Laura's society? Considering that he can only have acted from motives of pure charity, his conduct, under the circumstances, shows unusual good feeling and deserves extraordinary praise. Well! I give him extraordinary praise – and there's an end of it.

19TH – More discoveries in the inexhaustible mine of Sir Percival's virtues.

Today I approached the subject of my proposed sojourn under his wife's roof when he brings her back to England. I had hardly dropped my first hint in this direction before he caught me warmly by the hand, and said I had made the very offer to him which he had been, on his side, most anxious to make to me. I was the companion of all others whom he most sincerely longed to secure for his wife, and he begged me to believe that I had conferred a lasting favour on him by making the proposal to live with Laura after her marriage, exactly as I had always lived with her before it.

When I had thanked him in her name and mine for his considerate kindness to both of us, we passed next to the subject of his wedding tour, and began to talk of the English society in Rome to which Laura was to be introduced. He ran over the names of several friends whom he expected to meet abroad this winter. They were all English, as well as I can remember, with one exception. The one exception was Count Fosco.

The mention of the Count's name, and the discovery that he and his wife are likely to meet the bride and bridegroom on the continent, puts Laura's marriage, for the first time, in a distinctly favourable light. It is likely to be the means of healing a family feud. Hitherto Madame Fosco has chosen to forget her obligations as Laura's aunt out of sheer spite against the late Mr Fairlie for his conduct in the affair of the legacy. Now however, she can persist in this course of conduct no longer. Sir Percival and Count Fosco are old and fast friends, and their wives will have no choice but to meet on civil terms. Madame Fosco in her maiden days was one of the most impertinent women I ever met with – capricious, exacting, and vain to the last degree of absurdity. If her husband has succeeded in bringing her to her senses, he deserves the gratitude of every member of the family, and he may have mine to begin with.

I am becoming anxious to know the Count. He is the most intimate friend of Laura's husband, and in that capacity he excites my strongest interest. Neither Laura nor I have ever seen him. All I know of him is that his accidental presence, years ago, on the steps of the Trinitá del Monte at Rome, assisted Sir Percival's escape from robbery and assassination at the critical moment when he was wounded in the hand, and might the next instant have been wounded in the heart. I remember also that, at the time of the late Mr Fairlie's absurd objections to his sister's marriage, the Count wrote him a very temperate and sensible letter on the subject, which, I am ashamed to say, remained unanswered. This is all I know of Sir Percival's friend. I wonder if he will ever come to England? I wonder if I shall like him?

My pen is running away into mere speculation. Let me return to sober matter of fact. It is certain that Sir Percival's reception of my venturesome proposal to live with his wife was more than kind, it was almost affectionate. I am sure Laura's husband will have no reason to complain of me if I can only go on as I have begun. I have already declared him to be handsome, agreeable, full of good feeling towards the unfortunate and full of affectionate kindness towards me. Really, I hardly know myself again, in my new character of Sir Percival's warmest friend.

20TH – I hate Sir Percival! I flatly deny his good looks. I consider him to be eminently ill-tempered and disagreeable, and totally wanting in kindness and good feeling. Last night the cards for the married couple were sent home. Laura opened the packet and saw her future name in print for the first time.

Sir Percival looked over her shoulder familiarly at the new card which had already transformed Miss Fairlie into Lady Glyde – smiled with the most odious self-complacency, and whispered something in her ear. I don't know what it was – Laura has refused to tell me – but I saw her face turn to such a deadly whiteness that I thought she would have fainted. He took no notice of the change – he seemed to be barbarously unconscious that he had said anything to pain her. All my old feelings of hostility towards him revived on the instant, and all the hours that have passed since have done nothing to dissipate them. I am more unreasonable and more unjust than ever. In three words – how glibly my pen writes them! – in three words, I hate him.

21ST – Have the anxieties of this anxious time shaken me a little, at last? I have been writing, for the last few days, in a tone of levity which, Heaven knows, is far enough from my heart, and which it has rather shocked me to discover on looking back at the entries in my journal.

Perhaps I may have caught the feverish excitement of Laura's spirits for the last week. If so, the fit has already passed away from me, and has left me in a very strange state of mind. A persistent idea has been forcing itself on my attention, ever since last night, that something will yet happen to prevent the marriage. What has produced this singular fancy? Is it the indirect result of my apprehensions for Laura's future? Or has it been unconsciously suggested to me by the increasing restlessness and irritability which I have certainly observed in Sir Percival's manner as the wedding-day draws nearer and nearer? Impossible to say. I know that I have the idea – surely the wildest idea, under the circumstances, that ever entered a woman's head? – but try as I may, I cannot trace it back to its source.

This last day has been all confusion and wretchedness. How can I write about it? – and yet, I must write. Anything is better than brooding over my own gloomy thoughts.

Kind Mrs Vesey, whom we have all too much overlooked and forgotten of late, innocently caused us a sad morning to begin with. She has been, for months past, secretly making a warm Shetland shawl for her dear pupil – a most beautiful and surprising piece of work to be done by a woman at her age and with her habits. The gift was presented this morning, and poor warm-hearted Laura completely broke down when the shawl was put proudly on her shoulders by the loving old friend and guardian of her motherless childhood. I was hardly allowed time to quiet them both, or even to dry my own eyes, when I was sent for by Mr Fairlie, to be favoured with a long recital of his arrangements for the preservation of his own tranquillity on the wedding-day.

'Dear Laura' was to receive his present – a shabby ring, with her affectionate uncle's hair for an ornament, instead of a precious stone, and with a heartless French inscription inside, about congenial sentiments and eternal friendship – 'dear Laura' was to receive this tender tribute from my hands immediately, so that she might have plenty of time to recover from the agitation produced by the gift before she appeared in Mr Fairlie's presence. 'Dear Laura' was to pay him a little visit that evening, and to be kind enough not to make a scene. 'Dear Laura' was to pay him another little visit in her wedding-dress the next morning, and to be kind enough, again, not to make a scene. 'Dear Laura' was to look in once more, for the third time, before going away, but without harrowing his feelings by saying *when* she was going away, and without tears—'in the name of pity, in the name of everything, dear Marian, that is most affectionate and most domestic, and most delightfully and charmingly self-composed, *without tears!*' I was so exasperated by this miserable selfish trifling, at such a time, that I should certainly have shocked Mr Fairlie by some of the hardest and rudest truths he has ever heard in his life, if the arrival of Mr Arnold from Polesdean had not called me away to new duties downstairs.

The rest of the day is indescribable. I believe no one in the house really knew how it passed. The confusion of small events, all huddled together one on the other, bewildered everybody. There were dresses sent home that had been forgotten – there were trunks to be packed and unpacked and packed again – there were presents from friends far and near, friends high and low. We were all needlessly hurried, all nervously expectant of the morrow. Sir Percival, especially, was too restless now to remain five minutes together in the same place. That short, sharp cough of his troubled him more than ever. He was in and out of doors all day long, and he seemed to grow so inquisitive on a sudden, that he questioned the very strangers who came on small errands to the house. Add to all this, the one perpetual thought in Laura's mind and mine, that we were to part the next day, and the haunting dread, unexpressed by either of us, and yet ever present to both, that this deplorable marriage might prove to be the one fatal error of her life and the one hopeless sorrow of mine. For the first time in all the years of our close and happy intercourse we almost avoided looking each other in the face, and we refrained, by common consent, from speaking together in private through the whole evening. I can dwell on it no longer. Whatever future sorrows may be in store for me, I shall always look back on this twenty-first of December as the most comfortless and most miserable day of my life.

I am writing these lines in the solitude of my own room, long after midnight, having just come back from a stolen look at Laura in her pretty little white bed – the bed she has occupied since the days of her girlhood.

There she lay, unconscious that I was looking at her – quiet, more quiet than I had dared to hope, but not sleeping. The glimmer of the night-light showed me that her eyes were only partially closed – the traces of tears glistened between her eyelids. My little keepsake – only a brooch – lay on the table at her bedside, with her prayer-book, and the miniature portrait of her father which she takes with her wherever she goes. I waited a moment, looking at her from behind her pillow, as she lay beneath me, with one arm and hand resting on the white coverlid, so still, so quietly breathing, that the frill on her night-dress never moved – I waited, looking at her, as I have seen her thousands of times, as I shall never see her again – and then stole back to my room. My own love! with all your wealth, and all your beauty, how friendless you are! The one man who would give his heart's life to serve you is far away, tossing, this stormy night, on the awful sea. Who else is left to you? No father, no brother – no living creature but the helpless, useless woman who writes these sad lines, and watches by you for the morning, in sorrow that she cannot compose, in doubt that she cannot conquer. Oh, what a trust is to be placed in that man's hands tomorrow! If ever he forgets it – if ever he injures a hair of her head! –

THE TWENTY-SECOND OF DECEMBER. *Seven o'clock*. A wild, unsettled morning. She has just risen – better and calmer, now that the time has come, than she was yesterday.

Ten o'clock. She is dressed. We have kissed each other – we have promised each other not to lose courage. I am away for a moment in my own room. In the whirl and confusion of my thoughts, I can detect that strange fancy of some hindrance happening to stop the marriage still hanging about my mind. Is it hanging about *his* mind too? I see him from the window, moving hither and thither uneasily among the carriages at the door. – How can I write such folly! The marriage is a certainty. In less than half an hour we start for the church.

Eleven o'clock. It is all over. They are married.

Three o'clock. They are gone! I am blind with crying – I can write no more—

The First Epoch of the Story closes here.

THE SECOND EPOCH

THE STORY CONTINUED BY MARIAN HALCOMBE

I

BLACKWATER PARK, HAMPSHIRE

JUNE 11TH, 1860 – Six months to look back on – six long, lonely months since Laura and I last saw each other!

How many days have I still to wait? Only one! Tomorrow, the twelfth, the travellers return to England. I can hardly realise my own happiness – I can hardly believe that the next four-and-twenty hours will complete the last day of separation between Laura and me.

She and her husband have been in Italy all the winter, and afterwards in the Tyrol. They come back, accompanied by Count Fosco and his wife, who propose to settle somewhere in the neighbourhood of London, and who have engaged to stay at Blackwater Park for the summer months before deciding on a place of residence. So long as Laura returns, no matter who returns with her. Sir Percival may fill the house from floor to ceiling, if he likes, on condition that his wife and I inhabit it together.

Meanwhile, here I am, established at Blackwater Park, 'the ancient and interesting seat' (as the county history obligingly informs me) 'of Sir Percival Glyde, Bart.,' and the future abiding-place (as I may now venture to add on my account) of plain Marian Halcombe, spinster, now settled in a snug little sitting-room, with a cup of tea by her side, and all her earthly possessions ranged round her in three boxes and a bag.

I left Limmeridge yesterday, having received Laura's delightful letter from Paris the day before. I had been previously uncertain whether I was to meet them in London or in Hampshire, but this last letter informed me that Sir Percival proposed to land at Southampton, and to travel straight on to his country-house. He has spent so much money abroad that he has none left to defray the expenses of living in London for the remainder of the season, and he is economically resolved to pass the summer and autumn quietly at Blackwater. Laura has had more than enough of excitement and change of scene, and is pleased at the prospect of country tranquillity and retirement which her husband's prudence provides for her. As for me, I am ready to be happy anywhere in her society. We are all, therefore, well contented in our various ways, to begin with.

Last night I slept in London, and was delayed there so long today by various calls and commissions, that I did not reach Blackwater this evening till after dusk.

Judging by my vague impressions of the place thus far, it is the exact opposite of Limmeridge.

The house is situated on a dead flat, and seems to be shut in – almost suffocated, to my north-country notions, by trees. I have seen nobody but the man-servant who opened the door to me, and the housekeeper, a very civil person, who showed me the way to my own room, and got me my tea. I have a nice little boudoir and bedroom, at the end of a long passage on the first floor. The servants and some of the spare rooms are on the second floor, and all the living rooms are on the ground floor. I have not seen one of them yet, and I know nothing about the house, except that one wing of it is said to be five hundred years old, that it had a moat round it once, and that it gets its name of Blackwater from a lake in the park.

Eleven o'clock has just struck, in a ghostly and solemn manner, from a turret over the centre of the house, which I saw when I came in. A large dog has been woke, apparently by the sound of the bell, and is howling and yawning drearily, somewhere round a corner. I hear echoing footsteps in the passages below, and the iron thumping of bolts and bars at the house door. The servants are evidently going to bed. Shall I follow their example?

No, I am not half sleepy enough. Sleepy, did I say? I feel as if I should never close my eyes again. The bare anticipation of seeing that dear face, and hearing that well-known voice tomorrow, keeps me in a perpetual fever of excitement. If I only had the privileges of a man, I would order out Sir Percival's best horse instantly, and tear away on a night-gallop, eastward, to meet the rising sun – a long, hard, heavy, ceaseless gallop of hours and hours, like the famous highwayman's ride to York. Being, however, nothing but a woman, condemned to patience, propriety, and petticoats for life, I must respect the house-keeper's opinions, and try to compose myself in some feeble and feminine way.

Reading is out of the question – I can't fix my attention on books. Let me try if I can write myself into sleepiness and fatigue. My journal has been very much neglected of late. What can I recall – standing, as I now do, on the threshold of a new life – of persons and events, of chances and changes, during the past six months – the long, weary, empty interval since Laura's wedding-day?

Walter Hartright is uppermost in my memory, and he passes first in the shadowy procession of my absent friends. I received a few lines from him, after the landing of the expedition in Honduras, written more cheerfully and hopefully than he has written yet. A month or six weeks later I saw an extract from an American newspaper, describing the departure of the adventurers on their inland journey. They were last seen entering a wild primeval forest, each man with his rifle on his shoulder and his baggage at his back. Since that time, civilisation has lost all trace of them. Not a line more have I received from Walter, not a fragment of news from the expedition has appeared in any of the public journals.

The same dense, disheartening obscurity hangs over the fate and fortunes of Anne Catherick, and her companion, Mrs Clements. Nothing whatever has been heard of either of them. Whether they are in the country or out of it, whether they are living or dead, no one knows. Even Sir Percival's solicitor has lost all hope, and has ordered the useless search after the fugitives to be finally given up.

Our good old friend Mr Gilmore has met with a sad check in his active professional career. Early in the spring we were alarmed by hearing that he had been found insensible at his desk, and that the seizure was pronounced to be an apoplectic fit. He had been long complaining of fulness and oppression in the head, and his doctor had warned him of the consequences that would follow his persistency in continuing to work, early and late, as if he were still a young man. The result now is that he has been positively ordered to keep out of his office for a year to come, at least, and to seek repose of body and relief of mind by altogether changing his usual mode of life. The business is left, accordingly, to be carried on by his partner, and he is himself, at this moment, away in Germany, visiting some relations who are settled there in mercantile pursuits. Thus another true friend and trustworthy adviser is lost to us – lost, I earnestly hope and trust, for a time only.

Poor Mrs Vesey travelled with me as far as London. It was impossible to abandon her to solitude at Limmeridge after Laura and I had both left the house, and we have arranged that she is to live with an unmarried younger sister of hers, who keeps a school at Clapham. She is to come here this autumn to visit her pupil – I might almost say her adopted child. I saw the good old lady safe to her destination, and left her in the care of her relative, quietly happy at the prospect of seeing Laura again in a few months' time.

As for Mr Fairlie, I believe I am guilty of no injustice if I describe him as being unutterably relieved by having the house clear of us women. The idea of his missing his niece is simply preposterous – he used to let months pass in the old times without attempting to see her – and in my case and Mrs Vesey's, I take leave to consider his telling us both that he was half heart-broken at our departure, to be equivalent to a confession that he was secretly rejoiced to get rid of us. His last caprice has led him to keep two photographers incessantly employed in producing sun-pictures of all the treasures and curiosities in his possession. One complete copy of the collection of the photographs is to be presented to the Mechanics' Institution of Carlisle, mounted on the finest cardboard, with ostentatious red-letter inscriptions underneath, 'Madonna and Child by Raphael. In the possession of Frederick Fairlie, Esquire.' 'Copper coin of the period of Tiglath Pileser. In the possession of Frederick Fairlie, Esquire.' 'Unique Rembrandt etching. Known all over Europe as *The Smudge*, from a printer's blot in the corner which exists in no other copy. Valued at three hundred guineas. In the possession of Frederick Fairlie, Esq.' Dozens of photographs of this sort, and all inscribed in this manner, were completed before I left Cumberland, and hundreds more remain to be done. With this new interest to occupy him, Mr Fairlie will be a happy man for months and months to come, and the two unfortunate photographers will share the social martyrdom which he has hitherto inflicted on his valet alone.

So much for the persons and events which hold the foremost place in my memory. What next of the one person who holds the foremost place in my heart? Laura has been present to my thoughts all the while I have been writing these lines. What can I recall of her during the past six months, before I close my journal for the night? I have only her letters to guide me, and on the most important of all the questions which our correspondence can discuss, every one of those letters leaves me in the dark.

Does he treat her kindly? Is she happier now than she was when I parted with her on the wedding-day? All my letters have contained these two inquiries, put more or less directly, now in one form, and now in another, and all, on that point only, have remained without reply, or have been answered as if my questions merely related to the state of her health. She informs me, over and over again, that she is perfectly well – that travelling agrees with her – that she is getting through the winter, for the first time in her life, without catching cold – but not a word can I find anywhere which tells me plainly that she is reconciled to her marriage, and that she can now look back to the twenty-second of December without any bitter feelings of repentance and regret. The name of her husband is only mentioned in her letters, as she might mention the name of a friend who was travelling with them, and who had undertaken to make all the arrangements for the journey. 'Sir Percival' has settled that we leave on such a day—'Sir Percival' has decided that we travel by such a road. Sometimes she writes 'Percival' only, but very seldom – in nine cases out of ten she gives him his title.

I cannot find that his habits and opinions have changed and coloured hers in any single particular. The usual moral transformation which is insensibly wrought in a young, fresh, sensitive woman by her marriage, seems never to have taken place in Laura. She writes of her own thoughts and impressions, amid all the wonders she has seen, exactly as she might have written to some one else, if I had been travelling with her instead of her husband. I see no betrayal anywhere of sympathy of any kind existing between them. Even when she wanders from the subject of her travels, and occupies herself with the prospects that await her in England, her speculations are busied with her future as my sister, and persistently neglect to notice her future as Sir Percival's wife. In all this there is no undertone of complaint to warn me that she is absolutely unhappy in her married life. The impression I have derived from our correspondence does not, thank God, lead me to any such distressing conclusion as that. I only see a sad torpor, an unchangeable indifference, when I turn my mind from her in the old character of a sister, and look at her, through the medium of her letters, in the new character of a wife. In other words, it is always Laura Fairlie who has been writing to me for the last six months, and never Lady Glyde.

The strange silence which she maintains on the subject of her husband's character and conduct, she preserves with almost equal resolution in the few references which her later letters contain to the name of her husband's bosom friend, Count Fosco.

For some unexplained reason the Count and his wife appear to have changed their plans abruptly, at the end of last autumn, and to have gone to Vienna instead of going to Rome, at which latter place Sir Percival had expected to find them when he left England. They only quitted Vienna in the spring, and travelled as far as the Tyrol to meet the bride and bridegroom on their homeward journey. Laura writes readily enough about the meeting with Madame Fosco, and assures me that she has found her aunt so much changed for the better – so much quieter, and so much more sensible as a wife than she was as a single woman – that I shall hardly know her again when I see her here. But on the subject of Count Fosco (who interests me infinitely more than his wife), Laura is provokingly circumspect and silent. She only says that he puzzles her, and that she will not tell me what her impression of him is until I have seen him, and formed my own opinion first.

This, to my mind, looks ill for the Count. Laura has preserved, far more perfectly than most people do in later life, the child's subtle faculty of knowing a friend by instinct, and if I am right in assuming that her first impression of Count Fosco has not been favourable, I for one am in some danger of doubting and distrusting that illustrious foreigner before I have so much as set eyes on him. But, patience, patience – this uncertainty, and many uncertainties more, cannot last much longer. Tomorrow will see all my doubts in a fair way of being cleared up, sooner or later.

Twelve o'clock has struck, and I have just come back to close these pages, after looking out at my open window.

It is a still, sultry, moonless night. The stars are dull and few. The trees that shut out the view on all sides look dimly black and solid in the distance, like a great wall of rock. I hear the croaking of frogs, faint and far off, and the echoes of the great clock hum in the airless calm long after the strokes have ceased. I wonder how Blackwater Park will look in the daytime? I don't altogether like it by night.

12TH – A day of investigations and discoveries – a more interesting day, for many reasons, than I had ventured to anticipate.

I began my sight-seeing, of course, with the house.

The main body of the building is of the time of that highly-overrated woman, Queen Elizabeth. On the ground floor there are two hugely long galleries, with low ceilings lying parallel with each other, and rendered additionally dark and dismal by hideous family portraits – every one of which I should like to burn. The rooms on the floor above the two galleries are kept in tolerable repair, but are very seldom used. The civil housekeeper, who acted as my guide, offered to show me over them, but considerately added that she feared I should find them rather out of order. My respect for the integrity of my own petticoats and stockings infinitely exceeds my respect for all the Elizabethan bedrooms in the kingdom, so I positively declined exploring the upper regions of dust and dirt at the risk of soiling my nice clean clothes. The housekeeper said, 'I am quite of your opinion, miss,' and appeared to think me the most sensible woman she had met with for a long time past.

So much, then, for the main building. Two wings are added at either end of it. The half-ruined wing on the left (as you approach the house) was once a place of residence standing by itself, and was built in the fourteenth century. One of Sir Percival's maternal ancestors – I don't remember, and don't care which – tacked on the main building, at right angles to it, in the aforesaid Queen Elizabeth's time. The housekeeper told me that the architecture of 'the old wing,' both outside and inside, was considered remarkably fine by good judges. On further investigation I discovered that good judges could only exercise their abilities on Sir Percival's piece of antiquity by previously dismissing from their minds all fear of damp, darkness, and rats. Under these circumstances, I unhesitatingly acknowledged myself to be no judge at all, and suggested that we should treat 'the old wing' precisely as we had previously treated the Elizabethan bedrooms. Once more the housekeeper said, 'I am quite of your opinion, miss,' and once more she looked at me with undisguised admiration of my extraordinary common-sense.

We went next to the wing on the right, which was built, by way of completing the wonderful architectural jumble at Blackwater Park, in the time of George the Second.

This is the habitable part of the house, which has been repaired and redeco-
rated inside on Laura's account. My two rooms, and all the good bedrooms
besides, are on the first floor, and the basement contains a drawing-room, a
dining-room, a morning-room, a library, and a pretty little boudoir for Laura,
all very nicely ornamented in the bright modern way, and all very elegantly
furnished with the delightful modern luxuries. None of the rooms are anything
like so large and airy as our rooms at Limmeridge, but they all look pleasant
to live in. I was terribly afraid, from what I had heard of Blackwater Park, of
fatiguing antique chairs, and dismal stained glass, and musty, frouzy hangings,
and all the barbarous lumber which people born without a sense of comfort
accumulate about them, in defiance of the consideration due to the convenience
of their friends. It is an inexpressible relief to find that the nineteenth century
has invaded this strange future home of mine, and has swept the dirty 'good
old times' out of the way of our daily life.

I dawdled away the morning – part of the time in the rooms downstairs,
and part out of doors in the great square which is formed by the three sides
of the house, and by the lofty iron railings and gates which protect it in
front. A large circular fish-pond with stone sides, and an allegorical leaden
monster in the middle, occupies the centre of the square. The pond itself is
full of gold and silver fish, and is encircled by a broad belt of the softest
turf I ever walked on. I loitered here on the shady side pleasantly enough
till luncheon-time, and after that took my broad straw hat and wandered out
alone in the warm lovely sunlight to explore the grounds.

Daylight confirmed the impression which I had felt the night before, of there
being too many trees at Blackwater. The house is stifled by them. They are, for
the most part, young, and planted far too thickly. I suspect there must have
been a ruinous cutting down of timber all over the estate before Sir Percival's
time, and an angry anxiety on the part of the next possessor to fill up all the
gaps as thickly and rapidly as possible. After looking about me in front of the
house, I observed a flower-garden on my left hand, and walked towards it to
see what I could discover in that direction.

On a nearer view the garden proved to be small and poor and ill kept. I
left it behind me, opened a little gate in a ring fence, and found myself in
a plantation of fir-trees.

A pretty winding path, artificially made, led me on among the trees, and
my north-country experience soon informed me that I was approaching sandy,
heathy ground. After a walk of more than half a mile, I should think, among
the firs, the path took a sharp turn – the trees abruptly ceased to appear on
either side of me, and I found myself standing suddenly on the margin of a
vast open space, and looking down at the Blackwater lake from which the
house takes its name.

The ground, shelving away below me, was all sand, with a few little heathy hillocks to break the monotony of it in certain places. The lake itself had evidently once flowed to the spot on which I stood, and had been gradually wasted and dried up to less than a third of its former size. I saw its still, stagnant waters, a quarter of a mile away from me in the hollow, separated into pools and ponds by twining reeds and rushes, and little knolls of earth. On the farther bank from me the trees rose thickly again, and shut out the view, and cast their black shadows on the sluggish, shallow water. As I walked down to the lake, I saw that the ground on its farther side was damp and marshy, overgrown with rank grass and dismal willows. The water, which was clear enough on the open sandy side, where the sun shone, looked black and poisonous opposite to me, where it lay deeper under the shade of the spongy banks, and the rank overhanging thickets and tangled trees. The frogs were croaking, and the rats were slipping in and out of the shadowy water, like live shadows themselves, as I got nearer to the marshy side of the lake. I saw here, lying half in and half out of the water, the rotten wreck of an old overturned boat, with a sickly spot of sunlight glimmering through a gap in the trees on its dry surface, and a snake basking in the midst of the spot, fantastically coiled and treacherously still. Far and near the view suggested the same dreary impressions of solitude and decay, and the glorious brightness of the summer sky overhead seemed only to deepen and harden the gloom and barrenness of the wilderness on which it shone. I turned and retraced my steps to the high heathy ground, directing them a little aside from my former path towards a shabby old wooden shed, which stood on the outer skirt of the fir plantation, and which had hitherto been too unimportant to share my notice with the wide, wild prospect of the lake.

On approaching the shed I found that it had once been a boathouse, and that an attempt had apparently been made to convert it afterwards into a sort of rude arbour, by placing inside it a firwood seat, a few stools, and a table. I entered the place, and sat down for a little while to rest and get my breath again.

I had not been in the boathouse more than a minute when it struck me that the sound of my own quick breathing was very strangely echoed by something beneath me. I listened intently for a moment, and heard a low, thick, sobbing breath that seemed to come from the ground under the seat which I was occupying. My nerves are not easily shaken by trifles, but on this occasion I started to my feet in a fright – called out – received no answer – summoned back my recreant courage, and looked under the seat.

There, crouched up in the farthest corner, lay the forlorn cause of my terror, in the shape of a poor little dog – a black and white spaniel. The creature moaned feebly when I looked at it and called to it, but never stirred. I moved away the seat and looked closer. The poor little dog's eyes were glazing fast, and there were spots of blood on its glossy white side. The misery of a weak, helpless, dumb creature is surely one of the saddest of all the mournful sights which this world can show. I lifted the poor dog in my arms as gently as I could, and contrived a sort of make-shift hammock for him to lie in, by gathering up the front of my dress all round him. In this way I took the creature, as painlessly as possible, and as fast as possible, back to the house.

Finding no one in the hall I went up at once to my own sitting-room, made a bed for the dog with one of my old shawls, and rang the bell. The largest and fattest of all possible house-maids answered it, in a state of cheerful stupidity which would have provoked the patience of a saint. The girl's fat, shapeless face actually stretched into a broad grin at the sight of the wounded creature on the floor.

'What do you see there to laugh at?' I asked, as angrily as if she had been a servant of my own. 'Do you know whose dog it is?'

'No, miss, that I certainly don't.' She stooped, and looked down at the spaniel's injured side – brightened suddenly with the irradiation of a new idea – and pointing to the wound with a chuckle of satisfaction, said, 'That's Baxter's doings, that is.'

I was so exasperated that I could have boxed her ears. 'Baxter?' I said. 'Who is the brute you call Baxter?'

The girl grinned again more cheerfully than ever. 'Bless you, miss! Baxter's the keeper, and when he finds strange dogs hunting about, he takes and shoots 'em. It's keeper's dooty miss, I think that dog will die. Here's where he's been shot, ain't it? That's Baxter's doings, that is. Baxter's doings, miss, and Baxter's dooty.'

I was almost wicked enough to wish that Baxter had shot the housemaid instead of the dog. Seeing that it was quite useless to expect this densely impenetrable personage to give me any help in relieving the suffering creature at our feet, I told her to request the housekeeper's attendance with my compliments. She went out exactly as she had come in, grinning from ear to ear. As the door closed on her she said to herself softly, 'It's Baxter's doings and Baxter's dooty – that's what it is.'

The housekeeper, a person of some education and intelligence, thoughtfully brought upstairs with her some milk and some warm water. The instant she saw the dog on the floor she started and changed colour.

'Why, Lord bless me,' cried the housekeeper, 'that must be Mrs Catherick's dog!'

'Whose?' I asked, in the utmost astonishment.

'Mrs Catherick's. You seem to know Mrs Catherick, Miss Halcombe?'

'Not personally, but I have heard of her. Does she live here? Has she had any news of her daughter?'

'No, Miss Halcombe, she came here to ask for news.'

'When?'

'Only yesterday. She said some one had reported that a stranger answering to the description of her daughter had been seen in our neighbourhood. No such report has reached us here, and no such report was known in the village, when I sent to make inquiries there on Mrs Catherick's account. She certainly brought this poor little dog with her when she came, and I saw it trot out after her when she went away. I suppose the creature strayed into the plantations, and got shot. Where did you find it, Miss Halcombe?'

'In the old shed that looks out on the lake.'

'Ah, yes, that is the plantation side, and the poor thing dragged itself, I suppose, to the nearest shelter, as dogs will, to die. If you can moisten its lips with the milk, Miss Halcombe, I will wash the clotted hair from the wound. I am very much afraid it is too late to do any good. However, we can but try.'

Mrs Catherick! The name still rang in my ears, as if the housekeeper had only that moment surprised me by uttering it. While we were attending to the dog, the words of Walter Hartright's caution to me returned to my memory: 'If ever Anne Catherick crosses your path, make better use of the opportunity, Miss Halcombe, than I made of it.' The finding of the wounded spaniel had led me already to the discovery of Mrs Catherick's visit to Blackwater Park, and that event might lead in its turn, to something more. I determined to make the most of the chance which was now offered to me, and to gain as much information as I could.

'Did you say that Mrs Catherick lived anywhere in this neighbourhood?' I asked.

'Oh dear, no,' said the housekeeper. 'She lives at Welmingham, quite at the other end of the county – five-and-twenty miles off, at least.'

'I suppose you have known Mrs Catherick for some years?'

'On the contrary, Miss Halcombe, I never saw her before she came here yesterday. I had heard of her, of course, because I had heard of Sir Percival's kindness in putting her daughter under medical care. Mrs Catherick is rather a strange person in her manners, but extremely respectable-looking. She seemed sorely put out when she found that there was no foundation – none, at least, that any of us could discover – for the report of her daughter having been seen in this neighbourhood.'

'I am rather interested about Mrs Catherick,' I went on, continuing the conversation as long as possible. 'I wish I had arrived here soon enough to see her yesterday. Did she stay for any length of time?'

'Yes,' said the housekeeper, 'she stayed for some time; and I think she would have remained longer, if I had not been called away to speak to a strange gentleman – a gentleman who came to ask when Sir Percival was expected back. Mrs Catherick got up and left at once, when she heard the maid tell me what the visitor's errand was. She said to me, at parting, that there was no need to tell Sir Percival of her coming here. I thought that rather an odd remark to make, especially to a person in my responsible situation.'

I thought it an odd remark too. Sir Percival had certainly led me to believe, at Limmeridge, that the most perfect confidence existed between himself and Mrs Catherick. If that was the case, why should she be anxious to have her visit at Blackwater Park kept a secret from him?

'Probably,' I said, seeing that the housekeeper expected me to give my opinion on Mrs Catherick's parting words, 'probably she thought the announcement of her visit might vex Sir Percival to no purpose, by reminding him that her lost daughter was not found yet. Did she talk much on that subject?'

'Very little,' replied the housekeeper. 'She talked principally of Sir Percival, and asked a great many questions about where he had been travelling, and what sort of lady his new wife was. She seemed to be more soured and put out than distressed, by failing to find any traces of her daughter in these parts. "I give her up," were the last words she said that I can remember; "I give her up, ma'am, for lost." And from that she passed at once to her questions about Lady Glyde, wanting to know if she was a handsome, amiable lady, comely and healthy and young – Ah, dear! I thought how it would end. Look, Miss Halcombe, the poor thing is out of its misery at last!'

The dog was dead. It had given a faint, sobbing cry, it had suffered an instant's convulsion of the limbs, just as those last words, 'comely and healthy and young,' dropped from the housekeeper's lips. The change had happened with startling suddenness – in one moment the creature lay lifeless under our hands.

Eight o'clock. I have just returned from dining downstairs, in solitary state. The sunset is burning redly on the wilderness of trees that I see from my window, and I am poring over my journal again, to calm my impatience for the return of the travellers. They ought to have arrived, by my calculations, before this. How still and lonely the house is in the drowsy evening quiet! Oh me! how many minutes more before I hear the carriage wheels and run downstairs to find myself in Laura's arms?

The poor little dog! I wish my first day at Blackwater Park had not been associated with death, though it is only the death of a stray animal.

Welmingham – I see, on looking back through these private pages of mine, that Welmingham is the name of the place where Mrs Catherick lives. Her note is still in my possession, the note in answer to that letter about her unhappy daughter which Sir Percival obliged me to write. One of these days, when I can find a safe opportunity, I will take the note with me by way of introduction, and try what I can make of Mrs Catherick at a personal interview. I don't understand her wishing to conceal her visit to this place from Sir Percival's knowledge, and I don't feel half so sure, as the housekeeper seems to do, that her daughter Anne is not in the neighbourhood after all. What would Walter Hartright have said in this emergency? Poor, dear Hartright! I am beginning to feel the want of his honest advice and his willing help already.

Surely I heard something. Was it a bustle of footsteps below stairs? Yes! I hear the horses' feet – I hear the rolling wheels—

II

JUNE 15TH – The confusion of their arrival has had time to subside. Two days have elapsed since the return of the travellers, and that interval has sufficed to put the new machinery of our lives at Blackwater Park in fair working order. I may now return to my journal, with some little chance of being able to continue the entries in it as collectedly as usual.

I think I must begin by putting down an odd remark which has suggested itself to me since Laura came back.

When two members of a family or two intimate friends are separated, and one goes abroad and one remains at home, the return of the relative or friend who has been travelling always seems to place the relative or friend who has been staying at home at a painful disadvantage when the two first meet. The sudden encounter of the new thoughts and new habits eagerly gained in the one case, with the old thoughts and old habits passively preserved in the other, seems at first to part the sympathies of the most loving relatives and the fondest friends, and to set a sudden strangeness, unexpected by both and uncontrollable by both, between them on either side. After the first happiness of my meeting with Laura was over, after we had sat down together hand in hand to recover breath enough and calmness enough to talk, I felt this strangeness instantly, and I could see that she felt it too. It has partially worn away, now that we have fallen back into most of our old habits, and it will probably disappear before long. But it has certainly had an influence over the first impressions that I have formed of her, now that we are living together again – for which reason only I have thought fit to mention it here.

She has found me unaltered, but I have found her changed.

Changed in person, and in one respect changed in character. I cannot absolutely say that she is less beautiful than she used to be – I can only say that she is less beautiful to *me*.

Others, who do not look at her with my eyes and my recollections, would probably think her improved. There is more colour and more decision and roundness of outline in her face than there used to be, and her figure seems more firmly set and more sure and easy in all its movements than it was in her maiden days. But I miss something when I look at her – something that once belonged to the happy, innocent life of Laura Fairlie, and that I cannot find in Lady Glyde. There was in the old times a freshness, a softness, an ever-varying and yet ever-remaining tenderness of beauty in her face, the charm of which it is not possible to express in words, or, as poor Hartright used often to say, in painting either. This is gone. I thought I saw the faint reflection of it for a moment when she turned pale under the agitation of our sudden meeting on the evening of her return, but it has never reappeared since. None of her letters had prepared me for a personal change in her. On the contrary, they had led me to expect that her marriage had left her, in appearance at least, quite unaltered. Perhaps I read her letters wrongly in the past, and am now reading her face wrongly in the present? No matter! Whether her beauty has gained or whether it has lost in the last six months, the separation either way has made her own dear self more precious to me than ever, and that is one good result of her marriage, at any rate!

The second change, the change that I have observed in her character, has not surprised me, because I was prepared for it in this case by the tone of her letters. Now that she is at home again, I find her just as unwilling to enter into any details on the subject of her married life as I had previously found her all through the time of our separation, when we could only communicate with each other by writing. At the first approach I made to the forbidden topic she put her hand on my lips with a look and gesture which touchingly, almost painfully, recalled to my memory the days of her girlhood and the happy bygone time when there were no secrets between us.

'Whenever you and I are together, Marian,' she said, 'we shall both be happier and easier with one another, if we accept my married life for what it is, and say and think as little about it as possible. I would tell you every-thing, darling, about myself,' she went on, nervously buckling and unbuckling the ribbon round my waist, 'if my confidences could only end there. But they could not – they would lead me into confidences about my husband too; and now I am married, I think I had better avoid them, for his sake, and for your sake, and for mine. I don't say that they would distress you, or distress me – I wouldn't have you think that for the world. But – I want to be so happy, now I have got you back again, and I want you to be so happy too—' She broke off abruptly, and looked round the room, my own

sitting-room, in which we were talking. 'Ah!' she cried, clapping her hands
with a bright smile of recognition, 'another old friend found already! Your
book-case, Marian – your dear-little-shabby-old-satin-wood bookcase – how
glad I am you brought it with you from Limmeridge! And the horrid heavy
man's umbrella, that you always would walk out with when it rained! And
first and foremost of all, your own dear, dark, clever, gipsy-face, looking
at me just as usual! It is so like home again to be here. How can we make
it more like home still? I will put my father's portrait in your room instead
of in mine – and I will keep all my little treasures from Limmeridge here
– and we will pass hours and hours every day with these four friendly walls
round us. Oh, Marian!' she said, suddenly seating herself on a footstool at
my knees, and looking up earnestly in my face, 'promise you will never
marry, and leave me. It is selfish to say so, but you are so much better off
as a single woman – unless – unless you are very fond of your husband
– but you won't be very fond of anybody but me, will you?' She stopped
again, crossed my hands on my lap, and laid her face on them. 'Have you
been writing many letters, and receiving many letters lately?' she asked, in
low, suddenly-altered tones. I understood what the question meant, but I
thought it my duty not to encourage her by meeting her half way. 'Have
you heard from him?' she went on, coaxing me to forgive the more direct
appeal on which she now ventured, by kissing my hands, upon which her
face still rested. 'Is he well and happy, and getting on in his profession?
Has he recovered himself – and forgotten *me*?'

She should not have asked those questions. She should have remembered
her own resolution, on the morning when Sir Percival held her to her marriage
engagement, and when she resigned the book of Hartright's drawings into
my hands for ever. But, ah me! where is the faultless human creature who
can persevere in a good resolution, without sometimes failing and falling
back? Where is the woman who has ever really torn from her heart the image
that has been once fixed in it by a true love? Books tell us that such unearthly
creatures have existed – but what does our own experience say in answer
to books?

I made no attempt to remonstrate with her: perhaps, because I sincerely
appreciated the fearless candour which let me see, what other women in her
position might have had reasons for concealing even from their dearest friends
– perhaps, because I felt, in my own heart and conscience, that in her place
I should have asked the same questions and had the same thoughts. All I
could honestly do was to reply that I had not written to him or heard from
him lately, and then to turn the conversation to less dangerous topics.

There has been much to sadden me in our interview – my first confidential
interview with her since her return. The change which her marriage has

produced in our relations towards each other, by placing a forbidden subject between us, for the first time in our lives; the melancholy conviction of the dearth of all warmth of feeling, of all close sympathy, between her husband and herself, which her own unwilling words now force on my mind; the distressing discovery that the influence of that ill-fated attachment still remains (no matter how innocently, how harmlessly) rooted as deeply as ever in her heart – all these are disclosures to sadden any woman who loves her as dearly, and feels for her as acutely, as I do.

There is only one consolation to set against them – a consolation that ought to comfort me, and that does comfort me. All the graces and gentleness of her character – all the frank affection of her nature – all the sweet, simple, womanly charms which used to make her the darling and delight of every one who approached her, have come back to me with herself. Of my other impressions I am sometimes a little inclined to doubt. Of this last, best, happiest of all impressions, I grow more and more certain every hour in the day.

Let me turn, now, from her to her travelling companions. Her husband must engage my attention first. What have I observed in Sir Percival, since his return, to improve my opinion of him?

I can hardly say. Small vexations and annoyances seem to have beset him since he came back, and no man, under those circumstances, is ever presented at his best. He looks, as I think, thinner than he was when he left England. His wearisome cough and his comfortless restlessness have certainly increased. His manner – at least his manner towards me – is much more abrupt than it used to be. He greeted me, on the evening of his return, with little or nothing of the ceremony and civility of former times – no polite speeches of welcome – no appearance of extraordinary gratification at seeing me – nothing but a short shake of the hand, and a sharp 'How-d'ye-do, Miss Halcombe – glad to see you again.' He seemed to accept me as one of the necessary fixtures of Blackwater Park, to be satisfied at finding me established in my proper place, and then to pass me over altogether.

Most men show something of their disposition in their own houses, which they have concealed elsewhere, and Sir Percival has already displayed a mania for order and regularity, which is quite a new revelation of him, so far as my previous knowledge of his character is concerned. If I take a book from the library and leave it on the table, he follows me and puts it back again. If I rise from a chair, and let it remain where I have been sitting, he carefully restores it to its proper place against the wall. He picks up stray flower-blossoms from the carpet, and mutters to himself as discontentedly as if they were hot cinders burning holes in it, and he storms at the servants if there is a crease in the tablecloth, or a knife missing from its place at the dinner-table, as fiercely as if they had personally insulted him.

I have already referred to the small annoyances which appear to have troubled him since his return. Much of the alteration for the worse which I have noticed in him may be due to these. I try to persuade myself that it is so, because I am anxious not to be disheartened already about the future. It is certainly trying to any man's temper to be met by a vexation the moment he sets foot in his own house again, after a long absence, and this annoying circumstance did really happen to Sir Percival in my presence.

On the evening of their arrival the housekeeper followed me into the hall to receive her master and mistress and their guests. The instant he saw her, Sir Percival asked if any one had called lately. The housekeeper mentioned to him, in reply, what she had previously mentioned to me, the visit of the strange gentleman to make inquiries about the time of her master's return. He asked immediately for the gentleman's name. No name had been left. The gentleman's business? No business had been mentioned. What was the gentleman like? The housekeeper tried to describe him, but failed to distinguish the nameless visitor by any personal peculiarity which her master could recognise. Sir Percival frowned, stamped angrily on the floor, and walked on into the house, taking no notice of anybody. Why he should have been so discomposed by a trifle I cannot say – but he was seriously discomposed, beyond all doubt.

Upon the whole, it will be best, perhaps, if I abstain from forming a decisive opinion of his manners, language, and conduct in his own house, until time has enabled him to shake off the anxieties, whatever they may be, which now evidently troubled his mind in secret. I will turn over to a new page, and my pen shall let Laura's husband alone for the present.

The two guests – the Count and Countess Fosco – come next in my catalogue. I will dispose of the Countess first, so as to have done with the woman as soon as possible.

Laura was certainly not chargeable with any exaggeration, in writing me word that I should hardly recognise her aunt again when we met. Never before have I beheld such a change produced in a woman by her marriage as has been produced in Madame Fosco.

As Eleanor Fairlie (aged seven-and-thirty), she was always talking pretentious nonsense, and always worrying the unfortunate men with every small exaction which a vain and foolish woman can impose on long-suffering male humanity. As Madame Fosco (aged three-and-forty), she sits for hours together without saying a word, frozen up in the strangest manner in herself. The hideously ridiculous love-locks which used to hang on either side of her face are now replaced by stiff little rows of very short curls, of the sort one sees in old-fashioned wigs. A plain, matronly cap covers her head, and makes her look, for the first time in her life since I remember her, like a decent woman. Nobody (putting her husband out of the question, of course) now sees in her, what everybody once saw – I mean the structure of the female skeleton, in the upper regions of the collar-bones and the shoulder-blades. Clad in quiet black or grey gowns, made high round the throat – dresses that she would have laughed at, or screamed at, as the whim of the moment inclined her, in her maiden days – she sits speechless in corners; her dry white hands (so dry that the pores of her skin look chalky) incessantly engaged, either in monotonous embroidery work or in rolling up endless cigarettes for the Count's own particular smoking. On the few occasions when her cold blue eyes are off her work, they are generally turned on her husband, with the look of mute submissive inquiry which we are all familiar with in the eyes of a faithful dog. The only approach to an inward thaw which I have yet detected under her outer covering of icy constraint, has betrayed itself, once or twice, in the form of a suppressed tigerish jealousy of any woman in the house (the maids included) to whom the Count speaks, or on whom he looks with anything approaching to special interest or atten-tion. Except in this one particular, she is always, morning, noon, and night, indoors and out, fair weather or foul, as cold as a statue, and as impenetrable as the stone out of which it is cut. For the common purposes of society the extraordinary change thus produced in her is, beyond all doubt, a change for the better, seeing that it has transformed her into a civil, silent, unobtrusive woman, who is never in the way. How far she is really reformed or deterio-rated in her secret self, is another question. I have once or twice seen sudden changes of expression on her pinched lips, and heard sudden inflexions of tone in her calm voice, which have led me to suspect that her present state of suppression may have sealed up something dangerous in her nature, which used to evaporate harmlessly in the freedom of her former life. It is quite possible that I may be altogether wrong in this idea. My own impression, however, is, that I am right. Time will show.

And the magician who has wrought this wonderful transformation – the foreign husband who has tamed this once wayward English woman till her own relations hardly know her again – the Count himself? What of the Count?

This in two words: He looks like a man who could tame anything. If he had married a tigress, instead of a woman, he would have tamed the tigress. If he had married me, I should have made his cigarettes, as his wife does – I should have held my tongue when he looked at me, as she holds hers.

I am almost afraid to confess it, even to these secret pages. The man has interested me, has attracted me, has forced me to like him. In two short days he has made his way straight into my favourable estimation, and how he has worked the miracle is more than I can tell.

It absolutely startles me, now he is in my mind, to find how plainly I see him! – how much more plainly than I see Sir Percival, or Mr Fairlie, or Walter Hartright, or any other absent person of whom I think, with the one exception of Laura herself! I can hear his voice, as if he was speaking at this moment. I know what his conversation was yesterday, as well as if I was hearing it now. How am I to describe him? There are peculiarities in his personal appearance, his habits, and his amusements, which I should blame in the boldest terms, or ridicule in the most merciless manner, if I had seen them in another man. What is it that makes me unable to blame them, or to ridicule them in *him*?

For example, he is immensely fat. Before this time I have always especially disliked corpulent humanity. I have always maintained that the popular notion of connecting excessive grossness of size and excessive good-humour as inseparable allies was equivalent to declaring, either that no people but amiable people ever get fat, or that the accidental addition of so many pounds of flesh has a directly favourable influence over the disposition of the person on whose body they accumulate. I have invariably combated both these absurd assertions by quoting examples of fat people who were as mean, vicious, and cruel as the leanest and the worst of their neighbours. I have asked whether Henry the Eighth was an amiable character? Whether Pope Alexander the Sixth was a good man? Whether Mr Murderer and Mrs Murderess Manning were not both unusually stout people? Whether hired nurses, proverbially as cruel a set of women as are to be found in all England, were not, for the most part, also as fat a set of women as are to be found in all England? – and so on, through dozens of other examples, modern and ancient, native and foreign, high and low. Holding these strong opinions on the subject with might and main as I do at this moment, here, nevertheless, is Count Fosco, as fat as Henry the Eighth himself, established in my favour, at one day's notice, without let or hindrance from his own odious corpulence. Marvellous indeed!

Is it his face that has recommended him?

It may be his face. He is a most remarkable likeness, on a large scale, of the great Napoleon. His features have Napoleon's magnificent regularity – his expression recalls the grandly calm, immovable power of the Great Soldier's face. This striking resemblance certainly impressed me, to begin with; but there is something in him besides the resemblance, which has impressed me more. I think the influence I am now trying to find is in his eyes. They are the most unfathomable grey eyes I ever saw, and they have at times a cold, clear, beautiful, irresistible glitter in them which forces me to look at him, and yet causes me sensations, when I do look, which I would rather not feel. Other parts of his face and head have their strange peculiarities. His complexion, for instance, has a singular sallow-fairness, so much at variance with the dark-brown colour of his hair, that I suspect the hair of being a wig, and his face, closely shaven all over, is smoother and freer from all marks and wrinkles than mine, though (according to Sir Percival's account of him) he is close on sixty years of age. But these are not the prominent personal characteristics which distinguish him, to my mind, from all the other men I have ever seen. The marked peculiarity which singles him out from the rank and file of humanity lies entirely, so far as I can tell at present, in the extraordinary expression and extraordinary power of his eyes.

His manner and his command of our language may also have assisted him, in some degree, to establish himself in my good opinion. He has that quiet deference, that look of pleased, attentive interest in listening to a woman, and that secret gentleness in his voice in speaking to a woman, which, say what we may, we can none of us resist. Here, too, his unusual command of the English language necessarily helps him. I had often heard of the extraordinary aptitude which many Italians show in mastering our strong, hard, Northern speech; but, until I saw Count Fosco, I had never supposed it possible that any foreigner could have spoken English as he speaks it. There are times when it is almost impossible to detect, by his accent that he is not a countryman of our own, and as for fluency, there are very few born Englishmen who can talk with as few stoppages and repetitions as the Count. He may construct his sentences more or less in the foreign way, but I have never yet heard him use a wrong expression, or hesitate for a moment in his choice of a word.

All the smallest characteristics of this strange man have something strikingly original and perplexingly contradictory in them. Fat as he is and old as he is, his movements are astonishingly light and easy. He is as noiseless in a room as any of us women, and more than that, with all his look of unmistakable mental firmness and power, he is as nervously sensitive as the weakest of us. He starts at chance noises as inveterately as Laura herself. He winced and shuddered yesterday, when Sir Percival beat one of the spaniels, so that I felt ashamed of my own want of tenderness and sensibility by comparison with the Count.

The relation of this last incident reminds me of one of his most curious peculiarities, which I have not yet mentioned – his extraordinary fondness for pet animals.

Some of these he has left on the Continent, but he has brought with him to this house a cockatoo, two canary-birds, and a whole family of white mice. He attends to all the necessities of these strange favourites himself, and he has taught the creatures to be surprisingly fond of him and familiar with him. The cockatoo, a most vicious and treacherous bird towards every one else, absolutely seems to love him. When he lets it out of its cage, it hops on to his knee, and claws its way up his great big body, and rubs its top-knot against his sallow double chin in the most caressing manner imaginable. He has only to set the doors of the canaries' cages open, and to call them, and the pretty little cleverly trained creatures perch fearlessly on his hand, mount his fat outstretched fingers one by one, when he tells them to 'go upstairs,' and sing together as if they would burst their throats with delight when they get to the top finger. His white mice live in a little pagoda of gaily-painted wirework, designed and made by himself. They are almost as tame as the canaries, and they are perpetually let out like the canaries. They crawl all over him, popping in and out of his waistcoat, and sitting in couples, white as snow, on his capacious shoulders. He seems to be even fonder of his mice than of his other pets, smiles at them, and kisses them, and calls them by all sorts of endearing names. If it be possible to suppose an Englishman with any taste for such childish interests and amusements as these, that Englishman would certainly feel rather ashamed of them, and would be anxious to apologise for them, in the company of grown-up people. But the Count, apparently, sees nothing ridiculous in the amazing contrast between his colossal self and his frail little pets. He would blandly kiss his white mice and twitter to his canary-birds amid an assembly of English fox-hunters, and would only pity them as barbarians when they were all laughing their loudest at him.

It seems hardly credible while I am writing it down, but it is certainly true, that this same man, who has all the fondness of an old maid for his cockatoo, and all the small dexterities of an organ-boy in managing his white mice, can talk, when anything happens to rouse him, with a daring independence of thought, a knowledge of books in every language, and an experience of society in half the capitals of Europe, which would make him the prominent personage of any assembly in the civilised world. This trainer of canary-birds, this architect of a pagoda for white mice, is (as Sir Percival himself has told me) one of the first experimental chemists living, and has discovered, among other wonderful inventions, a means of petrifying the body after death, so as to preserve it, as hard as marble, to the end of time. This fat, indolent, elderly man, whose nerves are so finely strung that he starts at chance noises, and winces when he sees a house-spaniel get a whipping, went into the stable-yard on the morning after his arrival, and put his hand on the head of a chained bloodhound – a beast so savage that the very groom who feeds him keeps out of his reach. His wife and I were present, and I shall not forget the scene that followed, short as it was.

'Mind that dog, sir,' said the groom; 'he flies at everybody!' 'He does that, my friend,' replied the Count quietly, 'because everybody is afraid of him. Let us see if he flies at *me*.' And he laid his plump, yellow-white fingers, on which the canary-birds had been perching ten minutes before, upon the formidable brute's head, and looked him straight in the eyes. 'You big dogs are all cowards,' he said, addressing the animal contemptuously, with his face and the dog's within an inch of each other. 'You would kill a poor cat, you infernal coward. You would fly at a starving beggar, you infernal coward. Anything that you can surprise unawares – anything that is afraid of your big body, and your wicked white teeth, and your slobbering, bloodthirsty mouth, is the thing you like to fly at. You could throttle me at this moment, you mean, miserable bully, and you daren't so much as look me in the face, because I'm not afraid of you. Will you think better of it, and try your teeth in my fat neck? Bah! not you!' He turned away, laughing at the astonishment of the men in the yard, and the dog crept back meekly to his kennel. 'Ah! my nice waistcoat!' he said pathetically. 'I am sorry I came here. Some of that brute's slobber has got on my pretty clean waistcoat.' Those words express another of his incomprehensible oddities. He is as fond of fine clothes as the veriest fool in existence, and has appeared in four magnificent waist-coats already – all of light garish colours, and all immensely large even for him – in the two days of his residence at Blackwater Park.

His tact and cleverness in small things are quite as noticeable as the singular inconsistencies in his character, and the childish triviality of his ordinary tastes and pursuits.

I can see already that he means to live on excellent terms with all of us during the period of his sojourn in this place. He has evidently discov-ered that Laura secretly dislikes him (she confessed as much to me when I pressed her on the subject) – but he has also found out that she is extrava-gantly fond of flowers. Whenever she wants a nosegay he has got one to give her, gathered and arranged by himself, and greatly to my amusement, he is always cunningly provided with a duplicate, composed of exactly the same flowers, grouped in exactly the same way, to appease his icily jealous wife before she can so much as think herself aggrieved. His management of the Countess (in public) is a sight to see. He bows to her, he habitually addresses her as 'my angel,' he carries his canaries to pay her little visits on his fingers and to sing to her, he kisses her hand when she gives him his cigarettes; he presents her with sugar-plums in return, which he puts into her mouth playfully, from a box in his pocket. The rod of iron with which he rules her never appears in company – it is a private rod, and is always kept upstairs.

His method of recommending himself to *me* is entirely different. He flat-ters my vanity by talking to me as seriously and sensibly as if I was a man. Yes! I can find him out when I am away from him – I know he flatters my vanity, when I think of him up here in my own room – and yet, when I go downstairs, and get into his company again, he will blind me again, and I shall be flattered again, just as if I had never found him out at all! He can manage me as he manages his wife and Laura, as he managed the bloodhound in the stable-yard, as he manages Sir Percival himself, every hour in the day. 'My good Percival! how I like your rough English humour!'—'My good Percival! how I enjoy your solid English sense!' He puts the rudest remarks Sir Percival can make on his effeminate tastes and amusements quietly away from him in that manner – always calling the baronet by his Christian name, smiling at him with the calmest superiority, patting him on the shoulder, and bearing with him benignantly, as a good-humoured father bears with a wayward son.

The interest which I really cannot help feeling in this strangely original man has led me to question Sir Percival about his past life.

Sir Percival either knows little, or will tell me little, about it. He and the Count first met many years ago, at Rome, under the dangerous circumstances to which I have alluded elsewhere. Since that time they have been perpetually together in London, in Paris, and in Vienna – but never in Italy again; the Count having, oddly enough, not crossed the frontiers of his native country for years past. Perhaps he has been made the victim of some political persecution? At all events, he seems to be patriotically anxious not to lose sight of any of his own countrymen who may happen to be in England. On the evening of his arrival he asked how far we were from the nearest town, and whether we knew of any Italian gentlemen who might happen to be settled there. He is certainly in correspondence with people on the Continent, for his letters have all sorts of odd stamps on them, and I saw one for him this morning, waiting in his place at the breakfast-table, with a huge, official-looking seal on it. Perhaps he is in correspondence with his government? And yet, that is hardly to be reconciled either with my other idea that he may be a political exile.

How much I seem to have written about Count Fosco! And what does it all amount to? – as poor, dear Mr Gilmore would ask, in his impenetrable business-like way. I can only repeat that I do assuredly feel, even on this short acquaintance, a strange, half-willing, half-unwilling liking for the Count. He seems to have established over me the same sort of ascendency which he has evidently gained over Sir Percival. Free, and even rude, as he may occasionally be in his manner towards his fat friend, Sir Percival is nevertheless afraid, as I can plainly see, of giving any serious offence to the Count. I wonder whether I am afraid too? I certainly never saw a man, in all my experience, whom I should be so sorry to have for an enemy. Is this because I like him, or because I am afraid of him? *Chi sa?* – as Count Fosco might say in his own language. Who knows?

JUNE 16TH – Something to chronicle today besides my own ideas and impressions. A visitor has arrived – quite unknown to Laura and to me, and apparently quite unexpected by Sir Percival.

We were all at lunch, in the room with the new French windows that open into the verandah, and the Count (who devours pastry as I have never yet seen it devoured by any human beings but girls at boarding-schools) had just amused us by asking gravely for his fourth tart – when the servant entered to announce the visitor.

'Mr Merriman has just come, Sir Percival, and wishes to see you immediately.'

Sir Percival started, and looked at the man with an expression of angry alarm.

'Mr Merriman!' he repeated, as if he thought his own ears must have deceived him.

'Yes, Sir Percival – Mr Merriman, from London.'

'Where is he?'

'In the library, Sir Percival.'

He left the table the instant the last answer was given, and hurried out of the room without saying a word to any of us.

'Who is Mr Merriman?' asked Laura, appealing to me.

'I have not the least idea,' was all I could say in reply.

The Count had finished his fourth tart, and had gone to a side-table to look after his vicious cockatoo. He turned round to us with the bird perched on his shoulder.

'Mr Merriman is Sir Percival's solicitor,' he said quietly.

Sir Percival's solicitor. It was a perfectly straightforward answer to Laura's question, and yet, under the circumstances, it was not satisfactory. If Mr Merriman had been specially sent for by his client, there would have been nothing very wonderful in his leaving town to obey the summons. But when a lawyer travels from London to Hampshire without being sent for, and when his arrival at a gentleman's house seriously startles the gentleman himself, it may be safely taken for granted that the legal visitor is the bearer of some very important and very unexpected news – news which may be either very good or very bad, but which cannot, in either case, be of the common everyday kind.

Laura and I sat silent at the table for a quarter of an hour or more, wondering uneasily what had happened, and waiting for the chance of Sir Percival's speedy return. There were no signs of his return, and we rose to leave the room.

The Count, attentive as usual, advanced from the corner in which he had been feeding his cockatoo, with the bird still perched on his shoulder, and opened the door for us. Laura and Madame Fosco went out first. Just as I was on the point of following them he made a sign with his hand, and spoke to me, before I passed him, in the oddest manner.

'Yes,' he said, quietly answering the unexpressed idea at that moment in my mind, as if I had plainly confided it to him in so many words—'yes, Miss Halcombe, something *has* happened.'

I was on the point of answering, 'I never said so,' but the vicious cockatoo ruffled his clipped wings and gave a screech that set all my nerves on edge in an instant, and made me only too glad to get out of the room.

I joined Laura at the foot of the stairs. The thought in her mind was the same as the thought in mine, which Count Fosco had surprised, and when she spoke her words were almost the echo of his. She, too, said to me secretly that she was afraid something had happened.

III

JUNE 16TH – I have a few lines more to add to this day's entry before I go to bed tonight.

About two hours after Sir Percival rose from the luncheon-table to receive his solicitor, Mr Merriman, in the library, I left my room alone to take a walk in the plantations. Just as I was at the end of the landing the library door opened and the two gentlemen came out. Thinking it best not to disturb them by appearing on the stairs, I resolved to defer going down till they had crossed the hall. Although they spoke to each other in guarded tones, their words were pronounced with sufficient distinctness of utterance to reach my ears.

'Make your mind easy, Sir Percival,' I heard the lawyer say; 'it all rests with Lady Glyde.'

I had turned to go back to my own room for a minute or two, but the sound of Laura's name on the lips of a stranger stopped me instantly. I daresay it was very wrong and very discreditable to listen, but where is the woman, in the whole range of our sex, who can regulate her actions by the abstract principles of honour, when those principles point one way, and when her affections, and the interests which grow out of them, point the other?

I listened – and under similar circumstances I would listen again – yes! with my ear at the keyhole, if I could not possibly manage it in any other way.

'You quite understand, Sir Percival,' the lawyer went on. 'Lady Glyde is to sign her name in the presence of a witness – or of two witnesses, if you wish to be particularly careful – and is then to put her finger on the seal and say, "I deliver this as my act and deed." If that is done in a week's time the arrangement will be perfectly successful, and the anxiety will be all over. If not—'

'What do you mean by "if not"?' asked Sir Percival angrily. 'If the thing must be done it *shall* be done. I promise you that, Merriman.'

'Just so, Sir Percival – just so; but there are two alternatives in all trans-actions, and we lawyers like to look both of them in the face boldly. If through any extraordinary circumstance the arrangement should not be made, I think I may be able to get the parties to accept bills at three months. But how the money is to be raised when the bills fall due—'

'Damn the bills! The money is only to be got in one way, and in that way, I tell you again, it *shall* be got. Take a glass of wine, Merriman, before you go.'

'Much obliged, Sir Percival, I have not a moment to lose if I am to catch the up-train. You will let me know as soon as the arrangement is complete? and you will not forget the caution I recommended—'

'Of course I won't. There's the dog-cart at the door for you. My groom will get you to the station in no time. Benjamin, drive like mad! Jump in. If Mr Merriman misses the train you lose your place. Hold fast, Merriman, and if you are upset trust to the devil to save his own.' With that parting benediction the baronet turned about and walked back to the library.

I had not heard much, but the little that had reached my ears was enough to make me feel uneasy. The 'something' that 'had happened' was but too plainly a serious money embarrassment, and Sir Percival's relief from it depended upon Laura. The prospect of seeing her involved in her husband's secret difficulties filled me with dismay, exaggerated, no doubt, by my igno-rance of business and my settled distrust of Sir Percival. Instead of going out, as I proposed, I went back immediately to Laura's room to tell her what I had heard.

She received my bad news so composedly as to surprise me. She evidently knows more of her husband's character and her husband's embarrassments than I have suspected up to this time.

'I feared as much,' she said, 'when I heard of that strange gentleman who called, and declined to leave his name.'

'Who do you think the gentleman was, then?' I asked.

'Some person who has heavy claims on Sir Percival,' she answered, 'and who has been the cause of Mr Merriman's visit here today.'

'Do you know anything about those claims?'

'No, I know no particulars.'

'You will sign nothing, Laura, without first looking at it?'

'Certainly not, Marian. Whatever I can harmlessly and honestly do to help him I will do – for the sake of making your life and mine, love, as easy and as happy as possible. But I will do nothing ignorantly, which we might, one day, have reason to feel ashamed of. Let us say no more about it now. You have got your hat on – suppose we go and dream away the afternoon in the grounds?'

On leaving the house we directed our steps to the nearest shade.

As we passed an open space among the trees in front of the house, there was Count Fosco, slowly walking backwards and forwards on the grass, sunning himself in the full blaze of the hot June afternoon. He had a broad straw hat on, with a violet-coloured ribbon round it. A blue blouse, with profuse white fancy-work over the bosom, covered his prodigious body, and was girt about the place where his waist might once have been with a broad scarlet leather belt. Nankeen trousers, displaying more white fancy-work over the ankles, and purple morocco slippers, adorned his lower extremities. He was singing Figaro's famous song in the Barber of Seville, with that crisply fluent vocalisation which is never heard from any other than an Italian throat, accompanying himself on the concertina, which he played with ecstatic throwings-up of his arms, and graceful twistings and turnings of his head, like a fat St Cecilia masquerading in male attire. 'Figaro quà! Figaro là! Figaro sù! Figaro giù!' sang the Count, jauntily tossing up the concertina at arm's length, and bowing to us, on one side of the instrument, with the airy grace and elegance of Figaro himself at twenty years of age.

'Take my word for it, Laura, that man knows something of Sir Percival's embarrassments,' I said, as we returned the Count's salutation from a safe distance.

'What makes you think that?' she asked.

'How should he have known, otherwise, that Mr Merriman was Sir Percival's solicitor?' I rejoined. 'Besides, when I followed you out of the luncheon-room, he told me, without a single word of inquiry on my part, that something had happened. Depend upon it, he knows more than we do.'

'Don't ask him any questions if he does. Don't take him into our confidence!'

'You seem to dislike him, Laura, in a very determined manner. What has he said or done to justify you?'

'Nothing, Marian. On the contrary, he was all kindness and attention on our journey home, and he several times checked Sir Percival's outbreaks of temper, in the most considerate manner towards me. Perhaps I dislike him because he has so much more power over my husband than I have. Perhaps it hurts my pride to be under any obligations to his interference. All I know is, that I *do* dislike him.'

The rest of the day and evening passed quietly enough. The Count and I played at chess. For the first two games he politely allowed me to conquer him, and then, when he saw that I had found him out, begged my pardon, and at the third game checkmated me in ten minutes. Sir Percival never once referred, all through the evening, to the lawyer's visit. But either that event, or something else, had produced a singular alteration for the better in him. He was as polite and agreeable to all of us, as he used to be in the days of his probation at Limmeridge, and he was so amazingly attentive and kind to his wife, that even icy Madame Fosco was roused into looking at him with a grave surprise. What does this mean? I think I can guess – I am afraid Laura can guess – and I am sure Count Fosco knows. I caught Sir Percival looking at him for approval more than once in the course of the evening.

JUNE 17TH – A day of events. I most fervently hope I may not have to add, a day of disasters as well.

Sir Percival was as silent at breakfast as he had been the evening before, on the subject of the mysterious 'arrangement' (as the lawyer called it) which is hanging over our heads. An hour afterwards, however, he suddenly entered the morning-room, where his wife and I were waiting, with our hats on, for Madame Fosco to join us, and inquired for the Count.

'We expect to see him here directly,' I said.

'The fact is,' Sir Percival went on, walking nervously about the room, 'I want Fosco and his wife in the library, for a mere business formality, and I want you there, Laura, for a minute too.' He stopped, and appeared to notice, for the first time, that we were in our walking costume. 'Have you just come in?' he asked, 'or were you just going out?'

'We were all thinking of going to the lake this morning,' said Laura. 'But if you have any other arrangement to propose—'

'No, no,' he answered hastily. 'My arrangement can wait. After lunch will do as well for it as after breakfast. All going to the lake, eh? A good idea. Let's have an idle morning – I'll be one of the party.'

There was no mistaking his manner, even if it had been possible to mistake the uncharacteristic readiness which his words expressed, to submit his own plans and projects to the convenience of others. He was evidently relieved at finding any excuse for delaying the business formality in the library, to which his own words had referred. My heart sank within me as I drew the inevitable inference.

The Count and his wife joined us at that moment. The lady had her husband's embroidered tobacco-pouch, and her store of paper in her hand, for the manufacture of the eternal cigarettes. The gentleman, dressed, as usual, in his blouse and straw hat, carried the gay little pagoda-cage, with his darling white mice in it, and smiled on them, and on us, with a bland amiability which it was impossible to resist.

'With your kind permission,' said the Count, 'I will take my small family here – my poor-little-harmless-pretty-Mouseys, out for an airing along with us. There are dogs about the house, and shall I leave my forlorn white children at the mercies of the dogs? Ah, never!'

He chirruped paternally at his small white children through the bars of the pagoda, and we all left the house for the lake.

In the plantation Sir Percival strayed away from us. It seems to be part of his restless disposition always to separate himself from his companions on these occasions, and always to occupy himself when he is alone in cutting new walking-sticks for his own use. The mere act of cutting and lopping at hazard appears to please him. He has filled the house with walking-sticks of his own making, not one of which he ever takes up for a second time. When they have been once used his interest in them is all exhausted, and he thinks of nothing but going on and making more.

At the old boathouse he joined us again. I will put down the conversation that ensued when we were all settled in our places exactly as it passed. It is an important conversation, so far as I am concerned, for it has seriously disposed me to distrust the influence which Count Fosco has exercised over my thoughts and feelings, and to resist it for the future as resolutely as I can.

The boathouse was large enough to hold us all, but Sir Percival remained outside trimming the last new stick with his pocket-axe. We three women found plenty of room on the large seat. Laura took her work, and Madame Fosco began her cigarettes. I, as usual, had nothing to do. My hands always were, and always will be, as awkward as a man's. The Count good-humouredly took a stool many sizes too small for him, and balanced himself on it with his back against the side of the shed, which creaked and groaned under his weight. He put the pagoda-cage on his lap, and let out the mice to crawl over him as usual. They are pretty, innocent-looking little creatures, but the sight of them creeping about a man's body is for some reason not pleasant to me. It excites a strange responsive creeping in my own nerves, and suggests hideous ideas of men dying in prison with the crawling creatures of the dungeon preying on them undisturbed.

The morning was windy and cloudy, and the rapid alternations of shadow and sunlight over the waste of the lake made the view look doubly wild, weird, and gloomy.

'Some people call that picturesque,' said Sir Percival, pointing over the wide prospect with his half-finished walking-stick. 'I call it a blot on a gentleman's property. In my great-grandfather's time the lake flowed to this place. Look at it now! It is not four feet deep anywhere, and it is all puddles and pools. I wish I could afford to drain it, and plant it all over. My bailiff (a superstitious idiot) says he is quite sure the lake has a curse on it, like the Dead Sea. What do you think, Fosco? It looks just the place for a murder, doesn't it?'

'My good Percival,' remonstrated the Count. 'What is your solid English sense thinking of? The water is too shallow to hide the body, and there is sand everywhere to print off the murderer's footsteps. It is, upon the whole, the very worst place for a murder that I ever set my eyes on.'

'Humbug!' said Sir Percival, cutting away fiercely at his stick. 'You know what I mean. The dreary scenery, the lonely situation. If you choose to understand me, you can – if you don't choose, I am not going to trouble myself to explain my meaning.'

'And why not,' asked the Count, 'when your meaning can be explained by anybody in two words? If a fool was going to commit a murder, your lake is the first place he would choose for it. If a wise man was going to commit a murder, your lake is the last place he would choose for it. Is that your meaning? If it is, there is your explanation for you ready made. Take it, Percival, with your good Fosco's blessing.'

Laura looked at the Count with her dislike for him appearing a little too plainly in her face. He was so busy with his mice that he did not notice her.

'I am sorry to hear the lake-view connected with anything so horrible as the idea of murder,' she said. 'And if Count Fosco must divide murderers into classes, I think he has been very unfortunate in his choice of expressions. To describe them as fools only seems like treating them with an indulgence to which they have no claim. And to describe them as wise men sounds to me like a downright contradiction in terms. I have always heard that truly wise men are truly good men, and have a horror of crime.'

'My dear lady,' said the Count, 'those are admirable sentiments, and I have seen them stated at the tops of copy-books.' He lifted one of the white mice in the palm of his hand, and spoke to it in his whimsical way. 'My pretty little smooth white rascal,' he said, 'here is a moral lesson for you. A truly wise mouse is a truly good mouse. Mention that, if you please, to your companions, and never gnaw at the bars of your cage again as long as you live.'

'It is easy to turn everything into ridicule,' said Laura resolutely; 'but you will not find it quite so easy, Count Fosco, to give me an instance of a wise man who has been a great criminal.'

The Count shrugged his huge shoulders, and smiled on Laura in the friendliest manner.

'Most true!' he said. 'The fool's crime is the crime that is found out, and the wise man's crime is the crime that is *not* found out. If I could give you an instance, it would not be the instance of a wise man. Dear Lady Glyde, your sound English common sense has been too much for me. It is checkmate for me this time, Miss Halcombe – ha?'

'Stand to your guns, Laura,' sneered Sir Percival, who had been listening in his place at the door. 'Tell him next, that crimes cause their own detection. There's another bit of copy-book morality for you, Fosco. Crimes cause their own detection. What infernal humbug!'

'I believe it to be true,' said Laura quietly.

Sir Percival burst out laughing, so violently, so outrageously, that he quite startled us all – the Count more than any of us.

'I believe it too,' I said, coming to Laura's rescue.

Sir Percival, who had been unaccountably amused at his wife's remark, was just as unaccountably irritated by mine. He struck the new stick savagely on the sand, and walked away from us.

'Poor dear Percival!' cried Count Fosco, looking after him gaily, 'he is the victim of English spleen. But, my dear Miss Halcombe, my dear Lady Glyde, do you really believe that crimes cause their own detection? And you, my angel,' he continued, turning to his wife, who had not uttered a word yet, 'do you think so too?'

'I wait to be instructed,' replied the Countess, in tones of freezing reproof, intended for Laura and me, 'before I venture on giving my opinion in the presence of well-informed men.'

'Do you, indeed?' I said. 'I remember the time, Countess, when you advocated the Rights of Women, and freedom of female opinion was one of them.'

'What is your view of the subject, Count?' asked Madame Fosco, calmly proceeding with her cigarettes, and not taking the least notice of me.

The Count stroked one of his white mice reflectively with his chubby little finger before he answered.

'It is truly wonderful,' he said, 'how easily Society can console itself for the worst of its shortcomings with a little bit of clap-trap. The machinery it has set up for the detection of crime is miserably ineffective – and yet only invent a moral epigram, saying that it works well, and you blind everybody to its blunders from that moment. Crimes cause their own detection, do they? And murder will out (another moral epigram), will it? Ask Coroners who sit at inquests in large towns if that is true, Lady Glyde. Ask secretaries of life-assurance companies if that is true, Miss Halcombe. Read your own public journals. In the few cases that get into the newspapers, are there not instances of slain bodies found, and no murderers ever discovered? Multiply the cases that are reported by the cases that are *not* reported, and the bodies that are found by the bodies that are *not* found, and what conclusion do you come to? This. That there are foolish criminals who are discovered, and wise criminals who escape. The hiding of a crime, or the detection of a crime, what is it? A trial of skill between the police on one side, and the individual on the other. When the criminal is a brutal, ignorant fool, the police in nine cases out of ten win. When the criminal is a resolute, educated, highly-intelligent man, the police in nine cases out of ten lose. If the police win, you generally hear all about it. If the police lose, you generally hear nothing. And on this tottering foundation you build up your comfortable moral maxim that Crime causes its own detection! Yes – all the crime you know of. And what of the rest?'

'Devilish true, and very well put,' cried a voice at the entrance of the boathouse. Sir Percival had recovered his equanimity, and had come back while we were listening to the Count.

'Some of it may be true,' I said, 'and all of it may be very well put. But I don't see why Count Fosco should celebrate the victory of the criminal over Society with so much exultation, or why you, Sir Percival, should applaud him so loudly for doing it.'

'Do you hear that, Fosco?' asked Sir Percival. 'Take my advice, and make your peace with your audience. Tell them virtue's a fine thing – they like that, I can promise you.'

The Count laughed inwardly and silently, and two of the white mice in his waistcoat, alarmed by the internal convulsion going on beneath them, darted out in a violent hurry, and scrambled into their cage again.

'The ladies, my good Percival, shall tell me about virtue,' he said. 'They are better authorities than I am, for they know what virtue is, and I don't.'

'You hear him?' said Sir Percival. 'Isn't it awful?'

'It is true,' said the Count quietly. 'I am a citizen of the world, and I have met, in my time, with so many different sorts of virtue, that I am puzzled, in my old age, to say which is the right sort and which is the wrong. Here, in England, there is one virtue. And there, in China, there is another virtue. And John Englishman says my virtue is the genuine virtue. And John Chinaman says my virtue is the genuine virtue. And I say Yes to one, or No to the other, and am just as much bewildered about it in the case of John with the top-boots as I am in the case of John with the pigtail. Ah, nice little Mousey! come, kiss me. What is your own private notion of a virtuous man, my pret-pret-pretty? A man who keeps you warm, and gives you plenty to eat. And a good notion, too, for it is intelligible, at the least.'

'Stay a minute, Count,' I interposed. 'Accepting your illustration, surely we have one unquestionable virtue in England which is wanting in China. The Chinese authorities kill thousands of innocent people on the most frivo-lous pretexts. We in England are free from all guilt of that kind – we commit no such dreadful crime – we abhor reckless bloodshed with all our hearts.'

'Quite right, Marian,' said Laura. 'Well thought of, and well expressed.'

'Pray allow the Count to proceed,' said Madame Fosco, with stern civility. 'You will find, young ladies, that *he* never speaks without having excellent reasons for all that he says.'

'Thank you, my angel,' replied the Count. 'Have a bon-bon?' He took out of his pocket a pretty little inlaid box, and placed it open on the table. 'Chocolat à la Vanille,' cried the impenetrable man, cheerfully rattling the sweetmeats in the box, and bowing all round. 'Offered by Fosco as an act of homage to the charming society.'

'Be good enough to go on, Count,' said his wife, with a spiteful reference to myself. 'Oblige me by answering Miss Halcombe.'

'Miss Halcombe is unanswerable,' replied the polite Italian; 'that is to say, so far as she goes. Yes! I agree with her. John Bull does abhor the crimes of John Chinaman. He is the quickest old gentleman at finding out faults that are his neighbours', and the slowest old gentleman at finding out the faults that are his own, who exists on the face of creation. Is he so very much better in this way than the people whom he condemns in their way? English Society, Miss Halcombe, is as often the accomplice as it is the enemy of crime. Yes! yes! Crime is in this country what crime is in other countries – a good friend to a man and to those about him as often as it is an enemy. A great rascal provides for his wife and family. The worse he is the more he makes them the objects for your sympathy. He often provides also for himself. A profligate spendthrift who is always borrowing money will get more from his friends than the rigidly honest man who only borrows of them once, under pressure of the direst want. In the one case the friends will not be at all surprised, and they will give. In the other case they will be very much surprised, and they will hesitate. Is the prison that Mr Scoundrel lives in at the end of his career a more uncomfortable place than the workhouse that Mr Honesty lives in at the end of his career? When John-Howard-Philanthropist wants to relieve misery he goes to find it in prisons, where crime is wretched – not in huts and hovels, where virtue is wretched too. Who is the English poet who has won the most universal sympathy – who makes the easiest of all subjects for pathetic writing and pathetic painting? That nice young person who began life with a forgery, and ended it by a suicide – your dear, romantic, interesting Chatterton. Which gets on best, do you think, of two poor starving dressmakers – the woman who resists temptation and is honest, or the woman who falls under temptation and steals? You all know that the stealing is the making of that second woman's fortune – it advertises her from length to breadth of good-humoured, charitable England – and she is relieved, as the breaker of a commandment, when she would have been left to starve, as the keeper of it. Come here, my jolly little Mouse! Hey! presto! pass! I transform you, for the time being, into a respectable lady. Stop there, in the palm of my great big hand, my dear, and listen. You marry the poor man whom you love, Mouse, and one half your friends pity, and the other half blame you. And now, on the contrary, you sell yourself for gold to a man you don't care for, and all your friends rejoice over you, and a minister of public worship sanctions the base horror of the vilest of all human bargains, and smiles and smirks afterwards at your table, if you are polite enough to ask him to breakfast. Hey! presto! pass! Be a mouse again, and squeak. If you continue to be a lady much longer, I shall have you telling me that Society abhors crime – and then, Mouse, I shall doubt if your own eyes and ears are really of any use to you. Ah! I am a bad man, Lady Glyde, am I not? I say what other people only think, and when all the rest of the world is in a conspiracy to accept the mask for the true face, mine is the rash hand that tears off the plump pasteboard, and shows the bare bones beneath. I will get up on my big elephant's legs, before I do myself any more harm in your amiable estimations – I will get up and take a little airy walk of my own. Dear ladies, as your excellent Sheridan said, I go   and leave my character behind me.'

He got up, put the cage on the table, and paused for a moment to count the mice in it. 'One, two, three, four – Ha!' he cried, with a look of horror, 'where, in the name of Heaven, is the fifth – the youngest, the whitest, the most amiable of all – my Benjamin of mice!'

Neither Laura nor I were in any favorable disposition to be amused. The Count's glib cynicism had revealed a new aspect of his nature from which we both recoiled. But it was impossible to resist the comical distress of so very large a man at the loss of so very small a mouse. We laughed in spite of ourselves; and when Madame Fosco rose to set the example of leaving the boathouse empty, so that her husband might search it to its remotest corners, we rose also to follow her out.

Before we had taken three steps, the Count's quick eye discovered the lost mouse under the seat that we had been occupying. He pulled aside the bench, took the little animal up in his hand, and then suddenly stopped, on his knees, looking intently at a particular place on the ground just beneath him.

When he rose to his feet again, his hand shook so that he could hardly put the mouse back in the cage, and his face was of a faint livid yellow hue all over.

'Percival!' he said, in a whisper. 'Percival! come here.'

Sir Percival had paid no attention to any of us for the last ten minutes. He had been entirely absorbed in writing figures on the sand, and then rubbing them out again with the point of his stick.

'What's the matter now?' he asked, lounging carelessly into the boathouse.

'Do you see nothing there?' said the Count, catching him nervously by the collar with one hand, and pointing with the other to the place near which he had found the mouse.

'I see plenty of dry sand,' answered Sir Percival, 'and a spot of dirt in the middle of it.'

'Not dirt,' whispered the Count, fastening the other hand suddenly on Sir Percival's collar, and shaking it in his agitation. 'Blood.'

Laura was near enough to hear the last word, softly as he whispered it. She turned to me with a look of terror.

'Nonsense, my dear,' I said. 'There is no need to be alarmed. It is only the blood of a poor little stray dog.'

Everybody was astonished, and everybody's eyes were fixed on me inquiringly.

'How do you know that?' asked Sir Percival, speaking first.

'I found the dog here, dying, on the day when you all returned from abroad,' I replied. 'The poor creature had strayed into the plantation, and had been shot by your keeper.'

'Whose dog was it?' inquired Sir Percival. 'Not one of mine?'

'Did you try to save the poor thing?' asked Laura earnestly. 'Surely you tried to save it, Marian?'

'Yes,' I said, 'the housekeeper and I both did our best – but the dog was mortally wounded, and he died under our hands.'

'Whose dog was it?' persisted Sir Percival, repeating his question a little irritably. 'One of mine?'

'No, not one of yours.'

'Whose then? Did the housekeeper know?'

The housekeeper's report of Mrs Catherick's desire to conceal her visit to Blackwater Park from Sir Percival's knowledge recurred to my memory the moment he put that last question, and I half doubted the discretion of answering it; but in my anxiety to quiet the general alarm, I had thoughtlessly advanced too far to draw back, except at the risk of exciting suspicion, which might only make matters worse. There was nothing for it but to answer at once, without reference to results.

'Yes,' I said. 'The housekeeper knew. She told me it was Mrs Catherick's dog.'

Sir Percival had hitherto remained at the inner end of the boathouse with Count Fosco, while I spoke to him from the door. But the instant Mrs Catherick's name passed my lips he pushed by the Count roughly, and placed himself face to face with me under the open daylight.

'How came the housekeeper to know it was Mrs Catherick's dog?' he asked, fixing his eyes on mine with a frowning interest and attention, which half angered, half startled me.

'She knew it,' I said quietly, 'because Mrs Catherick brought the dog with her.'

'Brought it with her? Where did she bring it with her?'

'To this house.'

'What the devil did Mrs Catherick want at this house?'

The manner in which he put the question was even more offensive than the language in which he expressed it. I marked my sense of his want of common politeness by silently turning away from him.

Just as I moved the Count's persuasive hand was laid on his shoulder, and the Count's mellifluous voice interposed to quiet him.

'My dear Percival! – gently – gently!'

Sir Percival looked round in his angriest manner. The Count only smiled and repeated the soothing application.

'Gently, my good friend – gently!'

Sir Percival hesitated, followed me a few steps, and, to my great surprise, offered me an apology.

'I beg your pardon, Miss Halcombe,' he said. 'I have been out of order lately, and I am afraid I am a little irritable. But I should like to know what Mrs Catherick could possibly want here. When did she come? Was the housekeeper the only person who saw her?'

'The only person,' I answered, 'so far as I know.'

The Count interposed again.

'In that case why not question the housekeeper?' he said. 'Why not go, Percival, to the fountain-head of information at once?'

'Quite right!' said Sir Percival. 'Of course the housekeeper is the first person to question. Excessively stupid of me not to see it myself.' With those words he instantly left us to return to the house.

The motive of the Count's interference, which had puzzled me at first, betrayed itself when Sir Percival's back was turned. He had a host of questions to put to me about Mrs Catherick, and the cause of her visit to Blackwater Park, which he could scarcely have asked in his friend's presence. I made my answers as short as I civilly could, for I had already determined to check the least approach to any exchanging of confidences between Count Fosco and myself. Laura, however, unconsciously helped him to extract all my information, by making inquiries herself, which left me no alternative but to reply to her, or to appear in the very unenviable and very false character of a depositary of Sir Percival's secrets. The end of it was, that, in about ten minutes' time, the Count knew as much as I know of Mrs Catherick, and of the events which have so strangely connected us with her daughter, Anne, from the time when Hartright met with her to this day.

The effect of my information on him was, in one respect, curious enough.

Intimately as he knows Sir Percival, and closely as he appears to be associated with Sir Percival's private affairs in general, he is certainly as far as I am from knowing anything of the true story of Anne Catherick. The unsolved mystery in connection with this unhappy woman is now rendered doubly suspicious, in my eyes, by the absolute conviction which I feel, that the clue to it has been hidden by Sir Percival from the most intimate friend he has in the world. It was impossible to mistake the eager curiosity of the Count's look and manner while he drank in greedily every word that fell from my lips. There are many kinds of curiosity, I know – but there is no misinterpreting the curiosity of blank surprise: if I ever saw it in my life I saw it in the Count's face.

While the questions and answers were going on, we had all been strolling quietly back through the plantation. As soon as we reached the house the first object that we saw in front of it was Sir Percival's dog-cart, with the horse put to and the groom waiting by it in his stable-jacket. If these unexpected appearances were to be trusted, the examination of the house-keeper had produced important results already.

'A fine horse, my friend,' said the Count, addressing the groom with the most engaging familiarity of manner, 'You are going to drive out?'

'I am not going, sir,' replied the man, looking at his stable-jacket, and evidently wondering whether the foreign gentleman took it for his livery. 'My master drives himself.'

'Aha!' said the Count, 'does he indeed? I wonder he gives himself the trouble when he has got you to drive for him. Is he going to fatigue that nice, shining, pretty horse by taking him very far today?'

'I don't know, sir,' answered the man. 'The horse is a mare, if you please, sir. She's the highest-couraged thing we've got in the stables. Her name's Brown Molly, sir, and she'll go till she drops. Sir Percival usually takes Isaac of York for the short distances.'

'And your shining courageous Brown Molly for the long?'

'Logical inference, Miss Halcombe,' continued the Count, wheeling round briskly, and addressing me. 'Sir Percival is going a long distance today.'

I made no reply. I had my own inferences to draw, from what I knew through the housekeeper and from what I saw before me, and I did not choose to share them with Count Fosco.

When Sir Percival was in Cumberland (I thought to myself), he walked away a long distance, on Anne's account, to question the family at Todd's

Corner. Now he is in Hampshire, is he going to drive away a long distance, on Anne's account again, to question Mrs Catherick at Welmingham?

We all entered the house. As we crossed the hall Sir Percival came out from the library to meet us. He looked hurried and pale and anxious – but for all that, he was in his most polite mood when he spoke to us.

'I am sorry to say I am obliged to leave you,' he began – 'a long drive – a matter that I can't very well put off. I shall be back in good time tomorrow – but before I go I should like that little business-formality, which I spoke of this morning, to be settled. Laura, will you come into the library? It won't take a minute – a mere formality. Countess, may I trouble you also? I want you and the Countess, Fosco, to be witnesses to a signature – nothing more. Come in at once and get it over.'

He held the library door open until they had passed in, followed them, and shut it softly.

I remained, for a moment afterwards, standing alone in the hall, with my heart beating fast and my mind misgiving me sadly. Then I went on to the staircase, and ascended slowly to my own room.

IV

JUNE 17TH – Just as my hand was on the door of my room, I heard Sir Percival's voice calling to me from below.

'I must beg you to come downstairs again,' he said. 'It is Fosco's fault, Miss Halcombe, not mine. He has started some nonsensical objection to his wife being one of the witnesses, and has obliged me to ask you to join us in the library.'

I entered the room immediately with Sir Percival. Laura was waiting by the writing-table, twisting and turning her garden hat uneasily in her hands. Madame Fosco sat near her, in an arm-chair, imperturbably admiring her husband, who stood by himself at the other end of the library, picking off the dead leaves from the flowers in the window.

The moment I appeared the Count advanced to meet me, and to offer his explanations.

'A thousand pardons, Miss Halcombe,' he said. 'You know the character which is given to my countrymen by the English? We Italians are all wily and suspicious by nature, in the estimation of the good John Bull. Set me down, if you please, as being no better than the rest of my race. I am a wily Italian and a suspicious Italian. You have thought so yourself, dear lady, have you not? Well! it is part of my wiliness and part of my suspicion to object to Madame Fosco being a witness to Lady Glyde's signature, when I am also a witness myself.'

'There is not the shadow of a reason for his objection,' interposed Sir Percival. 'I have explained to him that the law of England allows Madame Fosco to witness a signature as well as her husband.'

'I admit it,' resumed the Count. 'The law of England says, Yes, but the conscience of Fosco says, No.' He spread out his fat fingers on the bosom of his blouse, and bowed solemnly, as if he wished to introduce his conscience to us all, in the character of an illustrious addition to the society. 'What this document which Lady Glyde is about to sign may be,' he continued, 'I neither know nor desire to know. I only say this, circumstances may happen in the future which may oblige Percival, or his representatives, to appeal to the two witnesses, in which case it is certainly desirable that those witnesses should represent two opinions which are perfectly independent the one of the other. This cannot be if my wife signs as well as myself, because we have but one opinion between us, and that opinion is mine. I will not have it cast in my teeth, at some future day, that Madame Fosco acted under my coercion, and was, in plain fact, no witness at all. I speak in Percival's interest, when I propose that my name shall appear (as the nearest friend of the husband), and your name, Miss Halcombe (as the nearest friend of the wife). I am a Jesuit, if you please to think so – a splitter of straws – a man of trifles and crochets and scruples – but you will humour me, I hope, in merciful consideration for my suspicious Italian character, and my uneasy Italian conscience.' He bowed again, stepped back a few paces, and withdrew his conscience from our society as politely as he had introduced it.

The Count's scruples might have been honourable and reasonable enough, but there was something in his manner of expressing them which increased my unwillingness to be concerned in the business of the signature. No consideration of less importance than my consideration for Laura would have induced me to consent to be a witness at all. One look, however, at her anxious face decided me to risk anything rather than desert her.

'I will readily remain in the room,' I said. 'And if I find no reason for starting any small scruples on my side, you may rely on me as a witness.'

Sir Percival looked at me sharply, as if he was about to say something. But at the same moment, Madame Fosco attracted his attention by rising from her chair. She had caught her husband's eye, and had evidently received her orders to leave the room.

'You needn't go,' said Sir Percival.

Madame Fosco looked for her orders again, got them again, said she would prefer leaving us to our business, and resolutely walked out. The Count lit a cigarette, went back to the flowers in the window, and puffed little jets of smoke at the leaves, in a state of the deepest anxiety about killing the insects.

Meanwhile Sir Percival unlocked a cupboard beneath one of the book-cases, and produced from it a piece of parchment, folded longwise, many times over. He placed it on the table, opened the last fold only, and kept his hand on the rest. The last fold displayed a strip of blank parchment with little wafers stuck on it at certain places. Every line of the writing was hidden in the part which he still held folded up under his hand. Laura and I looked at each other. Her face was pale, but it showed no indecision and no fear.

Sir Percival dipped a pen in ink, and handed it to his wife. 'Sign your name there,' he said, pointing to the place. 'You and Fosco are to sign after-wards, Miss Halcombe, opposite those two wafers. Come here, Fosco! witnessing a signature is not to be done by mooning out of window and smoking into the flowers.'

The Count threw away his cigarette, and joined us at the table, with his hands carelessly thrust into the scarlet belt of his blouse, and his eyes steadily fixed on Sir Percival's face. Laura, who was on the other side of her husband, with the pen in her hand, looked at him too. He stood between them holding the folded parchment down firmly on the table, and glancing across at me, as I sat opposite to him, with such a sinister mixture of suspi-cion and embarrassment on his face that he looked more like a prisoner at the bar than a gentleman in his own house.

'Sign there,' he repeated, turning suddenly on Laura, and pointing once more to the place on the parchment.

'What is it I am to sign?' she asked quietly.

'I have no time to explain,' he answered. 'The dog-cart is at the door, and I must go directly. Besides, if I had time, you wouldn't understand. It is a purely formal document, full of legal technicalities, and all that sort of thing. Come! come! sign your name, and let us have done as soon as possible.'

'I ought surely to know what I am signing, Sir Percival, before I write my name?'

'Nonsense! What have women to do with business? I tell you again, you can't understand it.'

'At any rate, let me try to understand it. Whenever Mr Gilmore had any business for me to do, he always explained it first, and I always understood him.'

'I dare say he did. He was your servant, and was obliged to explain. I am your husband, and am *not* obliged. How much longer do you mean to keep me here? I tell you again, there is no time for reading anything – the dog-cart is waiting at the door. Once for all, will you sign or will you not?'

She still had the pen in her hand, but she made no approach to signing her name with it.

'If my signature pledges me to anything,' she said, 'surely I have some claim to know what that pledge is?'

He lifted up the parchment, and struck it angrily on the table.

'Speak out!' he said. 'You were always famous for telling the truth. Never mind Miss Halcombe, never mind Fosco – say, in plain terms, you distrust me.'

The Count took one of his hands out of his belt and laid it on Sir Percival's shoulder. Sir Percival shook it off irritably. The Count put it on again with unruffled composure.

'Control your unfortunate temper, Percival,' he said. 'Lady Glyde is right.'

'Right!' cried Sir Percival. 'A wife right in distrusting her husband!'

'It is unjust and cruel to accuse me of distrusting you,' said Laura. 'Ask Marian if I am not justified in wanting to know what this writing requires of me before I sign it.'

'I won't have any appeals made to Miss Halcombe,' retorted Sir Percival. 'Miss Halcombe has nothing to do with the matter.'

I had not spoken hitherto, and I would much rather not have spoken now. But the expression of distress in Laura's face when she turned it towards me, and the insolent injustice of her husband's conduct, left me no other alternative than to give my opinion, for her sake, as soon as I was asked for it.

'Excuse me, Sir Percival,' I said—'but as one of the witnesses to the signature, I venture to think that I *have* something to do with the matter. Laura's objection seems to me a perfectly fair one, and speaking for myself only, I cannot assume the responsibility of witnessing her signature, unless she first understands what the writing is which you wish her to sign.'

'A cool declaration, upon my soul!' cried Sir Percival. 'The next time you invite yourself to a man's house, Miss Halcombe, I recommend you not to repay his hospitality by taking his wife's side against him in a matter that doesn't concern you.'

I started to my feet as suddenly as if he had struck me. If I had been a man, I would have knocked him down on the threshold of his own door, and have left his house, never on any earthly consideration to enter it again. But I was only a woman – and I loved his wife so dearly!

Thank God, that faithful love helped me, and I sat down again without saying a word. *She* knew what I had suffered and what I had suppressed. She ran round to me, with the tears streaming from her eyes. 'Oh, Marian!' she whispered softly. 'If my mother had been alive, she could have done no more for me!'

'Come back and sign!' cried Sir Percival from the other side of the table.

'Shall I?' she asked in my ear; 'I will, if you tell me.'

'No,' I answered. 'The right and the truth are with you – sign nothing, unless you have read it first.'

'Come back and sign!' he reiterated, in his loudest and angriest tones.

The Count, who had watched Laura and me with a close and silent attention, interposed for the second time.

'Percival!' he said. 'I remember that I am in the presence of ladies. Be good enough, if you please, to remember it too.'

Sir Percival turned on him speechless with passion. The Count's firm hand slowly tightened its grasp on his shoulder, and the Count's steady voice quietly repeated, 'Be good enough, if you please, to remember it too.'

They both looked at each other. Sir Percival slowly drew his shoulder from under the Count's hand, slowly turned his face away from the Count's eyes, doggedly looked down for a little while at the parchment on the table, and then spoke, with the sullen submission of a tamed animal, rather than the becoming resignation of a convinced man.

'I don't want to offend anybody,' he said, 'but my wife's obstinacy is enough to try the patience of a saint. I have told her this is merely a formal document – and what more can she want? You may say what you please, but it is no part of a woman's duty to set her husband at defiance. Once more, Lady Glyde, and for the last time, will you sign or will you not?'

Laura returned to his side of the table, and took up the pen again.

'I will sign with pleasure,' she said, 'if you will only treat me as a responsible being. I care little what sacrifice is required of me, if it will affect no one else, and lead to no ill results—'

'Who talked of a sacrifice being required of you?' he broke in, with a half-suppressed return of his former violence.

'I only meant,' she resumed, 'that I would refuse no concession which I could honourably make. If I have a scruple about signing my name to an engagement of which I know nothing, why should you visit it on me so severely? It is rather hard, I think, to treat Count Fosco's scruples so much more indulgently than you have treated mine.'

This unfortunate, yet most natural, reference to the Count's extraordinary power over her husband, indirect as it was, set Sir Percival's smouldering temper on fire again in an instant.

'Scruples!' he repeated. '*Your* scruples! It is rather late in the day for you to be scrupulous. I should have thought you had got over all weakness of that sort, when you made a virtue of necessity by marrying *me*.'

The instant he spoke those words, Laura threw down the pen – looked at him with an expression in her eyes which, throughout all my experience of her, I had never seen in them before, and turned her back on him in dead silence.

This strong expression of the most open and the most bitter contempt was so entirely unlike herself, so utterly out of her character, that it silenced us all. There was something hidden, beyond a doubt, under the mere surface-brutality of the words which her husband had just addressed to her. There was some lurking insult beneath them, of which I was wholly ignorant, but which had left the mark of its profanation so plainly on her face that even a stranger might have seen it.

The Count, who was no stranger, saw it as distinctly as I did. When I left my chair to join Laura, I heard him whisper under his breath to Sir Percival, 'You idiot!'

Laura walked before me to the door as I advanced, and at the same time her husband spoke to her once more.

'You positively refuse, then, to give me your signature?' he said, in the altered tone of a man who was conscious that he had let his own licence of language seriously injure him.

'After what you have just said to me,' she replied firmly, 'I refuse my signature until I have read every line in that parchment from the first word to the last. Come away, Marian, we have remained here long enough.'

'One moment!' interposed the Count before Sir Percival could speak again—'one moment, Lady Glyde, I implore you!'

Laura would have left the room without noticing him, but I stopped her.

'Don't make an enemy of the Count!' I whispered. 'Whatever you do, don't make an enemy of the Count!'

She yielded to me. I closed the door again, and we stood near it waiting. Sir Percival sat down at the table, with his elbow on the folded parchment, and his head resting on his clenched fist. The Count stood between us – master of the dreadful position in which we were placed, as he was master of everything else.

'Lady Glyde,' he said, with a gentleness which seemed to address itself to our forlorn situation instead of to ourselves, 'pray pardon me if I venture to offer one suggestion, and pray believe that I speak out of my profound respect and my friendly regard for the mistress of this house.' He turned sharply towards Sir Percival. 'Is it absolutely necessary,' he asked 'that this thing here, under your elbow, should be signed today?'

'It is necessary to my plans and wishes,' returned the other sulkily. 'But that consideration, as you may have noticed, has no influence with Lady Glyde.'

'Answer my plain question plainly. Can the business of the signature be put off till tomorrow – Yes or No?'

'Yes, if you will have it so.'

'Then what are you wasting your time for here? Let the signature wait till tomorrow – let it wait till you come back.'

Sir Percival looked up with a frown and an oath.

'You are taking a tone with me that I don't like,' he said. 'A tone I won't bear from any man.'

'I am advising you for your good,' returned the Count, with a smile of quiet contempt. 'Give yourself time – give Lady Glyde time. Have you forgotten that your dog-cart is waiting at the door? My tone surprises you – ha? I dare say it does – it is the tone of a man who can keep his temper. How many doses of good advice have I given you in my time? More than you can count. Have I ever been wrong? I defy you to quote me an instance of it. Go! take your drive. The matter of the signature can wait till tomorrow. Let it wait – and renew it when you come back.'

Sir Percival hesitated and looked at his watch. His anxiety about the secret journey which he was to take that day, revived by the Count's words, was now evidently disputing possession of his mind with his anxiety to obtain Laura's signature. He considered for a little while, and then got up from his chair.

'It is easy to argue me down,' he said, 'when I have no time to answer you. I will take your advice, Fosco – not because I want it, or believe in it, but because I can't stop here any longer.' He paused, and looked round darkly at his wife. 'If you don't give me your signature when I come back tomorrow!' The rest was lost in the noise of his opening the book-case cupboard again, and locking up the parchment once more. He took his hat and gloves off the table, and made for the door. Laura and I drew back to let him pass. 'Remember tomorrow!' he said to his wife, and went out.

We waited to give him time to cross the hall and drive away. The Count approached us while we were standing near the door.

'You have just seen Percival at his worst, Miss Halcombe,' he said. 'As his old friend, I am sorry for him and ashamed of him. As his old friend, I promise you that he shall not break out tomorrow in the same disgraceful manner in which he has broken out today.'

Laura had taken my arm while he was speaking and she pressed it significantly when he had done. It would have been a hard trial to any woman to stand by and see the office of apologist for her husband's misconduct quietly assumed by his male friend in her own house – and it was a trial to *her*. I thanked the Count civilly, and let her out. Yes! I thanked him: for I felt already, with a sense of inexpressible helplessness and humiliation, that it was either his interest or his caprice to make sure of my continuing to reside at Blackwater Park, and I knew after Sir Percival's conduct to me, that without the support of the Count's influence, I could not hope to remain there. His influence, the influence of all others that I dreaded most, was actually the one tie which now held me to Laura in the hour of her utmost need!

We heard the wheels of the dog-cart crashing on the gravel of the drive as we came into the hall. Sir Percival had started on his journey.

'Where is he going to, Marian?' Laura whispered. 'Every fresh thing he does seems to terrify me about the future. Have you any suspicions?'

After what she had undergone that morning, I was unwilling to tell her my suspicions.

'How should I know his secrets?' I said evasively.

'I wonder if the housekeeper knows?' she persisted.

'Certainly not,' I replied. 'She must be quite as ignorant as we are.'

Laura shook her head doubtfully.

'Did you not hear from the housekeeper that there was a report of Anne Catherick having been seen in this neighbourhood? Don't you think he may have gone away to look for her?'

'I would rather compose myself, Laura, by not thinking about it at all, and after what has happened, you had better follow my example. Come into my room, and rest and quiet yourself a little.'

We sat down together close to the window, and let the fragrant summer air breathe over our faces.

'I am ashamed to look at you, Marian,' she said, 'after what you submitted to downstairs, for my sake. Oh, my own love, I am almost heartbroken when I think of it! But I will try to make it up to you – I will indeed!'

'Hush! hush!' I replied; 'don't talk so. What is the trifling mortification of my pride compared to the dreadful sacrifice of your happiness?'

'You heard what he said to me?' she went on quickly and vehemently. 'You heard the words – but you don't know what they meant – you don't know why I threw down the pen and turned my back on him.' She rose in sudden agitation, and walked about the room. 'I have kept many things from your knowledge, Marian, for fear of distressing you, and making you unhappy at the outset of our new lives. You don't know how he has used me. And yet you ought to know, for you saw how he used me today. You heard him sneer at my presuming to be scrupulous – you heard him say I had made a virtue of necessity in marrying him.' She sat down again, her face flushed deeply, and her hands twisted and twined together in her lap. 'I can't tell you about it now,' she said; 'I shall burst out crying if I tell you now – later, Marian, when I am more sure of myself. My poor head aches, darling – aches, aches, aches. Where is your smelling-bottle? Let me talk to you about yourself. I wish I had given him my signature, for your sake. Shall I give it to him tomorrow? I would rather compromise myself than compromise you. After your taking my part against him, he will lay all the blame on you if I refuse again. What shall we do? Oh, for a friend to help us and advise us! – a friend we could really trust!'

She sighed bitterly. I saw in her face that she was thinking of Hartright – saw it the more plainly because her last words set me thinking of him too. In six months only from her marriage we wanted the faithful service he had offered to us in his farewell words. How little I once thought that we should ever want it at all!

'We must do what we can to help ourselves,' I said. 'Let us try to talk it over calmly, Laura – let us do all in our power to decide for the best.'

Putting what she knew of her husband's embarrassments and what I had heard of his conversation with the lawyer together, we arrived necessarily at the conclusion that the parchment in the library had been drawn up for the purpose of borrowing money, and that Laura's signature was absolutely necessary to fit it for the attainment of Sir Percival's object.

The second question, concerning the nature of the legal contract by which the money was to be obtained, and the degree of personal responsibility to which Laura might subject herself if she signed it in the dark, involved considerations which lay far beyond any knowledge and experience that either of us possessed. My own convictions led me to believe that the hidden contents of the parchment concealed a transaction of the meanest and the most fraudulent kind.

I had not formed this conclusion in consequence of Sir Percival's refusal to show the writing or to explain it, for that refusal might well have proceeded from his obstinate disposition and his domineering temper alone. My sole motive for distrusting his honesty sprang from the change which I had observed in his language and his manners at Blackwater Park, a change which convinced me that he had been acting a part throughout the whole period of his probation at Limmeridge House. His elaborate delicacy, his ceremonious politeness which harmonised so agreeably with Mr Gilmore's old-fashioned notions, his modesty with Laura, his candour with me, his moderation with Mr Fairlie – all these were the artifices of a mean, cunning, and brutal man, who had dropped his disguise when his practised duplicity had gained its end, and had openly shown himself in the library on that very day. I say nothing of the grief which this discovery caused me on Laura's account, for it is not to be expressed by any words of mine. I only refer to it at all, because it decided me to oppose her signing the parchment, whatever the consequences might be, unless she was first made acquainted with the contents.

Under these circumstances, the one chance for us when tomorrow came was to be provided with an objection to giving the signature, which might rest on sufficiently firm commercial or legal grounds to shake Sir Percival's resolution, and to make him suspect that we two women understood the laws and obligations of business as well as himself.

After some pondering, I determined to write to the only honest man within reach whom we could trust to help us discreetly in our forlorn situation. That man was Mr Gilmore's partner, Mr Kyrle, who conducted the business now that our old friend had been obliged to withdraw from it, and to leave London on account of his health. I explained to Laura that I had Mr Gilmore's own authority for placing implicit confidence in his partner's integrity, discretion, and accurate knowledge of all her affairs, and with her full approval I sat down at once to write the letter.

I began by stating our position to Mr Kyrle exactly as it was, and then asked for his advice in return, expressed in plain, downright terms which he could comprehend without any danger of misinterpretations and mistakes. My letter was as short as I could possibly make it, and was, I hope, unencumbered by needless apologies and needless details.

Just as I was about to put the address on the envelope an obstacle was discovered by Laura, which in the effort and preoccupation of writing had escaped my mind altogether.

'How are we to get the answer in time?' she asked. 'Your letter will not be delivered in London before tomorrow morning, and the post will not bring the reply here till the morning after.'

The only way of overcoming this difficulty was to have the answer brought to us from the lawyer's office by a special messenger. I wrote a postscript to that effect, begging that the messenger might be despatched with the reply by the eleven o'clock morning train, which would bring him to our station at twenty minutes past one, and so enable him to reach Blackwater Park by two o'clock at the latest. He was to be directed to ask for me, to answer no questions addressed to him by any one else, and to deliver his letter into no hands but mine.

'In case Sir Percival should come back tomorrow before two o'clock,' I said to Laura, 'the wisest plan for you to adopt is to be out in the grounds all the morning with your book or your work, and not to appear at the house till the messenger has had time to arrive with the letter. I will wait here for him all the morning, to guard against any misadventures or mistakes. By following this arrangement I hope and believe we shall avoid being taken by surprise. Let us go down to the drawing-room now. We may excite suspicion if we remain shut up together too long.'

'Suspicion?' she repeated. 'Whose suspicion can we excite, now that Sir Percival has left the house? Do you mean Count Fosco?'

'Perhaps I do, Laura.'

'You are beginning to dislike him as much as I do, Marian.'

'No, not to dislike him. Dislike is always more or less associated with contempt – I can see nothing in the Count to despise.'

'You are not afraid of him, are you?'

'Perhaps I am – a little.'

'Afraid of him, after his interference in our favour today!'

'Yes. I am more afraid of his interference than I am of Sir Percival's violence. Remember what I said to you in the library. Whatever you do, Laura, don't make an enemy of the Count!'

We went downstairs. Laura entered the drawing-room, while I proceeded across the hall, with my letter in my hand, to put it into the post-bag, which hung against the wall opposite to me.

The house door was open, and as I crossed past it, I saw Count Fosco and his wife standing talking together on the steps outside, with their faces turned towards me.

The Countess came into the hall rather hastily, and asked if I had leisure enough for five minutes' private conversation. Feeling a little surprised by such an appeal from such a person, I put my letter into the bag, and replied that I was quite at her disposal. She took my arm with unaccustomed friendliness and familiarity, and instead of leading me into an empty room, drew me out with her to the belt of turf which surrounded the large fish-pond.

As we passed the Count on the steps he bowed and smiled, and then went at once into the house, pushing the hall door to after him, but not actually closing it.

The Countess walked me gently round the fish-pond. I expected to be made the depositary of some extraordinary confidence, and I was astonished to find that Madame Fosco's communication for my private ear was nothing more than a polite assurance of her sympathy for me, after what had happened in the library. Her husband had told her of all that had passed, and of the insolent manner in which Sir Percival had spoken to me. This information had so shocked and distressed her, on my account and on Laura's, that she had made up her mind, if anything of the sort happened again, to mark her sense of Sir Percival's outrageous conduct by leaving the house. The Count had approved of her idea, and she now hoped that I approved of it too.

I thought this a very strange proceeding on the part of such a remarkably reserved woman as Madame Fosco, especially after the interchange of sharp speeches which had passed between us during the conversation in the boat-house on that very morning. However, it was my plain duty to meet a polite and friendly advance on the part of one of my elders with a polite and friendly reply. I answered the Countess accordingly in her own tone, and then, thinking we had said all that was necessary on either side, made an attempt to get back to the house.

But Madame Fosco seemed resolved not to part with me, and to my unspeakable amazement, resolved also to talk. Hitherto the most silent of women, she now persecuted me with fluent conventionalities on the subject of married life, on the subject of Sir Percival and Laura, on the subject of her own happiness, on the subject of the late Mr Fairlie's conduct to her in the matter of her legacy, and on half a dozen other subjects besides, until she had detained me walking round and round the fish-pond for more than half an hour, and had quite wearied me out. Whether she discovered this or not, I cannot say, but she stopped as abruptly as she had begun – looked towards the house door, resumed her icy manner in a moment, and dropped my arm of her own accord before I could think of an excuse for accomplishing my own release from her.

As I pushed open the door and entered the hall, I found myself suddenly face to face with the Count again. He was just putting a letter into the post-bag.

After he had dropped it in and had closed the bag, he asked me where I had left Madame Fosco. I told him, and he went out at the hall door immediately to join his wife. His manner when he spoke to me was so unusually quiet and subdued that I turned and looked after him, wondering if he were ill or out of spirits.

Why my next proceeding was to go straight up to the post-bag and take out my own letter and look at it again, with a vague distrust on me, and why the looking at it for the second time instantly suggested the idea to my mind of sealing the envelope for its greater security – are mysteries which are either too deep or too shallow for me to fathom. Women, as everybody knows, constantly act on impulses which they cannot explain even to themselves, and I can only suppose that one of those impulses was the hidden cause of my unaccountable conduct on this occasion.

Whatever influence animated me, I found cause to congratulate myself on having obeyed it as soon as I prepared to seal the letter in my own room. I had originally closed the envelope in the usual way by moistening the adhesive point and pressing it on the paper beneath, and when I now tried it with my finger, after a lapse of full three-quarters of an hour, the envelope opened on the instant, without sticking or tearing. Perhaps I had fastened it insufficiently? Perhaps there might have been some defect in the adhesive gum?

Or, perhaps – No! it is quite revolting enough to feel that third conjecture stirring in my mind. I would rather not see it confronting me in plain black and white.

I almost dread tomorrow – so much depends on my discretion and self-control. There are two precautions, at all events, which I am sure not to forget. I must be careful to keep up friendly appearances with the Count, and I must be well on my guard when the messenger from the office comes here with the answer to my letter.

V

JUNE 17TH – When the dinner hour brought us together again, Count Fosco was in his usual excellent spirits. He exerted himself to interest and amuse us, as if he was determined to efface from our memories all recollection of what had passed in the library that afternoon. Lively descriptions of his adventures in travelling, amusing anecdotes of remarkable people whom he had met with abroad, quaint comparisons between the social customs of various nations, illustrated by examples drawn from men and women indiscriminately all over Europe, humorous confessions of the innocent follies of his own early life, when he ruled the fashions of a second-rate Italian town, and wrote preposterous romances on the French model for a second-rate Italian newspaper – all flowed in succession so easily and so gaily from his lips, and all addressed our various curiosities and various interests so directly and so delicately, that Laura and I listened to him with as much attention and, inconsistent as it may seem, with as much admiration also, as Madame Fosco herself. Women can resist a man's love, a man's fame, a man's personal appearance, and a man's money, but they cannot resist a man's tongue when he knows how to talk to them.

After dinner, while the favourable impression which he had produced on us was still vivid in our minds, the Count modestly withdrew to read in the library.

Laura proposed a stroll in the grounds to enjoy the close of the long evening. It was necessary in common politeness to ask Madame Fosco to join us, but this time she had apparently received her orders beforehand, and she begged we would kindly excuse her. 'The Count will probably want a fresh supply of cigarettes,' she remarked by way of apology, 'and nobody can make them to his satisfaction but myself.' Her cold blue eyes almost warmed as she spoke the words – she looked actually proud of being the officiating medium through which her lord and master composed himself with tobacco-smoke!

Laura and I went out together alone.

It was a misty, heavy evening. There was a sense of blight in the air; the flowers were drooping in the garden, and the ground was parched and dewless. The western heaven, as we saw it over the quiet trees, was of a pale yellow hue, and the sun was setting faintly in a haze. Coming rain seemed near – it would fall probably with the fall of night.

'Which way shall we go?' I asked.

'Towards the lake, Marian, if you like,' she answered.

'You seem unaccountably fond, Laura, of that dismal lake.'

'No, not of the lake but of the scenery about it. The sand and heath and the fir-trees are the only objects I can discover, in all this large place, to remind me of Limmeridge. But we will walk in some other direction if you prefer it.'

'I have no favourite walks at Blackwater Park, my love. One is the same as another to me. Let us go to the lake – we may find it cooler in the open space than we find it here.'

We walked through the shadowy plantation in silence. The heaviness in the evening air oppressed us both, and when we reached the boathouse we were glad to sit down and rest inside.

A white fog hung low over the lake. The dense brown line of the trees on the opposite bank appeared above it, like a dwarf forest floating in the sky. The sandy ground, shelving downward from where we sat, was lost mysteriously in the outward layers of the fog. The silence was horrible. No rustling of the leaves – no bird's note in the wood – no cry of water-fowl from the pools of the hidden lake. Even the croaking of the frogs had ceased tonight.

'It is very desolate and gloomy,' said Laura. 'But we can be more alone here than anywhere else.'

She spoke quietly and looked at the wilderness of sand and mist with steady, thoughtful eyes. I could see that her mind was too much occupied to feel the dreary impressions from without which had fastened themselves already on mine.

'I promised, Marian, to tell you the truth about my married life, instead of leaving you any longer to guess it for yourself,' she began. 'That secret is the first I have ever had from you, love, and I am determined it shall be the last. I was silent, as you know, for your sake – and perhaps a little for my own sake as well. It is very hard for a woman to confess that the man to whom she has given her whole life is the man of all others who cares least for the gift. If you were married yourself, Marian – and especially if you were happily married – you would feel for me as no single woman *can* feel, however kind and true she may be.'

What answer could I make? I could only take her hand and look at her with my whole heart as well as my eyes would let me.

'How often,' she went on, 'I have heard you laughing over what you used to call your "poverty!" how often you have made me mock-speeches of congratulation on my wealth! Oh, Marian, never laugh again. Thank God for your poverty – it has made you your own mistress, and has saved you from the lot that has fallen on *me*.'

A sad beginning on the lips of a young wife! – sad in its quiet plain-spoken truth. The few days we had all passed together at Blackwater Park had been many enough to show me – to show any one – what her husband had married her for.

'You shall not be distressed,' she said, 'by hearing how soon my disappointments and my trials began – or even by knowing what they were. It is bad enough to have them on *my* memory. If I tell you how he received the first and last attempt at remonstrance that I ever made, you will know how he has always treated me, as well as if I had described it in so many words. It was one day at Rome when we had ridden out together to the tomb of Cecilia Metella. The sky was calm and lovely, and the grand old ruin looked beautiful, and the remembrance that a husband's love had raised it in the old time to a wife's memory, made me feel more tenderly and more anxiously towards my husband than I had ever felt yet. "Would you build such a tomb for *me*, Percival?" I asked him. "You said you loved me dearly before we were married, and yet, since that time—" I could get no farther. Marian! he was not even looking at me! I pulled down my veil, thinking it best not to let him see that the tears were in my eyes. I fancied he had not paid any attention to me, but he had. He said, "Come away," and laughed to himself as he helped me on to my horse. He mounted his own horse and laughed again as we rode away. "If I do build you a tomb," he said, "it will be done with your own money. I wonder whether Cecilia Metella had a fortune and paid for hers." I made no reply – how could I, when I was crying behind my veil? "Ah, you light-complexioned women are all sulky," he said. "What do you want? compliments and soft speeches? Well! I'm in a good humour this morning. Consider the compliments paid and the speeches said." Men little know when they say hard things to us how well we remember them, and how much harm they do us. It would have been better for me if I had gone on crying, but his contempt dried up my tears and hardened my heart. From that time, Marian, I never checked myself again in thinking of Walter Hartright. I let the memory of those happy days, when we were so fond of each other in secret, come back and comfort me. What else had I to look to for consolation? If we had been together you would have helped me to better things. I know it was wrong, darling, but tell me if I was wrong without any excuse.'

I was obliged to turn my face from her. 'Don't ask me!' I said. 'Have I suffered as you have suffered? What right have I to decide?'

'I used to think of him,' she pursued, dropping her voice and moving closer to me, 'I used to think of him when Percival left me alone at night to go among the Opera people. I used to fancy what I might have been if it had pleased God to bless me with poverty, and if I had been his wife. I used to see myself in my neat cheap gown, sitting at home and waiting for him while he was earning our bread – sitting at home and working for him and loving him all the better because I *had* to work for him – seeing him come in tired and taking off his hat and coat for him, and, Marian, pleasing him with little dishes at dinner that I had learnt to make for his sake. Oh! I hope he is never lonely enough and sad enough to think of me and see me as I have thought of *him* and see *him*!'

As she said those melancholy words, all the lost tenderness returned to her voice, and all the lost beauty trembled back into her face. Her eyes rested as lovingly on the blighted, solitary, ill-omened view before us, as if they saw the friendly hills of Cumberland in the dim and threatening sky.

'Don't speak of Walter any more,' I said, as soon as I could control myself. 'Oh, Laura, spare us both the wretchedness of talking of him now!'

She roused herself, and looked at me tenderly.

'I would rather be silent about him for ever,' she answered, 'than cause you a moment's pain.'

'It is in your interests,' I pleaded; 'it is for your sake that I speak. If your husband heard you—'

'It would not surprise him if he did hear me.'

She made that strange reply with a weary calmness and coldness. The change in her manner, when she gave the answer, startled me almost as much as the answer itself.

'Not surprise him!' I repeated. 'Laura! remember what you are saying – you frighten me!'

'It is true,' she said; 'it is what I wanted to tell you today, when we were talking in your room. My only secret when I opened my heart to him at Limmeridge was a harmless secret, Marian – you said so yourself. The name was all I kept from him, and he has discovered it.'

I heard her, but I could say nothing. Her last words had killed the little hope that still lived in me.

'It happened at Rome,' she went on, as wearily calm and cold as ever. 'We were at a little party given to the English by some friends of Sir Percival's – Mr and Mrs Markland. Mrs Markland had the reputation of sketching very beautifully, and some of the guests prevailed on her to show us her drawings. We all admired them, but something I said attracted her attention particularly to me. "Surely you draw yourself?" she asked. "I used to draw a little once," I answered, "but I have given it up." "If you have once drawn," she said, "you may take to it again one of these days, and if you do, I wish you would let me recommend you a master." I said nothing – you know why, Marian – and tried to change the conversation. But Mrs Markland persisted. "I have had all sorts of teachers," she went on, "but the best of all, the most intelligent and the most attentive, was a Mr Hartright. If you ever take up your drawing again, do try him as a master. He is a young man – modest and gentlemanlike – I am sure you will like him." Think of those words being spoken to me publicly, in the presence of strangers – strangers who had been invited to meet the bride and bridegroom! I did all I could to control myself – I said nothing, and looked down close at the drawings. When I ventured to raise my head again, my eyes and my husband's eyes met, and I knew, by his look, that my face had betrayed me. "We will see about Mr Hartright," he said, looking at me all the time, "when we get back to England. I agree with you, Mrs Markland – I think Lady Glyde is sure to like him." He laid an emphasis on the last words which made my cheeks burn, and set my heart beating as if it would stifle me. Nothing more was said. We came away early. He was silent in the carriage driving back to the hotel. He helped me out, and followed me upstairs as usual. But the moment we were in the drawing-room, he locked the door, pushed me down into a chair, and stood over me with his hands on my shoulders. "Ever since that morning when you made your audacious confession to me at Limmeridge," he said, "I have wanted to find out the man, and I found him in your face tonight. Your drawing-master was the man, and his name is Hartright. You shall repent it, and he shall repent it, to the last hour of your lives. Now go to bed and dream of him if you like, with the marks of my horsewhip on his shoulders." Whenever he is angry with me now he refers to what I acknowledged to him in your presence with a sneer or a threat. I have no power to prevent him from putting his own horrible construction on the confidence I placed in him. I have no influence to make him believe me, or to keep him silent. You looked surprised today when you heard him tell me that I had made a virtue of necessity in marrying him. You will not be surprised again when you hear him repeat it, the next time he is out of temper – Oh, Marian! don't! don't! you hurt me!'

I had caught her in my arms, and the sting and torment of my remorse had closed them round her like a vice. Yes! my remorse. The white despair of Walter's face, when my cruel words struck him to the heart in the summer-house at Limmeridge, rose before me in mute, unendurable reproach. My hand had pointed the way which led the man my sister loved, step by step, far from his country and his friends. Between those two young hearts I had stood, to sunder them for ever, the one from the other, and his life and her life lay wasted before me alike in witness of the deed. I had done this, and done it for Sir Percival Glyde.

For Sir Percival Glyde.

*   *   *

I heard her speaking, and I knew by the tone of her voice that she was comforting me – I, who deserved nothing but the reproach of her silence! How long it was before I mastered the absorbing misery of my own thoughts, I cannot tell. I was first conscious that she was kissing me, and then my eyes seemed to wake on a sudden to their sense of outward things, and I knew that I was looking mechanically straight before me at the prospect of the lake.

'It is late,' I heard her whisper. 'It will be dark in the plantation.' She shook my arm and repeated, 'Marian! it will be dark in the plantation.'

'Give me a minute longer,' I said – 'a minute, to get better in.'

I was afraid to trust myself to look at her yet, and I kept my eyes fixed on the view.

It *was* late. The dense brown line of trees in the sky had faded in the gathering darkness to the faint resemblance of a long wreath of smoke. The mist over the lake below had stealthily enlarged, and advanced on us. The silence was as breathless as ever, but the horror of it had gone, and the solemn mystery of its stillness was all that remained.

'We are far from the house,' she whispered. 'Let us go back.'

She stopped suddenly, and turned her face from me towards the entrance of the boathouse.

'Marian!' she said, trembling violently. 'Do you see nothing? Look!'

'Where?'

'Down there, below us.'

She pointed. My eyes followed her hand, and I saw it too.

A living figure was moving over the waste of heath in the distance. It crossed our range of view from the boathouse, and passed darkly along the outer edge of the mist. It stopped far off, in front of us – waited – and passed on; moving slowly, with the white cloud of mist behind it and above it – slowly, slowly, till it glided by the edge of the boathouse, and we saw it no more.

We were both unnerved by what had passed between us that evening. Some minutes elapsed before Laura would venture into the plantation, and before I could make up my mind to lead her back to the house.

'Was it a man or a woman?' she asked in a whisper, as we moved at last into the dark dampness of the outer air.

'I am not certain.'

'Which do you think?'

'It looked like a woman.'

'I was afraid it was a man in a long cloak.'

'It may be a man. In this dim light it is not possible to be certain.'

'Wait, Marian! I'm frightened – I don't see the path. Suppose the figure should follow us?'

'Not at all likely, Laura. There is really nothing to be alarmed about. The shores of the lake are not far from the village, and they are free to any one to walk on by day or night. It is only wonderful we have seen no living creature there before.'

We were now in the plantation. It was very dark – so dark, that we found some difficulty in keeping the path. I gave Laura my arm, and we walked as fast as we could on our way back.

Before we were half-way through she stopped, and forced me to stop with her. She was listening.

'Hush,' she whispered. 'I hear something behind us.'

'Dead leaves,' I said to cheer her, 'or a twig blown off the trees.'

'It is summer time, Marian, and there is not a breath of wind. Listen!'

I heard the sound too – a sound like a light footstep following us.

'No matter who it is, or what it is,' I said, 'let us walk on. In another minute, if there is anything to alarm us, we shall be near enough to the house to be heard.'

We went on quickly – so quickly, that Laura was breathless by the time we were nearly through the plantation, and within sight of the lighted windows.

I waited a moment to give her breathing-time. Just as we were about to proceed she stopped me again, and signed to me with her hand to listen once more. We both heard distinctly a long, heavy sigh behind us, in the black depths of the trees.

'Who's there?' I called out.

There was no answer.

'Who's there?' I repeated.

An instant of silence followed, and then we heard the light fall of the footsteps again, fainter and fainter – sinking away into the darkness – sinking, sinking, sinking – till they were lost in the silence.

We hurried out from the trees to the open lawn beyond, crossed it rapidly, and without another word passing between us, reached the house.

In the light of the hall-lamp Laura looked at me, with white cheeks and startled eyes.

'I am half dead with fear,' she said. 'Who could it have been?'

'We will try to guess tomorrow,' I replied. 'In the meantime say nothing to any one of what we have heard and seen.'

'Why not?'

'Because silence is safe, and we have need of safety in this house.'

I sent Laura upstairs immediately, waited a minute to take off my hat and put my hair smooth, and then went at once to make my first investigations in the library, on pretence of searching for a book.

There sat the Count, filling out the largest easy-chair in the house, smoking and reading calmly, with his feet on an ottoman, his cravat across his knees, and his shirt collar wide open. And there sat Madame Fosco, like a quiet child, on a stool by his side, making cigarettes. Neither husband nor wife could, by any possibility, have been out late that evening, and have just got back to the house in a hurry. I felt that my object in visiting the library was answered the moment I set eyes on them.

Count Fosco rose in polite confusion and tied his cravat on when I entered the room.

'Pray don't let me disturb you,' I said. 'I have only come here to get a book.'

'All unfortunate men of my size suffer from the heat,' said the Count, refreshing himself gravely with a large green fan. 'I wish I could change places with my excellent wife. She is as cool at this moment as a fish in the pond outside.'

The Countess allowed herself to thaw under the influence of her husband's quaint comparison. 'I am never warm, Miss Halcombe,' she remarked, with the modest air of a woman who was confessing to one of her own merits.

'Have you and Lady Glyde been out this evening?' asked the Count, while I was taking a book from the shelves to preserve appearances.

'Yes, we went out to get a little air.'

'May I ask in what direction?'

'In the direction of the lake – as far as the boathouse.'

'Aha? As far as the boathouse?'

Under other circumstances I might have resented his curiosity. But tonight I hailed it as another proof that neither he nor his wife were connected with the mysterious appearance at the lake.

'No more adventures, I suppose, this evening?' he went on. 'No more discoveries, like your discovery of the wounded dog?'

He fixed his unfathomable grey eyes on me, with that cold, clear, irresistible glitter in them which always forces me to look at him, and always makes me uneasy while I do look. An unutterable suspicion that his mind is prying into mine overcomes me at these times, and it overcame me now.

'No,' I said shortly; 'no adventures – no discoveries.'

I tried to look away from him and leave the room. Strange as it seems, I hardly think I should have succeeded in the attempt if Madame Fosco had not helped me by causing him to move and look away first.

'Count, you are keeping Miss Halcombe standing,' she said.

The moment he turned round to get me a chair, I seized my opportunity – thanked him – made my excuses – and slipped out.

An hour later, when Laura's maid happened to be in her mistress's room,

I took occasion to refer to the closeness of the night, with a view to ascertaining next how the servants had been passing their time.

'Have you been suffering much from the heat downstairs?' I asked.

'No, miss,' said the girl, 'we have not felt it to speak of.'

'You have been out in the woods then, I suppose?'

'Some of us thought of going, miss. But cook said she should take her chair into the cool court-yard, outside the kitchen door, and on second thoughts, all the rest of us took our chairs out there too.'

The housekeeper was now the only person who remained to be accounted for.

'Is Mrs Michelson gone to bed yet?' I inquired.

'I should think not, miss,' said the girl, smiling. 'Mrs Michelson is more likely to be getting up just now than going to bed.'

'Why? What do you mean? Has Mrs Michelson been taking to her bed in the daytime?'

'No, miss, not exactly, but the next thing to it. She's been asleep all the evening on the sofa in her own room.'

Putting together what I observed for myself in the library, and what I have just heard from Laura's maid, one conclusion seems inevitable. The figure we saw at the lake was not the figure of Madame Fosco, of her husband, or of any of the servants. The footsteps we heard behind us were not the footsteps of any one belonging to the house.

Who could it have been?

It seems useless to inquire. I cannot even decide whether the figure was a man's or a woman's. I can only say that I think it was a woman's.

VI

JUNE 18TH – The misery of self-reproach which I suffered yesterday evening, on hearing what Laura told me in the boathouse, returned in the loneliness of the night, and kept me waking and wretched for hours.

I lighted my candle at last, and searched through my old journals to see what my share in the fatal error of her marriage had really been, and what I might have once done to save her from it. The result soothed me a little for it showed that, however blindly and ignorantly I acted, I acted for the best. Crying generally does me harm; but it was not so last night – I think it relieved me. I rose this morning with a settled resolution and a quiet mind. Nothing Sir Percival can say or do shall ever irritate me again, or make me forget for one moment that I am staying here in defiance of mortifications, insults, and threats, for Laura's service and for Laura's sake.

The speculations in which we might have indulged this morning, on the subject of the figure at the lake and the footsteps in the plantation, have been all suspended by a trifling accident which has caused Laura great regret. She has lost the little brooch I gave her for a keepsake on the day before her marriage. As she wore it when we went out yesterday evening we can only suppose that it must have dropped from her dress, either in the boathouse or on our way back. The servants have been sent to search, and have returned unsuccessful. And now Laura herself has gone to look for it. Whether she finds it or not the loss will help to excuse her absence from the house, if Sir Percival returns before the letter from Mr Gilmore's partner is placed in my hands.

One o'clock has just struck. I am considering whether I had better wait here for the arrival of the messenger from London, or slip away quietly, and watch for him outside the lodge gate.

My suspicion of everybody and everything in this house inclines me to think that the second plan may be the best. The Count is safe in the breakfast-room. I heard him, through the door, as I ran upstairs ten minutes since, exercising his canary-birds at their tricks:—'Come out on my little finger, my pret-pret-pretties! Come out, and hop upstairs! One, two, three – and up! Three, two, one – and down! One, two, three – twit-twit-twit-tweet!' The birds burst into their usual ecstasy of singing, and the Count chirruped and whistled at them in return, as if he was a bird himself. My room door is open, and I can hear the shrill singing and whistling at this very moment. If I am really to slip out without being observed, now is my time.

Four o'clock. The three hours that have passed since I made my last entry have turned the whole march of events at Blackwater Park in a new direction. Whether for good or for evil, I cannot and dare not decide.

Let me get back first to the place at which I left off, or I shall lose myself in the confusion of my own thoughts.

I went out, as I had proposed, to meet the messenger with my letter from London at the lodge gate. On the stairs I saw no one. In the hall I heard the Count still exercising his birds. But on crossing the quadrangle outside, I passed Madame Fosco, walking by herself in her favourite circle, round and round the great fish-pond. I at once slackened my pace, so as to avoid all appearance of being in a hurry, and even went the length, for caution's sake, of inquiring if she thought of going out before lunch. She smiled at me in the friendliest manner – said she preferred remaining near the house, nodded pleasantly, and re-entered the hall. I looked back, and saw that she had closed the door before I had opened the wicket by the side of the carriage gates.

In less than a quarter of an hour I reached the lodge.

The lane outside took a sudden turn to the left, ran on straight for a hundred yards or so, and then took another sharp turn to the right to join the high-road. Between these two turns, hidden from the lodge on one side, and from the way to the station on the other, I waited, walking backwards and forwards. High hedges were on either side of me, and for twenty minutes, by my watch, I neither saw nor heard anything. At the end of that time the sound of a carriage caught my ear, and I was met, as I advanced towards the second turning, by a fly from the railway. I made a sign to the driver to stop. As he obeyed me a respectable-looking man put his head out of the window to see what was the matter.

'I beg your pardon,' I said, 'but am I right in supposing that you are going to Blackwater Park?'

'Yes, ma'am.'

'With a letter for any one?'

'With a letter for Miss Halcombe, ma'am.'

'You may give me the letter. I am Miss Halcombe.'

The man touched his hat, got out of the fly immediately, and gave me the letter.

I opened it at once and read these lines. I copy them here, thinking it best to destroy the original for caution's sake.

DEAR MADAM, – Your letter received this morning has caused me very great anxiety. I will reply to it as briefly and plainly as possible.

My careful consideration of the statement made by yourself, and my knowledge of Lady Glyde's position, as defined in the settlement, lead me, I regret to say, to the conclusion that a loan of the trust money to Sir Percival (or, in other words, a loan of some portion of the twenty thousand pounds of Lady Glyde's fortune) is in contemplation, and that she is made a party to the deed, in order to secure her approval of a flagrant breach of trust, and to have her signature produced against her if she should complain hereafter. It is impossible, on any other supposition, to account, situated as she is, for her execution to a deed of any kind being wanted at all.

In the event of Lady Glyde's signing such a document, as I am compelled to suppose the deed in question to be, her trustees would be at liberty to advance money to Sir Percival out of her twenty thousand pounds. If the amount so lent should not be paid back, and if Lady Glyde should have children, their fortune will then be diminished by the sum, large or small, so advanced. In plainer terms still, the transaction, for anything that Lady Glyde knows to the contrary, may be a fraud upon her unborn children.

Under these serious circumstances, I would recommend Lady Glyde to assign as a reason for withholding her signature, that she wishes the deed to be first submitted to myself, as her family solicitor (in the absence of my partner, Mr Gilmore). No reasonable objection can be made to taking this course – for, if the transaction is an honourable one, there will necessarily be no difficulty in my giving my approval.

Sincerely assuring you of my readiness to afford any additional help or advice that may be wanted, I beg to remain, Madam, your faithful servant,

WILLIAM KYRLE.

I read this kind and sensible letter very thankfully. It supplied Laura with a reason for objecting to the signature which was unanswerable, and which we could both of us understand. The messenger waited near me while I was reading to receive his directions when I had done.

'Will you be good enough to say that I understand the letter, and that I am very much obliged?' I said. 'There is no other reply necessary at present.'

Exactly at the moment when I was speaking those words, holding the letter open in my hand, Count Fosco turned the corner of the lane from the high-road, and stood before me as if he had sprung up out of the earth.

The suddenness of his appearance, in the very last place under heaven in which I should have expected to see him, took me completely by surprise. The messenger wished me good-morning, and got into the fly again. I could not say a word to him – I was not even able to return his bow. The conviction that I was discovered – and by that man, of all others – absolutely petrified me.

'Are you going back to the house, Miss Halcombe?' he inquired, without showing the least surprise on his side, and without even looking after the fly, which drove off while he was speaking to me.

I collected myself sufficiently to make a sign in the affirmative.

'I am going back too,' he said. 'Pray allow me the pleasure of accompanying you. Will you take my arm? You look surprised at seeing me!'

I took his arm. The first of my scattered senses that came back was the sense that warned me to sacrifice anything rather than make an enemy of him.

'You look surprised at seeing me!' he repeated in his quietly pertinacious way.

'I thought, Count, I heard you with your birds in the breakfast-room,' I answered, as quietly and firmly as I could.

'Surely. But my little feathered children, dear lady, are only too like other children. They have their days of perversity, and this morning was one of them.

My wife came in as I was putting them back in their cage, and said she had left you going out alone for a walk. You told her so, did you not?'

'Certainly.'

'Well, Miss Halcombe, the pleasure of accompanying you was too great a temptation for me to resist. At my age there is no harm in confessing so much as that, is there? I seized my hat, and set off to offer myself as your escort. Even so fat an old man as Fosco is surely better than no escort at all? I took the wrong path – I came back in despair, and here I am, arrived (may I say it?) at the height of my wishes.'

He talked on in this complimentary strain with a fluency which left me no exertion to make beyond the effort of maintaining my composure. He never referred in the most distant manner to what he had seen in the lane, or to the letter which I still had in my hand. This ominous discretion helped to convince me that he must have surprised, by the most dishonourable means, the secret of my application in Laura's interest to the lawyer; and that, having now assured himself of the private manner in which I had received the answer, he had discovered enough to suit his purposes, and was only bent on trying to quiet the suspicions which he knew he must have aroused in my mind. I was wise enough, under these circumstances, not to attempt to deceive him by plausible explanations, and woman enough, notwithstanding my dread of him, to feel as if my hand was tainted by resting on his arm.

On the drive in front of the house we met the dog-cart being taken round to the stables. Sir Percival had just returned. He came out to meet us at the house-door. Whatever other results his journey might have had, it had not ended in softening his savage temper.

'Oh! here are two of you come back,' he said, with a lowering face. 'What is the meaning of the house being deserted in this way? Where is Lady Glyde?'

I told him of the loss of the brooch, and said that Laura had gone into the plantation to look for it.

'Brooch or no brooch,' he growled sulkily, 'I recommend her not to forget her appointment in the library this afternoon. I shall expect to see her in half an hour.'

I took my hand from the Count's arm, and slowly ascended the steps. He honoured me with one of his magnificent bows, and then addressed himself gaily to the scowling master of the house.

'Tell me, Percival,' he said, 'have you had a pleasant drive? And has your pretty shining Brown Molly come back at all tired?'

'Brown Molly be hanged – and the drive too! I want my lunch.'

'And I want five minutes' talk with you, Percival, first,' returned the Count. 'Five minutes' talk, my friend, here on the grass.'

'What about?'

'About business that very much concerns you.'

I lingered long enough in passing through the hall-door to hear this question and answer, and to see Sir Percival thrust his hands into his pockets in sullen hesitation.

'If you want to badger me with any more of your infernal scruples,' he said, 'I for one won't hear them. I want my lunch.'

'Come out here and speak to me,' repeated the Count, still perfectly uninfluenced by the rudest speech that his friend could make to him.

Sir Percival descended the steps. The Count took him by the arm, and walked him away gently. The 'business,' I was sure, referred to the question of the signature. They were speaking of Laura and of me beyond a doubt. I felt heart-sick and faint with anxiety. It might be of the last importance to both of us to know what they were saying to each other at that moment, and not one word of it could by any possibility reach my ears.

I walked about the house, from room to room, with the lawyer's letter in my bosom (I was afraid by this time even to trust it under lock and key), till the oppression of my suspense half maddened me. There were no signs of Laura's return, and I thought of going out to look for her. But my strength was so exhausted by the trials and anxieties of the morning that the heat of the day quite overpowered me, and after an attempt to get to the door I was obliged to return to the drawing-room and lie down on the nearest sofa to recover.

I was just composing myself when the door opened softly and the Count looked in.

'A thousand pardons, Miss Halcombe,' he said; 'I only venture to disturb you because I am the bearer of good news. Percival – who is capricious in everything, as you know – has seen fit to alter his mind at the last moment, and the business of the signature is put off for the present. A great relief to all of us, Miss Halcombe, as I see with pleasure in your face. Pray present my best respects and felicitations, when you mention this pleasant change of circumstances to Lady Glyde.'

He left me before I had recovered my astonishment. There could be no doubt that this extraordinary alteration of purpose in the matter of the signature was due to his influence, and that his discovery of my application to London yesterday, and of my having received an answer to it today, had offered him the means of interfering with certain success.

I felt these impressions, but my mind seemed to share the exhaustion of my body, and I was in no condition to dwell on them with any useful reference to the doubtful present or the threatening future. I tried a second time to run out and find Laura, but my head was giddy and my knees trembled under me. There was no choice but to give it up again and return to the sofa, sorely against my will.

The quiet in the house, and the low murmuring hum of summer insects outside the open window, soothed me. My eyes closed of themselves, and I passed gradually into a strange condition, which was not waking – for I knew nothing of what was going on about me, and not sleeping – for I was conscious of my own repose. In this state my fevered mind broke loose from me, while my weary body was at rest, and in a trance, or day-dream of my fancy – I know not what to call it – I saw Walter Hartright. I had not thought of him since I rose that morning – Laura had not said one word to me either directly or indirectly referring to him – and yet I saw him now as plainly as if the past time had returned, and we were both together again at Limmeridge House.

He appeared to me as one among many other men, none of whose faces I could plainly discern. They were all lying on the steps of an immense ruined temple. Colossal tropical trees – with rank creepers twining endlessly about their trunks, and hideous stone idols glimmering and grinning at intervals behind leaves and stalks and branches – surrounded the temple and shut out the sky, and threw a dismal shadow over the forlorn band of men on the steps. White exhalations twisted and curled up stealthily from the ground, approached the men in wreaths like smoke, touched them, and stretched them out dead, one by one, in the places where they lay. An agony of pity and fear for Walter loosened my tongue, and I implored him to escape. 'Come back, come back!' I said. 'Remember your promise to *her* and to *me*. Come back to us before the Pestilence reaches you and lays you dead like the rest!'

He looked at me with an unearthly quiet in his face. 'Wait,' he said, 'I shall come back. The night when I met the lost Woman on the highway was the night which set my life apart to be the instrument of a Design that is yet unseen. Here, lost in the wilderness, or there, welcomed back in the land of my birth, I am still walking on the dark road which leads me, and you, and the sister of your love and mine, to the unknown Retribution and the inevitable End. Wait and look. The Pestilence which touches the rest will pass *me*.'

I saw him again. He was still in the forest, and the numbers of his lost companions had dwindled to very few. The temple was gone, and the idols were gone – and in their place the figures of dark, dwarfish men lurked murderously among the trees, with bows in their hands, and arrows fitted to the string. Once more I feared for Walter, and cried out to warn him. Once more he turned to me, with the immovable quiet in his face.

'Another step,' he said, 'on the dark road. Wait and look. The arrows that strike the rest will spare me.'

I saw him for the third time in a wrecked ship, stranded on a wild, sandy shore. The overloaded boats were making away from him for the land, and he alone was left to sink with the ship. I cried to him to hail the hindmost boat, and to make a last effort for his life. The quiet face looked at me in return, and the unmoved voice gave me back the changeless reply. 'Another step on the journey. Wait and look. The Sea which drowns the rest will spare me.'

I saw him for the last time. He was kneeling by a tomb of white marble, and the shadow of a veiled woman rose out of the grave beneath and waited by his side. The unearthly quiet of his face had changed to an unearthly sorrow. But the terrible certainty of his words remained the same. 'Darker and darker,' he said; 'farther and farther yet. Death takes the good, the beautiful, and the young – and spares me. The Pestilence that wastes, the Arrow that strikes, the Sea that drowns, the Grave that closes over Love and Hope, are steps of my journey, and take me nearer and nearer to the End.'

My heart sank under a dread beyond words, under a grief beyond tears. The darkness closed round the pilgrim at the marble tomb – closed round the veiled woman from the grave – closed round the dreamer who looked on them. I saw and heard no more.

I was aroused by a hand laid on my shoulder. It was Laura's.

She had dropped on her knees by the side of the sofa. Her face was flushed and agitated, and her eyes met mine in a wild bewildered manner. I started the instant I saw her.

'What has happened?' I asked. 'What has frightened you?'

She looked round at the half-open door, put her lips close to my ear, and answered in a whisper –

'Marian! – the figure at the lake – the footsteps last night – I've just seen her! I've just spoken to her!'

'Who, for Heaven's sake?'

'Anne Catherick.'

I was so startled by the disturbance in Laura's face and manner, and so dismayed by the first waking impressions of my dream, that I was not fit to bear the revelation which burst upon me when that name passed her lips. I could only stand rooted to the floor, looking at her in breathless silence.

She was too much absorbed by what had happened to notice the effect which her reply had produced on me. 'I have seen Anne Catherick! I have spoken to Anne Catherick!' she repeated as if I had not heard her. 'Oh, Marian, I have such things to tell you! Come away – we may be interrupted here – come at once into my room.'

With those eager words she caught me by the hand, and led me through the library, to the end room on the ground floor, which had been fitted up for her own especial use. No third person, except her maid, could have any excuse for surprising us here. She pushed me in before her, locked the door, and drew the chintz curtains that hung over the inside.

The strange, stunned feeling which had taken possession of me still remained. But a growing conviction that the complications which had long threatened to gather about her, and to gather about me, had suddenly closed fast round us both, was now beginning to penetrate my mind. I could not express it in words – I could hardly even realise it dimly in my own thoughts. 'Anne Catherick!' I whispered to myself, with useless, helpless reiteration—'Anne Catherick!'

Laura drew me to the nearest seat, an ottoman in the middle of the room. 'Look!' she said, 'look here!' – and pointed to the bosom of her dress.

I saw, for the first time, that the lost brooch was pinned in its place again. There was something real in the sight of it, something real in the touching of it afterwards, which seemed to steady the whirl and confusion in my thoughts, and to help me to compose myself.

'Where did you find your brooch?' The first words I could say to her were the words which put that trivial question at that important moment.

'*She* found it, Marian.'

'Where?'

'On the floor of the boathouse. Oh, how shall I begin – how shall I tell you about it! She talked to me so strangely – she looked so fearfully ill – she left me so suddenly!'

Her voice rose as the tumult of her recollections pressed upon her mind. The inveterate distrust which weighs, night and day, on my spirits in this house, instantly roused me to warn her – just as the sight of the brooch had roused me to question her, the moment before.

'Speak low,' I said. 'The window is open, and the garden path runs beneath it. Begin at the beginning, Laura. Tell me, word for word, what passed between that woman and you.'

'Shall I close the window?'

'No, only speak low – only remember that Anne Catherick is a dangerous subject under your husband's roof. Where did you first see her?'

'At the boathouse, Marian. I went out, as you know, to find my brooch, and I walked along the path through the plantation, looking down on the ground carefully at every step. In that way I got on, after a long time, to the boathouse, and as soon as I was inside it, I went on my knees to hunt over the floor. I was still searching with my back to the doorway, when I heard a soft, strange voice behind me say, "Miss Fairlie."'

'Miss Fairlie!'

'Yes, my old name – the dear, familiar name that I thought I had parted from for ever. I started up – not frightened, the voice was too kind and gentle to frighten anybody – but very much surprised. There, looking at me from the doorway, stood a woman, whose face I never remembered to have seen before—'

'How was she dressed?'

'She had a neat, pretty white gown on, and over it a poor worn thin dark shawl. Her bonnet was of brown straw, as poor and worn as the shawl. I was struck by the difference between her gown and the rest of her dress, and she saw that I noticed it. "Don't look at my bonnet and shawl," she said, speaking in a quick, breathless, sudden way; "if I mustn't wear white, I don't care what I wear. Look at my gown as much as you please – I'm not ashamed of that." Very strange, was it not? Before I could say anything to soothe her, she held out one of her hands, and I saw my brooch in it. I was so pleased and so grateful, that I went quite close to her to say what I really felt. "Are you thankful enough to do me one little kindness?" she asked. "Yes, indeed," I answered, "any kindness in my power I shall be glad to show you." "Then let me pin your brooch on for you, now I have found it." Her request was so unexpected, Marian, and she made it with such extraordinary eagerness, that I drew back a step or two, not well knowing what to do. "Ah!" she said, "your mother would have let me pin on the brooch." There was something in her voice and her look, as well as in her mentioning my mother in that reproachful manner, which made me ashamed of my distrust. I took her hand with the brooch in it, and put it up gently on the bosom of my dress. "You knew my mother?" I said. "Was it very long ago? have I ever seen you before?" Her hands were busy fastening the brooch: she stopped and pressed them against my breast. "You don't remember a fine spring day at Limmeridge," she said, "and your mother walking down the path that led to the school, with a little girl on each side of her? I have had nothing else to think of since, and I remember it. You were one of the little girls, and I was the other. Pretty, clever Miss Fairlie, and poor dazed Anne Catherick were nearer to each other then than they are now!"'

'Did you remember her, Laura, when she told you her name?'

'Yes, I remembered your asking me about Anne Catherick at Limmeridge, and your saying that she had once been considered like me.'

'What reminded you of that, Laura?'

'*She* reminded me. While I was looking at her, while she was very close to me, it came over my mind suddenly that we were like each other! Her face was pale and thin and weary – but the sight of it startled me, as if it had been the sight of my own face in the glass after a long illness. The discovery – I don't know why – gave me such a shock, that I was perfectly incapable of speaking to her for the moment.'

'Did she seem hurt by your silence?'

'I am afraid she was hurt by it. "You have not got your mother's face," she said, "or your mother's heart. Your mother's face was dark, and your mother's heart, Miss Fairlie, was the heart of an angel." "I am sure I feel kindly towards you," I said, "though I may not be able to express it as I ought. Why do you call me Miss Fairlie?—" "Because I love the name of Fairlie and hate the name of Glyde," she broke out violently. I had seen nothing like madness in her before this, but I fancied I saw it now in her eyes. "I only thought you might not know I was married," I said, remembering the wild letter she wrote to me at Limmeridge, and trying to quiet her. She sighed bitterly, and turned away from me. "Not know you were married?" she repeated. "I am here *because* you are married. I am here to make atonement to you, before I meet your mother in the world beyond the grave." She drew farther and farther away from me, till she was out of the boathouse, and then she watched and listened for a little while. When she turned round to speak again, instead of coming back, she stopped where she was, looking in at me, with a hand on each side of the entrance. "Did you see me at the lake last night?" she said. "Did you hear me following you in the wood? I have been waiting for days together to speak to you alone – I have left the only friend I have in the world, anxious and frightened about me – I have risked being shut up again in the mad-house – and all for your sake, Miss Fairlie, all for your sake." Her words alarmed me, Marian, and yet there was something in the way she spoke that made me pity her with all my heart. I am sure my pity must have been sincere, for it made me bold enough to ask the poor creature to come in, and sit down in the boathouse, by my side.'

'Did she do so?'

'No. She shook her head, and told me she must stop where she was, to watch and listen, and see that no third person surprised us. And from first to last, there she waited at the entrance, with a hand on each side of it, sometimes bending in suddenly to speak to me, sometimes drawing back suddenly to look about her. "I was here yesterday," she said, "before it came dark, and I heard you, and the lady with you, talking together. I heard you tell her about your husband. I heard you say you had no influence to make him believe you, and no influence to keep him silent. Ah! I knew what those words meant – my conscience told me while I was listening. Why did I ever let you marry him! Oh, my fear – my mad, miserable, wicked fear!" She covered up her face in her poor worn shawl, and moaned and murmured to herself behind it. I began to be afraid she might break out into some terrible despair which neither she nor I could master. "Try to quiet yourself," I said; "try to tell me how you might have prevented my marriage." She took the shawl from her face, and looked at me vacantly. "I ought to have had heart enough to stop at Limmeridge," she answered. "I ought never to have let the news of his coming there frighten me away. I ought to have warned you and saved you before it was too late. Why did I only have courage enough to write you that letter? Why did I only do harm, when I wanted and meant to do good? Oh, my fear – my mad, miserable, wicked fear!" She repeated those words again, and hid her face again in the end of her poor worn shawl. It was dreadful to see her, and dreadful to hear her.'

'Surely, Laura, you asked what the fear was which she dwelt on so earnestly?'

'Yes, I asked that.'

'And what did she say?'

'She asked me in return, if I should not be afraid of a man who had shut me up in a mad-house, and who would shut me up again, if he could? I said, "Are you afraid still? Surely you would not be here if you were afraid now?" "No," she said, "I am not afraid now." I asked why not. She suddenly bent forward into the boathouse, and said, "Can't you guess why?" I shook my head. "Look at me," she went on. I told her I was grieved to see that she looked very sorrowful and very ill. She smiled for the first time. "Ill?" she repeated; "I'm dying. You know why I'm not afraid of him now. Do you think I shall meet your mother in heaven? Will she forgive me if I do?" I was so shocked and so startled, that I could make no reply. "I have been thinking of it," she went on, "all the time I have been in hiding from your husband, all the time I lay ill. My thoughts have driven me here – I want to make atonement – I want to undo all I can of the harm I once did." I begged her as earnestly as I could to tell me what she meant. She still looked at me with fixed vacant eyes. "*Shall* I undo the harm?" she said to herself doubtfully. "You have friends to take your part. If *you* know his Secret, he will be afraid of you, he won't dare use you as he used me. He must treat you mercifully for his own sake, if he is afraid of you and your friends. And if he treats you mercifully, and if I can say it was my doing—" I listened eagerly for more, but she stopped at those words.'

'You tried to make her go on?'

'I tried, but she only drew herself away from me again, and leaned her face and arms against the side of the boathouse. "Oh!" I heard her say, with a dreadful, distracted tenderness in her voice, "oh! if I could only be buried with your mother! If I could only wake at her side, when the angel's trumpet sounds, and the graves give up their dead at the resurrection!" – Marian! I trembled from head to foot – it was horrible to hear her. "But there is no hope of that," she said, moving a little, so as to look at me again, "no hope for a poor stranger like me. I shall not rest under the marble cross that I washed with my own hands, and made so white and pure for her sake. Oh no! oh no! God's mercy, not man's, will take me to her, where the wicked cease from troubling and the weary are at rest." She spoke those words quietly and sorrowfully, with a heavy, hopeless sigh, and then waited a little. Her face was confused and troubled, she seemed to be thinking, or trying to think. "What was it I said just now?" she asked after a while. "When your mother is in my mind, everything else goes out of it. What was I saying? what was I saying?" I reminded the poor creature, as kindly and delicately as I could. "Ah, yes, yes," she said, still in a vacant, perplexed manner. "You are helpless with your wicked husband. Yes. And I must do what I have come to do here – I must make it up to you for having been afraid to speak out at a better time." "What is it you have to tell me?" I asked. "The Secret that your cruel husband is afraid of," she answered. "I once threatened him with the Secret, and frightened him. You shall threaten him with the Secret, and frighten him too." Her face darkened, and a hard, angry stare fixed itself in her eyes. She began waving her hand at me in a vacant, unmeaning manner. "My mother knows the Secret," she said. "My mother has wasted under the Secret half her lifetime. One day, when I was grown up, she said something to *me*. And the next day your husband—'"

'Yes! yes! Go on. What did she tell you about your husband?'

'She stopped again, Marian, at that point—'

'And said no more?'

'And listened eagerly. "Hush!" she whispered, still waving her hand at me. "Hush!" She moved aside out of the doorway, moved slowly and stealthily, step by step, till I lost her past the edge of the boathouse.'

'Surely you followed her?'

'Yes, my anxiety made me bold enough to rise and follow her. Just as I reached the entrance, she appeared again suddenly, round the side of the boathouse. "The Secret," I whispered to her – "wait and tell me the Secret!" She caught hold of my arm, and looked at me with wild frightened eyes. "Not now," she said, "we are not alone – we are watched. Come here tomorrow at this time – by yourself – mind – by yourself." She pushed me roughly into the boathouse again, and I saw her no more.'

'Oh, Laura, Laura, another chance lost! If I had only been near you she should not have escaped us. On which side did you lose sight of her?'

'On the left side, where the ground sinks and the wood is thickest.'

'Did you run out again? did you call after her?'

'How could I? I was too terrified to move or speak.'

'But when you *did* move – when you came out?'

'I ran back here, to tell you what had happened.'

'Did you see any one, or hear any one, in the plantation?'

'No, it seemed to be all still and quiet when I passed through it.'

I waited for a moment to consider. Was this third person, supposed to have been secretly present at the interview, a reality, or the creature of Anne Catherick's excited fancy? It was impossible to determine. The one thing certain was, that we had failed again on the very brink of discovery – failed utterly and irretrievably, unless Anne Catherick kept her appointment at the boathouse for the next day.

'Are you quite sure you have told me everything that passed? Every word that was said?' I inquired.

'I think so,' she answered. 'My powers of memory, Marian, are not like yours. But I was so strongly impressed, so deeply interested, that nothing of any importance can possibly have escaped me.'

'My dear Laura, the merest trifles are of importance where Anne Catherick is concerned. Think again. Did no chance reference escape her as to the place in which she is living at the present time?'

'None that I can remember.'

'Did she not mention a companion and friend – a woman named Mrs Clements?'

'Oh yes! yes! I forgot that. She told me Mrs Clements wanted sadly to go with her to the lake and take care of her, and begged and prayed that she would not venture into this neighbourhood alone.'

'Was that all she said about Mrs Clements?'

'Yes, that was all.'

'She told you nothing about the place in which she took refuge after leaving Todd's Corner?'

'Nothing – I am quite sure.'

'Nor where she has lived since? Nor what her illness had been?'

'No, Marian, not a word. Tell me, pray tell me, what you think about it. I don't know what to think, or what to do next.'

'You must do this, my love: You must carefully keep the appointment at the boathouse tomorrow. It is impossible to say what interests may not depend on your seeing that woman again. You shall not be left to yourself a second time. I will follow you at a safe distance. Nobody shall see me, but I will keep within hearing of your voice, if anything happens. Anne Catherick has escaped Walter Hartright, and has escaped you. Whatever happens, she shall not escape *me*.'

Laura's eyes read mine attentively.

'You believe,' she said, 'in this secret that my husband is afraid of? Suppose, Marian, it should only exist after all in Anne Catherick's fancy? Suppose she only wanted to see me and to speak to me, for the sake of old remembrances? Her manner was so strange – I almost doubted her. Would you trust her in other things?'

'I trust nothing, Laura, but my own observation of your husband's conduct. I judge Anne Catherick's words by his actions, and I believe there is a secret.'

I said no more, and got up to leave the room. Thoughts were troubling me which I might have told her if we had spoken together longer, and which it might have been dangerous for her to know. The influence of the terrible dream from which she had awakened me hung darkly and heavily over every fresh impression which the progress of her narrative produced on my mind. I felt the ominous future coming close, chilling me with an unutterable awe, forcing on me the conviction of an unseen design in the long series of complications which had now fastened round us. I thought of Hartright – as I saw him in the body when he said farewell; as I saw him in the spirit in my dream – and I too began to doubt now whether we were not advancing blindfold to an appointed and an inevitable end.

Leaving Laura to go upstairs alone, I went out to look about me in the walks near the house. The circumstances under which Anne Catherick had parted from her had made me secretly anxious to know how Count Fosco was passing the afternoon, and had rendered me secretly distrustful of the results of that solitary journey from which Sir Percival had returned but a few hours since.

After looking for them in every direction and discovering nothing, I returned to the house, and entered the different rooms on the ground floor one after another. They were all empty. I came out again into the hall, and went upstairs to return to Laura. Madame Fosco opened her door as I passed it in my way along the passage, and I stopped to see if she could inform me of the whereabouts of her husband and Sir Percival. Yes, she had seen them both from her window more than an hour since. The Count had looked up with his customary kindness, and had mentioned with his habitual attention to her in the smallest trifles, that he and his friend were going out together for a long walk.

For a long walk! They had never yet been in each other's company with that object in my experience of them. Sir Percival cared for no exercise but riding, and the Count (except when he was polite enough to be my escort) cared for no exercise at all.

When I joined Laura again, I found that she had called to mind in my absence the impending question of the signature to the deed, which, in the interest of discussing her interview with Anne Catherick, we had hitherto overlooked. Her first words when I saw her expressed her surprise at the absence of the expected summons to attend Sir Percival in the library.

'You may make your mind easy on that subject,' I said. 'For the present, at least, neither your resolution nor mine will be exposed to any further trial. Sir Percival has altered his plans – the business of the signature is put off.'

'Put off?' Laura repeated amazedly. 'Who told you so?'

'My authority is Count Fosco. I believe it is to his interference that we are indebted for your husband's sudden change of purpose.'

'It seems impossible, Marian. If the object of my signing was, as we suppose, to obtain money for Sir Percival that he urgently wanted, how can the matter be put off?'

'I think, Laura, we have the means at hand of setting that doubt at rest. Have you forgotten the conversation that I heard between Sir Percival and the lawyer as they were crossing the hall?'

'No, but I don't remember—'

'I do. There were two alternatives proposed. One was to obtain your signature to the parchment. The other was to gain time by giving bills at three months. The last resource is evidently the resource now adopted, and we may fairly hope to be relieved from our share in Sir Percival's embarrassments for some time to come.'

'Oh, Marian, it sounds too good to be true!'

'Does it, my love? You complimented me on my ready memory not long since, but you seem to doubt it now. I will get my journal, and you shall see if I am right or wrong.'

I went away and got the book at once.

On looking back to the entry referring to the lawyer's visit, we found that my recollection of the two alternatives presented was accurately correct. It was almost as great a relief to my mind as to Laura's, to find that my memory had served me, on this occasion, as faithfully as usual. In the perilous uncertainty of our present situation, it is hard to say what future interests may not depend upon the regularity of the entries in my journal, and upon the reliability of my recollection at the time when I make them.

Laura's face and manner suggested to me that this last consideration had occurred to her as well as to myself. Anyway, it is only a trifling matter, and I am almost ashamed to put it down here in writing – it seems to set the forlornness of our situation in such a miserably vivid light. We must have little indeed to depend on, when the discovery that my memory can still be trusted to serve us is hailed as if it was the discovery of a new friend!

The first bell for dinner separated us. Just as it had done ringing, Sir Percival and the Count returned from their walk. We heard the master of the house storming at the servants for being five minutes late, and the master's guest interposing, as usual, in the interests of propriety, patience, and peace.

The evening has come and gone. No extraordinary event has happened. But I have noticed certain peculiarities in the conduct of Sir Percival and the

Count, which have sent me to my bed feeling very anxious and uneasy about Anne Catherick, and about the results which tomorrow may produce.

I know enough by this time, to be sure, that the aspect of Sir Percival which is the most false, and which, therefore, means the worst, is his polite aspect. That long walk with his friend had ended in improving his manners, especially towards his wife. To Laura's secret surprise and to my secret alarm, he called her by her Christian name, asked if she had heard lately from her uncle, inquired when Mrs Vesey was to receive her invitation to Blackwater, and showed her so many other little attentions that he almost recalled the days of his hateful courtship at Limmeridge House. This was a bad sign to begin with, and I thought it more ominous still that he should pretend after dinner to fall asleep in the drawing-room, and that his eyes should cunningly follow Laura and me when he thought we neither of us suspected him. I have never had any doubt that his sudden journey by himself took him to Welmingham to question Mrs Catherick – but the experience of tonight has made me fear that the expedition was not undertaken in vain, and that he has got the information which he unquestionably left us to collect. If I knew where Anne Catherick was to be found, I would be up tomorrow with sunrise and warn her.

While the aspect under which Sir Percival presented himself tonight was unhappily but too familiar to me, the aspect under which the Count appeared was, on the other hand, entirely new in my experience of him. He permitted me, this evening, to make his acquaintance, for the first time, in the character of a Man of Sentiment – of sentiment, as I believe, really felt, not assumed for the occasion.

For instance, he was quiet and subdued – his eyes and his voice expressed a restrained sensibility. He wore (as if there was some hidden connection between his showiest finery and his deepest feeling) the most magnificent waistcoat he has yet appeared in – it was made of pale sea-green silk, and delicately trimmed with fine silver braid. His voice sank into the tenderest inflections, his smile expressed a thoughtful, fatherly admiration, whenever he spoke to Laura or to me. He pressed his wife's hand under the table when she thanked him for trifling little attentions at dinner. He took wine with her. 'Your health and happiness, my angel!' he said, with fond glistening eyes. He ate little or nothing, and sighed, and said 'Good Percival!' when his friend laughed at him. After dinner, he took Laura by the hand, and asked her if she would be 'so sweet as to play to him.' She complied, through sheer astonishment. He sat by the piano, with his watch-chain resting in folds, like a golden serpent, on the sea-green protuberance of his waistcoat. His immense head lay languidly on one side, and he gently beat time with two of his yellow-white fingers. He highly approved of the music, and tenderly admired

Laura's manner of playing – not as poor Hartright used to praise it, with an innocent enjoyment of the sweet sounds, but with a clear, cultivated, practical knowledge of the merits of the composition, in the first place, and of the merits of the player's touch in the second. As the evening closed in, he begged that the lovely dying light might not be profaned, just yet, by the appearance of the lamps. He came, with his horribly silent tread, to the distant window at which I was standing, to be out of his way and to avoid the very sight of him – he came to ask me to support his protest against the lamps. If any one of them could only have burnt him up at that moment, I would have gone down to the kitchen and fetched it myself.

'Surely you like this modest, trembling English twilight?' he said softly. 'Ah! I love it. I feel my inborn admiration of all that is noble, and great, and good, purified by the breath of heaven on an evening like this. Nature has such imperishable charms, such inextinguishable tenderness for me! – I am an old, fat man – talk which would become your lips, Miss Halcombe, sounds like a derision and a mockery on mine. It is hard to be laughed at in my moments of sentiment, as if my soul was like myself, old and overgrown. Observe, dear lady, what a light is dying on the trees! Does it penetrate your heart, as it penetrates mine?'

He paused, looked at me, and repeated the famous lines of Dante on the Evening-time, with a melody and tenderness which added a charm of their own to the matchless beauty of the poetry itself.

'Bah!' he cried suddenly, as the last cadence of those noble Italian words died away on his lips; 'I make an old fool of myself, and only weary you all! Let us shut up the window in our bosoms and get back to the matter-of-fact world. Percival! I sanction the admission of the lamps. Lady Glyde – Miss Halcombe – Eleanor, my good wife – which of you will indulge me with a game at dominoes?'

He addressed us all, but he looked especially at Laura.

She had learnt to feel my dread of offending him, and she accepted his proposal. It was more than I could have done at that moment. I could not have sat down at the same table with him for any consideration. His eyes seemed to reach my inmost soul through the thickening obscurity of the twilight. His voice trembled along every nerve in my body, and turned me hot and cold alternately. The mystery and terror of my dream, which had haunted me at intervals all through the evening, now oppressed my mind with an unendurable foreboding and an unutterable awe. I saw the white tomb again, and the veiled woman rising out of it by Hartright's side. The thought of Laura welled up like a spring in the depths of my heart, and filled it with waters of bitterness, never, never known to it before. I caught her by the hand as she passed me on her way to the table, and kissed her as if that

night was to part us for ever. While they were all gazing at me in astonishment, I ran out through the low window which was open before me to the
ground – ran out to hide from them in the darkness, to hide even from myself.

We separated that evening later than usual. Towards midnight the summer
silence was broken by the shuddering of a low, melancholy wind among the
trees. We all felt the sudden chill in the atmosphere, but the Count was the
first to notice the stealthy rising of the wind. He stopped while he was lighting
my candle for me, and held up his hand warningly –

'Listen!' he said. 'There will be a change tomorrow.'

VII

JUNE 19TH – The events of yesterday warned me to be ready, sooner or later,
to meet the worst. Today is not yet at an end, and the worst has come.

Judging by the closest calculation of time that Laura and I could make,
we arrived at the conclusion that Anne Catherick must have appeared at the
boathouse at half-past two o'clock on the afternoon of yesterday. I accordingly arranged that Laura should just show herself at the luncheon-table
today, and should then slip out at the first opportunity, leaving me behind to
preserve appearances, and to follow her as soon as I could safely do so. This
mode of proceeding, if no obstacles occurred to thwart us, would enable her
to be at the boathouse before half-past two, and (when I left the table, in
my turn) would take me to a safe position in the plantation before three.

The change in the weather, which last night's wind warned us to expect,
came with the morning. It was raining heavily when I got up, and it continued
to rain until twelve o'clock – when the clouds dispersed, the blue sky appeared,
and the sun shone again with the bright promise of a fine afternoon.

My anxiety to know how Sir Percival and the Count would occupy the
early part of the day was by no means set at rest, so far as Sir Percival was
concerned, by his leaving us immediately after breakfast, and going out by
himself, in spite of the rain. He neither told us where he was going nor when
we might expect him back. We saw him pass the breakfast-room window
hastily, with his high boots and his waterproof coat on – and that was all.

The Count passed the morning quietly indoors, some part of it in the
library, some part in the drawing-room, playing odds and ends of music on
the piano, and humming to himself. Judging by appearances, the sentimental
side of his character was persistently inclined to betray itself still. He was
silent and sensitive, and ready to sigh and languish ponderously (as only fat
men *can* sigh and languish) on the smallest provocation.

Luncheon-time came and Sir Percival did not return. The Count took his friend's place at the table, plaintively devoured the greater part of a fruit tart, submerged under a whole jugful of cream, and explained the full merit of the achievement to us as soon as he had done. 'A taste for sweets,' he said in his softest tones and his tenderest manner, 'is the innocent taste of women and children. I love to share it with them – it is another bond, dear ladies, between you and me.'

Laura left the table in ten minutes' time. I was sorely tempted to accompany her. But if we had both gone out together we must have excited suspicion, and worse still, if we allowed Anne Catherick to see Laura, accompanied by a second person who was a stranger to her, we should in all probability forfeit her confidence from that moment, never to regain it again.

I waited, therefore, as patiently as I could, until the servant came in to clear the table. When I quitted the room, there were no signs, in the house or out of it, of Sir Percival's return. I left the Count with a piece of sugar between his lips, and the vicious cockatoo scrambling up his waistcoat to get at it, while Madame Fosco, sitting opposite to her husband, watched the proceedings of his bird and himself as attentively as if she had never seen anything of the sort before in her life. On my way to the plantation I kept carefully beyond the range of view from the luncheon-room window. Nobody saw me and nobody followed me. It was then a quarter to three o'clock by my watch.

Once among the trees I walked rapidly, until I had advanced more than half-way through the plantation. At that point I slackened my pace and proceeded cautiously, but I saw no one, and heard no voices. By little and little I came within view of the back of the boathouse – stopped and listened – then went on, till I was close behind it, and must have heard any persons who were talking inside. Still the silence was unbroken – still far and near no sign of a living creature appeared anywhere.

After skirting round by the back of the building, first on one side and then on the other, and making no discoveries, I ventured in front of it, and fairly looked in. The place was empty.

I called, 'Laura!' – at first softly, then louder and louder. No one answered and no one appeared. For all that I could see and hear, the only human creature in the neighbourhood of the lake and the plantation was myself.

My heart began to beat violently, but I kept my resolution, and searched, first the boathouse and then the ground in front of it, for any signs which might show me whether Laura had really reached the place or not. No mark of her presence appeared inside the building, but I found traces of her outside it, in footsteps on the sand.

I detected the footsteps of two persons – large footsteps like a man's, and small footsteps, which, by putting my own feet into them and testing their size in that manner, I felt certain were Laura's. The ground was confusedly marked in this way just before the boathouse. Close against one side of it, under shelter of the projecting roof, I discovered a little hole in the sand – a hole artificially made, beyond a doubt. I just noticed it, and then turned away immediately to trace the footsteps as far as I could, and to follow the direction in which they might lead me.

They led me, starting from the left-hand side of the boathouse, along the edge of the trees, a distance, I should think, of between two and three hundred yards, and then the sandy ground showed no further trace of them. Feeling that the persons whose course I was tracking must necessarily have entered the plantation at this point, I entered it too. At first I could find no path, but I discovered one afterwards, just faintly traced among the trees, and followed it. It took me, for some distance, in the direction of the village, until I stopped at a point where another foot-track crossed it. The brambles grew thickly on either side of this second path. I stood looking down it, uncertain which way to take next, and while I looked I saw on one thorny branch some fragments of fringe from a woman's shawl. A closer examination of the fringe satisfied me that it had been torn from a shawl of Laura's, and I instantly followed the second path. It brought me out at last, to my great relief, at the back of the house. I say to my great relief, because I inferred that Laura must, for some unknown reason, have returned before me by this roundabout way. I went in by the court-yard and the offices. The first person whom I met in crossing the servants' hall was Mrs Michelson, the housekeeper.

'Do you know,' I asked, 'whether Lady Glyde has come in from her walk or not?'

'My lady came in a little while ago with Sir Percival,' answered the housekeeper. 'I am afraid, Miss Halcombe, something very distressing has happened.'

My heart sank within me. 'You don't mean an accident?' I said faintly.

'No, no – thank God, no accident. But my lady ran upstairs to her own room in tears, and Sir Percival has ordered me to give Fanny warning to leave in an hour's time.'

Fanny was Laura's maid – a good affectionate girl who had been with her for years – the only person in the house whose fidelity and devotion we could both depend upon.

'Where is Fanny?' I inquired.

'In my room, Miss Halcombe. The young woman is quite overcome, and I told her to sit down and try to recover herself.'

I went to Mrs Michelson's room, and found Fanny in a corner, with her box by her side, crying bitterly.

She could give me no explanation whatever of her sudden dismissal. Sir

Percival had ordered that she should have a month's wages, in place of a month's warning, and go. No reason had been assigned – no objection had been made to her conduct. She had been forbidden to appeal to her mistress, forbidden even to see her for a moment to say good-bye. She was to go without explanations or farewells, and to go at once.

After soothing the poor girl by a few friendly words, I asked where she proposed to sleep that night. She replied that she thought of going to the little inn in the village, the landlady of which was a respectable woman, known to the servants at Blackwater Park. The next morning, by leaving early, she might get back to her friends in Cumberland without stopping in London, where she was a total stranger.

I felt directly that Fanny's departure offered us a safe means of communication with London and with Limmeridge House, of which it might be very important to avail ourselves. Accordingly, I told her that she might expect to hear from her mistress or from me in the course of the evening, and that she might depend on our both doing all that lay in our power to help her, under the trial of leaving us for the present. Those words said, I shook hands with her and went upstairs.

The door which led to Laura's room was the door of an ante-chamber opening on to the passage. When I tried it, it was bolted on the inside.

I knocked, and the door was opened by the same heavy, overgrown housemaid whose lumpish insensibility had tried my patience so severely on the day when I found the wounded dog.

I had, since that time, discovered that her name was Margaret Porcher, and that she was the most awkward, slatternly, and obstinate servant in the house.

On opening the door she instantly stepped out to the threshold, and stood grinning at me in stolid silence.

'Why do you stand there?' I said. 'Don't you see that I want to come in?'

'Ah, but you mustn't come in,' was the answer, with another and a broader grin still.

'How dare you talk to me in that way? Stand back instantly!'

She stretched out a great red hand and arm on each side of her, so as to bar the doorway, and slowly nodded her addle head at me.

'Master's orders,' she said, and nodded again.

I had need of all my self-control to warn me against contesting the matter with *her*, and to remind me that the next words I had to say must be addressed to her master. I turned my back on her, and instantly went downstairs to find him. My resolution to keep my temper under all the irritations that Sir Percival could offer was, by this time, as completely forgotten – I say so to my shame – as if I had never made it. It did me good, after all I had suffered and suppressed in that house – it actually did me good to feel how angry I was.

The drawing-room and the breakfast-room were both empty. I went on to the library, and there I found Sir Percival, the Count, and Madame Fosco. They were all three standing up, close together, and Sir Percival had a little slip of paper in his hand. As I opened the door I heard the Count say to him, 'No – a thousand times over, no.'

I walked straight up to him, and looked him full in the face.

'Am I to understand, Sir Percival, that your wife's room is a prison, and that your housemaid is the gaoler who keeps it?' I asked.

'Yes, that *is* what you are to understand,' he answered. 'Take care my gaoler hasn't got double duty to do – take care your room is not a prison too.'

'Take *you* care how you treat your wife, and how you threaten *me*,' I broke out in the heat of my anger. 'There are laws in England to protect women from cruelty and outrage. If you hurt a hair of Laura's head, if you dare to interfere with my freedom, come what may, to those laws I will appeal.'

Instead of answering me he turned round to the Count.

'What did I tell you?' he asked. 'What do you say now?'

'What I said before,' replied the Count—'No.'

Even in the vehemence of my anger I felt his calm, cold, grey eyes on my face. They turned away from me as soon as he had spoken, and looked significantly at his wife. Madame Fosco immediately moved close to my side, and in that position addressed Sir Percival before either of us could speak again.

'Favour me with your attention for one moment,' she said, in her clear icily-suppressed tones. 'I have to thank you, Sir Percival, for your hospitality, and to decline taking advantage of it any longer. I remain in no house in which ladies are treated as your wife and Miss Halcombe have been treated here today!'

Sir Percival drew back a step, and stared at her in dead silence. The declaration he had just heard – a declaration which he well knew, as I well knew, Madame Fosco would not have ventured to make without her husband's permission – seemed to petrify him with surprise. The Count stood by, and looked at his wife with the most enthusiastic admiration.

'She is sublime!' he said to himself. He approached her while he spoke, and drew her hand through his arm. 'I am at your service, Eleanor,' he went on, with a quiet dignity that I had never noticed in him before. 'And at Miss Halcombe's service, if she will honour me by accepting all the assistance I can offer her.'

'Damn it! what do you mean?' cried Sir Percival, as the Count quietly moved away with his wife to the door.

'At other times I mean what I say, but at this time I mean what my wife says,' replied the impenetrable Italian. 'We have changed places, Percival, for once, and Madame Fosco's opinion is – mine.'

Sir Percival crumpled up the paper in his hand, and pushing past the Count, with another oath, stood between him and the door.

'Have your own way,' he said, with baffled rage in his low, half-whispering tones. 'Have your own way – and see what comes of it.' With those words he left the room.

Madame Fosco glanced inquiringly at her husband. 'He has gone away very suddenly,' she said. 'What does it mean?'

'It means that you and I together have brought the worst-tempered man in all England to his senses,' answered the Count. 'It means, Miss Halcombe, that Lady Glyde is relieved from a gross indignity, and you from the repetition of an unpardonable insult. Suffer me to express my admiration of your conduct and your courage at a very trying moment.'

'Sincere admiration,' suggested Madame Fosco.

'Sincere admiration,' echoed the Count.

I had no longer the strength of my first angry resistance to outrage and injury to support me. My heart-sick anxiety to see Laura, my sense of my own helpless ignorance of what had happened at the boathouse, pressed on me with an intolerable weight. I tried to keep up appearances by speaking to the Count and his wife in the tone which they had chosen to adopt in speaking to me, but the words failed on my lips – my breath came short and thick – my eyes looked longingly, in silence, at the door. The Count, understanding my anxiety, opened it, went out, and pulled it to after him. At the same time Sir Percival's heavy step descended the stairs. I heard them whispering together outside, while Madame Fosco was assuring me, in her calmest and most conventional manner, that she rejoiced, for all our sakes, that Sir Percival's conduct had not obliged her husband and herself to leave Blackwater Park. Before she had done speaking the whispering ceased, the door opened, and the Count looked in.

'Miss Halcombe,' he said, 'I am happy to inform you that Lady Glyde is mistress again in her own house. I thought it might be more agreeable to you to hear of this change for the better from me than from Sir Percival, and I have therefore expressly returned to mention it.'

'Admirable delicacy!' said Madame Fosco, paying back her husband's tribute of admiration with the Count's own coin, in the Count's own manner. He smiled and bowed as if he had received a formal compliment from a polite stranger, and drew back to let me pass out first.

Sir Percival was standing in the hall. As I hurried to the stairs I heard him call impatiently to the Count to come out of the library.

'What are you waiting there for?' he said. 'I want to speak to you.'

'And I want to think a little by myself,' replied the other. 'Wait till later, Percival, wait till later.'

Neither he nor his friend said any more. I gained the top of the stairs and ran along the passage. In my haste and my agitation I left the door of the ante-chamber open, but I closed the door of the bedroom the moment I was inside it.

Laura was sitting alone at the far end of the room, her arms resting wearily on a table, and her face hidden in her hands. She started up with a cry of delight when she saw me.

'How did you get here?' she asked. 'Who gave you leave? Not Sir Percival?'

In my overpowering anxiety to hear what she had to tell me, I could not answer her – I could only put questions on my side. Laura's eagerness to know what had passed downstairs proved, however, too strong to be resisted. She persistently repeated her inquiries.

'The Count, of course,' I answered impatiently. 'Whose influence in the house—'

She stopped me with a gesture of disgust.

'Don't speak of him,' she cried. 'The Count is the vilest creature breathing! The Count is a miserable Spy—!'

Before we could either of us say another word we were alarmed by a soft knocking at the door of the bedroom.

I had not yet sat down, and I went first to see who it was. When I opened the door Madame Fosco confronted me with my handkerchief in her hand.

'You dropped this downstairs, Miss Halcombe,' she said, 'and I thought I could bring it to you, as I was passing by to my own room.'

Her face, naturally pale, had turned to such a ghastly whiteness that I started at the sight of it. Her hands, so sure and steady at all other times, trembled violently, and her eyes looked wolfishly past me through the open door, and fixed on Laura.

She had been listening before she knocked! I saw it in her white face, I saw it in her trembling hands, I saw it in her look at Laura.

After waiting an instant she turned from me in silence, and slowly walked away.

I closed the door again. 'Oh, Laura! Laura! We shall both rue the day when you called the Count a Spy!'

'You would have called him so yourself, Marian, if you had known what I know. Anne Catherick was right. There *was* a third person watching us in the plantation yesterday, and that third person—'

'Are you sure it was the Count?'

'I am absolutely certain. He was Sir Percival's spy – he was Sir Percival's informer – he set Sir Percival watching and waiting, all the morning through, for Anne Catherick and for me.'

'Is Anne found? Did you see her at the lake?'

'No. She has saved herself by keeping away from the place. When I got to the boathouse no one was there.'

'Yes? Yes?'

'I went in and sat waiting for a few minutes. But my restlessness made me get up again, to walk about a little. As I passed out I saw some marks on the sand, close under the front of the boathouse. I stooped down to examine them, and discovered a word written in large letters on the sand. The word was – *look*.'

'And you scraped away the sand, and dug a hollow place in it?'

'How do you know that, Marian?'

'I saw the hollow place myself when I followed you to the boathouse. Go on – go on!'

'Yes, I scraped away the sand on the surface, and in a little while I came to a strip of paper hidden beneath, which had writing on it. The writing was signed with Anne Catherick's initials.'

'Where is it?'

'Sir Percival has taken it from me.'

'Can you remember what the writing was? Do you think you can repeat it to me?'

'In substance I can, Marian. It was very short. You would have remembered it, word for word.'

'Try to tell me what the substance was before we go any further.'

She complied. I write the lines down here exactly as she repeated them to me. They ran thus –

I was seen with you, yesterday, by a tall, stout old man, and had to run to save myself. He was not quick enough on his feet to follow me, and he lost me among the trees. I dare not risk coming back here today at the same time. I write this, and hide it in the sand, at six in the morning, to tell you so. When we speak next of your wicked husband's Secret we must speak safely, or not at all. Try to have patience. I promise you shall see me again and that soon. – A. C.

The reference to the 'tall, stout old man' (the terms of which Laura was certain that she had repeated to me correctly) left no doubt as to who the intruder had been. I called to mind that I had told Sir Percival, in the Count's presence the day before, that Laura had gone to the boathouse to look for her brooch. In all probability he had followed her there, in his officious way, to relieve her mind about the matter of the signature, immediately after he had mentioned the change in Sir Percival's plans to me in the drawing-room. In this case he could only have got to the neighbourhood of the boathouse at the very moment when Anne Catherick discovered him. The suspiciously hurried manner in which she parted from Laura had no doubt prompted his useless attempt to follow her. Of the conversation which had previously taken place between them he could have heard nothing. The distance between the house and the lake, and the time at which he left me in the drawing-room, as compared with the time at which Laura and Anne Catherick had been speaking together, proved that fact to us at any rate, beyond a doubt.

Having arrived at something like a conclusion so far, my next great interest was to know what discoveries Sir Percival had made after Count Fosco had given him his information.

'How came you to lose possession of the letter?' I asked. 'What did you do with it when you found it in the sand?'

'After reading it once through,' she replied, 'I took it into the boathouse with me to sit down and look over it a second time. While I was reading a shadow fell across the paper. I looked up, and saw Sir Percival standing in the doorway watching me.'

'Did you try to hide the letter?'

'I tried, but he stopped me. "You needn't trouble to hide that," he said. "I happen to have read it." I could only look at him helplessly – I could say nothing. "You understand?" he went on; "I have read it. I dug it up out of the sand two hours since, and buried it again, and wrote the word above it again, and left it ready to your hands. You can't lie yourself out of the scrape now. You saw Anne Catherick in secret yesterday, and you have got her letter in your hand at this moment. I have not caught *her* yet, but I have caught *you*. Give me the letter." He stepped close up to me – I was alone with him, Marian – what could I do? – I gave him the letter.'

'What did he say when you gave it to him?'

'At first he said nothing. He took me by the arm, and led me out of the boathouse, and looked about him on all sides, as if he was afraid of our being seen or heard. Then he clasped his hand fast round my arm, and whispered to me, "What did Anne Catherick say to you yesterday? I insist on hearing every word, from first to last."'

'Did you tell him?'

'I was alone with him, Marian – his cruel hand was bruising my arm – what could I do?'

'Is the mark on your arm still? Let me see it.'

'Why do you want to see it?'

'I want to see it, Laura, because our endurance must end, and our resistance must begin today. That mark is a weapon to strike him with. Let me
see it now – I may have to swear to it at some future time.'

'Oh, Marian, don't look so – don't talk so! It doesn't hurt me now!'

'Let me see it!'

She showed me the marks. I was past grieving over them, past crying
over them, past shuddering over them. They say we are either better than
men, or worse. If the temptation that has fallen in some women's way, and
made them worse, had fallen in mine at that moment – Thank God! my face
betrayed nothing that his wife could read. The gentle, innocent, affectionate
creature thought I was frightened for her and sorry for her, and thought
no more.

'Don't think too seriously of it, Marian,' she said simply, as she pulled
her sleeve down again. 'It doesn't hurt me now.'

'I will try to think quietly of it, my love, for your sake. – Well! well!
And you told him all that Anne Catherick had said to you – all that you told
me?'

'Yes, all. He insisted on it – I was alone with him – I could conceal
nothing.'

'Did he say anything when you had done?'

'He looked at me, and laughed to himself in a mocking, bitter way.
"I mean to have the rest out of you," he said, "do you hear? – the rest." I
declared to him solemnly that I had told him everything I knew. "Not you,"
he answered, "you know more than you choose to tell. Won't you tell it?
You shall! I'll wring it out of you at home if I can't wring it out of you
here." He led me away by a strange path through the plantation – a path
where there was no hope of our meeting *you* – and he spoke no more till
we came within sight of the house. Then he stopped again, and said, "Will
you take a second chance, if I give it to you? Will you think better of it, and
tell me the rest?" I could only repeat the same words I had spoken before.
He cursed my obstinacy, and went on, and took me with him to the house.
"You can't deceive me," he said, "you know more than you choose to tell.
I'll have your secret out of you, and I'll have it out of that sister of yours
as well. There shall be no more plotting and whispering between you. Neither
you nor she shall see each other again till you have confessed the truth. I'll
have you watched morning, noon, and night, till you confess the truth." He
was deaf to everything I could say. He took me straight upstairs into my
own room. Fanny was sitting there, doing some work for me, and he instantly
ordered her out. "I'll take good care *you're* not mixed up in the conspiracy,"
he said. "You shall leave this house today. If your mistress wants a maid,
she shall have one of my choosing." He pushed me into the room, and locked

the door on me. He set that senseless woman to watch me outside, Marian! He looked and spoke like a madman. You may hardly understand it – he did indeed.'

'I do understand it, Laura. He is mad – mad with the terrors of a guilty conscience. Every word you have said makes me positively certain that when Anne Catherick left you yesterday you were on the eve of discovering a secret which might have been your vile husband's ruin, and he thinks you *have* discovered it. Nothing you can say or do will quiet that guilty distrust, and convince his false nature of your truth. I don't say this, my love, to alarm you. I say it to open your eyes to your position, and to convince you of the urgent necessity of letting me act, as I best can, for your protection while the chance is our own. Count Fosco's interference has secured me access to you today, but he may withdraw that interference tomorrow. Sir Percival has already dismissed Fanny because she is a quick-witted girl, and devotedly attached to you, and has chosen a woman to take her place who cares nothing for your interests, and whose dull intelligence lowers her to the level of the watch-dog in the yard. It is impossible to say what violent measures he may take next, unless we make the most of our opportunities while we have them.'

'What can we do, Marian? Oh, if we could only leave this house, never to see it again!'

'Listen to me, my love, and try to think that you are not quite helpless so long as I am here with you.'

'I will think so – I do think so. Don't altogether forget poor Fanny in thinking of me. She wants help and comfort too.'

'I will not forget her. I saw her before I came up here, and I have arranged to communicate with her tonight. Letters are not safe in the post-bag at Blackwater Park, and I shall have two to write today, in your interests, which must pass through no hands but Fanny's.'

'What letters?'

'I mean to write first, Laura, to Mr Gilmore's partner, who has offered to help us in any fresh emergency. Little as I know of the law, I am certain that it can protect a woman from such treatment as that ruffian has inflicted on you today. I will go into no details about Anne Catherick, because I have no certain information to give. But the lawyer shall know of those bruises on your arm, and of the violence offered to you in this room – he shall, before I rest tonight!'

'But think of the exposure, Marian!'

'I am calculating on the exposure. Sir Percival has more to dread from it than you have. The prospect of an exposure may bring him to terms when nothing else will.'

I rose as I spoke, but Laura entreated me not to leave her. 'You will drive him to desperation,' she said, 'and increase our dangers tenfold.'

I felt the truth – the disheartening truth – of those words. But I could not bring myself plainly to acknowledge it to her. In our dreadful position there was no help and no hope for us but in risking the worst. I said so in guarded terms. She sighed bitterly, but did not contest the matter. She only asked about the second letter that I had proposed writing. To whom was it to be addressed?

'To Mr Fairlie,' I said. 'Your uncle is your nearest male relative, and the head of the family. He must and shall interfere.'

Laura shook her head sorrowfully.

'Yes, yes,' I went on, 'your uncle is a weak, selfish, worldly man, I know, but he is not Sir Percival Glyde, and he has no such friend about him as Count Fosco. I expect nothing from his kindness or his tenderness of feeling towards you or towards me, but he will do anything to pamper his own indolence, and to secure his own quiet. Let me only persuade him that his interference at this moment will save him inevitable trouble and wretchedness and responsibility hereafter, and he will bestir himself for his own sake. I know how to deal with him, Laura – I have had some practice.'

'If you could only prevail on him to let me go back to Limmeridge for a little while and stay there quietly with you, Marian, I could be almost as happy again as I was before I was married!'

Those words set me thinking in a new direction. Would it be possible to place Sir Percival between the two alternatives of either exposing himself to the scandal of legal interference on his wife's behalf, or of allowing her to be quietly separated from him for a time under pretext of a visit to her uncle's house? And could he, in that case, be reckoned on as likely to accept the last resource? It was doubtful – more than doubtful. And yet, hopeless as the experiment seemed, surely it was worth trying. I resolved to try it in sheer despair of knowing what better to do.

'Your uncle shall know the wish you have just expressed,' I said, 'and I will ask the lawyer's advice on the subject as well. Good may come of it – and will come of it, I hope.'

Saying that I rose again, and again Laura tried to make me resume my seat.

'Don't leave me,' she said uneasily. 'My desk is on that table. You can write here.'

It tried me to the quick to refuse her, even in her own interests. But we had been too long shut up alone together already. Our chance of seeing each other again might entirely depend on our not exciting any fresh suspicions. It was full time to show myself, quietly and unconcernedly, among the wretches who were at that very moment, perhaps, thinking of us and talking of us downstairs. I explained the miserable necessity to Laura, and prevailed on her to recognise it as I did.

'I will come back again, love, in an hour or less,' I said. 'The worst is over for today. Keep yourself quiet and fear nothing.'

'Is the key in the door, Marian? Can I lock it on the inside?'

'Yes, here is the key. Lock the door, and open it to nobody until I come upstairs again.'

I kissed her and left her. It was a relief to me as I walked away to hear the key turned in the lock, and to know that the door was at her own command.

VIII

JUNE 19TH – I had only got as far as the top of the stairs when the locking of Laura's door suggested to me the precaution of also locking my own door, and keeping the key safely about me while I was out of the room. My journal was already secured with other papers in the table drawer, but my writing materials were left out. These included a seal bearing the common device of two doves drinking out of the same cup, and some sheets of blotting-paper, which had the impression on them of the closing lines of my writing in these pages traced during the past night. Distorted by the suspicion which had now become a part of myself, even such trifles as these looked too dangerous to be trusted without a guard – even the locked table drawer seemed to be not sufficiently protected in my absence until the means of access to it had been carefully secured as well.

I found no appearance of any one having entered the room while I had been talking with Laura. My writing materials (which I had given the servant instructions never to meddle with) were scattered over the table much as usual. The only circumstance in connection with them that at all struck me was that the seal lay tidily in the tray with the pencils and the wax. It was not in my careless habits (I am sorry to say) to put it there, neither did I remember putting it there. But as I could not call to mind, on the other hand, where else I had thrown it down, and as I was also doubtful whether I might not for once have laid it mechanically in the right place, I abstained from adding to the perplexity with which the day's events had filled my mind by troubling it afresh about a trifle. I locked the door, put the key in my pocket, and went downstairs.

Madame Fosco was alone in the hall looking at the weather-glass.

'Still falling,' she said. 'I am afraid we must expect more rain.'

Her face was composed again to its customary expression and its customary colour. But the hand with which she pointed to the dial of the weather-glass still trembled.

Could she have told her husband already that she had overheard Laura reviling him, in my company, as a 'spy?' My strong suspicion that she must have told him, my irresistible dread (all the more overpowering from its very vagueness) of the consequences which might follow, my fixed conviction, derived from various little self-betrayals which women notice in each other, that Madame Fosco, in spite of her well-assumed external civility, had not forgiven her niece for innocently standing between her and the legacy of ten thousand pounds – all rushed upon my mind together, all impelled me to speak in the vain hope of using my own influence and my own powers of persuasion for the atonement of Laura's offence.

'May I trust to your kindness to excuse me, Madame Fosco, if I venture to speak to you on an exceedingly painful subject?'

She crossed her hands in front of her and bowed her head solemnly, without uttering a word, and without taking her eyes off mine for a moment.

'When you were so good as to bring me back my handkerchief,' I went on, 'I am very, very much afraid you must have accidentally heard Laura say something which I am unwilling to repeat, and which I will not attempt to defend. I will only venture to hope that you have not thought it of sufficient importance to be mentioned to the Count?'

'I think it of no importance whatever,' said Madame Fosco sharply and suddenly. 'But,' she added, resuming her icy manner in a moment, 'I have no secrets from my husband even in trifles. When he noticed just now that I looked distressed, it was my painful duty to tell him why I was distressed, and I frankly acknowledge to you, Miss Halcombe, that I *have* told him.'

I was prepared to hear it, and yet she turned me cold all over when she said those words.

'Let me earnestly entreat you, Madame Fosco – let me earnestly entreat the Count – to make some allowances for the sad position in which my sister is placed. She spoke while she was smarting under the insult and injustice inflicted on her by her husband, and she was not herself when she said those rash words. May I hope that they will be considerately and generously forgiven?'

'Most assuredly,' said the Count's quiet voice behind me. He had stolen on us with his noiseless tread and his book in his hand from the library.

'When Lady Glyde said those hasty words,' he went on, 'she did me an injustice which I lament – and forgive. Let us never return to the subject, Miss Halcombe; let us all comfortably combine to forget it from this moment.'

'You are very kind,' I said, 'you relieve me inexpressibly—'

I tried to continue, but his eyes were on me; his deadly smile that hides everything was set, hard, and unwavering on his broad, smooth face. My distrust of his unfathomable falseness, my sense of my own degradation in stooping to conciliate his wife and himself, so disturbed and confused me, that the next words failed on my lips, and I stood there in silence.

'I beg you on my knees to say no more, Miss Halcombe – I am truly shocked that you should have thought it necessary to say so much.' With that polite speech he took my hand – oh, how I despise myself! oh, how little comfort there is even in knowing that I submitted to it for Laura's sake! – he took my hand and put it to his poisonous lips. Never did I know all my horror of him till then. That innocent familiarity turned my blood as if it had been the vilest insult that a man could offer me. Yet I hid my disgust from him – I tried to smile – I, who once mercilessly despised deceit in other women, was as false as the worst of them, as false as the Judas whose lips had touched my hand.

I could not have maintained my degrading self-control – it is all that redeems me in my own estimation to know that I could not – if he had still continued to keep his eyes on my face. His wife's tigerish jealousy came to my rescue and forced his attention away from me the moment he possessed himself of my hand. Her cold blue eyes caught light, her dull white cheeks flushed into bright colour, she looked years younger than her age in an instant.

'Count!' she said. 'Your foreign forms of politeness are not understood by Englishwomen.'

'Pardon me, my angel! The best and dearest Englishwoman in the world understands them.' With those words he dropped my hand and quietly raised his wife's hand to his lips in place of it.

I ran back up the stairs to take refuge in my own room. If there had been time to think, my thoughts, when I was alone again, would have caused me bitter suffering. But there was no time to think. Happily for the preservation of my calmness and my courage there was time for nothing but action.

The letters to the lawyer and to Mr Fairlie were still to be written, and I sat down at once without a moment's hesitation to devote myself to them.

There was no multitude of resources to perplex me – there was absolutely no one to depend on, in the first instance, but myself. Sir Percival had neither friends nor relatives in the neighbourhood whose intercession I could attempt to employ. He was on the coldest terms – in some cases on the worst terms with the families of his own rank and station who lived near him. We two women had neither father nor brother to come to the house and take our parts. There was no choice but to write those two doubtful letters, or to put Laura in the wrong and myself in the wrong, and to make all peaceable negotiation in the future impossible by secretly escaping from Blackwater Park. Nothing but the most imminent personal peril could justify our taking that second course. The letters must be tried first, and I wrote them.

I said nothing to the lawyer about Anne Catherick, because (as I had already hinted to Laura) that topic was connected with a mystery which we could not yet explain, and which it would therefore be useless to write about to a professional man. I left my correspondent to attribute Sir Percival's disgraceful conduct, if he pleased, to fresh disputes about money matters, and simply consulted him on the possibility of taking legal proceedings for Laura's protection in the event of her husband's refusal to allow her to leave Blackwater Park for a time and return with me to Limmeridge. I referred him to Mr Fairlie for the details of this last arrangement – I assured him that I wrote with Laura's authority – and I ended by entreating him to act in her name to the utmost extent of his power and with the least possible loss of time.

The letter to Mr Fairlie occupied me next. I appealed to him on the terms which I had mentioned to Laura as the most likely to make him bestir himself; I enclosed a copy of my letter to the lawyer to show him how serious the case was, and I represented our removal to Limmeridge as the only compromise which would prevent the danger and distress of Laura's present position from inevitably affecting her uncle as well as herself at no very distant time.

When I had done, and had sealed and directed the two envelopes, I went back with the letters to Laura's room, to show her that they were written.

'Has anybody disturbed you?' I asked, when she opened the door to me.

'Nobody has knocked,' she replied. 'But I heard some one in the outer room.'

'Was it a man or a woman?'

'A woman. I heard the rustling of her gown.'

'A rustling like silk?'

'Yes, like silk.'

Madame Fosco had evidently been watching outside. The mischief she might do by herself was little to be feared. But the mischief she might do, as a willing instrument in her husband's hands, was too formidable to be overlooked.

'What became of the rustling of the gown when you no longer heard it in the ante-room?' I inquired. 'Did you hear it go past your wall, along the passage?'

'Yes. I kept still and listened, and just heard it.'

'Which way did it go?'

'Towards your room.'

I considered again. The sound had not caught my ears. But I was then deeply absorbed in my letters, and I write with a heavy hand and a quill pen, scraping and scratching noisily over the paper. It was more likely that Madame Fosco would hear the scraping of my pen than that I should hear the rustling of her dress. Another reason (if I had wanted one) for not trusting my letters to the post-bag in the hall.

Laura saw me thinking. 'More difficulties!' she said wearily; 'more difficulties and more dangers!'

'No dangers,' I replied. 'Some little difficulty, perhaps. I am thinking of the safest way of putting my two letters into Fanny's hands.'

'You have really written them, then? Oh, Marian, run no risks – pray, pray run no risks!'

'No, no – no fear. Let me see – what o'clock is it now?'

It was a quarter to six. There would be time for me to get to the village inn, and to come back again before dinner. If I waited till the evening I might find no second opportunity of safely leaving the house.

'Keep the key turned in the lock, Laura,' I said, 'and don't be afraid about me. If you hear any inquiries made, call through the door, and say that I am gone out for a walk.'

'When shall you be back?'

'Before dinner, without fail. Courage, my love. By this time tomorrow you will have a clear-headed, trustworthy man acting for your good. Mr Gilmore's partner is our next best friend to Mr Gilmore himself.'

A moment's reflection, as soon as I was alone, convinced me that I had better not appear in my walking-dress until I had first discovered what was going on in the lower part of the house. I had not ascertained yet whether Sir Percival was indoors or out.

The singing of the canaries in the library, and the smell of tobacco-smoke that came through the door, which was not closed, told me at once where the Count was. I looked over my shoulder as I passed the doorway, and saw to my surprise that he was exhibiting the docility of the birds in his most engagingly polite manner to the housekeeper. He must have specially invited her to see them – for she would never have thought of going into the library of her own accord. The man's slightest actions had a purpose of some kind at the bottom of every one of them. What could be his purpose here?

It was no time then to inquire into his motives. I looked about for Madame Fosco next, and found her following her favourite circle round and round the fish-pond.

I was a little doubtful how she would meet me, after the outbreak of jealousy of which I had been the cause so short a time since. But her husband had tamed her in the interval, and she now spoke to me with the same civility as usual. My only object in addressing myself to her was to ascertain if she knew what had become of Sir Percival. I contrived to refer to him indirectly, and after a little fencing on either side she at last mentioned that he had gone out.

'Which of the horses has he taken?' I asked carelessly.

'None of them,' she replied. 'He went away two hours since on foot. As

I understood it, his object was to make fresh inquiries about the woman named Anne Catherick. He appears to be unreasonably anxious about tracing her. Do you happen to know if she is dangerously mad, Miss Halcombe?'

'I do not, Countess.'

'Are you going in?'

'Yes, I think so. I suppose it will soon be time to dress for dinner.'

We entered the house together. Madame Fosco strolled into the library, and closed the door. I went at once to fetch my hat and shawl. Every moment was of importance, if I was to get to Fanny at the inn and be back before dinner.

When I crossed the hall again no one was there, and the singing of the birds in the library had ceased. I could not stop to make any fresh investigations. I could only assure myself that the way was clear, and then leave the house with the two letters safe in my pocket.

On my way to the village I prepared myself for the possibility of meeting Sir Percival. As long as I had him to deal with alone I felt certain of not losing my presence of mind. Any woman who is sure of her own wits is a match at any time for a man who is not sure of his own temper. I had no such fear of Sir Percival as I had of the Count. Instead of fluttering, it had composed me, to hear of the errand on which he had gone out. While the tracing of Anne Catherick was the great anxiety that occupied him, Laura and I might hope for some cessation of any active persecution at his hands. For our sakes now, as well as for Anne's, I hoped and prayed fervently that she might still escape him.

I walked on as briskly as the heat would let me till I reached the cross-road which led to the village, looking back from time to time to make sure that I was not followed by any one.

Nothing was behind me all the way but an empty country waggon. The noise made by the lumbering wheels annoyed me, and when I found that the waggon took the road to the village, as well as myself, I stopped to let it go by and pass out of hearing. As I looked toward it, more attentively than before, I thought I detected at intervals the feet of a man walking close behind it, the carter being in front, by the side of his horses. The part of the cross-road which I had just passed over was so narrow that the waggon coming after me brushed the trees and thickets on either side, and I had to wait until it went by before I could test the correctness of my impression. Apparently that impression was wrong, for when the waggon had passed me the road behind it was quite clear.

I reached the inn without meeting Sir Percival, and without noticing anything more, and was glad to find that the landlady had received Fanny with all possible kindness. The girl had a little parlour to sit in, away from the noise of the taproom, and a clean bedchamber at the top of the house. She began crying again at the sight of me, and said, poor soul, truly enough, that it was dreadful to feel herself turned out into the world as if she had committed some unpardonable fault, when no blame could be laid at her door by anybody – not even by her master, who had sent her away.

'Try to make the best of it, Fanny,' I said. 'Your mistress and I will stand your friends, and will take care that your character shall not suffer. Now, listen to me. I have very little time to spare, and I am going to put a great trust in your hands. I wish you to take care of these two letters. The one with the stamp on it you are to put into the post when you reach London tomorrow. The other, directed to Mr Fairlie, you are to deliver to him yourself as soon as you get home. Keep both the letters about you and give them up to no one. They are of the last importance to your mistress's interests.'

Fanny put the letters into the bosom of her dress. 'There they shall stop, miss,' she said, 'till I have done what you tell me.'

'Mind you are at the station in good time tomorrow morning,' I continued. 'And when you see the housekeeper at Limmeridge give her my compliments, and say that you are in my service until Lady Glyde is able to take you back. We may meet again sooner than you think. So keep a good heart, and don't miss the seven o'clock train.'

'Thank you, miss – thank you kindly. It gives one courage to hear your voice again. Please to offer my duty to my lady, and say I left all the things as tidy as I could in the time. Oh, dear! dear! who will dress her for dinner today? It really breaks my heart, miss, to think of it.'

When I got back to the house I had only a quarter of an hour to spare to put myself in order for dinner, and to say two words to Laura before I went downstairs.

'The letters are in Fanny's hands,' I whispered to her at the door. 'Do you mean to join us at dinner?'

'Oh, no, no – not for the world.'

'Has anything happened? Has any one disturbed you?'

'Yes – just now – Sir Percival—'

'Did he come in?'

'No, he frightened me by a thump on the door outside. I said, "Who's there?" "You know," he answered. "Will you alter your mind, and tell me the rest? You shall! Sooner or later I'll wring it out of you. You know where Anne Catherick is at this moment." "Indeed, indeed," I said, "I don't." "You do!" he called back. "I'll crush your obstinacy – mind that! – I'll wring it out of you!" He went away with those words – went away, Marian, hardly five minutes ago.'

He had not found Anne! We were safe for that night – he had not found her yet.

'You are going downstairs, Marian? Come up again in the evening.'

'Yes, yes. Don't be uneasy if I am a little late – I must be careful not to give offence by leaving them too soon.'

The dinner-bell rang and I hastened away.

Sir Percival took Madame Fosco into the dining-room, and the Count gave me his arm. He was hot and flushed, and was not dressed with his customary care and completeness. Had he, too, been out before dinner, and been late in getting back? or was he only suffering from the heat a little more severely than usual?

However this might be, he was unquestionably troubled by some secret annoyance or anxiety, which, with all his powers of deception, he was not able entirely to conceal. Through the whole of dinner he was almost as silent as Sir Percival himself, and he, every now and then, looked at his wife with an expression of furtive uneasiness which was quite new in my experience of him. The one social obligation which he seemed to be self-possessed enough to perform as carefully as ever was the obligation of being persistently civil and attentive to me. What vile object he has in view I cannot still discover, but be the design what it may, invariable politeness towards myself, invariable humility towards Laura, and invariable suppression (at any cost) of Sir Percival's clumsy violence, have been the means he has resolutely and impenetrably used to get to his end ever since he set foot in this house. I suspected it when he first interfered in our favour, on the day when the deed was produced in the library, and I feel certain of it now.

When Madame Fosco and I rose to leave the table, the Count rose also to accompany us back to the drawing-room.

'What are you going away for?' asked Sir Percival—'I mean you, Fosco.'

'I am going away because I have had dinner enough, and wine enough,' answered the Count. 'Be so kind, Percival, as to make allowances for my foreign habit of going out with the ladies, as well as coming in with them.'

'Nonsense! Another glass of claret won't hurt you. Sit down again like an Englishman. I want half an hour's quiet talk with you over our wine.'

'A quiet talk, Percival, with all my heart, but not now, and not over the wine. Later in the evening, if you please – later in the evening.'

'Civil!' said Sir Percival savagely. 'Civil behaviour, upon my soul, to a man in his own house!'

I had more than once seen him look at the Count uneasily during dinner-time, and had observed that the Count carefully abstained from looking at him in return. This circumstance, coupled with the host's anxiety for a little quiet talk over the wine, and the guest's obstinate resolution not to sit down again at the table, revived in my memory the request which Sir Percival had vainly addressed to his friend earlier in the day to come out of the library and speak to him. The Count had deferred granting that private interview, when it was first asked for in the afternoon, and had again deferred granting it, when it was a second time asked for at the dinner-table. Whatever the coming subject of discussion between them might be, it was clearly an important subject in Sir Percival's estimation – and perhaps (judging from his evident reluctance to approach it) a dangerous subject as well, in the estimation of the Count.

These considerations occurred to me while we were passing from the dining-room to the drawing-room. Sir Percival's angry commentary on his friend's desertion of him had not produced the slightest effect. The Count obstinately accompanied us to the tea-table – waited a minute or two in the room – went out into the hall – and returned with the post-bag in his hands. It was then eight o'clock – the hour at which the letters were always despatched from Blackwater Park.

'Have you any letter for the post, Miss Halcombe?' he asked, approaching me with the bag.

I saw Madame Fosco, who was making the tea, pause, with the sugar-tongs in her hand, to listen for my answer.

'No, Count, thank you. No letters today.'

He gave the bag to the servant, who was then in the room; sat down at the piano, and played the air of the lively Neapolitan street-song, 'La mia Carolina,' twice over. His wife, who was usually the most deliberate of women in all her movements, made the tea as quickly as I could have made it myself – finished her own cup in two minutes, and quietly glided out of the room.

I rose to follow her example – partly because I suspected her of attempting some treachery upstairs with Laura, partly because I was resolved not to remain alone in the same room with her husband.

Before I could get to the door the Count stopped me, by a request for a cup of tea. I gave him the cup of tea, and tried a second time to get away. He stopped me again – this time by going back to the piano, and suddenly appealing to me on a musical question in which he declared that the honour of his country was concerned.

I vainly pleaded my own total ignorance of music, and total want of taste in that direction. He only appealed to me again with a vehemence which set all further protest on my part at defiance. 'The English and the Germans (he indignantly declared) were always reviling the Italians for their inability to cultivate the higher kinds of music. We were perpetually talking of our Oratorios, and they were perpetually talking of their Symphonies. Did we forget and did they forget his immortal friend and countryman, Rossini? What was Moses in Egypt but a sublime oratorio, which was acted on the stage instead of being coldly sung in a concert-room? What was the overture to Guillaume Tell but a symphony under another name? Had I heard Moses in Egypt? Would I listen to this, and this, and this, and say if anything more sublimely sacred and grand had ever been composed by mortal man?' – And without waiting for a word of assent or dissent on my part, looking me hard in the face all the time, he began thundering on the piano, and singing to it with loud and lofty enthusiasm – only interrupting himself, at intervals, to announce to me fiercely the titles of the different pieces of music: 'Chorus of Egyptians in the Plague of Darkness, Miss Halcombe!'—'Recitativo of Moses with the tables of the Law.'—'Prayer of Israelites, at the passage of the Red Sea. Aha! Aha! Is that sacred? is that sublime?' The piano trembled under his powerful hands, and the teacups on the table rattled, as his big bass voice thundered out the notes, and his heavy foot beat time on the floor.

There was something horrible – something fierce and devilish – in the outburst of his delight at his own singing and playing, and in the triumph with which he watched its effect upon me as I shrank nearer and nearer to the door. I was released at last, not by my own efforts, but by Sir Percival's interposition. He opened the dining-room door, and called out angrily to know what 'that infernal noise' meant. The Count instantly got up from the piano. 'Ah! if Percival is coming,' he said, 'harmony and melody are both at an end. The Muse of Music, Miss Halcombe, deserts us in dismay, and I, the fat old minstrel, exhale the rest of my enthusiasm in the open air!' He stalked out into the verandah, put his hands in his pockets, and resumed the Recitativo of Moses, *sotto voce*, in the garden.

I heard Sir Percival call after him from the dining-room window. But he took no notice – he seemed determined not to hear. That long-deferred quiet talk between them was still to be put off, was still to wait for the Count's absolute will and pleasure.

He had detained me in the drawing-room nearly half an hour from the time when his wife left us. Where had she been, and what had she been doing in that interval?

I went upstairs to ascertain, but I made no discoveries, and when I questioned Laura, I found that she had not heard anything. Nobody had disturbed her, no faint rustling of the silk dress had been audible, either in the ante-room or in the passage.

It was then twenty minutes to nine. After going to my room to get my journal, I returned, and sat with Laura, sometimes writing, sometimes stopping to talk with her. Nobody came near us, and nothing happened. We remained together till ten o'clock. I then rose, said my last cheering words, and wished her good-night. She locked her door again after we had arranged that I should come in and see her the first thing in the morning.

I had a few sentences more to add to my diary before going to bed myself, and as I went down again to the drawing-room after leaving Laura for the last time that weary day, I resolved merely to show myself there, to make my excuses, and then to retire an hour earlier than usual for the night.

Sir Percival, and the Count and his wife, were sitting together. Sir Percival was yawning in an easy-chair, the Count was reading, Madame Fosco was fanning herself. Strange to say, *her* face was flushed now. She, who never suffered from the heat, was most undoubtedly suffering from it tonight.

'I am afraid, Countess, you are not quite so well as usual?' I said.

'The very remark I was about to make to you,' she replied. 'You are looking pale, my dear.'

My dear! It was the first time she had ever addressed me with that familiarity! There was an insolent smile too on her face when she said the words.

'I am suffering from one of my bad headaches,' I answered coldly.

'Ah, indeed? Want of exercise, I suppose? A walk before dinner would have been just the thing for you.' She referred to the 'walk' with a strange emphasis. Had she seen me go out? No matter if she had. The letters were safe now in Fanny's hands.

'Come and have a smoke, Fosco,' said Sir Percival, rising, with another uneasy look at his friend.

'With pleasure, Percival, when the ladies have gone to bed,' replied the Count.

'Excuse me, Countess, if I set you the example of retiring,' I said. 'The only remedy for such a headache as mine is going to bed.'

I took my leave. There was the same insolent smile on the woman's face when I shook hands with her. Sir Percival paid no attention to me. He was looking impatiently at Madame Fosco, who showed no signs of leaving the room with me. The Count smiled to himself behind his book. There was yet another delay to that quiet talk with Sir Percival – and the Countess was the impediment this time.

IX

JUNE 19TH – Once safely shut into my own room, I opened these pages, and prepared to go on with that part of the day's record which was still left to write.

For ten minutes or more I sat idle, with the pen in my hand, thinking over the events of the last twelve hours. When I at last addressed myself to my task, I found a difficulty in proceeding with it which I had never experienced before. In spite of my efforts to fix my thoughts on the matter in hand, they wandered away with the strangest persistency in the one direction of Sir Percival and the Count, and all the interest which I tried to concentrate on my journal centred instead in that private interview between them which had been put off all through the day, and which was now to take place in the silence and solitude of the night.

In this perverse state of my mind, the recollection of what had passed since the morning would not come back to me, and there was no resource but to close my journal and to get away from it for a little while.

I opened the door which led from my bedroom into my sitting-room, and having passed through, pulled it to again, to prevent any accident in case of draught with the candle left on the dressing-table. My sitting-room window was wide open, and I leaned out listlessly to look at the night.

It was dark and quiet. Neither moon nor stars were visible. There was a smell like rain in the still, heavy air, and I put my hand out of the window. No. The rain was only threatening, it had not come yet.

I remained leaning on the window-sill for nearly a quarter of an hour, looking out absently into the black darkness, and hearing nothing, except now and then the voices of the servants, or the distant sound of a closing door, in the lower part of the house.

Just as I was turning away wearily from the window to go back to the bedroom and make a second attempt to complete the unfinished entry in my journal, I smelt the odour of tobacco-smoke stealing towards me on the heavy night air. The next moment I saw a tiny red spark advancing from the farther end of the house in the pitch darkness. I heard no footsteps, and I could see nothing but the spark. It travelled along in the night, passed the window at which I was standing, and stopped opposite my bedroom window, inside which I had left the light burning on the dressing-table.

The spark remained stationary for a moment, then moved back again in the direction from which it had advanced. As I followed its progress I saw a second red spark, larger than the first, approaching from the distance. The two met together in the darkness. Remembering who smoked cigarettes and who smoked cigars, I inferred immediately that the Count had come out first to look and listen under my window, and that Sir Percival had afterwards joined him. They must both have been walking on the lawn – or I should certainly have heard Sir Percival's heavy footfall, though the Count's soft step might have escaped me, even on the gravel walk.

I waited quietly at the window, certain that they could neither of them see me in the darkness of the room.

'What's the matter?' I heard Sir Percival say in a low voice. 'Why don't you come in and sit down?'

'I want to see the light out of that window,' replied the Count softly.

'What harm does the light do?'

'It shows she is not in bed yet. She is sharp enough to suspect something, and bold enough to come downstairs and listen, if she can get the chance. Patience, Percival – patience.'

'Humbug! You're always talking of patience.'

'I shall talk of something else presently. My good friend, you are on the edge of your domestic precipice, and if I let you give the women one other chance, on my sacred word of honour they will push you over it!'

'What the devil do you mean?'

'We will come to our explanations, Percival, when the light is out of that window, and when I have had one little look at the rooms on each side of the library, and a peep at the staircase as well.'

They slowly moved away, and the rest of the conversation between them (which had been conducted throughout in the same low tones) ceased to be audible. It was no matter. I had heard enough to determine me on justifying the Count's opinion of my sharpness and my courage. Before the red sparks were out of sight in the darkness I had made up my mind that there should be a listener when those two men sat down to their talk – and that the listener, in spite of all the Count's precautions to the contrary, should be myself. I wanted but one motive to sanction the act to my own conscience, and to give me courage enough for performing it – and that motive I had. Laura's honour, Laura's happiness – Laura's life itself – might depend on my quick ears and my faithful memory tonight.

I had heard the Count say that he meant to examine the rooms on each side of the library, and the staircase as well, before he entered on any explanation with Sir Percival. This expression of his intentions was necessarily sufficient to inform me that the library was the room in which he proposed that the conversation should take place. The one moment of time which was long enough to bring me to that conclusion was also the moment which showed me a means of baffling his precautions – or, in other words, of hearing what he and Sir Percival said to each other, without the risk of descending at all into the lower regions of the house.

In speaking of the rooms on the ground floor I have mentioned incidentally the verandah outside them, on which they all opened by means of French windows, extending from the cornice to the floor. The top of this verandah was flat, the rain-water being carried off from it by pipes into tanks which helped to supply the house. On the narrow leaden roof, which ran along past the bedrooms, and which was rather less, I should think, than three feet below the sills of the window, a row of flower-pots was ranged, with wide intervals between each pot – the whole being protected from falling in high winds by an ornamental iron railing along the edge of the roof.

The plan which had now occurred to me was to get out at my sitting-room window on to this roof, to creep along noiselessly till I reached that part of it which was immediately over the library window, and to crouch down between the flower-pots, with my ear against the outer railing. If Sir Percival and the Count sat and smoked tonight, as I had seen them sitting and smoking many nights before, with their chairs close at the open window, and their feet stretched on the zinc garden seats which were placed under the verandah, every word they said to each other above a whisper (and no long conversation, as we all know by experience, can be carried on *in* a whisper) must inevitably reach my ears. If, on the other hand, they chose tonight to sit far back inside the room, then the chances were that I should hear little or nothing – and in that case, I must run the far more serious risk of trying to outwit them downstairs.

Strongly as I was fortified in my resolution by the desperate nature of our situation, I hoped most fervently that I might escape this last emergency. My courage was only a woman's courage after all, and it was very near to failing me when I thought of trusting myself on the ground floor, at the dead of night, within reach of Sir Percival and the Count.

I went softly back to my bedroom to try the safer experiment of the verandah roof first.

A complete change in my dress was imperatively necessary for many reasons. I took off my silk gown to begin with, because the slightest noise from it on that still night might have betrayed me. I next removed the white and cumbersome parts of my underclothing, and replaced them by a petticoat of dark flannel. Over this I put my black travelling cloak, and pulled the hood on to my head. In my ordinary evening costume I took up the room of three men at least. In my present dress, when it was held close about me, no man could have passed through the narrowest spaces more easily than I. The little breadth left on the roof of the verandah, between the flower-pots on one side and the wall and the windows of the house on the other, made this a serious consideration. If I knocked anything down, if I made the least noise, who could say what the consequences might be?

I only waited to put the matches near the candle before I extinguished it, and groped my way back into the sitting-room. I locked that door, as I had locked my bedroom door – then quietly got out of the window, and cautiously set my feet on the leaden roof of the verandah.

My two rooms were at the inner extremity of the new wing of the house in which we all lived, and I had five windows to pass before I could reach the position it was necessary to take up immediately over the library. The first window belonged to a spare room which was empty. The second and third windows belonged to Laura's room. The fourth window belonged to Sir Percival's room. The fifth belonged to the Countess's room. The others, by which it was not necessary for me to pass, were the windows of the Count's dressing-room, of the bathroom, and of the second empty spare room.

No sound reached my ears – the black blinding darkness of the night was all round me when I first stood on the verandah, except at that part of it which Madame Fosco's window overlooked. There, at the very place above the library to which my course was directed – there I saw a gleam of light! The Countess was not yet in bed.

It was too late to draw back – it was no time to wait. I determined to go on at all hazards, and trust for security to my own caution and to the darkness of the night. 'For Laura's sake!' I thought to myself, as I took the first step forward on the roof, with one hand holding my cloak close round me, and the other groping against the wall of the house. It was better to brush close by the wall than to risk striking my feet against the flower-pots within a few inches of me, on the other side.

I passed the dark window of the spare room, trying the leaden roof at each step with my foot before I risked resting my weight on it. I passed the dark windows of Laura's room ('God bless her and keep her tonight!'). I passed the dark window of Sir Percival's room. Then I waited a moment, knelt down with my hands to support me, and so crept to my position, under the protection of the low wall between the bottom of the lighted window and the verandah roof.

When I ventured to look up at the window itself I found that the top of it only was open, and that the blind inside was drawn down. While I was looking I saw the shadow of Madame Fosco pass across the white field of the blind – then pass slowly back again. Thus far she could not have heard me, or the shadow would surely have stopped at the blind, even if she had wanted courage enough to open the window and look out?

I placed myself sideways against the railing of the verandah – first ascertaining, by touching them, the position of the flower-pots on either side of me. There was room enough for me to sit between them and no more. The sweet-scented leaves of the flower on my left hand just brushed my cheek as I lightly rested my head against the railing.

The first sounds that reached me from below were caused by the opening or closing (most probably the latter) of three doors in succession – the doors, no doubt, leading into the hall and into the rooms on each side of the library, which the Count had pledged himself to examine. The first object that I saw was the red spark again travelling out into the night from under the verandah, moving away towards my window, waiting a moment, and then returning to the place from which it had set out.

'The devil take your restlessness! When do you mean to sit down?' growled Sir Percival's voice beneath me.

'Ouf! how hot it is!' said the Count, sighing and puffing wearily.

His exclamation was followed by the scraping of the garden chairs on the tiled pavement under the verandah – the welcome sound which told me they were going to sit close at the window as usual. So far the chance was mine. The clock in the turret struck the quarter to twelve as they settled themselves in their chairs. I heard Madame Fosco through the open window yawning, and saw her shadow pass once more across the white field of the blind.

Meanwhile, Sir Percival and the Count began talking together below, now and then dropping their voices a little lower than usual, but never sinking them to a whisper. The strangeness and peril of my situation, the dread, which I could not master, of Madame Fosco's lighted window, made it difficult, almost impossible, for me, at first, to keep my presence of mind, and to fix my attention solely on the conversation beneath. For some minutes I could only succeed in gathering the general substance of it. I understood the Count to say that the one window alight was his wife's, that the ground floor of the house was quite clear, and that they might now speak to each other without fear of accidents. Sir Percival merely answered by upbraiding his friend with having unjustifiably slighted his wishes and neglected his interests all through the day. The Count thereupon defended himself by declaring that he had been beset by certain troubles and anxieties which had absorbed all his attention, and that the only safe time to come to an explanation was a time when they could feel certain of being neither interrupted nor overheard. 'We are at a serious crisis in our affairs, Percival,' he said, 'and if we are to decide on the future at all, we must decide secretly tonight.'

That sentence of the Count's was the first which my attention was ready enough to master exactly as it was spoken. From this point, with certain breaks and interruptions, my whole interest fixed breathlessly on the conversation, and I followed it word for word.

'Crisis?' repeated Sir Percival. 'It's a worse crisis than you think for, I can tell you.'

'So I should suppose, from your behaviour for the last day or two,' returned the other coolly. 'But wait a little. Before we advance to what I do *not* know, let us be quite certain of what I *do* know. Let us first see if I am right about the time that is past, before I make any proposal to you for the time that is to come.'

'Stop till I get the brandy and water. Have some yourself.'

'Thank you, Percival. The cold water with pleasure, a spoon, and the basin of sugar. Eau sucrée, my friend – nothing more.'

'Sugar-and-water for a man of your age! – There! mix your sickly mess. You foreigners are all alike.'

'Now listen, Percival. I will put our position plainly before you, as I understand it, and you shall say if I am right or wrong. You and I both came back to this house from the Continent with our affairs very seriously embarrassed—'

'Cut it short! I wanted some thousands and you some hundreds, and without the money we were both in a fair way to go to the dogs together. There's the situation. Make what you can of it. Go on.'

'Well, Percival, in your own solid English words, you wanted some thousands and I wanted some hundreds, and the only way of getting them was for you to raise the money for your own necessity (with a small margin beyond for my poor little hundreds) by the help of your wife. What did I tell you about your wife on our way to England? – and what did I tell you again when we had come here, and when I had seen for myself the sort of woman Miss Halcombe was?'

'How should I know? You talked nineteen to the dozen, I suppose, just as usual.'

'I said this: Human ingenuity, my friend, has hitherto only discovered two ways in which a man can manage a woman. One way is to knock her down – a method largely adopted by the brutal lower orders of the people, but utterly abhorrent to the refined and educated classes above them. The other way (much longer, much more difficult, but in the end not less certain) is never to accept a provocation at a woman's hands. It holds with animals, it holds with children, and it holds with women, who are nothing but children grown up. Quiet resolution is the one quality the animals, the children, and the women all fail in. If they can once shake this superior quality in their master, they get the better of *him*. If they can never succeed in disturbing it, he gets the better of *them*. I said to you, Remember that plain truth when you want your wife to help you to the money. I said, Remember it doubly and trebly in the presence of your wife's sister, Miss Halcombe. Have you remembered it? Not once in all the complications that have twisted themselves about us in this house. Every provocation that your wife and her sister could offer to you, you instantly accepted from them. Your mad temper lost the signature to the deed, lost the ready money, set Miss Halcombe writing to the lawyer for the first time.'

'First time! Has she written again?'

'Yes, she has written again today.'

A chair fell on the pavement of the verandah – fell with a crash, as if it had been kicked down.

It was well for me that the Count's revelation roused Sir Percival's anger as it did. On hearing that I had been once more discovered I started so that the railing against which I leaned cracked again. Had he followed me to the inn? Did he infer that I must have given my letters to Fanny when I told him I had none for the post-bag. Even if it was so, how could he have examined the letters when they had gone straight from my hand to the bosom of the girl's dress?

'Thank your lucky star,' I heard the Count say next, 'that you have me in the house to undo the harm as fast as you do it. Thank your lucky star that I said No when you were mad enough to talk of turning the key today on Miss Halcombe, as you turned it in your mischievous folly on your wife. Where are your eyes? Can you look at Miss Halcombe and not see that she has the foresight and the resolution of a man? With that woman for my friend I would snap these fingers of mine at the world. With that woman for my enemy, I, with all my brains and experience – I, Fosco, cunning as the devil himself, as you have told me a hundred times – I walk, in your English phrase, upon egg-shells! And this grand creature – I drink her health in my sugar-and-water – this grand creature, who stands in the strength of her love and her courage, firm as a rock, between us two and that poor, flimsy, pretty blonde wife of yours – this magnificent woman, whom I admire with all my soul, though I oppose her in your interests and in mine, you drive to extremities as if she was no sharper and no bolder than the rest of her sex. Percival! Percival! you deserve to fail, and you *have* failed.'

There was a pause. I write the villain's words about myself because I mean to remember them – because I hope yet for the day when I may speak out once for all in his presence, and cast them back one by one in his teeth.

Sir Percival was the first to break the silence again.

'Yes, yes, bully and bluster as much as you like,' he said sulkily; 'the difficulty about the money is not the only difficulty. You would be for taking strong measures with the women yourself – if you knew as much as I do.'

'We will come to that second difficulty all in good time,' rejoined the Count. 'You may confuse yourself, Percival, as much as you please, but you shall not confuse me. Let the question of the money be settled first. Have I convinced your obstinacy? have I shown you that your temper will not let you help yourself? – Or must I go back, and (as you put it in your dear straightforward English) bully and bluster a little more?'

'Pooh! It's easy enough to grumble at *me*. Say what is to be done – that's a little harder.'

'Is it? Bah! This is what is to be done: You give up all direction in the business from tonight – you leave it for the future in my hands only. I am talking to a Practical British man – ha? Well, Practical, will that do for you?'

'What do you propose if I leave it all to you?'

'Answer me first. Is it to be in my hands or not?'

'Say it is in your hands – what then?'

'A few questions, Percival, to begin with. I must wait a little yet, to let circumstances guide me, and I must know, in every possible way, what those circumstances are likely to be. There is no time to lose. I have told you already that Miss Halcombe has written to the lawyer today for the second time.'

'How did you find it out? What did she say?'

'If I told you, Percival, we should only come back at the end to where we are now. Enough that I have found it out – and the finding has caused that trouble and anxiety which made me so inaccessible to you all through today. Now, to refresh my memory about your affairs – it is some time since I talked them over with you. The money has been raised, in the absence of your wife's signature, by means of bills at three months – raised at a cost that makes my poverty-stricken foreign hair stand on end to think of it! When the bills are due, is there really and truly no earthly way of paying them but by the help of your wife?'

'None.'

'What! You have no money at the bankers?'

'A few hundreds, when I want as many thousands.'

'Have you no other security to borrow upon?'

'Not a shred.'

'What have you actually got with your wife at the present moment?'

'Nothing but the interest of her twenty thousand pounds – barely enough to pay our daily expenses.'

'What do you expect from your wife?'

'Three thousand a year when her uncle dies.'

'A fine fortune, Percival. What sort of a man is this uncle? Old?'

'No – neither old nor young.'

'A good-tempered, freely-living man? Married? No – I think my wife told me, not married.'

'Of course not. If he was married, and had a son, Lady Glyde would not be next heir to the property. I'll tell you what he is. He's a maudlin, twaddling, selfish fool, and bores everybody who comes near him about the state of his health.'

'Men of that sort, Percival, live long, and marry malevolently when you least expect it. I don't give you much, my friend, for your chance of the three thousand a year. Is there nothing more that comes to you from your wife?'

'Nothing.'

'Absolutely nothing?'

'Absolutely nothing – except in case of her death.'

'Aha! in the case of her death.'

There was another pause. The Count moved from the verandah to the gravel walk outside. I knew that he had moved by his voice. 'The rain has come at last,' I heard him say. It had come. The state of my cloak showed that it had been falling thickly for some little time.

The Count went back under the verandah – I heard the chair creak beneath his weight as he sat down in it again.

'Well, Percival,' he said, 'and in the case of Lady Glyde's death, what do you get then?'

'If she leaves no children—'

'Which she is likely to do?'

'Which she is not in the least likely to do—'

'Yes?'

'Why, then I get her twenty thousand pounds.'

'Paid down?'

'Paid down.'

They were silent once more. As their voices ceased Madame Fosco's shadow darkened the blind again. Instead of passing this time, it remained, for a moment, quite still. I saw her fingers steal round the corner of the blind, and draw it on one side. The dim white outline of her face, looking out straight over me, appeared behind the window. I kept still, shrouded from head to foot in my black cloak. The rain, which was fast wetting me, dripped over the glass, blurred it, and prevented her from seeing anything. 'More rain!' I heard her say to herself. She dropped the blind, and I breathed again freely.

The talk went on below me, the Count resuming it this time.

'Percival! do you care about your wife?'

'Fosco! that's rather a downright question.'

'I am a downright man, and I repeat it.'

'Why the devil do you look at me in that way?'

'You won't answer me? Well, then, let us say your wife dies before the summer is out—'

'Drop it, Fosco!'

'Let us say your wife dies—'

'Drop it, I tell you!'

'In that case, you would gain twenty thousand pounds, and you would lose—'

'I should lose the chance of three thousand a year.'

'The *remote* chance, Percival – the remote chance only. And you want money, at once. In your position the gain is certain – the loss doubtful.'

'Speak for yourself as well as for me. Some of the money I want has been borrowed for you. And if you come to gain, my wife's death would be ten thousand pounds in your wife's pocket. Sharp as you are, you seem to have conveniently forgotten Madame Fosco's legacy. Don't look at me in that way! I won't have it! What with your looks and your questions, upon my soul, you make my flesh creep!'

'Your flesh? Does flesh mean conscience in English? I speak of your wife's death as I speak of a possibility. Why not? The respectable lawyers who scribble-scrabble your deeds and your wills look the deaths of living people in the face. Do lawyers make your flesh creep? Why should I? It is my business tonight to clear up your position beyond the possibility of mistake, and I have now done it. Here is your position. If your wife lives, you pay those bills with her signature to the parchment. If your wife dies, you pay them with her death.'

As he spoke the light in Madame Fosco's room was extinguished, and the whole second floor of the house was now sunk in darkness.

'Talk! talk!' grumbled Sir Percival. 'One would think, to hear you, that my wife's signature to the deed was got already.'

'You have left the matter in my hands,' retorted the Count, 'and I have more than two months before me to turn round in. Say no more about it, if you please, for the present. When the bills are due, you will see for yourself if my "talk! talk!" is worth something, or if it is not. And now, Percival, having done with the money matters for tonight, I can place my attention at your disposal, if you wish to consult me on that second difficulty which has mixed itself up with our little embarrassments, and which has so altered you for the worse, that I hardly know you again. Speak, my friend – and pardon me if I shock your fiery national tastes by mixing myself a second glass of sugar-and-water.'

'It's very well to say speak,' replied Sir Percival, in a far more quiet and more polite tone than he had yet adopted, 'but it's not so easy to know how to begin.'

'Shall I help you?' suggested the Count. 'Shall I give this private difficulty of yours a name? What if I call it – Anne Catherick?'

'Look here, Fosco, you and I have known each other for a long time, and if you have helped me out of one or two scrapes before this, I have done the best I could to help you in return, as far as money would go. We have made as many friendly sacrifices, on both sides, as men could, but we have had our secrets from each other, of course – haven't we?'

'You have had a secret from me, Percival. There is a skeleton in your cupboard here at Blackwater Park that has peeped out in these last few days at other people besides yourself.'

'Well, suppose it has. If it doesn't concern you, you needn't be curious about it, need you?'

'Do I look curious about it?'

'Yes, you do.'

'So! so! my face speaks the truth, then? What an immense foundation of good there must be in the nature of a man who arrives at my age, and whose face has not yet lost the habit of speaking the truth! – Come, Glyde! let us be candid one with the other. This secret of yours has sought *me*: I have not sought it. Let us say I am curious – do you ask me, as your old friend, to respect your secret, and to leave it, once for all, in your own keeping?'

'Yes – that's just what I do ask.'

'Then my curiosity is at an end. It dies in me from this moment.'

'Do you really mean that?'

'What makes you doubt me?'

'I have had some experience, Fosco, of your roundabout ways, and I am not so sure that you won't worm it out of me after all.'

The chair below suddenly creaked again – I felt the trellis-work pillar under me shake from top to bottom. The Count had started to his feet, and had struck it with his hand in indignation.

'Percival! Percival!' he cried passionately, 'do you know me no better than that? Has all your experience shown you nothing of my character yet? I am a man of the antique type! I am capable of the most exalted acts of virtue – when I have the chance of performing them. It has been the misfortune of my life that I have had few chances. My conception of friendship is sublime! Is it my fault that your skeleton has peeped out at me? Why do I confess my curiosity? You poor superficial Englishman, it is to magnify my own self-control. I could draw your secret out of you, if I liked, as I draw this finger out of the palm of my hand – you know I could! But you have appealed to my friendship, and the duties of friendship are sacred to me. See! I trample my base curiosity under my feet. My exalted sentiments lift me above it. Recognise them, Percival! imitate them, Percival! Shake hands – I forgive you.'

His voice faltered over the last words – faltered, as if he were actually shedding tears!

Sir Percival confusedly attempted to excuse himself, but the Count was too magnanimous to listen to him.

'No!' he said. 'When my friend has wounded me, I can pardon him without apologies. Tell me, in plain words, do you want my help?'

'Yes, badly enough.'

'And you can ask for it without compromising yourself?'

'I can try, at any rate.'

'Try, then.'

'Well, this is how it stands: – I told you today that I had done my best to find Anne Catherick, and failed.'

'Yes, you did.'

'Fosco! I'm a lost man if I *don't* find her.'

'Ha! Is it so serious as that?'

A little stream of light travelled out under the verandah, and fell over the gravel-walk. The Count had taken the lamp from the inner part of the room to see his friend clearly by the light of it.

'Yes!' he said. '*Your* face speaks the truth this time. Serious, indeed – as serious as the money matters themselves.'

'More serious. As true as I sit here, more serious!'

The light disappeared again and the talk went on.

'I showed you the letter to my wife that Anne Catherick hid in the sand,' Sir Percival continued. 'There's no boasting in that letter, Fosco – she *does* know the Secret.'

'Say as little as possible, Percival, in my presence, of the Secret. Does she know it from you?'

'No, from her mother.'

'Two women in possession of your private mind – bad, bad, bad, my friend! One question here, before we go any farther. The motive of your shutting up the daughter in the asylum is now plain enough to me, but the manner of her escape is not quite so clear. Do you suspect the people in charge of her of closing their eyes purposely, at the instance of some enemy who could afford to make it worth their while?'

'No, she was the best-behaved patient they had – and, like fools, they trusted her. She's just mad enough to be shut up, and just sane enough to ruin me when she's at large – if you understand that?'

'I do understand it. Now, Percival, come at once to the point, and then I shall know what to do. Where is the danger of your position at the present moment?'

'Anne Catherick is in this neighbourhood, and in communication with Lady Glyde – there's the danger, plain enough. Who can read the letter she hid in the sand, and not see that my wife is in possession of the Secret, deny it as she may?'

'One moment, Percival. If Lady Glyde does know the Secret, she must know also that it is a compromising secret for you. As your wife, surely it is her interest to keep it?'

'Is it? I'm coming to that. It might be her interest if she cared two straws about me. But I happen to be an encumbrance in the way of another man. She was in love with him before she married me – she's in love with him now – an infernal vagabond of a drawing-master, named Hartright.'

'My dear friend! what is there extraordinary in that? They are all in love with some other man. Who gets the first of a woman's heart? In all my experience I have never yet met with the man who was Number One. Number Two, sometimes. Number Three, Four, Five, often. Number One, never! He exists, of course – but I have not met with him.'

'Wait! I haven't done yet. Who do you think helped Anne Catherick to get the start, when the people from the mad-house were after her? Hartright. Who do you think saw her again in Cumberland? Hartright. Both times he spoke to her alone. Stop! don't interrupt me. The scoundrel's as sweet on my wife as she is on him. He knows the Secret, and she knows the Secret. Once let them both get together again, and it's her interest and his interest to turn their information against me.'

'Gently, Percival – gently! Are you insensible to the virtue of Lady Glyde?'

'That for the virtue of Lady Glyde! I believe in nothing about her but her money. Don't you see how the case stands? She might be harmless enough by herself; but if she and that vagabond Hartright—'

'Yes, yes, I see. Where is Mr Hartright?'

'Out of the country. If he means to keep a whole skin on his bones, I recommend him not to come back in a hurry.'

'Are you sure he is out of the country?'

'Certain. I had him watched from the time he left Cumberland to the time he sailed. Oh, I've been careful, I can tell you! Anne Catherick lived with some people at a farmhouse near Limmeridge. I went there myself, after she had given me the slip, and made sure that they knew nothing. I gave her mother a form of letter to write to Miss Halcombe, exonerating me from any bad motive in putting her under restraint. I've spent, I'm afraid to say how much, in trying to trace her, and in spite of it all, she turns up here and escapes me on my own property! How do I know who else may see her, who else may speak to her? That prying scoundrel, Hartright, may come back without my knowing it, and may make use of her tomorrow—'

'Not he, Percival! While I am on the spot, and while that woman is in the neighbourhood, I will answer for our laying hands on her before Mr Hartright – even if he does come back. I see! yes, yes, I see! The finding of Anne Catherick is the first necessity – make your mind easy about the rest. Your wife is here, under your thumb – Miss Halcombe is inseparable from her, and is, therefore, under your thumb also – and Mr Hartright is out of the country. This invisible Anne of yours is all we have to think of for the present. You have made your inquiries?'

'Yes. I have been to her mother, I have ransacked the village – and all to no purpose.'

'Is her mother to be depended on?'

'Yes.'

'She has told your secret once.'

'She won't tell it again.'

'Why not? Are her own interests concerned in keeping it, as well as yours?'

'Yes – deeply concerned.'

'I am glad to hear it, Percival, for your sake. Don't be discouraged, my friend. Our money matters, as I told you, leave me plenty of time to turn round in, and I may search for Anne Catherick tomorrow to better purpose than you. One last question before we go to bed.'

'What is it?'

'It is this. When I went to the boathouse to tell Lady Glyde that the little difficulty of her signature was put off, accident took me there in time to see a strange woman parting in a very suspicious manner from your wife. But accident did not bring me near enough to see this same woman's face plainly. I must know how to recognise our invisible Anne. What is she like?'

'Like? Come! I'll tell you in two words. She's a sickly likeness of my wife.'

The chair creaked, and the pillar shook once more. The Count was on his feet again – this time in astonishment.

'What!!!' he exclaimed eagerly.

'Fancy my wife, after a bad illness, with a touch of something wrong in her head – and there is Anne Catherick for you,' answered Sir Percival.

'Are they related to each other?'

'Not a bit of it.'

'And yet so like?'

'Yes, so like. What are you laughing about?'

There was no answer, and no sound of any kind. The Count was laughing in his smooth silent internal way.

'What are you laughing about?' reiterated Sir Percival.

'Perhaps at my own fancies, my good friend. Allow me my Italian humour – do I not come of the illustrious nation which invented the exhibition of Punch? Well, well, well, I shall know Anne Catherick when I see her – and so enough for tonight. Make your mind easy, Percival. Sleep, my son, the sleep of the just, and see what I will do for you when daylight comes to help us both. I have my projects and my plans here in my big head. You shall pay those bills and find Anne Catherick – my sacred word of honour on it, but you shall! Am I a friend to be treasured in the best corner of your heart, or am I not? Am I worth those loans of money which you so delicately reminded me of a little while since? Whatever you do, never wound me in my sentiments any more. Recognise them, Percival! imitate them, Percival! I forgive you again – I shake hands again. Good-night!'

Not another word was spoken. I heard the Count close the library door. I heard Sir Percival barring up the window-shutters. It had been raining, raining all the time. I was cramped by my position and chilled to the bones. When I first tried to move, the effort was so painful to me that I was obliged to desist. I tried a second time, and succeeded in rising to my knees on the wet roof.

As I crept to the wall, and raised myself against it, I looked back, and saw the window of the Count's dressing-room gleam into light. My sinking courage flickered up in me again, and kept my eyes fixed on his window, as I stole my way back, step by step, past the wall of the house.

The clock struck the quarter after one, when I laid my hands on the window-sill of my own room. I had seen nothing and heard nothing which could lead me to suppose that my retreat had been discovered.

X

JUNE 20TH – *Eight o'clock*. The sun is shining in a clear sky. I have not been near my bed – I have not once closed my weary wakeful eyes. From the same window at which I looked out into the darkness of last night, I look out now at the bright stillness of the morning.

I count the hours that have passed since I escaped to the shelter of this room by my own sensations – and those hours seem like weeks.

How short a time, and yet how long to *me* – since I sank down in the darkness, here, on the floor – drenched to the skin, cramped in every limb, cold to the bones, a useless, helpless, panic-stricken creature.

I hardly know when I roused myself. I hardly know when I groped my way back to the bedroom, and lighted the candle, and searched (with a strange ignorance, at first, of where to look for them) for dry clothes to warm me. The doing of these things is in my mind, but not the time when they were done.

Can I even remember when the chilled, cramped feeling left me, and the throbbing heat came in its place?

Surely it was before the sun rose? Yes, I heard the clock strike three. I remember the time by the sudden brightness and clearness, the feverish strain and excitement of all my faculties which came with it. I remember my resolution to control myself, to wait patiently hour after hour, till the chance offered of removing Laura from this horrible place, without the danger of immediate discovery and pursuit. I remember the persuasion settling itself in my mind that the words those two men had said to each other would furnish us, not only with our justification for leaving the house, but with our weapons of defence against them as well. I recall the impulse that awakened in me to preserve those words in writing, exactly as they were spoken, while the time was my own, and while my memory vividly retained them. All this I remember plainly: there is no confusion in my head yet. The coming in here from the bedroom, with my pen and ink and paper, before sunrise – the sitting down at the widely-opened window to get all the air I could to cool me – the ceaseless writing, faster and faster, hotter and hotter, driving on more and more wakefully, all through the dreadful interval before the house was astir again – how clearly I recall it, from the beginning by candle-light, to the end on the page before this, in the sunshine of the new day!

Why do I sit here still? Why do I weary my hot eyes and my burning head by writing more? Why not lie down and rest myself, and try to quench the fever that consumes me, in sleep?

I dare not attempt it. A fear beyond all other fears has got possession of me. I am afraid of this heat that parches my skin. I am afraid of the creeping and throbbing that I feel in my head. If I lie down now, how do I know that I may have the sense and the strength to rise again?

Oh, the rain, the rain – the cruel rain that chilled me last night!

Nine o'clock. Was it nine struck, or eight? Nine, surely? I am shivering again – shivering, from head to foot, in the summer air. Have I been sitting here asleep? I don't know what I have been doing.

Oh, my God! am I going to be ill?

Ill, at such a time as this!

My head – I am sadly afraid of my head. I can write, but the lines all run together. I see the words. Laura – I can write Laura, and see I write it. Eight or nine – which was it?

So cold, so cold – oh, that rain last night! – and the strokes of the clock, the strokes I can't count, keep striking in my head –

NOTE

At this place the entry in the Diary ceases to be legible. The two or three lines which follow contain fragments of words only, mingled with blots and scratches of the pen. The last marks on the paper bear some resemblance to the first two letters (L and A) of the name of Lady Glyde.

On the next page of the Diary, another entry appears. It is in a man's handwriting, large, bold, and firmly regular, and the date is 'June the 21st.' It contains these lines –

POSTSCRIPT BY A SINCERE FRIEND

The illness of our excellent Miss Halcombe has afforded me the opportunity of enjoying an unexpected intellectual pleasure.

I refer to the perusal (which I have just completed) of this interesting Diary.

There are many hundred pages here. I can lay my hand on my heart, and declare that every page has charmed, refreshed, delighted me.

To a man of my sentiments it is unspeakably gratifying to be able to say this.

Admirable woman!

I allude to Miss Halcombe.

Stupendous effort!

I refer to the Diary.

Yes! these pages are amazing. The tact which I find here, the discretion, the rare courage, the wonderful power of memory, the accurate observation of character, the easy grace of style, the charming outbursts of womanly feeling, have all inexpressibly increased my admiration of this sublime creature, of this magnificent Marian. The presentation of my own character is masterly in the extreme. I certify, with my whole heart, to the fidelity of the portrait. I feel how vivid an impression I must have produced to have been painted in such strong, such rich, such massive colours as these. I lament afresh the cruel necessity which sets our interests at variance, and opposes us to each other. Under happier circumstances how worthy I should have been of Miss Halcombe – how worthy Miss Halcombe would have been of *me*.

The sentiments which animate my heart assure me that the lines I have just written express a Profound Truth.

Those sentiments exalt me above all merely personal considerations. I bear witness, in the most disinterested manner, to the excellence of the stratagem by which this unparalleled woman surprised the private interview between Percival and myself – also to the marvellous accuracy of her report of the whole conversation from its beginning to its end.

Those sentiments have induced me to offer to the unimpressionable doctor who attends on her my vast knowledge of chemistry, and my luminous experience of the more subtle resources which medical and magnetic science have placed at the disposal of mankind. He has hitherto declined to avail himself of my assistance. Miserable man!

Finally, those sentiments dictate the lines – grateful, sympathetic, paternal lines – which appear in this place. I close the book. My strict sense of propriety restores it (by the hands of my wife) to its place on the writer's table. Events are hurrying me away. Circumstances are guiding me to serious issues. Vast perspectives of success unroll themselves before my eyes. I accomplish my destiny with a calmness which is terrible to myself. Nothing but the homage of my admiration is my own. I deposit it with respectful tenderness at the feet of Miss Halcombe.

I breathe my wishes for her recovery.

I condole with her on the inevitable failure of every plan that she has formed for her sister's benefit. At the same time, I entreat her to believe that the information which I have derived from her Diary will in no respect help me to contribute to that failure. It simply confirms the plan of conduct which I had previously arranged. I have to thank these pages for awakening the finest sensibilities in my nature – nothing more.

To a person of similar sensibility this simple assertion will explain and excuse everything.

Miss Halcombe is a person of similar sensibility.

In that persuasion I sign myself,

FOSCO.

THE STORY CONTINUED BY FREDERICK FAIRLIE, ESQ., OF LIMMERIDGE HOUSE*

It is the grand misfortune of my life that nobody will let me alone.

Why – I ask everybody – why worry *me*? Nobody answers that question, and nobody lets me alone. Relatives, friends, and strangers all combine to annoy me. What have I done? I ask myself, I ask my servant, Louis, fifty times a day – what have I done? Neither of us can tell. Most extraordinary!

The last annoyance that has assailed me is the annoyance of being called upon to write this Narrative. Is a man in my state of nervous wretchedness capable of writing narratives? When I put this extremely reasonable objection, I am told that certain very serious events relating to my niece have happened within my experience, and that I am the fit person to describe them on that account. I am threatened if I fail to exert myself in the manner required, with consequences which I cannot so much as think of without perfect prostration. There is really no need to threaten me. Shattered by my miserable health and my family troubles, I am incapable of resistance. If you insist, you take your unjust advantage of me, and I give way immediately. I will endeavour to remember what I can (under protest), and to write what I can (also under protest), and what I can't remember and can't write, Louis must remember and write for me. He is an ass, and I am an invalid, and we are likely to make all sorts of mistakes between us. How humiliating!

I am told to remember dates. Good heavens! I never did such a thing in my life – how am I to begin now?

I have asked Louis. He is not quite such an ass as I have hitherto supposed. He remembers the date of the event, within a week or two – and I remember the name of the person. The date was towards the end of June, or the beginning of July, and the name (in my opinion a remarkably vulgar one) was Fanny.

At the end of June, or the beginning of July, then, I was reclining in my customary state, surrounded by the various objects of Art which I have collected about me to improve the taste of the barbarous people in my neighbourhood. That is to say, I had the photographs of my pictures, and prints, and coins, and so forth, all about me, which I intend, one of these days, to present (the photographs, I mean, if the clumsy English language will let me mean anything) to present to the institution at Carlisle (horrid place!), with a view to improving the tastes of the members (Goths and Vandals to a man). It might be supposed that a gentleman who was in

---

*The manner in which Mr Fairlie's Narrative and other Narratives that are shortly to follow it, were originally obtained, forms the subject of an explanation which will appear at a later period.

course of conferring a great national benefit on his countrymen was the last gentleman in the world to be unfeelingly worried about private difficulties and family affairs. Quite a mistake, I assure you, in my case.

However, there I was, reclining, with my art-treasures about me, and wanting a quiet morning. Because I wanted a quiet morning, of course Louis came in. It was perfectly natural that I should inquire what the deuce he meant by making his appearance when I had not rung my bell. I seldom swear – it is such an ungentlemanlike habit – but when Louis answered by a grin, I think it was also perfectly natural that I should damn him for grinning. At any rate, I did.

This rigorous mode of treatment, I have observed, invariably brings persons in the lower class of life to their senses. It brought Louis to *his* senses. He was so obliging as to leave off grinning, and inform me that a Young Person was outside wanting to see me. He added (with the odious talkativeness of servants), that her name was Fanny.

'Who is Fanny?'

'Lady Glyde's maid, sir.'

'What does Lady Glyde's maid want with me?'

'A letter, sir—'

'Take it.'

'She refuses to give it to anybody but you, sir.'

'Who sends the letter?'

'Miss Halcombe, sir.'

The moment I heard Miss Halcombe's name I gave up. It is a habit of mine always to give up to Miss Halcombe. I find, by experience, that it saves noise. I gave up on this occasion. Dear Marian!

'Let Lady Glyde's maid come in, Louis. Stop! Do her shoes creak?'

I was obliged to ask the question. Creaking shoes invariably upset me for the day. I was resigned to see the Young Person, but I was *not* resigned to let the Young Person's shoes upset me. There is a limit even to my endurance.

Louis affirmed distinctly that her shoes were to be depended upon. I waved my hand. He introduced her. Is it necessary to say that she expressed her sense of embarrassment by shutting up her mouth and breathing through her nose? To the student of female human nature in the lower orders, surely not.

Let me do the girl justice. Her shoes did *not* creak. But why do Young Persons in service all perspire at the hands? Why have they all got fat noses and hard cheeks? And why are their faces so sadly unfinished, especially about the corners of the eyelids? I am not strong enough to think deeply myself on any subject, but I appeal to professional men, who are. Why have we no variety in our breed of Young Persons?

'You have a letter for me, from Miss Halcombe? Put it down on the table, please, and don't upset anything. How is Miss Halcombe?'

'Very well, thank you, sir.'

'And Lady Glyde?'

I received no answer. The Young Person's face became more unfinished than ever, and I think she began to cry. I certainly saw something moist about her eyes. Tears or perspiration? Louis (whom I have just consulted) is inclined to think, tears. He is in her class of life, and he ought to know best. Let us say, tears.

Except when the refining process of Art judiciously removes from them all resemblance to Nature, I distinctly object to tears. Tears are scientifically described as a Secretion. I can understand that a secretion may be healthy or unhealthy, but I cannot see the interest of a secretion from a sentimental point of view. Perhaps my own secretions being all wrong together, I am a little prejudiced on the subject. No matter. I behaved, on this occasion, with all possible propriety and feeling. I closed my eyes and said to Louis –

'Endeavour to ascertain what she means.'

Louis endeavoured, and the Young Person endeavoured. They succeeded in confusing each other to such an extent that I am bound in common grati-tude to say, they really amused me. I think I shall send for them again when I am in low spirits. I have just mentioned this idea to Louis. Strange to say, it seems to make him uncomfortable. Poor devil!

Surely I am not expected to repeat my niece's maid's explanation of her tears, interpreted in the English of my Swiss valet? The thing is manifestly impossible. I can give my own impressions and feelings perhaps. Will that do as well? Please say, Yes.

My idea is that she began by telling me (through Louis) that her master had dismissed her from her mistress's service. (Observe, throughout, the strange irrelevancy of the Young Person. Was it my fault that she had lost her place?) On her dismissal, she had gone to the inn to sleep. (I don't keep the inn – why mention it to *me*?) Between six o'clock and seven Miss Halcombe had come to say good-bye, and had given her two letters, one for me, and one for a gentleman in London. (I am not a gentleman in London – hang the gentleman in London!) She had carefully put the two letters into her bosom (what have I to do with her bosom?); she had been very unhappy, when Miss Halcombe had gone away again; she had not had the heart to put bit or drop between her lips till it was near bedtime, and then, when it was close on nine o'clock, she had thought she should like a cup of tea. (Am I responsible for any of these vulgar fluctuations, which begin with unhappiness and end with tea?) Just as she was *warming the pot* (I give the words on the authority of Louis, who says he knows what they mean, and wishes to explain, but I snub him on principle) – just as she was warming the pot the door opened, and she was *struck of a heap* (her own words again, and perfectly unintelligible this time to Louis, as well as to myself) by the appearance in the inn parlour of her ladyship the Countess. I give my niece's maid's description of my sister's title with a sense of the highest relish. My poor dear sister is a tiresome woman who married a foreigner. To resume: the door opened, her ladyship the Countess appeared in the parlour, and the Young Person was struck of a heap. Most remarkable!

I must really rest a little before I can get on any farther. When I have reclined for a few minutes, with my eyes closed, and when Louis has refreshed my poor aching temples with a little eau-de-Cologne, I may be able to proceed.

Her ladyship the Countess –

No. I am able to proceed, but not to sit up. I will recline and dictate. Louis has a horrid accent, but he knows the language, and can write. How very convenient!

Her ladyship, the Countess, explained her unexpected appearance at the inn by telling Fanny that she had come to bring one or two little messages which Miss Halcombe in her hurry had forgotten. The Young Person thereupon waited anxiously to hear what the messages were, but the Countess seemed disinclined to mention them (so like my sister's tiresome way!) until Fanny had had her tea. Her ladyship was surprisingly kind and thoughtful about it (extremely unlike my sister), and said, 'I am sure, my poor girl, you must want your tea. We can let the messages wait till afterwards. Come, come, if nothing else will put you at your ease, I'll make the tea and have a cup with you.' I think those were the words, as reported excitably, in my presence, by the Young Person. At any rate, the Countess insisted on making the tea, and carried her ridiculous ostentation of humility so far as to take one cup herself, and to insist on the girl's taking the other. The girl drank the tea, and according to her own account, solemnised the extraordinary occasion five minutes afterwards by fainting dead away for the first time in her life. Here again I use her own words. Louis thinks they were accompanied by an increased secretion of tears. I can't say myself. The effort of listening being quite as much as I could manage, my eyes were closed.

Where did I leave off? Ah, yes – she fainted after drinking a cup of tea with the Countess – a proceeding which might have interested me if I had been her medical man, but being nothing of the sort I felt bored by hearing of it, nothing more. When she came to herself in half an hour's time she was on the sofa, and nobody was with her but the landlady. The Countess, finding it too late to remain any longer at the inn, had gone away as soon as the girl showed signs of recovering, and the landlady had been good enough to help her upstairs to bed.

Left by herself, she had felt in her bosom (I regret the necessity of referring to this part of the subject a second time), and had found the two letters there quite safe, but strangely crumpled. She had been giddy in the night, but had got up well enough to travel in the morning. She had put the letter addressed to that obtrusive stranger, the gentleman in London into the post, and had now delivered the other letter into my hands as she was told. This was the plain truth, and though she could not blame herself for any intentional neglect, she was sadly troubled in her mind, and sadly in want of a word of advice. At this point Louis thinks the secretions appeared again. Perhaps they did, but it is of infinitely greater importance to mention that at this point also I lost my patience, opened my eyes, and interfered.

'What is the purport of all this?' I inquired.

My niece's irrelevant maid stared, and stood speechless.

'Endeavour to explain,' I said to my servant. 'Translate me, Louis.'

Louis endeavoured and translated. In other words, he descended immediately into a bottomless pit of confusion, and the Young Person followed him down. I really don't know when I have been so amused. I left them at the bottom of the pit as long as they diverted me. When they ceased to divert me, I exerted my intelligence, and pulled them up again.

It is unnecessary to say that my interference enabled me, in due course of time, to ascertain the purport of the Young Person's remarks.

I discovered that she was uneasy in her mind, because the train of events that she had just described to me had prevented her from receiving those supplementary messages which Miss Halcombe had intrusted to the Countess to deliver. She was afraid the messages might have been of great importance to her mistress's interests. Her dread of Sir Percival had deterred her from going to Blackwater Park late at night to inquire about them, and Miss Halcombe's own directions to her, on no account to miss the train in the morning, had prevented her from waiting at the inn the next day. She was most anxious that the misfortune of her fainting-fit should not lead to the second misfortune of making her mistress think her neglectful, and she would humbly beg to ask me whether I would advise her to write her explanations and excuses to Miss Halcombe, requesting to receive the messages by letter, if it was not too late. I make no apologies for this extremely prosy paragraph. I have been ordered to write it. There are people, unaccountable as it may appear, who actually take more interest in what my niece's maid said to me on this occasion than in what I said to my niece's maid. Amusing perversity!

'I should feel very much obliged to you, sir, if you would kindly tell me what I had better do,' remarked the Young Person.

'Let things stop as they are,' I said, adapting my language to my listener. 'I invariably let things stop as they are. Yes. Is that all?'

'If you think it would be a liberty in me, sir, to write, of course I wouldn't venture to do so. But I am so very anxious to do all I can to serve my mistress faithfully—'

People in the lower class of life never know when or how to go out of a room. They invariably require to be helped out by their betters. I thought it high time to help the Young Person out. I did it with two judicious words –

'Good-morning.'

Something outside or inside this singular girl suddenly creaked. Louis, who was looking at her (which I was not), says she creaked when she curt-seyed. Curious. Was it her shoes, her stays, or her bones? Louis thinks it was her stays. Most extraordinary!

As soon as I was left by myself I had a little nap – I really wanted it. When I awoke again I noticed dear Marian's letter. If I had had the least idea of what it contained I should certainly not have attempted to open it. Being, unfortunately for myself, quite innocent of all suspicion, I read the letter. It immediately upset me for the day.

I am, by nature, one of the most easy-tempered creatures that ever lived – I make allowances for everybody, and I take offence at nothing. But as I have before remarked, there are limits to my endurance. I laid down Marian's letter, and felt myself – justly felt myself – an injured man.

I am about to make a remark. It is, of course, applicable to the very serious matter now under notice, or I should not allow it to appear in this place.

Nothing, in my opinion, sets the odious selfishness of mankind in such a repulsively vivid light as the treatment, in all classes of society, which the Single people receive at the hands of the Married people. When you have once shown yourself too considerate and self-denying to add a family of your own to an already overcrowded population, you are vindictively marked out by your married friends, who have no similar consideration and no similar self-denial, as the recipient of half their conjugal troubles, and the born friend of all their children. Husbands and wives *talk* of the cares of matrimony, and bachelors and spinsters *bear* them. Take my own case. I considerately remain single, and my poor dear brother Philip inconsiderately marries. What does he do when he dies? He leaves his daughter to *me*. She is a sweet girl – she is also a dreadful responsibility. Why lay her on my shoulders? Because I am bound, in the harmless character of a single man, to relieve my married connections of all their own troubles. I do my best with my brother's respon-sibility – I marry my niece, with infinite fuss and difficulty, to the man her father wanted her to marry. She and her husband disagree, and unpleasant

consequences follow. What does she do with those consequences? She trans-
fers them to *me*. Why transfer them to *me*? Because I am bound, in the
harmless character of a single man, to relieve my married connections of all
their own troubles. Poor single people! Poor human nature!

It is quite unnecessary to say that Marian's letter threatened me. Everybody
threatens me. All sorts of horrors were to fall on my devoted head if I
hesitated to turn Limmeridge House into an asylum for my niece and her
misfortunes. I did hesitate, nevertheless.

I have mentioned that my usual course, hitherto, had been to submit to
dear Marian, and save noise. But on this occasion, the consequences involved
in her extremely inconsiderate proposal were of a nature to make me pause.
If I opened Limmeridge House as an asylum to Lady Glyde, what security
had I against Sir Percival Glyde's following her here in a state of violent
resentment against *me* for harbouring his wife? I saw such a perfect labyrinth
of troubles involved in this proceeding that I determined to feel my ground,
as it were. I wrote, therefore, to dear Marian to beg (as she had no husband
to lay claim to her) that she would come here by herself, first, and talk the
matter over with me. If she could answer my objections to my own perfect
satisfaction, then I assured her that I would receive our sweet Laura with
the greatest pleasure, but not otherwise.

I felt, of course, at the time, that this temporising on my part would probably end in bringing Marian here in a state of virtuous indignation, banging
doors. But then, the other course of proceeding might end in bringing Sir
Percival here in a state of virtuous indignation, banging doors also, and of
the two indignations and bangings I preferred Marian's, because I was used
to her. Accordingly I despatched the letter by return of post. It gained me
time, at all events – and, oh dear me! what a point that was to begin with.

When I am totally prostrated (did I mention that I was totally prostrated
by Marian's letter?) it always takes me three days to get up again. I was very
unreasonable – I expected three days of quiet. Of course I didn't get them.

The third day's post brought me a most impertinent letter from a person
with whom I was totally unacquainted. He described himself as the acting
partner of our man of business – our dear, pig-headed old Gilmore – and he
informed me that he had lately received, by the post, a letter addressed to
him in Miss Halcombe's handwriting. On opening the envelope, he had
discovered, to his astonishment, that it contained nothing but a blank sheet
of note-paper. This circumstance appeared to him so suspicious (as suggesting
to his restless legal mind that the letter had been tampered with) that he had
at once written to Miss Halcombe, and had received no answer by return of
post. In this difficulty, instead of acting like a sensible man and letting things
take their proper course, his next absurd proceeding, on his own showing,

was to pester me by writing to inquire if I knew anything about it. What the deuce should I know about it? Why alarm me as well as himself? I wrote back to that effect. It was one of my keenest letters. I have produced nothing with a sharper epistolary edge to it since I tendered his dismissal in writing to that extremely troublesome person, Mr Walter Hartright.

My letter produced its effect. I heard nothing more from the lawyer.

This perhaps was not altogether surprising. But it was certainly a remarkable circumstance that no second letter reached me from Marian, and that no warning signs appeared of her arrival. Her unexpected absence did me amazing good. It was so very soothing and pleasant to infer (as I did of course) that my married connections had made it up again. Five days of undisturbed tranquillity, of delicious single blessedness, quite restored me. On the sixth day I felt strong enough to send for my photographer, and to set him at work again on the presentation copies of my art-treasures, with a view, as I have already mentioned, to the improvement of taste in this barbarous neighbourhood. I had just dismissed him to his workshop, and had just begun coquetting with my coins, when Louis suddenly made his appearance with a card in his hand.

'Another Young Person?' I said. 'I won't see her. In my state of health Young Persons disagree with me. Not at home.'

'It is a gentleman this time, sir.'

A gentleman of course made a difference. I looked at the card.

Gracious Heaven! my tiresome sister's foreign husband, Count Fosco.

Is it necessary to say what my first impression was when I looked at my visitor's card? Surely not! My sister having married a foreigner, there was but one impression that any man in his senses could possibly feel. Of course the Count had come to borrow money of me.

'Louis,' I said, 'do you think he would go away if you gave him five shillings?'

Louis looked quite shocked. He surprised me inexpressibly by declaring that my sister's foreign husband was dressed superbly, and looked the picture of prosperity. Under these circumstances my first impression altered to a certain extent. I now took it for granted that the Count had matrimonial difficulties of his own to contend with, and that he had come, like the rest of the family, to cast them all on my shoulders.

'Did he mention his business?' I asked.

'Count Fosco said he had come here, sir, because Miss Halcombe was unable to leave Blackwater Park.'

Fresh troubles, apparently. Not exactly his own, as I had supposed, but dear Marian's. Troubles, anyway. Oh dear!

'Show him in,' I said resignedly.

The Count's first appearance really startled me. He was such an alarmingly large person that I quite trembled. I felt certain that he would shake the floor and knock down my art-treasures. He did neither the one nor the other. He was refreshingly dressed in summer costume – his manner was delightfully self-possessed and quiet – he had a charming smile. My first impression of him was highly favourable. It is not creditable to my penetration – as the sequel will show – to acknowledge this, but I am a naturally candid man, and I *do* acknowledge it notwithstanding.

'Allow me to present myself, Mr Fairlie,' he said. 'I come from Blackwater Park, and I have the honour and the happiness of being Madame Fosco's husband. Let me take my first and last advantage of that circumstance by entreating you not to make a stranger of me. I beg you will not disturb yourself – I beg you will not move.'

'You are very good,' I replied. 'I wish I was strong enough to get up. Charmed to see you at Limmeridge. Please take a chair.'

'I am afraid you are suffering today,' said the Count.

'As usual,' I said. 'I am nothing but a bundle of nerves dressed up to look like a man.'

'I have studied many subjects in my time,' remarked this sympathetic person. 'Among others the inexhaustible subject of nerves. May I make a suggestion, at once the simplest and the most profound? Will you let me alter the light in your room?'

'Certainly – if you will be so very kind as not to let any of it in on me.'

He walked to the window. Such a contrast to dear Marian! so extremely considerate in all his movements!

'Light,' he said, in that delightfully confidential tone which is so soothing to an invalid, 'is the first essential. Light stimulates, nourishes, preserves. You can no more do without it, Mr Fairlie, than if you were a flower. Observe. Here, where you sit, I close the shutters to compose you. There, where you do *not* sit, I draw up the blind and let in the invigorating sun. Admit the light into your room if you cannot bear it on yourself. Light, sir, is the grand decree of Providence. You accept Providence with your own restrictions. Accept light on the same terms.'

I thought this very convincing and attentive. He had taken me in up to that point about the light, he had certainly taken me in.

'You see me confused,' he said, returning to his place—'on my word of honour, Mr Fairlie, you see me confused in your presence.'

'Shocked to hear it, I am sure. May I inquire why?'

'Sir, can I enter this room (where you sit a sufferer), and see you surrounded by these admirable objects of Art, without discovering that you are a man whose feelings are acutely impressionable, whose sympathies are perpetually alive? Tell me, can I do this?'

If I had been strong enough to sit up in my chair I should, of course, have bowed. Not being strong enough, I smiled my acknowledgments instead. It did just as well, we both understood one another.

'Pray follow my train of thought,' continued the Count. 'I sit here, a man of refined sympathies myself, in the presence of another man of refined sympathies also. I am conscious of a terrible necessity for lacerating those sympathies by referring to domestic events of a very melancholy kind. What is the inevitable consequence? I have done myself the honour of pointing it out to you already. I sit confused.'

Was it at this point that I began to suspect he was going to bore me? I rather think it was.

'Is it absolutely necessary to refer to these unpleasant matters?' I inquired. 'In our homely English phrase, Count Fosco, won't they keep?'

The Count, with the most alarming solemnity, sighed and shook his head.

'Must I really hear them?'

He shrugged his shoulders (it was the first foreign thing he had done since he had been in the room), and looked at me in an unpleasantly penetrating manner. My instincts told me that I had better close my eyes. I obeyed my instincts.

'Please break it gently,' I pleaded. 'Anybody dead?'

'Dead!' cried the Count, with unnecessary foreign fierceness. 'Mr Fairlie, your national composure terrifies me. In the name of Heaven, what have I said or done to make you think me the messenger of death?'

'Pray accept my apologies,' I answered. 'You have said and done nothing. I make it a rule in these distressing cases always to anticipate the worst. It breaks the blow by meeting it half-way, and so on. Inexpressibly relieved, I am sure, to hear that nobody is dead. Anybody ill?'

I opened my eyes and looked at him. Was he very yellow when he came in, or had he turned very yellow in the last minute or two? I really can't say, and I can't ask Louis, because he was not in the room at the time.

'Anybody ill?' I repeated, observing that my national composure still appeared to affect him.

'That is part of my bad news, Mr Fairlie. Yes. Somebody is ill.'

'Grieved, I am sure. Which of them is it?'

'To my profound sorrow, Miss Halcombe. Perhaps you were in some degree prepared to hear this? Perhaps when you found that Miss Halcombe did not come here by herself, as you proposed, and did not write a second time, your affectionate anxiety may have made you fear that she was ill?'

I have no doubt my affectionate anxiety had led to that melancholy apprehension at some time or other, but at the moment my wretched memory entirely failed to remind me of the circumstance. However, I said yes, in justice to myself. I was much shocked. It was so very uncharacteristic of such a robust person as dear Marian to be ill, that I could only suppose she had met with an accident. A horse, or a false step on the stairs, or something of that sort.

'Is it serious?' I asked.

'Serious – beyond a doubt,' he replied. 'Dangerous – I hope and trust not. Miss Halcombe unhappily exposed herself to be wetted through by a heavy rain. The cold that followed was of an aggravated kind, and it has now brought with it the worst consequence – fever.'

When I heard the word fever, and when I remembered at the same moment that the unscrupulous person who was now addressing me had just come from Blackwater Park, I thought I should have fainted on the spot.

'Good God!' I said. 'Is it infectious?'

'Not at present,' he answered, with detestable composure. 'It may turn to infection – but no such deplorable complication had taken place when I left Blackwater Park. I have felt the deepest interest in the case, Mr Fairlie – I have endeavoured to assist the regular medical attendant in watching it – accept my personal assurances of the uninfectious nature of the fever when I last saw it.'

Accept his assurances! I never was farther from accepting anything in my life. I would not have believed him on his oath. He was too yellow to be believed. He looked like a walking-West-Indian-epidemic. He was big enough to carry typhus by the ton, and to dye the very carpet he walked on with scarlet fever. In certain emergencies my mind is remarkably soon made up. I instantly determined to get rid of him.

'You will kindly excuse an invalid,' I said—'but long conferences of any kind invariably upset me. May I beg to know exactly what the object is to which I am indebted for the honour of your visit?'

I fervently hoped that this remarkably broad hint would throw him off his balance – confuse him – reduce him to polite apologies – in short, get him out of the room. On the contrary, it only settled him in his chair. He became additionally solemn, and dignified, and confidential. He held up two of his horrid fingers and gave me another of his unpleasantly penetrating looks. What was I to do? I was not strong enough to quarrel with him. Conceive my situation, if you please. Is language adequate to describe it? I think not.

'The objects of my visit,' he went on, quite irrepressibly, 'are numbered on my fingers. They are two. First, I come to bear my testimony, with profound sorrow, to the lamentable disagreements between Sir Percival and Lady Glyde. I am Sir Percival's oldest friend – I am related to Lady Glyde by marriage – I am an eye-witness of all that has happened at Blackwater

Park. In those three capacities I speak with authority, with confidence, with honourable regret. Sir, I inform you, as the head of Lady Glyde's family, that Miss Halcombe has exaggerated nothing in the letter which she wrote to your address. I affirm that the remedy which that admirable lady has proposed is the only remedy that will spare you the horrors of public scandal. A temporary separation between husband and wife is the one peaceable solution of this difficulty. Part them for the present, and when all causes of irritation are removed, I, who have now the honour of addressing you – I will undertake to bring Sir Percival to reason. Lady Glyde is innocent, Lady Glyde is injured, but – follow my thought here! – she is, on that very account (I say it with shame), the cause of irritation while she remains under her husband's roof. No other house can receive her with propriety but yours. I invite you to open it.'

Cool. Here was a matrimonial hailstorm pouring in the South of England, and I was invited, by a man with fever in every fold of his coat, to come out from the North of England and take my share of the pelting. I tried to put the point forcibly, just as I have put it here. The Count deliberately lowered one of his horrid fingers, kept the other up, and went on – rode over me, as it were, without even the common coach-manlike attention of crying 'Hi!' before he knocked me down.

'Follow my thought once more, if you please,' he resumed. 'My first object you have heard. My second object in coming to this house is to do what Miss Halcombe's illness has prevented her from doing for herself. My large experience is consulted on all difficult matters at Blackwater Park, and my friendly advice was requested on the interesting subject of your letter to Miss Halcombe. I understood at once – for my sympathies are your sympathies – why you wished to see her here before you pledged yourself to inviting Lady Glyde. You are most right, sir, in hesitating to receive the wife until you are quite certain that the husband will not exert his authority to reclaim her. I agree to that. I also agree that such delicate explanations as this difficulty involves are not explanations which can be properly disposed of by writing only. My presence here (to my own great inconvenience) is the proof that I speak sincerely. As for the explanations themselves, I – Fosco – I, who know Sir Percival much better than Miss Halcombe knows him, affirm to you, on my honour and my word, that he will not come near this house, or attempt to communicate with this house, while his wife is living in it. His affairs are embarrassed. Offer him his freedom by means of the absence of Lady Glyde. I promise you he will take his freedom, and go back to the Continent at the earliest moment when he can get away. Is this clear to you as crystal? Yes, it is. Have you questions to address to me? Be it so, I am here to answer. Ask, Mr Fairlie – oblige me by asking to your heart's content.'

He had said so much already in spite of me, and he looked so dreadfully capable of saying a great deal more also in spite of me, that I declined his amiable invitation in pure self-defence.

'Many thanks,' I replied. 'I am sinking fast. In my state of health I must take things for granted. Allow me to do so on this occasion. We quite understand each other. Yes. Much obliged, I am sure, for your kind interference. If I ever get better, and ever have a second opportunity of improving our acquaintance—'

He got up. I thought he was going. No. More talk, more time for the development of infectious influences – in *my* room, too – remember that, in *my* room!

'One moment yet,' he said, 'one moment before I take my leave. I ask permission at parting to impress on you an urgent necessity. It is this, sir. You must not think of waiting till Miss Halcombe recovers before you receive Lady Glyde. Miss Halcombe has the attendance of the doctor, of the housekeeper at Blackwater Park, and of an experienced nurse as well – three persons for whose capacity and devotion I answer with my life. I tell you that. I tell you, also, that the anxiety and alarm of her sister's illness has already affected the health and spirits of Lady Glyde, and has made her totally unfit to be of use in the sick-room. Her position with her husband grows more and more deplorable and dangerous every day. If you leave her any longer at Blackwater Park, you do nothing whatever to hasten her sister's recovery, and at the same time, you risk the public scandal, which you and I, and all of us, are bound in the sacred interests of the family to avoid. With all my soul, I advise you to remove the serious responsibility of delay from your own shoulders by writing to Lady Glyde to come here at once. Do your affectionate, your honourable, your inevitable duty, and whatever happens in the future, no one can lay the blame on you. I speak from my large experience – I offer my friendly advice. Is it accepted – Yes, or No?'

I looked at him – merely looked at him – with my sense of his amazing assurance, and my dawning resolution to ring for Louis and have him shown out of the room expressed in every line of my face. It is perfectly incredible, but quite true, that my face did not appear to produce the slightest impression on him. Born without nerves – evidently born without nerves.

'You hesitate?' he said. 'Mr Fairlie! I understand that hesitation. You object – see, sir, how my sympathies look straight down into your thoughts! – you object that Lady Glyde is not in health and not in spirits to take the long journey, from Hampshire to this place, by herself. Her own maid is removed from her, as you know, and of other servants fit to travel with her, from one end of England to another, there are none at Blackwater Park. You object, again, that she cannot comfortably stop and rest in London, on her way here, because she cannot comfortably go alone to a public hotel where she is a total stranger. In one breath, I grant both objections – in another breath, I remove them. Follow me, if you please, for the last time. It was my intention, when I returned to England with Sir Percival, to settle myself in the neighbourhood of London. That purpose has just been happily accomplished. I have taken, for six months, a little furnished house in the quarter called St John's Wood. Be so obliging as to keep this fact in your mind, and observe the programme I now propose. Lady Glyde travels to London (a short journey) – I myself meet her at the station – I take her to rest and sleep at my house, which is also the house of her aunt – when she is restored I escort her to the station again – she travels to this place, and her own maid (who is now under your roof) receives her at the carriage-door. Here is comfort consulted – here are the interests of propriety consulted – here is your own duty – duty of hospitality, sympathy, protection, to an unhappy lady in need of all three – smoothed and made easy, from the beginning to the end. I cordially invite you, sir, to second my efforts in the sacred interests of the family. I seriously advise you to write, by my hands, offering the hospitality of your house (and heart), and the hospitality of my house (and heart), to that injured and unfortunate lady whose cause I plead today.'

He waved his horrid hand at me – he struck his infectious breast – he addressed me oratorically, as if I was laid up in the House of Commons. It was high time to take a desperate course of some sort. It was also high time to send for Louis, and adopt the precaution of fumigating the room.

In this trying emergency an idea occurred to me – an inestimable idea which, so to speak, killed two intrusive birds with one stone. I determined to get rid of the Count's tiresome eloquence, and of Lady Glyde's tiresome troubles, by complying with this odious foreigner's request, and writing the letter at once. There was not the least danger of the invitation being accepted, for there was not the least chance that Laura would consent to leave Blackwater Park while Marian was lying there ill. How this charmingly convenient obstacle could have escaped the officious penetration of the Count, it was impossible to conceive – but it *had* escaped him. My dread that he might yet discover it, if I allowed him any more time to think, stimulated me to such an amazing degree, that I struggled into a sitting position – seized, really seized, the writing materials by my side, and produced the letter as rapidly as if I had been a common clerk in an office. 'Dearest Laura, Please come, whenever you like. Break the journey by sleeping in London at your aunt's house. Grieved to hear of dear Marian's illness. Ever affectionately yours.' I handed these lines, at arm's length, to the Count – I sank back in my chair – I said, 'Excuse me – I am entirely prostrated – I can do no more. Will you rest and lunch downstairs? Love to all, and sympathy, and so on. *Good*-morning.'

He made another speech – the man was absolutely inexhaustible. I closed my eyes – I endeavoured to hear as little as possible. In spite of my endeavours I was obliged to hear a great deal. My sister's endless husband congratulated himself, and congratulated me, on the result of our interview – he mentioned a great deal more about his sympathies and mine – he deplored my miserable health – he offered to write me a prescription – he impressed on me the necessity of not forgetting what he had said about the importance of light – he accepted my obliging invitation to rest and lunch – he recommended me to expect Lady Glyde in two or three days' time – he begged my permission to look forward to our next meeting, instead of paining himself and paining me, by saying farewell – he added a great deal more, which, I rejoice to think, I did not attend to at the time, and do not remember now. I heard his sympathetic voice travelling away from me by degrees – but, large as he was, I never heard him. He had the negative merit of being absolutely noiseless. I don't know when he opened the door, or when he shut it. I ventured to make use of my eyes again, after an interval of silence – and he was gone.

I rang for Louis, and retired to my bathroom. Tepid water, strengthened with aromatic vinegar, for myself, and copious fumigation for my study, were the obvious precautions to take, and of course I adopted them. I rejoice to say they proved successful. I enjoyed my customary siesta. I awoke moist and cool.

My first inquiries were for the Count. Had we really got rid of him? Yes – he had gone away by the afternoon train. Had he lunched, and if so, upon what? Entirely upon fruit-tart and cream. What a man! What a digestion!

Am I expected to say anything more? I believe not. I believe I have reached the limits assigned to me. The shocking circumstances which happened at a later period did not, I am thankful to say, happen in my presence. I do beg and entreat that nobody will be so very unfeeling as to lay any part of the blame of those circumstances on me. I did everything for the best. I am not answerable for a deplorable calamity, which it was quite impossible to foresee. I am shattered by it – I have suffered under it, as nobody else has suffered. My servant, Louis (who is really attached to me in his unintelligent way), thinks I shall never get over it. He sees me dictating at this moment, with my handkerchief to my eyes. I wish to mention, in justice to myself, that it was not my fault, and that I am quite exhausted and heartbroken. Need I say more?

THE STORY CONTINUED BY ELIZA MICHELSON
(Housekeeper at Blackwater Park)

I

I am asked to state plainly what I know of the progress of Miss Halcombe's illness and of the circumstances under which Lady Glyde left Blackwater Park for London.

The reason given for making this demand on me is, that my testimony is wanted in the interests of truth. As the widow of a clergyman of the Church of England (reduced by misfortune to the necessity of accepting a situation), I have been taught to place the claims of truth above all other considerations. I therefore comply with a request which I might otherwise, through reluctance to connect myself with distressing family affairs, have hesitated to grant.

I made no memorandum at the time, and I cannot therefore be sure to a day of the date, but I believe I am correct in stating that Miss Halcombe's serious illness began during the last fortnight or ten days in June. The breakfast hour was late at Blackwater Park – sometimes as late as ten, never earlier than half-past nine. On the morning to which I am now referring, Miss Halcombe (who was usually the first to come down) did not make her appearance at the table. After the family had waited a quarter of an hour, the upper housemaid was sent to see after her, and came running out of the room dreadfully frightened. I met the servant on the stairs, and went at once to Miss Halcombe to see what was the matter. The poor lady was incapable of telling me. She was walking about her room with a pen in her hand, quite light-headed, in a state of burning fever.

Lady Glyde (being no longer in Sir Percival's service, I may, without impropriety, mention my former mistress by her name, instead of calling her my lady) was the first to come in from her own bedroom. She was so dreadfully alarmed and distressed that she was quite useless. The Count Fosco, and his lady, who came upstairs immediately afterwards, were both most serviceable and kind. Her ladyship assisted me to get Miss Halcombe to her bed. His lordship the Count remained in the sitting-room, and having sent for my medicine-chest, made a mixture for Miss Halcombe, and a cooling lotion to be applied to her head, so as to lose no time before the doctor came. We applied the lotion, but we could not get her to take the mixture. Sir Percival undertook to send for the doctor. He despatched a groom, on horseback, for the nearest medical man, Mr Dawson, of Oak Lodge.

Mr Dawson arrived in less than an hour's time. He was a respectable elderly man, well known all round the country, and we were much alarmed when we found that he considered the case to be a very serious one.

His lordship the Count affably entered into conversation with Mr Dawson, and gave his opinions with a judicious freedom. Mr Dawson, not over-courteously, inquired if his lordship's advice was the advice of a doctor, and being informed that it was the advice of one who had studied medicine unprofessionally, replied that he was not accustomed to consult with amateur physicians. The Count, with truly Christian meekness of temper, smiled and left the room. Before he went out he told me that he might be found, in case he was wanted in the course of the day, at the boathouse on the banks of the lake. Why he should have gone there, I cannot say. But he did go, remaining away the whole day till seven o'clock, which was dinner-time. Perhaps he wished to set the example of keeping the house as quiet as possible. It was entirely in his character to do so. He was a most considerate nobleman.

Miss Halcombe passed a very bad night, the fever coming and going, and getting worse towards the morning instead of better. No nurse fit to wait on her being at hand in the neighbourhood, her ladyship the Countess and myself undertook the duty, relieving each other. Lady Glyde, most unwisely, insisted on sitting up with us. She was much too nervous and too delicate in health to bear the anxiety of Miss Halcombe's illness calmly. She only did herself harm, without being of the least real assistance. A more gentle and affectionate lady never lived – but she cried, and she was frightened, two weaknesses which made her entirely unfit to be present in a sick-room.

Sir Percival and the Count came in the morning to make their inquiries.

Sir Percival (from distress, I presume, at his lady's affliction and at Miss Halcombe's illness) appeared much confused and unsettled in his mind. His lordship testified, on the contrary, a becoming composure and interest. He had his straw hat in one hand, and his book in the other, and he mentioned to Sir Percival in my hearing that he would go out again and study at the lake. 'Let us keep the house quiet,' he said. 'Let us not smoke indoors, my friend, now Miss Halcombe is ill. You go your way, and I will go mine. When I study I like to be alone. Good-morning, Mrs Michelson.'

Sir Percival was not civil enough – perhaps I ought in justice to say, not composed enough – to take leave of me with the same polite attention. The only person in the house, indeed, who treated me, at that time or at any other, on the footing of a lady in distressed circumstances, was the Count. He had the manners of a true nobleman – he was considerate towards every one. Even the young person (Fanny by name) who attended on Lady Glyde was not beneath his notice. When she was sent away by Sir Percival, his lordship (showing me his sweet little birds at the time) was most kindly anxious to know what had become of her, where she was to go the day she left Blackwater Park, and so on. It is in such little delicate attentions that the advantages of aristocratic birth always show themselves. I make no apology for introducing these particulars – they are brought forward in justice to his lordship, whose character, I have reason to know, is viewed rather harshly in certain quarters. A nobleman who can respect a lady in distressed circumstances, and can take a fatherly interest in the fortunes of an humble servant girl, shows principles and feelings of too high an order to be lightly called in question. I advance no opinions – I offer facts only. My endeavour through life is to judge not that I be not judged. One of my beloved husband's finest sermons was on that text. I read it constantly – in my own copy of the edition printed by subscription, in the first days of my widowhood – and at every fresh perusal I derive an increase of spiritual benefit and edification.

There was no improvement in Miss Halcombe, and the second night was even worse than the first. Mr Dawson was constant in his attendance. The practical duties of nursing were still divided between the Countess and myself, Lady Glyde persisting in sitting up with us, though we both entreated her to take some rest. 'My place is by Marian's bedside,' was her only answer. 'Whether I am ill, or well, nothing will induce me to lose sight of her.'

Towards midday I went downstairs to attend to some of my regular duties. An hour afterwards, on my way back to the sick-room, I saw the Count (who had gone out again early, for the third time) entering the hall, to all appearance in the highest good spirits. Sir Percival, at the same moment, put his head out of the library door, and addressed his noble friend, with extreme eagerness, in these words –

'Have you found her?'

His lordship's large face became dimpled all over with placid smiles, but he made no reply in words. At the same time Sir Percival turned his head, observed that I was approaching the stairs, and looked at me in the most rudely angry manner possible.

'Come in here and tell me about it,' he said to the Count. 'Whenever there are women in a house they're always sure to be going up or down stairs.' 'My dear Percival,' observed his lordship kindly, 'Mrs Michelson has duties. Pray recognise her admirable performance of them as sincerely as I do! How is the sufferer, Mrs Michelson?'

'No better, my lord, I regret to say.'

'Sad – most sad!' remarked the Count. 'You look fatigued, Mrs Michelson. It is certainly time you and my wife had some help in nursing. I think I may be the means of offering you that help. Circumstances have happened which will oblige Madame Fosco to travel to London either tomorrow or the day after. She will go away in the morning and return at night, and she will bring back with her, to relieve you, a nurse of excellent conduct and capacity, who is now disengaged. The woman is known to my wife as a person to be trusted. Before she comes here say nothing about her, if you please, to the doctor, because he will look with an evil eye on any nurse of my providing. When she appears in this house she will speak for herself, and Mr Dawson will be obliged to acknowledge that there is no excuse for not employing her. Lady Glyde will say the same. Pray present my best respects and sympathies to Lady Glyde.'

I expressed my grateful acknowledgments for his lordship's kind consideration. Sir Percival cut them short by calling to his noble friend (using, I regret to say, a profane expression) to come into the library, and not to keep him waiting there any longer.

I proceeded upstairs. We are poor erring creatures, and however well established a woman's principles may be she cannot always keep on her guard against the temptation to exercise an idle curiosity. I am ashamed to say that an idle curiosity, on this occasion, got the better of my principles, and made me unduly inquisitive about the question which Sir Percival had addressed to his noble friend at the library door. Who was the Count expected to find in the course of his studious morning rambles at Blackwater Park? A woman, it was to be presumed, from the terms of Sir Percival's inquiry. I did not suspect the Count of any impropriety – I knew his moral character too well. The only question I asked myself was – Had he found her?

To resume. The night passed as usual without producing any change for the better in Miss Halcombe. The next day she seemed to improve a little. The day after that her ladyship the Countess, without mentioning the object of her journey to any one in my hearing, proceeded by the morning train to London – her noble husband, with his customary attention, accompanying her to the station.

I was now left in sole charge of Miss Halcombe, with every apparent chance, in consequence of her sister's resolution not to leave the bedside, of having Lady Glyde herself to nurse next.

The only circumstance of any importance that happened in the course of the day was the occurrence of another unpleasant meeting between the doctor and the Count.

His lordship, on returning from the station, stepped up into Miss Halcombe's sitting-room to make his inquiries. I went out from the bedroom to speak to him, Mr Dawson and Lady Glyde being both with the patient at the time. The Count asked me many questions about the treatment and the symptoms. I informed him that the treatment was of the kind described as 'saline,' and that the symptoms, between the attacks of fever, were certainly those of increasing weakness and exhaustion. Just as I was mentioning these last particulars, Mr Dawson came out from the bedroom.

'Good-morning, sir,' said his lordship, stepping forward in the most urbane manner, and stopping the doctor, with a high-bred resolution impossible to resist, 'I greatly fear you find no improvement in the symptoms today?'

'I find decided improvement,' answered Mr Dawson.

'You still persist in your lowering treatment of this case of fever?' continued his lordship.

'I persist in the treatment which is justified by my own professional experience,' said Mr Dawson.

'Permit me to put one question to you on the vast subject of professional experience,' observed the Count. 'I presume to offer no more advice – I only presume to make an inquiry. You live at some distance, sir, from the gigantic centres of scientific activity – London and Paris. Have you ever heard of the wasting effects of fever being reasonably and intelligibly repaired by fortifying the exhausted patient with brandy, wine, ammonia, and quinine? Has that new heresy of the highest medical authorities ever reached your ears – Yes or No?'

'When a professional man puts that question to me I shall be glad to answer him,' said the doctor, opening the door to go out. 'You are not a professional man, and I beg to decline answering you.'

Buffeted in this inexcusably uncivil way on one cheek, the Count, like a practical Christian, immediately turned the other, and said, in the sweetest manner, 'Good-morning, Mr Dawson.'

If my late beloved husband had been so fortunate as to know his lordship, how highly he and the Count would have esteemed each other!

Her ladyship the Countess returned by the last train that night, and brought with her the nurse from London. I was instructed that this person's name was Mrs Rubelle. Her personal appearance, and her imperfect English when she spoke, informed me that she was a foreigner.

I have always cultivated a feeling of humane indulgence for foreigners. They do not possess our blessings and advantages, and they are, for the most part, brought up in the blind errors of Popery. It has also always been my precept and practice, as it was my dear husband's precept and practice before me (see Sermon XXIX in the Collection by the late Rev. Samuel Michelson, M.A.), to do as I would be done by. On both these accounts I will not say that Mrs Rubelle struck me as being a small, wiry, sly person, of fifty or thereabouts, with a dark brown or Creole complexion and watchful light grey eyes. Nor will I mention, for the reasons just alleged, that I thought her dress, though it was of the plainest black silk, inappropriately costly in texture and unnecessarily refined in trimming and finish, for a person in her position in

life. I should not like these things to be said of me, and therefore it is my
duty not to say them of Mrs Rubelle. I will merely mention that her manners
were, not perhaps unpleasantly reserved, but only remarkably quiet and
retiring – that she looked about her a great deal, and said very little, which
might have arisen quite as much from her own modesty as from distrust of
her position at Blackwater Park; and that she declined to partake of supper
(which was curious perhaps, but surely not suspicious?), although I myself
politely invited her to that meal in my own room.

At the Count's particular suggestion (so like his lordship's forgiving kindness!), it was arranged that Mrs Rubelle should not enter on her duties until
she had been seen and approved by the doctor the next morning. I sat up
that night. Lady Glyde appeared to be very unwilling that the new nurse
should be employed to attend on Miss Halcombe. Such want of liberality
towards a foreigner on the part of a lady of her education and refinement
surprised me. I ventured to say, 'My lady, we must all remember not to be
hasty in our judgments on our inferiors – especially when they come from
foreign parts.' Lady Glyde did not appear to attend to me. She only sighed,
and kissed Miss Halcombe's hand as it lay on the counterpane. Scarcely a
judicious proceeding in a sick-room, with a patient whom it was highly
desirable not to excite. But poor Lady Glyde knew nothing of nursing –
nothing whatever, I am sorry to say.

The next morning Mrs Rubelle was sent to the sitting-room, to be approved
by the doctor on his way through to the bedroom.

I left Lady Glyde with Miss Halcombe, who was slumbering at the time,
and joined Mrs Rubelle, with the object of kindly preventing her from feeling
strange and nervous in consequence of the uncertainty of her situation. She
did not appear to see it in that light. She seemed to be quite satisfied, beforehand, that Mr Dawson would approve of her, and she sat calmly looking out
of window, with every appearance of enjoying the country air. Some people
might have thought such conduct suggestive of brazen assurance. I beg to
say that I more liberally set it down to extraordinary strength of mind.

Instead of the doctor coming up to us, I was sent for to see the doctor. I
thought this change of affairs rather odd, but Mrs Rubelle did not appear to
be affected by it in any way. I left her still calmly looking out of the window,
and still silently enjoying the country air.

Mr Dawson was waiting for me by himself in the breakfast-room.

'About this new nurse, Mrs Michelson,' said the doctor.

'Yes, sir?'

'I find that she has been brought here from London by the wife of that
fat old foreigner, who is always trying to interfere with me. Mrs Michelson,
the fat old foreigner is a quack.'

This was very rude. I was naturally shocked at it.

'Are you aware, sir,' I said, 'that you are talking of a nobleman?'

'Pooh! He isn't the first quack with a handle to his name. They're all Counts – hang 'em!'

'He would not be a friend of Sir Percival Glyde's, sir, if he was not a member of the highest aristocracy – excepting the English aristocracy, of course.'

'Very well, Mrs Michelson, call him what you like, and let us get back to the nurse. I have been objecting to her already.'

'Without having seen her, sir?'

'Yes, without having seen her. She may be the best nurse in existence, but she is not a nurse of my providing. I have put that objection to Sir Percival, as the master of the house. He doesn't support me. He says a nurse of my providing would have been a stranger from London also, and he thinks the woman ought to have a trial, after his wife's aunt has taken the trouble to fetch her from London. There is some justice in that, and I can't decently say No. But I have made it a condition that she is to go at once, if I find reason to complain of her. This proposal being one which I have some right to make, as medical attendant, Sir Percival has consented to it. Now, Mrs Michelson, I know I can depend on you, and I want you to keep a sharp eye on the nurse for the first day or two, and to see that she gives Miss Halcombe no medicines but mine. This foreign nobleman of yours is dying to try his quack remedies (mesmerism included) on my patient, and a nurse who is brought here by his wife may be a little too willing to help him. You understand? Very well, then, we may go upstairs. Is the nurse there? I'll say a word to her before she goes into the sick-room.'

We found Mrs Rubelle still enjoying herself at the window. When I introduced her to Mr Dawson, neither the doctor's doubtful looks nor the doctor's searching questions appeared to confuse her in the least. She answered him quietly in her broken English, and though he tried hard to puzzle her, she never betrayed the least ignorance, so far, about any part of her duties. This was doubtless the result of strength of mind, as I said before, and not of brazen assurance, by any means.

We all went into the bedroom.

Mrs Rubelle looked very attentively at the patient, curtseyed to Lady Glyde, set one or two little things right in the room, and sat down quietly in a corner to wait until she was wanted. Her ladyship seemed startled and annoyed by the appearance of the strange nurse. No one said anything, for fear of rousing Miss Halcombe, who was still slumbering, except the doctor, who whispered a question about the night. I softly answered, 'Much as usual,' and then Mr Dawson went out. Lady Glyde followed him, I suppose to speak about Mrs Rubelle. For my own part, I had made up my mind already that this quiet foreign person would keep her situation. She had all her wits about her, and she certainly understood her business. So far, I could hardly have done much better by the bedside myself.

Remembering Mr Dawson's caution to me, I subjected Mrs Rubelle to a severe scrutiny at certain intervals for the next three or four days. I over and over again entered the room softly and suddenly, but I never found her out in any suspicious action. Lady Glyde, who watched her as attentively as I did, discovered nothing either. I never detected a sign of the medicine bottles being tampered with, I never saw Mrs Rubelle say a word to the Count, or the Count to her. She managed Miss Halcombe with unquestionable care and discretion. The poor lady wavered backwards and forwards between a sort of sleepy exhaustion, which was half faintness and half slumbering, and attacks of fever which brought with them more or less of wandering in her mind. Mrs Rubelle never disturbed her in the first case, and never startled her in the second, by appearing too suddenly at the bedside in the character of a stranger. Honour to whom honour is due (whether foreign or English) – and I give her privilege impartially to Mrs Rubelle. She was remarkably uncommunicative about herself, and she was too quietly independent of all advice from experienced persons who understood the duties of a sick-room – but with these drawbacks, she was a good nurse, and she never gave either Lady Glyde or Mr Dawson the shadow of a reason for complaining of her.

The next circumstance of importance that occurred in the house was the temporary absence of the Count, occasioned by business which took him to London. He went away (I think) on the morning of the fourth day after the arrival of Mrs Rubelle, and at parting he spoke to Lady Glyde very seriously, in my presence, on the subject of Miss Halcombe.

'Trust Mr Dawson,' he said, 'for a few days more, if you please. But if there is not some change for the better in that time, send for advice from London, which this mule of a doctor must accept in spite of himself. Offend Mr Dawson, and save Miss Halcombe. I say this seriously, on my word of honour and from the bottom of my heart.'

His lordship spoke with extreme feeling and kindness. But poor Lady Glyde's nerves were so completely broken down that she seemed quite frightened at him. She trembled from head to foot, and allowed him to take his leave without uttering a word on her side. She turned to me when he had gone, and said, 'Oh, Mrs Michelson, I am heartbroken about my sister, and I have no friend to advise me! Do you think Mr Dawson is wrong? He told me himself this morning that there was no fear, and no need to send for another doctor.'

'With all respect to Mr Dawson,' I answered, 'in your ladyship's place I should remember the Count's advice.'

Lady Glyde turned away from me suddenly, with an appearance of despair, for which I was quite unable to account.

'*His* advice!' she said to herself. 'God help us – *his* advice!'

The Count was away from Blackwater Park, as nearly as I remember, a week.

Sir Percival seemed to feel the loss of his lordship in various ways, and appeared also, I thought, much depressed and altered by the sickness and sorrow in the house. Occasionally he was so very restless that I could not help noticing it, coming and going, and wandering here and there and everywhere in the grounds. His inquiries about Miss Halcombe, and about his lady (whose failing health seemed to cause him sincere anxiety), were most attentive. I think his heart was much softened. If some kind clerical friend – some such friend as he might have found in my late excellent husband – had been near him at this time, cheering moral progress might have been made with Sir Percival. I seldom find myself mistaken on a point of this sort, having had experience to guide me in my happy married days.

Her ladyship the Countess, who was now the only company for Sir Percival downstairs, rather neglected him, as I considered – or, perhaps, it might have been that he neglected her. A stranger might almost have supposed that they were bent, now they were left together alone, on actually avoiding one another. This, of course, could not be. But it did so happen, nevertheless, that the Countess made her dinner at luncheon-time, and that she always came upstairs towards evening, although Mrs Rubelle had taken the nursing duties entirely off her hands. Sir Percival dined by himself, and William (the man out of livery) made the remark, in my hearing, that his master had put himself on half rations of food and on a double allowance of drink. I attach no importance to such an insolent observation as this on the part of a servant. I reprobated it at the time, and I wish to be understood as reprobating it once more on this occasion.

In the course of the next few days Miss Halcombe did certainly seem to all of us to be mending a little. Our faith in Mr Dawson revived. He appeared to be very confident about the case, and he assured Lady Glyde, when she spoke to him on the subject, that he would himself propose to send for a physician the moment he felt so much as the shadow of a doubt crossing his own mind.

The only person among us who did not appear to be relieved by these words was the Countess. She said to me privately, that she could not feel easy about Miss Halcombe on Mr Dawson's authority, and that she should wait anxiously for her husband's opinion on his return. That return, his letters informed her, would take place in three days' time. The Count and Countess corresponded regularly every morning during his lordship's absence. They were in that respect, as in all others, a pattern to married people.

On the evening of the third day I noticed a change in Miss Halcombe, which caused me serious apprehension. Mrs Rubelle noticed it too. We said nothing on the subject to Lady Glyde, who was then lying asleep, completely overpowered by exhaustion, on the sofa in the sitting-room.

Mr Dawson did not pay his evening visit till later than usual. As soon as he set eyes on his patient I saw his face alter. He tried to hide it, but he looked both confused and alarmed. A messenger was sent to his residence for his medicine-chest, disinfecting preparations were used in the room, and a bed was made up for him in the house by his own directions. 'Has the fever turned to infection?' I whispered to him. 'I am afraid it has,' he answered; 'we shall know better tomorrow morning.'

By Mr Dawson's own directions Lady Glyde was kept in ignorance of this change for the worse. He himself absolutely forbade her, on account of her health, to join us in the bedroom that night. She tried to resist – there was a sad scene – but he had his medical authority to support him, and he carried his point.

The next morning one of the men-servants was sent to London at eleven o'clock, with a letter to a physician in town, and with orders to bring the new doctor back with him by the earliest possible train. Half an hour after the messenger had gone the Count returned to Blackwater Park.

The Countess, on her own responsibility, immediately brought him in to see the patient. There was no impropriety that I could discover in her taking this course. His lordship was a married man, he was old enough to be Miss Halcombe's father, and he saw her in the presence of a female relative, Lady Glyde's aunt. Mr Dawson nevertheless protested against his presence in the room, but I could plainly remark the doctor was too much alarmed to make any serious resistance on this occasion.

The poor suffering lady was past knowing any one about her. She seemed to take her friends for enemies. When the Count approached her bedside her eyes, which had been wandering incessantly round and round the room before, settled on his face with a dreadful stare of terror, which I shall remember to my dying day. The Count sat down by her, felt her pulse and her temples, looked at her very attentively, and then turned round upon the doctor with such an expression of indignation and contempt in his face, that the words failed on Mr Dawson's lips, and he stood for a moment, pale with anger and alarm – pale and perfectly speechless.

His lordship looked next at me.

'When did the change happen?' he asked.

I told him the time.

'Has Lady Glyde been in the room since?'

I replied that she had not. The doctor had absolutely forbidden her to come into the room on the evening before, and had repeated the order again in the morning.

'Have you and Mrs Rubelle been made aware of the full extent of the mischief?' was his next question.

We were aware, I answered, that the malady was considered infectious. He stopped me before I could add anything more.

'It is typhus fever,' he said.

In the minute that passed, while these questions and answers were going on, Mr Dawson recovered himself, and addressed the Count with his customary firmness.

'It is *not* typhus fever,' he remarked sharply. 'I protest against this intrusion, sir. No one has a right to put questions here but me. I have done my duty to the best of my ability—'

The Count interrupted him – not by words, but only by pointing to the bed. Mr Dawson seemed to feel that silent contradiction to his assertion of his own ability, and to grow only the more angry under it.

'I say I have done my duty,' he reiterated. 'A physician has been sent for from London. I will consult on the nature of the fever with him, and with no one else. I insist on your leaving the room.'

'I entered this room, sir, in the sacred interests of humanity,' said the Count. 'And in the same interests, if the coming of the physician is delayed, I will enter it again. I warn you once more that the fever has turned to typhus, and that your treatment is responsible for this lamentable change. If that unhappy lady dies, I will give my testimony in a court of justice that your ignorance and obstinacy have been the cause of her death.'

Before Mr Dawson could answer, before the Count could leave us, the door was opened from the sitting-room, and we saw Lady Glyde on the threshold.

'I *must* and *will* come in,' she said, with extraordinary firmness.

Instead of stopping her, the Count moved into the sitting-room, and made way for her to go in. On all other occasions he was the last man in the world to forget anything, but in the surprise of the moment he apparently forgot the danger of infection from typhus, and the urgent necessity of forcing Lady Glyde to take proper care of herself.

To my astonishment Mr Dawson showed more presence of mind. He stopped her ladyship at the first step she took towards the bedside. 'I am sincerely sorry, I am sincerely grieved,' he said. 'The fever may, I fear, be infectious. Until I am certain that it is not, I entreat you to keep out of the room.'

She struggled for a moment, then suddenly dropped her arms and sank forward. She had fainted. The Countess and I took her from the doctor and carried her into her own room. The Count preceded us, and waited in the passage till I came out and told him that we had recovered her from the swoon.

I went back to the doctor to tell him, by Lady Glyde's desire, that she insisted on speaking to him immediately. He withdrew at once to quiet her ladyship's agitation, and to assure her of the physician's arrival in the course of a few hours. Those hours passed very slowly. Sir Percival and the Count were together downstairs, and sent up from time to time to make their inquiries. At last, between five and six o'clock, to our great relief, the physician came.

He was a younger man than Mr Dawson, very serious and very decided. What he thought of the previous treatment I cannot say, but it struck me as curious that he put many more questions to myself and to Mrs Rubelle than he put to the doctor, and that he did not appear to listen with much interest to what Mr Dawson said, while he was examining Mr Dawson's patient. I began to suspect, from what I observed in this way, that the Count had been right about the illness all the way through, and I was naturally confirmed in that idea when Mr Dawson, after some little delay, asked the one important question which the London doctor had been sent for to set at rest.

'What is your opinion of the fever?' he inquired.

'Typhus,' replied the physician. 'Typhus fever beyond all doubt.'

That quiet foreign person, Mrs Rubelle, crossed her thin brown hands in front of her, and looked at me with a very significant smile. The Count himself could hardly have appeared more gratified if he had been present in the room and had heard the confirmation of his own opinion.

After giving us some useful directions about the management of the patient, and mentioning that he would come again in five days' time, the physician withdrew to consult in private with Mr Dawson. He would offer no opinion on Miss Halcombe's chances of recovery – he said it was impossible at that stage of the illness to pronounce one way or the other.

The five days passed anxiously.

Countess Fosco and myself took it by turns to relieve Mrs Rubelle, Miss Halcombe's condition growing worse and worse, and requiring our utmost care and attention. It was a terribly trying time. Lady Glyde (supported, as Mr Dawson said, by the constant strain of her suspense on her sister's account) rallied in the most extraordinary manner, and showed a firmness and determination for which I should myself never have given her credit. She insisted on coming into the sick-room two or three times every day, to look at Miss Halcombe with her own eyes, promising not to go too close to the bed, if the doctor would consent to her wishes so far. Mr Dawson very unwillingly made the concession required of him – I think he saw that it was hopeless to dispute with her. She came in every day, and she self-denyingly kept her promise. I felt it personally so distressing (as reminding me of my own affliction during my husband's last illness) to see how she suffered under these circumstances, that I must beg not to dwell on this part of the subject any longer. It is more agreeable to me to mention that no fresh disputes took place between Mr Dawson and the Count. His lordship made all his inquiries by deputy, and remained continually in company with Sir Percival downstairs.

On the fifth day the physician came again and gave us a little hope. He said the tenth day from the first appearance of the typhus would probably decide the result of the illness, and he arranged for his third visit to take place on that date. The interval passed as before – except that the Count went to London again one morning and returned at night.

On the tenth day it pleased a merciful Providence to relieve our household from all further anxiety and alarm. The physician positively assured us that Miss Halcombe was out of danger. 'She wants no doctor now – all she requires is careful watching and nursing for some time to come, and that I see she has.' Those were his own words. That evening I read my husband's touching sermon on Recovery from Sickness, with more happiness and advantage (in a spiritual point of view) than I ever remember to have derived from it before.

The effect of the good news on poor Lady Glyde was, I grieve to say, quite overpowering. She was too weak to bear the violent reaction, and in another day or two she sank into a state of debility and depression which obliged her to keep her room. Rest and quiet, and change of air afterwards, were the best remedies which Mr Dawson could suggest for her benefit. It was fortunate that matters were no worse, for, on the very day after she took to her room, the Count and the doctor had another disagreement – and this time the dispute between them was of so serious a nature that Mr Dawson left the house.

I was not present at the time, but I understood that the subject of dispute was the amount of nourishment which it was necessary to give to assist Miss Halcombe's convalescence after the exhaustion of the fever. Mr Dawson, now that his patient was safe, was less inclined than ever to submit to unprofessional interference, and the Count (I cannot imagine why) lost all the self-control which he had so judiciously preserved on former occasions, and taunted the doctor, over and over again, with his mistake about the fever when it changed to typhus. The unfortunate affair ended in Mr Dawson's appealing to Sir Percival, and threatening (now that he could leave without absolute danger to Miss Halcombe) to withdraw from his attendance at Blackwater Park if the Count's interference was not peremptorily suppressed from that moment. Sir Percival's reply (though not designedly uncivil) had only resulted in making matters worse, and Mr Dawson had thereupon withdrawn from the house in a state of extreme indignation at Count Fosco's usage of him, and had sent in his bill the next morning.

We were now, therefore, left without the attendance of a medical man. Although there was no actual necessity for another doctor – nursing and watching being, as the physician had observed, all that Miss Halcombe required – I should still, if my authority had been consulted, have obtained professional assistance from some other quarter, for form's sake.

The matter did not seem to strike Sir Percival in that light. He said it would be time enough to send for another doctor if Miss Halcombe showed any signs of a relapse. In the meanwhile we had the Count to consult in any minor difficulty, and we need not unnecessarily disturb our patient in her present weak and nervous condition by the presence of a stranger at her bedside. There was much that was reasonable, no doubt, in these considerations, but they left me a little anxious nevertheless. Nor was I quite satisfied in my own mind of the propriety of our concealing the doctor's absence as we did from Lady Glyde. It was a merciful deception, I admit – for she was in no state to bear any fresh anxieties. But still it was a deception, and, as such, to a person of my principles, at best a doubtful proceeding.

A second perplexing circumstance which happened on the same day, and which took me completely by surprise, added greatly to the sense of uneasiness that was now weighing on my mind.

I was sent for to see Sir Percival in the library. The Count, who was with him when I went in, immediately rose and left us alone together. Sir Percival civilly asked me to take a seat, and then, to my great astonishment, addressed me in these terms –

'I want to speak to you, Mrs Michelson, about a matter which I decided on some time ago, and which I should have mentioned before, but for the sickness and trouble in the house. In plain words, I have reasons for wishing to break up my establishment immediately at this place – leaving you in charge, of course, as usual. As soon as Lady Glyde and Miss Halcombe can travel they must both have change of air. My friends, Count Fosco and the Countess, will leave us before that time to live in the neighbourhood of London, and I have reasons for not opening the house to any more company, with a view to economising as carefully as I can. I don't blame you, but my expenses here are a great deal too heavy. In short, I shall sell the horses, and get rid of all the servants at once. I never do things by halves, as you know, and I mean to have the house clear of a pack of useless people by this time tomorrow.'

I listened to him, perfectly aghast with astonishment.

'Do you mean, Sir Percival, that I am to dismiss the indoor servants under my charge without the usual month's warning?' I asked.

'Certainly I do. We may all be out of the house before another month, and I am not going to leave the servants here in idleness, with no master to wait on.'

'Who is to do the cooking, Sir Percival, while you are still staying here?'

'Margaret Porcher can roast and boil – keep her. What do I want with a cook if I don't mean to give any dinner-parties?'

'The servant you have mentioned is the most unintelligent servant in the house, Sir Percival.'

'Keep her, I tell you, and have a woman in from the village to do the cleaning and go away again. My weekly expenses must and shall be lowered immediately. I don't send for you to make objections, Mrs Michelson – I send for you to carry out my plans of economy. Dismiss the whole lazy pack of indoor servants tomorrow, except Porcher. She is as strong as a horse – and we'll make her work like a horse.'

'You will excuse me for reminding you, Sir Percival, that if the servants go tomorrow they must have a month's wages in lieu of a month's warning.'

'Let them! A month's wages saves a month's waste and gluttony in the servants' hall.'

This last remark conveyed an aspersion of the most offensive kind on my management. I had too much self-respect to defend myself under so gross an imputation. Christian consideration for the helpless position of Miss Halcombe and Lady Glyde, and for the serious inconvenience which my sudden absence might inflict on them, alone prevented me from resigning my situation on the spot. I rose immediately. It would have lowered me in my own estimation to have permitted the interview to continue a moment longer.

'After that last remark, Sir Percival, I have nothing more to say. Your directions shall be attended to.' Pronouncing those words, I bowed my head with the most distant respect, and went out of the room.

The next day the servants left in a body. Sir Percival himself dismissed the grooms and stablemen, sending them, with all the horses but one, to London. Of the whole domestic establishment, indoors and out, there now remained only myself, Margaret Porcher, and the gardener – this last living in his own cottage, and being wanted to take care of the one horse that remained in the stables.

With the house left in this strange and lonely condition – with the mistress of it ill in her room – with Miss Halcombe still as helpless as a child – and with the doctor's attendance withdrawn from us in enmity – it was surely not unnatural that my spirits should sink, and my customary composure be very hard to maintain. My mind was ill at ease. I wished the poor ladies both well again, and I wished myself away from Blackwater Park.

II

The next event that occurred was of so singular a nature that it might have caused me a feeling of superstitious surprise, if my mind had not been fortified by principle against any pagan weakness of that sort. The uneasy sense of something wrong in the family which had made me wish myself away from Blackwater Park, was actually followed, strange to say, by my departure from the house. It is true that my absence was for a temporary period only, but the coincidence was, in my opinion, not the less remarkable on that account.

My departure took place under the following circumstances –

A day or two after the servants all left I was again sent for to see Sir Percival. The undeserved slur which he had cast on my management of the household did not, I am happy to say, prevent me from returning good for evil to the best of my ability, by complying with his request as readily and respectfully as ever. It cost me a struggle with that fallen nature, which we all share in common, before I could suppress my feelings. Being accustomed to self-discipline, I accomplished the sacrifice.

I found Sir Percival and Count Fosco sitting together again. On this occasion his lordship remained present at the interview, and assisted in the development of Sir Percival's views.

The subject to which they now requested my attention related to the healthy change of air by which we all hoped that Miss Halcombe and Lady Glyde might soon be enabled to profit. Sir Percival mentioned that both the ladies would probably pass the autumn (by invitation of Frederick Fairlie, Esquire) at Limmeridge House, Cumberland. But before they went there, it was his opinion, confirmed by Count Fosco (who here took up the conversation and continued it to the end), that they would benefit by a short residence first in the genial climate of Torquay. The great object, therefore, was to engage lodgings at that place, affording all the comforts and advantages of which they stood in need, and the great difficulty was to find an experienced person capable of choosing the sort of residence which they wanted. In this emergency the Count begged to inquire, on Sir Percival's behalf, whether I would object to give the ladies the benefit of my assistance, by proceeding myself to Torquay in their interests.

It was impossible for a person in my situation to meet any proposal, made in these terms, with a positive objection.

I could only venture to represent the serious inconvenience of my leaving Blackwater Park in the extraordinary absence of all the indoor servants, with the one exception of Margaret Porcher. But Sir Percival and his lordship declared that they were both willing to put up with inconvenience for the sake of the invalids. I next respectfully suggested writing to an agent at Torquay, but I was met here by being reminded of the imprudence of taking lodgings without first seeing them. I was also informed that the Countess (who would otherwise have gone to Devonshire herself) could not, in Lady Glyde's present condition, leave her niece, and that Sir Percival and the Count had business to transact together which would oblige them to remain at Blackwater Park. In short, it was clearly shown me that if I did not undertake the errand, no one else could be trusted with it. Under these circumstances, I could only inform Sir Percival that my services were at the disposal of Miss Halcombe and Lady Glyde.

It was thereupon arranged that I should leave the next morning, that I should occupy one or two days in examining all the most convenient houses in Torquay, and that I should return with my report as soon as I conveniently could. A memorandum was written for me by his lordship, stating the requisites which the place I was sent to take must be found to possess, and a note of the pecuniary limit assigned to me was added by Sir Percival.

My own idea on reading over these instructions was, that no such residence as I saw described could be found at any watering-place in England, and that, even if it could by chance be discovered, it would certainly not be parted with for any period on such terms as I was permitted to offer. I hinted at these difficulties to both the gentlemen, but Sir Percival (who undertook to answer me) did not appear to feel them. It was not for me to dispute the question. I said no more, but I felt a very strong conviction that the business on which I was sent away was so beset by difficulties that my errand was almost hopeless at starting.

Before I left I took care to satisfy myself that Miss Halcombe was going on favourably.

There was a painful expression of anxiety in her face which made me fear that her mind, on first recovering itself, was not at ease. But she was certainly strengthening more rapidly than I could have ventured to anticipate, and she was able to send kind messages to Lady Glyde, saying that she was fast getting well, and entreating her ladyship not to exert herself again too soon. I left her in charge of Mrs Rubelle, who was still as quietly independent of every one else in the house as ever. When I knocked at Lady Glyde's door before going away, I was told that she was still sadly weak and depressed, my informant being the Countess, who was then keeping her company in her room. Sir Percival and the Count were walking on the road to the lodge as I was driven by in the chaise. I bowed to them and quitted the house, with not a living soul left in the servants' offices but Margaret Porcher.

Every one must feel what I have felt myself since that time, that these circumstances were more than unusual – they were almost suspicious. Let me, however, say again that it was impossible for me, in my dependent position, to act otherwise than I did.

The result of my errand at Torquay was exactly what I had foreseen. No such lodgings as I was instructed to take could be found in the whole place, and the terms I was permitted to give were much too low for the purpose, even if I had been able to discover what I wanted. I accordingly returned to Blackwater Park, and informed Sir Percival, who met me at the door, that my journey had been taken in vain. He seemed too much occupied with some other subject to care about the failure of my errand, and his first words informed me that even in the short time of my absence another remarkable change had taken place in the house.

The Count and Countess Fosco had left Blackwater Park for their new residence in St John's Wood.

I was not made aware of the motive for this sudden departure – I was only told that the Count had been very particular in leaving his kind compliments to me. When I ventured on asking Sir Percival whether Lady Glyde had any one to attend to her comforts in the absence of the Countess, he replied that she had Margaret Porcher to wait on her, and he added that a woman from the village had been sent for to do the work downstairs.

The answer really shocked me – there was such a glaring impropriety in permitting an under-housemaid to fill the place of confidential attendant on Lady Glyde. I went upstairs at once, and met Margaret on the bedroom landing. Her services had not been required (naturally enough), her mistress having sufficiently recovered that morning to be able to leave her bed. I asked next after Miss Halcombe, but I was answered in a slouching, sulky way, which left me no wiser than I was before.

I did not choose to repeat the question, and perhaps provoke an impertinent reply. It was in every respect more becoming to a person in my position to present myself immediately in Lady Glyde's room.

I found that her ladyship had certainly gained in health during the last few days. Although still sadly weak and nervous, she was able to get up without assistance, and to walk slowly about her room, feeling no worse effect from the exertion than a slight sensation of fatigue. She had been made a little anxious that morning about Miss Halcombe, through having received no news of her from any one. I thought this seemed to imply a blamable want of attention on the part of Mrs Rubelle, but I said nothing, and remained with Lady Glyde to assist her to dress. When she was ready we both left the room together to go to Miss Halcombe.

We were stopped in the passage by the appearance of Sir Percival. He looked as if he had been purposely waiting there to see us.

'Where are you going?' he said to Lady Glyde.

'To Marian's room,' she answered.

'It may spare you a disappointment,' remarked Sir Percival, 'if I tell you at once that you will not find her there.'

'Not find her there!'

'No. She left the house yesterday morning with Fosco and his wife.'

Lady Glyde was not strong enough to bear the surprise of this extra-ordinary statement. She turned fearfully pale, and leaned back against the wall, looking at her husband in dead silence.

I was so astonished myself that I hardly knew what to say. I asked Sir Percival if he really meant that Miss Halcombe had left Blackwater Park.

'I certainly mean it,' he answered.

'In her state, Sir Percival! Without mentioning her intentions to Lady Glyde!'

Before he could reply her ladyship recovered herself a little and spoke.

'Impossible!' she cried out in a loud, frightened manner, taking a step or two forward from the wall. 'Where was the doctor? where was Mr Dawson when Marian went away?'

'Mr Dawson wasn't wanted, and wasn't here,' said Sir Percival. 'He left of his own accord, which is enough of itself to show that she was strong enough to travel. How you stare! If you don't believe she has gone, look for yourself. Open her room door, and all the other room doors if you like.'

She took him at his word, and I followed her. There was no one in Miss Halcombe's room but Margaret Porcher, who was busy setting it to rights. There was no one in the spare rooms or the dressing-rooms when we looked into them afterwards. Sir Percival still waited for us in the passage. As we were leaving the last room that we had examined Lady Glyde whispered, 'Don't go, Mrs Michelson! don't leave me, for God's sake!' Before I could say anything in return she was out again in the passage, speaking to her husband.

'What does it mean, Sir Percival? I insist – I beg and pray you will tell me what it means.'

'It means,' he answered, 'that Miss Halcombe was strong enough yesterday morning to sit up and be dressed, and that she insisted on taking advantage of Fosco's going to London to go there too.'

'To London!'

'Yes – on her way to Limmeridge.'

Lady Glyde turned and appealed to me.

'You saw Miss Halcombe last,' she said. 'Tell me plainly, Mrs Michelson, did you think she looked fit to travel?'

'Not in *my* opinion, your ladyship.'

Sir Percival, on his side, instantly turned and appealed to me also.

'Before you went away,' he said, 'did you, or did you not, tell the nurse that Miss Halcombe looked much stronger and better?'

'I certainly made the remark, Sir Percival.'

He addressed her ladyship again the moment I offered that reply.

'Set one of Mrs Michelson's opinions fairly against the other,' he said, 'and try to be reasonable about a perfectly plain matter. If she had not been well enough to be moved do you think we should any of us have risked letting her go? She has got three competent people to look after her – Fosco and your aunt, and Mrs Rubelle, who went away with them expressly for that purpose. They took a whole carriage yesterday, and made a bed for her on the seat in case she felt tired. Today, Fosco and Mrs Rubelle go on with her themselves to Cumberland.'

'Why does Marian go to Limmeridge and leave me here by myself?' said her ladyship, interrupting Sir Percival.

'Because your uncle won't receive you till he has seen your sister first,' he replied. 'Have you forgotten the letter he wrote to her at the beginning of her illness? It was shown to you, you read it yourself, and you ought to remember it.'

'I do remember it.'

'If you do, why should you be surprised at her leaving you? You want to be back at Limmeridge, and she has gone there to get your uncle's leave for you on his own terms.'

Poor Lady Glyde's eyes filled with tears.

'Marian never left me before,' she said, 'without bidding me good-bye.'

'She would have bid you good-bye this time,' returned Sir Percival, 'if she had not been afraid of herself and of you. She knew you would try to stop her, she knew you would distress her by crying. Do you want to make any more objections? If you do, you must come downstairs and ask questions in the dining-room. These worries upset me. I want a glass of wine.'

He left us suddenly.

His manner all through this strange conversation had been very unlike what it usually was. He seemed to be almost as nervous and fluttered, every now and then, as his lady herself. I should never have supposed that his health had been so delicate, or his composure so easy to upset.

I tried to prevail on Lady Glyde to go back to her room, but it was useless.

She stopped in the passage, with the look of a woman whose mind was panic-stricken.

'Something has happened to my sister!' she said.

'Remember, my lady, what surprising energy there is in Miss Halcombe,' I suggested. 'She might well make an effort which other ladies in her situation would be unfit for. I hope and believe there is nothing wrong – I do indeed.'

'I must follow Marian,' said her ladyship, with the same panic-stricken look. 'I must go where she has gone, I must see that she is alive and well with my own eyes. Come! come down with me to Sir Percival.'

I hesitated, fearing that my presence might be considered an intrusion. I attempted to represent this to her ladyship, but she was deaf to me. She held my arm fast enough to force me to go downstairs with her, and she still clung to me with all the little strength she had at the moment when I opened the dining-room door.

Sir Percival was sitting at the table with a decanter of wine before him. He raised the glass to his lips as we went in and drained it at a draught. Seeing that he looked at me angrily when he put it down again, I attempted to make some apology for my accidental presence in the room.

'Do you suppose there are any secrets going on here?' he broke out suddenly; 'there are none – there is nothing underhand, nothing kept from you or from any one.' After speaking those strange words loudly and sternly, he filled himself another glass of wine and asked Lady Glyde what she wanted of him.

'If my sister is fit to travel I am fit to travel,' said her ladyship, with more firmness than she had yet shown. 'I come to beg you will make allowances for my anxiety about Marian, and let me follow her at once by the afternoon train.'

'You must wait till tomorrow,' replied Sir Percival, 'and then if you don't hear to the contrary you can go. I don't suppose you are at all likely to hear to the contrary, so I shall write to Fosco by tonight's post.'

He said those last words holding his glass up to the light, and looking at the wine in it instead of at Lady Glyde. Indeed he never once looked at her throughout the conversation. Such a singular want of good breeding in a gentleman of his rank impressed me, I own, very painfully.

'Why should you write to Count Fosco?' she asked, in extreme surprise.

'To tell him to expect you by the midday train,' said Sir Percival. 'He will meet you at the station when you get to London, and take you on to sleep at your aunt's in St John's Wood.'

Lady Glyde's hand began to tremble violently round my arm – why I could not imagine.

'There is no necessity for Count Fosco to meet me,' she said. 'I would rather not stay in London to sleep.'

'You must. You can't take the whole journey to Cumberland in one day. You must rest a night in London – and I don't choose you to go by yourself to an hotel. Fosco made the offer to your uncle to give you house-room on the way down, and your uncle has accepted it. Here! here is a letter from him addressed to yourself. I ought to have sent it up this morning, but I forgot. Read it and see what Mr Fairlie himself says to you.'

Lady Glyde looked at the letter for a moment and then placed it in my hands.

'Read it,' she said faintly. 'I don't know what is the matter with me. I can't read it myself.'

It was a note of only four lines – so short and so careless that it quite struck me. If I remember correctly it contained no more than these words –

'Dearest Laura, Please come whenever you like. Break the journey by sleeping at your aunt's house. Grieved to hear of dear Marian's illness. Affectionately yours, Frederick Fairlie.'

'I would rather not go there – I would rather not stay a night in London,' said her ladyship, breaking out eagerly with those words before I had quite done reading the note, short as it was. 'Don't write to Count Fosco! Pray, pray don't write to him!'

Sir Percival filled another glass from the decanter so awkwardly that he upset it and spilt all the wine over the table. 'My sight seems to be failing me,' he muttered to himself, in an odd, muffled voice. He slowly set the glass up again, refilled it, and drained it once more at a draught. I began to fear, from his look and manner, that the wine was getting into his head.

'Pray don't write to Count Fosco,' persisted Lady Glyde, more earnestly than ever.

'Why not, I should like to know?' cried Sir Percival, with a sudden burst of anger that startled us both. 'Where can you stay more properly in London than at the place your uncle himself chooses for you – at your aunt's house? Ask Mrs Michelson.'

The arrangement proposed was so unquestionably the right and the proper one, that I could make no possible objection to it. Much as I sympathised with Lady Glyde in other respects, I could not sympathise with her in her unjust prejudices against Count Fosco. I never before met with any lady of her rank and station who was so lamentably narrow-minded on the subject of foreigners. Neither her uncle's note nor Sir Percival's increasing impatience seemed to have the least effect on her. She still objected to staying a night in London, she still implored her husband not to write to the Count.

'Drop it!' said Sir Percival, rudely turning his back on us. 'If you haven't

sense enough to know what is best for yourself other people must know it
for you. The arrangement is made and there is an end of it. You are only
wanted to do what Miss Halcombe has done for you –'

'Marian?' repeated her Ladyship, in a bewildered manner; 'Marian sleeping
in Count Fosco's house!'

'Yes, in Count Fosco's house. She slept there last night to break the
journey, and you are to follow her example, and do what your uncle tells
you. You are to sleep at Fosco's tomorrow night, as your sister did, to break
the journey. Don't throw too many obstacles in my way! don't make me
repent of letting you go at all!'

He started to his feet, and suddenly walked out into the verandah through
the open glass doors.

'Will your ladyship excuse me,' I whispered, 'if I suggest that we had
better not wait here till Sir Percival comes back? I am very much afraid he
is over-excited with wine.'

She consented to leave the room in a weary, absent manner.

As soon as we were safe upstairs again, I did all I could to compose her
ladyship's spirits. I reminded her that Mr Fairlie's letters to Miss Halcombe
and to herself did certainly sanction, and even render necessary, sooner or
later, the course that had been taken. She agreed to this, and even admitted,
of her own accord, that both letters were strictly in character with her uncle's
peculiar disposition – but her fears about Miss Halcombe, and her unaccountable dread of sleeping at the Count's house in London, still remained
unshaken in spite of every consideration that I could urge. I thought it my
duty to protest against Lady Glyde's unfavourable opinion of his lordship,
and I did so, with becoming forbearance and respect.

'Your ladyship will pardon my freedom,' I remarked, in conclusion, 'but
it is said, "by their fruits ye shall know them." I am sure the Count's constant
kindness and constant attention, from the very beginning of Miss Halcombe's
illness, merit our best confidence and esteem. Even his lordship's serious
misunderstanding with Mr Dawson was entirely attributable to his anxiety
on Miss Halcombe's account.'

'What misunderstanding?' inquired her ladyship, with a look of sudden
interest.

I related the unhappy circumstances under which Mr Dawson had withdrawn his attendance – mentioning them all the more readily because I
disapproved of Sir Percival's continuing to conceal what had happened (as
he had done in my presence) from the knowledge of Lady Glyde.

Her ladyship started up, with every appearance of being additionally
agitated and alarmed by what I had told her.

'Worse! worse than I thought!' she said, walking about the room, in a bewildered manner. 'The Count knew Mr Dawson would never consent to Marian's taking a journey – he purposely insulted the doctor to get him out of the house.'

'Oh, my lady! my lady!' I remonstrated.

'Mrs Michelson!' she went on vehemently, 'no words that ever were spoken will persuade me that my sister is in that man's power and in that man's house with her own consent. My horror of him is such, that nothing Sir Percival could say and no letters my uncle could write, would induce me, if I had only my own feelings to consult, to eat, drink, or sleep under his roof. But my misery of suspense about Marian gives me the courage to follow her anywhere, to follow her even into Count Fosco's house.'

I thought it right, at this point, to mention that Miss Halcombe had already gone on to Cumberland, according to Sir Percival's account of the matter.

'I am afraid to believe it!' answered her ladyship. 'I am afraid she is still in that man's house. If I am wrong, if she has really gone on to Limmeridge, I am resolved I will not sleep tomorrow night under Count Fosco's roof. My dearest friend in the world, next to my sister, lives near London. You have heard me, you have heard Miss Halcombe, speak of Mrs Vesey? I mean to write, and propose to sleep at her house. I don't know how I shall get there – I don't know how I shall avoid the Count – but to that refuge I will escape in some way, if my sister has gone to Cumberland. All I ask of you to do, is to see yourself that my letter to Mrs Vesey goes to London tonight, as certainly as Sir Percival's letter goes to Count Fosco. I have reasons for not trusting the post-bag downstairs. Will you keep my secret, and help me in this? it is the last favour, perhaps, that I shall ever ask of you.'

I hesitated, I thought it all very strange, I almost feared that her ladyship's mind had been a little affected by recent anxiety and suffering. At my own risk, however, I ended by giving my consent. If the letter had been addressed to a stranger, or to any one but a lady so well known to me by report as Mrs Vesey, I might have refused. I thank God – looking to what happened afterwards – I thank God I never thwarted that wish, or any other, which Lady Glyde expressed to me, on the last day of her residence at Blackwater Park.

The letter was written and given into my hands. I myself put it into the post-box in the village that evening.

We saw nothing more of Sir Percival for the rest of the day.

I slept, by Lady Glyde's own desire, in the next room to hers, with the door open between us. There was something so strange and dreadful in the loneliness and emptiness of the house, that I was glad, on my side, to have a companion near me. Her ladyship sat up late, reading letters and burning them, and emptying her drawers and cabinets of little things she prized, as if she never expected to return to Blackwater Park. Her sleep was sadly disturbed when she at last went to bed – she cried out in it several times, once so loud that she woke herself. Whatever her dreams were, she did not think fit to communicate them to me. Perhaps, in my situation, I had no right to expect that she should do so. It matters little now. I was sorry for her, I was indeed heartily sorry for her all the same.

The next day was fine and sunny. Sir Percival came up, after breakfast, to tell us that the chaise would be at the door at a quarter to twelve – the train to London stopping at our station at twenty minutes after. He informed Lady Glyde that he was obliged to go out, but added that he hoped to be back before she left. If any unforeseen accident delayed him, I was to accompany her to the station, and to take special care that she was in time for the train. Sir Percival communicated these directions very hastily – walking here and there about the room all the time. Her ladyship looked attentively after him wherever he went. He never once looked at her in return.

She only spoke when he had done, and then she stopped him as he approached the door, by holding out her hand.

'I shall see you no more,' she said, in a very marked manner. 'This is our parting – our parting, it may be for ever. Will you try to forgive me, Percival, as heartily as I forgive *you*?'

His face turned of an awful whiteness all over, and great beads of perspiration broke out on his bald forehead. 'I shall come back,' he said, and made for the door, as hastily as if his wife's farewell words had frightened him out of the room.

I had never liked Sir Percival, but the manner in which he left Lady Glyde made me feel ashamed of having eaten his bread and lived in his service. I thought of saying a few comforting and Christian words to the poor lady, but there was something in her face, as she looked after her husband when the door closed on him, that made me alter my mind and keep silence.

At the time named the chaise drew up at the gates. Her ladyship was right – Sir Percival never came back. I waited for him till the last moment, and waited in vain.

No positive responsibility lay on my shoulders, and yet I did not feel easy in my mind. 'It is of your own free will,' I said, as the chaise drove through the lodge-gates, 'that your ladyship goes to London?'

'I will go anywhere,' she answered, 'to end the dreadful suspense that I am suffering at this moment.'

She had made me feel almost as anxious and as uncertain about Miss Halcombe as she felt herself. I presumed to ask her to write me a line, if all went well in London. She answered, 'Most willingly, Mrs Michelson.'

'We all have our crosses to bear, my lady,' I said, seeing her silent and thoughtful, after she had promised to write.

She made no reply – she seemed to be too much wrapped up in her own thoughts to attend to me.

'I fear your ladyship rested badly last night,' I remarked, after waiting a little.

'Yes,' she said, 'I was terribly disturbed by dreams.'

'Indeed, my lady?' I thought she was going to tell me her dreams, but no, when she spoke next it was only to ask a question.

'You posted the letter to Mrs Vesey with your own hands?'

'Yes, my lady.'

'Did Sir Percival say, yesterday, that Count Fosco was to meet me at the terminus in London?'

'He did, my lady.'

She sighed heavily when I answered that last question, and said no more.

We arrived at the station, with hardly two minutes to spare. The gardener (who had driven us) managed about the luggage, while I took the ticket. The whistle of the train was sounding when I joined her ladyship on the platform. She looked very strangely, and pressed her hand over her heart, as if some sudden pain or fright had overcome her at that moment.

'I wish you were going with me!' she said, catching eagerly at my arm when I gave her the ticket.

If there had been time, if I had felt the day before as I felt then, I would have made my arrangements to accompany her, even though the doing so had obliged me to give Sir Percival warning on the spot. As it was, her wishes, expressed at the last moment only, were expressed too late for me to comply with them. She seemed to understand this herself before I could explain it, and did not repeat her desire to have me for a travelling companion. The train drew up at the platform. She gave the gardener a present for his children, and took my hand, in her simple hearty manner, before she got into the carriage.

'You have been very kind to me and to my sister,' she said—'kind when we were both friendless. I shall remember you gratefully, as long as I live to remember any one. Good-bye – and God bless you!'

She spoke those words with a tone and a look which brought the tears into my eyes – she spoke them as if she was bidding me farewell for ever.

'Good-bye, my lady,' I said, putting her into the carriage, and trying to cheer her; 'good-bye, for the present only; good-bye, with my best and kindest wishes for happier times.'

She shook her head, and shuddered as she settled herself in the carriage. The guard closed the door. 'Do you believe in dreams?' she whispered to me at the window. 'My dreams, last night, were dreams I have never had before. The terror of them is hanging over me still.' The whistle sounded before I could answer, and the train moved. Her pale quiet face looked at me for the last time – looked sorrowfully and solemnly from the window. She waved her hand, and I saw her no more.

Towards five o'clock on the afternoon of that same day, having a little time to myself in the midst of the household duties which now pressed upon me, I sat down alone in my own room, to try and compose my mind with the volume of my husband's Sermons. For the first time in my life I found my attention wandering over those pious and cheering words. Concluding that Lady Glyde's departure must have disturbed me far more seriously than I had myself supposed, I put the book aside, and went out to take a turn in the garden. Sir Percival had not yet returned, to my knowledge, so I could feel no hesitation about showing myself in the grounds.

On turning the corner of the house, and gaining a view of the garden, I was startled by seeing a stranger walking in it. The stranger was a woman – she was lounging along the path with her back to me, and was gathering the flowers.

As I approached she heard me, and turned round.

My blood curdled in my veins. The strange woman in the garden was Mrs Rubelle!

I could neither move nor speak. She came up to me, as composedly as ever, with her flowers in her hand.

'What is the matter, ma'am?' she said quietly.

'You here!' I gasped out. 'Not gone to London! Not gone to Cumberland!'

Mrs Rubelle smelt at her flowers with a smile of malicious pity.

'Certainly not,' she said. 'I have never left Blackwater Park.'

I summoned breath enough and courage enough for another question.

'Where is Miss Halcombe?'

Mrs Rubelle fairly laughed at me this time, and replied in these words –

'Miss Halcombe, ma'am, has not left Blackwater Park either.'

When I heard that astounding answer, all my thoughts were startled back on the instant to my parting with Lady Glyde. I can hardly say I reproached myself, but at that moment I think I would have given many a year's hard savings to have known four hours earlier what I knew now.

Mrs Rubelle waited, quietly arranging her nosegay, as if she expected me to say something.

I could say nothing. I thought of Lady Glyde's worn-out energies and weakly health, and I trembled for the time when the shock of the discovery that I had made would fall on her. For a minute or more my fears for the poor ladies silenced me. At the end of that time Mrs Rubelle looked up sideways from her flowers, and said, 'Here is Sir Percival, ma'am, returned from his ride.'

I saw him as soon as she did. He came towards us, slashing viciously at the flowers with his riding-whip. When he was near enough to see my face he stopped, struck at his boot with the whip, and burst out laughing, so harshly and so violently that the birds flew away, startled, from the tree by which he stood.

'Well, Mrs Michelson,' he said, 'you have found it out at last, have you?'

I made no reply. He turned to Mrs Rubelle.

'When did you show yourself in the garden?'

'I showed myself about half an hour ago, sir. You said I might take my liberty again as soon as Lady Glyde had gone away to London.'

'Quite right. I don't blame you – I only asked the question.' He waited a moment, and then addressed himself once more to me. 'You can't believe it, can you?' he said mockingly. 'Here! come along and see for yourself.'

He led the way round to the front of the house. I followed him, and Mrs Rubelle followed me. After passing through the iron gates he stopped, and pointed with his whip to the disused middle wing of the building.

'There!' he said. 'Look up at the first floor. You know the old Elizabethan bedrooms? Miss Halcombe is snug and safe in one of the best of them at this moment. Take her in, Mrs Rubelle (you have got your key?); take Mrs Michelson in, and let her own eyes satisfy her that there is no deception this time.'

The tone in which he spoke to me, and the minute or two that had passed since we left the garden, helped me to recover my spirits a little. What I might have done at this critical moment, if all my life had been passed in service, I cannot say. As it was, possessing the feelings, the principles, and the bringing up of a lady, I could not hesitate about the right course to pursue. My duty to myself, and my duty to Lady Glyde, alike forbade me to remain in the employment of a man who had shamefully deceived us both by a series of atrocious falsehoods.

'I must beg permission, Sir Percival, to speak a few words to you in private,' I said. 'Having done so, I shall be ready to proceed with this person to Miss Halcombe's room.'

Mrs Rubelle, whom I had indicated by a slight turn of my head, insolently sniffed at her nosegay and walked away, with great deliberation, towards the house door.

'Well,' said Sir Percival sharply, 'what is it now?'

'I wish to mention, sir, that I am desirous of resigning the situation I now hold at Blackwater Park.' That was literally how I put it. I was resolved that the first words spoken in his presence should be words which expressed my intention to leave his service.

He eyed me with one of his blackest looks, and thrust his hands savagely into the pockets of his riding-coat.

'Why?' he said, 'why, I should like to know?'

'It is not for me, Sir Percival, to express an opinion on what has taken place in this house. I desire to give no offence. I merely wish to say that I do not feel it consistent with my duty to Lady Glyde and to myself to remain any longer in your service.'

'Is it consistent with your duty to me to stand there, casting suspicion on me to my face?' he broke out in his most violent manner. 'I see what you're driving at. You have taken your own mean, underhand view of an innocent deception practised on Lady Glyde for her own good. It was essential to her health that she should have a change of air immediately, and you know as well as I do she would never have gone away if she had been told Miss Halcombe was still left here. She has been deceived in her own interests – and I don't care who knows it. Go, if you like – there are plenty of house-keepers as good as you to be had for the asking. Go when you please – but take care how you spread scandals about me and my affairs when you're out of my service. Tell the truth, and nothing but the truth, or it will be the worse for you! See Miss Halcombe for yourself – see if she hasn't been as well taken care of in one part of the house as in the other. Remember the doctor's own orders that Lady Glyde was to have a change of air at the earliest possible opportunity. Bear all that well in mind, and then say anything against me and my proceedings if you dare!'

He poured out these words fiercely, all in a breath, walking backwards and forwards, and striking about him in the air with his whip.

Nothing that he said or did shook my opinion of the disgraceful series of falsehoods that he had told in my presence the day before, or of the cruel deception by which he had separated Lady Glyde from her sister, and had sent her uselessly to London, when she was half distracted with anxiety on Miss Halcombe's account. I naturally kept these thoughts to myself, and said nothing more to irritate him; but I was not the less resolved to persist in my purpose. A soft answer turneth away wrath, and I suppressed my own feelings accordingly when it was my turn to reply.

'While I am in your service, Sir Percival,' I said, 'I hope I know my duty well enough not to inquire into your motives. When I am out of your service, I hope I know my own place well enough not to speak of matters which don't concern me—'

'When do you want to go?' he asked, interrupting me without ceremony. 'Don't suppose I am anxious to keep you – don't suppose I care about your leaving the house. I am perfectly fair and open in this matter, from first to last. When do you want to go?'

'I should wish to leave at your earliest convenience, Sir Percival.'

'My convenience has nothing to do with it. I shall be out of the house for good and all tomorrow morning, and I can settle your accounts tonight. If you want to study anybody's convenience, it had better be Miss Halcombe's. Mrs Rubelle's time is up today, and she has reasons for wishing to be in London tonight. If you go at once, Miss Halcombe won't have a soul left here to look after her.'

I hope it is unnecessary for me to say that I was quite incapable of deserting Miss Halcombe in such an emergency as had now befallen Lady Glyde and herself. After first distinctly ascertaining from Sir Percival that Mrs Rubelle was certain to leave at once if I took her place, and after also obtaining permission to arrange for Mr Dawson's resuming his attendance on his patient, I willingly consented to remain at Blackwater Park until Miss Halcombe no longer required my services. It was settled that I should give Sir Percival's solicitor a week's notice before I left, and that he was to undertake the necessary arrangements for appointing my successor. The matter was discussed in very few words. At its conclusion Sir Percival abruptly turned on his heel, and left me free to join Mrs Rubelle. That singular foreign person had been sitting composedly on the door-step all this time, waiting till I could follow her to Miss Halcombe's room.

I had hardly walked half-way towards the house when Sir Percival, who had withdrawn in the opposite direction, suddenly stopped and called me back.

'Why are you leaving my service?' he asked.

The question was so extraordinary, after what had just passed between us, that I hardly knew what to say in answer to it.

'Mind! I don't know why you are going,' he went on. 'You must give a reason for leaving me, I suppose, when you get another situation. What reason? The breaking up of the family? Is that it?'

'There can be no positive objection, Sir Percival, to that reason—'

'Very well! That's all I want to know. If people apply for your character, that's your reason, stated by yourself. You go in consequence of the breaking up of the family.'

He turned away again before I could say another word, and walked out rapidly into the grounds. His manner was as strange as his language. I acknowledge he alarmed me.

Even the patience of Mrs Rubelle was getting exhausted, when I joined her at the house door.

'At last!' she said, with a shrug of her lean foreign shoulders. She led the way into the inhabited side of the house, ascended the stairs, and opened with her key the door at the end of the passage, which communicated with the old Elizabethan rooms – a door never previously used, in my time, at Blackwater Park. The rooms themselves I knew well, having entered them myself on various occasions from the other side of the house. Mrs Rubelle stopped at the third door along the old gallery, handed me the key of it, with the key of the door of communication, and told me I should find Miss Halcombe in that room. Before I went in I thought it desirable to make her understand that her attendance had ceased. Accordingly, I told her in plain words that the charge of the sick lady henceforth devolved entirely on myself.

'I am glad to hear it, ma'am,' said Mrs Rubelle. 'I want to go very much.'

'Do you leave today?' I asked, to make sure of her.

'Now that you have taken charge, ma'am, I leave in half an hour's time. Sir Percival has kindly placed at my disposition the gardener, and the chaise, whenever I want them. I shall want them in half an hour's time to go to the station. I am packed up in anticipation already. I wish you good-day, ma'am.'

She dropped a brisk curtsey, and walked back along the gallery, humming a little tune, and keeping time to it cheerfully with the nosegay in her hand. I am sincerely thankful to say that was the last I saw of Mrs Rubelle.

When I went into the room Miss Halcombe was asleep. I looked at her anxiously, as she lay in the dismal, high, old-fashioned bed. She was certainly not in any respect altered for the worse since I had seen her last. She had not been neglected, I am bound to admit, in any way that I could perceive. The room was dreary, and dusty, and dark, but the window (looking on a solitary court-yard at the back of the house) was opened to let in the fresh air, and all that could be done to make the place comfortable had been done. The whole cruelty of Sir Percival's deception had fallen on poor Lady Glyde. The only ill-usage which either he or Mrs Rubelle had inflicted on Miss Halcombe consisted, so far as I could see, in the first offence of hiding her away.

I stole back, leaving the sick lady still peacefully asleep, to give the gardener instructions about bringing the doctor. I begged the man, after he had taken Mrs Rubelle to the station, to drive round by Mr Dawson's, and leave a message in my name, asking him to call and see me. I knew he would come on my account, and I knew he would remain when he found Count Fosco had left the house.

In due course of time the gardener returned, and said that he had driven round by Mr Dawson's residence, after leaving Mrs Rubelle at the station. The doctor sent me word that he was poorly in health himself, but that he would call, if possible, the next morning.

Having delivered his message the gardener was about to withdraw, but I stopped him to request that he would come back before dark, and sit up that night, in one of the empty bedrooms, so as to be within call in case I wanted him. He understood readily enough my unwillingness to be left alone all night in the most desolate part of that desolate house, and we arranged that he should come in between eight and nine.

He came punctually, and I found cause to be thankful that I had adopted the precaution of calling him in. Before midnight Sir Percival's strange temper broke out in the most violent and most alarming manner, and if the gardener had not been on the spot to pacify him on the instant, I am afraid to think what might have happened.

Almost all the afternoon and evening he had been walking about the house and grounds in an unsettled, excitable manner, having, in all probability, as I thought, taken an excessive quantity of wine at his solitary dinner. However that may be, I heard his voice calling loudly and angrily in the new wing of the house, as I 'was taking a turn backwards and forwards along the gallery the last thing at night. The gardener immediately ran down to him, and I closed the door of communication, to keep the alarm, if possible, from reaching Miss Halcombe's ears. It was full half an hour before the gardener came back. He declared that his master was quite out of his senses – not through the excitement of drink, as I had supposed, but through a kind of panic or frenzy of mind, for which it was impossible to account. He had found Sir Percival walking backwards and forwards by himself in the hall, swearing, with every appearance of the most violent passion, that he would not stop another minute alone in such a dungeon as his own house, and that he would take the first stage of his journey immediately in the middle of the night. The gardener, on approaching him, had been hunted out, with oaths and threats, to get the horse and chaise ready instantly. In a quarter of an hour Sir Percival had joined him in the yard, had jumped into the chaise, and, lashing the horse into a gallop, had driven himself away, with his face as pale as ashes in the moonlight. The gardener had heard him shouting and cursing at the lodge-keeper to get up and open the gate – had heard the wheels roll furiously on again in the still night, when the gate was unlocked – and knew no more.

The next day, or a day or two after, I forget which, the chaise was brought back from Knowlesbury, our nearest town, by the ostler at the old inn. Sir Percival had stopped there, and had afterwards left by the train – for what destination the man could not tell. I never received any further information, either from himself or from any one else, of Sir Percival's proceedings, and I am not even aware, at this moment, whether he is in England or out of it. He and I have not met since he drove away like an escaped criminal from his own house, and it is my fervent hope and prayer that we may never meet again.

*   *   *

My own part of this sad family story is now drawing to an end.

I have been informed that the particulars of Miss Halcombe's waking, and of what passed between us when she found me sitting by her bedside, are not material to the purpose which is to be answered by the present narrative. It will be sufficient for me to say in this place, that she was not herself conscious of the means adopted to remove her from the inhabited to the uninhabited part of the house. She was in a deep sleep at the time, whether naturally or artificially produced she could not say. In my absence at Torquay, and in the absence of all the resident servants except Margaret Porcher (who was perpetually eating, drinking, or sleeping, when she was not at work), the secret transfer of Miss Halcombe from one part of the house to the other was no doubt easily performed. Mrs Rubelle (as I discovered for myself, in looking about the room) had provisions, and all other necessaries, together with the means of heating water, broth, and so on, without kindling a fire, placed at her disposal during the few days of her imprisonment with the sick lady. She had declined to answer the questions which Miss Halcombe naturally put, but had not, in other respects, treated her with unkindness or neglect. The disgrace of lending herself to a vile deception is the only disgrace with which I can conscientiously charge Mrs Rubelle.

I need write no particulars (and I am relieved to know it) of the effect produced on Miss Halcombe by the news of Lady Glyde's departure, or by the far more melancholy tidings which reached us only too soon afterwards at Blackwater Park. In both cases I prepared her mind beforehand as gently and as carefully as possible, having the doctor's advice to guide me, in the last case only, through Mr Dawson's being too unwell to come to the house for some days after I had sent for him. It was a sad time, a time which it afflicts me to think of or to write of now. The precious blessings of religious consolation which I endeavoured to convey were long in reaching Miss Halcombe's heart, but I hope and believe they came home to her at last. I never left her till her strength was restored. The train which took me away from that miserable house was the train which took her away also. We parted very mournfully in London. I remained with a relative at Islington, and she went on to Mr Fairlie's house in Cumberland.

I have only a few lines more to write before I close this painful statement. They are dictated by a sense of duty.

In the first place, I wish to record my own personal conviction that no blame whatever, in connection with the events which I have now related, attaches to Count Fosco. I am informed that a dreadful suspicion has been raised, and that some very serious constructions are placed upon his lordship's conduct. My persuasion of the Count's innocence remains, however, quite unshaken. If he assisted Sir Percival in sending me to Torquay, he assisted under a delusion, for which, as a foreigner and a stranger, he was not to blame. If he was concerned in bringing Mrs Rubelle to Blackwater Park, it was his misfortune and not his fault, when that foreign person was base enough to assist a deception planned and carried out by the master of the house. I protest, in the interests of morality, against blame being gratuitously and wantonly attached to the proceedings of the Count.

In the second place, I desire to express my regret at my own inability to remember the precise day on which Lady Glyde left Blackwater Park for London. I am told that it is of the last importance to ascertain the exact date of that lamentable journey, and I have anxiously taxed my memory to recall it. The effort has been in vain. I can only remember now that it was towards the latter part of July. We all know the difficulty, after a lapse of time, of fixing precisely on a past date unless it has been previously written down. That difficulty is greatly increased in my case by the alarming and confusing events which took place about the period of Lady Glyde's departure. I heartily wish I had made a memorandum at the time. I heartily wish my memory of the date was as vivid as my memory of that poor lady's face, when it looked at me sorrowfully for the last time from the carriage window.

THE STORY CONTINUED IN SEVERAL NARRATIVES

I

THE NARRATIVE OF HESTER PINHORN, COOK IN THE SERVICE OF COUNT FOSCO
Taken down from her own statement

I am sorry to say that I have never learnt to read or write. I have been a hard-working woman all my life, and have kept a good character. I know that it is a sin and wickedness to say the thing which is not, and I will truly beware of doing so on this occasion. All that I know I will tell, and I humbly beg the gentleman who takes this down to put my language right as he goes on, and to make allowances for my being no scholar.

In this last summer I happened to be out of place (through no fault of my own), and I heard of a situation as plain cook, at Number Five, Forest Road, St John's Wood. I took the place on trial. My master's name was Fosco. My mistress was an English lady. He was Count and she was Countess. There was a girl to do housemaid's work when I got there. She was not over-clean or tidy, but there was no harm in her. I and she were the only servants in the house.

Our master and mistress came after we got in; and as soon as they did come we were told, downstairs, that company was expected from the country.

The company was my mistress's niece, and the back bedroom on the first floor was got ready for her. My mistress mentioned to me that Lady Glyde (that was her name) was in poor health, and that I must be particular in my cooking accordingly. She was to come that day, as well as I can remember – but whatever you do, don't trust my memory in the matter. I am sorry to say it's no use asking me about days of the month, and such-like. Except Sundays, half my time I take no heed of them, being a hard-working woman and no scholar. All I know is Lady Glyde came, and when she did come, a fine fright she gave us all surely. I don't know how master brought her to the house, being hard at work at the time. But he did bring her in the afternoon, I think, and the housemaid opened the door to them, and showed them into the parlour. Before she had been long down in the kitchen again with me, we heard a hurry-skurry upstairs, and the parlour bell ringing like mad, and my mistress's voice calling out for help.

We both ran up, and there we saw the lady laid on the sofa, with her face ghastly white, and her hands fast clenched, and her head drawn down to one side. She had been taken with a sudden fright, my mistress said, and master he told us she was in a fit of convulsions. I ran out, knowing the neighbourhood a little better than the rest of them, to fetch the nearest doctor's help. The nearest help was at Goodricke's and Garth's, who worked together as partners, and had a good name and connection, as I have heard, all round St John's Wood. Mr Goodricke was in, and he came back with me directly.

It was some time before he could make himself of much use. The poor unfortunate lady fell out of one fit into another, and went on so till she was quite wearied out, and as helpless as a new-born babe. We then got her to bed. Mr Goodricke went away to his house for medicine, and came back again in a quarter of an hour or less. Besides the medicine he brought a bit of hollow mahogany wood with him, shaped like a kind of trumpet, and after waiting a little while, he put one end over the lady's heart and the other to his ear, and listened carefully.

When he had done he says to my mistress, who was in the room, 'This is a very serious case,' he says, 'I recommend you to write to Lady Glyde's friends directly.' My mistress says to him, 'Is it heart-disease?' And he says, 'Yes, heart-disease of a most dangerous kind.' He told her exactly what he thought was the matter, which I was not clever enough to understand. But I know this, he ended by saying that he was afraid neither his help nor any other doctor's help was likely to be of much service.

My mistress took this ill news more quietly than my master. He was a big, fat, odd sort of elderly man, who kept birds and white mice, and spoke to them as if they were so many Christian children. He seemed terribly cut up by what had happened. 'Ah! poor Lady Glyde! poor dear Lady Glyde!' he says, and went stalking about, wringing his fat hands more like a play-actor than a gentleman. For one question my mistress asked the doctor about the lady's chances of getting round, he asked a good fifty at least. I declare he quite tormented us all, and when he was quiet at last, out he went into the bit of back garden, picking trumpery little nosegays, and asking me to take them upstairs and make the sick-room look pretty with them. As if *that* did any good. I think he must have been, at times, a little soft in his head. But he was not a bad master – he had a monstrous civil tongue of his own, and a jolly, easy, coaxing way with him. I liked him a deal better than my mistress. She was a hard one, if ever there was a hard one yet.

Towards night-time the lady roused up a little. She had been so wearied out, before that, by the convulsions, that she never stirred hand or foot, or spoke a word to anybody. She moved in the bed now, and stared about her at the room and us in it. She must have been a nice-looking lady when well, with light hair, and blue eyes and all that. Her rest was troubled at night – at least so I heard from my mistress, who sat up alone with her. I only went in once before going to bed to see if I could be of any use, and then she was talking to herself in a confused, rambling manner. She seemed to want sadly to speak to somebody who was absent from her somewhere. I couldn't catch the name the first time, and the second time master knocked at the door, with his regular mouthful of questions, and another of his trumpery nosegays.

When I went in early the next morning, the lady was clean worn out again, and lay in a kind of faint sleep. Mr Goodricke brought his partner, Mr Garth, with him to advise. They said she must not be disturbed out of her rest on any account. They asked my mistress many questions, at the other end of the room, about what the lady's health had been in past times, and who had attended her, and whether she had ever suffered much and long together under distress of mind. I remember my mistress said 'Yes' to that last question. And Mr Goodricke looked at Mr Garth, and shook his head; and Mr Garth looked at Mr Goodricke, and shook his head. They seemed to think that the distress might have something to do with the mischief at the lady's heart. She was but a frail thing to look at, poor creature! Very little strength at any time, I should say – very little strength.

Later on the same morning, when she woke, the lady took a sudden turn, and got seemingly a great deal better. I was not let in again to see her, no more was the housemaid, for the reason that she was not to be disturbed by strangers. What I heard of her being better was through my master. He was in wonderful good spirits about the change, and looked in at the kitchen window from the garden, with his great big curly-brimmed white hat on, to go out.

'Good Mrs Cook,' says he, 'Lady Glyde is better. My mind is more easy than it was, and I am going out to stretch my big legs with a sunny little summer walk. Shall I order for you, shall I market for you, Mrs Cook? What are you making there? A nice tart for dinner? Much crust, if you please – much crisp crust, my dear, that melts and crumbles delicious in the mouth.' That was his way. He was past sixty, and fond of pastry. Just think of that!

The doctor came again in the forenoon, and saw for himself that Lady Glyde had woke up better. He forbid us to talk to her, or to let her talk to us, in case she was that way disposed, saying she must be kept quiet before all things, and encouraged to sleep as much as possible. She did not seem to want to talk whenever I saw her, except overnight, when I couldn't make out what she was saying – she seemed too much worn down. Mr Goodricke was not nearly in such good spirits about her as master. He said nothing when he came downstairs, except that he would call again at five o'clock.

About that time (which was before master came home again) the bell rang hard from the bedroom, and my mistress ran out into the landing, and called to me to go for Mr Goodricke, and tell him the lady had fainted. I got on my bonnet and shawl, when, as good luck would have it, the doctor himself came to the house for his promised visit.

I let him in, and went upstairs along with him. 'Lady Glyde was just as usual,' says my mistress to him at the door; 'she was awake, and looking about her in a strange, forlorn manner, when I heard her give a sort of half cry, and she fainted in a moment.' The doctor went up to the bed, and stooped down over the sick lady. He looked very serious, all on a sudden, at the sight of her, and put his hand on her heart.

My mistress stared hard in Mr Goodricke's face. 'Not dead!' says she, whispering, and turning all of a tremble from head to foot.

'Yes,' says the doctor, very quiet and grave. 'Dead. I was afraid it would happen suddenly when I examined her heart yesterday.' My mistress stepped back from the bedside while he was speaking, and trembled and trembled again. 'Dead!' she whispers to herself; 'dead so suddenly! dead so soon! What will the Count say?' Mr Goodricke advised her to go downstairs, and quiet herself a little. 'You have been sitting up all night,' says he, 'and your nerves are shaken. This person,' says he, meaning me, 'this person will stay in the room till I can send for the necessary assistance.' My mistress did as he told her. 'I must prepare the Count,' she says. 'I must carefully prepare the Count.' And so she left us, shaking from head to foot, and went out.

'Your master is a foreigner,' says Mr Goodricke, when my mistress had left us. 'Does he understand about registering the death?' 'I can't rightly tell, sir,' says I, 'but I should think not.' The doctor considered a minute, and then says he, 'I don't usually do such things,' says he, 'but it may save the family trouble in this case if I register the death myself. I shall pass the district office in half an hour's time, and I can easily look in. Mention, if you please, that I will do so.' 'Yes, sir,' says I, 'with thanks, I'm sure, for your kindness in thinking of it.' 'You don't mind staying here till I can send you the proper person?' says he. 'No, sir,' says I; 'I'll stay with the poor lady till then. I suppose nothing more could be done, sir, than was done?' says I. 'No,' says he, 'nothing; she must have suffered sadly before ever I saw her – the case was hopeless when I was called in.' 'Ah, dear me! we all come to it, sooner or later, don't we, sir?' says I. He gave no answer to that – he didn't seem to care about talking. He said, 'Good-day,' and went out.

I stopped by the bedside from that time till the time when Mr Goodricke sent the person in, as he had promised. She was, by name, Jane Gould. I considered her to be a respectable-looking woman. She made no remark, except to say that she understood what was wanted of her, and that she had winded a many of them in her time.

How master bore the news, when he first heard it, is more than I can tell, not having been present. When I did see him he looked awfully overcome by it, to be sure. He sat quiet in a corner, with his fat hands hanging over his thick knees, and his head down, and his eyes looking at nothing. He seemed not so much sorry, as scared and dazed like, by what had happened.

My mistress managed all that was to be done about the funeral. It must have cost a sight of money – the coffin, in particular, being most beautiful. The dead lady's husband was away, as we heard, in foreign parts. But my mistress (being her aunt) settled it with her friends in the country (Cumberland, I think) that she should be buried there, in the same grave along with her mother. Everything was done handsomely, in respect of the funeral, I say again, and master went down to attend the burying in the country himself. He looked grand in his deep mourning, with his big solemn face, and his slow walk, and his broad hatband – that he did!

In conclusion, I have to say, in answer to questions put to me –

(1) That neither I nor my fellow-servant ever saw my master give Lady Glyde any medicine himself.

(2) That he was never, to my knowledge and belief, left alone in the room with Lady Glyde.

(3) That I am not able to say what caused the sudden fright, which my mistress informed me had seized the lady on her first coming into the house. The cause was never explained, either to me or to my fellow-servant.

The above statement has been read over in my presence. I have nothing to add to it, or to take away from it. I say, on my oath as a Christian woman, this is the truth.

(Signed) HESTER PINHORN, Her + Mark.

II

THE NARRATIVE OF THE DOCTOR

To the Registrar of the Sub-District in which the undermentioned death took place. – I hereby certify that I attended Lady Glyde, aged Twenty-One last Birthday; that I last saw her on Thursday the 25th July 1850; that she died on the same day at No. 5 Forest Road, St John's Wood, and that the cause of her death was Aneurism. Duration of disease not known.

(Signed) ALFRED GOODRICKE
Profl. Title. *M.R.C.S. Eng., L.S.A.* Address: *12 Croydon Gardens St John's Wood.*

III

THE NARRATIVE OF JANE GOULD

I was the person sent in by Mr Goodricke to do what was right and needful by the remains of a lady who had died at the house named in the certificate which precedes this. I found the body in charge of the servant, Hester Pinhorn.

I remained with it, and prepared it at the proper time for the grave. It was laid in the coffin in my presence, and I afterwards saw the coffin screwed down previous to its removal. When that had been done, and not before, I received what was due to me and left the house. I refer persons who may wish to investigate my character to Mr Goodricke. He will bear witness that I can be trusted to tell the truth.

(Signed) JANE GOULD

IV

THE NARRATIVE OF THE TOMBSTONE

Sacred to the Memory of Laura, Lady Glyde, wife of Sir Percival Glyde, Bart., of Blackwater Park, Hampshire, and daughter of the late Philip Fairlie, Esq., of Limmeridge House, in this parish. Born March 27th, 1829; married December 22nd, 1849; died July 25th, 1850.

V

THE NARRATIVE OF WALTER HARTRIGHT

Early in the summer of 1850 I and my surviving companions left the wilds and forests of Central America for home. Arrived at the coast, we took ship there for England. The vessel was wrecked in the Gulf of Mexico – I was among the few saved from the sea. It was my third escape from peril of death. Death by disease, death by the Indians, death by drowning – all three had approached me; all three had passed me by.

The survivors of the wreck were rescued by an American vessel bound for Liverpool. The ship reached her port on the thirteenth day of October 1850. We landed late in the afternoon, and I arrived in London the same night.

These pages are not the record of my wanderings and my dangers away from home. The motives which led me from my country and my friends to a new world of adventure and peril are known. From that self-imposed exile I came back, as I had hoped, prayed, believed I should come back – a changed man. In the waters of a new life I had tempered my nature afresh. In the stern school of extremity and danger my will had learnt to be strong, my heart to be resolute, my mind to rely on itself. I had gone out to fly from my own future. I came back to face it, as a man should.

To face it with that inevitable suppression of myself which I knew it would demand from me. I had parted with the worst bitterness of the past, but not with my heart's remembrance of the sorrow and the tenderness of

that memorable time. I had not ceased to feel the one irreparable disappointment of my life – I had only learnt to bear it. Laura Fairlie was in all my
thoughts when the ship bore me away, and I looked my last at England.
Laura Fairlie was in all my thoughts when the ship brought me back, and
the morning light showed the friendly shore in view.

My pen traces the old letters as my heart goes back to the old love. I
write of her as Laura Fairlie still. It is hard to think of her, it is hard to speak
of her, by her husband's name.

There are no more words of explanation to add on my appearance for
the second time in these pages. This narrative, if I have the strength and the
courage to write it, may now go on.

My first anxieties and first hopes when the morning came centred in my mother
and my sister. I felt the necessity of preparing them for the joy and surprise
of my return, after an absence during which it had been impossible for them
to receive any tidings of me for months past. Early in the morning I sent a
letter to the Hampstead Cottage, and followed it myself in an hour's time.

When the first meeting was over, when our quiet and composure of other
days began gradually to return to us, I saw something in my mother's face
which told me that a secret oppression lay heavy on her heart. There was
more than love – there was sorrow in the anxious eyes that looked on me so
tenderly – there was pity in the kind hand that slowly and fondly strengthened
its hold on mine. We had no concealments from each other. She knew how
the hope of my life had been wrecked – she knew why I had left her. It was
on my lips to ask as composedly as I could if any letter had come for me
from Miss Halcombe, if there was any news of her sister that I might hear.
But when I looked in my mother's face I lost courage to put the question
even in that guarded form. I could only say, doubtingly and restrainedly –

'You have something to tell me.'

My sister, who had been sitting opposite to us, rose suddenly without a
word of explanation – rose and left the room.

My mother moved closer to me on the sofa and put her arms round my
neck. Those fond arms trembled – the tears flowed fast over the faithful
loving face.

'Walter!' she whispered, 'my own darling! my heart is heavy for you. Oh,
my son! my son! try to remember that I am still left!'

My head sank on her bosom. She had said all in saying those words.

It was the morning of the third day since my return – the morning of the
sixteenth of October.

I had remained with them at the cottage – I had tried hard not to embitter the happiness of my return to *them* as it was embittered to *me*. I had done all man could to rise after the shock, and accept my life resignedly – to let my great sorrow come in tenderness to my heart, and not in despair. It was useless and hopeless. No tears soothed my aching eyes, no relief came to me from my sister's sympathy or my mother's love.

On that third morning I opened my heart to them. At last the words passed my lips which I had longed to speak on the day when my mother told me of her death.

'Let me go away alone for a little while,' I said. 'I shall bear it better when I have looked once more at the place where I first saw her – when I have knelt and prayed by the grave where they have laid her to rest.'

I departed on my journey – my journey to the grave of Laura Fairlie.

It was a quiet autumn afternoon when I stopped at the solitary station, and set forth alone on foot by the well-remembered road. The waning sun was shining faintly through thin white clouds – the air was warm and still – the peacefulness of the lonely country was overshadowed and saddened by the influence of the falling year.

I reached the moor – I stood again on the brow of the hill – I looked on along the path – and there were the familiar garden trees in the distance, the clear sweeping semicircle of the drive, the high white walls of Limmeridge House. The chances and changes, the wanderings and dangers of months and months past, all shrank and shrivelled to nothing in my mind. It was like yesterday since my feet had last trodden the fragrant heathy ground. I thought I should see her coming to meet me, with her little straw hat shading her face, her simple dress fluttering in the air, and her well-filled sketch-book ready in her hand.

Oh death, thou hast thy sting! oh, grave, thou hast thy victory!

I turned aside, and there below me in the glen was the lonesome grey church, the porch where I had waited for the coming of the woman in white, the hills encircling the quiet burial-ground, the brook bubbling cold over its stony bed. There was the marble cross, fair and white, at the head of the tomb – the tomb that now rose over mother and daughter alike.

I approached the grave. I crossed once more the low stone stile, and bared my head as I touched the sacred ground. Sacred to gentleness and goodness, sacred to reverence and grief.

I stopped before the pedestal from which the cross rose. On one side of it, on the side nearest to me, the newly-cut inscription met my eyes – the hard, clear, cruel black letters which told the story of her life and death. I tried to read them. I did read as far as the name. 'Sacred to the Memory of Laura—' The kind blue eyes dim with tears – the fair head drooping wearily – the innocent parting words which implored me to leave her – oh, for a happier last memory of her than this; the memory I took away with me, the memory I bring back with me to her grave!

A second time I tried to read the inscription. I saw at the end the date of her death, and above it –

Above it there were lines on the marble – there was a name among them which disturbed my thoughts of her. I went round to the other side of the grave, where there was nothing to read, nothing of earthly vileness to force its way between her spirit and mine.

I knelt down by the tomb. I laid my hands, I laid my head on the broad white stone, and closed my weary eyes on the earth around, on the light above. I let her come back to me. Oh, my love! my love! my heart may speak to you *now*! It is yesterday again since we parted – yesterday, since your dear hand lay in mine – yesterday, since my eyes looked their last on you. My love! my love!

Time had flowed on, and silence had fallen like thick night over its course.

The first sound that came after the heavenly peace rustled faintly like a passing breath of air over the grass of the burial-ground. I heard it nearing me slowly, until it came changed to my ear – came like footsteps moving onward – then stopped.

I looked up.

The sunset was near at hand. The clouds had parted – the slanting light fell mellow over the hills. The last of the day was cold and clear and still in the quiet valley of the dead.

Beyond me, in the burial-ground, standing together in the cold clearness of the lower light, I saw two women. They were looking towards the tomb, looking towards me.

Two.

They came a little on, and stopped again. Their veils were down, and hid their faces from me. When they stopped, one of them raised her veil. In the still evening light I saw the face of Marian Halcombe.

Changed, changed as if years had passed over it! The eyes large and wild, and looking at me with a strange terror in them. The face worn and wasted piteously. Pain and fear and grief written on her as with a brand.

I took one step towards her from the grave. She never moved – she never spoke. The veiled woman with her cried out faintly. I stopped. The springs of my life fell low, and the shuddering of an unutterable dread crept over me from head to foot.

The woman with the veiled face moved away from her companion, and came towards me slowly. Left by herself, standing by herself, Marian

Halcombe spoke. It was the voice that I remembered – the voice not changed, like the frightened eyes and the wasted face.

'My dream! my dream!' I heard her say those words softly in the awful silence. She sank on her knees, and raised her clasped hands to heaven. 'Father! strengthen him. Father! help him in his hour of need.'

The woman came on, slowly and silently came on. I looked at her – at her, and at none other, from that moment.

The voice that was praying for me faltered and sank low – then rose on a sudden, and called affrightedly, called despairingly to me to come away.

But the veiled woman had possession of me, body and soul. She stopped on one side of the grave. We stood face to face with the tombstone between us. She was close to the inscription on the side of the pedestal. Her gown touched the black letters.

The voice came nearer, and rose and rose more passionately still. 'Hide your face! don't look at her! Oh, for God's sake, spare him—'

The woman lifted her veil.

'Sacred to the Memory of Laura, Lady Glyde—'

Laura, Lady Glyde, was standing by the inscription, and was looking at me over the grave.

The Second Epoch of the Story closes here.

THE THIRD EPOCH

THE STORY CONTINUED BY
WALTER HARTRIGHT

I

I open a new page. I advance my narrative by one week.

The history of the interval which I thus pass over must remain unrecorded. My heart turns faint, my mind sinks in darkness and confusion when I think of it. This must not be, if I who write am to guide, as I ought, you who read. This must not be, if the clue that leads through the windings of the story is to remain from end to end untangled in my hands.

A life suddenly changed – its whole purpose created afresh, its hopes and fears, its struggles, its interests, and its sacrifices all turned at once and for ever into a new direction – this is the prospect which now opens before me, like the burst of view from a mountain's top. I left my narrative in the quiet shadow of Limmeridge church – I resume it, one week later, in the stir and turmoil of a London street.

The street is in a populous and a poor neighbourhood. The ground floor of one of the houses in it is occupied by a small newsvendor's shop, and the first floor and the second are let as furnished lodgings of the humblest kind.

I have taken those two floors in an assumed name. On the upper floor I live, with a room to work in, a room to sleep in. On the lower floor, under the same assumed name, two women live, who are described as my sisters. I get my bread by drawing and engraving on wood for the cheap periodicals. My sisters are supposed to help me by taking in a little needle-work. Our poor place of abode, our humble calling, our assumed relationship, and our assumed name, are all used alike as a means of hiding us in the house-forest of London. We are numbered no longer with the people whose lives are open and known. I am an obscure, unnoticed man, without patron or friend to help me. Marian Halcombe is nothing now but my eldest sister, who provides for our household wants by the toil of her own hands. We two, in the estimation of others, are at once the dupes and the agents of a daring imposture. We are supposed to be the accomplices of mad Anne Catherick, who claims the name, the place, and the living personality of dead Lady Glyde.

That is our situation. That is the changed aspect in which we three must appear, henceforth, in this narrative, for many and many a page to come.

In the eye of reason and of law, in the estimation of relatives and friends,

according to every received formality of civilised society, 'Laura, Lady Glyde,'
lay buried with her mother in Limmeridge churchyard. Torn in her own
lifetime from the list of the living, the daughter of Philip Fairlie and the wife
of Percival Glyde might still exist for her sister, might still exist for me, but
to all the world besides she was dead. Dead to her uncle, who had renounced
her; dead to the servants of the house, who had failed to recognise her; dead
to the persons in authority, who had transmitted her fortune to her husband
and her aunt; dead to my mother and my sister, who believed me to be the
dupe of an adventuress and the victim of a fraud; socially, morally, legally
– dead.

And yet alive! Alive in poverty and in hiding. Alive, with the poor drawing-
master to fight her battle, and to win the way back for her to her place in
the world of living beings.

Did no suspicion, excited by my own knowledge of Anne Catherick's
resemblance to her, cross my mind, when her face was first revealed to me?
Not the shadow of a suspicion, from the moment when she lifted her veil
by the side of the inscription which recorded her death.

Before the sun of that day had set, before the last glimpse of the home
which was closed against her had passed from our view, the farewell words
I spoke, when we parted at Limmeridge House, had been recalled by both
of us – repeated by me, recognised by her. 'If ever the time comes, when
the devotion of my whole heart and soul and strength will give you a moment's
happiness, or spare you a moment's sorrow, will you try to remember the
poor drawing-master who has taught you?' She, who now remembered so
little of the trouble and terror of a later time, remembered those words, and
laid her poor head innocently and trustingly on the bosom of the man who
had spoken them. In that moment, when she called me by my name, when
she said, 'They have tried to make me forget everything, Walter; but I
remember Marian, and I remember *you*' – in that moment, I, who had long
since given her my love, gave her my life, and thanked God that it was mine
to bestow on her. Yes! the time had come. From thousands on thousands of
miles away – through forest and wilderness, where companions stronger than
I had fallen by my side, through peril of death thrice renewed, and thrice
escaped, the Hand that leads men on the dark road to the future had led me
to meet that time. Forlorn and disowned, sorely tried and sadly changed – her
beauty faded, her mind clouded – robbed of her station in the world, of her
place among living creatures – the devotion I had promised, the devotion of
my whole heart and soul and strength, might be laid blamelessly now at
those dear feet. In the right of her calamity, in the right of her friendlessness,
she was mine at last! Mine to support, to protect, to cherish, to restore. Mine
to love and honour as father and brother both. Mine to vindicate through all

risks and all sacrifices – through the hopeless struggle against Rank and Power, through the long fight with armed deceit and fortified Success, through the waste of my reputation, through the loss of my friends, through the hazard of my life.

II

My position is defined – my motives are acknowledged. The story of Marian and the story of Laura must come next.

I shall relate both narratives, not in the words (often interrupted, often inevitably confused) of the speakers themselves, but in the words of the brief, plain, studiously simple abstract which I committed to writing for my own guidance, and for the guidance of my legal adviser. So the tangled web will be most speedily and most intelligibly unrolled.

The story of Marian begins where the narrative of the housekeeper at Blackwater Park left off.

On Lady Glyde's departure from her husband's house, the fact of that departure, and the necessary statement of the circumstances under which it had taken place, were communicated to Miss Halcombe by the housekeeper. It was not till some days afterwards (how many days exactly, Mrs Michelson, in the absence of any written memorandum on the subject, could not undertake to say) that a letter arrived from Madame Fosco announcing Lady Glyde's sudden death in Count Fosco's house. The letter avoided mentioning dates, and left it to Mrs Michelson's discretion to break the news at once to Miss Halcombe, or to defer doing so until that lady's health should be more firmly established.

Having consulted Mr Dawson (who had been himself delayed, by ill health, in resuming his attendance at Blackwater Park), Mrs Michelson, by the doctor's advice, and in the doctor's presence, communicated the news, either on the day when the letter was received, or on the day after. It is not necessary to dwell here upon the effect which the intelligence of Lady Glyde's sudden death produced on her sister. It is only useful to the present purpose to say that she was not able to travel for more than three weeks afterwards. At the end of that time she proceeded to London accompanied by the housekeeper. They parted there – Mrs Michelson previously informing Miss Halcombe of her address, in case they might wish to communicate at a future period.

On parting with the housekeeper Miss Halcombe went at once to the office of Messrs Gilmore & Kyrle to consult with the latter gentleman in Mr Gilmore's absence. She mentioned to Mr Kyrle what she had thought it desirable to conceal from every one else (Mrs Michelson included) – her suspicion of the circumstances under which Lady Glyde was said to have met her death. Mr Kyrle, who had previously given friendly proof of his anxiety to serve Miss Halcombe, at once undertook to make such inquiries as the delicate and dangerous nature of the investigation proposed to him would permit.

To exhaust this part of the subject before going farther, it may be mentioned that Count Fosco offered every facility to Mr Kyrle, on that gentleman's stating that he was sent by Miss Halcombe to collect such particulars as had not yet reached her of Lady Glyde's decease. Mr Kyrle was placed in communication with the medical man, Mr Goodricke, and with the two servants. In the absence of any means of ascertaining the exact date of Lady Glyde's departure from Blackwater Park, the result of the doctor's and the servants' evidence, and of the volunteered statements of Count Fosco and his wife, was conclusive to the mind of Mr Kyrle. He could only assume that the intensity of Miss Halcombe's suffering, under the loss of her sister, had misled her judgment in a most deplorable manner, and he wrote her word that the shocking suspicion to which she had alluded in his presence was, in his opinion, destitute of the smallest fragment of foundation in truth. Thus the investigation by Mr Gilmore's partner began and ended.

Meanwhile, Miss Halcombe had returned to Limmeridge House, and had there collected all the additional information which she was able to obtain.

Mr Fairlie had received his first intimation of his niece's death from his sister, Madame Fosco, this letter also not containing any exact reference to dates. He had sanctioned his sister's proposal that the deceased lady should be laid in her mother's grave in Limmeridge churchyard. Count Fosco had accompanied the remains to Cumberland, and had attended the funeral at Limmeridge, which took place on the 30th of July. It was followed, as a mark of respect, by all the inhabitants of the village and the neighbourhood. On the next day the inscription (originally drawn out, it was said, by the aunt of the deceased lady, and submitted for approval to her brother, Mr Fairlie) was engraved on one side of the monument over the tomb.

On the day of the funeral, and for one day after it, Count Fosco had been received as a guest at Limmeridge House, but no interview had taken place between Mr Fairlie and himself, by the former gentleman's desire. They had communicated by writing, and through this medium Count Fosco had made Mr Fairlie acquainted with the details of his niece's last illness and death. The letter presenting this information added no new facts to the facts already known, but one very remarkable paragraph was contained in the postscript. It referred to Anne Catherick.

The substance of the paragraph in question was as follows –

It first informed Mr Fairlie that Anne Catherick (of whom he might hear full particulars from Miss Halcombe when she reached Limmeridge) had been traced and recovered in the neighbourhood of Blackwater Park, and had been for the second time placed under the charge of the medical man from whose custody she had once escaped.

This was the first part of the postscript. The second part warned Mr Fairlie that Anne Catherick's mental malady had been aggravated by her long freedom from control, and that the insane hatred and distrust of Sir Percival Glyde, which had been one of her most marked delusions in former times, still existed under a newly-acquired form. The unfortunate woman's last idea in connection with Sir Percival was the idea of annoying and distressing him, and of elevating herself, as she supposed, in the estimation of the patients and nurses, by assuming the character of his deceased wife, the scheme of this personation having evidently occurred to her after a stolen interview which she had succeeded in obtaining with Lady Glyde, and at which she had observed the extraordinary accidental likeness between the deceased lady and herself. It was to the last degree improbable that she would succeed a second time in escaping from the Asylum, but it was just possible she might find some means of annoying the late Lady Glyde's relatives with letters, and in that case Mr Fairlie was warned beforehand how to receive them.

The postscript, expressed in these terms, was shown to Miss Halcombe when she arrived at Limmeridge. There were also placed in her possession the clothes Lady Glyde had worn, and the other effects she had brought with her to her aunt's house. They had been carefully collected and sent to Cumberland by Madame Fosco.

Such was the posture of affairs when Miss Halcombe reached Limmeridge in the early part of September.

Shortly afterwards she was confined to her room by a relapse, her weakened physical energies giving way under the severe mental affliction from which she was now suffering. On getting stronger again, in a month's time, her suspicion of the circumstances described as attending her sister's death still remained unshaken. She had heard nothing in the interim of Sir Percival Glyde, but letters had reached her from Madame Fosco, making the most affectionate inquiries on the part of her husband and herself. Instead of answering these letters, Miss Halcombe caused the house in St John's Wood, and the proceedings of its inmates, to be privately watched.

Nothing doubtful was discovered. The same result attended the next investigations, which were secretly instituted on the subject of Mrs Rubelle. She had arrived in London about six months before with her husband. They had come from Lyons, and they had taken a house in the neighbourhood of Leicester Square, to be fitted up as a boarding-house for foreigners, who were expected to visit England in large numbers to see the Exhibition of 1851. Nothing was known against husband or wife in the neighbourhood. They were quiet people, and they had paid their way honestly up to the present time. The final inquiries related to Sir Percival Glyde. He was settled in Paris, and living there quietly in a small circle of English and French friends.

Foiled at all points, but still not able to rest, Miss Halcombe next determined to visit the Asylum in which she then supposed Anne Catherick to be for the second time confined. She had felt a strong curiosity about the woman in former days, and she was now doubly interested – first, in ascertaining whether the report of Anne Catherick's attempted personation of Lady Glyde was true, and secondly (if it proved to be true), in discovering for herself what the poor creature's real motives were for attempting the deceit. Although Count Fosco's letter to Mr Fairlie did not mention the address of the Asylum, that important omission cast no difficulties in Miss Halcombe's way. When Mr Hartright had met Anne Catherick at Limmeridge, she had informed him of the locality in which the house was situated, and Miss Halcombe had noted down the direction in her diary, with all the other particulars of the interview exactly as she heard them from Mr Hartright's own lips. Accordingly she looked back at the entry and extracted the address – furnished herself with the Count's letter to Mr Fairlie as a species of credential which might be useful to her, and started by herself for the Asylum on the eleventh of October.

She passed the night of the eleventh in London. It had been her intention to sleep at the house inhabited by Lady Glyde's old governess, but Mrs Vesey's agitation at the sight of her lost pupil's nearest and dearest friend was so distressing that Miss Halcombe considerately refrained from remaining in her presence, and removed to a respectable boarding-house in the neighbourhood, recommended by Mrs Vesey's married sister. The next day she proceeded to the Asylum, which was situated not far from London on the northern side of the metropolis.

She was immediately admitted to see the proprietor.

At first he appeared to be decidedly unwilling to let her communicate with his patient. But on her showing him the postscript to Count Fosco's letter – on her reminding him that she was the 'Miss Halcombe' there referred to – that she was a near relative of the deceased Lady Glyde – and that she was therefore naturally interested, for family reasons, in observing for herself the extent of Anne Catherick's delusion in relation to her late sister – the tone and manner of the owner of the Asylum altered, and he withdrew his objections. He probably felt that a continued refusal, under these circumstances, would not only be an act of discourtesy in itself, but would also imply that the proceedings in his establishment were not of a nature to bear investigation by respectable strangers.

Miss Halcombe's own impression was that the owner of the Asylum had not been received into the confidence of Sir Percival and the Count. His consenting at all to let her visit his patient seemed to afford one proof of this, and his readiness in making admissions which could scarcely have escaped the lips of an accomplice, certainly appeared to furnish another.

For example, in the course of the introductory conversation which took place, he informed Miss Halcombe that Anne Catherick had been brought back to him with the necessary order and certificates by Count Fosco on the twenty-seventh of July – the Count also producing a letter of explanations and instructions signed by Sir Percival Glyde. On receiving his inmate again, the proprietor of the Asylum acknowledged that he had observed some curious personal changes in her. Such changes no doubt were not without precedent in his experience of persons mentally afflicted. Insane people were often at one time, outwardly as well as inwardly, unlike what they were at another – the change from better to worse, or from worse to better, in the madness having a necessary tendency to produce alterations of appearance externally. He allowed for these, and he allowed also for the modification in the form of Anne Catherick's delusion, which was reflected no doubt in her manner and expression. But he was still perplexed at times by certain differences between his patient before she had escaped and his patient since she had been brought back. Those differences were too minute to be described. He could not say of course that she was absolutely altered in height or shape or complexion, or in the colour of her hair and eyes, or in the general form of her face – the change was something that he felt more than something that he saw. In short, the case had been a puzzle from the first, and one more perplexity was added to it now.

It cannot be said that this conversation led to the result of even partially preparing Miss Halcombe's mind for what was to come. But it produced, nevertheless, a very serious effect upon her. She was so completely unnerved by it, that some little time elapsed before she could summon composure enough to follow the proprietor of the Asylum to that part of the house in which the inmates were confined.

On inquiry, it turned out that the supposed Anne Catherick was then taking exercise in the grounds attached to the establishment. One of the nurses volunteered to conduct Miss Halcombe to the place, the proprietor of the Asylum remaining in the house for a few minutes to attend to a case which required his services, and then engaging to join his visitor in the grounds.

The nurse led Miss Halcombe to a distant part of the property, which was prettily laid out, and after looking about her a little, turned into a turf walk, shaded by a shrubbery on either side. About half-way down this walk two women were slowly approaching. The nurse pointed to them and said, 'There is Anne Catherick, ma'am, with the attendant who waits on her. The attendant will answer any questions you wish to put.' With those words the nurse left her to return to the duties of the house.

Miss Halcombe advanced on her side, and the women advanced on theirs. When they were within a dozen paces of each other, one of the women stopped for an instant, looked eagerly at the strange lady, shook off the nurse's grasp on her, and the next moment rushed into Miss Halcombe's arms. In that moment Miss Halcombe recognised her sister – recognised the dead-alive.

Fortunately for the success of the measures taken subsequently, no one was present at that moment but the nurse. She was a young woman, and she was so startled that she was at first quite incapable of interfering. When she was able to do so her whole services were required by Miss Halcombe, who had for the moment sunk altogether in the effort to keep her own senses under the shock of the discovery. After waiting a few minutes in the fresh air and the cool shade, her natural energy and courage helped her a little, and she became sufficiently mistress of herself to feel the necessity of recalling her presence of mind for her unfortunate sister's sake.

She obtained permission to speak alone with the patient, on condition that they both remained well within the nurse's view. There was no time for questions – there was only time for Miss Halcombe to impress on the unhappy lady the necessity of controlling herself, and to assure her of immediate help and rescue if she did so. The prospect of escaping from the Asylum by obedience to her sister's directions was sufficient to quiet Lady Glyde, and to make her understand what was required of her. Miss Halcombe next returned to the nurse, placed all the gold she then had in her pocket (three sovereigns) in the nurse's hands, and asked when and where she could speak to her alone.

The woman was at first surprised and distrustful. But on Miss Halcombe's declaring that she only wanted to put some questions which she was too much agitated to ask at that moment, and that she had no intention of misleading the nurse into any dereliction of duty, the woman took the money, and proposed three o'clock on the next day as the time for the interview. She might then slip out for half an hour, after the patients had dined, and she would meet the lady in a retired place, outside the high north wall which screened the grounds of the house. Miss Halcombe had only time to assent, and to whisper to her sister that she should hear from her on the next day, when the proprietor of the Asylum joined them. He noticed his visitor's agitation, which Miss Halcombe accounted for by saying that her interview with Anne Catherick had a little startled her at first. She took her leave as soon after as possible – that is to say, as soon as she could summon courage to force herself from the presence of her unfortunate sister.

A very little reflection, when the capacity to reflect returned, convinced her that any attempt to identify Lady Glyde and to rescue her by legal means, would, even if successful, involve a delay that might be fatal to her sister's intellects, which were shaken already by the horror of the situation to which she had been consigned. By the time Miss Halcombe had got back to London, she had determined to effect Lady Glyde's escape privately, by means of the nurse.

She went at once to her stockbroker, and sold out of the funds all the little property she possessed, amounting to rather less than seven hundred pounds. Determined, if necessary, to pay the price of her sister's liberty with every farthing she had in the world, she repaired the next day, having the whole sum about her in bank-notes, to her appointment outside the Asylum wall.

The nurse was there. Miss Halcombe approached the subject cautiously by many preliminary questions. She discovered, among other particulars, that the nurse who had in former times attended on the true Anne Catherick had been held responsible (although she was not to blame for it) for the patient's escape, and had lost her place in consequence. The same penalty, it was added, would attach to the person then speaking to her, if the supposed Anne Catherick was missing a second time; and, moreover, the nurse in this case had an especial interest in keeping her place. She was engaged to be married, and she and her future husband were waiting till they could save, together, between two and three hundred pounds to start in business. The nurse's wages were good, and she might succeed, by strict economy, in contributing her small share towards the sum required in two years' time.

On this hint Miss Halcombe spoke. She declared that the supposed Anne Catherick was nearly related to her, that she had been placed in the Asylum under a fatal mistake, and that the nurse would be doing a good and a Christian action in being the means of restoring them to one another. Before there was time to start a single objection, Miss Halcombe took four bank-notes of a hundred pounds each from her pocket-book, and offered them to the woman, as a compensation for the risk she was to run, and for the loss of her place.

The nurse hesitated, through sheer incredulity and surprise. Miss Halcombe pressed the point on her firmly.

'You will be doing a good action,' she repeated; 'you will be helping the most injured and unhappy woman alive. There is your marriage portion for a reward. Bring her safely to me here, and I will put these four bank-notes into your hand before I claim her.'

'Will you give me a letter saying those words, which I can show to my sweetheart when he asks how I got the money?' inquired the woman.

'I will bring the letter with me, ready written and signed,' answered Miss Halcombe.

'Then I'll risk it,' said the nurse.

'When?'

'Tomorrow.'

It was hastily agreed between them that Miss Halcombe should return early the next morning and wait out of sight among the trees – always, however, keeping near the quiet spot of ground under the north wall. The nurse could fix no time for her appearance, caution requiring that she should wait and be guided by circumstances. On that understanding they separated.

Miss Halcombe was at her place, with the promised letter and the promised bank-notes, before ten the next morning. She waited more than an hour and a half. At the end of that time the nurse came quickly round the corner of the wall holding Lady Glyde by the arm. The moment they met Miss Halcombe put the bank-notes and the letter into her hand, and the sisters were united again.

The nurse had dressed Lady Glyde, with excellent forethought, in a bonnet, veil, and shawl of her own. Miss Halcombe only detained her to suggest a means of turning the pursuit in a false direction, when the escape was discovered at the Asylum. She was to go back to the house, to mention in the hearing of the other nurses that Anne Catherick had been inquiring latterly about the distance from London to Hampshire, to wait till the last moment, before discovery was inevitable, and then to give the alarm that Anne was missing. The supposed inquiries about Hampshire, when communicated to the owner of the Asylum, would lead him to imagine that his patient had returned to Blackwater Park, under the influence of the delusion which made her persist in asserting herself to be Lady Glyde, and the first pursuit would, in all probability, be turned in that direction.

The nurse consented to follow these suggestions, the more readily as they offered her the means of securing herself against any worse consequences than the loss of her place, by remaining in the Asylum, and so maintaining the appearance of innocence, at least. She at once returned to the house, and Miss Halcombe lost no time in taking her sister back with her to London. They caught the afternoon train to Carlisle the same afternoon, and arrived at Limmeridge, without accident or difficulty of any kind, that night.

During the latter part of their journey they were alone in the carriage, and Miss Halcombe was able to collect such remembrances of the past as her sister's confused and weakened memory was able to recall. The terrible story of the conspiracy so obtained was presented in fragments, sadly incoherent in themselves, and widely detached from each other. Imperfect as the revelation was, it must nevertheless be recorded here before this explanatory narrative closes with the events of the next day at Limmeridge House.

Lady Glyde's recollection of the events which followed her departure from Blackwater Park began with her arrival at the London terminus of the South Western Railway. She had omitted to make a memorandum beforehand of the day on which she took the journey. All hope of fixing that important date by any evidence of hers, or of Mrs Michelson's, must be given up for lost.

On the arrival of the train at the platform Lady Glyde found Count Fosco waiting for her. He was at the carriage door as soon as the porter could open it. The train was unusually crowded, and there was great confusion in getting the luggage. Some person whom Count Fosco brought with him procured the luggage which belonged to Lady Glyde. It was marked with her name. She drove away alone with the Count in a vehicle which she did not particularly notice at the time.

Her first question, on leaving the terminus, referred to Miss Halcombe. The Count informed her that Miss Halcombe had not yet gone to Cumberland, after-consideration having caused him to doubt the prudence of her taking so long a journey without some days' previous rest.

Lady Glyde next inquired whether her sister was then staying in the Count's house. Her recollection of the answer was confused, her only distinct impression in relation to it being that the Count declared he was then taking her to see Miss Halcombe. Lady Glyde's experience of London was so limited that she could not tell, at the time, through what streets they were driving. But they never left the streets, and they never passed any gardens or trees. When the carriage stopped, it stopped in a small street behind a square – a square in which there were shops, and public buildings, and many people. From these recollections (of which Lady Glyde was certain) it seems quite clear that Count Fosco did not take her to his own residence in the suburb of St John's Wood.

They entered the house, and went upstairs to a back room, either on the first or second floor. The luggage was carefully brought in. A female servant opened the door, and a man with a dark beard, apparently a foreigner, met them in the hall, and with great politeness showed them the way upstairs. In answer to Lady Glyde's inquiries, the Count assured her that Miss Halcombe was in the house, and that she should be immediately informed of her sister's arrival. He and the foreigner then went away and left her by herself in the room. It was poorly furnished as a sitting-room, and it looked out on the backs of houses.

The place was remarkably quiet – no footsteps went up or down the stairs – she only heard in the room beneath her a dull, rumbling sound of men's voices talking. Before she had been long left alone the Count returned, to explain that Miss Halcombe was then taking rest, and could not be disturbed for a little while. He was accompanied into the room by a gentleman (an Englishman), whom he begged to present as a friend of his.

After this singular introduction – in the course of which no names, to the best of Lady Glyde's recollection, had been mentioned – she was left alone with the stranger. He was perfectly civil, but he startled and confused her by some odd questions about herself, and by looking at her, while he asked them, in a strange manner. After remaining a short time he went out, and a minute or two afterwards a second stranger – also an Englishman – came in. This person introduced himself as another friend of Count Fosco's, and he, in his turn, looked at her very oddly, and asked some curious questions – never, as well as she could remember, addressing her by name, and going out again, after a little while, like the first man. By this time she was so frightened about herself, and so uneasy about her sister, that she had thoughts of venturing downstairs again, and claiming the protection and assistance of the only woman she had seen in the house – the servant who answered the door.

Just as she had risen from her chair, the Count came back into the room.

The moment he appeared she asked anxiously how long the meeting between her sister and herself was to be still delayed. At first he returned an evasive answer, but on being pressed, he acknowledged, with great apparent reluctance, that Miss Halcombe was by no means so well as he had hitherto represented her to be. His tone and manner, in making this reply, so alarmed Lady Glyde, or rather so painfully increased the uneasiness which she had felt in the company of the two strangers, that a sudden faintness overcame her, and she was obliged to ask for a glass of water. The Count called from the door for water, and for a bottle of smelling-salts. Both were brought in by the foreign-looking man with the beard. The water, when Lady Glyde attempted to drink it, had so strange a taste that it increased her faintness, and she hastily took the bottle of salts from Count Fosco, and smelt at it. Her head became giddy on the instant. The Count caught the bottle as it dropped out of her hand, and the last impression of which she was conscious was that he held it to her nostrils again.

From this point her recollections were found to be confused, fragmentary, and difficult to reconcile with any reasonable probability.

Her own impression was that she recovered her senses later in the evening, that she then left the house, that she went (as she had previously arranged to go, at Blackwater Park) to Mrs Vesey's – that she drank tea there, and that she passed the night under Mrs Vesey's roof. She was totally unable to say how, or when, or in what company she left the house to which Count Fosco had brought her. But she persisted in asserting that she had been to Mrs Vesey's, and still more extraordinary, that she had been helped to undress and get to bed by Mrs Rubelle! She could not remember what the conversation was at Mrs Vesey's or whom she saw there besides that lady, or why Mrs Rubelle should have been present in the house to help her.

Her recollection of what happened to her the next morning was still more vague and unreliable.

She had some dim idea of driving out (at what hour she could not say) with Count Fosco, and with Mrs Rubelle again for a female attendant. But when, and why, she left Mrs Vesey she could not tell; neither did she know what direction the carriage drove in, or where it set her down, or whether the Count and Mrs Rubelle did or did not remain with her all the time she was out. At this point in her sad story there was a total blank. She had no impressions of the faintest kind to communicate – no idea whether one day, or more than one day, had passed – until she came to herself suddenly in a strange place, surrounded by women who were all unknown to her.

This was the Asylum. Here she first heard herself called by Anne Catherick's name, and here, as a last remarkable circumstance in the story of the conspiracy, her own eyes informed her that she had Anne Catherick's clothes on. The nurse, on the first night in the Asylum, had shown her the marks on each article of her underclothing as it was taken off, and had said, not at all irritably or unkindly, 'Look at your own name on your own clothes, and don't worry us all any more about being Lady Glyde. She's dead and buried, and you're alive and hearty. Do look at your clothes now! There it is, in good marking ink, and there you will find it on all your old things, which we have kept in the house – Anne Catherick, as plain as print!' And there it was, when Miss Halcombe examined the linen her sister wore, on the night of their arrival at Limmeridge House.

These were the only recollections – all of them uncertain, and some of them contradictory – which could be extracted from Lady Glyde by careful questioning on the journey to Cumberland. Miss Halcombe abstained from pressing her with any inquiries relating to events in the Asylum – her mind being but too evidently unfit to bear the trial of reverting to them. It was known, by the voluntary admission of the owner of the mad-house, that she was received there on the twenty-seventh of July. From that date until the fifteenth of October (the day of her rescue) she had been under restraint, her identity with Anne Catherick systematically asserted, and her sanity, from first to last, practically denied. Faculties less delicately balanced, constitutions less tenderly organised, must have suffered under such an ordeal as this. No man could have gone through it and come out of it unchanged.

Arriving at Limmeridge late on the evening of the fifteenth, Miss Halcombe wisely resolved not to attempt the assertion of Lady Glyde's identity until the next day.

The first thing in the morning she went to Mr Fairlie's room, and using all possible cautions and preparations beforehand, at last told him in so many words what had happened. As soon as his first astonishment and alarm had subsided, he angrily declared that Miss Halcombe had allowed herself to be duped by Anne Catherick. He referred her to Count Fosco's letter, and to what she had herself told him of the personal resemblance between Anne and his deceased niece, and he positively declined to admit to his presence, even for one minute only, a madwoman, whom it was an insult and an outrage to have brought into his house at all.

Miss Halcombe left the room – waited till the first heat of her indignation had passed away – decided on reflection that Mr Fairlie should see his niece in the interests of common humanity before he closed his doors on her as a stranger – and thereupon, without a word of previous warning, took Lady Glyde with her to his room. The servant was posted at the door to prevent their entrance, but Miss Halcombe insisted on passing him, and made her way into Mr Fairlie's presence, leading her sister by the hand.

The scene that followed, though it only lasted for a few minutes, was too painful to be described – Miss Halcombe herself shrank from referring to it. Let it be enough to say that Mr Fairlie declared, in the most positive terms, that he did not recognise the woman who had been brought into his room – that he saw nothing in her face and manner to make him doubt for a moment that his niece lay buried in Limmeridge churchyard, and that he would call on the law to protect him if before the day was over she was not removed from the house.

Taking the very worst view of Mr Fairlie's selfishness, indolence, and habitual want of feeling, it was manifestly impossible to suppose that he was capable of such infamy as secretly recognising and openly disowning his brother's child. Miss Halcombe humanely and sensibly allowed all due force to the influence of prejudice and alarm in preventing him from fairly exercising his perceptions, and accounted for what had happened in that way. But when she next put the servants to the test, and found that they too were, in every case, uncertain, to say the least of it, whether the lady presented to them was their young mistress or Anne Catherick, of whose resemblance to her they had all heard, the sad conclusion was inevitable that the change produced in Lady Glyde's face and manner by her imprisonment in the Asylum was far more serious than Miss Halcombe had at first supposed.

The vile deception which had asserted her death defied exposure even in the house where she was born, and among the people with whom she had lived.

In a less critical situation the effort need not have been given up as hopeless even yet.

For example, the maid, Fanny, who happened to be then absent from Limmeridge, was expected back in two days, and there would be a chance of gaining her recognition to start with, seeing that she had been in much more constant communication with her mistress, and had been much more heartily attached to her than the other servants. Again, Lady Glyde might have been privately kept in the house or in the village to wait until her health was a little recovered and her mind was a little steadied again. When her memory could be once more trusted to serve her, she would naturally refer to persons and events in the past with a certainty and a familiarity which no impostor could simulate, and so the fact of her identity, which her own appearance had failed to establish, might subsequently be proved, with time to help her, by the surer test of her own words.

But the circumstances under which she had regained her freedom rendered all recourse to such means as these simply impracticable. The pursuit from the Asylum, diverted to Hampshire for the time only, would infallibly next take the direction of Cumberland. The persons appointed to seek the fugitive might arrive at Limmeridge House at a few hours' notice, and in Mr Fairlie's present temper of mind they might count on the immediate exertion of his local influence and authority to assist them. The commonest consideration for Lady Glyde's safety forced on Miss Halcombe the necessity of resigning the struggle to do her justice, and of removing her at once from the place of all others that was now most dangerous to her – the neighbourhood of her own home.

An immediate return to London was the first and wisest measure of security which suggested itself. In the great city all traces of them might be most speedily and most surely effaced. There were no preparations to make – no farewell words of kindness to exchange with any one. On the afternoon of that memorable day of the sixteenth Miss Halcombe roused her sister to a last exertion of courage, and without a living soul to wish them well at parting, the two took their way into the world alone, and turned their backs for ever on Limmeridge House.

They had passed the hill above the churchyard, when Lady Glyde insisted on turning back to look her last at her mother's grave. Miss Halcombe tried to shake her resolution, but, in this one instance, tried in vain. She was immovable. Her dim eyes lit with a sudden fire, and flashed through the veil that hung over them – her wasted fingers strengthened moment by moment round the friendly arm by which they had held so listlessly till this time. I believe in my soul that the hand of God was pointing their way back to them, and that the most innocent and the most afflicted of His creatures was chosen in that dread moment to see it.

They retraced their steps to the burial-ground, and by that act sealed the future of our three lives.

III

This was the story of the past – the story so far as we knew it then.

Two obvious conclusions presented themselves to my mind after hearing it. In the first place, I saw darkly what the nature of the conspiracy had been, how chances had been watched, and how circumstances had been handled to ensure impunity to a daring and an intricate crime. While all details were still a mystery to me, the vile manner in which the personal resemblance between the woman in white and Lady Glyde had been turned to account was clear beyond a doubt. It was plain that Anne Catherick had been introduced into Count Fosco's house as Lady Glyde – it was plain that Lady Glyde had taken the dead woman's place in the Asylum – the substitution having been so managed as to make innocent people (the doctor and the two servants certainly, and the owner of the mad-house in all probability) accomplices in the crime.

The second conclusion came as the necessary consequence of the first. We three had no mercy to expect from Count Fosco and Sir Percival Glyde. The success of the conspiracy had brought with it a clear gain to those two men of thirty thousand pounds – twenty thousand to one, ten thousand to the other through his wife. They had that interest, as well as other interests, in ensuring their impunity from exposure, and they would leave no stone unturned, no sacrifice unattempted, no treachery untried, to discover the place in which their victim was concealed, and to part her from the only friends she had in the world – Marian Halcombe and myself.

The sense of this serious peril – a peril which every day and every hour might bring nearer and nearer to us – was the one influence that guided me in fixing the place of our retreat. I chose it in the far east of London, where there were fewest idle people to lounge and look about them in the streets. I chose it in a poor and a populous neighbourhood – because the harder the struggle for existence among the men and women about us, the less the risk of their having the time or taking the pains to notice chance strangers who came among them. These were the great advantages I looked to, but our locality was a gain to us also in another and a hardly less important respect. We could live cheaply by the daily work of my hands, and could save every farthing we possessed to forward the purpose, the righteous purpose, of redressing an infamous wrong – which, from first to last, I now kept steadily in view.

In a week's time Marian Halcombe and I had settled how the course of our new lives should be directed.

There were no other lodgers in the house, and we had the means of going in and out without passing through the shop. I arranged, for the present at least, that neither Marian nor Laura should stir outside the door without my being with them, and that in my absence from home they should let no one into their rooms on any pretence whatever. This rule established, I went to a friend whom I had known in former days – a wood engraver in large practice – to seek for employment, telling him, at the same time, that I had reasons for wishing to remain unknown.

He at once concluded that I was in debt, expressed his regret in the usual forms, and then promised to do what he could to assist me. I left his false impression undisturbed, and accepted the work he had to give. He knew that he could trust my experience and my industry. I had what he wanted, steadiness and facility, and though my earnings were but small, they sufficed for our necessities. As soon as we could feel certain of this, Marian Halcombe and I put together what we possessed. She had between two and three hundred pounds left of her own property, and I had nearly as much remaining from the purchase-money obtained by the sale of my drawing-master's practice before I left England. Together we made up between us more than four hundred pounds. I deposited this little fortune in a bank, to be kept for the expense of those secret inquiries and investigations which I was determined to set on foot, and to carry on by myself if I could find no one to help me. We calculated our weekly expenditure to the last farthing, and we never touched our little fund except in Laura's interests and for Laura's sake.

The house-work, which, if we had dared trust a stranger near us, would have been done by a servant, was taken on the first day, taken as her own right, by Marian Halcombe. 'What a woman's hands *are* fit for,' she said, 'early and late, these hands of mine shall do.' They trembled as she held them out. The wasted arms told their sad story of the past, as she turned up the sleeves of the poor plain dress that she wore for safety's sake; but the unquenchable spirit of the woman burnt bright in her even yet. I saw the big tears rise thick in her eyes, and fall slowly over her cheeks as she looked at me. She dashed them away with a touch of her old energy, and smiled with a faint reflection of her old good spirits. 'Don't doubt my courage, Walter,' she pleaded, 'it's my weakness that cries, not *me*. The house-work shall conquer it if I can't.' And she kept her word – the victory was won when we met in the evening, and she sat down to rest. Her large steady black eyes looked at me with a flash of their bright firmness of bygone days. 'I am not quite broken down yet,' she said. 'I am worth trusting with my share of the work.' Before I could answer, she added in a whisper, 'And worth trusting with my share in the risk and the danger too. Remember that, if the time comes!'

I did remember it when the time came.

As early as the end of October the daily course of our lives had assumed its settled direction, and we three were as completely isolated in our place of concealment as if the house we lived in had been a desert island, and the great network of streets and the thousands of our fellow-creatures all round us the waters of an illimitable sea. I could now reckon on some leisure time for considering what my future plan of action should be, and how I might arm myself most securely at the outset for the coming struggle with Sir Percival and the Count.

I gave up all hope of appealing to my recognition of Laura, or to Marian's recognition of her, in proof of her identity. If we had loved her less dearly, if the instinct implanted in us by that love had not been far more certain than any exercise of reasoning, far keener than any process of observation, even we might have hesitated on first seeing her.

The outward changes wrought by the suffering and the terror of the past had fearfully, almost hopelessly, strengthened the fatal resemblance between Anne Catherick and herself. In my narrative of events at the time of my residence in Limmeridge House, I have recorded, from my own observation of the two, how the likeness, striking as it was when viewed generally, failed in many important points of similarity when tested in detail. In those former days, if they had both been seen together side by side, no person could for a moment have mistaken them one for the other – as has happened often in the instances of twins. I could not say this now. The sorrow and suffering which I had once blamed myself for associating even by a passing thought with the future of Laura Fairlie, *had* set their profaning marks on the youth and beauty of her face; and the fatal resemblance which I had once seen and shuddered at seeing, in idea only, was now a real and living resemblance which asserted itself before my own eyes. Strangers, acquaintances, friends even who could not look at her as we looked, if she had been shown to them in the first days of her rescue from the Asylum, might have doubted if she were the Laura Fairlie they had once seen, and doubted without blame.

The one remaining chance, which I had at first thought might be trusted to serve us – the chance of appealing to her recollection of persons and events with which no impostor could be familiar, was proved, by the sad test of our later experience, to be hopeless. Every little caution that Marian and I practised towards her – every little remedy we tried, to strengthen and steady slowly the weakened, shaken faculties, was a fresh protest in itself against the risk of turning her mind back on the troubled and the terrible past.

The only events of former days which we ventured on encouraging her to recall were the little trivial domestic events of that happy time at Limmeridge, when I first went there and taught her to draw. The day when I roused those remembrances by showing her the sketch of the summer-house which she had given me on the morning of our farewell, and which had never been separated from me since, was the birthday of our first hope. Tenderly and gradually, the memory of the old walks and drives dawned upon her, and the poor weary pining eyes looked at Marian and at me with a new interest, with a faltering thoughtfulness in them, which from that moment we cherished and kept alive. I bought her a little box of colours, and a sketch-book like the old sketch-book which I had seen in her hands on the morning that we first met. Once again – oh me, once again! – at spare hours saved from my work, in the dull London light, in the poor London room, I sat by her side to guide the faltering touch, to help the feeble hand. Day by day I raised and raised the new interest till its place in the blank of her existence was at last assured – till she could think of her drawing and talk of it, and patiently practise it by herself, with some faint reflection of the innocent pleasure in my encouragement, the growing enjoyment in her own progress, which belonged to the lost life and the lost happiness of past days.

We helped her mind slowly by this simple means, we took her out between us to walk on fine days, in a quiet old City square near at hand, where there was nothing to confuse or alarm her – we spared a few pounds from the fund at the banker's to get her wine, and the delicate strengthening food that she required – we amused her in the evenings with children's games at cards, with scrap-books full of prints which I borrowed from the engraver who employed me – by these, and other trifling attentions like them, we composed her and steadied her, and hoped all things, as cheerfully as we could from time and care, and love that never neglected and never despaired of her. But to take her mercilessly from seclusion and repose – to confront her with strangers, or with acquaintances who were little better than strangers – to rouse the painful impressions of her past life which we had so carefully hushed to rest – this, even in her own interests, we dared not do. Whatever sacrifices it cost, whatever long, weary, heartbreaking delays it involved, the wrong that had been inflicted on her, if mortal means could grapple it, must be redressed without her knowledge and without her help.

This resolution settled, it was next necessary to decide how the first risk should be ventured, and what the first proceedings should be.

After consulting with Marian, I resolved to begin by gathering together as many facts as could be collected – then to ask the advice of Mr Kyrle (whom we knew we could trust), and to ascertain from him, in the first instance, if the legal remedy lay fairly within our reach. I owed it to Laura's interests not to stake her whole future on my own unaided exertions, so long as there was the faintest prospect of strengthening our position by obtaining reliable assistance of any kind.

The first source of information to which I applied was the journal kept at Blackwater Park by Marian Halcombe. There were passages in this diary relating to myself which she thought it best that I should not see. Accordingly, she read to me from the manuscript, and I took the notes I wanted as she went on. We could only find time to pursue this occupation by sitting up late at night. Three nights were devoted to the purpose, and were enough to put me in possession of all that Marian could tell.

My next proceeding was to gain as much additional evidence as I could procure from other people without exciting suspicion. I went myself to Mrs Vesey to ascertain if Laura's impression of having slept there was correct or not. In this case, from consideration for Mrs Vesey's age and infirmity, and in all subsequent cases of the same kind from considerations of caution, I kept our real position a secret, and was always careful to speak of Laura as 'the late Lady Glyde.'

Mrs Vesey's answer to my inquiries only confirmed the apprehensions which I had previously felt. Laura had certainly written to say she would pass the night under the roof of her old friend – but she had never been near the house.

Her mind in this instance, and, as I feared, in other instances besides, confusedly presented to her something which she had only intended to do in the false light of something which she had really done. The unconscious contradiction of herself was easy to account for in this way – but it was likely to lead to serious results. It was a stumble on the threshold at starting – it was a flaw in the evidence which told fatally against us.

When I next asked for the letter which Laura had written to Mrs Vesey from Blackwater Park, it was given to me without the envelope, which had been thrown into the wastepaper basket, and long since destroyed. In the letter itself no date was mentioned – not even the day of the week. It only contained these lines:—'Dearest Mrs Vesey, I am in sad distress and anxiety, and I may come to your house tomorrow night, and ask for a bed. I can't tell you what is the matter in this letter – I write it in such fear of being found out that I can fix my mind on nothing. Pray be at home to see me. I will give you a thousand kisses, and tell you everything. Your affectionate Laura.' What help was there in those lines? None.

On returning from Mrs Vesey's, I instructed Marian to write (observing the same caution which I practised myself) to Mrs Michelson. She was to express, if she pleased, some general suspicion of Count Fosco's conduct, and she was to ask the housekeeper to supply us with a plain statement of events, in the interests of truth. While we were waiting for the answer, which reached us in a week's time, I went to the doctor in St John's Wood, introducing myself as sent by Miss Halcombe to collect, if possible, more particulars of her sister's last illness than Mr Kyrle had found the time to procure. By Mr Goodricke's assistance, I obtained a copy of the certificate of death, and an interview with the woman (Jane Gould) who had been employed to prepare the body for the grave. Through this person I also discovered a means of communicating with the servant, Hester Pinhorn. She had recently left her place in consequence of a disagreement with her mistress, and she was lodging with some people in the neighbourhood whom Mrs Gould knew. In the manner here indicated I obtained the Narratives of the housekeeper, of the doctor, of Jane Gould, and of Hester Pinhorn, exactly as they are presented in these pages.

Furnished with such additional evidence as these documents afforded, I considered myself to be sufficiently prepared for a consultation with Mr Kyrle, and Marian wrote accordingly to mention my name to him, and to specify the day and hour at which I requested to see him on private business.

There was time enough in the morning for me to take Laura out for her walk as usual, and to see her quietly settled at her drawing afterwards. She looked up at me with a new anxiety in her face as I rose to leave the room, and her fingers began to toy doubtfully, in the old way, with the brushes and pencils on the table.

'You are not tired of me yet?' she said. 'You are not going away because you are tired of me? I will try to do better – I will try to get well. Are you as fond of me, Walter as you used to be, now I am so pale and thin, and so slow in learning to draw?'

She spoke as a child might have spoken, she showed me her thoughts as a child might have shown them. I waited a few minutes longer – waited to tell her that she was dearer to me now than she had ever been in the past times. 'Try to get well again,' I said, encouraging the new hope in the future which I saw dawning in her mind, 'try to get well again, for Marian's sake and for mine.'

'Yes,' she said to herself, returning to her drawing. 'I must try, because they are both so fond of me.' She suddenly looked up again. 'Don't be gone long! I can't get on with my drawing, Walter, when you are not here to help me.'

'I shall soon be back, my darling – soon be back to see how you are getting on.'

My voice faltered a little in spite of me. I forced myself from the room. It was no time, then, for parting with the self-control which might yet serve me in my need before the day was out.

As I opened the door, I beckoned to Marian to follow me to the stairs. It was necessary to prepare her for a result which I felt might sooner or later follow my showing myself openly in the streets.

'I shall, in all probability, be back in a few hours,' I said, 'and you will take care, as usual, to let no one inside the doors in my absence. But if anything happens—'

'What can happen?' she interposed quickly. 'Tell me plainly, Walter, if there is any danger, and I shall know how to meet it.'

'The only danger,' I replied, 'is that Sir Percival Glyde may have been recalled to London by the news of Laura's escape. You are aware that he had me watched before I left England, and that he probably knows me by sight, although I don't know him?'

She laid her hand on my shoulder and looked at me in anxious silence. I saw she understood the serious risk that threatened us.

'It is not likely,' I said, 'that I shall be seen in London again so soon, either by Sir Percival himself or by the persons in his employ. But it is barely possible that an accident may happen. In that case, you will not be alarmed if I fail to return tonight, and you will satisfy any inquiry of Laura's with the best excuse that you can make for me? If I find the least reason to suspect that I am watched, I will take good care that no spy follows me back to this house. Don't doubt my return, Marian, however it may be delayed – and fear nothing.'

'Nothing!' she answered firmly. 'You shall not regret, Walter, that you have only a woman to help you.' She paused, and detained me for a moment longer. 'Take care!' she said, pressing my hand anxiously—'take care!'

I left her, and set forth to pave the way for discovery – the dark and doubtful way, which began at the lawyer's door.

IV

No circumstance of the slightest importance happened on my way to the offices of Messrs Gilmore & Kyrle, in Chancery Lane.

While my card was being taken in to Mr Kyrle, a consideration occurred to me which I deeply regretted not having thought of before. The information derived from Marian's diary made it a matter of certainty that Count Fosco had opened her first letter from Blackwater Park to Mr Kyrle, and had, by means of his wife, intercepted the second. He was therefore well aware of the address of the office, and he would naturally infer that if Marian wanted advice and assistance, after Laura's escape from the Asylum, she would apply once more to the experience of Mr Kyrle. In this case the office in Chancery Lane was the very first place which he and Sir Percival would cause to be watched, and if the same persons were chosen for the purpose who had been employed to follow me, before my departure from England, the fact of my return would in all probability be ascertained on that very day. I had thought, generally, of the chances of my being recognised in the streets, but the special risk connected with the office had never occurred to me until the present moment. It was too late now to repair this unfortunate error in judgment – too late to wish that I had made arrangements for meeting the lawyer in some place privately appointed beforehand. I could only resolve to be cautious on leaving Chancery Lane, and not to go straight home again under any circumstances whatever.

After waiting a few minutes I was shown into Mr Kyrle's private room. He was a pale, thin, quiet, self-possessed man, with a very attentive eye, a very low voice, and a very undemonstrative manner – not (as I judged) ready with his sympathy where strangers were concerned, and not at all easy to disturb in his professional composure. A better man for my purpose could hardly have been found. If he committed himself to a decision at all, and if the decision was favourable, the strength of our case was as good as proved from that moment.

'Before I enter on the business which brings me here,' I said, 'I ought to warn you, Mr Kyrle, that the shortest statement I can make of it may occupy some little time.'

'My time is at Miss Halcombe's disposal,' he replied. 'Where any interests of hers are concerned, I represent my partner personally, as well as professionally. It was his request that I should do so, when he ceased to take an active part in business.'

'May I inquire whether Mr Gilmore is in England?'

'He is not, he is living with his relatives in Germany. His health has improved, but the period of his return is still uncertain.'

While we were exchanging these few preliminary words, he had been searching among the papers before him, and he now produced from them a sealed letter. I thought he was about to hand the letter to me, but, apparently changing his mind, he placed it by itself on the table, settled himself in his chair, and silently waited to hear what I had to say.

Without wasting a moment in prefatory words of any sort, I entered on my narrative, and put him in full possession of the events which have already been related in these pages.

Lawyer as he was to the very marrow of his bones, I startled him out of his professional composure. Expressions of incredulity and surprise, which he could not repress, interrupted me several times before I had done. I persevered, however, to the end, and as soon as I reached it, boldly asked the one important question –

'What is your opinion, Mr Kyrle?'

He was too cautious to commit himself to an answer without taking time to recover his self-possession first.

'Before I give my opinion,' he said, 'I must beg permission to clear the ground by a few questions.'

He put the questions – sharp, suspicious, unbelieving questions, which clearly showed me, as they proceeded, that he thought I was the victim of a delusion, and that he might even have doubted, but for my introduction to him by Miss Halcombe, whether I was not attempting the perpetration of a cunningly-designed fraud.

'Do you believe that I have spoken the truth, Mr Kyrle?' I asked, when he had done examining me.

'So far as your own convictions are concerned, I am certain you have spoken the truth,' he replied. 'I have the highest esteem for Miss Halcombe, and I have therefore every reason to respect a gentleman whose mediation she trusts in a matter of this kind. I will even go farther, if you like, and admit, for courtesy's sake and for argument's sake, that the identity of Lady Glyde as a living person is a proved fact to Miss Halcombe and yourself. But you come to me for a legal opinion. As a lawyer, and as a lawyer only, it is my duty to tell you, Mr Hartright, that you have not the shadow of a case.'

'You put it strongly, Mr Kyrle.'

'I will try to put it plainly as well. The evidence of Lady Glyde's death is, on the face of it, clear and satisfactory. There is her aunt's testimony to prove that she came to Count Fosco's house, that she fell ill, and that she died. There is the testimony of the medical certificate to prove the death, and to show that it took place under natural circumstances. There is the fact of the funeral at Limmeridge, and there is the assertion of the inscription on the tomb. That is the case you want to overthrow. What evidence have you to support the declaration on your side that the person who died and was buried was not Lady Glyde? Let us run through the main points of your statement and see what they are worth. Miss Halcombe goes to a certain private Asylum, and there sees a certain female patient. It is known that a woman named Anne Catherick, and bearing an extraordinary personal resemblance to Lady Glyde, escaped from the Asylum; it is known that the person received there last July was received as Anne Catherick brought back; it is

known that the gentleman who brought her back warned Mr Fairlie that it
was part of her insanity to be bent on personating his dead niece; and it is
known that she did repeatedly declare herself in the Asylum (where no one
believed her) to be Lady Glyde. These are all facts. What have you to set
against them? Miss Halcombe's recognition of the woman, which recognition
after-events invalidate or contradict. Does Miss Halcombe assert her supposed
sister's identity to the owner of the Asylum, and take legal means for rescuing
her? No, she secretly bribes a nurse to let her escape. When the patient has
been released in this doubtful manner, and is taken to Mr Fairlie, does he
recognise her? Is he staggered for one instant in his belief of his niece's
death? No. Do the servants recognise her? No. Is she kept in the neighbourhood to assert her own identity, and to stand the test of further proceedings?
No, she is privately taken to London. In the meantime you have recognised
her also, but you are not a relative – you are not even an old friend of the
family. The servants contradict you, and Mr Fairlie contradicts Miss
Halcombe, and the supposed Lady Glyde contradicts herself. She declares
she passed the night in London at a certain house. Your own evidence shows
that she has never been near that house, and your own admission is that her
condition of mind prevents you from producing her anywhere to submit to
investigation, and to speak for herself. I pass over minor points of evidence
on both sides to save time, and I ask you, if this case were to go now into
a court of law – to go before a jury, bound to take facts as they reasonably
appear – where are your proofs?'

I was obliged to wait and collect myself before I could answer him. It
was the first time the story of Laura and the story of Marian had been
presented to me from a stranger's point of view – the first time the terrible
obstacles that lay across our path had been made to show themselves in their
true character.

'There can be no doubt,' I said, 'that the facts, as you have stated them,
appear to tell against us, but—'

'But you think those facts can be explained away,' interposed Mr Kyrle.
'Let me tell you the result of my experience on that point. When an English
jury has to choose between a plain fact *on* the surface and a long explanation *under* the surface, it always takes the fact in preference to the
explanation. For example, Lady Glyde (I call the lady you represent by
that name for argument's sake) declares she has slept at a certain house,
and it is proved that she has not slept at that house. You explain this
circumstance by entering into the state of her mind, and deducing from it
a metaphysical conclusion. I don't say the conclusion is wrong – I only
say that the jury will take the fact of her contradicting herself in preference
to any reason for the contradiction that you can offer.'

'But is it not possible,' I urged, 'by dint of patience and exertion, to discover additional evidence? Miss Halcombe and I have a few hundred pounds—'

He looked at me with a half-suppressed pity, and shook his head.

'Consider the subject, Mr Hartright, from your own point of view,' he said. 'If you are right about Sir Percival Glyde and Count Fosco (which I don't admit, mind), every imaginable difficulty would be thrown in the way of your getting fresh evidence. Every obstacle of litigation would be raised – every point in the case would be systematically contested – and by the time we had spent our thousands instead of our hundreds, the final result would, in all probability, be against us. Questions of identity, where instances of personal resemblance are concerned, are, in themselves, the hardest of all questions to settle – the hardest, even when they are free from the complications which beset the case we are now discussing. I really see no prospect of throwing any light whatever on this extraordinary affair. Even if the person buried in Limmeridge churchyard be not Lady Glyde, she was, in life, on your own showing, so like her, that we should gain nothing, if we applied for the necessary authority to have the body exhumed. In short, there is no case, Mr Hartright – there is really no case.'

I was determined to believe that there *was* a case, and in that determination shifted my ground, and appealed to him once more.

'Are there not other proofs that we might produce besides the proof of identity?' I asked.

'Not as you are situated,' he replied. 'The simplest and surest of all proofs, the proof by comparison of dates, is, as I understand, altogether out of your reach. If you could show a discrepancy between the date of the doctor's certificate and the date of Lady Glyde's journey to London, the matter would wear a totally different aspect, and I should be the first to say, Let us go on.'

'That date may yet be recovered, Mr Kyrle.'

'On the day when it is recovered, Mr Hartright, you will have a case. If you have any prospect, at this moment, of getting at it – tell me, and we shall see if I can advise you.'

I considered. The housekeeper could not help us – Laura could not help us – Marian could not help us. In all probability, the only persons in existence who knew the date were Sir Percival and the Count.

'I can think of no means of ascertaining the date at present,' I said, 'because I can think of no persons who are sure to know it, but Count Fosco and Sir Percival Glyde.'

Mr Kyrle's calmly attentive face relaxed, for the first time, into a smile.

'With your opinion of the conduct of those two gentlemen,' he said, 'you don't expect help in that quarter, I presume? If they have combined to gain large sums of money by a conspiracy, they are not likely to confess it, at any rate.'

'They may be forced to confess it, Mr Kyrle.'

'By whom?'

'By me.'

We both rose. He looked me attentively in the face with more appearance of interest than he had shown yet. I could see that I had perplexed him a little.

'You are very determined,' he said. 'You have, no doubt, a personal motive for proceeding, into which it is not my business to inquire. If a case can be produced in the future, I can only say, my best assistance is at your service. At the same time I must warn you, as the money question always enters into the law question, that I see little hope, even if you ultimately established the fact of Lady Glyde's being alive, of recovering her fortune. The foreigner would probably leave the country before proceedings were commenced, and Sir Percival's embarrassments are numerous enough and pressing enough to transfer almost any sum of money he may possess from himself to his creditors. You are of course aware—'

I stopped him at that point.

'Let me beg that we may not discuss Lady Glyde's affairs,' I said. 'I have never known anything about them in former times, and I know nothing of them now – except that her fortune is lost. You are right in assuming that I have personal motives for stirring in this matter. I wish those motives to be always as disinterested as they are at the present moment—'

He tried to interpose and explain. I was a little heated, I suppose, by feeling that he had doubted me, and I went on bluntly, without waiting to hear him.

'There shall be no money motive,' I said, 'no idea of personal advantage in the service I mean to render to Lady Glyde. She has been cast out as a stranger from the house in which she was born – a lie which records her death has been written on her mother's tomb – and there are two men, alive and unpunished, who are responsible for it. That house shall open again to receive her in the presence of every soul who followed the false funeral to the grave – that lie shall be publicly erased from the tombstone by the authority of the head of the family, and those two men shall answer for their crime to *me*, though the justice that sits in tribunals is powerless to pursue them. I have given my life to that purpose, and, alone as I stand, if God spares me, I will accomplish it.'

He drew back towards his table, and said nothing. His face showed plainly that he thought my delusion had got the better of my reason, and that he considered it totally useless to give me any more advice.

'We each keep our opinion, Mr Kyrle,' I said, 'and we must wait till the events of the future decide between us. In the meantime, I am much obliged to you for the attention you have given to my statement. You have shown me that the legal remedy lies, in every sense of the word, beyond our means. We cannot produce the law proof, and we are not rich enough to pay the law expenses. It is something gained to know that.'

I bowed and walked to the door. He called me back and gave me the letter which I had seen him place on the table by itself at the beginning of our interview.

'This came by post a few days ago,' he said. 'Perhaps you will not mind delivering it? Pray tell Miss Halcombe, at the same time, that I sincerely regret being, thus far, unable to help her, except by advice, which will not be more welcome, I am afraid, to her than to you.'

I looked at the letter while he was speaking. It was addressed to 'Miss Halcombe. Care of Messrs Gilmore & Kyrle, Chancery Lane.' The hand-writing was quite unknown to me.

On leaving the room I asked one last question.

'Do you happen to know,' I said, 'if Sir Percival Glyde is still in Paris?'

'He has returned to London,' replied Mr Kyrle. 'At least I heard so from his solicitor, whom I met yesterday.'

After that answer I went out.

On leaving the office the first precaution to be observed was to abstain from attracting attention by stopping to look about me. I walked towards one of the quietest of the large squares on the north of Holborn, then suddenly stopped and turned round at a place where a long stretch of pavement was left behind me.

There were two men at the corner of the square who had stopped also, and who were standing talking together. After a moment's reflection I turned back so as to pass them. One moved as I came near, and turned the corner leading from the square into the street. The other remained stationary. I looked at him as I passed and instantly recognised one of the men who had watched me before I left England.

If I had been free to follow my own instincts, I should probably have begun by speaking to the man, and have ended by knocking him down. But I was bound to consider consequences. If I once placed myself publicly in the wrong, I put the weapons at once into Sir Percival's hands. There was no choice but to oppose cunning by cunning. I turned into the street down which the second man had disappeared, and passed him, waiting in a doorway. He was a stranger to me, and I was glad to make sure of his personal appear-ance in case of future annoyance. Having done this, I again walked northward till I reached the New Road. There I turned aside to the west (having the men behind me all the time), and waited at a point where I knew myself to be at some distance from a cab-stand, until a fast two-wheel cab, empty, should happen to pass me. One passed in a few minutes. I jumped in and told the man to drive rapidly towards Hyde Park. There was no second fast cab for the spies behind me. I saw them dart across to the other side of the road, to follow me by running, until a cab or a cab-stand came in their way. But I had the start of them, and when I stopped the driver and got out, they were nowhere in sight. I crossed Hyde Park and made sure, on the open ground, that I was free. When I at last turned my steps homewards, it was not till many hours later – not till after dark.

I found Marian waiting for me alone in the little sitting-room. She had persuaded Laura to go to rest, after first promising to show me her drawing the moment I came in. The poor little dim faint sketch – so trifling in itself, so touching in its associations – was propped up carefully on the table with two books, and was placed where the faint light of the one candle we allowed ourselves might fall on it to the best advantage. I sat down to look at the drawing, and to tell Marian, in whispers, what had happened. The partition which divided us from the next room was so thin that we could almost hear Laura's breathing, and we might have disturbed her if we had spoken aloud.

Marian preserved her composure while I described my interview with Mr Kyrle. But her face became troubled when I spoke next of the men who had followed me from the lawyer's office, and when I told her of the discovery of Sir Percival's return.

'Bad news, Walter,' she said, 'the worst news you could bring. Have you nothing more to tell me?'

'I have something to give you,' I replied, handing her the note which Mr Kyrle had confided to my care.

She looked at the address and recognised the handwriting instantly.

'You know your correspondent?' I said.

'Too well,' she answered. 'My correspondent is Count Fosco.'

With that reply she opened the note. Her face flushed deeply while she read it – her eyes brightened with anger as she handed it to me to read in my turn.

The note contained these lines –

Impelled by honourable admiration – honourable to myself, honourable to you – I write, magnificent Marian, in the interests of your tranquillity, to say two consoling words –

Fear nothing!

Exercise your fine natural sense and remain in retirement. Dear and admirable woman, invite no dangerous publicity. Resignation is sublime – adopt it. The modest repose of home is eternally fresh – enjoy it. The storms of life pass harmless over the valley of Seclusion – dwell, dear lady, in the valley.

Do this and I authorise you to fear nothing. No new calamity shall lacerate your sensibilities – sensibilities precious to me as my own. You shall not be molested, the fair companion of your retreat shall not be pursued. She has found a new asylum in your heart. Priceless asylum! – I envy her and leave her there.

One last word of affectionate warning, of paternal caution, and I tear myself from the charm of addressing you – I close these fervent lines.

Advance no farther than you have gone already, compromise no serious interests, threaten nobody. Do not, I implore you, force me into action – *me*, the Man of Action – when it is the cherished object of my ambition to be passive, to restrict the vast reach of my energies and my combinations for your sake. If you have rash friends, moderate their deplorable ardour. If Mr Hartright returns to England, hold no communication with him. I walk on a path of my own, and Percival follows at my heels. On the day when Mr Hartright crosses that path, he is a lost man.

The only signature to these lines was the initial letter F, surrounded by a circle of intricate flourishes. I threw the letter on the table with all the contempt that I felt for it.

'He is trying to frighten you – a sure sign that he is frightened himself,' I said.

She was too genuine a woman to treat the letter as I treated it. The insolent familiarity of the language was too much for her self-control. As she looked at me across the table, her hands clenched themselves in her lap, and the old quick fiery temper flamed out again brightly in her cheeks and her eyes.

'Walter!' she said, 'if ever those two men are at your mercy, and if you are obliged to spare one of them, don't let it be the Count.'

'I will keep this letter, Marian, to help my memory when the time comes.'

She looked at me attentively as I put the letter away in my pocket-book.

'When the time comes?' she repeated. 'Can you speak of the future as if you were certain of it? – certain after what you have heard in Mr Kyrle's office, after what has happened to you today?'

'I don't count the time from today, Marian. All I have done today is to ask another man to act for me. I count from tomorrow—'

'Why from tomorrow?'

'Because tomorrow I mean to act for myself.'

'How?'

'I shall go to Blackwater by the first train, and return, I hope, at night.'

'To Blackwater!'

'Yes. I have had time to think since I left Mr Kyrle. His opinion on one point confirms my own. We must persist to the last in hunting down the date of Laura's journey. The one weak point in the conspiracy, and probably the one chance of proving that she is a living woman, centre in the discovery of that date.'

'You mean,' said Marian, 'the discovery that Laura did not leave Blackwater Park till after the date of her death on the doctor's certificate?'

'Certainly.'

'What makes you think it might have been *after*? Laura can tell us nothing of the time she was in London.'

'But the owner of the Asylum told you that she was received there on the twenty-seventh of July. I doubt Count Fosco's ability to keep her in London, and to keep her insensible to all that was passing around her, more than one night. In that case, she must have started on the twenty-sixth, and must have come to London one day after the date of her own death on the doctor's certificate. If we can prove that date, we prove our case against Sir Percival and the Count.'

'Yes, yes – I see! But how is the proof to be obtained?'

'Mrs Michelson's narrative has suggested to me two ways of trying to obtain it. One of them is to question the doctor, Mr Dawson, who must know when he resumed his attendance at Blackwater Park after Laura left the house. The other is to make inquiries at the inn to which Sir Percival drove away by himself at night. We know that his departure followed Laura's after the lapse of a few hours, and we may get at the date in that way. The attempt is at least worth making, and tomorrow I am determined it shall be made.'

'And suppose it fails – I look at the worst now, Walter; but I will look at the best if disappointments come to try us – suppose no one can help you at Blackwater?'

'There are two men who can help me, and shall help me in London – Sir Percival and the Count. Innocent people may well forget the date – but *they* are guilty, and *they* know it. If I fail everywhere else, I mean to force a confession out of one or both of them on my own terms.'

All the woman flushed up in Marian's face as I spoke.

'Begin with the Count,' she whispered eagerly. 'For my sake, begin with the Count.'

'We must begin, for Laura's sake, where there is the best chance of success,' I replied.

The colour faded from her face again, and she shook her head sadly.

'Yes,' she said, 'you are right – it was mean and miserable of me to say that. I try to be patient, Walter, and succeed better now than I did in happier times. But I have a little of my old temper still left, and it *will* get the better of me when I think of the Count!'

'His turn will come,' I said. 'But, remember, there is no weak place in his life that we know of yet.' I waited a little to let her recover her self-possession, and then spoke the decisive words –

'Marian! There is a weak place we both know of in Sir Percival's life—'

'You mean the Secret!'

'Yes: the Secret. It is our only sure hold on him. I can force him from his position of security, I can drag him and his villainy into the face of day, by no other means. Whatever the Count may have done, Sir Percival has consented to the conspiracy against Laura from another motive besides the motive of gain. You heard him tell the Count that he believed his wife knew enough to ruin him? You heard him say that he was a lost man if the secret of Anne Catherick was known?'

'Yes! yes! I did.'

'Well, Marian, when our other resources have failed us, I mean to know the Secret. My old superstition clings to me, even yet. I say again the woman in white is a living influence in our three lives. The End is appointed – the End is drawing us on – and Anne Catherick, dead in her grave, points the way to it still!'

V

The story of my first inquiries in Hampshire is soon told.

My early departure from London enabled me to reach Mr Dawson's house in the forenoon. Our interview, so far as the object of my visit was concerned, led to no satisfactory result.

Mr Dawson's books certainly showed when he had resumed his attendance on Miss Halcombe at Blackwater Park, but it was not possible to calculate back from this date with any exactness, without such help from Mrs Michelson as I knew she was unable to afford. She could not say from memory (who, in similar cases, ever can?) how many days had elapsed between the renewal of the doctor's attendance on his patient and the previous departure of Lady Glyde. She was almost certain of having mentioned the circumstance of the departure to Miss Halcombe, on the day after it happened – but then she was no more able to fix the date of the day on which this disclosure took place, than to fix the date of the day before, when Lady Glyde had left for London. Neither could she calculate, with any nearer

approach to exactness, the time that had passed from the departure of her
mistress, to the period when the undated letter from Madame Fosco arrived.
Lastly, as if to complete the series of difficulties, the doctor himself, having
been ill at the time, had omitted to make his usual entry of the day of the
week and month when the gardener from Blackwater Park had called on
him to deliver Mrs Michelson's message.

Hopeless of obtaining assistance from Mr Dawson, I resolved to try next
if I could establish the date of Sir Percival's arrival at Knowlesbury.

It seemed like a fatality! When I reached Knowlesbury the inn was shut
up, and bills were posted on the walls. The speculation had been a bad one,
as I was informed, ever since the time of the railway. The new hotel at the
station had gradually absorbed the business, and the old inn (which we knew
to be the inn at which Sir Percival had put up), had been closed about two
months since. The proprietor had left the town with all his goods and
chattels, and where he had gone I could not positively ascertain from any
one. The four people of whom I inquired gave me four different accounts
of his plans and projects when he left Knowlesbury.

There were still some hours to spare before the last train left for London,
and I drove back again in a fly from the Knowlesbury station to Blackwater
Park, with the purpose of questioning the gardener and the person who kept
the lodge. If they, too, proved unable to assist me, my resources for the
present were at an end, and I might return to town.

I dismissed the fly a mile distant from the park, and getting my directions
from the driver, proceeded by myself to the house.

As I turned into the lane from the high-road, I saw a man, with a carpet-
bag, walking before me rapidly on the way to the lodge. He was a little man,
dressed in shabby black, and wearing a remarkably large hat. I set him down
(as well as it was possible to judge) for a lawyer's clerk, and stopped at once
to widen the distance between us. He had not heard me, and he walked on
out of sight, without looking back. When I passed through the gates myself,
a little while afterwards, he was not visible – he had evidently gone on to
the house.

There were two women in the lodge. One of them was old, the other I
knew at once, by Marian's description of her, to be Margaret Porcher.

I asked first if Sir Percival was at the Park, and receiving a reply in the
negative, inquired next when he had left it. Neither of the women could tell
me more than that he had gone away in the summer. I could extract nothing
from Margaret Porcher but vacant smiles and shakings of the head. The old
woman was a little more intelligent, and I managed to lead her into speaking
of the manner of Sir Percival's departure, and of the alarm that it caused
her. She remembered her master calling her out of bed, and remembered his

frightening her by swearing – but the date at which the occurrence happened was, as she honestly acknowledged, 'quite beyond her.'

On leaving the lodge I saw the gardener at work not far off. When I first addressed him, he looked at me rather distrustfully, but on my using Mrs Michelson's name, with a civil reference to himself, he entered into conversation readily enough. There is no need to describe what passed between us – it ended, as all my other attempts to discover the date had ended. The gardener knew that his master had driven away, at night, 'some time in July, the last fortnight or the last ten days in the month' – and knew no more.

While we were speaking together I saw the man in black, with the large hat, come out from the house, and stand at some little distance observing us.

Certain suspicions of his errand at Blackwater Park had already crossed my mind. They were now increased by the gardener's inability (or unwillingness) to tell me who the man was, and I determined to clear the way before me, if possible, by speaking to him. The plainest question I could put as a stranger would be to inquire if the house was allowed to be shown to visitors. I walked up to the man at once, and accosted him in those words.

His look and manner unmistakably betrayed that he knew who I was, and that he wanted to irritate me into quarrelling with him. His reply was insolent enough to have answered the purpose, if I had been less determined to control myself. As it was, I met him with the most resolute politeness, apologised for my involuntary intrusion (which he called a 'trespass,') and left the grounds. It was exactly as I suspected. The recognition of me when I left Mr Kyrle's office had been evidently communicated to Sir Percival Glyde, and the man in black had been sent to the Park in anticipation of my making inquiries at the house or in the neighbourhood. If I had given him the least chance of lodging any sort of legal complaint against me, the interference of the local magistrate would no doubt have been turned to account as a clog on my proceedings, and a means of separating me from Marian and Laura for some days at least.

I was prepared to be watched on the way from Blackwater Park to the station, exactly as I had been watched in London the day before. But I could not discover at the time, whether I was really followed on this occasion or not. The man in black might have had means of tracking me at his disposal of which I was not aware, but I certainly saw nothing of him, in his own person, either on the way to the station, or afterwards on my arrival at the London terminus in the evening. I reached home on foot, taking the precaution, before I approached our own door, of walking round by the loneliest street in the neighbourhood, and there stopping and looking back more than once over the open space behind me. I had first learnt to use this stratagem against suspected treachery in the wilds of Central America – and now I was practising it again, with the same purpose and with even greater caution, in the heart of civilised London!

Nothing had happened to alarm Marian during my absence. She asked eagerly what success I had met with. When I told her she could not conceal her surprise at the indifference with which I spoke of the failure of my investigations thus far.

The truth was, that the ill-success of my inquiries had in no sense daunted me. I had pursued them as a matter of duty, and I had expected nothing from them. In the state of my mind at that time, it was almost a relief to me to know that the struggle was now narrowed to a trial of strength between myself and Sir Percival Glyde. The vindictive motive had mingled itself all along with my other and better motives, and I confess it was a satisfaction to me to feel that the surest way, the only way left, of serving Laura's cause, was to fasten my hold firmly on the villain who had married her.

While I acknowledge that I was not strong enough to keep my motives above the reach of this instinct of revenge, I can honestly say something in my own favour on the other side. No base speculation on the future relations of Laura and myself, and on the private and personal concessions which I might force from Sir Percival if I once had him at my mercy, ever entered my mind. I never said to myself, 'If I do succeed, it shall be one result of my success that I put it out of her husband's power to take her from me again.' I could not look at her and think of the future with such thoughts as those. The sad sight of the change in her from her former self, made the one interest of my love an interest of tenderness and compassion which her father or her brother might have felt, and which I felt, God knows, in my inmost heart. All my hopes looked no farther on now than to the day of her recovery. There, till she was strong again and happy again – there, till she could look at me as she had once looked, and speak to me as she had once spoken – the future of my happiest thoughts and my dearest wishes ended.

These words are written under no prompting of idle self-contemplation. Passages in this narrative are soon to come which will set the minds of others in judgment on my conduct. It is right that the best and the worst of me should be fairly balanced before that time.

On the morning after my return from Hampshire I took Marian upstairs into my working-room, and there laid before her the plan that I had matured thus far, for mastering the one assailable point in the life of Sir Percival Glyde.

The way to the Secret lay through the mystery, hitherto impenetrable to all of us, of the woman in white. The approach to that in its turn might be gained by obtaining the assistance of Anne Catherick's mother, and the only ascertainable means of prevailing on Mrs Catherick to act or to speak in the matter depended on the chance of my discovering local particulars and family particulars first of all from Mrs Clements. After thinking the subject over carefully, I felt certain that I could only begin the new inquiries by placing myself in communication with the faithful friend and protectress of Anne Catherick.

The first difficulty then was to find Mrs Clements.

I was indebted to Marian's quick perception for meeting this necessity at once by the best and simplest means. She proposed to write to the farm near Limmeridge (Todd's Corner), to inquire whether Mrs Clements had communicated with Mrs Todd during the past few months. How Mrs Clements had been separated from Anne it was impossible for us to say, but that separation once effected, it would certainly occur to Mrs Clements to inquire after the missing woman in the neighbourhood of all others to which she was known to be most attached – the neighbourhood of Limmeridge. I saw directly that Marian's proposal offered us a prospect of success, and she wrote to Mrs Todd accordingly by that day's post.

While we were waiting for the reply, I made myself master of all the information Marian could afford on the subject of Sir Percival's family, and of his early life. She could only speak on these topics from hearsay, but she was reasonably certain of the truth of what little she had to tell.

Sir Percival was an only child. His father, Sir Felix Glyde, had suffered from his birth under a painful and incurable deformity, and had shunned all society from his earliest years. His sole happiness was in the enjoyment of music, and he had married a lady with tastes similar to his own, who was said to be a most accomplished musician. He inherited the Blackwater property while still a young man. Neither he nor his wife after taking possession, made advances of any sort towards the society of the neighbourhood, and no one endeavoured to tempt them into abandoning their reserve, with the one disastrous exception of the rector of the parish.

The rector was the worst of all innocent mischief-makers – an over-zealous man. He had heard that Sir Felix had left College with the character of being little better than a revolutionist in politics and an infidel in religion, and he arrived conscientiously at the conclusion that it was his bounden duty to summon the lord of the manor to hear sound views enunciated in the parish church. Sir Felix fiercely resented the clergyman's well-meant but ill-directed interference, insulting him so grossly and so publicly, that the families in the neighbourhood sent letters of indignant remonstrance to the Park, and even the tenants of the Blackwater property expressed their opinion as strongly as they dared. The baronet, who had no country tastes of any kind, and no attachment to the estate or to any one living on it, declared that society at Blackwater should never have a second chance of annoying him, and left the place from that moment.

After a short residence in London he and his wife departed for the Continent, and never returned to England again. They lived part of the time in France and part in Germany – always keeping themselves in the strict retirement which the morbid sense of his own personal deformity had made a necessity to Sir Felix. Their son, Percival, had been born abroad, and had been educated there by private tutors. His mother was the first of his parents whom he lost. His father had died a few years after her, either in 1825 or 1826. Sir Percival had been in England, as a young man, once or twice before that period, but his acquaintance with the late Mr Fairlie did not begin till after the time of his father's death. They soon became very intimate, although Sir Percival was seldom, or never, at Limmeridge House in those days. Mr Frederick Fairlie might have met him once or twice in Mr Philip Fairlie's company, but he could have known little of him at that or at any other time. Sir Percival's only intimate friend in the Fairlie family had been Laura's father.

These were all the particulars that I could gain from Marian. They suggested nothing which was useful to my present purpose, but I noted them down carefully, in the event of their proving to be of importance at any future period.

Mrs Todd's reply (addressed, by our own wish, to a post-office at some distance from us) had arrived at its destination when I went to apply for it. The chances, which had been all against us hitherto, turned from this moment in our favour. Mrs Todd's letter contained the first item of information of which we were in search.

Mrs Clements, it appeared, had (as we had conjectured) written to Todd's Corner, asking pardon in the first place for the abrupt manner in which she and Anne had left their friends at the farm-house (on the morning after I had met the woman in white in Limmeridge churchyard), and then informing Mrs Todd of Anne's disappearance, and entreating that she would cause inquiries to be made in the neighbourhood, on the chance that the lost woman might have strayed back to Limmeridge. In making this request, Mrs Clements had been careful to add to it the address at which she might always be heard of, and that address Mrs Todd now transmitted to Marian. It was in London, and within half an hour's walk of our own lodging.

In the words of the proverb, I was resolved not to let the grass grow under my feet. The next morning I set forth to seek an interview with Mrs Clements.

This was my first step forward in the investigation. The story of the desperate attempt to which I now stood committed begins here.

VI

The address communicated by Mrs Todd took me to a lodging-house situated in a respectable street near the Gray's Inn Road.

When I knocked the door was opened by Mrs Clements herself. She did not appear to remember me, and asked what my business was. I recalled to her our meeting in Limmeridge churchyard at the close of my interview there with the woman in white, taking special care to remind her that I was the person who assisted Anne Catherick (as Anne had herself declared) to escape the pursuit from the Asylum. This was my only claim to the confidence of Mrs Clements. She remembered the circumstance the moment I spoke of it, and asked me into the parlour, in the greatest anxiety to know if I had brought her any news of Anne.

It was impossible for me to tell her the whole truth without, at the same time, entering into particulars on the subject of the conspiracy, which it would have been dangerous to confide to a stranger. I could only abstain most carefully from raising any false hopes, and then explain that the object of my visit was to discover the persons who were really responsible for Anne's disappearance. I even added, so as to exonerate myself from any after-reproach of my own conscience, that I entertained not the least hope of being able to trace her – that I believed we should never see her alive again – and that my main interest in the affair was to bring to punishment two men whom I suspected to be concerned in luring her away, and at whose hands I and some dear friends of mine had suffered a grievous wrong. With this explanation I left it to Mrs Clements to say whether our interest in the matter (whatever difference there might be in the motives which actuated us) was not the same, and whether she felt any reluctance to forward my object by giving me such information on the subject of my inquiries as she happened to possess.

The poor woman was at first too much confused and agitated to understand thoroughly what I said to her. She could only reply that I was welcome to anything she could tell me in return for the kindness I had shown to Anne; but as she was not very quick and ready, at the best of times, in talking to strangers, she would beg me to put her in the right way, and to say where I wished her to begin.

Knowing by experience that the plainest narrative attainable from persons who are not accustomed to arrange their ideas, is the narrative which goes far enough back at the beginning to avoid all impediments of retrospection in its course, I asked Mrs Clements to tell me first what had happened after she had left Limmeridge, and so, by watchful questioning, carried her on from point to point, till we reached the period of Anne's disappearance.

The substance of the information which I thus obtained was as follows: –

On leaving the farm at Todd's Corner, Mrs Clements and Anne had travelled that day as far as Derby, and had remained there a week on Anne's account. They had then gone on to London, and had lived in the lodging occupied by Mrs Clements at that time for a month or more, when circumstances connected with the house and the landlord had obliged them to change their quarters. Anne's terror of being discovered in London or its neighbourhood, whenever they ventured to walk out, had gradually communicated itself to Mrs Clements, and she had determined on removing to one of the most out-of-the-way places in England – to the town of Grimsby in Lincolnshire, where her deceased husband had passed all his early life. His relatives were respectable people settled in the town – they had always treated Mrs Clements with great kindness, and she thought it impossible to do better than go there and take the advice of her husband's friends. Anne would not hear of returning to her mother at Welmingham, because she had been removed to the Asylum from that place, and because Sir Percival would be certain to go back there and find her again. There was serious weight in this objection, and Mrs Clements felt that it was not to be easily removed.

At Grimsby the first serious symptoms of illness had shown themselves in Anne. They appeared soon after the news of Lady Glyde's marriage had been made public in the newspapers, and had reached her through that medium.

The medical man who was sent for to attend the sick woman discovered at once that she was suffering from a serious affection of the heart. The illness lasted long, left her very weak, and returned at intervals, though with mitigated severity, again and again. They remained at Grimsby, in consequence, during the first half of the new year, and there they might probably have stayed much longer, but for the sudden resolution which Anne took at this time to venture back to Hampshire, for the purpose of obtaining a private interview with Lady Glyde.

Mrs Clements did all in her power to oppose the execution of this hazardous and unaccountable project. No explanation of her motives was offered by Anne, except that she believed the day of her death was not far off, and that she had something on her mind which must be communicated to Lady Glyde, at any risk, in secret. Her resolution to accomplish this purpose was so firmly settled that she declared her intention of going to Hampshire by herself if Mrs Clements felt any unwillingness to go with her. The doctor, on being consulted, was of opinion that serious opposition to her wishes would, in all probability, produce another and perhaps a fatal fit of illness, and Mrs Clements, under this advice, yielded to necessity, and once more, with sad forebodings of trouble and danger to come, allowed Anne Catherick to have her own way.

On the journey from London to Hampshire Mrs Clements discovered that one of their fellow-passengers was well acquainted with the neighbourhood of Blackwater, and could give her all the information she needed on the subject of localities. In this way she found out that the only place they could go to, which was not dangerously near to Sir Percival's residence, was a large village called Sandon. The distance here from Blackwater Park was between three and four miles – and that distance, and back again, Anne had walked on each occasion when she had appeared in the neighbourhood of the lake.

For the few days during which they were at Sandon without being discovered they had lived a little away from the village, in the cottage of a decent widow-woman who had a bedroom to let, and whose discreet silence Mrs Clements had done her best to secure, for the first week at least. She had also tried hard to induce Anne to be content with writing to Lady Glyde, in the first instance; but the failure of the warning contained in the anonymous letter sent to Limmeridge had made Anne resolute to speak this time, and obstinate in the determination to go on her errand alone.

Mrs Clements, nevertheless, followed her privately on each occasion when she went to the lake, without, however, venturing near enough to the boat-house to be witness of what took place there. When Anne returned for the last time from the dangerous neighbourhood, the fatigue of walking, day after day, distances which were far too great for her strength, added to the exhausting effect of the agitation from which she had suffered, produced the result which Mrs Clements had dreaded all along. The old pain over the heart and the other symptoms of the illness at Grimsby returned, and Anne was confined to her bed in the cottage.

In this emergency the first necessity, as Mrs Clements knew by experience, was to endeavour to quiet Anne's anxiety of mind, and for this purpose the good woman went herself the next day to the lake, to try if she could find Lady Glyde (who would be sure, as Anne said, to take her daily walk to the boathouse), and prevail on her to come back privately to the cottage near Sandon. On reaching the outskirts of the plantation Mrs Clements encountered, not Lady Glyde, but a tall, stout, elderly gentleman, with a book in his hand – in other words, Count Fosco.

The Count, after looking at her very attentively for a moment, asked if she expected to see any one in that place, and added, before she could reply, that he was waiting there with a message from Lady Glyde, but that he was not quite certain whether the person then before him answered the description of the person with whom he was desired to communicate.

Upon this Mrs Clements at once confided her errand to him, and entreated that he would help to allay Anne's anxiety by trusting his message to her. The Count most readily and kindly complied with her request. The message, he said, was a very important one. Lady Glyde entreated Anne and her good friend to return immediately to London, as she felt certain that Sir Percival would discover them if they remained any longer in the neighbourhood of Blackwater. She was herself going to London in a short time, and if Mrs Clements and Anne would go there first, and would let her know what their address was, they should hear from her and see her in a fortnight or less. The Count added that he had already attempted to give a friendly warning to Anne herself, but that she had been too much startled by seeing that he was a stranger to let him approach and speak to her.

To this Mrs Clements replied, in the greatest alarm and distress, that she asked nothing better than to take Anne safely to London, but that there was no present hope of removing her from the dangerous neighbourhood, as she lay ill in her bed at that moment. The Count inquired if Mrs Clements had sent for medical advice, and hearing that she had hitherto hesitated to do so, from the fear of making their position publicly known in the village, informed her that he was himself a medical man, and that he would go back with her if she pleased, and see what could be done for Anne. Mrs Clements (feeling a natural confidence in the Count, as a person trusted with a secret message from Lady Glyde) gratefully accepted the offer, and they went back together to the cottage.

Anne was asleep when they got there. The Count started at the sight of her (evidently from astonishment at her resemblance to Lady Glyde). Poor Mrs Clements supposed that he was only shocked to see how ill she was. He would not allow her to be awakened – he was contented with putting questions to Mrs Clements about her symptoms, with looking at her, and with lightly touching her pulse. Sandon was a large enough place to have a grocer's and druggist's shop in it, and thither the Count went to write his prescription and to get the medicine made up. He brought it back himself, and told Mrs Clements that the medicine was a powerful stimulant, and that it would certainly give Anne strength to get up and bear the fatigue of a journey to London of only a few hours. The remedy was to be administered at stated times on that day and on the day after. On the third day she would be well enough to travel, and he arranged to meet Mrs Clements at the Blackwater station, and to see them off by the midday train. If they did not appear he would assume that Anne was worse, and would proceed at once to the cottage.

As events turned out, no such emergency as this occurred.

This medicine had an extraordinary effect on Anne, and the good results of it were helped by the assurance Mrs Clements could now give her that she would soon see Lady Glyde in London. At the appointed day and time (when they had not been quite so long as a week in Hampshire altogether), they arrived at the station. The Count was waiting there for them, and was talking to an elderly lady, who appeared to be going to travel by the train to London also. He most kindly assisted them, and put them into the carriage himself, begging Mrs Clements not to forget to send her address to Lady Glyde. The elderly lady did not travel in the same compartment, and they did not notice what became of her on reaching the London terminus. Mrs Clements secured respectable lodgings in a quiet neighbourhood, and then wrote, as she had engaged to do, to inform Lady Glyde of the address.

A little more than a fortnight passed, and no answer came.

At the end of that time a lady (the same elderly lady whom they had seen at the station) called in a cab, and said that she came from Lady Glyde, who was then at an hotel in London, and who wished to see Mrs Clements, for the purpose of arranging a future interview with Anne. Mrs Clements expressed her willingness (Anne being present at the time, and entreating her to do so) to forward the object in view, especially as she was not required to be away from the house for more than half an hour at the most. She and the elderly lady (clearly Madame Fosco) then left in the cab. The lady stopped the cab, after it had driven some distance, at a shop before they got to the hotel, and begged Mrs Clements to wait for her for a few minutes while she made a purchase that had been forgotten. She never appeared again.

After waiting some time Mrs Clements became alarmed, and ordered the cabman to drive back to her lodgings. When she got there, after an absence of rather more than half an hour, Anne was gone.

The only information to be obtained from the people of the house was derived from the servant who waited on the lodgers. She had opened the door to a boy from the street, who had left a letter for 'the young woman who lived on the second floor' (the part of the house which Mrs Clements occupied). The servant had delivered the letter, had then gone downstairs, and five minutes afterwards had observed Anne open the front door and go out, dressed in her bonnet and shawl. She had probably taken the letter with her, for it was not to be found, and it was therefore impossible to tell what inducement had been offered to make her leave the house. It must have been a strong one, for she would never stir out alone in London of her own accord. If Mrs Clements had not known this by experience nothing would have induced her to go away in the cab, even for so short a time as half an hour only.

As soon as she could collect her thoughts, the first idea that naturally occurred to Mrs Clements was to go and make inquiries at the Asylum, to which she dreaded that Anne had been taken back.

She went there the next day, having been informed of the locality in which the house was situated by Anne herself. The answer she received (her application having in all probability been made a day or two before the false Anne Catherick had really been consigned to safe keeping in the Asylum) was, that no such person had been brought back there. She had then written to Mrs Catherick at Welmingham to know if she had seen or heard anything of her daughter, and had received an answer in the negative. After that reply had reached her, she was at the end of her resources, and perfectly ignorant where else to inquire or what else to do. From that time to this she had remained in total ignorance of the cause of Anne's disappearance and of the end of Anne's story.

VII

Thus far the information which I had received from Mrs Clements – though it established facts of which I had not previously been aware – was of a preliminary character only.

It was clear that the series of deceptions which had removed Anne Catherick to London, and separated her from Mrs Clements, had been accomplished solely by Count Fosco and the Countess, and the question whether any part of the conduct of husband or wife had been of a kind to place either of them within reach of the law might be well worthy of future consideration. But the purpose I had now in view led me in another direction than this. The immediate object of my visit to Mrs Clements was to make some approach at least to the discovery of Sir Percival's secret, and she had said nothing as yet which advanced me on my way to that important end. I felt the necessity of trying to awaken her recollections of other times, persons, and events than those on which her memory had hitherto been employed, and when I next spoke I spoke with that object indirectly in view.

'I wish I could be of any help to you in this sad calamity,' I said. 'All I can do is to feel heartily for your distress. If Anne had been your own child, Mrs Clements, you could have shown her no truer kindness – you could have made no readier sacrifices for her sake.'

'There's no great merit in that, sir,' said Mrs Clements simply. 'The poor thing was as good as my own child to me. I nursed her from a baby, sir, bringing her up by hand – and a hard job it was to rear her. It wouldn't go to my heart so to lose her if I hadn't made her first short clothes and taught her to walk. I always said she was sent to console me for never having

chick or child of my own. And now she's lost the old times keep coming
back to my mind, and even at my age I can't help crying about her – I can't
indeed, sir!'

I waited a little to give Mrs Clements time to compose herself. Was the
light that I had been looking for so long glimmering on me – far off, as yet
– in the good woman's recollections of Anne's early life?

'Did you know Mrs Catherick before Anne was born?' I asked.

'Not very long, sir – not above four months. We saw a great deal of each
other in that time, but we were never very friendly together.'

Her voice was steadier as she made that reply. Painful as many of her
recollections might be, I observed that it was unconsciously a relief to
her mind to revert to the dimly-seen troubles of the past, after dwelling so
long on the vivid sorrows of the present.

'Were you and Mrs Catherick neighbours?' I inquired, leading her memory
on as encouragingly as I could.

'Yes, sir – neighbours at Old Welmingham.'

'*Old* Welmingham? There are two places of that name, then, in Hampshire?'

'Well, sir, there used to be in those days – better than three-and-twenty
years ago. They built a new town about two miles off, convenient to the river
– and Old Welmingham, which was never much more than a village, got
in time to be deserted. The new town is the place they call Welmingham
now – but the old parish church is the parish church still. It stands by itself,
with the houses pulled down or gone to ruin all round it. I've lived to see
sad changes. It was a pleasant, pretty place in my time.'

'Did you live there before your marriage, Mrs Clements?'

'No, sir – I'm a Norfolk woman. It wasn't the place my husband belonged
to either. He was from Grimsby, as I told you, and he served his apprenticeship
there. But having friends down south, and hearing of an opening, he got into
business at Southampton. It was in a small way, but he made enough for a
plain man to retire on, and settled at Old Welmingham. I went there with him
when he married me. We were neither of us young, but we lived very happy
together – happier than our neighbour, Mr Catherick, lived along with his wife
when they came to Old Welmingham a year or two afterwards.'

'Was your husband acquainted with them before that?'

'With Catherick, sir – not with his wife. She was a stranger to both of
us. Some gentlemen had made interest for Catherick, and he got the situation
of clerk at Welmingham church, which was the reason of his coming to settle
in our neighbourhood. He brought his newly-married wife along with him,
and we heard in course of time she had been lady's-maid in a family that
lived at Varneck Hall, near Southampton. Catherick had found it a hard matter
to get her to marry him, in consequence of her holding herself uncommonly

high. He had asked and asked, and given the thing up at last, seeing she was so contrary about it. When he *had* given it up she turned contrary just the other way, and came to him of her own accord, without rhyme or reason seemingly. My poor husband always said that was the time to have given her a lesson. But Catherick was too fond of her to do anything of the sort – he never checked her either before they were married or after. He was a quick man in his feelings, letting them carry him a deal too far, now in one way and now in another, and he would have spoilt a better wife than Mrs Catherick if a better had married him. I don't like to speak ill of any one, sir, but she was a heartless woman, with a terrible will of her own – fond of foolish admiration and fine clothes, and not caring to show so much as decent outward respect to Catherick, kindly as he always treated her. My husband said he thought things would turn out badly when they first came to live near us, and his words proved true. Before they had been quite four months in our neighbourhood there was a dreadful scandal and a miserable break-up in their household. Both of them were in fault – I am afraid both of them were equally in fault.'

'You mean both husband and wife?'

'Oh, no, sir! I don't mean Catherick – he was only to be pitied. I meant his wife and the person—'

'And the person who caused the scandal?'

'Yes, sir. A gentleman born and brought up, who ought to have set a better example. You know him, sir – and my poor dear Anne knew him only too well.'

'Sir Percival Glyde?'

'Yes, Sir Percival Glyde.'

My heart beat fast – I thought I had my hand on the clue. How little I knew then of the windings of the labyrinths which were still to mislead me!

'Did Sir Percival live in your neighbourhood at that time?' I asked.

'No, sir. He came among us as a stranger. His father had died not long before in foreign parts. I remember he was in mourning. He put up at the little inn on the river (they have pulled it down since that time), where gentlemen used to go to fish. He wasn't much noticed when he first came – it was a common thing enough for gentlemen to travel from all parts of England to fish in our river.'

'Did he make his appearance in the village before Anne was born?'

'Yes, sir. Anne was born in the June month of eighteen hundred and twenty-seven – and I think he came at the end of April or the beginning of May.'

'Came as a stranger to all of you? A stranger to Mrs Catherick as well as to the rest of the neighbours?'

'So we thought at first, sir. But when the scandal broke out, nobody believed they were strangers. I remember how it happened as well as if it was yesterday. Catherick came into our garden one night, and woke us by throwing up a handful of gravel from the walk at our window. I heard him beg my husband, for the Lord's sake, to come down and speak to him. They were a long time together talking in the porch. When my husband came back upstairs he was all of a tremble. He sat down on the side of the bed and he says to me, "Lizzie! I always told you that woman was a bad one – I always said she would end ill, and I'm afraid in my own mind that the end has come already. Catherick has found a lot of lace handkerchiefs, and two fine rings, and a new gold watch and chain, hid away in his wife's drawer – things that nobody but a born lady ought ever to have – and his wife won't say how she came by them." "Does he think she stole them?" says I. "No," says he, "stealing would be bad enough. But it's worse than that, she's had no chance of stealing such things as those, and she's not a woman to take them if she had. They're gifts, Lizzie – there's her own initials engraved inside the watch – and Catherick has seen her talking privately, and carrying on as no married woman should, with that gentleman in mourning, Sir Percival Glyde. Don't you say anything about it – I've quieted Catherick for tonight. I've told him to keep his tongue to himself, and his eyes and his ears open, and to wait a day or two, till he can be quite certain." "I believe you are both of you wrong," says I. "It's not in nature, comfortable and respectable as she is here, that Mrs Catherick should take up with a chance stranger like Sir Percival Glyde." "Ay, but is he a stranger to her?" says my husband. "You forget how Catherick's wife came to marry him. She went to him of her own accord, after saying No over and over again when he asked her. There have been wicked women before her time, Lizzie, who have used honest men who loved them as a means of saving their characters, and I'm sorely afraid this Mrs Catherick is as wicked as the worst of them. We shall see," says my husband, "we shall soon see." And only two days afterwards we did see.'

Mrs Clements waited for a moment before she went on. Even in that moment, I began to doubt whether the clue that I thought I had found was really leading me to the central mystery of the labyrinth after all. Was this common, too common, story of a man's treachery and a woman's frailty the key to a secret which had been the lifelong terror of Sir Percival Glyde?

'Well, sir, Catherick took my husband's advice and waited,' Mrs Clements continued. 'And as I told you, he hadn't long to wait. On the second day he found his wife and Sir Percival whispering together quite familiar, close under the vestry of the church. I suppose they thought the neighbourhood of the vestry was the last place in the world where anybody would think of looking after them, but, however that may be, there they were. Sir Percival, being seemingly surprised and confounded, defended himself in such a guilty way that poor Catherick (whose quick temper I have told you of already) fell into a kind of frenzy at his own disgrace, and struck Sir Percival. He was no match (and I am sorry to say it) for the man who had wronged him, and he was beaten in the cruelest manner, before the neighbours, who had come to the place on hearing the disturbance, could run in to part them. All this happened towards evening, and before nightfall, when my husband went to Catherick's house, he was gone, nobody knew where. No living soul in the village ever saw him again. He knew too well, by that time, what his wife's vile reason had been for marrying him, and he felt his misery and disgrace, especially after what had happened to him with Sir Percival, too keenly. The clergyman of the parish put an advertisement in the paper begging him to come back, and saying that he should not lose his situation or his friends. But Catherick had too much pride and spirit, as some people said – too much feeling, as I think, sir – to face his neighbours again, and try to live down the memory of his disgrace. My husband heard from him when he had left England, and heard a second time, when he was settled and doing well in America. He is alive there now, as far as I know, but none of us in the old country – his wicked wife least of all – are ever likely to set eyes on him again.'

'What became of Sir Percival?' I inquired. 'Did he stay in the neighbourhood?'

'Not he, sir. The place was too hot to hold him. He was heard at high words with Mrs Catherick the same night when the scandal broke out, and the next morning he took himself off.'

'And Mrs Catherick? Surely she never remained in the village among the people who knew of her disgrace?'

'She did, sir. She was hard enough and heartless enough to set the opinions of all her neighbours at flat defiance. She declared to everybody, from the clergyman downwards, that she was the victim of a dreadful mistake, and that all the scandal-mongers in the place should not drive her out of it, as if she was a guilty woman. All through my time she lived at Old Welmingham, and after my time, when the new town was building, and the respectable neighbours began moving to it, she moved too, as if she was determined to live among them and scandalise them to the very last. There she is now, and there she will stop, in defiance of the best of them, to her dying day.'

'But how has she lived through all these years?' I asked. 'Was her husband able and willing to help her?'

'Both able and willing, sir,' said Mrs Clements. 'In the second letter he wrote to my good man, he said she had borne his name, and lived in his home, and, wicked as she was, she must not starve like a beggar in the street. He could afford to make her some small allowance, and she might draw for it quarterly at a place in London.'

'Did she accept the allowance?'

'Not a farthing of it, sir. She said she would never be beholden to Catherick for bit or drop, if she lived to be a hundred. And she has kept her word ever since. When my poor dear husband died, and left all to me, Catherick's letter was put in my possession with the other things, and I told her to let me know if she was ever in want. "I'll let all England know I'm in want," she said, "before I tell Catherick, or any friend of Catherick's. Take that for your answer, and give it to *him* for an answer, if he ever writes again."'

'Do you suppose that she had money of her own?'

'Very little, if any, sir. It was said, and said truly, I am afraid, that her means of living came privately from Sir Percival Glyde.'

After that last reply I waited a little, to reconsider what I had heard. If I unreservedly accepted the story so far, it was now plain that no approach, direct or indirect, to the Secret had yet been revealed to me, and that the pursuit of my object had ended again in leaving me face to face with the most palpable and the most disheartening failure.

But there was one point in the narrative which made me doubt the propriety of accepting it unreservedly, and which suggested the idea of something hidden below the surface.

I could not account to myself for the circumstance of the clerk's guilty wife voluntarily living out all her after-existence on the scene of her disgrace. The woman's own reported statement that she had taken this strange course as a practical assertion of her innocence did not satisfy me. It seemed, to my mind, more natural and more probable to assume that she was not so completely a free agent in this matter as she had herself asserted. In that case, who was the likeliest person to possess the power of compelling her to remain at Welmingham? The person unquestionably from whom she derived the means of living. She had refused assistance from her husband, she had no adequate resources of her own, she was a friendless, degraded woman – from what source should she derive help but from the source at which report pointed – Sir Percival Glyde?

Reasoning on these assumptions, and always bearing in mind the one certain fact to guide me, that Mrs Catherick was in possession of the Secret, I easily understood that it was Sir Percival's interest to keep her at Welmingham, because her character in that place was certain to isolate her from all communication with female neighbours, and to allow her no opportunities of talking incautiously in moments of free intercourse with inquisitive bosom friends. But what was the mystery to be concealed? Not Sir Percival's infamous connection with Mrs Catherick's disgrace, for the neighbours were the very people who knew of it – not the suspicion that he was Anne's father, for Welmingham was the place in which that suspicion must inevitably exist. If I accepted the guilty appearances described to me as unreservedly as others had accepted them, if I drew from them the same superficial conclusion which Mr Catherick and all his neighbours had drawn, where was the suggestion, in all that I had heard, of a dangerous secret between Sir Percival and Mrs Catherick, which had been kept hidden from that time to this?

And yet, in those stolen meetings, in those familiar whisperings between the clerk's wife and 'the gentleman in mourning,' the clue to discovery existed beyond a doubt.

Was it possible that appearances in this case had pointed one way while the truth lay all the while unsuspected in another direction? Could Mrs Catherick's assertion, that she was the victim of a dreadful mistake, by any possibility be true? Or, assuming it to be false, could the conclusion which associated Sir Percival with her guilt have been founded in some inconceivable error? Had Sir Percival, by any chance, courted the suspicion that was wrong for the sake of diverting from himself some other suspicion that was right? Here – if I could find it – here was the approach to the Secret, hidden deep under the surface of the apparently unpromising story which I had just heard.

My next questions were now directed to the one object of ascertaining whether Mr Catherick had or had not arrived truly at the conviction of his wife's misconduct. The answers I received from Mrs Clements left me in no doubt whatever on that point. Mrs Catherick had, on the clearest evidence, compromised her reputation, while a single woman, with some person unknown, and had married to save her character. It had been positively ascertained, by calculations of time and place into which I need not enter particularly, that the daughter who bore her husband's name was not her husband's child.

The next object of inquiry, whether it was equally certain that Sir Percival must have been the father of Anne, was beset by far greater difficulties. I was in no position to try the probabilities on one side or on the other in this instance by any better test than the test of personal resemblance.

'I suppose you often saw Sir Percival when he was in your village?' I said.

'Yes, sir, very often,' replied Mrs Clements.

'Did you ever observe that Anne was like him?'

'She was not at all like him, sir.'

'Was she like her mother, then?'

'Not like her mother either, sir. Mrs Catherick was dark, and full in the face.'

Not like her mother and not like her (supposed) father. I knew that the test by personal resemblance was not to be implicitly trusted, but, on the other hand, it was not to be altogether rejected on that account. Was it possible to strengthen the evidence by discovering any conclusive facts in relation to the lives of Mrs Catherick and Sir Percival before they either of them appeared at Old Welmingham? When I asked my next questions I put them with this view.

'When Sir Percival first arrived in your neighbourhood,' I said, 'did you hear where he had come from last?'

'No, sir. Some said from Blackwater Park, and some said from Scotland – but nobody knew.'

'Was Mrs Catherick living in service at Varneck Hall immediately before her marriage?'

'Yes, sir.'

'And had she been long in her place?'

'Three or four years, sir; I am not quite certain which.'

'Did you ever hear the name of the gentleman to whom Varneck Hall belonged at that time?'

'Yes, sir. His name was Major Donthorne.'

'Did Mr Catherick, or did any one else you knew, ever hear that Sir Percival was a friend of Major Donthorne's, or ever see Sir Percival in the neighbourhood of Varneck Hall?'

'Catherick never did, sir, that I can remember – nor any one else either, that I know of.'

I noted down Major Donthorne's name and address, on the chance that he might still be alive, and that it might be useful at some future time to apply to him. Meanwhile, the impression on my mind was now decidedly adverse to the opinion that Sir Percival was Anne's father, and decidedly favourable to the conclusion that the secret of his stolen interviews with Mrs Catherick was entirely unconnected with the disgrace which the woman had inflicted on her husband's good name. I could think of no further inquiries which I might make to strengthen this impression – I could only encourage Mrs Clements to speak next of Anne's early days, and watch for any chance suggestion which might in this way offer itself to me.

'I have not heard yet,' I said, 'how the poor child, born in all this sin and misery, came to be trusted, Mrs Clements, to your care.'

'There was nobody else, sir, to take the little helpless creature in hand,' replied Mrs Clements. 'The wicked mother seemed to hate it – as if the poor baby was in fault! – from the day it was born. My heart was heavy for the child, and I made the offer to bring it up as tenderly as if it was my own.'

'Did Anne remain entirely under your care from that time?'

'Not quite entirely, sir. Mrs Catherick had her whims and fancies about it at times, and used now and then to lay claim to the child, as if she wanted to spite me for bringing it up. But these fits of hers never lasted for long. Poor little Anne was always returned to me, and was always glad to get back

– though she led but a gloomy life in my house, having no playmates, like other children, to brighten her up. Our longest separation was when her mother took her to Limmeridge. Just at that time I lost my husband, and I felt it was as well, in that miserable affliction, that Anne should not be in the house. She was between ten and eleven years old then, slow at her lessons, poor soul, and not so cheerful as other children – but as pretty a little girl to look at as you would wish to see. I waited at home till her mother brought her back, and then I made the offer to take her with me to London – the truth being, sir, that I could not find it in my heart to stop at Old Welmingham after my husband's death, the place was so changed and so dismal to me.'

'And did Mrs Catherick consent to your proposal?'

'No, sir. She came back from the north harder and bitterer than ever. Folks did say that she had been obliged to ask Sir Percival's leave to go, to begin with; and that she only went to nurse her dying sister at Limmeridge because the poor woman was reported to have saved money – the truth being that she hardly left enough to bury her. These things may have soured Mrs Catherick likely enough, but however that may be, she wouldn't hear of my taking the child away. She seemed to like distressing us both by parting us. All I could do was to give Anne my direction, and to tell her privately, if she was ever in trouble, to come to me. But years passed before she was free to come. I never saw her again, poor soul, till the night she escaped from the mad-house.'

'You know, Mrs Clements, why Sir Percival Glyde shut her up?'

'I only know what Anne herself told me, sir. The poor thing used to ramble and wander about it sadly. She said her mother had got some secret of Sir Percival's to keep, and had let it out to her long after I left Hampshire – and when Sir Percival found she knew it, he shut her up. But she never could say what it was when I asked her. All she could tell me was, that her mother might be the ruin and destruction of Sir Percival if she chose. Mrs Catherick may have let out just as much as that, and no more. I'm next to certain I should have heard the whole truth from Anne, if she had really known it as she pretended to do, and as she very likely fancied she did, poor soul.'

This idea had more than once occurred to my own mind. I had already told Marian that I doubted whether Laura was really on the point of making any important discovery when she and Anne Catherick were disturbed by Count Fosco at the boathouse. It was perfectly in character with Anne's mental affliction that she should assume an absolute knowledge of the secret on no better grounds than vague suspicion, derived from hints which her mother had incautiously let drop in her presence. Sir Percival's guilty distrust would, in that case, infallibly inspire him with the false idea that Anne knew all from her mother, just as it had afterwards fixed in his mind the equally false suspicion that his wife knew all from Anne.

The time was passing, the morning was wearing away. It was doubtful, if I stayed longer, whether I should hear anything more from Mrs Clements that would be at all useful to my purpose. I had already discovered those local and family particulars, in relation to Mrs Catherick, of which I had been in search, and I had arrived at certain conclusions, entirely new to me, which might immensely assist in directing the course of my future proceedings. I rose to take my leave, and to thank Mrs Clements for the friendly readiness she had shown in affording me information.

'I am afraid you must have thought me very inquisitive,' I said. 'I have troubled you with more questions than many people would have cared to answer.'

'You are heartily welcome, sir, to anything I can tell you,' answered Mrs Clements. She stopped and looked at me wistfully. 'But I do wish,' said the poor woman, 'you could have told me a little more about Anne, sir. I thought I saw something in your face when you came in which looked as if you could. You can't think how hard it is not even to know whether she is living or dead. I could bear it better if I was only certain. You said you never expected we should see her alive again. Do you know, sir – do you know for truth – that it has pleased God to take her?'

I was not proof against this appeal, it would have been unspeakably mean and cruel of me if I had resisted it.

'I am afraid there is no doubt of the truth,' I answered gently; 'I have the certainty in my own mind that her troubles in this world are over.'

The poor woman dropped into her chair and hid her face from me. 'Oh, sir,' she said, 'how do you know it? Who can have told you?'

'No one has told me, Mrs Clements. But I have reasons for feeling sure of it – reasons which I promise you shall know as soon as I can safely explain them. I am certain she was not neglected in her last moments – I am certain the heart complaint from which she suffered so sadly was the true cause of her death. You shall feel as sure of this as I do, soon – you shall know, before long, that she is buried in a quiet country churchyard – in a pretty, peaceful place, which you might have chosen for her yourself.'

'Dead!' said Mrs Clements, 'dead so young, and I am left to hear it! I made her first short frocks. I taught her to walk. The first time she ever said Mother she said it to me – and now I am left and Anne is taken! Did you say, sir,' said the poor woman, removing the handkerchief from her face, and looking up at me for the first time, 'did you say that she had been nicely buried? Was it the sort of funeral she might have had if she had really been my own child?'

I assured her that it was. She seemed to take an inexplicable pride in my answer – to find a comfort in it which no other and higher considerations could afford. 'It would have broken my heart,' she said simply, 'if Anne had not been nicely buried – but how do you know it, sir? who told you?' I once more entreated her to wait until I could speak to her unreservedly. 'You are sure to see me again,' I said, 'for I have a favour to ask when you are a little more composed – perhaps in a day or two.'

'Don't keep it waiting, sir, on my account,' said Mrs Clements. 'Never mind my crying if I can be of use. If you have anything on your mind to say to me, sir, please to say it now.'

'I only wish to ask you one last question,' I said. 'I only want to know Mrs Catherick's address at Welmingham.'

My request so startled Mrs Clements, that, for the moment, even the tidings of Anne's death seemed to be driven from her mind. Her tears suddenly ceased to flow, and she sat looking at me in blank amazement.

'For the Lord's sake, sir!' she said, 'what do you want with Mrs Catherick!'

'I want this, Mrs Clements,' I replied, 'I want to know the secret of those private meetings of hers with Sir Percival Glyde. There is something more in what you have told me of that woman's past conduct, and of that man's past relations with her, than you or any of your neighbours ever suspected. There is a secret we none of us know between those two, and I am going to Mrs Catherick with the resolution to find it out.'

'Think twice about it, sir!' said Mrs Clements, rising in her earnestness and laying her hand on my arm. 'She's an awful woman – you don't know her as I do. Think twice about it.'

'I am sure your warning is kindly meant, Mrs Clements. But I am determined to see the woman, whatever comes of it.'

Mrs Clements looked me anxiously in the face.

'I see your mind is made up, sir,' she said. 'I will give you the address.'

I wrote it down in my pocket-book and then took her hand to say farewell.

'You shall hear from me soon,' I said; 'you shall know all that I have promised to tell you.'

Mrs Clements sighed and shook her head doubtfully.

'An old woman's advice is sometimes worth taking, sir,' she said. 'Think twice before you go to Welmingham.'

VIII

When I reached home again after my interview with Mrs Clements, I was struck by the appearance of a change in Laura.

The unvarying gentleness and patience which long misfortune had tried so cruelly and had never conquered yet, seemed now to have suddenly failed her. Insensible to all Marian's attempts to soothe and amuse her, she sat, with her neglected drawing pushed away on the table, her eyes resolutely cast down, her fingers twining and untwining themselves restlessly in her lap. Marian rose when I came in, with a silent distress in her face, waited for a moment to see if Laura would look up at my approach, whispered to me, 'Try if you can rouse her,' and left the room.

I sat down in the vacant chair – gently unclasped the poor, worn, restless fingers, and took both her hands in mine.

'What are you thinking of, Laura? Tell me, my darling – try and tell me what it is.'

She struggled with herself, and raised her eyes to mine. 'I can't feel happy,' she said, 'I can't help thinking—' She stopped, bent forward a little, and laid her head on my shoulder, with a terrible mute helplessness that struck me to the heart.

'Try to tell me,' I repeated gently; 'try to tell me why you are not happy.'

'I am so useless – I am such a burden on both of you,' she answered, with a weary, hopeless sigh. 'You work and get money, Walter, and Marian helps you. Why is there nothing I can do? You will end in liking Marian better than you like me – you will, because I am so helpless! Oh, don't, don't, don't treat me like a child!'

I raised her head, and smoothed away the tangled hair that fell over her face, and kissed her – my poor, faded flower! my lost, afflicted sister! 'You shall help us, Laura,' I said, 'you shall begin, my darling, today.'

She looked at me with a feverish eagerness, with a breathless interest, that made me tremble for the new life of hope which I had called into being by those few words.

I rose, and set her drawing materials in order, and placed them near her again.

'You know that I work and get money by drawing,' I said. 'Now you have taken such pains, now you are so much improved, you shall begin to work and get money too. Try to finish this little sketch as nicely and prettily as you can. When it is done I will take it away with me, and the same person will buy it who buys all that I do. You shall keep your own earnings in your own purse, and Marian shall come to you to help us, as often as she comes to me. Think how useful you are going to make yourself to both of us, and you will soon be as happy, Laura, as the day is long.'

Her face grew eager, and brightened into a smile. In the moment while it lasted, in the moment when she again took up the pencils that had been laid aside, she almost looked like the Laura of past days.

I had rightly interpreted the first signs of a new growth and strength in her mind, unconsciously expressing themselves in the notice she had taken

of the occupations which filled her sister's life and mine. Marian (when I
told her what had passed) saw, as I saw, that she was longing to assume her
own little position of importance, to raise herself in her own estimation and
in ours – and, from that day, we tenderly helped the new ambition which
gave promise of the hopeful, happier future, that might now not be far off.
Her drawings, as she finished them, or tried to finish them, were placed in
my hands. Marian took them from me and hid them carefully, and I set aside
a little weekly tribute from my earnings, to be offered to her as the price
paid by strangers for the poor, faint, valueless sketches, of which I was the
only purchaser. It was hard sometimes to maintain our innocent deception,
when she proudly brought out her purse to contribute her share towards the
expenses, and wondered with serious interest, whether I or she had earned
the most that week. I have all those hidden drawings in my possession still
– they are my treasures beyond price – the dear remembrances that I love
to keep alive – the friends in past adversity that my heart will never part
from, my tenderness never forget.

Am I trifling, here, with the necessities of my task? am I looking forward
to the happier time which my narrative has not yet reached? Yes. Back again
– back to the days of doubt and dread, when the spirit within me struggled
hard for its life, in the icy stillness of perpetual suspense. I have paused and
rested for a while on my forward course. It is not, perhaps, time wasted, if
the friends who read these pages have paused and rested too.

I took the first opportunity I could find of speaking to Marian in private, and
of communicating to her the result of the inquiries which I had made that
morning. She seemed to share the opinion on the subject of my proposed
journey to Welmingham, which Mrs Clements had already expressed to me.

'Surely, Walter,' she said, 'you hardly know enough yet to give you any
hope of claiming Mrs Catherick's confidence? Is it wise to proceed to these
extremities, before you have really exhausted all safer and simpler means of
attaining your object? When you told me that Sir Percival and the Count
were the only two people in existence who knew the exact date of Laura's
journey, you forgot, and I forgot, that there was a third person who must
surely know it – I mean Mrs Rubelle. Would it not be far easier, and far less
dangerous, to insist on a confession from her, than to force it from Sir
Percival?'

'It might be easier,' I replied, 'but we are not aware of the full extent of
Mrs Rubelle's connivance and interest in the conspiracy, and we are therefore
not certain that the date has been impressed on her mind, as it has been
assuredly impressed on the minds of Sir Percival and the Count. It is too
late, now, to waste the time on Mrs Rubelle, which may be all-important to the

discovery of the one assailable point in Sir Percival's life. Are you thinking a little too seriously, Marian, of the risk I may run in returning to Hampshire? Are you beginning to doubt whether Sir Percival Glyde may not in the end be more than a match for me?'

'He will not be more than your match,' she replied decidedly, 'because he will not be helped in resisting you by the impenetrable wickedness of the Count.'

'What has led you to that conclusion?' I replied, in some surprise.

'My own knowledge of Sir Percival's obstinacy and impatience of the Count's control,' she answered. 'I believe he will insist on meeting you single-handed – just as he insisted at first on acting for himself at Blackwater Park. The time for suspecting the Count's interference will be the time when you have Sir Percival at your mercy. His own interests will then be directly threatened, and he will act, Walter, to terrible purpose in his own defence.'

'We may deprive him of his weapons beforehand,' I said. 'Some of the particulars I have heard from Mrs Clements may yet be turned to account against him, and other means of strengthening the case may be at our disposal. There are passages in Mrs Michelson's narrative which show that the Count found it necessary to place himself in communication with Mr Fairlie, and there may be circumstances which compromise him in that proceeding. While I am away, Marian, write to Mr Fairlie and say that you want an answer describing exactly what passed between the Count and himself, and informing you also of any particulars that may have come to his knowledge at the same time in connection with his niece. Tell him that the statement you request will, sooner or later, be insisted on, if he shows any reluctance to furnish you with it of his own accord.'

'The letter shall be written, Walter. But are you really determined to go to Welmingham?'

'Absolutely determined. I will devote the next two days to earning what we want for the week to come, and on the third day I go to Hampshire.'

When the third day came I was ready for my journey.

As it was possible that I might be absent for some little time, I arranged with Marian that we were to correspond every day – of course addressing each other by assumed names, for caution's sake. As long as I heard from her regularly, I should assume that nothing was wrong. But if the morning came and brought me no letter, my return to London would take place, as a matter of course, by the first train. I contrived to reconcile Laura to my departure by telling her that I was going to the country to find new purchasers for her drawings and for mine, and I left her occupied and happy. Marian followed me downstairs to the street door.

'Remember what anxious hearts you leave here,' she whispered, as we stood together in the passage. 'Remember all the hopes that hang on your safe return. If strange things happen to you on this journey – if you and Sir Percival meet—'

'What makes you think we shall meet?' I asked.

'I don't know – I have fears and fancies that I cannot account for. Laugh at them, Walter, if you like – but, for God's sake, keep your temper if you come in contact with that man!'

'Never fear, Marian! I answer for my self-control.'

With those words we parted.

I walked briskly to the station. There was a glow of hope in me. There was a growing conviction in my mind that my journey this time would not be taken in vain. It was a fine, clear, cold morning. My nerves were firmly strung, and I felt all the strength of my resolution stirring in me vigorously from head to foot.

As I crossed the railway platform, and looked right and left among the people congregated on it, to search for any faces among them that I knew, the doubt occurred to me whether it might not have been to my advantage if I had adopted a disguise before setting out for Hampshire. But there was something so repellent to me in the idea – something so meanly like the common herd of spies and informers in the mere act of adopting a disguise – that I dismissed the question from consideration almost as soon as it had risen in my mind. Even as a mere matter of expediency the proceeding was doubtful in the extreme. If I tried the experiment at home the landlord of the house would sooner or later discover me, and would have his suspicions aroused immediately. If I tried it away from home the same persons might see me, by the commonest accident, with the disguise and without it, and I should in that way be inviting the notice and distrust which it was my most pressing interest to avoid. In my own character I had acted thus far – and in my own character I was resolved to continue to the end.

The train left me at Welmingham early in the afternoon.

Is there any wilderness of sand in the deserts of Arabia, is there any prospect of desolation among the ruins of Palestine, which can rival the repelling effect on the eye, and the depressing influence on the mind, of an English country town in the first stage of its existence, and in the transition state of its prosperity? I asked myself that question as I passed through the clean desolation, the neat ugliness, the prim torpor of the streets of Welmingham. And the tradesmen who stared after me from their lonely shops – the trees that drooped helpless in their arid exile of unfinished crescents and squares – the dead house-carcasses that waited in vain for the vivifying human element to animate them with the breath of life – every creature that I saw, every object that I passed, seemed to answer with one accord: The deserts of Arabia are innocent of our civilised desolation – the ruins of Palestine are incapable of our modern gloom!

I inquired my way to the quarter of the town in which Mrs Catherick lived, and on reaching it found myself in a square of small houses, one story high. There was a bare little plot of grass in the middle, protected by a cheap wire fence. An elderly nursemaid and two children were standing in a corner of the enclosure, looking at a lean goat tethered to the grass. Two foot-passengers were talking together on one side of the pavement before the houses, and an idle little boy was leading an idle little dog along by a string on the other. I heard the dull tinkling of a piano at a distance, accompanied by the intermittent knocking of a hammer nearer at hand. These were all the sights and sounds of life that encountered me when I entered the square.

I walked at once to the door of Number Thirteen – the number of Mrs Catherick's house – and knocked, without waiting to consider beforehand how I might best present myself when I got in. The first necessity was to see Mrs Catherick. I could then judge, from my own observation, of the safest and easiest manner of approaching the object of my visit.

The door was opened by a melancholy middle-aged woman servant. I gave her my card, and asked if I could see Mrs Catherick. The card was taken into the front parlour, and the servant returned with a message requesting me to mention what my business was.

'Say, if you please, that my business relates to Mrs Catherick's daughter,' I replied. This was the best pretext I could think of, on the spur of the moment, to account for my visit.

The servant again retired to the parlour, again returned, and this time begged me, with a look of gloomy amazement, to walk in.

I entered a little room, with a flaring paper of the largest pattern on the walls. Chairs, tables, cheffonier, and sofa, all gleamed with the glutinous brightness of cheap upholstery. On the largest table, in the middle of the room, stood a smart Bible, placed exactly in the centre on a red and yellow woollen mat and at the side of the table nearest to the window, with a little knitting-basket on her lap, and a wheezing, blear-eyed old spaniel crouched at her feet, there sat an elderly woman, wearing a black net cap and a black silk gown, and having slate-coloured mittens on her hands. Her iron-grey hair hung in heavy bands on either side of her face – her dark eyes looked straight forward, with a hard, defiant, implacable stare. She had full square cheeks, a long, firm chin, and thick, sensual, colourless lips. Her figure was stout and sturdy, and her manner aggressively self-possessed. This was Mrs Catherick.

'You have come to speak to me about my daughter,' she said, before I could utter a word on my side. 'Be so good as to mention what you have to say.'

The tone of her voice was as hard, as defiant, as implacable as the expression of her eyes. She pointed to a chair, and looked me all over attentively, from head to foot, as I sat down in it. I saw that my only chance with this woman was to speak to her in her own tone, and to meet her, at the outset of our interview, on her own ground.

'You are aware,' I said, 'that your daughter has been lost?'

'I am perfectly aware of it.'

'Have you felt any apprehension that the misfortune of her loss might be followed by the misfortune of her death?'

'Yes. Have you come here to tell me she is dead?'

'I have.'

'Why?'

She put that extraordinary question without the slightest change in her voice, her face, or her manner. She could not have appeared more perfectly unconcerned if I had told her of the death of the goat in the enclosure outside.

'Why?' I repeated. 'Do you ask why I come here to tell you of your daughter's death?'

'Yes. What interest have you in me, or in her? How do you come to know anything about my daughter?'

'In this way. I met her on the night when she escaped from the Asylum, and I assisted her in reaching a place of safety.'

'You did very wrong.'

'I am sorry to hear her mother say so.'

'Her mother does say so. How do you know she is dead?'

'I am not at liberty to say how I know it – but I *do* know it.'

'Are you at liberty to say how you found out my address?'

'Certainly. I got your address from Mrs Clements.'

'Mrs Clements is a foolish woman. Did she tell you to come here?'

'She did not.'

'Then, I ask you again, why did you come?'

As she was determined to have her answer, I gave it to her in the plainest possible form.

'I came,' I said, 'because I thought Anne Catherick's mother might have some natural interest in knowing whether she was alive or dead.'

'Just so,' said Mrs Catherick, with additional self-possession. 'Had you no other motive?'

I hesitated. The right answer to that question was not easy to find at a moment's notice.

'If you have no other motive,' she went on, deliberately taking off her slate-coloured mittens, and rolling them up, 'I have only to thank you for your visit, and to say that I will not detain you here any longer. Your information would be more satisfactory if you were willing to explain how you became possessed of it. However, it justifies me, I suppose, in going into mourning. There is not much alteration necessary in my dress, as you see. When I have changed my mittens, I shall be all in black.'

She searched in the pocket of her gown, drew out a pair of black lace mittens, put them on with the stoniest and steadiest composure, and then quietly crossed her hands in her lap.

'I wish you good morning,' she said.

The cool contempt of her manner irritated me into directly avowing that the purpose of my visit had not been answered yet.

'I *have* another motive in coming here,' I said.

'Ah! I thought so,' remarked Mrs Catherick.

'Your daughter's death—'

'What did she die of?'

'Of disease of the heart.'

'Yes. Go on.'

'Your daughter's death has been made the pretext for inflicting serious injury on a person who is very dear to me. Two men have been concerned, to my certain knowledge, in doing that wrong. One of them is Sir Percival Glyde.'

'Indeed!'

I looked attentively to see if she flinched at the sudden mention of that name. Not a muscle of her stirred – the hard, defiant, implacable stare in her eyes never wavered for an instant.

'You may wonder,' I went on, 'how the event of your daughter's death can have been made the means of inflicting injury on another person.'

'No,' said Mrs Catherick; 'I don't wonder at all. This appears to be your affair. You are interested in my affairs. I am not interested in yours.'

'You may ask, then,' I persisted, 'why I mention the matter in your presence.'

'Yes, I *do* ask that.'

'I mention it because I am determined to bring Sir Percival Glyde to account for the wickedness he has committed.'

'What have I to do with your determination?'

'You shall hear. There are certain events in Sir Percival's past life which it is necessary for my purpose to be fully acquainted with. *You* know them – and for that reason I come to *you*.'

'What events do you mean?'

'Events that occurred at Old Welmingham when your husband was parish-clerk at that place, and before the time when your daughter was born.'

I had reached the woman at last through the barrier of impenetrable reserve that she had tried to set up between us. I saw her temper smouldering in her eyes – as plainly as I saw her hands grow restless, then unclasp themselves, and begin mechanically smoothing her dress over her knees.

'What do you know of those events?' she asked.

'All that Mrs Clements could tell me,' I answered.

There was a momentary flush on her firm square face, a momentary stillness in her restless hands, which seemed to betoken a coming outburst of anger that might throw her off her guard. But no – she mastered the rising irritation, leaned back in her chair, crossed her arms on her broad bosom, and with a smile of grim sarcasm on her thick lips, looked at me as steadily as ever.

'Ah! I begin to understand it all now,' she said, her tamed and disciplined anger only expressing itself in the elaborate mockery of her tone and manner. 'You have got a grudge of your own against Sir Percival Glyde, and I must help you to wreak it. I must tell you this, that, and the other about Sir Percival and myself, must I? Yes, indeed? You have been prying into my private affairs. You think you have found a lost woman to deal with, who lives here on sufferance, and who will do anything you ask for fear you may injure her in the opinions of the town's-people. I see through you and your precious speculation – I do! and it amuses me. Ha! ha!'

She stopped for a moment, her arms tightened over her bosom, and she laughed to herself – a hard, harsh, angry laugh.

'You don't know how I have lived in this place, and what I have done in this place, Mr What's-your-name,' she went on. 'I'll tell you, before I ring the bell and have you shown out. I came here a wronged woman – I came here robbed of my character and determined to claim it back. I've been years and years about it – and I *have* claimed it back. I have matched the respectable people fairly and openly on their own ground. If they say anything against me now they must say it in secret – they can't say it, they daren't say it, openly. I stand high enough in this town to be out of your reach. *The clergyman bows to me.* Aha! you didn't bargain for that when you came here. Go to the church and inquire about me – you will find Mrs Catherick has her sitting like the rest of them, and pays the rent on the day it's due. Go to the town-hall. There's a petition lying there – a petition of the respectable inhabitants against allowing a circus to come and perform here and corrupt our morals – yes! *our* morals. I signed that petition this morning. Go to the bookseller's shop. The clergyman's Wednesday evening Lectures on Justification by Faith are publishing there by subscription – I'm down on the list. The doctor's wife only put a shilling in the plate at our last charity sermon – I put half-a-crown. Mr Churchwarden Soward held the plate, and bowed to me. Ten years ago he told Pigrum the chemist I ought to be whipped out of the town at the cart's tail. Is your mother alive? Has she got a better Bible on her table than I have got on mine? Does she stand better with her trades-people than I do with mine? Has she always lived within her income? I have always lived within mine. Ah! there *is* the clergyman coming along the square. Look, Mr What's-your-name – look, if you please!'

She started up with the activity of a young woman, went to the window, waited till the clergyman passed, and bowed to him solemnly. The clergyman ceremoniously raised his hat, and walked on. Mrs Catherick returned to her chair, and looked at me with a grimmer sarcasm than ever.

'There!' she said. 'What do you think of that for a woman with a lost character? How does your speculation look now?'

The singular manner in which she had chosen to assert herself, the extraordinary practical vindication of her position in the town which she had just offered, had so perplexed me that I listened to her in silent surprise. I was not the less resolved, however, to make another effort to throw her off her guard. If the woman's fierce temper once got beyond her control, and once flamed out on me, she might yet say the words which would put the clue in my hands.

'How does your speculation look now?' she repeated.

'Exactly as it looked when I first came in,' I answered. 'I don't doubt the position you have gained in the town, and I don't wish to assail it even if I could. I came here because Sir Percival Glyde is, to my certain knowledge, your enemy, as well as mine. If I have a grudge against him, you have a grudge against him too. You may deny it if you like, you may distrust me as much as you please, you may be as angry as you will – but, of all the women in England, you, if you have any sense of injury, are the woman who ought to help me to crush that man.'

'Crush him for yourself,' she said; 'then come back here, and see what I say to you.'

She spoke those words as she had not spoken yet, quickly, fiercely, vindictively. I had stirred in its lair the serpent-hatred of years, but only for a moment. Like a lurking reptile it leaped up at me as she eagerly bent forward towards the place in which I was sitting. Like a lurking reptile it dropped out of sight again as she instantly resumed her former position in the chair.

'You won't trust me?' I said.

'No.'

'You are afraid?'

'Do I look as if I was?'

'You are afraid of Sir Percival Glyde?'

'Am I?'

Her colour was rising, and her hands were at work again smoothing her gown. I pressed the point farther and farther home, I went on without allowing her a moment of delay.

'Sir Percival has a high position in the world,' I said; 'it would be no wonder if you were afraid of him. Sir Percival is a powerful man, a baronet, the possessor of a fine estate, the descendant of a great family—'

She amazed me beyond expression by suddenly bursting out laughing.

'Yes,' she repeated, in tones of the bitterest, steadiest contempt. 'A baronet, the possessor of a fine estate, the descendant of a great family. Yes, indeed! A great family – especially by the mother's side.'

There was no time to reflect on the words that had just escaped her, there was only time to feel that they were well worth thinking over the moment I left the house.

'I am not here to dispute with you about family questions,' I said. 'I know nothing of Sir Percival's mother—'

'And you know as little of Sir Percival himself,' she interposed sharply.

'I advise you not to be too sure of that,' I rejoined. 'I know some things about him, and I suspect many more.'

'What do you suspect?'

'I'll tell you what I *don't* suspect. I *don't* suspect him of being Anne's father.'

She started to her feet, and came close up to me with a look of fury.

'How dare you talk to me about Anne's father! How dare you say who was her father, or who wasn't!' she broke out, her face quivering, her voice trembling with passion.

'The secret between you and Sir Percival is not *that* secret,' I persisted. 'The mystery which darkens Sir Percival's life was not born with your daughter's birth, and has not died with your daughter's death.'

She drew back a step. 'Go!' she said, and pointed sternly to the door.

'There was no thought of the child in your heart or in his,' I went on, determined to press her back to her last defences. 'There was no bond of guilty love between you and him when you held those stolen meetings, when your husband found you whispering together under the vestry of the church.'

Her pointing hand instantly dropped to her side, and the deep flush of anger faded from her face while I spoke. I saw the change pass over her – I saw that hard, firm, fearless, self-possessed woman quail under a terror which her utmost resolution was not strong enough to resist when I said those five last words, 'the vestry of the church.'

For a minute or more we stood looking at each other in silence. I spoke first.

'Do you still refuse to trust me?' I asked.

She could not call the colour that had left it back to her face, but she had steadied her voice, she had recovered the defiant self-possession of her manner when she answered me.

'I do refuse,' she said.

'Do you still tell me to go?'

'Yes. Go – and never come back.'

I walked to the door, waited a moment before I opened it, and turned round to look at her again.

'I may have news to bring you of Sir Percival which you don't expect,' I said, 'and in that case I shall come back.'

'There is no news of Sir Percival that I don't expect, except—'

She stopped, her pale face darkened, and she stole back with a quiet, stealthy, cat-like step to her chair.

'Except the news of his death,' she said, sitting down again, with the mockery of a smile just hovering on her cruel lips, and the furtive light of hatred lurking deep in her steady eyes.

As I opened the door of the room to go out, she looked round at me quickly. The cruel smile slowly widened her lips – she eyed me, with a strange stealthy interest, from head to foot – an unutterable expectation showed itself wickedly all over her face. Was she speculating, in the secrecy of her own heart, on my youth and strength, on the force of my sense of injury and the limits of my self-control, and was she considering the lengths to which they might carry me, if Sir Percival and I ever chanced to meet? The bare doubt that it might be so drove me from her presence, and silenced even the common forms of farewell on my lips. Without a word more, on my side or on hers, I left the room.

As I opened the outer door, I saw the same clergyman who had already passed the house once, about to pass it again, on his way back through the square. I waited on the door-step to let him go by, and looked round, as I did so, at the parlour window.

Mrs Catherick had heard his footsteps approaching, in the silence of that lonely place, and she was on her feet at the window again, waiting for him. Not all the strength of all the terrible passions I had roused in that woman's heart, could loosen her desperate hold on the one fragment of social consideration which years of resolute effort had just dragged within her grasp. There she was again, not a minute after I had left her, placed purposely in a position which made it a matter of common courtesy on the part of the clergyman to bow to her for a second time. He raised his hat once more.

I saw the hard ghastly face behind the window soften, and light up with gratified pride – I saw the head with the grim black cap bend ceremoniously in return. The clergyman had bowed to her, and in my presence, twice in one day!

IX

I left the house, feeling that Mrs Catherick had helped me a step forward, in spite of herself. Before I had reached the turning which led out of the square, my attention was suddenly aroused by the sound of a closing door behind me.

I looked round, and saw an undersized man in black on the door-step of a house, which, as well as I could judge, stood next to Mrs Catherick's place of abode – next to it, on the side nearest to me. The man did not hesitate a moment about the direction he should take. He advanced rapidly towards the turning at which I had stopped. I recognised him as the lawyer's clerk, who had preceded me in my visit to Blackwater Park, and who had tried to pick a quarrel with me, when I asked him if I could see the house.

I waited where I was, to ascertain whether his object was to come to close quarters and speak on this occasion. To my surprise he passed on rapidly, without saying a word, without even looking up in my face as he went by. This was such a complete inversion of the course of proceeding which I had every reason to expect on his part, that my curiosity, or rather my suspicion, was aroused, and I determined on my side to keep him cautiously in view, and to discover what the business might be in which he was now employed. Without caring whether he saw me or not, I walked after him. He never looked back, and he led me straight through the streets to the railway station.

The train was on the point of starting, and two or three passengers who were late were clustering round the small opening through which the tickets were issued. I joined them, and distinctly heard the lawyer's clerk demand a ticket for the Blackwater station. I satisfied myself that he had actually left by the train before I came away.

There was only one interpretation that I could place on what I had just seen and heard. I had unquestionably observed the man leaving a house which closely adjoined Mrs Catherick's residence. He had been probably placed there, by Sir Percival's directions, as a lodger, in anticipation of my inquiries leading me, sooner or later, to communicate with Mrs Catherick. He had doubtless seen me go in and come out, and he had hurried away by the first train to make his report at Blackwater Park, to which place Sir Percival would naturally betake himself (knowing what he evidently knew of my movements), in order to be ready on the spot, if I returned to Hampshire. Before many days were over, there seemed every likelihood now that he and I might meet.

Whatever result events might be destined to produce, I resolved to pursue my own course, straight to the end in view, without stopping or turning aside for Sir Percival or for any one. The great responsibility which weighed on me heavily in London – the responsibility of so guiding my slightest actions as to prevent them from leading accidentally to the discovery of Laura's place of refuge – was removed, now that I was in Hampshire. I could go and come as I pleased at Welmingham, and if I chanced to fail in observing any necessary precautions, the immediate results, at least, would affect no one but myself.

When I left the station the winter evening was beginning to close in. There was little hope of continuing my inquiries after dark to any useful purpose in a neighbourhood that was strange to me. Accordingly, I made my way to the nearest hotel, and ordered my dinner and my bed. This done, I wrote to Marian, to tell her that I was safe and well, and that I had fair prospects of success. I had directed her, on leaving home, to address the first letter she wrote to me (the letter I expected to receive the next morning) to 'The Post-Office, Welmingham,' and I now begged her to send her second day's letter to the same address. I could easily receive it by writing to the postmaster if I happened to be away from the town when it arrived.

The coffee-room of the hotel, as it grew late in the evening, became a perfect solitude. I was left to reflect on what I had accomplished that afternoon as uninterruptedly as if the house had been my own. Before I retired to rest I had attentively thought over my extraordinary interview with Mrs Catherick from beginning to end, and had verified at my leisure the conclusions which I had hastily drawn in the earlier part of the day.

The vestry of Old Welmingham church was the starting-point from which my mind slowly worked its way back through all that I had heard Mrs Catherick say, and through all I had seen Mrs Catherick do.

At the time when the neighbourhood of the vestry was first referred to in my presence by Mrs Clements, I had thought it the strangest and most unaccountable of all places for Sir Percival to select for a clandestine meeting with the clerk's wife. Influenced by this impression, and by no other, I had mentioned 'the vestry of the church' before Mrs Catherick on pure speculation – it represented one of the minor peculiarities of the story which occurred to me while I was speaking. I was prepared for her answering me confusedly or angrily, but the blank terror that seized her when I said the words took me completely by surprise. I had long before associated Sir Percival's Secret with the concealment of a serious crime which Mrs Catherick knew of, but I had gone no further than this. Now the woman's paroxysm of terror associated the crime, either directly or indirectly, with the vestry, and convinced me that she had been more than the mere witness of it – she was also the accomplice, beyond a doubt.

What had been the nature of the crime? Surely there was a contemptible side to it, as well as a dangerous side, or Mrs Catherick would not have repeated my own words, referring to Sir Percival's rank and power, with such marked disdain as she had certainly displayed. It was a contemptible crime then and a dangerous crime, and she had shared in it, and it was associated with the vestry of the church.

The next consideration to be disposed of led me a step farther from this point.

Mrs Catherick's undisguised contempt for Sir Percival plainly extended to his mother as well. She had referred with the bitterest sarcasm to the great family he had descended from—'especially by the mother's side.' What did this mean?

There appeared to be only two explanations of it. Either his mother's birth had been low, or his mother's reputation was damaged by some hidden flaw with which Mrs Catherick and Sir Percival were both privately acquainted? I could only put the first explanation to the test by looking at the register of her marriage, and so ascertaining her maiden name and her parentage as a preliminary to further inquiries.

On the other hand, if the second case supposed were the true one, what had been the flaw in her reputation? Remembering the account which Marian had given me of Sir Percival's father and mother, and of the suspiciously unsocial secluded life they had both led, I now asked myself whether it might not be possible that his mother had never been married at all. Here again the register might, by offering written evidence of the marriage, prove to me, at any rate, that this doubt had no foundation in truth. But where was the register to be found? At this point I took up the conclusions which I had previously formed, and the same mental process which had discovered the locality of the concealed crime, now lodged the register also in the vestry of Old Welmingham church.

These were the results of my interview with Mrs Catherick – these were the various considerations, all steadily converging to one point, which decided the course of my proceedings on the next day.

The morning was cloudy and lowering, but no rain fell. I left my bag at the hotel to wait there till I called for it, and, after inquiring the way, set forth on foot for Old Welmingham church.

It was a walk of rather more than two miles, the ground rising slowly all the way.

On the highest point stood the church – an ancient, weather-beaten building, with heavy buttresses at its sides, and a clumsy square tower in front. The vestry at the back was built out from the church, and seemed to be of the same age. Round the building at intervals appeared the remains of the village which Mrs Clements had described to me as her husband's place of abode in former years, and which the principal inhabitants had long since deserted for the new town. Some of the empty houses had been dismantled to their outer walls, some had been left to decay with time, and some were still inhabited by persons evidently of the poorest class. It was a dreary scene, and yet, in the worst aspect of its ruin, not so dreary as the modern town that I had just left. Here there was the brown, breezy sweep of surrounding fields for the eye to repose on – here the trees, leafless as they were, still varied the monotony of the prospect, and helped the mind to look forward to summer-time and shade.

As I moved away from the back of the church, and passed some of the dismantled cottages in search of a person who might direct me to the clerk, I saw two men saunter out after me from behind a wall. The tallest of the two – a stout muscular man in the dress of a gamekeeper – was a stranger to me. The other was one of the men who had followed me in London on the day when I left Mr Kyrle's office. I had taken particular notice of him at the time; and I felt sure that I was not mistaken in identifying the fellow on this occasion.

Neither he nor his companion attempted to speak to me, and both kept themselves at a respectful distance, but the motive of their presence in the neighbourhood of the church was plainly apparent. It was exactly as I had supposed – Sir Percival was already prepared for me. My visit to Mrs Catherick had been reported to him the evening before, and those two men had been placed on the look-out near the church in anticipation of my appearance at Old Welmingham. If I had wanted any further proof that my investigations had taken the right direction at last, the plan now adopted for watching me would have supplied it.

I walked on away from the church till I reached one of the inhabited houses, with a patch of kitchen garden attached to it on which a labourer was at work. He directed me to the clerk's abode, a cottage at some little distance off, standing by itself on the outskirts of the forsaken village. The clerk was indoors, and was just putting on his greatcoat. He was a cheerful, familiar, loudly-talkative old man, with a very poor opinion (as I soon discovered) of the place in which he lived, and a happy sense of superiority to his neighbours in virtue of the great personal distinction of having once been in London.

'It's well you came so early, sir,' said the old man, when I had mentioned the object of my visit. 'I should have been away in ten minutes more. Parish business, sir, and a goodish long trot before it's all done for a man at my age. But, bless you, I'm strong on my legs still! As long as a man don't give at his legs, there's a deal of work left in him. Don't you think so yourself, sir?'

He took his keys down while he was talking from a hook behind the fireplace, and locked his cottage door behind us.

'Nobody at home to keep house for me,' said the clerk, with a cheerful sense of perfect freedom from all family encumbrances. 'My wife's in the churchyard there, and my children are all married. A wretched place this, isn't it, sir? But the parish is a large one – every man couldn't get through the business as I do. It's learning does it, and I've had my share, and a little more. I can talk the Queen's English (God bless the Queen!), and that's more than most of the people about here can do. You're from London, I suppose, sir? I've been in London a matter of five-and-twenty year ago. What's the news there now, if you please?'

Chattering on in this way, he led me back to the vestry. I looked about to see if the two spies were still in sight. They were not visible anywhere. After having discovered my application to the clerk, they had probably concealed themselves where they could watch my next proceedings in perfect freedom.

The vestry door was of stout old oak, studded with strong nails, and the clerk put his large heavy key into the lock with the air of a man who knew that he had a difficulty to encounter, and who was not quite certain of creditably conquering it.

'I'm obliged to bring you this way, sir,' he said, 'because the door from the vestry to the church is bolted on the vestry side. We might have got in through the church otherwise. This is a perverse lock, if ever there was one yet. It's big enough for a prison-door – it's been hampered over and over again, and it ought to be changed for a new one. I've mentioned that to the churchwarden fifty times over at least – he's always saying, "I'll see about it" – and he never does see. Ah, it's a sort of lost corner, this place. Not like London – is it, sir? Bless you, we are all asleep here! *We* don't march with the times.'

After some twisting and turning of the key, the heavy lock yielded, and he opened the door.

The vestry was larger than I should have supposed it to be, judging from the outside only. It was a dim, mouldy, melancholy old room, with a low, raftered ceiling. Round two sides of it, the sides nearest to the interior of the church, ran heavy wooden presses, worm-eaten and gaping with age. Hooked to the inner corner of one of these presses hung several surplices, all bulging out at their lower ends in an irreverent-looking bundle of limp drapery. Below the surplices, on the floor, stood three packing-cases, with the lids half off, half on, and the straw profusely bursting out of their cracks and crevices in every direction. Behind them, in a corner, was a litter of dusty papers, some large and rolled up like architects' plans, some loosely strung together on files like bills or letters. The room had once been lighted by a small side window, but this had been bricked up, and a lantern skylight was now substituted for it. The atmosphere of the place was heavy and mouldy, being rendered additionally oppressive by the closing of the door which led into the church. This door also was composed of solid oak, and was bolted at the top and bottom on the vestry side.

'We might be tidier, mightn't we, sir?' said the cheerful clerk; 'but when you're in a lost corner of a place like this, what are you to do? Why, look here now, just look at these packing-cases. There they've been, for a year or more, ready to go down to London – there they are, littering the place, and there they'll stop as long as the nails hold them together. I'll tell you what, sir, as I said before, this is not London. We are all asleep here. Bless you, *we* don't march with the times!'

'What is there in the packing-cases?' I asked.

'Bits of old wood carvings from the pulpit, and panels from the chancel, and images from the organ-loft,' said the clerk. 'Portraits of the twelve apostles in wood, and not a whole nose among 'em. All broken, and worm-eaten, and crumbling to dust at the edges. As brittle as crockery, sir, and as old as the church, if not older.'

'And why were they going to London? To be repaired?'

'That's it, sir, to be repaired, and where they were past repair, to be copied in sound wood. But, bless you, the money fell short, and there they are, waiting for new subscriptions, and nobody to subscribe. It was all done a year ago, sir. Six gentlemen dined together about it, at the hotel in the new town. They made speeches, and passed resolutions, and put their names down, and printed off thousands of prospectuses. Beautiful prospectuses, sir, all flourished over with Gothic devices in red ink, saying it was a disgrace not to restore the church and repair the famous carvings, and so on. There are the prospectuses that couldn't be distributed, and the architect's plans and estimates, and the whole correspondence which set everybody at logger-heads and ended in a dispute, all down together in that corner, behind the packing-cases. The money dribbled in a little at first – but what *can* you expect out of London? There was just enough, you know, to pack the broken carvings, and get the estimates, and pay the printer's bill, and after that there wasn't a halfpenny left. There the things are, as I said before. We have nowhere else to put them – nobody in the new town cares about accommodating us – we're in a lost corner – and this is an untidy vestry – and who's to help it? – that's what I want to know.'

My anxiety to examine the register did not dispose me to offer much encouragement to the old man's talkativeness. I agreed with him that nobody could help the untidiness of the vestry, and then suggested that we should proceed to our business without more delay.

'Ay, ay, the marriage-register, to be sure,' said the clerk, taking a little bunch of keys from his pocket. 'How far do you want to look back, sir?'

Marian had informed me of Sir Percival's age at the time when we had spoken together of his marriage engagement with Laura. She had then described him as being forty-five years old. Calculating back from this, and making due allowance for the year that had passed since I had gained my information, I found that he must have been born in eighteen hundred and four, and that I might safely start on my search through the register from that date.

'I want to begin with the year eighteen hundred and four,' I said.

'Which way after that, sir?' asked the clerk. 'Forwards to our time or backwards away from us?'

'Backwards from eighteen hundred and four.'

He opened the door of one of the presses – the press from the side of which the surplices were hanging – and produced a large volume bound in greasy brown leather. I was struck by the insecurity of the place in which the register was kept. The door of the press was warped and cracked with age, and the lock was of the smallest and commonest kind. I could have forced it easily with the walking-stick I carried in my hand.

'Is that considered a sufficiently secure place for the register?' I inquired. 'Surely a book of such importance as this ought to be protected by a better lock, and kept carefully in an iron safe?'

'Well, now, that's curious!' said the clerk, shutting up the book again, just after he had opened it, and smacking his hand cheerfully on the cover. 'Those were the very words my old master was always saying years and years ago, when I was a lad. "Why isn't the register" (meaning this register here, under my hand)—"why isn't it kept in an iron safe?" If I've heard him say that once, I've heard him say it a hundred times. He was the solicitor in those days, sir, who had the appointment of vestry-clerk to this church. A fine hearty old gentleman, and the most particular man breathing. As long as he lived he kept a copy of this book in his office at Knowlesbury, and had it posted up regular, from time to time, to correspond with the fresh entries here. You would hardly think it, but he had his own appointed days, once or twice in every quarter, for riding over to this church on his old white pony, to check the copy, by the register, with his own eyes and hands. "How do I know?" (he used to say) "how do I know that the register in this vestry may not be stolen or destroyed? Why isn't it kept in an iron safe? Why can't I make other people as careful as I am myself? Some of these days there will be an accident happen, and when the register's lost, then the parish will find out the value of my copy." He used to take his pinch of snuff after that, and look about him as bold as a lord. Ah! the like of him for doing business isn't easy to find now. You may go to London and not match him, even *there*. Which year did you say, sir? Eighteen hundred and what?'

'Eighteen hundred and four,' I replied, mentally resolving to give the old man no more opportunities of talking, until my examination of the register was over.

The clerk put on his spectacles, and turned over the leaves of the register, carefully wetting his finger and thumb at every third page. 'There it is, sir,' said he, with another cheerful smack on the open volume. 'There's the year you want.'

As I was ignorant of the month in which Sir Percival was born, I began my backward search with the early part of the year. The register-book was of the old-fashioned kind, the entries being all made on blank pages in manuscript, and the divisions which separated them being indicated by ink lines drawn across the page at the close of each entry.

I reached the beginning of the year eighteen hundred and four without encountering the marriage, and then travelled back through December eighteen hundred and three – through November and October – through –

No! not through September also. Under the heading of that month in the year I found the marriage.

I looked carefully at the entry. It was at the bottom of a page, and was for want of room compressed into a smaller space than that occupied by the marriages above. The marriage immediately before it was impressed on my attention by the circumstance of the bridegroom's Christian name being the same as my own. The entry immediately following it (on the top of the next page) was noticeable in another way from the large space it occupied, the record in this case registering the marriages of two brothers at the same time. The register of the marriage of Sir Felix Glyde was in no respect remarkable except for the narrowness of the space into which it was compressed at the bottom of the page. The information about his wife was the usual information given in such cases. She was described as 'Cecilia Jane Elster, of Park-View Cottages, Knowlesbury, only daughter of the late Patrick Elster, Esq., formerly of Bath.'

I noted down these particulars in my pocket-book, feeling as I did so both doubtful and disheartened about my next proceedings. The Secret which I had believed until this moment to be within my grasp seemed now farther from my reach than ever.

What suggestions of any mystery unexplained had arisen out of my visit to the vestry? I saw no suggestions anywhere. What progress had I made towards discovering the suspected stain on the reputation of Sir Percival's mother? The one fact I had ascertained vindicated her reputation. Fresh doubts, fresh difficulties, fresh delays began to open before me in interminable prospect. What was I to do next? The one immediate resource left to me appeared to be this. I might institute inquiries about 'Miss Elster of Knowlesbury,' on the chance of advancing towards the main object of my investigation, by first discovering the secret of Mrs Catherick's contempt for Sir Percival's mother.

'Have you found what you wanted, sir?' said the clerk, as I closed the register-book.

'Yes,' I replied, 'but I have some inquiries still to make. I suppose the clergyman who officiated here in the year eighteen hundred and three is no longer alive?'

'No, no, sir, he was dead three or four years before I came here, and that was as long ago as the year twenty-seven. I got this place, sir,' persisted my talkative old friend, 'through the clerk before me leaving it. They say he was driven out of house and home by his wife – and she's living still down in the new town there. I don't know the rights of the story myself – all I know is I got the place. Mr Wansborough got it for me – the son of my old master that I was telling you of. He's a free, pleasant gentleman as ever lived – rides to the hounds, keeps his pointers and all that. He's vestry-clerk here now as his father was before him.'

'Did you not tell me your former master lived at Knowlesbury?' I asked, calling to mind the long story about the precise gentleman of the old school with which my talkative friend had wearied me before he opened the register-book.

'Yes, to be sure, sir,' replied the clerk. 'Old Mr Wansborough lived at Knowlesbury, and young Mr Wansborough lives there too.'

'You said just now he was vestry-clerk, like his father before him. I am not quite sure that I know what a vestry-clerk is.'

'Don't you indeed, sir? – and you come from London too! Every parish church, you know, has a vestry-clerk and a parish-clerk. The parish-clerk is a man like me (except that I've got a deal more learning than most of them – though I don't boast of it). The vestry-clerk is a sort of an appointment that the lawyers get, and if there's any business to be done for the vestry, why there they are to do it. It's just the same in London. Every parish church there has got its vestry-clerk – and you may take my word for it he's sure to be a lawyer.'

'Then young Mr Wansborough is a lawyer, I suppose?'

'Of course he is, sir! A lawyer in High Street, Knowlesbury – the old offices that his father had before him. The number of times I've swept those offices out, and seen the old gentleman come trotting in to business on his white pony, looking right and left all down the street and nodding to everybody! Bless you, he was a popular character! – he'd have done in London!'

'How far is it to Knowlesbury from this place?'

'A long stretch, sir,' said the clerk, with that exaggerated idea of distances, and that vivid perception of difficulties in getting from place to place, which is peculiar to all country people. 'Nigh on five mile, I can tell you!'

It was still early in the forenoon. There was plenty of time for a walk to Knowlesbury and back again to Welmingham; and there was no person probably in the town who was fitter to assist my inquiries about the character and position of Sir Percival's mother before her marriage than the local solicitor. Resolving to go at once to Knowlesbury on foot, I led the way out of the vestry.

'Thank you kindly, sir,' said the clerk, as I slipped my little present into his hand. 'Are you really going to walk all the way to Knowlesbury and back? Well! you're strong on your legs, too – and what a blessing that is, isn't it? There's the road, you can't miss it. I wish I was going your way – it's pleasant to meet with gentlemen from London in a lost corner like this. One hears the news. Wish you good-morning, sir, and thank you kindly once more.'

We parted. As I left the church behind me I looked back, and there were the two men again on the road below, with a third in their company, that third person being the short man in black whom I had traced to the railway the evening before.

The three stood talking together for a little while, then separated. The man in black went away by himself towards Welmingham – the other two remained together, evidently waiting to follow me as soon as I walked on.

I proceeded on my way without letting the fellows see that I took any special notice of them. They caused me no conscious irritation of feeling at that moment – on the contrary, they rather revived my sinking hopes. In the surprise of discovering the evidence of the marriage, I had forgotten the inference I had drawn on first perceiving the men in the neighbourhood of the vestry. Their reappearance reminded me that Sir Percival had anticipated my visit to Old Welmingham church as the next result of my interview with Mrs Catherick – otherwise he would never have placed his spies there to wait for me. Smoothly and fairly as appearances looked in the vestry, there was something wrong beneath them – there was something in the register-book, for aught I knew, that I had not discovered yet.

X

Once out of sight of the church, I pressed forward briskly on my way to Knowlesbury.

The road was, for the most part, straight and level. Whenever I looked back over it I saw the two spies steadily following me. For the greater part of the way they kept at a safe distance behind. But once or twice they quickened their pace, as if with the purpose of overtaking me, then stopped, consulted together, and fell back again to their former position. They had some special object evidently in view, and they seemed to be hesitating or differing about the best means of accomplishing it. I could not guess exactly what their design might be, but I felt serious doubts of reaching Knowlesbury without some mischance happening to me on the way. These doubts were realised.

I had just entered on a lonely part of the road, with a sharp turn at some distance ahead, and had just concluded (calculating by time) that I must be getting near to the town, when I suddenly heard the steps of the men close behind me.

Before I could look round, one of them (the man by whom I had been followed in London) passed rapidly on my left side and hustled me with his shoulder. I had been more irritated by the manner in which he and his companion had dogged my steps all the way from Old Welmingham than I was myself aware of, and I unfortunately pushed the fellow away smartly with my open hand. He instantly shouted for help. His companion, the tall man in the gamekeeper's clothes, sprang to my right side, and the next moment the two scoundrels held me pinioned between them in the middle of the road.

The conviction that a trap had been laid for me, and the vexation of knowing that I had fallen into it, fortunately restrained me from making my position still worse by an unavailing struggle with two men, one of whom would, in all probability, have been more than a match for me single-handed. I repressed the first natural movement by which I had attempted to shake them off, and looked about to see if there was any person near to whom I could appeal.

A labourer was at work in an adjoining field who must have witnessed all that had passed. I called to him to follow us to the town. He shook his head with stolid obstinacy, and walked away in the direction of a cottage which stood back from the high-road. At the same time the men who held me between them declared their intention of charging me with an assault. I was cool enough and wise enough now to make no opposition. 'Drop your hold of my arms,' I said, 'and I will go with you to the town.' The man in the gamekeeper's dress roughly refused. But the shorter man was sharp enough to look to consequences, and not to let his companion commit himself by unnecessary violence. He made a sign to the other, and I walked on between them with my arms free.

We reached the turning in the road, and there, close before us, were the suburbs of Knowlesbury. One of the local policemen was walking along the path by the roadside. The men at once appealed to him. He replied that the magistrate was then sitting at the town-hall, and recommended that we should appear before him immediately.

We went on to the town-hall. The clerk made out a formal summons, and the charge was preferred against me, with the customary exaggeration and the customary perversion of the truth on such occasions. The magistrate (an ill-tempered man, with a sour enjoyment in the exercise of his own power) inquired if any one on or near the road had witnessed the assault, and, greatly to my surprise, the complainant admitted the presence of the labourer in the field. I was enlightened, however, as to the object of the admission by the magistrate's next words. He remanded me at once for the production of the witness, expressing, at the same time, his willingness to take bail for my reappearance if I could produce one responsible surety to offer it. If I had been known in the town he would have liberated me on my own recognisances, but as I was a total stranger it was necessary that I should find responsible bail.

The whole object of the stratagem was now disclosed to me. It had been so managed as to make a remand necessary in a town where I was a perfect stranger, and where I could not hope to get my liberty on bail. The remand merely extended over three days, until the next sitting of the magistrate. But in that time, while I was in confinement, Sir Percival might use any means he pleased to embarrass my future proceedings – perhaps to screen himself from detection altogether – without the slightest fear of any hindrance on my part. At the end of the three days the charge would, no doubt, be withdrawn, and the attendance of the witness would be perfectly useless.

My indignation, I may almost say, my despair, at this mischievous check to all further progress – so base and trifling in itself, and yet so disheartening and so serious in its probable results – quite unfitted me at first to reflect on the best means of extricating myself from the dilemma in which I now stood. I had the folly to call for writing materials, and to think of privately communicating my real position to the magistrate. The hopelessness and the imprudence of this proceeding failed to strike me before I had actually written the opening lines of the letter. It was not till I had pushed the paper away – not till, I am ashamed to say, I had almost allowed the vexation of my helpless position to conquer me – that a course of action suddenly occurred to my mind, which Sir Percival had probably not anticipated, and which might set me free again in a few hours. I determined to communicate the situation in which I was placed to Mr Dawson, of Oak Lodge.

I had visited this gentleman's house, it may be remembered, at the time of my first inquiries in the Blackwater Park neighbourhood, and I had presented to him a letter of introduction from Miss Halcombe, in which she recommended me to his friendly attention in the strongest terms. I now wrote, referring to this letter, and to what I had previously told Mr Dawson of the delicate and dangerous nature of my inquiries. I had not revealed to him the truth about Laura, having merely described my errand as being of the utmost importance to private family interests with which Miss Halcombe was concerned. Using the same caution still, I now accounted for my presence at Knowlesbury in the same manner, and I put it to the doctor to say whether the trust reposed in me by a lady whom he well knew, and the hospitality I had myself received in his house, justified me or not in asking him to come to my assistance in a place where I was quite friendless.

I obtained permission to hire a messenger to drive away at once with my letter in a conveyance which might be used to bring the doctor back immediately. Oak Lodge was on the Knowlesbury side of Blackwater. The man declared he could drive there in forty minutes, and could bring Mr Dawson back in forty more. I directed him to follow the doctor wherever he might happen to be, if he was not at home, and then sat down to wait for the result with all the patience and all the hope that I could summon to help me.

It was not quite half-past one when the messenger departed. Before half-past three he returned, and brought the doctor with him. Mr Dawson's kindness, and the delicacy with which he treated his prompt assistance quite as a matter of course, almost overpowered me. The bail required was offered, and accepted immediately. Before four o'clock, on that afternoon, I was shaking hands warmly with the good old doctor – a free man again – in the streets of Knowlesbury.

Mr Dawson hospitably invited me to go back with him to Oak Lodge, and take up my quarters there for the night. I could only reply that my time was not my own, and I could only ask him to let me pay my visit in a few days, when I might repeat my thanks, and offer to him all the explanations which I felt to be only his due, but which I was not then in a position to make. We parted with friendly assurances on both sides, and I turned my steps at once to Mr Wansborough's office in the High Street.

Time was now of the last importance.

The news of my being free on bail would reach Sir Percival, to an absolute certainty, before night. If the next few hours did not put me in a position to justify his worst fears, and to hold him helpless at my mercy, I might lose every inch of the ground I had gained, never to recover it again. The unscrupulous nature of the man, the local influence he possessed, the desperate peril of exposure with which my blindfold inquiries threatened him – all warned me to press on to positive discovery, without the useless waste of a single minute. I had found time to think while I was waiting for Mr Dawson's arrival, and I had well employed it. Certain portions of the conversation of the talkative old clerk, which had wearied me at the time, now recurred to my memory with a new significance, and a suspicion crossed my mind darkly which had not occurred to me while I was in the vestry. On my way to Knowlesbury, I had only proposed to apply to Mr Wansborough for information on the subject of Sir Percival's mother. My object now was to examine the duplicate register of Old Welmingham Church.

Mr Wansborough was in his office when I inquired for him.

He was a jovial, red-faced, easy-looking man – more like a country squire than a lawyer – and he seemed to be both surprised and amused by my application. He had heard of his father's copy of the register, but had not even seen it himself. It had never been inquired after, and it was no doubt in the strong room among other papers that had not been disturbed since his father's death. It was a pity (Mr Wansborough said) that the old gentleman was not alive to hear his precious copy asked for at last. He would have ridden his favourite hobby harder than ever now. How had I come to hear of the copy? was it through anybody in the town?

I parried the question as well as I could. It was impossible at this stage of the investigation to be too cautious, and it was just as well not to let Mr Wansborough know prematurely that I had already examined the original register. I described myself, therefore, as pursuing a family inquiry, to the object of which every possible saving of time was of great importance. I was anxious to send certain particulars to London by that day's post, and one look at the duplicate register (paying, of course, the necessary fees) might supply what I required, and save me a further journey to Old Welmingham. I added that, in the event of my subsequently requiring a copy of the original register, I should make application to Mr Wansborough's office to furnish me with the document.

After this explanation no objection was made to producing the copy. A clerk was sent to the strong room, and after some delay returned with the volume. It was of exactly the same size as the volume in the vestry, the only difference being that the copy was more smartly bound. I took it with me to an unoccupied desk. My hands were trembling – my head was burning hot – I felt the necessity of concealing my agitation as well as I could from the persons about me in the room, before I ventured on opening the book.

On the blank page at the beginning, to which I first turned, were traced some lines in faded ink. They contained these words –

'Copy of the Marriage Register of Welmingham Parish Church. Executed under my orders, and afterwards compared, entry by entry, with the original, by myself. (Signed) Robert Wansborough, vestry-clerk.' Below this note there was a line added, in another handwriting, as follows: 'Extending from the first of January, 1800, to the thirtieth of June, 1815.'

I turned to the month of September, eighteen hundred and three. I found the marriage of the man whose Christian name was the same as my own. I found the double register of the marriages of the two brothers. And between these entries, at the bottom of the page?

Nothing! Not a vestige of the entry which recorded the marriage of Sir Felix Glyde and Cecilia Jane Elster in the register of the church!

My heart gave a great bound, and throbbed as if it would stifle me. I looked again – I was afraid to believe the evidence of my own eyes. No! not a doubt. The marriage was not there. The entries on the copy occupied exactly the same places on the page as the entries in the original. The last entry on one page recorded the marriage of the man with my Christian name. Below it there was a blank space – a space evidently left because it was too narrow to contain the entry of the marriages of the two brothers, which in the copy, as in the original, occupied the top of the next page. That space told the whole story! There it must have remained in the church register from eighteen hundred and three (when the marriages had been solemnised and the copy had been made) to eighteen hundred and twenty-seven, when Sir Percival appeared at Old Welmingham. Here, at Knowlesbury, was the chance of committing the forgery shown to me in the copy, and there, at Old Welmingham, was the forgery committed in the register of the church.

My head turned giddy – I held by the desk to keep myself from falling. Of all the suspicions which had struck me in relation to that desperate man, not one had been near the truth.

The idea that he was not Sir Percival Glyde at all, that he had no more claim to the baronetcy and to Blackwater Park than the poorest labourer who worked on the estate, had never once occurred to my mind. At one time I had thought he might be Anne Catherick's father – at another time I had thought he might have been Anne Catherick's husband – the offence of which he was really guilty had been, from first to last, beyond the widest reach of my imagination.

The paltry means by which the fraud had been effected, the magnitude and daring of the crime that it represented, the horror of the consequences involved in its discovery, overwhelmed me. Who could wonder now at the brute-restlessness of the wretch's life – at his desperate alternations between abject duplicity and reckless violence – at the madness of guilty distrust which had made him imprison Anne Catherick in the Asylum, and had given him over to the vile conspiracy against his wife, on the bare suspicion that the one and the other knew his terrible secret? The disclosure of that secret might, in past years, have hanged him – might now transport him for life. The disclosure of that secret, even if the sufferers by his deception spared him the penalties of the law, would deprive him at one blow of the name, the rank, the estate, the whole social existence that he had usurped. This was the Secret, and it was mine! A word from me, and house, lands, baronetcy, were gone from him for ever – a word from me, and he was driven out into the world, a nameless, penniless, friendless outcast! The man's whole future hung on my lips – and he knew it by this time as certainly as I did!

That last thought steadied me. Interests far more precious than my own depended on the caution which must now guide my slightest actions. There was no possible treachery which Sir Percival might not attempt against me. In the danger and desperation of his position he would be staggered by no risks, he would recoil at no crime – he would literally hesitate at nothing to save himself.

I considered for a minute. My first necessity was to secure positive evidence in writing of the discovery that I had just made, and in the event of any personal misadventure happening to me, to place that evidence beyond Sir Percival's reach. The copy of the register was sure to be safe in Mr Wansborough's strong room. But the position of the original in the vestry was, as I had seen with my own eyes, anything but secure.

In this emergency I resolved to return to the church, to apply again to the clerk, and to take the necessary extract from the register before I slept that night. I was not then aware that a legally-certified copy was necessary, and that no document merely drawn out by myself could claim the proper importance as a proof. I was not aware of this, and my determination to keep my present proceedings a secret prevented me from asking any questions which might have procured the necessary information. My one anxiety was the anxiety to get back to Old Welmingham. I made the best excuses I could for the discomposure in my face and manner which Mr Wansborough had already noticed, laid the necessary fee on his table, arranged that I should write to him in a day or two, and left the office, with my head in a whirl and my blood throbbing through my veins at fever heat.

It was just getting dark. The idea occurred to me that I might be followed again and attacked on the high-road.

My walking-stick was a light one, of little or no use for purposes of defence. I stopped before leaving Knowlesbury and bought a stout country cudgel, short, and heavy at the head. With this homely weapon, if any one man tried to stop me I was a match for him. If more than one attacked me I could trust to my heels. In my school-days I had been a noted runner, and I had not wanted for practice since in the later time of my experience in Central America.

I started from the town at a brisk pace, and kept the middle of the road.

A small misty rain was falling, and it was impossible for the first half of the way to make sure whether I was followed or not. But at the last half of my journey, when I supposed myself to be about two miles from the church, I saw a man run by me in the rain, and then heard the gate of a field by the roadside shut to sharply. I kept straight on, with my cudgel ready in my hand, my ears on the alert, and my eyes straining to see through the mist and the darkness. Before I had advanced a hundred yards there was a rustling in the hedge on my right, and three men sprang out into the road.

I drew aside on the instant to the footpath. The two foremost men were carried beyond me before they could check themselves. The third was as quick as lightning. He stopped, half turned, and struck at me with his stick. The blow was aimed at hazard, and was not a severe one. It fell on my left shoulder. I returned it heavily on his head. He staggered back and jostled his two companions just as they were both rushing at me. This circumstance gave me a moment's start. I slipped by them, and took to the middle of the road again at the top of my speed.

The two unhurt men pursued me. They were both good runners – the road was smooth and level, and for the first five minutes or more I was conscious that I did not gain on them. It was perilous work to run for long in the darkness. I could barely see the dim black line of the hedges on either side, and any chance obstacle in the road would have thrown me down to a certainty. Ere long I felt the ground changing – it descended from the level at a turn, and then rose again beyond. Downhill the men rather gained on me, but uphill I began to distance them. The rapid, regular thump of their feet grew fainter on my ear, and I calculated by the sound that I was far enough in advance to take to the fields with a good chance of their passing me in the darkness. Diverging to the footpath, I made for the first break that I could guess at, rather than see, in the hedge. It proved to be a closed gate. I vaulted over, and finding myself in a field, kept across it steadily with my back to the road. I heard the men pass the gate, still running, then in a minute more heard one of them call to the other to come back. It was no matter what they did now, I was out of their sight and out of their hearing. I kept straight across the field, and when I had reached the farther extremity of it, waited there for a minute to recover my breath.

It was impossible to venture back to the road, but I was determined nevertheless to get to Old Welmingham that evening.

Neither moon nor stars appeared to guide me. I only knew that I had kept the wind and rain at my back on leaving Knowlesbury, and if I now kept them at my back still, I might at least be certain of not advancing altogether in the wrong direction.

Proceeding on this plan, I crossed the country – meeting with no worse obstacles than hedges, ditches, and thickets, which every now and then obliged me to alter my course for a little while – until I found myself on a hill-side, with the ground sloping away steeply before me. I descended to the bottom of the hollow, squeezed my way through a hedge, and got out into a lane. Having turned to the right on leaving the road, I now turned to the left, on the chance of regaining the line from which I had wandered. After following the muddy windings of the lane for ten minutes or more, I saw a cottage with a light in one of the windows. The garden gate was open to the lane, and I went in at once to inquire my way.

Before I could knock at the door it was suddenly opened, and a man came running out with a lighted lantern in his hand. He stopped and held it up at the sight of me. We both started as we saw each other. My wanderings had led me round the outskirts of the village, and had brought me out at the lower end of it. I was back at Old Welmingham, and the man with the lantern was no other than my acquaintance of the morning, the parish clerk.

His manner appeared to have altered strangely in the interval since I had last seen him. He looked suspicious and confused – his ruddy cheeks were deeply flushed – and his first words, when he spoke, were quite unintelligible to me.

'Where are the keys?' he asked. 'Have you taken them?'

'What keys?' I repeated. 'I have this moment come from Knowlesbury. What keys do you mean?'

'The keys of the vestry. Lord save us and help us! what shall I do? The keys are gone! Do you hear?' cried the old man, shaking the lantern at me in his agitation, 'the keys are gone!'

'How? When? Who can have taken them?'

'I don't know,' said the clerk, staring about him wildly in the darkness. 'I've only just got back. I told you I had a long day's work this morning – I locked the door and shut the window down – it's open now, the window's open. Look! somebody has got in there and taken the keys.'

He turned to the casement window to show me that it was wide open. The door of the lantern came loose from its fastening as he swayed it round, and the wind blew the candle out instantly.

'Get another light,' I said, 'and let us both go to the vestry together. Quick! quick!'

I hurried him into the house. The treachery that I had every reason to expect, the treachery that might deprive me of every advantage I had gained, was at that moment, perhaps, in process of accomplishment. My impatience to reach the church was so great that I could not remain inactive in the cottage while the clerk lit the lantern again. I walked out, down the garden path, into the lane.

Before I had advanced ten paces a man approached me from the direction leading to the church. He spoke respectfully as we met. I could not see his face, but judging by his voice only, he was a perfect stranger to me.

'I beg your pardon, Sir Percival—' he began.

I stopped him before he could say more.

'The darkness misleads you,' I said. 'I am not Sir Percival.'

The man drew back directly.

'I thought it was my master,' he muttered, in a confused, doubtful way.

'You expected to meet your master here?'

'I was told to wait in the lane.'

With that answer he retraced his steps. I looked back at the cottage and saw the clerk coming out, with the lantern lighted once more. I took the old man's arm to help him on the more quickly. We hastened along the lane, and passed the person who had accosted me. As well as I could see by the light of the lantern, he was a servant out of livery.

'Who's that?' whispered the clerk. 'Does he know anything about the keys?'

'We won't wait to ask him,' I replied. 'We will go on to the vestry first.'

The church was not visible, even by daytime, until the end of the lane was reached. As we mounted the rising ground which led to the building from that point, one of the village children – a boy – came close up to us, attracted by the light we carried, and recognised the clerk.

'I say, measter,' said the boy, pulling officiously at the clerk's coat, 'there be summun up yander in the church. I heerd un lock the door on hisself – I heerd un strike a loight wi' a match.'

The clerk trembled and leaned against me heavily.

'Come! come!' I said encouragingly. 'We are not too late. We will catch the man, whoever he is. Keep the lantern, and follow me as fast as you can.'

I mounted the hill rapidly. The dark mass of the church-tower was the first object I discerned dimly against the night sky. As I turned aside to get round to the vestry, I heard heavy footsteps close to me. The servant had ascended to the church after us. 'I don't mean any harm,' he said, when I turned round on him, 'I'm only looking for my master.' The tones in which he spoke betrayed unmistakable fear. I took no notice of him and went on.

The instant I turned the corner and came in view of the vestry, I saw the lantern-skylight on the roof brilliantly lit up from within. It shone out with dazzling brightness against the murky, starless sky.

I hurried through the churchyard to the door.

As I got near there was a strange smell stealing out on the damp night air. I heard a snapping noise inside – I saw the light above grow brighter and brighter – a pane of the glass cracked – I ran to the door and put my hand on it. The vestry was on fire!

Before I could move, before I could draw my breath after that discovery, I was horror-struck by a heavy thump against the door from the inside. I heard the key worked violently in the lock – I heard a man's voice behind the door, raised to a dreadful shrillness, screaming for help.

The servant who had followed me staggered back shuddering, and dropped to his knees. 'Oh, my God!' he said, 'it's Sir Percival!'

As the words passed his lips the clerk joined us, and at the same moment there was another and a last grating turn of the key in the lock.

'The Lord have mercy on his soul!' said the old man. 'He is doomed and dead. He has hampered the lock.'

I rushed to the door. The one absorbing purpose that had filled all my thoughts, that had controlled all my actions, for weeks and weeks past, vanished in an instant from my mind. All remembrance of the heartless injury the man's crimes had inflicted – of the love, the innocence, the happiness he had pitilessly laid waste – of the oath I had sworn in my own heart to summon him to the terrible reckoning that he deserved – passed from my memory like a dream. I remembered nothing but the horror of his situation. I felt nothing but the natural human impulse to save him from a frightful death.

'Try the other door!' I shouted. 'Try the door into the church! The lock's hampered. You're a dead man if you waste another moment on it.'

There had been no renewed cry for help when the key was turned for the last time. There was no sound now of any kind, to give token that he was still alive. I heard nothing but the quickening crackle of the flames, and the sharp snap of the glass in the skylight above.

I looked round at my two companions. The servant had risen to his feet – he had taken the lantern, and was holding it up vacantly at the door. Terror seemed to have struck him with downright idiocy – he waited at my heels, he followed me about when I moved like a dog. The clerk sat crouched up on one of the tombstones, shivering, and moaning to himself. The one moment in which I looked at them was enough to show me that they were both helpless.

Hardly knowing what I did, acting desperately on the first impulse that occurred to me, I seized the servant and pushed him against the vestry wall. 'Stoop!' I said, 'and hold by the stones. I am going to climb over you to the roof – I am going to break the skylight, and give him some air!'

The man trembled from head to foot, but he held firm. I got on his back, with my cudgel in my mouth, seized the parapet with both hands, and was instantly on the roof. In the frantic hurry and agitation of the moment, it never struck me that I might let out the flame instead of letting in the air. I struck at the skylight, and battered in the cracked, loosened glass at a blow. The fire leaped out like a wild beast from its lair. If the wind had not chanced, in the position I occupied, to set it away from me, my exertions might have ended then and there. I crouched on the roof as the smoke poured out above me with the flame. The gleams and flashes of the light showed me the serv-ant's face staring up vacantly under the wall – the clerk risen to his feet on the tombstone, wringing his hands in despair – and the scanty population of the village, haggard men and terrified women, clustered beyond in the church-yard – all appearing and disappearing, in the red of the dreadful glare, in the black of the choking smoke. And the man beneath my feet! – the man, suffocating, burning, dying so near us all, so utterly beyond our reach!

The thought half maddened me. I lowered myself from the roof, by my hands, and dropped to the ground.

'The key of the church!' I shouted to the clerk. 'We must try it that way – we may save him yet if we can burst open the inner door.'

'No, no, no!' cried the old man. 'No hope! the church key and the vestry key are on the same ring – both inside there! Oh, sir, he's past saving – he's dust and ashes by this time!'

'They'll see the fire from the town,' said a voice from among the men behind me. 'There's a ingine in the town. They'll save the church.'

I called to that man – *he* had his wits about him – I called to him to come and speak to me. It would be a quarter of an hour at least before the town engine could reach us. The horror of remaining inactive all that time was more than I could face. In defiance of my own reason I persuaded myself that the doomed and lost wretch in the vestry might still be lying senseless on the floor, might not be dead yet. If we broke open the door, might we save him? I knew the strength of the heavy lock – I knew the thickness of the nailed oak – I knew the hopelessness of assailing the one and the other by ordinary means. But surely there were beams still left in the dismantled cottages near the church? What if we got one, and used it as a battering-ram against the door?

The thought leaped through me like the fire leaping out of the shattered skylight. I appealed to the man who had spoken first of the fire-engine in the town. 'Have you got your pickaxes handy?' Yes, they had. 'And a hatchet, and a saw, and a bit of rope?' Yes! yes! yes! I ran down among the villagers, with the lantern in my hand. 'Five shillings apiece to every man who helps me!' They started into life at the words. That ravenous second hunger of poverty

– the hunger for money – roused them into tumult and activity in a moment. 'Two of you for more lanterns, if you have them! Two of you for the pickaxes and the tools! The rest after me to find the beam!' They cheered – with shrill starveling voices they cheered. The women and the children fled back on either side. We rushed in a body down the churchyard path to the first empty cottage. Not a man was left behind but the clerk – the poor old clerk standing on the flat tombstone sobbing and wailing over the church. The servant was still at my heels – his white, helpless, panic-stricken face was close over my shoulder as we pushed into the cottage. There were rafters from the torn-down floor above, lying loose on the ground – but they were too light. A beam ran across over our heads, but not out of reach of our arms and our pickaxes – a beam fast at each end in the ruined wall, with ceiling and flooring all ripped away, and a great gap in the roof above, open to the sky. We attacked the beam at both ends at once. God! how it held – how the brick and mortar of the wall resisted us! We struck, and tugged, and tore. The beam gave at one end – it came down with a lump of brickwork after it. There was a scream from the women all huddled in the doorway to look at us – a shout from the men – two of them down but not hurt. Another tug all together – and the beam was loose at both ends. We raised it, and gave the word to clear the doorway. Now for the work! now for the rush at the door! There is the fire streaming into the sky, streaming brighter than ever to light us! Steady along the churchyard path – steady with the beam for a rush at the door. One, two, three – and off. Out rings the cheering again, irrepressibly. We have shaken it already, the hinges must give if the lock won't. Another run with the beam! One, two, three – and off. It's loose! the stealthy fire darts at us through the crevice all round it. Another, and a last rush! The door falls in with a crash. A great hush of awe, a stillness of breathless expectation, possesses every living soul of us. We look for the body. The scorching heat on our faces drives us back: we see nothing – above, below, all through the room, we see nothing but a sheet of living fire.

'Where is he?' whispered the servant, staring vacantly at the flames.

'He's dust and ashes,' said the clerk. 'And the books are dust and ashes – and oh, sirs! the church will be dust and ashes soon.'

Those were the only two who spoke. When they were silent again, nothing stirred in the stillness but the bubble and the crackle of the flames.

Hark!

A harsh rattling sound in the distance – then the hollow beat of horses' hoofs at full gallop – then the low roar, the all-predominant tumult of hundreds of human voices clamouring and shouting together. The engine at last.

The people about me all turned from the fire, and ran eagerly to the brow of the hill. The old clerk tried to go with the rest, but his strength was exhausted. I saw him holding by one of the tombstones. 'Save the church!' he cried out faintly, as if the firemen could hear him already.

Save the church!

The only man who never moved was the servant. There he stood, his eyes still fastened on the flames in a changeless, vacant stare. I spoke to him, I shook him by the arm. He was past rousing. He only whispered once more, 'Where is he?'

In ten minutes the engine was in position, the well at the back of the church was feeding it, and the hose was carried to the doorway of the vestry. If help had been wanted from me I could not have afforded it now. My energy of will was gone – my strength was exhausted – the turmoil of my thoughts was fearfully and suddenly stilled, now I knew that he was dead.

I stood useless and helpless – looking, looking, looking into the burning room.

I saw the fire slowly conquered. The brightness of the glare faded – the steam rose in white clouds, and the smouldering heaps of embers showed red and black through it on the floor. There was a pause – then an advance all together of the firemen and the police which blocked up the doorway – then a consultation in low voices – and then two men were detached from the rest, and sent out of the churchyard through the crowd. The crowd drew back on either side in dead silence to let them pass.

After a while a great shudder ran through the people, and the living lane widened slowly. The men came back along it with a door from one of the empty houses. They carried it to the vestry and went in. The police closed again round the doorway, and men stole out from among the crowd by twos and threes and stood behind them to be the first to see. Others waited near to be the first to hear. Women and children were among these last.

The tidings from the vestry began to flow out among the crowd – they dropped slowly from mouth to mouth till they reached the place where I was standing. I heard the questions and answers repeated again and again in low, eager tones all round me.

'Have they found him?' 'Yes.'—'Where?' 'Against the door, on his face.'—'Which door?' 'The door that goes into the church. His head was against it – he was down on his face.'—'Is his face burnt?' 'No.' 'Yes, it is.' 'No, scorched, not burnt – he lay on his face, I tell you.'—'Who was he? A lord, they say.' 'No, not a lord. *Sir* Something; Sir means Knight.' 'And Baronight, too.' 'No.' 'Yes, it does.'—'What did he want in there?' 'No good, you may depend on it.'—'Did he do it on purpose?'—'Burn himself on purpose!'—'I don't mean himself, I mean the vestry.'—'Is he dreadful to look at?' 'Dreadful!'—'Not about the face, though?' 'No, no, not so much about the face. Don't anybody know him?' 'There's a man says he does.'—'Who?' 'A servant, they say. But he's struck stupid-like, and the police don't believe him.'—'Don't anybody else know who it is?' 'Hush—!'

The loud, clear voice of a man in authority silenced the low hum of talking all round me in an instant.

'Where is the gentleman who tried to save him?' said the voice.

'Here, sir – here he is!' Dozens of eager faces pressed about me – dozens of eager arms parted the crowd. The man in authority came up to me with a lantern in his hand.

'This way, sir, if you please,' he said quietly.

I was unable to speak to him, I was unable to resist him when he took my arm. I tried to say that I had never seen the dead man in his lifetime – that there was no hope of identifying him by means of a stranger like me. But the words failed on my lips. I was faint, and silent, and helpless.

'Do you know him, sir?'

I was standing inside a circle of men. Three of them opposite to me were holding lanterns low down to the ground. Their eyes, and the eyes of all the rest, were fixed silently and expectantly on my face. I knew what was at my feet – I knew why they were holding the lanterns so low to the ground.

'Can you identify him, sir?'

My eyes dropped slowly. At first I saw nothing under them but a coarse canvas cloth. The dripping of the rain on it was audible in the dreadful silence. I looked up, along the cloth, and there at the end, stark and grim and black, in the yellow light – there was his dead face.

So, for the first and last time, I saw him. So the Visitation of God ruled it that he and I should meet.

XI

The inquest was hurried for certain local reasons which weighed with the coroner and the town authorities. It was held on the afternoon of the next day. I was necessarily one among the witnesses summoned to assist the objects of the investigation.

My first proceeding in the morning was to go to the post-office, and inquire for the letter which I expected from Marian. No change of circumstances, however extraordinary, could affect the one great anxiety which weighed on my mind while I was away from London. The morning's letter, which was the only assurance I could receive that no misfortune had happened in my absence, was still the absorbing interest with which my day began.

To my relief, the letter from Marian was at the office waiting for me.

Nothing had happened – they were both as safe and as well as when I had left them. Laura sent her love, and begged that I would let her know of my return a day beforehand. Her sister added, in explanation of this message, that she had saved 'nearly a sovereign' out of her own private purse, and that she had claimed the privilege of ordering the dinner and giving the dinner which was to celebrate the day of my return. I read these little domestic confidences in the bright morning with the terrible recollection of what had happened the evening before vivid in my memory. The necessity of sparing Laura any sudden knowledge of the truth was the first consideration which the letter suggested to me. I wrote at once to Marian to tell her what I have told in these pages – presenting the tidings as gradually and gently as I could, and warning her not to let any such thing as a newspaper fall in Laura's way while I was absent. In the case of any other woman, less courageous and less reliable, I might have hesitated before I ventured on unreservedly disclosing the whole truth. But I owed it to Marian to be faithful to my past experience of her, and to trust her as I trusted myself.

My letter was necessarily a long one. It occupied me until the time came for proceeding to the inquest.

The objects of the legal inquiry were necessarily beset by peculiar complications and difficulties. Besides the investigation into the manner in which the deceased had met his death, there were serious questions to be settled relating to the cause of the fire, to the abstraction of the keys, and to the presence of a stranger in the vestry at the time when the flames broke out. Even the identification of the dead man had not yet been accomplished. The helpless condition of the servant had made the police distrustful of his asserted recognition of his master. They had sent to Knowlesbury overnight to secure the attendance of witnesses who were well acquainted with the personal appearance of Sir Percival Glyde, and they had communicated, the first thing in the morning, with Blackwater Park. These precautions enabled the coroner and jury to settle the question of identity, and to confirm the correctness of the servant's assertion; the evidence offered by competent witnesses, and by the discovery of certain facts, being subsequently strengthened by an examination of the dead man's watch. The crest and the name of Sir Percival Glyde were engraved inside it.

The next inquiries related to the fire.

The servant and I, and the boy who had heard the light struck in the vestry, were the first witnesses called. The boy gave his evidence clearly enough, but the servant's mind had not yet recovered the shock inflicted on it – he was plainly incapable of assisting the objects of the inquiry, and he was desired to stand down.

To my own relief, my examination was not a long one. I had not known the deceased – I had never seen him – I was not aware of his presence at

Old Welmingham – and I had not been in the vestry at the finding of the body. All I could prove was that I had stopped at the clerk's cottage to ask my way – that I had heard from him of the loss of the keys – that I had accompanied him to the church to render what help I could – that I had seen the fire – that I had heard some person unknown, inside the vestry, trying vainly to unlock the door – and that I had done what I could, from motives of humanity, to save the man. Other witnesses, who had been acquainted with the deceased, were asked if they could explain the mystery of his presumed abstraction of the keys, and his presence in the burning room. But the coroner seemed to take it for granted, naturally enough, that I, as a total stranger in the neighbourhood, and a total stranger to Sir Percival Glyde, could not be in a position to offer any evidence on these two points.

The course that I was myself bound to take, when my formal examination had closed, seemed clear to me. I did not feel called on to volunteer any statement of my own private convictions; in the first place, because my doing so could serve no practical purpose, now that all proof in support of any surmises of mine was burnt with the burnt register; in the second place, because I could not have intelligibly stated my opinion – my unsupported opinion – without disclosing the whole story of the conspiracy, and producing beyond a doubt the same unsatisfactory effect on the minds of the coroner and the jury, which I had already produced on the mind of Mr Kyrle.

In these pages, however, and after the time that has now elapsed, no such cautions and restraints as are here described need fetter the free expression of my opinion. I will state briefly, before my pen occupies itself with other events, how my own convictions lead me to account for the abstraction of the keys, for the outbreak of the fire, and for the death of the man.

The news of my being free on bail drove Sir Percival, as I believe, to his last resources. The attempted attack on the road was one of those resources, and the suppression of all practical proof of his crime, by destroying the page of the register on which the forgery had been committed, was the other, and the surest of the two. If I could produce no extract from the original book to compare with the certified copy at Knowlesbury, I could produce no positive evidence, and could threaten him with no fatal exposure. All that was necessary to the attainment of his end was, that he should get into the vestry unperceived, that he should tear out the page in the register, and that he should leave the vestry again as privately as he had entered it.

On this supposition, it is easy to understand why he waited until nightfall before he made the attempt, and why he took advantage of the clerk's absence to possess himself of the keys. Necessity would oblige him to strike a light to find his way to the right register, and common caution would suggest his locking the door on the inside in case of intrusion on the part of any inquisitive stranger, or on my part, if I happened to be in the neighbourhood at the time.

I cannot believe that it was any part of his intention to make the destruction of the register appear to be the result of accident, by purposely setting the vestry on fire. The bare chance that prompt assistance might arrive, and that the books might, by the remotest possibility, be saved, would have been enough, on a moment's consideration, to dismiss any idea of this sort from his mind. Remembering the quantity of combustible objects in the vestry – the straw, the papers, the packing-cases, the dry wood, the old worm-eaten presses – all the probabilities, in my estimation, point to the fire as the result of an accident with his matches or his light.

His first impulse, under these circumstances, was doubtless to try to extinguish the flames, and failing in that, his second impulse (ignorant as he was of the state of the lock) had been to attempt to escape by the door which had given him entrance. When I had called to him, the flames must have reached across the door leading into the church, on either side of which the presses extended, and close to which the other combustible objects were placed. In all probability, the smoke and flame (confined as they were to the room) had been too much for him when he tried to escape by the inner door. He must have dropped in his death-swoon – he must have sunk in the place where he was found – just as I got on the roof to break the skylight window. Even if we had been able, afterwards, to get into the church, and to burst open the door from that side, the delay must have been fatal. He would have been past saving, long past saving, by that time. We should only have given the flames free ingress into the church – the church, which was now preserved, but which, in that event, would have shared the fate of the vestry. There is no doubt in my mind, there can be no doubt in the mind of any one, that he was a dead man before ever we got to the empty cottage, and worked with might and main to tear down the beam.

This is the nearest approach that any theory of mine can make towards accounting for a result which was visible matter of fact. As I have described them, so events passed to us outside. As I have related it, so his body was found.

The inquest was adjourned over one day – no explanation that the eye of the law could recognise having been discovered thus far to account for the mysterious circumstances of the case.

It was arranged that more witnesses should be summoned, and that the London solicitor of the deceased should be invited to attend. A medical man was also charged with the duty of reporting on the mental condition of the servant, which appeared at present to debar him from giving any evidence of the least importance. He could only declare, in a dazed way, that he had been ordered, on the night of the fire, to wait in the lane, and that he knew nothing else, except that the deceased was certainly his master.

My own impression was, that he had been first used (without any guilty knowledge on his own part) to ascertain the fact of the clerk's absence from home on the previous day, and that he had been afterwards ordered to wait near the church (but out of sight of the vestry) to assist his master, in the event of my escaping the attack on the road, and of a collision occurring between Sir Percival and myself. It is necessary to add, that the man's own testimony was never obtained to confirm this view. The medical report of him declared that what little mental faculty he possessed was seriously shaken; nothing satisfactory was extracted from him at the adjourned inquest, and for aught I know to the contrary, he may never have recovered to this day.

I returned to the hotel at Welmingham so jaded in body and mind, so weakened and depressed by all that I had gone through, as to be quite unfit to endure the local gossip about the inquest, and to answer the trivial questions that the talkers addressed to me in the coffee-room. I withdrew from my scanty dinner to my cheap garret-chamber to secure myself a little quiet, and to think undisturbed of Laura and Marian.

If I had been a richer man I would have gone back to London, and would have comforted myself with a sight of the two dear faces again that night. But I was bound to appear, if called on, at the adjourned inquest, and doubly bound to answer my bail before the magistrate at Knowlesbury. Our slender resources had suffered already, and the doubtful future – more doubtful than ever now – made me dread decreasing our means unnecessarily by allowing myself an indulgence even at the small cost of a double railway journey in the carriages of the second class.

The next day – the day immediately following the inquest – was left at my own disposal. I began the morning by again applying at the post-office for my regular report from Marian. It was waiting for me as before, and it was written throughout in good spirits. I read the letter thankfully, and then set forth with my mind at ease for the day to go to Old Welmingham, and to view the scene of the fire by the morning light.

What changes met me when I got there!

Through all the ways of our unintelligible world the trivial and the terrible walk hand in hand together. The irony of circumstances holds no mortal catastrophe in respect. When I reached the church, the trampled condition of the burial-ground was the only serious trace left to tell of the fire and the death. A rough hoarding of boards had been knocked up before the vestry doorway. Rude caricatures were scrawled on it already, and the village

children were fighting and shouting for the possession of the best peep-hole
to see through. On the spot where I had heard the cry for help from the
burning room, on the spot where the panic-stricken servant had dropped on
his knees, a fussy flock of poultry was now scrambling for the first choice
of worms after the rain; and on the ground at my feet, where the door and
its dreadful burden had been laid, a workman's dinner was waiting for him,
tied up in a yellow basin, and his faithful cur in charge was yelping at me
for coming near the food. The old clerk, looking idly at the slow commencement of the repairs, had only one interest that he could talk about now – the
interest of escaping all blame for his own part on account of the accident
that had happened. One of the village women, whose white wild face I
remembered the picture of terror when we pulled down the beam, was giggling
with another woman, the picture of inanity, over an old washing-tub. There
is nothing serious in mortality! Solomon in all his glory was Solomon with
the elements of the contemptible lurking in every fold of his robes and in
every corner of his palace.

As I left the place, my thoughts turned, not for the first time, to the
complete overthrow that all present hope of establishing Laura's identity had
now suffered through Sir Percival's death. He was gone – and with him the
chance was gone which had been the one object of all my labours and all
my hopes.

Could I look at my failure from no truer point of view than this?

Suppose he had lived, would that change of circumstance have altered
the result? Could I have made my discovery a marketable commodity, even
for Laura's sake, after I had found out that robbery of the rights of others
was the essence of Sir Percival's crime? Could I have offered the price of
my silence for *his* confession of the conspiracy, when the effect of that silence
must have been to keep the right heir from the estates, and the right owner
from the name? Impossible! If Sir Percival had lived, the discovery, from
which (in my ignorance of the true nature of the Secret) I had hoped so
much, could not have been mine to suppress or to make public, as I thought
best, for the vindication of Laura's rights. In common honesty and common
honour I must have gone at once to the stranger whose birthright had been
usurped – I must have renounced the victory at the moment when it was
mine by placing my discovery unreservedly in that stranger's hands – and I
must have faced afresh all the difficulties which stood between me and the
one object of my life, exactly as I was resolved in my heart of hearts to face
them now!

I returned to Welmingham with my mind composed, feeling more sure
of myself and my resolution than I had felt yet.

On my way to the hotel I passed the end of the square in which Mrs

Catherick lived. Should I go back to the house, and make another attempt to see her. No. That news of Sir Percival's death, which was the last news she ever expected to hear, must have reached her hours since. All the proceedings at the inquest had been reported in the local paper that morning – there was nothing I could tell her which she did not know already. My interest in making her speak had slackened. I remembered the furtive hatred in her face when she said, 'There is no news of Sir Percival that I don't expect – except the news of his death.' I remembered the stealthy interest in her eyes when they settled on me at parting, after she had spoken those words. Some instinct, deep in my heart, which I felt to be a true one, made the prospect of again entering her presence repulsive to me – I turned away from the square, and went straight back to the hotel.

Some hours later, while I was resting in the coffee-room, a letter was placed in my hands by the waiter. It was addressed to me by name, and I found on inquiry that it had been left at the bar by a woman just as it was near dusk, and just before the gas was lighted. She had said nothing, and she had gone away again before there was time to speak to her, or even to notice who she was.

I opened the letter. It was neither dated nor signed, and the handwriting was palpably disguised. Before I had read the first sentence, however, I knew who my correspondent was – Mrs Catherick.

The letter ran as follows – I copy it exactly, word for word.

THE STORY CONTINUED BY MRS CATHERICK

Sir, – You have not come back, as you said you would. No matter – I know the news, and I write to tell you so. Did you see anything particular in my face when you left me? I was wondering, in my own mind, whether the day of his downfall had come at last, and whether you were the chosen instrument for working it. You were, and you *have* worked it.

You were weak enough, as I have heard, to try and save his life. If you had succeeded, I should have looked upon you as my enemy. Now you have failed, I hold you as my friend. Your inquiries frightened him into the vestry by night – your inquiries, without your privity and against your will, have served the hatred and wreaked the vengeance of three-and-twenty years. Thank you, sir, in spite of yourself.

I owe something to the man who has done this. How can I pay my debt? If I was a young woman still I might say, 'Come, put your arm round my waist, and kiss me, if you like.' I should have been fond enough of you even to go that length, and you would have accepted my invitation – you would, sir, twenty years ago! But I am an old woman now. Well! I can satisfy your curiosity, and pay my debt in that way. You *had* a great curiosity to know certain private affairs of mine when you came to see me – private affairs which all your sharpness could not look into without my help – private affairs which you have not discovered, even now. You *shall* discover them – your curiosity shall be satisfied. I will take any trouble to please you, my estimable young friend!

You were a little boy, I suppose, in the year twenty-seven? I was a handsome young woman at that time, living at Old Welmingham. I had a contemptible fool for a husband. I had also the honour of being acquainted (never mind how) with a certain gentleman (never mind whom). I shall not call him by his name. Why should I? It was not his own. He never had a name: you know that, by this time, as well as I do.

It will be more to the purpose to tell you how he worked himself into my good graces. I was born with the tastes of a lady, and he gratified them – in other words, he admired me, and he made me presents. No woman can resist admiration and presents – especially presents, provided they happen to be just the thing she wants. He was sharp enough to know that – most men are. Naturally he wanted something in return – all men do. And what do you think was the something? The merest trifle. Nothing but the key of the vestry, and the key of the press inside it, when my husband's back was turned. Of course he lied when I asked him why he wished me to get him the keys in that private way. He might have saved himself the trouble – I didn't believe him. But I liked my presents, and I wanted more. So I got him the keys, without my husband's knowledge, and I watched him, without his own knowledge. Once, twice, four times I watched him, and the fourth time I found him out.

I was never over-scrupulous where other people's affairs were concerned, and I was not over-scrupulous about his adding one to the marriages in the register on his own account.

Of course I knew it was wrong, but it did no harm to me, which was one good reason for not making a fuss about it. And I had not got a gold watch and chain, which was another, still better – and he had promised me one from London only the day before, which was a third, best of all. If I had known what the law considered the crime to be, and how the law punished it, I should have taken proper care of myself, and have exposed him then and there. But I knew nothing, and I longed for the gold watch. All the conditions I insisted on were that he should take me into his confidence and tell me everything. I was as curious about his affairs then as you are about mine now. He granted my conditions – why, you will see presently.

This, put in short, is what I heard from him. He did not willingly tell me all that I tell you here. I drew some of it from him by persuasion and some of it by questions. I was determined to have all the truth, and I believe I got it.

He knew no more than any one else of what the state of things really was between his father and mother till after his mother's death. Then his father confessed it, and promised to do what he could for his son. He died having done nothing – not having even made a will. The son (who can blame him?) wisely provided for himself. He came to England at once, and took possession of the property. There was no one to suspect him, and no one to say him nay. His father and mother had always lived as man and wife – none of the few people who were acquainted with them ever supposed them to be anything else. The right person to claim the property (if the truth had been known) was a distant relation, who had no idea of ever getting it, and who was away at sea when his father died. He had no difficulty so far – he took possession, as a matter of course. But he could not borrow money on the property as a matter of course. There were two things wanted of him before he could do this. One was a certificate of his birth, and the other was a certificate of his parents' marriage. The certificate of his birth was easily got – he was born abroad, and the certificate was there in due form. The other matter was a difficulty, and that difficulty brought him to Old Welmingham.

But for one consideration he might have gone to Knowlesbury instead.

His mother had been living there just before she met with his father – living under her maiden name, the truth being that she was really a married woman, married in Ireland, where her husband had ill-used her, and had afterwards gone off with some other person. I give you this fact on good authority – Sir Felix mentioned it to his son as the reason why he had not married. You may wonder why the son, knowing that his parents had met each other at Knowlesbury, did not play his first tricks with the register of that church, where it might have been fairly presumed his father and mother were married. The reason was that the clergyman who did duty at Knowlesbury church, in the year eighteen hundred and three (when, according to his birth certificate, his father and mother *ought* to have been married), was alive still when he took possession of the property in the New Year of eighteen hundred and twenty-seven. This awkward circumstance forced him to extend his inquiries to our neighbourhood. There no such danger existed, the former clergyman at our church having been dead for some years.

Old Welmingham suited his purpose as well as Knowlesbury. His father had removed his mother from Knowlesbury, and had lived with her at a cottage on the river, a little distance from our village. People who had known his solitary ways when he was single did not wonder at his solitary ways when he was supposed to be married. If he had not been a hideous creature to look at, his retired life with the lady might have raised suspicions; but, as things were, his hiding his ugliness and his deformity in the strictest privacy surprised nobody. He lived in our neighbourhood till he came in possession of the Park. After three or four and twenty years had passed, who was to say (the clergyman being dead) that his marriage had not been as private as the rest of his life, and that it had not taken place at Old Welmingham church? So, as I told you, the son found our neighbourhood the surest place he could choose to set things right secretly in his own interests. It may surprise you to hear that what he really did to the marriage register was done on the spur of the moment – done on second thoughts.

His first notion was only to tear the leaf out (in the right year and month), to destroy it privately, to go back to London, and to tell the lawyers to get him the necessary certificate of his father's marriage, innocently referring them of course to the date on the leaf that was gone. Nobody could say his father and mother had *not* been married after that, and whether, under the circumstances, they would stretch a point or not about lending him the money (he thought they would), he had his answer ready at all events, if a question was ever raised about his right to the name and the estate.

But when he came to look privately at the register for himself, he found at the bottom of one of the pages for the year eighteen hundred and three a blank space left, seemingly through there being no room to make a long entry there, which was made instead at the top of the next page. The sight of this chance altered all his plans. It was an opportunity he had never hoped for, or thought of – and he took it – you know how. The blank space, to have exactly tallied with his birth certificate, ought to have occurred in the July part of the register. It occurred in the September part instead. However, in this case, if suspicious questions were asked, the answer was not hard to find. He had only to describe himself as a seven months' child.

I was fool enough, when he told me his story, to feel some interest and some pity for him – which was just what he calculated on, as you will see. I thought him hardly used. It was not his fault that his father and mother were not married, and it was not his father's and mother's fault either. A more scrupulous woman than I was – a woman who had not set her heart on a gold watch and chain – would have found some excuses for him. At all events, I held my tongue, and helped to screen what he was about.

He was some time getting the ink the right colour (mixing it over and over again in pots and bottles of mine), and some time afterwards in prac- tising the handwriting. But he succeeded in the end, and made an honest woman of his mother after she was dead in her grave! So far, I don't deny that he behaved honourably enough to myself. He gave me my watch and chain, and spared no expense in buying them; both were of superior work- manship, and very expensive. I have got them still – the watch goes beautifully.

You said the other day that Mrs Clements had told you everything she knew. In that case there is no need for me to write about the trumpery scandal by which I was the sufferer – the innocent sufferer, I positively assert. You must know as well as I do what the notion was which my husband took into his head when he found me and my fine-gentleman acquaintance meeting each other privately and talking secrets together. But what you don't know is how it ended between that same gentleman and myself. You shall read and see how he behaved to me.

The first words I said to him, when I saw the turn things had taken, were, 'Do me justice – clear my character of a stain on it which you know I don't deserve. I don't want you to make a clean breast of it to my husband – only tell him, on your word of honour as a gentleman, that he is wrong, and that I am not to blame in the way he thinks I am. Do me that justice, at least, after all I have done for you.' He flatly refused, in so many words. He told me plainly that it was his interest to let my husband and all my neighbours believe the falsehood – because, as long as they did so they were quite certain never to suspect the truth. I had a spirit of my own, and I told him they should know the truth from my lips. His reply was short, and to the point. If I spoke, I was a lost woman, as certainly as he was a lost man.

Yes! it had come to that. He had deceived me about the risk I ran in helping him. He had practised on my ignorance, he had tempted me with his gifts, he had interested me with his story – and the result of it was that he made me his accomplice. He owned this coolly, and he ended by telling me, for the first time, what the frightful punishment really was for his offence, and for any one who helped him to commit it. In those days the law was not so tender-hearted as I hear it is now. Murderers were not the only people liable to be hanged, and women convicts were not treated like ladies in undeserved distress. I confess he frightened me – the mean impostor! the cowardly blackguard! Do you understand now how I hated him? Do you understand why I am taking all this trouble – thankfully taking it – to gratify the curiosity of the meritorious young gentleman who hunted him down?

Well, to go on. He was hardly fool enough to drive me to downright desperation. I was not the sort of woman whom it was quite safe to hunt into a corner – he knew that, and wisely quieted me with proposals for the future.

I deserved some reward (he was kind enough to say) for the service I had done him, and some compensation (he was so obliging as to add) for what I had suffered. He was quite willing – generous scoundrel! – to make me a handsome yearly allowance, payable quarterly, on two conditions. First, I was to hold my tongue – in my own interests as well as in his. Secondly, I was not to stir away from Welmingham without first letting him know, and waiting till I had obtained his permission. In my own neighbourhood, no virtuous female friends would tempt me into dangerous gossiping at the tea-table. In my own neighbourhood, he would always know where to find me. A hard condition, that second one – but I accepted it.

What else was I to do? I was left helpless, with the prospect of a coming incumbrance in the shape of a child. What else was I to do? Cast myself on the mercy of my runaway idiot of a husband who had raised the scandal against me? I would have died first. Besides, the allowance *was* a handsome one. I had a better income, a better house over my head, better carpets on my floors, than half the women who turned up the whites of their eyes at the sight of me. The dress of Virtue, in our parts, was cotton print. I had silk.

So I accepted the conditions he offered me, and made the best of them, and fought my battle with my respectable neighbours on their own ground, and won it in course of time – as you saw yourself. How I kept his Secret (and mine) through all the years that have passed from that time to this, and whether my late daughter, Anne, ever really crept into my confidence, and got the keeping of the Secret too – are questions, I dare say, to which you are curious to find an answer. Well! my gratitude refuses you nothing. I will turn to a fresh page and give you the answer immediately. But you must excuse one thing – you must excuse my beginning, Mr Hartright, with an expression of surprise at the interest which you appear to have felt in my late daughter. It is quite unaccountable to me. If that interest makes you anxious for any particulars of her early life, I must refer you to Mrs Clements, who knows more of the subject than I do. Pray understand that I do not profess to have been at all overfond of my late daughter. She was a worry to me from first to last, with the additional disadvantage of being always weak in the head. You like candour, and I hope this satisfies you.

There is no need to trouble you with many personal particulars relating to those past times. It will be enough to say that I observed the terms of the bargain on my side, and that I enjoyed my comfortable income in return, paid quarterly.

Now and then I got away and changed the scene for a short time, always asking leave of my lord and master first, and generally getting it. He was not, as I have already told you, fool enough to drive me too hard, and he could reasonably rely on my holding my tongue for my own sake, if not for his. One of my longest trips away from home was the trip I took to Limmeridge to nurse a half-sister there, who was dying. She was reported to have saved money, and I thought it as well (in case any accident happened to stop my allowance) to look after my own interests in that direction. As things turned out, however, my pains were all thrown away, and I got nothing, because nothing was to be had.

I had taken Anne to the north with me, having my whims and fancies, occasionally, about my child, and getting, at such times, jealous of Mrs Clements' influence over her. I never liked Mrs Clements. She was a poor, empty-headed, spiritless woman – what you call a born drudge – and I was now and then not averse to plaguing her by taking Anne away. Not knowing what else to do with my girl while I was nursing in Cumberland, I put her to school at Limmeridge. The lady of the manor, Mrs Fairlie (a remarkably plain-looking woman, who had entrapped one of the handsomest men in England into marrying her), amused me wonderfully by taking a violent fancy to my girl. The consequence was, she learnt nothing at school, and was petted and spoilt at Limmeridge House. Among other whims and fancies which they taught her there, they put some nonsense into her head about always wearing white. Hating white and liking colours myself, I determined to take the nonsense out of her head as soon as we got home again.

Strange to say, my daughter resolutely resisted me. When she *had* got a notion once fixed in her mind she was, like other half-witted people, as obstinate as a mule in keeping it. We quarrelled finely, and Mrs Clements, not liking to see it, I suppose, offered to take Anne away to live in London with her. I should have said Yes, if Mrs Clements had not sided with my daughter about her dressing herself in white. But being determined she should *not* dress herself in white, and disliking Mrs Clements more than ever for taking part against me, I said No, and meant No, and stuck to No. The consequence was, my daughter remained with me, and the consequence of that, in its turn, was the first serious quarrel that happened about the Secret.

The circumstance took place long after the time I have just been writing of. I had been settled for years in the new town, and was steadily living down my bad character and slowly gaining ground among the respectable inhabitants. It helped me forward greatly towards this object to have my daughter with me. Her harmlessness and her fancy for dressing in white excited a certain amount of sympathy. I left off opposing her favourite whim on that account, because some of the sympathy was sure, in course of time, to fall to my share. Some of it did fall. I date my getting a choice of the two best sittings to let in the church from that time, and I date the clergy-man's first bow from my getting the sittings.

Well, being settled in this way, I received a letter one morning from that highly born gentleman (now deceased) in answer to one of mine, warning him, according to agreement, of my wishing to leave the town for a little change of air and scene.

The ruffianly side of him must have been uppermost, I suppose, when he got my letter, for he wrote back, refusing me in such abominably insolent language, that I lost all command over myself, and abused him, in my daughter's presence, as 'a low impostor whom I could ruin for life if I chose to open my lips and let out his Secret.' I said no more about him than that, being brought to my senses as soon as those words had escaped me by the sight of my daughter's face looking eagerly and curiously at mine. I instantly ordered her out of the room until I had composed myself again.

My sensations were not pleasant, I can tell you, when I came to reflect on my own folly. Anne had been more than usually crazy and queer that year, and when I thought of the chance there might be of her repeating my words in the town, and mentioning *his* name in connection with them, if inquisitive people got hold of her, I was finely terrified at the possible conse-quences. My worst fears for myself, my worst dread of what he might do, led me no farther than this. I was quite unprepared for what really did happen only the next day.

On that next day, without any warning to me to expect him, he came to the house.

His first words, and the tone in which he spoke them, surly as it was, showed me plainly enough that he had repented already of his insolent answer to my application, and that he had come in a mighty bad temper to try and set matters right again before it was too late. Seeing my daughter in the room with me (I had been afraid to let her out of my sight after what had happened the day before) he ordered her away. They neither of them liked each other, and he vented the ill-temper on *her* which he was afraid to show to *me*.

'Leave us,' he said, looking at her over his shoulder. She looked back over *her* shoulder and waited as if she didn't care to go. 'Do you hear?' he roared out, 'leave the room.' 'Speak to me civilly,' says she, getting red in the face. 'Turn the idiot out,' says he, looking my way. She had always had crazy notions of her own about her dignity, and that word 'idiot' upset her in a moment. Before I could interfere she stepped up to him in a fine passion. 'Beg my pardon, directly,' says she, 'or I'll make it the worse for you. I'll let out your Secret. I can ruin you for life if I choose to open my lips.' My own words! – repeated exactly from what I had said the day before – repeated, in his presence, as if they had come from herself. He sat speechless, as white as the paper I am writing on, while I pushed her out of the room. When he recovered himself –

No! I am too respectable a woman to mention what he said when he recovered himself. My pen is the pen of a member of the rector's congregation, and a subscriber to the 'Wednesday Lectures on Justification by Faith' – how can you expect me to employ it in writing bad language? Suppose, for yourself, the raging, swearing frenzy of the lowest ruffian in England, and let us get on together, as fast as may be, to the way in which it all ended.

It ended, as you probably guess by this time, in his insisting on securing his own safety by shutting her up.

I tried to set things right. I told him that she had merely repeated, like a parrot, the words she had heard me say and that she knew no particulars whatever, because I had mentioned none. I explained that she had affected, out of crazy spite against him, to know what she really did *not* know – that she only wanted to threaten him and aggravate him for speaking to her as he had just spoken – and that my unlucky words gave her just the chance of doing mischief of which she was in search. I referred him to other queer ways of hers, and to his own experience of the vagaries of half-witted people – it was all to no purpose – he would not believe me on my oath – he was absolutely certain I had betrayed the whole Secret. In short, he would hear of nothing but shutting her up.

Under these circumstances, I did my duty as a mother. 'No pauper Asylum,' I said, 'I won't have her put in a pauper Asylum. A Private Establishment, if you please. I have my feelings as a mother, and my character to preserve in the town, and I will submit to nothing but a Private Establishment, of the sort which my genteel neighbours would choose for afflicted relatives of their own.' Those were my words. It is gratifying to me to reflect that I did my duty. Though never overfond of my late daughter, I had a proper pride about her. No pauper stain – thanks to my firmness and resolution – ever rested on *my* child.

Having carried my point (which I did the more easily, in consequence of the facilities offered by private Asylums), I could not refuse to admit that there were certain advantages gained by shutting her up. In the first place, she was taken excellent care of – being treated (as I took care to mention in the town) on the footing of a lady. In the second place, she was kept away from Welmingham, where she might have set people suspecting and inquiring, by repeating my own incautious words.

The only drawback of putting her under restraint was a very slight one. We merely turned her empty boast about knowing the Secret into a fixed delusion. Having first spoken in sheer crazy spitefulness against the man who had offended her, she was cunning enough to see that she had seriously frightened him, and sharp enough afterwards to discover that *he* was concerned in shutting her up. The consequence was she flamed out into a perfect frenzy of passion against him, going to the Asylum, and the first words she said to the nurses, after they had quieted her, were, that she was put in confinement for knowing his Secret, and that she meant to open her lips and ruin him, when the right time came.

She may have said the same thing to you, when you thoughtlessly assisted her escape. She certainly said it (as I heard last summer) to the unfortunate woman who married our sweet-tempered, nameless gentleman lately deceased. If either you, or that unlucky lady, had questioned my daughter closely, and had insisted on her explaining what she really meant, you would have found her lose all her self-importance suddenly, and get vacant, and restless, and confused – you would have discovered that I am writing nothing here but the plain truth. She knew that there was a Secret – she knew who was connected with it – she knew who would suffer by its being known – and beyond that, whatever airs of importance she may have given herself, whatever crazy boasting she may have indulged in with strangers, she never to her dying day knew more.

Have I satisfied your curiosity? I have taken pains enough to satisfy it at any rate. There is really nothing else I have to tell you about myself or my daughter. My worst responsibilities, so far as she was concerned, were all over when she was secured in the Asylum. I had a form of letter relating to the circumstances under which she was shut up, given me to write, in answer to one Miss Halcombe, who was curious in the matter, and who must have heard plenty of lies about me from a certain tongue well accustomed to the telling of the same. And I did what I could afterwards to trace my runaway daughter, and prevent her from doing mischief by making inquiries myself in the neighbourhood where she was falsely reported to have been seen. But these, and other trifles like them, are of little or no interest to you after what you have heard already.

So far, I have written in the friendliest possible spirit. But I cannot close this letter without adding a word here of serious remonstrance and reproof, addressed to yourself.

In the course of your personal interview with me, you audaciously referred to my late daughter's parentage on the father's side, as if that parentage was a matter of doubt. This was highly improper and very ungentlemanlike on your part! If we see each other again, remember, if you please, that I will allow no liberties to be taken with my reputation, and that the moral atmosphere of Welmingham (to use a favourite expression of my friend the rector's) must not be tainted by loose conversation of any kind. If you allow yourself to doubt that my husband was Anne's father, you personally insult me in the grossest manner. If you have felt, and if you still continue to feel, an unhallowed curiosity on this subject, I recommend you, in your own interests, to check it at once, and for ever. On this side of the grave, Mr Hartright, whatever may happen on the other, *that* curiosity will never be gratified.

Perhaps, after what I have just said, you will see the necessity of writing me an apology. Do so, and I will willingly receive it. I will, afterwards, if your wishes point to a second interview with me, go a step farther, and receive you. My circumstances only enable me to invite you to tea – not that they are at all altered for the worse by what has happened. I have always lived, as I think I told you, well within my income, and I have saved enough, in the last twenty years, to make me quite comfortable for the rest of my life. It is not my intention to leave Welmingham. There are one or two little advantages which I have still to gain in the town. The clergyman bows to me – as you saw. He is married, and his wife is not quite so civil. I propose to join the Dorcas Society, and I mean to make the clergyman's wife bow to me next.

If you favour me with your company, pray understand that the conversation must be entirely on general subjects. Any attempted reference to this letter will be quite useless – I am determined not to acknowledge having written it. The evidence has been destroyed in the fire, I know, but I think it desirable to err on the side of caution, nevertheless.

On this account no names are mentioned here, nor is any signature attached to these lines: the handwriting is disguised throughout, and I mean to deliver the letter myself, under circumstances which will prevent all fear of its being traced to my house. You can have no possible cause to complain of these precautions, seeing that they do not affect the information I here communicate, in consideration of the special indulgence which you have deserved at my hands. My hour for tea is half-past five, and my buttered toast waits for nobody.

THE STORY CONTINUED BY
WALTER HARTRIGHT

I

My first impulse, after reading Mrs Catherick's extraordinary narrative, was to destroy it. The hardened shameless depravity of the whole composition, from beginning to end – the atrocious perversity of mind which persistently associated me with a calamity for which I was in no sense answerable, and with a death which I had risked my life in trying to avert – so disgusted me, that I was on the point of tearing the letter, when a consideration suggested itself which warned me to wait a little before I destroyed it.

This consideration was entirely unconnected with Sir Percival. The information communicated to me, so far as it concerned him, did little more than confirm the conclusions at which I had already arrived.

He had committed his offence, as I had supposed him to have committed it, and the absence of all reference, on Mrs Catherick's part, to the duplicate register at Knowlesbury, strengthened my previous conviction that the existence of the book, and the risk of detection which it implied, must have been necessarily unknown to Sir Percival. My interest in the question of the forgery was now at an end, and my only object in keeping the letter was to make it of some future service in clearing up the last mystery that still remained to baffle me – the parentage of Anne Catherick on the father's side. There were one or two sentences dropped in her mother's narrative, which it might be useful to refer to again, when matters of more immediate importance allowed me leisure to search for the missing evidence. I did not despair of still finding that evidence, and I had lost none of my anxiety to discover it, for I had lost none of my interest in tracing the father of the poor creature who now lay at rest in Mrs Fairlie's grave.

Accordingly, I sealed up the letter and put it away carefully in my pocket-book, to be referred to again when the time came.

The next day was my last in Hampshire. When I had appeared again before the magistrate at Knowlesbury, and when I had attended at the adjourned inquest, I should be free to return to London by the afternoon or the evening train.

My first errand in the morning was, as usual, to the post-office. The letter from Marian was there, but I thought when it was handed to me that it felt unusually light. I anxiously opened the envelope. There was nothing inside but a small strip of paper folded in two. The few blotted hurriedly-written lines which were traced on it contained these words:

Come back as soon as you can. I have been obliged to move. Come to Gower's Walk, Fulham (number five). I will be on the look-out for you. Don't be alarmed about us, we are both safe and well. But come back. – Marian.

The news which those lines contained – news which I instantly associated with some attempted treachery on the part of Count Fosco – fairly overwhelmed me. I stood breathless with the paper crumpled up in my hand. What had happened? What subtle wickedness had the Count planned and executed in my absence? A night had passed since Marian's note was written – hours must elapse still before I could get back to them – some new disaster might have happened already of which I was ignorant. And here, miles and miles away from them, here I must remain – held, doubly held, at the disposal of the law!

I hardly know to what forgetfulness of my obligations anxiety and alarm might not have tempted me, but for the quieting influence of my faith in Marian. My absolute reliance on her was the one earthly consideration which helped me to restrain myself, and gave me courage to wait. The inquest was the first of the impediments in the way of my freedom of action. I attended it at the appointed time, the legal formalities requiring my presence in the room, but as it turned out, not calling on me to repeat my evidence. This useless delay was a hard trial, although I did my best to quiet my impatience by following the course of the proceedings as closely as I could.

The London solicitor of the deceased (Mr Merriman) was among the persons present. But he was quite unable to assist the objects of the inquiry. He could only say that he was inexpressibly shocked and astonished, and that he could throw no light whatever on the mysterious circumstances of the case. At intervals during the adjourned investigation, he suggested questions which the Coroner put, but which led to no results. After a patient inquiry, which lasted nearly three hours, and which exhausted every available source of information, the jury pronounced the customary verdict in cases of sudden death by accident. They added to the formal decision a statement, that there had been no evidence to show how the keys had been abstracted, how the fire had been caused, or what the purpose was for which the deceased had entered the vestry. This act closed the proceedings. The legal representative of the dead man was left to provide for the necessities of the interment, and the witnesses were free to retire.

Resolved not to lose a minute in getting to Knowlesbury, I paid my bill at the hotel, and hired a fly to take me to the town. A gentleman who heard me give the order, and who saw that I was going alone, informed me that he lived in the neighbourhood of Knowlesbury, and asked if I would have any objection to his getting home by sharing the fly with me. I accepted his proposal as a matter of course.

Our conversation during the drive was naturally occupied by the one absorbing subject of local interest.

My new acquaintance had some knowledge of the late Sir Percival's solicitor, and he and Mr Merriman had been discussing the state of the deceased gentleman's affairs and the succession to the property. Sir Percival's embarrassments were so well known all over the county that his solicitor could only make a virtue of necessity and plainly acknowledge them. He had died without leaving a will, and he had no personal property to bequeath, even if he had made one, the whole fortune which he had derived from his wife having been swallowed up by his creditors. The heir to the estate (Sir Percival having left no issue) was a son of Sir Felix Glyde's first cousin, an officer in command of an East Indiaman. He would find his unexpected inheritance sadly encumbered, but the property would recover with time, and, if 'the captain' was careful, he might be a rich man yet before he died.

Absorbed as I was in the one idea of getting to London, this information (which events proved to be perfectly correct) had an interest of its own to attract my attention. I thought it justified me in keeping secret my discovery of Sir Percival's fraud. The heir, whose rights he had usurped, was the heir who would now have the estate. The income from it, for the last three-and-twenty years, which should properly have been his, and which the dead man had squandered to the last farthing, was gone beyond recall. If I spoke, my speaking would confer advantage on no one. If I kept the secret, my silence concealed the character of the man who had cheated Laura into marrying him. For her sake, I wished to conceal it – for her sake, still, I tell this story under feigned names.

I parted with my chance companion at Knowlesbury, and went at once to the town-hall. As I had anticipated, no one was present to prosecute the case against me – the necessary formalities were observed, and I was discharged. On leaving the court a letter from Mr Dawson was put into my hand. It informed me that he was absent on professional duty, and it reiterated the offer I had already received from him of any assistance which I might require at his hands. I wrote back, warmly acknowledging my obligations to his kindness, and apologising for not expressing my thanks personally, in consequence of my immediate recall on pressing business to town.

Half an hour later I was speeding back to London by the express train.

II

It was between nine and ten o'clock before I reached Fulham, and found my way to Gower's Walk.

Both Laura and Marian came to the door to let me in. I think we had hardly known how close the tie was which bound us three together, until the evening came which united us again. We met as if we had been parted for months instead of for a few days only. Marian's face was sadly worn and anxious. I saw who had known all the danger and borne all the trouble in my absence the moment I looked at her. Laura's brighter looks and better spirits told me how carefully she had been spared all knowledge of the dreadful death at Welmingham, and of the true reason of our change of abode.

The stir of the removal seemed to have cheered and interested her. She only spoke of it as a happy thought of Marian's to surprise me on my return with a change from the close, noisy street to the pleasant neighbourhood of trees and fields and the river. She was full of projects for the future – of the drawings she was to finish – of the purchasers I had found in the country who were to buy them – of the shillings and sixpences she had saved, till her purse was so heavy that she proudly asked me to weigh it in my own hand. The change for the better which had been wrought in her during the few days of my absence was a surprise to me for which I was quite unprepared – and for all the unspeakable happiness of seeing it, I was indebted to Marian's courage and to Marian's love.

When Laura had left us, and when we could speak to one another without restraint, I tried to give some expression to the gratitude and the admiration which filled my heart. But the generous creature would not wait to hear me. That sublime self-forgetfulness of women, which yields so much and asks so little, turned all her thoughts from herself to me.

'I had only a moment left before post-time,' she said, 'or I should have written less abruptly. You look worn and weary, Walter. I am afraid my letter must have seriously alarmed you?'

'Only at first,' I replied. 'My mind was quieted, Marian, by my trust in you. Was I right in attributing this sudden change of place to some threatened annoyance on the part of Count Fosco?'

'Perfectly right,' she said. 'I saw him yesterday, and worse than that, Walter – I spoke to him.'

'Spoke to him? Did he know where we lived? Did he come to the house?'

'He did. To the house – but not upstairs. Laura never saw him – Laura suspects nothing. I will tell you how it happened: the danger, I believe and hope, is over now. Yesterday, I was in the sitting-room, at our old lodgings. Laura was drawing at the table, and I was walking about and setting things to rights. I passed the window, and as I passed it, looked out into the street. There, on the opposite side of the way, I saw the Count, with a man talking to him—'

'Did he notice you at the window?'

'No – at least, I thought not. I was too violently startled to be quite sure.'

'Who was the other man? A stranger?'

'Not a stranger, Walter. As soon as I could draw my breath again, I recognised him. He was the owner of the Lunatic Asylum.'

'Was the Count pointing out the house to him?'

'No, they were talking together as if they had accidentally met in the street. I remained at the window looking at them from behind the curtain. If I had turned round, and if Laura had seen my face at that moment – Thank God, she was absorbed over her drawing! They soon parted. The man from the Asylum went one way, and the Count the other. I began to hope they were in the street by chance, till I saw the Count come back, stop opposite to us again, take out his card-case and pencil, write something, and then cross the road to the shop below us. I ran past Laura before she could see me, and said I had forgotten something upstairs. As soon as I was out of the room I went down to the first landing and waited – I was determined to stop him if he tried to come upstairs. He made no such attempt. The girl from the shop came through the door into the passage, with his card in her hand – a large gilt card with his name, and a coronet above it, and these lines underneath in pencil: "Dear lady" (yes! the villain could address me in that way still)—"dear lady, one word, I implore you, on a matter serious to us both." If one can think at all, in serious difficulties, one thinks quick. I felt directly that it might be a fatal mistake to leave myself and to leave you in the dark, where such a man as the Count was concerned. I felt that the doubt of what he might do, in your absence, would be ten times more trying to me if I declined to see him than if I consented. "Ask the gentleman to wait in the shop," I said. "I will be with him in a moment." I ran upstairs for my bonnet, being determined not to let him speak to me indoors. I knew his deep ringing voice, and I was afraid Laura might hear it, even in the shop. In less than a minute I was down again in the passage, and had opened the door into the street. He came round to meet me from the shop. There he was in deep mourning, with his smooth bow and his deadly smile, and some idle boys and women near him, staring at his great size, his fine black clothes, and his large cane with the gold knob to it. All the horrible time at Blackwater came back to me the moment I set eyes on him. All the old loathing crept and crawled through me, when he took off his hat with a flourish and spoke to me, as if we had parted on the friendliest terms hardly a day since.'

'You remember what he said?'

'I can't repeat it, Walter. You shall know directly what he said about you – but I can't repeat what he said to me. It was worse than the polite insolence of his letter. My hands tingled to strike him, as if I had been a man! I only kept them quiet by tearing his card to pieces under my shawl. Without saying a word on my side, I walked away from the house (for fear of Laura seeing us), and he followed, protesting softly all the way. In the first by-street I turned, and asked him what he wanted with me. He wanted two things. First, if I had no objection, to express his sentiments. I declined to hear them. Secondly, to repeat the warning in his letter. I asked, what occasion there was for repeating it. He bowed and smiled, and said he would explain. The explanation exactly confirmed the fears I expressed before you left us. I told you, if you remember, that Sir Percival would be too headstrong to take his friend's advice where you were concerned, and that there was no danger to be dreaded from the Count till his own interests were threatened, and he was roused into acting for himself?'

'I recollect, Marian.'

'Well, so it has really turned out. The Count offered his advice, but it was refused. Sir Percival would only take counsel of his own violence, his own obstinacy, and his own hatred of you. The Count let him have his way, first privately ascertaining, in case of his own interests being threatened next, where we lived. You were followed, Walter, on returning here, after your first journey to Hampshire, by the lawyer's men for some distance from the railway, and by the Count himself to the door of the house. How he contrived to escape being seen by you he did not tell me, but he found us out on that occasion, and in that way. Having made the discovery, he took no advantage of it till the news reached him of Sir Percival's death, and then, as I told you, he acted for himself, because he believed you would next proceed against the dead man's partner in the conspiracy. He at once made his arrangements to meet the owner of the Asylum in London, and to take him to the place where his runaway patient was hidden, believing that the results, whichever way they ended, would be to involve you in interminable legal disputes and difficulties, and to tie your hands for all purposes of offence, so far as he was concerned. That was his purpose, on his own confession to me. The only consideration which made him hesitate, at the last moment—'

'Yes?'

'It is hard to acknowledge it, Walter, and yet I must. I was the only consideration. No words can say how degraded I feel in my own estimation when I think of it, but the one weak point in that man's iron character is the horrible admiration he feels for me. I have tried, for the sake of my own self-respect, to disbelieve it as long as I could; but his looks, his actions, force on me the shameful conviction of the truth. The eyes of that monster of wickedness moistened while he was speaking to me – they did, Walter! He declared that at the moment of pointing out the house to the doctor, he thought of my misery if I was separated from Laura, of my responsibility if

I was called on to answer for effecting her escape, and he risked the worst that you could do to him, the second time, for my sake. All he asked was that I would remember the sacrifice, and restrain your rashness, in my own interests – interests which he might never be able to consult again. I made no such bargain with him – I would have died first. But believe him or not, whether it is true or false that he sent the doctor away with an excuse, one thing is certain, I saw the man leave him without so much as a glance at our window, or even at our side of the way.'

'I believe it, Marian. The best men are not consistent in good – why should the worst men be consistent in evil? At the same time, I suspect him of merely attempting to frighten you, by threatening what he cannot really do. I doubt his power of annoying us, by means of the owner of the Asylum, now that Sir Percival is dead, and Mrs Catherick is free from all control. But let me hear more. What did the Count say of me?'

'He spoke last of you. His eyes brightened and hardened, and his manner changed to what I remember it in past times – to that mixture of pitiless resolution and mountebank mockery which makes it so impossible to fathom him. "Warn Mr Hartright!" he said in his loftiest manner. "He has a man of brains to deal with, a man who snaps his big fingers at the laws and conventions of society, when he measures himself with *me*. If my lamented friend had taken my advice, the business of the inquest would have been with the body of Mr Hartright. But my lamented friend was obstinate. See! I mourn his loss – inwardly in my soul, outwardly on my hat. This trivial crape expresses sensibilities which I summon Mr Hartright to respect. They may be transformed to immeasurable enmities if he ventures to disturb them. Let him be content with what he has got – with what I leave unmolested, for your sake, to him and to you. Say to him (with my compliments), if he stirs me, he has Fosco to deal with. In the English of the Popular Tongue, I inform him – Fosco sticks at nothing. Dear lady, good morning." His cold grey eyes settled on my face – he took off his hat solemnly – bowed, bare-headed – and left me.'

'Without returning? without saying more last words?'

'He turned at the corner of the street, and waved his hand, and then struck it theatrically on his breast. I lost sight of him after that. He disappeared in the opposite direction to our house, and I ran back to Laura. Before I was indoors again, I had made up my mind that we must go. The house (especially in your absence) was a place of danger instead of a place of safety, now that the Count had discovered it. If I could have felt certain of your return, I should have risked waiting till you came back. But I was certain of nothing, and I acted at once on my own impulse. You had spoken, before leaving us, of moving into a quieter neighbourhood and purer air, for the sake of Laura's health. I had only to remind her of that, and to suggest surprising you and saving you trouble by managing the move in your absence, to make her quite as anxious for the change as I was. She helped me to pack up your things, and she has arranged them all for you in your new working-room here.'

'What made you think of coming to this place?'

'My ignorance of other localities in the neighbourhood of London. I felt the necessity of getting as far away as possible from our old lodgings, and I knew something of Fulham, because I had once been at school there. I despatched a messenger with a note, on the chance that the school might still be in existence. It was in existence – the daughters of my old mistress were carrying it on for her, and they engaged this place from the instructions I had sent. It was just post-time when the messenger returned to me with the address of the house. We moved after dark – we came here quite unobserved. Have I done right, Walter? Have I justified your trust in me?'

I answered her warmly and gratefully, as I really felt. But the anxious look still remained on her face while I was speaking, and the first question she asked, when I had done, related to Count Fosco.

I saw that she was thinking of him now with a changed mind. No fresh outbreak of anger against him, no new appeal to me to hasten the day of reckoning escaped her. Her conviction that the man's hateful admiration of herself was really sincere, seemed to have increased a hundredfold her distrust of his unfathomable cunning, her inborn dread of the wicked energy and vigilance of all his faculties. Her voice fell low, her manner was hesitating, her eyes searched into mine with an eager fear when she asked me what I thought of his message, and what I meant to do next after hearing it.

'Not many weeks have passed, Marian,' I answered, 'since my interview with Mr Kyrle. When he and I parted, the last words I said to him about Laura were these: "Her uncle's house shall open to receive her, in the presence of every soul who followed the false funeral to the grave; the lie that records her death shall be publicly erased from the tombstone by the authority of the head of the family, and the two men who have wronged her shall answer for their crime to *me*, though the justice that sits in tribunals is powerless to pursue them." One of those men is beyond mortal reach. The other remains, and my resolution remains.'

Her eyes lit up – her colour rose. She said nothing, but I saw all her sympathies gathering to mine in her face.

'I don't disguise from myself, or from you,' I went on, 'that the prospect before us is more than doubtful. The risks we have run already are, it may be, trifles compared with the risks that threaten us in the future, but the venture shall be tried, Marian, for all that. I am not rash enough to measure myself against such a man as the Count before I am well prepared for him.

I have learnt patience – I can wait my time. Let him believe that his message has produced its effect – let him know nothing of us, and hear nothing of us – let us give him full time to feel secure – his own boastful nature, unless I seriously mistake him, will hasten that result. This is one reason for waiting, but there is another more important still. My position, Marian, towards you and towards Laura ought to be a stronger one than it is now before I try our last chance.'

She leaned near to me, with a look of surprise.

'How can it be stronger?' she asked.

'I will tell you,' I replied, 'when the time comes. It has not come yet – it may never come at all. I may be silent about it to Laura for ever – I must be silent now, even to *you*, till I see for myself that I can harmlessly and honourably speak. Let us leave that subject. There is another which has more pressing claims on our attention. You have kept Laura, mercifully kept her, in ignorance of her husband's death—'

'Oh, Walter, surely it must be long yet before we tell her of it?'

'No, Marian. Better that you should reveal it to her now, than that accident, which no one can guard against, should reveal it to her at some future time. Spare her all the details – break it to her very tenderly, but tell her that he is dead.'

'You have a reason, Walter, for wishing her to know of her husband's death besides the reason you have just mentioned?'

'I have.'

'A reason connected with that subject which must not be mentioned between us yet? – which may never be mentioned to Laura at all?'

She dwelt on the last words meaningly. When I answered her in the affirmative, I dwelt on them too.

Her face grew pale. For a while she looked at me with a sad, hesitating interest. An unaccustomed tenderness trembled in her dark eyes and softened her firm lips, as she glanced aside at the empty chair in which the dear companion of all our joys and sorrows had been sitting.

'I think I understand,' she said. 'I think I owe it to her and to you, Walter, to tell her of her husband's death.'

She sighed, and held my hand fast for a moment – then dropped it abruptly, and left the room. On the next day Laura knew that his death had released her, and that the error and the calamity of her life lay buried in his tomb.

His name was mentioned among us no more. Thenceforward, we shrank from the slightest approach to the subject of his death, and in the same scrupulous manner, Marian and I avoided all further reference to that other subject, which, by her consent and mine, was not to be mentioned between us yet. It was not the less present in our minds – it was rather kept alive in them by the restraint which we had imposed on ourselves. We both watched Laura more anxiously than ever, sometimes waiting and hoping, sometimes waiting and fearing, till the time came.

By degrees we returned to our accustomed way of life. I resumed the daily work, which had been suspended during my absence in Hampshire. Our new lodgings cost us more than the smaller and less convenient rooms which we had left, and the claim thus implied on my increased exertions was strengthened by the doubtfulness of our future prospects. Emergencies might yet happen which would exhaust our little fund at the banker's, and the work of my hands might be, ultimately, all we had to look to for support. More permanent and more lucrative employment than had yet been offered to me was a necessity of our position – a necessity for which I now diligently set myself to provide.

It must not be supposed that the interval of rest and seclusion of which I am now writing, entirely suspended, on my part, all pursuit of the one absorbing purpose with which my thoughts and actions are associated in these pages. That purpose was, for months and months yet, never to relax its claims on me. The slow ripening of it still left me a measure of precaution to take, an obligation of gratitude to perform, and a doubtful question to solve.

The measure of precaution related, necessarily, to the Count. It was of the last importance to ascertain, if possible, whether his plans committed him to remaining in England – or, in other words, to remaining within my reach. I contrived to set this doubt at rest by very simple means. His address in St John's Wood being known to me, I inquired in the neighbourhood, and having found out the agent who had the disposal of the furnished house in which he lived, I asked if number five, Forest Road, was likely to be let within a reasonable time. The reply was in the negative. I was informed that the foreign gentleman then residing in the house had renewed his term of occupation for another six months, and would remain in possession until the end of June in the following year. We were then at the beginning of December only. I left the agent with my mind relieved from all present fear of the Count's escaping me.

The obligation I had to perform took me once more into the presence of Mrs Clements. I had promised to return, and to confide to her those particulars relating to the death and burial of Anne Catherick which I had been obliged to withhold at our first interview. Changed as circumstances now were, there was no hindrance to my trusting the good woman with as much of the story of the conspiracy as it was necessary to tell. I had every reason that sympathy and friendly feeling could suggest to urge on me the speedy performance of my promise, and I did conscientiously and carefully perform it. There is no need to burden these pages with any statement of what passed at the interview. It will be more to the purpose to say, that the interview itself necessarily brought to my mind the one doubtful question still remaining to be solved – the question of Anne Catherick's parentage on the father's side.

A multitude of small considerations in connection with this subject – trifling enough in themselves, but strikingly important when massed together – had latterly led my mind to a conclusion which I resolved to verify. I obtained Marian's permission to write to Major Donthorne, of Varneck Hall (where Mrs Catherick had lived in service for some years previous to her marriage), to ask him certain questions. I made the inquiries in Marian's name, and described them as relating to matters of personal history in her family, which might explain and excuse my application. When I wrote the letter I had no certain knowledge that Major Donthorne was still alive – I despatched it on the chance that he might be living, and able and willing to reply.

After a lapse of two days proof came, in the shape of a letter, that the Major was living, and that he was ready to help us.

The idea in my mind when I wrote to him, and the nature of my inquiries will be easily inferred from his reply. His letter answered my questions by communicating these important facts –

In the first place, 'the late Sir Percival Glyde, of Blackwater Park,' had never set foot in Varneck Hall. The deceased gentleman was a total stranger to Major Donthorne, and to all his family.

In the second place, 'the late Mr Philip Fairlie, of Limmeridge House,' had been, in his younger days, the intimate friend and constant guest of Major Donthorne. Having refreshed his memory by looking back to old letters and other papers, the Major was in a position to say positively that Mr Philip Fairlie was staying at Varneck Hall in the month of August, eighteen hundred and twenty-six, and that he remained there for the shooting during the month of September and part of October following. He then left, to the best of the Major's belief, for Scotland, and did not return to Varneck Hall till after a lapse of time, when he reappeared in the character of a newly-married man.

Taken by itself, this statement was, perhaps, of little positive value, but taken in connection with certain facts, every one of which either Marian or I knew to be true, it suggested one plain conclusion that was, to our minds, irresistible.

Knowing, now, that Mr Philip Fairlie had been at Varneck Hall in the autumn of eighteen hundred and twenty-six, and that Mrs Catherick had been living there in service at the same time, we knew also – first, that Anne had been born in June, eighteen hundred and twenty-seven; secondly, that she had always presented an extraordinary personal resemblance to Laura; and, thirdly, that Laura herself was strikingly like her father. Mr Philip Fairlie had been one of the notoriously handsome men of his time. In disposition entirely unlike his brother Frederick, he was the spoilt darling of society, especially of the women – an easy, light-hearted, impulsive, affectionate man – generous to a fault – constitutionally lax in his principles, and notoriously thoughtless of moral obligations where women were concerned. Such were the facts we knew – such was the character of the man. Surely the plain inference that follows needs no pointing out?

Read by the new light which had now broken upon me, even Mrs Catherick's letter, in despite of herself, rendered its mite of assistance towards strengthening the conclusion at which I had arrived. She had described Mrs Fairlie (in writing to me) as 'plain-looking,' and as having 'entrapped the handsomest man in England into marrying her.' Both assertions were gratuitously made, and both were false. Jealous dislike (which, in such a woman as Mrs Catherick, would express itself in petty malice rather than not express itself at all) appeared to me to be the only assignable cause for the peculiar insolence of her reference to Mrs Fairlie, under circumstances which did not necessitate any reference at all.

The mention here of Mrs Fairlie's name naturally suggests one other question. Did she ever suspect whose child the little girl brought to her at Limmeridge might be?

Marian's testimony was positive on this point. Mrs Fairlie's letter to her husband, which had been read to me in former days – the letter describing Anne's resemblance to Laura, and acknowledging her affectionate interest in the little stranger – had been written, beyond all question, in perfect innocence of heart. It even seemed doubtful, on consideration, whether Mr Philip Fairlie himself had been nearer than his wife to any suspicion of the truth. The disgracefully deceitful circumstances under which Mrs Catherick had married, the purpose of concealment which the marriage was intended to answer, might well keep her silent for caution's sake, perhaps for her own pride's sake also, even assuming that she had the means, in his absence, of communicating with the father of her unborn child.

As this surmise floated through my mind, there rose on my memory the remembrance of the Scripture denunciation which we have all thought of in our time with wonder and with awe: 'The sins of the fathers shall be visited on the children.' But for the fatal resemblance between the two daughters of one father, the conspiracy of which Anne had been the innocent instrument and Laura the innocent victim could never have been planned. With what unerring and terrible directness the long chain of circumstances led down from the thoughtless wrong committed by the father to the heartless injury inflicted on the child!

These thoughts came to me, and others with them, which drew my mind away to the little Cumberland churchyard where Anne Catherick now lay buried. I thought of the bygone days when I had met her by Mrs Fairlie's grave, and met her for the last time. I thought of her poor helpless hands beating on the tombstone, and her weary, yearning words, murmured to the dead remains of her protectress and her friend: 'Oh, if I could die, and be hidden and at rest with *you*!' Little more than a year had passed since she breathed that wish; and how inscrutably, how awfully, it had been fulfilled! The words she had spoken to Laura by the shores of the lake, the very words had now come true. 'Oh, if I could only be buried with your mother! If I could only wake at her side when the angel's trumpet sounds and the graves give up their dead at the resurrection!' Through what mortal crime and horror, through what darkest windings of the way down to death – the lost creature had wandered in God's leading to the last home that, living, she never hoped to reach! In that sacred rest I leave her – in that dread companionship let her remain undisturbed.

So the ghostly figure which has haunted these pages, as it haunted my life, goes down into the impenetrable gloom. Like a shadow she first came to me in the loneliness of the night. Like a shadow she passes away in the loneliness of the dead.

III

Four months elapsed. April came – the month of spring – the month of change.

The course of time had flowed through the interval since the winter peacefully and happily in our new home. I had turned my long leisure to good account, had largely increased my sources of employment, and had placed our means of subsistence on surer grounds. Freed from the suspense and the anxiety which had tried her so sorely and hung over her so long, Marian's spirits rallied, and her natural energy of character began to assert itself again, with something, if not all, of the freedom and the vigour of former times.

More pliable under change than her sister, Laura showed more plainly the progress made by the healing influences of her new life. The worn and wasted look which had prematurely aged her face was fast leaving it, and the expression which had been the first of its charms in past days was the first of its beauties that now returned. My closest observations of her detected but one serious result of the conspiracy which had once threatened her reason and her life. Her memory of events, from the period of her leaving Blackwater Park to the period of our meeting in the burial-ground of Limmeridge Church, was lost beyond all hope of recovery. At the slightest reference to that time she changed and trembled still, her words became confused, her memory wandered and lost itself as helplessly as ever. Here, and here only, the traces of the past lay deep – too deep to be effaced.

In all else she was now so far on the way to recovery that, on her best and brightest days, she sometimes looked and spoke like the Laura of old times. The happy change wrought its natural result in us both. From their long slumber, on her side and on mine, those imperishable memories of our past life in Cumberland now awoke, which were one and all alike, the memories of our love.

Gradually and insensibly our daily relations towards each other became constrained. The fond words which I had spoken to her so naturally, in the days of her sorrow and her suffering, faltered strangely on my lips. In the time when my dread of losing her was most present to my mind, I had always kissed her when she left me at night and when she met me in the morning. The kiss seemed now to have dropped between us – to be lost out of our lives. Our hands began to tremble again when they met. We hardly ever looked long at one another out of Marian's presence. The talk often flagged between us when we were alone. When I touched her by accident I felt my heart beating fast, as it used to beat at Limmeridge House – I saw the lovely answering flush glowing again in her cheeks, as if we were back among the Cumberland Hills in our past characters of master and pupil once more. She had long intervals of silence and thoughtfulness, and denied she had been thinking when Marian asked her the question. I surprised myself one day neglecting my work to dream over the little water-colour portrait of her which I had taken in the summer-house where we first met – just as I used to neglect Mr Fairlie's drawings to dream over the same likeness when it was newly finished in the bygone time. Changed as all the circumstances now were, our position towards each other in the golden days of our first companionship seemed to be revived with the revival of our love. It was as if Time had drifted us back on the wreck of our early hopes to the old familiar shore!

To any other woman I could have spoken the decisive words which I still hesitated to speak to *her*. The utter helplessness of her position – her friendless dependence on all the forbearing gentleness that I could show her – my fear of touching too soon some secret sensitiveness in her which my instinct as a man might not have been fine enough to discover – these considerations, and others like them, kept me self-distrustfully silent. And yet I knew that the restraint on both sides must be ended, that the relations in which we stood towards one another must be altered in some settled manner for the future, and that it rested with me, in the first instance, to recognise the necessity for a change.

The more I thought of our position, the harder the attempt to alter it appeared, while the domestic conditions on which we three had been living together since the winter remained undisturbed. I cannot account for the capricious state of mind in which this feeling originated, but the idea nevertheless possessed me that some previous change of place and circumstances, some sudden break in the quiet monotony of our lives, so managed as to vary the home aspect under which we had been accustomed to see each other, might prepare the way for me to speak, and might make it easier and less embarrassing for Laura and Marian to hear.

With this purpose in view, I said, one morning, that I thought we had all earned a little holiday and a change of scene. After some consideration, it was decided that we should go for a fortnight to the sea-side.

On the next day we left Fulham for a quiet town on the south coast. At that early season of the year we were the only visitors in the place. The cliffs, the beach, and the walks inland were all in the solitary condition which was most welcome to us. The air was mild – the prospects over hill and wood and down were beautifully varied by the shifting April light and shade, and the restless sea leapt under our windows, as if it felt, like the land, the glow and freshness of spring.

I owed it to Marian to consult her before I spoke to Laura, and to be guided afterwards by her advice.

On the third day from our arrival I found a fit opportunity of speaking to her alone. The moment we looked at one another, her quick instinct detected the thought in my mind before I could give it expression. With her customary energy and directness she spoke at once, and spoke first.

'You are thinking of that subject which was mentioned between us on the evening of your return from Hampshire,' she said. 'I have been expecting you to allude to it for some time past. There must be a change in our little household, Walter, we cannot go on much longer as we are now. I see it as plainly as you do – as plainly as Laura sees it, though she says nothing. How strangely the old times in Cumberland seem to have come back! You and I are together again, and the one subject of interest between us is Laura once more. I could almost fancy that this room is the summer-house at Limmeridge, and that those waves beyond us are beating on our sea-shore.'

'I was guided by your advice in those past days,' I said, 'and now, Marian, with reliance tenfold greater I will be guided by it again.'

She answered by pressing my hand. I saw that she was deeply touched by my reference to the past. We sat together near the window, and while I

spoke and she listened, we looked at the glory of the sunlight shining on the
majesty of the sea.

'Whatever comes of this confidence between us,' I said, 'whether it ends
happily or sorrowfully for *me*, Laura's interests will still be the interests of
my life. When we leave this place, on whatever terms we leave it, my determination to wrest from Count Fosco the confession which I failed to obtain
from his accomplice, goes back with me to London, as certainly as I go back
myself. Neither you nor I can tell how that man may turn on me, if I bring
him to bay; we only know, by his own words and actions, that he is capable
of striking at me through Laura, without a moment's hesitation, or a moment's
remorse. In our present position I have no claim on her which society sanctions, which the law allows, to strengthen me in resisting him, and in protecting
her. This places me at a serious disadvantage. If I am to fight our cause with
the Count, strong in the consciousness of Laura's safety, I must fight it for
my Wife. Do you agree to that, Marian, so far?'

'To every word of it,' she answered.

'I will not plead out of my own heart,' I went on; 'I will not appeal to
the love which has survived all changes and all shocks – I will rest my only
vindication of myself for thinking of her, and speaking of her as my wife,
on what I have just said. If the chance of forcing a confession from the
Count is, as I believe it to be, the last chance left of publicly establishing
the fact of Laura's existence, the least selfish reason that I can advance for
our marriage is recognised by us both. But I may be wrong in my conviction
– other means of achieving our purpose may be in our power, which are less
uncertain and less dangerous. I have searched anxiously, in my own mind,
for those means, and I have not found them. Have you?'

'No. I have thought about it too, and thought in vain.'

'In all likelihood,' I continued, 'the same questions have occurred to you,
in considering this difficult subject, which have occurred to me. Ought we
to return with her to Limmeridge, now that she is like herself again, and
trust to the recognition of her by the people of the village, or by the children
at the school? Ought we to appeal to the practical test of her handwriting?
Suppose we did so. Suppose the recognition of her obtained, and the identity
of the handwriting established. Would success in both those cases do more
than supply an excellent foundation for a trial in a court of law? Would the
recognition and the handwriting prove her identity to Mr Fairlie and take
her back to Limmeridge House, against the evidence of her aunt, against
the evidence of the medical certificate, against the fact of the funeral and
the fact of the inscription on the tomb? No! We could only hope to succeed
in throwing a serious doubt on the assertion of her death, a doubt which
nothing short of a legal inquiry can settle. I will assume that we possess

(what we have certainly not got) money enough to carry this inquiry on through all its stages. I will assume that Mr Fairlie's prejudices might be reasoned away – that the false testimony of the Count and his wife, and all the rest of the false testimony, might be confuted – that the recognition could not possibly be ascribed to a mistake between Laura and Anne Catherick, or the handwriting be declared by our enemies to be a clever fraud – all these are assumptions which, more or less, set plain probabilities at defiance; but let them pass – and let us ask ourselves what would be the first consequence or the first questions put to Laura herself on the subject of the conspiracy. We know only too well what the consequence would be, for we know that she has never recovered her memory of what happened to her in London. Examine her privately, or examine her publicly, she is utterly incapable of assisting the assertion of her own case. If you don't see this, Marian, as plainly as I see it, we will go to Limmeridge and try the experiment tomorrow.'

'I *do* see it, Walter. Even if we had the means of paying all the law expenses, even if we succeeded in the end, the delays would be unendurable, the perpetual suspense, after what we have suffered already, would be heart-breaking. You are right about the hopelessness of going to Limmeridge. I wish I could feel sure that you are right also in determining to try that last chance with the Count. *Is* it a chance at all?'

'Beyond a doubt, Yes. It is the chance of recovering the lost date of Laura's journey to London. Without returning to the reasons I gave you some time since, I am still as firmly persuaded as ever that there is a discrepancy between the date of that journey and the date on the certificate of death. There lies the weak point of the whole conspiracy – it crumbles to pieces if we attack it in that way, and the means of attacking it are in possession of the Count. If I succeed in wresting them from him, the object of your life and mine is fulfilled. If I fail, the wrong that Laura has suffered will, in this world, never be redressed.'

'Do you fear failure yourself, Walter?'

'I dare not anticipate success, and for that very reason, Marian, I speak openly and plainly as I have spoken now. In my heart and my conscience I can say it, Laura's hopes for the future are at their lowest ebb. I know that her fortune is gone – I know that the last chance of restoring her to her place in the world lies at the mercy of her worst enemy, of a man who is now absolutely unassailable, and who may remain unassailable to the end. With every worldly advantage gone from her, with all prospect of recovering her rank and station more than doubtful, with no clearer future before her than the future which her husband can provide, the poor drawing-master may harmlessly open his heart at last. In the days of her prosperity, Marian, I was only the teacher who guided her hand – I ask for it, in her adversity, as the hand of my wife!'

Marian's eyes met mine affectionately – I could say no more. My heart was full, my lips were trembling. In spite of myself I was in danger of appealing to her pity. I got up to leave the room. She rose at the same moment, laid her hand gently on my shoulder, and stopped me.

'Walter!' she said, 'I once parted you both, for your good and for hers. Wait here, my brother! – wait, my dearest, best friend, till Laura comes, and tells you what I have done now!'

For the first time since the farewell morning at Limmeridge she touched my forehead with her lips. A tear dropped on my face as she kissed me. She turned quickly, pointed to the chair from which I had risen, and left the room.

I sat down alone at the window to wait through the crisis of my life. My mind in that breathless interval felt like a total blank. I was conscious of nothing but a painful intensity of all familiar perceptions. The sun grew blinding bright, the white sea birds chasing each other far beyond me seemed to be flitting before my face, the mellow murmur of the waves on the beach was like thunder in my ears.

The door opened, and Laura came in alone. So she had entered the breakfast-room at Limmeridge House on the morning when we parted. Slowly and falteringly, in sorrow and in hesitation, she had once approached me. Now she came with the haste of happiness in her feet, with the light of happiness radiant in her face. Of their own accord those dear arms clasped themselves round me, of their own accord the sweet lips came to meet mine. 'My darling!' she whispered, 'we may own we love each other now?' Her head nestled with a tender contentedness on my bosom. 'Oh,' she said innocently, 'I am so happy at last!'

Ten days later we were happier still. We were married.

IV

The course of this narrative, steadily flowing on, bears me away from the morning-time of our married life, and carries me forward to the end.

In a fortnight more we three were back in London, and the shadow was stealing over us of the struggle to come.

Marian and I were careful to keep Laura in ignorance of the cause that had hurried us back – the necessity of making sure of the Count. It was now the beginning of May, and his term of occupation at the house in Forest Road expired in June. If he renewed it (and I had reasons, shortly to be mentioned, for anticipating that he would), I might be certain of his not escaping me. But if by any chance he disappointed my expectations and left the country, then I had no time to lose in arming myself to meet him as I best might.

In the first fulness of my new happiness, there had been moments when my resolution faltered – moments when I was tempted to be safely content, now that the dearest aspiration of my life was fulfilled in the possession of Laura's love. For the first time I thought faint-heartedly of the greatness of the risk, of the adverse chances arrayed against me, of the fair promise of our new life, and of the peril in which I might place the happiness which we had so hardly earned. Yes! let me own it honestly. For a brief time I wandered, in the sweet guiding of love, far from the purpose to which I had been true under sterner discipline and in darker days. Innocently Laura had tempted me aside from the hard path – innocently she was destined to lead me back again.

At times, dreams of the terrible past still disconnectedly recalled to her, in the mystery of sleep, the events of which her waking memory had lost all trace. One night (barely two weeks after our marriage), when I was watching her at rest, I saw the tears come slowly through her closed eyelids, I heard the faint murmuring words escape her which told me that her spirit was back again on the fatal journey from Blackwater Park. That unconscious appeal, so touching and so awful in the sacredness of her sleep, ran through me like fire. The next day was the day we came back to London – the day when my resolution returned to me with tenfold strength.

The first necessity was to know something of the man. Thus far, the true story of his life was an impenetrable mystery to me.

I began with such scanty sources of information as were at my own disposal. The important narrative written by Mr Frederick Fairlie (which Marian had obtained by following the directions I had given to her in the winter) proved to be of no service to the special object with which I now looked at it. While reading it I reconsidered the disclosure revealed to me by Mrs Clements of the series of deceptions which had brought Anne Catherick to London, and which had there devoted her to the interests of the conspiracy. Here, again, the Count had not openly committed himself – here, again, he was, to all practical purpose, out of my reach.

I next returned to Marian's journal at Blackwater Park. At my request she read to me again a passage which referred to her past curiosity about the Count, and to the few particulars which she had discovered relating to him.

The passage to which I allude occurs in that part of her journal which delineates his character and his personal appearance. She describes him as 'not having crossed the frontiers of his native country for years past' – as 'anxious to know if any Italian gentlemen were settled in the nearest town to Blackwater Park' – as 'receiving letters with all sorts of odd stamps on them, and one with a large official-looking seal on it.' She is inclined to consider that his long absence from his native country may be accounted for by assuming that he is a political exile. But she is, on the other hand, unable to reconcile this idea with the reception of the letter from abroad bearing 'the large official-looking seal' – letters from the Continent addressed to political exiles being usually the last to court attention from foreign post-offices in that way.

The considerations thus presented to me in the diary, joined to certain surmises of my own that grew out of them, suggested a conclusion which I wondered I had not arrived at before. I now said to myself – what Laura had once said to Marian at Blackwater Park, what Madame Fosco had overheard by listening at the door – the Count is a spy!

Laura had applied the word to him at hazard, in natural anger at his proceedings towards herself. I applied it to him with the deliberate conviction that his vocation in life was the vocation of a spy. On this assumption, the reason for his extraordinary stay in England so long after the objects of the conspiracy had been gained, became, to my mind, quite intelligible.

The year of which I am now writing was the year of the famous Crystal Palace Exhibition in Hyde Park. Foreigners in unusually large numbers had arrived already, and were still arriving in England. Men were among us by hundreds whom the ceaseless distrustfulness of their governments had followed privately, by means of appointed agents, to our shores. My surmises did not for a moment class a man of the Count's abilities and social position with the ordinary rank and file of foreign spies. I suspected him of holding a position of authority, of being entrusted by the government which he secretly served with the organisation and management of agents specially employed in this country, both men and women, and I believed Mrs Rubelle, who had been so opportunely found to act as nurse at Blackwater Park, to be, in all probability, one of the number.

Assuming that this idea of mine had a foundation in truth, the position of the Count might prove to be more assailable than I had hitherto ventured to hope. To whom could I apply to know something more of the man's history and of the man himself than I knew now?

In this emergency it naturally occurred to my mind that a countryman of his own, on whom I could rely, might be the fittest person to help me. The first man whom I thought of under these circumstances was also the only Italian with whom I was intimately acquainted – my quaint little friend, Professor Pesca.

* * *

The professor has been so long absent from these pages that he has run some risk of being forgotten altogether.

It is the necessary law of such a story as mine that the persons concerned in it only appear when the course of events takes them up – they come and go, not by favour of my personal partiality, but by right of their direct connection with the circumstances to be detailed. For this reason, not Pesca alone, but my mother and sister as well, have been left far in the background of the narrative. My visits to the Hampstead cottage, my mother's belief in the denial of Laura's identity which the conspiracy had accomplished, my vain efforts to overcome the prejudice on her part and on my sister's to which, in their jealous affection for me, they both continued to adhere, the painful necessity which that prejudice imposed on me of concealing my marriage from them till they had learnt to do justice to my wife – all these little domestic occurrences have been left unrecorded because they were not essential to the main interest of the story. It is nothing that they added to my anxieties and embittered my disappointments – the steady march of events has inexorably passed them by.

For the same reason I have said nothing here of the consolation that I found in Pesca's brotherly affection for me, when I saw him again after the sudden cessation of my residence at Limmeridge House. I have not recorded the fidelity with which my warm-hearted little friend followed me to the place of embarkation when I sailed for Central America, or the noisy transport of joy with which he received me when we next met in London. If I had felt justified in accepting the offers of service which he made to me on my return, he would have appeared again long ere this. But, though I knew that his honour and his courage were to be implicitly relied on, I was not so sure that his discretion was to be trusted, and, for that reason only, I followed the course of all my inquiries alone. It will now be sufficiently understood that Pesca was not separated from all connection with me and my interests, although he has hitherto been separated from all connection with the progress of this narrative. He was as true and as ready a friend of mine still as ever he had been in his life.

Before I summoned Pesca to my assistance it was necessary to see for myself what sort of man I had to deal with. Up to this time I had never once set eyes on Count Fosco.

Three days after my return with Laura and Marian to London, I set forth alone for Forest Road, St John's Wood, between ten and eleven o'clock in the morning. It was a fine day – I had some hours to spare – and I thought it likely, if I waited a little for him, that the Count might be tempted out. I had no great reason to fear the chance of his recognising me in the daytime, for the only occasion when I had been seen by him was the occasion on which he had followed me home at night.

No one appeared at the windows in the front of the house. I walked down a turning which ran past the side of it, and looked over the low garden wall. One of the back windows on the lower floor was thrown up and a net was stretched across the opening. I saw nobody, but I heard, in the room, first a shrill whistling and singing of birds, then the deep ringing voice which Marian's description had made familiar to me. 'Come out on my little finger, my pret-pret-pretties!' cried the voice. 'Come out and hop upstairs! One, two, three – and up! Three, two, one – and down! One, two, three – twit-twit-twit-tweet!' The Count was exercising his canaries as he used to exercise them in Marian's time at Blackwater Park.

I waited a little while, and the singing and the whistling ceased. 'Come, kiss me, my pretties!' said the deep voice. There was a responsive twittering and chirping – a low, oily laugh – a silence of a minute or so, and then I heard the opening of the house door. I turned and retraced my steps. The magnificent melody of the Prayer in Rossini's Moses, sung in a sonorous bass voice, rose grandly through the suburban silence of the place. The front garden gate opened and closed. The Count had come out.

He crossed the road and walked towards the western boundary of the Regent's Park. I kept on my own side of the way, a little behind him, and walked in that direction also.

Marian had prepared me for his high stature, his monstrous corpulence, and his ostentatious mourning garments, but not for the horrible freshness and cheerfulness and vitality of the man. He carried his sixty years as if they had been fewer than forty. He sauntered along, wearing his hat a little on one side, with a light jaunty step, swinging his big stick, humming to himself, looking up from time to time at the houses and gardens on either side of him with superb, smiling patronage. If a stranger had been told that the whole neighbourhood belonged to him, that stranger would not have been surprised to hear it. He never looked back, he paid no apparent attention to me, no apparent attention to any one who passed him on his own side of the road, except now and then, when he smiled and smirked, with an easy paternal good humour, at the nursery-maids and the children whom he met. In this way he led me on, till we reached a colony of shops outside the western terraces of the Park.

Here he stopped at a pastrycook's, went in (probably to give an order), and came out again immediately with a tart in his hand. An Italian was grinding an organ before the shop, and a miserable little shrivelled monkey was sitting on the instrument. The Count stopped, bit a piece for himself out of the tart, and gravely handed the rest to the monkey. 'My poor little man!'

he said, with grotesque tenderness, 'you look hungry. In the sacred name of humanity, I offer you some lunch!' The organ-grinder piteously put in his claim to a penny from the benevolent stranger. The Count shrugged his shoulders contemptuously, and passed on.

We reached the streets and the better class of shops between the New Road and Oxford Street. The Count stopped again and entered a small optician's shop, with an inscription in the window announcing that repairs were neatly executed inside. He came out again with an opera-glass in his hand, walked a few paces on, and stopped to look at a bill of the opera placed outside a music-seller's shop. He read the bill attentively, considered a moment, and then hailed an empty cab as it passed him. 'Opera Box-office,' he said to the man, and was driven away.

I crossed the road, and looked at the bill in my turn. The performance announced was Lucrezia Borgia, and it was to take place that evening. The opera-glass in the Count's hand, his careful reading of the bill, and his direction to the cabman, all suggested that he proposed making one of the audience. I had the means of getting an admission for myself and a friend to the pit by applying to one of the scene-painters attached to the theatre, with whom I had been well acquainted in past times. There was a chance at least that the Count might be easily visible among the audience to me and to any one with me, and in this case I had the means of ascertaining whether Pesca knew his countryman or not that very night.

This consideration at once decided the disposal of my evening. I procured the tickets, leaving a note at the Professor's lodgings on the way. At a quarter to eight I called to take him with me to the theatre. My little friend was in a state of the highest excitement, with a festive flower in his button-hole, and the largest opera-glass I ever saw hugged up under his arm.

'Are you ready?' I asked.

'Right-all-right,' said Pesca.

We started for the theatre.

V

The last notes of the introduction to the opera were being played, and the seats in the pit were all filled, when Pesca and I reached the theatre.

There was plenty of room, however, in the passage that ran round the pit – precisely the position best calculated to answer the purpose for which I was attending the performance. I went first to the barrier separating us from the stalls, and looked for the Count in that part of the theatre. He was not there. Returning along the passage, on the left-hand side from the stage, and looking about me attentively, I discovered him in the pit. He occupied an excellent place, some twelve or fourteen seats from the end of a bench, within three rows of the stalls. I placed myself exactly on a line with him, Pesca standing by my side. The Professor was not yet aware of the purpose for which I had brought him to the theatre, and he was rather surprised that we did not move nearer to the stage.

The curtain rose, and the opera began.

Throughout the whole of the first act we remained in our position – the Count, absorbed by the orchestra and the stage, never casting so much as a chance glance at us. Not a note of Donizetti's delicious music was lost on him. There he sat, high above his neighbours, smiling, and nodding his great head enjoyingly from time to time. When the people near him applauded the close of an air (as an English audience in such circumstances always *will* applaud), without the least consideration for the orchestral movement which immediately followed it, he looked round at them with an expression of compassionate remonstrance, and held up one hand with a gesture of polite entreaty. At the more refined passages of the singing, at the more delicate phases of the music, which passed unapplauded by others, his fat hands, adorned with perfectly-fitting black kid gloves, softly patted each other, in token of the cultivated appreciation of a musical man. At such times, his oily murmur of approval, 'Bravo! Bra-a-a-a!' hummed through the silence, like the purring of a great cat. His immediate neighbours on either side – hearty, ruddy-faced people from the country, basking amazedly in the sunshine of fashionable London – seeing and hearing him, began to follow his lead. Many a burst of applause from the pit that night started from the soft, comfortable patting of the black-gloved hands. The man's voracious vanity devoured this implied tribute to his local and critical supremacy with an appearance of the highest relish. Smiles rippled continuously over his fat face. He looked about him, at the pauses in the music, serenely satisfied with himself and his fellow-creatures. 'Yes! yes! these barbarous English people are learning something from *me*. Here, there, and everywhere, I – Fosco – am an influence that is felt, a man who sits supreme!' If ever face spoke, his face spoke then, and that was its language.

The curtain fell on the first act, and the audience rose to look about them. This was the time I had waited for – the time to try if Pesca knew him.

He rose with the rest, and surveyed the occupants of the boxes grandly with his opera-glass. At first his back was towards us, but he turned round in time, to our side of the theatre, and looked at the boxes above us, using his glass for a few minutes – then removing it, but still continuing to look up. This was the moment I chose, when his full face was in view, for directing Pesca's attention to him.

'Do you know that man?' I asked.

'Which man, my friend?'

'The tall, fat man, standing there, with his face towards us.'

Pesca raised himself on tiptoe, and looked at the Count.

'No,' said the Professor. 'The big fat man is a stranger to me. Is he famous? Why do you point him out?'

'Because I have particular reasons for wishing to know something of him. He is a countryman of yours – his name is Count Fosco. Do you know that name?'

'Not I, Walter. Neither the name nor the man is known to me.'

'Are you quite sure you don't recognise him? Look again – look carefully. I will tell you why I am so anxious about it when we leave the theatre. Stop! let me help you up here, where you can see him better.'

I helped the little man to perch himself on the edge of the raised dais upon which the pit-seats were all placed. His small stature was no hindrance to him – here he could see over the heads of the ladies who were seated near the outermost part of the bench.

A slim, light-haired man standing by us, whom I had not noticed before – a man with a scar on his left cheek – looked attentively at Pesca as I helped him up, and then looked still more attentively, following the direction of Pesca's eyes, at the Count. Our conversation might have reached his ears, and might, as it struck me, have roused his curiosity.

Meanwhile, Pesca fixed his eyes earnestly on the broad, full, smiling face turned a little upward, exactly opposite to him.

'No,' he said, 'I have never set my two eyes on that big fat man before in all my life.'

As he spoke the Count looked downwards towards the boxes behind us on the pit tier.

The eyes of the two Italians met.

The instant before I had been perfectly satisfied, from his own reiterated assertion, that Pesca did not know the Count. The instant afterwards I was equally certain that the Count knew Pesca!

Knew him, and – more surprising still – *feared* him as well! There was no mistaking the change that passed over the villain's face. The leaden hue that altered his yellow complexion in a moment, the sudden rigidity of all his features, the furtive scrutiny of his cold grey eyes, the motionless stillness of him from head to foot told their own tale. A mortal dread had mastered him body and soul – and his own recognition of Pesca was the cause of it!

The slim man with the scar on his cheek was still close by us. He had apparently drawn his inference from the effect produced on the Count by the sight of Pesca as I had drawn mine. He was a mild, gentlemanlike man, looking like a foreigner, and his interest in our proceedings was not expressed in anything approaching to an offensive manner.

For my own part I was so startled by the change in the Count's face, so astounded at the entirely unexpected turn which events had taken, that I knew neither what to say or do next. Pesca roused me by stepping back to his former place at my side and speaking first.

'How the fat man stares!' he exclaimed. 'Is it *me*? Am I famous? How can he know me when I don't know him?'

I kept my eye still on the Count. I saw him move for the first time when Pesca moved, so as not to lose sight of the little man in the lower position in which he now stood. I was curious to see what would happen if Pesca's attention under these circumstances was withdrawn from him, and I accordingly asked the Professor if he recognised any of his pupils that evening among the ladies in the boxes. Pesca immediately raised the large opera-glass to his eyes, and moved it slowly all round the upper part of the theatre, searching for his pupils with the most conscientious scrutiny.

The moment he showed himself to be thus engaged the Count turned round, slipped past the persons who occupied seats on the farther side of him from where we stood, and disappeared in the middle passage down the centre of the pit. I caught Pesca by the arm, and to his inexpressible astonishment, hurried him round with me to the back of the pit to intercept the Count before he could get to the door. Somewhat to my surprise, the slim man hastened out before us, avoiding a stoppage caused by some people on our side of the pit leaving their places, by which Pesca and myself were delayed. When we reached the lobby the Count had disappeared, and the foreigner with the scar was gone too.

'Come home,' I said; 'come home, Pesca, to your lodgings. I must speak to you in private – I must speak directly.'

'My-soul-bless-my-soul!' cried the Professor, in a state of the extremest bewilderment. 'What on earth is the matter?'

I walked on rapidly without answering. The circumstances under which the Count had left the theatre suggested to me that his extraordinary anxiety to escape Pesca might carry him to further extremities still. He might escape *me*, too, by leaving London. I doubted the future if I allowed him so much as a day's freedom to act as he pleased. And I doubted that foreign stranger, who had got the start of us, and whom I suspected of intentionally following him out.

With this double distrust in my mind, I was not long in making Pesca understand what I wanted. As soon as we two were alone in his room, I increased his confusion and amazement a hundredfold by telling him what my purpose was as plainly and unreservedly as I have acknowledged it here.

'My friend, what can I do?' cried the Professor, piteously appealing to me with both hands. 'Deuce-what-the-deuce! how can I help you, Walter, when I don't know the man?'

'*He* knows *you* – he is afraid of you – he has left the theatre to escape you. Pesca! there must be a reason for this. Look back into your own life before you came to England. You left Italy, as you have told me yourself, for political reasons. You have never mentioned those reasons to me, and I don't inquire into them now. I only ask you to consult your own recollections, and to say if they suggest no past cause for the terror which the first sight of you produced in that man.'

To my unutterable surprise, these words, harmless as they appeared to *me*, produced the same astounding effect on Pesca which the sight of Pesca had produced on the Count. The rosy face of my little friend whitened in an instant, and he drew back from me slowly, trembling from head to foot.

'Walter!' he said. 'You don't know what you ask.'

He spoke in a whisper – he looked at me as if I had suddenly revealed to him some hidden danger to both of us. In less than one minute of time he was so altered from the easy, lively, quaint little man of all my past experience, that if I had met him in the street, changed as I saw him now, I should most certainly not have known him again.

'Forgive me, if I have unintentionally pained and shocked you,' I replied. 'Remember the cruel wrong my wife has suffered at Count Fosco's hands. Remember that the wrong can never be redressed, unless the means are in my power of forcing him to do her justice. I spoke in *her* interests, Pesca – I ask you again to forgive me – I can say no more.'

I rose to go. He stopped me before I reached the door.

'Wait,' he said. 'You have shaken me from head to foot. You don't know how I left my country, and why I left my country. Let me compose myself, let me think, if I can.'

I returned to my chair. He walked up and down the room, talking to himself incoherently in his own language. After several turns backwards and forwards, he suddenly came up to me, and laid his little hands with a strange tenderness and solemnity on my breast.

'On your heart and soul, Walter,' he said, 'is there no other way to get to that man but the chance-way through *me*?'

'There is no other way,' I answered.

He left me again, opened the door of the room and looked out cautiously into the passage, closed it once more, and came back.

'You won your right over me, Walter,' he said, 'on the day when you saved my life. It was yours from that moment, when you pleased to take it.

Take it now. Yes! I mean what I say. My next words, as true as the good God is above us, will put my life into your hands.'

The trembling earnestness with which he uttered this extraordinary warning, carried with it, to my mind, the conviction that he spoke the truth.

'Mind this!' he went on, shaking his hands at me in the vehemence of his agitation. 'I hold no thread, in my own mind, between that man Fosco, and the past time which I call back to me for your sake. If you find the thread, keep it to yourself – tell me nothing – on my knees I beg and pray, let me be ignorant, let me be innocent, let me be blind to all the future as I am now!'

He said a few words more, hesitatingly and disconnectedly, then stopped again.

I saw that the effort of expressing himself in English, on an occasion too serious to permit him the use of the quaint turns and phrases of his ordinary vocabulary, was painfully increasing the difficulty he had felt from the first in speaking to me at all. Having learnt to read and understand his native language (though not to speak it), in the earlier days of our intimate companionship, I now suggested to him that he should express himself in Italian, while I used English in putting any questions which might be necessary to my enlightenment. He accepted the proposal. In his smooth-flowing language, spoken with a vehement agitation which betrayed itself in the perpetual working of his features, in the wildness and the suddenness of his foreign gesticulations, but never in the raising of his voice, I now heard the words which armed me to meet the last struggle, that is left for this story to record.*

'You know nothing of my motive for leaving Italy,' he began, 'except that it was for political reasons. If I had been driven to this country by the persecution of my government, I should not have kept those reasons a secret from you or from any one. I have concealed them because no government authority has pronounced the sentence of my exile. You have heard, Walter, of the political societies that are hidden in every great city on the continent of Europe? To one of those societies I belonged in Italy – and belong still in England. When I came to this country, I came by the direction of my chief. I was over-zealous in my younger time – I ran the risk of compromising myself and others. For those reasons I was ordered to emigrate to England and to wait. I emigrated – I have waited – I wait still. Tomorrow I may be called away – ten years hence I may be called away. It is all one to me – I

---

* It is only right to mention here, that I repeat Pesco's statement to me with the careful suppressions and alterations which the serious nature of the subject and my own sense of duty to my friend demand. My first and last concealments from the reader are those which caution renders absolutely necessary in this portion of the narrative.

am here, I support myself by teaching, and I wait. I violate no oath (you shall hear why presently) in making my confidence complete by telling you the name of the society to which I belong. All I do is to put my life in your hands. If what I say to you now is ever known by others to have passed my lips, as certainly as we two sit here, I am a dead man.'

He whispered the next words in my ear. I keep the secret which he thus communicated. The society to which he belonged will be sufficiently individualised for the purpose of these pages, if I call it 'The Brotherhood,' on the few occasions when any reference to the subject will be needed in this place.

'The object of the Brotherhood,' Pesca went on, 'is, briefly, the object of other political societies of the same sort – the destruction of tyranny and the assertion of the rights of the people. The principles of the Brotherhood are two. So long as a man's life is useful, or even harmless only, he has the right to enjoy it. But, if his life inflicts injury on the well-being of his fellow-men, from that moment he forfeits the right, and it is not only no crime, but a positive merit, to deprive him of it. It is not for me to say in what frightful circumstances of oppression and suffering this society took its rise. It is not for you to say – you Englishmen, who have conquered your freedom so long ago, that you have conveniently forgotten what blood you shed, and what extremities you proceeded to in the conquering – it is not for you to say how far the worst of all exasperations may, or may not, carry the maddened men of an enslaved nation. The iron that has entered into our souls has gone too deep for you to find it. Leave the refugee alone! Laugh at him, distrust him, open your eyes in wonder at that secret self which smoulders in him, sometimes under the everyday respectability and tranquillity of a man like me – sometimes under the grinding poverty, the fierce squalor, of men less lucky, less pliable, less patient than I am – but judge us not! In the time of your first Charles you might have done us justice – the long luxury of your own freedom has made you incapable of doing us justice now.'

All the deepest feelings of his nature seemed to force themselves to the surface in those words – all his heart was poured out to me for the first time in our lives – but still his voice never rose, still his dread of the terrible revelation he was making to me never left him.

'So far,' he resumed, 'you think the society like other societies. Its object (in your English opinion) is anarchy and revolution. It takes the life of a bad king or a bad minister, as if the one and the other were dangerous wild beasts to be shot at the first opportunity. I grant you this. But the laws of the Brotherhood are the laws of no other political society on the face of the earth. The members are not known to one another. There is a president in Italy; there are presidents abroad. Each of these has his secretary. The presidents and the secretaries know the members, but the members, among themselves, are all strangers, until their chiefs see fit, in the political necessity of the time, or in the private necessity of the society, to make them known to each other. With such a safeguard as this there is no oath among us on admittance. We are identified with the Brotherhood by a secret mark, which we all bear, which lasts while our lives last. We are told to go about our ordinary business, and to report ourselves to the president, or the secretary, four times a year, in the event of our services being required. We are warned, if we betray the Brotherhood, or if we injure it by serving other interests, that we die by the principles of the Brotherhood – die by the hand of a stranger who may be sent from the other end of the world to strike the blow – or by the hand of our own bosom-friend, who may have been a member unknown to us through all the years of our intimacy. Sometimes the death is delayed – sometimes it follows close on the treachery. It is our first business to know how to wait – our second business to know how to obey when the word is spoken. Some of us may wait our lives through, and may not be wanted. Some of us may be called to the work, or to the preparation for the work, the very day of our admission. I myself – the little, easy, cheerful man you know, who, of his own accord, would hardly lift up his handkerchief to strike down the fly that buzzes about his face – I, in my younger time, under provocation so dreadful that I will not tell you of it, entered the Brotherhood by an impulse, as I might have killed myself by an impulse. I must remain in it now – it has got me, whatever I may think of it in my better circumstances and my cooler manhood, to my dying day. While I was still in Italy I was chosen secretary, and all the members of that time, who were brought face to face with my president, were brought face to face also with *me*.'

I began to understand him – I saw the end towards which his extraordinary disclosure was now tending. He waited a moment, watching me earnestly – watching till he had evidently guessed what was passing in my mind before he resumed.

'You have drawn your own conclusion already,' he said. 'I see it in your face. Tell me nothing – keep me out of the secret of your thoughts. Let me make my one last sacrifice of myself, for your sake, and then have done with this subject, never to return to it again.'

He signed to me not to answer him – rose – removed his coat – and rolled up the shirt-sleeve on his left arm.

'I promised you that this confidence should be complete,' he whispered, speaking close at my ear, with his eyes looking watchfully at the door. 'Whatever comes of it you shall not reproach me with having hidden anything from you which it was necessary to your interests to know. I have said that the Brotherhood identifies its members by a mark that lasts for life. See the place, and the mark on it for yourself.'

He raised his bare arm, and showed me, high on the upper part of it and in the inner side, a brand deeply burnt in the flesh and stained of a bright blood-red colour. I abstain from describing the device which the brand represented. It will be sufficient to say that it was circular in form, and so small that it would have been completely covered by a shilling coin.

'A man who has this mark, branded in this place,' he said, covering his arm again, 'is a member of the Brotherhood. A man who has been false to the Brotherhood is discovered sooner or later by the chiefs who know him – presidents or secretaries, as the case may be. And a man discovered by the chiefs is dead. *No human laws can protect him.* Remember what you have seen and heard – draw what conclusions *you* like – act as you please. But, in the name of God, whatever you discover, whatever you do, tell me nothing! Let me remain free from a responsibility which it horrifies me to think of – which I know, in my conscience, is not my responsibility now. For the last time I say it – on my honour as a gentleman, on my oath as a Christian, if the man you pointed out at the Opera knows *me*, he is so altered, or so disguised, that I do not know *him*. I am ignorant of his proceedings or his purposes in England. I never saw him, I never heard the name he goes by, to my knowledge, before tonight. I say no more. Leave me a little, Walter. I am overpowered by what has happened – I am shaken by what I have said. Let me try to be like myself again when we meet next.'

He dropped into a chair, and turning away from me, hid his face in his hands. I gently opened the door so as not to disturb him, and spoke my few parting words in low tones, which he might hear or not, as he pleased.

'I will keep the memory of tonight in my heart of hearts,' I said. 'You shall never repent the trust you have reposed in me. May I come to you tomorrow? May I come as early as nine o'clock?'

'Yes, Walter,' he replied, looking up at me kindly, and speaking in English once more, as if his one anxiety now was to get back to our former relations towards each other. 'Come to my little bit of breakfast before I go my ways among the pupils that I teach.'

'Good-night, Pesca.'

'Good-night, my friend.'

VI

My first conviction as soon as I found myself outside the house, was that no alternative was left me but to act at once on the information I had received – to make sure of the Count that night, or to risk the loss, if I only delayed till the morning, of Laura's last chance. I looked at my watch – it was ten o'clock.

Not the shadow of a doubt crossed my mind of the purpose for which the Count had left the theatre. His escape from us, that evening, was beyond all question the preliminary only to his escape from London. The mark of the Brotherhood was on his arm – I felt as certain of it as if he had shown me the brand; and the betrayal of the Brotherhood was on his conscience – I had seen it in his recognition of Pesca.

It was easy to understand why that recognition had not been mutual. A man of the Count's character would never risk the terrible consequences of turning spy without looking to his personal security quite as carefully as he looked to his golden reward. The shaven face, which I had pointed out at the Opera, might have been covered by a beard in Pesca's time – his dark brown hair might be a wig – his name was evidently a false one. The accident of time might have helped him as well – his immense corpulence might have come with his later years. There was every reason why Pesca should not have known him again – every reason also why he should have known Pesca, whose singular personal appearance made a marked man of him, go where he might.

I have said that I felt certain of the purpose in the Count's mind when he escaped us at the theatre. How could I doubt it, when I saw, with my own eyes, that he believed himself, in spite of the change in his appearance, to have been recognised by Pesca, and to be therefore in danger of his life? If I could get speech of him that night, if I could show him that I, too knew of the mortal peril in which he stood, what result would follow? Plainly this. One of us must be master of the situation – one of us must inevitably be at the mercy of the other.

I owed it to myself to consider the chances against me before I confronted them. I owed it to my wife to do all that lay in my power to lessen the risk.

The chances against me wanted no reckoning up – they were all merged in one. If the Count discovered, by my own avowal, that the direct way to his safety lay through my life, he was probably the last man in existence who would shrink from throwing me off my guard and taking that way, when he had me alone within his reach. The only means of defence against him on which I could at all rely to lessen the risk, presented themselves, after a little careful thinking, clearly enough. Before I made any personal acknowledgment of my discovery in his presence, I must place the discovery itself where it would be ready for instant use against him, and safe from any attempt at suppression on his part. If I laid the mine under his feet before I approached him, and if I left instructions with a third person to fire it on the expiration of a certain time, unless directions to the contrary were previously received under my own hand, or from my own lips – in that event the Count's security was absolutely dependent upon mine, and I might hold the vantage ground over him securely, even in his own house.

This idea occurred to me when I was close to the new lodgings which we had taken on returning from the sea-side. I went in without disturbing any one, by the help of my key. A light was in the hall, and I stole up with it to my workroom to make my preparations, and absolutely to commit myself to an interview with the Count, before either Laura or Marian could have the slightest suspicion of what I intended to do.

A letter addressed to Pesca represented the surest measure of precaution which it was now possible for me to take. I wrote as follows –

The man whom I pointed out to you at the Opera is a member of the Brotherhood, and has been false to his trust. Put both these assertions to the test instantly. You know the name he goes by in England. His address is No. 5 Forest Road, St John's Wood. On the love you once bore me, use the power entrusted to you without mercy and without delay against that man. I have risked all and lost all – and the forfeit of my failure has been paid with my life.

I signed and dated these lines, enclosed them in an envelope, and sealed it up. On the outside I wrote this direction: 'Keep the enclosure unopened until nine o'clock tomorrow morning. If you do not hear from me, or see me, before that time, break the seal when the clock strikes, and read the contents.' I added my initials, and protected the whole by enclosing it in a second sealed envelope, addressed to Pesca at his lodgings.

Nothing remained to be done after this but to find the means of sending my letter to its destination immediately. I should then have accomplished all that lay in my power. If anything happened to me in the Count's house, I had now provided for his answering it with his life.

That the means of preventing his escape, under any circumstances whatever, were at Pesca's disposal, if he chose to exert them, I did not for an instant doubt. The extraordinary anxiety which he had expressed to remain unenlightened as to the Count's identity – or, in other words, to be left uncertain enough about facts to justify him to his own conscience in remaining passive – betrayed plainly that the means of exercising the terrible justice of the Brotherhood were ready to his hand, although, as a naturally humane man, he had shrunk from plainly saying as much in my presence. The deadly certainty with which the vengeance of foreign political societies can hunt down a traitor to the cause, hide himself where he may, had been too often exemplified, even in my superficial experience, to allow of any doubt. Considering the subject only as a reader of newspapers, cases recurred to my memory, both in London and in Paris, of foreigners found stabbed in the streets, whose assassins could never be traced – of bodies and parts of bodies thrown into the Thames and the Seine, by hands that could never be discovered – of deaths by secret violence which could only be accounted for in one way. I have disguised nothing relating to myself in these pages, and I do not disguise here that I believed I had written Count Fosco's death-warrant, if the fatal emergency happened which authorised Pesca to open my enclosure.

I left my room to go down to the ground floor of the house, and speak to the landlord about finding me a messenger. He happened to be ascending the stairs at the time, and we met on the landing. His son, a quick lad, was the messenger he proposed to me on hearing what I wanted. We had the boy upstairs, and I gave him his directions. He was to take the letter in a cab, to put it into Professor Pesca's own hands, and to bring me back a line of acknowledgment from that gentleman – returning in the cab, and keeping it at the door for my use. It was then nearly half-past ten. I calculated that the boy might be back in twenty minutes, and that I might drive to St John's Wood, on his return, in twenty minutes more.

When the lad had departed on his errand I returned to my own room for a little while, to put certain papers in order, so that they might be easily found in case of the worst. The key of the old-fashioned bureau in which the papers were kept I sealed up, and left it on my table, with Marian's name written on the outside of the little packet. This done, I went downstairs to the sitting-room, in which I expected to find Laura and Marian awaiting my return from the Opera. I felt my hand trembling for the first time when I laid it on the lock of the door.

No one was in the room but Marian. She was reading, and she looked at her watch, in surprise, when I came in.

'How early you are back!' she said. 'You must have come away before the Opera was over.'

'Yes,' I replied, 'neither Pesca nor I waited for the end. Where is Laura?'

'She had one of her bad headaches this evening, and I advised her to go to bed when we had done tea.'

I left the room again on the pretext of wishing to see whether Laura was asleep. Marian's quick eyes were beginning to look inquiringly at my face – Marian's quick instinct was beginning to discover that I had something weighing on my mind.

When I entered the bedchamber, and softly approached the bedside by the dim flicker of the night-lamp, my wife was asleep.

We had not been married quite a month yet. If my heart was heavy, if my resolution for a moment faltered again, when I looked at her face turned faithfully to *my* pillow in her sleep – when I saw her hand resting open on the coverlid, as if it was waiting unconsciously for mine – surely there was some excuse for me? I only allowed myself a few minutes to kneel down at the bedside, and to look close at her – so close that her breath, as it came and went, fluttered on my face. I only touched her hand and her cheek with my lips at parting. She stirred in her sleep and murmured my name, but without waking. I lingered for an instant at the door to look at her again. 'God bless and keep you, my darling!' I whispered, and left her.

Marian was at the stairhead waiting for me. She had a folded slip of paper in her hand.

'The landlord's son has brought this for you,' she said. 'He has got a cab at the door – he says you ordered him to keep it at your disposal.'

'Quite right, Marian. I want the cab – I am going out again.'

I descended the stairs as I spoke, and looked into the sitting-room to read the slip of paper by the light on the table. It contained these two sentences in Pesca's handwriting –

'Your letter is received. If I don't see you before the time you mention, I will break the seal when the clock strikes.'

I placed the paper in my pocket-book, and made for the door. Marian met me on the threshold, and pushed me back into the room, where the candle-light fell full on my face. She held me by both hands, and her eyes fastened searchingly on mine.

'I see!' she said, in a low eager whisper. 'You are trying the last chance tonight.'

'Yes, the last chance and the best,' I whispered back.

'Not alone! Oh, Walter, for God's sake, not alone! Let me go with you. Don't refuse me because I'm only a woman. I must go! I will go! I'll wait outside in the cab!'

It was my turn now to hold *her*. She tried to break away from me and get down first to the door.

'If you want to help me,' I said, 'stop here and sleep in my wife's room tonight. Only let me go away with my mind easy about Laura, and I answer for everything else. Come, Marian, give me a kiss, and show that you have the courage to wait till I come back.'

I dared not allow her time to say a word more. She tried to hold me again. I unclasped her hands, and was out of the room in a moment. The boy below heard me on the stairs, and opened the hall-door. I jumped into the cab before the driver could get off the box. 'Forest Road, St John's Wood,' I called to him through the front window. 'Double fare if you get there in a quarter of an hour.' 'I'll do it, sir.' I looked at my watch. Eleven o'clock. Not a minute to lose.

The rapid motion of the cab, the sense that every instant now was bringing me nearer to the Count, the conviction that I was embarked at last, without let or hindrance, on my hazardous enterprise, heated me into such a fever of excitement that I shouted to the man to go faster and faster.

As we left the streets, and crossed St John's Wood Road, my impatience so completely overpowered me that I stood up in the cab and stretched my head out of the window, to see the end of the journey before we reached it. Just as a church clock in the distance struck the quarter past, we turned into the Forest Road. I stopped the driver a little away from the Count's house, paid and dismissed him, and walked on to the door.

As I approached the garden gate, I saw another person advancing towards it also from the direction opposite to mine. We met under the gas lamp in the road, and looked at each other. I instantly recognised the light-haired foreigner with the scar on his cheek, and I thought he recognised me. He said nothing, and instead of stopping at the house, as I did, he slowly walked on. Was he in the Forest Road by accident? Or had he followed the Count home from the Opera?

I did not pursue those questions. After waiting a little till the foreigner had slowly passed out of sight, I rang the gate bell. It was then twenty minutes past eleven – late enough to make it quite easy for the Count to get rid of me by the excuse that he was in bed.

The only way of providing against this contingency was to send in my name without asking any preliminary questions, and to let him know, at the same time, that I had a serious motive for wishing to see him at that late hour. Accordingly, while I was waiting, I took out my card and wrote under my name 'On important business.' The maid-servant answered the door while I was writing the last word in pencil, and asked me distrustfully what I 'pleased to want.'

'Be so good as to take that to your master,' I replied, giving her the card.

I saw, by the girl's hesitation of manner, that if I had asked for the Count in the first instance she would only have followed her instructions by telling me he was not at home. She was staggered by the confidence with which I gave her the card. After staring at me, in great perturbation, she went back into the house with my message, closing the door, and leaving me to wait in the garden.

In a minute or so she reappeared. 'Her master's compliments, and would I be so obliging as to say what my business was?' 'Take my compliments back,' I replied, 'and say that the business cannot be mentioned to any one but your master.' She left me again, again returned, and this time asked me to walk in.

I followed her at once. In another moment I was inside the Count's house.

VII

There was no lamp in the hall, but by the dim light of the kitchen candle, which the girl had brought upstairs with her, I saw an elderly lady steal noiselessly out of a back room on the ground floor. She cast one viperish look at me as I entered the hall, but said nothing, and went slowly upstairs without returning my bow. My familiarity with Marian's journal sufficiently assured me that the elderly lady was Madame Fosco.

The servant led me to the room which the Countess had just left. I entered it, and found myself face to face with the Count.

He was still in his evening dress, except his coat, which he had thrown across a chair. His shirt-sleeves were turned up at the wrists, but no higher. A carpet-bag was on one side of him, and a box on the other. Books, papers, and articles of wearing apparel were scattered about the room. On a table, at one side of the door, stood the cage, so well known to me by description, which contained his white mice. The canaries and the cockatoo were probably in some other room. He was seated before the box, packing it, when I went in, and rose with some papers in his hand to receive me. His face still betrayed plain traces of the shock that had overwhelmed him at the Opera. His fat cheeks hung loose, his cold grey eyes were furtively vigilant, his voice, look, and manner were all sharply suspicious alike, as he advanced a step to meet me, and requested, with distant civility, that I would take a chair.

'You come here on business, sir?' he said. 'I am at a loss to know what that business can possibly be.'

The unconcealed curiosity, with which he looked hard in my face while he spoke, convinced me that I had passed unnoticed by him at the Opera. He had seen Pesca first, and from that moment till he left the theatre he had evidently seen nothing else. My name would necessarily suggest to him that I had not come into his house with other than a hostile purpose towards himself, but he appeared to be utterly ignorant thus far of the real nature of my errand.

'I am fortunate in finding you here tonight,' I said. 'You seem to be on the point of taking a journey?'

'Is your business connected with my journey?'

'In some degree.'

'In what degree? Do you know where I am going to?'

'No. I only know why you are leaving London.'

He slipped by me with the quickness of thought, locked the door, and put the key in his pocket.

'You and I, Mr Hartright, are excellently well acquainted with one another by reputation,' he said. 'Did it, by any chance, occur to you when you came to this house that I was not the sort of man you could trifle with?'

'It did occur to me,' I replied. 'And I have not come to trifle with you. I am here on a matter of life and death, and if that door which you have locked was open at this moment, nothing you could say or do would induce me to pass through it.'

I walked farther into the room, and stood opposite to him on the rug before the fireplace. He drew a chair in front of the door, and sat down on it, with his left arm resting on the table. The cage with the white mice was close to him, and the little creatures scampered out of their sleeping-place as his heavy arm shook the table, and peered at him through the gaps in the smartly painted wires.

'On a matter of life and death,' he repeated to himself. 'Those words are more serious, perhaps, than you think. What do you mean?'

'What I say.'

The perspiration broke out thickly on his broad forehead. His left hand stole over the edge of the table. There was a drawer in it, with a lock, and the key was in the lock. His finger and thumb closed over the key, but did not turn it.

'So you know why I am leaving London?' he went on. 'Tell me the reason, if you please.' He turned the key, and unlocked the drawer as he spoke.

'I can do better than that,' I replied. 'I can *show* you the reason, if you like.'

'How can you show it?'

'You have got your coat off,' I said. 'Roll up the shirt-sleeve on your left arm, and you will see it there.'

The same livid leaden change passed over his face which I had seen pass over it at the theatre. The deadly glitter in his eyes shone steady and straight into mine. He said nothing. But his left hand slowly opened the table-drawer, and softly slipped into it. The harsh grating noise of something heavy that he was moving unseen to me sounded for a moment, then ceased. The silence that followed was so intense that the faint ticking nibble of the white mice at their wires was distinctly audible where I stood.

My life hung by a thread, and I knew it. At that final moment I thought with *his* mind, I felt with *his* fingers – I was as certain as if I had seen it of what he kept hidden from me in the drawer.

'Wait a little,' I said. 'You have got the door locked – you see I don't move – you see my hands are empty. Wait a little. I have something more to say.'

'You have said enough,' he replied, with a sudden composure so unnatural and so ghastly that it tried my nerves as no outbreak of violence could have tried them. 'I want one moment for my own thoughts, if you please. Do you guess what I am thinking about?'

'Perhaps I do.'

'I am thinking,' he remarked quietly, 'whether I shall add to the disorder in this room by scattering your brains about the fireplace.'

If I had moved at that moment, I saw in his face that he would have done it.

'I advise you to read two lines of writing which I have about me,' I rejoined, 'before you finally decide that question.'

The proposal appeared to excite his curiosity. He nodded his head. I took Pesca's acknowledgment of the receipt of my letter out of my pocket-book, handed it to him at arm's length, and returned to my former position in front of the fireplace.

He read the lines aloud: 'Your letter is received. If I don't hear from you before the time you mention, I will break the seal when the clock strikes.'

Another man in his position would have needed some explanation of those words – the Count felt no such necessity. One reading of the note showed him the precaution that I had taken as plainly as if he had been present at the time when I adopted it. The expression of his face changed on the instant, and his hand came out of the drawer empty.

'I don't lock up my drawer, Mr Hartright,' he said, 'and I don't say that I may not scatter your brains about the fireplace yet. But I am a just man even to my enemy, and I will acknowledge beforehand that they are cleverer brains than I thought them. Come to the point, sir! You want something of me?'

'I do, and I mean to have it.'

'On conditions?'

'On no conditions.'

His hand dropped into the drawer again.

'Bah! we are travelling in a circle,' he said, 'and those clever brains of yours are in danger again. Your tone is deplorably imprudent, sir – moderate it on the spot! The risk of shooting you on the place where you stand is less to me than the risk of letting you out of this house, except on conditions that I dictate and approve. You have not got my lamented friend to deal with now – you are face to face with Fosco! If the lives of twenty Mr Hartrights were the stepping-stones to my safety, over all those stones I would go, sustained by my sublime indifference, self-balanced by my impenetrable calm. Respect me, if you love your own life! I summon you to answer three questions before you open your lips again. Hear them – they are necessary to this interview. Answer them – they are necessary to *me*.' He held up one finger of his right hand. 'First question!' he said. 'You come here possessed of information which may be true or may be false – where did you get it?'

'I decline to tell you.'

'No matter – I shall find out. If that information is true – mind I say, with the whole force of my resolution, if – you are making your market of it here by treachery of your own or by treachery of some other man. I note that circumstance for future use in my memory, which forgets nothing, and proceed.' He held up another finger. 'Second question! Those lines you invited me to read are without signature. Who wrote them?'

'A man whom I have every reason to depend on, and whom you have every reason to fear.'

My answer reached him to some purpose. His left hand trembled audibly in the drawer.

'How long do you give me,' he asked, putting his third question in a quieter tone, 'before the clock strikes and the seal is broken?'

'Time enough for you to come to my terms,' I replied.

'Give me a plainer answer, Mr Hartright. What hour is the clock to strike?'

'Nine, tomorrow morning.'

'Nine, tomorrow morning? Yes, yes – your trap is laid for me before I can get my passport regulated and leave London. It is not earlier, I suppose? We will see about that presently – I can keep you hostage here, and bargain with you to send for your letter before I let you go. In the meantime, be so good next as to mention your terms.'

'You shall hear them. They are simple, and soon stated. You know whose interests I represent in coming here?'

He smiled with the most supreme composure, and carelessly waved his right hand.

'I consent to hazard a guess,' he said jeeringly. 'A lady's interests, of course!'

'My Wife's interests.'

He looked at me with the first honest expression that had crossed his face in my presence – an expression of blank amazement. I could see that I sank in his estimation as a dangerous man from that moment. He shut up the drawer at once, folded his arms over his breast, and listened to me with a smile of satirical attention.

'You are well enough aware,' I went on, 'of the course which my inquiries have taken for many months past, to know that any attempted denial of plain facts will be quite useless in my presence. You are guilty of an infamous conspiracy! And the gain of a fortune of ten thousand pounds was your motive for it.'

He said nothing. But his face became overclouded suddenly by a lowering anxiety.

'Keep your gain,' I said. (His face lightened again immediately, and his eyes opened on me in wider and wider astonishment.) 'I am not here to disgrace myself by bargaining for money which has passed through your hands, and which has been the price of a vile crime.

'Gently, Mr Hartright. Your moral clap-traps have an excellent effect in England – keep them for yourself and your own countrymen, if you please. The ten thousand pounds was a legacy left to my excellent wife by the late Mr Fairlie. Place the affair on those grounds, and I will discuss it if you like. To a man of my sentiments, however, the subject is deplorably sordid.

I prefer to pass it over. I invite you to resume the discussion of your terms. What do you demand?'

'In the first place, I demand a full confession of the conspiracy, written and signed in my presence by yourself.'

He raised his finger again. 'One!' he said, checking me off with the steady attention of a practical man.

'In the second place, I demand a plain proof, which does not depend on your personal asseveration, of the date at which my wife left Blackwater Park and travelled to London.'

'So! so! you can lay your finger, I see, on the weak place,' he remarked composedly. 'Any more?'

'At present, no more.'

'Good! you have mentioned your terms, now listen to mine. The responsibility to myself of admitting what you are pleased to call the "conspiracy" is less, perhaps, upon the whole, than the responsibility of laying you dead on that hearthrug. Let us say that I meet your proposal – on my own conditions. The statement you demand of me shall be written, and the plain proof shall be produced. You call a letter from my late lamented friend informing me of the day and hour of his wife's arrival in London, written, signed, and dated by himself, a proof, I suppose? I can give you this. I can also send you to the man of whom I hired the carriage to fetch my visitor from the railway, on the day when she arrived – his order-book may help you to your date, even if his coachman who drove me proves to be of no use. These things I can do, and will do, on conditions. I recite them. First condition! Madame Fosco and I leave this house when and how we please, without interference of any kind on your part. Second condition! You wait here, in company with me, to see my agent, who is coming at seven o'clock in the morning to regulate my affairs. You give my agent a written order to the man who has got your sealed letter to resign his possession of it. You wait here till my agent places that letter unopened in my hands, and you then allow me one clear half-hour to leave the house – after which you resume your own freedom of action and go where you please. Third condition! You give me the satisfaction of a gentleman for your intrusion into my private affairs, and for the language you have allowed yourself to use to me at this conference. The time and place, abroad, to be fixed in a letter from my hand when I am safe on the Continent, and that letter to contain a strip of paper measuring accurately the length of my sword. Those are my terms. Inform me if you accept them – Yes or No.'

The extraordinary mixture of prompt decision, far-sighted cunning, and mountebank bravado in this speech, staggered me for a moment – and only for a moment. The one question to consider was, whether I was justified or not in possessing myself of the means of establishing Laura's identity at the cost of allowing the scoundrel who had robbed her of it to escape me with impunity. I knew that the motive of securing the just recognition of my wife in the birthplace from which she had been driven out as an impostor, and of publicly erasing the lie that still profaned her mother's tombstone, was far purer, in its freedom from all taint of evil passion, than the vindictive motive which had mingled itself with my purpose from the first. And yet I cannot honestly say that my own moral convictions were strong enough to decide the struggle in me by themselves. They were helped by my remembrance of Sir Percival's death. How awfully, at the last moment, had the working of the retribution *there* been snatched from my feeble hands! What right had I to decide, in my poor mortal ignorance of the future, that this man, too, must escape with impunity because he escaped *me*? I thought of these things – perhaps with the superstition inherent in my nature, perhaps with a sense worthier of me than superstition. It was hard, when I had fastened my hold on him at last, to loosen it again of my own accord – but I forced myself to make the sacrifice. In plainer words, I determined to be guided by the one higher motive of which I was certain, the motive of serving the cause of Laura and the cause of Truth.

'I accept your conditions,' I said. 'With one reservation on my part.'

'What reservation may that be?' he asked.

'It refers to the sealed letter,' I answered. 'I require you to destroy it unopened in my presence as soon as it is placed in your hands.'

My object in making this stipulation was simply to prevent him from carrying away written evidence of the nature of my communication with Pesca. The *fact* of my communication he would necessarily discover, when I gave the address to his agent in the morning. But he could make no use of it on his own unsupported testimony – even if he really ventured to try the experiment – which need excite in me the slightest apprehension on Pesca's account.

'I grant your reservation,' he replied, after considering the question gravely for a minute or two. 'It is not worth dispute – the letter shall be destroyed when it comes into my hands.'

He rose, as he spoke, from the chair in which he had been sitting opposite to me up to this time. With one effort he appeared to free his mind from the whole pressure on it of the interview between us thus far. 'Ouf!' he cried, stretching his arms luxuriously, 'the skirmish was hot while it lasted. Take a seat, Mr Hartright. We meet as mortal enemies hereafter – let us, like gallant gentlemen, exchange polite attentions in the meantime. Permit me to take the liberty of calling for my wife.'

He unlocked and opened the door. 'Eleanor!' he called out in his deep voice. The lady of the viperish face came in 'Madame Fosco – Mr Hartright,' said the Count, introducing us with easy dignity. 'My angel,' he went on, addressing his wife, 'will your labours of packing up allow you time to make me some nice strong coffee? I have writing business to transact with Mr Hartright – and I require the full possession of my intelligence to do justice to myself.'

Madame Fosco bowed her head twice – once sternly to me, once submissively to her husband, and glided out of the room.

The Count walked to a writing-table near the window, opened his desk, and took from it several quires of paper and a bundle of quill pens. He scattered the pens about the table, so that they might lie ready in all directions to be taken up when wanted, and then cut the paper into a heap of narrow slips, of the form used by professional writers for the press. 'I shall make this a remarkable document,' he said, looking at me over his shoulder. 'Habits of literary composition are perfectly familiar to me. One of the rarest of all the intellectual accomplishments that a man can possess is the grand faculty of arranging his ideas. Immense privilege! I possess it. Do you?'

He marched backwards and forwards in the room, until the coffee appeared, humming to himself, and marking the places at which obstacles occurred in the arrangement of his ideas, by striking his forehead from time to time with the palm of his hand. The enormous audacity with which he seized on the situation in which I placed him, and made it the pedestal on which his vanity mounted for the one cherished purpose of self-display, mastered my astonishment by main force. Sincerely as I loathed the man, the prodigious strength of his character, even in its most trivial aspects, impressed me in spite of myself.

The coffee was brought in by Madame Fosco. He kissed her hand in grateful acknowledgment, and escorted her to the door; returned, poured out a cup of coffee for himself, and took it to the writing-table.

'May I offer you some coffee, Mr Hartright?' he said, before he sat down. I declined.

'What! you think I shall poison you?' he said gaily. 'The English intellect is sound, so far as it goes,' he continued, seating himself at the table; 'but it has one grave defect – it is always cautious in the wrong place.'

He dipped his pen in the ink, placed the first slip of paper before him with a thump of his hand on the desk, cleared his throat, and began. He wrote with great noise and rapidity, in so large and bold a hand, and with such wide spaces between the lines, that he reached the bottom of the slip in not more than two minutes certainly from the time when he started at the top. Each slip as he finished it was paged, and tossed over his shoulder out of his way on the floor. When his first pen was worn out, *that* went over his shoulder too, and he pounced on a second from the supply scattered about the table. Slip after slip, by dozens, by fifties, by hundreds, flew over his shoulders on either side of him till he had snowed himself up in paper all round his chair. Hour after hour passed – and there I sat watching, there he sat writing. He never stopped, except to sip his coffee, and when that was exhausted, to smack his forehead from time to time. One o'clock struck, two, three, four – and still the slips flew about all round him; still the untiring pen scraped its way ceaselessly from top to bottom of the page, still the white chaos of paper rose higher and higher all round his chair. At four o'clock I heard a sudden splutter of the pen, indicative of the flourish with which he signed his name. 'Bravo!' he cried, springing to his feet with the activity of a young man, and looking me straight in the face with a smile of superb triumph.

'Done, Mr Hartright!' he announced with a self-renovating thump of his fist on his broad breast. 'Done, to my own profound satisfaction – to *your* profound astonishment, when you read what I have written. The subject is exhausted: the man – Fosco – is not. I proceed to the arrangement of my slips – to the revision of my slips – to the reading of my slips – addressed emphatically to your private ear. Four o'clock has just struck. Good! Arrangement, revision, reading, from four to five. Short snooze of restoration for myself from five to six. Final preparations from six to seven. Affair of agent and sealed letter from seven to eight. At eight, en route. Behold the programme!'

He sat down cross-legged on the floor among his papers, strung them together with a bodkin and a piece of string – revised them, wrote all the titles and honours by which he was personally distinguished at the head of the first page, and then read the manuscript to me with loud theatrical emphasis and profuse theatrical gesticulation. The reader will have an opportunity, ere long, of forming his own opinion of the document. It will be sufficient to mention here that it answered my purpose.

He next wrote me the address of the person from whom he had hired the fly, and handed me Sir Percival's letter. It was dated from Hampshire on the 25th of July, and it announced the journey of 'Lady Glyde' to London on the 26th. Thus, on the very day (the 25th) when the doctor's certificate declared that she had died in St John's Wood, she was alive, by Sir Percival's own showing, at Blackwater – and, on the day after, she was to take a journey! When the proof of that journey was obtained from the flyman, the evidence would be complete.

'A quarter-past five,' said the Count, looking at his watch. 'Time for my restorative snooze. I personally resemble Napoleon the Great, as you may have remarked, Mr Hartright – I also resemble that immortal man in my power of commanding sleep at will. Excuse me one moment. I will summon

Madame Fosco, to keep you from feeling dull.'

Knowing as well as he did, that he was summoning Madame Fosco to ensure my not leaving the house while he was asleep, I made no reply, and occupied myself in tying up the papers which he had placed in my possession.

The lady came in, cool, pale, and venomous as ever. 'Amuse Mr Hartright, my angel,' said the Count. He placed a chair for her, kissed her hand for the second time, withdrew to a sofa, and, in three minutes, was as peacefully and happily asleep as the most virtuous man in existence.

Madame Fosco took a book from the table, sat down, and looked at me, with the steady vindictive malice of a woman who never forgot and never forgave.

'I have been listening to your conversation with my husband,' she said. 'If I had been in *his* place – I would have laid you dead on the hearthrug.'

With those words she opened her book, and never looked at me or spoke to me from that time till the time when her husband woke.

He opened his eyes and rose from the sofa, accurately to an hour from the time when he had gone to sleep.

'I feel infinitely refreshed,' he remarked. 'Eleanor, my good wife, are you all ready upstairs? That is well. My little packing here can be completed in ten minutes – my travelling-dress assumed in ten minutes more. What remains before the agent comes?' He looked about the room, and noticed the cage with his white mice in it. 'Ah!' he cried piteously, 'a last laceration of my sympathies still remains. My innocent pets! my little cherished children! what am I to do with them? For the present we are settled nowhere; for the present we travel incessantly – the less baggage we carry the better for ourselves. My cockatoo, my canaries, and my little mice – who will cherish them when their good Papa is gone?'

He walked about the room deep in thought. He had not been at all troubled about writing his confession, but he was visibly perplexed and distressed about the far more important question of the disposal of his pets. After long consideration he suddenly sat down again at the writing-table.

'An idea!' he exclaimed. 'I will offer my canaries and my cockatoo to this vast Metropolis – my agent shall present them in my name to the Zoological Gardens of London. The Document that describes them shall be drawn out on the spot.'

He began to write, repeating the words as they flowed from his pen.

'Number one. Cockatoo of transcendent plumage: attraction, of himself, to all visitors of taste. Number two. Canaries of unrivalled vivacity and intelligence: worthy of the garden of Eden, worthy also of the garden in the Regent's Park. Homage to British Zoology. Offered by Fosco.'

The pen spluttered again, and the flourish was attached to his signature.

'Count! you have not included the mice,' said Madame Fosco

He left the table, took her hand, and placed it on his heart.

'All human resolution, Eleanor,' he said solemnly, 'has its limits. *My* limits are inscribed on that Document. I cannot part with my white mice. Bear with me, my angel, and remove them to their travelling cage upstairs.'

'Admirable tenderness!' said Madame Fosco, admiring her husband, with a last viperish look in my direction. She took up the cage carefully, and left the room.

The Count looked at his watch. In spite of his resolute assumption of composure, he was getting anxious for the agent's arrival. The candles had long since been extinguished, and the sunlight of the new morning poured into the room. It was not till five minutes past seven that the gate bell rang, and the agent made his appearance. He was a foreigner with a dark beard.

'Mr Hartright – Monsieur Rubelle,' said the Count, introducing us. He took the agent (a foreign spy, in every line of his face, if ever there was one yet) into a corner of the room, whispered some directions to him, and then left us together. 'Monsieur Rubelle,' as soon as we were alone, suggested with great politeness that I should favour him with his instructions. I wrote two lines to Pesca, authorising him to deliver my sealed letter 'to the bearer,' directed the note, and handed it to Monsieur Rubelle.

The agent waited with me till his employer returned, equipped in travelling costume. The Count examined the address of my letter before he dismissed the agent. 'I thought so!' he said, turning on me with a dark look, and altering again in his manner from that moment.

He completed his packing, and then sat consulting a travelling map, making entries in his pocket-book, and looking every now and then impatiently at his watch. Not another word, addressed to myself, passed his lips. The near approach of the hour for his departure, and the proof he had seen of the communication established between Pesca and myself, had plainly recalled his whole attention to the measures that were necessary for securing his escape.

A little before eight o'clock, Monsieur Rubelle came back with my unopened letter in his hand. The Count looked carefully at the superscription and the seal, lit a candle, and burnt the letter. 'I perform my promise,' he said, 'but this matter, Mr Hartright, shall not end here.'

The agent had kept at the door the cab in which he had returned. He and the maid-servant now busied themselves in removing the luggage. Madame Fosco came downstairs, thickly veiled, with the travelling cage of the white mice in her hand. She neither spoke to me nor looked towards me. Her husband escorted her to the cab. 'Follow me as far as the passage,' he whispered in my ear; 'I may want to speak to you at the last moment.'

I went out to the door, the agent standing below me in the front garden. The Count came back alone, and drew me a few steps inside the passage.

'Remember the Third condition!' he whispered. 'You shall hear from me, Mr Hartright – I may claim from you the satisfaction of a gentleman sooner than you think for.' He caught my hand before I was aware of him, and wrung it hard – then turned to the door, stopped, and came back to me again.

'One word more,' he said confidentially. 'When I last saw Miss Halcombe, she looked thin and ill. I am anxious about that admirable woman. Take care of her, sir! With my hand on my heart, I solemnly implore you, take care of Miss Halcombe!'

Those were the last words he said to me before he squeezed his huge body into the cab and drove off.

The agent and I waited at the door a few moments looking after him. While we were standing together, a second cab appeared from a turning a little way down the road. It followed the direction previously taken by the Count's cab, and as it passed the house and the open garden gate, a person inside looked at us out of the window. The stranger at the Opera again! – the foreigner with a scar on his left cheek.

'You wait here with me, sir, for half an hour more!' said Monsieur Rubelle.

'I do.'

We returned to the sitting-room. I was in no humour to speak to the agent, or to allow him to speak to me. I took out the papers which the Count had placed in my hands, and read the terrible story of the conspiracy told by the man who had planned and perpetrated it.

THE STORY CONTINUED BY ISIDOR OTTAVIO BALDASSARE FOSCO

(Count of the Holy Roman Empire, Knight Grand Cross of the Order of the Brazen Crown, Perpetual Arch-Master of the Rosicrucian Masons of Mesopotamia; Attached (in Honorary Capacities) to Societies Musical, Societies Medical, Societies Philosophical, and Societies General Benevolent, throughout Europe; etc. etc. etc.)

THE COUNT'S NARRATIVE

In the summer of eighteen hundred and fifty I arrived in England, charged with a delicate political mission from abroad. Confidential persons were semi-officially connected with me, whose exertions I was authorised to direct, Monsieur and Madame Rubelle being among the number. Some weeks of spare time were at my disposal, before I entered on my functions by establishing myself in the suburbs of London. Curiosity may stop here to ask for some explanation of those functions on my part. I entirely sympathise with the request. I also regret that diplomatic reserve forbids me to comply with it.

I arranged to pass the preliminary period of repose, to which I have just referred, in the superb mansion of my late lamented friend, Sir Percival Glyde. *He* arrived from the Continent with his wife. I arrived from the Continent with *mine*. England is the land of domestic happiness – how appropriately we entered it under these domestic circumstances!

The bond of friendship which united Percival and myself was strengthened, on this occasion, by a touching similarity in the pecuniary position on his side and on mine. We both wanted money. Immense necessity! Universal want! Is there a civilised human being who does not feel for us? How insensible must that man be! Or how rich!

I enter into no sordid particulars, in discussing this part of the subject. My mind recoils from them. With a Roman austerity, I show my empty purse and Percival's to the shrinking public gaze. Let us allow the deplorable fact to assert itself, once for all, in that manner, and pass on.

We were received at the mansion by the magnificent creature who is inscribed on my heart as 'Marian,' who is known in the colder atmosphere of society as 'Miss Halcombe.'

Just Heaven! with what inconceivable rapidity I learnt to adore that woman. At sixty, I worshipped her with the volcanic ardour of eighteen. All the gold of my rich nature was poured hopelessly at her feet. My wife – poor angel! – my wife, who adores me, got nothing but the shillings and the pennies. Such is the World, such Man, such Love. What are we (I ask) but puppets in a show-box? Oh, omnipotent Destiny, pull our strings gently! Dance us mercifully off our miserable little stage!

The preceding lines, rightly understood, express an entire system of philosophy. It is mine.

I resume.

The domestic position at the commencement of our residence at Blackwater Park has been drawn with amazing accuracy, with profound mental insight, by the hand of Marian herself. (Pass me the intoxicating familiarity of mentioning this sublime creature by her Christian name.) Accurate knowledge of the contents of her journal – to which I obtained access by clandestine means, unspeakably precious to me in the remembrance – warns my eager pen from topics which this essentially exhaustive woman has already made her own.

The interests – interests, breathless and immense! – with which I am here concerned, begin with the deplorable calamity of Marian's illness.

The situation at this period was emphatically a serious one. Large sums of money, due at a certain time, were wanted by Percival (I say nothing of the modicum equally necessary to myself), and the one source to look to for supplying them was the fortune of his wife, of which not one farthing was at his disposal until her death. Bad so far, and worse still farther on. My lamented friend had private troubles of his own, into which the delicacy of my disinterested attachment to him forbade me from inquiring too curiously. I knew nothing but that a woman, named Anne Catherick, was hidden in the neighbourhood, that she was in communication with Lady Glyde, and that the disclosure of a secret, which would be the certain ruin of Percival, might be the result. He had told me himself that he was a lost man, unless his wife was silenced, and unless Anne Catherick was found. If he was a lost man, what would become of our pecuniary interests? Courageous as I am by nature, I absolutely trembled at the idea!

The whole force of my intelligence was now directed to the finding of Anne Catherick. Our money affairs, important as they were, admitted of delay – but the necessity of discovering the woman admitted of none. I only knew her by description, as presenting an extraordinary personal resemblance to Lady Glyde. The statement of this curious fact – intended merely to assist me in identifying the person of whom we were in search – when coupled with the additional information that Anne Catherick had escaped from a mad-house, started the first immense conception in my mind, which subsequently led to such amazing results. That conception involved nothing less than the complete transformation of two separate identities. Lady Glyde and Anne Catherick were to change names, places, and destinies, the one with the other – the prodigious consequences contemplated by the change being the gain of thirty thousand pounds, and the eternal preservation of Sir Percival's secret.

My instincts (which seldom err) suggested to me, on reviewing the circumstances, that our invisible Anne would, sooner or later, return to the boathouse at the Blackwater lake. There I posted myself, previously mentioning to Mrs Michelson, the housekeeper, that I might be found when wanted, immersed in study, in that solitary place. It is my rule never to make unnecessary mysteries, and never to set people suspecting me for want of a little seasonable candour on my part. Mrs Michelson believed in me from first to last. This ladylike person (widow of a Protestant priest) overflowed with faith. Touched by such superfluity of simple confidence in a woman of her mature years, I opened the ample reservoirs of my nature and absorbed it all.

I was rewarded for posting myself sentinel at the lake by the appearance – not of Anne Catherick herself, but of the person in charge of her. This individual also overflowed with simple faith, which I absorbed in myself, as in the case already mentioned. I leave her to describe the circumstances (if she has not done so already) under which she introduced me to the object of her maternal care. When I first saw Anne Catherick she was asleep. I was electrified by the likeness between this unhappy woman and Lady Glyde. The details of the grand scheme which had suggested themselves in outline only, up to that period, occurred to me, in all their masterly combination, at the sight of the sleeping face. At the same time, my heart, always accessible to tender influences, dissolved in tears at the spectacle of suffering before me. I instantly set myself to impart relief. In other words, I provided the necessary stimulant for strengthening Anne Catherick to perform the journey to London.

At this point I enter a necessary protest, and correct a lamentable error.

The best years of my life have been passed in the ardent study of medical and chemical science. Chemistry especially has always had irresistible attractions for me from the enormous, the illimitable power which the knowledge of it confers. Chemists – I assert it emphatically – might sway, if they pleased, the destinies of humanity. Let me explain this before I go further.

Mind, they say, rules the world. But what rules the mind? The body (follow me closely here) lies at the mercy of the most omnipotent of all potentates – the Chemist. Give me – Fosco – chemistry; and when Shakespeare has conceived Hamlet, and sits down to execute the conception – with a few grains of powder dropped into his daily food, I will reduce his mind, by the action of his body, till his pen pours out the most abject drivel that has ever degraded paper. Under similar circumstances, revive me the illustrious Newton. I guarantee that when he sees the apple fall he shall *eat it*, instead of discovering the principle of gravitation. Nero's dinner shall transform Nero into the mildest of men before he has done digesting it, and the morning draught of Alexander the Great shall make Alexander run for his life at the first sight of the enemy the same afternoon. On my sacred word of honour it is lucky for Society that modern chemists are, by incomprehensible good fortune, the most harmless of mankind. The mass are worthy fathers of families, who keep shops. The few are philosophers besotted with admiration for the sound of their own lecturing voices, visionaries who waste their lives on fantastic impossibilities, or quacks whose ambition soars no higher than our corns. Thus Society escapes, and the illimitable power of Chemistry remains the slave of the most superficial and the most insignificant ends.

Why this outburst? Why this withering eloquence?

Because my conduct has been misrepresented, because my motives have been misunderstood. It has been assumed that I used my vast chemical resources against Anne Catherick, and that I would have used them if I could against the magnificent Marian herself. Odious insinuations both! All my interests were concerned (as will be seen presently) in the preservation of Anne Catherick's life. All my anxieties were concentrated on Marian's rescue from the hands of the licensed imbecile who attended her, and who found my advice confirmed from first to last by the physician from London. On two occasions only – both equally harmless to the individual on whom I practised – did I summon to myself the assistance of chemical knowledge. On the first of the two, after following Marian to the inn at Blackwater (studying, behind a convenient waggon which hid me from her, the poetry of motion, as embodied in her walk), I availed myself of the services of my invaluable wife, to copy one and to intercept the other of two letters which my adored enemy had entrusted to a discarded maid. In this case, the letters being in the bosom of the girl's dress, Madame Fosco could only open them, read them, perform her instructions, seal them, and put them back again by scientific assistance – which assistance I rendered in a half-ounce bottle. The second occasion, when the same means were employed, was the occasion (to which I shall soon refer) of Lady Glyde's arrival in London. Never at any other time was I indebted to my Art as distinguished from myself. To all other emergencies and complications my natural capacity for grappling, single-handed, with circumstances, was invariably equal. I affirm the all-pervading intelligence of that capacity. At the expense of the Chemist I vindicate the Man.

Respect this outburst of generous indignation. It has inexpressibly relieved me. *En route!* Let us proceed.

Having suggested to Mrs Clement (or Clements, I am not sure which) that the best method of keeping Anne out of Percival's reach was to remove her to London – having found that my proposal was eagerly received, and having appointed a day to meet the travellers at the station and to see them leave it, I was at liberty to return to the house and to confront the difficulties which still remained to be met.

My first proceeding was to avail myself of the sublime devotion of my wife. I had arranged with Mrs Clements that she should communicate her London address, in Anne's interests, to Lady Glyde. But this was not enough. Designing persons in my absence might shake the simple confidence of Mrs Clements, and she might not write after all. Who could I find capable of travelling to London by the train she travelled by, and of privately seeing her home? I asked myself this question. The conjugal part of me immediately answered – Madame Fosco.

After deciding on my wife's mission to London, I arranged that the journey should serve a double purpose. A nurse for the suffering Marian, equally devoted to the patient and to myself, was a necessity of my position. One of the most eminently confidential and capable women in existence was by good fortune at my disposal. I refer to that respectable matron, Madame Rubelle, to whom I addressed a letter, at her residence in London, by the hands of my wife.

On the appointed day Mrs Clements and Anne Catherick met me at the station. I politely saw them off, I politely saw Madame Fosco off by the same train. The last thing at night my wife returned to Blackwater, having followed her instructions with the most unimpeachable accuracy. She was accompanied by Madame Rubelle, and she brought me the London address of Mrs Clements. After-events proved this last precaution to have been unnecessary. Mrs Clements punctually informed Lady Glyde of her place of abode. With a wary eye on future emergencies, I kept the letter.

The same day I had a brief interview with the doctor, at which I protested, in the sacred interests of humanity, against his treatment of Marian's case. He was insolent, as all ignorant people are. I showed no resentment, I deferred quarrelling with him till it was necessary to quarrel to some purpose.

My next proceeding was to leave Blackwater myself. I had my London residence to take in anticipation of coming events. I had also a little business of the domestic sort to transact with Mr Frederick Fairlie. I found the house I wanted in St John's Wood. I found Mr Fairlie at Limmeridge, Cumberland.

My own private familiarity with the nature of Marian's correspondence had previously informed me that she had written to Mr Fairlie, proposing, as a relief to Lady Glyde's matrimonial embarrassments, to take her on a visit to her uncle in Cumberland. This letter I had wisely allowed to reach its destination, feeling at the time that it could do no harm, and might do good. I now presented myself before Mr Fairlie to support Marian's own proposal – with certain modifications which, happily for the success of my plans, were rendered really inevitable by her illness. It was necessary that Lady Glyde should leave Blackwater alone, by her uncle's invitation, and that she should rest a night on the journey at her aunt's house (the house I had in St John's Wood) by her uncle's express advice. To achieve these results, and to secure a note of invitation which could be shown to Lady Glyde, were the objects of my visit to Mr Fairlie. When I have mentioned that this gentleman was equally feeble in mind and body, and that I let loose the whole force of my character on him, I have said enough. I came, saw, and conquered Fairlie.

On my return to Blackwater Park (with the letter of invitation) I found that the doctor's imbecile treatment of Marian's case had led to the most alarming results. The fever had turned to typhus. Lady Glyde, on the day of my return, tried to force herself into the room to nurse her sister. She and I had no affinities of sympathy – she had committed the unpardonable outrage on my sensibilities of calling me a spy – she was a stumbling-block in my way and in Percival's – but, for all that, my magnanimity forbade me to put her in danger of infection with my own hand. At the same time I offered no hindrance to her putting herself in danger. If she had succeeded in doing so, the intricate knot which I was slowly and patiently operating on might perhaps have been cut by circumstances. As it was, the doctor interfered and she was kept out of the room.

I had myself previously recommended sending for advice to London. This course had been now taken. The physician, on his arrival, confirmed my view of the case. The crisis was serious. But we had hope of our charming patient on the fifth day from the appearance of the typhus. I was only once absent from Blackwater at this time – when I went to London by the morning train to make the final arrangements at my house in St John's Wood, to assure myself by private inquiry that Mrs Clements had not moved, and to settle one or two little preliminary matters with the husband of Madame Rubelle. I returned at night. Five days afterwards the physician pronounced our interesting Marian to be out of all danger, and to be in need of nothing but careful nursing. This was the time I had waited for. Now that medical attendance was no longer indispensable, I played the first move in the game by asserting myself against the doctor. He was one among many witnesses in my way whom it was necessary to remove. A lively altercation between us (in which

Percival, previously instructed by me, refused to interfere) served the purpose in view. I descended on the miserable man in an irresistible avalanche of indignation, and swept him from the house. The servants were the next encumbrances to get rid of. Again I instructed Percival (whose moral courage required perpetual stimulants), and Mrs Michelson was amazed, one day, by hearing from her master that the establishment was to be broken up. We cleared the house of all the servants but one, who was kept for domestic purposes, and whose lumpish stupidity we could trust to make no embarrassing discoveries. When they were gone, nothing remained but to relieve ourselves of Mrs Michelson – a result which was easily achieved by sending this amiable lady to find lodgings for her mistress at the sea-side.

The circumstances were now exactly what they were required to be. Lady Glyde was confined to her room by nervous illness, and the lumpish housemaid (I forget her name) was shut up there at night in attendance on her mistress. Marian, though fast recovering, still kept her bed, with Mrs Rubelle for nurse. No other living creatures but my wife, myself, and Percival were in the house. With all the chances thus in our favour I confronted the next emergency, and played the second move in the game.

The object of the second move was to induce Lady Glyde to leave Blackwater unaccompanied by her sister. Unless we could persuade her that Marian had gone on to Cumberland first, there was no chance of removing her, of her own free will, from the house. To produce this necessary operation in her mind, we concealed our interesting invalid in one of the uninhabited bedrooms at Blackwater. At the dead of night Madame Fosco, Madame Rubelle, and myself (Percival not being cool enough to be trusted) accomplished the concealment. The scene was picturesque, mysterious, dramatic in the highest degree. By my directions the bed had been made, in the morning, on a strong movable framework of wood. We had only to lift the framework gently at the head and foot, and to transport our patient where we pleased, without disturbing herself or her bed. No chemical assistance was needed or used in this case. Our interesting Marian lay in the deep repose of convalescence. We placed the candles and opened the doors beforehand. I, in right of my great personal strength, took the head of the framework – my wife and Madame Rubelle took the foot. I bore my share of that inestimably precious burden with a manly tenderness, with a fatherly care. Where is the modern Rembrandt who could depict our midnight procession? Alas for the Arts! alas for this most pictorial of subjects! The modern Rembrandt is nowhere to be found.

The next morning my wife and I started for London, leaving Marian secluded, in the uninhabited middle of the house, under care of Madame Rubelle, who kindly consented to imprison herself with her patient for two or three days. Before taking our departure I gave Percival Mr Fairlie's letter of invitation to his niece (instructing her to sleep on the journey to Cumberland at her aunt's house), with directions to show it to Lady Glyde on hearing from me. I also obtained from him the address of the Asylum in which Anne Catherick had been confined, and a letter to the proprietor, announcing to that gentleman the return of his runaway patient to medical care.

I had arranged, at my last visit to the metropolis, to have our modest domestic establishment ready to receive us when we arrived in London by the early train. In consequence of this wise precaution, we were enabled that same day to play the third move in the game – the getting possession of Anne Catherick.

Dates are of importance here. I combine in myself the opposite characteristics of a Man of Sentiment and a Man of Business. I have all the dates at my fingers' ends.

On Wednesday, the 24th of July 1850, I sent my wife in a cab to clear Mrs Clements out of the way, in the first place. A supposed message from Lady Glyde in London was sufficient to obtain this result. Mrs Clements was taken away in the cab, and was left in the cab, while my wife (on pretence of purchasing something at a shop) gave her the slip, and returned to receive her expected visitor at our house in St John's Wood. It is hardly necessary to add that the visitor had been described to the servants as 'Lady Glyde.'

In the meanwhile I had followed in another cab, with a note for Anne Catherick, merely mentioning that Lady Glyde intended to keep Mrs Clements to spend the day with her, and that she was to join them under care of the good gentleman waiting outside, who had already saved her from discovery in Hampshire by Sir Percival. The 'good gentleman' sent in this note by a street boy, and paused for results a door or two farther on. At the moment when Anne appeared at the house door and closed it this excellent man had the cab door open ready for her, absorbed her into the vehicle, and drove off.

(Pass me, here, one exclamation in parenthesis. How interesting this is!)

On the way to Forest Road my companion showed no fear. I can be paternal – no man more so – when I please, and I was intensely paternal on this occasion. What titles I had to her confidence! I had compounded the medicine which had done her good – I had warned her of her danger from Sir Percival. Perhaps I trusted too implicitly to these titles – perhaps I underrated the keenness of the lower instincts in persons of weak intellect – it is certain that I neglected to prepare her sufficiently for a disappointment on entering my house. When I took her into the drawing-room – when she saw no one present but Madame Fosco, who was a stranger to her – she exhibited the most violent agitation; if she had scented danger in the air, as a dog scents the presence of some creature unseen, her alarm could not have displayed itself more suddenly and more causelessly. I interposed in vain. The fear from which she was suffering I might have soothed, but the serious heart-disease, under which she laboured, was beyond the reach of all moral palliatives. To my unspeakable horror she was seized with convulsions – a shock to the system, in her condition, which might have laid her dead at any moment at our feet.

The nearest doctor was sent for, and was told that 'Lady Glyde' required his immediate services. To my infinite relief, he was a capable man. I represented my visitor to him as a person of weak intellect, and subject to delusions, and I arranged that no nurse but my wife should watch in the sick-room. The unhappy woman was too ill, however, to cause any anxiety about what she might say. The one dread which now oppressed me was the dread that the false Lady Glyde might die before the true Lady Glyde arrived in London.

I had written a note in the morning to Madame Rubelle, telling her to join me at her husband's house on the evening of Friday the 26th, with another note to Percival, warning him to show his wife her uncle's letter of invitation, to assert that Marian had gone on before her, and to despatch her to town by the midday train, on the 26th, also. On reflection I had felt the necessity, in Anne Catherick's state of health, of precipitating events, and of having Lady Glyde at my disposal earlier than I had originally contemplated. What fresh directions, in the terrible uncertainty of my position, could I now issue? I could do nothing but trust to chance and the doctor. My emotions expressed themselves in pathetic apostrophes, which I was just self-possessed enough to couple, in the hearing of other people, with the name of 'Lady Glyde.' In all other respects Fosco, on that memorable day, was Fosco shrouded in total eclipse.

She passed a bad night, she awoke worn out, but later in the day she revived amazingly. My elastic spirits revived with her. I could receive no answers from Percival and Madame Rubelle till the morning of the next day, the 26th. In anticipation of their following my directions, which, accident apart, I knew they would do, I went to secure a fly to fetch Lady Glyde from the railway, directing it to be at my house on the 26th, at two o'clock. After seeing the order entered in the book, I went on to arrange matters with Monsieur Rubelle. I also procured the services of two gentlemen who could furnish me with the necessary certificates of lunacy. One of them I knew personally – the other was known to Monsieur Rubelle. Both were men whose vigorous minds soared superior to narrow scruples – both were labouring under temporary embarrassments – both believed in *me*.

It was past five o'clock in the afternoon before I returned from the performance of these duties. When I got back Anne Catherick was dead. Dead on the 25th, and Lady Glyde was not to arrive in London till the 26th!

I was stunned. Meditate on that. Fosco stunned!

It was too late to retrace our steps. Before my return the doctor had officiously undertaken to save me all trouble by registering the death, on the date when it happened, with his own hand. My grand scheme, unassailable hitherto, had its weak place now – no efforts on my part could alter the fatal event of the 25th. I turned manfully to the future. Percival's interests and mine being still at stake, nothing was left but to play the game through to the end. I recalled my impenetrable calm – and played it.

On the morning of the 26th Percival's letter reached me, announcing his wife's arrival by the midday train. Madame Rubelle also wrote to say she would follow in the evening. I started in the fly, leaving the false Lady Glyde dead in the house, to receive the true Lady Glyde on her arrival by the railway at three o'clock. Hidden under the seat of the carriage, I carried with me all the clothes Anne Catherick had worn on coming into my house – they were destined to assist the resurrection of the woman who was dead in the person of the woman who was living. What a situation! I suggest it to the rising romance writers of England. I offer it, as totally new, to the worn-out dramatists of France.

Lady Glyde was at the station. There was great crowding and confusion, and more delay than I liked (in case any of her friends had happened to be on the spot), in reclaiming her luggage. Her first questions, as we drove off, implored me to tell her news of her sister. I invented news of the most pacifying kind, assuring her that she was about to see her sister at my house. My house, on this occasion only, was in the neighbourhood of Leicester Square, and was in the occupation of Monsieur Rubelle, who received us in the hall.

I took my visitor upstairs into a back room, the two medical gentlemen being there in waiting on the floor beneath to see the patient, and to give me their certificates. After quieting Lady Glyde by the necessary assurances about her sister, I introduced my friends separately to her presence. They performed the formalities of the occasion briefly, intelligently, conscientiously. I entered the room again as soon as they had left it, and at once precipitated events by a reference of the alarming kind to 'Miss Halcombe's' state of health.

Results followed as I had anticipated. Lady Glyde became frightened, and turned faint. For the second time, and the last, I called Science to my assistance. A medicated glass of water and a medicated bottle of smelling-salts relieved her of all further embarrassment and alarm. Additional applications later in the evening procured her the inestimable blessing of a good night's rest. Madame Rubelle arrived in time to preside at Lady Glyde's toilet. Her own clothes were taken away from her at night, and Anne Catherick's were put on her in the morning, with the strictest regard to propriety, by the matronly hands of the good Rubelle. Throughout the day I kept our patient in a state of partially-suspended consciousness, until the dexterous assistance of my medical friends enabled me to procure the necessary order rather earlier than I had ventured to hope. That evening (the evening of the 27th) Madame Rubelle and I took our revived 'Anne Catherick' to the Asylum. She was received with great surprise, but without suspicion, thanks to the order and certificates, to Percival's letter, to the likeness, to the clothes, and to the patient's own confused mental condition at the time. I returned at once to assist Madame Fosco in the preparations for the burial of the False 'Lady Glyde,' having the clothes and luggage of the true 'Lady Glyde' in my possession. They were afterwards sent to Cumberland by the conveyance which was used for the funeral. I attended the funeral, with becoming dignity, attired in the deepest mourning.

My narrative of these remarkable events, written under equally remarkable circumstances, closes here. The minor precautions which I observed in communicating with Limmeridge House are already known, so is the magnificent success of my enterprise, so are the solid pecuniary results which followed it. I have to assert, with the whole force of my conviction, that the one weak place in my scheme would never have been found out if the one weak place in my heart had not been discovered first. Nothing but my fatal admiration for Marian restrained me from stepping in to my own rescue when she effected her sister's escape. I ran the risk, and trusted in the complete destruction of Lady Glyde's identity. If either Marian or Mr Hartright attempted to assert that identity, they would publicly expose themselves to the imputation of sustaining a rank deception, they would be distrusted and discredited accordingly, and they would therefore be powerless to place my interests or Percival's secret in jeopardy. I committed one error in trusting myself to such a blindfold calculation of chances as this. I committed another when Percival had paid the penalty of his own obstinacy and violence, by granting Lady Glyde a second reprieve from the mad-house, and allowing Mr Hartright a second chance of escaping me. In brief, Fosco, at this serious crisis, was untrue to himself. Deplorable and uncharacteristic fault! Behold the cause, in my heart – behold, in the image of Marian Halcombe, the first and last weakness of Fosco's life!

At the ripe age of sixty, I make this unparalleled confession. Youths! I invoke your sympathy. Maidens! I claim your tears.

A word more, and the attention of the reader (concentrated breathlessly on myself) shall be released.

My own mental insight informs me that three inevitable questions will be asked here by persons of inquiring minds. They shall be stated – they shall be answered.

First question. What is the secret of Madame Fosco's unhesitating devotion of herself to the fulfilment of my boldest wishes, to the furtherance of my deepest plans? I might answer this by simply referring to my own character, and by asking, in my turn, Where, in the history of the world, has a man of my order ever been found without a woman in the background self-immolated on the altar of his life? But I remember that I am writing in England, I remember that I was married in England, and I ask if a woman's marriage obligations in this country provide for her private opinion of her husband's principles? No! They charge her unreservedly to love, honour, and obey him. That is exactly what my wife has done. I stand here on a supreme moral elevation, and I loftily assert her accurate performance of her conjugal duties. Silence, Calumny! Your sympathy, Wives of England, for Madame Fosco!

Second question. If Anne Catherick had not died when she did, what should I have done? I should, in that case, have assisted worn-out Nature in finding permanent repose. I should have opened the doors of the Prison of Life, and have extended to the captive (incurably afflicted in mind and body both) a happy release.

Third question. On a calm revision of all the circumstances – Is my conduct worthy of any serious blame? Most emphatically, No! Have I not carefully avoided exposing myself to the odium of committing unnecessary crime? With my vast resources in chemistry, I might have taken Lady Glyde's life. At immense personal sacrifice I followed the dictates of my own ingenuity, my own humanity, my own caution, and took her identity instead. Judge me by what I might have done. How comparatively innocent! how indirectly virtuous I appear in what I really did!

I announced on beginning it that this narrative would be a remarkable document. It has entirely answered my expectations. Receive these fervid lines – my last legacy to the country I leave for ever. They are worthy of the occasion, and worthy of

FOSCO.

THE STORY CONCLUDED BY
WALTER HARTRIGHT

I

When I closed the last leaf of the Count's manuscript the half-hour during which I had engaged to remain at Forest Road had expired. Monsieur Rubelle looked at his watch and bowed. I rose immediately, and left the agent in possession of the empty house. I never saw him again – I never heard more of him or of his wife. Out of the dark byways of villainy and deceit they had crawled across our path – into the same byways they crawled back secretly and were lost.

In a quarter of an hour after leaving Forest Road I was at home again.

But few words sufficed to tell Laura and Marian how my desperate venture had ended, and what the next event in our lives was likely to be. I left all details to be described later in the day, and hastened back to St John's Wood, to see the person of whom Count Fosco had ordered the fly, when he went to meet Laura at the station.

The address in my possession led me to some 'livery stables,' about a quarter of a mile distant from Forest Road. The proprietor proved to be a civil and respectable man. When I explained that an important family matter obliged me to ask him to refer to his books for the purpose of ascertaining a date with which the record of his business transactions might supply me, he offered no objection to granting my request. The book was produced, and there, under the date of 'July 26th, 1850,' the order was entered in these words –

'Brougham to Count Fosco, 5 Forest Road. Two o'clock. (John Owen).'

I found on inquiry that the name of 'John Owen,' attached to the entry, referred to the man who had been employed to drive the fly. He was then at work in the stable-yard, and was sent for to see me at my request.

'Do you remember driving a gentleman, in the month of July last, from Number Five Forest Road to the Waterloo Bridge station?' I asked.

'Well, sir,' said the man, 'I can't exactly say I do.'

'Perhaps you remember the gentleman himself? Can you call to mind driving a foreigner last summer – a tall gentleman and remarkably fat?' The man's face brightened directly.

'I remember him, sir! The fattest gentleman as ever I see, and the heaviest customer as ever I drove. Yes, yes – I call him to mind, sir! We *did* go to the station, and it *was* from Forest Road. There was a parrot, or summat like it, screeching in the window. The gentleman was in a mortal hurry about the lady's luggage, and he gave me a handsome present for looking sharp and getting the boxes.'

Getting the boxes! I recollected immediately that Laura's own account of herself on her arrival in London described her luggage as being collected for her by some person whom Count Fosco brought with him to the station. This was the man.

'Did you see the lady?' I asked. 'What did she look like? Was she young or old?'

'Well, sir, what with the hurry and the crowd of people pushing about, I can't rightly say what the lady looked like. I can't call nothing to mind about her that I know of excepting her name.'

'You remember her name?'

'Yes, sir. Her name was Lady Glyde.'

'How do you come to remember that, when you have forgotten what she looked like?'

The man smiled, and shifted his feet in some little embarrassment.

'Why, to tell you the truth, sir,' he said, 'I hadn't been long married at that time, and my wife's name, before she changed it for mine, was the same as the lady's – meaning the name of Glyde, sir. The lady mentioned it herself. "Is your name on your boxes, ma'am?" says I. "Yes," says she, "my name is on my luggage – it is Lady Glyde." "Come!" I says to myself, "I've a bad head for gentlefolks' names in general – but *this* one comes like an old friend, at any rate." I can't say nothing about the time, sir, it might be nigh on a year ago, or it mightn't. But I can swear to the stout gentleman, and swear to the lady's name.'

There was no need that he should remember the time – the date was positively established by his master's order-book. I felt at once that the means were now in my power of striking down the whole conspiracy at a blow with the irresistible weapon of plain fact. Without a moment's hesitation, I took the proprietor of the livery stables aside and told him what the real importance was of the evidence of his order-book and the evidence of his driver. An arrangement to compensate him for the temporary loss of the man's services was easily made, and a copy of the entry in the book was taken by myself, and certified as true by the master's own signature. I left the livery stables, having settled that John Owen was to hold himself at my disposal for the next three days, or for a longer period if necessity required it. I now had in my possession all the papers that I wanted – the district registrar's own copy of the certificate of death, and Sir Percival's dated letter to the Count, being safe in my pocket-book.

With this written evidence about me, and with the coachman's answers fresh in my memory, I next turned my steps, for the first time since the beginning of all my inquiries, in the direction of Mr Kyrle's office. One of my objects in paying him this second visit was, necessarily, to tell him what I had done. The other was to warn him of my resolution to take my wife to Limmeridge the next morning, and to have her publicly received and recognised in her uncle's house. I left it to Mr Kyrle to decide under these circumstances, and in Mr Gilmore's absence, whether he was or was not bound, as the family solicitor, to be present on that occasion in the family interests.

I will say nothing of Mr Kyrle's amazement, or of the terms in which he expressed his opinion of my conduct from the first stage of the investigation to the last. It is only necessary to mention that he at once decided on accompanying us to Cumberland.

We started the next morning by the early train. Laura, Marian, Mr Kyrle, and myself in one carriage, and John Owen, with a clerk from Mr Kyrle's office, occupying places in another. On reaching the Limmeridge station we went first to the farmhouse at Todd's Corner. It was my firm determination that Laura should not enter her uncle's house till she appeared there publicly recognised as his niece. I left Marian to settle the question of accommodation with Mrs Todd, as soon as the good woman had recovered from the bewilderment of hearing what our errand was in Cumberland, and I arranged with her husband that John Owen was to be committed to the ready hospitality of the farm-servants. These preliminaries completed, Mr Kyrle and I set forth together for Limmeridge House.

I cannot write at any length of our interview with Mr Fairlie, for I cannot recall it to mind without feelings of impatience and contempt, which make the scene, even in remembrance only, utterly repulsive to me. I prefer to record simply that I carried my point. Mr Fairlie attempted to treat us on his customary plan. We passed without notice his polite insolence at the outset of the interview. We heard without sympathy the protestations with which he tried next to persuade us that the disclosure of the conspiracy had overwhelmed him. He absolutely whined and whimpered at last like a fretful child. 'How was he to know that his niece was alive when he was told that she was dead? He would welcome dear Laura with pleasure, if we would only allow him time to recover. Did we think he looked as if he wanted hurrying into his grave? No. Then, why hurry him?' He reiterated these remonstrances at every available opportunity, until I checked them once for all, by placing him firmly between two inevitable alternatives. I gave him his choice between doing his niece justice on my terms, or facing the consequence of a public assertion of her existence in a court of law. Mr Kyrle, to whom he turned for help, told him plainly that he must decide the question then and there. Characteristically choosing the alternative which promised soonest to release him from all personal anxiety, he announced with a sudden outburst of energy, that he was not strong enough to bear any more bullying, and that we might do as we pleased.

Mr Kyrle and I at once went downstairs, and agreed upon a form of letter which was to be sent round to the tenants who had attended the false funeral, summoning them, in Mr Fairlie's name, to assemble in Limmeridge House on the next day but one. An order referring to the same date was also written, directing a statuary in Carlisle to send a man to Limmeridge churchyard for the purpose of erasing an inscription – Mr Kyrle, who had arranged to sleep in the house, undertaking that Mr Fairlie should hear these letters read to him, and should sign them with his own hand.

I occupied the interval day at the farm in writing a plain narrative of the conspiracy, and in adding to it a statement of the practical contradiction which facts offered to the assertion of Laura's death. This I submitted to Mr Kyrle before I read it the next day to the assembled tenants. We also arranged the form in which the evidence should be presented at the close of the reading. After these matters were settled, Mr Kyrle endeavoured to turn the conversation next to Laura's affairs. Knowing, and desiring to know nothing of those affairs, and doubting whether he would approve, as a man of business, of my conduct in relation to my wife's life-interest in the legacy left to Madame Fosco, I begged Mr Kyrle to excuse me if I abstained from discussing the subject. It was connected, as I could truly tell him, with those sorrows and troubles of the past which we never referred to among ourselves, and which we instinctively shrank from discussing with others.

My last labour, as the evening approached, was to obtain 'The Narrative of the Tombstone,' by taking a copy of the false inscription on the grave before it was erased.

The day came – the day when Laura once more entered the familiar breakfast-room at Limmeridge House. All the persons assembled rose from their seats as Marian and I led her in. A perceptible shock of surprise, an audible murmur of interest ran through them, at the sight of her face. Mr Fairlie was present (by my express stipulation), with Mr Kyrle by his side. His valet stood behind him with a smelling-bottle ready in one hand, and a white handkerchief, saturated with eau-de-Cologne, in the other.

I opened the proceedings by publicly appealing to Mr Fairlie to say whether I appeared there with his authority and under his express sanction. He extended an arm, on either side, to Mr Kyrle and to his valet – was by them assisted to stand on his legs, and then expressed himself in these terms: 'Allow me to present Mr Hartright. I am as great an invalid as ever, and he is so very obliging as to speak for me. The subject is dreadfully embarrassing. Please hear him, and don't make a noise!' With those words he slowly sank back again into the chair, and took refuge in his scented pocket-handkerchief.

The disclosure of the conspiracy followed, after I had offered my preliminary explanation, first of all, in the fewest and the plainest words. I was there present (I informed my hearers) to declare, first, that my wife, then sitting by me, was the daughter of the late Mr Philip Fairlie; secondly, to prove by positive facts, that the funeral which they had attended in Limmeridge churchyard was the funeral of another woman; thirdly, to give them a plain account of how it had all happened. Without further preface, I at once read the narrative of the conspiracy, describing it in clear outline, and dwelling only upon the pecuniary motive for it, in order to avoid complicating my statement by unnecessary reference to Sir Percival's secret. This done, I reminded my audience of the date on the inscription in the churchyard (the 25th), and confirmed its correctness by producing the certificate of death. I then read them Sir Percival's letter of the 25th, announcing his wife's intended journey from Hampshire to London on the 26th. I next showed that she had taken that journey, by the personal testimony of the driver of the fly, and I proved that she had performed it on the appointed day, by the order-book at the livery stables. Marian then added her own statement of the meeting between Laura and herself at the mad-house, and of her sister's escape. After which I closed the proceedings by informing the persons present of Sir Percival's death and of my marriage.

Mr Kyrle rose when I resumed my seat, and declared, as the legal adviser of the family, that my case was proved by the plainest evidence he had ever heard in his life. As he spoke those words, I put my arm round Laura, and raised her so that she was plainly visible to every one in the room. 'Are you all of the same opinion?' I asked, advancing towards them a few steps, and pointing to my wife.

The effect of the question was electrical. Far down at the lower end of the room one of the oldest tenants on the estate started to his feet, and led the rest with him in an instant. I see the man now, with his honest brown face and his iron-grey hair, mounted on the window-seat, waving his heavy riding-whip over his head, and leading the cheers. 'There she is, alive and hearty – God bless her! Gi' it tongue, lads! Gi' it tongue!' The shout that answered him, reiterated again and again, was the sweetest music I ever heard. The labourers in the village and the boys from the school, assembled on the lawn, caught up the cheering and echoed it back on us. The farmers' wives clustered round Laura, and struggled which should be first to shake hands with her, and to implore her, with the tears pouring over their own cheeks, to bear up bravely and not to cry. She was so completely overwhelmed, that I was obliged to take her from them, and carry her to the door. There I gave her into Marian's care – Marian, who had never failed us yet, whose courageous self-control did not fail us now. Left by myself at the door, I invited all the persons present (after thanking them in Laura's name and mine) to follow me to the churchyard, and see the false inscription struck off the tombstone with their own eyes.

They all left the house, and all joined the throng of villagers collected round the grave, where the statuary's man was waiting for us. In a breathless silence, the first sharp stroke of the steel sounded on the marble. Not a voice was heard – not a soul moved, till those three words, 'Laura, Lady Glyde,' had vanished from sight. Then there was a great heave of relief among the crowd, as if they felt that the last fetters of the conspiracy had been struck off Laura herself, and the assembly slowly withdrew. It was late in the day before the whole inscription was erased. One line only was afterwards engraved in its place: 'Anne Catherick, July 25th, 1850.'

I returned to Limmeridge House early enough in the evening to take leave of Mr Kyrle. He and his clerk, and the driver of the fly, went back to London by the night train. On their departure an insolent message was delivered to me from Mr Fairlie – who had been carried from the room in a shattered condition, when the first outbreak of cheering answered my appeal to the tenantry. The message conveyed to us 'Mr Fairlie's best congratulations,' and requested to know whether 'we contemplated stopping in the house.' I sent back word that the only object for which we had entered his doors was accomplished – that I contemplated stopping in no man's house but my own – and that Mr Fairlie need not entertain the slightest apprehension of ever seeing us or hearing from us again. We went back to our friends at the farm to rest that night, and the next morning – escorted to the station, with the heartiest enthusiasm and good will, by the whole village and by all the farmers in the neighbourhood – we returned to London.

As our view of the Cumberland hills faded in the distance, I thought of the first disheartening circumstances under which the long struggle that was now past and over had been pursued. It was strange to look back and to see, now, that the poverty which had denied us all hope of assistance had been the indirect means of our success, by forcing me to act for myself. If we had been rich enough to find legal help, what would have been the result? The gain (on Mr Kyrle's own showing) would have been more than doubtful – the loss, judging by the plain test of events as they had really happened, certain. The law would never have obtained me my interview with Mrs

Catherick. The law would never have made Pesca the means of forcing a confession from the Count.

II

Two more events remain to be added to the chain before it reaches fairly from the outset of the story to the close.

While our new sense of freedom from the long oppression of the past was still strange to us, I was sent for by the friend who had given me my first employment in wood engraving, to receive from him a fresh testimony of his regard for my welfare. He had been commissioned by his employers to go to Paris, and to examine for them a fresh discovery in the practical application of his Art, the merits of which they were anxious to ascertain. His own engagements had not allowed him leisure time to undertake the errand, and he had most kindly suggested that it should be transferred to me. I could have no hesitation in thankfully accepting the offer, for if I acquitted myself of my commission as I hoped I should, the result would be a permanent engagement on the illustrated newspaper, to which I was now only occasionally attached.

I received my instructions and packed up for the journey the next day. On leaving Laura once more (under what changed circumstances!) in her sister's care, a serious consideration recurred to me, which had more than once crossed my wife's mind, as well as my own, already – I mean the consideration of Marian's future. Had we any right to let our selfish affection accept the devotion of all that generous life? Was it not our duty, our best expression of gratitude, to forget ourselves, and to think only of *her*? I tried to say this when we were alone for a moment, before I went away. She took my hand, and silenced me at the first words.

'After all that we three have suffered together,' she said 'there can be no parting between us till the last parting of all. My heart and my happiness, Walter, are with Laura and you. Wait a little till there are children's voices at your fireside. I will teach them to speak for me in *their* language, and the first lesson they say to their father and mother shall be – We can't spare our aunt!'

My journey to Paris was not undertaken alone. At the eleventh hour Pesca decided that he would accompany me. He had not recovered his customary cheerfulness since the night at the Opera, and he determined to try what a week's holiday would do to raise his spirits.

I performed the errand entrusted to me, and drew out the necessary report, on the fourth day from our arrival in Paris. The fifth day I arranged to devote to sight-seeing and amusements in Pesca's company.

Our hotel had been too full to accommodate us both on the same floor. My room was on the second story, and Pesca's was above me, on the third. On the morning of the fifth day I went upstairs to see if the Professor was ready to go out. Just before I reached the landing I saw his door opened from the inside – a long, delicate, nervous hand (not my friend's hand certainly) held it ajar. At the same time I heard Pesca's voice saying eagerly, in low tones, and in his own language—'I remember the name, but I don't know the man. You saw at the Opera he was so changed that I could not recognise him. I will forward the report – I can do no more.' 'No more need be done,' answered the second voice. The door opened wide, and the light-haired man with the scar on his cheek – the man I had seen following Count Fosco's cab a week before – came out. He bowed as I drew aside to let him pass – his face was fearfully pale – and he held fast by the banisters as he descended the stairs.

I pushed open the door and entered Pesca's room. He was crouched up, in the strangest manner, in a corner of the sofa. He seemed to shrink from me when I approached him.

'Am I disturbing you?' I asked. 'I did not know you had a friend with you till I saw him come out.'

'No friend,' said Pesca eagerly. 'I see him today for the first time and the last.'

'I am afraid he has brought you bad news?'

'Horrible news, Walter! Let us go back to London – I don't want to stop here – I am sorry I ever came. The misfortunes of my youth are very hard upon me,' he said, turning his face to the wall, 'very hard upon me in my later time. I try to forget them – and they will not forget *me*!'

'We can't return, I am afraid, before the afternoon,' I replied. 'Would you like to come out with me in the meantime?'

'No, my friend, I will wait here. But let us go back today – pray let us go back.'

I left him with the assurance that he should leave Paris that afternoon. We had arranged the evening before to ascend the Cathedral of Notre Dame, with Victor Hugo's noble romance for our guide. There was nothing in the French capital that I was more anxious to see, and I departed by myself for the church.

Approaching Notre Dame by the river-side, I passed on my way the terrible dead-house of Paris – the Morgue. A great crowd clamoured and heaved round the door. There was evidently something inside which excited the popular curiosity, and fed the popular appetite for horror.

I should have walked on to the church if the conversation of two men and a woman on the outskirts of the crowd had not caught my ear. They had just come out from seeing the sight in the Morgue, and the account they were giving of the dead body to their neighbours described it as the corpse of a man – a man of immense size, with a strange mark on his left arm.

The moment those words reached me I stopped and took my place with the crowd going in. Some dim foreshadowing of the truth had crossed my mind when I heard Pesca's voice through the open door, and when I saw the stranger's face as he passed me on the stairs of the hotel. Now the truth itself was revealed to me – revealed in the chance words that had just reached my ears. Other vengeance than mine had followed that fated man from the theatre to his own door – from his own door to his refuge in Paris. Other vengeance than mine had called him to the day of reckoning, and had exacted from him the penalty of his life. The moment when I had pointed him out to Pesca at the theatre in the hearing of that stranger by our side, who was looking for him too – was the moment that sealed his doom. I remembered the struggle in my own heart, when he and I stood face to face – the struggle before I could let him escape me – and shuddered as I recalled it.

Slowly, inch by inch, I pressed in with the crowd, moving nearer and nearer to the great glass screen that parts the dead from the living at the Morgue – nearer and nearer, till I was close behind the front row of spectators, and could look in.

There he lay, unowned, unknown, exposed to the flippant curiosity of a French mob! There was the dreadful end of that long life of degraded ability and heartless crime! Hushed in the sublime repose of death, the broad, firm, massive face and head fronted us so grandly that the chattering Frenchwomen about me lifted their hands in admiration, and cried in shrill chorus, 'Ah, what a handsome man!' The wound that had killed him had been struck with a knife or dagger exactly over his heart. No other traces of violence appeared about the body except on the left arm, and there, exactly in the place where I had seen the brand on Pesca's arm, were two deep cuts in the shape of the letter T, which entirely obliterated the mark of the Brotherhood. His clothes, hung above him, showed that he had been himself conscious of his danger – they were clothes that had disguised him as a French artisan. For a few moments, but not for longer, I forced myself to see these things through the glass screen. I can write of them at no greater length, for I saw no more.

The few facts in connection with his death which I subsequently ascertained (partly from Pesca and partly from other sources), may be stated here before the subject is dismissed from these pages.

His body was taken out of the Seine in the disguise which I have described, nothing being found on him which revealed his name, his rank, or his place of abode. The hand that struck him was never traced, and the circumstances under which he was killed were never discovered. I leave others to draw their own conclusions in reference to the secret of the assassination as I have drawn mine. When I have intimated that the foreigner with the scar was a member of the Brotherhood (admitted in Italy after Pesca's departure from his native country), and when I have further added that the two cuts, in the form of a T, on the left arm of the dead man, signified the Italian word 'Traditore,' and showed that justice had been done by the Brotherhood on a traitor, I have contributed all that I know towards elucidating the mystery of Count Fosco's death.

The body was identified the day after I had seen it by means of an anonymous letter addressed to his wife. He was buried by Madame Fosco in the cemetery of Père la Chaise. Fresh funeral wreaths continue to this day to be hung on the ornamental bronze railings round the tomb by the Countess's own hand. She lives in the strictest retirement at Versailles. Not long since she published a biography of her deceased husband. The work throws no light whatever on the name that was really his own or on the secret history of his life – it is almost entirely devoted to the praise of his domestic virtues, the assertion of his rare abilities, and the enumeration of the honours conferred on him. The circumstances attending his death are very briefly noticed, and are summed up on the last page in this sentence—'His life was one long assertion of the rights of the aristocracy and the sacred principles of Order, and he died a martyr to his cause.'

III

The summer and autumn passed after my return from Paris, and brought no changes with them which need be noticed here. We lived so simply and quietly that the income which I was now steadily earning sufficed for all our wants.

In the February of the new year our first child was born – a son. My mother and sister and Mrs Vesey were our guests at the little christening party, and Mrs Clements was present to assist my wife on the same occasion. Marian was our boy's godmother, and Pesca and Mr Gilmore (the latter acting by proxy) were his godfathers. I may add here that when Mr Gilmore returned to us a year later he assisted the design of these pages, at my request, by writing the Narrative which appears early in the story under his name, and which, though first in order of precedence, was thus, in order of time, the last that I received.

The only event in our lives which now remains to be recorded, occurred when our little Walter was six months old.

At that time I was sent to Ireland to make sketches for certain forthcoming illustrations in the newspaper to which I was attached. I was away for nearly a fortnight, corresponding regularly with my wife and Marian, except during the last three days of my absence, when my movements were too uncertain to enable me to receive letters. I performed the latter part of my journey back at night, and when I reached home in the morning, to my utter astonishment there was no one to receive me. Laura and Marian and the child had left the house on the day before my return.

A note from my wife, which was given to me by the servant, only increased my surprise, by informing me that they had gone to Limmeridge House. Marian had prohibited any attempt at written explanations – I was entreated to follow them the moment I came back – complete enlightenment awaited me on my arrival in Cumberland – and I was forbidden to feel the slightest anxiety in the meantime. There the note ended. It was still early enough to catch the morning train. I reached Limmeridge House the same afternoon.

My wife and Marian were both upstairs. They had established themselves (by way of completing my amazement) in the little room which had been once assigned to me for a studio, when I was employed on Mr Fairlie's drawings. On the very chair which I used to occupy when I was at work Marian was sitting now, with the child industriously sucking his coral upon her lap – while Laura was standing by the well-remembered drawing-table which I had so often used, with the little album that I had filled for her in past times open under her hand.

'What in the name of heaven has brought you here?' I asked. 'Does Mr Fairlie know—?'

Marian suspended the question on my lips by telling me that Mr Fairlie was dead. He had been struck by paralysis, and had never rallied after the shock. Mr Kyrle had informed them of his death, and had advised them to proceed immediately to Limmeridge House.

Some dim perception of a great change dawned on my mind. Laura spoke before I had quite realised it. She stole close to me to enjoy the surprise which was still expressed in my face.

'My darling Walter,' she said, 'must we really account for our boldness in coming here? I am afraid, love, I can only explain it by breaking through our rule, and referring to the past.'

'There is not the least necessity for doing anything of the kind,' said Marian. 'We can be just as explicit, and much more interesting, by referring to the future.' She rose and held up the child kicking and crowing in her arms. 'Do you know who this is, Walter?' she asked, with bright tears of happiness gathering in her eyes.

'Even *my* bewilderment has its limits,' I replied. 'I think I can still answer for knowing my own child.'

'Child!' she exclaimed, with all her easy gaiety of old times. 'Do you talk in that familiar manner of one of the landed gentry of England? Are you aware, when I present this illustrious baby to your notice, in whose presence you stand? Evidently not! Let me make two eminent personages known to one another: Mr Walter Hartright – *The Heir of Limmeridge.*'

So she spoke. In writing those last words, I have written all. The pen falters in my hand. The long, happy labour of many months is over. Marian was the good angel of our lives – let Marian end our Story.

METAMORPHOSIS

METAMORPHOSIS

FRANZ KAFKA

Translated from the German by
William Aaltonen

This edition published in 2019 by Arcturus Publishing Limited
26/27 Bickels Yard, 151–153 Bermondsey Street,
London SE1 3HA

Typesetting by Palimpsest Book Production Limited

Cover design: Peter Ridley
Cover illustration: Peter Gray
Design: Beatriz Custodio

AD005947UK

Printed in the UK

FSC

MIX
Paper from
responsible sources
FSC® C018072

www.fsc.org

Contents

Introduction 7

Chapter 1 15

Chapter 2 41

Chapter 3 69

Introduction

From Ovid's *Metamorphoses* to Marvel Comics' *X-Men*, it's hard to think of a shape-shifting story that isn't both violent and sensational. None is weirder or more wonderful than Franz Kafka's *Metamorphosis*, but Kafka's story is also richly comic. Born in Prague in 1883, Kafka grew up in a German-speaking family. He wrote the funny, poignant and unsettling *Metamorphosis* in 1912, creating a key text in the revolutionary spirit of 20th-century Modernism – and a classic of surrealist horror.

Metamorphosis tells the story of Gregor Samsa, a successful young travelling salesman who one day wakes to find that he has turned into 'a kind of giant bug'. Kafka's detailed description, of 'the arch of a brown abdomen, divided into stiff, domed segments... [and] a regiment of puny legs', conjures up something between a centipede and a cockroach.

Is the transformation a real, physical fact, or are we meant to understand it on some more profound level, a continuation of the 'troubled dreams' from which young Gregor has just woken? As the anti-hero himself states, 'It was no dream.' And Kafka's painfully funny and extremely realistic depiction of the bug-human struggling to get its ugly, ungainly carapace out of bed asks us to take the transformation at face value.

Any translator coming to Kafka's work sees at once that it is written in clear and concise language whose economy is a clever artistic counterpoint to the subtlety of its underlying themes. Sticking to this plain elegance without taking too many liberties with the original has been the overriding objective of this translation, but the close reader will find that there are a few well-intentioned minor departures.

Despite the disturbing strangeness of events, Kafka's powerful narrative manages to make us suspend disbelief, but at the same time the story works on a deeper level.

If Gregor's plight is a metaphor for the human condition, then how should we interpret it? Stuck in a 15-mile motorway tailback, or in voice-mail jail on the phone to an impenetrable utility company, we all know what it feels like to be Kafka's beetle. He has hit on something universal in human experience. Sadly, for a long time Gregor himself remains in denial about his fall from grace.

This is all the more poignant in that until the horror comes upon him, the young man has been a model of virtue: for several years, ever since his valetudinarian father's business failed, he has singlehandedly supported his parents and teenage sister, Grete. Sweet-natured to a fault – it really doesn't do to be too submissive in life – Samsa's first fear is not for himself, as might be expected, but that, having missed the five a.m. train, his bullying boss will sack him.

As he worries about losing his job, we learn that in fact Gregor hates his work. Is work the metaphoric beetle – the cockroach we all have to bear (unless we happen to enjoy our employment)? If so, it would again strike a pretty universal chord.

In fact, its critique of work is only the first in many levels of understanding that begin to unfold in Kafka's story. Next, he leads us to think about the truculence of youth, and the way in which family power can shift away from parents as their children come into their own. For a short while, Gregor and sister Grete, who takes charge of her bug-brother, enjoy a new and unaccustomed power as their parents struggle and fail to deal with the filthy, crawling nightmare in the bedroom beyond.

Now we have struck the mother lode of Kafka's metaphor – power. The theme will carry us much further, helped on its way by the author's repeated use of brilliant and sinister farce. The office manager comes to find out why Gregor is not at work. Afraid the man will leave before he can explain himself, and quite forgetting he is now a giant bug, the Gregor-monster panics. 'The manager had to be stopped, calmed, convinced and finally won over. His own and his family's future depended on it!... The manager was already on the stairs... Gregor sprang forward to try and stop him. The manager must have guessed what was coming, for he leapt down the steps in a single bound and vanished with a cry of "Aaagh!"... His rapid escape had the unfortunate effect of causing Gregor's father... to fly completely off the handle... he seized the manager's walking stick in his right hand... grabbed a large newspaper from the table to his left and began stamping his feet and brandishing the paper and the cane to drive Gregor back into his room. Gregor's pleas went unheard; he had not the slightest chance of being understood, no matter how submissively he lowered his head. The more meekly he behaved, the harder his father stamped.'

If you had to choose a scene that encapsulates Franz Kafka's real-life relationship with his own father, it might be this one. Kafka was perfectly open about how incurably bad things remained between them throughout his life. Hermann Kafka was by all accounts a loud, overbearing and impatient blunderbuss. A reasonably prosperous self-made businessman, Kafka senior was quite unable to understand why his first-born child, Franz, could possibly wish to do other than follow in his footsteps, and help run his ladies' clothing firm. Confronted with a slight, sensitive, artistic and voraciously bookish child, Hermann's reaction was to try to 'toughen him up – knock some sense into the boy'. What on earth was the point of an artist? Instead, the verbal – and perhaps physical – bullying young Franz endured gave rise to the theme that underpins and informs almost all of his work. A weak, innocent and naïve character is forced on a quest to understand, to reason with and, ultimately, to placate an implacable, uncaring force. Since this force is always beyond reason and knowledge, the quest is invariably doomed.

Always the defendant in a trial he can never win, Kafka's anti-hero lives in a kind of quiet, despairing hell, longing only for a peace and recon-ciliation that are forever denied by a faceless and merciless tyranny. One of his longer novellas is entitled *The Trial [Der Prozess]*, another *The Judgement [Das Urteil]*. It is not surprising, then, that Kafka's work, which seems to have prefigured and even predicted Nazi bestiality, enjoyed a huge resurgence after World War Two.

In *Metamorphosis,* once it becomes clear to the father that his son has become economically useless and a hideous social embarrassment, only the interventions of his mother and sister prevent Herr Samsa from beating him to death. 'He was caught fast and needed help. On one side, his little legs fluttered in the air; on the other they were squashed painfully against the floor. His father struck him a life-threatening blow from behind with the cane. Gregor was sent flying into the bedroom and fell, bleeding heavily. His father slammed the door shut with the stick, and then, at last, all was still.'

Increasingly violent and abusive, later on Gregor's father has another go at murdering him. In a scene of dark comic genius, he sets about Gregor with the contents of the fruit bowl. 'Suddenly something whizzed past him, fell to the ground and rolled away. It was an apple. It was followed immediately by a second one. Paralyzed with terror, Gregor froze.... A weakly thrown apple grazed his back and bounced off harmlessly, but the next one pierced it right through. Gregor's instinct was to drag himself away in the hope that a change of position might alleviate the shocking and unbelievable pain. But he seemed to be nailed fast to the spot and lay spread-eagled, head spinning.'

At the time, Sigmund Freud's theories of subconscious family hatred were being hotly discussed by an enthralled Europe. Kafka acknowledged that a Freudian interpretation of his stories had some value [Freud was a near neighbour in Prague], but insisted it was 'too facile'. He dismissed the value of psychoanalysis in overcoming childhood trauma. To Kafka the whole point of art – or at least his art – was that it stood outside and went beyond simple explanation, into realms of ethical enquiry that made Freud's 'scientific' solutions redundant.

A fan of the Danish theologian Kierkegaard, Kafka was also frank about his interest in the spiritual. Some have interpreted Kafka's work as a commentary on the unknowable divine. In this, much like Kafka's own father, the heavenly father stands eternally apart, all-powerful, unknowable and arbitrary. His workings are so mysterious and beyond the power of human understanding that, like Abraham ordered to slaughter his first-born son, we can only trust to the good and obey. For Kafka, The Book of Job, with its terrifying and whimsical God, was a defining text.

Not long before he died in 1924, Kafka wrote, 'The reason posterity's appraisal of a man is often more correct than that of his contemporaries is that he is dead. Only after death does a man's true nature emerge. In death, as on the chimney sweep's Saturday night, the soot gets washed from his body. Then it can be seen who did the more harm – his contemporaries to him, or he to his contemporaries. If the latter, he was a great man.'

Wriggling on the pin of sublime ignorance, humanity's attempts to make rational sense of the universe are, in Kafka's scheme of things, absurd. It is a mark of his compassion – and his genius – that he takes the cruel absurdities of life and makes us laugh at them. In so doing he keeps our hope in humanity alive.

William Aaltonen

Chapter 1

When Gregor Samsa woke one morning from troubled dreams, he found that he had been transformed – in his bed – into a kind of giant bug. He lay on his back, which had become as hard as armour. Raising his head a little, he saw the arch of a brown abdomen, divided into stiff, domed segments. The quilt was perched precariously on top, and looked as if it might slide off at any moment. A regiment of puny legs, horribly thin compared to the rest of him, quivered wretchedly before his eyes. 'What on earth has happened to me?' he wondered.

It was no dream. His room, which although too small was designed for human occupation, breathed peacefully within its four familiar walls. Above the table, where a collection of cloth samples lay scattered – Samsa was a commercial traveller – hung the picture that he had recently cut from an illustrated magazine and placed in a pretty gilded frame. It showed a lady sitting upright, wearing a fur hat and boa, with her forearm plunged up to the elbow in a heavy fur muff.

Gregor turned his gaze to the window. The dismal weather – raindrops rattled hard on the flashing – made him feel sad. 'What if I just go back to sleep for a bit and forget all this nonsense?' he thought. But with things as they stood that was impossible. He was used to sleeping on his right side, and in his present state there was no way he could adopt that position. The more he tried to force himself over on to his right, the more he kept falling on to his back. He tried a hundred times, closing his eyes so that he did not have to look at his quivering legs, and only gave up when he began to feel a slight, dull ache in his side, of a kind that he had never experienced before.

'God!' he thought. 'What an exhausting job I've chosen. On the road day in and day out – much more stressful than working from home! And apart from the demands of doing business, the actual travelling is so bad: struggling to catch connecting trains, terrible meals at all hours of the day and night, a sea of ever-changing faces and never any chance of making friends. To hell with it all!'

He felt a slight itch at the top of his stomach and slowly hauled himself up to the bedpost on his back, so he could lift his head. There was a scattering of small, white spots at the itchy place, but he had no idea what they meant. He went to explore the area with one of his legs, but drew it back at once – the contact made his blood run cold.

CHAPTER 1

He slid back down into his former position. 'Getting up at the crack of dawn like this,' he said to himself, 'is enough to drive anyone completely insane. A man must have his sleep. The other salesmen live like kept women. When I get back to the hotel in the morning to process my orders, I find these gentlemen still at their breakfast. I'd like to see what my boss would say if I tried that; I'd be out on my ear. Still, that might be a good thing! If I didn't have my parents to think of, I'd have handed in my notice long ago. I'd have gone to the boss and given him a piece of my mind. Knocked him off his perch! Ridiculous, the way he sits up high on his desk, so that he can talk down to us workers from a lofty height – especially when he's so hard of hearing and we all have to stand up close to him! Still, all hope is not lost. Once I've saved the money my parents owe him – which will be in five or six years – I'll definitely go through with it. Take the plunge! In the meantime, I'd better get up: my train goes at five.'

He looked at the alarm clock ticking on the chest. 'Good God!' he thought. It was already half past six, and the minute hand was still creeping steadily forwards – now it was almost a quarter to seven. Had the alarm simply failed? Even from bed he could see the clock was set correctly for four am. It had definitely gone off. Could he really have slept calmly through that earth-shattering

17

din? Calmly, no: his sleep had been anything but peaceful; and yet he had slept perfectly soundly. What exactly, though, was he supposed to do now?

The next train went at seven. To catch it he'd really have to get a move on, and he hadn't even packed his samples yet. The trouble was, he didn't feel in the least bit rested or inclined to get up. Even if he did catch the train, his boss would come down on him hard – the office messenger would have been waiting on the five o'clock train and would long since have told the boss Gregor hadn't turned up. The boy was the manager's creature, a wretched, snivelling toady.

Supposing he called in sick? But that would cause its own problems, and be suspicious, too: during the five years he'd been with the firm he had never once had the slightest illness. The manager would turn up with the Health Insurance doctor. He would reproach his parents for their son's idleness and cut short all objections by repeating the doctor's refrain: there are no sick people in the world, only the workshy. And would he be so far wrong in this case? Apart from the drowsiness that was entirely natural after such a long sleep, Gregor felt in fine form; he was even unusually hungry.

As all these thoughts were racing through his mind, but before he had actually made up his mind to get out of bed, the clock struck quarter to seven.

There was a timid knock on the door by the head of his bed. 'Gregor,' someone called – it was his mother – 'it's quarter to seven. Isn't it time you were on your way?'

What a sweet voice! Gregor trembled as he heard his own in reply. It was unmistakably his voice, but it came with a kind of nasty whining undertone, which meant his words only took proper shape for an instant and then were immediately muffled so that you wondered if you'd really heard them in the first place. Gregor wanted to explain the situation fully; but, given the circumstances, all he said was: 'Yes, yes, thank you, mother – I'm getting up now.' No doubt the door prevented his mother from noticing the change in Gregor's voice, for the explanation reassured her, and she shuffled away in her slippers. Even so, this little exchange had alerted the other members of the family to the fact that Gregor was still in the house. He'd never been this late before. His father started banging on one of the side doors, softly, but with his fists. 'Gregor, Gregor,' he called, 'what's the matter?' And, a moment later, in a louder voice, 'Gregor! Gregor!'

From behind the door on the other side of the room, Gregor's sister called softly, 'Gregor, are you ill? Do you need anything?'

'I'm just coming,' Gregor told them, forcing himself to enunciate carefully and separate each word with a long pause to keep his voice natural. His father went back to breakfast, but his sister kept whispering, 'Gregor, open the door, please!'

Gregor, however, had absolutely no intention of complying; on the contrary, he was pleased he'd got into the habit of always locking the door on his business trips. He wanted to get up and get dressed without anyone bothering him, and above all, he wanted his breakfast. After that, he'd take time to reflect. There was no way he could make any sensible decisions in bed. He remembered that he often got a mild ache or pain from sleeping awkwardly, which turned out to be imaginary and disappeared as soon as he rose. He was eager to see if this was true of his present condition. As for the change in his voice, he thought privately it must be the sign of a nasty cold, the occupational hazard of travelling salesmen.

He had no difficulty getting rid of the quilt; he only had to puff himself up slightly and it fell clear. But after that, things became much more difficult because his body was now so very much broader. To get up, he needed his arms and hands; but all he had were dozens of little legs, which persisted in wriggling uncontrollably. Before he could bend one leg, he first had to stretch it out; and even when he'd finally managed to make that one behave, all the other little legs kept thrashing about in the most unpleasant and disgusting way.

Chapter 1

'I mustn't just lie in bed like a useless lump,' Gregor told himself. To get himself going, he tried to shift the lower part of his body out of bed; but the problem was that this bit of him – which, by the way, he hadn't yet managed to see or even imagine with any clarity – proved too difficult to move.

Slowly beginning to panic, he gathered all his strength and launched himself forward but, getting his aim wrong, he banged hard into one of the bedposts. The searing pain taught him immediately that the lower part of his body was the most sensitive. Next, he tried to manoeuvre the upper part of his new body out of bed. Proceeding with great care, he rotated his head toward the edge of the bed. He managed this quite easily, and the rest of him, despite its mass and size, slowly followed in the same direction. But once his head had cleared the side of the bed and was hanging in mid-air, he was afraid to go any further; if he fell now, it would be a miracle if he didn't crack his skull. This was no time to knock himself unconscious. Better to stay in bed.

But when, panting with fatigue, he found himself stretched out exactly as before, and saw his little legs quivering away more chaotically than ever, he despaired of finding a way of imposing order and peace on all this mess. Again he was forced to the conclusion that he just could not stay in bed, and that if there was the slightest chance of success then the most reasonable course of action was to get up. At the same time, he felt that cool and wise reflection would be far better than rushing into any rash decisions.

At such moments he usually turned his eyes to the window for encouragement and hope. But the fog stopped him from seeing across to the other side of the narrow street, and the view through the glass neither lifted his morale nor gave him confidence. 'Seven o'clock already,' he said as the alarm clock struck the hour for the second time. 'Seven o'clock already, and the fog is still like pea soup!' He lay back again for a while, keeping his breathing shallow – as if, in the complete silence, he could wait calmly for everything, including himself, to return to normal.

Then he said to himself: 'Before it gets to a quarter past, I absolutely have to be up. In any case, they'll send someone from the office, which opens at seven, to look for me before then.' And he began to rock on his back in an effort to get his whole body out of bed in one go. That way, he would be able to protect his head by snapping it upwards as he fell. His back seemed to be nice and hard; no harm would come to him if he fell on that. His only fear was that the resulting crash, which everyone in the whole house would surely hear, might cause panic, or at the very least make the others anxious. It was a risk he would just have to take.

When Gregor had half his body out of bed –
this new way of going at it seemed more like a
game than a struggle, since all he had to do was
rock himself on his back – he began to think how
easily he could have done it if only he had had a
little help. Two strong people – his father and the
maid came to mind – would have managed it
easily. All they would have needed to do was get
their arms under his curved back, lift it up from
the bed, shift their weight – and his – quickly
forward and then simply wait, always taking due
care, until he was on the floor where he hoped
his feet would at last have found a way of behaving
sensibly. But even if the doors had not been closed,
would it have been wise for him to call for help?
In spite of the desperate circumstances, he couldn't
hold back a smile at this thought.

By now he was rocking so far and so hard that
he was very close to tipping over, and knew he
would have to take a serious decision: in five
minutes it would be a quarter to eight. Suddenly
there was a knock at the front door. 'Someone
from the office,' he thought, and he felt the blood
freeze in his veins, while his little legs danced faster
than ever. For a moment, all was quiet. 'They're
not answering,' Gregor thought with a wild surge
of hope. But then he heard the maid's usual heavy
footsteps as she went to the door and opened it.
Gregor had only to hear the visitor's first words

of greeting to know who it was – the office manager in person. Why was Gregor, of all people, condemned to work for a firm which invariably took the most suspicious view of its employees, and jumped hard on the first sign of any failing? Were all its employees really rogues? Was he the one good and faithful servant among them? Even if he had by chance missed a couple of hours work that morning, he was now so wracked with remorse that he simply couldn't get up.

Couldn't they just have sent one of the trainees to sort things out if they really had to come snooping round? Why did the manager himself have to come, as if to show the whole of Gregor's – entirely blameless – family that only someone of his stature could be trusted to clear up this regrettable affair?

These thoughts annoyed Gregor so much that he swung himself out of bed with a last, almighty heave. It made a loud thud, but not the terrible crash he had feared. The carpet had absorbed some of the impact, and Gregor's back was more flexible than he had imagined, so the noise wasn't too bad. He'd only given his head a bit of a bang. He hadn't kept it high enough, and it had taken a knock in the fall. Cross and in pain, he twisted his head and rubbed it on the carpet.

'Something has just fallen in there,' cried the manager in the room to the left. Gregor tried to imagine the look on his employer's face if *he* had been struck down by a misfortune like this. And why not? As if in brutal reply, the manager began to pace up and down in the next room, which made his patent leather boots creak. Gregor's sister whispered a warning from the room to the right: 'Gregor, your manager's here.'

'I know,' Gregor muttered, but didn't dare raise his voice enough for her to hear. 'Gregor,' said his father in the room on the left, 'the office manager has come to find out why you didn't catch the early train. We don't know what to say. He wants to speak to you in person. So please open the door. I'm sure he will be kind enough to excuse the untidiness of your room.'

'Good morning, Mr Samsa,' the manager said in a friendly tone.

'He is not well,' his mother said, while his father went on talking through the door. 'Believe me, sir, Gregor is not well. How else could he have missed the train? The boy thinks of nothing but his work! It upsets me to see how he never goes out in the evening. Do you know, he's just spent a whole week in town and he's been at home every night! He sits down with us at the table and stays there, quietly reading the paper or studying his timetables. His greatest relaxation is to do a little fretwork. Why, only the other day he made a small picture frame. He finished it in two or three evenings, and you'd be surprised to see how pretty it is. It's hanging in his room. As soon as Gregor opens his door, you'll be able to see it. I'm so glad you came, sir, as we haven't managed to get Gregor to open his door by ourselves; he is so obstinate. I'm sure he must be ill, even though he says he isn't.'

'I am just coming,' Gregor said slowly and carefully, but he continued to lie still so as not to miss a word of the conversation.

'My dear lady, I can offer no other suggestion,' the manager replied. 'Let us only hope it's nothing serious. But like it or not, we businessmen have to get on with our jobs and ignore our little indispositions.'

'Can the manager come in now?' his father asked impatiently, rapping on the door again.

'No,' Gregor said. There was a painful silence from the room to his left. His sister began to weep in the one on the right. Why didn't she join the others? Perhaps she'd only just got out of bed and wasn't dressed yet. And what was she crying for? Because her brother wouldn't get up to let the manager in? Because he risked losing his job, and because the company director would start pursuing his parents for their outstanding debts again? For the moment, these worries were misplaced. Gregor was still there and hadn't the slightest intention of letting his family down. But at this very moment he was stretched out on the carpet, and nobody seeing him in that state could seriously have asked him to let the manager into his room.

But it was not on account of this slight discourtesy – which in normal circumstances he would easily have found some reason to apologize for later – that Gregor would be dismissed. And he thought it better, for now, to leave the man alone rather than upset him with pleading and tears. But it was exactly his inaction that upset the others and, at the same time, justified their behaviour.

'Mr Samsa,' the manager cried, raising his voice. 'Whatever is the matter? You barricade yourself in your room, you refuse to give us a straight yes or no, you upset your parents needlessly and you neglect your professional duties in the most unheard-of manner. I speak for your employer and your parents when I demand an immediate explanation.

'I am astonished – astonished! I took you for a quiet, reasonable young man, and here you go suddenly giving yourself airs, behaving in a quite fantastic manner! Speaking to me this morning, the director suggested an explanation for your absence which I rejected – I mean the new sample collection we recently entrusted to your care. I all but gave him my word of honour that this had nothing to do with matters. But now that I have witnessed your stubbornness for myself, Mr

Samsa, I can assure you I no longer feel any wish to defend you. Your job is by no means safe. I had intended to tell you this in private but, since you oblige me to waste my time here to no purpose, I see no reason for showing discretion in front of your parents. I'll also have you know that your work has been far from satisfactory of late. We realize, of course, that this time of the year is not the best for business, but you must understand, Mr Samsa, that a period with no business at all cannot, and should not, be tolerated!'

'But, sir,' Gregor cried out to himself, forgetting everything else in his anxiety. 'I will open the door immediately. I will open it. I only felt a little unwell; a slight dizziness stopped me from getting up. I am still in bed. But I feel better already. I am just getting up, really. If you'll only be patient a moment. I am not quite so well as I thought. But I'm all right, really. I don't understand why I've suddenly fallen ill. Only yesterday I felt quite well, as my parents will tell you. And then yesterday evening I felt a bit odd. They must have noticed. Why didn't I tell the office! But then, you always think you'll be able to shake off an illness without having to stay home. Please spare my parents, sir. The complaints you made just now are really without any foundation. No one has even suggested them before. Perhaps you have not seen the last orders I sent in. I will leave on the eight o'clock train. These few moments of rest have done me the world of good. Please don't waste your time any longer, sir. I shall be at the office immediately. Please tell the director what has happened and put in a good word for me.'

While Gregor was hastily explaining all this, scarcely understanding a word he'd said, he had squirmed up to the wardrobe and begun trying to pull himself upright. His previous gymnastics helped. He wanted to open the door. He wanted to be seen and to speak with the manager. He wanted to know what these people – who kept on harassing him – would say when they saw him. If he frightened them, there would be nothing left to say and they could leave him be. If they took everything calmly, then he had no need to be upset.

If he hurried, he might still be in time to catch the eight o'clock train. The wardrobe was polished, and Gregor slipped several times but, with one final effort, he managed to stand upright. Ignoring the sharp pains in his stomach, he let himself tumble forward on to the top of a nearby chair and clung to it fast with his little legs. Then, finding himself in control of his body, he fell silent so that he could hear what the manager had to say.

'Did you understand a word of what he said?' the manager asked Gregor's parents. 'Is he trying to make fools of us, or what?'

'Merciful God!' Gregor's mother cried, already in tears. 'Perhaps he is seriously ill, and here we are torturing him all this while! Grete! Grete!' she called.

'Mother!' cried her daughter from the other side – they were talking across Gregor's room – 'Fetch a doctor immediately! Gregor is ill! A doctor, quickly! Did you hear him speak?'

'It was an animal's voice,' said the manager. After Mrs Samsa's shrieking, his voice sounded curiously gentle. 'Anna, Anna!' shouted Gregor's father down the hall into the kitchen, clapping his hands. 'Get a locksmith, quick!'

Already the two girls were racing down the hall, skirts rustling – how could his sister have managed to get dressed so quickly? – and tearing out through the front door. Gregor did not hear it close. Perhaps they'd left it open, as so often happens in houses that have suffered disaster.

Gregor felt much calmer. He realized they had not understood his speech, though the words had seemed clear enough to him – clearer, indeed, than before; perhaps because he was getting used to it. But at least they now understood there was something seriously wrong with him, and were ready to help.

The correctness and confident nature of these initial measures made him feel better. He felt as if he were back in the fold of human society, and looked forward to great and wonderful deeds from both the locksmith and the doctor. To clear his throat for the decisive conversation he would soon have to have, he coughed a little, but as quietly as possible, for he feared that even his coughing might not sound human. Meanwhile, in the next room, things had all gone quiet. Perhaps his parents were sitting at the table whispering with the manager; perhaps they were all leaning against the door, listening.

Gregor shuffled slowly towards the door with the chair, threw it aside at the last moment, flung himself at the door and clung upright to the woodwork. The soles of his feet secreted a sticky substance. He rested for a moment. Next, he tried to turn the key in the lock with his mouth. Unfortunately, it seemed he no longer had proper teeth. How could he take hold of the key? On the other hand, he did have a set of very strong jaws. Using these, and ignoring the injury he was probably doing to himself – a brown liquid dribbled from his mouth, trickled over the lock and dripped to the floor – he managed to get hold of the key.

'Listen!' said the manager in the next room. 'He's turning the key.' Gregor took heart at this. He would have liked his father, his mother, everybody to start cheering him on: 'Courage, Gregor, come on, give it all you've got!' Encouraged by the idea that everyone was egging him on, he twisted the key with every last ounce of power his jaws possessed, straining until he nearly passed out. As it turned, he twisted round with it, gripping the key with his mandibles and pressing back up against it with all his weight whenever it slipped. The loud click of the lock as it sprang brought Gregor back to reality. 'They won't need the lock-smith now,' he thought, and leaned his head against the handle to open one leaf of the double doors. It was the only way he could have done it, but it prevented the others from actually seeing him, even when the door panel stood almost wide open.

He had to shuffle his way around the edge of the partition with great care, so as not to spoil his entrance by falling flat on his back. He was concentrating on this to the exclusion of everything else when he heard the manager, who was nearest the door, utter a loud 'Oh!'. It sounded like a sudden rush of wind. Gregor saw him clap a hand over his open mouth and slowly stagger back, as if propelled by some invisible and intensely powerful force. His mother, whose hair was still a complete mess despite the manager's presence, shot her husband a look, clasped her hands, took a couple of steps in Gregor's direction and then toppled backward into the arms of her family in a wild confusion of skirts. Her face, which had fallen forward on to her chest, was obscured. Mr Samsa clenched his fists with a menacing air, as if to beat Gregor back into his room; then he cast around the room in bewilderment, covered his eyes with one hand and began weeping so hard the sobs shook his powerful chest.

Gregor stayed out of the room. He stood against the closed half of the double doors, so they could only see a part of his body and, above that, his head, which he now tilted to one side so that he could keep an eye on them. Meanwhile, it had grown much lighter: on either side of the street a part of the long, dark building opposite could clearly be seen – it was a hospital, its grey-black façade pierced by rows of identical, stark windows. It was still raining, in huge drops that smashed to the earth one by one. The breakfast crockery was spread across the table: for his father, breakfast was the most important meal of the day; he would keep it going for hours while he worked his way through various newspapers.

On the wall hung a photograph of Gregor in a lieutenant's uniform, taken while he was in military service; he was smiling, his hand on the hilt of his sword. He looked happy at being respected for his rank. The living-room door was ajar, and, as the front door was also open, there was a clear view out to the landing and the top of the stairs.

'Now,' Gregor said – he realized he was the only one to have kept calm – 'now I will get dressed, pack my samples, and go. Will you please let me go? Surely you can see now, sir, that I am not just being difficult and that I fully intend to work. Commercial travelling is tiresome, and no mistake, but without it I cannot live. Where are you going, sir? To the office? Yes? Will you tell them the truth about everything? Everybody has a day off now and again, and that's the time to review their work record: once things improve, they go back to the grindstone and work better than ever. I owe the director a great deal, as you know. And I have my parents and my sister to think about. I'm in an awkward position, but I shall return to work. Only, please do not make things more difficult for me – they're hard enough as it is. Speak up for me at the office. I know they don't like the salesmen. They think we earn too much money, and lead an easy life.

'The present situation doesn't exactly help overcome this prejudice; but you, sir, as manager, can judge the circumstances better than the rest of the staff, better than the director himself — between ourselves, as the boss he is often misled by unfair talk. You know quite well that the travelling salesman, who barely sets foot in the office from one year to the next, is often the victim of gossip, or of random sniping against which he is powerless to defend himself for the simple reason that he usually doesn't even know what he is being accused of. He only learns about it when he comes home exhausted at the end of a trip, or when the unfortunate consequences of some business he can no longer even remember return to haunt him. Don't leave without a word or two to show that you give me some credit.'

But as soon as Gregor started to speak the manager turned away, only glancing back with a twitch of his shoulder and pursed lips. He had not been idle while Gregor was speaking; instead, he had retreated furtively, step by step, towards the door – making sure he kept a close eye on Gregor at all times – sneaking off as if there were some unwritten law against leaving the room. Already he had reached the hall. He took his last steps out of the living-room as if the soles of his shoes were on fire. As he exited, he stretched his right hand out blindly towards the stairs as if some divine deliverance awaited him below.

Gregor realized that if he let the manager go as things stood, then he could probably kiss goodbye to his job. Unfortunately, his parents did not share in his moment of clarity; they'd long believed that Gregor was settled in the firm for life and were so consumed by their present grief that they had no idea what to make of it all. But Gregor was thinking ahead. The manager had to be stopped, calmed, convinced and finally won over. His own and his family's future depended on it!

If only his sister were there! She had understood; she had actually begun to cry while Gregor was still lying quietly on his back. The manager, who was a ladies' man, would have listened to her, let her guide him. She would have closed the living-room door and convinced him, out there on the landing, that his terror was unfounded. But there was no sign of her. Gregor would just have to deal with the problem himself. And without even stopping to wonder whether he was physically up to the task, or whether his little speech had even been understood, he let go of the partition, shoved himself out through the door in an effort to over-take the manager (by now he was clinging to the banisters with both hands in the most ridiculous manner), made a vain attempt to catch himself and then, with a sharp cry, fell forward on to his scurrying feet.

Suddenly, and for the first time that morning, he experienced a feeling of physical wellbeing. Not only were his feet now on firm ground, but he noticed with a pang of joy that his legs obeyed him wonderfully; they were eager to carry him wherever he wanted. Maybe his troubles were all behind him now. He scuttled up to his mother and began rocking back and forth. At this point he saw her suddenly snap out of her faint, jump up, throw her arms in the air and shout, 'Help! For God's sake, help!' She tilted her head to get a better look at Gregor. Then, as if thinking better of it, she began careering backwards, completely forgetting that the table, still covered with all the breakfast things, was directly behind her. She staggered right into it and sat down almost absent-mindedly, hardly noticing that the overturned coffee pot right next to her was belching its contents all over the carpet.

'Mother, mother,' Gregor said quietly, looking up at her. He had quite forgotten about the manager. Seeing the coffee spilling, without thinking Gregor found himself snapping his mandibles in the air.

At this, his mother started shrieking again, jumped up from the table and fell into the arms of her husband, who had rushed up behind her. But Gregor had no time to worry about them. The manager was already on the stairs; resting his chin on the banister, he was looking back for one last time.

Gregor sprang forward to try and stop him. The manager must have guessed what was coming, for he leapt down the steps in a single bound and vanished with a cry of 'Aaagh!' which echoed through the stairwell. His rapid escape had the unfortunate effect of causing Gregor's father – who until now had kept a hold of himself – to fly completely off the handle. Instead of running after the manager, or at least not trying to stop

Gregor from overhauling him, he seized the manager's walking stick in his right hand – he had left it behind on a chair, along with his overcoat and hat – grabbed a large newspaper from the table to his left and began stamping his feet and brandishing the paper and the cane to drive Gregor back into his room. Gregor's pleas went unheard; he had not the slightest chance of being understood no matter how submissively he lowered his head. The more meekly he behaved, the harder his father stamped.

Across from them, and despite the cold, Mrs Samsa had thrown the window open and was leaning out as far as possible, her face pressed into her hands. A great draught of air swept up the stairs from the street. The curtains billowed, the papers blew up and a few sheets flew across the room. Hissing savagely, Gregor's father came after him. Unused to moving backwards, Gregor beat a slow retreat. If only he'd been able to turn around he'd have reached his room in no time. But he was afraid that if the treacle slowness of his retreat made his father any more impatient, then his reward would be a lethal blow from the stick to the head or back.

Gregor quickly ran out of options. To his horror, he realized that he had no control when he was in reverse gear. Watching his parent fearfully out of the corner of his eye, he tried his hardest to speed up the turn. It was taking forever. Perhaps his father realized he meant well: instead of hindering him, he was now helping shove Gregor round with the tip of the stick. If only he would stop that unbearable hissing! It was driving Gregor mad. He had almost completed his turn when, confused by all the din, he lost his sense of direction and began lumbering back round to face his father. He was just celebrating the fact that he'd got his head through the half-opened double doors, when he discovered that without even more of a performance his body was too wide to go through them.

Naturally, in his present mood it never occurred to his father to open the other side of the door so that Gregor could pass through. The one idea in his head was to get the boy back into his room as quickly as possible.

His father didn't have the patience to wait for Gregor to haul himself upright and get into his room that way. Right on his heels and making enough noise for a hundred fathers, not one, his father badgered Gregor to get through the door as if that was the easiest thing in the world. This wasn't funny any more. Throwing caution to the winds, Gregor hurled himself at the gap. One side of his body stuck fast in the doorway, lacerated by the door jamb, whose white paint was now covered in horrible brown stains. He was caught fast and needed help.

On one side, his little legs fluttered helplessly in the air; on the other they were squashed painfully against the floor. His father struck him a life-threatening blow from behind with the cane. Gregor was sent flying into the bedroom and fell, bleeding heavily. His father slammed the door shut with the stick, and then, at last, all was still.

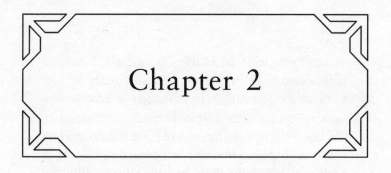

Chapter 2

It was dusk by the time Gregor woke from his heavy, swoon-like sleep. He would have woken up anyway even without any disturbance – he felt fully rested – but it seemed to him that he'd been spooked by the furtive rattle of a key in the lock of the hall door.

Here and there, the ceiling and furniture caught the muted play of light reflected from the electric tramway. But down where Gregor lay all was dark. He hauled himself slowly towards the door in an effort to work out what had happened, probing clumsily with the feelers which he was only now beginning to master. His left side seemed to him to be one long, painful scar, and he was limping on his double set of legs. One leg had been seriously injured in the course of the morning's events – it was a miracle more of them hadn't been damaged – and it dragged lifelessly behind him.

When he reached the door, he realized what had attracted him: the smell of food. There was a bowl of sweetened milk there, with little pieces of bread floating in it. He could have chuckled with delight; he was even hungrier than he had been in the morning. He plunged his head in the milk up to his eyes. Immediately, he withdrew it; his tender left side made eating difficult, and in fact he could only manage by contorting his whole body and snorting. But the thing was, he could no longer bear the smell of milk which had once been his favourite drink and which his sister had no doubt brought specially. He turned away from the bowl in disgust and dragged himself to the middle of the room.

The gas was lit in the living-room – he could see it through the cracks in the door. Under normal circumstances, this was the time of day when his father entertained the family by reading aloud from the evening paper; but for the moment all was quiet. Perhaps this ritual, which his sister always told him about in her letters, had recently died out. Everything was silent, and yet surely there had to be someone in the room? 'What a quiet life my family has led,' thought Gregor, staring into the darkness, and he felt very proud that he was the one who had provided his parents and his sister with their tranquil life and their lovely flat.

What would happen now, if this peace, this happiness, this wellbeing were to end in terror and disaster? To push away these gloomy thoughts,

Gregor began to take a little exercise, crawling backwards and forwards across the floor.

At one point during the evening he saw the door on the left open slightly, and another time it was the door on the right: someone seemed to think about coming in, but decided not to risk it. Gregor waited by the dining-room door, willing on the hesitant visitor as best he might, or at least hoping to see who it was; but it never opened again, and Gregor stood sentry in vain. That morning, when the door had been locked, everyone had tried to invade his room; but now that they had managed to open it, no one came to see him. They had even locked the doors on the outside.

The lights in the living-room stayed on until late, and Gregor knew his parents and sister were still up; he heard the three of them stealing away on tiptoe. That meant no one would come and see him before morning, which gave him plenty of time to think about how he was going to manage his new life. But now that he had to keep his stomach down flat to the floor, the enormous room he had lived in for the past five years frightened him in a way he could not comprehend.

Half-heartedly and somewhat ashamed, he fled under the sofa, where he soon found that he felt more comfortable, even though his back was slightly squashed and he could not raise his head fully. He was only sorry his body was too thick to fit right under it. He spent the whole night there in a half-sleep, broken by sharp pangs of hunger and vague hopes and worries. These led him to conclude that it was his duty to remain quiet and patient at all costs, and to try to make things as bearable as he could for his family, despite the unpleasant turn of events.

Early in the morning he had a chance to test the strength of his new resolution. It was only just growing light. His sister, who was already almost fully dressed, opened the hall door and looked in curiously. At first, she didn't see him, and must have thought, 'He must be somewhere, for heaven's sake, he can't just have flown away.' Then, when she spotted him under the sofa, she was so scared she rushed back out again, slamming the door behind her. A moment later, regretting her behaviour, she opened it for the second time and tiptoed in, as if entering the room of a stranger or someone who was seriously ill.

Gregor stuck his head out from the side of the sofa and watched her. Would she notice that he'd left the milk, and realize it was not because he wasn't hungry? Would she bring him some other food that suited him better? If she didn't do so of her own accord, he would rather have starved to death than draw her attention to it, despite his tremendous urge to shoot forward out of his hiding place, throw himself at his sister's feet and beg her for something nice to eat.

In fact his sister noticed the brimming bowl immediately. Her eyes widened. Some milk had spilled around it; using a piece of paper, of course, and not her bare hands, she picked the bowl up and carried it off to the kitchen. Gregor was extremely curious to see what she would bring him instead, and all kinds of things came into his mind. But he would never have guessed what his sister, in her kindness, actually did. To find out what her brother really liked to eat, she brought a whole range of options spread out on an old newspaper. There were half-rotten chunks of vegetables; bones from the family supper covered in congealed white sauce; a few currants and raisins; some almonds; some cheese that Gregor had recently decided was inedible; a stale loaf; a piece of salted bread and butter, and another slice of bread without the salt. She also set down the bowl again, the one which was almost certainly now earmarked for Gregor's exclusive use and which she had filled with water. Showing great consideration in understanding that her brother would prefer not to eat in front of her, she then left, closing and locking the door so that he could eat in peace and quiet.

As he headed for the food, Gregor felt all his little legs start to tremble beneath him. His wounds seemed to have healed, for he moved with complete freedom, which amazed him when he remembered that he'd cut his finger more than a month earlier, and that it had still been hurting as recently as two days before.

'Am I less vulnerable now?' he wondered. But he had already started sucking eagerly at the cheese, for which he had developed a singular and sudden craving. In quick succession, he devoured the cheese, the vegetables and the sauce, tears of pure joy streaming from his eyes. But he wouldn't go near the fresh food – the smell of it repelled him, and he pushed it further away so that it wouldn't put him off the rest.

Long after he'd finished, he was drowsing idly in the same spot when his sister turned the key in the lock, softly and slowly so that he'd have time to hide. Even though he was still half asleep, he got the wind up and hurried back to the sofa. It took all his self-control to stay under it for the short time his sister was in the room: the heavy meal had made him a bit fatter, so that he could scarcely breathe in the tight space. Struggling for breath, he watched tearfully as his sister, assuming he no longer wanted it, swept up the remains of his meal and the things that he hadn't touched, dropped the trash into a bucket, covered it with a wooden lid and took it away. Almost before she'd turned her back, Gregor struggled out from his hiding place, stretched and let his body expand to its proper size.

That's how he was fed every day. In the morning, before his parents and the maid were awake, and in the afternoon, when lunch was over and while his parents were taking a short nap – and his sister had given the maid a task to keep her busy. They certainly didn't want Gregor to die of hunger, but they probably didn't choose to know any more about how he ate his food than they were told. Perhaps, too, Gregor's sister wanted to spare them any more heartache than they were no doubt already enduring.

Gregor never learned what excuses they had made to get the doctor and the locksmith out of the apartment, because while he could understand what other people said, no one, not even his sister, imagined that he could do so. When she came into his room, he had to content himself with listening to her sighing and invoking the saints. It was only much later, when they had become a bit more used to the changed situation – obviously, they were never going to get used to it entirely – that Gregor would occasionally overhear a few words betraying what seemed to him like kindness. When he had eaten all the food off the newspaper she would say, 'He liked what I brought today.' At other times, when he had no appetite – and as time went on this became more frequent – she would tell them with a certain sadness, 'He didn't touch a thing today.'

Even if he couldn't get any direct news, Gregor overheard a good deal of what was said in the dining-room. As soon as he picked up the sound of voices, he would hurry to the appropriate door and press the length of his body tight up against it. In the early days, especially, there was little conversation, secret or otherwise, that did not bear more or less directly on his predicament. For two whole days, mealtimes were given over to discussions about the best way to handle things. Even between meals, the talk was mainly the same. At least two members of the family were always at home – none of them wanted to be there alone, but under no circumstances could they leave the apartment unattended.

It was not entirely clear how much the cook knew, but, on the very first day, she had fallen on her knees and begged Mrs Samsa to let her go at once. A quarter of an hour later, she thanked them tearfully on her way out, as if letting her quit was the greatest, kindest thing they had ever done for her. And without being asked to do so, she swore a terrible oath never to reveal even the slightest hint about what she knew to anyone.

Now Gregor's mother and sister had to do the cooking, but this wasn't too troublesome since no one was eating very much. Occasionally Gregor would hear one of them vainly exhorting another to eat. The reply was always more or less the same: 'I'm full, thanks.' They didn't really drink much, either. Often his sister would ask her father if he'd like some beer. She'd offer to fetch it, or, faced with his silence and to get round him, she'd suggest that the janitor's wife go for it. But each time her father replied with a loud 'No!' and that was the end of it.

On day one of the crisis, Mr Samsa had given his wife and daughter a clear account of their financial situation and future prospects. From time to time, he would get up from the table and hunt for some document or account book in his small Wertheim safe, which he'd rescued from the failure of his business five years earlier. They all heard him opening and closing the complicated locks, taking things out and relocking it. His father's announcement was the most heartening thing Gregor had heard since becoming a prisoner. He had always imagined that his father had been unable to save a penny from the ruins of his business. That's because his father had never said anything to the contrary, and Gregor had never asked. His only concern had been to do everything he could to help his family forget the financial disaster that had plunged them all into such despair as quickly as possible.

He had set to work with exemplary enthusiasm; almost overnight he had been promoted from junior clerk to commercial traveller, with all the benefits the new job entailed – not least the prospect of earning more money. And in very short order, his efforts were transformed into ready money, laid out on the table before his family's surprised and delighted eyes. Happy days, never since recaptured, even though later on Gregor had made so much money that he'd been able to shoulder the family's entire financial burden.

His family had grown to accept this state of affairs as much as Gregor. He gave the money willingly, they took it gratefully, but the arrangement no longer gave rise to any special warmth. Only his sister had kept a place in her heart for Gregor, who planned to pay for her to enter the Conservatory the following year, regardless of the high fees which he would just have to find some other way. Unlike Gregor, his sister was very fond of music and wanted to study the violin, which she played with some skill. The Conservatory often came up in the fleeting conversations they had when Gregor snatched a few hours at home, but almost always in the guise of happy daydreaming. Their parents didn't much like even these innocent reveries, but Gregor took the matter very seriously, and had set his heart on announcing the plan officially come Christmas Eve.

Even though they were pointless in his present situation, it was ideas like this that teemed in Gregor's thoughts when he was pressed up against the door listening. Sometimes, he grew so tired he could listen no more, and his head would accidentally bump against the panelling; but he would snatch it back at once, since they'd notice even the slightest noise in the room beyond and fall silent.

'What on earth is he up to now?' his father would say after a pause, no doubt with a nod at the door; and only then did they pick up the interrupted conversation. Since his father was often obliged to repeat his explanation in order to recall details he himself had long forgotten, or to make his wife understand – she did not always grasp things the first time around – Gregor discovered that, despite all their misfortunes, his parents had been able to save a small sum of money, and that the untouched interest on this had meantime helped it grow.

Neither had they spent all of the monthly wages that Gregor, keeping only a couple of shillings for himself, had handed over every week. This had enabled them to accumulate a little more capital. Behind the door, Gregor nodded approvingly, delighted at this unexpected foresight and thrift. It was true that his father could have paid off his debt to Gregor's employer with these savings much sooner, and so brought Gregor's release date nearer; but under the circumstances it was much better that his father had acted as he had.

Unfortunately, the interest on the capital wasn't enough for the family to live on: it would last a year, perhaps two, but no longer. That nest egg had to be kept for emergencies. They would have to earn the money to pay the bills.

Despite his good health, Mr Samsa was nonetheless an old man who hadn't worked for five years – no one could really expect too much of him. During these five years of retirement – his first holiday in a life dedicated to hard work and failure – he had become extremely fat and slow-moving. And suffering as she did from asthma, old Mrs Samsa wouldn't be able to earn much, either. In fact, nowadays, just getting around the house was an effort, and she spent every other day lying on the sofa, wheezing for breath by the open window. Was his sister – a child, still, at 17 – supposed to become the breadwinner? Her life so far – she was always nicely dressed and rested, helping a little about the house, enjoying a few modest amusements and above all devoted to her violin – had not prepared her for anything so taxing. Whenever the conversation turned to the subject of earning money, Gregor would leave his post by the door and fall back on to the nearby sofa, whose cool leather was so soothing to his body, burning as it was with anxiety and shame.

Often he lay sleepless the whole night, scratching at the leather for hours on end. At other times, he would eagerly push his armchair over to the window, pull himself up on the casement, wedge himself against the seat and lean forward against the panes; not so much to savour the view as to re-live the happiness he'd felt there before. In reality, he could now barely make out the hospital – whose unremitting bulk he had once cursed – directly opposite. If he hadn't been certain he lived in the quiet but entirely urban confines of Charlottenstrasse, he might well have believed his window looked out on to a wasteland, where the grey of the sky and the grey of the earth merged indistinguishably. His attentive sister had only to see the armchair by the window twice to understand; from then on, each time she tidied the room she would push the armchair up to the window, and leave the lower half of the casement open.

If only Gregor had been able to speak to her and thank her for doing so much for him, he could have accepted her services more easily. As it was, they both pained and embarrassed him. Naturally she tried to pass things off as lightly as possible, and as time went on she played her part even better; but she could not prevent her brother from understanding with increasing clarity how matters stood.

He began to dread her visits. The moment she came into the room – hurriedly shutting the door as if she wanted to spare the others the sight of what lay within – she would run to the window, fling it open and stick her head out, breathing deeply for a minute no matter how cold it was, as if to prevent imminent suffocation. Twice a day, while he lay trembling under the sofa, she terrified Gregor with all this rush and clatter. He knew his sister would have spared him this ordeal if she'd been able to stand being in the same room with him with the window shut.

One day – it must have been a good month after Gregor's metamorphosis, and his sister could hardly have had any reason to be surprised at his appearance – she came a little earlier than usual and found him looking out of the window. He was motionless, but something in the way he was standing struck fear into her heart. Gregor wouldn't have been surprised if she'd stayed out of the room – his position prevented her from opening the window. But not only would she not enter, she sprang back, slammed the door and locked it.

A stranger might have thought that Gregor was planning to bite her. Of course, Gregor hid under the sofa at once, but it was noon before his sister ventured back and, when she did turn up, she looked much more agitated than usual. From this, he deduced that his appearance still disgusted her, that it always would and that it was only by exercising the most terrific self-control that she stopped herself running from the room the moment she caught sight of the tiniest part of his body protruding from under the sofa. To spare her the awful sight, one day Gregor took a sheet on his back, dragged it to the sofa – it took him four hours – and arranged it in such a way that his sister couldn't see him even if she bent down. If she hadn't wanted this screen, then she could have removed it – it was clear he wasn't hiding for fun.

But his sister left the sheet where it was, and Gregor, prudently parting the fabric with his head to see how she was taking the new arrangement, thought he detected a look of gratitude on her face. During the first fortnight his parents had not been able to bring themselves to enter his room. He often heard them praising his sister's hard work, whereas before they had frequently complained that she was a useless young girl. But now, both his father and mother would often wait outside Gregor's door while she was tidying the room, and scarcely had she come out again than they would make her tell them in detail exactly how she had found things in there: what had Gregor eaten, exactly what was he doing and was there any sign of improvement, however slight? His mother had wanted to see Gregor almost from the first, but his father and sister had dissuaded her with sensible arguments, to which Gregor listened very attentively and with which he wholly agreed.

Later, however, they had to hold her back by force, and when his mother began to cry, 'Let me go to Gregor! My poor boy! Don't you understand that I have to see him!' Gregor thought that perhaps it might be a good thing after all if his mother came in, not every day, of course, but perhaps once a week: she would understand things better than his sister, who for all her courage was still only a child, and had in all likelihood only taken on such a difficult job out of naïve goodwill.

Gregor's hopes of seeing his mother were soon fulfilled. He avoided showing himself at the window during the day out of consideration for his parents; but he couldn't crawl very far on the few square metres of his bedroom floor, and found it hard to lie quietly at night. Since he no longer enjoyed eating, he took to scuttling around the room to distract himself: up and down the walls and across the ceiling, from which he liked to hang upside down. It was much better than crawling across the floor – he breathed more easily, his body vibrated with pleasure, and he sometimes lost himself so completely in the moment that much to his surprise he'd let go and come crashing down. But now that he had better control over his body, he managed to make these headlong plunges harmless.

His sister immediately noticed the new pastime Gregor had devised for himself – even at a crawl he left a trail of sticky marks everywhere – and took it into her head to help him beetle about as freely as possible by removing all the furniture that might get in his way, especially the wardrobe and the writing desk. Unfortunately, she was not strong enough to manage this on her own and didn't dare ask her father to lend a hand. As for the sixteen-year-old maid, there was no way she'd have agreed to help – the child had worked with a will since the former cook had been let go, but only on condition that she could keep the kitchen door locked, and open it only when specially requested. So his sister would just have to ask her mother to help one day when her father was out. Mrs Samsa consented gladly, but her loud cries of pleasure ceased abruptly when she reached Gregor's door.

Of course, his sister made sure everything in the room was in order first; then she allowed her mother to go in. In his extreme haste, Gregor had pulled the sheet down further than usual, and the folds made it look as if it had just been thrown over the sofa by chance. This first time, he stopped himself from peeping out under the sheet to see his mother, but he was delighted to have her nearby. 'Come in – you can't see him,' his sister said, and obviously taking her mother by the hand, she led her into the room. Then Gregor heard the two frail women struggling to move the heavy old wardrobe. His sister did most of the work, despite her mother's warnings that she might overstrain herself. It took a very long time.

They had been struggling with the monster wardrobe for about a quarter of an hour when Mrs Samsa declared it might be best to leave the thing where it was: in the first place, it was too heavy for them, and they wouldn't be able to finish moving it before Mr Samsa came back. Secondly, if they left the wardrobe in the middle of the room, then Gregor might find it got in his way. Finally, who knew whether or not he'd be pleased if they moved his furniture out? Mrs Samsa thought he wouldn't; the sight of the bare walls made her heart ache. How could Gregor not feel the same, when he'd lived with all this furniture for so long; how could he possibly not feel abandoned in a bare room? 'In any case,' she said in a low voice – she had spoken in whispers ever since she came in, not so much because Gregor, whose lair she had not yet discovered, might hear her words – she was convinced he couldn't understand these – but so he would not have to listen to the sound of her voice. 'In any case, if we move all the stuff out, aren't we more or less saying we've given up all hope of seeing him cured? Are we just going to leave him to his fate? I think it would be better to keep everything just as it was, so that when Gregor comes back to us he'll find everything the same – and it will be easier for him to forget what's happened.'

Hearing his mother's words, Gregor realized that the monotonous life he'd been leading for the past two months, in the course of which no one had spoken a single word to him, must have turned his mind. He could not otherwise explain his over-whelming desire for a nice empty room. Did he really want this warm, comfortable den filled with all the family furniture to be transformed into an empty cave, where he could crawl about to his heart's content – and wave a swift goodbye to his human past? Had he come so close to forget-ting it already? It had taken nothing less than his mother's voice, which he hadn't heard for so long, to wake him up. Nothing should be removed; everything had to remain as it was. The furniture had to stay because it was keeping him sane; if it prevented him from utterly losing his wits and crawling aimlessly around the place, then so much the better.

Unfortunately, his sister had other plans. She'd grown used to taking charge of her parents when it came to Gregor. There was good reason for all this, and now her mother's remarks were enough to make her decide to remove not only the writing desk and the wardrobe – which up till then had been her sole aim – but all of the other furniture as well, except of course for the indispensable sofa. This wasn't just out of childish contrariness, nor just because of the hard-won and recent self-confidence she had so unexpectedly acquired. No, she really believed that Gregor needed plenty of room to run about in, and that, as far as she could tell, he never used the furniture.

Perhaps, also, the passionate nature of girls her age played a part – her way was to seek out every opportunity for self-expression, and it now drove her to make her brother's life even more difficult, as she strove to do more and more on his behalf.

Only Grete dared enter and stay in the room over whose bare walls Gregor reigned supreme. She ignored her mother, who seemed ill-at-ease in there, and who now fell silent, doing her best to help move the wardrobe. Gregor could just about put up with that going, but the desk had to stay. And hardly had the women left the room, panting as they pushed the wardrobe, than Gregor stuck his head out from under the sofa to see if he might make a prudent and tactful intervention. But unfortunately it was his mother who returned first. Grete was next door, arms around the wardrobe, pulling and pushing it, but unable to get it into place.

Gregor knew his mother wasn't used to the sight of him; he didn't want her to pass out with fright. Terrified, he reversed hurriedly towards the other end of the sofa, but in doing so inadvertently knocked the sheet. His mother couldn't help but notice. She stopped short, stood stock still for a moment and then hurried back to Grete. Although Gregor kept telling himself that nothing out of the ordinary was happening – that they were just moving a few pieces of furniture – there was no doubt that the commotion the women were making, their muted cries, the scraping of the furniture, was unnerving him. However much he kept his head down, drew his legs up and pressed himself flat, he knew he couldn't bear all of this for much longer. They were emptying his room, taking everything he loved; they had already taken the wardrobe, where he kept his saw and his fretwork kit; now they were shifting his desk, which had stood so solidly in place all these years, the very same desk where he'd done his homework when he was in business college, at secondary school and even back in primary school.

He really didn't have any time left to worry about the good intentions of these two women. In any case he'd almost forgotten their existence: by now they were so tired they were working almost in silence, and the only sound he could hear was the thumping of their feet. So Gregor came out of his lair. The women were leaning against the desk in the next room taking a short breather – and he found himself so bewildered that he changed direction four times. He couldn't make up his mind what to try and save first; then he suddenly caught sight of his picture of the woman dressed in furs, stark on the bare wall. He scuttled up and pressed himself against the glass, which felt good stuck fast to his hot belly. At least no one could take the picture now that he was spread-eagled all over it. He turned his head toward the living-room door to watch them coming back.

They'd only taken a short break and now here they were. Grete had her arm round her mother and was almost dragging her along. 'Well, what shall we do next?' Grete said, looking around. Her gaze met Gregor's as he hung on the wall. It was probably only out of concern for her mother that she kept any composure. She leaned her head forward to stop her mother from seeing anything and said a little too quickly and in a trembling voice, 'Come on, let's go back to the living-room for a minute.'

Grete's eyes told Gregor what she had in mind: she was going to get her mother to safety and then come back and chase him down off the wall. Well, let her try! He lay over his picture, determined not to give it up. He would sooner leap into his sister's face. But Grete's words had served to upset her mother; at that very moment, Mrs Samsa turned, saw the gigantic brown blob on the wallpaper and, before she had time to take in the fact it was her son, screamed, 'O God! O God!' and fell back on to the sofa and lay motionless, arms flung wide in total horror.

'You – Gregor!' Grete cried, raising her fist and shooting him a withering look. They were the first words she'd spoken to him directly since his transformation. She ran through to the next room, to fetch something to revive her mother. Gregor decided to help – there was still time to save the picture – but found he was stuck fast to the glass and had to make a violent effort to break free. He hurried after his sister, meaning to give her more of the same good advice he'd handed out in the past. But he could only stand and watch as she rummaged among the bottles. Then he frightened her so terribly when she turned round that a bottle fell and shattered on the floor. A splinter from this wounded Gregor in the face, and he found himself covered in some kind of corrosive medicine. Grete snatched up as many bottles as she could carry and rushed in to her mother, slamming the door behind her with her foot.

Now there was no way Gregor could reach his mother, and it was his fault if she was at death's door. He didn't dare go and look in case he drove his sister away again; she had to stay with his mother. There was nothing he could do but wait. Gnawed by self-reproach and anxiety, he began crawling all over the place: across the walls, the furniture, the ceiling, until finally, in a torment of despair and, as his head began to spin, he fell heavily, slap bang on to the middle of the big table.

Some time passed while Gregor lay dazed where he'd fallen. Everything was quiet. Perhaps that was a good sign. Then the bell rang. With the maid barricaded in the kitchen as usual, Grete had to go and open the front door. His father was back. The first thing he said was, 'What happened?' Grete's expression told him everything he needed to know. In a stifled voice – she probably had her face buried in her father's chest – she said, 'Mother fainted, but she's much better now. Gregor has escaped.'

'Just what I expected,' her father replied. 'I told you all along, but you women will never listen.'

It was clear to Gregor that his father had misunderstood Grete's all too brief explanation and imagined that his son was guilty of some violent act. Since there was no time and no possibility of making him understand, he had to find some way of pacifying his father. He rushed to the bedroom door and pressed himself up against it, so that when he came in from the hallway his father would know he meant to go back into his own room immediately, and there was no need to drive him back by force. All he needed to do was open the door, and Gregor would shoot back inside.

But his father was in no mood for niceties. As he entered he cried, 'Ha!' in a tone that suggested he was both furious and pleased at the same time. Gregor drew his head back from the door and turned to look at his father. He was amazed. He had never imagined his father could look as he now did. It was true that Gregor had been so taken up with the lovely new sensation of crawling around that he hadn't really kept up with what was going on in the house, and had therefore not become aware of certain changes. And yet – and yet, was that really his father? Was this really the same man who once had lain buried wearily in bed when Gregor was setting off on his business trips? Who met him, on his return, still in his dressing gown, wedged into an armchair from which he couldn't even lift himself, or do any more than raise his arms to show how pleased he was? Was this that same old man who, on the rare walks they took together as a family, two or three Sundays a year and on special holidays, would hobble ever more slowly between Gregor and his mother – who in any case walked slowly enough – bundled up in an old coat, probing cautiously ahead with his walking stick as he struggled to make progress? And who, when he wanted to say something, would stop dead and gather his family around him?

Now here he was, a fine, upstanding citizen, dressed in a tight-fitting blue uniform with gold buttons of the kind worn by bank employees. His monumental double chin spread its imposing folds above a high, stiff collar; dark, watchful eyes peered keenly out from beneath the bushy eyebrows; normally untidy, his white hair now featured a painfully exact parting. He threw his cap, which seemed to be decorated with the gold monogram of some bank, in a neat arc across the room on to the sofa. Then, with his hands in his trouser pockets, the long tails of his coat turned back, he walked toward Gregor with a menacing air.

In fact, he was probably unsure about what he was going to do; but he lifted his feet quite immoderately high in the air. Gregor was astonished at the enormous size of his father's boot soles. But he had no time to dwell on that. From the very first day of his new life he'd known that his father believed he should be treated with the utmost severity. And so he scuttled ahead of him, stopping whenever he stopped and scurrying off again at his father's slightest movement. They circled the room several times in this way without matters coming to a head. Truth be told, their movements were so slow it didn't even look like a proper chase. Gregor stayed on the floor, not least because he was afraid that if his father saw him climbing about the walls or rushing across the ceiling he'd take it as a sign of particular malice. And yet, he knew things couldn't go on like this for very much longer.

In the short time it took his father to take one step, Gregor had to make a whole series of rippling gymnastic movements, and as he'd never had good lungs, he was already growing noticeably short of breath. He staggered along, concentrating all his strength on running away, scarcely able to keep his eyes open, so dazed that all he could think of was escape. He had almost forgotten that he could use the walls, although in this room all the finely carved furniture, with its serrations and sharp points, worked against him. Suddenly something whizzed past him, fell to the ground and rolled away. It was an apple. It was followed immediately by a second one.

Paralyzed with terror, Gregor froze. It was no good trying to run any more – his father had decided to bombard him. He had filled his pockets with the contents of the fruit bowl on the sideboard, and was flinging one apple after another, without – at least for the moment – even taking proper aim. The little red apples rolled about the floor, colliding with one another as if electrified. A weakly thrown apple grazed his back and bounced off harmlessly, but the next one pierced it right through. Gregor's instinct was to drag himself away in the hope that a change of position might alleviate the shocking and unbelievable pain. But he seemed to be nailed fast to the spot and lay spread-eagled, head spinning. With his last glance, he saw his bedroom door suddenly flung wide, and his mother dash out in front of his sister who was shouting at the top of her voice.

His mother was in her undergarments: to ease the grip of her fainting fit his sister had partly undressed her so that she could breathe more easily. Then he saw his mother run to his father, her untied petticoats slipping to the floor one after another. Tripping over her skirts, she fell forward against her husband, put her arms around him, hugged him tight and, clasping the back of his neck – at which point Gregor's eyesight failed him – begged him to spare Gregor's life.

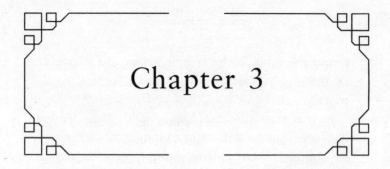

Chapter 3

The apple which no one dared remove from Gregor's back remained embedded in his flesh, and the terrible wound he'd now borne for more than a month was left as a permanent reminder. It seemed to make even his father realize that Gregor, despite all his troubles and his terrible transformation, was nonetheless still a member of the family, who should not be treated as an enemy. On the contrary, family duty demanded they swallow their disgust and be patient, always and only patient.

His injury had probably caused him to lose his mobility for good, and it now took him forever just to get across his room, his movements like those of an ageing invalid. Crawling anywhere high up was out of the question. But to Gregor, the fact that they now left the living-room door open every evening was some compensation for his worsening condition. He looked forward eagerly to this. Lying invisible in the darkness of his room, he could see the whole family gathered round the table in the lamplight and listen freely to their conversation. This was a radical and welcome change.

It was true they no longer held those lively conversations he'd thought of longingly each time he climbed between the damp sheets of some cramped little hotel room. Most of the time, now, they sat in silence. Directly after dinner, his father would settle down to doze in his armchair, while his mother and sister hushed each other. Leaning forward into the light, his mother would sew away at some fine needlework she was doing for a clothing store, while his sister, who now worked as a sales assistant, studied shorthand and French in the hope of finding a better job. Now and then his father would wake up and, not realizing he'd been asleep, say to his wife, 'You've been sewing for so long today!' and then go straight back to sleep, prompting Gregor's mother and sister to exchange a tired smile.

Out of some obstinate whim, his father invariably refused to take off his uniform when he came back in from work. His dressing gown hung unused on the hook, and he slept in his armchair in full livery, as if to keep himself always ready to carry out the orders of his superiors, even at home. As a result, the uniform, which had not been new even when it was issued to him, grew shabbier by the day despite the best efforts of the two women. Gregor passed long evenings staring at the old man as he slept uncomfortably but peacefully in his stained and spotted jacket with its brightly polished buttons.

As soon as the clock struck ten, his mother would quietly try to rouse her husband and encourage him to go to bed, as it was impossible for him, slumped in that way, to get the sleep he needed before returning to work at six the next morning. But, with the same obstinacy that had characterized him since he'd started working at the bank, he would insist on staying at the table even though he regularly dropped off to sleep, which made it more and more difficult to coax him out of his armchair and into bed. Try as they might to urge him to move with gentle encouragements, he would sit there with his eyes tight shut for fifteen minutes at a time, slowly nodding his head and refusing to get up. Well might his wife tug him by the sleeve and whisper sweet nothings in his ear, or his daughter lay her work aside to try and help. Nothing had any effect. The old man would simply sink deeper into his chair.

Only when the two women seized him under the arms would he open his eyes, gaze at each of them in turn and say, 'What a life! Is this the hard-earned rest of my old age?' and, leaning on the two women, haul himself up as if he weighed a ton and let himself be led to the door. Once there he would wave them away and continue alone, while his wife put down her needle, his daughter her pen and they both ran fussing after him. Who in this overworked and overtired family had time to attend to Gregor, except when it came to his most pressing needs?

The household budget dwindled to the point where they had to dismiss the maid. In her place, they took on a gigantic charwoman with bony features and white hair floating around her head to come in morning and evening to do the heavy work. His mother had to take care of everything else on top of her interminable needlework. His mother and sister even had to sell off some of the family jewellery they'd worn with so much pride on high days and holidays, as Gregor discovered one evening when he heard them discussing the prices they hoped to get. But the biggest complaint was always about the flat, which was much larger than they needed and which they now found too expensive to maintain. They couldn't leave, they said, because they couldn't think of any way of moving Gregor. In fact, Gregor knew he wasn't really what stopped them from moving; they could easily have transported him in a large wooden box pierced with a few air holes. The thing that really stopped them moving was their own despair, and the sense that they had been afflicted with a misfortune unlike any that had ever before occurred in their family or circle of acquaintance.

They were now under the cosh of crushing poverty: his father had to fetch breakfast for the bank underlings; his mother worked herself to the bone mending the linen of strangers; his sister ran about behind her counter at her customers' beck and call, until the whole family was at the end of its tether.

When his mother and sister came back from putting his father to bed, laid their work down and drew their chairs close until they were sitting almost cheek to cheek, Gregor would feel the wound in his back starting to hurt again. And then pointing at Gregor's bedroom, his mother would say, 'Close the door, Grete,' and he would once again be left in the darkness, while next door the two women either mingled their tears or sat dry-eyed, staring at the table.

For long days and nights Gregor could not sleep. Sometimes he thought that the next time they opened the door, he would find himself managing his family's affairs as he always had done. Much later, his boss, the manager, the clerks and the firm's apprentices bubbled up to the surface of his mind: the nitwit office boy, two or three friends from other firms, a chambermaid in a provincial hotel – a sweet, if fleeting memory – a till girl in a hat shop he'd courted seriously but too slowly.

They all paraded through his thoughts, jumbled up with strangers and long forgotten faces. But none of them could help either Gregor or his family, and he was glad when they all vanished.

He found he now no longer cared what happened to his family; on the contrary, he felt nothing but a sort of blind rage at the way they now neglected him; and even though there was no longer anything he fancied, he began to concoct elaborate plans for a raid on the larder, with a view to taking the food to which he was still entitled, even if he wasn't hungry.

Nowadays his sister no longer took the trouble to think of something he might like to eat. She shoved any old food in with her foot before hurrying off to work in the morning and at midday. In the evening, without even bothering to see whether he'd touched his meal or not – usually, he hadn't – she would sweep away the leftovers with a whisk of the broom.

As for cleaning his room, which she now did in the evenings, she could hardly have done it any faster. Great patches of dirt streaked the wall, and little heaps of dust and rubbish lay all over the place. At first, Gregor would position himself in the filthiest places when she appeared as a kind of reproach. But even if he'd stayed there for weeks at a time, it still wouldn't have changed anything: Grete saw the dirt as well as he did, but she'd made up her mind to ignore it. Showing the same oversensitivity that had now infected them all, none of this stopped her from taking more jealous care than ever to ensure that no one else should presume on her sole right to clean the room.

One day Gregor's mother, though, took it upon herself to give Gregor's room a thorough clean. This required several buckets of water. Crouched on his sofa in bitter immobility, the ensuing deluge upset Gregor deeply; but his mother soon had her punishment. No sooner had his sister arrived home that night and noticed the difference in Gregor's room than, feeling deeply offended, she ran into the living-room and, ignoring her mother's pleading, uplifted hands, burst into a flood of tears, which her parents – her father was frightened out of his chair – at first watched in helpless amazement. Gradually, she began to calm down. But then her father lost his temper, too. On the one hand, he began reproaching his wife for not leaving the care and cleaning of Gregor's room to Grete; on the other, he yelled at his daughter, insisting she would never again be allowed to go in and clean it. His wife tried to draw her husband, who was quite beside himself, into his bedroom. Wracked with sobs, Grete banged on the table with her little fists, while Gregor hissed loudly with rage at the idea that no one had the decency or consideration to close the door and spare him the sight of all these tear-floods and sigh-tempests.

But even if his sister, tired out by her work, could no longer be bothered to look after Gregor as diligently as before, there was no need for her mother to take up the task or for him to be neglected: they had a cleaning lady now. This elderly widow, whose big, bony frame had helped her out of worse trouble during her long life, could not really be said to feel any disgust for Gregor. One day, without being in the least curious, she opened his door. Gregor began scurrying about in alarm, although she made no move to chase him. Perfectly astonished at the sight, she froze, hands folded over her stomach.

From that moment on, she never failed morning and evening to open the door a little and peep in on him. At first she would call him over in a familiar tone with expressions like: 'Come on, you old dung beetle!' or, 'Hey, look at the old cockroach!' Gregor ignored her. He would stay motionless beneath his sofa as if no one was there. If only they'd told the woman to clean his room out every day, instead of allowing her to go on teasing and upsetting him when the mood took her!

Early one morning, when heavy rain – perhaps a sign of approaching spring – beat on the roof-tops, the old woman's taunts annoyed Gregor so much he began to turn, feebly and slowly, as if about to attack her. She was not in the least bit frightened. A chair stood by the door. She snatched it up and brandished it high in the air, opening her mouth wide: it was obvious she didn't intend closing it until she had brought the chair crashing down on Gregor's back. 'Is that it, then?' she asked, as he turned away, and she calmly put the chair back in the corner.

By this time, Gregor was hardly eating. Only when he happened on his scraps would he amuse himself by taking a piece of food in his mouth, keeping it there for hours but almost always spitting it out again. At first he thought it was his dejection over the state of his room that had made him lose his appetite, but in fact he quickly grew used to the changes. His family had fallen into the habit of throwing anything unwanted in there, and there was a great deal of this lumber now that one of the bedrooms had been let to three lodgers.

These earnest men – all three had full beards, as Gregor saw one day when he was peering through a crack in the door – were fanatically tidy. They insisted on order, not only in their own room, but also, once they were paying rent, throughout the whole flat, especially the kitchen. They had no time for useless, dirty junk. They had brought most of the things they needed with them, leaving a lot of stuff that couldn't be sold but that no one wanted to throw out. It was all chucked into Gregor's room, along with the ash bucket and the kitchen rubbish bin. The char-woman, always in a tearing hurry, dumped anything else that looked as if it might not be needed in there too.

Luckily, all Gregor usually saw was a hand flourishing the object in question before the door slammed shut again. Perhaps the cleaner intended retrieving it all when she got the time and the opportunity; perhaps she meant to throw the whole lot out in one go. But the reality was that the rubbish remained where it had first landed, unless Gregor disturbed it as he wandered through it – at first because he had to and then later because he enjoyed it. Even so, these excursions left him half dead with fatigue, and after them he sat without moving for hours.

As the lodgers sometimes also took their dinner in the living-room, its door was occasionally closed. But Gregor no longer cared. For some time now, even when his family left the door open he'd squat back in the darkest corner of his room, unnoticed and out of sight. One day the cleaner left the dining-room door standing slightly ajar, and it was still in that position when the lodgers came in and turned on the lights. They sat down in the places that had once been occupied by Gregor, his father and his mother, unfolded their napkins and took up their knives and forks.

Gregor's mother appeared in the doorway shortly afterwards with a plate of meat, followed immediately by his sister carrying a dish piled high with potatoes. The food sent up a great cloud of steam. The lodgers leaned over as if to examine it, and the one who was seated in the middle and appeared to have some authority over the others cut a piece of meat to see whether it was tender enough, or if he should send it back to the kitchen. He appeared satisfied, however, and the two women, who had been watching anxiously, breathed a sigh of relief. The family itself ate in the kitchen. Nevertheless, Gregor's father always came in, bowed once, and made the rounds of the table cap in hand before going back into the kitchen. The boarders rose as one, muttering something into their beards. Once they were alone, they ate in almost total silence. Gregor found it odd that he could hear the sound of their chewing over and above the clatter of the cutlery; it was as if they wanted to show him that you needed real teeth to eat properly, and that even with the finest toothless jaws in the world there was no chance of getting anything down. 'I am hungry,' thought Gregor sadly, 'but not for that kind of food. Look how those lodgers shovel it in, while I lie here wasting away.'

This whole weary time, he could not remember hearing his sister play her violin. But this evening, he heard music coming from the kitchen. The lodgers had just finished their meal; the middle one had produced a newspaper, handing a page of it to each of the others; now they were all three reading, leaning back in their chairs and smoking. The sound of the violin caught their attention, and they rose and tiptoed toward the hall door, where they halted in a tight group. Apparently, they had been heard in the kitchen: Gregor's father called, 'Does the violin upset you gentlemen? If so, we'll stop it immediately.' 'On the contrary,' the middle lodger said. 'Wouldn't the young lady like to come through and play to us here in the dining-room, where it is much nicer and more comfortable?' 'Oh, thank you,' said Mr Samsa as if he were the one playing.

The gentlemen walked back across the room and waited. Soon Gregor's father came in with the music stand, his mother with the sheets of music, and his sister with the violin. She calmly prepared to play. Her parents, who had never before let their rooms, treated the lodgers with exaggerated politeness and didn't dare sit in their own chairs. Mr Samsa leaned against the door, his right hand thrust between two buttons of his jacket. One of the gentlemen offered Gregor's mother a chair, and she sat exactly where he had placed it, off in the corner.

Gregor's sister began to play, while her father and mother, who were to either side, watched her hands as they moved over the instrument. Drawn by the music, Gregor had crawled forward a little and poked his head into the room. He was no longer surprised that he'd lost all consideration for others, the very consideration that once had been his pride and joy. Yet he had never had more reason to remain hidden: for now, as a result of all the dust in his room which flew up at the slightest disturbance, he was always covered in threads, hair and morsels of stale food, which stuck to his back and sides and trailed after him wherever he went. His apathy was now so great he no longer bothered turning on his back and rubbing himself clean on the carpet. And despite being in this filthy state, he had no qualms about crawling forward over the spotless floor.

So far, no one had noticed him. His family was wrapped up in the violin recital. Hands in their pockets, the lodgers, who had at first gathered round the music stand so that they could read the notes – putting Grete off her playing – soon moved back to the window, where they stood with their heads down talking in low tones, watched anxiously by Mr Samsa who stood nearby.

It was perfectly clear that they were disappointed in their expectations of a fine or at least amusing recital, were fed up with the whole thing and only tolerated this interruption to their peace and quiet out of politeness. Even the snooty way they blew cigar smoke out through their noses and mouths showed how unimpressed they were.

And yet Grete was playing so beautifully. Head tilted to one side, her gaze followed the score with sorrowful care. Gregor crawled a little further forward and lowered his head in an effort to catch her eye. Was he really just an animal when music stirred him so deeply? It seemed to him to open a pathway toward that unknown source of sustenance for which he so longed.

He resolved to creep up to his sister and tug at her dress, to make her understand that she must bring her violin into his room, for no one valued her playing as he did. He would never again let her out of his room – at least, not while he lived – and for once his horrible shape would come in useful. He would be at all the doors at once, keeping all intruders at bay with his fearsome hissing. There would be no question of force; his sister must live with him of her own accord. She would sit with him on the sofa and listen to what he said. He would tell her in confidence that, had this misfortune not so swiftly overtaken him, he had planned on telling everyone last Christmas – was Christmas really past? – that he was sending her to the Conservatory, whatever anyone said.

Moved by this explanation, his sister would surely weep pure tears of happiness, and Gregor, climbing up on her shoulder, would kiss her neck;

this would be all the easier, for she had worn neither collar nor ribbon since starting work in the shop.

'Mr Samsa!' cried the middle lodger. Wordlessly, he pointed his index finger at Gregor, who was advancing slowly into the room. Grete stopped playing. The middle lodger turned to his friends, grinned, shook his head and then looked back at Gregor. At first, Gregor's father seemed more concerned with reassuring the lodgers than with driving his son from the room. But the lodgers didn't seem all that upset by the spectacle: if anything, they found Gregor more entertaining than the violin. Mr Samsa hurried forward and, with outstretched arms, tried to guide them back into their room, while hiding Gregor from their eyes with his bulk. At this, they started to get annoyed, although it wasn't clear whether this was because of their landlord's behaviour or because, unwittingly, they had all been living right next door to a monster like Gregor.

Demanding Mr Samsa explain matters, they began waving their arms in the air, fiddling with their beards as they fell slowly back towards their room. In the meantime, Grete had recovered from this sudden and distressing interruption of her recital. After standing for a moment not knowing what to do – with the violin and bow dangling limply from her hands, and following the score as if she were still playing – she suddenly came back to life. She laid the violin in her mother's lap – Mrs Samsa was gasping for breath in her chair, lungs working overtime – and rushed through into the next room, towards which the lodgers were retreating ever more rapidly in the face of Mr Samsa's advance. Pillows and blankets flew under Grete's quick, practised hands as she set their beds to rights, and she had slipped out again before they came in.

Once again in the grip of his strange obstinacy, Mr Samsa had quite forgotten the respect due his lodgers. He kept pushing them back, until the middle lodger reached the door of his room, where he stopped dead and stamped hard on the floor. 'I hereby wish to inform you,' he said, raising a hand and letting his gaze sweep the two women, 'that in view of the disgusting circumstances prevailing in this family and this house' – at this he spat contemptuously on the floor – 'as of tomorrow morning, I am giving up my room. Naturally, you will not get a penny for the time I have been living here. On the contrary, I am seriously considering whether to sue you, given how easy the case would be to prove. I shall certainly look into the matter, believe me, sir.' He broke off and stared into space as if waiting for something. His two friends spoke up in their turn: 'We, too, give our notice.' At this, the middle lodger seized the door handle, and all three trooped inside.

The door slammed shut with a bang. Gregor's father staggered over to his armchair, rested his trembling hands on the arms, and stretched out as if he were settling in for his customary evening nap; but the rapid and apparently uncontrollable nodding of his head told a very different story.

All this time, Gregor had stuck fast on the spot where he had surprised the lodgers. The disappointment over the failure of his plans, combined perhaps also with the weakness of extreme hunger, meant he could not move a muscle. He feared some terrible catastrophe would befall him at any moment and stood there waiting for the axe to descend. Even the violin didn't startle him as it slipped from his mother's trembling fingers, fell off her lap and hit the floor with a hollow sound.

'My dear parents,' said his sister, beating the table with her hand to get their attention, 'things can't go on like this. Even if you don't see it, it's clear as day to me. I won't mention my brother's name in the same breath as this monster. All I have to say is that we must find some way of getting rid of it. We've done everything humanly possible to care for it and put up with it. No one can say that we're to blame.'

'She's right, a thousand times right,' her father said. But her mother, who still hadn't got her breath back, coughed into her hand with a wild look. Her daughter hurried over to her and held her forehead. Grete's words seemed to have made up her father's mind: he sat up and poked at his cap, which was lying on the table among the dishes left from the lodgers' dinner. From time to time he stared at Gregor.

'We must find a way of getting rid of it,' she repeated, now speaking only to her father. Her mother's coughing was making her deaf. 'It'll be the death of you both, I can see it coming. When people have to work all day, like us, they can't put up with constant torture at home. I certainly can't.' And she wept so bitterly that her tears, wiped mechanically away, fell on her mother's face. 'But what can we do, child?' her father said, demonstrating remarkable grasp and compassion. Grete merely shrugged her shoulders, as if to show that the confusion brought on by her emotional state had banished her former self-assurance. 'If only he could understand us,' her father said wonderingly. But Grete signalled through her tears that this was out of the question.

'If only he could understand us,' her father said again – and he shut his eyes as he spoke, as if to show that he agreed with Grete that such a thing was quite impossible. 'If only he could understand us, then perhaps we could come to some accommodation with him. But as it is...'

'That thing has to go!' Grete cried. 'It's the only way, Father. You have to stop believing it's Gregor.

We've believed that for far too long, that's why we're so unhappy. How could it be Gregor? If it were really him, he would have realized long since that he can't possibly live with human beings and would have left of his own free will. I no longer have a brother – but what we can do is go on living and respect his memory. Instead, this monster dogs our footsteps, drives our lodgers away and schemes to take over the whole flat. We'll be out on the streets, soon! Look, Father, look!' she screamed suddenly, 'He's off again!' And in a panic Gregor couldn't begin to understand, she jumped out of her chair, abandoning Mrs Samsa as if she would rather throw her own mother to the four winds than be anywhere near Gregor. She ran behind her father. Deeply upset by her behaviour, he stood up and spread his arms wide to protect her.

But Gregor had no desire to frighten anyone, least of all his sister. He had merely started to turn around in order to go back into his room. Given that in his weakened state Gregor had to keep bumping his head on the floor to help push himself around, this looked very peculiar. He stopped and looked back at them. They seemed to realize he meant well; the momentary panic had passed. They watched him in silent sorrow. Mrs Samsa lay back in her armchair, legs outstretched and pressed tightly together, eyelids drooping with fatigue. Grete sat beside her father with her arm around his neck. 'Now perhaps I can turn around,' Gregor thought, bending again to the task. He couldn't stop himself from wheezing loudly, and he was forced to rest from time to time. But no one hurried him, they left him to get on with it. His turn completed, he beat a hasty retreat. He was amazed at the great distance that now seemed to separate him from his bedroom.

Weak as he now felt, he couldn't understand how he had only recently covered the same ground with so little effort. Focused wholly on regaining his room, he failed to notice that his family hadn't uttered a single word between them. It was only when he had at long last reached his door that he thought of turning his head – not completely, because his neck had become very stiff – but enough to see that nothing behind him had changed. His sister was the only one standing. He reserved his last glance for his mother who by now was fast asleep.

The second he was back in his room someone slammed, locked and double-bolted the door. The loud, sudden crash from behind made Gregor's legs buckle in fright. It was his sister who had rushed to the door. She'd been standing ready, and at the right moment had raced forward on her toes so that he couldn't hear her. As she turned the key in the lock, she glanced back at her parents and cried, 'At last!'

'Now what?' Gregor wondered, peering round in the darkness. He soon discovered that he was unable to move. This didn't surprise him in the least: it seemed to him much more remarkable that his frail little legs had supported him up until now. But on the whole he felt quite comfortable. It was true that his whole body ached, but these pains seemed gradually to be fading away. By now he hardly felt the rotten apple in his back, or the inflamed, dust-covered area surrounding it. He thought tenderly and lovingly of his family. He knew he had to go; he was even more certain of it than his sister had been. He lay dreaming in a half-trance until the church clock struck three in the morning. He watched the world growing lighter through the window. Then, without his willing it, his head drooped and a last feeble breath left his nostrils in a soft stream.

The cleaner arrived early in the morning. Although she had often been asked not to do so, she slammed all the doors so loudly in her hustle and bustle that once she was in the house it was impossible to remain asleep. At first, she didn't notice anything out of the ordinary as she paid Gregor her usual quick morning visit. She thought he was lying motionless on purpose, feigning injury. She gave him every credit for intelligence. She had a long broom in her hand, and tried to tickle him from the doorway. When there was still no response she grew irritated and poked him a couple of times. It was only when this, too, failed to budge him that the truth hit her.

Grasping what had happened, she opened her eyes wide and whistled in astonishment. At once, she ran to the bedroom door and wrenched it open, shouting out into the darkness, 'Come and look! It's stone dead! It's lying there, absolutely dead as a doornail!'

Mr and Mrs Samsa sat up in bed. The cleaner had frightened them so much they could not at first make sense of her words. But now they hastily scrambled out of bed, Mr Samsa on one side, his wife on the other. Mr Samsa threw the quilt over his shoulders, while Mrs Samsa came out clad in nothing but her nightdress and they hurried into Gregor's room. Meanwhile, Grete had opened the living-room door. She had been sleeping there ever since the lodgers arrived. She was fully dressed, and the pallor of her skin suggested she hadn't slept a wink. 'Dead?' said Mrs Samsa, shooting the cleaner a questioning look, even though she could see perfectly well for herself what had happened. 'I should say so,' the cleaner replied, giving Gregor's corpse a hefty shove with her broom to prove it. Mrs Samsa made as if to stop her, but then faltered. 'Well,' Mr Samsa said, 'let's all thank God for that!' He crossed himself and the three women followed his example. Grete, whose eyes had never once left the corpse, said, 'Look how thin he was! It was such a long time since he'd eaten anything. The food came out of his room exactly as it went in.' Gregor's body was indeed quite flat and dry – they could only see this clearly now that his legs had collapsed, and there was nothing to distract them. 'Come in our room for a minute, Grete,' Mrs Samsa said with a sad smile, and Grete followed her parents into their bedroom, glancing continually back at the corpse as she went.

The cleaner shut the door and threw the window wide open. Despite the early hour, the fresh morning air held a certain warmth. It was already the end of March. The three lodgers came out of their room and cast round in astonishment for their breakfast, but everyone had forgotten them. 'Where's our breakfast?' the middle lodger asked the cleaner grumpily. But she put a finger to her lips and urged them silently to follow her to Gregor's bedroom.

They went in and stood around the corpse, hands in the pockets of their rather shabby coats, in the middle of a room already brilliant with sunlight. Then the bedroom door opened and Mr Samsa appeared in his uniform, with his wife on one side and his daughter on the other. They all looked as if they had been crying, and now and again Grete pressed her face against her father's arm.

'Leave my house immediately!' Mr Samsa barked, pointing to the door while holding on tight to his family.

'Whatever do you mean?' said the middle lodger with a timid smile, somewhat taken aback. The two others kept their hands behind their backs, rubbing the palms together as if looking forward to a row that must surely end in their favour. 'I mean exactly what I say!' Mr Samsa retorted, marching directly at the middle lodger and his companions. The lodger stood his ground, eyes fixed on the floor, as if he were contemplating the changed circumstances. 'Very well then, we'll go,' he said at last, raising his eyes to Mr Samsa as if, in a sudden access of humility, he sought approval for his words. Mr Samsa did no more than nod, glaring. At this, the principal lodger strode out into the hallway, his two friends – their hands now quite still – scurrying after him as if they were afraid Mr Samsa might get there before them and cut them off. In the hallway, they took their hats from the pegs, lifted their walking sticks from the umbrella stand, bowed silently and quit the apartment.

With a mistrust that was self-evidently and wholly unjustified, Mr Samsa and his wife and daughter followed the three men out on to the landing and leaned over the balustrade to watch as they slowly but steadily descended the long staircase, appearing and disappearing as they spiralled downwards floor by floor. The farther they went down, the more the Samsas lost interest, and when the lodgers had met and passed a butcher's boy climbing proudly up the stairs with his basket on his head, the family turned from the railing and went back indoors with a sigh of relief.

They decided to spend the remainder of the day resting and strolling. They not only deserved the break, they very much needed it. And so they sat down at the table to write three letters of apology: Mr Samsa to the bank manager, Mrs Samsa to her employer and Grete to her boss. While they were writing, the cleaner came in to say that she'd finished her work and was leaving. At first, the Samsas merely nodded without raising their eyes; it was only when the cleaner showed no signs of actually going that they looked crossly up at her. 'Well?' Mr Samsa demanded. The cleaner was standing in the doorway, smiling as if she had some good news, but would only spit it out if they questioned her in the right way. The little ostrich feather sticking up out of her hat, which had annoyed Mr Samsa from the moment she'd started cleaning for them, bobbed about merrily all over the place. Mrs Samsa, whom the cleaner had always respected the most asked, 'What is it?' 'What I wanted to say,' the woman replied, laughing so much she could hardly get the words out, 'is that you needn't worry about getting rid of that rubbish next door. I've already taken care of it.' Grete and her mother bent back to the table as if to resume their letter-writing. Realizing that the woman was about to launch into a more detailed explanation, Mr Samsa cut her short with a peremptory gesture. Cut off in mid-sentence, the cleaner suddenly remembered that she was in a great hurry and, calling, 'Goodbye, everyone,' in a furious voice, she turned on her heel and disappeared, slamming the door behind her with an almighty crash.

'This evening we must sack her,' Mr Samsa declared. But neither his wife nor his daughter replied. Even the cleaner had not been able to disturb their newfound tranquillity. The two of them rose, went to the window and stood there with their arms around each other. Turning towards them in his armchair, Mr Samsa stared over for a moment in silence. Then he said, 'Well, well, it's all water under the bridge now. So you can start paying me some attention.' The women hurried across to him, kissed him and finished off their letters as quickly as possible. Then they all left the apartment together, something they hadn't done for months, and took the tram out to the countryside.

There were no other passengers in the compartment, which was warm and bright in the sunlight.

Leaning comfortably back in their seats, they fell to discussing the future. On closer examination, they decided things weren't nearly as bad as they'd imagined. The fact was – and this was something they hadn't really discussed among themselves before – that they'd all three found reasonable jobs, which promised even better for the future. The greatest immediate improvement they could make to their circumstances was to move from their current apartment to a smaller, cheaper and more practical flat, and above all a place in a much better neighbourhood than the one Gregor had chosen for them.

As their daughter grew more and more animated, Mr and Mrs Samsa realized almost as one that, despite all the terrible things she'd been through over these past weeks which had left her looking so pale and wan, Grete was blossoming into a beautiful, full-figured young woman.

They fell quiet, and communicating via little more than meaningful glances, they both saw that the time had come to find her a good husband. And when, at the end of the journey, their daughter stood and stretched her young body before them, it came almost as a confirmation of their new hopes and dreams.

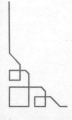
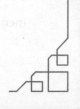